image comics presents

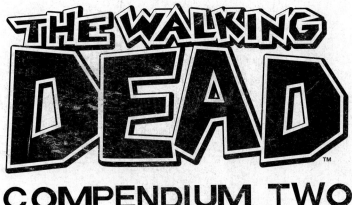

COMPENDIUM TWO

For SKYBOUND ENTERTAINMENT

Robert Kirkman - CEO
David Alpert - President
Sean Mackiewicz - Editorial Director
Shawn Kirkham - Director of Business Development
Brian Huntington - Online Editorial Director
June Alain - Publicity Director
Rachel Skidmore - Director of Media Development
Jon Moisan - Editor
Arielle Basich - Assistant Editor
Dan Petersen - Operations Manager
Nick Palmer - Operations Coordinator
Genevieve Jones - Production Coordinator
Andres Juarez - Graphic Designer
Stephan Murillo - Business Development Coordinator

For international rights inquiries,
please contact: foreign@skybound.com

WWW.SKYBOUND.COM

IMAGE COMICS, INC.
Robert Kirkman – Chief Operating Officer
Erik Larsen – Chief Financial Officer
Todd McFarlane – President
Marc Silvestri – Chief Executive Officer
Jim Valentino – Vice-President

Eric Stephenson – Publisher
Corey Murphy – Director of Sales
Jeff Boison – Director of Publishing Planning & Book Trade Sales
Jeremy Sullivan – Director of Digital Sales
Kat Salazar – Director of PR & Marketing
Emily Miller – Director of Operations
Branwyn Bigglestone – Senior Accounts Manager
Sarah Mello – Accounts Manager
Drew Gill – Art Director
Jonathan Chan – Production Manager
Meredith Wallace – Print Manager
Briah Skelly – Publicity Assistant
Sasha Head – Sales & Marketing Production Designer
Randy Okamura – Digital Production Designer
David Brothers – Branding Manager
Ally Power – Content Manager
Addison Duke – Production Artist
Vincent Kukua – Production Artist
Tricia Ramos – Production Artist
Jeff Stang – Direct Market Sales Representative
Emilio Bautista – Digital Sales Associate
Leanna Caunter – Accounting Assistant
Chloe Ramos-Peterson – Administrative Assistant
IMAGECOMICS.COM

THE WALKING DEAD COMPENDIUM, VOL. 2. Third Printing. Published by Image Comics, Inc. Office of publication: 2001 Center Street, 6th Floor, Berkeley, California 94704.

PRINTED IN THE U.S.A.

ISBN: 978-1-60706-596-8

ROBERT KIRKMAN
creator, writer

CHARLIE ADLARD
penciler, inker

CLIFF RATHBURN
gray tones

RUS WOOTON
letterer

SINA GRACE
editor

CHARLIE ADLARD
& CLIFF RATHBURN
cover

Chapter Nine:
Here We Remain

ROBERT KIRKMAN
creator, writer

CHARLIE ADLARD
penciler, inker

CLIFF RATHBURN
gray tones

RUS WOOTON
letterer

SINA GRACE
editor

CHARLIE ADLARD
& CLIFF RATHBURN
cover

Chapter Nine:
Here We Remain

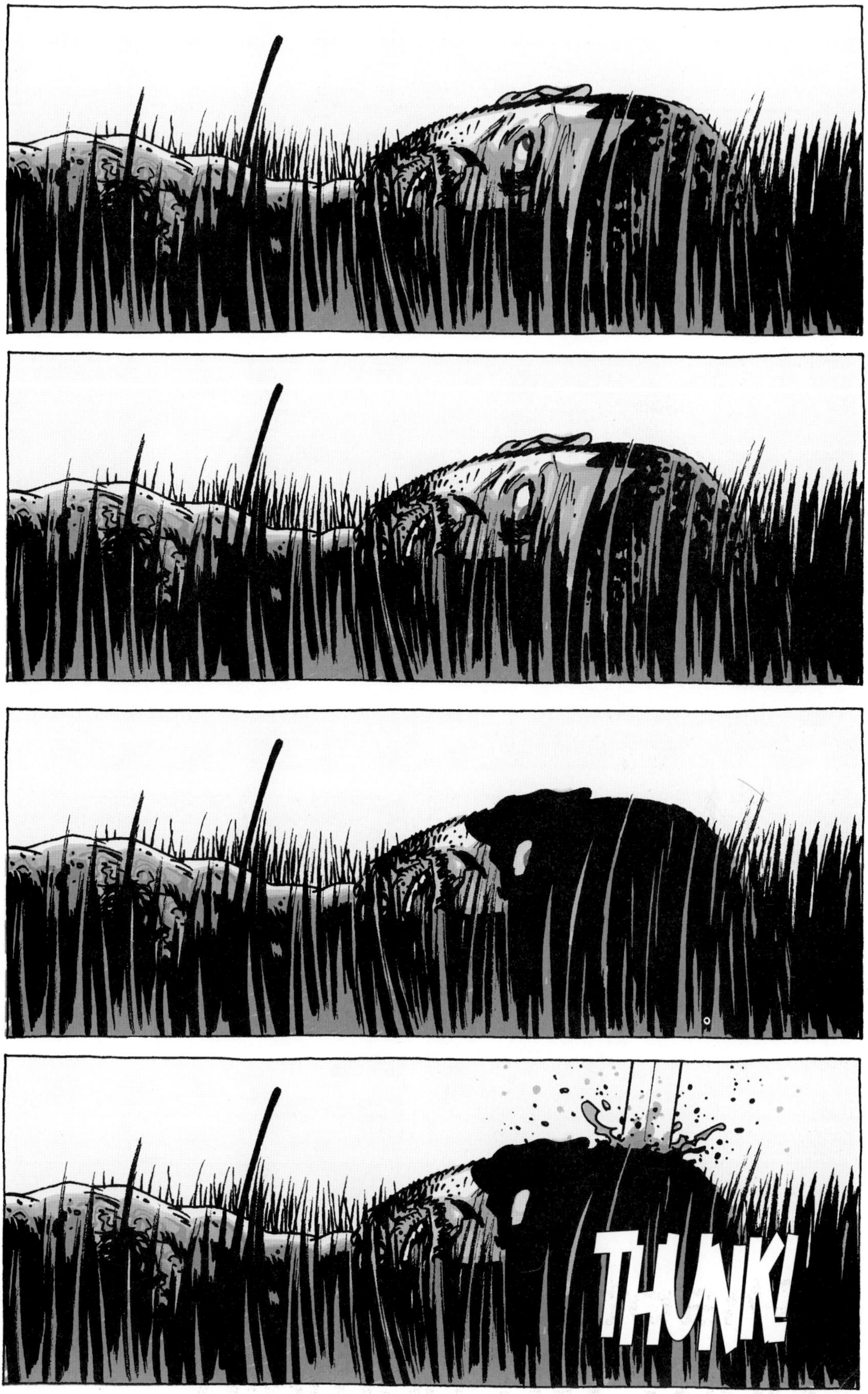
THUNK!

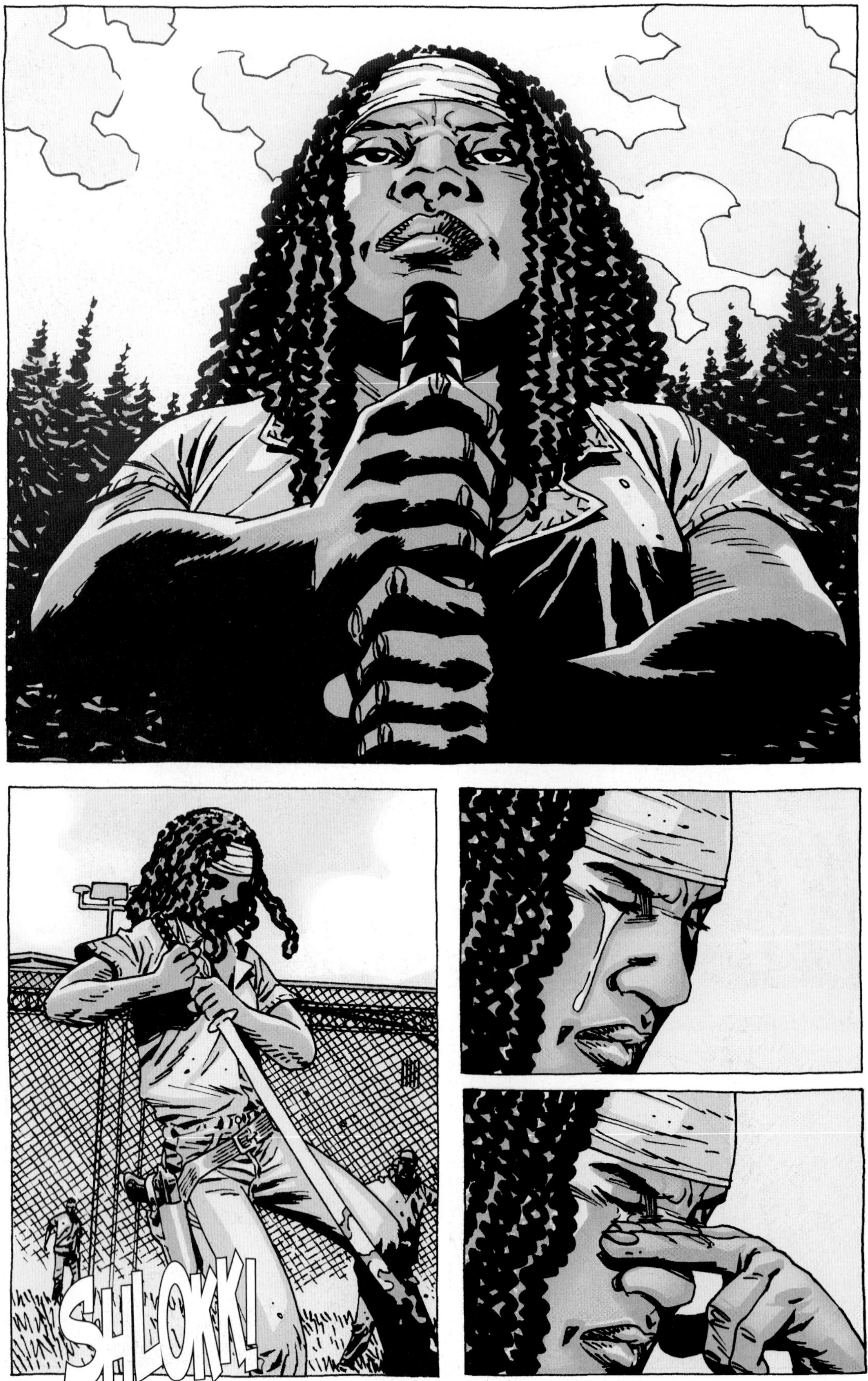
SHLOKK!

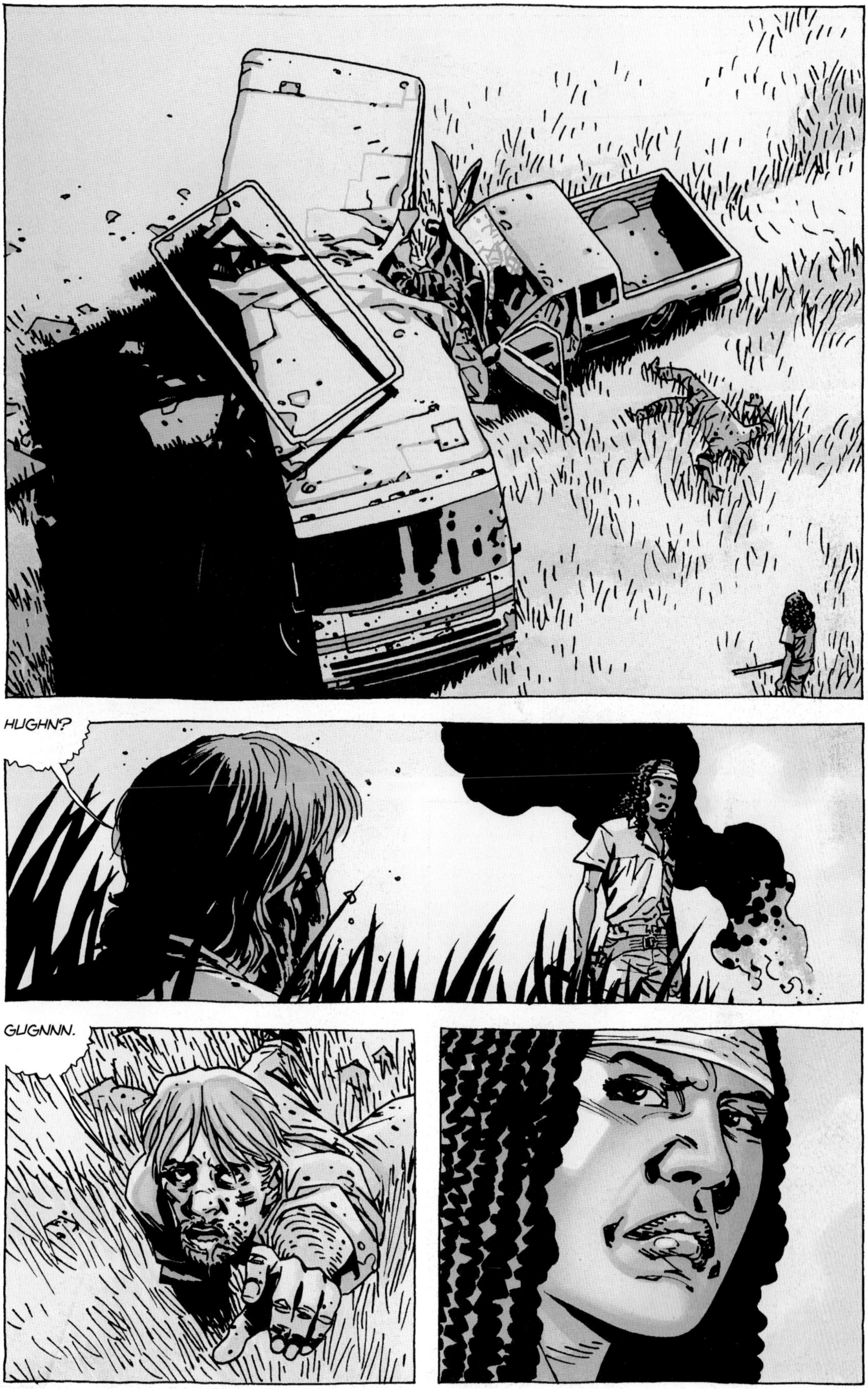
HUGHN?
GUGNNN.

WHRONK!

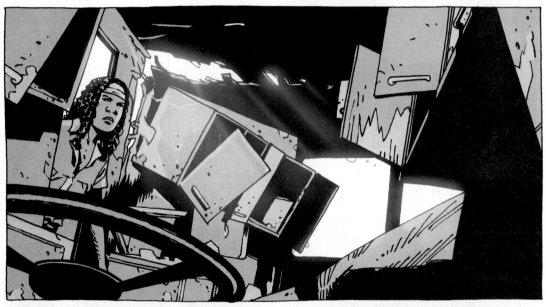

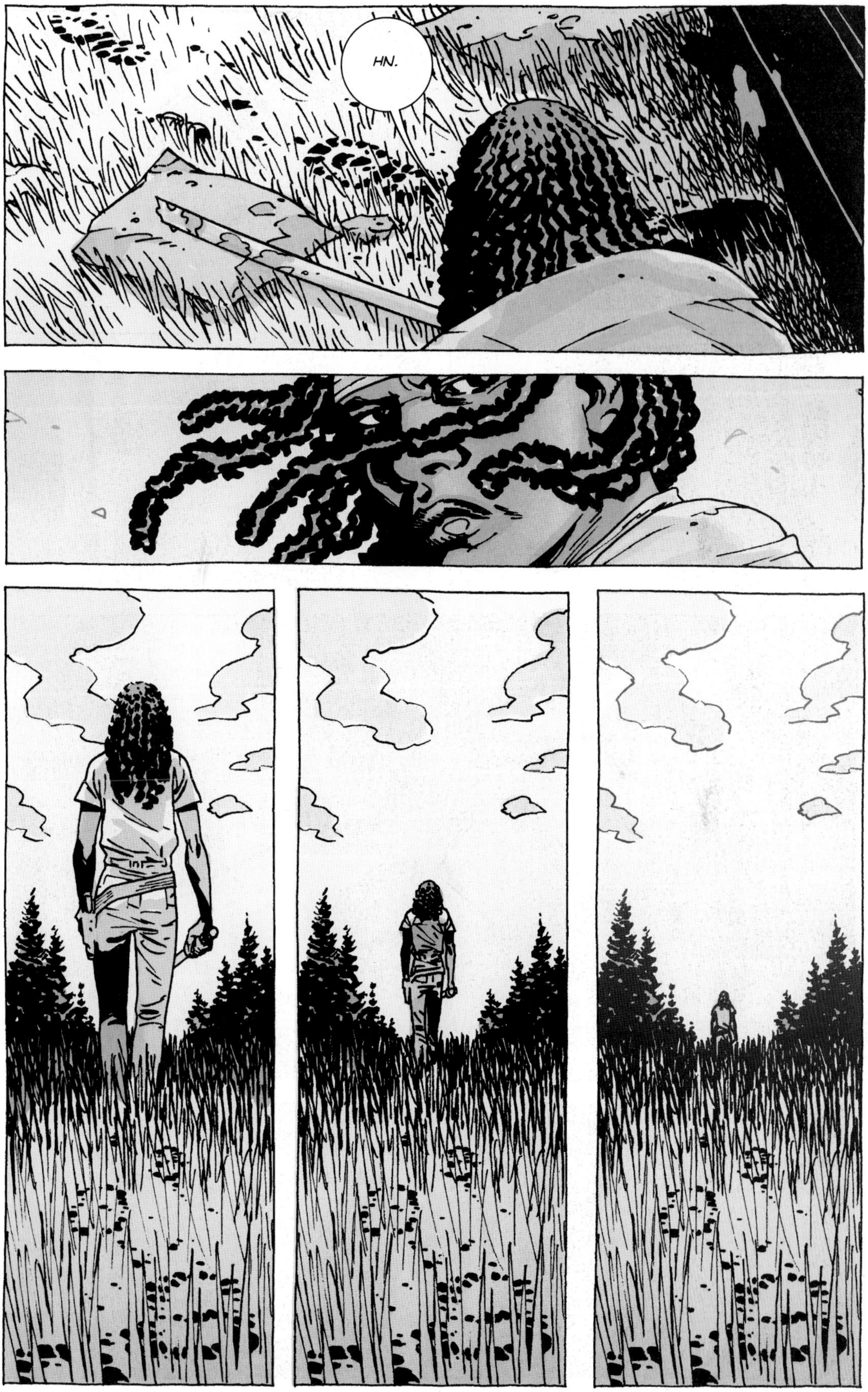
HN.

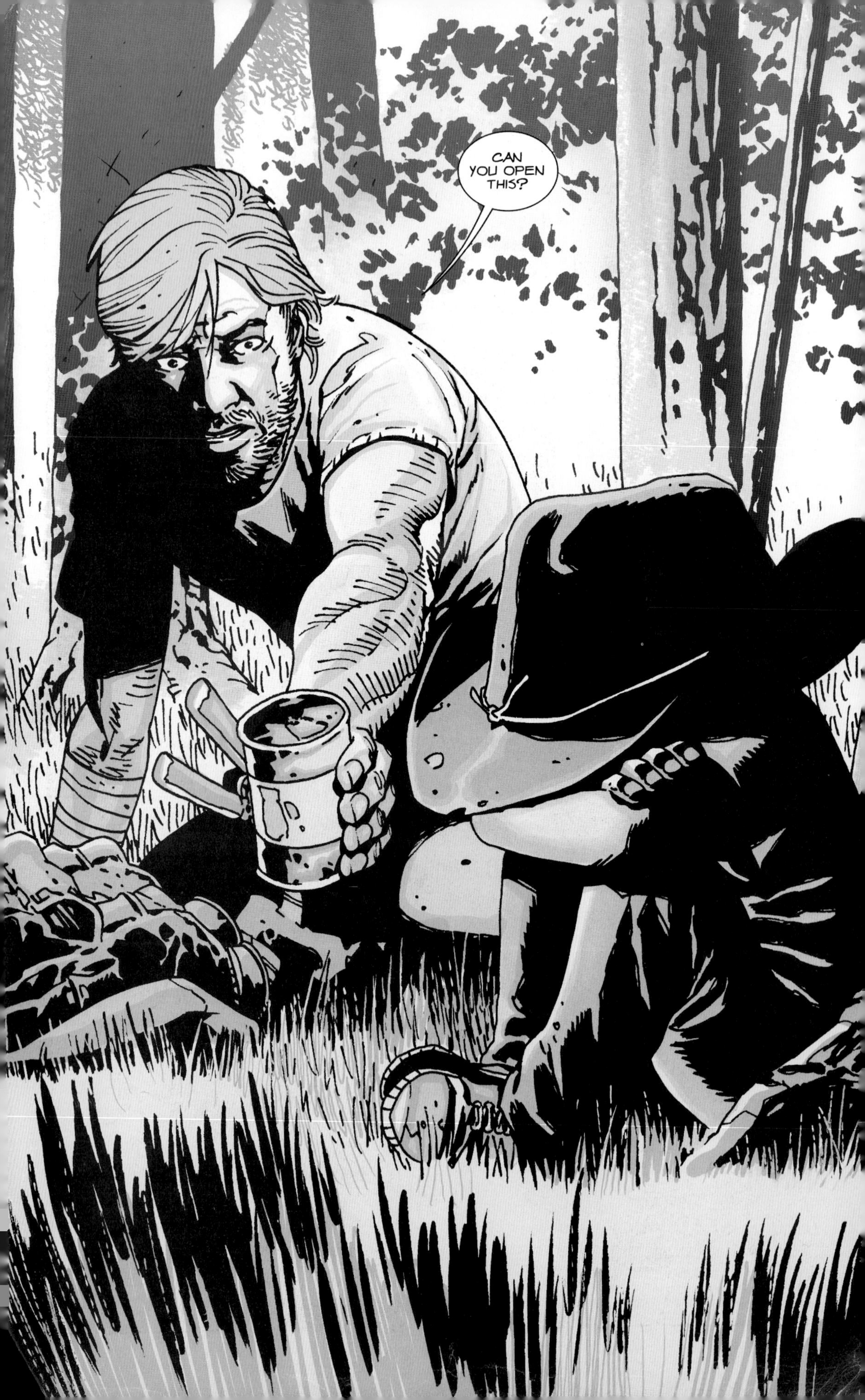
CAN YOU OPEN THIS?

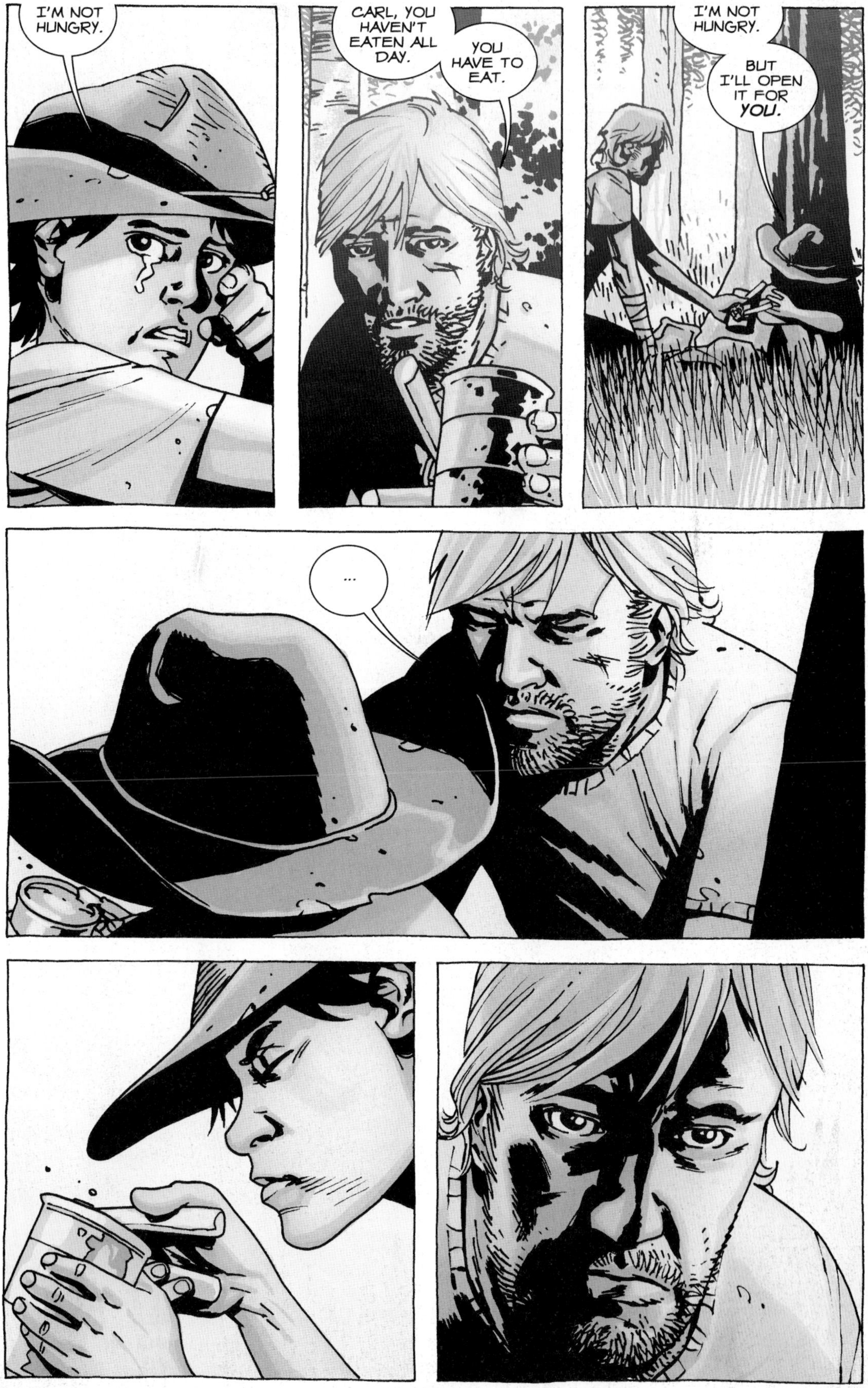
I'M NOT HUNGRY.
CARL, YOU HAVEN'T EATEN ALL DAY.
YOU HAVE TO EAT.
I'M NOT HUNGRY.
BUT I'LL OPEN IT FOR *YOU*.
...

THANKS.

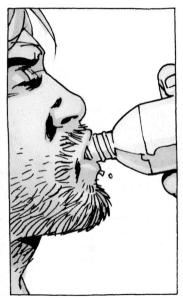

NO THANKS.

OKAY.

WE SHOULD PROBABLY GET MOVING ANYWAY-- FIND SOME SHELTER FOR THE NIGHT.

YOU GET HUNGRY, YOU LET ME KNOW. OKAY?

WE'LL STOP AGAIN-- WHENEVER YOU GET HUNGRY.

OKAY.

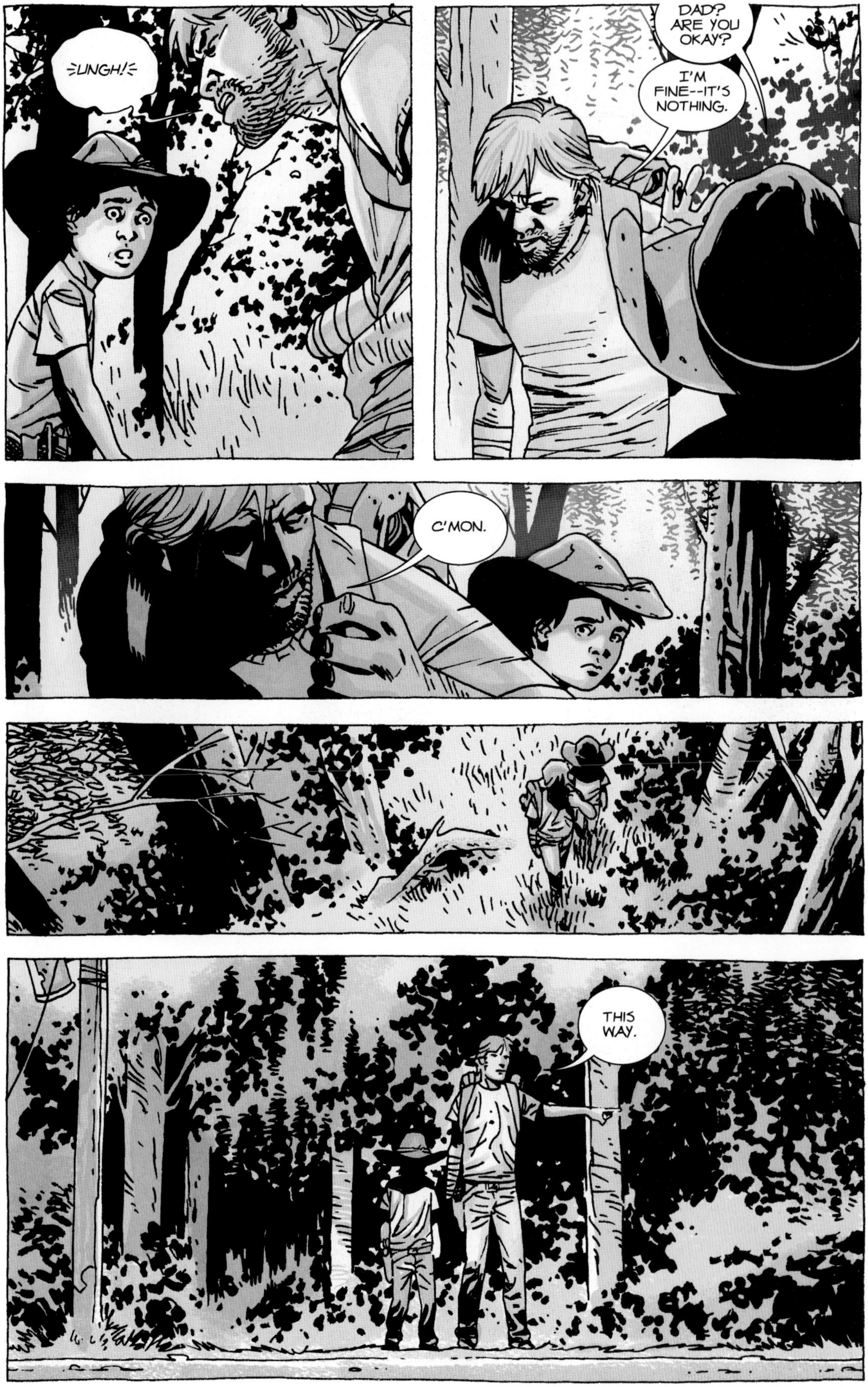

=UNGH!=
DAD? ARE YOU OKAY?
I'M FINE--IT'S NOTHING.
C'MON.
THIS WAY.

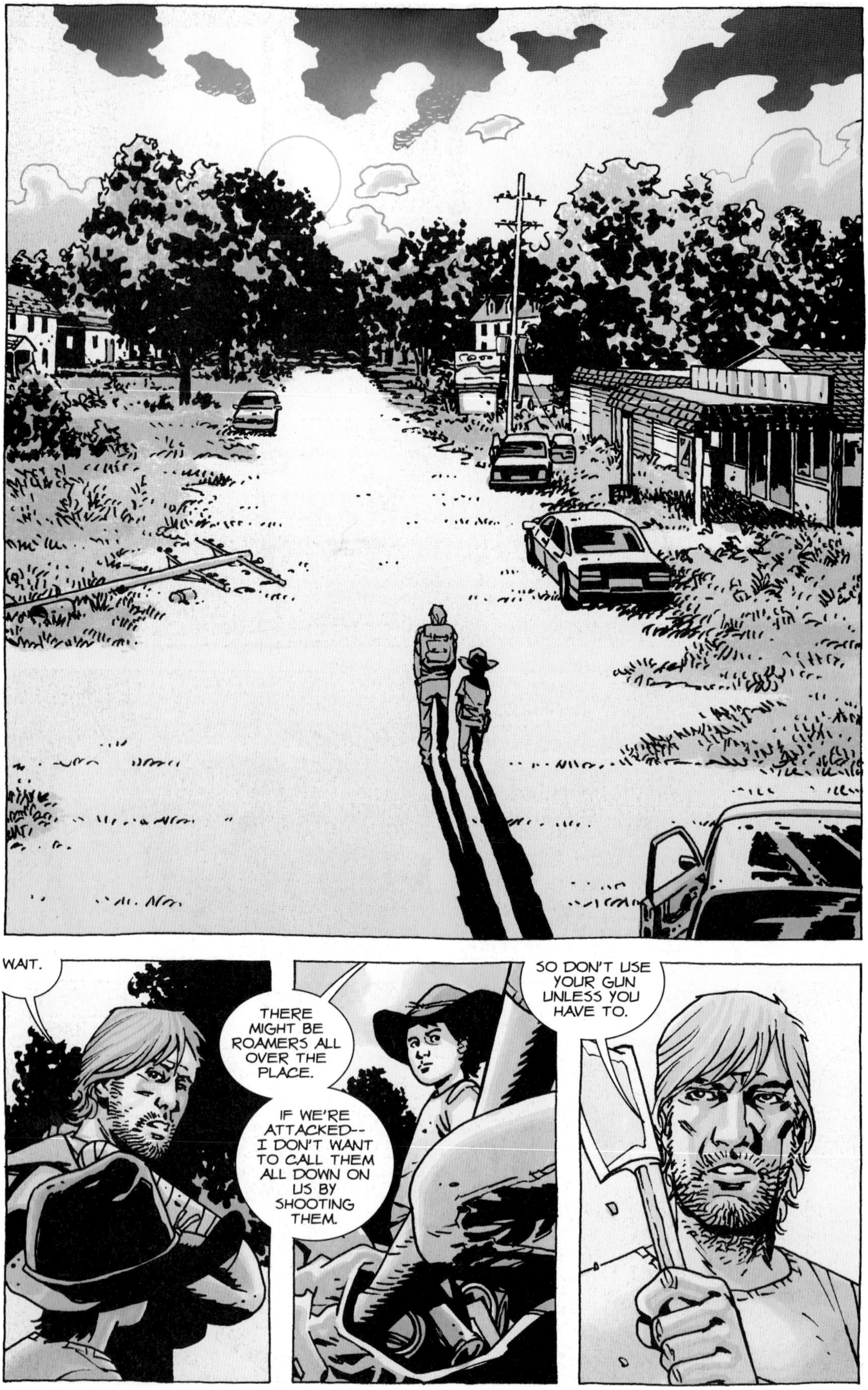

WAIT.
THERE MIGHT BE ROAMERS ALL OVER THE PLACE.
IF WE'RE ATTACKED-- I DON'T WANT TO CALL THEM ALL DOWN ON US BY SHOOTING THEM.
SO DON'T USE YOUR GUN UNLESS YOU HAVE TO.

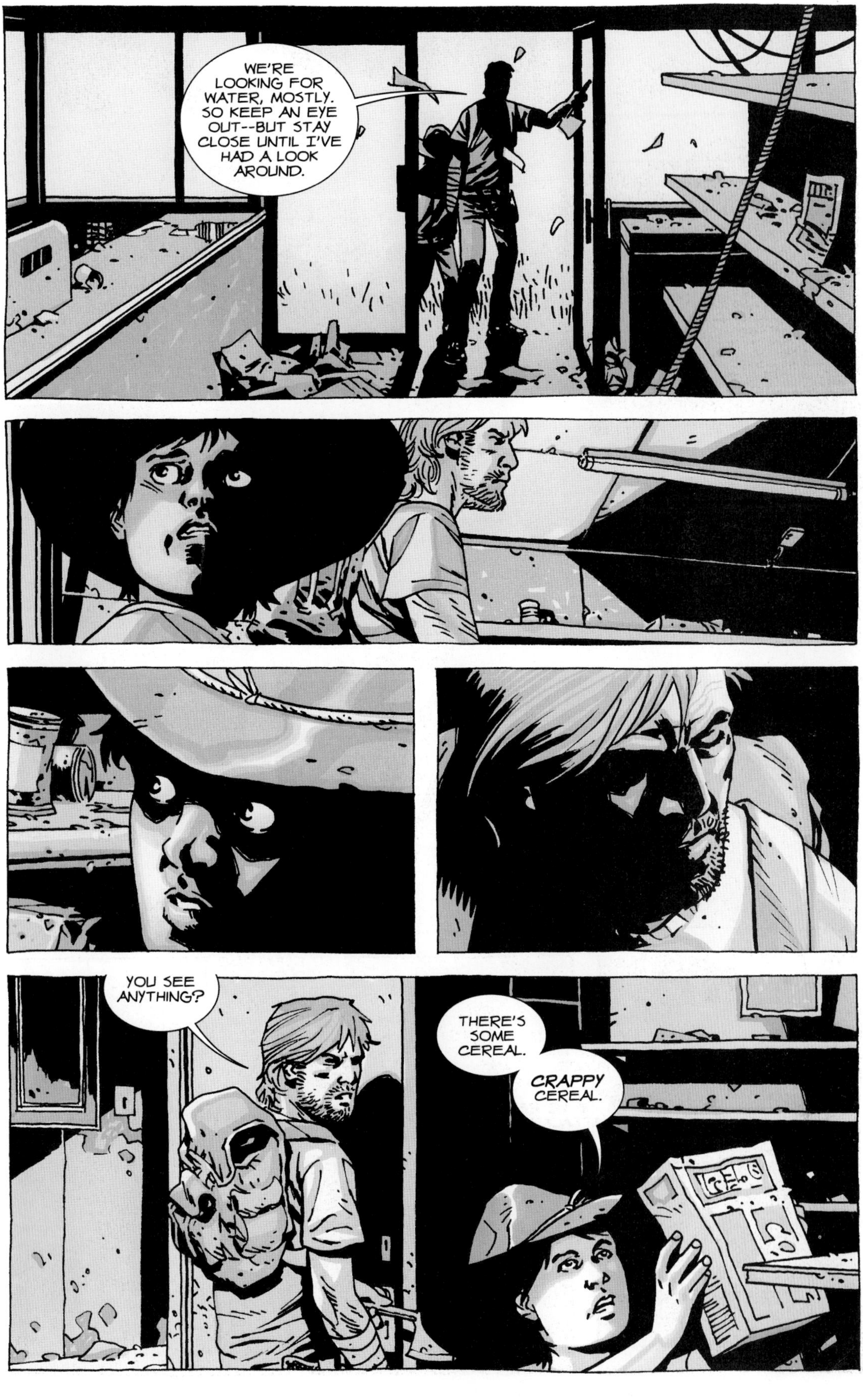
WE'RE LOOKING FOR WATER, MOSTLY. SO KEEP AN EYE OUT--BUT STAY CLOSE UNTIL I'VE HAD A LOOK AROUND.
YOU SEE ANYTHING?
THERE'S SOME CEREAL.
CRAPPY CEREAL.

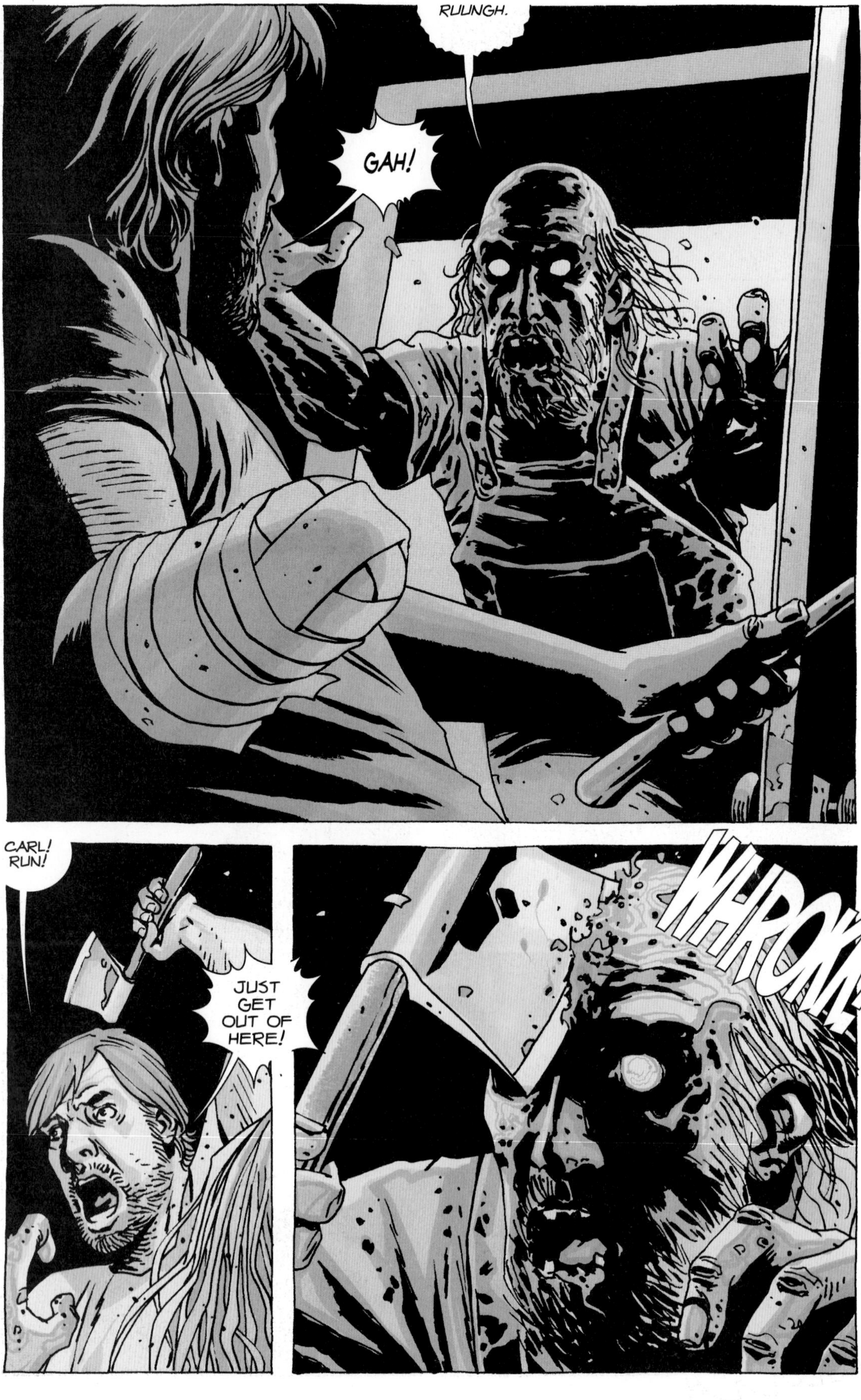
RUUNGH.
GAH!
CARL! RUN!
JUST GET OUT OF HERE!
WHROKK!

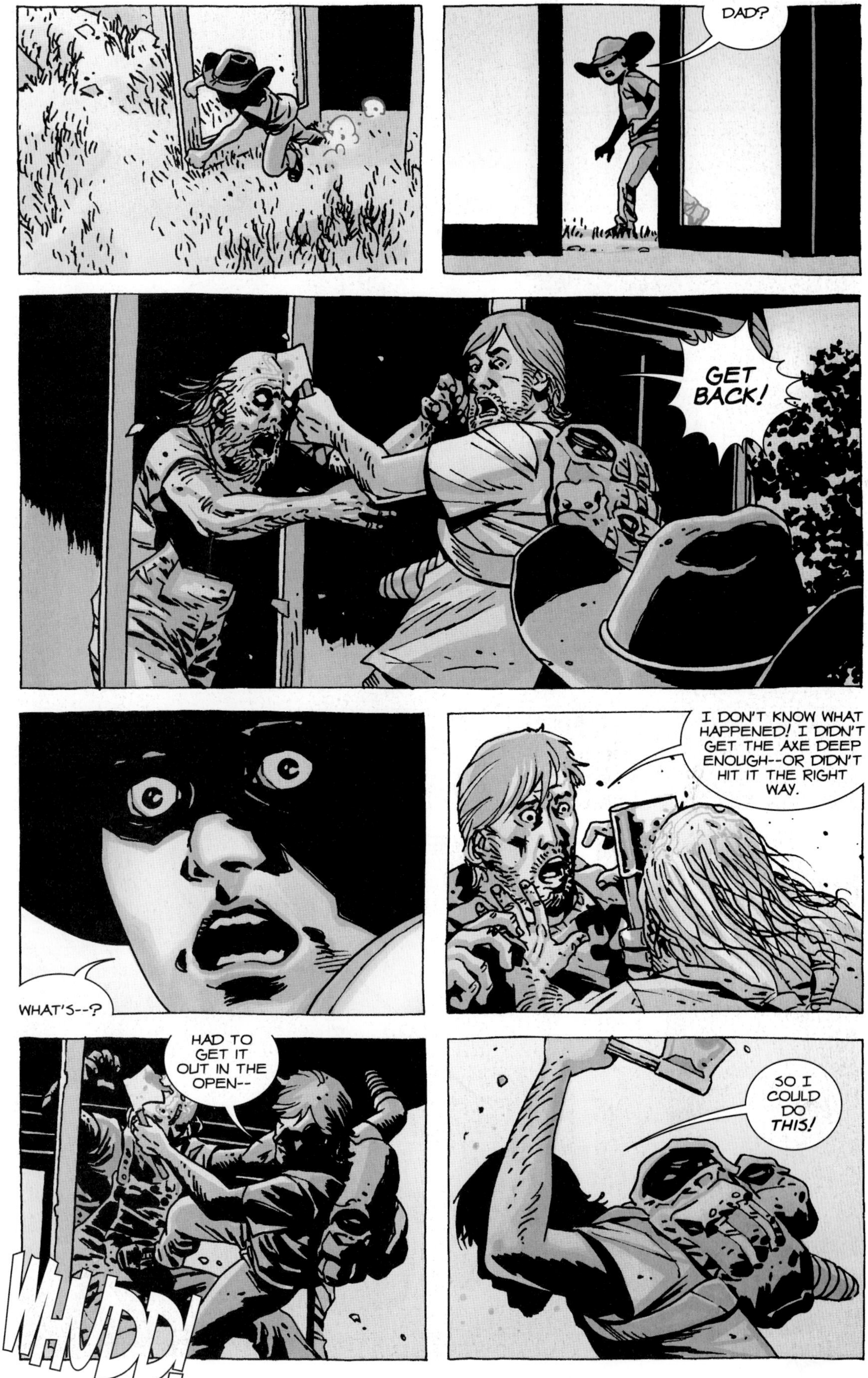

DAD?
GET BACK!
WHAT'S--?
I DON'T KNOW WHAT HAPPENED! I DIDN'T GET THE AXE DEEP ENOUGH--OR DIDN'T HIT IT THE RIGHT WAY.
HAD TO GET IT OUT IN THE OPEN--
WHUDD!
SO I COULD DO THIS!

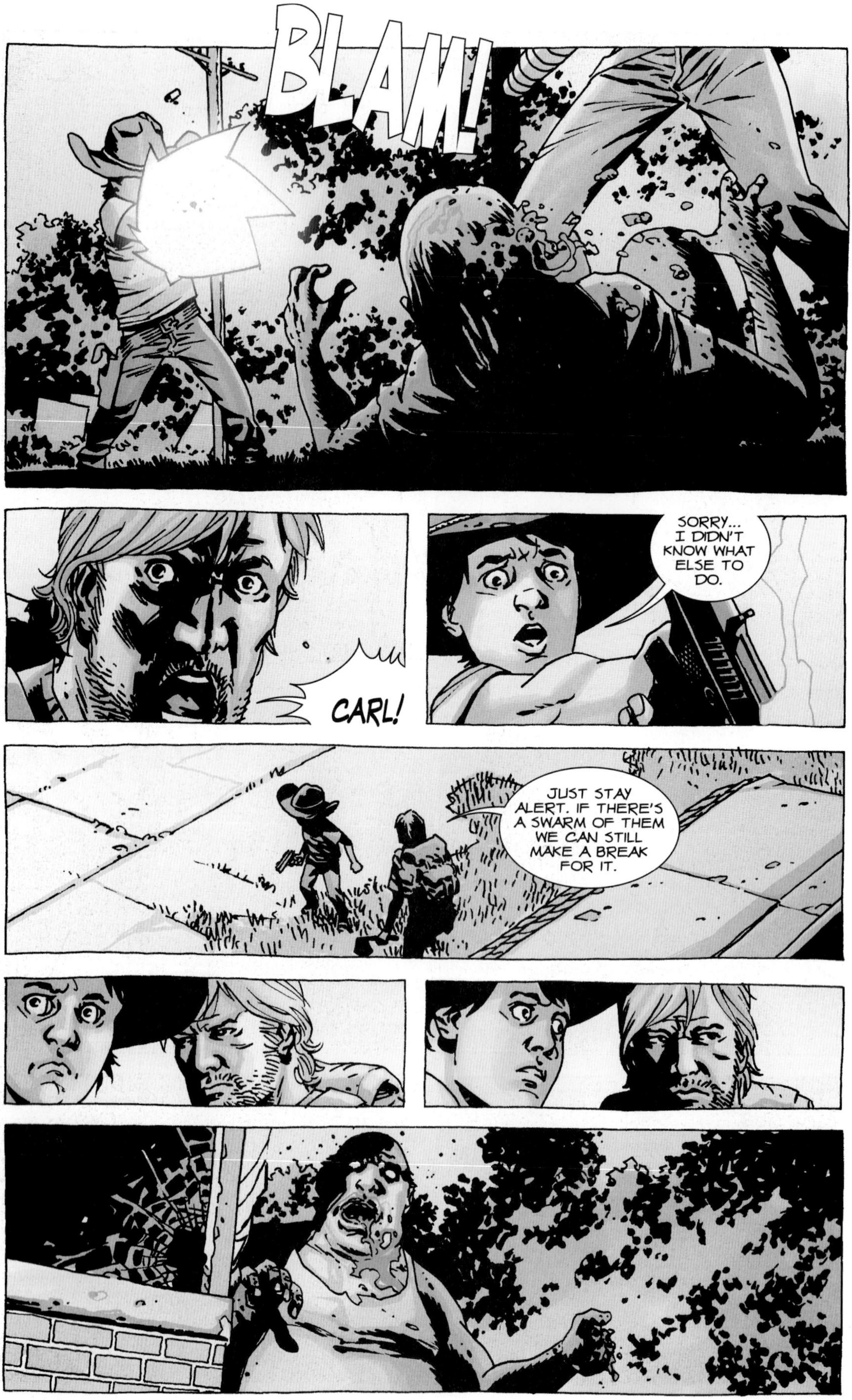
BLAM!
CARL!
SORRY... I DIDN'T KNOW WHAT ELSE TO DO.
JUST STAY ALERT. IF THERE'S A SWARM OF THEM WE CAN STILL MAKE A BREAK FOR IT.

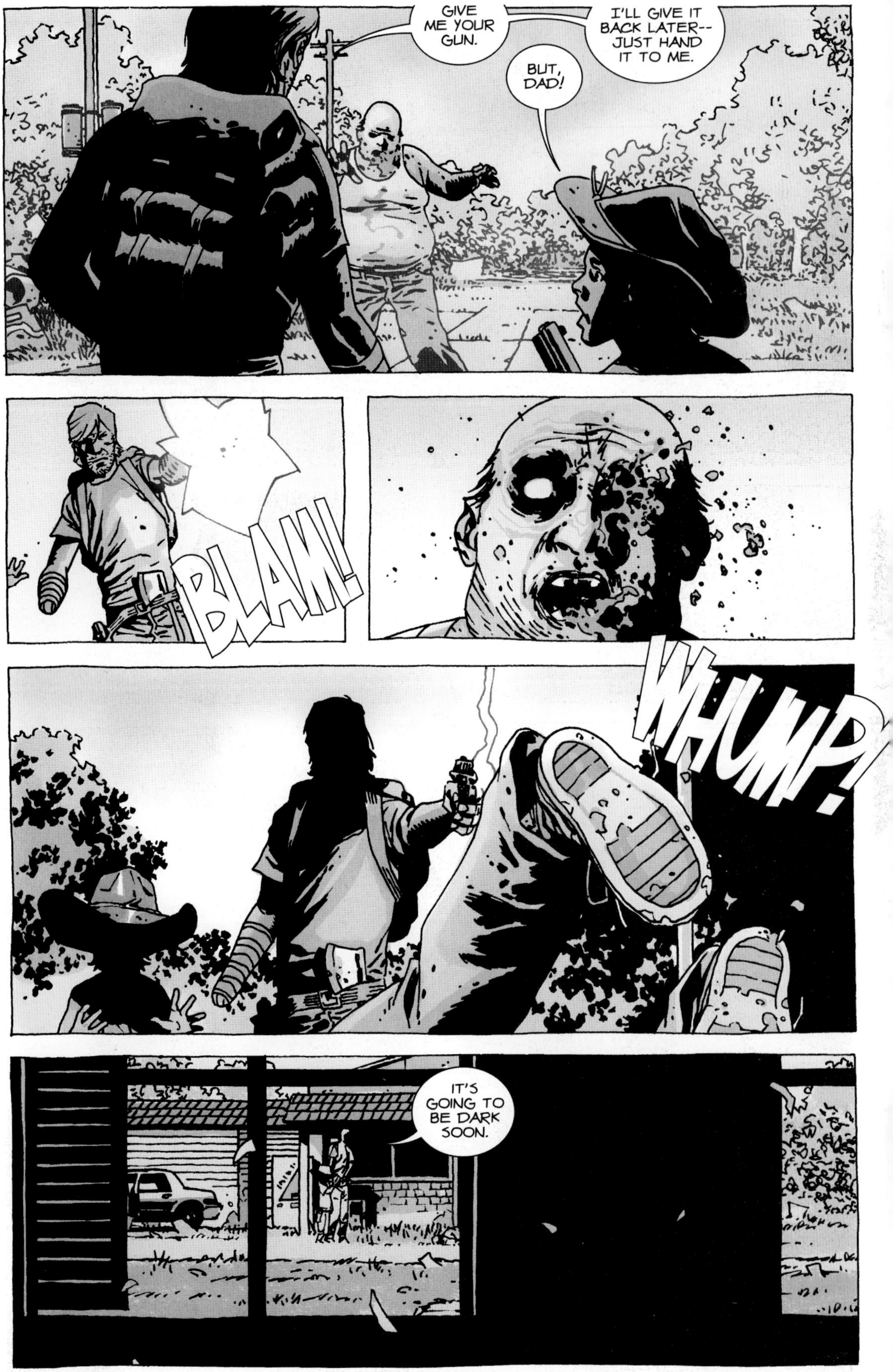
GIVE ME YOUR GUN.
I'LL GIVE IT BACK LATER-- JUST HAND IT TO ME.
BUT, DAD!
BLAM!
WHUMP!
IT'S GOING TO BE DARK SOON.

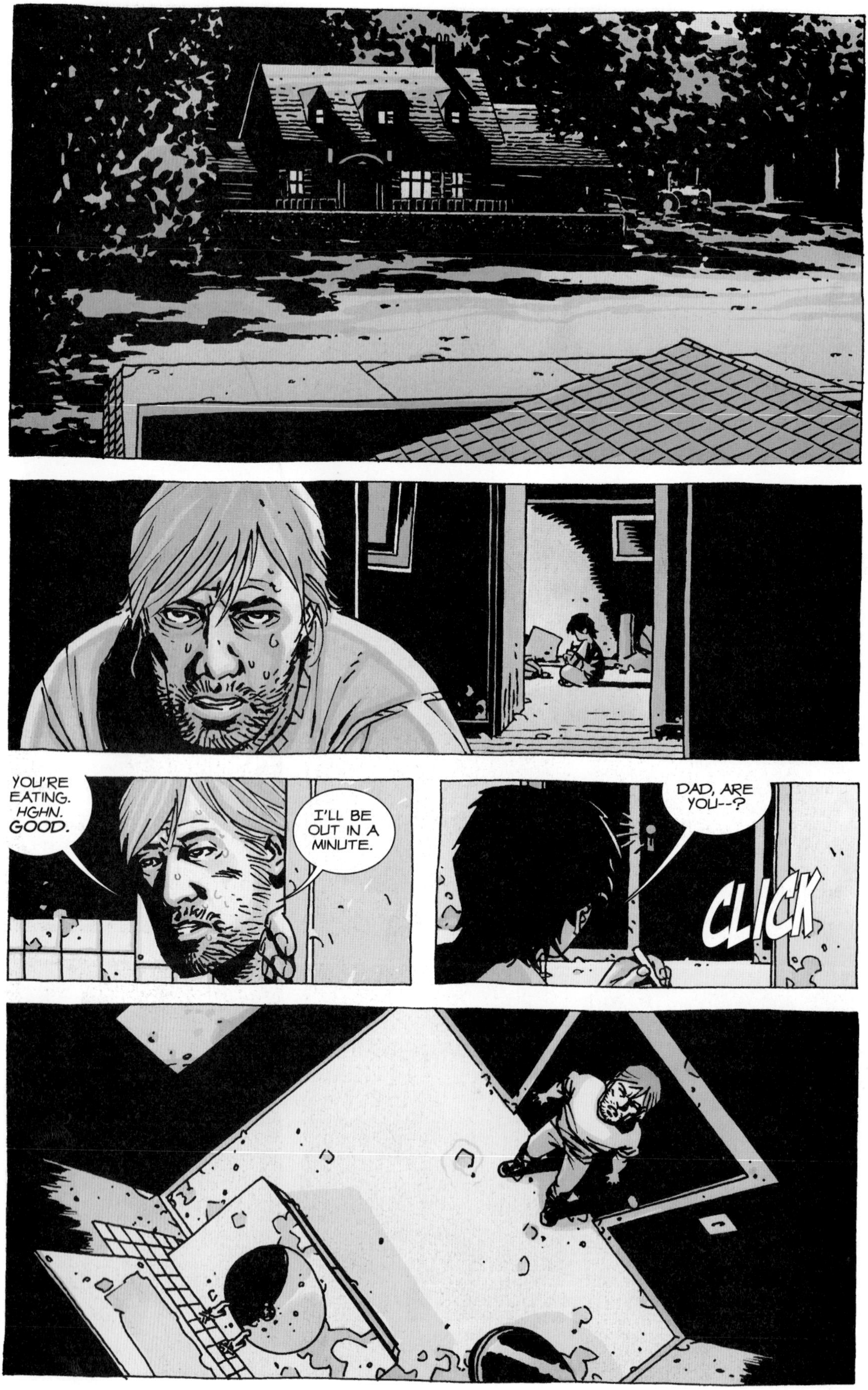
YOU'RE EATING. HGHN. GOOD.
I'LL BE OUT IN A MINUTE.
DAD, ARE YOU--?
CLICK

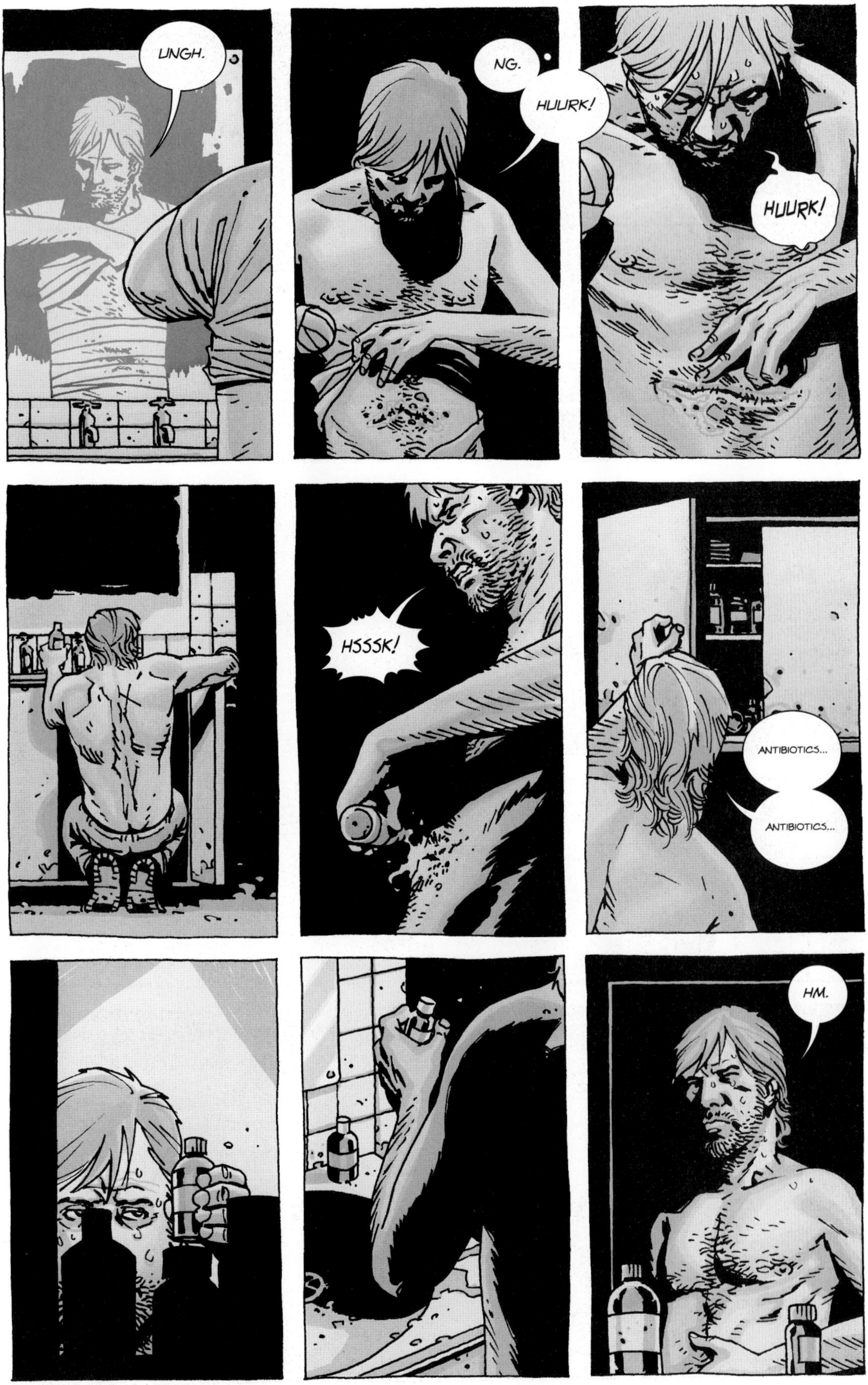
UNGH.
NG.
HUURK!
HUURK!
HSSSK!
ANTIBIOTICS...
ANTIBIOTICS...
HM.

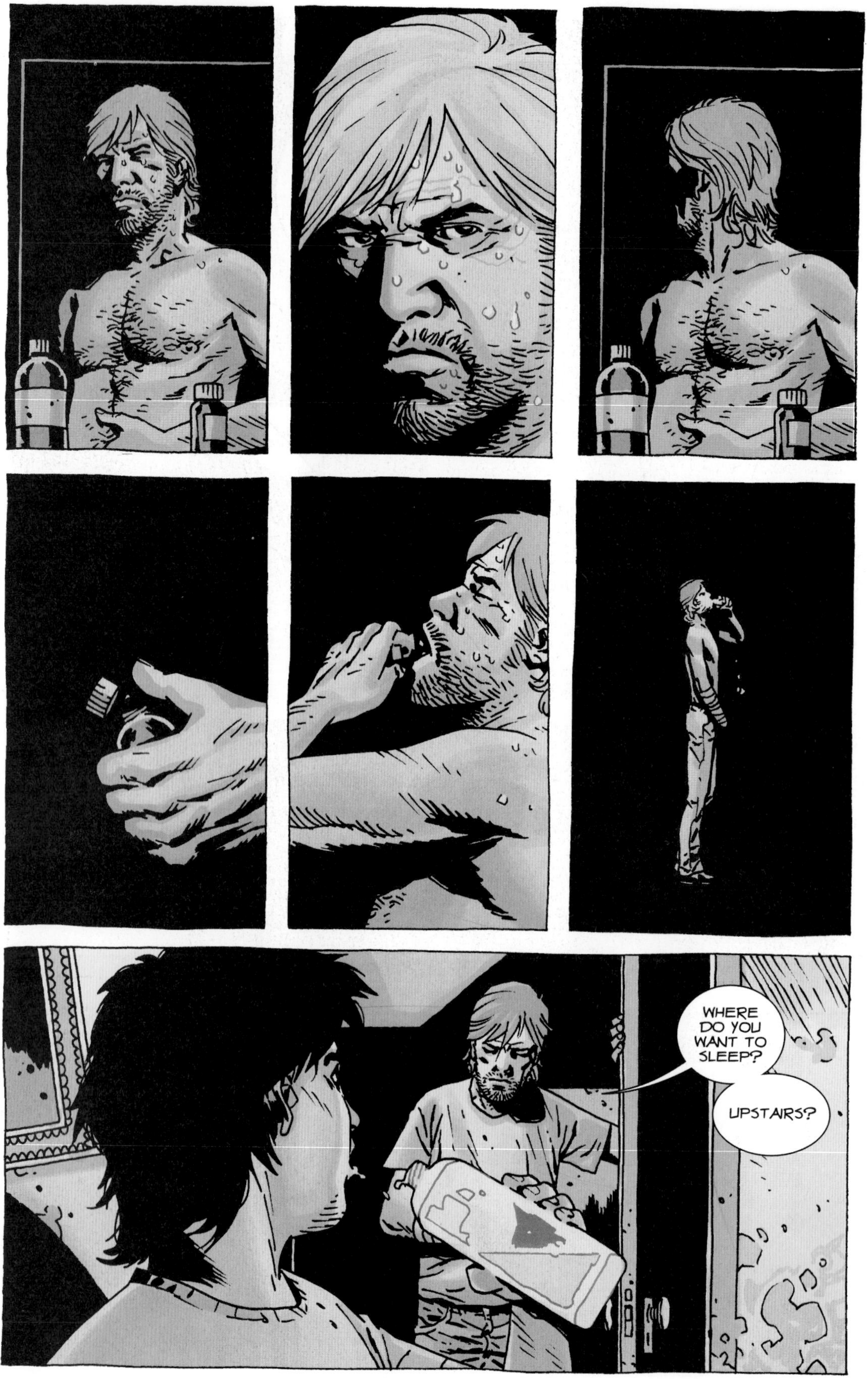
WHERE DO YOU WANT TO SLEEP?
UPSTAIRS?

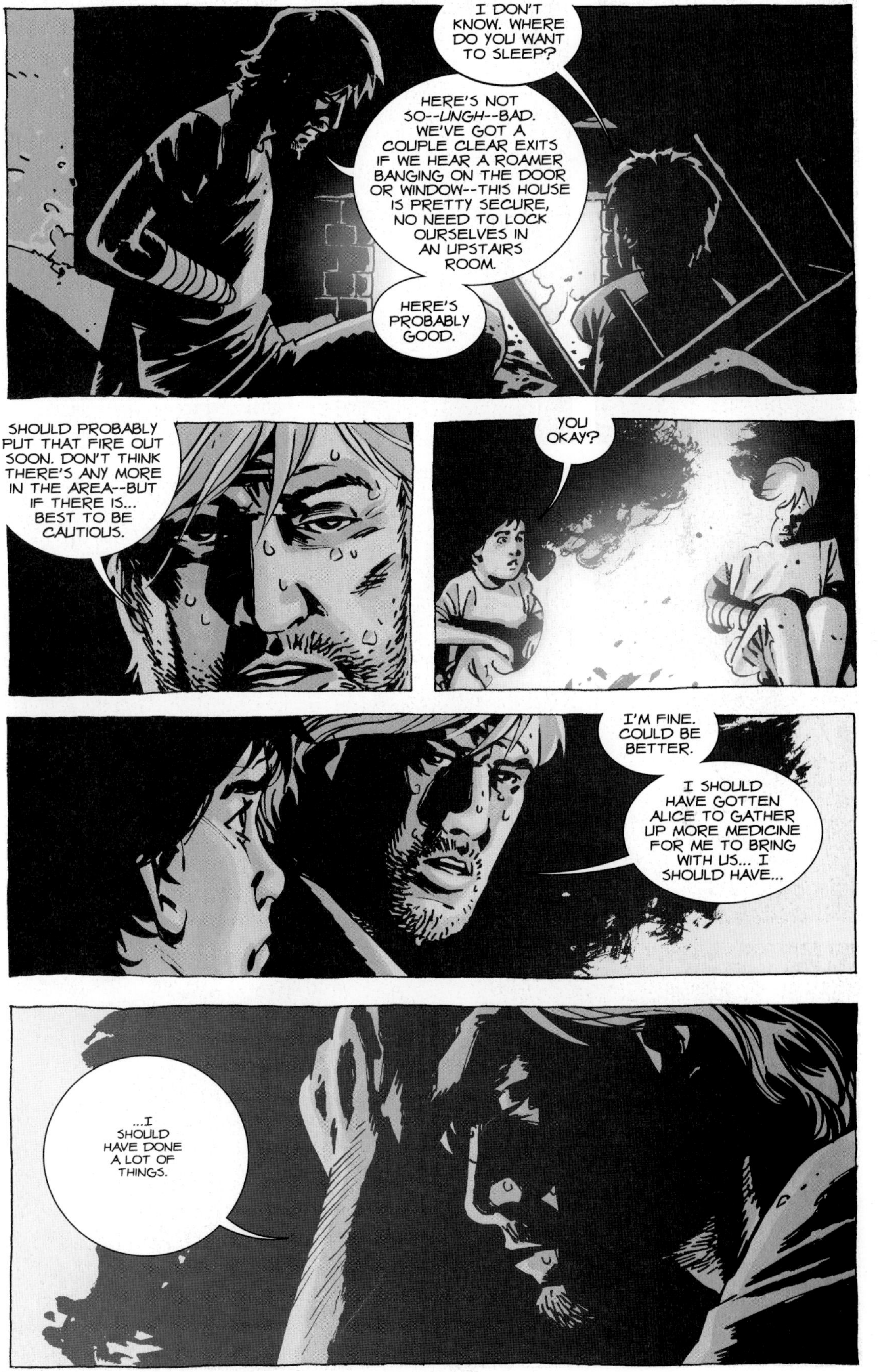
I DON'T KNOW. WHERE DO YOU WANT TO SLEEP?
HERE'S NOT SO--UNGH--BAD. WE'VE GOT A COUPLE CLEAR EXITS IF WE HEAR A ROAMER BANGING ON THE DOOR OR WINDOW--THIS HOUSE IS PRETTY SECURE, NO NEED TO LOCK OURSELVES IN AN UPSTAIRS ROOM.
HERE'S PROBABLY GOOD.
SHOULD PROBABLY PUT THAT FIRE OUT SOON. DON'T THINK THERE'S ANY MORE IN THE AREA--BUT IF THERE IS... BEST TO BE CAUTIOUS.
YOU OKAY?
I'M FINE. COULD BE BETTER.
I SHOULD HAVE GOTTEN ALICE TO GATHER UP MORE MEDICINE FOR ME TO BRING WITH US... I SHOULD HAVE...
...I SHOULD HAVE DONE A LOT OF THINGS.

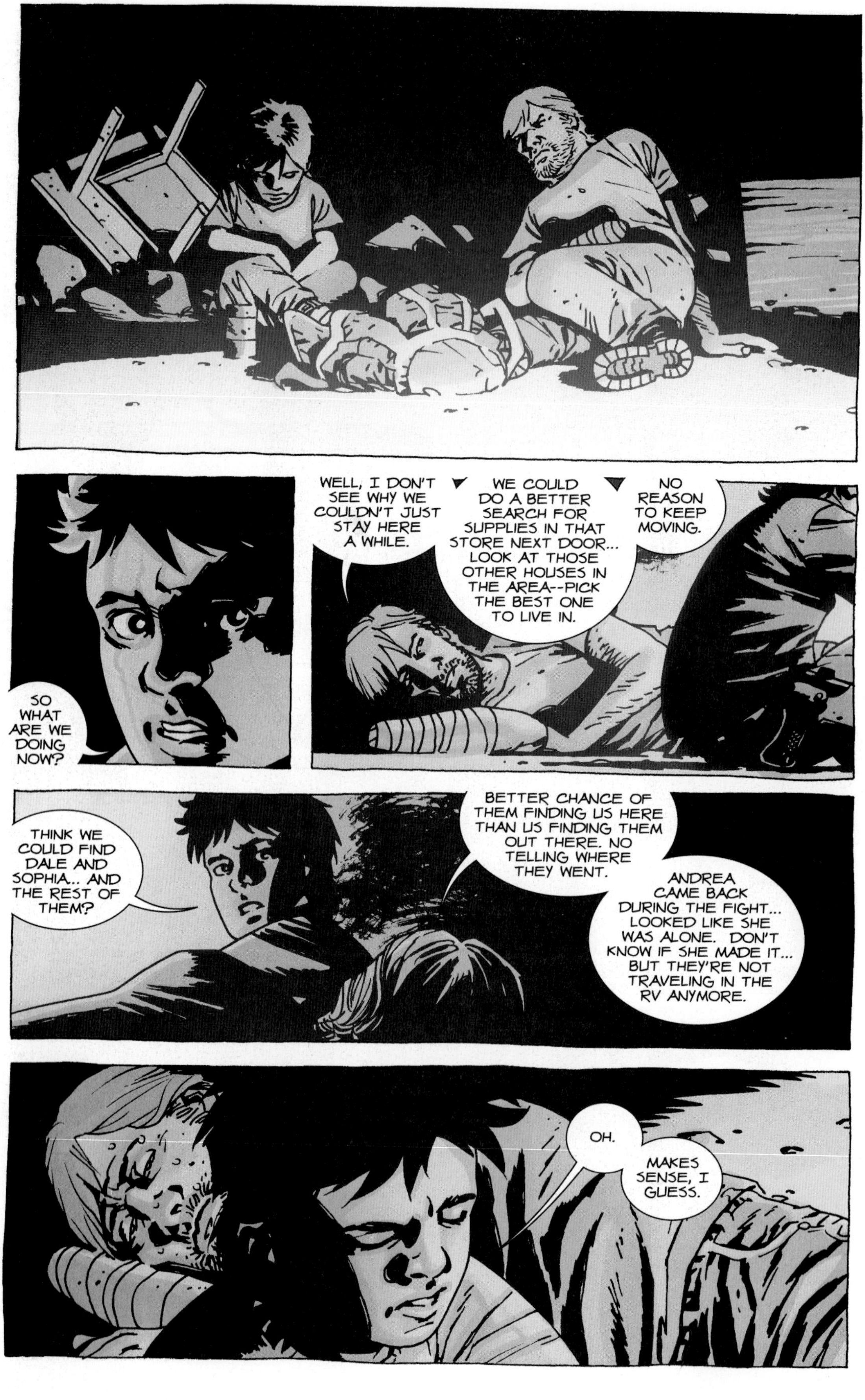
SO WHAT ARE WE DOING NOW?
WELL, I DON'T SEE WHY WE COULDN'T JUST STAY HERE A WHILE.
WE COULD DO A BETTER SEARCH FOR SUPPLIES IN THAT STORE NEXT DOOR... LOOK AT THOSE OTHER HOUSES IN THE AREA--PICK THE BEST ONE TO LIVE IN.
NO REASON TO KEEP MOVING.
THINK WE COULD FIND DALE AND SOPHIA... AND THE REST OF THEM?
BETTER CHANCE OF THEM FINDING US HERE THAN US FINDING THEM OUT THERE. NO TELLING WHERE THEY WENT.
ANDREA CAME BACK DURING THE FIGHT... LOOKED LIKE SHE WAS ALONE. DON'T KNOW IF SHE MADE IT... BUT THEY'RE NOT TRAVELING IN THE RV ANYMORE.
OH.
MAKES SENSE, I GUESS.

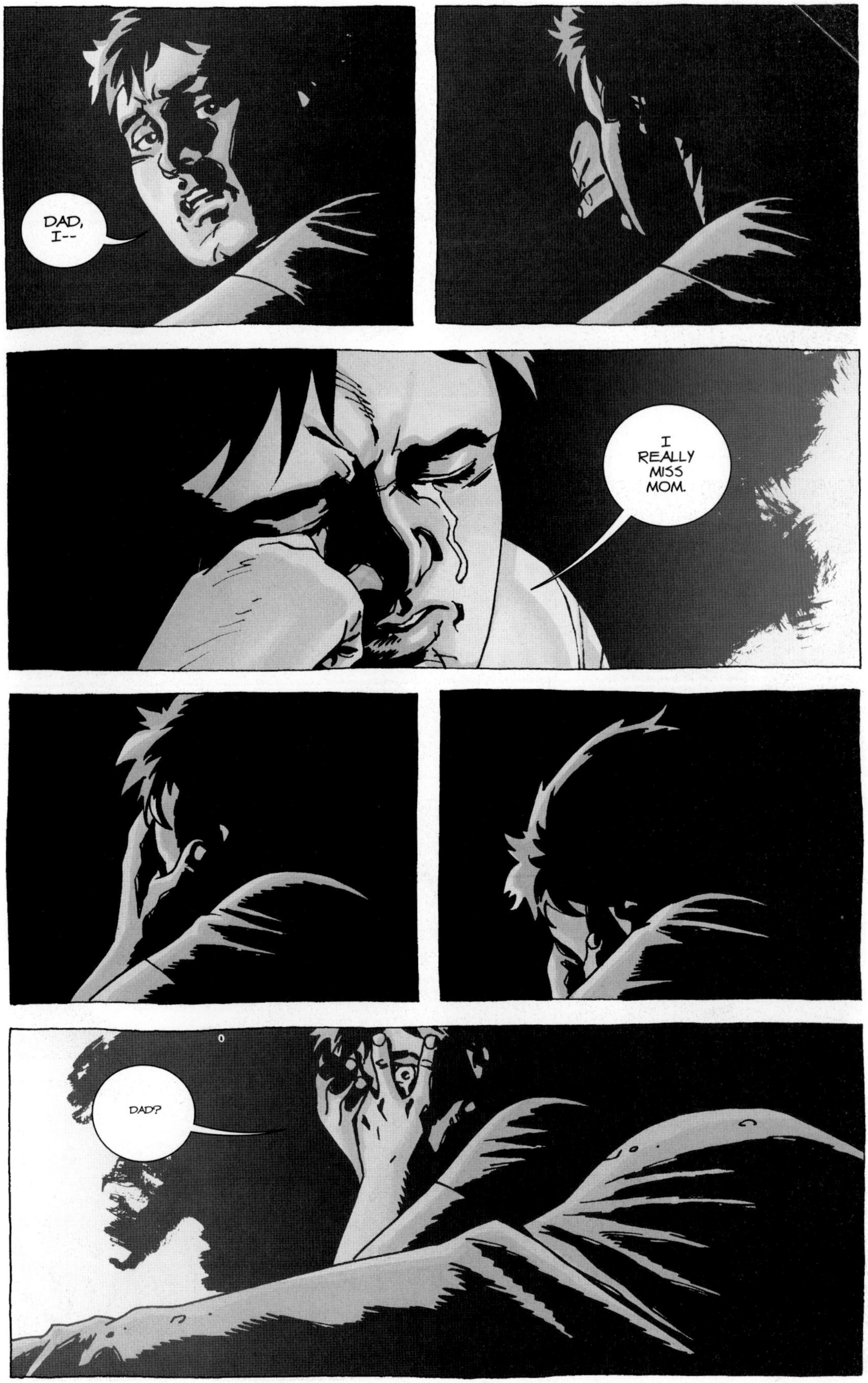
DAD, I--
I REALLY MISS MOM.
DAD?

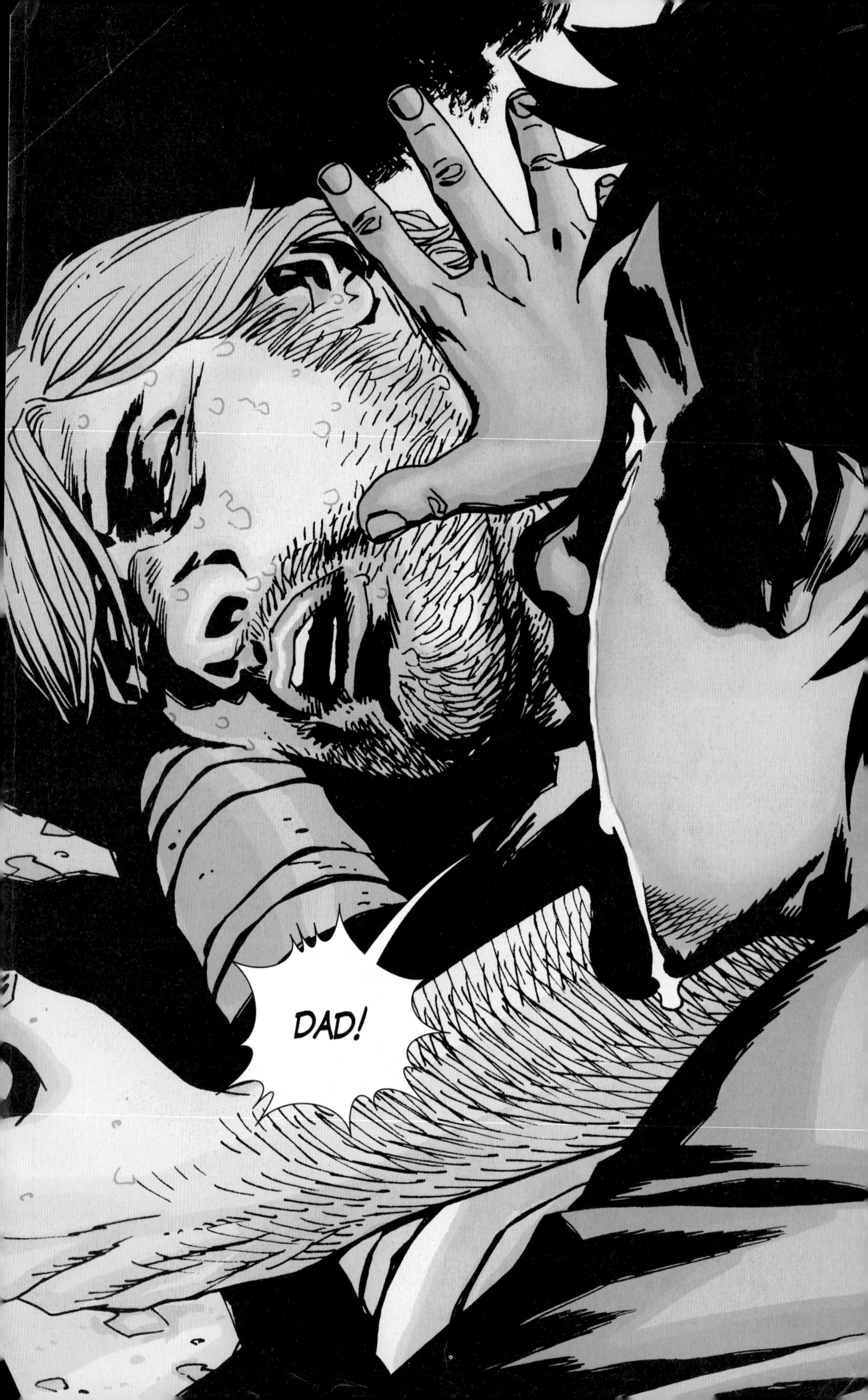
DAD!

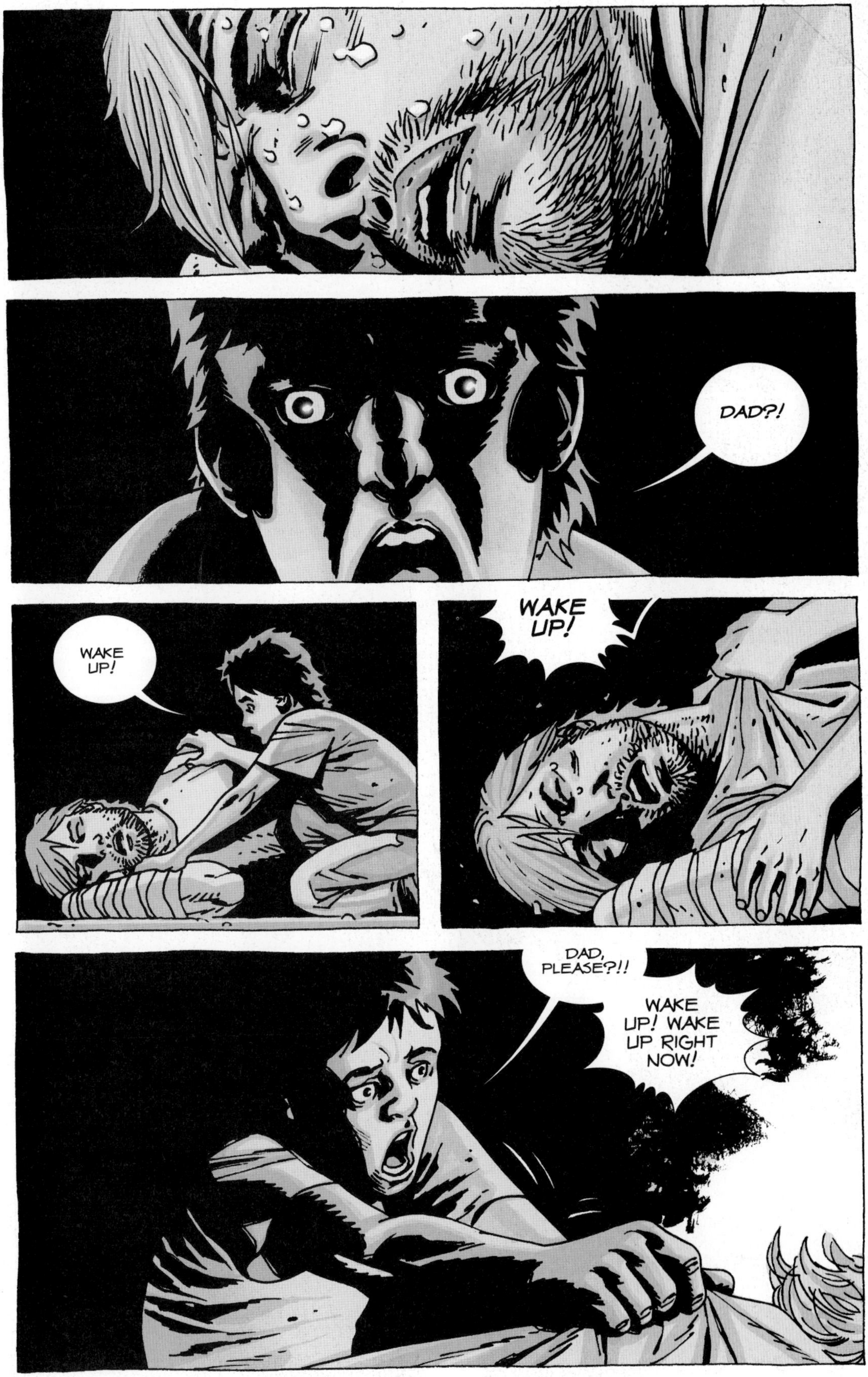
DAD?!
WAKE UP!
WAKE UP!
DAD, PLEASE?!!
WAKE UP! WAKE UP RIGHT NOW!

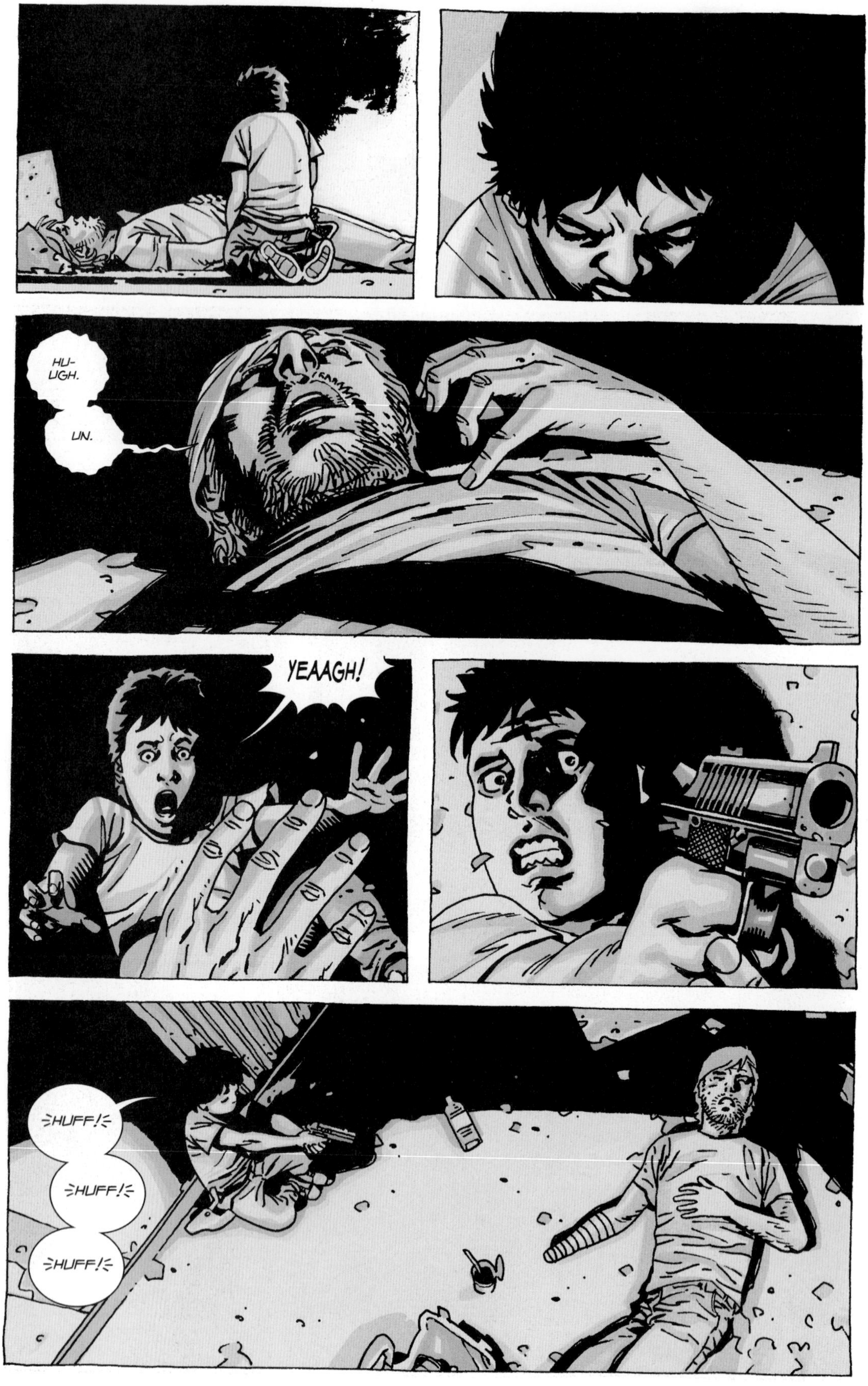
HU-
UGH.
UN.
YEAAGH!
HUFF!
HUFF!
HUFF!

HUFF!
HUFF!
NOT MOVING-- NOT DEAD.
YOU'RE STILL BREATHING.
YOU'RE JUST SICK.
IF YOU'RE SICK--I DON'T KNOW WHAT TO DO...
I DON'T KNOW WHAT TO DO, DAD.

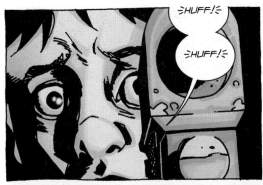

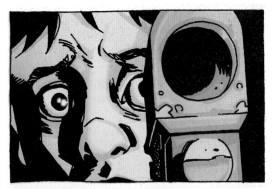

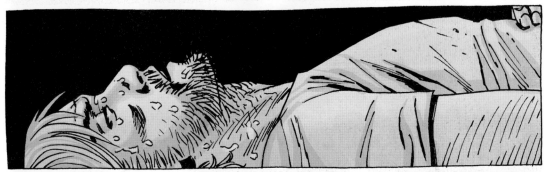

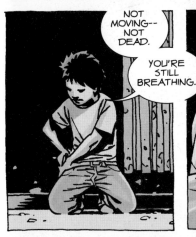

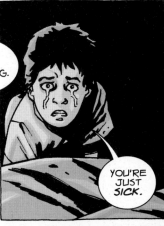

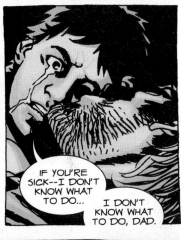

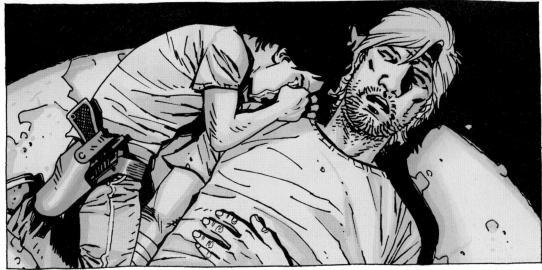

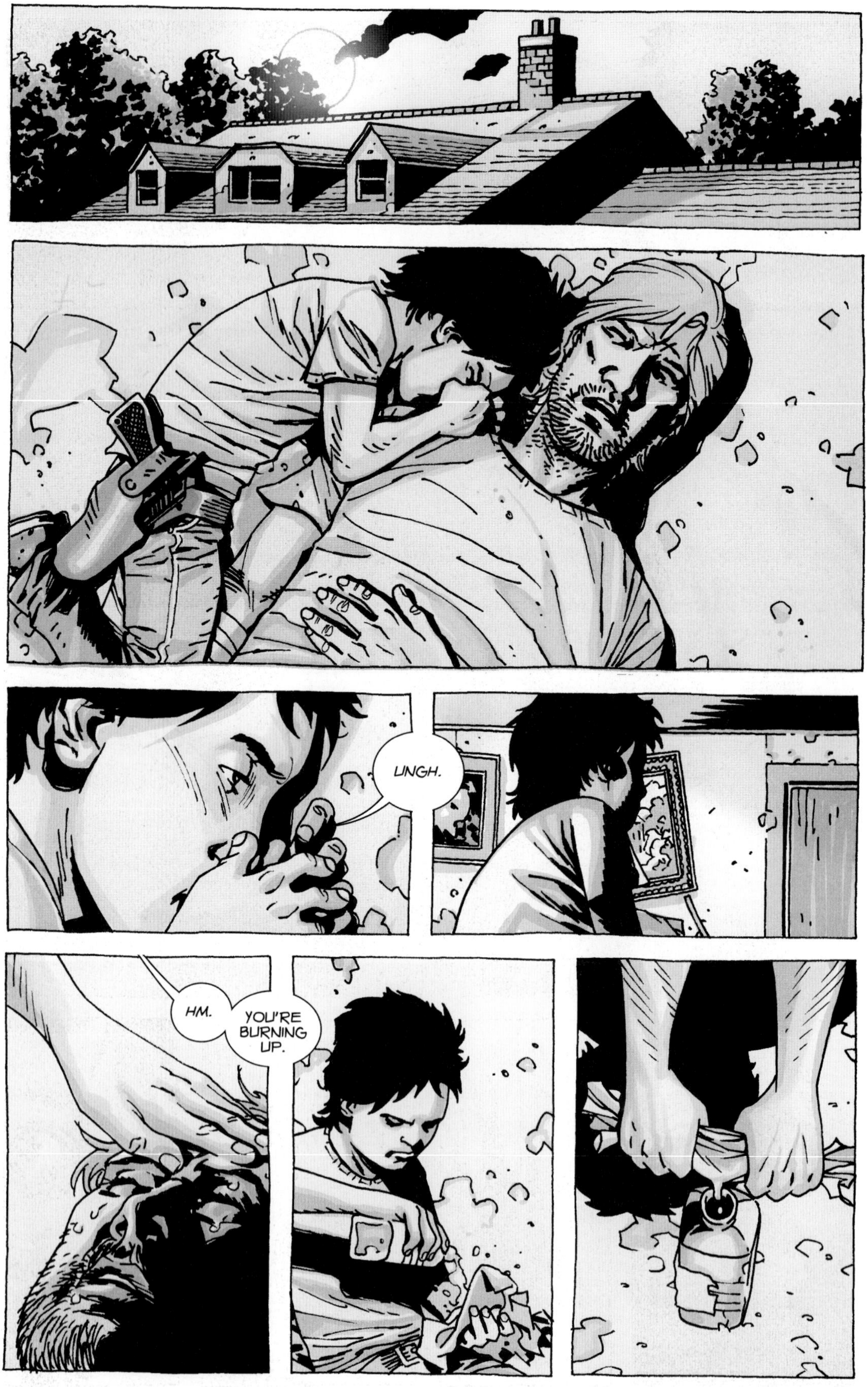
UNGH.
HM.
YOU'RE BURNING UP.

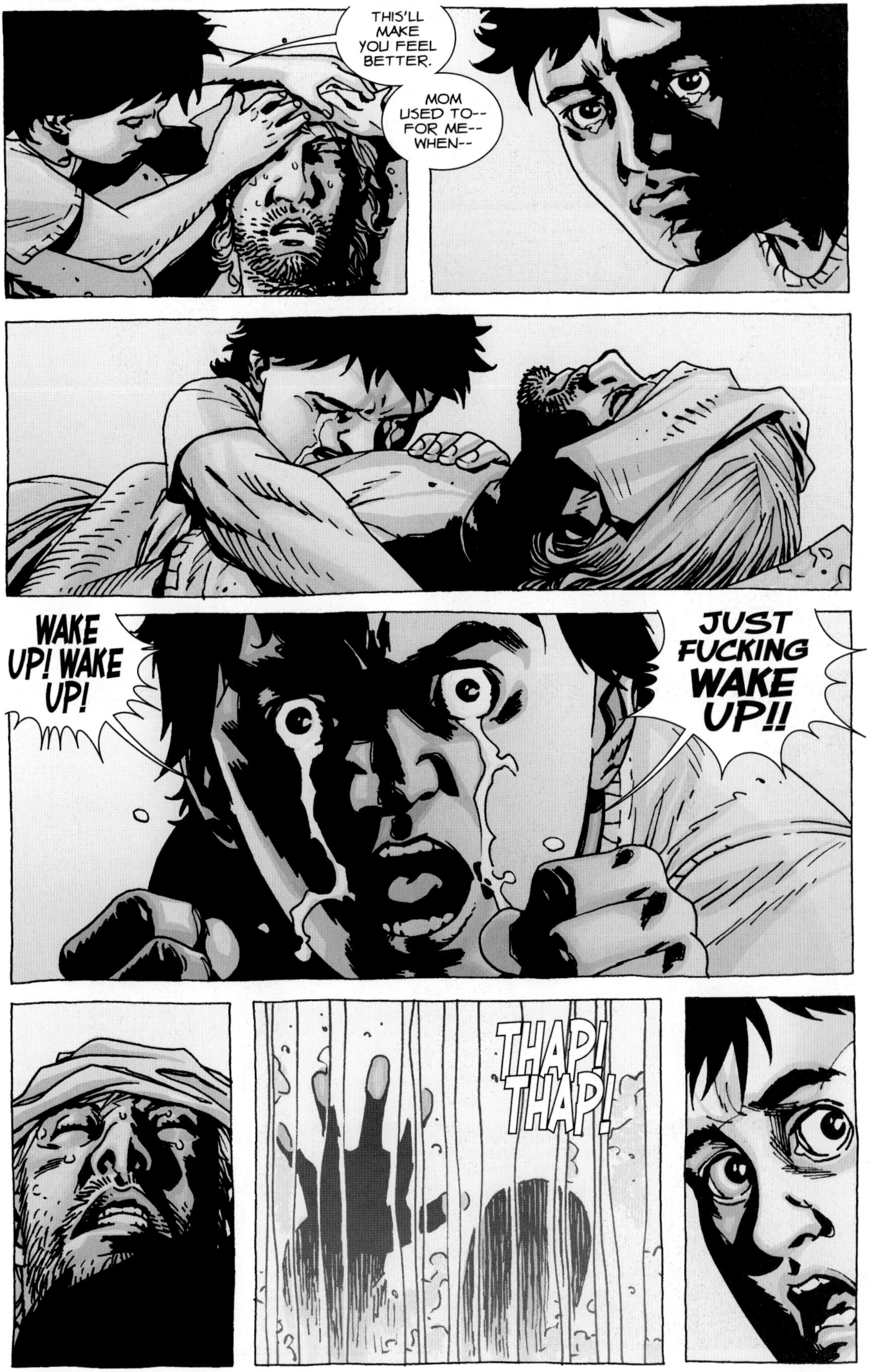
THIS'LL MAKE YOU FEEL BETTER.
MOM USED TO-- FOR ME-- WHEN--
WAKE UP! WAKE UP! WAKE UP!
JUST FUCKING WAKE UP!!
THAP! THAP!

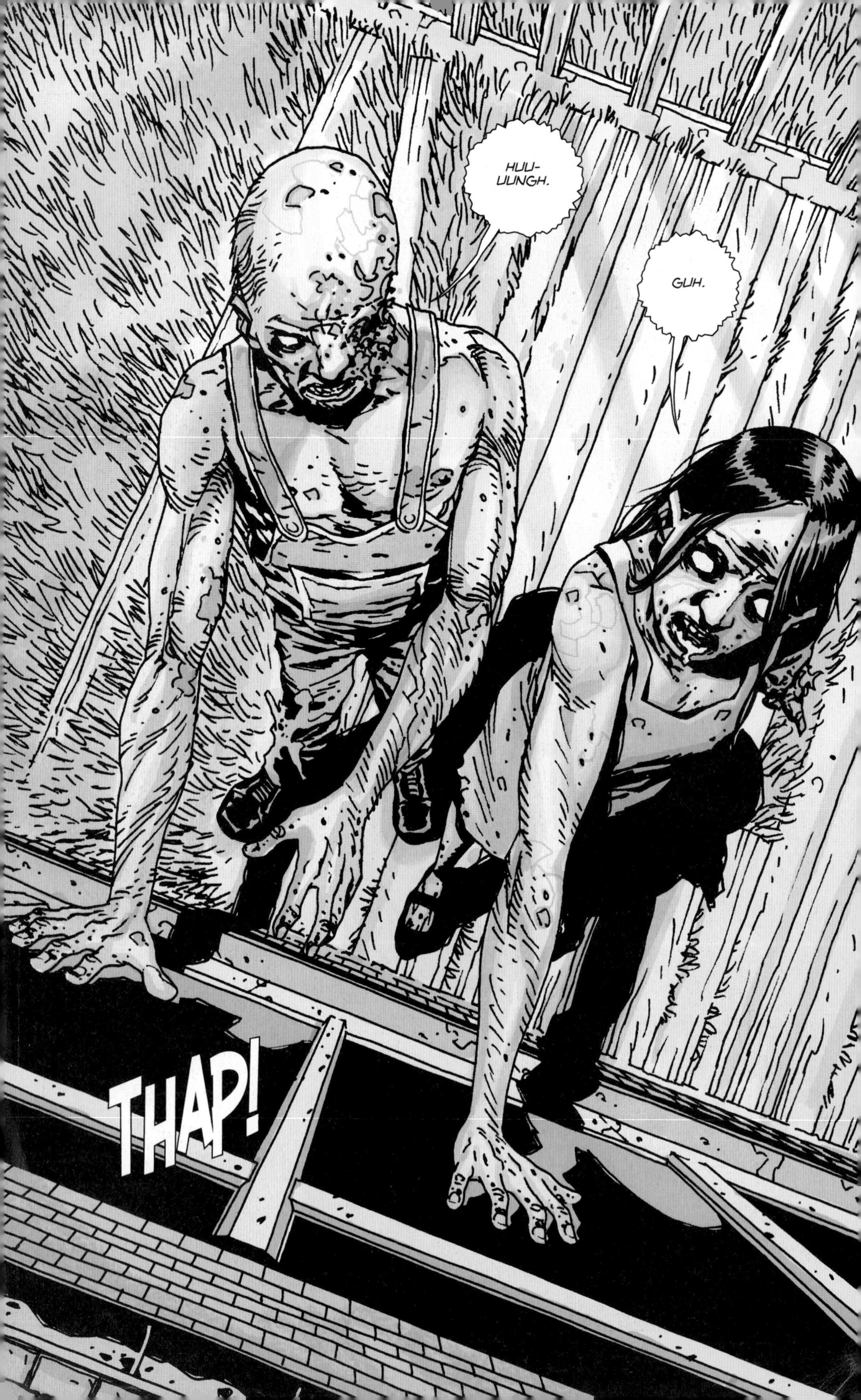
HUU-
UUNGH.
GUH.
THAP!

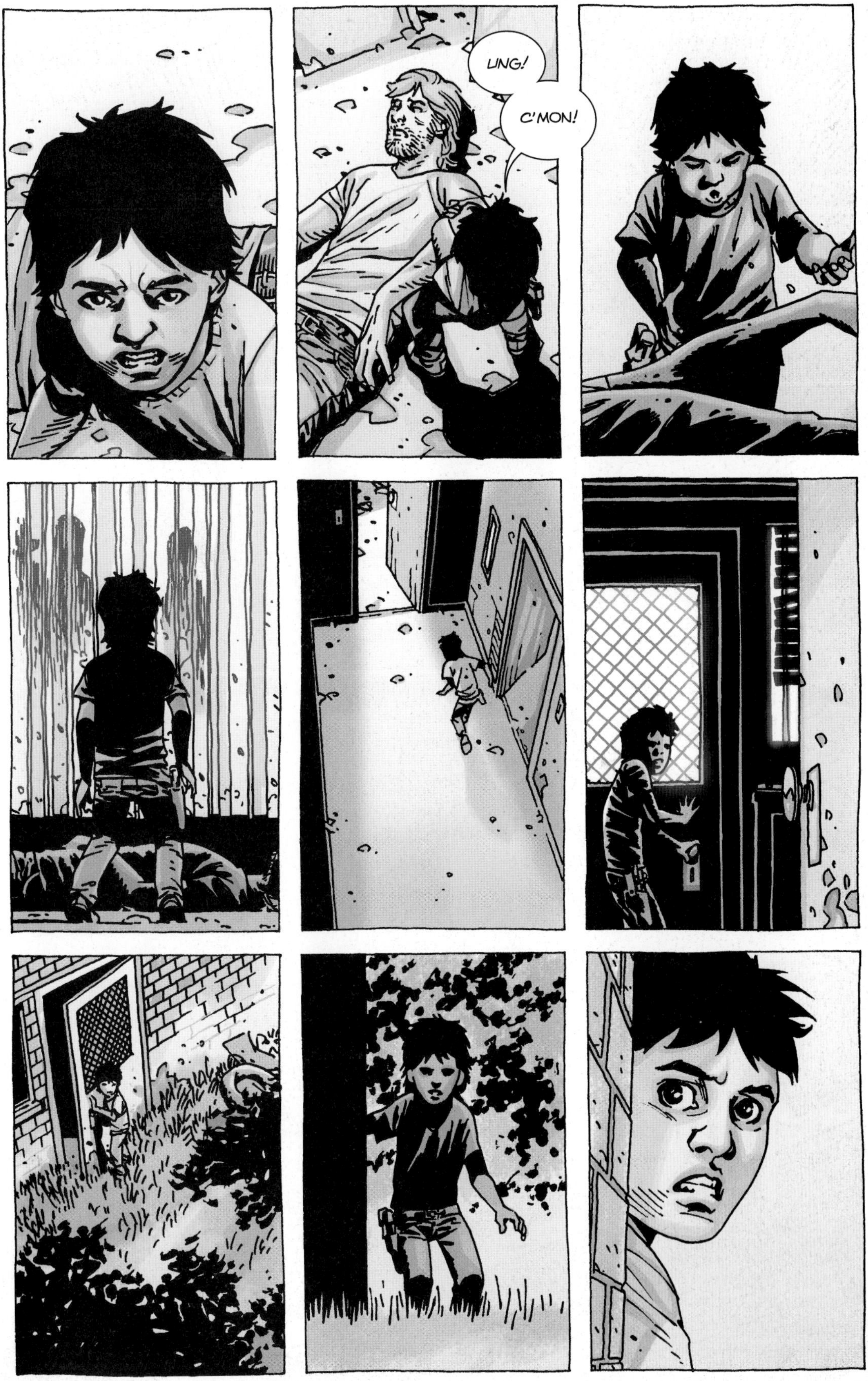
UNG!
C'MON!

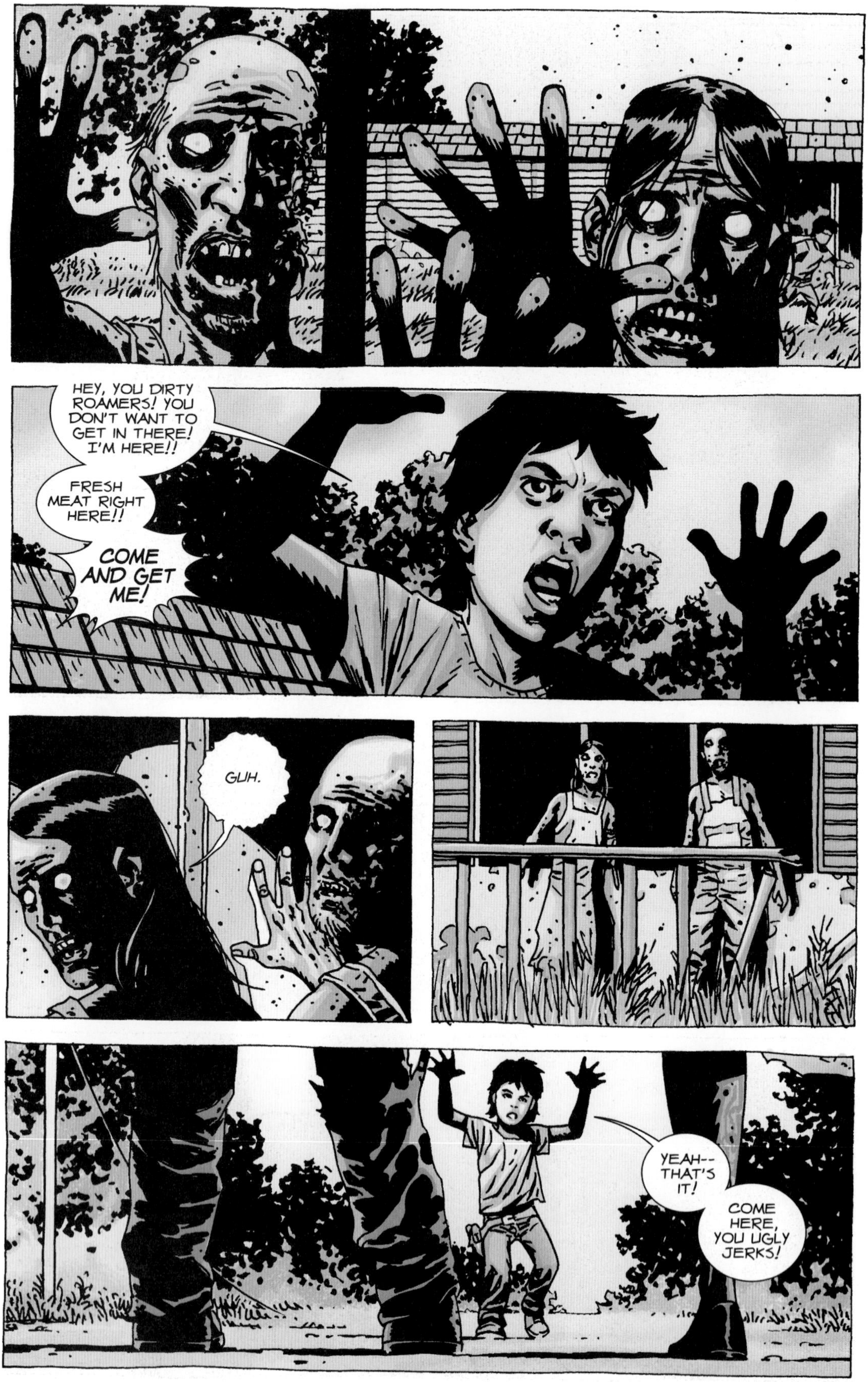
HEY, YOU DIRTY ROAMERS! YOU DON'T WANT TO GET IN THERE! I'M HERE!!
FRESH MEAT RIGHT HERE!!
COME AND GET ME!
GUH.
YEAH-- THAT'S IT!
COME HERE, YOU UGLY JERKS!

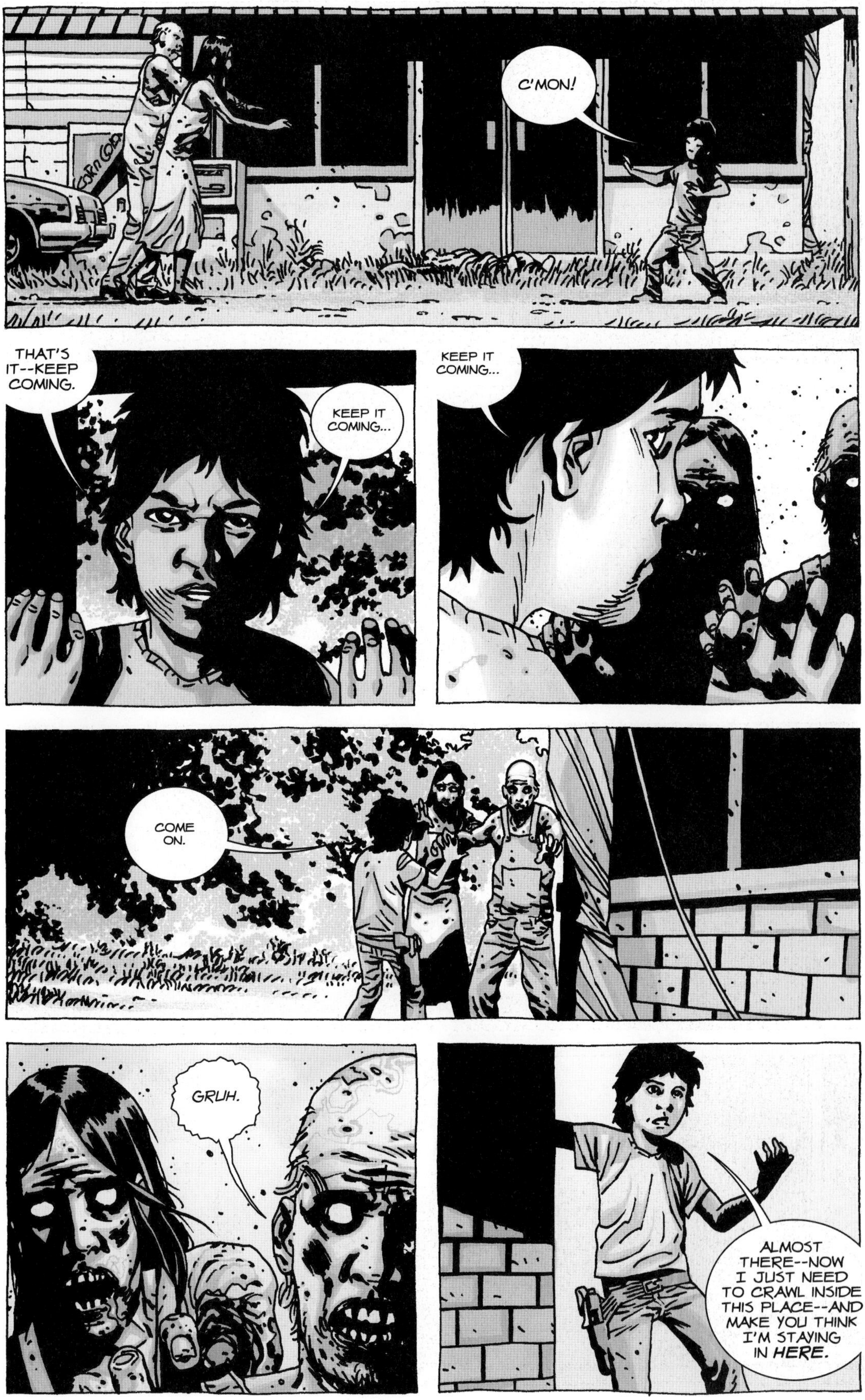
C'MON!
THAT'S IT--KEEP COMING.
KEEP IT COMING...
KEEP IT COMING...
COME ON.
GRUH.
ALMOST THERE--NOW I JUST NEED TO CRAWL INSIDE THIS PLACE--AND MAKE YOU THINK I'M STAYING IN *HERE.*

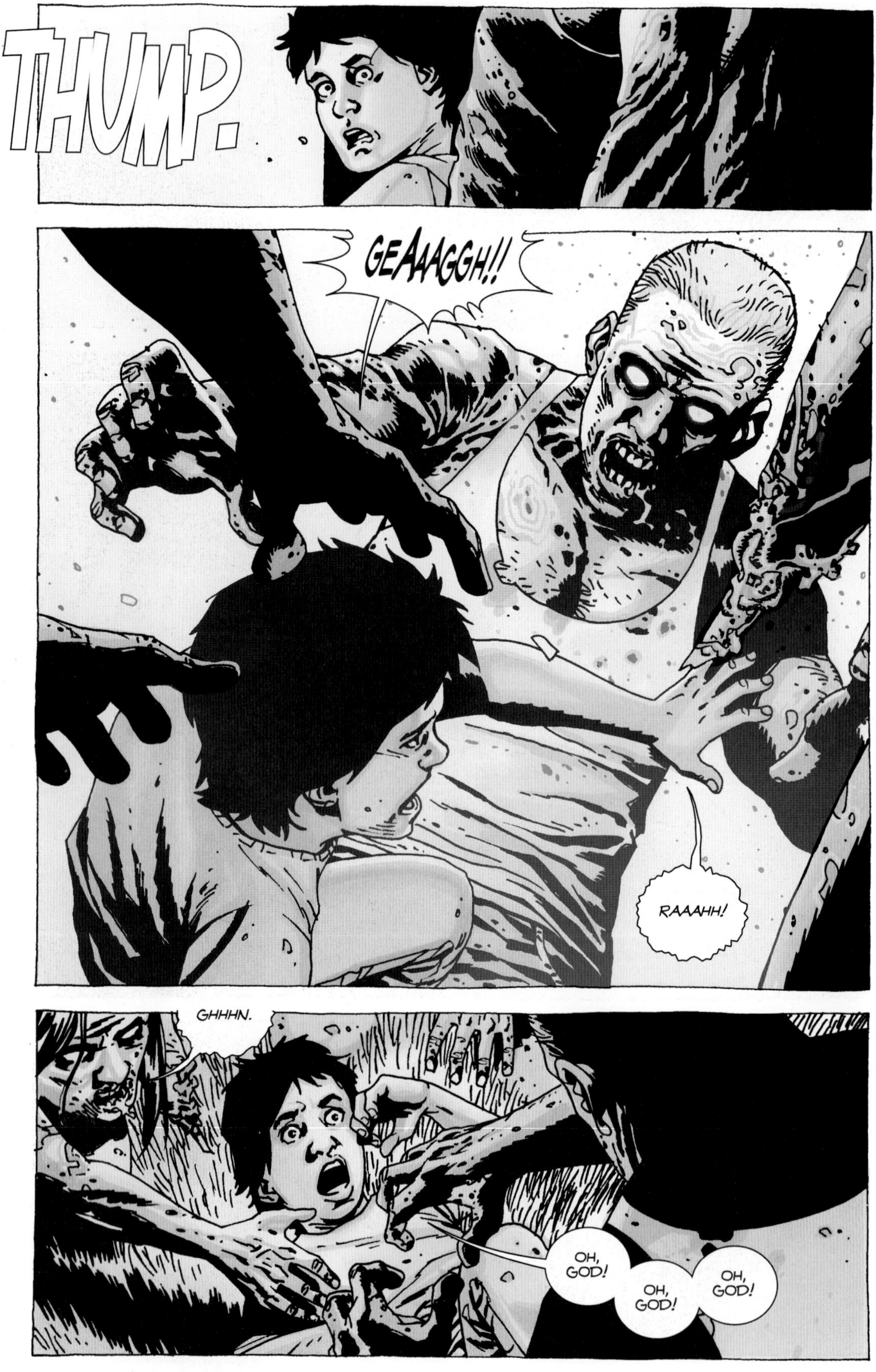
THUMP.
GEAAAGGH!!
RAAAHH!
GHHHN.
OH, GOD!
OH, GOD!
OH, GOD!

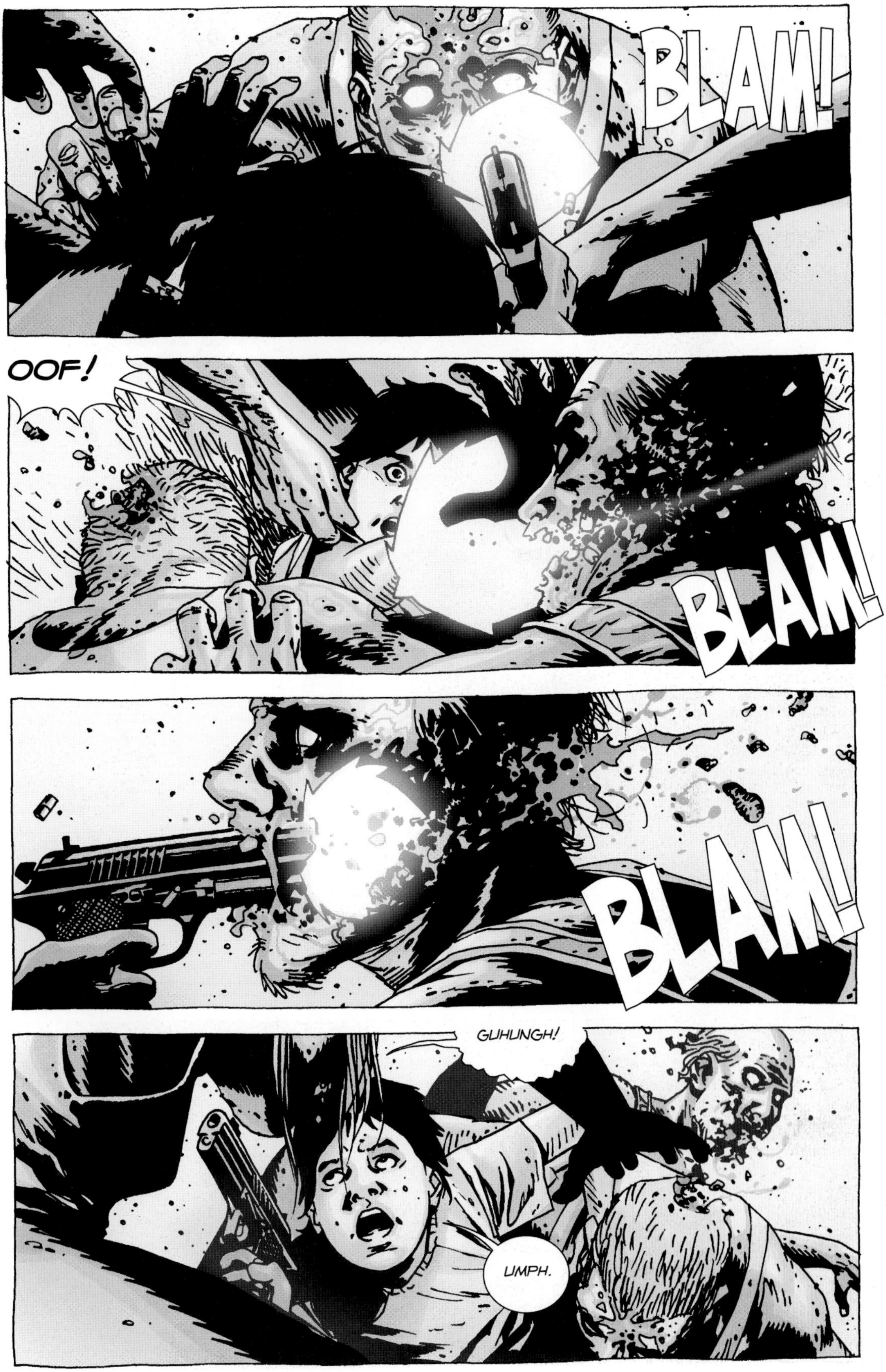
BLAM!
OOF!
BLAM!
BLAM!
GUHUNGH!
UMPH.

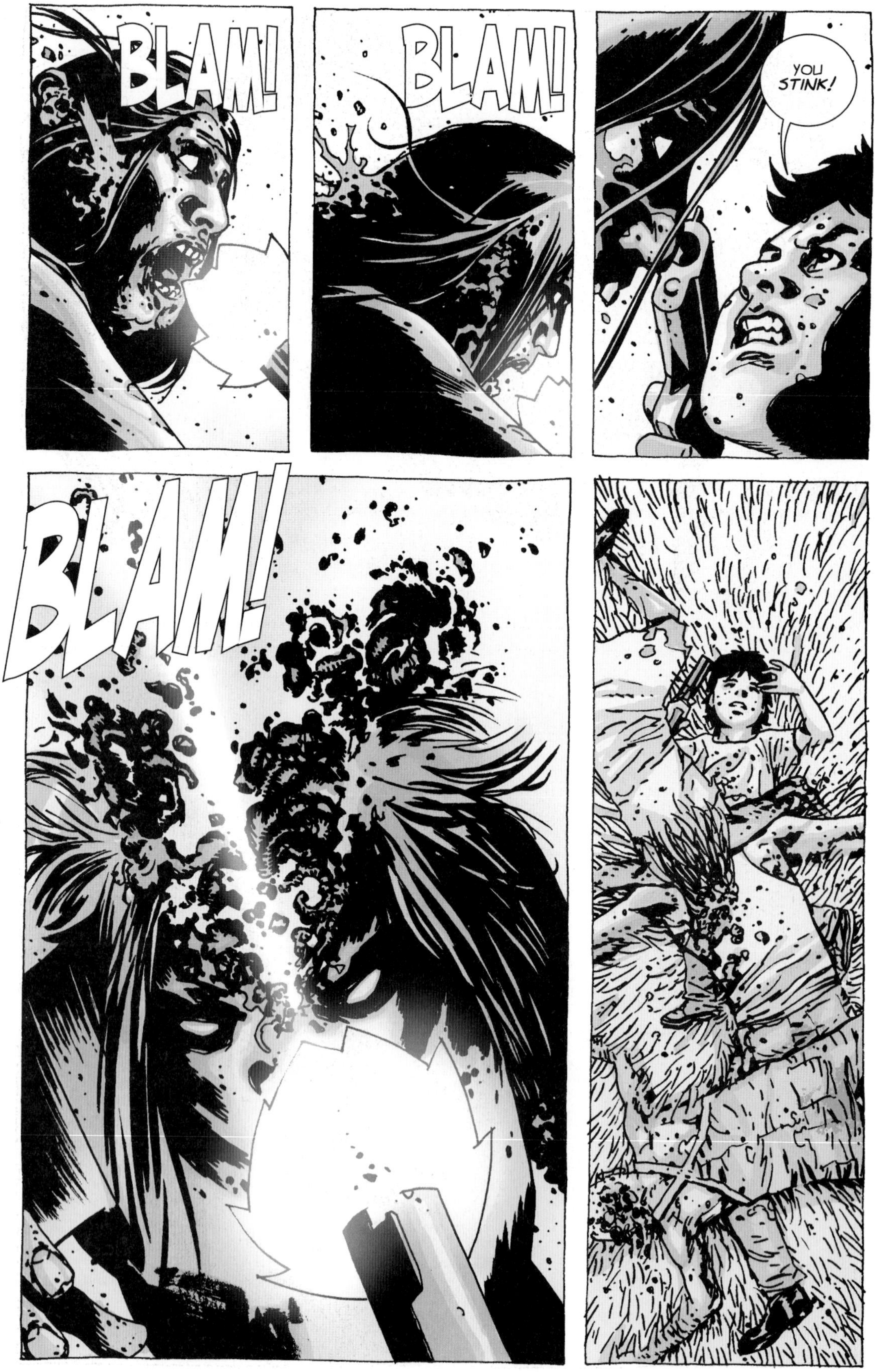
BLAM!
BLAM!
YOU STINK!
BLAM!

ULP!

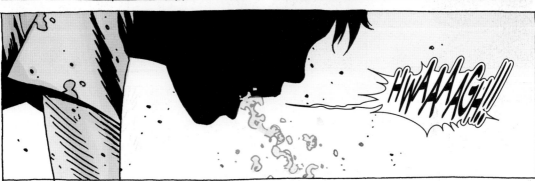

HWAAAAGH!!

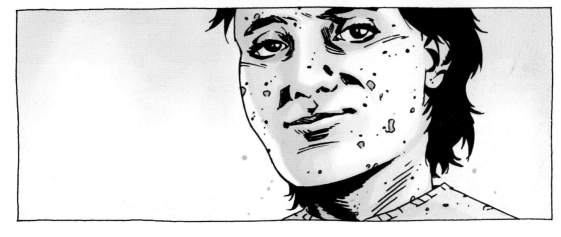

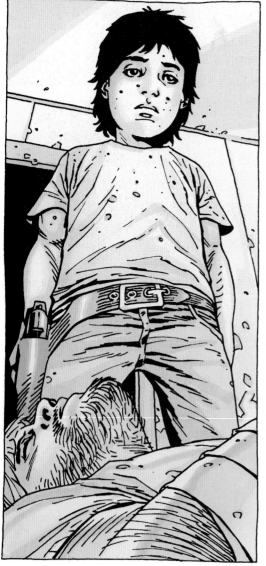

I JUST KILLED THREE ROAMERS, DAD.

THREE.

I KILLED THEM ALL BY MYSELF.

IT WAS JUST ME.

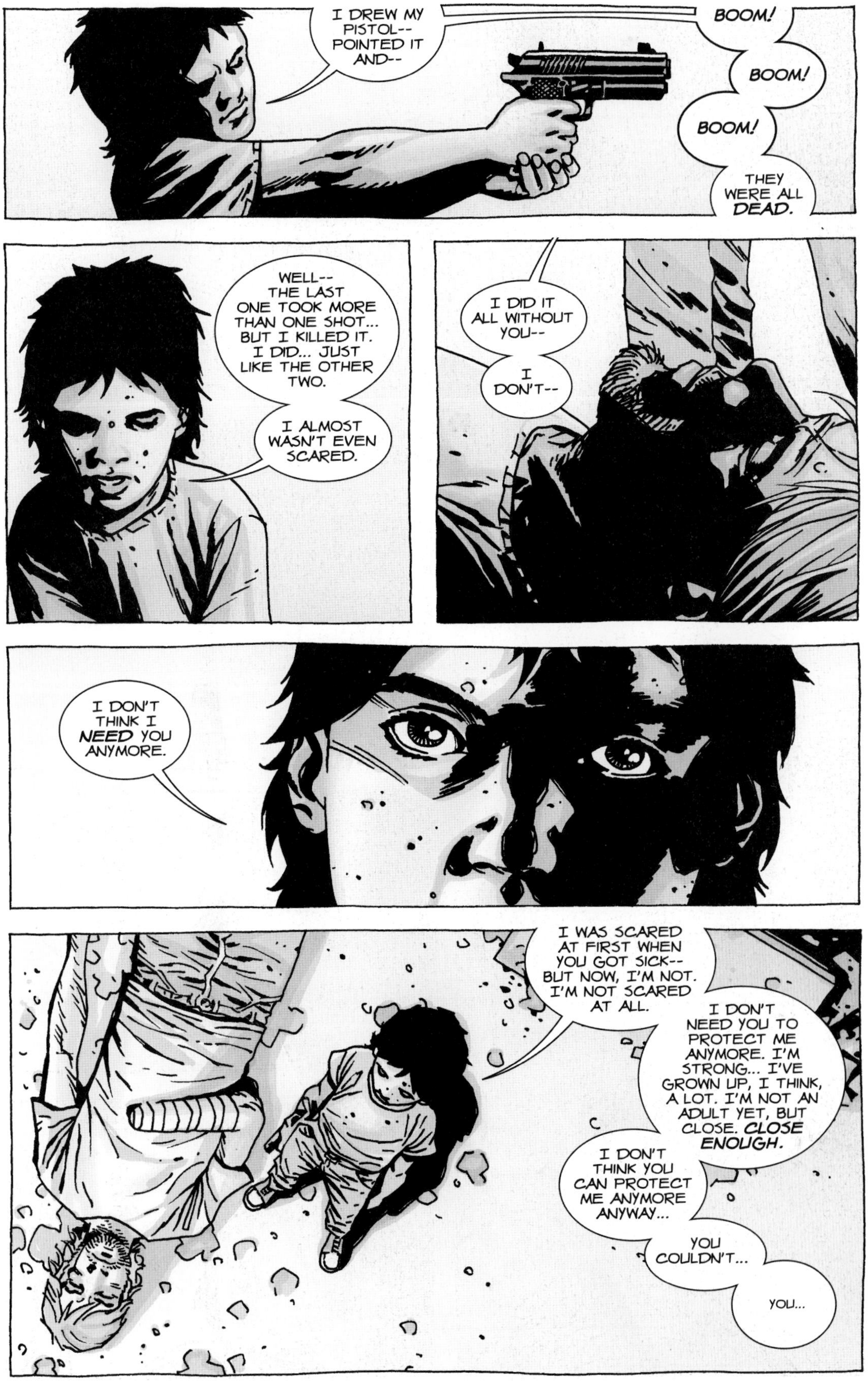

I DREW MY PISTOL-- POINTED IT AND--
BOOM!
BOOM!
BOOM!
THEY WERE ALL DEAD.
WELL-- THE LAST ONE TOOK MORE THAN ONE SHOT... BUT I KILLED IT. I DID... JUST LIKE THE OTHER TWO.
I ALMOST WASN'T EVEN SCARED.
I DID IT ALL WITHOUT YOU--
I DON'T--
I DON'T THINK I NEED YOU ANYMORE.
I WAS SCARED AT FIRST WHEN YOU GOT SICK-- BUT NOW, I'M NOT. I'M NOT SCARED AT ALL.
I DON'T NEED YOU TO PROTECT ME ANYMORE. I'M STRONG... I'VE GROWN UP, I THINK, A LOT. I'M NOT AN ADULT YET, BUT CLOSE. CLOSE ENOUGH.
I DON'T THINK YOU CAN PROTECT ME ANYMORE ANYWAY...
YOU COULDN'T...
YOU...

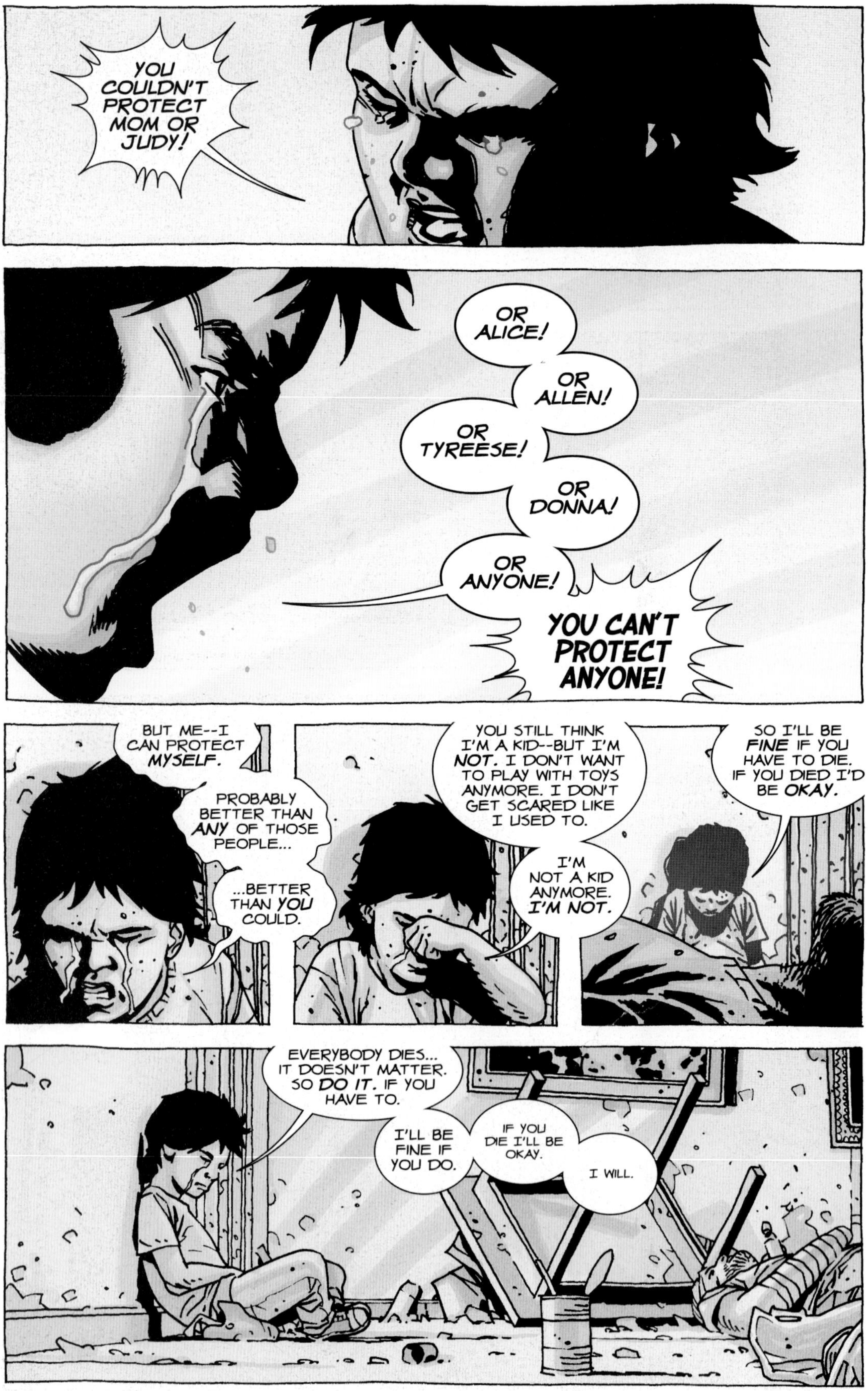
YOU COULDN'T PROTECT MOM OR JUDY!
OR ALICE!
OR ALLEN!
OR TYREESE!
OR DONNA!
OR ANYONE!
YOU CAN'T PROTECT ANYONE!
BUT ME--I CAN PROTECT MYSELF.
PROBABLY BETTER THAN ANY OF THOSE PEOPLE...
...BETTER THAN YOU COULD.
YOU STILL THINK I'M A KID--BUT I'M NOT. I DON'T WANT TO PLAY WITH TOYS ANYMORE. I DON'T GET SCARED LIKE I USED TO.
I'M NOT A KID ANYMORE. I'M NOT.
SO I'LL BE FINE IF YOU HAVE TO DIE. IF YOU DIED I'D BE OKAY.
EVERYBODY DIES... IT DOESN'T MATTER. SO DO IT. IF YOU HAVE TO.
I'LL BE FINE IF YOU DO.
IF YOU DIE I'LL BE OKAY.
I WILL.

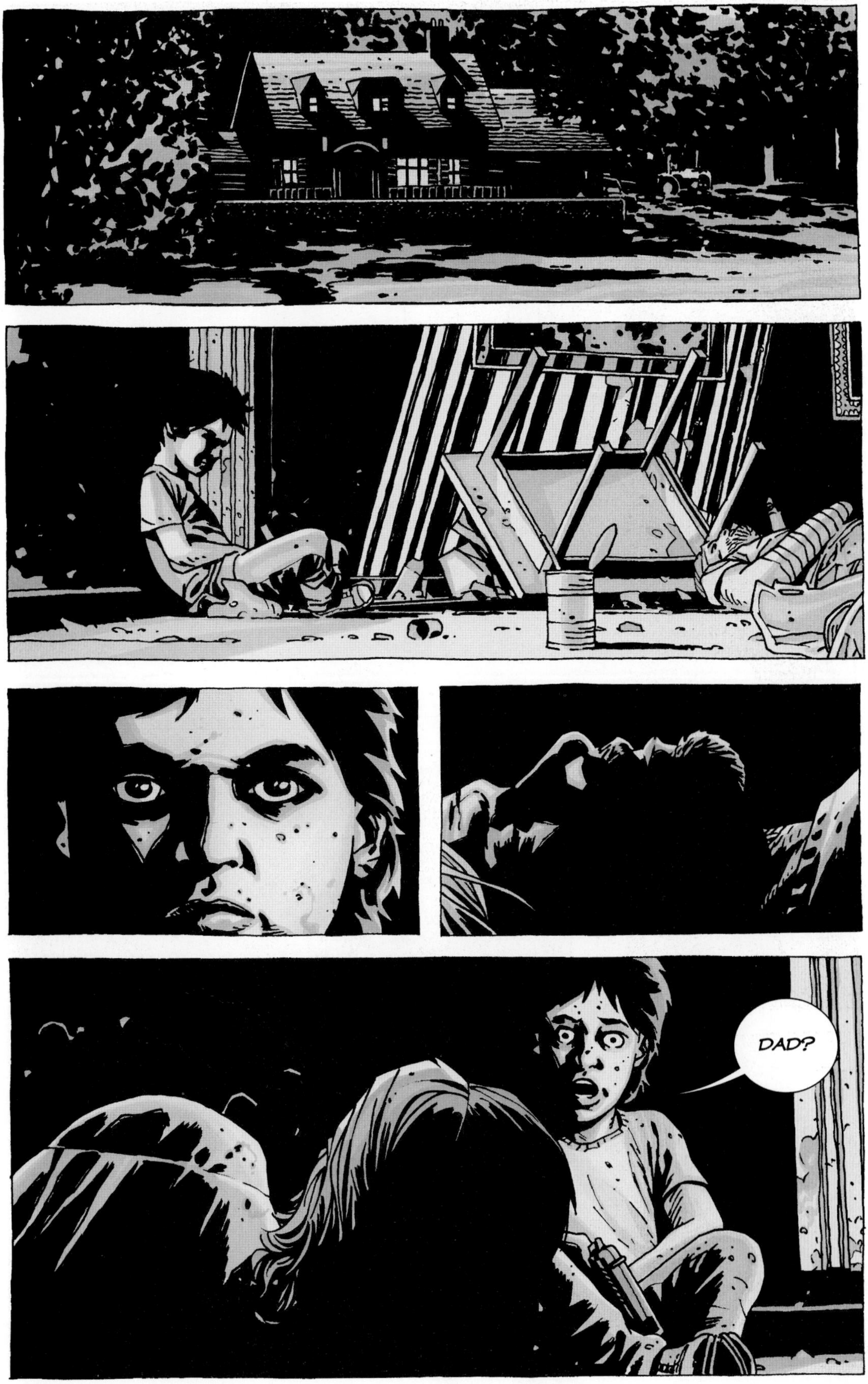
DAD?

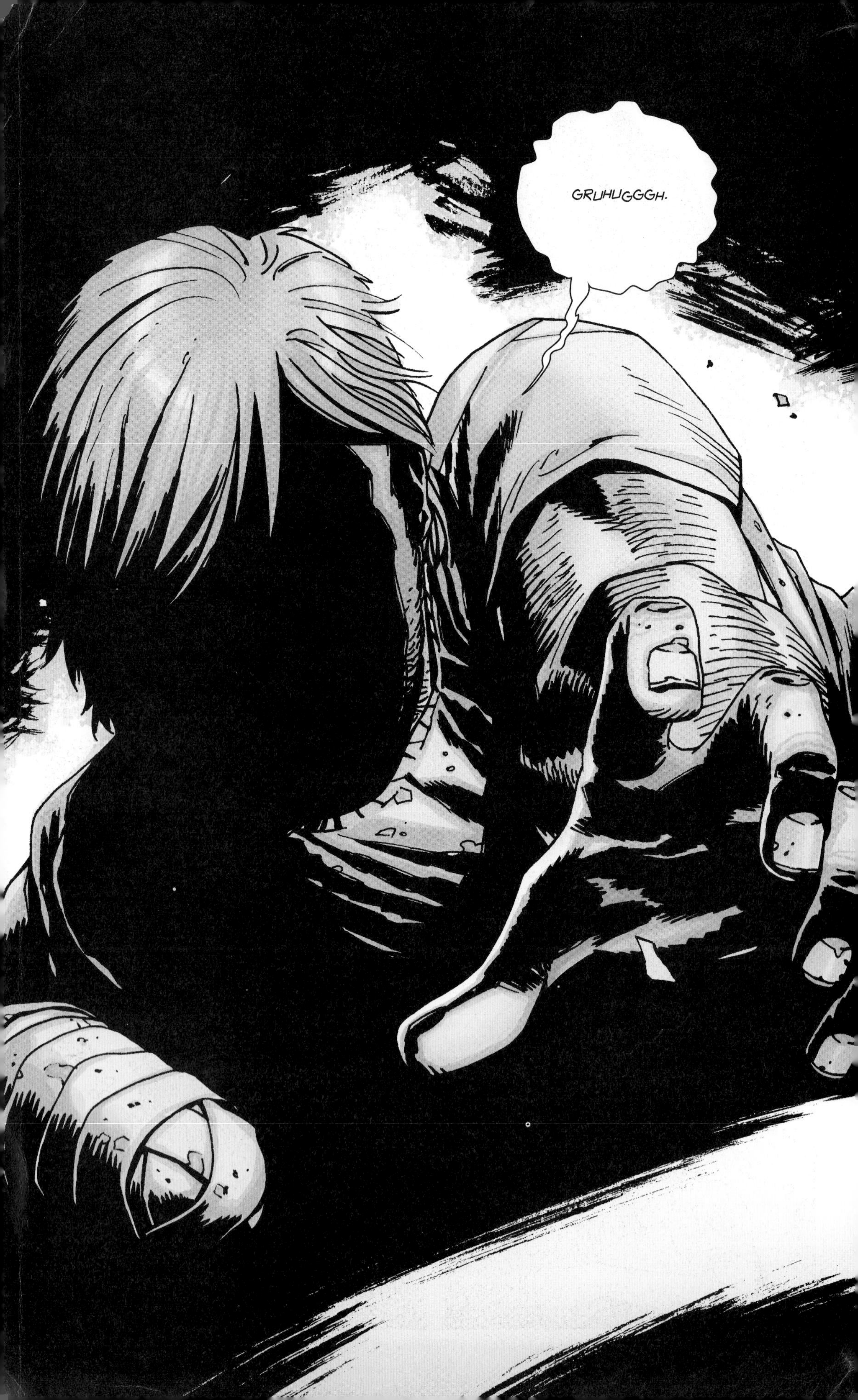
GRUHUGGGH.

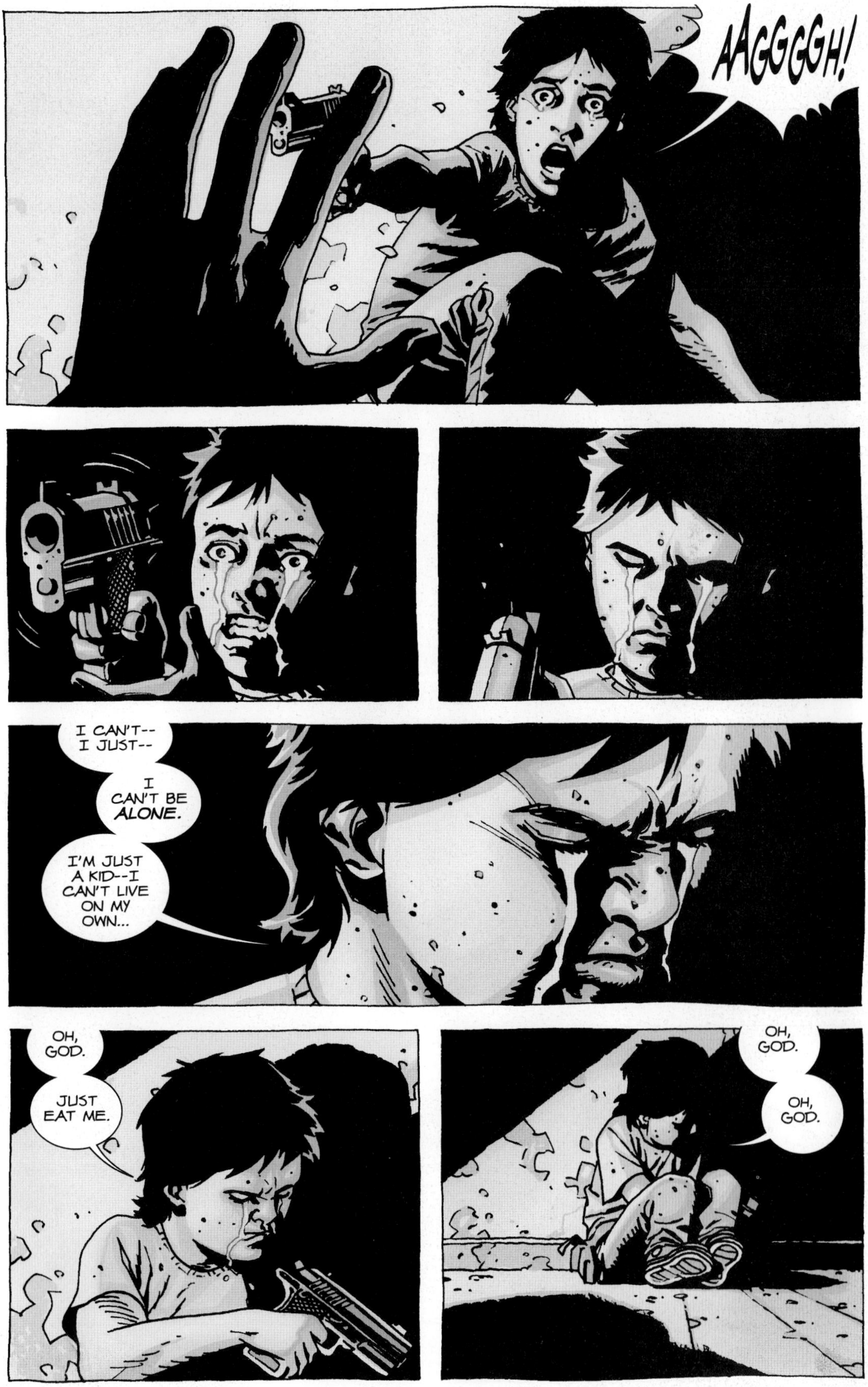
AAGGGGH!
I CAN'T-- I JUST--
I CAN'T BE ALONE.
I'M JUST A KID--I CAN'T LIVE ON MY OWN...
OH, GOD.
JUST EAT ME.
OH, GOD.
OH, GOD.

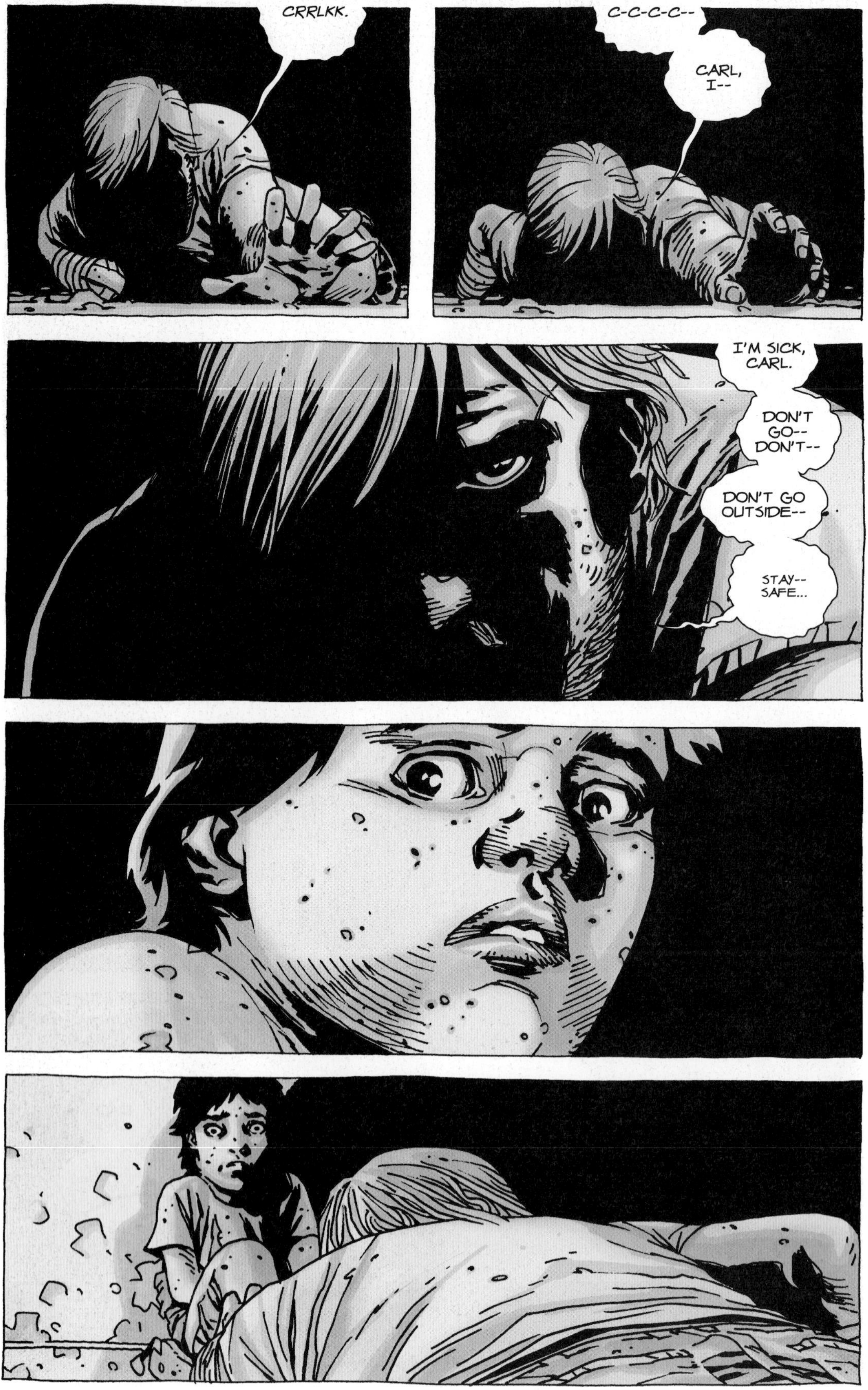
CRRLKK.
C-C-C-C--
CARL, I--
I'M SICK, CARL.
DON'T GO-- DON'T--
DON'T GO OUTSIDE--
STAY-- SAFE...

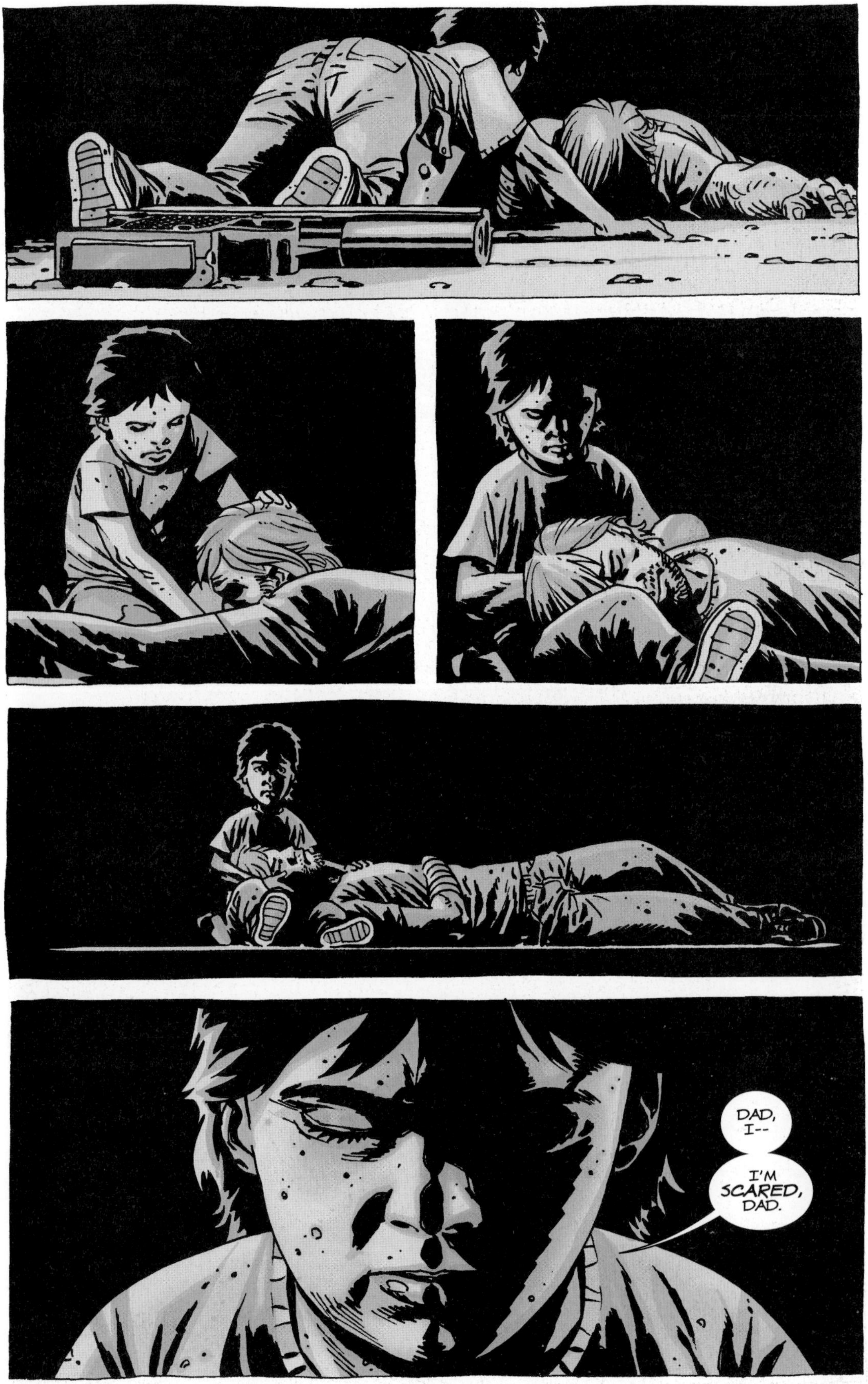
DAD, I--
I'M SCARED, DAD.

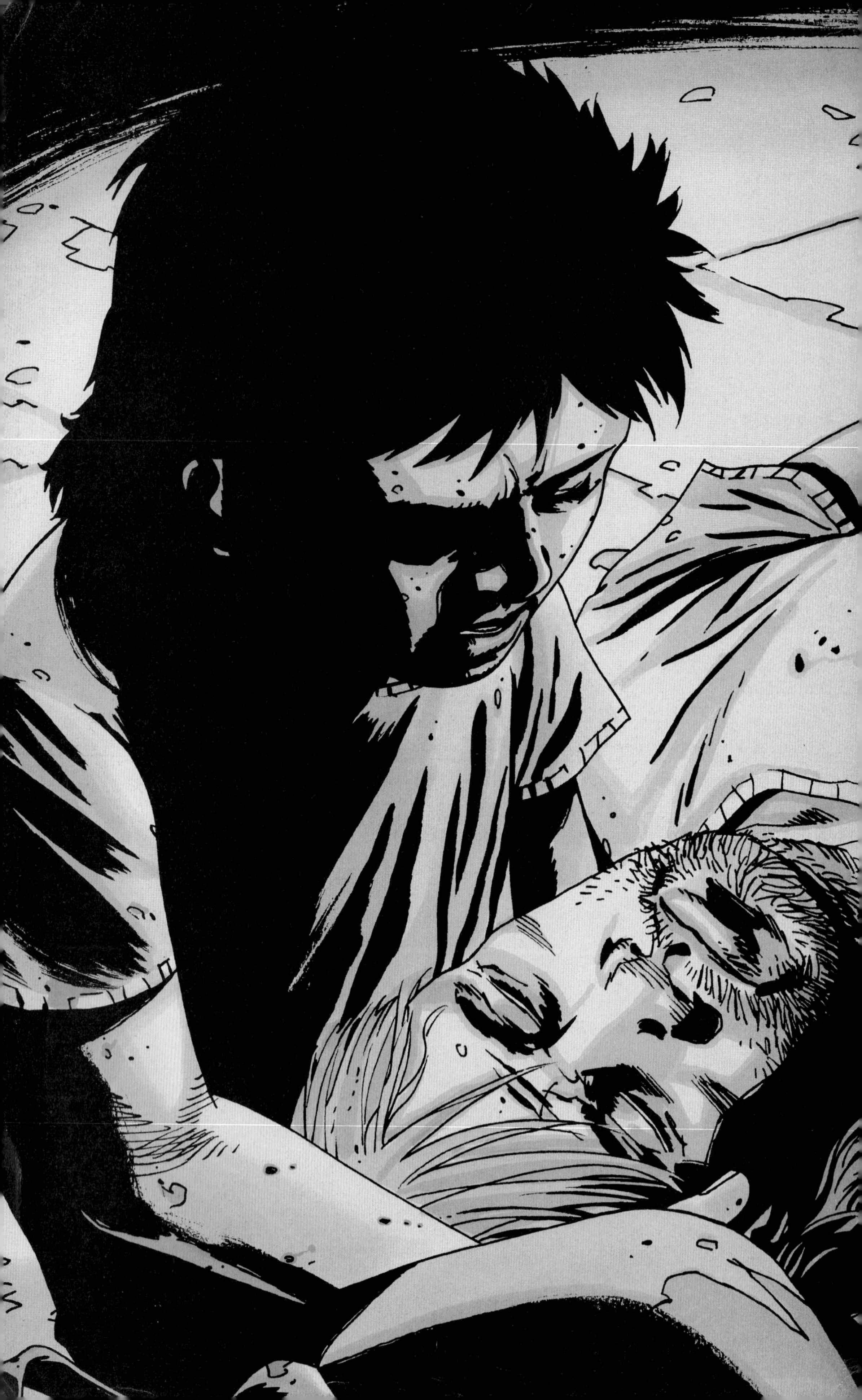

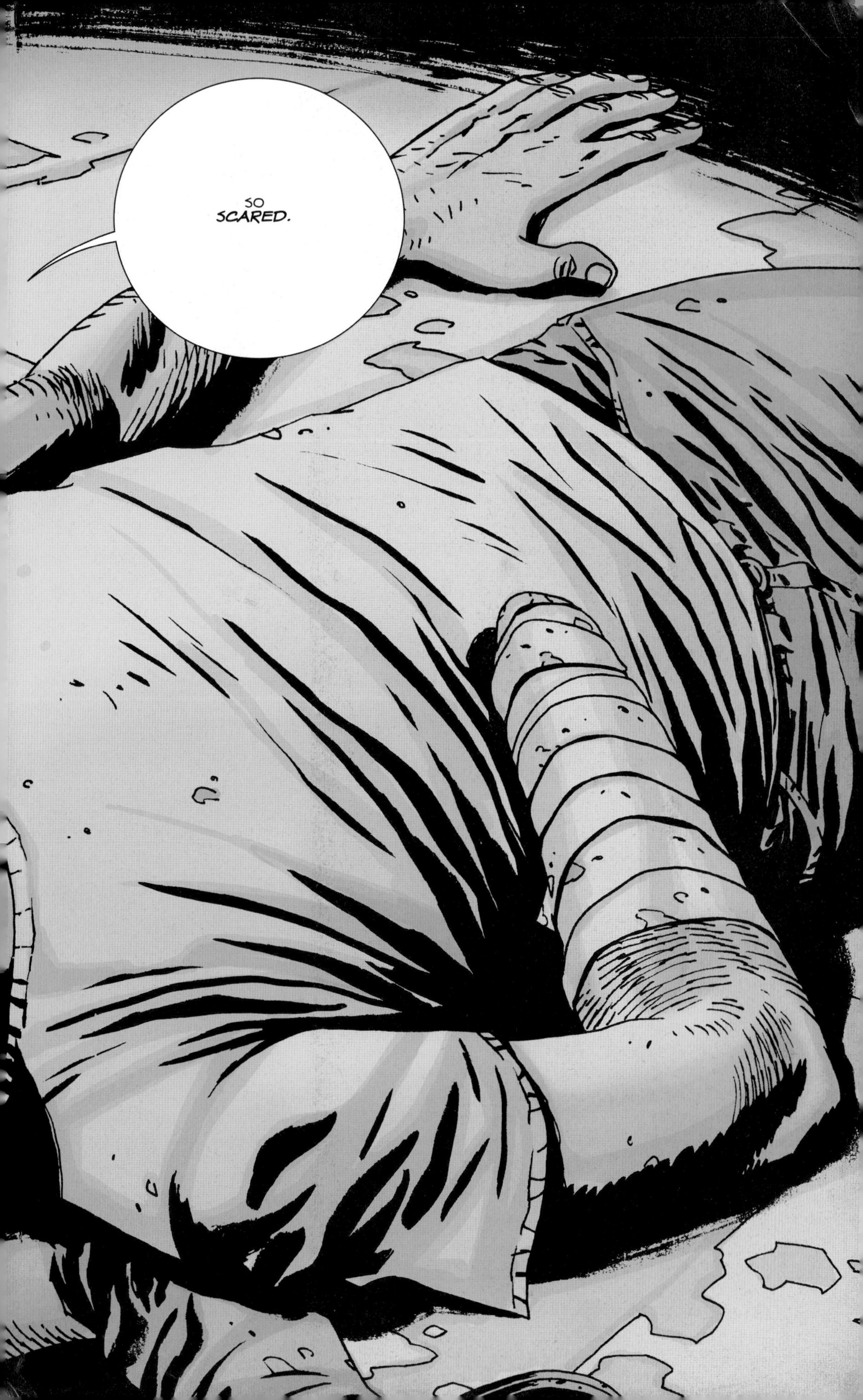
SO SCARED.

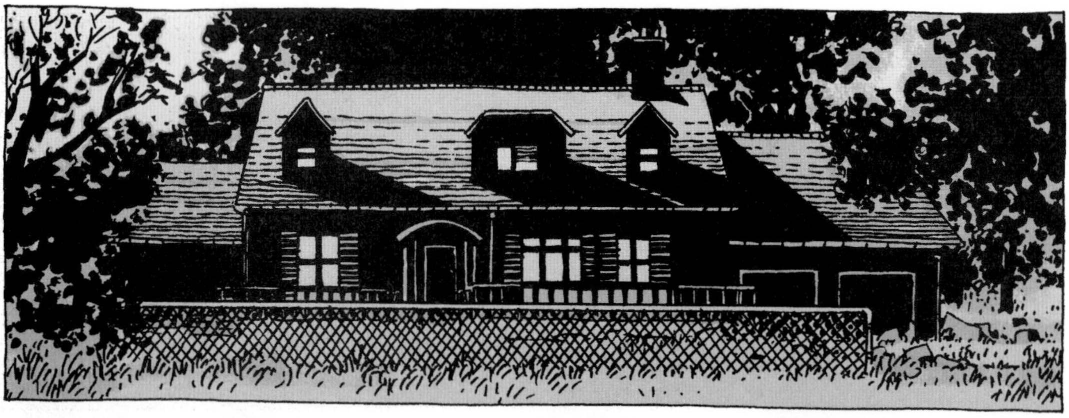
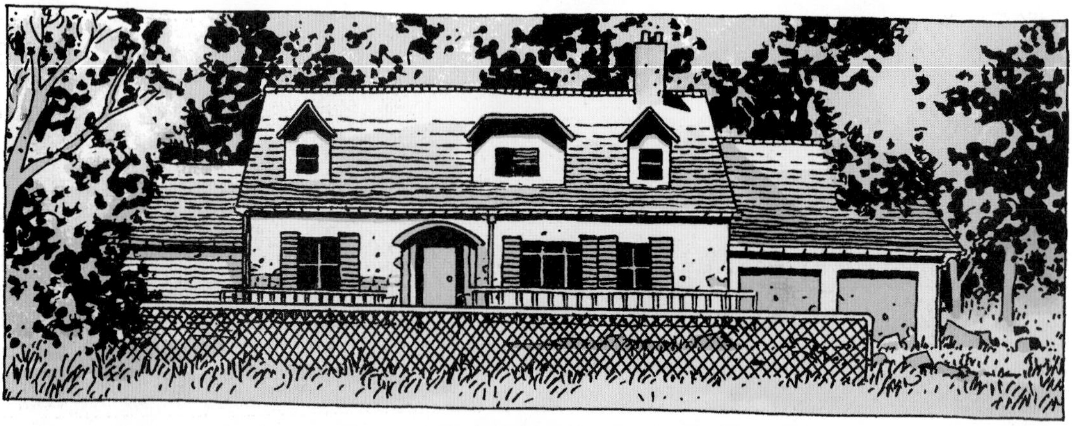
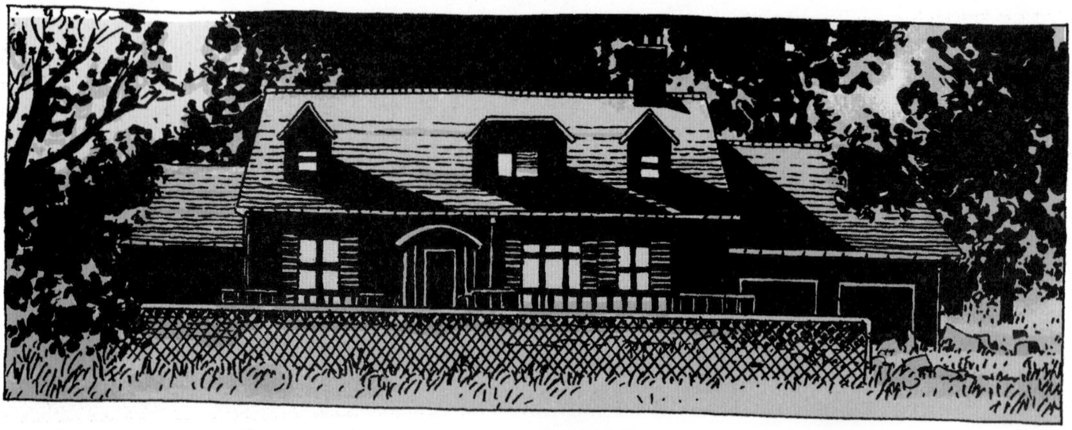
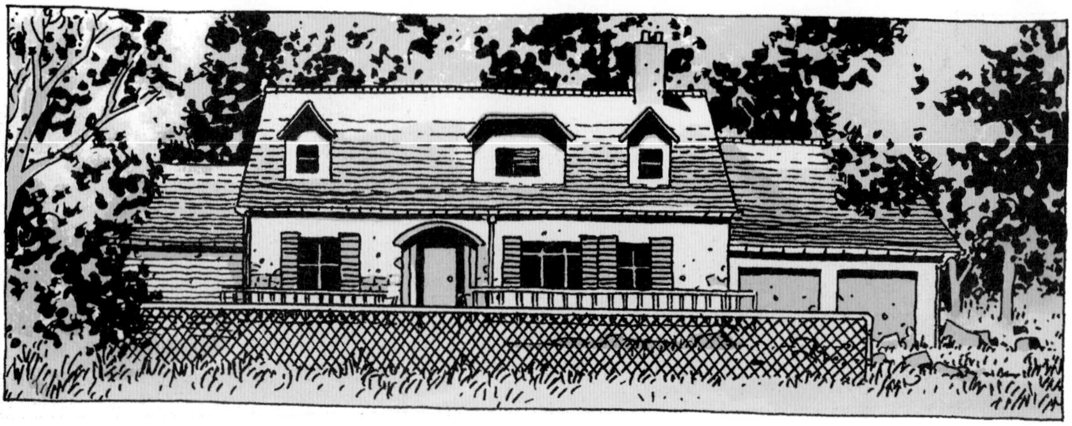

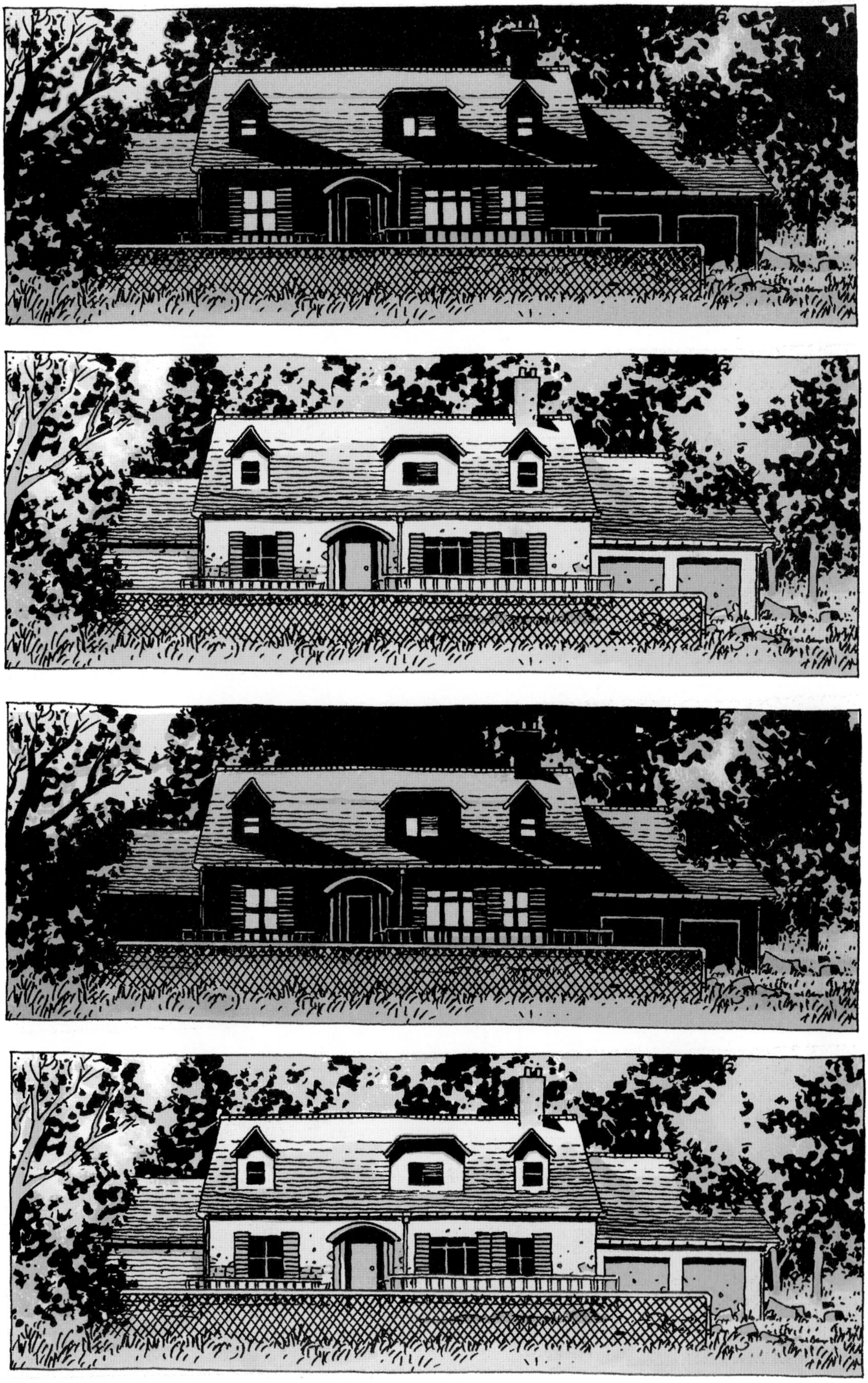

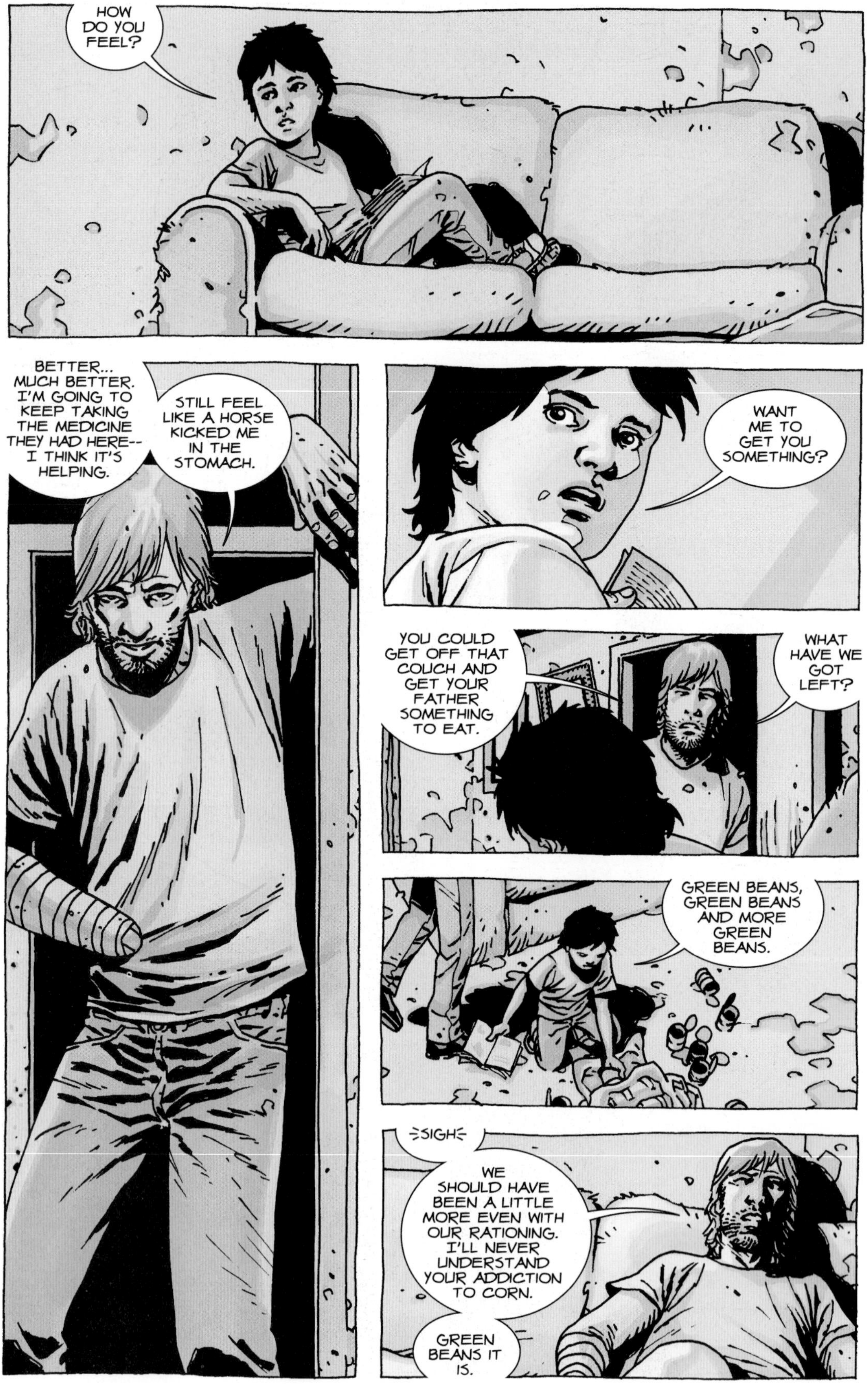
HOW DO YOU FEEL?
BETTER... MUCH BETTER. I'M GOING TO KEEP TAKING THE MEDICINE THEY HAD HERE-- I THINK IT'S HELPING.
STILL FEEL LIKE A HORSE KICKED ME IN THE STOMACH.
WANT ME TO GET YOU SOMETHING?
YOU COULD GET OFF THAT COUCH AND GET YOUR FATHER SOMETHING TO EAT.
WHAT HAVE WE GOT LEFT?
GREEN BEANS, GREEN BEANS AND MORE GREEN BEANS.
SIGH
WE SHOULD HAVE BEEN A LITTLE MORE EVEN WITH OUR RATIONING. I'LL NEVER UNDERSTAND YOUR ADDICTION TO CORN.
GREEN BEANS IT IS.

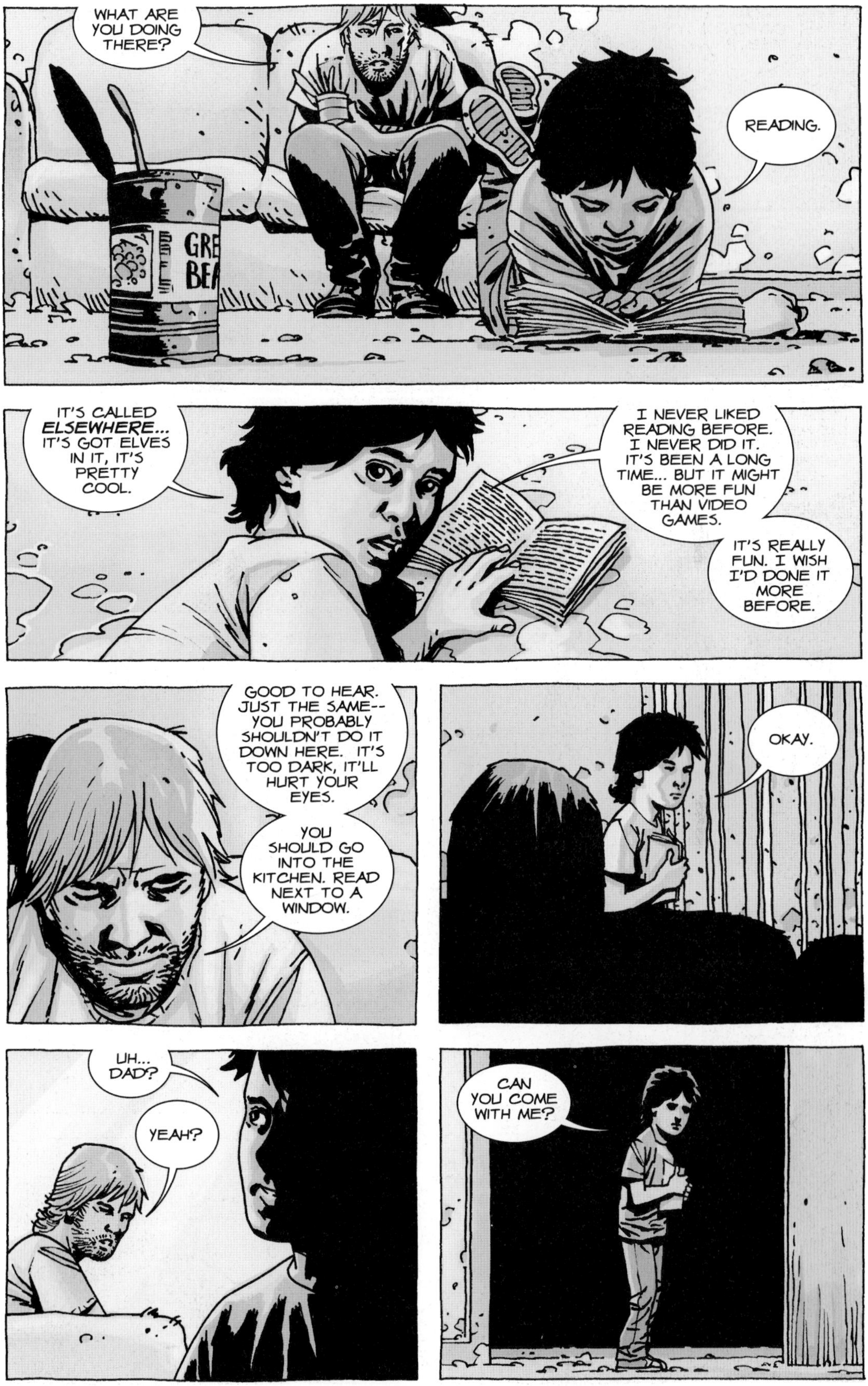
WHAT ARE YOU DOING THERE?
READING.
IT'S CALLED *ELSEWHERE*... IT'S GOT ELVES IN IT, IT'S PRETTY COOL.
I NEVER LIKED READING BEFORE. I NEVER DID IT. IT'S BEEN A LONG TIME... BUT IT MIGHT BE MORE FUN THAN VIDEO GAMES.
IT'S REALLY FUN. I WISH I'D DONE IT MORE BEFORE.
GOOD TO HEAR. JUST THE SAME-- YOU PROBABLY SHOULDN'T DO IT DOWN HERE. IT'S TOO DARK, IT'LL HURT YOUR EYES.
YOU SHOULD GO INTO THE KITCHEN. READ NEXT TO A WINDOW.
OKAY.
UH... DAD?
YEAH?
CAN YOU COME WITH ME?

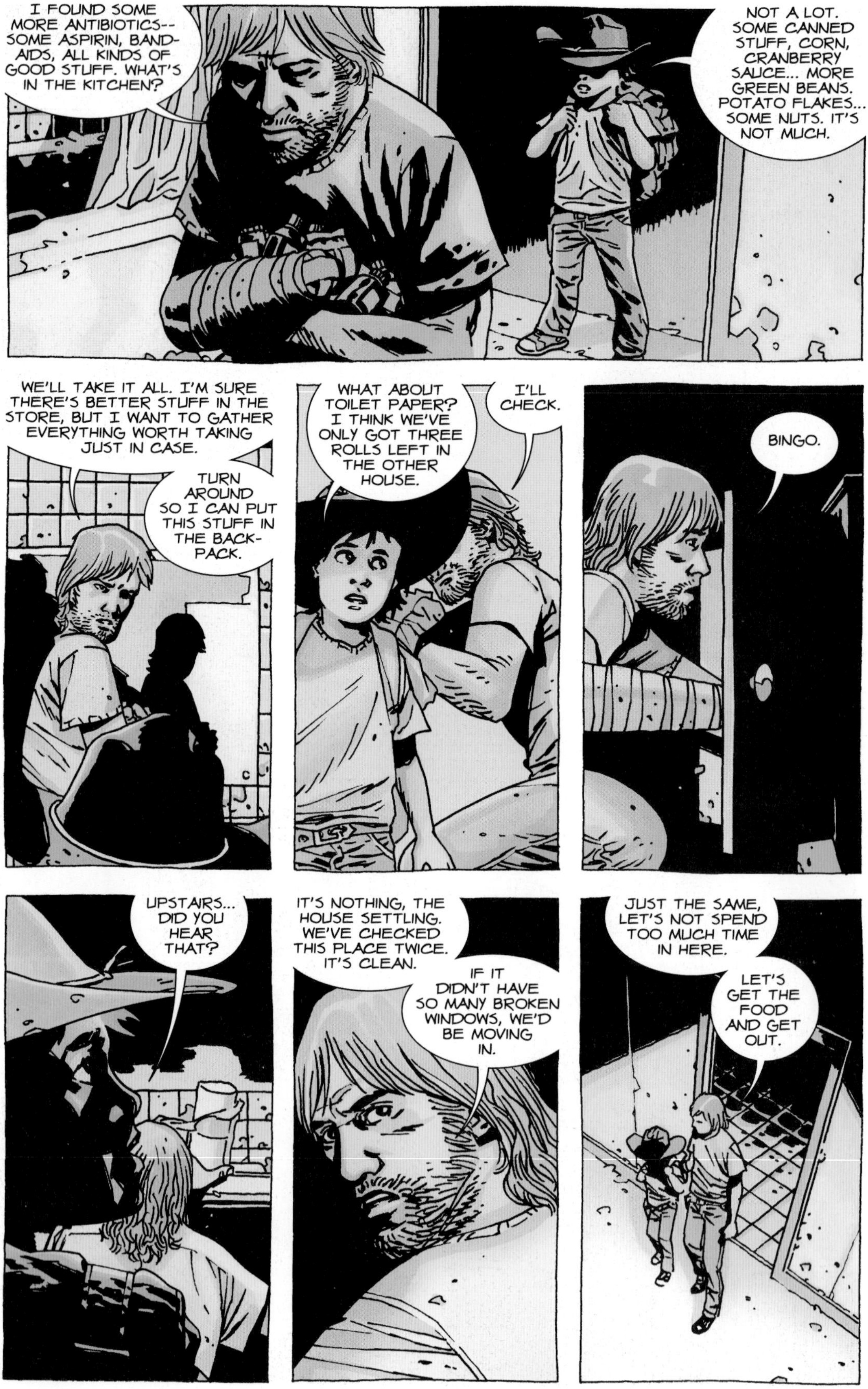
I FOUND SOME MORE ANTIBIOTICS-- SOME ASPIRIN, BAND-AIDS, ALL KINDS OF GOOD STUFF. WHAT'S IN THE KITCHEN?
NOT A LOT. SOME CANNED STUFF, CORN, CRANBERRY SAUCE... MORE GREEN BEANS. POTATO FLAKES... SOME NUTS. IT'S NOT MUCH.
WE'LL TAKE IT ALL. I'M SURE THERE'S BETTER STUFF IN THE STORE, BUT I WANT TO GATHER EVERYTHING WORTH TAKING JUST IN CASE.
TURN AROUND SO I CAN PUT THIS STUFF IN THE BACK-PACK.
WHAT ABOUT TOILET PAPER? I THINK WE'VE ONLY GOT THREE ROLLS LEFT IN THE OTHER HOUSE.
I'LL CHECK.
BINGO.
UPSTAIRS... DID YOU HEAR THAT?
IT'S NOTHING, THE HOUSE SETTLING. WE'VE CHECKED THIS PLACE TWICE. IT'S CLEAN.
IF IT DIDN'T HAVE SO MANY BROKEN WINDOWS, WE'D BE MOVING IN.
JUST THE SAME, LET'S NOT SPEND TOO MUCH TIME IN HERE.
LET'S GET THE FOOD AND GET OUT.

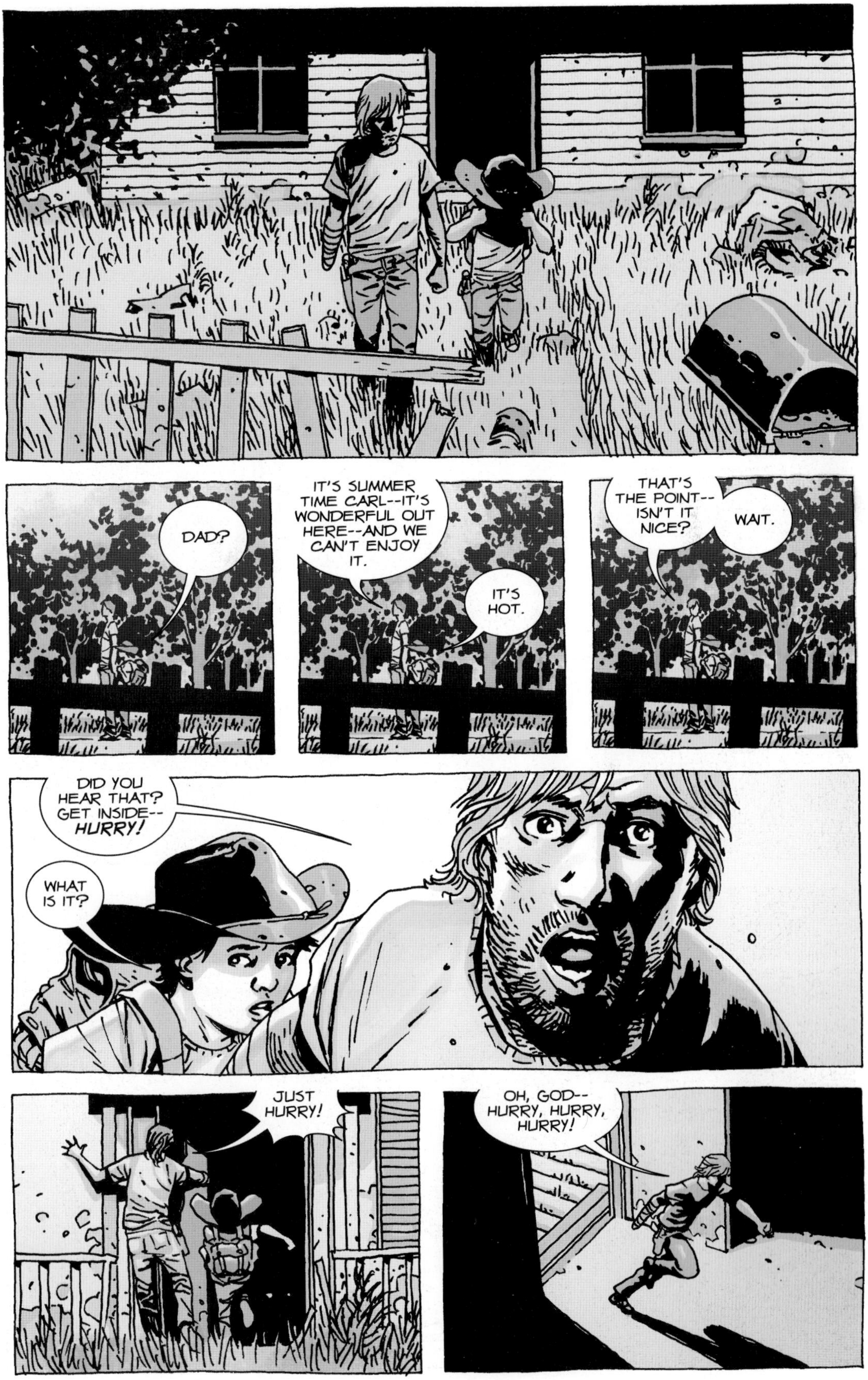
DAD?
IT'S SUMMER TIME CARL--IT'S WONDERFUL OUT HERE--AND WE CAN'T ENJOY IT.
IT'S HOT.
THAT'S THE POINT-- ISN'T IT NICE?
WAIT.
DID YOU HEAR THAT? GET INSIDE-- HURRY!
WHAT IS IT?
JUST HURRY!
OH, GOD-- HURRY, HURRY, HURRY!

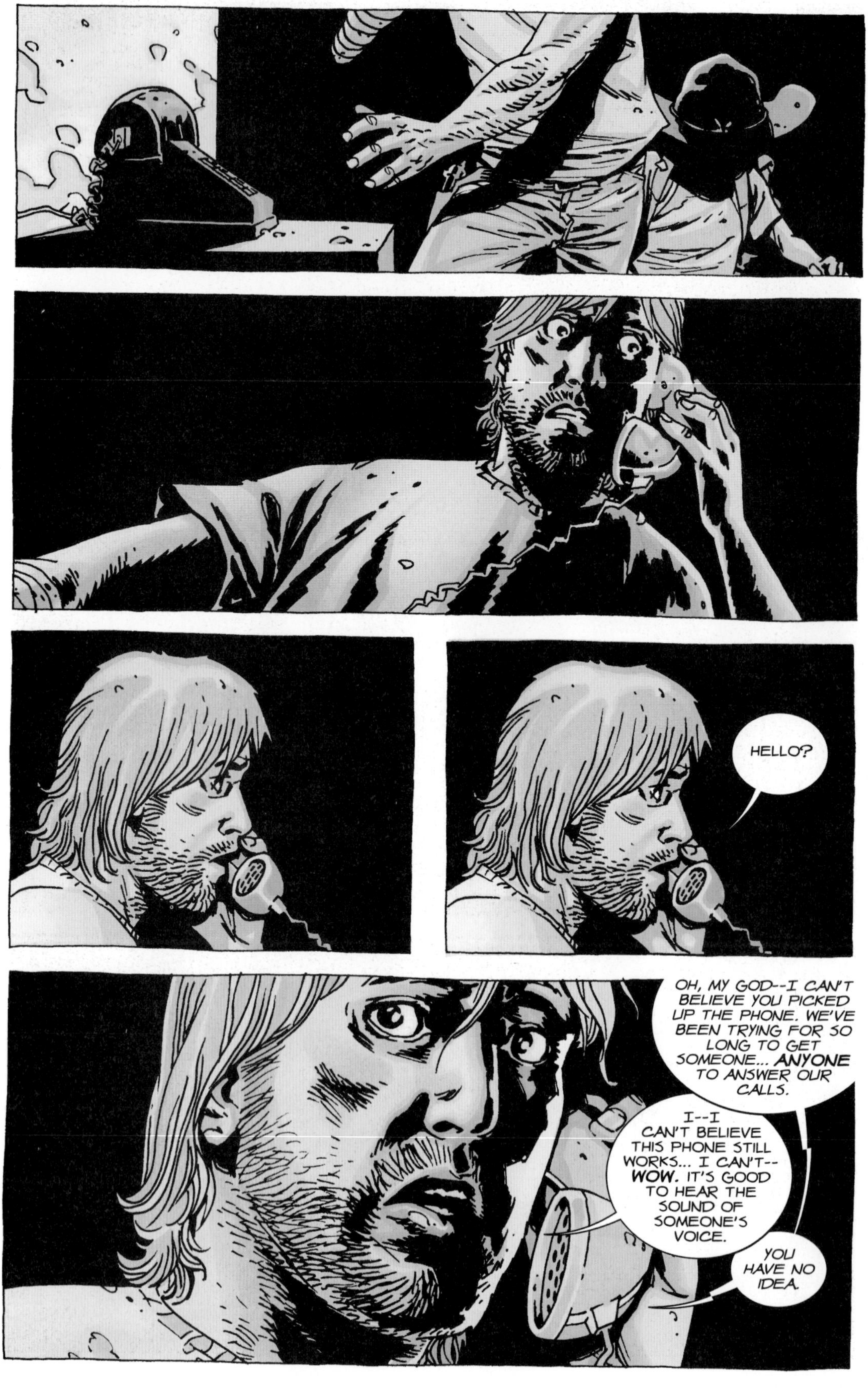
HELLO?
OH, MY GOD--I CAN'T BELIEVE YOU PICKED UP THE PHONE. WE'VE BEEN TRYING FOR SO LONG TO GET SOMEONE... **ANYONE** TO ANSWER OUR CALLS.
I--I CAN'T BELIEVE THIS PHONE STILL WORKS... I CAN'T-- **WOW.** IT'S GOOD TO HEAR THE SOUND OF SOMEONE'S VOICE.
YOU HAVE NO IDEA.

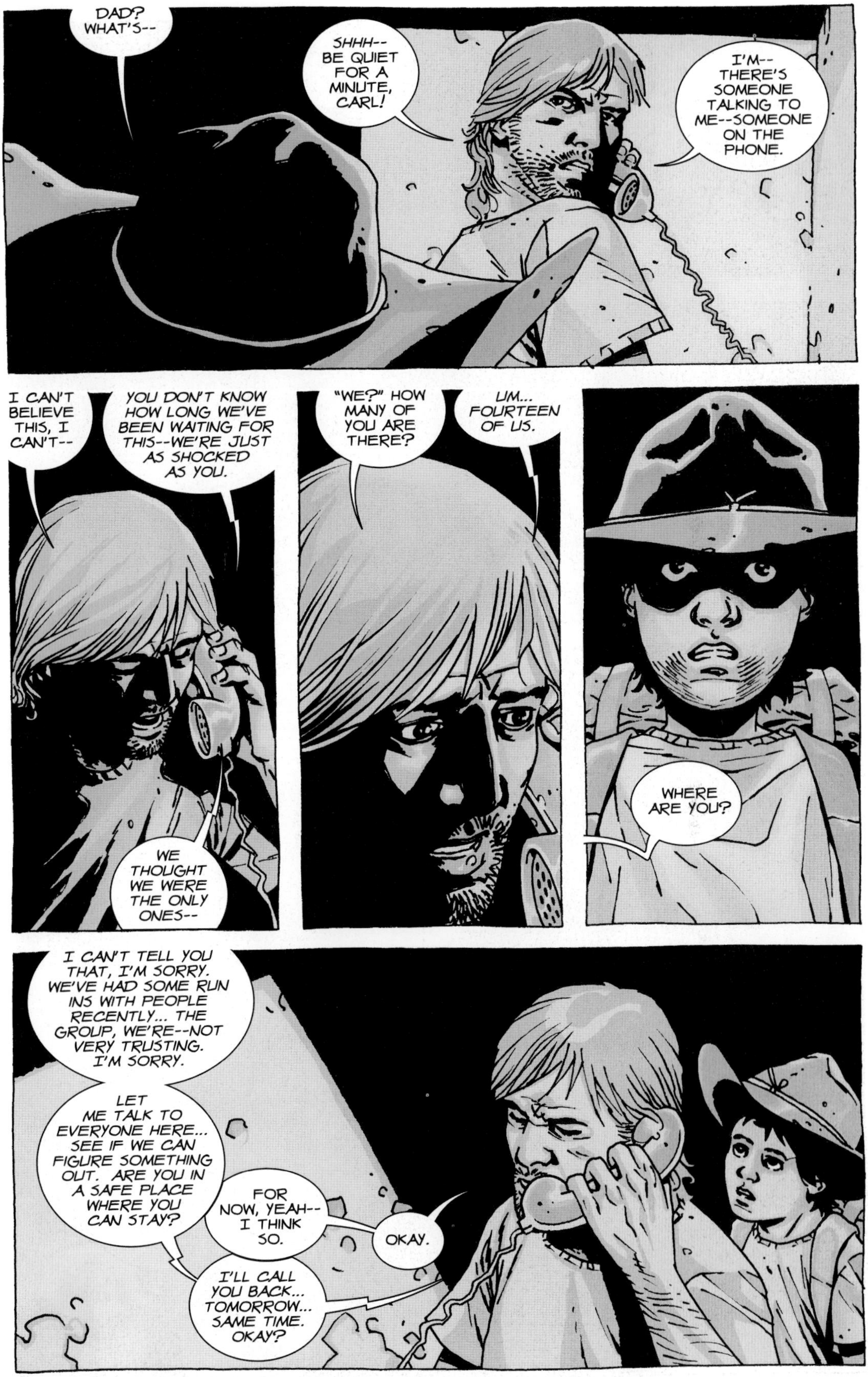

DAD? WHAT'S--
SHHH-- BE QUIET FOR A MINUTE, CARL!
I'M-- THERE'S SOMEONE TALKING TO ME--SOMEONE ON THE PHONE.
I CAN'T BELIEVE THIS, I CAN'T--
YOU DON'T KNOW HOW LONG WE'VE BEEN WAITING FOR THIS--WE'RE JUST AS SHOCKED AS YOU.
WE THOUGHT WE WERE THE ONLY ONES--
"WE?" HOW MANY OF YOU ARE THERE?
UM... FOURTEEN OF US.
WHERE ARE YOU?
I CAN'T TELL YOU THAT, I'M SORRY. WE'VE HAD SOME RUN INS WITH PEOPLE RECENTLY... THE GROUP, WE'RE--NOT VERY TRUSTING. I'M SORRY.
LET ME TALK TO EVERYONE HERE... SEE IF WE CAN FIGURE SOMETHING OUT. ARE YOU IN A SAFE PLACE WHERE YOU CAN STAY?
FOR NOW, YEAH-- I THINK SO.
OKAY.
I'LL CALL YOU BACK... TOMORROW... SAME TIME. OKAY?

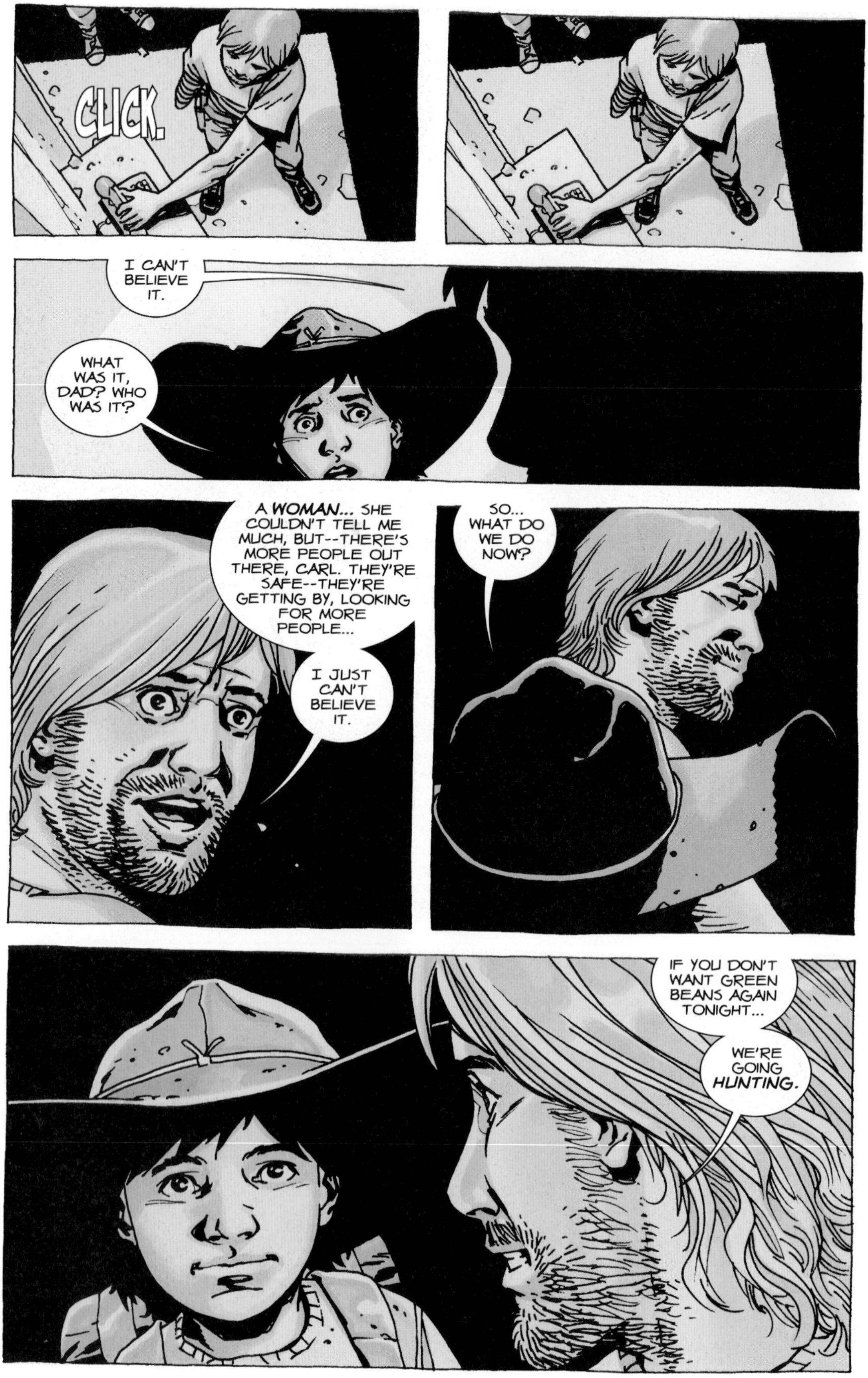
CLICK.
I CAN'T BELIEVE IT.
WHAT WAS IT, DAD? WHO WAS IT?
A *WOMAN...* SHE COULDN'T TELL ME MUCH, BUT--THERE'S MORE PEOPLE OUT THERE, CARL. THEY'RE SAFE--THEY'RE GETTING BY, LOOKING FOR MORE PEOPLE...
I JUST CAN'T BELIEVE IT.
SO... WHAT DO WE DO NOW?
IF YOU DON'T WANT GREEN BEANS AGAIN TONIGHT...
WE'RE GOING *HUNTING.*

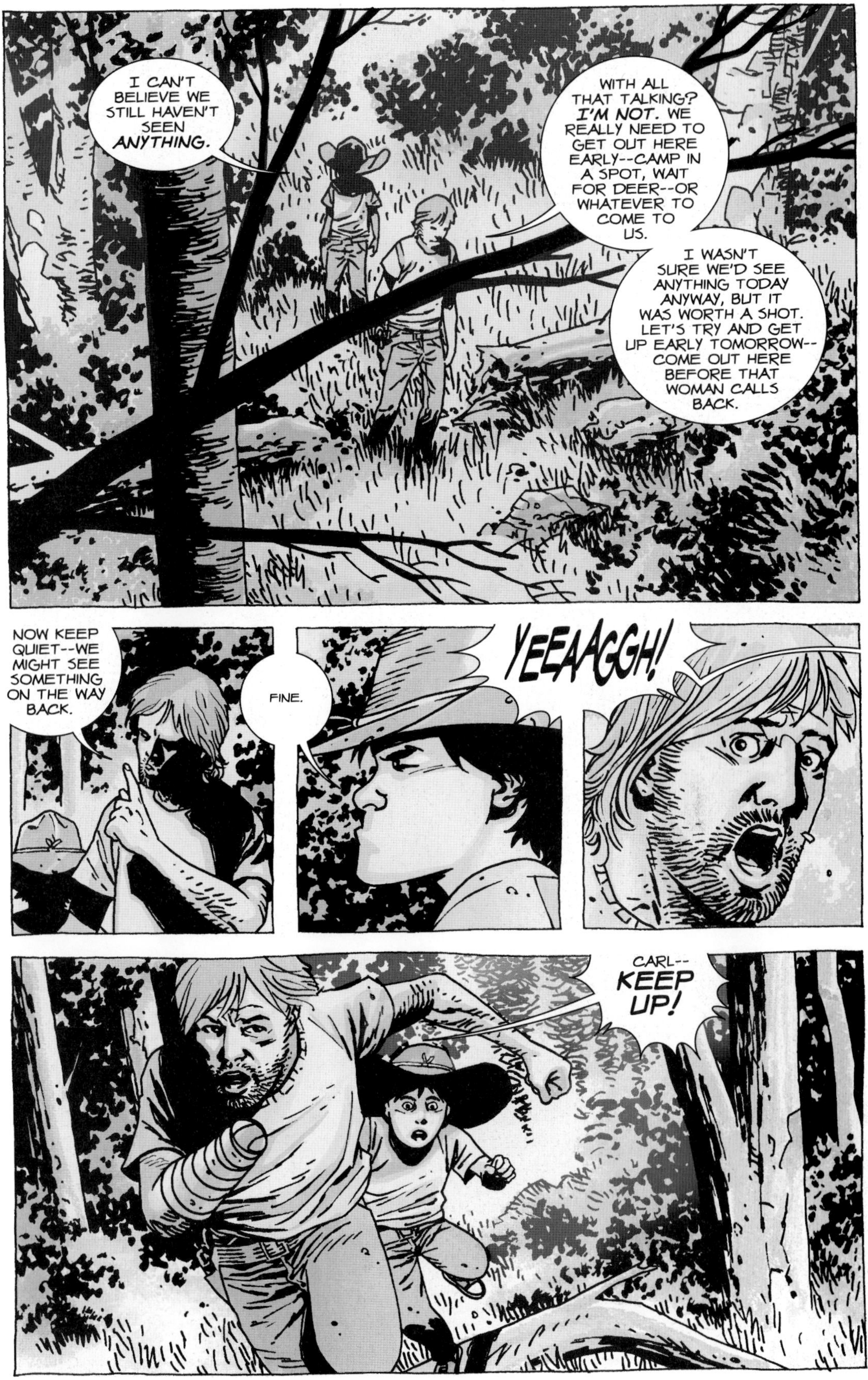
I CAN'T BELIEVE WE STILL HAVEN'T SEEN ANYTHING.
WITH ALL THAT TALKING? I'M NOT. WE REALLY NEED TO GET OUT HERE EARLY--CAMP IN A SPOT, WAIT FOR DEER--OR WHATEVER TO COME TO US.
I WASN'T SURE WE'D SEE ANYTHING TODAY ANYWAY, BUT IT WAS WORTH A SHOT. LET'S TRY AND GET UP EARLY TOMORROW--COME OUT HERE BEFORE THAT WOMAN CALLS BACK.
NOW KEEP QUIET--WE MIGHT SEE SOMETHING ON THE WAY BACK.
FINE.
YEEAAGGH!
CARL-- KEEP UP!

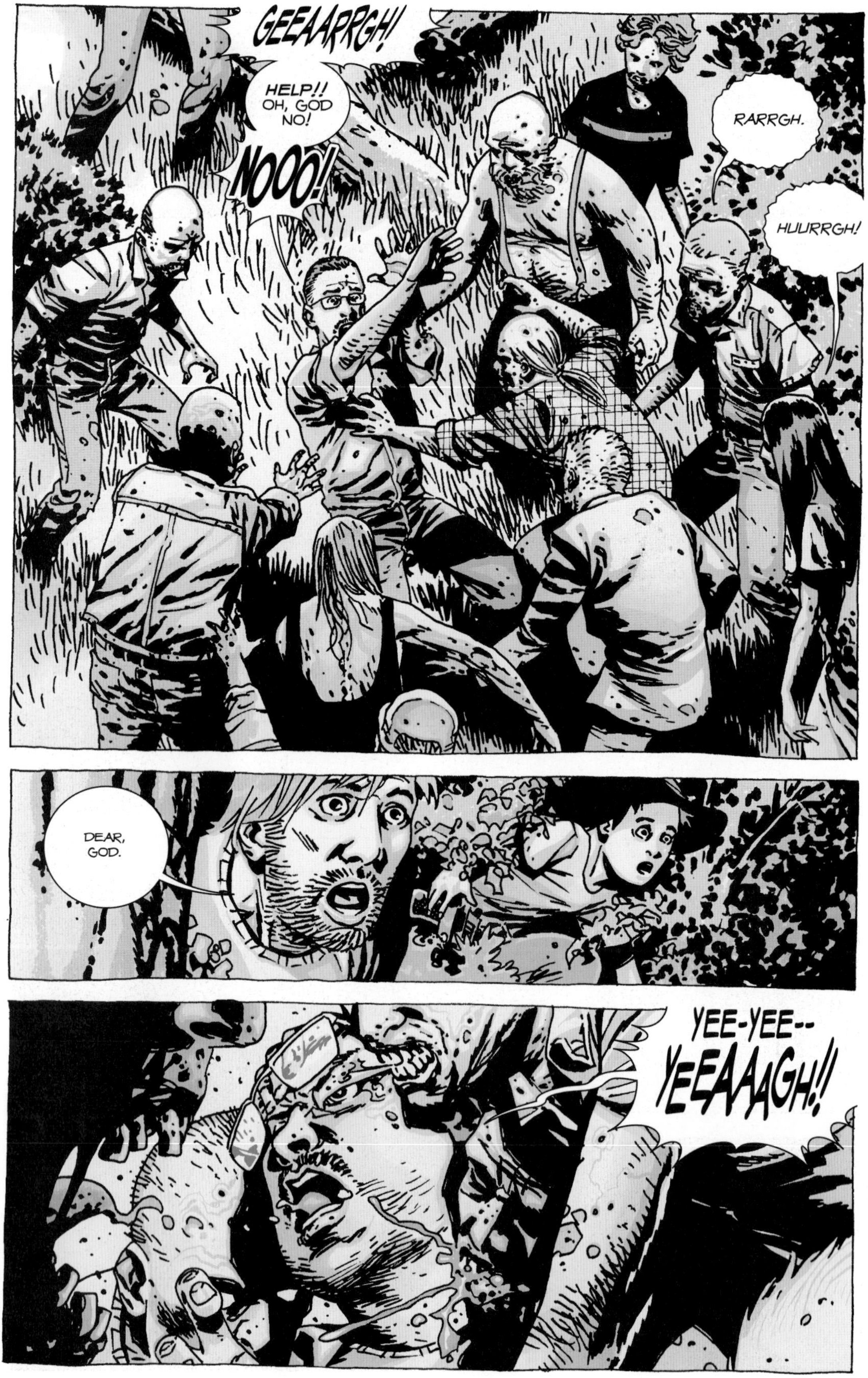
GEEAARRGH!
HELP!! OH, GOD NO!
NOOO!
RARRGH.
HUURRGH!
DEAR, GOD.
YEE-YEE-- YEEAAAGH!!

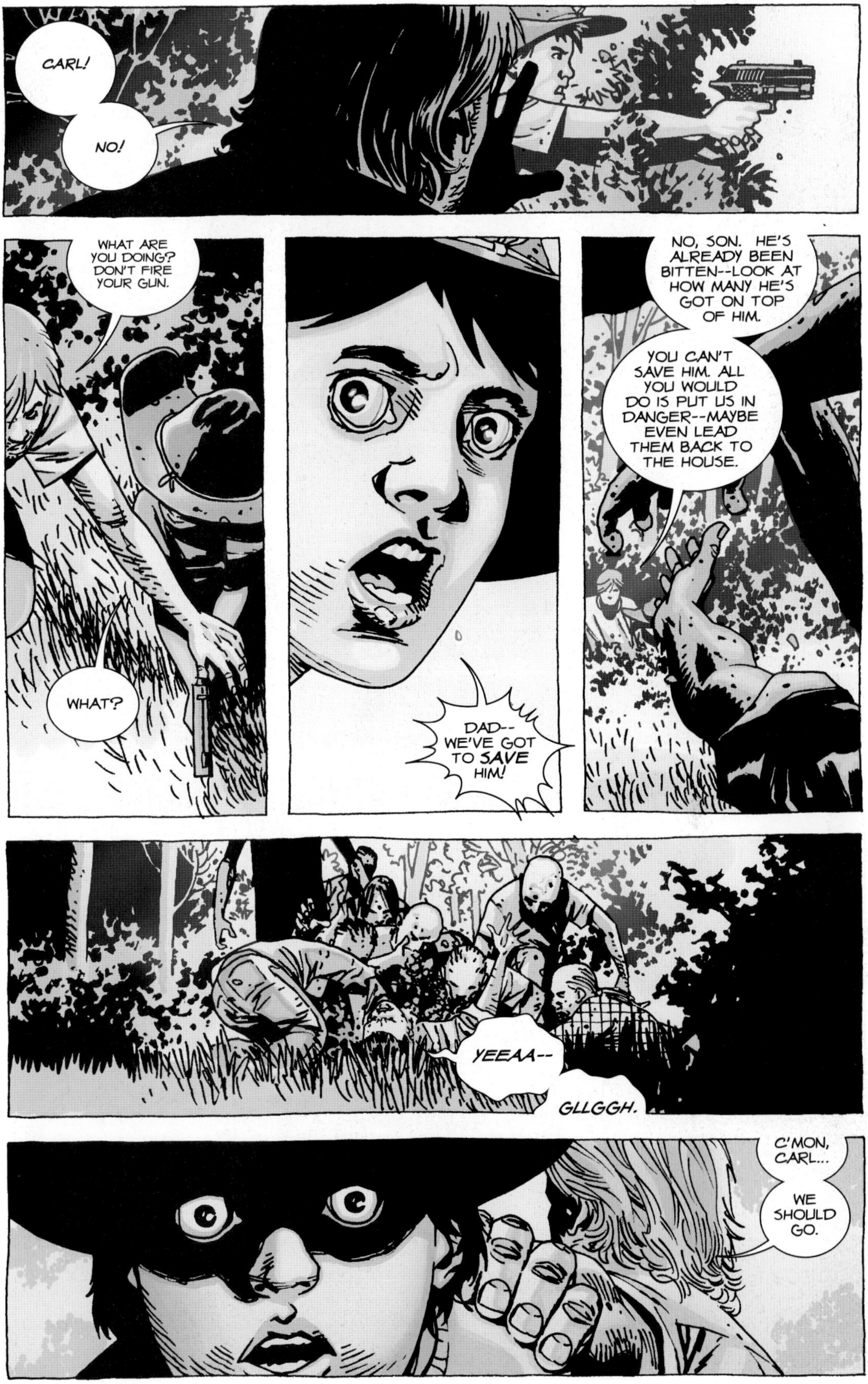
CARL!
NO!
WHAT ARE YOU DOING? DON'T FIRE YOUR GUN.
WHAT?
DAD--WE'VE GOT TO SAVE HIM!
NO, SON. HE'S ALREADY BEEN BITTEN--LOOK AT HOW MANY HE'S GOT ON TOP OF HIM.
YOU CAN'T SAVE HIM. ALL YOU WOULD DO IS PUT US IN DANGER--MAYBE EVEN LEAD THEM BACK TO THE HOUSE.
YEEAA--
GLLGGH.
C'MON, CARL...
WE SHOULD GO.

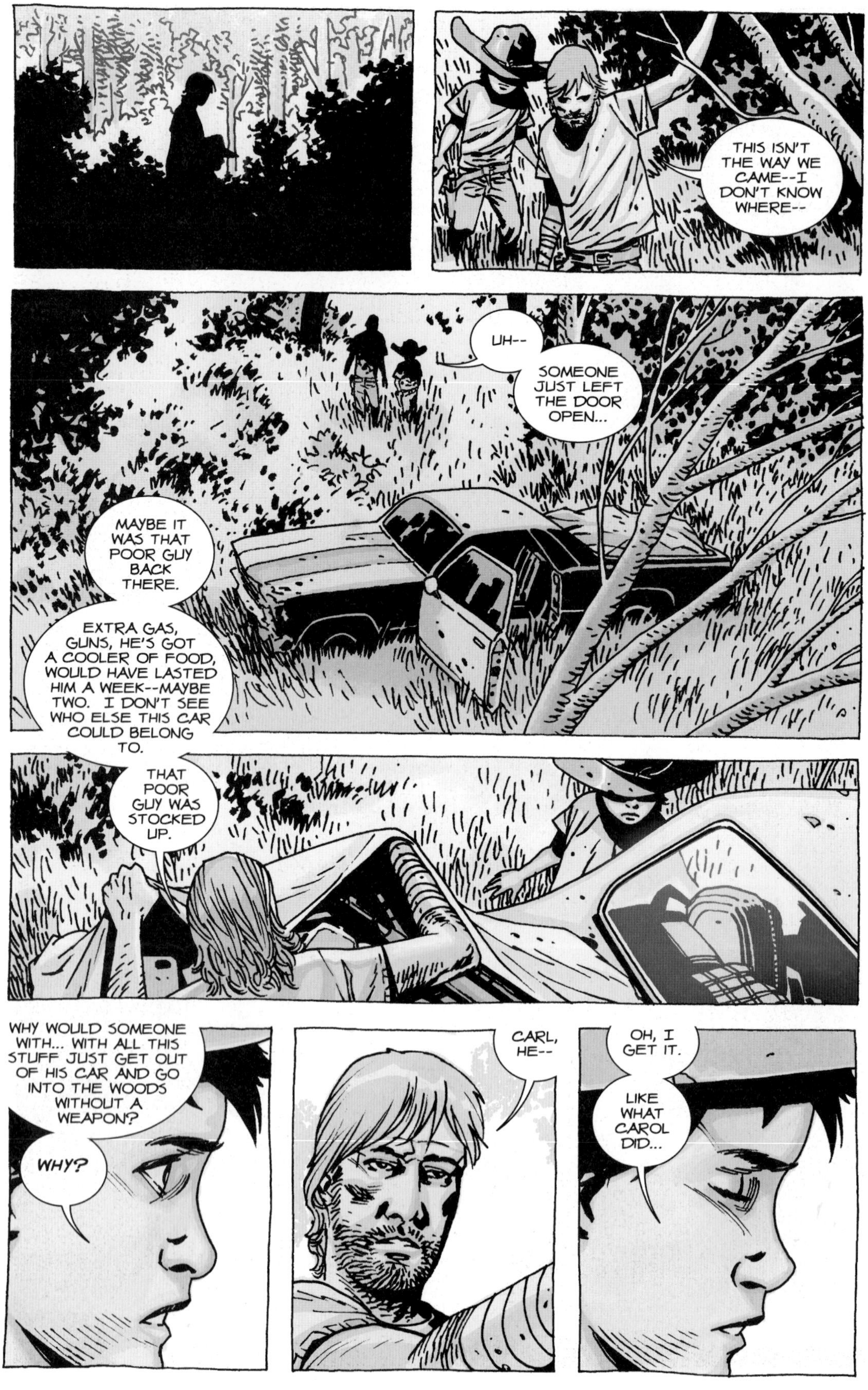

THIS ISN'T THE WAY WE CAME--I DON'T KNOW WHERE--
UH--
SOMEONE JUST LEFT THE DOOR OPEN...
MAYBE IT WAS THAT POOR GUY BACK THERE.
EXTRA GAS, GUNS, HE'S GOT A COOLER OF FOOD, WOULD HAVE LASTED HIM A WEEK--MAYBE TWO. I DON'T SEE WHO ELSE THIS CAR COULD BELONG TO.
THAT POOR GUY WAS STOCKED UP.
WHY WOULD SOMEONE WITH... WITH ALL THIS STUFF JUST GET OUT OF HIS CAR AND GO INTO THE WOODS WITHOUT A WEAPON?
WHY?
CARL, HE--
OH, I GET IT.
LIKE WHAT CAROL DID...

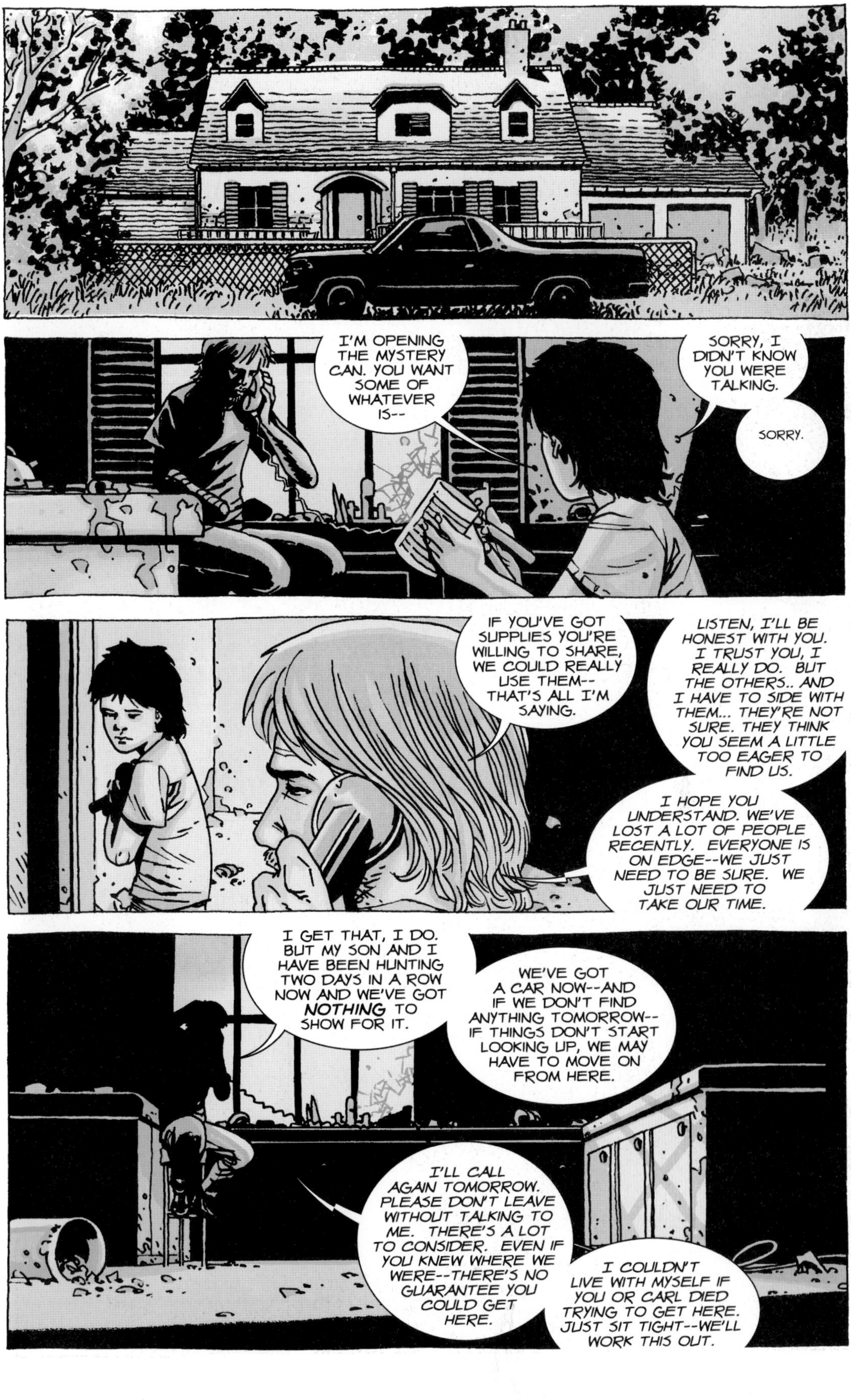
I'M OPENING THE MYSTERY CAN. YOU WANT SOME OF WHATEVER IS--
SORRY, I DIDN'T KNOW YOU WERE TALKING.
SORRY.
IF YOU'VE GOT SUPPLIES YOU'RE WILLING TO SHARE, WE COULD REALLY USE THEM-- THAT'S ALL I'M SAYING.
LISTEN, I'LL BE HONEST WITH YOU. I TRUST YOU, I REALLY DO. BUT THE OTHERS.. AND I HAVE TO SIDE WITH THEM... THEY'RE NOT SURE. THEY THINK YOU SEEM A LITTLE TOO EAGER TO FIND US.
I HOPE YOU UNDERSTAND. WE'VE LOST A LOT OF PEOPLE RECENTLY. EVERYONE IS ON EDGE--WE JUST NEED TO BE SURE. WE JUST NEED TO TAKE OUR TIME.
I GET THAT, I DO. BUT MY SON AND I HAVE BEEN HUNTING TWO DAYS IN A ROW NOW AND WE'VE GOT ***NOTHING*** TO SHOW FOR IT.
WE'VE GOT A CAR NOW--AND IF WE DON'T FIND ANYTHING TOMORROW-- IF THINGS DON'T START LOOKING UP, WE MAY HAVE TO MOVE ON FROM HERE.
I'LL CALL AGAIN TOMORROW. PLEASE DON'T LEAVE WITHOUT TALKING TO ME. THERE'S A LOT TO CONSIDER. EVEN IF YOU KNEW WHERE WE WERE--THERE'S NO GUARANTEE YOU COULD GET HERE.
I COULDN'T LIVE WITH MYSELF IF YOU OR CARL DIED TRYING TO GET HERE. JUST SIT TIGHT--WE'LL WORK THIS OUT.

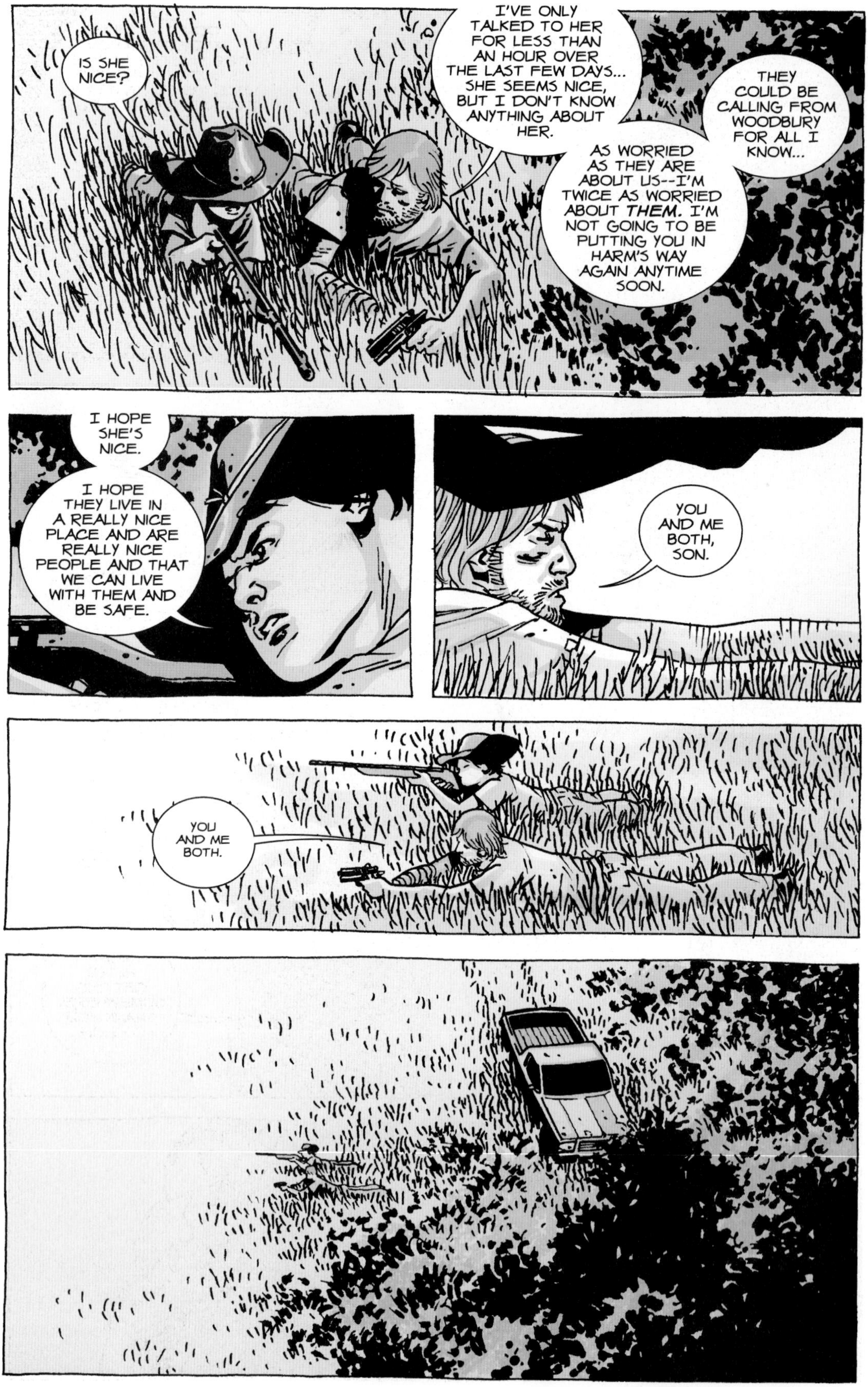
IS SHE NICE?
I'VE ONLY TALKED TO HER FOR LESS THAN AN HOUR OVER THE LAST FEW DAYS... SHE SEEMS NICE, BUT I DON'T KNOW ANYTHING ABOUT HER.
THEY COULD BE CALLING FROM WOODBURY FOR ALL I KNOW...
AS WORRIED AS THEY ARE ABOUT US--I'M TWICE AS WORRIED ABOUT **THEM.** I'M NOT GOING TO BE PUTTING YOU IN HARM'S WAY AGAIN ANYTIME SOON.
I HOPE SHE'S NICE.
I HOPE THEY LIVE IN A REALLY NICE PLACE AND ARE REALLY NICE PEOPLE AND THAT WE CAN LIVE WITH THEM AND BE SAFE.
YOU AND ME BOTH, SON.
YOU AND ME BOTH.

THERE'S LITTLE MORE THAN SCRAPS LEFT IN THE LITTLE GENERAL STORE NEXT DOOR. WE CAN'T FIND ANYTHING IN THE WAY OF ANIMALS WHEN WE GO OUT HUNTING.

I THINK WE'RE GOING TO HAVE TO MOVE ON.

PLEASE DON'T MISTAKE MY DESPERATION FOR SINISTER MOTIVE. I UNDERSTAND THE NEED TO BE CAUTIOUS... I DON'T EXACTLY TRUST YOU PEOPLE EITHER. IT'S JUST, I DON'T KNOW WHAT THE ODDS WERE ON YOU CONTACTING ME LIKE THIS. IF WE LEAVE HERE--WE'LL NEVER SPEAK AGAIN.

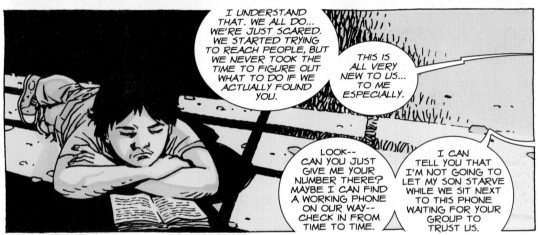

I UNDERSTAND THAT. WE ALL DO... WE'RE JUST SCARED. WE STARTED TRYING TO REACH PEOPLE, BUT WE NEVER TOOK THE TIME TO FIGURE OUT WHAT TO DO IF WE ACTUALLY FOUND YOU.

THIS IS ALL VERY NEW TO US... TO ME ESPECIALLY.

LOOK-- CAN YOU JUST GIVE ME YOUR NUMBER THERE? MAYBE I CAN FIND A WORKING PHONE ON OUR WAY-- CHECK IN FROM TIME TO TIME.

I CAN TELL YOU THAT I'M NOT GOING TO LET MY SON STARVE WHILE WE SIT NEXT TO THIS PHONE WAITING FOR YOUR GROUP TO TRUST US.

I DON'T KNOW, I'D HAVE TO CHECK WITH EVERYONE BEFORE I GAVE OUT THE NUMBER.

OH, WHAT'S THE PROBLEM? I CAN'T EXACTLY RUN A TRACE ON A PHONE NUMBER HERE, Y'KNOW.

OKAY, OKAY... YOU'RE RIGHT. LET ME GET THE NUMBER.

NOW WE'RE GETTING SOMEWHERE. THANK YOU SO MUCH...

...

Y'KNOW, IT JUST OCCURRED TO ME THAT I HAVEN'T EVEN ASKED YOU YOUR NAME.

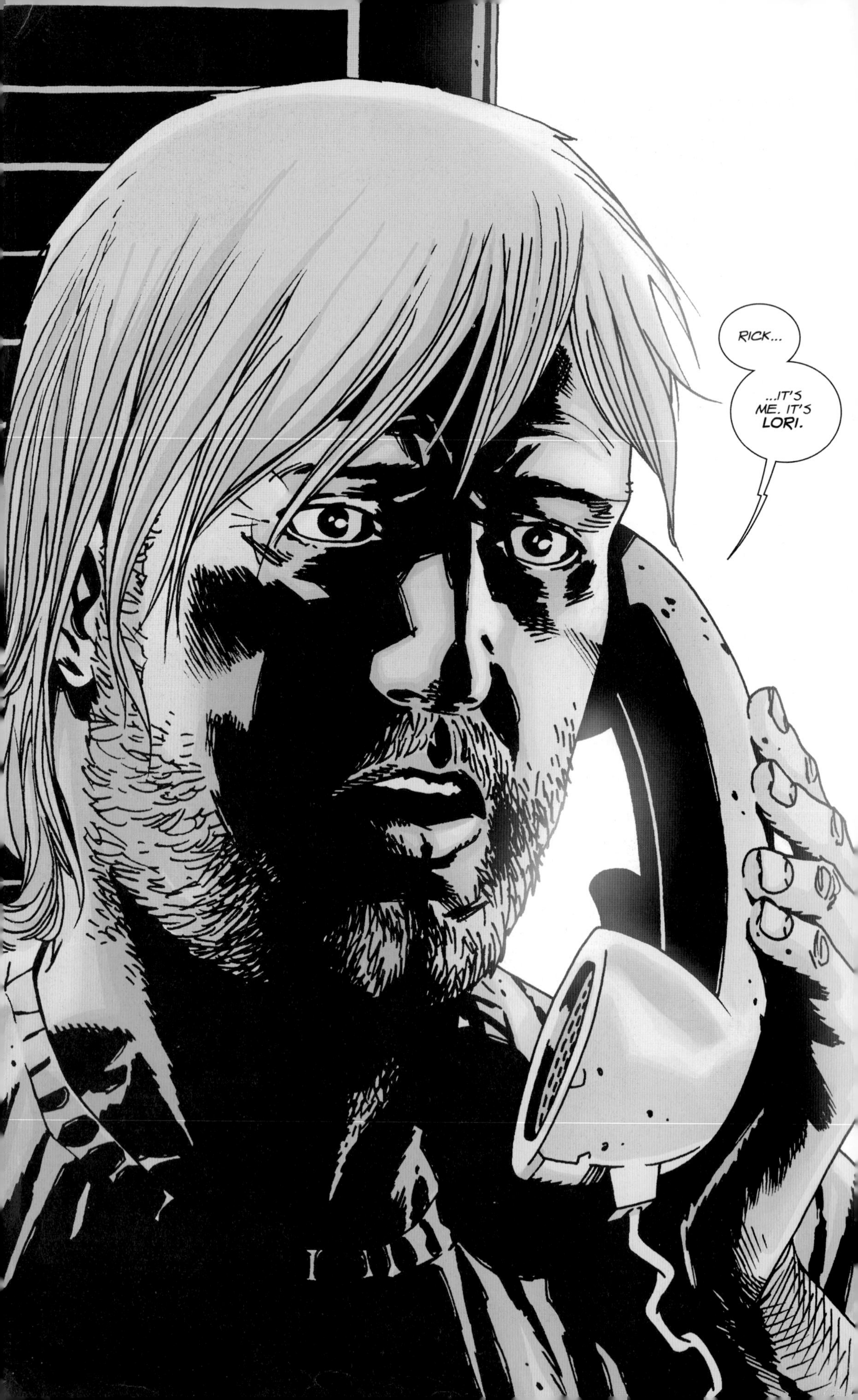
RICK...
...IT'S ME. IT'S LORI.

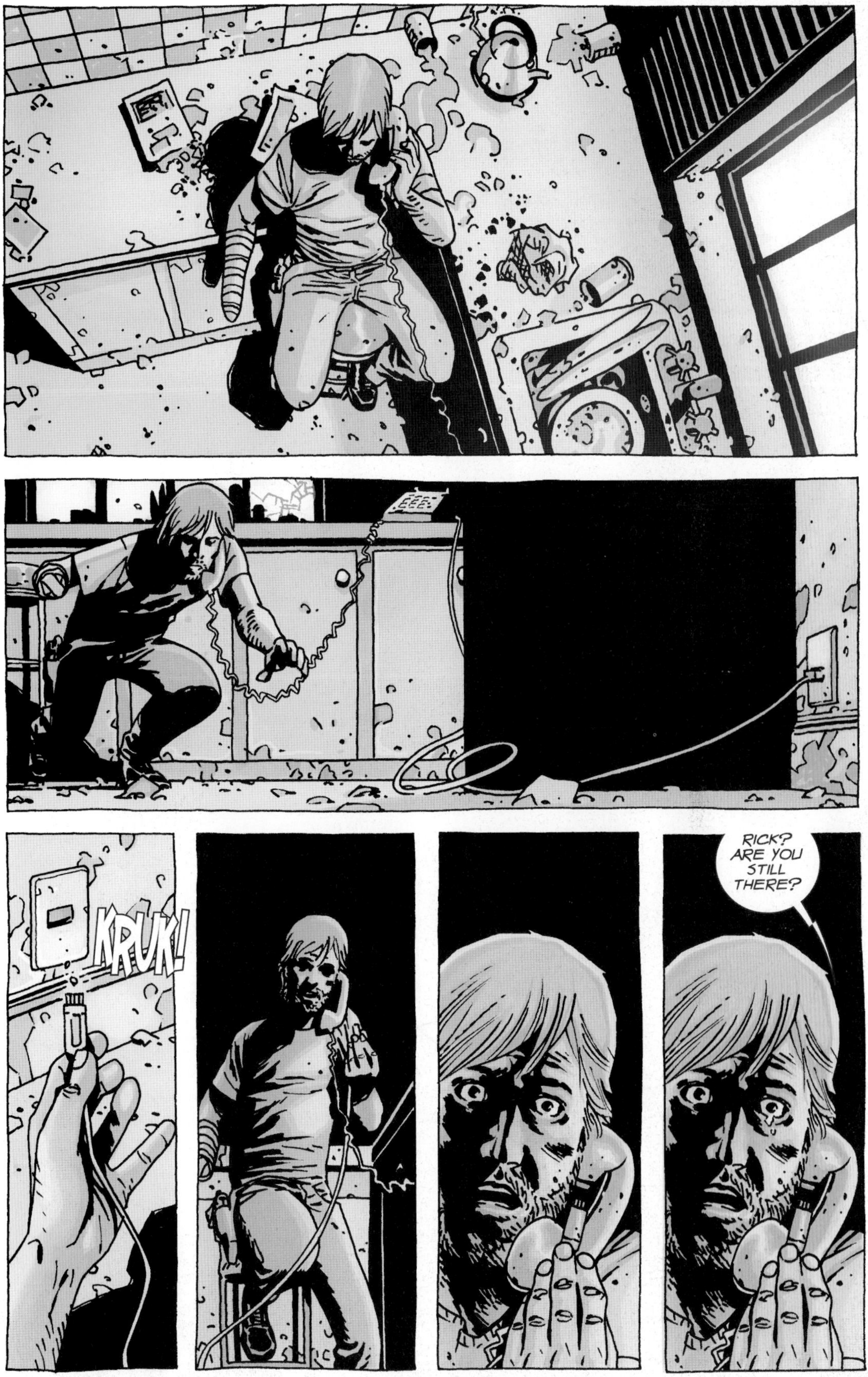
KRUK!
RICK? ARE YOU STILL THERE?

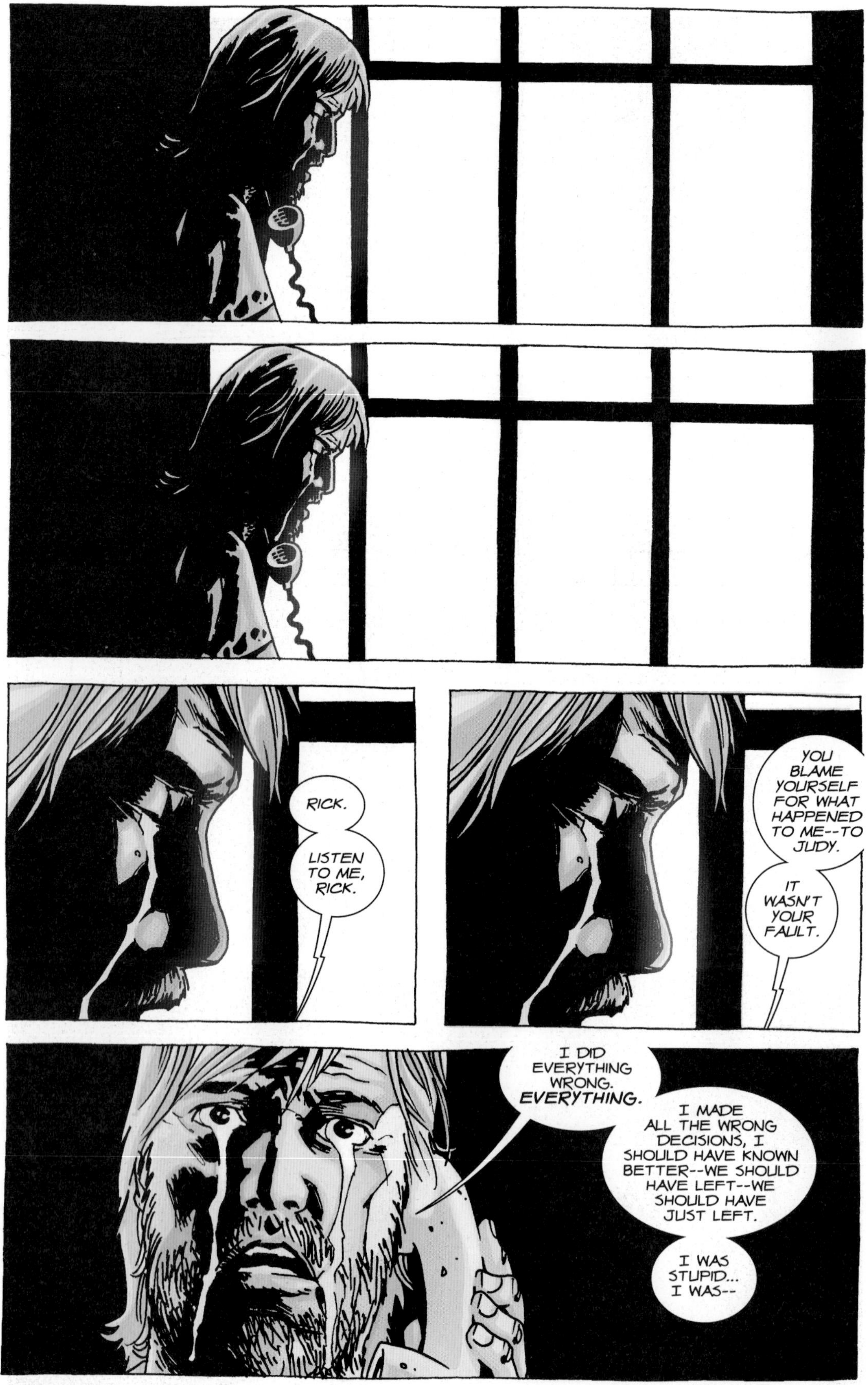
RICK.
LISTEN TO ME, RICK.
YOU BLAME YOURSELF FOR WHAT HAPPENED TO ME--TO JUDY.
IT WASN'T YOUR FAULT.
I DID EVERYTHING WRONG. EVERYTHING.
I MADE ALL THE WRONG DECISIONS, I SHOULD HAVE KNOWN BETTER--WE SHOULD HAVE LEFT--WE SHOULD HAVE JUST LEFT.
I WAS STUPID... I WAS--

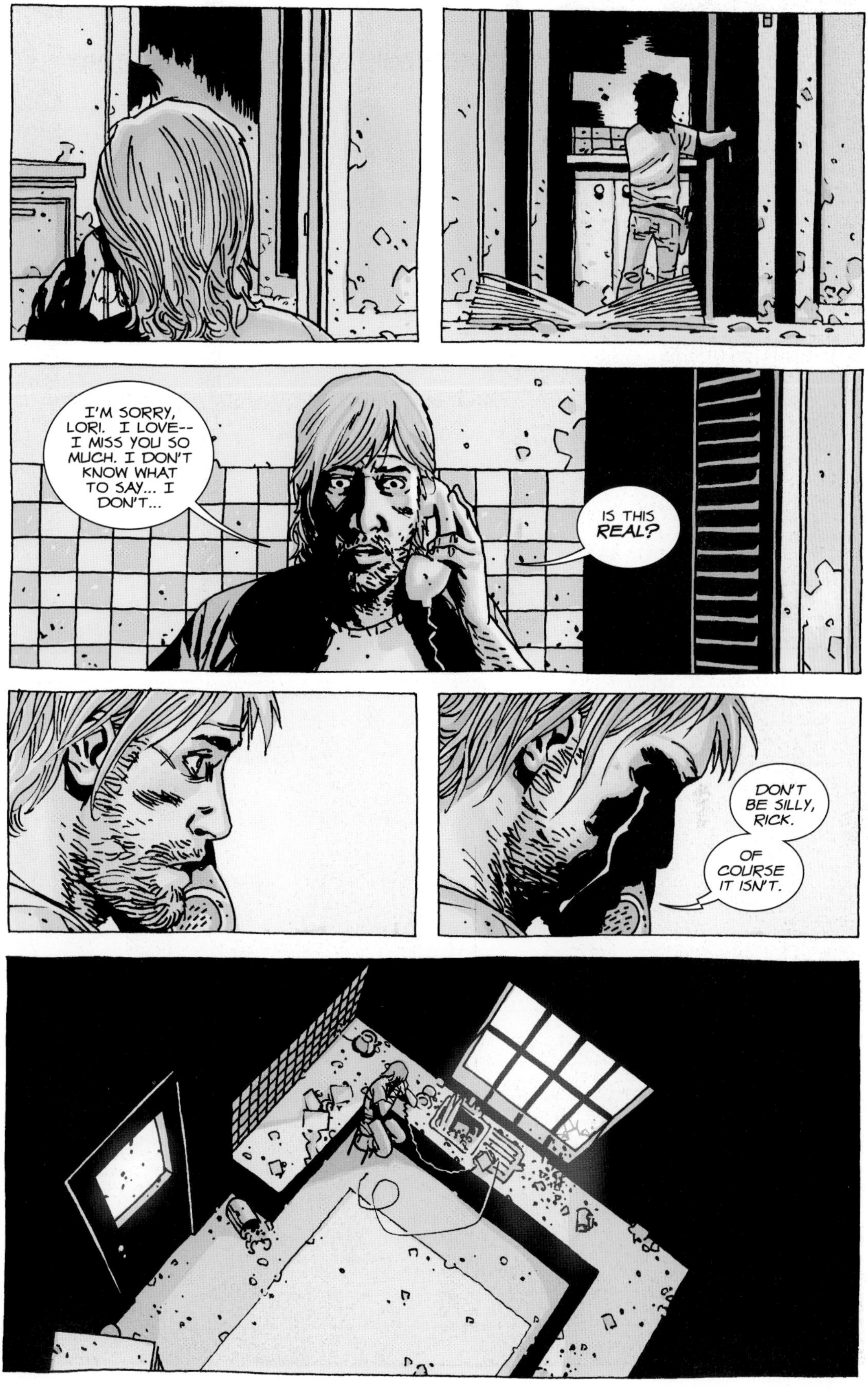
I'M SORRY, LORI. I LOVE-- I MISS YOU SO MUCH. I DON'T KNOW WHAT TO SAY... I DON'T...
IS THIS REAL?
DON'T BE SILLY, RICK.
OF COURSE IT ISN'T.

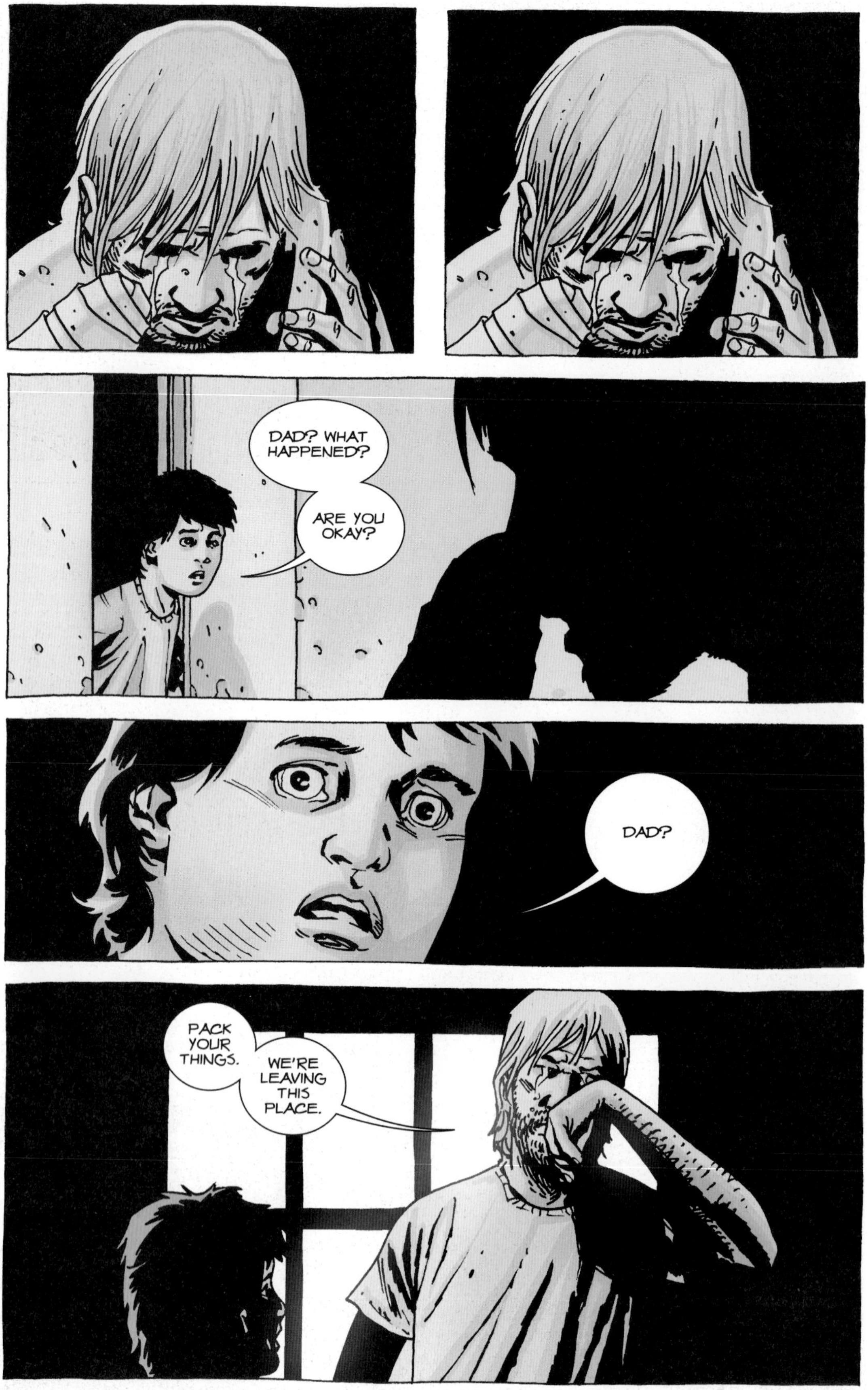
DAD? WHAT HAPPENED?
ARE YOU OKAY?
DAD?
PACK YOUR THINGS.
WE'RE LEAVING THIS PLACE.

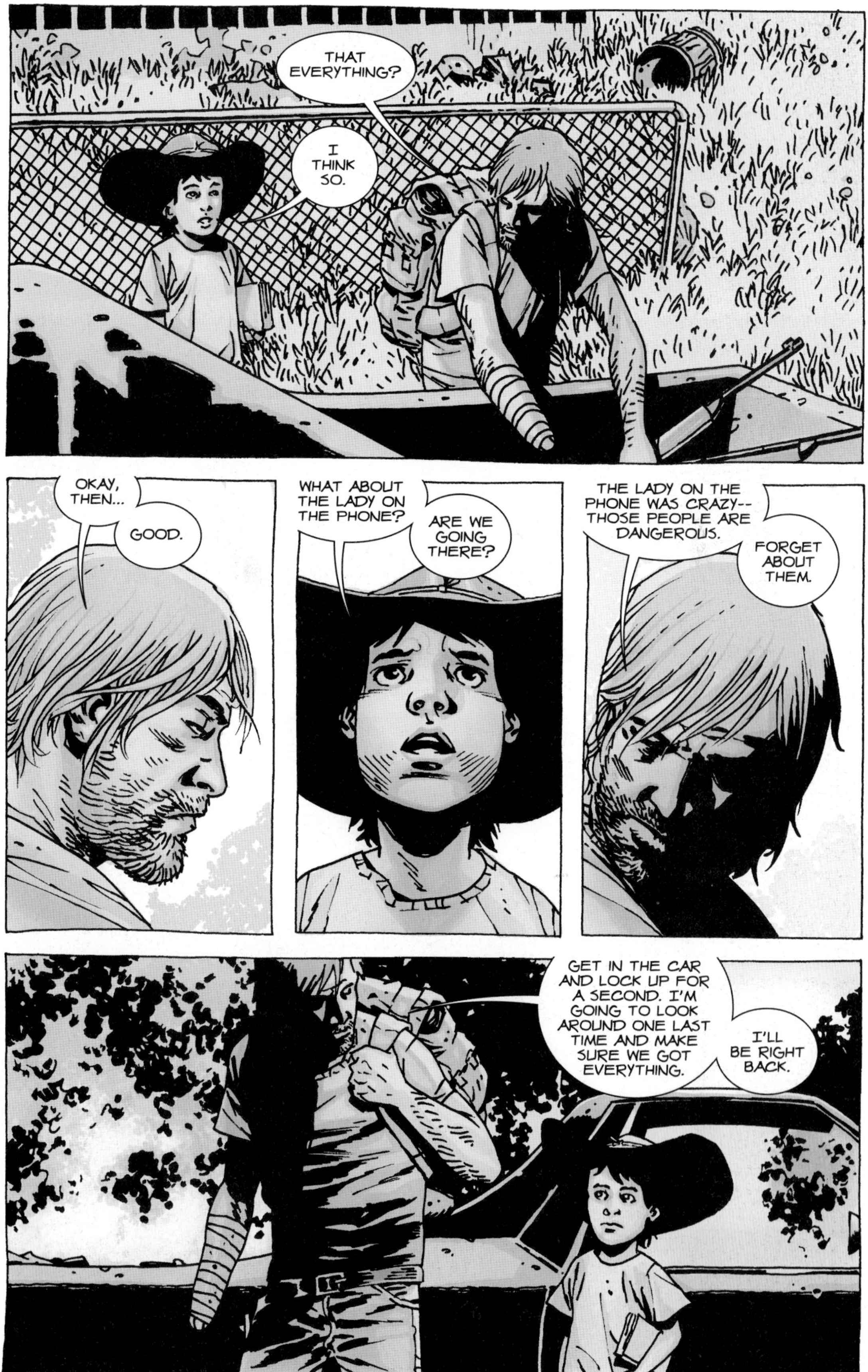
THAT EVERYTHING?
I THINK SO.
OKAY, THEN...
GOOD.
WHAT ABOUT THE LADY ON THE PHONE?
ARE WE GOING THERE?
THE LADY ON THE PHONE WAS CRAZY-- THOSE PEOPLE ARE DANGEROUS.
FORGET ABOUT THEM.
GET IN THE CAR AND LOCK UP FOR A SECOND. I'M GOING TO LOOK AROUND ONE LAST TIME AND MAKE SURE WE GOT EVERYTHING.
I'LL BE RIGHT BACK.

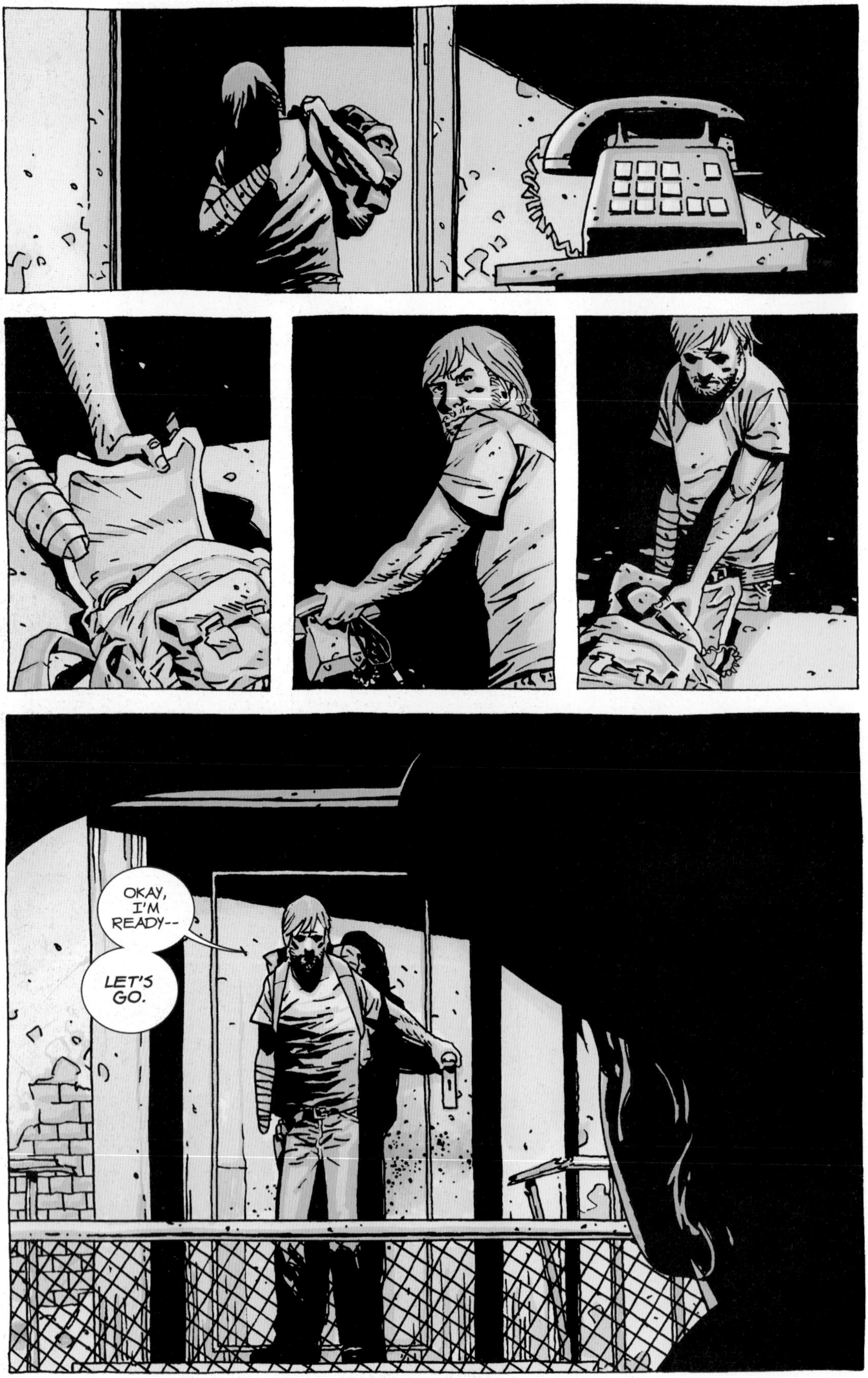
OKAY, I'M READY--
LET'S GO.

RNNK?

VMMMMMM!

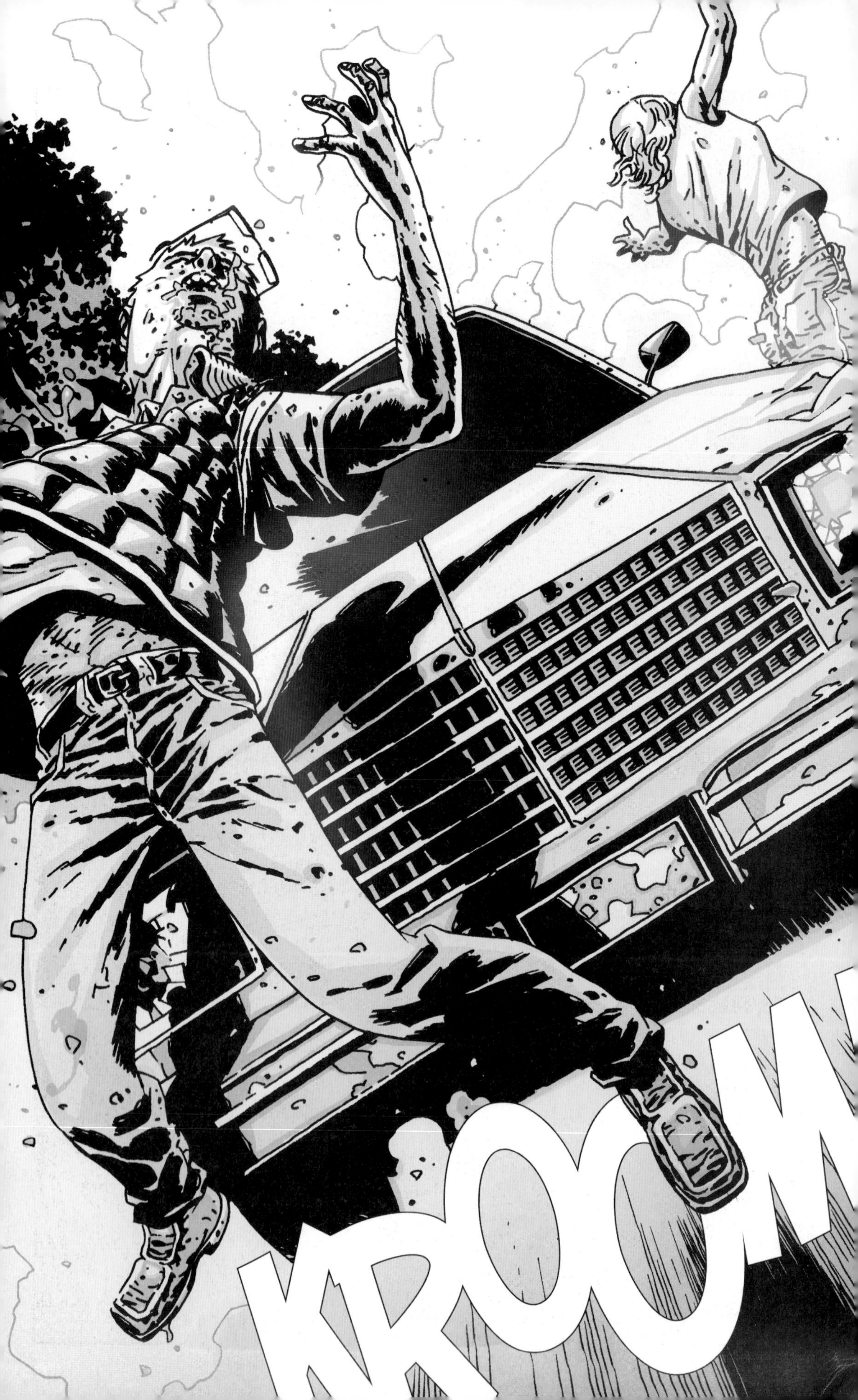

KROOM

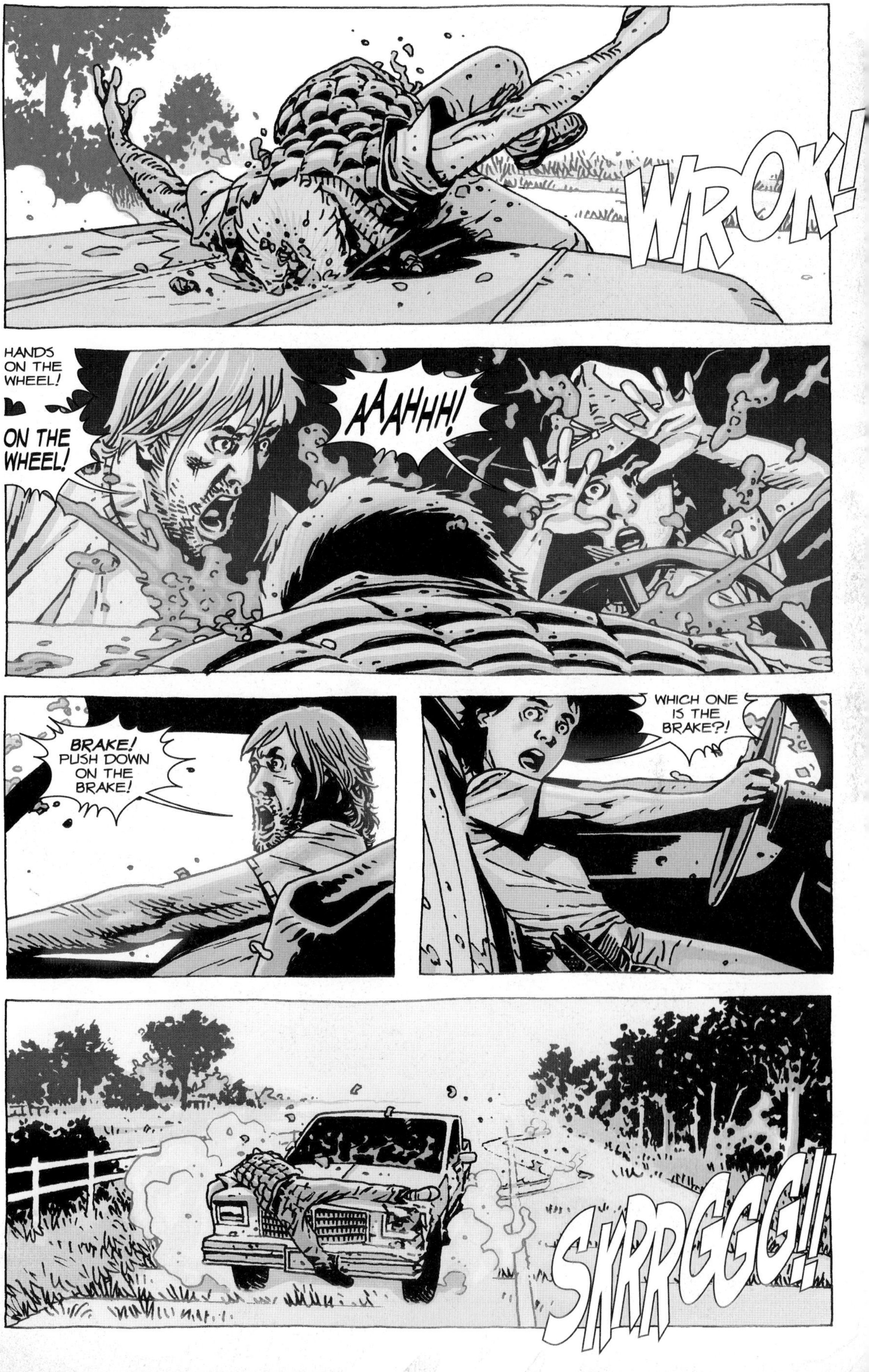
WROK!
HANDS ON THE WHEEL!
ON THE WHEEL!
AAAHHH!
BRAKE! PUSH DOWN ON THE BRAKE!
WHICH ONE IS THE BRAKE?!
SKRRGGG!!

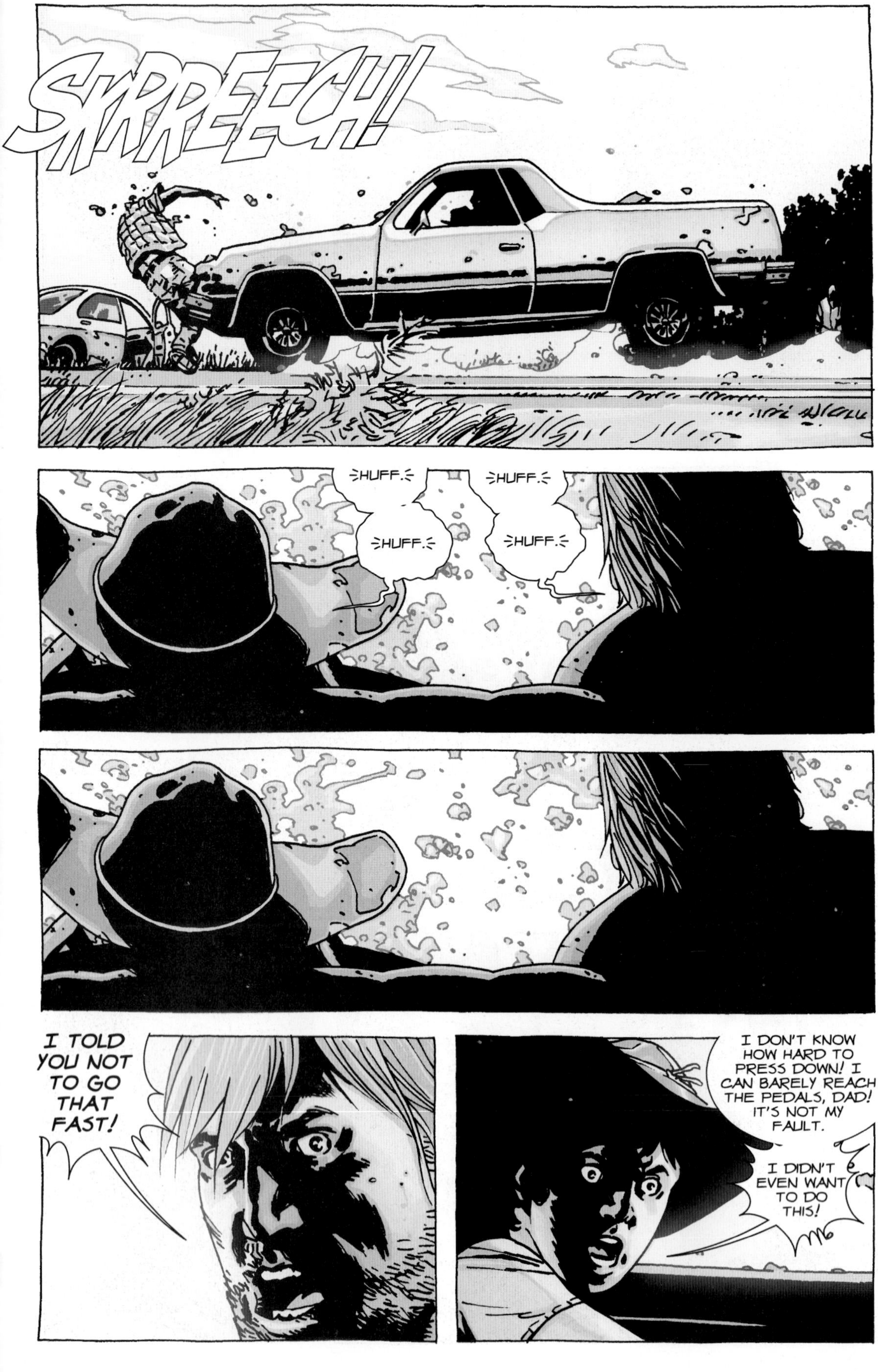
SKRREEECH!
HUFF.
HUFF.
HUFF.
HUFF.
I TOLD YOU NOT TO GO THAT FAST!
I DON'T KNOW HOW HARD TO PRESS DOWN! I CAN BARELY REACH THE PEDALS, DAD! IT'S NOT MY FAULT.
I DIDN'T EVEN WANT TO DO THIS!

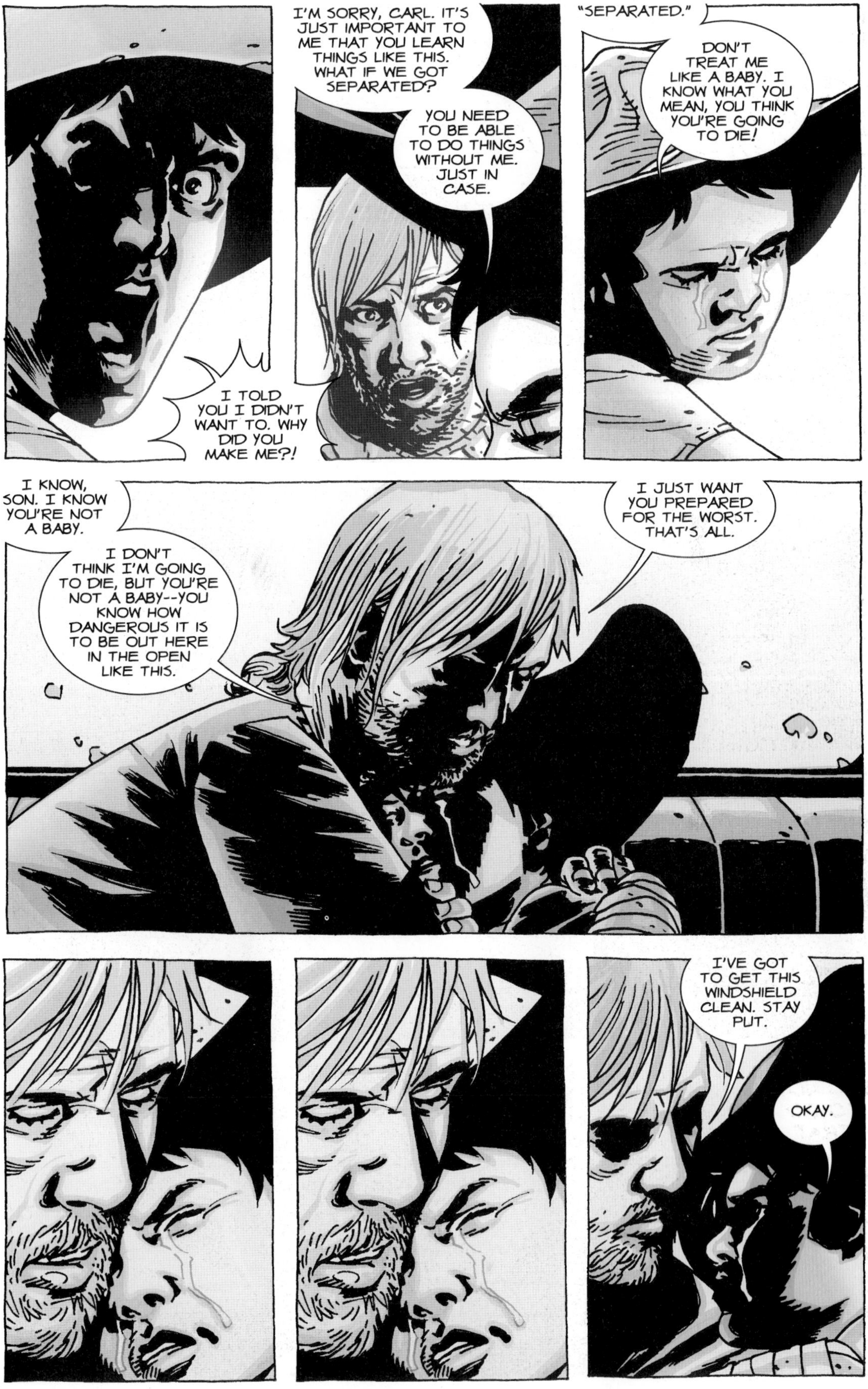
I TOLD YOU I DIDN'T WANT TO. WHY DID YOU MAKE ME?!
I'M SORRY, CARL. IT'S JUST IMPORTANT TO ME THAT YOU LEARN THINGS LIKE THIS. WHAT IF WE GOT SEPARATED?
YOU NEED TO BE ABLE TO DO THINGS WITHOUT ME. JUST IN CASE.
"SEPARATED."
DON'T TREAT ME LIKE A BABY. I KNOW WHAT YOU MEAN, YOU THINK YOU'RE GOING TO DIE!
I KNOW, SON. I KNOW YOU'RE NOT A BABY.
I DON'T THINK I'M GOING TO DIE, BUT YOU'RE NOT A BABY--YOU KNOW HOW DANGEROUS IT IS TO BE OUT HERE IN THE OPEN LIKE THIS.
I JUST WANT YOU PREPARED FOR THE WORST. THAT'S ALL.
I'VE GOT TO GET THIS WINDSHIELD CLEAN. STAY PUT.
OKAY.

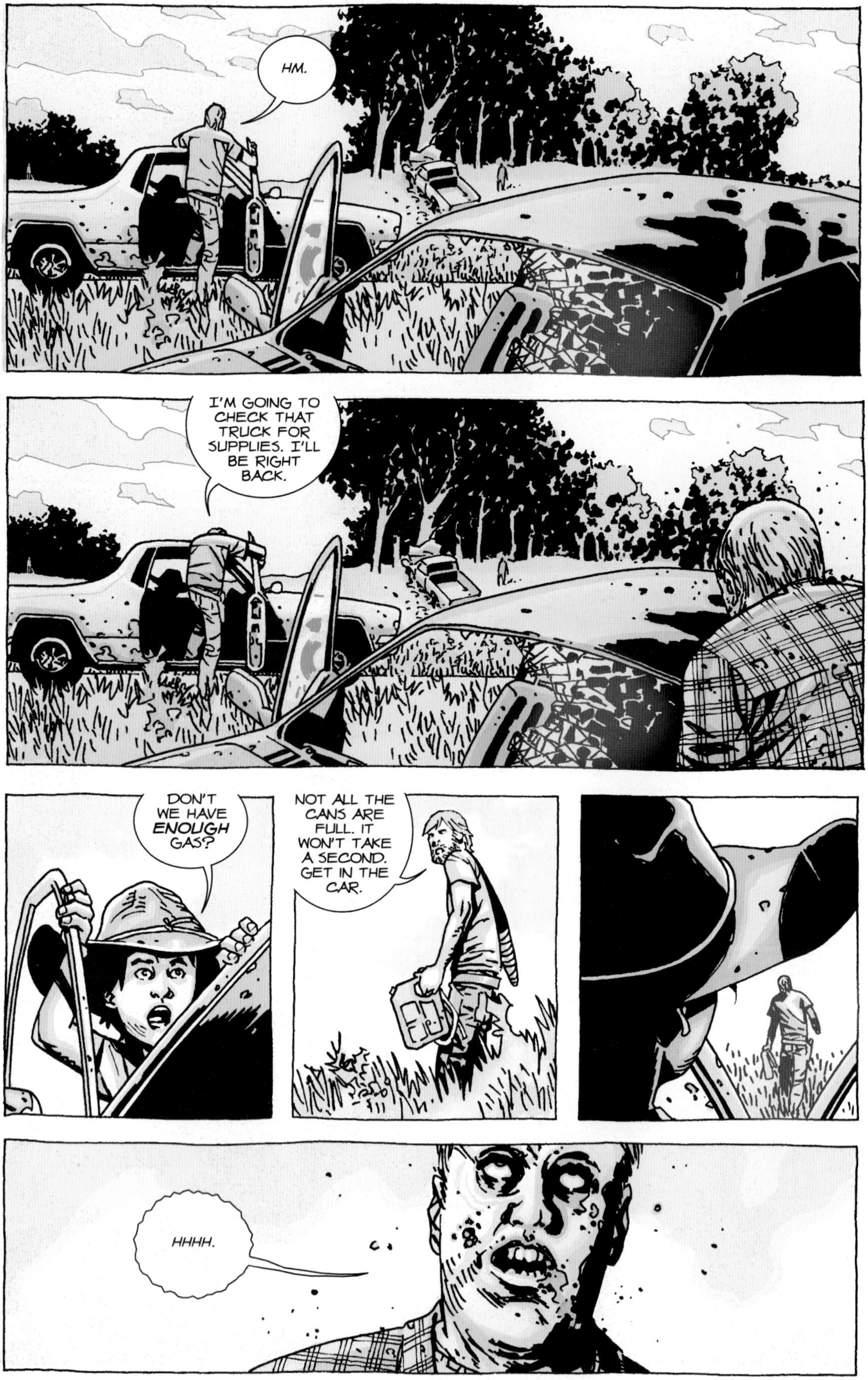
HM.
I'M GOING TO CHECK THAT TRUCK FOR SUPPLIES. I'LL BE RIGHT BACK.
DON'T WE HAVE ENOUGH GAS?
NOT ALL THE CANS ARE FULL. IT WON'T TAKE A SECOND. GET IN THE CAR.
HHHH.

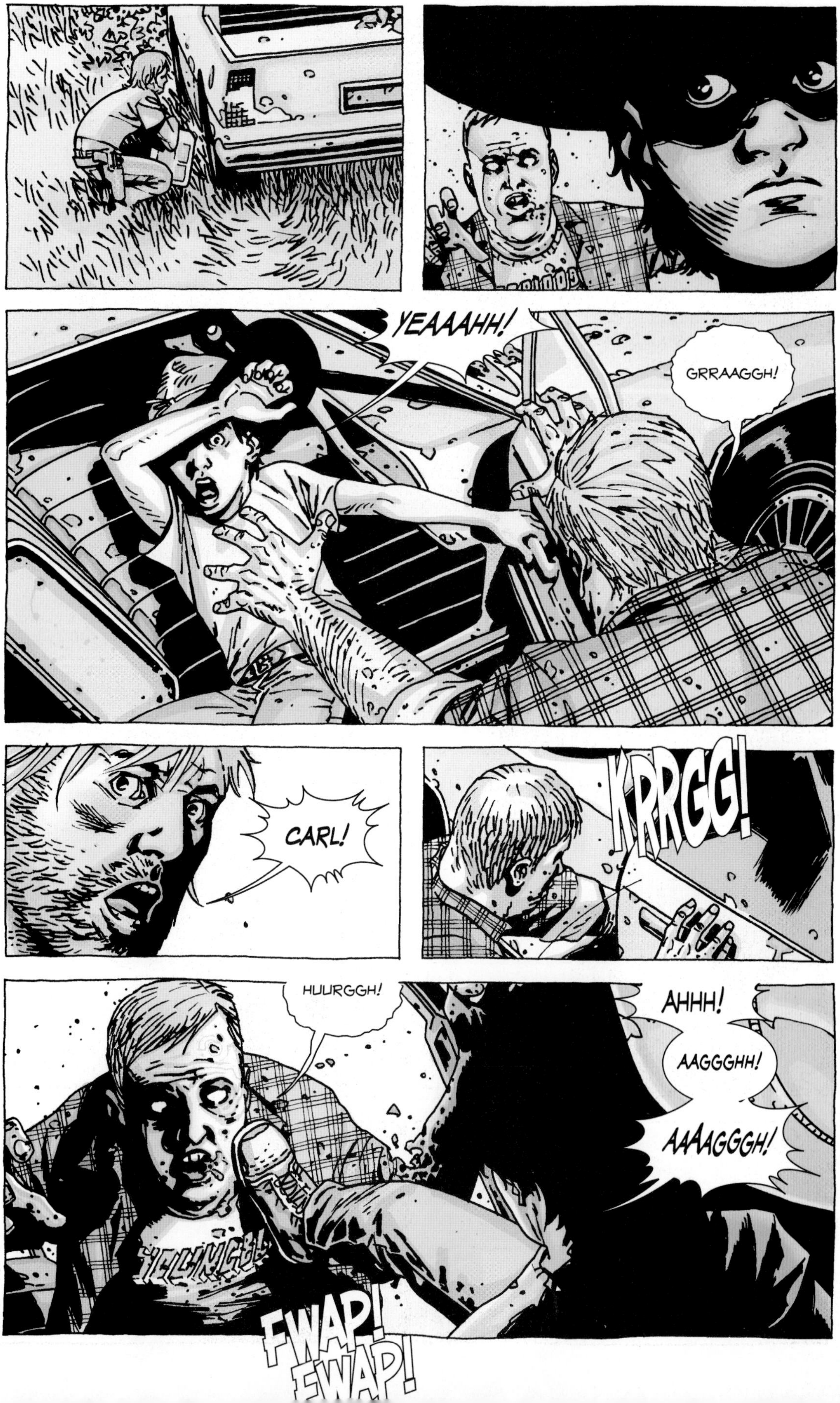
YEAAAHH!
GRRAAGGH!
CARL!
KRRGG!
HUURGGH!
AHHH!
AAGGGHH!
AAAAGGGH!
FWAP!
FWAP!

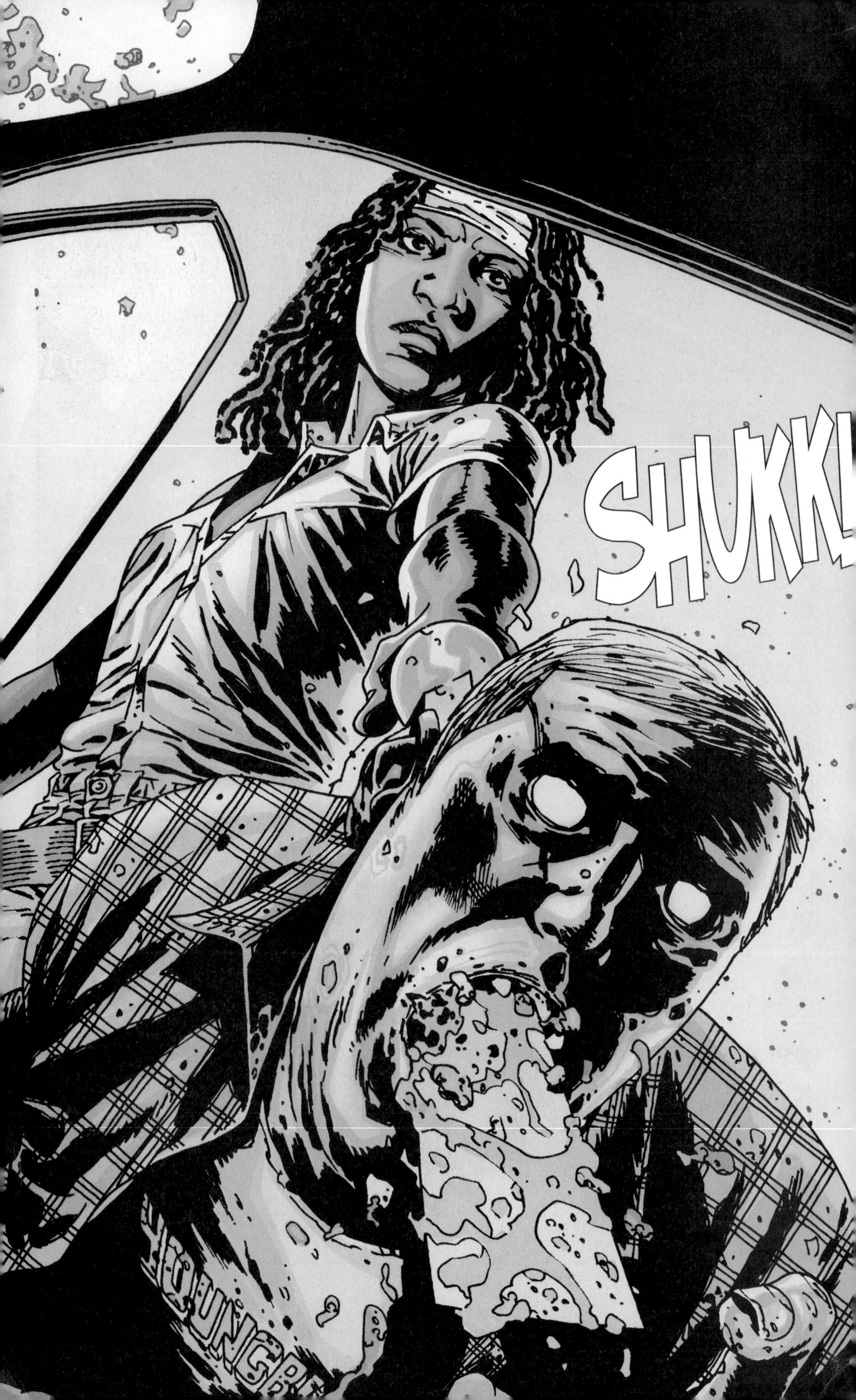
SHUKKL

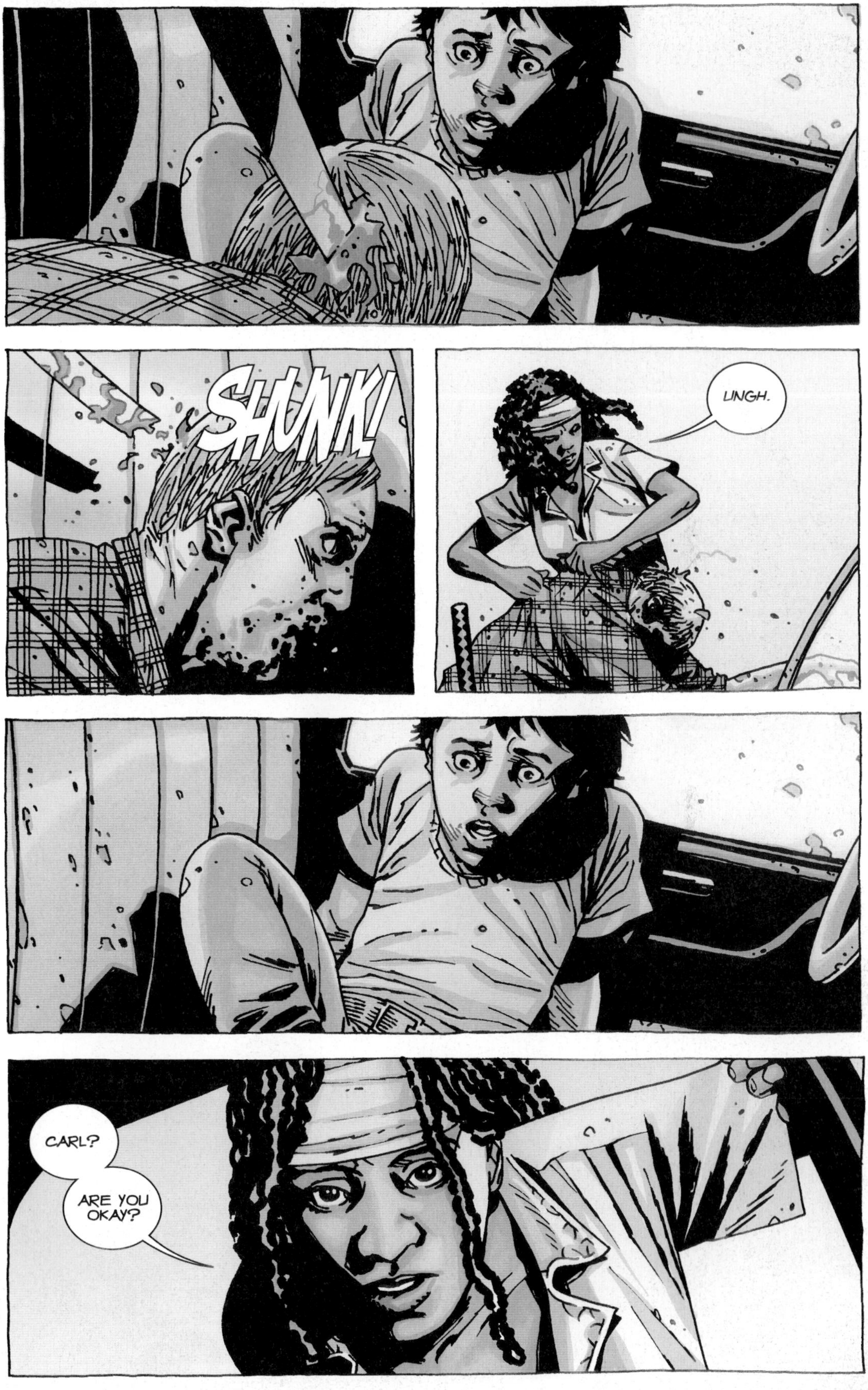
SHUNK!
UNGH.
CARL?
ARE YOU OKAY?

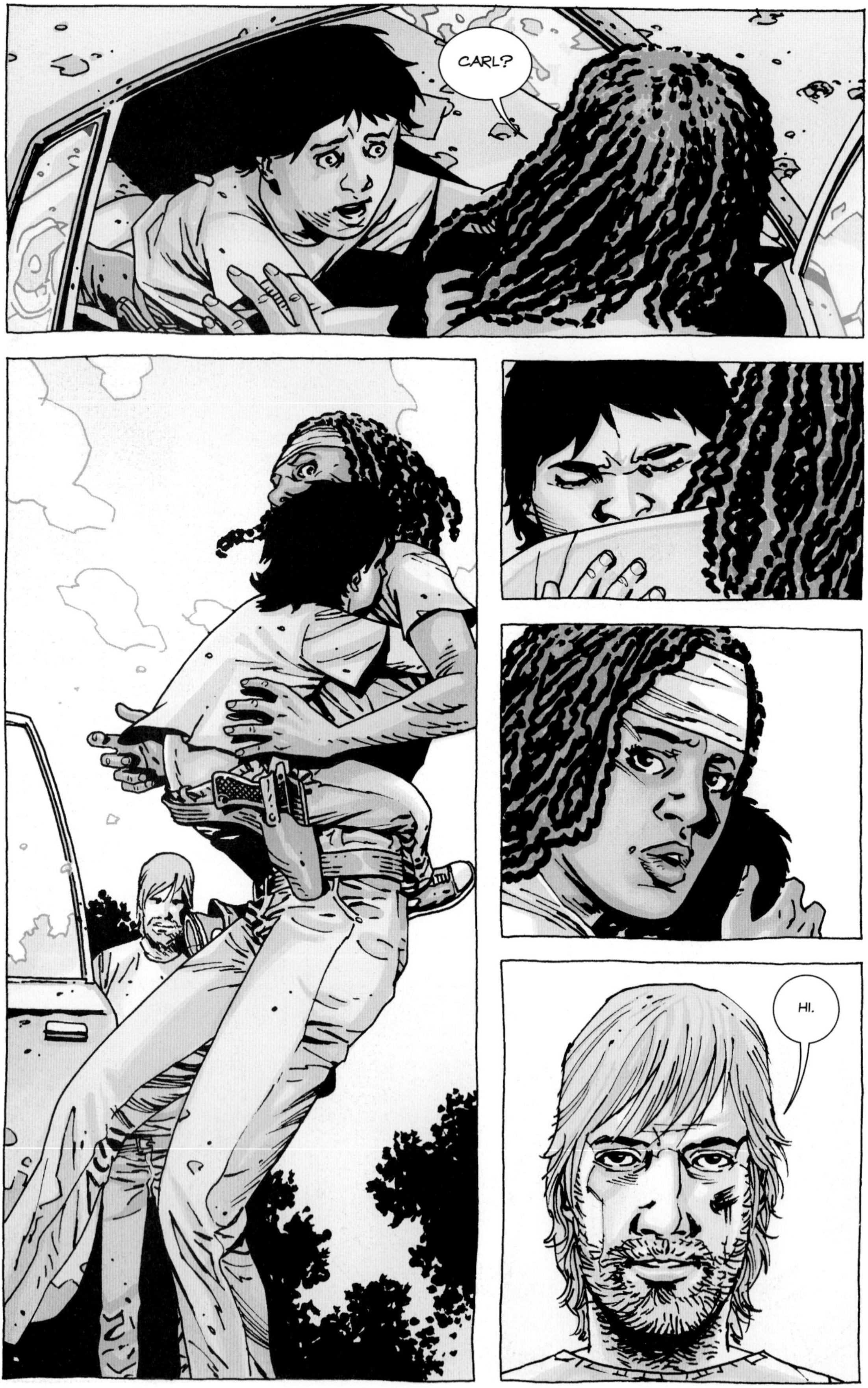
CARL?
HI.

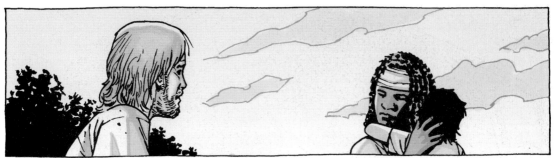

TYREESE, HE--

I KNOW.

I'M SORRY IF I'M TOO HEAVY.

I JUST-- THANKS FOR SAVING ME.

I'M GLAD YOU'RE OKAY.

I'M GLAD YOU'RE OKAY.

WHERE ARE YOU GUYS HEADED?

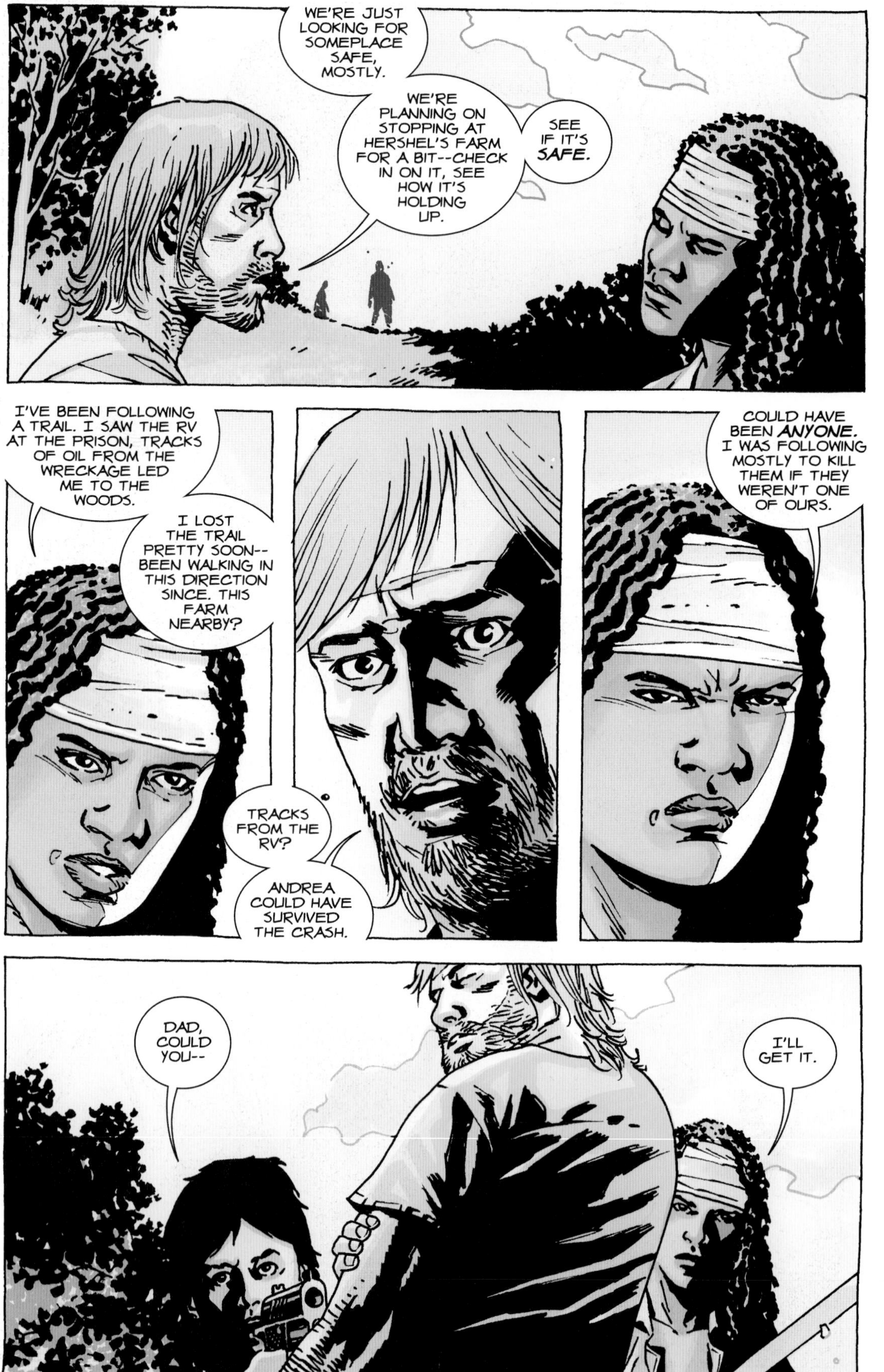

WE'RE JUST LOOKING FOR SOMEPLACE SAFE, MOSTLY.
WE'RE PLANNING ON STOPPING AT HERSHEL'S FARM FOR A BIT--CHECK IN ON IT, SEE HOW IT'S HOLDING UP.
SEE IF IT'S *SAFE.*
I'VE BEEN FOLLOWING A TRAIL. I SAW THE RV AT THE PRISON, TRACKS OF OIL FROM THE WRECKAGE LED ME TO THE WOODS.
I LOST THE TRAIL PRETTY SOON--BEEN WALKING IN THIS DIRECTION SINCE. THIS FARM NEARBY?
TRACKS FROM THE RV?
ANDREA COULD HAVE SURVIVED THE CRASH.
COULD HAVE BEEN *ANYONE.* I WAS FOLLOWING MOSTLY TO KILL THEM IF THEY WEREN'T ONE OF OURS.
DAD, COULD YOU--
I'LL GET IT.

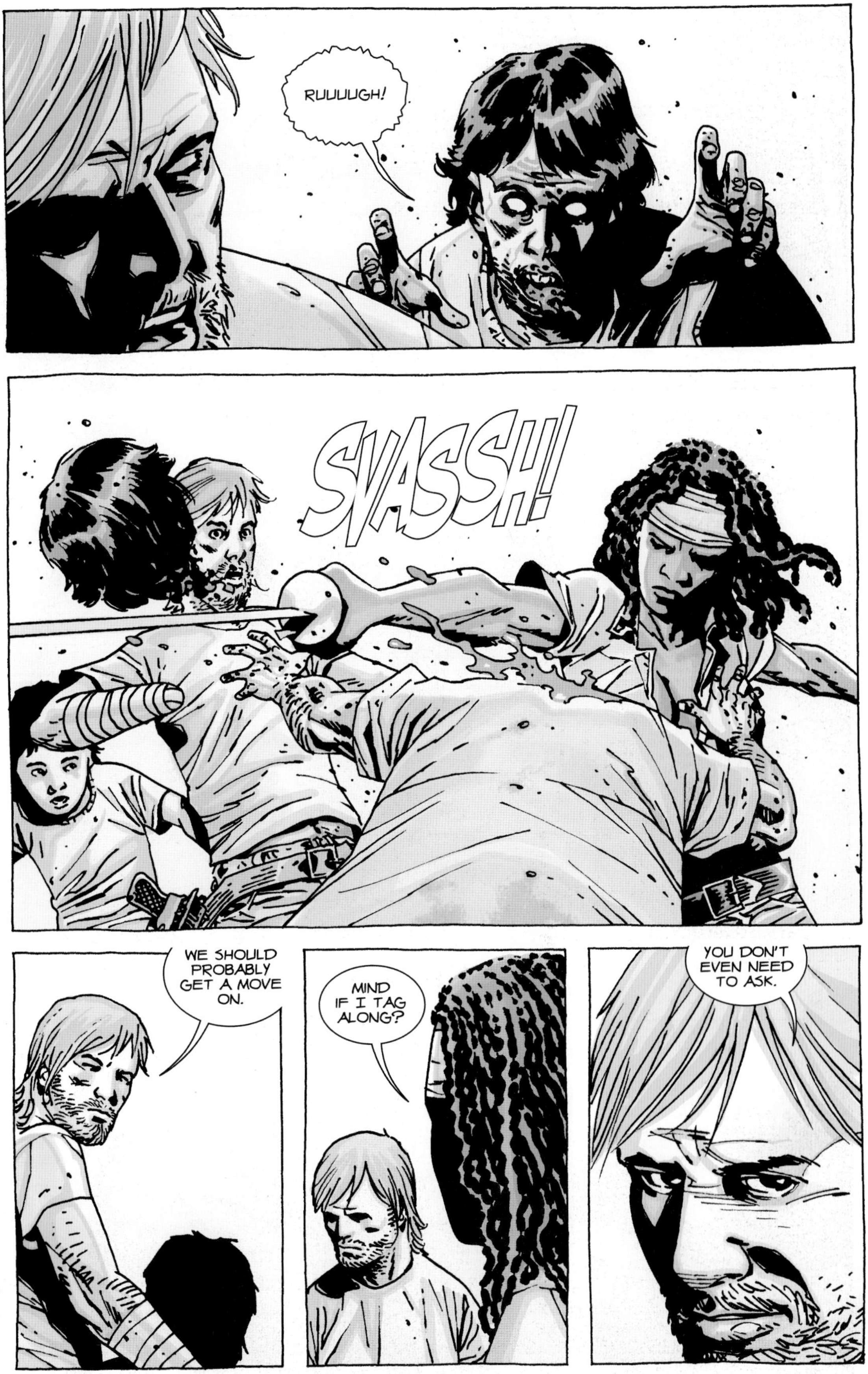

RUUUUGH!
SVASSH!
WE SHOULD PROBABLY GET A MOVE ON.
MIND IF I TAG ALONG?
YOU DON'T EVEN NEED TO ASK.

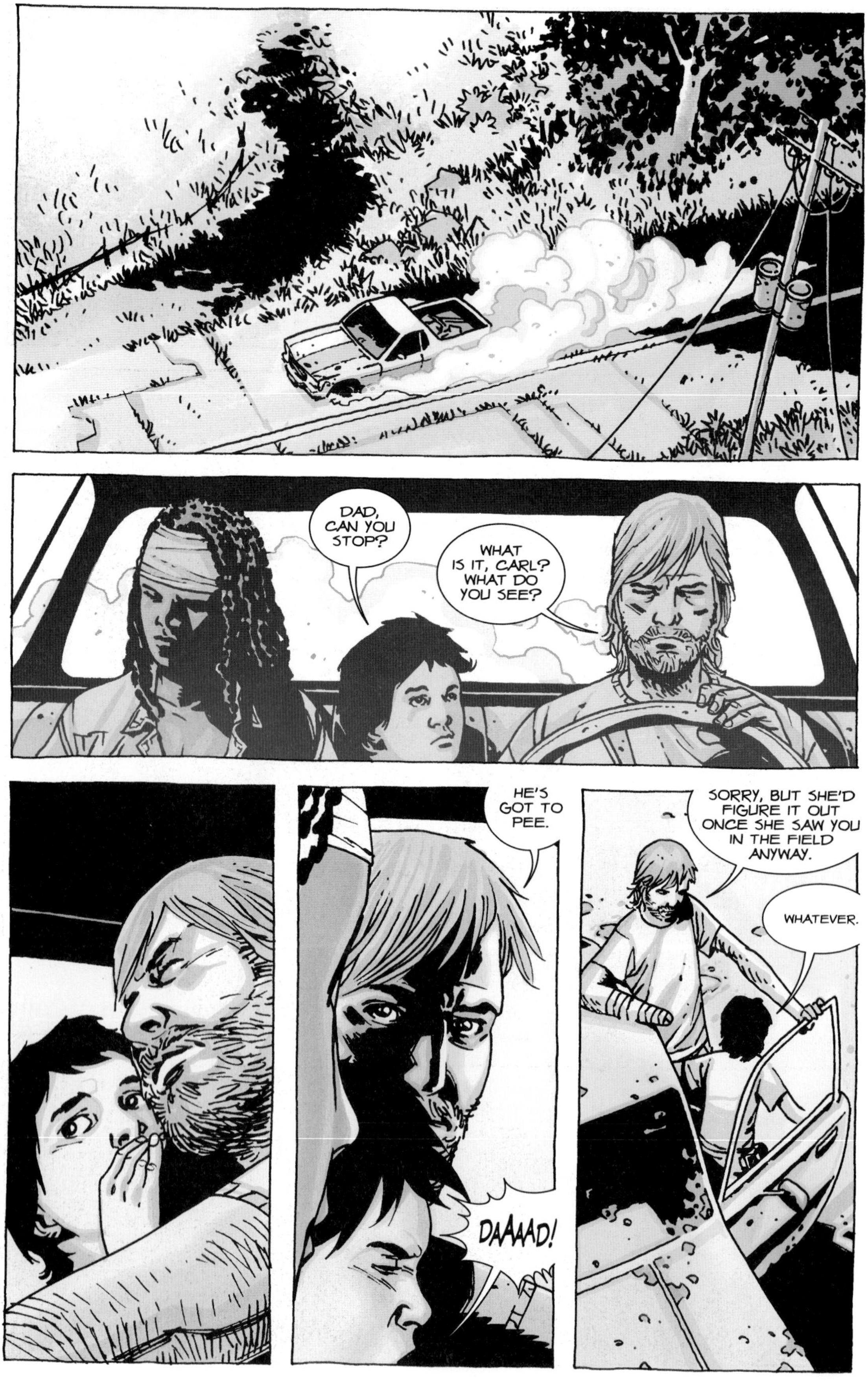

DAD, CAN YOU STOP?
WHAT IS IT, CARL? WHAT DO YOU SEE?
HE'S GOT TO PEE.
DAAAAD!
SORRY, BUT SHE'D FIGURE IT OUT ONCE SHE SAW YOU IN THE FIELD ANYWAY.
WHATEVER.

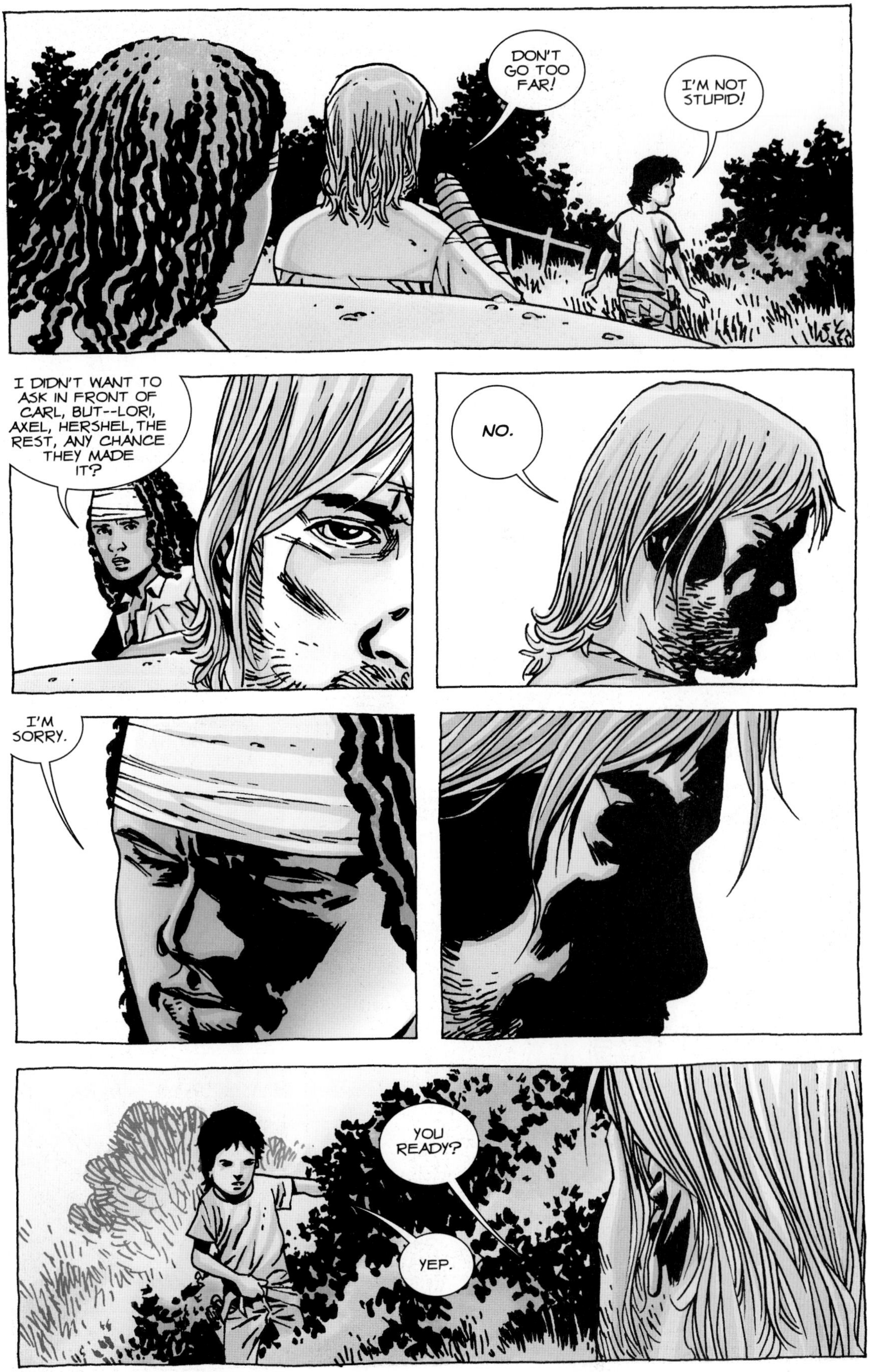
DON'T GO TOO FAR!
I'M NOT STUPID!
I DIDN'T WANT TO ASK IN FRONT OF CARL, BUT--LORI, AXEL, HERSHEL, THE REST, ANY CHANCE THEY MADE IT?
NO.
I'M SORRY.
YOU READY?
YEP.

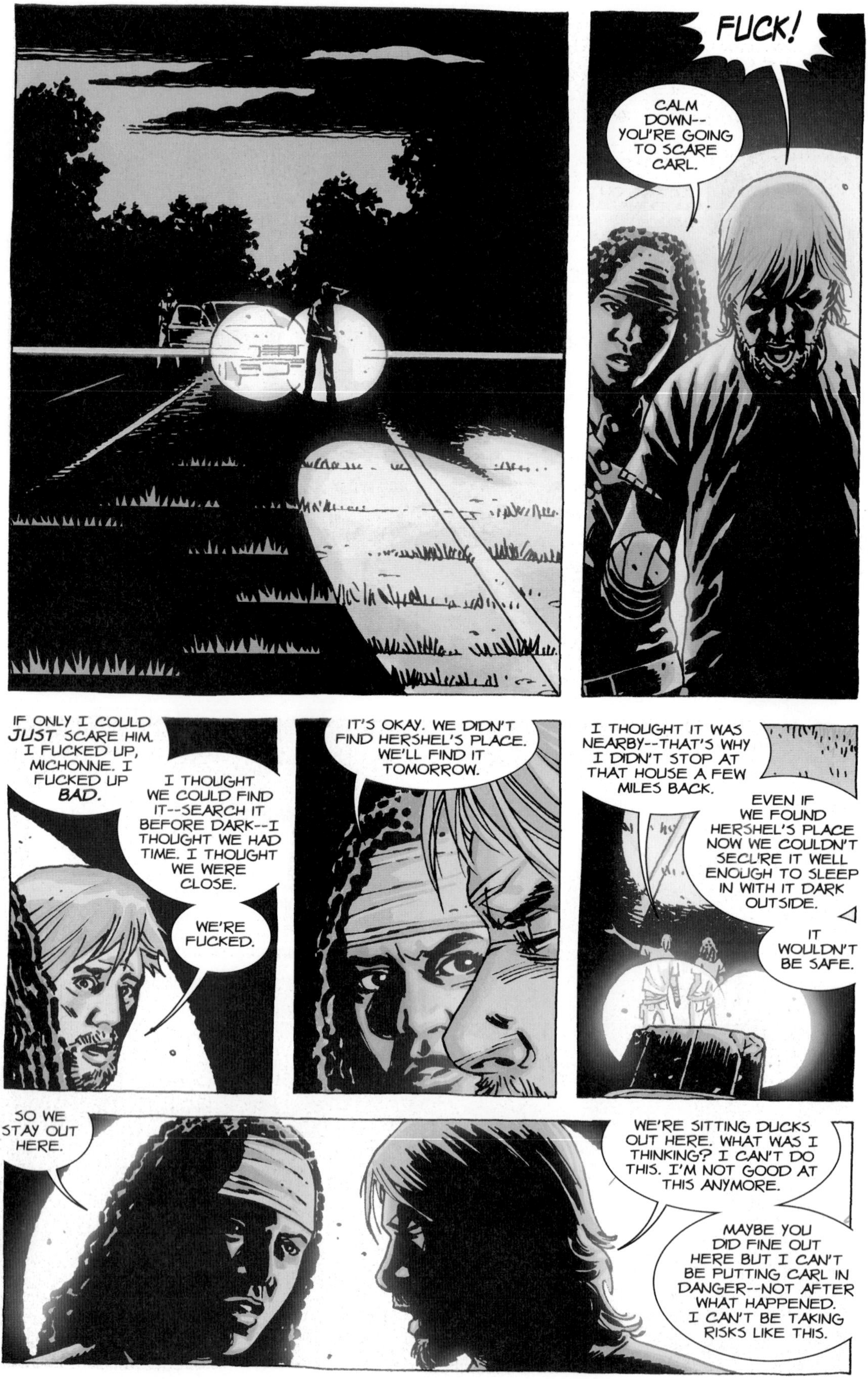
FUCK!
CALM DOWN-- YOU'RE GOING TO SCARE CARL.
IF ONLY I COULD JUST SCARE HIM. I FUCKED UP, MICHONNE. I FUCKED UP BAD.
I THOUGHT WE COULD FIND IT--SEARCH IT BEFORE DARK--I THOUGHT WE HAD TIME. I THOUGHT WE WERE CLOSE.
WE'RE FUCKED.
IT'S OKAY. WE DIDN'T FIND HERSHEL'S PLACE. WE'LL FIND IT TOMORROW.
I THOUGHT IT WAS NEARBY--THAT'S WHY I DIDN'T STOP AT THAT HOUSE A FEW MILES BACK.
EVEN IF WE FOUND HERSHEL'S PLACE NOW WE COULDN'T SECURE IT WELL ENOUGH TO SLEEP IN WITH IT DARK OUTSIDE.
IT WOULDN'T BE SAFE.
SO WE STAY OUT HERE.
WE'RE SITTING DUCKS OUT HERE. WHAT WAS I THINKING? I CAN'T DO THIS. I'M NOT GOOD AT THIS ANYMORE.
MAYBE YOU DID FINE OUT HERE BUT I CAN'T BE PUTTING CARL IN DANGER--NOT AFTER WHAT HAPPENED. I CAN'T BE TAKING RISKS LIKE THIS.

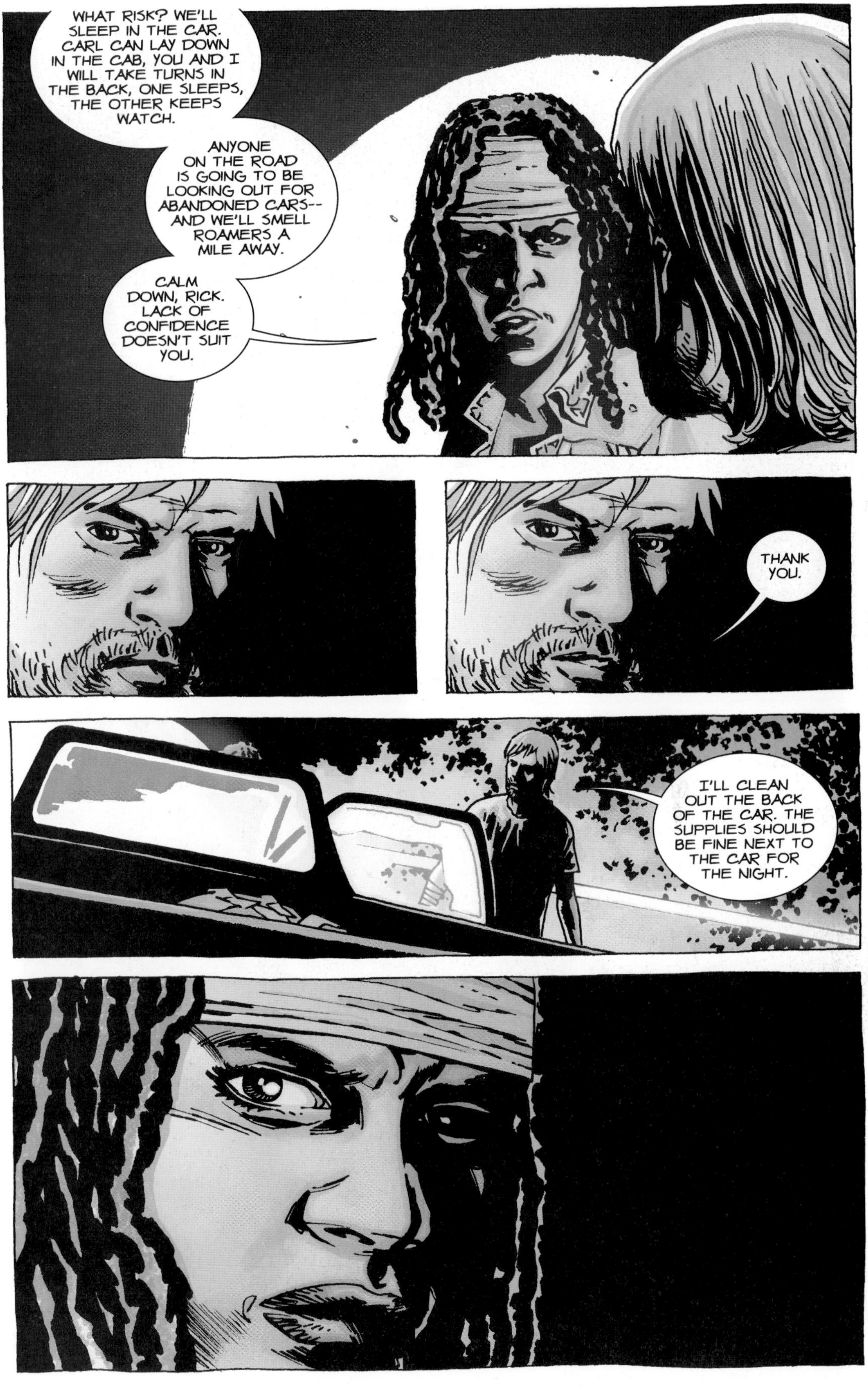
WHAT RISK? WE'LL SLEEP IN THE CAR. CARL CAN LAY DOWN IN THE CAB, YOU AND I WILL TAKE TURNS IN THE BACK, ONE SLEEPS, THE OTHER KEEPS WATCH.
ANYONE ON THE ROAD IS GOING TO BE LOOKING OUT FOR ABANDONED CARS-- AND WE'LL SMELL ROAMERS A MILE AWAY.
CALM DOWN, RICK. LACK OF CONFIDENCE DOESN'T SUIT YOU.
THANK YOU.
I'LL CLEAN OUT THE BACK OF THE CAR. THE SUPPLIES SHOULD BE FINE NEXT TO THE CAR FOR THE NIGHT.

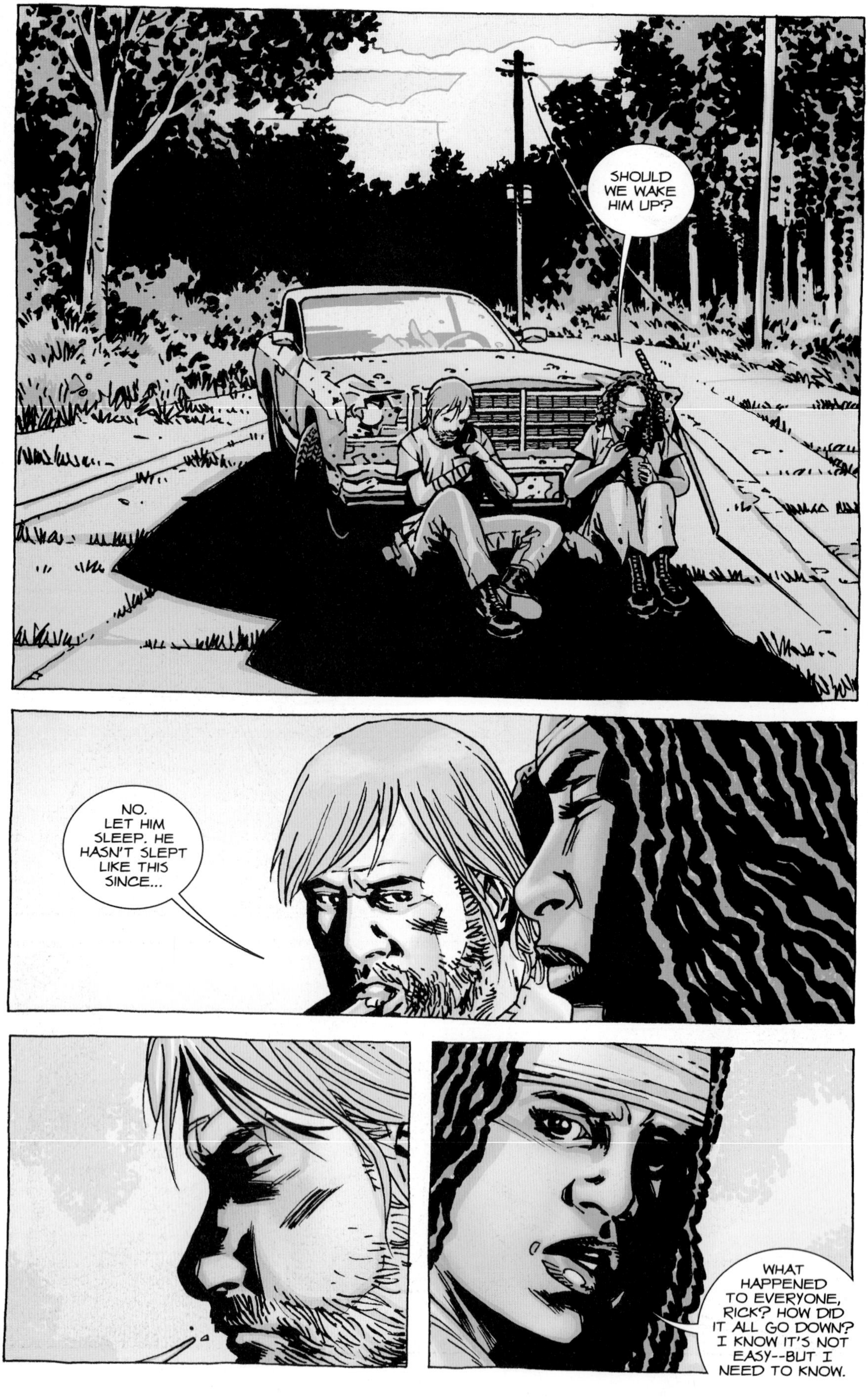
SHOULD WE WAKE HIM UP?
NO. LET HIM SLEEP. HE HASN'T SLEPT LIKE THIS SINCE...
WHAT HAPPENED TO EVERYONE, RICK? HOW DID IT ALL GO DOWN? I KNOW IT'S NOT EASY--BUT I NEED TO KNOW.

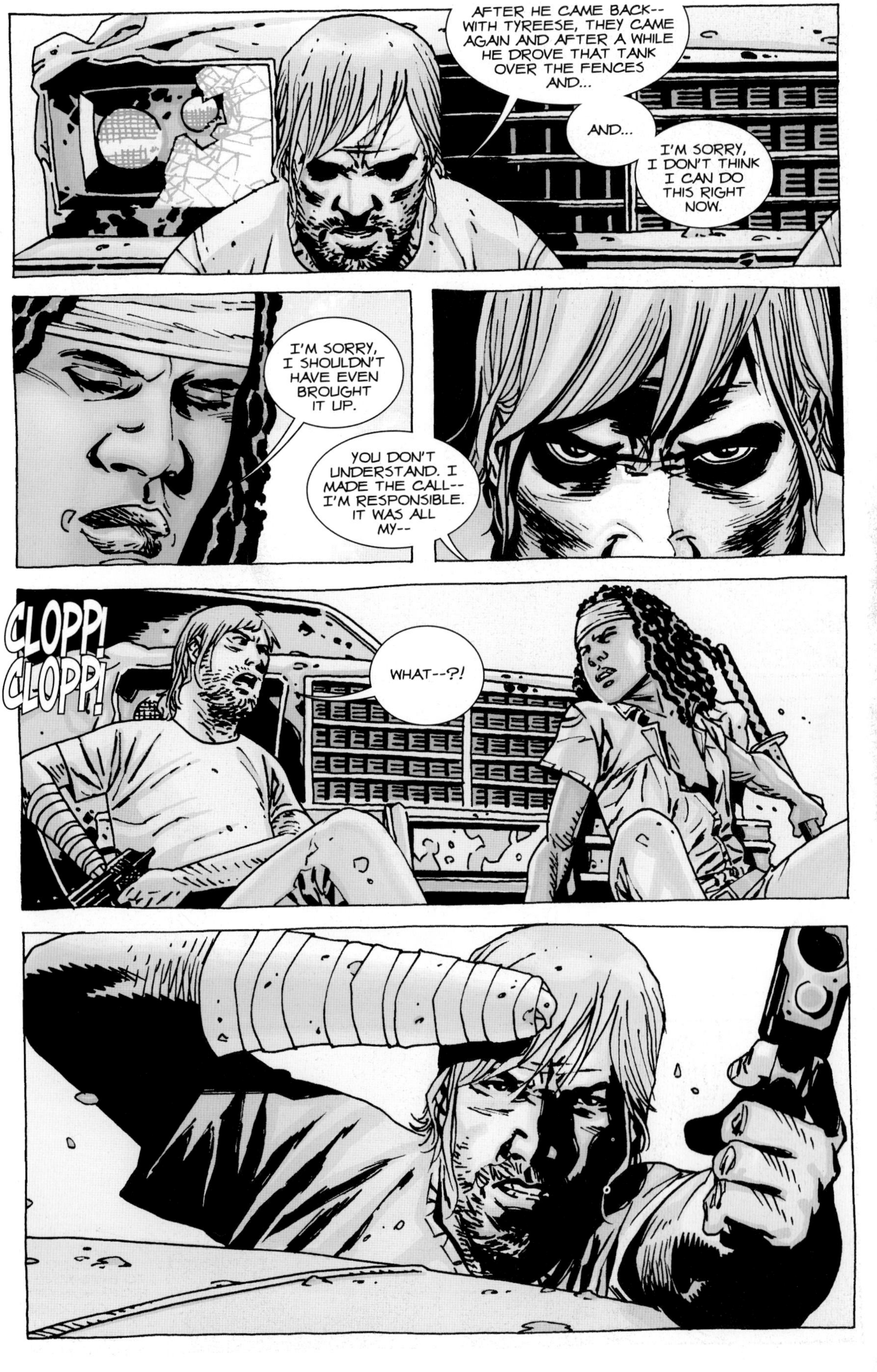
AFTER HE CAME BACK-- WITH TYREESE, THEY CAME AGAIN AND AFTER A WHILE HE DROVE THAT TANK OVER THE FENCES AND...
AND...
I'M SORRY, I DON'T THINK I CAN DO THIS RIGHT NOW.
I'M SORRY, I SHOULDN'T HAVE EVEN BROUGHT IT UP.
YOU DON'T UNDERSTAND. I MADE THE CALL-- I'M RESPONSIBLE. IT WAS ALL MY--
CLOPP! CLOPP!
WHAT--?!

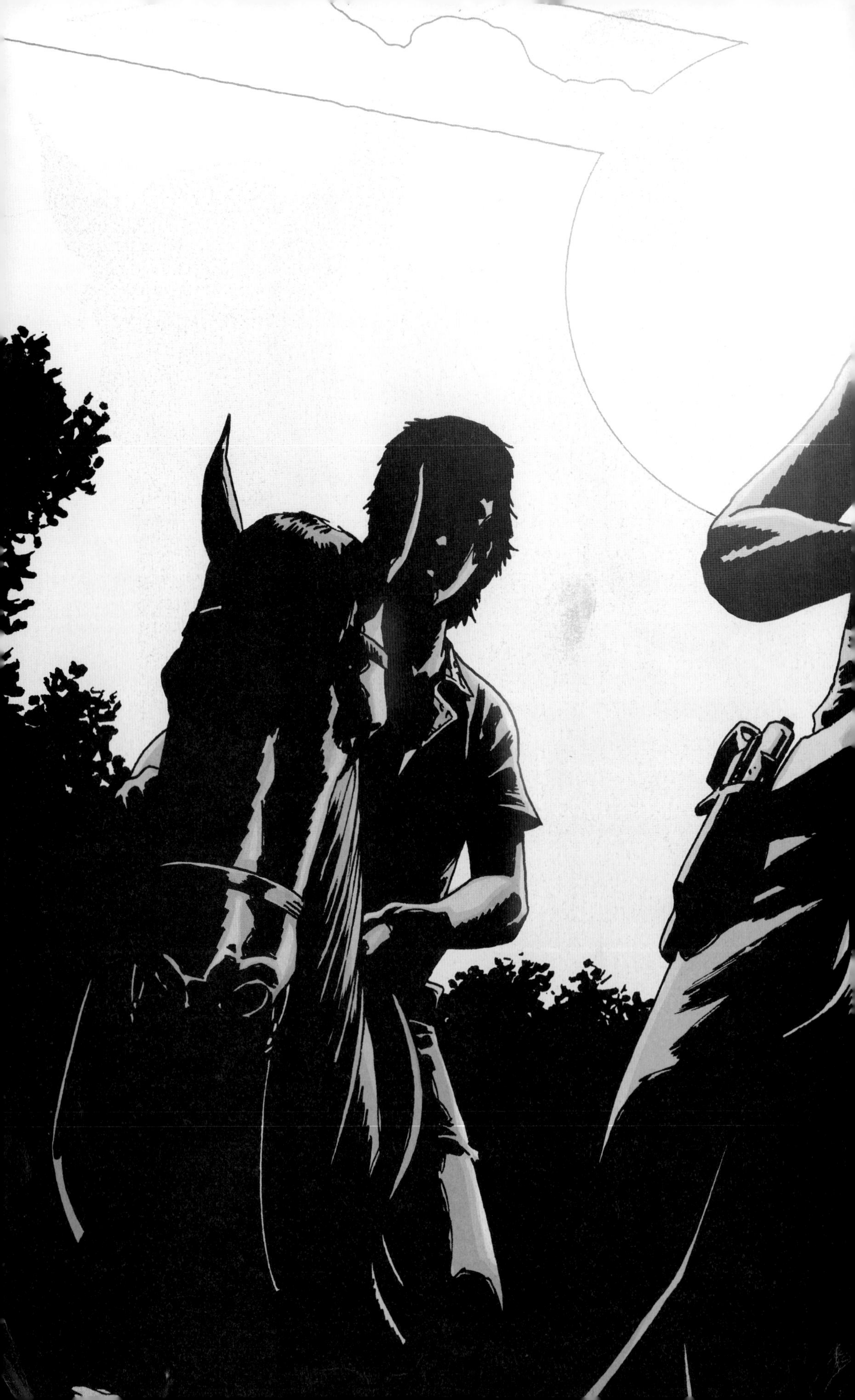

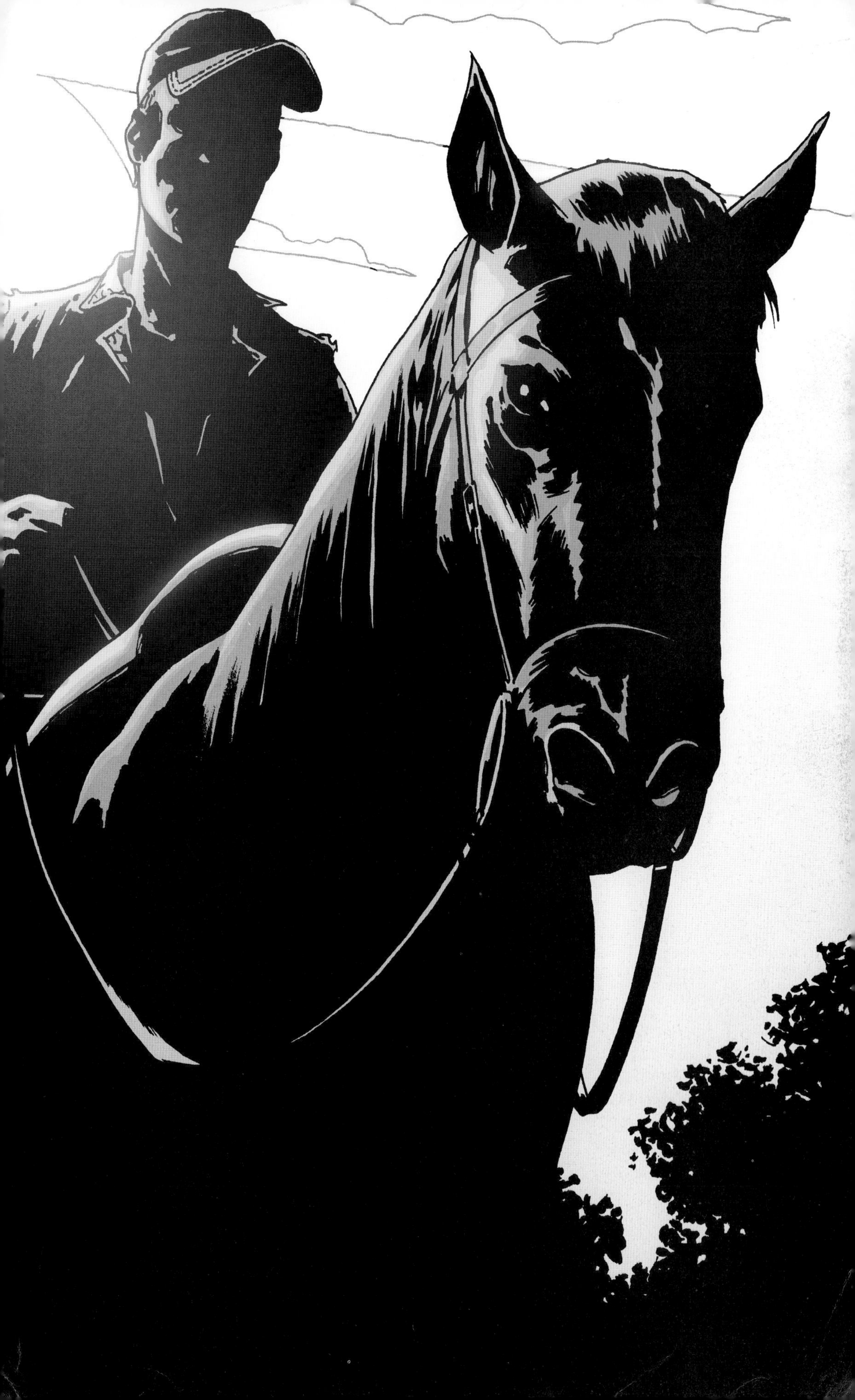

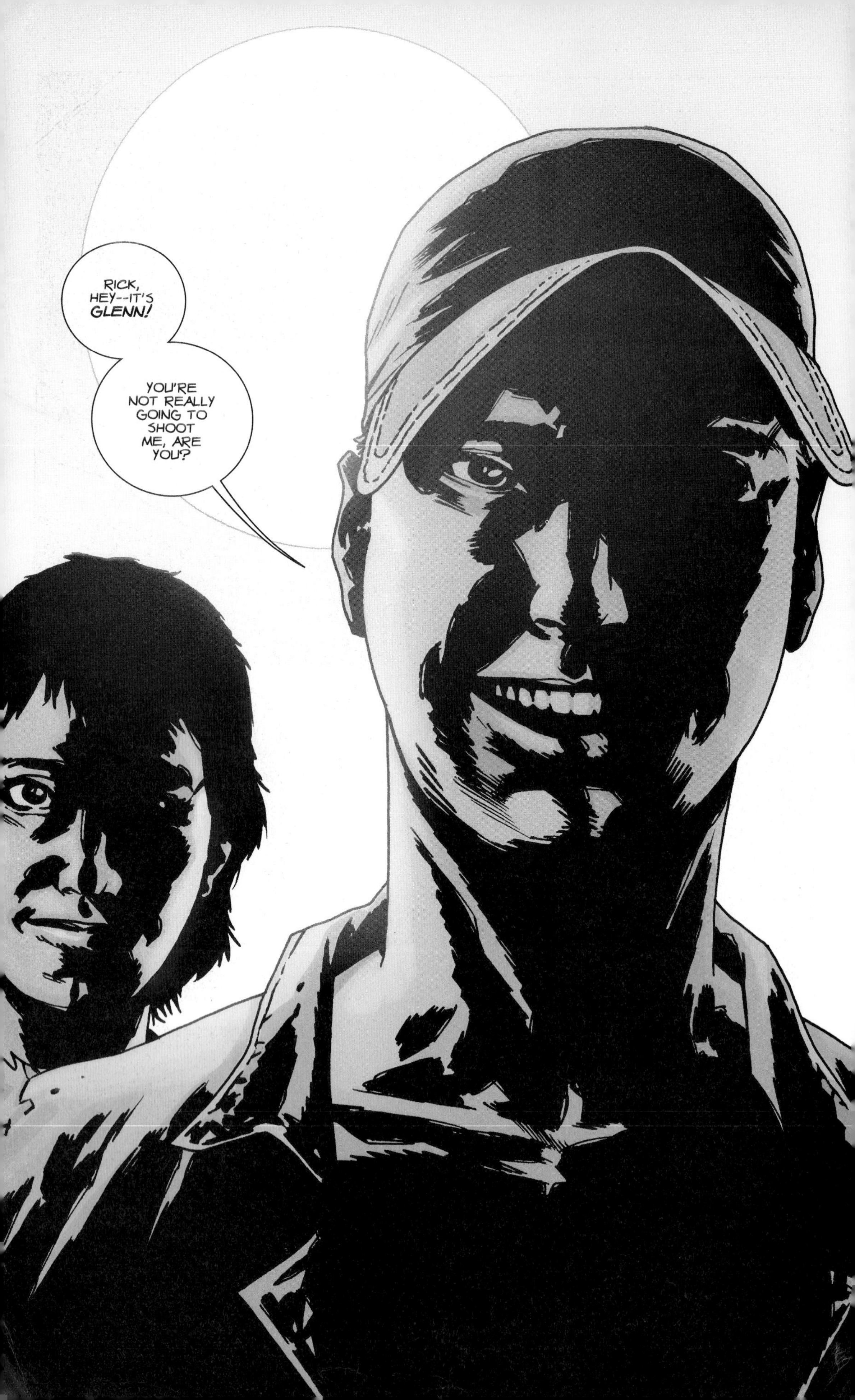
RICK, HEY--IT'S GLENN!
YOU'RE NOT REALLY GOING TO SHOOT ME, ARE YOU?

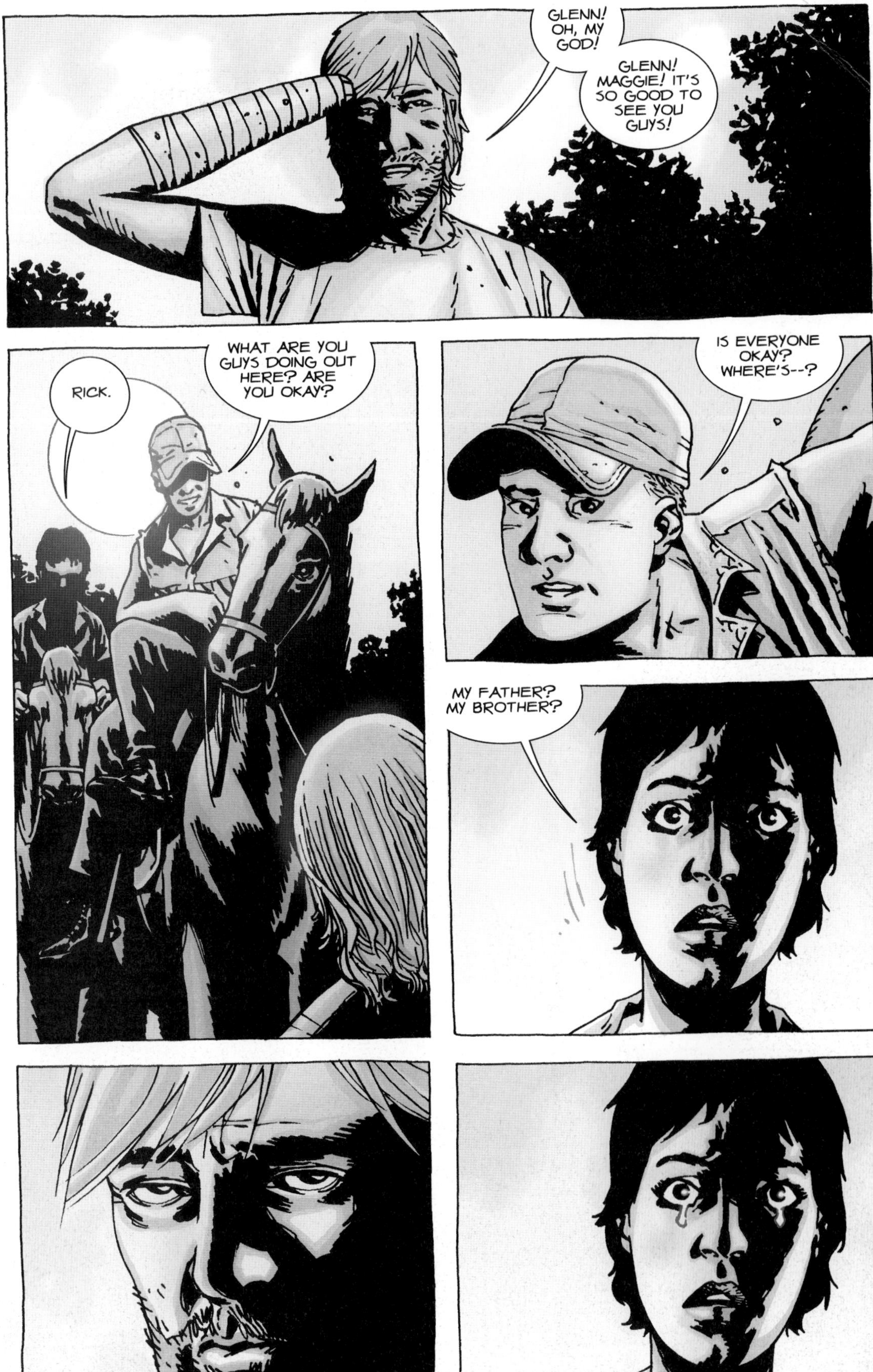
GLENN! OH, MY GOD!
GLENN! MAGGIE! IT'S SO GOOD TO SEE YOU GUYS!
RICK.
WHAT ARE YOU GUYS DOING OUT HERE? ARE YOU OKAY?
IS EVERYONE OKAY? WHERE'S--?
MY FATHER? MY BROTHER?

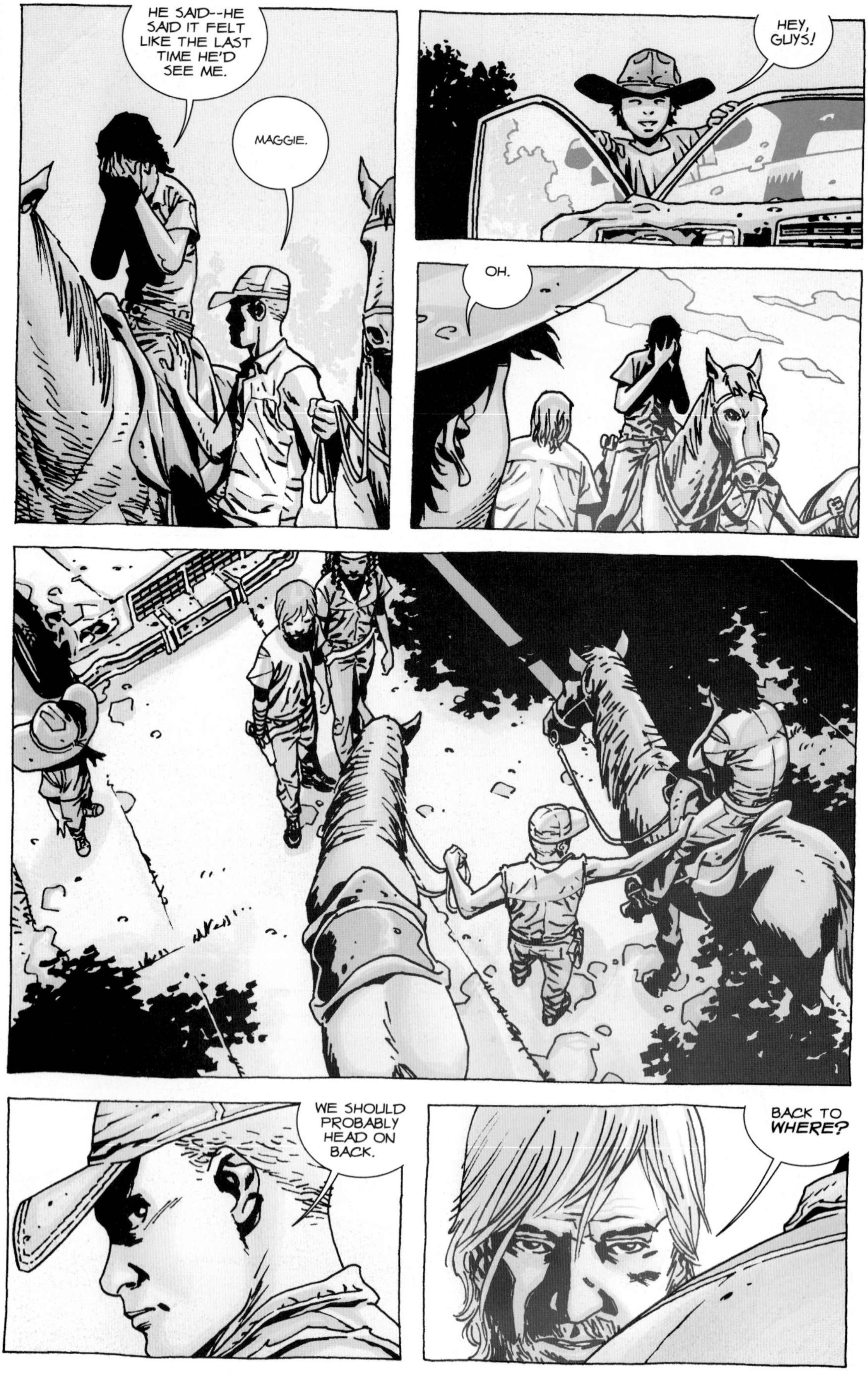
HE SAID--HE SAID IT FELT LIKE THE LAST TIME HE'D SEE ME.
MAGGIE.
HEY, GUYS!
OH.
WE SHOULD PROBABLY HEAD ON BACK.
BACK TO *WHERE?*

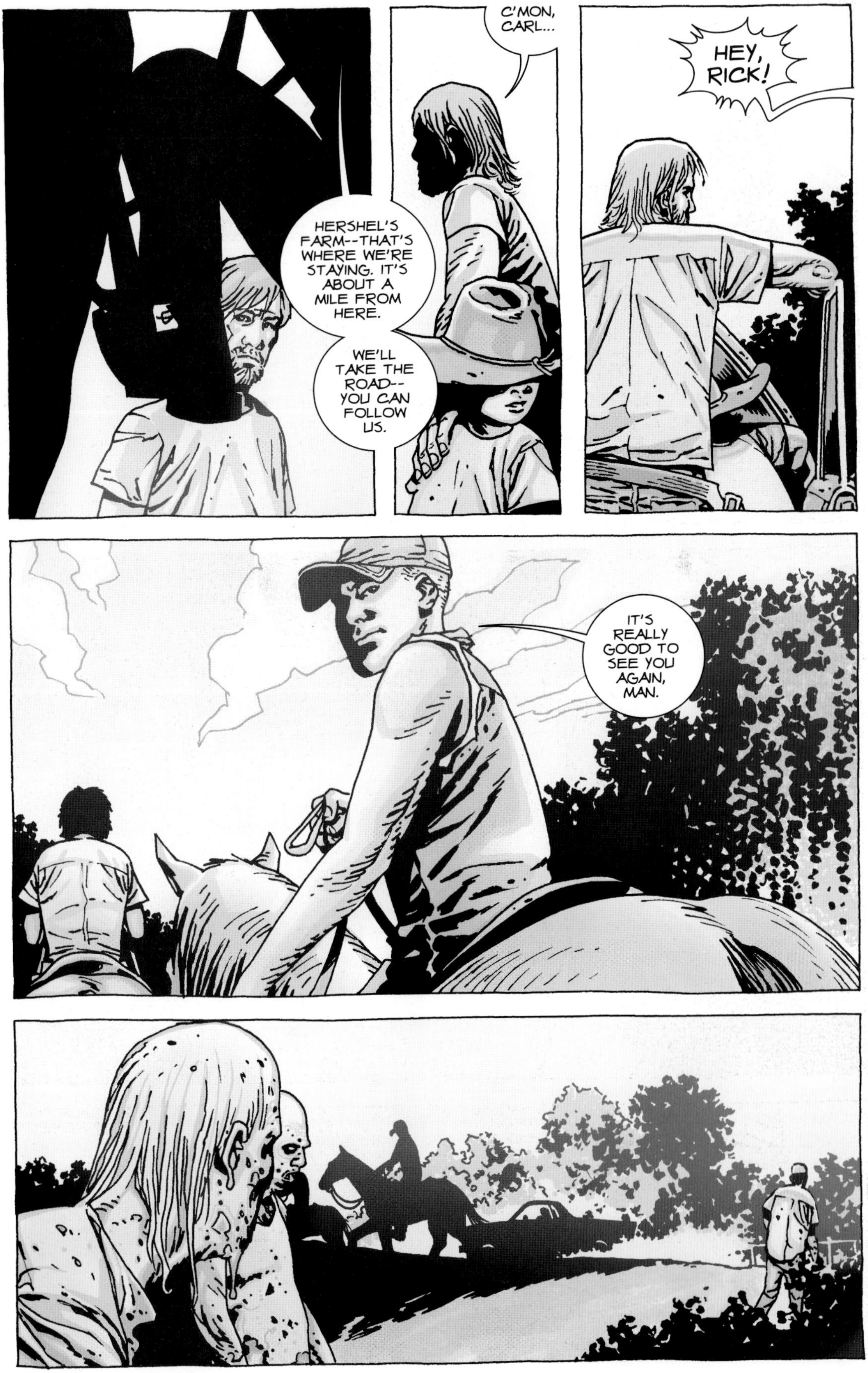
HERSHEL'S FARM--THAT'S WHERE WE'RE STAYING. IT'S ABOUT A MILE FROM HERE.
WE'LL TAKE THE ROAD--YOU CAN FOLLOW US.
C'MON, CARL...
HEY, RICK!
IT'S REALLY GOOD TO SEE YOU AGAIN, MAN.

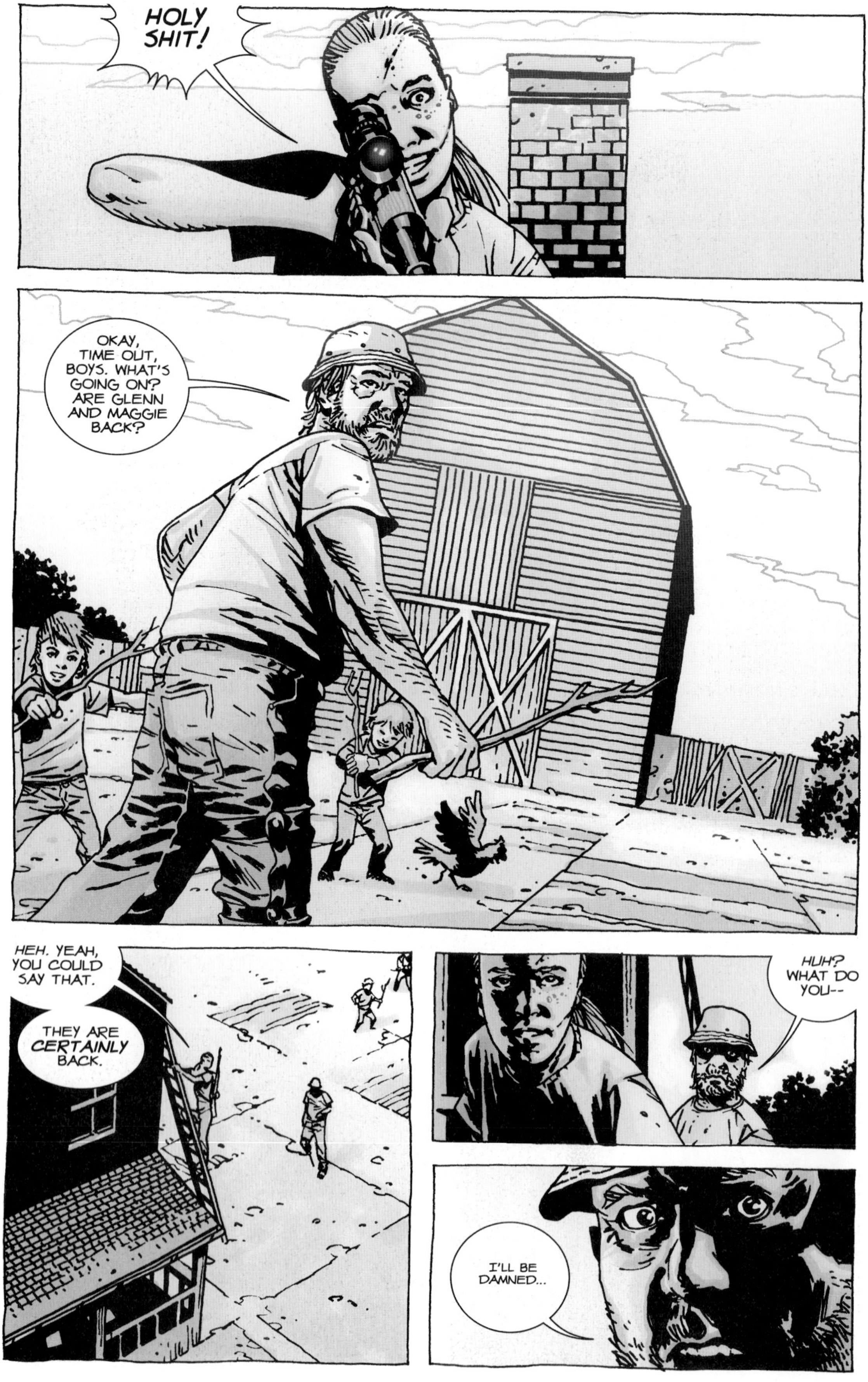
HOLY SHIT!
OKAY, TIME OUT, BOYS. WHAT'S GOING ON? ARE GLENN AND MAGGIE BACK?
HEH. YEAH, YOU COULD SAY THAT.
THEY ARE CERTAINLY BACK.
HUH? WHAT DO YOU--
I'LL BE DAMNED...

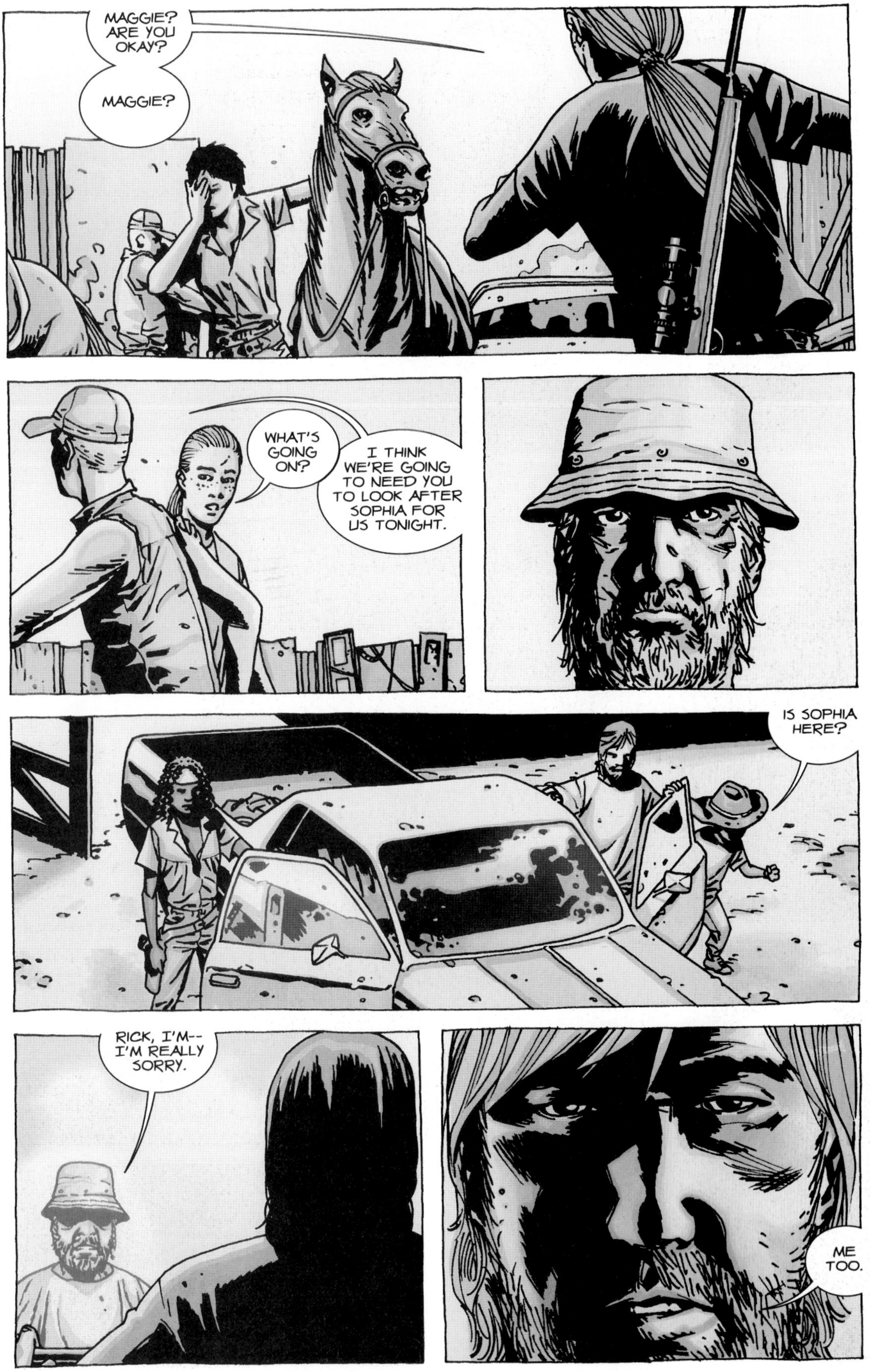
MAGGIE? ARE YOU OKAY?
MAGGIE?
WHAT'S GOING ON?
I THINK WE'RE GOING TO NEED YOU TO LOOK AFTER SOPHIA FOR US TONIGHT.
IS SOPHIA HERE?
RICK, I'M-- I'M REALLY SORRY.
ME TOO.

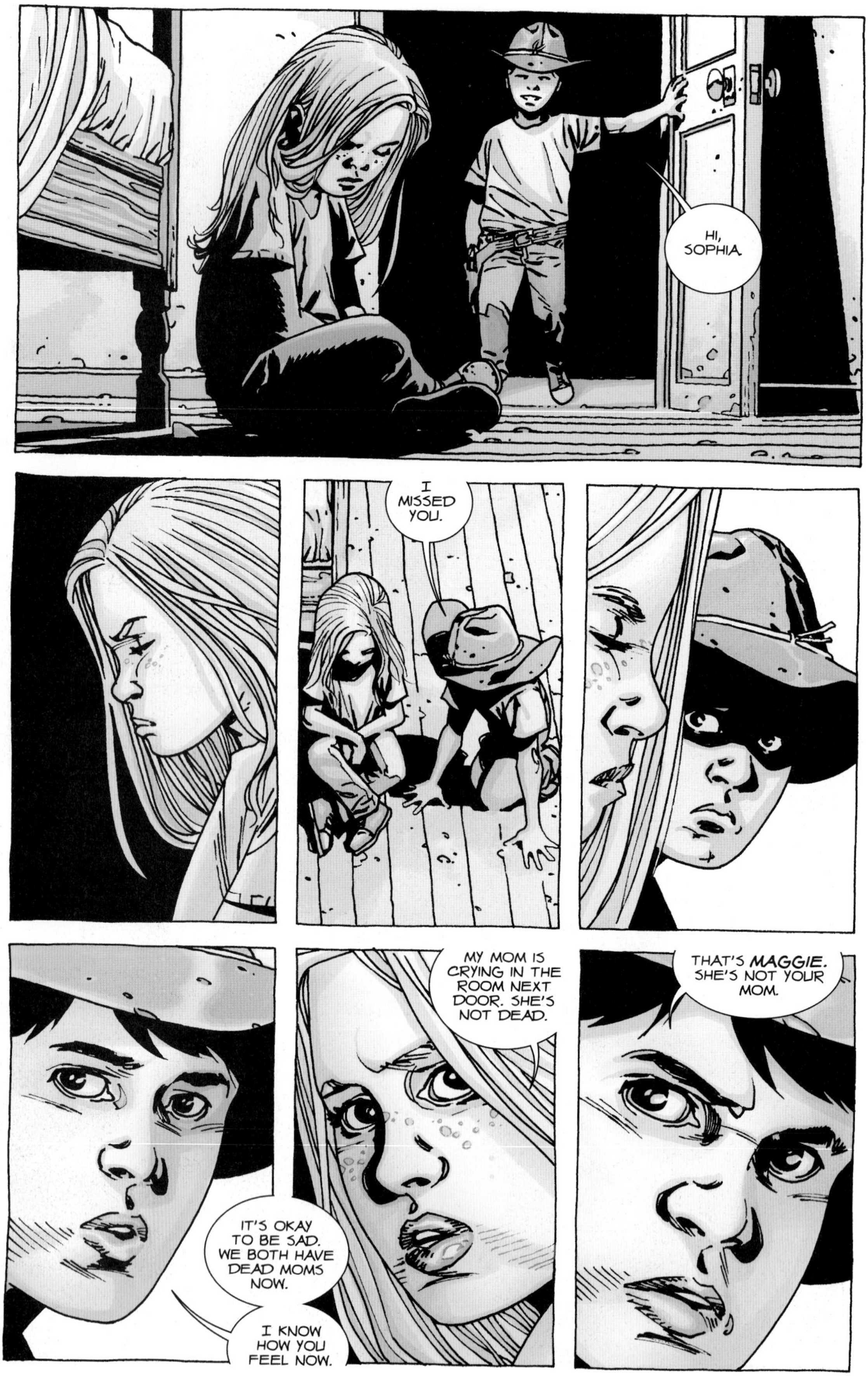
HI, SOPHIA.
I MISSED YOU.
IT'S OKAY TO BE SAD. WE BOTH HAVE DEAD MOMS NOW.
I KNOW HOW YOU FEEL NOW.
MY MOM IS CRYING IN THE ROOM NEXT DOOR. SHE'S NOT DEAD.
THAT'S MAGGIE. SHE'S NOT YOUR MOM.

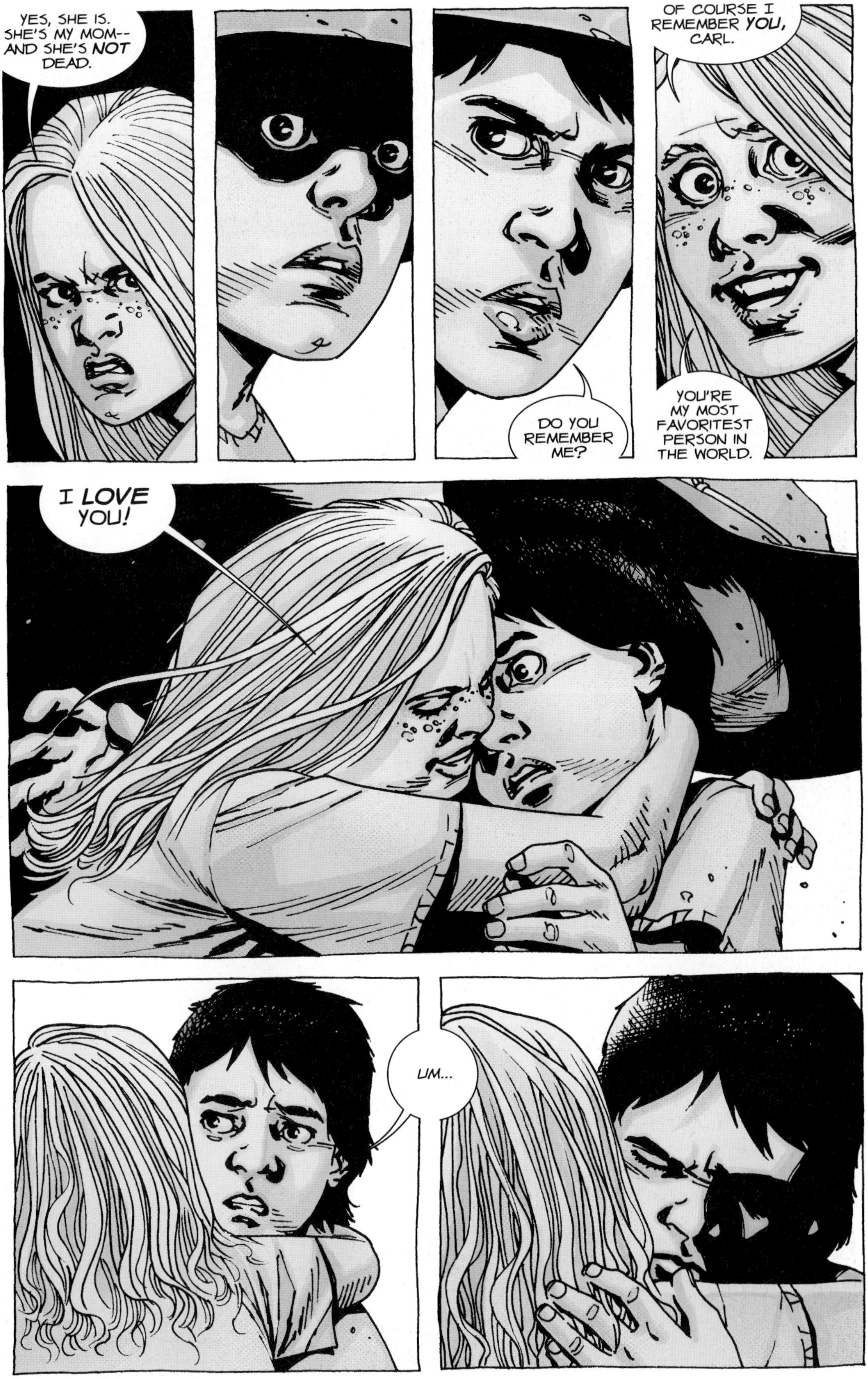
YES, SHE IS. SHE'S MY MOM-- AND SHE'S NOT DEAD.
OF COURSE I REMEMBER YOU, CARL.
DO YOU REMEMBER ME?
YOU'RE MY MOST FAVORITEST PERSON IN THE WORLD.
I LOVE YOU!
UM...

SOPHIA'S *CRAZY*.

MOST GIRLS ARE AT THAT AGE. YOU'LL GET USED TO IT... AND IT ONLY GETS WORSE.

NO. REALLY CRAZY. SHE THINKS MAGGIE IS HER REAL MOM. SHE DOESN'T EVEN *REMEMBER* HER MOM.

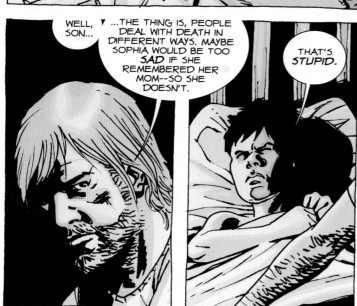

WELL, SON...

...THE THING IS, PEOPLE DEAL WITH DEATH IN DIFFERENT WAYS. MAYBE SOPHIA WOULD BE TOO *SAD* IF SHE REMEMBERED HER MOM--SO SHE DOESN'T.

THAT'S *STUPID*.

NO, DAMN IT... NO, IT *ISN'T*, AND YOU SURE AS HELL SHOULDN'T THINK IT IS.

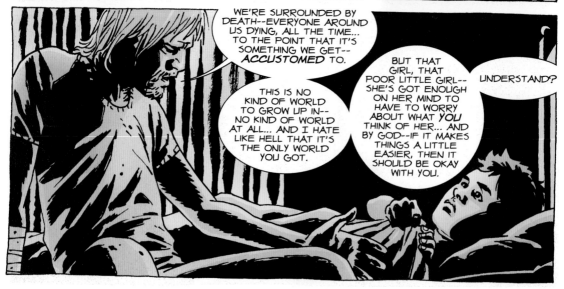

WE'RE SURROUNDED BY DEATH--EVERYONE AROUND US DYING, ALL THE TIME... TO THE POINT THAT IT'S SOMETHING WE GET-- *ACCUSTOMED* TO.

THIS IS NO KIND OF WORLD TO GROW UP IN-- NO KIND OF WORLD AT ALL... AND I HATE LIKE HELL THAT IT'S THE ONLY WORLD YOU GOT.

BUT THAT GIRL, THAT POOR LITTLE GIRL-- SHE'S GOT ENOUGH ON HER MIND TO HAVE TO WORRY ABOUT WHAT *YOU* THINK OF HER... AND BY GOD--IF IT MAKES THINGS A LITTLE EASIER, THEN IT SHOULD BE OKAY WITH YOU.

UNDERSTAND?

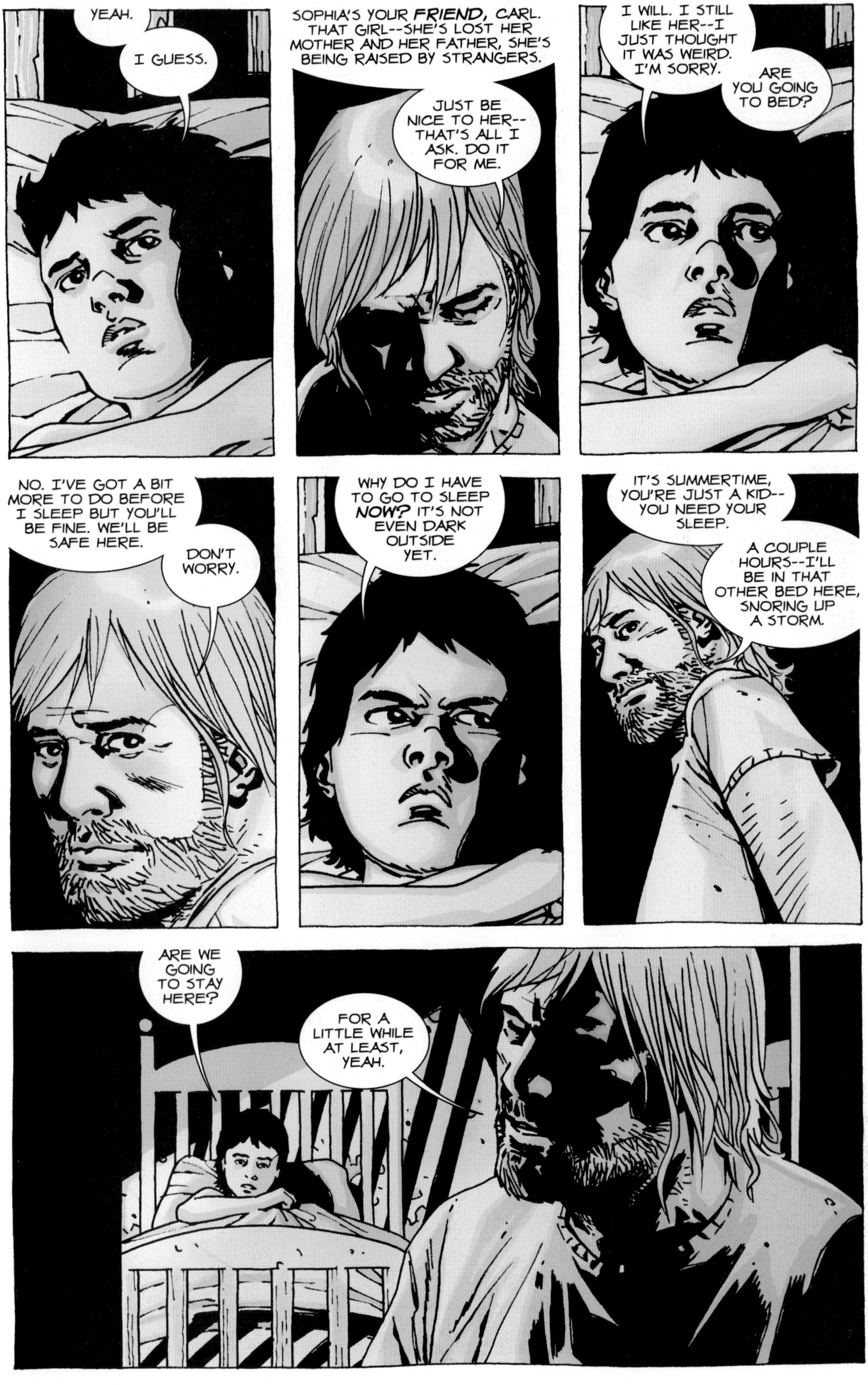
YEAH.
I GUESS.
SOPHIA'S YOUR FRIEND, CARL. THAT GIRL--SHE'S LOST HER MOTHER AND HER FATHER, SHE'S BEING RAISED BY STRANGERS.
JUST BE NICE TO HER--THAT'S ALL I ASK. DO IT FOR ME.
I WILL. I STILL LIKE HER--I JUST THOUGHT IT WAS WEIRD. I'M SORRY.
ARE YOU GOING TO BED?
NO. I'VE GOT A BIT MORE TO DO BEFORE I SLEEP BUT YOU'LL BE FINE. WE'LL BE SAFE HERE.
DON'T WORRY.
WHY DO I HAVE TO GO TO SLEEP NOW? IT'S NOT EVEN DARK OUTSIDE YET.
IT'S SUMMERTIME, YOU'RE JUST A KID--YOU NEED YOUR SLEEP.
A COUPLE HOURS--I'LL BE IN THAT OTHER BED HERE, SNORING UP A STORM.
ARE WE GOING TO STAY HERE?
FOR A LITTLE WHILE AT LEAST, YEAH.

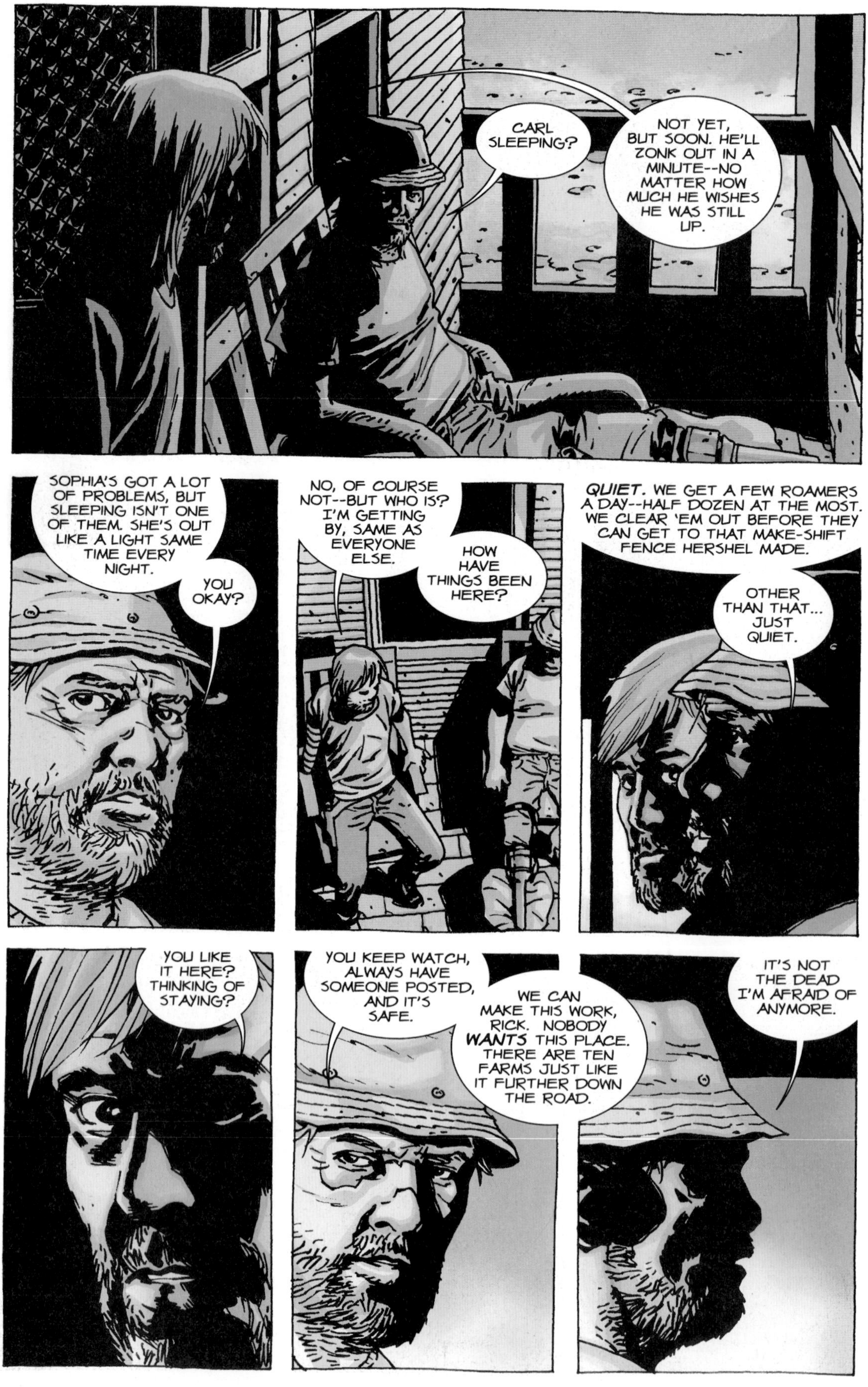
CARL SLEEPING?
NOT YET, BUT SOON. HE'LL ZONK OUT IN A MINUTE--NO MATTER HOW MUCH HE WISHES HE WAS STILL UP.
SOPHIA'S GOT A LOT OF PROBLEMS, BUT SLEEPING ISN'T ONE OF THEM. SHE'S OUT LIKE A LIGHT SAME TIME EVERY NIGHT.
YOU OKAY?
NO, OF COURSE NOT--BUT WHO IS? I'M GETTING BY, SAME AS EVERYONE ELSE.
HOW HAVE THINGS BEEN HERE?
QUIET. WE GET A FEW ROAMERS A DAY--HALF DOZEN AT THE MOST. WE CLEAR 'EM OUT BEFORE THEY CAN GET TO THAT MAKE-SHIFT FENCE HERSHEL MADE.
OTHER THAN THAT... JUST QUIET.
YOU LIKE IT HERE? THINKING OF STAYING?
YOU KEEP WATCH, ALWAYS HAVE SOMEONE POSTED, AND IT'S SAFE.
WE CAN MAKE THIS WORK, RICK. NOBODY WANTS THIS PLACE. THERE ARE TEN FARMS JUST LIKE IT FURTHER DOWN THE ROAD.
IT'S NOT THE DEAD I'M AFRAID OF ANYMORE.

WE WOULD HAVE BEEN OKAY IF WE'D JUST LEFT WITH YOU--

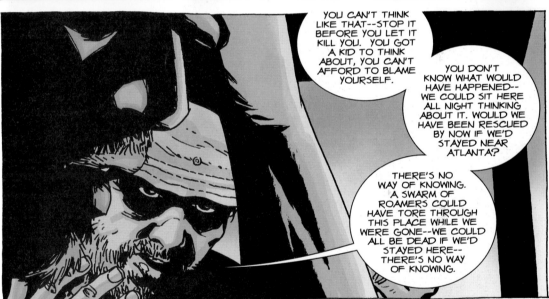

YOU CAN'T THINK LIKE THAT--STOP IT BEFORE YOU LET IT KILL YOU. YOU GOT A KID TO THINK ABOUT, YOU CAN'T AFFORD TO BLAME YOURSELF.

YOU DON'T KNOW WHAT WOULD HAVE HAPPENED-- WE COULD SIT HERE ALL NIGHT THINKING ABOUT IT. WOULD WE HAVE BEEN RESCUED BY NOW IF WE'D STAYED NEAR ATLANTA?

THERE'S NO WAY OF KNOWING. A SWARM OF ROAMERS COULD HAVE TORE THROUGH THIS PLACE WHILE WE WERE GONE--WE COULD ALL BE DEAD IF WE'D STAYED HERE-- THERE'S NO WAY OF KNOWING.

FORGET THE DEAD--FOCUS ON THE LIVING. I KNOW I'D BE DEAD RIGHT NOW IF NOT FOR YOU--SAME WITH YOUR SON--SAME WITH ALMOST ALL OF US.

YOU CAN'T KNOW YOU DIDN'T KILL THE DEAD--BUT I CAN ASSURE YOU--ANY OF US HERE STILL ALIVE, IT'S BECAUSE OF YOU. THAT'S A FACT.

THANKS, DALE.

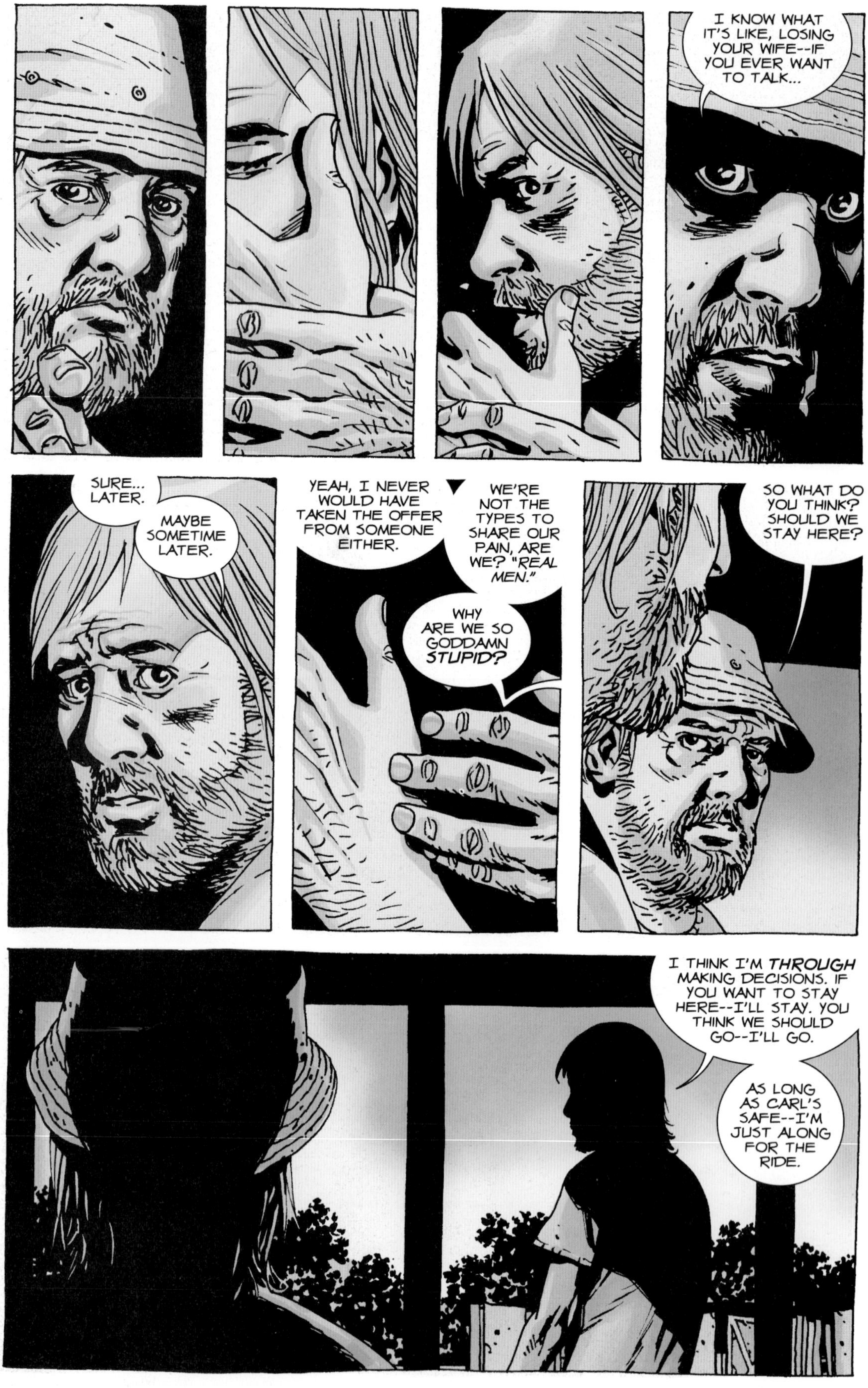
I KNOW WHAT IT'S LIKE, LOSING YOUR WIFE--IF YOU EVER WANT TO TALK...
SURE... LATER.
MAYBE SOMETIME LATER.
YEAH, I NEVER WOULD HAVE TAKEN THE OFFER FROM SOMEONE EITHER.
WE'RE NOT THE TYPES TO SHARE OUR PAIN, ARE WE? "REAL MEN."
WHY ARE WE SO GODDAMN STUPID?
SO WHAT DO YOU THINK? SHOULD WE STAY HERE?
I THINK I'M THROUGH MAKING DECISIONS. IF YOU WANT TO STAY HERE--I'LL STAY. YOU THINK WE SHOULD GO--I'LL GO.
AS LONG AS CARL'S SAFE--I'M JUST ALONG FOR THE RIDE.

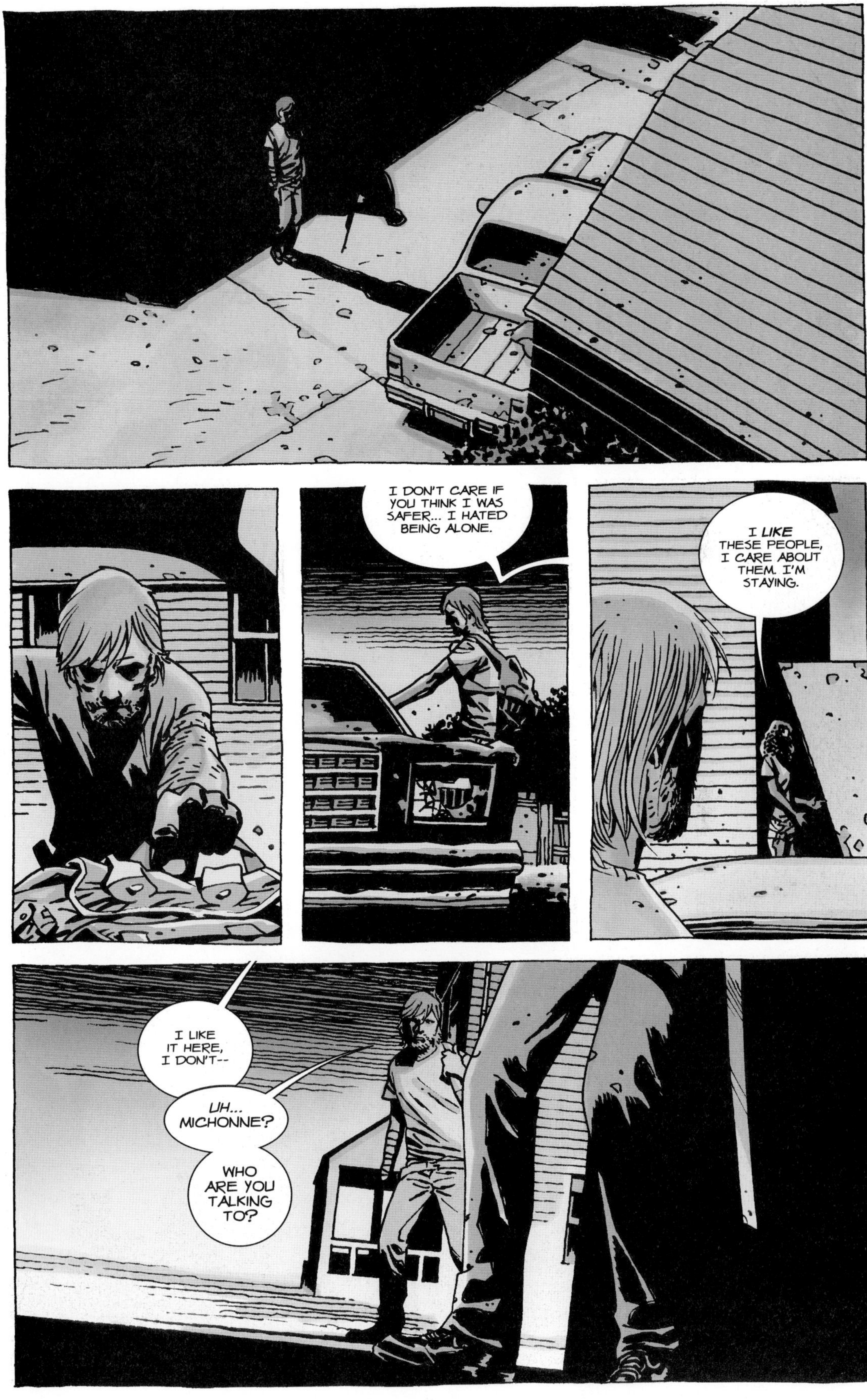
I DON'T CARE IF YOU THINK I WAS SAFER... I HATED BEING ALONE.
I *LIKE* THESE PEOPLE, I CARE ABOUT THEM. I'M STAYING.
I LIKE IT HERE, I DON'T--
UH... MICHONNE?
WHO ARE YOU TALKING TO?

NOBODY. I WASN'T SAYING ANYTHING.

MICHONNE--I *HEARD* YOU TALKING TO SOMEONE. ARE YOU *REALLY* GOING TO LIE TO ME?

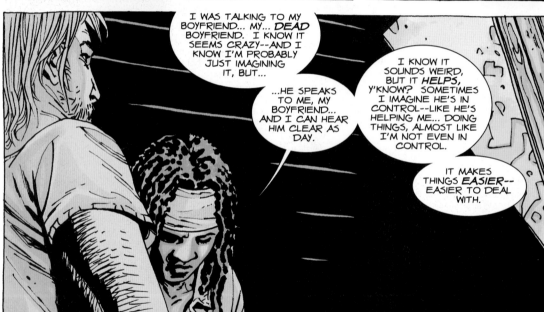

I WAS TALKING TO MY BOYFRIEND... MY... *DEAD* BOYFRIEND. I KNOW IT SEEMS CRAZY--AND I KNOW I'M PROBABLY JUST IMAGINING IT, BUT...

...HE SPEAKS TO ME, MY BOYFRIEND... AND I CAN HEAR HIM CLEAR AS DAY.

I KNOW IT SOUNDS WEIRD, BUT IT *HELPS*, Y'KNOW? SOMETIMES I IMAGINE HE'S IN CONTROL--LIKE HE'S HELPING ME... DOING THINGS, ALMOST LIKE I'M NOT EVEN IN CONTROL.

IT MAKES THINGS *EASIER*-- EASIER TO DEAL WITH.

YOU THINK I'M CRAZY.

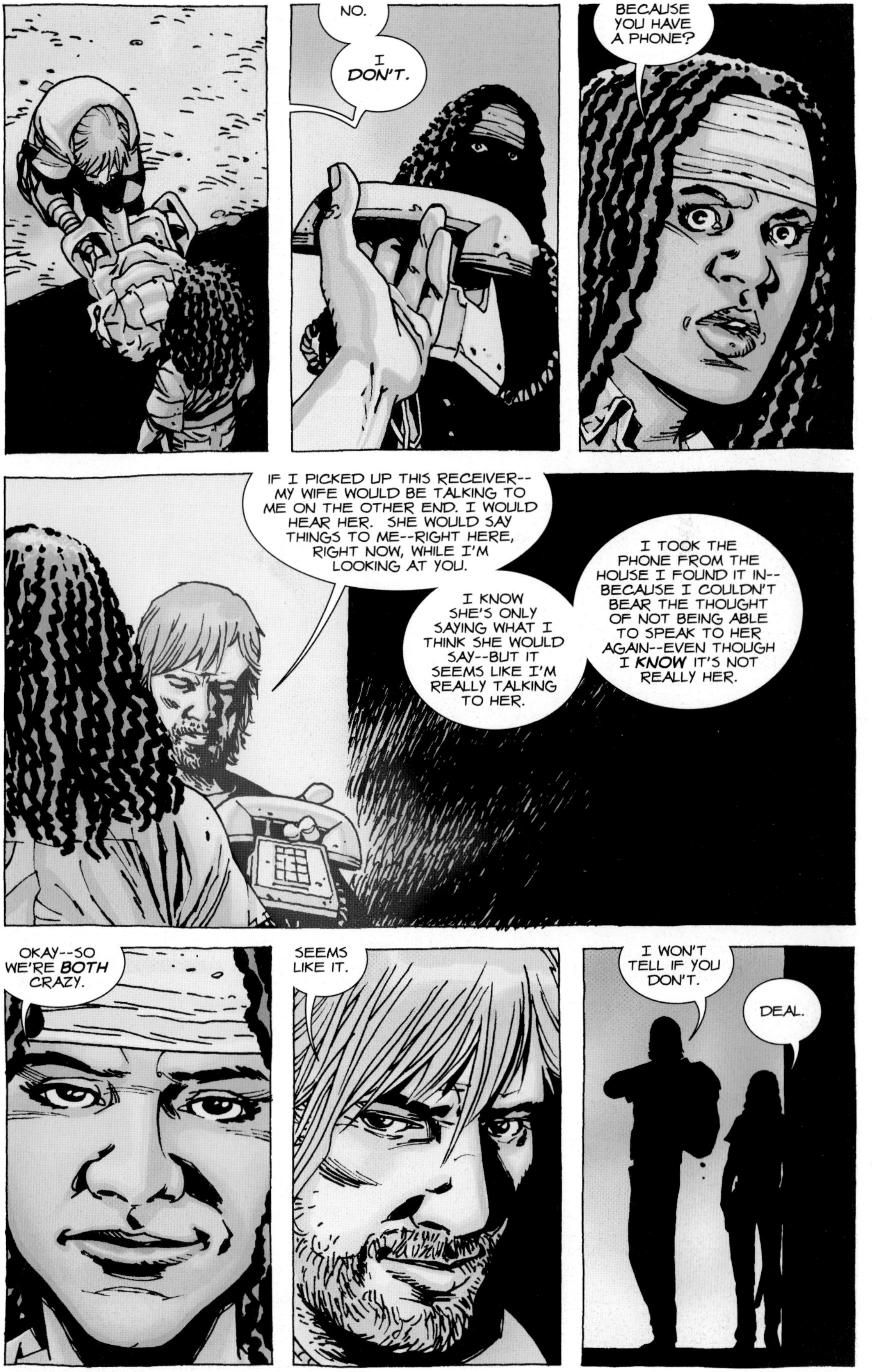
NO.
I DON'T.
BECAUSE YOU HAVE A PHONE?
IF I PICKED UP THIS RECEIVER-- MY WIFE WOULD BE TALKING TO ME ON THE OTHER END. I WOULD HEAR HER. SHE WOULD SAY THINGS TO ME--RIGHT HERE, RIGHT NOW, WHILE I'M LOOKING AT YOU.
I KNOW SHE'S ONLY SAYING WHAT I THINK SHE WOULD SAY--BUT IT SEEMS LIKE I'M REALLY TALKING TO HER.
I TOOK THE PHONE FROM THE HOUSE I FOUND IT IN-- BECAUSE I COULDN'T BEAR THE THOUGHT OF NOT BEING ABLE TO SPEAK TO HER AGAIN--EVEN THOUGH I KNOW IT'S NOT REALLY HER.
OKAY--SO WE'RE BOTH CRAZY.
SEEMS LIKE IT.
I WON'T TELL IF YOU DON'T.
DEAL.

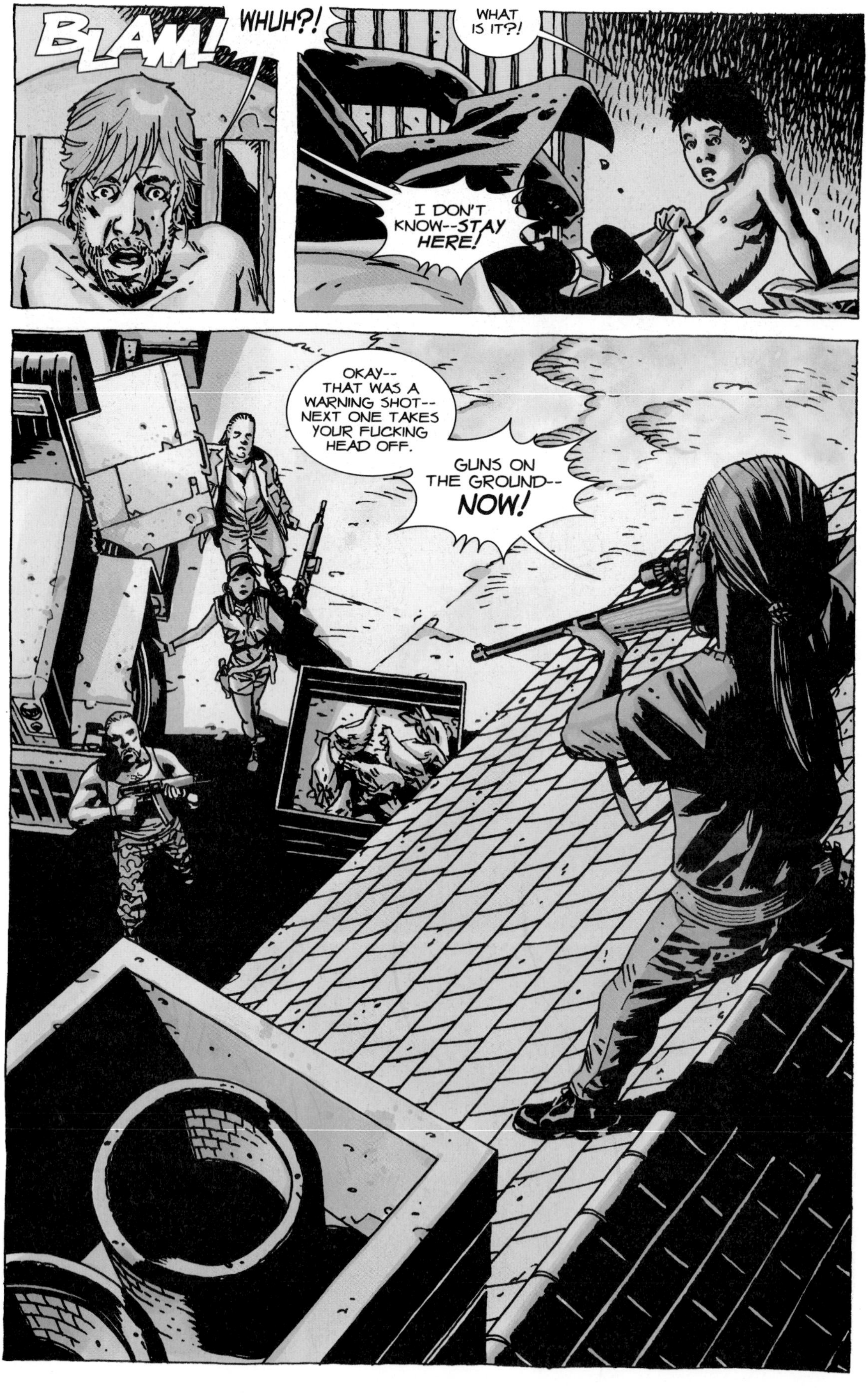
BLAM!
WHUH?!
WHAT IS IT?!
I DON'T KNOW--STAY HERE!
OKAY-- THAT WAS A WARNING SHOT-- NEXT ONE TAKES YOUR FUCKING HEAD OFF.
GUNS ON THE GROUND-- NOW!

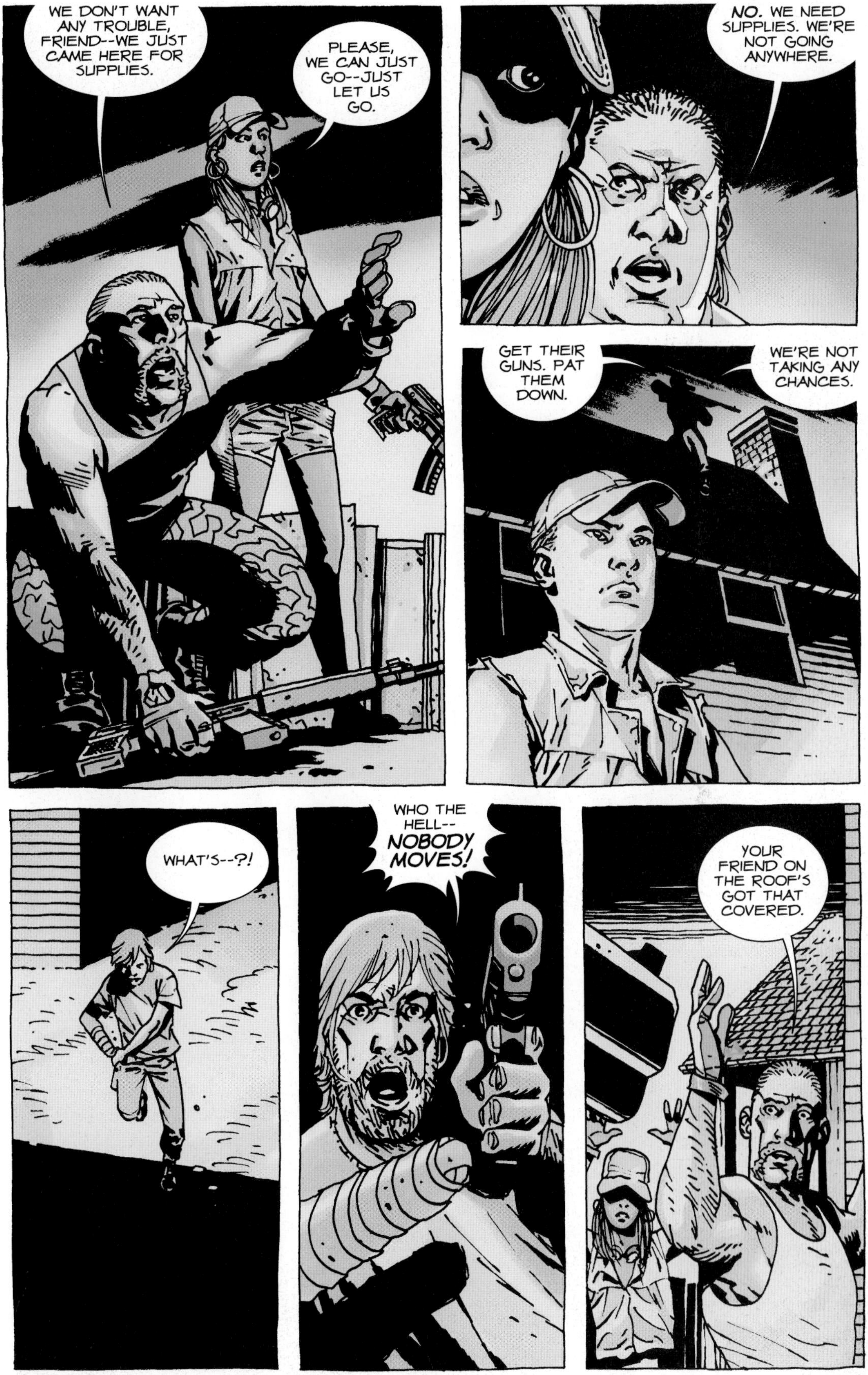
WE DON'T WANT ANY TROUBLE, FRIEND--WE JUST CAME HERE FOR SUPPLIES.
PLEASE, WE CAN JUST GO--JUST LET US GO.
NO. WE NEED SUPPLIES. WE'RE NOT GOING ANYWHERE.
GET THEIR GUNS. PAT THEM DOWN.
WE'RE NOT TAKING ANY CHANCES.
WHAT'S--?!
WHO THE HELL--
NOBODY MOVES!
YOUR FRIEND ON THE ROOF'S GOT THAT COVERED.

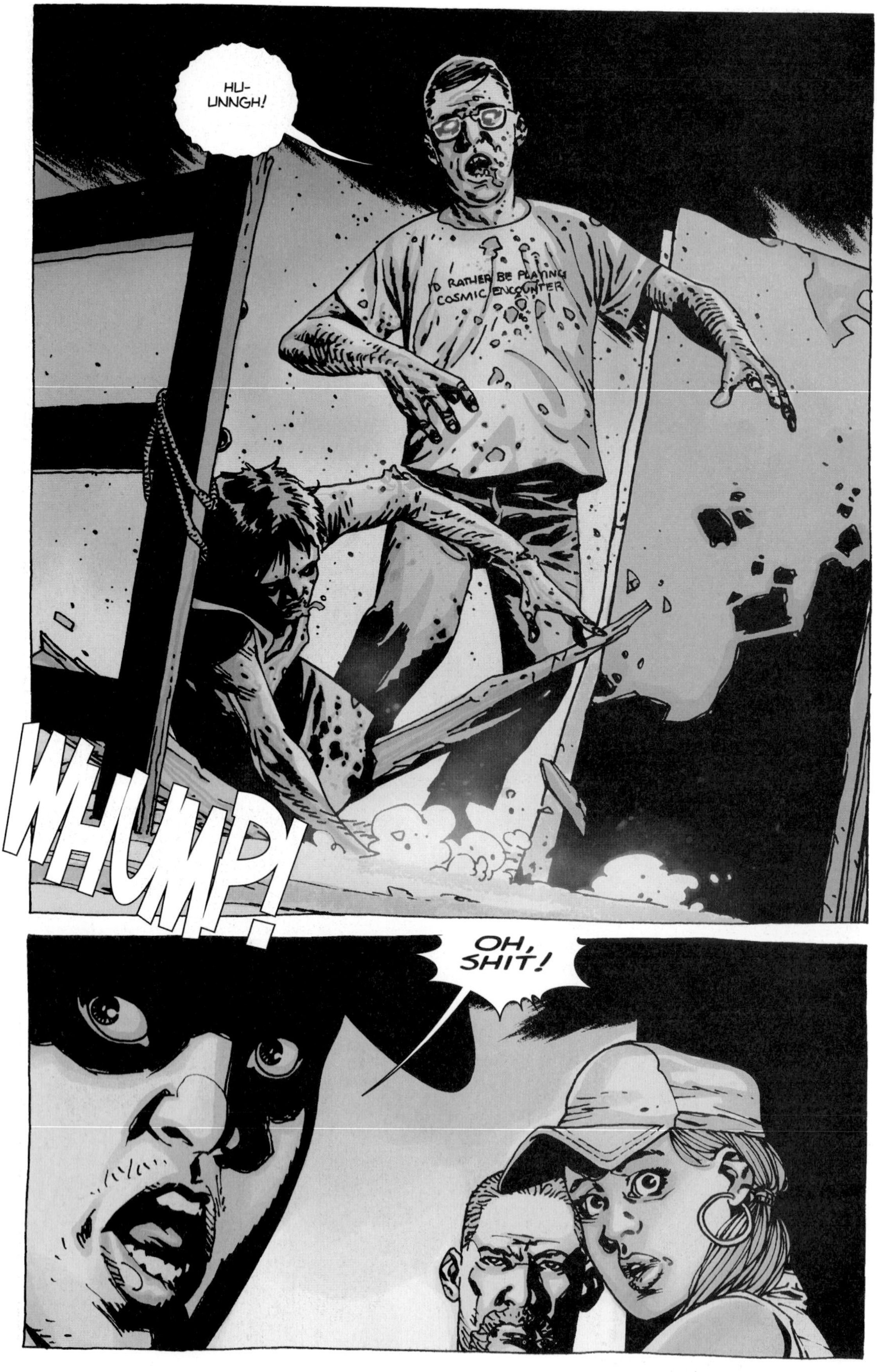
HU-
UNNGH!
I'D RATHER BE PLAYING
COSMIC ENCOUNTER
WHUMP!
OH,
SHIT!

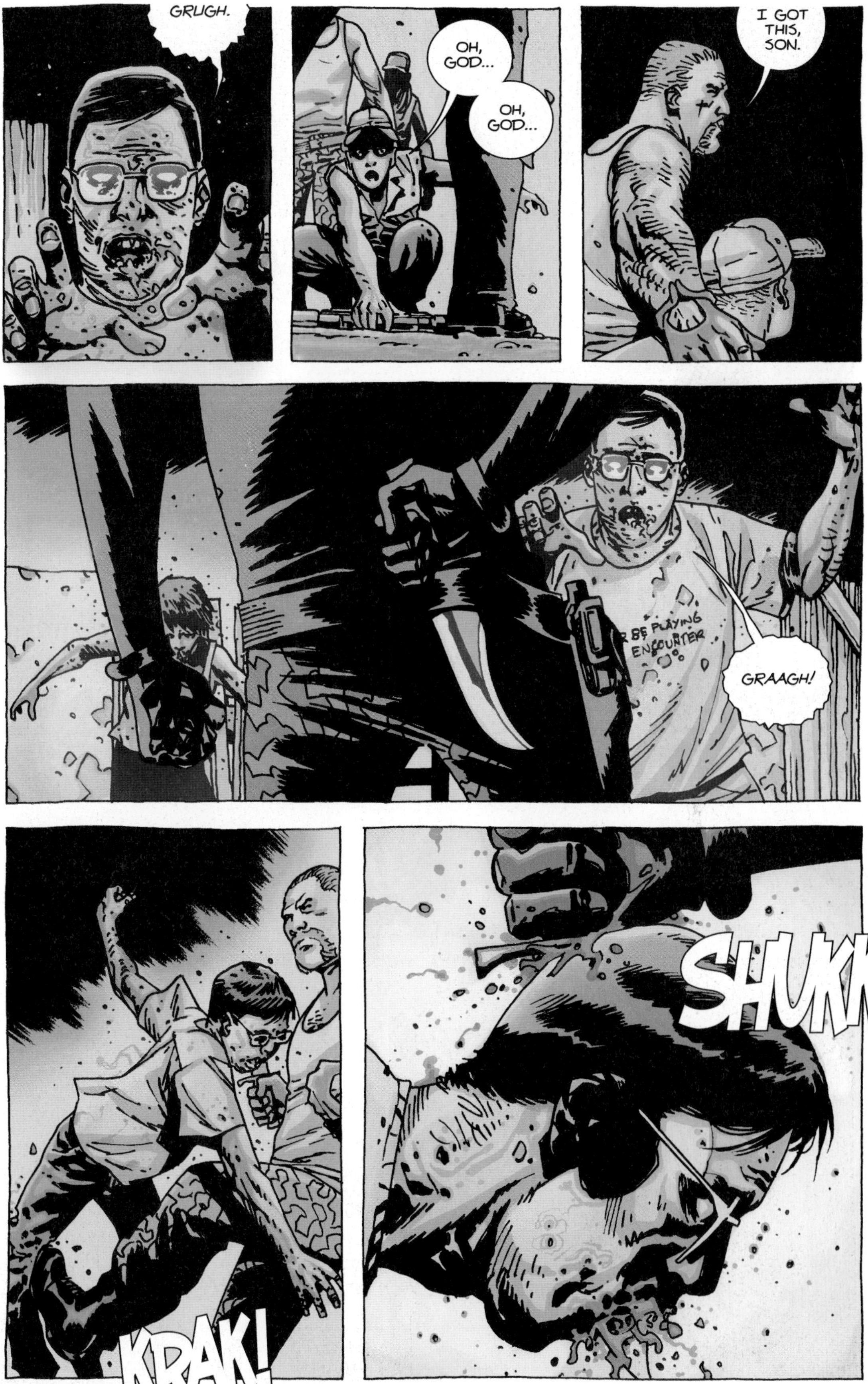
GRUGH.
OH, GOD...
OH, GOD...
I GOT THIS, SON.
GRAAGH!
KRAK!
SHUKK!

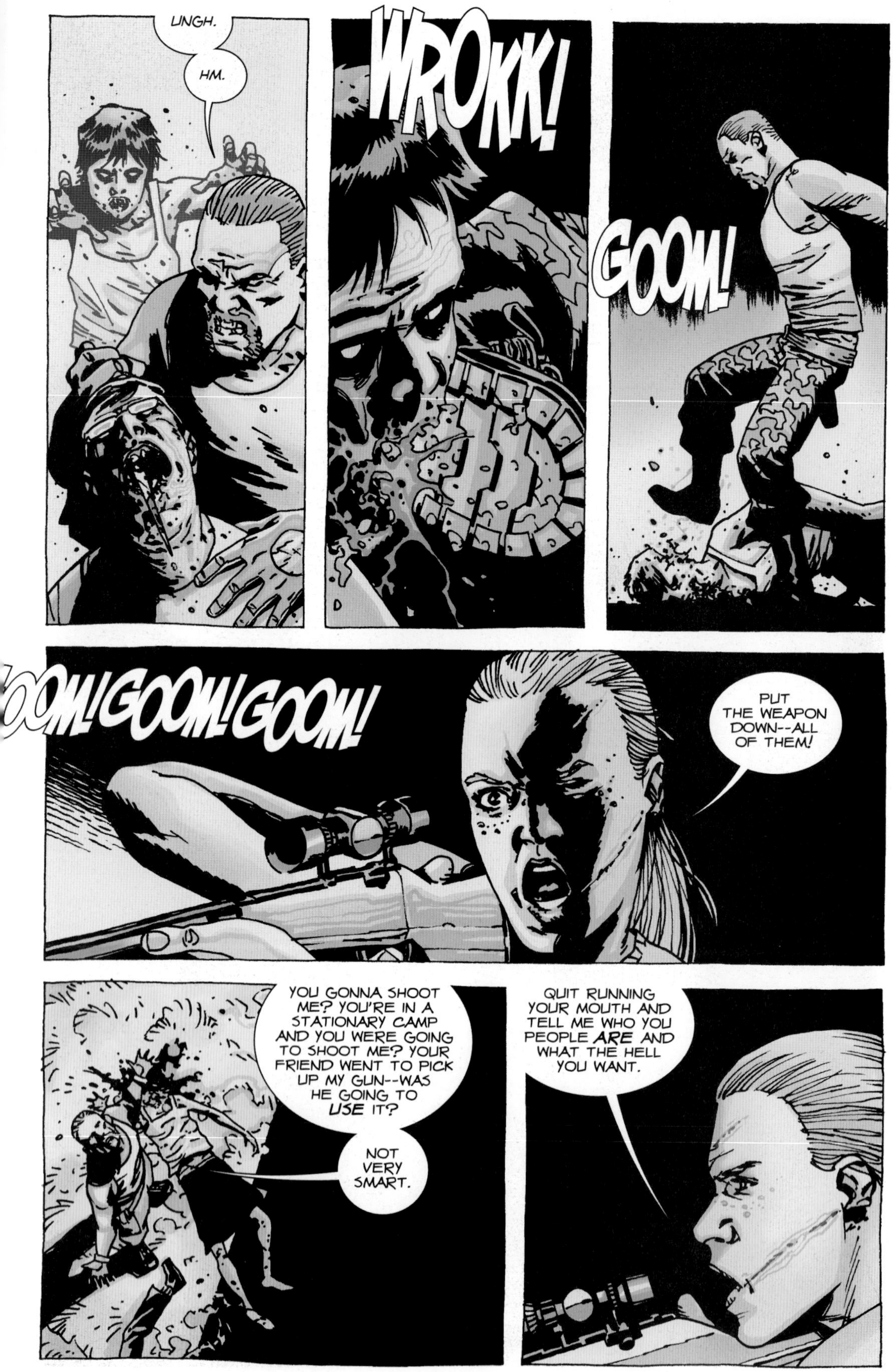

UNGH.
HM.
WROKK!
GOOM!
GOOM! GOOM! GOOM!
PUT THE WEAPON DOWN--ALL OF THEM!
YOU GONNA SHOOT ME? YOU'RE IN A STATIONARY CAMP AND YOU WERE GOING TO SHOOT ME? YOUR FRIEND WENT TO PICK UP MY GUN--WAS HE GOING TO USE IT?
NOT VERY SMART.
QUIT RUNNING YOUR MOUTH AND TELL ME WHO YOU PEOPLE ARE AND WHAT THE HELL YOU WANT.

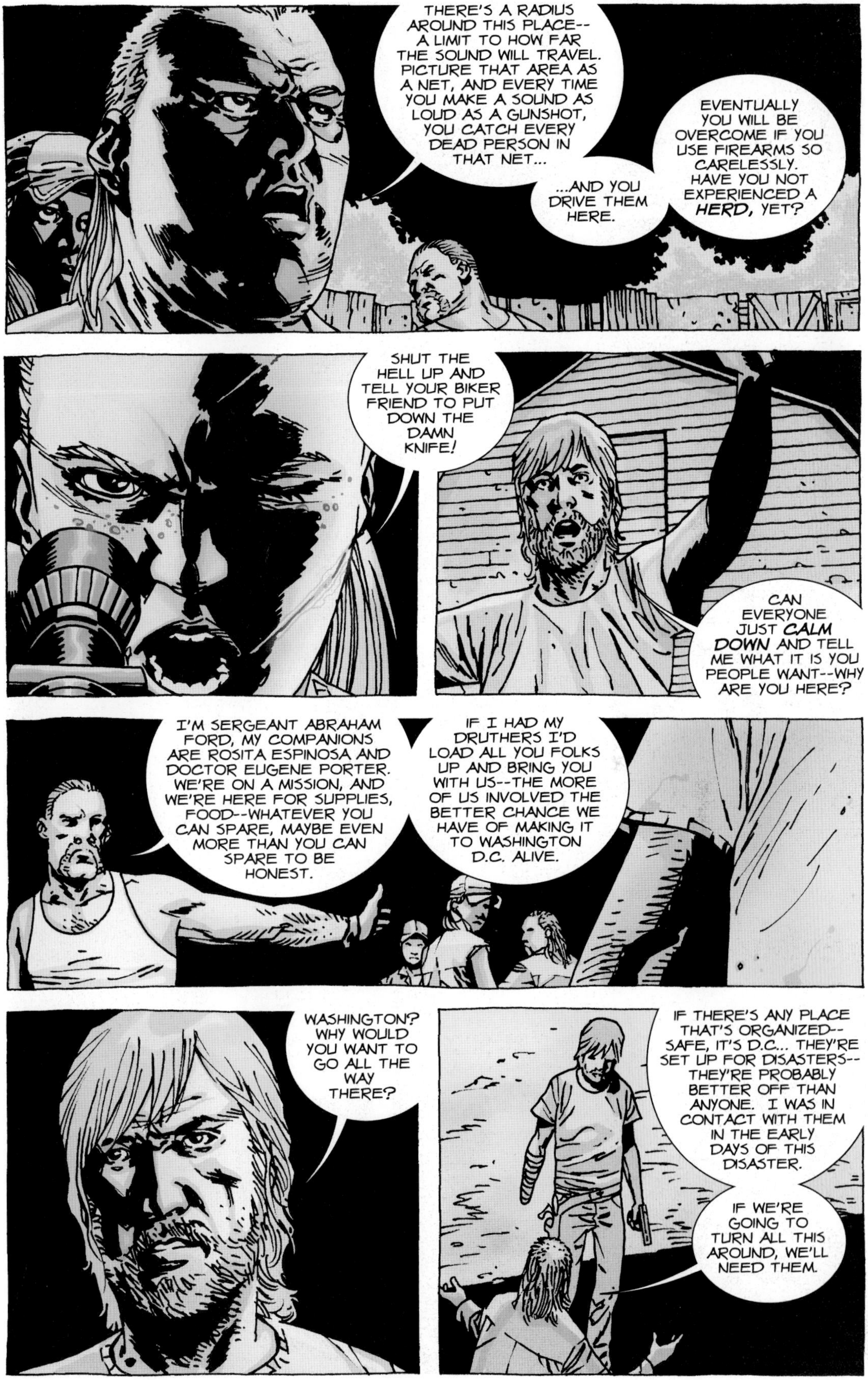

THERE'S A RADIUS AROUND THIS PLACE-- A LIMIT TO HOW FAR THE SOUND WILL TRAVEL. PICTURE THAT AREA AS A NET, AND EVERY TIME YOU MAKE A SOUND AS LOUD AS A GUNSHOT, YOU CATCH EVERY DEAD PERSON IN THAT NET...
...AND YOU DRIVE THEM HERE.
EVENTUALLY YOU WILL BE OVERCOME IF YOU USE FIREARMS SO CARELESSLY. HAVE YOU NOT EXPERIENCED A HERD, YET?
SHUT THE HELL UP AND TELL YOUR BIKER FRIEND TO PUT DOWN THE DAMN KNIFE!
CAN EVERYONE JUST CALM DOWN AND TELL ME WHAT IT IS YOU PEOPLE WANT--WHY ARE YOU HERE?
I'M SERGEANT ABRAHAM FORD, MY COMPANIONS ARE ROSITA ESPINOSA AND DOCTOR EUGENE PORTER. WE'RE ON A MISSION, AND WE'RE HERE FOR SUPPLIES, FOOD--WHATEVER YOU CAN SPARE, MAYBE EVEN MORE THAN YOU CAN SPARE TO BE HONEST.
IF I HAD MY DRUTHERS I'D LOAD ALL YOU FOLKS UP AND BRING YOU WITH US--THE MORE OF US INVOLVED THE BETTER CHANCE WE HAVE OF MAKING IT TO WASHINGTON D.C. ALIVE.
WASHINGTON? WHY WOULD YOU WANT TO GO ALL THE WAY THERE?
IF THERE'S ANY PLACE THAT'S ORGANIZED-- SAFE, IT'S D.C... THEY'RE SET UP FOR DISASTERS-- THEY'RE PROBABLY BETTER OFF THAN ANYONE. I WAS IN CONTACT WITH THEM IN THE EARLY DAYS OF THIS DISASTER.
IF WE'RE GOING TO TURN ALL THIS AROUND, WE'LL NEED THEM.

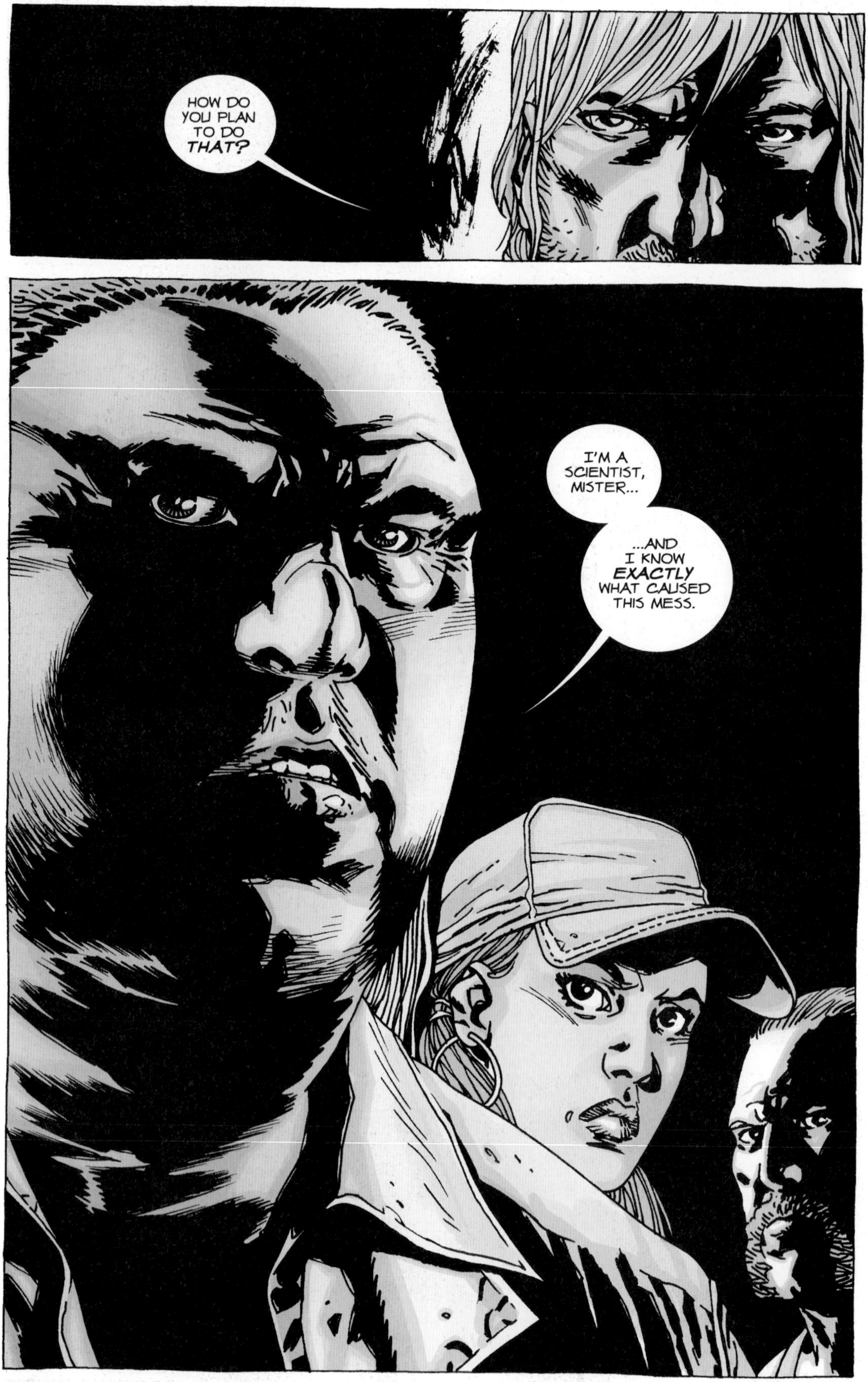
HOW DO YOU PLAN TO DO *THAT?*
I'M A SCIENTIST, MISTER...
...AND I KNOW ***EXACTLY*** WHAT CAUSED THIS MESS.

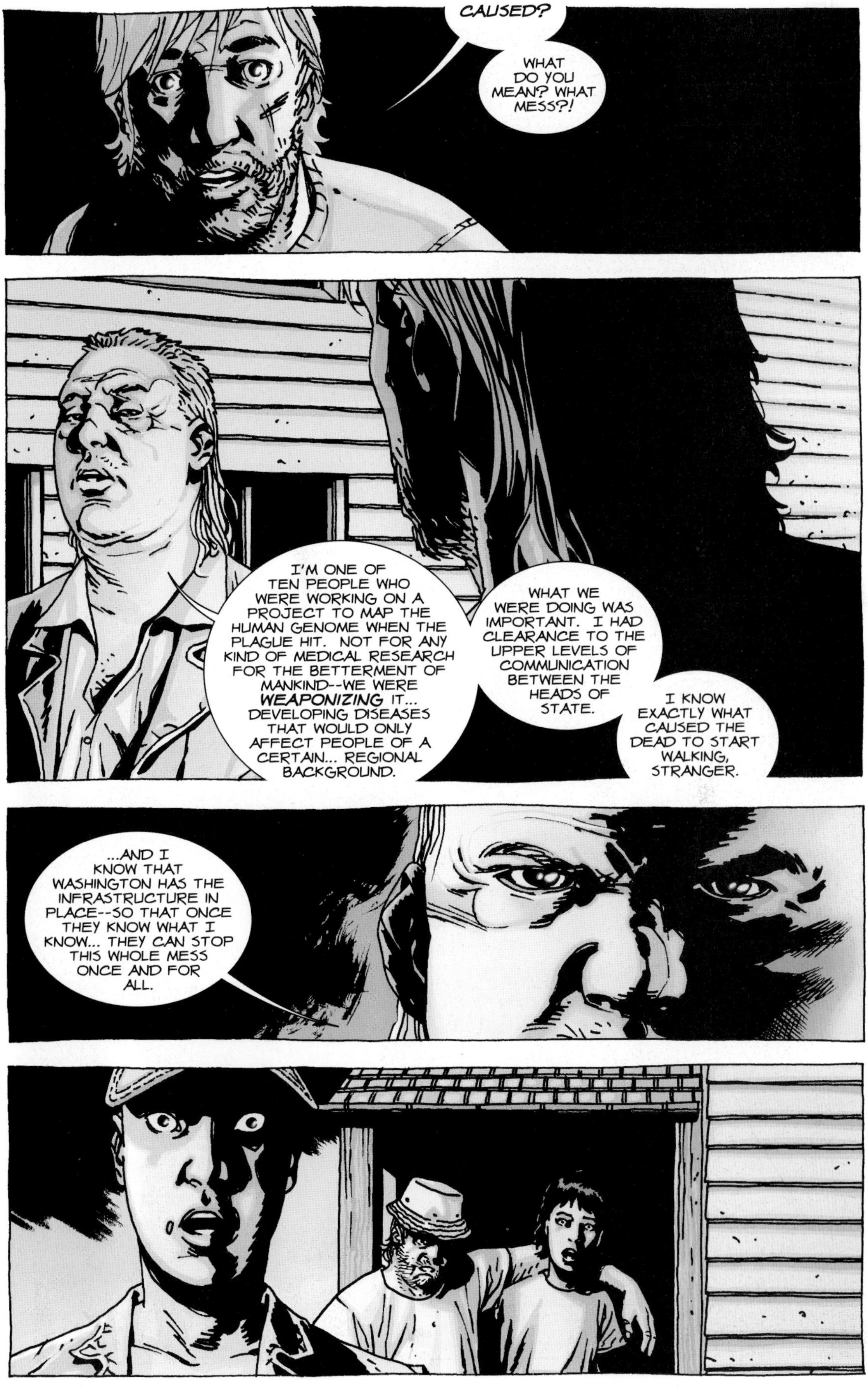

CAUSED?
WHAT DO YOU MEAN? WHAT MESS?!
I'M ONE OF TEN PEOPLE WHO WERE WORKING ON A PROJECT TO MAP THE HUMAN GENOME WHEN THE PLAGUE HIT. NOT FOR ANY KIND OF MEDICAL RESEARCH FOR THE BETTERMENT OF MANKIND--WE WERE *WEAPONIZING* IT... DEVELOPING DISEASES THAT WOULD ONLY AFFECT PEOPLE OF A CERTAIN... REGIONAL BACKGROUND.
WHAT WE WERE DOING WAS IMPORTANT. I HAD CLEARANCE TO THE UPPER LEVELS OF COMMUNICATION BETWEEN THE HEADS OF STATE.
I KNOW EXACTLY WHAT CAUSED THE DEAD TO START WALKING, STRANGER.
...AND I KNOW THAT WASHINGTON HAS THE INFRASTRUCTURE IN PLACE--SO THAT ONCE THEY KNOW WHAT I KNOW... THEY CAN STOP THIS WHOLE MESS ONCE AND FOR ALL.

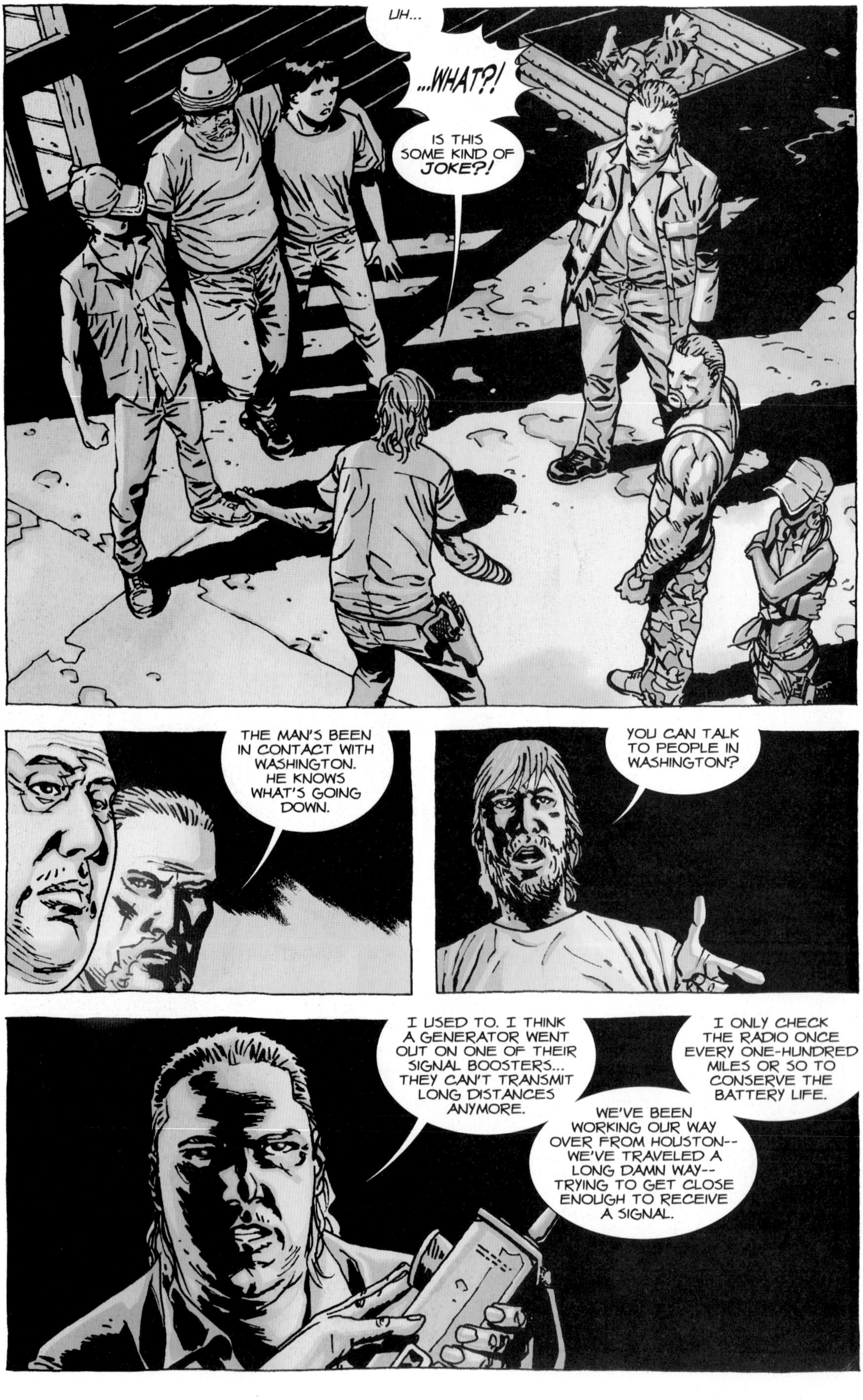

UH...
...WHAT?!
IS THIS SOME KIND OF JOKE?!
THE MAN'S BEEN IN CONTACT WITH WASHINGTON. HE KNOWS WHAT'S GOING DOWN.
YOU CAN TALK TO PEOPLE IN WASHINGTON?
I USED TO. I THINK A GENERATOR WENT OUT ON ONE OF THEIR SIGNAL BOOSTERS... THEY CAN'T TRANSMIT LONG DISTANCES ANYMORE.
I ONLY CHECK THE RADIO ONCE EVERY ONE-HUNDRED MILES OR SO TO CONSERVE THE BATTERY LIFE.
WE'VE BEEN WORKING OUR WAY OVER FROM HOUSTON-- WE'VE TRAVELED A LONG DAMN WAY-- TRYING TO GET CLOSE ENOUGH TO RECEIVE A SIGNAL.

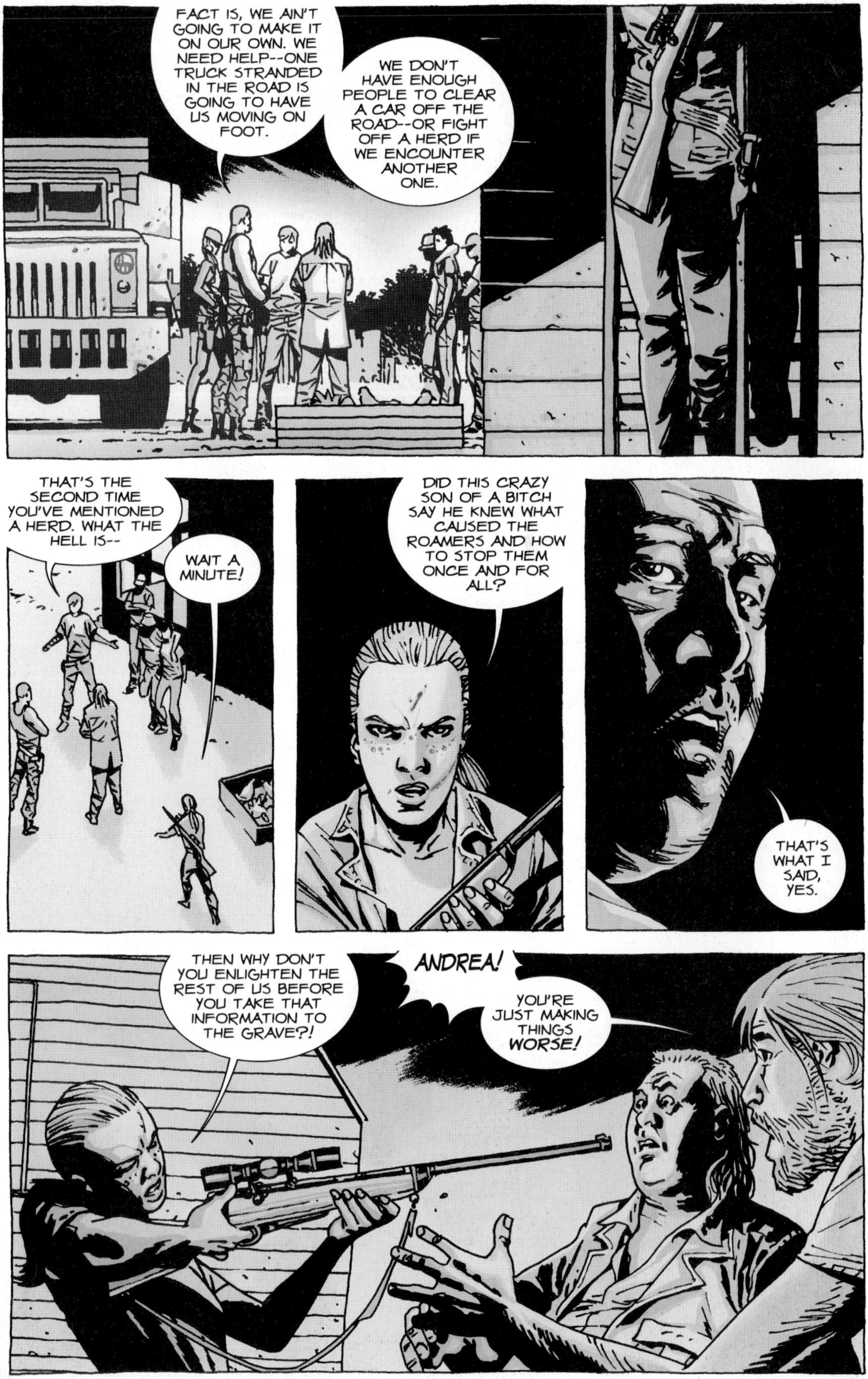
FACT IS, WE AIN'T GOING TO MAKE IT ON OUR OWN. WE NEED HELP--ONE TRUCK STRANDED IN THE ROAD IS GOING TO HAVE US MOVING ON FOOT.
WE DON'T HAVE ENOUGH PEOPLE TO CLEAR A CAR OFF THE ROAD--OR FIGHT OFF A HERD IF WE ENCOUNTER ANOTHER ONE.
THAT'S THE SECOND TIME YOU'VE MENTIONED A HERD. WHAT THE HELL IS--
WAIT A MINUTE!
DID THIS CRAZY SON OF A BITCH SAY HE KNEW WHAT CAUSED THE ROAMERS AND HOW TO STOP THEM ONCE AND FOR ALL?
THAT'S WHAT I SAID, YES.
THEN WHY DON'T YOU ENLIGHTEN THE REST OF US BEFORE YOU TAKE THAT INFORMATION TO THE GRAVE?!
ANDREA!
YOU'RE JUST MAKING THINGS WORSE!

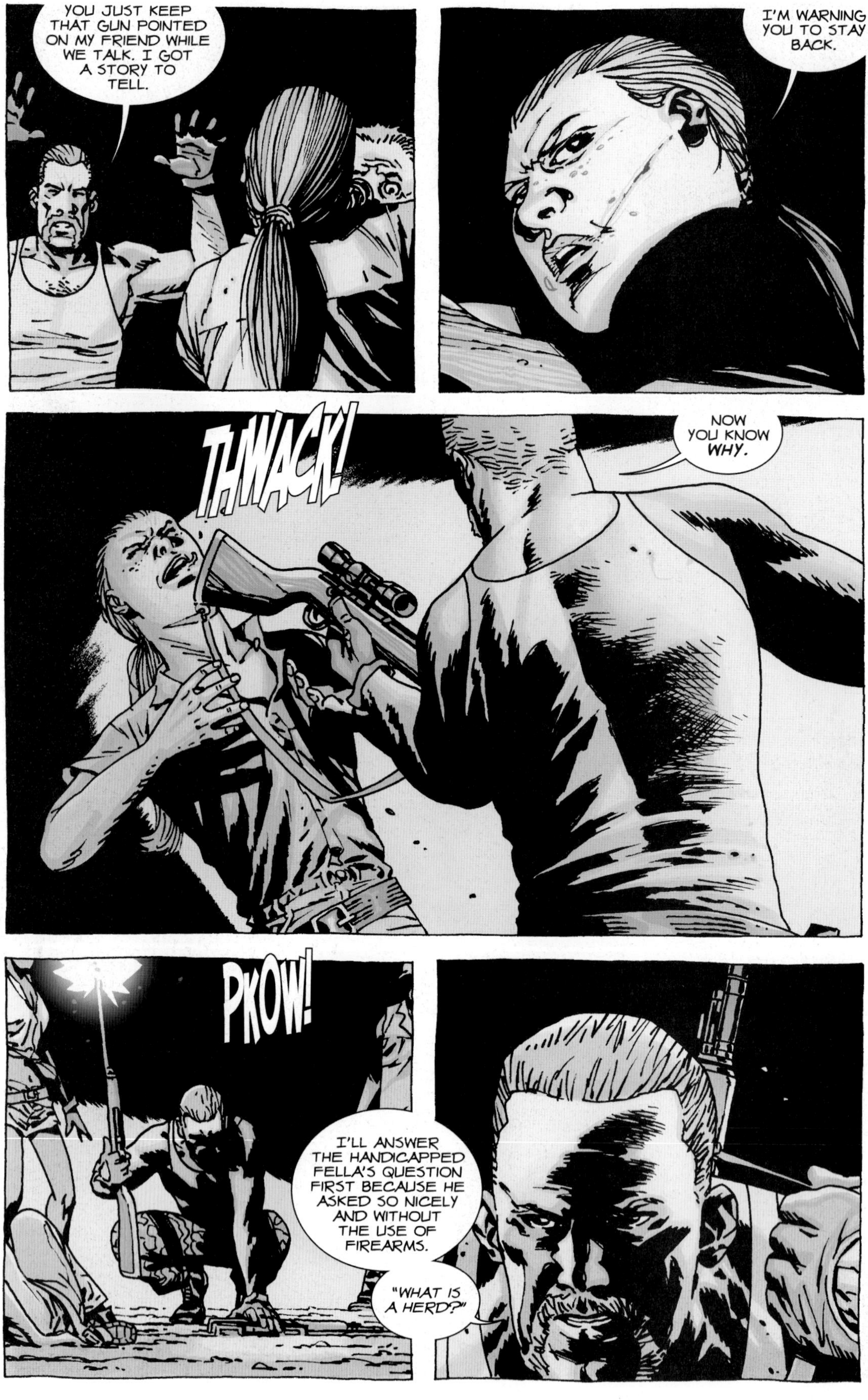
YOU JUST KEEP THAT GUN POINTED ON MY FRIEND WHILE WE TALK. I GOT A STORY TO TELL.
I'M WARNING YOU TO STAY BACK.
THWACK!
NOW YOU KNOW WHY.
PKOW!
I'LL ANSWER THE HANDICAPPED FELLA'S QUESTION FIRST BECAUSE HE ASKED SO NICELY AND WITHOUT THE USE OF FIREARMS.
"WHAT IS A HERD?"

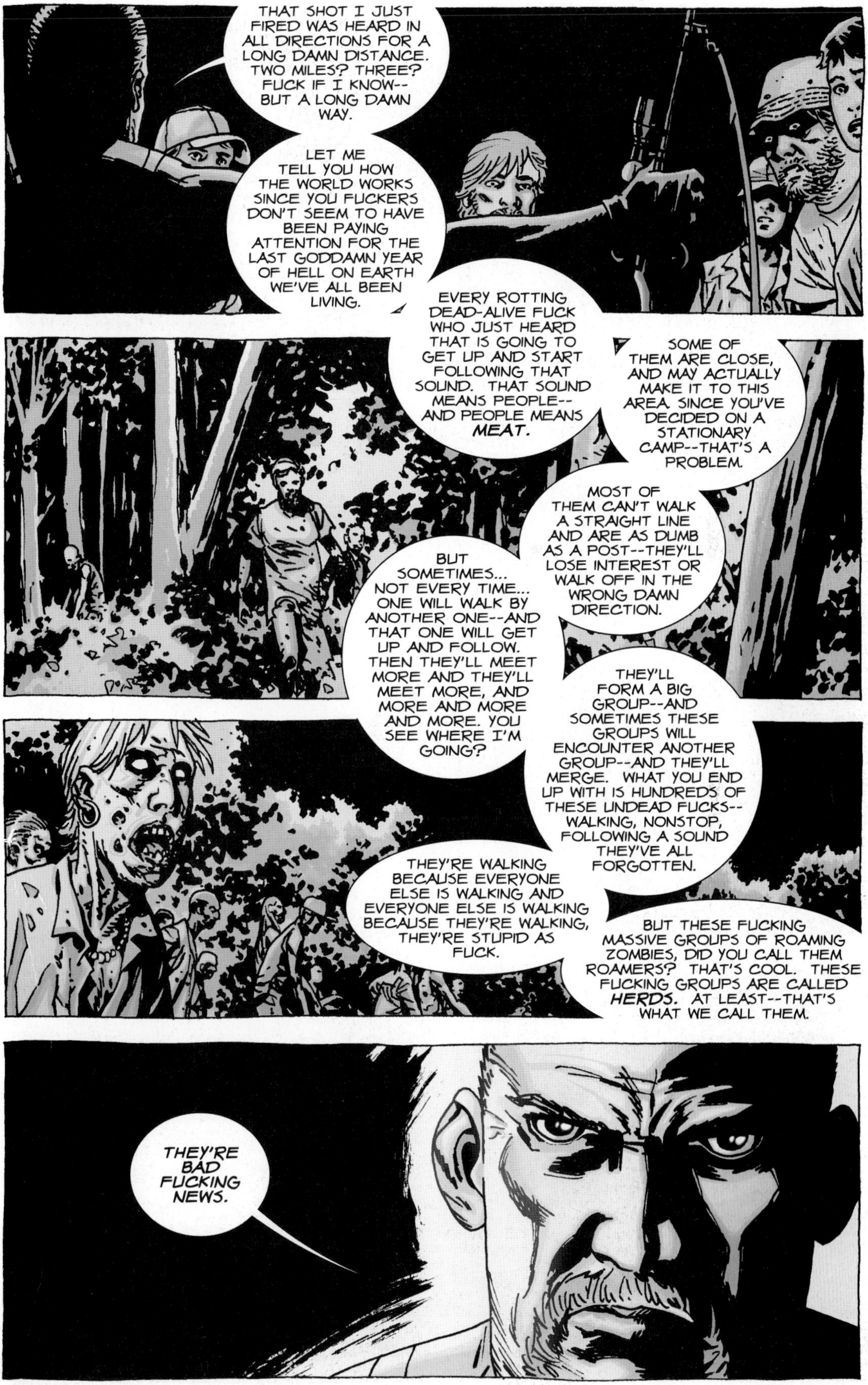
THAT SHOT I JUST FIRED WAS HEARD IN ALL DIRECTIONS FOR A LONG DAMN DISTANCE. TWO MILES? THREE? FUCK IF I KNOW-- BUT A LONG DAMN WAY.
LET ME TELL YOU HOW THE WORLD WORKS SINCE YOU FUCKERS DON'T SEEM TO HAVE BEEN PAYING ATTENTION FOR THE LAST GODDAMN YEAR OF HELL ON EARTH WE'VE ALL BEEN LIVING.
EVERY ROTTING DEAD-ALIVE FUCK WHO JUST HEARD THAT IS GOING TO GET UP AND START FOLLOWING THAT SOUND. THAT SOUND MEANS PEOPLE-- AND PEOPLE MEANS MEAT.
SOME OF THEM ARE CLOSE, AND MAY ACTUALLY MAKE IT TO THIS AREA. SINCE YOU'VE DECIDED ON A STATIONARY CAMP--THAT'S A PROBLEM.
MOST OF THEM CAN'T WALK A STRAIGHT LINE AND ARE AS DUMB AS A POST--THEY'LL LOSE INTEREST OR WALK OFF IN THE WRONG DAMN DIRECTION.
BUT SOMETIMES... NOT EVERY TIME... ONE WILL WALK BY ANOTHER ONE--AND THAT ONE WILL GET UP AND FOLLOW. THEN THEY'LL MEET MORE AND THEY'LL MEET MORE, AND MORE AND MORE AND MORE. YOU SEE WHERE I'M GOING?
THEY'LL FORM A BIG GROUP--AND SOMETIMES THESE GROUPS WILL ENCOUNTER ANOTHER GROUP--AND THEY'LL MERGE. WHAT YOU END UP WITH IS HUNDREDS OF THESE UNDEAD FUCKS-- WALKING, NONSTOP, FOLLOWING A SOUND THEY'VE ALL FORGOTTEN.
THEY'RE WALKING BECAUSE EVERYONE ELSE IS WALKING AND EVERYONE ELSE IS WALKING BECAUSE THEY'RE WALKING, THEY'RE STUPID AS FUCK.
BUT THESE FUCKING MASSIVE GROUPS OF ROAMING ZOMBIES, DID YOU CALL THEM ROAMERS? THAT'S COOL. THESE FUCKING GROUPS ARE CALLED HERDS. AT LEAST--THAT'S WHAT WE CALL THEM.
THEY'RE BAD FUCKING NEWS.

NOW TO ANSWER LITTLE MISS DEATH THREAT'S QUESTION...

FUCK YOU.

RIGHT BACK AT YOU. EUGENE-- WHAT WOULD YOUR ANSWER HAVE BEEN IF YOU HADN'T BEEN SO BUSY FOCUSING ON NOT SHITTING YOUR PANTS?

I CAN'T TELL HER ANYTHING. IT'S ALL CLASSIFIED.

IT'S CLASSIFIED-- HE NEVER TOLD US AND HE CAN'T FUCKING TELL *YOU*. NOW I KNOW WHAT YOU'RE THINKING--THIS GUY IS CRAZY--THESE PEOPLE ARE CRAZY--WHO THE FUCK WOULD FOLLOW THIS CRAZY ASSHOLE TO WASHINGTON D.C. WITHOUT HAVING ANY IDEA WHAT THE FUCK IT IS HE'S ACTUALLY TRYING TO TELL THEM.

AND RIGHTLY SO... BECAUSE THAT'S WHAT I THOUGHT ABOUT EUGENE WHEN I FIRST MET HIM. WHAT A CRAZY PIECE OF SHIT... THAT WAS MY ACTUAL THOUGHT.

BUT I WAS *WRONG*.

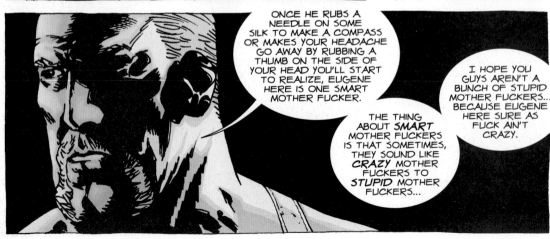

ONCE HE RUBS A NEEDLE ON SOME SILK TO MAKE A COMPASS OR MAKES YOUR HEADACHE GO AWAY BY RUBBING A THUMB ON THE SIDE OF YOUR HEAD YOU'LL START TO REALIZE, EUGENE HERE IS ONE SMART MOTHER FUCKER.

I HOPE YOU GUYS AREN'T A BUNCH OF STUPID MOTHER FUCKERS... BECAUSE EUGENE HERE SURE AS FUCK AIN'T CRAZY.

THE THING ABOUT *SMART* MOTHER FUCKERS IS THAT SOMETIMES, THEY SOUND LIKE *CRAZY* MOTHER FUCKERS TO *STUPID* MOTHER FUCKERS...

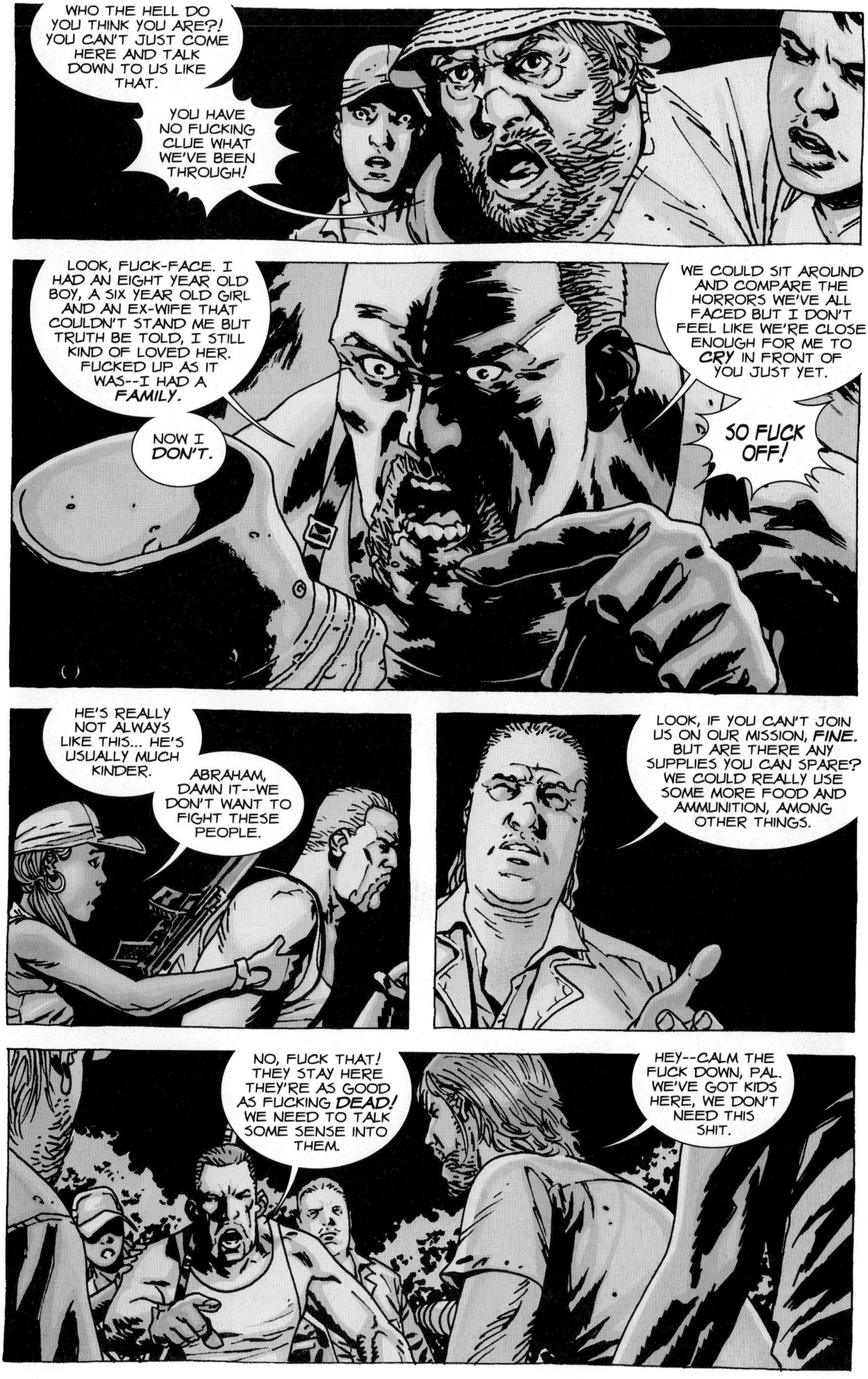
WHO THE HELL DO YOU THINK YOU ARE?! YOU CAN'T JUST COME HERE AND TALK DOWN TO US LIKE THAT.
YOU HAVE NO FUCKING CLUE WHAT WE'VE BEEN THROUGH!
LOOK, FUCK-FACE. I HAD AN EIGHT YEAR OLD BOY, A SIX YEAR OLD GIRL AND AN EX-WIFE THAT COULDN'T STAND ME BUT TRUTH BE TOLD, I STILL KIND OF LOVED HER. FUCKED UP AS IT WAS--I HAD A FAMILY.
NOW I DON'T.
WE COULD SIT AROUND AND COMPARE THE HORRORS WE'VE ALL FACED BUT I DON'T FEEL LIKE WE'RE CLOSE ENOUGH FOR ME TO CRY IN FRONT OF YOU JUST YET.
SO FUCK OFF!
HE'S REALLY NOT ALWAYS LIKE THIS... HE'S USUALLY MUCH KINDER.
ABRAHAM, DAMN IT--WE DON'T WANT TO FIGHT THESE PEOPLE.
LOOK, IF YOU CAN'T JOIN US ON OUR MISSION, FINE. BUT ARE THERE ANY SUPPLIES YOU CAN SPARE? WE COULD REALLY USE SOME MORE FOOD AND AMMUNITION, AMONG OTHER THINGS.
NO, FUCK THAT! THEY STAY HERE THEY'RE AS GOOD AS FUCKING DEAD! WE NEED TO TALK SOME SENSE INTO THEM.
HEY--CALM THE FUCK DOWN, PAL. WE'VE GOT KIDS HERE, WE DON'T NEED THIS SHIT.

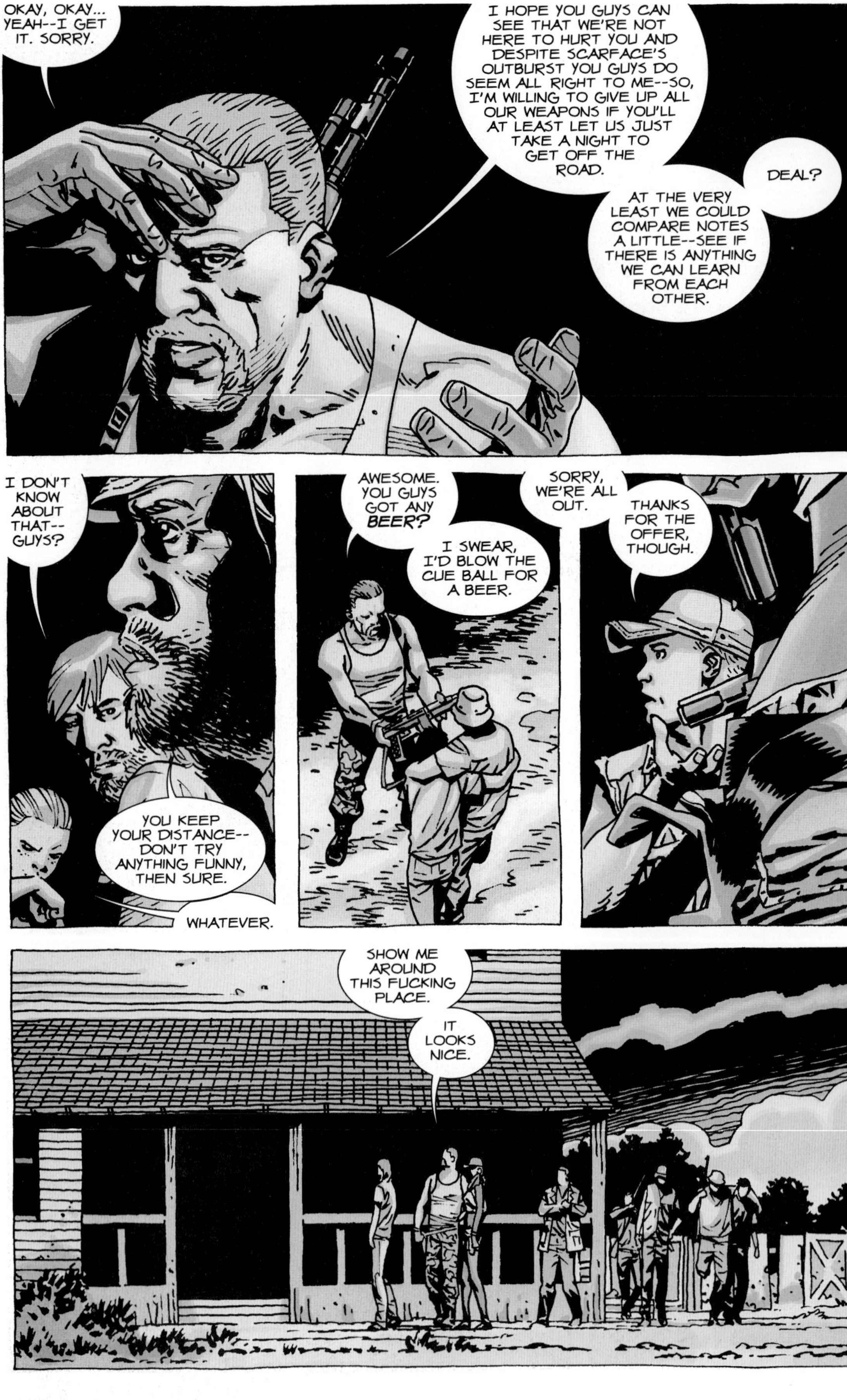
OKAY, OKAY... YEAH--I GET IT. SORRY.
I HOPE YOU GUYS CAN SEE THAT WE'RE NOT HERE TO HURT YOU AND DESPITE SCARFACE'S OUTBURST YOU GUYS DO SEEM ALL RIGHT TO ME--SO, I'M WILLING TO GIVE UP ALL OUR WEAPONS IF YOU'LL AT LEAST LET US JUST TAKE A NIGHT TO GET OFF THE ROAD.
AT THE VERY LEAST WE COULD COMPARE NOTES A LITTLE--SEE IF THERE IS ANYTHING WE CAN LEARN FROM EACH OTHER.
DEAL?
I DON'T KNOW ABOUT THAT-- GUYS?
YOU KEEP YOUR DISTANCE-- DON'T TRY ANYTHING FUNNY, THEN SURE.
WHATEVER.
AWESOME. YOU GUYS GOT ANY BEER?
I SWEAR, I'D BLOW THE CUE BALL FOR A BEER.
SORRY, WE'RE ALL OUT.
THANKS FOR THE OFFER, THOUGH.
SHOW ME AROUND THIS FUCKING PLACE.
IT LOOKS NICE.

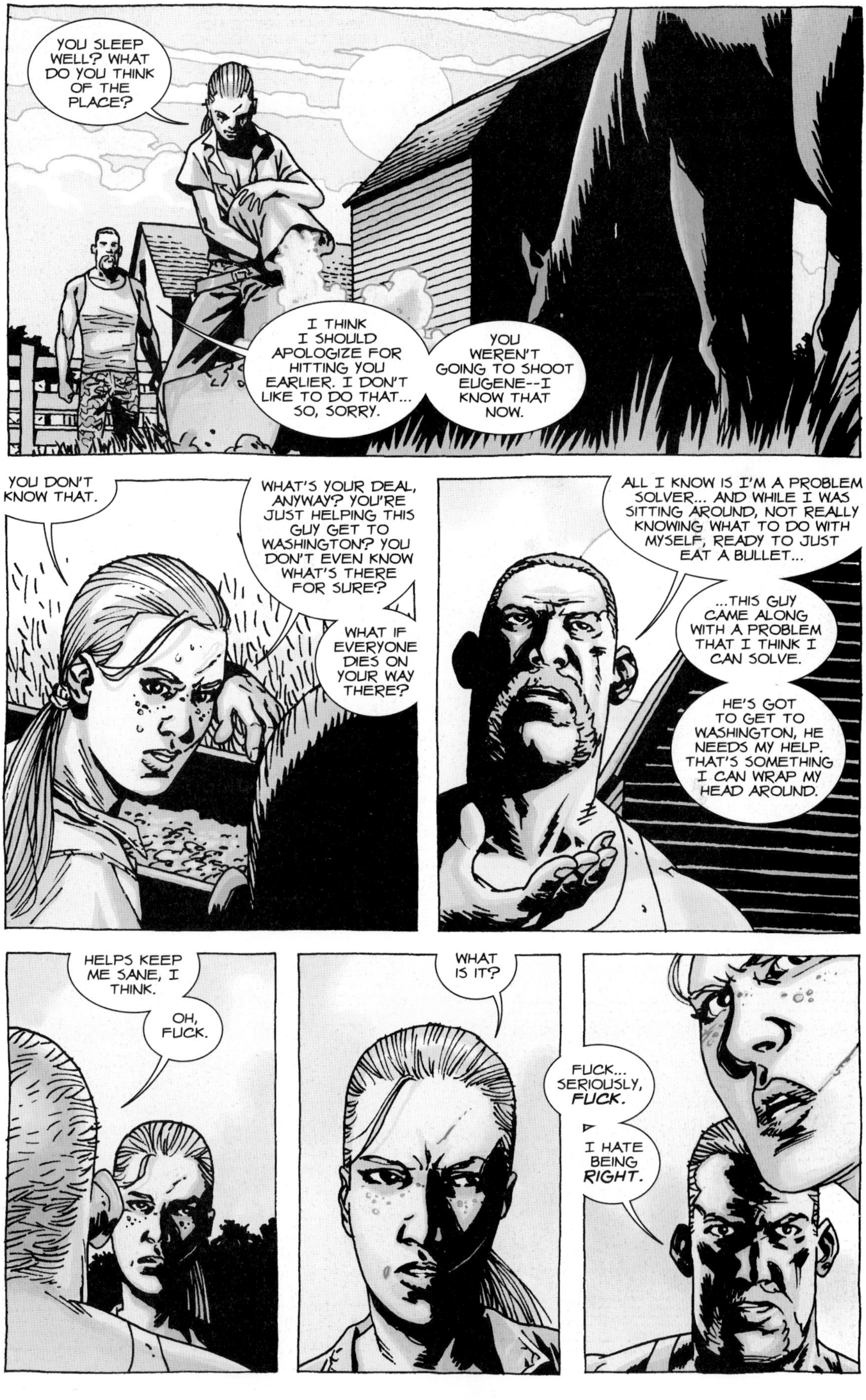
YOU SLEEP WELL? WHAT DO YOU THINK OF THE PLACE?
I THINK I SHOULD APOLOGIZE FOR HITTING YOU EARLIER. I DON'T LIKE TO DO THAT... SO, SORRY.
YOU WEREN'T GOING TO SHOOT EUGENE--I KNOW THAT NOW.
YOU DON'T KNOW THAT.
WHAT'S YOUR DEAL, ANYWAY? YOU'RE JUST HELPING THIS GUY GET TO WASHINGTON? YOU DON'T EVEN KNOW WHAT'S THERE FOR SURE?
WHAT IF EVERYONE DIES ON YOUR WAY THERE?
ALL I KNOW IS I'M A PROBLEM SOLVER... AND WHILE I WAS SITTING AROUND, NOT REALLY KNOWING WHAT TO DO WITH MYSELF, READY TO JUST EAT A BULLET...
...THIS GUY CAME ALONG WITH A PROBLEM THAT I THINK I CAN SOLVE.
HE'S GOT TO GET TO WASHINGTON, HE NEEDS MY HELP. THAT'S SOMETHING I CAN WRAP MY HEAD AROUND.
HELPS KEEP ME SANE, I THINK.
OH, FUCK.
WHAT IS IT?
FUCK... SERIOUSLY, *FUCK*.
I HATE BEING *RIGHT*.

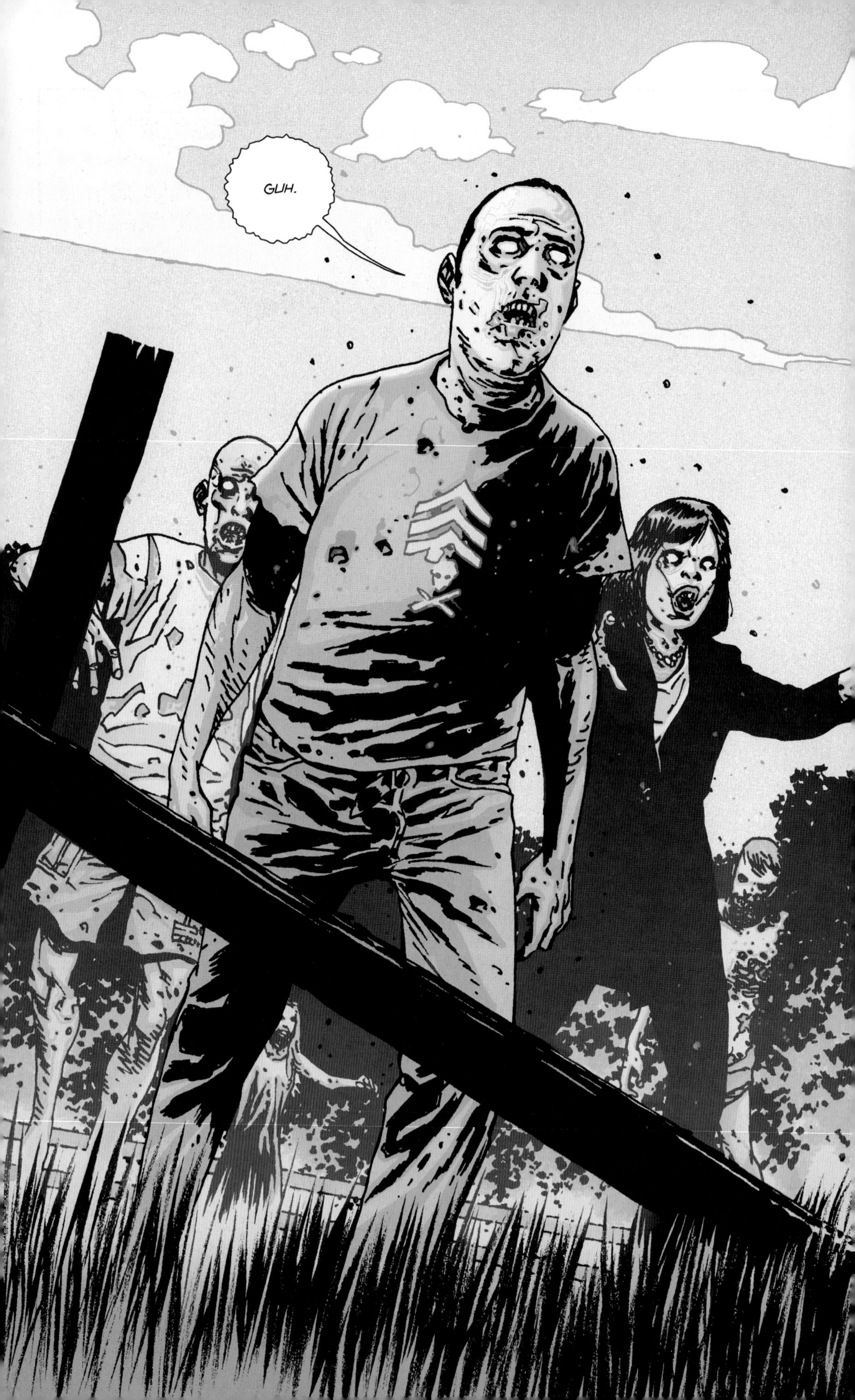
GUH.

GO GET YOUR FRIENDS, TELL THEM TO GRAB SOME HAMMERS OR AXES OR SOMETHING--JUST IN CASE I NEED HELP.

I'M GOING TO BORROW YOUR PITCH FORK.

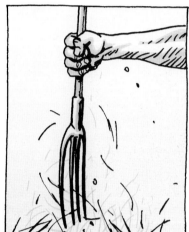

HU-UNGH!

WROKK!

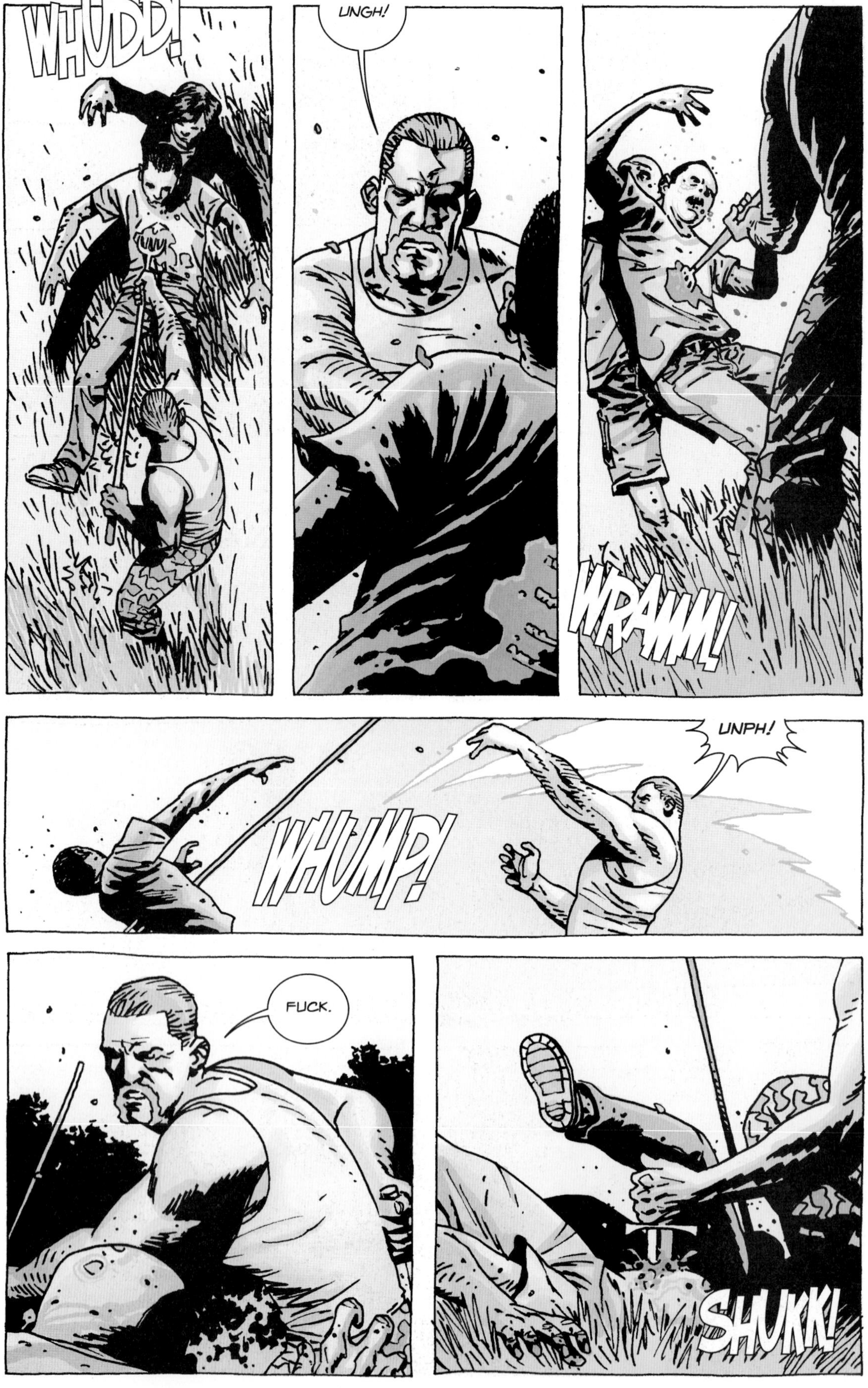
WHUDD!
UNGH!
WRAMM!
WHUMP!
UNPH!
FUCK.
SHUKK!

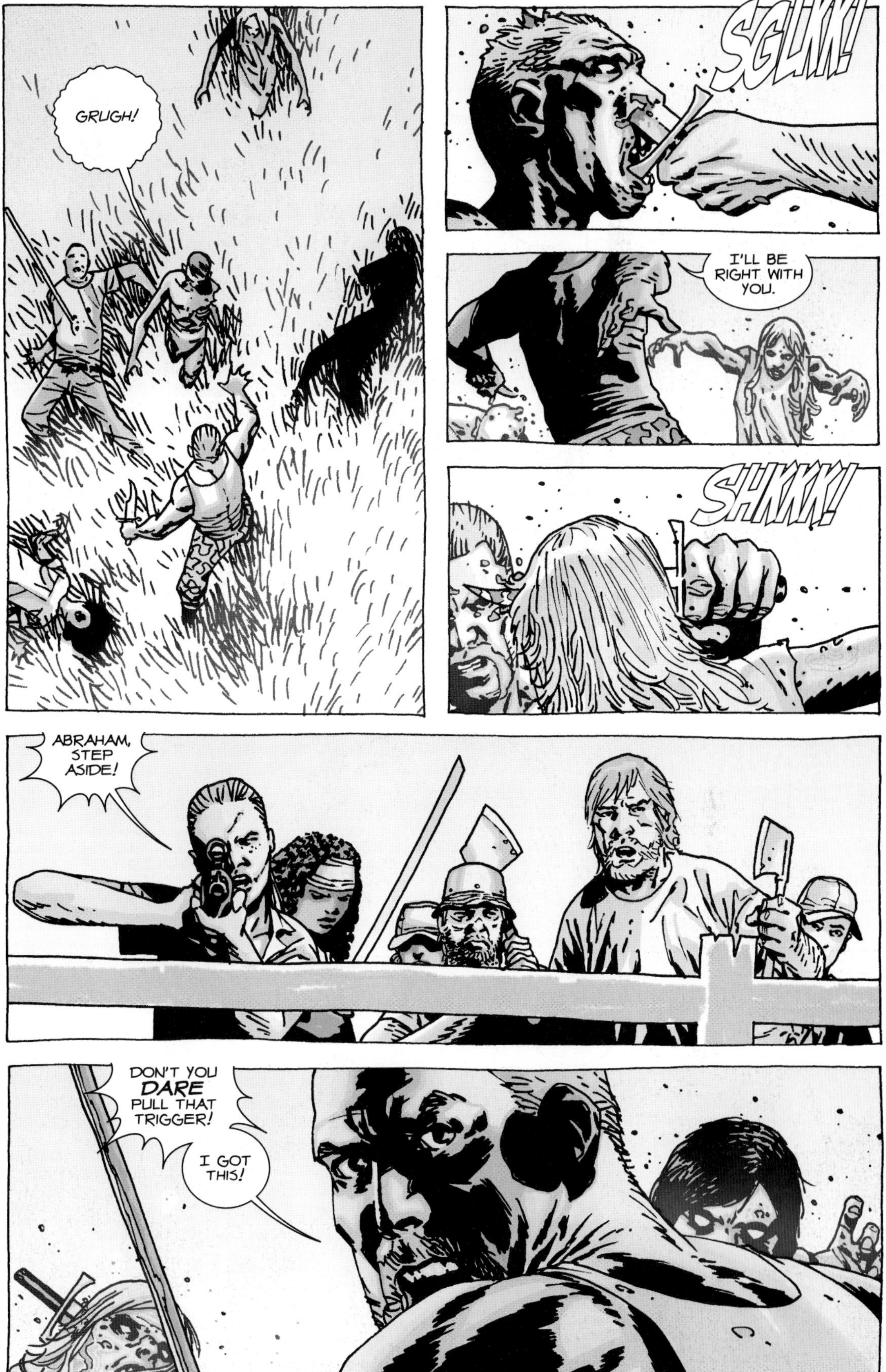
GRUGH!
SGLKK!
I'LL BE RIGHT WITH YOU.
SHKKK!
ABRAHAM, STEP ASIDE!
DON'T YOU DARE PULL THAT TRIGGER!
I GOT THIS!

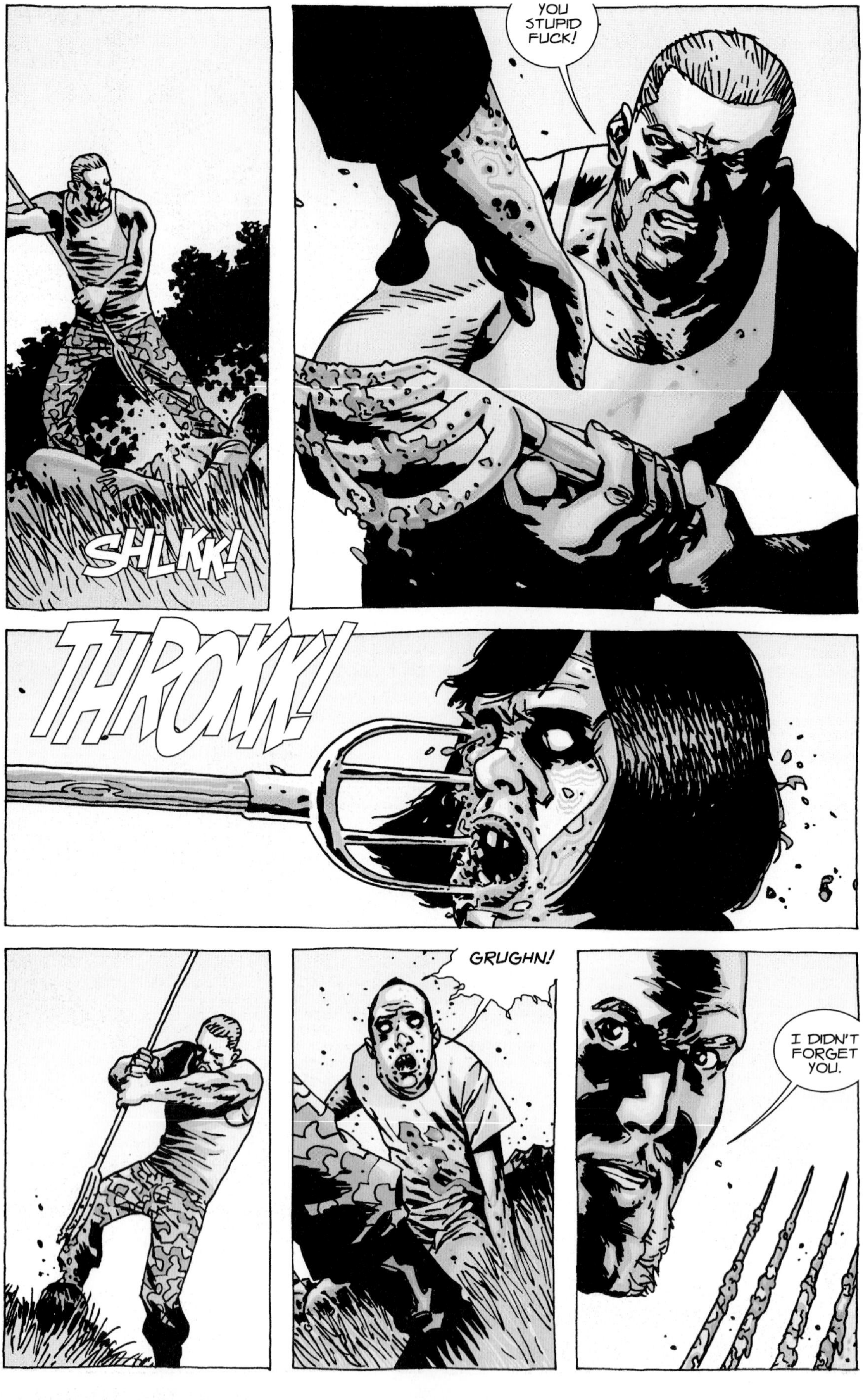
SHLKK!
YOU STUPID FUCK!
THROKK!
GRUGHN!
I DIDN'T FORGET YOU.

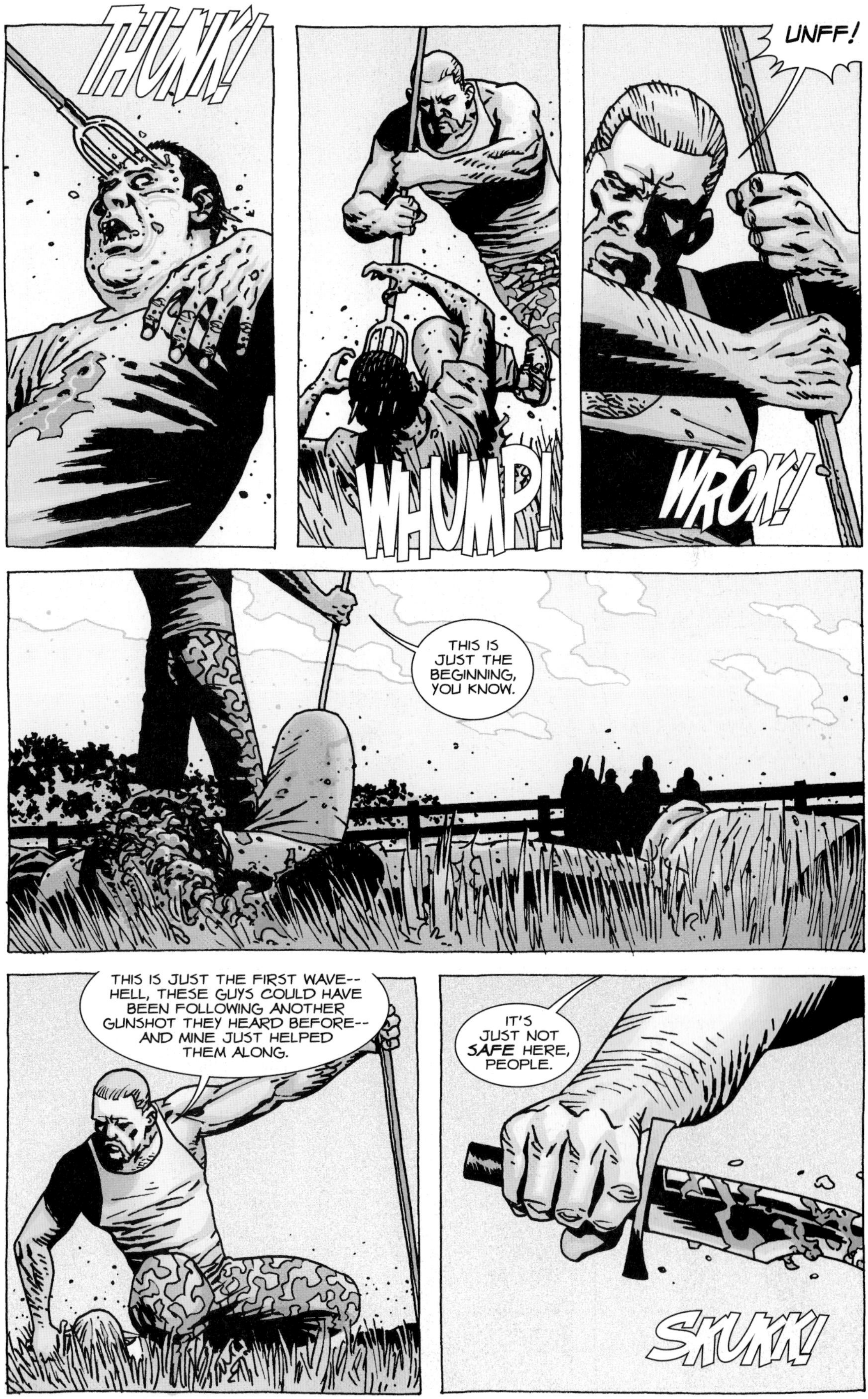
THUNK!
WHUMP!
UNFF!
WROK!
THIS IS JUST THE BEGINNING, YOU KNOW.
THIS IS JUST THE FIRST WAVE-- HELL, THESE GUYS COULD HAVE BEEN FOLLOWING ANOTHER GUNSHOT THEY HEARD BEFORE-- AND MINE JUST HELPED THEM ALONG.
IT'S JUST NOT SAFE HERE, PEOPLE.
SKUKK!

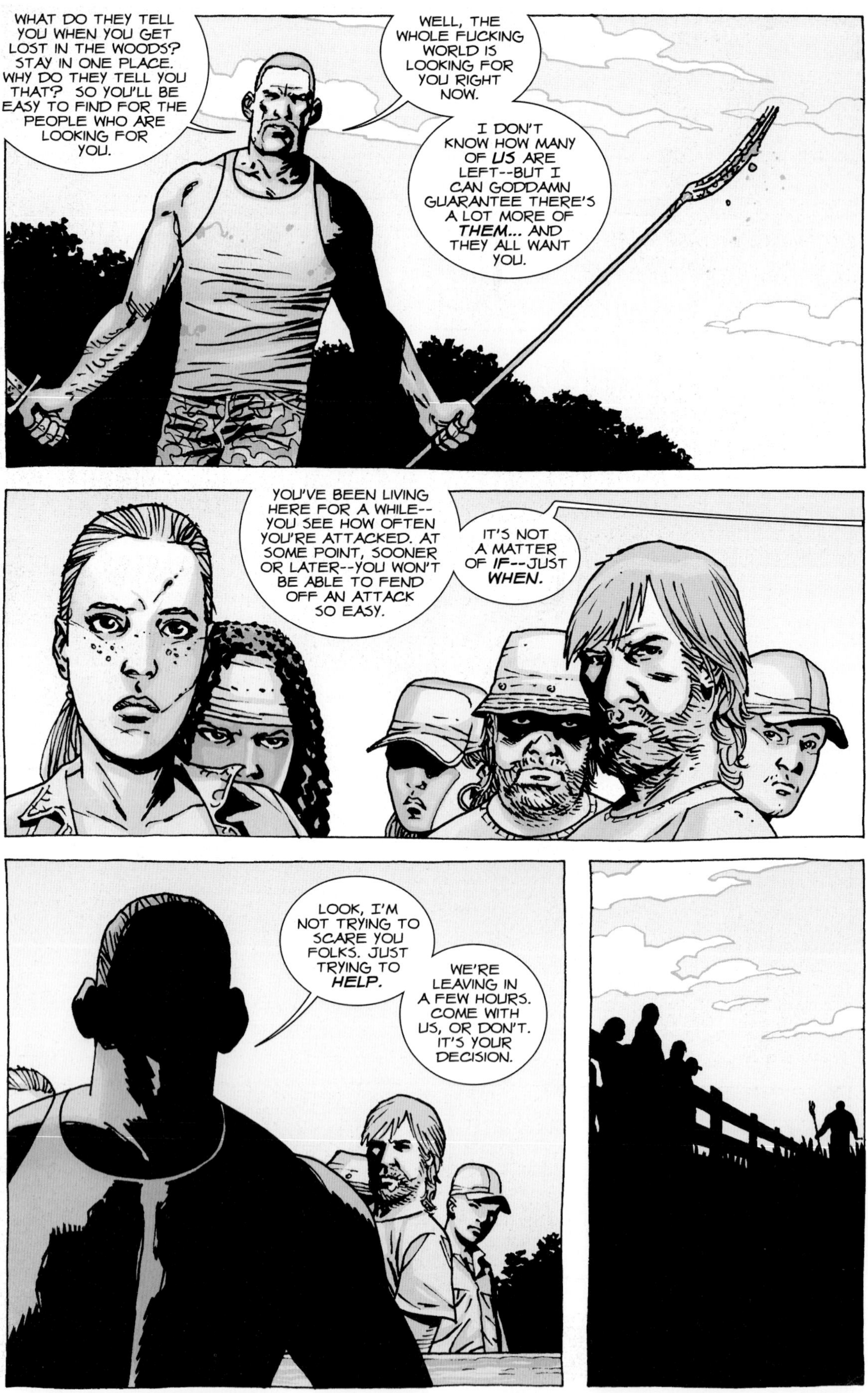
WHAT DO THEY TELL YOU WHEN YOU GET LOST IN THE WOODS? STAY IN ONE PLACE. WHY DO THEY TELL YOU THAT? SO YOU'LL BE EASY TO FIND FOR THE PEOPLE WHO ARE LOOKING FOR YOU.
WELL, THE WHOLE FUCKING WORLD IS LOOKING FOR YOU RIGHT NOW.
I DON'T KNOW HOW MANY OF US ARE LEFT--BUT I CAN GODDAMN GUARANTEE THERE'S A LOT MORE OF THEM... AND THEY ALL WANT YOU.
YOU'VE BEEN LIVING HERE FOR A WHILE--YOU SEE HOW OFTEN YOU'RE ATTACKED. AT SOME POINT, SOONER OR LATER--YOU WON'T BE ABLE TO FEND OFF AN ATTACK SO EASY.
IT'S NOT A MATTER OF IF--JUST WHEN.
LOOK, I'M NOT TRYING TO SCARE YOU FOLKS. JUST TRYING TO HELP.
WE'RE LEAVING IN A FEW HOURS. COME WITH US, OR DON'T. IT'S YOUR DECISION.

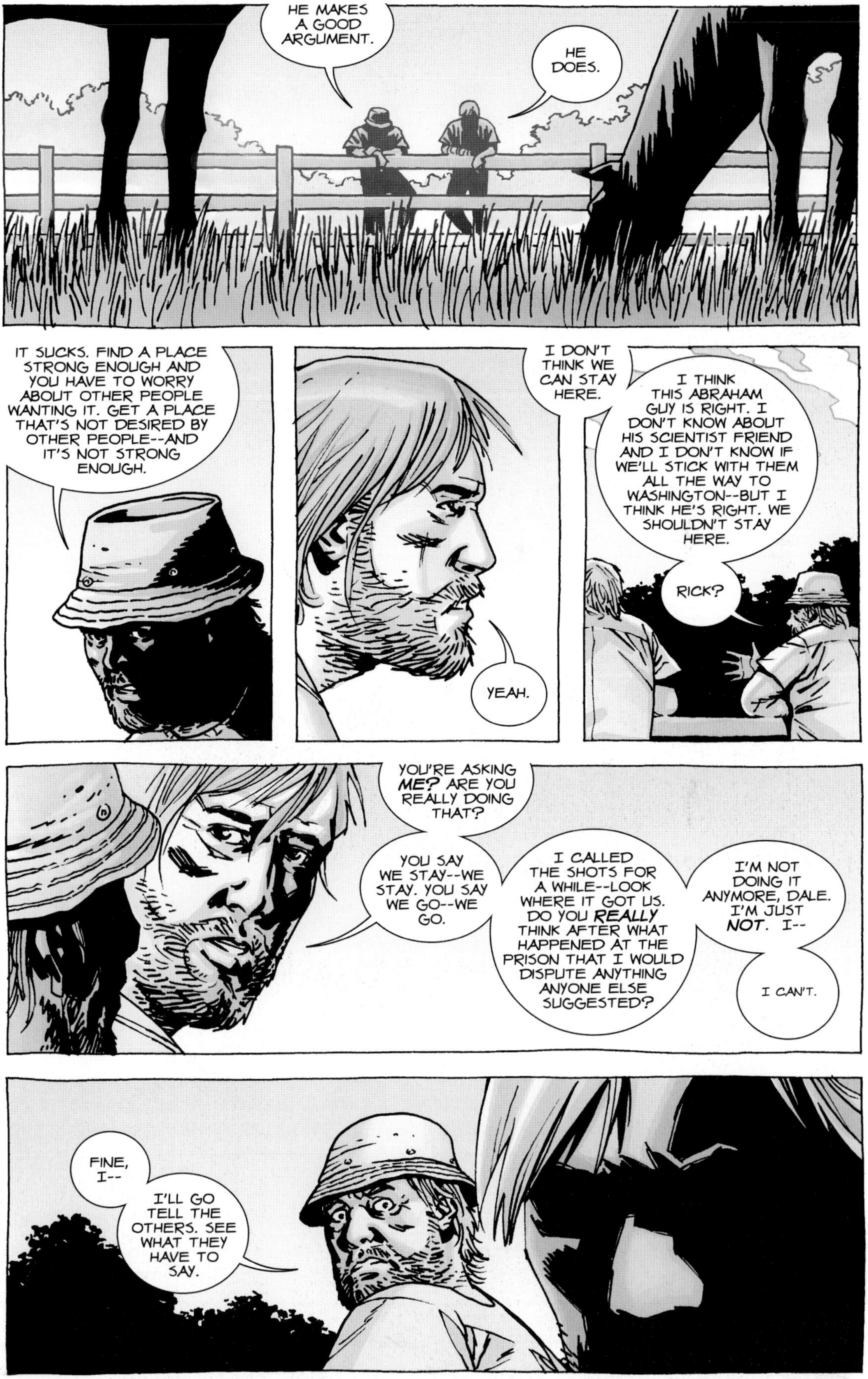
HE MAKES A GOOD ARGUMENT.
HE DOES.
IT SUCKS. FIND A PLACE STRONG ENOUGH AND YOU HAVE TO WORRY ABOUT OTHER PEOPLE WANTING IT. GET A PLACE THAT'S NOT DESIRED BY OTHER PEOPLE--AND IT'S NOT STRONG ENOUGH.
YEAH.
I DON'T THINK WE CAN STAY HERE.
I THINK THIS ABRAHAM GUY IS RIGHT. I DON'T KNOW ABOUT HIS SCIENTIST FRIEND AND I DON'T KNOW IF WE'LL STICK WITH THEM ALL THE WAY TO WASHINGTON--BUT I THINK HE'S RIGHT. WE SHOULDN'T STAY HERE.
RICK?
YOU'RE ASKING ME? ARE YOU REALLY DOING THAT?
YOU SAY WE STAY--WE STAY. YOU SAY WE GO--WE GO.
I CALLED THE SHOTS FOR A WHILE--LOOK WHERE IT GOT US. DO YOU REALLY THINK AFTER WHAT HAPPENED AT THE PRISON THAT I WOULD DISPUTE ANYTHING ANYONE ELSE SUGGESTED?
I'M NOT DOING IT ANYMORE, DALE. I'M JUST NOT. I--
I CAN'T.
FINE, I--
I'LL GO TELL THE OTHERS. SEE WHAT THEY HAVE TO SAY.

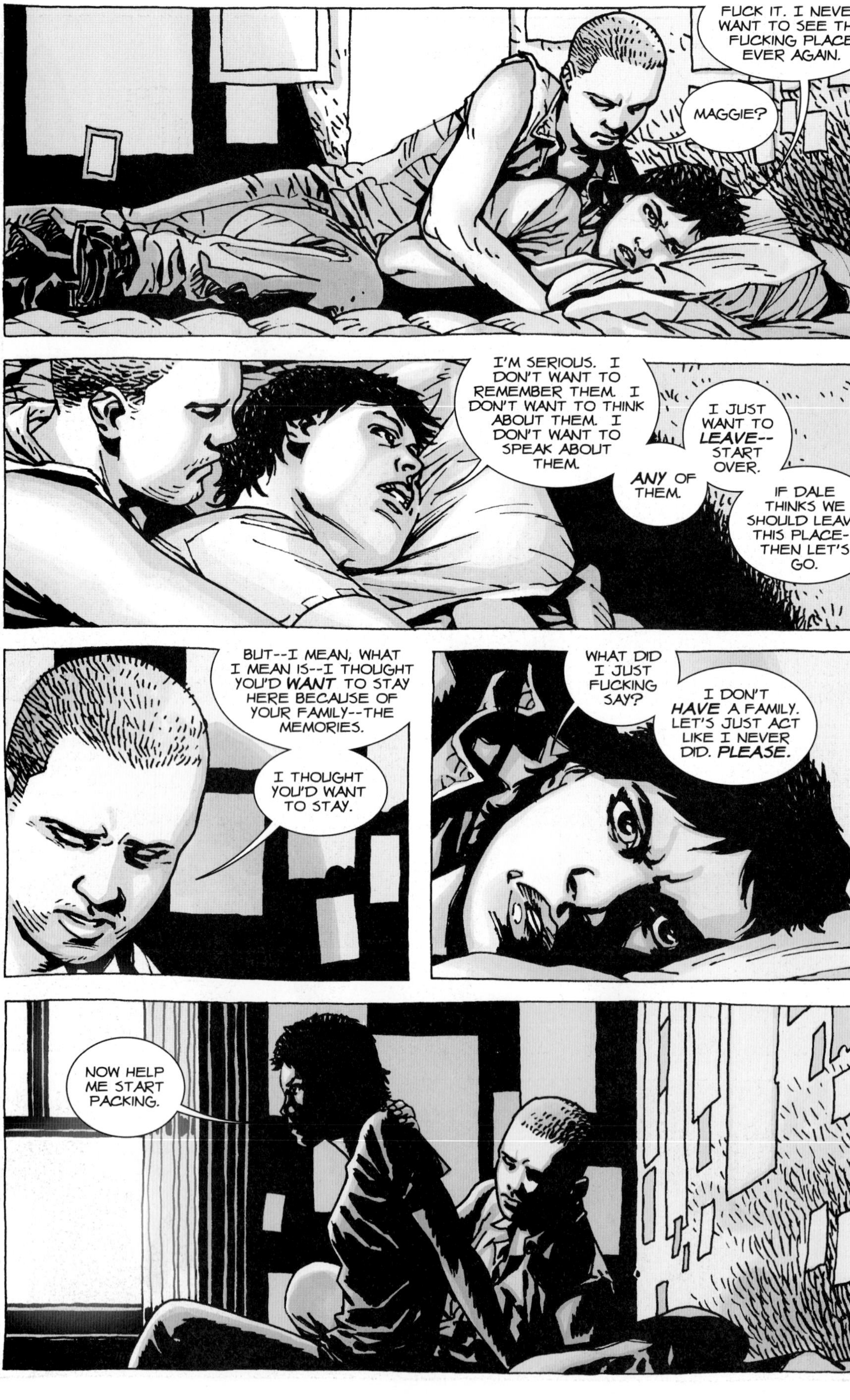
FUCK IT. I NEVER WANT TO SEE THIS FUCKING PLACE EVER AGAIN.
MAGGIE?
I'M SERIOUS. I DON'T WANT TO REMEMBER THEM. I DON'T WANT TO THINK ABOUT THEM. I DON'T WANT TO SPEAK ABOUT THEM.
ANY OF THEM.
I JUST WANT TO LEAVE-- START OVER.
IF DALE THINKS WE SHOULD LEAVE THIS PLACE-- THEN LET'S GO.
BUT--I MEAN, WHAT I MEAN IS--I THOUGHT YOU'D WANT TO STAY HERE BECAUSE OF YOUR FAMILY--THE MEMORIES.
I THOUGHT YOU'D WANT TO STAY.
WHAT DID I JUST FUCKING SAY?
I DON'T HAVE A FAMILY. LET'S JUST ACT LIKE I NEVER DID. PLEASE.
NOW HELP ME START PACKING.

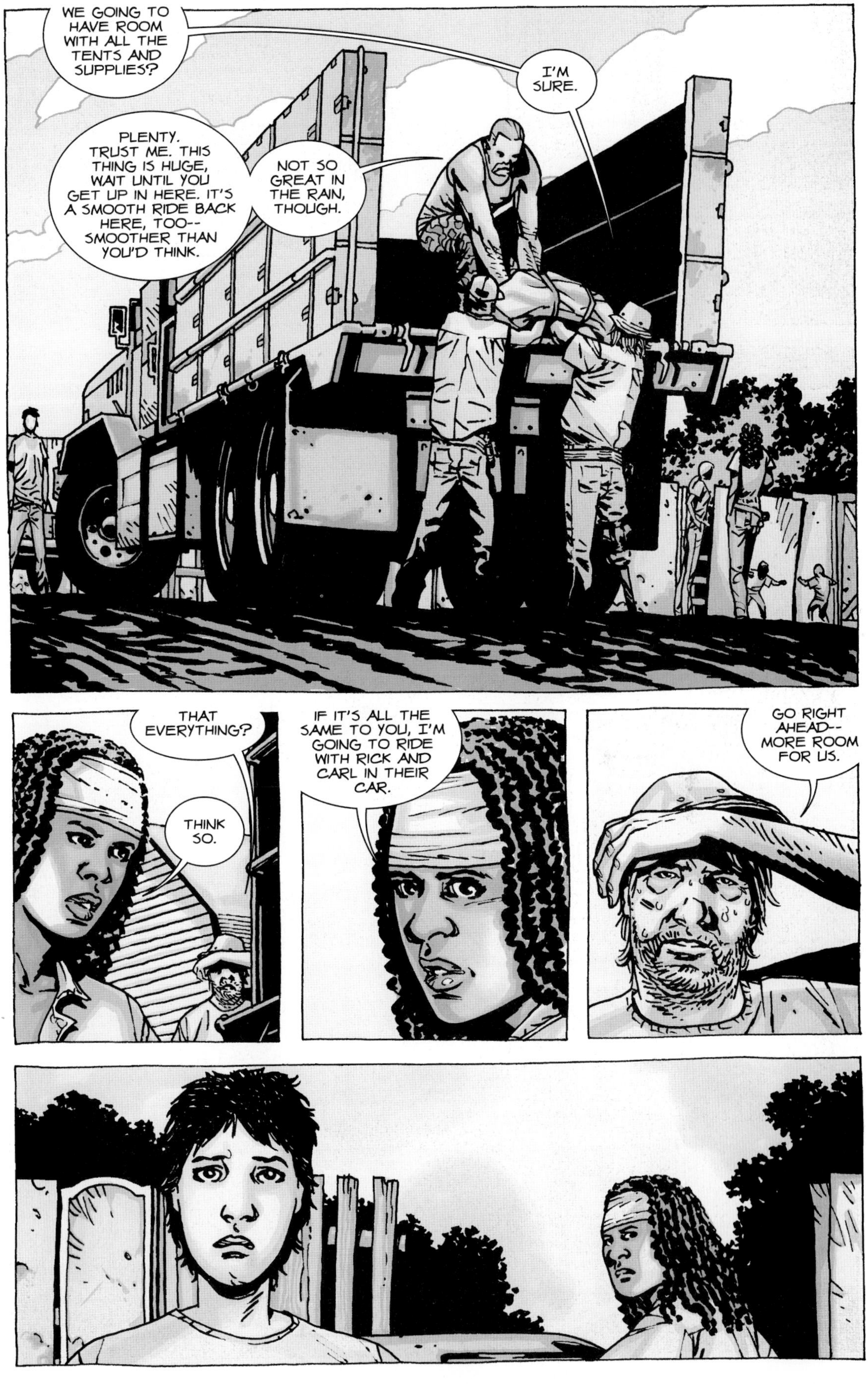
WE GOING TO HAVE ROOM WITH ALL THE TENTS AND SUPPLIES?
I'M SURE.
PLENTY. TRUST ME. THIS THING IS HUGE, WAIT UNTIL YOU GET UP IN HERE. IT'S A SMOOTH RIDE BACK HERE, TOO-- SMOOTHER THAN YOU'D THINK.
NOT SO GREAT IN THE RAIN, THOUGH.
THAT EVERYTHING?
THINK SO.
IF IT'S ALL THE SAME TO YOU, I'M GOING TO RIDE WITH RICK AND CARL IN THEIR CAR.
GO RIGHT AHEAD-- MORE ROOM FOR US.

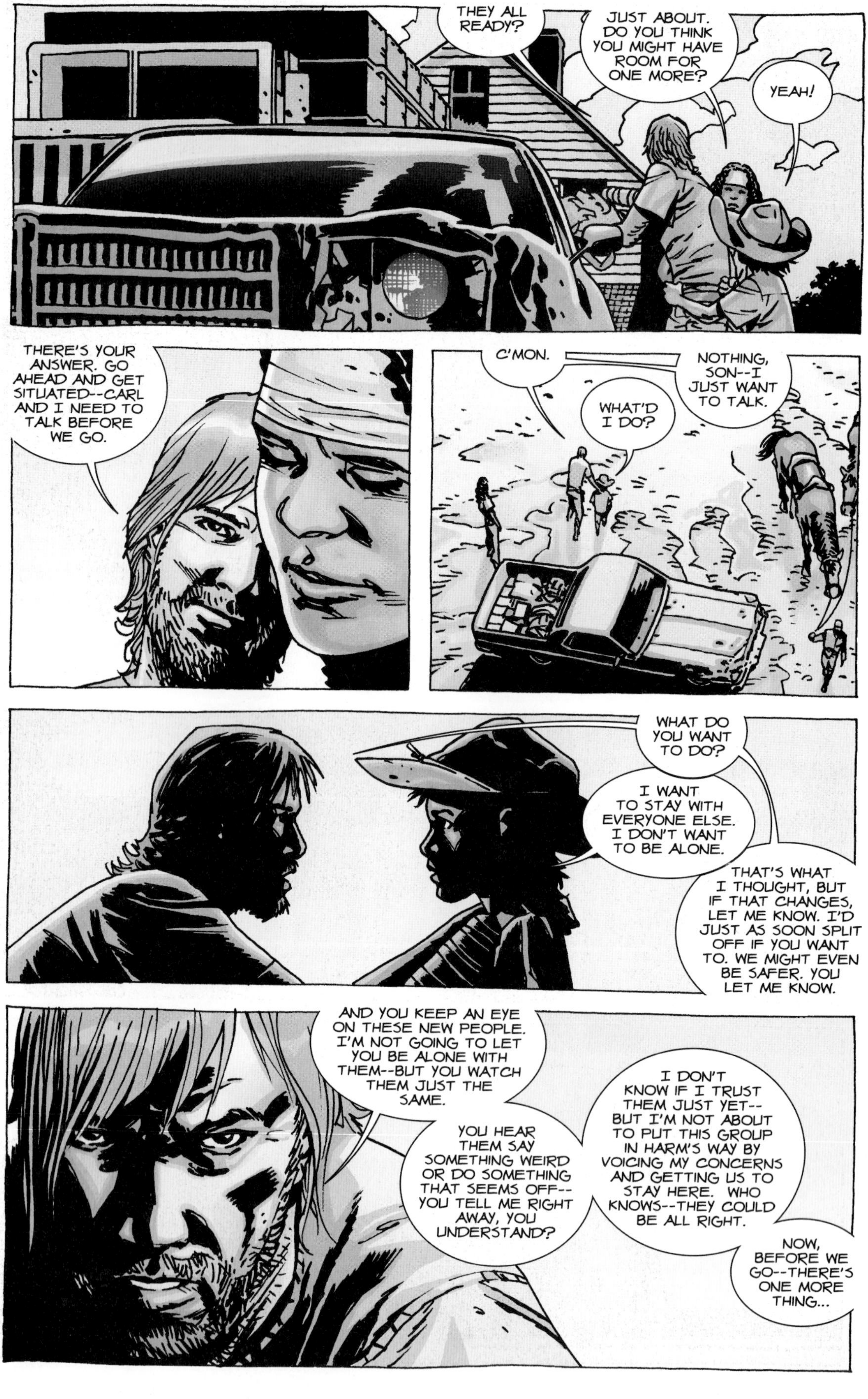
THEY ALL READY?
JUST ABOUT. DO YOU THINK YOU MIGHT HAVE ROOM FOR ONE MORE?
YEAH!
THERE'S YOUR ANSWER. GO AHEAD AND GET SITUATED--CARL AND I NEED TO TALK BEFORE WE GO.
C'MON.
WHAT'D I DO?
NOTHING, SON--I JUST WANT TO TALK.
WHAT DO YOU WANT TO DO?
I WANT TO STAY WITH EVERYONE ELSE. I DON'T WANT TO BE ALONE.
THAT'S WHAT I THOUGHT, BUT IF THAT CHANGES, LET ME KNOW. I'D JUST AS SOON SPLIT OFF IF YOU WANT TO. WE MIGHT EVEN BE SAFER. YOU LET ME KNOW.
AND YOU KEEP AN EYE ON THESE NEW PEOPLE. I'M NOT GOING TO LET YOU BE ALONE WITH THEM--BUT YOU WATCH THEM JUST THE SAME.
YOU HEAR THEM SAY SOMETHING WEIRD OR DO SOMETHING THAT SEEMS OFF--YOU TELL ME RIGHT AWAY, YOU UNDERSTAND?
I DON'T KNOW IF I TRUST THEM JUST YET--BUT I'M NOT ABOUT TO PUT THIS GROUP IN HARM'S WAY BY VOICING MY CONCERNS AND GETTING US TO STAY HERE. WHO KNOWS--THEY COULD BE ALL RIGHT.
NOW, BEFORE WE GO--THERE'S ONE MORE THING...

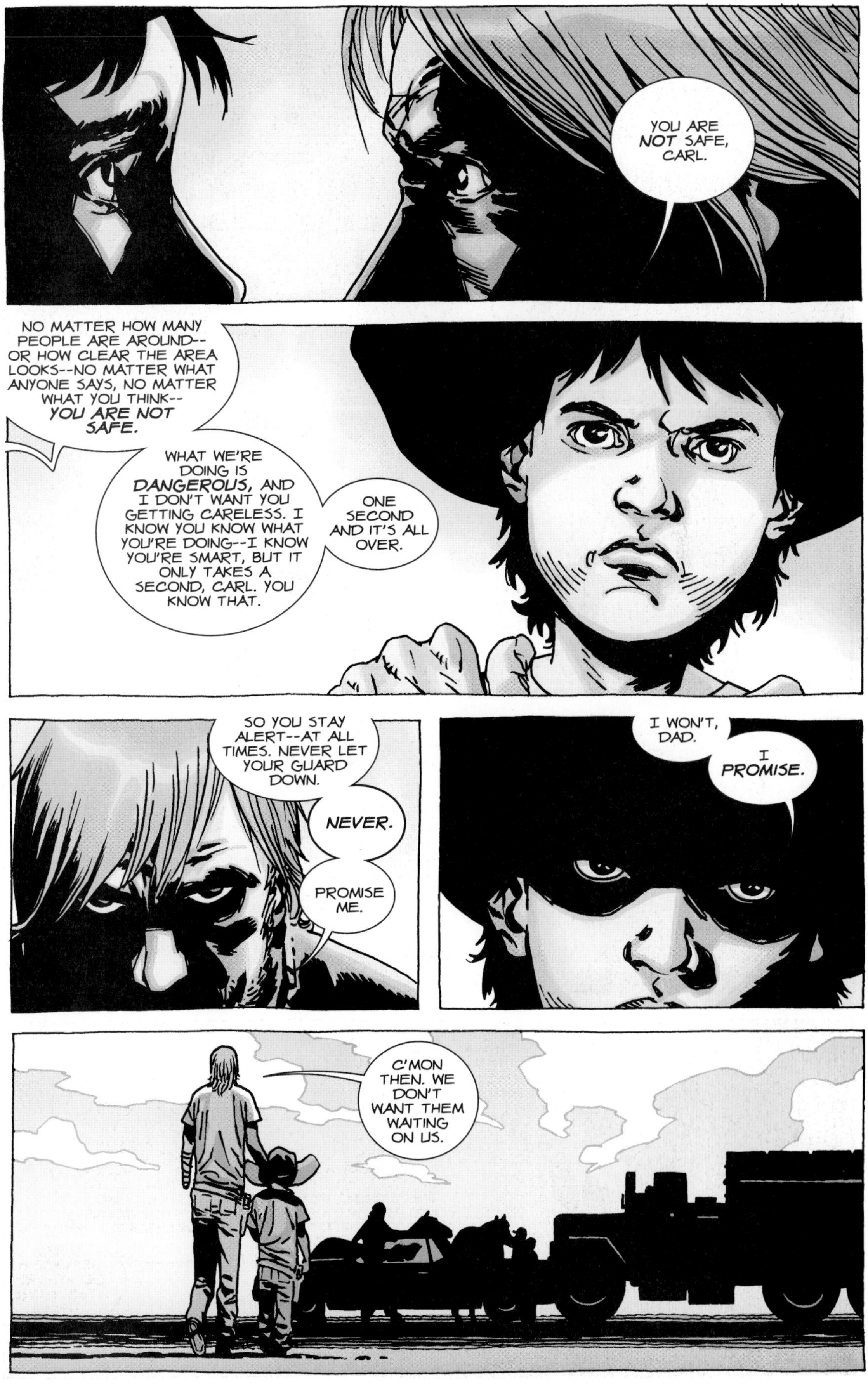

YOU ARE NOT SAFE, CARL.
NO MATTER HOW MANY PEOPLE ARE AROUND-- OR HOW CLEAR THE AREA LOOKS--NO MATTER WHAT ANYONE SAYS, NO MATTER WHAT YOU THINK-- YOU ARE NOT SAFE.
WHAT WE'RE DOING IS DANGEROUS, AND I DON'T WANT YOU GETTING CARELESS. I KNOW YOU KNOW WHAT YOU'RE DOING--I KNOW YOU'RE SMART, BUT IT ONLY TAKES A SECOND, CARL. YOU KNOW THAT.
ONE SECOND AND IT'S ALL OVER.
SO YOU STAY ALERT--AT ALL TIMES. NEVER LET YOUR GUARD DOWN.
NEVER.
PROMISE ME.
I WON'T, DAD.
I PROMISE.
C'MON THEN. WE DON'T WANT THEM WAITING ON US.

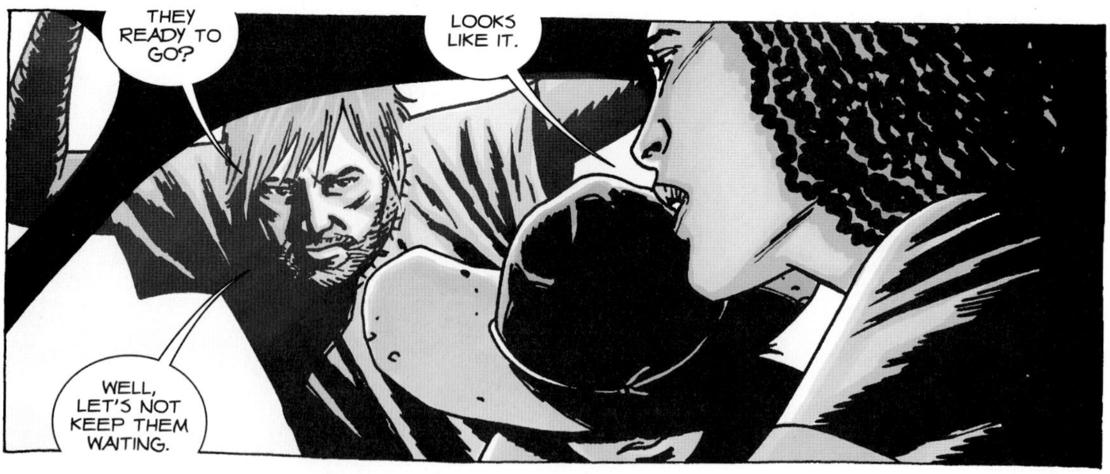
THEY READY TO GO?
LOOKS LIKE IT.
WELL, LET'S NOT KEEP THEM WAITING.

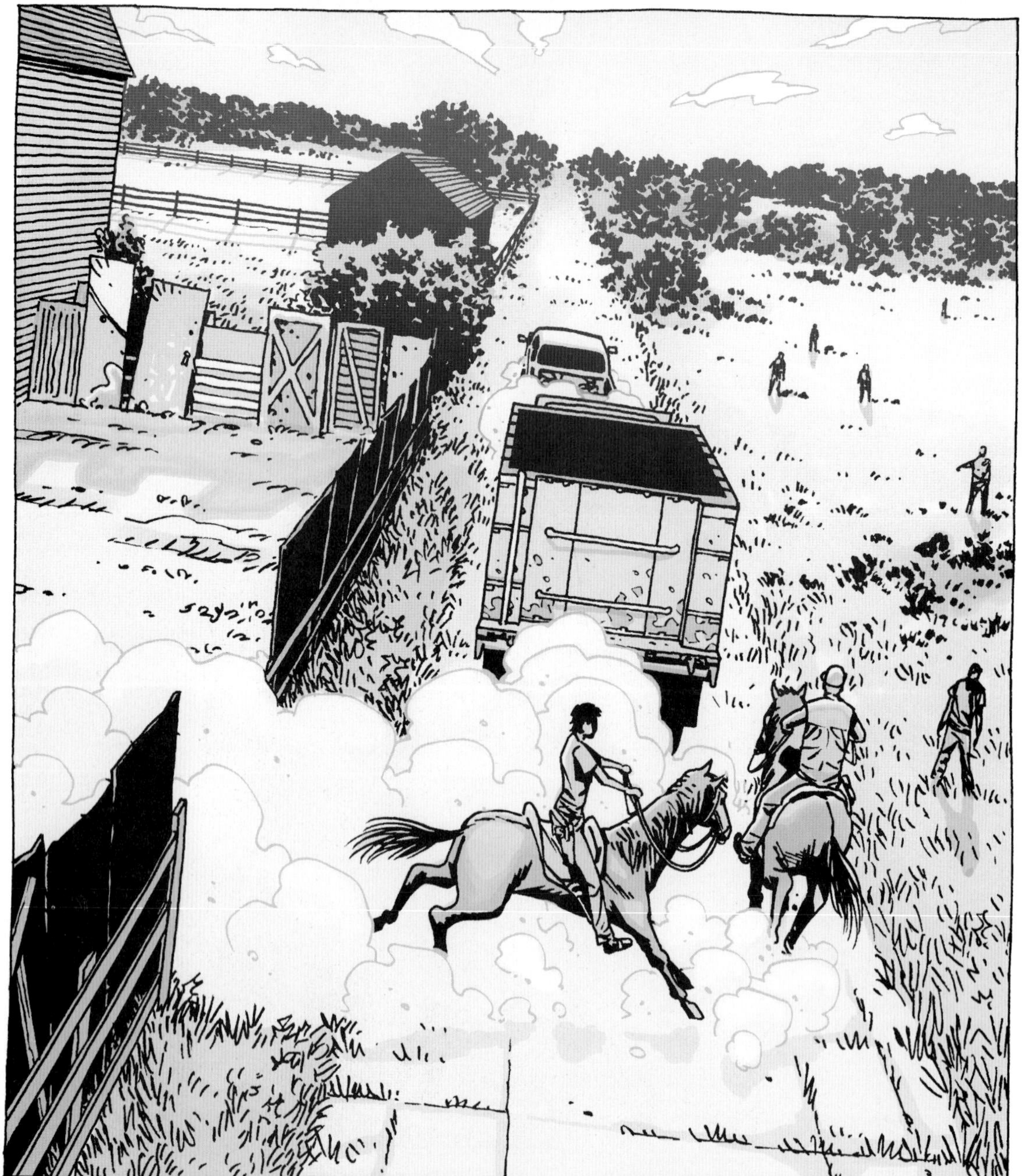

Chapter Ten:
What We Become

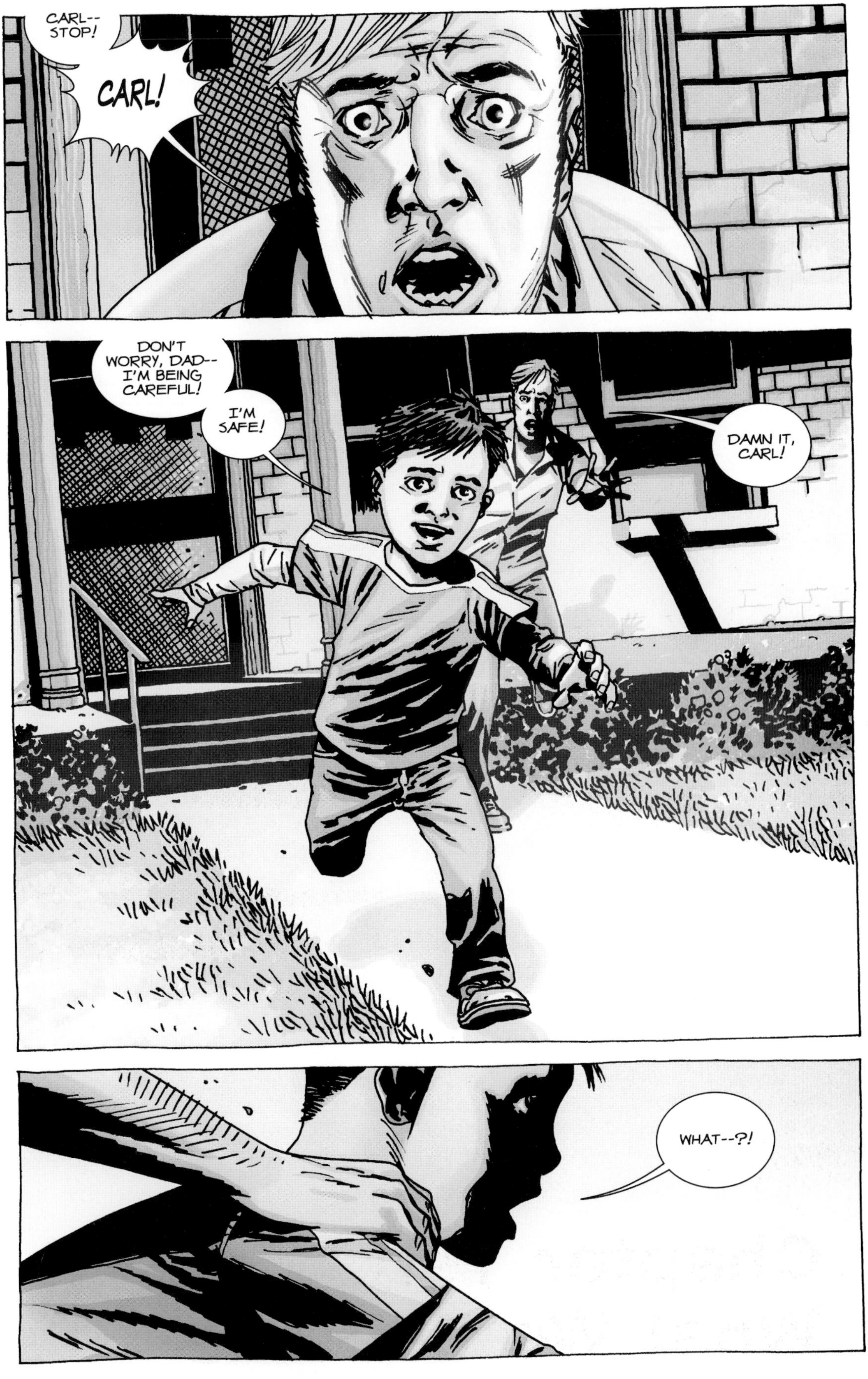
CARL--
STOP!
CARL!
DON'T WORRY, DAD-- I'M BEING CAREFUL!
I'M SAFE!
DAMN IT, CARL!
WHAT--?!

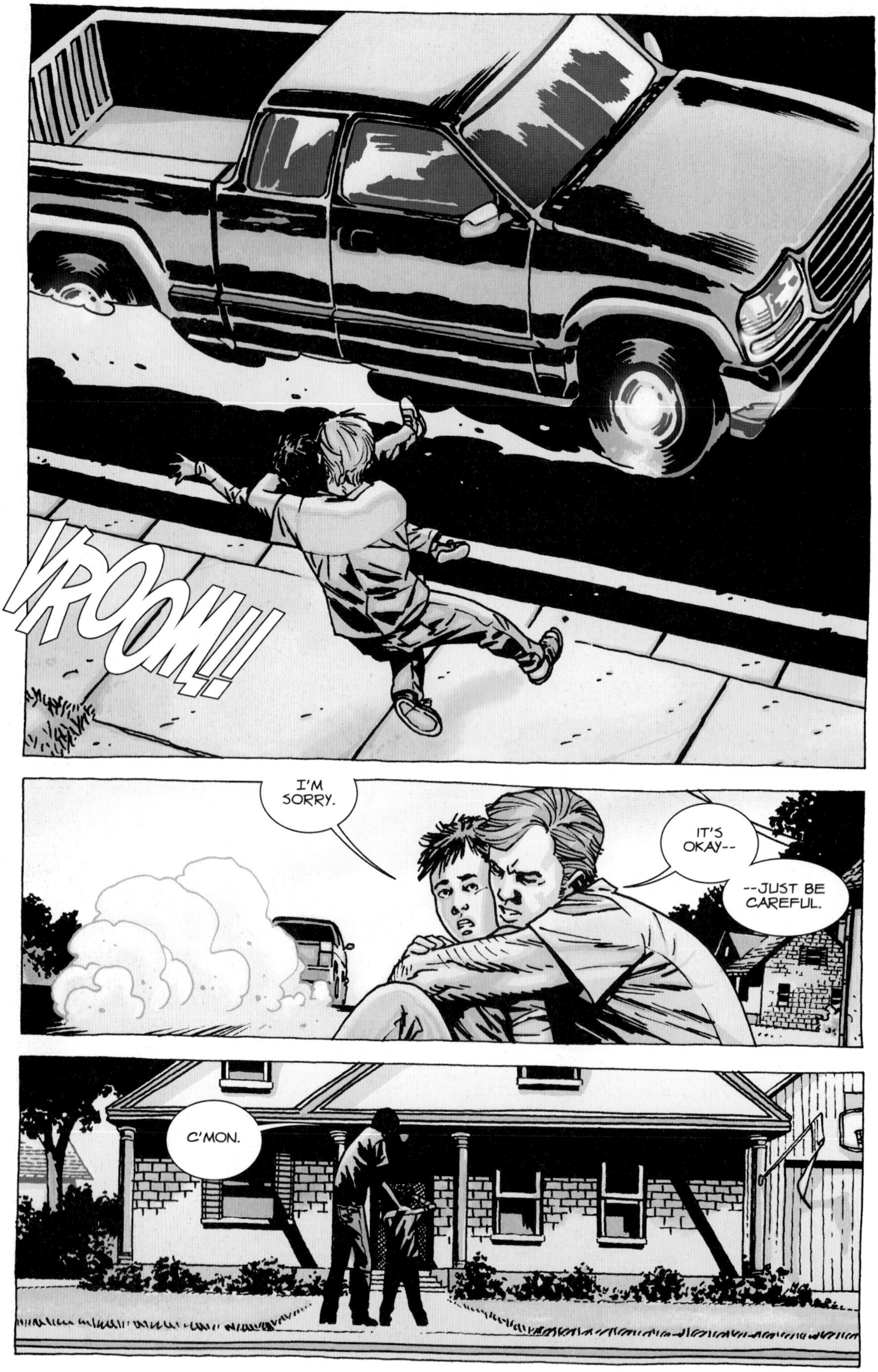
VROOM!!
I'M SORRY.
IT'S OKAY--
--JUST BE CAREFUL.
C'MON.

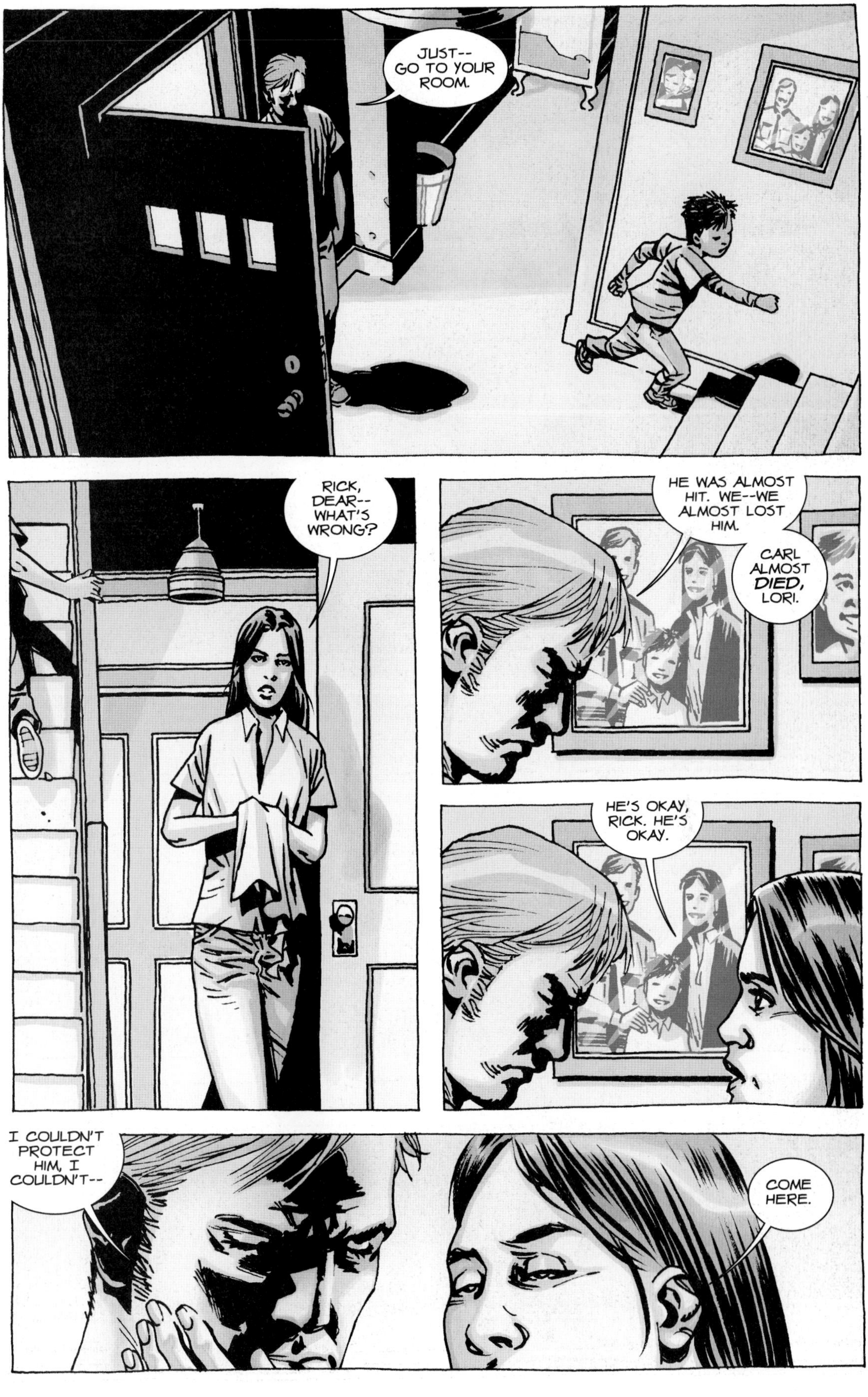
JUST-- GO TO YOUR ROOM.
RICK, DEAR-- WHAT'S WRONG?
HE WAS ALMOST HIT. WE--WE ALMOST LOST HIM.
CARL ALMOST DIED, LORI.
HE'S OKAY, RICK. HE'S OKAY.
I COULDN'T PROTECT HIM, I COULDN'T--
COME HERE.

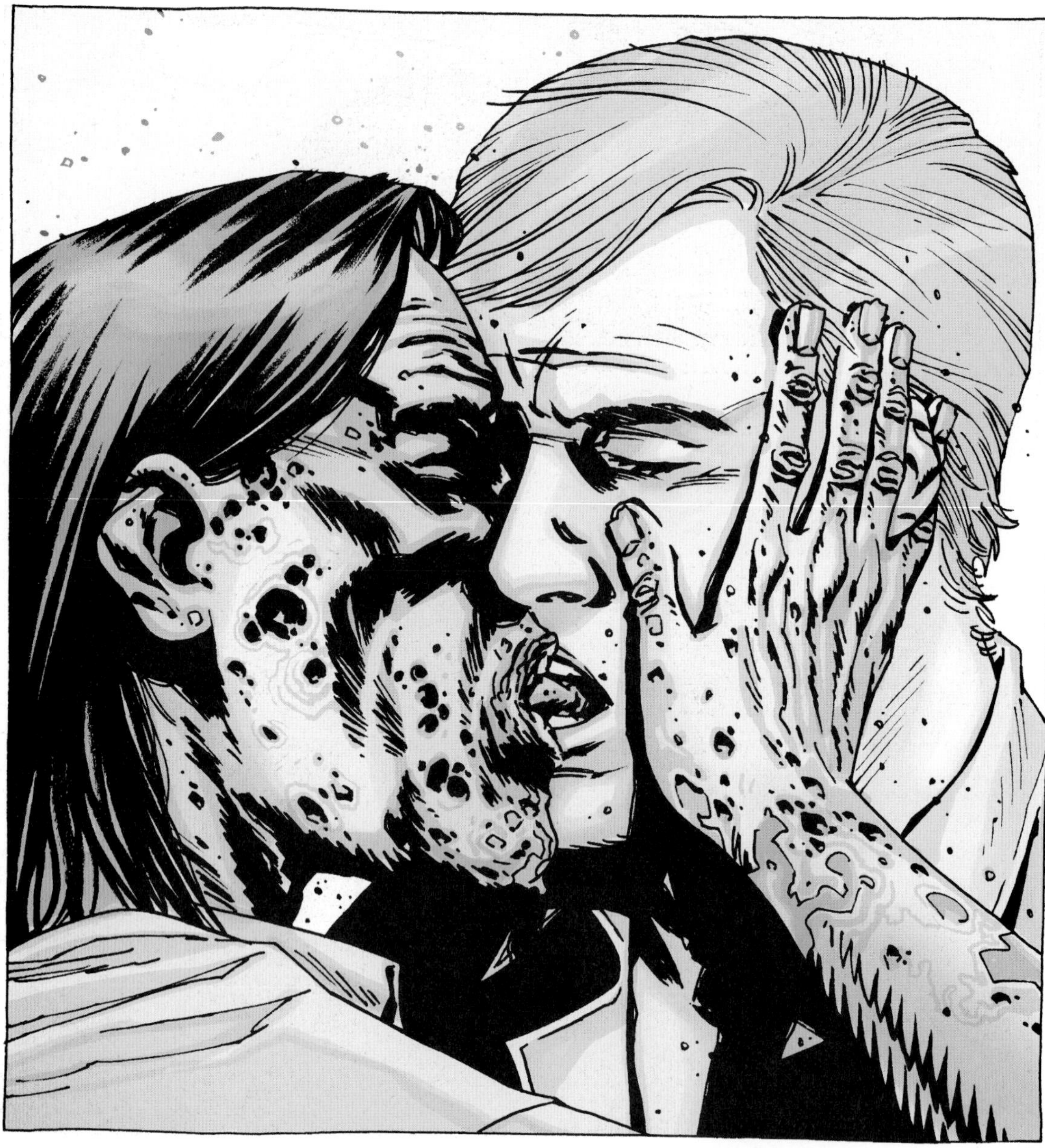

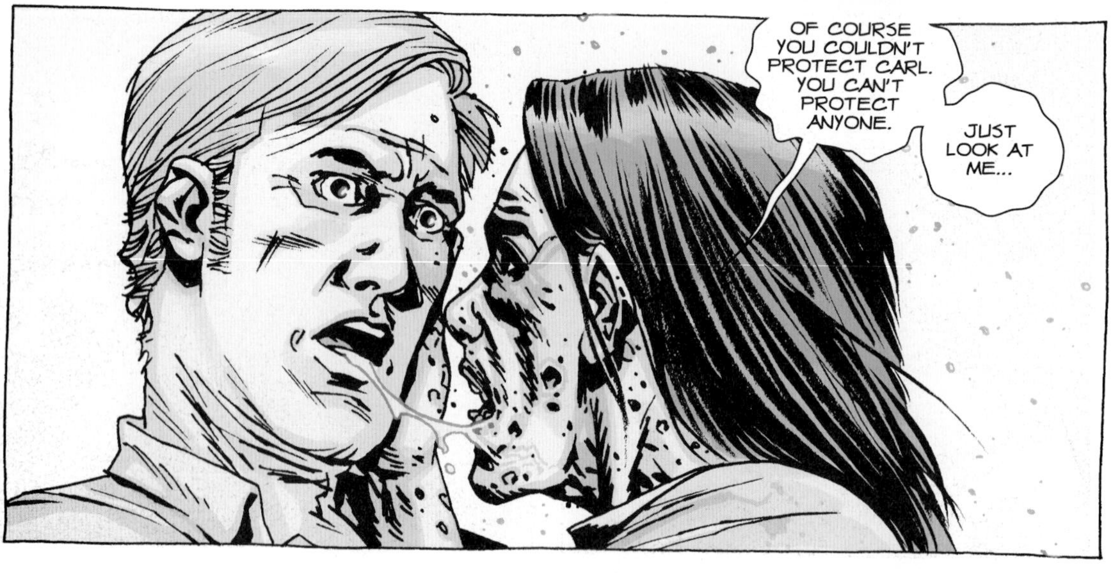
OF COURSE YOU COULDN'T PROTECT CARL. YOU CAN'T PROTECT ANYONE.
JUST LOOK AT ME...

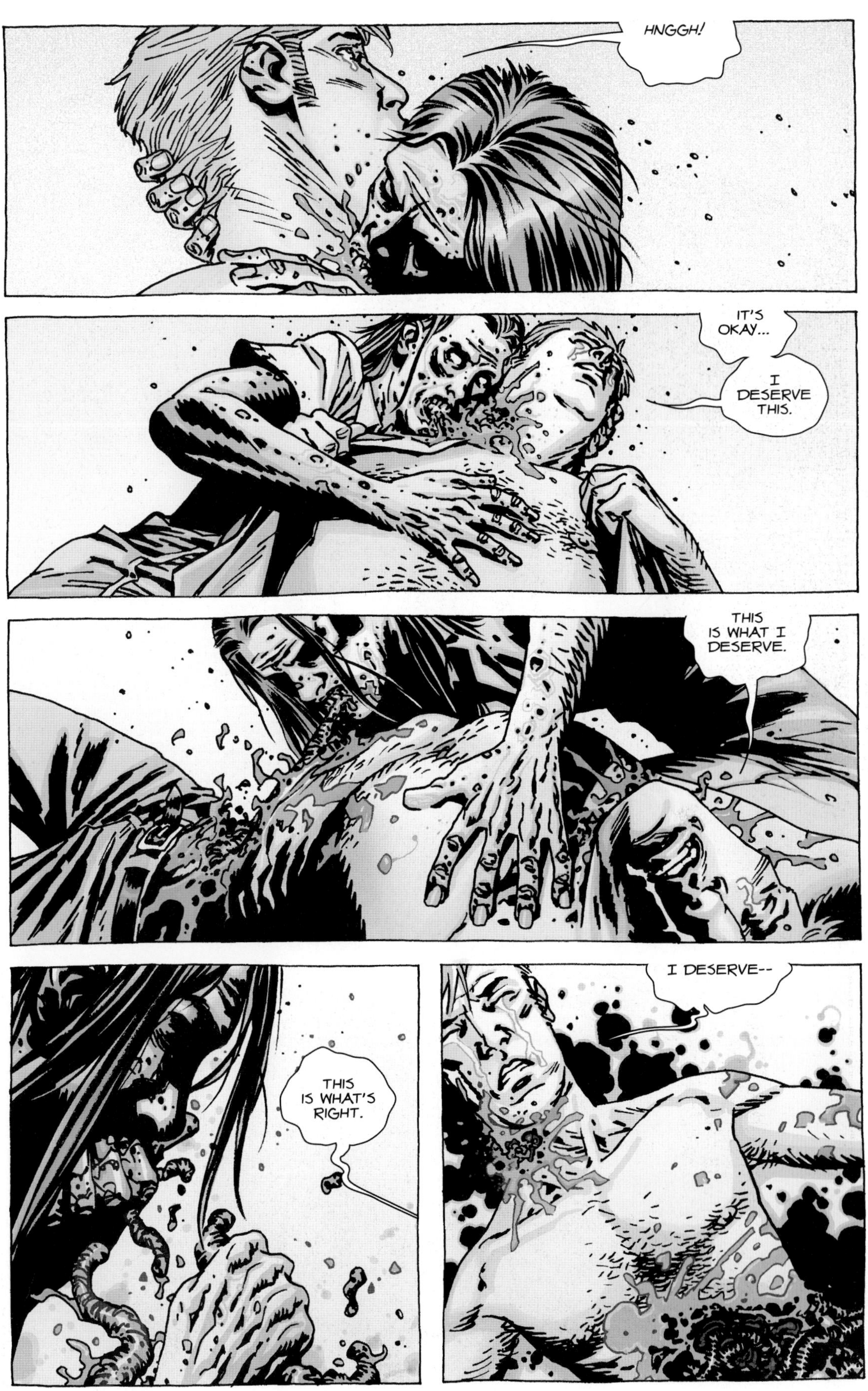
HNGGH!
IT'S OKAY...
I DESERVE THIS.
THIS IS WHAT I DESERVE.
THIS IS WHAT'S RIGHT.
I DESERVE--

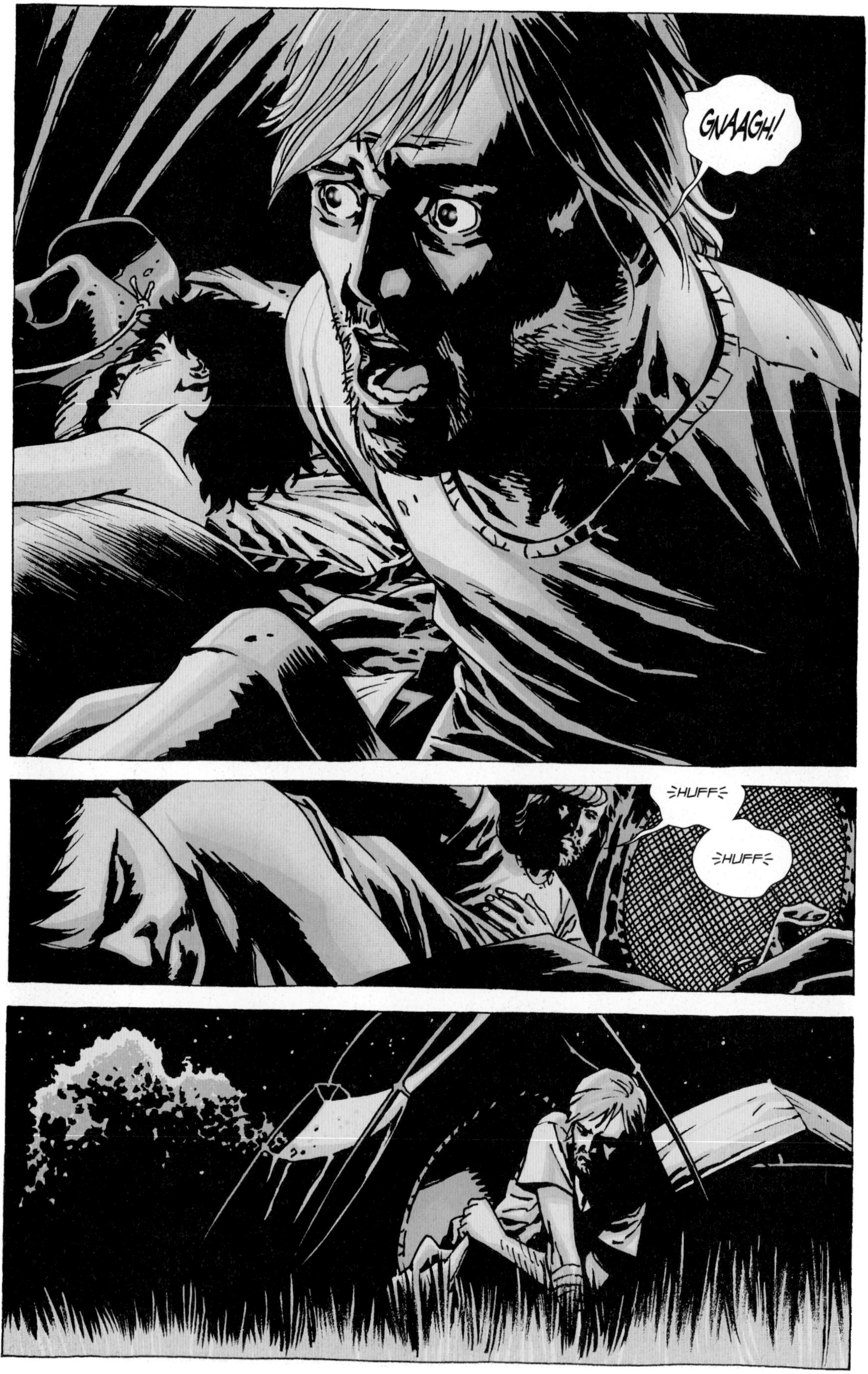
GNAAGH!
HUFF
HUFF

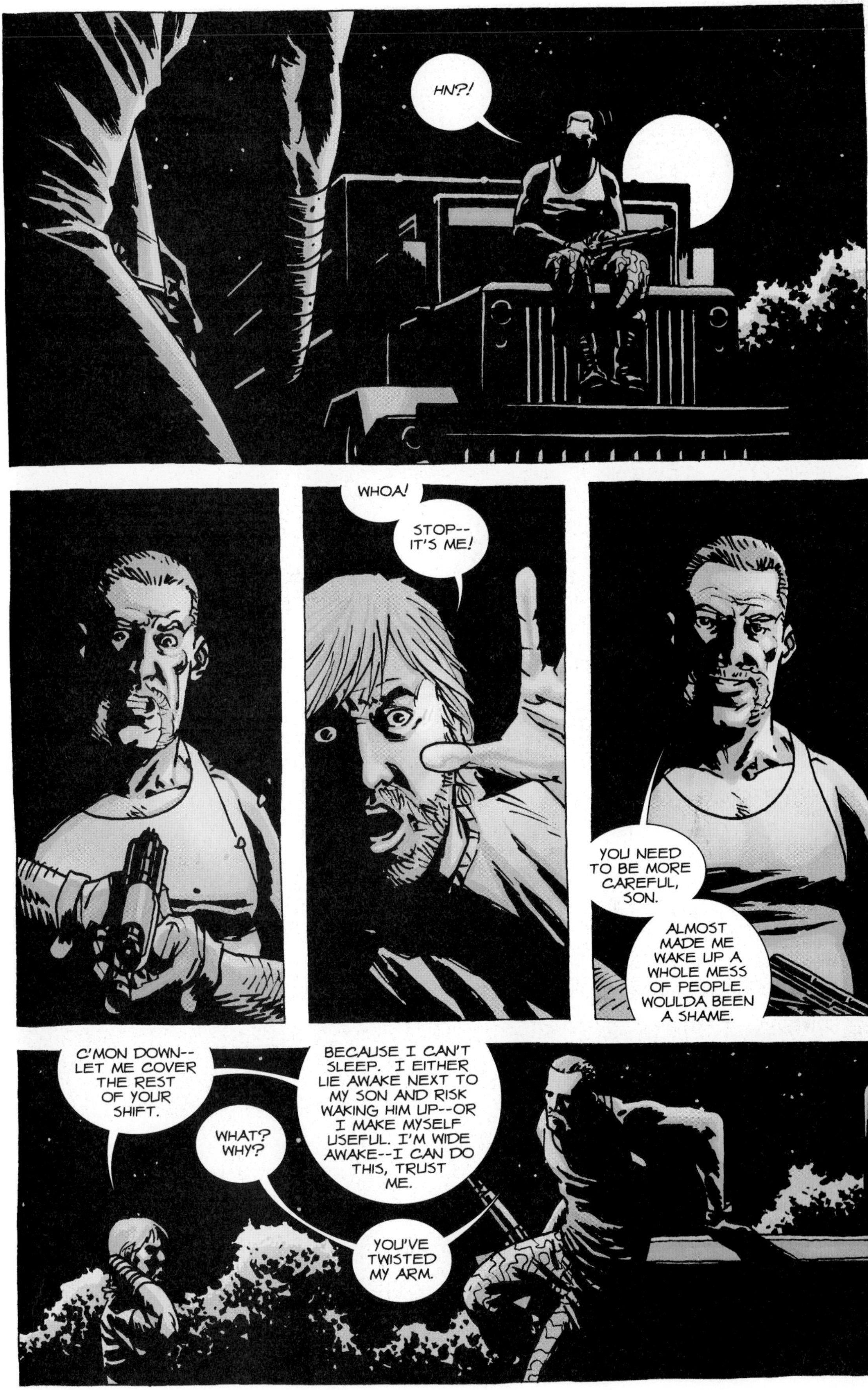
HN?!
WHOA!
STOP-- IT'S ME!
YOU NEED TO BE MORE CAREFUL, SON.
ALMOST MADE ME WAKE UP A WHOLE MESS OF PEOPLE. WOULDA BEEN A SHAME.
C'MON DOWN-- LET ME COVER THE REST OF YOUR SHIFT.
WHAT? WHY?
BECAUSE I CAN'T SLEEP. I EITHER LIE AWAKE NEXT TO MY SON AND RISK WAKING HIM UP--OR I MAKE MYSELF USEFUL. I'M WIDE AWAKE--I CAN DO THIS, TRUST ME.
YOU'VE TWISTED MY ARM.

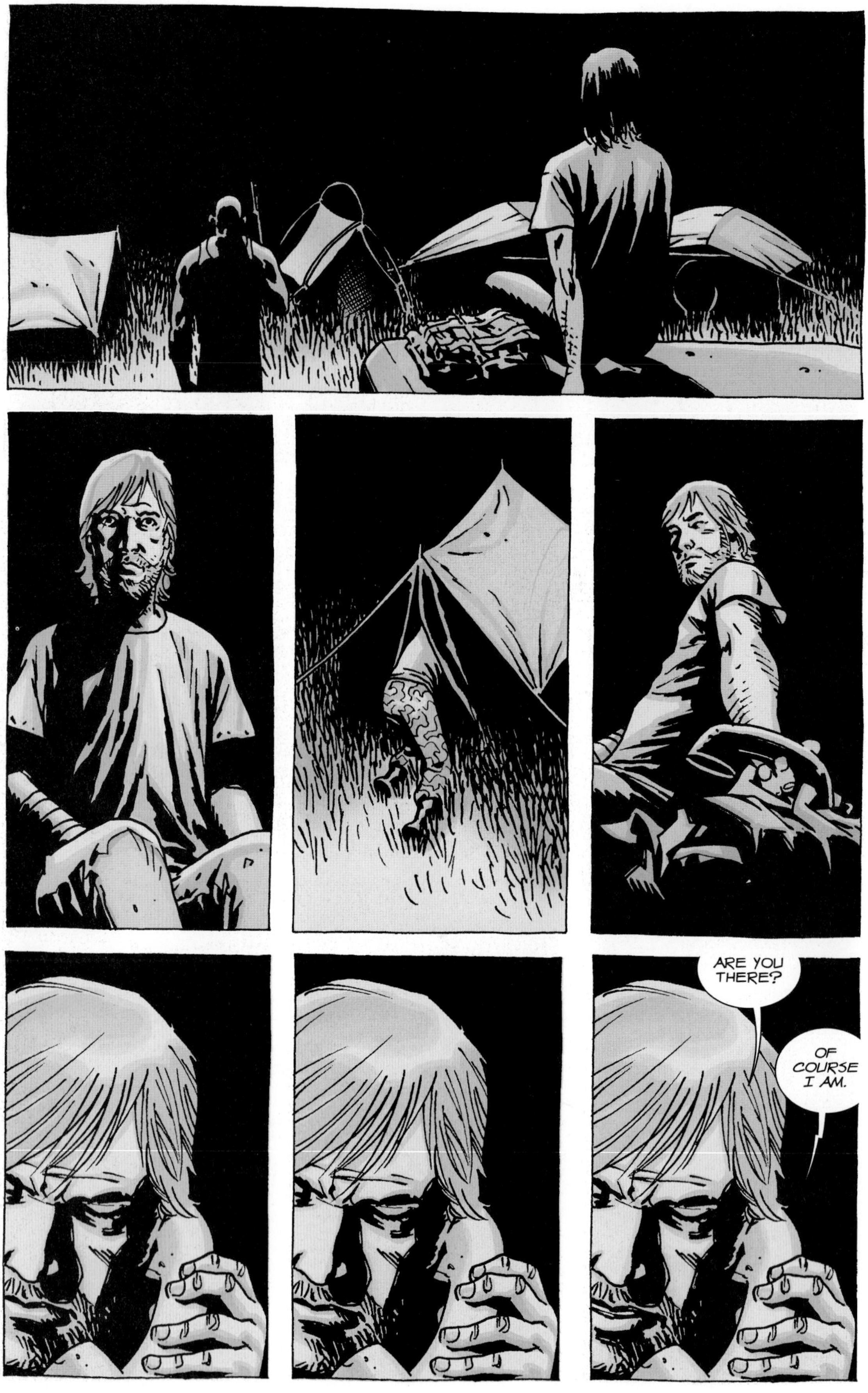
ARE YOU THERE?
OF COURSE I AM.

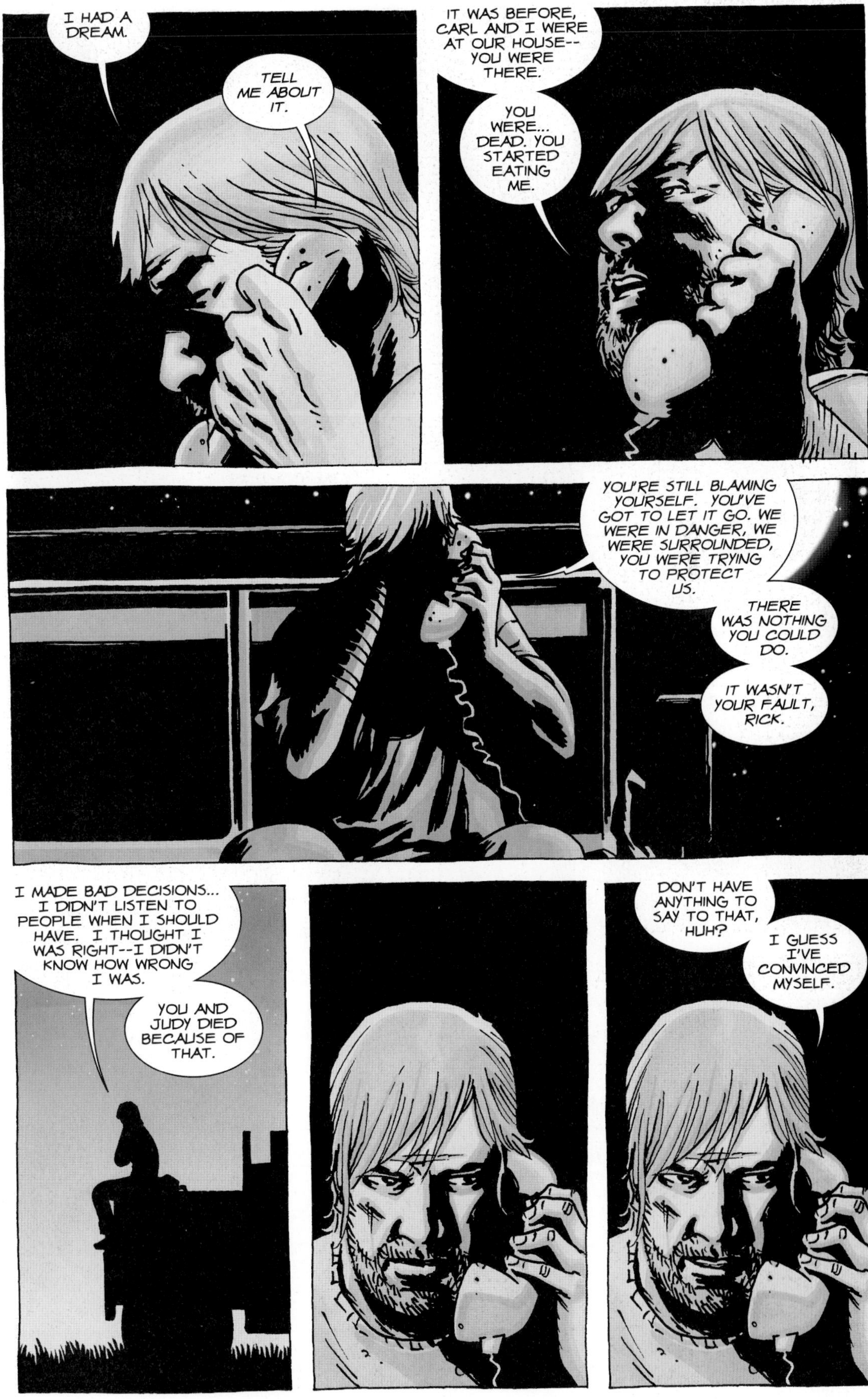
I HAD A DREAM.
TELL ME ABOUT IT.
IT WAS BEFORE, CARL AND I WERE AT OUR HOUSE-- YOU WERE THERE.
YOU WERE... DEAD. YOU STARTED EATING ME.
YOU'RE STILL BLAMING YOURSELF. YOU'VE GOT TO LET IT GO. WE WERE IN DANGER, WE WERE SURROUNDED, YOU WERE TRYING TO PROTECT US.
THERE WAS NOTHING YOU COULD DO.
IT WASN'T YOUR FAULT, RICK.
I MADE BAD DECISIONS... I DIDN'T LISTEN TO PEOPLE WHEN I SHOULD HAVE. I THOUGHT I WAS RIGHT--I DIDN'T KNOW HOW WRONG I WAS.
YOU AND JUDY DIED BECAUSE OF THAT.
DON'T HAVE ANYTHING TO SAY TO THAT, HUH?
I GUESS I'VE CONVINCED MYSELF.

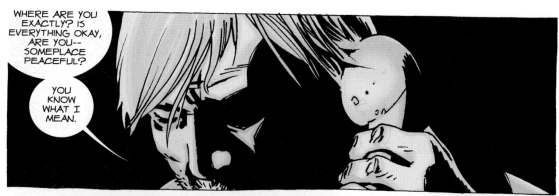

WHERE ARE YOU EXACTLY? IS EVERYTHING OKAY, ARE YOU-- SOMEPLACE PEACEFUL?

YOU KNOW WHAT I MEAN.

I DO.

IT'S NICE HERE. EVERYONE WE LOST CAME HERE. EVERYONE IS HERE TOGETHER, WE'RE ALL HAPPY.

IT'S PERFECT, THERE'S NO DANGER. IT'S EVERYTHING YOU'D THINK IT IS AND MORE.

I THINK WE'RE MUCH BETTER OFF HERE.

...

OF COURSE, I'M ONLY SAYING THESE THINGS BECAUSE YOU WANT ME TO MAKE YOU FEEL BETTER. OR DID YOU FORGET THAT I'M NOT REAL?

BESIDES, YOU NEVER WERE VERY RELIGIOUS.

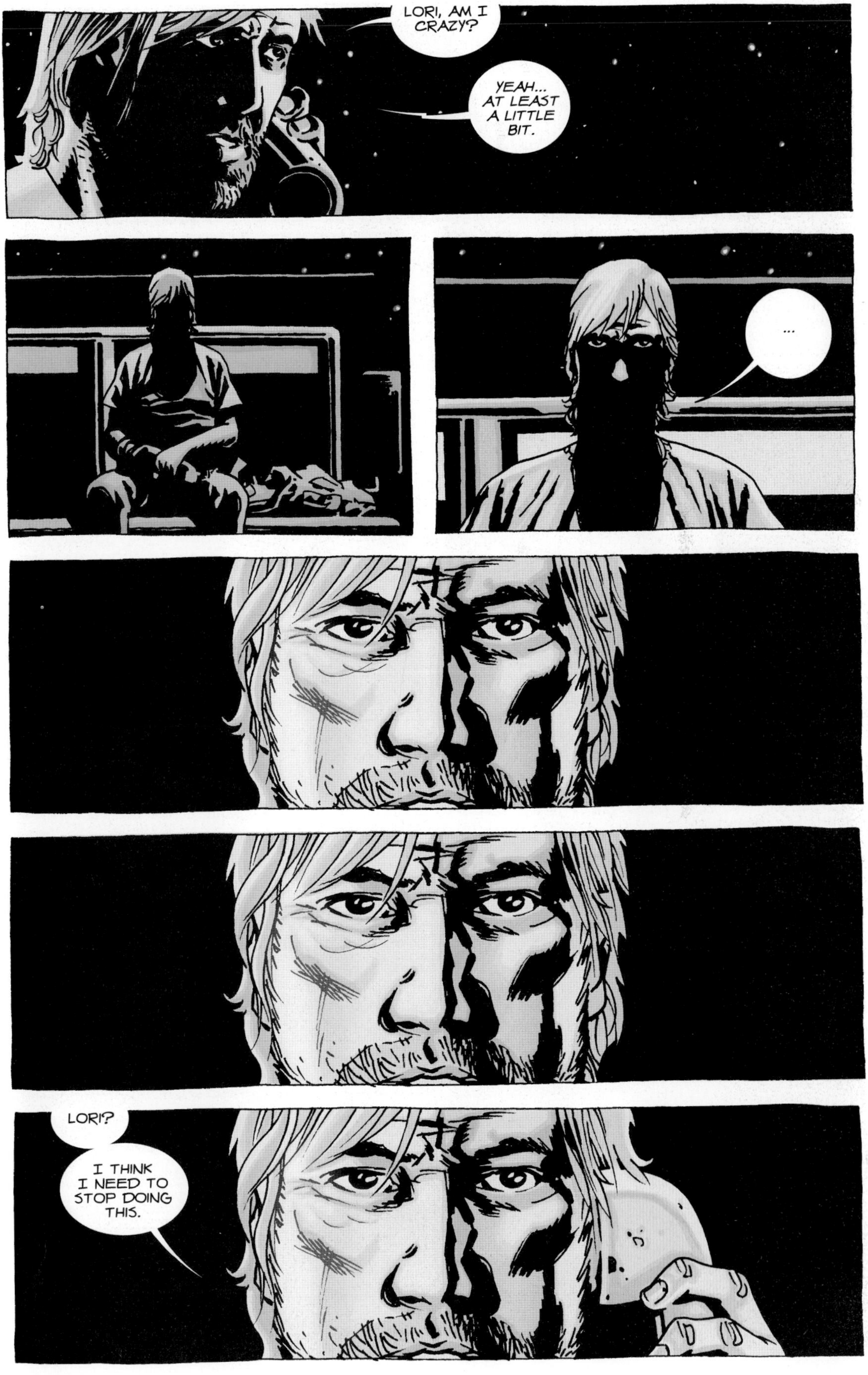
LORI, AM I CRAZY?
YEAH... AT LEAST A LITTLE BIT.
...
LORI?
I THINK I NEED TO STOP DOING THIS.

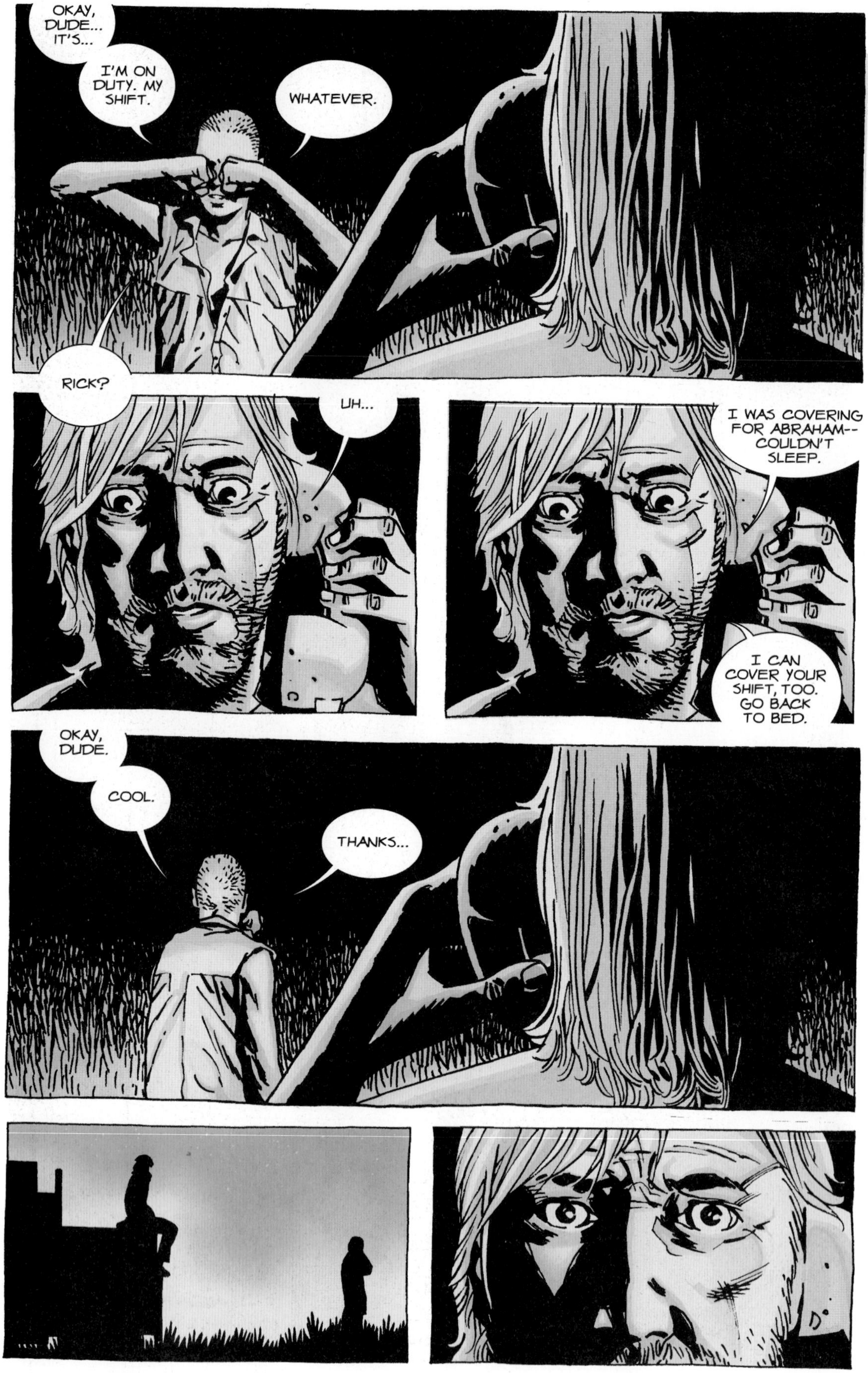
OKAY, DUDE... IT'S...
I'M ON DUTY. MY SHIFT.
WHATEVER.
RICK?
UH...
I WAS COVERING FOR ABRAHAM-- COULDN'T SLEEP.
I CAN COVER YOUR SHIFT, TOO. GO BACK TO BED.
OKAY, DUDE.
COOL.
THANKS...

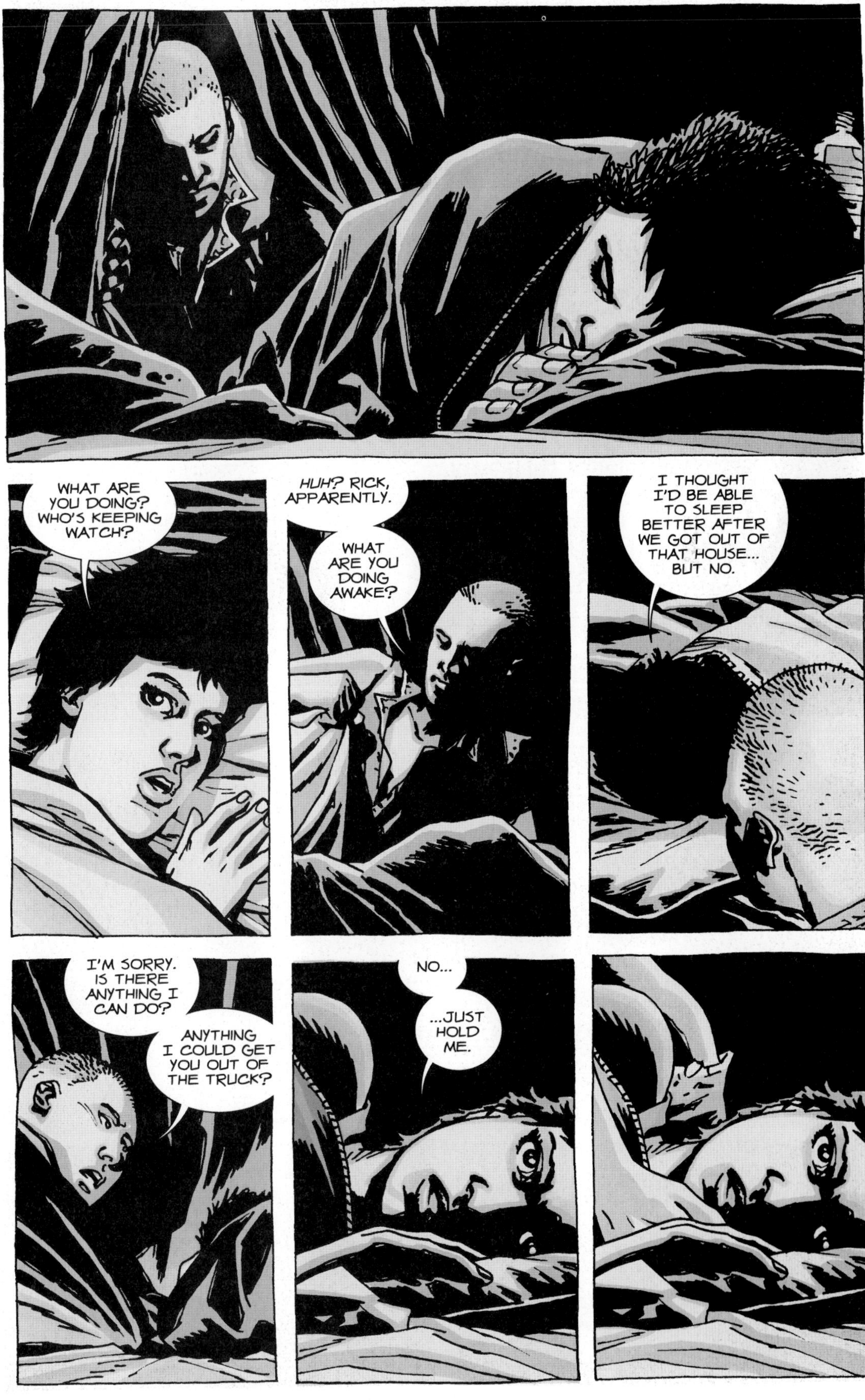
WHAT ARE YOU DOING? WHO'S KEEPING WATCH?
HUH? RICK, APPARENTLY.
WHAT ARE YOU DOING AWAKE?
I THOUGHT I'D BE ABLE TO SLEEP BETTER AFTER WE GOT OUT OF THAT HOUSE... BUT NO.
I'M SORRY. IS THERE ANYTHING I CAN DO?
ANYTHING I COULD GET YOU OUT OF THE TRUCK?
NO...
...JUST HOLD ME.

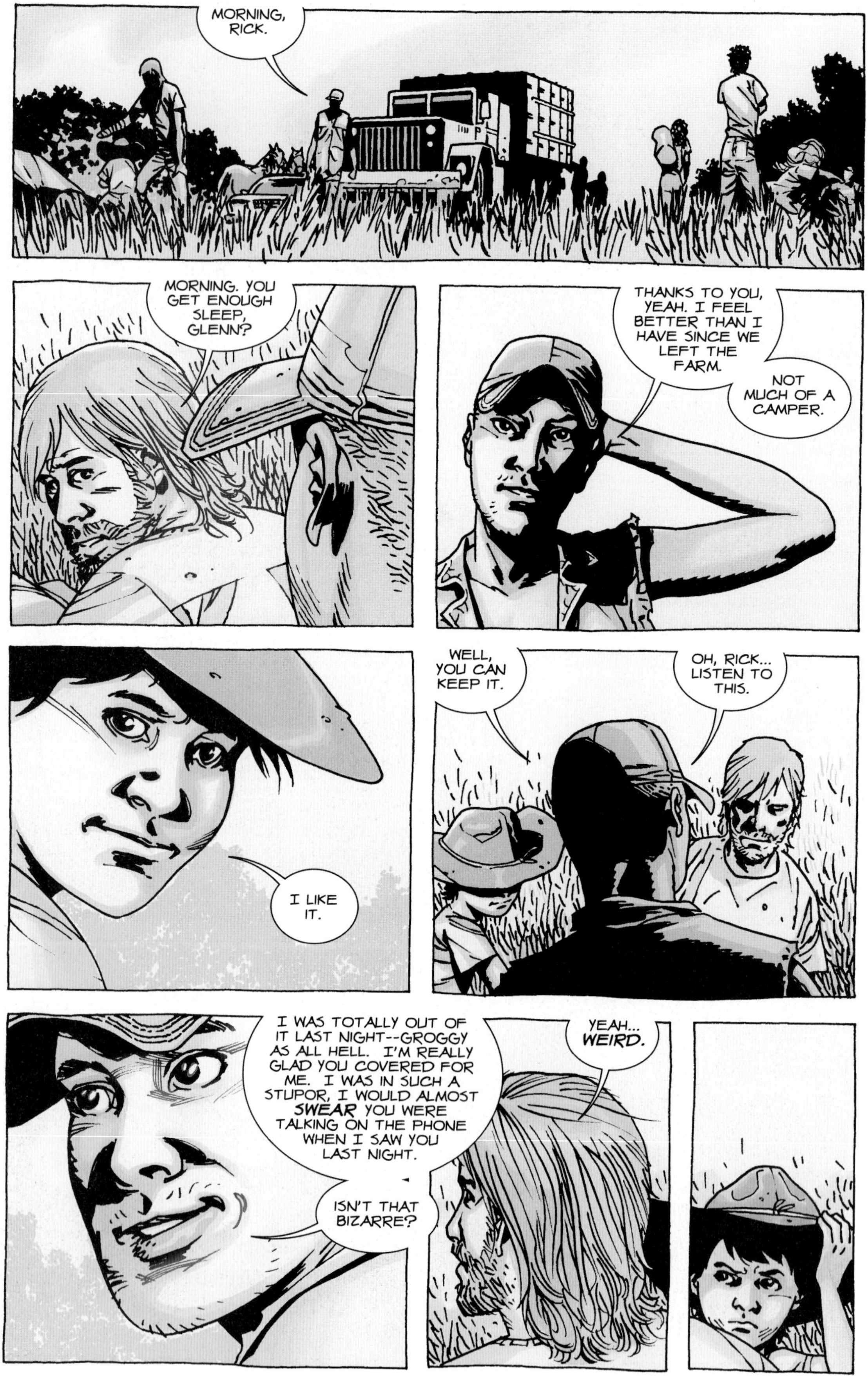
MORNING, RICK.
MORNING. YOU GET ENOUGH SLEEP, GLENN?
THANKS TO YOU, YEAH. I FEEL BETTER THAN I HAVE SINCE WE LEFT THE FARM.
NOT MUCH OF A CAMPER.
I LIKE IT.
WELL, YOU CAN KEEP IT.
OH, RICK... LISTEN TO THIS.
I WAS TOTALLY OUT OF IT LAST NIGHT--GROGGY AS ALL HELL. I'M REALLY GLAD YOU COVERED FOR ME. I WAS IN SUCH A STUPOR, I WOULD ALMOST SWEAR YOU WERE TALKING ON THE PHONE WHEN I SAW YOU LAST NIGHT.
ISN'T THAT BIZARRE?
YEAH... WEIRD.

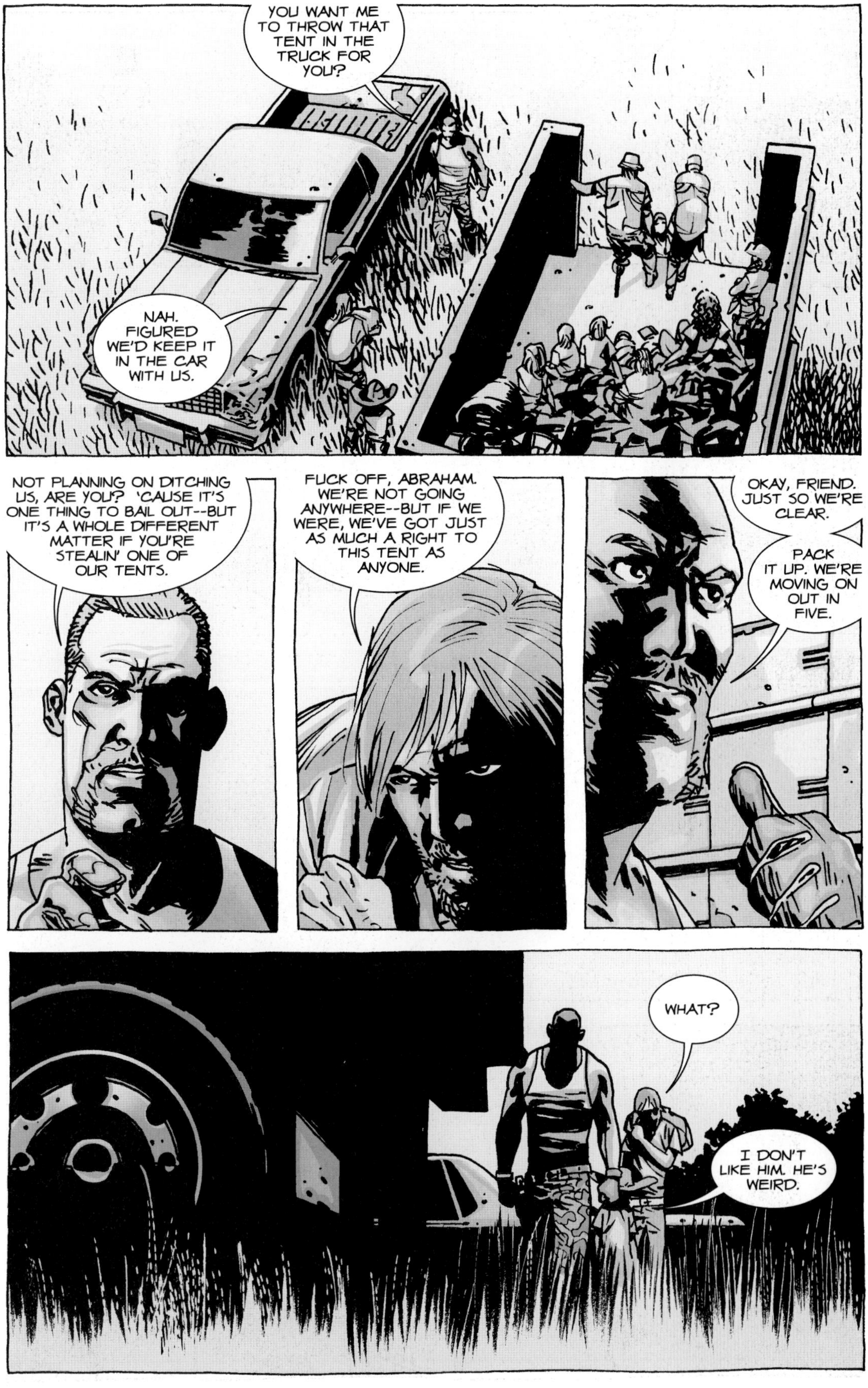
YOU WANT ME TO THROW THAT TENT IN THE TRUCK FOR YOU?
NAH. FIGURED WE'D KEEP IT IN THE CAR WITH US.
NOT PLANNING ON DITCHING US, ARE YOU? 'CAUSE IT'S ONE THING TO BAIL OUT--BUT IT'S A WHOLE DIFFERENT MATTER IF YOU'RE STEALIN' ONE OF OUR TENTS.
FUCK OFF, ABRAHAM. WE'RE NOT GOING ANYWHERE--BUT IF WE WERE, WE'VE GOT JUST AS MUCH A RIGHT TO THIS TENT AS ANYONE.
OKAY, FRIEND. JUST SO WE'RE CLEAR.
PACK IT UP. WE'RE MOVING ON OUT IN FIVE.
WHAT?
I DON'T LIKE HIM. HE'S WEIRD.

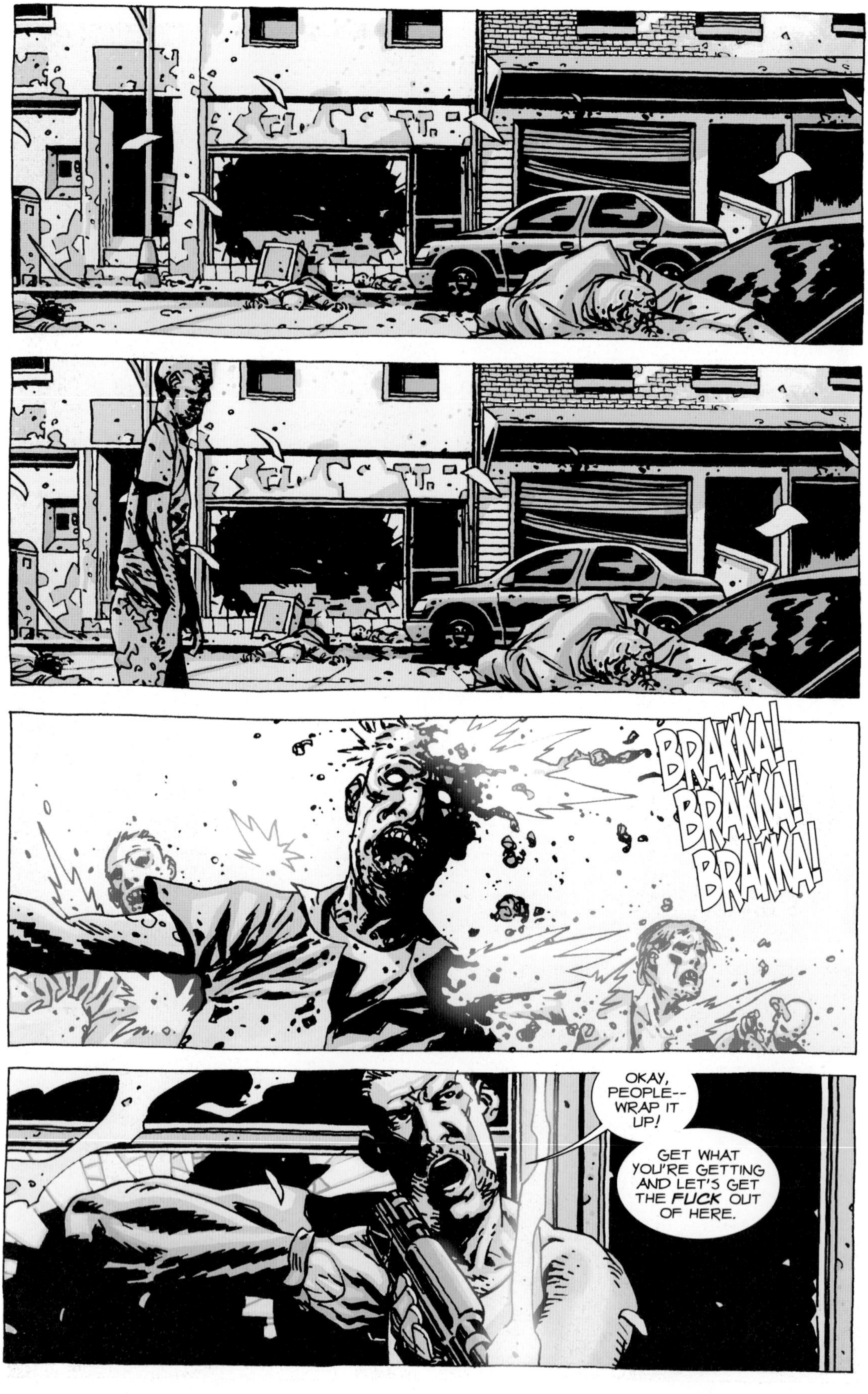
BRAKKA! BRAKKA! BRAKKA!
OKAY, PEOPLE-- WRAP IT UP!
GET WHAT YOU'RE GETTING AND LET'S GET THE FUCK OUT OF HERE.

CRAP-- ROAMERS! CARL, GET IN THE CAR NOW!

EVERY AXE AND KNIFE IN THE WHOLE DAMN PLACE IS GONE--BUT THE PLACE IS FULL OF SHARPENERS.

NOBODY THINKS AHEAD.

ANYONE ELSE IN THERE?

DALE IS IN THERE WITH GLENN AND MAGGIE BUT I THINK THEY'RE ALMOST DONE.

GET THEM OUT OF THERE!

TIME TO GO, LADIES. WE'VE GOT COMPANY!

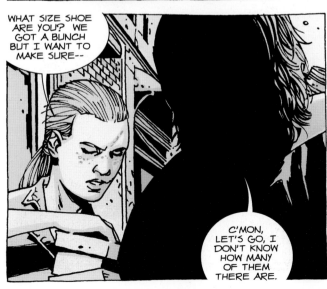

WHAT SIZE SHOE ARE YOU? WE GOT A BUNCH BUT I WANT TO MAKE SURE--

C'MON, LET'S GO, I DON'T KNOW HOW MANY OF THEM THERE ARE.

PLEASE. AIN'T A ONE OF THEM GETTING NEAR US. NOT WITH ABRAHAM ON THE JOB.

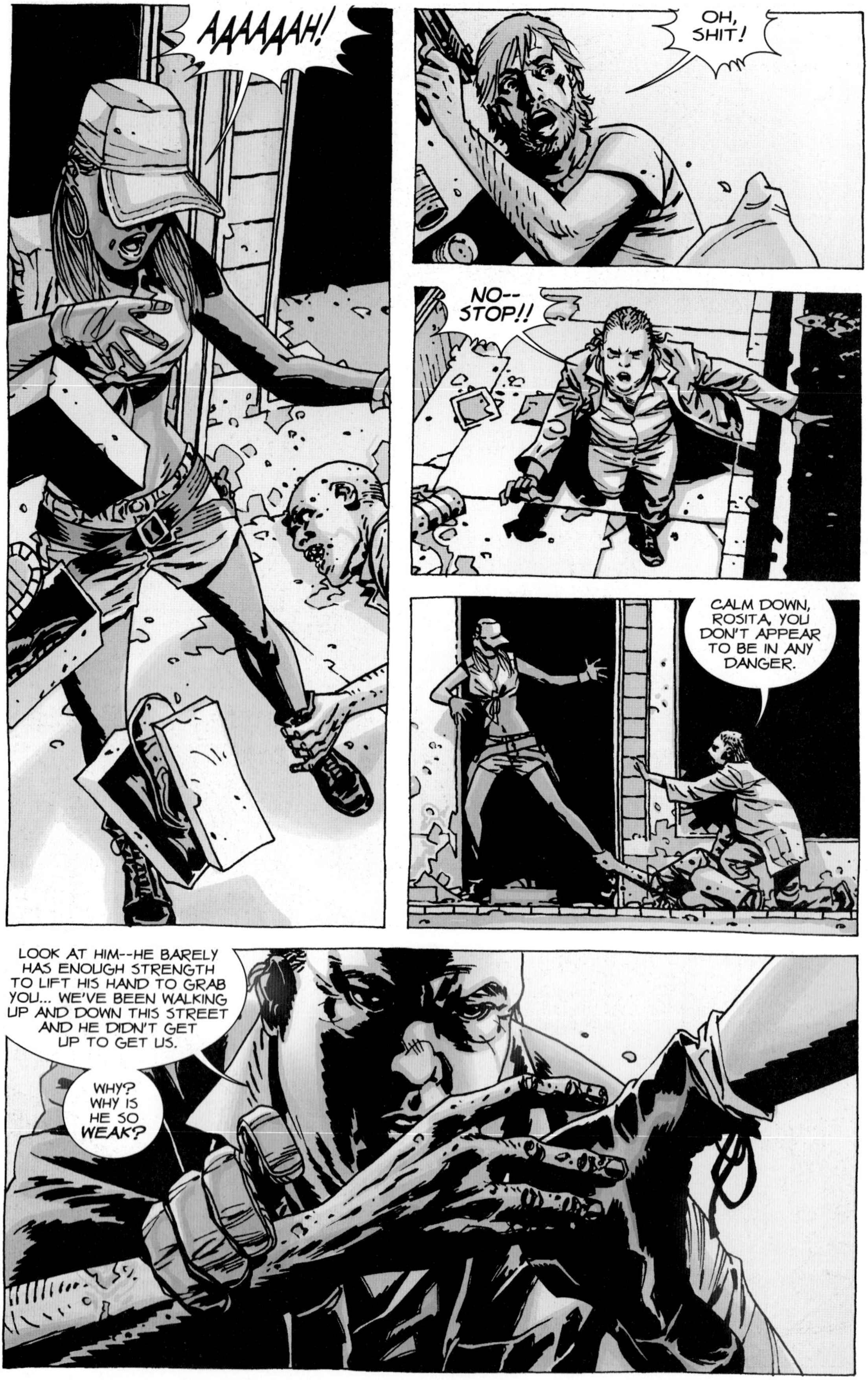
AAAAAAH!
OH, SHIT!
NO-- STOP!!
CALM DOWN, ROSITA, YOU DON'T APPEAR TO BE IN ANY DANGER.
LOOK AT HIM--HE BARELY HAS ENOUGH STRENGTH TO LIFT HIS HAND TO GRAB YOU... WE'VE BEEN WALKING UP AND DOWN THIS STREET AND HE DIDN'T GET UP TO GET US.
WHY? WHY IS HE SO WEAK?

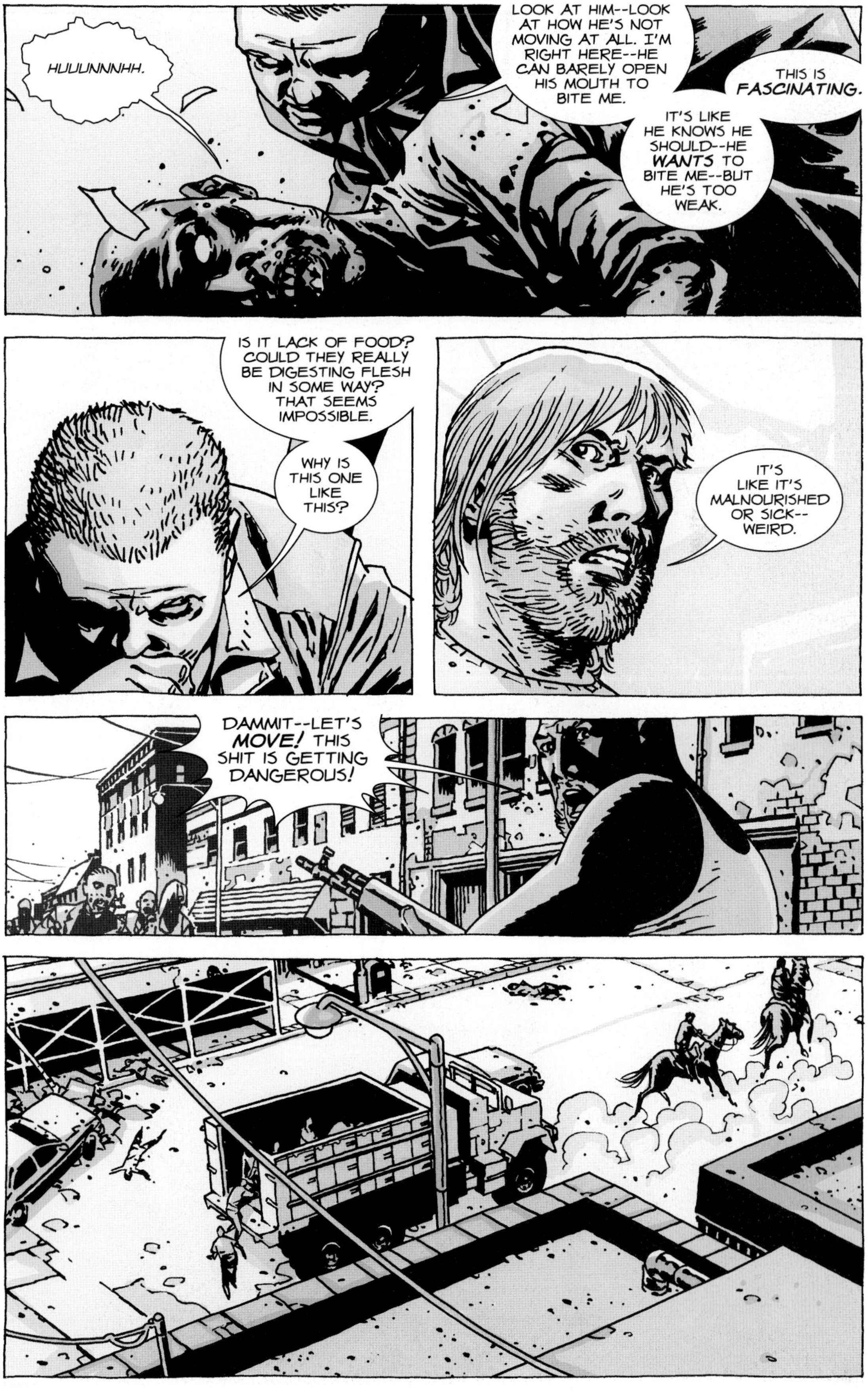
HUUUNNNHH.
LOOK AT HIM--LOOK AT HOW HE'S NOT MOVING AT ALL. I'M RIGHT HERE--HE CAN BARELY OPEN HIS MOUTH TO BITE ME.
THIS IS FASCINATING.
IT'S LIKE HE KNOWS HE SHOULD--HE WANTS TO BITE ME--BUT HE'S TOO WEAK.
IS IT LACK OF FOOD? COULD THEY REALLY BE DIGESTING FLESH IN SOME WAY? THAT SEEMS IMPOSSIBLE.
WHY IS THIS ONE LIKE THIS?
IT'S LIKE IT'S MALNOURISHED OR SICK-- WEIRD.
DAMMIT--LET'S MOVE! THIS SHIT IS GETTING DANGEROUS!

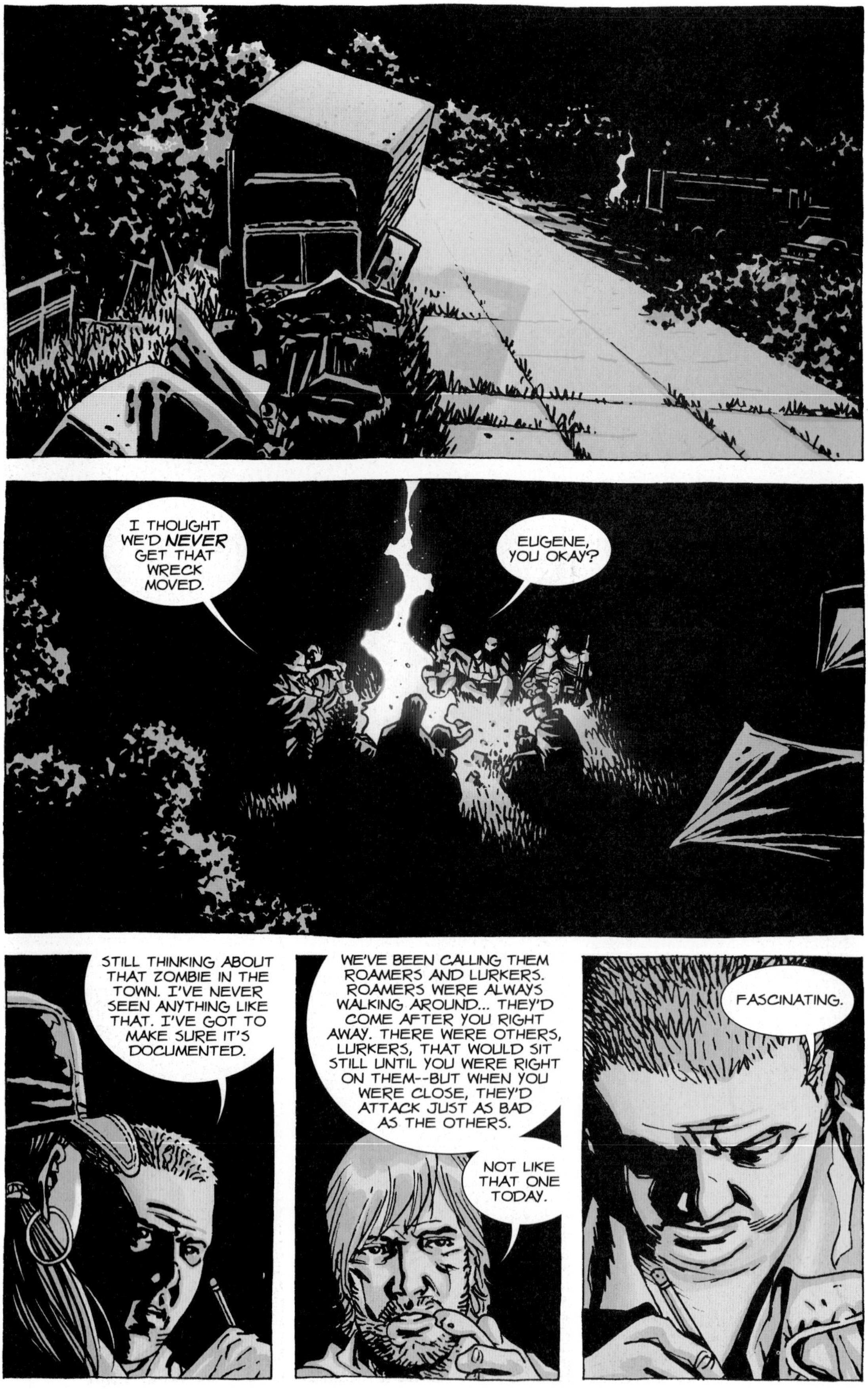
I THOUGHT WE'D NEVER GET THAT WRECK MOVED.
EUGENE, YOU OKAY?
STILL THINKING ABOUT THAT ZOMBIE IN THE TOWN. I'VE NEVER SEEN ANYTHING LIKE THAT. I'VE GOT TO MAKE SURE IT'S DOCUMENTED.
WE'VE BEEN CALLING THEM ROAMERS AND LURKERS. ROAMERS WERE ALWAYS WALKING AROUND... THEY'D COME AFTER YOU RIGHT AWAY. THERE WERE OTHERS, LURKERS, THAT WOULD SIT STILL UNTIL YOU WERE RIGHT ON THEM--BUT WHEN YOU WERE CLOSE, THEY'D ATTACK JUST AS BAD AS THE OTHERS.
NOT LIKE THAT ONE TODAY.
FASCINATING.

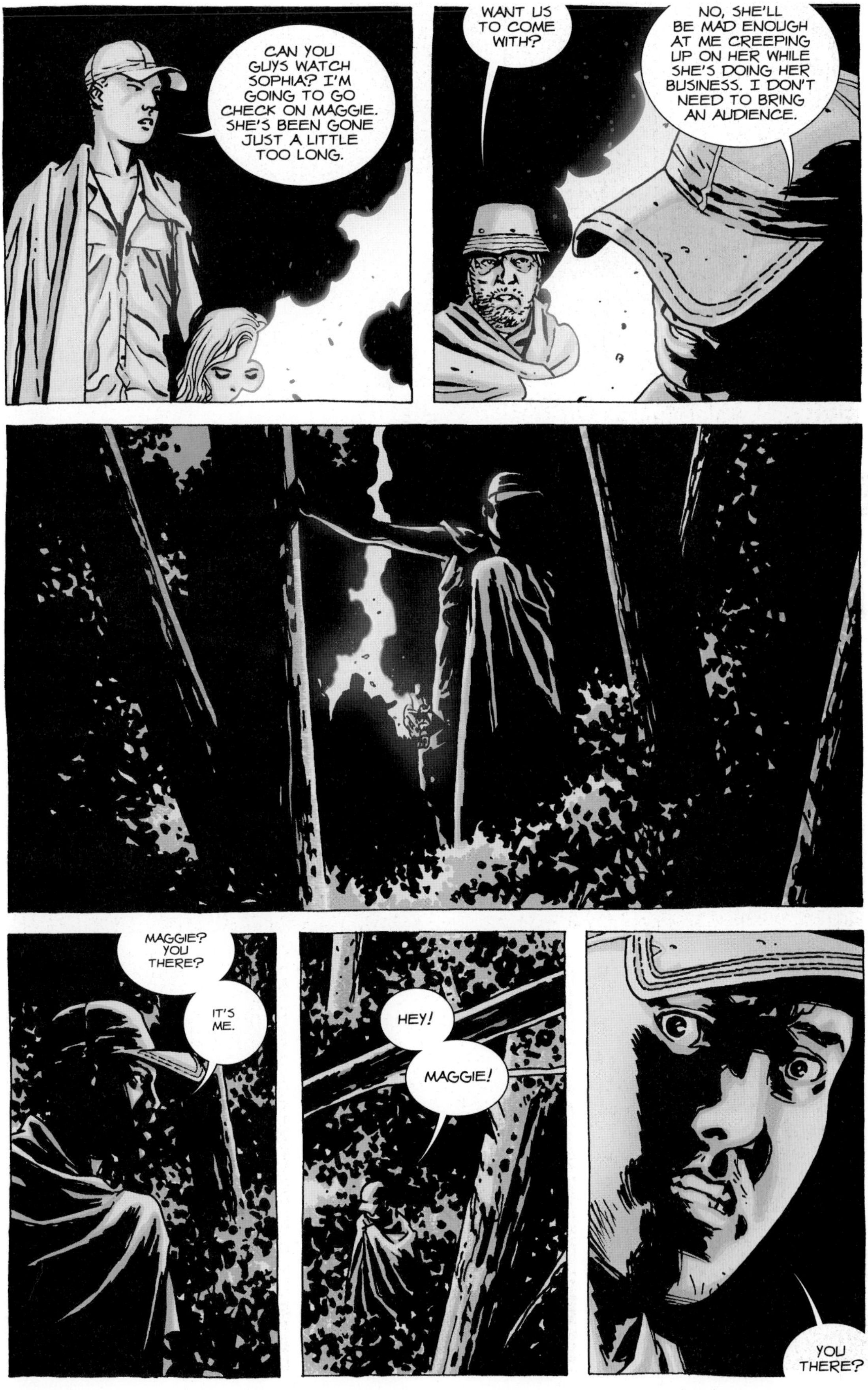

CAN YOU GUYS WATCH SOPHIA? I'M GOING TO GO CHECK ON MAGGIE. SHE'S BEEN GONE JUST A LITTLE TOO LONG.
WANT US TO COME WITH?
NO, SHE'LL BE MAD ENOUGH AT ME CREEPING UP ON HER WHILE SHE'S DOING HER BUSINESS. I DON'T NEED TO BRING AN AUDIENCE.
MAGGIE? YOU THERE?
IT'S ME.
HEY!
MAGGIE!
YOU THERE?

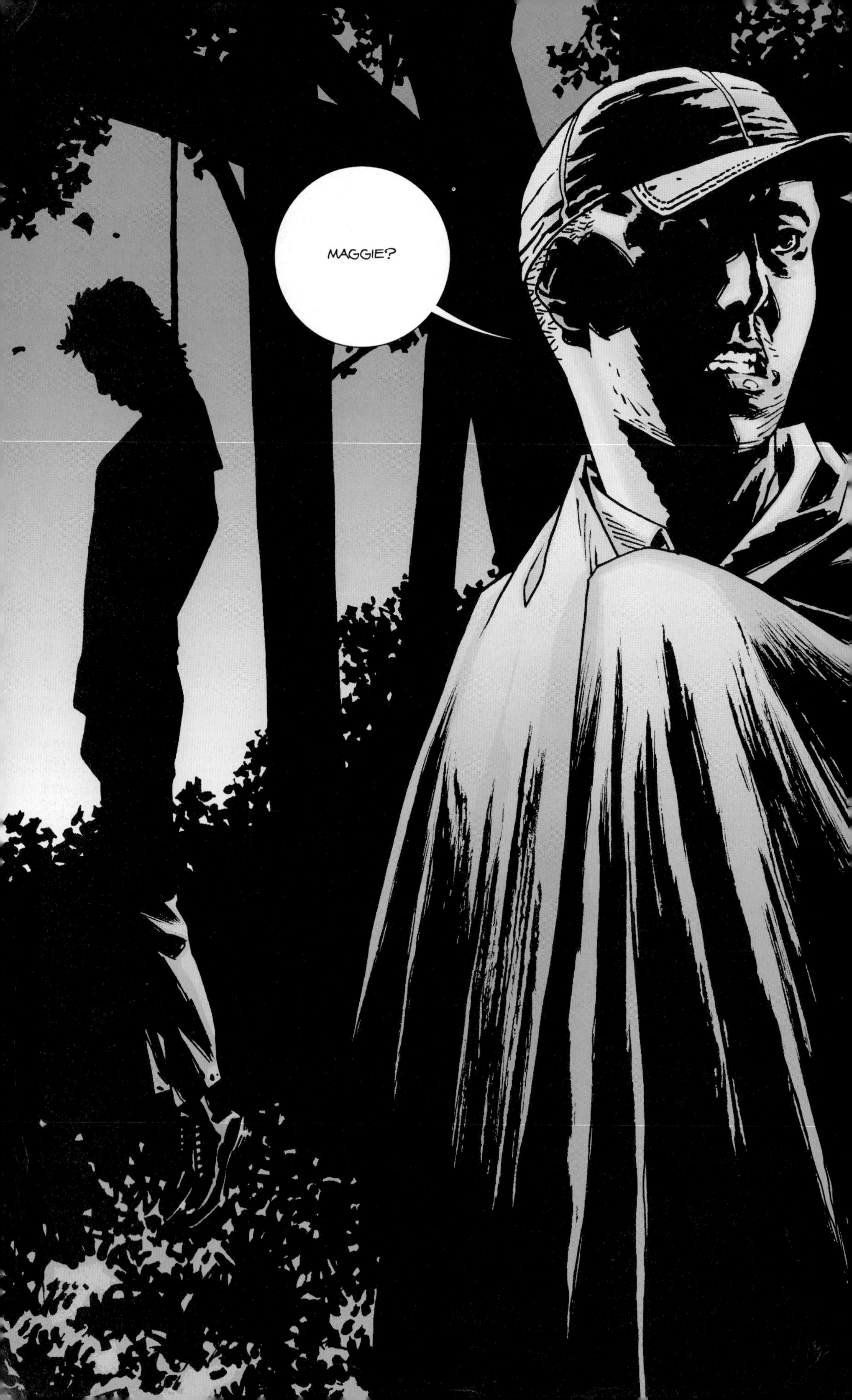
MAGGIE?

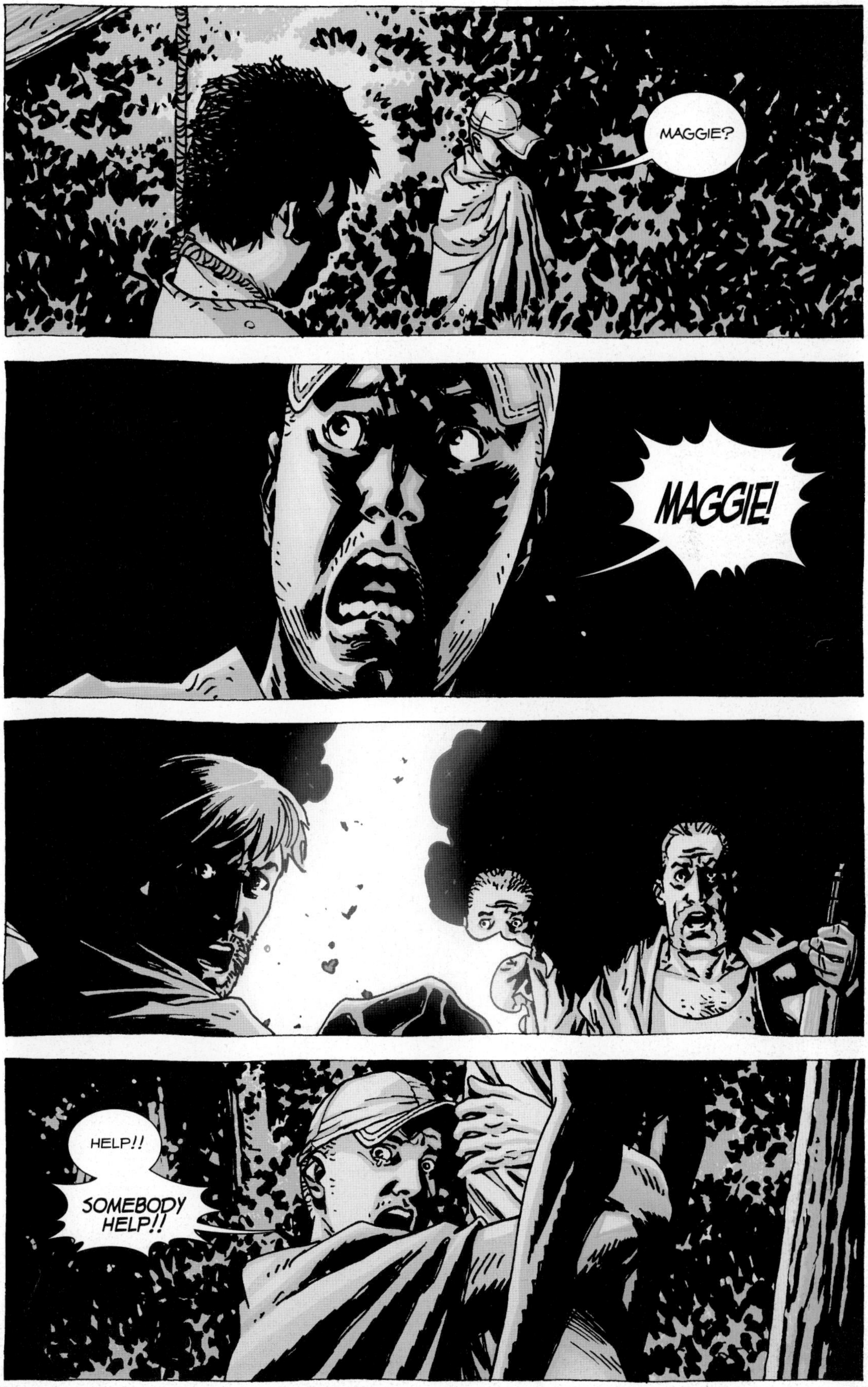
MAGGIE?
MAGGIE!
HELP!!
SOMEBODY HELP!!

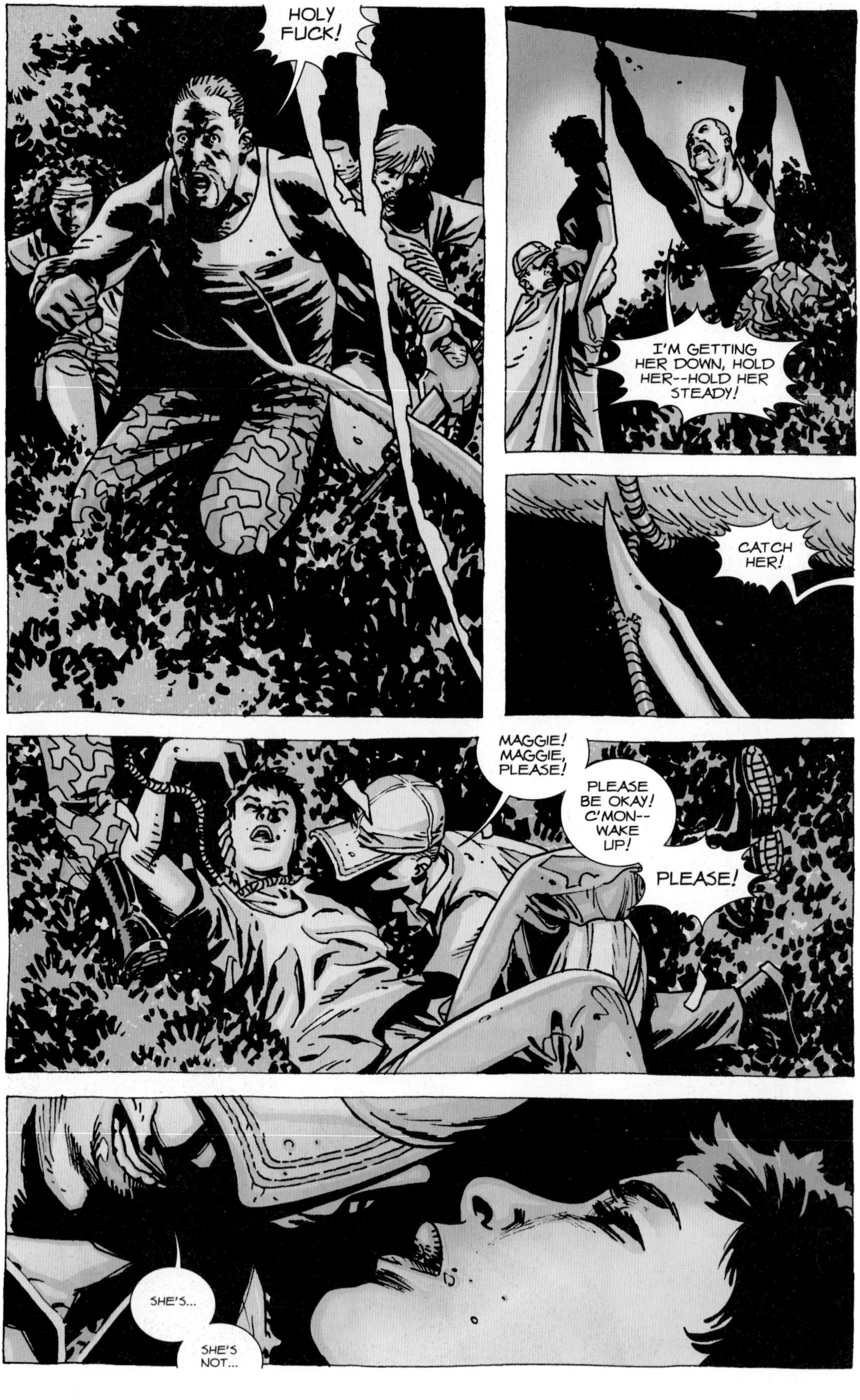
HOLY FUCK!
I'M GETTING HER DOWN, HOLD HER--HOLD HER STEADY!
CATCH HER!
MAGGIE! MAGGIE, PLEASE!
PLEASE BE OKAY! C'MON--WAKE UP!
PLEASE!
SHE'S...
SHE'S NOT...

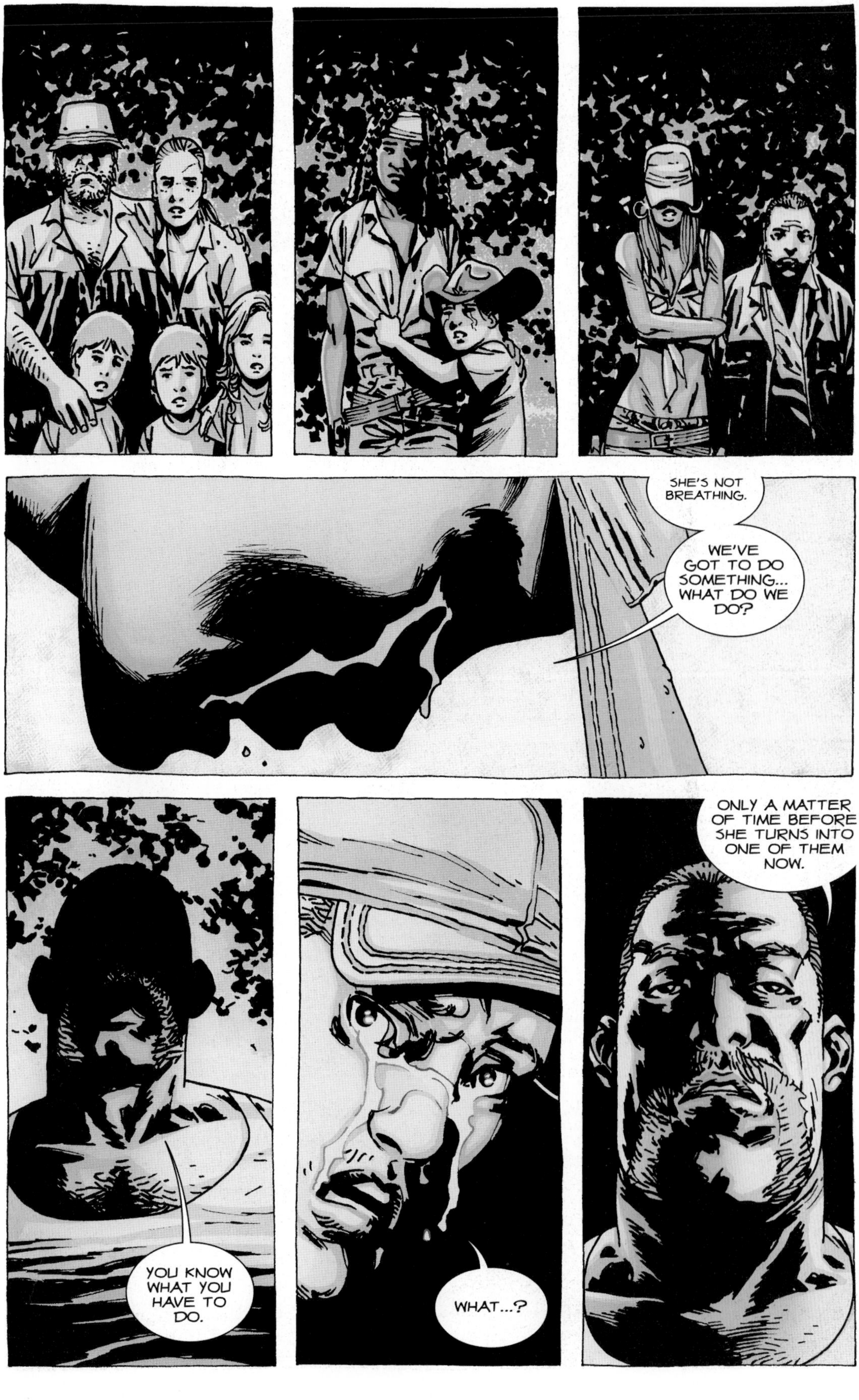
SHE'S NOT BREATHING.
WE'VE GOT TO DO SOMETHING... WHAT DO WE DO?
YOU KNOW WHAT YOU HAVE TO DO.
WHAT...?
ONLY A MATTER OF TIME BEFORE SHE TURNS INTO ONE OF THEM NOW.

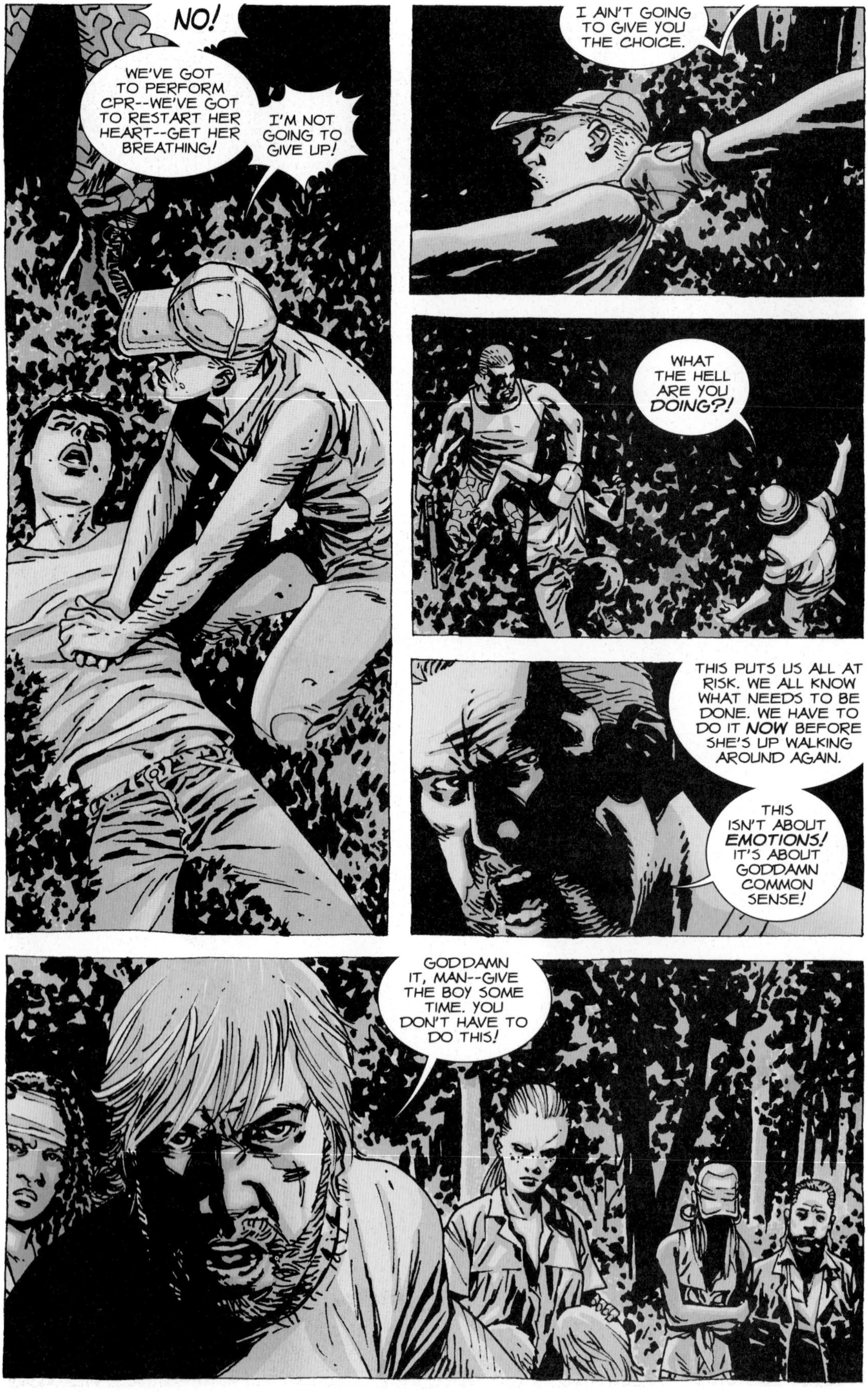
NO!
WE'VE GOT TO PERFORM CPR--WE'VE GOT TO RESTART HER HEART--GET HER BREATHING!
I'M NOT GOING TO GIVE UP!
I AIN'T GOING TO GIVE YOU THE CHOICE.
WHAT THE HELL ARE YOU DOING?!
THIS PUTS US ALL AT RISK. WE ALL KNOW WHAT NEEDS TO BE DONE. WE HAVE TO DO IT NOW BEFORE SHE'S UP WALKING AROUND AGAIN.
THIS ISN'T ABOUT EMOTIONS! IT'S ABOUT GODDAMN COMMON SENSE!
GODDAMN IT, MAN--GIVE THE BOY SOME TIME. YOU DON'T HAVE TO DO THIS!

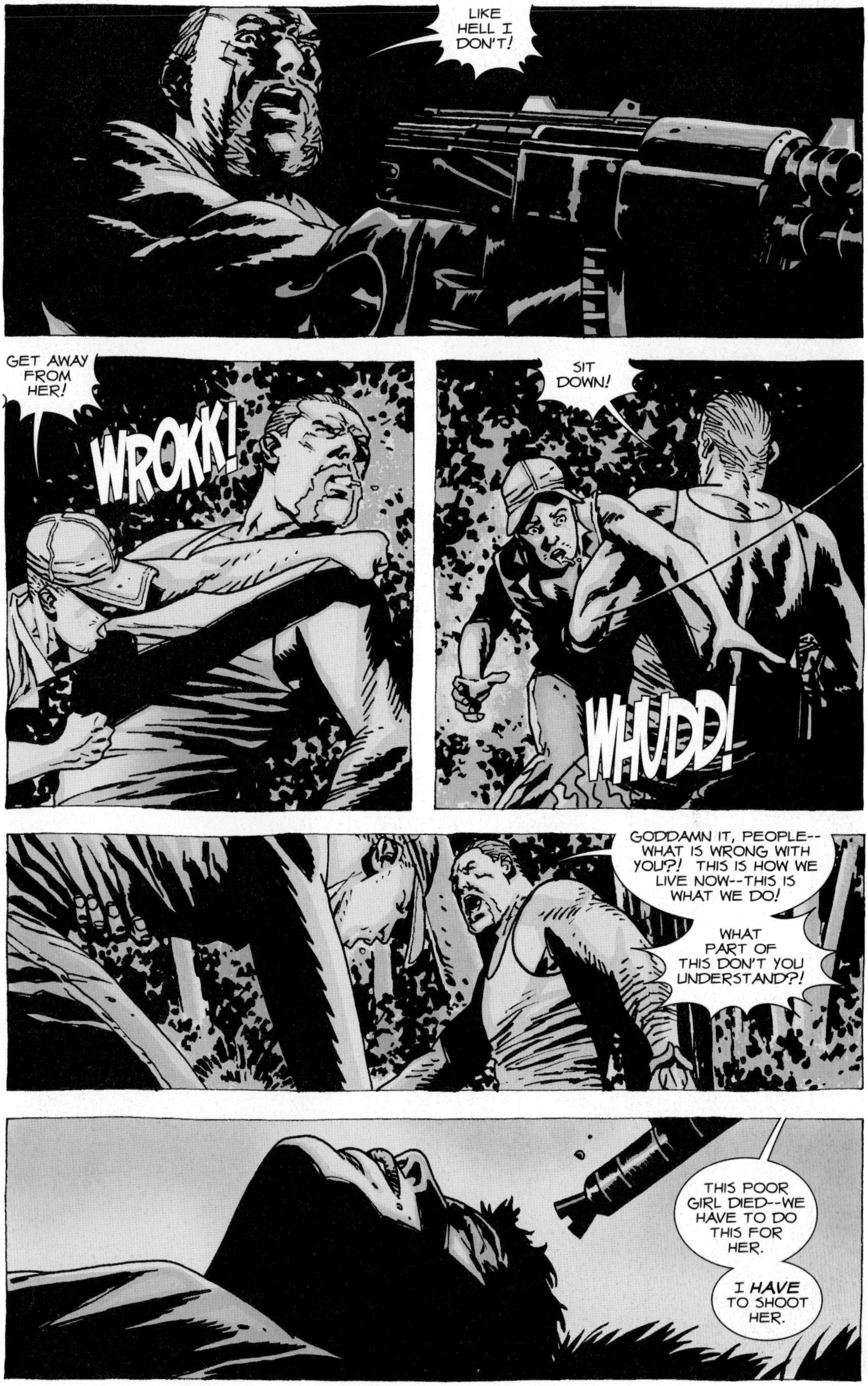
LIKE HELL I DON'T!
GET AWAY FROM HER!
WROKK!
SIT DOWN!
WHUDD!
GODDAMN IT, PEOPLE-- WHAT IS WRONG WITH YOU?! THIS IS HOW WE LIVE NOW--THIS IS WHAT WE DO!
WHAT PART OF THIS DON'T YOU UNDERSTAND?!
THIS POOR GIRL DIED--WE HAVE TO DO THIS FOR HER.
I HAVE TO SHOOT HER.

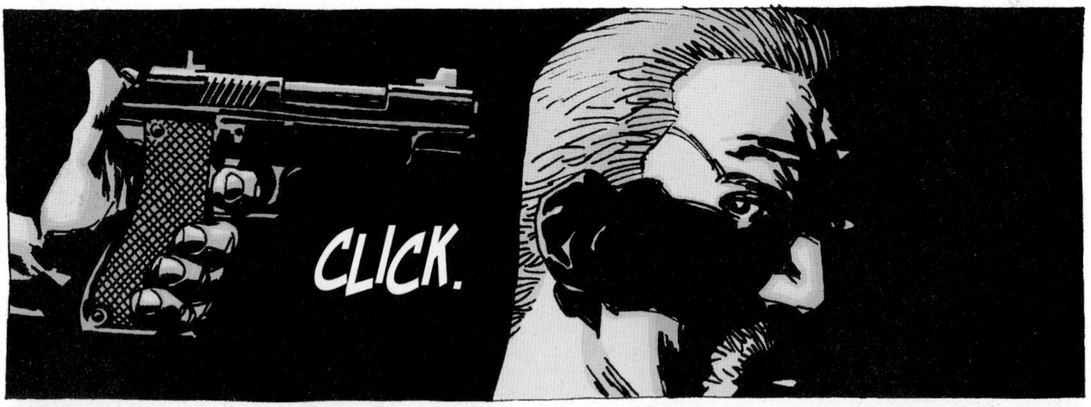
CLICK.

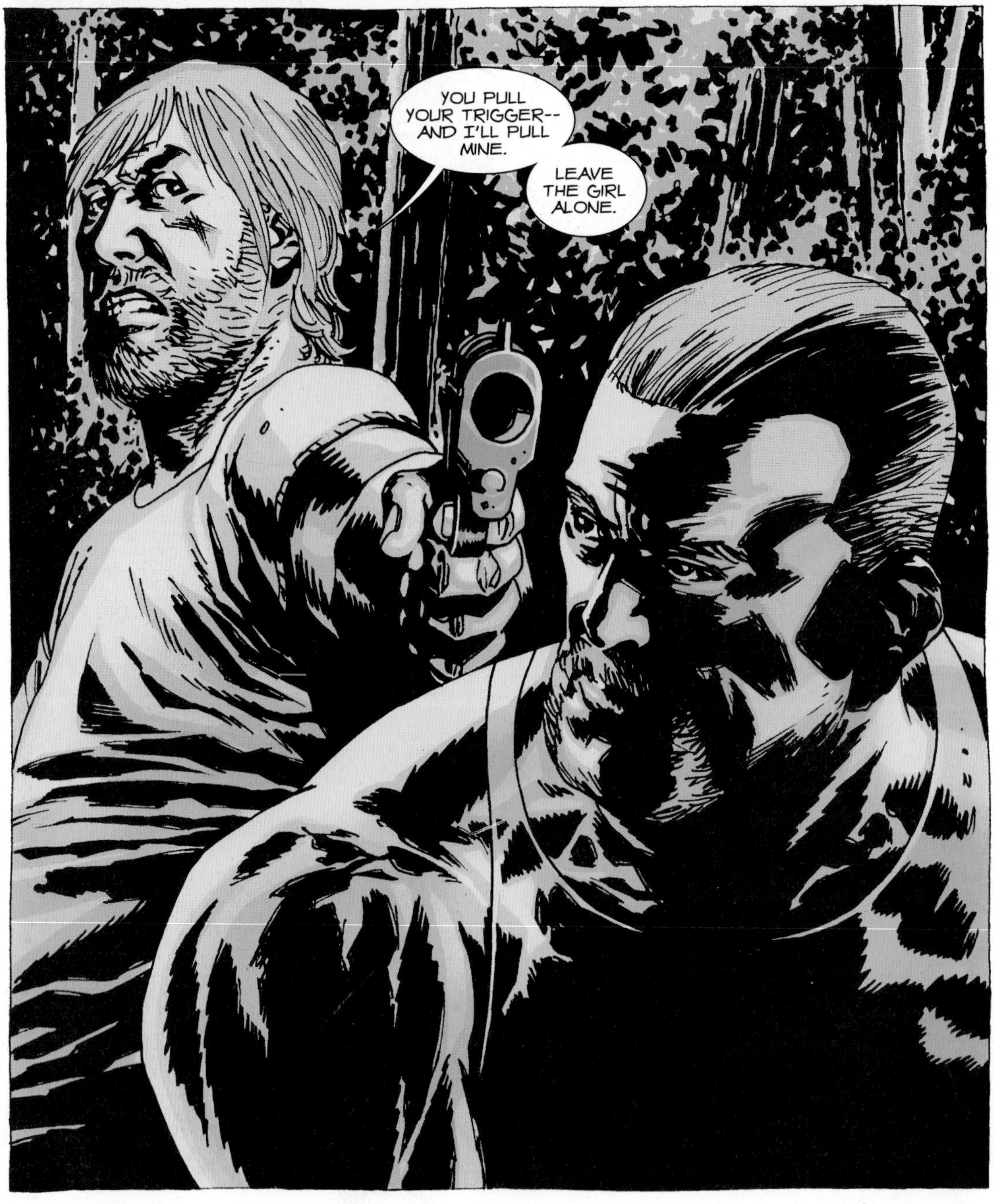
YOU PULL YOUR TRIGGER-- AND I'LL PULL MINE.
LEAVE THE GIRL ALONE.

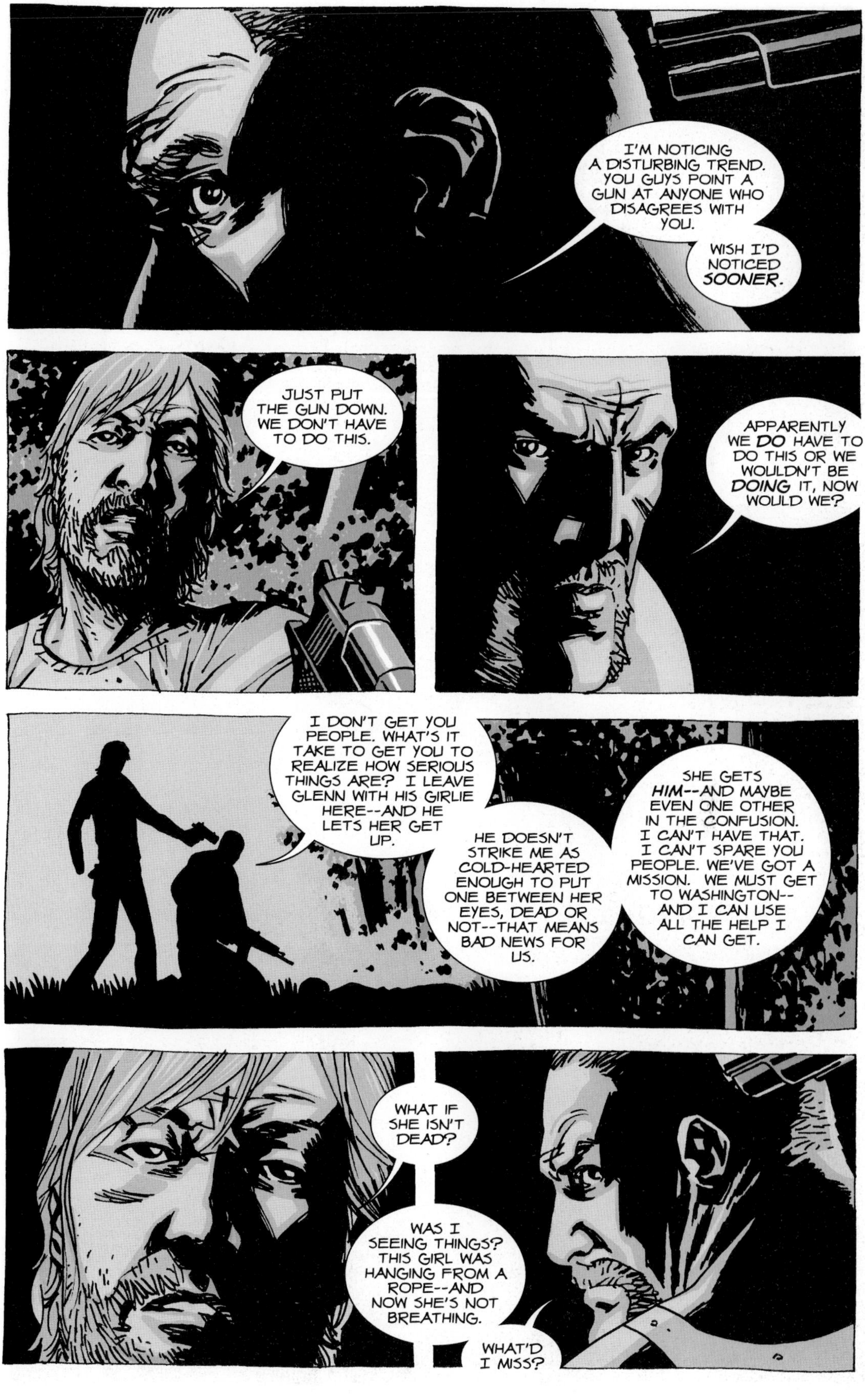
I'M NOTICING A DISTURBING TREND. YOU GUYS POINT A GUN AT ANYONE WHO DISAGREES WITH YOU.
WISH I'D NOTICED SOONER.
JUST PUT THE GUN DOWN. WE DON'T HAVE TO DO THIS.
APPARENTLY WE DO HAVE TO DO THIS OR WE WOULDN'T BE DOING IT, NOW WOULD WE?
I DON'T GET YOU PEOPLE. WHAT'S IT TAKE TO GET YOU TO REALIZE HOW SERIOUS THINGS ARE? I LEAVE GLENN WITH HIS GIRLIE HERE--AND HE LETS HER GET UP.
HE DOESN'T STRIKE ME AS COLD-HEARTED ENOUGH TO PUT ONE BETWEEN HER EYES, DEAD OR NOT--THAT MEANS BAD NEWS FOR US.
SHE GETS HIM--AND MAYBE EVEN ONE OTHER IN THE CONFUSION. I CAN'T HAVE THAT. I CAN'T SPARE YOU PEOPLE. WE'VE GOT A MISSION. WE MUST GET TO WASHINGTON--AND I CAN USE ALL THE HELP I CAN GET.
WHAT IF SHE ISN'T DEAD?
WAS I SEEING THINGS? THIS GIRL WAS HANGING FROM A ROPE--AND NOW SHE'S NOT BREATHING.
WHAT'D I MISS?

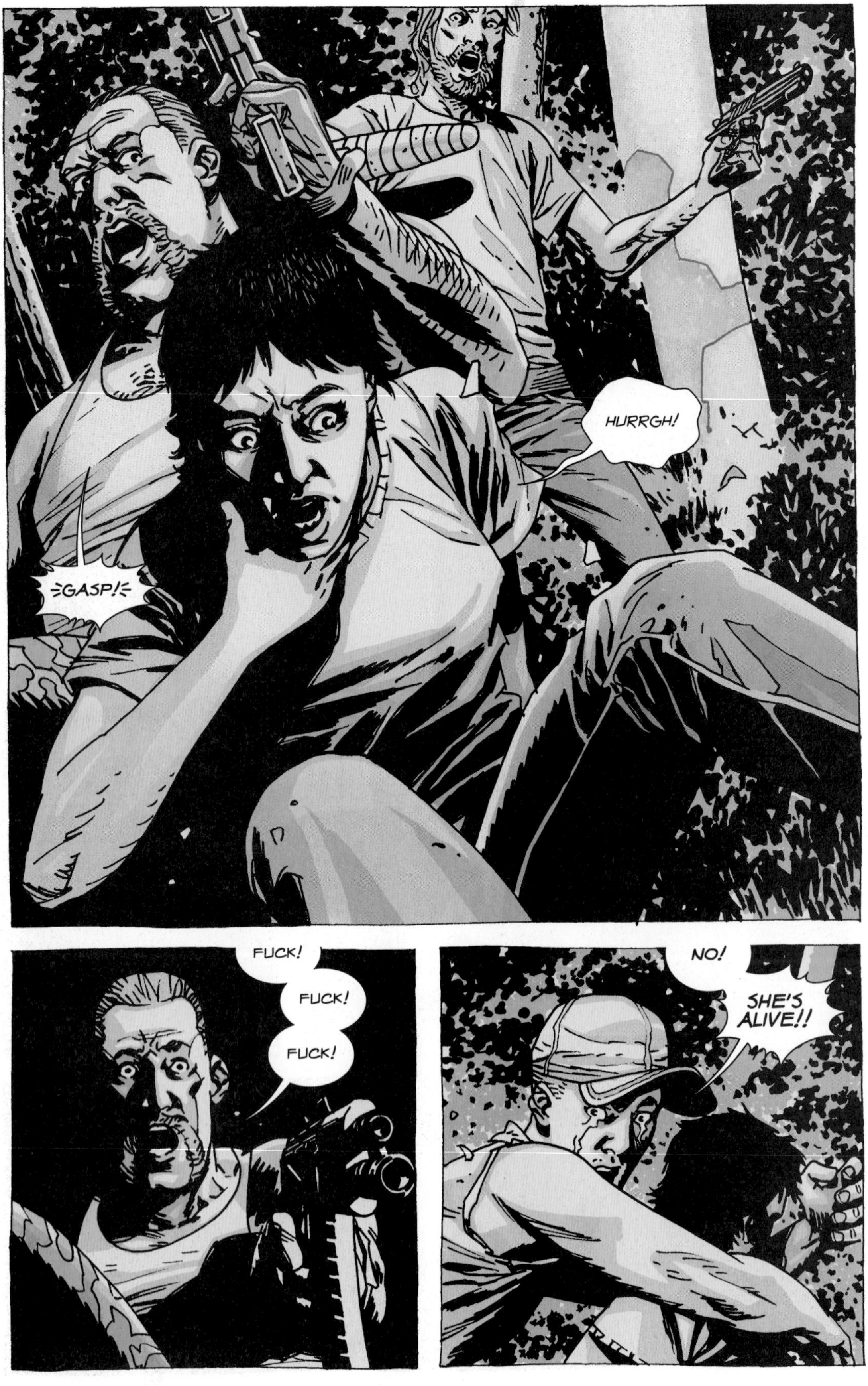
HURRGH!
=GASP!=
FUCK!
FUCK!
FUCK!
NO!
SHE'S ALIVE!!

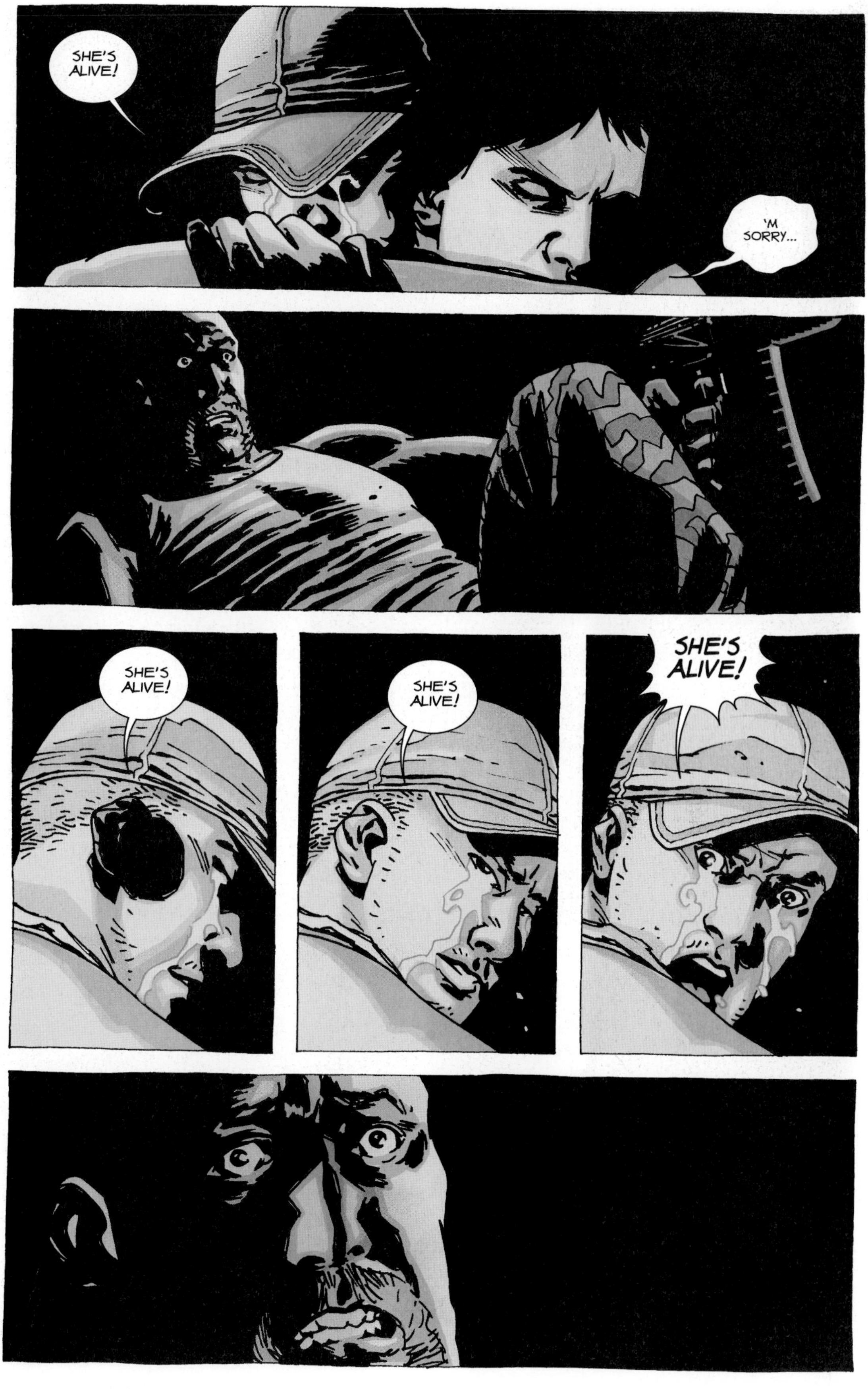
SHE'S ALIVE!
'M SORRY...
SHE'S ALIVE!
SHE'S ALIVE!
SHE'S ALIVE!

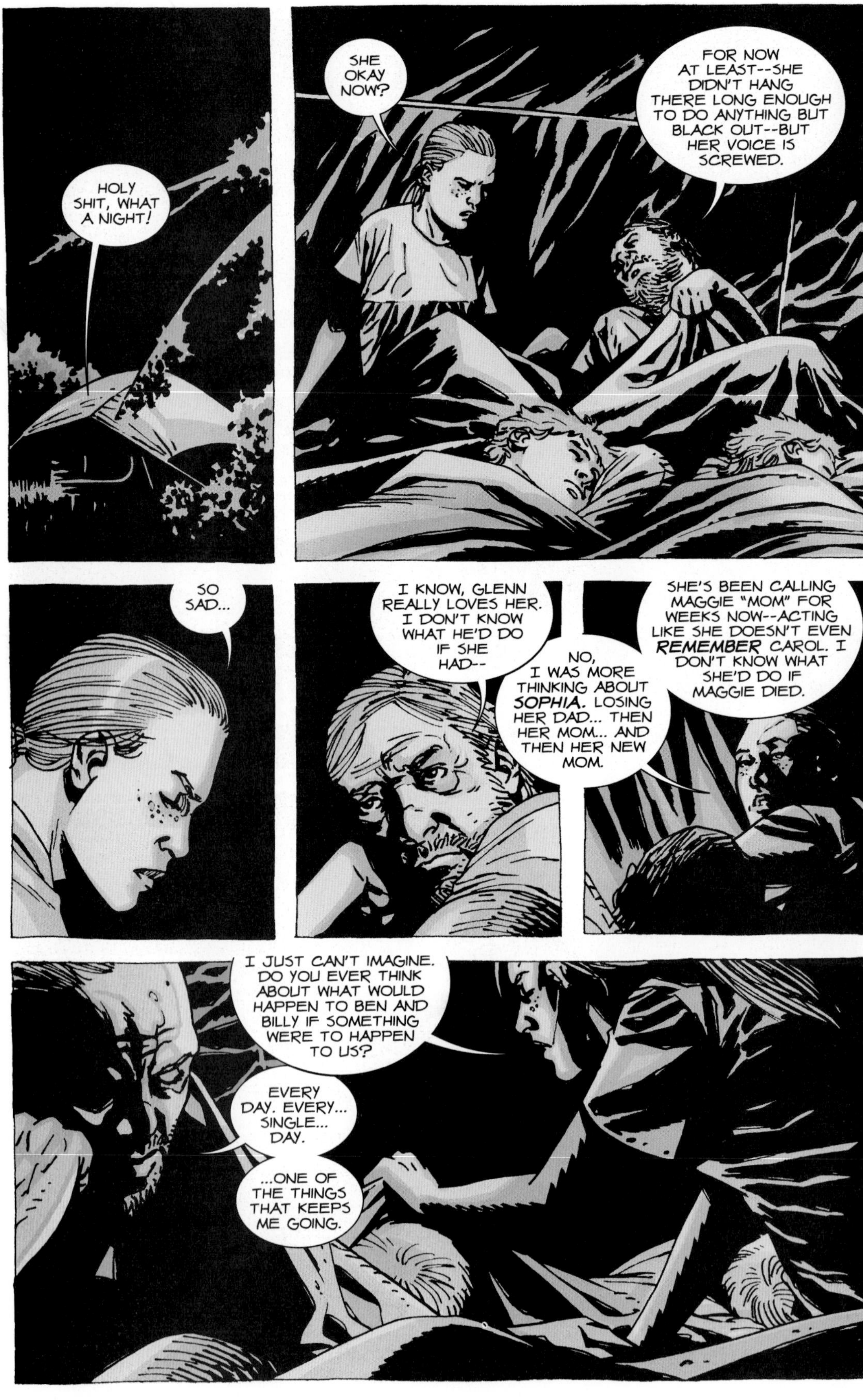
HOLY SHIT, WHAT A NIGHT!
SHE OKAY NOW?
FOR NOW AT LEAST--SHE DIDN'T HANG THERE LONG ENOUGH TO DO ANYTHING BUT BLACK OUT--BUT HER VOICE IS SCREWED.
SO SAD...
I KNOW, GLENN REALLY LOVES HER. I DON'T KNOW WHAT HE'D DO IF SHE HAD--
NO, I WAS MORE THINKING ABOUT SOPHIA. LOSING HER DAD... THEN HER MOM... AND THEN HER NEW MOM.
SHE'S BEEN CALLING MAGGIE "MOM" FOR WEEKS NOW--ACTING LIKE SHE DOESN'T EVEN REMEMBER CAROL. I DON'T KNOW WHAT SHE'D DO IF MAGGIE DIED.
I JUST CAN'T IMAGINE. DO YOU EVER THINK ABOUT WHAT WOULD HAPPEN TO BEN AND BILLY IF SOMETHING WERE TO HAPPEN TO US?
EVERY DAY. EVERY... SINGLE... DAY.
...ONE OF THE THINGS THAT KEEPS ME GOING.

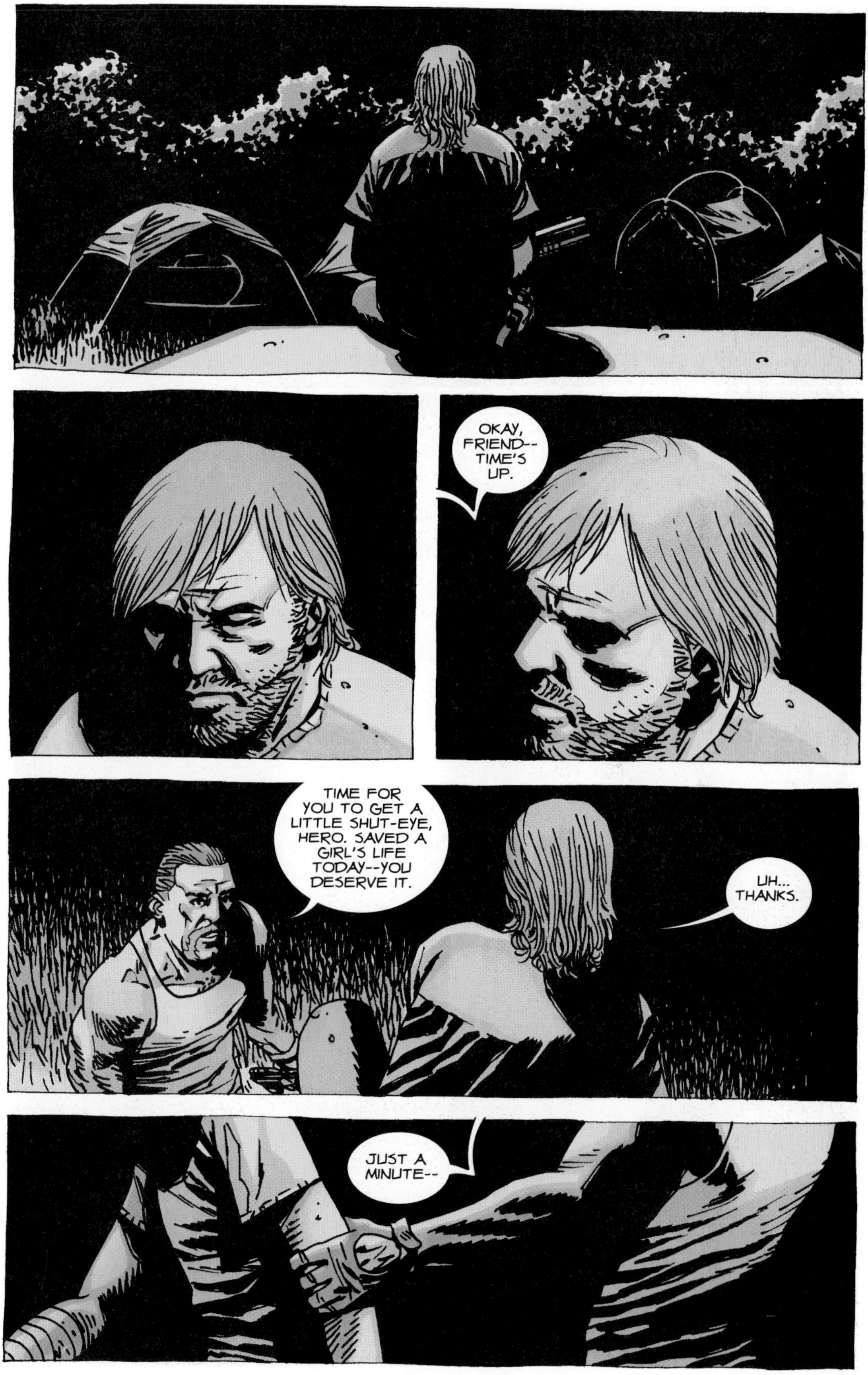
OKAY, FRIEND-- TIME'S UP.
TIME FOR YOU TO GET A LITTLE SHUT-EYE, HERO. SAVED A GIRL'S LIFE TODAY--YOU DESERVE IT.
UH... THANKS.
JUST A MINUTE--

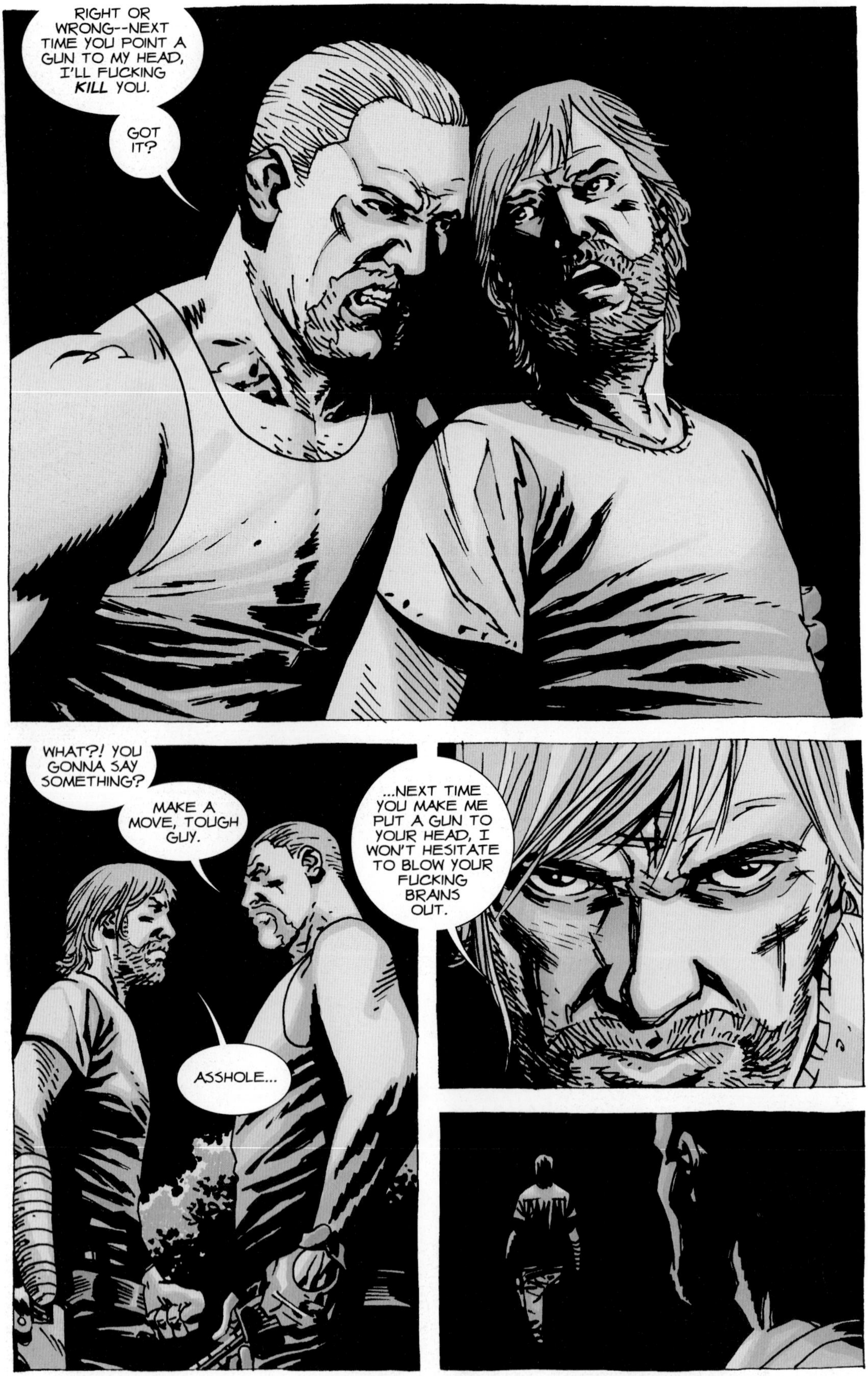
RIGHT OR WRONG--NEXT TIME YOU POINT A GUN TO MY HEAD, I'LL FUCKING **KILL** YOU.
GOT IT?
WHAT?! YOU GONNA SAY SOMETHING?
MAKE A MOVE, TOUGH GUY.
ASSHOLE...
...NEXT TIME YOU MAKE ME PUT A GUN TO YOUR HEAD, I WON'T HESITATE TO BLOW YOUR FUCKING BRAINS OUT.

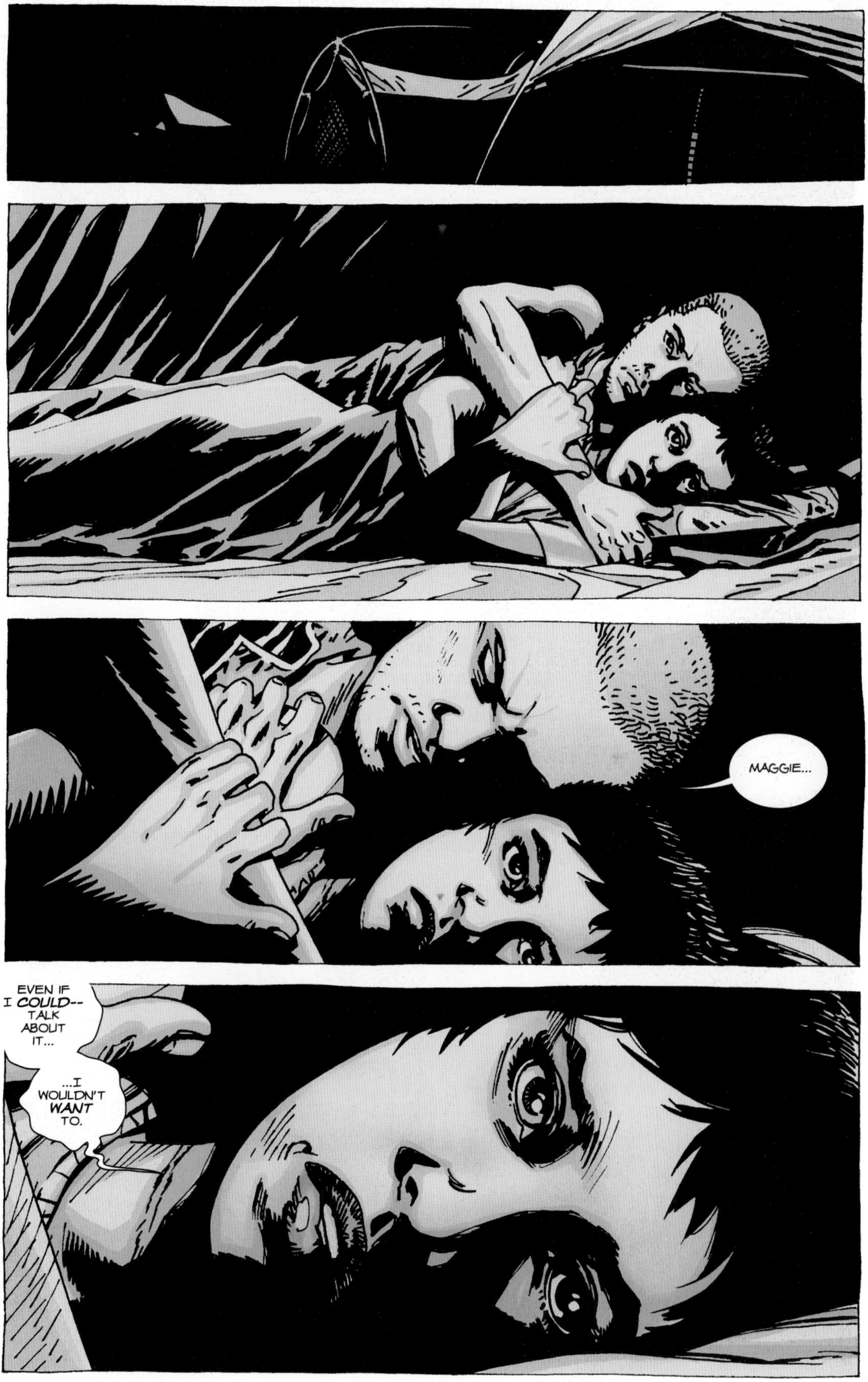
MAGGIE...
EVEN IF I COULD-- TALK ABOUT IT...
...I WOULDN'T WANT TO.

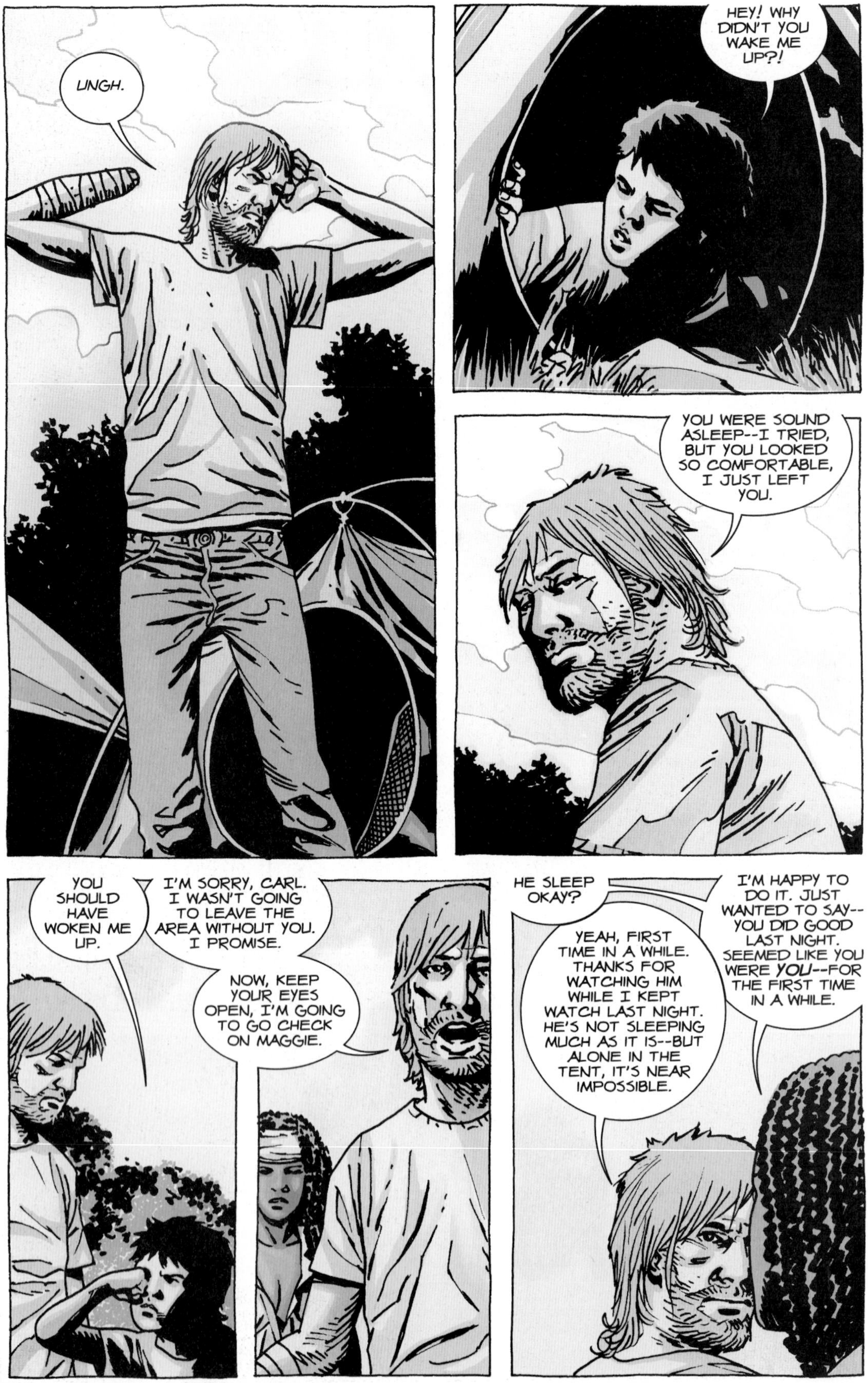
UNGH.
HEY! WHY DIDN'T YOU WAKE ME UP?!
YOU WERE SOUND ASLEEP--I TRIED, BUT YOU LOOKED SO COMFORTABLE, I JUST LEFT YOU.
YOU SHOULD HAVE WOKEN ME UP.
I'M SORRY, CARL. I WASN'T GOING TO LEAVE THE AREA WITHOUT YOU. I PROMISE.
NOW, KEEP YOUR EYES OPEN, I'M GOING TO GO CHECK ON MAGGIE.
HE SLEEP OKAY?
YEAH, FIRST TIME IN A WHILE. THANKS FOR WATCHING HIM WHILE I KEPT WATCH LAST NIGHT. HE'S NOT SLEEPING MUCH AS IT IS--BUT ALONE IN THE TENT, IT'S NEAR IMPOSSIBLE.
I'M HAPPY TO DO IT. JUST WANTED TO SAY-- YOU DID GOOD LAST NIGHT. SEEMED LIKE YOU WERE *YOU*--FOR THE FIRST TIME IN A WHILE.

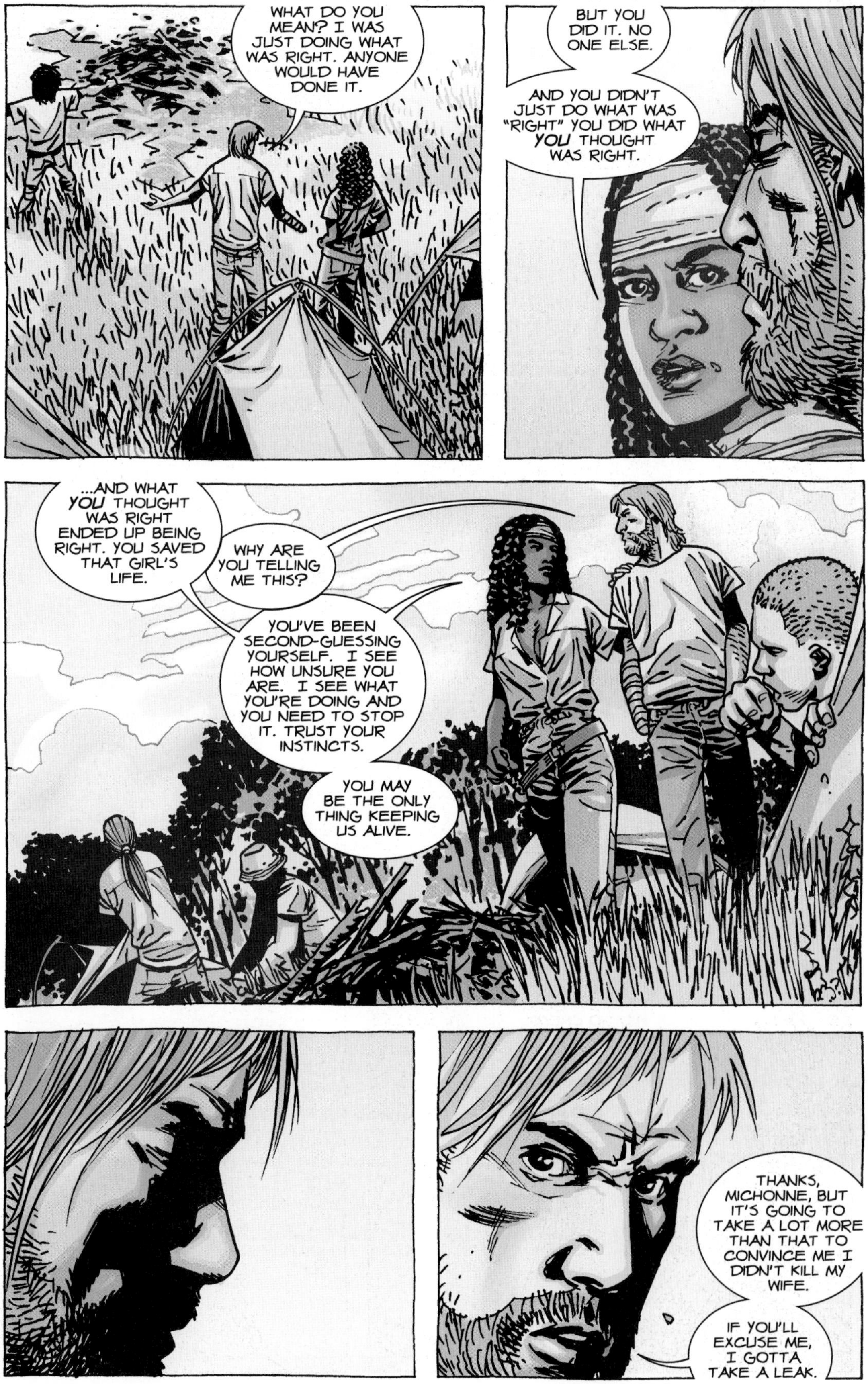
WHAT DO YOU MEAN? I WAS JUST DOING WHAT WAS RIGHT. ANYONE WOULD HAVE DONE IT.
BUT YOU DID IT. NO ONE ELSE.
AND YOU DIDN'T JUST DO WHAT WAS "RIGHT" YOU DID WHAT *YOU* THOUGHT WAS RIGHT.
...AND WHAT *YOU* THOUGHT WAS RIGHT ENDED UP BEING RIGHT. YOU SAVED THAT GIRL'S LIFE.
WHY ARE YOU TELLING ME THIS?
YOU'VE BEEN SECOND-GUESSING YOURSELF. I SEE HOW UNSURE YOU ARE. I SEE WHAT YOU'RE DOING AND YOU NEED TO STOP IT. TRUST YOUR INSTINCTS.
YOU MAY BE THE ONLY THING KEEPING US ALIVE.
THANKS, MICHONNE, BUT IT'S GOING TO TAKE A LOT MORE THAN THAT TO CONVINCE ME I DIDN'T KILL MY WIFE.
IF YOU'LL EXCUSE ME, I GOTTA TAKE A LEAK.

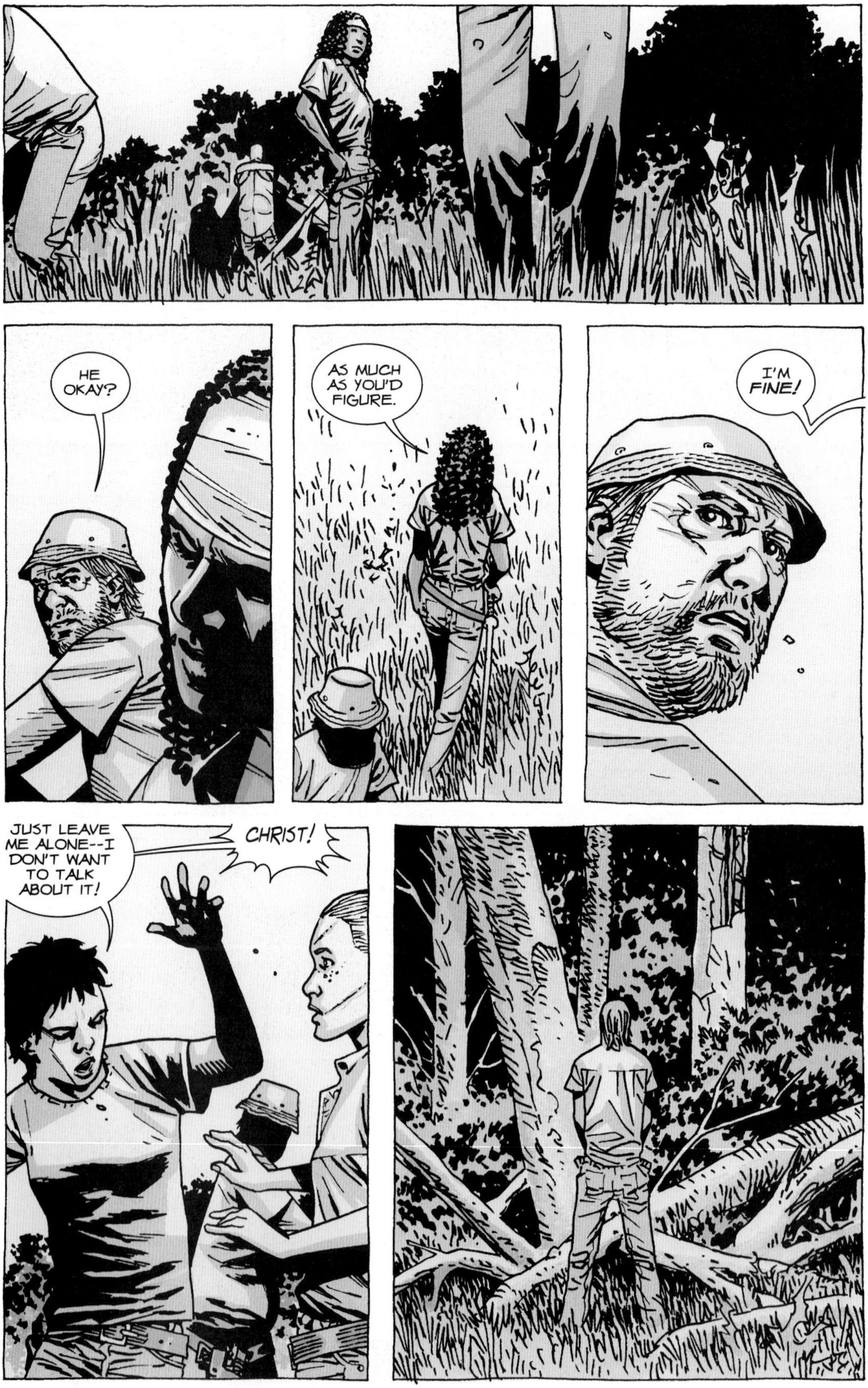
HE OKAY?
AS MUCH AS YOU'D FIGURE.
I'M FINE!
JUST LEAVE ME ALONE--I DON'T WANT TO TALK ABOUT IT!
CHRIST!

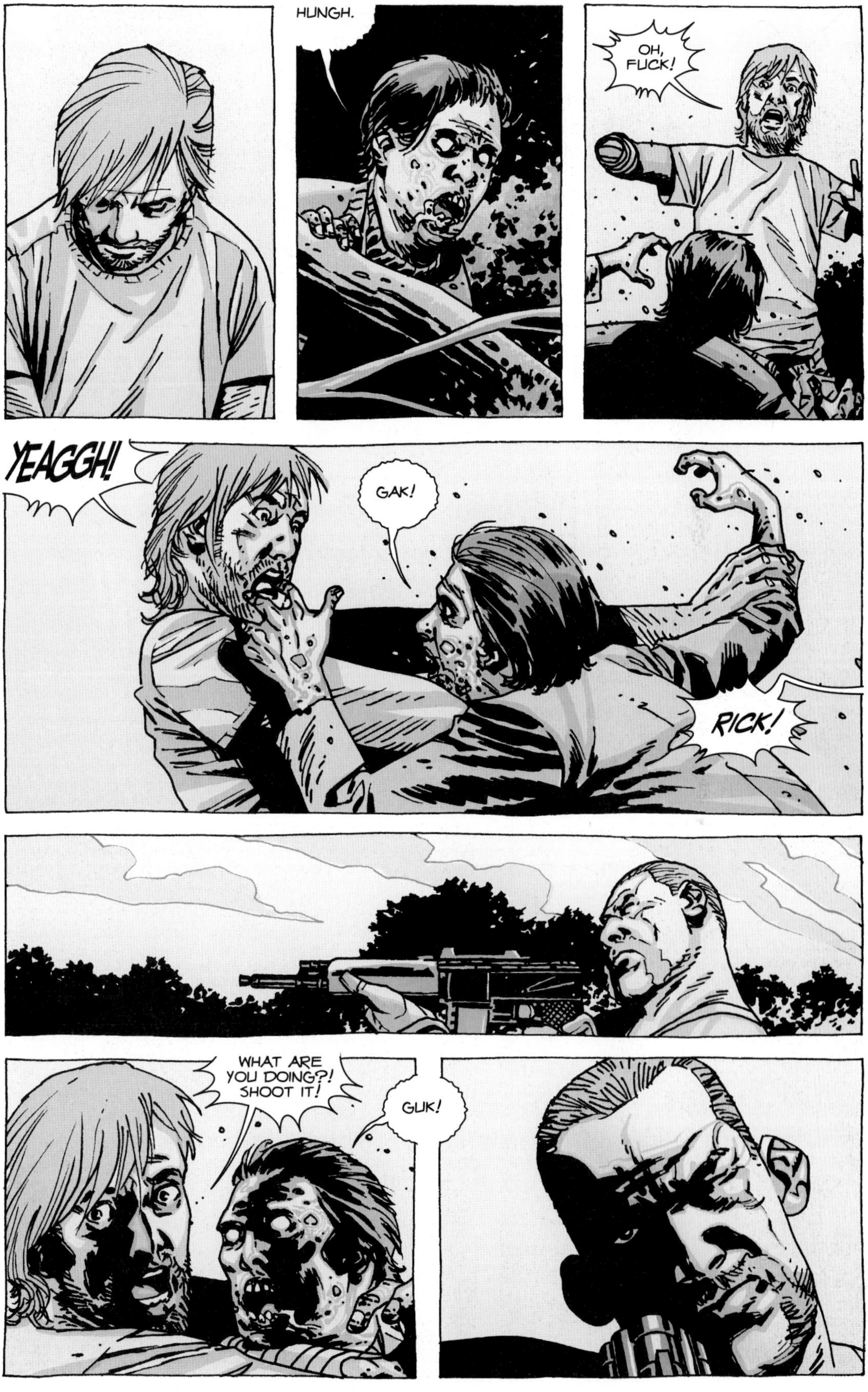
HUNGH.
OH, FUCK!
YEAGGH!
GAK!
RICK!
WHAT ARE YOU DOING?! SHOOT IT!
GUK!

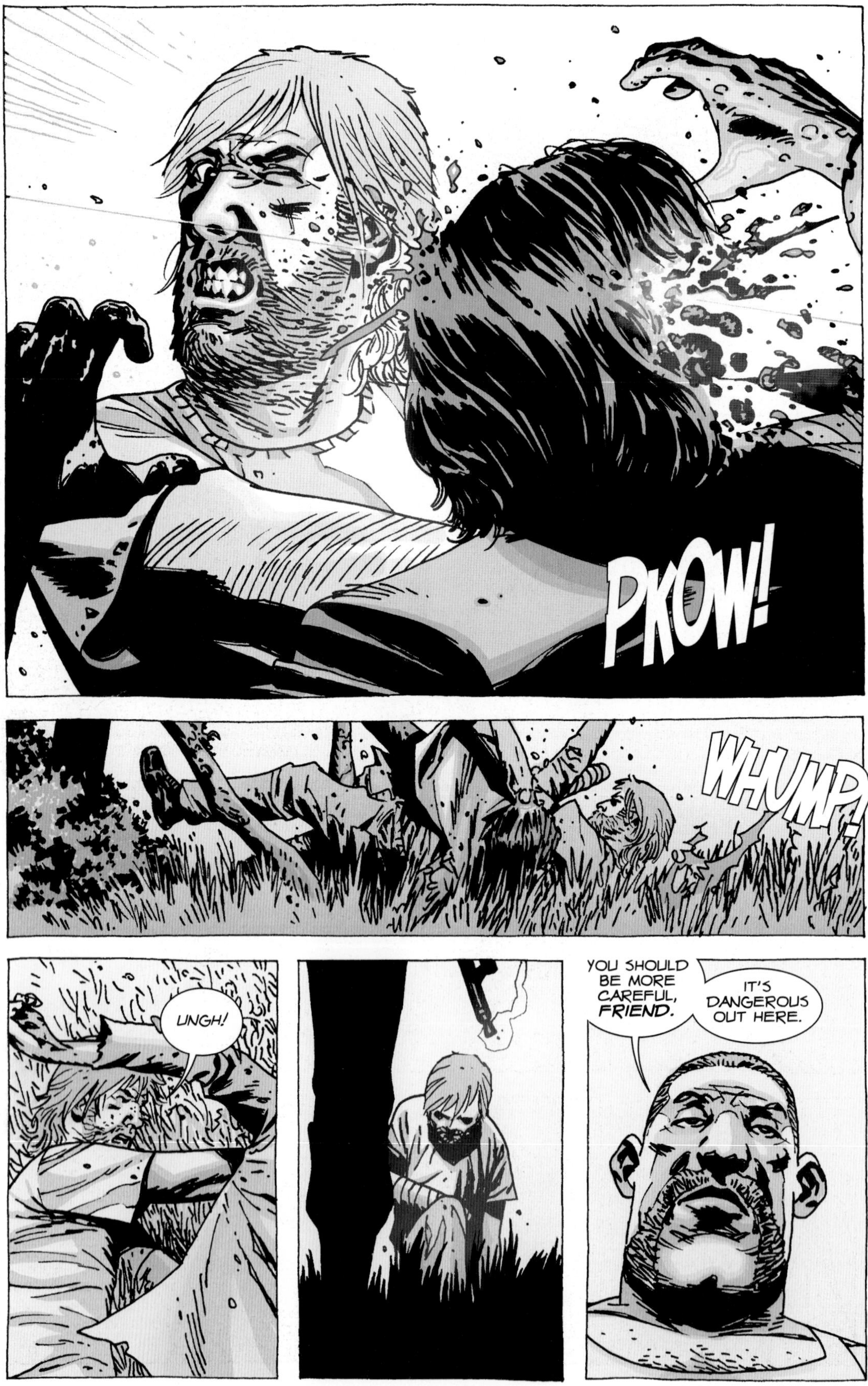
PKOW!
WHUMP!
UNGH!
YOU SHOULD BE MORE CAREFUL, FRIEND.
IT'S DANGEROUS OUT HERE.

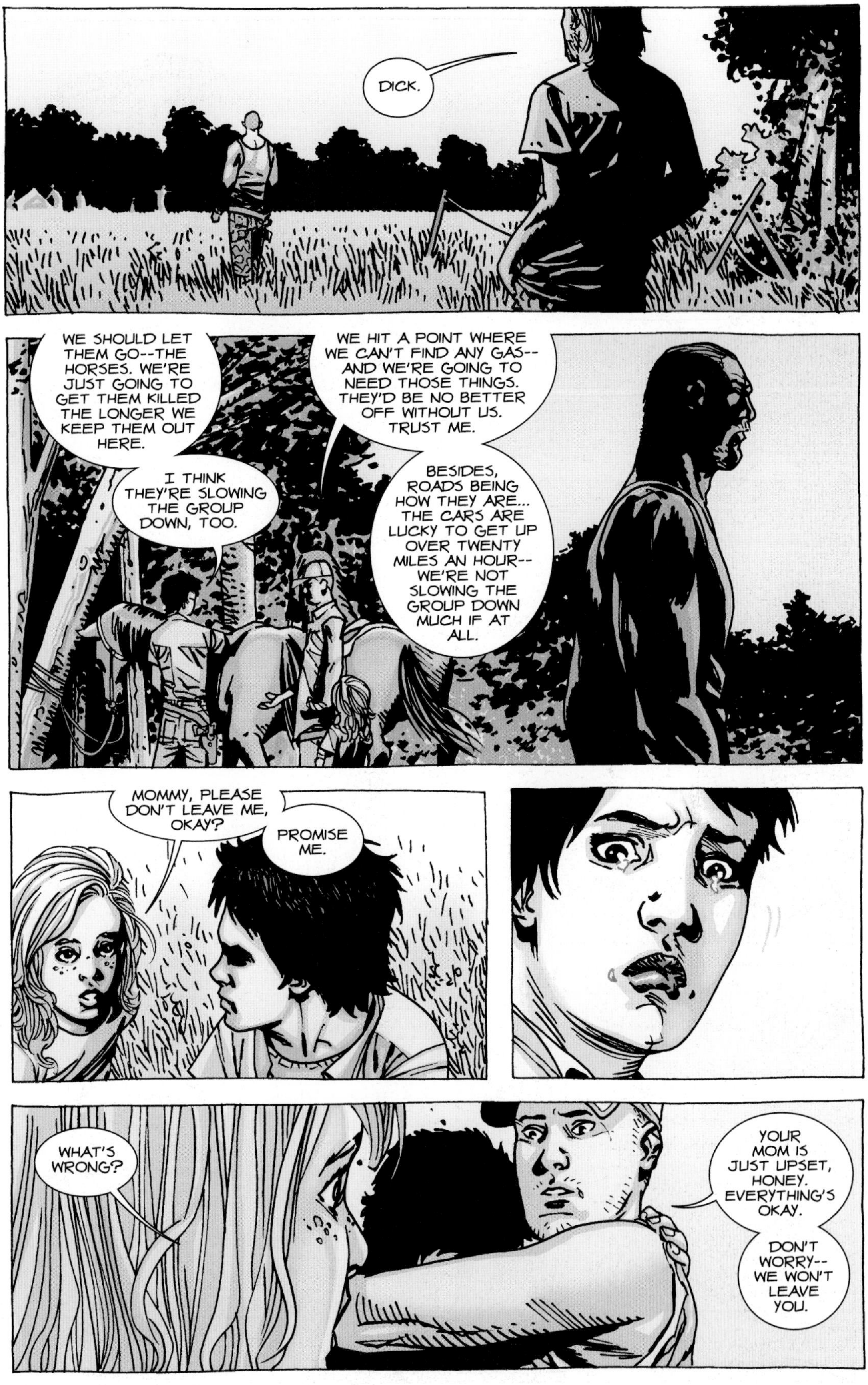
DICK.
WE SHOULD LET THEM GO--THE HORSES. WE'RE JUST GOING TO GET THEM KILLED THE LONGER WE KEEP THEM OUT HERE.
I THINK THEY'RE SLOWING THE GROUP DOWN, TOO.
WE HIT A POINT WHERE WE CAN'T FIND ANY GAS--AND WE'RE GOING TO NEED THOSE THINGS. THEY'D BE NO BETTER OFF WITHOUT US. TRUST ME.
BESIDES, ROADS BEING HOW THEY ARE... THE CARS ARE LUCKY TO GET UP OVER TWENTY MILES AN HOUR--WE'RE NOT SLOWING THE GROUP DOWN MUCH IF AT ALL.
MOMMY, PLEASE DON'T LEAVE ME, OKAY?
PROMISE ME.
WHAT'S WRONG?
YOUR MOM IS JUST UPSET, HONEY. EVERYTHING'S OKAY.
DON'T WORRY--WE WON'T LEAVE YOU.

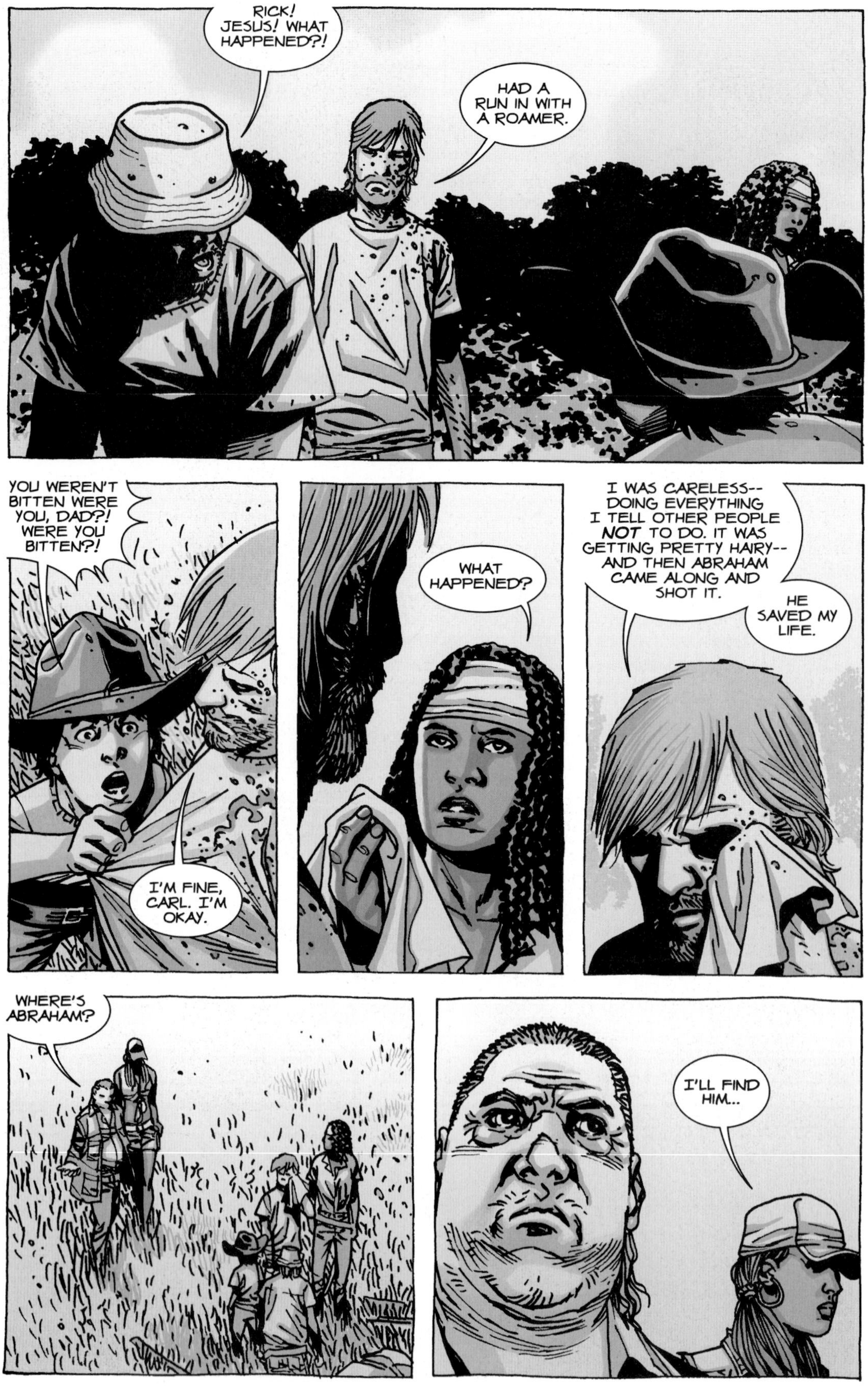
RICK! JESUS! WHAT HAPPENED?!
HAD A RUN IN WITH A ROAMER.
YOU WEREN'T BITTEN WERE YOU, DAD?! WERE YOU BITTEN?!
I'M FINE, CARL. I'M OKAY.
WHAT HAPPENED?
I WAS CARELESS-- DOING EVERYTHING I TELL OTHER PEOPLE NOT TO DO. IT WAS GETTING PRETTY HAIRY-- AND THEN ABRAHAM CAME ALONG AND SHOT IT.
HE SAVED MY LIFE.
WHERE'S ABRAHAM?
I'LL FIND HIM...

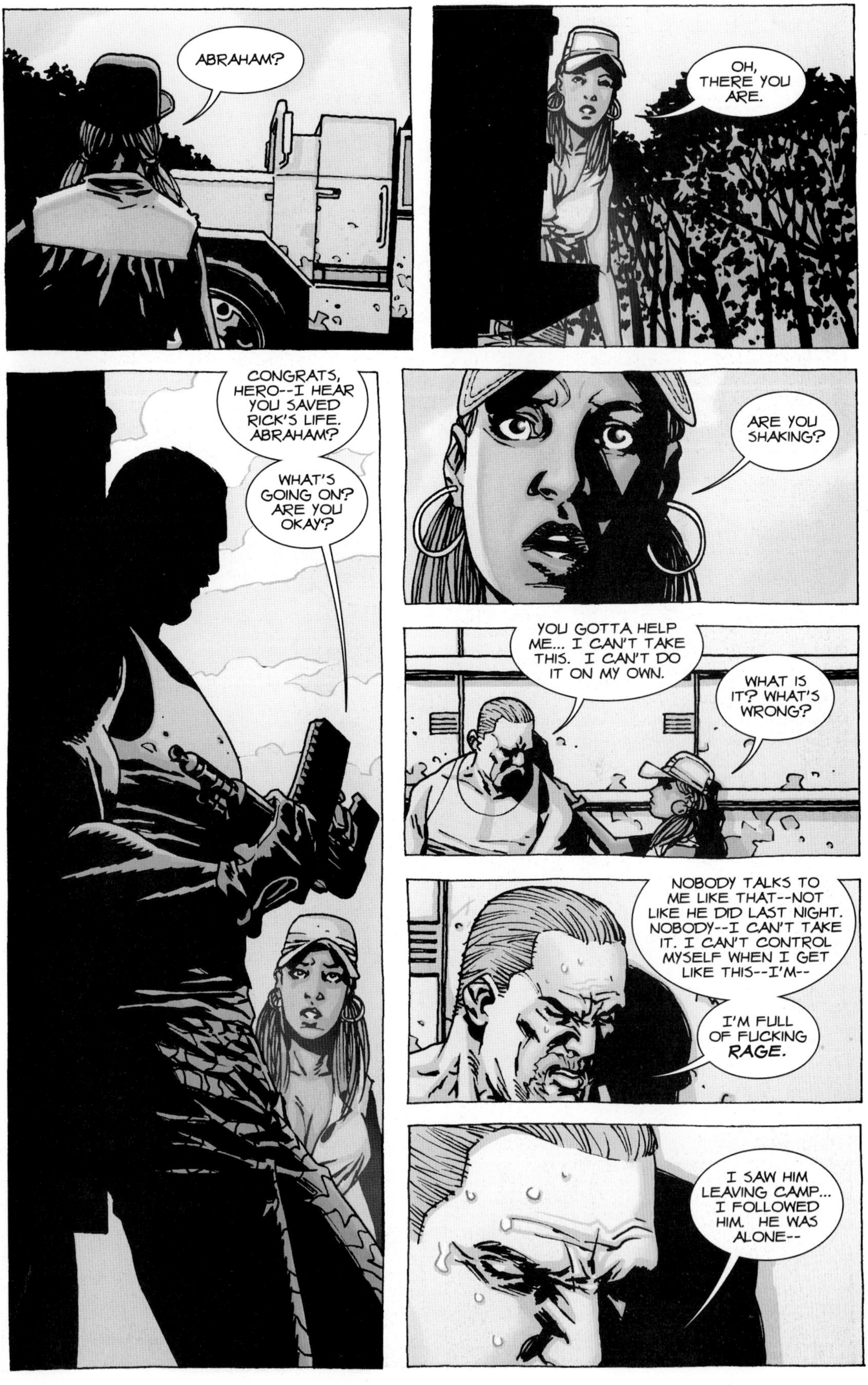
ABRAHAM?
OH, THERE YOU ARE.
CONGRATS, HERO--I HEAR YOU SAVED RICK'S LIFE. ABRAHAM?
WHAT'S GOING ON? ARE YOU OKAY?
ARE YOU SHAKING?
YOU GOTTA HELP ME... I CAN'T TAKE THIS. I CAN'T DO IT ON MY OWN.
WHAT IS IT? WHAT'S WRONG?
NOBODY TALKS TO ME LIKE THAT--NOT LIKE HE DID LAST NIGHT. NOBODY--I CAN'T TAKE IT. I CAN'T CONTROL MYSELF WHEN I GET LIKE THIS--I'M--
I'M FULL OF FUCKING RAGE.
I SAW HIM LEAVING CAMP... I FOLLOWED HIM. HE WAS ALONE--

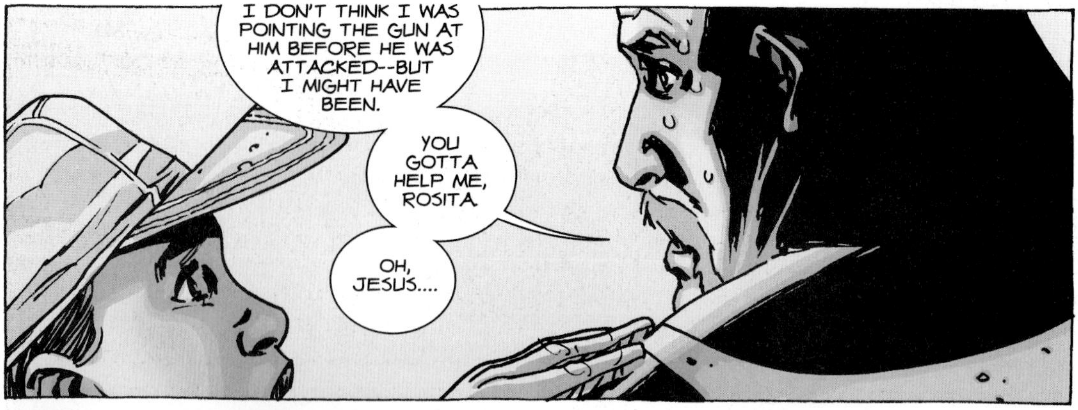
I DON'T THINK I WAS POINTING THE GUN AT HIM BEFORE HE WAS ATTACKED--BUT I MIGHT HAVE BEEN.
YOU GOTTA HELP ME, ROSITA.
OH, JESUS....

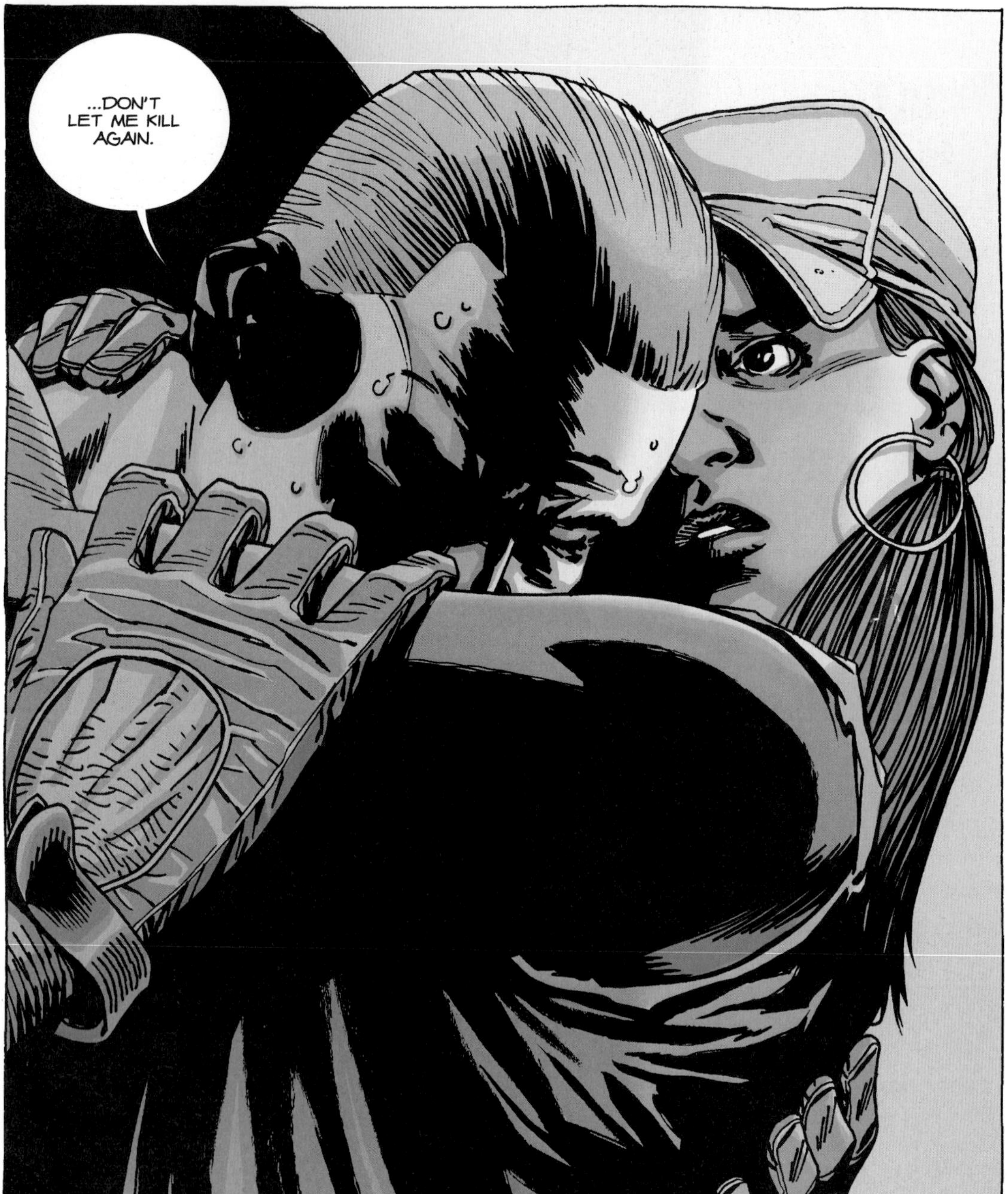
...DON'T LET ME KILL AGAIN.

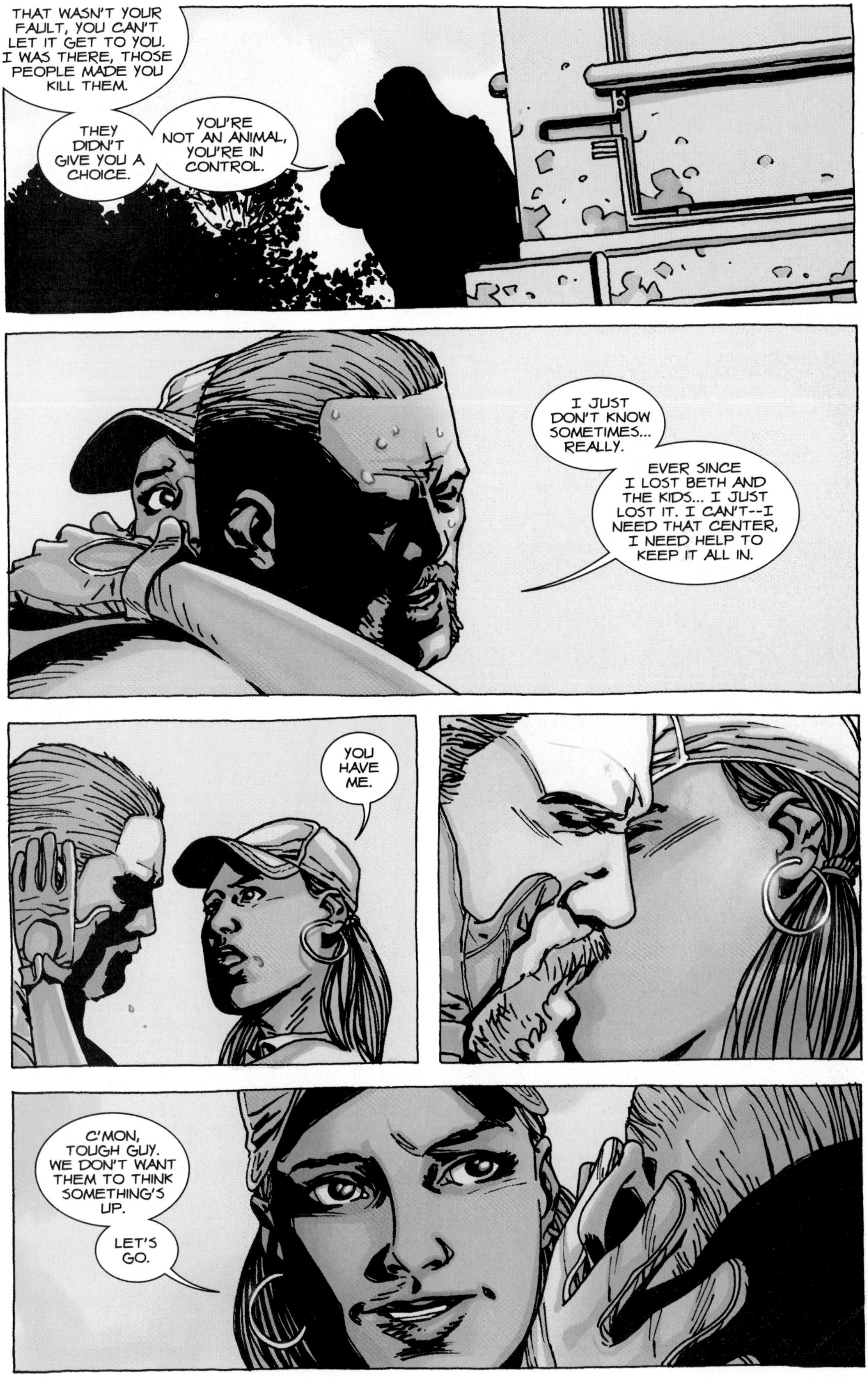
THAT WASN'T YOUR FAULT, YOU CAN'T LET IT GET TO YOU. I WAS THERE, THOSE PEOPLE MADE YOU KILL THEM.
THEY DIDN'T GIVE YOU A CHOICE.
YOU'RE NOT AN ANIMAL, YOU'RE IN CONTROL.
I JUST DON'T KNOW SOMETIMES... REALLY.
EVER SINCE I LOST BETH AND THE KIDS... I JUST LOST IT. I CAN'T--I NEED THAT CENTER, I NEED HELP TO KEEP IT ALL IN.
YOU HAVE ME.
C'MON, TOUGH GUY. WE DON'T WANT THEM TO THINK SOMETHING'S UP.
LET'S GO.

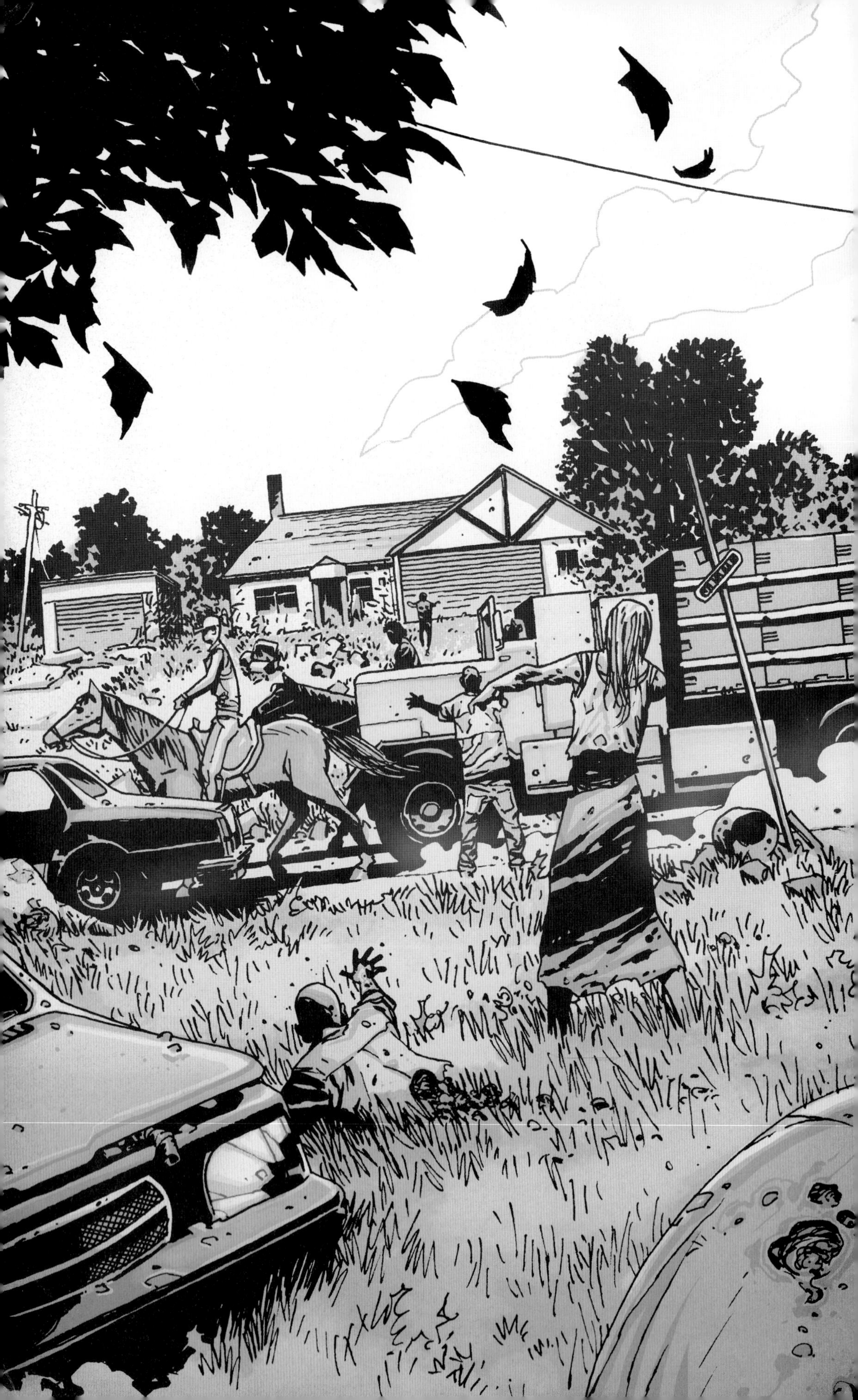

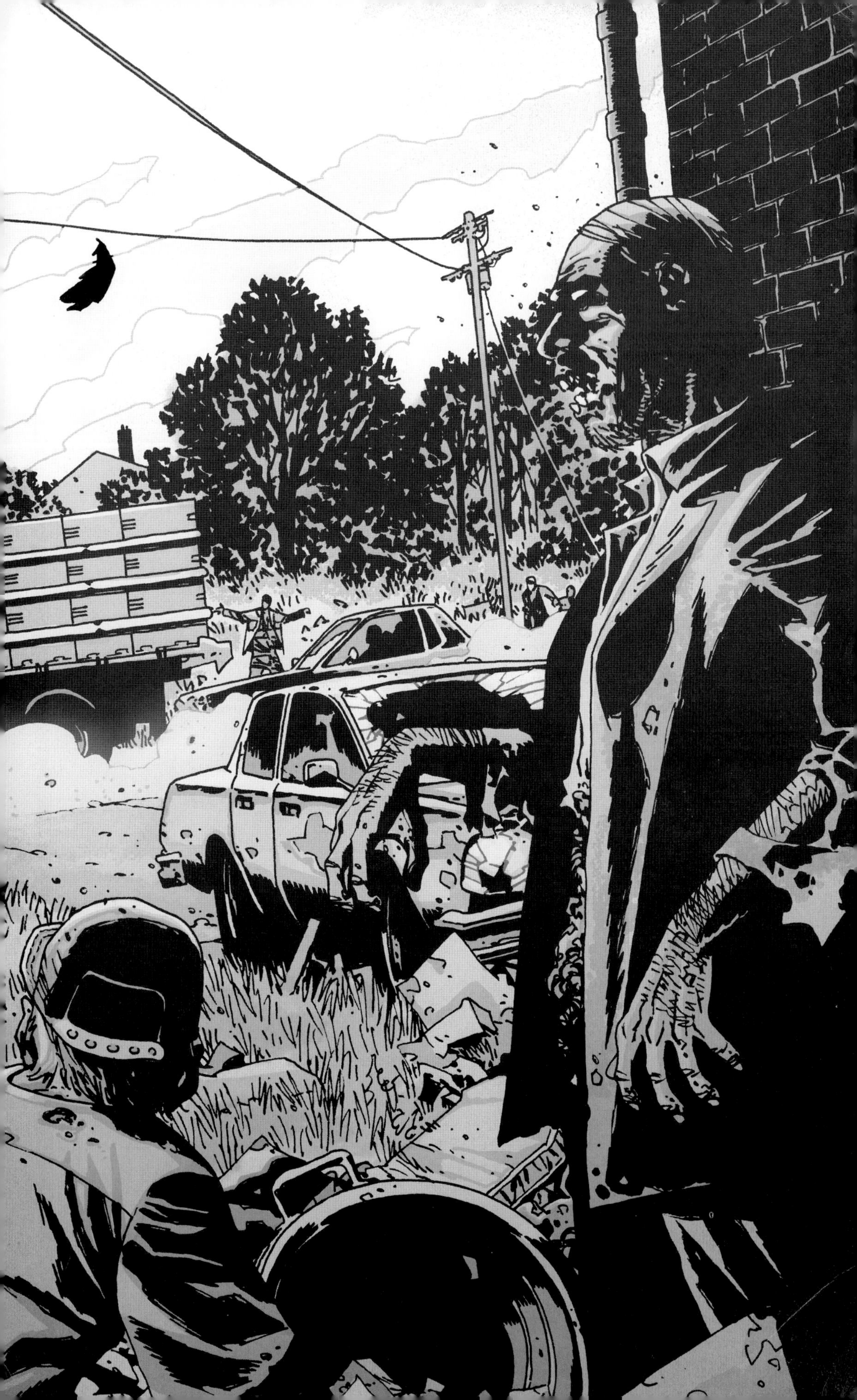

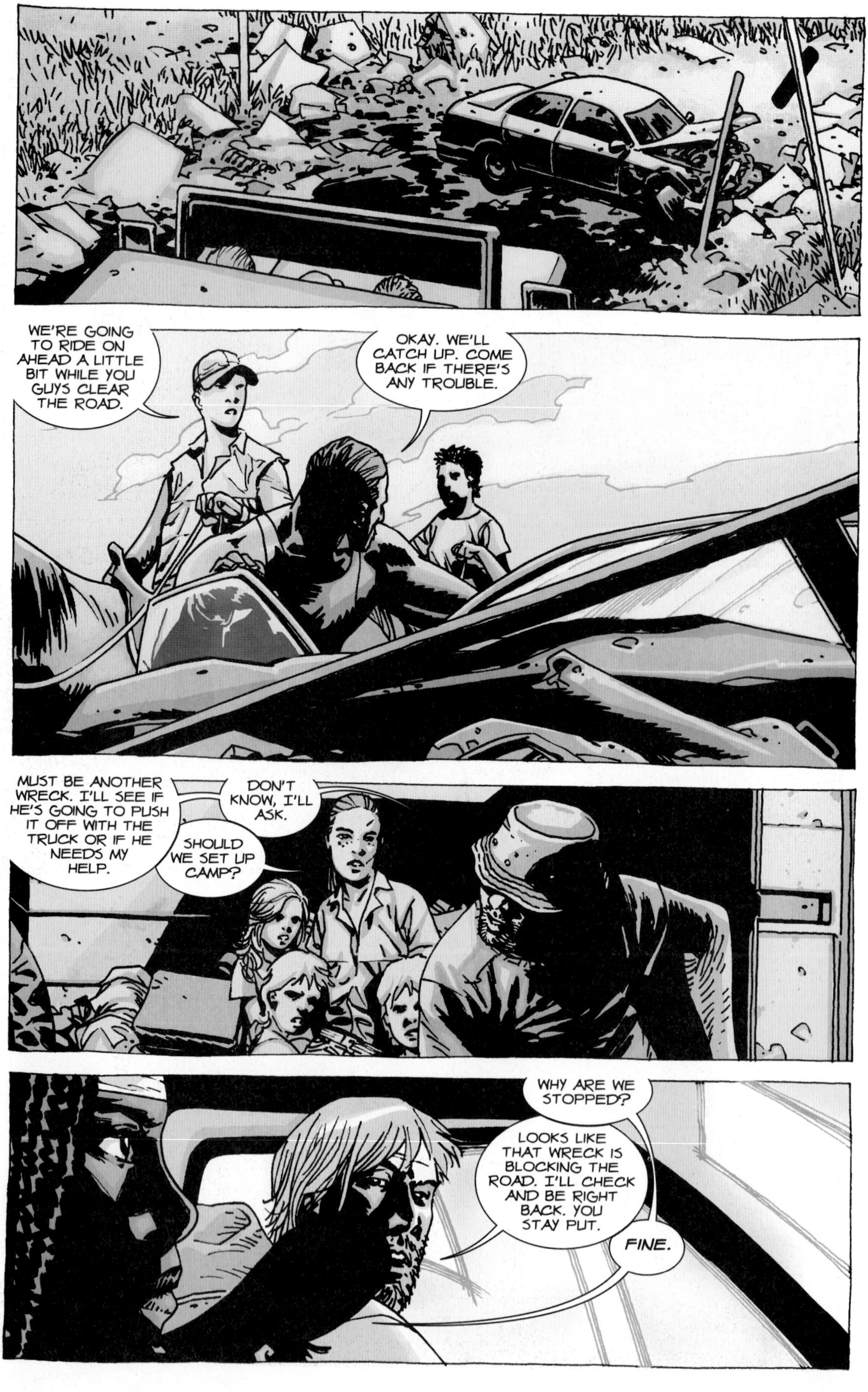

WE'RE GOING TO RIDE ON AHEAD A LITTLE BIT WHILE YOU GUYS CLEAR THE ROAD.
OKAY. WE'LL CATCH UP. COME BACK IF THERE'S ANY TROUBLE.
MUST BE ANOTHER WRECK. I'LL SEE IF HE'S GOING TO PUSH IT OFF WITH THE TRUCK OR IF HE NEEDS MY HELP.
DON'T KNOW, I'LL ASK.
SHOULD WE SET UP CAMP?
WHY ARE WE STOPPED?
LOOKS LIKE THAT WRECK IS BLOCKING THE ROAD. I'LL CHECK AND BE RIGHT BACK. YOU STAY PUT.
FINE.

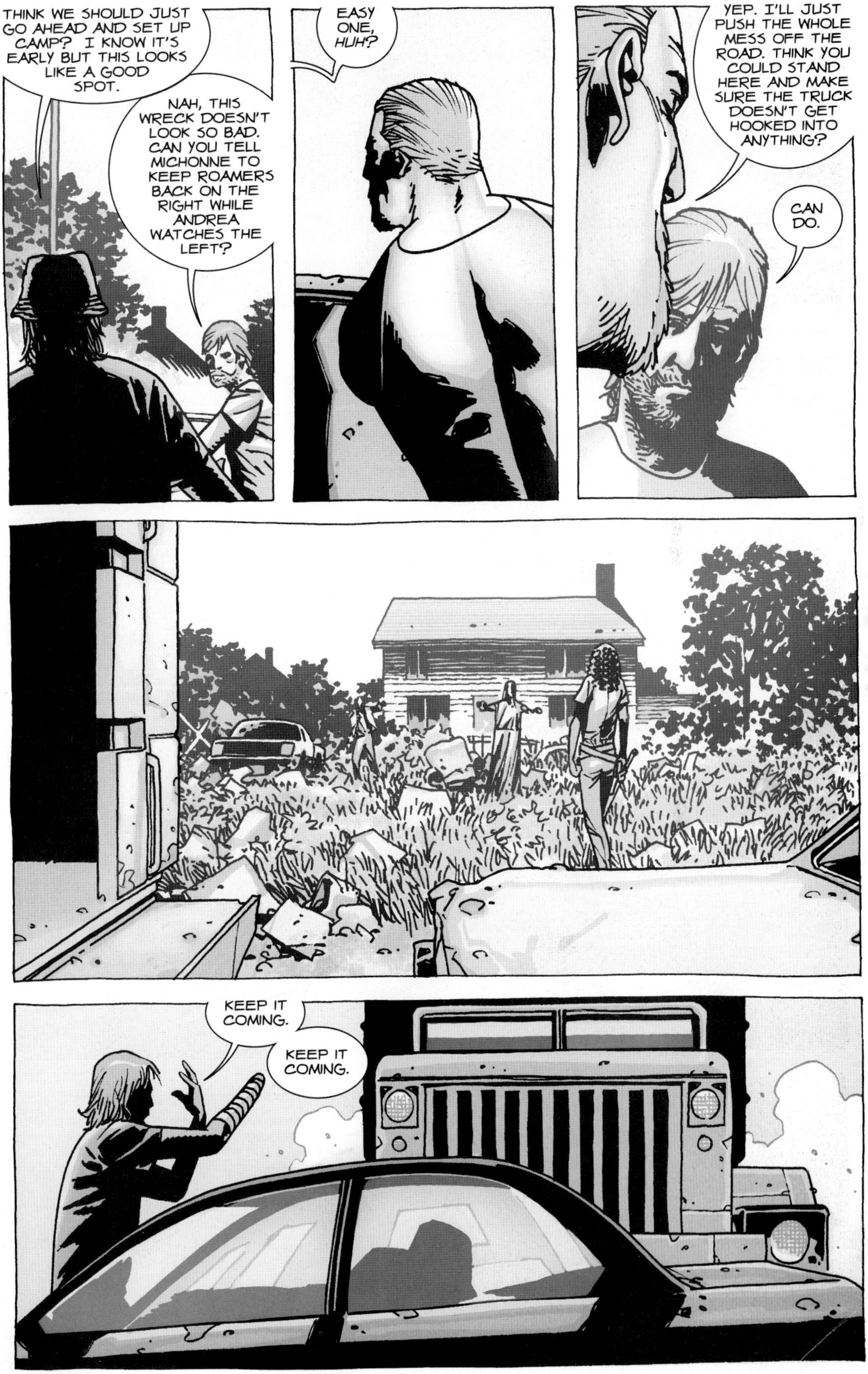
THINK WE SHOULD JUST GO AHEAD AND SET UP CAMP? I KNOW IT'S EARLY BUT THIS LOOKS LIKE A GOOD SPOT.
NAH, THIS WRECK DOESN'T LOOK SO BAD. CAN YOU TELL MICHONNE TO KEEP ROAMERS BACK ON THE RIGHT WHILE ANDREA WATCHES THE LEFT?
EASY ONE, *HUH?*
YEP. I'LL JUST PUSH THE WHOLE MESS OFF THE ROAD. THINK YOU COULD STAND HERE AND MAKE SURE THE TRUCK DOESN'T GET HOOKED INTO ANYTHING?
CAN DO.
KEEP IT COMING.
KEEP IT COMING.

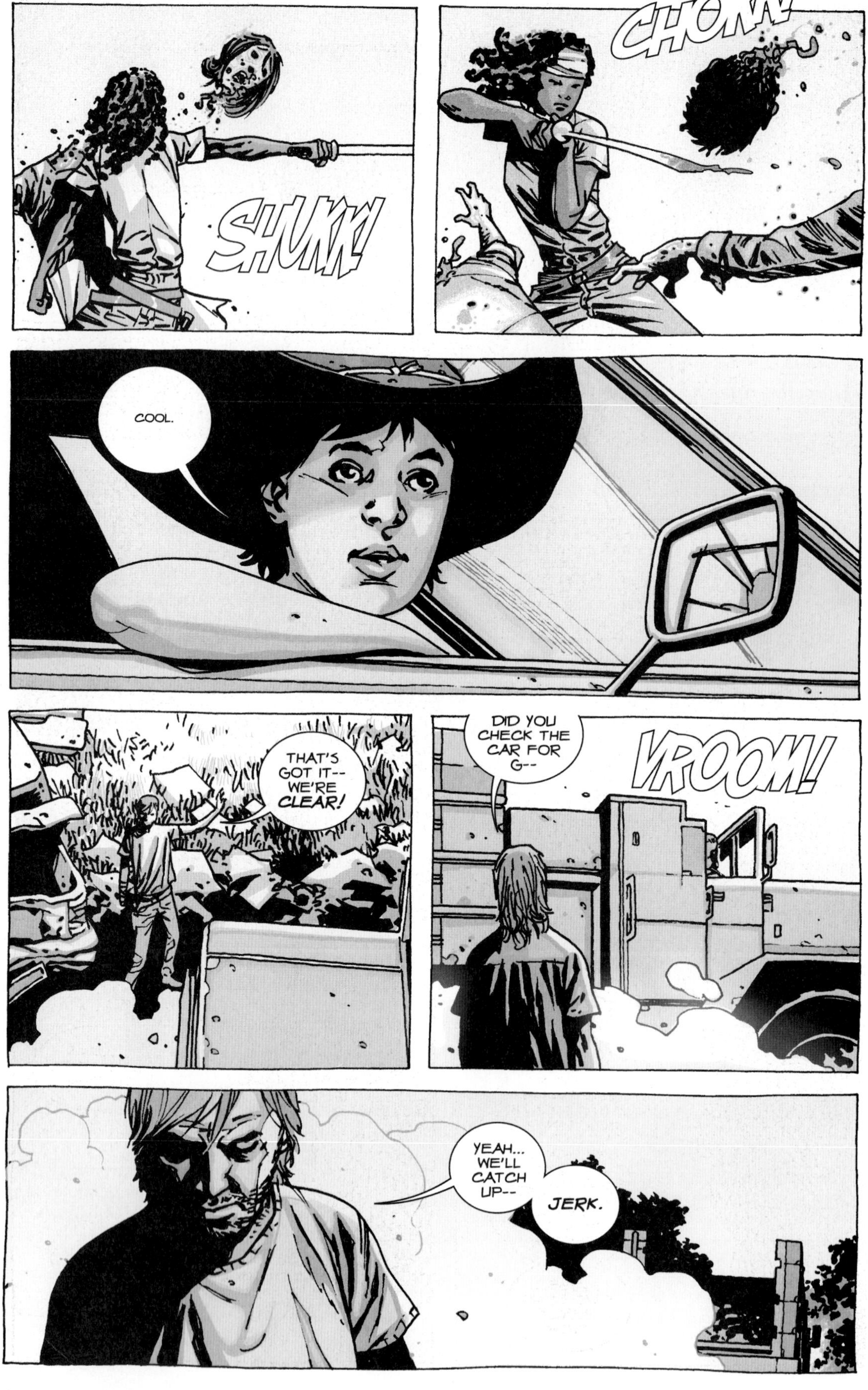
SHUKK!
CHOKK!
COOL.
THAT'S GOT IT-- WE'RE CLEAR!
DID YOU CHECK THE CAR FOR G--
VROOM!
YEAH... WE'LL CATCH UP--
JERK.

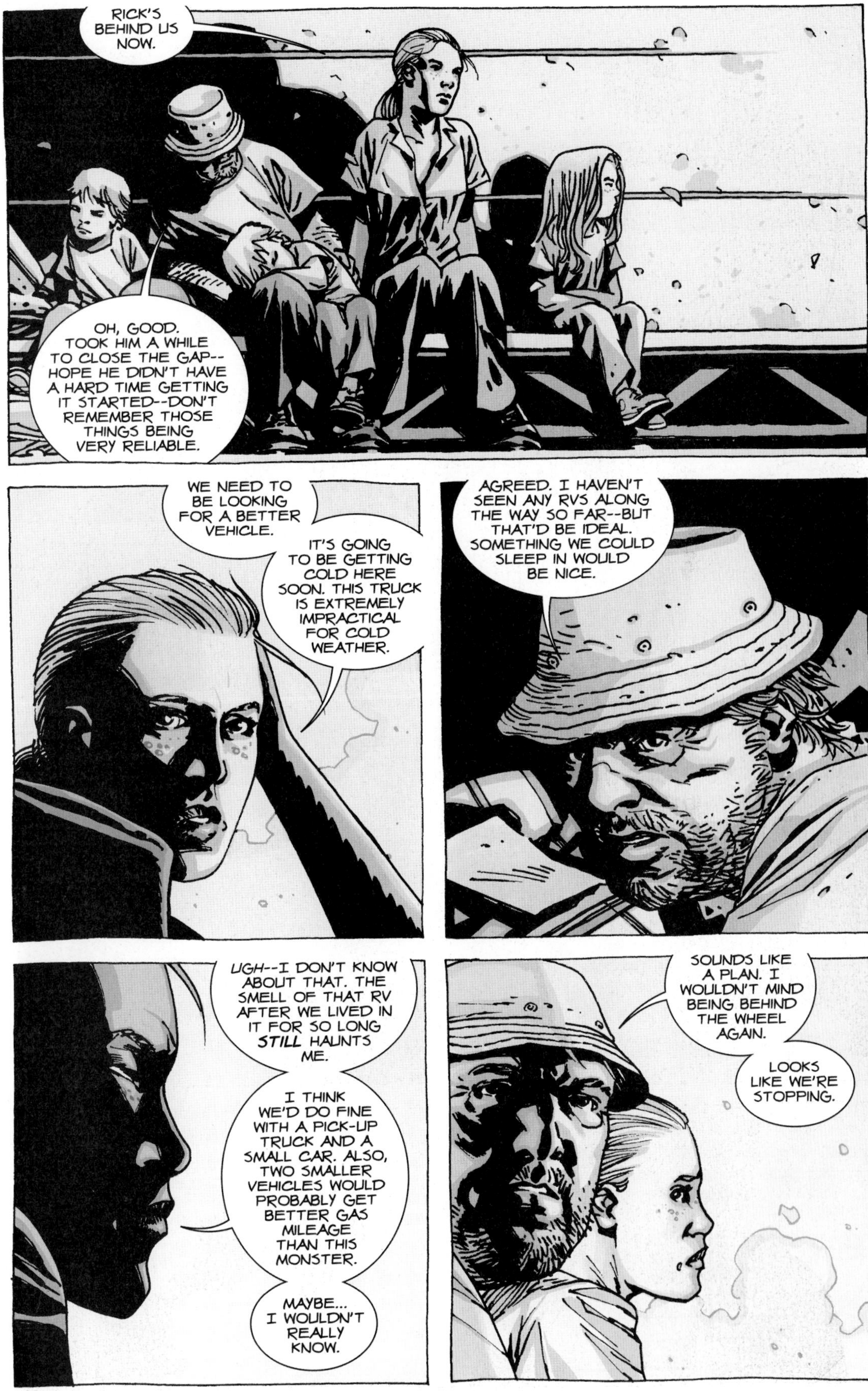
RICK'S BEHIND US NOW.
OH, GOOD. TOOK HIM A WHILE TO CLOSE THE GAP--HOPE HE DIDN'T HAVE A HARD TIME GETTING IT STARTED--DON'T REMEMBER THOSE THINGS BEING VERY RELIABLE.
WE NEED TO BE LOOKING FOR A BETTER VEHICLE.
IT'S GOING TO BE GETTING COLD HERE SOON. THIS TRUCK IS EXTREMELY IMPRACTICAL FOR COLD WEATHER.
AGREED. I HAVEN'T SEEN ANY RVS ALONG THE WAY SO FAR--BUT THAT'D BE IDEAL. SOMETHING WE COULD SLEEP IN WOULD BE NICE.
UGH--I DON'T KNOW ABOUT THAT. THE SMELL OF THAT RV AFTER WE LIVED IN IT FOR SO LONG STILL HAUNTS ME.
I THINK WE'D DO FINE WITH A PICK-UP TRUCK AND A SMALL CAR. ALSO, TWO SMALLER VEHICLES WOULD PROBABLY GET BETTER GAS MILEAGE THAN THIS MONSTER.
MAYBE... I WOULDN'T REALLY KNOW.
SOUNDS LIKE A PLAN. I WOULDN'T MIND BEING BEHIND THE WHEEL AGAIN.
LOOKS LIKE WE'RE STOPPING.

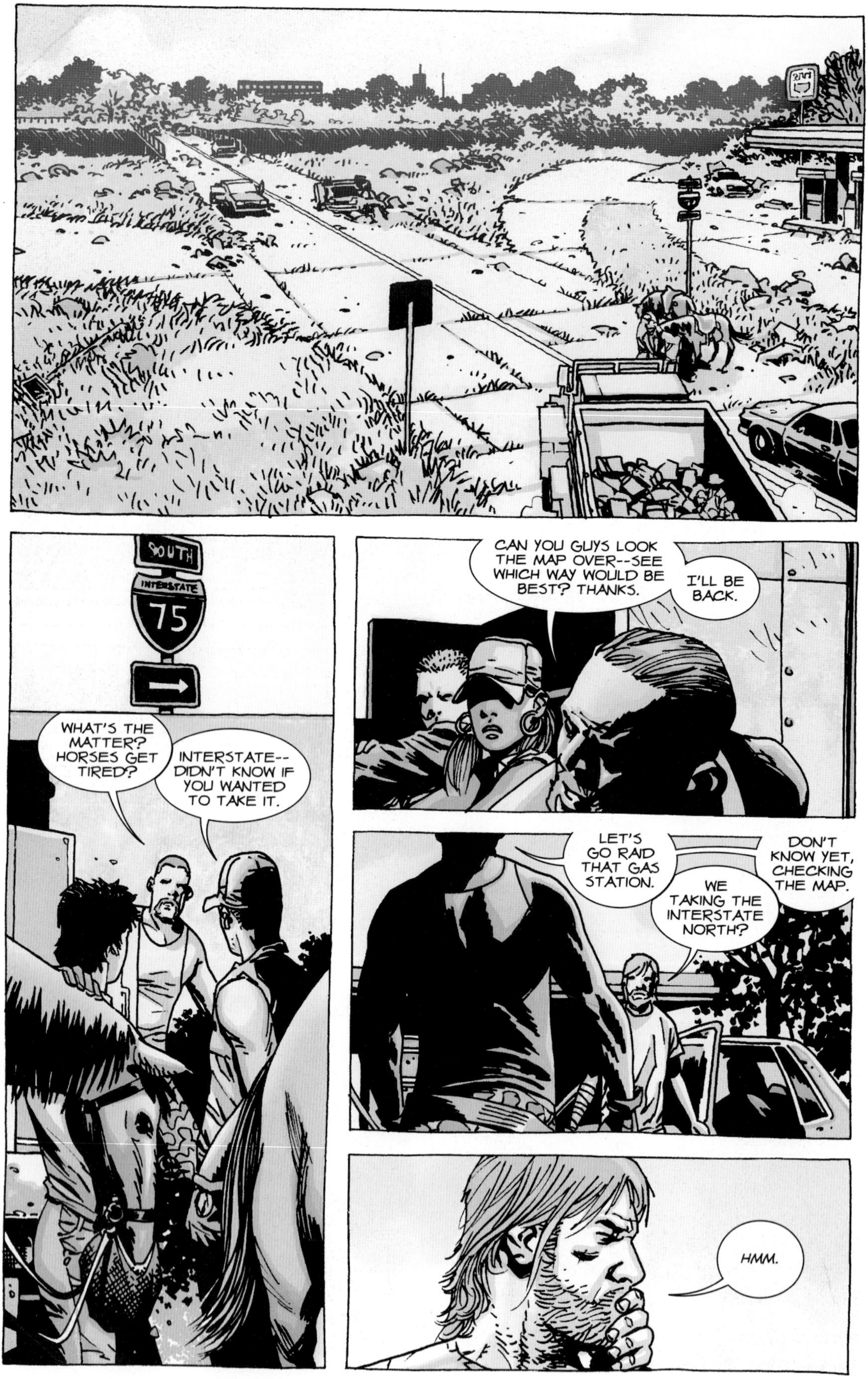
SOUTH
INTERSTATE
75
WHAT'S THE MATTER? HORSES GET TIRED?
INTERSTATE--DIDN'T KNOW IF YOU WANTED TO TAKE IT.
CAN YOU GUYS LOOK THE MAP OVER--SEE WHICH WAY WOULD BE BEST? THANKS.
I'LL BE BACK.
LET'S GO RAID THAT GAS STATION.
WE TAKING THE INTERSTATE NORTH?
DON'T KNOW YET, CHECKING THE MAP.
HMM.

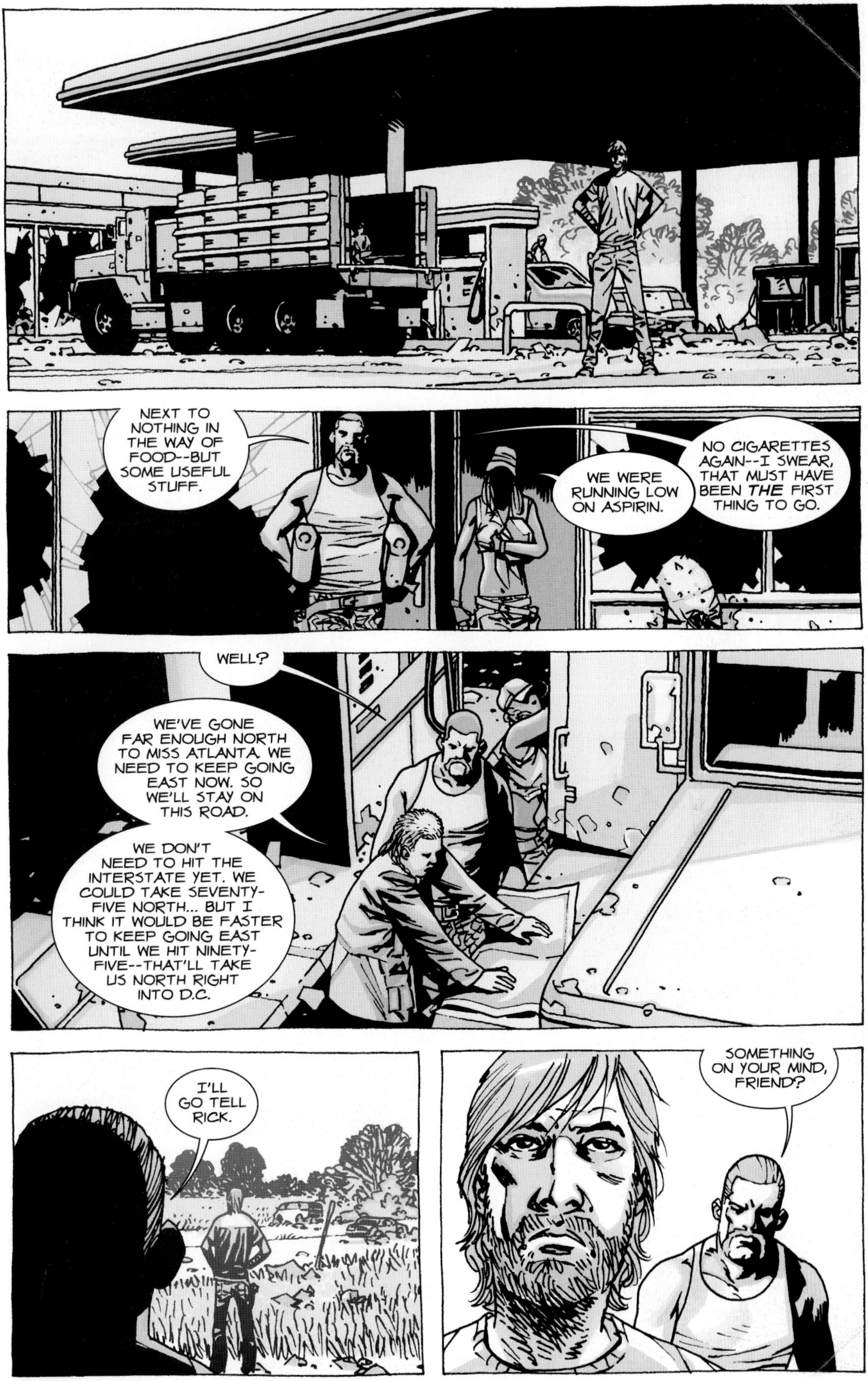
NEXT TO NOTHING IN THE WAY OF FOOD--BUT SOME USEFUL STUFF.
WE WERE RUNNING LOW ON ASPIRIN.
NO CIGARETTES AGAIN--I SWEAR, THAT MUST HAVE BEEN THE FIRST THING TO GO.
WELL?
WE'VE GONE FAR ENOUGH NORTH TO MISS ATLANTA. WE NEED TO KEEP GOING EAST NOW. SO WE'LL STAY ON THIS ROAD.
WE DON'T NEED TO HIT THE INTERSTATE YET. WE COULD TAKE SEVENTY-FIVE NORTH... BUT I THINK IT WOULD BE FASTER TO KEEP GOING EAST UNTIL WE HIT NINETY-FIVE--THAT'LL TAKE US NORTH RIGHT INTO D.C.
I'LL GO TELL RICK.
SOMETHING ON YOUR MIND, FRIEND?

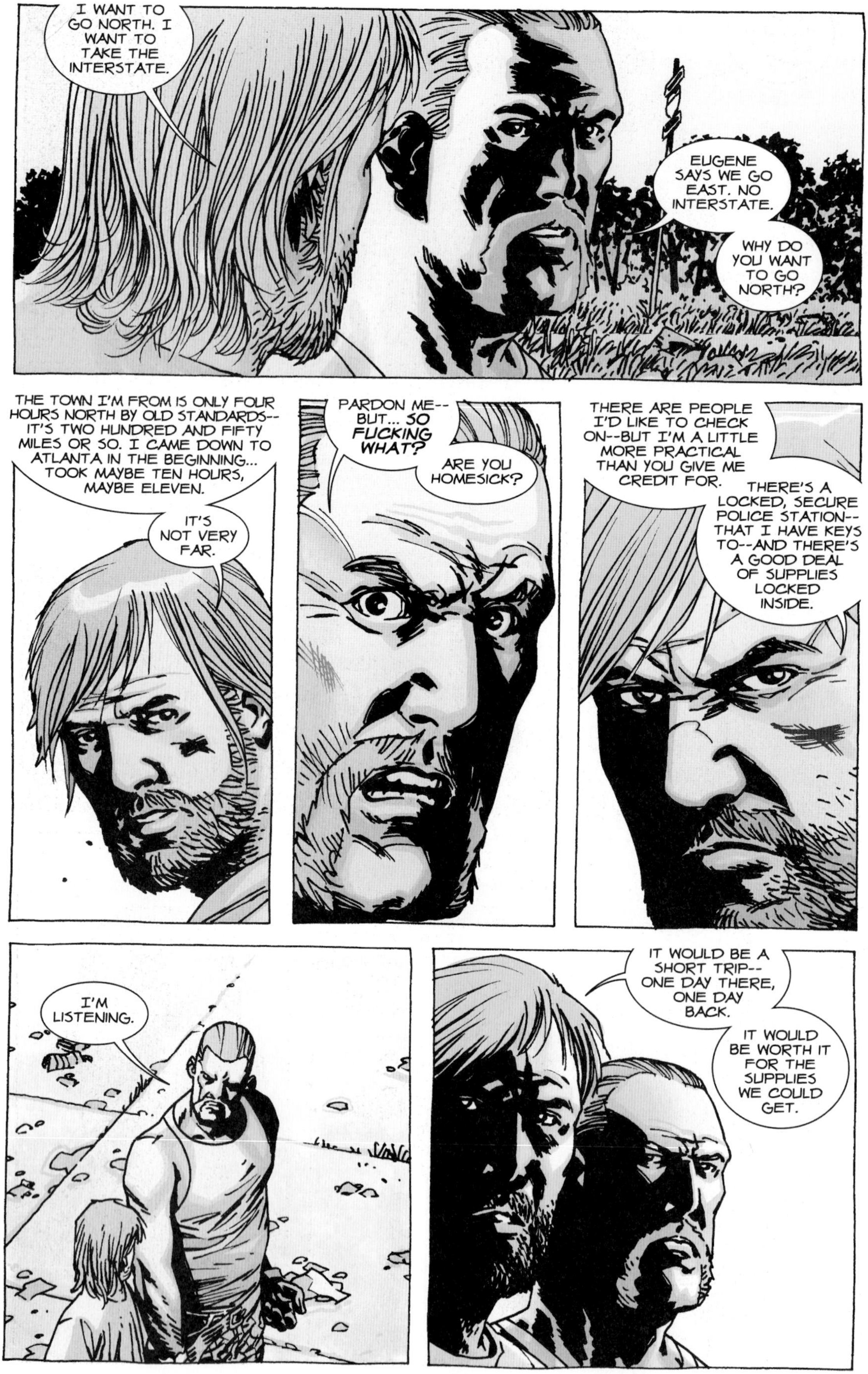

I WANT TO GO NORTH. I WANT TO TAKE THE INTERSTATE.
EUGENE SAYS WE GO EAST. NO INTERSTATE.
WHY DO YOU WANT TO GO NORTH?
THE TOWN I'M FROM IS ONLY FOUR HOURS NORTH BY OLD STANDARDS-- IT'S TWO HUNDRED AND FIFTY MILES OR SO. I CAME DOWN TO ATLANTA IN THE BEGINNING... TOOK MAYBE TEN HOURS, MAYBE ELEVEN.
IT'S NOT VERY FAR.
PARDON ME-- BUT... *SO FUCKING WHAT?*
ARE YOU HOMESICK?
THERE ARE PEOPLE I'D LIKE TO CHECK ON--BUT I'M A LITTLE MORE PRACTICAL THAN YOU GIVE ME CREDIT FOR.
THERE'S A LOCKED, SECURE POLICE STATION-- THAT I HAVE KEYS TO--AND THERE'S A GOOD DEAL OF SUPPLIES LOCKED INSIDE.
I'M LISTENING.
IT WOULD BE A SHORT TRIP-- ONE DAY THERE, ONE DAY BACK.
IT WOULD BE WORTH IT FOR THE SUPPLIES WE COULD GET.

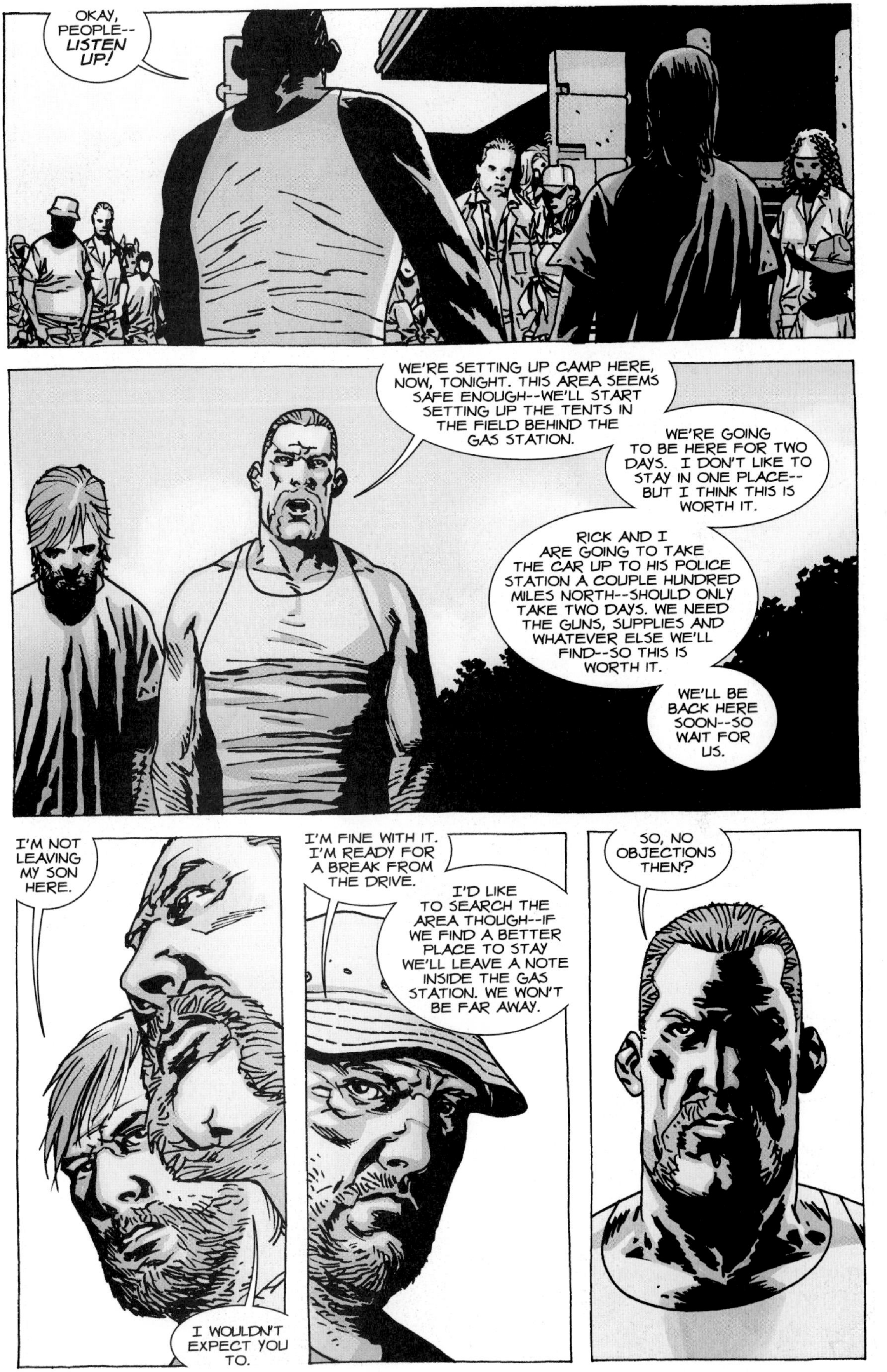
OKAY, PEOPLE-- LISTEN UP!
WE'RE SETTING UP CAMP HERE, NOW, TONIGHT. THIS AREA SEEMS SAFE ENOUGH--WE'LL START SETTING UP THE TENTS IN THE FIELD BEHIND THE GAS STATION.
WE'RE GOING TO BE HERE FOR TWO DAYS. I DON'T LIKE TO STAY IN ONE PLACE-- BUT I THINK THIS IS WORTH IT.
RICK AND I ARE GOING TO TAKE THE CAR UP TO HIS POLICE STATION A COUPLE HUNDRED MILES NORTH--SHOULD ONLY TAKE TWO DAYS. WE NEED THE GUNS, SUPPLIES AND WHATEVER ELSE WE'LL FIND--SO THIS IS WORTH IT.
WE'LL BE BACK HERE SOON--SO WAIT FOR US.
I'M NOT LEAVING MY SON HERE.
I WOULDN'T EXPECT YOU TO.
I'M FINE WITH IT. I'M READY FOR A BREAK FROM THE DRIVE.
I'D LIKE TO SEARCH THE AREA THOUGH--IF WE FIND A BETTER PLACE TO STAY WE'LL LEAVE A NOTE INSIDE THE GAS STATION. WE WON'T BE FAR AWAY.
SO, NO OBJECTIONS THEN?

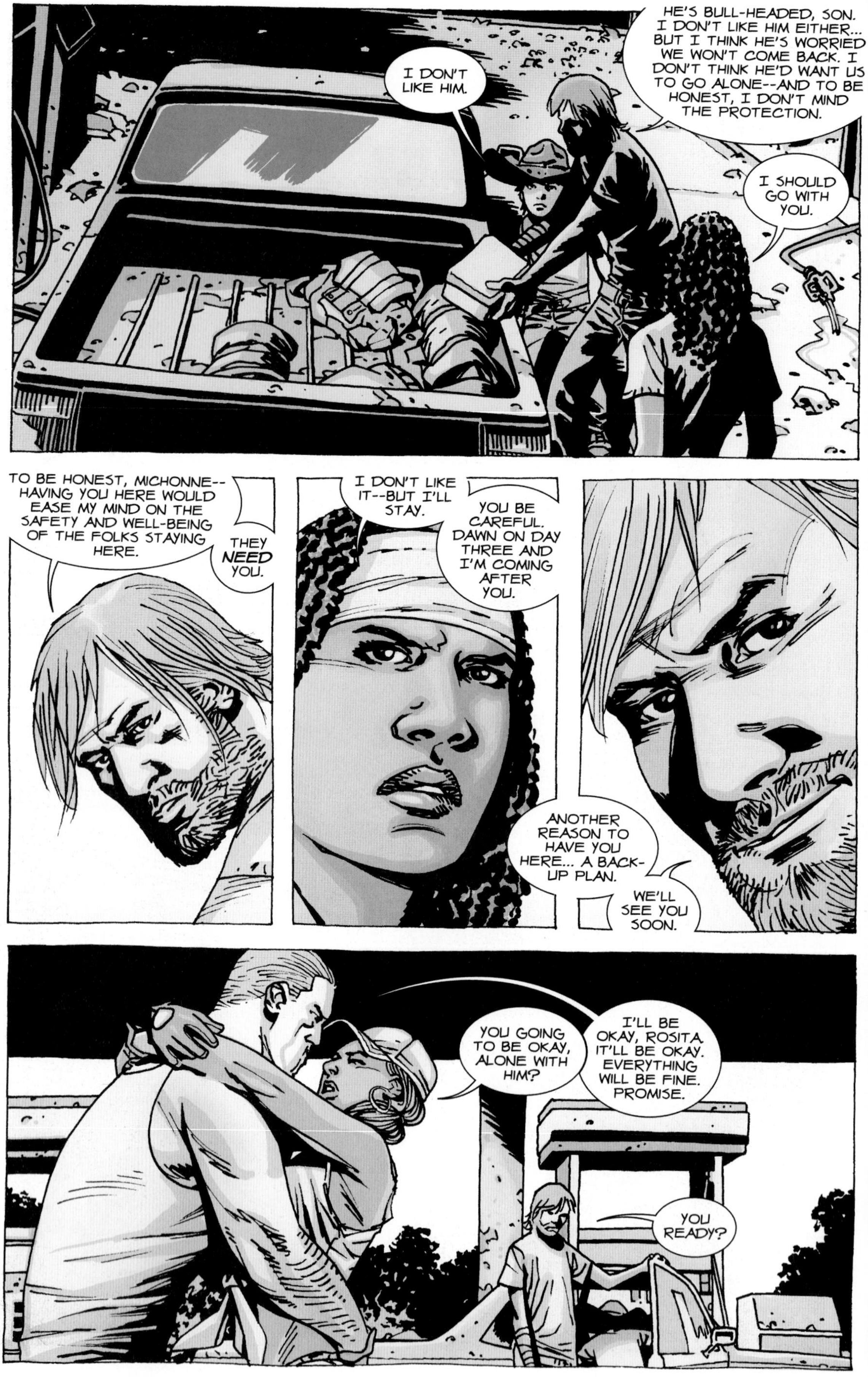
I DON'T LIKE HIM.
HE'S BULL-HEADED, SON. I DON'T LIKE HIM EITHER... BUT I THINK HE'S WORRIED WE WON'T COME BACK. I DON'T THINK HE'D WANT US TO GO ALONE--AND TO BE HONEST, I DON'T MIND THE PROTECTION.
I SHOULD GO WITH YOU.
TO BE HONEST, MICHONNE-- HAVING YOU HERE WOULD EASE MY MIND ON THE SAFETY AND WELL-BEING OF THE FOLKS STAYING HERE.
THEY *NEED* YOU.
I DON'T LIKE IT--BUT I'LL STAY.
YOU BE CAREFUL. DAWN ON DAY THREE AND I'M COMING AFTER YOU.
ANOTHER REASON TO HAVE YOU HERE... A BACK-UP PLAN.
WE'LL SEE YOU SOON.
YOU GOING TO BE OKAY, ALONE WITH HIM?
I'LL BE OKAY, ROSITA. IT'LL BE OKAY. EVERYTHING WILL BE FINE. PROMISE.
YOU READY?

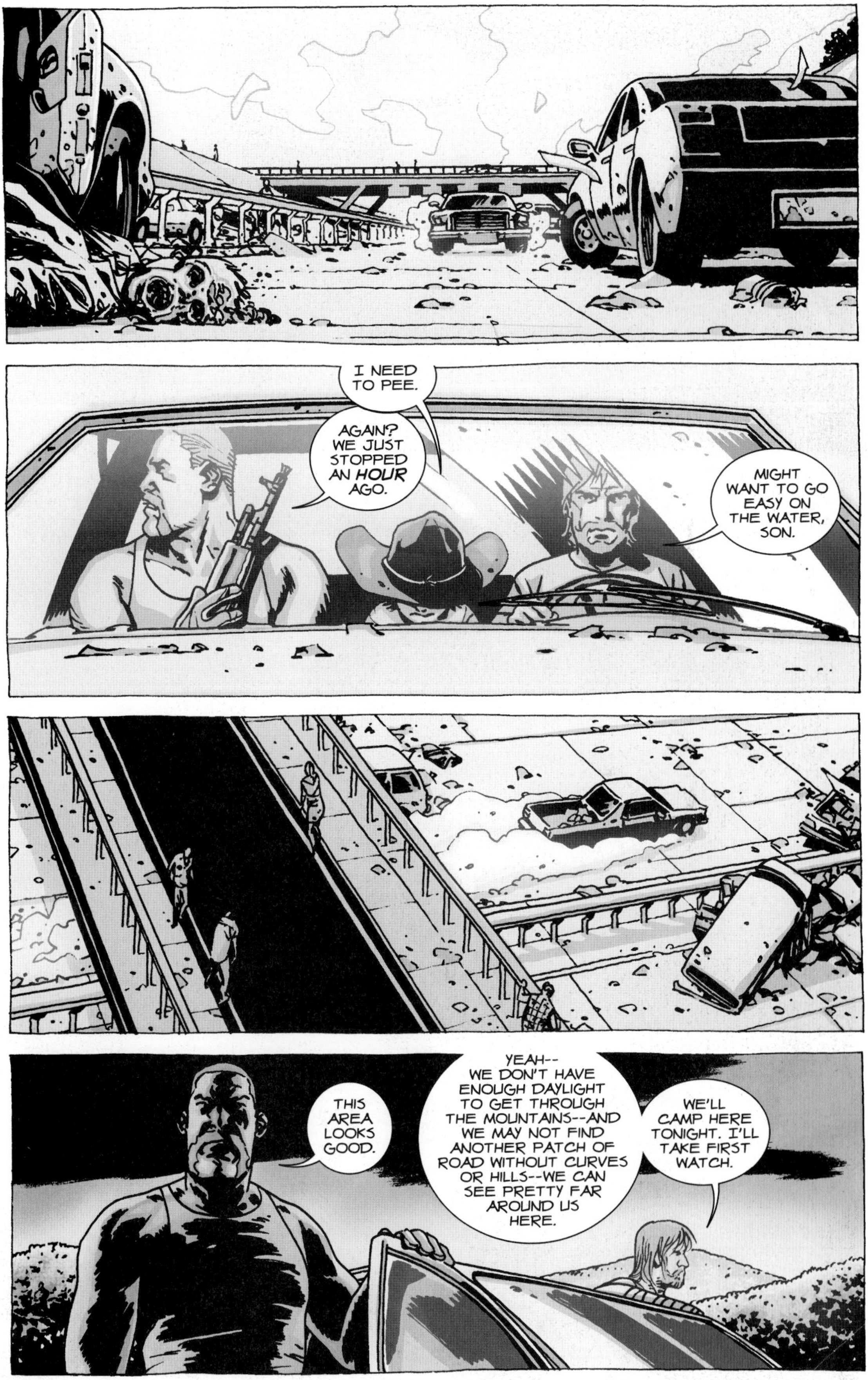
I NEED TO PEE.
AGAIN? WE JUST STOPPED AN HOUR AGO.
MIGHT WANT TO GO EASY ON THE WATER, SON.
THIS AREA LOOKS GOOD.
YEAH-- WE DON'T HAVE ENOUGH DAYLIGHT TO GET THROUGH THE MOUNTAINS--AND WE MAY NOT FIND ANOTHER PATCH OF ROAD WITHOUT CURVES OR HILLS--WE CAN SEE PRETTY FAR AROUND US HERE.
WE'LL CAMP HERE TONIGHT. I'LL TAKE FIRST WATCH.

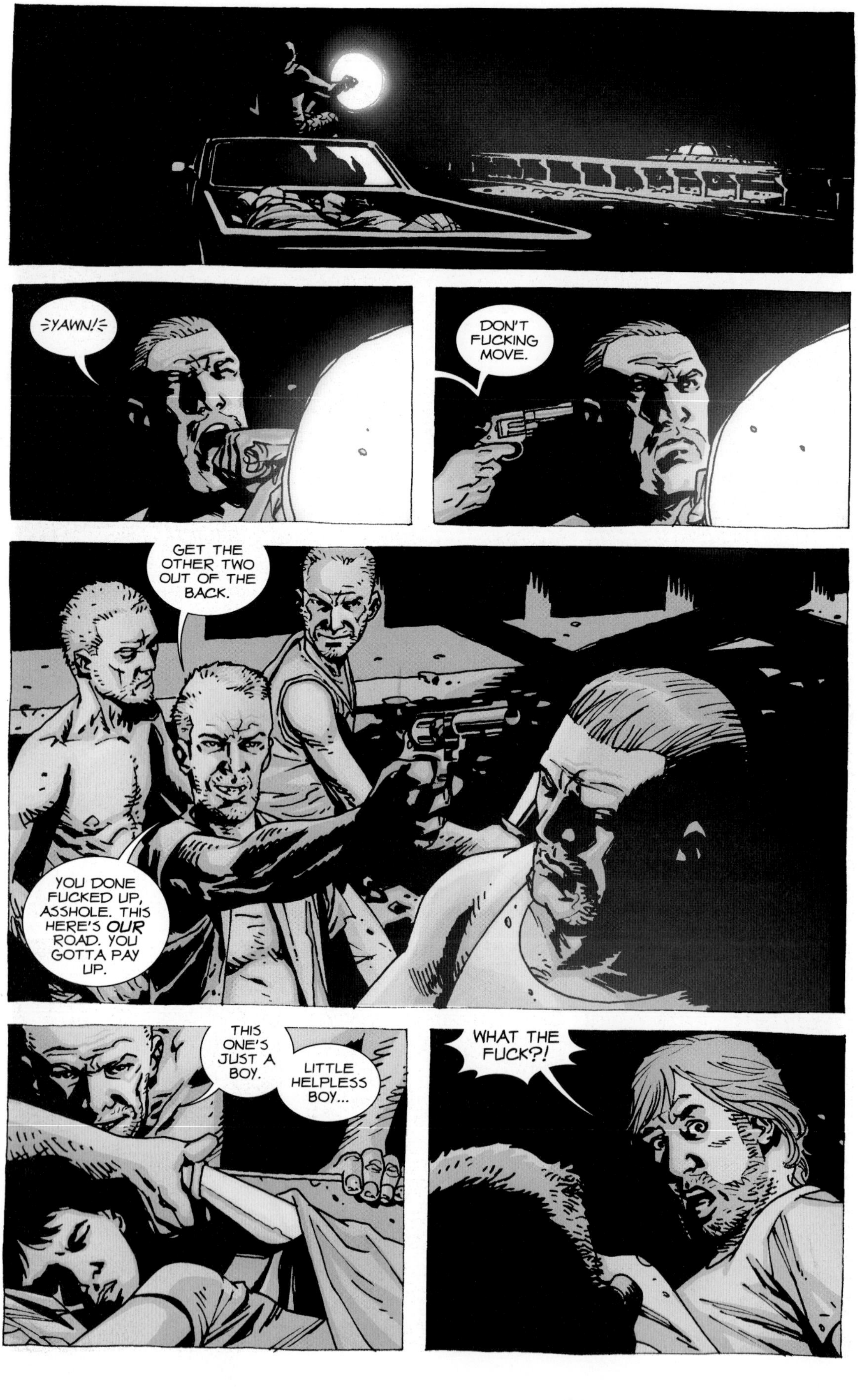
=YAWN!=
DON'T FUCKING MOVE.
GET THE OTHER TWO OUT OF THE BACK.
YOU DONE FUCKED UP, ASSHOLE. THIS HERE'S *OUR* ROAD. YOU GOTTA PAY UP.
THIS ONE'S JUST A BOY.
LITTLE HELPLESS BOY...
WHAT THE FUCK?!

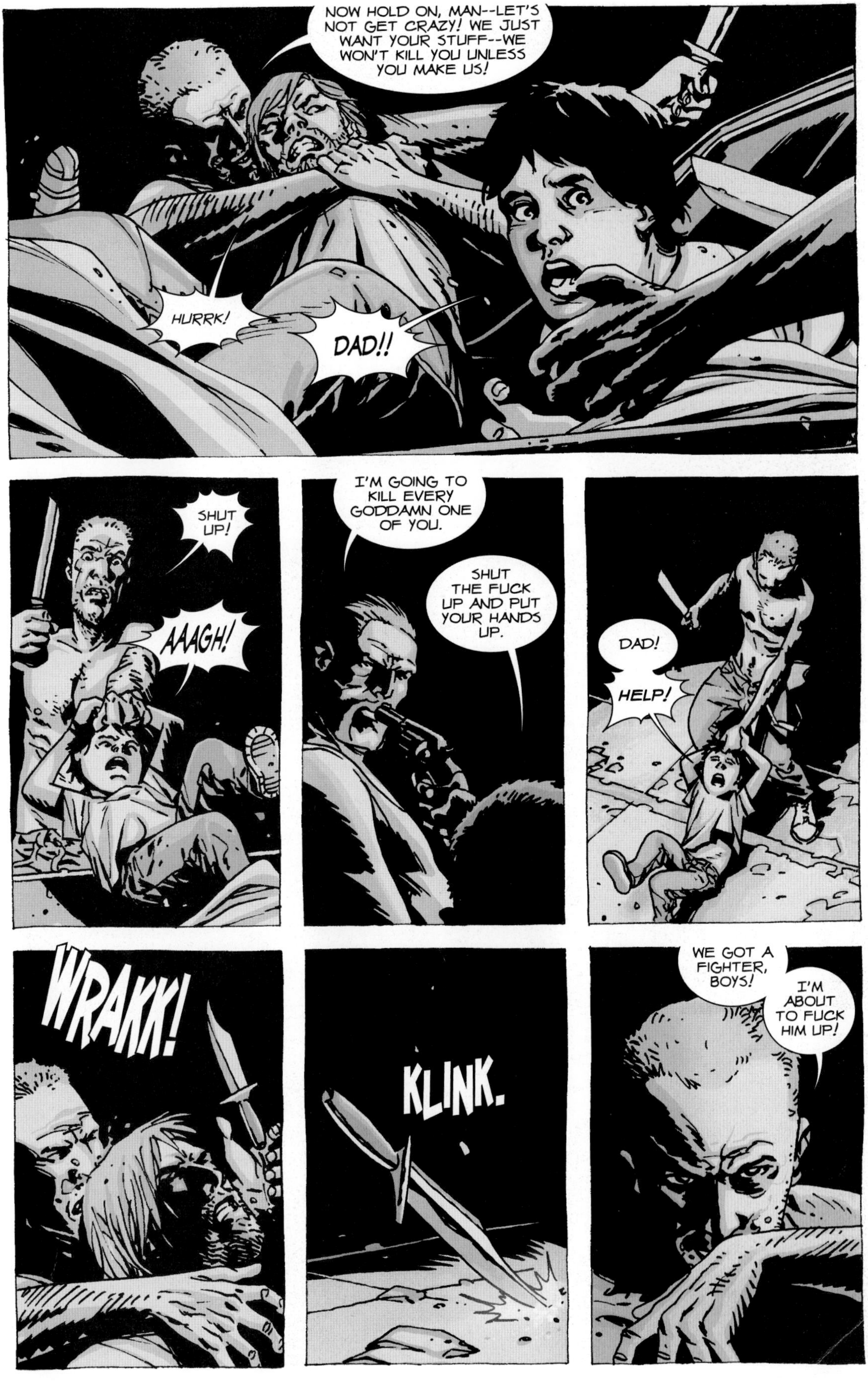
NOW HOLD ON, MAN--LET'S NOT GET CRAZY! WE JUST WANT YOUR STUFF--WE WON'T KILL YOU UNLESS YOU MAKE US!
HURRK!
DAD!!
SHUT UP!
AAAGH!
I'M GOING TO KILL EVERY GODDAMN ONE OF YOU.
SHUT THE FUCK UP AND PUT YOUR HANDS UP.
DAD!
HELP!
WRAKK!
KLINK.
WE GOT A FIGHTER, BOYS!
I'M ABOUT TO FUCK HIM UP!

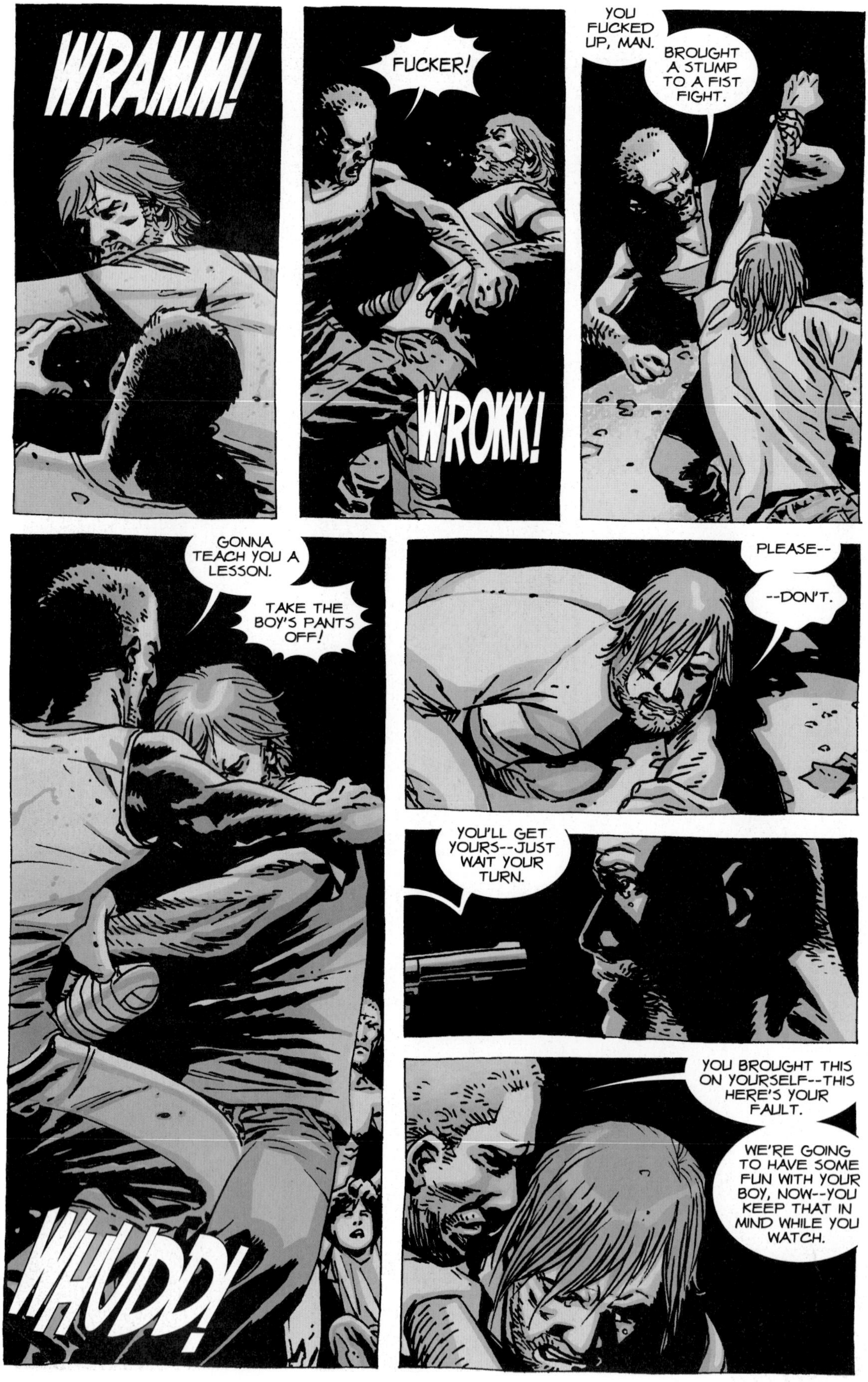

WRAMM!
FUCKER!
WROKK!
YOU FUCKED UP, MAN.
BROUGHT A STUMP TO A FIST FIGHT.
GONNA TEACH YOU A LESSON.
TAKE THE BOY'S PANTS OFF!
WHUDD!
PLEASE--
--DON'T.
YOU'LL GET YOURS--JUST WAIT YOUR TURN.
YOU BROUGHT THIS ON YOURSELF--THIS HERE'S YOUR FAULT.
WE'RE GOING TO HAVE SOME FUN WITH YOUR BOY, NOW--YOU KEEP THAT IN MIND WHILE YOU WATCH.

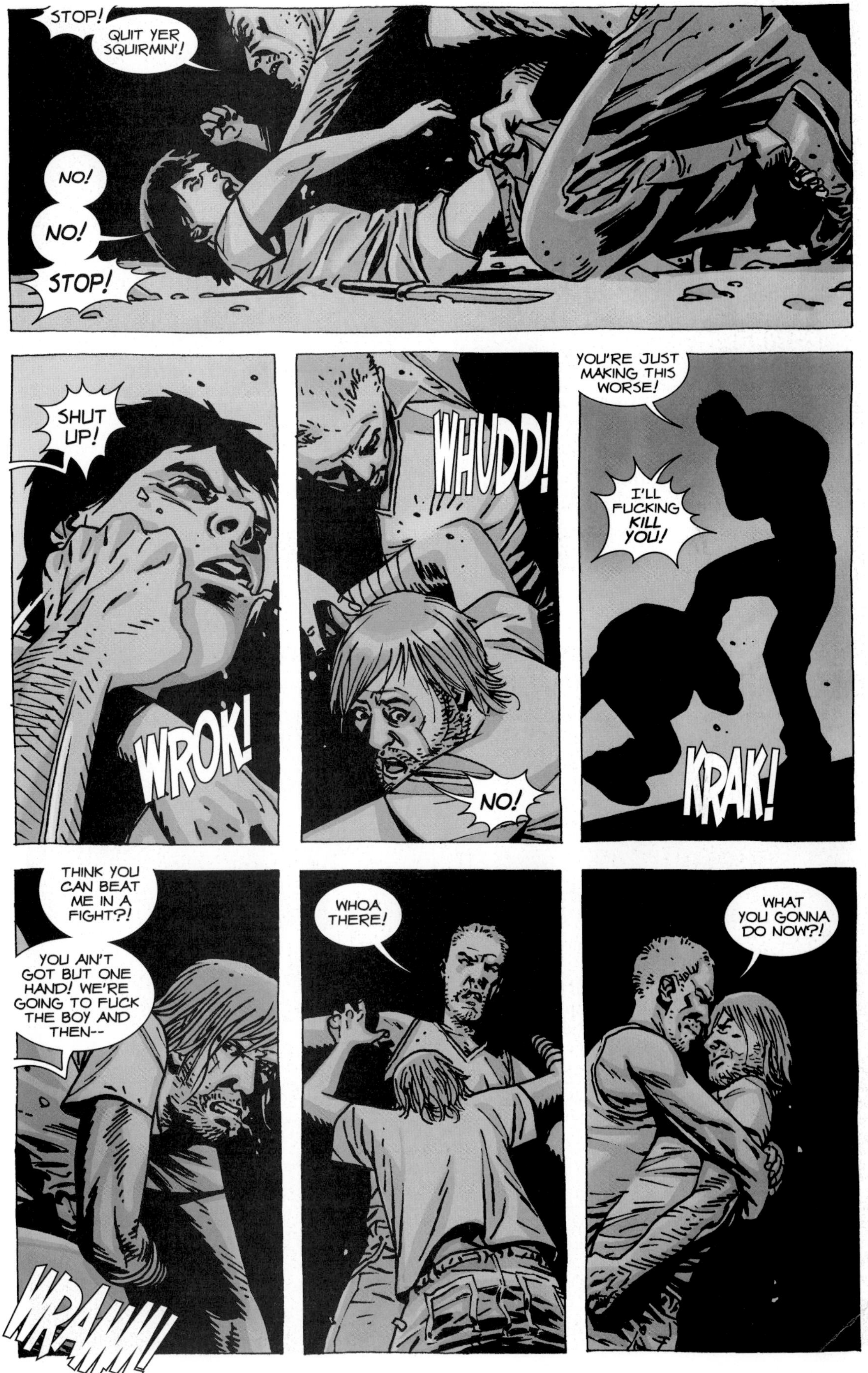

STOP!
QUIT YER SQUIRMIN'!
NO!
NO!
STOP!
SHUT UP!
WROK!
WHUDD!
NO!
YOU'RE JUST MAKING THIS WORSE!
I'LL FUCKING KILL YOU!
KRAK!
THINK YOU CAN BEAT ME IN A FIGHT?!
YOU AIN'T GOT BUT ONE HAND! WE'RE GOING TO FUCK THE BOY AND THEN--
WRAMM!
WHOA THERE!
WHAT YOU GONNA DO NOW?!

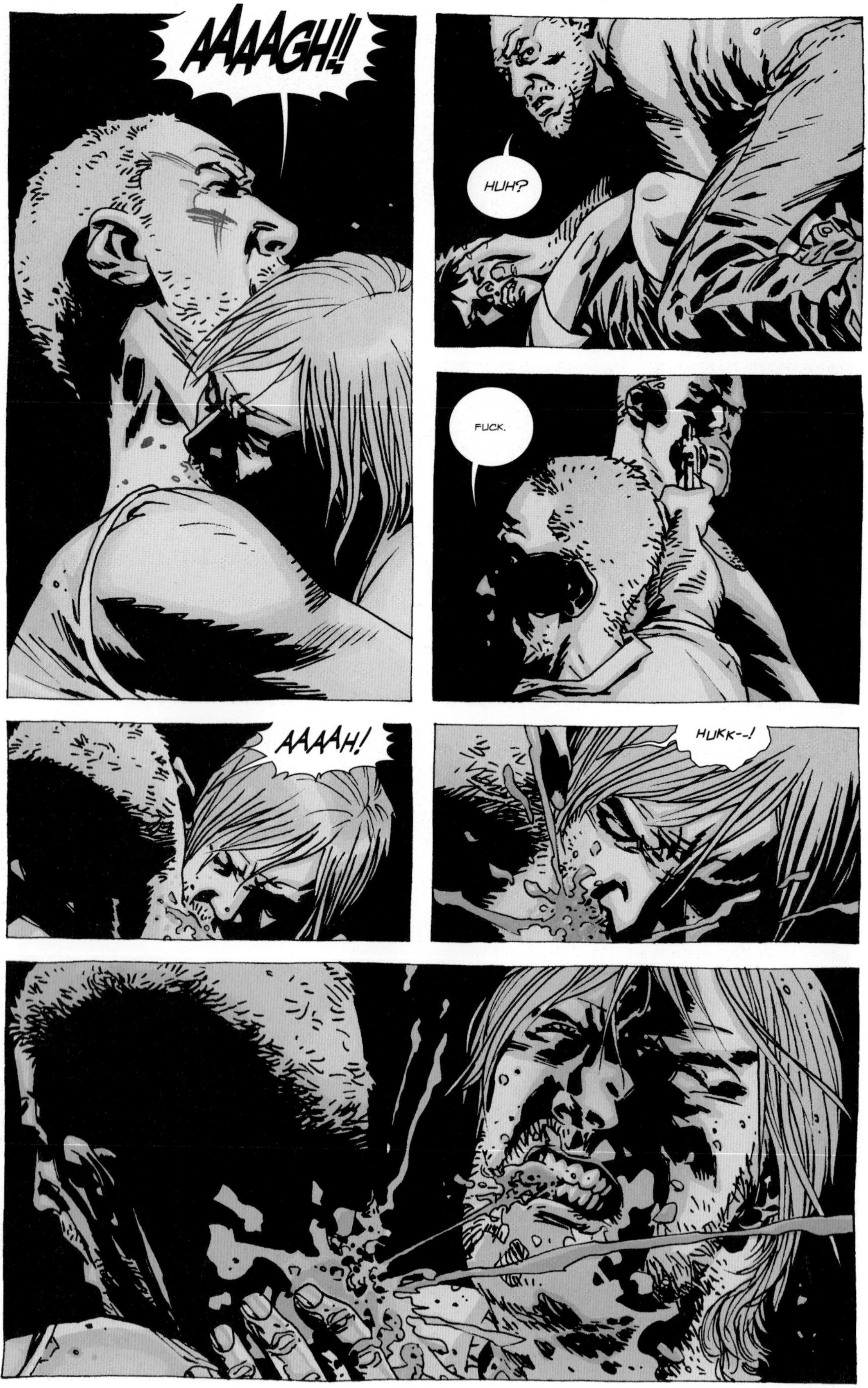
AAAAGH!!
HUH?
FUCK.
AAAAH!
HUKK--!

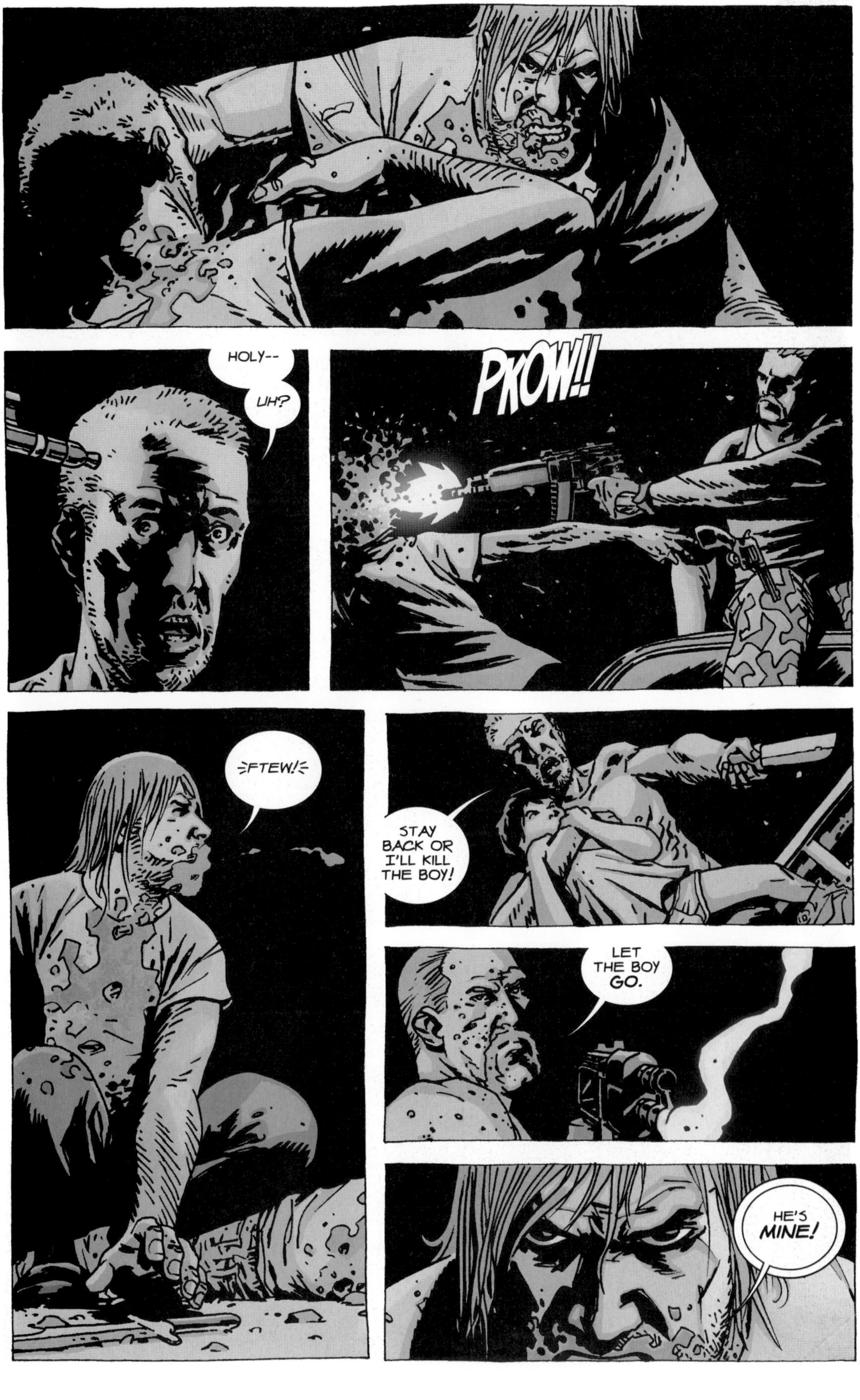
HOLY--
UH?
PKOW!!
FTEW!
STAY BACK OR I'LL KILL THE BOY!
LET THE BOY GO.
HE'S MINE!

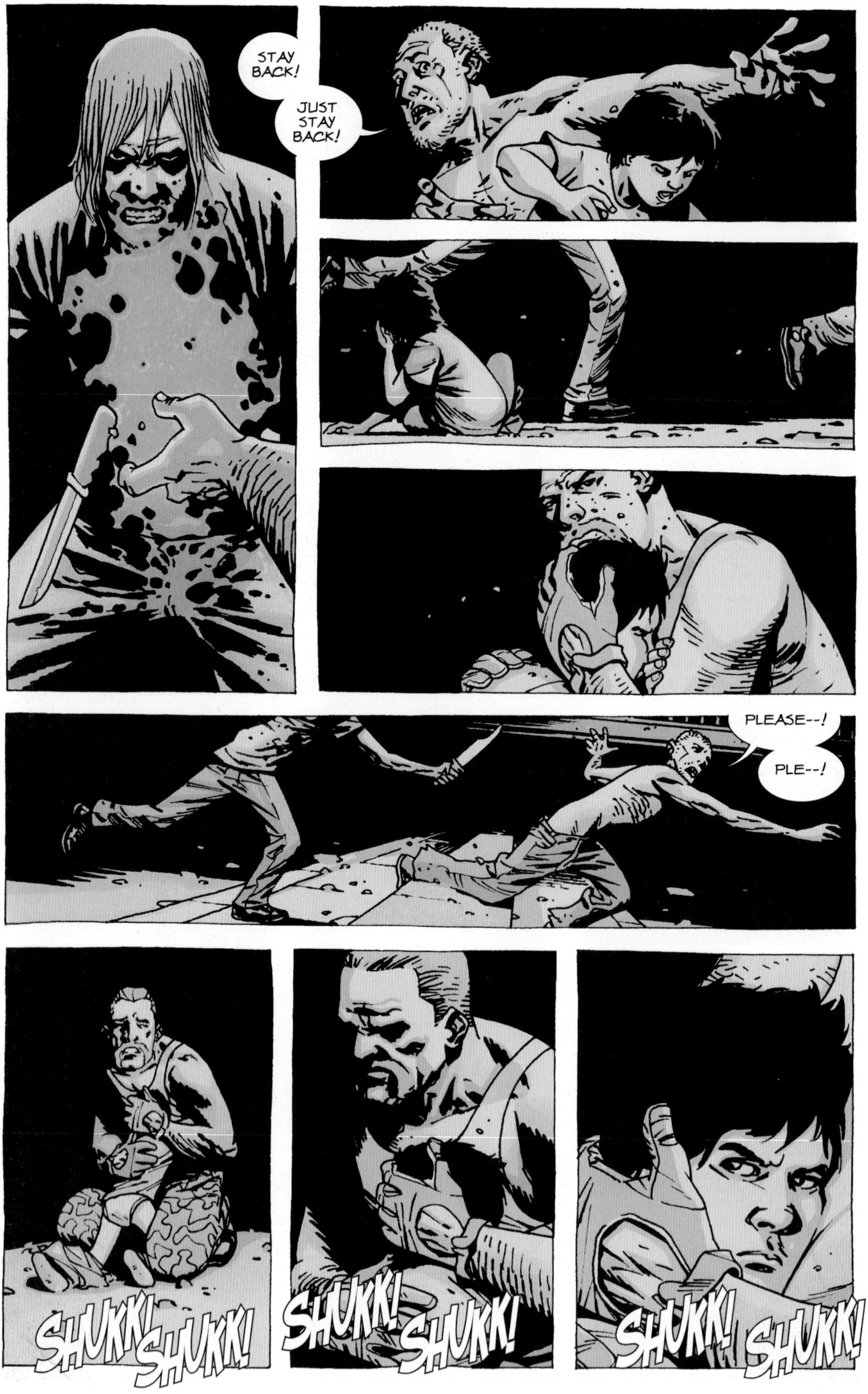
STAY BACK!
JUST STAY BACK!
PLEASE--!
PLE--!
SHUKK! SHUKK!
SHUKK! SHUKK!
SHUKK! SHUKK!

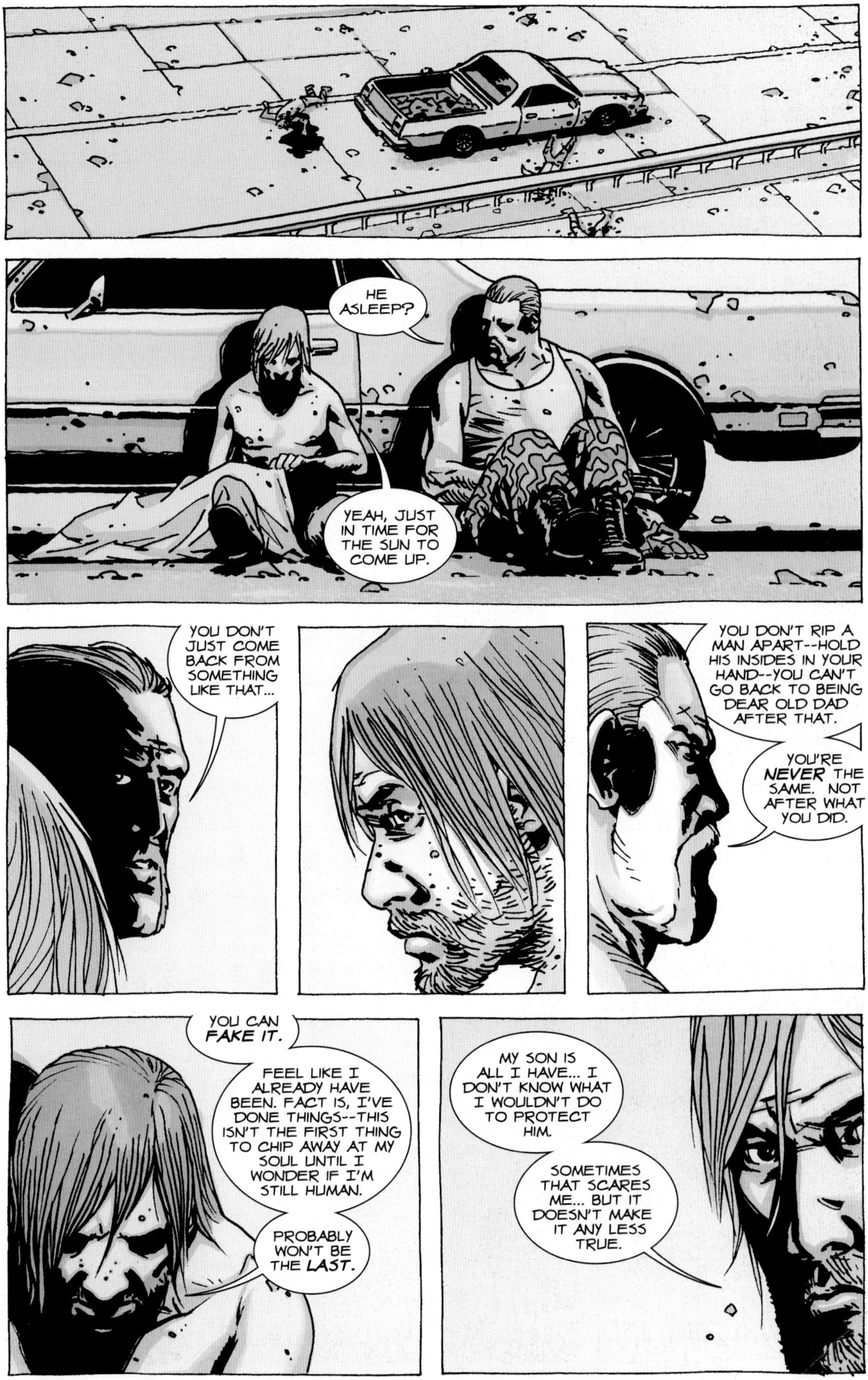

HE ASLEEP?
YEAH, JUST IN TIME FOR THE SUN TO COME UP.
YOU DON'T JUST COME BACK FROM SOMETHING LIKE THAT...
YOU DON'T RIP A MAN APART--HOLD HIS INSIDES IN YOUR HAND--YOU CAN'T GO BACK TO BEING DEAR OLD DAD AFTER THAT.
YOU'RE NEVER THE SAME. NOT AFTER WHAT YOU DID.
YOU CAN FAKE IT.
FEEL LIKE I ALREADY HAVE BEEN. FACT IS, I'VE DONE THINGS--THIS ISN'T THE FIRST THING TO CHIP AWAY AT MY SOUL UNTIL I WONDER IF I'M STILL HUMAN.
PROBABLY WON'T BE THE LAST.
MY SON IS ALL I HAVE... I DON'T KNOW WHAT I WOULDN'T DO TO PROTECT HIM.
SOMETIMES THAT SCARES ME... BUT IT DOESN'T MAKE IT ANY LESS TRUE.

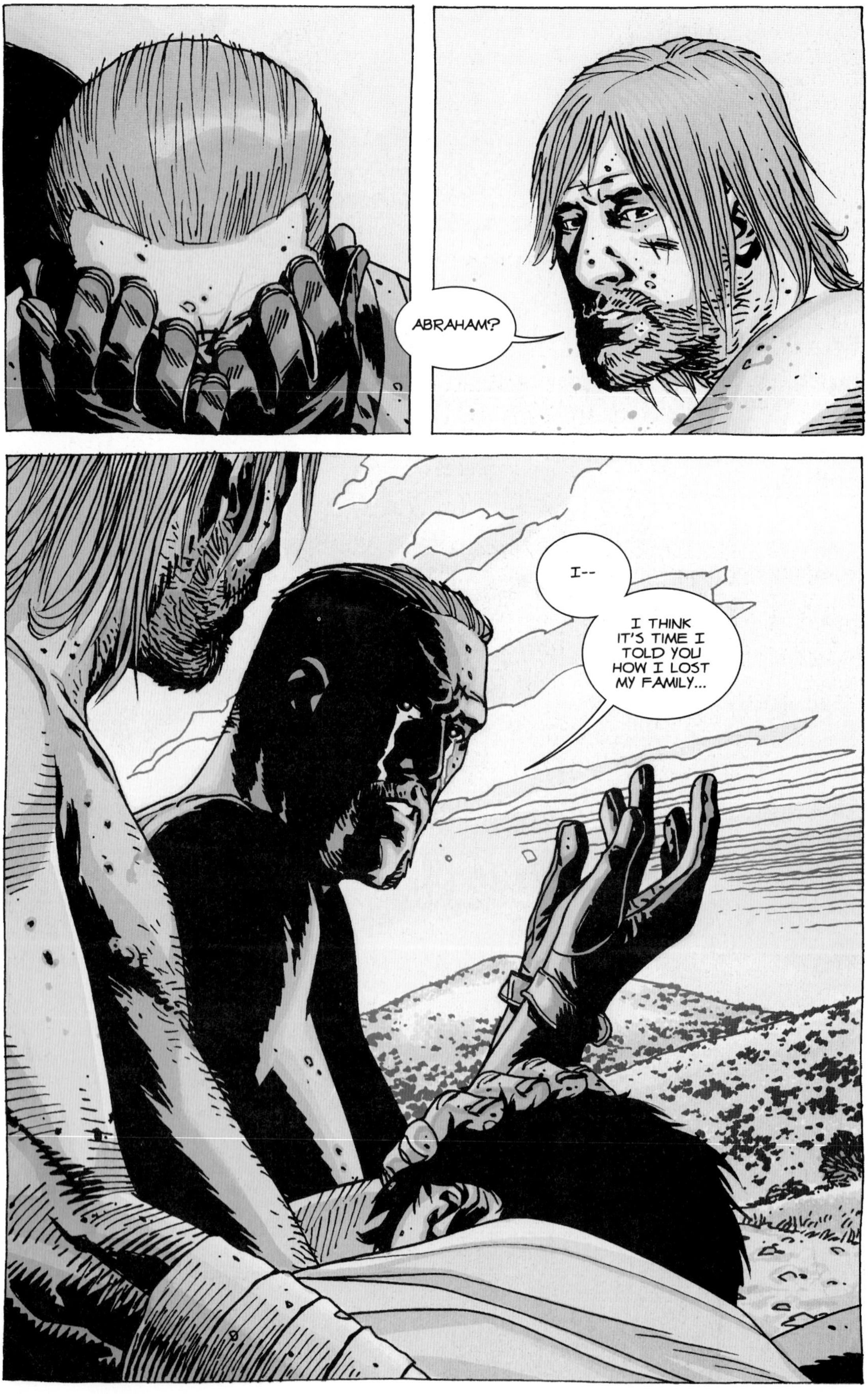
ABRAHAM?
I--
I THINK IT'S TIME I TOLD YOU HOW I LOST MY FAMILY...

...

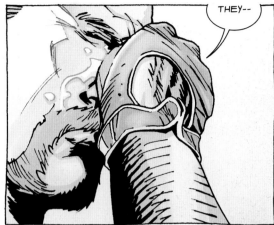
THEY--

IT'S OKAY, MAN... YOU DON'T HAVE TO--

AT FIRST, WHEN IT ALL STARTED, A GROUP OF SURVIVORS FORMED--LOCALS. WE BANDED TOGETHER FOR SECURITY.

FRIENDS... NEIGHBORS...

THEY *RAPED* MY WIFE AND DAUGHTER.

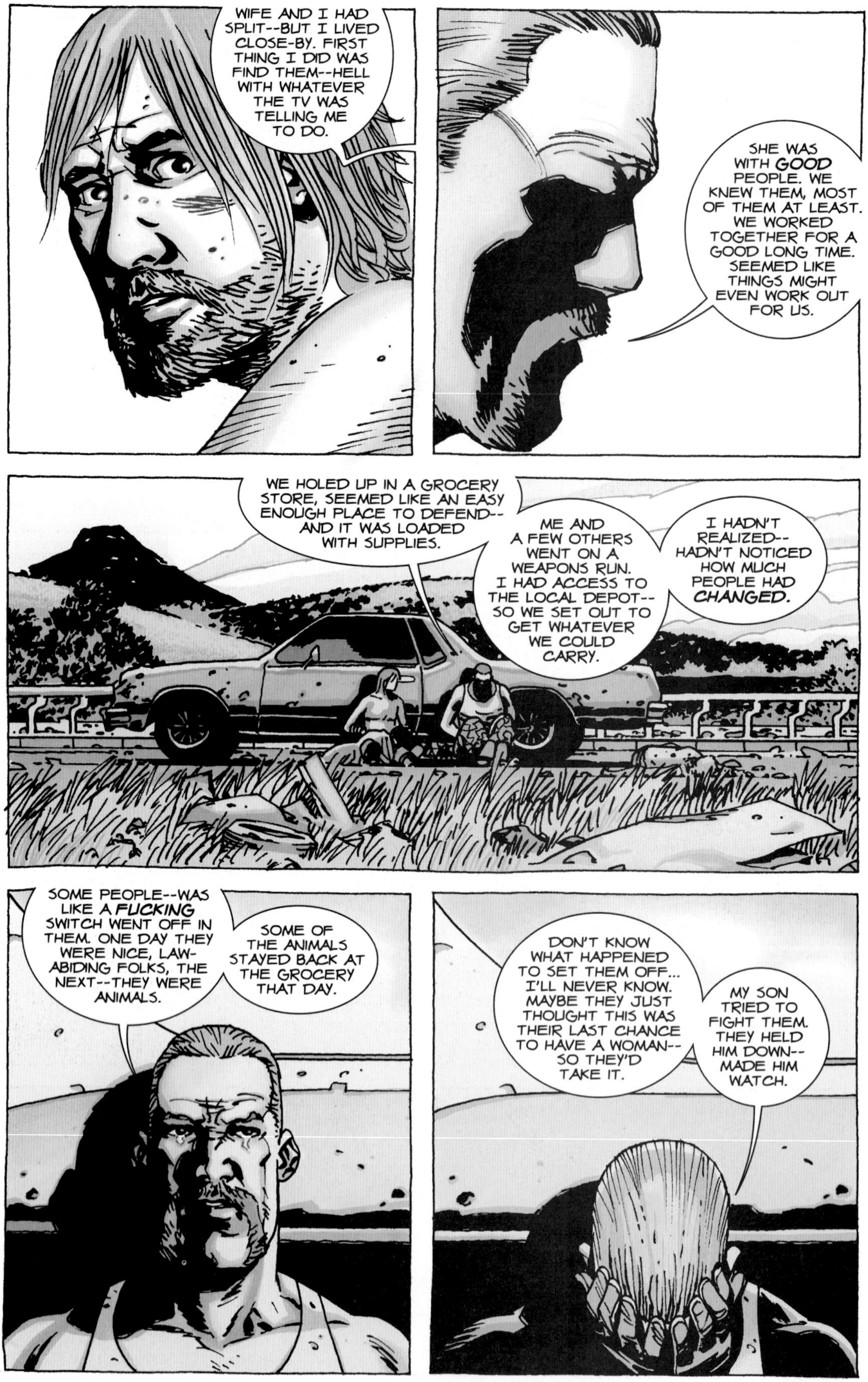
WIFE AND I HAD SPLIT--BUT I LIVED CLOSE-BY. FIRST THING I DID WAS FIND THEM--HELL WITH WHATEVER THE TV WAS TELLING ME TO DO.
SHE WAS WITH GOOD PEOPLE. WE KNEW THEM, MOST OF THEM AT LEAST. WE WORKED TOGETHER FOR A GOOD LONG TIME. SEEMED LIKE THINGS MIGHT EVEN WORK OUT FOR US.
WE HOLED UP IN A GROCERY STORE, SEEMED LIKE AN EASY ENOUGH PLACE TO DEFEND-- AND IT WAS LOADED WITH SUPPLIES.
ME AND A FEW OTHERS WENT ON A WEAPONS RUN. I HAD ACCESS TO THE LOCAL DEPOT-- SO WE SET OUT TO GET WHATEVER WE COULD CARRY.
I HADN'T REALIZED-- HADN'T NOTICED HOW MUCH PEOPLE HAD CHANGED.
SOME PEOPLE--WAS LIKE A FUCKING SWITCH WENT OFF IN THEM. ONE DAY THEY WERE NICE, LAW-ABIDING FOLKS, THE NEXT--THEY WERE ANIMALS.
SOME OF THE ANIMALS STAYED BACK AT THE GROCERY THAT DAY.
DON'T KNOW WHAT HAPPENED TO SET THEM OFF... I'LL NEVER KNOW. MAYBE THEY JUST THOUGHT THIS WAS THEIR LAST CHANCE TO HAVE A WOMAN-- SO THEY'D TAKE IT.
MY SON TRIED TO FIGHT THEM. THEY HELD HIM DOWN-- MADE HIM WATCH.

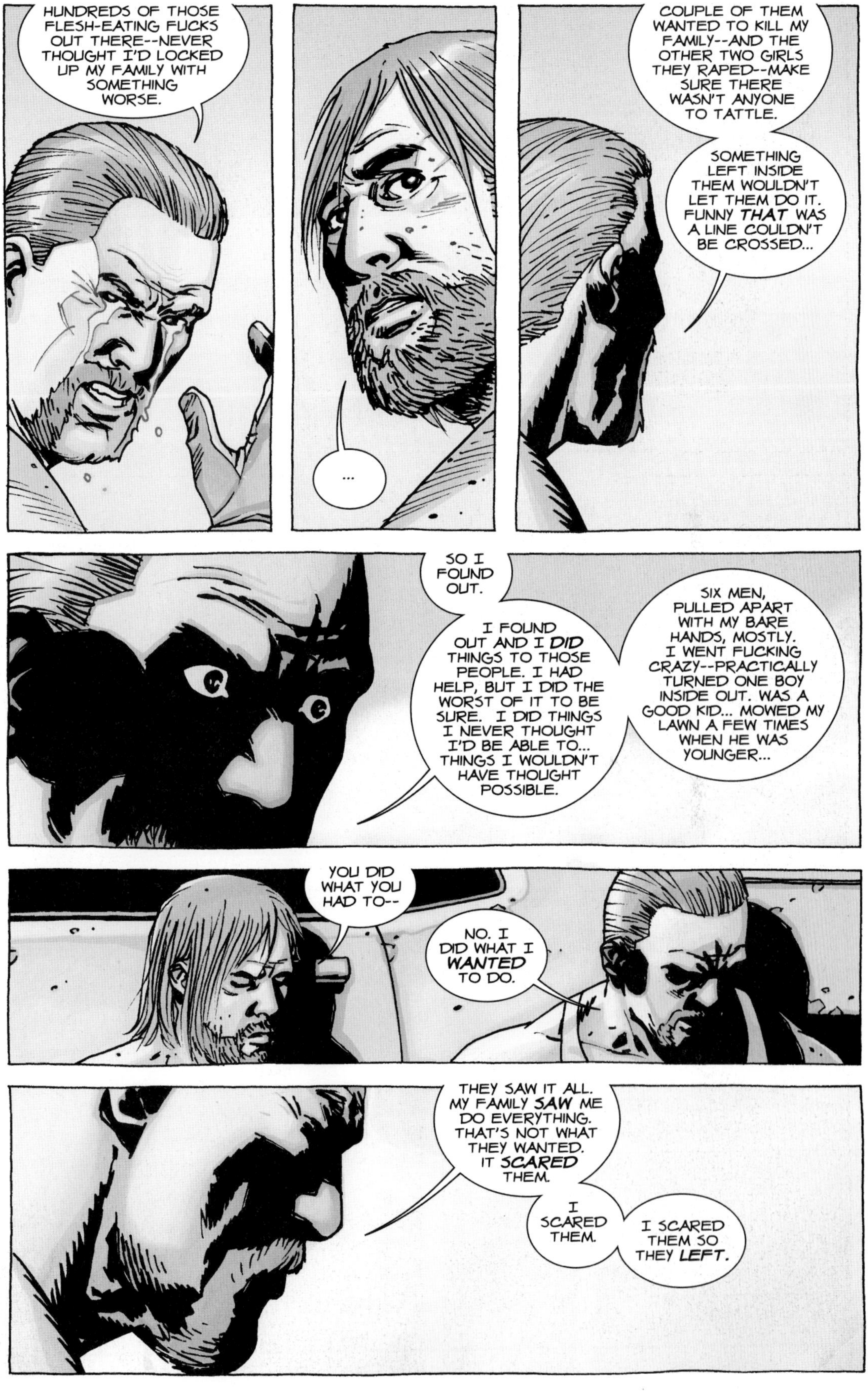
HUNDREDS OF THOSE FLESH-EATING FUCKS OUT THERE--NEVER THOUGHT I'D LOCKED UP MY FAMILY WITH SOMETHING WORSE.
...
COUPLE OF THEM WANTED TO KILL MY FAMILY--AND THE OTHER TWO GIRLS THEY RAPED--MAKE SURE THERE WASN'T ANYONE TO TATTLE.
SOMETHING LEFT INSIDE THEM WOULDN'T LET THEM DO IT. FUNNY THAT WAS A LINE COULDN'T BE CROSSED...
SO I FOUND OUT.
I FOUND OUT AND I DID THINGS TO THOSE PEOPLE. I HAD HELP, BUT I DID THE WORST OF IT TO BE SURE. I DID THINGS I NEVER THOUGHT I'D BE ABLE TO... THINGS I WOULDN'T HAVE THOUGHT POSSIBLE.
SIX MEN, PULLED APART WITH MY BARE HANDS, MOSTLY. I WENT FUCKING CRAZY--PRACTICALLY TURNED ONE BOY INSIDE OUT. WAS A GOOD KID... MOWED MY LAWN A FEW TIMES WHEN HE WAS YOUNGER...
YOU DID WHAT YOU HAD TO--
NO. I DID WHAT I WANTED TO DO.
THEY SAW IT ALL. MY FAMILY SAW ME DO EVERYTHING. THAT'S NOT WHAT THEY WANTED. IT SCARED THEM.
I SCARED THEM.
I SCARED THEM SO THEY LEFT.

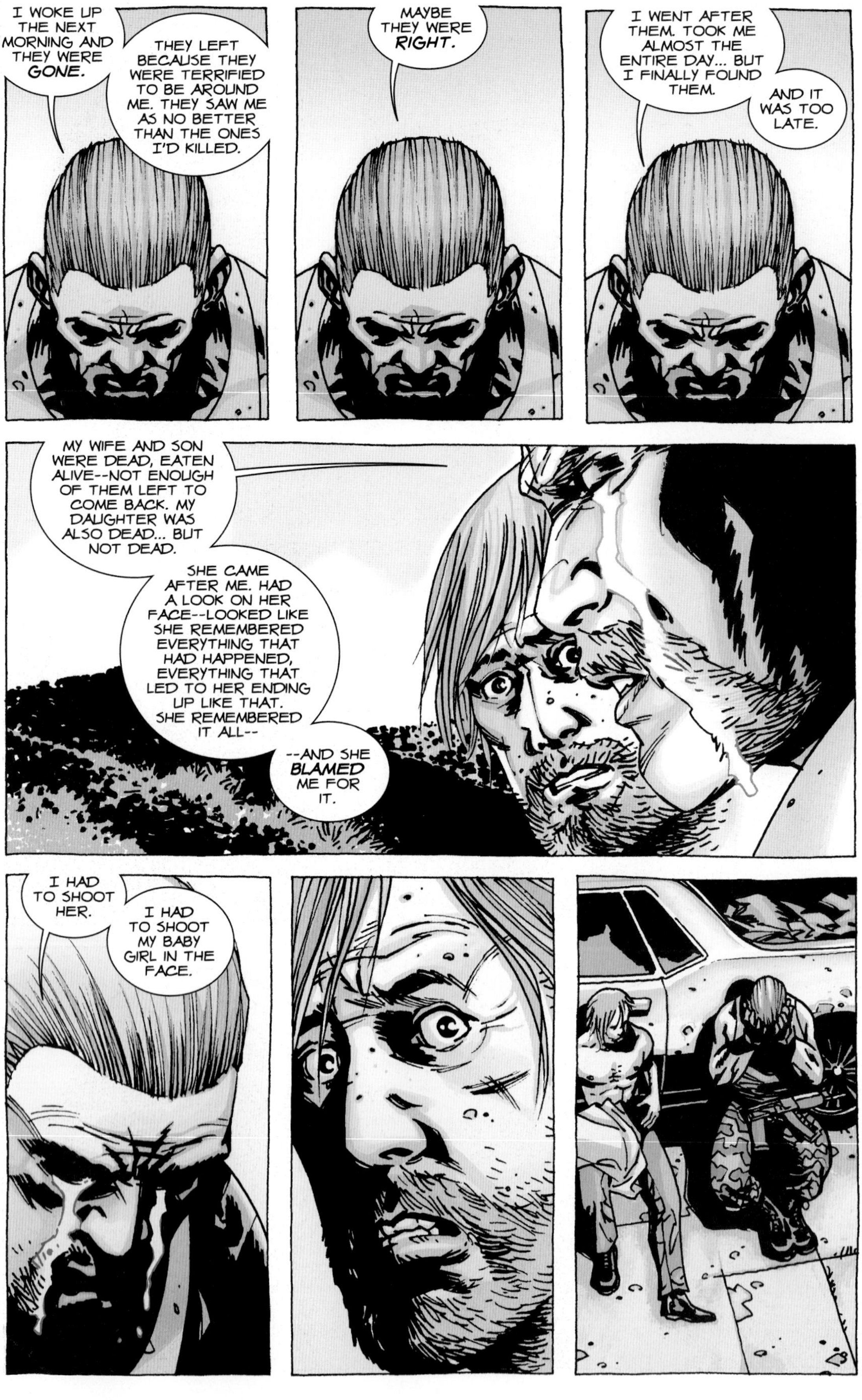

I WOKE UP THE NEXT MORNING AND THEY WERE GONE.
THEY LEFT BECAUSE THEY WERE TERRIFIED TO BE AROUND ME. THEY SAW ME AS NO BETTER THAN THE ONES I'D KILLED.
MAYBE THEY WERE RIGHT.
I WENT AFTER THEM. TOOK ME ALMOST THE ENTIRE DAY... BUT I FINALLY FOUND THEM.
AND IT WAS TOO LATE.
MY WIFE AND SON WERE DEAD, EATEN ALIVE--NOT ENOUGH OF THEM LEFT TO COME BACK. MY DAUGHTER WAS ALSO DEAD... BUT NOT DEAD.
SHE CAME AFTER ME. HAD A LOOK ON HER FACE--LOOKED LIKE SHE REMEMBERED EVERYTHING THAT HAD HAPPENED, EVERYTHING THAT LED TO HER ENDING UP LIKE THAT. SHE REMEMBERED IT ALL--
--AND SHE BLAMED ME FOR IT.
I HAD TO SHOOT HER.
I HAD TO SHOOT MY BABY GIRL IN THE FACE.

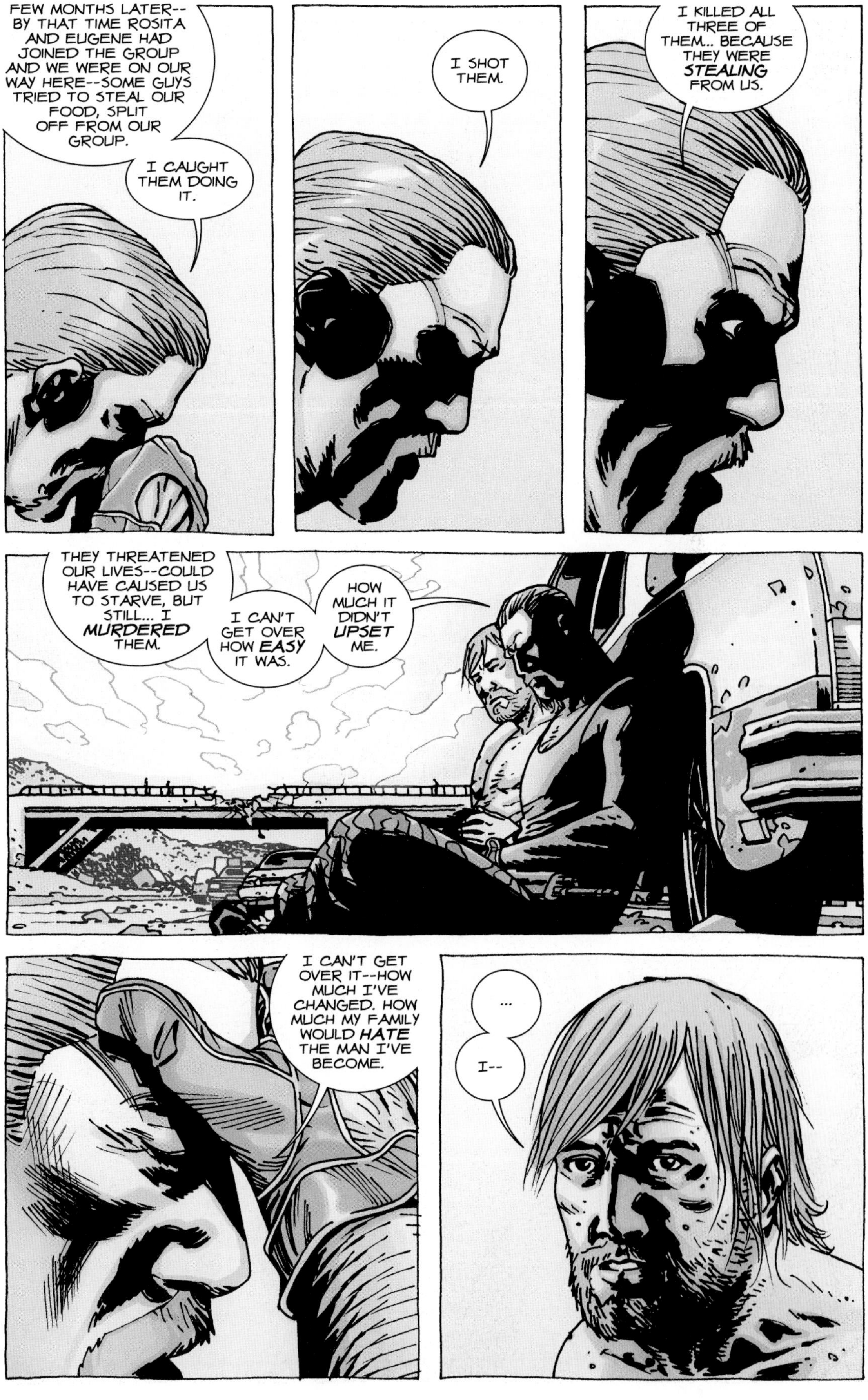
FEW MONTHS LATER-- BY THAT TIME ROSITA AND EUGENE HAD JOINED THE GROUP AND WE WERE ON OUR WAY HERE--SOME GUYS TRIED TO STEAL OUR FOOD, SPLIT OFF FROM OUR GROUP.
I CAUGHT THEM DOING IT.
I SHOT THEM.
I KILLED ALL THREE OF THEM... BECAUSE THEY WERE STEALING FROM US.
THEY THREATENED OUR LIVES--COULD HAVE CAUSED US TO STARVE, BUT STILL... I MURDERED THEM.
I CAN'T GET OVER HOW EASY IT WAS.
HOW MUCH IT DIDN'T UPSET ME.
I CAN'T GET OVER IT--HOW MUCH I'VE CHANGED. HOW MUCH MY FAMILY WOULD HATE THE MAN I'VE BECOME.
...
I--

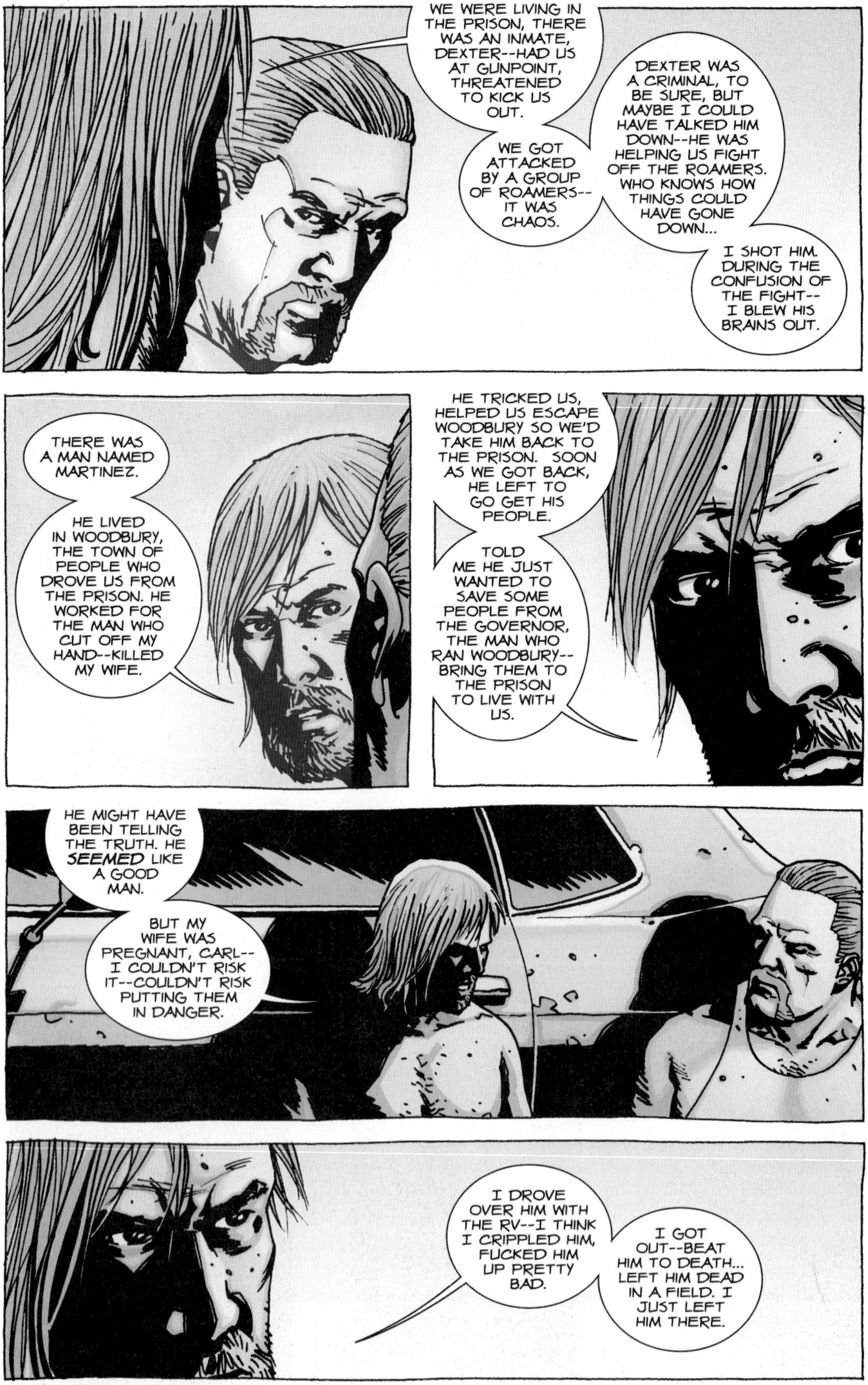

WE WERE LIVING IN THE PRISON, THERE WAS AN INMATE, DEXTER--HAD US AT GUNPOINT, THREATENED TO KICK US OUT.
WE GOT ATTACKED BY A GROUP OF ROAMERS-- IT WAS CHAOS.
DEXTER WAS A CRIMINAL, TO BE SURE, BUT MAYBE I COULD HAVE TALKED HIM DOWN--HE WAS HELPING US FIGHT OFF THE ROAMERS. WHO KNOWS HOW THINGS COULD HAVE GONE DOWN...
I SHOT HIM. DURING THE CONFUSION OF THE FIGHT-- I BLEW HIS BRAINS OUT.
THERE WAS A MAN NAMED MARTINEZ.
HE LIVED IN WOODBURY, THE TOWN OF PEOPLE WHO DROVE US FROM THE PRISON. HE WORKED FOR THE MAN WHO CUT OFF MY HAND--KILLED MY WIFE.
HE TRICKED US, HELPED US ESCAPE WOODBURY SO WE'D TAKE HIM BACK TO THE PRISON. SOON AS WE GOT BACK, HE LEFT TO GO GET HIS PEOPLE.
TOLD ME HE JUST WANTED TO SAVE SOME PEOPLE FROM THE GOVERNOR, THE MAN WHO RAN WOODBURY-- BRING THEM TO THE PRISON TO LIVE WITH US.
HE MIGHT HAVE BEEN TELLING THE TRUTH. HE *SEEMED* LIKE A GOOD MAN.
BUT MY WIFE WAS PREGNANT, CARL-- I COULDN'T RISK IT--COULDN'T RISK PUTTING THEM IN DANGER.
I DROVE OVER HIM WITH THE RV--I THINK I CRIPPLED HIM, FUCKED HIM UP PRETTY BAD.
I GOT OUT--BEAT HIM TO DEATH... LEFT HIM DEAD IN A FIELD. I JUST LEFT HIM THERE.

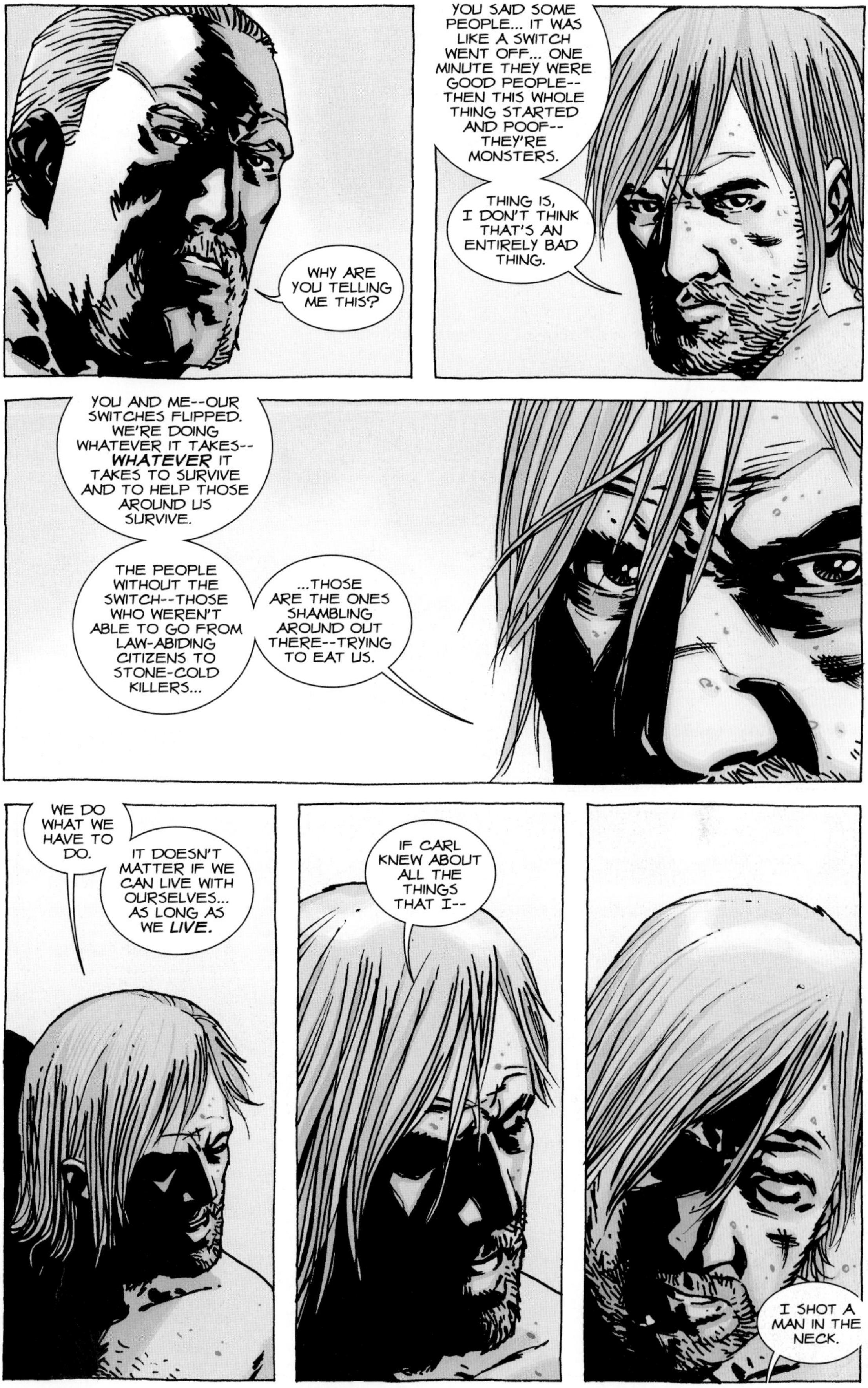
WHY ARE YOU TELLING ME THIS?
YOU SAID SOME PEOPLE... IT WAS LIKE A SWITCH WENT OFF... ONE MINUTE THEY WERE GOOD PEOPLE--THEN THIS WHOLE THING STARTED AND POOF--THEY'RE MONSTERS.
THING IS, I DON'T THINK THAT'S AN ENTIRELY BAD THING.
YOU AND ME--OUR SWITCHES FLIPPED. WE'RE DOING WHATEVER IT TAKES--*WHATEVER* IT TAKES TO SURVIVE AND TO HELP THOSE AROUND US SURVIVE.
THE PEOPLE WITHOUT THE SWITCH--THOSE WHO WEREN'T ABLE TO GO FROM LAW-ABIDING CITIZENS TO STONE-COLD KILLERS...
...THOSE ARE THE ONES SHAMBLING AROUND OUT THERE--TRYING TO EAT US.
WE DO WHAT WE HAVE TO DO.
IT DOESN'T MATTER IF WE CAN LIVE WITH OURSELVES... AS LONG AS WE *LIVE.*
IF CARL KNEW ABOUT ALL THE THINGS THAT I--
I SHOT A MAN IN THE NECK.

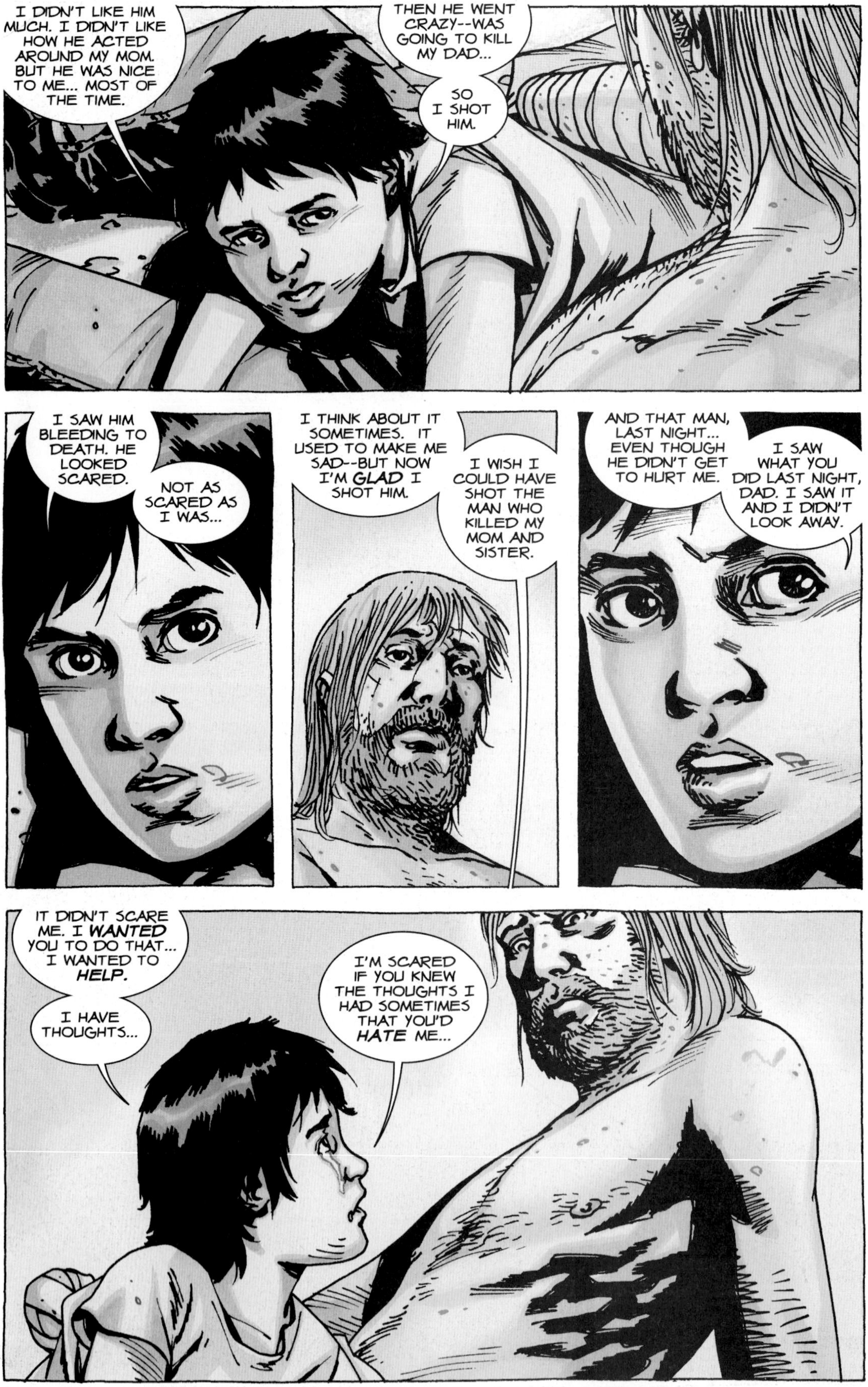
I DIDN'T LIKE HIM MUCH. I DIDN'T LIKE HOW HE ACTED AROUND MY MOM. BUT HE WAS NICE TO ME... MOST OF THE TIME.
THEN HE WENT CRAZY--WAS GOING TO KILL MY DAD...
SO I SHOT HIM.
I SAW HIM BLEEDING TO DEATH. HE LOOKED SCARED.
NOT AS SCARED AS I WAS...
I THINK ABOUT IT SOMETIMES. IT USED TO MAKE ME SAD--BUT NOW I'M GLAD I SHOT HIM.
I WISH I COULD HAVE SHOT THE MAN WHO KILLED MY MOM AND SISTER.
AND THAT MAN, LAST NIGHT... EVEN THOUGH HE DIDN'T GET TO HURT ME.
I SAW WHAT YOU DID LAST NIGHT, DAD. I SAW IT AND I DIDN'T LOOK AWAY.
IT DIDN'T SCARE ME. I WANTED YOU TO DO THAT... I WANTED TO HELP.
I HAVE THOUGHTS...
I'M SCARED IF YOU KNEW THE THOUGHTS I HAD SOMETIMES THAT YOU'D HATE ME...

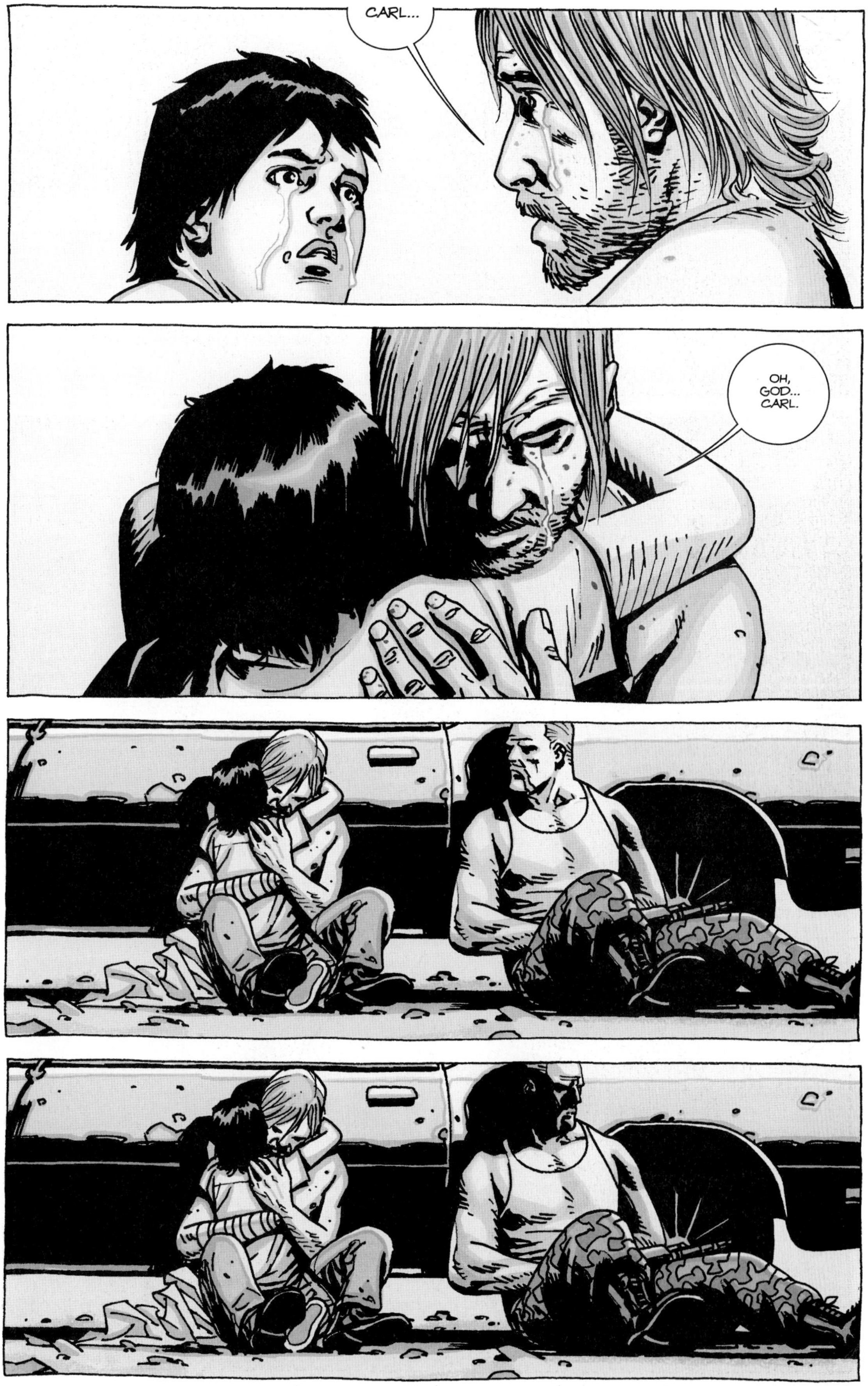
CARL...
OH, GOD... CARL.

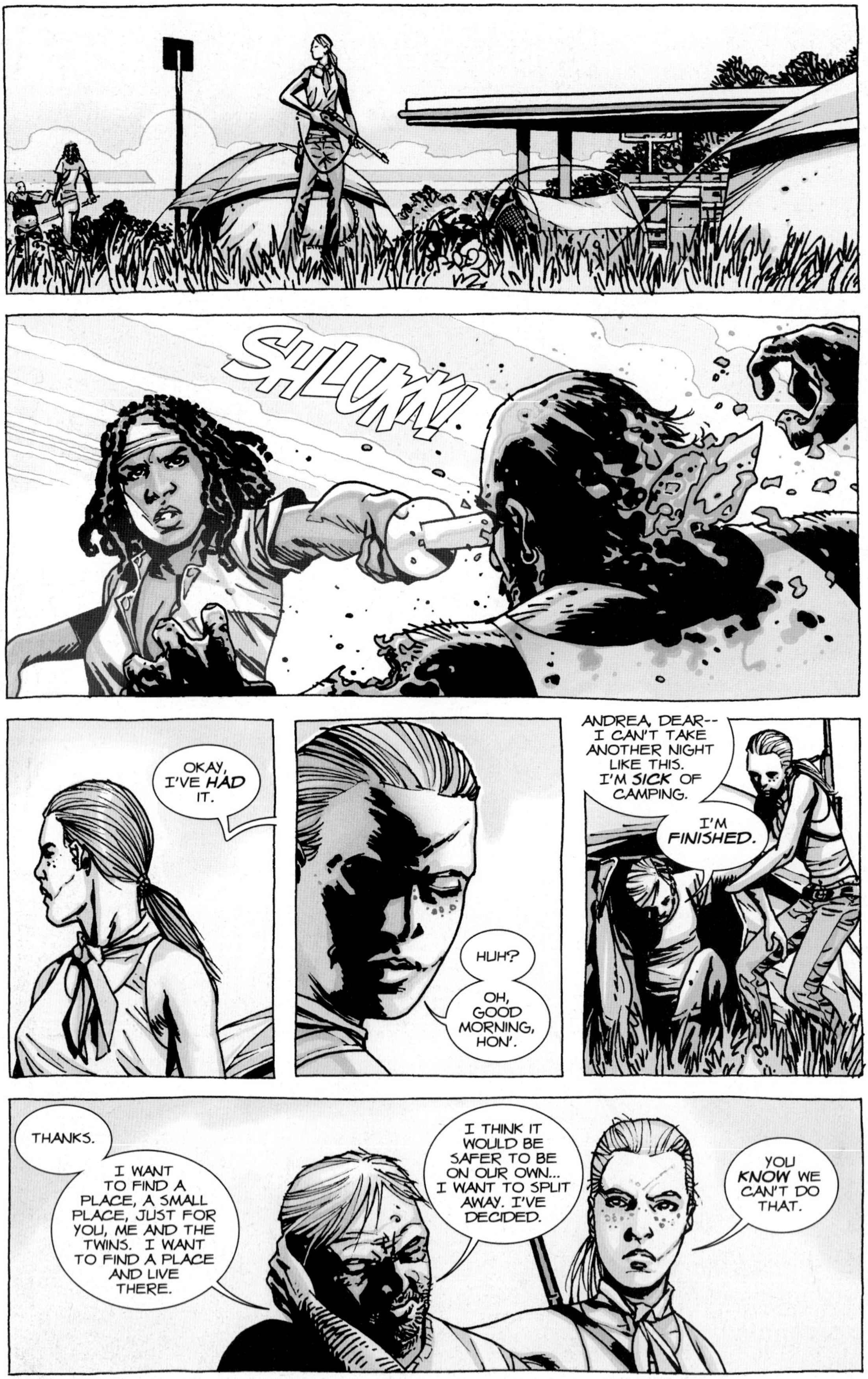
SHLUKK!
OKAY, I'VE HAD IT.
HUH?
OH, GOOD MORNING, HON'.
ANDREA, DEAR-- I CAN'T TAKE ANOTHER NIGHT LIKE THIS. I'M SICK OF CAMPING.
I'M FINISHED.
THANKS.
I WANT TO FIND A PLACE, A SMALL PLACE, JUST FOR YOU, ME AND THE TWINS. I WANT TO FIND A PLACE AND LIVE THERE.
I THINK IT WOULD BE SAFER TO BE ON OUR OWN... I WANT TO SPLIT AWAY. I'VE DECIDED.
YOU KNOW WE CAN'T DO THAT.

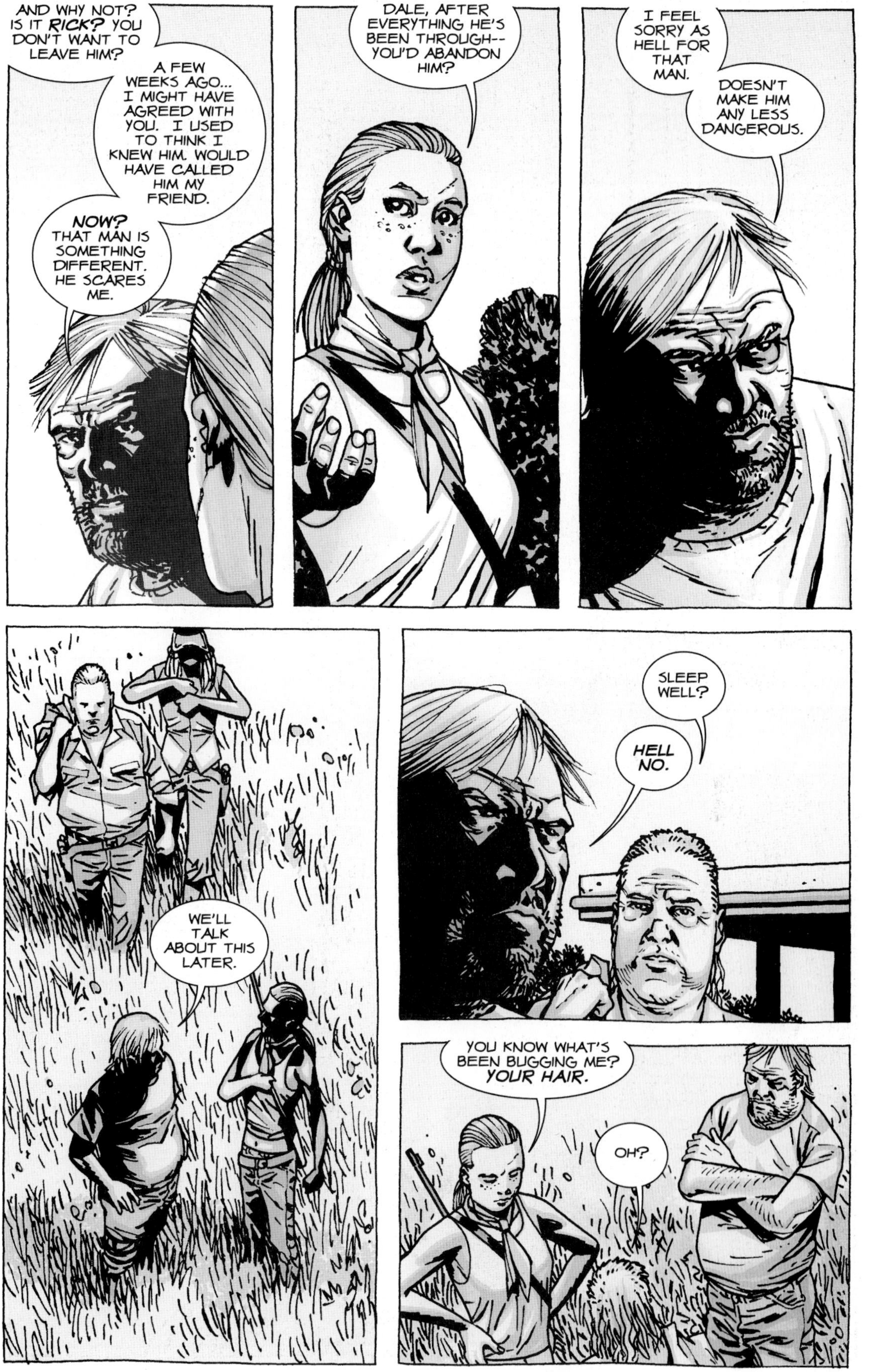
AND WHY NOT? IS IT RICK? YOU DON'T WANT TO LEAVE HIM?
A FEW WEEKS AGO... I MIGHT HAVE AGREED WITH YOU. I USED TO THINK I KNEW HIM. WOULD HAVE CALLED HIM MY FRIEND.
NOW? THAT MAN IS SOMETHING DIFFERENT. HE SCARES ME.
DALE, AFTER EVERYTHING HE'S BEEN THROUGH-- YOU'D ABANDON HIM?
I FEEL SORRY AS HELL FOR THAT MAN.
DOESN'T MAKE HIM ANY LESS DANGEROUS.
WE'LL TALK ABOUT THIS LATER.
SLEEP WELL?
HELL NO.
YOU KNOW WHAT'S BEEN BUGGING ME? YOUR HAIR.
OH?

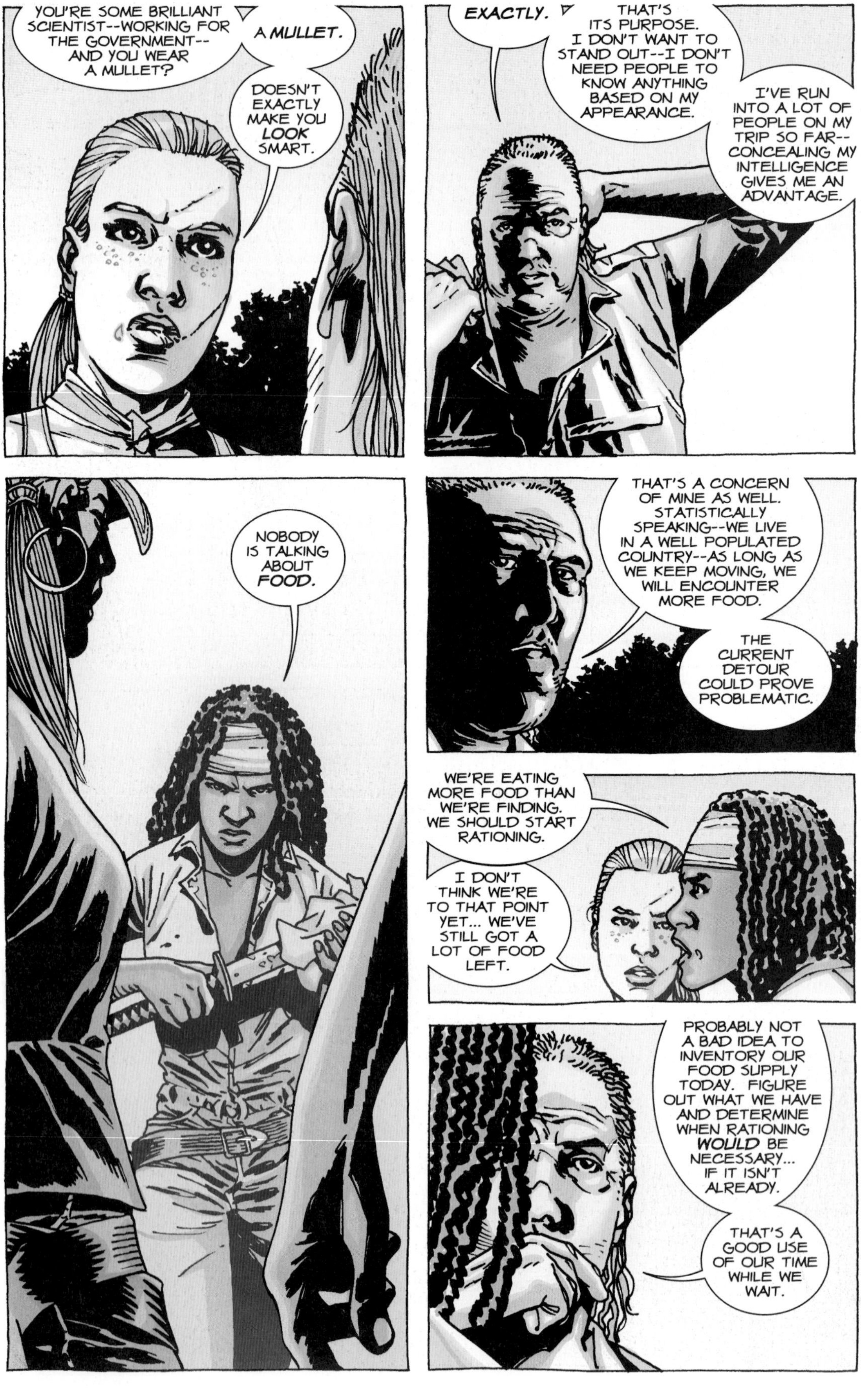
YOU'RE SOME BRILLIANT SCIENTIST--WORKING FOR THE GOVERNMENT--AND YOU WEAR A MULLET?
A MULLET.
DOESN'T EXACTLY MAKE YOU LOOK SMART.
EXACTLY.
THAT'S ITS PURPOSE. I DON'T WANT TO STAND OUT--I DON'T NEED PEOPLE TO KNOW ANYTHING BASED ON MY APPEARANCE.
I'VE RUN INTO A LOT OF PEOPLE ON MY TRIP SO FAR--CONCEALING MY INTELLIGENCE GIVES ME AN ADVANTAGE.
NOBODY IS TALKING ABOUT FOOD.
THAT'S A CONCERN OF MINE AS WELL. STATISTICALLY SPEAKING--WE LIVE IN A WELL POPULATED COUNTRY--AS LONG AS WE KEEP MOVING, WE WILL ENCOUNTER MORE FOOD.
THE CURRENT DETOUR COULD PROVE PROBLEMATIC.
WE'RE EATING MORE FOOD THAN WE'RE FINDING. WE SHOULD START RATIONING.
I DON'T THINK WE'RE TO THAT POINT YET... WE'VE STILL GOT A LOT OF FOOD LEFT.
PROBABLY NOT A BAD IDEA TO INVENTORY OUR FOOD SUPPLY TODAY. FIGURE OUT WHAT WE HAVE AND DETERMINE WHEN RATIONING WOULD BE NECESSARY... IF IT ISN'T ALREADY.
THAT'S A GOOD USE OF OUR TIME WHILE WE WAIT.

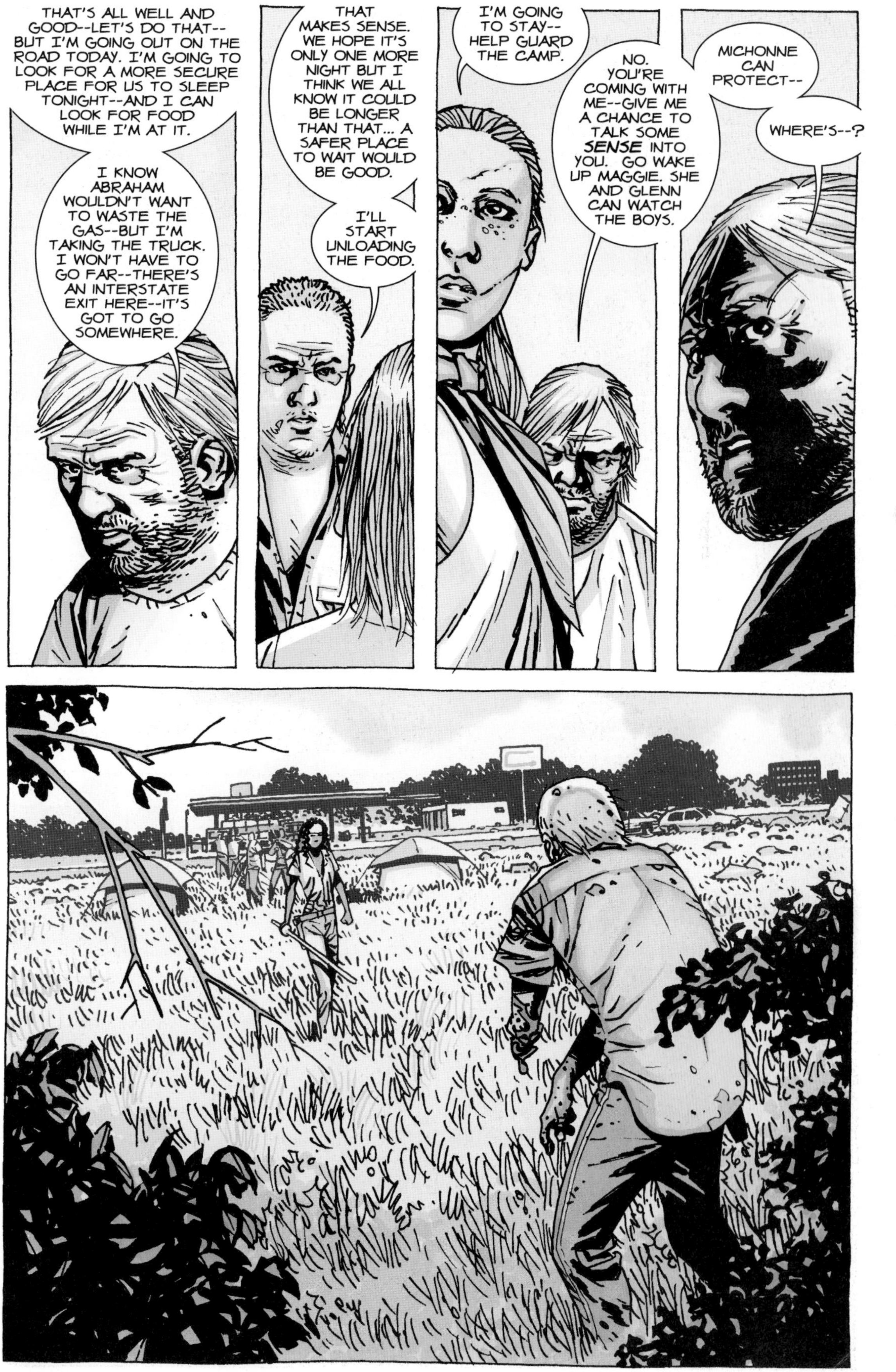
THAT'S ALL WELL AND GOOD--LET'S DO THAT--BUT I'M GOING OUT ON THE ROAD TODAY. I'M GOING TO LOOK FOR A MORE SECURE PLACE FOR US TO SLEEP TONIGHT--AND I CAN LOOK FOR FOOD WHILE I'M AT IT.
I KNOW ABRAHAM WOULDN'T WANT TO WASTE THE GAS--BUT I'M TAKING THE TRUCK. I WON'T HAVE TO GO FAR--THERE'S AN INTERSTATE EXIT HERE--IT'S GOT TO GO SOMEWHERE.
THAT MAKES SENSE. WE HOPE IT'S ONLY ONE MORE NIGHT BUT I THINK WE ALL KNOW IT COULD BE LONGER THAN THAT... A SAFER PLACE TO WAIT WOULD BE GOOD.
I'LL START UNLOADING THE FOOD.
I'M GOING TO STAY--HELP GUARD THE CAMP.
NO. YOU'RE COMING WITH ME--GIVE ME A CHANCE TO TALK SOME SENSE INTO YOU. GO WAKE UP MAGGIE. SHE AND GLENN CAN WATCH THE BOYS.
MICHONNE CAN PROTECT--
WHERE'S--?

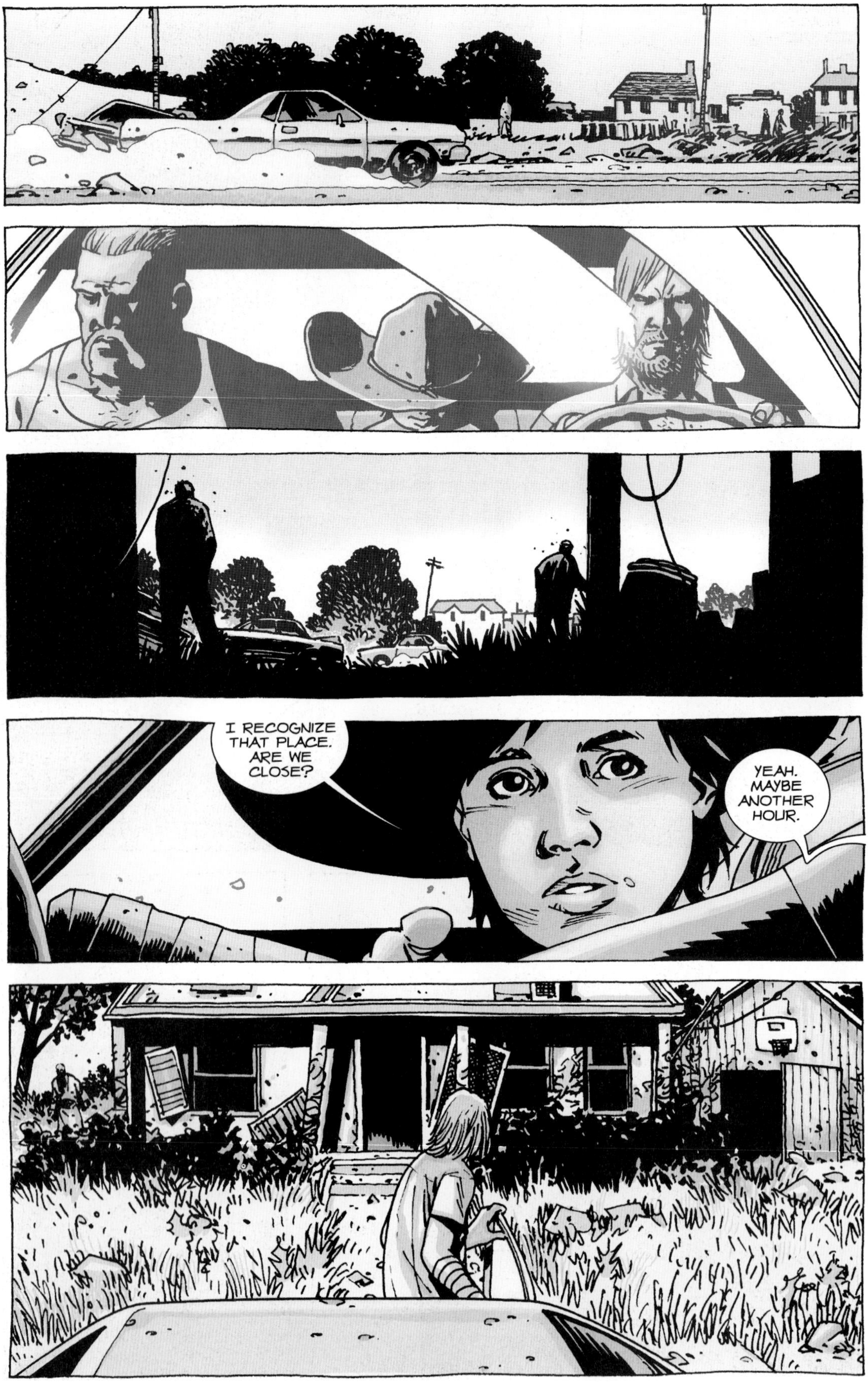
I RECOGNIZE THAT PLACE. ARE WE CLOSE?
YEAH. MAYBE ANOTHER HOUR.

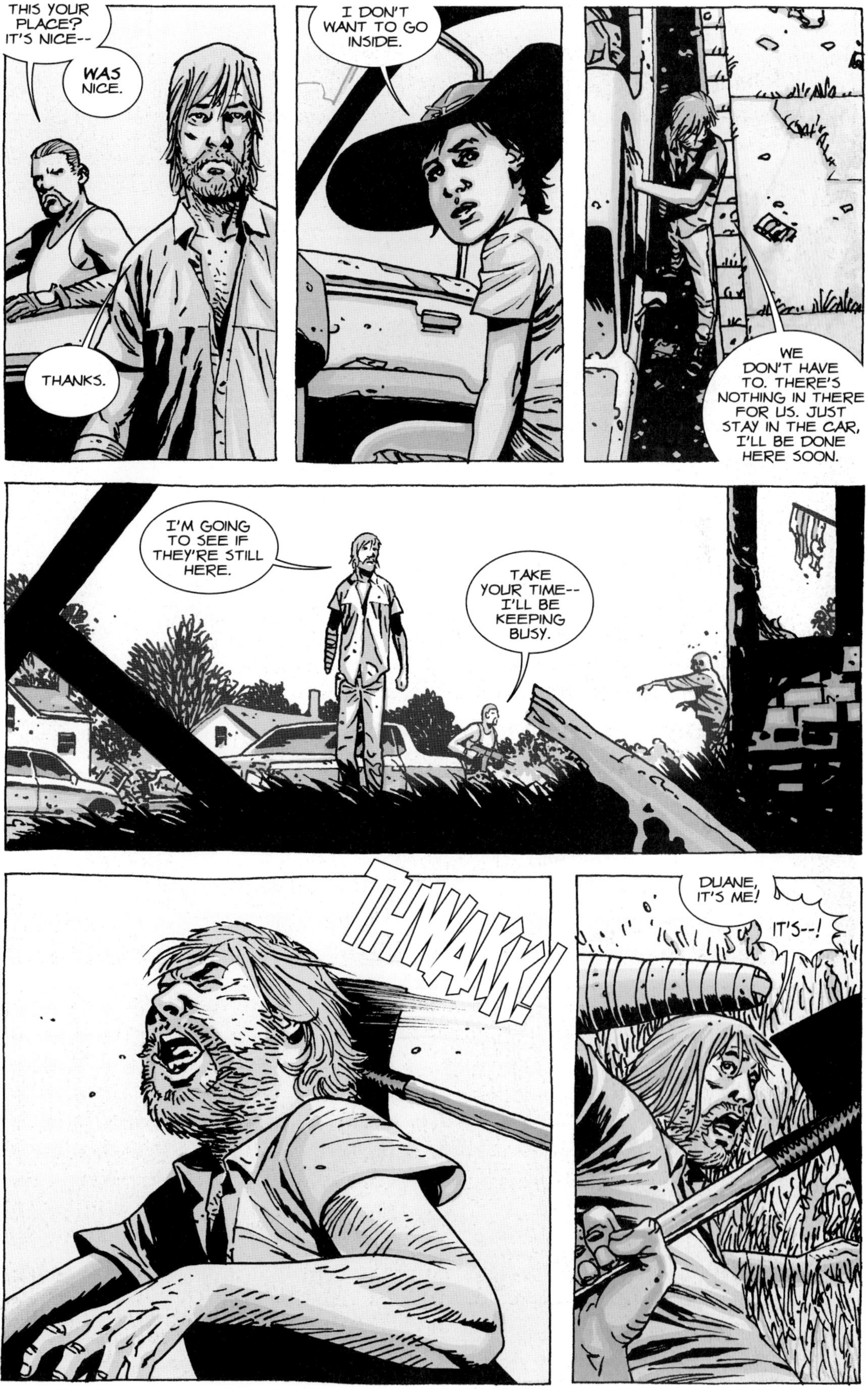
THIS YOUR PLACE? IT'S NICE--
WAS NICE.
THANKS.
I DON'T WANT TO GO INSIDE.
WE DON'T HAVE TO. THERE'S NOTHING IN THERE FOR US. JUST STAY IN THE CAR, I'LL BE DONE HERE SOON.
I'M GOING TO SEE IF THEY'RE STILL HERE.
TAKE YOUR TIME-- I'LL BE KEEPING BUSY.
THWAKK!
DUANE, IT'S ME!
IT'S--!

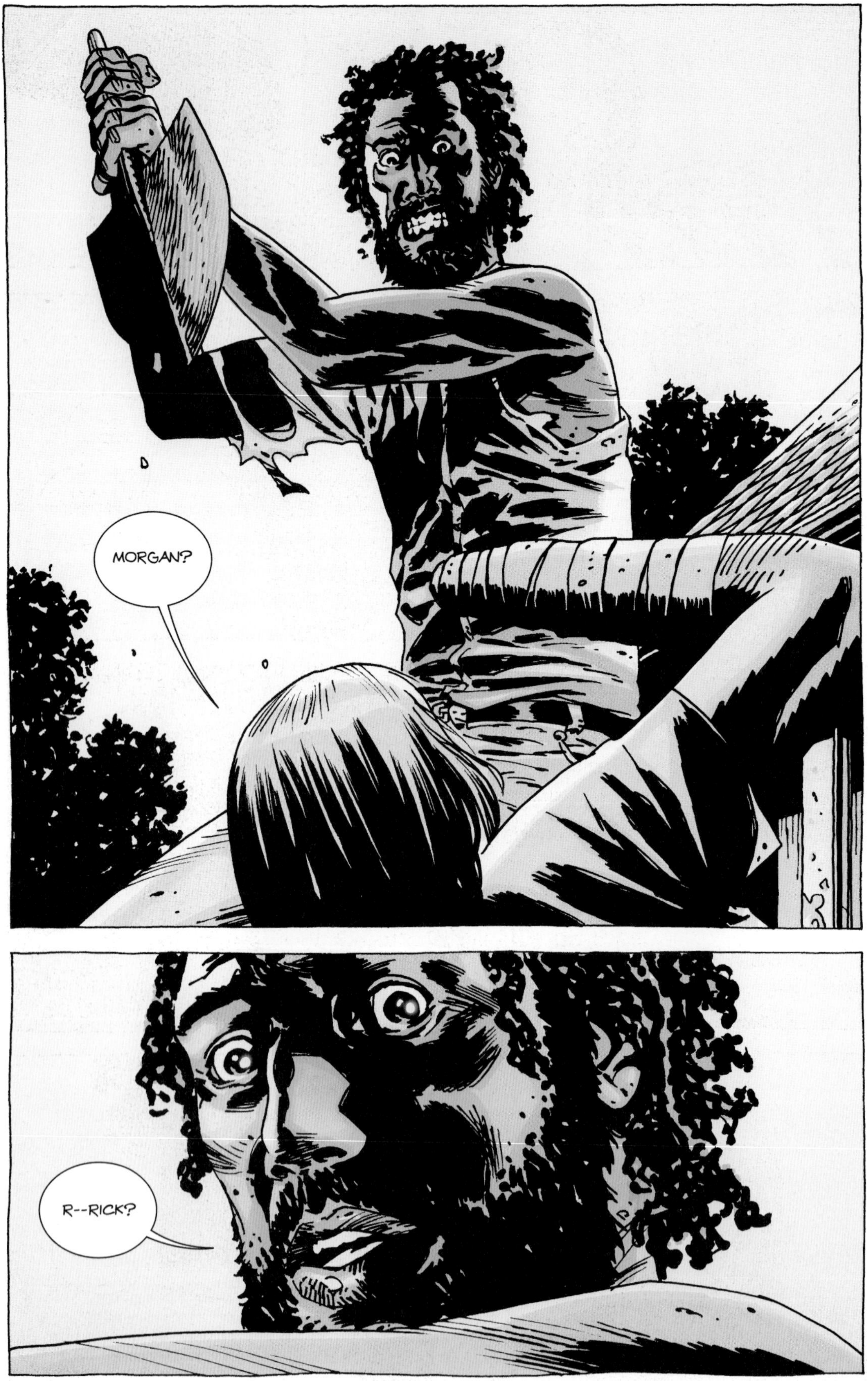
MORGAN?
R--RICK?

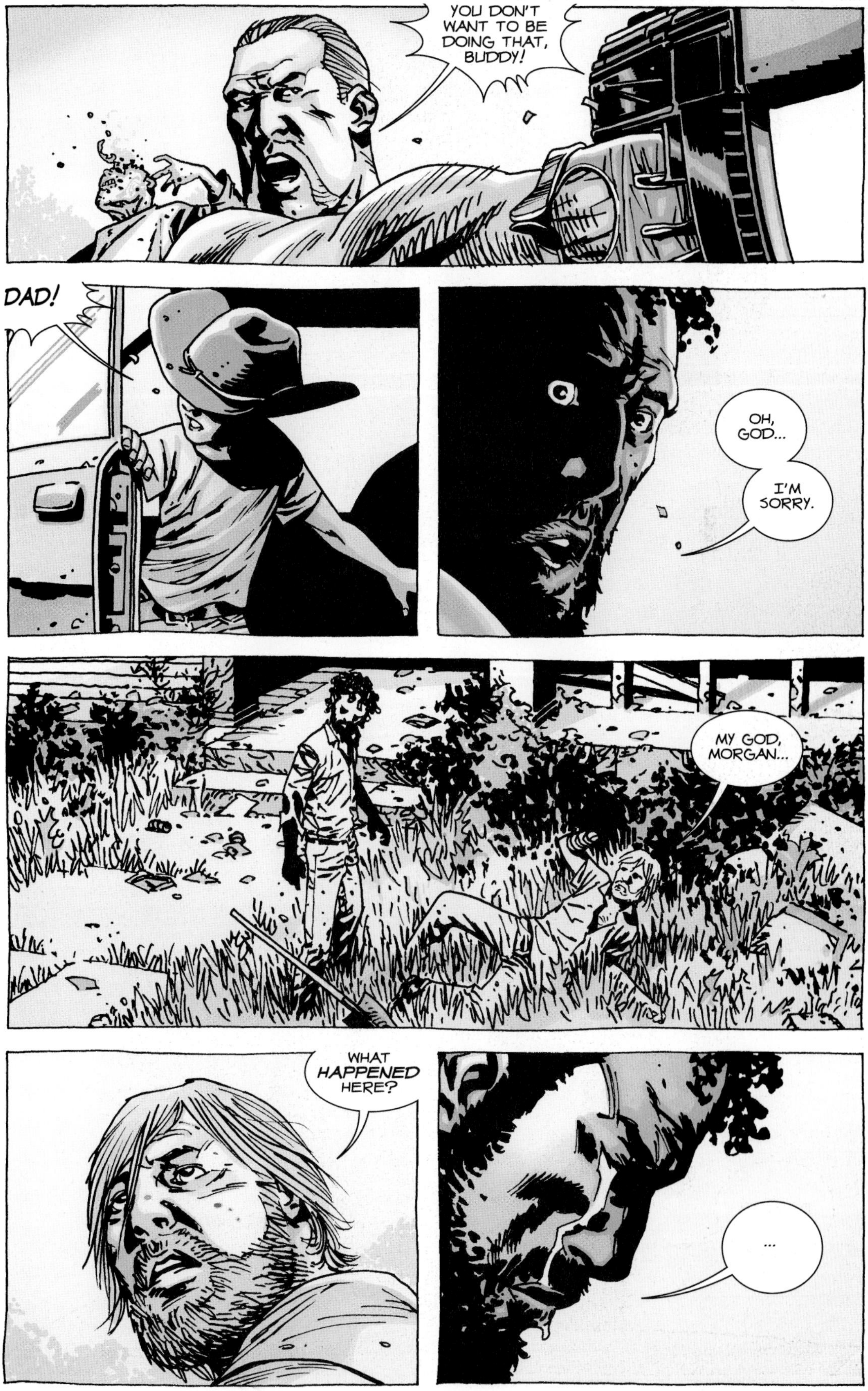

YOU DON'T WANT TO BE DOING THAT, BUDDY!
DAD!
OH, GOD...
I'M SORRY.
MY GOD, MORGAN...
WHAT HAPPENED HERE?
...

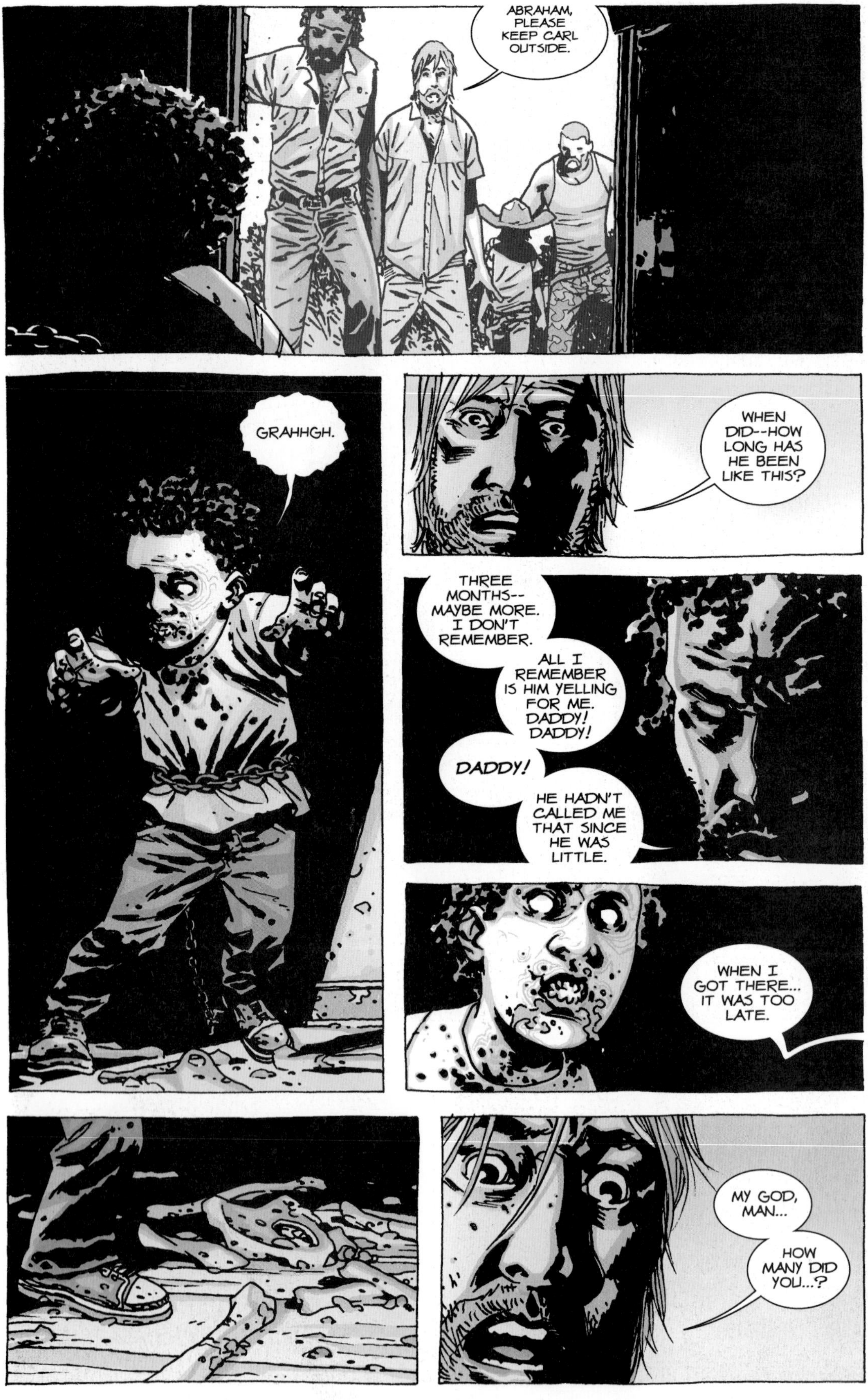
ABRAHAM, PLEASE KEEP CARL OUTSIDE.
GRAHHGH.
WHEN DID--HOW LONG HAS HE BEEN LIKE THIS?
THREE MONTHS-- MAYBE MORE. I DON'T REMEMBER.
ALL I REMEMBER IS HIM YELLING FOR ME. DADDY! DADDY!
DADDY!
HE HADN'T CALLED ME THAT SINCE HE WAS LITTLE.
WHEN I GOT THERE... IT WAS TOO LATE.
MY GOD, MAN...
HOW MANY DID YOU...?

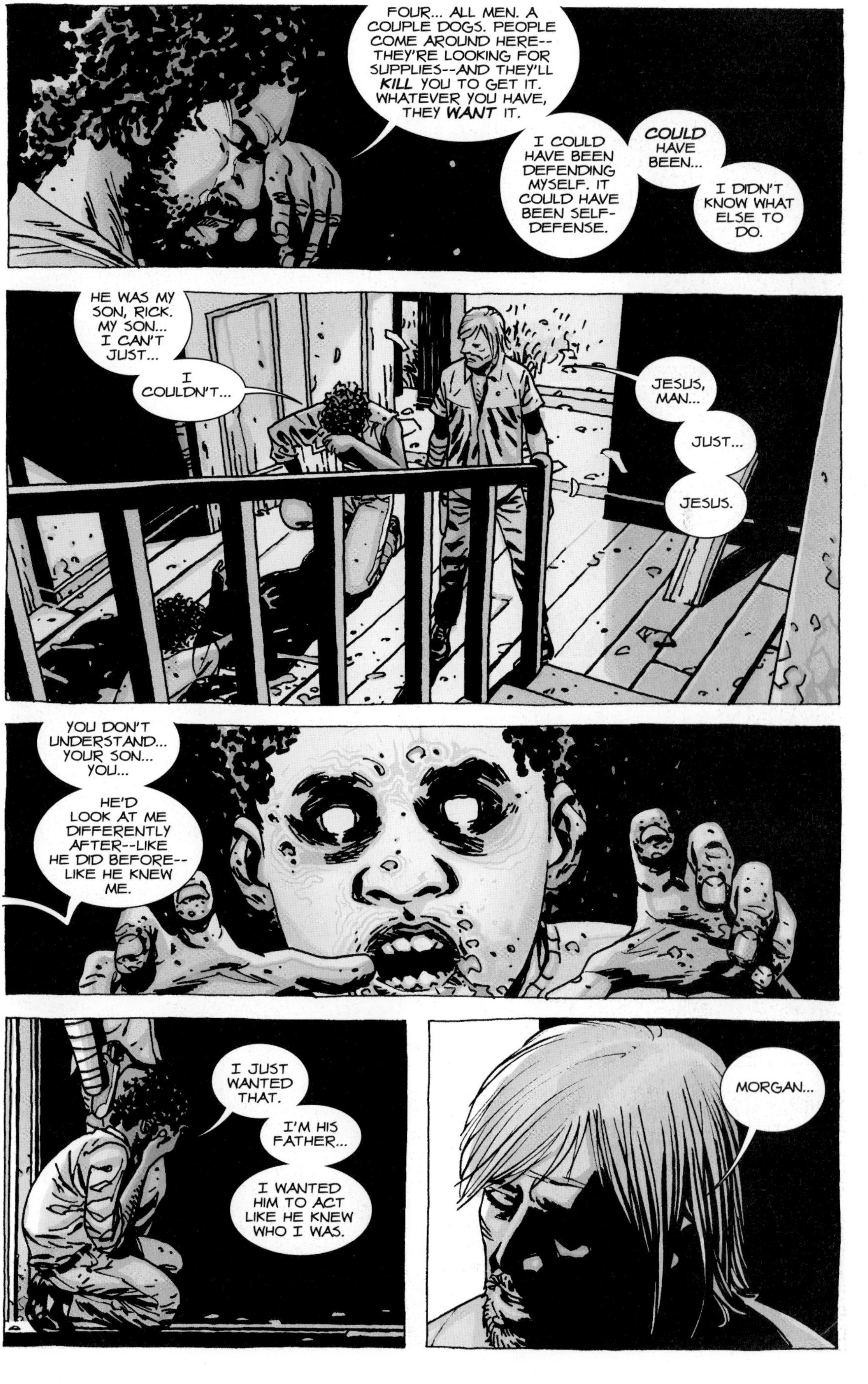
FOUR... ALL MEN. A COUPLE DOGS. PEOPLE COME AROUND HERE-- THEY'RE LOOKING FOR SUPPLIES--AND THEY'LL KILL YOU TO GET IT. WHATEVER YOU HAVE, THEY WANT IT.
I COULD HAVE BEEN DEFENDING MYSELF. IT COULD HAVE BEEN SELF-DEFENSE.
COULD HAVE BEEN...
I DIDN'T KNOW WHAT ELSE TO DO.
HE WAS MY SON, RICK. MY SON... I CAN'T JUST...
I COULDN'T...
JESUS, MAN...
JUST...
JESUS.
YOU DON'T UNDERSTAND... YOUR SON... YOU...
HE'D LOOK AT ME DIFFERENTLY AFTER--LIKE HE DID BEFORE-- LIKE HE KNEW ME.
I JUST WANTED THAT.
I'M HIS FATHER...
I WANTED HIM TO ACT LIKE HE KNEW WHO I WAS.
MORGAN...

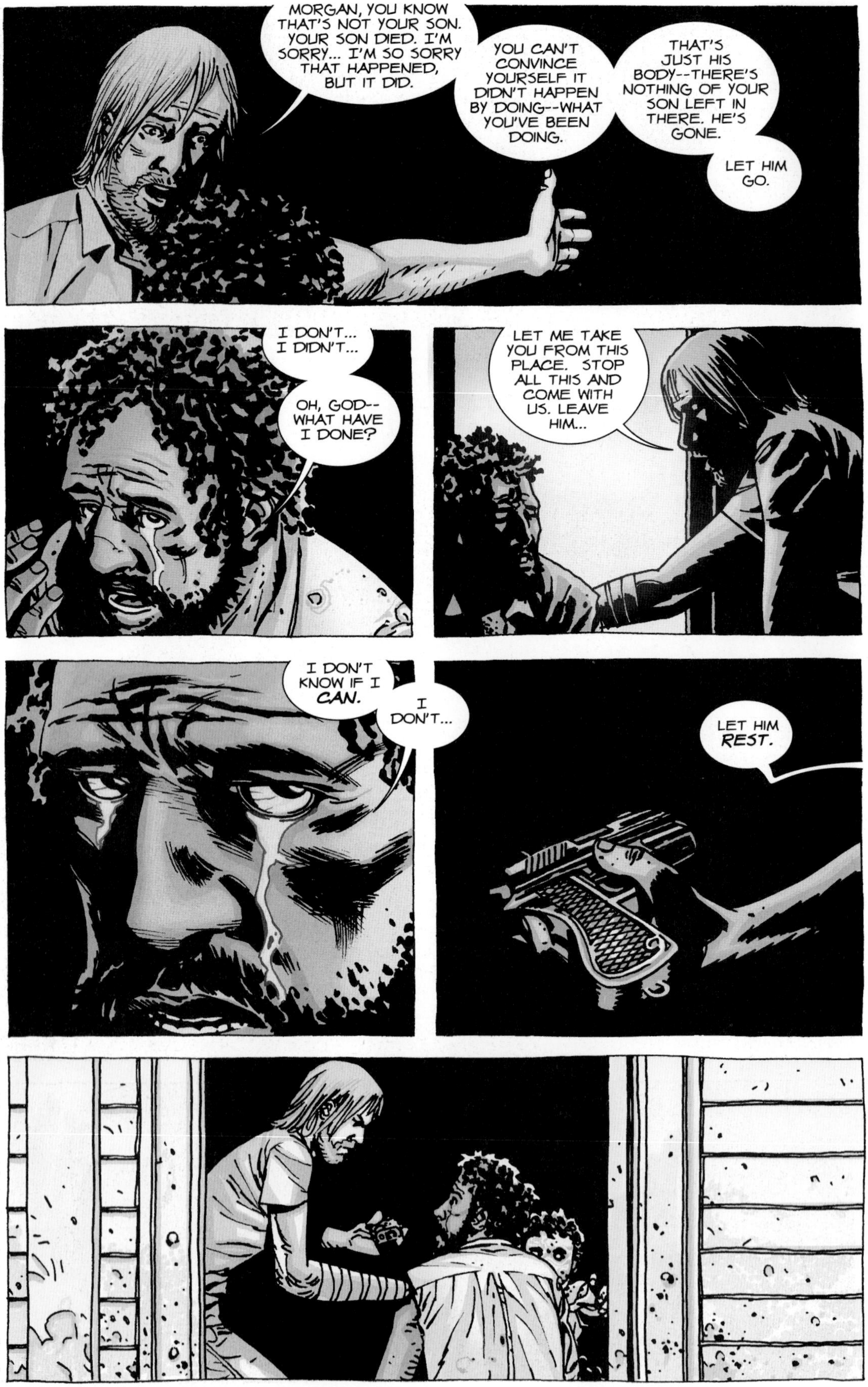
MORGAN, YOU KNOW THAT'S NOT YOUR SON. YOUR SON DIED. I'M SORRY... I'M SO SORRY THAT HAPPENED, BUT IT DID.
YOU CAN'T CONVINCE YOURSELF IT DIDN'T HAPPEN BY DOING--WHAT YOU'VE BEEN DOING.
THAT'S JUST HIS BODY--THERE'S NOTHING OF YOUR SON LEFT IN THERE. HE'S GONE.
LET HIM GO.
I DON'T... I DIDN'T...
OH, GOD-- WHAT HAVE I DONE?
LET ME TAKE YOU FROM THIS PLACE. STOP ALL THIS AND COME WITH US. LEAVE HIM...
I DON'T KNOW IF I CAN.
I DON'T...
LET HIM REST.

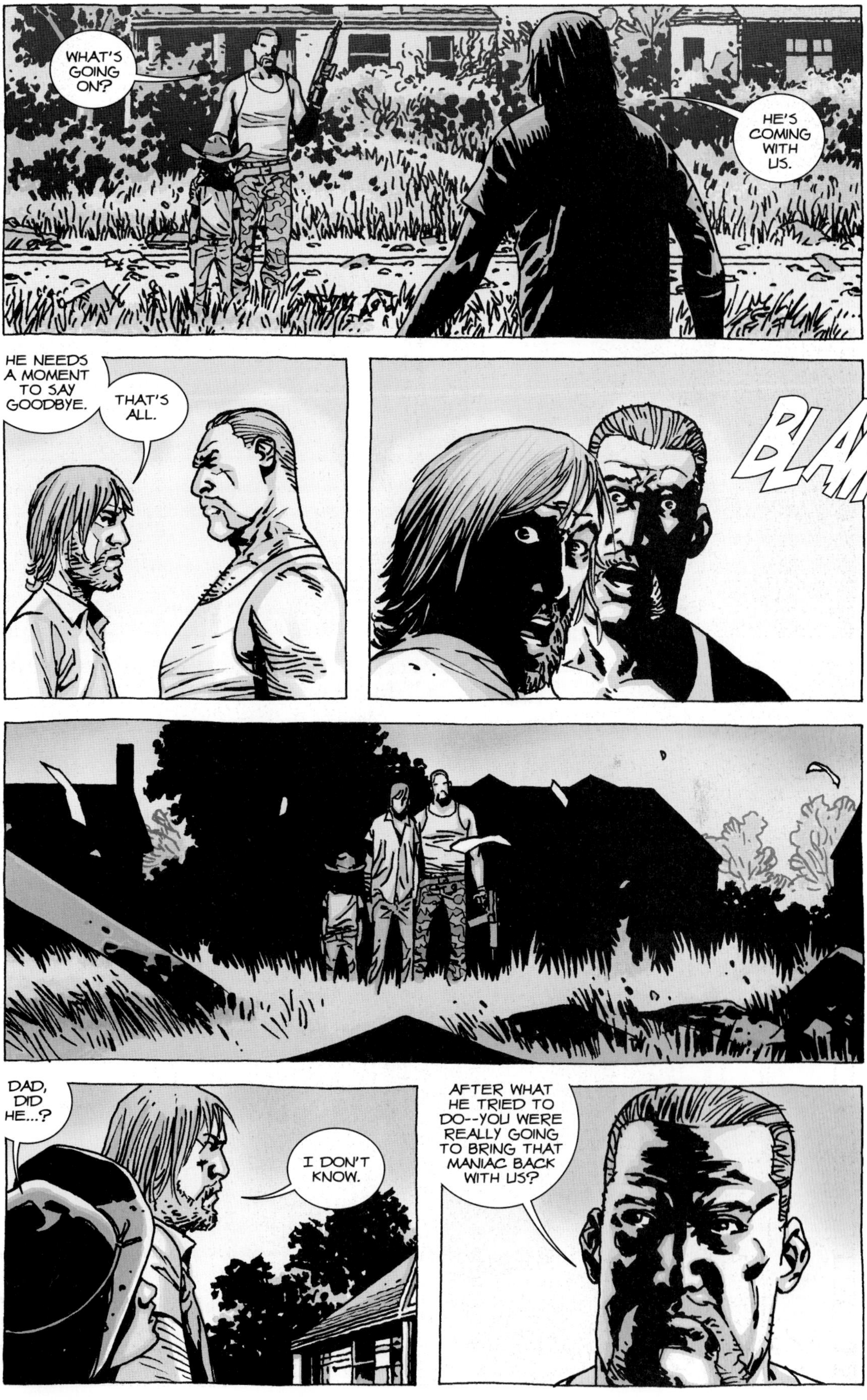

WHAT'S GOING ON?
HE'S COMING WITH US.
HE NEEDS A MOMENT TO SAY GOODBYE.
THAT'S ALL.
BLAM!
DAD, DID HE...?
I DON'T KNOW.
AFTER WHAT HE TRIED TO DO--YOU WERE REALLY GOING TO BRING THAT MANIAC BACK WITH US?

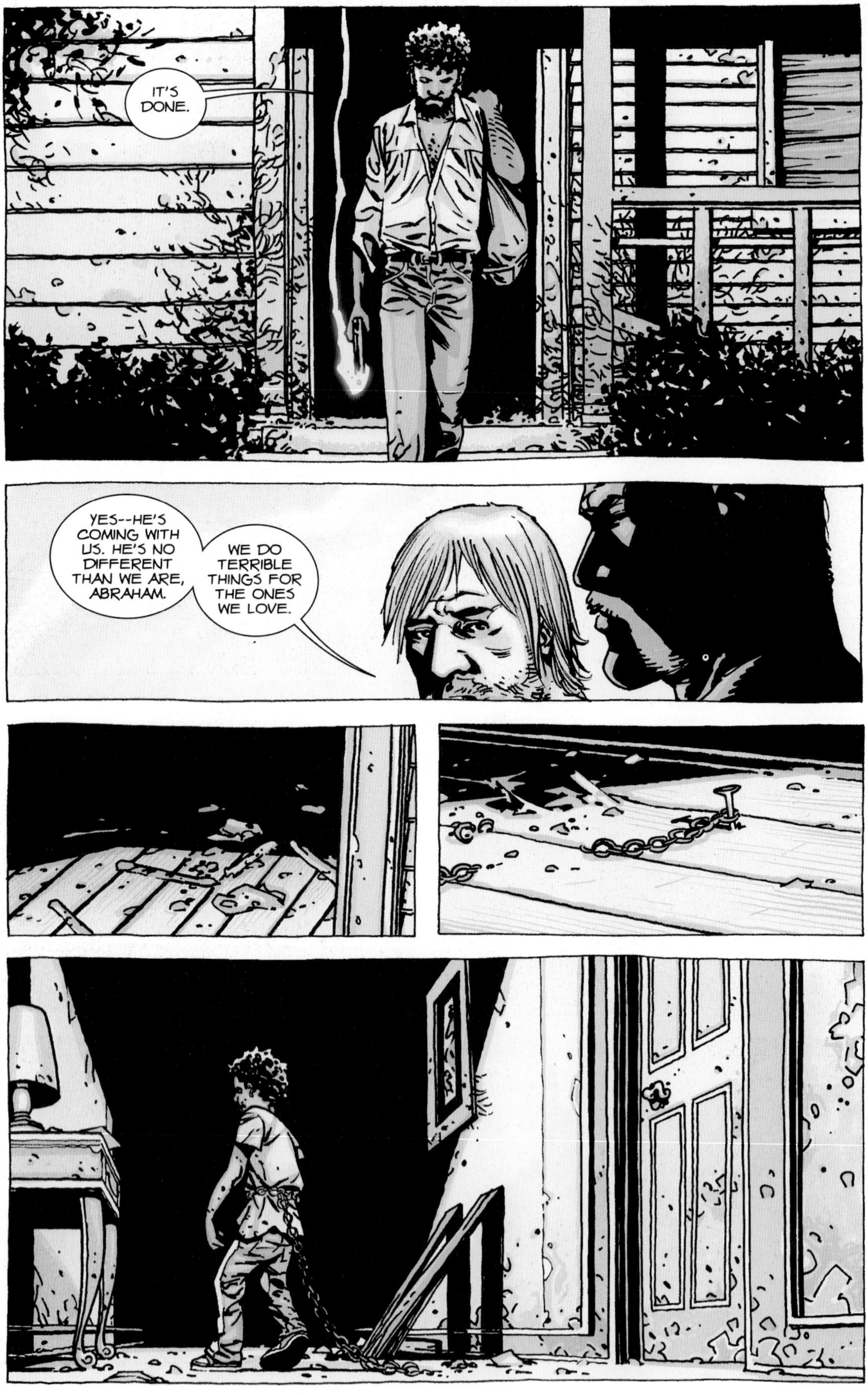
IT'S DONE.
YES--HE'S COMING WITH US. HE'S NO DIFFERENT THAN WE ARE, ABRAHAM.
WE DO TERRIBLE THINGS FOR THE ONES WE LOVE.

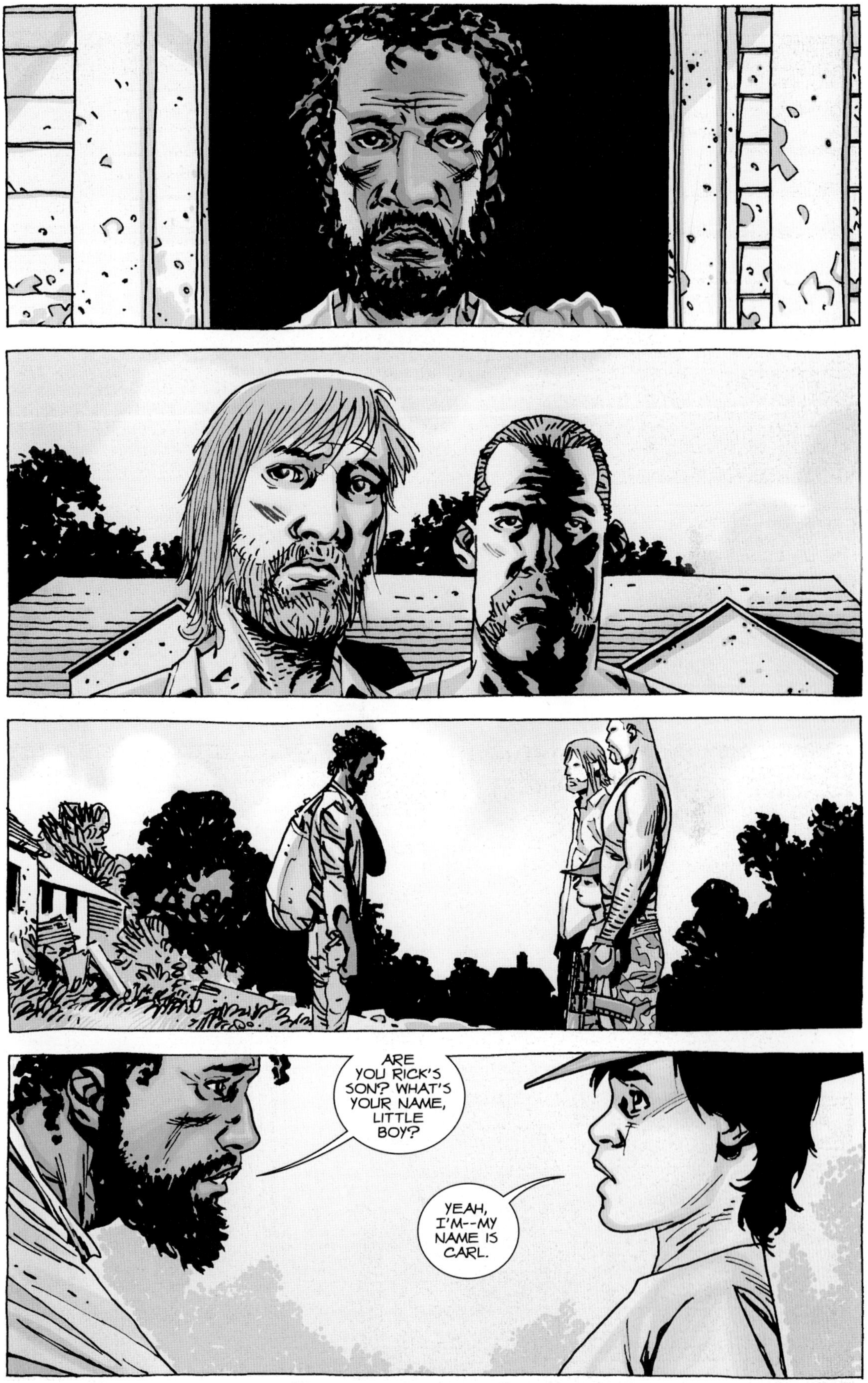
ARE YOU RICK'S SON? WHAT'S YOUR NAME, LITTLE BOY?
YEAH, I'M--MY NAME IS CARL.

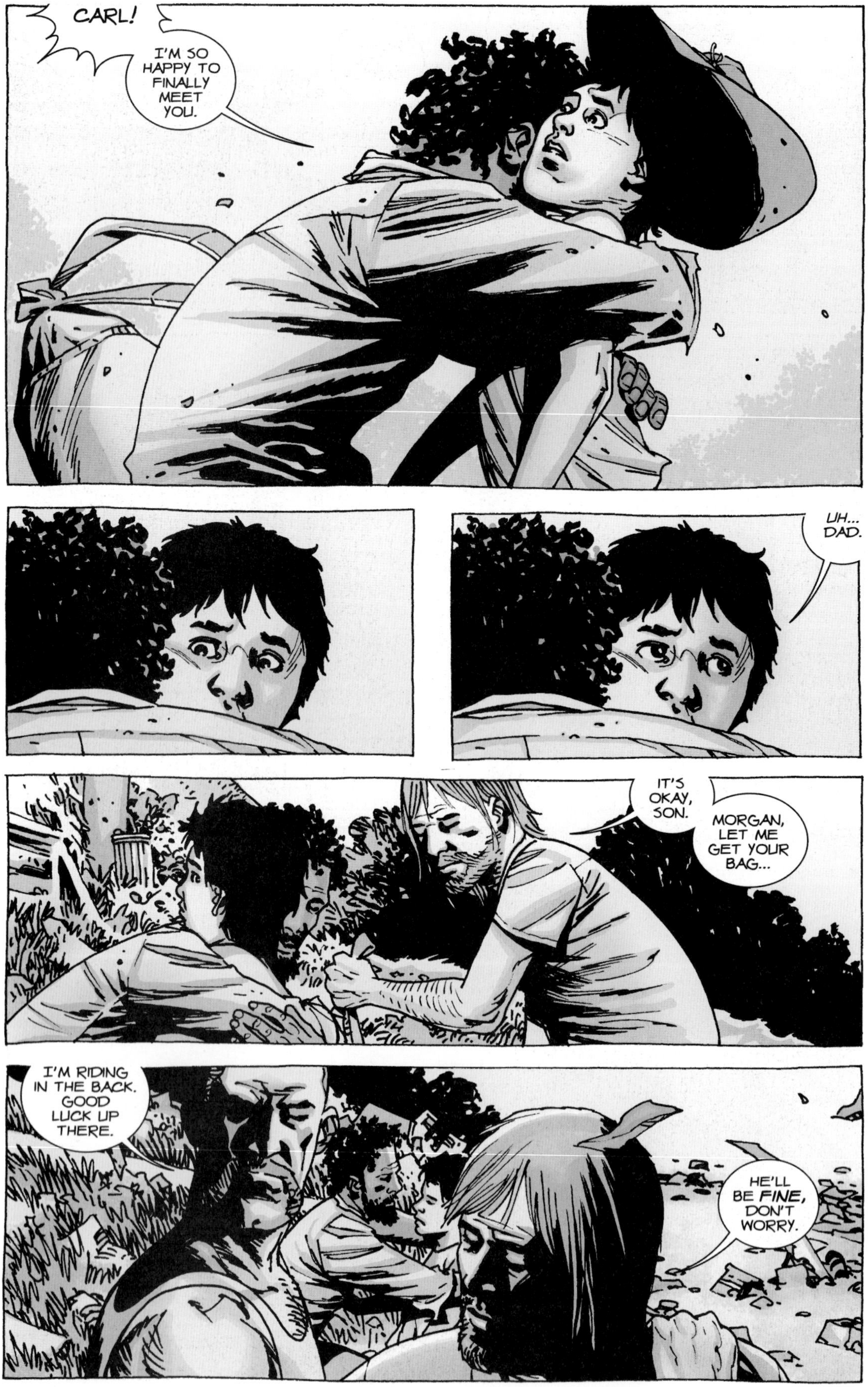
CARL!
I'M SO HAPPY TO FINALLY MEET YOU.
UH... DAD.
IT'S OKAY, SON.
MORGAN, LET ME GET YOUR BAG...
I'M RIDING IN THE BACK. GOOD LUCK UP THERE.
HE'LL BE *FINE,* DON'T WORRY.

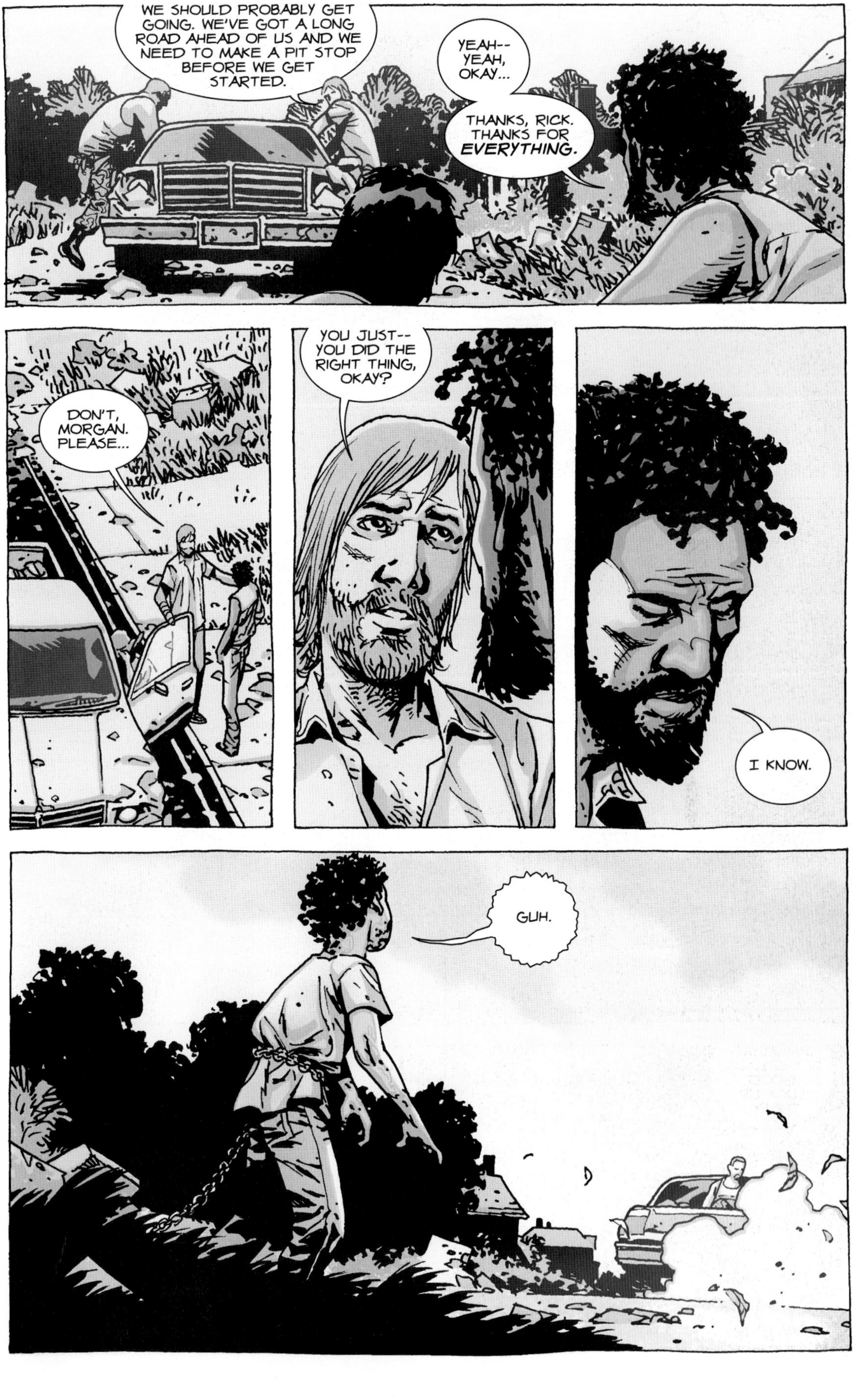
WE SHOULD PROBABLY GET GOING. WE'VE GOT A LONG ROAD AHEAD OF US AND WE NEED TO MAKE A PIT STOP BEFORE WE GET STARTED.
YEAH-- YEAH, OKAY...
THANKS, RICK. THANKS FOR *EVERYTHING.*
DON'T, MORGAN. PLEASE...
YOU JUST-- YOU DID THE RIGHT THING, OKAY?
I KNOW.
GUH.

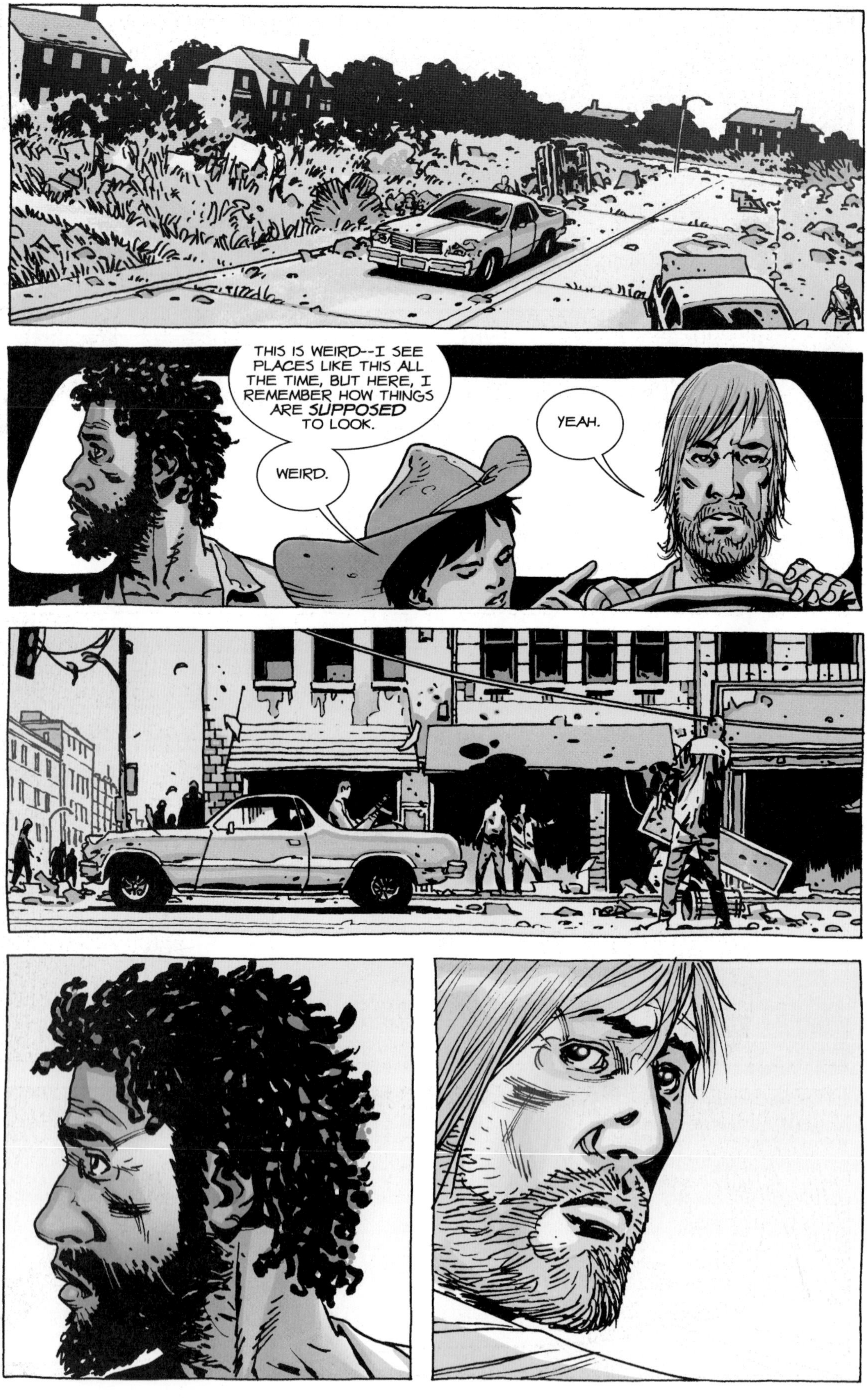
THIS IS WEIRD--I SEE PLACES LIKE THIS ALL THE TIME, BUT HERE, I REMEMBER HOW THINGS ARE SUPPOSED TO LOOK.
WEIRD.
YEAH.

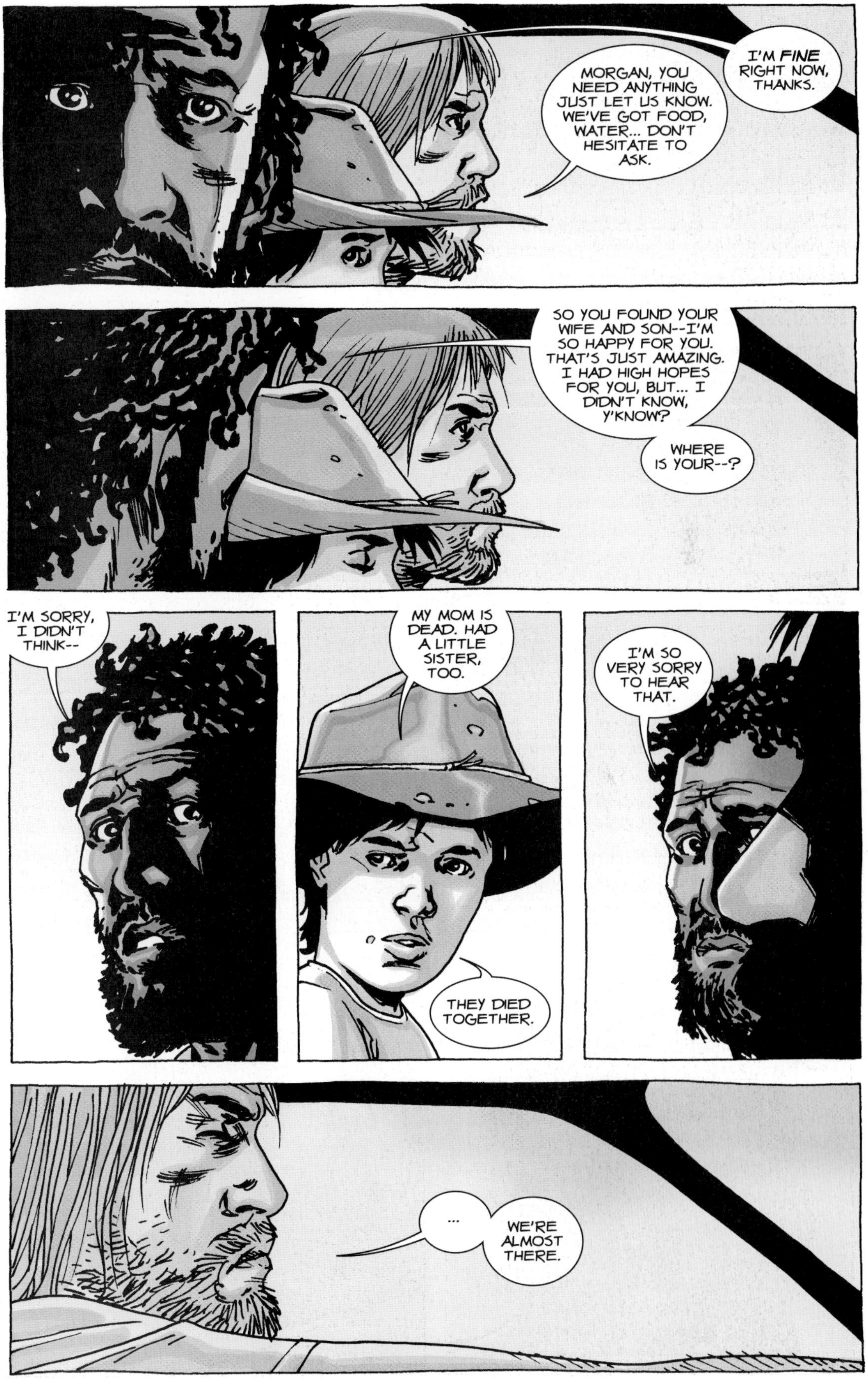

MORGAN, YOU NEED ANYTHING JUST LET US KNOW. WE'VE GOT FOOD, WATER... DON'T HESITATE TO ASK.
I'M FINE RIGHT NOW, THANKS.
SO YOU FOUND YOUR WIFE AND SON--I'M SO HAPPY FOR YOU. THAT'S JUST AMAZING. I HAD HIGH HOPES FOR YOU, BUT... I DIDN'T KNOW, Y'KNOW?
WHERE IS YOUR--?
I'M SORRY, I DIDN'T THINK--
MY MOM IS DEAD. HAD A LITTLE SISTER, TOO.
THEY DIED TOGETHER.
I'M SO VERY SORRY TO HEAR THAT.
...
WE'RE ALMOST THERE.

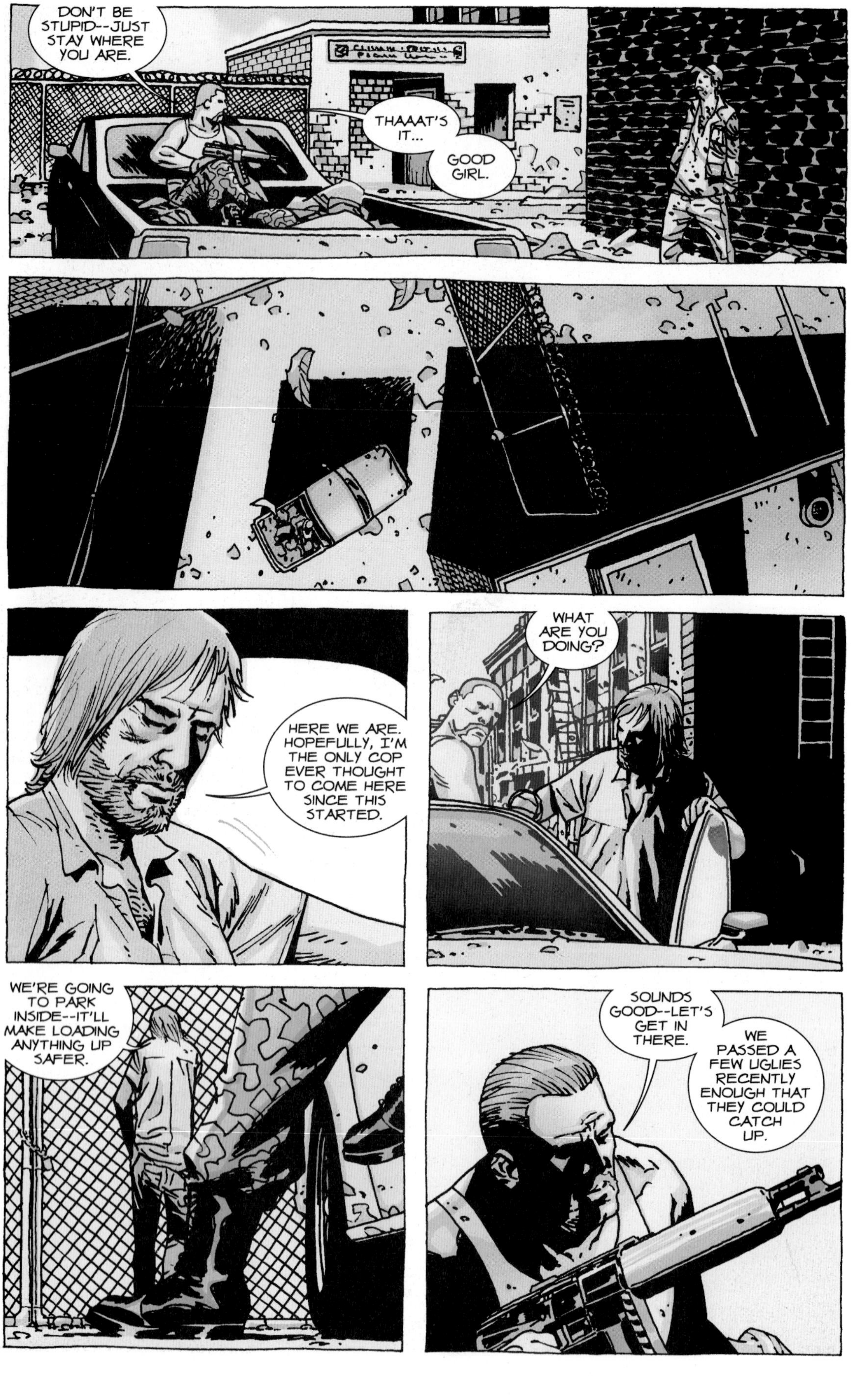
DON'T BE STUPID--JUST STAY WHERE YOU ARE.
THAAAT'S IT...
GOOD GIRL.
HERE WE ARE. HOPEFULLY, I'M THE ONLY COP EVER THOUGHT TO COME HERE SINCE THIS STARTED.
WHAT ARE YOU DOING?
WE'RE GOING TO PARK INSIDE--IT'LL MAKE LOADING ANYTHING UP SAFER.
SOUNDS GOOD--LET'S GET IN THERE.
WE PASSED A FEW UGLIES RECENTLY ENOUGH THAT THEY COULD CATCH UP.

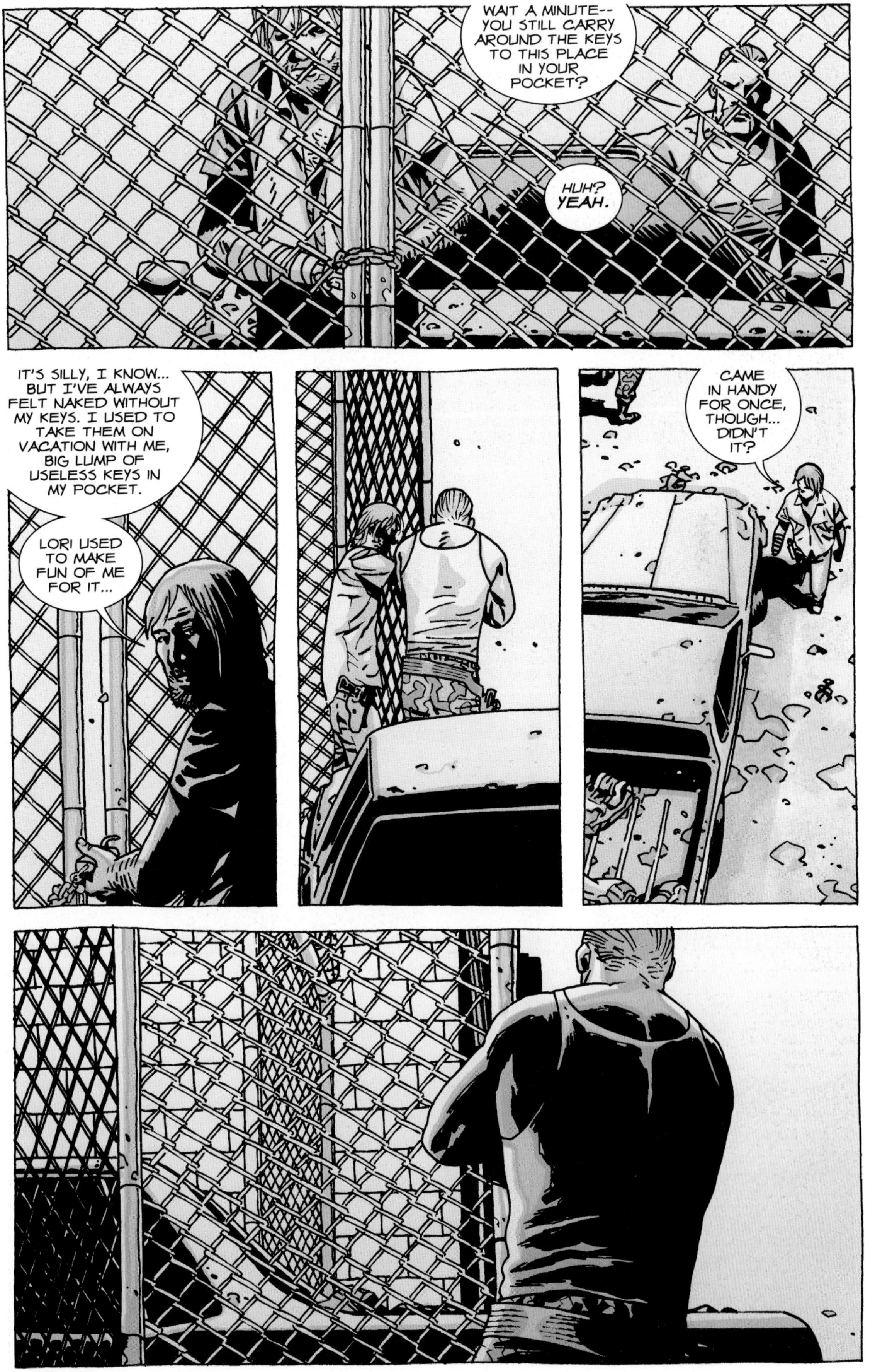

WAIT A MINUTE-- YOU STILL CARRY AROUND THE KEYS TO THIS PLACE IN YOUR POCKET?
HUH? YEAH.
IT'S SILLY, I KNOW... BUT I'VE ALWAYS FELT NAKED WITHOUT MY KEYS. I USED TO TAKE THEM ON VACATION WITH ME, BIG LUMP OF USELESS KEYS IN MY POCKET.
LORI USED TO MAKE FUN OF ME FOR IT...
CAME IN HANDY FOR ONCE, THOUGH... DIDN'T IT?

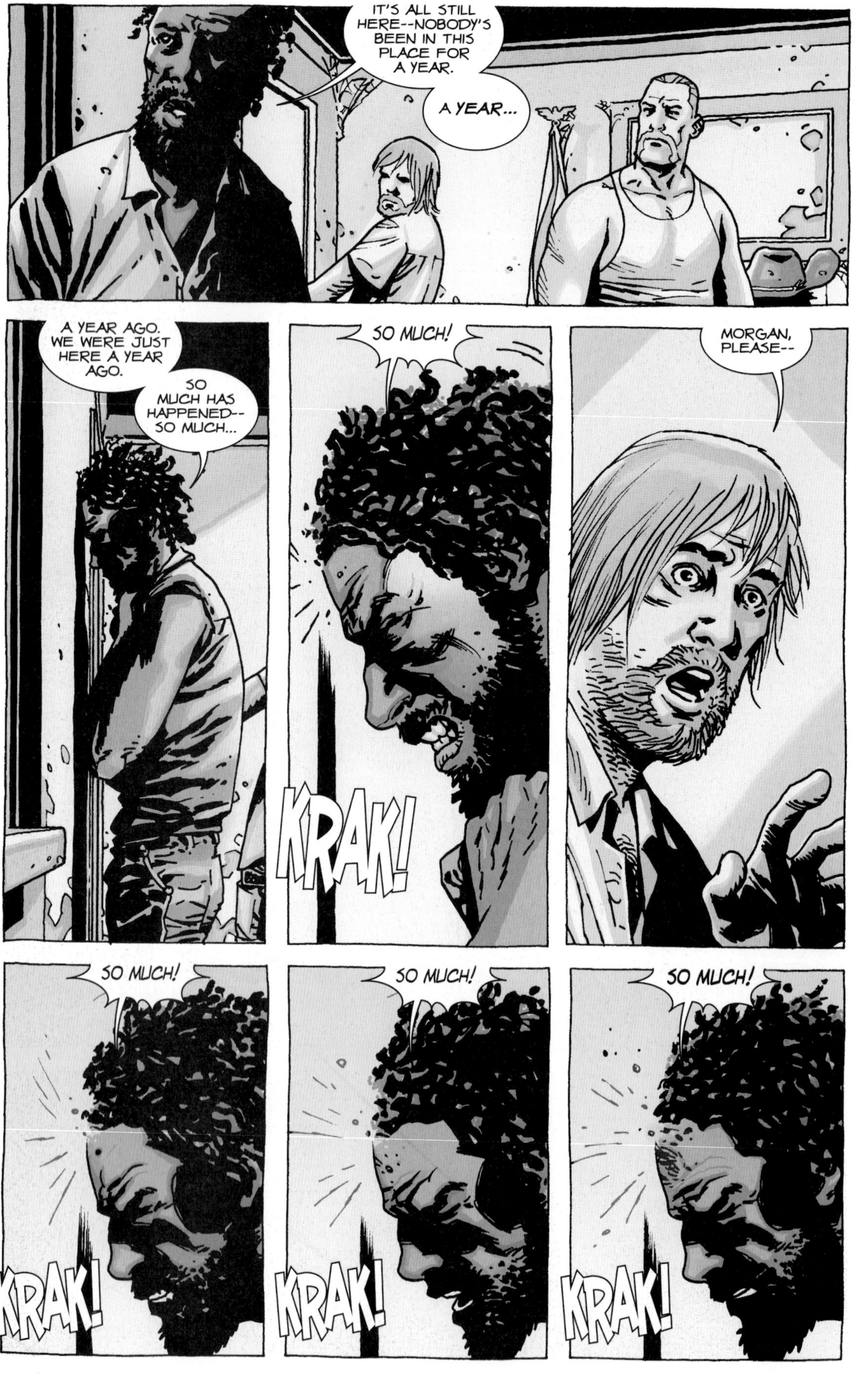

IT'S ALL STILL HERE--NOBODY'S BEEN IN THIS PLACE FOR A YEAR.
A YEAR...
A YEAR AGO. WE WERE JUST HERE A YEAR AGO.
SO MUCH HAS HAPPENED-- SO MUCH...
SO MUCH!
KRAK!
MORGAN, PLEASE--
SO MUCH!
KRAK!
SO MUCH!
KRAK!
SO MUCH!
KRAK!

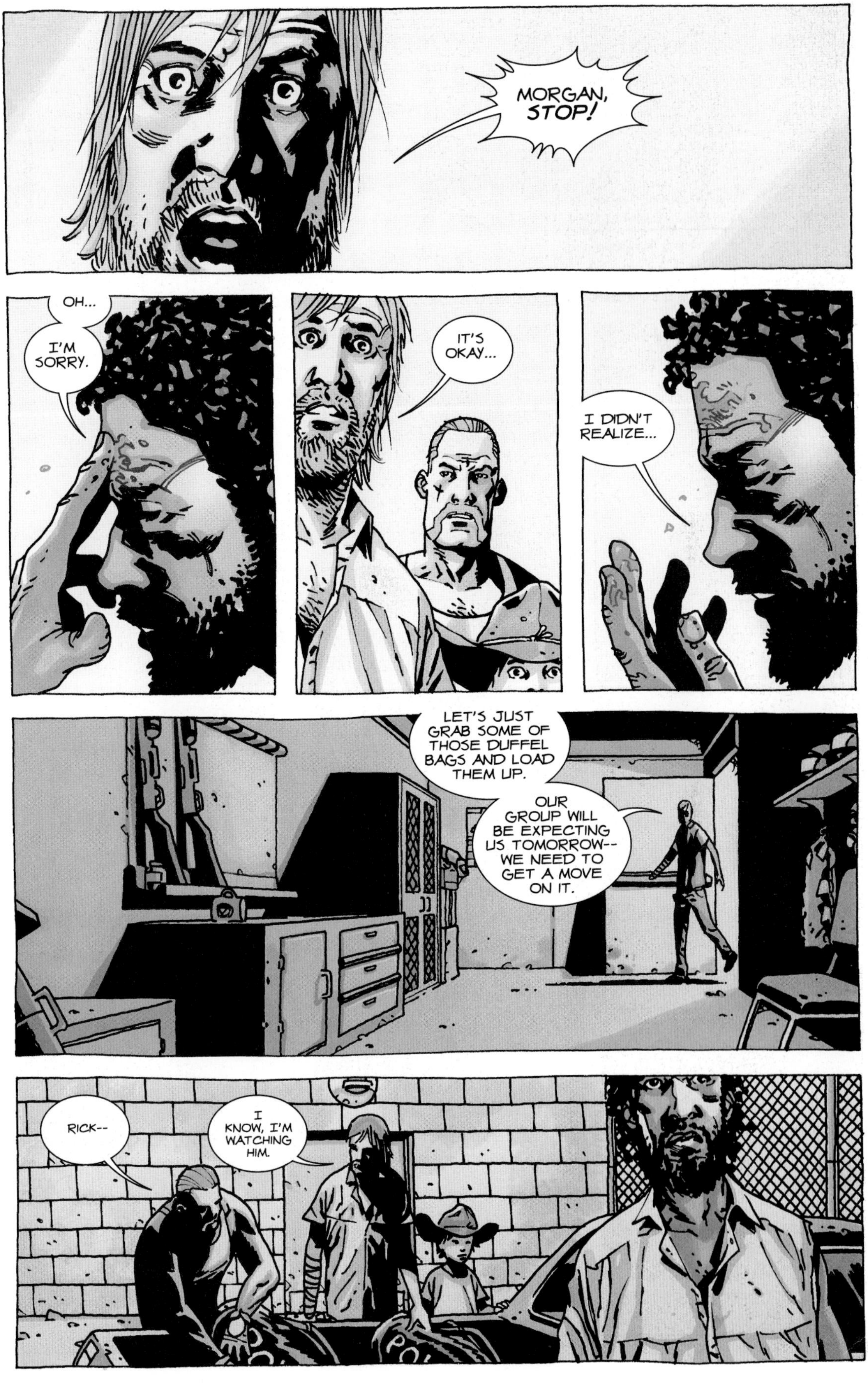
MORGAN, STOP!
OH...
I'M SORRY.
IT'S OKAY...
I DIDN'T REALIZE...
LET'S JUST GRAB SOME OF THOSE DUFFEL BAGS AND LOAD THEM UP.
OUR GROUP WILL BE EXPECTING US TOMORROW-- WE NEED TO GET A MOVE ON IT.
RICK--
I KNOW, I'M WATCHING HIM.

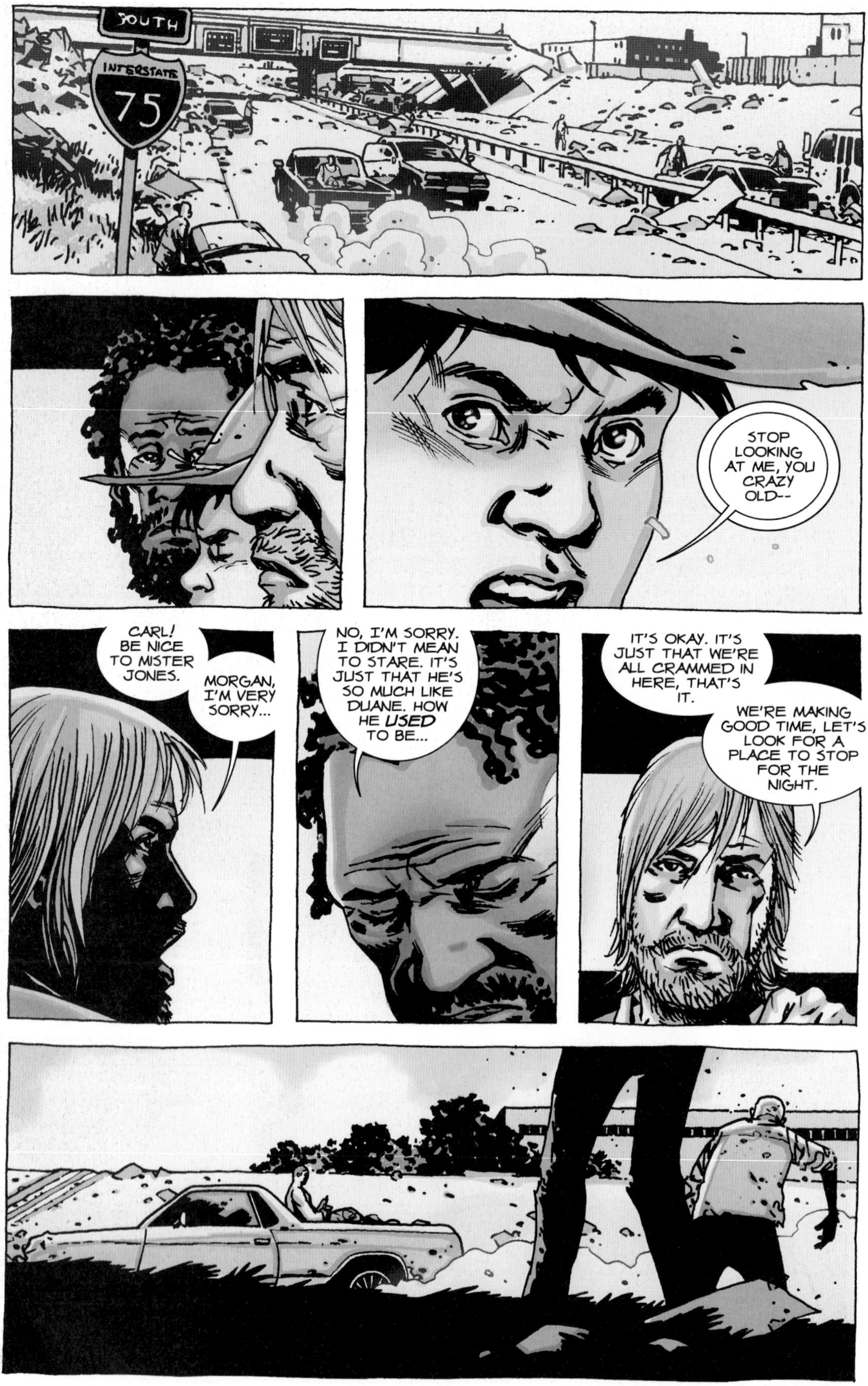
SOUTH
INTERSTATE
75
STOP LOOKING AT ME, YOU CRAZY OLD--
CARL! BE NICE TO MISTER JONES.
MORGAN, I'M VERY SORRY...
NO, I'M SORRY. I DIDN'T MEAN TO STARE. IT'S JUST THAT HE'S SO MUCH LIKE DUANE. HOW HE USED TO BE...
IT'S OKAY. IT'S JUST THAT WE'RE ALL CRAMMED IN HERE, THAT'S IT.
WE'RE MAKING GOOD TIME, LET'S LOOK FOR A PLACE TO STOP FOR THE NIGHT.

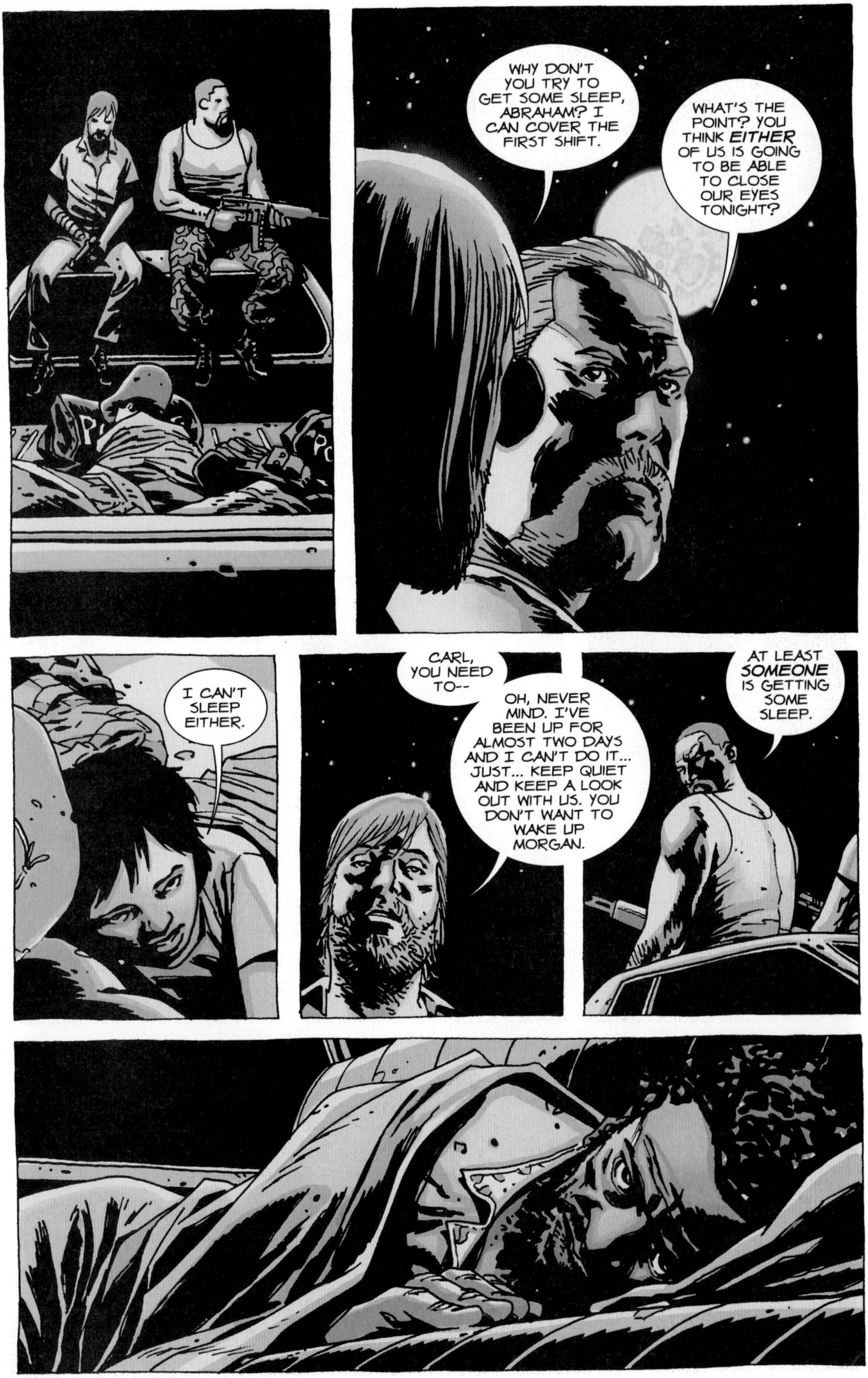
WHY DON'T YOU TRY TO GET SOME SLEEP, ABRAHAM? I CAN COVER THE FIRST SHIFT.
WHAT'S THE POINT? YOU THINK *EITHER* OF US IS GOING TO BE ABLE TO CLOSE OUR EYES TONIGHT?
I CAN'T SLEEP EITHER.
CARL, YOU NEED TO--
OH, NEVER MIND. I'VE BEEN UP FOR ALMOST TWO DAYS AND I CAN'T DO IT... JUST... KEEP QUIET AND KEEP A LOOK OUT WITH US. YOU DON'T WANT TO WAKE UP MORGAN.
AT LEAST *SOMEONE* IS GETTING SOME SLEEP.

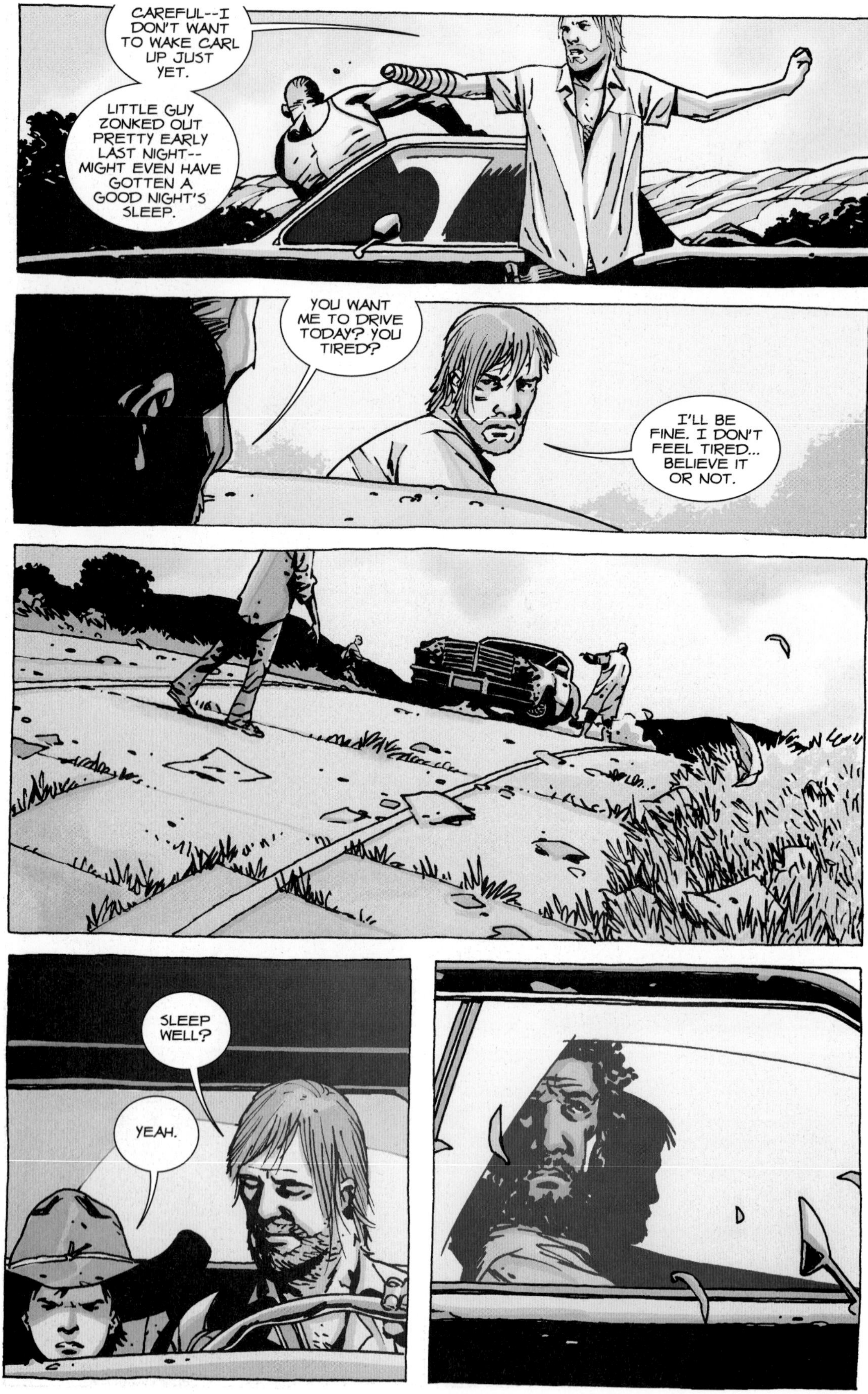
CAREFUL--I DON'T WANT TO WAKE CARL UP JUST YET.
LITTLE GUY ZONKED OUT PRETTY EARLY LAST NIGHT-- MIGHT EVEN HAVE GOTTEN A GOOD NIGHT'S SLEEP.
YOU WANT ME TO DRIVE TODAY? YOU TIRED?
I'LL BE FINE. I DON'T FEEL TIRED... BELIEVE IT OR NOT.
SLEEP WELL?
YEAH.

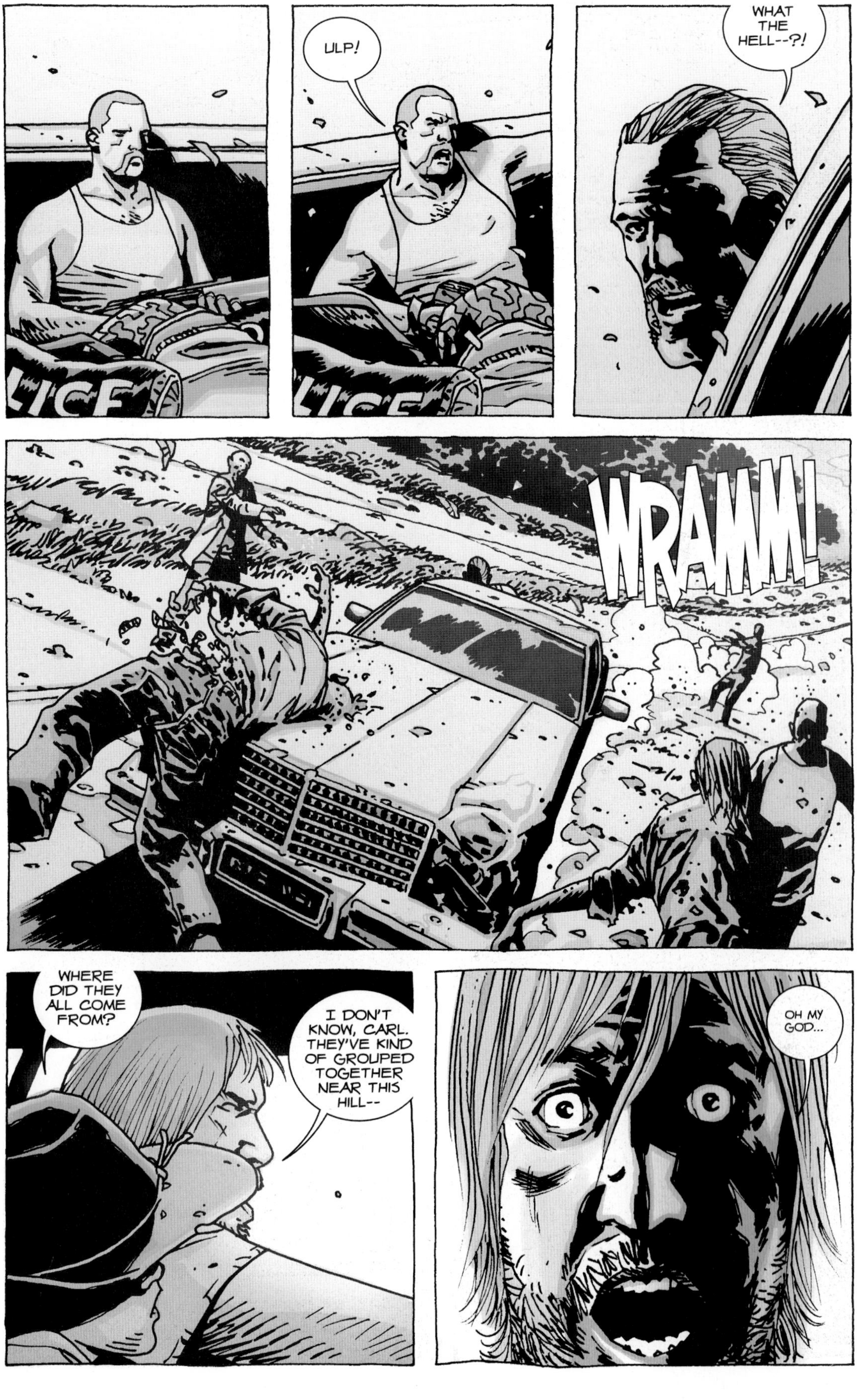
ULP!
WHAT THE HELL--?!
WRAMM!
WHERE DID THEY ALL COME FROM?
I DON'T KNOW, CARL. THEY'VE KIND OF GROUPED TOGETHER NEAR THIS HILL--
OH MY GOD...

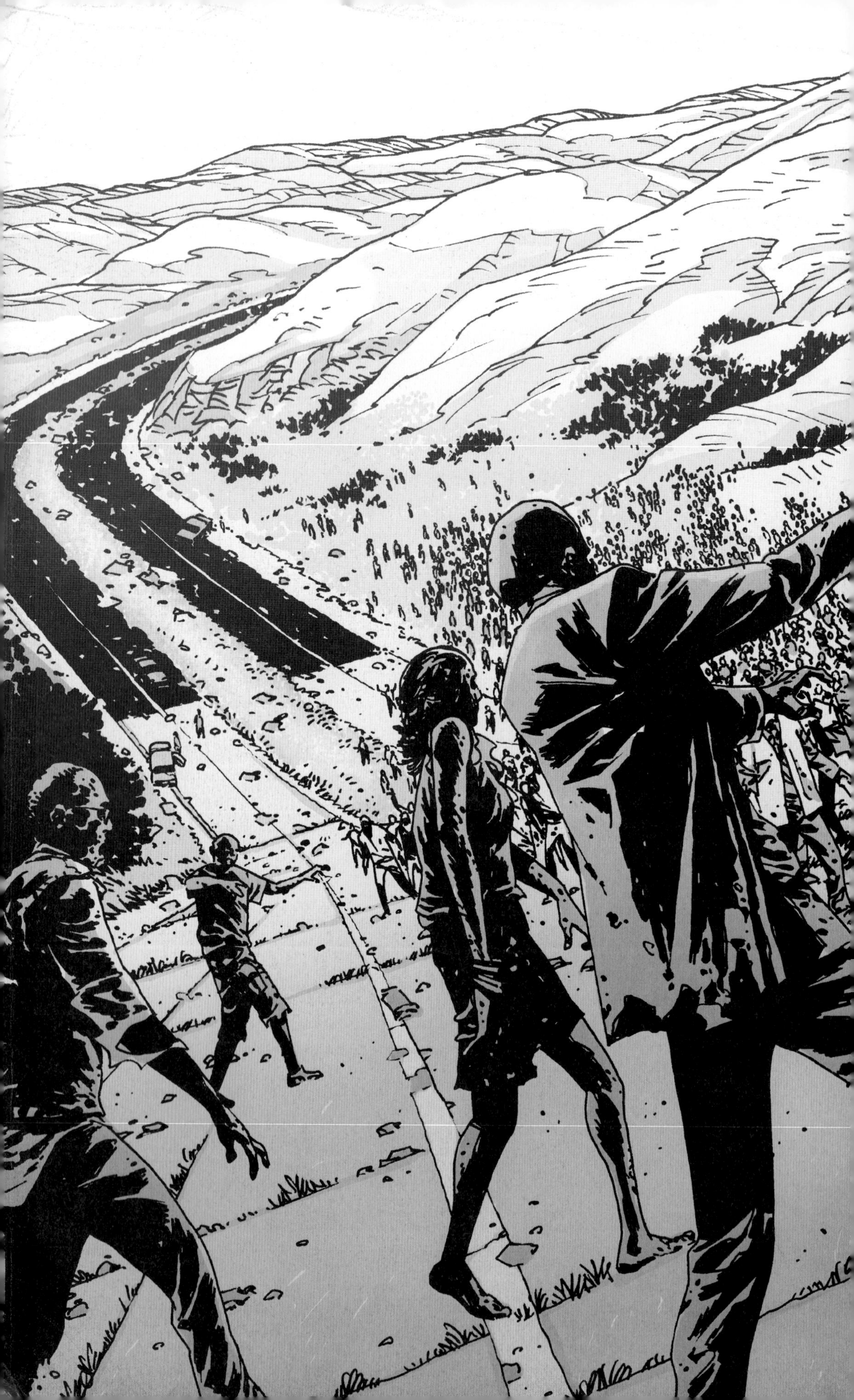

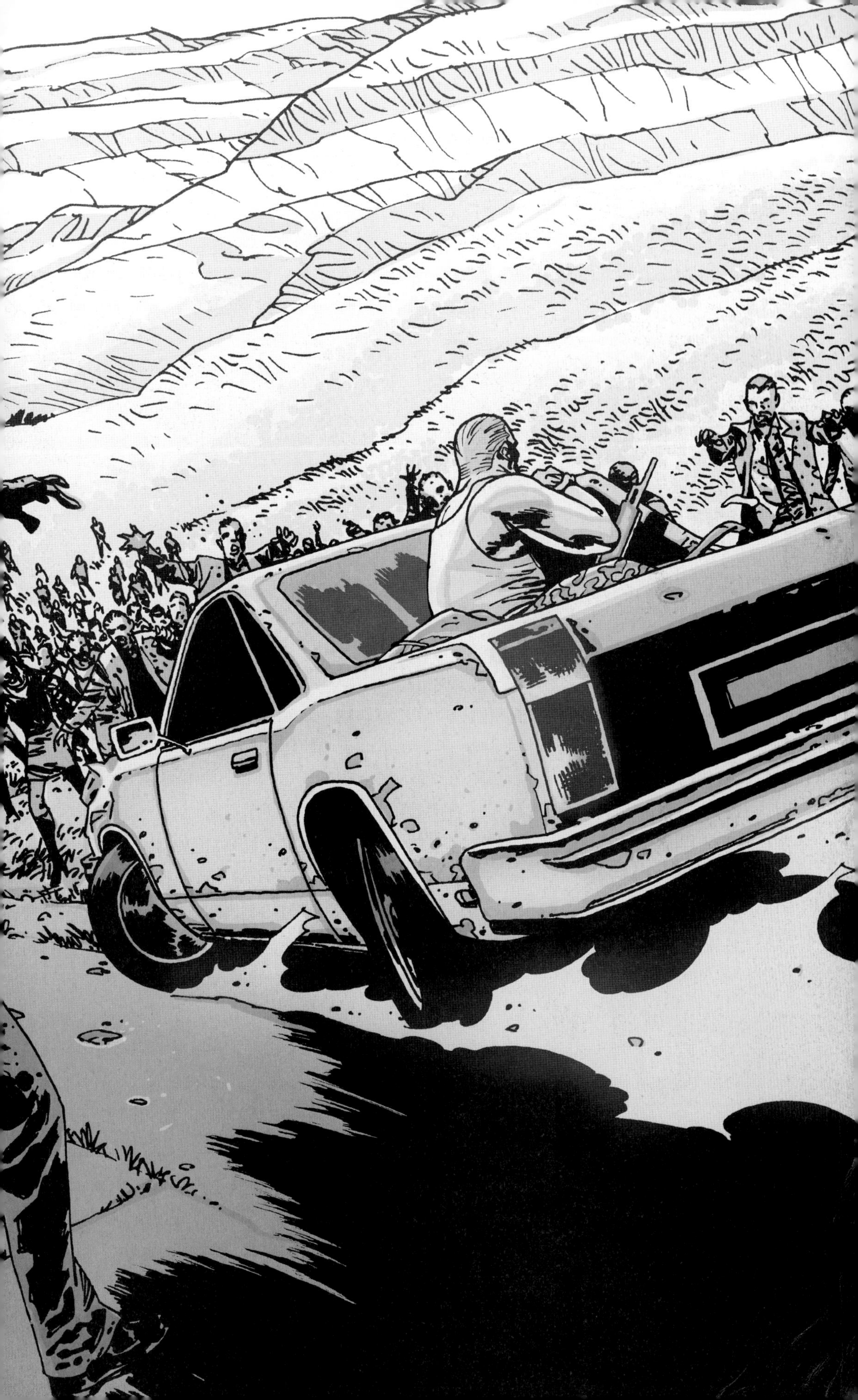

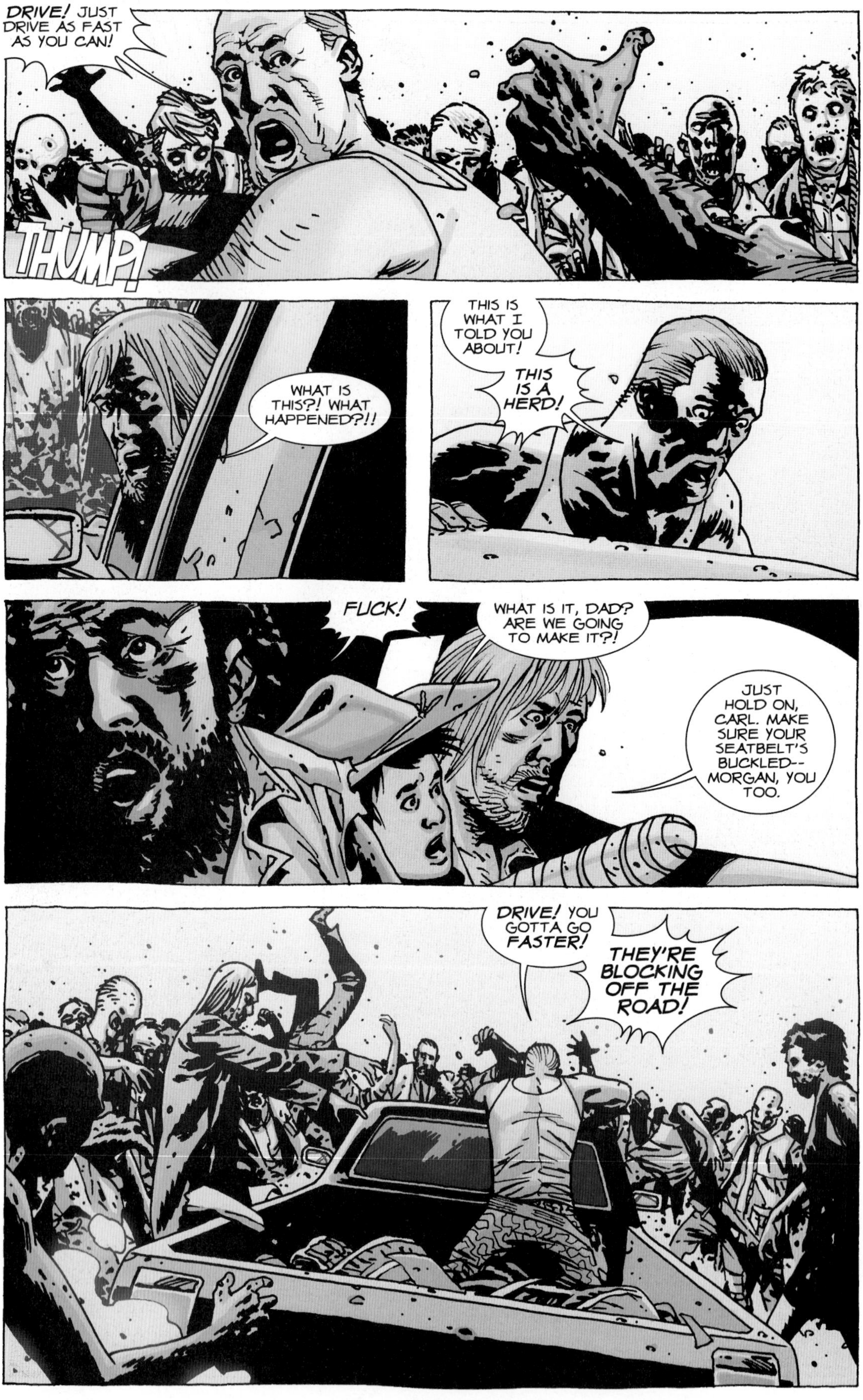
DRIVE! JUST DRIVE AS FAST AS YOU CAN!
THUMP!
WHAT IS THIS?! WHAT HAPPENED?!!
THIS IS WHAT I TOLD YOU ABOUT!
THIS IS A HERD!
FUCK!
WHAT IS IT, DAD? ARE WE GOING TO MAKE IT?!
JUST HOLD ON, CARL. MAKE SURE YOUR SEATBELT'S BUCKLED-- MORGAN, YOU TOO.
DRIVE! YOU GOTTA GO FASTER!
THEY'RE BLOCKING OFF THE ROAD!

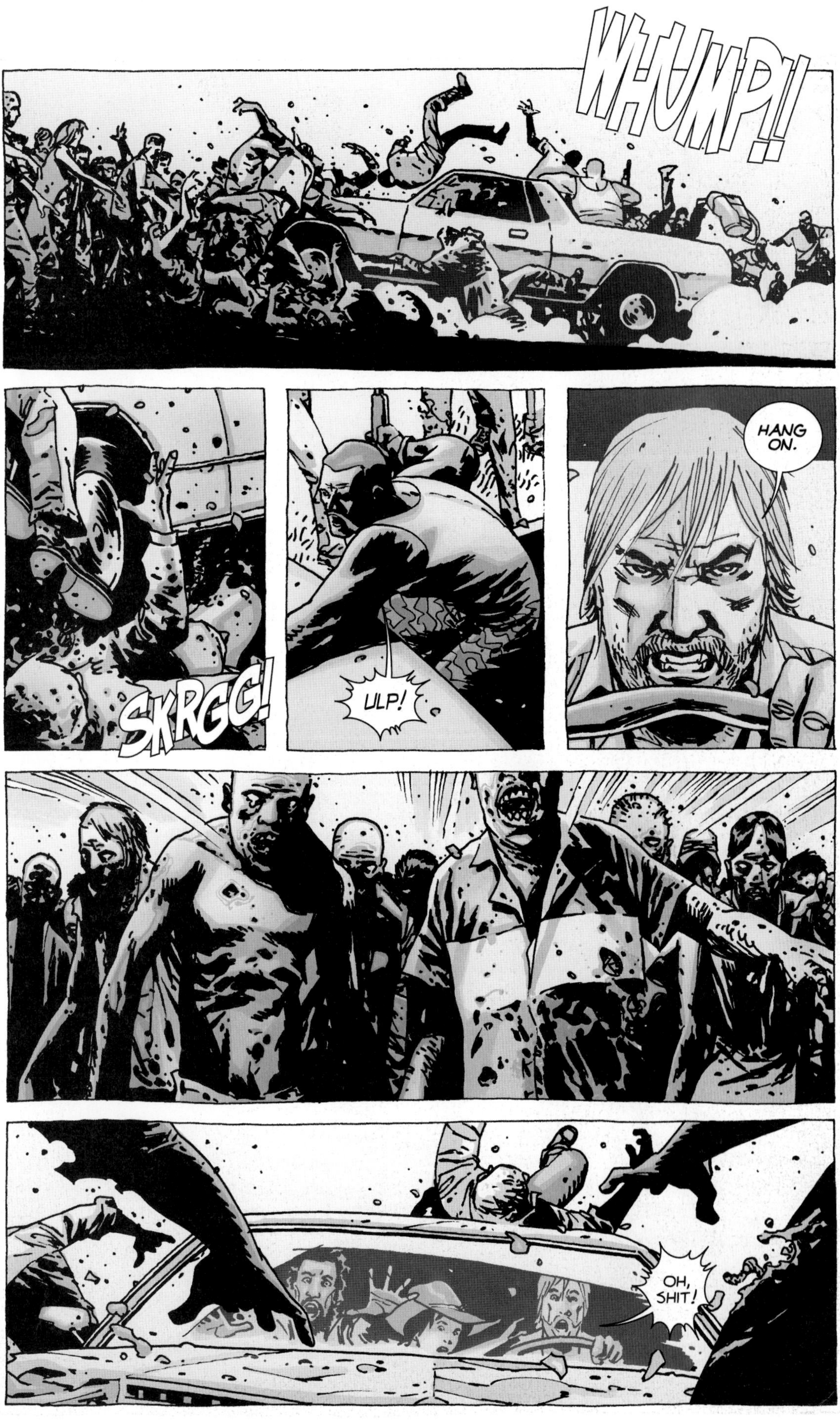
WHUMP!!
SKRGG!
ULP!
HANG ON.
OH, SHIT!

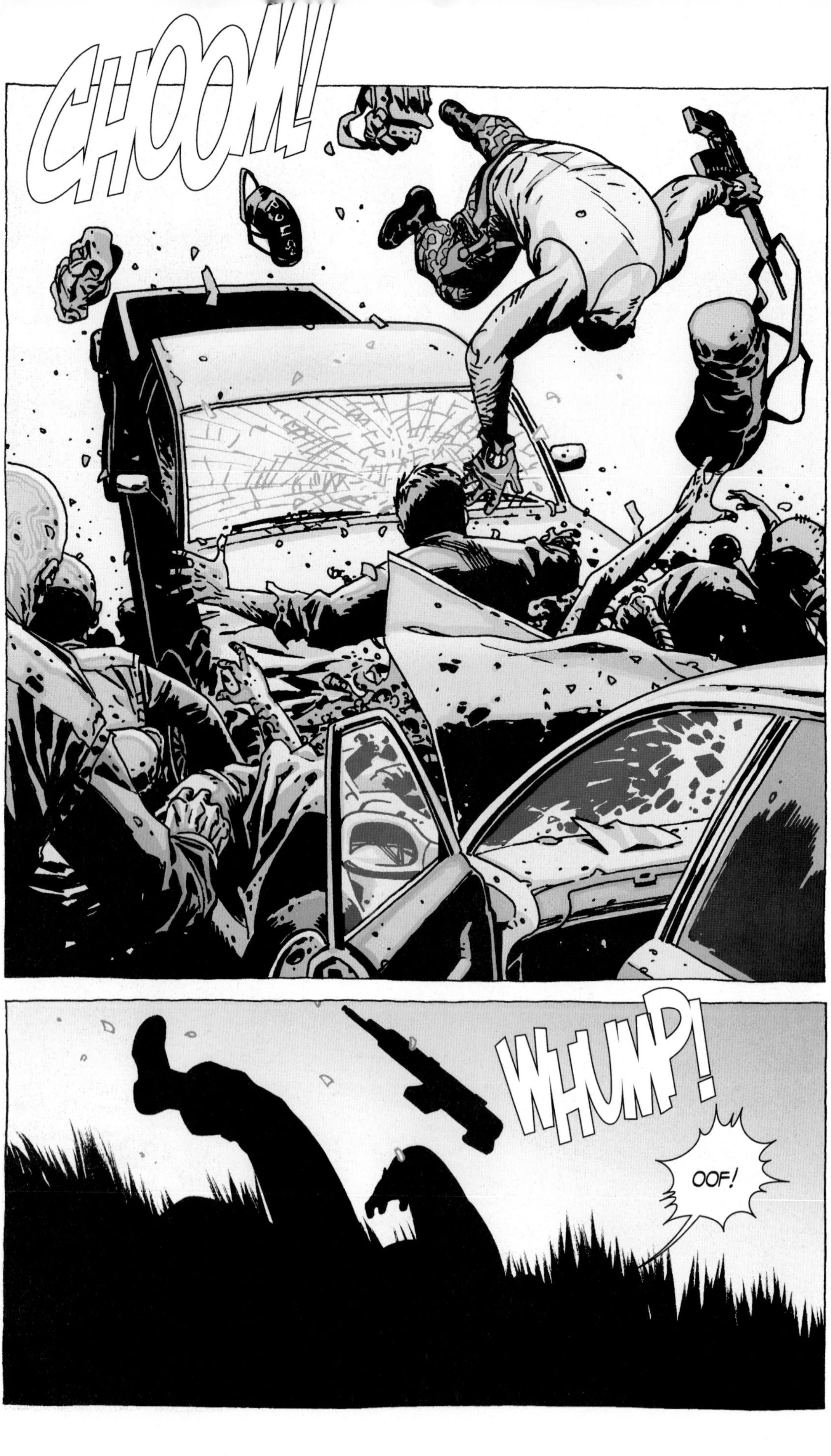
CHOOM!
WHUMP!
OOF!

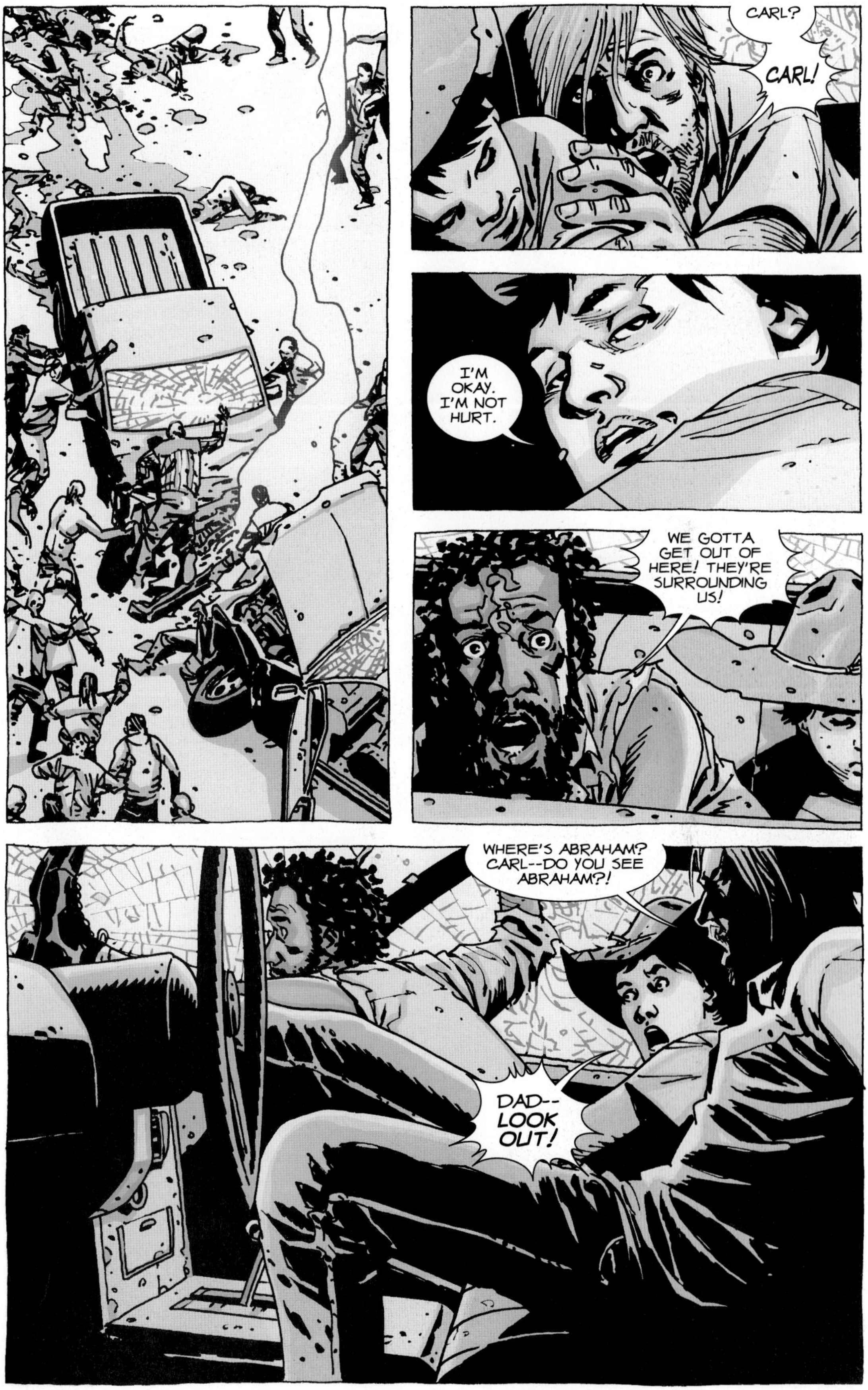
CARL?
CARL!
I'M OKAY. I'M NOT HURT.
WE GOTTA GET OUT OF HERE! THEY'RE SURROUNDING US!
WHERE'S ABRAHAM? CARL--DO YOU SEE ABRAHAM?!
DAD-- LOOK OUT!

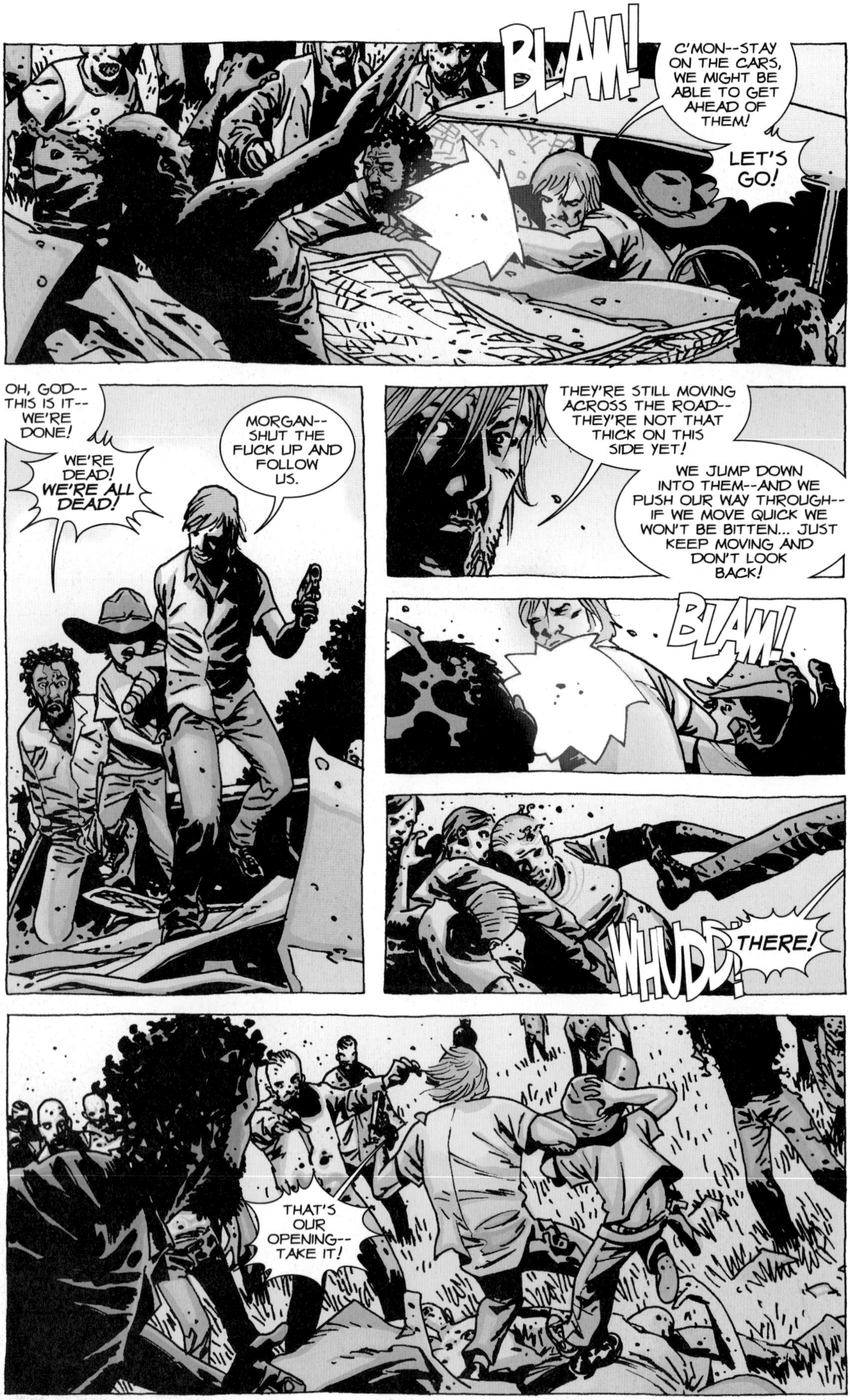
BLAM!
C'MON--STAY ON THE CARS, WE MIGHT BE ABLE TO GET AHEAD OF THEM!
LET'S GO!
OH, GOD--THIS IS IT--WE'RE DONE!
WE'RE DEAD! WE'RE ALL DEAD!
MORGAN--SHUT THE FUCK UP AND FOLLOW US.
THEY'RE STILL MOVING ACROSS THE ROAD--THEY'RE NOT THAT THICK ON THIS SIDE YET!
WE JUMP DOWN INTO THEM--AND WE PUSH OUR WAY THROUGH--IF WE MOVE QUICK WE WON'T BE BITTEN... JUST KEEP MOVING AND DON'T LOOK BACK!
BLAM!
WHUDD!
THERE!
THAT'S OUR OPENING--TAKE IT!

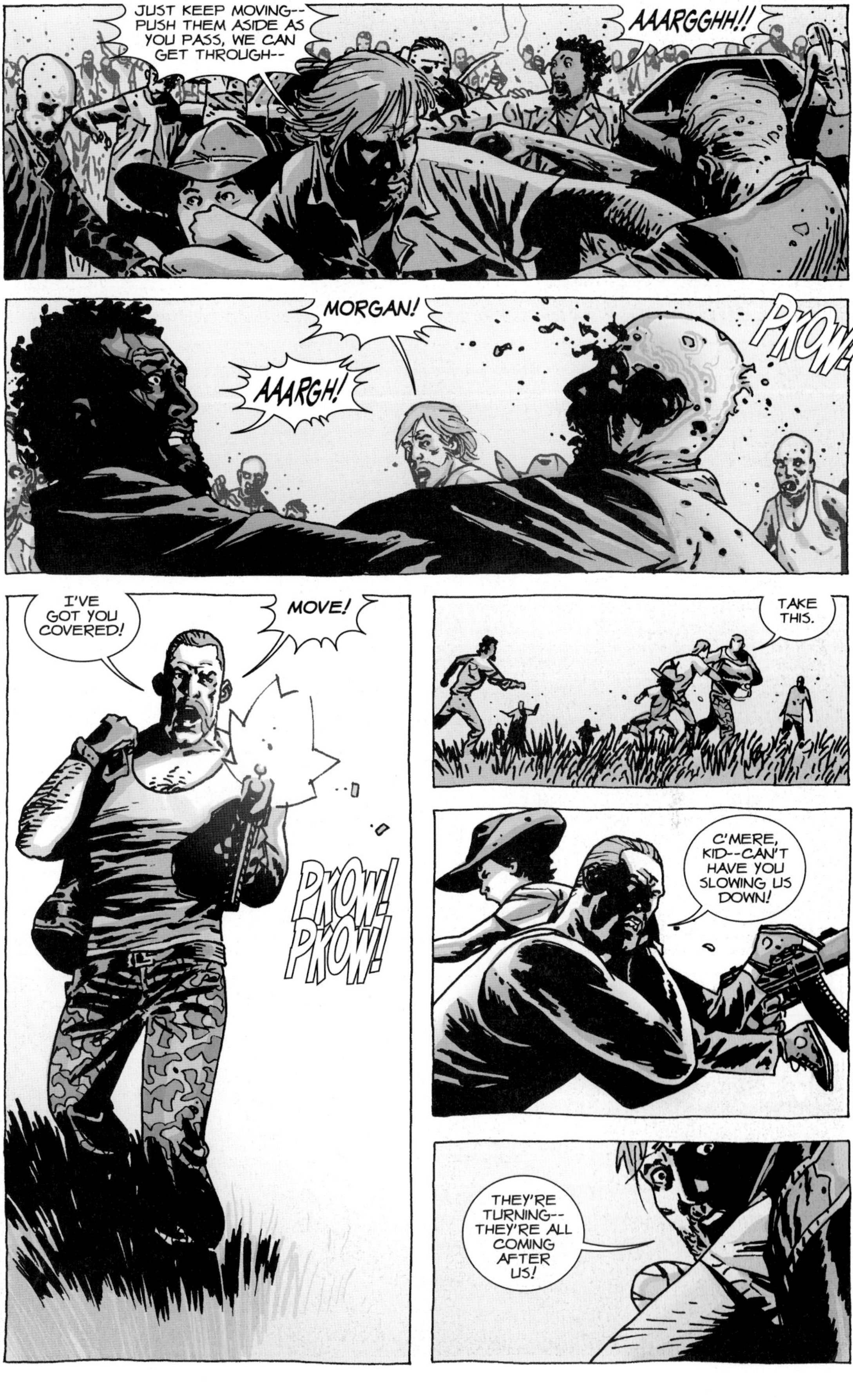
JUST KEEP MOVING-- PUSH THEM ASIDE AS YOU PASS, WE CAN GET THROUGH--
AAARGGHH!!
MORGAN!
AAARGH!
PKOW!
I'VE GOT YOU COVERED!
MOVE!
PKOW! PKOW!
TAKE THIS.
C'MERE, KID--CAN'T HAVE YOU SLOWING US DOWN!
THEY'RE TURNING-- THEY'RE ALL COMING AFTER US!

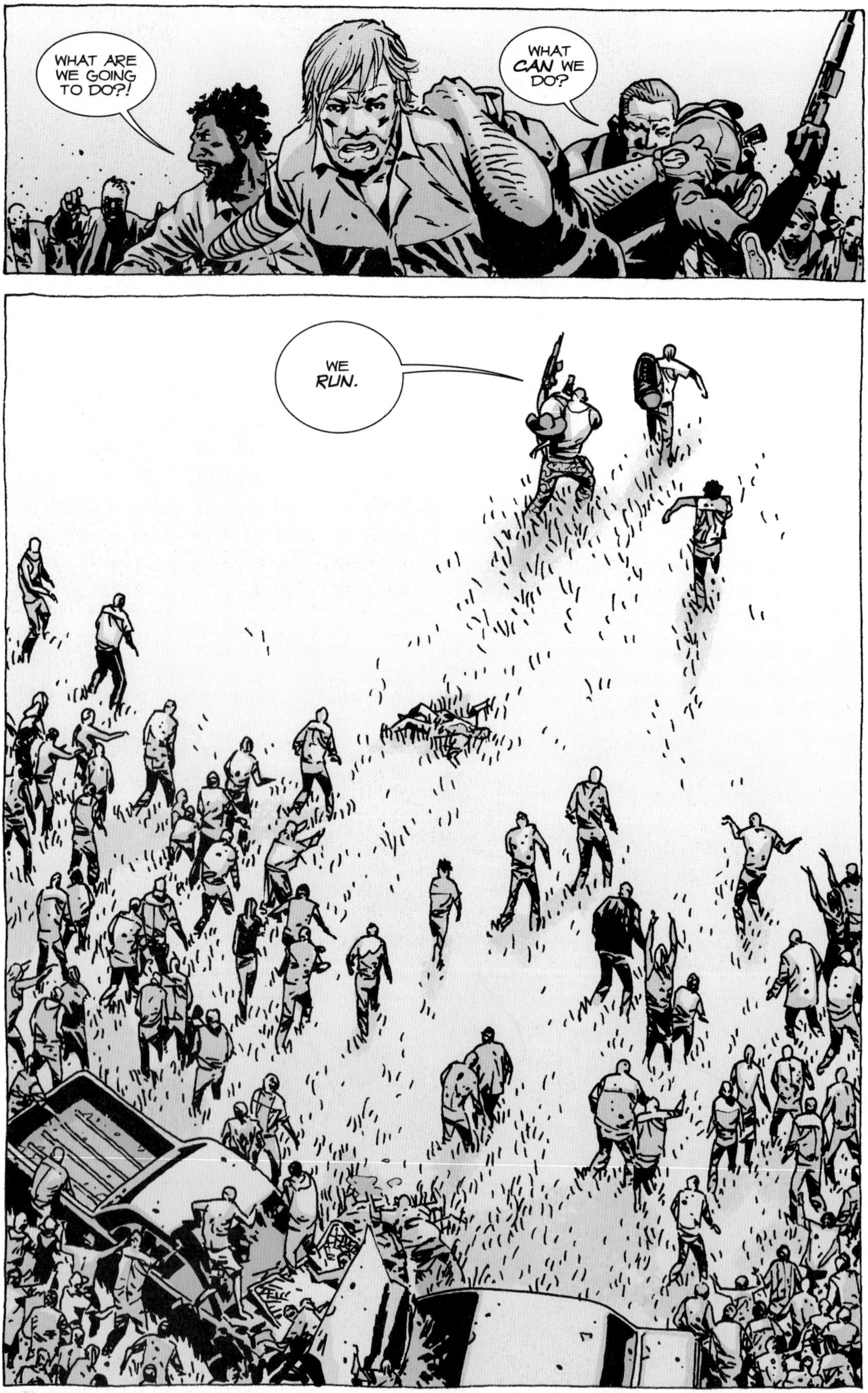
WHAT ARE WE GOING TO DO?!
WHAT CAN WE DO?
WE RUN.

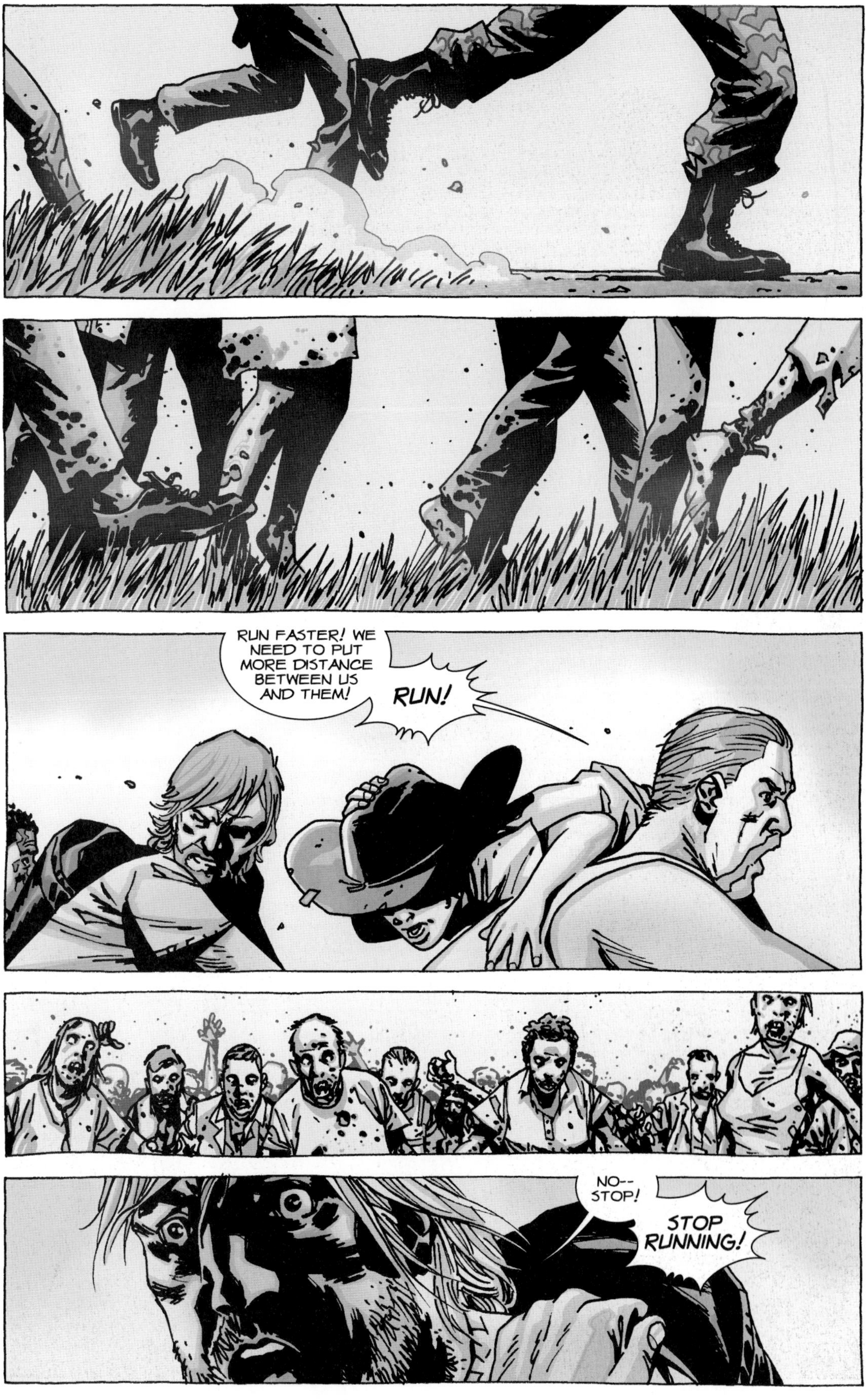
RUN FASTER! WE NEED TO PUT MORE DISTANCE BETWEEN US AND THEM!
RUN!
NO-- STOP!
STOP RUNNING!

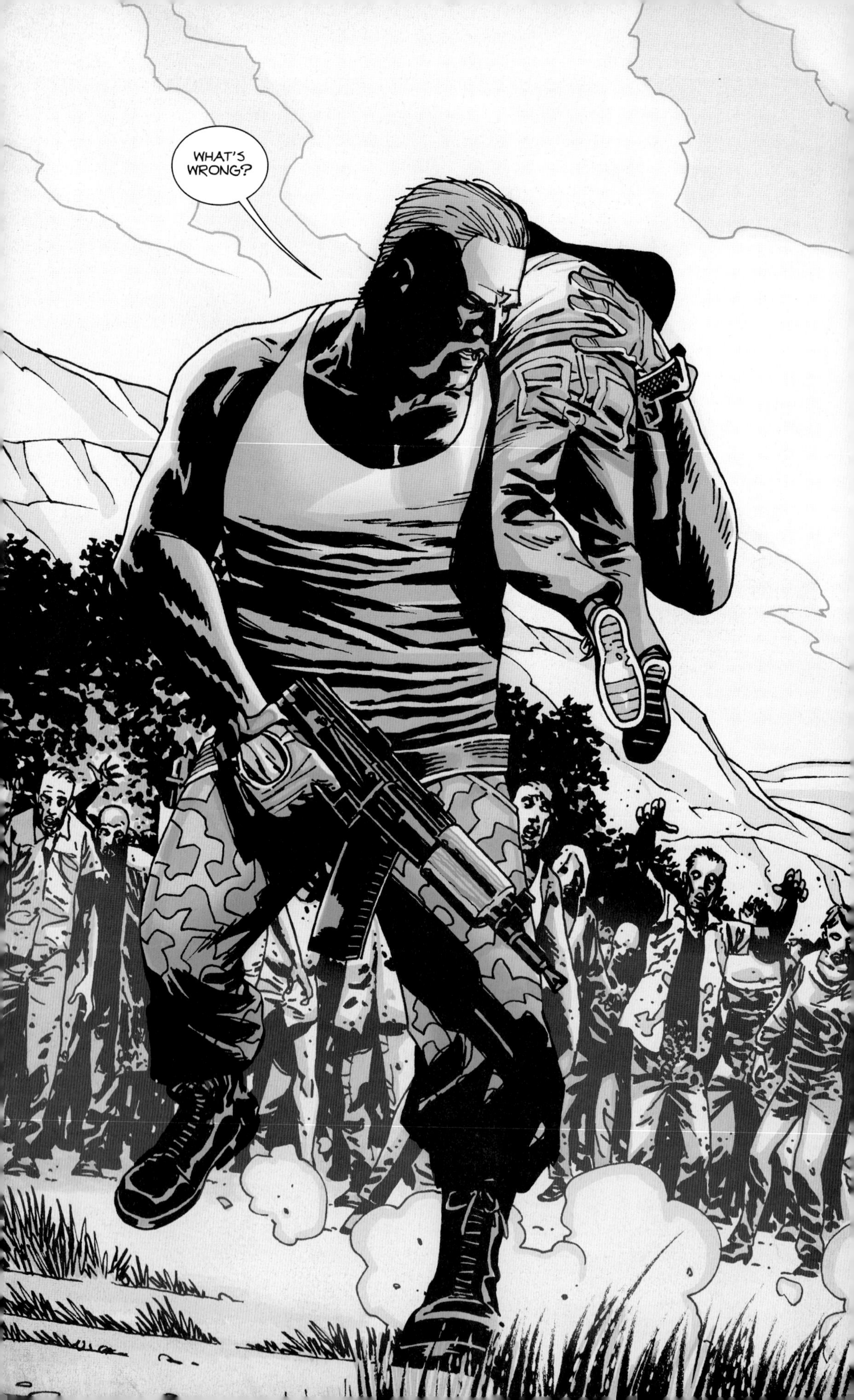
WHAT'S WRONG?

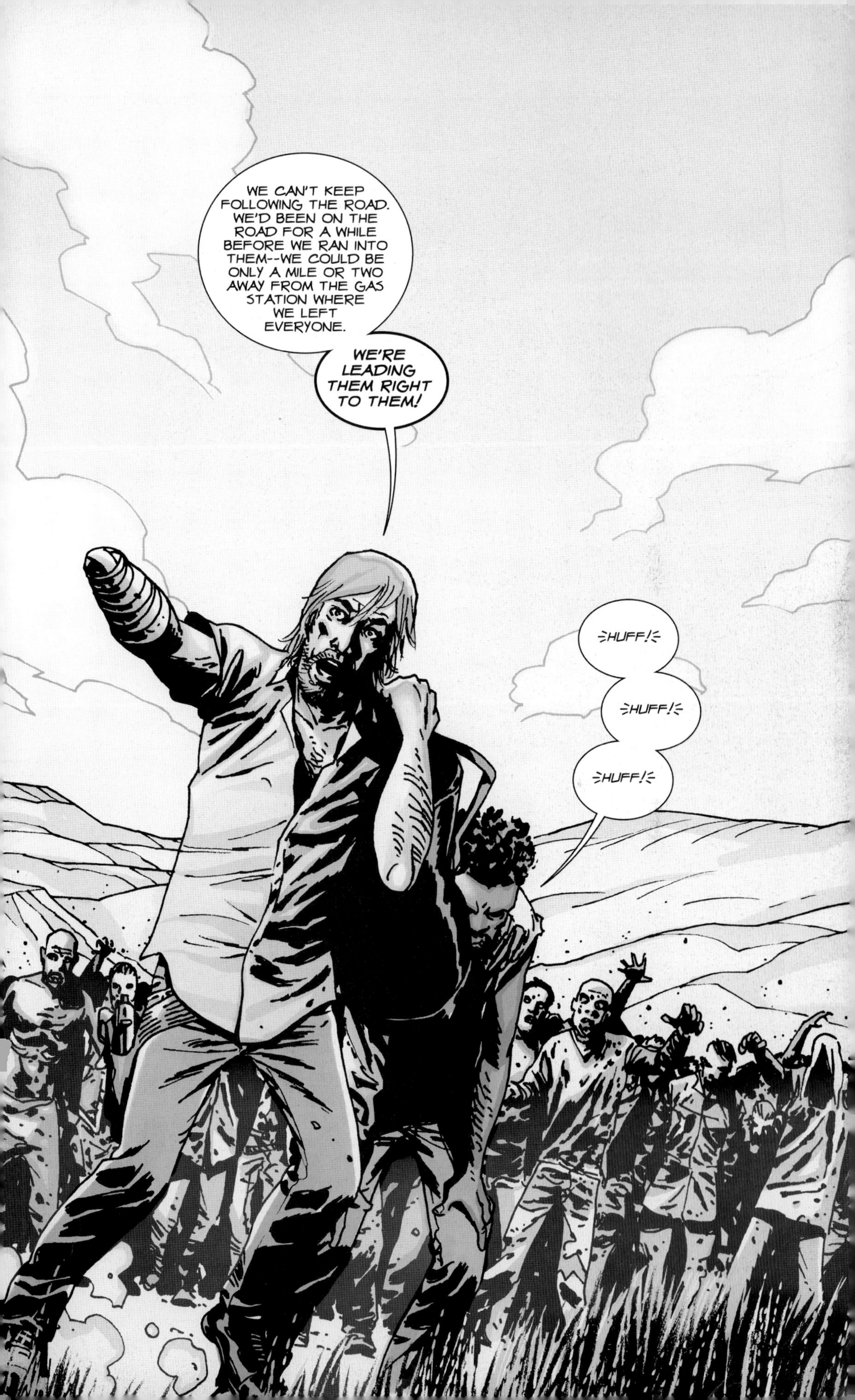
WE CAN'T KEEP FOLLOWING THE ROAD. WE'D BEEN ON THE ROAD FOR A WHILE BEFORE WE RAN INTO THEM--WE COULD BE ONLY A MILE OR TWO AWAY FROM THE GAS STATION WHERE WE LEFT EVERYONE.
WE'RE LEADING THEM RIGHT TO THEM!
HUFF!
HUFF!
HUFF!

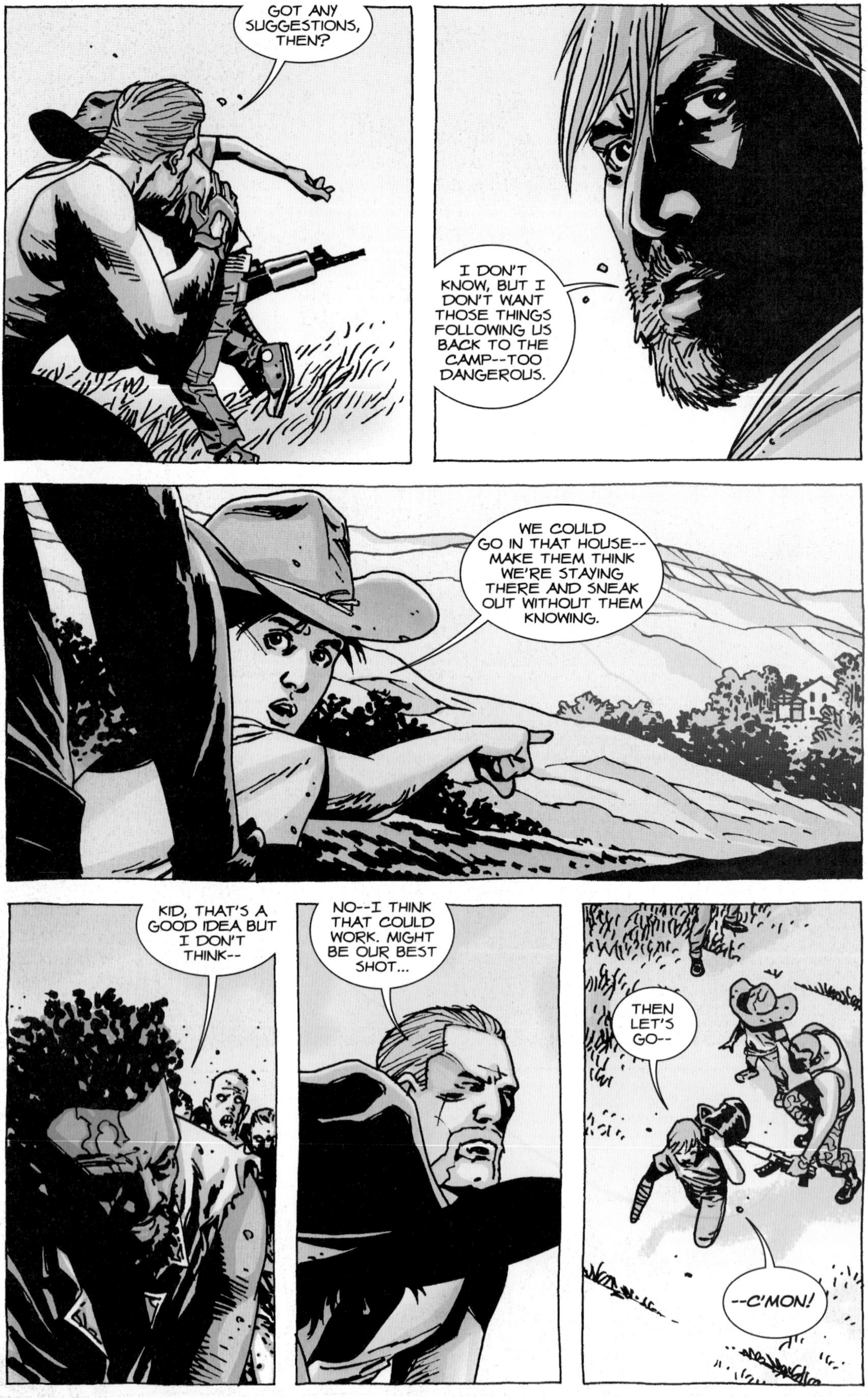
GOT ANY SUGGESTIONS, THEN?
I DON'T KNOW, BUT I DON'T WANT THOSE THINGS FOLLOWING US BACK TO THE CAMP--TOO DANGEROUS.
WE COULD GO IN THAT HOUSE-- MAKE THEM THINK WE'RE STAYING THERE AND SNEAK OUT WITHOUT THEM KNOWING.
KID, THAT'S A GOOD IDEA BUT I DON'T THINK--
NO--I THINK THAT COULD WORK. MIGHT BE OUR BEST SHOT...
THEN LET'S GO--
--C'MON!

KEEP RUNNING!

ALMOST THERE.

ONCE WE GET INSIDE... WE CAN JUST SNEAK OUT THE BACK--THEY'LL THINK WE STAYED INSIDE AND WON'T FOLLOW US.

WE'RE GOING TO NEED SOME WAY OF MAKING THEM THINK WE'RE STILL IN HERE SO WE HAVE ENOUGH TIME TO GET AWAY--

DAMN IT!

IT'S LOCKED.

MOVE.

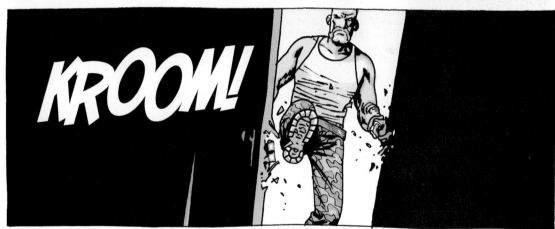

KROOM!

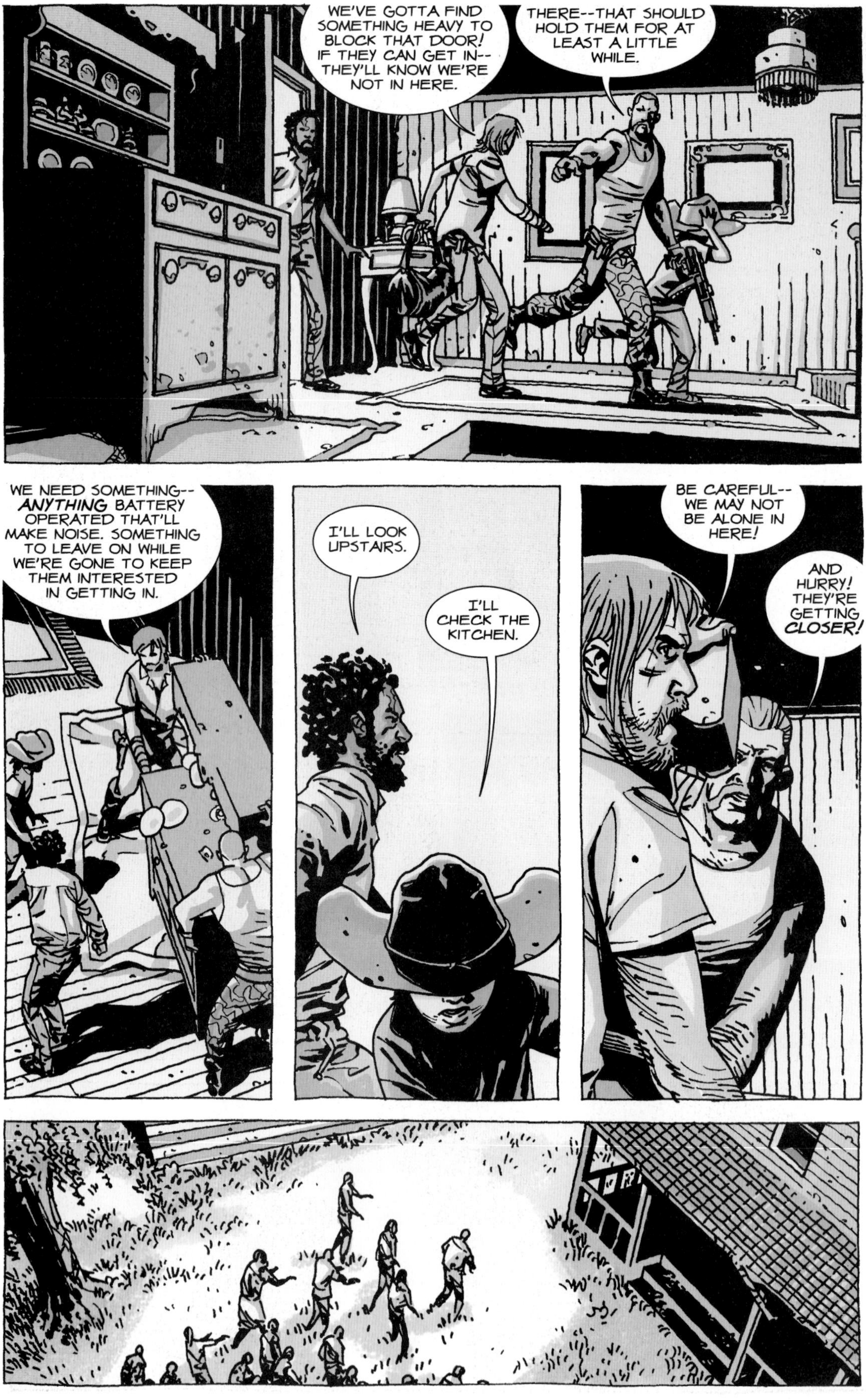
WE'VE GOTTA FIND SOMETHING HEAVY TO BLOCK THAT DOOR! IF THEY CAN GET IN-- THEY'LL KNOW WE'RE NOT IN HERE.
THERE--THAT SHOULD HOLD THEM FOR AT LEAST A LITTLE WHILE.
WE NEED SOMETHING-- ANYTHING BATTERY OPERATED THAT'LL MAKE NOISE. SOMETHING TO LEAVE ON WHILE WE'RE GONE TO KEEP THEM INTERESTED IN GETTING IN.
I'LL LOOK UPSTAIRS.
I'LL CHECK THE KITCHEN.
BE CAREFUL-- WE MAY NOT BE ALONE IN HERE!
AND HURRY! THEY'RE GETTING CLOSER!

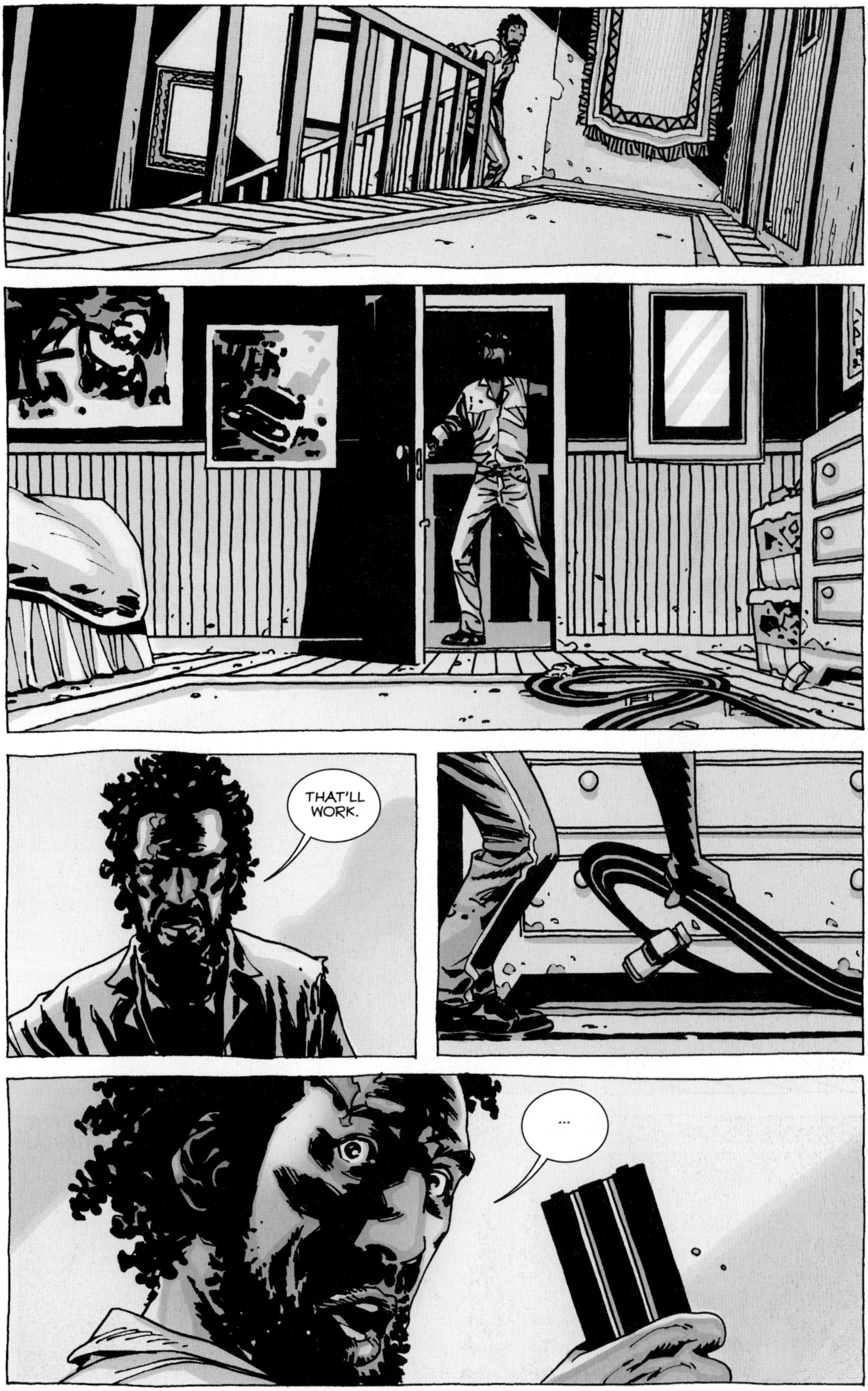

THAT'LL WORK.
...

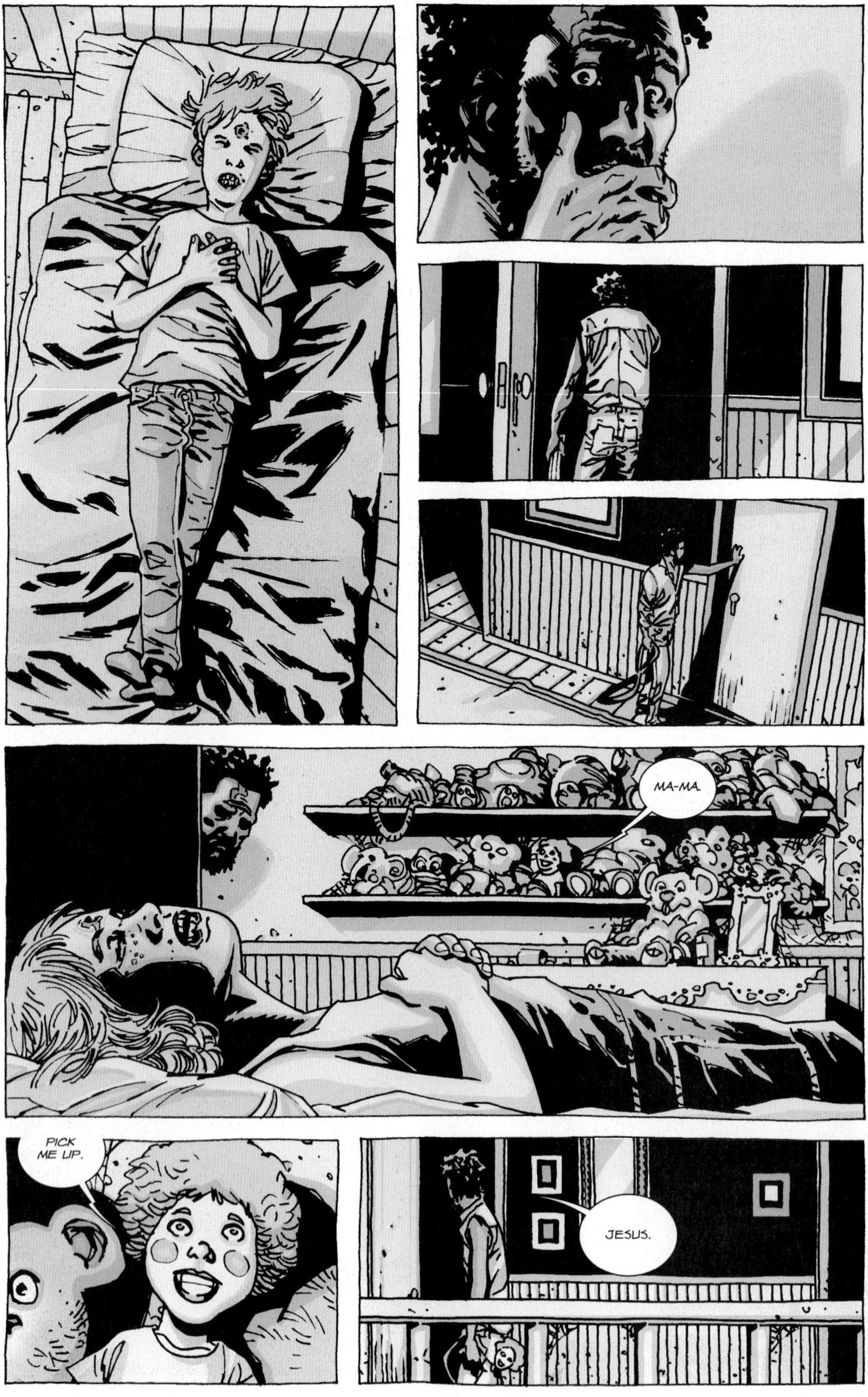
MA-MA
PICK ME UP.
JESUS.

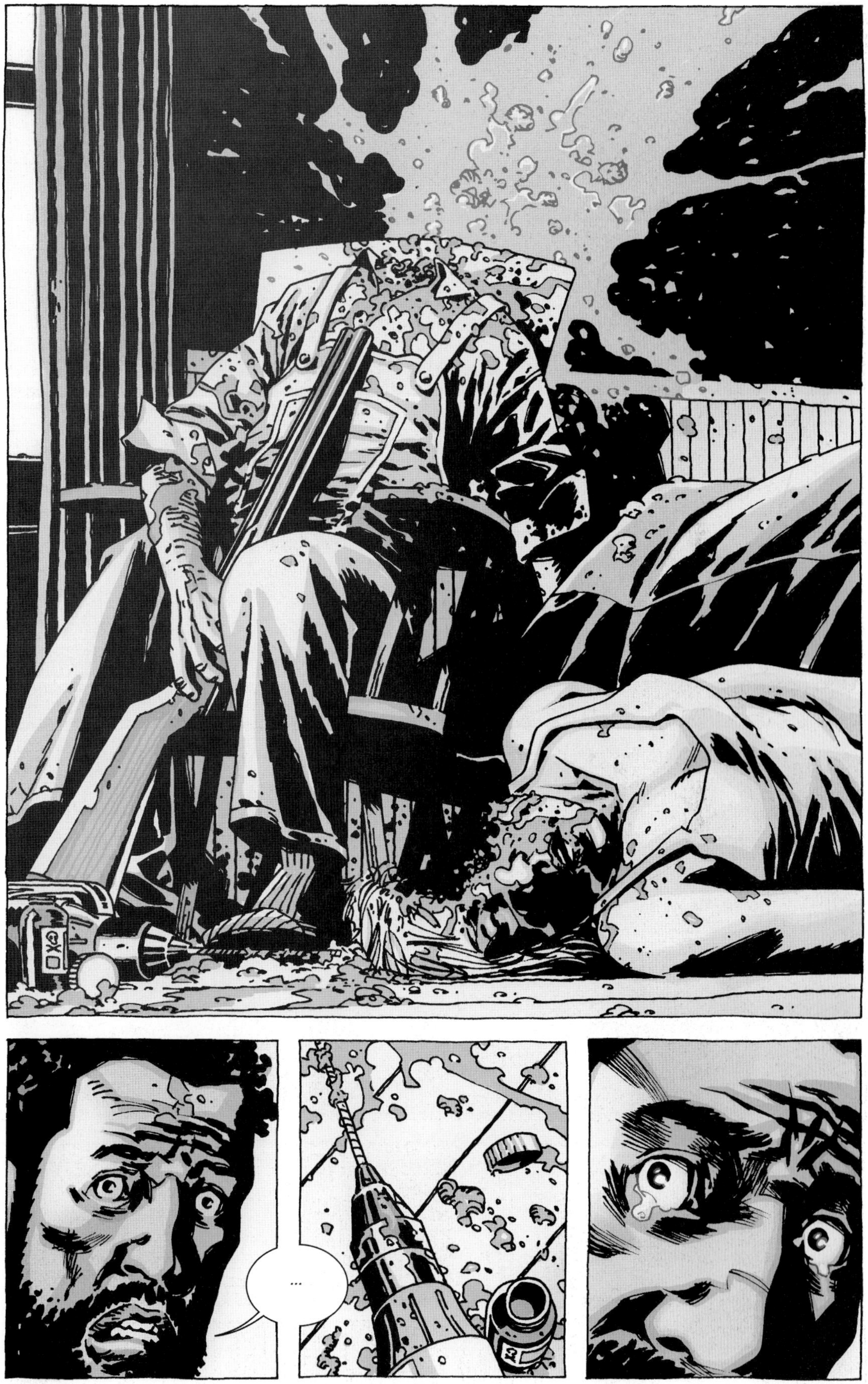
...

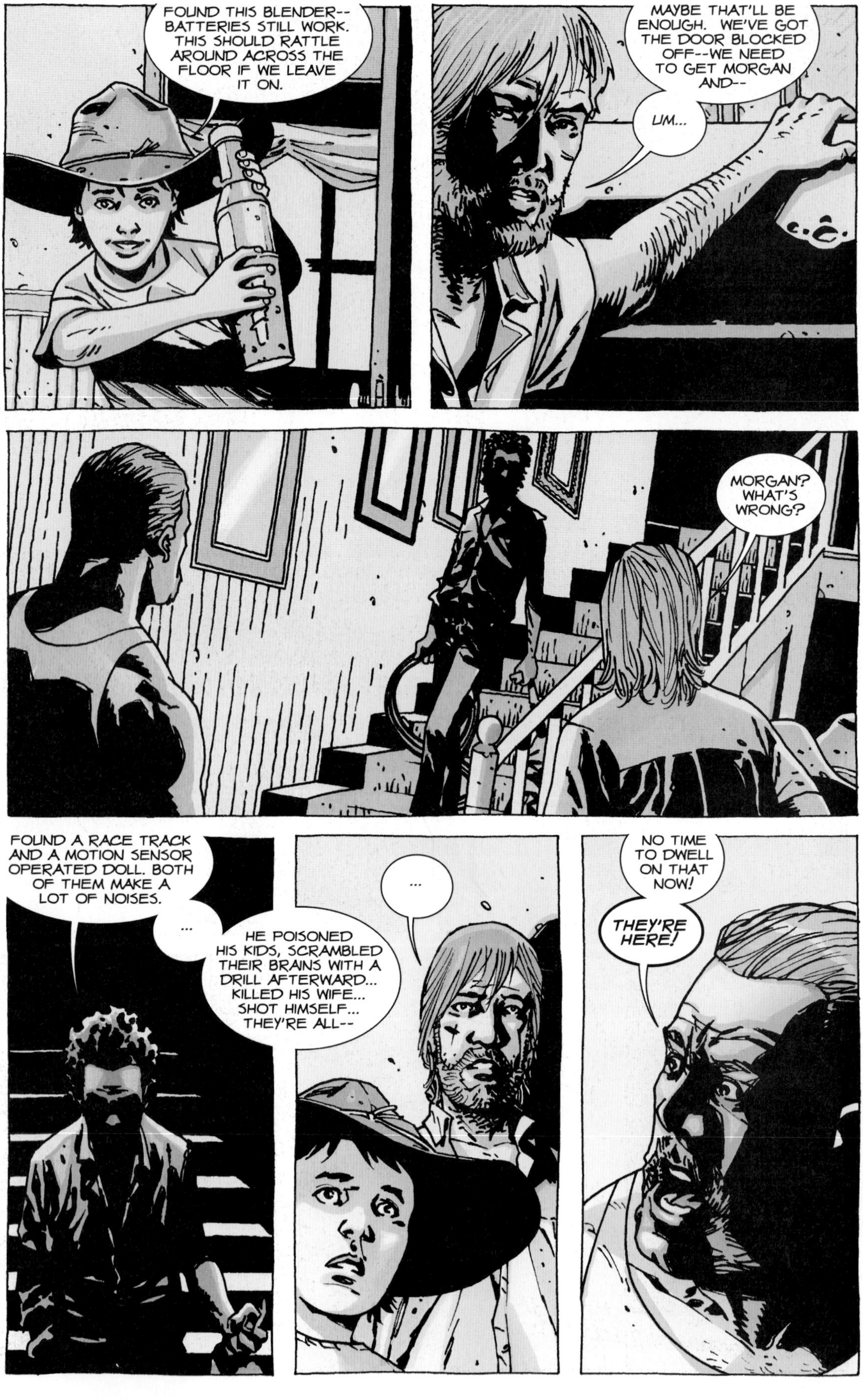
FOUND THIS BLENDER-- BATTERIES STILL WORK. THIS SHOULD RATTLE AROUND ACROSS THE FLOOR IF WE LEAVE IT ON.
MAYBE THAT'LL BE ENOUGH. WE'VE GOT THE DOOR BLOCKED OFF--WE NEED TO GET MORGAN AND--
UM...
MORGAN? WHAT'S WRONG?
FOUND A RACE TRACK AND A MOTION SENSOR OPERATED DOLL. BOTH OF THEM MAKE A LOT OF NOISES.
...
HE POISONED HIS KIDS, SCRAMBLED THEIR BRAINS WITH A DRILL AFTERWARD... KILLED HIS WIFE... SHOT HIMSELF... THEY'RE ALL--
...
NO TIME TO DWELL ON THAT NOW!
THEY'RE HERE!

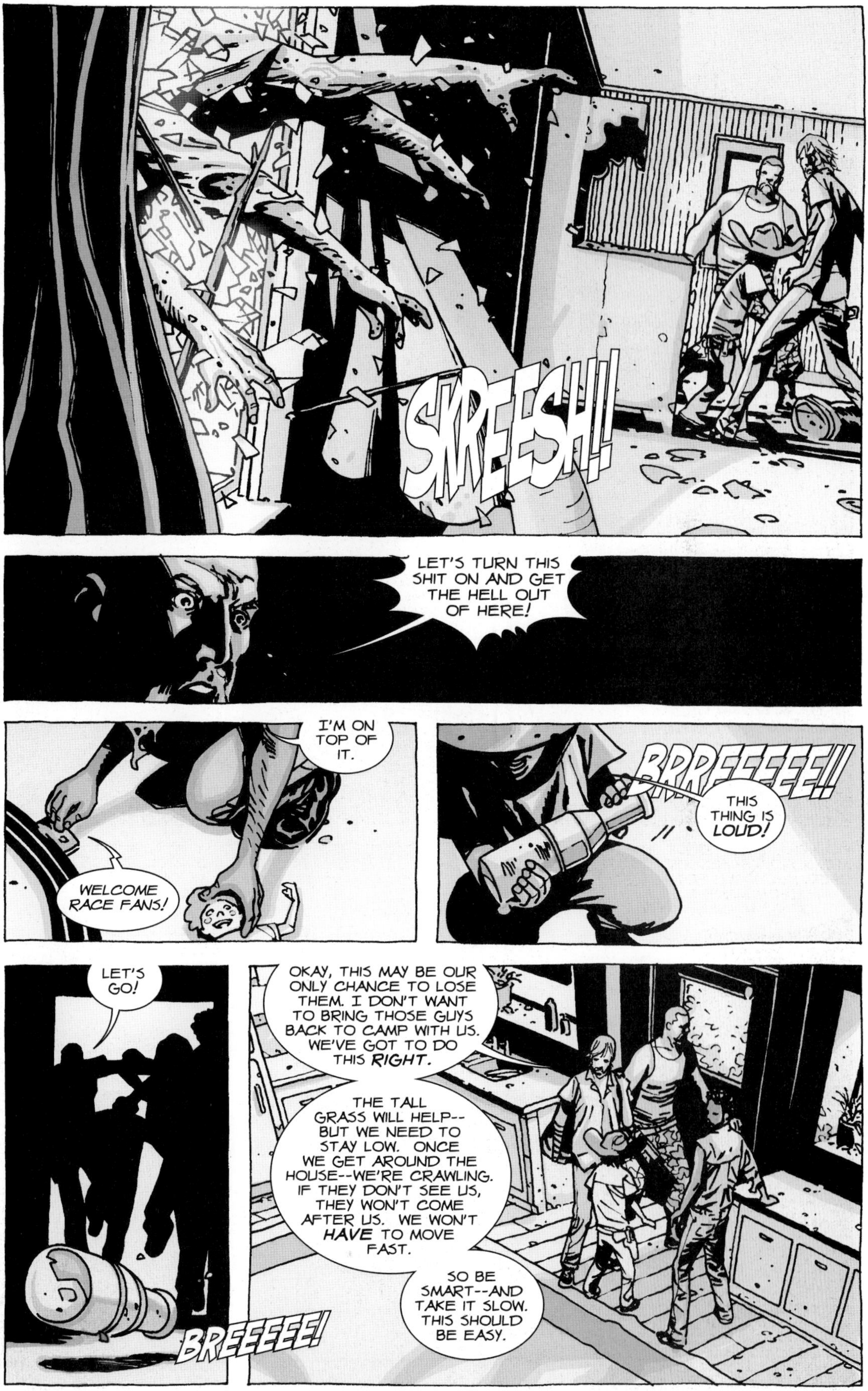

SKREESH!!
LET'S TURN THIS SHIT ON AND GET THE HELL OUT OF HERE!
I'M ON TOP OF IT.
WELCOME RACE FANS!
BRREEEEE!!
THIS THING IS LOUD!
LET'S GO!
BREEEEE!
OKAY, THIS MAY BE OUR ONLY CHANCE TO LOSE THEM. I DON'T WANT TO BRING THOSE GUYS BACK TO CAMP WITH US. WE'VE GOT TO DO THIS RIGHT.
THE TALL GRASS WILL HELP-- BUT WE NEED TO STAY LOW. ONCE WE GET AROUND THE HOUSE--WE'RE CRAWLING. IF THEY DON'T SEE US, THEY WON'T COME AFTER US. WE WON'T HAVE TO MOVE FAST.
SO BE SMART--AND TAKE IT SLOW. THIS SHOULD BE EASY.

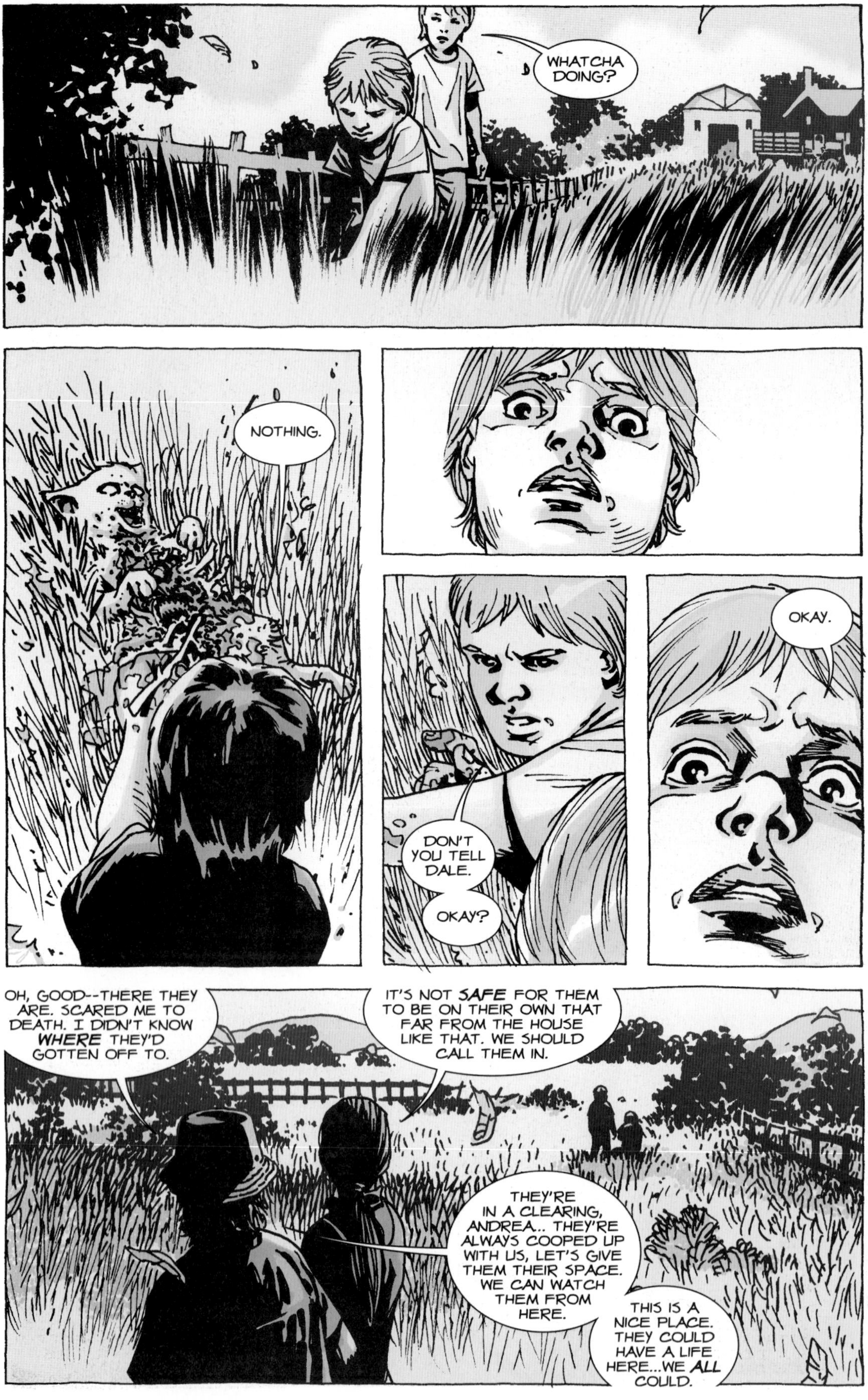
WHATCHA DOING?
NOTHING.
DON'T YOU TELL DALE.
OKAY?
OKAY.
OH, GOOD--THERE THEY ARE. SCARED ME TO DEATH. I DIDN'T KNOW WHERE THEY'D GOTTEN OFF TO.
IT'S NOT SAFE FOR THEM TO BE ON THEIR OWN THAT FAR FROM THE HOUSE LIKE THAT. WE SHOULD CALL THEM IN.
THEY'RE IN A CLEARING, ANDREA.. THEY'RE ALWAYS COOPED UP WITH US, LET'S GIVE THEM THEIR SPACE. WE CAN WATCH THEM FROM HERE.
THIS IS A NICE PLACE. THEY COULD HAVE A LIFE HERE...WE ALL COULD.

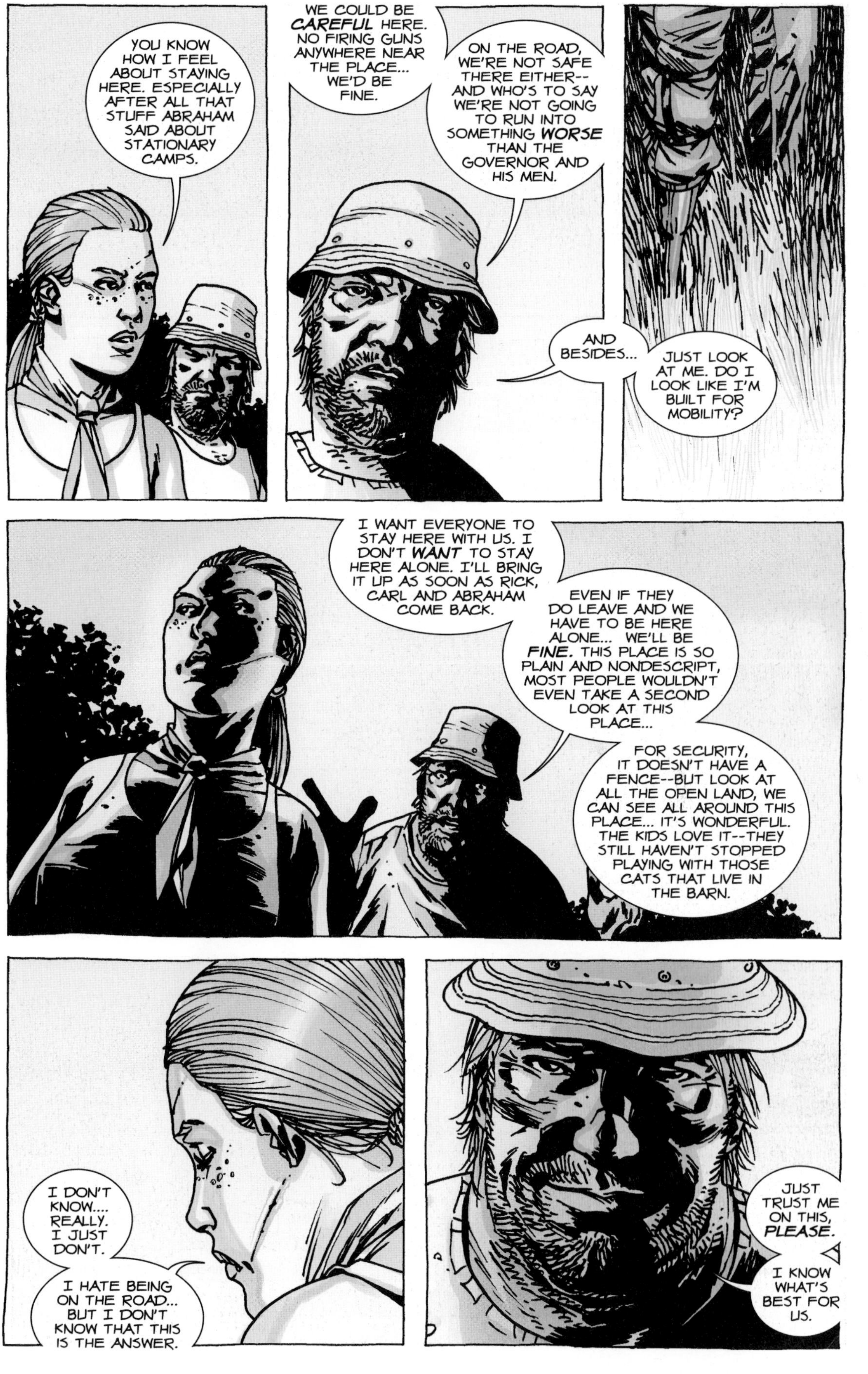

YOU KNOW HOW I FEEL ABOUT STAYING HERE. ESPECIALLY AFTER ALL THAT STUFF ABRAHAM SAID ABOUT STATIONARY CAMPS.
WE COULD BE CAREFUL HERE. NO FIRING GUNS ANYWHERE NEAR THE PLACE... WE'D BE FINE.
ON THE ROAD, WE'RE NOT SAFE THERE EITHER-- AND WHO'S TO SAY WE'RE NOT GOING TO RUN INTO SOMETHING WORSE THAN THE GOVERNOR AND HIS MEN.
AND BESIDES...
JUST LOOK AT ME. DO I LOOK LIKE I'M BUILT FOR MOBILITY?
I WANT EVERYONE TO STAY HERE WITH US. I DON'T WANT TO STAY HERE ALONE. I'LL BRING IT UP AS SOON AS RICK, CARL AND ABRAHAM COME BACK.
EVEN IF THEY DO LEAVE AND WE HAVE TO BE HERE ALONE... WE'LL BE FINE. THIS PLACE IS SO PLAIN AND NONDESCRIPT, MOST PEOPLE WOULDN'T EVEN TAKE A SECOND LOOK AT THIS PLACE...
FOR SECURITY, IT DOESN'T HAVE A FENCE--BUT LOOK AT ALL THE OPEN LAND, WE CAN SEE ALL AROUND THIS PLACE... IT'S WONDERFUL. THE KIDS LOVE IT--THEY STILL HAVEN'T STOPPED PLAYING WITH THOSE CATS THAT LIVE IN THE BARN.
I DON'T KNOW.... REALLY. I JUST DON'T.
I HATE BEING ON THE ROAD... BUT I DON'T KNOW THAT THIS IS THE ANSWER.
JUST TRUST ME ON THIS, PLEASE.
I KNOW WHAT'S BEST FOR US.

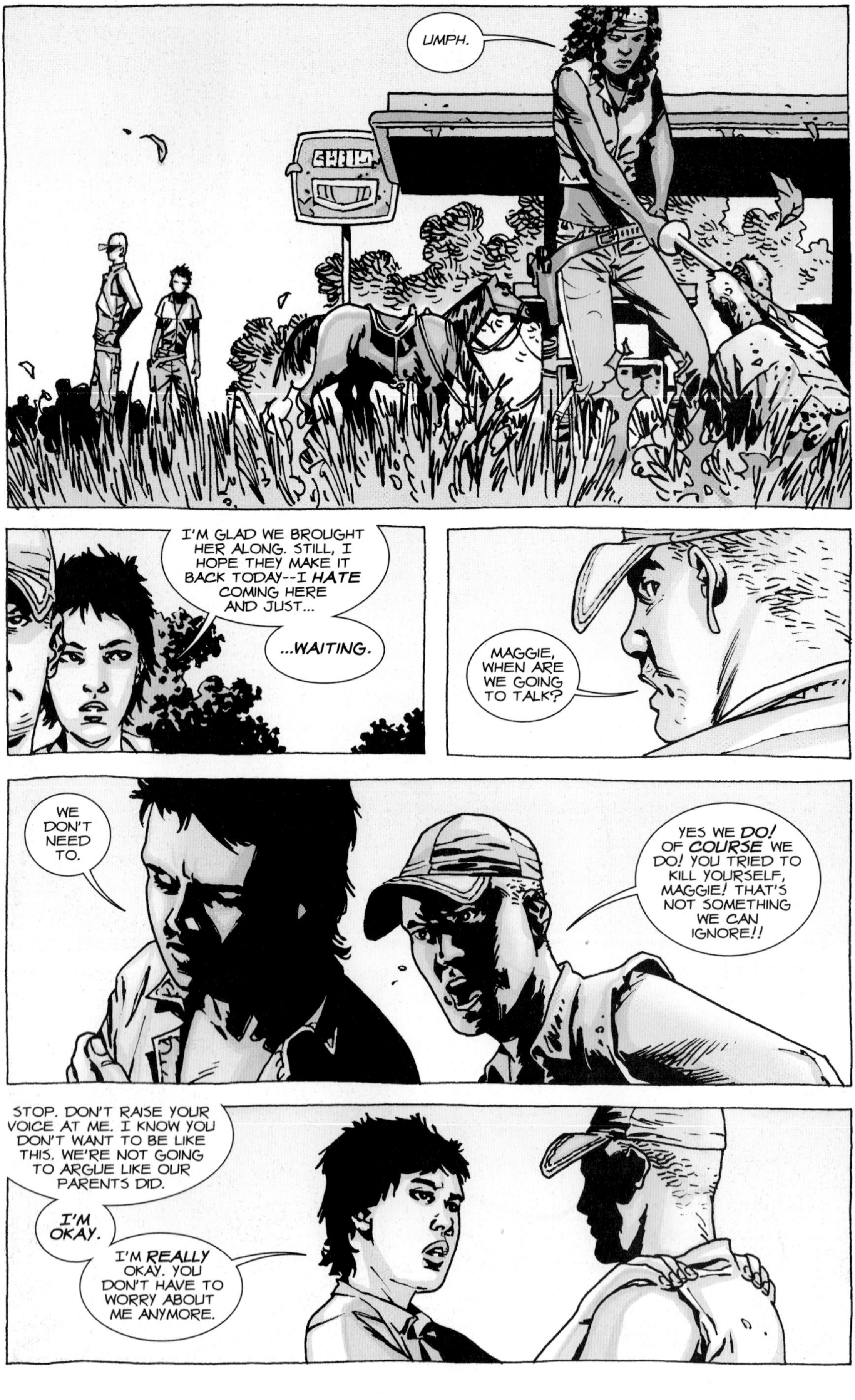
UMPH.
I'M GLAD WE BROUGHT HER ALONG. STILL, I HOPE THEY MAKE IT BACK TODAY--I HATE COMING HERE AND JUST...
...WAITING.
MAGGIE, WHEN ARE WE GOING TO TALK?
WE DON'T NEED TO.
YES WE DO! OF COURSE WE DO! YOU TRIED TO KILL YOURSELF, MAGGIE! THAT'S NOT SOMETHING WE CAN IGNORE!!
STOP. DON'T RAISE YOUR VOICE AT ME. I KNOW YOU DON'T WANT TO BE LIKE THIS. WE'RE NOT GOING TO ARGUE LIKE OUR PARENTS DID.
I'M OKAY.
I'M REALLY OKAY. YOU DON'T HAVE TO WORRY ABOUT ME ANYMORE.

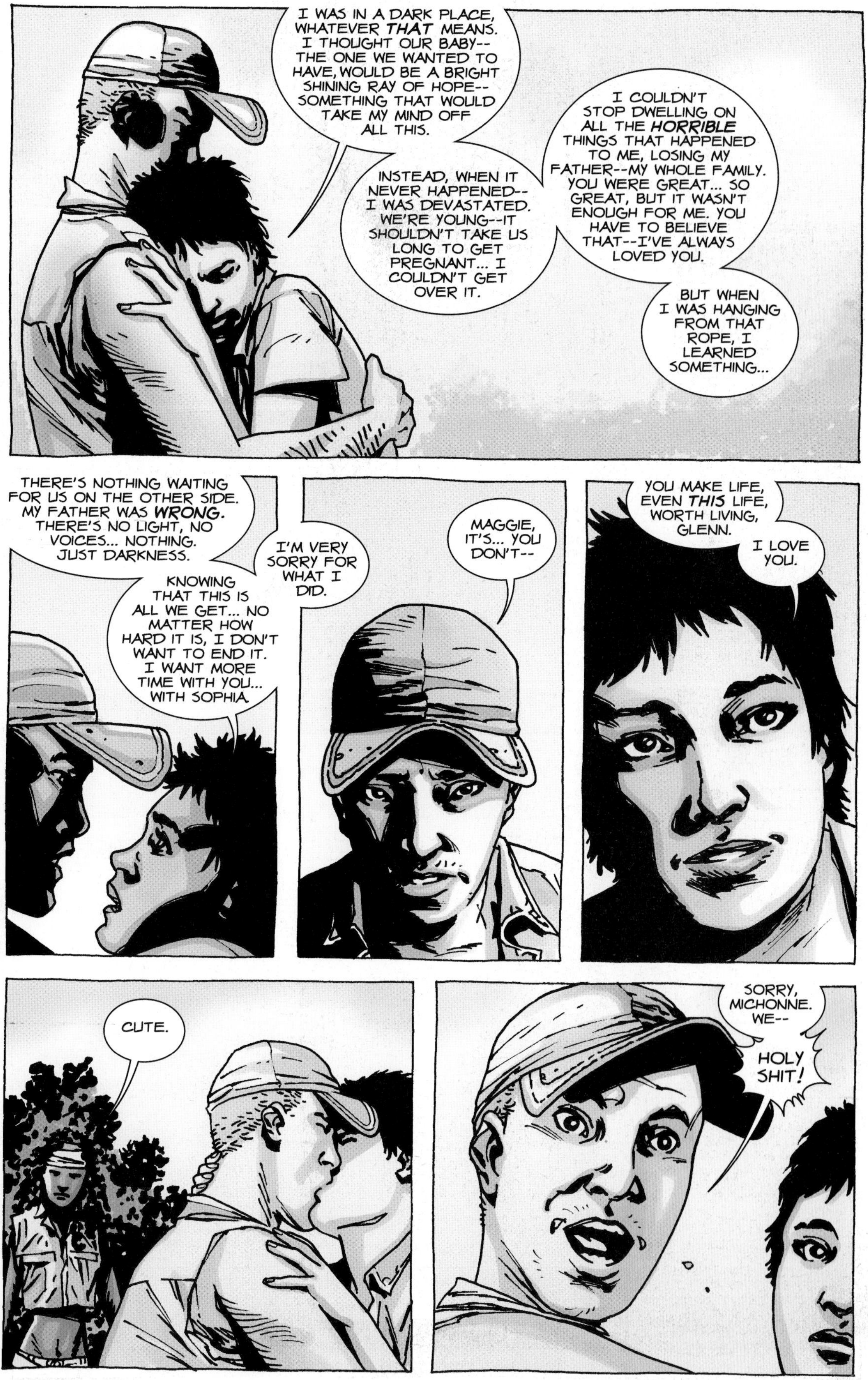

I WAS IN A DARK PLACE, WHATEVER THAT MEANS. I THOUGHT OUR BABY-- THE ONE WE WANTED TO HAVE, WOULD BE A BRIGHT SHINING RAY OF HOPE-- SOMETHING THAT WOULD TAKE MY MIND OFF ALL THIS.
INSTEAD, WHEN IT NEVER HAPPENED-- I WAS DEVASTATED. WE'RE YOUNG--IT SHOULDN'T TAKE US LONG TO GET PREGNANT... I COULDN'T GET OVER IT.
I COULDN'T STOP DWELLING ON ALL THE HORRIBLE THINGS THAT HAPPENED TO ME, LOSING MY FATHER--MY WHOLE FAMILY. YOU WERE GREAT... SO GREAT, BUT IT WASN'T ENOUGH FOR ME. YOU HAVE TO BELIEVE THAT--I'VE ALWAYS LOVED YOU.
BUT WHEN I WAS HANGING FROM THAT ROPE, I LEARNED SOMETHING...
THERE'S NOTHING WAITING FOR US ON THE OTHER SIDE. MY FATHER WAS WRONG. THERE'S NO LIGHT, NO VOICES... NOTHING. JUST DARKNESS.
KNOWING THAT THIS IS ALL WE GET... NO MATTER HOW HARD IT IS, I DON'T WANT TO END IT. I WANT MORE TIME WITH YOU... WITH SOPHIA.
I'M VERY SORRY FOR WHAT I DID.
MAGGIE, IT'S... YOU DON'T--
YOU MAKE LIFE, EVEN THIS LIFE, WORTH LIVING, GLENN.
I LOVE YOU.
CUTE.
SORRY, MICHONNE. WE--
HOLY SHIT!

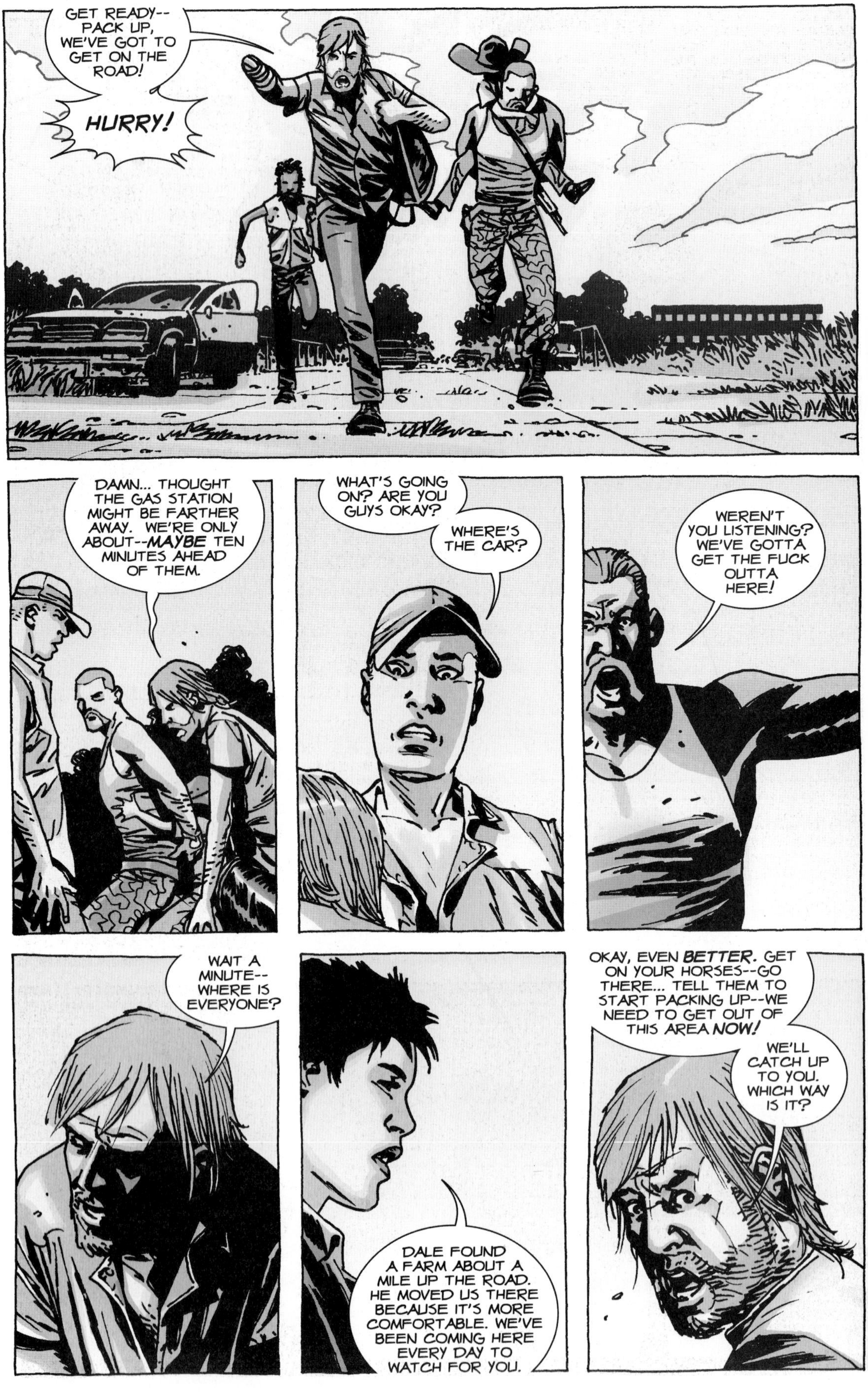
GET READY-- PACK UP, WE'VE GOT TO GET ON THE ROAD!
HURRY!
DAMN... THOUGHT THE GAS STATION MIGHT BE FARTHER AWAY. WE'RE ONLY ABOUT--MAYBE TEN MINUTES AHEAD OF THEM.
WHAT'S GOING ON? ARE YOU GUYS OKAY?
WHERE'S THE CAR?
WEREN'T YOU LISTENING? WE'VE GOTTA GET THE FUCK OUTTA HERE!
WAIT A MINUTE-- WHERE IS EVERYONE?
DALE FOUND A FARM ABOUT A MILE UP THE ROAD. HE MOVED US THERE BECAUSE IT'S MORE COMFORTABLE. WE'VE BEEN COMING HERE EVERY DAY TO WATCH FOR YOU.
OKAY, EVEN BETTER. GET ON YOUR HORSES--GO THERE... TELL THEM TO START PACKING UP--WE NEED TO GET OUT OF THIS AREA NOW!
WE'LL CATCH UP TO YOU. WHICH WAY IS IT?

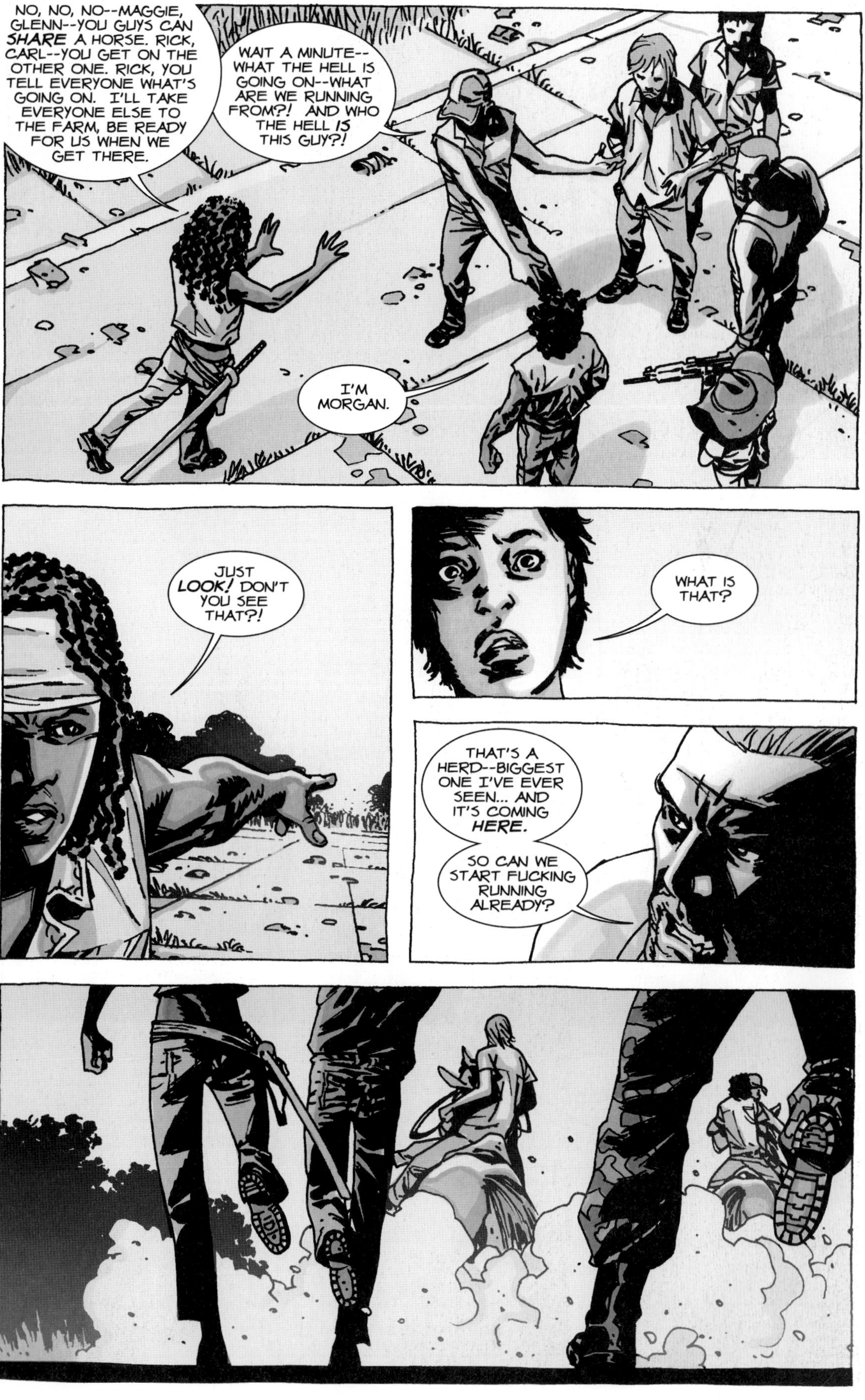
NO, NO, NO--MAGGIE, GLENN--YOU GUYS CAN *SHARE* A HORSE. RICK, CARL--YOU GET ON THE OTHER ONE. RICK, YOU TELL EVERYONE WHAT'S GOING ON. I'LL TAKE EVERYONE ELSE TO THE FARM, BE READY FOR US WHEN WE GET THERE.
WAIT A MINUTE-- WHAT THE HELL IS GOING ON--WHAT ARE WE RUNNING FROM?! AND WHO THE HELL *IS* THIS GUY?!
I'M MORGAN.
JUST *LOOK!* DON'T YOU SEE THAT?!
WHAT IS THAT?
THAT'S A HERD--BIGGEST ONE I'VE EVER SEEN... AND IT'S COMING *HERE.*
SO CAN WE START FUCKING RUNNING ALREADY?

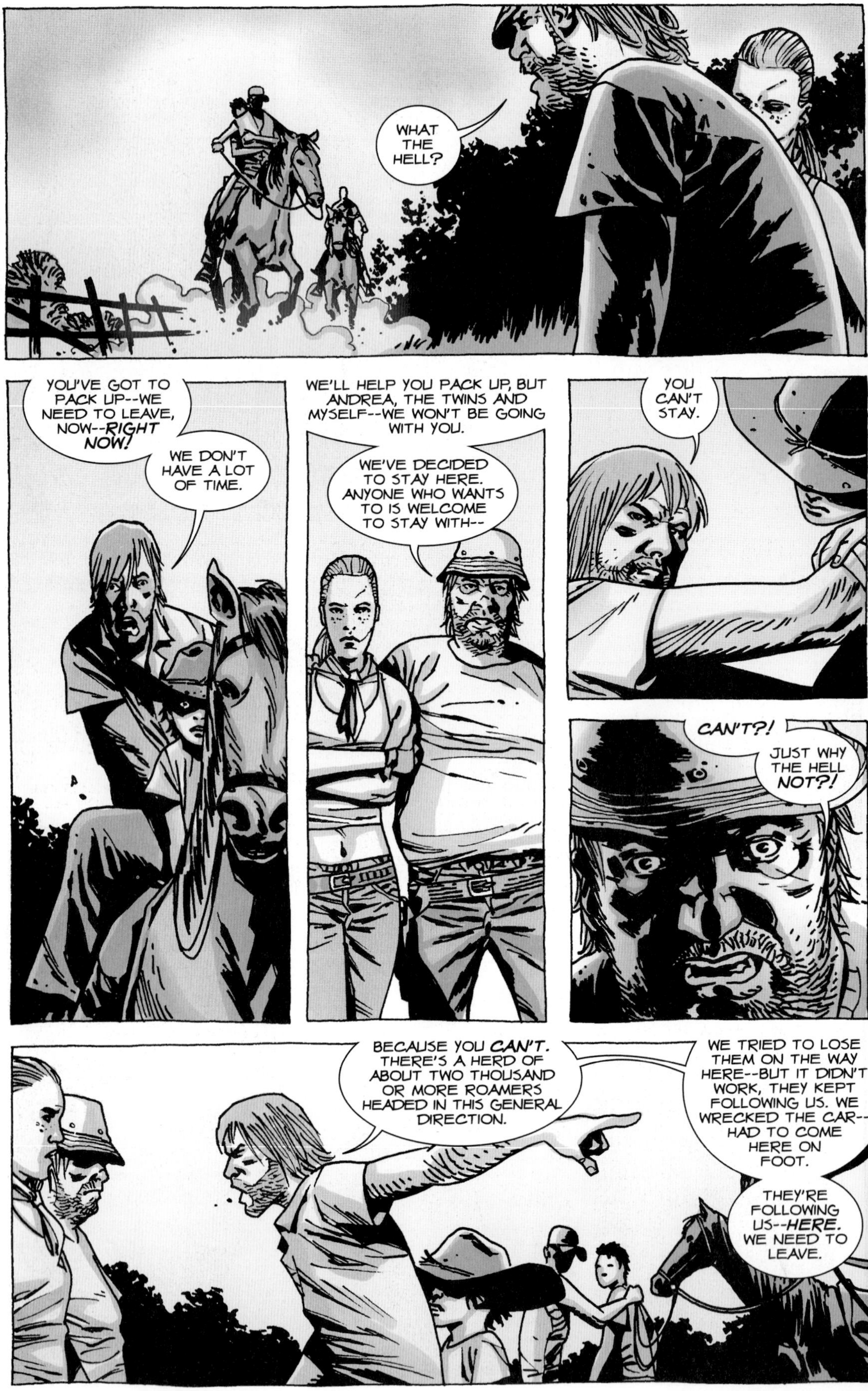
WHAT THE HELL?
YOU'VE GOT TO PACK UP--WE NEED TO LEAVE, NOW--RIGHT NOW!
WE DON'T HAVE A LOT OF TIME.
WE'LL HELP YOU PACK UP, BUT ANDREA, THE TWINS AND MYSELF--WE WON'T BE GOING WITH YOU.
WE'VE DECIDED TO STAY HERE. ANYONE WHO WANTS TO IS WELCOME TO STAY WITH--
YOU CAN'T STAY.
CAN'T?!
JUST WHY THE HELL NOT?!
BECAUSE YOU CAN'T. THERE'S A HERD OF ABOUT TWO THOUSAND OR MORE ROAMERS HEADED IN THIS GENERAL DIRECTION.
WE TRIED TO LOSE THEM ON THE WAY HERE--BUT IT DIDN'T WORK, THEY KEPT FOLLOWING US. WE WRECKED THE CAR--HAD TO COME HERE ON FOOT.
THEY'RE FOLLOWING US--HERE. WE NEED TO LEAVE.

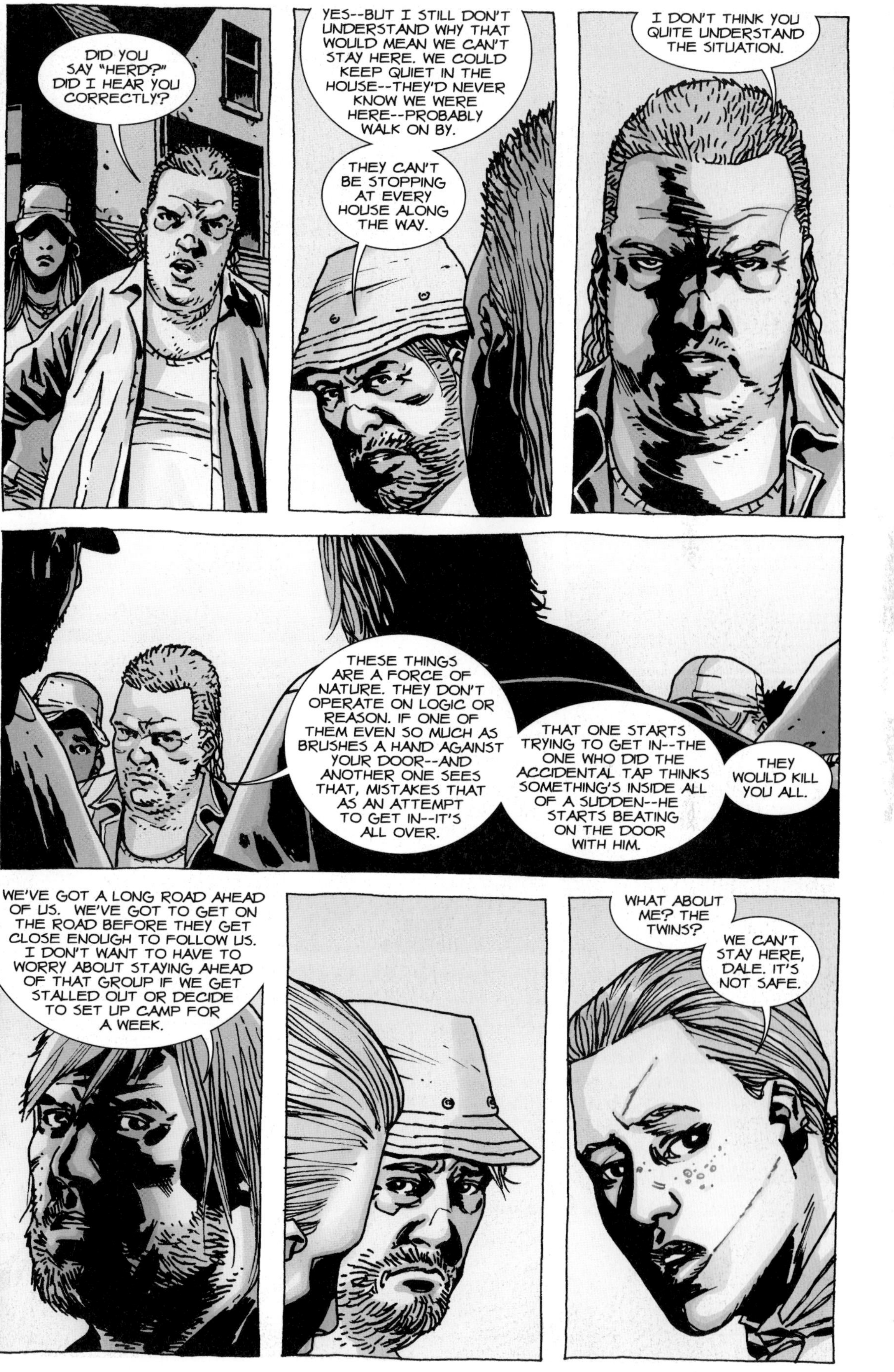
DID YOU SAY "HERD?" DID I HEAR YOU CORRECTLY?
YES--BUT I STILL DON'T UNDERSTAND WHY THAT WOULD MEAN WE CAN'T STAY HERE. WE COULD KEEP QUIET IN THE HOUSE--THEY'D NEVER KNOW WE WERE HERE--PROBABLY WALK ON BY.
THEY CAN'T BE STOPPING AT EVERY HOUSE ALONG THE WAY.
I DON'T THINK YOU QUITE UNDERSTAND THE SITUATION.
THESE THINGS ARE A FORCE OF NATURE. THEY DON'T OPERATE ON LOGIC OR REASON. IF ONE OF THEM EVEN SO MUCH AS BRUSHES A HAND AGAINST YOUR DOOR--AND ANOTHER ONE SEES THAT, MISTAKES THAT AS AN ATTEMPT TO GET IN--IT'S ALL OVER.
THAT ONE STARTS TRYING TO GET IN--THE ONE WHO DID THE ACCIDENTAL TAP THINKS SOMETHING'S INSIDE ALL OF A SUDDEN--HE STARTS BEATING ON THE DOOR WITH HIM.
THEY WOULD KILL YOU ALL.
WE'VE GOT A LONG ROAD AHEAD OF US. WE'VE GOT TO GET ON THE ROAD BEFORE THEY GET CLOSE ENOUGH TO FOLLOW US. I DON'T WANT TO HAVE TO WORRY ABOUT STAYING AHEAD OF THAT GROUP IF WE GET STALLED OUT OR DECIDE TO SET UP CAMP FOR A WEEK.
WHAT ABOUT ME? THE TWINS?
WE CAN'T STAY HERE, DALE. IT'S NOT SAFE.

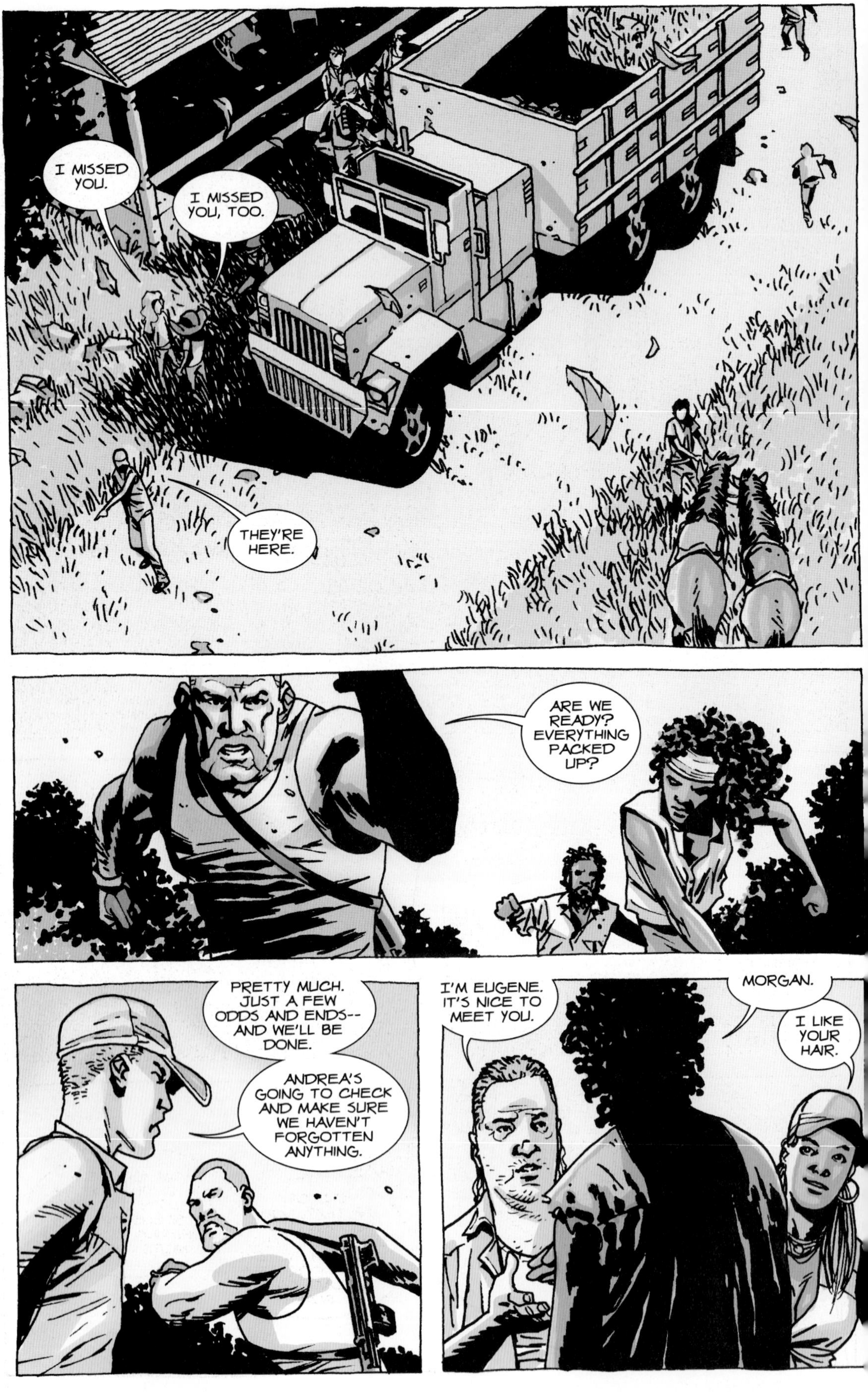

I MISSED YOU.
I MISSED YOU, TOO.
THEY'RE HERE.
ARE WE READY? EVERYTHING PACKED UP?
PRETTY MUCH. JUST A FEW ODDS AND ENDS-- AND WE'LL BE DONE.
ANDREA'S GOING TO CHECK AND MAKE SURE WE HAVEN'T FORGOTTEN ANYTHING.
I'M EUGENE. IT'S NICE TO MEET YOU.
MORGAN.
I LIKE YOUR HAIR.

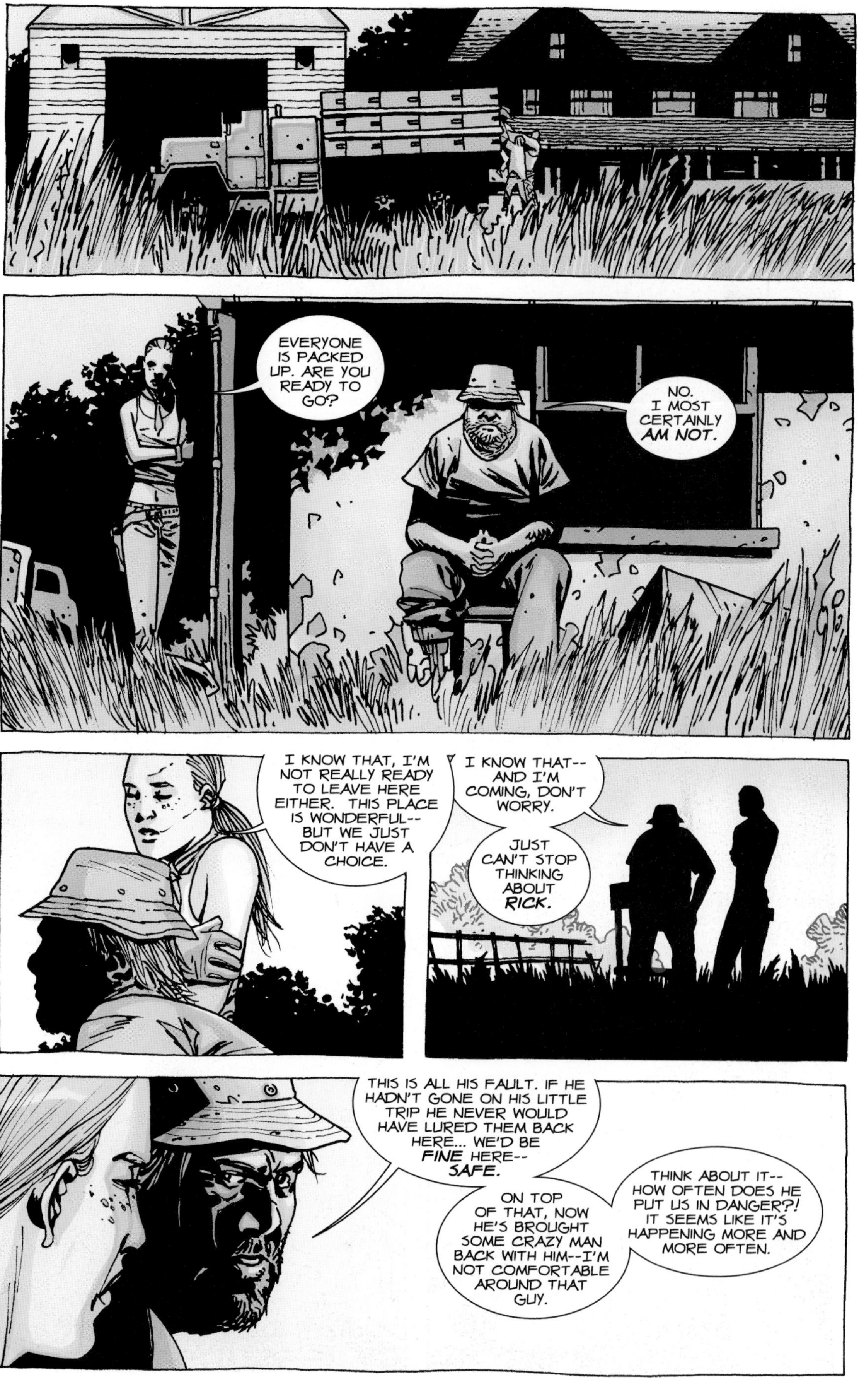
EVERYONE IS PACKED UP. ARE YOU READY TO GO?
NO. I MOST CERTAINLY AM NOT.
I KNOW THAT, I'M NOT REALLY READY TO LEAVE HERE EITHER. THIS PLACE IS WONDERFUL-- BUT WE JUST DON'T HAVE A CHOICE.
I KNOW THAT-- AND I'M COMING, DON'T WORRY.
JUST CAN'T STOP THINKING ABOUT RICK.
THIS IS ALL HIS FAULT. IF HE HADN'T GONE ON HIS LITTLE TRIP HE NEVER WOULD HAVE LURED THEM BACK HERE... WE'D BE FINE HERE-- SAFE.
ON TOP OF THAT, NOW HE'S BROUGHT SOME CRAZY MAN BACK WITH HIM--I'M NOT COMFORTABLE AROUND THAT GUY.
THINK ABOUT IT-- HOW OFTEN DOES HE PUT US IN DANGER?! IT SEEMS LIKE IT'S HAPPENING MORE AND MORE OFTEN.

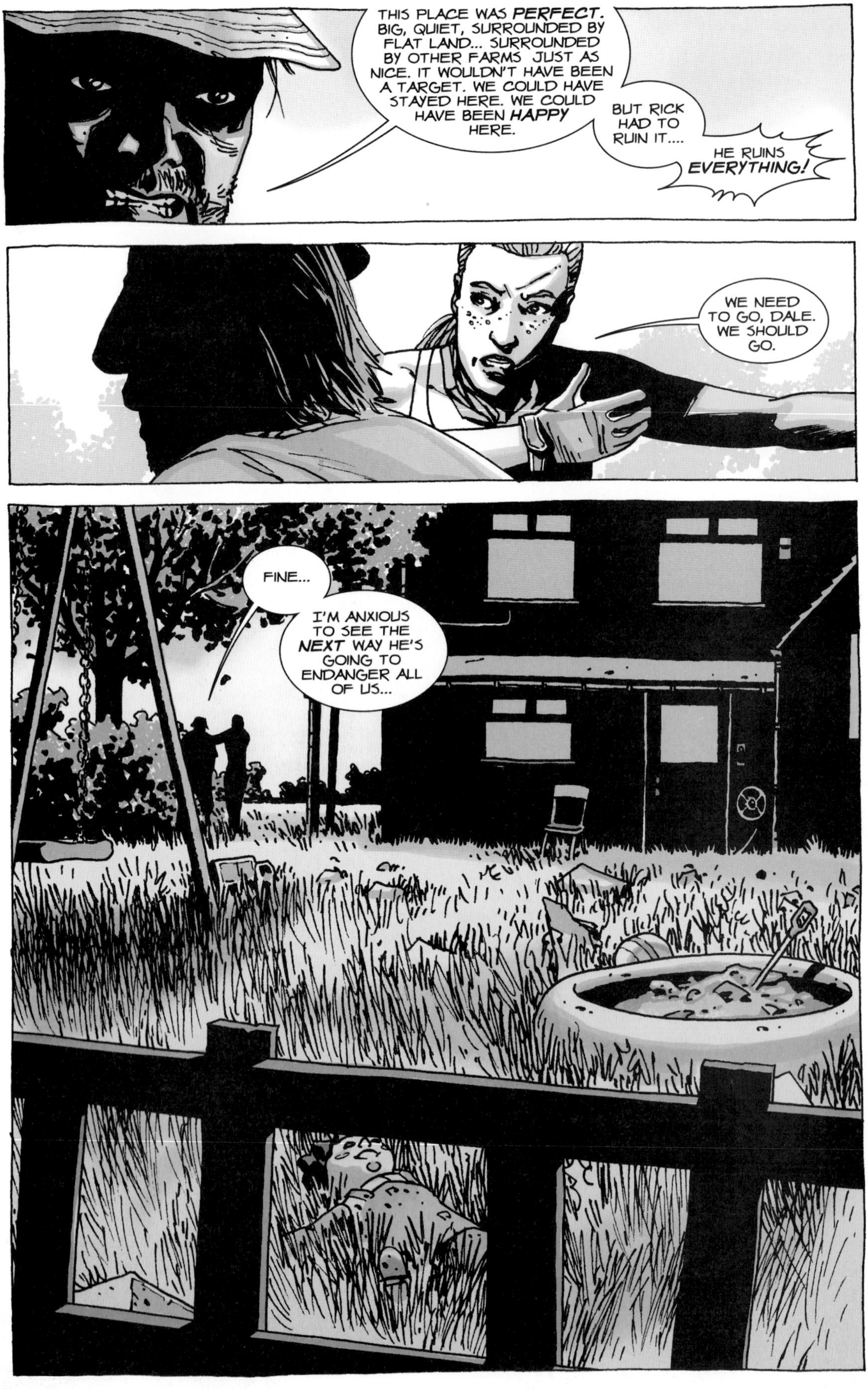
THIS PLACE WAS PERFECT. BIG, QUIET, SURROUNDED BY FLAT LAND... SURROUNDED BY OTHER FARMS JUST AS NICE. IT WOULDN'T HAVE BEEN A TARGET. WE COULD HAVE STAYED HERE. WE COULD HAVE BEEN HAPPY HERE.
BUT RICK HAD TO RUIN IT....
HE RUINS EVERYTHING!
WE NEED TO GO, DALE. WE SHOULD GO.
FINE...
I'M ANXIOUS TO SEE THE NEXT WAY HE'S GOING TO ENDANGER ALL OF US...

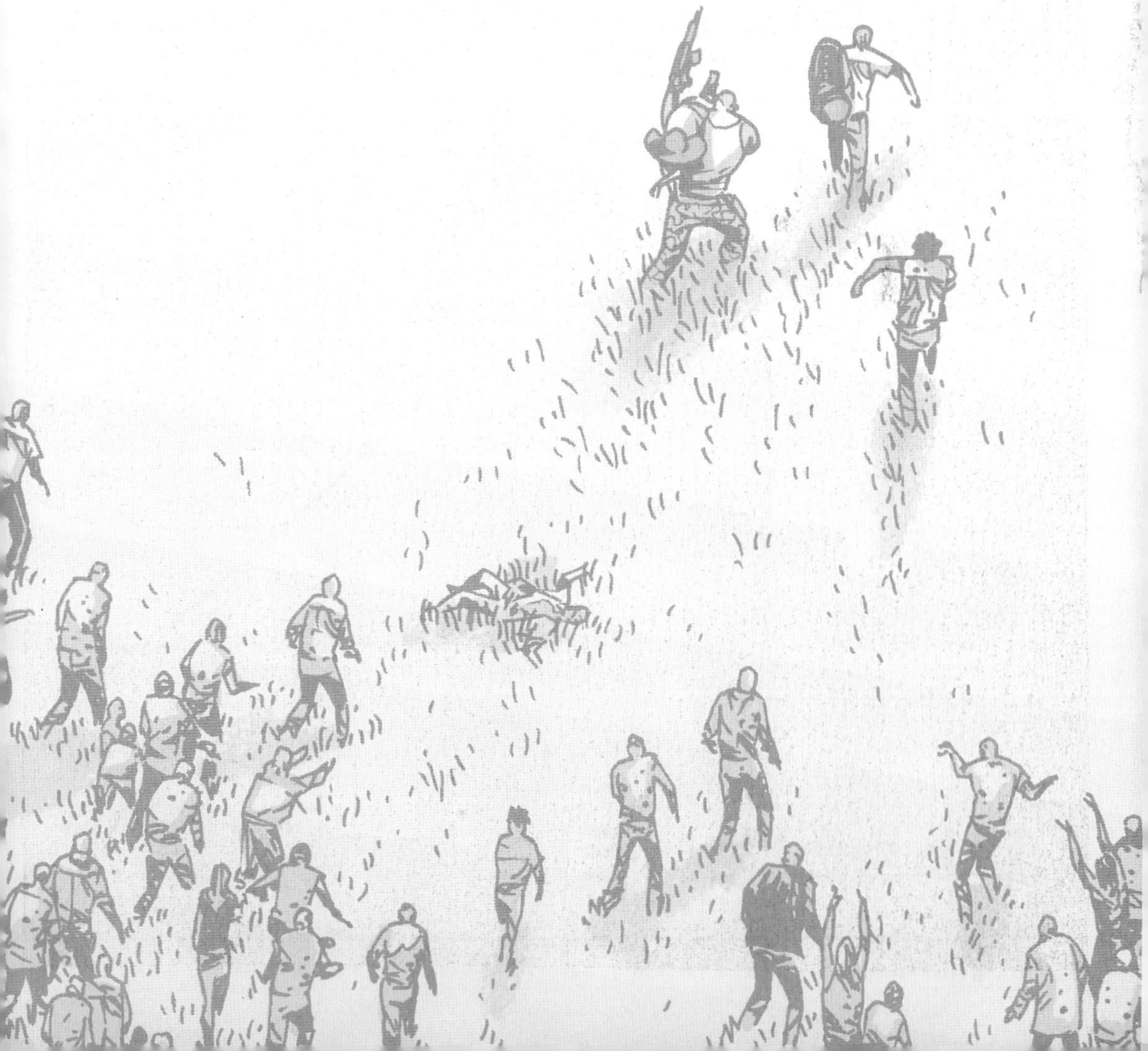

Chapter Eleven:
Fear The Hunters

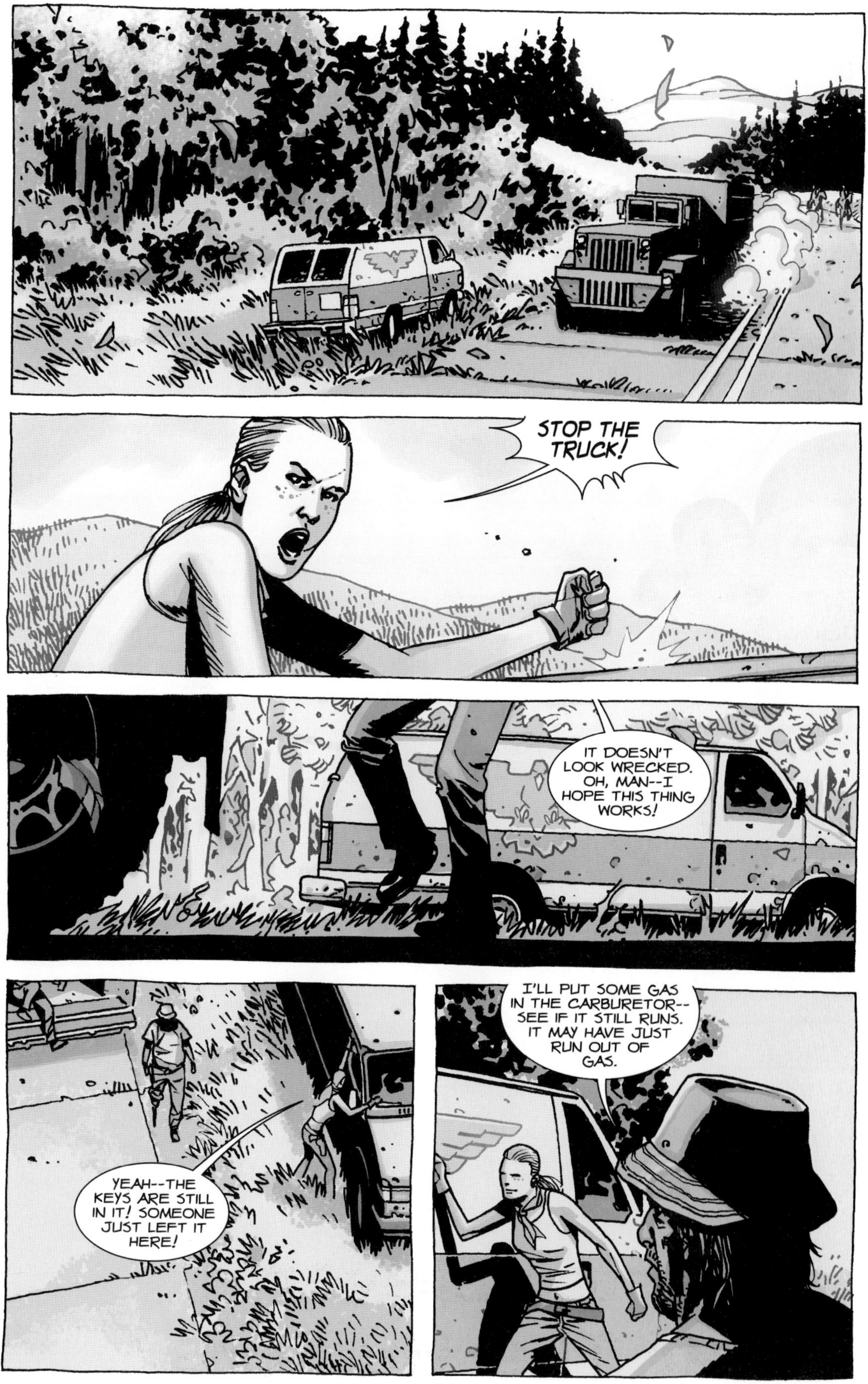
STOP THE TRUCK!
IT DOESN'T LOOK WRECKED. OH, MAN--I HOPE THIS THING WORKS!
YEAH--THE KEYS ARE STILL IN IT! SOMEONE JUST LEFT IT HERE!
I'LL PUT SOME GAS IN THE CARBURETOR--SEE IF IT STILL RUNS. IT MAY HAVE JUST RUN OUT OF GAS.

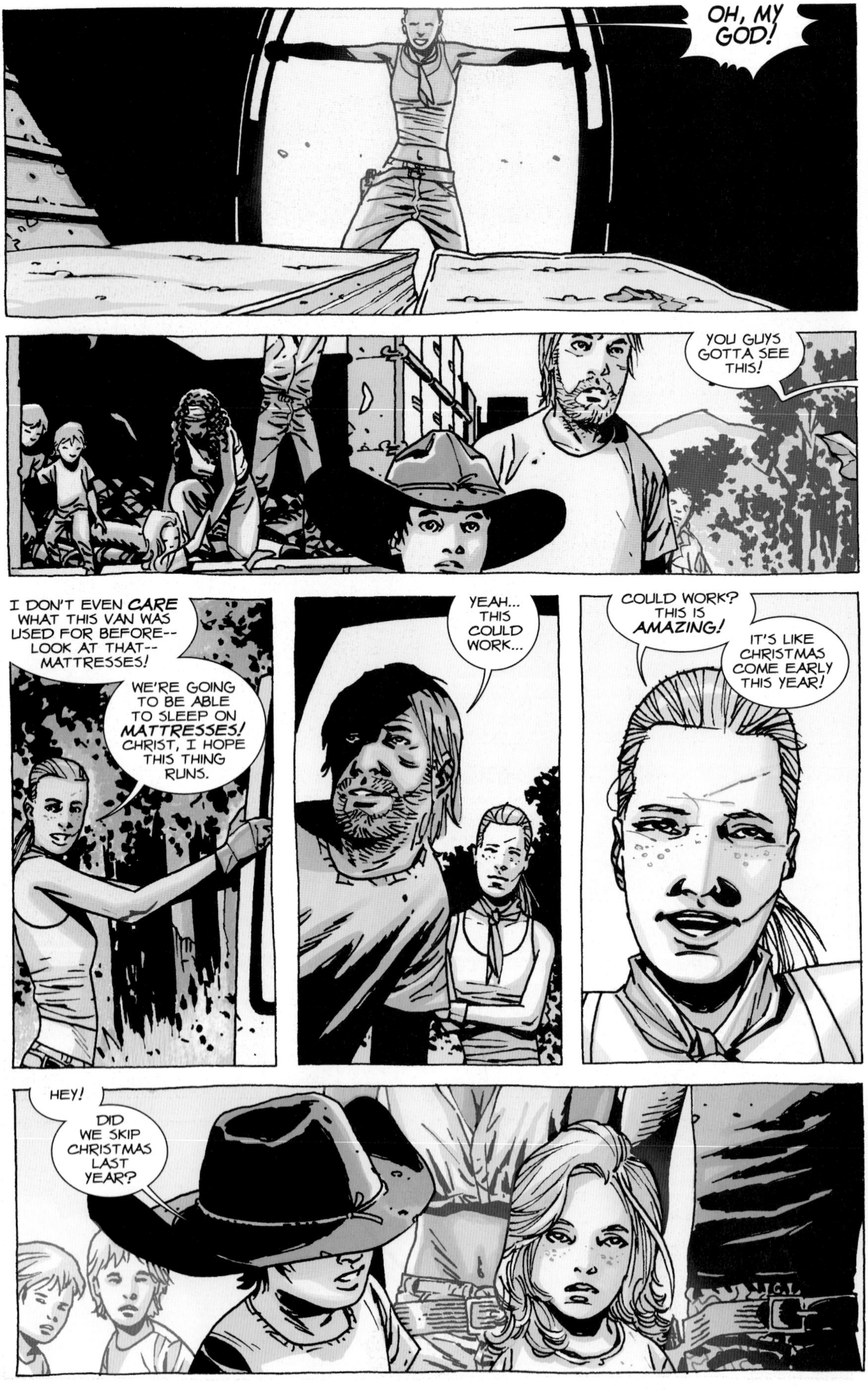
OH, MY GOD!
YOU GUYS GOTTA SEE THIS!
I DON'T EVEN CARE WHAT THIS VAN WAS USED FOR BEFORE-- LOOK AT THAT-- MATTRESSES!
WE'RE GOING TO BE ABLE TO SLEEP ON MATTRESSES! CHRIST, I HOPE THIS THING RUNS.
YEAH... THIS COULD WORK...
COULD WORK? THIS IS AMAZING!
IT'S LIKE CHRISTMAS COME EARLY THIS YEAR!
HEY!
DID WE SKIP CHRISTMAS LAST YEAR?

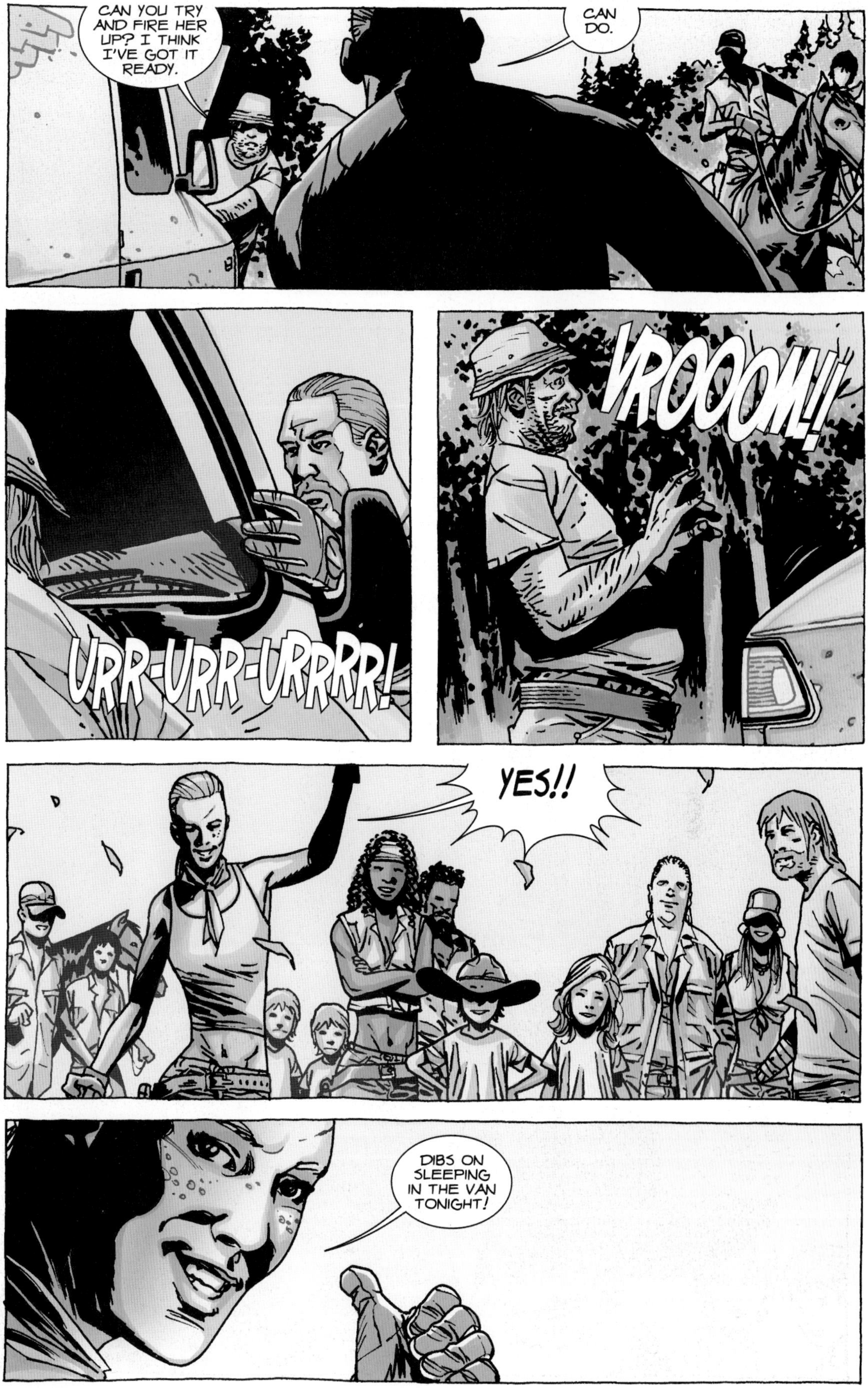
CAN YOU TRY AND FIRE HER UP? I THINK I'VE GOT IT READY.
CAN DO.
URR-URR-URRRR!
VROOOM!!
YES!!
DIBS ON SLEEPING IN THE VAN TONIGHT!

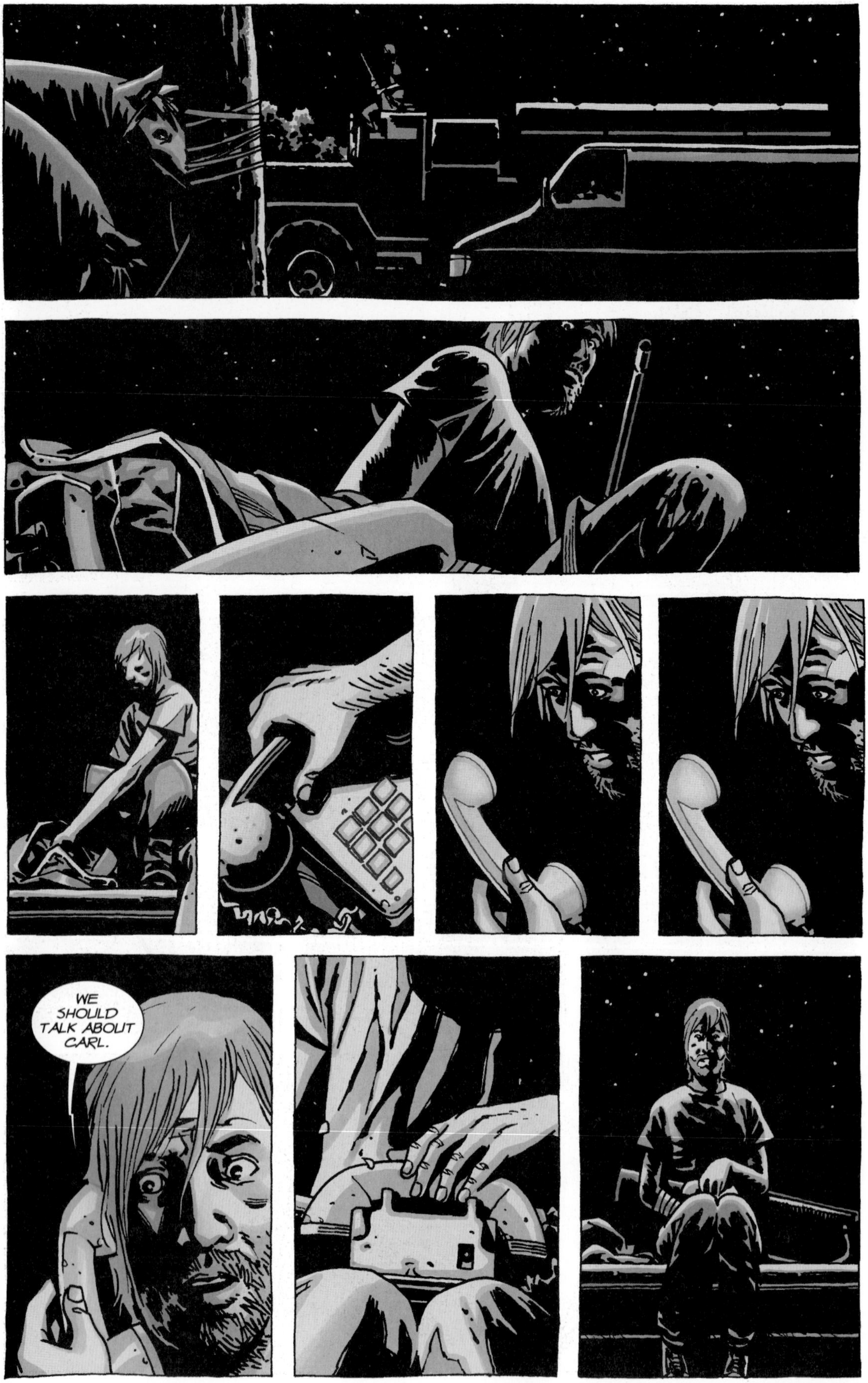
WE SHOULD TALK ABOUT CARL.

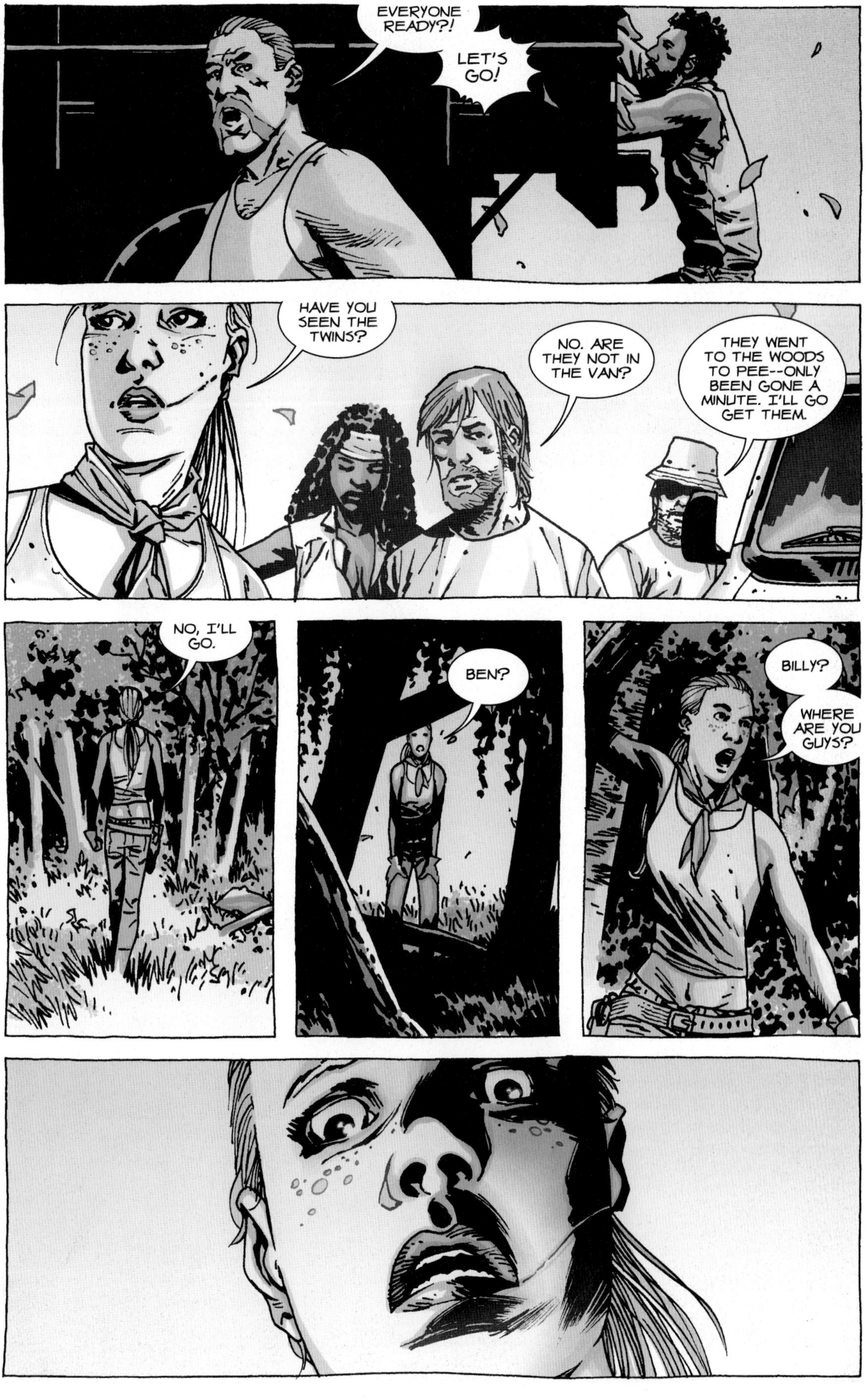
EVERYONE READY?!
LET'S GO!
HAVE YOU SEEN THE TWINS?
NO. ARE THEY NOT IN THE VAN?
THEY WENT TO THE WOODS TO PEE--ONLY BEEN GONE A MINUTE. I'LL GO GET THEM.
NO, I'LL GO.
BEN?
BILLY?
WHERE ARE YOU GUYS?

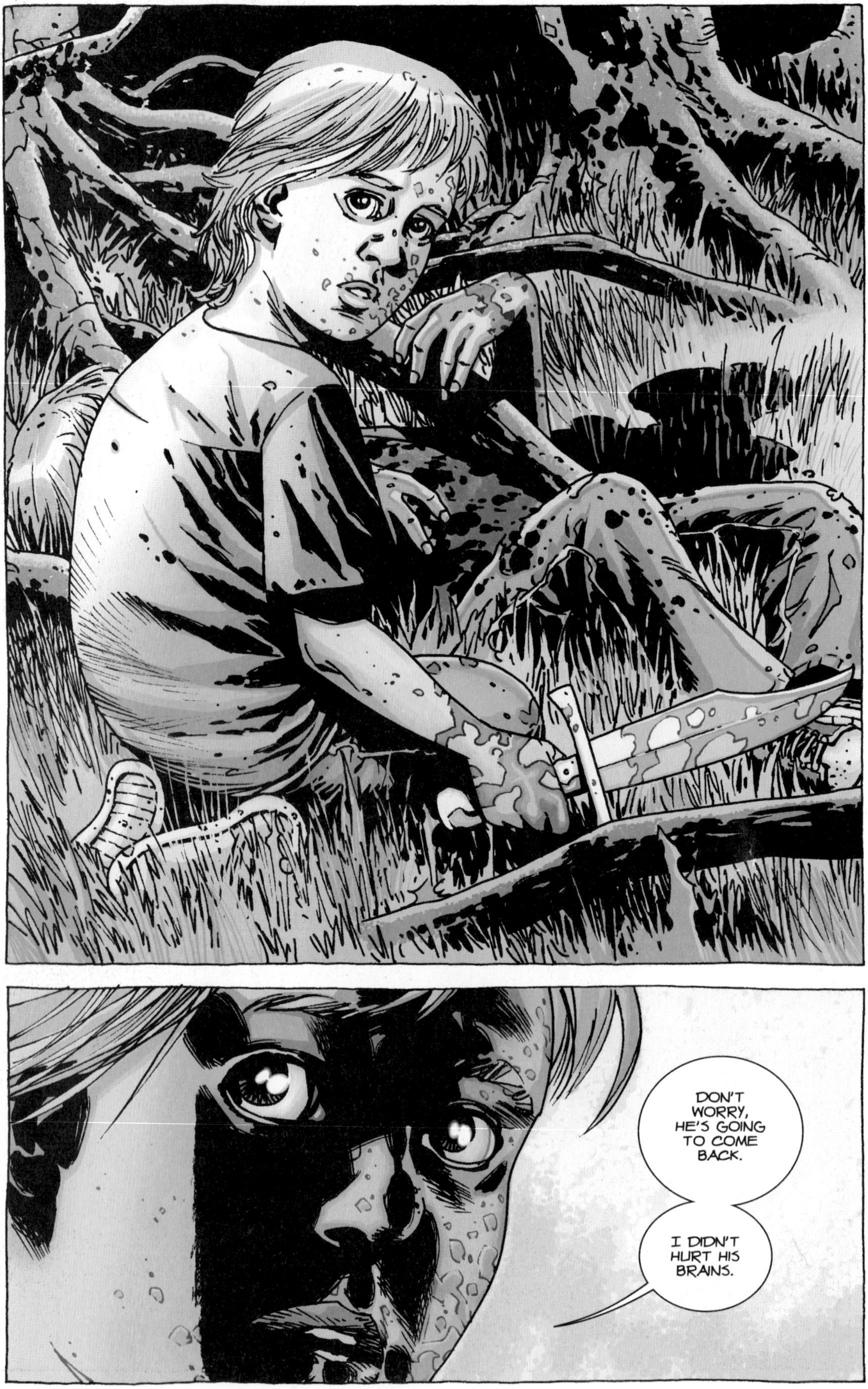
DON'T WORRY, HE'S GOING TO COME BACK.
I DIDN'T HURT HIS BRAINS.

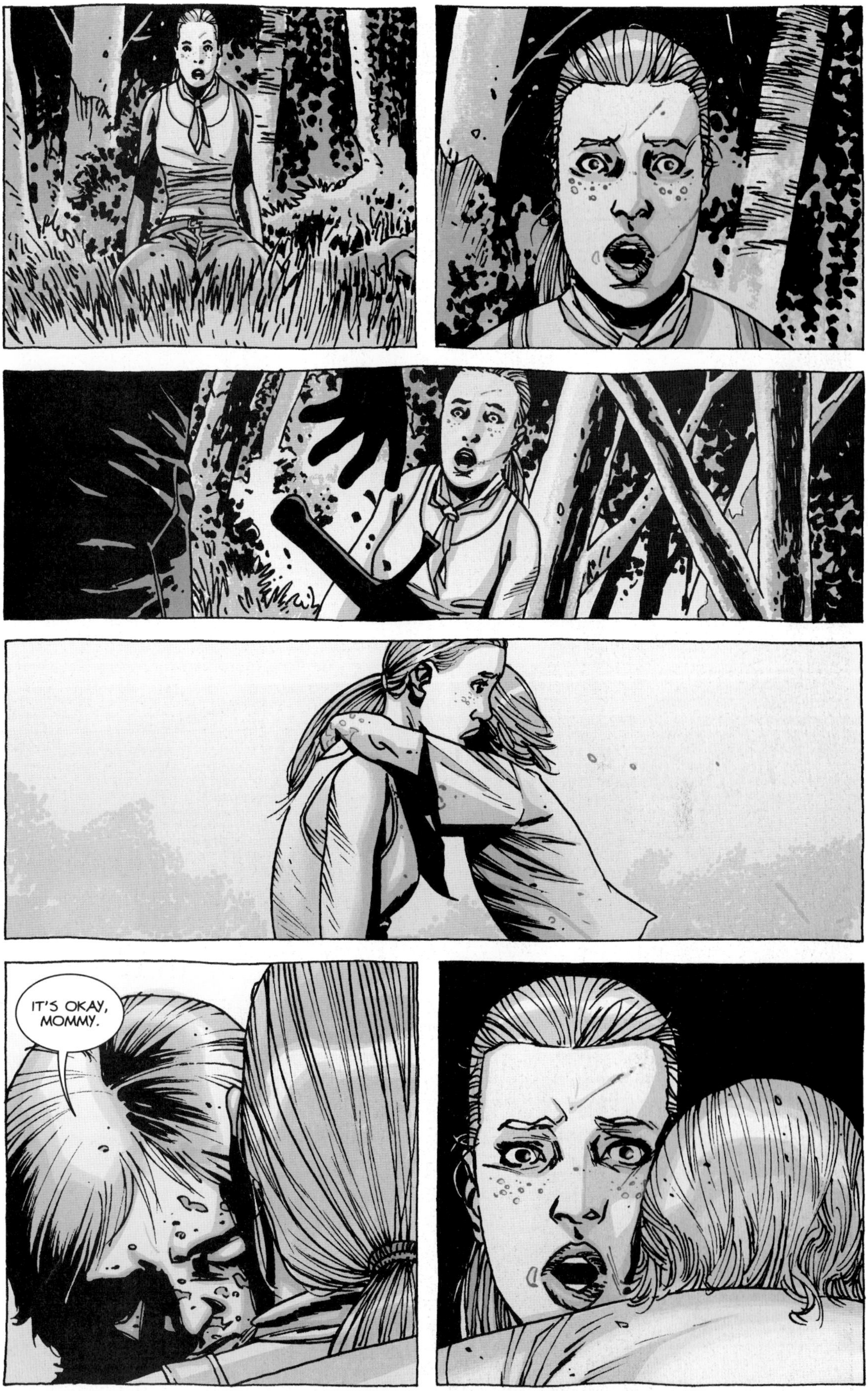
IT'S OKAY, MOMMY.

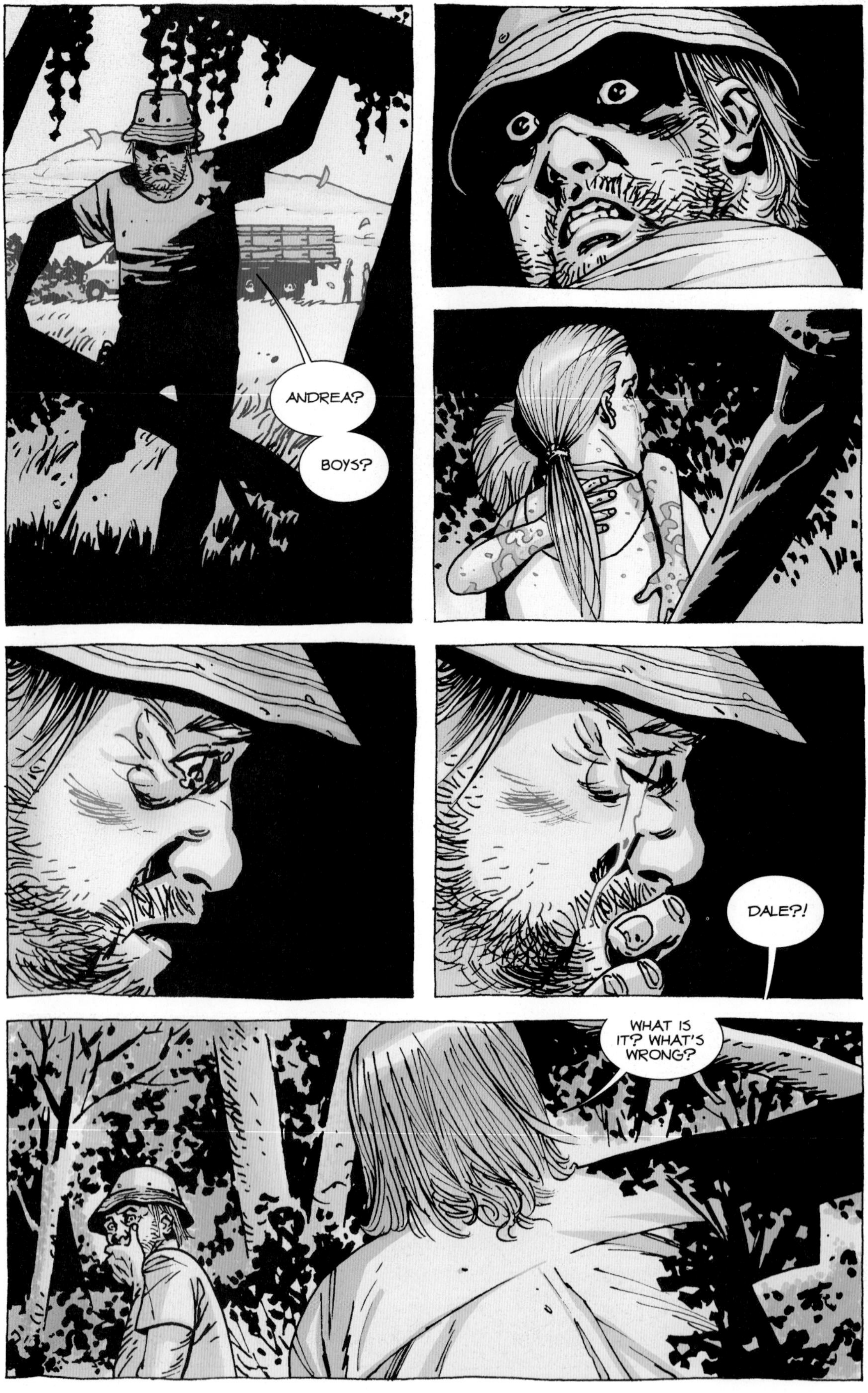
ANDREA?
BOYS?
DALE?!
WHAT IS IT? WHAT'S WRONG?

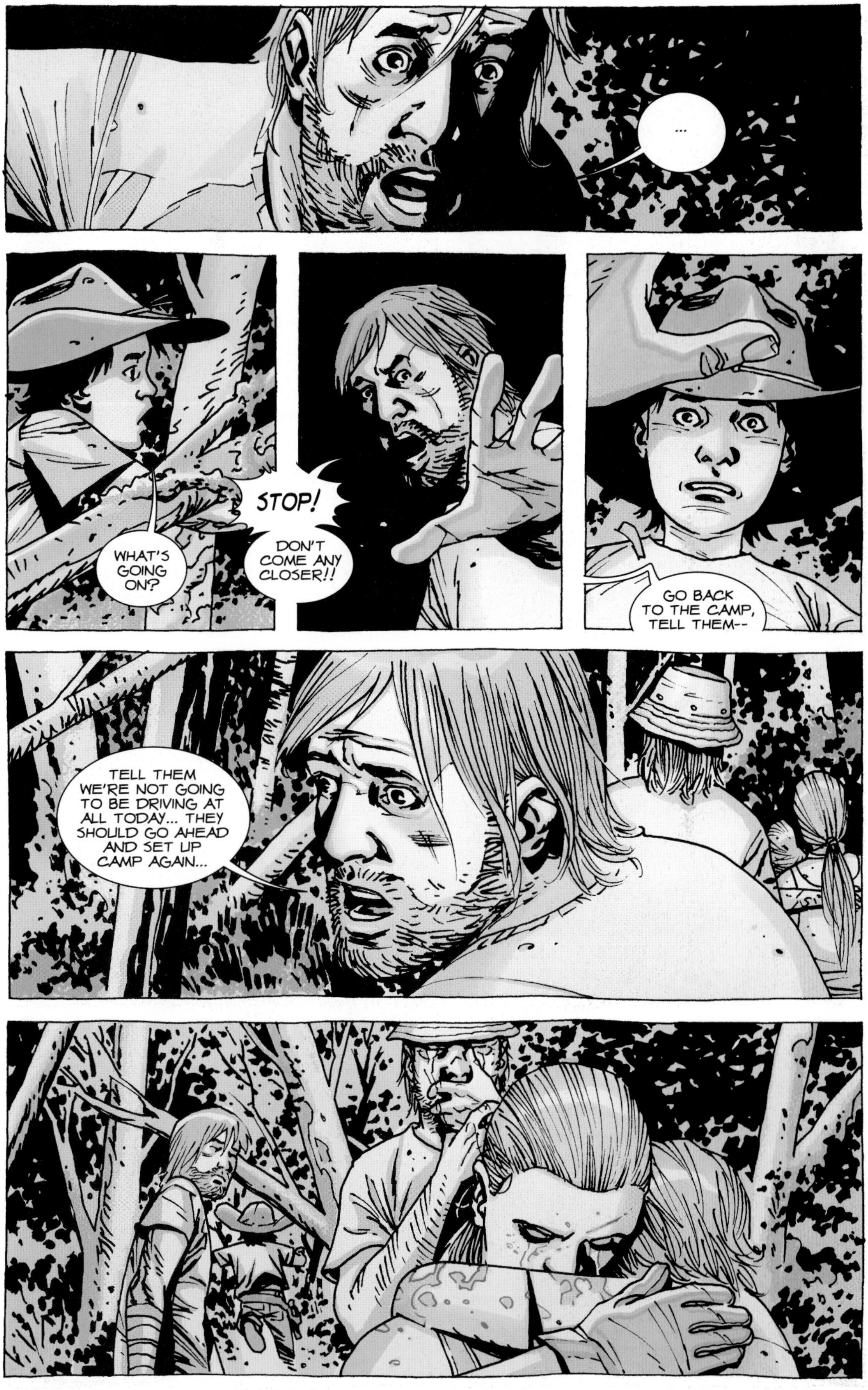
...
WHAT'S GOING ON?
STOP!
DON'T COME ANY CLOSER!!
GO BACK TO THE CAMP, TELL THEM--
TELL THEM WE'RE NOT GOING TO BE DRIVING AT ALL TODAY... THEY SHOULD GO AHEAD AND SET UP CAMP AGAIN...

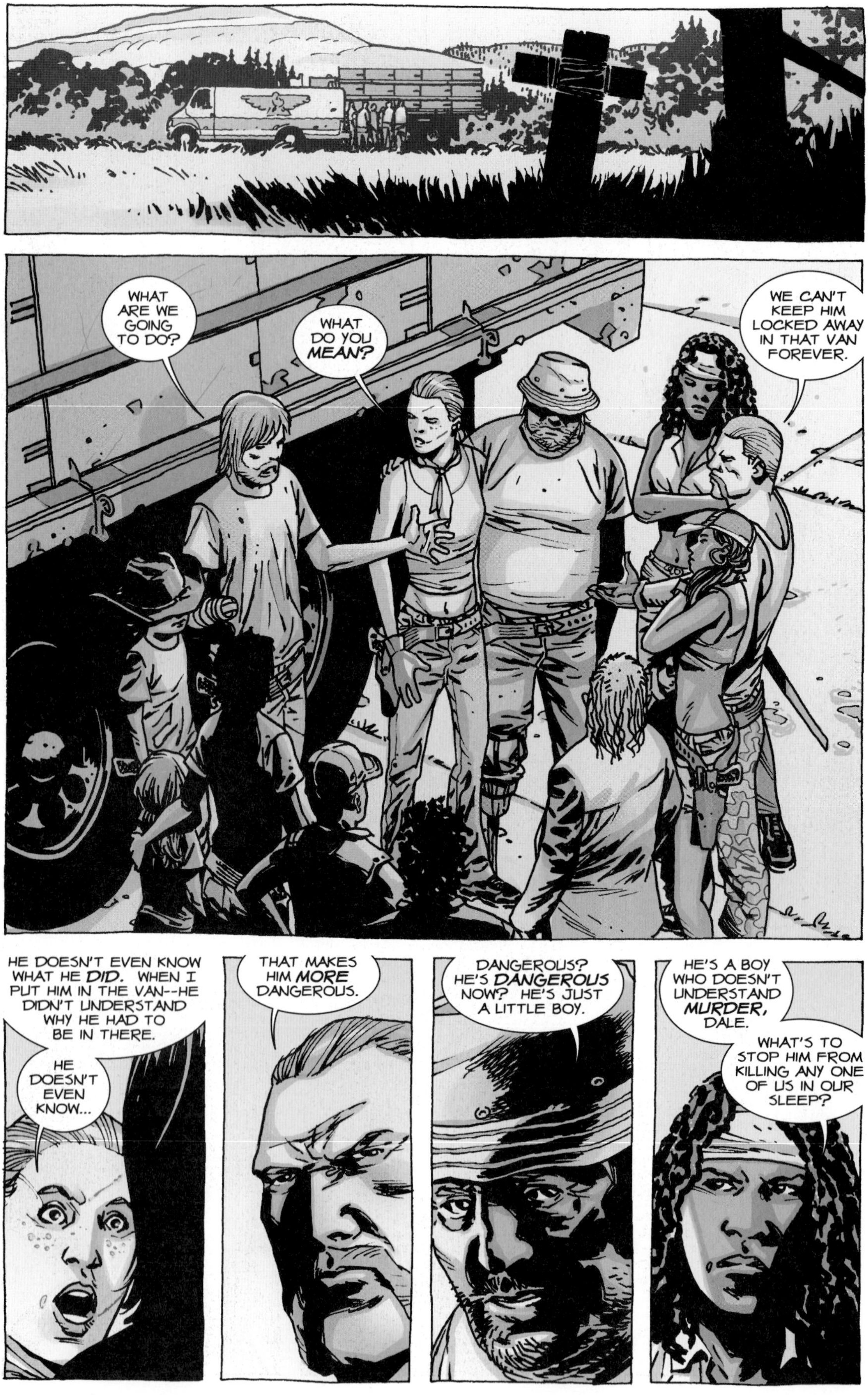
WHAT ARE WE GOING TO DO?
WHAT DO YOU MEAN?
WE CAN'T KEEP HIM LOCKED AWAY IN THAT VAN FOREVER.
HE DOESN'T EVEN KNOW WHAT HE DID. WHEN I PUT HIM IN THE VAN--HE DIDN'T UNDERSTAND WHY HE HAD TO BE IN THERE.
HE DOESN'T EVEN KNOW...
THAT MAKES HIM MORE DANGEROUS.
DANGEROUS? HE'S DANGEROUS NOW? HE'S JUST A LITTLE BOY.
HE'S A BOY WHO DOESN'T UNDERSTAND MURDER, DALE.
WHAT'S TO STOP HIM FROM KILLING ANY ONE OF US IN OUR SLEEP?

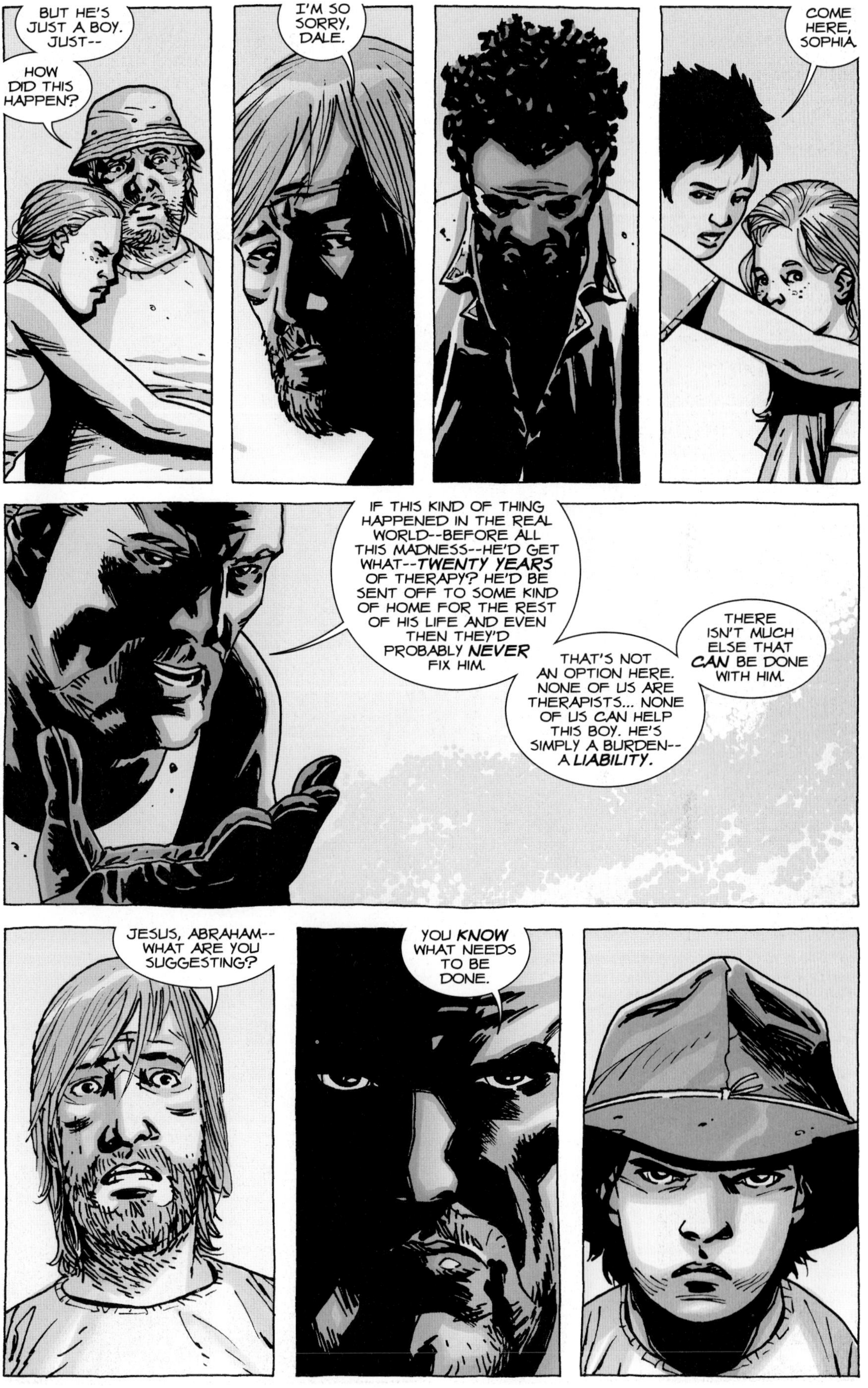

BUT HE'S JUST A BOY. JUST--
HOW DID THIS HAPPEN?
I'M SO SORRY, DALE.
COME HERE, SOPHIA.
IF THIS KIND OF THING HAPPENED IN THE REAL WORLD--BEFORE ALL THIS MADNESS--HE'D GET WHAT--TWENTY YEARS OF THERAPY? HE'D BE SENT OFF TO SOME KIND OF HOME FOR THE REST OF HIS LIFE AND EVEN THEN THEY'D PROBABLY NEVER FIX HIM.
THAT'S NOT AN OPTION HERE. NONE OF US ARE THERAPISTS... NONE OF US CAN HELP THIS BOY. HE'S SIMPLY A BURDEN--A LIABILITY.
THERE ISN'T MUCH ELSE THAT CAN BE DONE WITH HIM.
JESUS, ABRAHAM--WHAT ARE YOU SUGGESTING?
YOU KNOW WHAT NEEDS TO BE DONE.

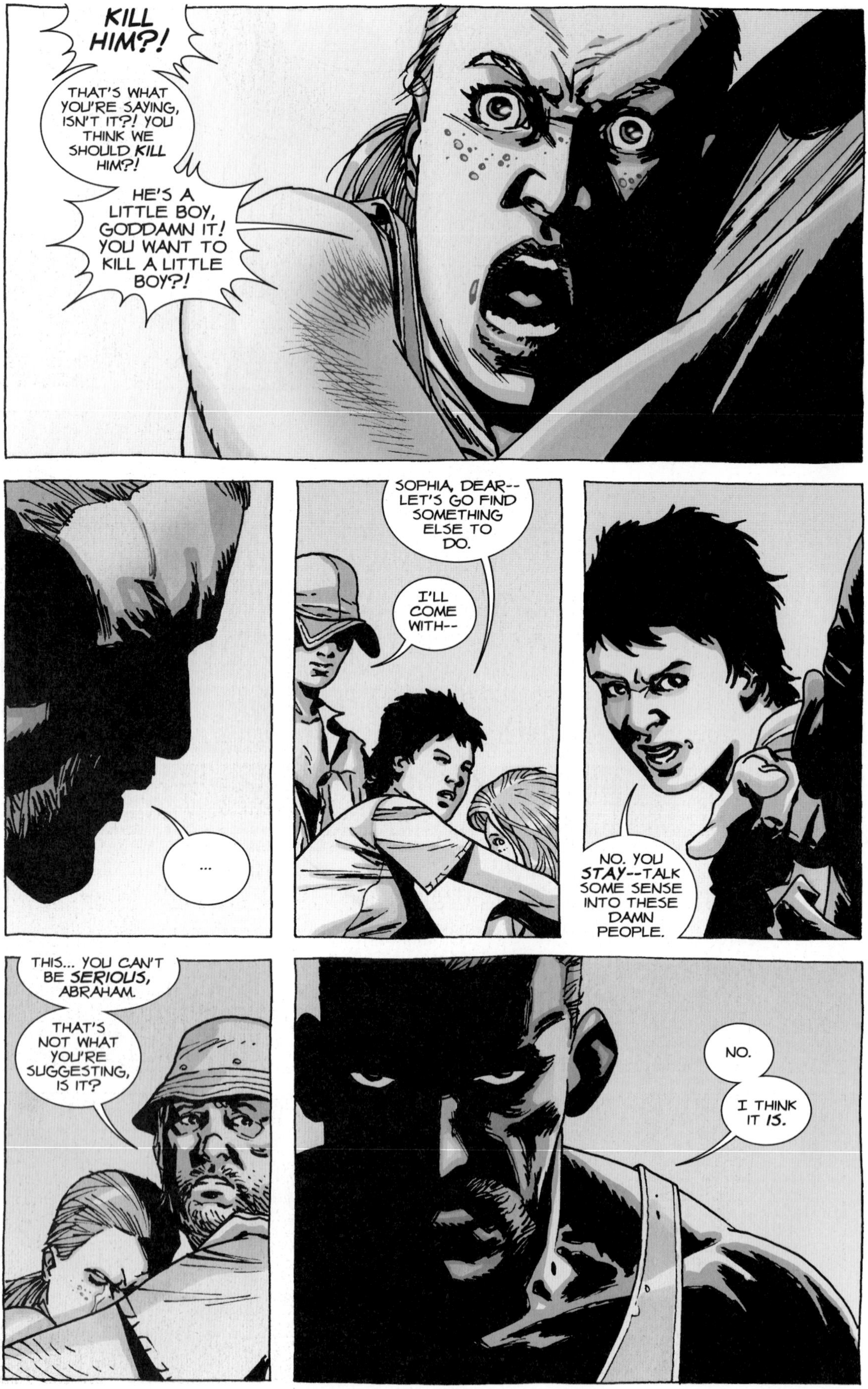
KILL HIM?!
THAT'S WHAT YOU'RE SAYING, ISN'T IT?! YOU THINK WE SHOULD KILL HIM?!
HE'S A LITTLE BOY, GODDAMN IT! YOU WANT TO KILL A LITTLE BOY?!
...
SOPHIA, DEAR-- LET'S GO FIND SOMETHING ELSE TO DO.
I'LL COME WITH--
NO. YOU STAY--TALK SOME SENSE INTO THESE DAMN PEOPLE.
THIS... YOU CAN'T BE SERIOUS, ABRAHAM.
THAT'S NOT WHAT YOU'RE SUGGESTING, IS IT?
NO.
I THINK IT IS.

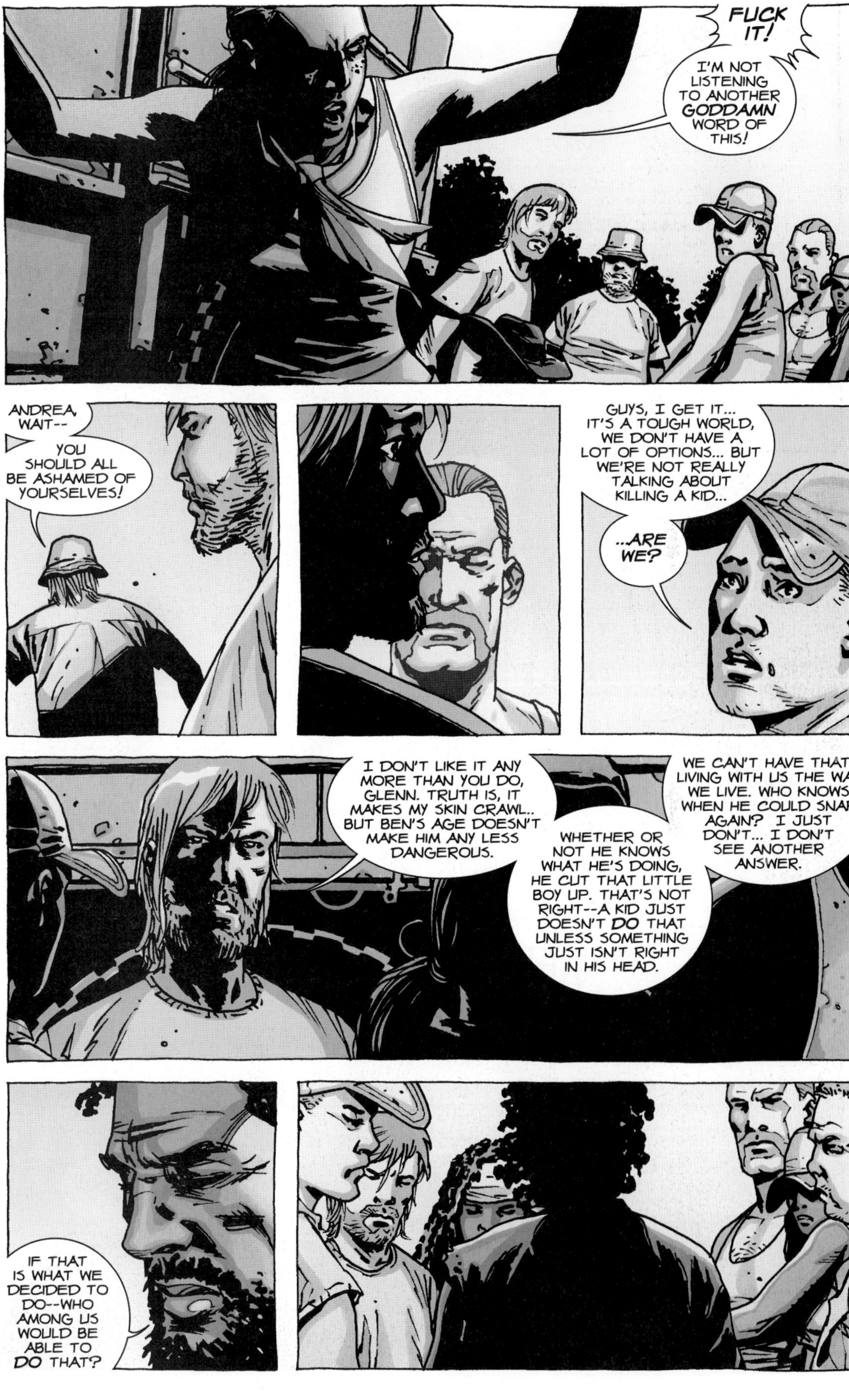
FUCK IT!
I'M NOT LISTENING TO ANOTHER GODDAMN WORD OF THIS!
ANDREA, WAIT--
YOU SHOULD ALL BE ASHAMED OF YOURSELVES!
GUYS, I GET IT... IT'S A TOUGH WORLD, WE DON'T HAVE A LOT OF OPTIONS... BUT WE'RE NOT REALLY TALKING ABOUT KILLING A KID...
...ARE WE?
I DON'T LIKE IT ANY MORE THAN YOU DO, GLENN. TRUTH IS, IT MAKES MY SKIN CRAWL.. BUT BEN'S AGE DOESN'T MAKE HIM ANY LESS DANGEROUS.
WHETHER OR NOT HE KNOWS WHAT HE'S DOING, HE CUT THAT LITTLE BOY UP. THAT'S NOT RIGHT--A KID JUST DOESN'T DO THAT UNLESS SOMETHING JUST ISN'T RIGHT IN HIS HEAD.
WE CAN'T HAVE THAT, LIVING WITH US THE WAY WE LIVE. WHO KNOWS WHEN HE COULD SNAP AGAIN? I JUST DON'T... I DON'T SEE ANOTHER ANSWER.
IF THAT IS WHAT WE DECIDED TO DO--WHO AMONG US WOULD BE ABLE TO DO THAT?

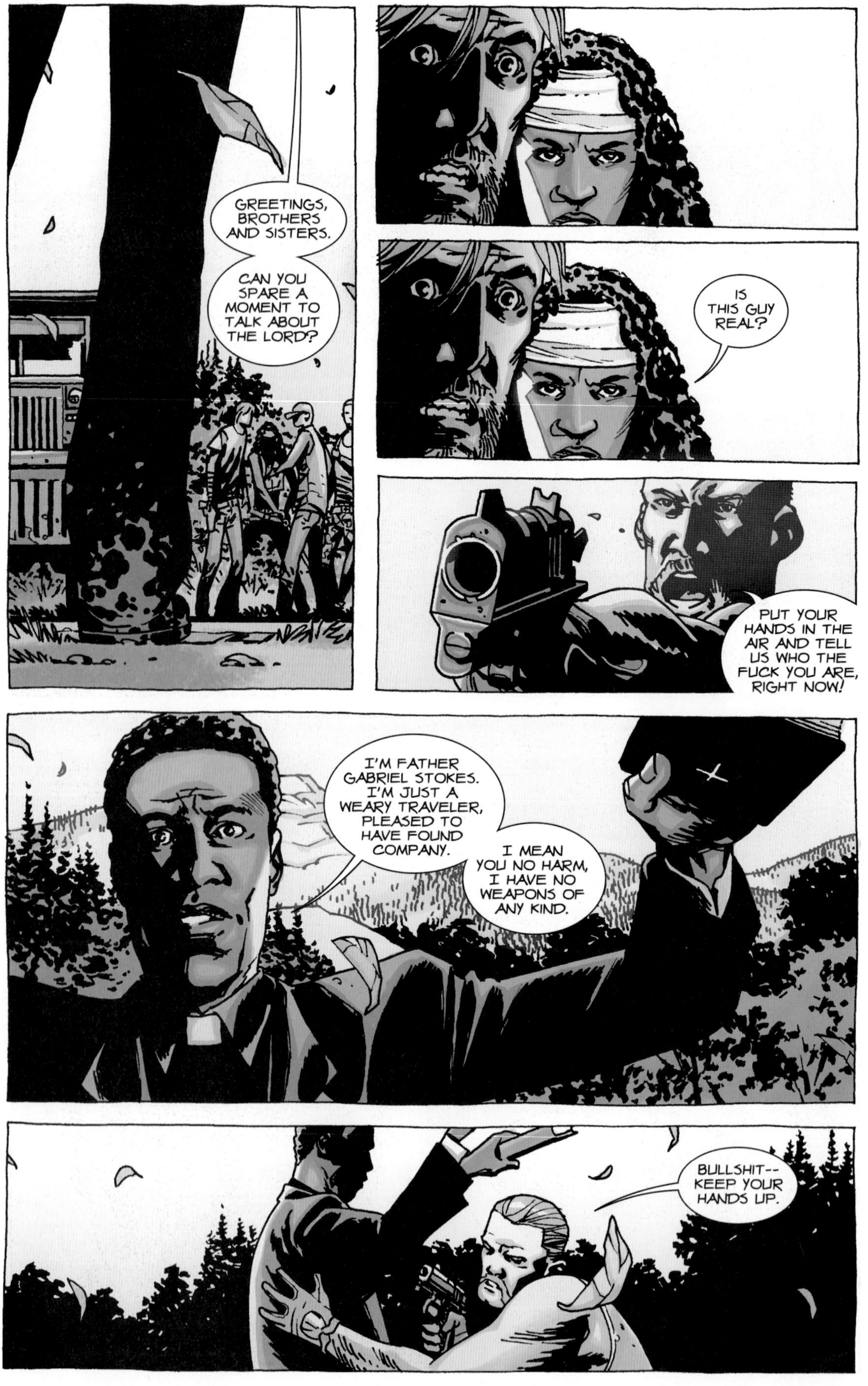
GREETINGS, BROTHERS AND SISTERS.
CAN YOU SPARE A MOMENT TO TALK ABOUT THE LORD?
IS THIS GUY REAL?
PUT YOUR HANDS IN THE AIR AND TELL US WHO THE FUCK YOU ARE, RIGHT NOW!
I'M FATHER GABRIEL STOKES. I'M JUST A WEARY TRAVELER, PLEASED TO HAVE FOUND COMPANY.
I MEAN YOU NO HARM, I HAVE NO WEAPONS OF ANY KIND.
BULLSHIT-- KEEP YOUR HANDS UP.

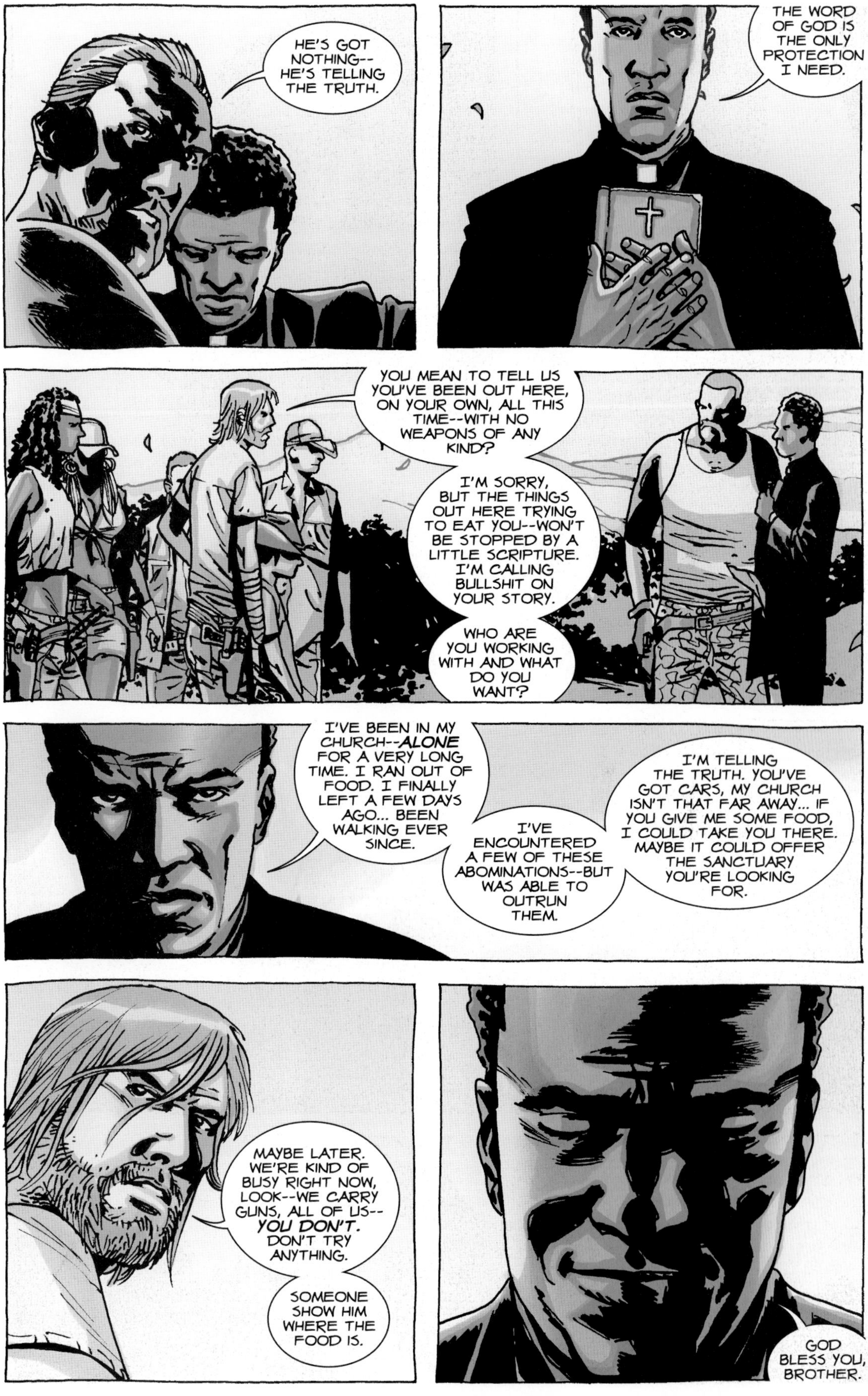

HE'S GOT NOTHING-- HE'S TELLING THE TRUTH.
THE WORD OF GOD IS THE ONLY PROTECTION I NEED.
YOU MEAN TO TELL US YOU'VE BEEN OUT HERE, ON YOUR OWN, ALL THIS TIME--WITH NO WEAPONS OF ANY KIND?
I'M SORRY, BUT THE THINGS OUT HERE TRYING TO EAT YOU--WON'T BE STOPPED BY A LITTLE SCRIPTURE. I'M CALLING BULLSHIT ON YOUR STORY.
WHO ARE YOU WORKING WITH AND WHAT DO YOU WANT?
I'VE BEEN IN MY CHURCH--*ALONE* FOR A VERY LONG TIME. I RAN OUT OF FOOD. I FINALLY LEFT A FEW DAYS AGO... BEEN WALKING EVER SINCE.
I'VE ENCOUNTERED A FEW OF THESE ABOMINATIONS--BUT WAS ABLE TO OUTRUN THEM.
I'M TELLING THE TRUTH. YOU'VE GOT CARS, MY CHURCH ISN'T THAT FAR AWAY... IF YOU GIVE ME SOME FOOD, I COULD TAKE YOU THERE. MAYBE IT COULD OFFER THE SANCTUARY YOU'RE LOOKING FOR.
MAYBE LATER. WE'RE KIND OF BUSY RIGHT NOW, LOOK--WE CARRY GUNS, ALL OF US-- *YOU DON'T.* DON'T TRY ANYTHING.
SOMEONE SHOW HIM WHERE THE FOOD IS.
GOD BLESS YOU, BROTHER.

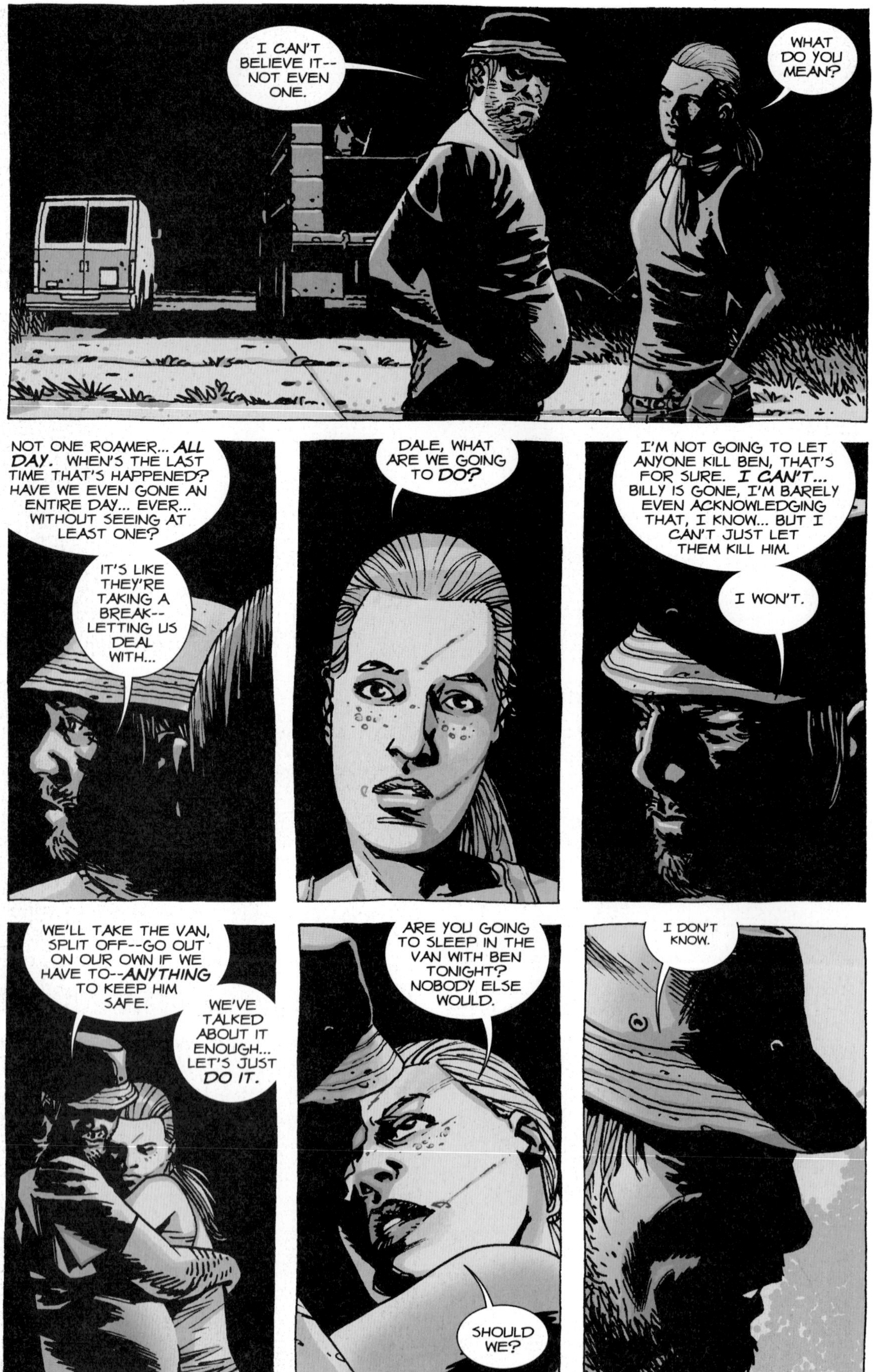
I CAN'T BELIEVE IT-- NOT EVEN ONE.
WHAT DO YOU MEAN?
NOT ONE ROAMER... ALL DAY. WHEN'S THE LAST TIME THAT'S HAPPENED? HAVE WE EVEN GONE AN ENTIRE DAY... EVER... WITHOUT SEEING AT LEAST ONE?
IT'S LIKE THEY'RE TAKING A BREAK-- LETTING US DEAL WITH...
DALE, WHAT ARE WE GOING TO DO?
I'M NOT GOING TO LET ANYONE KILL BEN, THAT'S FOR SURE. I CAN'T... BILLY IS GONE, I'M BARELY EVEN ACKNOWLEDGING THAT, I KNOW... BUT I CAN'T JUST LET THEM KILL HIM.
I WON'T.
WE'LL TAKE THE VAN, SPLIT OFF--GO OUT ON OUR OWN IF WE HAVE TO--ANYTHING TO KEEP HIM SAFE.
WE'VE TALKED ABOUT IT ENOUGH... LET'S JUST DO IT.
ARE YOU GOING TO SLEEP IN THE VAN WITH BEN TONIGHT? NOBODY ELSE WOULD.
SHOULD WE?
I DON'T KNOW.

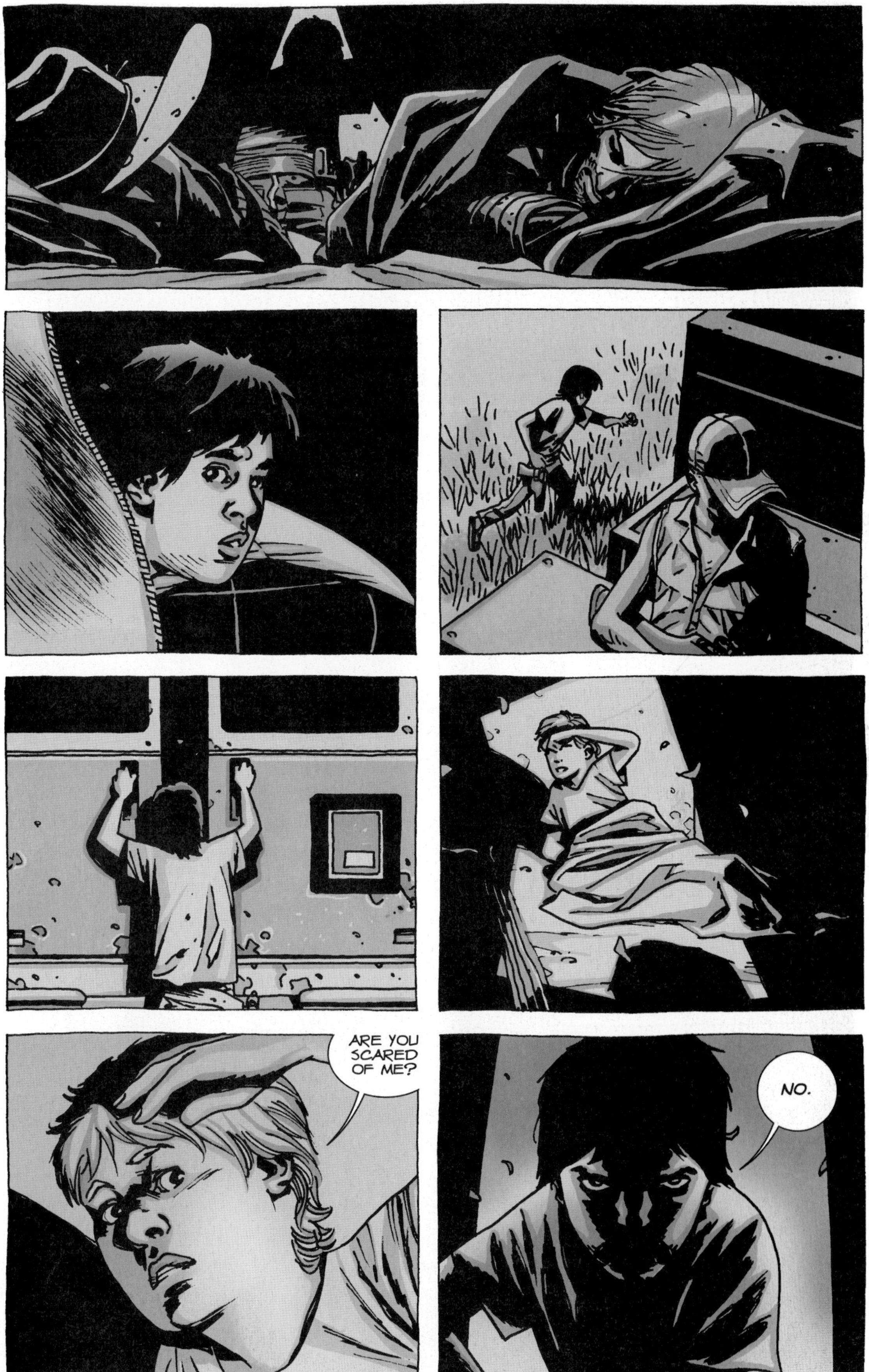
ARE YOU SCARED OF ME?
NO.

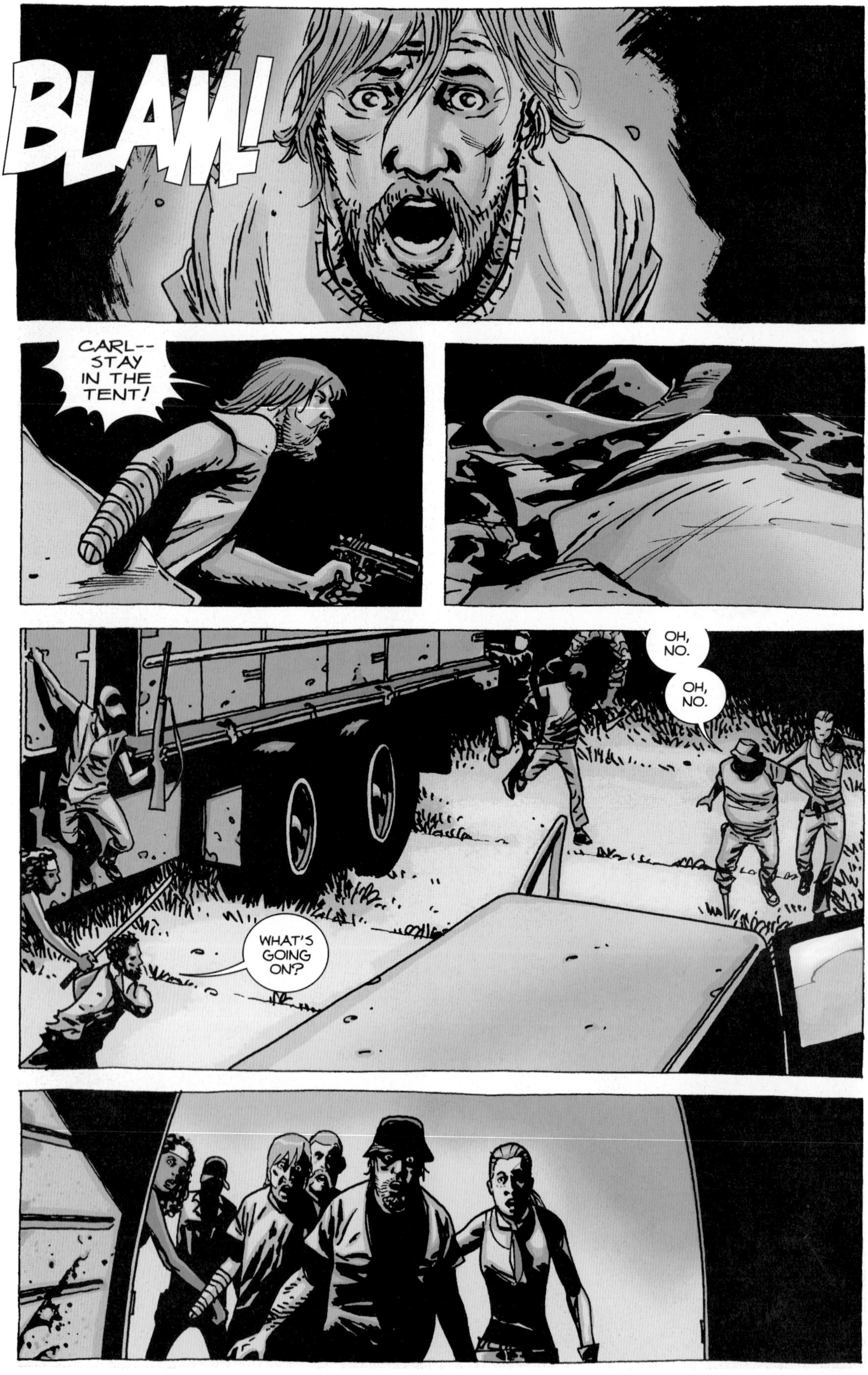
BLAM!
CARL-- STAY IN THE TENT!
OH, NO.
OH, NO.
WHAT'S GOING ON?

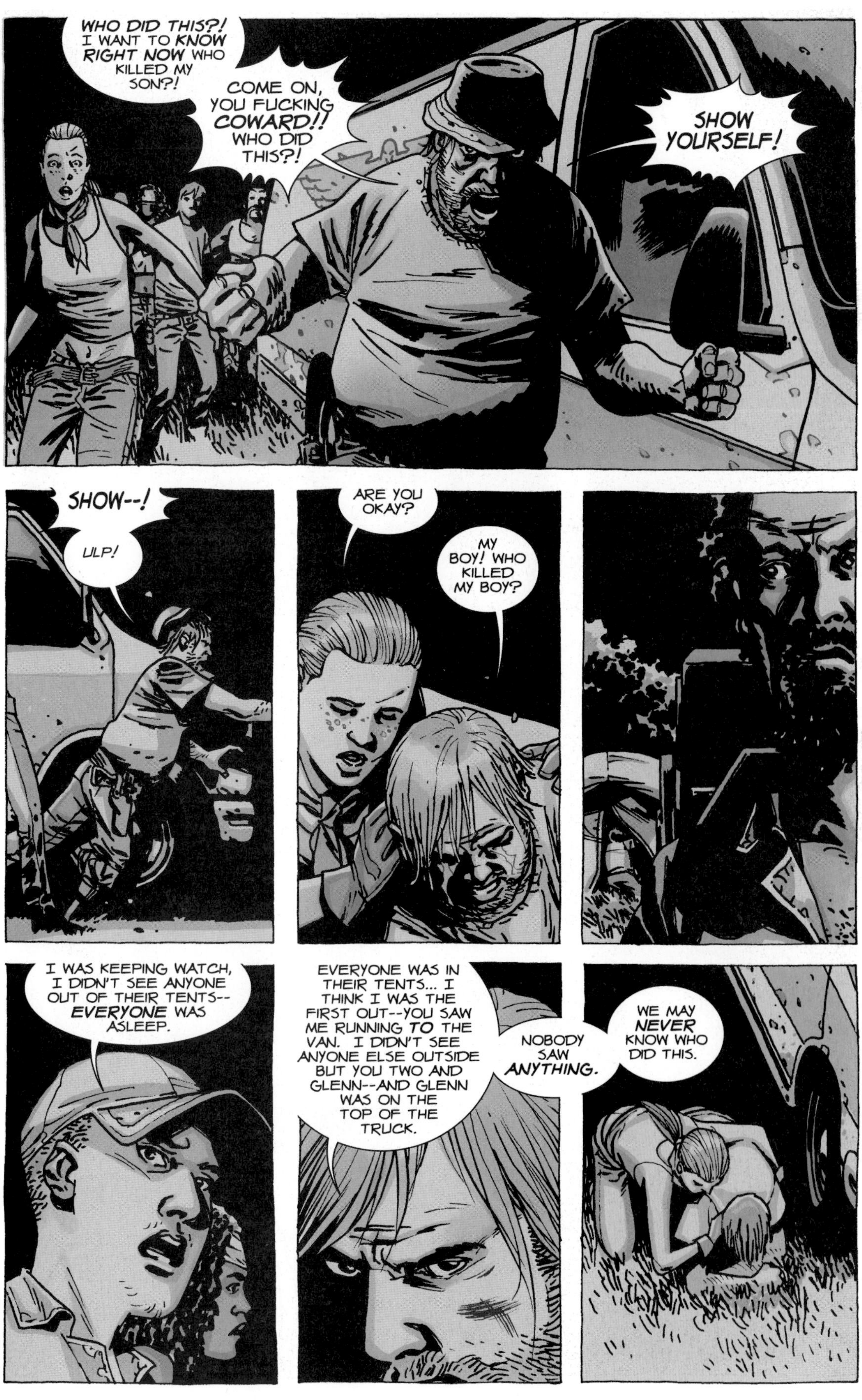
WHO DID THIS?! I WANT TO KNOW RIGHT NOW WHO KILLED MY SON?!
COME ON, YOU FUCKING COWARD!! WHO DID THIS?!
SHOW YOURSELF!
SHOW--!
ULP!
ARE YOU OKAY?
MY BOY! WHO KILLED MY BOY?
I WAS KEEPING WATCH, I DIDN'T SEE ANYONE OUT OF THEIR TENTS-- EVERYONE WAS ASLEEP.
EVERYONE WAS IN THEIR TENTS... I THINK I WAS THE FIRST OUT--YOU SAW ME RUNNING TO THE VAN. I DIDN'T SEE ANYONE ELSE OUTSIDE BUT YOU TWO AND GLENN--AND GLENN WAS ON THE TOP OF THE TRUCK.
NOBODY SAW ANYTHING.
WE MAY NEVER KNOW WHO DID THIS.

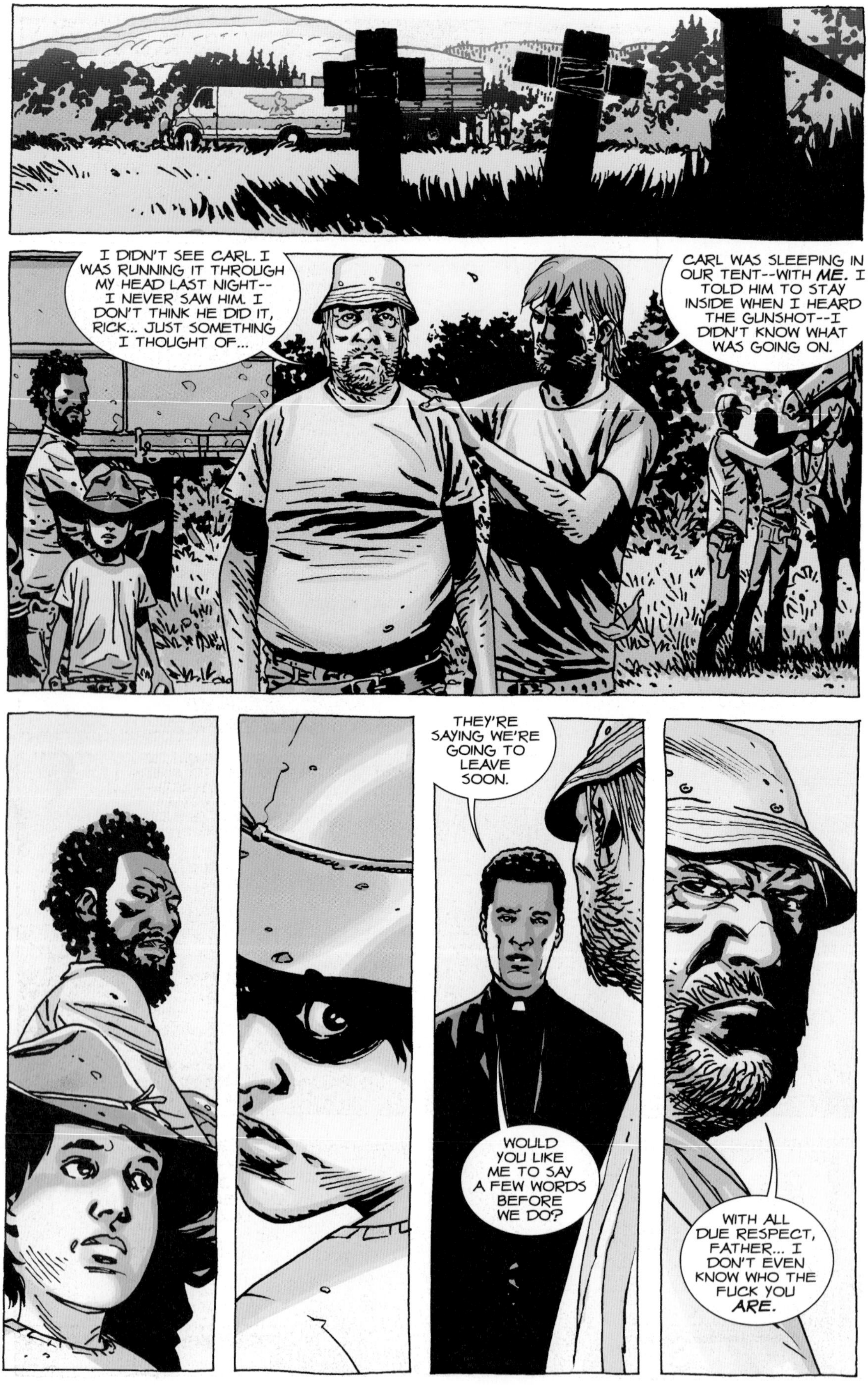
I DIDN'T SEE CARL. I WAS RUNNING IT THROUGH MY HEAD LAST NIGHT-- I NEVER SAW HIM. I DON'T THINK HE DID IT, RICK... JUST SOMETHING I THOUGHT OF...
CARL WAS SLEEPING IN OUR TENT--WITH ME. I TOLD HIM TO STAY INSIDE WHEN I HEARD THE GUNSHOT--I DIDN'T KNOW WHAT WAS GOING ON.
THEY'RE SAYING WE'RE GOING TO LEAVE SOON.
WOULD YOU LIKE ME TO SAY A FEW WORDS BEFORE WE DO?
WITH ALL DUE RESPECT, FATHER... I DON'T EVEN KNOW WHO THE FUCK YOU ARE.

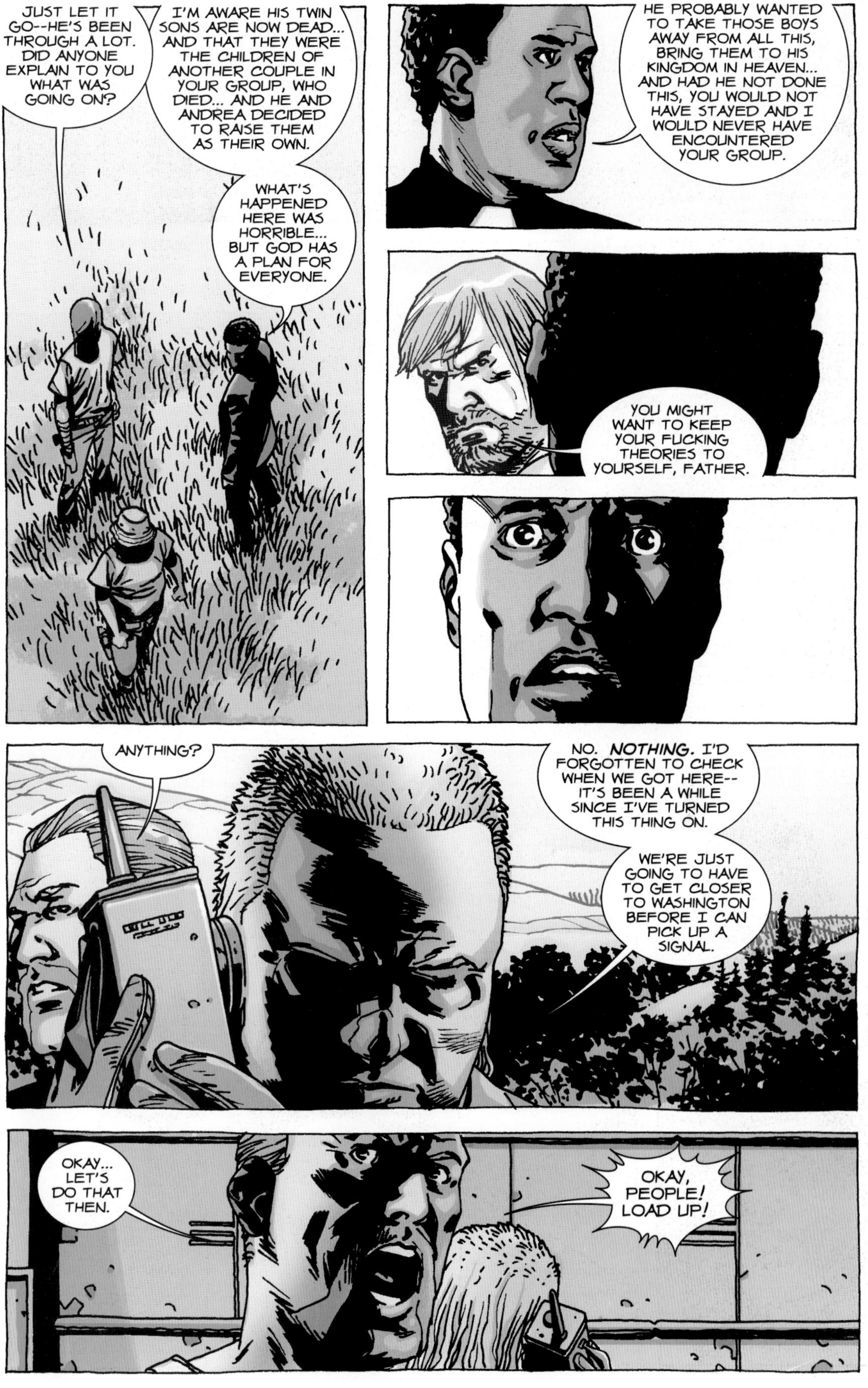
JUST LET IT GO--HE'S BEEN THROUGH A LOT. DID ANYONE EXPLAIN TO YOU WHAT WAS GOING ON?
I'M AWARE HIS TWIN SONS ARE NOW DEAD... AND THAT THEY WERE THE CHILDREN OF ANOTHER COUPLE IN YOUR GROUP, WHO DIED... AND HE AND ANDREA DECIDED TO RAISE THEM AS THEIR OWN.
WHAT'S HAPPENED HERE WAS HORRIBLE... BUT GOD HAS A PLAN FOR EVERYONE.
HE PROBABLY WANTED TO TAKE THOSE BOYS AWAY FROM ALL THIS, BRING THEM TO HIS KINGDOM IN HEAVEN... AND HAD HE NOT DONE THIS, YOU WOULD NOT HAVE STAYED AND I WOULD NEVER HAVE ENCOUNTERED YOUR GROUP.
YOU MIGHT WANT TO KEEP YOUR FUCKING THEORIES TO YOURSELF, FATHER.
ANYTHING?
NO. NOTHING. I'D FORGOTTEN TO CHECK WHEN WE GOT HERE-- IT'S BEEN A WHILE SINCE I'VE TURNED THIS THING ON.
WE'RE JUST GOING TO HAVE TO GET CLOSER TO WASHINGTON BEFORE I CAN PICK UP A SIGNAL.
OKAY... LET'S DO THAT THEN.
OKAY, PEOPLE! LOAD UP!

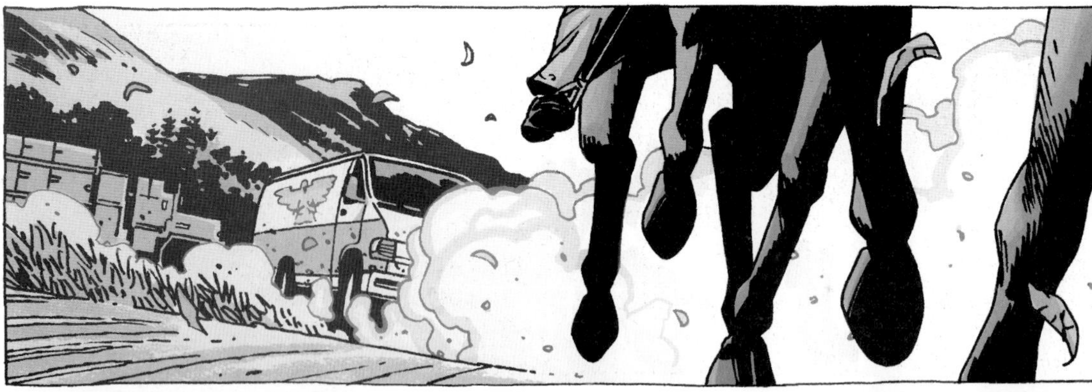

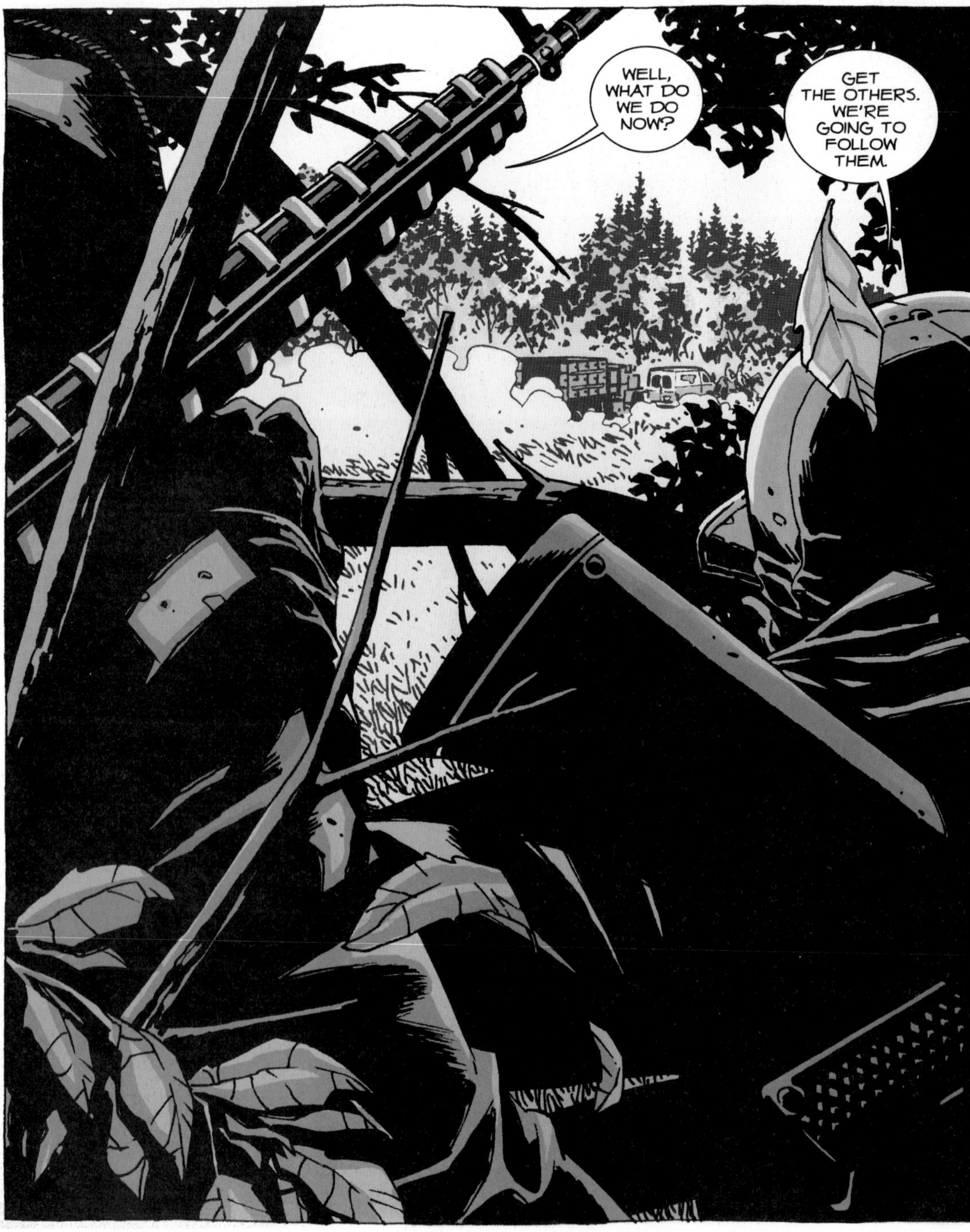

WELL, WHAT DO WE DO NOW?
GET THE OTHERS. WE'RE GOING TO FOLLOW THEM.

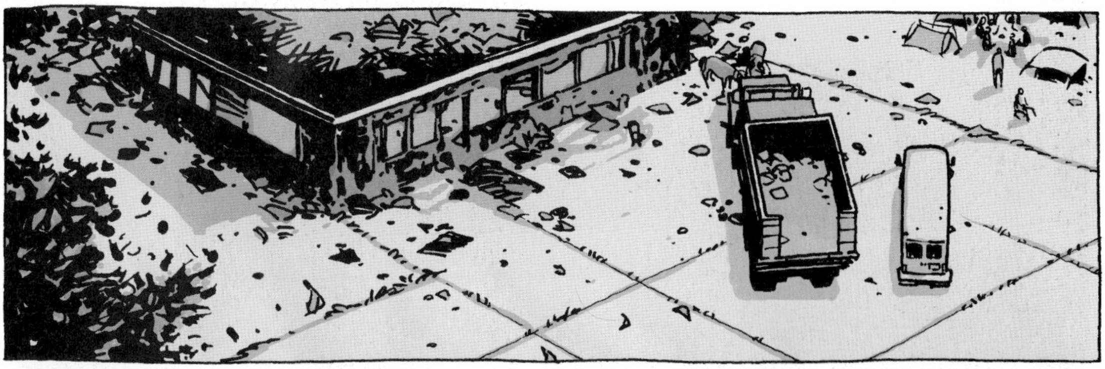

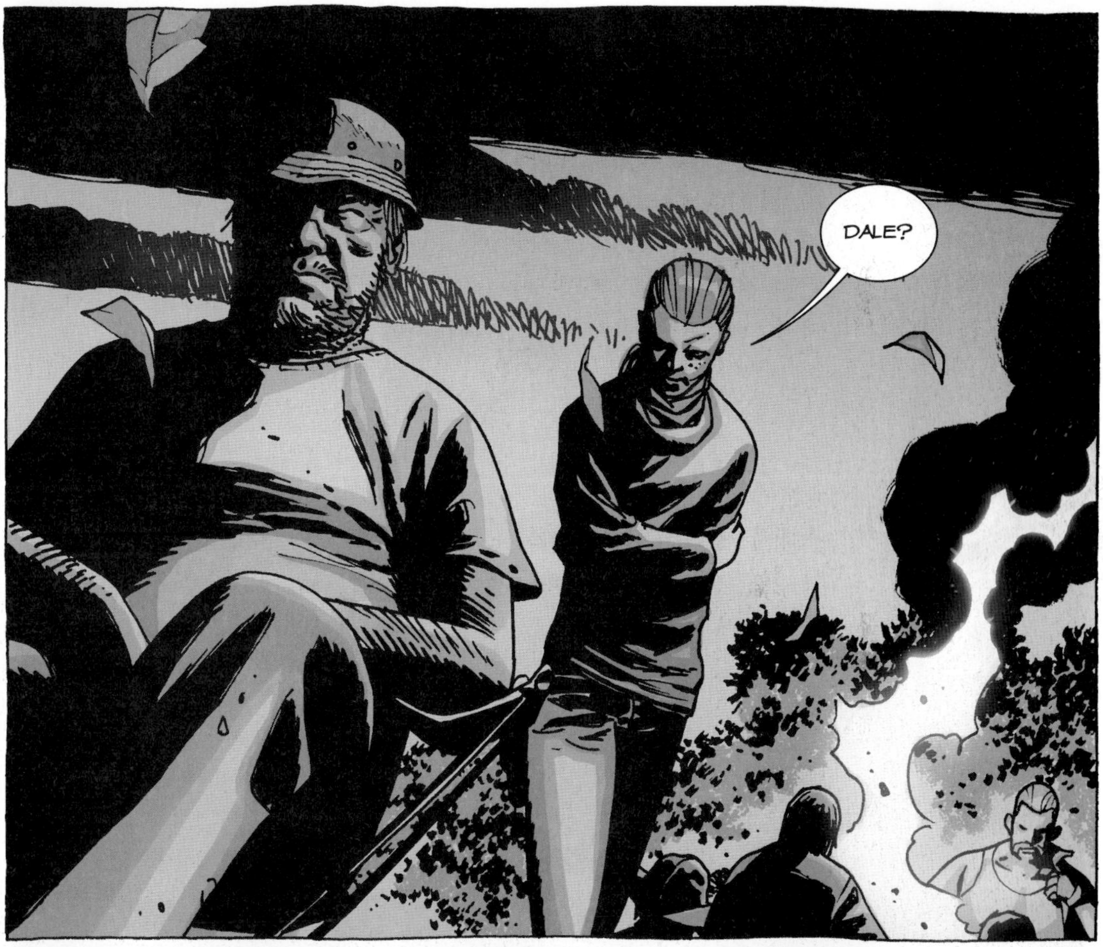
DALE?

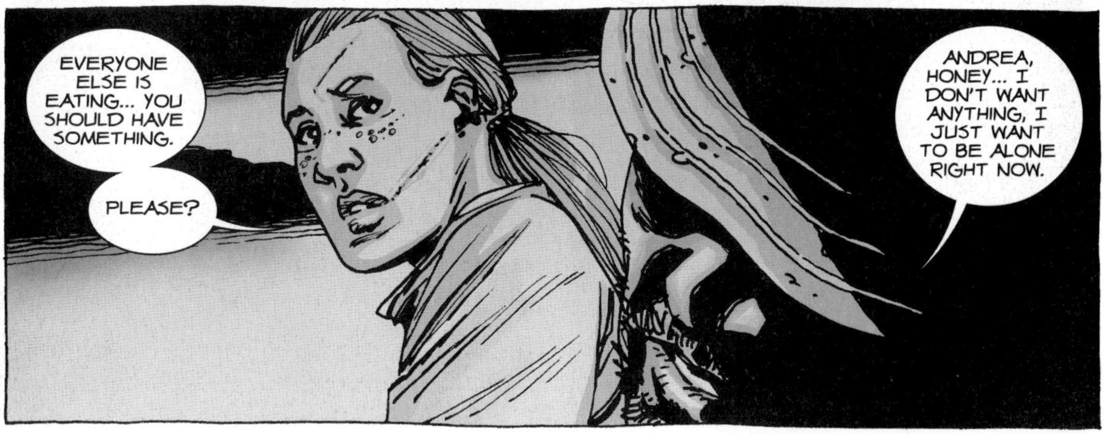
EVERYONE ELSE IS EATING... YOU SHOULD HAVE SOMETHING.
PLEASE?
ANDREA, HONEY... I DON'T WANT ANYTHING, I JUST WANT TO BE ALONE RIGHT NOW.

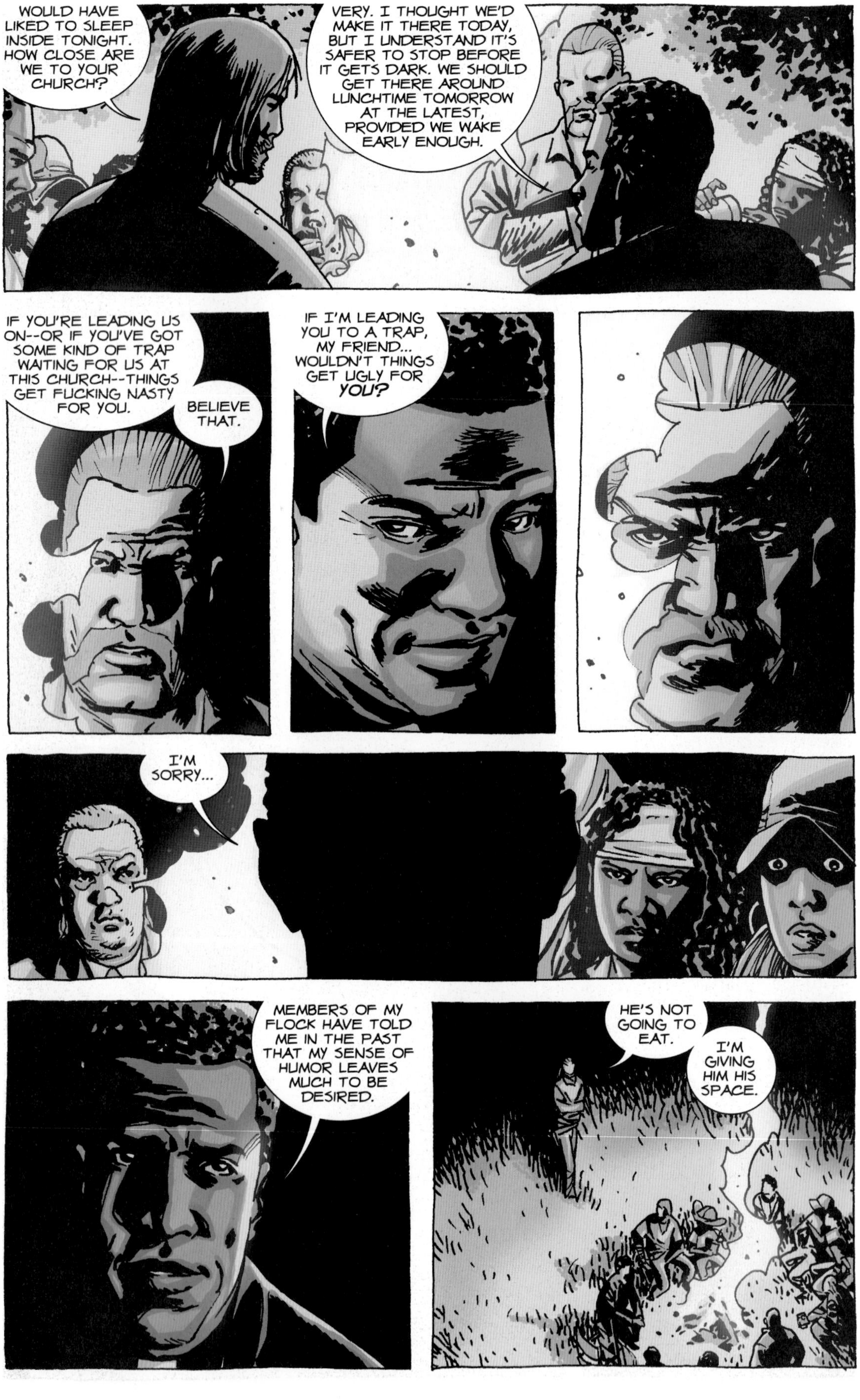
WOULD HAVE LIKED TO SLEEP INSIDE TONIGHT. HOW CLOSE ARE WE TO YOUR CHURCH?
VERY. I THOUGHT WE'D MAKE IT THERE TODAY, BUT I UNDERSTAND IT'S SAFER TO STOP BEFORE IT GETS DARK. WE SHOULD GET THERE AROUND LUNCHTIME TOMORROW AT THE LATEST, PROVIDED WE WAKE EARLY ENOUGH.
IF YOU'RE LEADING US ON--OR IF YOU'VE GOT SOME KIND OF TRAP WAITING FOR US AT THIS CHURCH--THINGS GET FUCKING NASTY FOR YOU.
BELIEVE THAT.
IF I'M LEADING YOU TO A TRAP, MY FRIEND... WOULDN'T THINGS GET UGLY FOR YOU?
I'M SORRY...
MEMBERS OF MY FLOCK HAVE TOLD ME IN THE PAST THAT MY SENSE OF HUMOR LEAVES MUCH TO BE DESIRED.
HE'S NOT GOING TO EAT.
I'M GIVING HIM HIS SPACE.

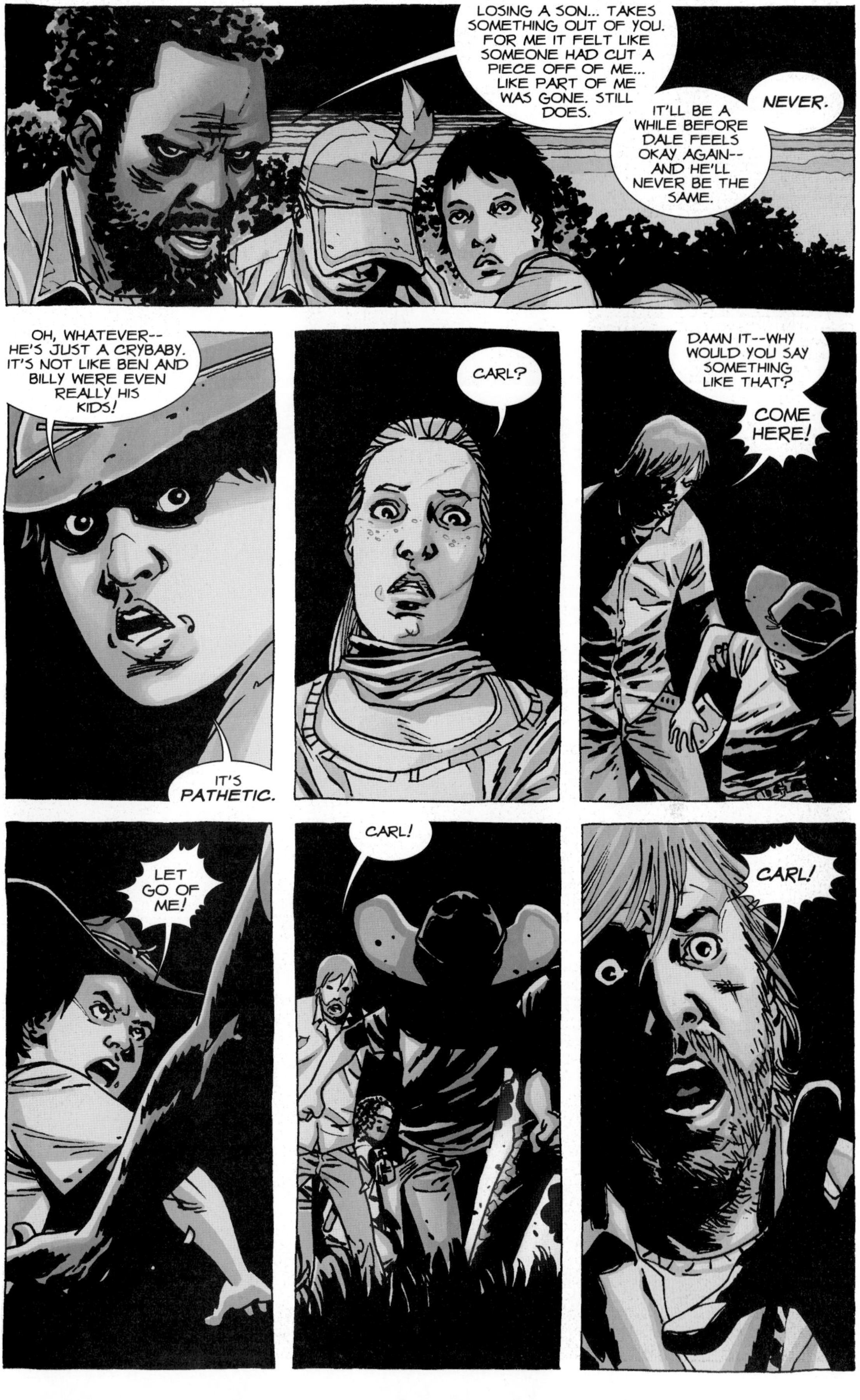
LOSING A SON... TAKES SOMETHING OUT OF YOU. FOR ME IT FELT LIKE SOMEONE HAD CUT A PIECE OFF OF ME... LIKE PART OF ME WAS GONE. STILL DOES.
IT'LL BE A WHILE BEFORE DALE FEELS OKAY AGAIN-- AND HE'LL NEVER BE THE SAME.
NEVER.
OH, WHATEVER-- HE'S JUST A CRYBABY. IT'S NOT LIKE BEN AND BILLY WERE EVEN REALLY HIS KIDS!
IT'S PATHETIC.
CARL?
DAMN IT--WHY WOULD YOU SAY SOMETHING LIKE THAT?
COME HERE!
LET GO OF ME!
CARL!
CARL!

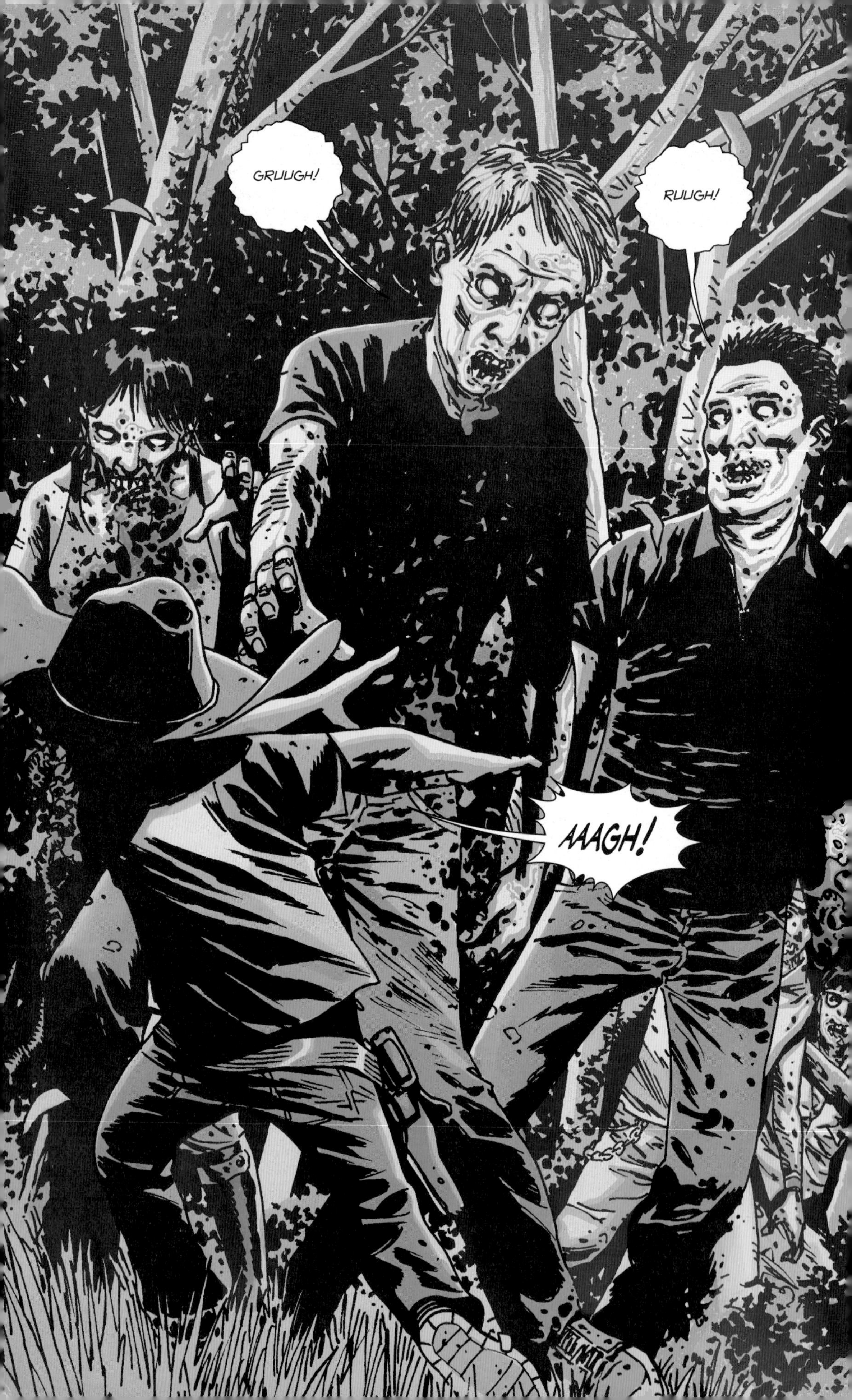
GRUUGH!
RUUGH!
AAAGH!

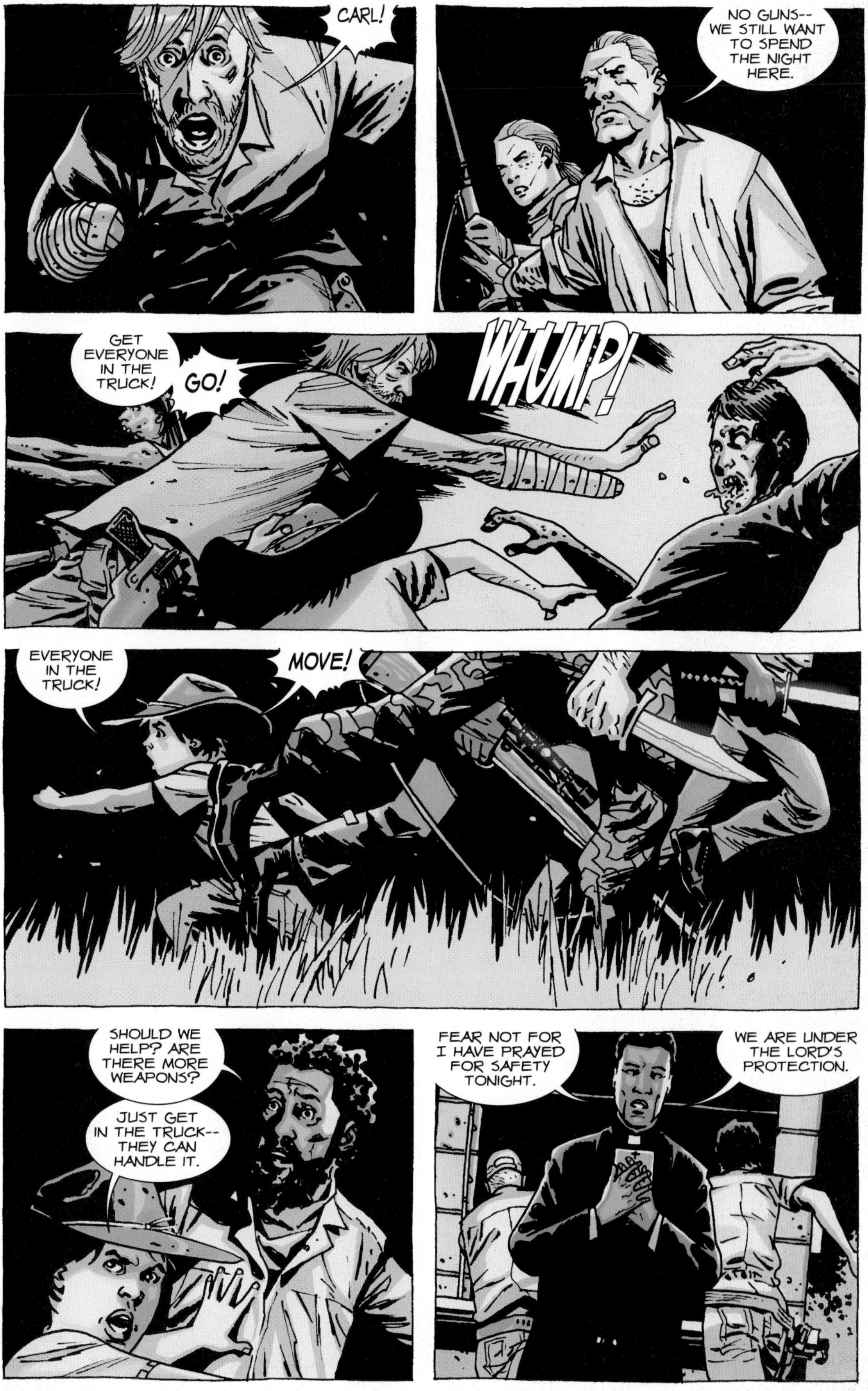

CARL!
NO GUNS-- WE STILL WANT TO SPEND THE NIGHT HERE.
GET EVERYONE IN THE TRUCK!
GO!
WHUMP!
EVERYONE IN THE TRUCK!
MOVE!
SHOULD WE HELP? ARE THERE MORE WEAPONS?
JUST GET IN THE TRUCK-- THEY CAN HANDLE IT.
FEAR NOT FOR I HAVE PRAYED FOR SAFETY TONIGHT.
WE ARE UNDER THE LORD'S PROTECTION.

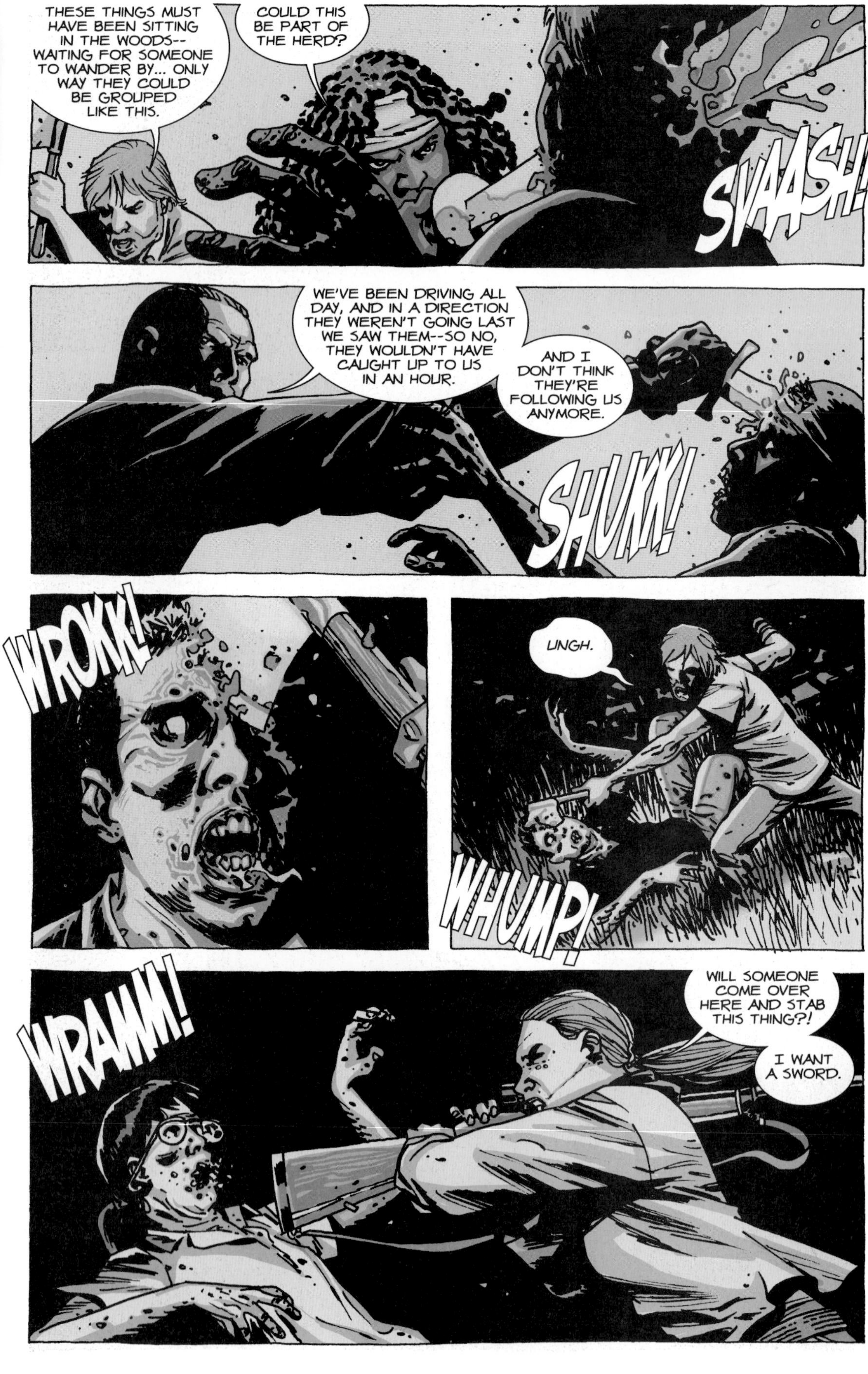
THESE THINGS MUST HAVE BEEN SITTING IN THE WOODS-- WAITING FOR SOMEONE TO WANDER BY... ONLY WAY THEY COULD BE GROUPED LIKE THIS.
COULD THIS BE PART OF THE HERD?
SVAASH!
WE'VE BEEN DRIVING ALL DAY, AND IN A DIRECTION THEY WEREN'T GOING LAST WE SAW THEM--SO NO, THEY WOULDN'T HAVE CAUGHT UP TO US IN AN HOUR.
AND I DON'T THINK THEY'RE FOLLOWING US ANYMORE.
SHUKK!
WROKK!
UNGH.
WHUMP!
WRAMM!
WILL SOMEONE COME OVER HERE AND STAB THIS THING?!
I WANT A SWORD.

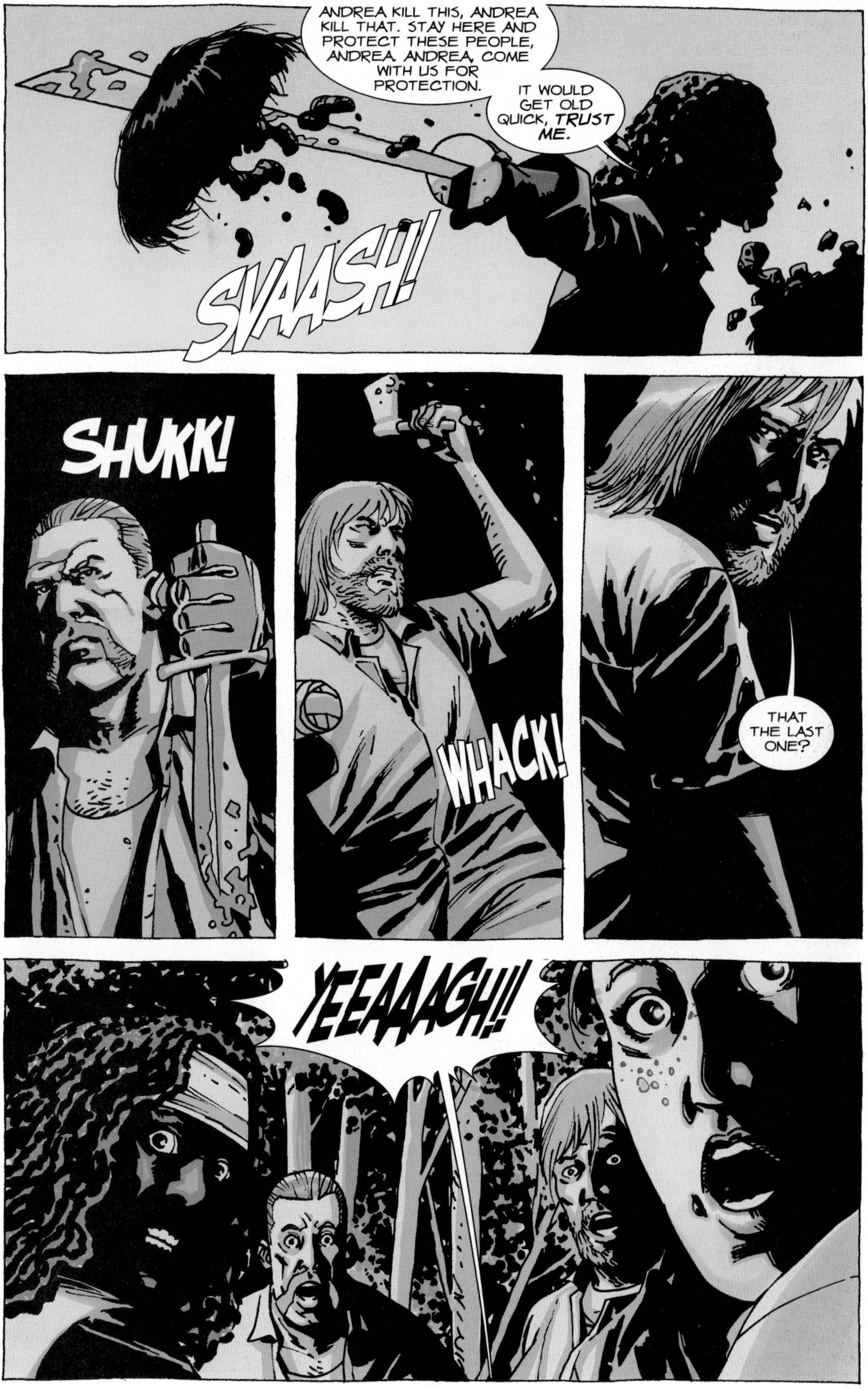
ANDREA KILL THIS, ANDREA KILL THAT. STAY HERE AND PROTECT THESE PEOPLE, ANDREA. ANDREA, COME WITH US FOR PROTECTION.
IT WOULD GET OLD QUICK, TRUST ME.
SVAASH!
SHUKK!
WHACK!
THAT THE LAST ONE?
YEEAAAGH!!

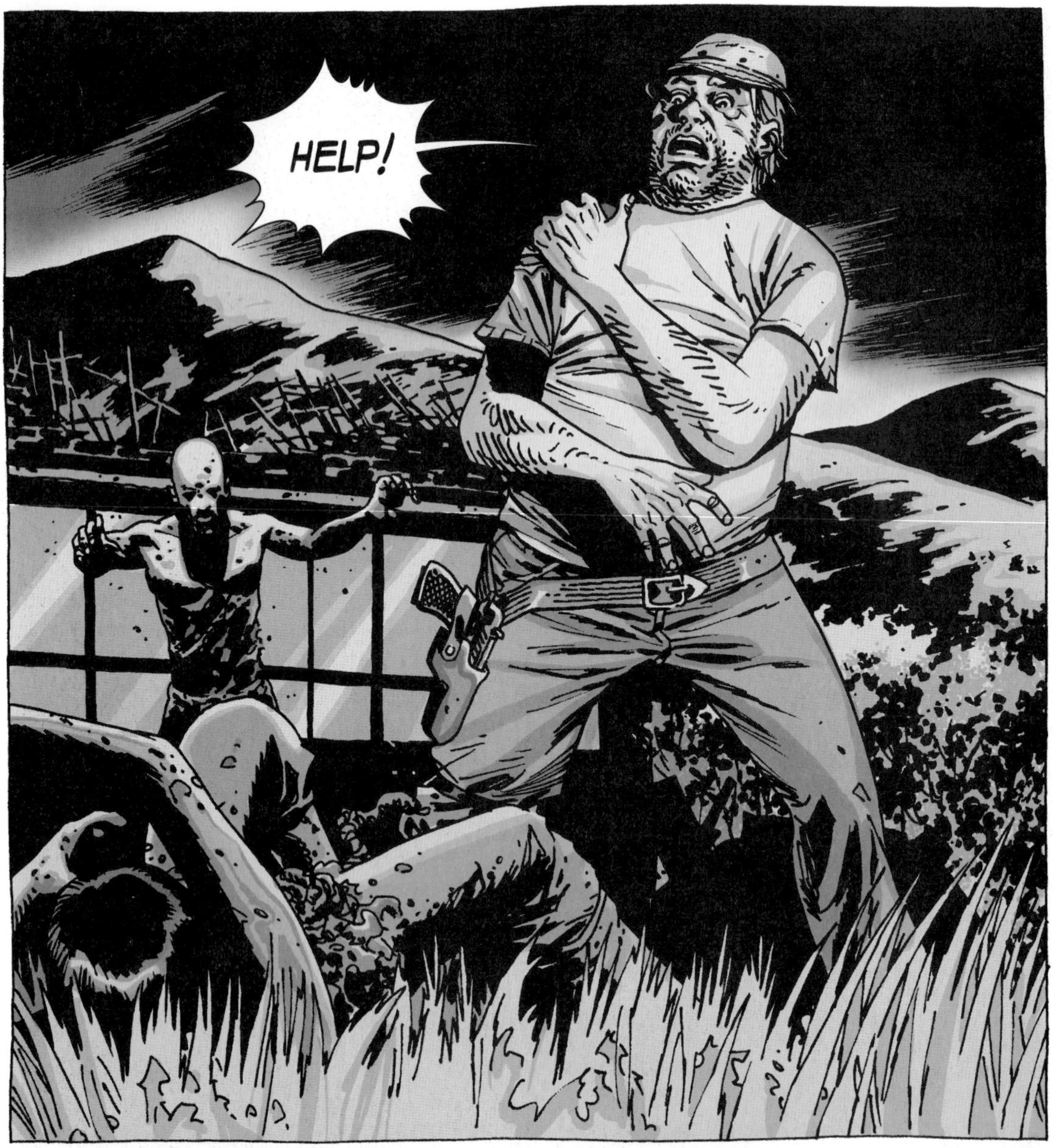
HELP!

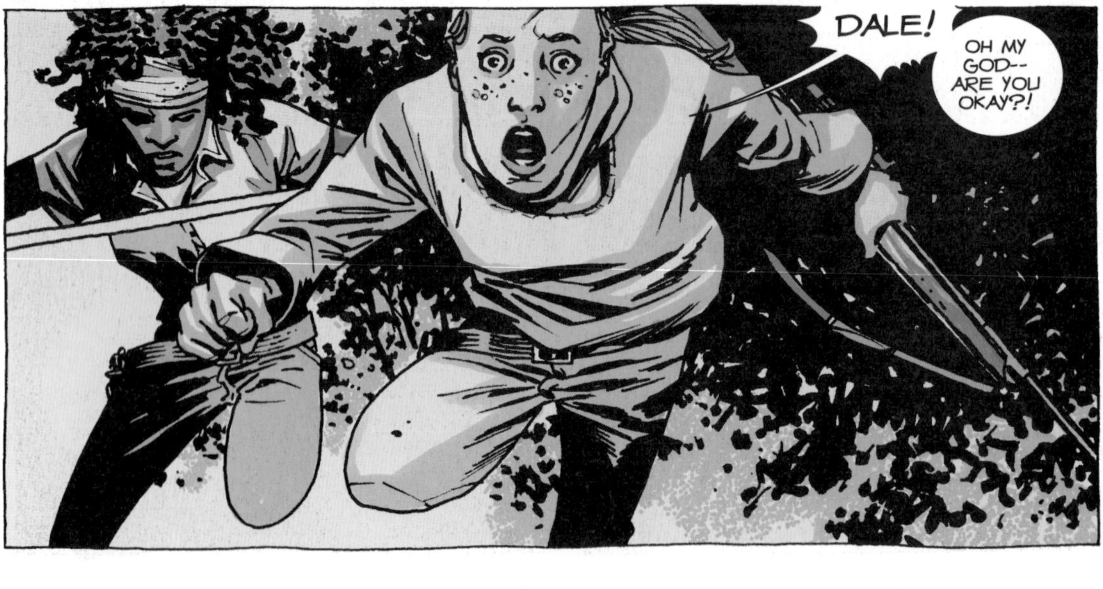
DALE!
OH MY GOD-- ARE YOU OKAY?!

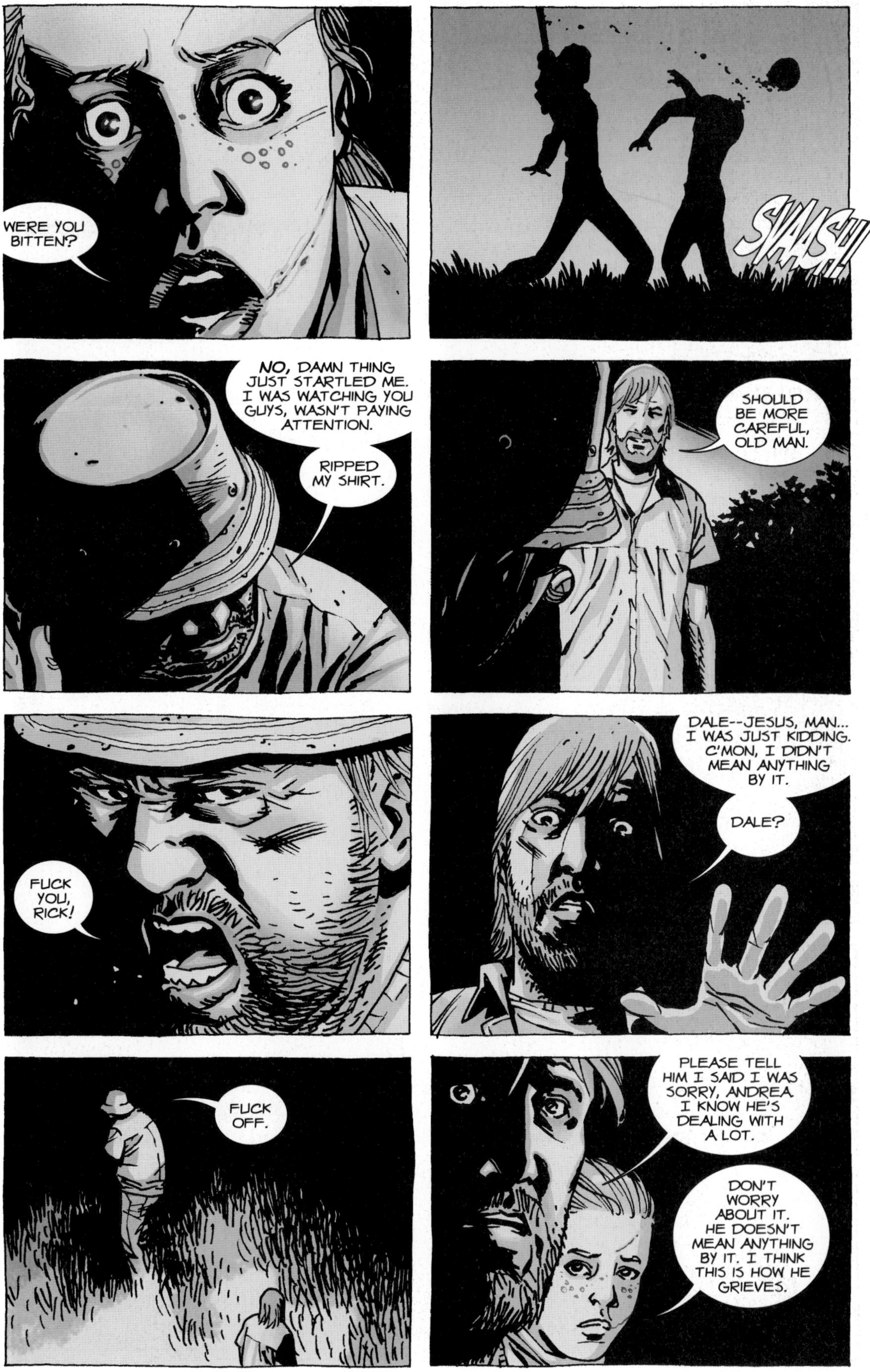
WERE YOU BITTEN?
SWASH!!
NO, DAMN THING JUST STARTLED ME. I WAS WATCHING YOU GUYS, WASN'T PAYING ATTENTION.
RIPPED MY SHIRT.
SHOULD BE MORE CAREFUL, OLD MAN.
FUCK YOU, RICK!
DALE--JESUS, MAN... I WAS JUST KIDDING. C'MON, I DIDN'T MEAN ANYTHING BY IT.
DALE?
FUCK OFF.
PLEASE TELL HIM I SAID I WAS SORRY, ANDREA. I KNOW HE'S DEALING WITH A LOT.
DON'T WORRY ABOUT IT. HE DOESN'T MEAN ANYTHING BY IT. I THINK THIS IS HOW HE GRIEVES.

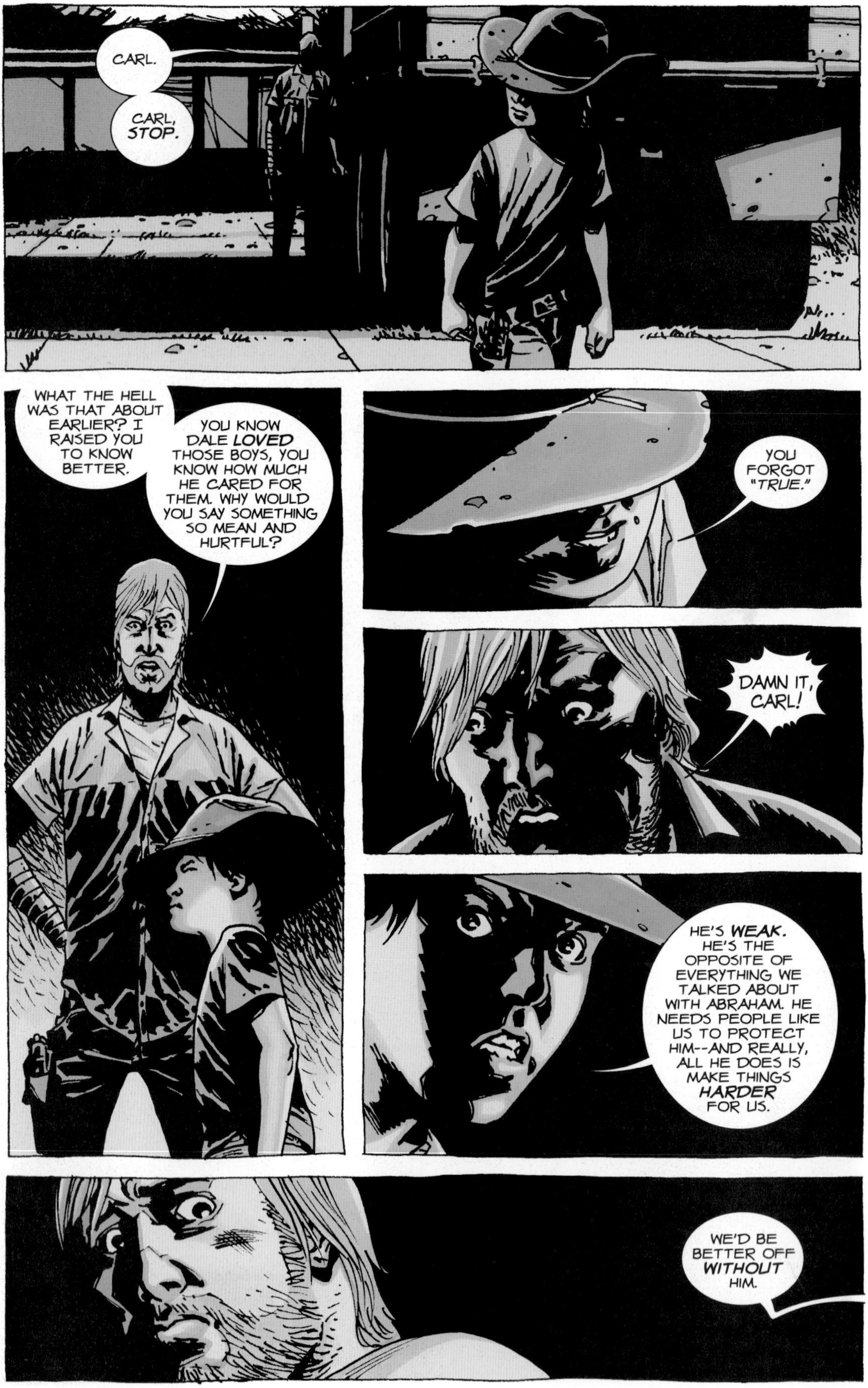
CARL.
CARL, STOP.
WHAT THE HELL WAS THAT ABOUT EARLIER? I RAISED YOU TO KNOW BETTER.
YOU KNOW DALE LOVED THOSE BOYS, YOU KNOW HOW MUCH HE CARED FOR THEM. WHY WOULD YOU SAY SOMETHING SO MEAN AND HURTFUL?
YOU FORGOT "TRUE."
DAMN IT, CARL!
HE'S WEAK. HE'S THE OPPOSITE OF EVERYTHING WE TALKED ABOUT WITH ABRAHAM. HE NEEDS PEOPLE LIKE US TO PROTECT HIM--AND REALLY, ALL HE DOES IS MAKE THINGS HARDER FOR US.
WE'D BE BETTER OFF WITHOUT HIM.

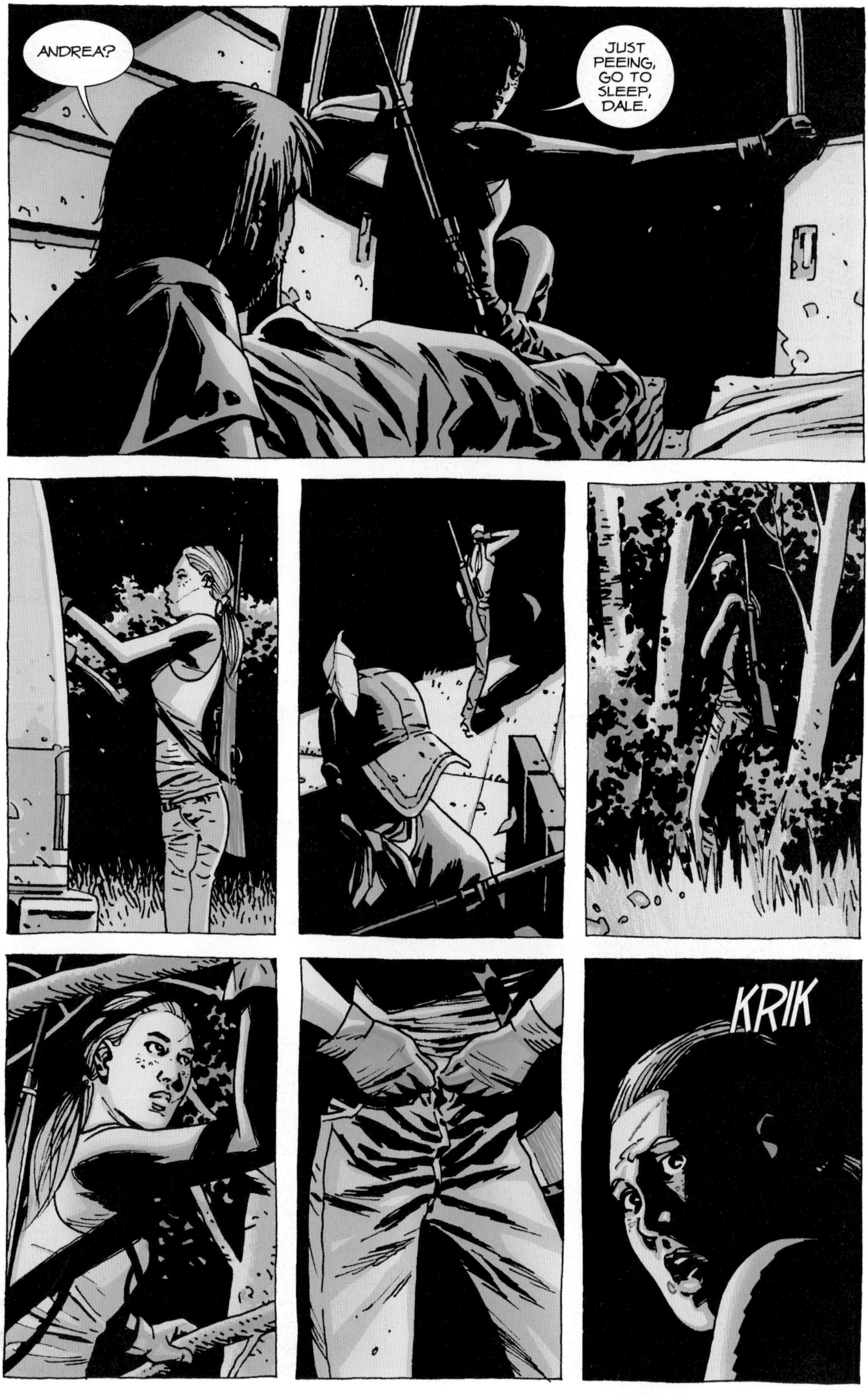
ANDREA?
JUST PEEING, GO TO SLEEP, DALE.
KRIK

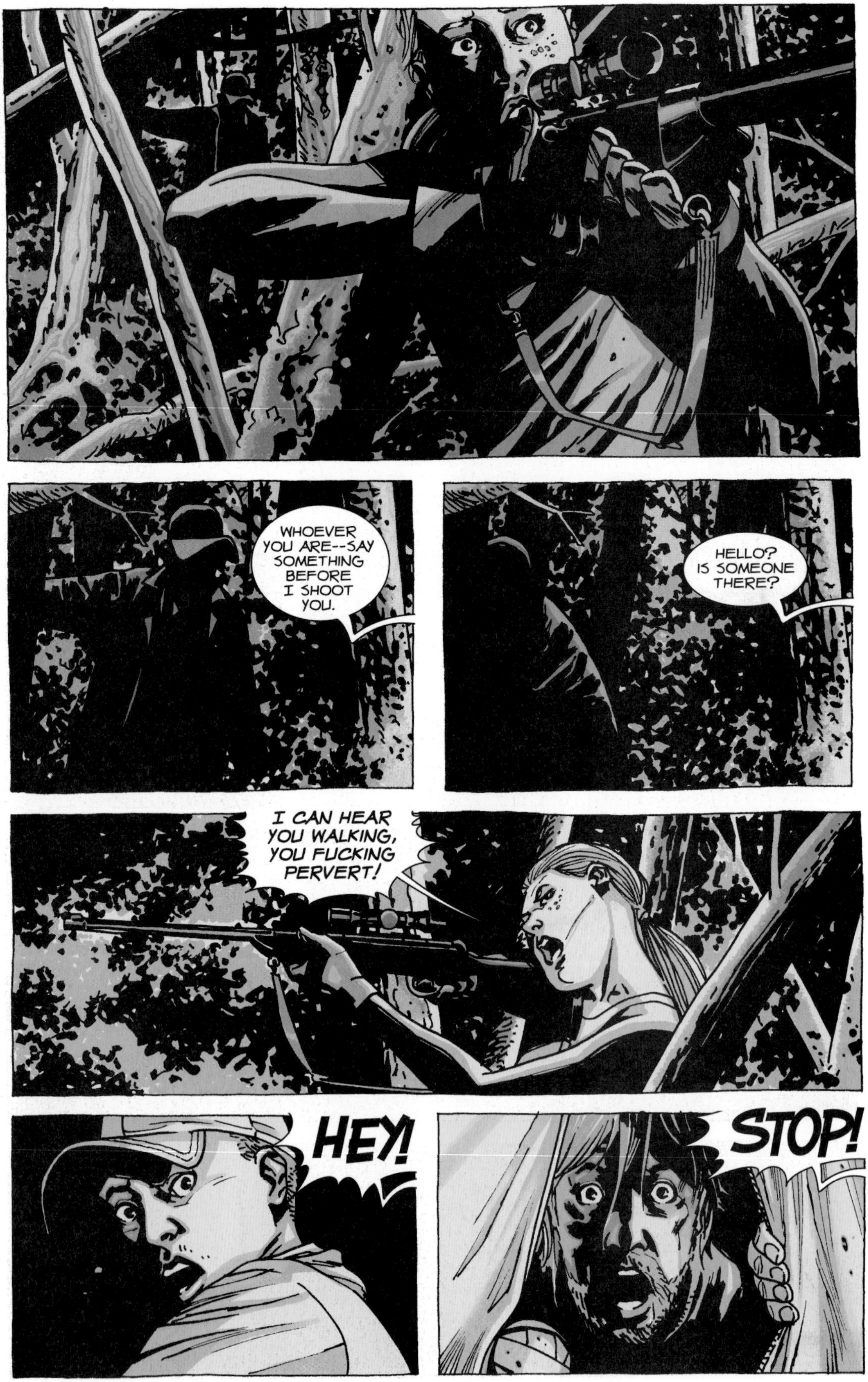
WHOEVER YOU ARE--SAY SOMETHING BEFORE I SHOOT YOU.
HELLO? IS SOMEONE THERE?
I CAN HEAR YOU WALKING, YOU FUCKING PERVERT!
HEY!
STOP!

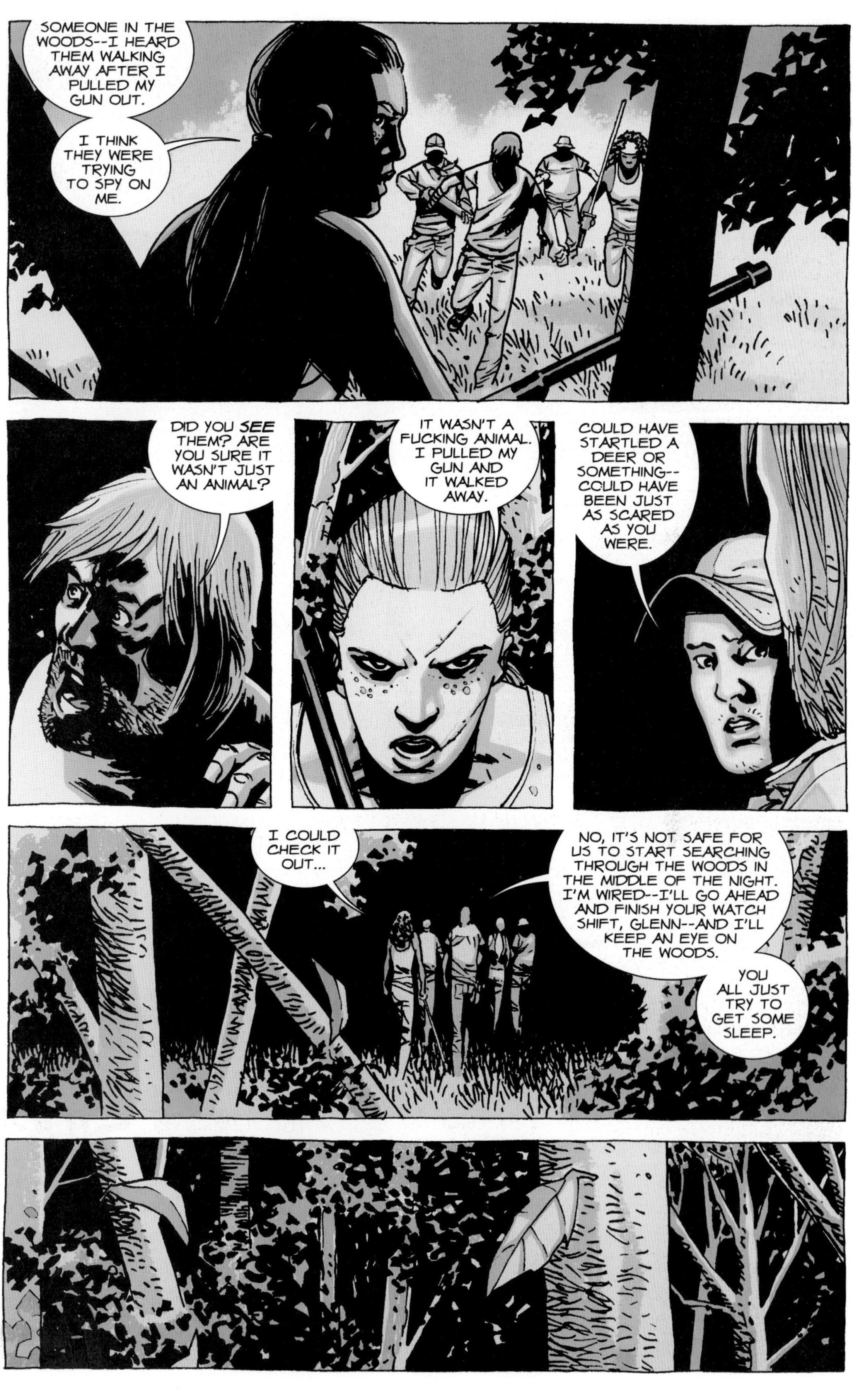

SOMEONE IN THE WOODS--I HEARD THEM WALKING AWAY AFTER I PULLED MY GUN OUT.
I THINK THEY WERE TRYING TO SPY ON ME.
DID YOU SEE THEM? ARE YOU SURE IT WASN'T JUST AN ANIMAL?
IT WASN'T A FUCKING ANIMAL. I PULLED MY GUN AND IT WALKED AWAY.
COULD HAVE STARTLED A DEER OR SOMETHING--COULD HAVE BEEN JUST AS SCARED AS YOU WERE.
I COULD CHECK IT OUT...
NO, IT'S NOT SAFE FOR US TO START SEARCHING THROUGH THE WOODS IN THE MIDDLE OF THE NIGHT. I'M WIRED--I'LL GO AHEAD AND FINISH YOUR WATCH SHIFT, GLENN--AND I'LL KEEP AN EYE ON THE WOODS.
YOU ALL JUST TRY TO GET SOME SLEEP.

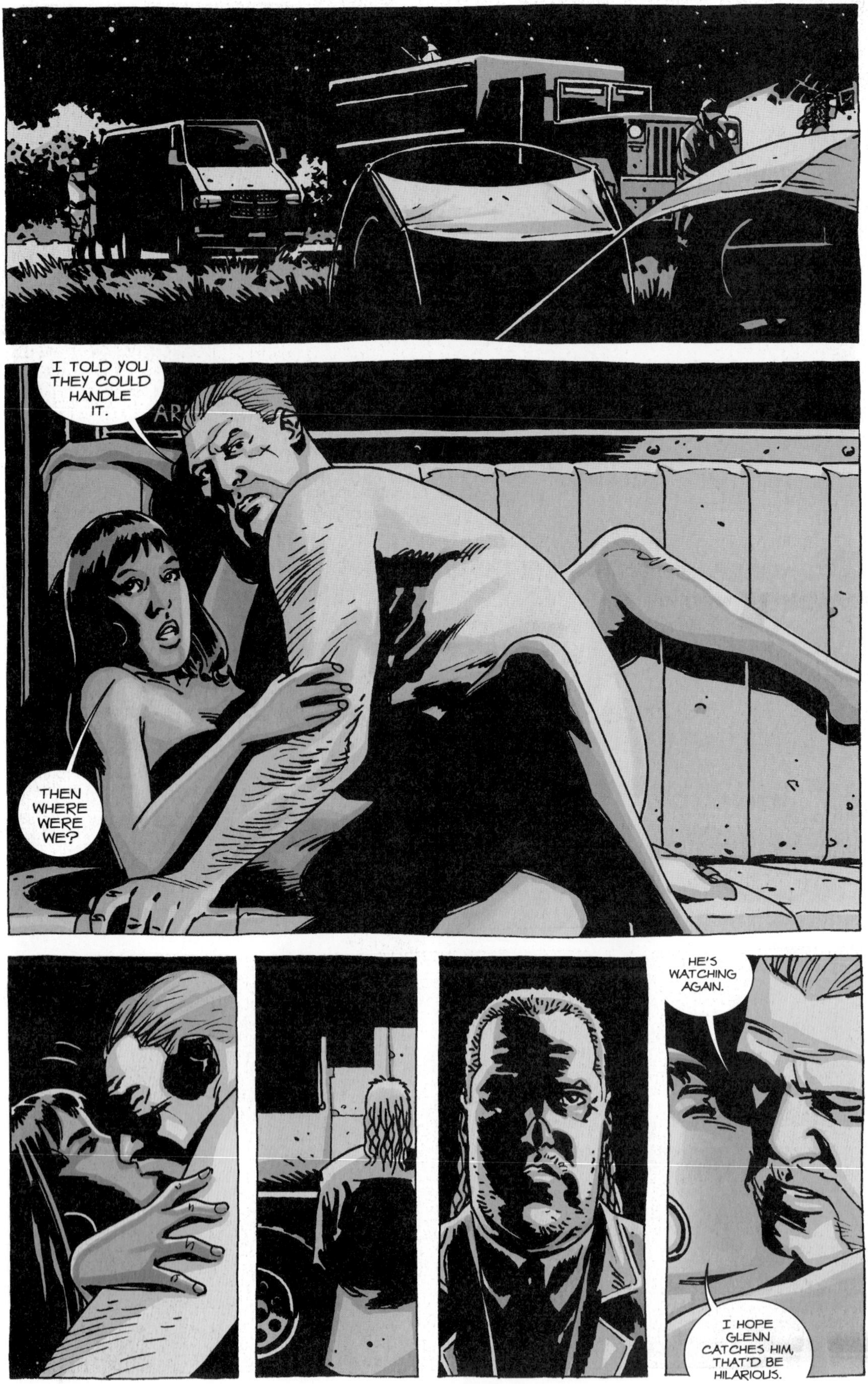
I TOLD YOU THEY COULD HANDLE IT.
THEN WHERE WERE WE?
HE'S WATCHING AGAIN.
I HOPE GLENN CATCHES HIM, THAT'D BE HILARIOUS.

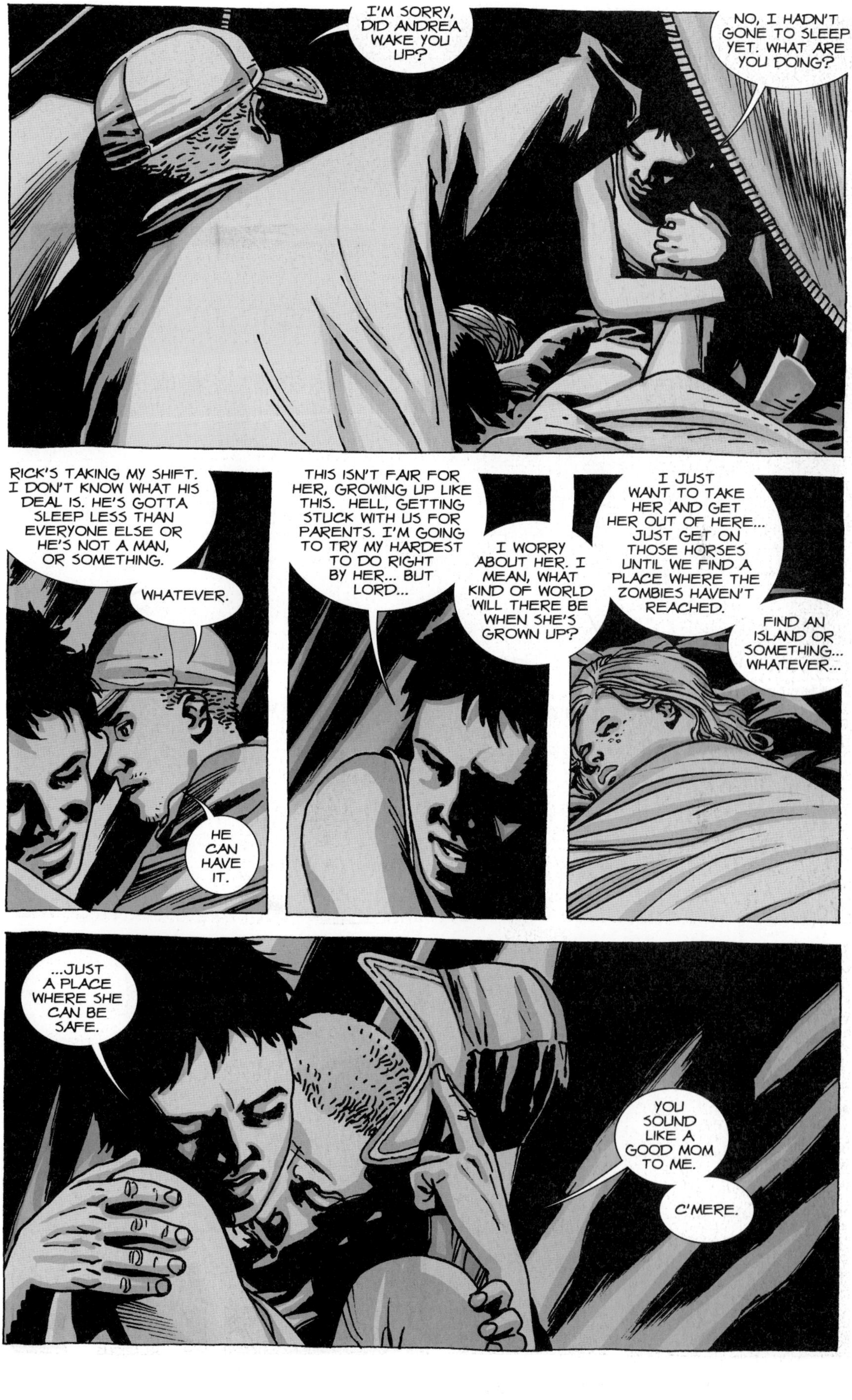
I'M SORRY, DID ANDREA WAKE YOU UP?
NO, I HADN'T GONE TO SLEEP YET. WHAT ARE YOU DOING?
RICK'S TAKING MY SHIFT. I DON'T KNOW WHAT HIS DEAL IS. HE'S GOTTA SLEEP LESS THAN EVERYONE ELSE OR HE'S NOT A MAN, OR SOMETHING.
WHATEVER.
HE CAN HAVE IT.
THIS ISN'T FAIR FOR HER, GROWING UP LIKE THIS. HELL, GETTING STUCK WITH US FOR PARENTS. I'M GOING TO TRY MY HARDEST TO DO RIGHT BY HER... BUT LORD...
I WORRY ABOUT HER. I MEAN, WHAT KIND OF WORLD WILL THERE BE WHEN SHE'S GROWN UP?
I JUST WANT TO TAKE HER AND GET HER OUT OF HERE... JUST GET ON THOSE HORSES UNTIL WE FIND A PLACE WHERE THE ZOMBIES HAVEN'T REACHED.
FIND AN ISLAND OR SOMETHING... WHATEVER...
...JUST A PLACE WHERE SHE CAN BE SAFE.
YOU SOUND LIKE A GOOD MOM TO ME.
C'MERE.

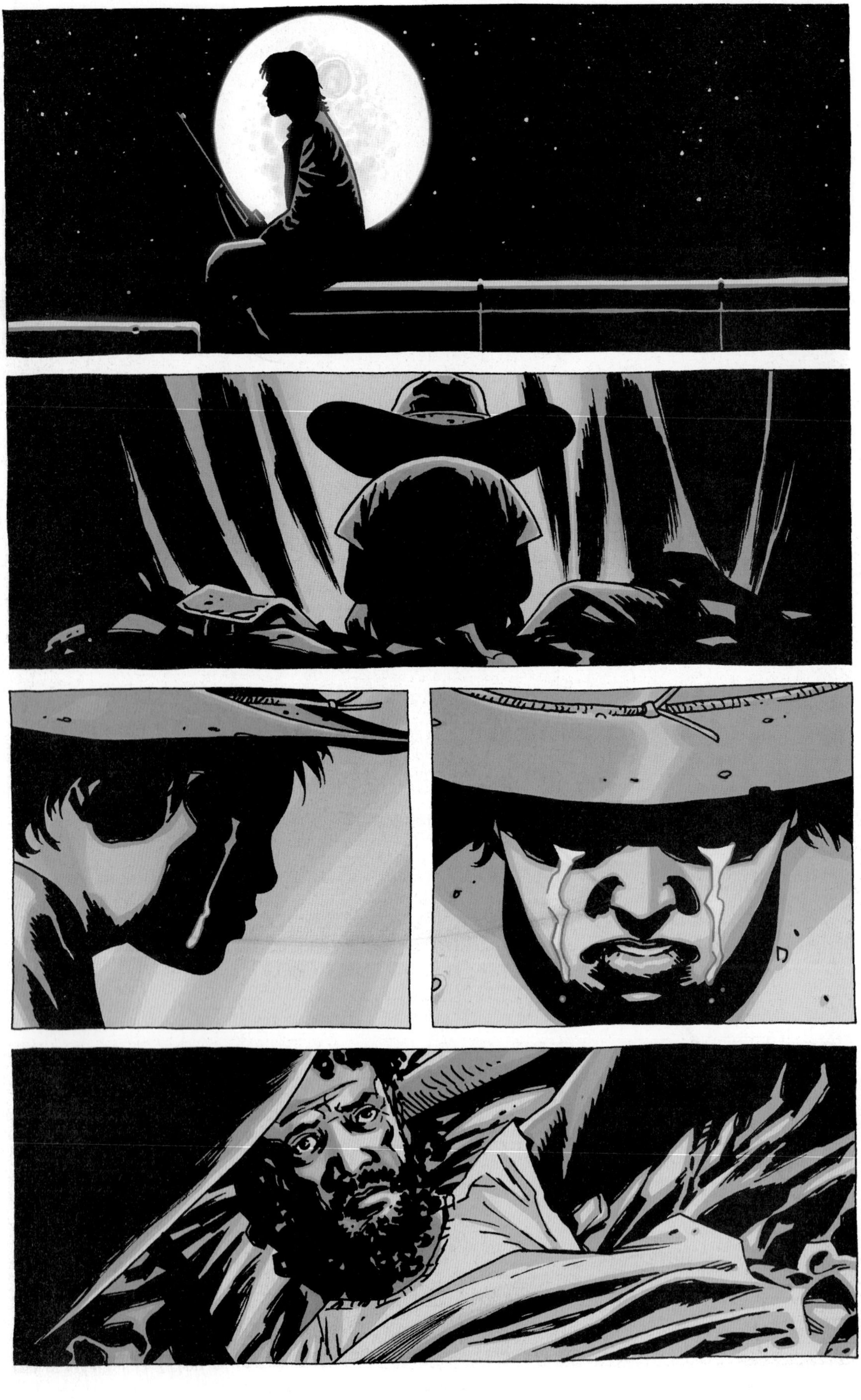

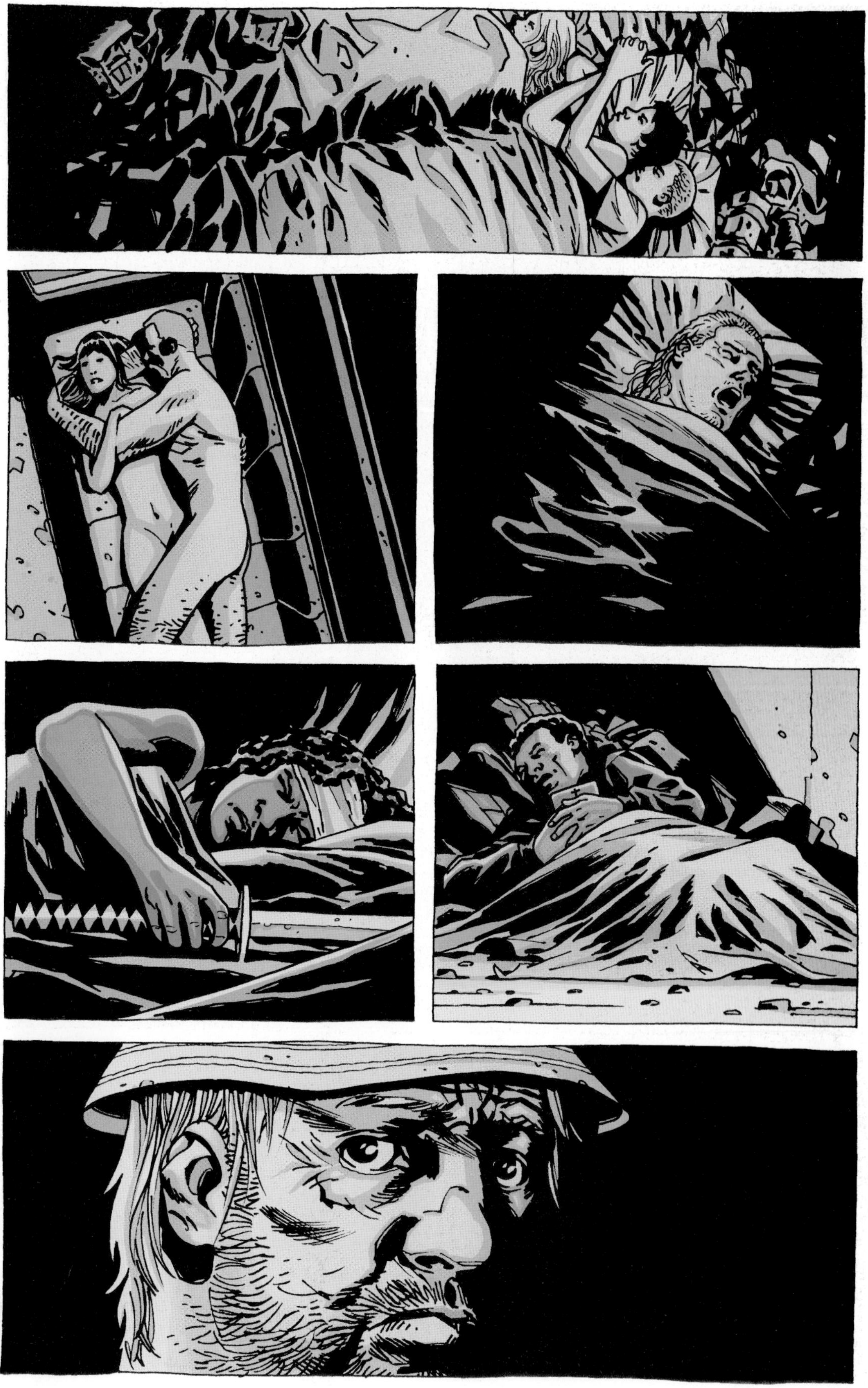

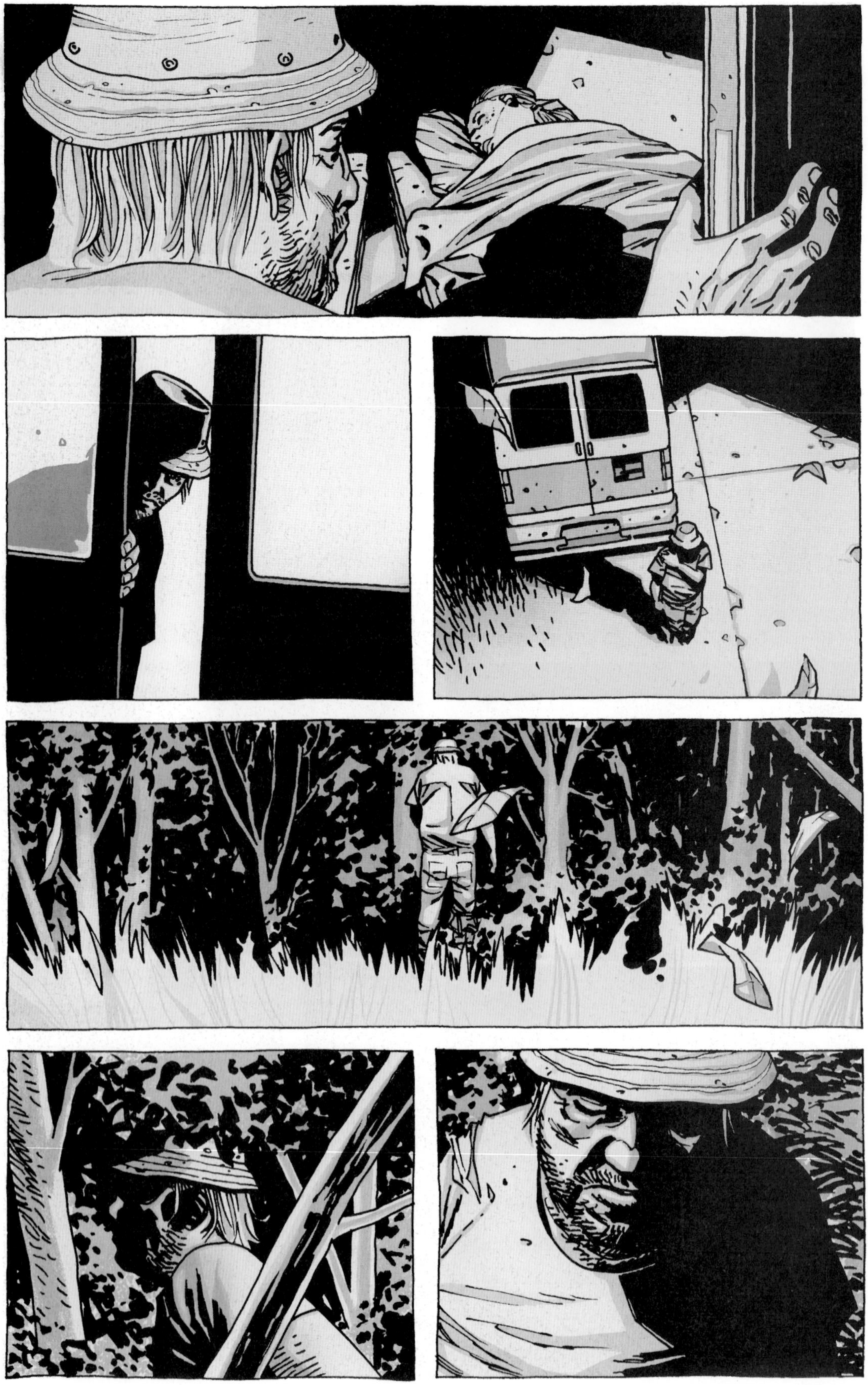

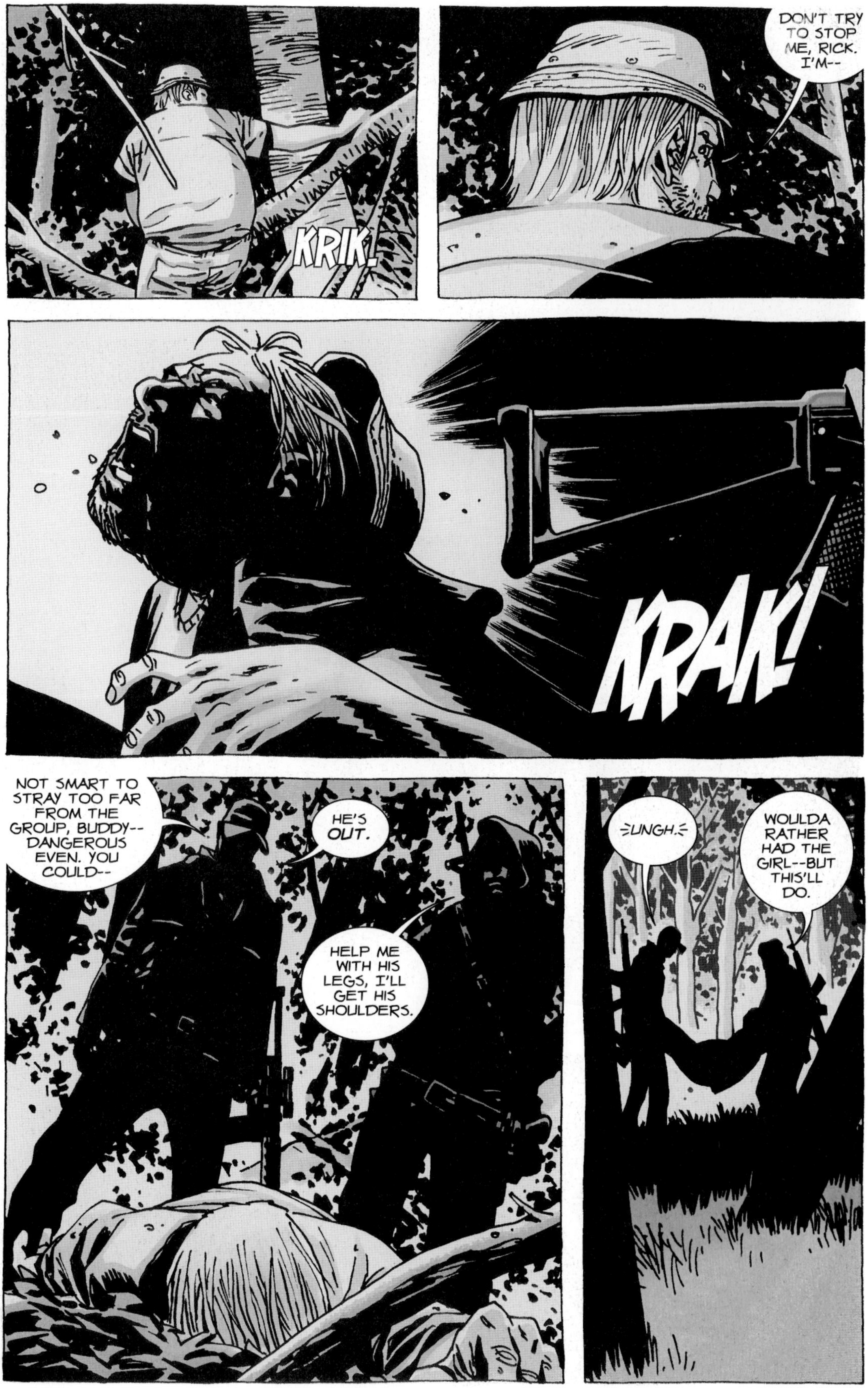
KRIK.
DON'T TRY TO STOP ME, RICK. I'M--
KRAK!
NOT SMART TO STRAY TOO FAR FROM THE GROUP, BUDDY--DANGEROUS EVEN. YOU COULD--
HE'S OUT.
HELP ME WITH HIS LEGS, I'LL GET HIS SHOULDERS.
=UNGH.=
WOULDA RATHER HAD THE GIRL--BUT THIS'LL DO.

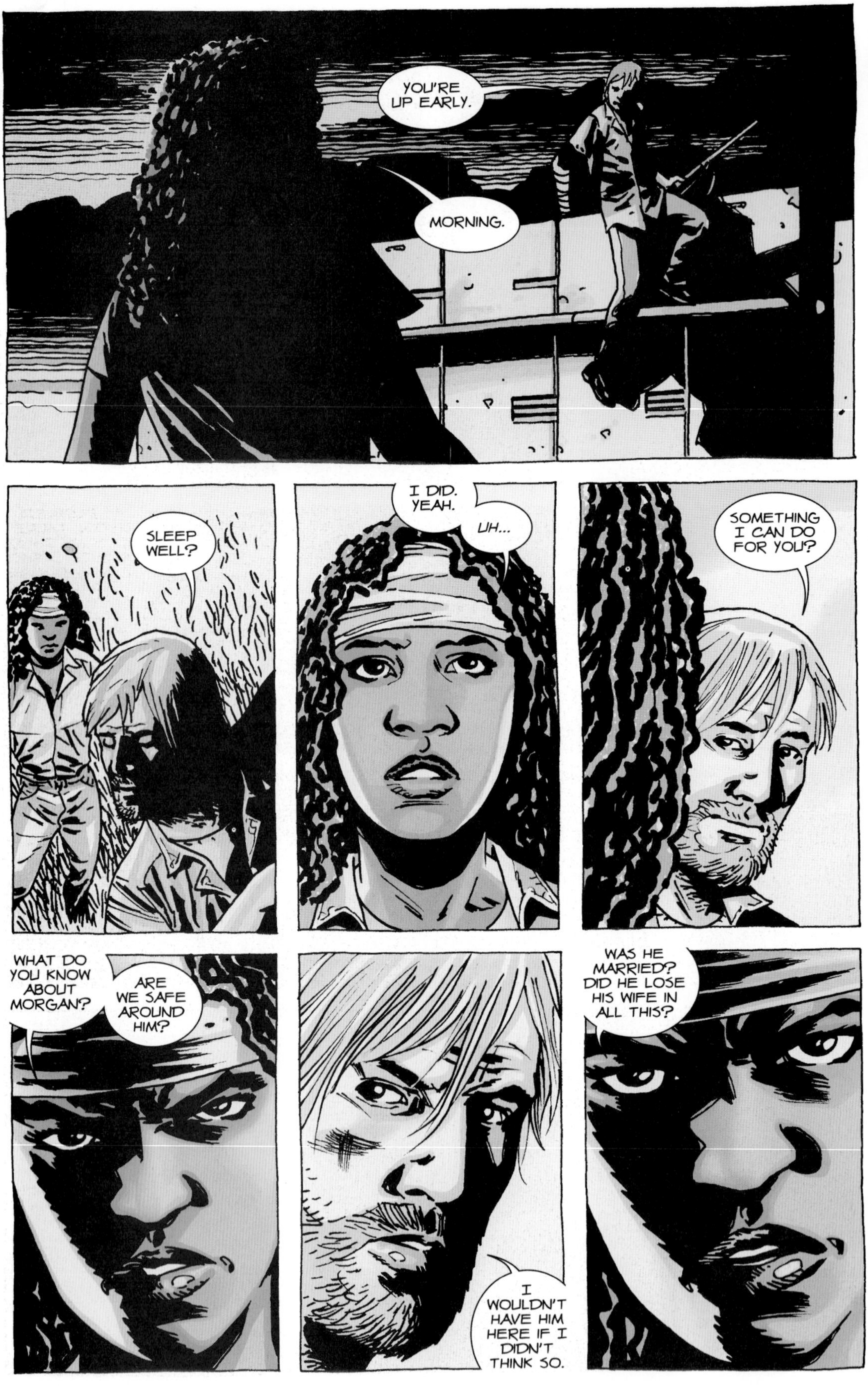
YOU'RE UP EARLY.
MORNING.
SLEEP WELL?
I DID. YEAH.
UH...
SOMETHING I CAN DO FOR YOU?
WHAT DO YOU KNOW ABOUT MORGAN?
ARE WE SAFE AROUND HIM?
I WOULDN'T HAVE HIM HERE IF I DIDN'T THINK SO.
WAS HE MARRIED? DID HE LOSE HIS WIFE IN ALL THIS?

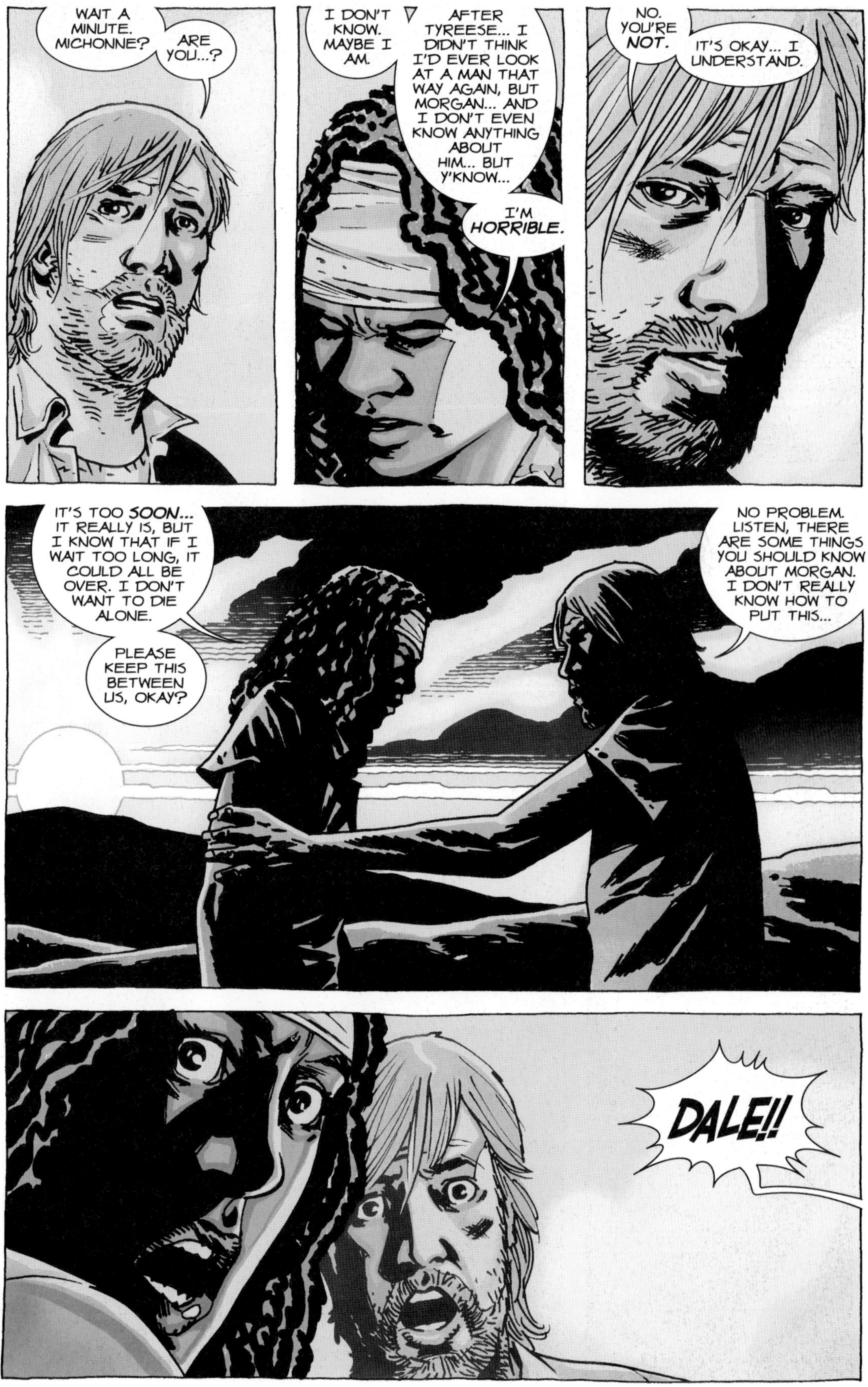
WAIT A MINUTE. MICHONNE?
ARE YOU...?
I DON'T KNOW. MAYBE I AM.
AFTER TYREESE... I DIDN'T THINK I'D EVER LOOK AT A MAN THAT WAY AGAIN, BUT MORGAN... AND I DON'T EVEN KNOW ANYTHING ABOUT HIM... BUT Y'KNOW...
I'M HORRIBLE.
NO. YOU'RE NOT.
IT'S OKAY... I UNDERSTAND.
IT'S TOO SOON... IT REALLY IS, BUT I KNOW THAT IF I WAIT TOO LONG, IT COULD ALL BE OVER. I DON'T WANT TO DIE ALONE.
PLEASE KEEP THIS BETWEEN US, OKAY?
NO PROBLEM. LISTEN, THERE ARE SOME THINGS YOU SHOULD KNOW ABOUT MORGAN. I DON'T REALLY KNOW HOW TO PUT THIS...
DALE!!

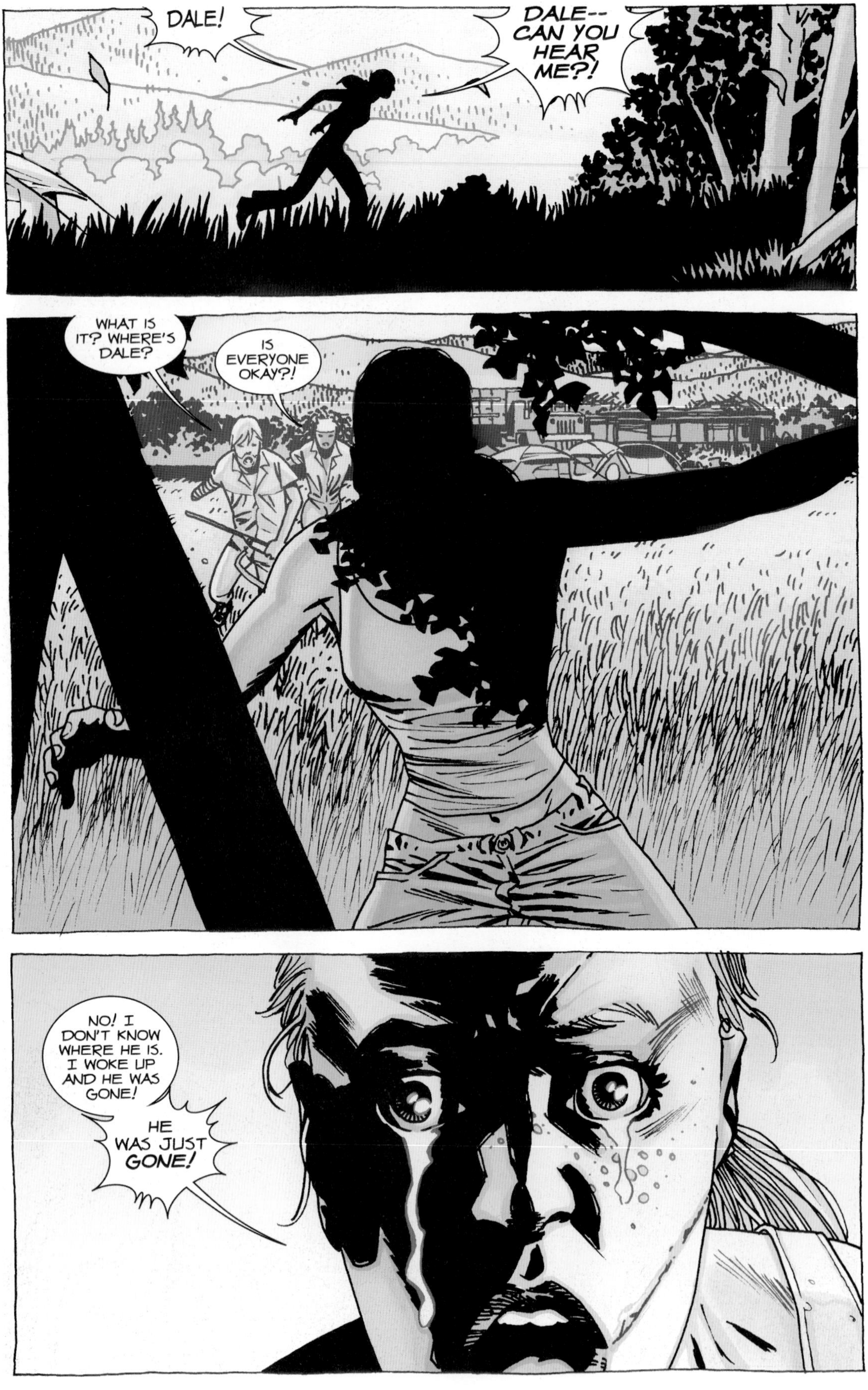

DALE!
DALE-- CAN YOU HEAR ME?!
WHAT IS IT? WHERE'S DALE?
IS EVERYONE OKAY?!
NO! I DON'T KNOW WHERE HE IS. I WOKE UP AND HE WAS GONE!
HE WAS JUST GONE!

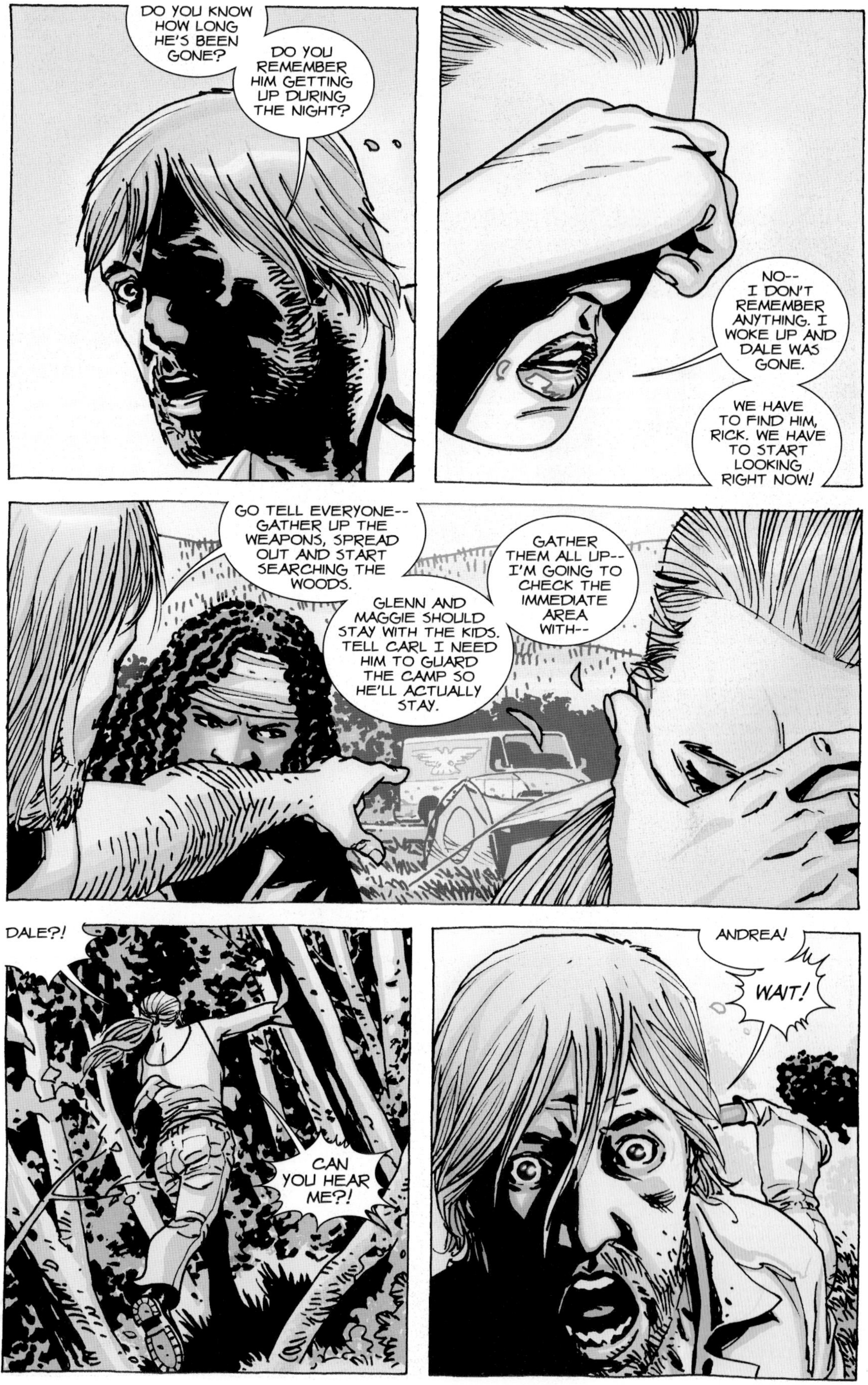
DO YOU KNOW HOW LONG HE'S BEEN GONE?
DO YOU REMEMBER HIM GETTING UP DURING THE NIGHT?
NO-- I DON'T REMEMBER ANYTHING. I WOKE UP AND DALE WAS GONE.
WE HAVE TO FIND HIM, RICK. WE HAVE TO START LOOKING RIGHT NOW!
GO TELL EVERYONE-- GATHER UP THE WEAPONS, SPREAD OUT AND START SEARCHING THE WOODS.
GLENN AND MAGGIE SHOULD STAY WITH THE KIDS. TELL CARL I NEED HIM TO GUARD THE CAMP SO HE'LL ACTUALLY STAY.
GATHER THEM ALL UP-- I'M GOING TO CHECK THE IMMEDIATE AREA WITH--
DALE?!
CAN YOU HEAR ME?!
ANDREA!
WAIT!

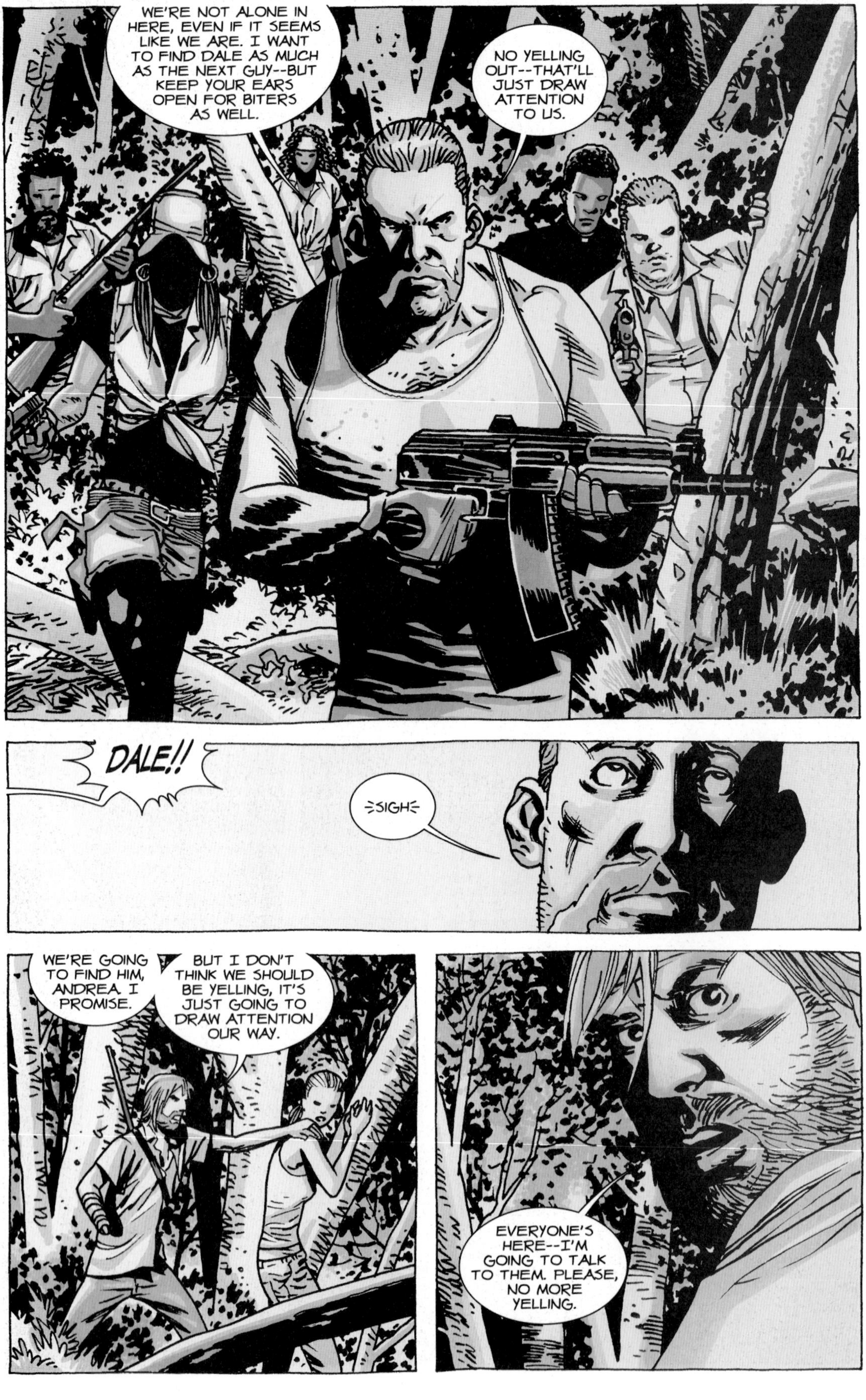
WE'RE NOT ALONE IN HERE, EVEN IF IT SEEMS LIKE WE ARE. I WANT TO FIND DALE AS MUCH AS THE NEXT GUY--BUT KEEP YOUR EARS OPEN FOR BITERS AS WELL.
NO YELLING OUT--THAT'LL JUST DRAW ATTENTION TO US.
DALE!!
SIGH
WE'RE GOING TO FIND HIM, ANDREA. I PROMISE.
BUT I DON'T THINK WE SHOULD BE YELLING, IT'S JUST GOING TO DRAW ATTENTION OUR WAY.
EVERYONE'S HERE--I'M GOING TO TALK TO THEM. PLEASE, NO MORE YELLING.

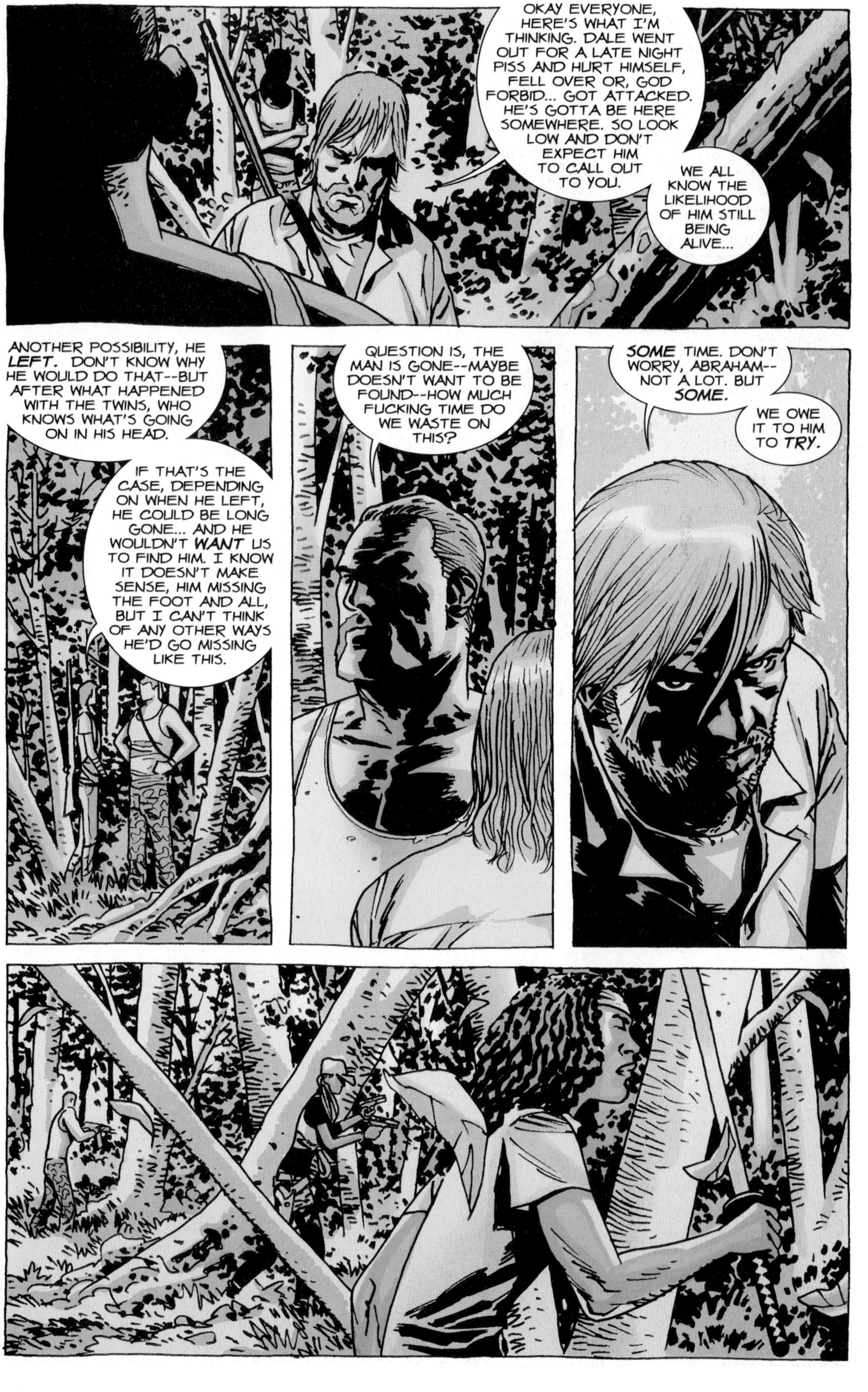
OKAY EVERYONE, HERE'S WHAT I'M THINKING. DALE WENT OUT FOR A LATE NIGHT PISS AND HURT HIMSELF, FELL OVER OR, GOD FORBID... GOT ATTACKED. HE'S GOTTA BE HERE SOMEWHERE. SO LOOK LOW AND DON'T EXPECT HIM TO CALL OUT TO YOU.
WE ALL KNOW THE LIKELIHOOD OF HIM STILL BEING ALIVE...
ANOTHER POSSIBILITY, HE LEFT. DON'T KNOW WHY HE WOULD DO THAT--BUT AFTER WHAT HAPPENED WITH THE TWINS, WHO KNOWS WHAT'S GOING ON IN HIS HEAD.
IF THAT'S THE CASE, DEPENDING ON WHEN HE LEFT, HE COULD BE LONG GONE... AND HE WOULDN'T WANT US TO FIND HIM. I KNOW IT DOESN'T MAKE SENSE, HIM MISSING THE FOOT AND ALL, BUT I CAN'T THINK OF ANY OTHER WAYS HE'D GO MISSING LIKE THIS.
QUESTION IS, THE MAN IS GONE--MAYBE DOESN'T WANT TO BE FOUND--HOW MUCH FUCKING TIME DO WE WASTE ON THIS?
SOME TIME. DON'T WORRY, ABRAHAM-- NOT A LOT. BUT SOME.
WE OWE IT TO HIM TO TRY.

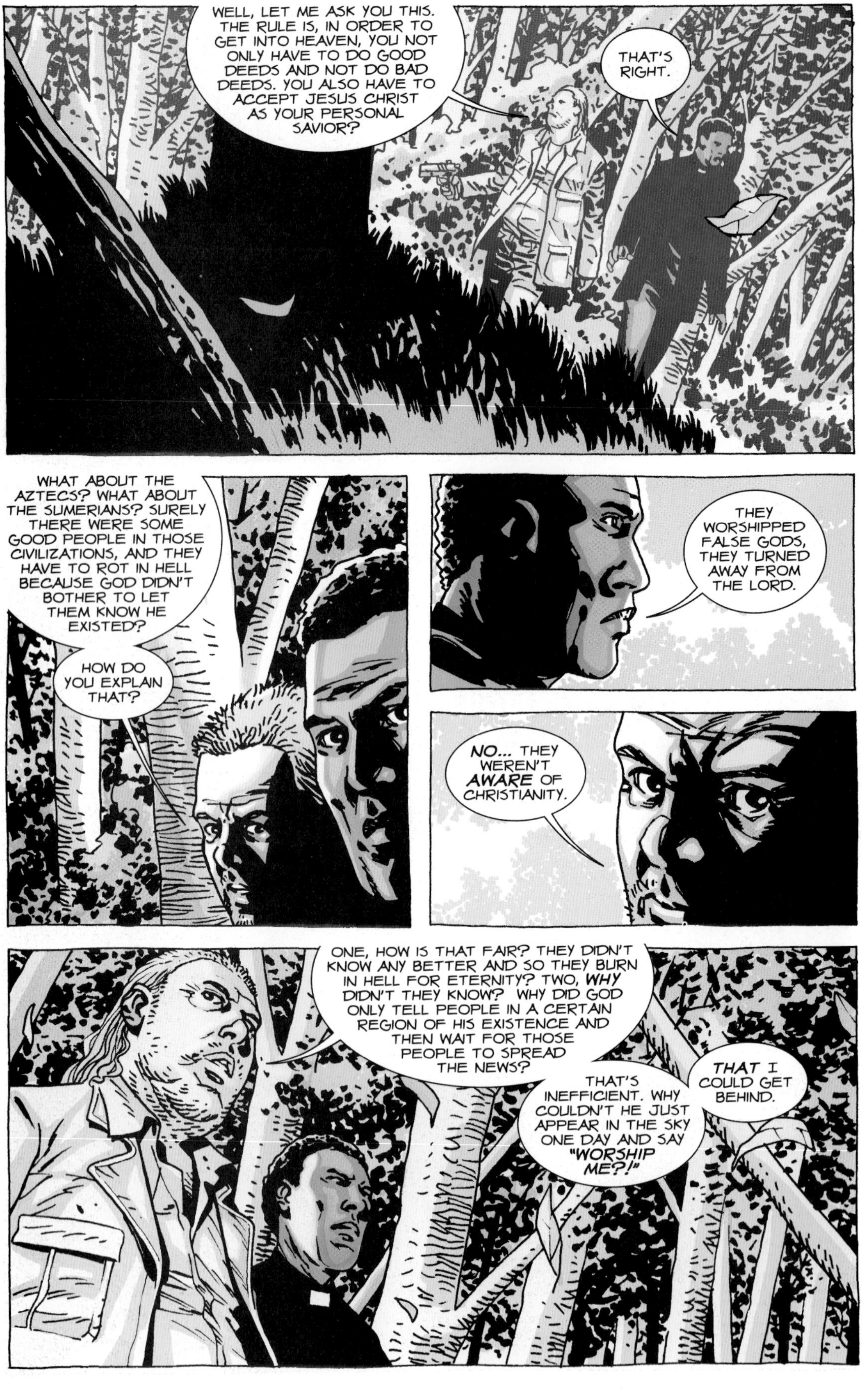
WELL, LET ME ASK YOU THIS. THE RULE IS, IN ORDER TO GET INTO HEAVEN, YOU NOT ONLY HAVE TO DO GOOD DEEDS AND NOT DO BAD DEEDS. YOU ALSO HAVE TO ACCEPT JESUS CHRIST AS YOUR PERSONAL SAVIOR?
THAT'S RIGHT.
WHAT ABOUT THE AZTECS? WHAT ABOUT THE SUMERIANS? SURELY THERE WERE SOME GOOD PEOPLE IN THOSE CIVILIZATIONS, AND THEY HAVE TO ROT IN HELL BECAUSE GOD DIDN'T BOTHER TO LET THEM KNOW HE EXISTED?
HOW DO YOU EXPLAIN THAT?
THEY WORSHIPPED FALSE GODS, THEY TURNED AWAY FROM THE LORD.
NO... THEY WEREN'T AWARE OF CHRISTIANITY.
ONE, HOW IS THAT FAIR? THEY DIDN'T KNOW ANY BETTER AND SO THEY BURN IN HELL FOR ETERNITY? TWO, WHY DIDN'T THEY KNOW? WHY DID GOD ONLY TELL PEOPLE IN A CERTAIN REGION OF HIS EXISTENCE AND THEN WAIT FOR THOSE PEOPLE TO SPREAD THE NEWS?
THAT'S INEFFICIENT. WHY COULDN'T HE JUST APPEAR IN THE SKY ONE DAY AND SAY "WORSHIP ME?!"
THAT I COULD GET BEHIND.

LET US JUST TAKE INTO CONSIDERATION, FOR A MOMENT, THAT WE ARE TWO MORTALS, WITH OUR LIMITED KNOWLEDGE OF THE UNIVERSE, DISCUSSING THE INNER WORKINGS OF THE MIND OF GOD.

HE WORKS IN MYSTERIOUS WAYS.

AND THAT'S NOT MEANT TO BE A DISMISSIVE ANSWER. I'M JUST ACKNOWLEDGING THAT HE EXISTS AT A LEVEL *BEYOND* OUR COMPREHENSION. HE HAS A PLAN... IT'S NOT OUR JOB TO UNDERSTAND IT, IT'S OUR JOB TO *BELIEVE* IN HIM.

IS IT SO HARD TO BELIEVE, BROTHER EUGENE?

I BELIEVE YOUR BELIEFS ARE ABSURD.

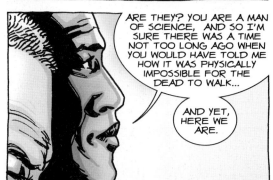

ARE THEY? YOU ARE A MAN OF SCIENCE, AND SO I'M SURE THERE WAS A TIME NOT TOO LONG AGO WHEN YOU WOULD HAVE TOLD ME HOW IT WAS PHYSICALLY IMPOSSIBLE FOR THE DEAD TO WALK...

AND YET, HERE WE ARE.

POINT TAKEN. BUT THE LIVING DEAD DOESN'T MAKE ME BELIEVE IN THE EXISTENCE OF A GOD.

NO... BUT IT'S A START.

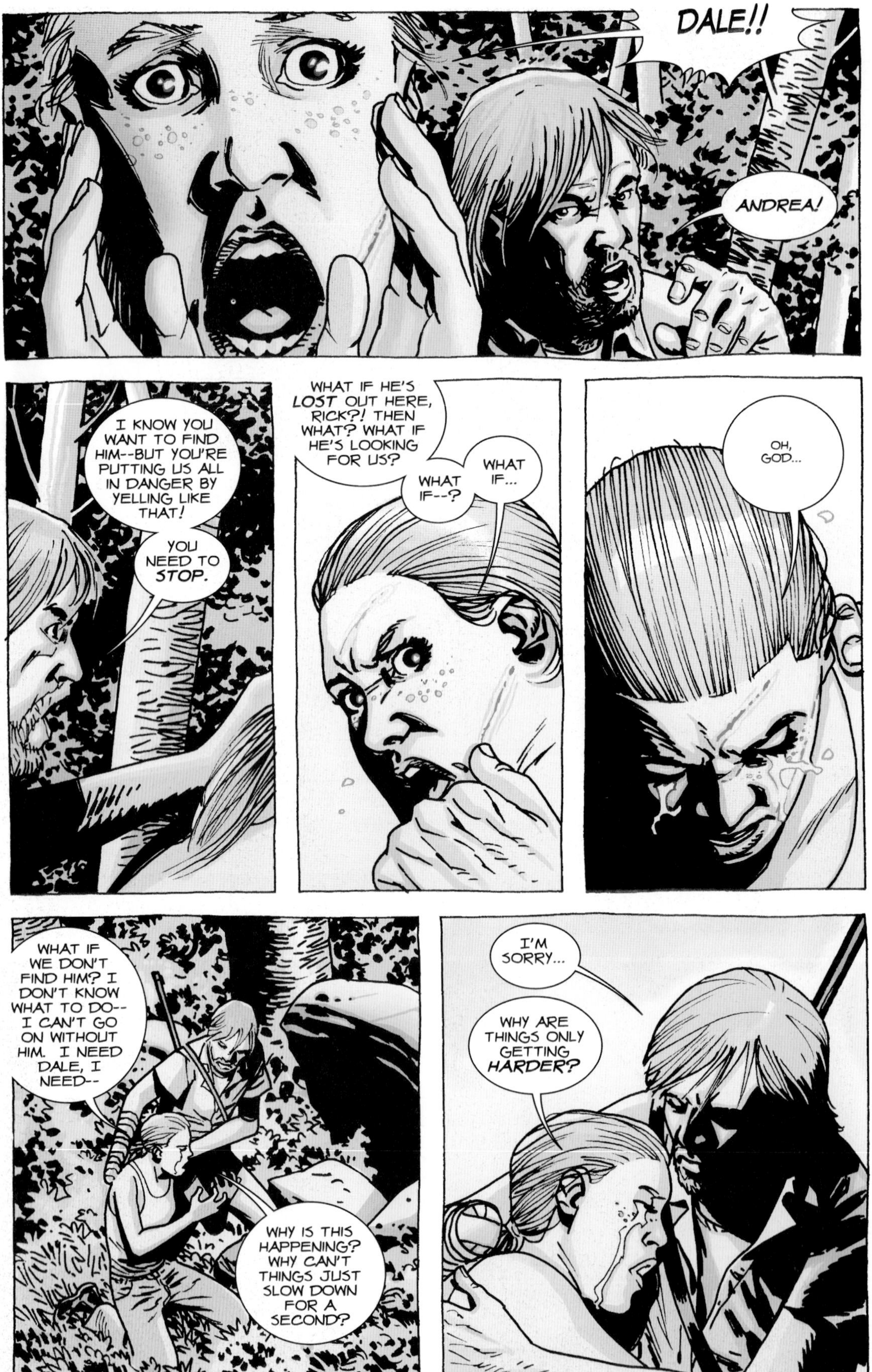
DALE!!
ANDREA!
I KNOW YOU WANT TO FIND HIM--BUT YOU'RE PUTTING US ALL IN DANGER BY YELLING LIKE THAT!
YOU NEED TO STOP.
WHAT IF HE'S LOST OUT HERE, RICK?! THEN WHAT? WHAT IF HE'S LOOKING FOR US?
WHAT IF--?
WHAT IF...
OH, GOD...
WHAT IF WE DON'T FIND HIM? I DON'T KNOW WHAT TO DO-- I CAN'T GO ON WITHOUT HIM. I NEED DALE, I NEED--
WHY IS THIS HAPPENING? WHY CAN'T THINGS JUST SLOW DOWN FOR A SECOND?
I'M SORRY...
WHY ARE THINGS ONLY GETTING HARDER?

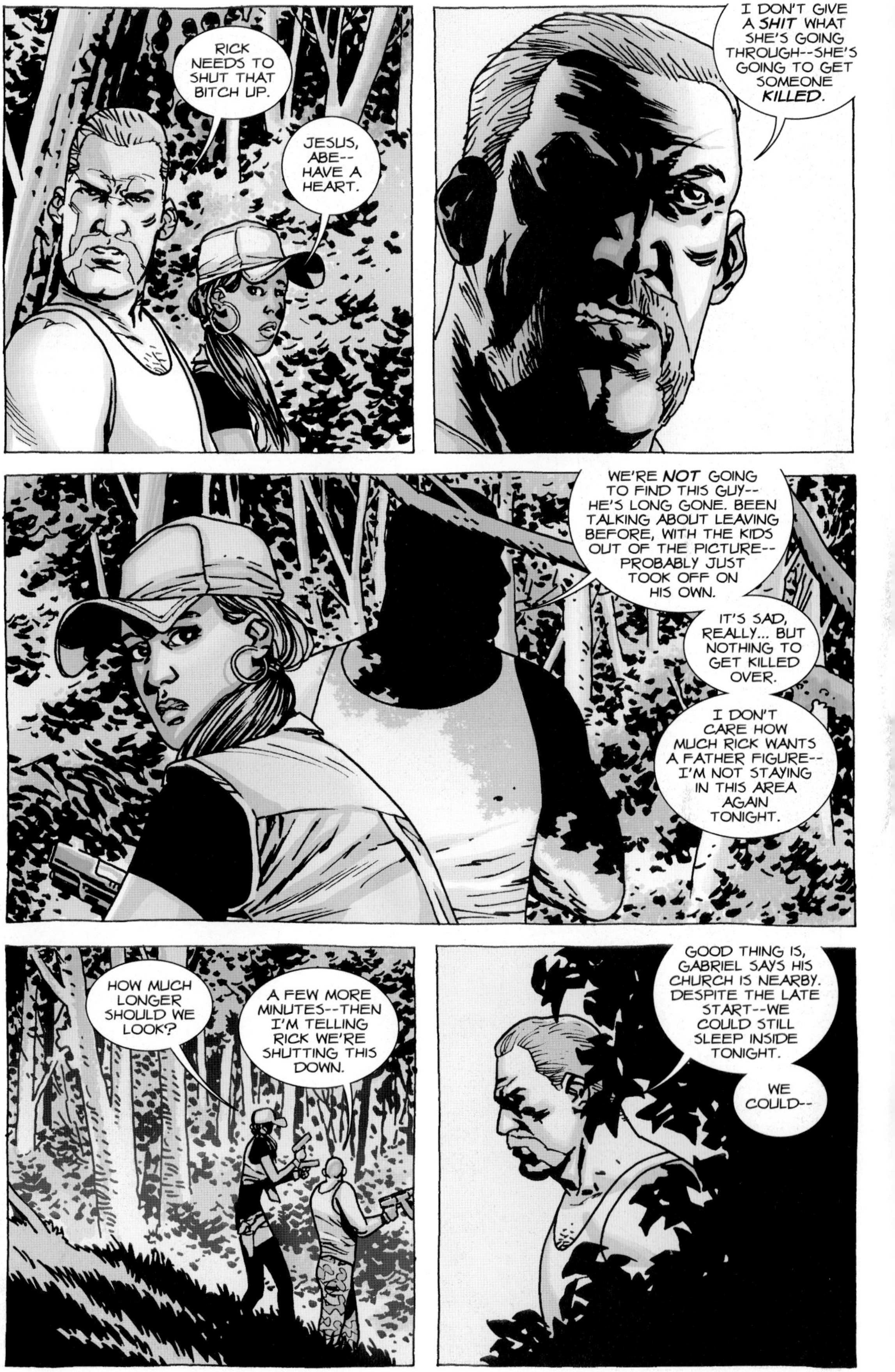
RICK NEEDS TO SHUT THAT BITCH UP.
JESUS, ABE-- HAVE A HEART.
I DON'T GIVE A SHIT WHAT SHE'S GOING THROUGH--SHE'S GOING TO GET SOMEONE KILLED.
WE'RE NOT GOING TO FIND THIS GUY-- HE'S LONG GONE. BEEN TALKING ABOUT LEAVING BEFORE, WITH THE KIDS OUT OF THE PICTURE-- PROBABLY JUST TOOK OFF ON HIS OWN.
IT'S SAD, REALLY... BUT NOTHING TO GET KILLED OVER.
I DON'T CARE HOW MUCH RICK WANTS A FATHER FIGURE-- I'M NOT STAYING IN THIS AREA AGAIN TONIGHT.
HOW MUCH LONGER SHOULD WE LOOK?
A FEW MORE MINUTES--THEN I'M TELLING RICK WE'RE SHUTTING THIS DOWN.
GOOD THING IS, GABRIEL SAYS HIS CHURCH IS NEARBY. DESPITE THE LATE START--WE COULD STILL SLEEP INSIDE TONIGHT.
WE COULD--

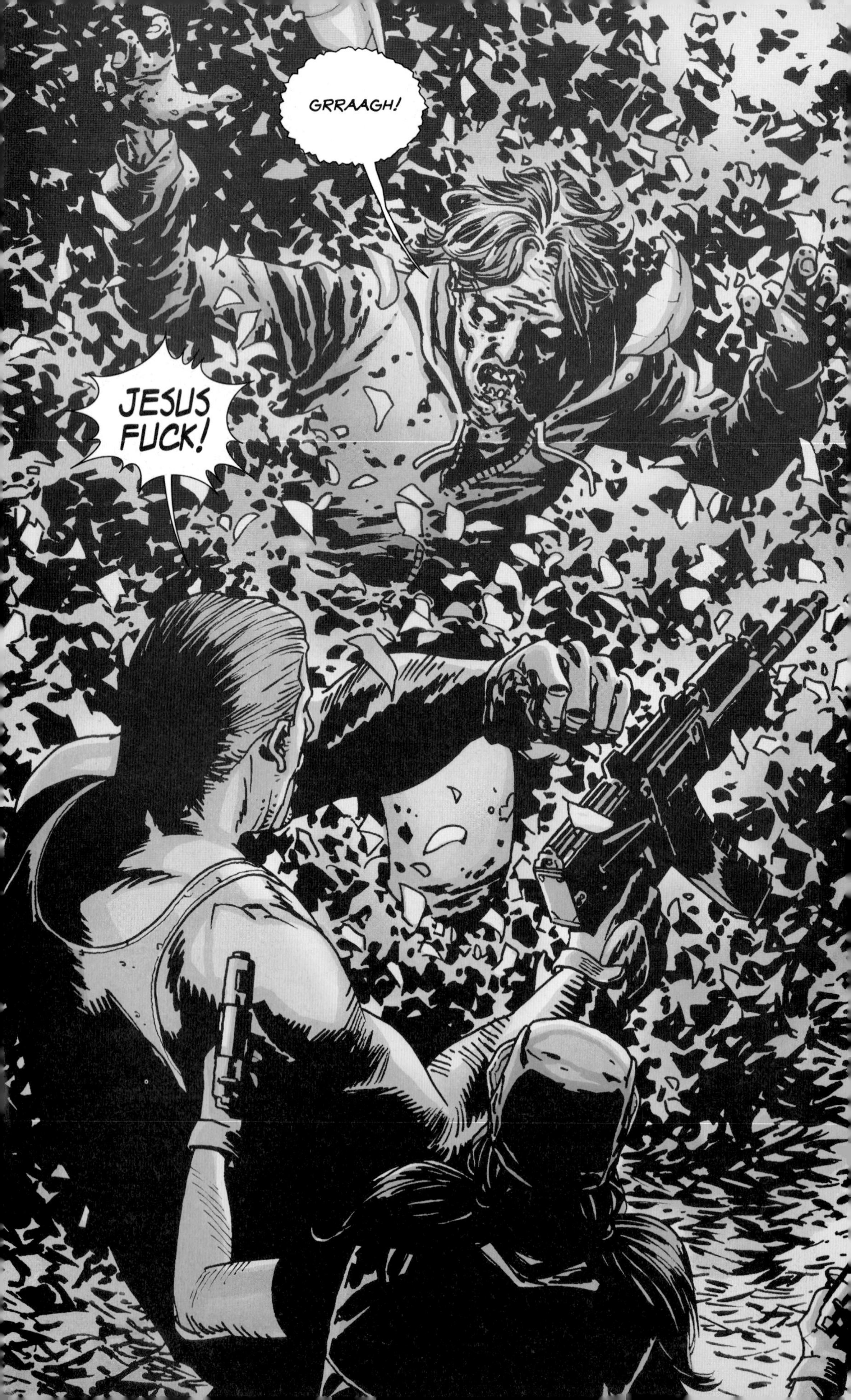
GRRAAGH!
JESUS FUCK!

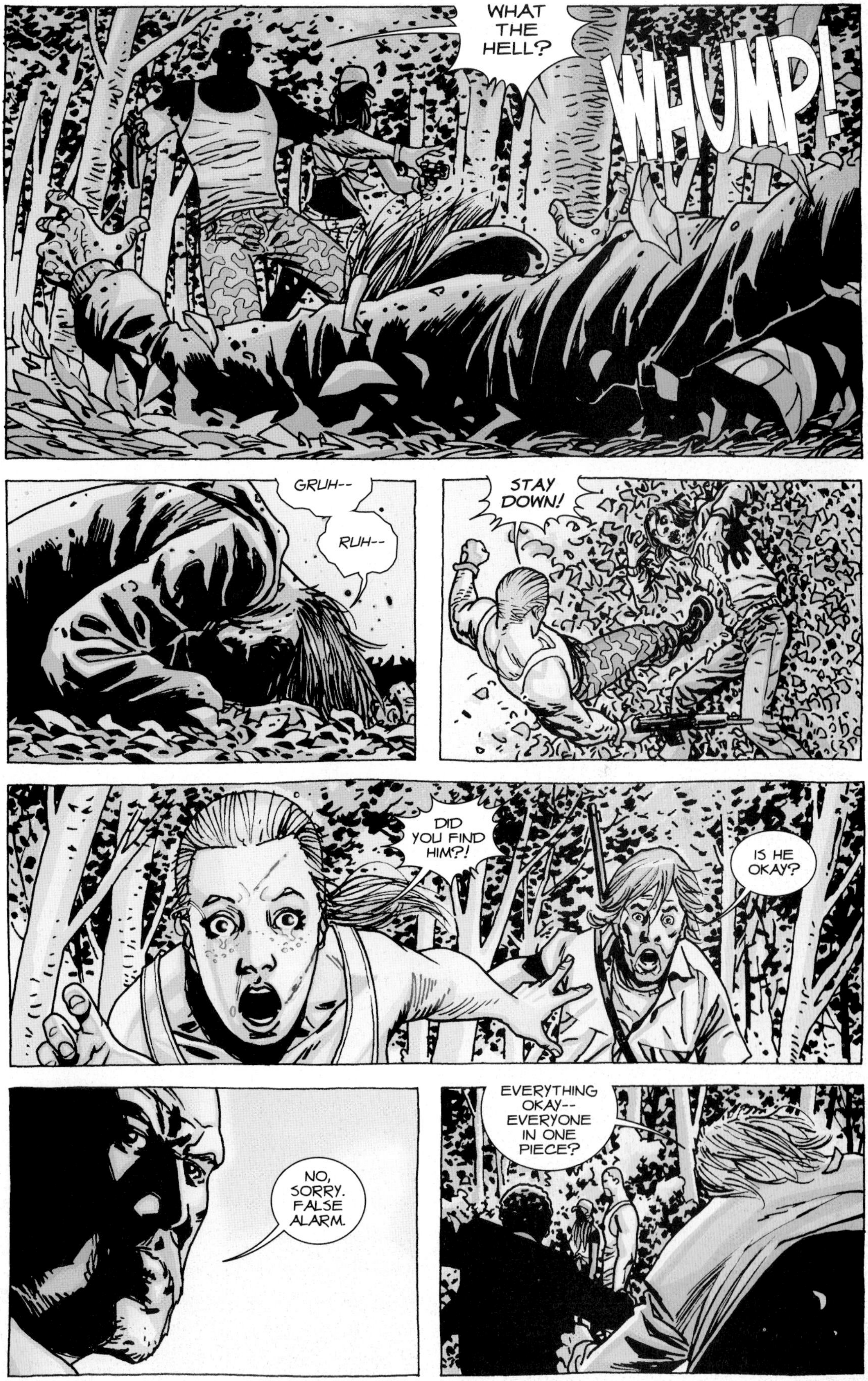
WHAT THE HELL?
WHUMP!
GRUH--
RUH--
STAY DOWN!
DID YOU FIND HIM?!
IS HE OKAY?
NO, SORRY. FALSE ALARM.
EVERYTHING OKAY-- EVERYONE IN ONE PIECE?

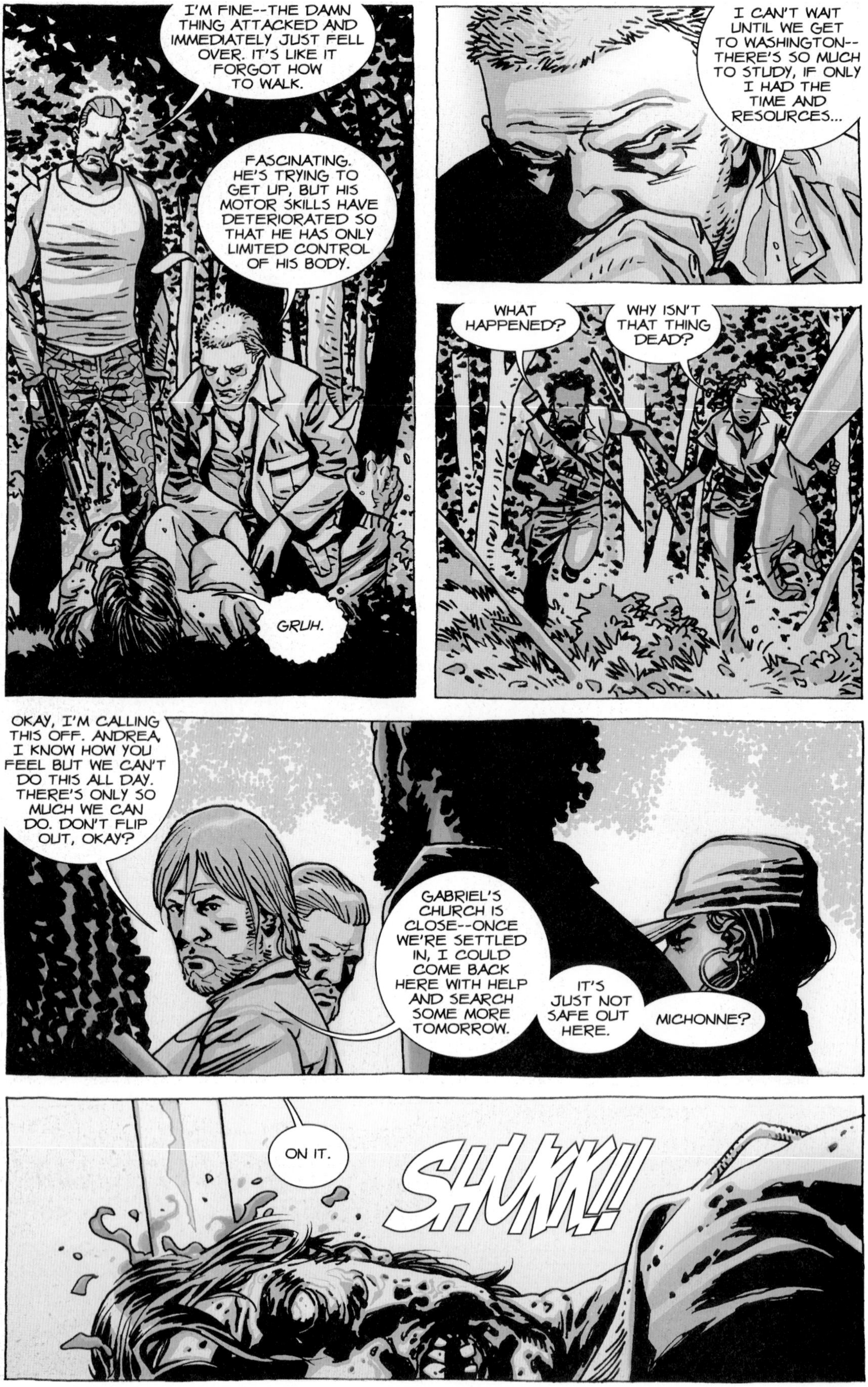
I'M FINE--THE DAMN THING ATTACKED AND IMMEDIATELY JUST FELL OVER. IT'S LIKE IT FORGOT HOW TO WALK.
FASCINATING. HE'S TRYING TO GET UP, BUT HIS MOTOR SKILLS HAVE DETERIORATED SO THAT HE HAS ONLY LIMITED CONTROL OF HIS BODY.
GRUH.
I CAN'T WAIT UNTIL WE GET TO WASHINGTON-- THERE'S SO MUCH TO STUDY, IF ONLY I HAD THE TIME AND RESOURCES...
WHAT HAPPENED?
WHY ISN'T THAT THING DEAD?
OKAY, I'M CALLING THIS OFF. ANDREA, I KNOW HOW YOU FEEL BUT WE CAN'T DO THIS ALL DAY. THERE'S ONLY SO MUCH WE CAN DO. DON'T FLIP OUT, OKAY?
GABRIEL'S CHURCH IS CLOSE--ONCE WE'RE SETTLED IN, I COULD COME BACK HERE WITH HELP AND SEARCH SOME MORE TOMORROW.
IT'S JUST NOT SAFE OUT HERE.
MICHONNE?
ON IT.
SHUKK!!

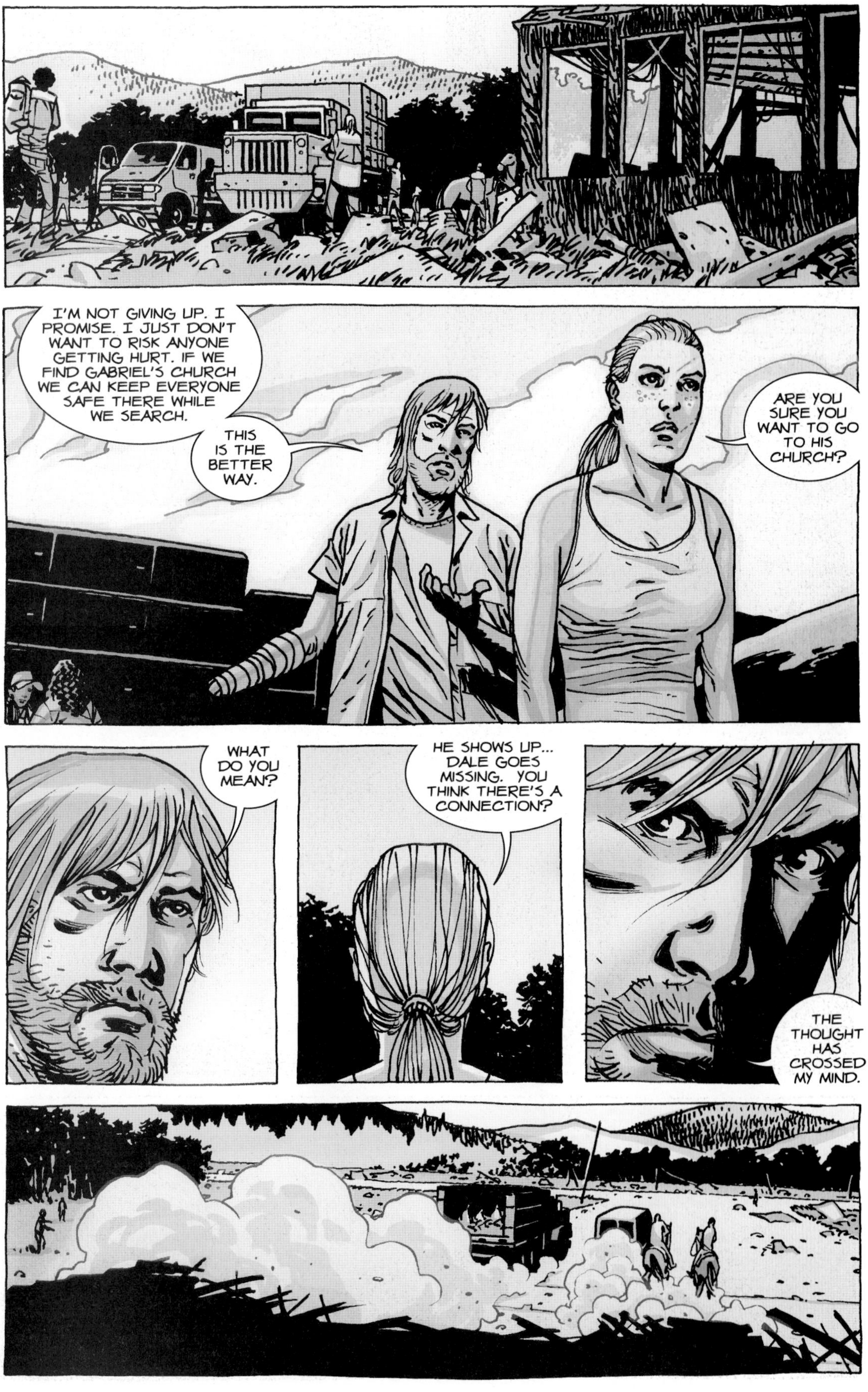
I'M NOT GIVING UP. I PROMISE. I JUST DON'T WANT TO RISK ANYONE GETTING HURT. IF WE FIND GABRIEL'S CHURCH WE CAN KEEP EVERYONE SAFE THERE WHILE WE SEARCH.
THIS IS THE BETTER WAY.
ARE YOU SURE YOU WANT TO GO TO HIS CHURCH?
WHAT DO YOU MEAN?
HE SHOWS UP... DALE GOES MISSING. YOU THINK THERE'S A CONNECTION?
THE THOUGHT HAS CROSSED MY MIND.

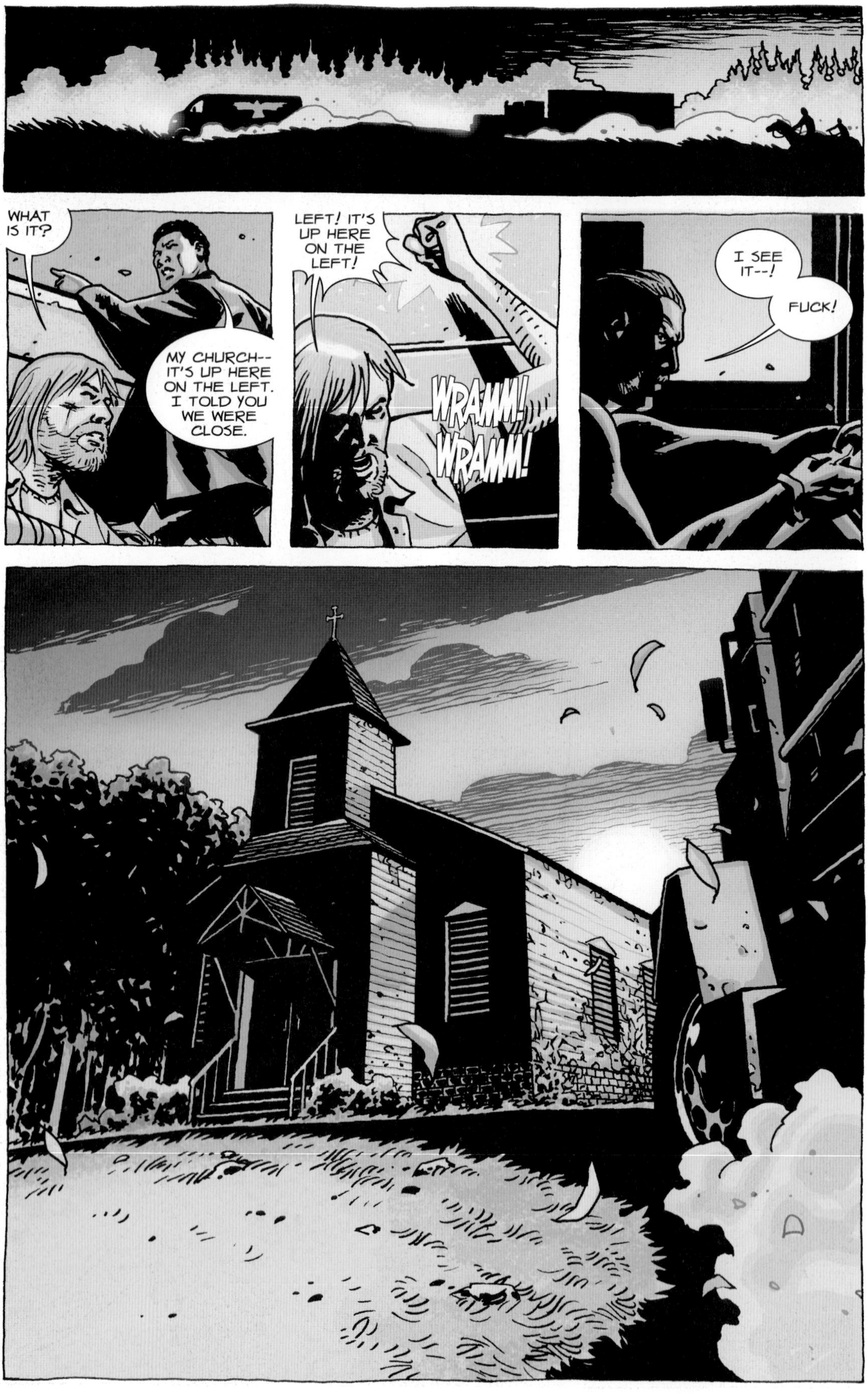
WHAT IS IT?
MY CHURCH-- IT'S UP HERE ON THE LEFT. I TOLD YOU WE WERE CLOSE.
LEFT! IT'S UP HERE ON THE LEFT!
WRAMM! WRAMM!
I SEE IT--!
FUCK!

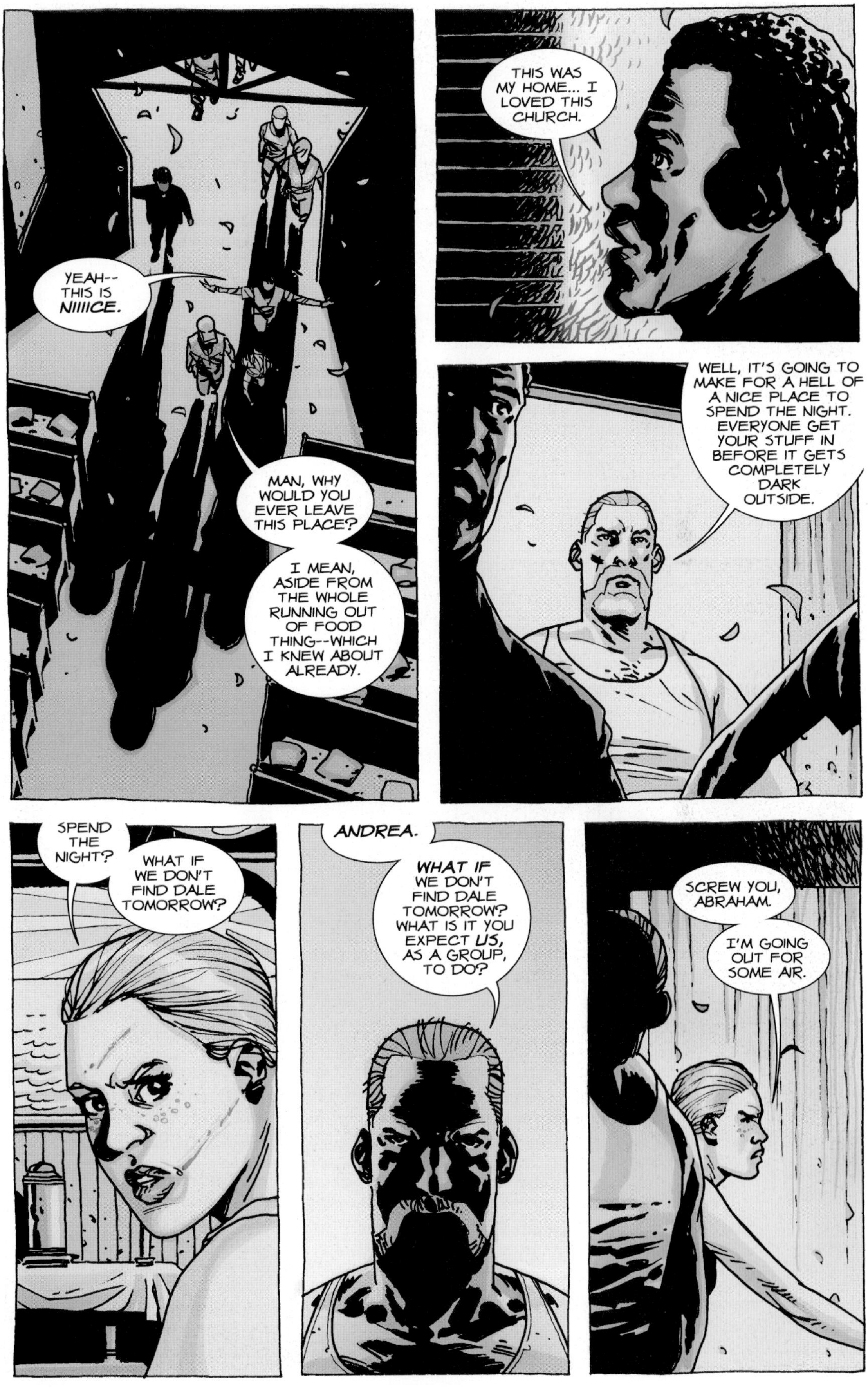
YEAH-- THIS IS NIIIICE.
MAN, WHY WOULD YOU EVER LEAVE THIS PLACE?
I MEAN, ASIDE FROM THE WHOLE RUNNING OUT OF FOOD THING--WHICH I KNEW ABOUT ALREADY.
THIS WAS MY HOME... I LOVED THIS CHURCH.
WELL, IT'S GOING TO MAKE FOR A HELL OF A NICE PLACE TO SPEND THE NIGHT. EVERYONE GET YOUR STUFF IN BEFORE IT GETS COMPLETELY DARK OUTSIDE.
SPEND THE NIGHT?
WHAT IF WE DON'T FIND DALE TOMORROW?
ANDREA.
WHAT IF WE DON'T FIND DALE TOMORROW? WHAT IS IT YOU EXPECT US, AS A GROUP, TO DO?
SCREW YOU, ABRAHAM.
I'M GOING OUT FOR SOME AIR.

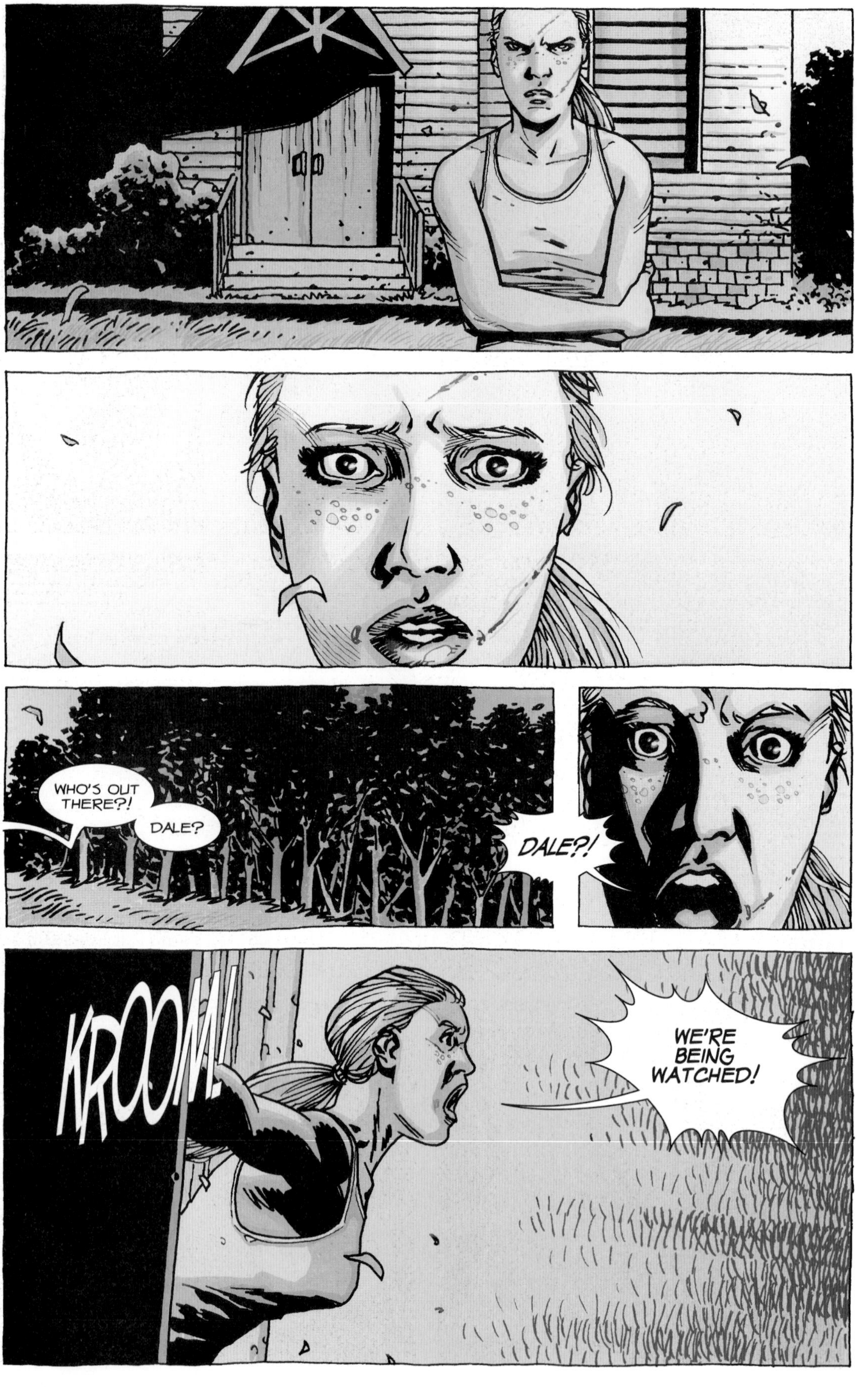
WHO'S OUT THERE?!
DALE?
DALE?!
KROOM!
WE'RE BEING WATCHED!

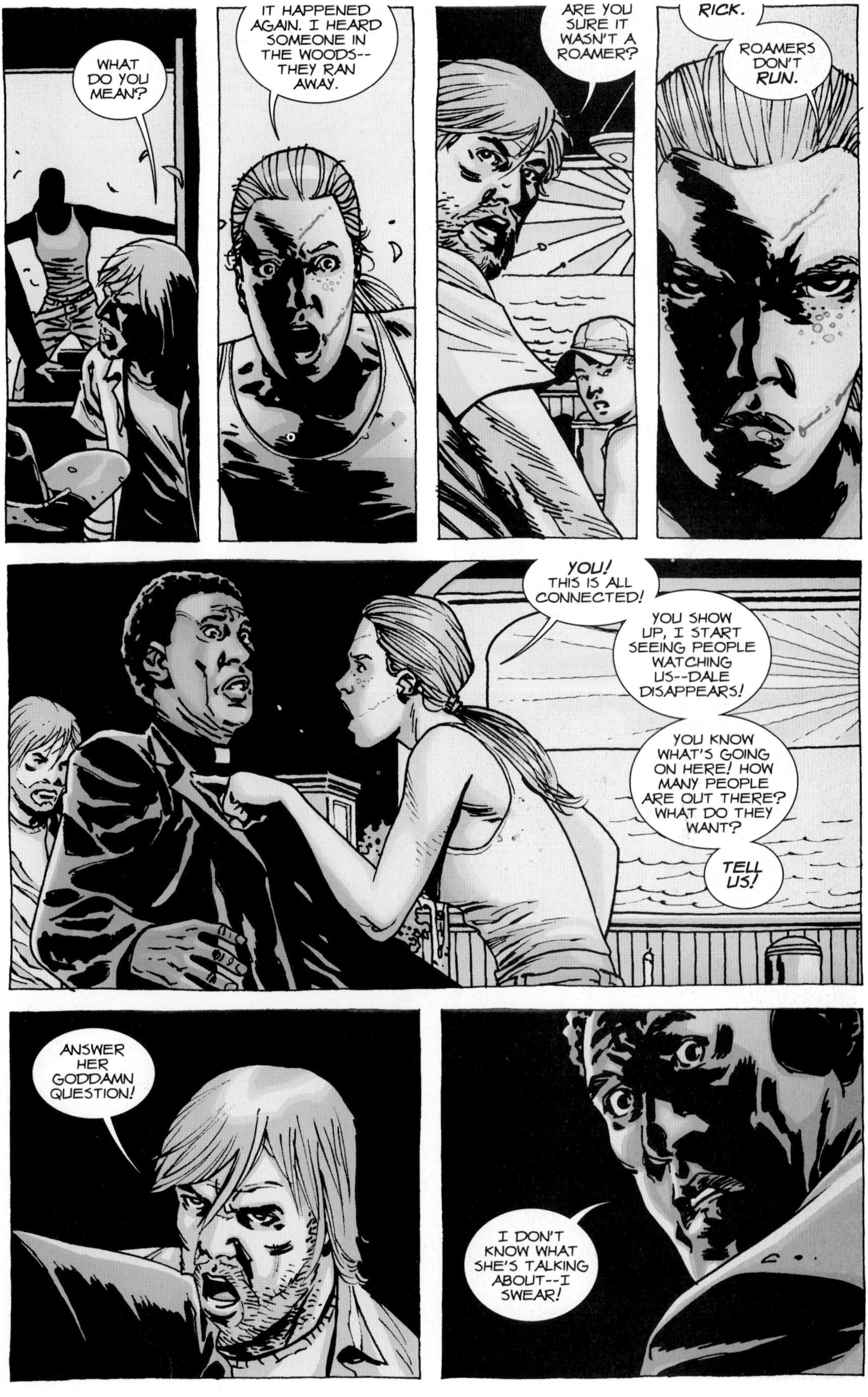
WHAT DO YOU MEAN?
IT HAPPENED AGAIN. I HEARD SOMEONE IN THE WOODS-- THEY RAN AWAY.
ARE YOU SURE IT WASN'T A ROAMER?
RICK.
ROAMERS DON'T RUN.
YOU! THIS IS ALL CONNECTED!
YOU SHOW UP, I START SEEING PEOPLE WATCHING US--DALE DISAPPEARS!
YOU KNOW WHAT'S GOING ON HERE! HOW MANY PEOPLE ARE OUT THERE? WHAT DO THEY WANT?
TELL US!
ANSWER HER GODDAMN QUESTION!
I DON'T KNOW WHAT SHE'S TALKING ABOUT--I SWEAR!

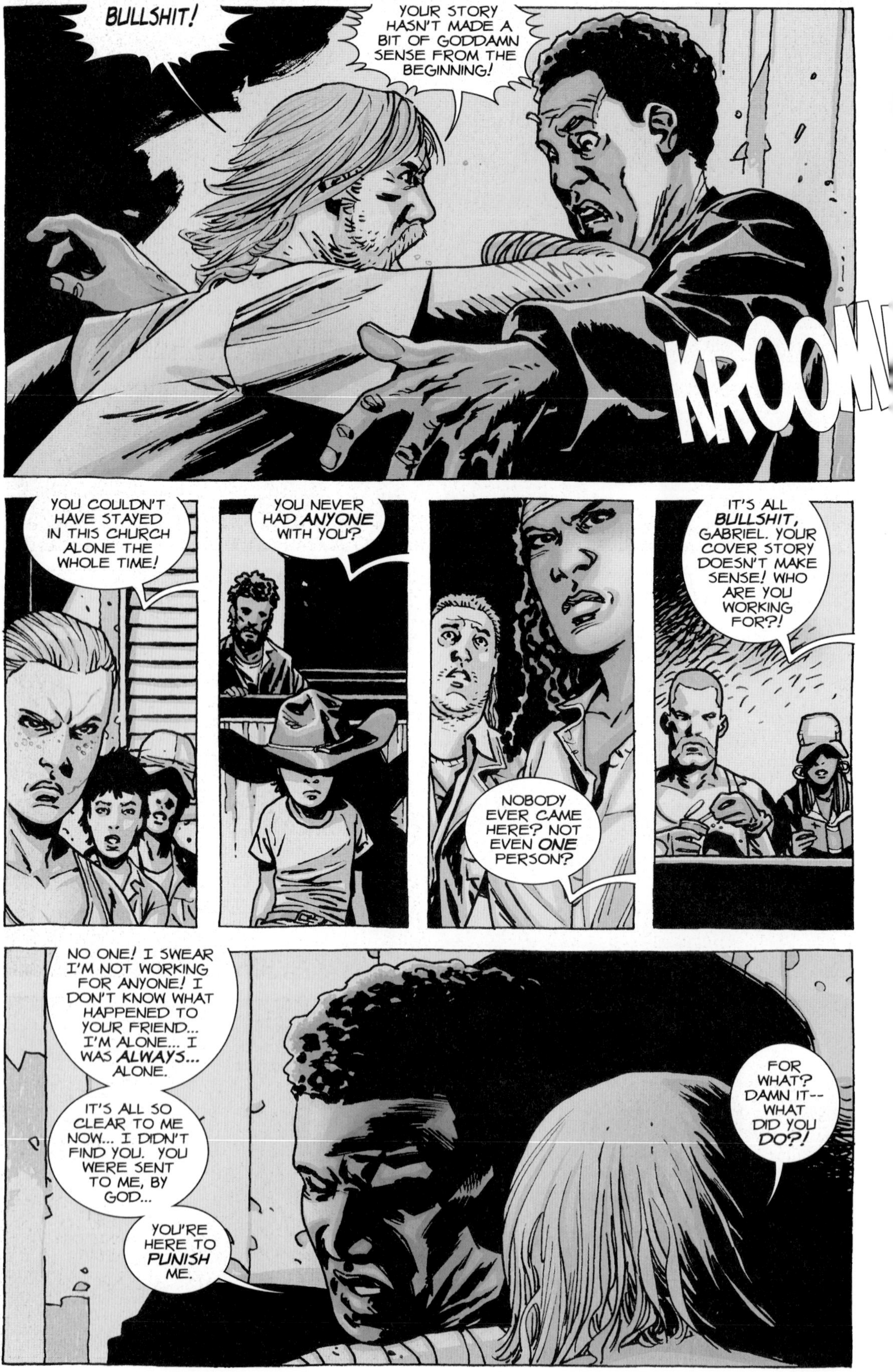

BULLSHIT!
YOUR STORY HASN'T MADE A BIT OF GODDAMN SENSE FROM THE BEGINNING!
KROOM
YOU COULDN'T HAVE STAYED IN THIS CHURCH ALONE THE WHOLE TIME!
YOU NEVER HAD ANYONE WITH YOU?
NOBODY EVER CAME HERE? NOT EVEN ONE PERSON?
IT'S ALL BULLSHIT, GABRIEL. YOUR COVER STORY DOESN'T MAKE SENSE! WHO ARE YOU WORKING FOR?!
NO ONE! I SWEAR I'M NOT WORKING FOR ANYONE! I DON'T KNOW WHAT HAPPENED TO YOUR FRIEND... I'M ALONE... I WAS ALWAYS... ALONE.
IT'S ALL SO CLEAR TO ME NOW... I DIDN'T FIND YOU. YOU WERE SENT TO ME, BY GOD...
YOU'RE HERE TO PUNISH ME.
FOR WHAT? DAMN IT-- WHAT DID YOU DO?!

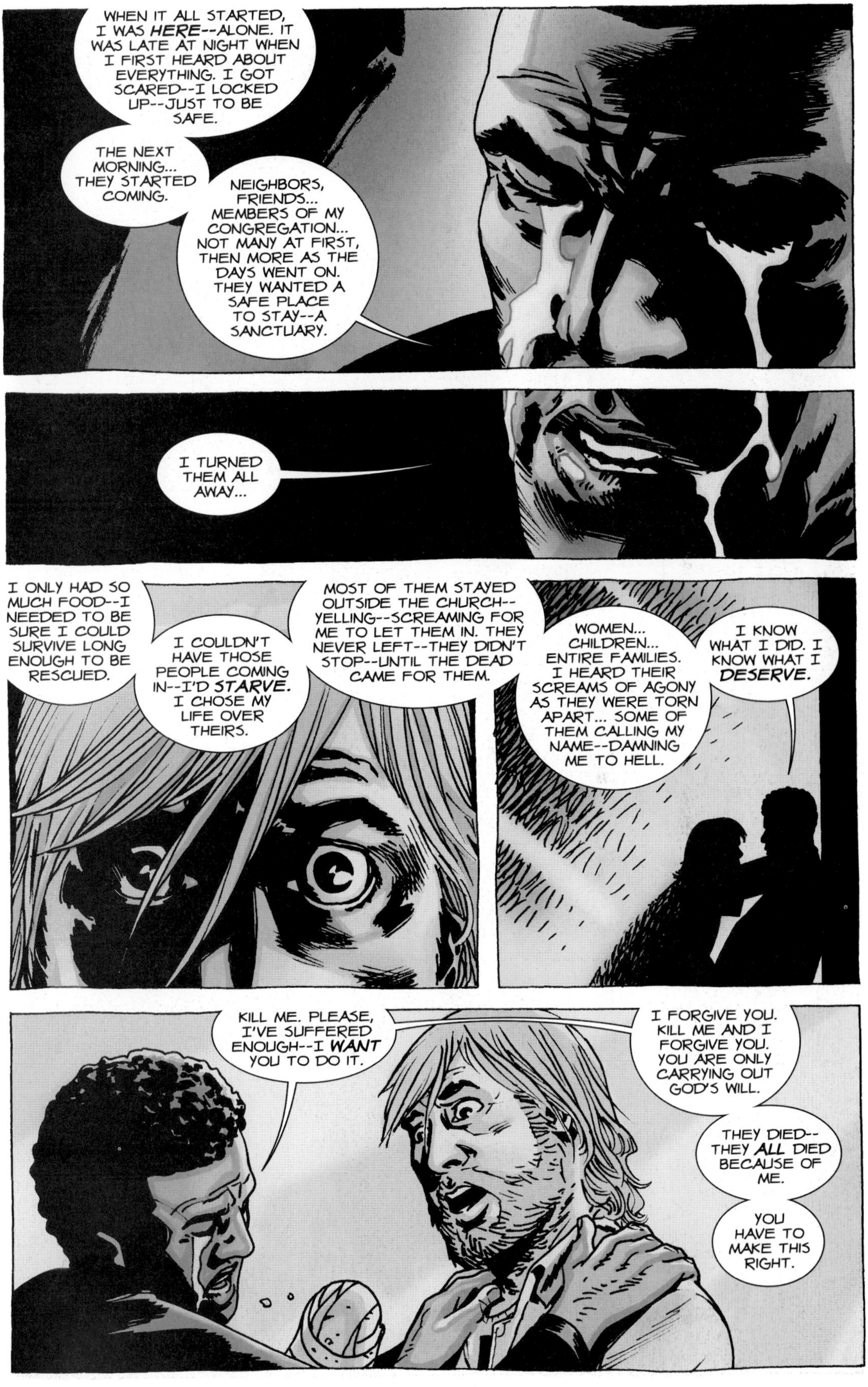

WHEN IT ALL STARTED, I WAS HERE--ALONE. IT WAS LATE AT NIGHT WHEN I FIRST HEARD ABOUT EVERYTHING. I GOT SCARED--I LOCKED UP--JUST TO BE SAFE.
THE NEXT MORNING... THEY STARTED COMING.
NEIGHBORS, FRIENDS... MEMBERS OF MY CONGREGATION... NOT MANY AT FIRST, THEN MORE AS THE DAYS WENT ON. THEY WANTED A SAFE PLACE TO STAY--A SANCTUARY.
I TURNED THEM ALL AWAY...
I ONLY HAD SO MUCH FOOD--I NEEDED TO BE SURE I COULD SURVIVE LONG ENOUGH TO BE RESCUED.
I COULDN'T HAVE THOSE PEOPLE COMING IN--I'D STARVE. I CHOSE MY LIFE OVER THEIRS.
MOST OF THEM STAYED OUTSIDE THE CHURCH--YELLING--SCREAMING FOR ME TO LET THEM IN. THEY NEVER LEFT--THEY DIDN'T STOP--UNTIL THE DEAD CAME FOR THEM.
WOMEN... CHILDREN... ENTIRE FAMILIES. I HEARD THEIR SCREAMS OF AGONY AS THEY WERE TORN APART... SOME OF THEM CALLING MY NAME--DAMNING ME TO HELL.
I KNOW WHAT I DID. I KNOW WHAT I DESERVE.
KILL ME. PLEASE, I'VE SUFFERED ENOUGH--I WANT YOU TO DO IT.
I FORGIVE YOU. KILL ME AND I FORGIVE YOU. YOU ARE ONLY CARRYING OUT GOD'S WILL.
THEY DIED--THEY ALL DIED BECAUSE OF ME.
YOU HAVE TO MAKE THIS RIGHT.

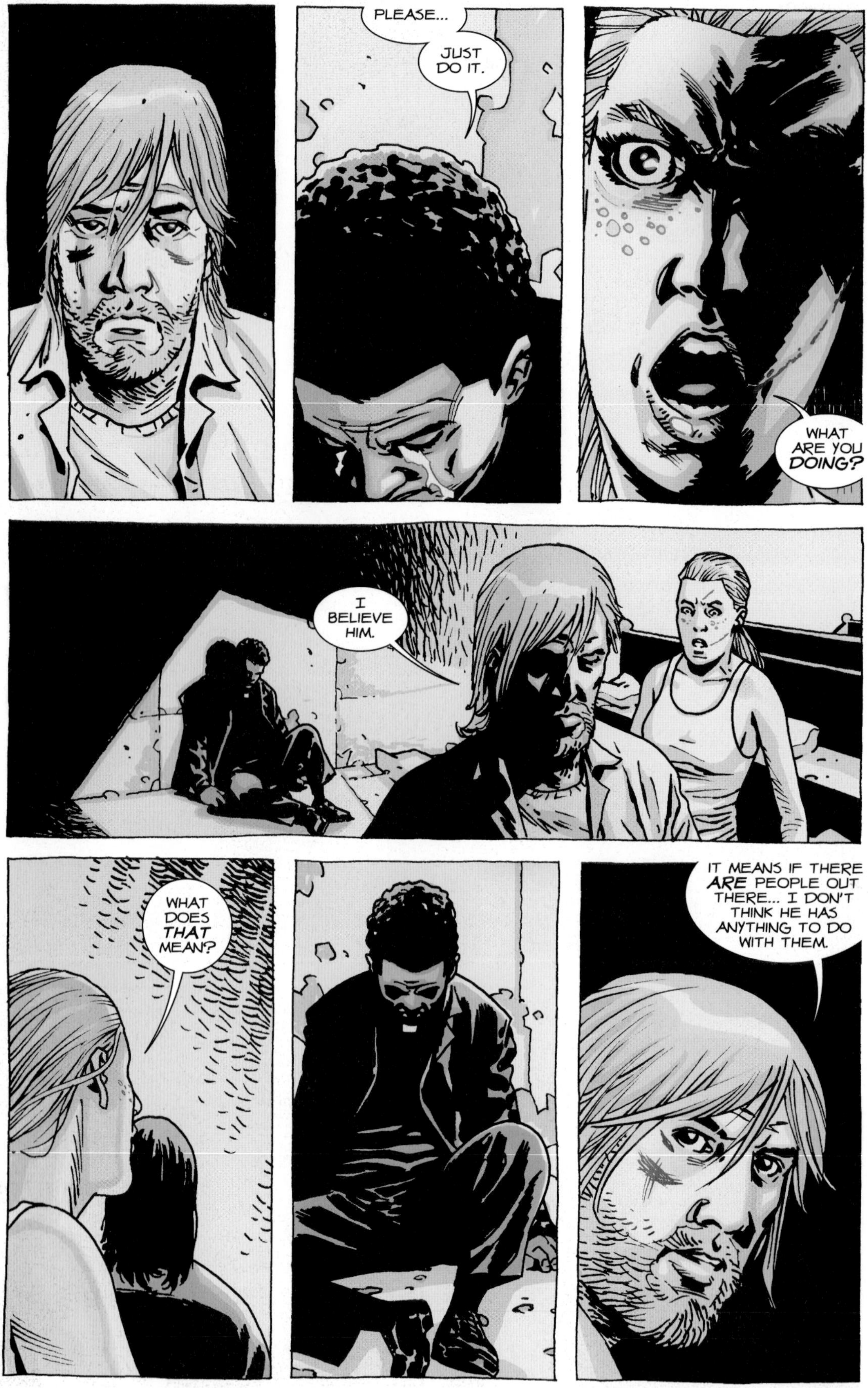
PLEASE...
JUST DO IT.
WHAT ARE YOU DOING?
I BELIEVE HIM.
WHAT DOES THAT MEAN?
IT MEANS IF THERE ARE PEOPLE OUT THERE... I DON'T THINK HE HAS ANYTHING TO DO WITH THEM.

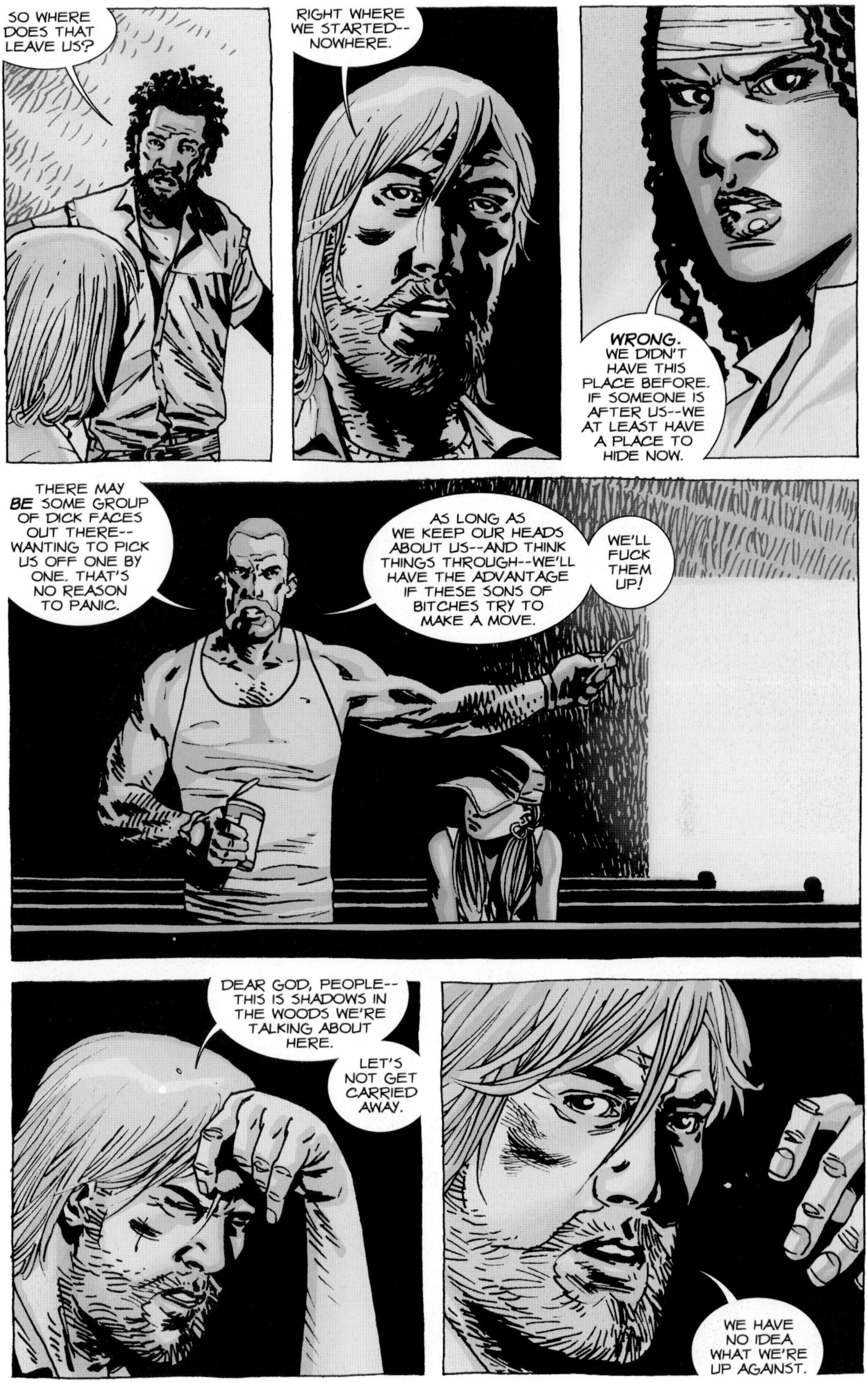
SO WHERE DOES THAT LEAVE US?
RIGHT WHERE WE STARTED-- NOWHERE.
WRONG. WE DIDN'T HAVE THIS PLACE BEFORE. IF SOMEONE IS AFTER US--WE AT LEAST HAVE A PLACE TO HIDE NOW.
THERE MAY BE SOME GROUP OF DICK FACES OUT THERE-- WANTING TO PICK US OFF ONE BY ONE. THAT'S NO REASON TO PANIC.
AS LONG AS WE KEEP OUR HEADS ABOUT US--AND THINK THINGS THROUGH--WE'LL HAVE THE ADVANTAGE IF THESE SONS OF BITCHES TRY TO MAKE A MOVE.
WE'LL FUCK THEM UP!
DEAR GOD, PEOPLE-- THIS IS SHADOWS IN THE WOODS WE'RE TALKING ABOUT HERE.
LET'S NOT GET CARRIED AWAY.
WE HAVE NO IDEA WHAT WE'RE UP AGAINST.

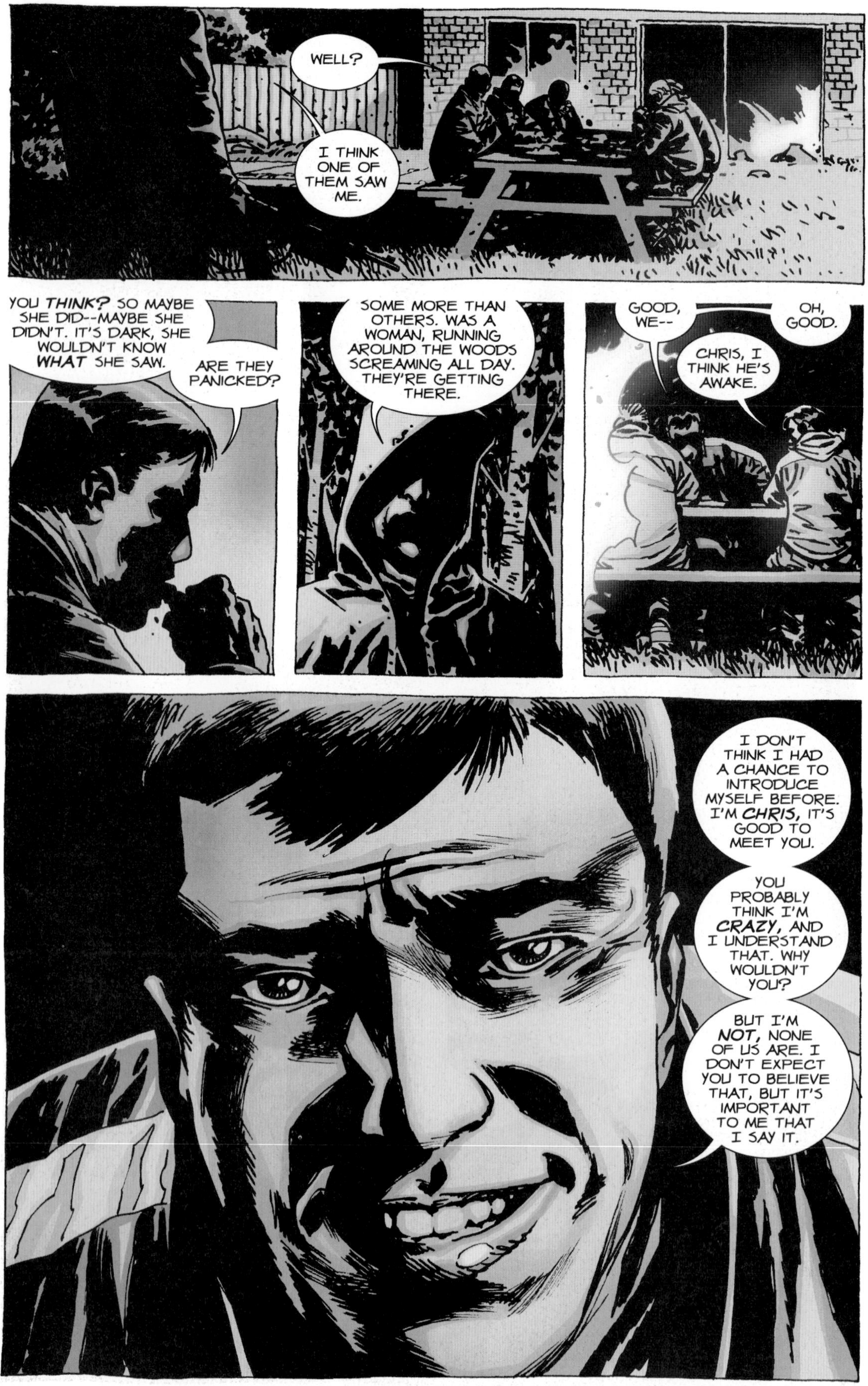
WELL?
I THINK ONE OF THEM SAW ME.
YOU THINK? SO MAYBE SHE DID--MAYBE SHE DIDN'T. IT'S DARK, SHE WOULDN'T KNOW WHAT SHE SAW.
ARE THEY PANICKED?
SOME MORE THAN OTHERS. WAS A WOMAN, RUNNING AROUND THE WOODS SCREAMING ALL DAY. THEY'RE GETTING THERE.
GOOD, WE--
OH, GOOD.
CHRIS, I THINK HE'S AWAKE.
I DON'T THINK I HAD A CHANCE TO INTRODUCE MYSELF BEFORE. I'M CHRIS, IT'S GOOD TO MEET YOU.
YOU PROBABLY THINK I'M CRAZY, AND I UNDERSTAND THAT. WHY WOULDN'T YOU?
BUT I'M NOT, NONE OF US ARE. I DON'T EXPECT YOU TO BELIEVE THAT, BUT IT'S IMPORTANT TO ME THAT I SAY IT.

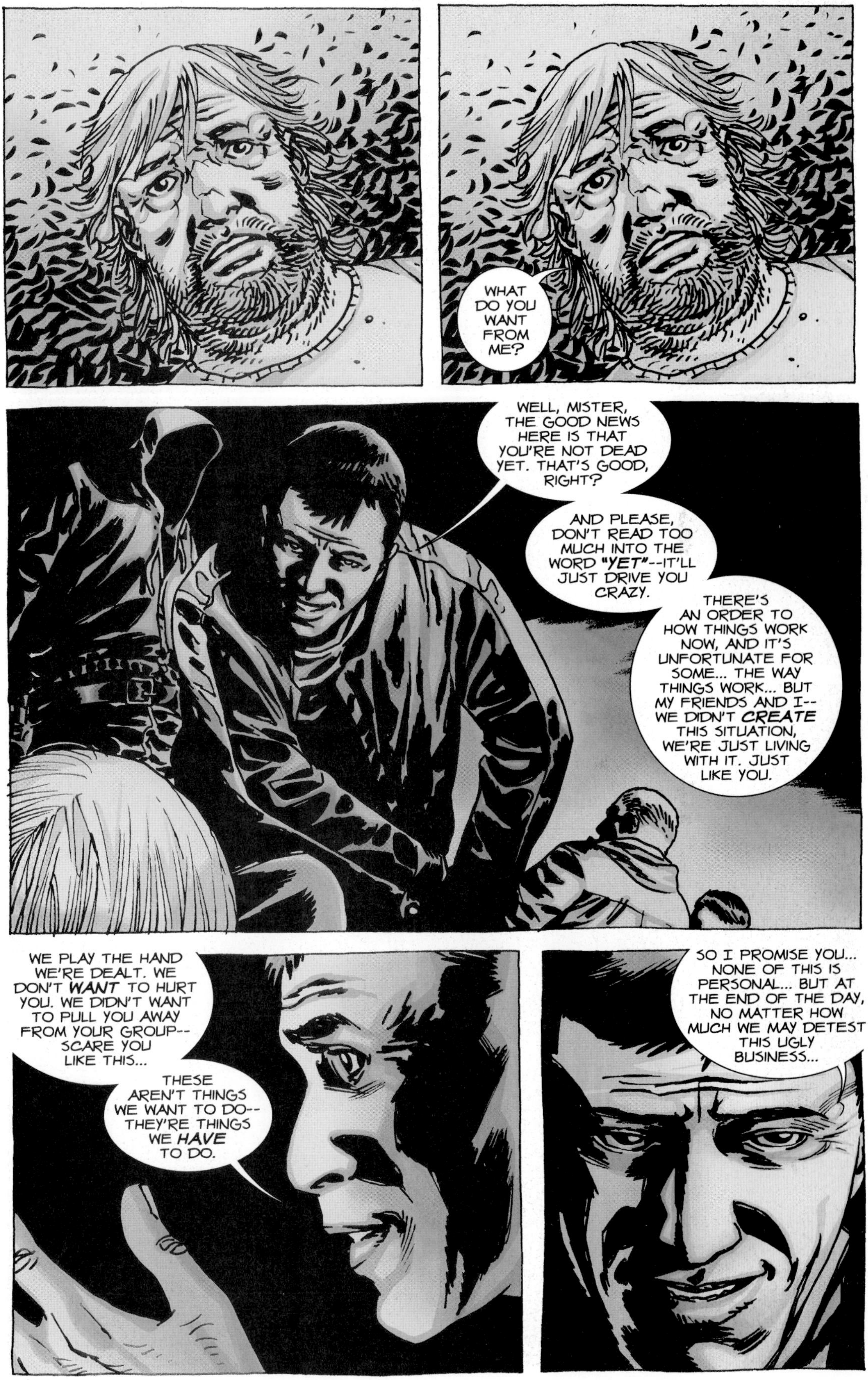
WHAT DO YOU WANT FROM ME?
WELL, MISTER, THE GOOD NEWS HERE IS THAT YOU'RE NOT DEAD YET. THAT'S GOOD, RIGHT?
AND PLEASE, DON'T READ TOO MUCH INTO THE WORD "YET"--IT'LL JUST DRIVE YOU CRAZY.
THERE'S AN ORDER TO HOW THINGS WORK NOW, AND IT'S UNFORTUNATE FOR SOME... THE WAY THINGS WORK... BUT MY FRIENDS AND I-- WE DIDN'T CREATE THIS SITUATION, WE'RE JUST LIVING WITH IT. JUST LIKE YOU.
WE PLAY THE HAND WE'RE DEALT. WE DON'T WANT TO HURT YOU. WE DIDN'T WANT TO PULL YOU AWAY FROM YOUR GROUP-- SCARE YOU LIKE THIS...
THESE AREN'T THINGS WE WANT TO DO-- THEY'RE THINGS WE HAVE TO DO.
SO I PROMISE YOU... NONE OF THIS IS PERSONAL... BUT AT THE END OF THE DAY, NO MATTER HOW MUCH WE MAY DETEST THIS UGLY BUSINESS...

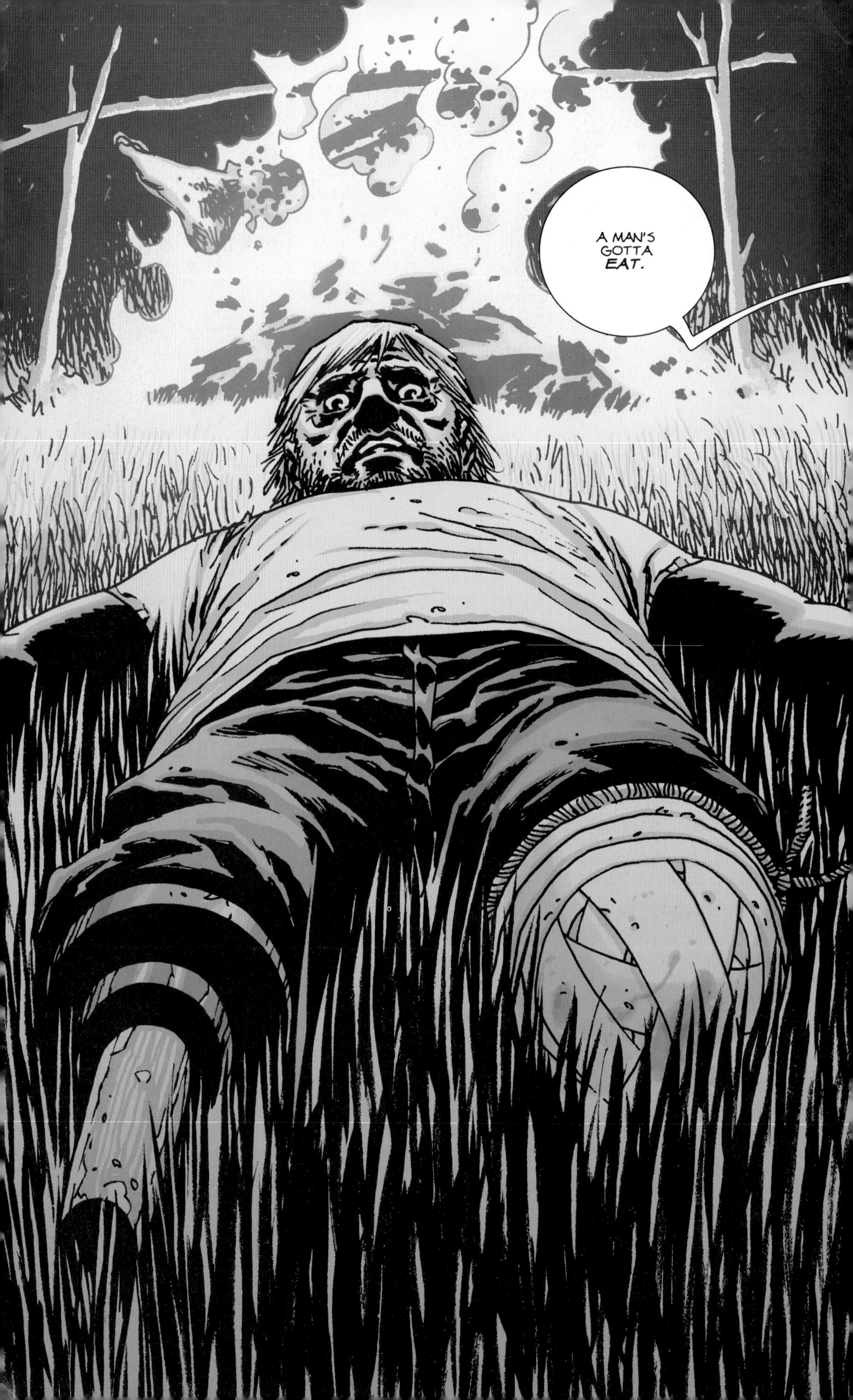
A MAN'S GOTTA EAT.

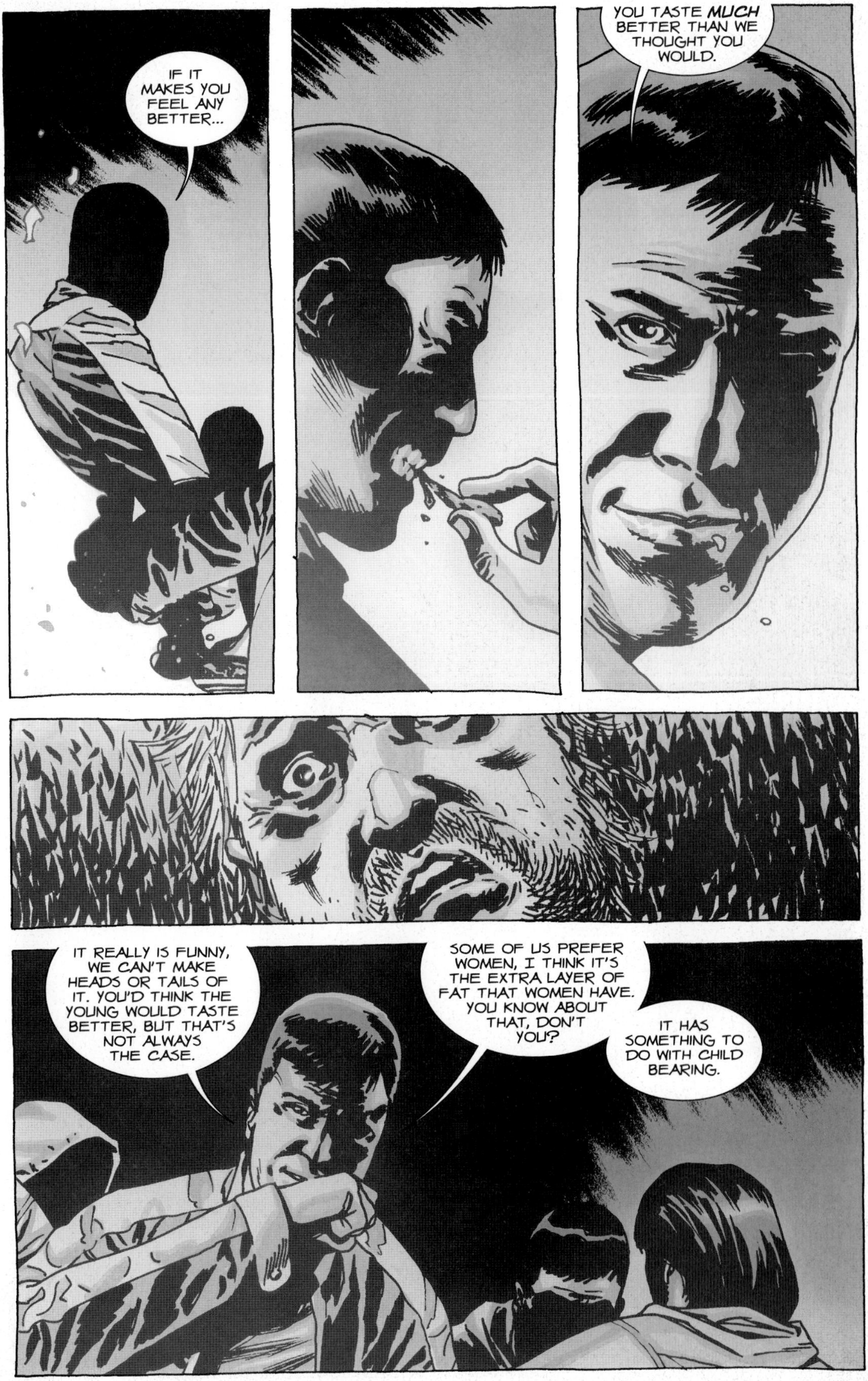
IF IT MAKES YOU FEEL ANY BETTER...
YOU TASTE MUCH BETTER THAN WE THOUGHT YOU WOULD.
IT REALLY IS FUNNY, WE CAN'T MAKE HEADS OR TAILS OF IT. YOU'D THINK THE YOUNG WOULD TASTE BETTER, BUT THAT'S NOT ALWAYS THE CASE.
SOME OF US PREFER WOMEN, I THINK IT'S THE EXTRA LAYER OF FAT THAT WOMEN HAVE. YOU KNOW ABOUT THAT, DON'T YOU?
IT HAS SOMETHING TO DO WITH CHILD BEARING.

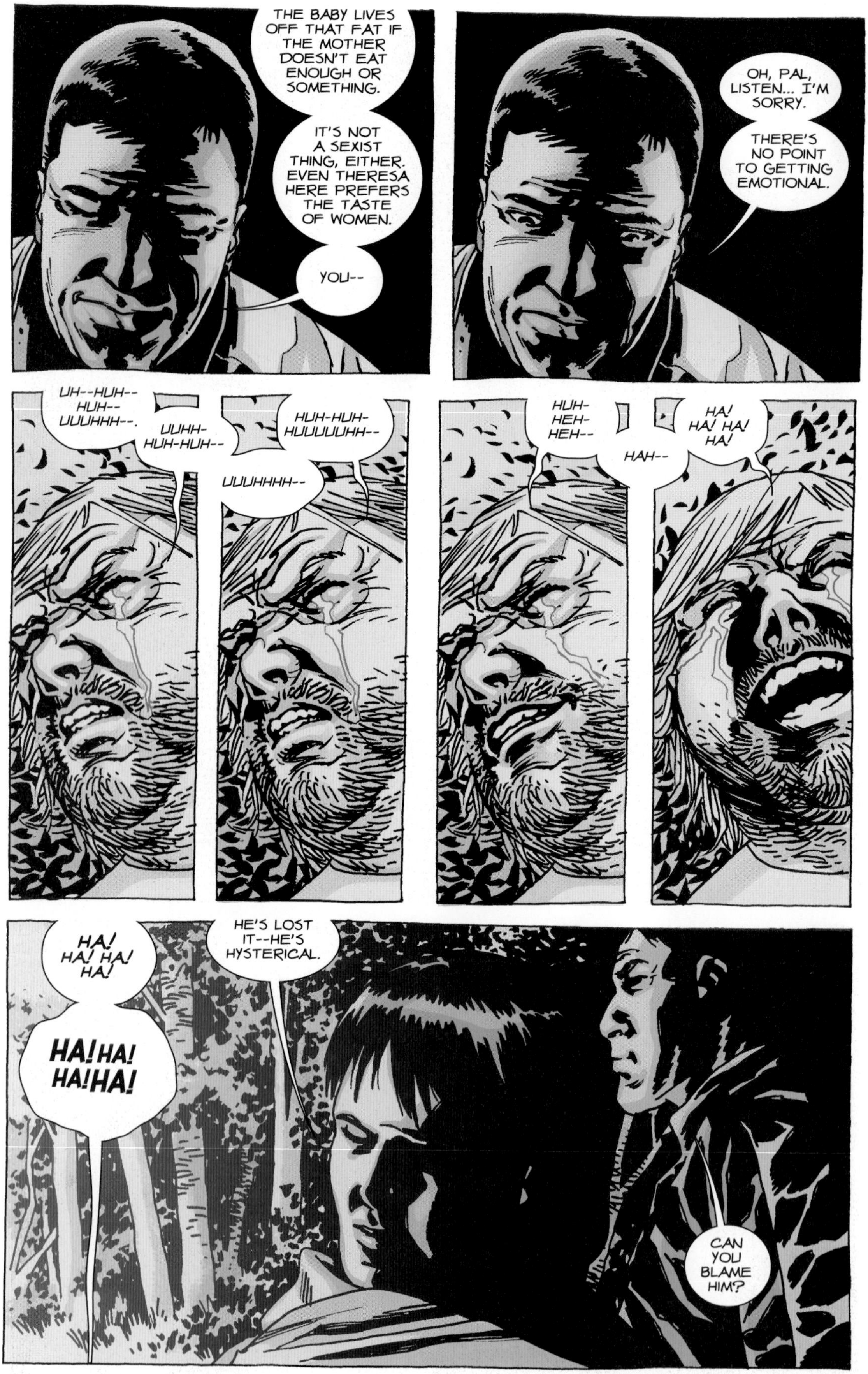
THE BABY LIVES OFF THAT FAT IF THE MOTHER DOESN'T EAT ENOUGH OR SOMETHING.
IT'S NOT A SEXIST THING, EITHER. EVEN THERESA HERE PREFERS THE TASTE OF WOMEN.
YOU--
OH, PAL, LISTEN... I'M SORRY.
THERE'S NO POINT TO GETTING EMOTIONAL.
UH--HUH--HUH--UUUHHH--.
UUHH-HUH-HUH--
HUH-HUH-HUUUUUHH--
UUUHHHH--
HUH-HEH-HEH--
HAH--
HA! HA! HA! HA!
HA! HA! HA! HA!
HE'S LOST IT--HE'S HYSTERICAL.
HA! HA! HA! HA!
CAN YOU BLAME HIM?

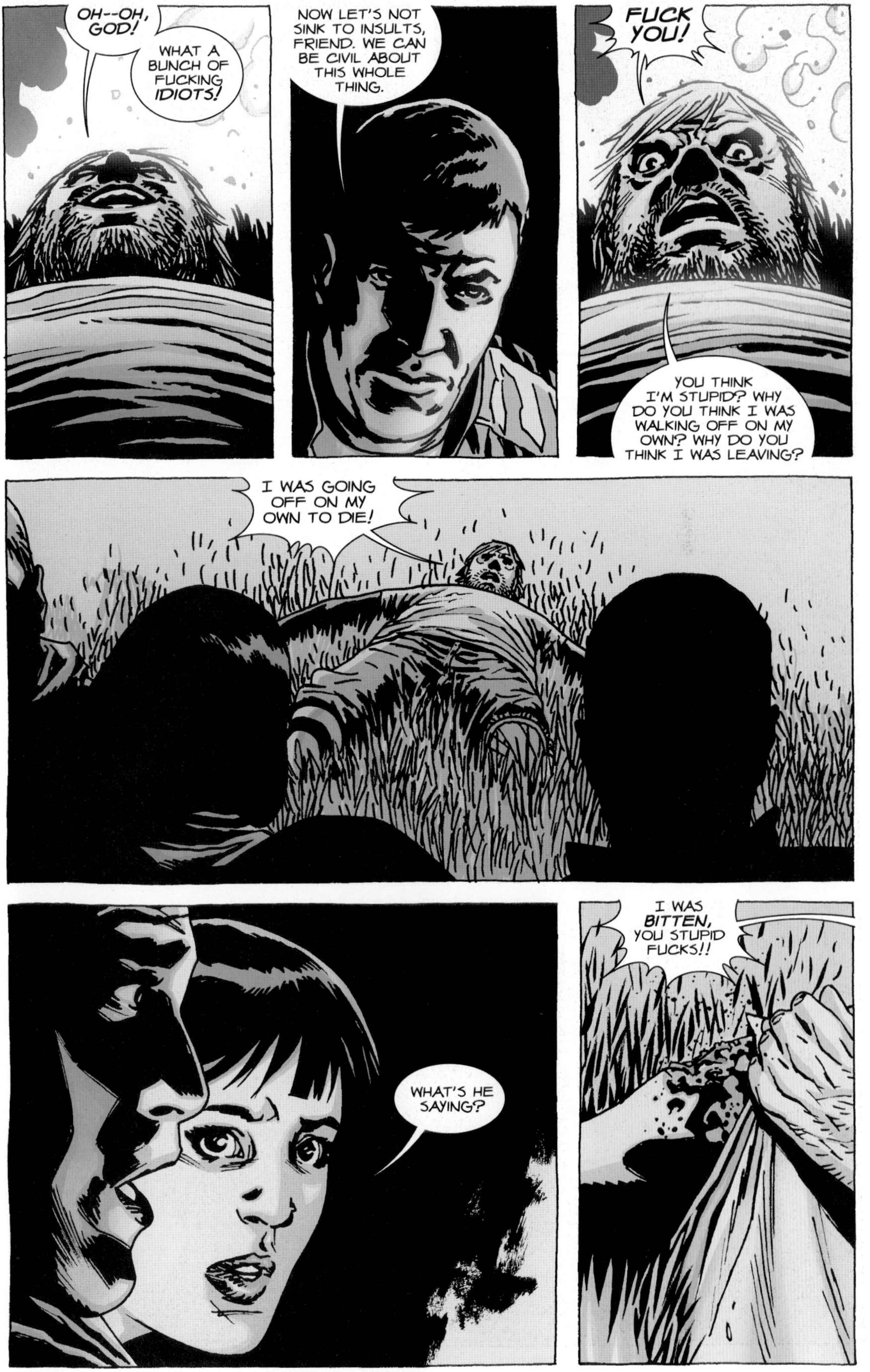
OH--OH, GOD!
WHAT A BUNCH OF FUCKING IDIOTS!
NOW LET'S NOT SINK TO INSULTS, FRIEND. WE CAN BE CIVIL ABOUT THIS WHOLE THING.
FUCK YOU!
YOU THINK I'M STUPID? WHY DO YOU THINK I WAS WALKING OFF ON MY OWN? WHY DO YOU THINK I WAS LEAVING?
I WAS GOING OFF ON MY OWN TO DIE!
WHAT'S HE SAYING?
I WAS BITTEN, YOU STUPID FUCKS!!

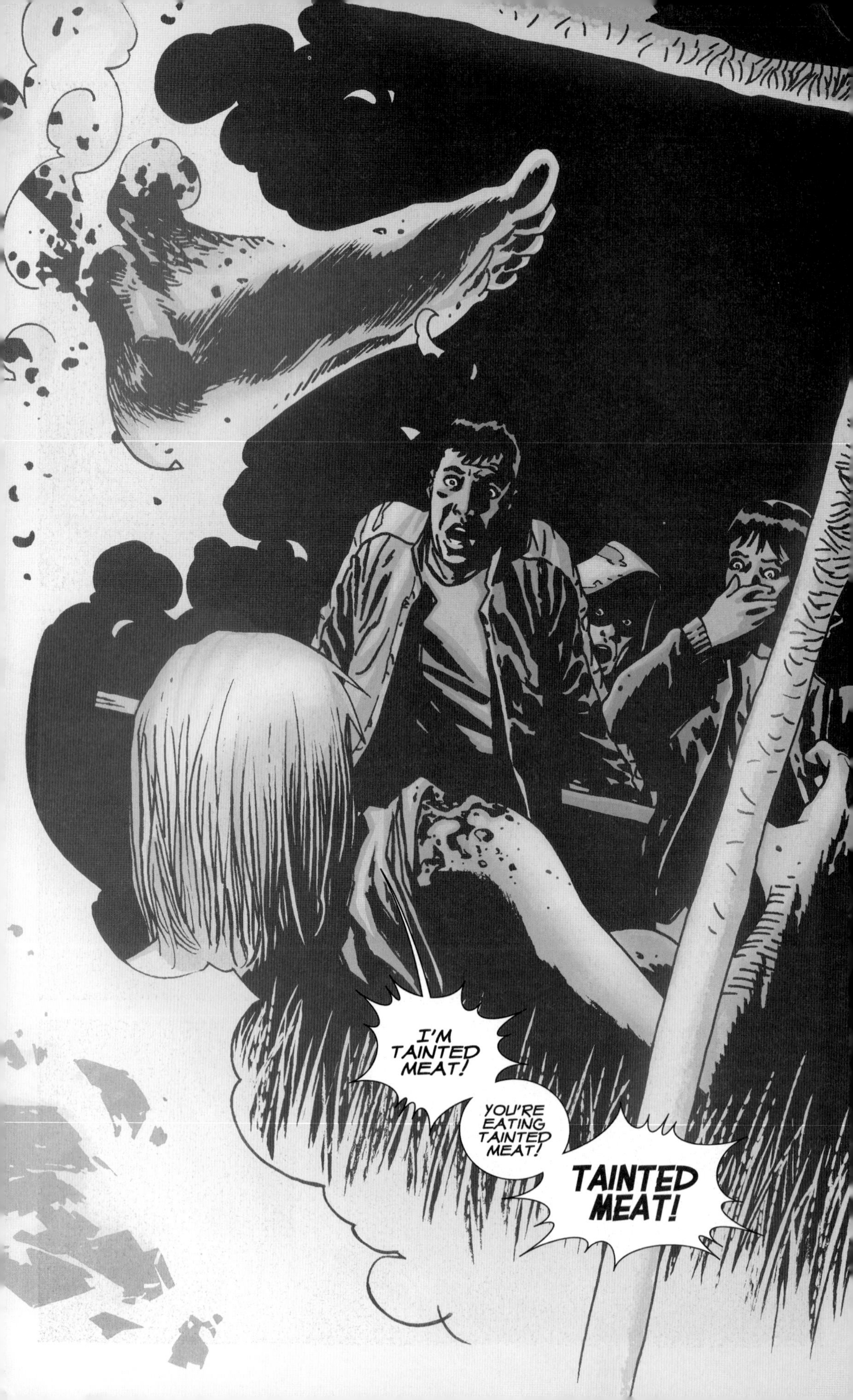

I'M TAINTED MEAT!
YOU'RE EATING TAINTED MEAT!
TAINTED MEAT!

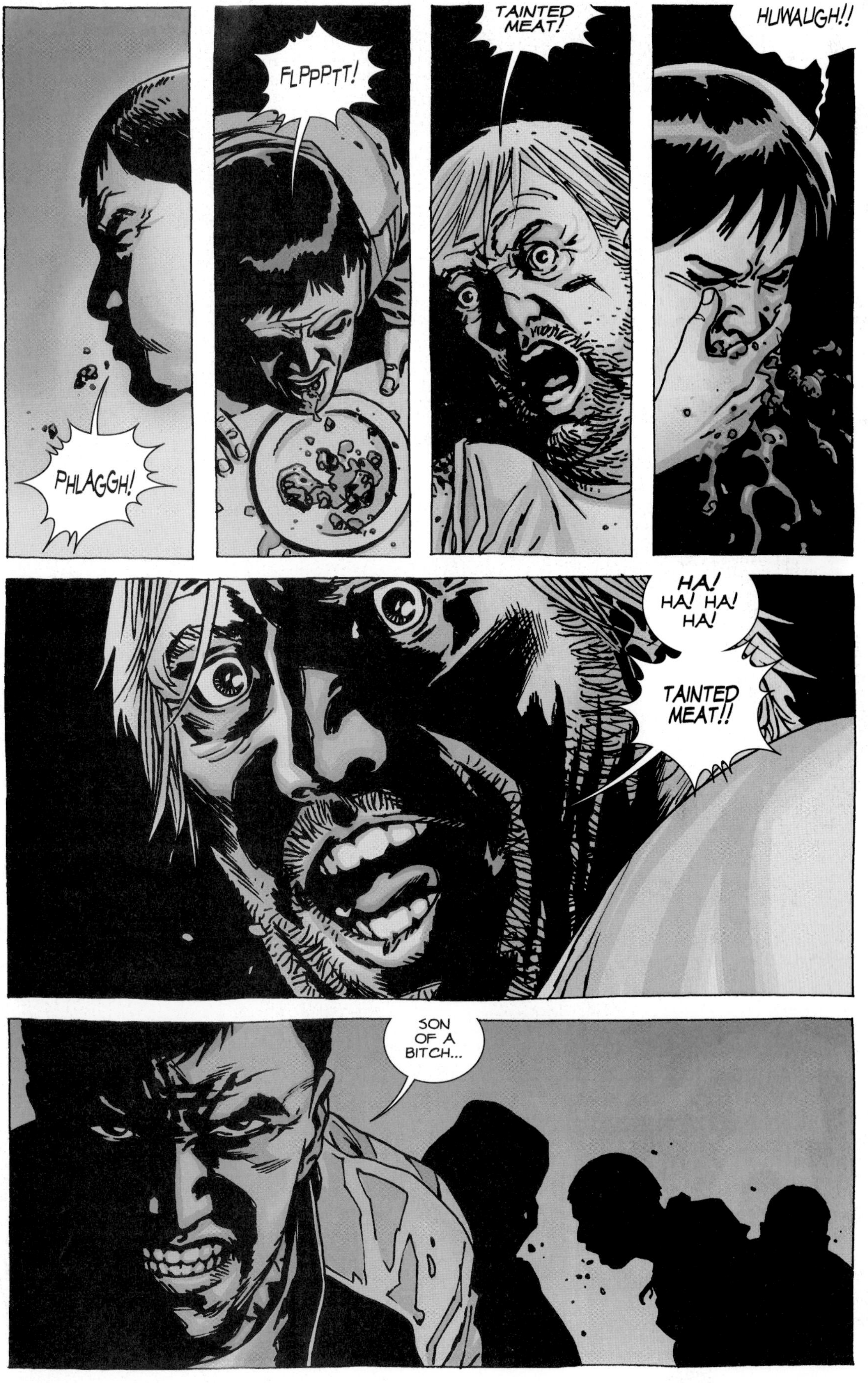
PHLAGGH!
FLPPPTT!
TAINTED MEAT!
HUWAUGH!!
HA! HA! HA! HA!
TAINTED MEAT!!
SON OF A BITCH...

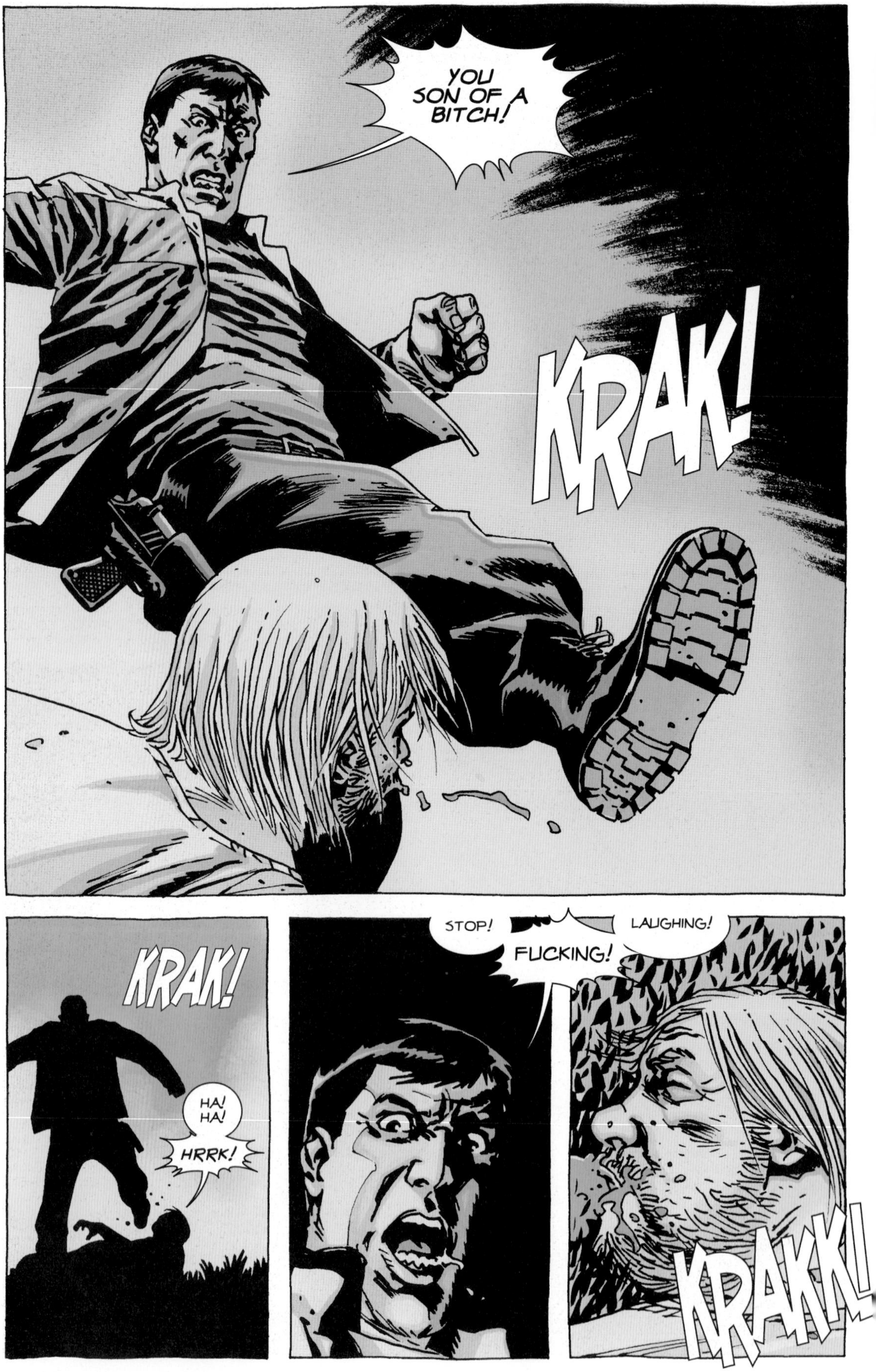
YOU SON OF A BITCH!
KRAK!
KRAK!
HA! HA!
HRRK!
STOP!
FUCKING!
LAUGHING!
KRAKK!

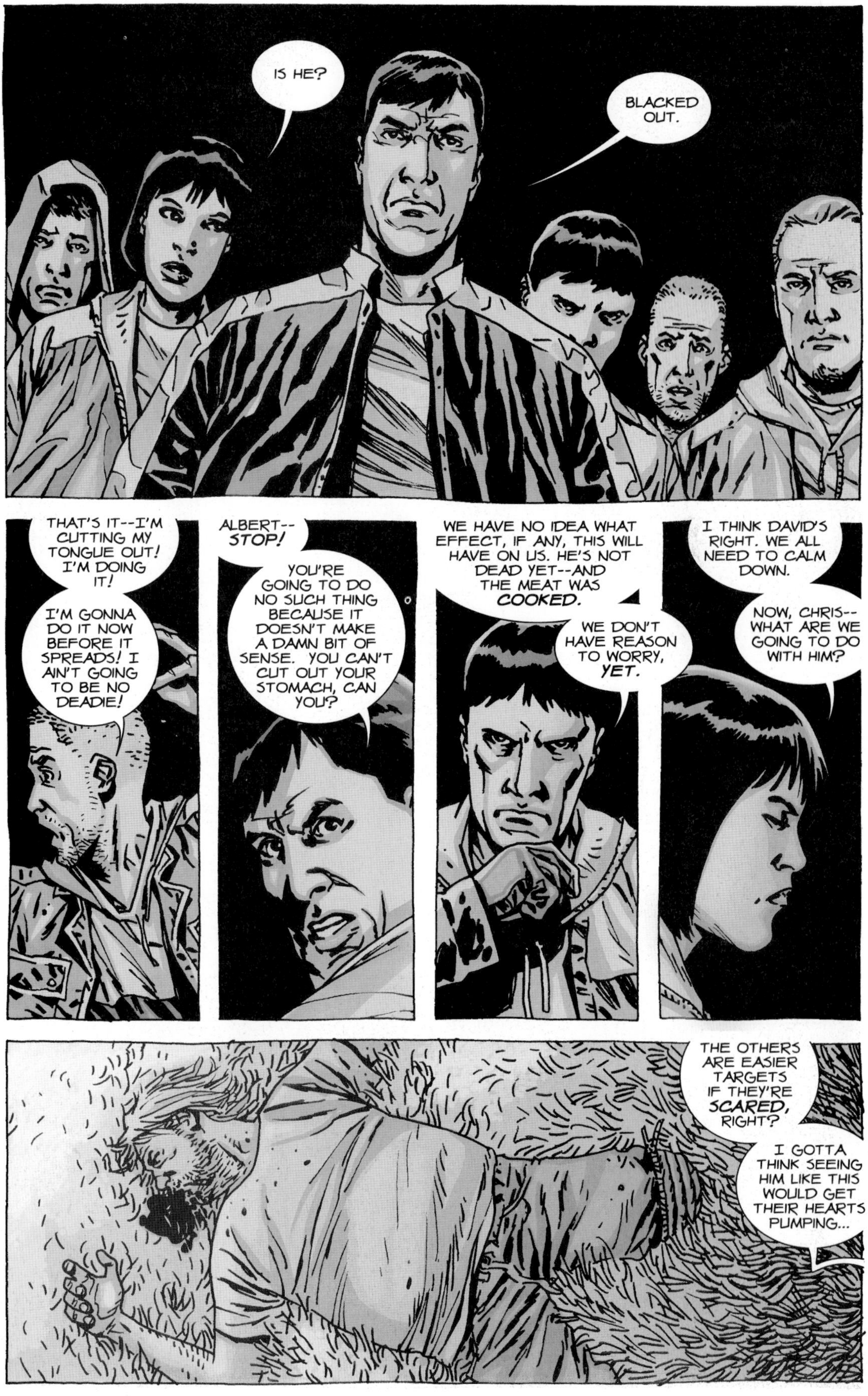
IS HE?
BLACKED OUT.
THAT'S IT--I'M CUTTING MY TONGUE OUT! I'M DOING IT!
I'M GONNA DO IT NOW BEFORE IT SPREADS! I AIN'T GOING TO BE NO DEADIE!
ALBERT-- STOP!
YOU'RE GOING TO DO NO SUCH THING BECAUSE IT DOESN'T MAKE A DAMN BIT OF SENSE. YOU CAN'T CUT OUT YOUR STOMACH, CAN YOU?
WE HAVE NO IDEA WHAT EFFECT, IF ANY, THIS WILL HAVE ON US. HE'S NOT DEAD YET--AND THE MEAT WAS COOKED.
WE DON'T HAVE REASON TO WORRY, YET.
I THINK DAVID'S RIGHT. WE ALL NEED TO CALM DOWN.
NOW, CHRIS-- WHAT ARE WE GOING TO DO WITH HIM?
THE OTHERS ARE EASIER TARGETS IF THEY'RE SCARED, RIGHT?
I GOTTA THINK SEEING HIM LIKE THIS WOULD GET THEIR HEARTS PUMPING...

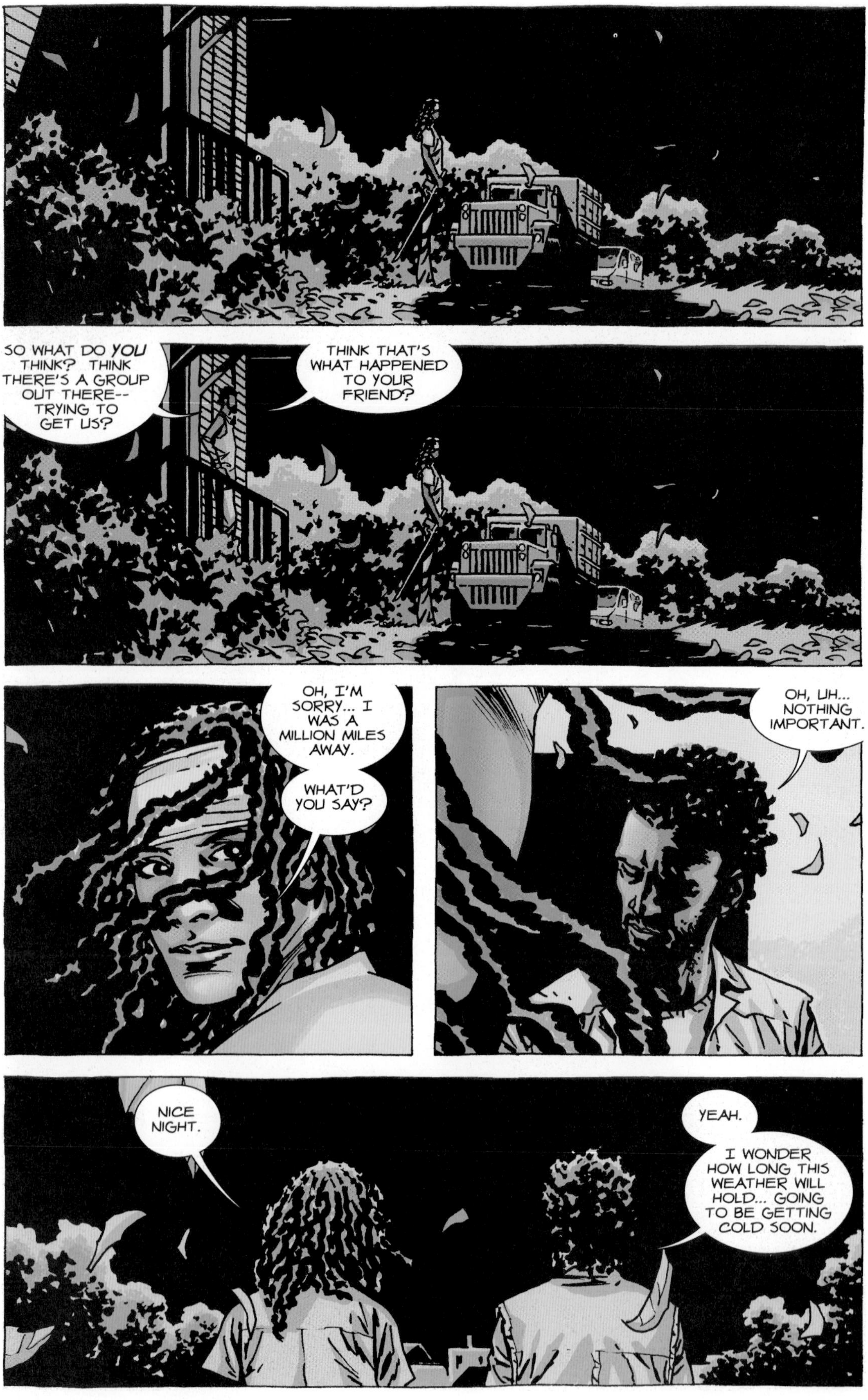

SO WHAT DO *YOU* THINK? THINK THERE'S A GROUP OUT THERE-- TRYING TO GET US?
THINK THAT'S WHAT HAPPENED TO YOUR FRIEND?
OH, I'M SORRY... I WAS A MILLION MILES AWAY.
WHAT'D YOU SAY?
OH, UH... NOTHING IMPORTANT.
NICE NIGHT.
YEAH.
I WONDER HOW LONG THIS WEATHER WILL HOLD... GOING TO BE GETTING COLD SOON.

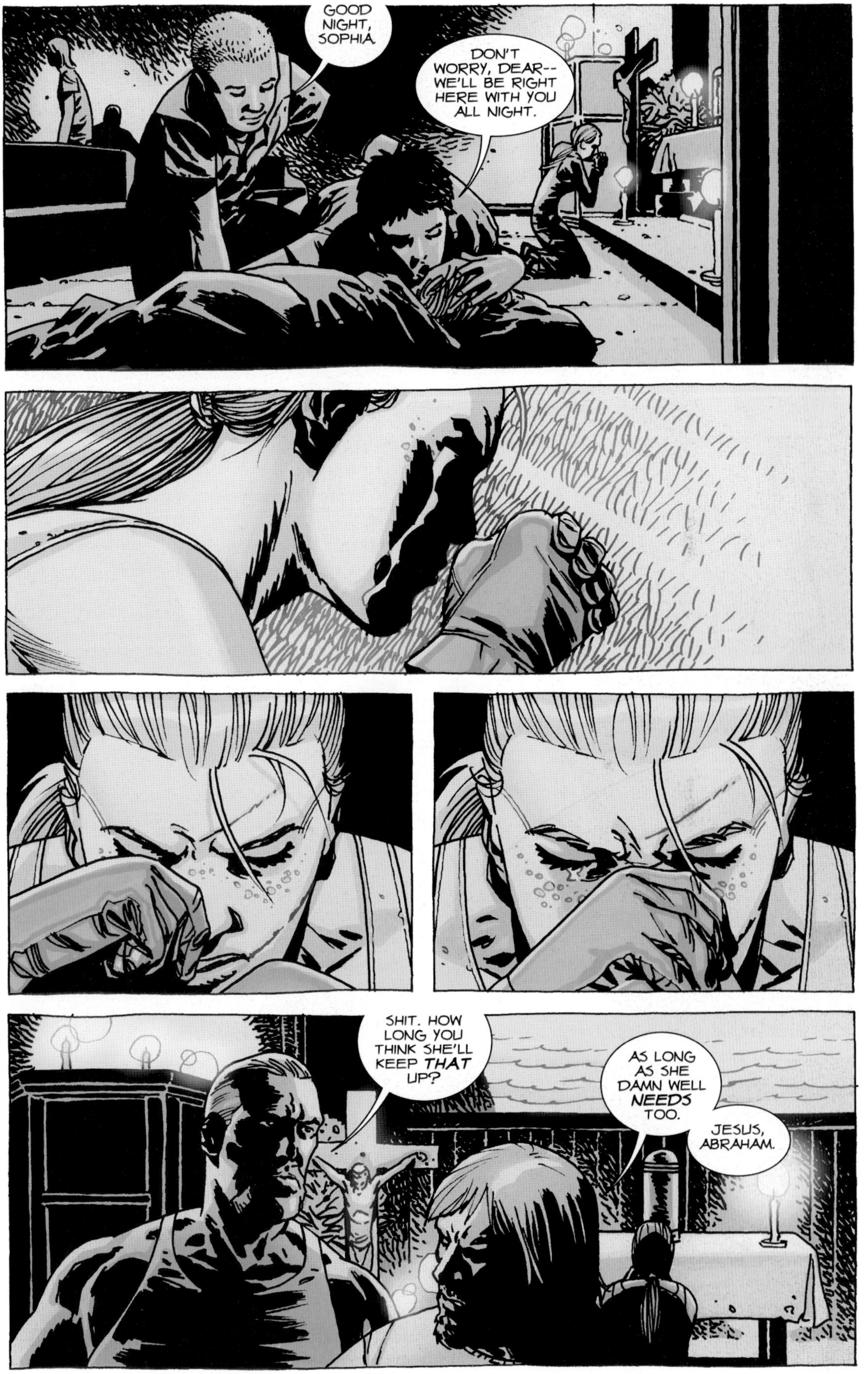
GOOD NIGHT, SOPHIA.
DON'T WORRY, DEAR-- WE'LL BE RIGHT HERE WITH YOU ALL NIGHT.
SHIT. HOW LONG YOU THINK SHE'LL KEEP THAT UP?
AS LONG AS SHE DAMN WELL NEEDS TOO.
JESUS, ABRAHAM.

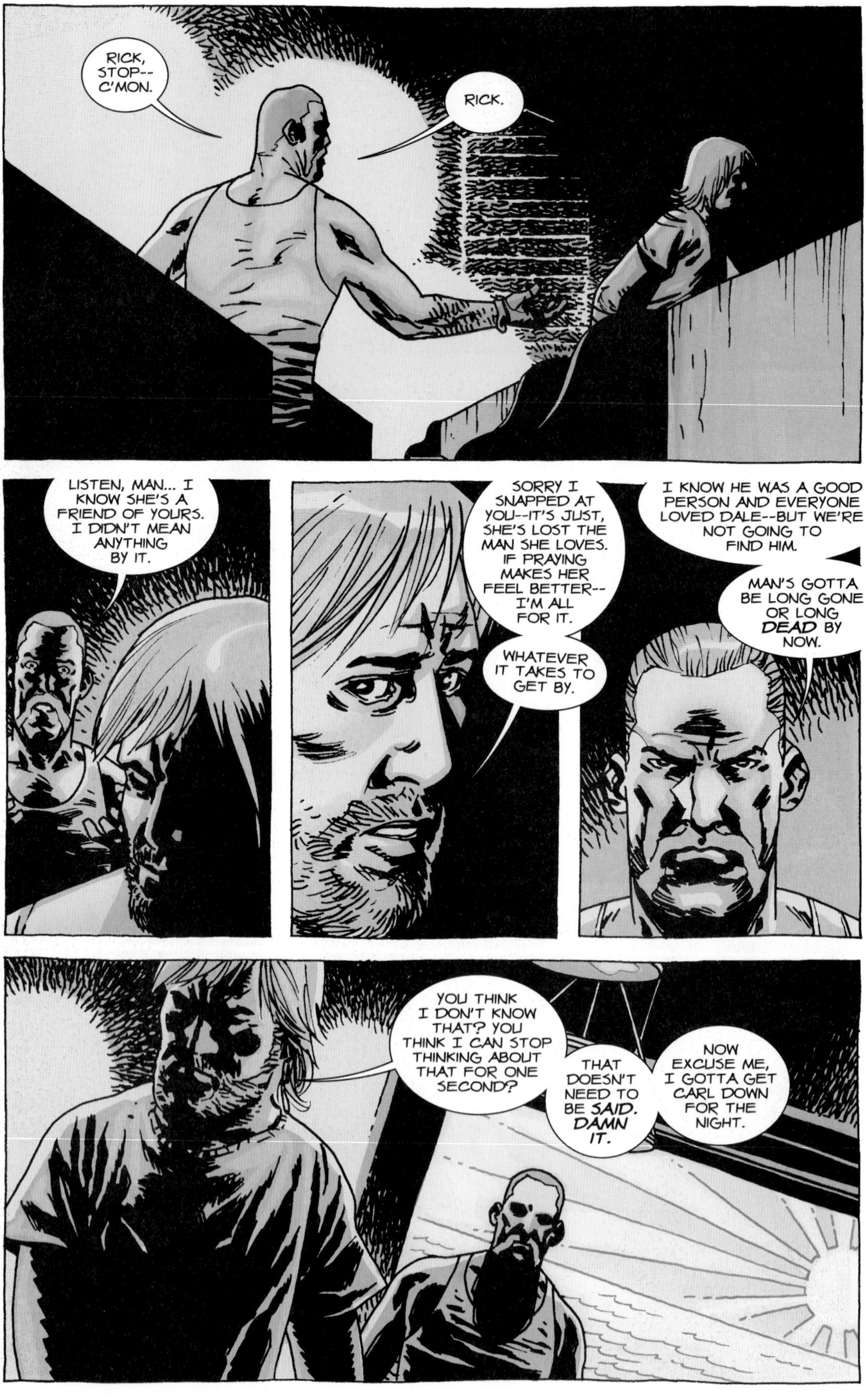
RICK, STOP-- C'MON.
RICK.
LISTEN, MAN... I KNOW SHE'S A FRIEND OF YOURS. I DIDN'T MEAN ANYTHING BY IT.
SORRY I SNAPPED AT YOU--IT'S JUST, SHE'S LOST THE MAN SHE LOVES. IF PRAYING MAKES HER FEEL BETTER-- I'M ALL FOR IT.
WHATEVER IT TAKES TO GET BY.
I KNOW HE WAS A GOOD PERSON AND EVERYONE LOVED DALE--BUT WE'RE NOT GOING TO FIND HIM.
MAN'S GOTTA BE LONG GONE OR LONG DEAD BY NOW.
YOU THINK I DON'T KNOW THAT? YOU THINK I CAN STOP THINKING ABOUT THAT FOR ONE SECOND?
THAT DOESN'T NEED TO BE SAID. DAMN IT.
NOW EXCUSE ME, I GOTTA GET CARL DOWN FOR THE NIGHT.

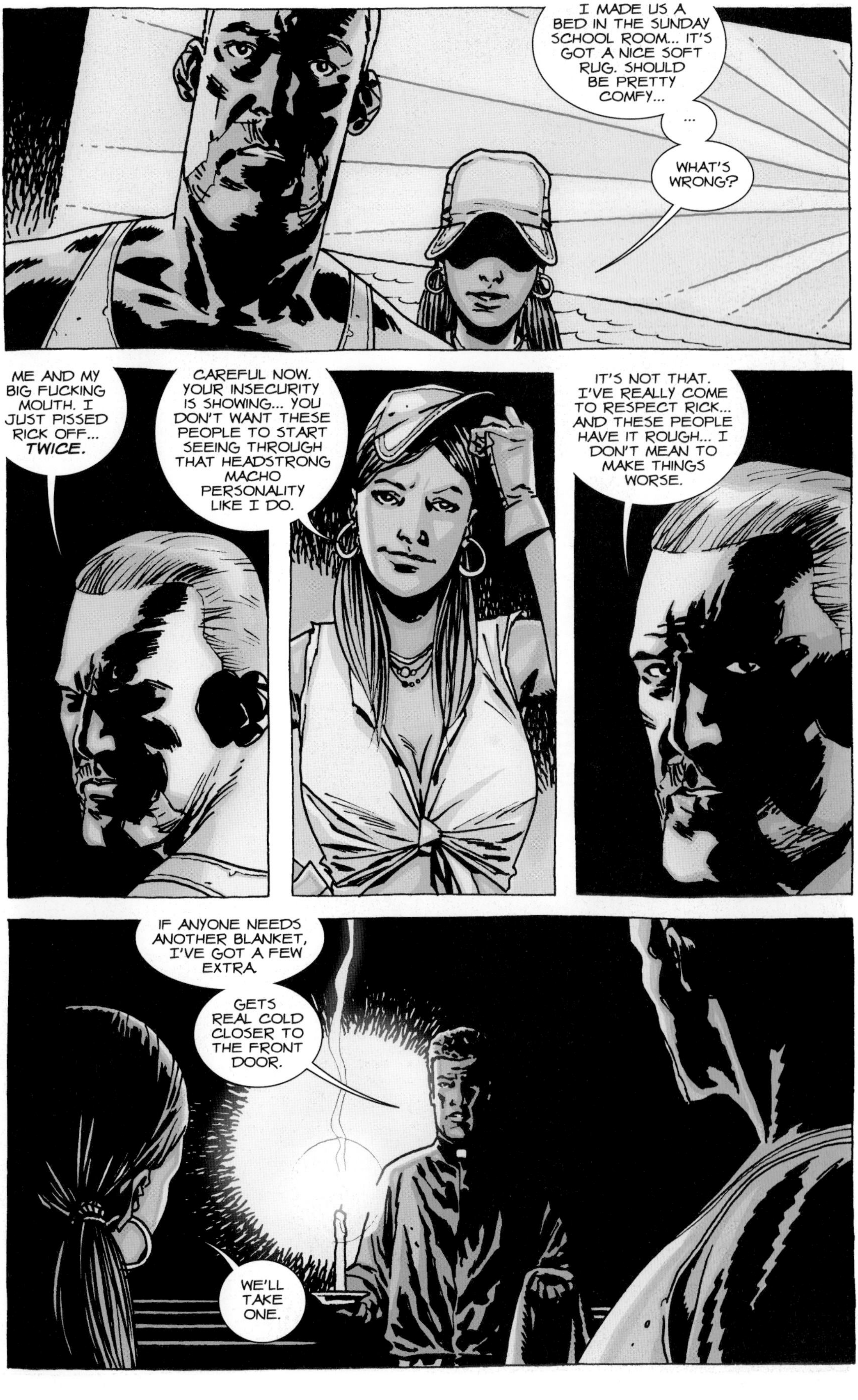
I MADE US A BED IN THE SUNDAY SCHOOL ROOM... IT'S GOT A NICE SOFT RUG. SHOULD BE PRETTY COMFY...
...
WHAT'S WRONG?
ME AND MY BIG FUCKING MOUTH. I JUST PISSED RICK OFF... *TWICE.*
CAREFUL NOW. YOUR INSECURITY IS SHOWING... YOU DON'T WANT THESE PEOPLE TO START SEEING THROUGH THAT HEADSTRONG MACHO PERSONALITY LIKE I DO.
IT'S NOT THAT. I'VE REALLY COME TO RESPECT RICK... AND THESE PEOPLE HAVE IT ROUGH... I DON'T MEAN TO MAKE THINGS WORSE.
IF ANYONE NEEDS ANOTHER BLANKET, I'VE GOT A FEW EXTRA
GETS REAL COLD CLOSER TO THE FRONT DOOR.
WE'LL TAKE ONE.

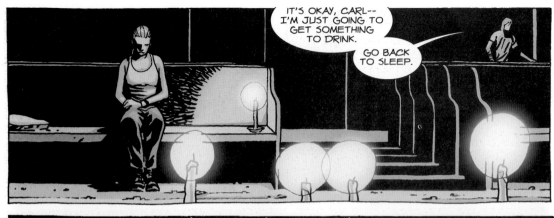

IT'S OKAY, CARL-- I'M JUST GOING TO GET SOMETHING TO DRINK.

GO BACK TO SLEEP.

I'M SORRY, ANDREA.

I REALLY AM.

I CAN'T STOP THINKING ABOUT HIM, RICK.

THAT'S UNDERSTANDABLE. THERE'S NOTHING **WRONG** WITH THAT, ANDREA.

NO, YOU DON'T UNDERSTAND...

AT FIRST, IT WASN'T ANYTHING SERIOUS. AMY AND I WERE TAKING ADVANTAGE, FRANKLY. FLIRT WITH THE OLD MAN, GET TO SLEEP IN THE BIG SAFE RV.

IT WAS A SURVIVAL THING. NEITHER OF US WERE ACTUALLY ATTRACTED TO HIM.

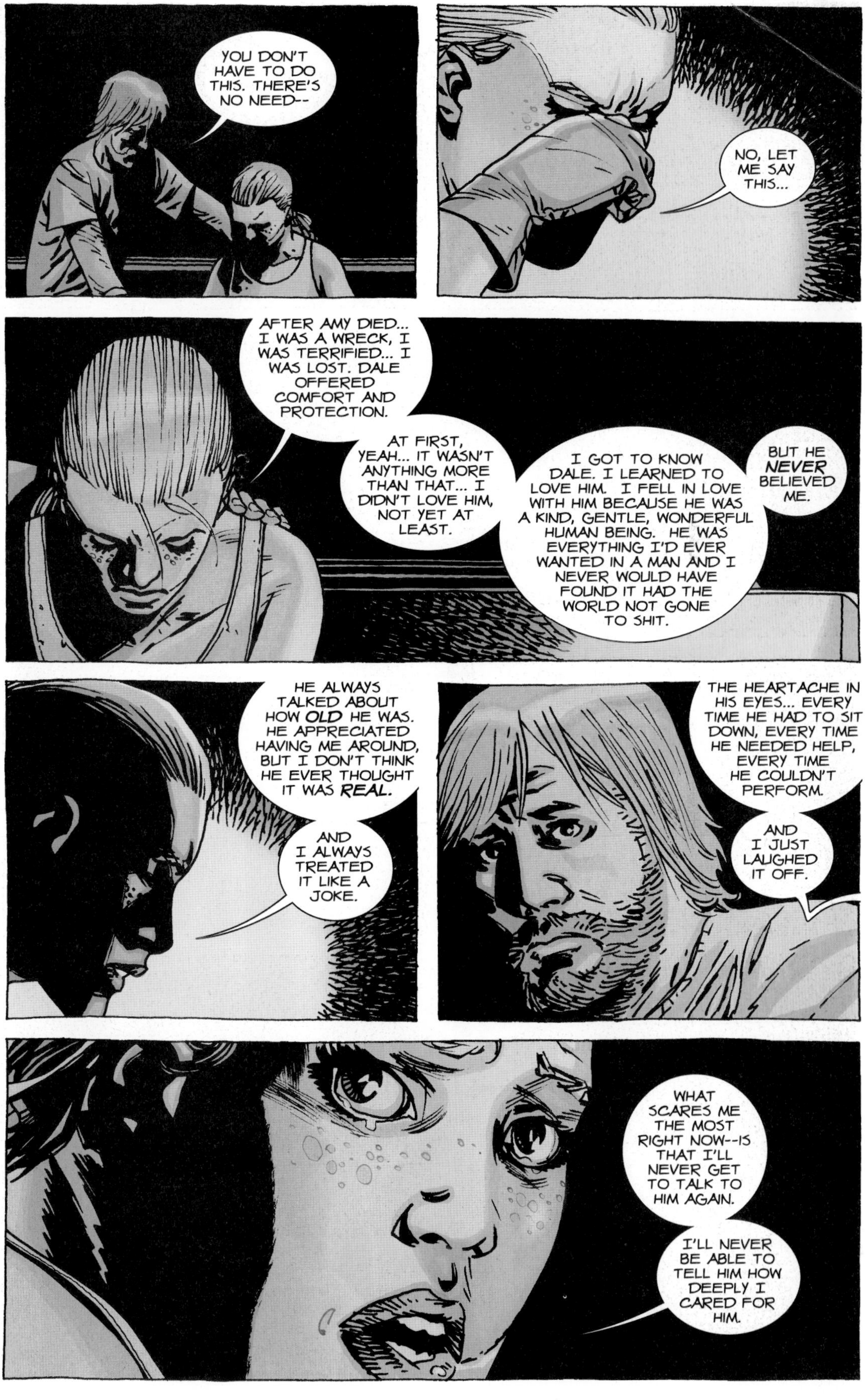

YOU DON'T HAVE TO DO THIS. THERE'S NO NEED--
NO, LET ME SAY THIS...
AFTER AMY DIED... I WAS A WRECK, I WAS TERRIFIED... I WAS LOST. DALE OFFERED COMFORT AND PROTECTION.
AT FIRST, YEAH... IT WASN'T ANYTHING MORE THAN THAT... I DIDN'T LOVE HIM, NOT YET AT LEAST.
I GOT TO KNOW DALE. I LEARNED TO LOVE HIM. I FELL IN LOVE WITH HIM BECAUSE HE WAS A KIND, GENTLE, WONDERFUL HUMAN BEING. HE WAS EVERYTHING I'D EVER WANTED IN A MAN AND I NEVER WOULD HAVE FOUND IT HAD THE WORLD NOT GONE TO SHIT.
BUT HE NEVER BELIEVED ME.
HE ALWAYS TALKED ABOUT HOW OLD HE WAS. HE APPRECIATED HAVING ME AROUND, BUT I DON'T THINK HE EVER THOUGHT IT WAS REAL.
AND I ALWAYS TREATED IT LIKE A JOKE.
THE HEARTACHE IN HIS EYES... EVERY TIME HE HAD TO SIT DOWN, EVERY TIME HE NEEDED HELP, EVERY TIME HE COULDN'T PERFORM.
AND I JUST LAUGHED IT OFF.
WHAT SCARES ME THE MOST RIGHT NOW--IS THAT I'LL NEVER GET TO TALK TO HIM AGAIN.
I'LL NEVER BE ABLE TO TELL HIM HOW DEEPLY I CARED FOR HIM.

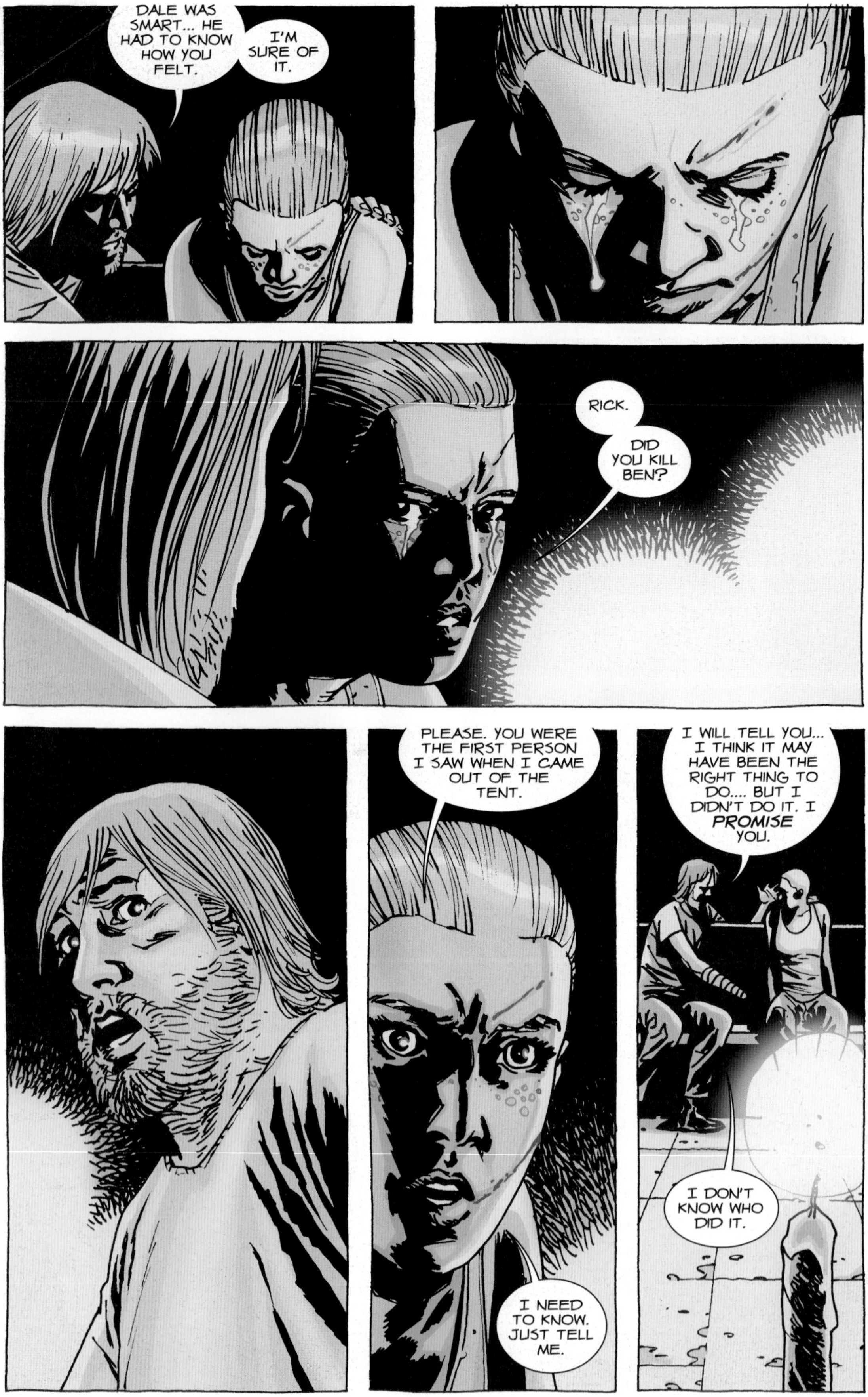
DALE WAS SMART... HE HAD TO KNOW HOW YOU FELT.
I'M SURE OF IT.
RICK.
DID YOU KILL BEN?
PLEASE. YOU WERE THE FIRST PERSON I SAW WHEN I CAME OUT OF THE TENT.
I NEED TO KNOW. JUST TELL ME.
I WILL TELL YOU... I THINK IT MAY HAVE BEEN THE RIGHT THING TO DO.... BUT I DIDN'T DO IT. I PROMISE YOU.
I DON'T KNOW WHO DID IT.

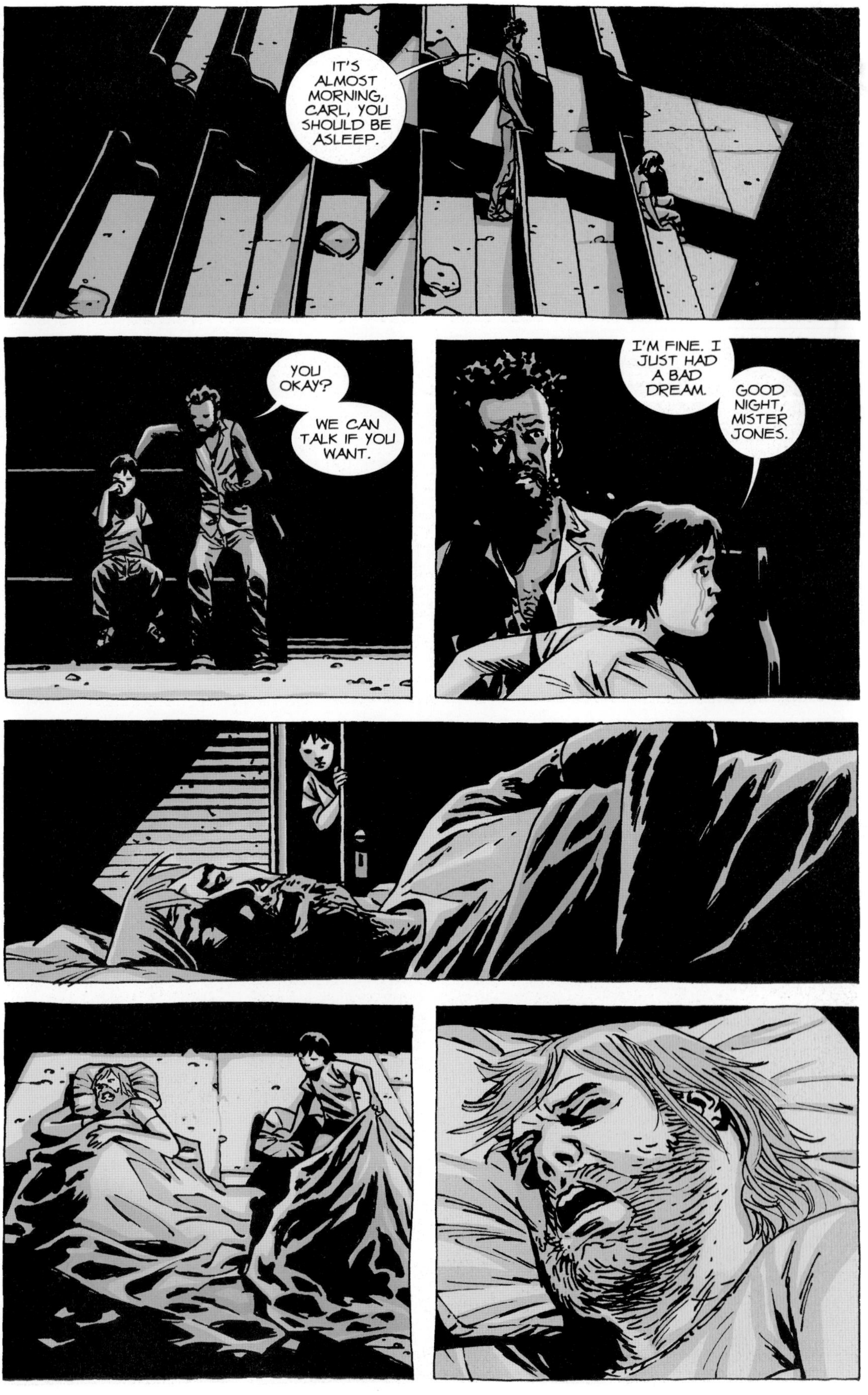
IT'S ALMOST MORNING, CARL, YOU SHOULD BE ASLEEP.
YOU OKAY?
WE CAN TALK IF YOU WANT.
I'M FINE. I JUST HAD A BAD DREAM.
GOOD NIGHT, MISTER JONES.

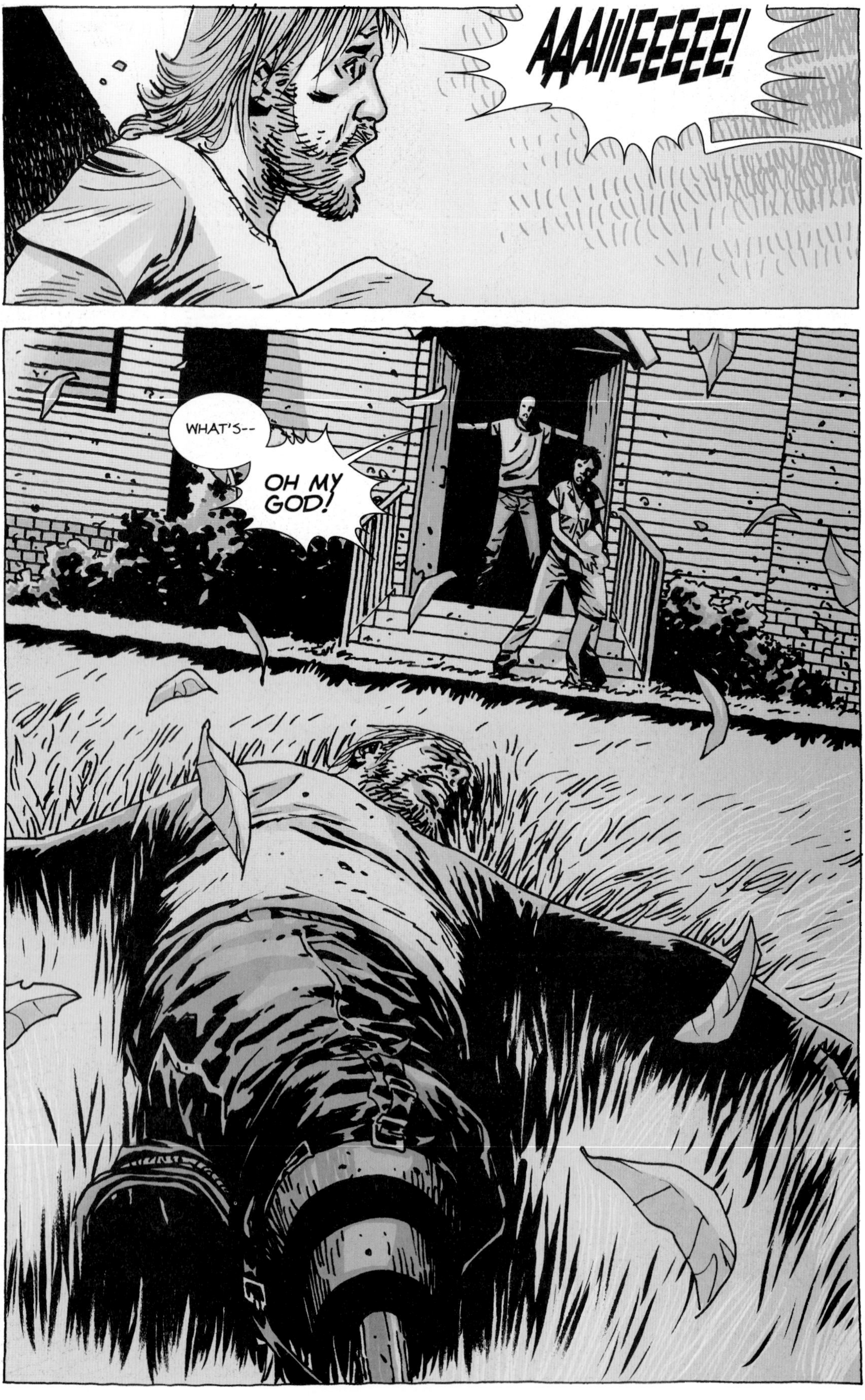
AAAIIIIEEEEEE!
WHAT'S--
OH MY GOD!

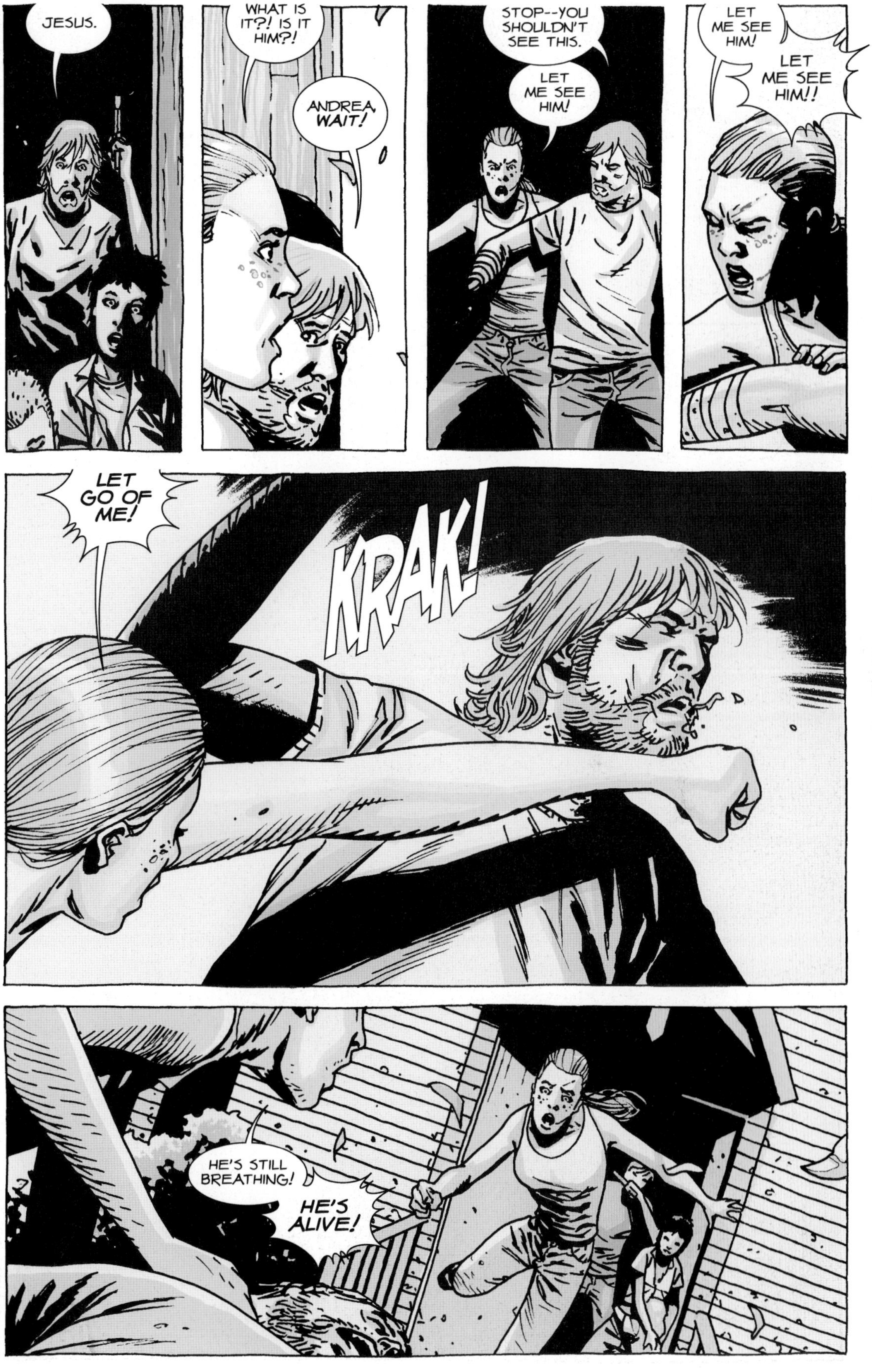

JESUS.
WHAT IS IT?! IS IT HIM?!
ANDREA, WAIT!
STOP--YOU SHOULDN'T SEE THIS.
LET ME SEE HIM!
LET ME SEE HIM!
LET ME SEE HIM!!
LET GO OF ME!
KRAK!
HE'S STILL BREATHING!
HE'S ALIVE!

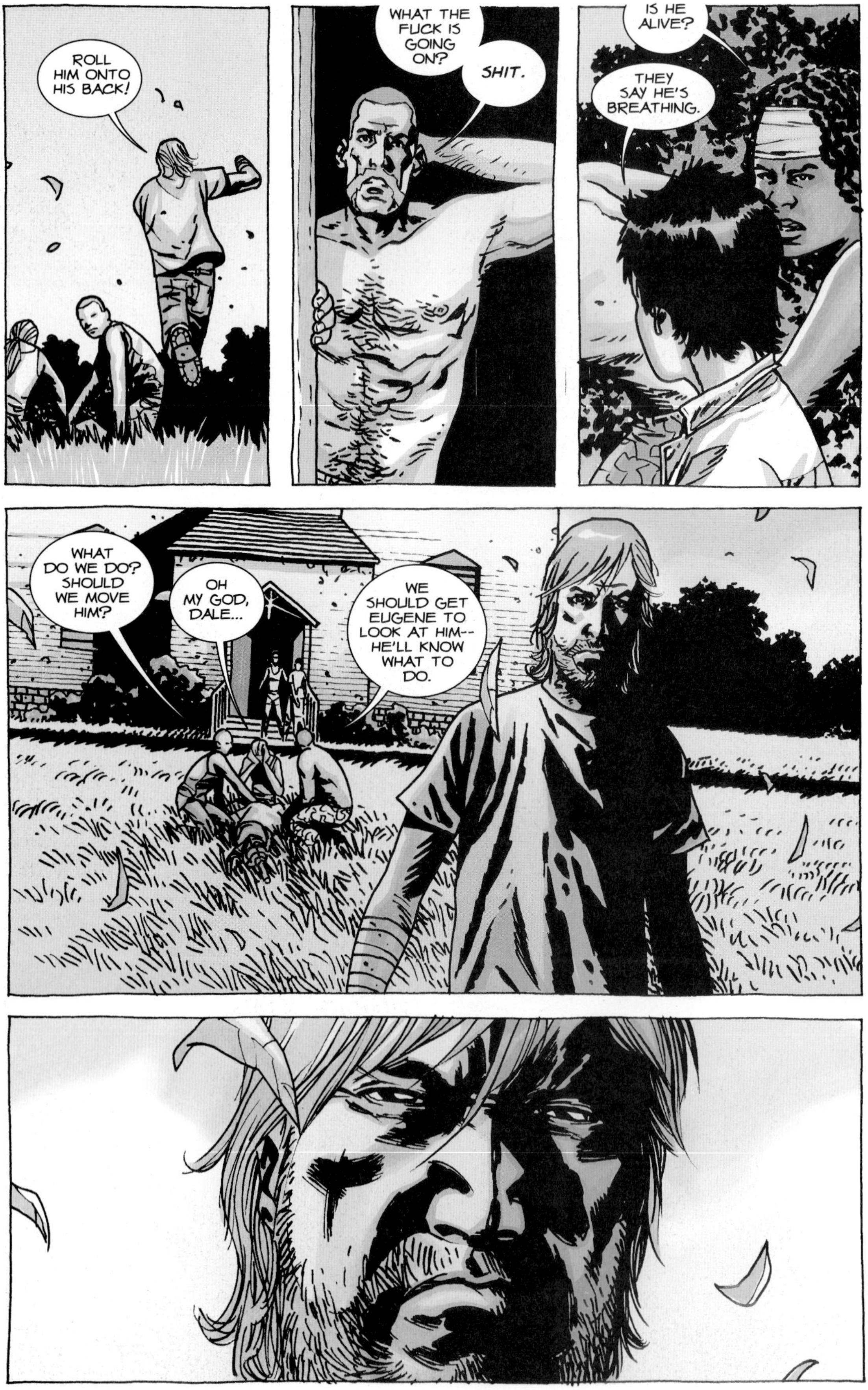
ROLL HIM ONTO HIS BACK!
WHAT THE FUCK IS GOING ON?
SHIT.
IS HE ALIVE?
THEY SAY HE'S BREATHING.
WHAT DO WE DO? SHOULD WE MOVE HIM?
OH MY GOD, DALE...
WE SHOULD GET EUGENE TO LOOK AT HIM-- HE'LL KNOW WHAT TO DO.

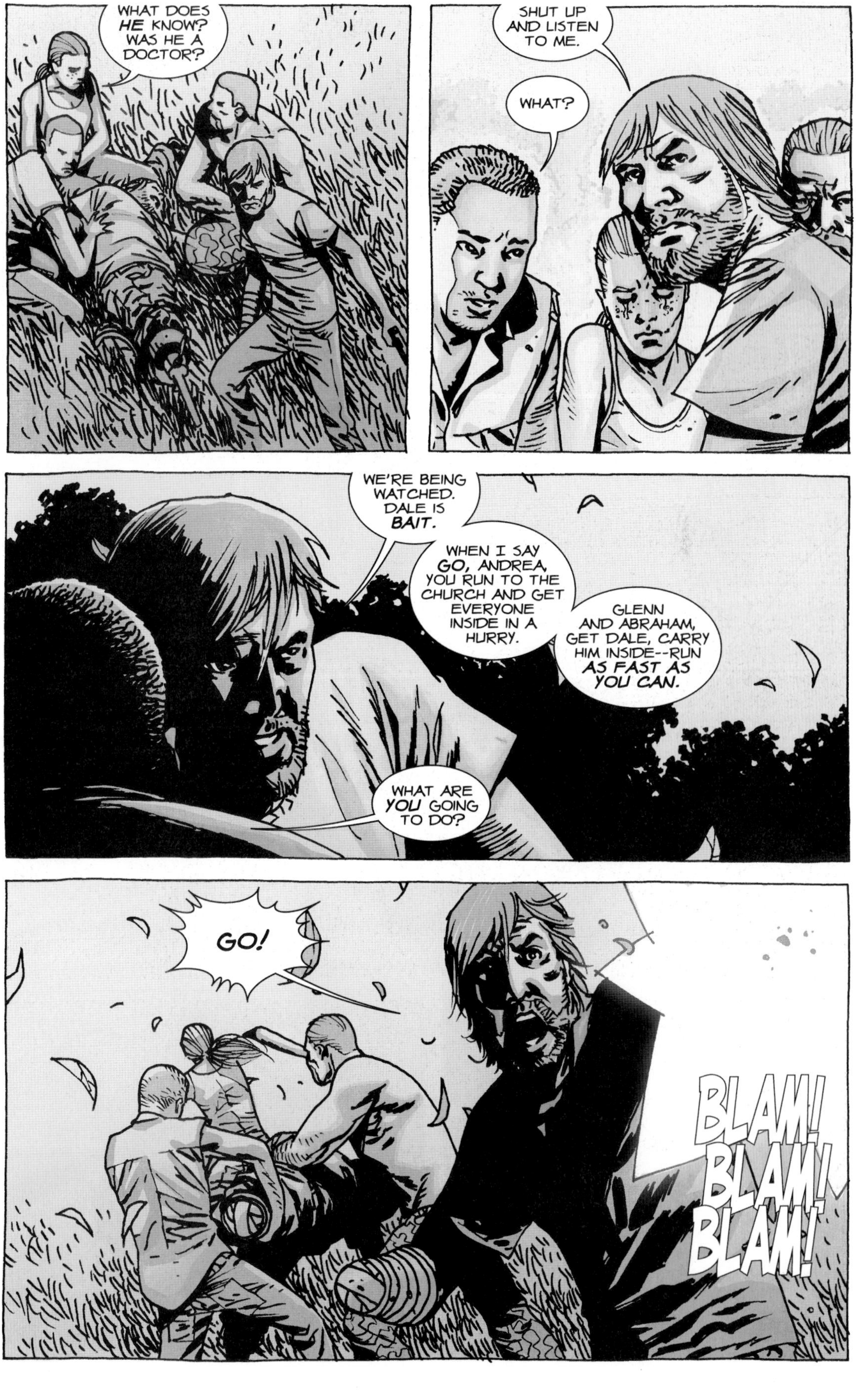

WHAT DOES HE KNOW? WAS HE A DOCTOR?
SHUT UP AND LISTEN TO ME.
WHAT?
WE'RE BEING WATCHED. DALE IS BAIT.
WHEN I SAY GO, ANDREA, YOU RUN TO THE CHURCH AND GET EVERYONE INSIDE IN A HURRY.
GLENN AND ABRAHAM, GET DALE, CARRY HIM INSIDE--RUN AS FAST AS YOU CAN.
WHAT ARE YOU GOING TO DO?
GO!
BLAM! BLAM! BLAM!

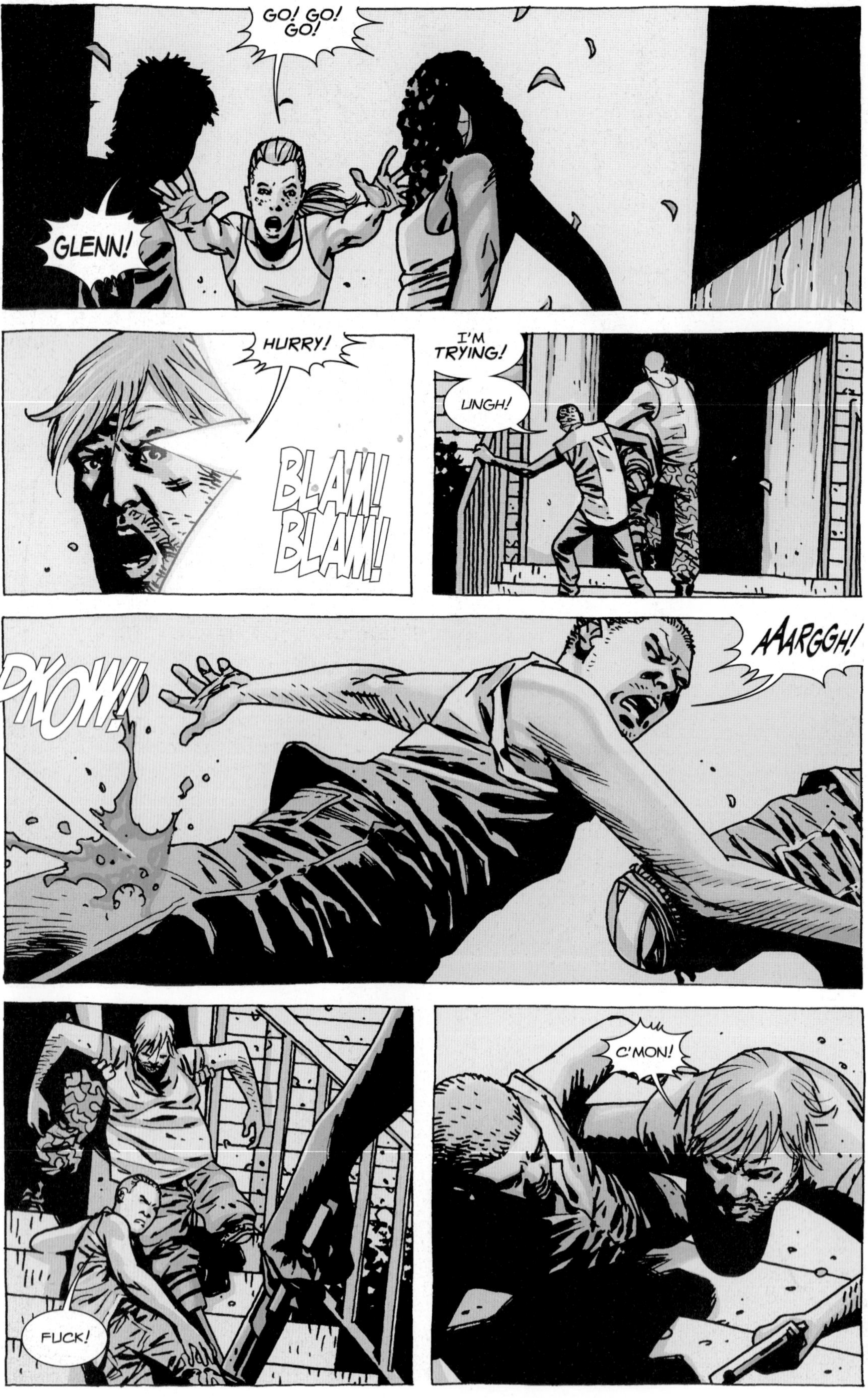
GO! GO! GO!
GLENN!
HURRY!
BLAM! BLAM!
I'M TRYING!
UNGH!
PKOW!
AAARGGH!
FUCK!
C'MON!

SHUT THE DOORS! LOCK THEM!

UNG.

EVERYONE GET DOWN. STAY AWAY FROM THE WINDOWS.

THEY'RE STILL OUT THERE!

EUGENE--CLEAN UP GLENN'S LEG AND THEN CHECK OUT DALE. EVERYONE--CLOSE THE WINDOWS AND STAY AWAY--BUT WE DON'T NEED TO BE HUGGING THE FLOOR.

ABRAHAM-- WHAT ARE YOU DOING?!

THEY ONLY FIRED ONE SHOT, RICK.

WHAT DO YOU MEAN?

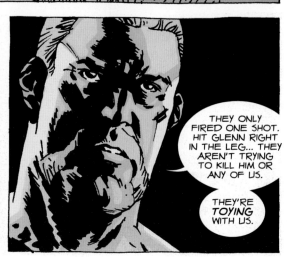

THEY ONLY FIRED ONE SHOT. HIT GLENN RIGHT IN THE LEG... THEY AREN'T TRYING TO KILL HIM OR ANY OF US.

THEY'RE TOYING WITH US.

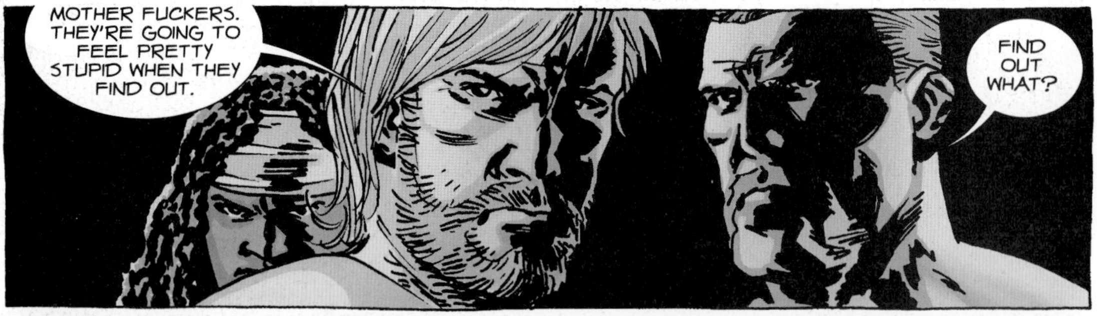
MOTHER FUCKERS. THEY'RE GOING TO FEEL PRETTY STUPID WHEN THEY FIND OUT.
FIND OUT WHAT?

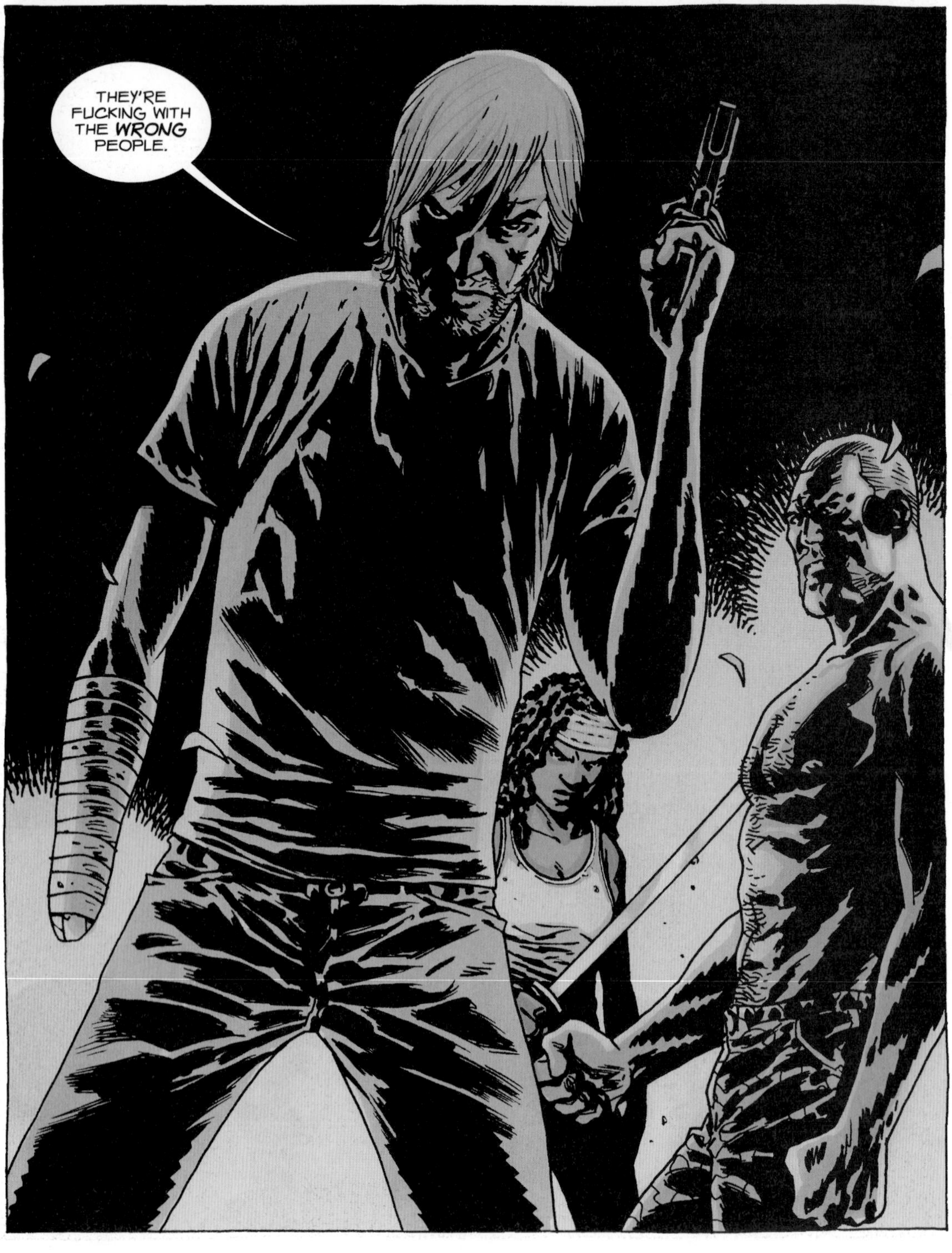
THEY'RE FUCKING WITH THE **WRONG** PEOPLE.

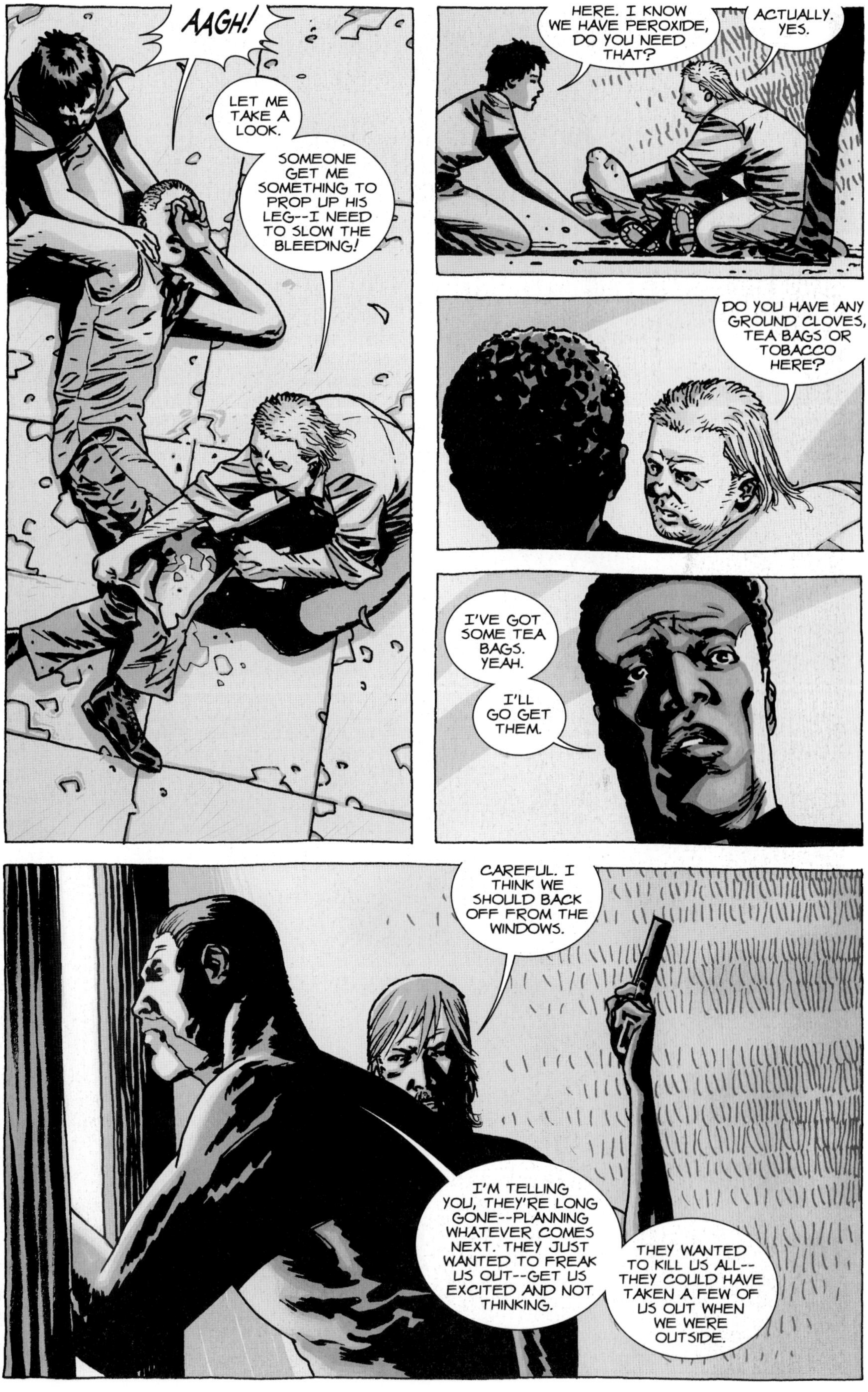
AAGH!
LET ME TAKE A LOOK.
SOMEONE GET ME SOMETHING TO PROP UP HIS LEG--I NEED TO SLOW THE BLEEDING!
HERE. I KNOW WE HAVE PEROXIDE, DO YOU NEED THAT?
ACTUALLY. YES.
DO YOU HAVE ANY GROUND CLOVES, TEA BAGS OR TOBACCO HERE?
I'VE GOT SOME TEA BAGS. YEAH.
I'LL GO GET THEM.
CAREFUL. I THINK WE SHOULD BACK OFF FROM THE WINDOWS.
I'M TELLING YOU, THEY'RE LONG GONE--PLANNING WHATEVER COMES NEXT. THEY JUST WANTED TO FREAK US OUT--GET US EXCITED AND NOT THINKING.
THEY WANTED TO KILL US ALL--THEY COULD HAVE TAKEN A FEW OF US OUT WHEN WE WERE OUTSIDE.

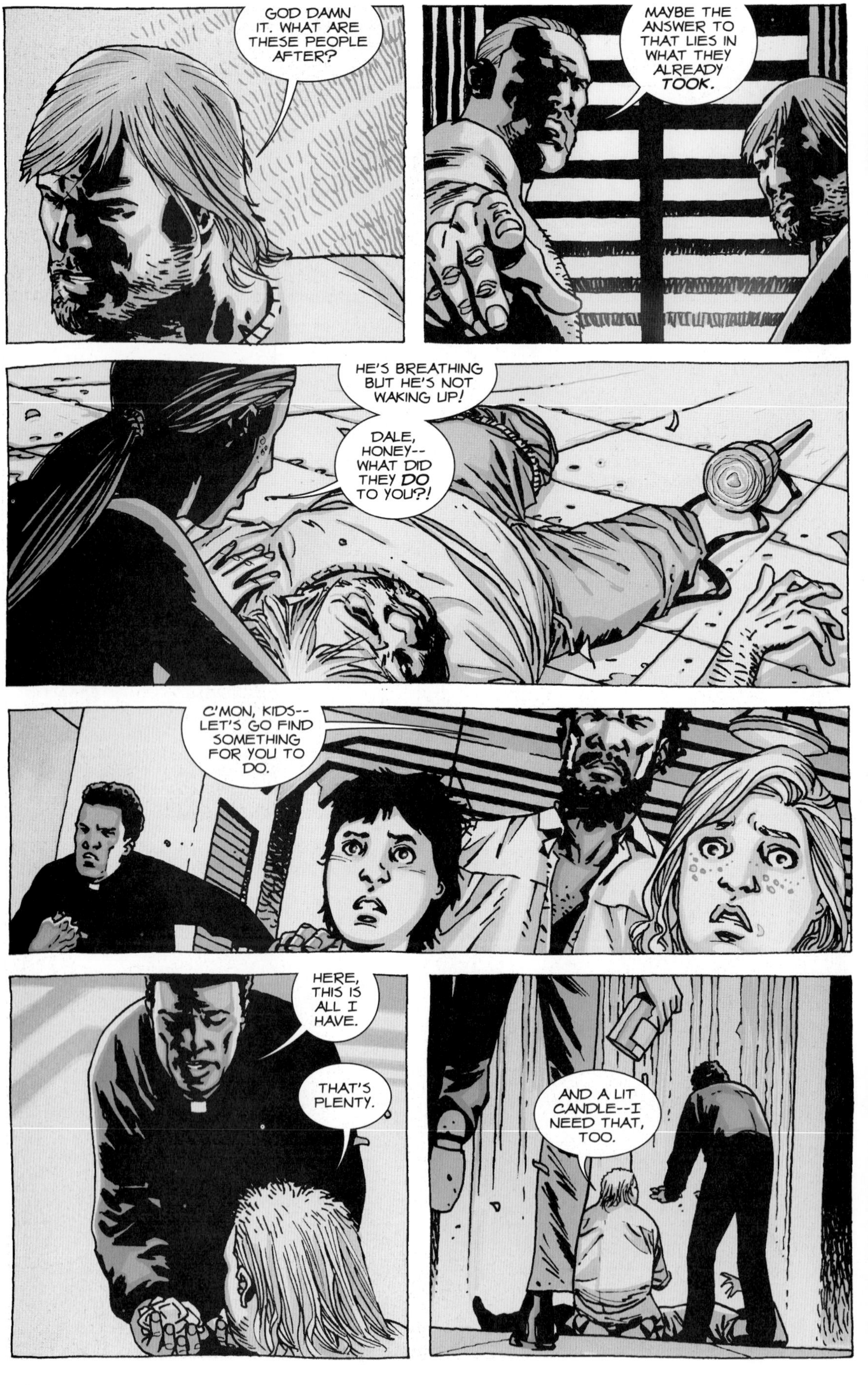

GOD DAMN IT. WHAT ARE THESE PEOPLE AFTER?
MAYBE THE ANSWER TO THAT LIES IN WHAT THEY ALREADY TOOK.
HE'S BREATHING BUT HE'S NOT WAKING UP!
DALE, HONEY-- WHAT DID THEY DO TO YOU?!
C'MON, KIDS-- LET'S GO FIND SOMETHING FOR YOU TO DO.
HERE, THIS IS ALL I HAVE.
THAT'S PLENTY.
AND A LIT CANDLE--I NEED THAT, TOO.

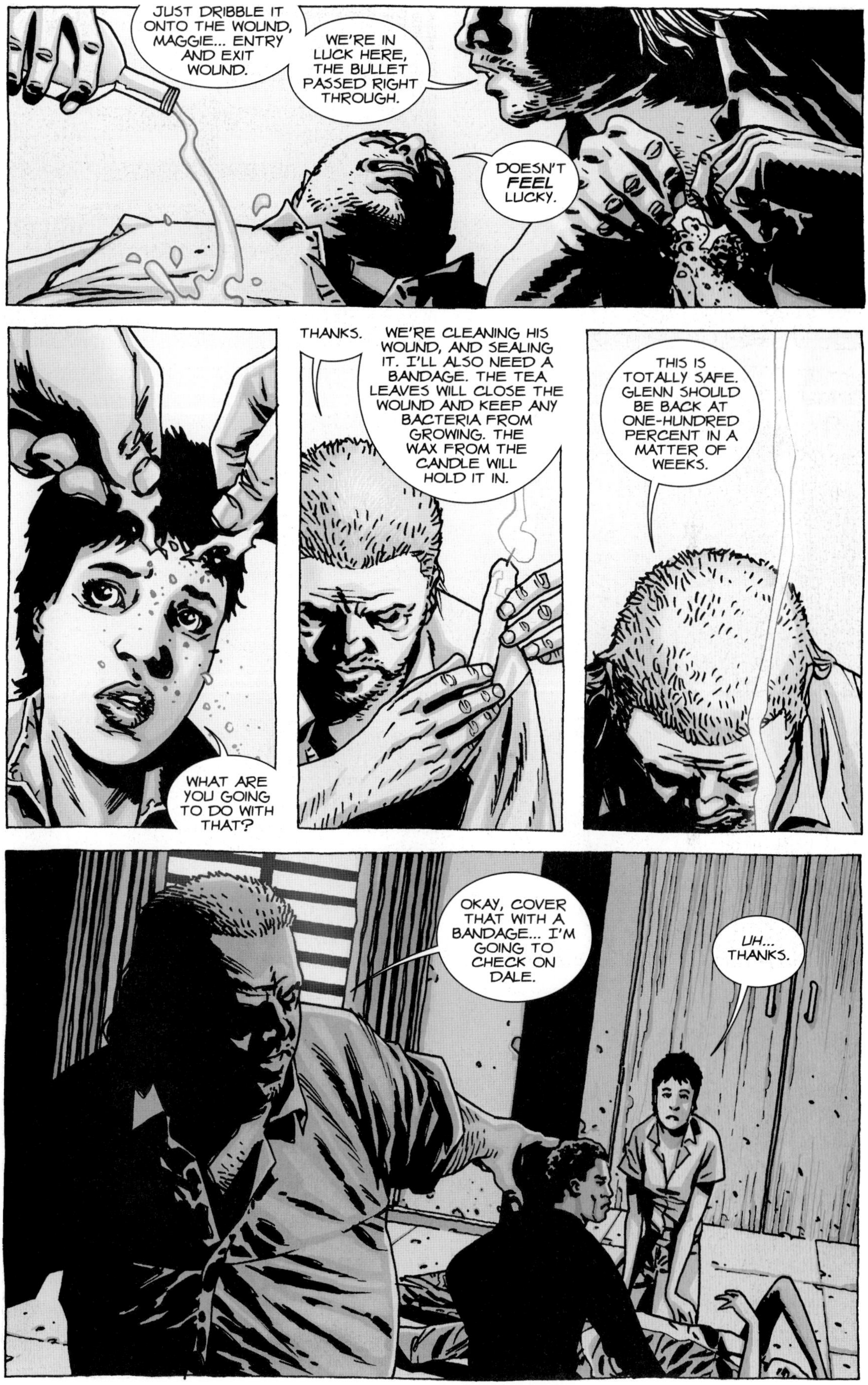

JUST DRIBBLE IT ONTO THE WOUND, MAGGIE... ENTRY AND EXIT WOUND.
WE'RE IN LUCK HERE, THE BULLET PASSED RIGHT THROUGH.
DOESN'T *FEEL* LUCKY.
WHAT ARE YOU GOING TO DO WITH THAT?
THANKS.
WE'RE CLEANING HIS WOUND, AND SEALING IT. I'LL ALSO NEED A BANDAGE. THE TEA LEAVES WILL CLOSE THE WOUND AND KEEP ANY BACTERIA FROM GROWING. THE WAX FROM THE CANDLE WILL HOLD IT IN.
THIS IS TOTALLY SAFE. GLENN SHOULD BE BACK AT ONE-HUNDRED PERCENT IN A MATTER OF WEEKS.
OKAY, COVER THAT WITH A BANDAGE... I'M GOING TO CHECK ON DALE.
UH... THANKS.

ANDREA? HOW DID I GET BACK--?

YOU WERE *BROUGHT* HERE.

YOU HAVE TO TELL RICK TO GET EVERYONE OUT OF HERE.

THESE ARE DANGEROUS PEOPLE WE'RE DEALING WITH. YOU HAVE NO IDEA WHAT THEY'RE CAPABLE OF.

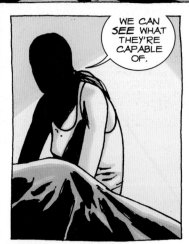

WE CAN *SEE* WHAT THEY'RE CAPABLE OF.

WHY DIDN'T YOU *TELL* ME YOU'D BEEN BITTEN?

...

I'M SORRY, ANDREA. I AM. I NEVER EXPECTED TO HAVE TO SEE YOU AGAIN, NOT LIKE *THIS*.

I SAW MY WIFE BITTEN, I DIDN'T EXACTLY KNOW WHAT WAS HAPPENING... BUT I WATCHED HER GET SICK. I SAW HER WASTE AWAY TO NOTHING AND DIE.

THIS IS AN UGLY PROCESS... I DIDN'T WANT YOU TO HAVE TO SEE THAT.

I WANTED TO SPARE YOU THAT MISERY.

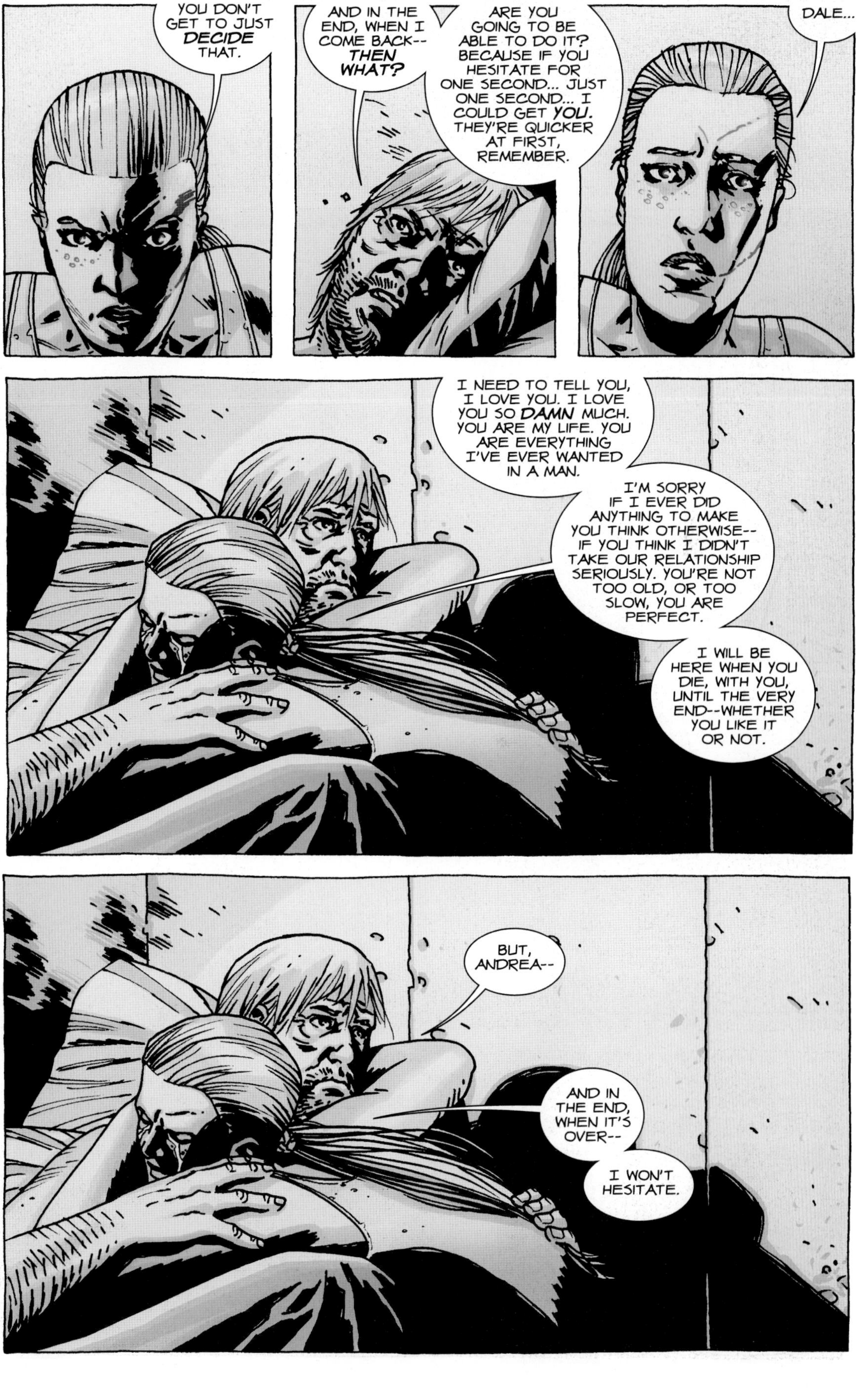

YOU DON'T GET TO JUST DECIDE THAT.
AND IN THE END, WHEN I COME BACK-- THEN WHAT?
ARE YOU GOING TO BE ABLE TO DO IT? BECAUSE IF YOU HESITATE FOR ONE SECOND... JUST ONE SECOND... I COULD GET YOU. THEY'RE QUICKER AT FIRST, REMEMBER.
DALE...
I NEED TO TELL YOU, I LOVE YOU. I LOVE YOU SO DAMN MUCH. YOU ARE MY LIFE. YOU ARE EVERYTHING I'VE EVER WANTED IN A MAN.
I'M SORRY IF I EVER DID ANYTHING TO MAKE YOU THINK OTHERWISE-- IF YOU THINK I DIDN'T TAKE OUR RELATIONSHIP SERIOUSLY. YOU'RE NOT TOO OLD, OR TOO SLOW, YOU ARE PERFECT.
I WILL BE HERE WHEN YOU DIE, WITH YOU, UNTIL THE VERY END--WHETHER YOU LIKE IT OR NOT.
BUT, ANDREA--
AND IN THE END, WHEN IT'S OVER--
I WON'T HESITATE.

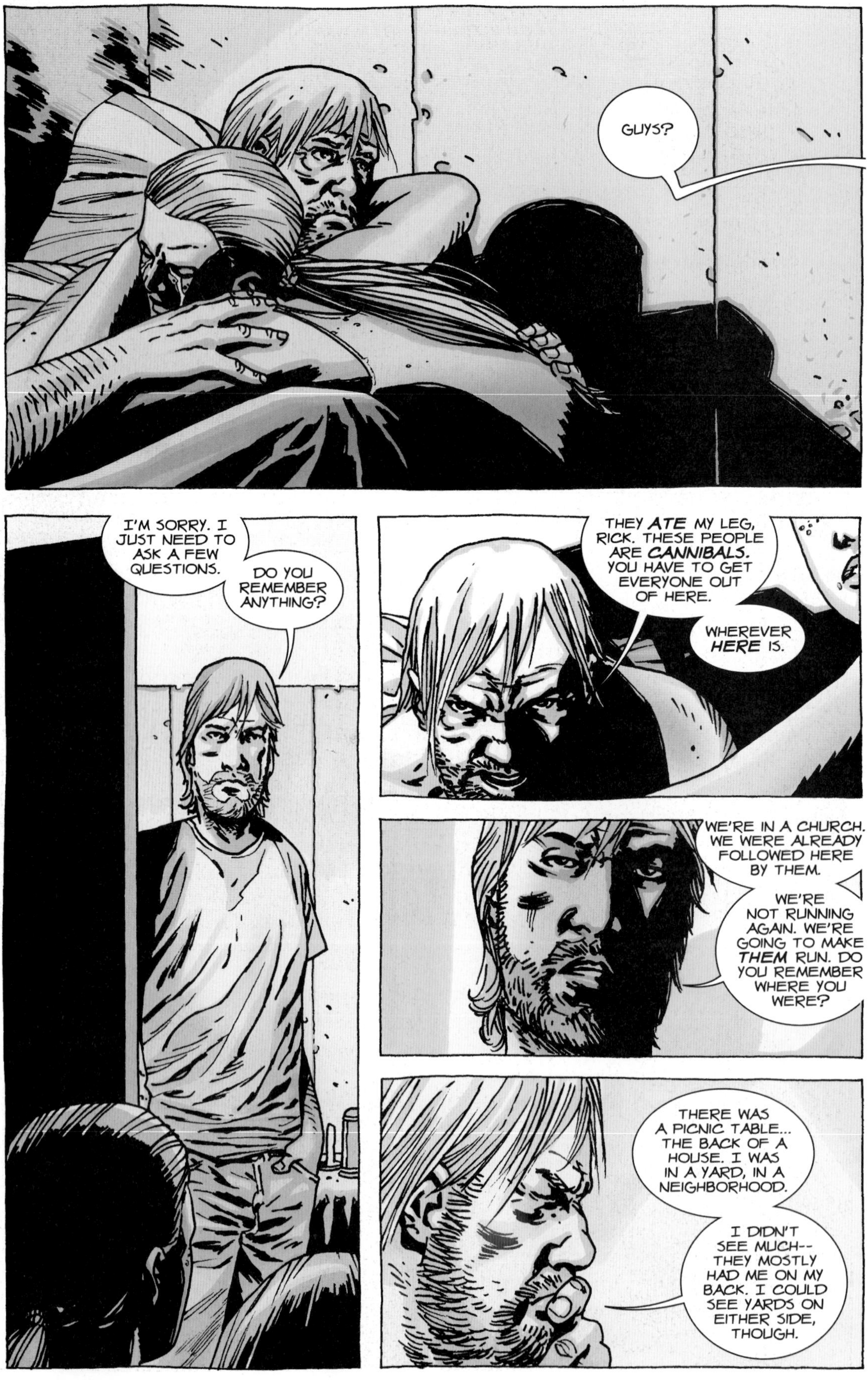
GUYS?
I'M SORRY. I JUST NEED TO ASK A FEW QUESTIONS.
DO YOU REMEMBER ANYTHING?
THEY ATE MY LEG, RICK. THESE PEOPLE ARE CANNIBALS. YOU HAVE TO GET EVERYONE OUT OF HERE.
WHEREVER HERE IS.
WE'RE IN A CHURCH. WE WERE ALREADY FOLLOWED HERE BY THEM.
WE'RE NOT RUNNING AGAIN. WE'RE GOING TO MAKE THEM RUN. DO YOU REMEMBER WHERE YOU WERE?
THERE WAS A PICNIC TABLE... THE BACK OF A HOUSE. I WAS IN A YARD, IN A NEIGHBORHOOD.
I DIDN'T SEE MUCH-- THEY MOSTLY HAD ME ON MY BACK. I COULD SEE YARDS ON EITHER SIDE, THOUGH.

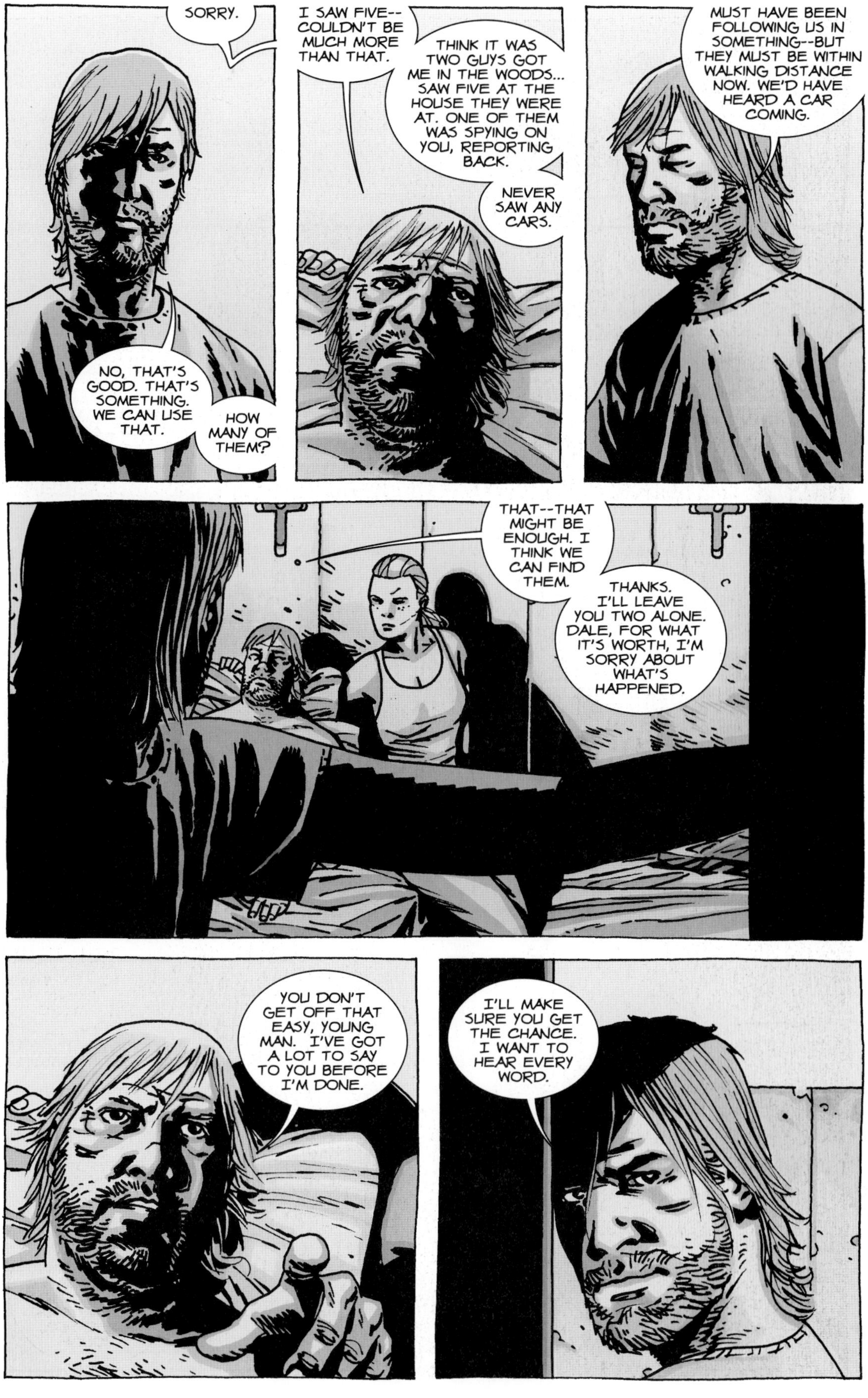
SORRY.
NO, THAT'S GOOD. THAT'S SOMETHING. WE CAN USE THAT.
HOW MANY OF THEM?
I SAW FIVE-- COULDN'T BE MUCH MORE THAN THAT.
THINK IT WAS TWO GUYS GOT ME IN THE WOODS... SAW FIVE AT THE HOUSE THEY WERE AT. ONE OF THEM WAS SPYING ON YOU, REPORTING BACK.
NEVER SAW ANY CARS.
MUST HAVE BEEN FOLLOWING US IN SOMETHING--BUT THEY MUST BE WITHIN WALKING DISTANCE NOW. WE'D HAVE HEARD A CAR COMING.
THAT--THAT MIGHT BE ENOUGH. I THINK WE CAN FIND THEM.
THANKS. I'LL LEAVE YOU TWO ALONE. DALE, FOR WHAT IT'S WORTH, I'M SORRY ABOUT WHAT'S HAPPENED.
YOU DON'T GET OFF THAT EASY, YOUNG MAN. I'VE GOT A LOT TO SAY TO YOU BEFORE I'M DONE.
I'LL MAKE SURE YOU GET THE CHANCE. I WANT TO HEAR EVERY WORD.

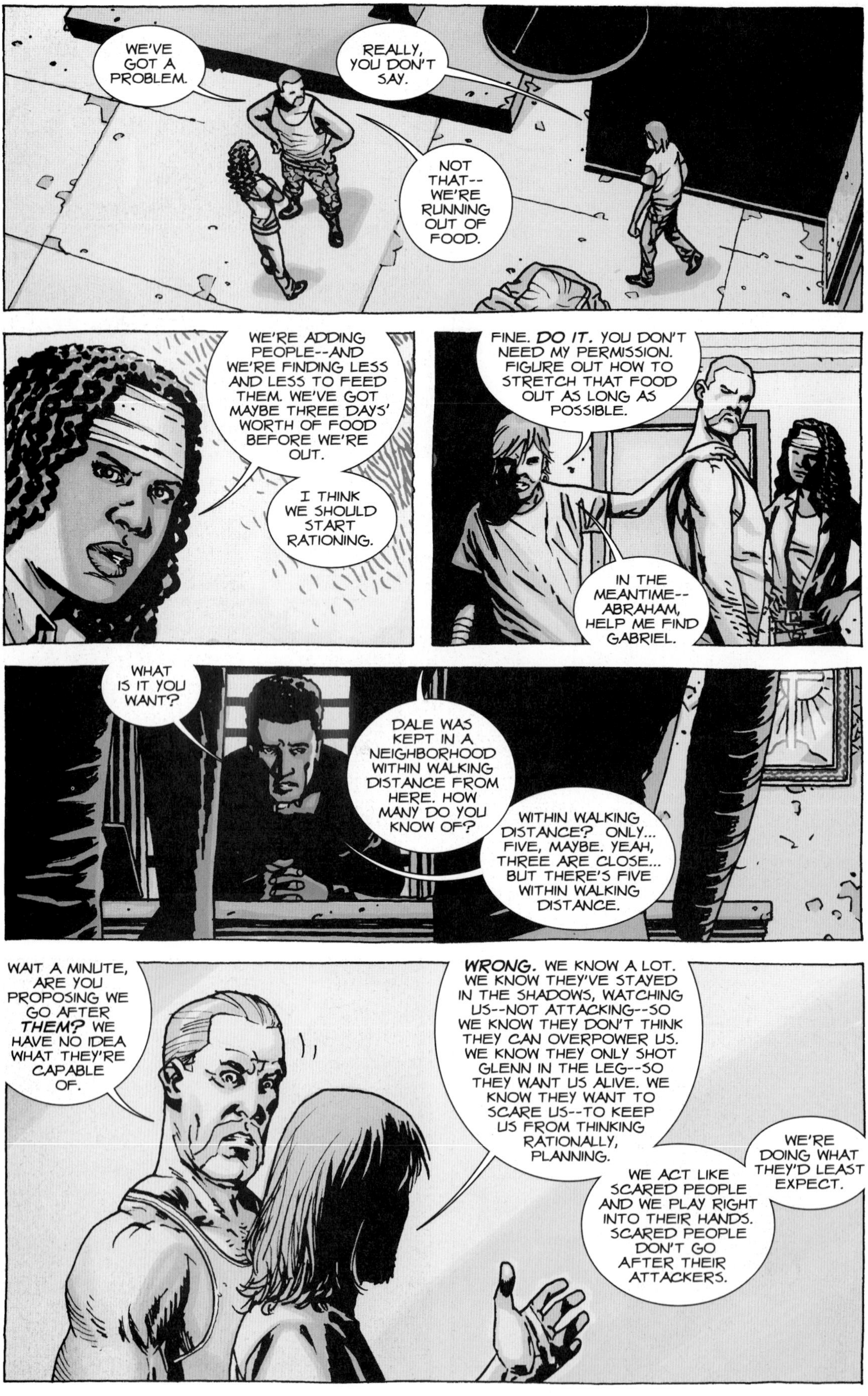

WE'VE GOT A PROBLEM.
REALLY, YOU DON'T SAY.
NOT THAT-- WE'RE RUNNING OUT OF FOOD.
WE'RE ADDING PEOPLE--AND WE'RE FINDING LESS AND LESS TO FEED THEM. WE'VE GOT MAYBE THREE DAYS' WORTH OF FOOD BEFORE WE'RE OUT.
I THINK WE SHOULD START RATIONING.
FINE. DO IT. YOU DON'T NEED MY PERMISSION. FIGURE OUT HOW TO STRETCH THAT FOOD OUT AS LONG AS POSSIBLE.
IN THE MEANTIME-- ABRAHAM, HELP ME FIND GABRIEL.
WHAT IS IT YOU WANT?
DALE WAS KEPT IN A NEIGHBORHOOD WITHIN WALKING DISTANCE FROM HERE. HOW MANY DO YOU KNOW OF?
WITHIN WALKING DISTANCE? ONLY... FIVE, MAYBE. YEAH, THREE ARE CLOSE... BUT THERE'S FIVE WITHIN WALKING DISTANCE.
WAIT A MINUTE, ARE YOU PROPOSING WE GO AFTER THEM? WE HAVE NO IDEA WHAT THEY'RE CAPABLE OF.
WRONG. WE KNOW A LOT. WE KNOW THEY'VE STAYED IN THE SHADOWS, WATCHING US--NOT ATTACKING--SO WE KNOW THEY DON'T THINK THEY CAN OVERPOWER US. WE KNOW THEY ONLY SHOT GLENN IN THE LEG--SO THEY WANT US ALIVE. WE KNOW THEY WANT TO SCARE US--TO KEEP US FROM THINKING RATIONALLY, PLANNING.
WE ACT LIKE SCARED PEOPLE AND WE PLAY RIGHT INTO THEIR HANDS. SCARED PEOPLE DON'T GO AFTER THEIR ATTACKERS.
WE'RE DOING WHAT THEY'D LEAST EXPECT.

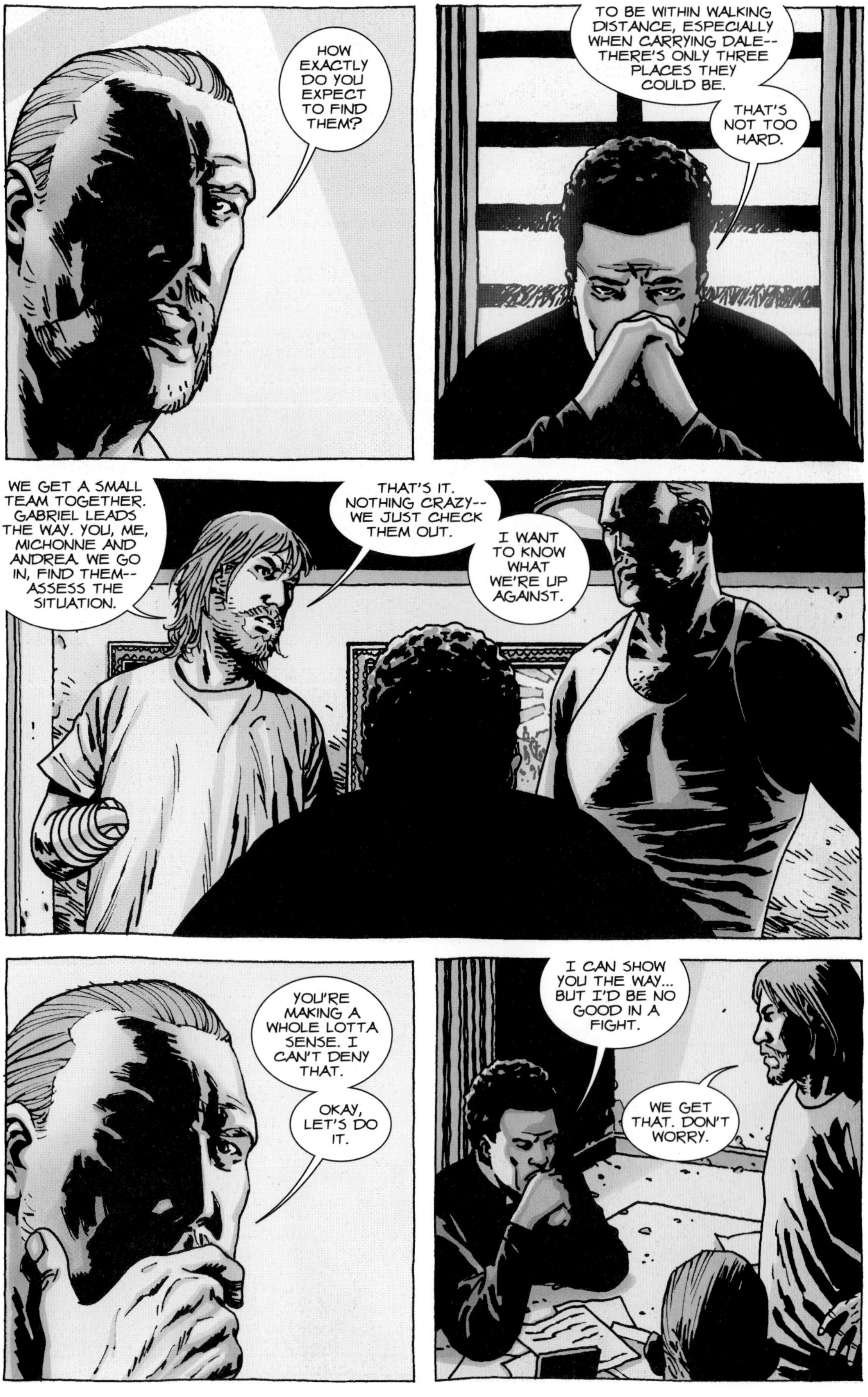

HOW EXACTLY DO YOU EXPECT TO FIND THEM?
TO BE WITHIN WALKING DISTANCE, ESPECIALLY WHEN CARRYING DALE-- THERE'S ONLY THREE PLACES THEY COULD BE.
THAT'S NOT TOO HARD.
WE GET A SMALL TEAM TOGETHER. GABRIEL LEADS THE WAY. YOU, ME, MICHONNE AND ANDREA WE GO IN, FIND THEM-- ASSESS THE SITUATION.
THAT'S IT. NOTHING CRAZY-- WE JUST CHECK THEM OUT.
I WANT TO KNOW WHAT WE'RE UP AGAINST.
YOU'RE MAKING A WHOLE LOTTA SENSE. I CAN'T DENY THAT.
OKAY, LET'S DO IT.
I CAN SHOW YOU THE WAY... BUT I'D BE NO GOOD IN A FIGHT.
WE GET THAT. DON'T WORRY.

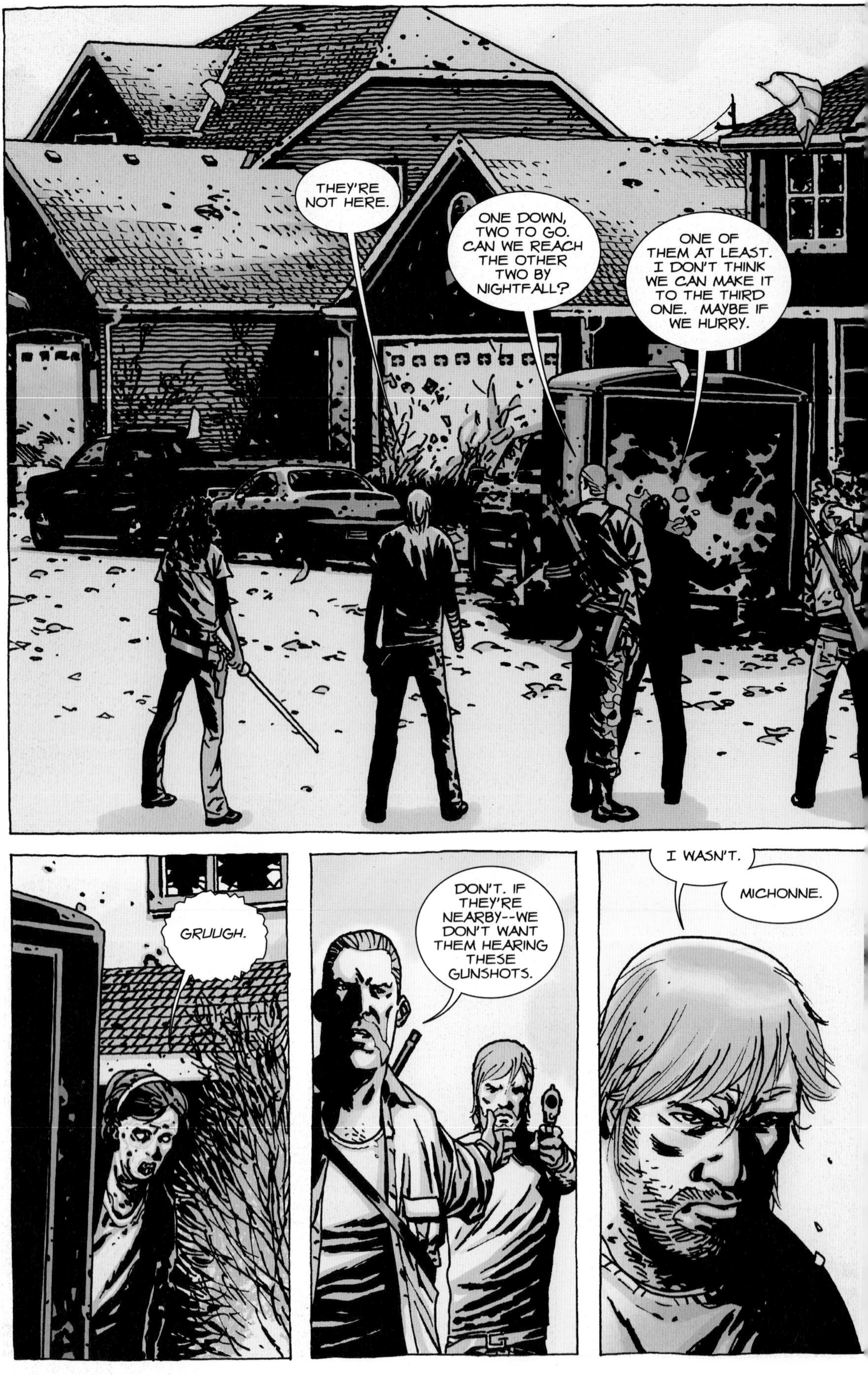

THEY'RE NOT HERE.
ONE DOWN, TWO TO GO. CAN WE REACH THE OTHER TWO BY NIGHTFALL?
ONE OF THEM AT LEAST. I DON'T THINK WE CAN MAKE IT TO THE THIRD ONE. MAYBE IF WE HURRY.
GRUUGH.
DON'T. IF THEY'RE NEARBY--WE DON'T WANT THEM HEARING THESE GUNSHOTS.
I WASN'T.
MICHONNE.

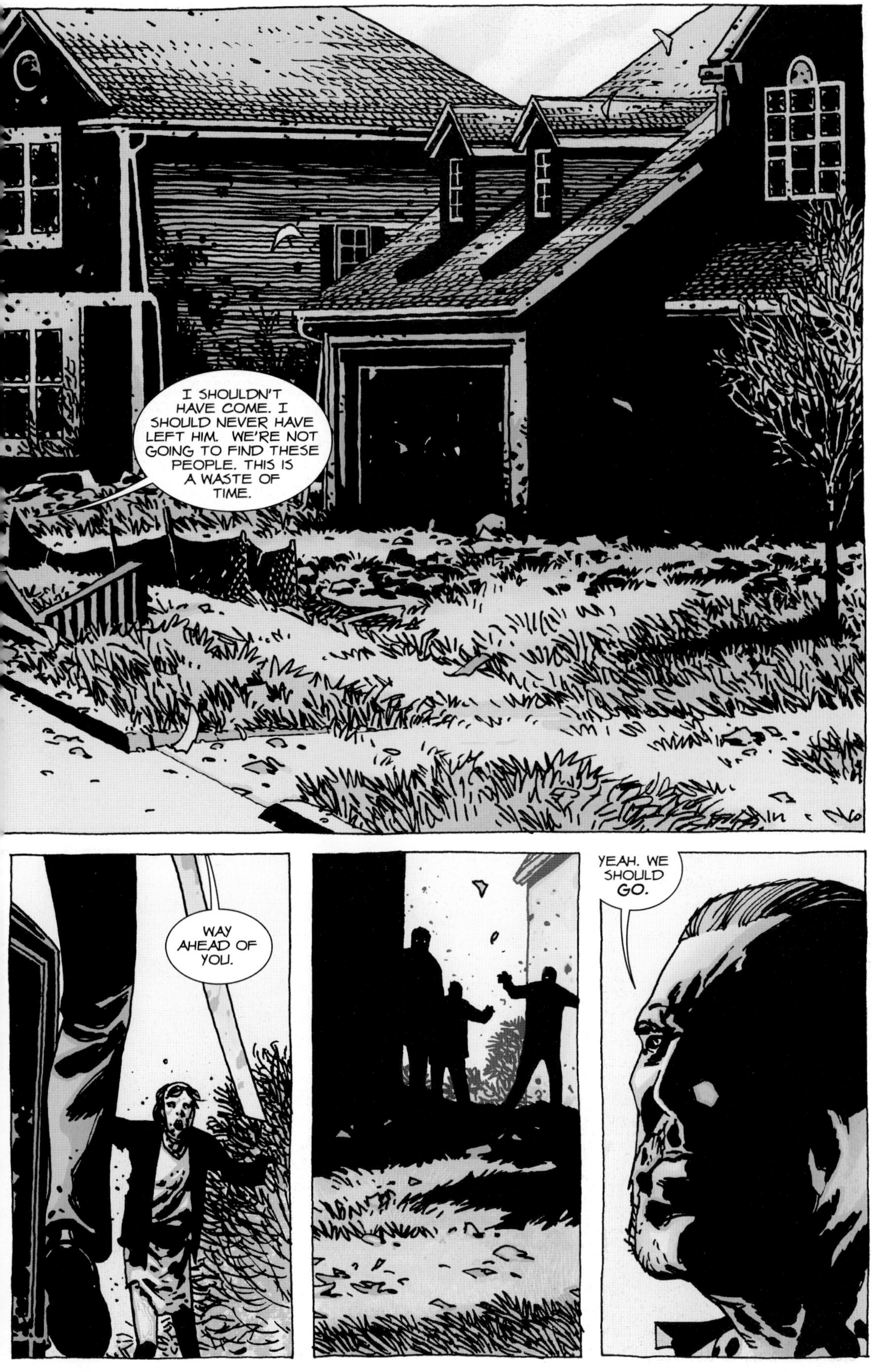
I SHOULDN'T HAVE COME. I SHOULD NEVER HAVE LEFT HIM. WE'RE NOT GOING TO FIND THESE PEOPLE. THIS IS A WASTE OF TIME.
WAY AHEAD OF YOU.
YEAH. WE SHOULD GO.

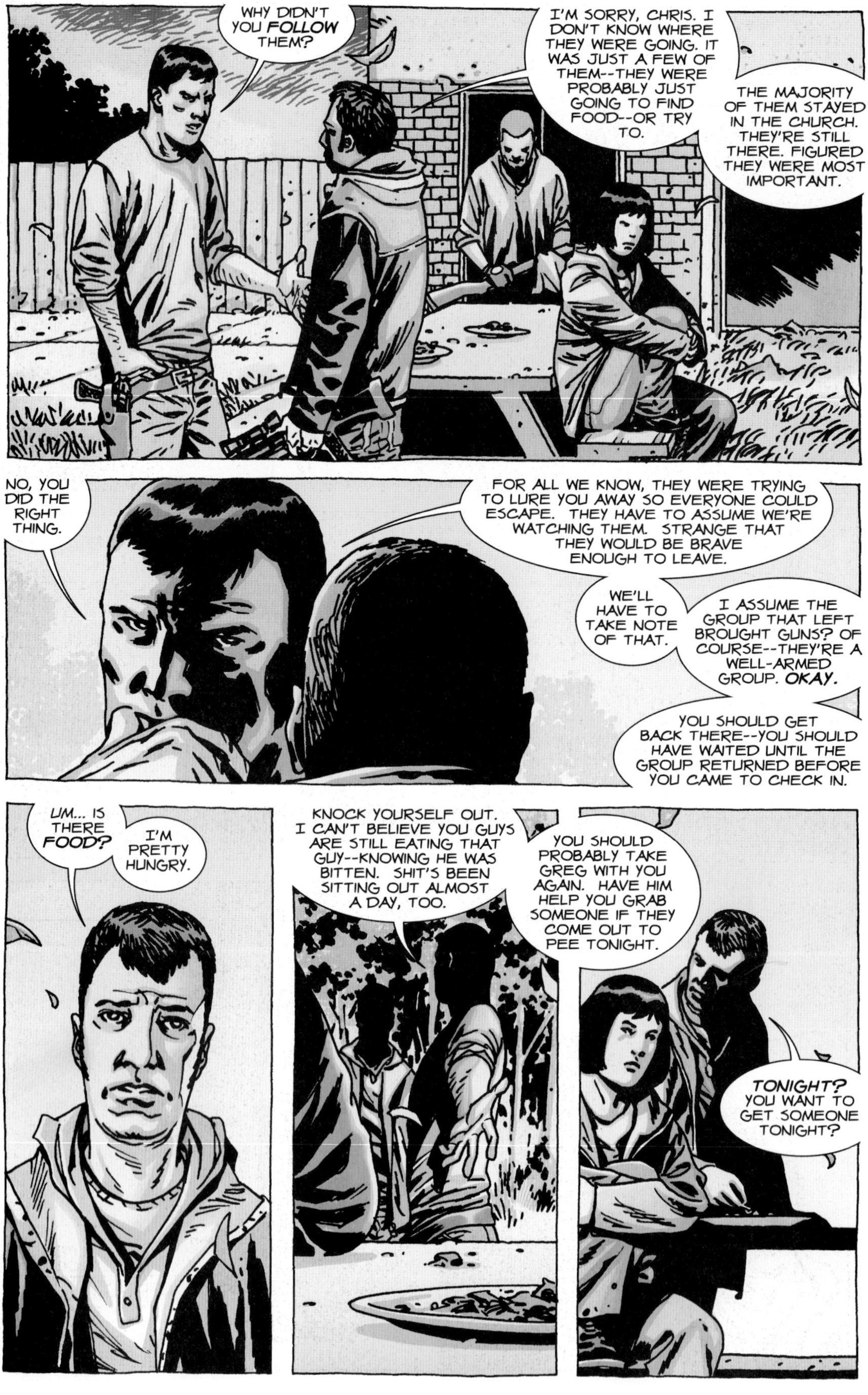
WHY DIDN'T YOU FOLLOW THEM?
I'M SORRY, CHRIS. I DON'T KNOW WHERE THEY WERE GOING. IT WAS JUST A FEW OF THEM--THEY WERE PROBABLY JUST GOING TO FIND FOOD--OR TRY TO.
THE MAJORITY OF THEM STAYED IN THE CHURCH. THEY'RE STILL THERE. FIGURED THEY WERE MOST IMPORTANT.
NO, YOU DID THE RIGHT THING.
FOR ALL WE KNOW, THEY WERE TRYING TO LURE YOU AWAY SO EVERYONE COULD ESCAPE. THEY HAVE TO ASSUME WE'RE WATCHING THEM. STRANGE THAT THEY WOULD BE BRAVE ENOUGH TO LEAVE.
WE'LL HAVE TO TAKE NOTE OF THAT.
I ASSUME THE GROUP THAT LEFT BROUGHT GUNS? OF COURSE--THEY'RE A WELL-ARMED GROUP. OKAY.
YOU SHOULD GET BACK THERE--YOU SHOULD HAVE WAITED UNTIL THE GROUP RETURNED BEFORE YOU CAME TO CHECK IN.
UM... IS THERE FOOD?
I'M PRETTY HUNGRY.
KNOCK YOURSELF OUT. I CAN'T BELIEVE YOU GUYS ARE STILL EATING THAT GUY--KNOWING HE WAS BITTEN. SHIT'S BEEN SITTING OUT ALMOST A DAY, TOO.
YOU SHOULD PROBABLY TAKE GREG WITH YOU AGAIN. HAVE HIM HELP YOU GRAB SOMEONE IF THEY COME OUT TO PEE TONIGHT.
TONIGHT? YOU WANT TO GET SOMEONE TONIGHT?

YOU KNOW THE DRILL--WE'VE GOT TO KEEP THESE PEOPLE SCARED SHITLESS. I KNOW WE'VE NEVER DONE A GROUP THIS LARGE BEFORE, BUT IT'S THE SAME DEAL.

WE SHOULD ACTUALLY PICK THEM OFF SOONER, THIN THEIR NUMBERS OUT AND MAKE THEM FEAR FOR THEIR LIVES.

WISH THEY HADN'T FOUND THAT CHURCH. IT'D BE EASIER IF THEY WERE ON THE MOVE. WE'D HAVE MORE OPPORTUNITIES TO SNAG SOMEONE.

WHAT IF THEY STAY IN THAT CHURCH ALL NIGHT? MIGHT NOT HAVE TO GO OUTSIDE TO USE THE JOHN. WHAT DO I DO THEN?

JUST WAIT. SOMEONE WILL GET STUPID SOONER OR LATER. THEY ALWAYS DO.

WE'VE BOUGHT OURSELVES A LITTLE TIME BY DROPPING OFF THE OLD MAN. HE'LL BE A CONSTANT REMINDER OF THE DEEP SHIT THEY'RE IN.

SEEING THEIR MAN LIKE THAT... THAT SHOULD DRIVE THEM CRAZY.

BETWEEN THAT AND ALBERT SHOOTING THEIR OTHER MAN IN THE LEG--WE COULD DRAG THIS OUT FOR AT LEAST ANOTHER DAY OR TWO WITHOUT GRABBING SOMEONE IF WE HAVE TO.

AND THEY'VE GOTTA BE LOW ON FOOD.

HELL, THAT GROUP LEAVING... MAYBE THEY WERE MAKING A BREAK FOR IT.

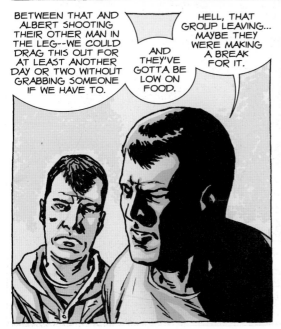

THEY'RE ALL PROBABLY SHITTING THEMSELVES RIGHT NOW.

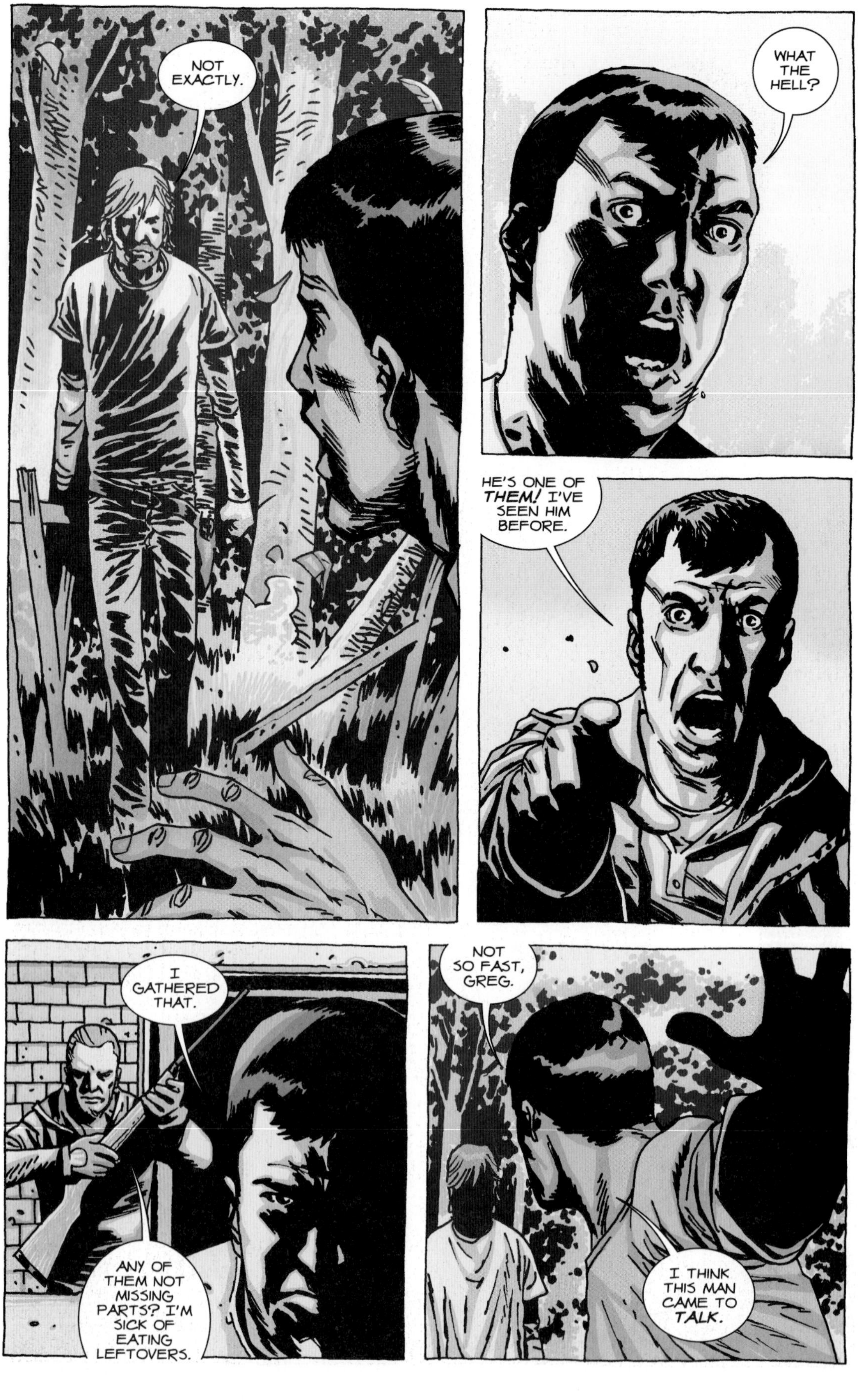
NOT EXACTLY.
WHAT THE HELL?
HE'S ONE OF THEM! I'VE SEEN HIM BEFORE.
I GATHERED THAT.
ANY OF THEM NOT MISSING PARTS? I'M SICK OF EATING LEFTOVERS.
NOT SO FAST, GREG.
I THINK THIS MAN CAME TO TALK.

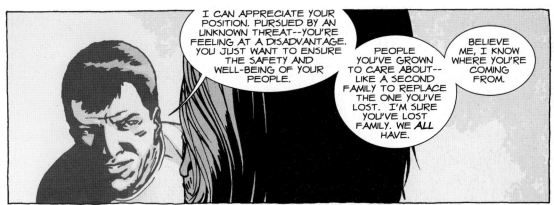

I CAN APPRECIATE YOUR POSITION. PURSUED BY AN UNKNOWN THREAT--YOU'RE FEELING AT A DISADVANTAGE. YOU JUST WANT TO ENSURE THE SAFETY AND WELL-BEING OF YOUR PEOPLE.

PEOPLE YOU'VE GROWN TO CARE ABOUT-- LIKE A SECOND FAMILY TO REPLACE THE ONE YOU'VE LOST. I'M SURE YOU'VE LOST FAMILY. WE ALL HAVE.

BELIEVE ME, I KNOW WHERE YOU'RE COMING FROM.

IS THAT SO?

YES, YES IT IS.

YOU CAME HERE ALONE, TO TRY AND NEGOTIATE WITH US. THAT'S VERY VERY BRAVE OF YOU BY THE WAY.

THAT'S ADMIRABLE.

JUST CAME TO ASK YOU THIS.

ANY AMOUNT OF TALKING GOING TO GET YOU TO BACK OFF? WILL YOU STOP COMING AFTER MY PEOPLE?

IN ALL HONESTY?

PROBABLY NOT.

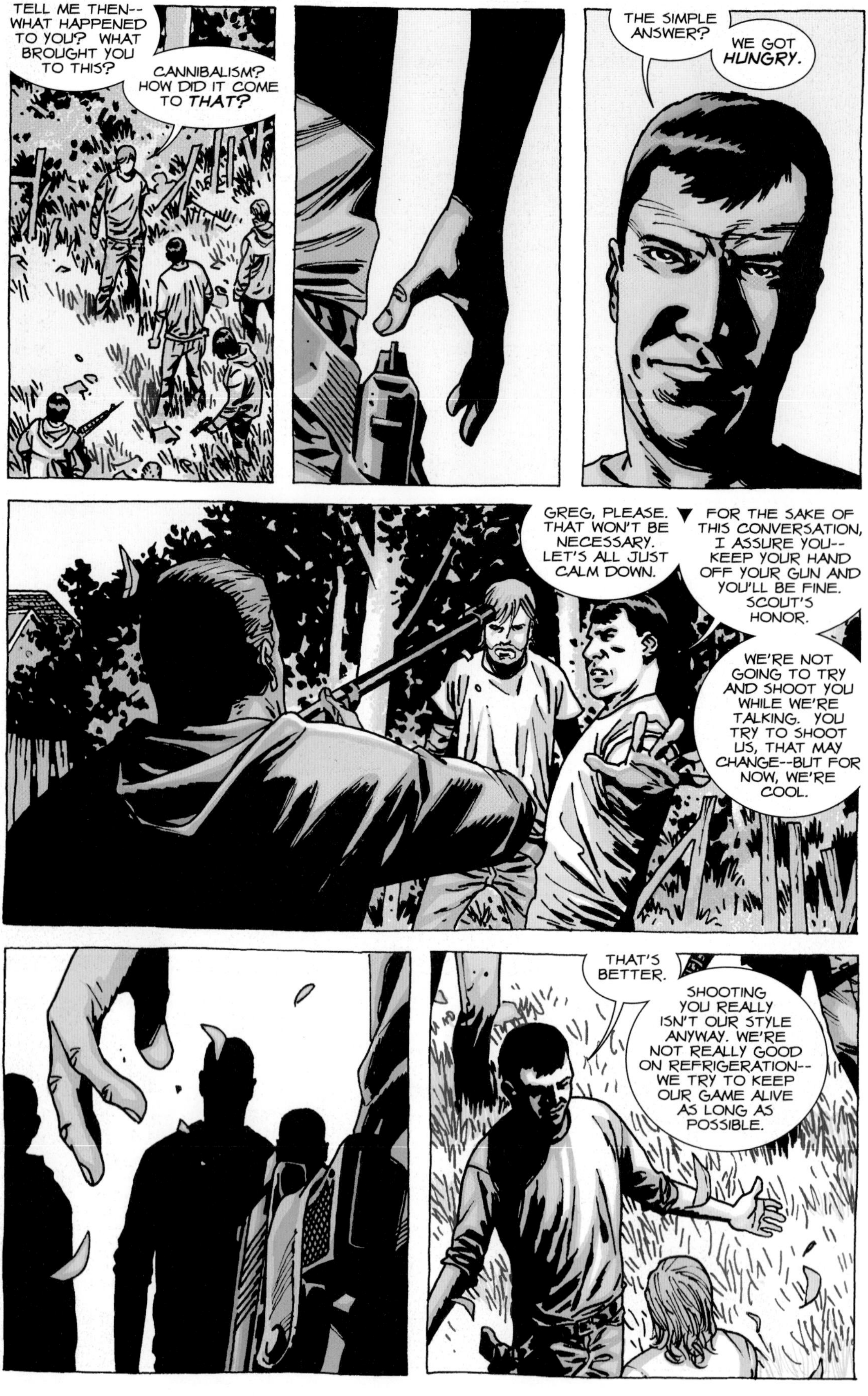

TELL ME THEN-- WHAT HAPPENED TO YOU? WHAT BROUGHT YOU TO THIS?
CANNIBALISM? HOW DID IT COME TO *THAT?*
THE SIMPLE ANSWER?
WE GOT *HUNGRY.*
GREG, PLEASE. THAT WON'T BE NECESSARY. LET'S ALL JUST CALM DOWN.
FOR THE SAKE OF THIS CONVERSATION, I ASSURE YOU-- KEEP YOUR HAND OFF YOUR GUN AND YOU'LL BE FINE. SCOUT'S HONOR.
WE'RE NOT GOING TO TRY AND SHOOT YOU WHILE WE'RE TALKING. YOU TRY TO SHOOT US, THAT MAY CHANGE--BUT FOR NOW, WE'RE COOL.
THAT'S BETTER.
SHOOTING YOU REALLY ISN'T OUR STYLE ANYWAY. WE'RE NOT REALLY GOOD ON REFRIGERATION-- WE TRY TO KEEP OUR GAME ALIVE AS LONG AS POSSIBLE.

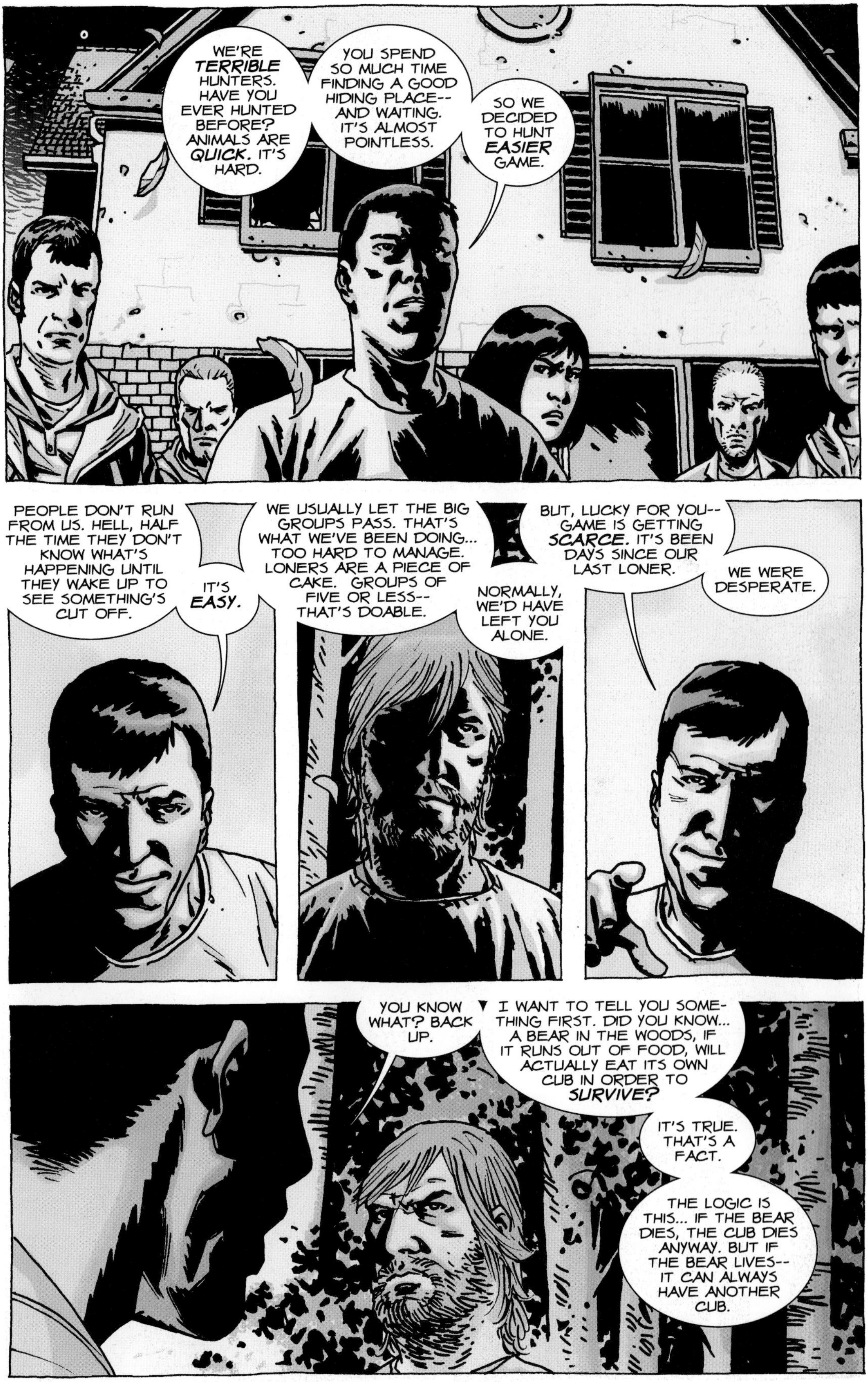
WE'RE TERRIBLE HUNTERS. HAVE YOU EVER HUNTED BEFORE? ANIMALS ARE QUICK. IT'S HARD.
YOU SPEND SO MUCH TIME FINDING A GOOD HIDING PLACE-- AND WAITING. IT'S ALMOST POINTLESS.
SO WE DECIDED TO HUNT EASIER GAME.
PEOPLE DON'T RUN FROM US. HELL, HALF THE TIME THEY DON'T KNOW WHAT'S HAPPENING UNTIL THEY WAKE UP TO SEE SOMETHING'S CUT OFF.
IT'S EASY.
WE USUALLY LET THE BIG GROUPS PASS. THAT'S WHAT WE'VE BEEN DOING... TOO HARD TO MANAGE. LONERS ARE A PIECE OF CAKE. GROUPS OF FIVE OR LESS-- THAT'S DOABLE.
NORMALLY, WE'D HAVE LEFT YOU ALONE.
BUT, LUCKY FOR YOU-- GAME IS GETTING SCARCE. IT'S BEEN DAYS SINCE OUR LAST LONER.
WE WERE DESPERATE.
YOU KNOW WHAT? BACK UP.
I WANT TO TELL YOU SOMETHING FIRST. DID YOU KNOW... A BEAR IN THE WOODS, IF IT RUNS OUT OF FOOD, WILL ACTUALLY EAT ITS OWN CUB IN ORDER TO SURVIVE?
IT'S TRUE. THAT'S A FACT.
THE LOGIC IS THIS... IF THE BEAR DIES, THE CUB DIES ANYWAY. BUT IF THE BEAR LIVES-- IT CAN ALWAYS HAVE ANOTHER CUB.

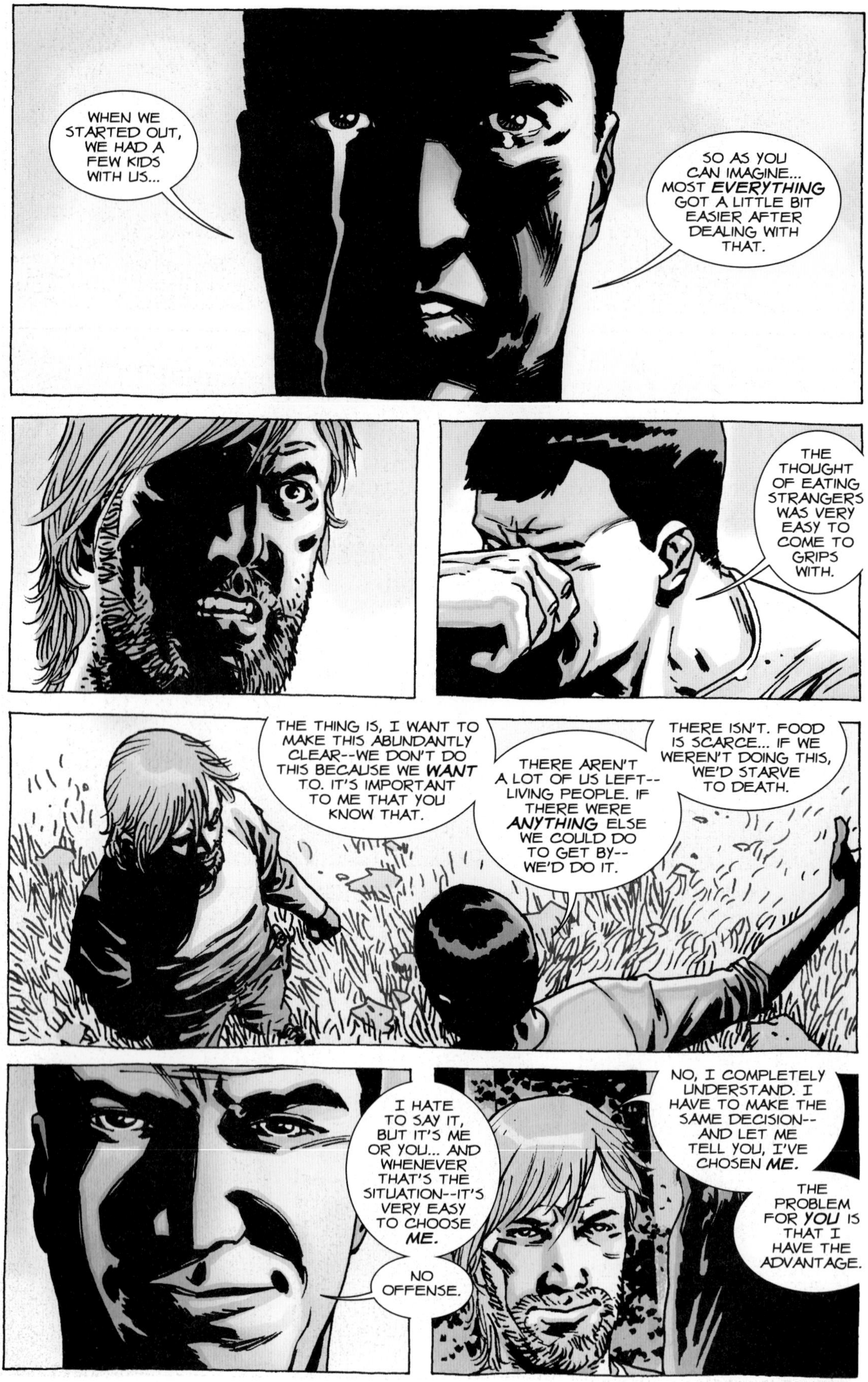

WHEN WE STARTED OUT, WE HAD A FEW KIDS WITH US...
SO AS YOU CAN IMAGINE... MOST EVERYTHING GOT A LITTLE BIT EASIER AFTER DEALING WITH THAT.
THE THOUGHT OF EATING STRANGERS WAS VERY EASY TO COME TO GRIPS WITH.
THE THING IS, I WANT TO MAKE THIS ABUNDANTLY CLEAR--WE DON'T DO THIS BECAUSE WE WANT TO. IT'S IMPORTANT TO ME THAT YOU KNOW THAT.
THERE AREN'T A LOT OF US LEFT-- LIVING PEOPLE. IF THERE WERE ANYTHING ELSE WE COULD DO TO GET BY-- WE'D DO IT.
THERE ISN'T. FOOD IS SCARCE... IF WE WEREN'T DOING THIS, WE'D STARVE TO DEATH.
I HATE TO SAY IT, BUT IT'S ME OR YOU... AND WHENEVER THAT'S THE SITUATION--IT'S VERY EASY TO CHOOSE ME.
NO OFFENSE.
NO, I COMPLETELY UNDERSTAND. I HAVE TO MAKE THE SAME DECISION-- AND LET ME TELL YOU, I'VE CHOSEN ME.
THE PROBLEM FOR YOU IS THAT I HAVE THE ADVANTAGE.

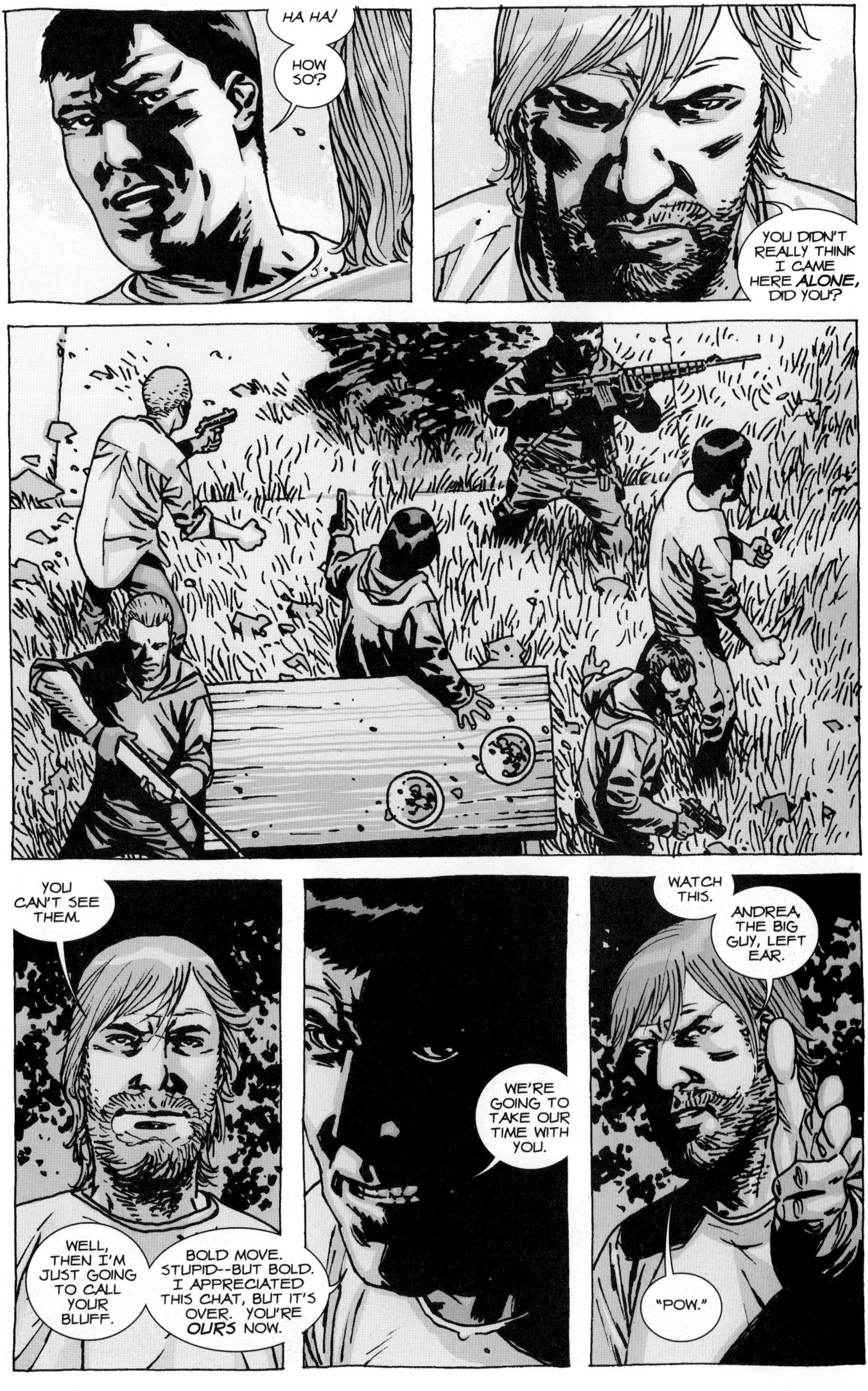
HA HA!
HOW SO?
YOU DIDN'T REALLY THINK I CAME HERE ALONE, DID YOU?
YOU CAN'T SEE THEM.
WELL, THEN I'M JUST GOING TO CALL YOUR BLUFF.
BOLD MOVE. STUPID--BUT BOLD. I APPRECIATED THIS CHAT, BUT IT'S OVER. YOU'RE OURS NOW.
WE'RE GOING TO TAKE OUR TIME WITH YOU.
WATCH THIS.
ANDREA, THE BIG GUY, LEFT EAR.
"POW."

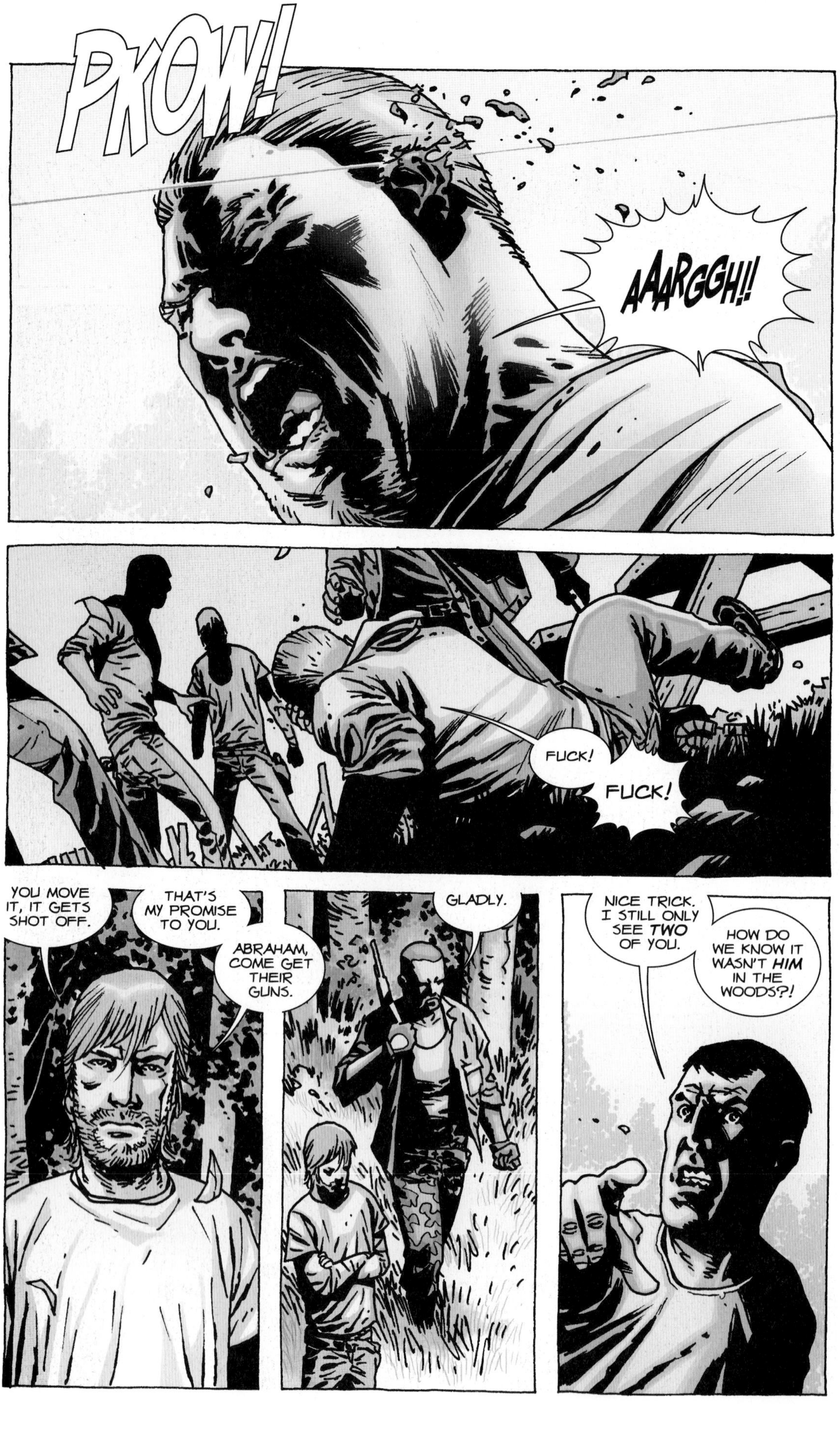
PKOW!
AAARGGH!!
FUCK!
FUCK!
YOU MOVE IT, IT GETS SHOT OFF.
THAT'S MY PROMISE TO YOU.
ABRAHAM, COME GET THEIR GUNS.
GLADLY.
NICE TRICK. I STILL ONLY SEE TWO OF YOU.
HOW DO WE KNOW IT WASN'T HIM IN THE WOODS?!

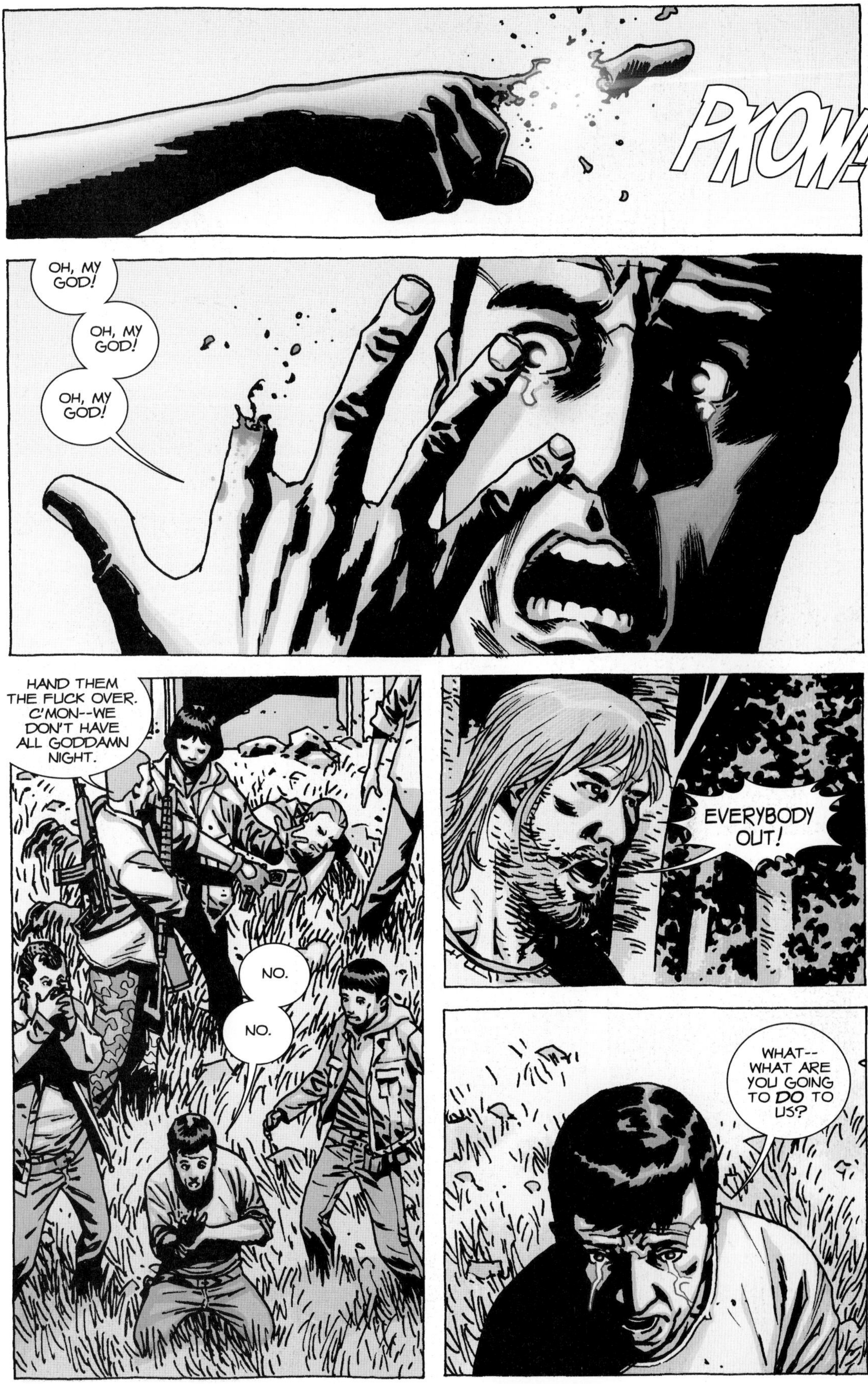

PKOW!!
OH, MY GOD!
OH, MY GOD!
OH, MY GOD!
HAND THEM THE FUCK OVER. C'MON--WE DON'T HAVE ALL GODDAMN NIGHT.
NO.
NO.
EVERYBODY OUT!
WHAT-- WHAT ARE YOU GOING TO DO TO US?

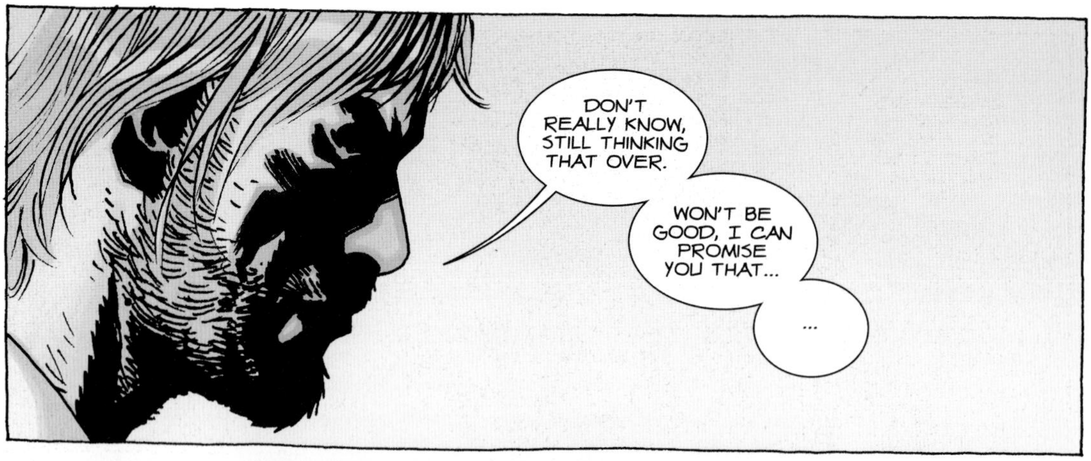
DON'T REALLY KNOW, STILL THINKING THAT OVER.
WON'T BE GOOD, I CAN PROMISE YOU THAT...
...

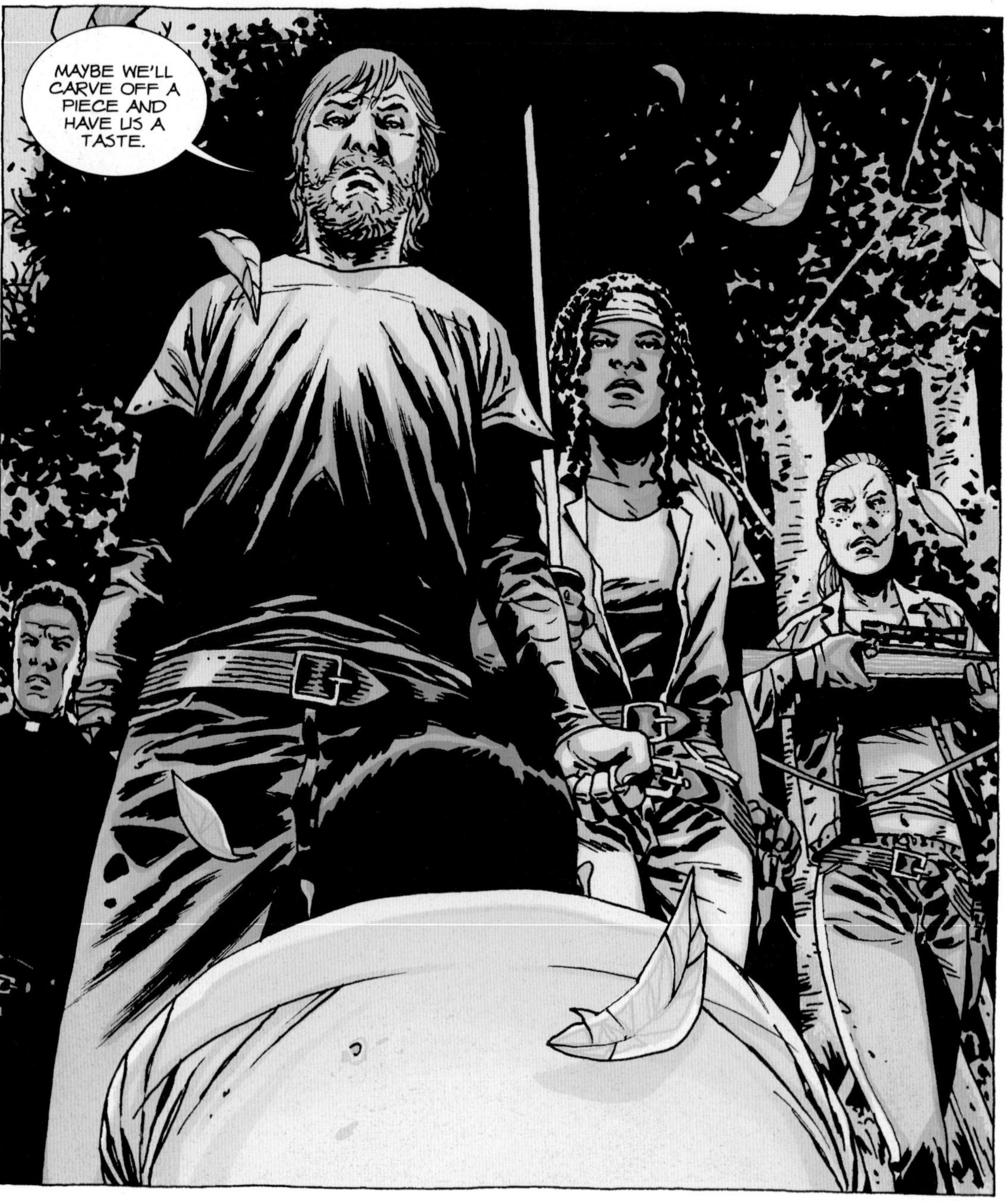
MAYBE WE'LL CARVE OFF A PIECE AND HAVE US A TASTE.

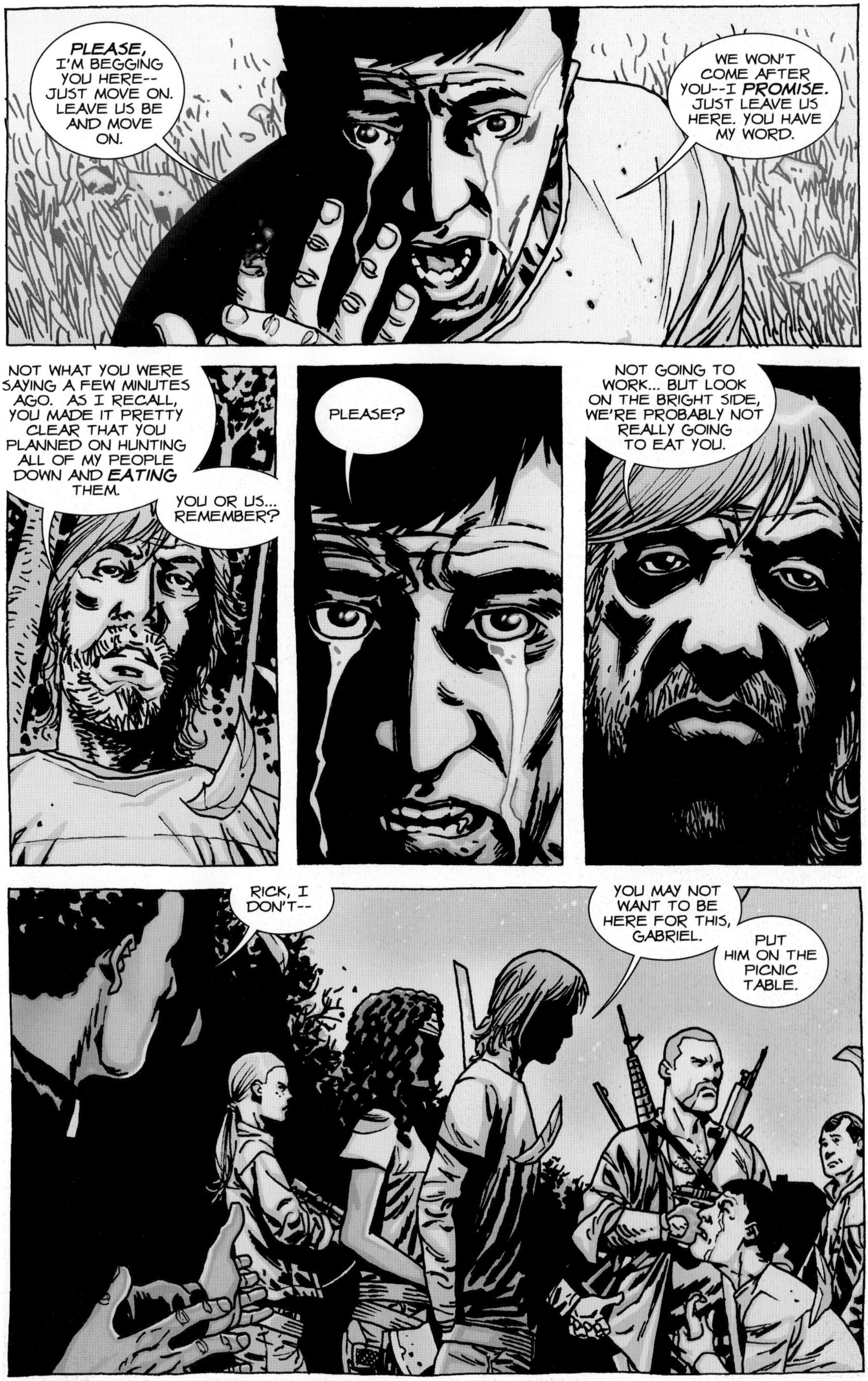
PLEASE, I'M BEGGING YOU HERE-- JUST MOVE ON. LEAVE US BE AND MOVE ON.
WE WON'T COME AFTER YOU--I PROMISE. JUST LEAVE US HERE. YOU HAVE MY WORD.
NOT WHAT YOU WERE SAYING A FEW MINUTES AGO. AS I RECALL, YOU MADE IT PRETTY CLEAR THAT YOU PLANNED ON HUNTING ALL OF MY PEOPLE DOWN AND EATING THEM.
YOU OR US... REMEMBER?
PLEASE?
NOT GOING TO WORK... BUT LOOK ON THE BRIGHT SIDE, WE'RE PROBABLY NOT REALLY GOING TO EAT YOU.
RICK, I DON'T--
YOU MAY NOT WANT TO BE HERE FOR THIS, GABRIEL.
PUT HIM ON THE PICNIC TABLE.

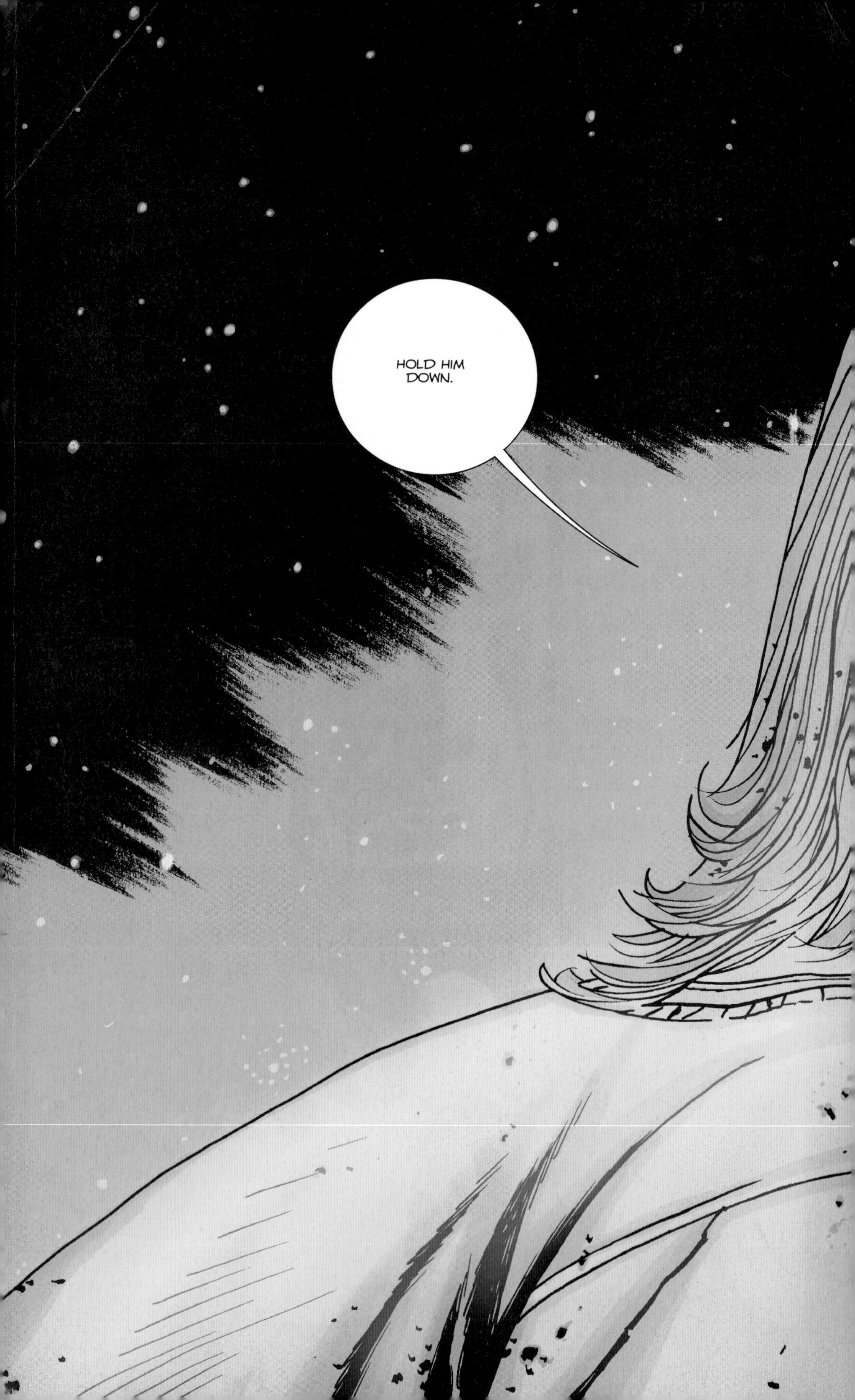
HOLD HIM DOWN.

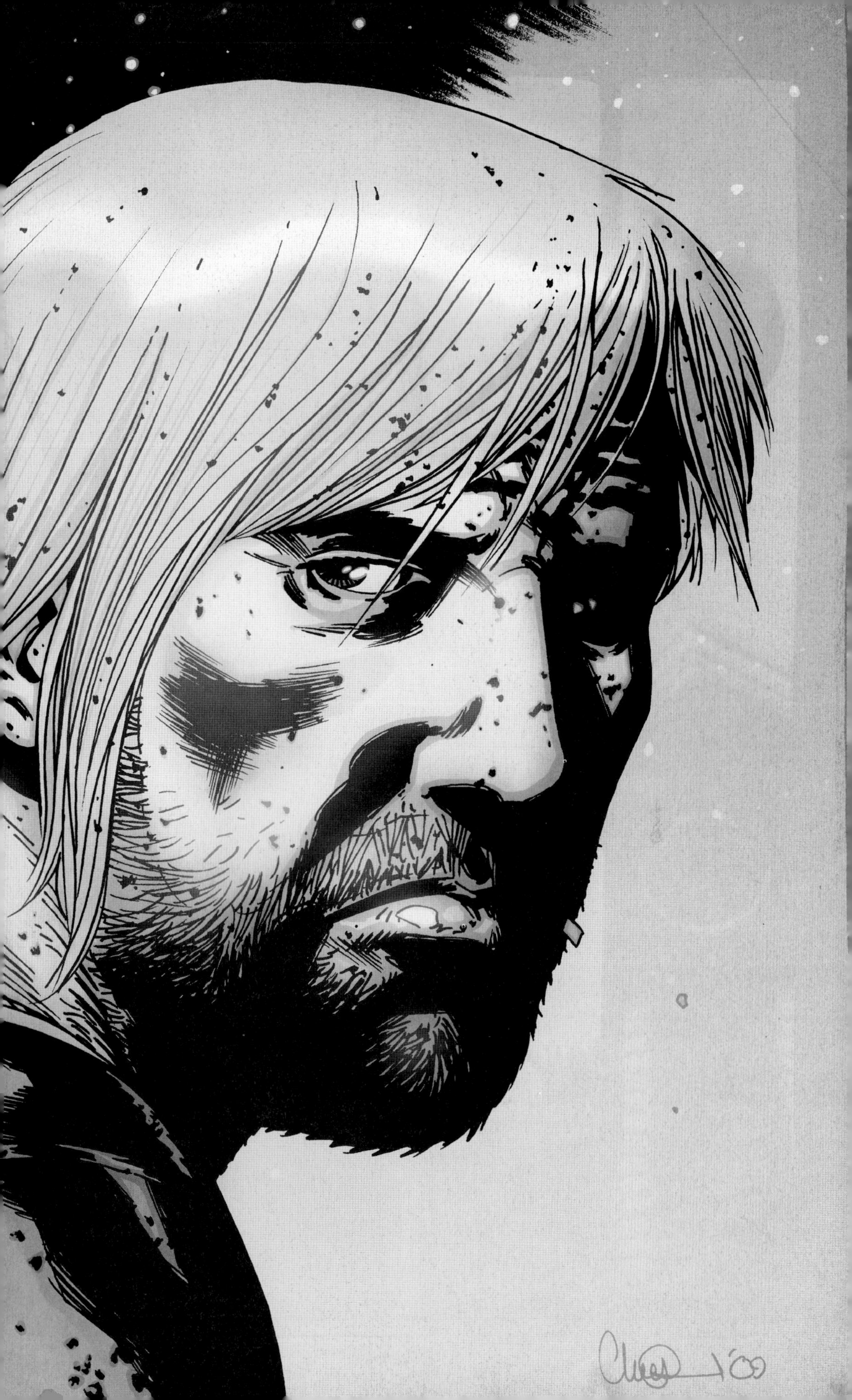

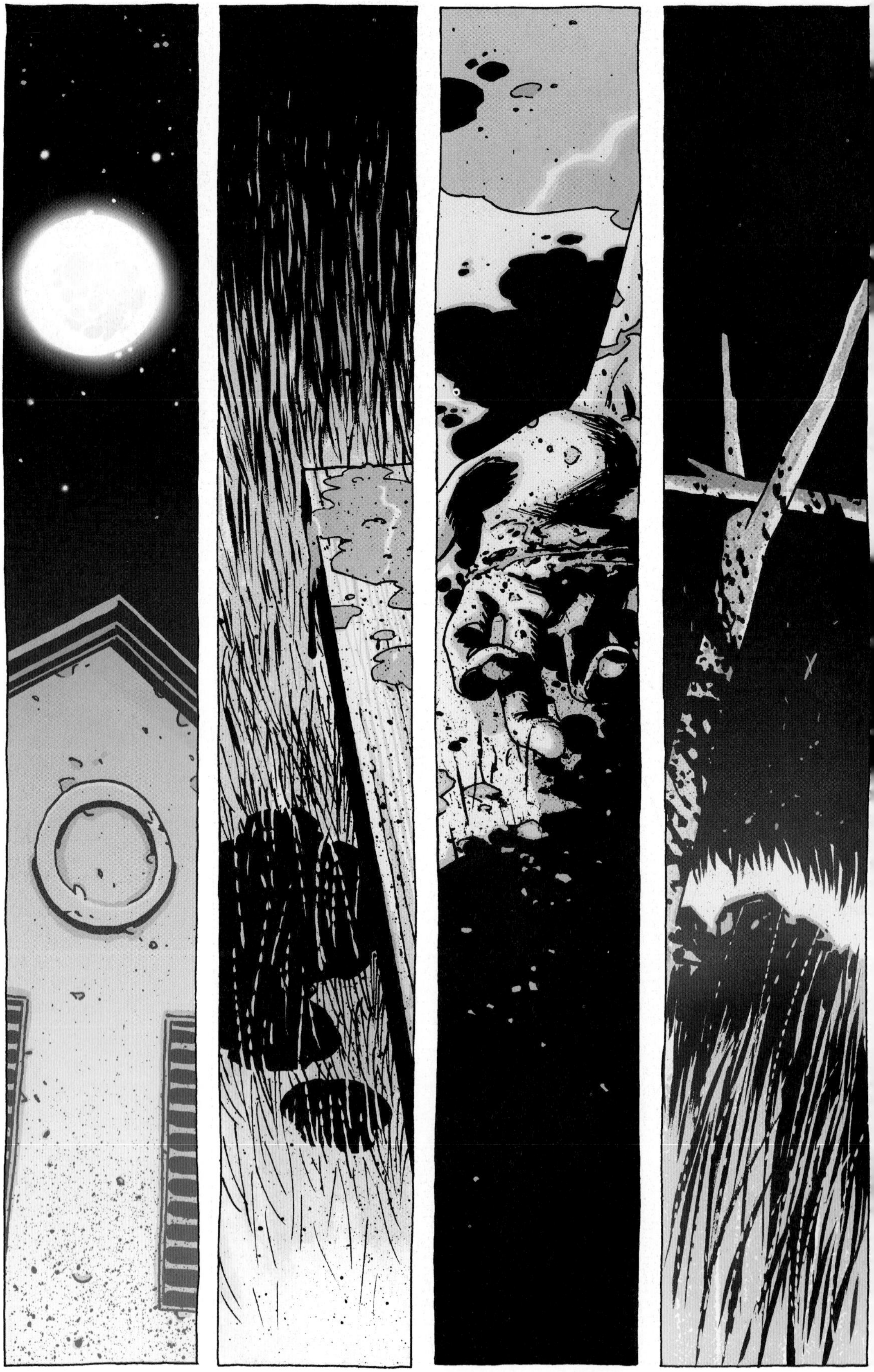

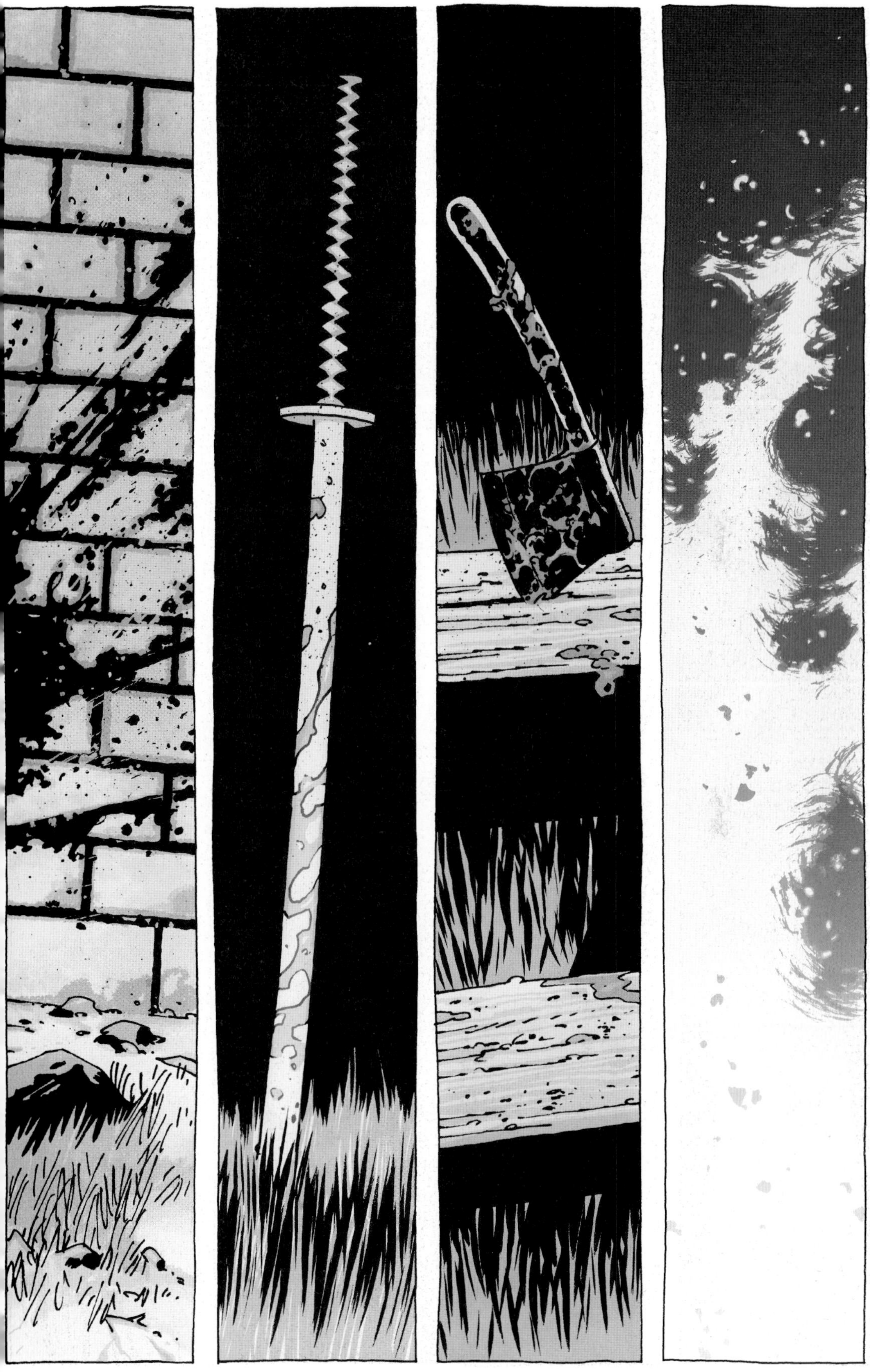

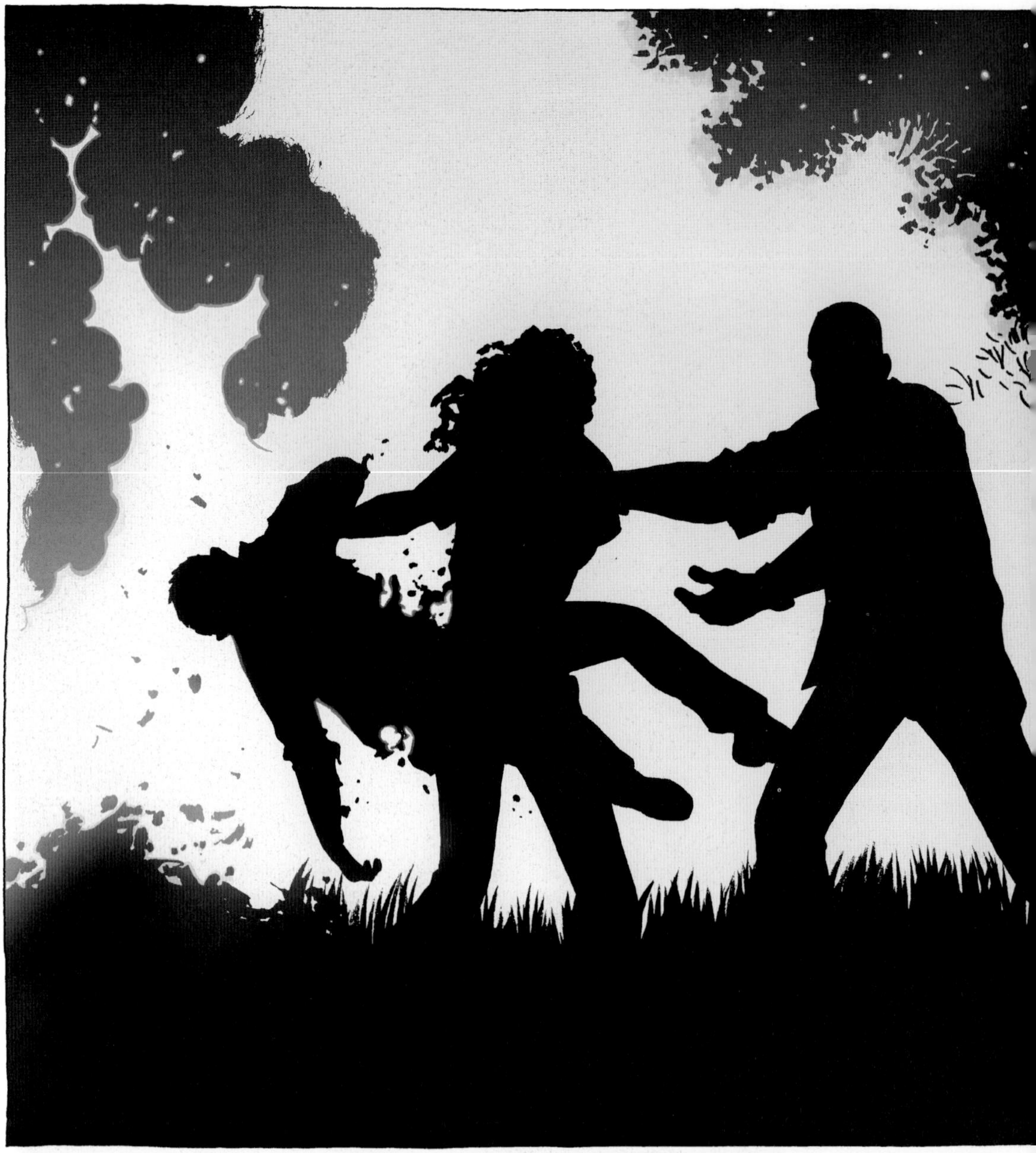
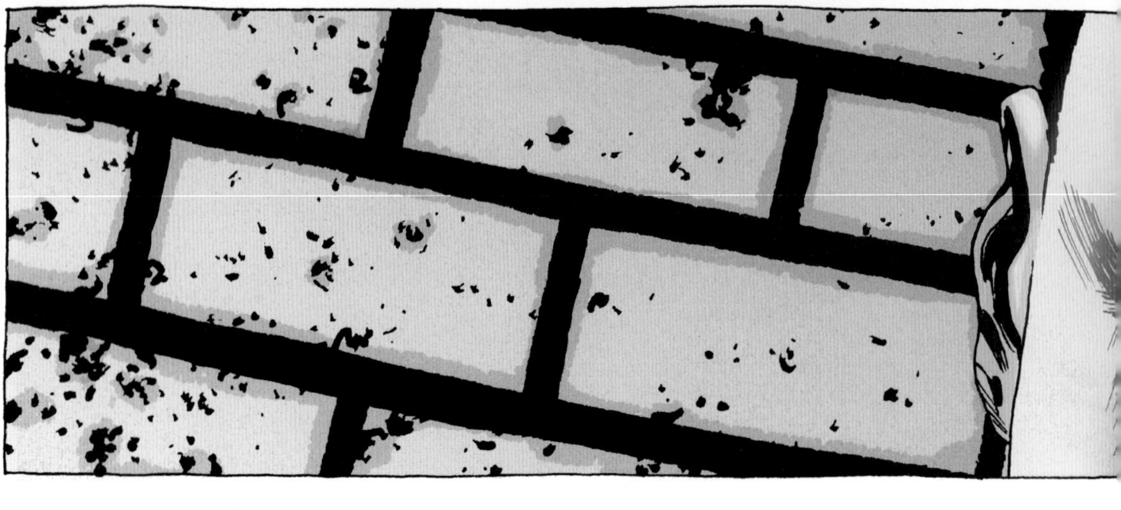

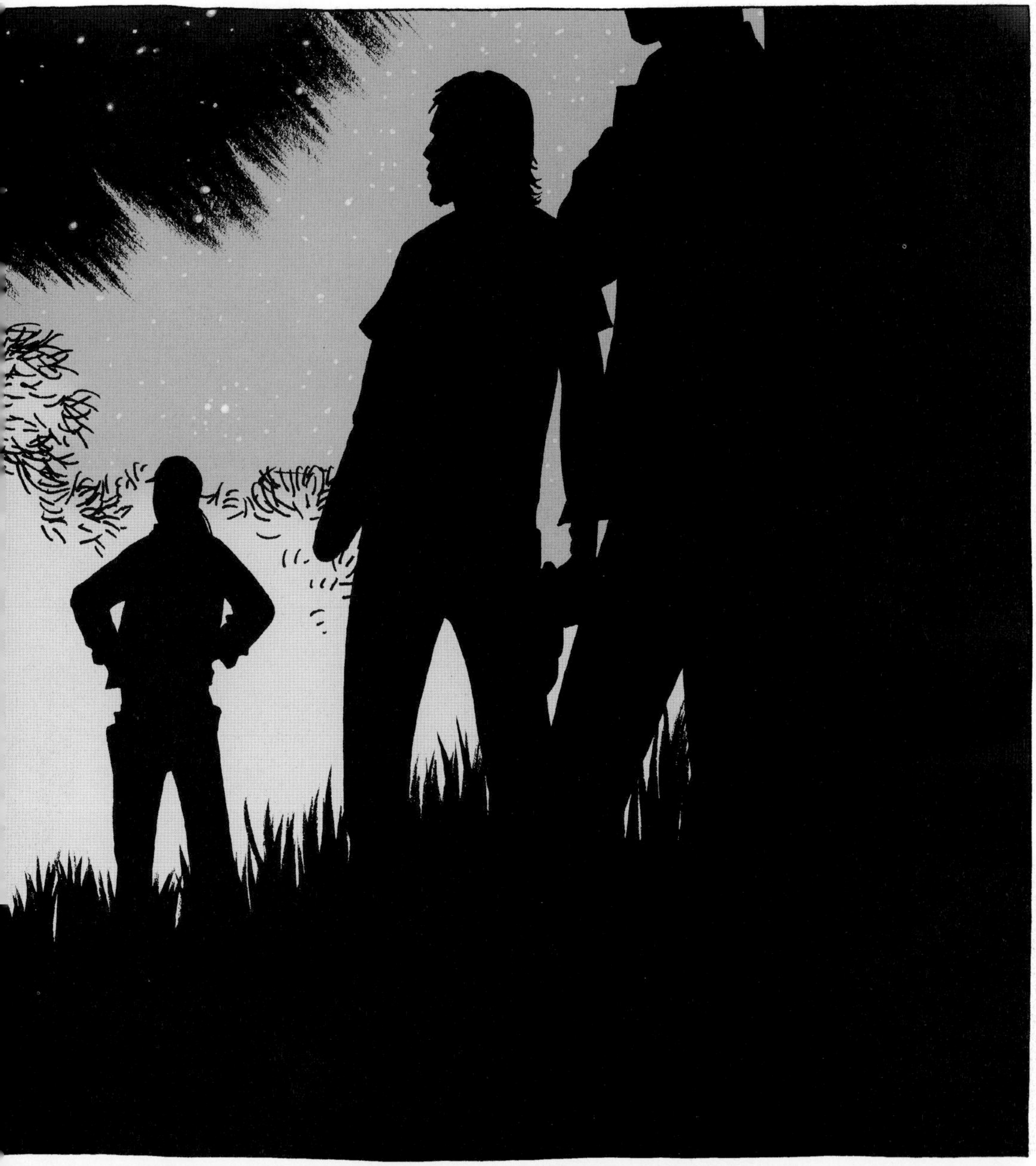

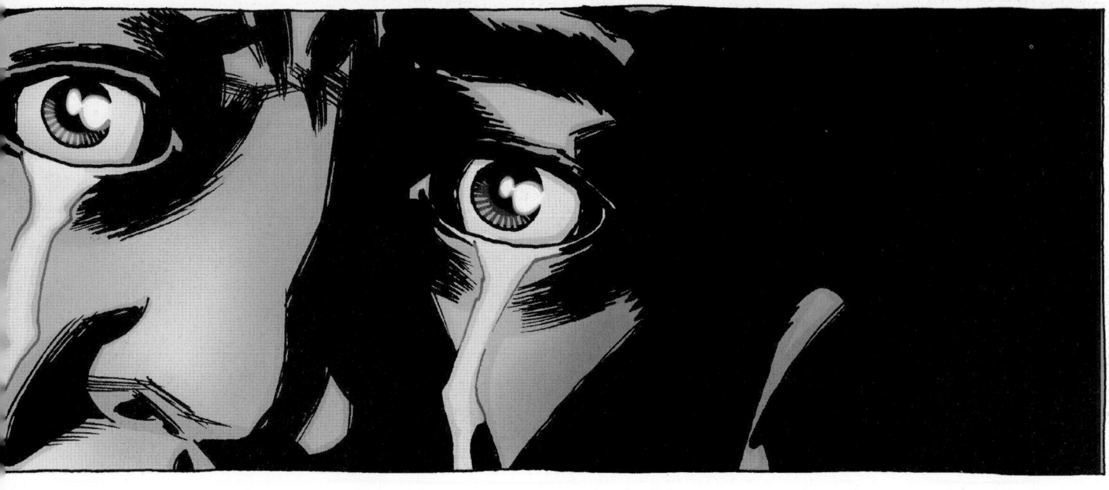

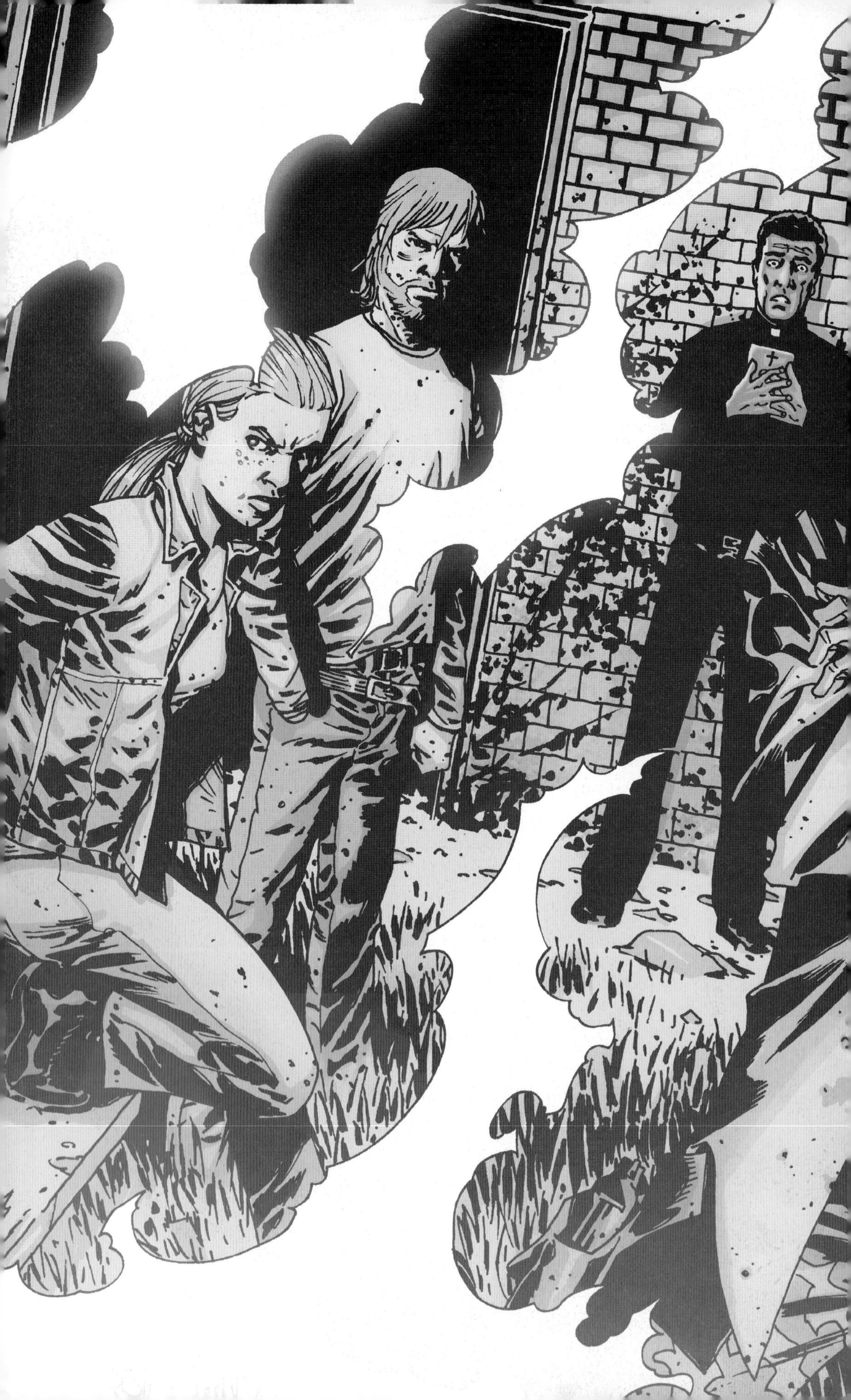

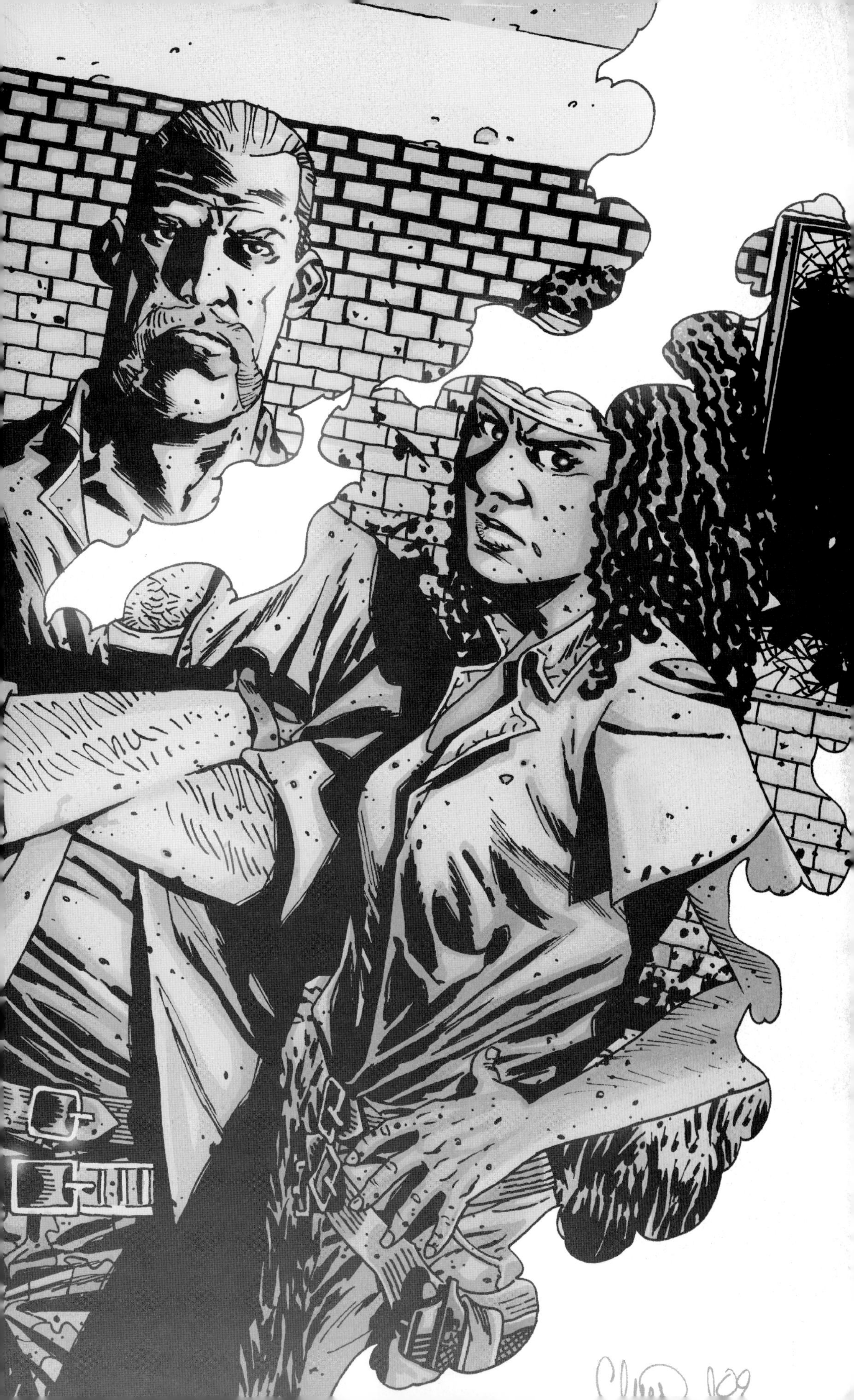

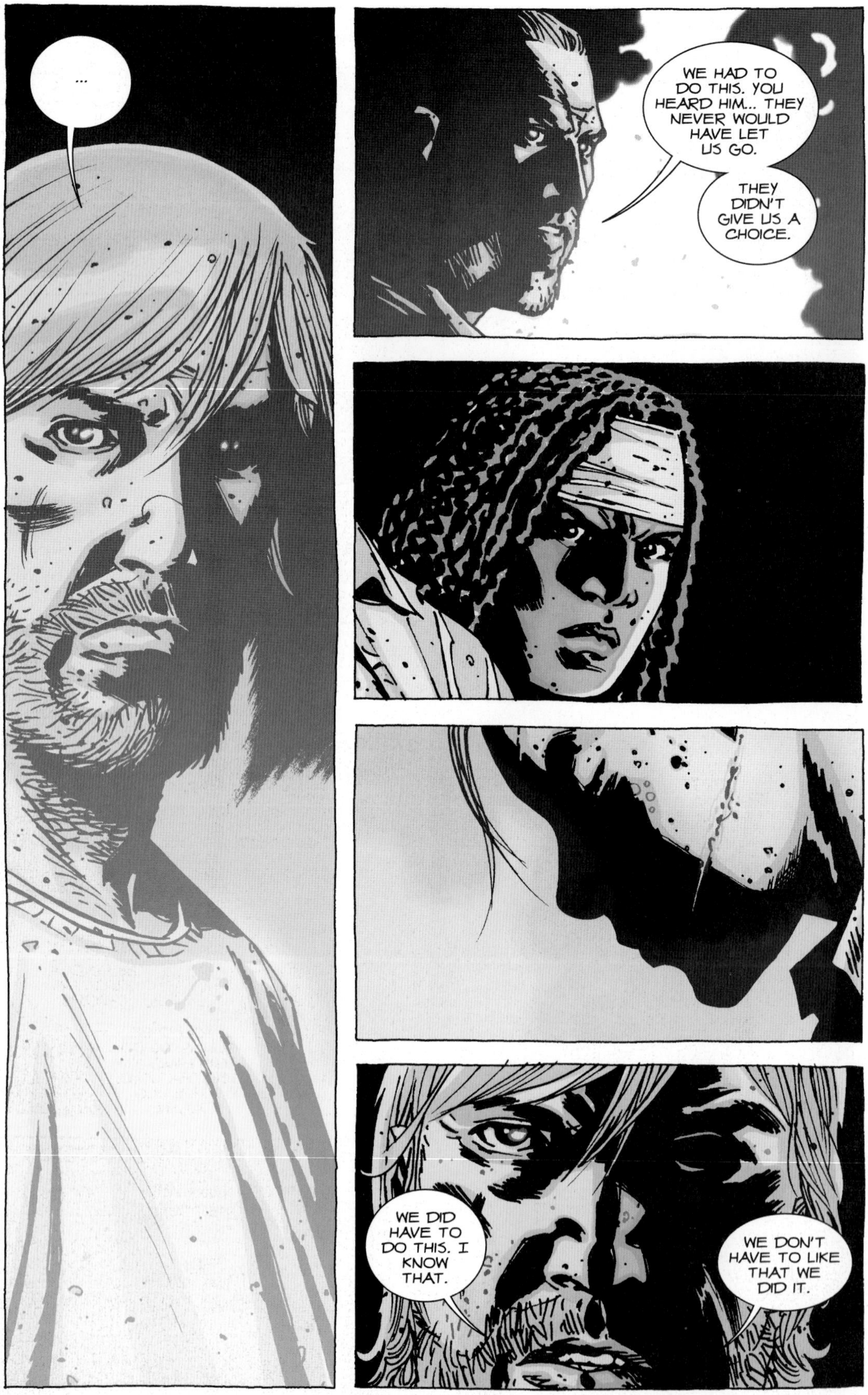
...
WE HAD TO DO THIS. YOU HEARD HIM... THEY NEVER WOULD HAVE LET US GO.
THEY DIDN'T GIVE US A CHOICE.
WE DID HAVE TO DO THIS. I KNOW THAT.
WE DON'T HAVE TO LIKE THAT WE DID IT.

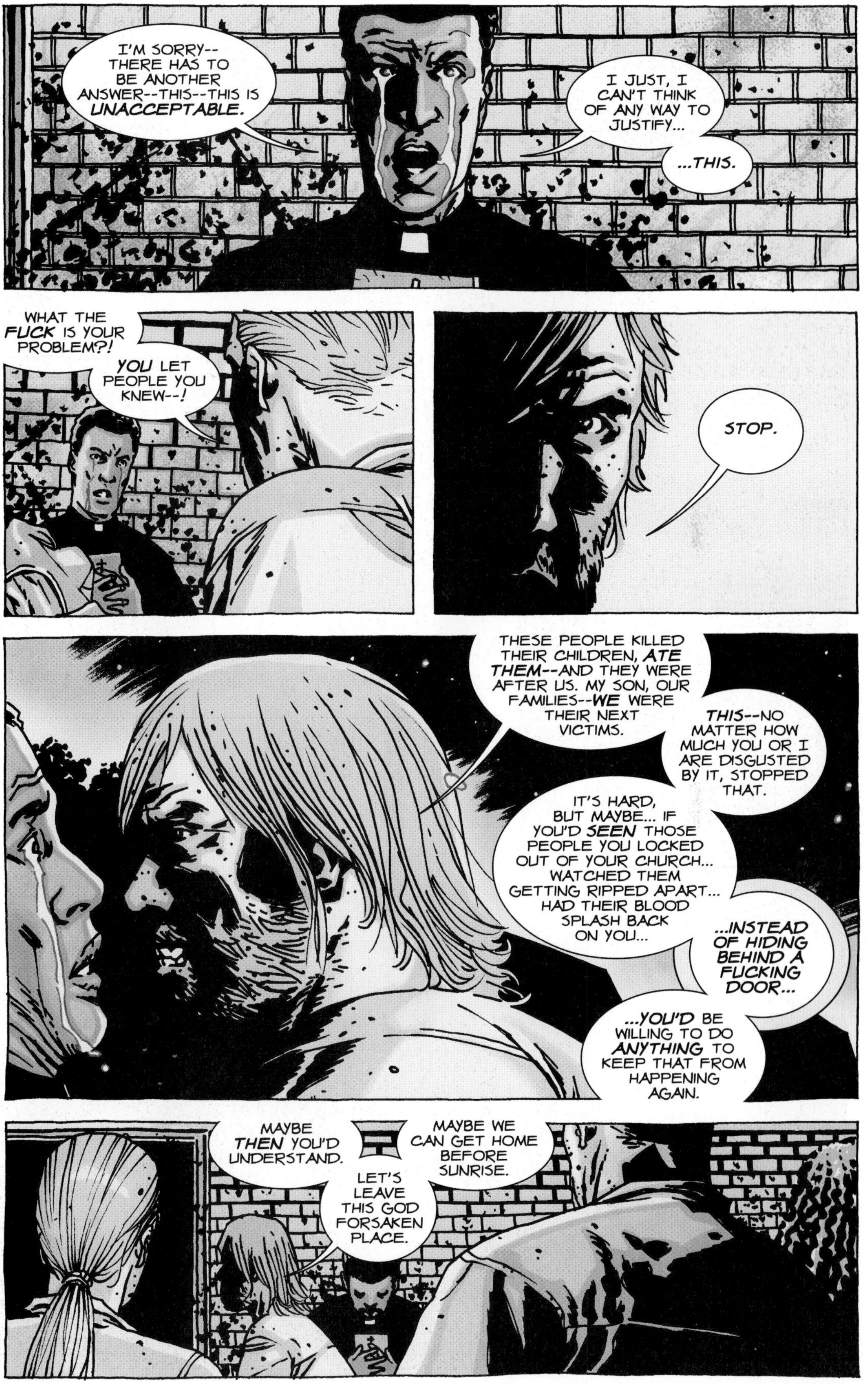
I'M SORRY-- THERE HAS TO BE ANOTHER ANSWER--THIS--THIS IS UNACCEPTABLE.
I JUST, I CAN'T THINK OF ANY WAY TO JUSTIFY...
...THIS.
WHAT THE FUCK IS YOUR PROBLEM?!
YOU LET PEOPLE YOU KNEW--!
STOP.
THESE PEOPLE KILLED THEIR CHILDREN, ATE THEM--AND THEY WERE AFTER US. MY SON, OUR FAMILIES--WE WERE THEIR NEXT VICTIMS.
THIS--NO MATTER HOW MUCH YOU OR I ARE DISGUSTED BY IT, STOPPED THAT.
IT'S HARD, BUT MAYBE... IF YOU'D SEEN THOSE PEOPLE YOU LOCKED OUT OF YOUR CHURCH... WATCHED THEM GETTING RIPPED APART... HAD THEIR BLOOD SPLASH BACK ON YOU...
...INSTEAD OF HIDING BEHIND A FUCKING DOOR...
...YOU'D BE WILLING TO DO ANYTHING TO KEEP THAT FROM HAPPENING AGAIN.
MAYBE THEN YOU'D UNDERSTAND.
LET'S LEAVE THIS GOD FORSAKEN PLACE.
MAYBE WE CAN GET HOME BEFORE SUNRISE.

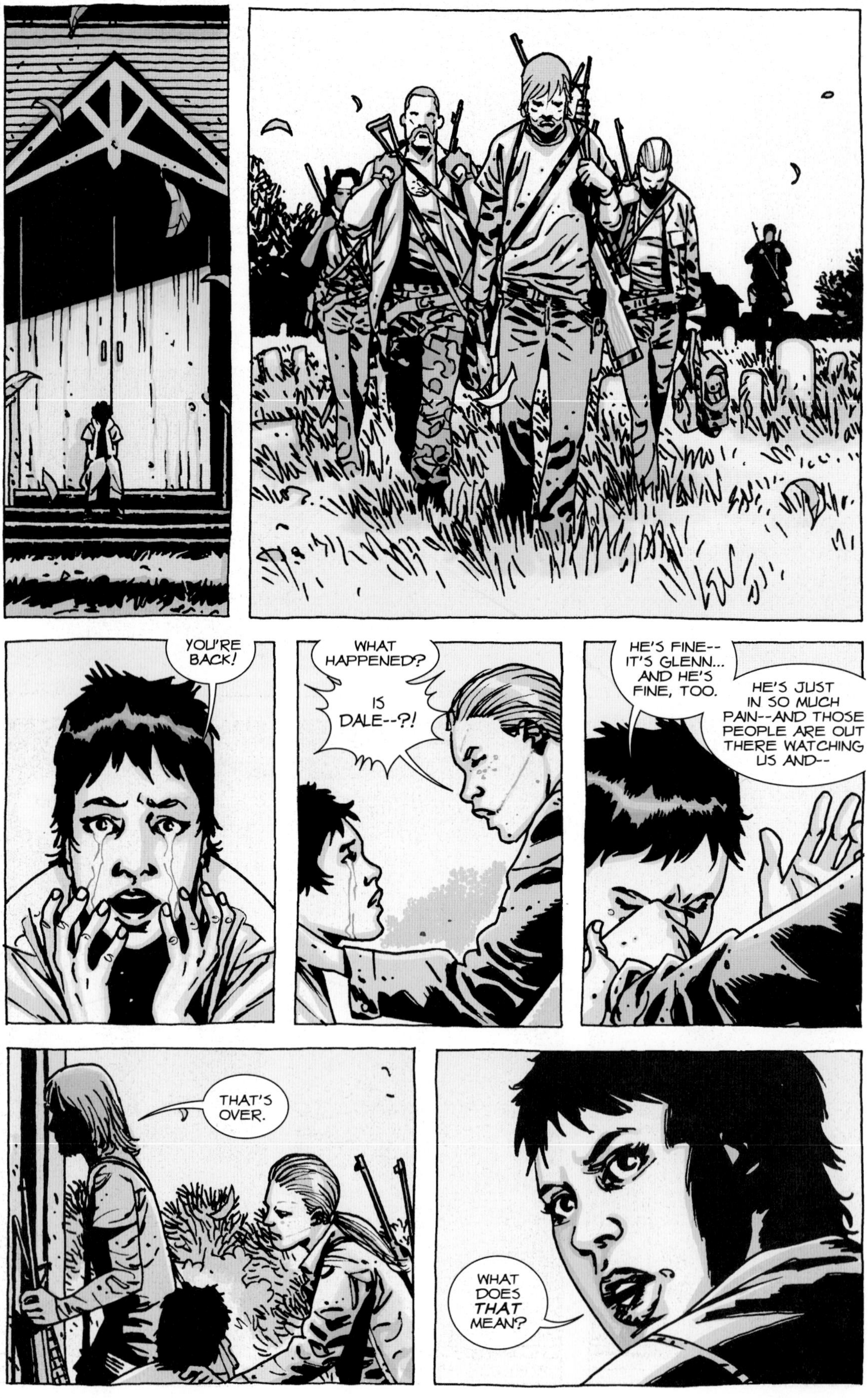

YOU'RE BACK!
WHAT HAPPENED?
IS DALE--?!
HE'S FINE-- IT'S GLENN... AND HE'S FINE, TOO.
HE'S JUST IN SO MUCH PAIN--AND THOSE PEOPLE ARE OUT THERE WATCHING US AND--
THAT'S OVER.
WHAT DOES THAT MEAN?

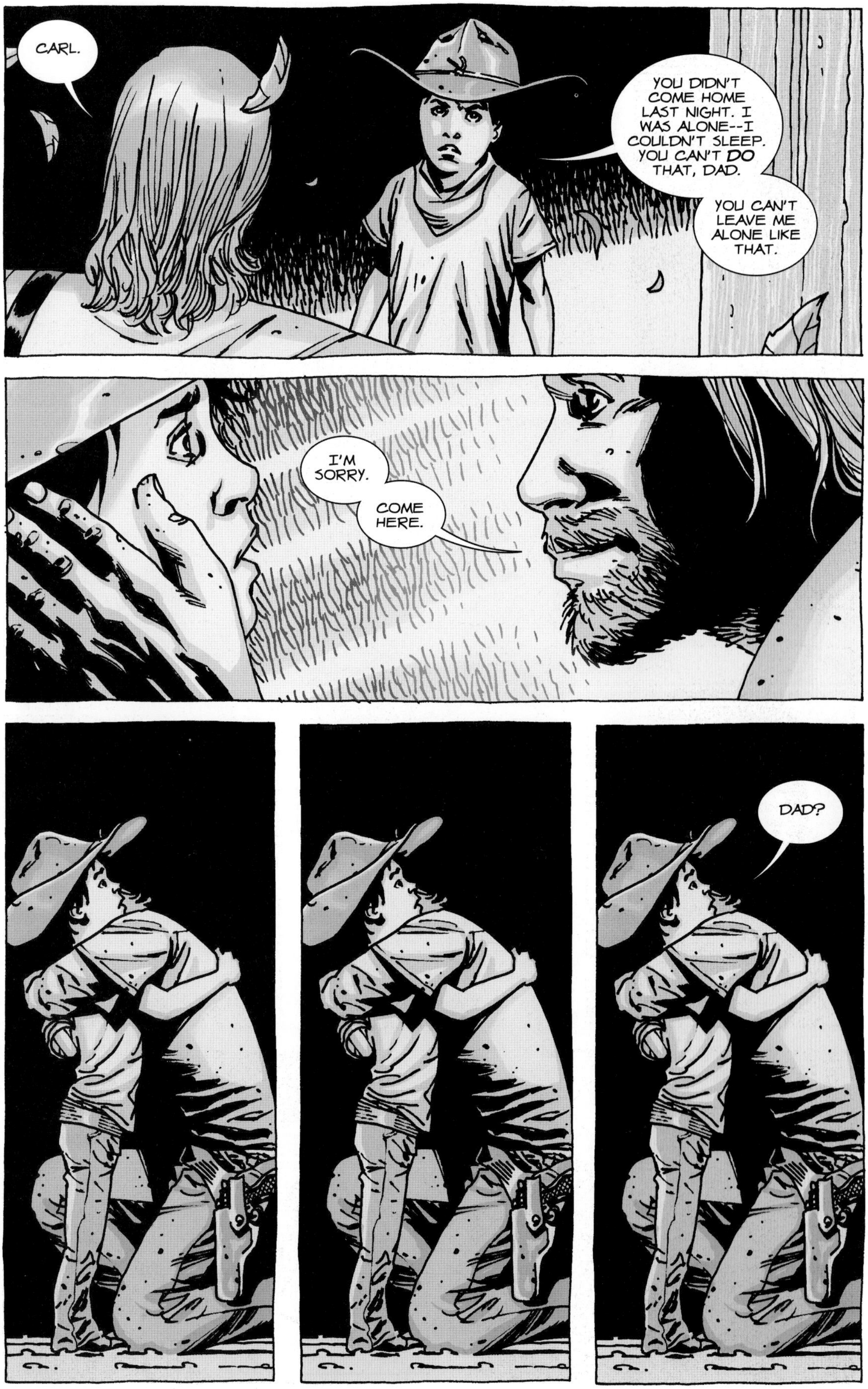
CARL.
YOU DIDN'T COME HOME LAST NIGHT. I WAS ALONE--I COULDN'T SLEEP. YOU CAN'T DO THAT, DAD.
YOU CAN'T LEAVE ME ALONE LIKE THAT.
I'M SORRY.
COME HERE.
DAD?

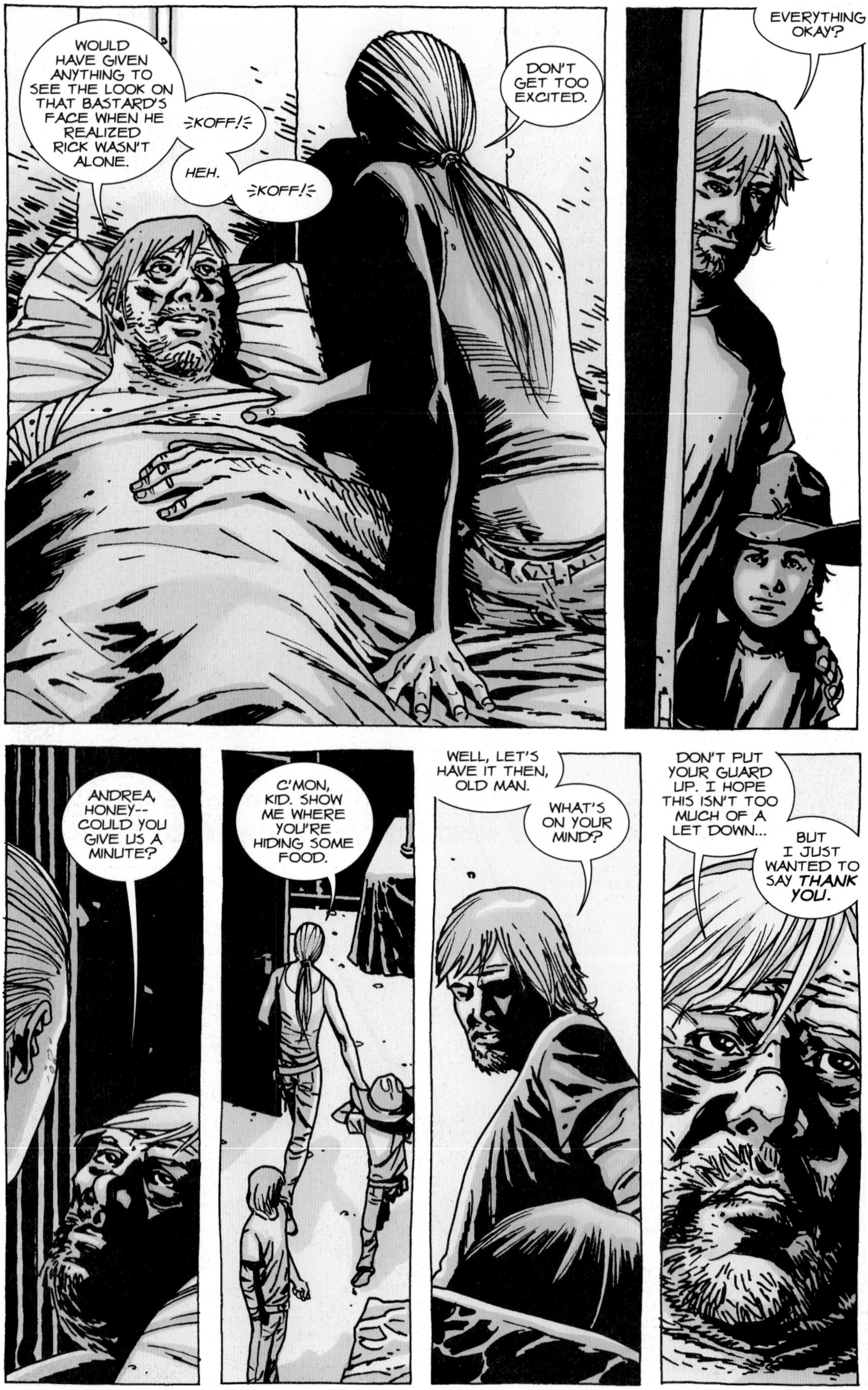

WOULD HAVE GIVEN ANYTHING TO SEE THE LOOK ON THAT BASTARD'S FACE WHEN HE REALIZED RICK WASN'T ALONE.
KOFF!
HEH.
KOFF!
DON'T GET TOO EXCITED.
EVERYTHING OKAY?
ANDREA, HONEY-- COULD YOU GIVE US A MINUTE?
C'MON, KID. SHOW ME WHERE YOU'RE HIDING SOME FOOD.
WELL, LET'S HAVE IT THEN, OLD MAN.
WHAT'S ON YOUR MIND?
DON'T PUT YOUR GUARD UP. I HOPE THIS ISN'T TOO MUCH OF A LET DOWN...
BUT I JUST WANTED TO SAY *THANK YOU*.

FOR WHAT?

FOR--

≠KOFF!≠

"FOR WHAT?" HE SAYS!

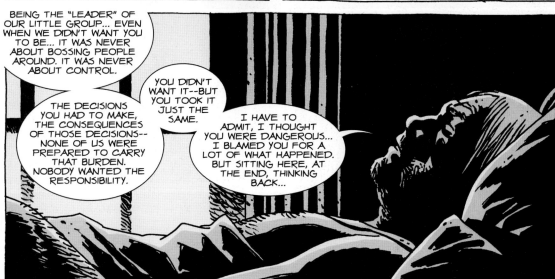

BEING THE "LEADER" OF OUR LITTLE GROUP... EVEN WHEN WE DIDN'T WANT YOU TO BE... IT WAS NEVER ABOUT BOSSING PEOPLE AROUND. IT WAS NEVER ABOUT CONTROL.

YOU DIDN'T WANT IT--BUT YOU TOOK IT JUST THE SAME.

THE DECISIONS YOU HAD TO MAKE, THE CONSEQUENCES OF THOSE DECISIONS-- NONE OF US WERE PREPARED TO CARRY THAT BURDEN. NOBODY WANTED THE RESPONSIBILITY.

I HAVE TO ADMIT, I THOUGHT YOU WERE DANGEROUS... I BLAMED YOU FOR A LOT OF WHAT HAPPENED. BUT SITTING HERE, AT THE END, THINKING BACK...

IT'S EASY TO BLAME YOU FOR WHAT HAPPENED AT TIMES--AND THAT'S YOUR BURDEN FOR TAKING CONTROL--FOR TAKING CARE OF STRANGERS-- TRYING TO PROTECT US.

IT'S NOT AS EASY TO GIVE YOU CREDIT FOR THINGS THAT DIDN'T HAPPEN.

A LOT OF PEOPLE ARE DEAD... BUT LOOK AT HOW LONG THIS GROUP HAS LASTED.

I THINK THAT'S YOUR FAULT, TOO.

YOU HELPED ME LAST THIS LONG, GAVE ME THE TIME I HAD WITH THE BOYS, WITH ANDREA... AND I APPRECIATE THAT VERY VERY MUCH...

SO THANK YOU.

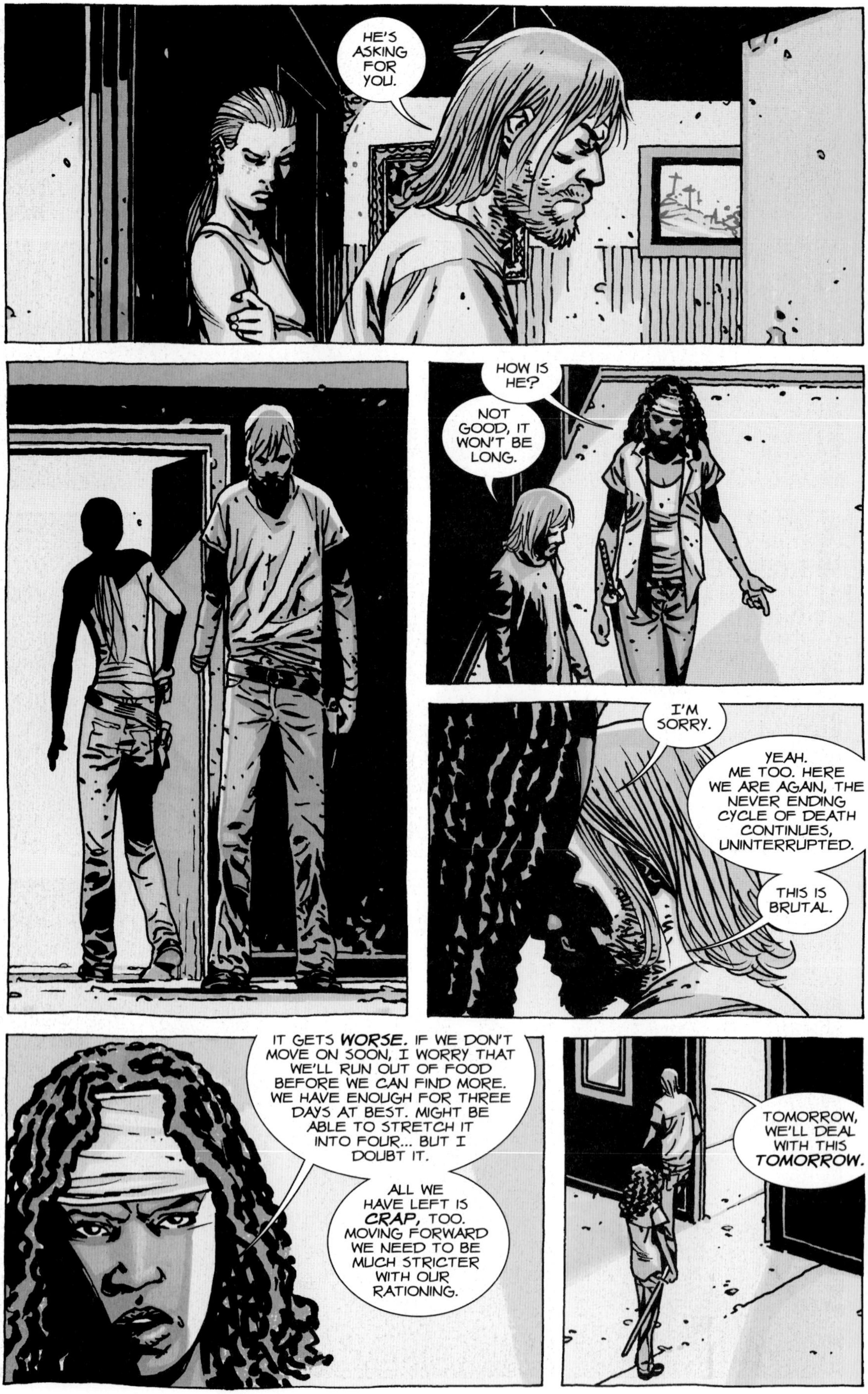
HE'S ASKING FOR YOU.
HOW IS HE?
NOT GOOD, IT WON'T BE LONG.
I'M SORRY.
YEAH. ME TOO. HERE WE ARE AGAIN, THE NEVER ENDING CYCLE OF DEATH CONTINUES, UNINTERRUPTED.
THIS IS BRUTAL.
IT GETS WORSE. IF WE DON'T MOVE ON SOON, I WORRY THAT WE'LL RUN OUT OF FOOD BEFORE WE CAN FIND MORE. WE HAVE ENOUGH FOR THREE DAYS AT BEST. MIGHT BE ABLE TO STRETCH IT INTO FOUR... BUT I DOUBT IT.
ALL WE HAVE LEFT IS CRAP, TOO. MOVING FORWARD WE NEED TO BE MUCH STRICTER WITH OUR RATIONING.
TOMORROW, WE'LL DEAL WITH THIS TOMORROW.

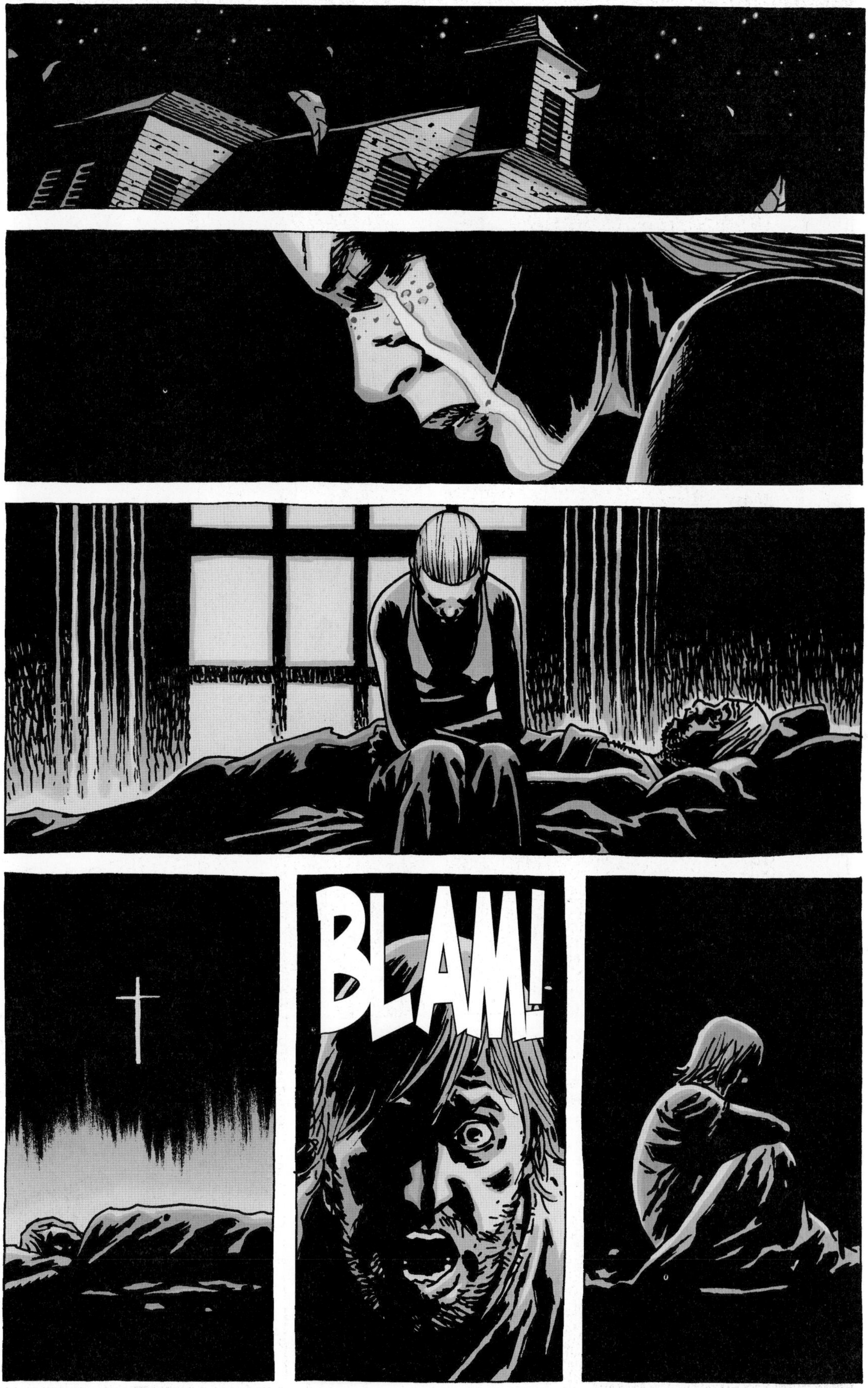
BLAM!

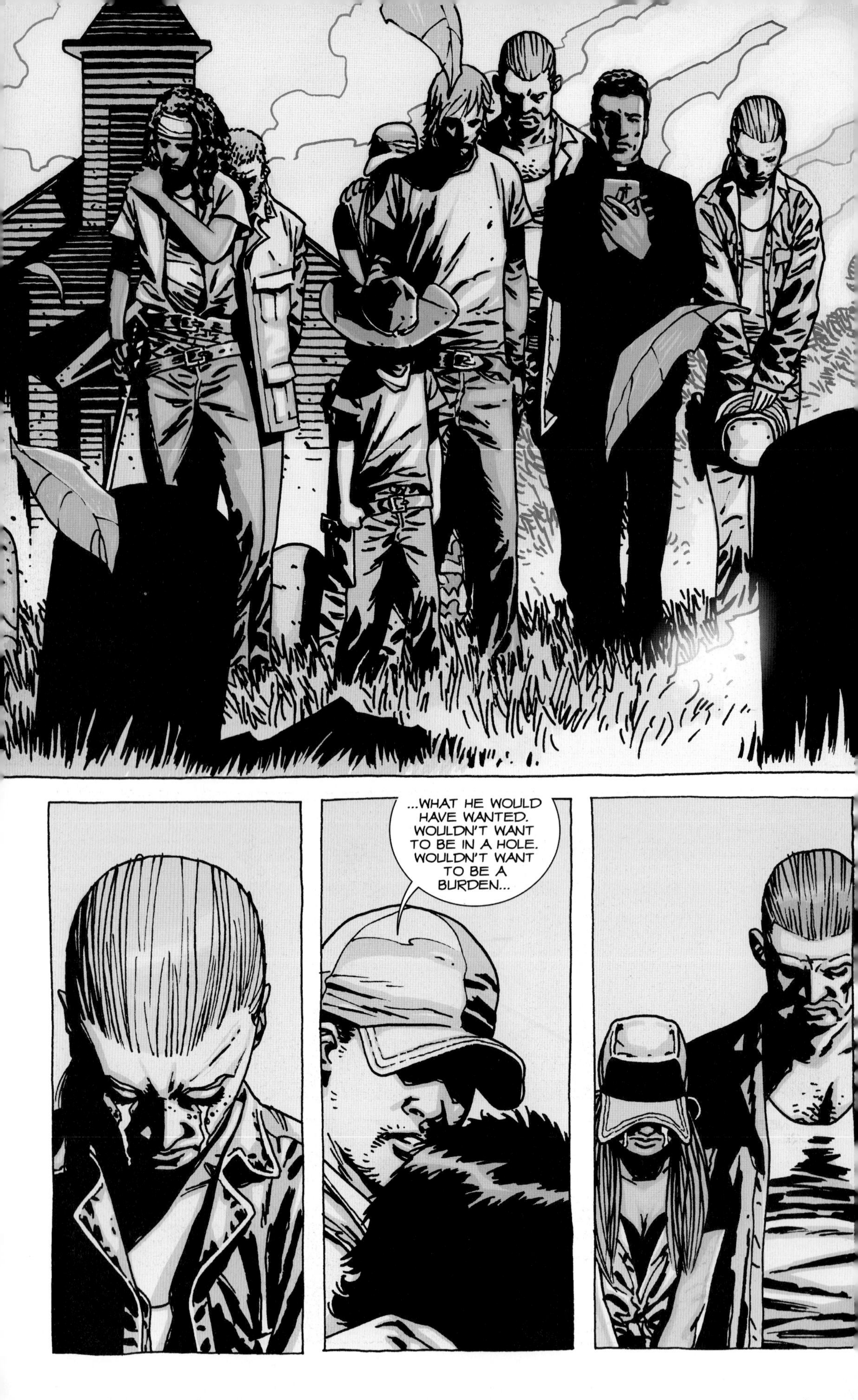
...WHAT HE WOULD HAVE WANTED. WOULDN'T WANT TO BE IN A HOLE. WOULDN'T WANT TO BE A BURDEN...

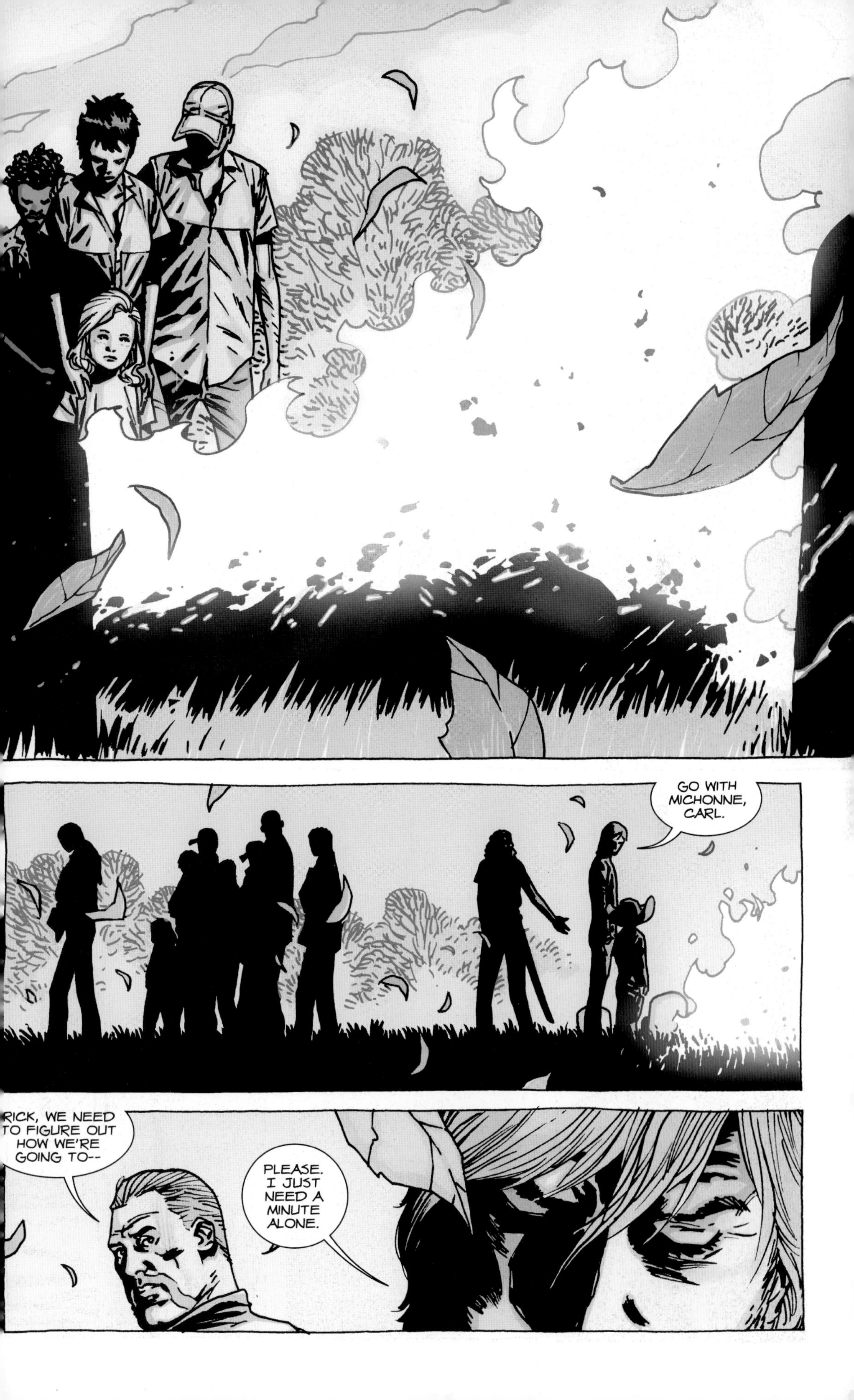
GO WITH MICHONNE, CARL.
RICK, WE NEED TO FIGURE OUT HOW WE'RE GOING TO--
PLEASE. I JUST NEED A MINUTE ALONE.

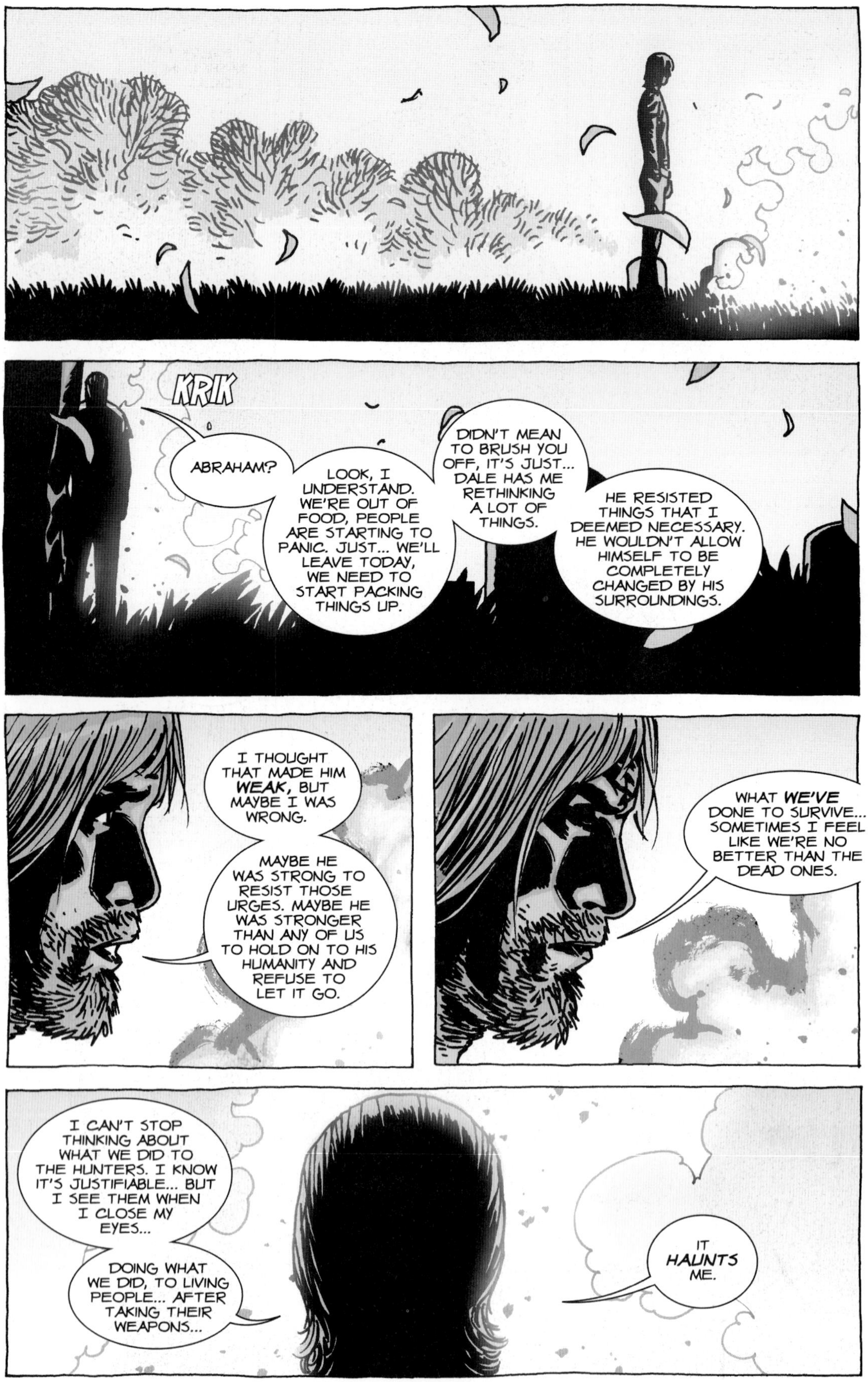
KRIK
ABRAHAM?
LOOK, I UNDERSTAND. WE'RE OUT OF FOOD, PEOPLE ARE STARTING TO PANIC. JUST... WE'LL LEAVE TODAY, WE NEED TO START PACKING THINGS UP.
DIDN'T MEAN TO BRUSH YOU OFF, IT'S JUST... DALE HAS ME RETHINKING A LOT OF THINGS.
HE RESISTED THINGS THAT I DEEMED NECESSARY. HE WOULDN'T ALLOW HIMSELF TO BE COMPLETELY CHANGED BY HIS SURROUNDINGS.
I THOUGHT THAT MADE HIM WEAK, BUT MAYBE I WAS WRONG.
MAYBE HE WAS STRONG TO RESIST THOSE URGES. MAYBE HE WAS STRONGER THAN ANY OF US TO HOLD ON TO HIS HUMANITY AND REFUSE TO LET IT GO.
WHAT WE'VE DONE TO SURVIVE... SOMETIMES I FEEL LIKE WE'RE NO BETTER THAN THE DEAD ONES.
I CAN'T STOP THINKING ABOUT WHAT WE DID TO THE HUNTERS. I KNOW IT'S JUSTIFIABLE... BUT I SEE THEM WHEN I CLOSE MY EYES...
DOING WHAT WE DID, TO LIVING PEOPLE... AFTER TAKING THEIR WEAPONS...
IT HAUNTS ME.

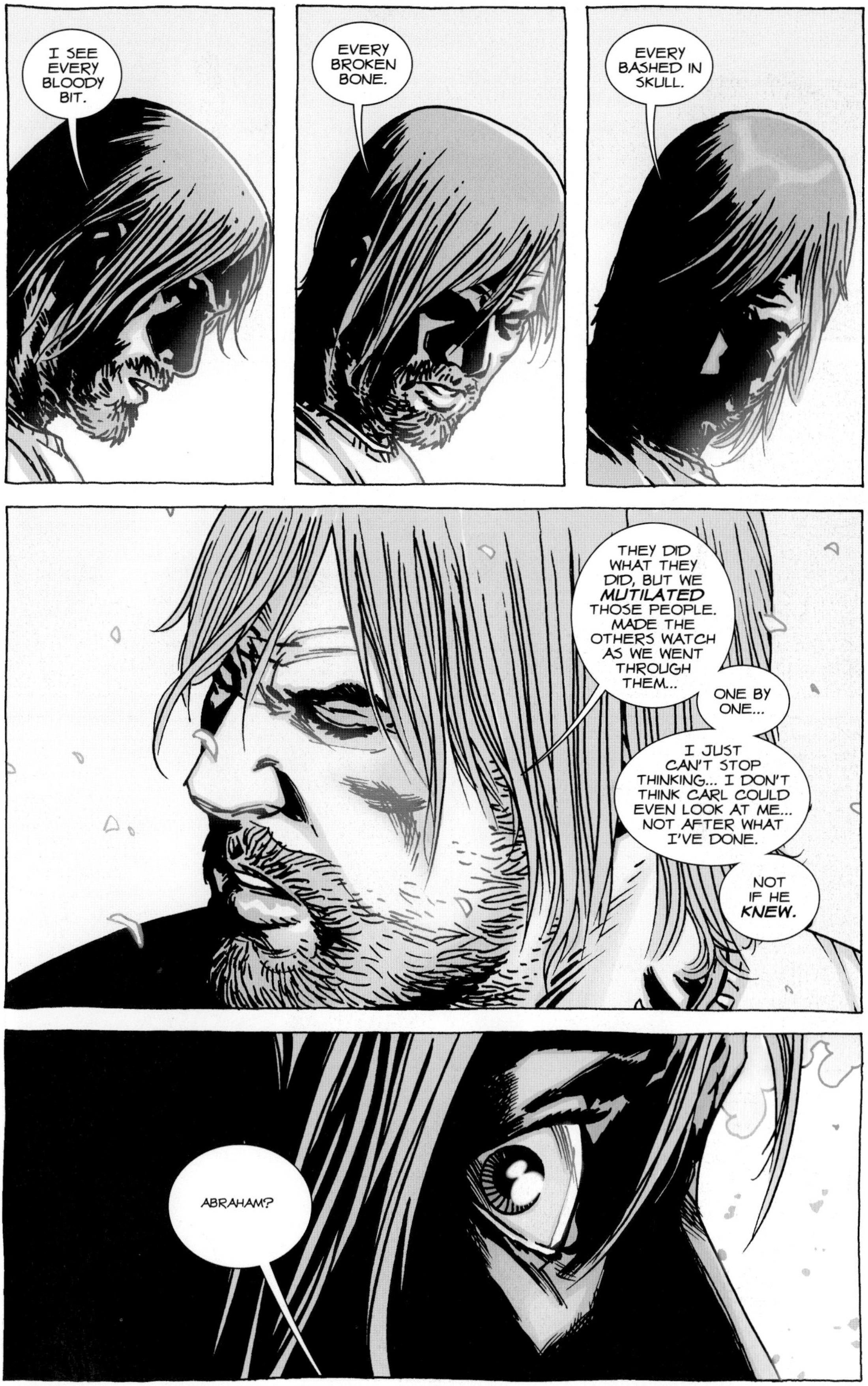
I SEE EVERY BLOODY BIT.
EVERY BROKEN BONE.
EVERY BASHED IN SKULL.
THEY DID WHAT THEY DID, BUT WE MUTILATED THOSE PEOPLE. MADE THE OTHERS WATCH AS WE WENT THROUGH THEM...
ONE BY ONE...
I JUST CAN'T STOP THINKING... I DON'T THINK CARL COULD EVEN LOOK AT ME... NOT AFTER WHAT I'VE DONE.
NOT IF HE KNEW.
ABRAHAM?

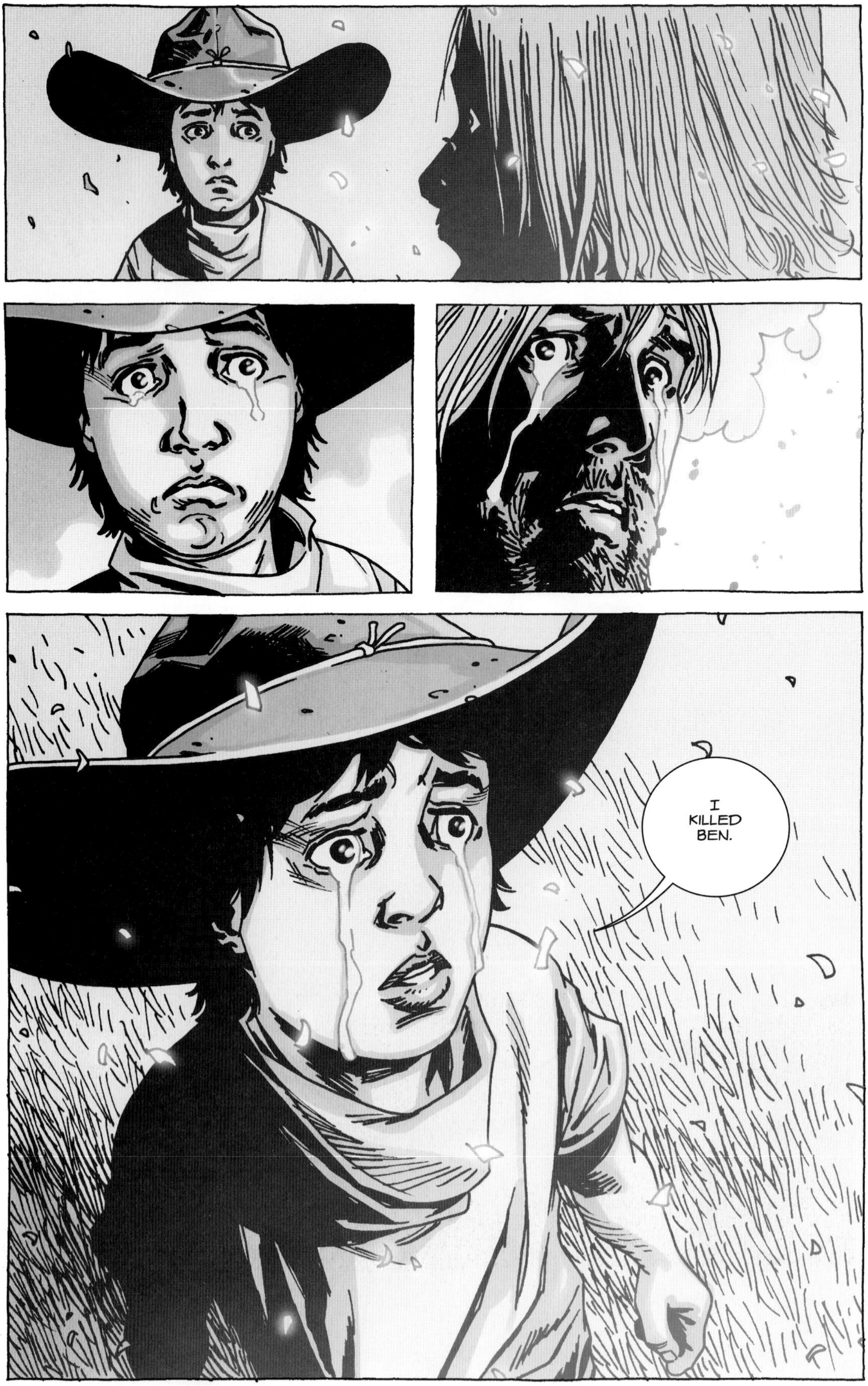
I KILLED BEN.

Chapter Twelve:
Life Among Them

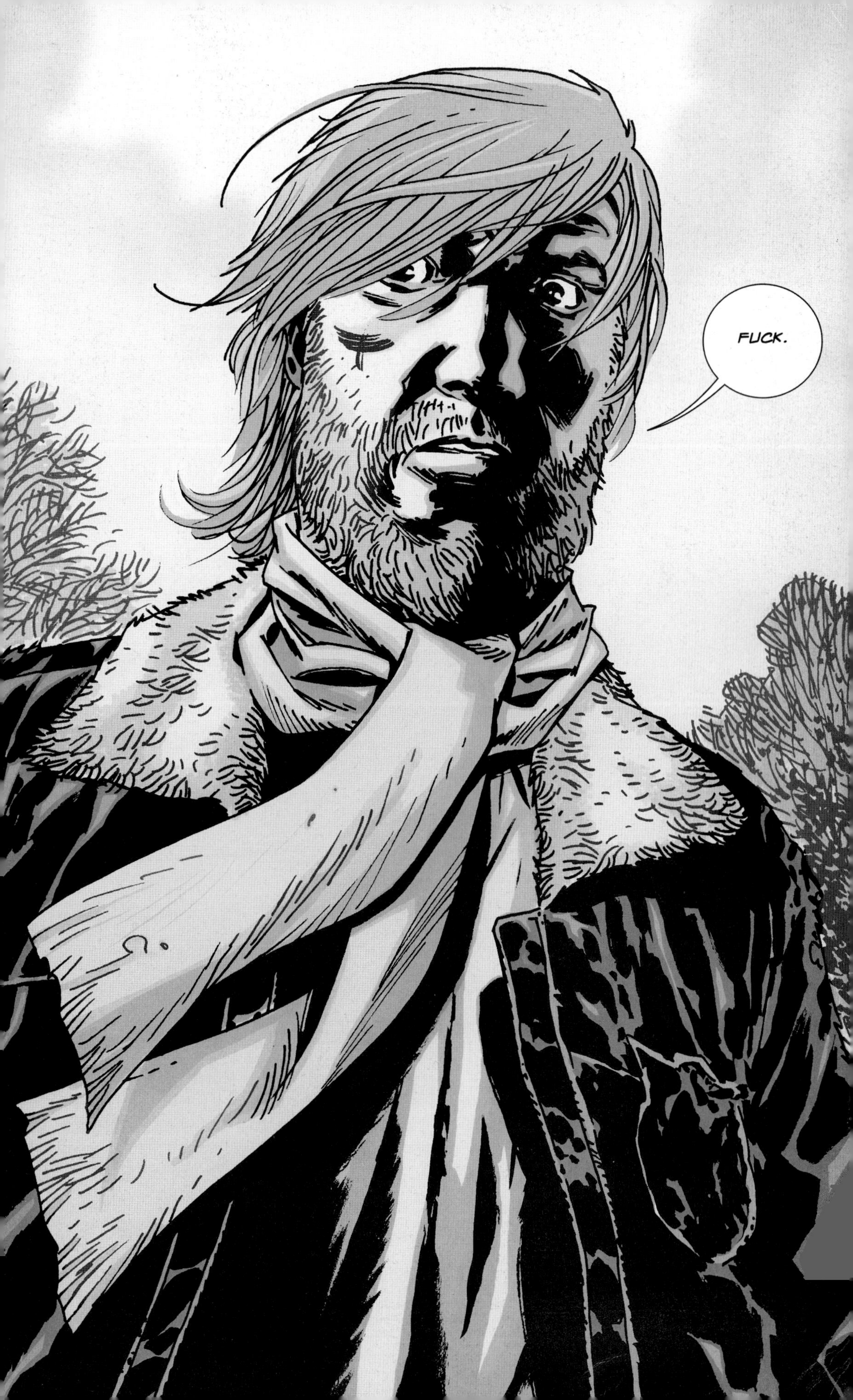
FUCK.

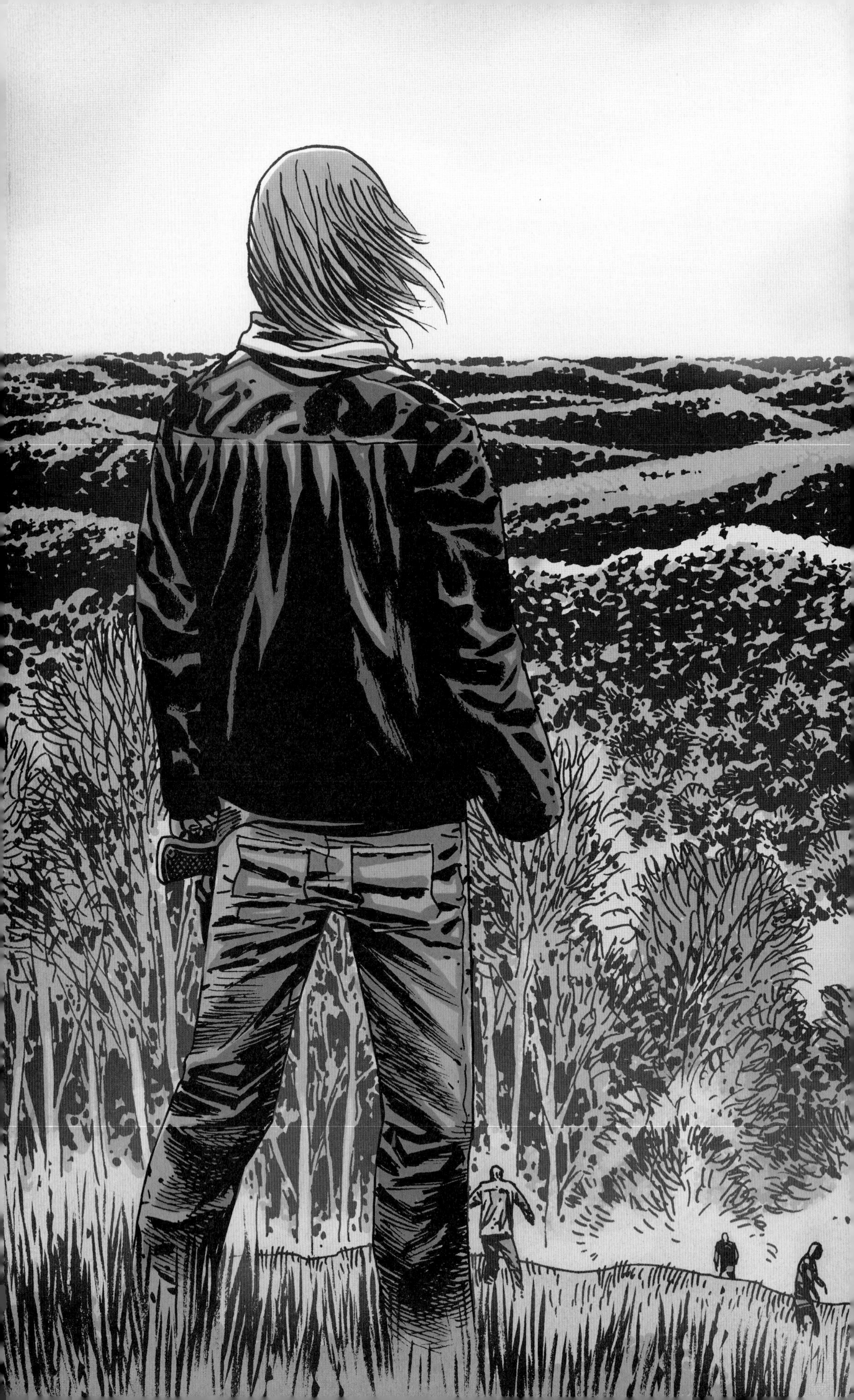

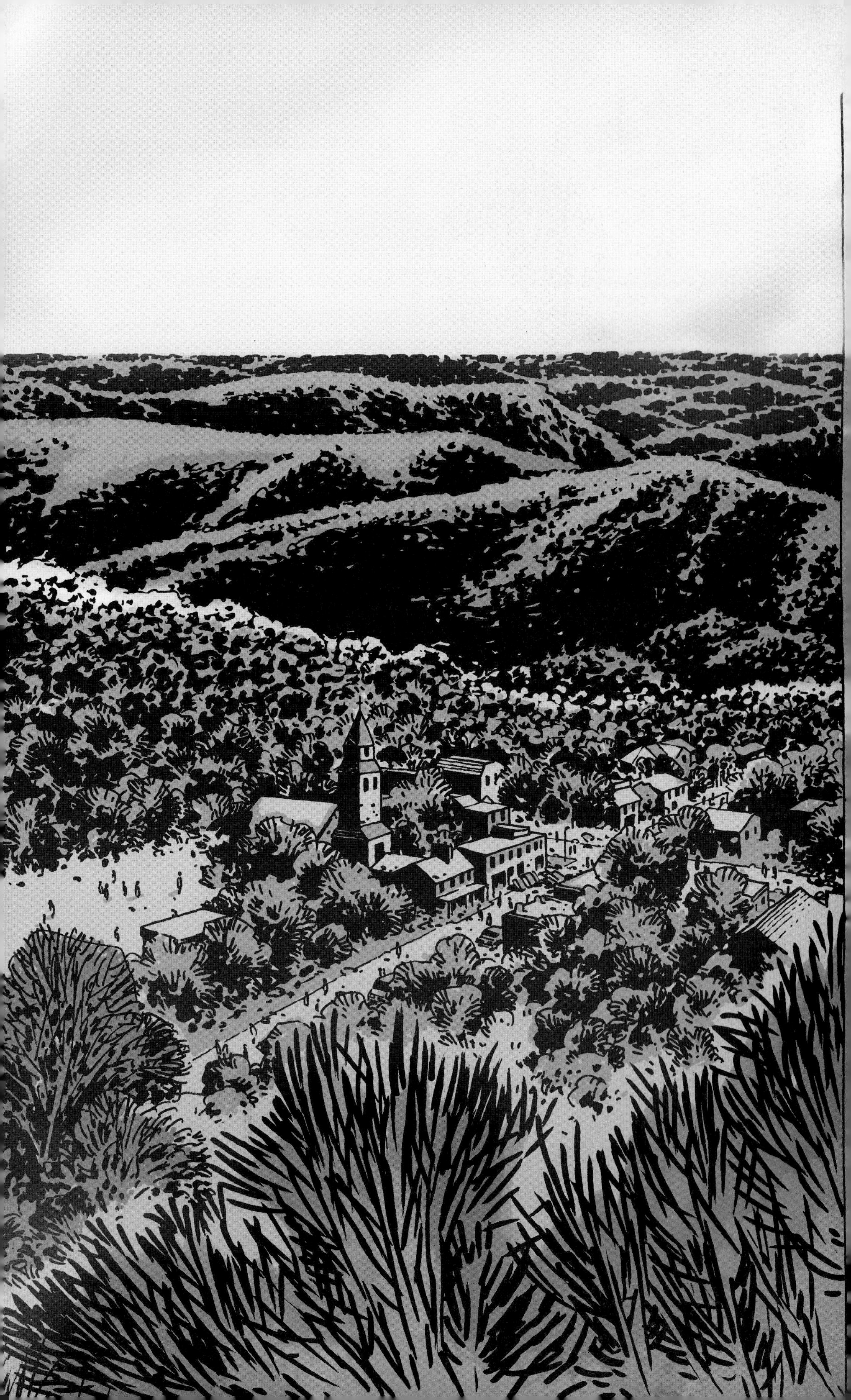

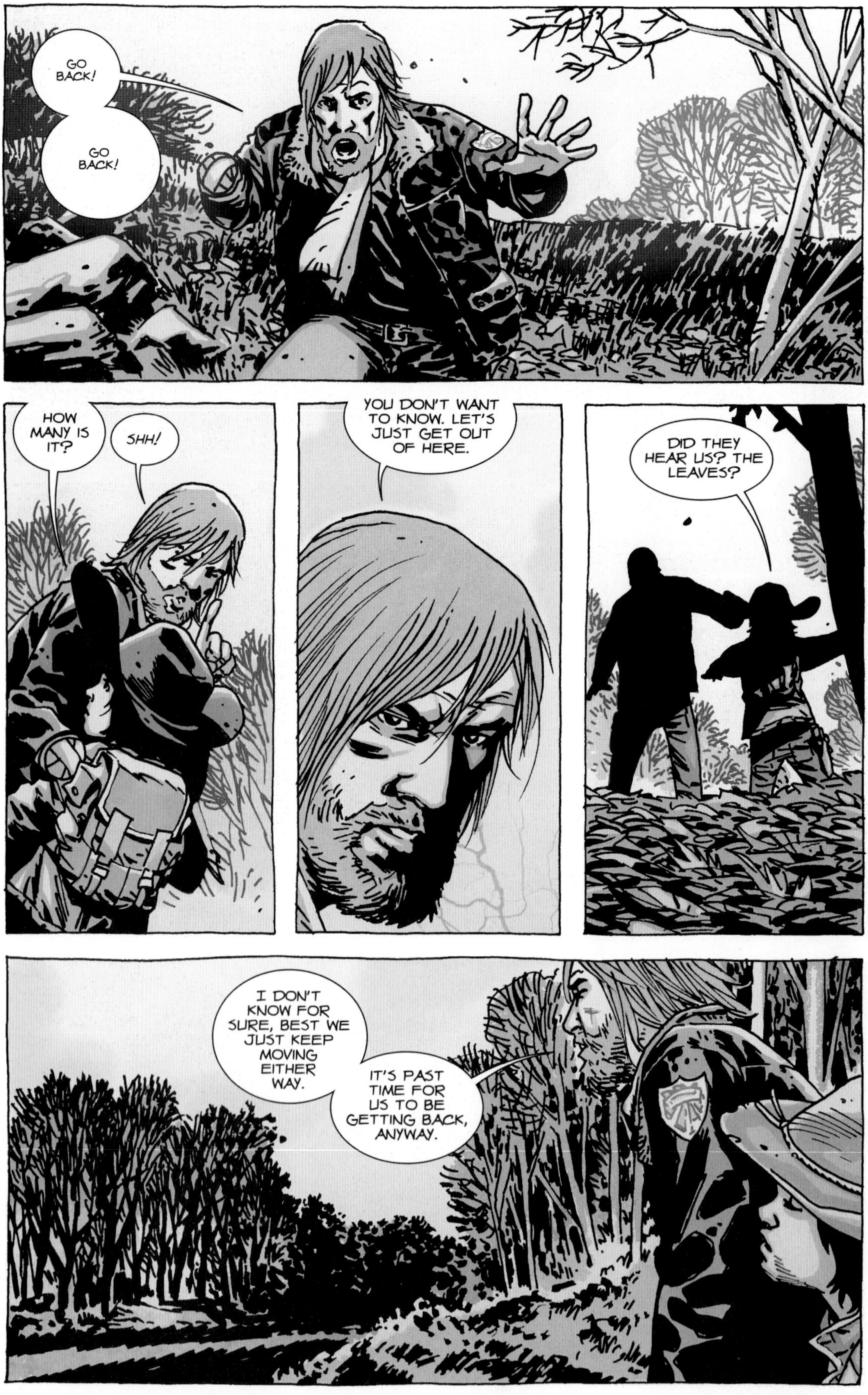

GO BACK!
GO BACK!
HOW MANY IS IT?
SHH!
YOU DON'T WANT TO KNOW. LET'S JUST GET OUT OF HERE.
DID THEY HEAR US? THE LEAVES?
I DON'T KNOW FOR SURE, BEST WE JUST KEEP MOVING EITHER WAY.
IT'S PAST TIME FOR US TO BE GETTING BACK, ANYWAY.

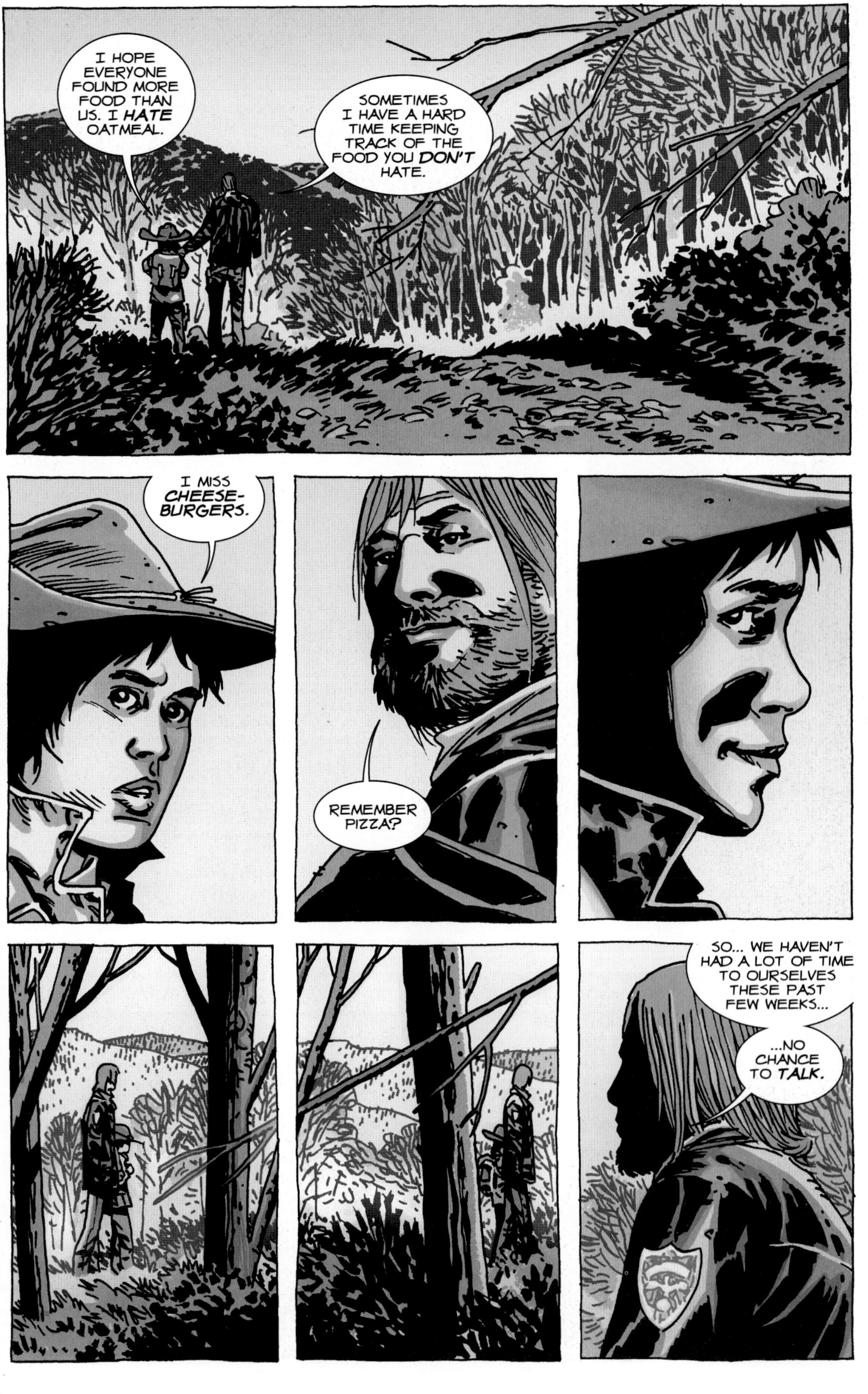
I HOPE EVERYONE FOUND MORE FOOD THAN US. I HATE OATMEAL.
SOMETIMES I HAVE A HARD TIME KEEPING TRACK OF THE FOOD YOU DON'T HATE.
I MISS CHEESE-BURGERS.
REMEMBER PIZZA?
SO... WE HAVEN'T HAD A LOT OF TIME TO OURSELVES THESE PAST FEW WEEKS...
...NO CHANCE TO TALK.

WHY DID YOU KILL BEN?

WHY?

YOU KNOW WHY. SAME REASON *YOU* HAVE TO DO EVERYTHING.

BECAUSE IT NEEDED TO BE DONE. AND BECAUSE NO ONE ELSE WOULD.

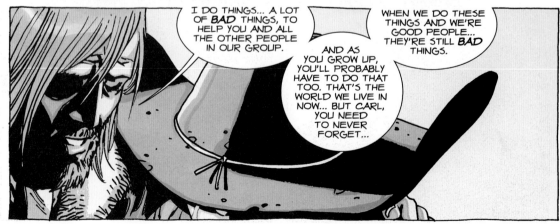

I DO THINGS... A LOT OF *BAD* THINGS, TO HELP YOU AND ALL THE OTHER PEOPLE IN OUR GROUP.

AND AS YOU GROW UP, YOU'LL PROBABLY HAVE TO DO THAT TOO. THAT'S THE WORLD WE LIVE IN NOW... BUT CARL, YOU NEED TO NEVER FORGET...

WHEN WE DO THESE THINGS AND WE'RE GOOD PEOPLE... THEY'RE STILL *BAD* THINGS.

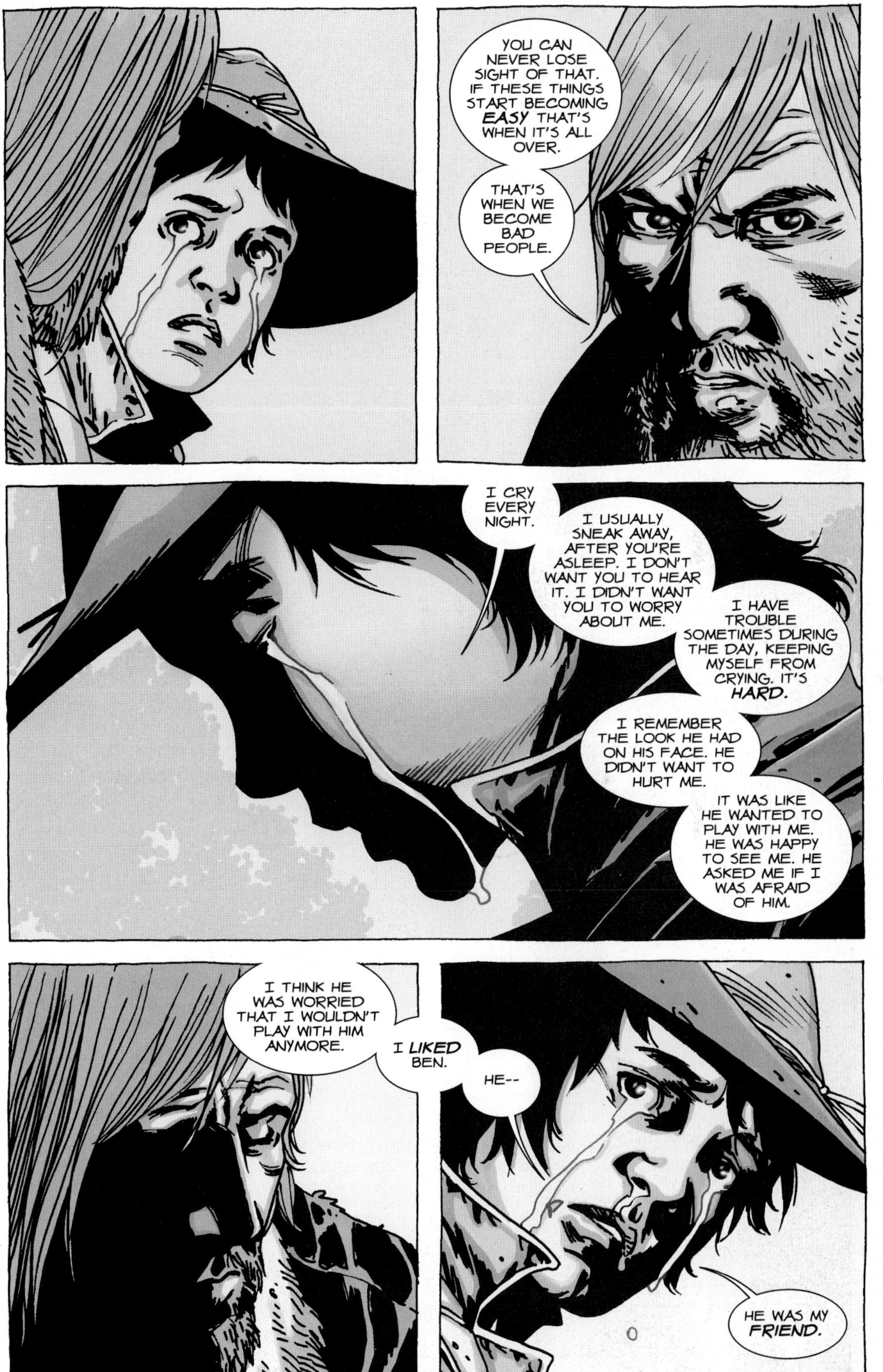
YOU CAN NEVER LOSE SIGHT OF THAT. IF THESE THINGS START BECOMING *EASY* THAT'S WHEN IT'S ALL OVER.
THAT'S WHEN WE BECOME BAD PEOPLE.
I CRY EVERY NIGHT.
I USUALLY SNEAK AWAY, AFTER YOU'RE ASLEEP. I DON'T WANT YOU TO HEAR IT. I DIDN'T WANT YOU TO WORRY ABOUT ME.
I HAVE TROUBLE SOMETIMES DURING THE DAY, KEEPING MYSELF FROM CRYING. IT'S *HARD.*
I REMEMBER THE LOOK HE HAD ON HIS FACE. HE DIDN'T WANT TO HURT ME.
IT WAS LIKE HE WANTED TO PLAY WITH ME. HE WAS HAPPY TO SEE ME. HE ASKED ME IF I WAS AFRAID OF HIM.
I THINK HE WAS WORRIED THAT I WOULDN'T PLAY WITH HIM ANYMORE.
I *LIKED* BEN.
HE--
HE WAS MY *FRIEND.*

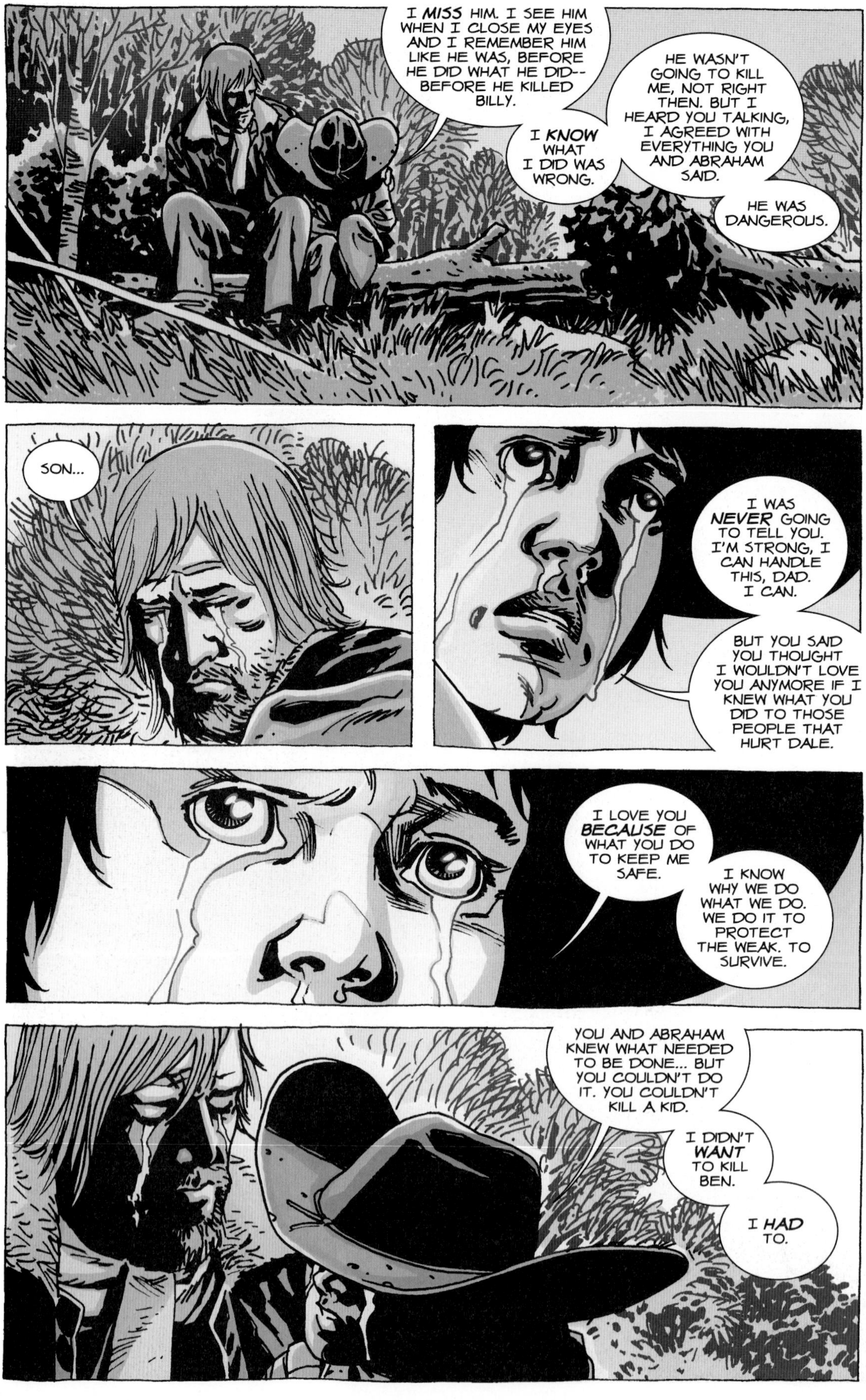

I MISS HIM. I SEE HIM WHEN I CLOSE MY EYES AND I REMEMBER HIM LIKE HE WAS, BEFORE HE DID WHAT HE DID-- BEFORE HE KILLED BILLY.
I KNOW WHAT I DID WAS WRONG.
HE WASN'T GOING TO KILL ME, NOT RIGHT THEN. BUT I HEARD YOU TALKING, I AGREED WITH EVERYTHING YOU AND ABRAHAM SAID.
HE WAS DANGEROUS.
SON...
I WAS NEVER GOING TO TELL YOU. I'M STRONG, I CAN HANDLE THIS, DAD. I CAN.
BUT YOU SAID YOU THOUGHT I WOULDN'T LOVE YOU ANYMORE IF I KNEW WHAT YOU DID TO THOSE PEOPLE THAT HURT DALE.
I LOVE YOU BECAUSE OF WHAT YOU DO TO KEEP ME SAFE.
I KNOW WHY WE DO WHAT WE DO. WE DO IT TO PROTECT THE WEAK. TO SURVIVE.
YOU AND ABRAHAM KNEW WHAT NEEDED TO BE DONE... BUT YOU COULDN'T DO IT. YOU COULDN'T KILL A KID.
I DIDN'T WANT TO KILL BEN.
I HAD TO.

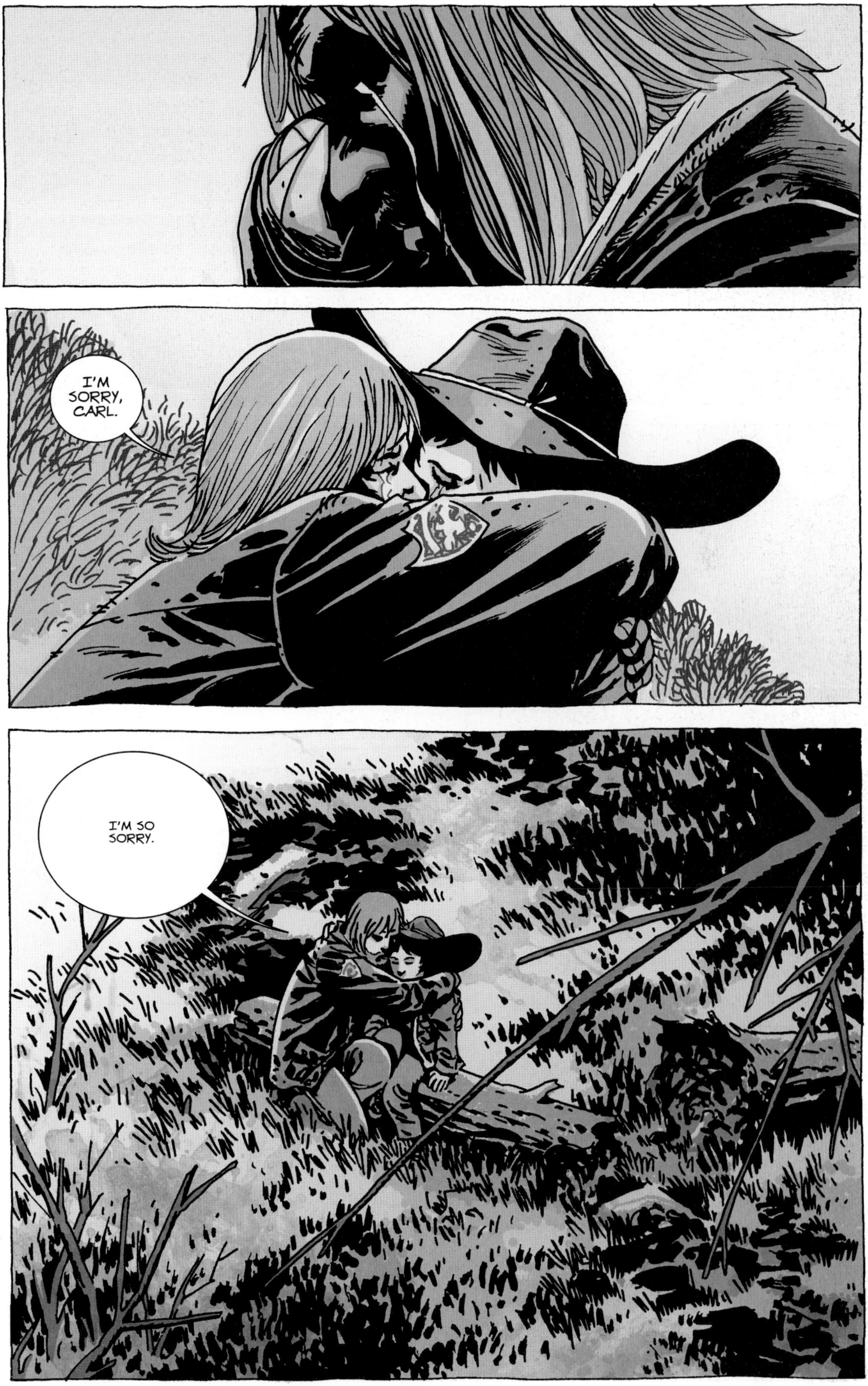
I'M SORRY, CARL.
I'M SO SORRY.

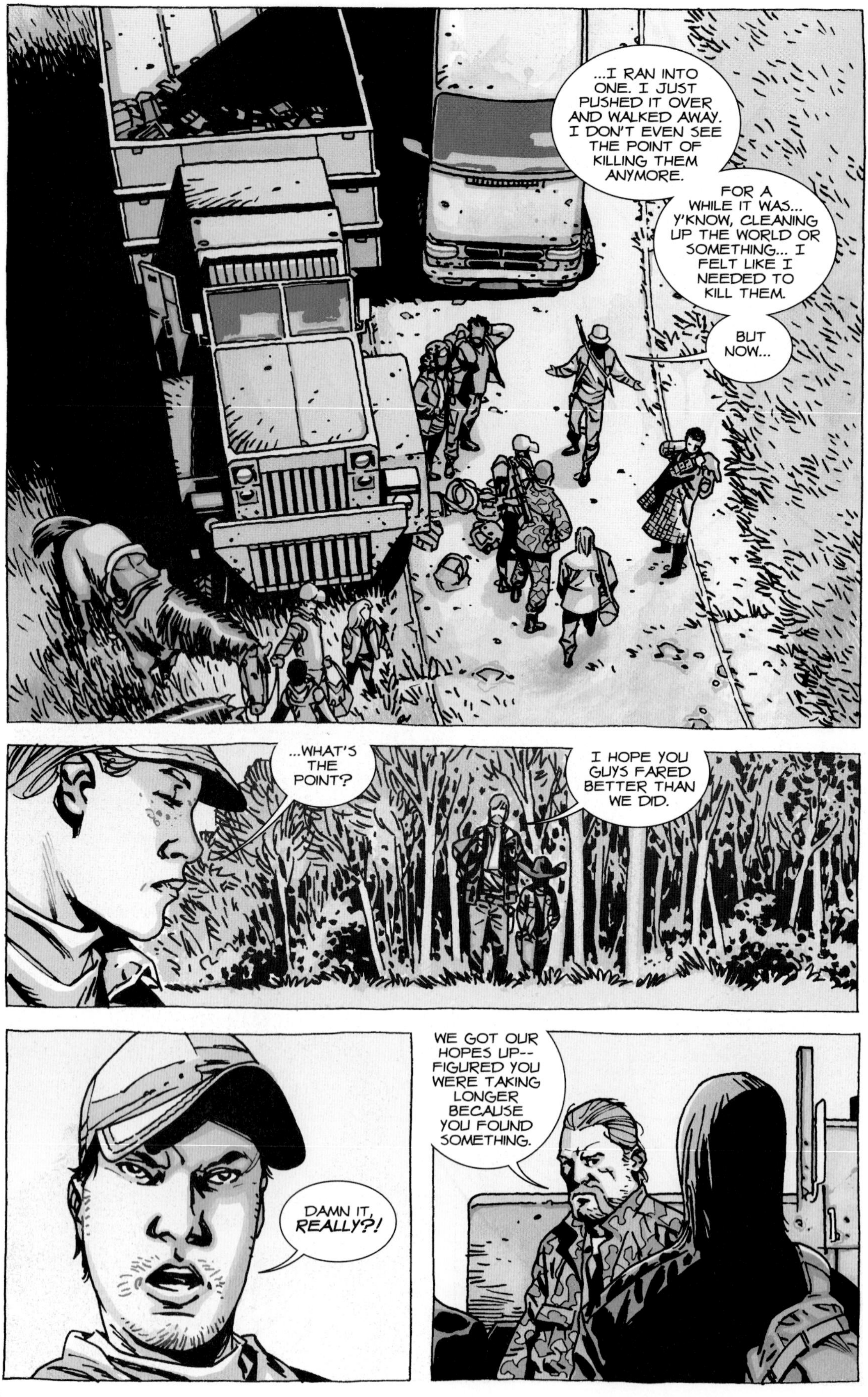
...I RAN INTO ONE. I JUST PUSHED IT OVER AND WALKED AWAY. I DON'T EVEN SEE THE POINT OF KILLING THEM ANYMORE.
FOR A WHILE IT WAS... Y'KNOW, CLEANING UP THE WORLD OR SOMETHING... I FELT LIKE I NEEDED TO KILL THEM.
BUT NOW...
...WHAT'S THE POINT?
I HOPE YOU GUYS FARED BETTER THAN WE DID.
WE GOT OUR HOPES UP-- FIGURED YOU WERE TAKING LONGER BECAUSE YOU FOUND SOMETHING.
DAMN IT, *REALLY?!*

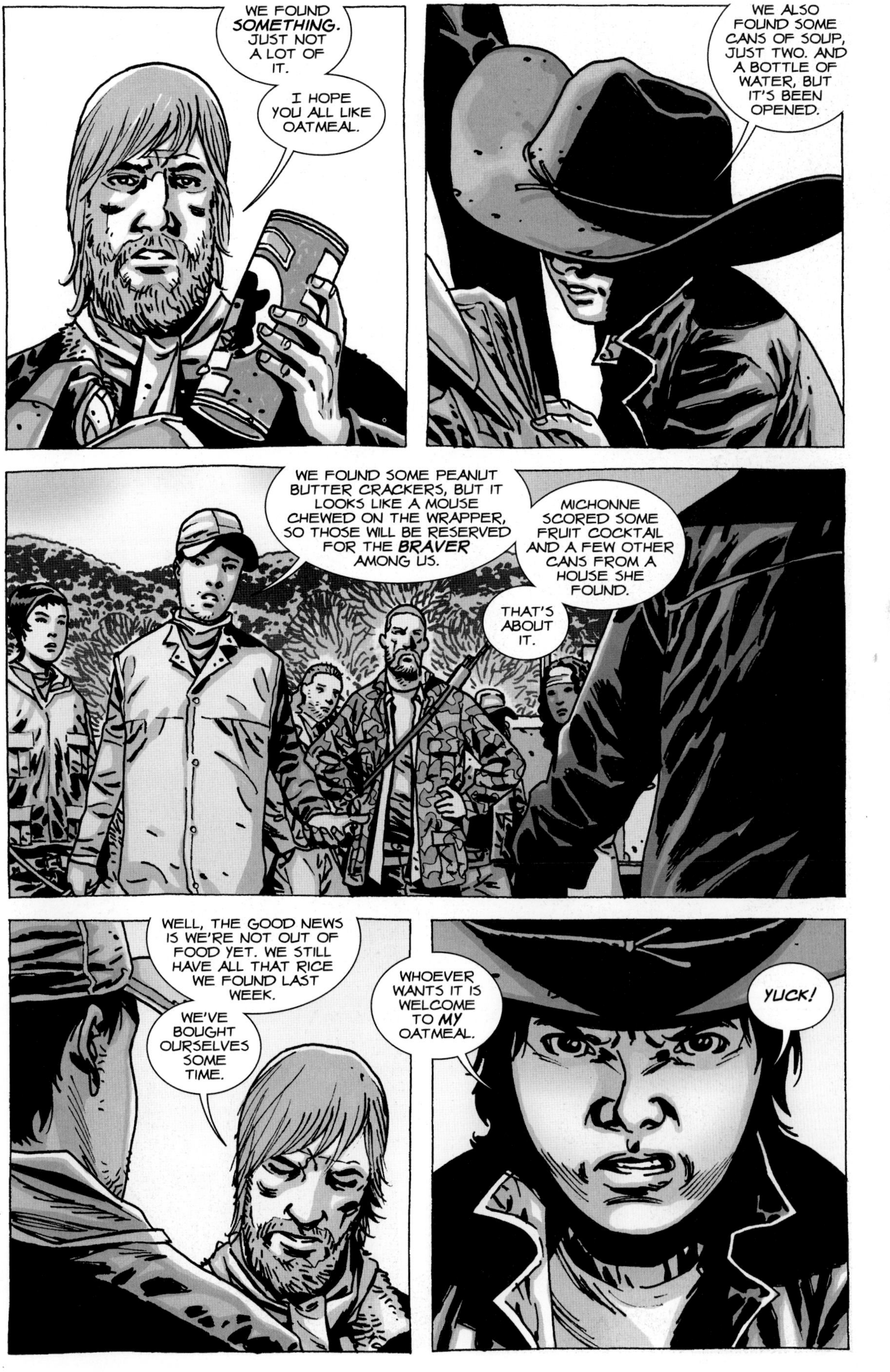

WE FOUND SOMETHING. JUST NOT A LOT OF IT.
I HOPE YOU ALL LIKE OATMEAL.
WE ALSO FOUND SOME CANS OF SOUP, JUST TWO. AND A BOTTLE OF WATER, BUT IT'S BEEN OPENED.
WE FOUND SOME PEANUT BUTTER CRACKERS, BUT IT LOOKS LIKE A MOUSE CHEWED ON THE WRAPPER, SO THOSE WILL BE RESERVED FOR THE BRAVER AMONG US.
MICHONNE SCORED SOME FRUIT COCKTAIL AND A FEW OTHER CANS FROM A HOUSE SHE FOUND.
THAT'S ABOUT IT.
WELL, THE GOOD NEWS IS WE'RE NOT OUT OF FOOD YET. WE STILL HAVE ALL THAT RICE WE FOUND LAST WEEK.
WE'VE BOUGHT OURSELVES SOME TIME.
WHOEVER WANTS IT IS WELCOME TO MY OATMEAL.
YUCK!

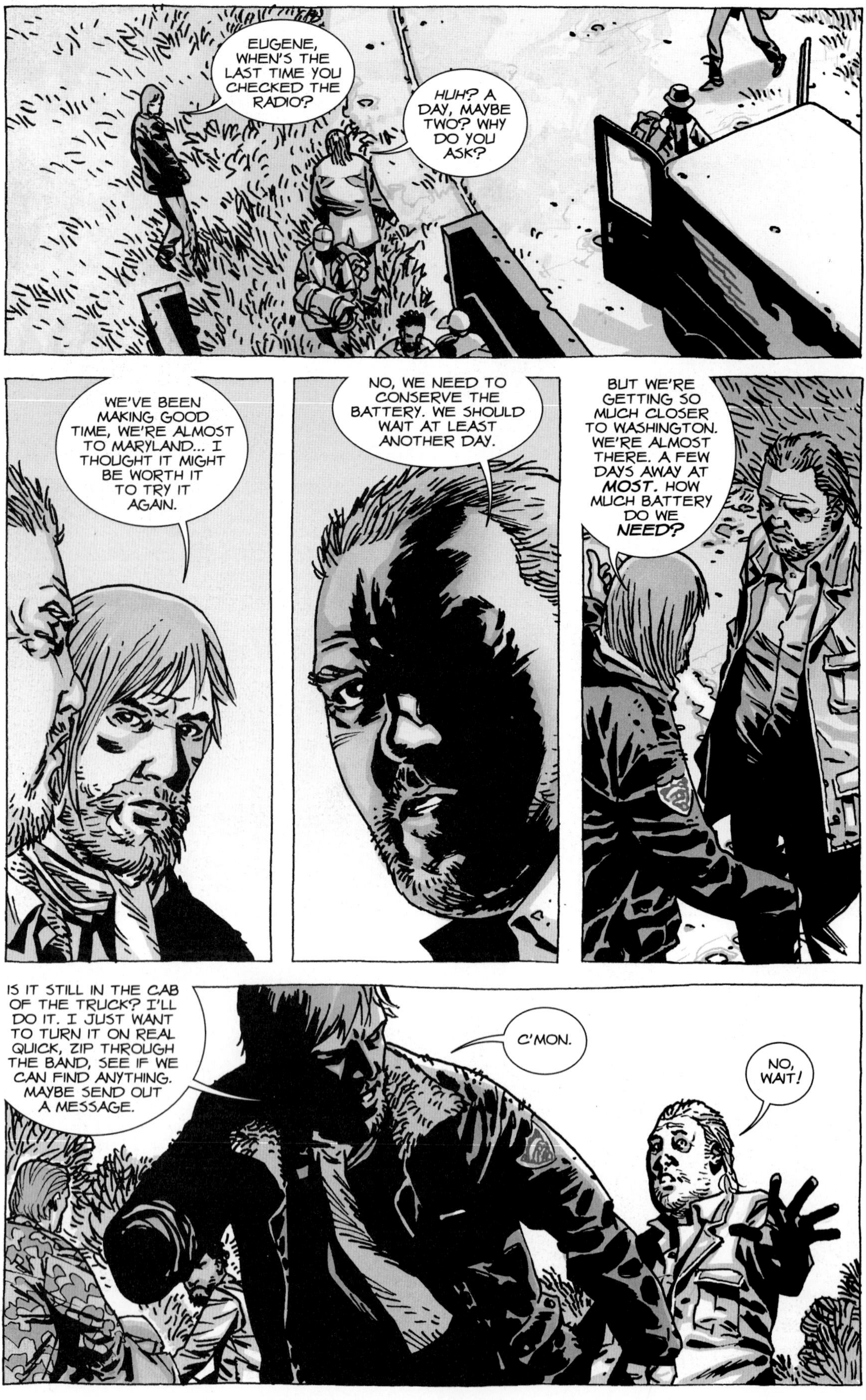
EUGENE, WHEN'S THE LAST TIME YOU CHECKED THE RADIO?
HUH? A DAY, MAYBE TWO? WHY DO YOU ASK?
WE'VE BEEN MAKING GOOD TIME, WE'RE ALMOST TO MARYLAND... I THOUGHT IT MIGHT BE WORTH IT TO TRY IT AGAIN.
NO, WE NEED TO CONSERVE THE BATTERY. WE SHOULD WAIT AT LEAST ANOTHER DAY.
BUT WE'RE GETTING SO MUCH CLOSER TO WASHINGTON. WE'RE ALMOST THERE. A FEW DAYS AWAY AT MOST. HOW MUCH BATTERY DO WE NEED?
IS IT STILL IN THE CAB OF THE TRUCK? I'LL DO IT. I JUST WANT TO TURN IT ON REAL QUICK, ZIP THROUGH THE BAND, SEE IF WE CAN FIND ANYTHING. MAYBE SEND OUT A MESSAGE.
C'MON.
NO, WAIT!

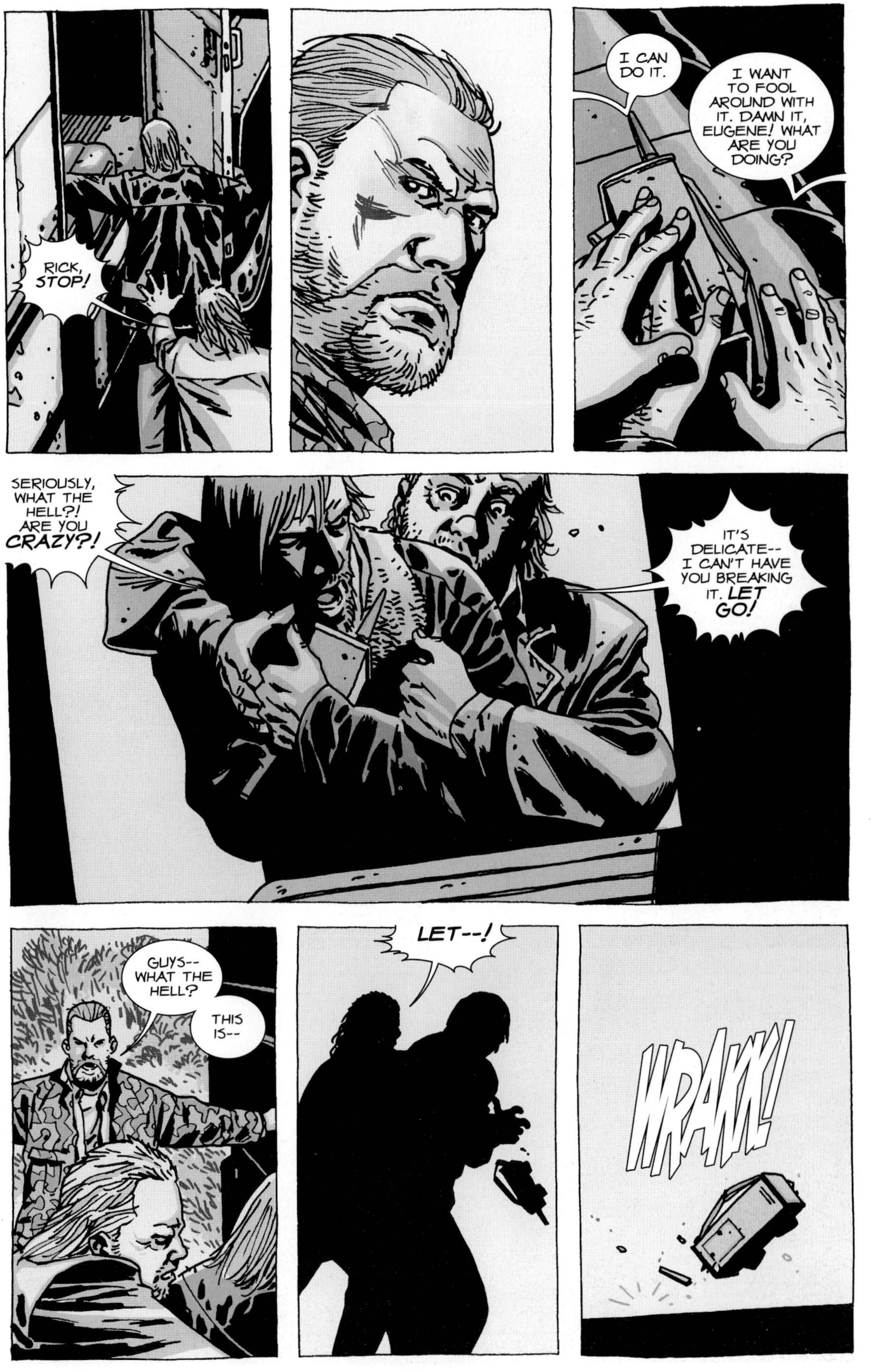
RICK, STOP!
I CAN DO IT.
I WANT TO FOOL AROUND WITH IT. DAMN IT, EUGENE! WHAT ARE YOU DOING?
SERIOUSLY, WHAT THE HELL?! ARE YOU CRAZY?!
IT'S DELICATE-- I CAN'T HAVE YOU BREAKING IT. LET GO!
GUYS-- WHAT THE HELL?
THIS IS--
LET--!
WRAKK!

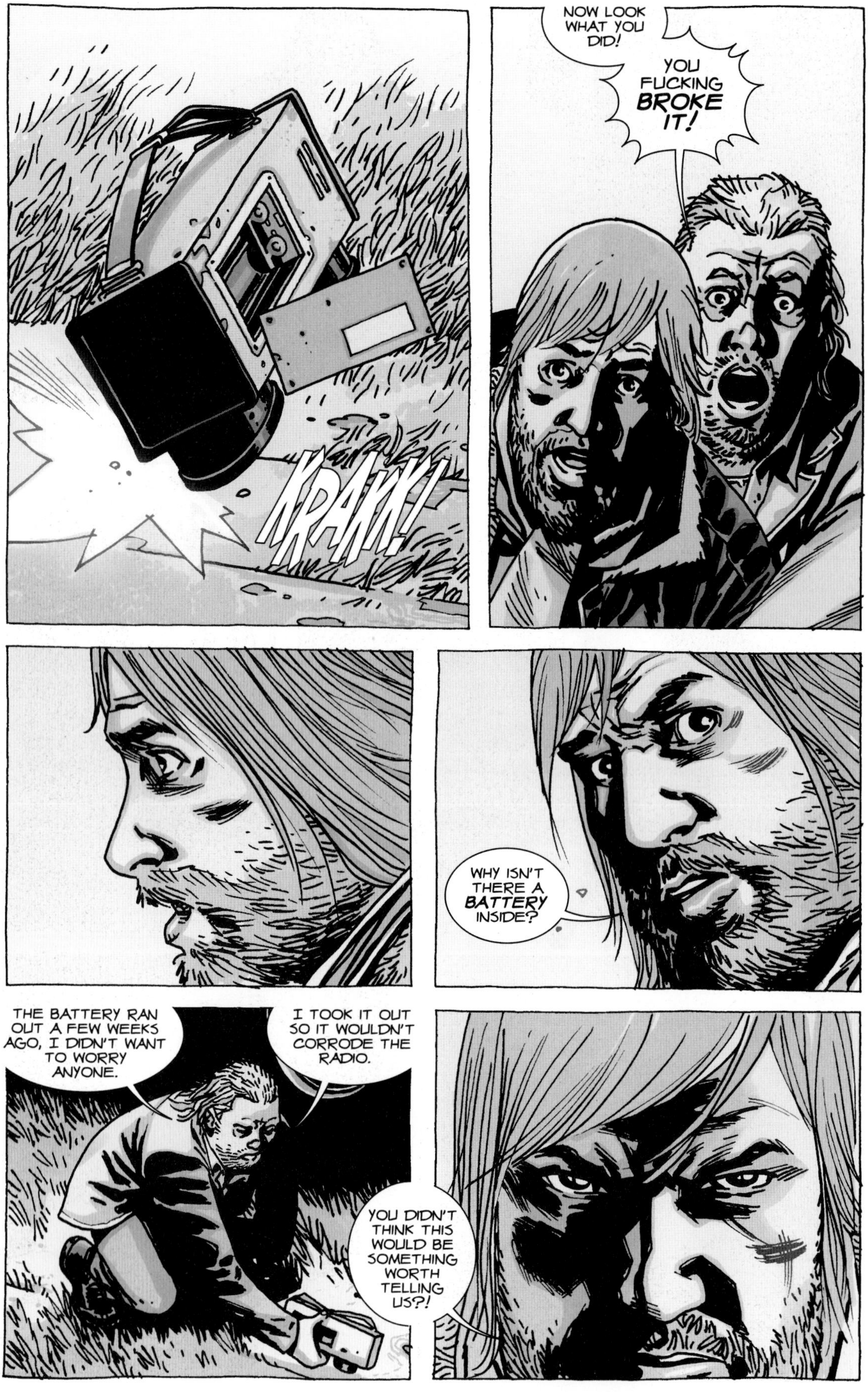
KRAKK!
NOW LOOK WHAT YOU DID!
YOU FUCKING BROKE IT!
WHY ISN'T THERE A BATTERY INSIDE?
THE BATTERY RAN OUT A FEW WEEKS AGO, I DIDN'T WANT TO WORRY ANYONE.
I TOOK IT OUT SO IT WOULDN'T CORRODE THE RADIO.
YOU DIDN'T THINK THIS WOULD BE SOMETHING WORTH TELLING US?!

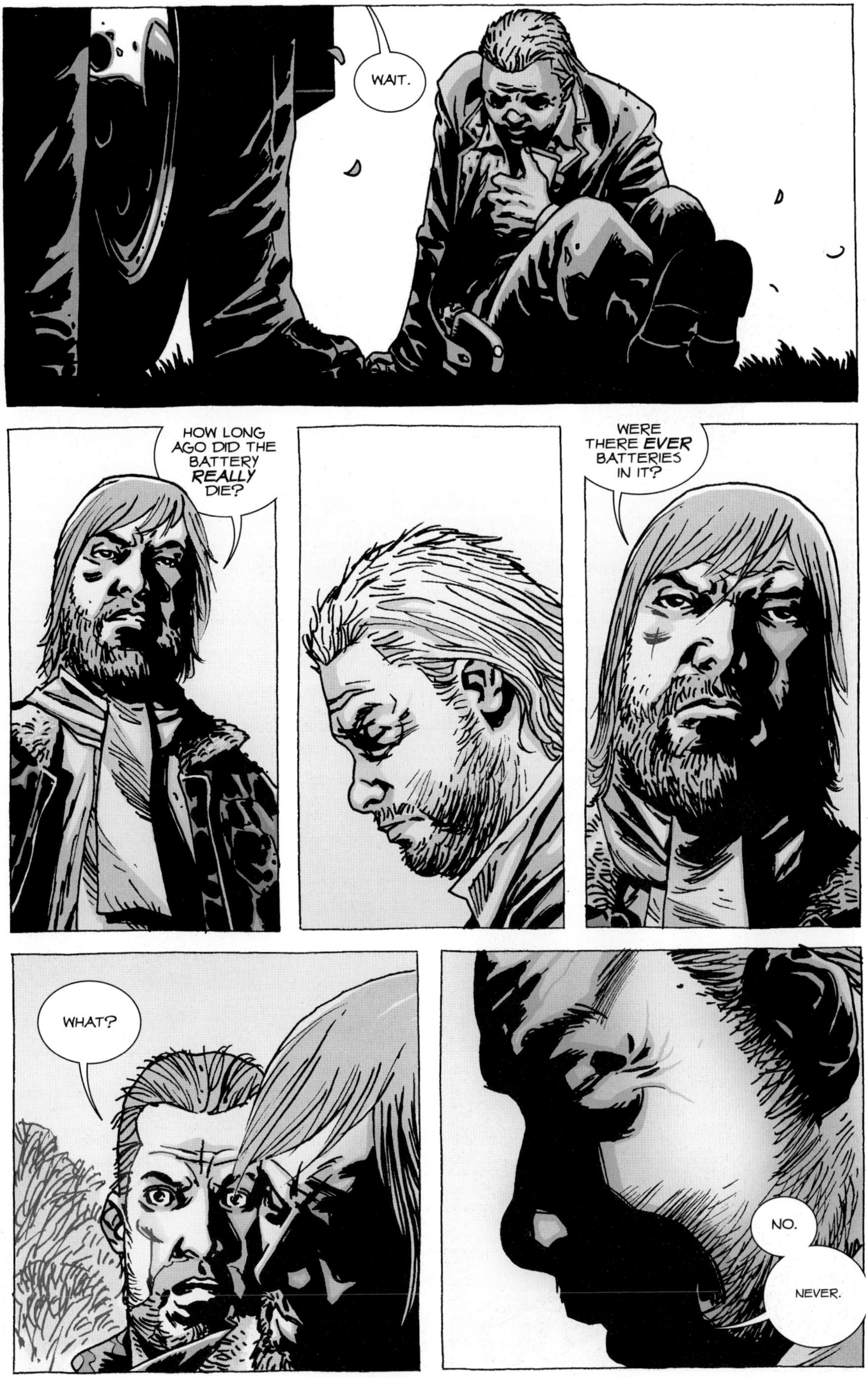
WAIT.
HOW LONG AGO DID THE BATTERY REALLY DIE?
WERE THERE EVER BATTERIES IN IT?
WHAT?
NO.
NEVER.

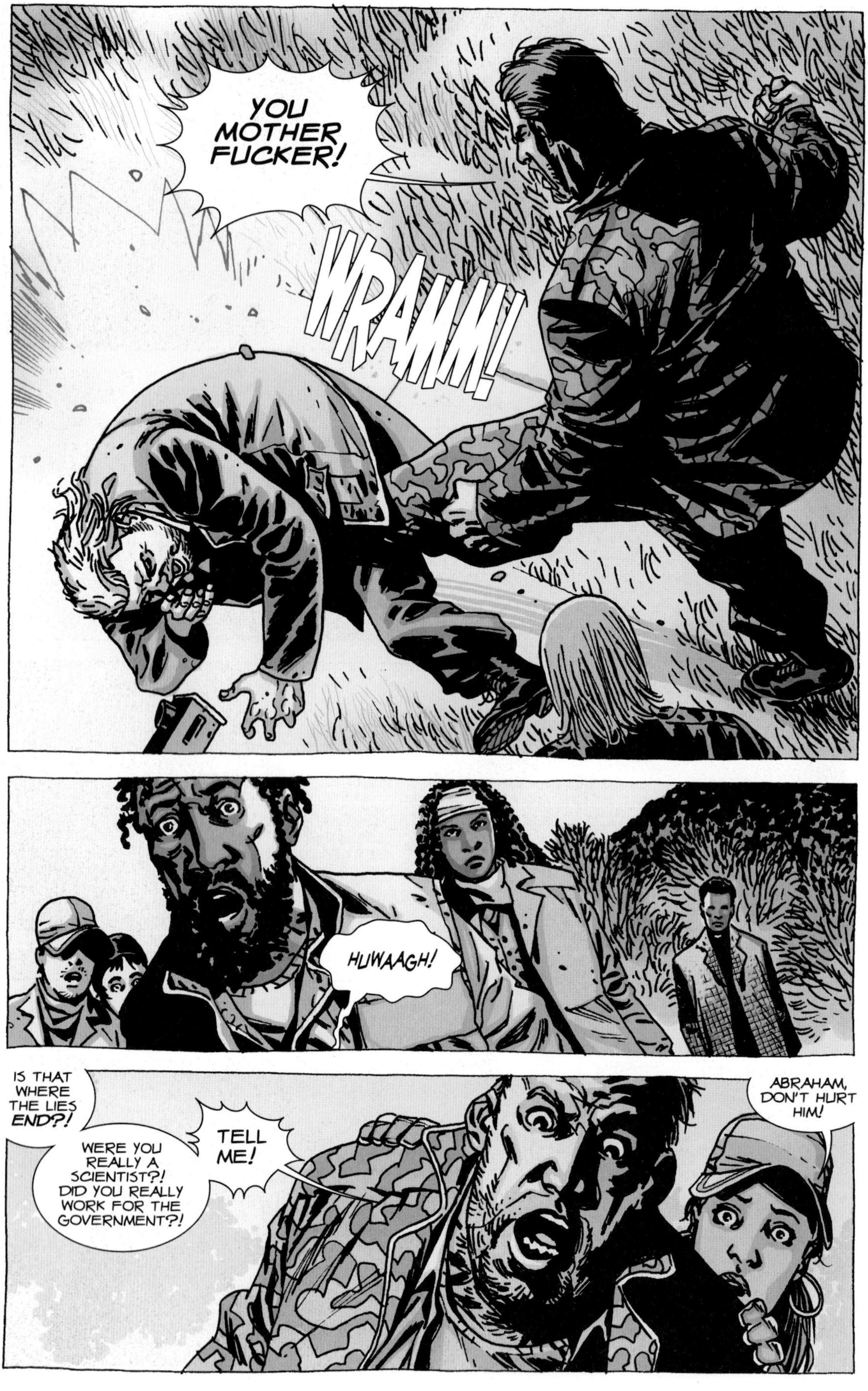

YOU MOTHER FUCKER!
WRAMM!
HUWAAGH!
IS THAT WHERE THE LIES END?!
WERE YOU REALLY A SCIENTIST?! DID YOU REALLY WORK FOR THE GOVERNMENT?!
TELL ME!
ABRAHAM, DON'T HURT HIM!

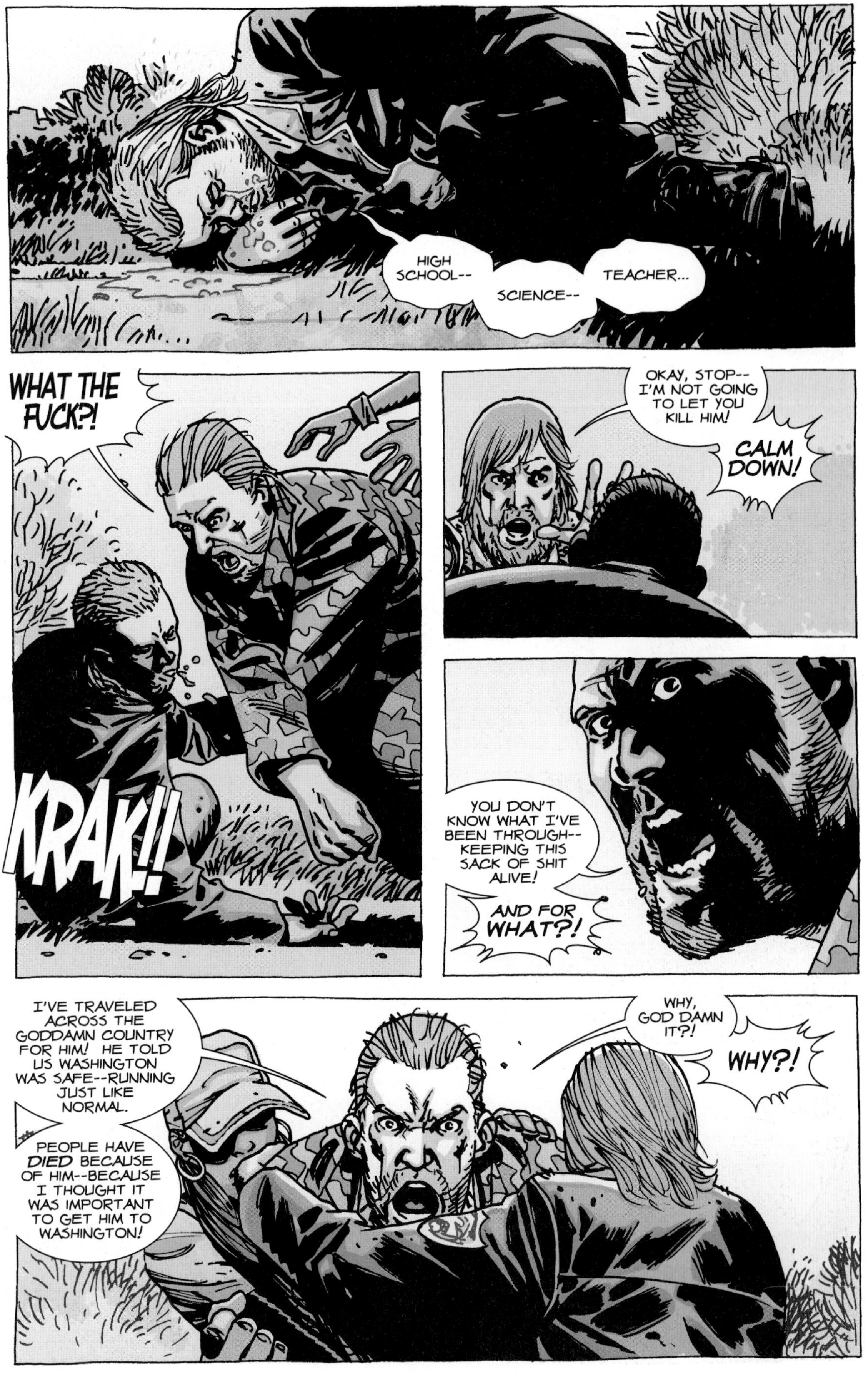
HIGH SCHOOL--
SCIENCE--
TEACHER...
WHAT THE FUCK?!
KRAK!!
OKAY, STOP-- I'M NOT GOING TO LET YOU KILL HIM!
CALM DOWN!
YOU DON'T KNOW WHAT I'VE BEEN THROUGH-- KEEPING THIS SACK OF SHIT ALIVE!
AND FOR WHAT?!
I'VE TRAVELED ACROSS THE GODDAMN COUNTRY FOR HIM! HE TOLD US WASHINGTON WAS SAFE--RUNNING JUST LIKE NORMAL.
PEOPLE HAVE DIED BECAUSE OF HIM--BECAUSE I THOUGHT IT WAS IMPORTANT TO GET HIM TO WASHINGTON!
WHY, GOD DAMN IT?!
WHY?!

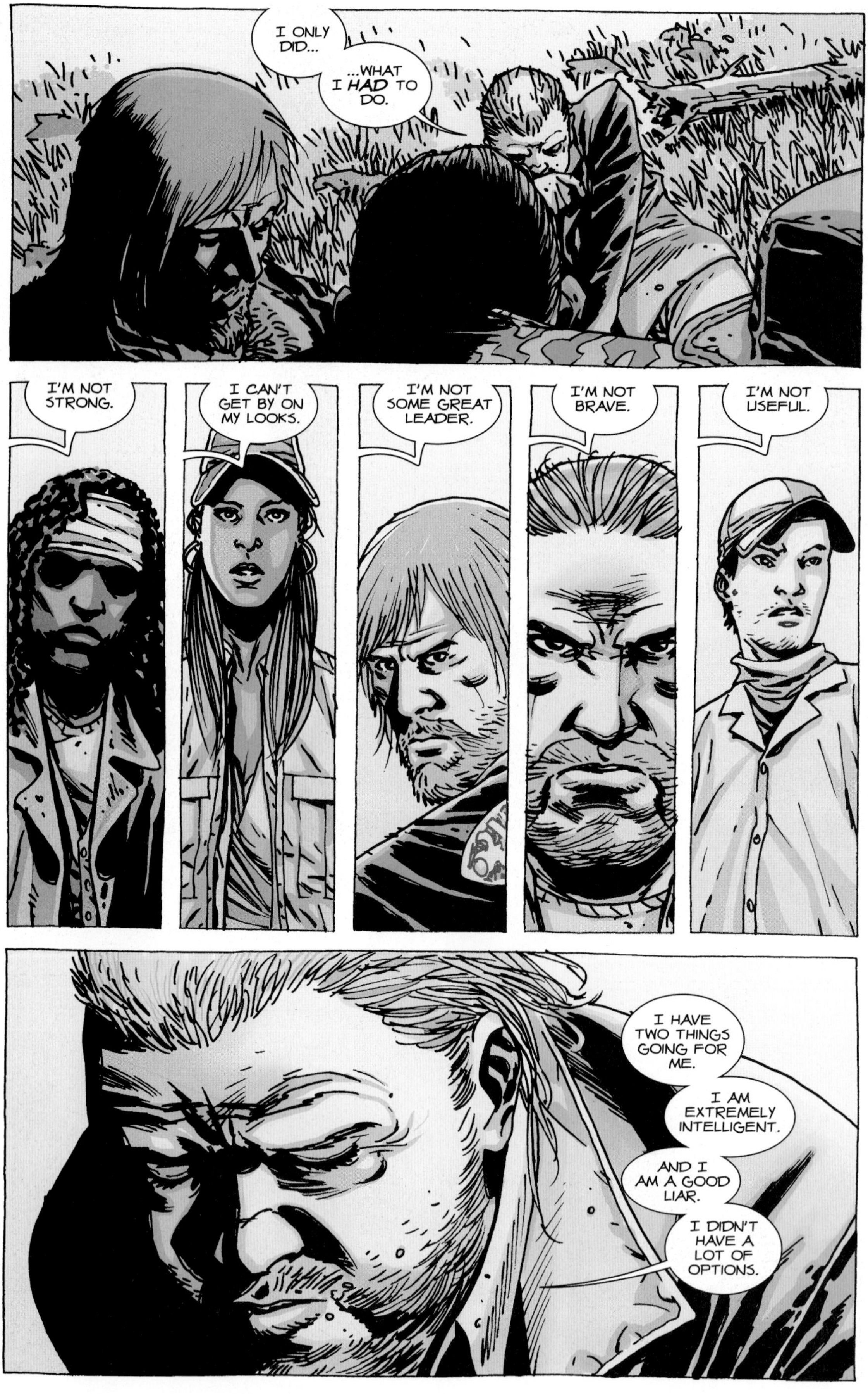

I ONLY DID...
...WHAT I HAD TO DO.
I'M NOT STRONG.
I CAN'T GET BY ON MY LOOKS.
I'M NOT SOME GREAT LEADER.
I'M NOT BRAVE.
I'M NOT USEFUL.
I HAVE TWO THINGS GOING FOR ME.
I AM EXTREMELY INTELLIGENT.
AND I AM A GOOD LIAR.
I DIDN'T HAVE A LOT OF OPTIONS.

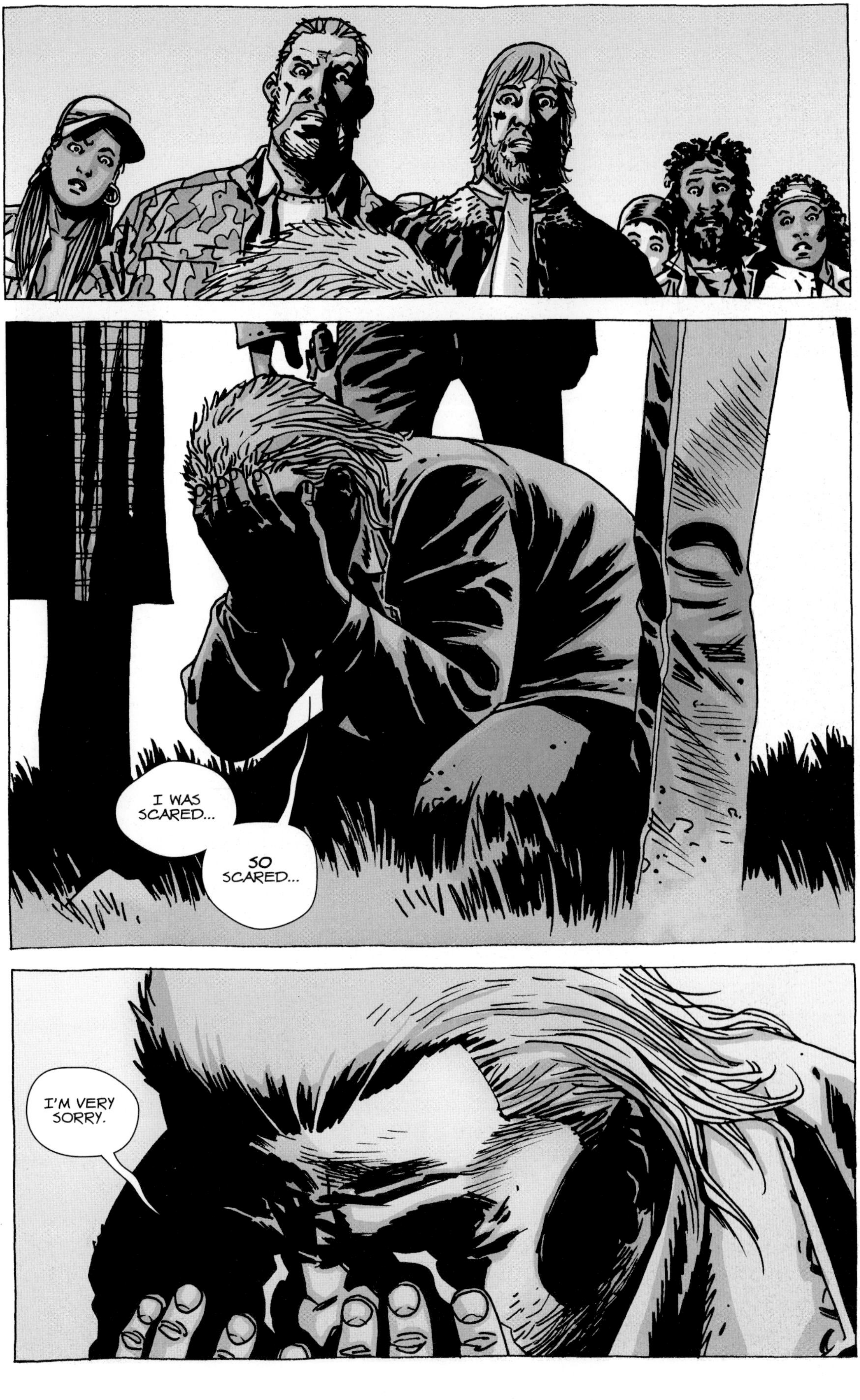
I WAS SCARED...
SO SCARED...
I'M VERY SORRY.

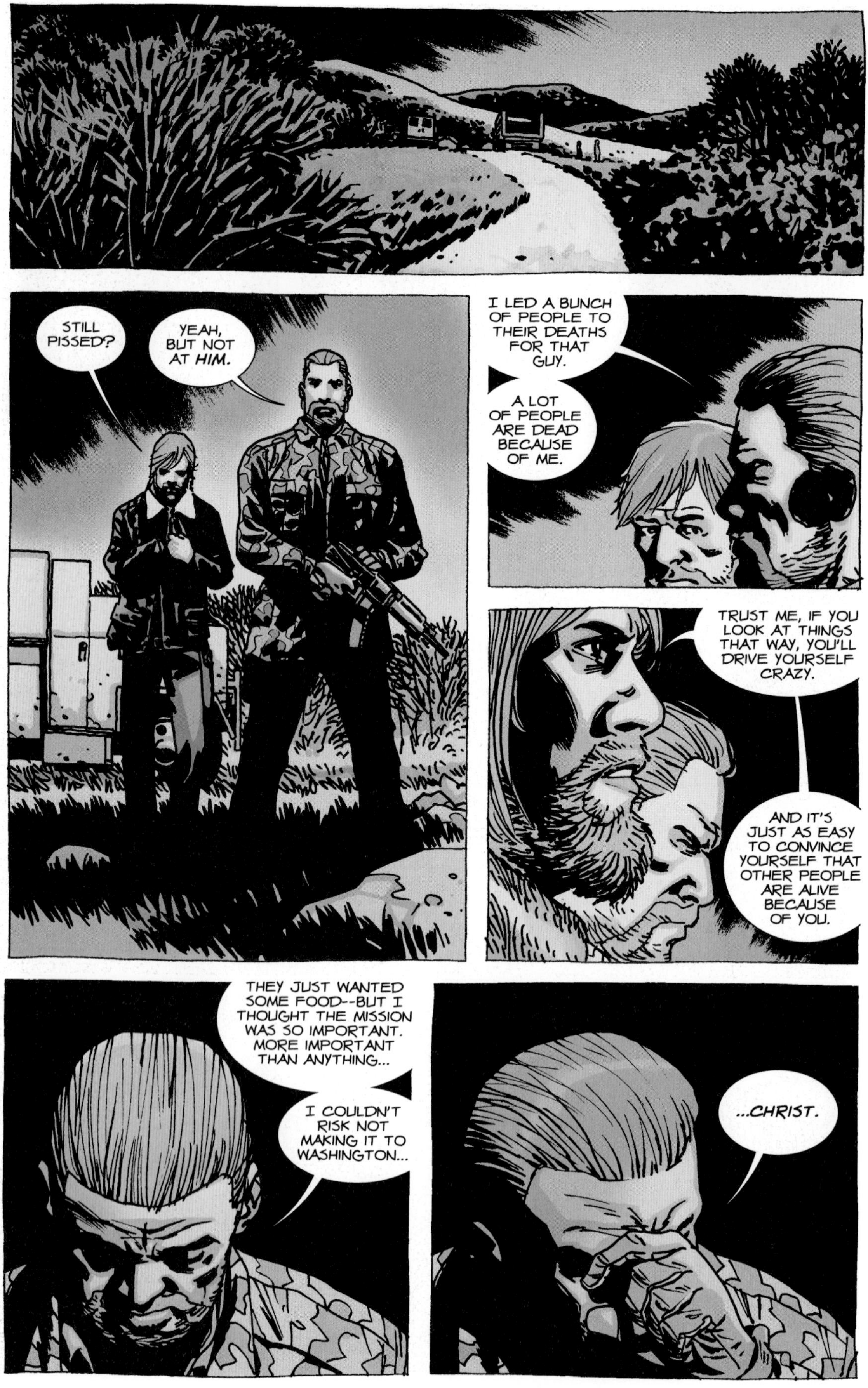
STILL PISSED?
YEAH, BUT NOT AT *HIM.*
I LED A BUNCH OF PEOPLE TO THEIR DEATHS FOR THAT GUY.
A LOT OF PEOPLE ARE DEAD BECAUSE OF ME.
TRUST ME, IF YOU LOOK AT THINGS THAT WAY, YOU'LL DRIVE YOURSELF CRAZY.
AND IT'S JUST AS EASY TO CONVINCE YOURSELF THAT OTHER PEOPLE ARE ALIVE BECAUSE OF YOU.
THEY JUST WANTED SOME FOOD--BUT I THOUGHT THE MISSION WAS SO IMPORTANT. MORE IMPORTANT THAN ANYTHING...
I COULDN'T RISK NOT MAKING IT TO WASHINGTON...
...CHRIST.

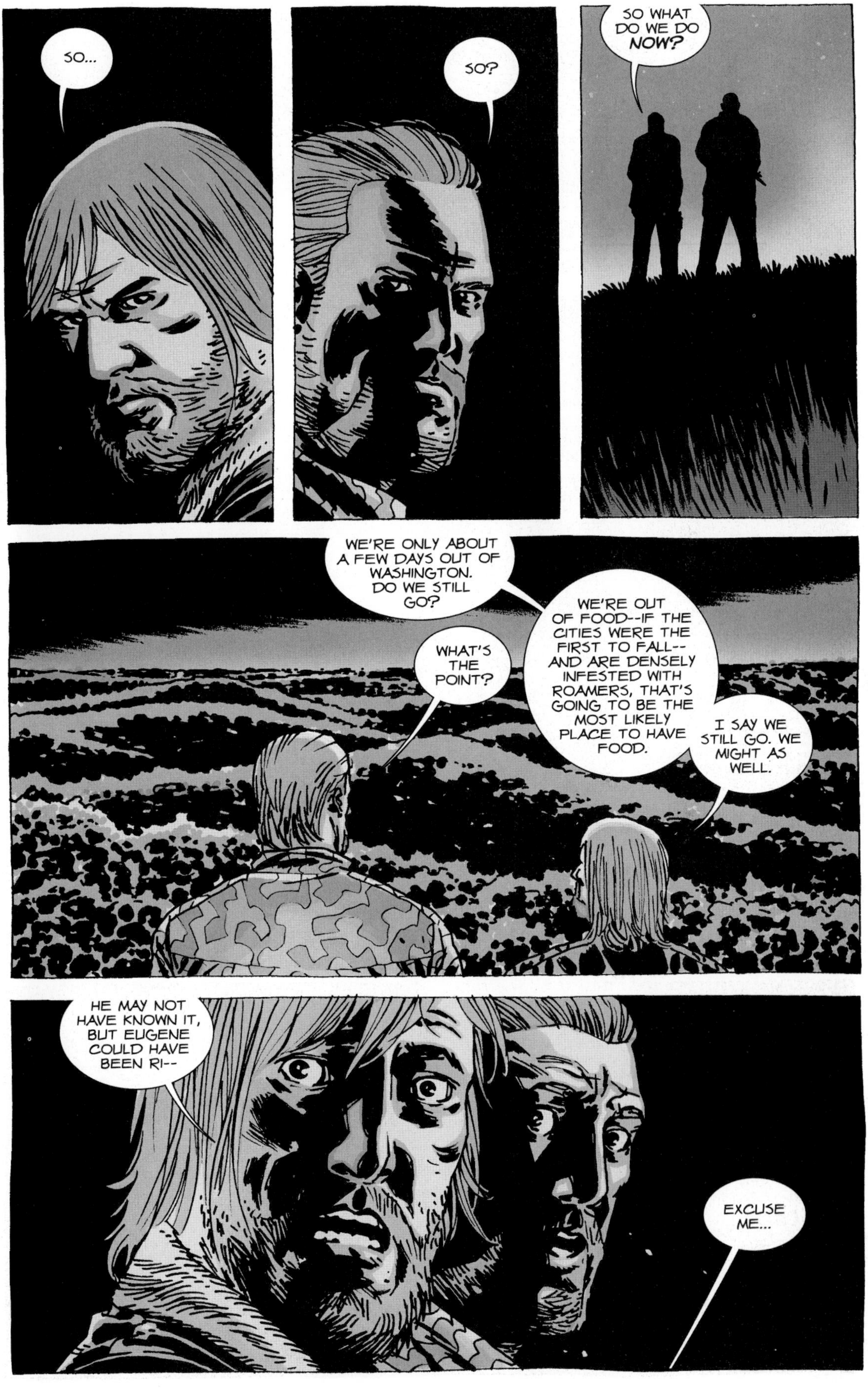
SO...
SO?
SO WHAT DO WE DO NOW?
WE'RE ONLY ABOUT A FEW DAYS OUT OF WASHINGTON. DO WE STILL GO?
WHAT'S THE POINT?
WE'RE OUT OF FOOD--IF THE CITIES WERE THE FIRST TO FALL--AND ARE DENSELY INFESTED WITH ROAMERS, THAT'S GOING TO BE THE MOST LIKELY PLACE TO HAVE FOOD.
I SAY WE STILL GO. WE MIGHT AS WELL.
HE MAY NOT HAVE KNOWN IT, BUT EUGENE COULD HAVE BEEN RI--
EXCUSE ME...

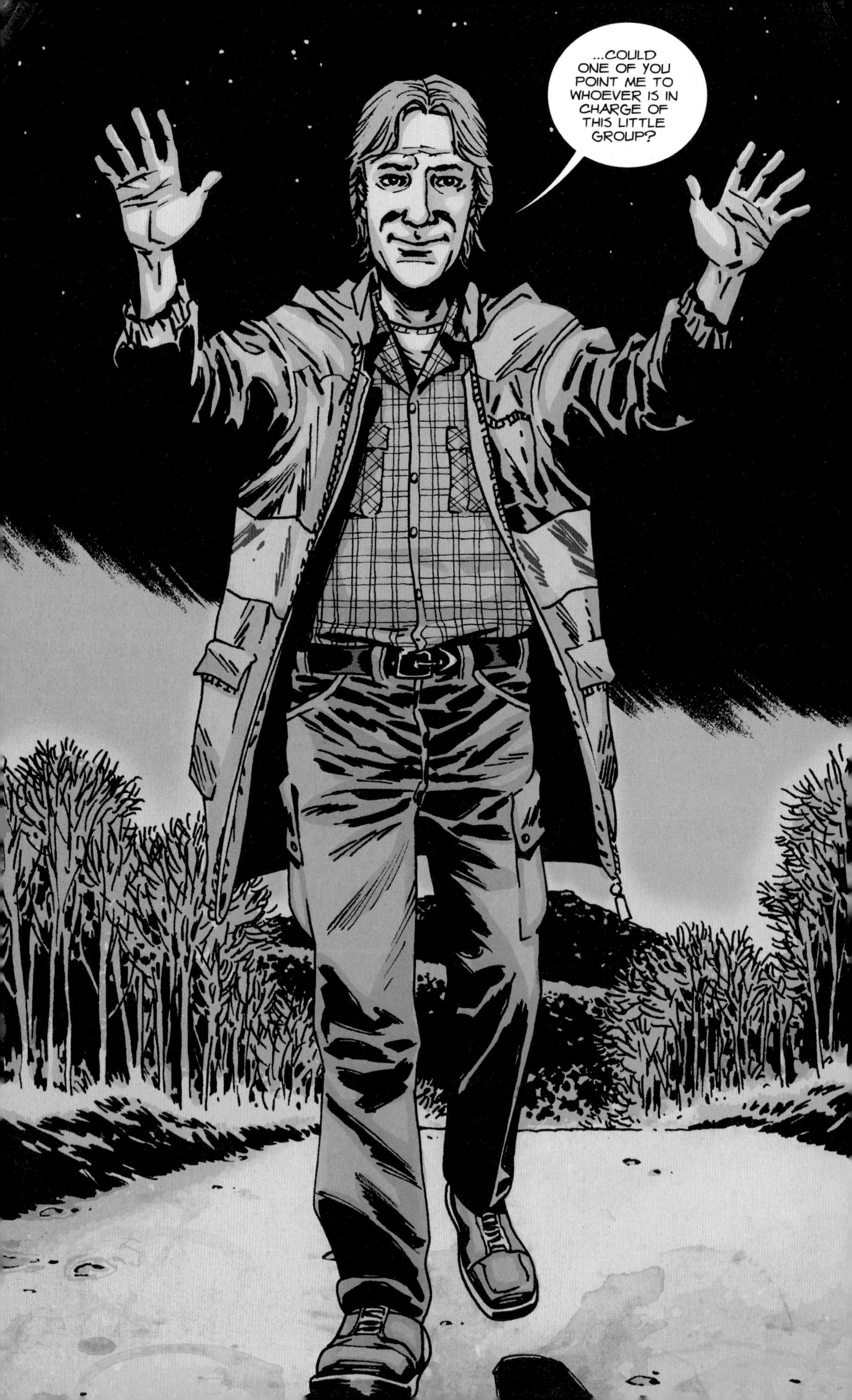
...COULD ONE OF YOU POINT ME TO WHOEVER IS IN CHARGE OF THIS LITTLE GROUP?

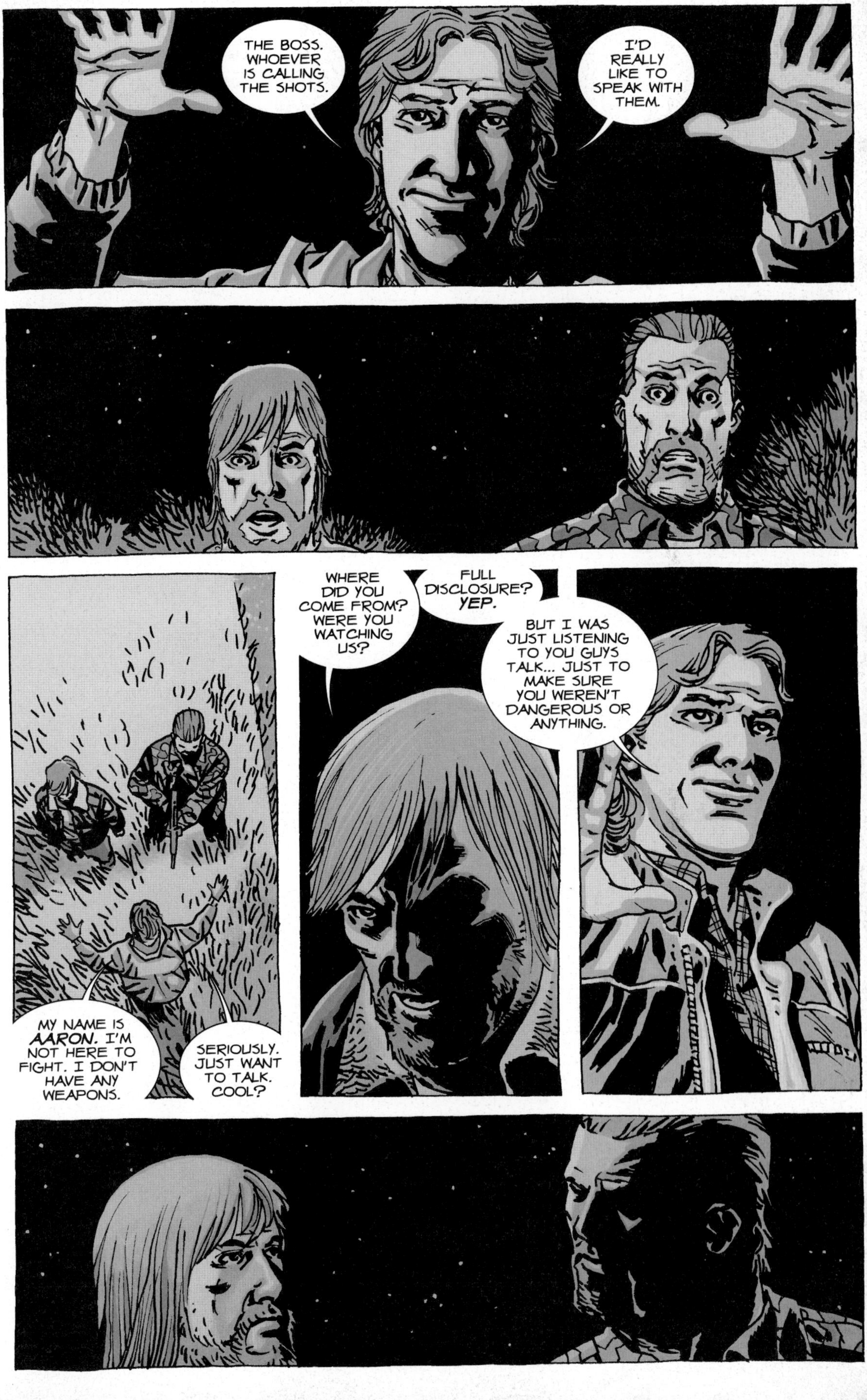
THE BOSS. WHOEVER IS CALLING THE SHOTS.
I'D REALLY LIKE TO SPEAK WITH THEM.
MY NAME IS AARON. I'M NOT HERE TO FIGHT. I DON'T HAVE ANY WEAPONS.
SERIOUSLY. JUST WANT TO TALK. COOL?
WHERE DID YOU COME FROM? WERE YOU WATCHING US?
FULL DISCLOSURE? YEP.
BUT I WAS JUST LISTENING TO YOU GUYS TALK... JUST TO MAKE SURE YOU WEREN'T DANGEROUS OR ANYTHING.

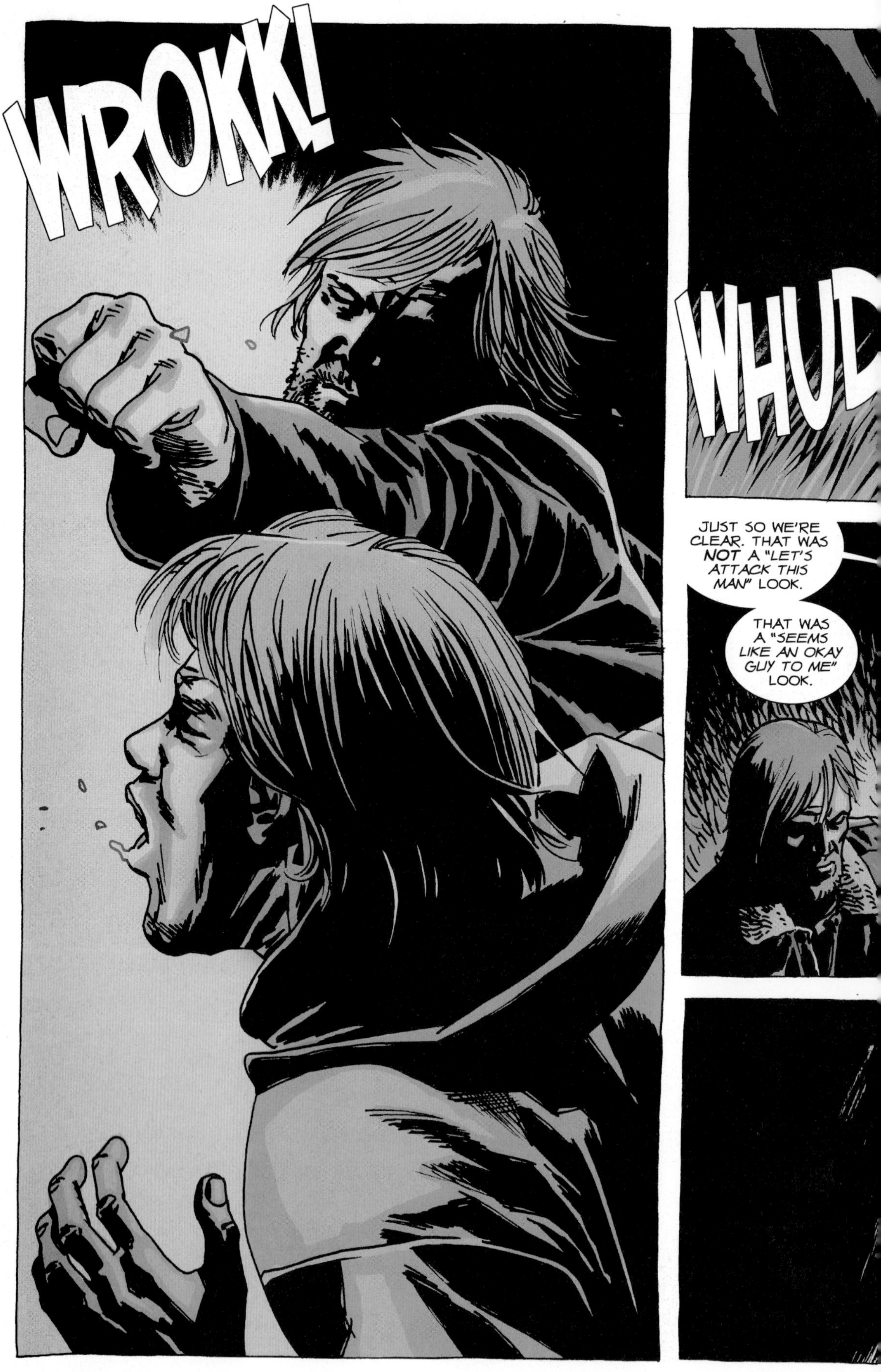
WROKK!
WHUD
JUST SO WE'RE CLEAR. THAT WAS NOT A "LET'S ATTACK THIS MAN" LOOK.
THAT WAS A "SEEMS LIKE AN OKAY GUY TO ME" LOOK.

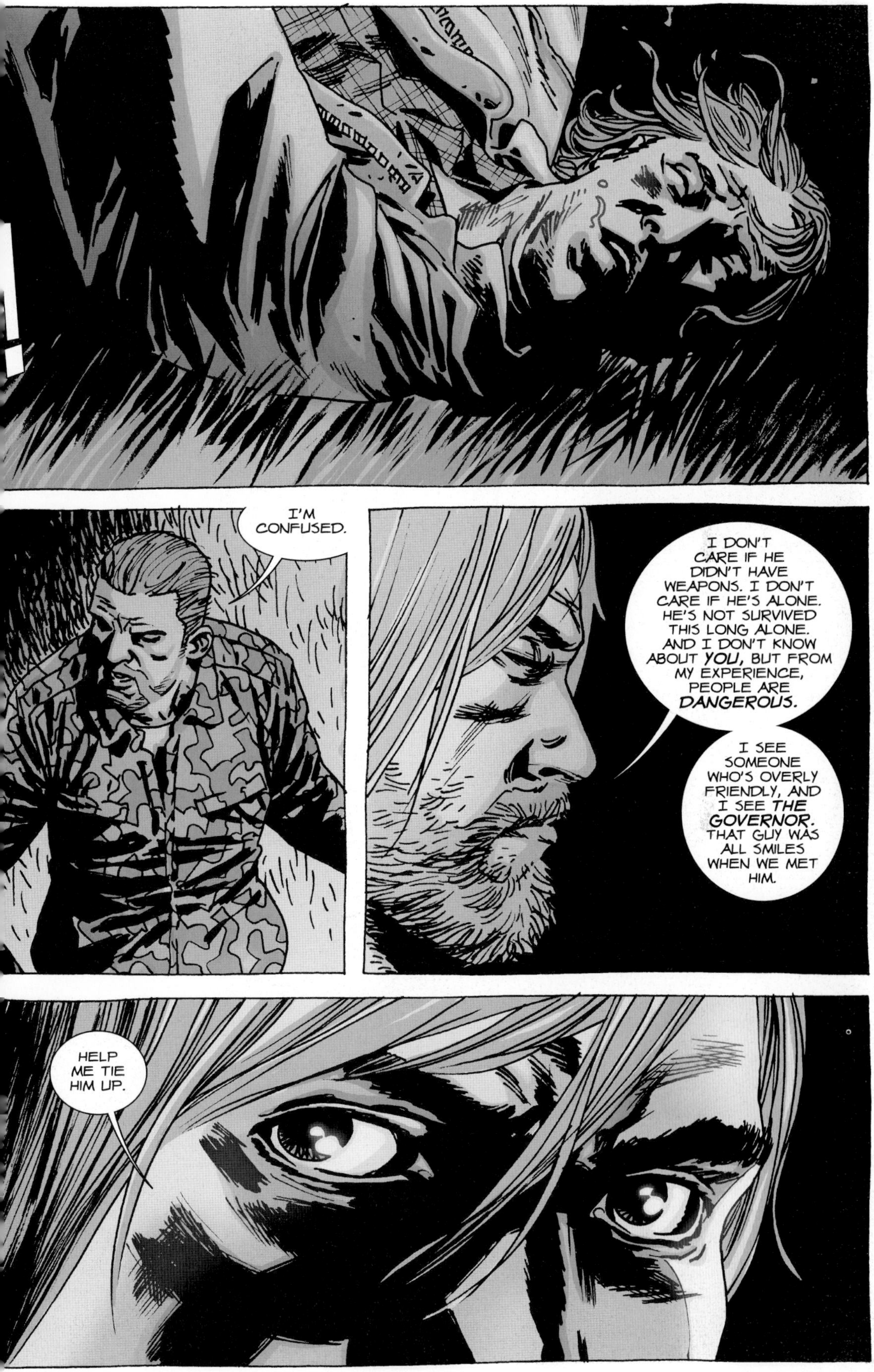
I'M CONFUSED.
I DON'T CARE IF HE DIDN'T HAVE WEAPONS. I DON'T CARE IF HE'S ALONE. HE'S NOT SURVIVED THIS LONG ALONE. AND I DON'T KNOW ABOUT YOU, BUT FROM MY EXPERIENCE, PEOPLE ARE DANGEROUS.
I SEE SOMEONE WHO'S OVERLY FRIENDLY, AND I SEE THE GOVERNOR. THAT GUY WAS ALL SMILES WHEN WE MET HIM.
HELP ME TIE HIM UP.

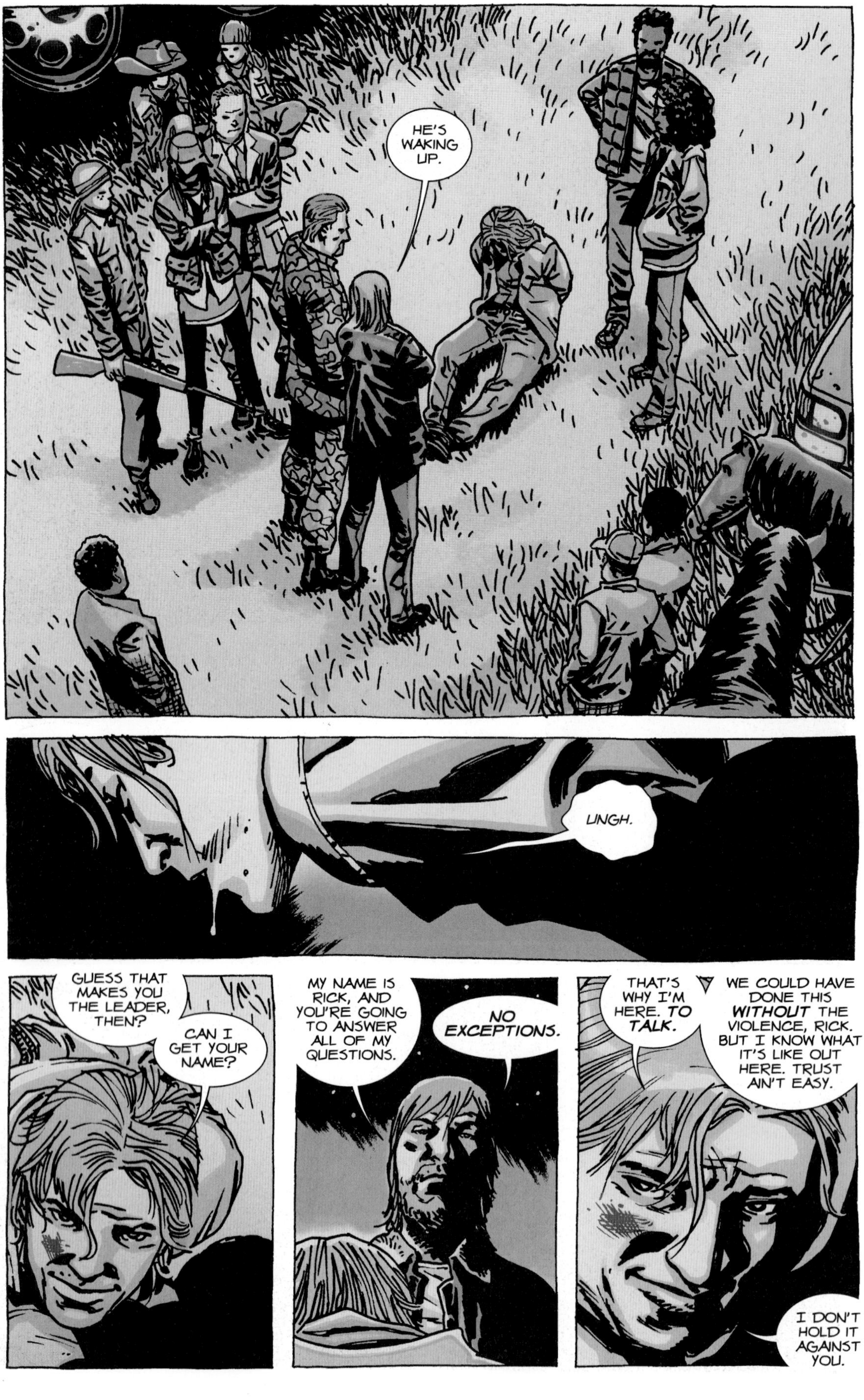
HE'S WAKING UP.
UNGH.
GUESS THAT MAKES YOU THE LEADER, THEN?
CAN I GET YOUR NAME?
MY NAME IS RICK, AND YOU'RE GOING TO ANSWER ALL OF MY QUESTIONS.
NO EXCEPTIONS.
THAT'S WHY I'M HERE. TO TALK.
WE COULD HAVE DONE THIS WITHOUT THE VIOLENCE, RICK. BUT I KNOW WHAT IT'S LIKE OUT HERE. TRUST AIN'T EASY.
I DON'T HOLD IT AGAINST YOU.

GOOD MAN. I APPRECIATE THAT.

HOW MANY PEOPLE ARE IN YOUR GROUP?

I DON'T KNOW, THIRTY-FOUR OR SO. I THINK WE'RE STILL UNDER FORTY.

THAT MANY? WHERE ARE THEY?

IN OUR COMMUNITY, IT'S ON THE OTHER SIDE OF D.C. ABOUT TWENTY MILES AWAY.

WHY ARE YOU *HERE?*

I'M A KIND OF RECRUITER, I GUESS. I PROMISE I WAS ONLY SPYING ON YOU TO MAKE SURE THAT YOUR GROUP WOULD... FIT IN? I THINK THAT'S WHAT I MEAN TO SAY.

BEEN WATCHING YOU FOR A WHILE. YOU SEEM LIKE A NICE BUNCH OF FOLKS. THE KID DOESN'T LIKE OATMEAL. IT'S FUNNY.

I KNOW YOU'RE HAVING TROUBLE FINDING FOOD--THAT'S COMMON AROUND HERE. WE'VE PRETTY MUCH EXHAUSTED ALL THE SUPPLIES IN THIS AREA.

WE HAVE STOCKPILES OF FOOD. WE HAVE SECURITY WALLS. WE HAVE ROOM FOR ALL OF YOU. I PROMISE YOU, OUR COMMUNITY IS EVERYTHING YOU'VE BEEN LOOKING FOR.

I'M HERE TO INVITE YOU TO... AUDITION FOR MEMBERSHIP.

YOU'VE GOT A SAFE, SECURE PLACE TO LIVE AND YOU'RE JUST TRAVELING AROUND INVITING PEOPLE IN?

WHAT'S IN IT FOR *YOU?*

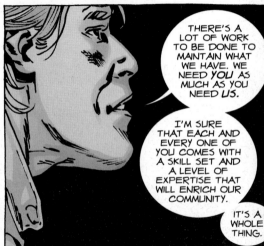

THERE'S A LOT OF WORK TO BE DONE TO MAINTAIN WHAT WE HAVE. WE NEED *YOU* AS MUCH AS YOU NEED *US.*

I'M SURE THAT EACH AND EVERY ONE OF YOU COMES WITH A SKILL SET AND A LEVEL OF EXPERTISE THAT WILL ENRICH OUR COMMUNITY.

IT'S A WHOLE THING.

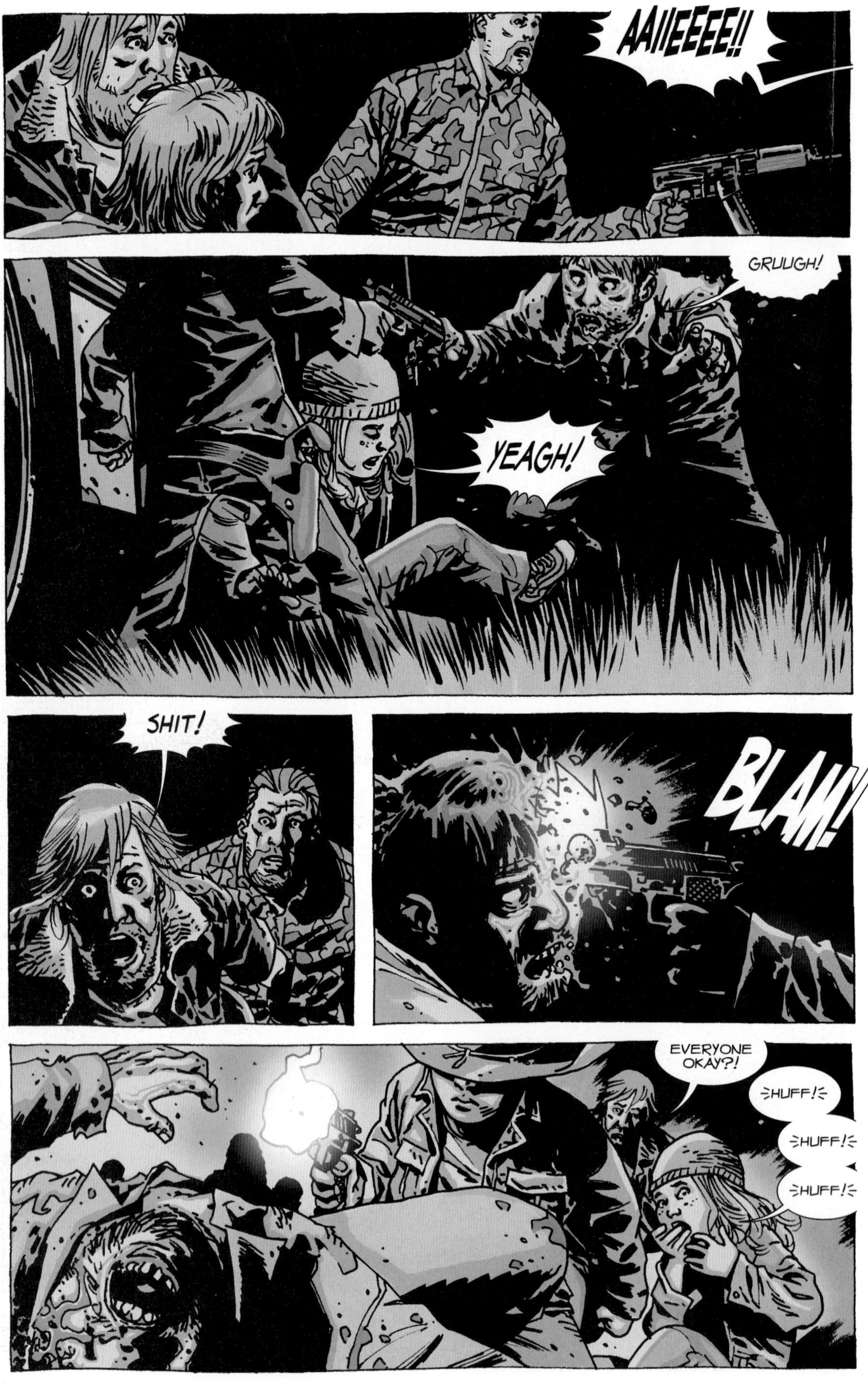
AAIIEEEE!!
GRUUGH!
YEAGH!
SHIT!
BLAM!
EVERYONE OKAY?!
HUFF!
HUFF!
HUFF!

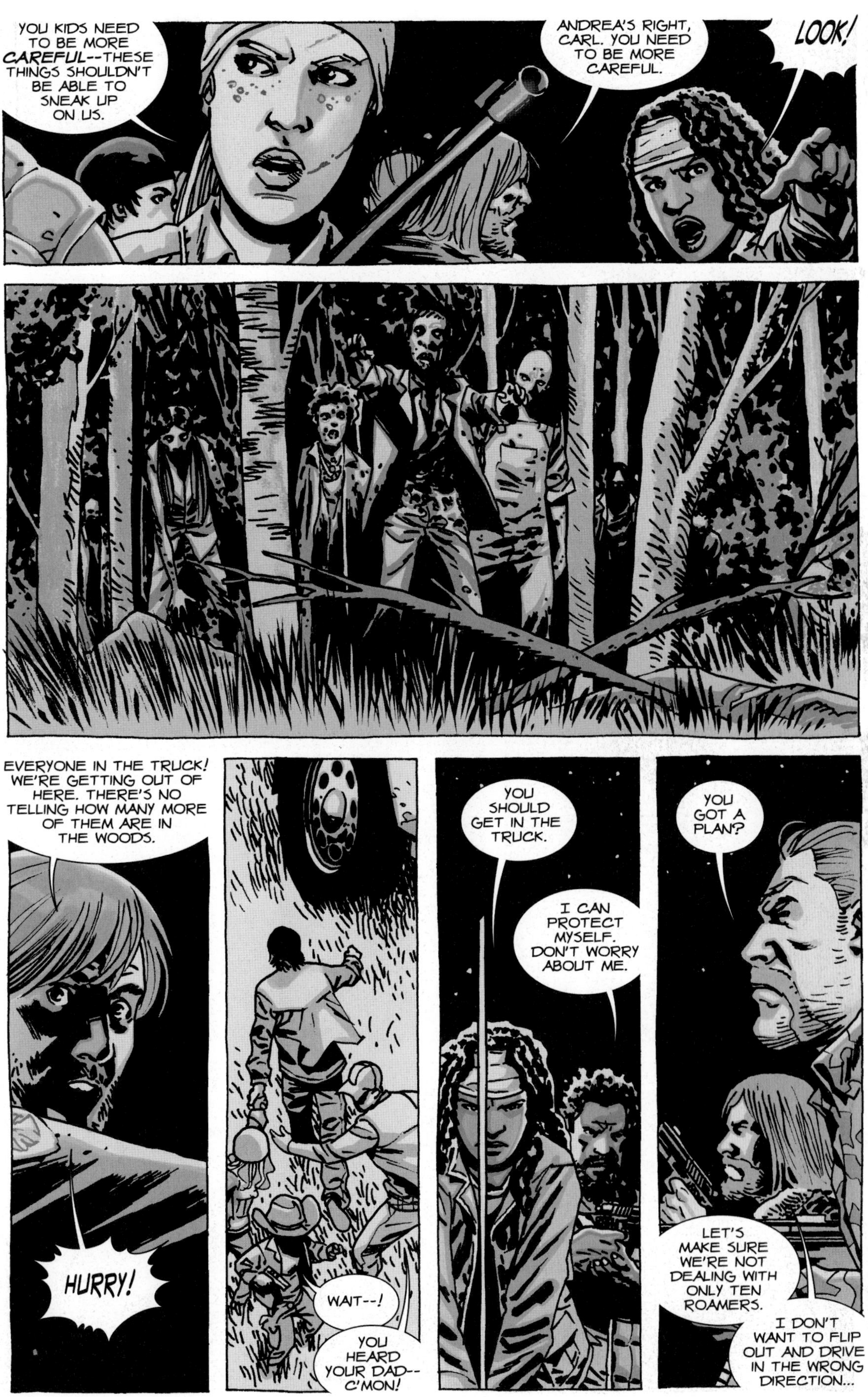
YOU KIDS NEED TO BE MORE CAREFUL--THESE THINGS SHOULDN'T BE ABLE TO SNEAK UP ON US.
ANDREA'S RIGHT, CARL. YOU NEED TO BE MORE CAREFUL.
LOOK!
EVERYONE IN THE TRUCK! WE'RE GETTING OUT OF HERE. THERE'S NO TELLING HOW MANY MORE OF THEM ARE IN THE WOODS.
HURRY!
WAIT--!
YOU HEARD YOUR DAD--C'MON!
YOU SHOULD GET IN THE TRUCK.
I CAN PROTECT MYSELF. DON'T WORRY ABOUT ME.
YOU GOT A PLAN?
LET'S MAKE SURE WE'RE NOT DEALING WITH ONLY TEN ROAMERS.
I DON'T WANT TO FLIP OUT AND DRIVE IN THE WRONG DIRECTION...

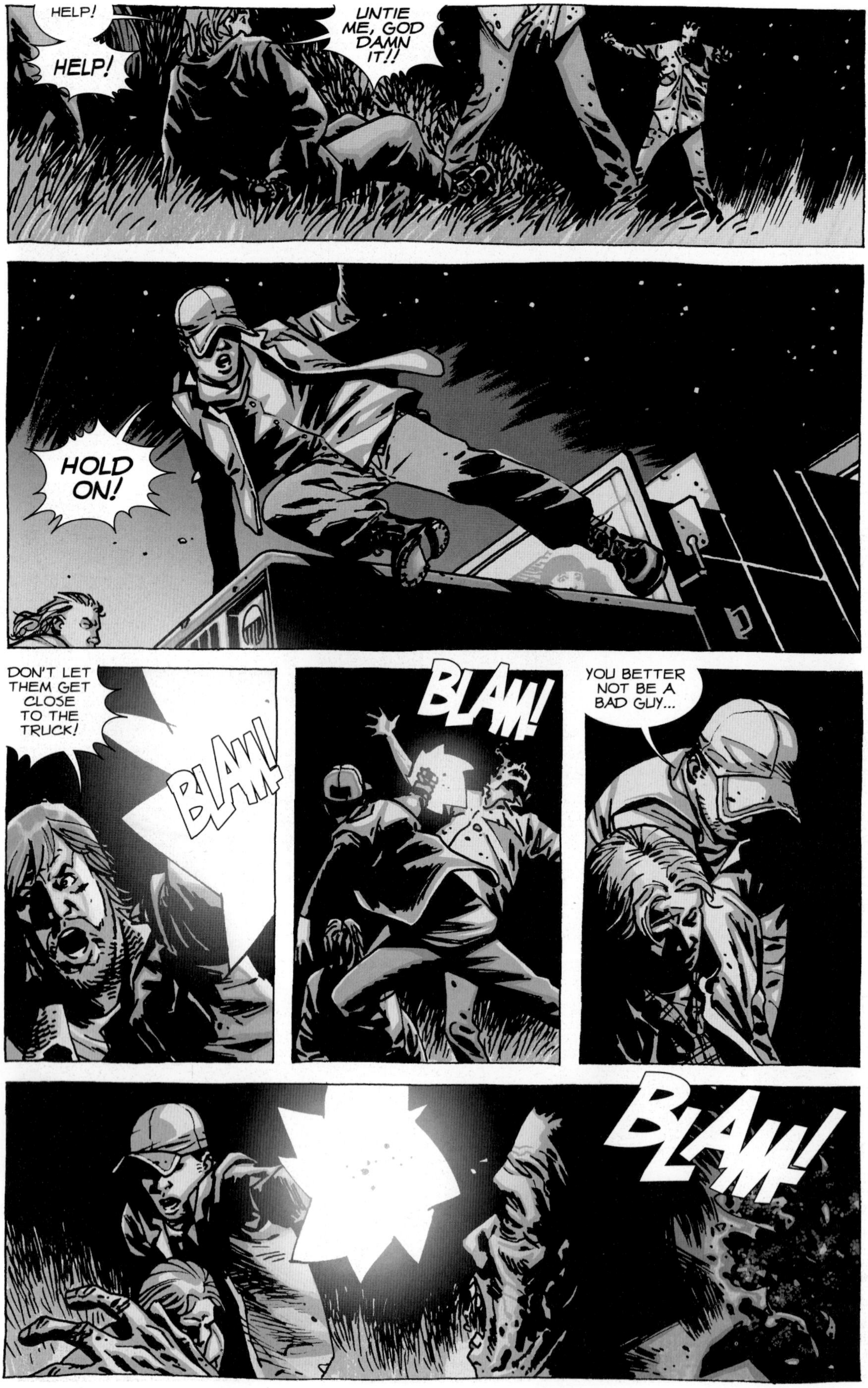

HELP!
HELP!
UNTIE ME, GOD DAMN IT!!
HOLD ON!
DON'T LET THEM GET CLOSE TO THE TRUCK!
BLAM!
BLAM!
YOU BETTER NOT BE A BAD GUY...
BLAM!

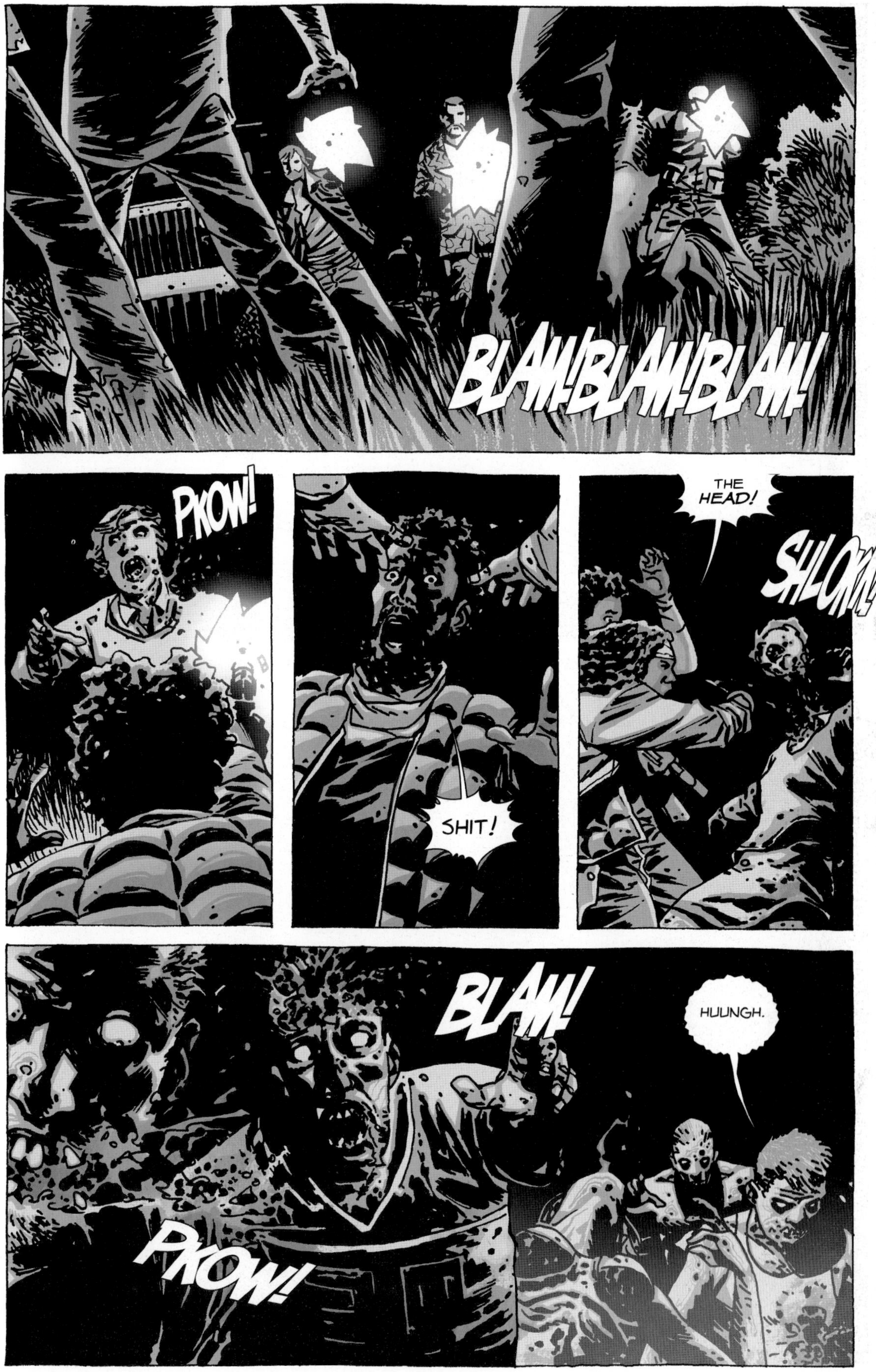
BLAM-BLAM-BLAM!
PKOW!
SHIT!
THE HEAD!
SHLORK!
BLAM!
HUUNGH.
PKOW!

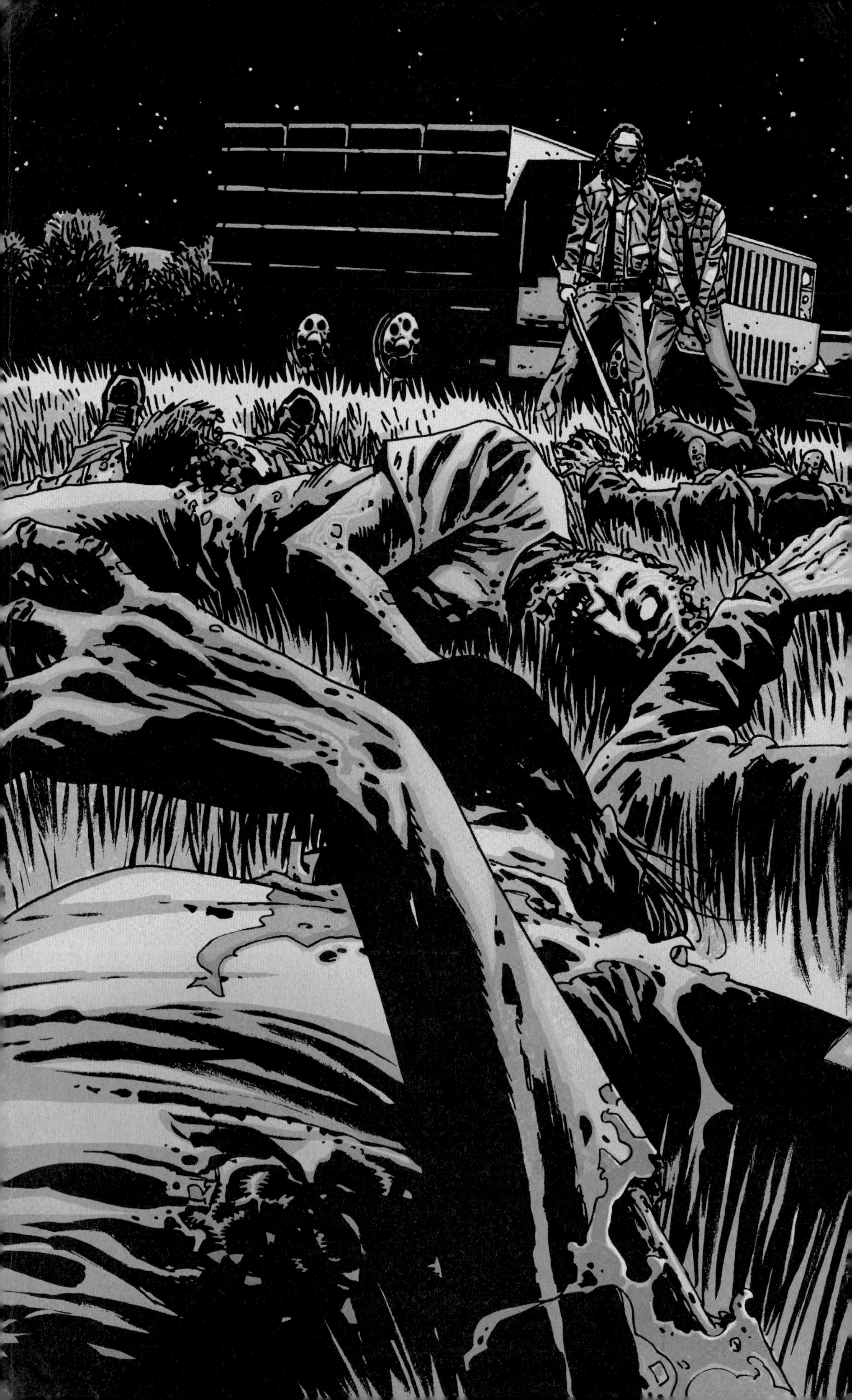

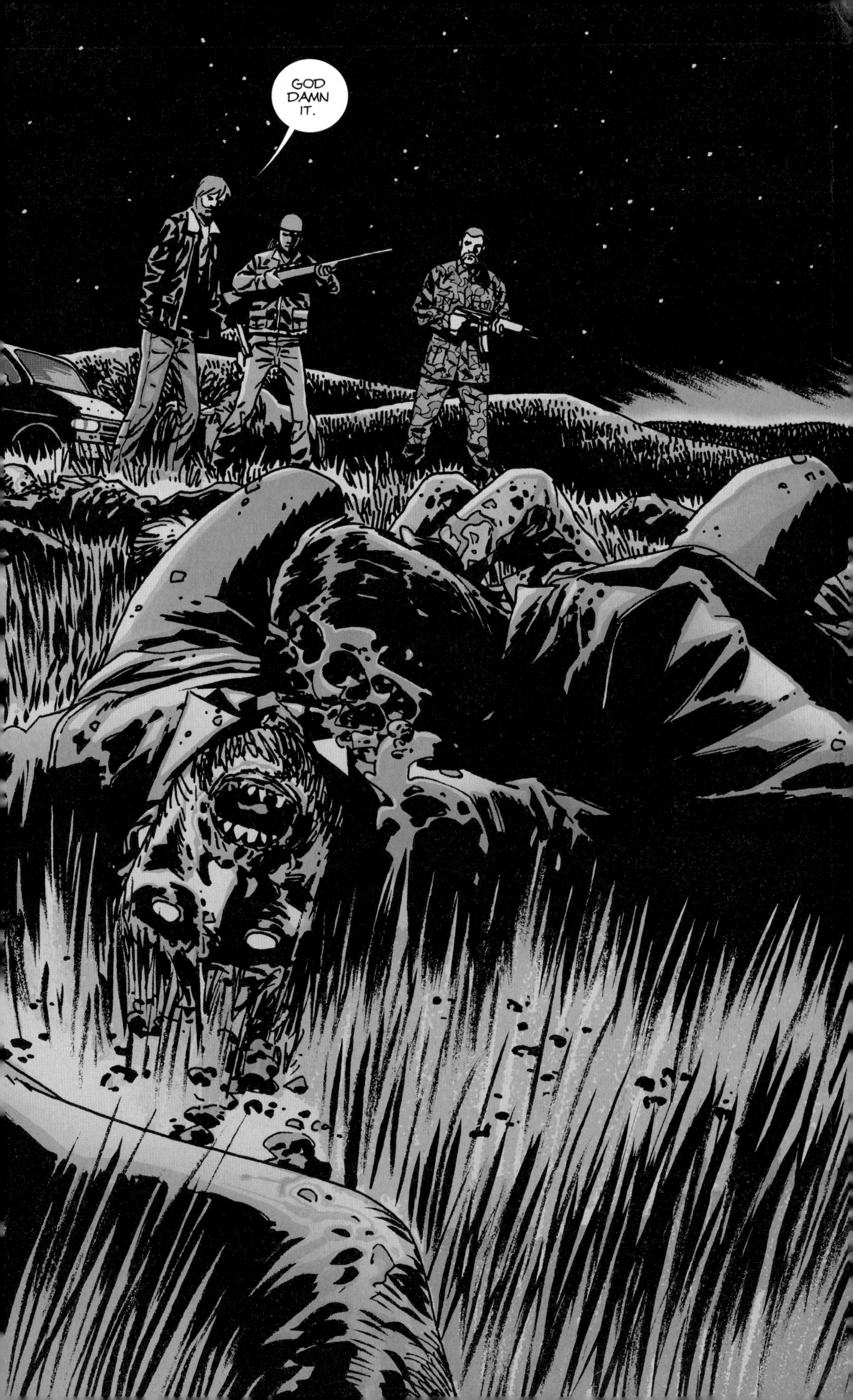
GOD DAMN IT.

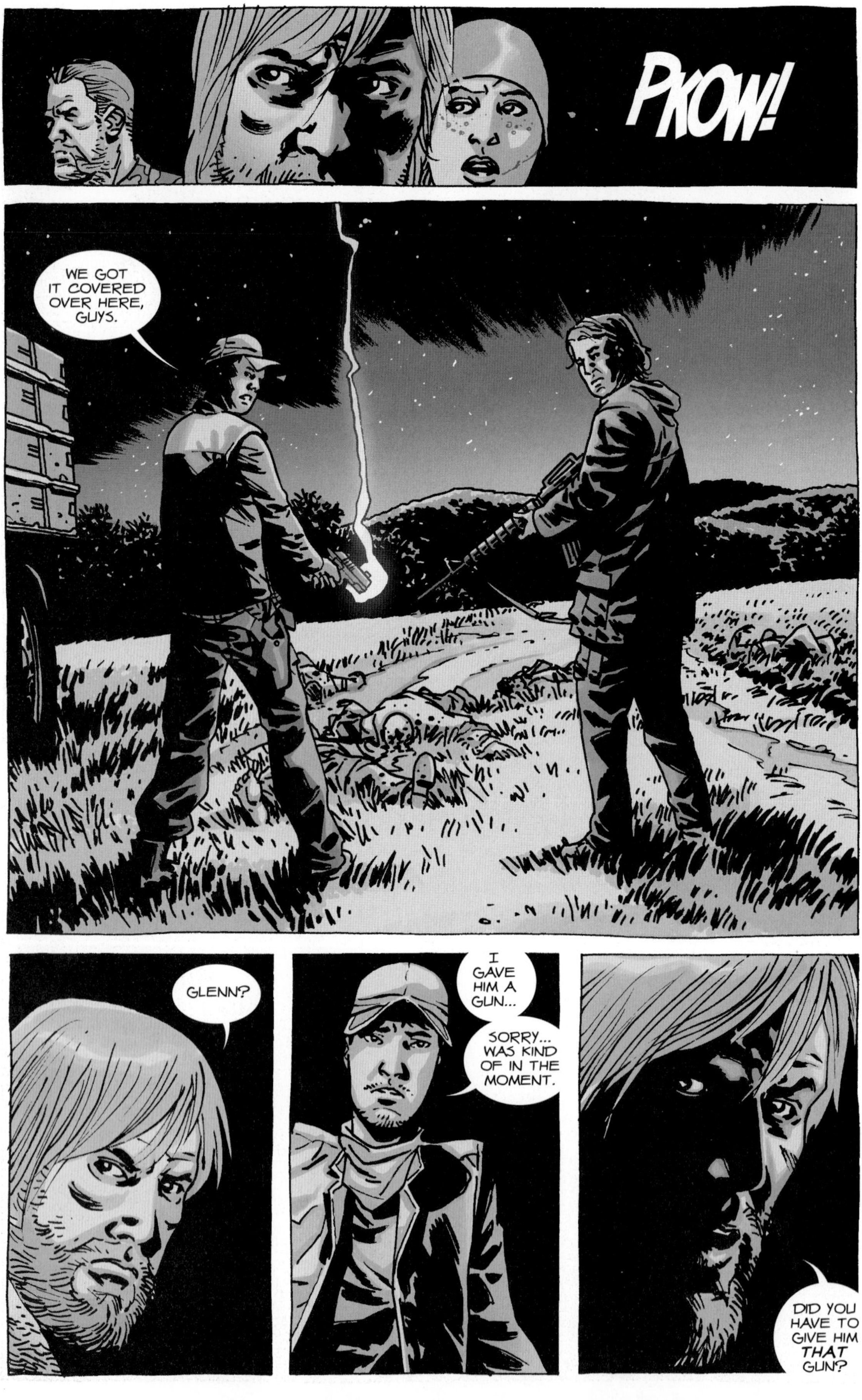
PKOW!
WE GOT IT COVERED OVER HERE, GUYS.
GLENN?
I GAVE HIM A GUN...
SORRY... WAS KIND OF IN THE MOMENT.
DID YOU HAVE TO GIVE HIM THAT GUN?

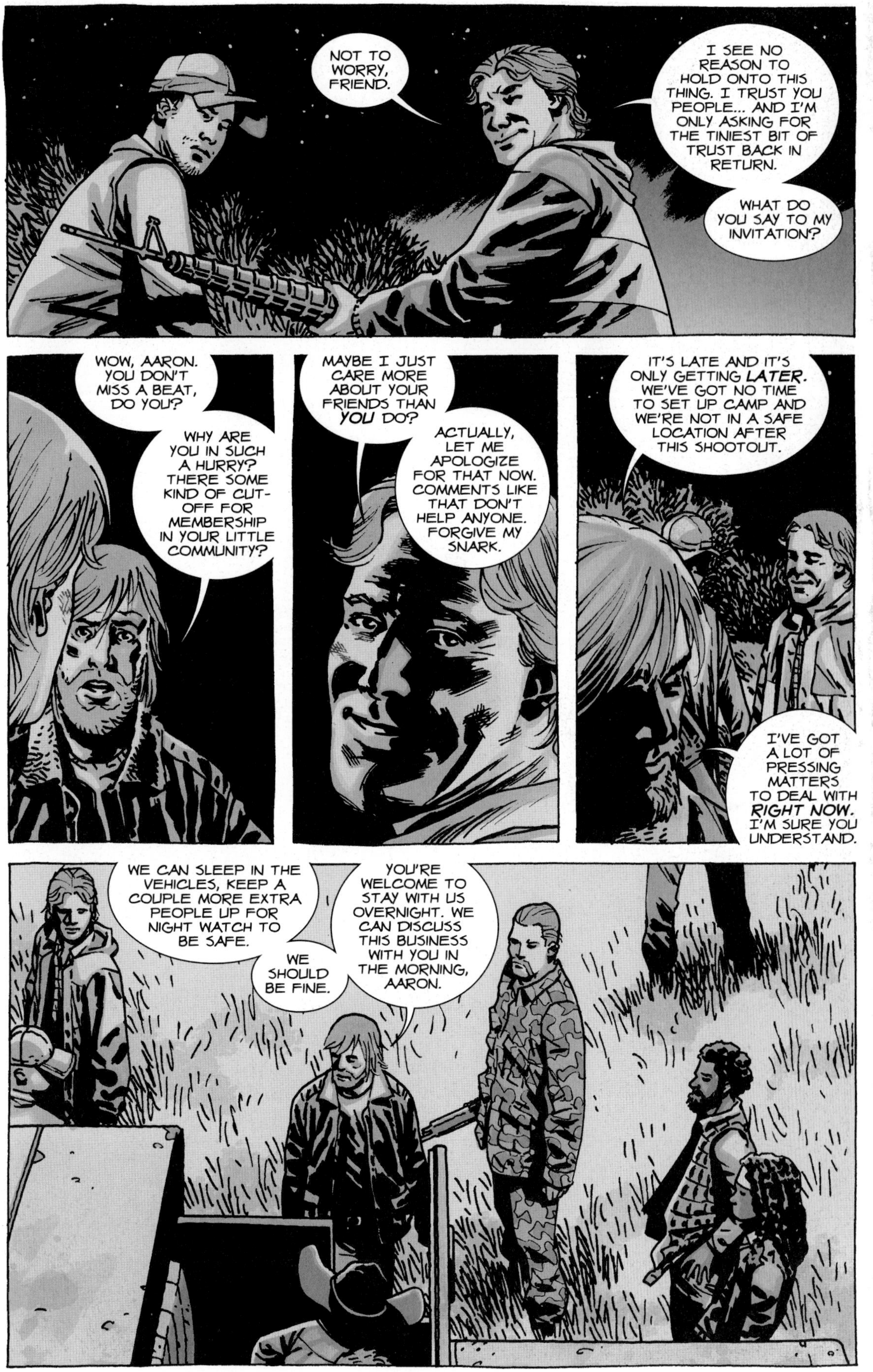
NOT TO WORRY, FRIEND.
I SEE NO REASON TO HOLD ONTO THIS THING. I TRUST YOU PEOPLE... AND I'M ONLY ASKING FOR THE TINIEST BIT OF TRUST BACK IN RETURN.
WHAT DO YOU SAY TO MY INVITATION?
WOW, AARON. YOU DON'T MISS A BEAT, DO YOU?
WHY ARE YOU IN SUCH A HURRY? THERE SOME KIND OF CUT-OFF FOR MEMBERSHIP IN YOUR LITTLE COMMUNITY?
MAYBE I JUST CARE MORE ABOUT YOUR FRIENDS THAN YOU DO?
ACTUALLY, LET ME APOLOGIZE FOR THAT NOW. COMMENTS LIKE THAT DON'T HELP ANYONE. FORGIVE MY SNARK.
IT'S LATE AND IT'S ONLY GETTING LATER. WE'VE GOT NO TIME TO SET UP CAMP AND WE'RE NOT IN A SAFE LOCATION AFTER THIS SHOOTOUT.
I'VE GOT A LOT OF PRESSING MATTERS TO DEAL WITH RIGHT NOW. I'M SURE YOU UNDERSTAND.
YOU'RE WELCOME TO STAY WITH US OVERNIGHT. WE CAN DISCUSS THIS BUSINESS WITH YOU IN THE MORNING, AARON.
WE SHOULD BE FINE.
WE CAN SLEEP IN THE VEHICLES, KEEP A COUPLE MORE EXTRA PEOPLE UP FOR NIGHT WATCH TO BE SAFE.

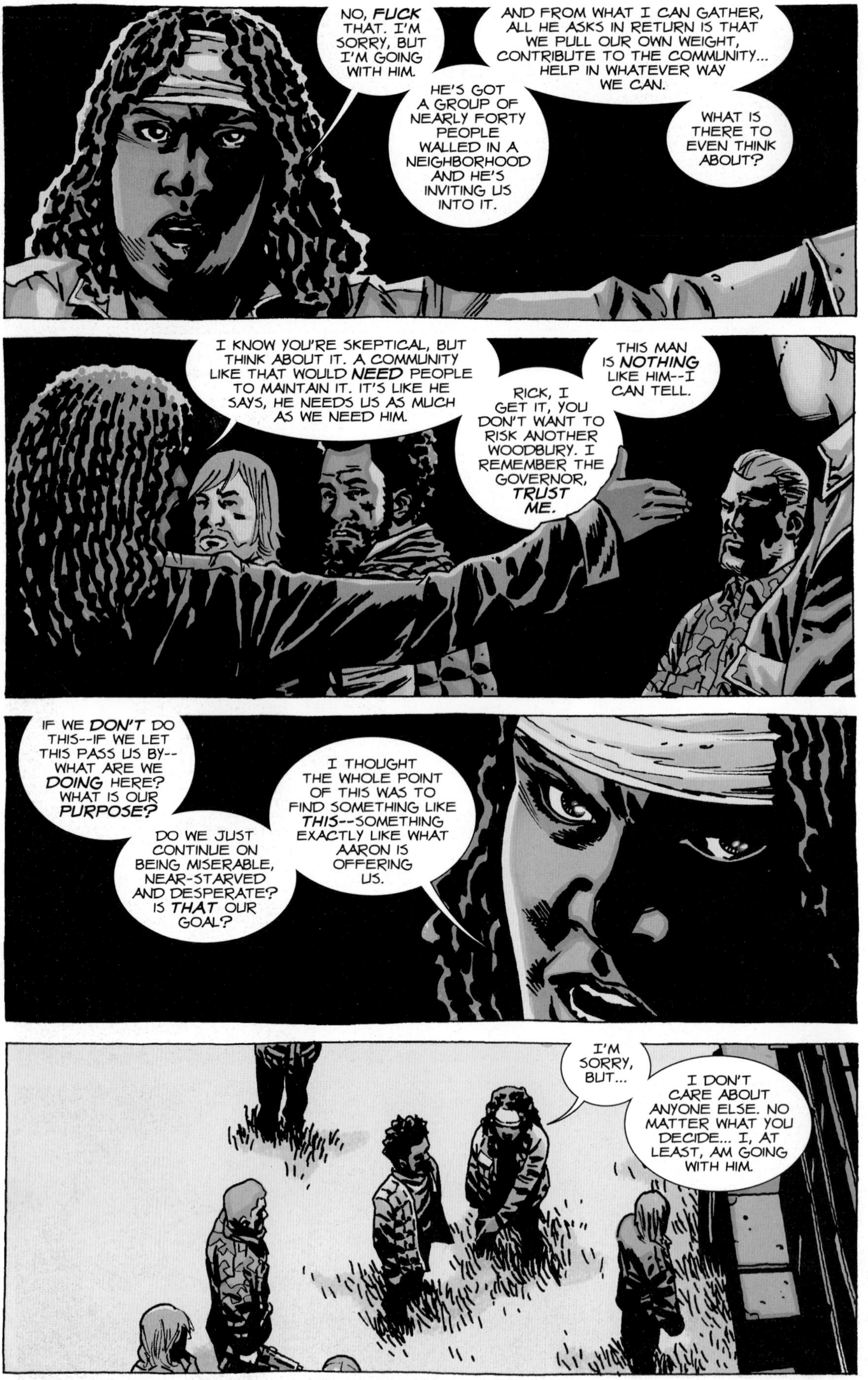

NO, FUCK THAT. I'M SORRY, BUT I'M GOING WITH HIM.
HE'S GOT A GROUP OF NEARLY FORTY PEOPLE WALLED IN A NEIGHBORHOOD AND HE'S INVITING US INTO IT.
AND FROM WHAT I CAN GATHER, ALL HE ASKS IN RETURN IS THAT WE PULL OUR OWN WEIGHT, CONTRIBUTE TO THE COMMUNITY... HELP IN WHATEVER WAY WE CAN.
WHAT IS THERE TO EVEN THINK ABOUT?
I KNOW YOU'RE SKEPTICAL, BUT THINK ABOUT IT. A COMMUNITY LIKE THAT WOULD NEED PEOPLE TO MAINTAIN IT. IT'S LIKE HE SAYS, HE NEEDS US AS MUCH AS WE NEED HIM.
RICK, I GET IT, YOU DON'T WANT TO RISK ANOTHER WOODBURY. I REMEMBER THE GOVERNOR, TRUST ME.
THIS MAN IS NOTHING LIKE HIM--I CAN TELL.
IF WE DON'T DO THIS--IF WE LET THIS PASS US BY--WHAT ARE WE DOING HERE? WHAT IS OUR PURPOSE?
DO WE JUST CONTINUE ON BEING MISERABLE, NEAR-STARVED AND DESPERATE? IS THAT OUR GOAL?
I THOUGHT THE WHOLE POINT OF THIS WAS TO FIND SOMETHING LIKE THIS--SOMETHING EXACTLY LIKE WHAT AARON IS OFFERING US.
I'M SORRY, BUT...
I DON'T CARE ABOUT ANYONE ELSE. NO MATTER WHAT YOU DECIDE... I, AT LEAST, AM GOING WITH HIM.

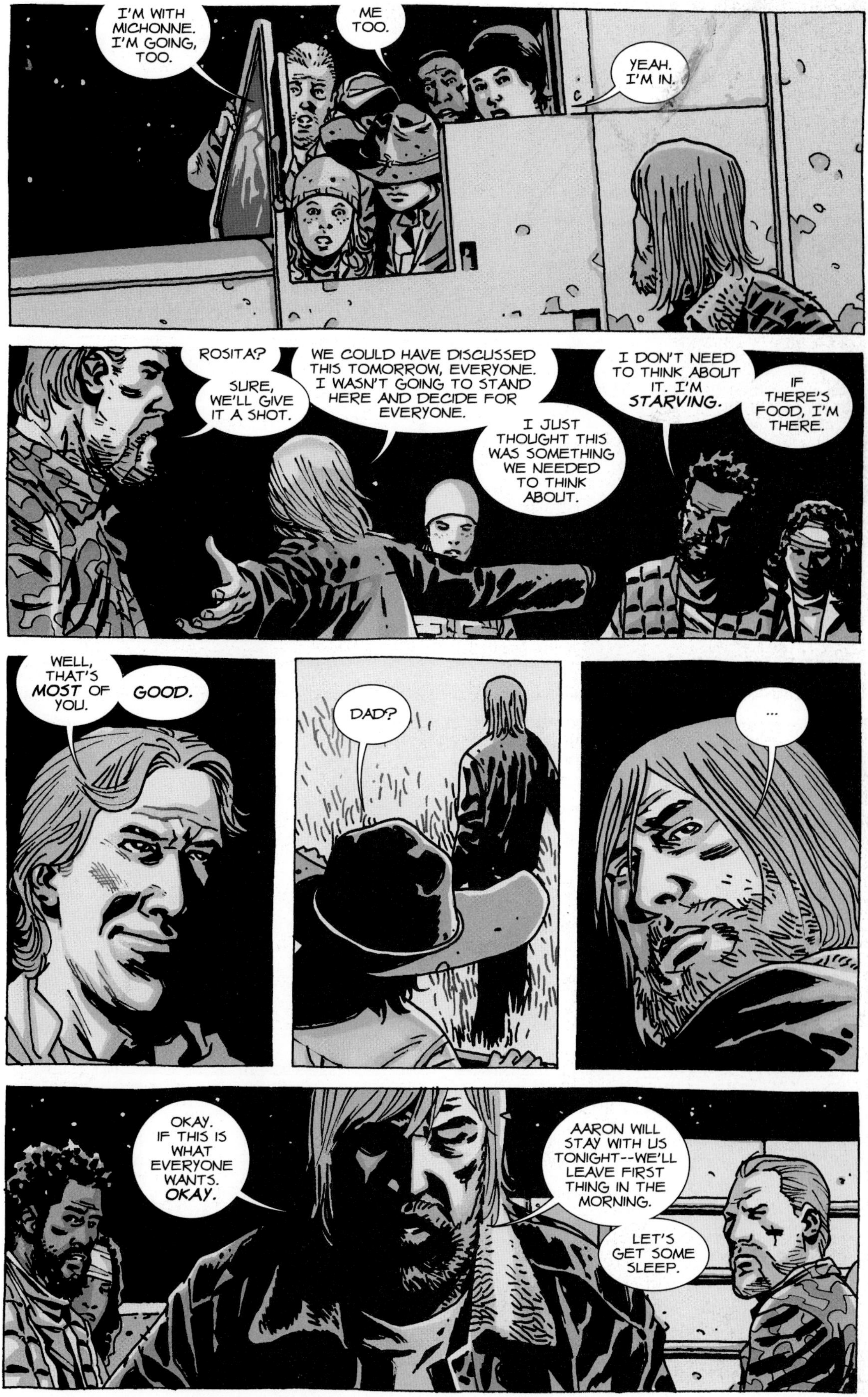

I'M WITH MICHONNE. I'M GOING, TOO.
ME TOO.
YEAH. I'M IN.
ROSITA?
SURE, WE'LL GIVE IT A SHOT.
WE COULD HAVE DISCUSSED THIS TOMORROW, EVERYONE. I WASN'T GOING TO STAND HERE AND DECIDE FOR EVERYONE.
I JUST THOUGHT THIS WAS SOMETHING WE NEEDED TO THINK ABOUT.
I DON'T NEED TO THINK ABOUT IT. I'M STARVING.
IF THERE'S FOOD, I'M THERE.
WELL, THAT'S MOST OF YOU.
GOOD.
DAD?
...
OKAY. IF THIS IS WHAT EVERYONE WANTS. OKAY.
AARON WILL STAY WITH US TONIGHT--WE'LL LEAVE FIRST THING IN THE MORNING.
LET'S GET SOME SLEEP.

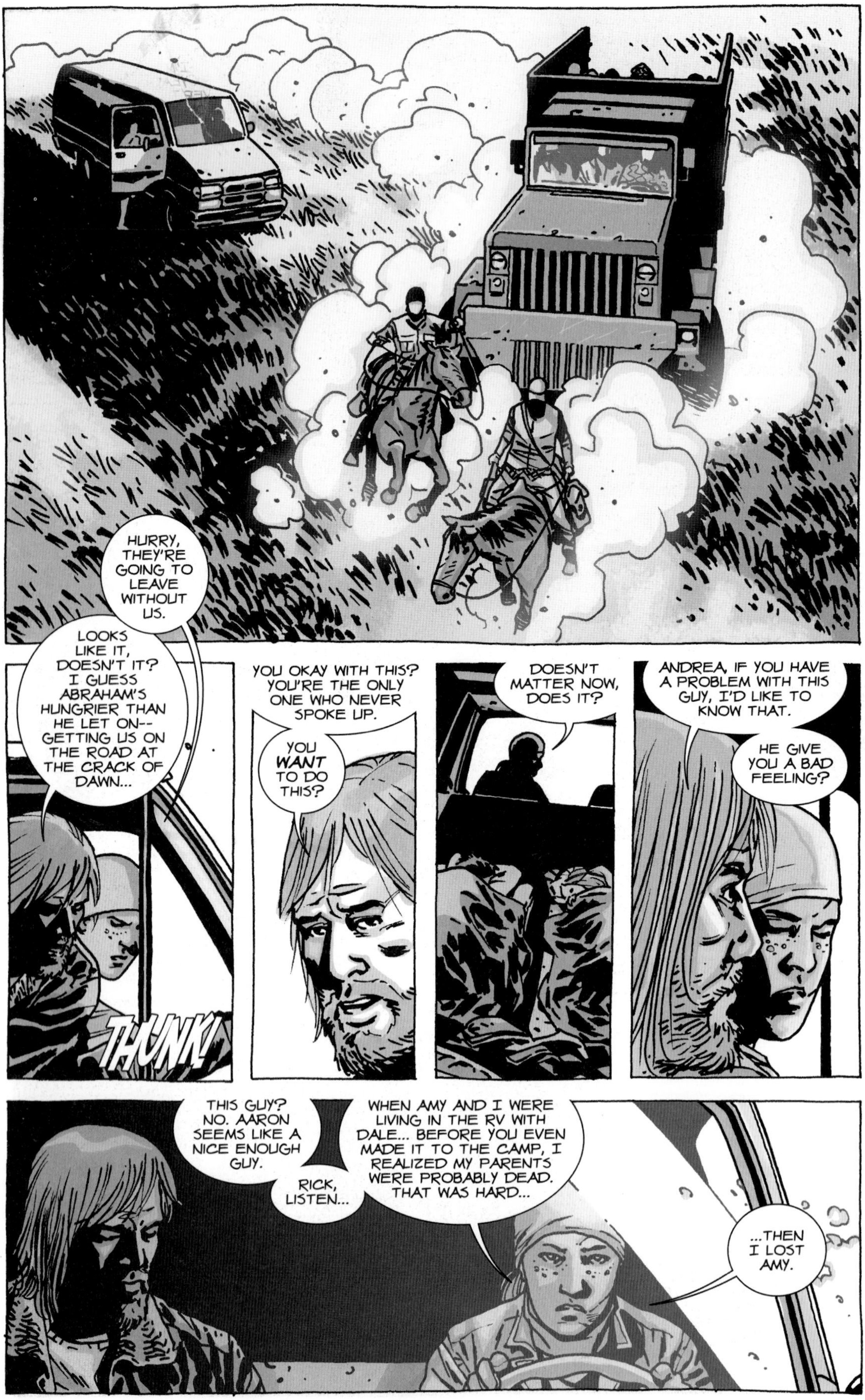

HURRY, THEY'RE GOING TO LEAVE WITHOUT US.
LOOKS LIKE IT, DOESN'T IT? I GUESS ABRAHAM'S HUNGRIER THAN HE LET ON-- GETTING US ON THE ROAD AT THE CRACK OF DAWN...
THUNK!
YOU OKAY WITH THIS? YOU'RE THE ONLY ONE WHO NEVER SPOKE UP.
YOU WANT TO DO THIS?
DOESN'T MATTER NOW, DOES IT?
ANDREA, IF YOU HAVE A PROBLEM WITH THIS GUY, I'D LIKE TO KNOW THAT.
HE GIVE YOU A BAD FEELING?
THIS GUY? NO. AARON SEEMS LIKE A NICE ENOUGH GUY.
RICK, LISTEN...
WHEN AMY AND I WERE LIVING IN THE RV WITH DALE... BEFORE YOU EVEN MADE IT TO THE CAMP, I REALIZED MY PARENTS WERE PROBABLY DEAD. THAT WAS HARD...
...THEN I LOST AMY.

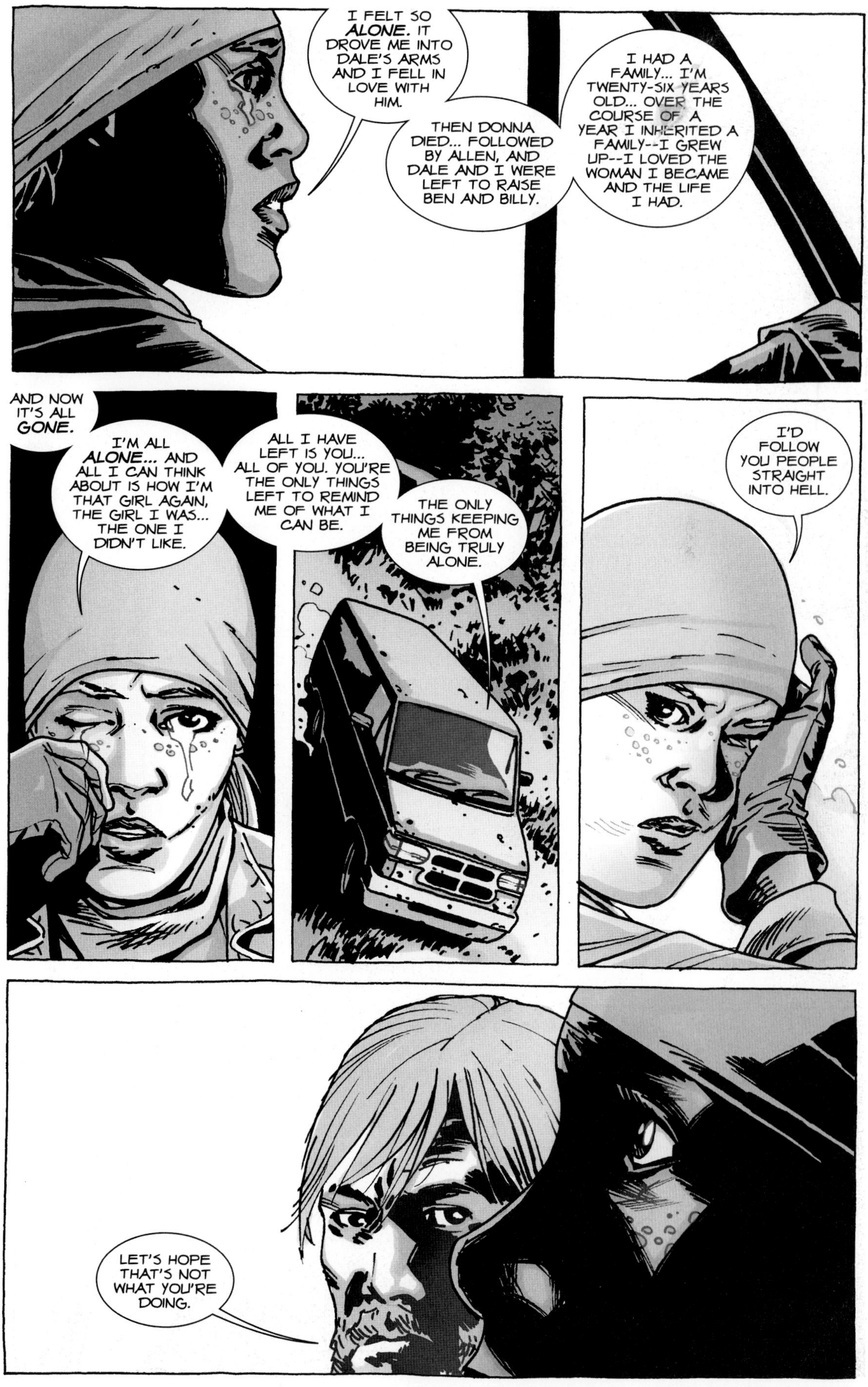
I FELT SO ALONE. IT DROVE ME INTO DALE'S ARMS AND I FELL IN LOVE WITH HIM.
THEN DONNA DIED... FOLLOWED BY ALLEN, AND DALE AND I WERE LEFT TO RAISE BEN AND BILLY.
I HAD A FAMILY... I'M TWENTY-SIX YEARS OLD... OVER THE COURSE OF A YEAR I INHERITED A FAMILY--I GREW UP--I LOVED THE WOMAN I BECAME AND THE LIFE I HAD.
AND NOW IT'S ALL GONE.
I'M ALL ALONE... AND ALL I CAN THINK ABOUT IS HOW I'M THAT GIRL AGAIN, THE GIRL I WAS... THE ONE I DIDN'T LIKE.
ALL I HAVE LEFT IS YOU... ALL OF YOU. YOU'RE THE ONLY THINGS LEFT TO REMIND ME OF WHAT I CAN BE.
THE ONLY THINGS KEEPING ME FROM BEING TRULY ALONE.
I'D FOLLOW YOU PEOPLE STRAIGHT INTO HELL.
LET'S HOPE THAT'S NOT WHAT YOU'RE DOING.

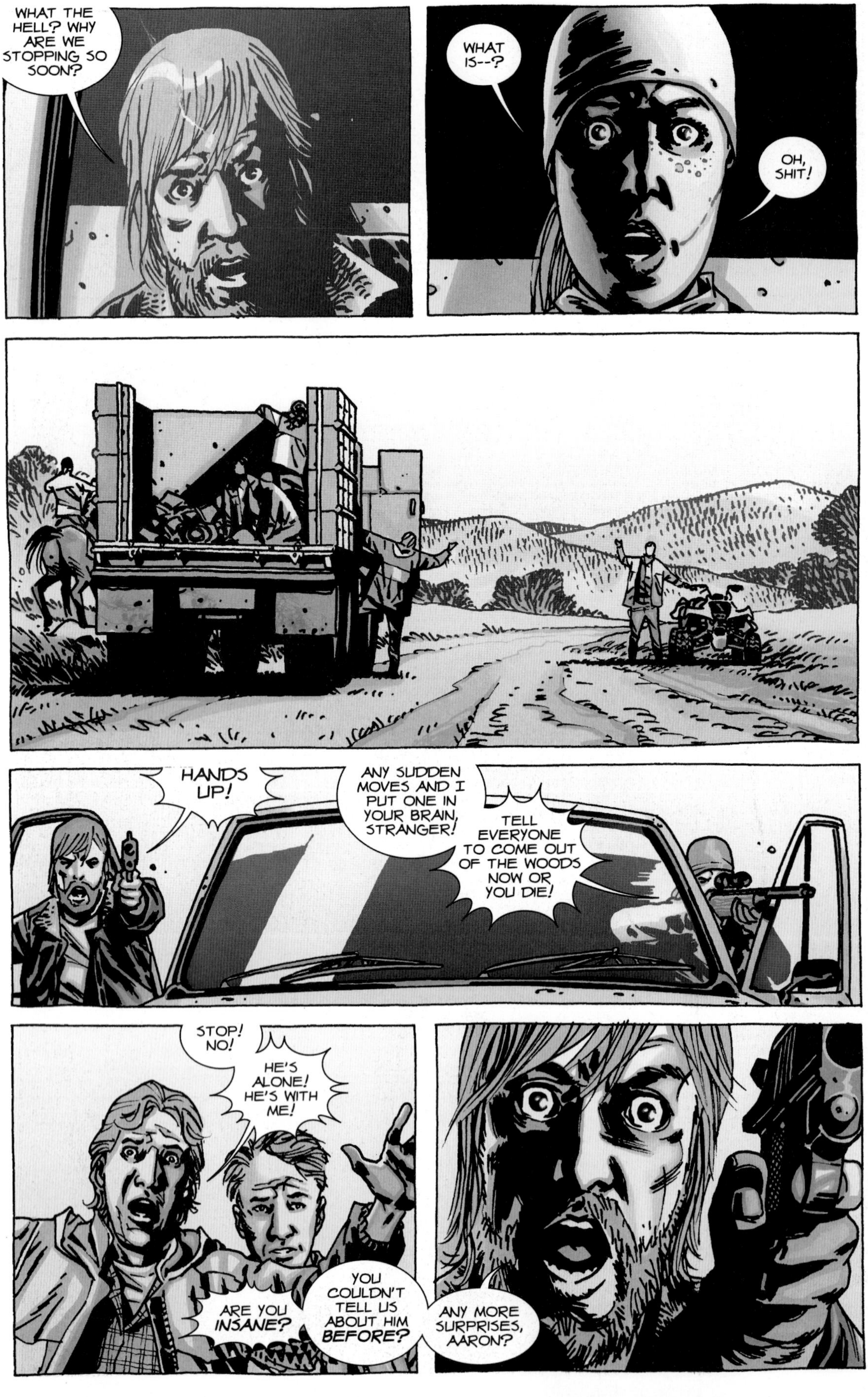

WHAT THE HELL? WHY ARE WE STOPPING SO SOON?
WHAT IS--?
OH, SHIT!
HANDS UP!
ANY SUDDEN MOVES AND I PUT ONE IN YOUR BRAIN, STRANGER!
TELL EVERYONE TO COME OUT OF THE WOODS NOW OR YOU DIE!
STOP! NO!
HE'S ALONE! HE'S WITH ME!
ARE YOU INSANE?
YOU COULDN'T TELL US ABOUT HIM BEFORE?
ANY MORE SURPRISES, AARON?

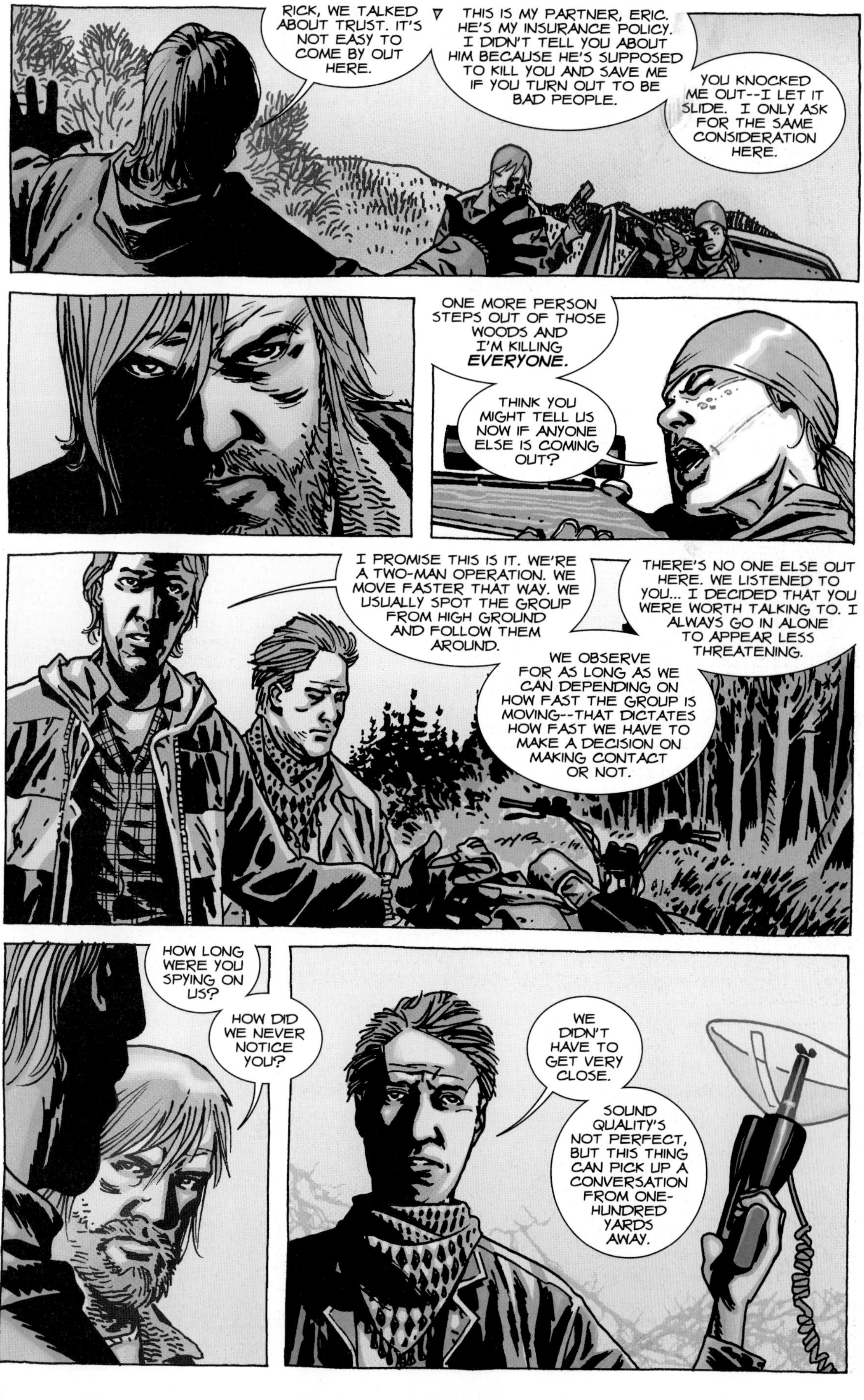
RICK, WE TALKED ABOUT TRUST. IT'S NOT EASY TO COME BY OUT HERE.
THIS IS MY PARTNER, ERIC. HE'S MY INSURANCE POLICY. I DIDN'T TELL YOU ABOUT HIM BECAUSE HE'S SUPPOSED TO KILL YOU AND SAVE ME IF YOU TURN OUT TO BE BAD PEOPLE.
YOU KNOCKED ME OUT--I LET IT SLIDE. I ONLY ASK FOR THE SAME CONSIDERATION HERE.
ONE MORE PERSON STEPS OUT OF THOSE WOODS AND I'M KILLING EVERYONE.
THINK YOU MIGHT TELL US NOW IF ANYONE ELSE IS COMING OUT?
I PROMISE THIS IS IT. WE'RE A TWO-MAN OPERATION. WE MOVE FASTER THAT WAY. WE USUALLY SPOT THE GROUP FROM HIGH GROUND AND FOLLOW THEM AROUND.
WE OBSERVE FOR AS LONG AS WE CAN DEPENDING ON HOW FAST THE GROUP IS MOVING--THAT DICTATES HOW FAST WE HAVE TO MAKE A DECISION ON MAKING CONTACT OR NOT.
THERE'S NO ONE ELSE OUT HERE. WE LISTENED TO YOU... I DECIDED THAT YOU WERE WORTH TALKING TO. I ALWAYS GO IN ALONE TO APPEAR LESS THREATENING.
HOW LONG WERE YOU SPYING ON US?
HOW DID WE NEVER NOTICE YOU?
WE DIDN'T HAVE TO GET VERY CLOSE.
SOUND QUALITY'S NOT PERFECT, BUT THIS THING CAN PICK UP A CONVERSATION FROM ONE-HUNDRED YARDS AWAY.

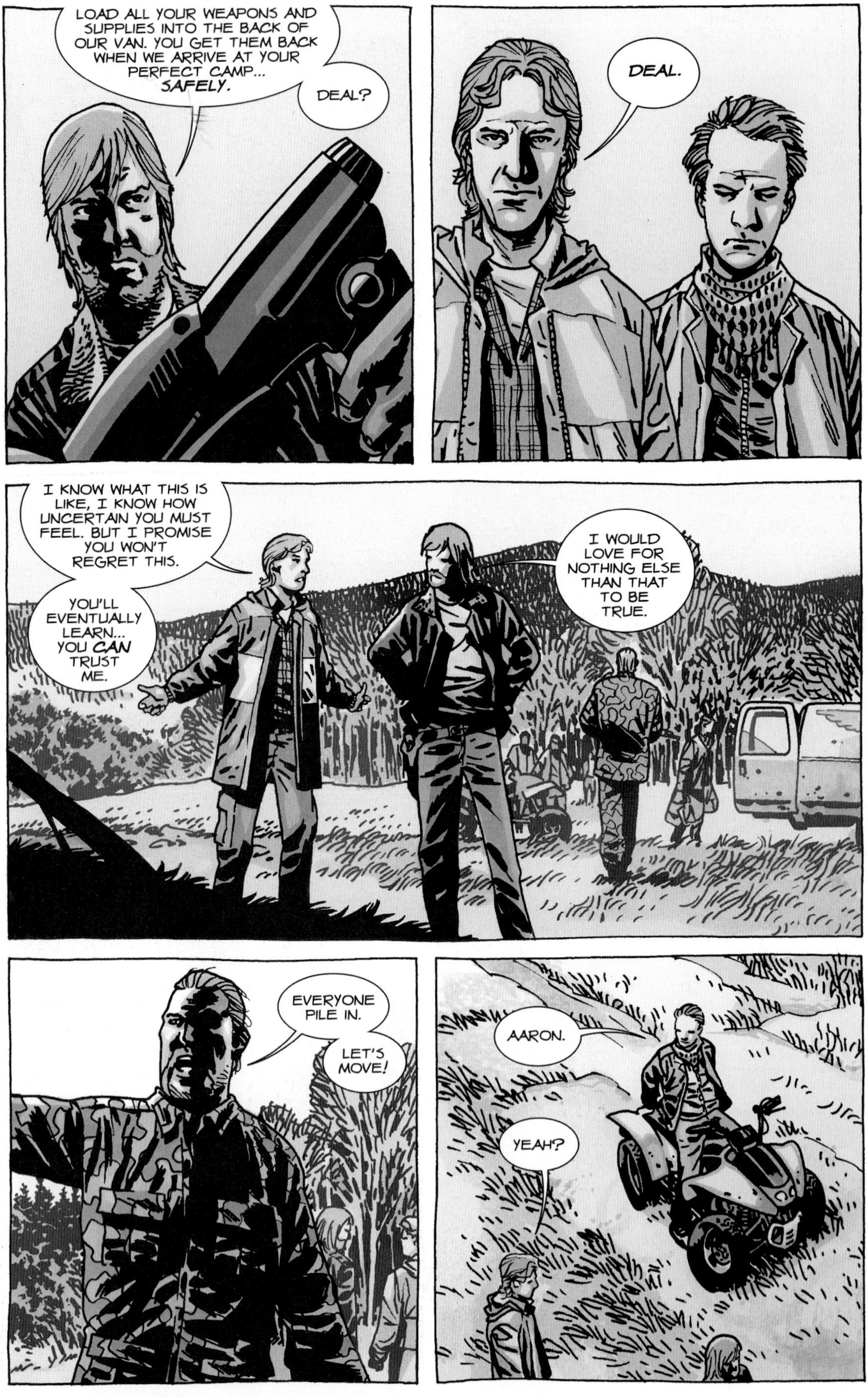

LOAD ALL YOUR WEAPONS AND SUPPLIES INTO THE BACK OF OUR VAN. YOU GET THEM BACK WHEN WE ARRIVE AT YOUR PERFECT CAMP... SAFELY.
DEAL?
DEAL.
I KNOW WHAT THIS IS LIKE, I KNOW HOW UNCERTAIN YOU MUST FEEL. BUT I PROMISE YOU WON'T REGRET THIS.
YOU'LL EVENTUALLY LEARN... YOU CAN TRUST ME.
I WOULD LOVE FOR NOTHING ELSE THAN THAT TO BE TRUE.
EVERYONE PILE IN.
LET'S MOVE!
AARON.
YEAH?

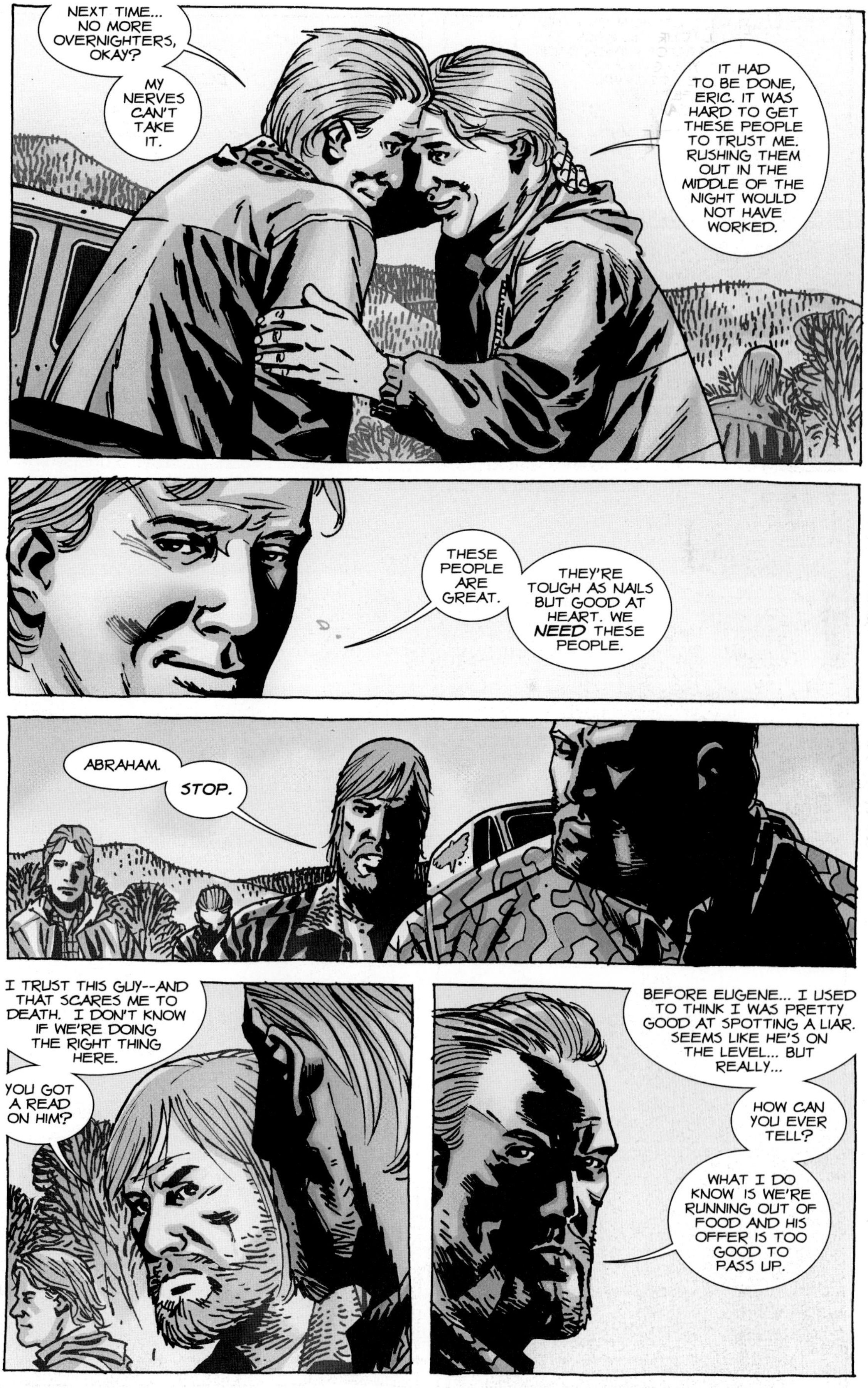
NEXT TIME... NO MORE OVERNIGHTERS, OKAY?
MY NERVES CAN'T TAKE IT.
IT HAD TO BE DONE, ERIC. IT WAS HARD TO GET THESE PEOPLE TO TRUST ME. RUSHING THEM OUT IN THE MIDDLE OF THE NIGHT WOULD NOT HAVE WORKED.
THESE PEOPLE ARE GREAT.
THEY'RE TOUGH AS NAILS BUT GOOD AT HEART. WE NEED THESE PEOPLE.
ABRAHAM.
STOP.
I TRUST THIS GUY--AND THAT SCARES ME TO DEATH. I DON'T KNOW IF WE'RE DOING THE RIGHT THING HERE.
YOU GOT A READ ON HIM?
BEFORE EUGENE... I USED TO THINK I WAS PRETTY GOOD AT SPOTTING A LIAR. SEEMS LIKE HE'S ON THE LEVEL... BUT REALLY...
HOW CAN YOU EVER TELL?
WHAT I DO KNOW IS WE'RE RUNNING OUT OF FOOD AND HIS OFFER IS TOO GOOD TO PASS UP.

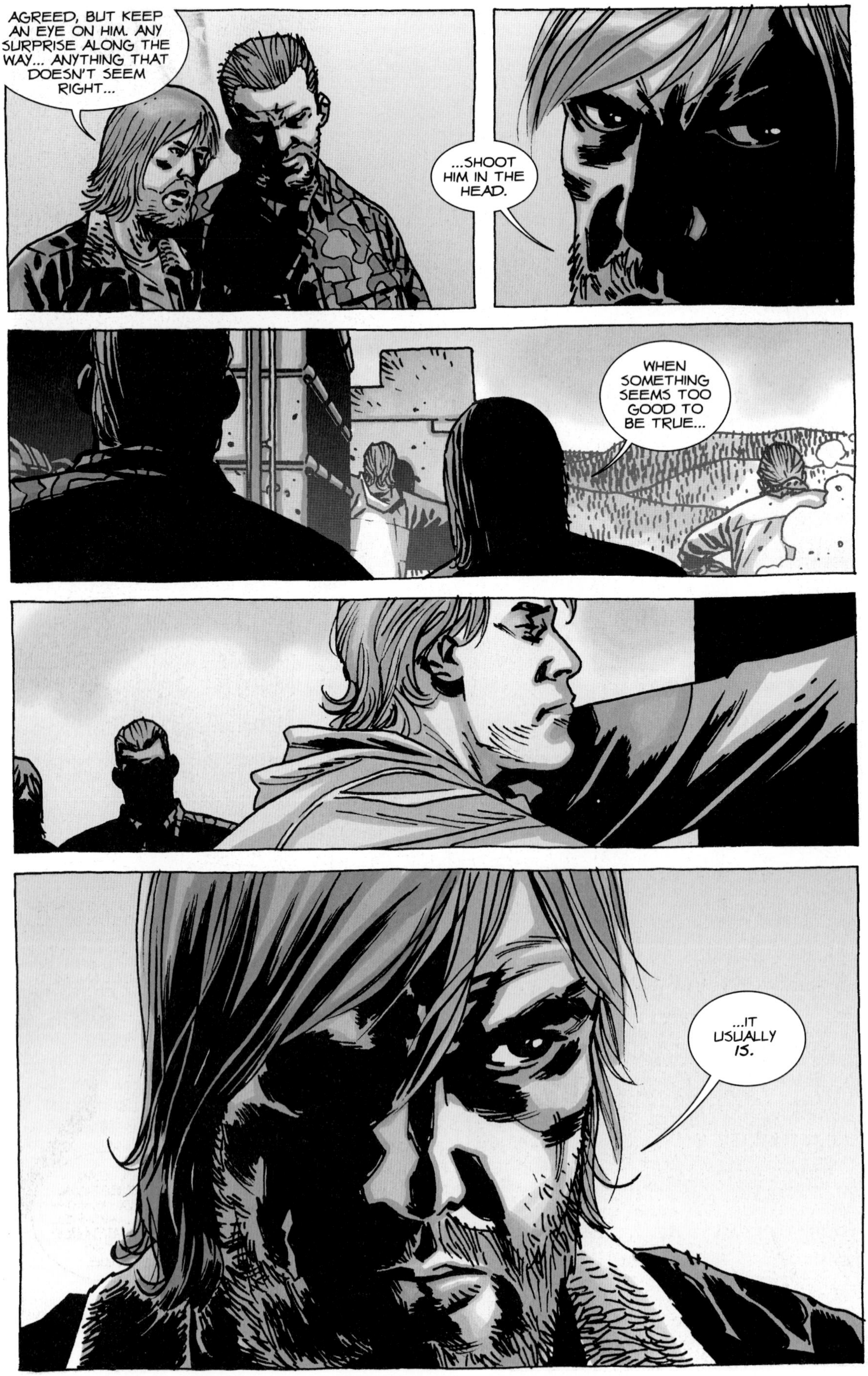
AGREED, BUT KEEP AN EYE ON HIM. ANY SURPRISE ALONG THE WAY... ANYTHING THAT DOESN'T SEEM RIGHT...
...SHOOT HIM IN THE HEAD.
WHEN SOMETHING SEEMS TOO GOOD TO BE TRUE...
...IT USUALLY IS.

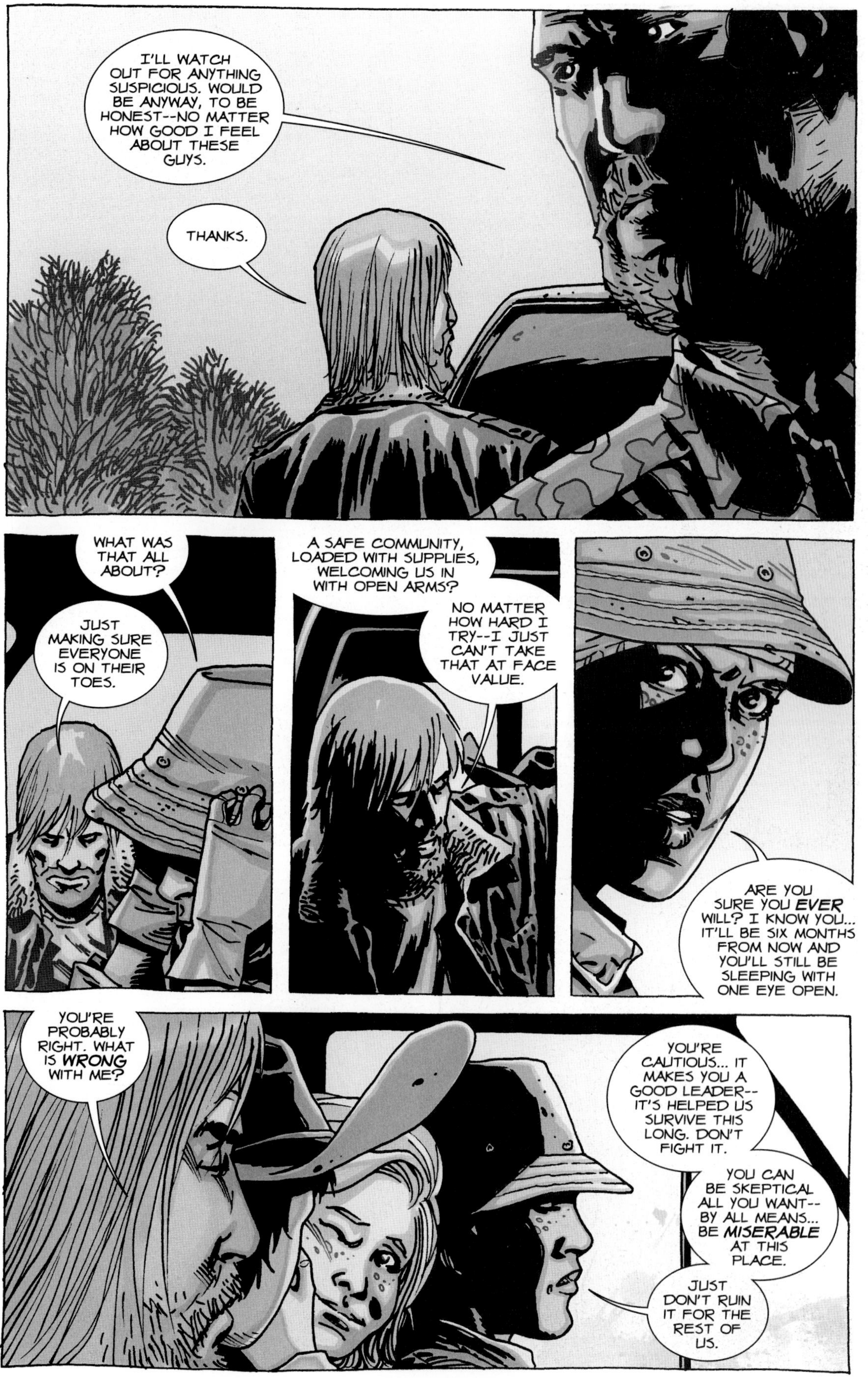

I'LL WATCH OUT FOR ANYTHING SUSPICIOUS. WOULD BE ANYWAY, TO BE HONEST--NO MATTER HOW GOOD I FEEL ABOUT THESE GUYS.
THANKS.
WHAT WAS THAT ALL ABOUT?
JUST MAKING SURE EVERYONE IS ON THEIR TOES.
A SAFE COMMUNITY, LOADED WITH SUPPLIES, WELCOMING US IN WITH OPEN ARMS?
NO MATTER HOW HARD I TRY--I JUST CAN'T TAKE THAT AT FACE VALUE.
ARE YOU SURE YOU EVER WILL? I KNOW YOU... IT'LL BE SIX MONTHS FROM NOW AND YOU'LL STILL BE SLEEPING WITH ONE EYE OPEN.
YOU'RE PROBABLY RIGHT. WHAT IS WRONG WITH ME?
YOU'RE CAUTIOUS... IT MAKES YOU A GOOD LEADER-- IT'S HELPED US SURVIVE THIS LONG. DON'T FIGHT IT.
YOU CAN BE SKEPTICAL ALL YOU WANT-- BY ALL MEANS... BE MISERABLE AT THIS PLACE.
JUST DON'T RUIN IT FOR THE REST OF US.

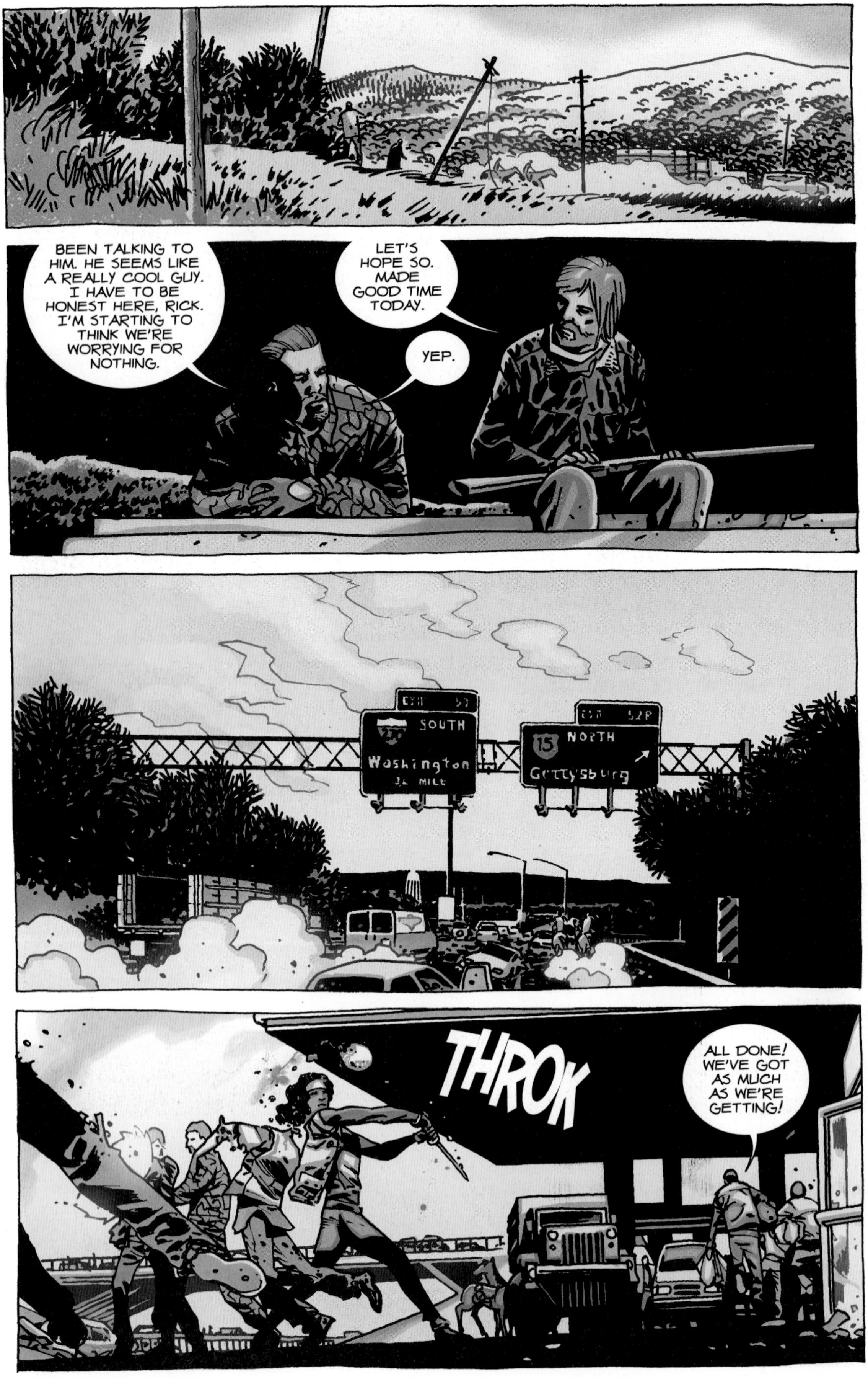
BEEN TALKING TO HIM. HE SEEMS LIKE A REALLY COOL GUY. I HAVE TO BE HONEST HERE, RICK. I'M STARTING TO THINK WE'RE WORRYING FOR NOTHING.
LET'S HOPE SO. MADE GOOD TIME TODAY.
YEP.
SOUTH
Washington
15
NORTH
Gettysburg
THROK
ALL DONE! WE'VE GOT AS MUCH AS WE'RE GETTING!

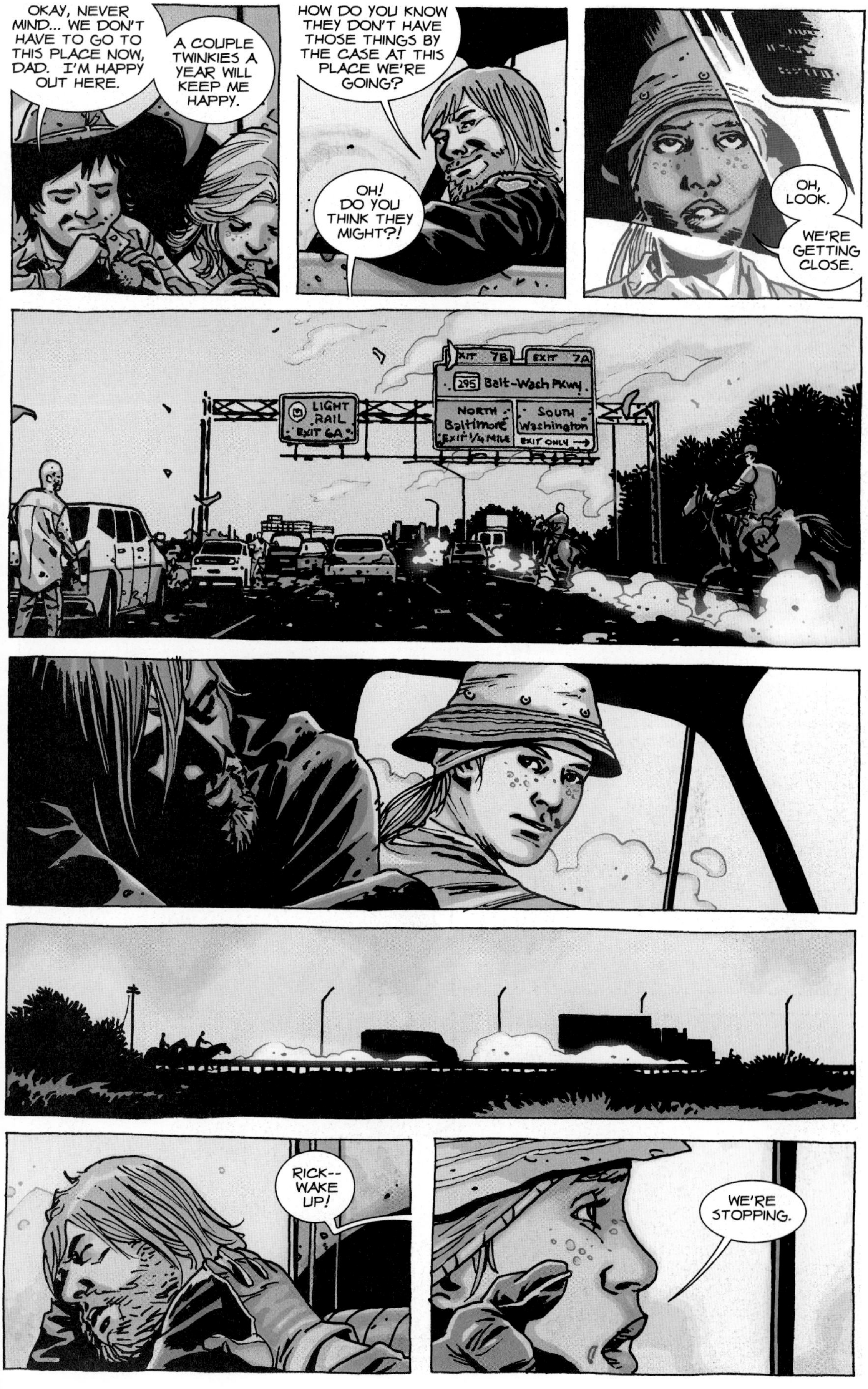
OKAY, NEVER MIND... WE DON'T HAVE TO GO TO THIS PLACE NOW, DAD. I'M HAPPY OUT HERE.
A COUPLE TWINKIES A YEAR WILL KEEP ME HAPPY.
HOW DO YOU KNOW THEY DON'T HAVE THOSE THINGS BY THE CASE AT THIS PLACE WE'RE GOING?
OH! DO YOU THINK THEY MIGHT?!
OH, LOOK.
WE'RE GETTING CLOSE.
EXIT 7B
EXIT 7A
295 Balt-Wash Pkwy
LIGHT RAIL
EXIT 6A
NORTH Baltimore
EXIT 1/4 MILE
SOUTH Washington
EXIT ONLY
RICK-- WAKE UP!
WE'RE STOPPING.

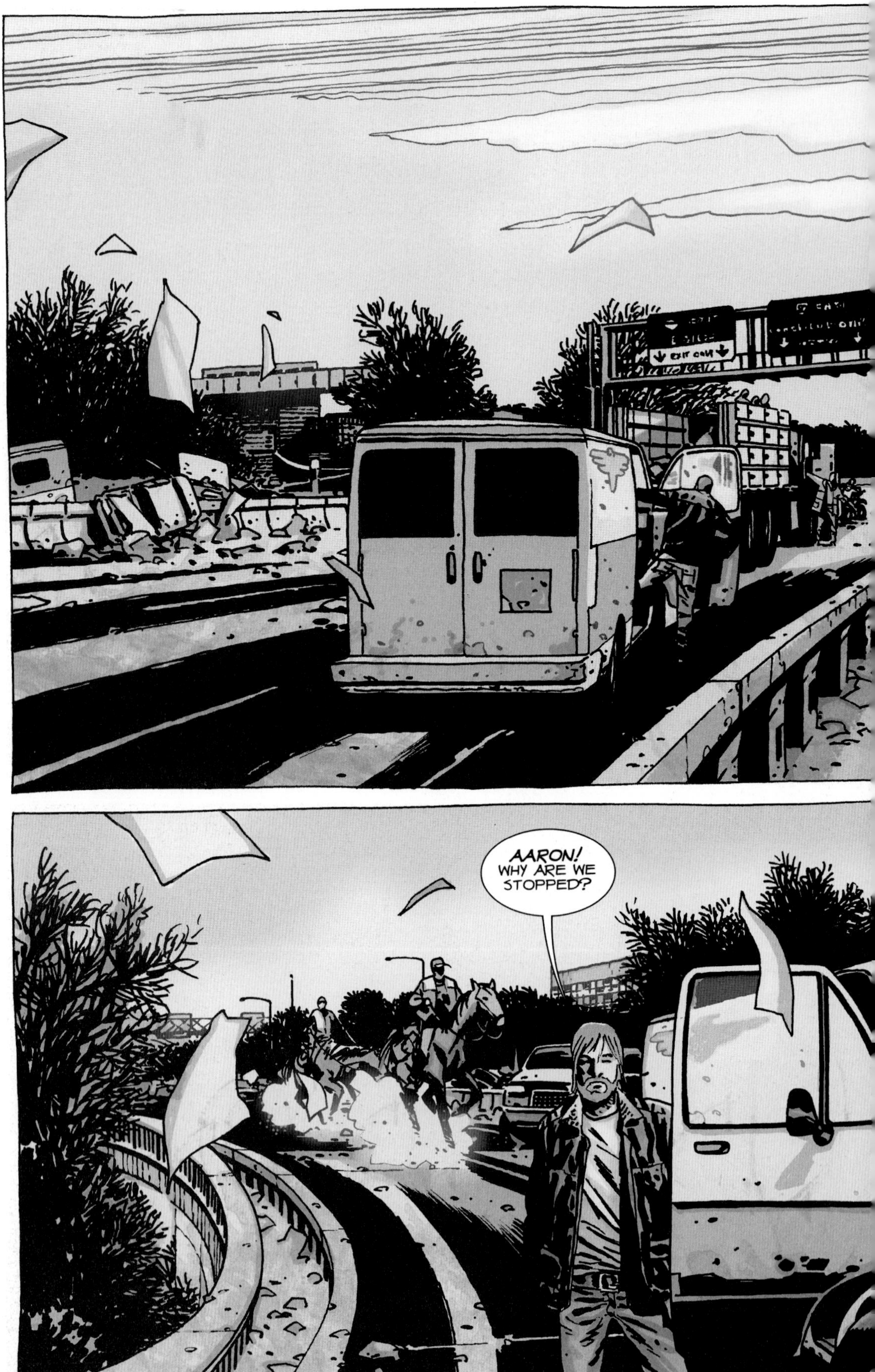
AARON! WHY ARE WE STOPPED?

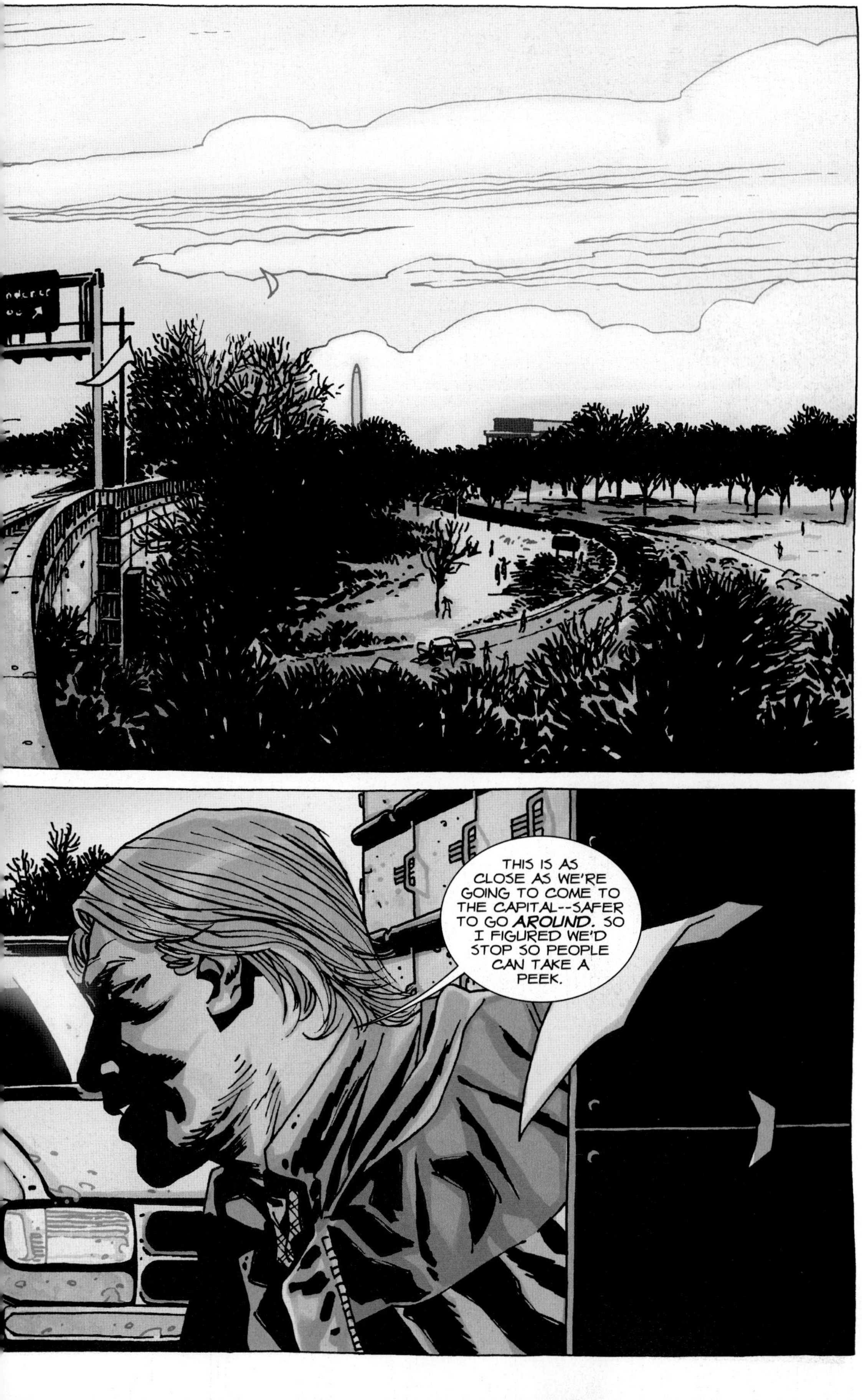
THIS IS AS CLOSE AS WE'RE GOING TO COME TO THE CAPITAL--SAFER TO GO AROUND. SO I FIGURED WE'D STOP SO PEOPLE CAN TAKE A PEEK.

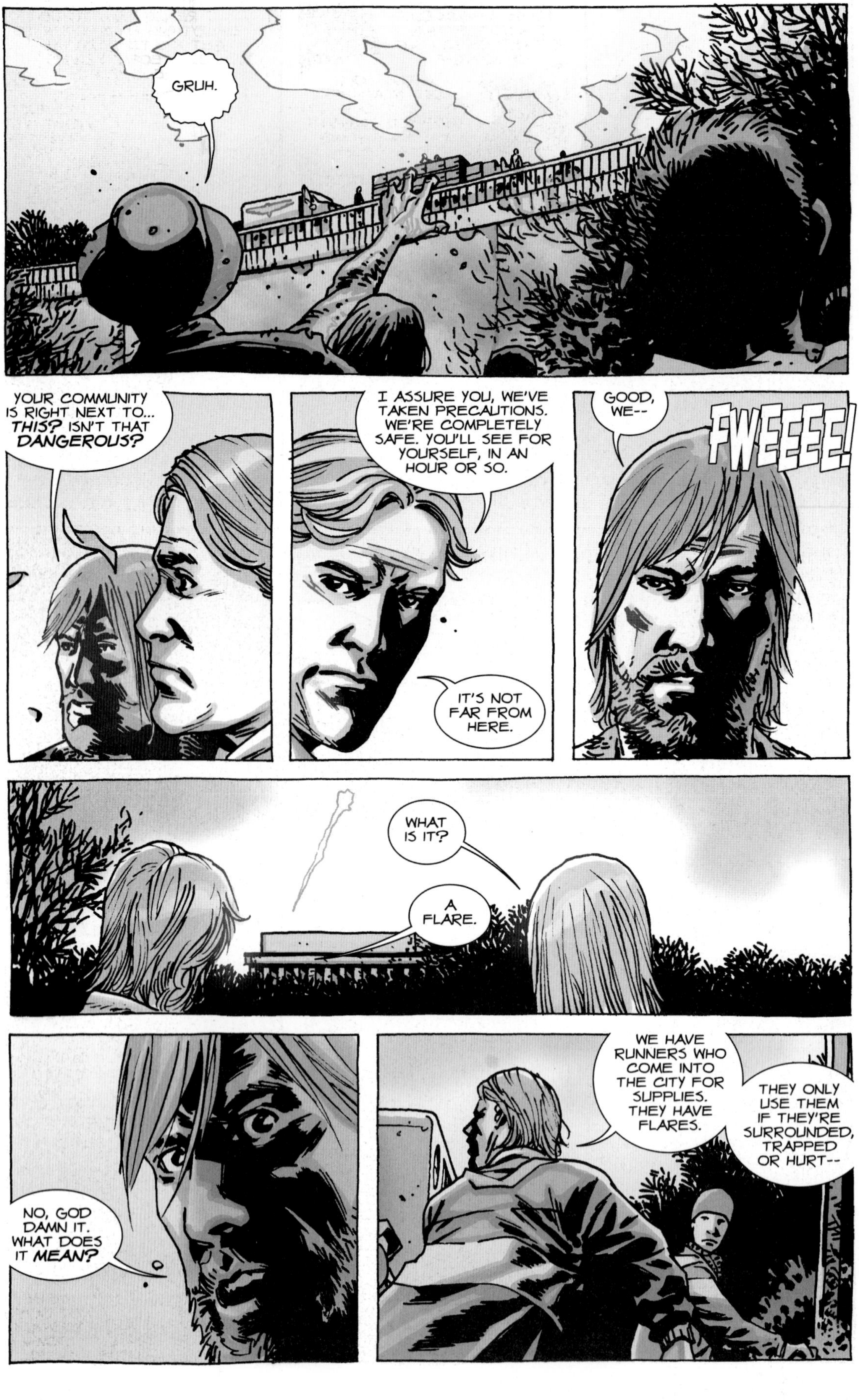
GRUH.
YOUR COMMUNITY IS RIGHT NEXT TO... THIS? ISN'T THAT DANGEROUS?
I ASSURE YOU, WE'VE TAKEN PRECAUTIONS. WE'RE COMPLETELY SAFE. YOU'LL SEE FOR YOURSELF, IN AN HOUR OR SO.
IT'S NOT FAR FROM HERE.
GOOD, WE--
FWEEEE!
WHAT IS IT?
A FLARE.
NO, GOD DAMN IT. WHAT DOES IT MEAN?
WE HAVE RUNNERS WHO COME INTO THE CITY FOR SUPPLIES. THEY HAVE FLARES.
THEY ONLY USE THEM IF THEY'RE SURROUNDED, TRAPPED OR HURT--

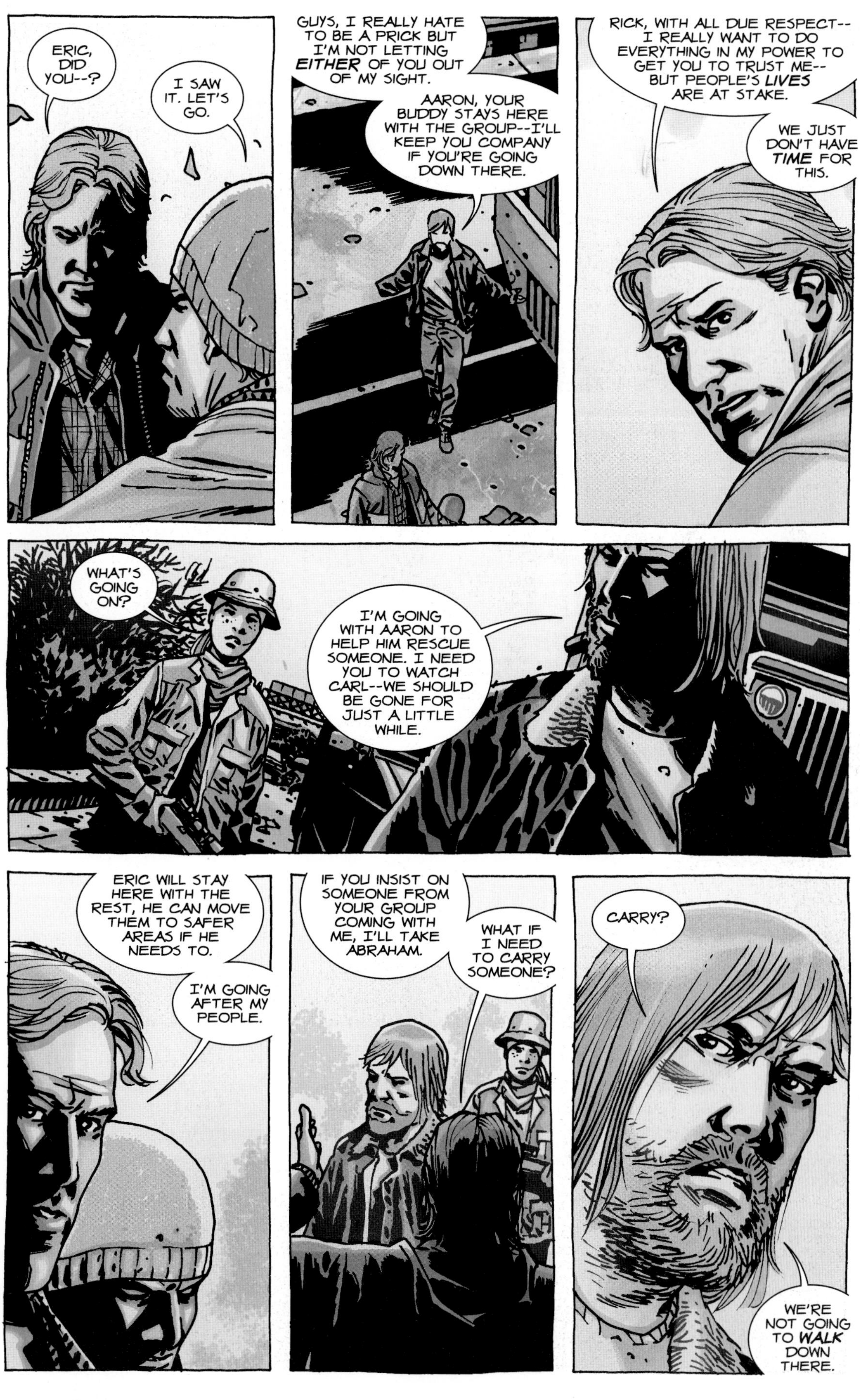
ERIC, DID YOU--?
I SAW IT. LET'S GO.
GUYS, I REALLY HATE TO BE A PRICK BUT I'M NOT LETTING *EITHER* OF YOU OUT OF MY SIGHT.
AARON, YOUR BUDDY STAYS HERE WITH THE GROUP--I'LL KEEP YOU COMPANY IF YOU'RE GOING DOWN THERE.
RICK, WITH ALL DUE RESPECT-- I REALLY WANT TO DO EVERYTHING IN MY POWER TO GET YOU TO TRUST ME-- BUT PEOPLE'S *LIVES* ARE AT STAKE.
WE JUST DON'T HAVE *TIME* FOR THIS.
WHAT'S GOING ON?
I'M GOING WITH AARON TO HELP HIM RESCUE SOMEONE. I NEED YOU TO WATCH CARL--WE SHOULD BE GONE FOR JUST A LITTLE WHILE.
ERIC WILL STAY HERE WITH THE REST, HE CAN MOVE THEM TO SAFER AREAS IF HE NEEDS TO.
I'M GOING AFTER MY PEOPLE.
IF YOU INSIST ON SOMEONE FROM YOUR GROUP COMING WITH ME, I'LL TAKE ABRAHAM.
WHAT IF I NEED TO CARRY SOMEONE?
CARRY?
WE'RE NOT GOING TO *WALK* DOWN THERE.

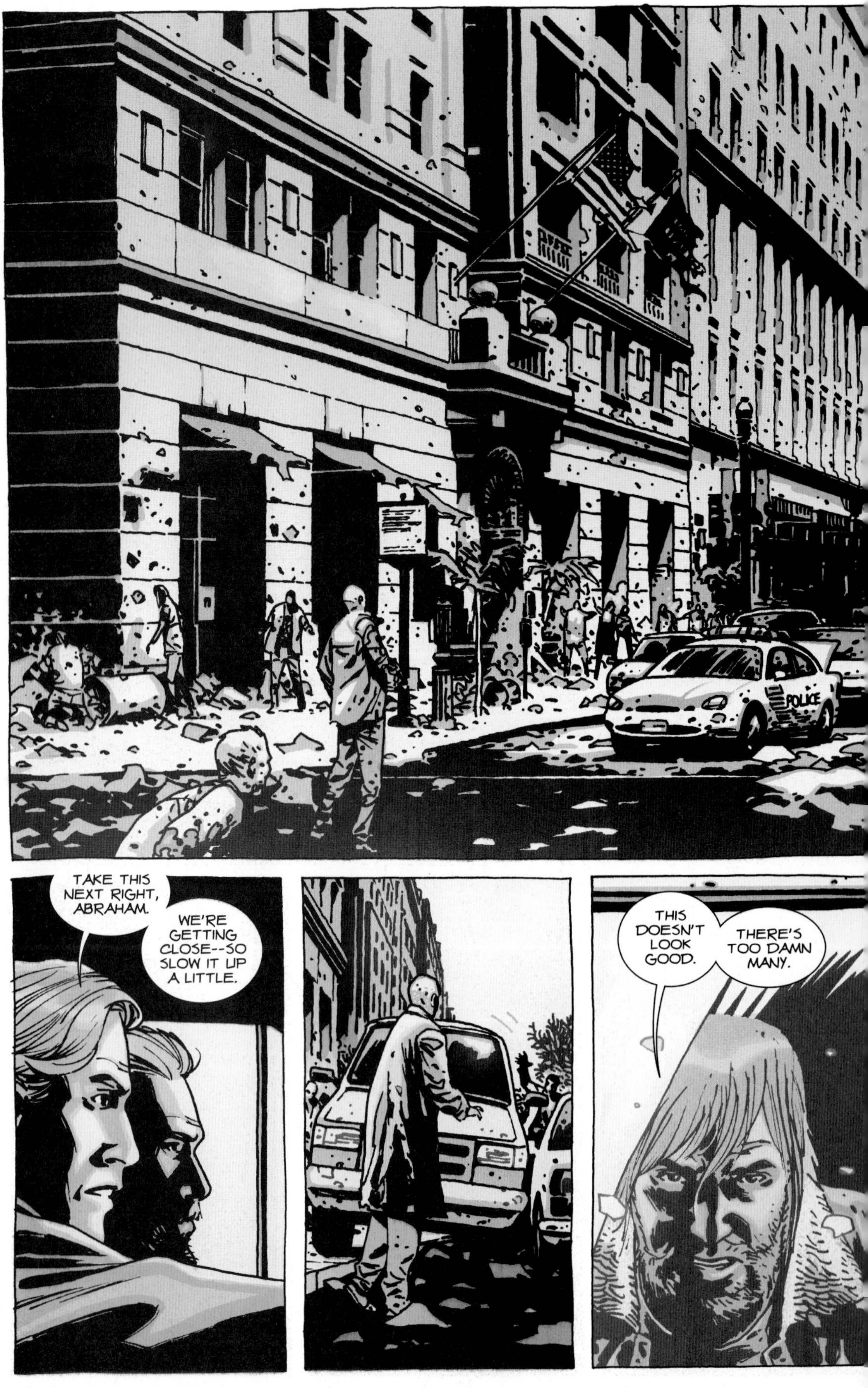

TAKE THIS NEXT RIGHT, ABRAHAM.
WE'RE GETTING CLOSE--SO SLOW IT UP A LITTLE.
THIS DOESN'T LOOK GOOD.
THERE'S TOO DAMN MANY.
POLICE

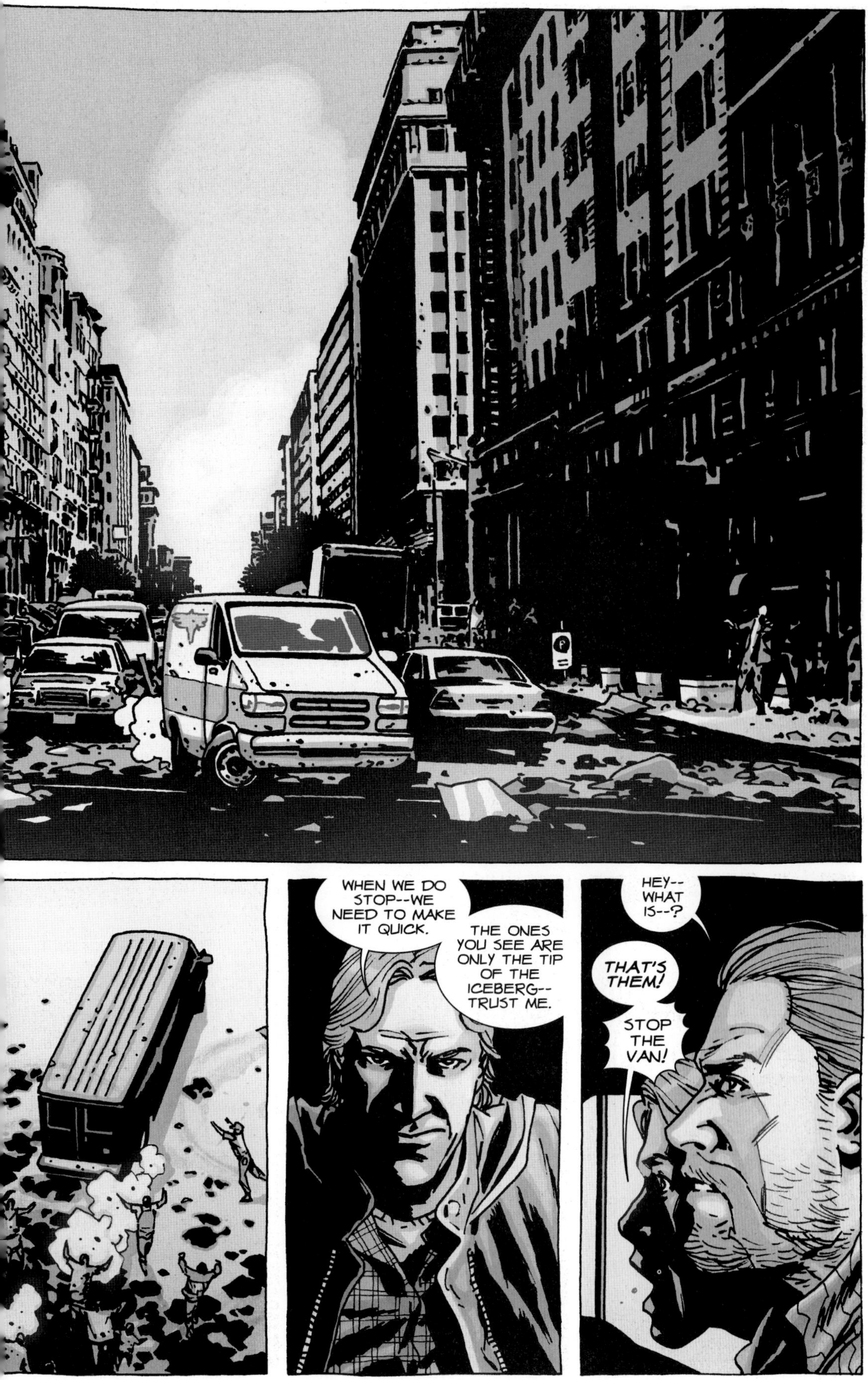
WHEN WE DO STOP--WE NEED TO MAKE IT QUICK.
THE ONES YOU SEE ARE ONLY THE TIP OF THE ICEBERG-- TRUST ME.
HEY-- WHAT IS--?
THAT'S THEM!
STOP THE VAN!

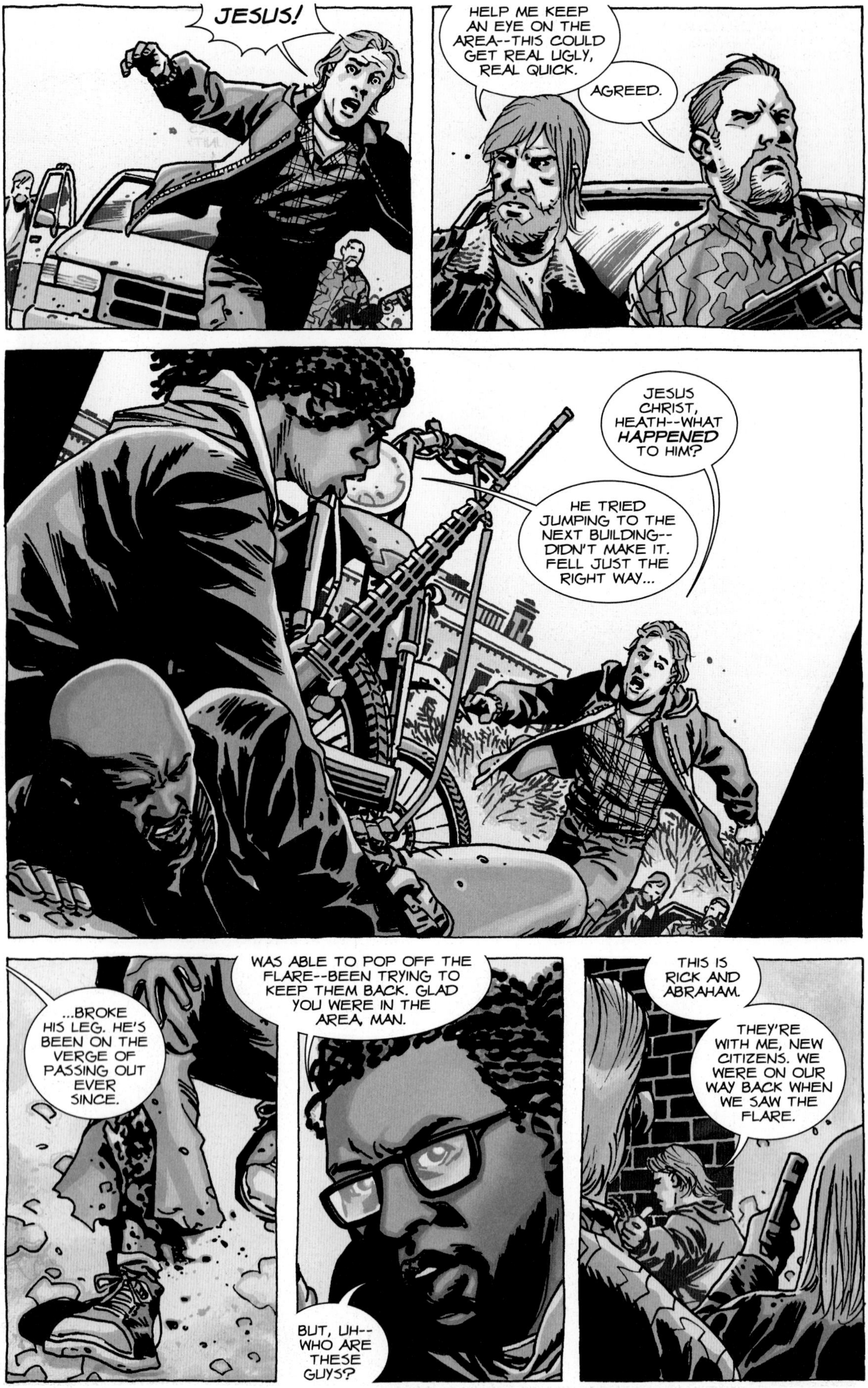
JESUS!
HELP ME KEEP AN EYE ON THE AREA--THIS COULD GET REAL UGLY, REAL QUICK.
AGREED.
JESUS CHRIST, HEATH--WHAT *HAPPENED* TO HIM?
HE TRIED JUMPING TO THE NEXT BUILDING-- DIDN'T MAKE IT. FELL JUST THE RIGHT WAY...
...BROKE HIS LEG. HE'S BEEN ON THE VERGE OF PASSING OUT EVER SINCE.
WAS ABLE TO POP OFF THE FLARE--BEEN TRYING TO KEEP THEM BACK. GLAD YOU WERE IN THE AREA, MAN.
BUT, UH-- WHO ARE THESE GUYS?
THIS IS RICK AND ABRAHAM.
THEY'RE WITH ME, NEW CITIZENS. WE WERE ON OUR WAY BACK WHEN WE SAW THE FLARE.

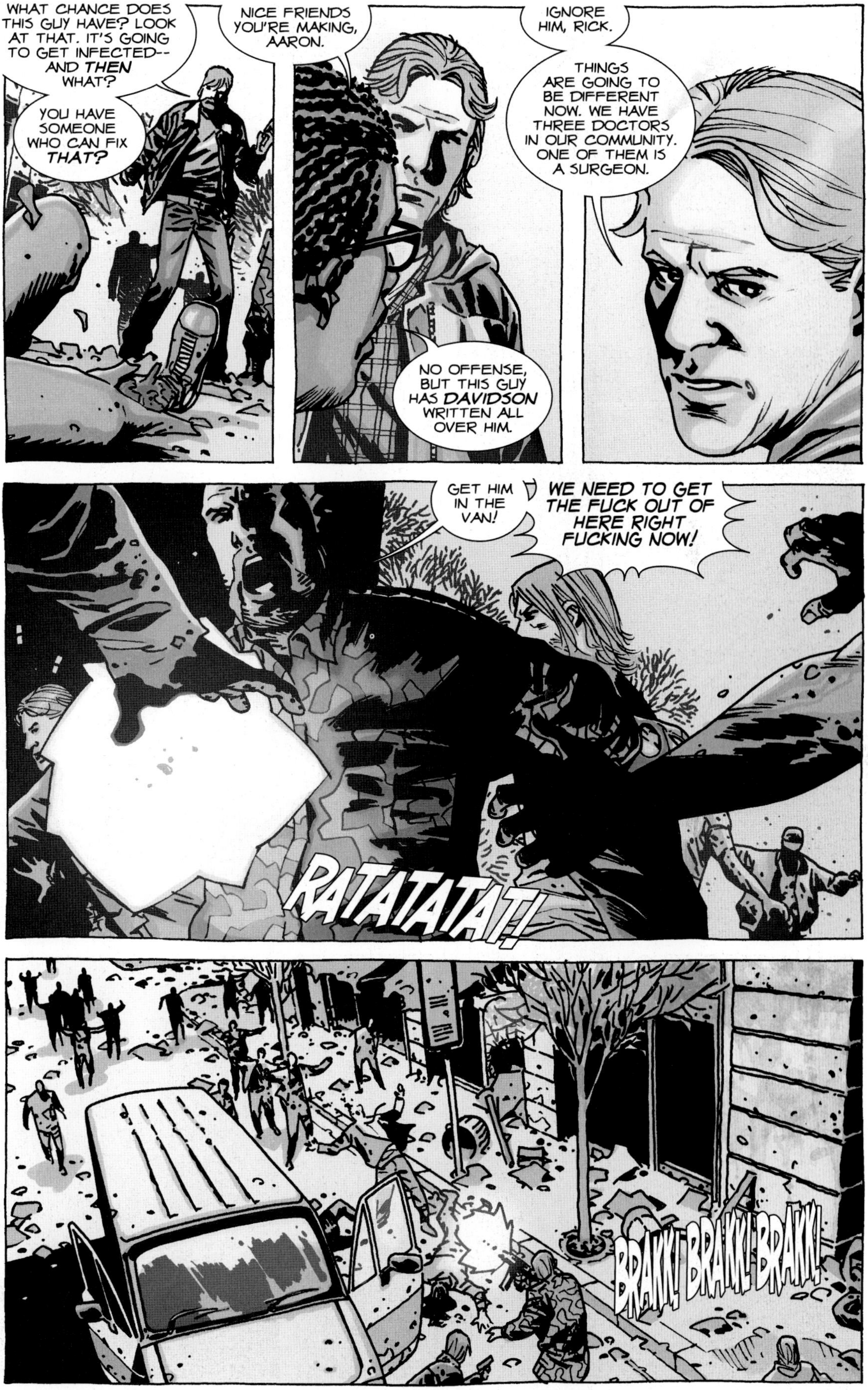
WHAT CHANCE DOES THIS GUY HAVE? LOOK AT THAT. IT'S GOING TO GET INFECTED-- AND THEN WHAT?
YOU HAVE SOMEONE WHO CAN FIX THAT?
NICE FRIENDS YOU'RE MAKING, AARON.
NO OFFENSE, BUT THIS GUY HAS DAVIDSON WRITTEN ALL OVER HIM.
IGNORE HIM, RICK.
THINGS ARE GOING TO BE DIFFERENT NOW. WE HAVE THREE DOCTORS IN OUR COMMUNITY. ONE OF THEM IS A SURGEON.
GET HIM IN THE VAN!
WE NEED TO GET THE FUCK OUT OF HERE RIGHT FUCKING NOW!
RATATATAT!
BRAKK! BRAKK! BRAKK!

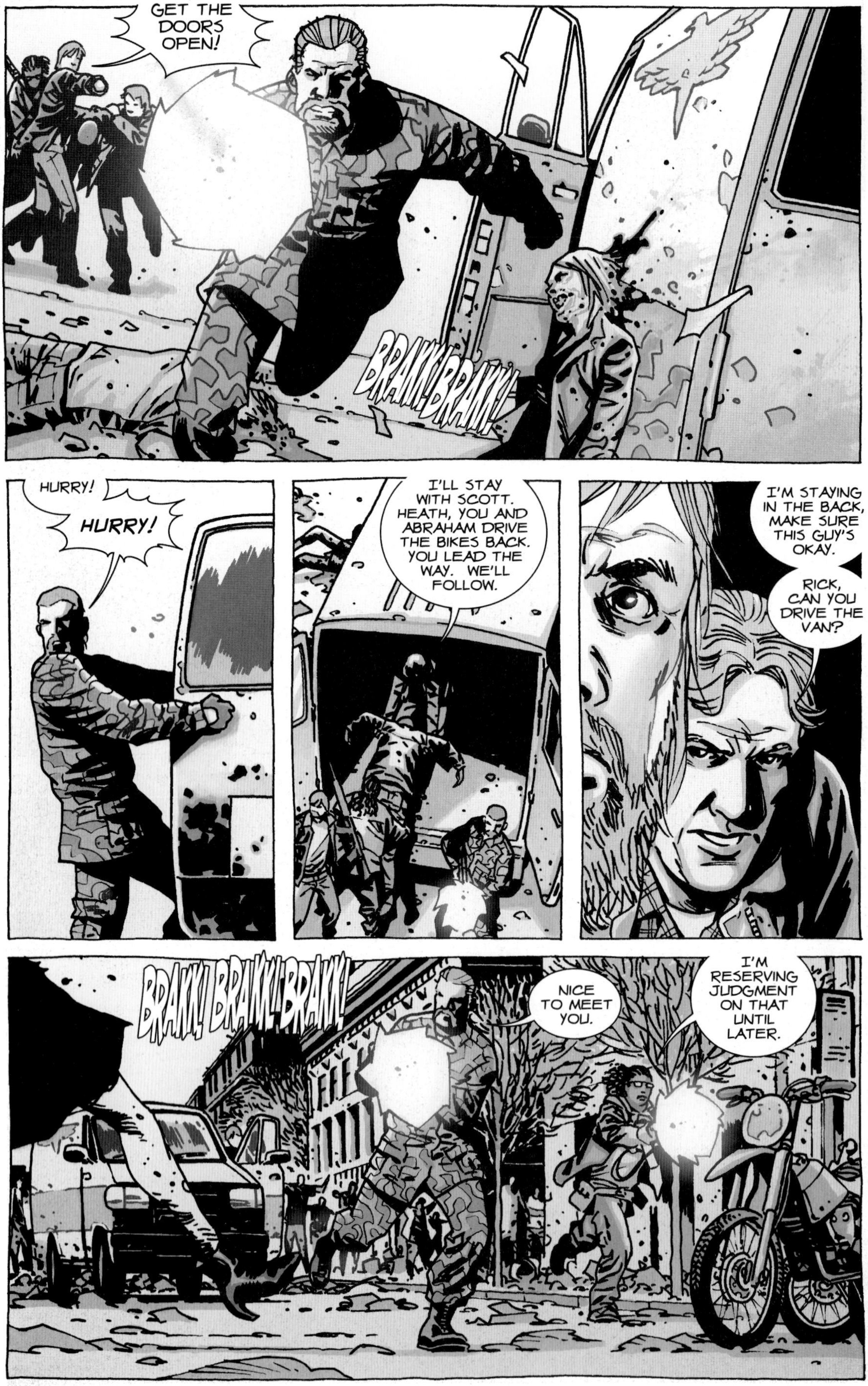

GET THE DOORS OPEN!
BRAKK! BRAKK!
HURRY!
HURRY!
I'LL STAY WITH SCOTT. HEATH, YOU AND ABRAHAM DRIVE THE BIKES BACK. YOU LEAD THE WAY. WE'LL FOLLOW.
I'M STAYING IN THE BACK, MAKE SURE THIS GUY'S OKAY.
RICK, CAN YOU DRIVE THE VAN?
BRAKK! BRAKK! BRAKK!
NICE TO MEET YOU.
I'M RESERVING JUDGMENT ON THAT UNTIL LATER.

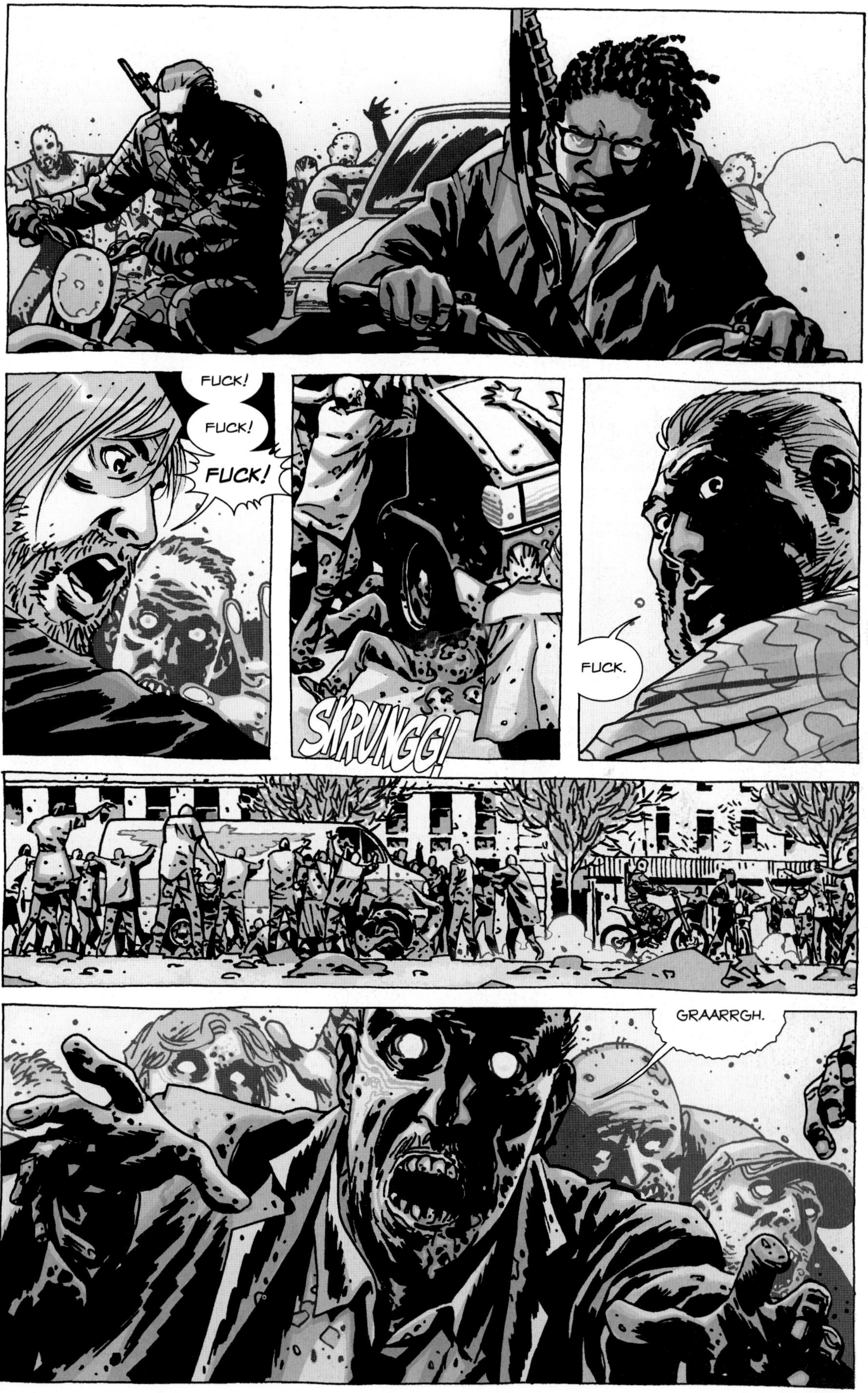
FUCK!
FUCK!
FUCK!
SKRUNGG!
FUCK.
GRAARRGH.

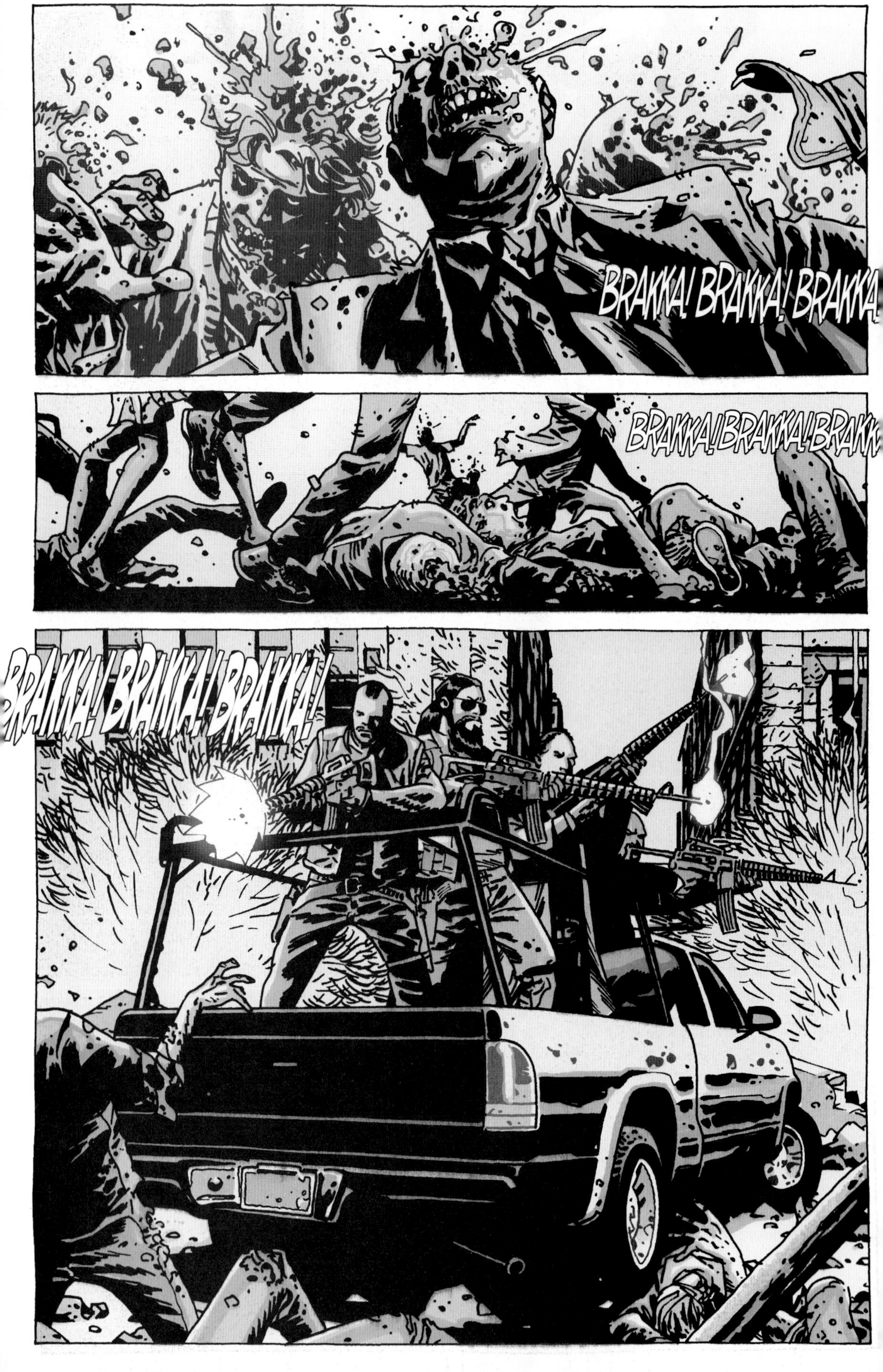
BRAKKA! BRAKKA! BRAKKA!
BRAKKA! BRAKKA! BRAKK
BRAKKA! BRAKKA! BRAKKA!

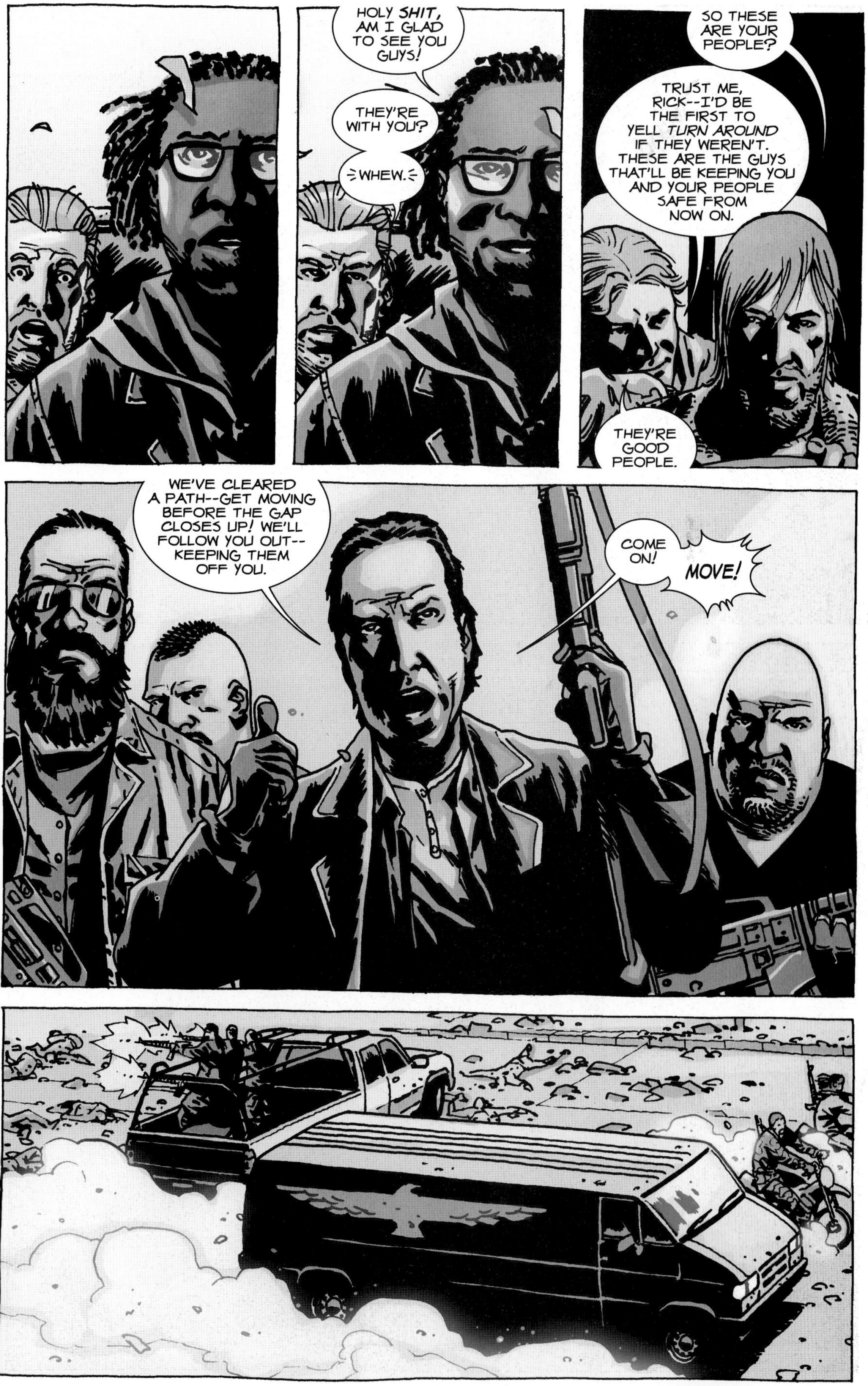
HOLY SHIT, AM I GLAD TO SEE YOU GUYS!
THEY'RE WITH YOU?
WHEW.
SO THESE ARE YOUR PEOPLE?
TRUST ME, RICK--I'D BE THE FIRST TO YELL TURN AROUND IF THEY WEREN'T. THESE ARE THE GUYS THAT'LL BE KEEPING YOU AND YOUR PEOPLE SAFE FROM NOW ON.
THEY'RE GOOD PEOPLE.
WE'VE CLEARED A PATH--GET MOVING BEFORE THE GAP CLOSES UP! WE'LL FOLLOW YOU OUT--KEEPING THEM OFF YOU.
COME ON!
MOVE!

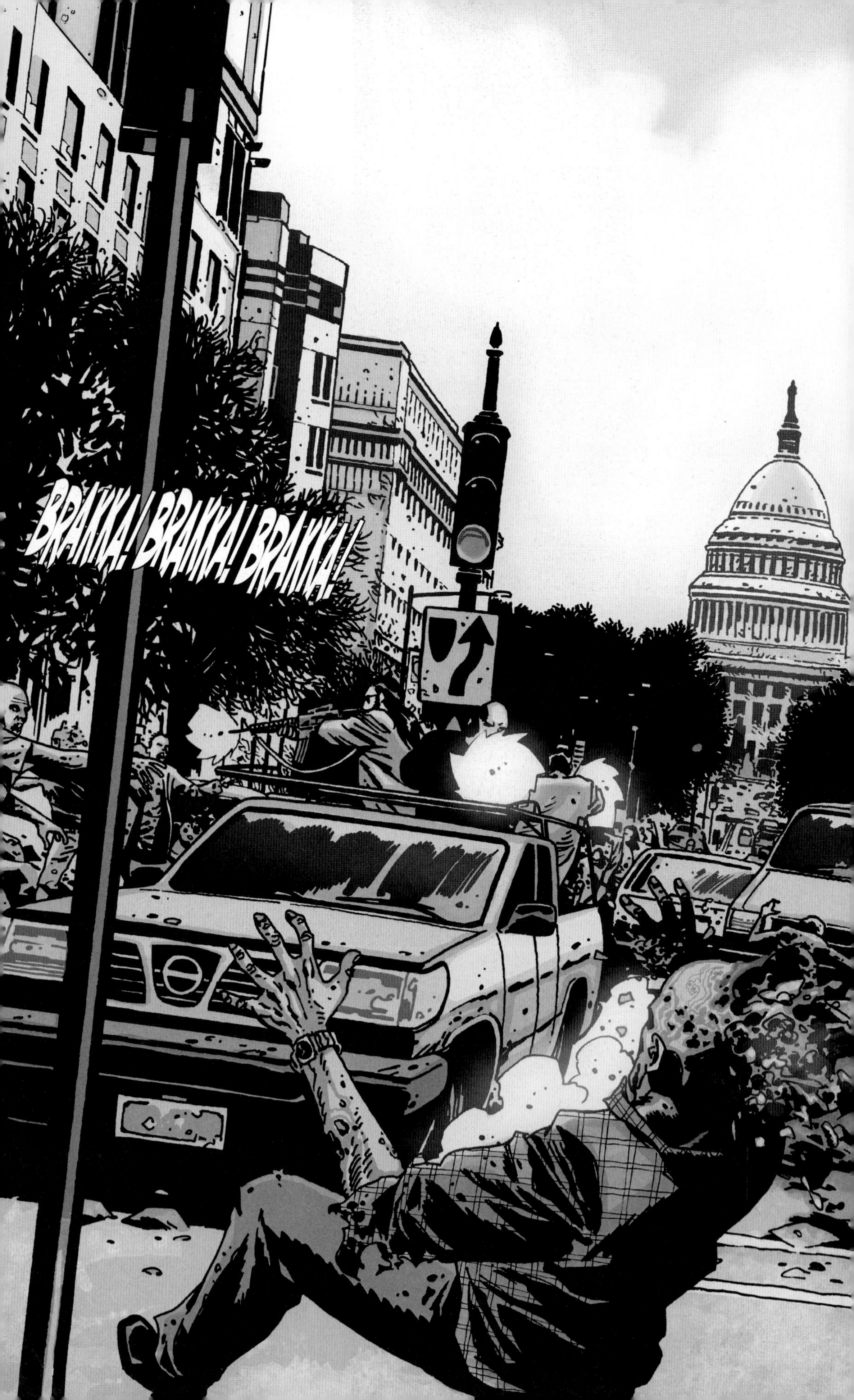
BRAKKA! BRAKKA! BRAKKA!

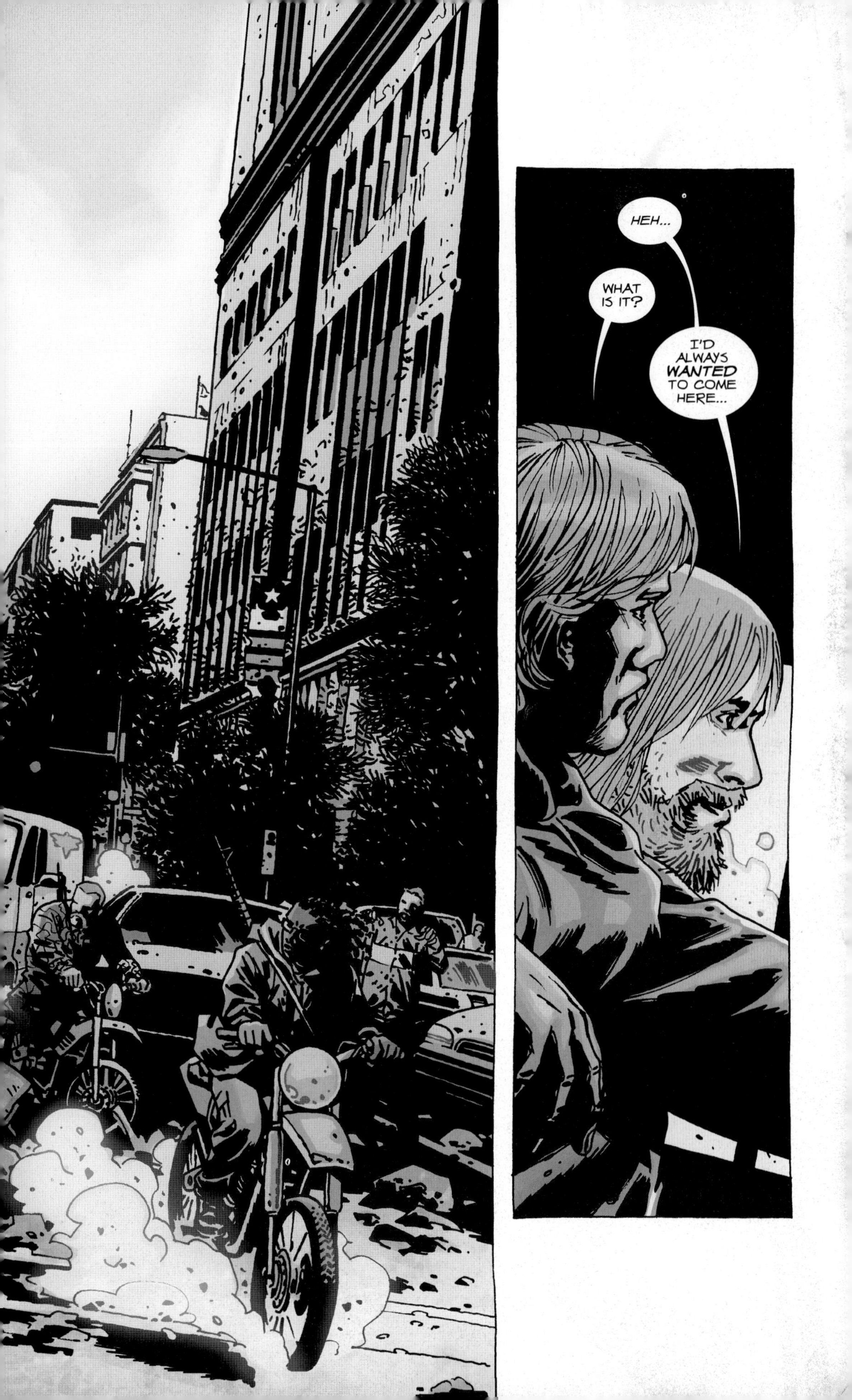
HEH...
WHAT IS IT?
I'D ALWAYS WANTED TO COME HERE...

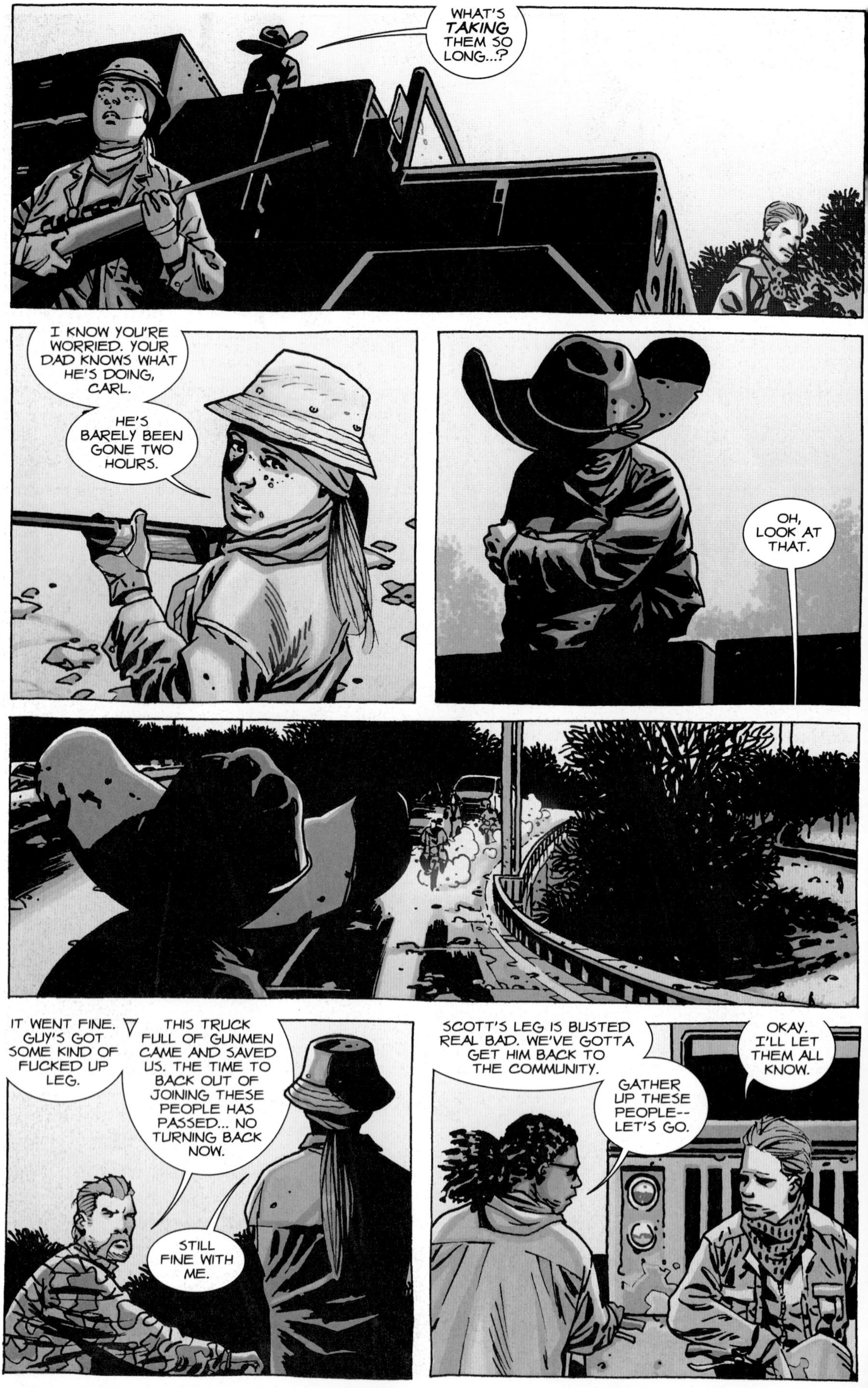

WHAT'S *TAKING* THEM SO LONG...?
I KNOW YOU'RE WORRIED. YOUR DAD KNOWS WHAT HE'S DOING, CARL.
HE'S BARELY BEEN GONE TWO HOURS.
OH, LOOK AT THAT.
IT WENT FINE. GUY'S GOT SOME KIND OF FUCKED UP LEG.
THIS TRUCK FULL OF GUNMEN CAME AND SAVED US. THE TIME TO BACK OUT OF JOINING THESE PEOPLE HAS PASSED... NO TURNING BACK NOW.
STILL FINE WITH ME.
SCOTT'S LEG IS BUSTED REAL BAD. WE'VE GOTTA GET HIM BACK TO THE COMMUNITY.
GATHER UP THESE PEOPLE-- LET'S GO.
OKAY. I'LL LET THEM ALL KNOW.

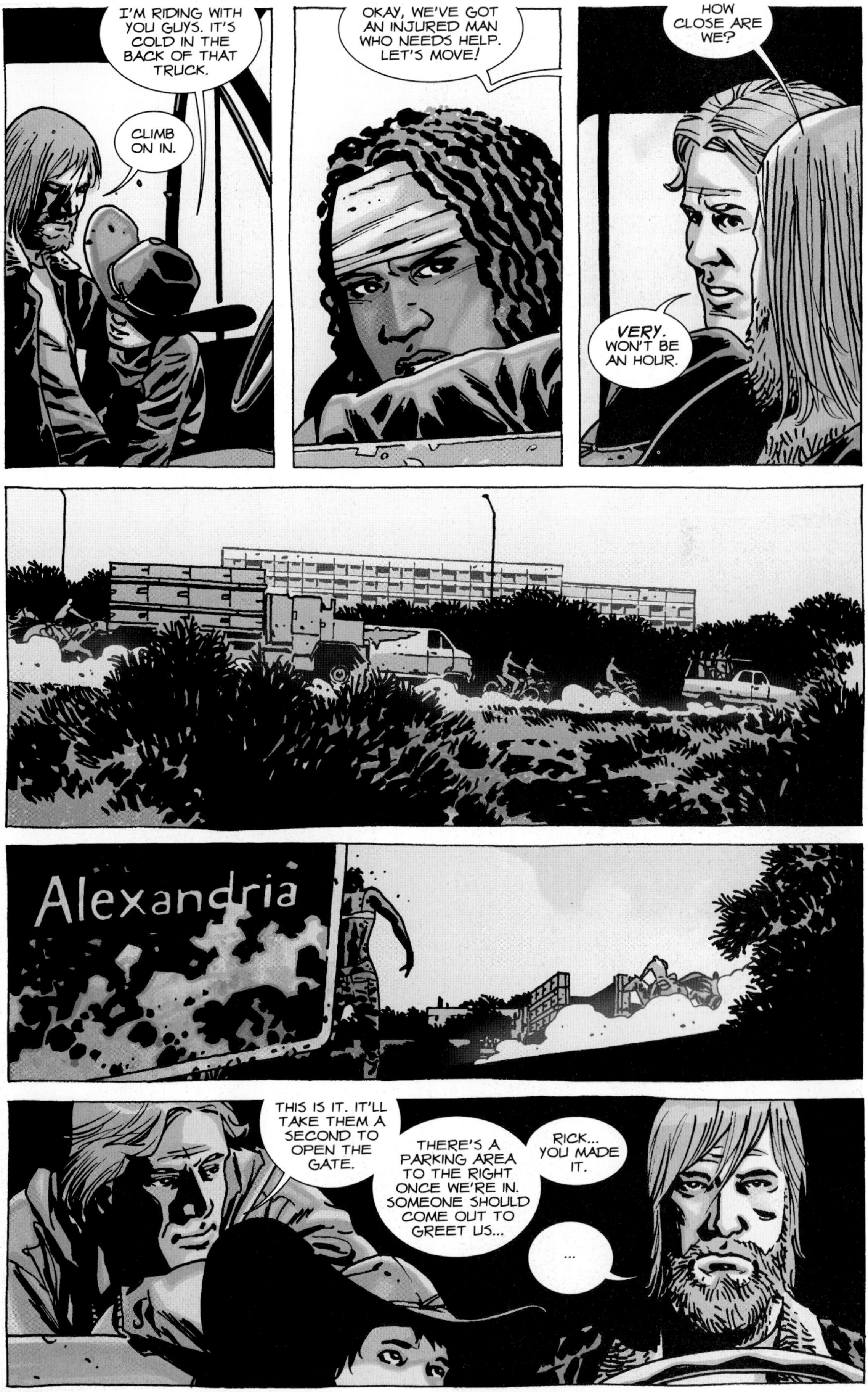
I'M RIDING WITH YOU GUYS. IT'S COLD IN THE BACK OF THAT TRUCK.
CLIMB ON IN.
OKAY, WE'VE GOT AN INJURED MAN WHO NEEDS HELP. LET'S MOVE!
HOW CLOSE ARE WE?
VERY. WON'T BE AN HOUR.
Alexandria
THIS IS IT. IT'LL TAKE THEM A SECOND TO OPEN THE GATE.
THERE'S A PARKING AREA TO THE RIGHT ONCE WE'RE IN. SOMEONE SHOULD COME OUT TO GREET US...
RICK... YOU MADE IT.
...

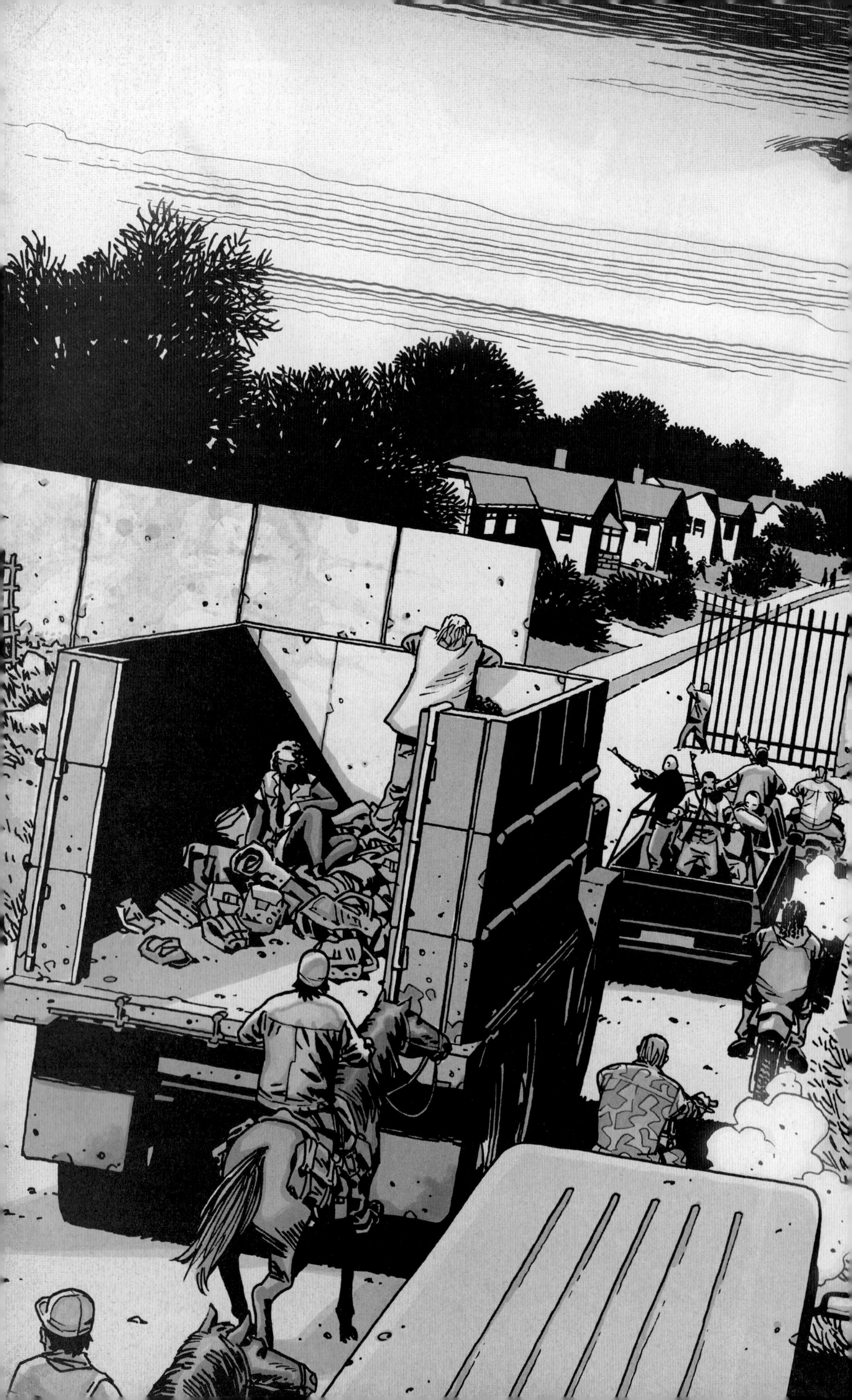

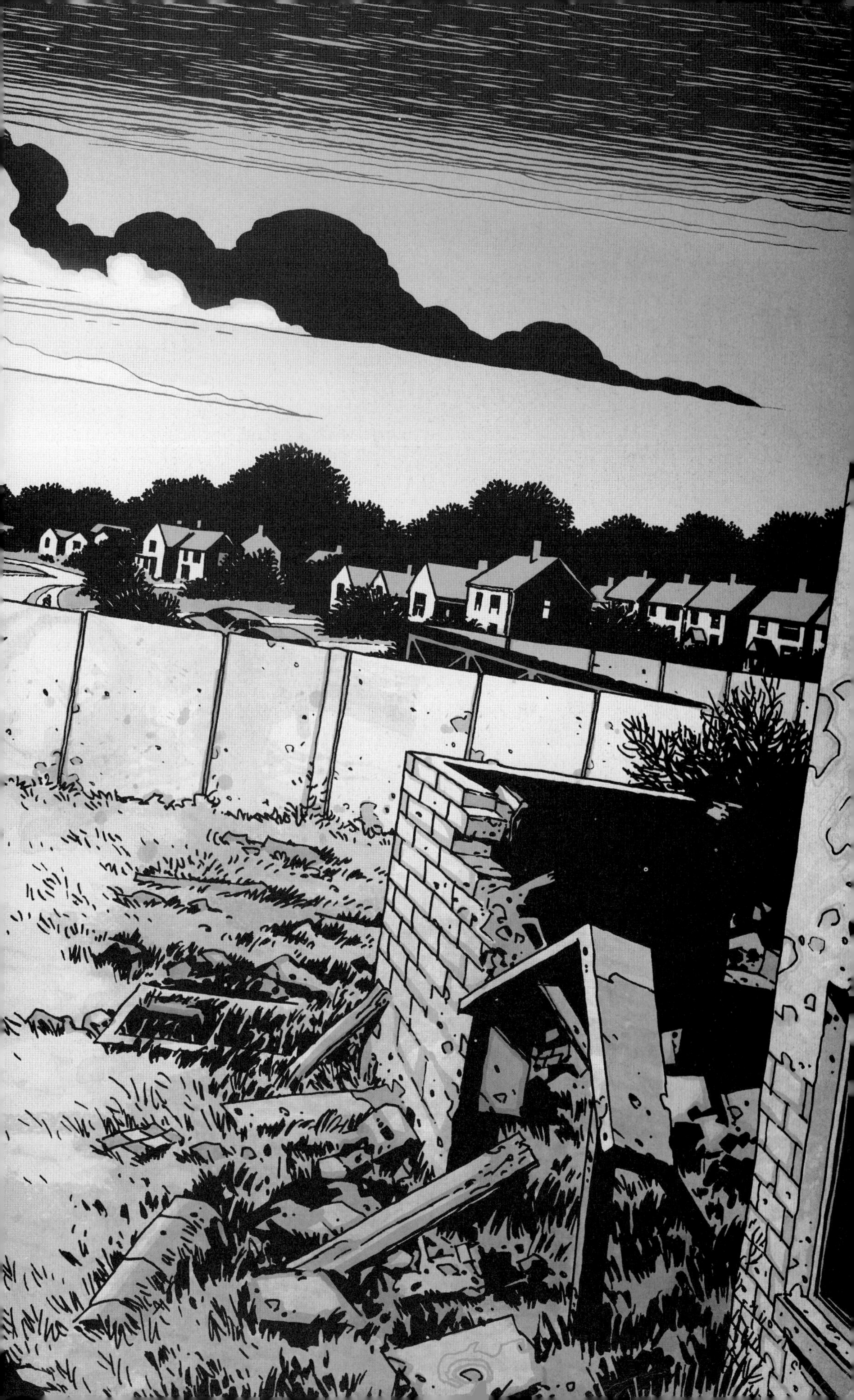

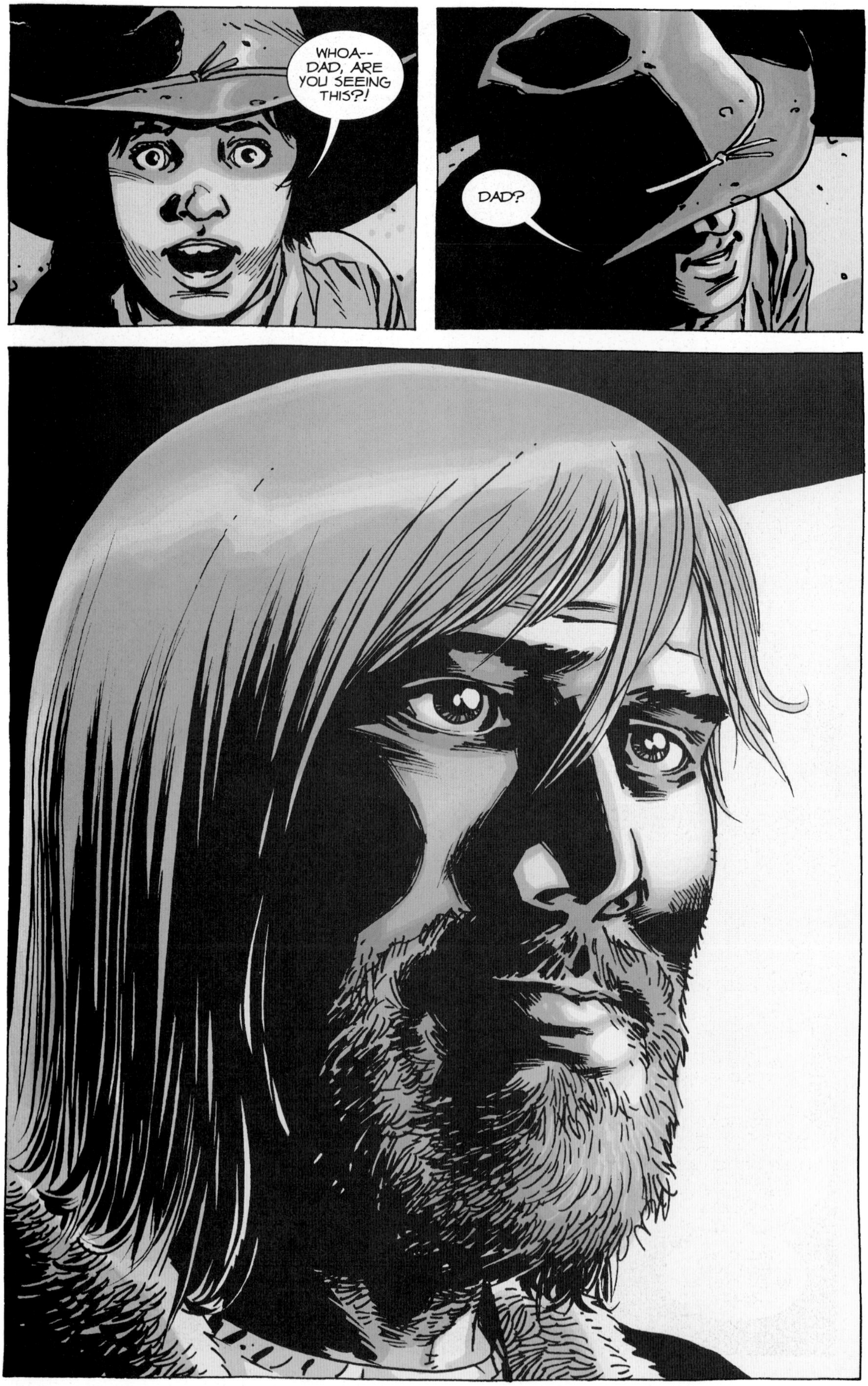
WHOA-- DAD, ARE YOU SEEING THIS?!
DAD?

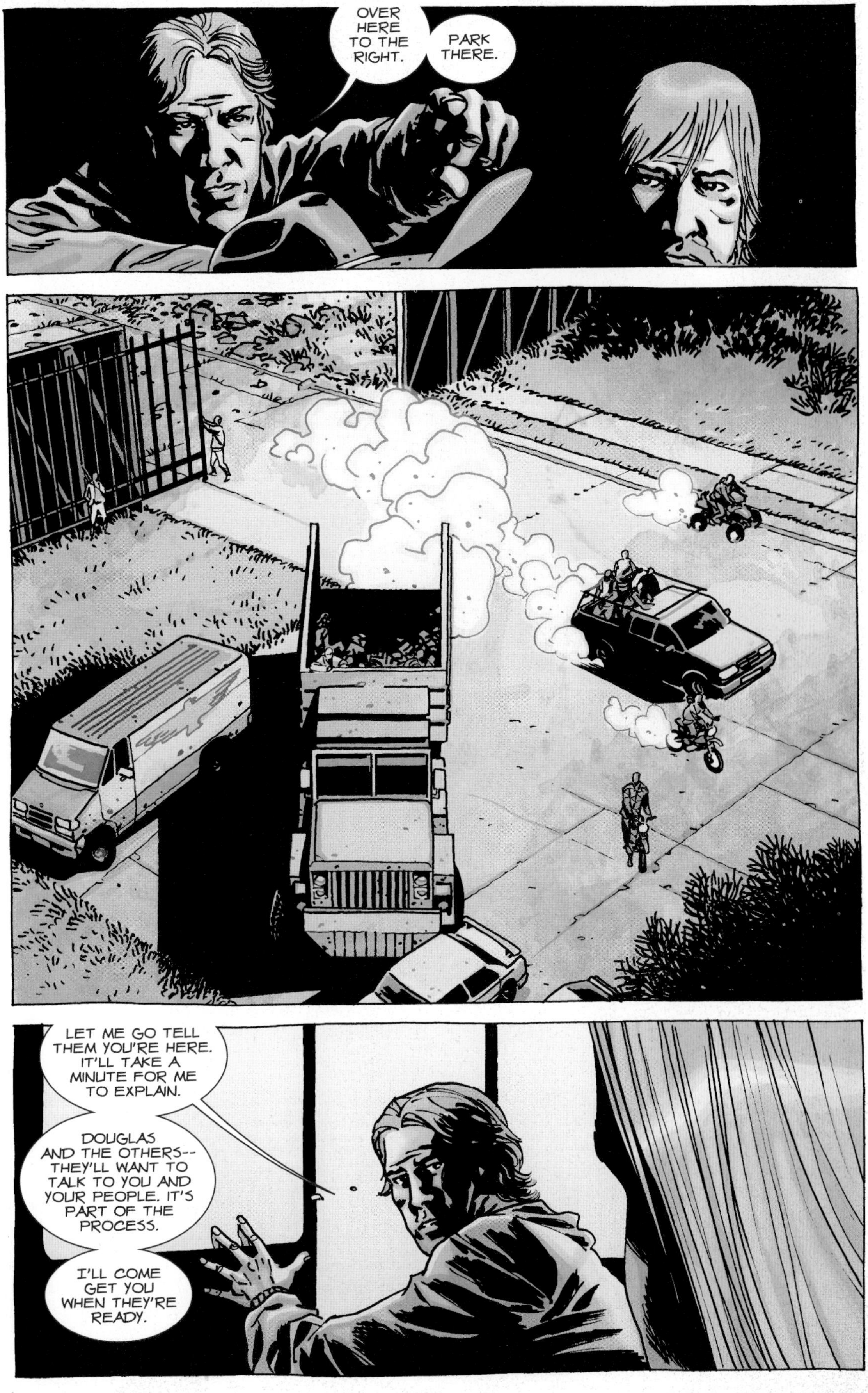
OVER HERE TO THE RIGHT.
PARK THERE.
LET ME GO TELL THEM YOU'RE HERE. IT'LL TAKE A MINUTE FOR ME TO EXPLAIN.
DOUGLAS AND THE OTHERS-- THEY'LL WANT TO TALK TO YOU AND YOUR PEOPLE. IT'S PART OF THE PROCESS.
I'LL COME GET YOU WHEN THEY'RE READY.

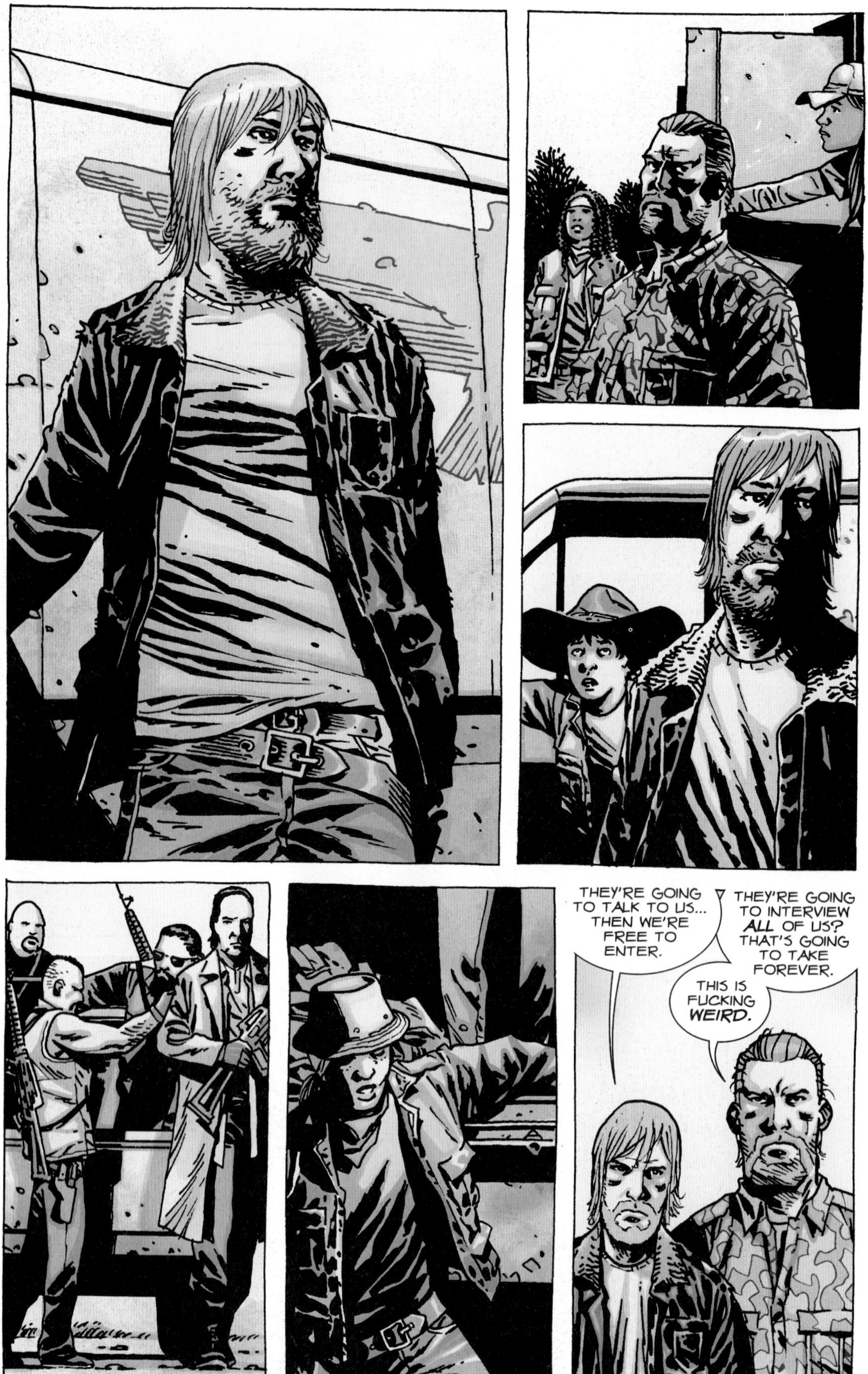
THEY'RE GOING TO TALK TO US... THEN WE'RE FREE TO ENTER.
THEY'RE GOING TO INTERVIEW ALL OF US? THAT'S GOING TO TAKE FOREVER.
THIS IS FUCKING WEIRD.

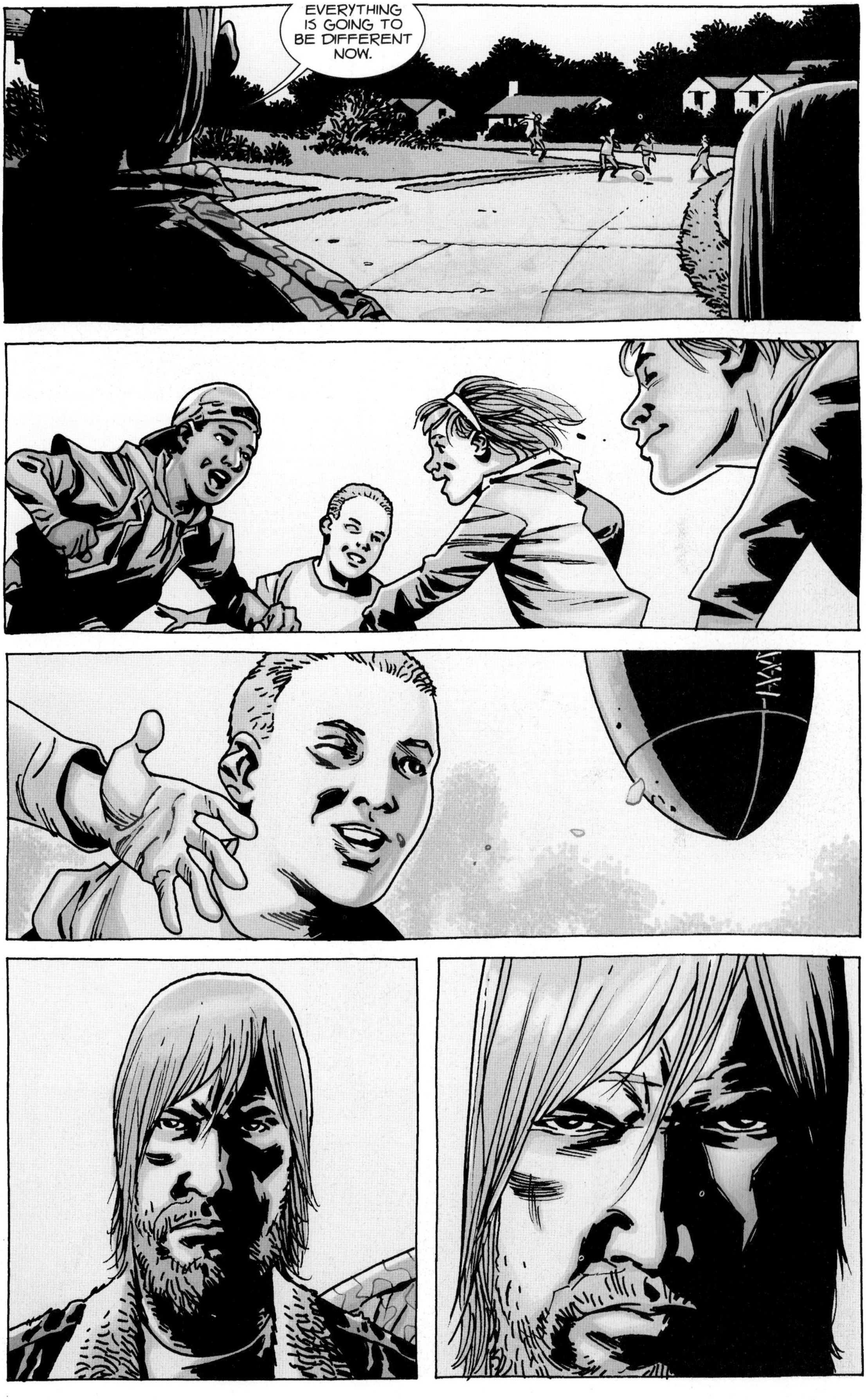
EVERYTHING IS GOING TO BE DIFFERENT NOW.

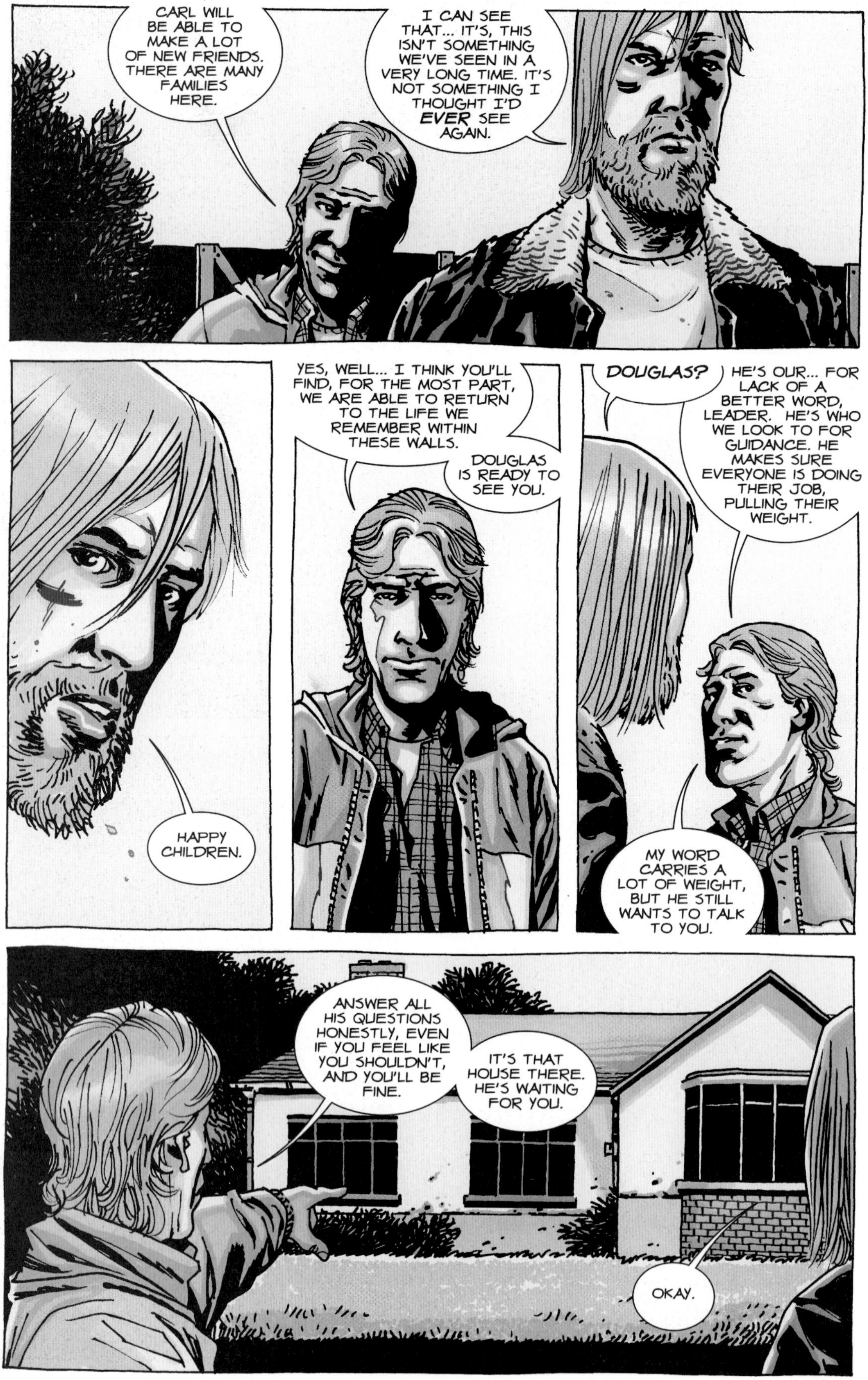
CARL WILL BE ABLE TO MAKE A LOT OF NEW FRIENDS. THERE ARE MANY FAMILIES HERE.
I CAN SEE THAT... IT'S, THIS ISN'T SOMETHING WE'VE SEEN IN A VERY LONG TIME. IT'S NOT SOMETHING I THOUGHT I'D EVER SEE AGAIN.
HAPPY CHILDREN.
YES, WELL... I THINK YOU'LL FIND, FOR THE MOST PART, WE ARE ABLE TO RETURN TO THE LIFE WE REMEMBER WITHIN THESE WALLS.
DOUGLAS IS READY TO SEE YOU.
DOUGLAS?
HE'S OUR... FOR LACK OF A BETTER WORD, LEADER. HE'S WHO WE LOOK TO FOR GUIDANCE. HE MAKES SURE EVERYONE IS DOING THEIR JOB, PULLING THEIR WEIGHT.
MY WORD CARRIES A LOT OF WEIGHT, BUT HE STILL WANTS TO TALK TO YOU.
ANSWER ALL HIS QUESTIONS HONESTLY, EVEN IF YOU FEEL LIKE YOU SHOULDN'T, AND YOU'LL BE FINE.
IT'S THAT HOUSE THERE. HE'S WAITING FOR YOU.
OKAY.

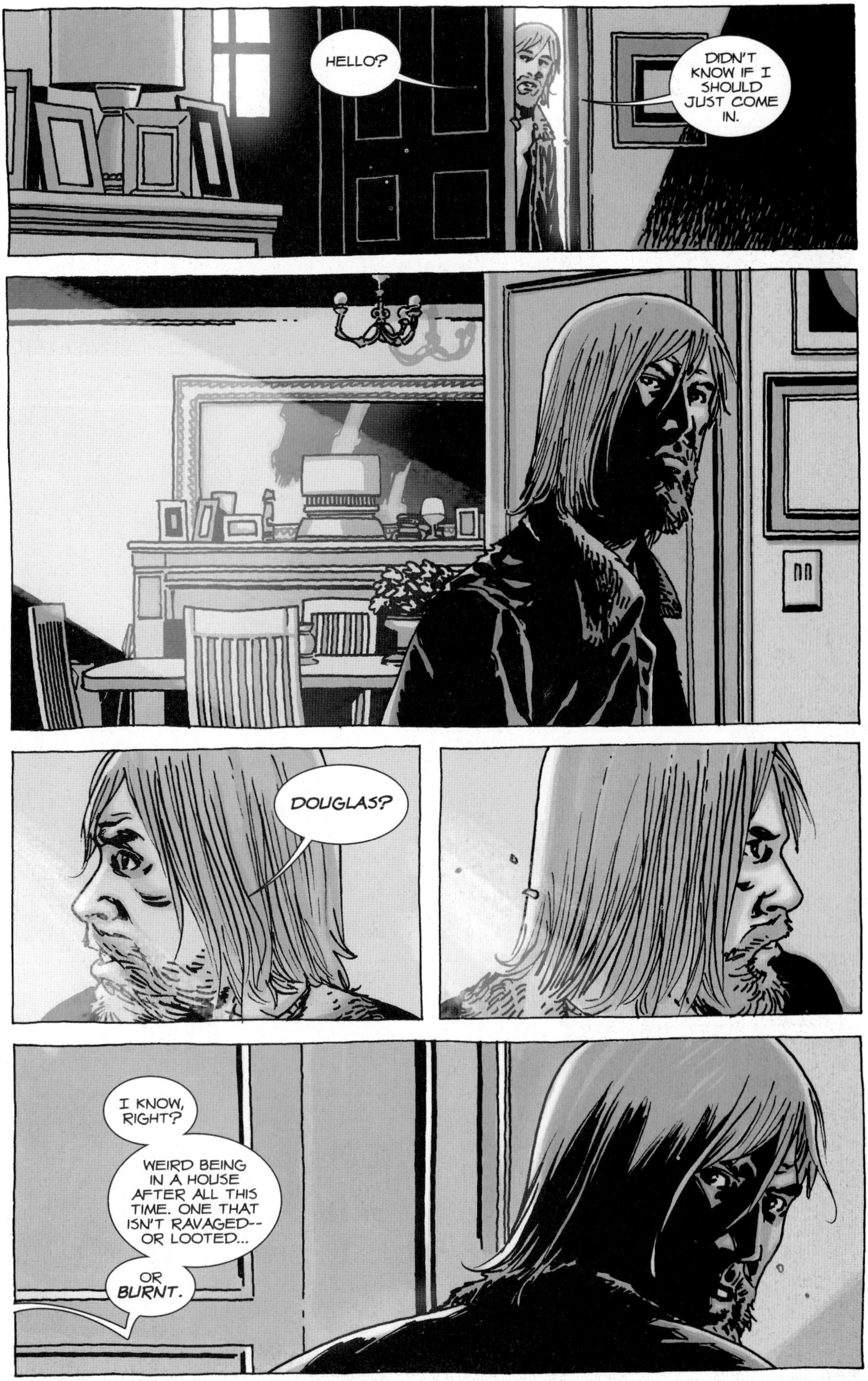
HELLO?
DIDN'T KNOW IF I SHOULD JUST COME IN.
DOUGLAS?
I KNOW, RIGHT?
WEIRD BEING IN A HOUSE AFTER ALL THIS TIME. ONE THAT ISN'T RAVAGED-- OR LOOTED...
OR BURNT.

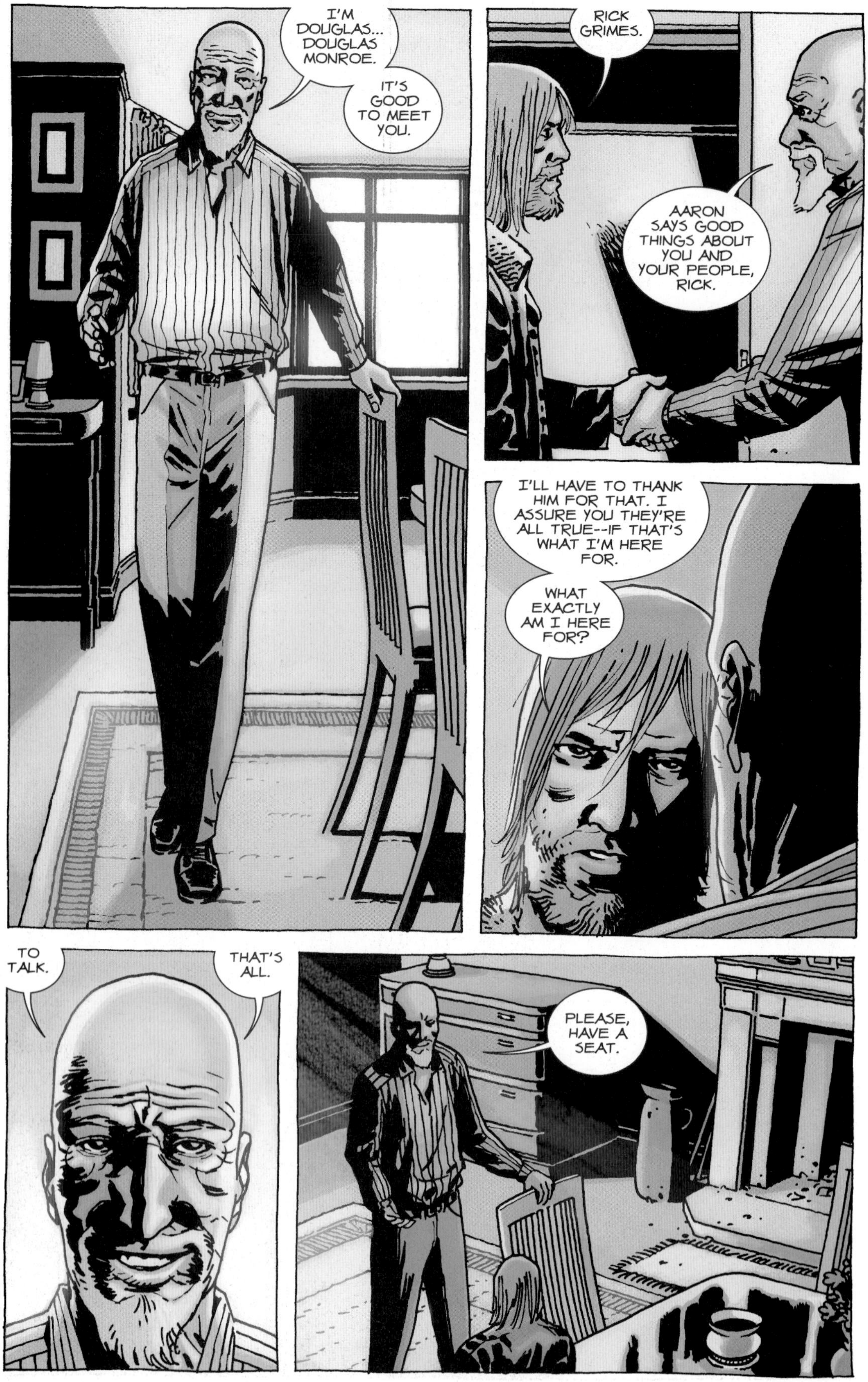
I'M DOUGLAS... DOUGLAS MONROE.
IT'S GOOD TO MEET YOU.
RICK GRIMES.
AARON SAYS GOOD THINGS ABOUT YOU AND YOUR PEOPLE, RICK.
I'LL HAVE TO THANK HIM FOR THAT. I ASSURE YOU THEY'RE ALL TRUE--IF THAT'S WHAT I'M HERE FOR.
WHAT EXACTLY AM I HERE FOR?
TO TALK.
THAT'S ALL.
PLEASE, HAVE A SEAT.

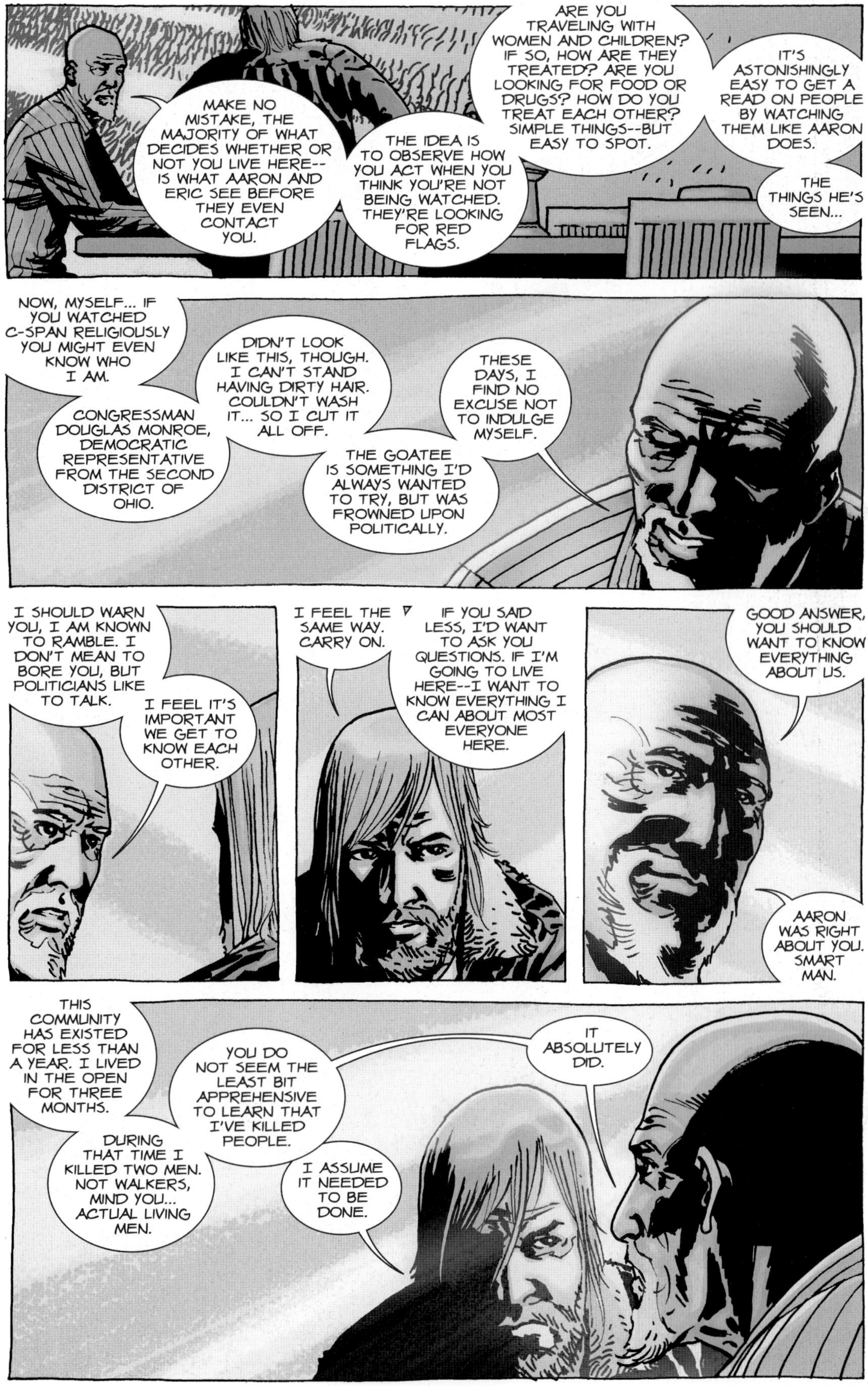
MAKE NO MISTAKE, THE MAJORITY OF WHAT DECIDES WHETHER OR NOT YOU LIVE HERE-- IS WHAT AARON AND ERIC SEE BEFORE THEY EVEN CONTACT YOU.
THE IDEA IS TO OBSERVE HOW YOU ACT WHEN YOU THINK YOU'RE NOT BEING WATCHED. THEY'RE LOOKING FOR RED FLAGS.
ARE YOU TRAVELING WITH WOMEN AND CHILDREN? IF SO, HOW ARE THEY TREATED? ARE YOU LOOKING FOR FOOD OR DRUGS? HOW DO YOU TREAT EACH OTHER? SIMPLE THINGS--BUT EASY TO SPOT.
IT'S ASTONISHINGLY EASY TO GET A READ ON PEOPLE BY WATCHING THEM LIKE AARON DOES.
THE THINGS HE'S SEEN...
NOW, MYSELF... IF YOU WATCHED C-SPAN RELIGIOUSLY YOU MIGHT EVEN KNOW WHO I AM.
CONGRESSMAN DOUGLAS MONROE, DEMOCRATIC REPRESENTATIVE FROM THE SECOND DISTRICT OF OHIO.
DIDN'T LOOK LIKE THIS, THOUGH. I CAN'T STAND HAVING DIRTY HAIR. COULDN'T WASH IT... SO I CUT IT ALL OFF.
THE GOATEE IS SOMETHING I'D ALWAYS WANTED TO TRY, BUT WAS FROWNED UPON POLITICALLY.
THESE DAYS, I FIND NO EXCUSE NOT TO INDULGE MYSELF.
I SHOULD WARN YOU, I AM KNOWN TO RAMBLE. I DON'T MEAN TO BORE YOU, BUT POLITICIANS LIKE TO TALK.
I FEEL IT'S IMPORTANT WE GET TO KNOW EACH OTHER.
I FEEL THE SAME WAY. CARRY ON.
IF YOU SAID LESS, I'D WANT TO ASK YOU QUESTIONS. IF I'M GOING TO LIVE HERE--I WANT TO KNOW EVERYTHING I CAN ABOUT MOST EVERYONE HERE.
GOOD ANSWER, YOU SHOULD WANT TO KNOW EVERYTHING ABOUT US.
AARON WAS RIGHT ABOUT YOU. SMART MAN.
THIS COMMUNITY HAS EXISTED FOR LESS THAN A YEAR. I LIVED IN THE OPEN FOR THREE MONTHS.
DURING THAT TIME I KILLED TWO MEN. NOT WALKERS, MIND YOU... ACTUAL LIVING MEN.
YOU DO NOT SEEM THE LEAST BIT APPREHENSIVE TO LEARN THAT I'VE KILLED PEOPLE.
I ASSUME IT NEEDED TO BE DONE.
IT ABSOLUTELY DID.

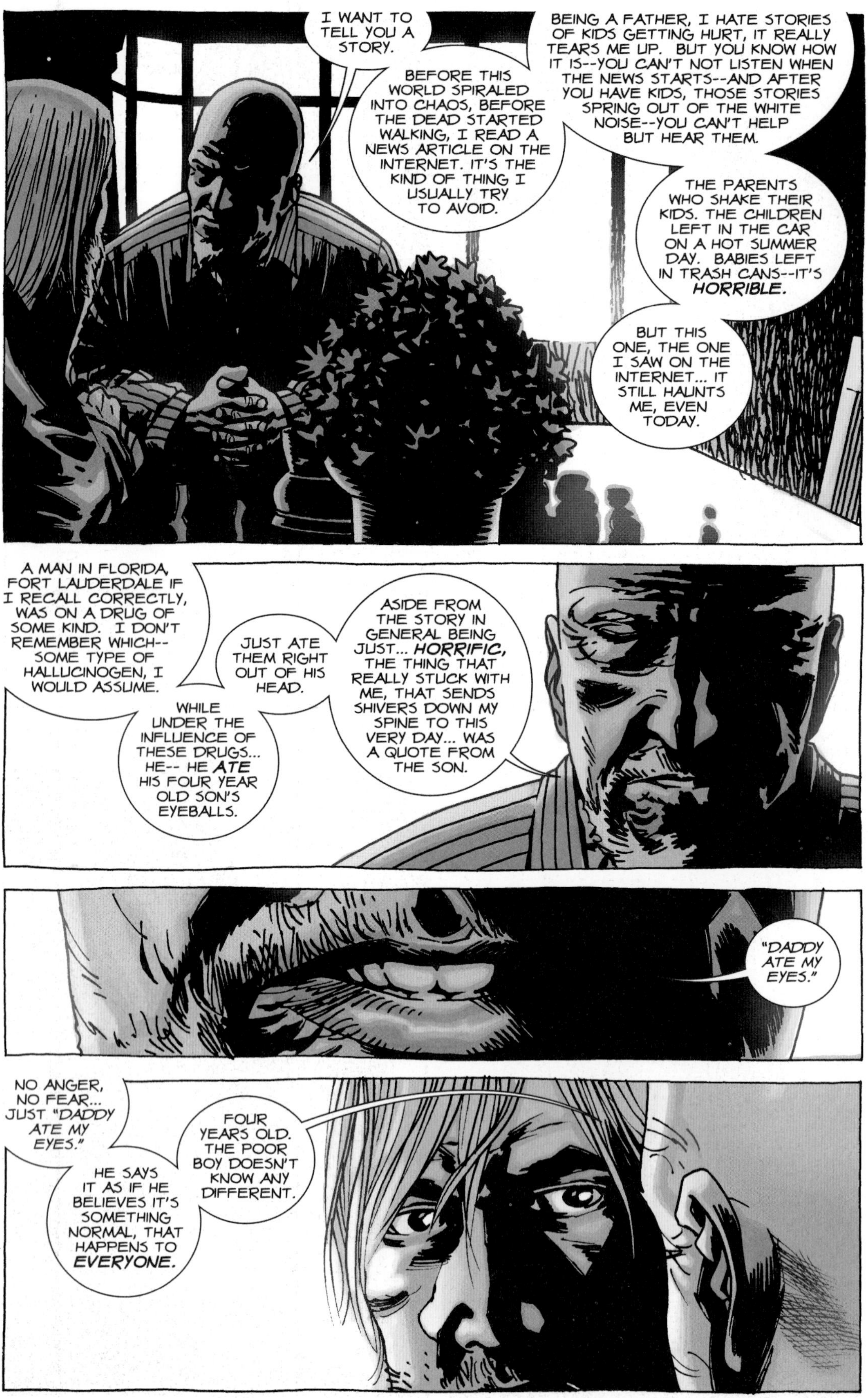
I WANT TO TELL YOU A STORY.
BEFORE THIS WORLD SPIRALED INTO CHAOS, BEFORE THE DEAD STARTED WALKING, I READ A NEWS ARTICLE ON THE INTERNET. IT'S THE KIND OF THING I USUALLY TRY TO AVOID.
BEING A FATHER, I HATE STORIES OF KIDS GETTING HURT, IT REALLY TEARS ME UP. BUT YOU KNOW HOW IT IS--YOU CAN'T NOT LISTEN WHEN THE NEWS STARTS--AND AFTER YOU HAVE KIDS, THOSE STORIES SPRING OUT OF THE WHITE NOISE--YOU CAN'T HELP BUT HEAR THEM.
THE PARENTS WHO SHAKE THEIR KIDS. THE CHILDREN LEFT IN THE CAR ON A HOT SUMMER DAY. BABIES LEFT IN TRASH CANS--IT'S ***HORRIBLE.***
BUT THIS ONE, THE ONE I SAW ON THE INTERNET... IT STILL HAUNTS ME, EVEN TODAY.
A MAN IN FLORIDA, FORT LAUDERDALE IF I RECALL CORRECTLY, WAS ON A DRUG OF SOME KIND. I DON'T REMEMBER WHICH-- SOME TYPE OF HALLUCINOGEN, I WOULD ASSUME.
WHILE UNDER THE INFLUENCE OF THESE DRUGS... HE-- HE ***ATE*** HIS FOUR YEAR OLD SON'S EYEBALLS.
JUST ATE THEM RIGHT OUT OF HIS HEAD.
ASIDE FROM THE STORY IN GENERAL BEING JUST... ***HORRIFIC,*** THE THING THAT REALLY STUCK WITH ME, THAT SENDS SHIVERS DOWN MY SPINE TO THIS VERY DAY... WAS A QUOTE FROM THE SON.
"DADDY ATE MY EYES."
NO ANGER, NO FEAR... JUST *"DADDY ATE MY EYES."*
HE SAYS IT AS IF HE BELIEVES IT'S SOMETHING NORMAL, THAT HAPPENS TO ***EVERYONE.***
FOUR YEARS OLD. THE POOR BOY DOESN'T KNOW ANY DIFFERENT.

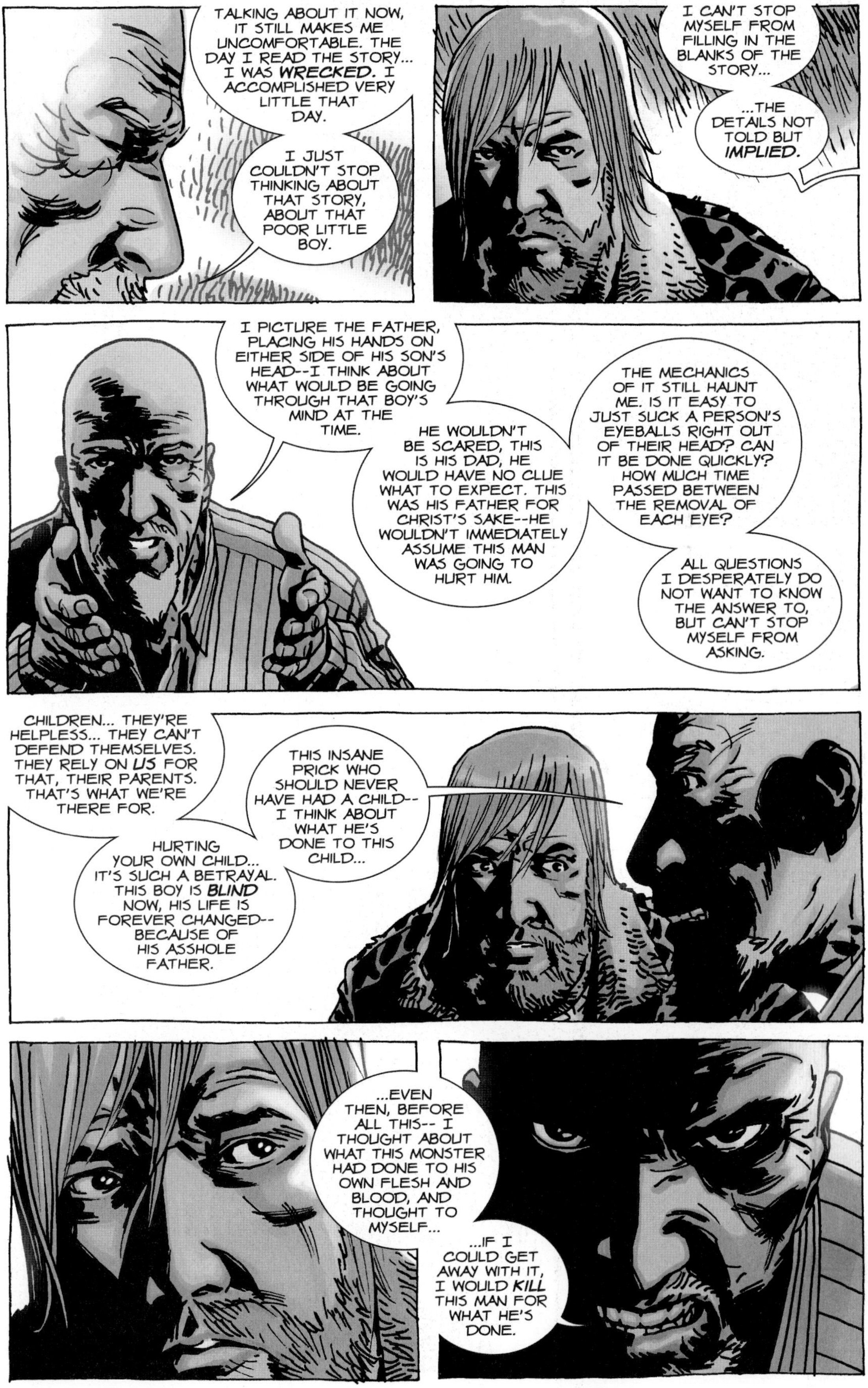
TALKING ABOUT IT NOW, IT STILL MAKES ME UNCOMFORTABLE. THE DAY I READ THE STORY... I WAS WRECKED. I ACCOMPLISHED VERY LITTLE THAT DAY.
I JUST COULDN'T STOP THINKING ABOUT THAT STORY, ABOUT THAT POOR LITTLE BOY.
I CAN'T STOP MYSELF FROM FILLING IN THE BLANKS OF THE STORY...
...THE DETAILS NOT TOLD BUT IMPLIED.
I PICTURE THE FATHER, PLACING HIS HANDS ON EITHER SIDE OF HIS SON'S HEAD--I THINK ABOUT WHAT WOULD BE GOING THROUGH THAT BOY'S MIND AT THE TIME.
HE WOULDN'T BE SCARED, THIS IS HIS DAD, HE WOULD HAVE NO CLUE WHAT TO EXPECT. THIS WAS HIS FATHER FOR CHRIST'S SAKE--HE WOULDN'T IMMEDIATELY ASSUME THIS MAN WAS GOING TO HURT HIM.
THE MECHANICS OF IT STILL HAUNT ME. IS IT EASY TO JUST SUCK A PERSON'S EYEBALLS RIGHT OUT OF THEIR HEAD? CAN IT BE DONE QUICKLY? HOW MUCH TIME PASSED BETWEEN THE REMOVAL OF EACH EYE?
ALL QUESTIONS I DESPERATELY DO NOT WANT TO KNOW THE ANSWER TO, BUT CAN'T STOP MYSELF FROM ASKING.
CHILDREN... THEY'RE HELPLESS... THEY CAN'T DEFEND THEMSELVES. THEY RELY ON US FOR THAT, THEIR PARENTS. THAT'S WHAT WE'RE THERE FOR.
HURTING YOUR OWN CHILD... IT'S SUCH A BETRAYAL. THIS BOY IS BLIND NOW, HIS LIFE IS FOREVER CHANGED-- BECAUSE OF HIS ASSHOLE FATHER.
THIS INSANE PRICK WHO SHOULD NEVER HAVE HAD A CHILD-- I THINK ABOUT WHAT HE'S DONE TO THIS CHILD...
...EVEN THEN, BEFORE ALL THIS-- I THOUGHT ABOUT WHAT THIS MONSTER HAD DONE TO HIS OWN FLESH AND BLOOD, AND THOUGHT TO MYSELF...
...IF I COULD GET AWAY WITH IT, I WOULD KILL THIS MAN FOR WHAT HE'S DONE.

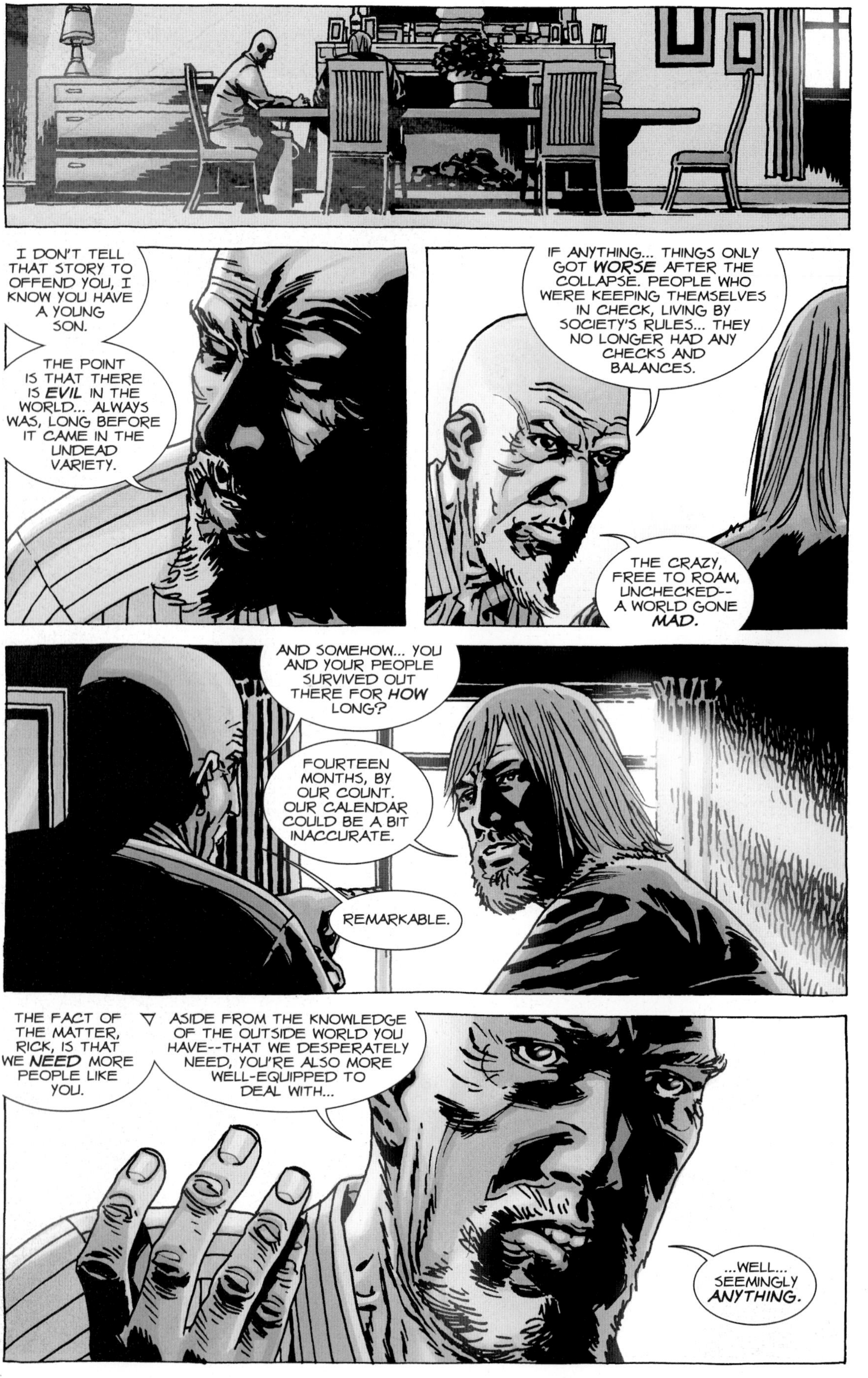

I DON'T TELL THAT STORY TO OFFEND YOU, I KNOW YOU HAVE A YOUNG SON.
THE POINT IS THAT THERE IS EVIL IN THE WORLD... ALWAYS WAS, LONG BEFORE IT CAME IN THE UNDEAD VARIETY.
IF ANYTHING... THINGS ONLY GOT WORSE AFTER THE COLLAPSE. PEOPLE WHO WERE KEEPING THEMSELVES IN CHECK, LIVING BY SOCIETY'S RULES... THEY NO LONGER HAD ANY CHECKS AND BALANCES.
THE CRAZY, FREE TO ROAM, UNCHECKED-- A WORLD GONE MAD.
AND SOMEHOW... YOU AND YOUR PEOPLE SURVIVED OUT THERE FOR HOW LONG?
FOURTEEN MONTHS, BY OUR COUNT. OUR CALENDAR COULD BE A BIT INACCURATE.
REMARKABLE.
THE FACT OF THE MATTER, RICK, IS THAT WE NEED MORE PEOPLE LIKE YOU.
ASIDE FROM THE KNOWLEDGE OF THE OUTSIDE WORLD YOU HAVE--THAT WE DESPERATELY NEED, YOU'RE ALSO MORE WELL-EQUIPPED TO DEAL WITH...
...WELL... SEEMINGLY ANYTHING.

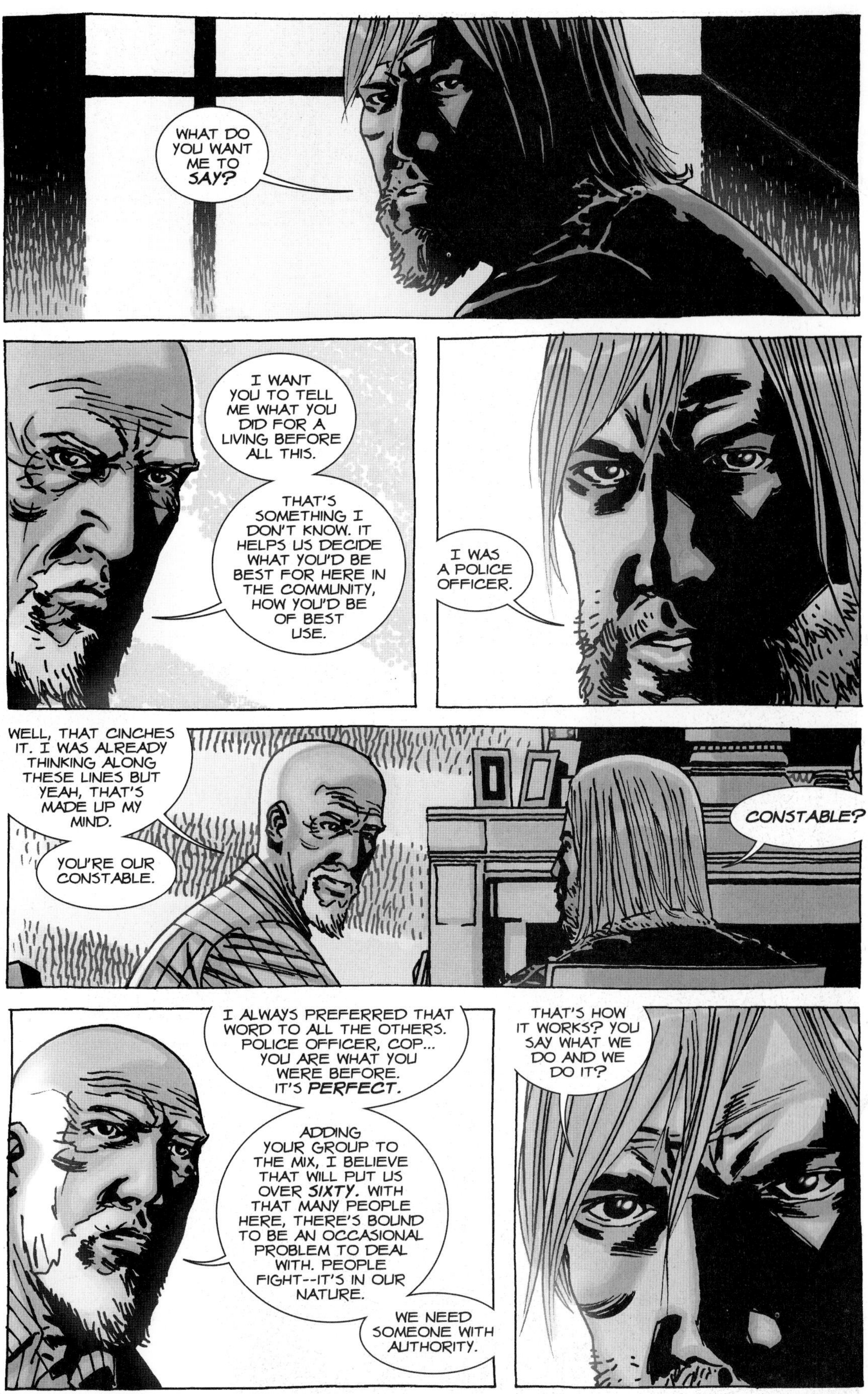
WHAT DO YOU WANT ME TO SAY?
I WANT YOU TO TELL ME WHAT YOU DID FOR A LIVING BEFORE ALL THIS.
THAT'S SOMETHING I DON'T KNOW. IT HELPS US DECIDE WHAT YOU'D BE BEST FOR HERE IN THE COMMUNITY, HOW YOU'D BE OF BEST USE.
I WAS A POLICE OFFICER.
WELL, THAT CINCHES IT. I WAS ALREADY THINKING ALONG THESE LINES BUT YEAH, THAT'S MADE UP MY MIND.
YOU'RE OUR CONSTABLE.
CONSTABLE?
I ALWAYS PREFERRED THAT WORD TO ALL THE OTHERS. POLICE OFFICER, COP... YOU ARE WHAT YOU WERE BEFORE. IT'S PERFECT.
ADDING YOUR GROUP TO THE MIX, I BELIEVE THAT WILL PUT US OVER SIXTY. WITH THAT MANY PEOPLE HERE, THERE'S BOUND TO BE AN OCCASIONAL PROBLEM TO DEAL WITH. PEOPLE FIGHT--IT'S IN OUR NATURE.
WE NEED SOMEONE WITH AUTHORITY.
THAT'S HOW IT WORKS? YOU SAY WHAT WE DO AND WE DO IT?

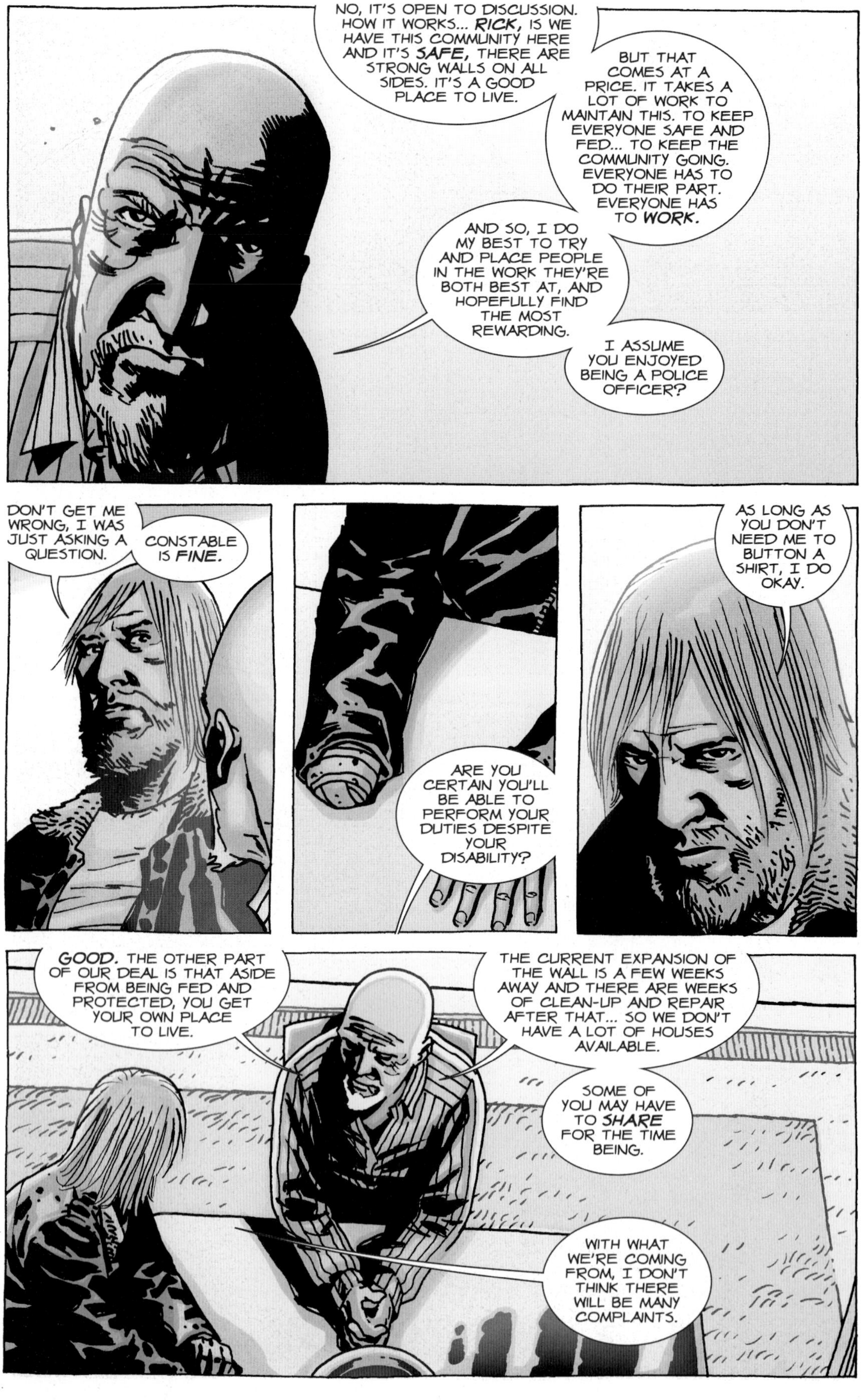
NO, IT'S OPEN TO DISCUSSION. HOW IT WORKS... RICK, IS WE HAVE THIS COMMUNITY HERE AND IT'S SAFE, THERE ARE STRONG WALLS ON ALL SIDES. IT'S A GOOD PLACE TO LIVE.
BUT THAT COMES AT A PRICE. IT TAKES A LOT OF WORK TO MAINTAIN THIS. TO KEEP EVERYONE SAFE AND FED... TO KEEP THE COMMUNITY GOING. EVERYONE HAS TO DO THEIR PART. EVERYONE HAS TO WORK.
AND SO, I DO MY BEST TO TRY AND PLACE PEOPLE IN THE WORK THEY'RE BOTH BEST AT, AND HOPEFULLY FIND THE MOST REWARDING.
I ASSUME YOU ENJOYED BEING A POLICE OFFICER?
DON'T GET ME WRONG, I WAS JUST ASKING A QUESTION.
CONSTABLE IS FINE.
ARE YOU CERTAIN YOU'LL BE ABLE TO PERFORM YOUR DUTIES DESPITE YOUR DISABILITY?
AS LONG AS YOU DON'T NEED ME TO BUTTON A SHIRT, I DO OKAY.
GOOD. THE OTHER PART OF OUR DEAL IS THAT ASIDE FROM BEING FED AND PROTECTED, YOU GET YOUR OWN PLACE TO LIVE.
THE CURRENT EXPANSION OF THE WALL IS A FEW WEEKS AWAY AND THERE ARE WEEKS OF CLEAN-UP AND REPAIR AFTER THAT... SO WE DON'T HAVE A LOT OF HOUSES AVAILABLE.
SOME OF YOU MAY HAVE TO SHARE FOR THE TIME BEING.
WITH WHAT WE'RE COMING FROM, I DON'T THINK THERE WILL BE MANY COMPLAINTS.

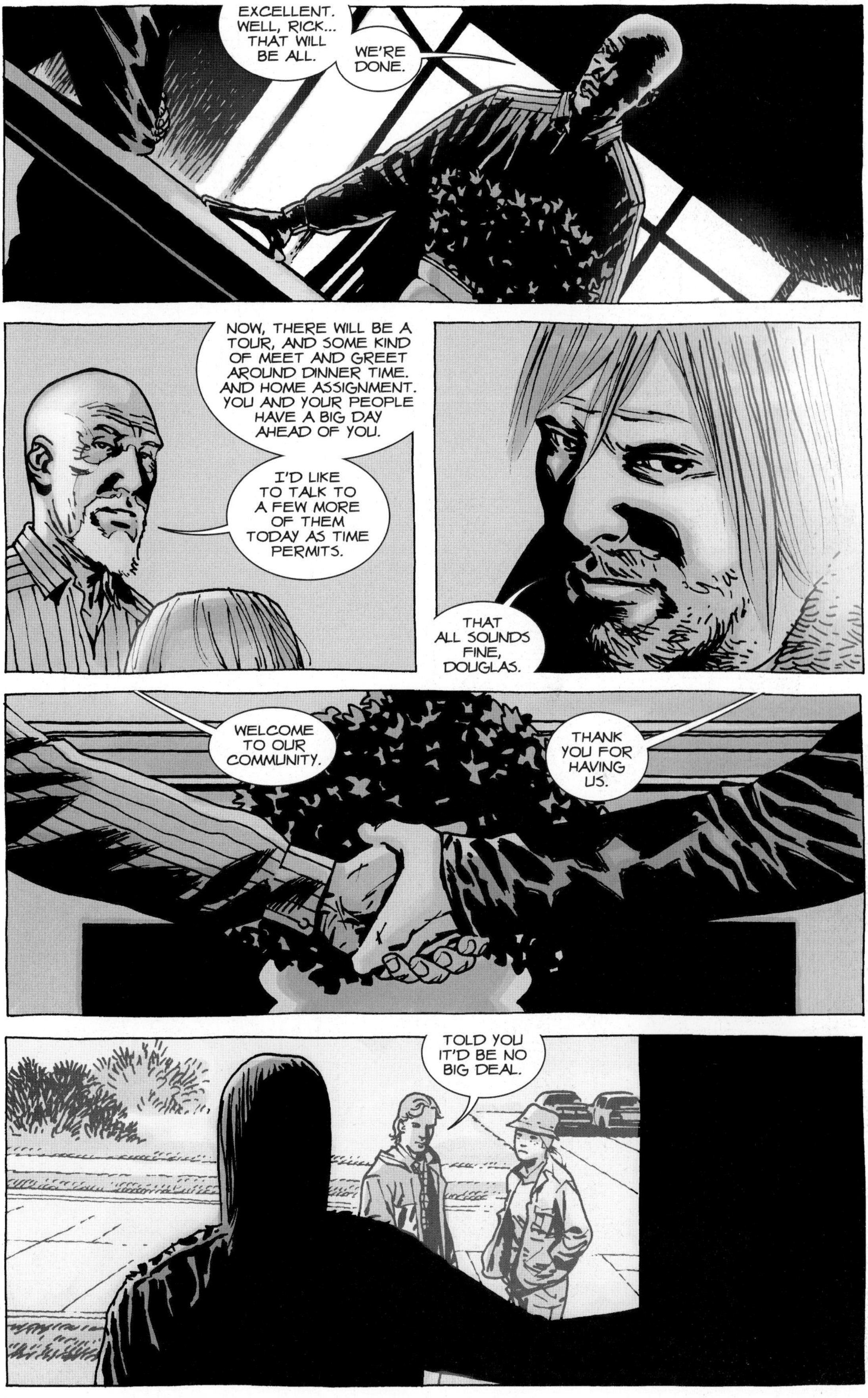

EXCELLENT. WELL, RICK... THAT WILL BE ALL.
WE'RE DONE.
NOW, THERE WILL BE A TOUR, AND SOME KIND OF MEET AND GREET AROUND DINNER TIME. AND HOME ASSIGNMENT. YOU AND YOUR PEOPLE HAVE A BIG DAY AHEAD OF YOU.
I'D LIKE TO TALK TO A FEW MORE OF THEM TODAY AS TIME PERMITS.
THAT ALL SOUNDS FINE, DOUGLAS.
WELCOME TO OUR COMMUNITY.
THANK YOU FOR HAVING US.
TOLD YOU IT'D BE NO BIG DEAL.

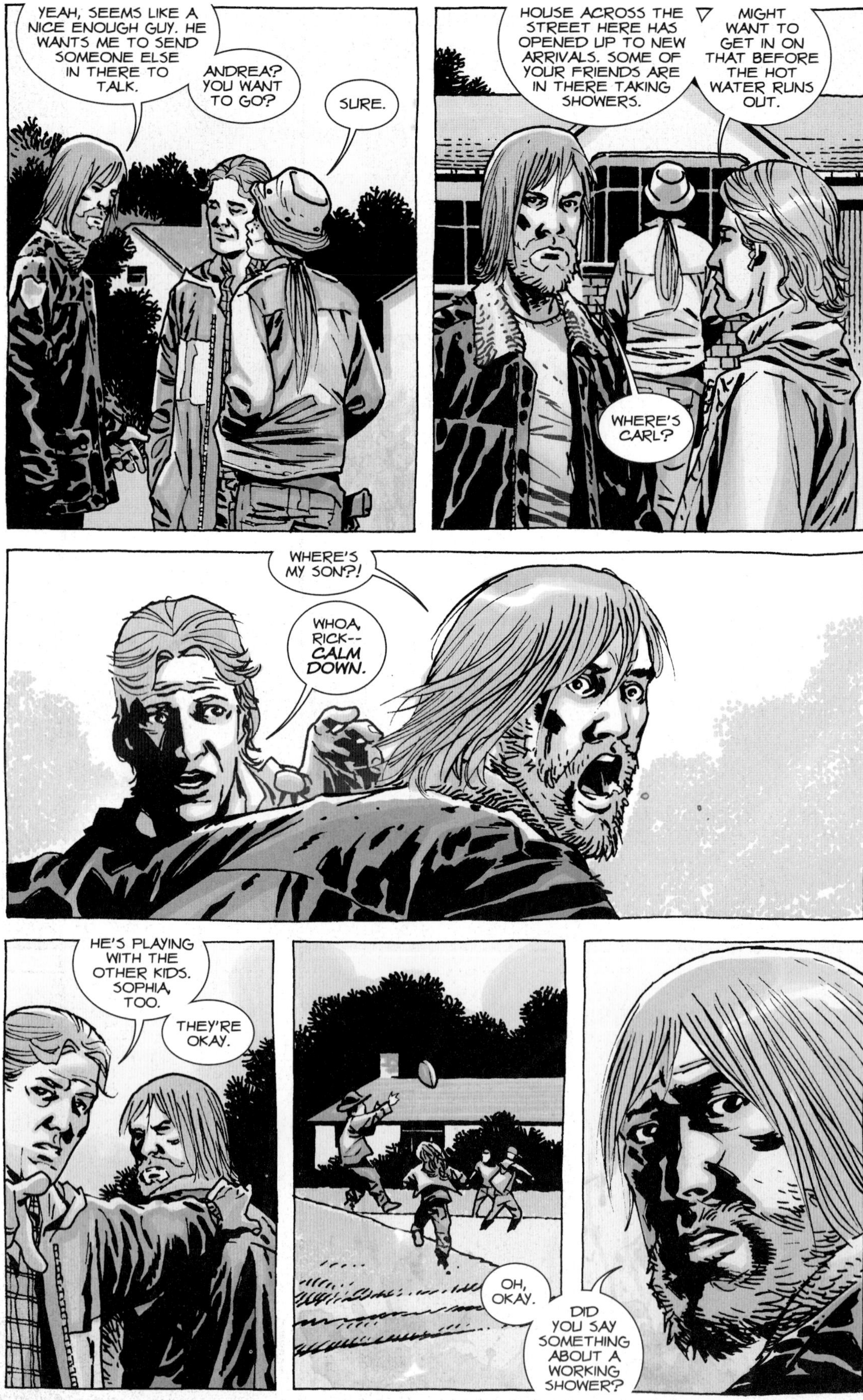

YEAH, SEEMS LIKE A NICE ENOUGH GUY. HE WANTS ME TO SEND SOMEONE ELSE IN THERE TO TALK.
ANDREA? YOU WANT TO GO?
SURE.
HOUSE ACROSS THE STREET HERE HAS OPENED UP TO NEW ARRIVALS. SOME OF YOUR FRIENDS ARE IN THERE TAKING SHOWERS.
MIGHT WANT TO GET IN ON THAT BEFORE THE HOT WATER RUNS OUT.
WHERE'S CARL?
WHERE'S MY SON?!
WHOA, RICK-- CALM DOWN.
HE'S PLAYING WITH THE OTHER KIDS. SOPHIA, TOO.
THEY'RE OKAY.
OH, OKAY.
DID YOU SAY SOMETHING ABOUT A WORKING SHOWER?

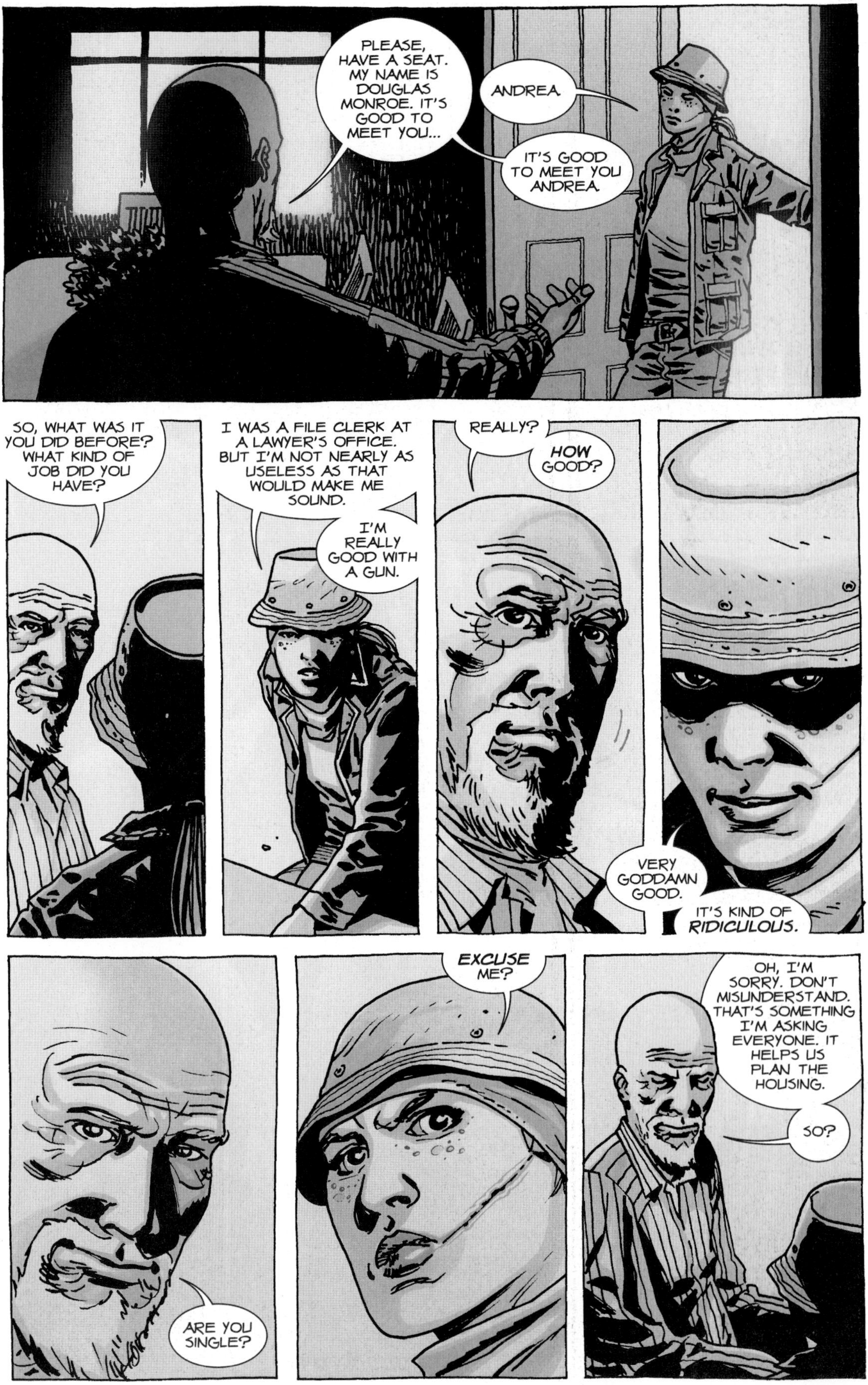
PLEASE, HAVE A SEAT. MY NAME IS DOUGLAS MONROE. IT'S GOOD TO MEET YOU...
ANDREA.
IT'S GOOD TO MEET YOU ANDREA.
SO, WHAT WAS IT YOU DID BEFORE? WHAT KIND OF JOB DID YOU HAVE?
I WAS A FILE CLERK AT A LAWYER'S OFFICE. BUT I'M NOT NEARLY AS USELESS AS THAT WOULD MAKE ME SOUND.
I'M REALLY GOOD WITH A GUN.
REALLY?
HOW GOOD?
VERY GODDAMN GOOD.
IT'S KIND OF RIDICULOUS.
ARE YOU SINGLE?
EXCUSE ME?
OH, I'M SORRY. DON'T MISUNDERSTAND. THAT'S SOMETHING I'M ASKING EVERYONE. IT HELPS US PLAN THE HOUSING.
SO?

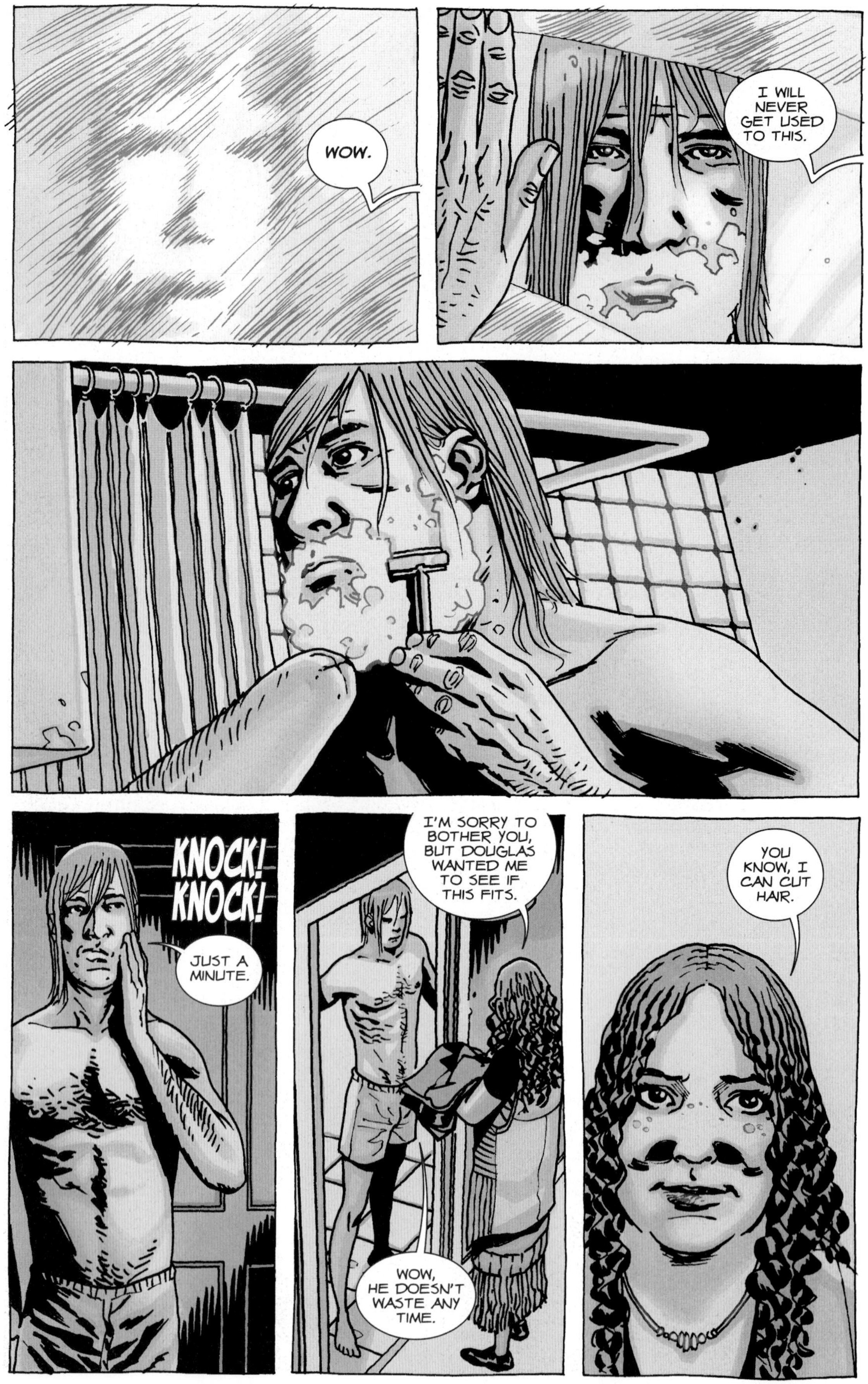
WOW.
I WILL NEVER GET USED TO THIS.
KNOCK! KNOCK!
JUST A MINUTE.
I'M SORRY TO BOTHER YOU, BUT DOUGLAS WANTED ME TO SEE IF THIS FITS.
WOW, HE DOESN'T WASTE ANY TIME.
YOU KNOW, I CAN CUT HAIR.

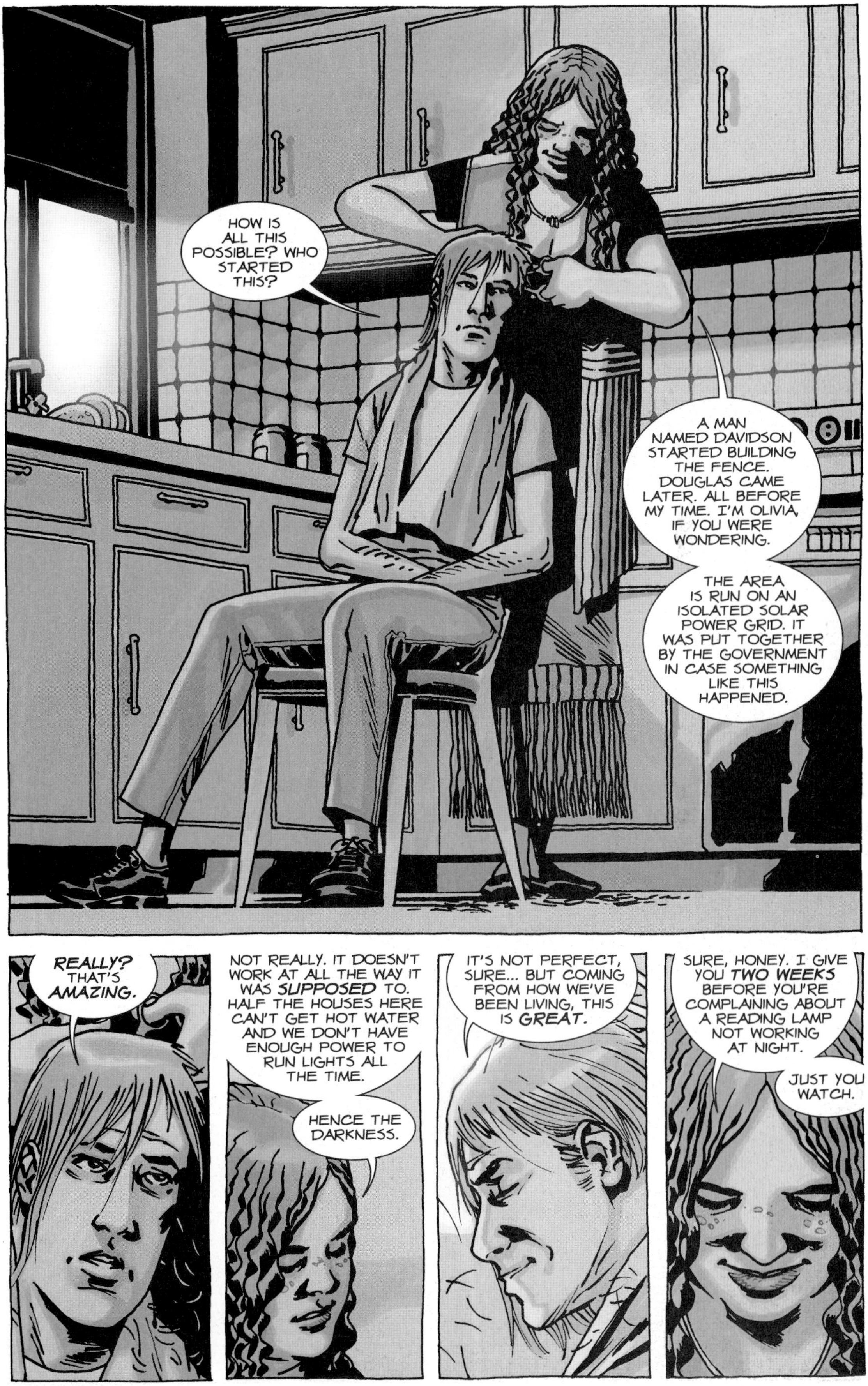
HOW IS ALL THIS POSSIBLE? WHO STARTED THIS?
A MAN NAMED DAVIDSON STARTED BUILDING THE FENCE. DOUGLAS CAME LATER. ALL BEFORE MY TIME. I'M OLIVIA, IF YOU WERE WONDERING.
THE AREA IS RUN ON AN ISOLATED SOLAR POWER GRID. IT WAS PUT TOGETHER BY THE GOVERNMENT IN CASE SOMETHING LIKE THIS HAPPENED.
REALLY? THAT'S AMAZING.
NOT REALLY. IT DOESN'T WORK AT ALL THE WAY IT WAS SUPPOSED TO. HALF THE HOUSES HERE CAN'T GET HOT WATER AND WE DON'T HAVE ENOUGH POWER TO RUN LIGHTS ALL THE TIME.
HENCE THE DARKNESS.
IT'S NOT PERFECT, SURE... BUT COMING FROM HOW WE'VE BEEN LIVING, THIS IS GREAT.
SURE, HONEY. I GIVE YOU TWO WEEKS BEFORE YOU'RE COMPLAINING ABOUT A READING LAMP NOT WORKING AT NIGHT.
JUST YOU WATCH.

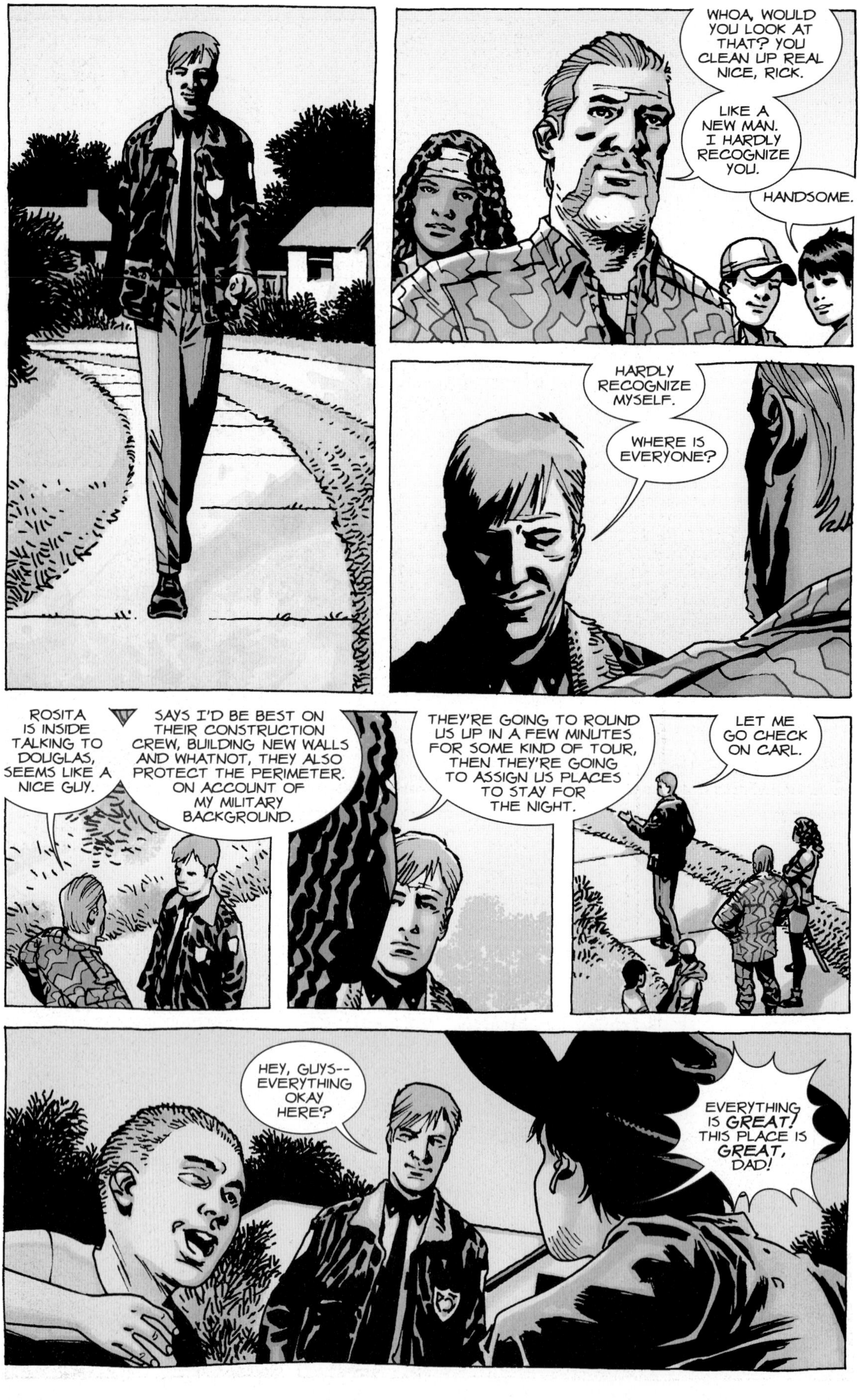
WHOA, WOULD YOU LOOK AT THAT? YOU CLEAN UP REAL NICE, RICK.
LIKE A NEW MAN. I HARDLY RECOGNIZE YOU.
HANDSOME.
HARDLY RECOGNIZE MYSELF.
WHERE IS EVERYONE?
ROSITA IS INSIDE TALKING TO DOUGLAS, SEEMS LIKE A NICE GUY.
SAYS I'D BE BEST ON THEIR CONSTRUCTION CREW, BUILDING NEW WALLS AND WHATNOT, THEY ALSO PROTECT THE PERIMETER. ON ACCOUNT OF MY MILITARY BACKGROUND.
THEY'RE GOING TO ROUND US UP IN A FEW MINUTES FOR SOME KIND OF TOUR, THEN THEY'RE GOING TO ASSIGN US PLACES TO STAY FOR THE NIGHT.
LET ME GO CHECK ON CARL.
HEY, GUYS-- EVERYTHING OKAY HERE?
EVERYTHING IS *GREAT!* THIS PLACE IS *GREAT,* DAD!

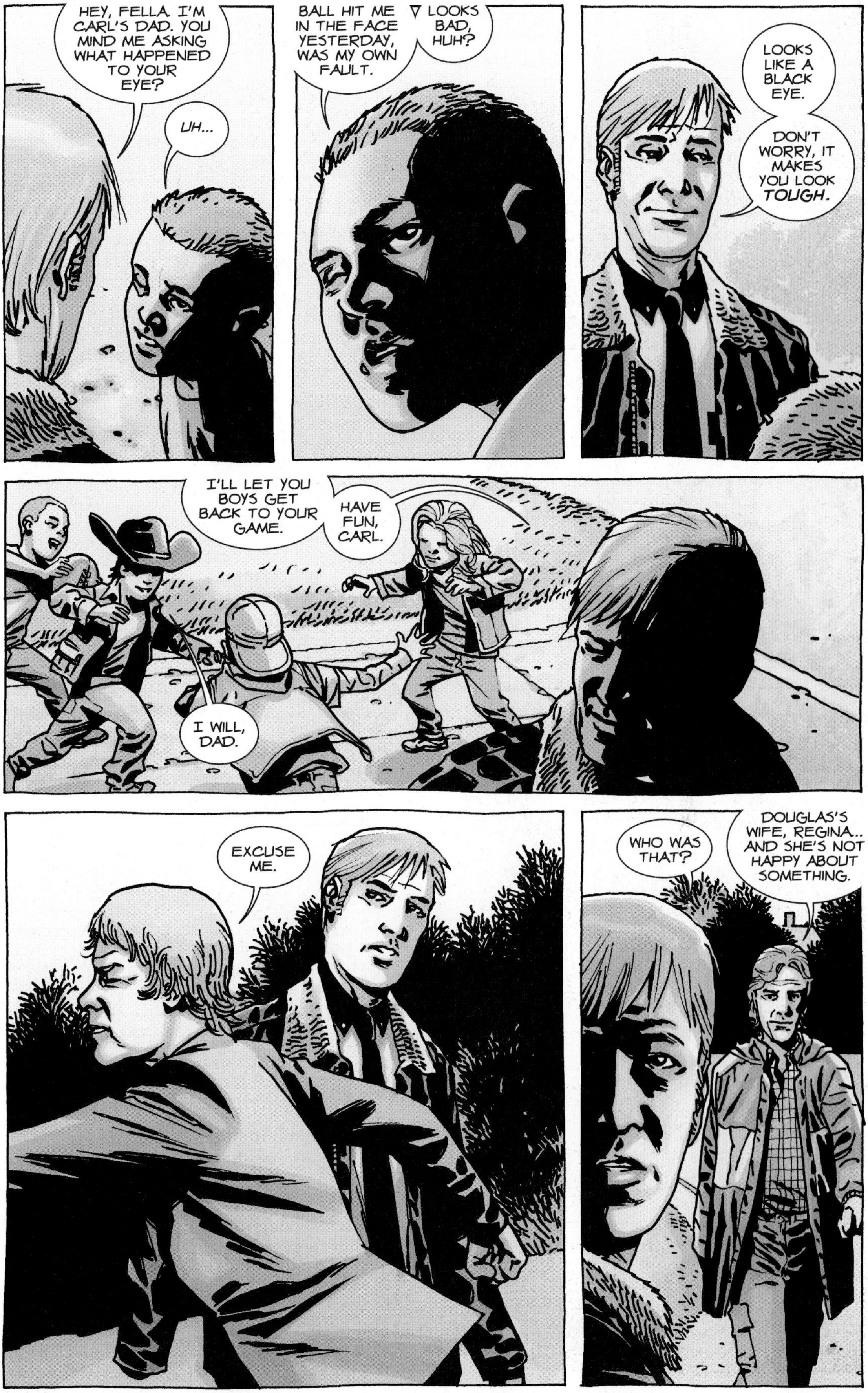
HEY, FELLA. I'M CARL'S DAD. YOU MIND ME ASKING WHAT HAPPENED TO YOUR EYE?
UH...
BALL HIT ME IN THE FACE YESTERDAY, WAS MY OWN FAULT.
LOOKS BAD, HUH?
LOOKS LIKE A BLACK EYE.
DON'T WORRY, IT MAKES YOU LOOK *TOUGH.*
I'LL LET YOU BOYS GET BACK TO YOUR GAME.
HAVE FUN, CARL.
I WILL, DAD.
EXCUSE ME.
WHO WAS THAT?
DOUGLAS'S WIFE, REGINA... AND SHE'S NOT HAPPY ABOUT SOMETHING.

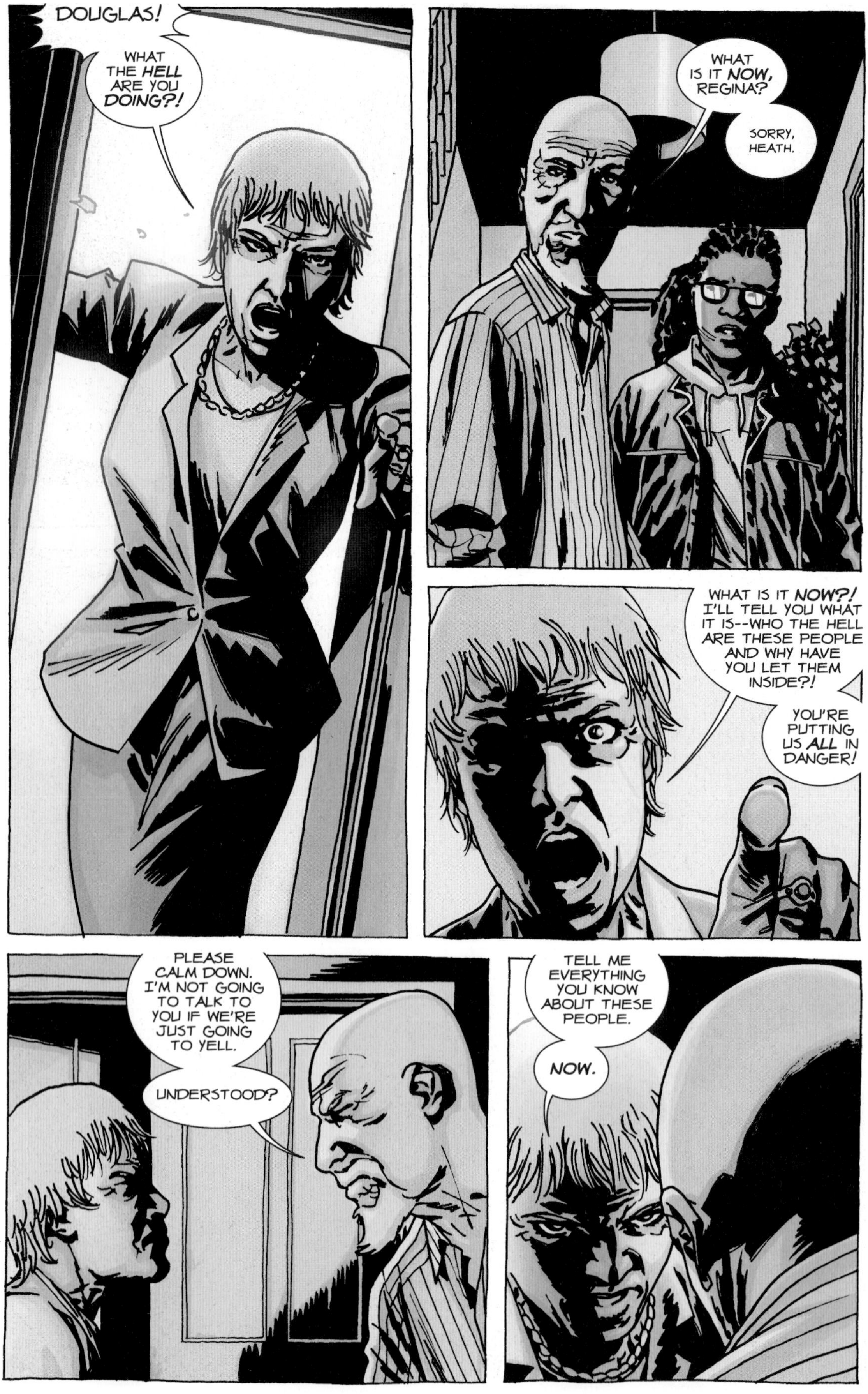
DOUGLAS!
WHAT THE HELL ARE YOU DOING?!
WHAT IS IT NOW, REGINA?
SORRY, HEATH.
WHAT IS IT NOW?! I'LL TELL YOU WHAT IT IS--WHO THE HELL ARE THESE PEOPLE AND WHY HAVE YOU LET THEM INSIDE?!
YOU'RE PUTTING US ALL IN DANGER!
PLEASE CALM DOWN. I'M NOT GOING TO TALK TO YOU IF WE'RE JUST GOING TO YELL.
UNDERSTOOD?
TELL ME EVERYTHING YOU KNOW ABOUT THESE PEOPLE.
NOW.

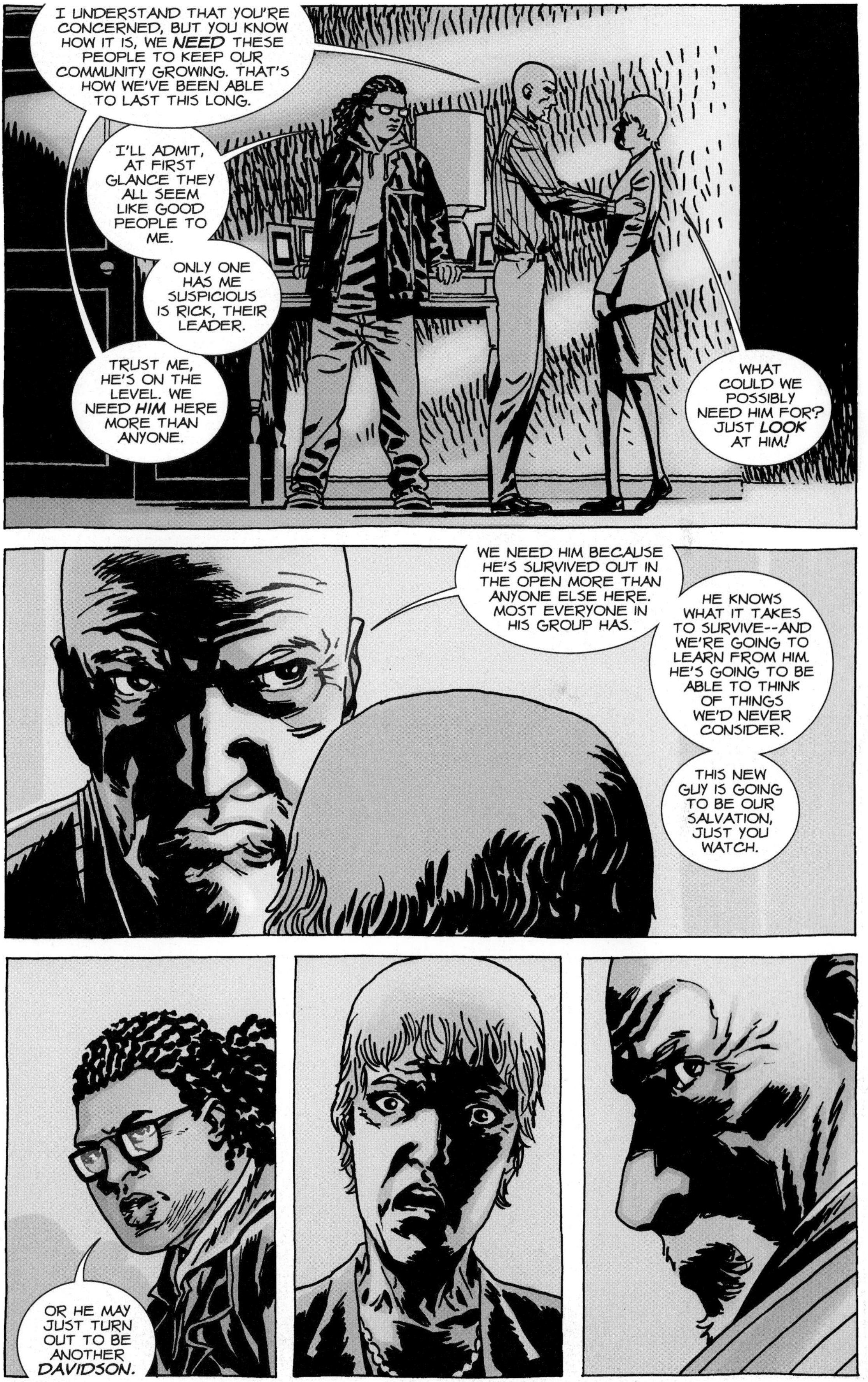
I UNDERSTAND THAT YOU'RE CONCERNED, BUT YOU KNOW HOW IT IS, WE NEED THESE PEOPLE TO KEEP OUR COMMUNITY GROWING. THAT'S HOW WE'VE BEEN ABLE TO LAST THIS LONG.
I'LL ADMIT, AT FIRST GLANCE THEY ALL SEEM LIKE GOOD PEOPLE TO ME.
ONLY ONE HAS ME SUSPICIOUS IS RICK, THEIR LEADER.
TRUST ME, HE'S ON THE LEVEL. WE NEED HIM HERE MORE THAN ANYONE.
WHAT COULD WE POSSIBLY NEED HIM FOR? JUST LOOK AT HIM!
WE NEED HIM BECAUSE HE'S SURVIVED OUT IN THE OPEN MORE THAN ANYONE ELSE HERE. MOST EVERYONE IN HIS GROUP HAS.
HE KNOWS WHAT IT TAKES TO SURVIVE--AND WE'RE GOING TO LEARN FROM HIM. HE'S GOING TO BE ABLE TO THINK OF THINGS WE'D NEVER CONSIDER.
THIS NEW GUY IS GOING TO BE OUR SALVATION, JUST YOU WATCH.
OR HE MAY JUST TURN OUT TO BE ANOTHER DAVIDSON.

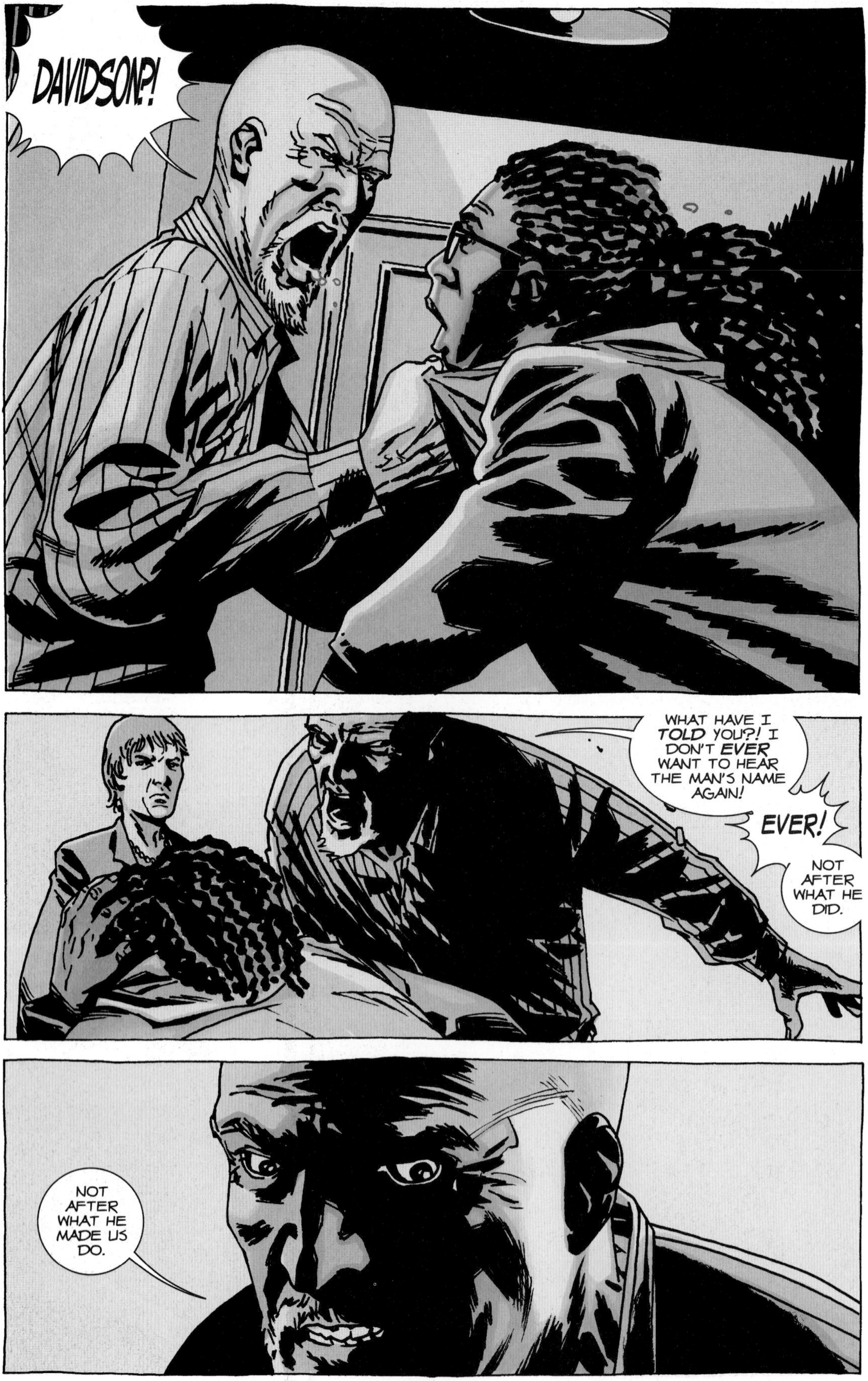
DAVIDSON?!
WHAT HAVE I TOLD YOU?! I DON'T EVER WANT TO HEAR THE MAN'S NAME AGAIN!
EVER!
NOT AFTER WHAT HE DID.
NOT AFTER WHAT HE MADE US DO.

DOUGLAS.

SERIOUSLY, MAN. WHAT THE HELL?

I KNOW. I'M SORRY.

YOU KNOW HOW I FEEL, YOU KNOW WHAT I'VE SAID. I DIDN'T MEAN TO OVERREACT.

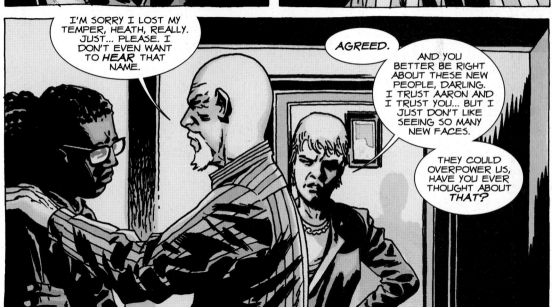

I'M SORRY I LOST MY TEMPER, HEATH, REALLY. JUST... PLEASE. I DON'T EVEN WANT TO *HEAR* THAT NAME.

AGREED.

AND YOU BETTER BE RIGHT ABOUT THESE NEW PEOPLE, DARLING. I TRUST AARON AND I TRUST YOU... BUT I JUST DON'T LIKE SEEING SO MANY NEW FACES.

THEY COULD OVERPOWER US, HAVE YOU EVER THOUGHT ABOUT *THAT?*

REGINA, DEAR-- WITH ALL DUE RESPECT, CALM DOWN. WE'VE THROWN THESE PEOPLE A LIFE RAFT. THEY'RE HAPPY TO BE HERE.

JUST THE SAME, EVERYONE HERE WILL KEEP AN EYE OUT FOR ANYTHING WEIRD OR OFF IN ANY WAY.

NOW IF YOU'LL EXCUSE ME. I'M GOING TO GIVE OUR NEW FRIENDS A QUICK TOUR AROUND THE COMMUNITY.

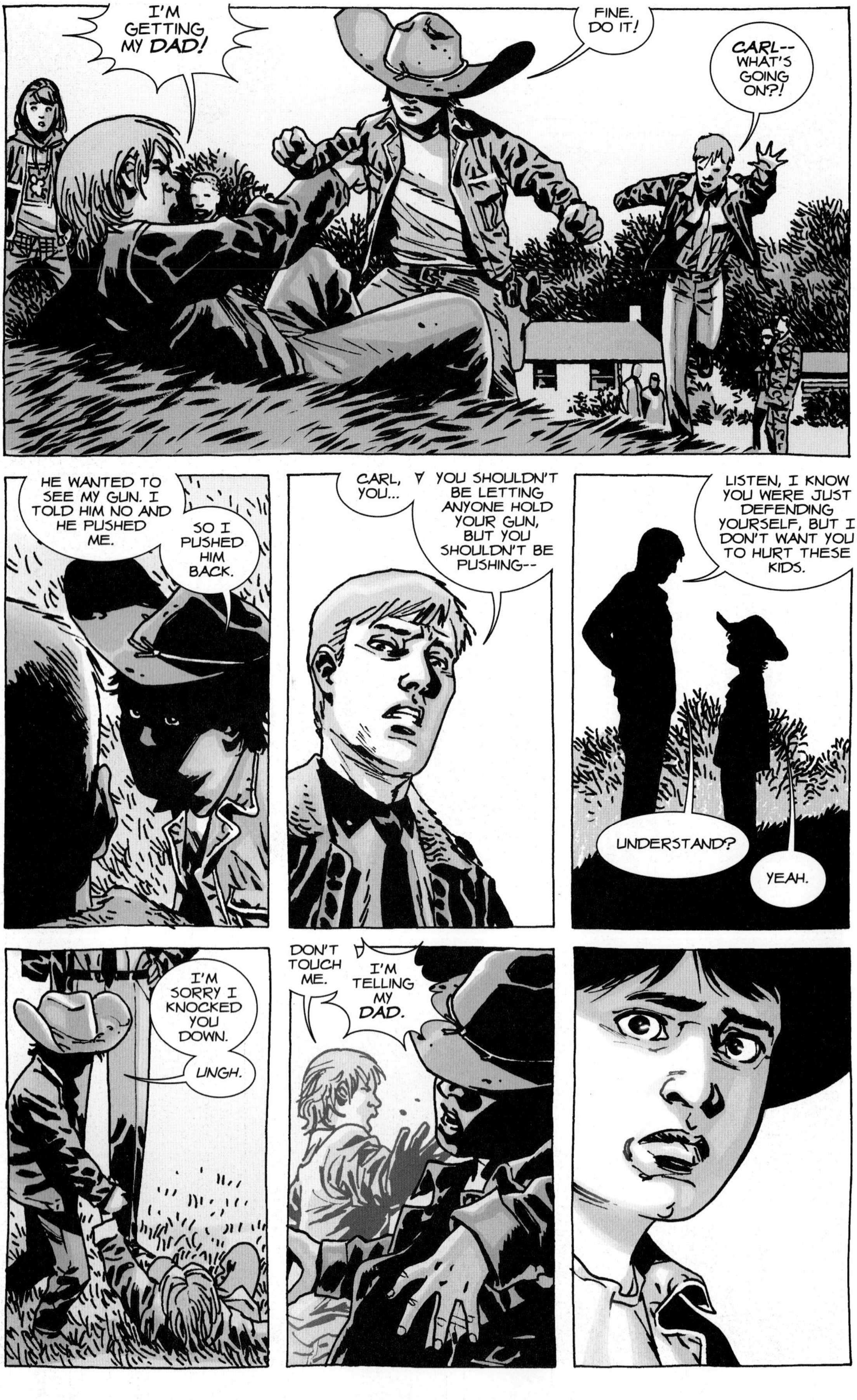
I'M GETTING MY DAD!
FINE. DO IT!
CARL-- WHAT'S GOING ON?!
HE WANTED TO SEE MY GUN. I TOLD HIM NO AND HE PUSHED ME.
SO I PUSHED HIM BACK.
CARL, YOU...
YOU SHOULDN'T BE LETTING ANYONE HOLD YOUR GUN, BUT YOU SHOULDN'T BE PUSHING--
LISTEN, I KNOW YOU WERE JUST DEFENDING YOURSELF, BUT I DON'T WANT YOU TO HURT THESE KIDS.
UNDERSTAND?
YEAH.
I'M SORRY I KNOCKED YOU DOWN.
UNGH.
DON'T TOUCH ME.
I'M TELLING MY DAD.

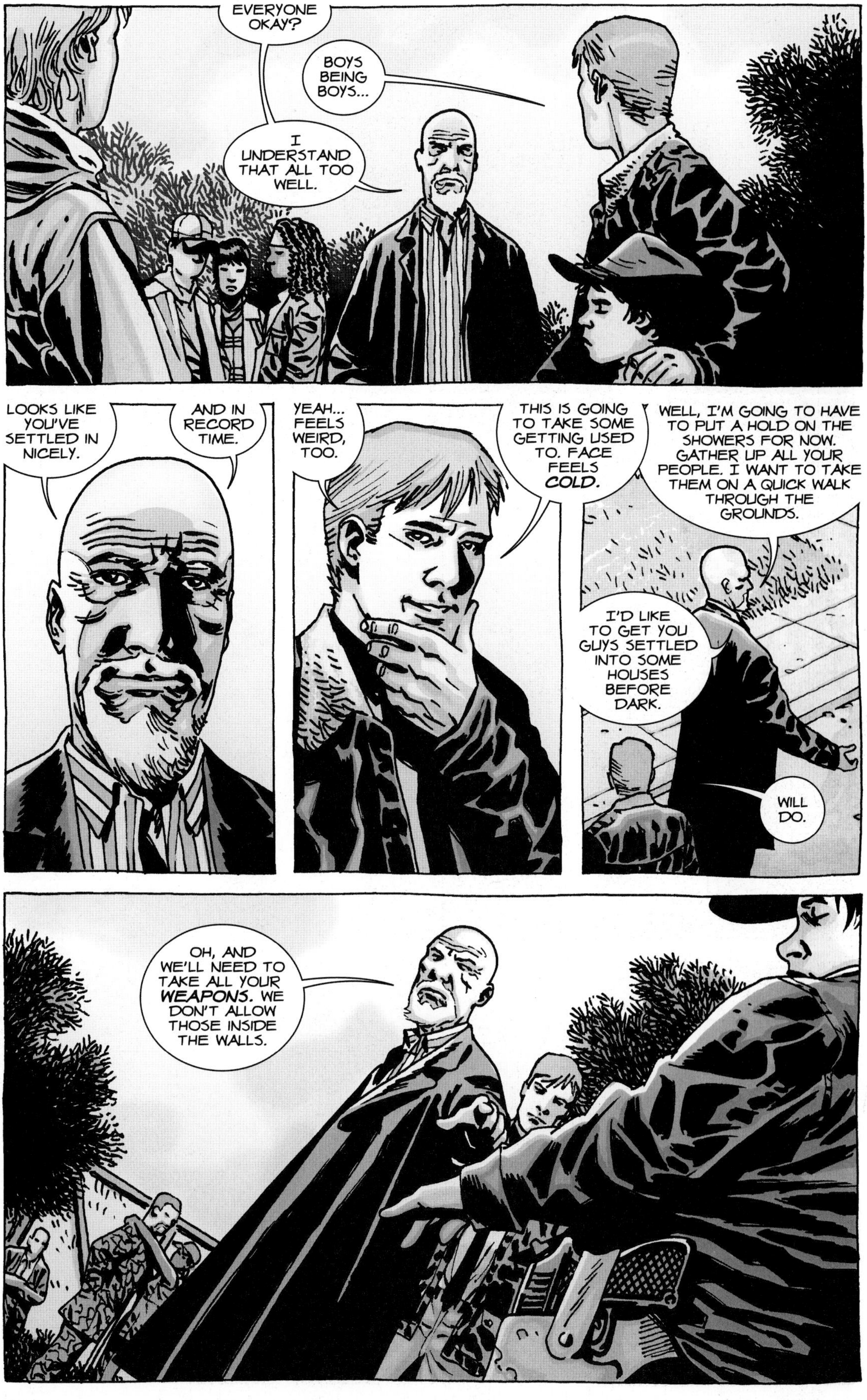
EVERYONE OKAY?
BOYS BEING BOYS...
I UNDERSTAND THAT ALL TOO WELL.
LOOKS LIKE YOU'VE SETTLED IN NICELY.
AND IN RECORD TIME.
YEAH... FEELS WEIRD, TOO.
THIS IS GOING TO TAKE SOME GETTING USED TO. FACE FEELS COLD.
WELL, I'M GOING TO HAVE TO PUT A HOLD ON THE SHOWERS FOR NOW. GATHER UP ALL YOUR PEOPLE. I WANT TO TAKE THEM ON A QUICK WALK THROUGH THE GROUNDS.
I'D LIKE TO GET YOU GUYS SETTLED INTO SOME HOUSES BEFORE DARK.
WILL DO.
OH, AND WE'LL NEED TO TAKE ALL YOUR WEAPONS. WE DON'T ALLOW THOSE INSIDE THE WALLS.

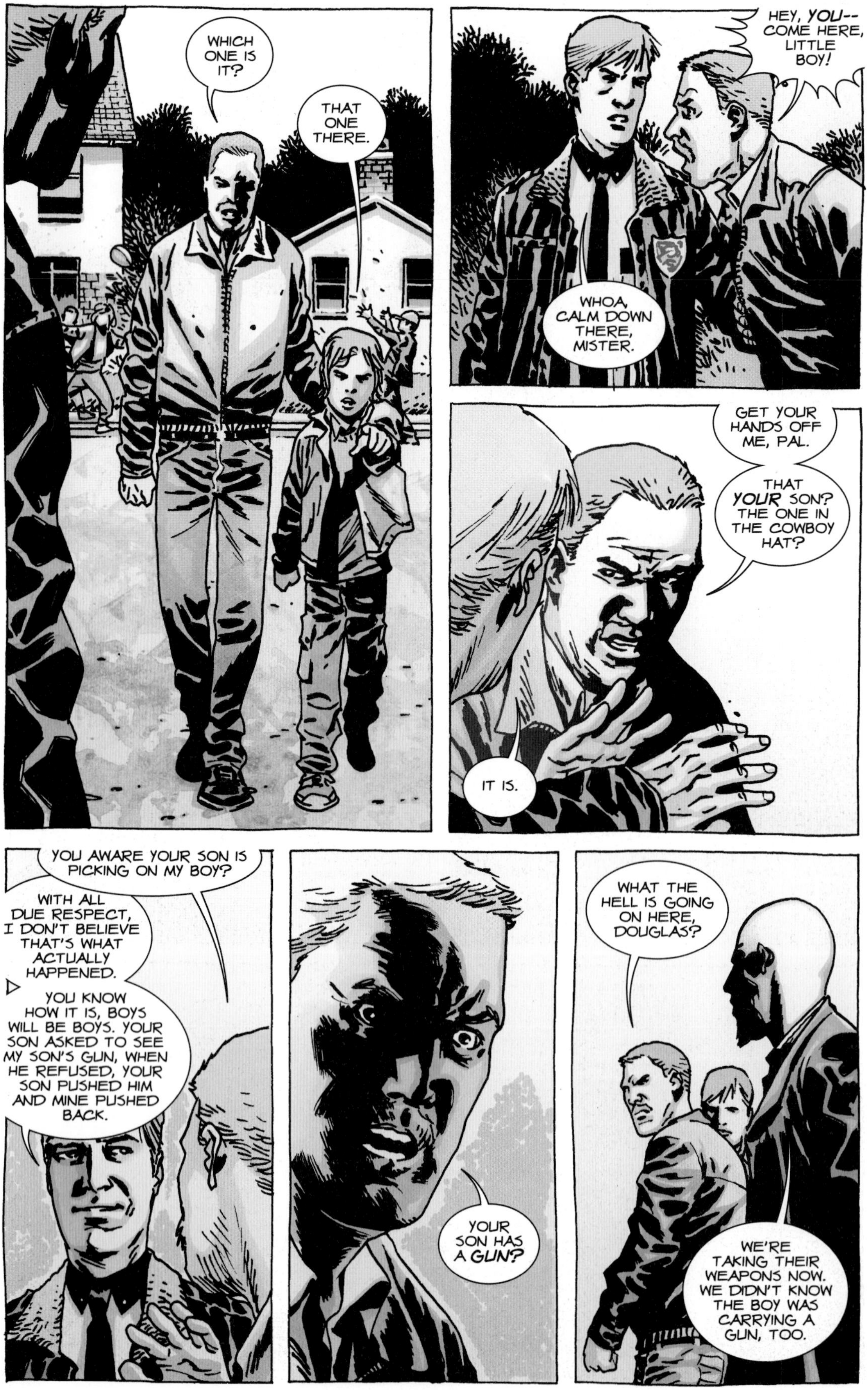

WHICH ONE IS IT?
THAT ONE THERE.
HEY, YOU-- COME HERE, LITTLE BOY!
WHOA, CALM DOWN THERE, MISTER.
GET YOUR HANDS OFF ME, PAL.
THAT YOUR SON? THE ONE IN THE COWBOY HAT?
IT IS.
YOU AWARE YOUR SON IS PICKING ON MY BOY?
WITH ALL DUE RESPECT, I DON'T BELIEVE THAT'S WHAT ACTUALLY HAPPENED.
YOU KNOW HOW IT IS, BOYS WILL BE BOYS. YOUR SON ASKED TO SEE MY SON'S GUN, WHEN HE REFUSED, YOUR SON PUSHED HIM AND MINE PUSHED BACK.
YOUR SON HAS A GUN?
WHAT THE HELL IS GOING ON HERE, DOUGLAS?
WE'RE TAKING THEIR WEAPONS NOW. WE DIDN'T KNOW THE BOY WAS CARRYING A GUN, TOO.

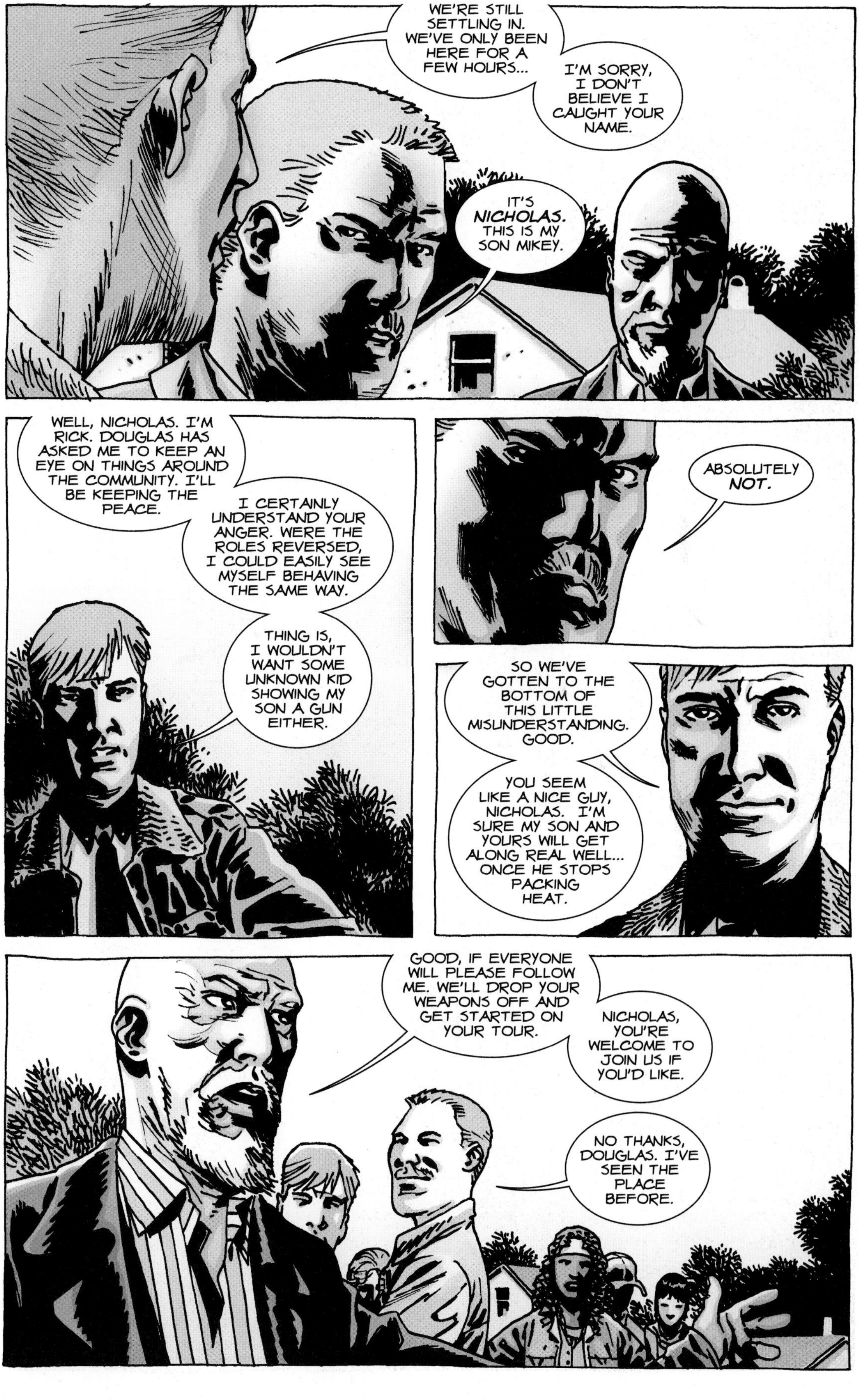
WE'RE STILL SETTLING IN. WE'VE ONLY BEEN HERE FOR A FEW HOURS...
I'M SORRY, I DON'T BELIEVE I CAUGHT YOUR NAME.
IT'S NICHOLAS. THIS IS MY SON MIKEY.
WELL, NICHOLAS. I'M RICK. DOUGLAS HAS ASKED ME TO KEEP AN EYE ON THINGS AROUND THE COMMUNITY. I'LL BE KEEPING THE PEACE.
I CERTAINLY UNDERSTAND YOUR ANGER. WERE THE ROLES REVERSED, I COULD EASILY SEE MYSELF BEHAVING THE SAME WAY.
THING IS, I WOULDN'T WANT SOME UNKNOWN KID SHOWING MY SON A GUN EITHER.
ABSOLUTELY NOT.
SO WE'VE GOTTEN TO THE BOTTOM OF THIS LITTLE MISUNDERSTANDING. GOOD.
YOU SEEM LIKE A NICE GUY, NICHOLAS. I'M SURE MY SON AND YOURS WILL GET ALONG REAL WELL... ONCE HE STOPS PACKING HEAT.
GOOD, IF EVERYONE WILL PLEASE FOLLOW ME. WE'LL DROP YOUR WEAPONS OFF AND GET STARTED ON YOUR TOUR.
NICHOLAS, YOU'RE WELCOME TO JOIN US IF YOU'D LIKE.
NO THANKS, DOUGLAS. I'VE SEEN THE PLACE BEFORE.

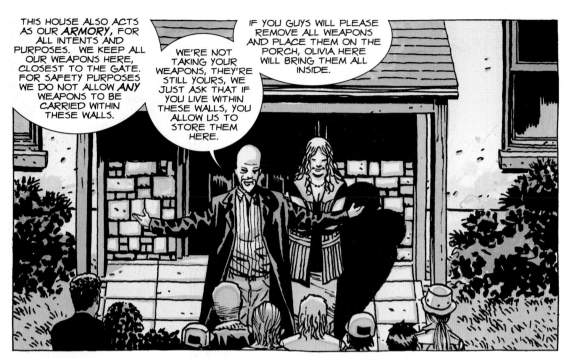

THIS HOUSE ALSO ACTS AS OUR *ARMORY*, FOR ALL INTENTS AND PURPOSES. WE KEEP ALL OUR WEAPONS HERE, CLOSEST TO THE GATE. FOR SAFETY PURPOSES WE DO NOT ALLOW *ANY* WEAPONS TO BE CARRIED WITHIN THESE WALLS.

WE'RE NOT TAKING YOUR WEAPONS, THEY'RE STILL YOURS, WE JUST ASK THAT IF YOU LIVE WITHIN THESE WALLS, YOU ALLOW US TO STORE THEM HERE.

IF YOU GUYS WILL PLEASE REMOVE ALL WEAPONS AND PLACE THEM ON THE PORCH, OLIVIA HERE WILL BRING THEM ALL INSIDE.

I'D LIKE TO KEEP MY SWORD WITH ME. IT HAS SENTIMENTAL VALUE.

AGAIN, WE'RE NOT *TAKING* YOUR WEAPONS, JUST STORING THEM HERE. AND I'M SORRY, BUT A WEAPON IS A WEAPON...

...AND I'M TOLD YOU'RE QUITE DEADLY WITH THAT SWORD.

OH, DOUGLAS. A WEAPON IS A WEAPON? *ANYTHING* CAN BE A WEAPON. TO MOST PEOPLE A HAMMER'D BE MORE DEADLY THAN THAT SWORD, YOU LET PEOPLE KEEP THOSE.

I'VE GOT KNIVES IN MY KITCHEN AREN'T MUCH SMALLER THAN THAT. LET THE WOMAN KEEP HER SWORD.

YOU *DO NOT* CARRY IT WITH YOU. KEEP IT IN YOUR HOUSE.

IN FACT, I WANT TO SEE IT HANGING OVER YOUR MANTEL. IT'S RETIRED AS LONG AS YOU'RE WITHIN THESE WALLS.

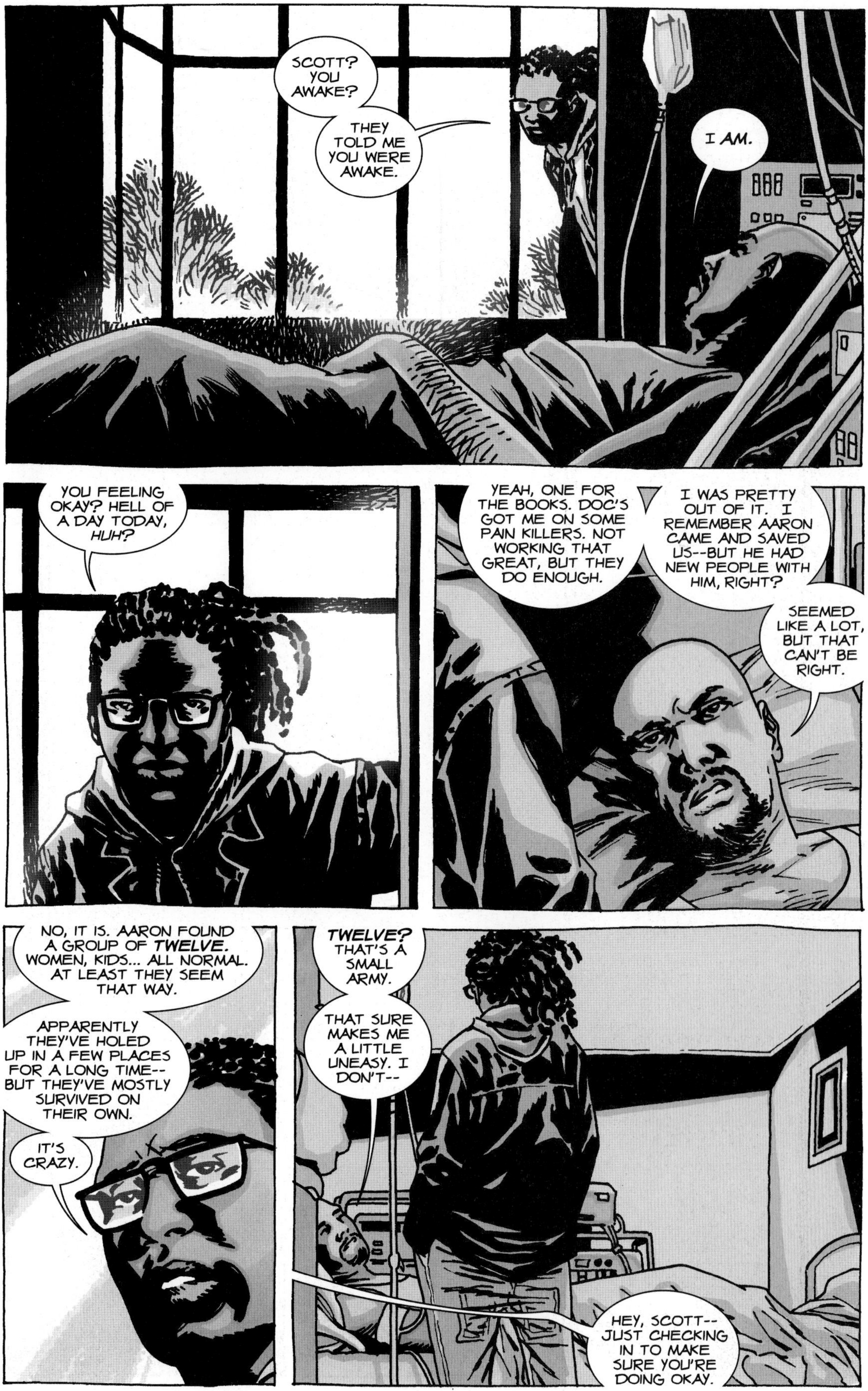

SCOTT? YOU AWAKE?
THEY TOLD ME YOU WERE AWAKE.
I AM.
YOU FEELING OKAY? HELL OF A DAY TODAY, *HUH?*
YEAH, ONE FOR THE BOOKS. DOC'S GOT ME ON SOME PAIN KILLERS. NOT WORKING THAT GREAT, BUT THEY DO ENOUGH.
I WAS PRETTY OUT OF IT. I REMEMBER AARON CAME AND SAVED US--BUT HE HAD NEW PEOPLE WITH HIM, RIGHT?
SEEMED LIKE A LOT, BUT THAT CAN'T BE RIGHT.
NO, IT IS. AARON FOUND A GROUP OF ***TWELVE.*** WOMEN, KIDS... ALL NORMAL. AT LEAST THEY SEEM THAT WAY.
APPARENTLY THEY'VE HOLED UP IN A FEW PLACES FOR A LONG TIME-- BUT THEY'VE MOSTLY SURVIVED ON THEIR OWN.
IT'S CRAZY.
TWELVE? THAT'S A SMALL ARMY.
THAT SURE MAKES ME A LITTLE UNEASY. I DON'T--
HEY, SCOTT-- JUST CHECKING IN TO MAKE SURE YOU'RE DOING OKAY.

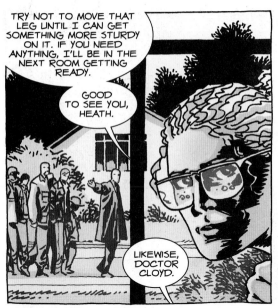

TRY NOT TO MOVE THAT LEG UNTIL I CAN GET SOMETHING MORE STURDY ON IT. IF YOU NEED ANYTHING, I'LL BE IN THE NEXT ROOM GETTING READY.

GOOD TO SEE YOU, HEATH.

LIKEWISE, DOCTOR CLOYD.

THIS HOUSE IS THE INFIRMARY. WE ACTUALLY HAVE THREE DOCTORS HERE IN THE COMMUNITY, ONE A SURGEON.

THANKS TO HEATH AND THE OTHER RUNNERS, WE HAVE SOME STATE OF THE ART EQUIPMENT. IT'S QUITE NICE.

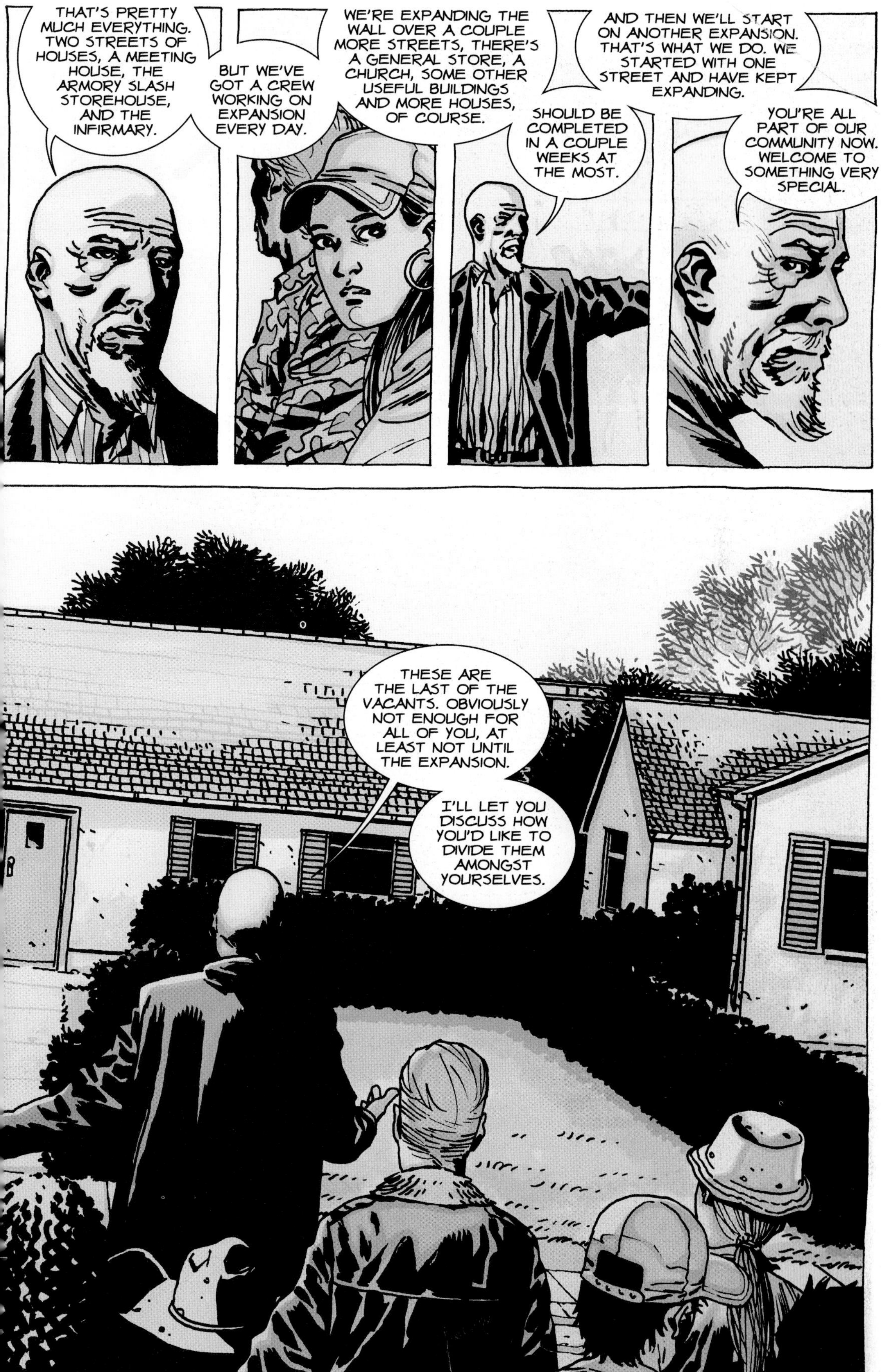
THAT'S PRETTY MUCH EVERYTHING. TWO STREETS OF HOUSES, A MEETING HOUSE, THE ARMORY SLASH STOREHOUSE, AND THE INFIRMARY.
BUT WE'VE GOT A CREW WORKING ON EXPANSION EVERY DAY.
WE'RE EXPANDING THE WALL OVER A COUPLE MORE STREETS, THERE'S A GENERAL STORE, A CHURCH, SOME OTHER USEFUL BUILDINGS AND MORE HOUSES, OF COURSE.
SHOULD BE COMPLETED IN A COUPLE WEEKS AT THE MOST.
AND THEN WE'LL START ON ANOTHER EXPANSION. THAT'S WHAT WE DO. WE STARTED WITH ONE STREET AND HAVE KEPT EXPANDING.
YOU'RE ALL PART OF OUR COMMUNITY NOW. WELCOME TO SOMETHING VERY SPECIAL.
THESE ARE THE LAST OF THE VACANTS. OBVIOUSLY NOT ENOUGH FOR ALL OF YOU, AT LEAST NOT UNTIL THE EXPANSION.
I'LL LET YOU DISCUSS HOW YOU'D LIKE TO DIVIDE THEM AMONGST YOURSELVES.

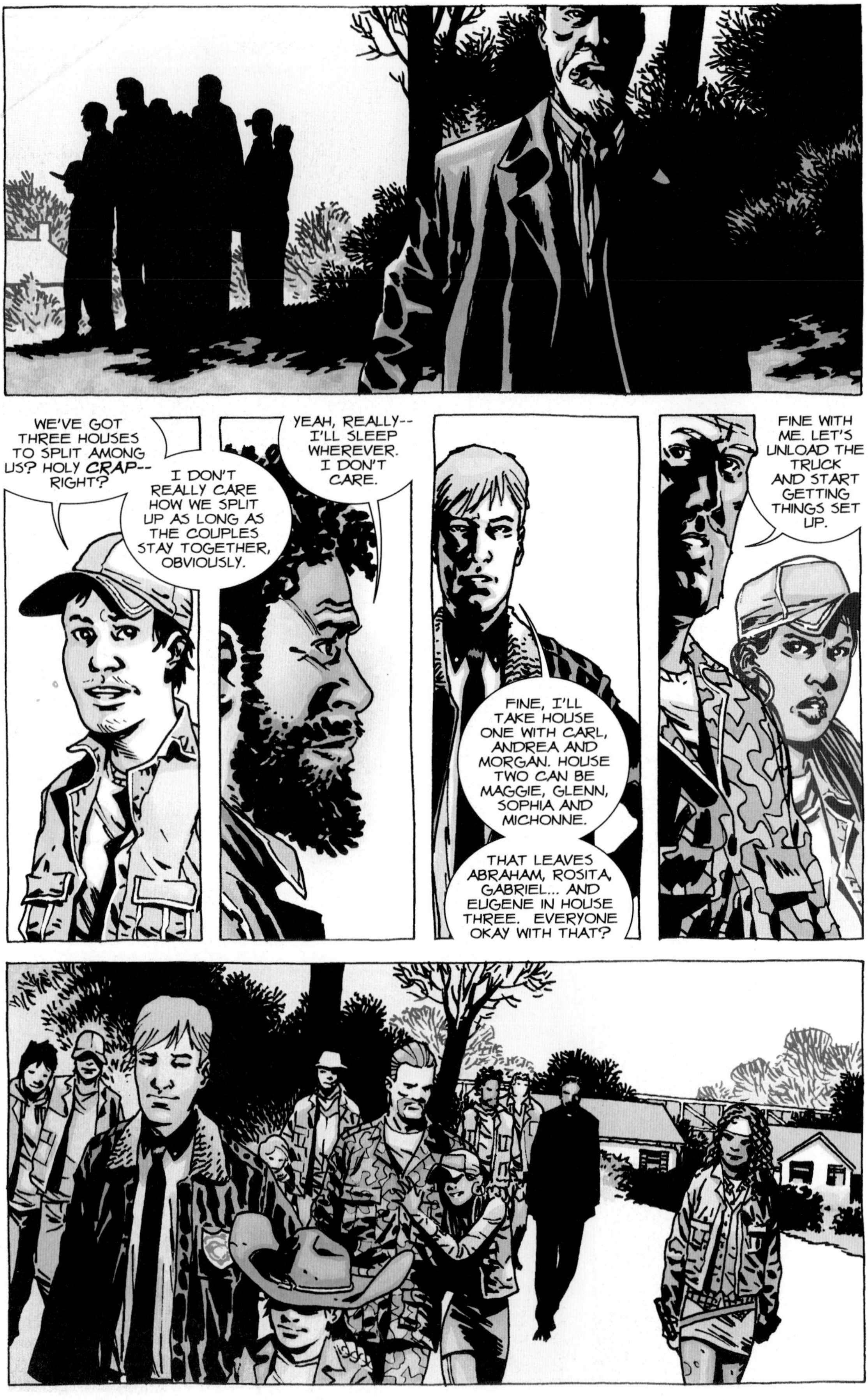
WE'VE GOT THREE HOUSES TO SPLIT AMONG US? HOLY CRAP-- RIGHT?
I DON'T REALLY CARE HOW WE SPLIT UP AS LONG AS THE COUPLES STAY TOGETHER, OBVIOUSLY.
YEAH, REALLY-- I'LL SLEEP WHEREVER. I DON'T CARE.
FINE, I'LL TAKE HOUSE ONE WITH CARL, ANDREA AND MORGAN. HOUSE TWO CAN BE MAGGIE, GLENN, SOPHIA AND MICHONNE.
THAT LEAVES ABRAHAM, ROSITA, GABRIEL... AND EUGENE IN HOUSE THREE. EVERYONE OKAY WITH THAT?
FINE WITH ME. LET'S UNLOAD THE TRUCK AND START GETTING THINGS SET UP.

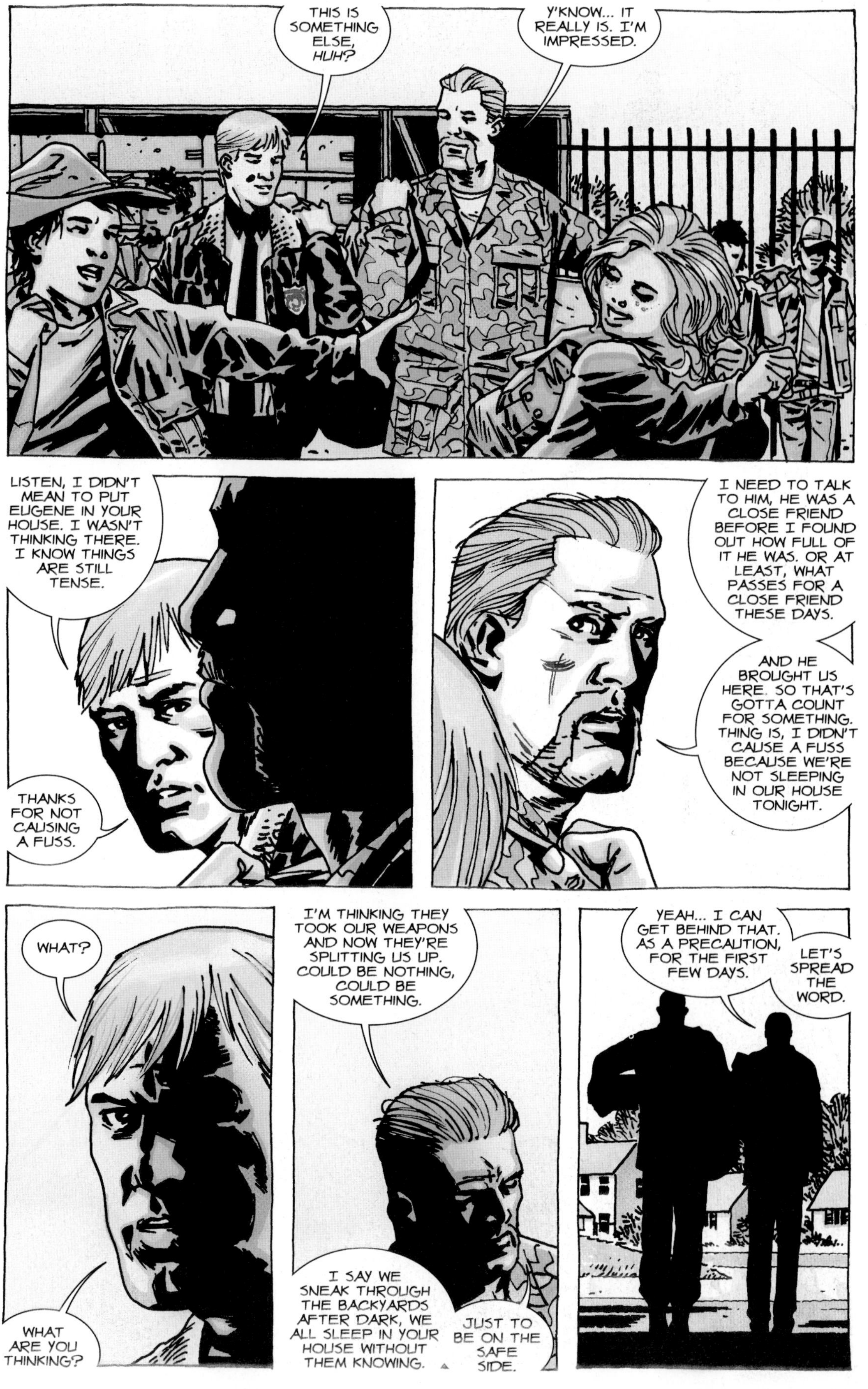

THIS IS SOMETHING ELSE, HUH?
Y'KNOW... IT REALLY IS. I'M IMPRESSED.
LISTEN, I DIDN'T MEAN TO PUT EUGENE IN YOUR HOUSE. I WASN'T THINKING THERE. I KNOW THINGS ARE STILL TENSE.
THANKS FOR NOT CAUSING A FUSS.
I NEED TO TALK TO HIM, HE WAS A CLOSE FRIEND BEFORE I FOUND OUT HOW FULL OF IT HE WAS. OR AT LEAST, WHAT PASSES FOR A CLOSE FRIEND THESE DAYS.
AND HE BROUGHT US HERE. SO THAT'S GOTTA COUNT FOR SOMETHING. THING IS, I DIDN'T CAUSE A FUSS BECAUSE WE'RE NOT SLEEPING IN OUR HOUSE TONIGHT.
WHAT?
WHAT ARE YOU THINKING?
I'M THINKING THEY TOOK OUR WEAPONS AND NOW THEY'RE SPLITTING US UP. COULD BE NOTHING, COULD BE SOMETHING.
I SAY WE SNEAK THROUGH THE BACKYARDS AFTER DARK, WE ALL SLEEP IN YOUR HOUSE WITHOUT THEM KNOWING.
JUST TO BE ON THE SAFE SIDE.
YEAH... I CAN GET BEHIND THAT. AS A PRECAUTION, FOR THE FIRST FEW DAYS.
LET'S SPREAD THE WORD.

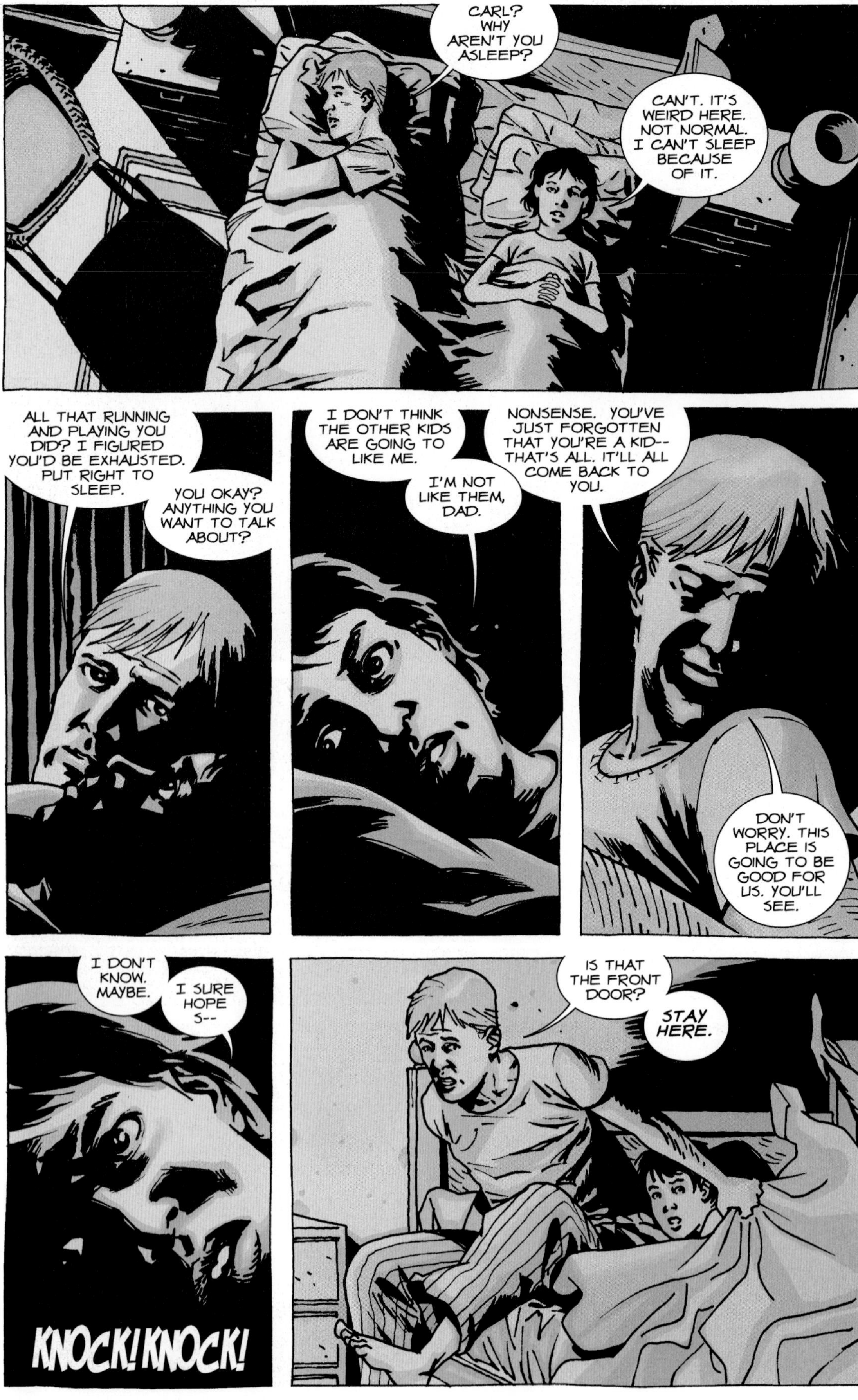
CARL? WHY AREN'T YOU ASLEEP?
CAN'T. IT'S WEIRD HERE. NOT NORMAL. I CAN'T SLEEP BECAUSE OF IT.
ALL THAT RUNNING AND PLAYING YOU DID? I FIGURED YOU'D BE EXHAUSTED. PUT RIGHT TO SLEEP.
YOU OKAY? ANYTHING YOU WANT TO TALK ABOUT?
I DON'T THINK THE OTHER KIDS ARE GOING TO LIKE ME.
I'M NOT LIKE THEM, DAD.
NONSENSE. YOU'VE JUST FORGOTTEN THAT YOU'RE A KID-- THAT'S ALL. IT'LL ALL COME BACK TO YOU.
DON'T WORRY. THIS PLACE IS GOING TO BE GOOD FOR US. YOU'LL SEE.
I DON'T KNOW. MAYBE.
I SURE HOPE S--
KNOCK! KNOCK!
IS THAT THE FRONT DOOR?
STAY HERE.

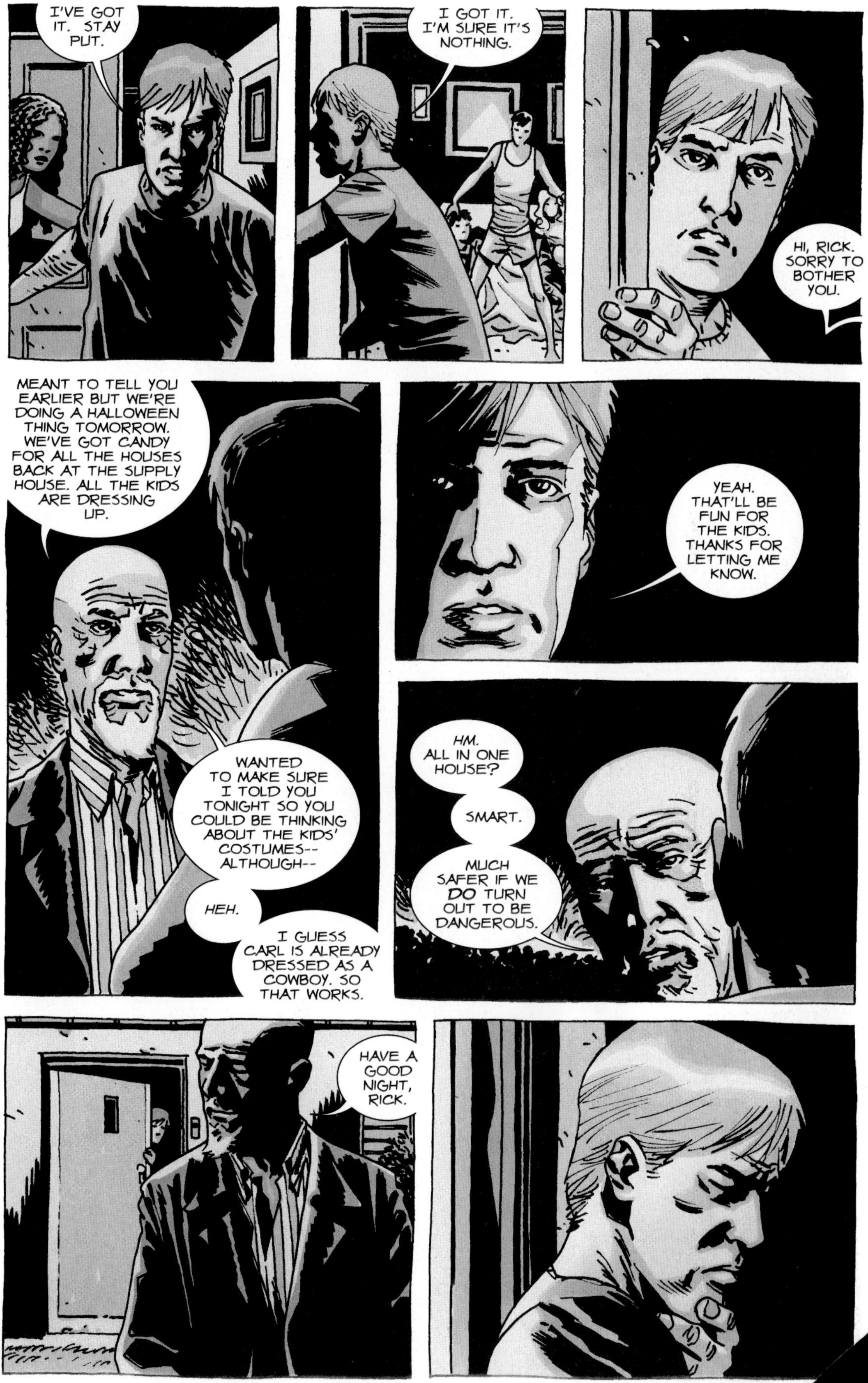
I'VE GOT IT. STAY PUT.
I GOT IT. I'M SURE IT'S NOTHING.
HI, RICK. SORRY TO BOTHER YOU.
MEANT TO TELL YOU EARLIER BUT WE'RE DOING A HALLOWEEN THING TOMORROW. WE'VE GOT CANDY FOR ALL THE HOUSES BACK AT THE SUPPLY HOUSE. ALL THE KIDS ARE DRESSING UP.
WANTED TO MAKE SURE I TOLD YOU TONIGHT SO YOU COULD BE THINKING ABOUT THE KIDS' COSTUMES-- ALTHOUGH--
HEH.
I GUESS CARL IS ALREADY DRESSED AS A COWBOY. SO THAT WORKS.
YEAH. THAT'LL BE FUN FOR THE KIDS. THANKS FOR LETTING ME KNOW.
HM. ALL IN ONE HOUSE?
SMART.
MUCH SAFER IF WE DO TURN OUT TO BE DANGEROUS.
HAVE A GOOD NIGHT, RICK.

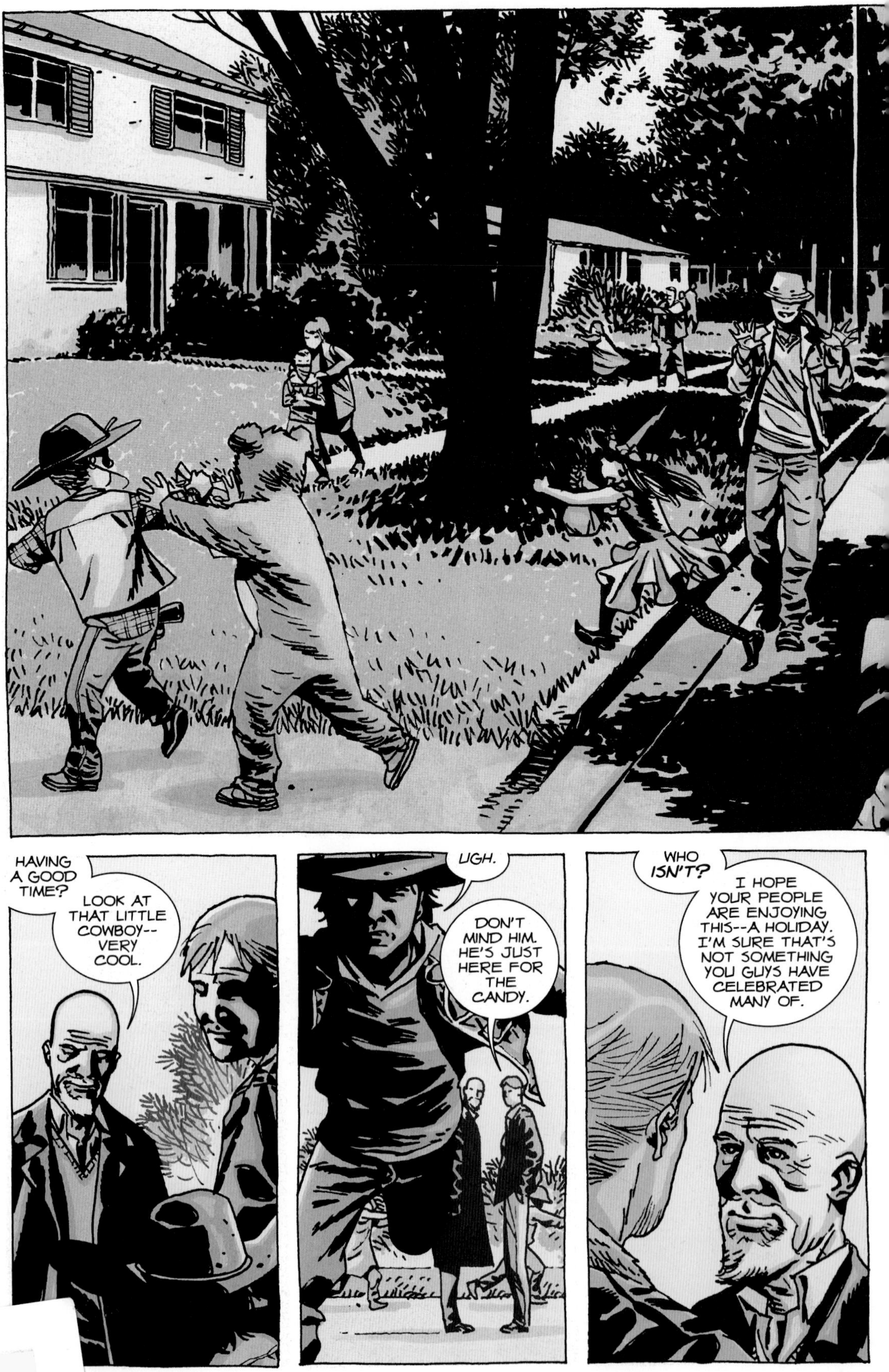

HAVING A GOOD TIME?
LOOK AT THAT LITTLE COWBOY-- VERY COOL.
UGH.
DON'T MIND HIM. HE'S JUST HERE FOR THE CANDY.
WHO ISN'T?
I HOPE YOUR PEOPLE ARE ENJOYING THIS--A HOLIDAY. I'M SURE THAT'S NOT SOMETHING YOU GUYS HAVE CELEBRATED MANY OF.

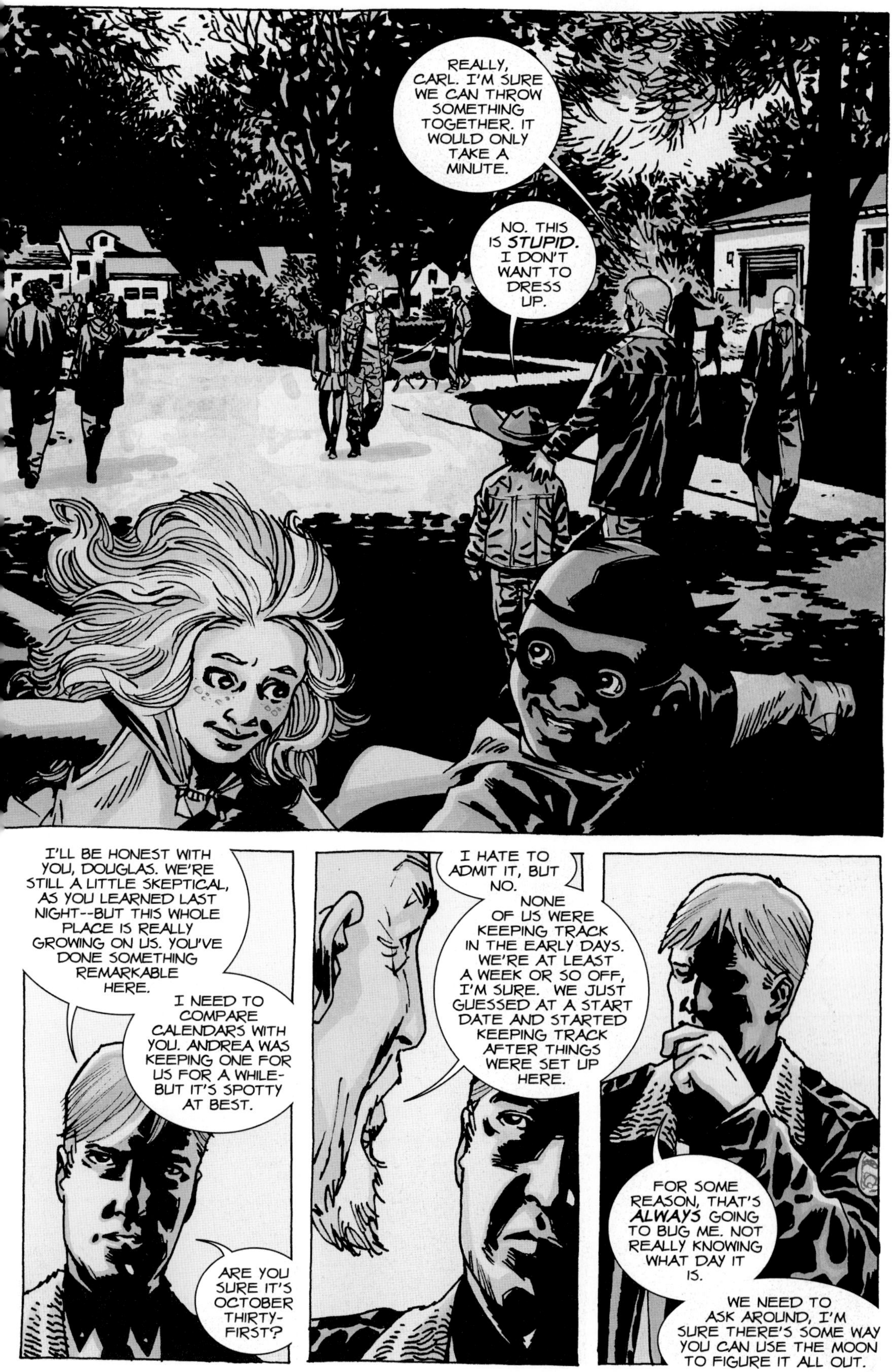
REALLY, CARL. I'M SURE WE CAN THROW SOMETHING TOGETHER. IT WOULD ONLY TAKE A MINUTE.
NO. THIS IS STUPID. I DON'T WANT TO DRESS UP.
I'LL BE HONEST WITH YOU, DOUGLAS. WE'RE STILL A LITTLE SKEPTICAL, AS YOU LEARNED LAST NIGHT--BUT THIS WHOLE PLACE IS REALLY GROWING ON US. YOU'VE DONE SOMETHING REMARKABLE HERE.
I NEED TO COMPARE CALENDARS WITH YOU. ANDREA WAS KEEPING ONE FOR US FOR A WHILE-BUT IT'S SPOTTY AT BEST.
ARE YOU SURE IT'S OCTOBER THIRTY-FIRST?
I HATE TO ADMIT IT, BUT NO.
NONE OF US WERE KEEPING TRACK IN THE EARLY DAYS. WE'RE AT LEAST A WEEK OR SO OFF, I'M SURE. WE JUST GUESSED AT A START DATE AND STARTED KEEPING TRACK AFTER THINGS WERE SET UP HERE.
FOR SOME REASON, THAT'S ALWAYS GOING TO BUG ME. NOT REALLY KNOWING WHAT DAY IT IS.
WE NEED TO ASK AROUND, I'M SURE THERE'S SOME WAY YOU CAN USE THE MOON TO FIGURE IT ALL OUT.

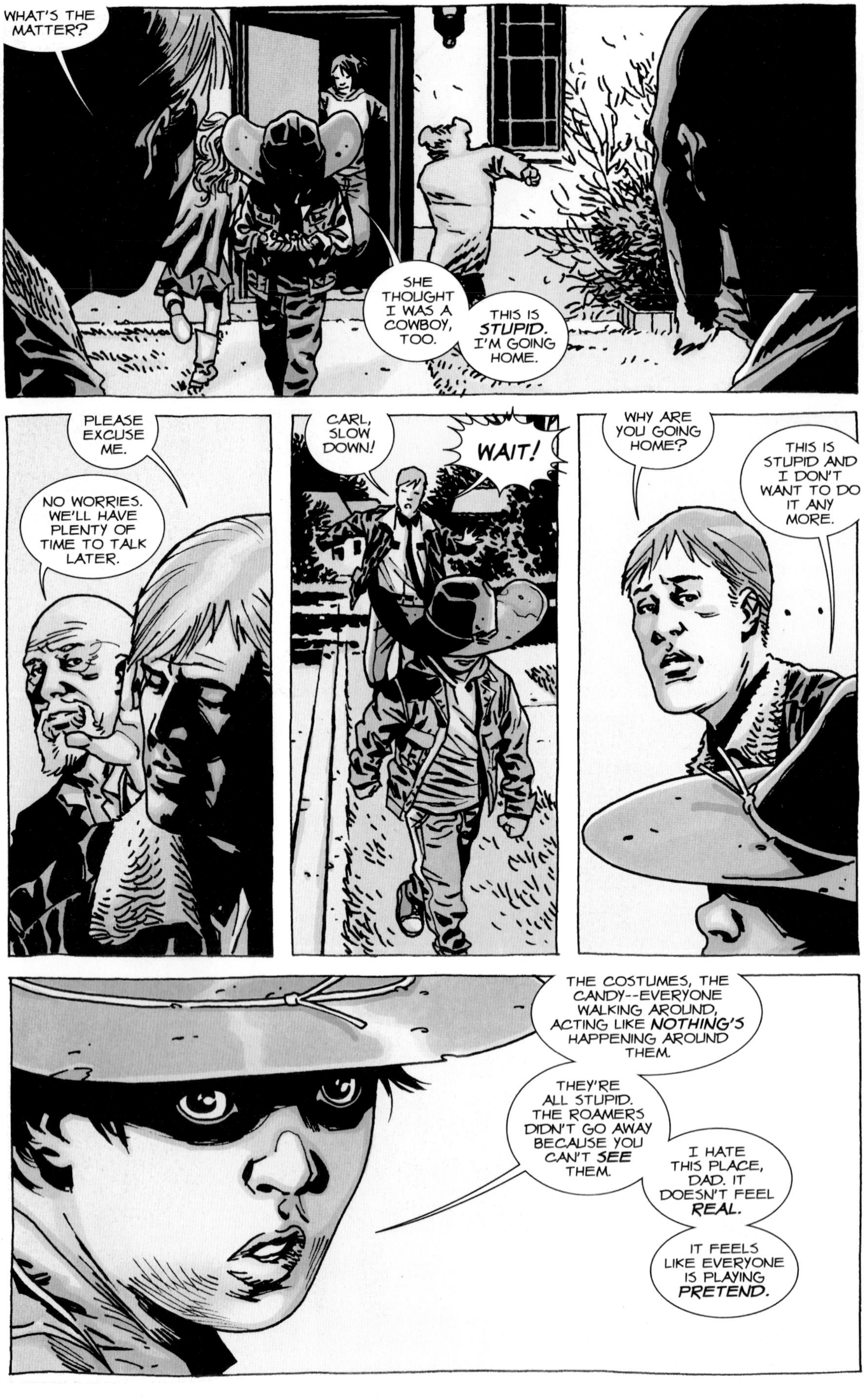
WHAT'S THE MATTER?
SHE THOUGHT I WAS A COWBOY, TOO.
THIS IS STUPID. I'M GOING HOME.
PLEASE EXCUSE ME.
NO WORRIES. WE'LL HAVE PLENTY OF TIME TO TALK LATER.
CARL, SLOW DOWN!
WAIT!
WHY ARE YOU GOING HOME?
THIS IS STUPID AND I DON'T WANT TO DO IT ANY MORE.
THE COSTUMES, THE CANDY--EVERYONE WALKING AROUND, ACTING LIKE NOTHING'S HAPPENING AROUND THEM.
THEY'RE ALL STUPID. THE ROAMERS DIDN'T GO AWAY BECAUSE YOU CAN'T SEE THEM.
I HATE THIS PLACE, DAD. IT DOESN'T FEEL REAL.
IT FEELS LIKE EVERYONE IS PLAYING PRETEND.

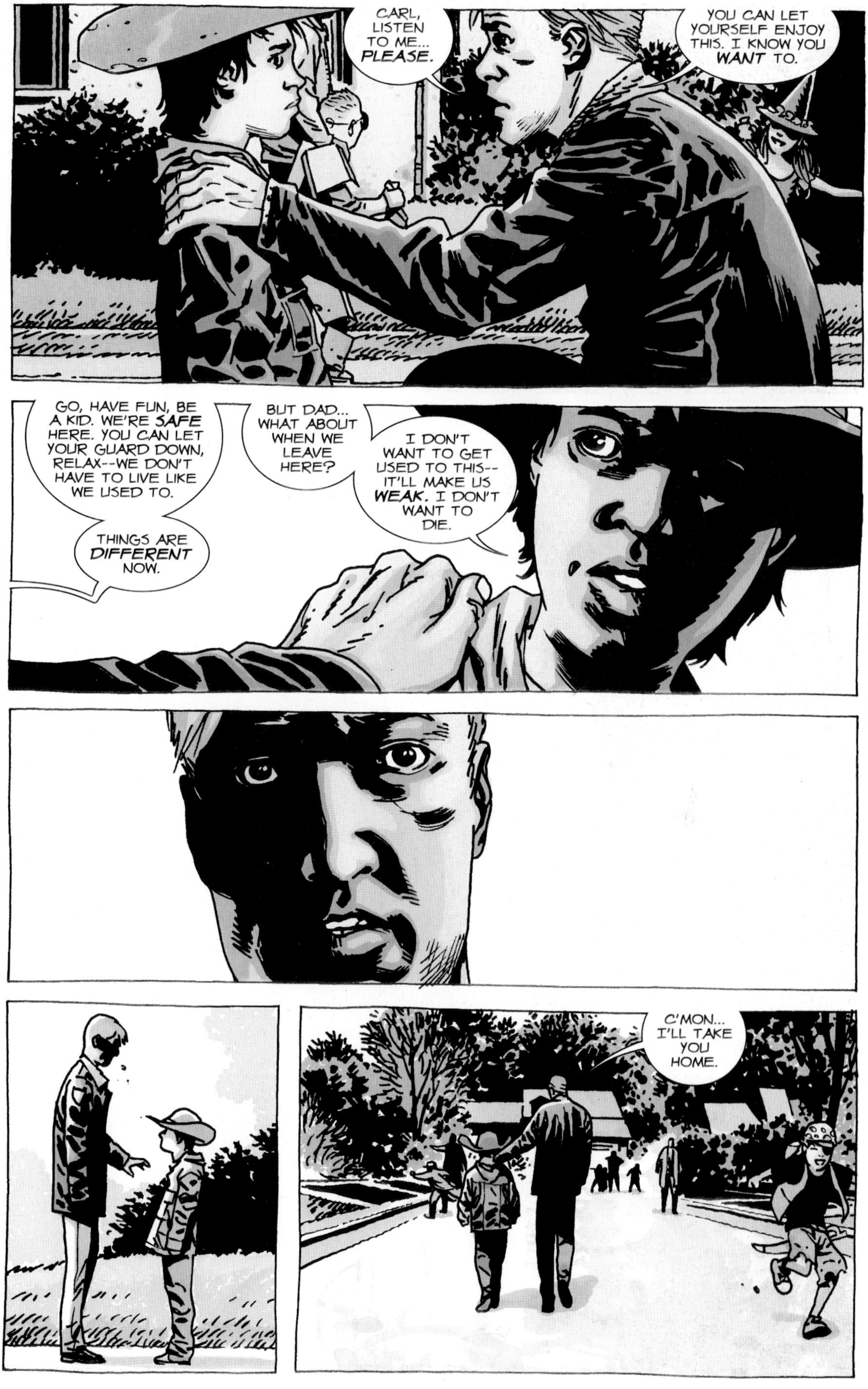
CARL, LISTEN TO ME... PLEASE.
YOU CAN LET YOURSELF ENJOY THIS. I KNOW YOU WANT TO.
GO, HAVE FUN, BE A KID. WE'RE SAFE HERE. YOU CAN LET YOUR GUARD DOWN, RELAX--WE DON'T HAVE TO LIVE LIKE WE USED TO.
THINGS ARE DIFFERENT NOW.
BUT DAD... WHAT ABOUT WHEN WE LEAVE HERE?
I DON'T WANT TO GET USED TO THIS-- IT'LL MAKE US WEAK. I DON'T WANT TO DIE.
C'MON... I'LL TAKE YOU HOME.

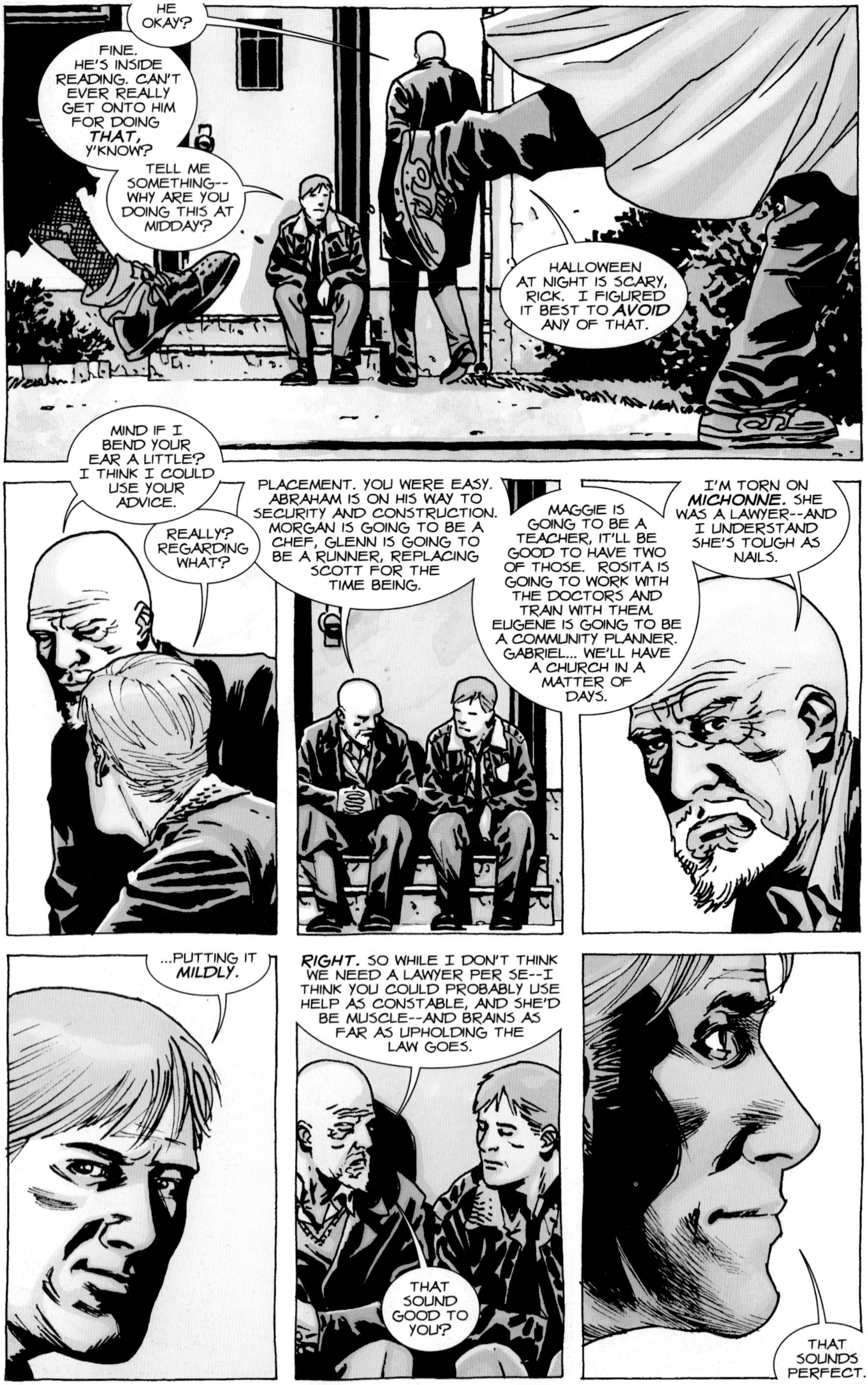
HE OKAY?
FINE. HE'S INSIDE READING. CAN'T EVER REALLY GET ONTO HIM FOR DOING *THAT,* Y'KNOW?
TELL ME SOMETHING-- WHY ARE YOU DOING THIS AT MIDDAY?
HALLOWEEN AT NIGHT IS SCARY, RICK. I FIGURED IT BEST TO *AVOID* ANY OF THAT.
MIND IF I BEND YOUR EAR A LITTLE? I THINK I COULD USE YOUR ADVICE.
REALLY? REGARDING WHAT?
PLACEMENT. YOU WERE EASY. ABRAHAM IS ON HIS WAY TO SECURITY AND CONSTRUCTION. MORGAN IS GOING TO BE A CHEF, GLENN IS GOING TO BE A RUNNER, REPLACING SCOTT FOR THE TIME BEING.
MAGGIE IS GOING TO BE A TEACHER, IT'LL BE GOOD TO HAVE TWO OF THOSE. ROSITA IS GOING TO WORK WITH THE DOCTORS AND TRAIN WITH THEM. EUGENE IS GOING TO BE A COMMUNITY PLANNER. GABRIEL... WE'LL HAVE A CHURCH IN A MATTER OF DAYS.
I'M TORN ON *MICHONNE.* SHE WAS A LAWYER--AND I UNDERSTAND SHE'S TOUGH AS NAILS.
...PUTTING IT *MILDLY.*
RIGHT. SO WHILE I DON'T THINK WE NEED A LAWYER PER SE--I THINK YOU COULD PROBABLY USE HELP AS CONSTABLE, AND SHE'D BE MUSCLE--AND BRAINS AS FAR AS UPHOLDING THE LAW GOES.
THAT SOUND GOOD TO YOU?
THAT SOUNDS PERFECT.

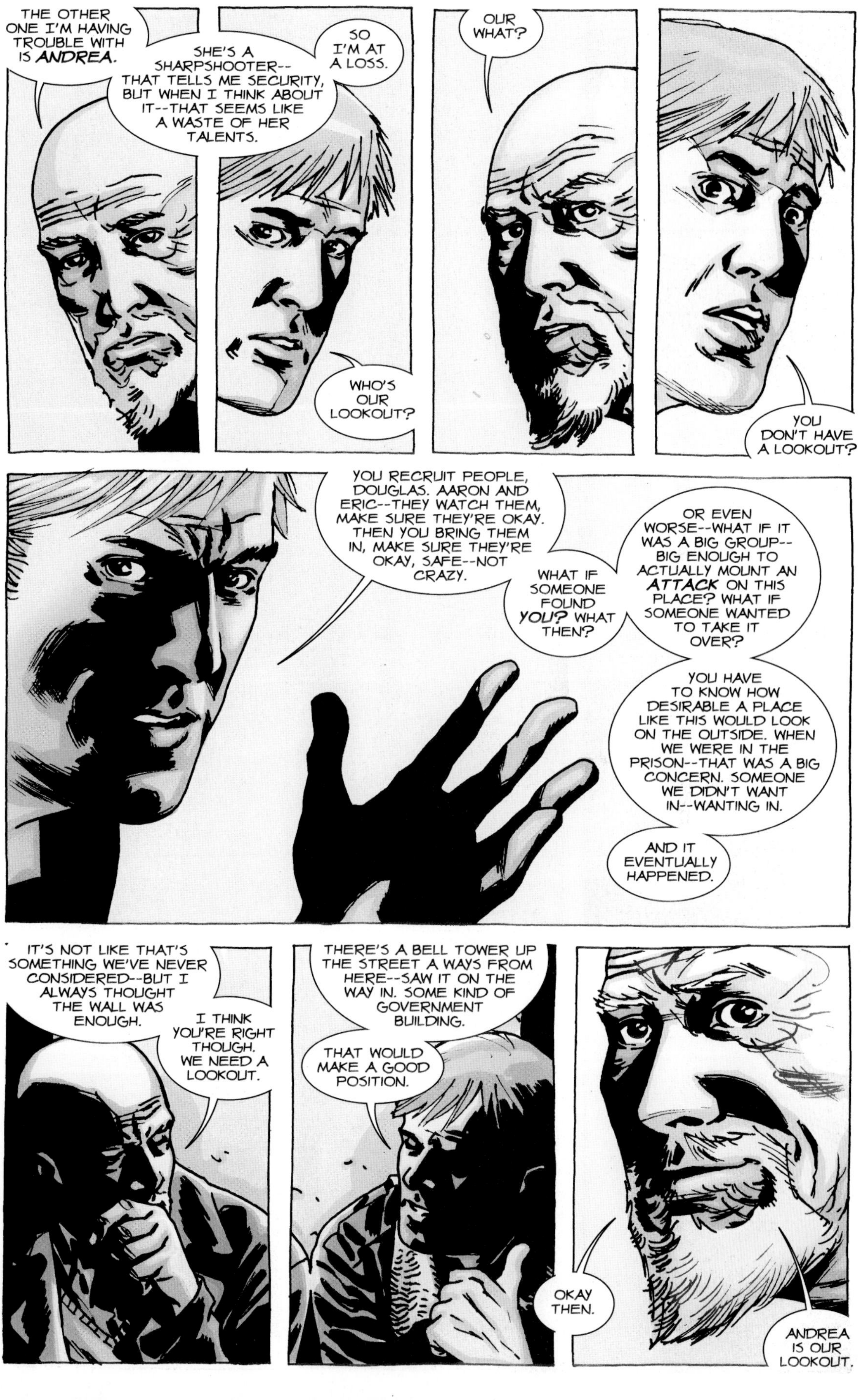
THE OTHER ONE I'M HAVING TROUBLE WITH IS ANDREA.
SHE'S A SHARPSHOOTER-- THAT TELLS ME SECURITY, BUT WHEN I THINK ABOUT IT--THAT SEEMS LIKE A WASTE OF HER TALENTS.
SO I'M AT A LOSS.
WHO'S OUR LOOKOUT?
OUR WHAT?
YOU DON'T HAVE A LOOKOUT?
YOU RECRUIT PEOPLE, DOUGLAS. AARON AND ERIC--THEY WATCH THEM, MAKE SURE THEY'RE OKAY. THEN YOU BRING THEM IN, MAKE SURE THEY'RE OKAY, SAFE--NOT CRAZY.
WHAT IF SOMEONE FOUND YOU? WHAT THEN?
OR EVEN WORSE--WHAT IF IT WAS A BIG GROUP-- BIG ENOUGH TO ACTUALLY MOUNT AN ATTACK ON THIS PLACE? WHAT IF SOMEONE WANTED TO TAKE IT OVER?
YOU HAVE TO KNOW HOW DESIRABLE A PLACE LIKE THIS WOULD LOOK ON THE OUTSIDE. WHEN WE WERE IN THE PRISON--THAT WAS A BIG CONCERN. SOMEONE WE DIDN'T WANT IN--WANTING IN.
AND IT EVENTUALLY HAPPENED.
IT'S NOT LIKE THAT'S SOMETHING WE'VE NEVER CONSIDERED--BUT I ALWAYS THOUGHT THE WALL WAS ENOUGH.
I THINK YOU'RE RIGHT THOUGH. WE NEED A LOOKOUT.
THERE'S A BELL TOWER UP THE STREET A WAYS FROM HERE--SAW IT ON THE WAY IN. SOME KIND OF GOVERNMENT BUILDING.
THAT WOULD MAKE A GOOD POSITION.
OKAY THEN.
ANDREA IS OUR LOOKOUT.

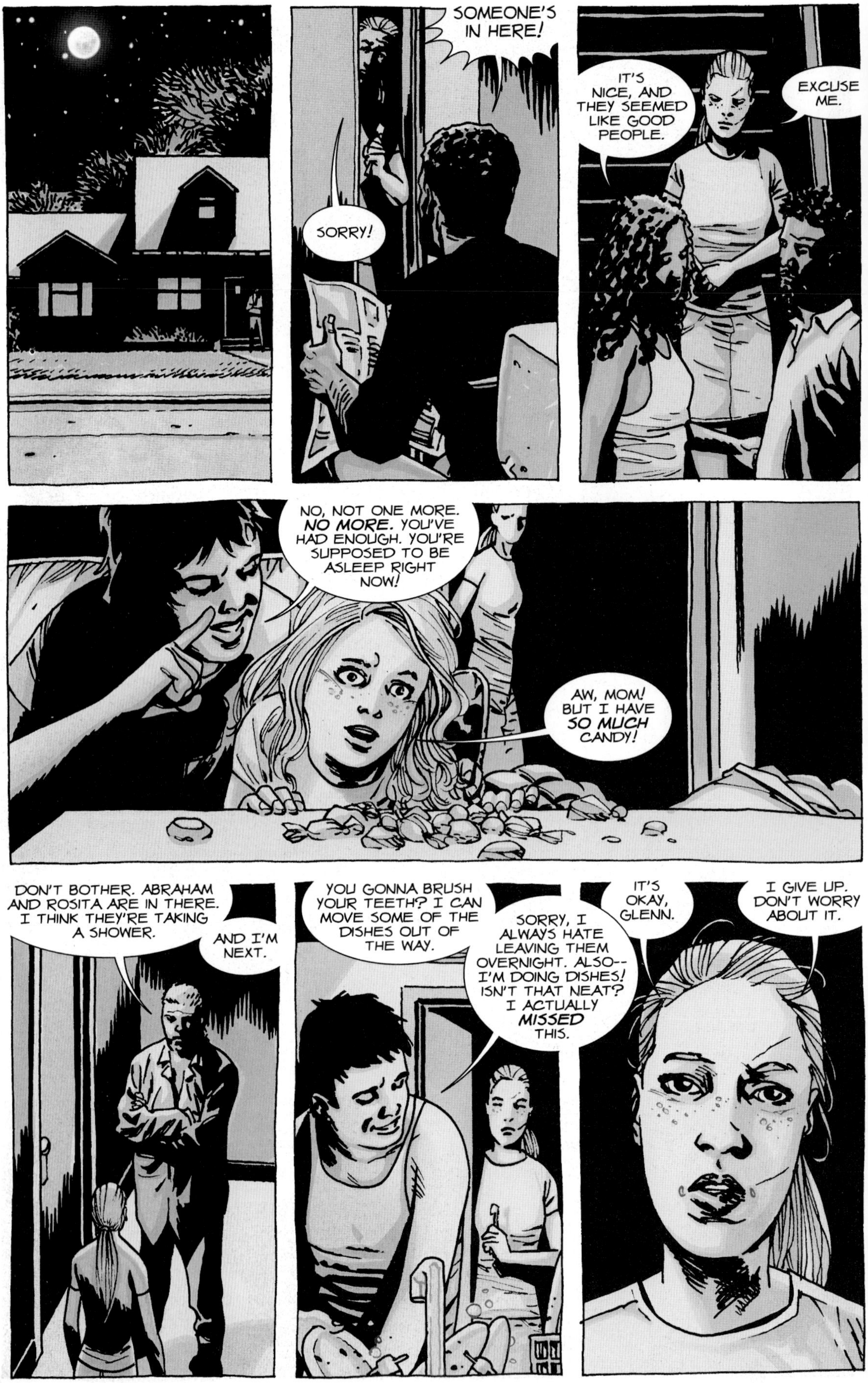
SOMEONE'S IN HERE!
SORRY!
IT'S NICE, AND THEY SEEMED LIKE GOOD PEOPLE.
EXCUSE ME.
NO, NOT ONE MORE. NO MORE. YOU'VE HAD ENOUGH. YOU'RE SUPPOSED TO BE ASLEEP RIGHT NOW!
AW, MOM! BUT I HAVE SO MUCH CANDY!
DON'T BOTHER. ABRAHAM AND ROSITA ARE IN THERE. I THINK THEY'RE TAKING A SHOWER.
AND I'M NEXT.
YOU GONNA BRUSH YOUR TEETH? I CAN MOVE SOME OF THE DISHES OUT OF THE WAY.
SORRY, I ALWAYS HATE LEAVING THEM OVERNIGHT. ALSO-- I'M DOING DISHES! ISN'T THAT NEAT? I ACTUALLY MISSED THIS.
IT'S OKAY, GLENN.
I GIVE UP. DON'T WORRY ABOUT IT.

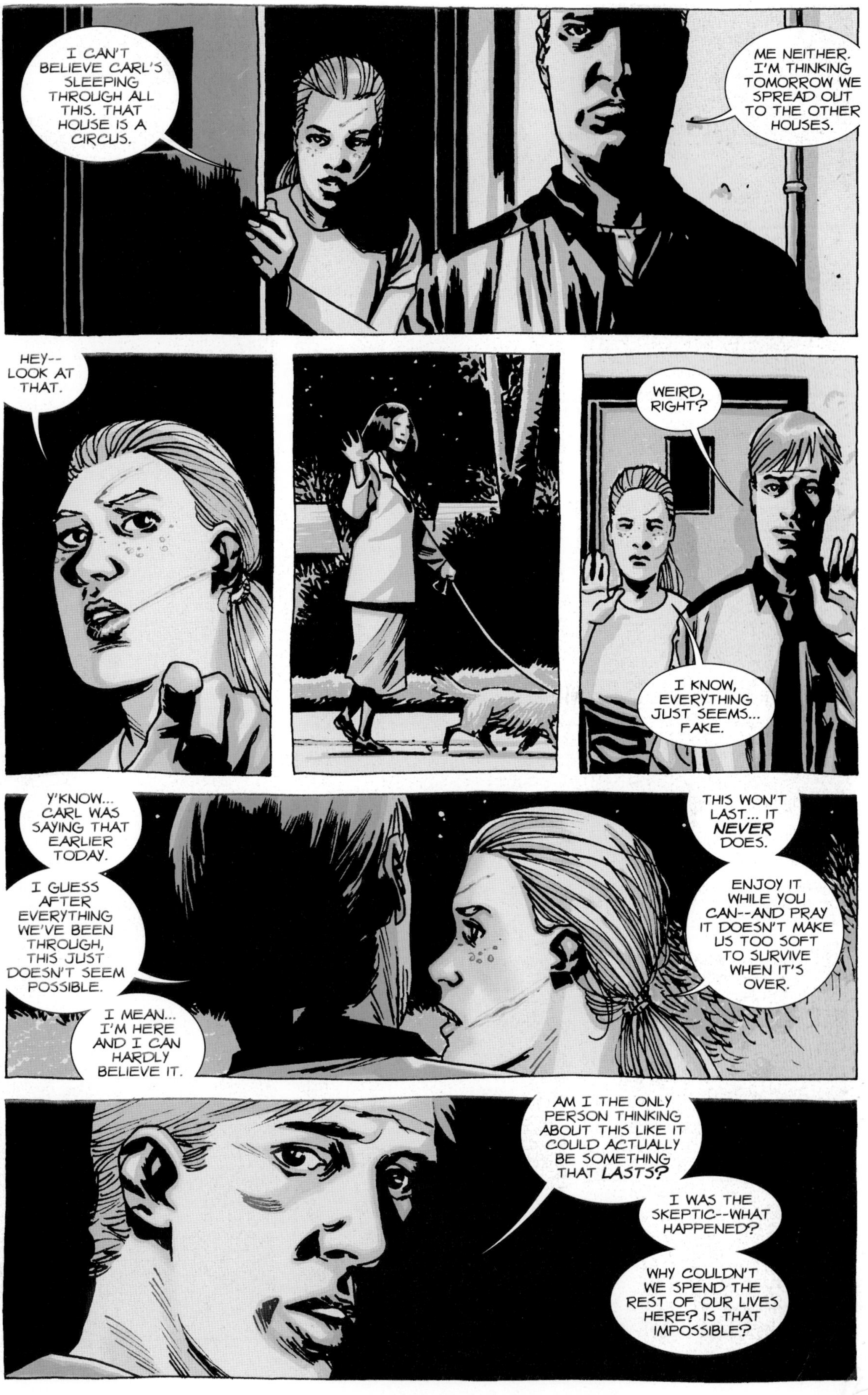
I CAN'T BELIEVE CARL'S SLEEPING THROUGH ALL THIS. THAT HOUSE IS A CIRCUS.
ME NEITHER. I'M THINKING TOMORROW WE SPREAD OUT TO THE OTHER HOUSES.
HEY-- LOOK AT THAT.
WEIRD, RIGHT?
I KNOW, EVERYTHING JUST SEEMS... FAKE.
Y'KNOW... CARL WAS SAYING THAT EARLIER TODAY.
I GUESS AFTER EVERYTHING WE'VE BEEN THROUGH, THIS JUST DOESN'T SEEM POSSIBLE.
I MEAN... I'M HERE AND I CAN HARDLY BELIEVE IT.
THIS WON'T LAST... IT NEVER DOES.
ENJOY IT WHILE YOU CAN--AND PRAY IT DOESN'T MAKE US TOO SOFT TO SURVIVE WHEN IT'S OVER.
AM I THE ONLY PERSON THINKING ABOUT THIS LIKE IT COULD ACTUALLY BE SOMETHING THAT LASTS?
I WAS THE SKEPTIC--WHAT HAPPENED?
WHY COULDN'T WE SPEND THE REST OF OUR LIVES HERE? IS THAT IMPOSSIBLE?

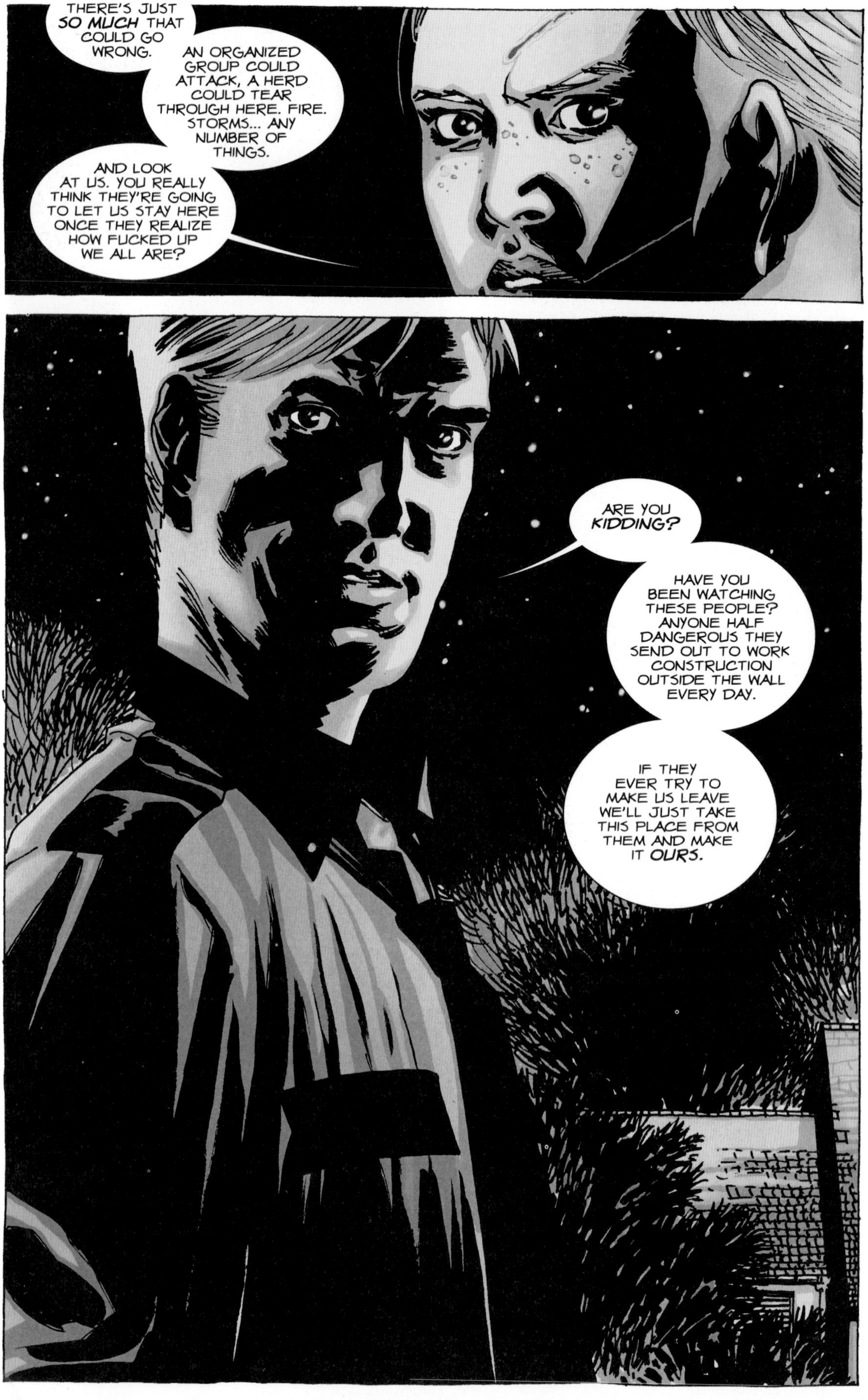
THERE'S JUST SO MUCH THAT COULD GO WRONG.
AN ORGANIZED GROUP COULD ATTACK, A HERD COULD TEAR THROUGH HERE. FIRE. STORMS... ANY NUMBER OF THINGS.
AND LOOK AT US. YOU REALLY THINK THEY'RE GOING TO LET US STAY HERE ONCE THEY REALIZE HOW FUCKED UP WE ALL ARE?
ARE YOU KIDDING?
HAVE YOU BEEN WATCHING THESE PEOPLE? ANYONE HALF DANGEROUS THEY SEND OUT TO WORK CONSTRUCTION OUTSIDE THE WALL EVERY DAY.
IF THEY EVER TRY TO MAKE US LEAVE WE'LL JUST TAKE THIS PLACE FROM THEM AND MAKE IT OURS.

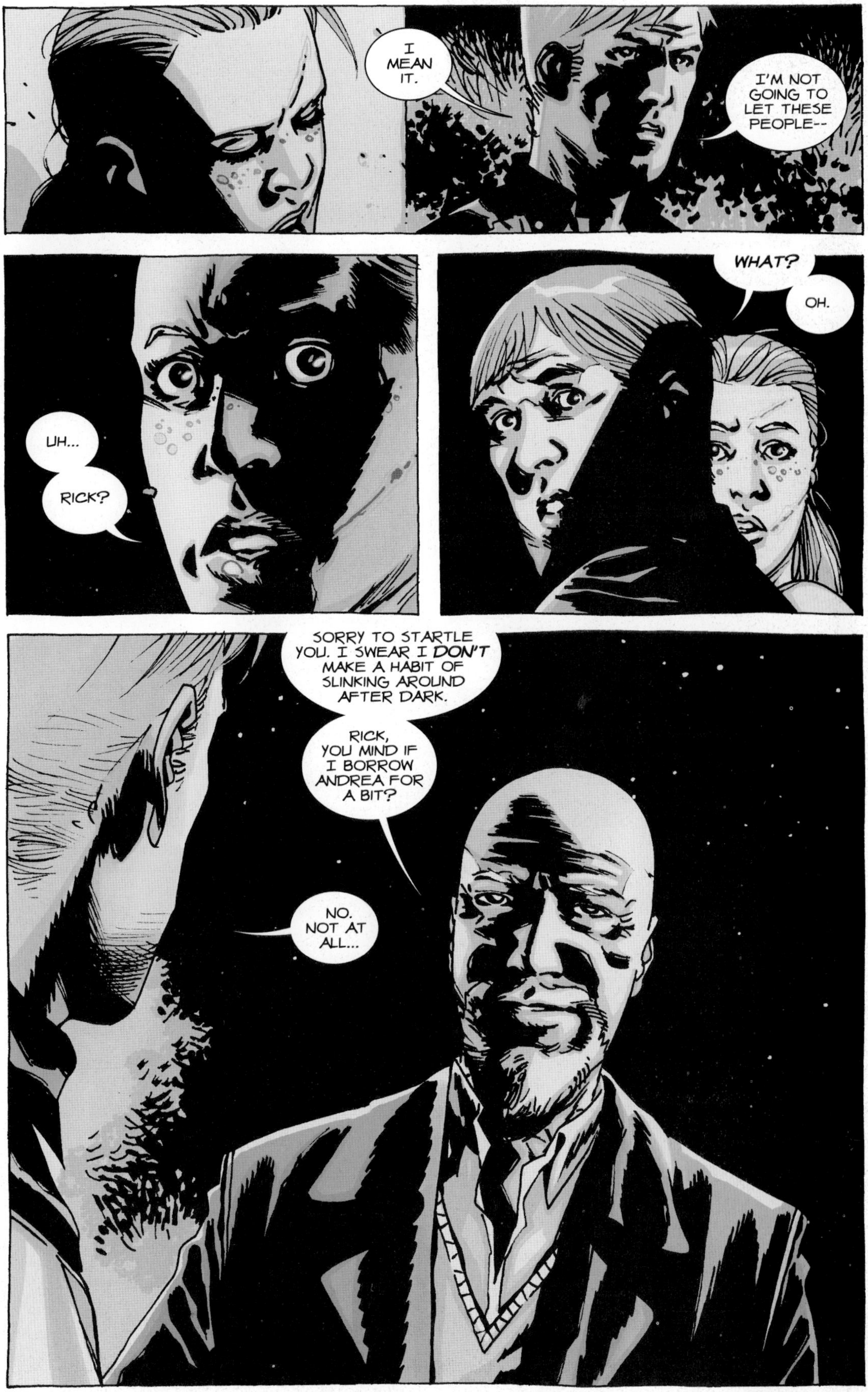
I MEAN IT.
I'M NOT GOING TO LET THESE PEOPLE--
UH...
RICK?
WHAT?
OH.
SORRY TO STARTLE YOU. I SWEAR I DON'T MAKE A HABIT OF SLINKING AROUND AFTER DARK.
RICK, YOU MIND IF I BORROW ANDREA FOR A BIT?
NO. NOT AT ALL...

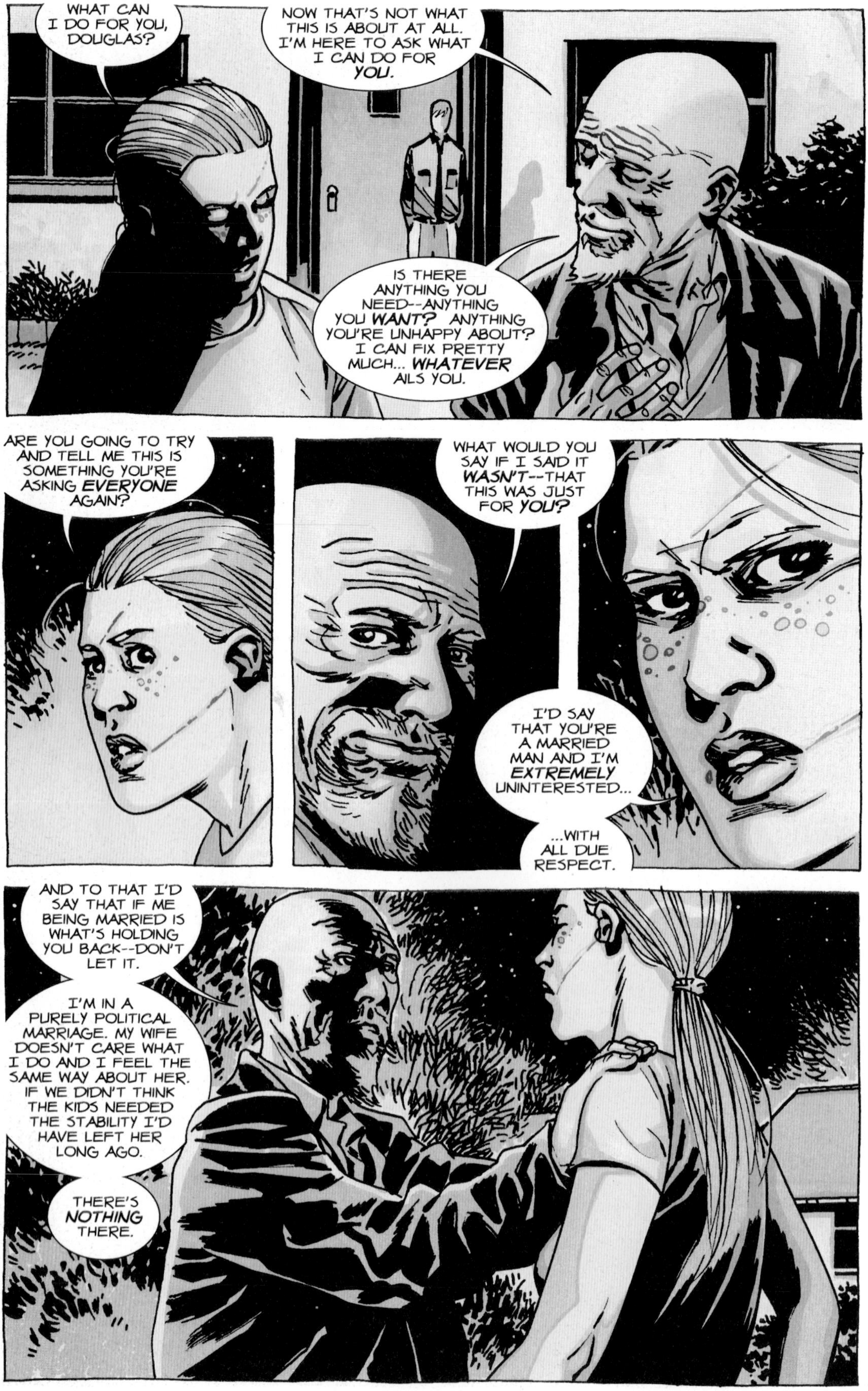
WHAT CAN I DO FOR YOU, DOUGLAS?
NOW THAT'S NOT WHAT THIS IS ABOUT AT ALL. I'M HERE TO ASK WHAT I CAN DO FOR YOU.
IS THERE ANYTHING YOU NEED--ANYTHING YOU WANT? ANYTHING YOU'RE UNHAPPY ABOUT? I CAN FIX PRETTY MUCH... WHATEVER AILS YOU.
ARE YOU GOING TO TRY AND TELL ME THIS IS SOMETHING YOU'RE ASKING EVERYONE AGAIN?
WHAT WOULD YOU SAY IF I SAID IT WASN'T--THAT THIS WAS JUST FOR YOU?
I'D SAY THAT YOU'RE A MARRIED MAN AND I'M EXTREMELY UNINTERESTED...
...WITH ALL DUE RESPECT.
AND TO THAT I'D SAY THAT IF ME BEING MARRIED IS WHAT'S HOLDING YOU BACK--DON'T LET IT.
I'M IN A PURELY POLITICAL MARRIAGE. MY WIFE DOESN'T CARE WHAT I DO AND I FEEL THE SAME WAY ABOUT HER. IF WE DIDN'T THINK THE KIDS NEEDED THE STABILITY I'D HAVE LEFT HER LONG AGO.
THERE'S NOTHING THERE.

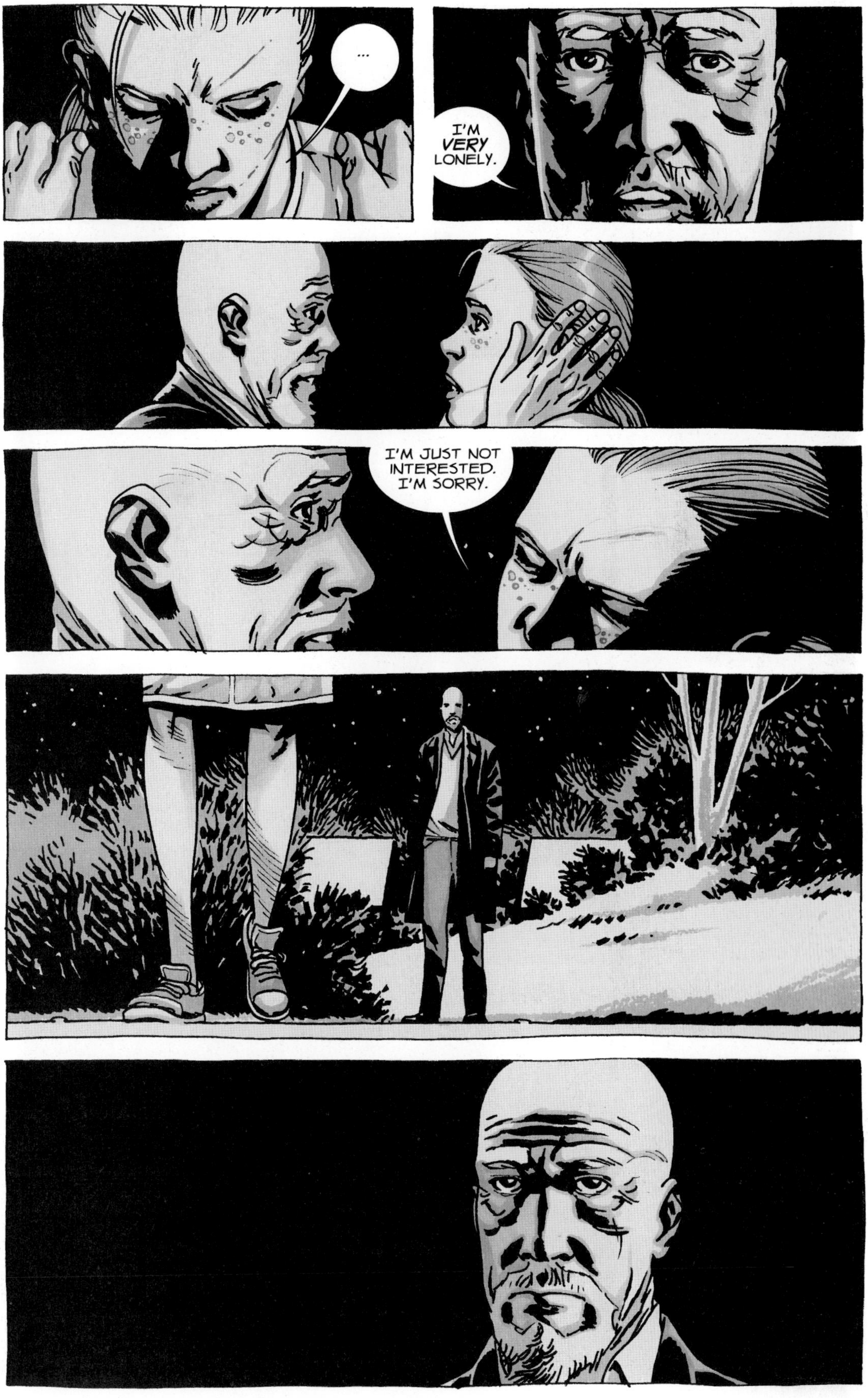

...
I'M VERY LONELY.
I'M JUST NOT INTERESTED. I'M SORRY.

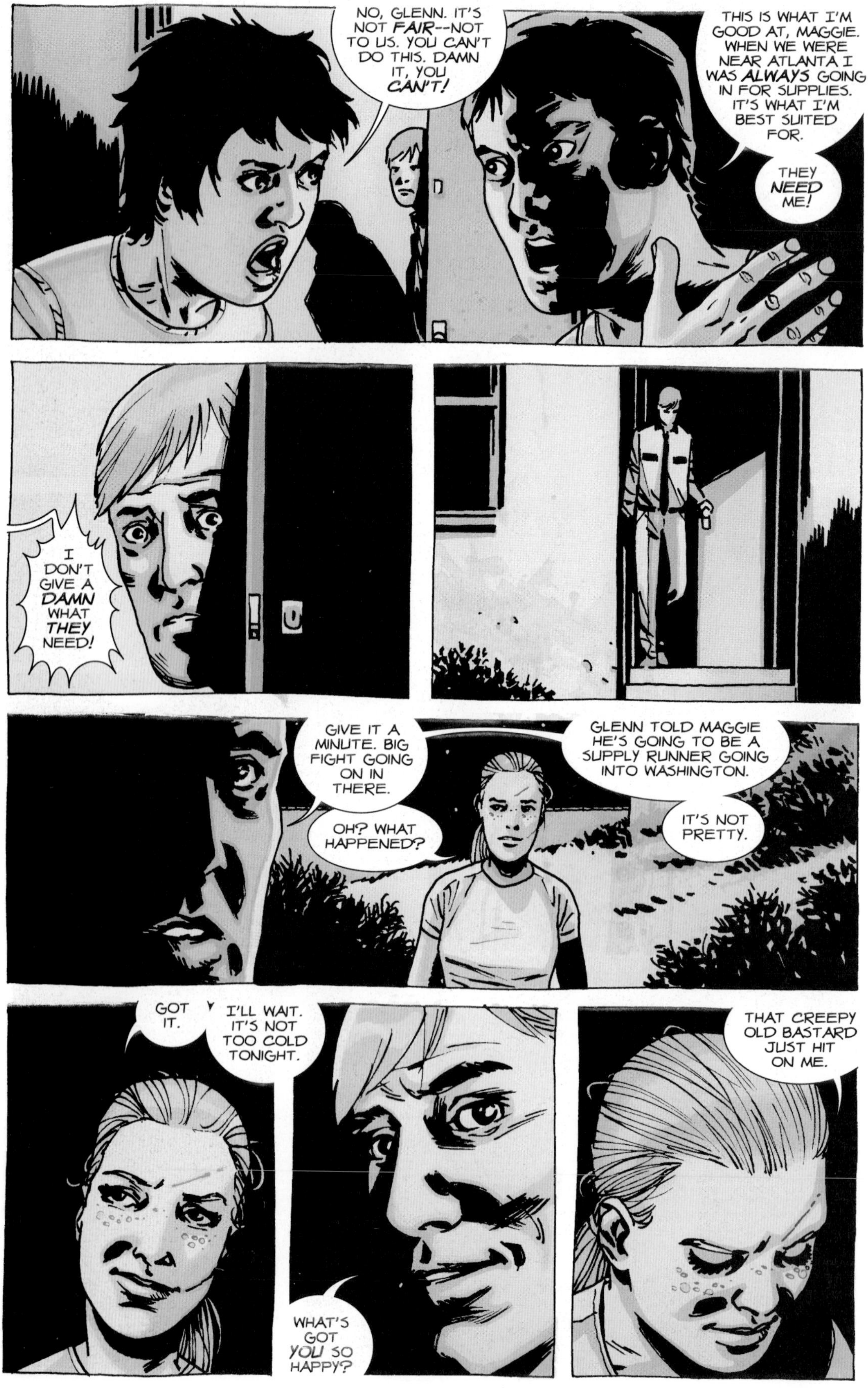
NO, GLENN. IT'S NOT FAIR--NOT TO US. YOU CAN'T DO THIS. DAMN IT, YOU CAN'T!
THIS IS WHAT I'M GOOD AT, MAGGIE. WHEN WE WERE NEAR ATLANTA I WAS ALWAYS GOING IN FOR SUPPLIES. IT'S WHAT I'M BEST SUITED FOR.
THEY NEED ME!
I DON'T GIVE A DAMN WHAT THEY NEED!
GIVE IT A MINUTE. BIG FIGHT GOING ON IN THERE.
OH? WHAT HAPPENED?
GLENN TOLD MAGGIE HE'S GOING TO BE A SUPPLY RUNNER GOING INTO WASHINGTON.
IT'S NOT PRETTY.
GOT IT.
I'LL WAIT. IT'S NOT TOO COLD TONIGHT.
WHAT'S GOT YOU SO HAPPY?
THAT CREEPY OLD BASTARD JUST HIT ON ME.

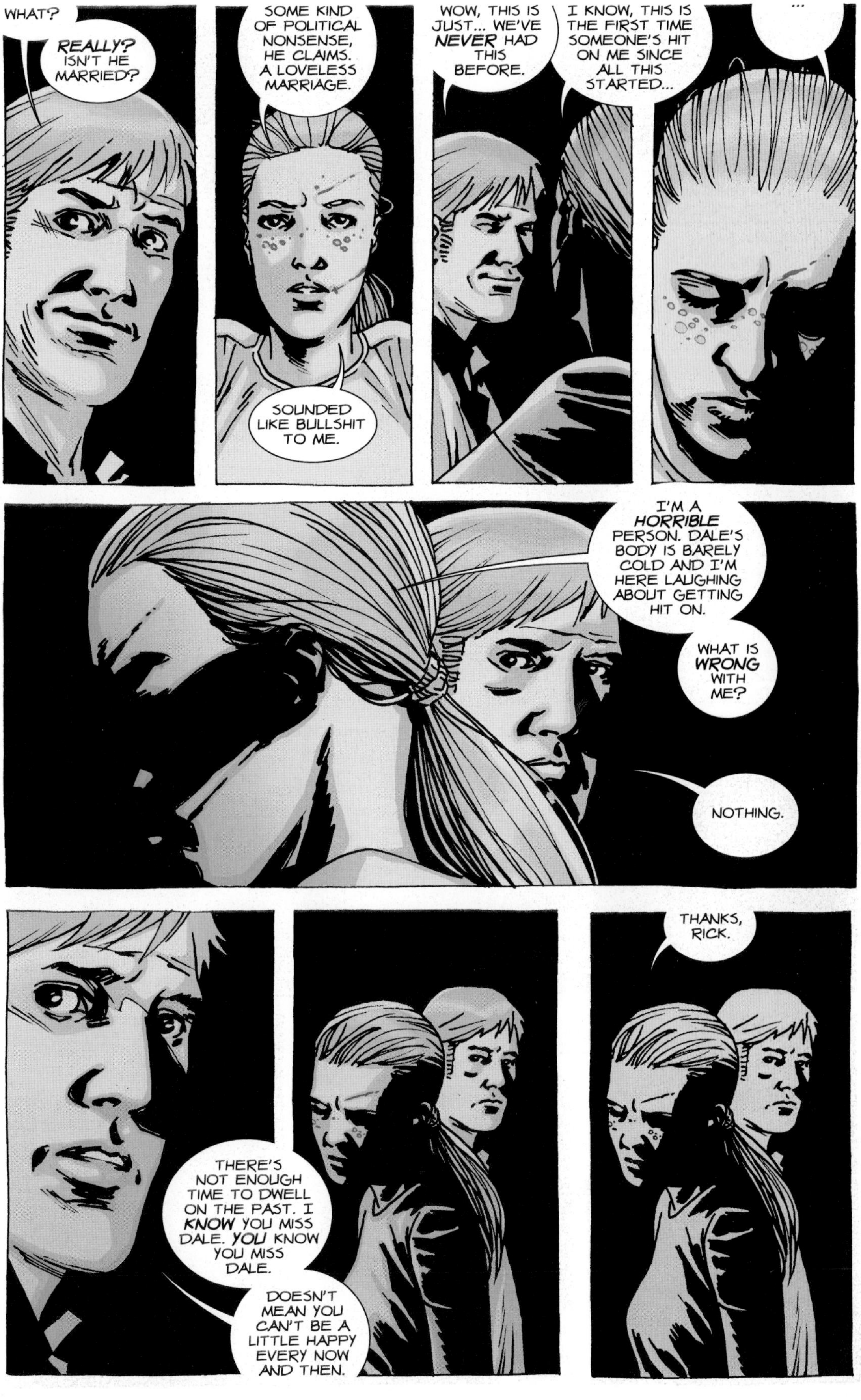
WHAT?
REALLY? ISN'T HE MARRIED?
SOME KIND OF POLITICAL NONSENSE, HE CLAIMS. A LOVELESS MARRIAGE.
SOUNDED LIKE BULLSHIT TO ME.
WOW, THIS IS JUST... WE'VE NEVER HAD THIS BEFORE.
I KNOW, THIS IS THE FIRST TIME SOMEONE'S HIT ON ME SINCE ALL THIS STARTED...
...
I'M A HORRIBLE PERSON. DALE'S BODY IS BARELY COLD AND I'M HERE LAUGHING ABOUT GETTING HIT ON.
WHAT IS WRONG WITH ME?
NOTHING.
THERE'S NOT ENOUGH TIME TO DWELL ON THE PAST. I KNOW YOU MISS DALE. YOU KNOW YOU MISS DALE.
DOESN'T MEAN YOU CAN'T BE A LITTLE HAPPY EVERY NOW AND THEN.
THANKS, RICK.

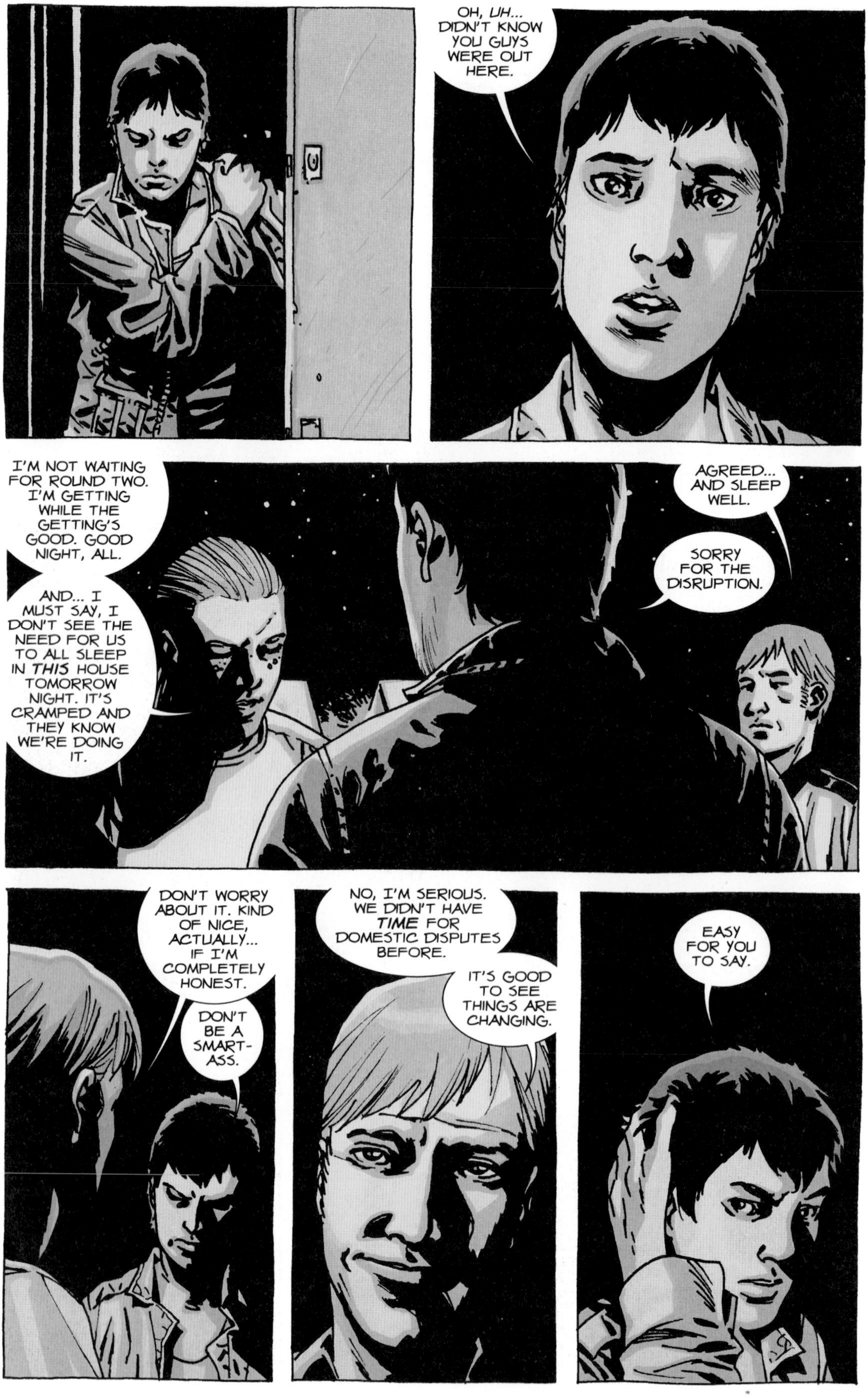
OH, UH... DIDN'T KNOW YOU GUYS WERE OUT HERE.
I'M NOT WAITING FOR ROUND TWO. I'M GETTING WHILE THE GETTING'S GOOD. GOOD NIGHT, ALL.
AND... I MUST SAY, I DON'T SEE THE NEED FOR US TO ALL SLEEP IN THIS HOUSE TOMORROW NIGHT. IT'S CRAMPED AND THEY KNOW WE'RE DOING IT.
AGREED... AND SLEEP WELL.
SORRY FOR THE DISRUPTION.
DON'T WORRY ABOUT IT. KIND OF NICE, ACTUALLY... IF I'M COMPLETELY HONEST.
DON'T BE A SMART-ASS.
NO, I'M SERIOUS. WE DIDN'T HAVE TIME FOR DOMESTIC DISPUTES BEFORE.
IT'S GOOD TO SEE THINGS ARE CHANGING.
EASY FOR YOU TO SAY.

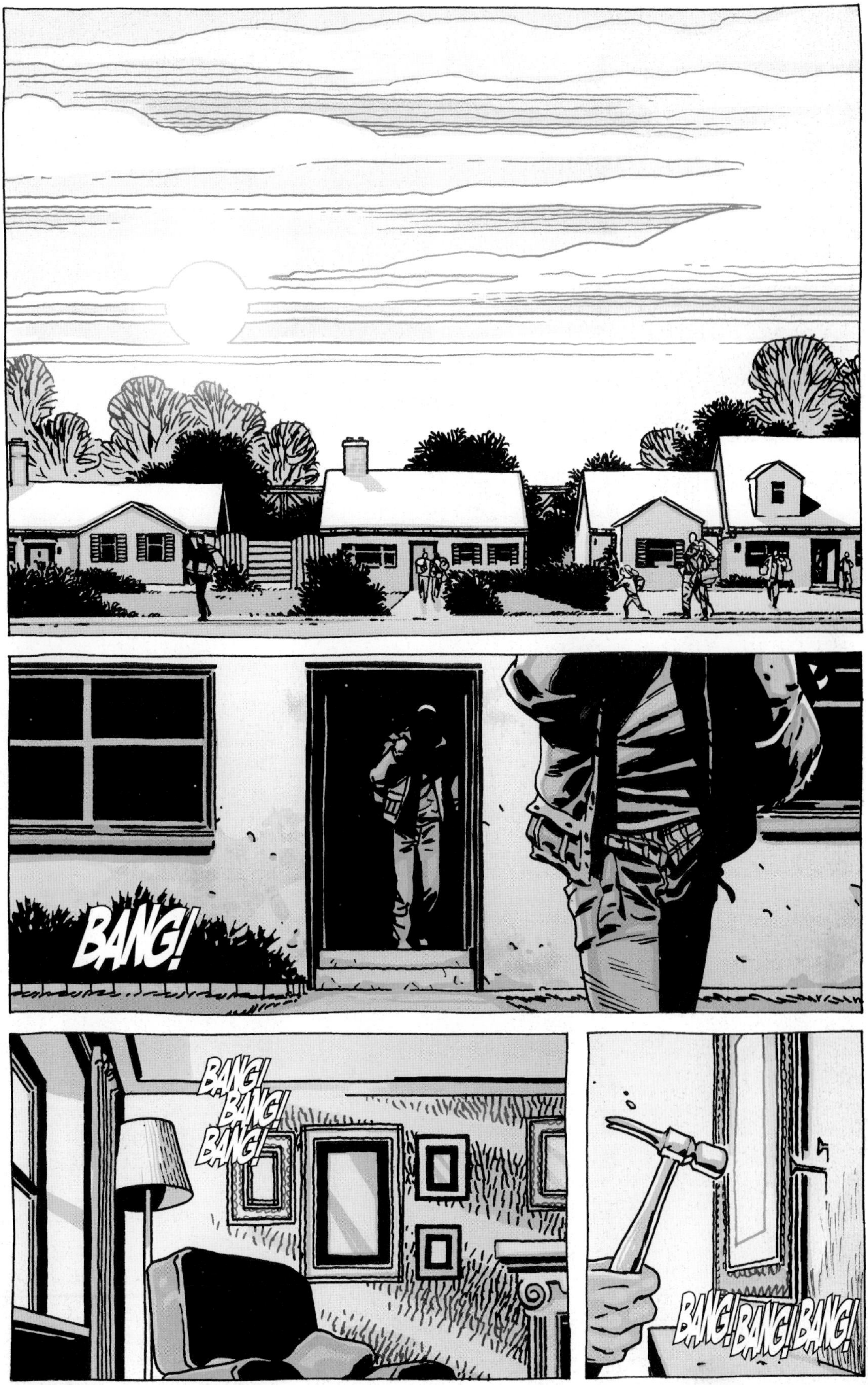
BANG!
BANG!
BANG!
BANG!
BANG! BANG! BANG!

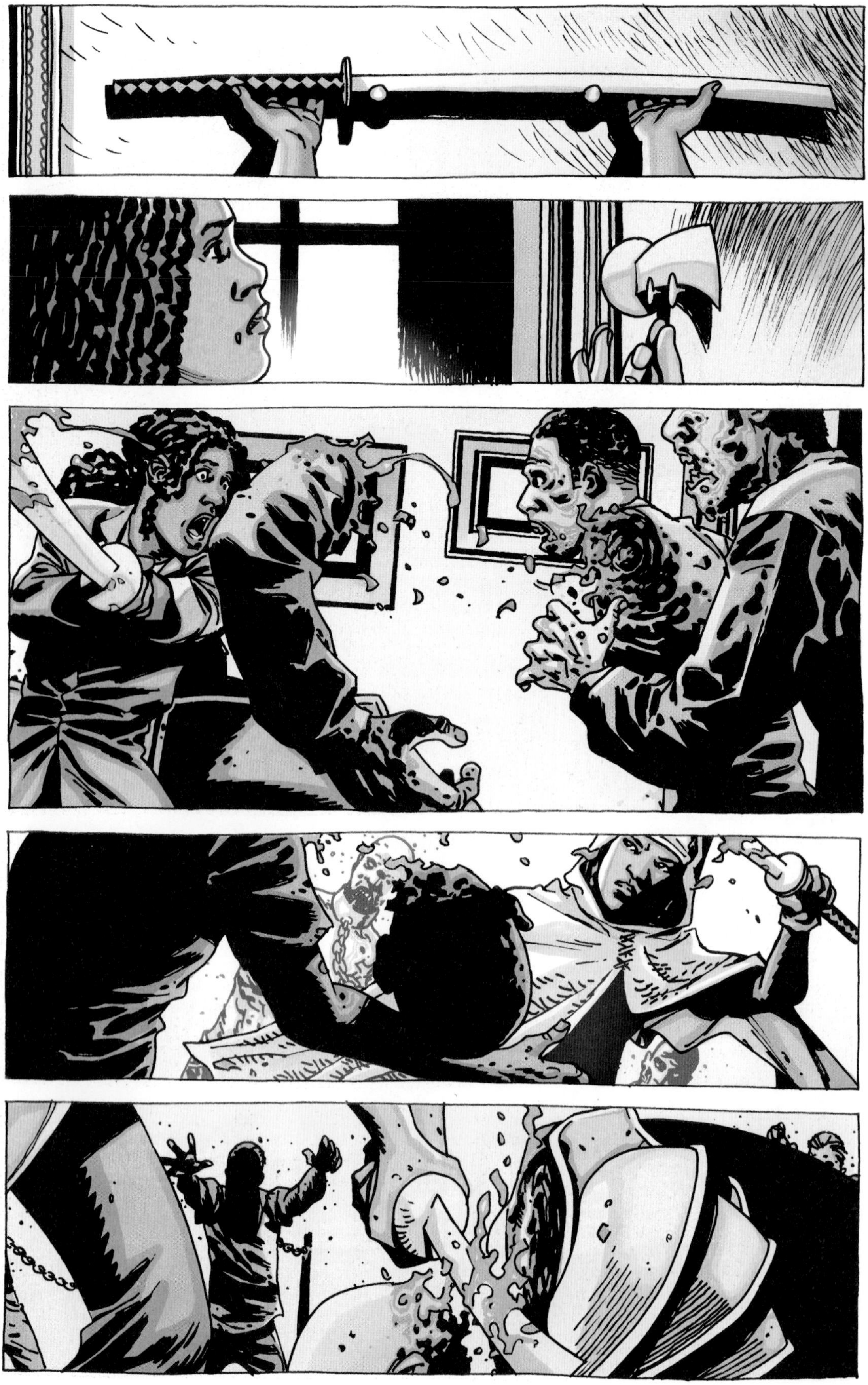

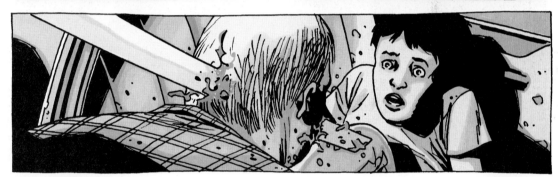

I'M THROUGH WITH YOU.

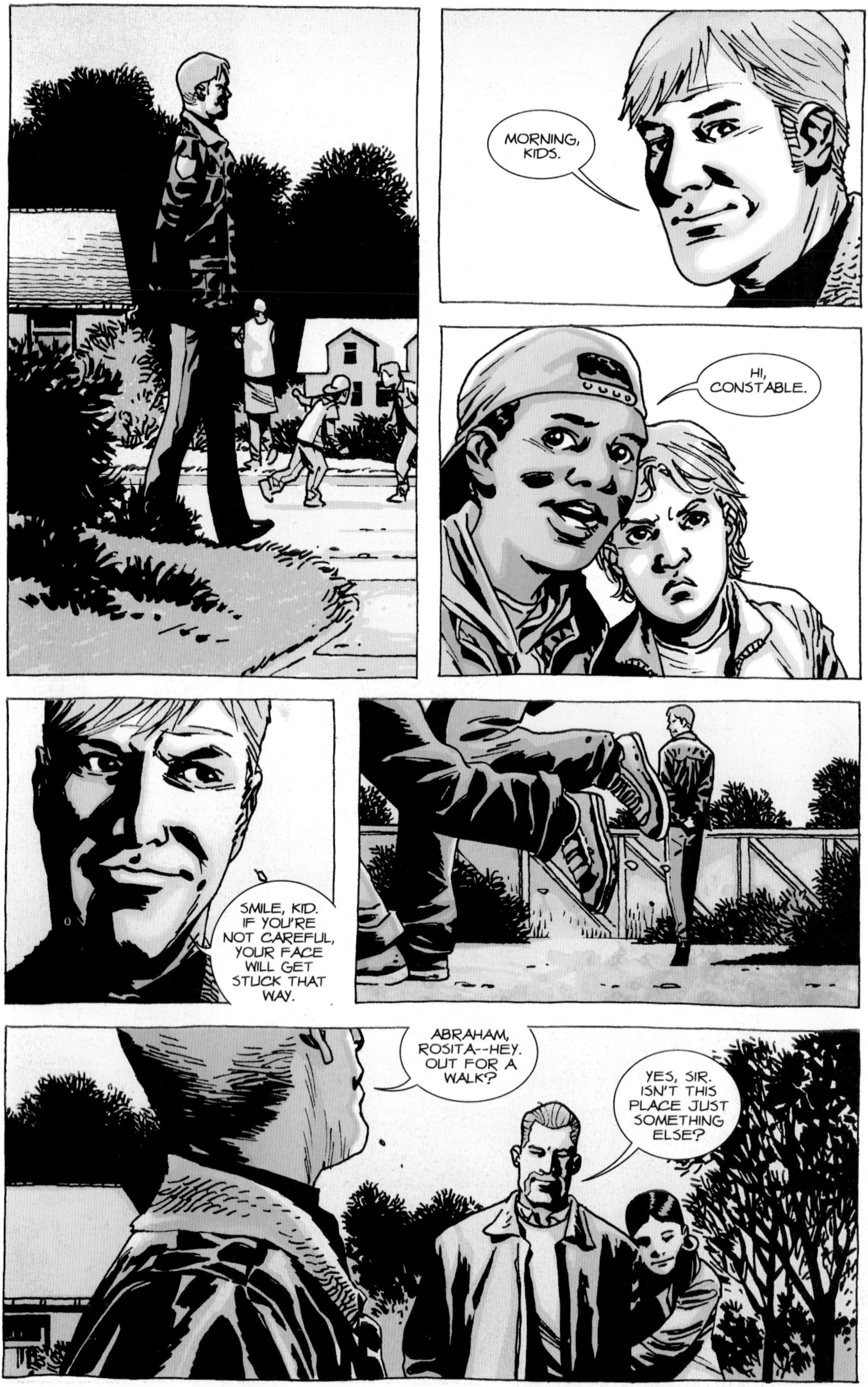

MORNING, KIDS.
HI, CONSTABLE.
SMILE, KID. IF YOU'RE NOT CAREFUL, YOUR FACE WILL GET STUCK THAT WAY.
ABRAHAM, ROSITA--HEY. OUT FOR A WALK?
YES, SIR. ISN'T THIS PLACE JUST SOMETHING ELSE?

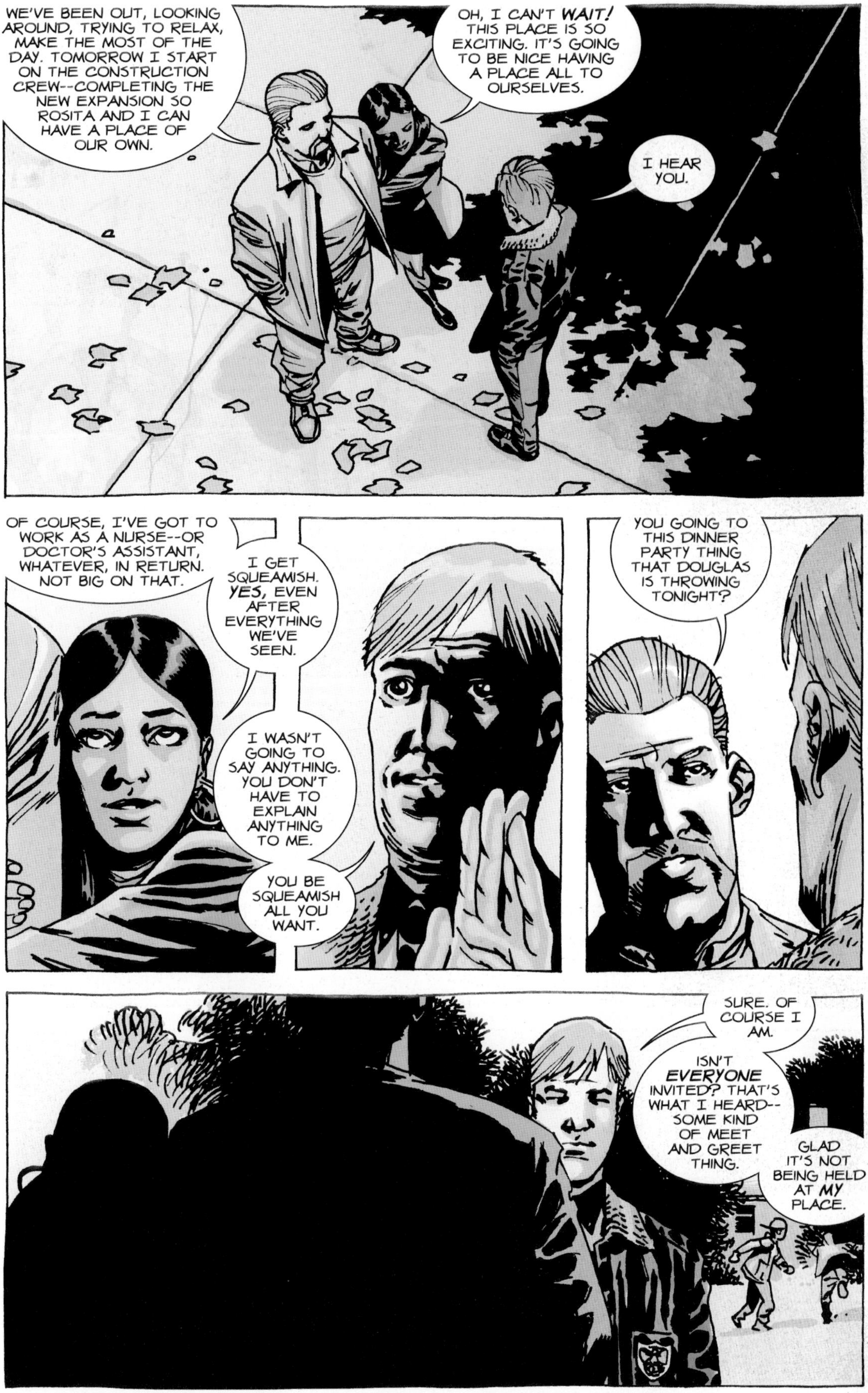
WE'VE BEEN OUT, LOOKING AROUND, TRYING TO RELAX, MAKE THE MOST OF THE DAY. TOMORROW I START ON THE CONSTRUCTION CREW--COMPLETING THE NEW EXPANSION SO ROSITA AND I CAN HAVE A PLACE OF OUR OWN.
OH, I CAN'T *WAIT!* THIS PLACE IS SO EXCITING. IT'S GOING TO BE NICE HAVING A PLACE ALL TO OURSELVES.
I HEAR YOU.
OF COURSE, I'VE GOT TO WORK AS A NURSE--OR DOCTOR'S ASSISTANT, WHATEVER, IN RETURN. NOT BIG ON THAT.
I GET SQUEAMISH. *YES,* EVEN AFTER EVERYTHING WE'VE SEEN.
I WASN'T GOING TO SAY ANYTHING. YOU DON'T HAVE TO EXPLAIN ANYTHING TO ME.
YOU BE SQUEAMISH ALL YOU WANT.
YOU GOING TO THIS DINNER PARTY THING THAT DOUGLAS IS THROWING TONIGHT?
SURE. OF COURSE I AM.
ISN'T *EVERYONE* INVITED? THAT'S WHAT I HEARD-- SOME KIND OF MEET AND GREET THING.
GLAD IT'S NOT BEING HELD AT *MY* PLACE.

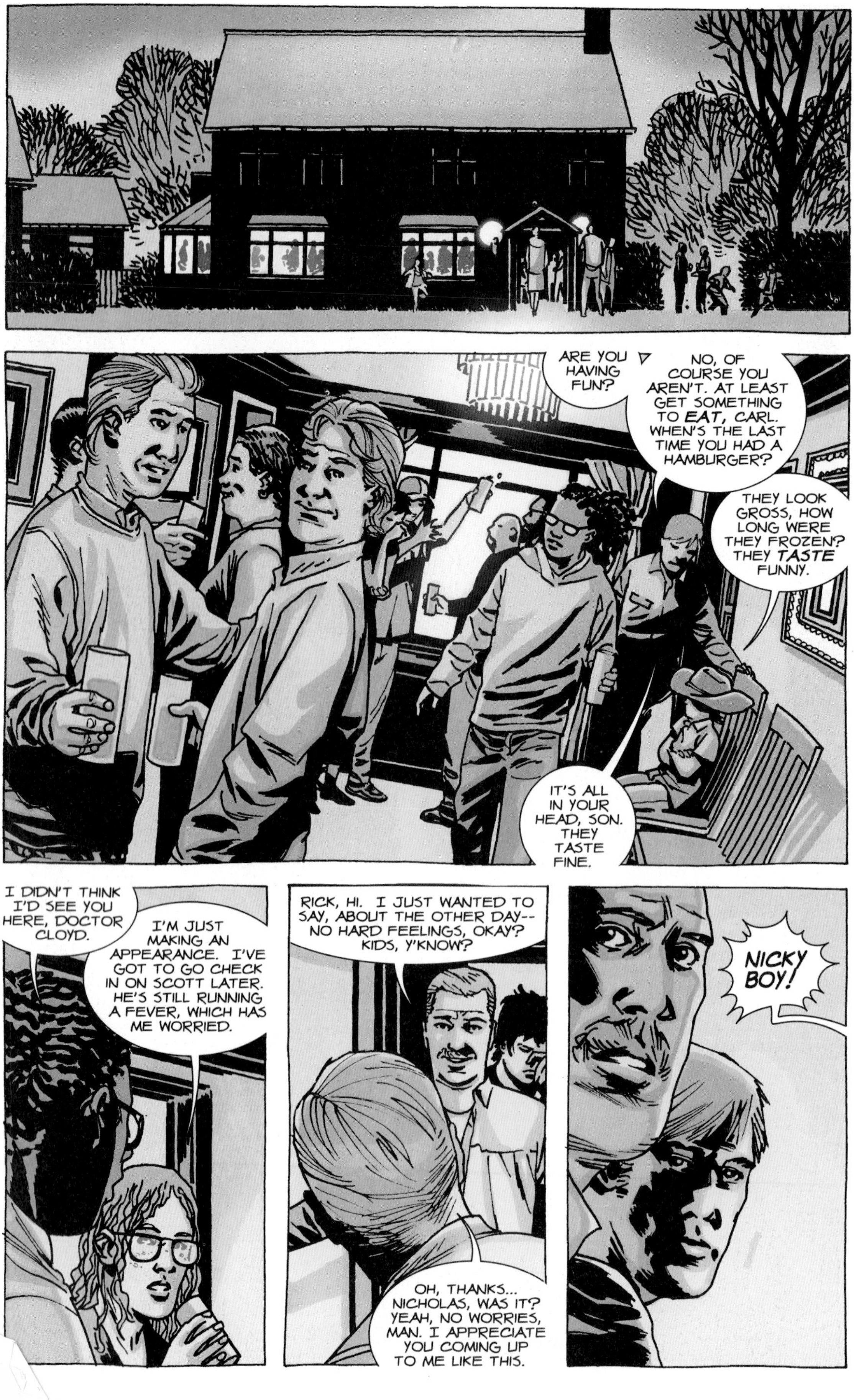

ARE YOU HAVING FUN?
NO, OF COURSE YOU AREN'T. AT LEAST GET SOMETHING TO EAT, CARL. WHEN'S THE LAST TIME YOU HAD A HAMBURGER?
THEY LOOK GROSS, HOW LONG WERE THEY FROZEN? THEY TASTE FUNNY.
IT'S ALL IN YOUR HEAD, SON. THEY TASTE FINE.
I DIDN'T THINK I'D SEE YOU HERE, DOCTOR CLOYD.
I'M JUST MAKING AN APPEARANCE. I'VE GOT TO GO CHECK IN ON SCOTT LATER. HE'S STILL RUNNING A FEVER, WHICH HAS ME WORRIED.
RICK, HI. I JUST WANTED TO SAY, ABOUT THE OTHER DAY-- NO HARD FEELINGS, OKAY? KIDS, Y'KNOW?
OH, THANKS... NICHOLAS, WAS IT? YEAH, NO WORRIES, MAN. I APPRECIATE YOU COMING UP TO ME LIKE THIS.
NICKY BOY!

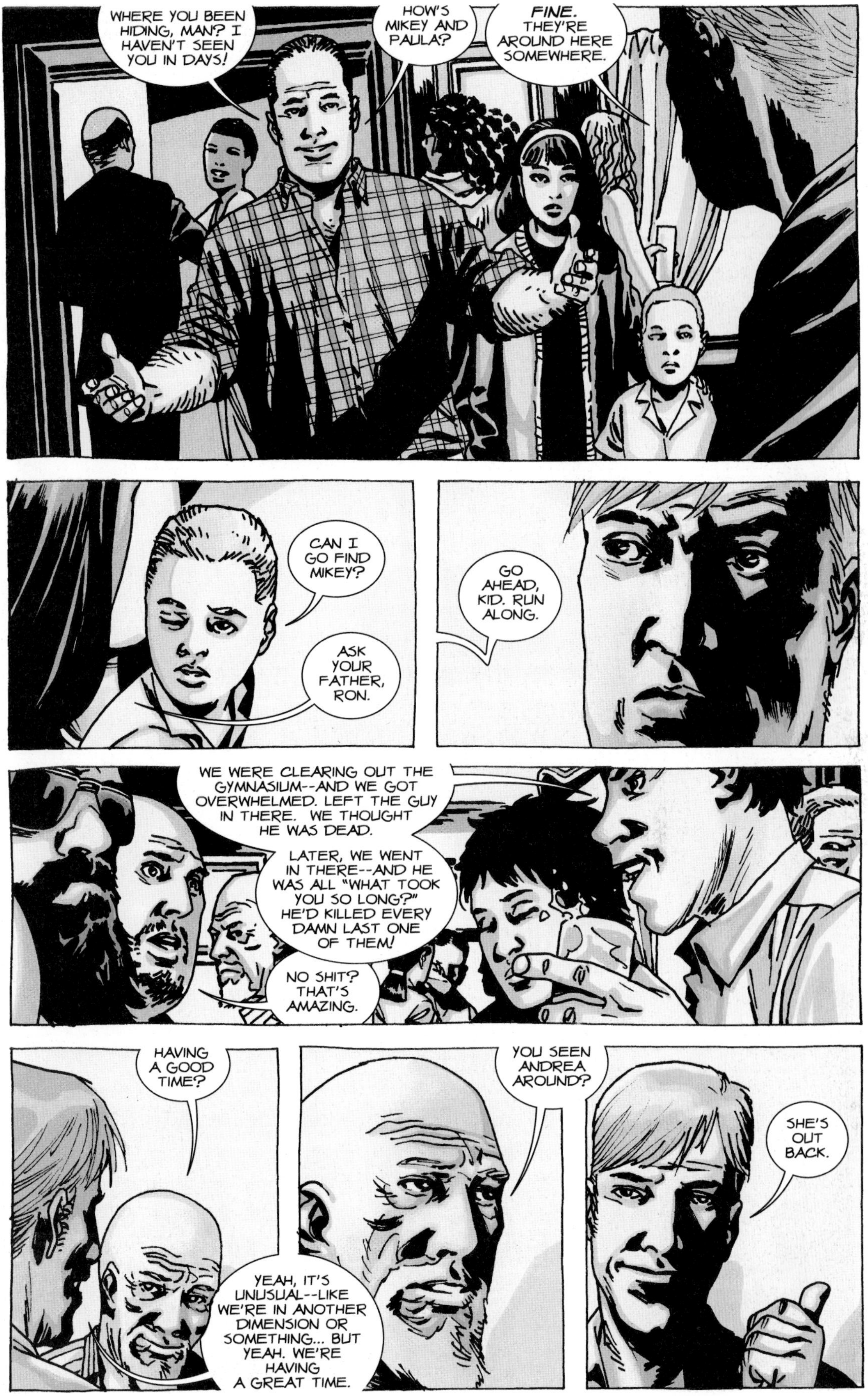

WHERE YOU BEEN HIDING, MAN? I HAVEN'T SEEN YOU IN DAYS!
HOW'S MIKEY AND PAULA?
FINE. THEY'RE AROUND HERE SOMEWHERE.
CAN I GO FIND MIKEY?
ASK YOUR FATHER, RON.
GO AHEAD, KID. RUN ALONG.
WE WERE CLEARING OUT THE GYMNASIUM--AND WE GOT OVERWHELMED. LEFT THE GUY IN THERE. WE THOUGHT HE WAS DEAD.
LATER, WE WENT IN THERE--AND HE WAS ALL "WHAT TOOK YOU SO LONG?" HE'D KILLED EVERY DAMN LAST ONE OF THEM!
NO SHIT? THAT'S AMAZING.
HAVING A GOOD TIME?
YEAH, IT'S UNUSUAL--LIKE WE'RE IN ANOTHER DIMENSION OR SOMETHING... BUT YEAH. WE'RE HAVING A GREAT TIME.
YOU SEEN ANDREA AROUND?
SHE'S OUT BACK.

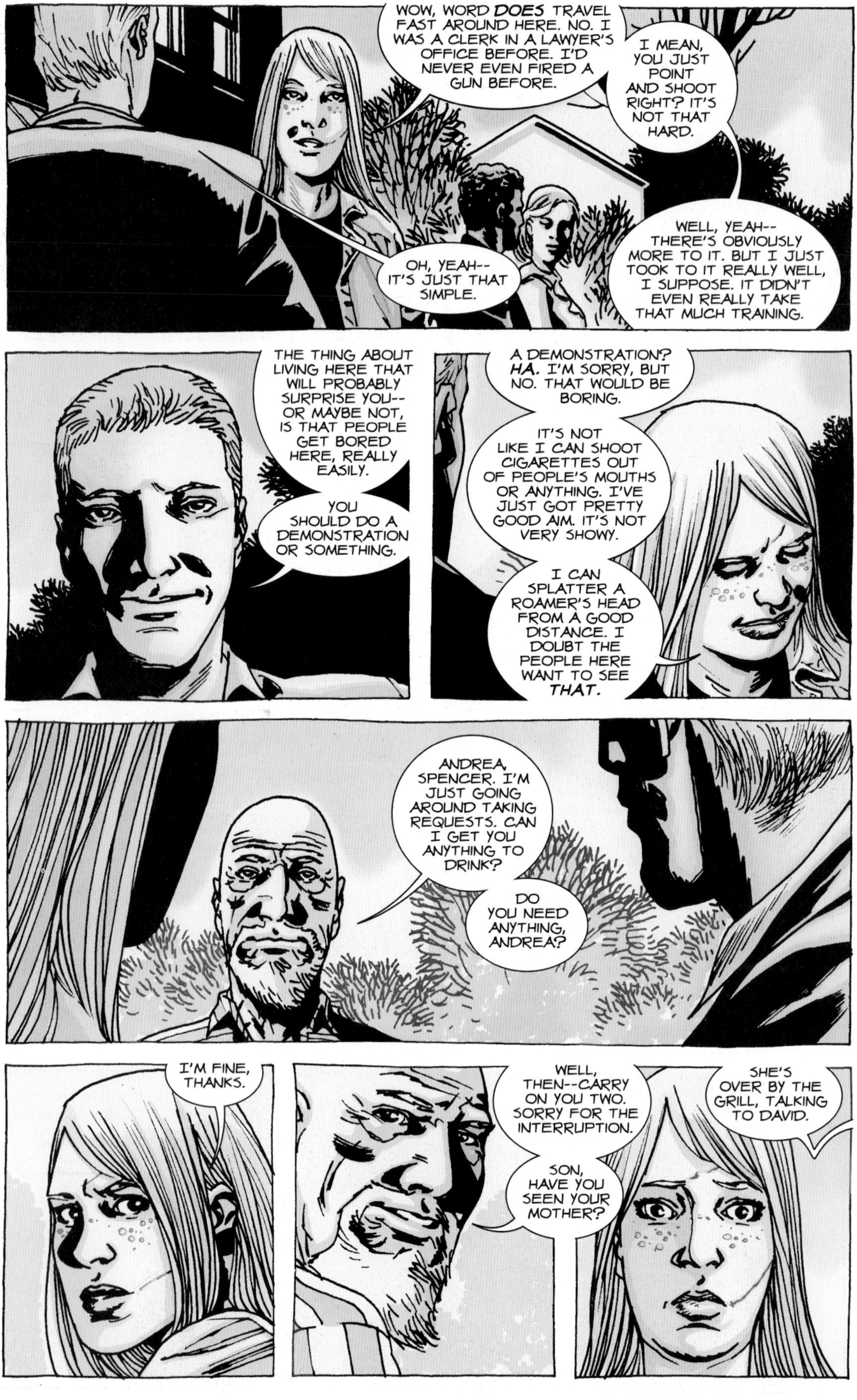
WOW, WORD DOES TRAVEL FAST AROUND HERE. NO. I WAS A CLERK IN A LAWYER'S OFFICE BEFORE. I'D NEVER EVEN FIRED A GUN BEFORE.
I MEAN, YOU JUST POINT AND SHOOT RIGHT? IT'S NOT THAT HARD.
OH, YEAH-- IT'S JUST THAT SIMPLE.
WELL, YEAH-- THERE'S OBVIOUSLY MORE TO IT. BUT I JUST TOOK TO IT REALLY WELL, I SUPPOSE. IT DIDN'T EVEN REALLY TAKE THAT MUCH TRAINING.
THE THING ABOUT LIVING HERE THAT WILL PROBABLY SURPRISE YOU-- OR MAYBE NOT, IS THAT PEOPLE GET BORED HERE, REALLY EASILY.
YOU SHOULD DO A DEMONSTRATION OR SOMETHING.
A DEMONSTRATION? HA. I'M SORRY, BUT NO. THAT WOULD BE BORING.
IT'S NOT LIKE I CAN SHOOT CIGARETTES OUT OF PEOPLE'S MOUTHS OR ANYTHING. I'VE JUST GOT PRETTY GOOD AIM. IT'S NOT VERY SHOWY.
I CAN SPLATTER A ROAMER'S HEAD FROM A GOOD DISTANCE. I DOUBT THE PEOPLE HERE WANT TO SEE THAT.
ANDREA, SPENCER. I'M JUST GOING AROUND TAKING REQUESTS. CAN I GET YOU ANYTHING TO DRINK?
DO YOU NEED ANYTHING, ANDREA?
I'M FINE, THANKS.
WELL, THEN--CARRY ON YOU TWO. SORRY FOR THE INTERRUPTION.
SON, HAVE YOU SEEN YOUR MOTHER?
SHE'S OVER BY THE GRILL, TALKING TO DAVID.

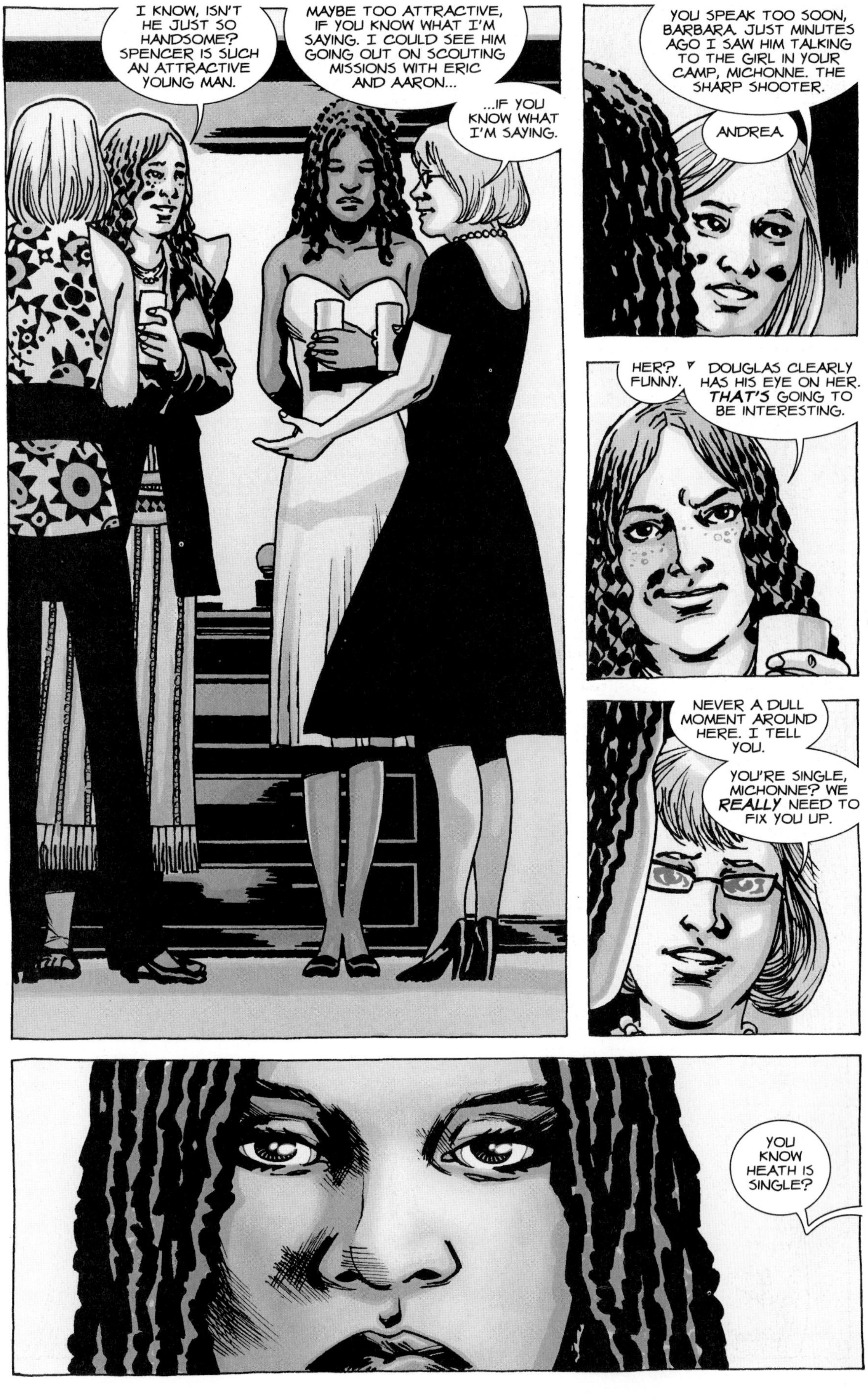
I KNOW, ISN'T HE JUST SO HANDSOME? SPENCER IS SUCH AN ATTRACTIVE YOUNG MAN.
MAYBE TOO ATTRACTIVE, IF YOU KNOW WHAT I'M SAYING. I COULD SEE HIM GOING OUT ON SCOUTING MISSIONS WITH ERIC AND AARON...
...IF YOU KNOW WHAT I'M SAYING.
YOU SPEAK TOO SOON, BARBARA. JUST MINUTES AGO I SAW HIM TALKING TO THE GIRL IN YOUR CAMP, MICHONNE. THE SHARP SHOOTER.
ANDREA.
HER? FUNNY.
DOUGLAS CLEARLY HAS HIS EYE ON HER. *THAT'S* GOING TO BE INTERESTING.
NEVER A DULL MOMENT AROUND HERE. I TELL YOU.
YOU'RE SINGLE, MICHONNE? WE *REALLY* NEED TO FIX YOU UP.
YOU KNOW HEATH IS SINGLE?

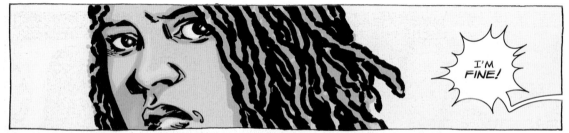

I'M FINE!

COME ON, WE'RE LEAVING.

I SAID I'M FINE! I'M NOT GOING ANYWHERE!

COULD YOU PLEASE--

I'VE GOT IT UNDER CONTROL.

I'LL TAKE CARE OF THIS.

GLENN, C'MON. WE'RE GOING OUTSIDE.

ALL OUR KIDS ARE HERE, GLENN. JESUS.

I'M SORRY.

I'M SORRY.

JUST... GET HIM HOME. I'LL MAKE SURE SOPHIA MAKES IT BACK OKAY.

OKAY, THANKS, RICK.

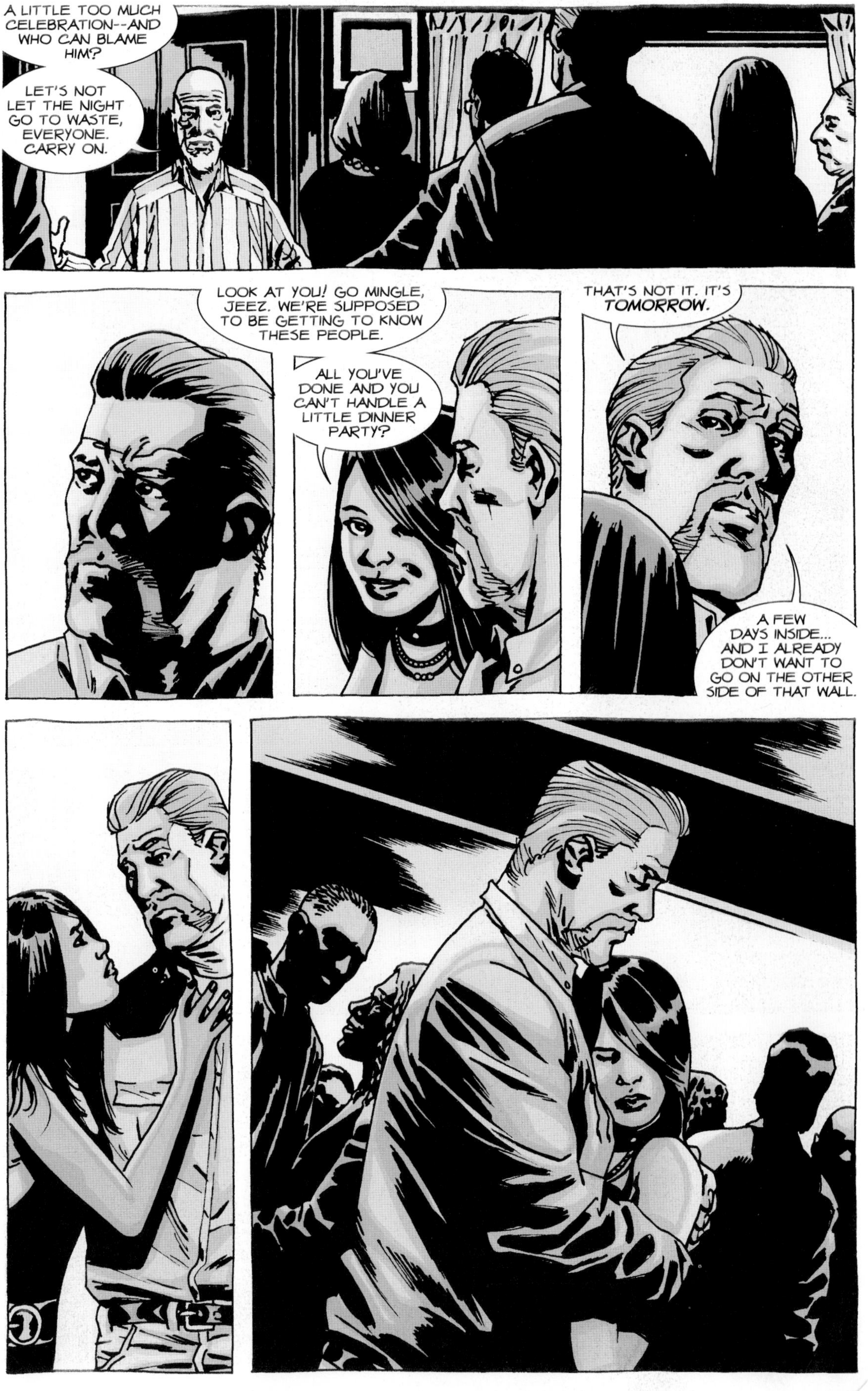
A LITTLE TOO MUCH CELEBRATION--AND WHO CAN BLAME HIM?
LET'S NOT LET THE NIGHT GO TO WASTE, EVERYONE. CARRY ON.
LOOK AT YOU! GO MINGLE, JEEZ. WE'RE SUPPOSED TO BE GETTING TO KNOW THESE PEOPLE.
ALL YOU'VE DONE AND YOU CAN'T HANDLE A LITTLE DINNER PARTY?
THAT'S NOT IT. IT'S *TOMORROW.*
A FEW DAYS INSIDE... AND I ALREADY DON'T WANT TO GO ON THE OTHER SIDE OF THAT WALL.

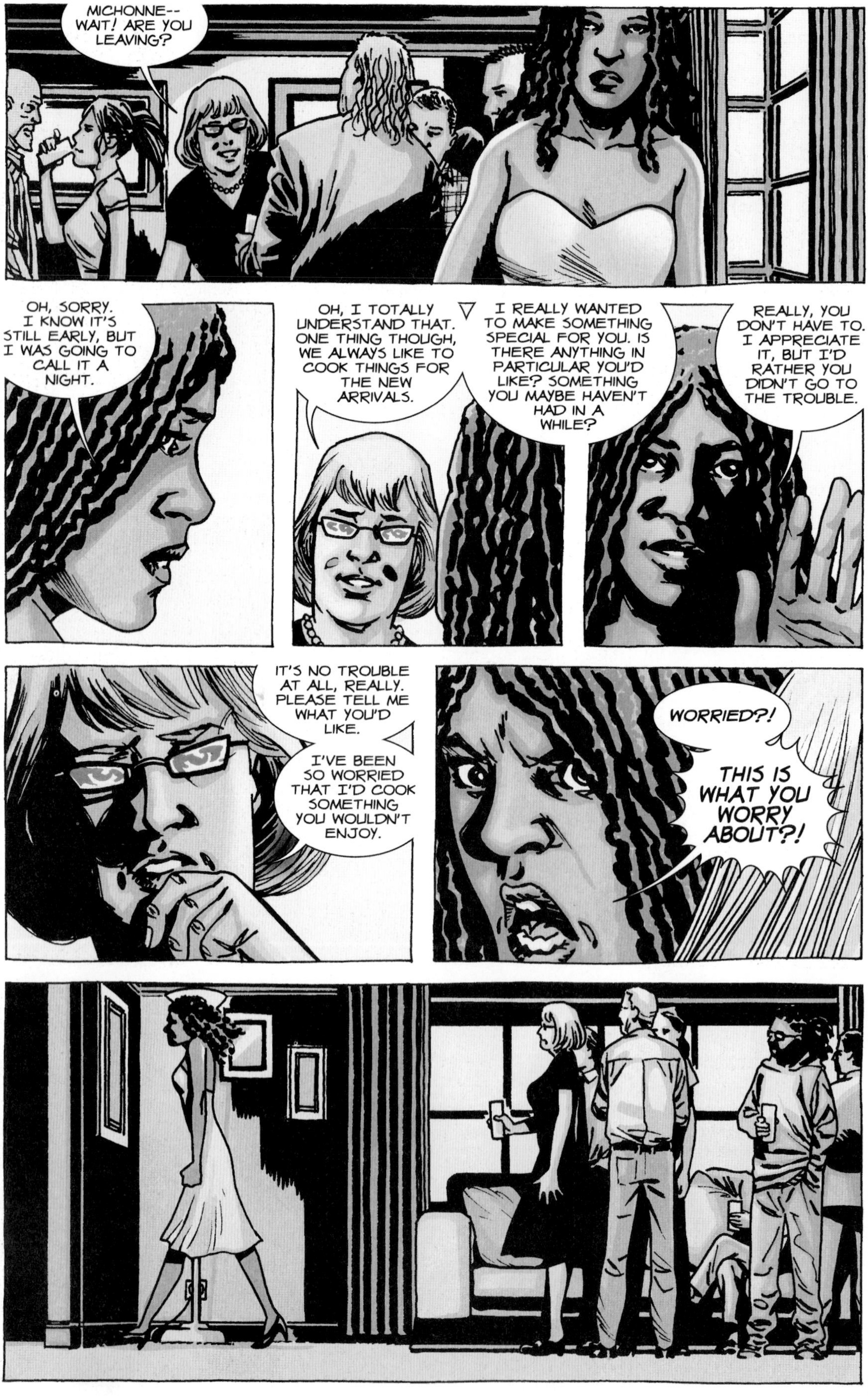
MICHONNE-- WAIT! ARE YOU LEAVING?
OH, SORRY. I KNOW IT'S STILL EARLY, BUT I WAS GOING TO CALL IT A NIGHT.
OH, I TOTALLY UNDERSTAND THAT. ONE THING THOUGH, WE ALWAYS LIKE TO COOK THINGS FOR THE NEW ARRIVALS.
I REALLY WANTED TO MAKE SOMETHING SPECIAL FOR YOU. IS THERE ANYTHING IN PARTICULAR YOU'D LIKE? SOMETHING YOU MAYBE HAVEN'T HAD IN A WHILE?
REALLY, YOU DON'T HAVE TO. I APPRECIATE IT, BUT I'D RATHER YOU DIDN'T GO TO THE TROUBLE.
IT'S NO TROUBLE AT ALL, REALLY. PLEASE TELL ME WHAT YOU'D LIKE.
I'VE BEEN SO WORRIED THAT I'D COOK SOMETHING YOU WOULDN'T ENJOY.
WORRIED?!
THIS IS WHAT YOU WORRY ABOUT?!

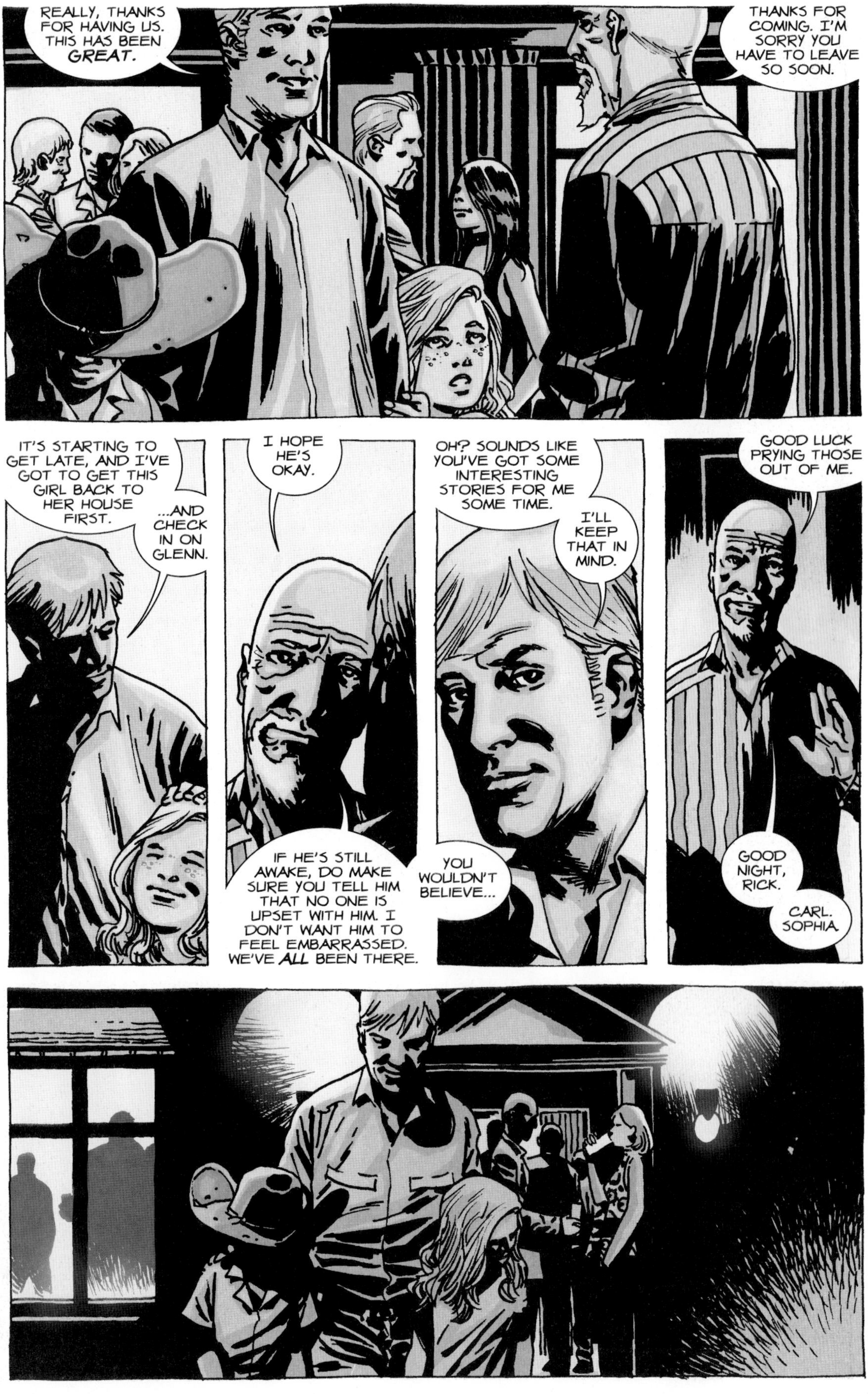
REALLY, THANKS FOR HAVING US. THIS HAS BEEN GREAT.
THANKS FOR COMING. I'M SORRY YOU HAVE TO LEAVE SO SOON.
IT'S STARTING TO GET LATE, AND I'VE GOT TO GET THIS GIRL BACK TO HER HOUSE FIRST.
...AND CHECK IN ON GLENN.
I HOPE HE'S OKAY.
IF HE'S STILL AWAKE, DO MAKE SURE YOU TELL HIM THAT NO ONE IS UPSET WITH HIM. I DON'T WANT HIM TO FEEL EMBARRASSED. WE'VE ALL BEEN THERE.
YOU WOULDN'T BELIEVE...
OH? SOUNDS LIKE YOU'VE GOT SOME INTERESTING STORIES FOR ME SOME TIME.
I'LL KEEP THAT IN MIND.
GOOD LUCK PRYING THOSE OUT OF ME.
GOOD NIGHT, RICK.
CARL. SOPHIA.

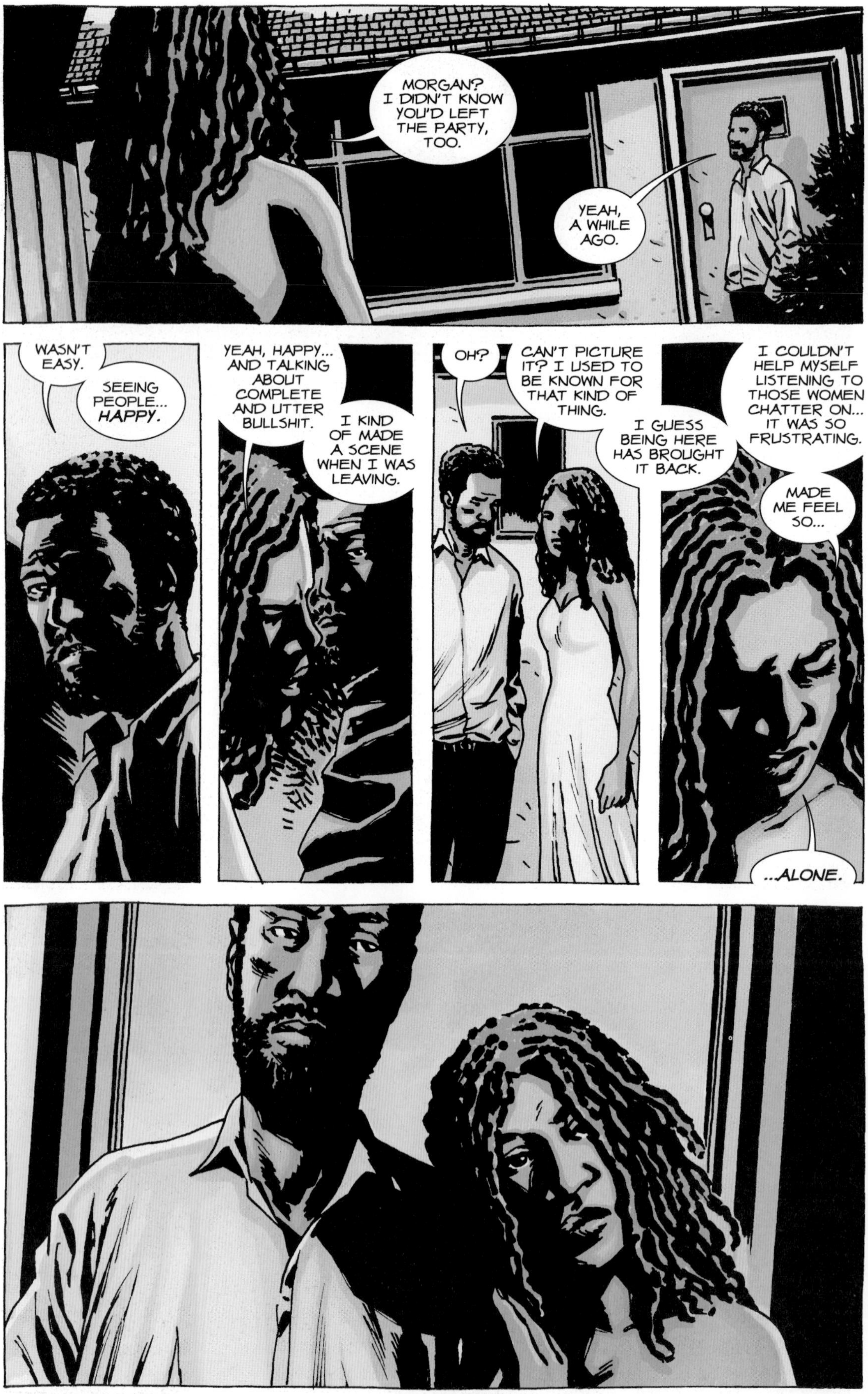
MORGAN? I DIDN'T KNOW YOU'D LEFT THE PARTY, TOO.
YEAH, A WHILE AGO.
WASN'T EASY.
SEEING PEOPLE... *HAPPY.*
YEAH, HAPPY... AND TALKING ABOUT COMPLETE AND UTTER BULLSHIT.
I KIND OF MADE A SCENE WHEN I WAS LEAVING.
OH?
CAN'T PICTURE IT? I USED TO BE KNOWN FOR THAT KIND OF THING.
I GUESS BEING HERE HAS BROUGHT IT BACK.
I COULDN'T HELP MYSELF LISTENING TO THOSE WOMEN CHATTER ON... IT WAS SO FRUSTRATING.
MADE ME FEEL SO...
...ALONE.

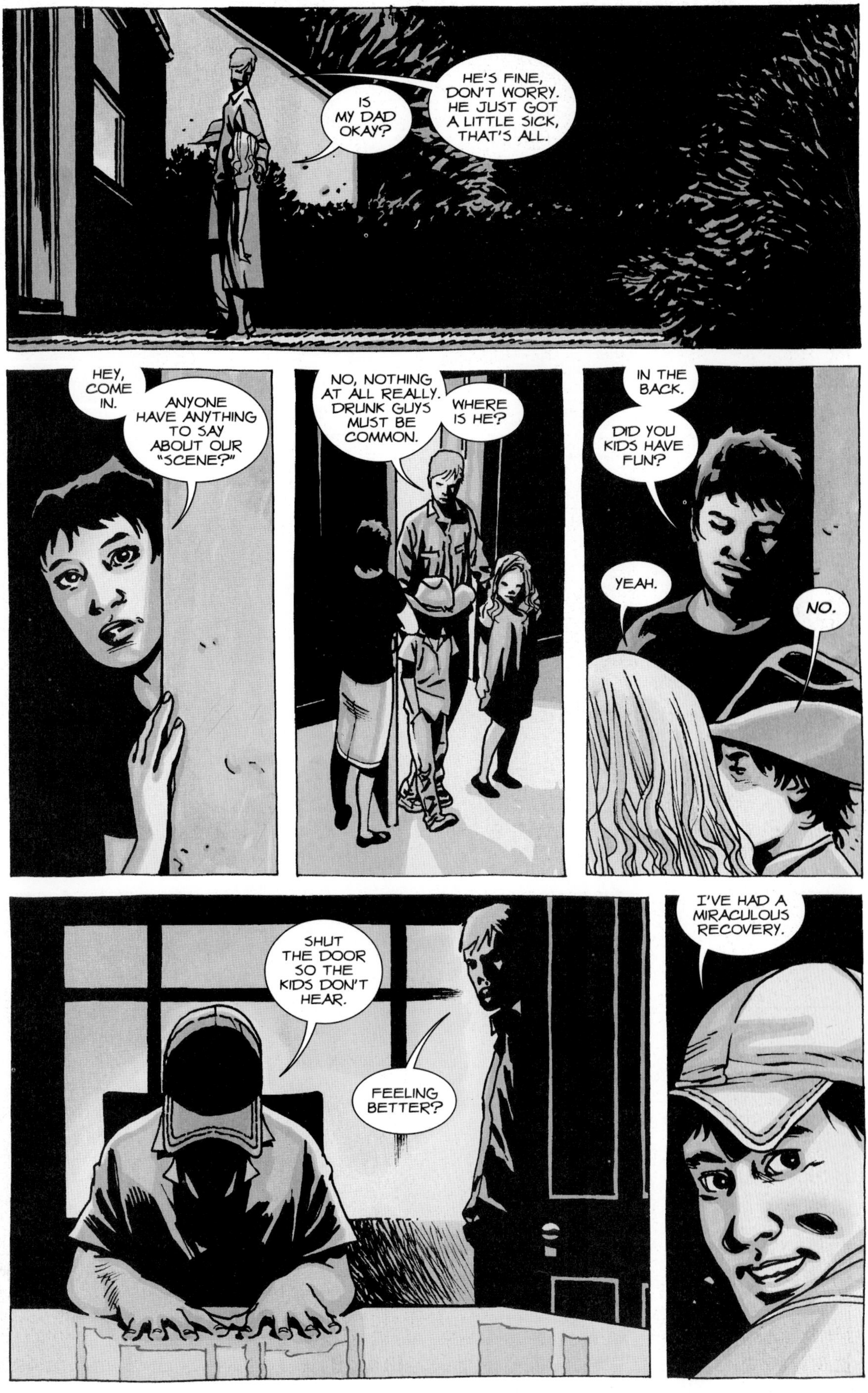
IS MY DAD OKAY?
HE'S FINE, DON'T WORRY. HE JUST GOT A LITTLE SICK, THAT'S ALL.
HEY, COME IN.
ANYONE HAVE ANYTHING TO SAY ABOUT OUR "SCENE?"
NO, NOTHING AT ALL REALLY. DRUNK GUYS MUST BE COMMON.
WHERE IS HE?
IN THE BACK.
DID YOU KIDS HAVE FUN?
YEAH.
NO.
SHUT THE DOOR SO THE KIDS DON'T HEAR.
FEELING BETTER?
I'VE HAD A MIRACULOUS RECOVERY.

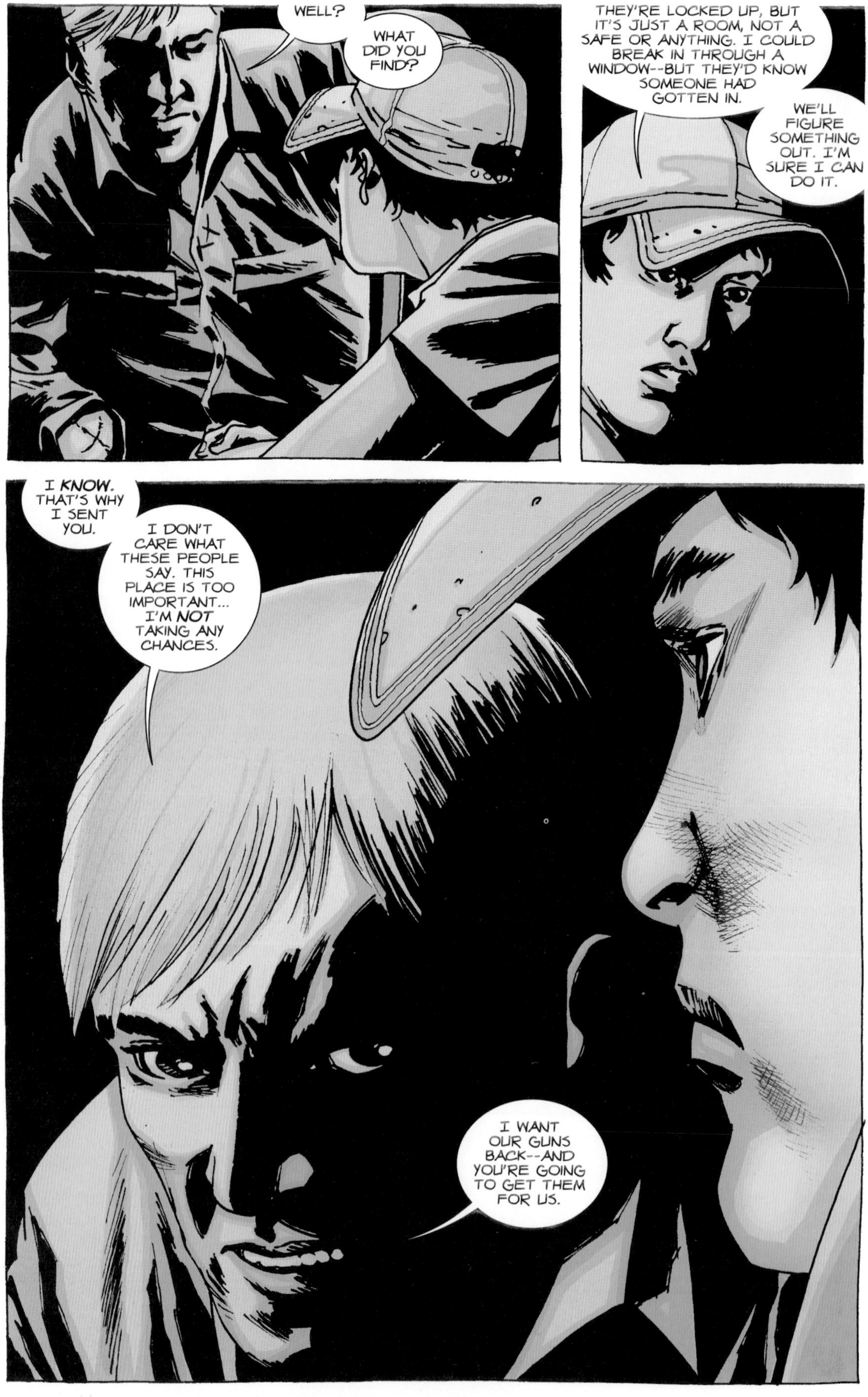
WELL?
WHAT DID YOU FIND?
THEY'RE LOCKED UP, BUT IT'S JUST A ROOM, NOT A SAFE OR ANYTHING. I COULD BREAK IN THROUGH A WINDOW--BUT THEY'D KNOW SOMEONE HAD GOTTEN IN.
WE'LL FIGURE SOMETHING OUT. I'M SURE I CAN DO IT.
I KNOW. THAT'S WHY I SENT YOU.
I DON'T CARE WHAT THESE PEOPLE SAY. THIS PLACE IS TOO IMPORTANT... I'M NOT TAKING ANY CHANCES.
I WANT OUR GUNS BACK--AND YOU'RE GOING TO GET THEM FOR US.

Chapter Thirteen: Too Far Gone

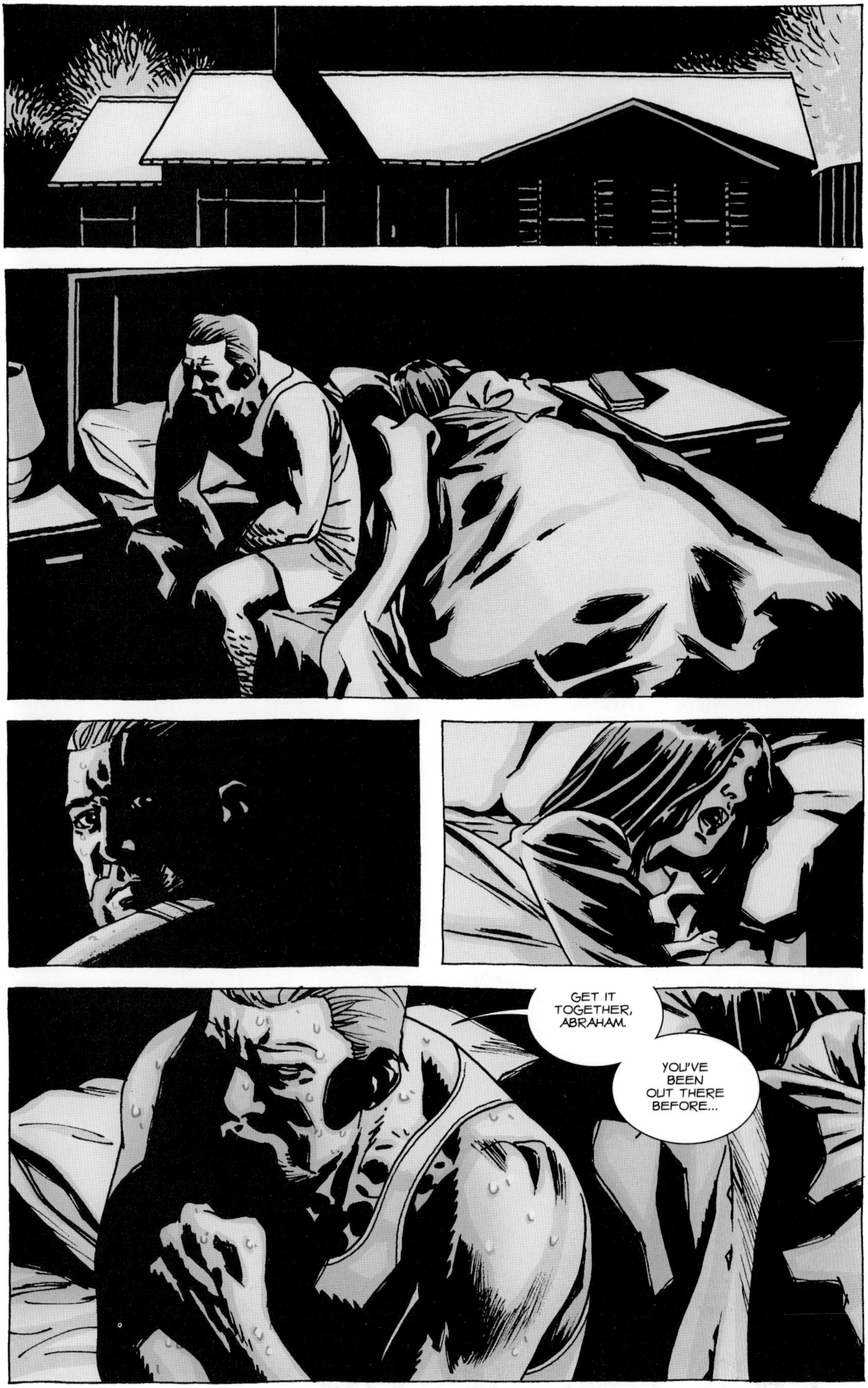
GET IT TOGETHER, ABRAHAM.
YOU'VE BEEN OUT THERE BEFORE...

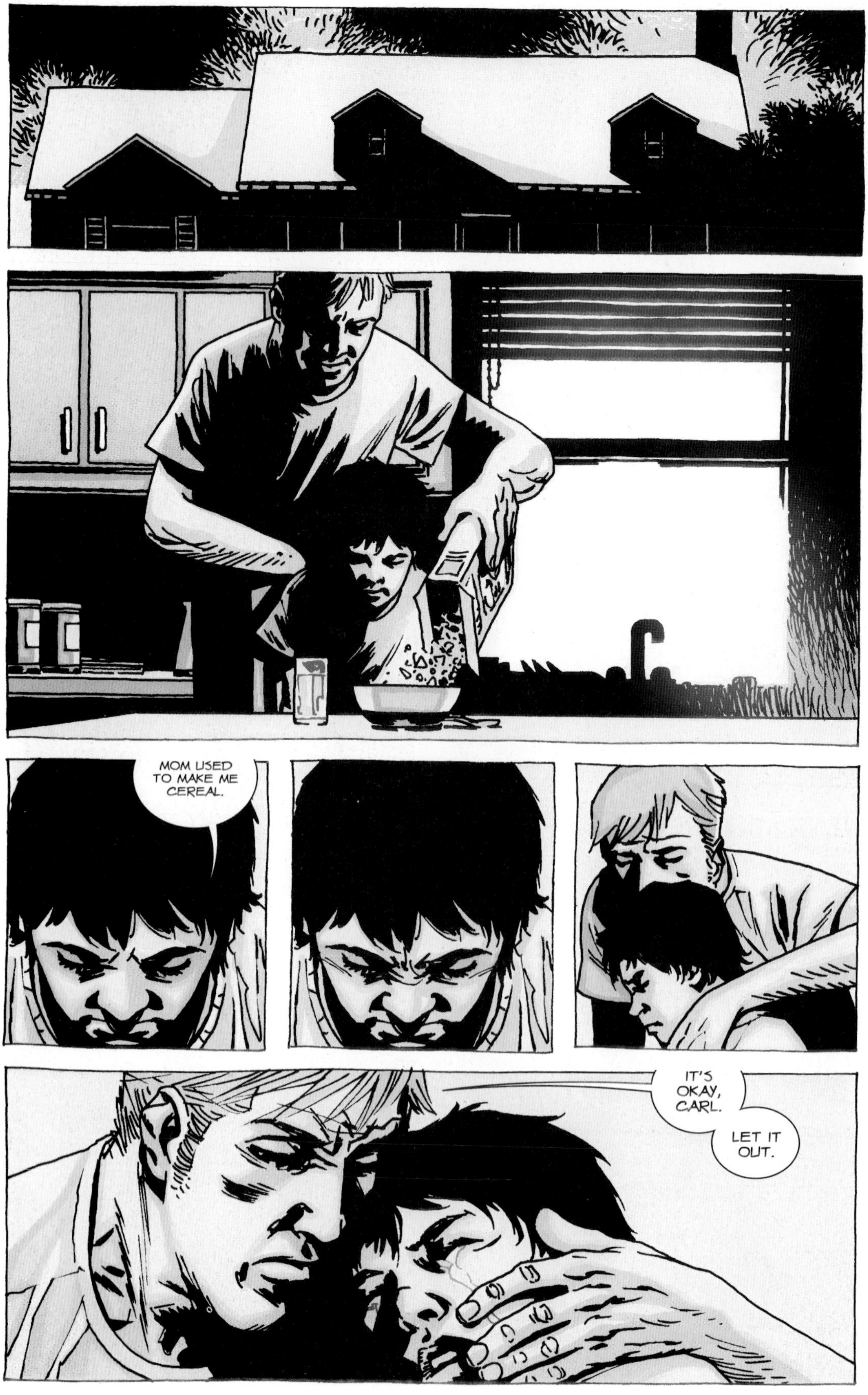

MOM USED TO MAKE ME CEREAL.
IT'S OKAY, CARL.
LET IT OUT.

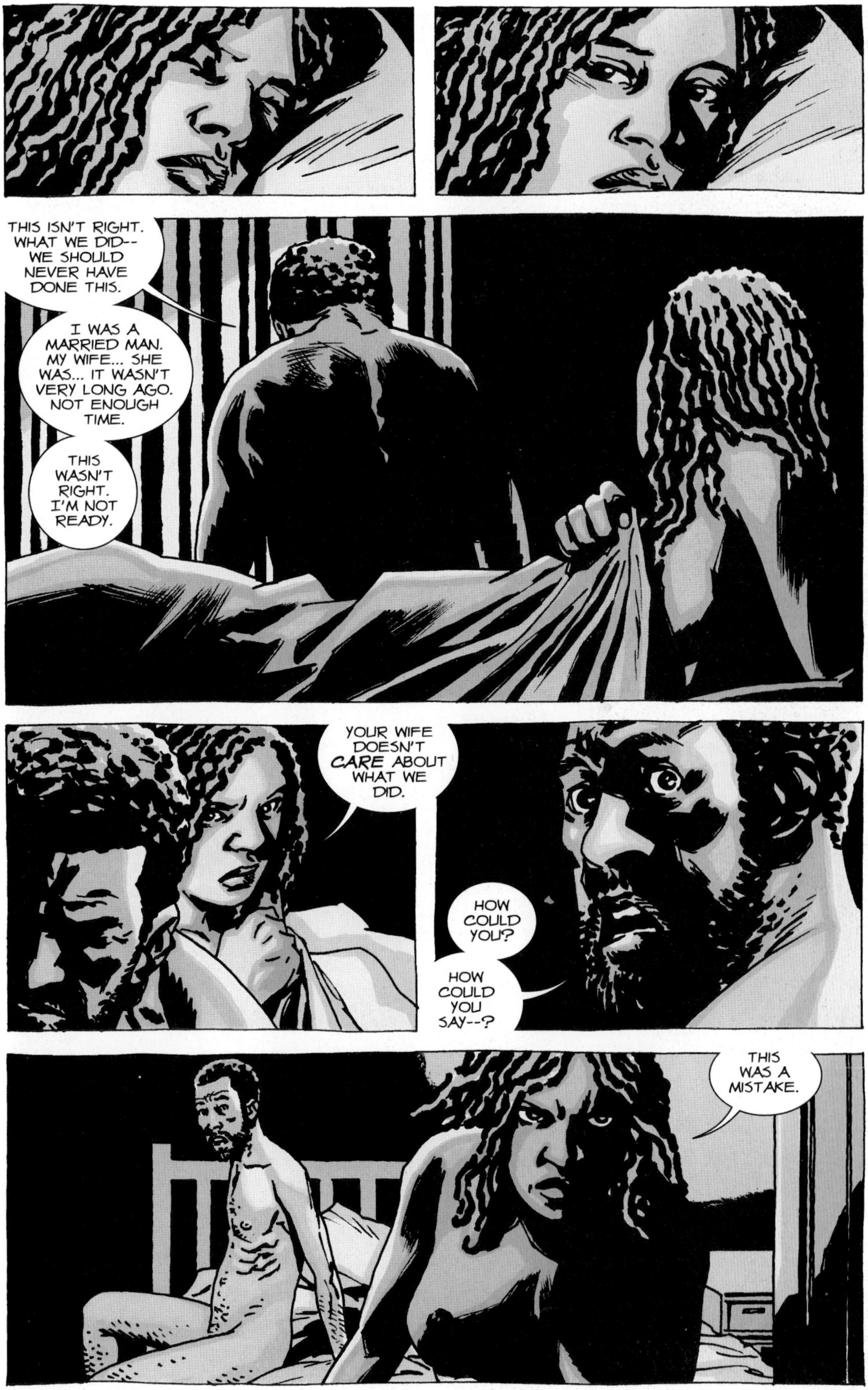
THIS ISN'T RIGHT. WHAT WE DID-- WE SHOULD NEVER HAVE DONE THIS.
I WAS A MARRIED MAN. MY WIFE... SHE WAS... IT WASN'T VERY LONG AGO. NOT ENOUGH TIME.
THIS WASN'T RIGHT. I'M NOT READY.
YOUR WIFE DOESN'T CARE ABOUT WHAT WE DID.
HOW COULD YOU?
HOW COULD YOU SAY--?
THIS WAS A MISTAKE.

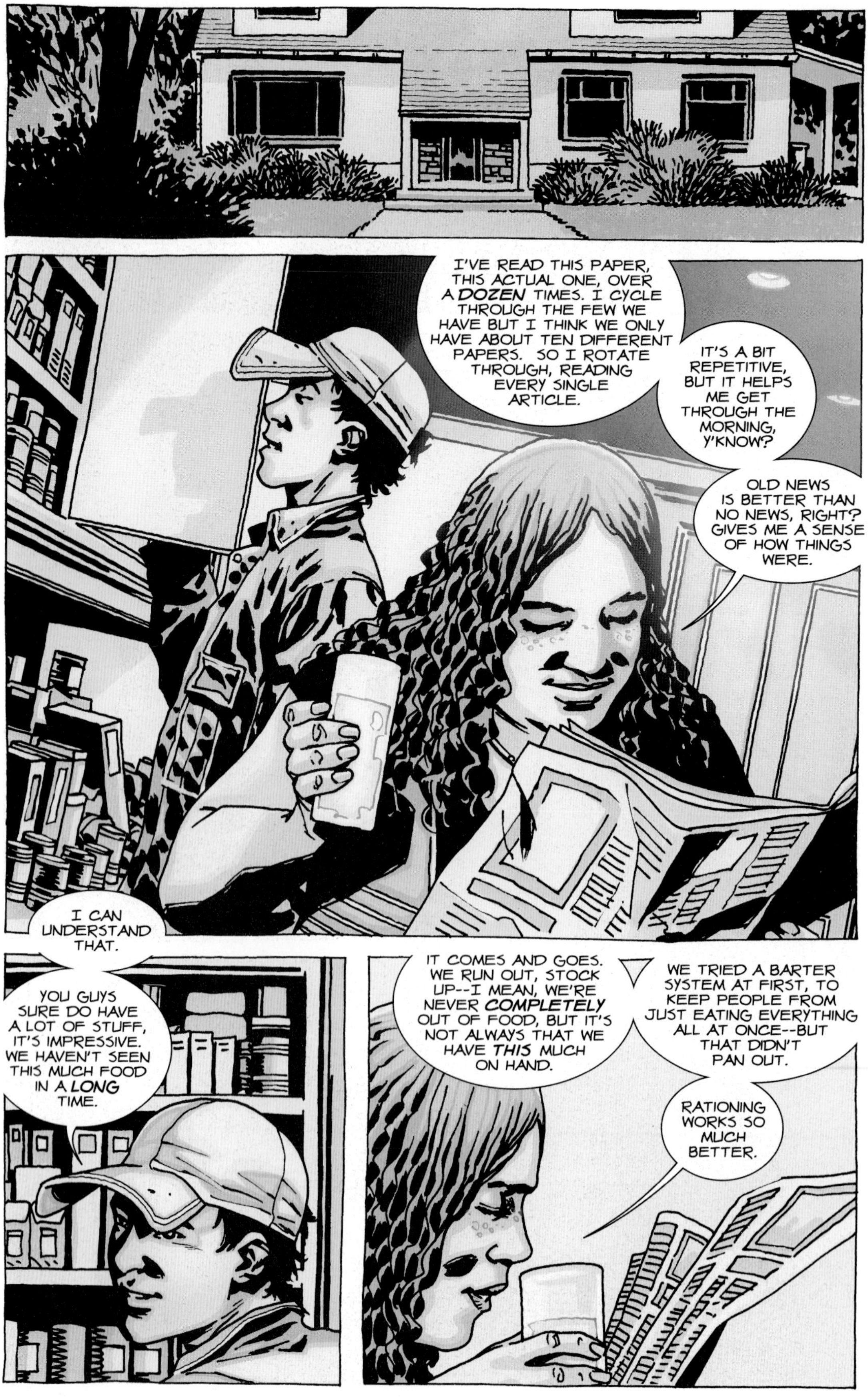
I'VE READ THIS PAPER, THIS ACTUAL ONE, OVER A DOZEN TIMES. I CYCLE THROUGH THE FEW WE HAVE BUT I THINK WE ONLY HAVE ABOUT TEN DIFFERENT PAPERS. SO I ROTATE THROUGH, READING EVERY SINGLE ARTICLE.
IT'S A BIT REPETITIVE, BUT IT HELPS ME GET THROUGH THE MORNING, Y'KNOW?
OLD NEWS IS BETTER THAN NO NEWS, RIGHT? GIVES ME A SENSE OF HOW THINGS WERE.
I CAN UNDERSTAND THAT.
YOU GUYS SURE DO HAVE A LOT OF STUFF, IT'S IMPRESSIVE. WE HAVEN'T SEEN THIS MUCH FOOD IN A LONG TIME.
IT COMES AND GOES. WE RUN OUT, STOCK UP--I MEAN, WE'RE NEVER COMPLETELY OUT OF FOOD, BUT IT'S NOT ALWAYS THAT WE HAVE THIS MUCH ON HAND.
WE TRIED A BARTER SYSTEM AT FIRST, TO KEEP PEOPLE FROM JUST EATING EVERYTHING ALL AT ONCE--BUT THAT DIDN'T PAN OUT.
RATIONING WORKS SO MUCH BETTER.

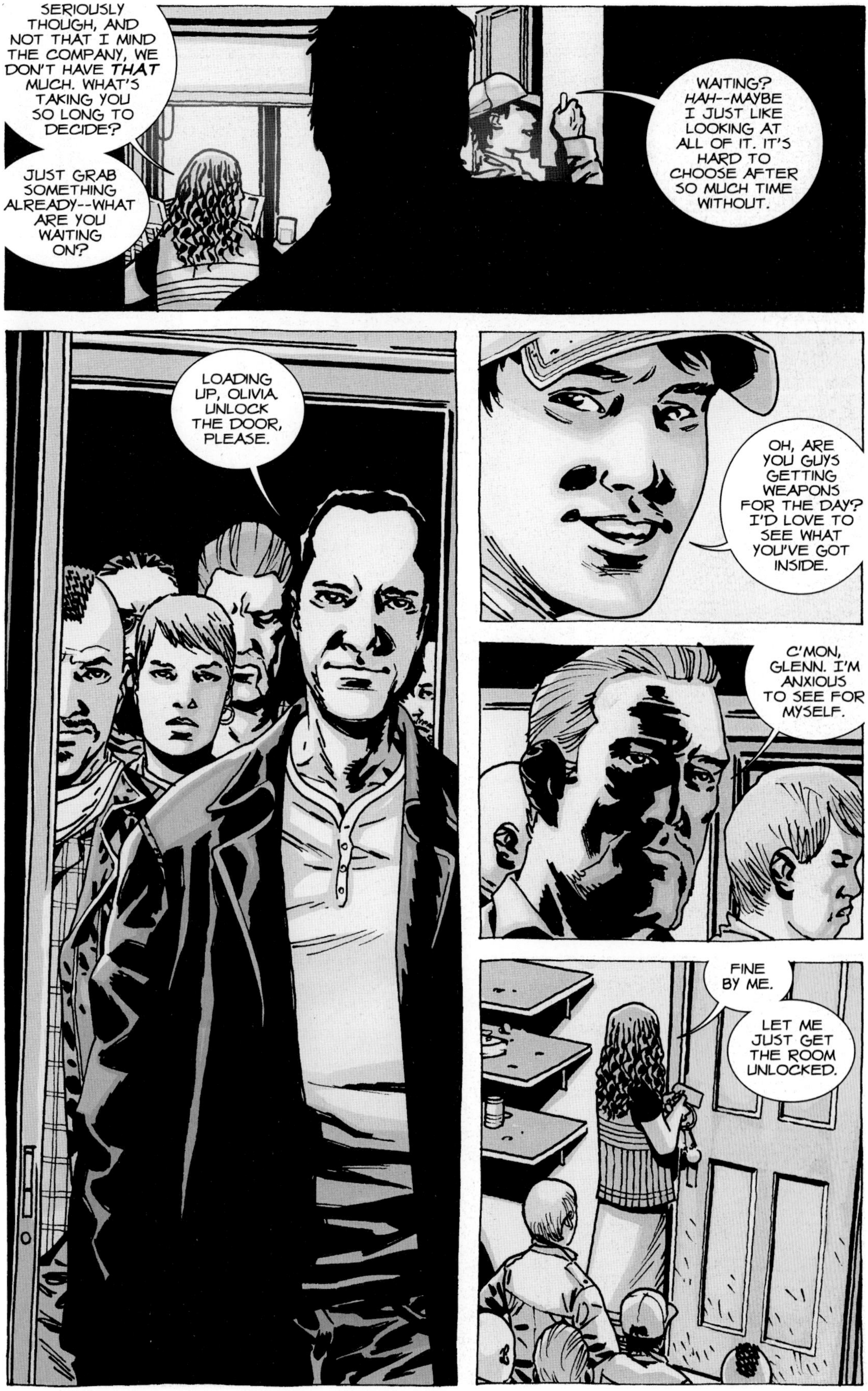
SERIOUSLY THOUGH, AND NOT THAT I MIND THE COMPANY, WE DON'T HAVE *THAT* MUCH. WHAT'S TAKING YOU SO LONG TO DECIDE?
JUST GRAB SOMETHING ALREADY--WHAT ARE YOU WAITING ON?
WAITING? *HAH*--MAYBE I JUST LIKE LOOKING AT ALL OF IT. IT'S HARD TO CHOOSE AFTER SO MUCH TIME WITHOUT.
LOADING UP, OLIVIA. UNLOCK THE DOOR, PLEASE.
OH, ARE YOU GUYS GETTING WEAPONS FOR THE DAY? I'D LOVE TO SEE WHAT YOU'VE GOT INSIDE.
C'MON, GLENN. I'M ANXIOUS TO SEE FOR MYSELF.
FINE BY ME.
LET ME JUST GET THE ROOM UNLOCKED.

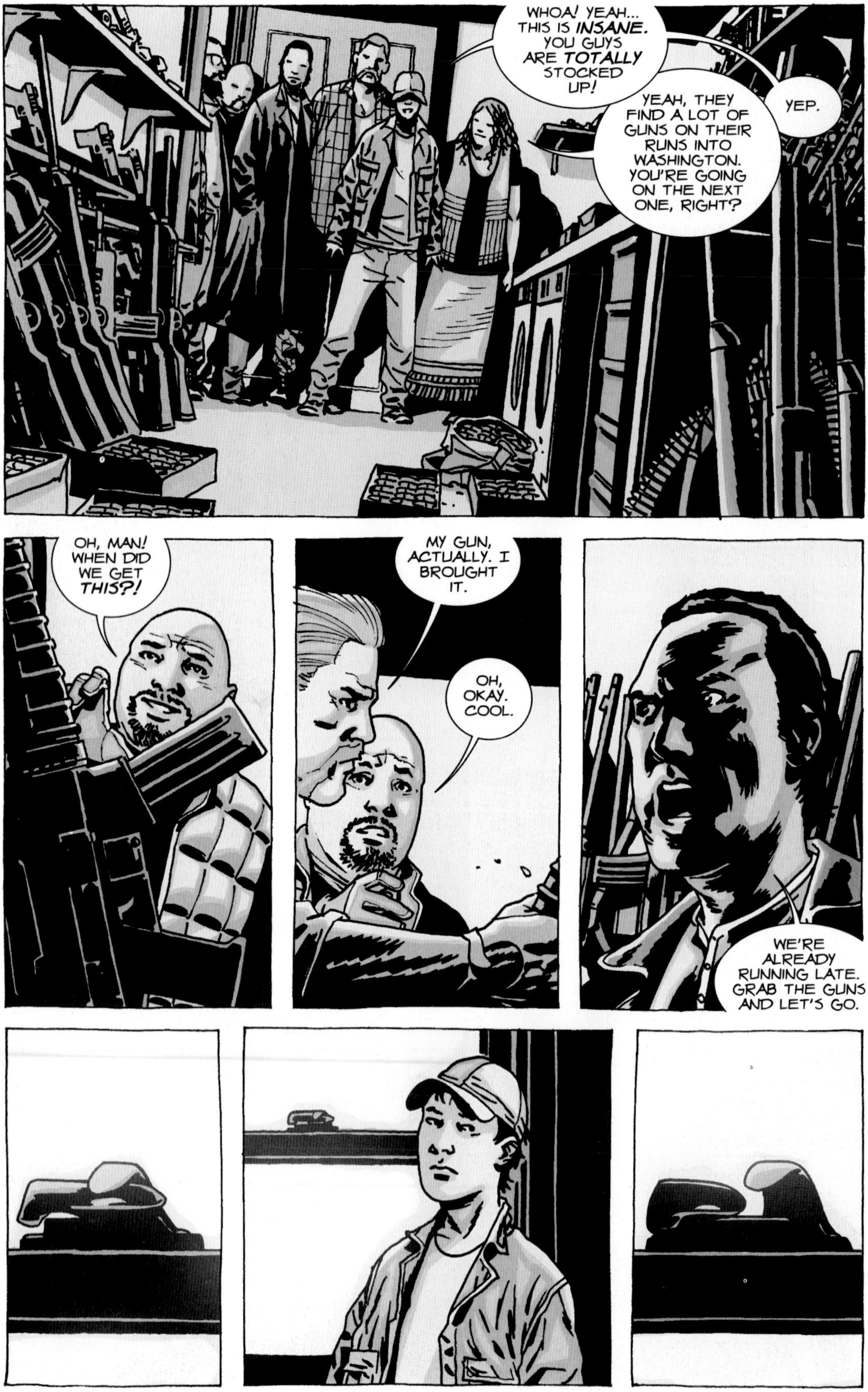
WHOA! YEAH... THIS IS INSANE. YOU GUYS ARE TOTALLY STOCKED UP!
YEAH, THEY FIND A LOT OF GUNS ON THEIR RUNS INTO WASHINGTON. YOU'RE GOING ON THE NEXT ONE, RIGHT?
YEP.
OH, MAN! WHEN DID WE GET THIS?!
MY GUN, ACTUALLY. I BROUGHT IT.
OH, OKAY. COOL.
WE'RE ALREADY RUNNING LATE. GRAB THE GUNS AND LET'S GO.

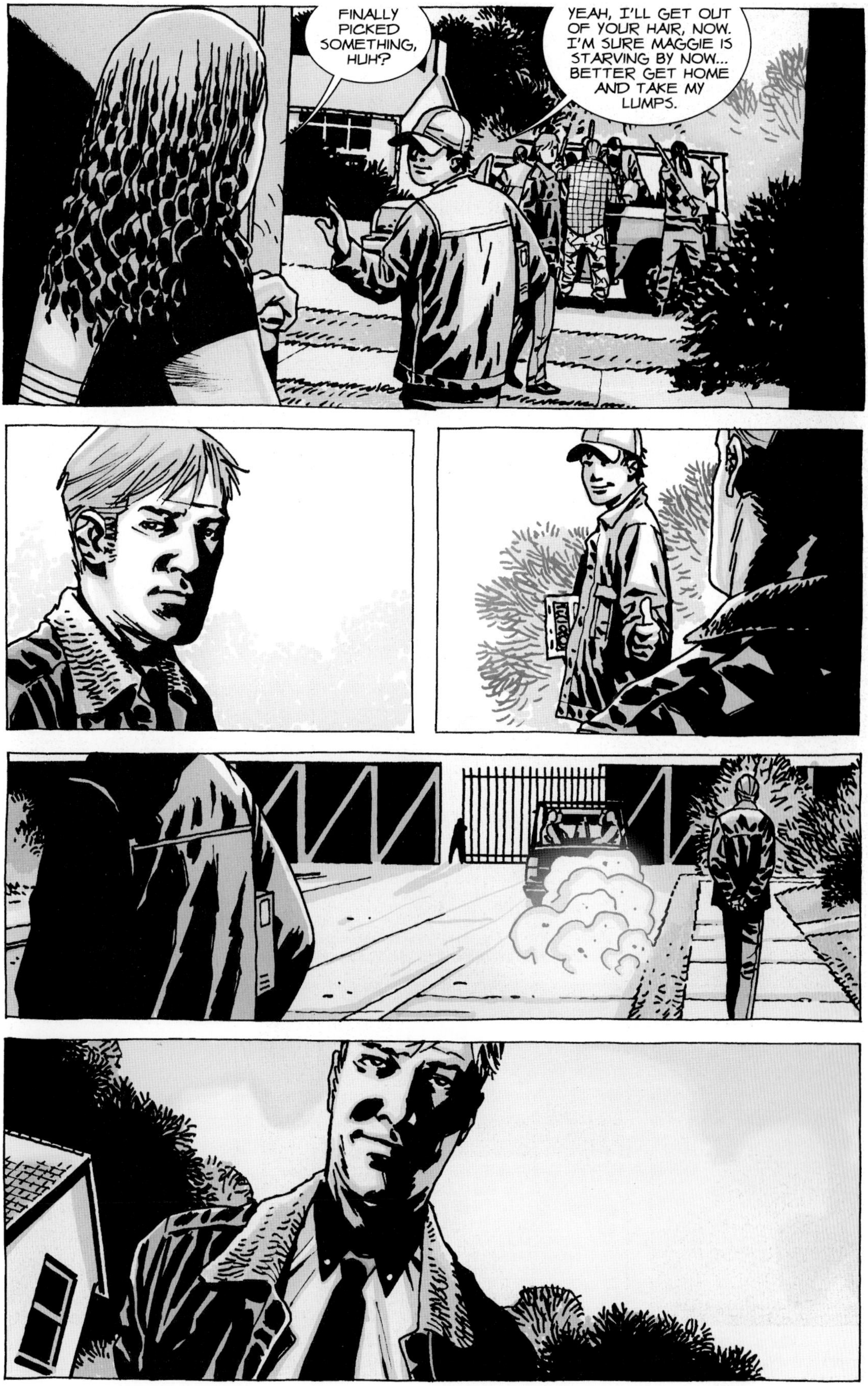
FINALLY PICKED SOMETHING, HUH?
YEAH, I'LL GET OUT OF YOUR HAIR, NOW. I'M SURE MAGGIE IS STARVING BY NOW... BETTER GET HOME AND TAKE MY LUMPS.

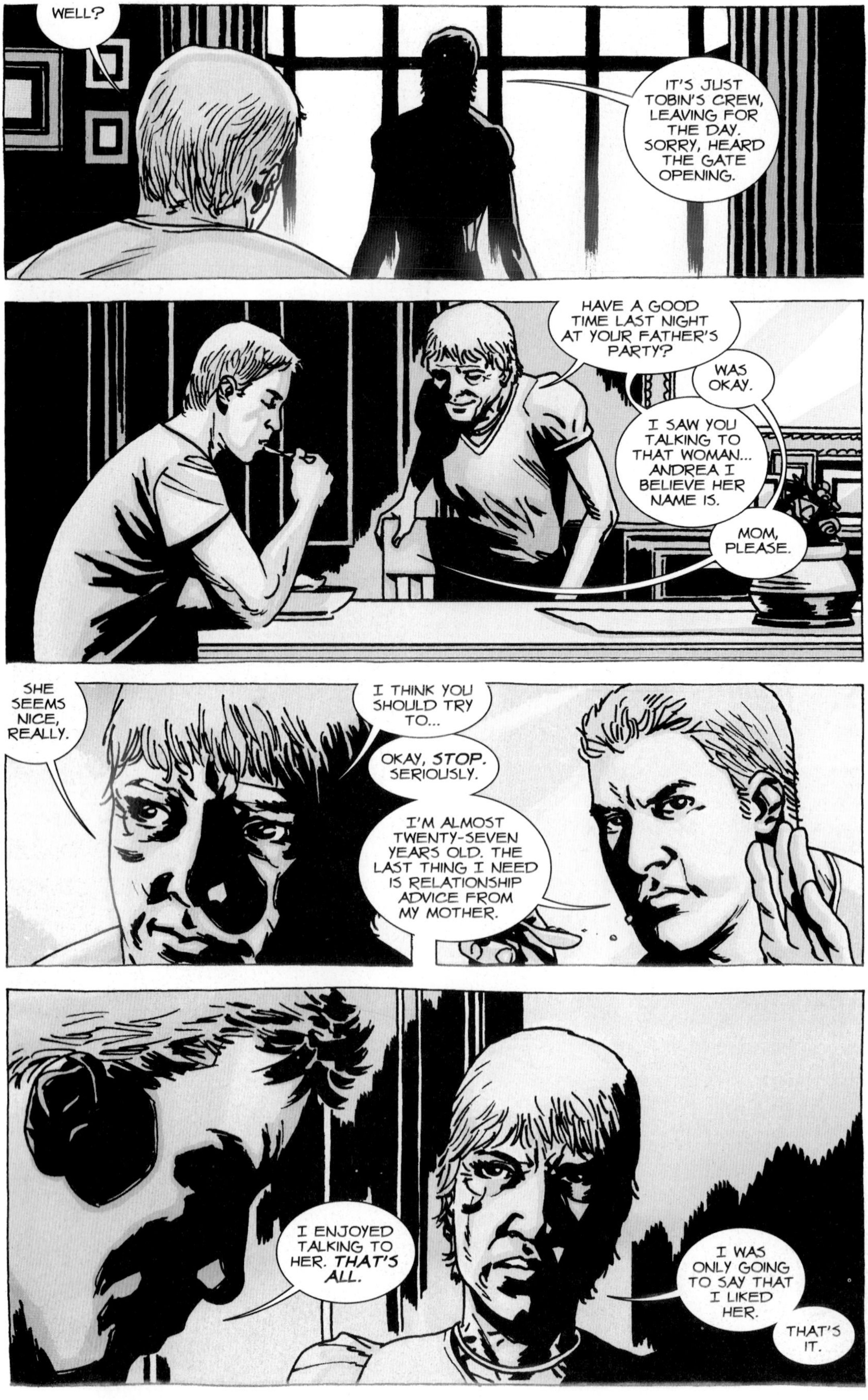
WELL?
IT'S JUST TOBIN'S CREW, LEAVING FOR THE DAY. SORRY, HEARD THE GATE OPENING.
HAVE A GOOD TIME LAST NIGHT AT YOUR FATHER'S PARTY?
WAS OKAY.
I SAW YOU TALKING TO THAT WOMAN... ANDREA I BELIEVE HER NAME IS.
MOM, PLEASE.
SHE SEEMS NICE, REALLY.
I THINK YOU SHOULD TRY TO...
OKAY, STOP. SERIOUSLY.
I'M ALMOST TWENTY-SEVEN YEARS OLD. THE LAST THING I NEED IS RELATIONSHIP ADVICE FROM MY MOTHER.
I ENJOYED TALKING TO HER. THAT'S ALL.
I WAS ONLY GOING TO SAY THAT I LIKED HER.
THAT'S IT.

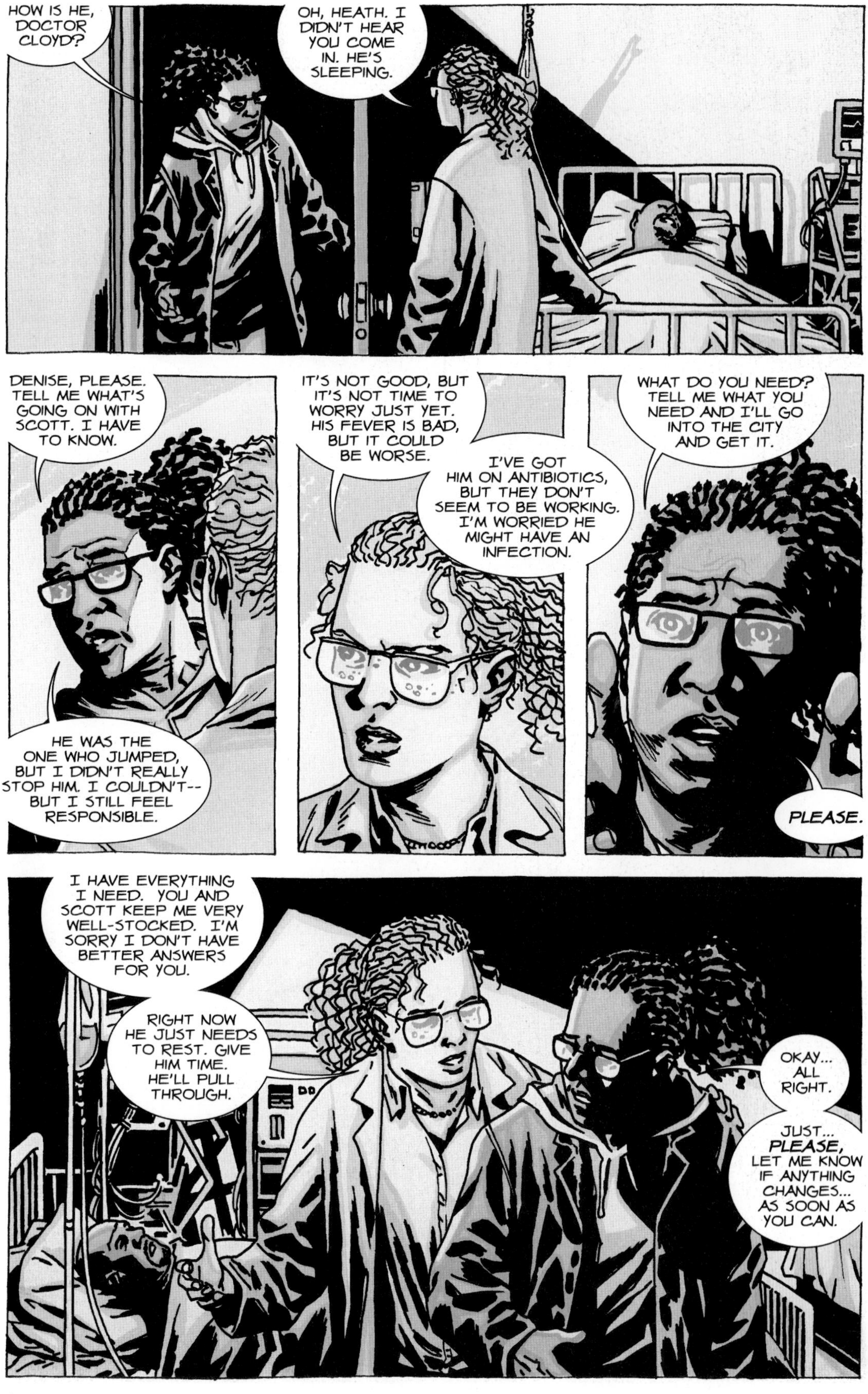
HOW IS HE, DOCTOR CLOYD?
OH, HEATH. I DIDN'T HEAR YOU COME IN. HE'S SLEEPING.
DENISE, PLEASE. TELL ME WHAT'S GOING ON WITH SCOTT. I HAVE TO KNOW.
HE WAS THE ONE WHO JUMPED, BUT I DIDN'T REALLY STOP HIM. I COULDN'T-- BUT I STILL FEEL RESPONSIBLE.
IT'S NOT GOOD, BUT IT'S NOT TIME TO WORRY JUST YET. HIS FEVER IS BAD, BUT IT COULD BE WORSE.
I'VE GOT HIM ON ANTIBIOTICS, BUT THEY DON'T SEEM TO BE WORKING. I'M WORRIED HE MIGHT HAVE AN INFECTION.
WHAT DO YOU NEED? TELL ME WHAT YOU NEED AND I'LL GO INTO THE CITY AND GET IT.
PLEASE.
I HAVE EVERYTHING I NEED. YOU AND SCOTT KEEP ME VERY WELL-STOCKED. I'M SORRY I DON'T HAVE BETTER ANSWERS FOR YOU.
RIGHT NOW HE JUST NEEDS TO REST. GIVE HIM TIME. HE'LL PULL THROUGH.
OKAY... ALL RIGHT.
JUST... PLEASE, LET ME KNOW IF ANYTHING CHANGES... AS SOON AS YOU CAN.

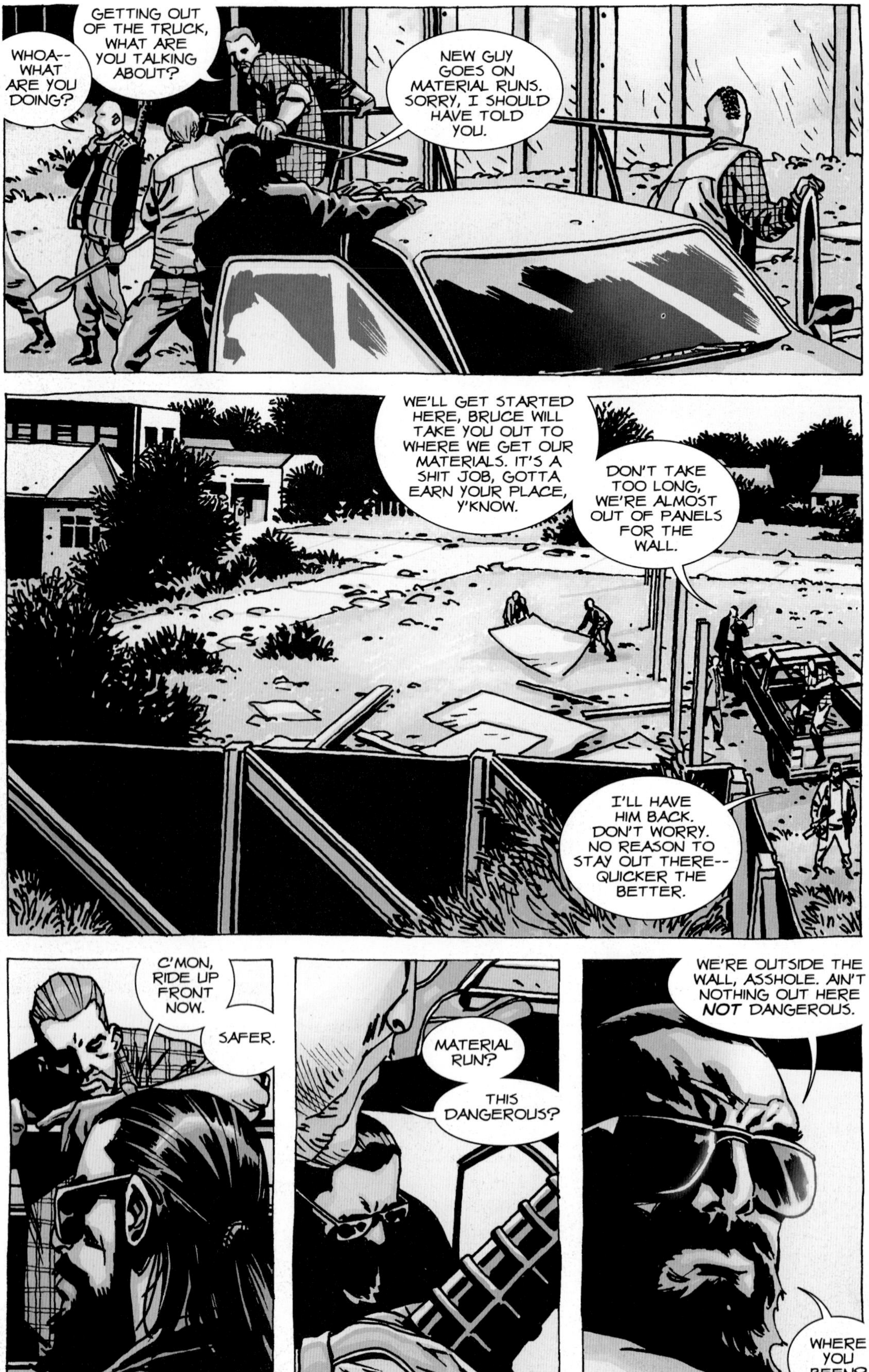
WHOA-- WHAT ARE YOU DOING?
GETTING OUT OF THE TRUCK, WHAT ARE YOU TALKING ABOUT?
NEW GUY GOES ON MATERIAL RUNS. SORRY, I SHOULD HAVE TOLD YOU.
WE'LL GET STARTED HERE, BRUCE WILL TAKE YOU OUT TO WHERE WE GET OUR MATERIALS. IT'S A SHIT JOB, GOTTA EARN YOUR PLACE, Y'KNOW.
DON'T TAKE TOO LONG, WE'RE ALMOST OUT OF PANELS FOR THE WALL.
I'LL HAVE HIM BACK. DON'T WORRY. NO REASON TO STAY OUT THERE-- QUICKER THE BETTER.
C'MON, RIDE UP FRONT NOW.
SAFER.
MATERIAL RUN?
THIS DANGEROUS?
WE'RE OUTSIDE THE WALL, ASSHOLE. AIN'T NOTHING OUT HERE *NOT* DANGEROUS.
WHERE YOU BEEN?

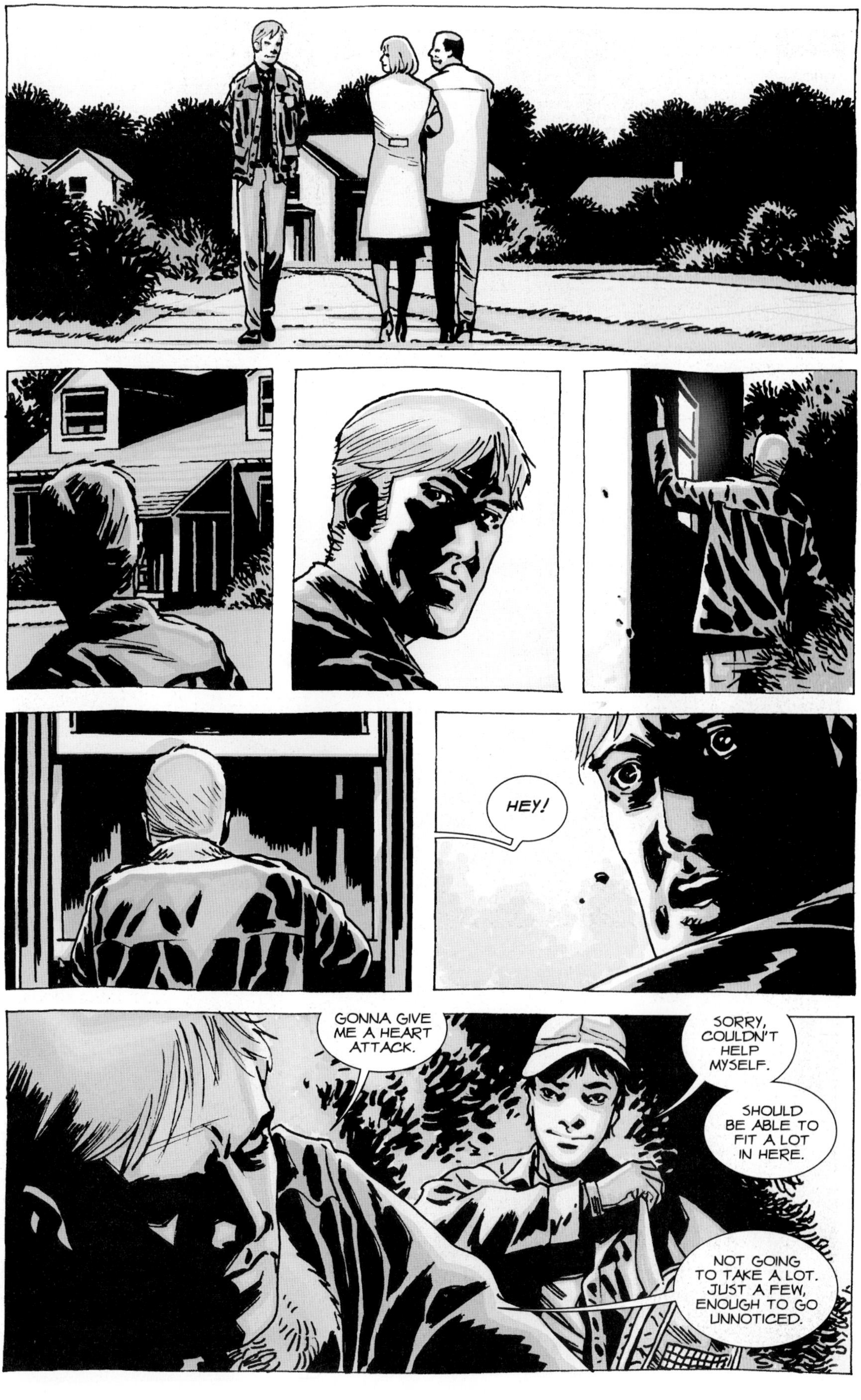

HEY!
GONNA GIVE ME A HEART ATTACK.
SORRY, COULDN'T HELP MYSELF.
SHOULD BE ABLE TO FIT A LOT IN HERE.
NOT GOING TO TAKE A LOT. JUST A FEW, ENOUGH TO GO UNNOTICED.

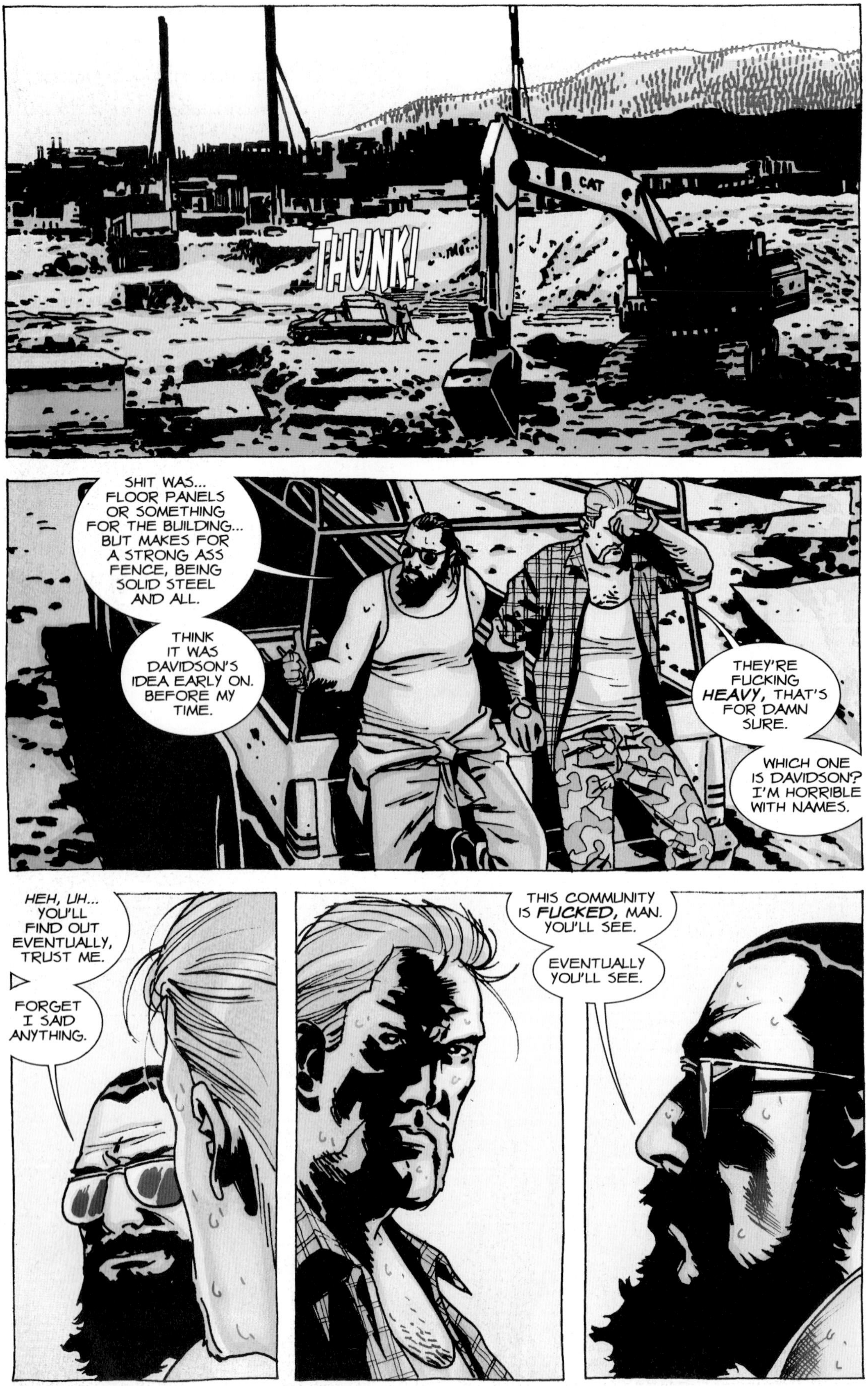
THUNK!
CAT
SHIT WAS... FLOOR PANELS OR SOMETHING FOR THE BUILDING... BUT MAKES FOR A STRONG ASS FENCE, BEING SOLID STEEL AND ALL.
THINK IT WAS DAVIDSON'S IDEA EARLY ON. BEFORE MY TIME.
THEY'RE FUCKING HEAVY, THAT'S FOR DAMN SURE.
WHICH ONE IS DAVIDSON? I'M HORRIBLE WITH NAMES.
HEH, UH... YOU'LL FIND OUT EVENTUALLY, TRUST ME.
FORGET I SAID ANYTHING.
THIS COMMUNITY IS FUCKED, MAN. YOU'LL SEE.
EVENTUALLY YOU'LL SEE.

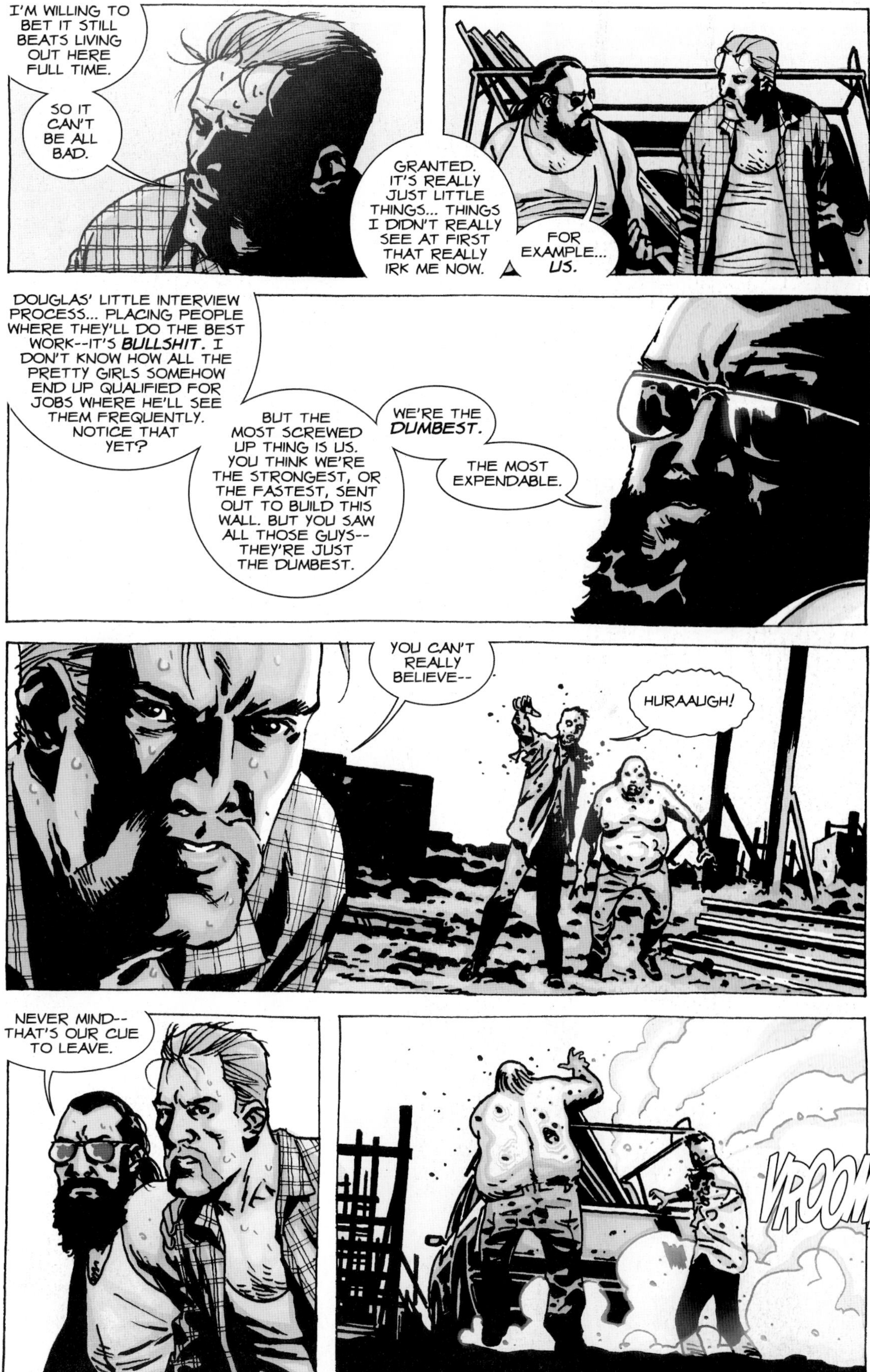
I'M WILLING TO BET IT STILL BEATS LIVING OUT HERE FULL TIME.
SO IT CAN'T BE ALL BAD.
GRANTED. IT'S REALLY JUST LITTLE THINGS... THINGS I DIDN'T REALLY SEE AT FIRST THAT REALLY IRK ME NOW.
FOR EXAMPLE... US.
DOUGLAS' LITTLE INTERVIEW PROCESS... PLACING PEOPLE WHERE THEY'LL DO THE BEST WORK--IT'S BULLSHIT. I DON'T KNOW HOW ALL THE PRETTY GIRLS SOMEHOW END UP QUALIFIED FOR JOBS WHERE HE'LL SEE THEM FREQUENTLY. NOTICE THAT YET?
BUT THE MOST SCREWED UP THING IS US. YOU THINK WE'RE THE STRONGEST, OR THE FASTEST, SENT OUT TO BUILD THIS WALL. BUT YOU SAW ALL THOSE GUYS--THEY'RE JUST THE DUMBEST.
WE'RE THE DUMBEST.
THE MOST EXPENDABLE.
YOU CAN'T REALLY BELIEVE--
HURAAUGH!
NEVER MIND--THAT'S OUR CUE TO LEAVE.
VROOM!!

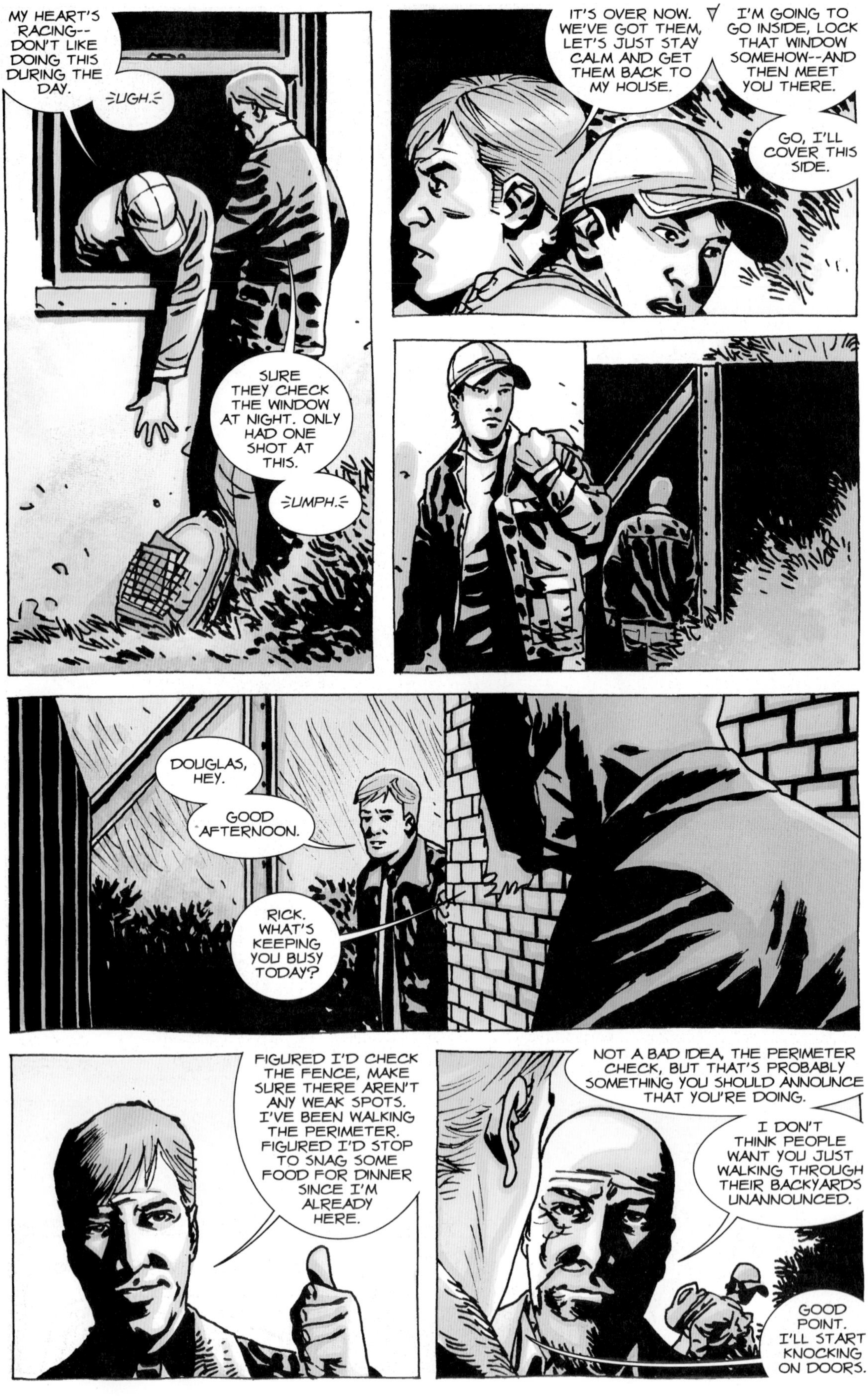
MY HEART'S RACING-- DON'T LIKE DOING THIS DURING THE DAY.
UGH.
SURE THEY CHECK THE WINDOW AT NIGHT. ONLY HAD ONE SHOT AT THIS.
UMPH.
IT'S OVER NOW. WE'VE GOT THEM, LET'S JUST STAY CALM AND GET THEM BACK TO MY HOUSE.
I'M GOING TO GO INSIDE, LOCK THAT WINDOW SOMEHOW--AND THEN MEET YOU THERE.
GO, I'LL COVER THIS SIDE.
DOUGLAS, HEY.
GOOD AFTERNOON.
RICK. WHAT'S KEEPING YOU BUSY TODAY?
FIGURED I'D CHECK THE FENCE, MAKE SURE THERE AREN'T ANY WEAK SPOTS. I'VE BEEN WALKING THE PERIMETER. FIGURED I'D STOP TO SNAG SOME FOOD FOR DINNER SINCE I'M ALREADY HERE.
NOT A BAD IDEA, THE PERIMETER CHECK, BUT THAT'S PROBABLY SOMETHING YOU SHOULD ANNOUNCE THAT YOU'RE DOING.
I DON'T THINK PEOPLE WANT YOU JUST WALKING THROUGH THEIR BACKYARDS UNANNOUNCED.
GOOD POINT. I'LL START KNOCKING ON DOORS.

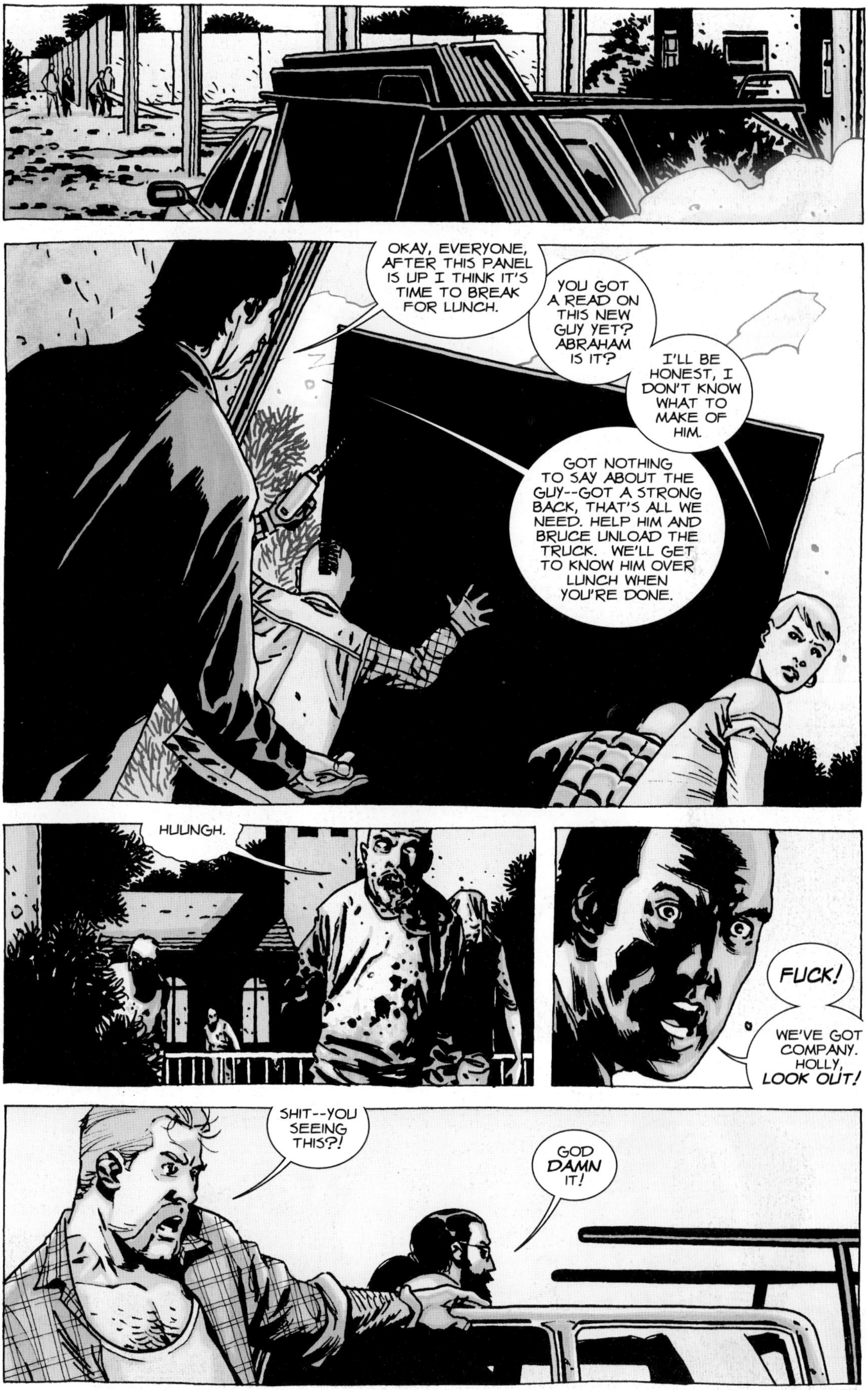

OKAY, EVERYONE, AFTER THIS PANEL IS UP I THINK IT'S TIME TO BREAK FOR LUNCH.
YOU GOT A READ ON THIS NEW GUY YET? ABRAHAM IS IT?
I'LL BE HONEST, I DON'T KNOW WHAT TO MAKE OF HIM.
GOT NOTHING TO SAY ABOUT THE GUY--GOT A STRONG BACK, THAT'S ALL WE NEED. HELP HIM AND BRUCE UNLOAD THE TRUCK. WE'LL GET TO KNOW HIM OVER LUNCH WHEN YOU'RE DONE.
HUUNGH.
FUCK!
WE'VE GOT COMPANY. HOLLY, LOOK OUT!
SHIT--YOU SEEING THIS?!
GOD DAMN IT!

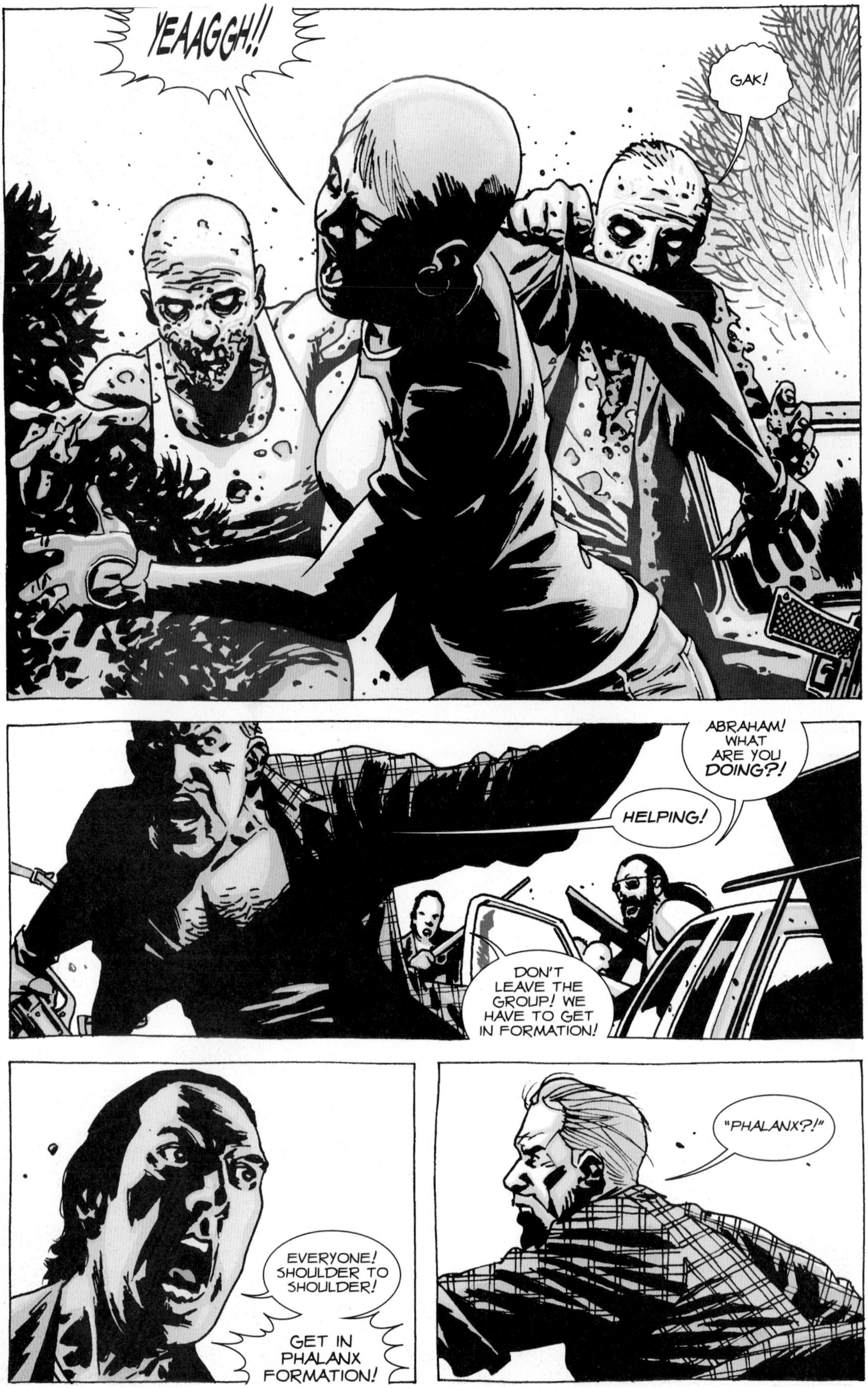
YEAAGGH!!
GAK!
ABRAHAM! WHAT ARE YOU DOING?!
HELPING!
DON'T LEAVE THE GROUP! WE HAVE TO GET IN FORMATION!
EVERYONE! SHOULDER TO SHOULDER!
GET IN PHALANX FORMATION!
"PHALANX?!"

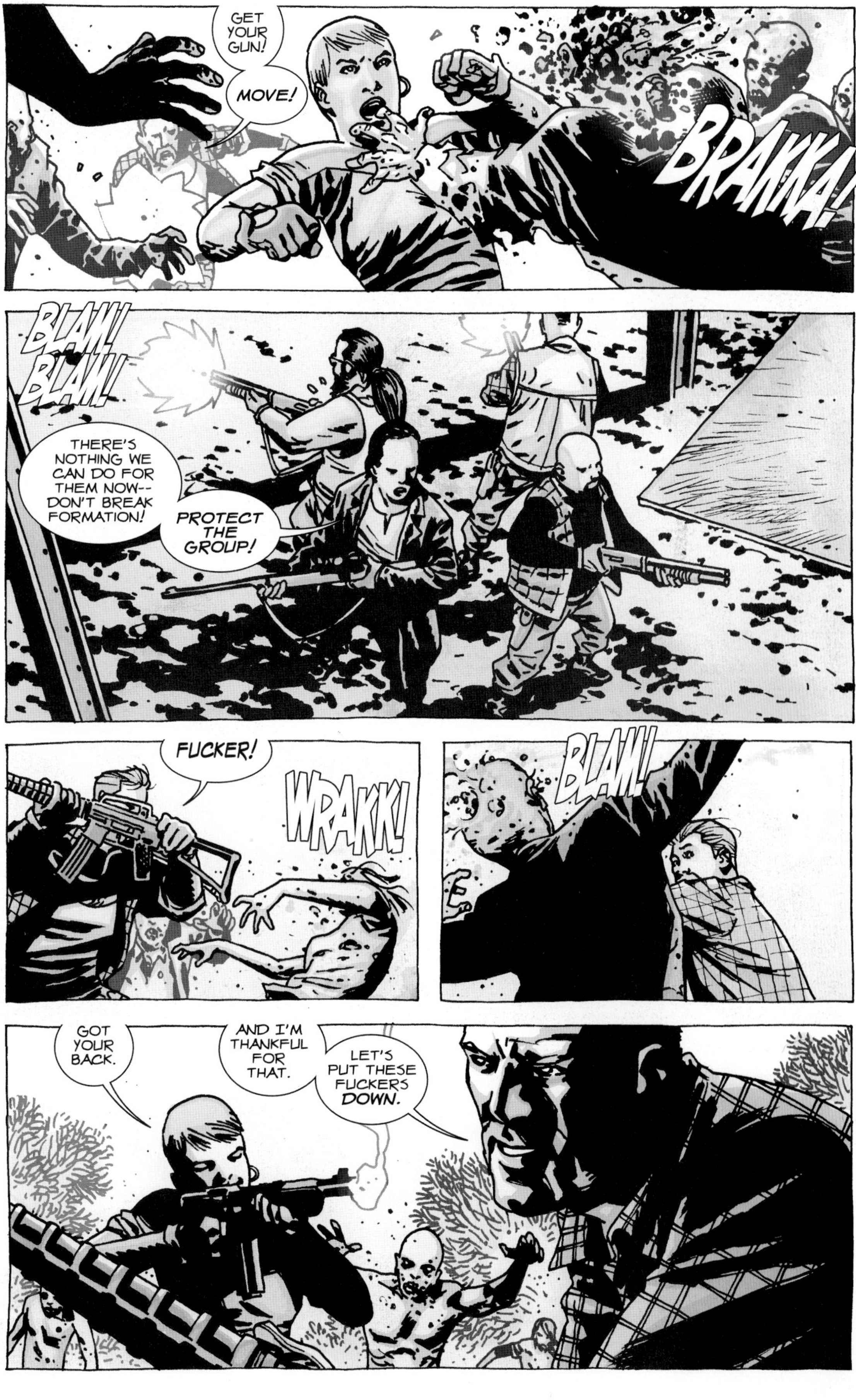

GET YOUR GUN!
MOVE!
BRAKKA!
BLAM! BLAM!
THERE'S NOTHING WE CAN DO FOR THEM NOW-- DON'T BREAK FORMATION!
PROTECT THE GROUP!
FUCKER!
WRAKK!
BLAM!
GOT YOUR BACK.
AND I'M THANKFUL FOR THAT.
LET'S PUT THESE FUCKERS DOWN.

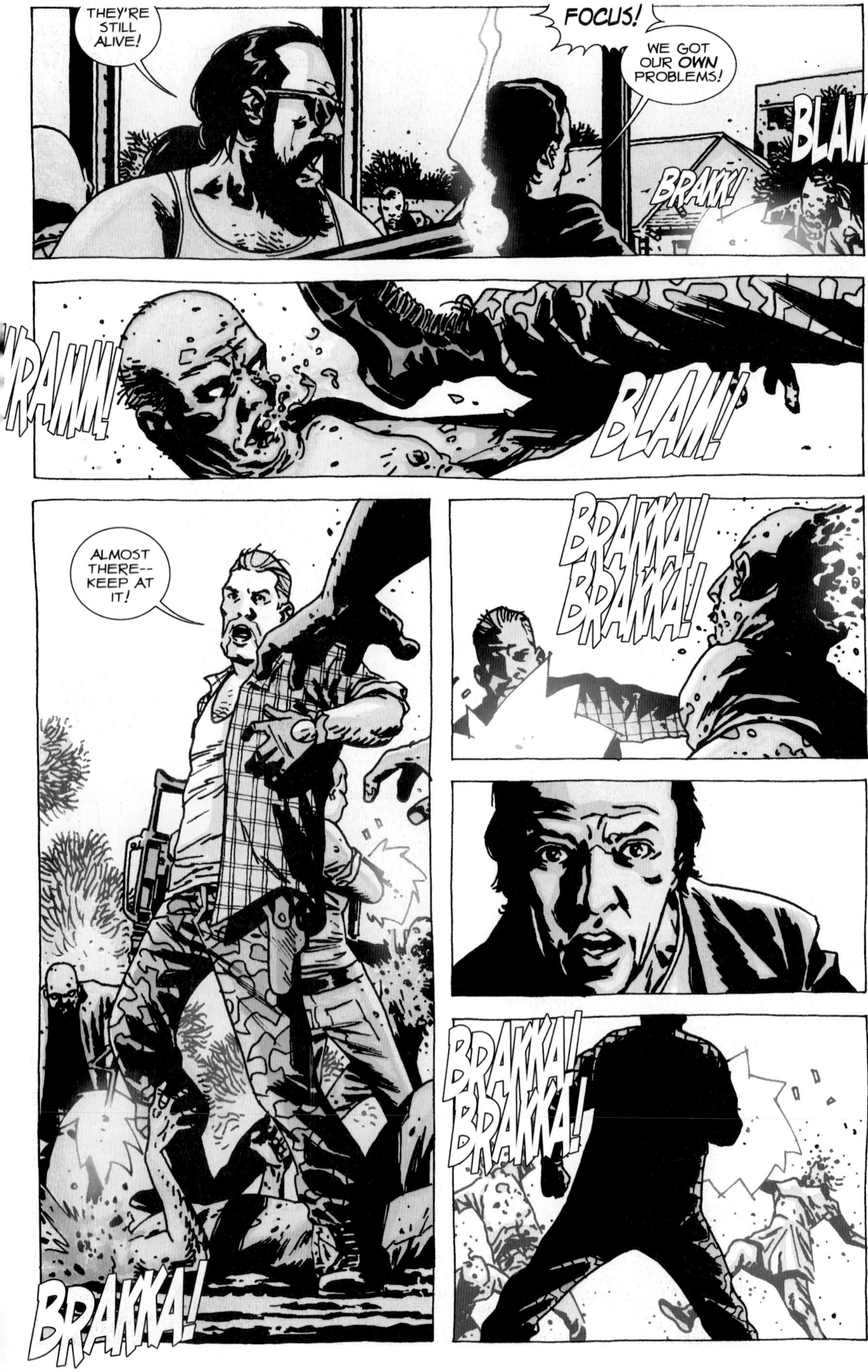
THEY'RE STILL ALIVE!
FOCUS!
WE GOT OUR OWN PROBLEMS!
BLAM!
BRAKK!
BLAM!
ALMOST THERE-- KEEP AT IT!
BRAKKA!
BRAKKA! BRAKKA!
BRAKKA! BRAKKA!

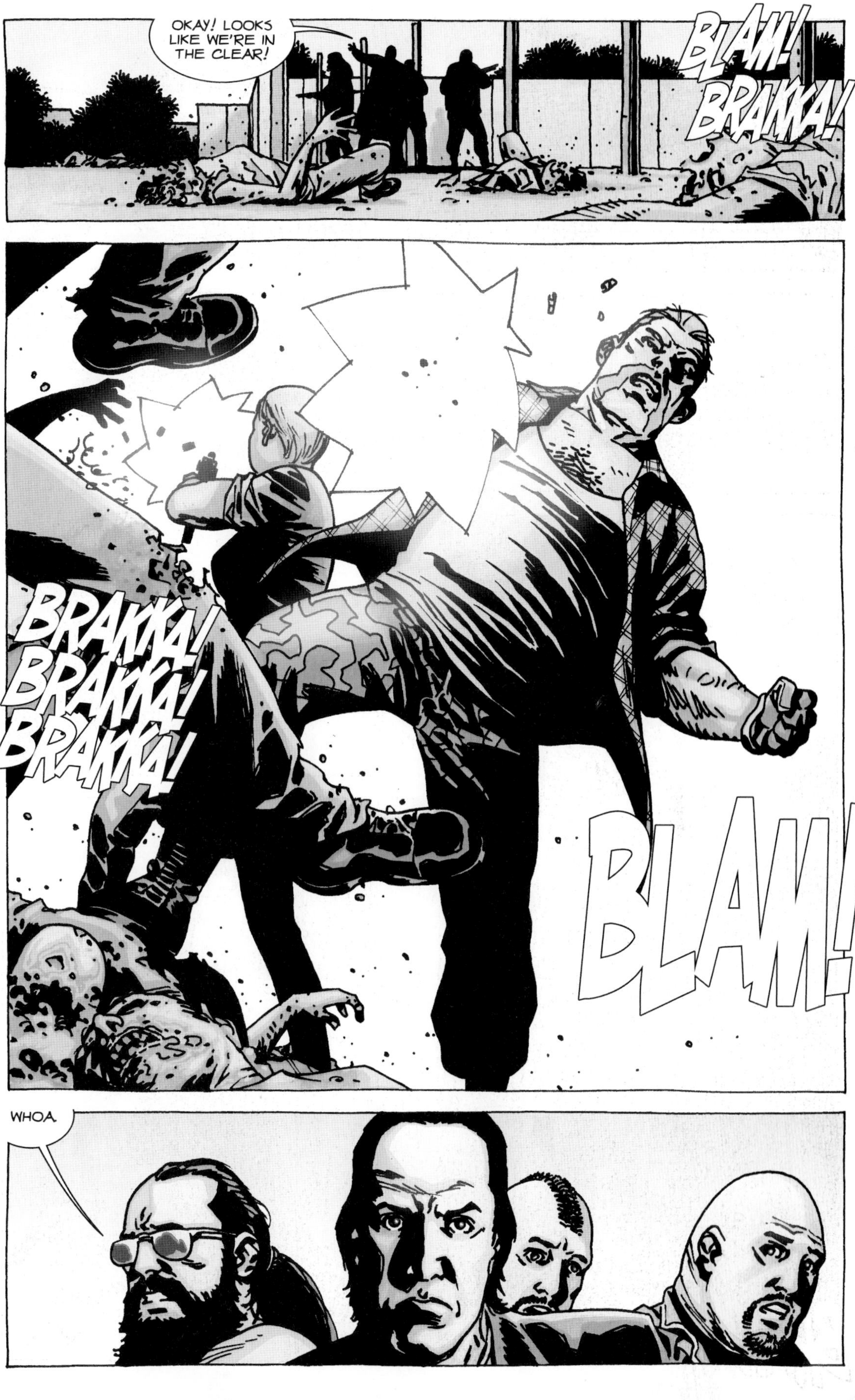
OKAY! LOOKS LIKE WE'RE IN THE CLEAR!
BLAM! BRAKKA!
BRAKKA! BRAKKA! BRAKKA!
BLAM!
WHOA.

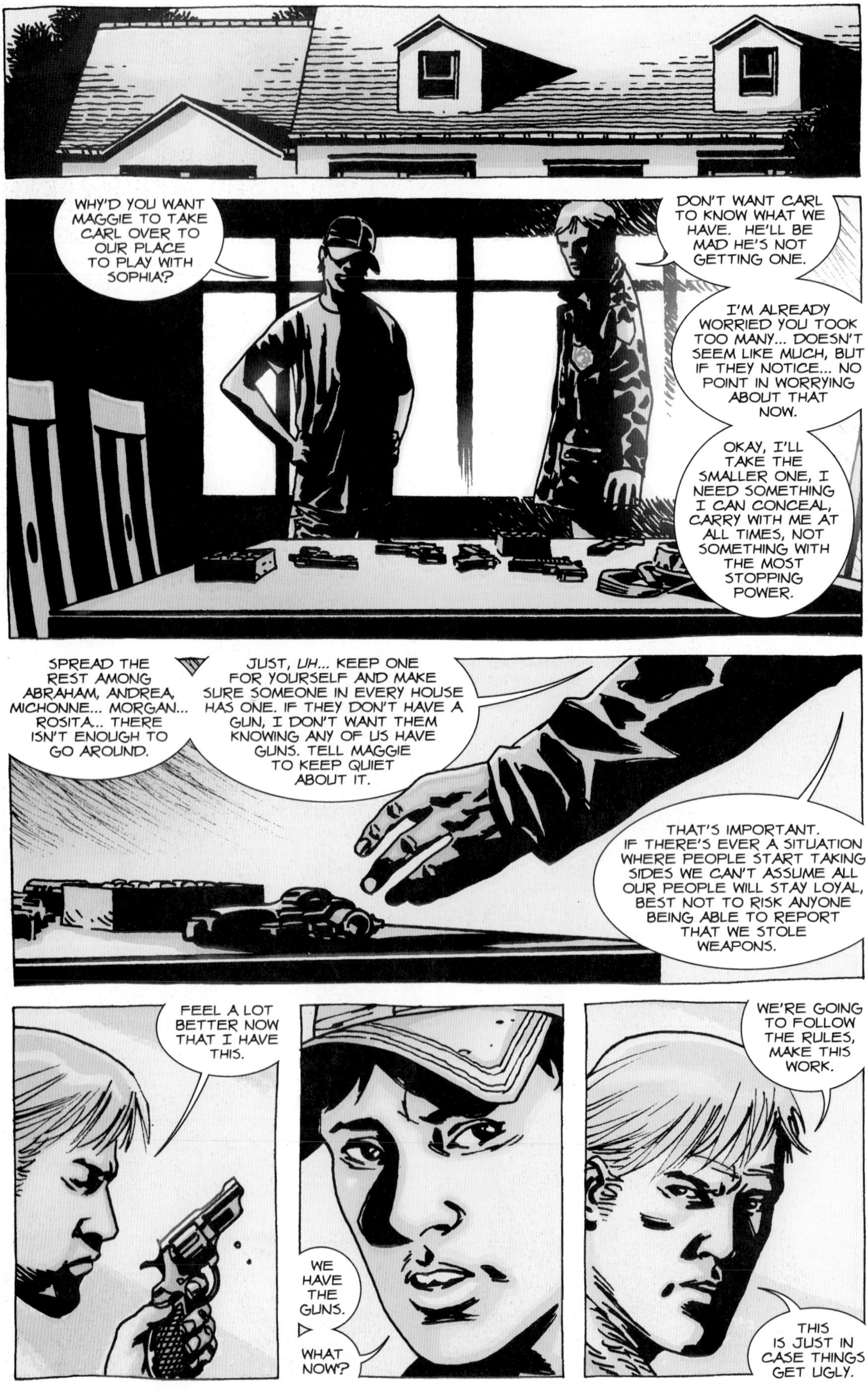
WHY'D YOU WANT MAGGIE TO TAKE CARL OVER TO OUR PLACE TO PLAY WITH SOPHIA?
DON'T WANT CARL TO KNOW WHAT WE HAVE. HE'LL BE MAD HE'S NOT GETTING ONE.
I'M ALREADY WORRIED YOU TOOK TOO MANY... DOESN'T SEEM LIKE MUCH, BUT IF THEY NOTICE... NO POINT IN WORRYING ABOUT THAT NOW.
OKAY, I'LL TAKE THE SMALLER ONE, I NEED SOMETHING I CAN CONCEAL, CARRY WITH ME AT ALL TIMES, NOT SOMETHING WITH THE MOST STOPPING POWER.
SPREAD THE REST AMONG ABRAHAM, ANDREA, MICHONNE... MORGAN... ROSITA... THERE ISN'T ENOUGH TO GO AROUND.
JUST, *UH*... KEEP ONE FOR YOURSELF AND MAKE SURE SOMEONE IN EVERY HOUSE HAS ONE. IF THEY DON'T HAVE A GUN, I DON'T WANT THEM KNOWING ANY OF US HAVE GUNS. TELL MAGGIE TO KEEP QUIET ABOUT IT.
THAT'S IMPORTANT. IF THERE'S EVER A SITUATION WHERE PEOPLE START TAKING SIDES WE CAN'T ASSUME ALL OUR PEOPLE WILL STAY LOYAL, BEST NOT TO RISK ANYONE BEING ABLE TO REPORT THAT WE STOLE WEAPONS.
FEEL A LOT BETTER NOW THAT I HAVE THIS.
WE HAVE THE GUNS.
WHAT NOW?
WE'RE GOING TO FOLLOW THE RULES, MAKE THIS WORK.
THIS IS JUST IN CASE THINGS GET UGLY.

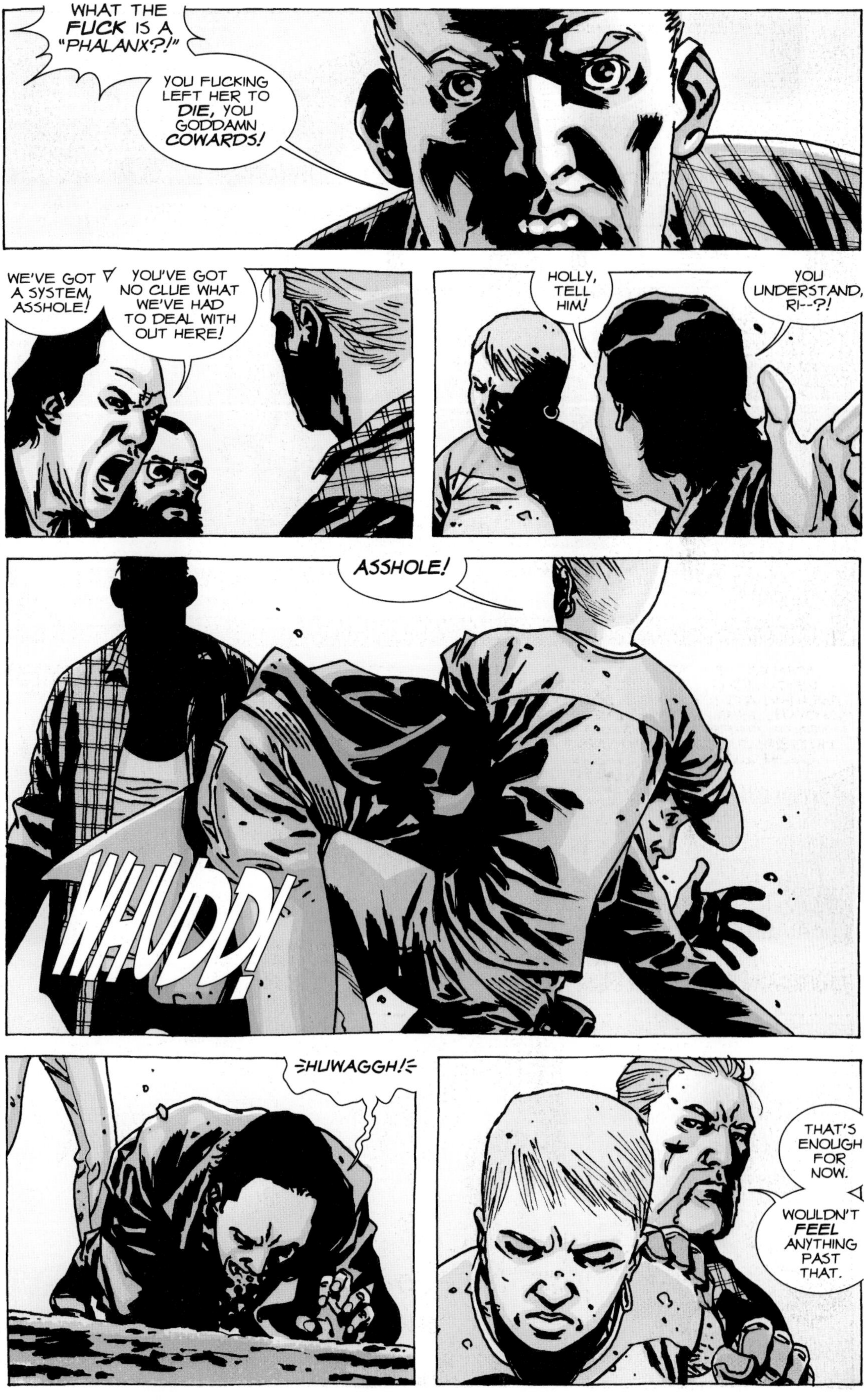
WHAT THE FUCK IS A "PHALANX?!"
YOU FUCKING LEFT HER TO DIE, YOU GODDAMN COWARDS!
WE'VE GOT A SYSTEM, ASSHOLE!
YOU'VE GOT NO CLUE WHAT WE'VE HAD TO DEAL WITH OUT HERE!
HOLLY, TELL HIM!
YOU UNDERSTAND, RI--?!
ASSHOLE!
WHUDD!
HUWAGGH!
THAT'S ENOUGH FOR NOW.
WOULDN'T FEEL ANYTHING PAST THAT.

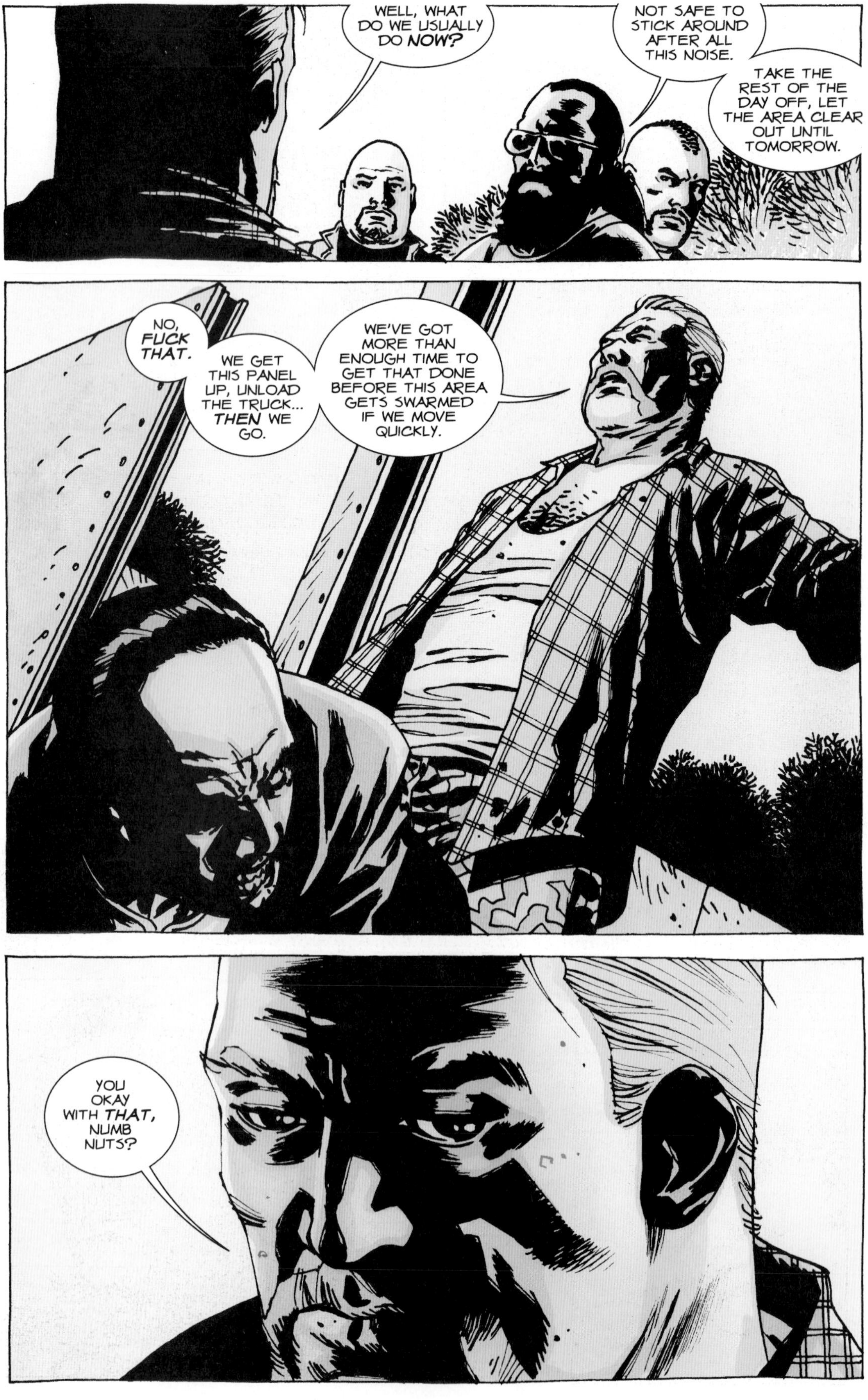
WELL, WHAT DO WE USUALLY DO NOW?
NOT SAFE TO STICK AROUND AFTER ALL THIS NOISE.
TAKE THE REST OF THE DAY OFF, LET THE AREA CLEAR OUT UNTIL TOMORROW.
NO, FUCK THAT.
WE GET THIS PANEL UP, UNLOAD THE TRUCK... THEN WE GO.
WE'VE GOT MORE THAN ENOUGH TIME TO GET THAT DONE BEFORE THIS AREA GETS SWARMED IF WE MOVE QUICKLY.
YOU OKAY WITH THAT, NUMB NUTS?

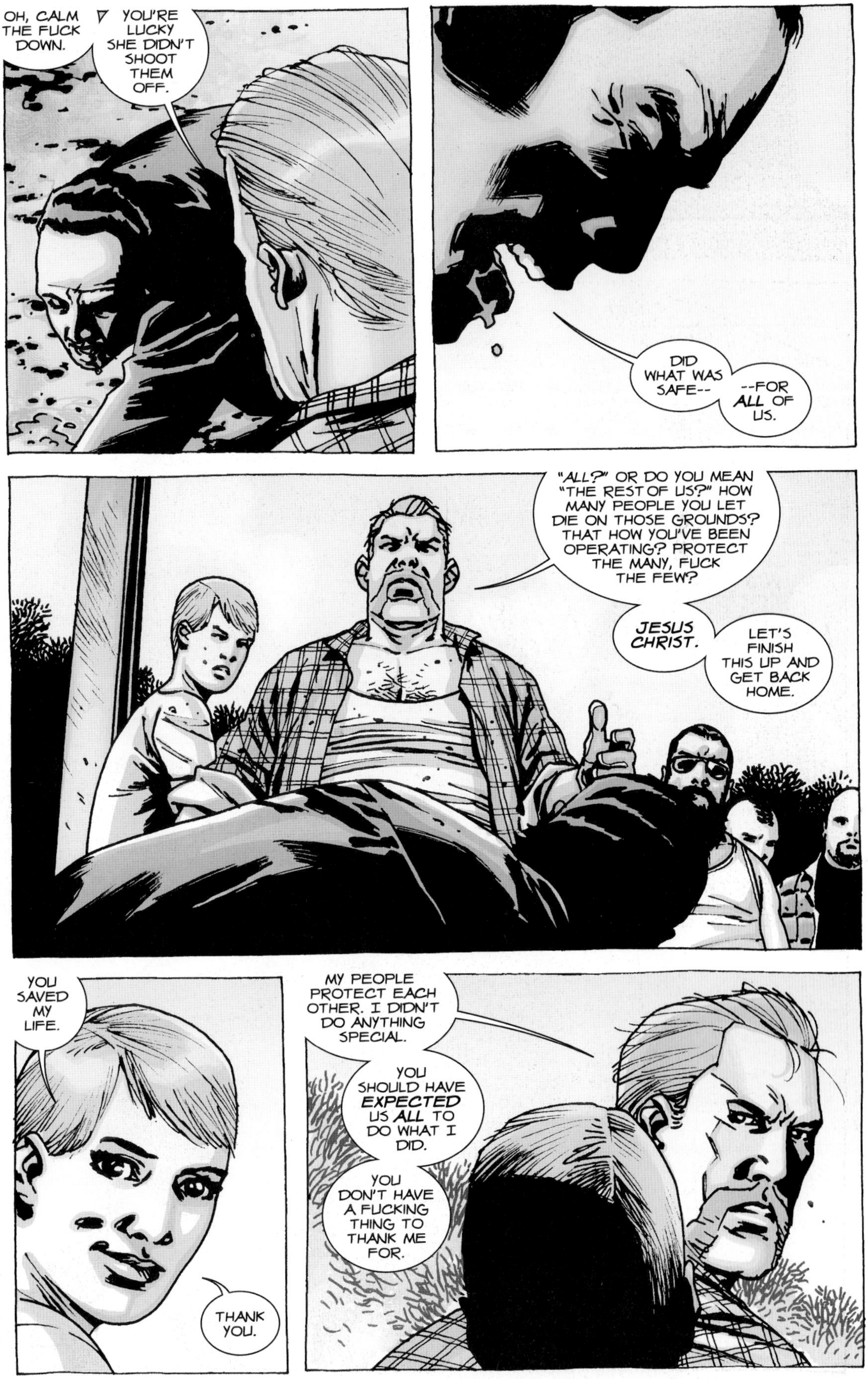
OH, CALM THE FUCK DOWN.
YOU'RE LUCKY SHE DIDN'T SHOOT THEM OFF.
DID WHAT WAS SAFE--
--FOR ALL OF US.
"ALL?" OR DO YOU MEAN "THE REST OF US?" HOW MANY PEOPLE YOU LET DIE ON THOSE GROUNDS? THAT HOW YOU'VE BEEN OPERATING? PROTECT THE MANY, FUCK THE FEW?
JESUS CHRIST.
LET'S FINISH THIS UP AND GET BACK HOME.
YOU SAVED MY LIFE.
THANK YOU.
MY PEOPLE PROTECT EACH OTHER. I DIDN'T DO ANYTHING SPECIAL.
YOU SHOULD HAVE EXPECTED US ALL TO DO WHAT I DID.
YOU DON'T HAVE A FUCKING THING TO THANK ME FOR.

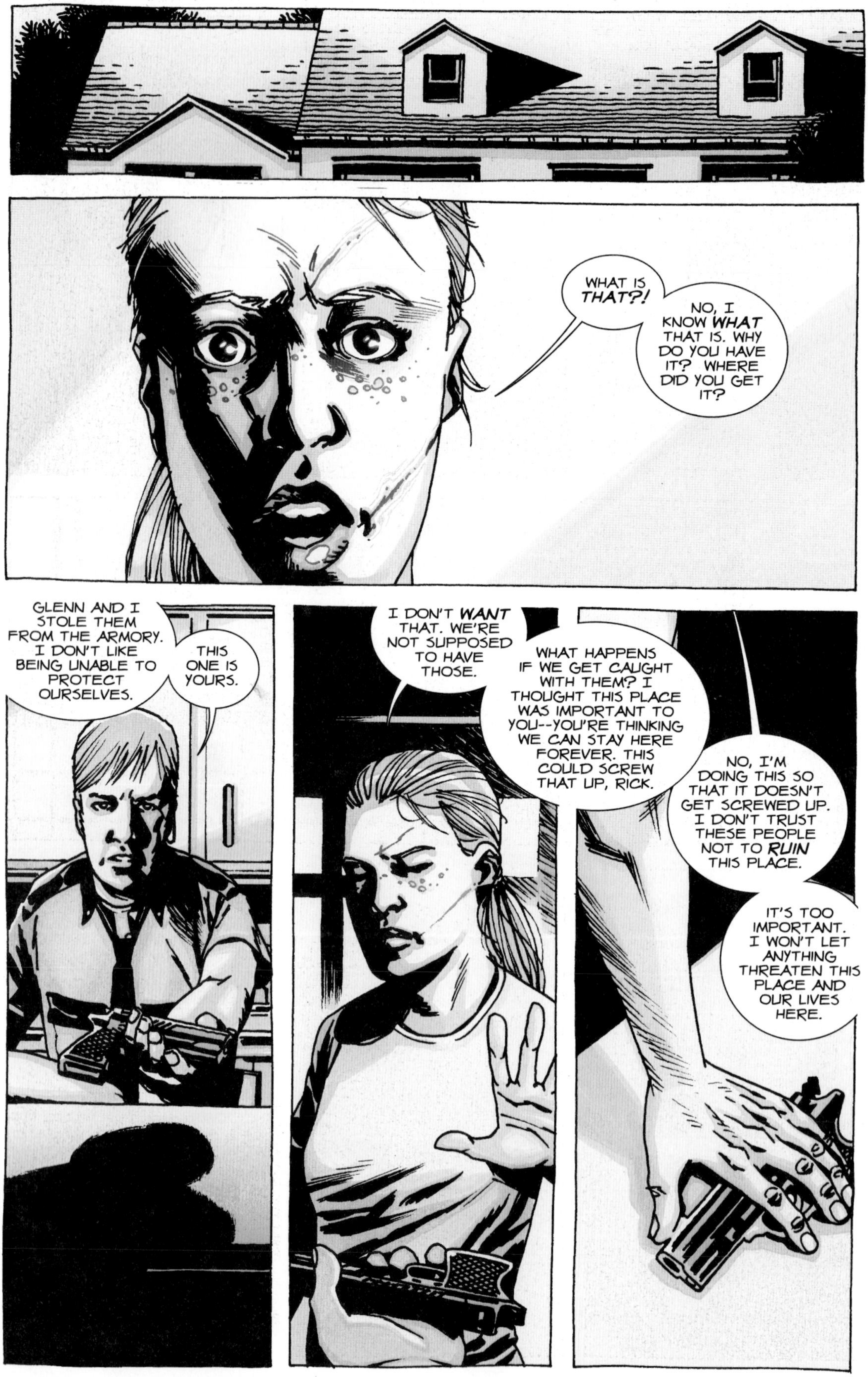

WHAT IS THAT?!
NO, I KNOW WHAT THAT IS. WHY DO YOU HAVE IT? WHERE DID YOU GET IT?
GLENN AND I STOLE THEM FROM THE ARMORY. I DON'T LIKE BEING UNABLE TO PROTECT OURSELVES.
THIS ONE IS YOURS.
I DON'T WANT THAT. WE'RE NOT SUPPOSED TO HAVE THOSE.
WHAT HAPPENS IF WE GET CAUGHT WITH THEM? I THOUGHT THIS PLACE WAS IMPORTANT TO YOU--YOU'RE THINKING WE CAN STAY HERE FOREVER. THIS COULD SCREW THAT UP, RICK.
NO, I'M DOING THIS SO THAT IT DOESN'T GET SCREWED UP. I DON'T TRUST THESE PEOPLE NOT TO RUIN THIS PLACE.
IT'S TOO IMPORTANT. I WON'T LET ANYTHING THREATEN THIS PLACE AND OUR LIVES HERE.

SO YOU'RE GOING TO TAKE OVER? THAT IT? I REMEMBER WHEN YOU DIDN'T **WANT** TO BE THE LEADER. THAT'S WHAT MADE YOU A GOOD ONE.

WHAT IS GOING ON, RICK? WHAT IS IT ABOUT THIS PLACE THAT'S BROUGHT THIS OUT OF YOU?

IT'S **CARL.**

I CAN'T SHAKE THE FEELING THAT THIS PLACE IS HIS LAST CHANCE.

LAST CHANCE FOR **WHAT?**

RICK, LISTEN TO ME. CARL IS **FINE.**

IS HE?

HE CAN'T EVEN ENJOY HIMSELF HERE. HE JUST LOST HIS MOTHER, HIS... NEW BABY SISTER. HIS DAD IS A **WRECK.** I ALMOST DIED RIGHT AFTER THEY DID--AND HE WAS THERE FOR THAT.

HE THOUGHT I **WAS** DEAD FOR A BIT THERE.

FOR GOD'S SAKE, ANDREA, YOU **KNOW** WHAT HE DI--

...

WHAT?

I KNOW WHAT CARL **WHAT?**

WHAT?

I KNOW WHAT CARL **WHAT?**

YOU KNOW WHAT CARL'S BEEN THROUGH.

I HAVE TO MAKE THINGS **WORK** HERE. I HAVE TO BE READY FOR ANYTHING... I HAVE TO THINK THREE STEPS AHEAD OF EVERYONE.

IF YOU DON'T WANT THE GUN, I'LL GIVE IT TO SOMEONE ELSE-- BUT PLEASE, KEEP THIS BETWEEN THE TWO OF US.

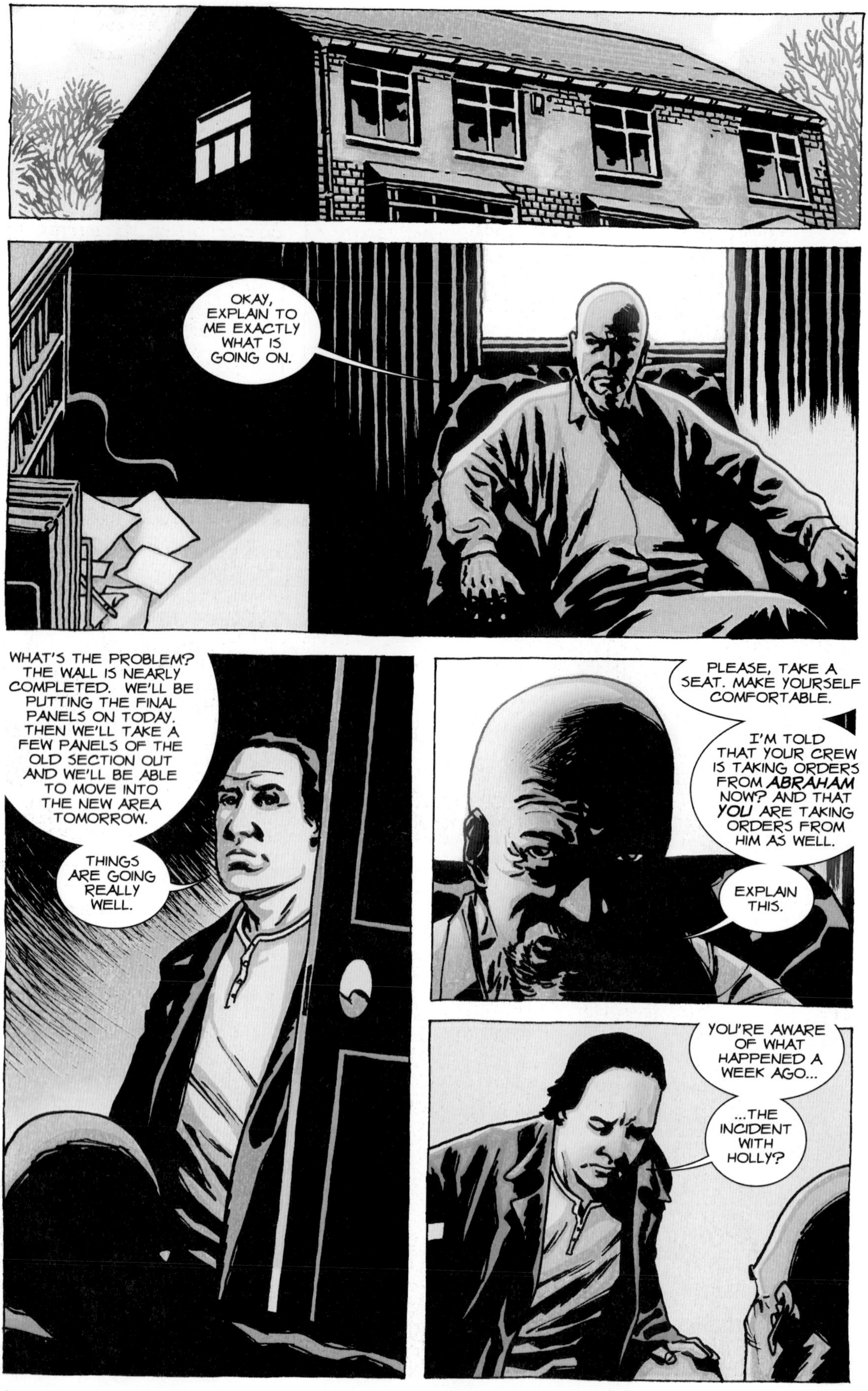
OKAY, EXPLAIN TO ME EXACTLY WHAT IS GOING ON.
WHAT'S THE PROBLEM? THE WALL IS NEARLY COMPLETED. WE'LL BE PUTTING THE FINAL PANELS ON TODAY. THEN WE'LL TAKE A FEW PANELS OF THE OLD SECTION OUT AND WE'LL BE ABLE TO MOVE INTO THE NEW AREA TOMORROW.
THINGS ARE GOING REALLY WELL.
PLEASE, TAKE A SEAT. MAKE YOURSELF COMFORTABLE.
I'M TOLD THAT YOUR CREW IS TAKING ORDERS FROM ABRAHAM NOW? AND THAT YOU ARE TAKING ORDERS FROM HIM AS WELL.
EXPLAIN THIS.
YOU'RE AWARE OF WHAT HAPPENED A WEEK AGO...
...THE INCIDENT WITH HOLLY?

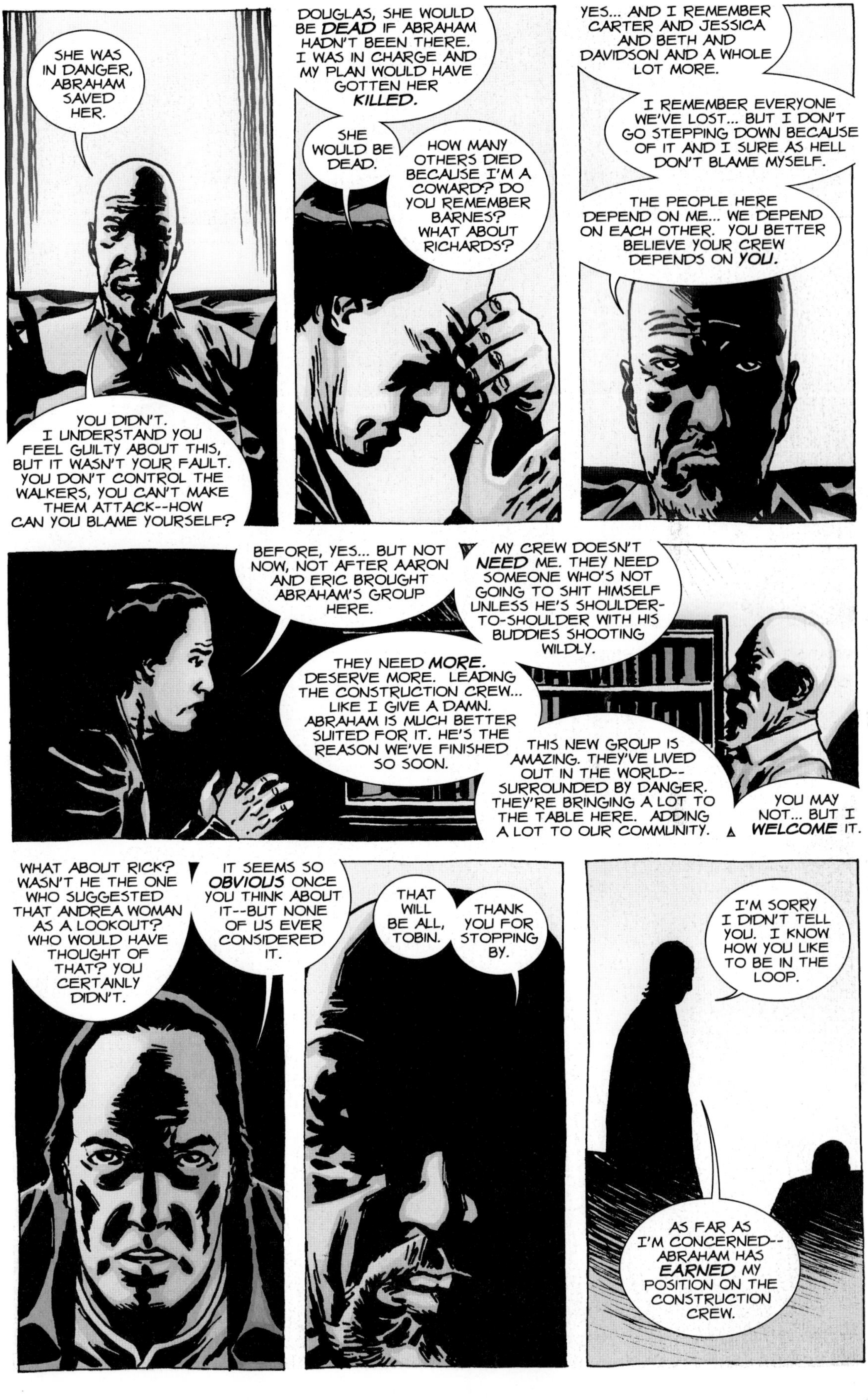
SHE WAS IN DANGER, ABRAHAM SAVED HER.
YOU DIDN'T. I UNDERSTAND YOU FEEL GUILTY ABOUT THIS, BUT IT WASN'T YOUR FAULT. YOU DON'T CONTROL THE WALKERS, YOU CAN'T MAKE THEM ATTACK--HOW CAN YOU BLAME YOURSELF?
DOUGLAS, SHE WOULD BE DEAD IF ABRAHAM HADN'T BEEN THERE. I WAS IN CHARGE AND MY PLAN WOULD HAVE GOTTEN HER KILLED.
SHE WOULD BE DEAD.
HOW MANY OTHERS DIED BECAUSE I'M A COWARD? DO YOU REMEMBER BARNES? WHAT ABOUT RICHARDS?
YES... AND I REMEMBER CARTER AND JESSICA AND BETH AND DAVIDSON AND A WHOLE LOT MORE.
I REMEMBER EVERYONE WE'VE LOST... BUT I DON'T GO STEPPING DOWN BECAUSE OF IT AND I SURE AS HELL DON'T BLAME MYSELF.
THE PEOPLE HERE DEPEND ON ME... WE DEPEND ON EACH OTHER. YOU BETTER BELIEVE YOUR CREW DEPENDS ON YOU.
BEFORE, YES... BUT NOT NOW, NOT AFTER AARON AND ERIC BROUGHT ABRAHAM'S GROUP HERE.
MY CREW DOESN'T NEED ME. THEY NEED SOMEONE WHO'S NOT GOING TO SHIT HIMSELF UNLESS HE'S SHOULDER-TO-SHOULDER WITH HIS BUDDIES SHOOTING WILDLY.
THEY NEED MORE. DESERVE MORE. LEADING THE CONSTRUCTION CREW... LIKE I GIVE A DAMN. ABRAHAM IS MUCH BETTER SUITED FOR IT. HE'S THE REASON WE'VE FINISHED SO SOON.
THIS NEW GROUP IS AMAZING. THEY'VE LIVED OUT IN THE WORLD-- SURROUNDED BY DANGER. THEY'RE BRINGING A LOT TO THE TABLE HERE. ADDING A LOT TO OUR COMMUNITY.
YOU MAY NOT... BUT I WELCOME IT.
WHAT ABOUT RICK? WASN'T HE THE ONE WHO SUGGESTED THAT ANDREA WOMAN AS A LOOKOUT? WHO WOULD HAVE THOUGHT OF THAT? YOU CERTAINLY DIDN'T.
IT SEEMS SO OBVIOUS ONCE YOU THINK ABOUT IT--BUT NONE OF US EVER CONSIDERED IT.
THAT WILL BE ALL, TOBIN.
THANK YOU FOR STOPPING BY.
I'M SORRY I DIDN'T TELL YOU. I KNOW HOW YOU LIKE TO BE IN THE LOOP.
AS FAR AS I'M CONCERNED-- ABRAHAM HAS EARNED MY POSITION ON THE CONSTRUCTION CREW.

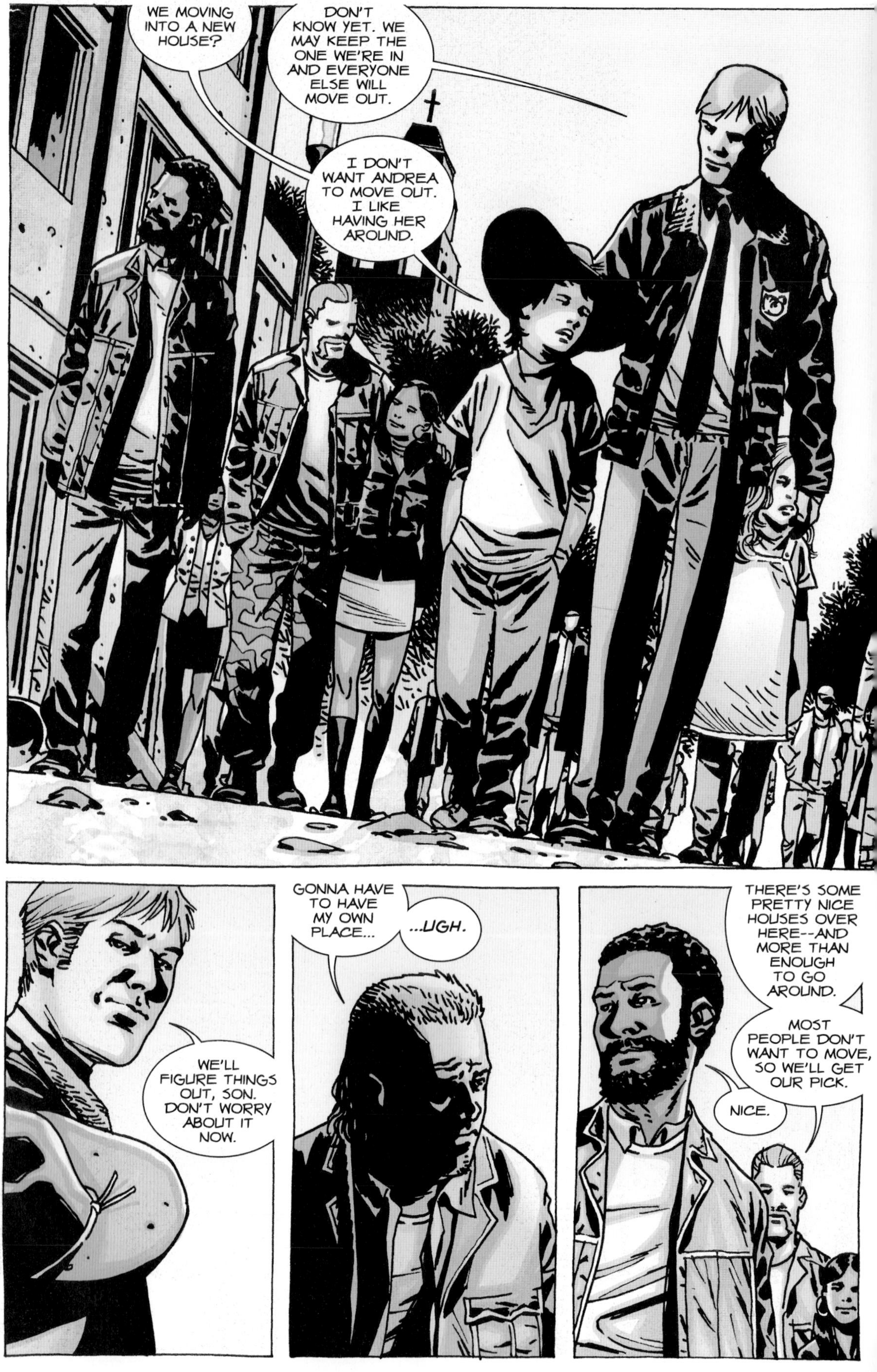
WE MOVING INTO A NEW HOUSE?
DON'T KNOW YET. WE MAY KEEP THE ONE WE'RE IN AND EVERYONE ELSE WILL MOVE OUT.
I DON'T WANT ANDREA TO MOVE OUT. I LIKE HAVING HER AROUND.
WE'LL FIGURE THINGS OUT, SON. DON'T WORRY ABOUT IT NOW.
GONNA HAVE TO HAVE MY OWN PLACE...
...UGH.
THERE'S SOME PRETTY NICE HOUSES OVER HERE--AND MORE THAN ENOUGH TO GO AROUND.
MOST PEOPLE DON'T WANT TO MOVE, SO WE'LL GET OUR PICK.
NICE.

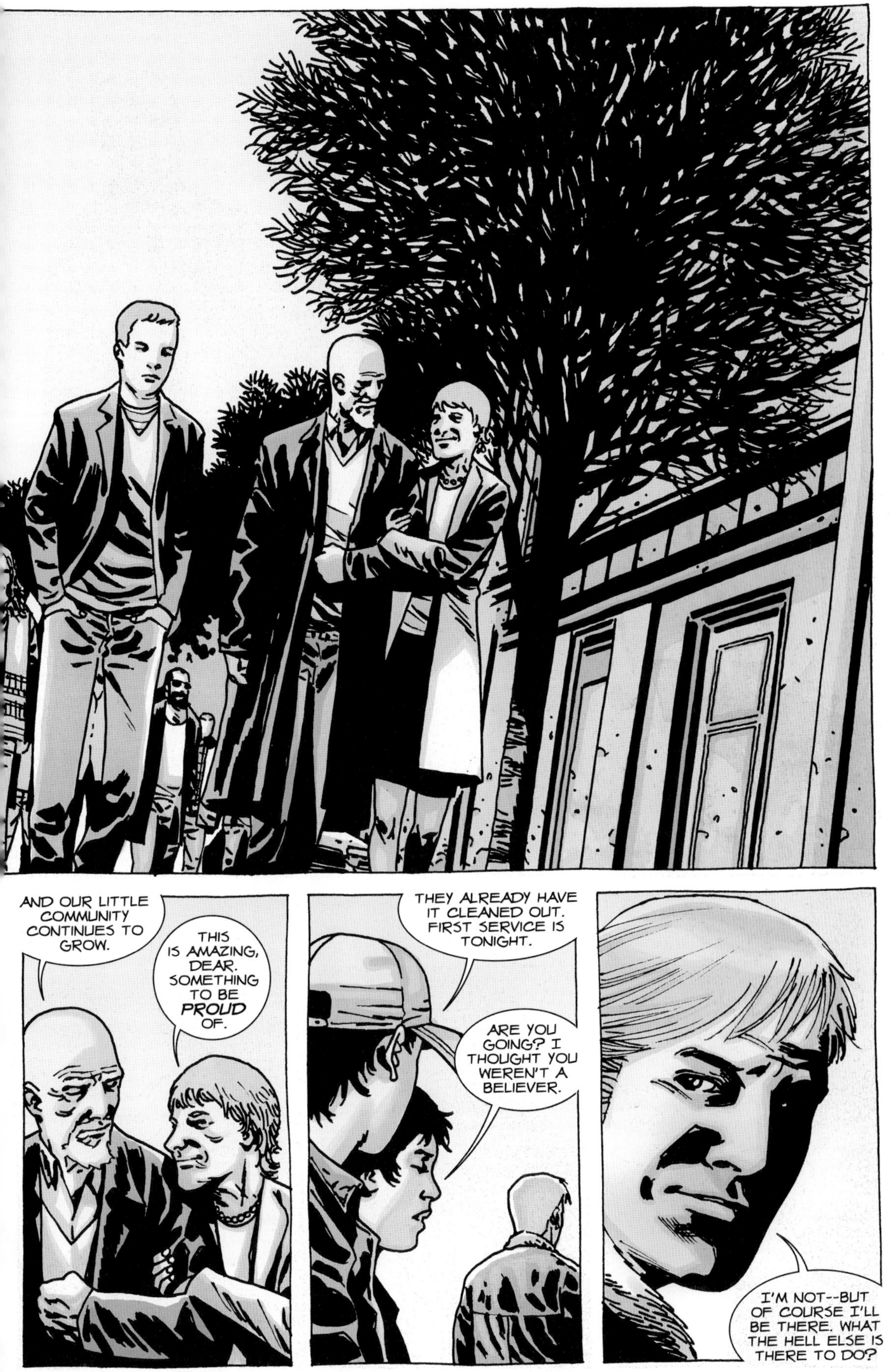

AND OUR LITTLE COMMUNITY CONTINUES TO GROW.
THIS IS AMAZING, DEAR. SOMETHING TO BE PROUD OF.
THEY ALREADY HAVE IT CLEANED OUT. FIRST SERVICE IS TONIGHT.
ARE YOU GOING? I THOUGHT YOU WEREN'T A BELIEVER.
I'M NOT--BUT OF COURSE I'LL BE THERE. WHAT THE HELL ELSE IS THERE TO DO?

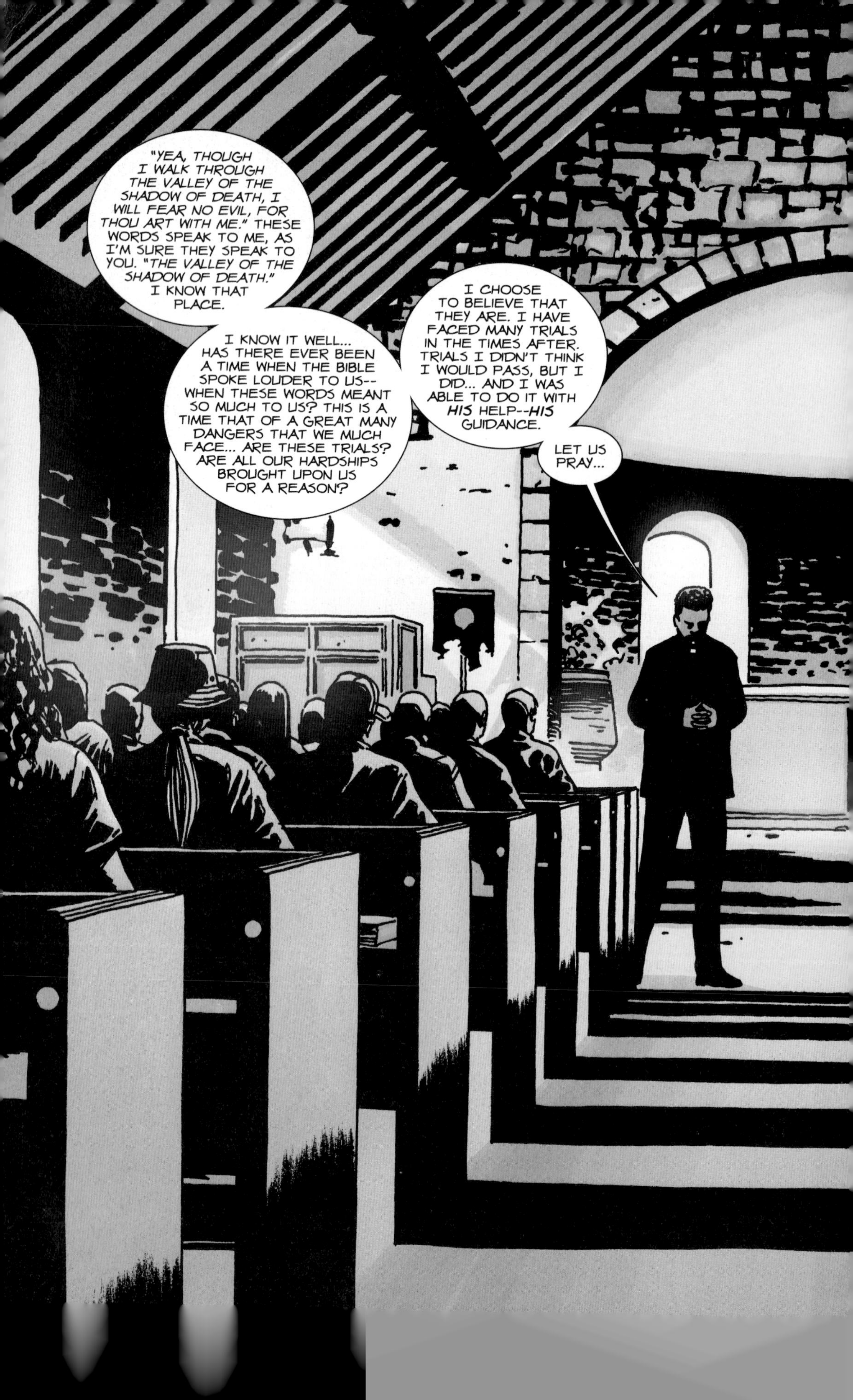
"YEA, THOUGH I WALK THROUGH THE VALLEY OF THE SHADOW OF DEATH, I WILL FEAR NO EVIL, FOR THOU ART WITH ME." THESE WORDS SPEAK TO ME, AS I'M SURE THEY SPEAK TO YOU. "THE VALLEY OF THE SHADOW OF DEATH." I KNOW THAT PLACE.
I KNOW IT WELL... HAS THERE EVER BEEN A TIME WHEN THE BIBLE SPOKE LOUDER TO US-- WHEN THESE WORDS MEANT SO MUCH TO US? THIS IS A TIME THAT OF A GREAT MANY DANGERS THAT WE MUCH FACE... ARE THESE TRIALS? ARE ALL OUR HARDSHIPS BROUGHT UPON US FOR A REASON?
I CHOOSE TO BELIEVE THAT THEY ARE. I HAVE FACED MANY TRIALS IN THE TIMES AFTER. TRIALS I DIDN'T THINK I WOULD PASS, BUT I DID... AND I WAS ABLE TO DO IT WITH HIS HELP--HIS GUIDANCE.
LET US PRAY...

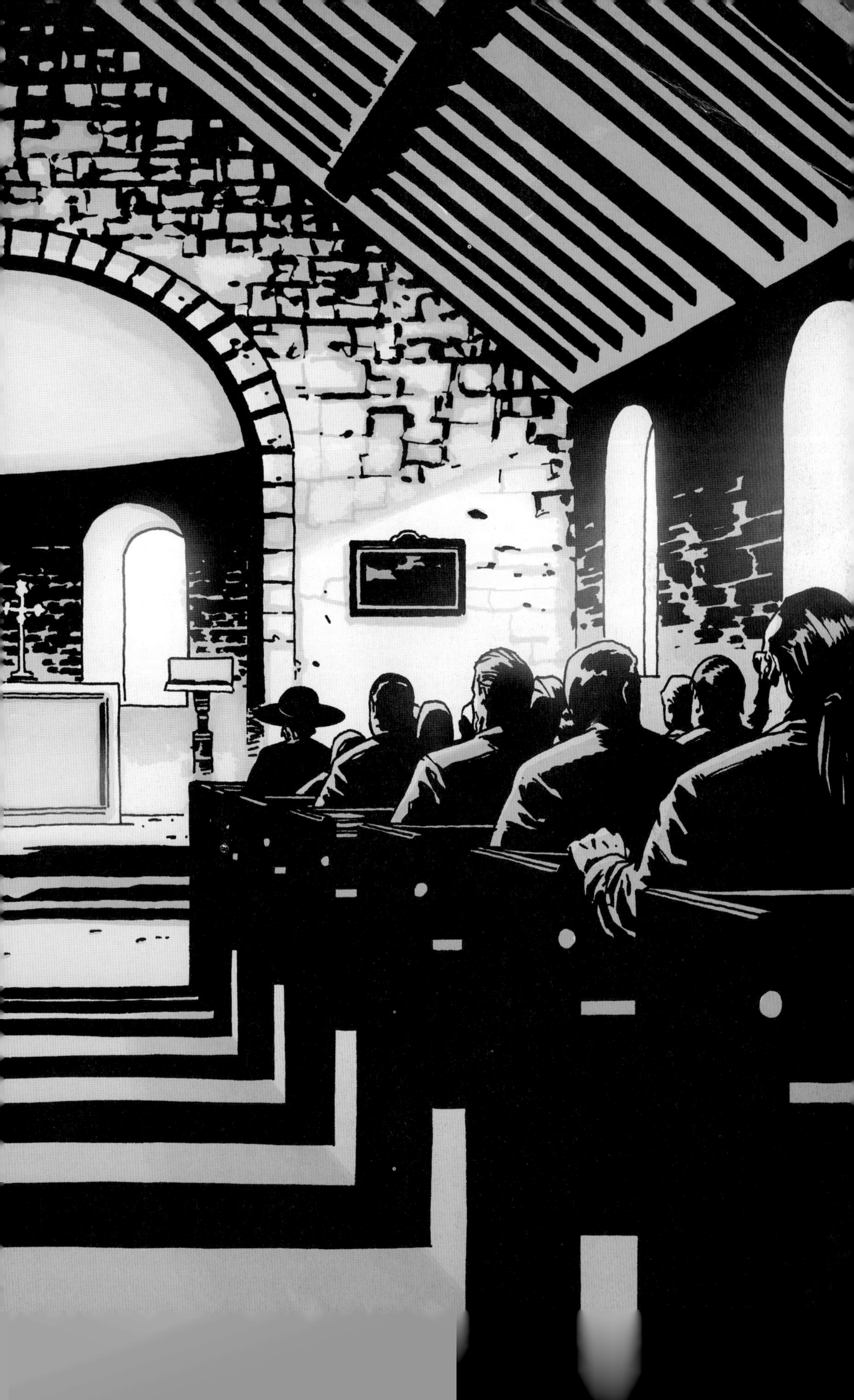

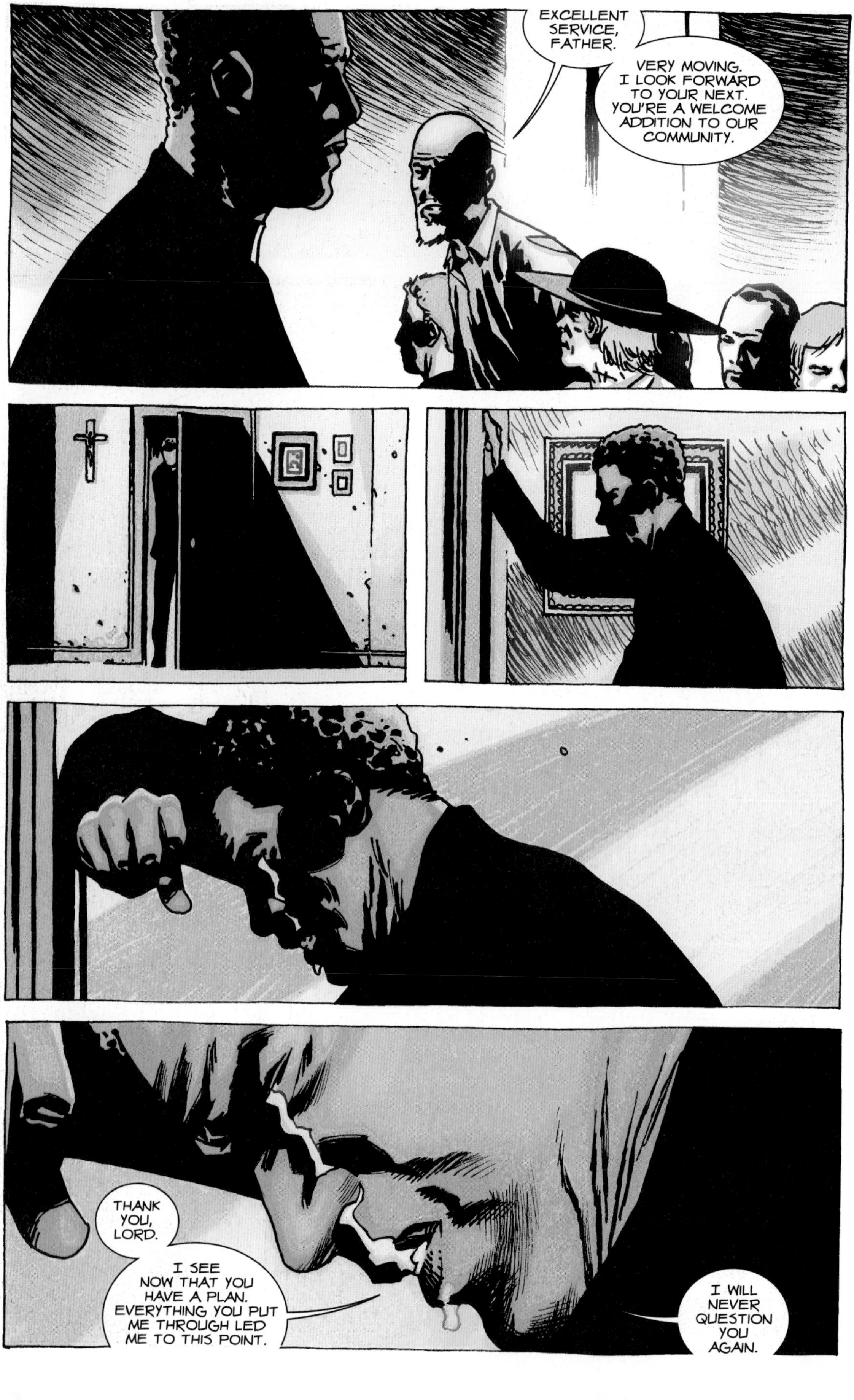
EXCELLENT SERVICE, FATHER.
VERY MOVING. I LOOK FORWARD TO YOUR NEXT. YOU'RE A WELCOME ADDITION TO OUR COMMUNITY.
THANK YOU, LORD.
I SEE NOW THAT YOU HAVE A PLAN. EVERYTHING YOU PUT ME THROUGH LED ME TO THIS POINT.
I WILL NEVER QUESTION YOU AGAIN.

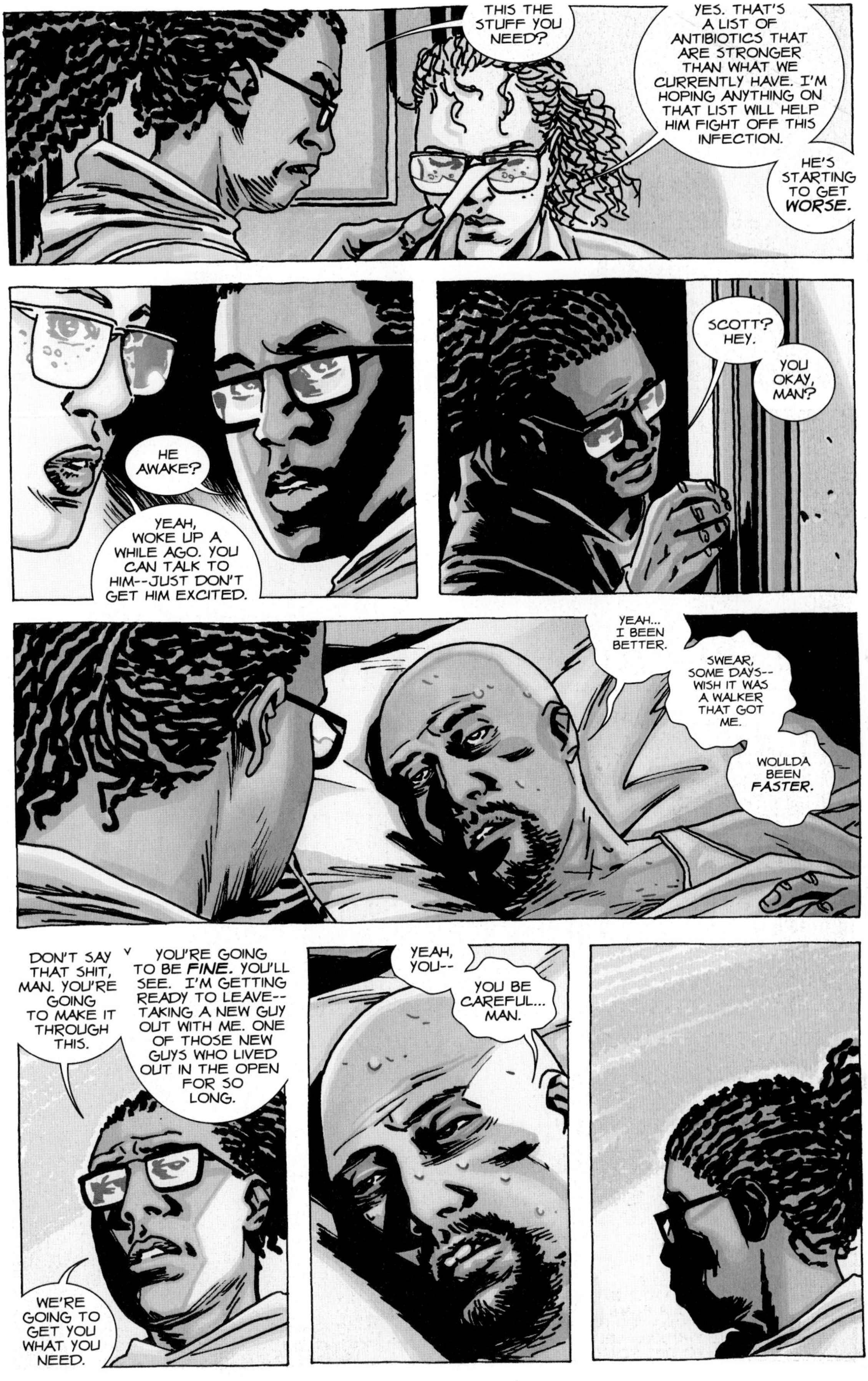

THIS THE STUFF YOU NEED?
YES. THAT'S A LIST OF ANTIBIOTICS THAT ARE STRONGER THAN WHAT WE CURRENTLY HAVE. I'M HOPING ANYTHING ON THAT LIST WILL HELP HIM FIGHT OFF THIS INFECTION.
HE'S STARTING TO GET WORSE.
HE AWAKE?
YEAH, WOKE UP A WHILE AGO. YOU CAN TALK TO HIM--JUST DON'T GET HIM EXCITED.
SCOTT? HEY.
YOU OKAY, MAN?
YEAH... I BEEN BETTER.
SWEAR, SOME DAYS-- WISH IT WAS A WALKER THAT GOT ME.
WOULDA BEEN FASTER.
DON'T SAY THAT SHIT, MAN. YOU'RE GOING TO MAKE IT THROUGH THIS.
YOU'RE GOING TO BE FINE. YOU'LL SEE. I'M GETTING READY TO LEAVE-- TAKING A NEW GUY OUT WITH ME. ONE OF THOSE NEW GUYS WHO LIVED OUT IN THE OPEN FOR SO LONG.
WE'RE GOING TO GET YOU WHAT YOU NEED.
YEAH, YOU--
YOU BE CAREFUL... MAN.

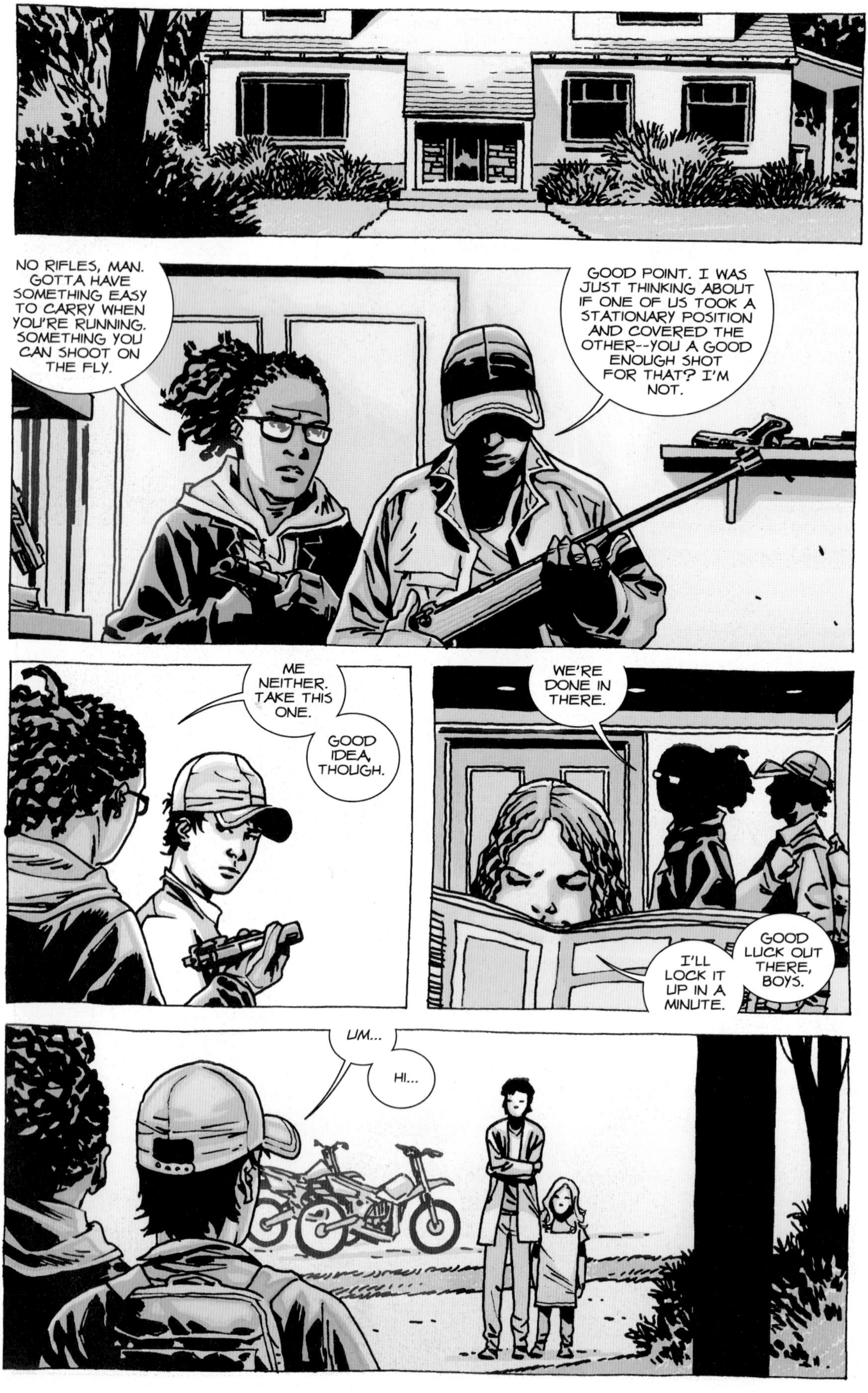
NO RIFLES, MAN. GOTTA HAVE SOMETHING EASY TO CARRY WHEN YOU'RE RUNNING. SOMETHING YOU CAN SHOOT ON THE FLY.
GOOD POINT. I WAS JUST THINKING ABOUT IF ONE OF US TOOK A STATIONARY POSITION AND COVERED THE OTHER--YOU A GOOD ENOUGH SHOT FOR THAT? I'M NOT.
ME NEITHER. TAKE THIS ONE.
GOOD IDEA, THOUGH.
WE'RE DONE IN THERE.
I'LL LOCK IT UP IN A MINUTE.
GOOD LUCK OUT THERE, BOYS.
UM...
HI...

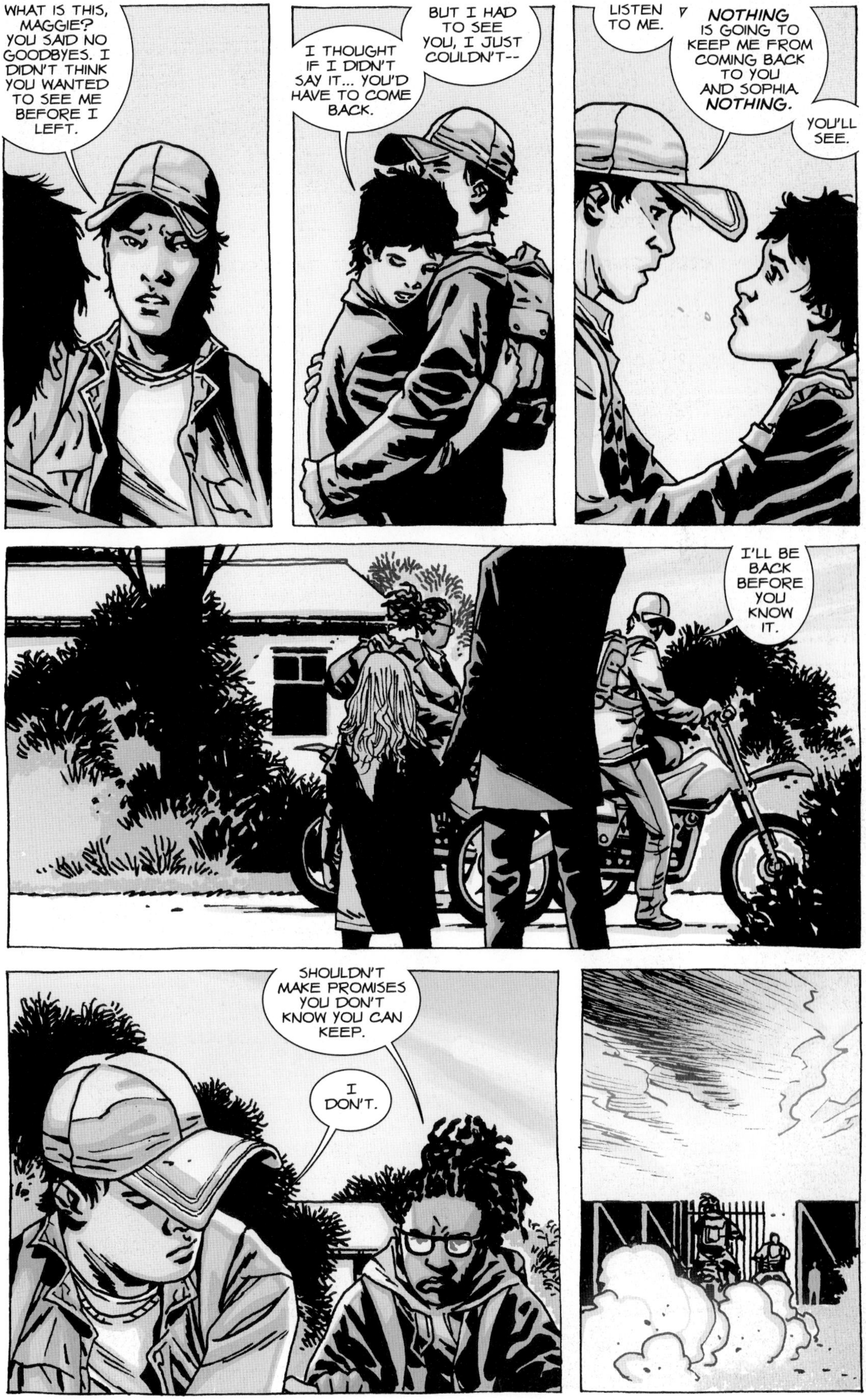
WHAT IS THIS, MAGGIE? YOU SAID NO GOODBYES. I DIDN'T THINK YOU WANTED TO SEE ME BEFORE I LEFT.
I THOUGHT IF I DIDN'T SAY IT... YOU'D HAVE TO COME BACK.
BUT I HAD TO SEE YOU, I JUST COULDN'T--
LISTEN TO ME.
NOTHING IS GOING TO KEEP ME FROM COMING BACK TO YOU AND SOPHIA. NOTHING.
YOU'LL SEE.
I'LL BE BACK BEFORE YOU KNOW IT.
SHOULDN'T MAKE PROMISES YOU DON'T KNOW YOU CAN KEEP.
I DON'T.

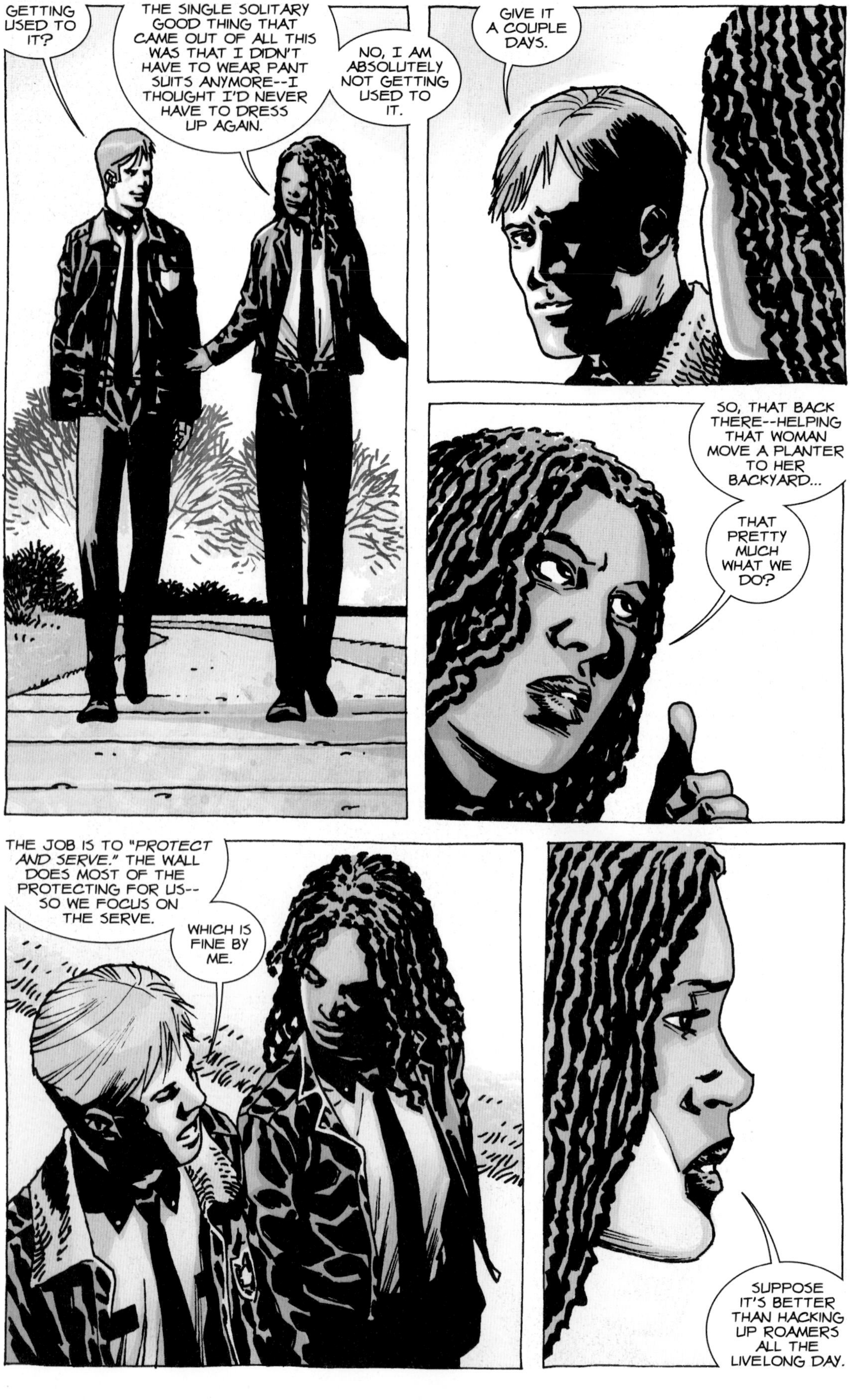
GETTING USED TO IT?
THE SINGLE SOLITARY GOOD THING THAT CAME OUT OF ALL THIS WAS THAT I DIDN'T HAVE TO WEAR PANT SUITS ANYMORE--I THOUGHT I'D NEVER HAVE TO DRESS UP AGAIN.
NO, I AM ABSOLUTELY NOT GETTING USED TO IT.
GIVE IT A COUPLE DAYS.
SO, THAT BACK THERE--HELPING THAT WOMAN MOVE A PLANTER TO HER BACKYARD...
THAT PRETTY MUCH WHAT WE DO?
THE JOB IS TO "PROTECT AND SERVE." THE WALL DOES MOST OF THE PROTECTING FOR US--SO WE FOCUS ON THE SERVE.
WHICH IS FINE BY ME.
SUPPOSE IT'S BETTER THAN HACKING UP ROAMERS ALL THE LIVELONG DAY.

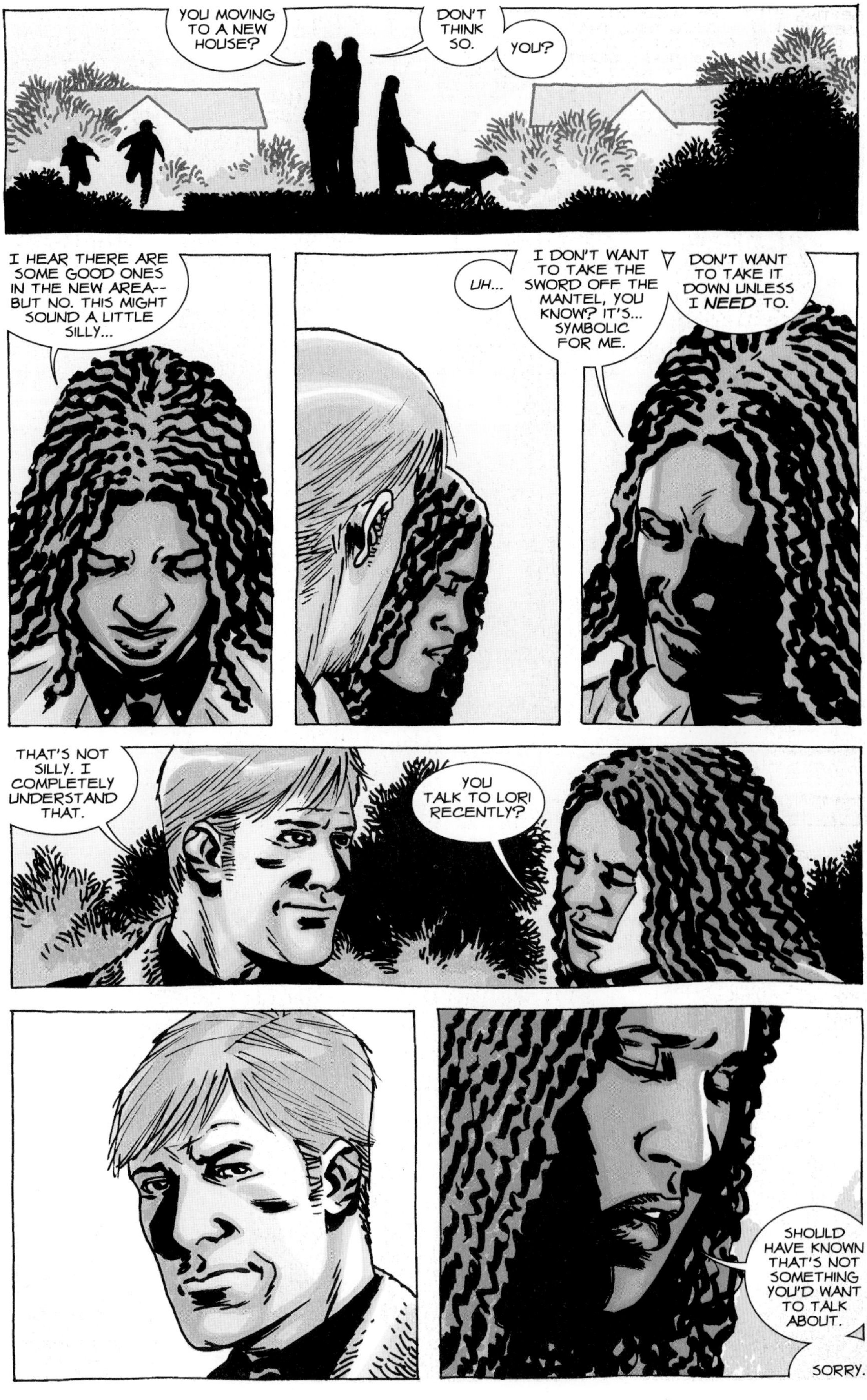

YOU MOVING TO A NEW HOUSE?
DON'T THINK SO.
YOU?
I HEAR THERE ARE SOME GOOD ONES IN THE NEW AREA-- BUT NO. THIS MIGHT SOUND A LITTLE SILLY...
UH...
I DON'T WANT TO TAKE THE SWORD OFF THE MANTEL, YOU KNOW? IT'S... SYMBOLIC FOR ME.
DON'T WANT TO TAKE IT DOWN UNLESS I NEED TO.
THAT'S NOT SILLY. I COMPLETELY UNDERSTAND THAT.
YOU TALK TO LORI RECENTLY?
SHOULD HAVE KNOWN THAT'S NOT SOMETHING YOU'D WANT TO TALK ABOUT.
SORRY.

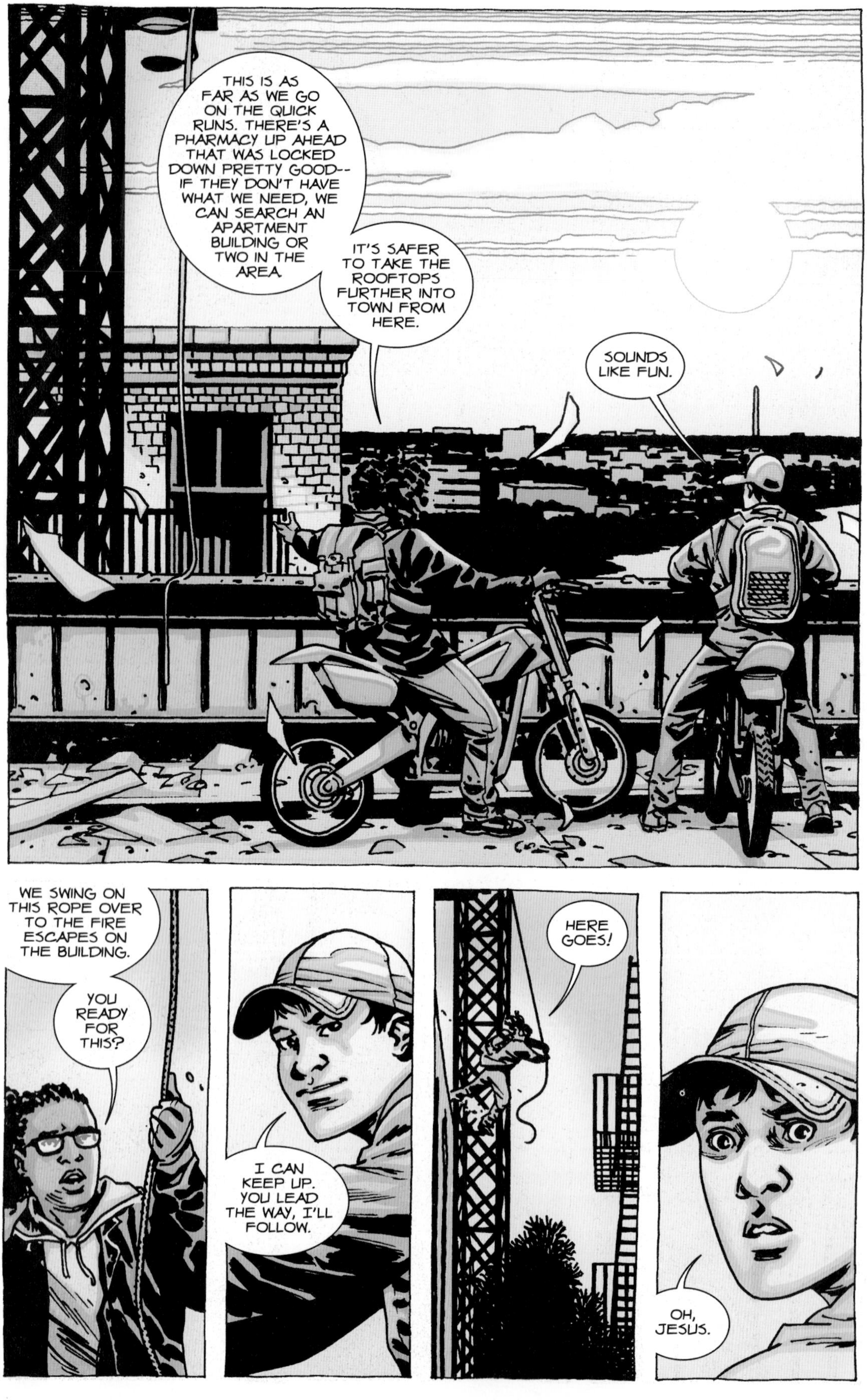
THIS IS AS FAR AS WE GO ON THE QUICK RUNS. THERE'S A PHARMACY UP AHEAD THAT WAS LOCKED DOWN PRETTY GOOD-- IF THEY DON'T HAVE WHAT WE NEED, WE CAN SEARCH AN APARTMENT BUILDING OR TWO IN THE AREA.
IT'S SAFER TO TAKE THE ROOFTOPS FURTHER INTO TOWN FROM HERE.
SOUNDS LIKE FUN.
WE SWING ON THIS ROPE OVER TO THE FIRE ESCAPES ON THE BUILDING.
YOU READY FOR THIS?
I CAN KEEP UP. YOU LEAD THE WAY, I'LL FOLLOW.
HERE GOES!
OH, JESUS.

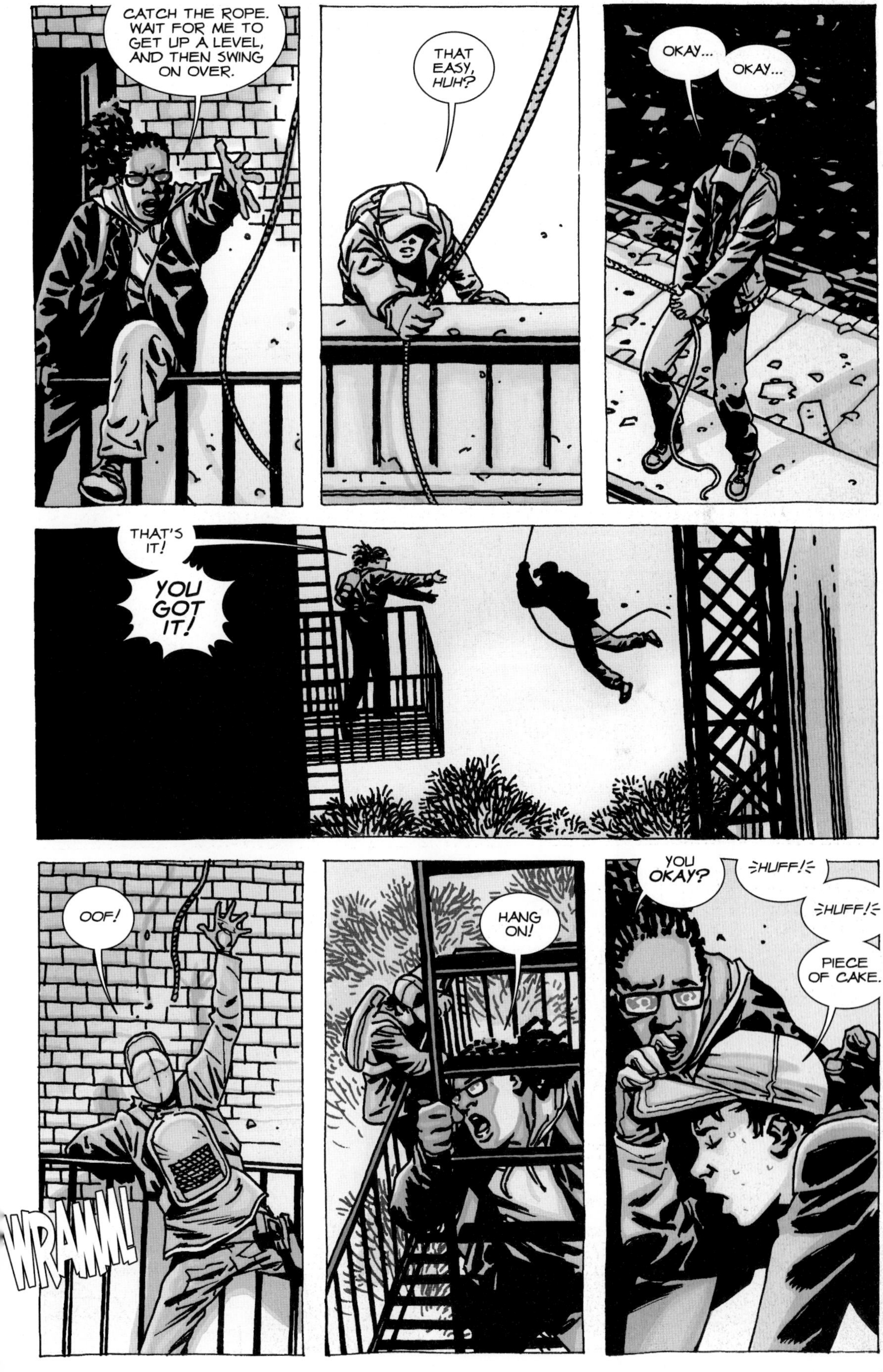
CATCH THE ROPE. WAIT FOR ME TO GET UP A LEVEL, AND THEN SWING ON OVER.
THAT EASY, HUH?
OKAY...
OKAY...
THAT'S IT!
YOU GOT IT!
OOF!
WRAMM!
HANG ON!
YOU OKAY?
HUFF!
HUFF!
PIECE OF CAKE.

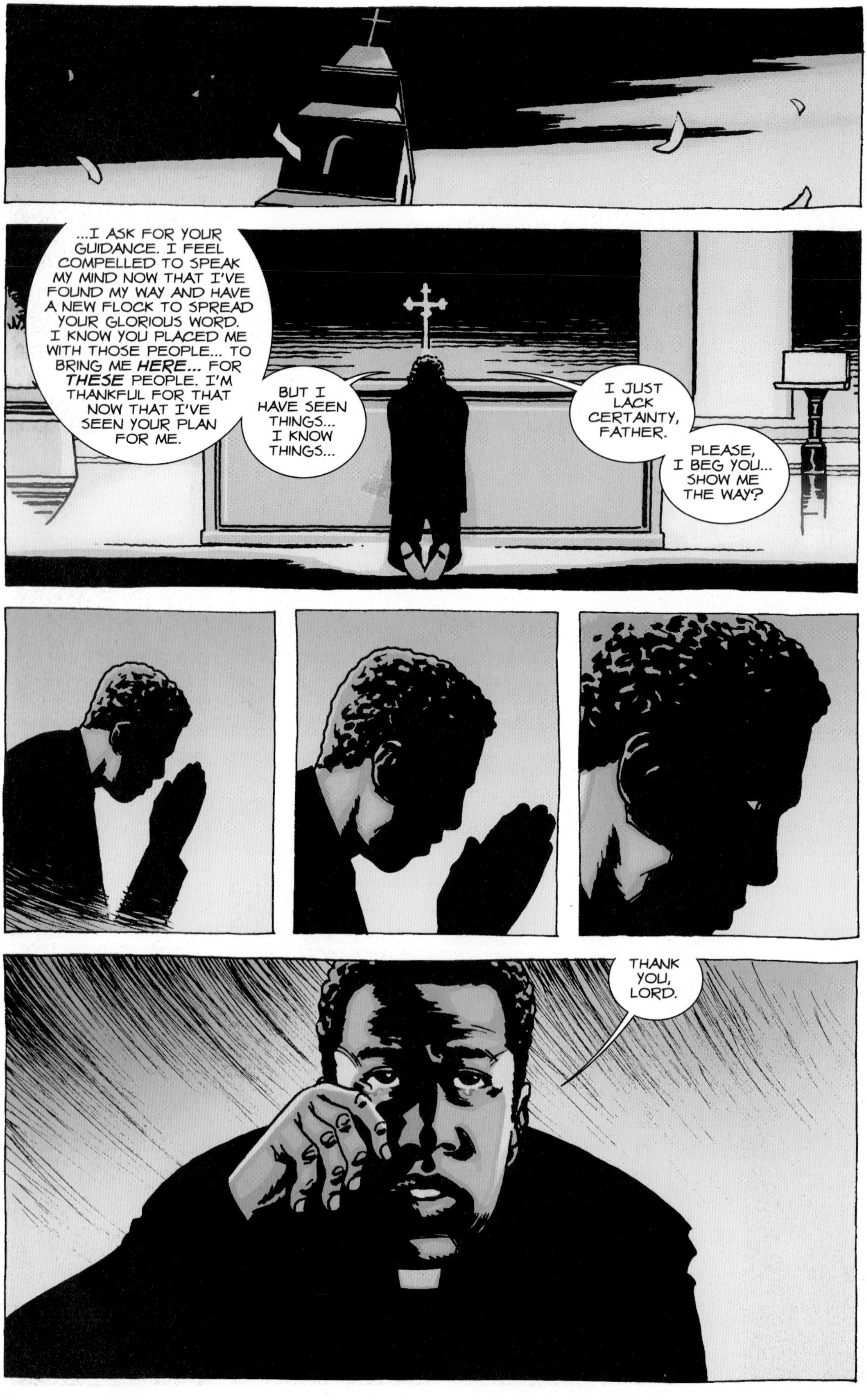
...I ASK FOR YOUR GUIDANCE. I FEEL COMPELLED TO SPEAK MY MIND NOW THAT I'VE FOUND MY WAY AND HAVE A NEW FLOCK TO SPREAD YOUR GLORIOUS WORD. I KNOW YOU PLACED ME WITH THOSE PEOPLE... TO BRING ME HERE... FOR THESE PEOPLE. I'M THANKFUL FOR THAT NOW THAT I'VE SEEN YOUR PLAN FOR ME.
BUT I HAVE SEEN THINGS... I KNOW THINGS...
I JUST LACK CERTAINTY, FATHER.
PLEASE, I BEG YOU... SHOW ME THE WAY?
THANK YOU, LORD.

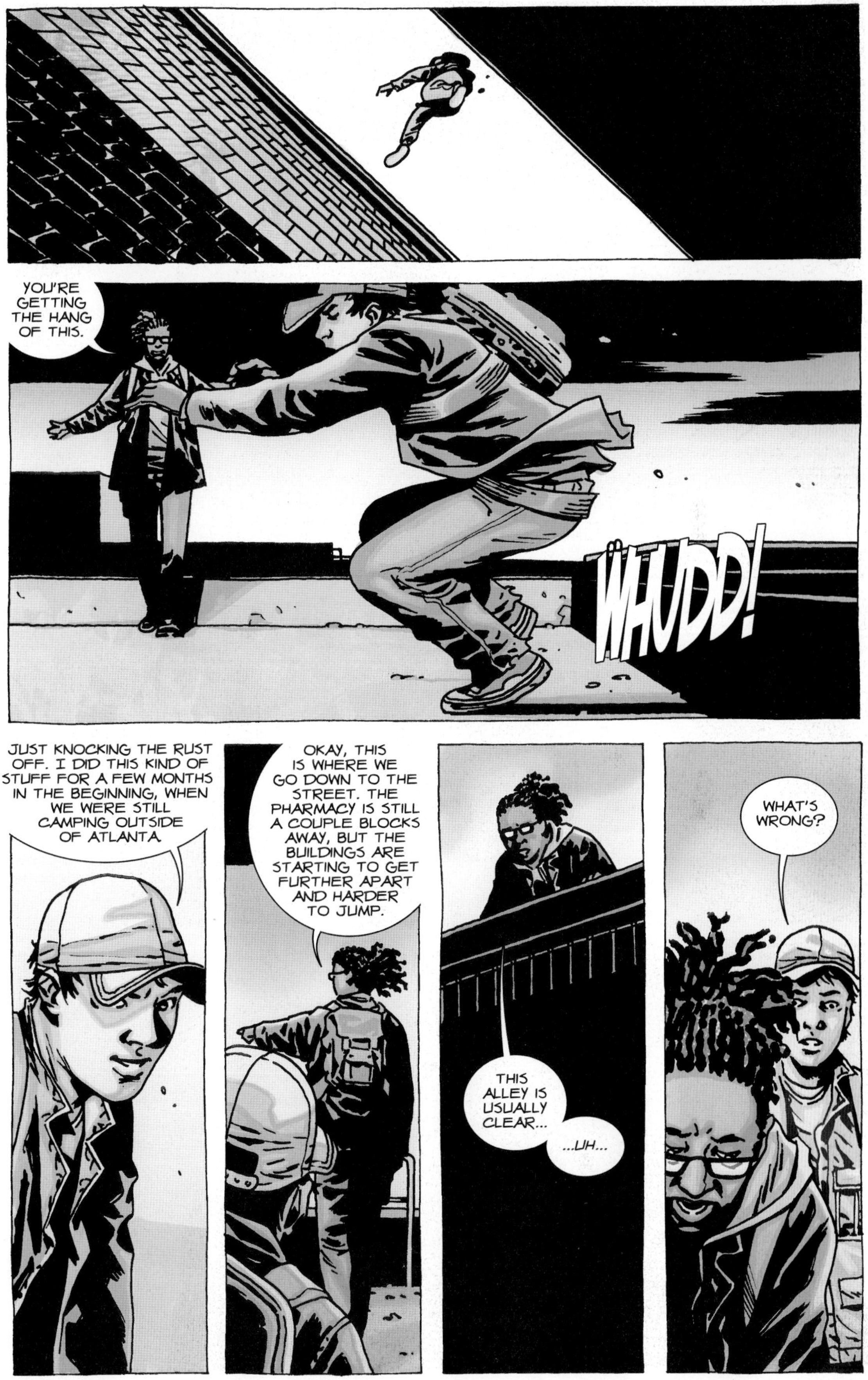
YOU'RE GETTING THE HANG OF THIS.
WHUDD!
JUST KNOCKING THE RUST OFF. I DID THIS KIND OF STUFF FOR A FEW MONTHS IN THE BEGINNING, WHEN WE WERE STILL CAMPING OUTSIDE OF ATLANTA.
OKAY, THIS IS WHERE WE GO DOWN TO THE STREET. THE PHARMACY IS STILL A COUPLE BLOCKS AWAY, BUT THE BUILDINGS ARE STARTING TO GET FURTHER APART AND HARDER TO JUMP.
THIS ALLEY IS USUALLY CLEAR...
...UH...
WHAT'S WRONG?

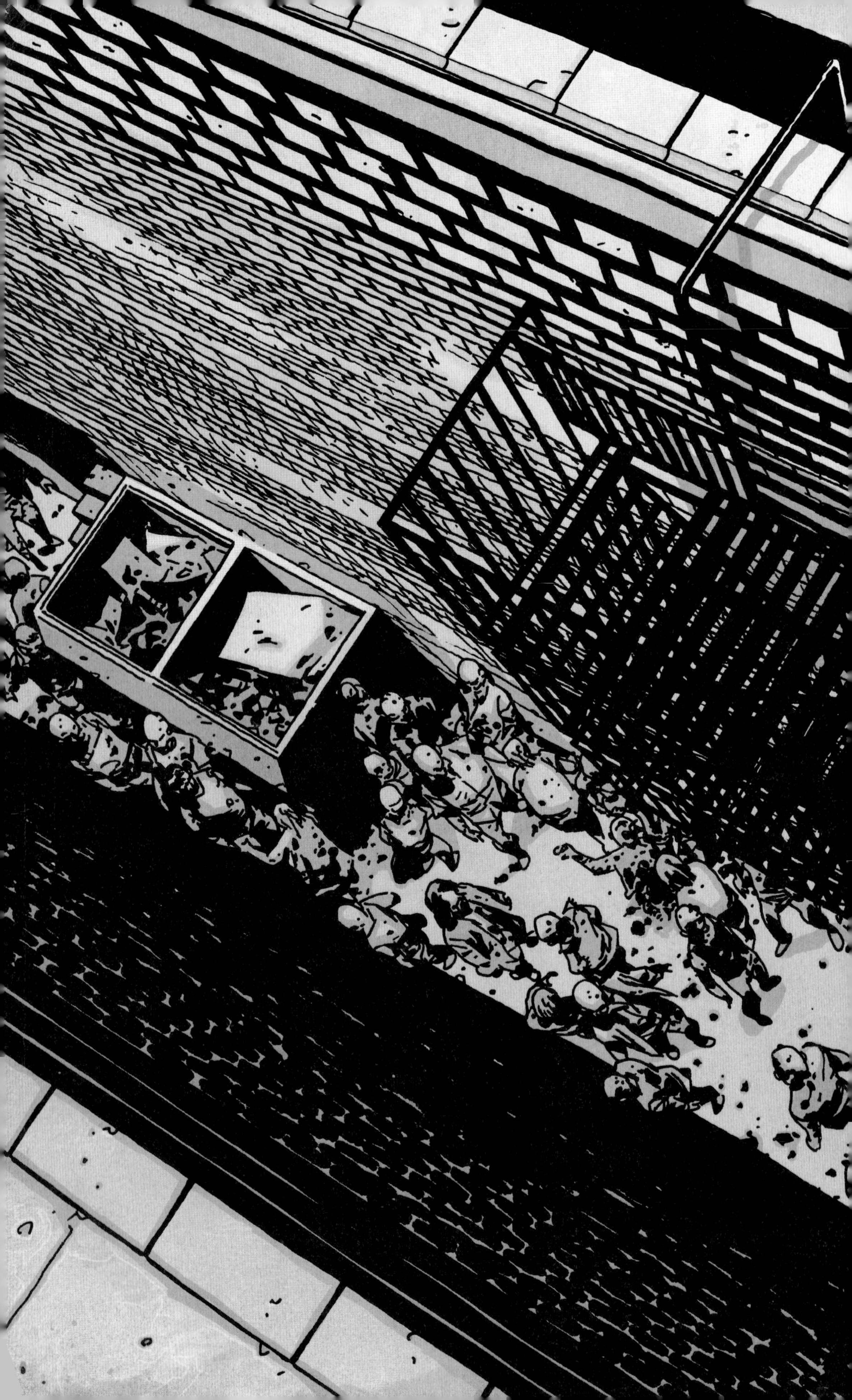

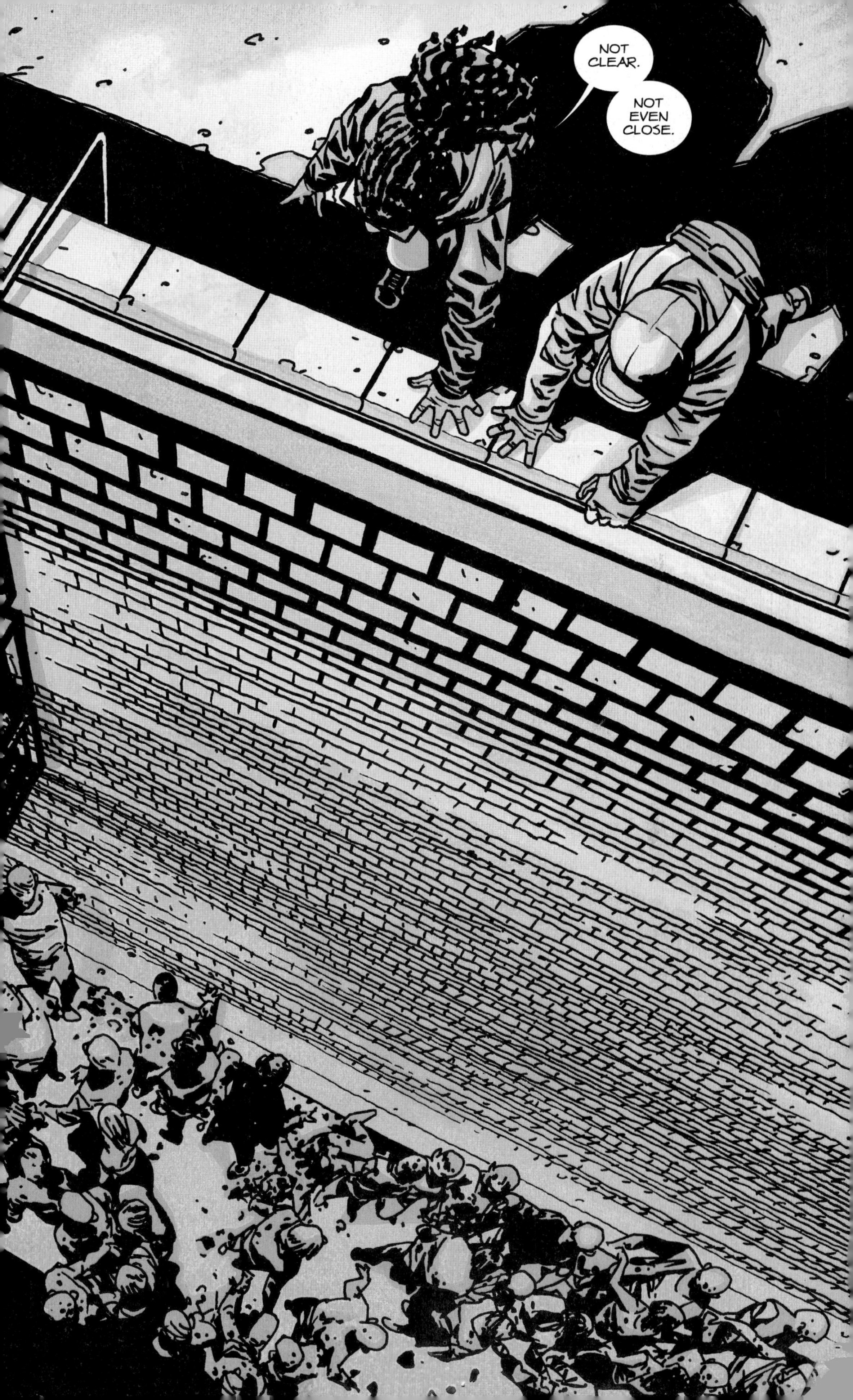
NOT CLEAR.
NOT EVEN CLOSE.

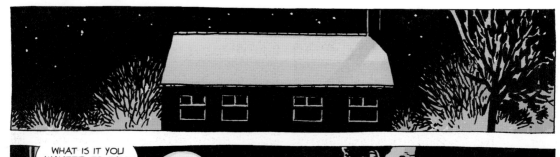

WHAT IS IT YOU WANTED TO TALK TO ME ABOUT, GABRIEL?

I'M SORRY, SIR. THIS JUST COULDN'T WAIT.

I'M SO VERY THANKFUL YOU'VE ALLOWED US TO COME LIVE HERE. THE PEOPLE HERE ARE SO KIND AND ACCEPTING.

AS HAPPY AS I AM THAT YOU LET US IN, I FEAR YOU MAY HAVE MADE A GRAVE MISTAKE IN DOING SO.

THESE PEOPLE WHO WERE WITH ME, ARE *NOT* GOOD PEOPLE. THEY'VE DONE THINGS... *HORRIBLE* THINGS...

...UNSPEAKABLE THINGS.

THEY SIMPLY DON'T *BELONG* HERE.

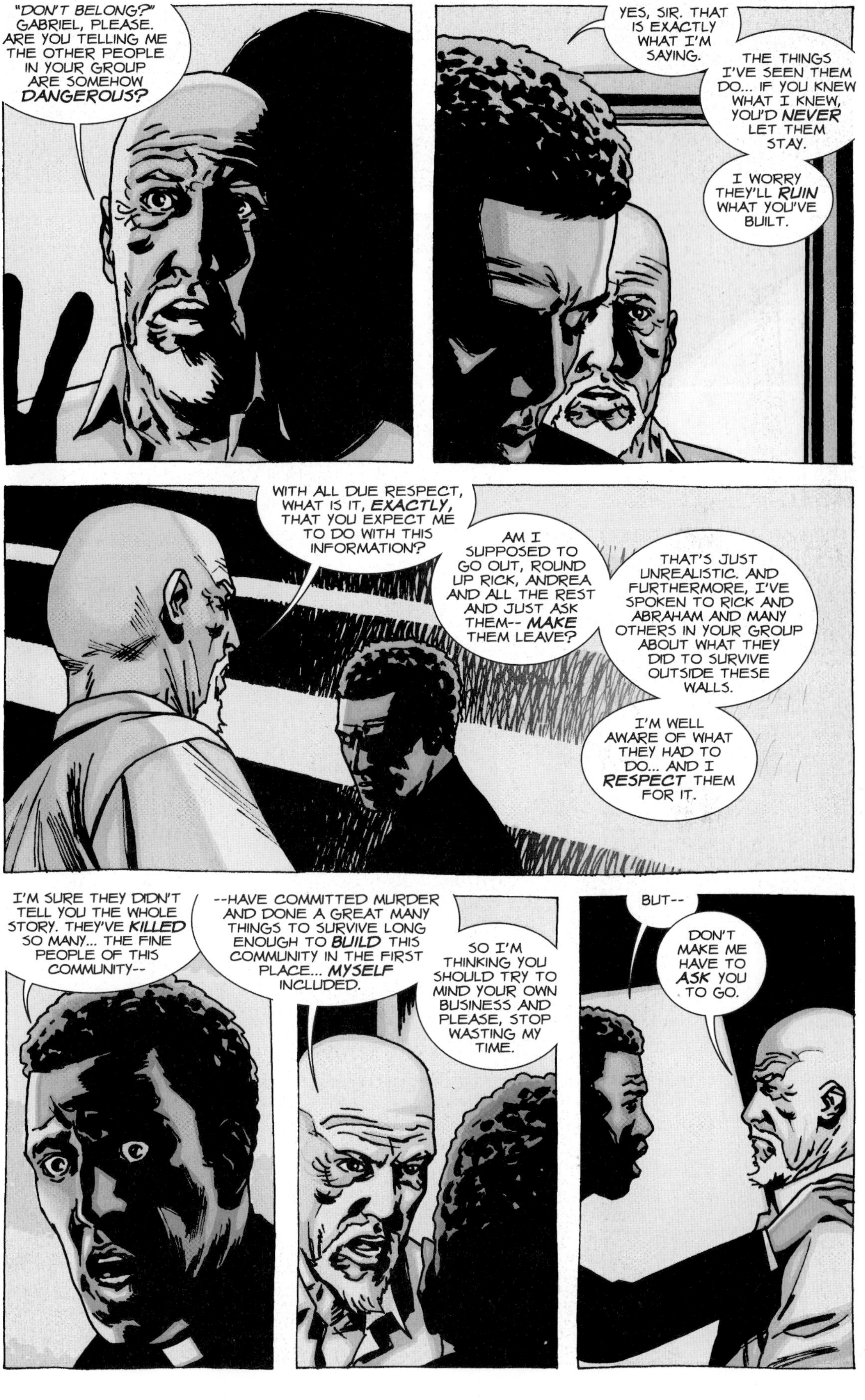
"DON'T BELONG?" GABRIEL, PLEASE. ARE YOU TELLING ME THE OTHER PEOPLE IN YOUR GROUP ARE SOMEHOW DANGEROUS?
YES, SIR. THAT IS EXACTLY WHAT I'M SAYING.
THE THINGS I'VE SEEN THEM DO... IF YOU KNEW WHAT I KNEW, YOU'D NEVER LET THEM STAY.
I WORRY THEY'LL RUIN WHAT YOU'VE BUILT.
WITH ALL DUE RESPECT, WHAT IS IT, EXACTLY, THAT YOU EXPECT ME TO DO WITH THIS INFORMATION?
AM I SUPPOSED TO GO OUT, ROUND UP RICK, ANDREA AND ALL THE REST AND JUST ASK THEM-- MAKE THEM LEAVE?
THAT'S JUST UNREALISTIC. AND FURTHERMORE, I'VE SPOKEN TO RICK AND ABRAHAM AND MANY OTHERS IN YOUR GROUP ABOUT WHAT THEY DID TO SURVIVE OUTSIDE THESE WALLS.
I'M WELL AWARE OF WHAT THEY HAD TO DO... AND I RESPECT THEM FOR IT.
I'M SURE THEY DIDN'T TELL YOU THE WHOLE STORY. THEY'VE KILLED SO MANY... THE FINE PEOPLE OF THIS COMMUNITY--
--HAVE COMMITTED MURDER AND DONE A GREAT MANY THINGS TO SURVIVE LONG ENOUGH TO BUILD THIS COMMUNITY IN THE FIRST PLACE... MYSELF INCLUDED.
SO I'M THINKING YOU SHOULD TRY TO MIND YOUR OWN BUSINESS AND PLEASE, STOP WASTING MY TIME.
BUT--
DON'T MAKE ME HAVE TO ASK YOU TO GO.

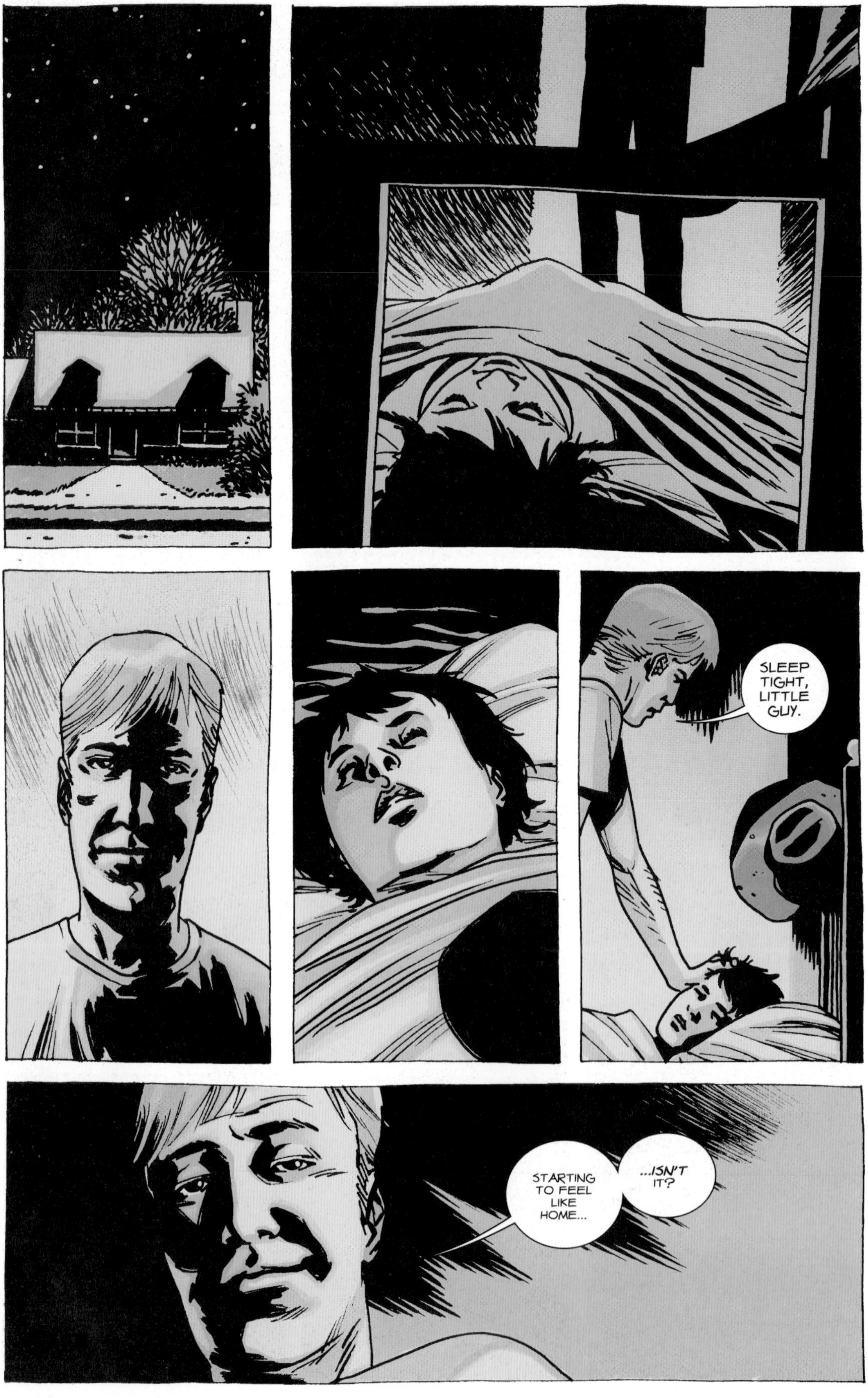
SLEEP TIGHT, LITTLE GUY.
STARTING TO FEEL LIKE HOME...
...ISN'T IT?

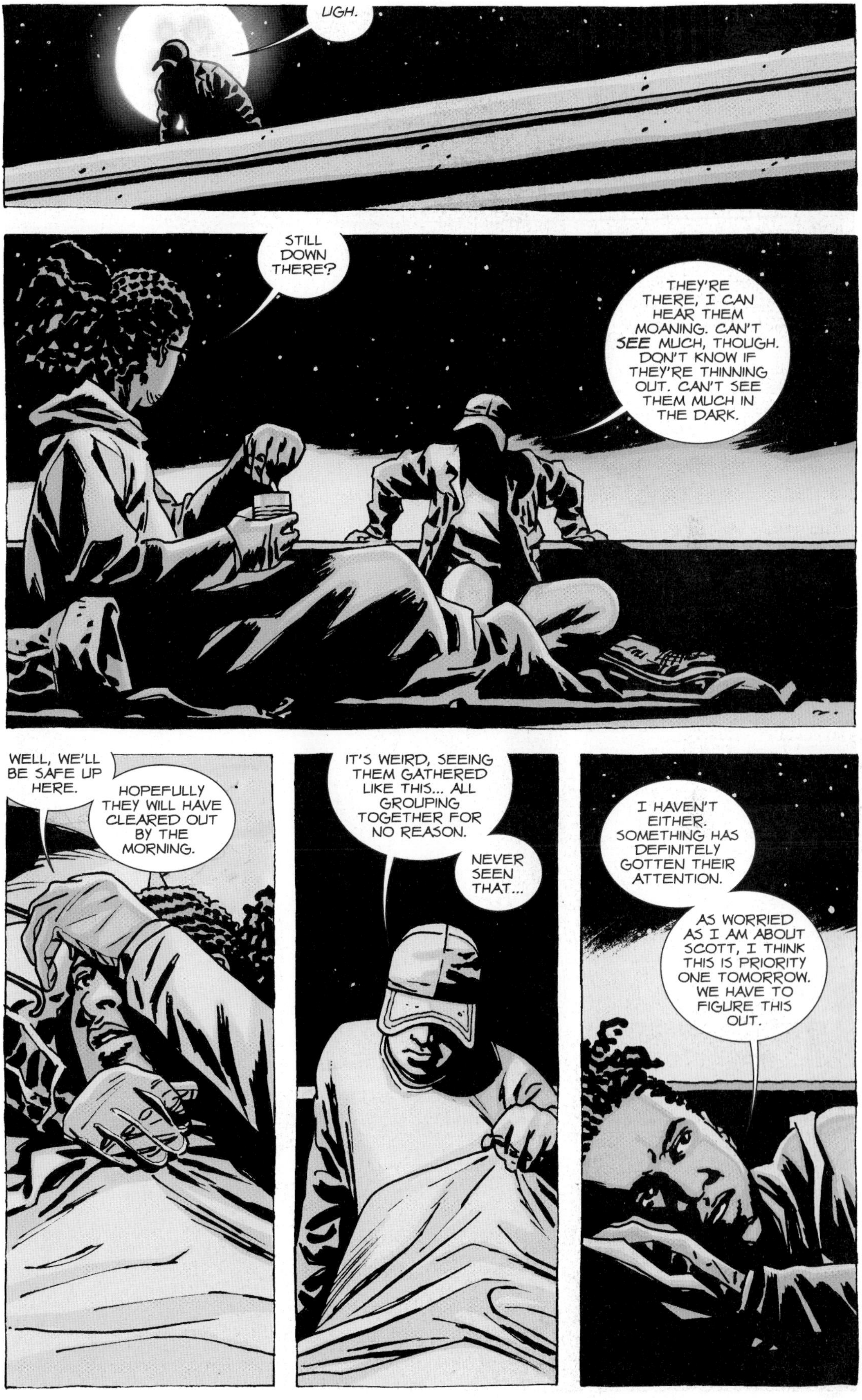
UGH.
STILL DOWN THERE?
THEY'RE THERE, I CAN HEAR THEM MOANING. CAN'T SEE MUCH, THOUGH. DON'T KNOW IF THEY'RE THINNING OUT. CAN'T SEE THEM MUCH IN THE DARK.
WELL, WE'LL BE SAFE UP HERE.
HOPEFULLY THEY WILL HAVE CLEARED OUT BY THE MORNING.
IT'S WEIRD, SEEING THEM GATHERED LIKE THIS... ALL GROUPING TOGETHER FOR NO REASON.
NEVER SEEN THAT...
I HAVEN'T EITHER. SOMETHING HAS DEFINITELY GOTTEN THEIR ATTENTION.
AS WORRIED AS I AM ABOUT SCOTT, I THINK THIS IS PRIORITY ONE TOMORROW. WE HAVE TO FIGURE THIS OUT.

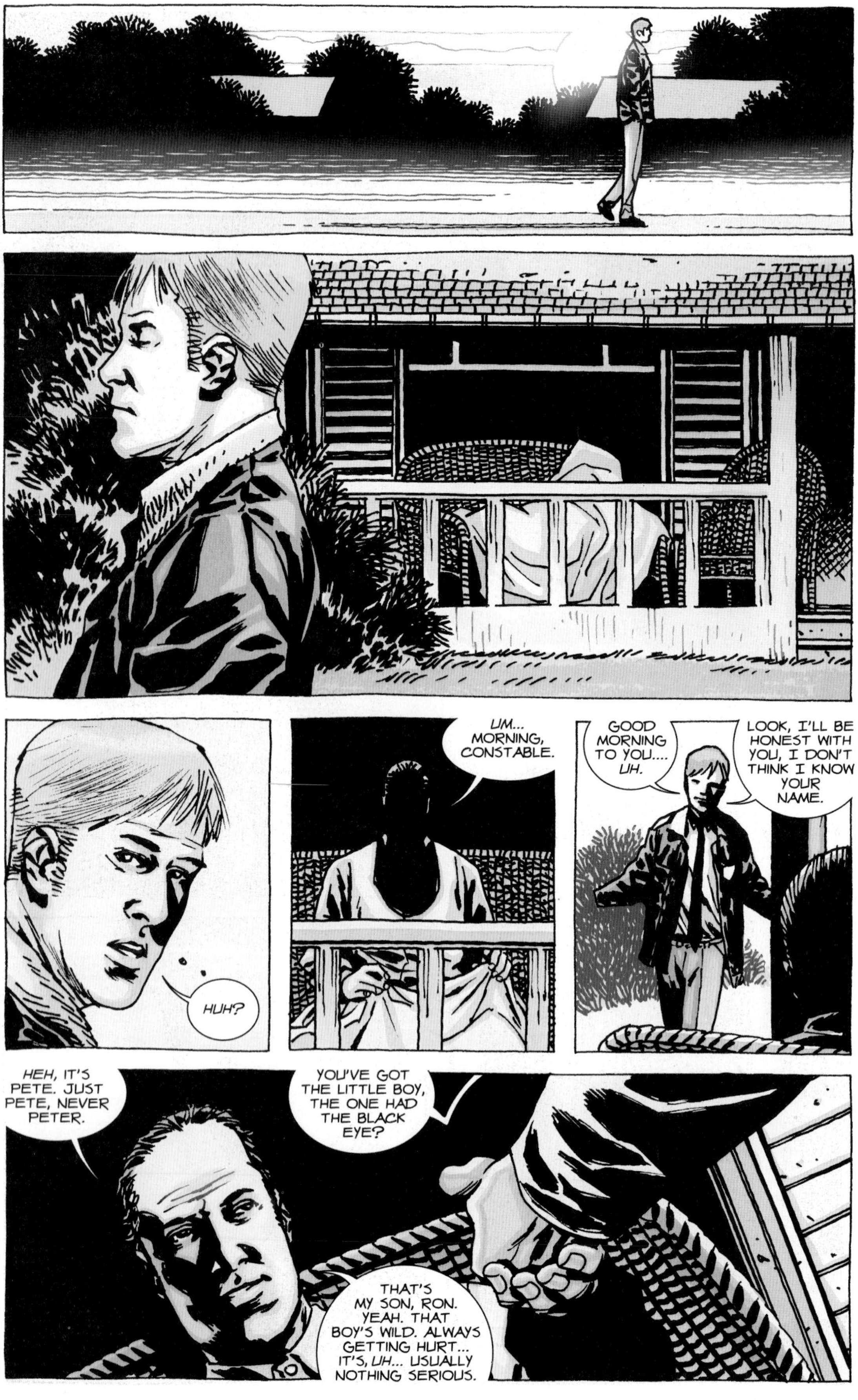
HUH?
UM... MORNING, CONSTABLE.
GOOD MORNING TO YOU.... UH.
LOOK, I'LL BE HONEST WITH YOU, I DON'T THINK I KNOW YOUR NAME.
HEH, IT'S PETE. JUST PETE, NEVER PETER.
YOU'VE GOT THE LITTLE BOY, THE ONE HAD THE BLACK EYE?
THAT'S MY SON, RON. YEAH. THAT BOY'S WILD. ALWAYS GETTING HURT... IT'S, UH... USUALLY NOTHING SERIOUS.

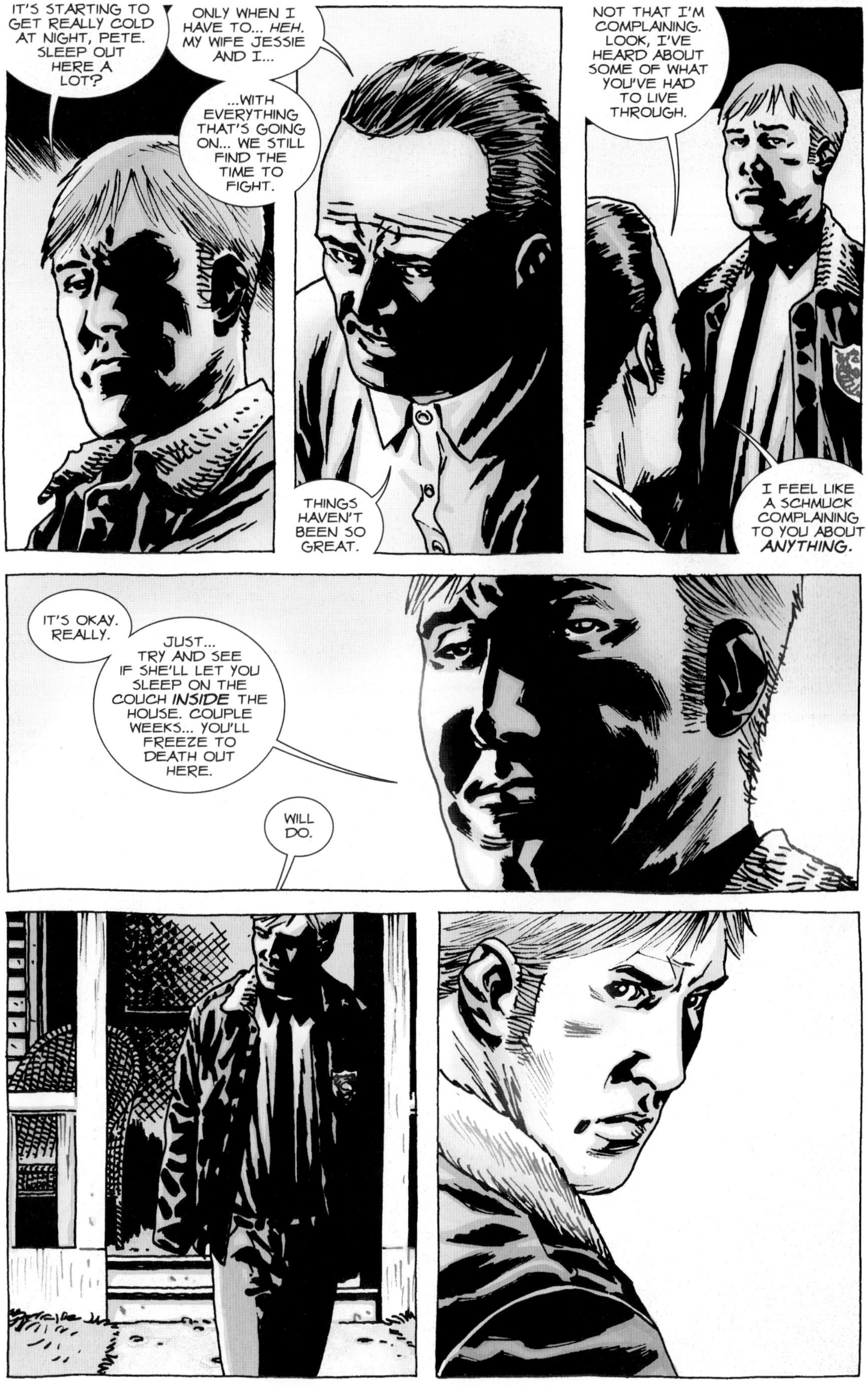
IT'S STARTING TO GET REALLY COLD AT NIGHT, PETE. SLEEP OUT HERE A LOT?
ONLY WHEN I HAVE TO... HEH. MY WIFE JESSIE AND I...
...WITH EVERYTHING THAT'S GOING ON... WE STILL FIND THE TIME TO FIGHT.
THINGS HAVEN'T BEEN SO GREAT.
NOT THAT I'M COMPLAINING. LOOK, I'VE HEARD ABOUT SOME OF WHAT YOU'VE HAD TO LIVE THROUGH.
I FEEL LIKE A SCHMUCK COMPLAINING TO YOU ABOUT ANYTHING.
IT'S OKAY. REALLY.
JUST... TRY AND SEE IF SHE'LL LET YOU SLEEP ON THE COUCH INSIDE THE HOUSE. COUPLE WEEKS... YOU'LL FREEZE TO DEATH OUT HERE.
WILL DO.

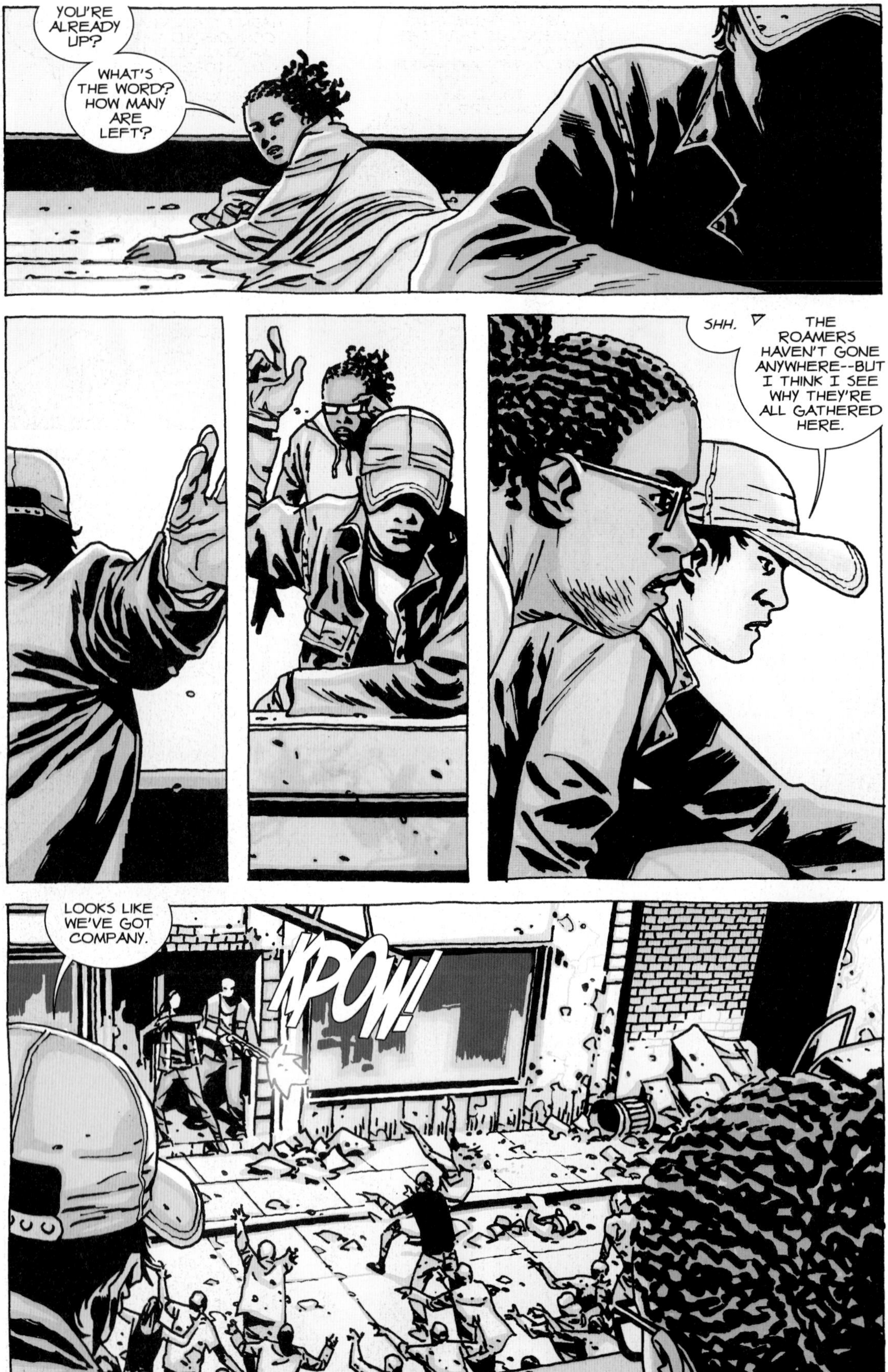
YOU'RE ALREADY UP?
WHAT'S THE WORD? HOW MANY ARE LEFT?
SHH.
THE ROAMERS HAVEN'T GONE ANYWHERE--BUT I THINK I SEE WHY THEY'RE ALL GATHERED HERE.
LOOKS LIKE WE'VE GOT COMPANY.
KPOW!

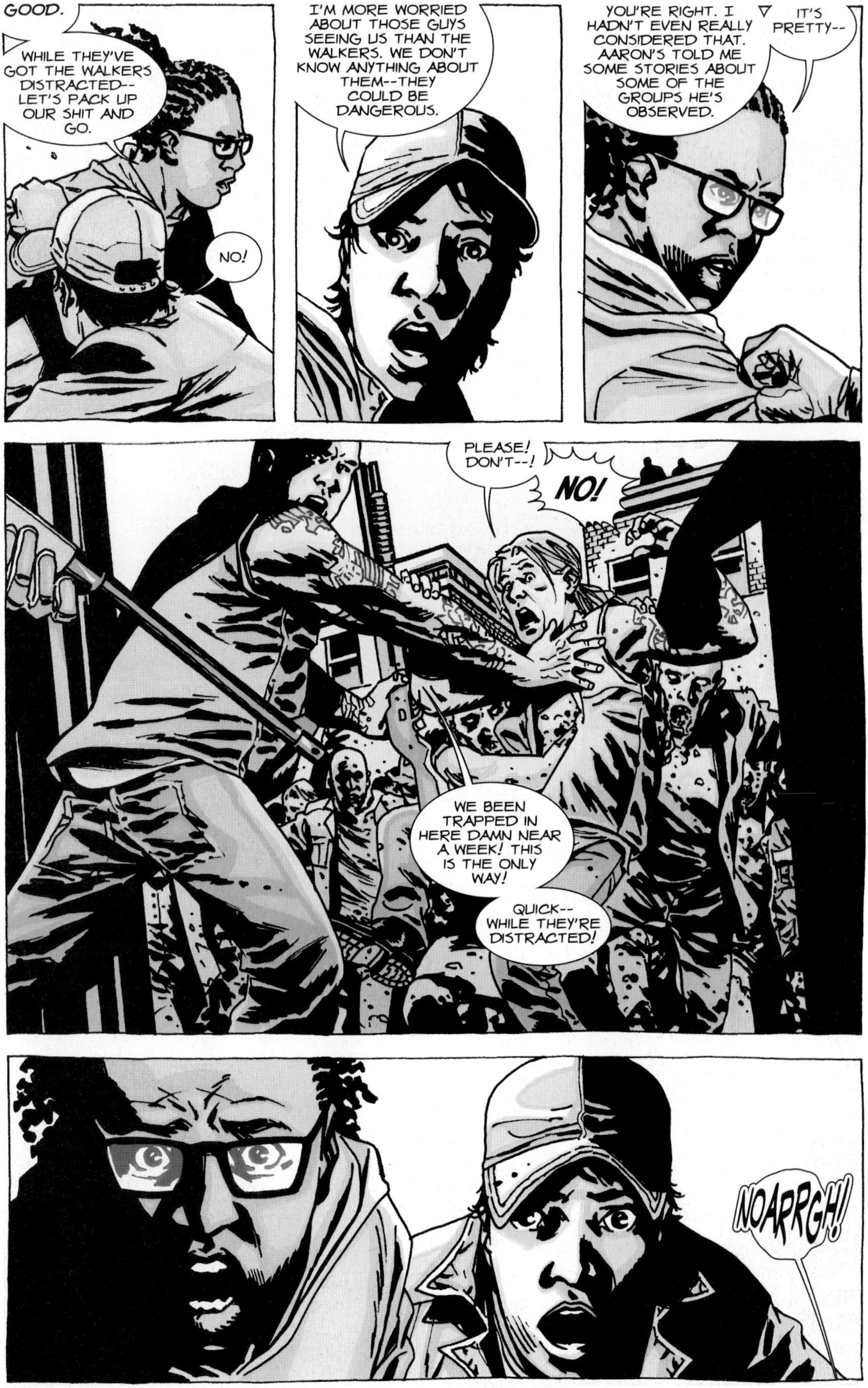
GOOD.
WHILE THEY'VE GOT THE WALKERS DISTRACTED-- LET'S PACK UP OUR SHIT AND GO.
NO!
I'M MORE WORRIED ABOUT THOSE GUYS SEEING US THAN THE WALKERS. WE DON'T KNOW ANYTHING ABOUT THEM--THEY COULD BE DANGEROUS.
YOU'RE RIGHT. I HADN'T EVEN REALLY CONSIDERED THAT. AARON'S TOLD ME SOME STORIES ABOUT SOME OF THE GROUPS HE'S OBSERVED.
IT'S PRETTY--
PLEASE! DON'T--!
NO!
WE BEEN TRAPPED IN HERE DAMN NEAR A WEEK! THIS IS THE ONLY WAY!
QUICK-- WHILE THEY'RE DISTRACTED!
NOARRGH!

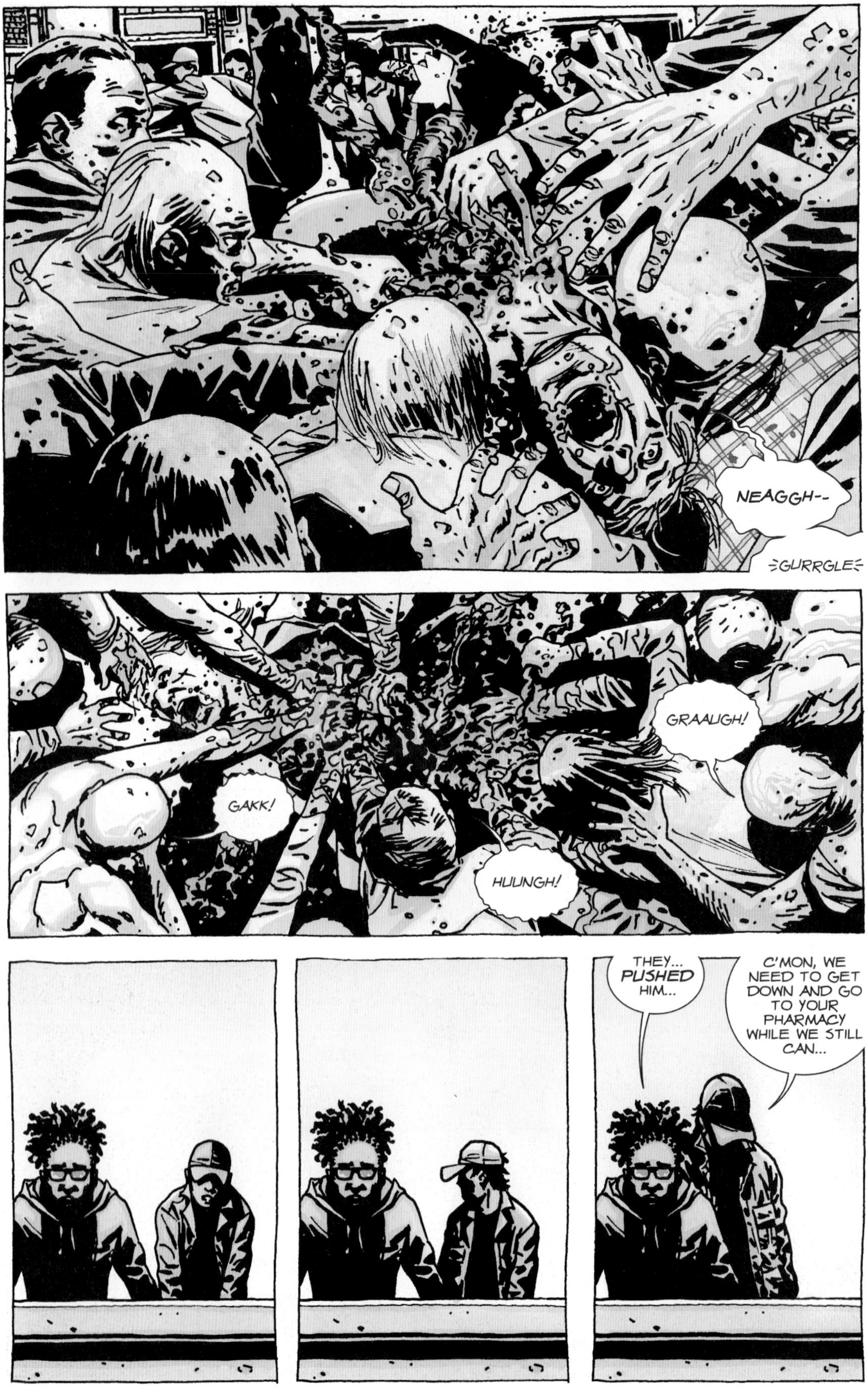
NEAGGH--
GURRGLE
GRAAUGH!
GAKK!
HUUNGH!
THEY... PUSHED HIM...
C'MON, WE NEED TO GET DOWN AND GO TO YOUR PHARMACY WHILE WE STILL CAN...

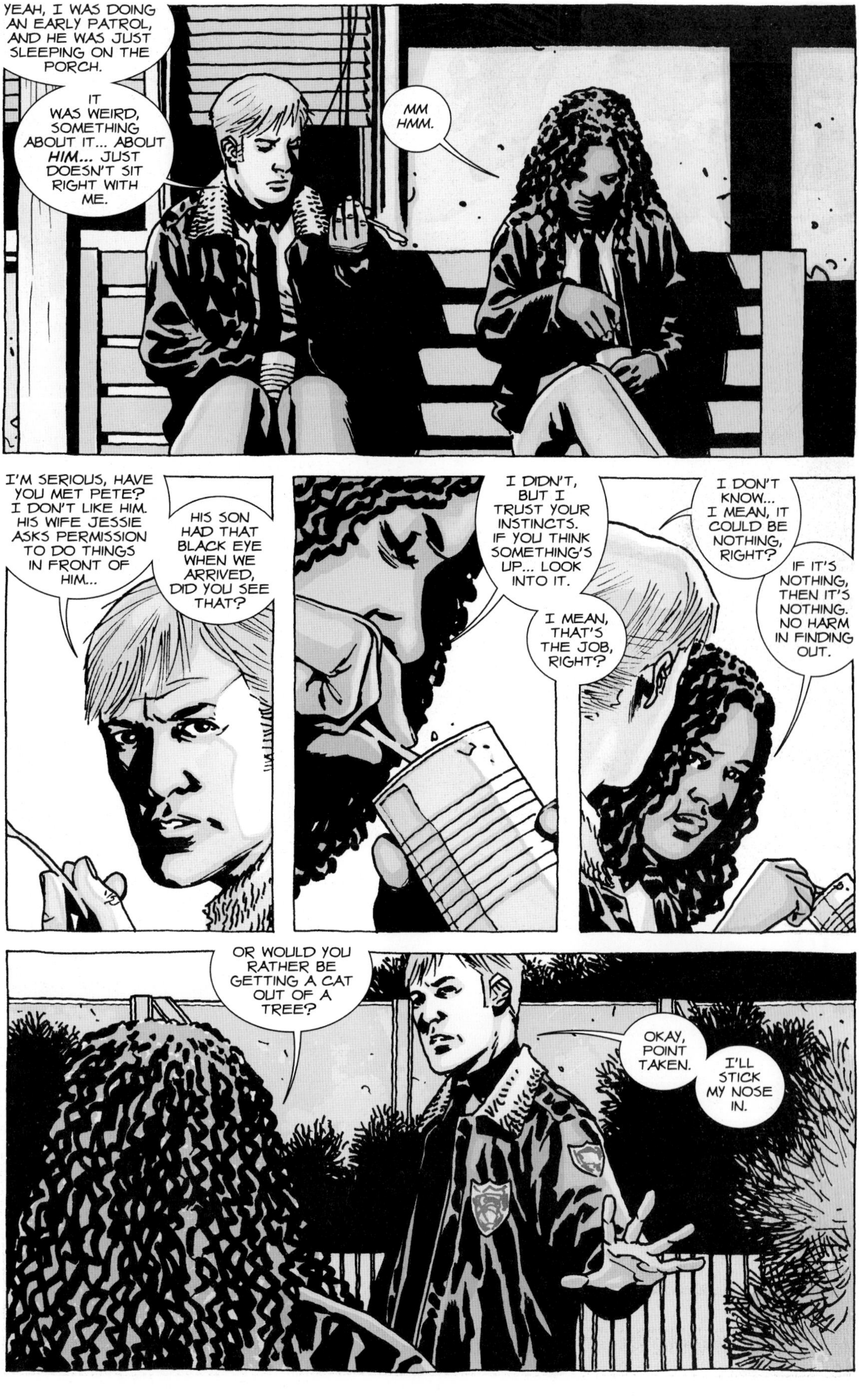
YEAH, I WAS DOING AN EARLY PATROL, AND HE WAS JUST SLEEPING ON THE PORCH.
IT WAS WEIRD, SOMETHING ABOUT IT... ABOUT HIM... JUST DOESN'T SIT RIGHT WITH ME.
MM HMM.
I'M SERIOUS, HAVE YOU MET PETE? I DON'T LIKE HIM. HIS WIFE JESSIE ASKS PERMISSION TO DO THINGS IN FRONT OF HIM...
HIS SON HAD THAT BLACK EYE WHEN WE ARRIVED, DID YOU SEE THAT?
I DIDN'T, BUT I TRUST YOUR INSTINCTS. IF YOU THINK SOMETHING'S UP... LOOK INTO IT.
I MEAN, THAT'S THE JOB, RIGHT?
I DON'T KNOW... I MEAN, IT COULD BE NOTHING, RIGHT?
IF IT'S NOTHING, THEN IT'S NOTHING. NO HARM IN FINDING OUT.
OR WOULD YOU RATHER BE GETTING A CAT OUT OF A TREE?
OKAY, POINT TAKEN.
I'LL STICK MY NOSE IN.

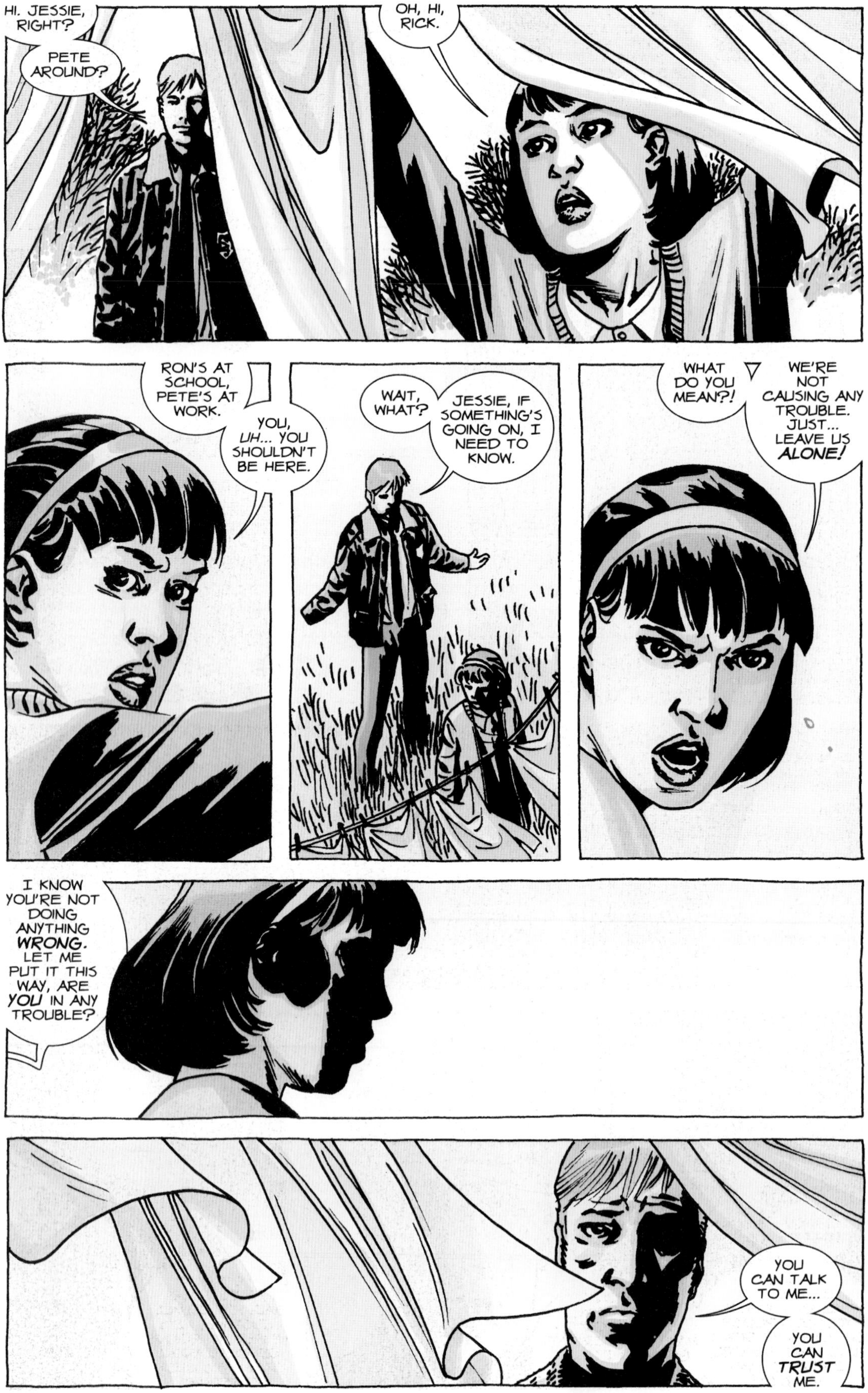

HI. JESSIE, RIGHT?
PETE AROUND?
OH, HI, RICK.
RON'S AT SCHOOL, PETE'S AT WORK.
YOU, UH... YOU SHOULDN'T BE HERE.
WAIT, WHAT?
JESSIE, IF SOMETHING'S GOING ON, I NEED TO KNOW.
WHAT DO YOU MEAN?!
WE'RE NOT CAUSING ANY TROUBLE. JUST... LEAVE US ALONE!
I KNOW YOU'RE NOT DOING ANYTHING WRONG. LET ME PUT IT THIS WAY, ARE YOU IN ANY TROUBLE?
YOU CAN TALK TO ME...
YOU CAN TRUST ME.

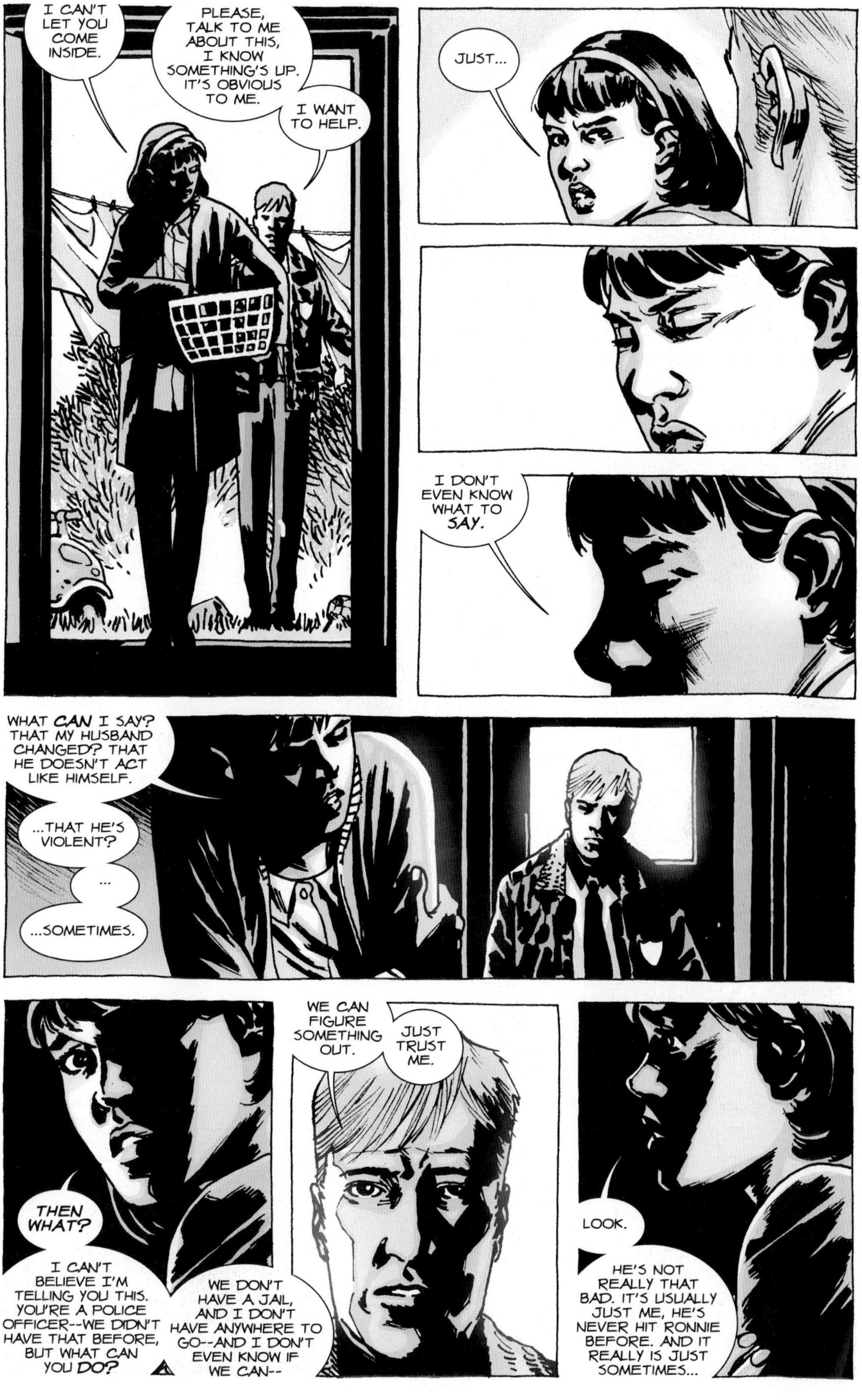

I CAN'T LET YOU COME INSIDE.
PLEASE, TALK TO ME ABOUT THIS, I KNOW SOMETHING'S UP. IT'S OBVIOUS TO ME.
I WANT TO HELP.
JUST...
I DON'T EVEN KNOW WHAT TO SAY.
WHAT CAN I SAY? THAT MY HUSBAND CHANGED? THAT HE DOESN'T ACT LIKE HIMSELF.
...THAT HE'S VIOLENT?
...
...SOMETIMES.
THEN WHAT?
I CAN'T BELIEVE I'M TELLING YOU THIS. YOU'RE A POLICE OFFICER--WE DIDN'T HAVE THAT BEFORE, BUT WHAT CAN YOU DO?
WE CAN FIGURE SOMETHING OUT.
JUST TRUST ME.
WE DON'T HAVE A JAIL, AND I DON'T HAVE ANYWHERE TO GO--AND I DON'T EVEN KNOW IF WE CAN--
LOOK.
HE'S NOT REALLY THAT BAD. IT'S USUALLY JUST ME, HE'S NEVER HIT RONNIE BEFORE. AND IT REALLY IS JUST SOMETIMES...

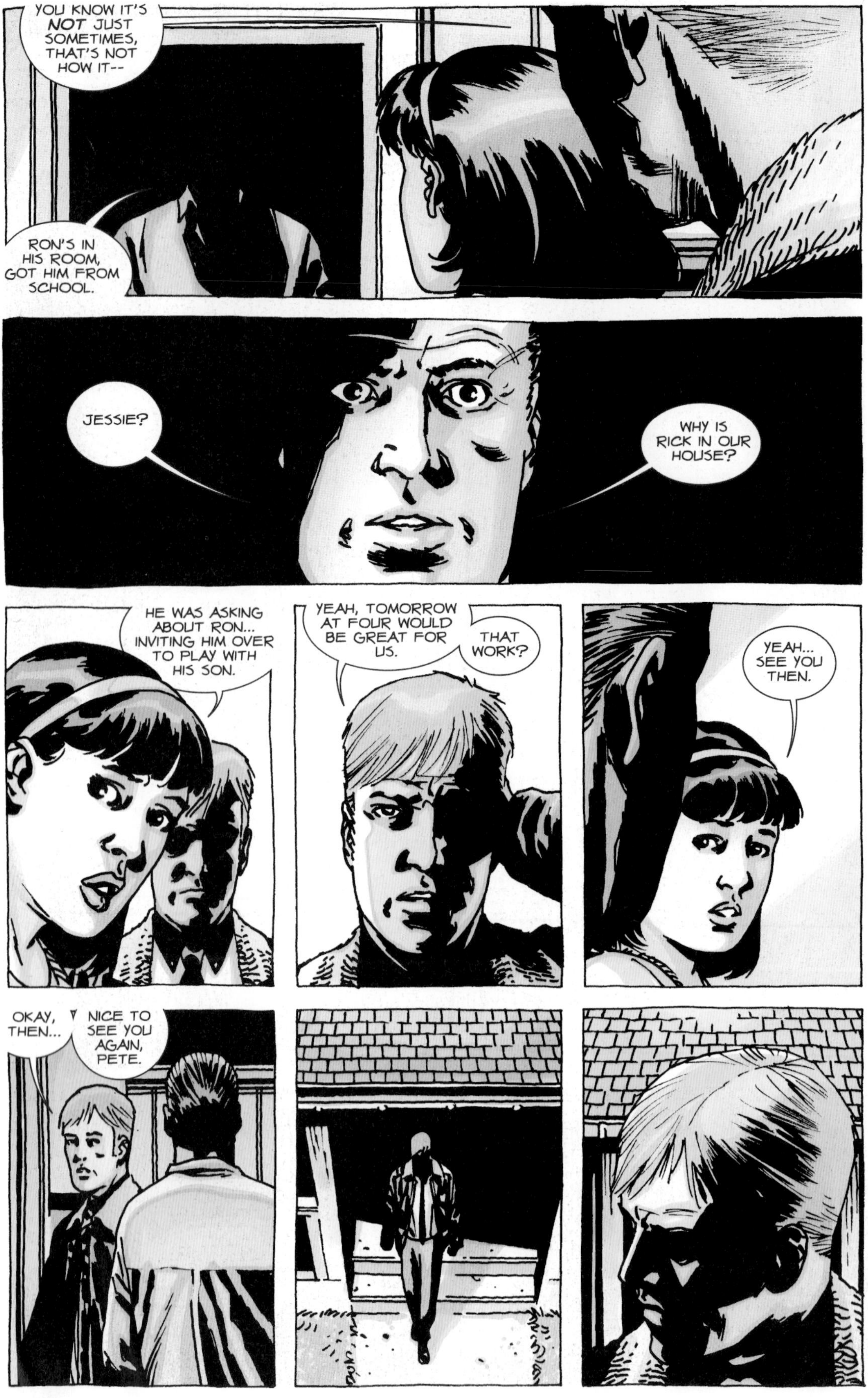
YOU KNOW IT'S *NOT* JUST SOMETIMES, THAT'S NOT HOW IT--
RON'S IN HIS ROOM, GOT HIM FROM SCHOOL.
JESSIE?
WHY IS RICK IN OUR HOUSE?
HE WAS ASKING ABOUT RON... INVITING HIM OVER TO PLAY WITH HIS SON.
YEAH, TOMORROW AT FOUR WOULD BE GREAT FOR US.
THAT WORK?
YEAH... SEE YOU THEN.
OKAY, THEN...
NICE TO SEE YOU AGAIN, PETE.

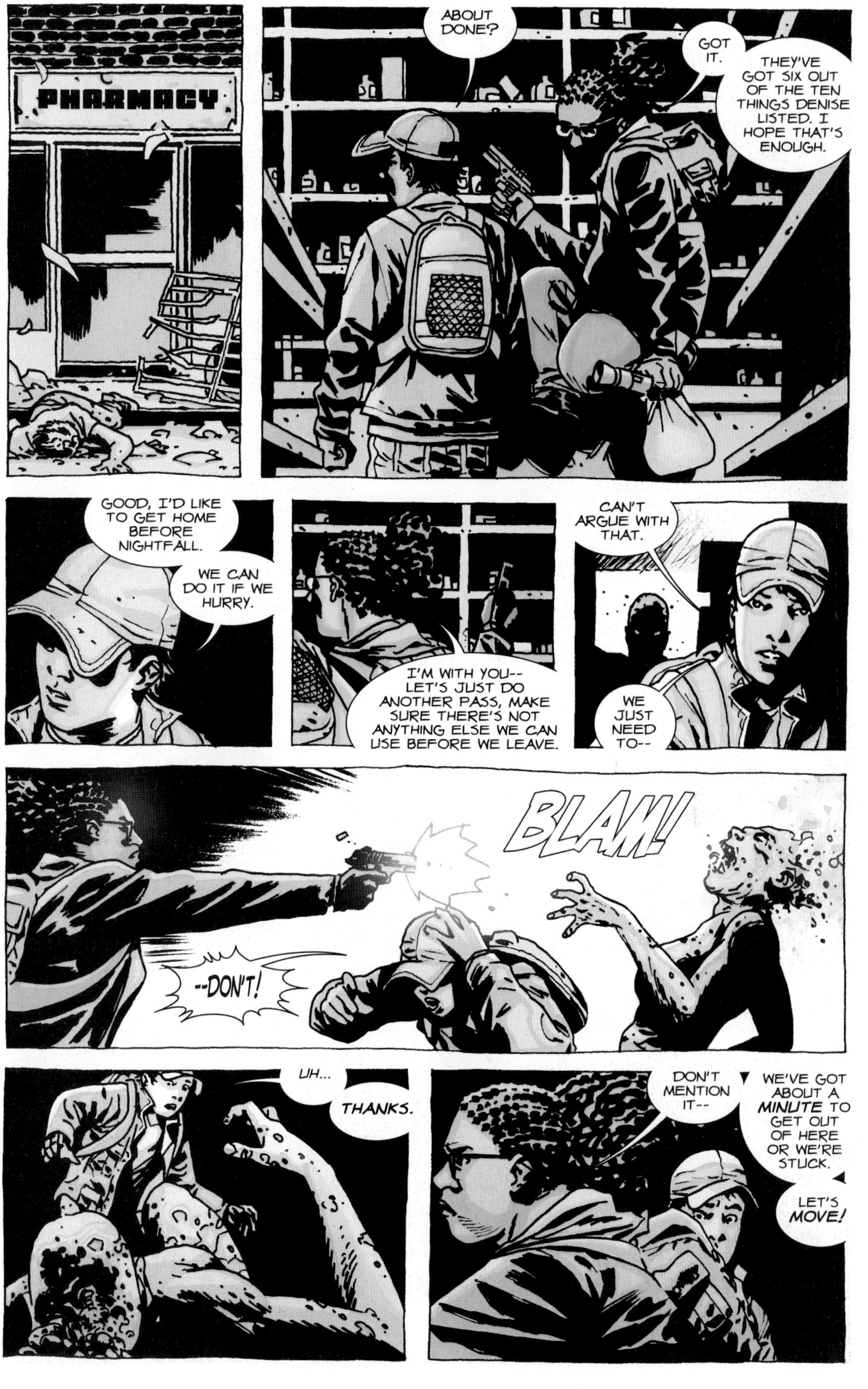
PHARMACY
ABOUT DONE?
GOT IT.
THEY'VE GOT SIX OUT OF THE TEN THINGS DENISE LISTED. I HOPE THAT'S ENOUGH.
GOOD, I'D LIKE TO GET HOME BEFORE NIGHTFALL.
WE CAN DO IT IF WE HURRY.
I'M WITH YOU-- LET'S JUST DO ANOTHER PASS, MAKE SURE THERE'S NOT ANYTHING ELSE WE CAN USE BEFORE WE LEAVE.
CAN'T ARGUE WITH THAT.
WE JUST NEED TO--
BLAM!
--DON'T!
UH...
THANKS.
DON'T MENTION IT--
WE'VE GOT ABOUT A MINUTE TO GET OUT OF HERE OR WE'RE STUCK.
LET'S MOVE!

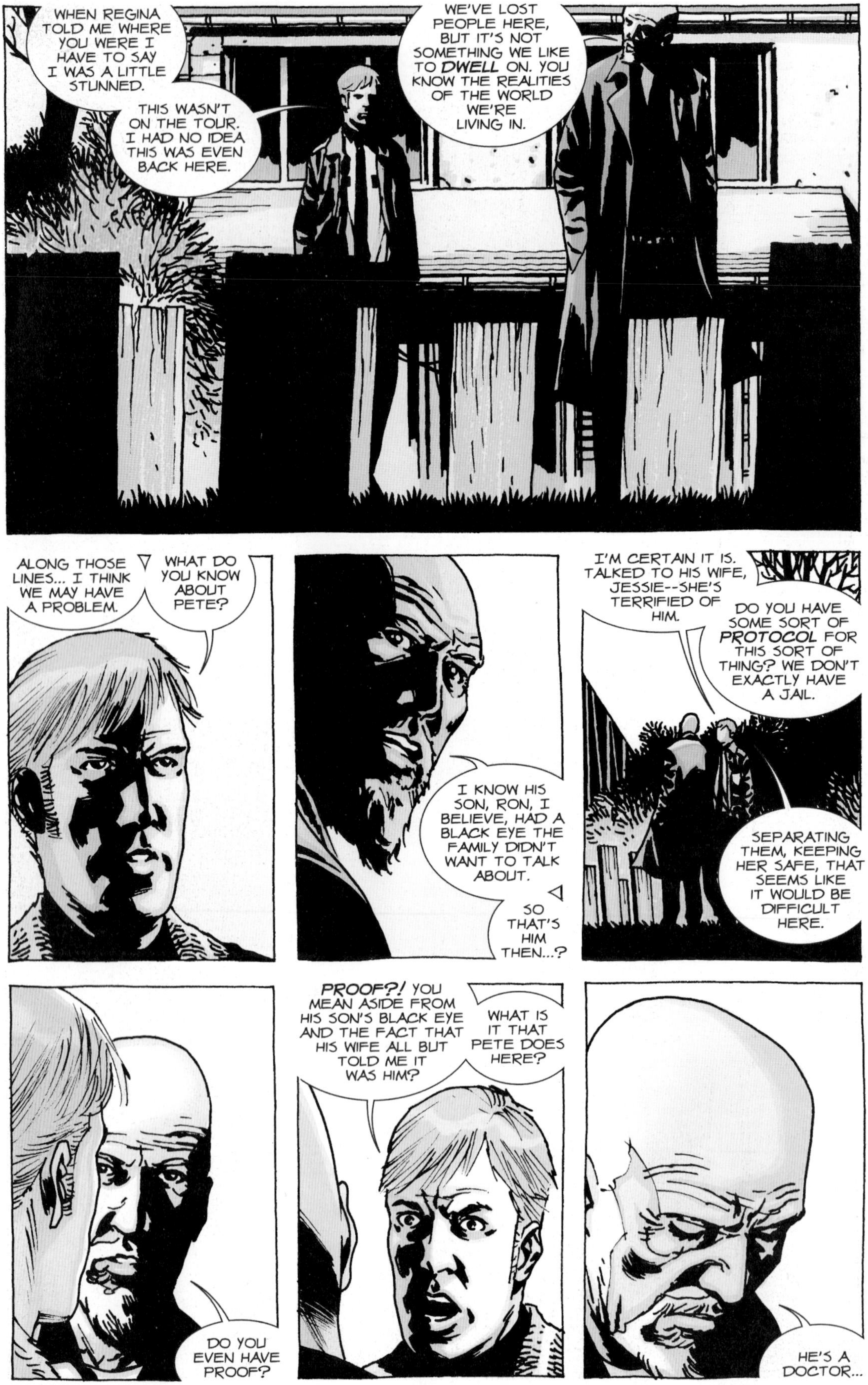

WHEN REGINA TOLD ME WHERE YOU WERE I HAVE TO SAY I WAS A LITTLE STUNNED.
THIS WASN'T ON THE TOUR. I HAD NO IDEA THIS WAS EVEN BACK HERE.
WE'VE LOST PEOPLE HERE, BUT IT'S NOT SOMETHING WE LIKE TO DWELL ON. YOU KNOW THE REALITIES OF THE WORLD WE'RE LIVING IN.
ALONG THOSE LINES... I THINK WE MAY HAVE A PROBLEM.
WHAT DO YOU KNOW ABOUT PETE?
I KNOW HIS SON, RON, I BELIEVE, HAD A BLACK EYE THE FAMILY DIDN'T WANT TO TALK ABOUT.
SO THAT'S HIM THEN...?
I'M CERTAIN IT IS. TALKED TO HIS WIFE, JESSIE--SHE'S TERRIFIED OF HIM.
DO YOU HAVE SOME SORT OF PROTOCOL FOR THIS SORT OF THING? WE DON'T EXACTLY HAVE A JAIL.
SEPARATING THEM, KEEPING HER SAFE, THAT SEEMS LIKE IT WOULD BE DIFFICULT HERE.
DO YOU EVEN HAVE PROOF?
PROOF?! YOU MEAN ASIDE FROM HIS SON'S BLACK EYE AND THE FACT THAT HIS WIFE ALL BUT TOLD ME IT WAS HIM?
WHAT IS IT THAT PETE DOES HERE?
HE'S A DOCTOR...

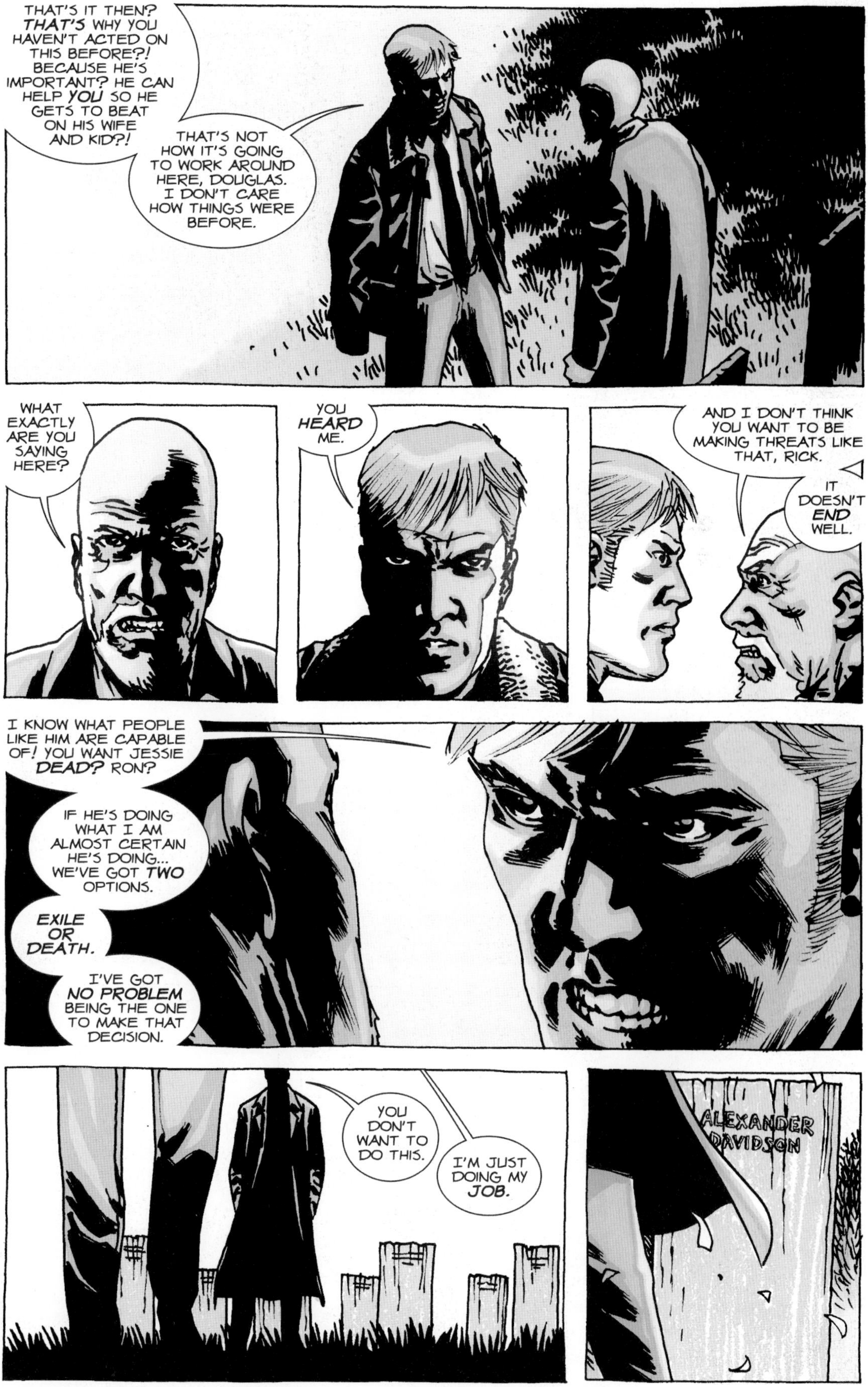
THAT'S IT THEN? THAT'S WHY YOU HAVEN'T ACTED ON THIS BEFORE?! BECAUSE HE'S IMPORTANT? HE CAN HELP YOU SO HE GETS TO BEAT ON HIS WIFE AND KID?!
THAT'S NOT HOW IT'S GOING TO WORK AROUND HERE, DOUGLAS. I DON'T CARE HOW THINGS WERE BEFORE.
WHAT EXACTLY ARE YOU SAYING HERE?
YOU HEARD ME.
AND I DON'T THINK YOU WANT TO BE MAKING THREATS LIKE THAT, RICK.
IT DOESN'T END WELL.
I KNOW WHAT PEOPLE LIKE HIM ARE CAPABLE OF! YOU WANT JESSIE DEAD? RON?
IF HE'S DOING WHAT I AM ALMOST CERTAIN HE'S DOING... WE'VE GOT TWO OPTIONS.
EXILE OR DEATH.
I'VE GOT NO PROBLEM BEING THE ONE TO MAKE THAT DECISION.
YOU DON'T WANT TO DO THIS.
I'M JUST DOING MY JOB.
ALEXANDER DAVIDSON

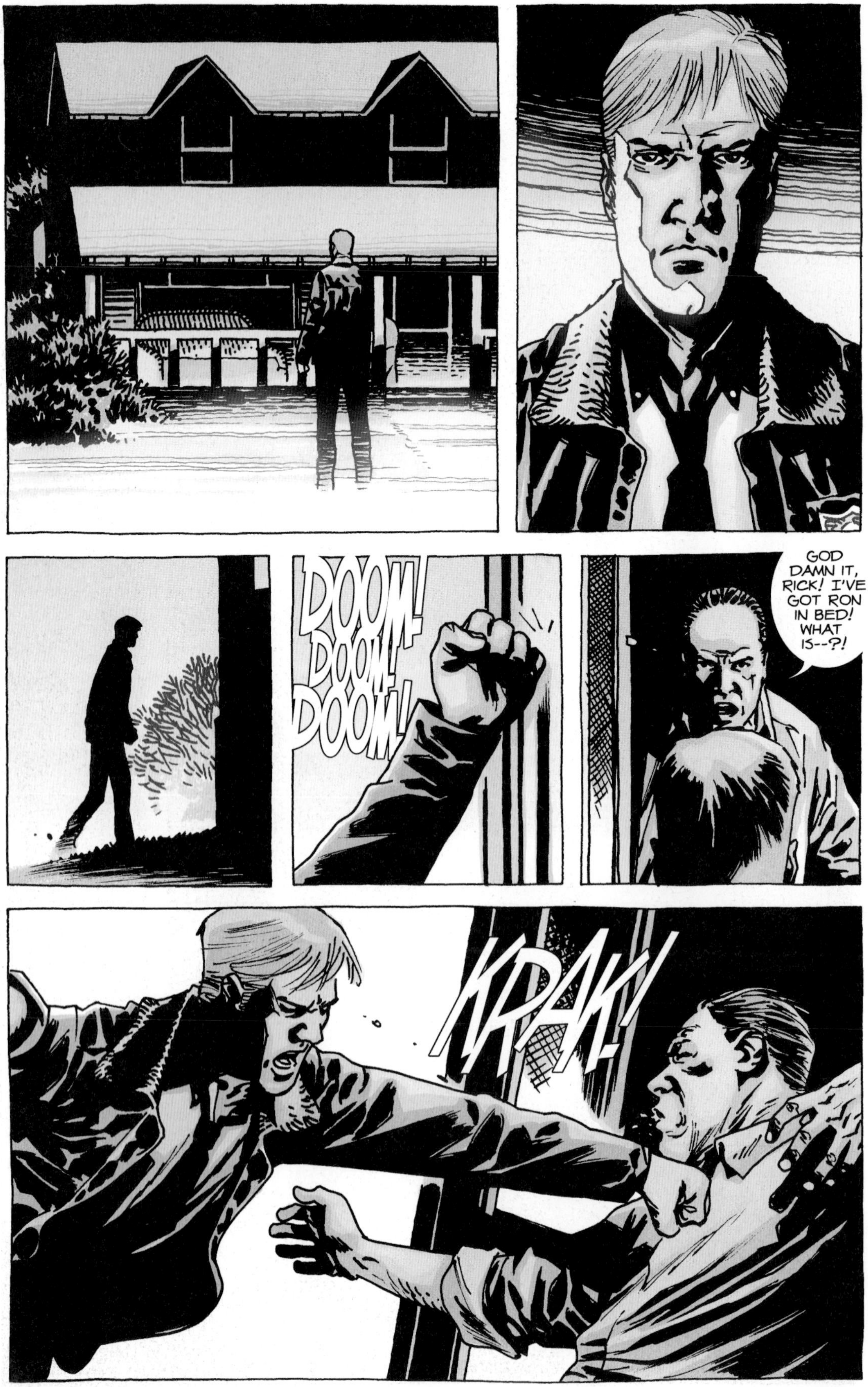
DOOM! DOOM! DOOM!
GOD DAMN IT, RICK! I'VE GOT RON IN BED! WHAT IS--?!
KRAK!

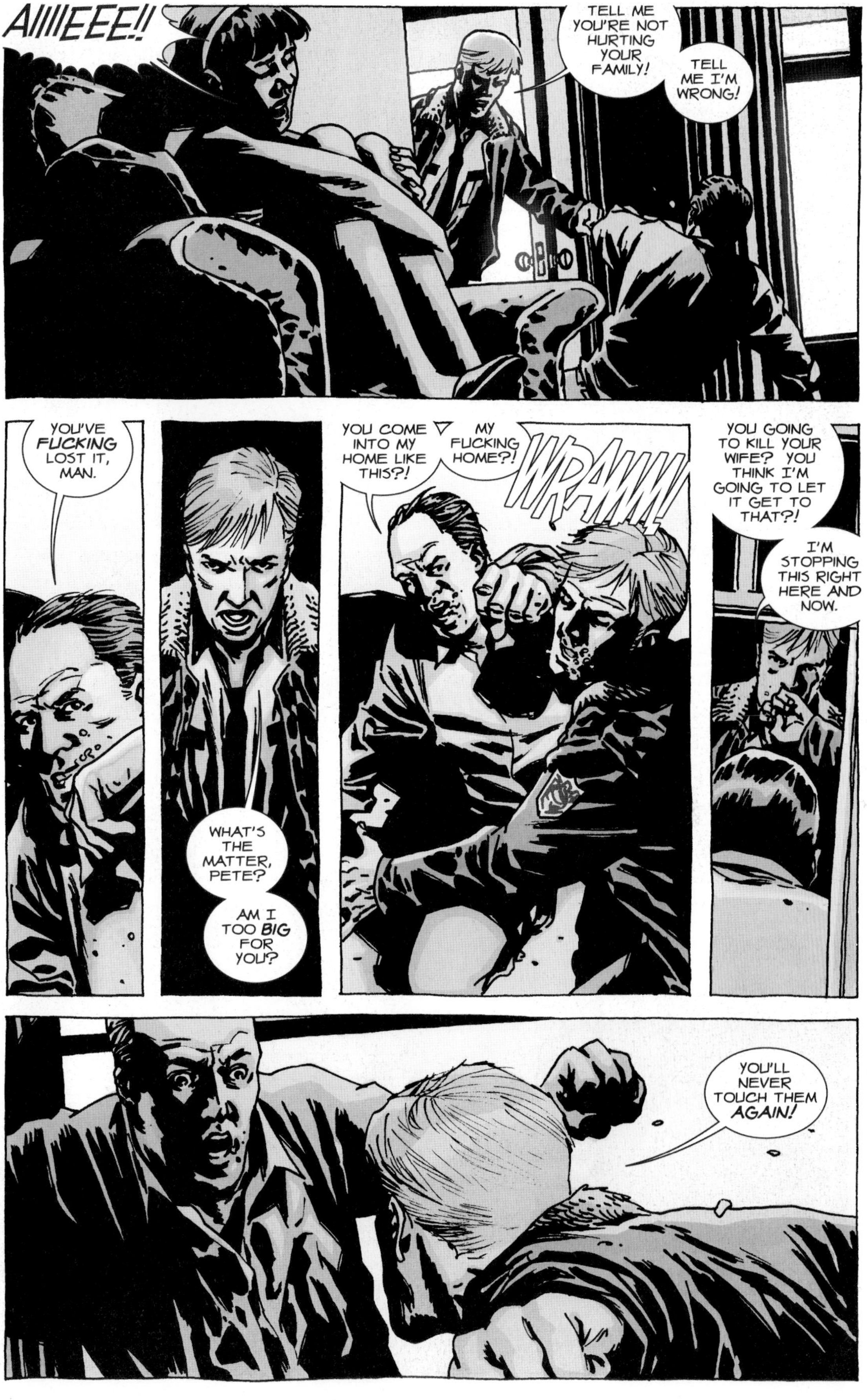

AIIIIEEE!!
TELL ME YOU'RE NOT HURTING YOUR FAMILY!
TELL ME I'M WRONG!
YOU'VE FUCKING LOST IT, MAN.
WHAT'S THE MATTER, PETE?
AM I TOO BIG FOR YOU?
YOU COME INTO MY HOME LIKE THIS?!
MY FUCKING HOME?!
WRAMM!
YOU GOING TO KILL YOUR WIFE? YOU THINK I'M GOING TO LET IT GET TO THAT?!
I'M STOPPING THIS RIGHT HERE AND NOW.
YOU'LL NEVER TOUCH THEM AGAIN!

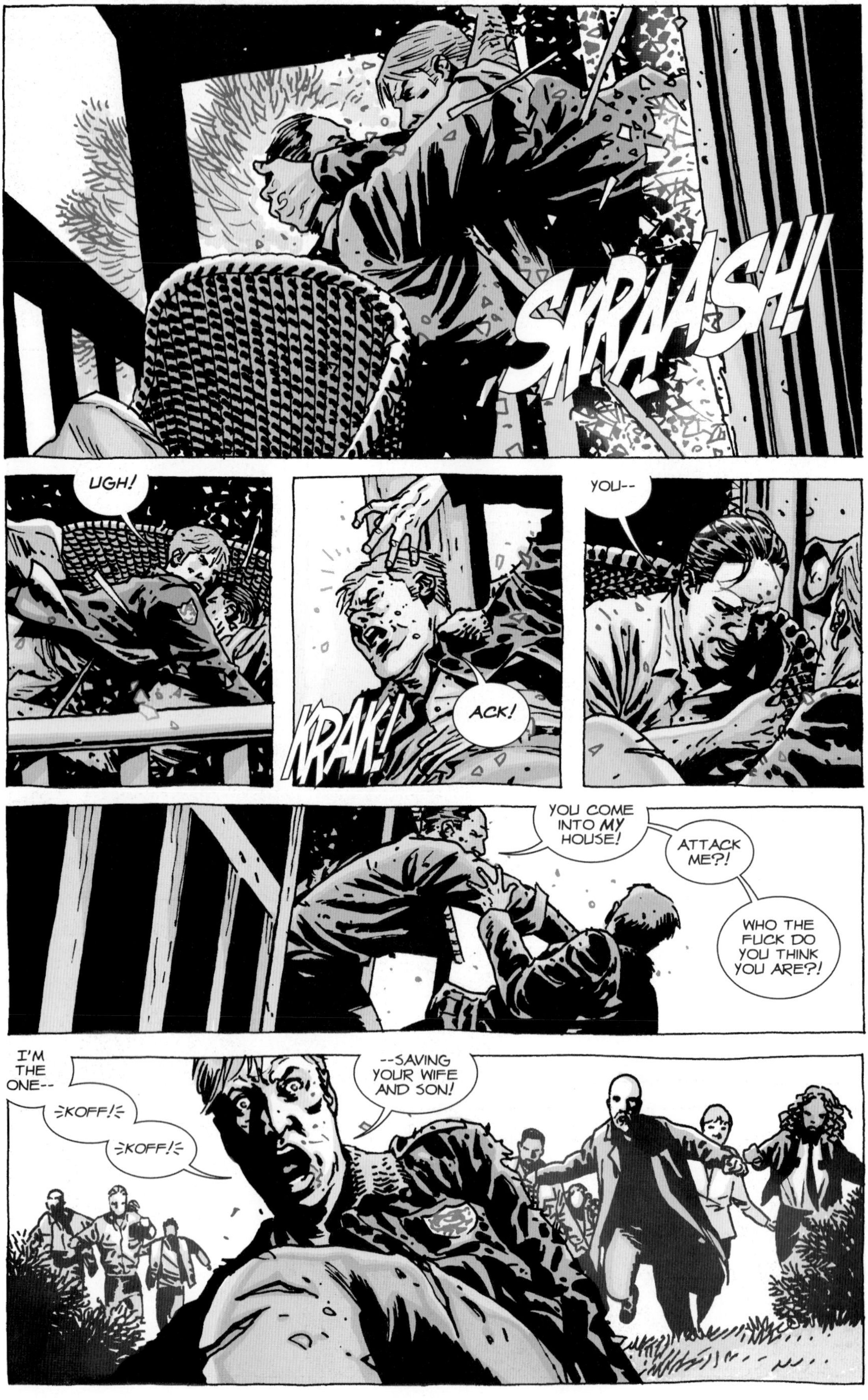
SKRAASH!
UGH!
KRAK!
ACK!
YOU--
YOU COME INTO MY HOUSE!
ATTACK ME?!
WHO THE FUCK DO YOU THINK YOU ARE?!
I'M THE ONE--
KOFF!
KOFF!
--SAVING YOUR WIFE AND SON!

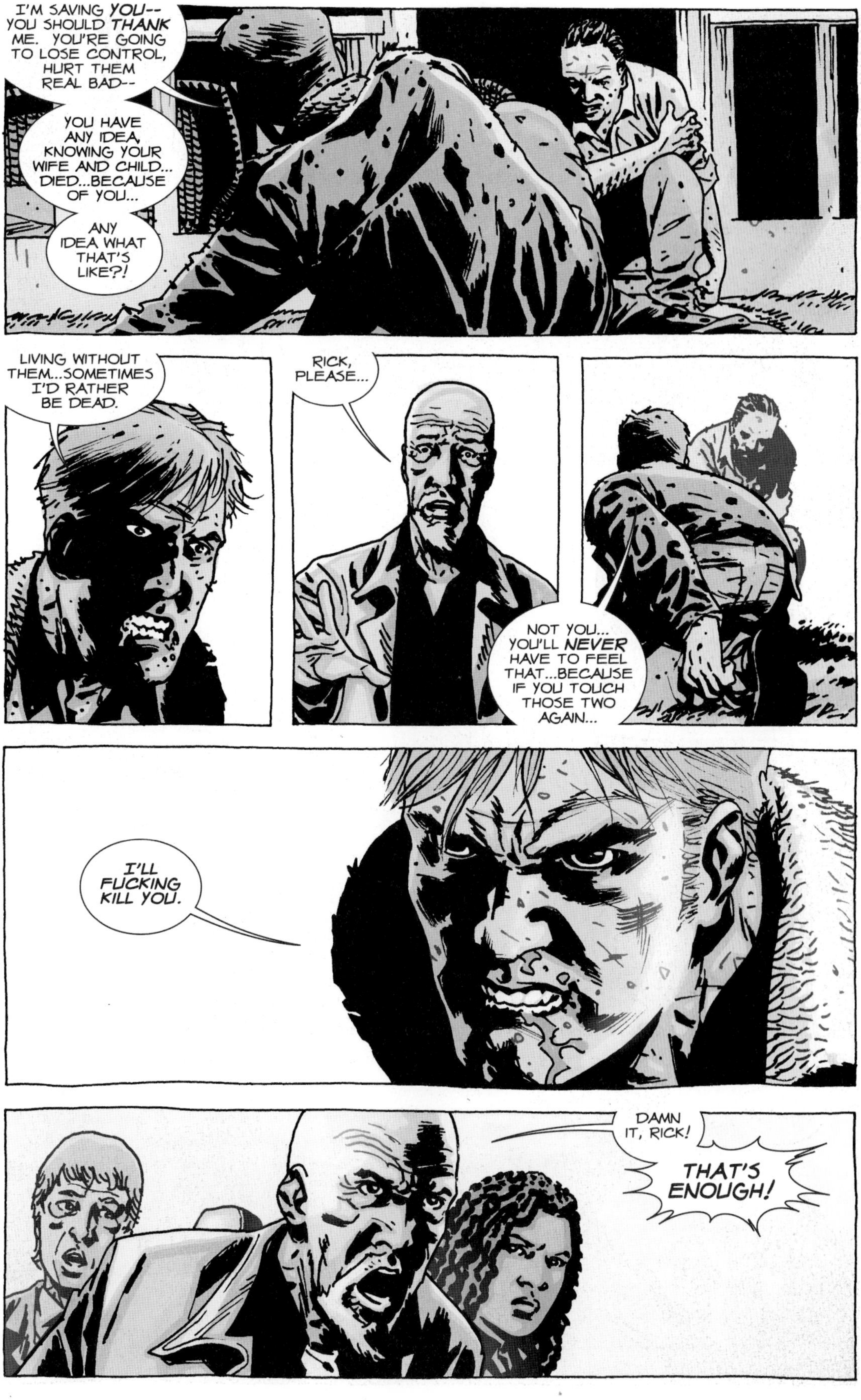
I'M SAVING YOU-- YOU SHOULD THANK ME. YOU'RE GOING TO LOSE CONTROL, HURT THEM REAL BAD--
YOU HAVE ANY IDEA, KNOWING YOUR WIFE AND CHILD... DIED...BECAUSE OF YOU...
ANY IDEA WHAT THAT'S LIKE?!
LIVING WITHOUT THEM...SOMETIMES I'D RATHER BE DEAD.
RICK, PLEASE...
NOT YOU... YOU'LL NEVER HAVE TO FEEL THAT...BECAUSE IF YOU TOUCH THOSE TWO AGAIN...
I'LL FUCKING KILL YOU.
DAMN IT, RICK!
THAT'S ENOUGH!

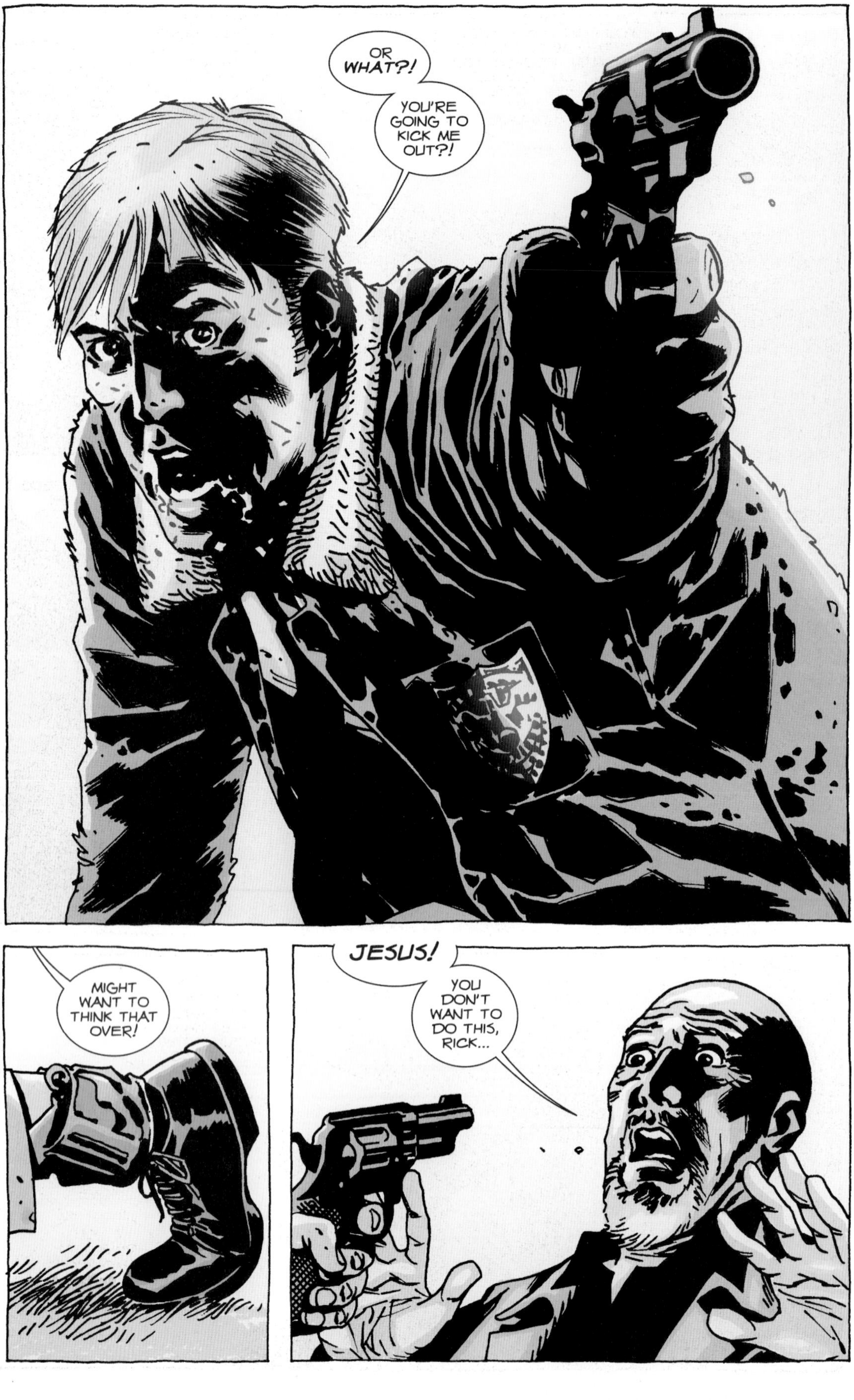
OR WHAT?!
YOU'RE GOING TO KICK ME OUT?!
MIGHT WANT TO THINK THAT OVER!
JESUS!
YOU DON'T WANT TO DO THIS, RICK...

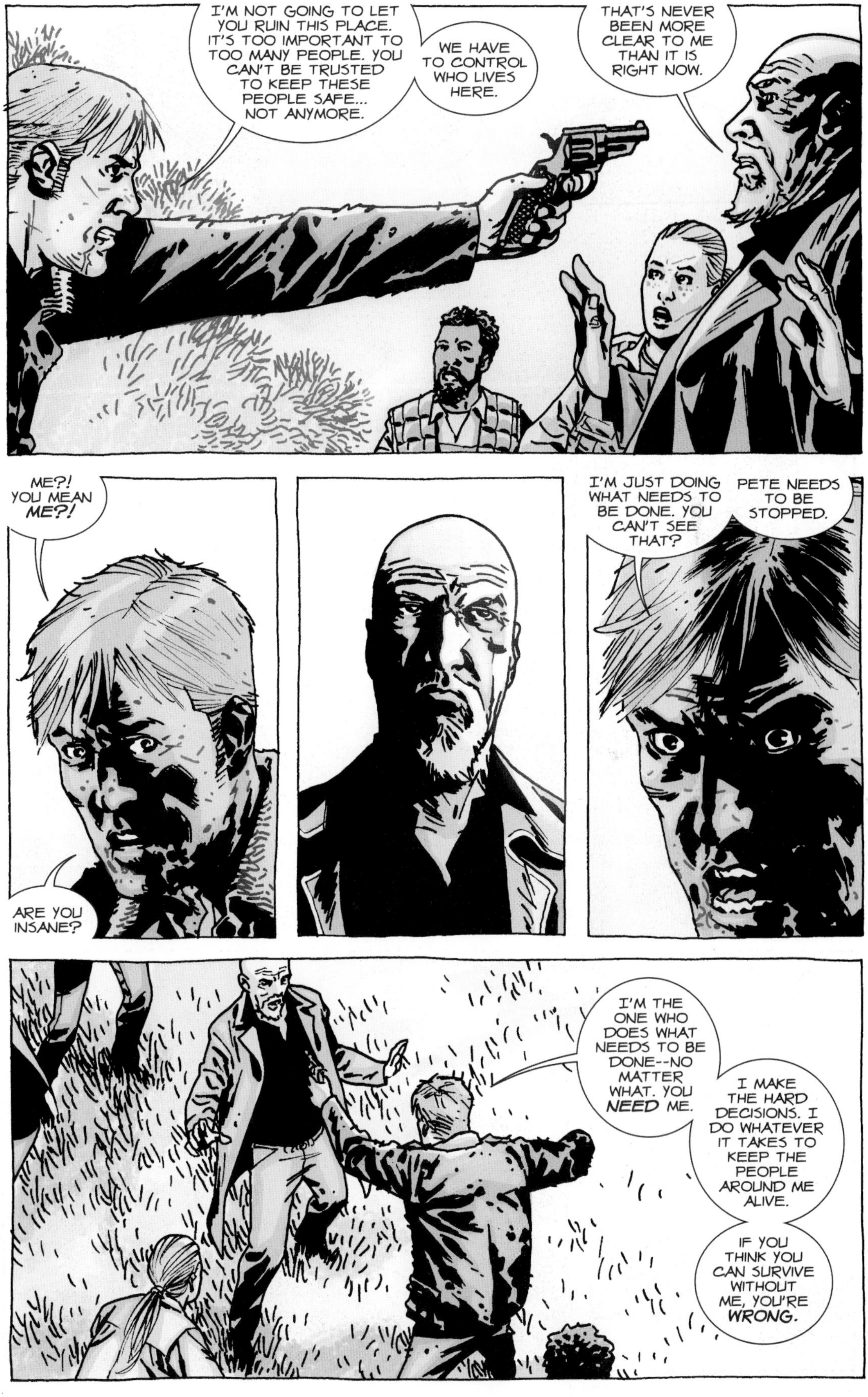
I'M NOT GOING TO LET YOU RUIN THIS PLACE. IT'S TOO IMPORTANT TO TOO MANY PEOPLE. YOU CAN'T BE TRUSTED TO KEEP THESE PEOPLE SAFE... NOT ANYMORE.
WE HAVE TO CONTROL WHO LIVES HERE.
THAT'S NEVER BEEN MORE CLEAR TO ME THAN IT IS RIGHT NOW.
ME?! YOU MEAN *ME?!*
ARE YOU INSANE?
I'M JUST DOING WHAT NEEDS TO BE DONE. YOU CAN'T SEE THAT?
PETE NEEDS TO BE STOPPED.
I'M THE ONE WHO DOES WHAT NEEDS TO BE DONE--NO MATTER WHAT. YOU *NEED* ME.
I MAKE THE HARD DECISIONS. I DO WHATEVER IT TAKES TO KEEP THE PEOPLE AROUND ME ALIVE.
IF YOU THINK YOU CAN SURVIVE WITHOUT ME, YOU'RE *WRONG.*

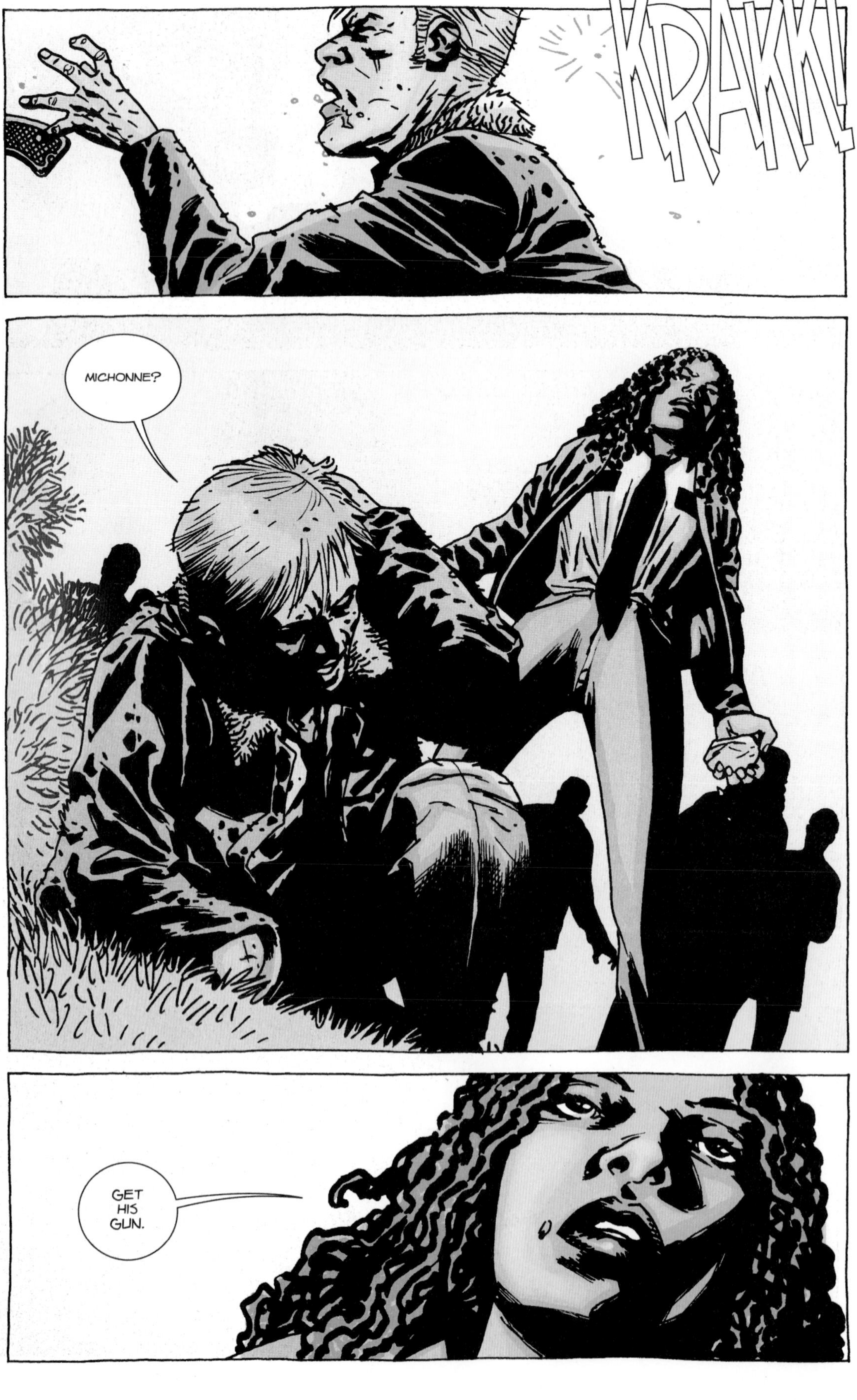
KRAKK!
MICHONNE?
GET HIS GUN.

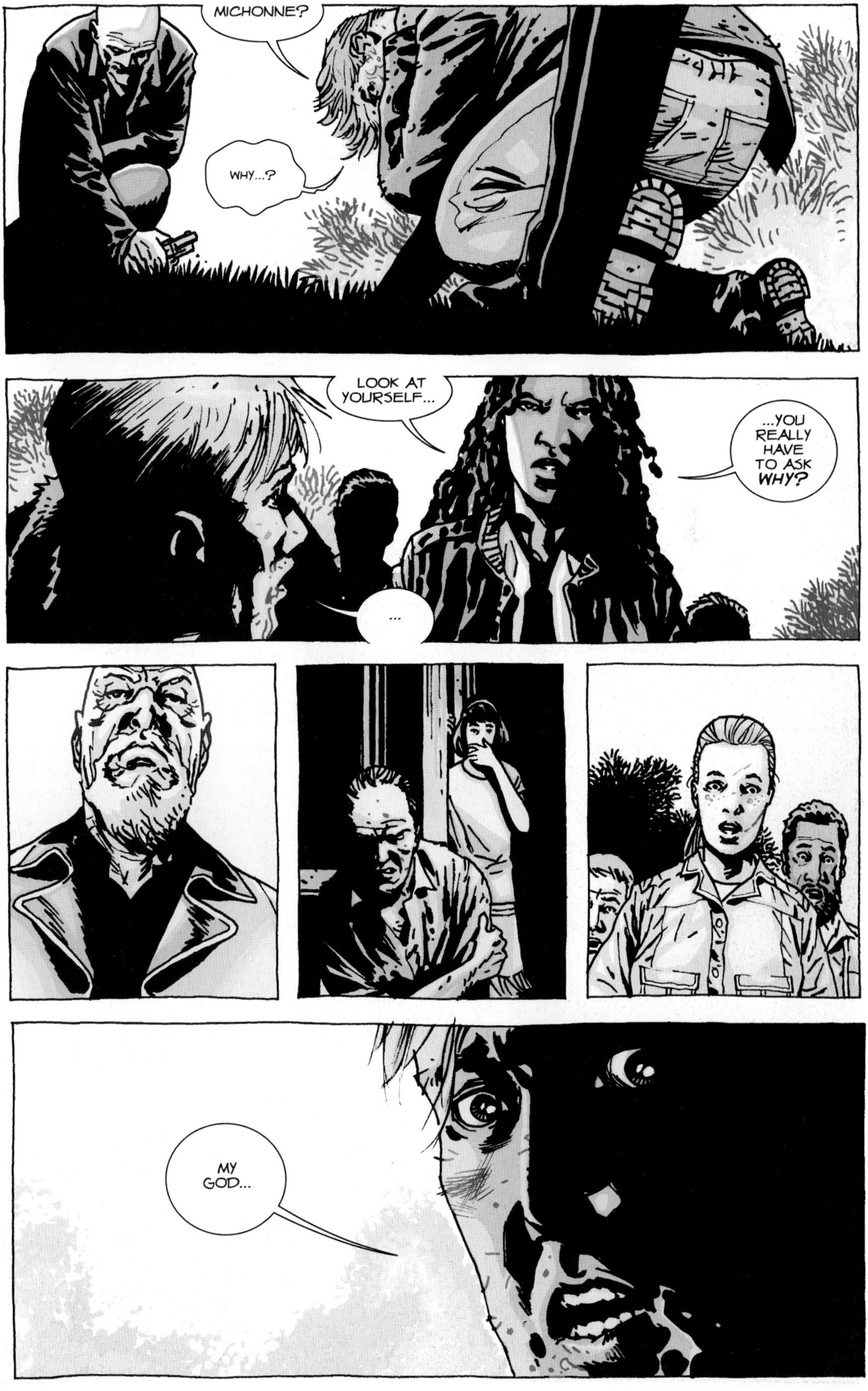
MICHONNE?
WHY...?
LOOK AT YOURSELF...
...YOU REALLY HAVE TO ASK WHY?
...
MY GOD...

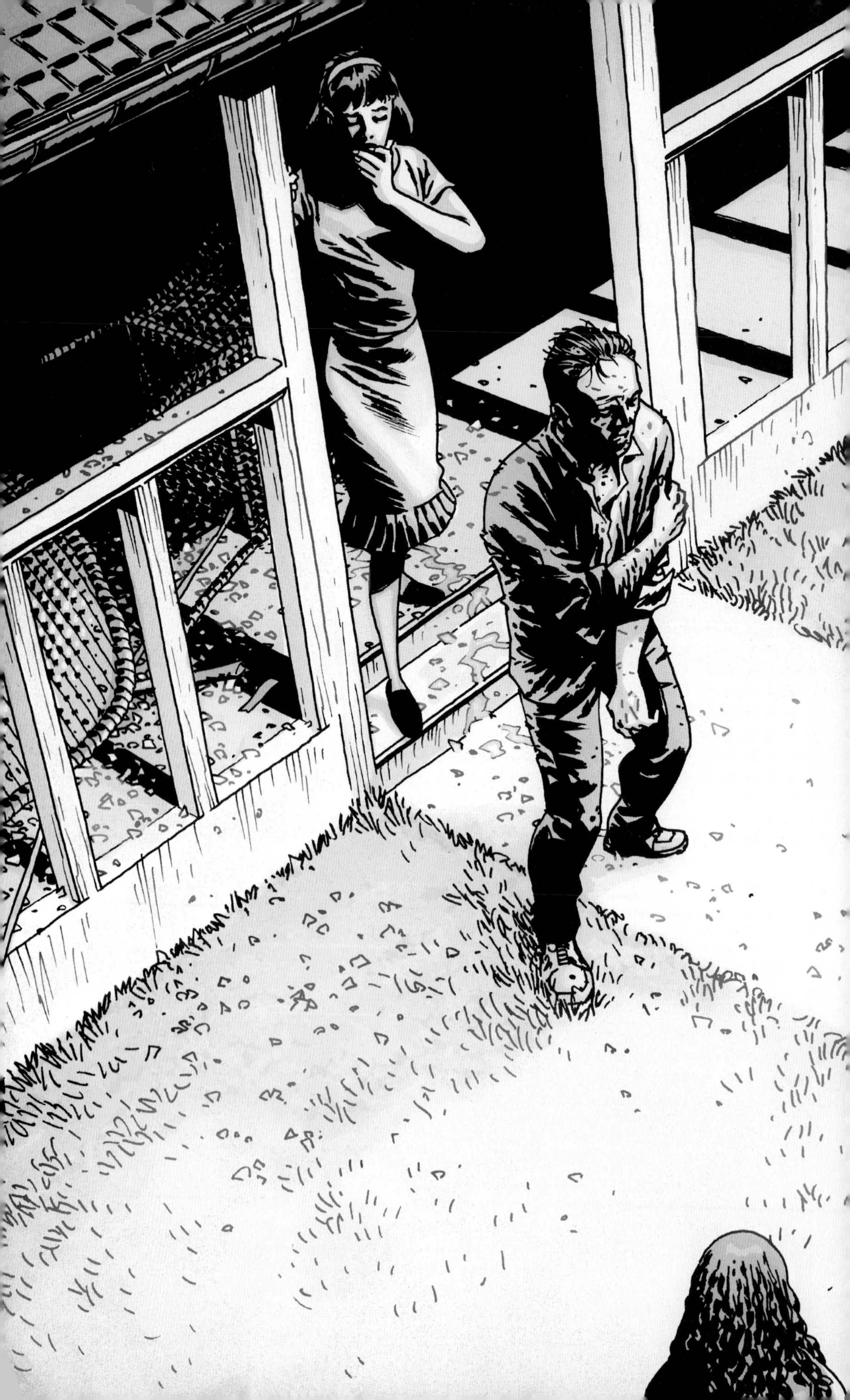

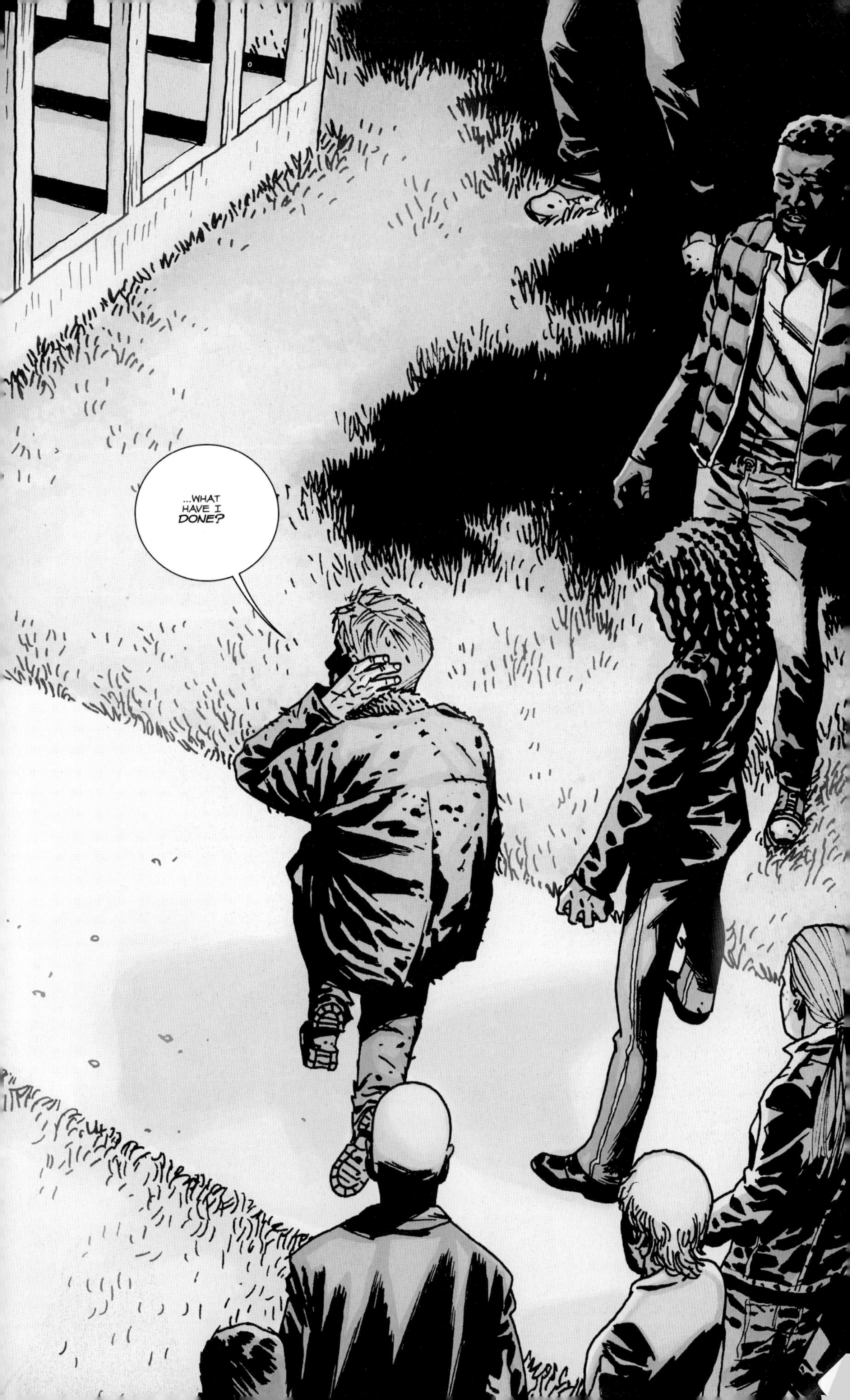
...WHAT HAVE I DONE?

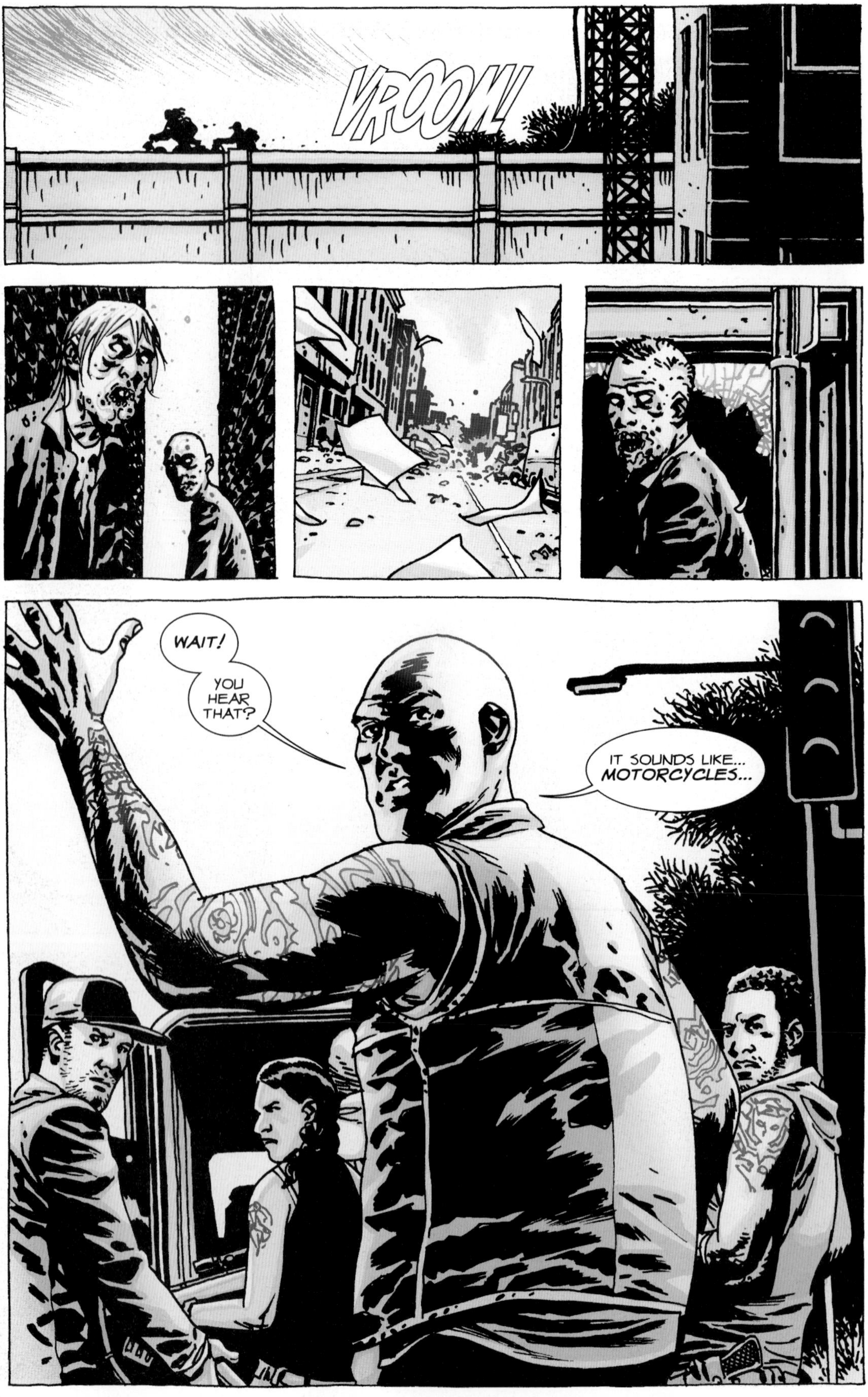
VROOM!
WAIT!
YOU HEAR THAT?
IT SOUNDS LIKE... MOTORCYCLES...

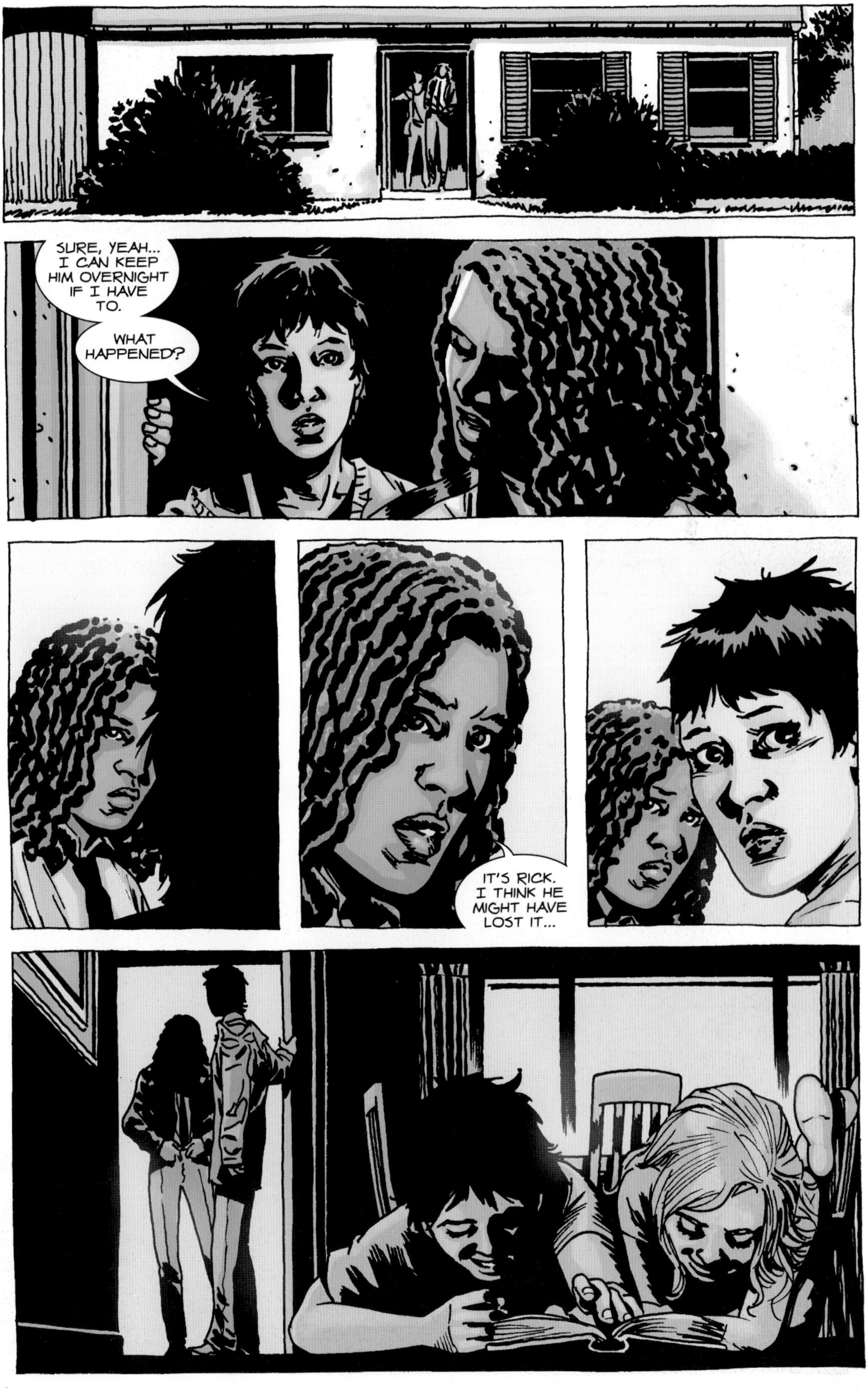
SURE, YEAH... I CAN KEEP HIM OVERNIGHT IF I HAVE TO.
WHAT HAPPENED?
IT'S RICK. I THINK HE MIGHT HAVE LOST IT...

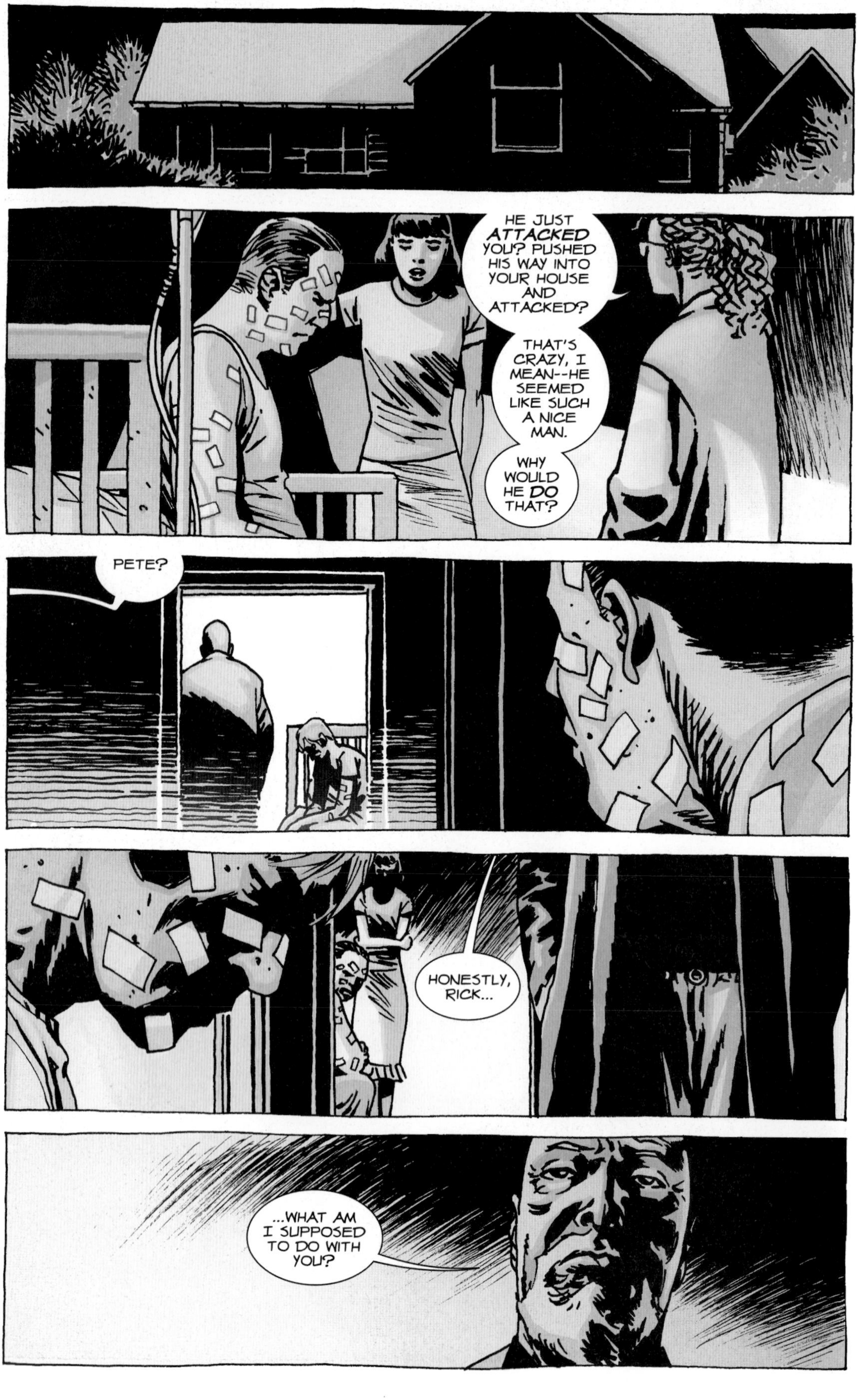
HE JUST ATTACKED YOU? PUSHED HIS WAY INTO YOUR HOUSE AND ATTACKED?
THAT'S CRAZY, I MEAN--HE SEEMED LIKE SUCH A NICE MAN.
WHY WOULD HE DO THAT?
PETE?
HONESTLY, RICK...
...WHAT AM I SUPPOSED TO DO WITH YOU?

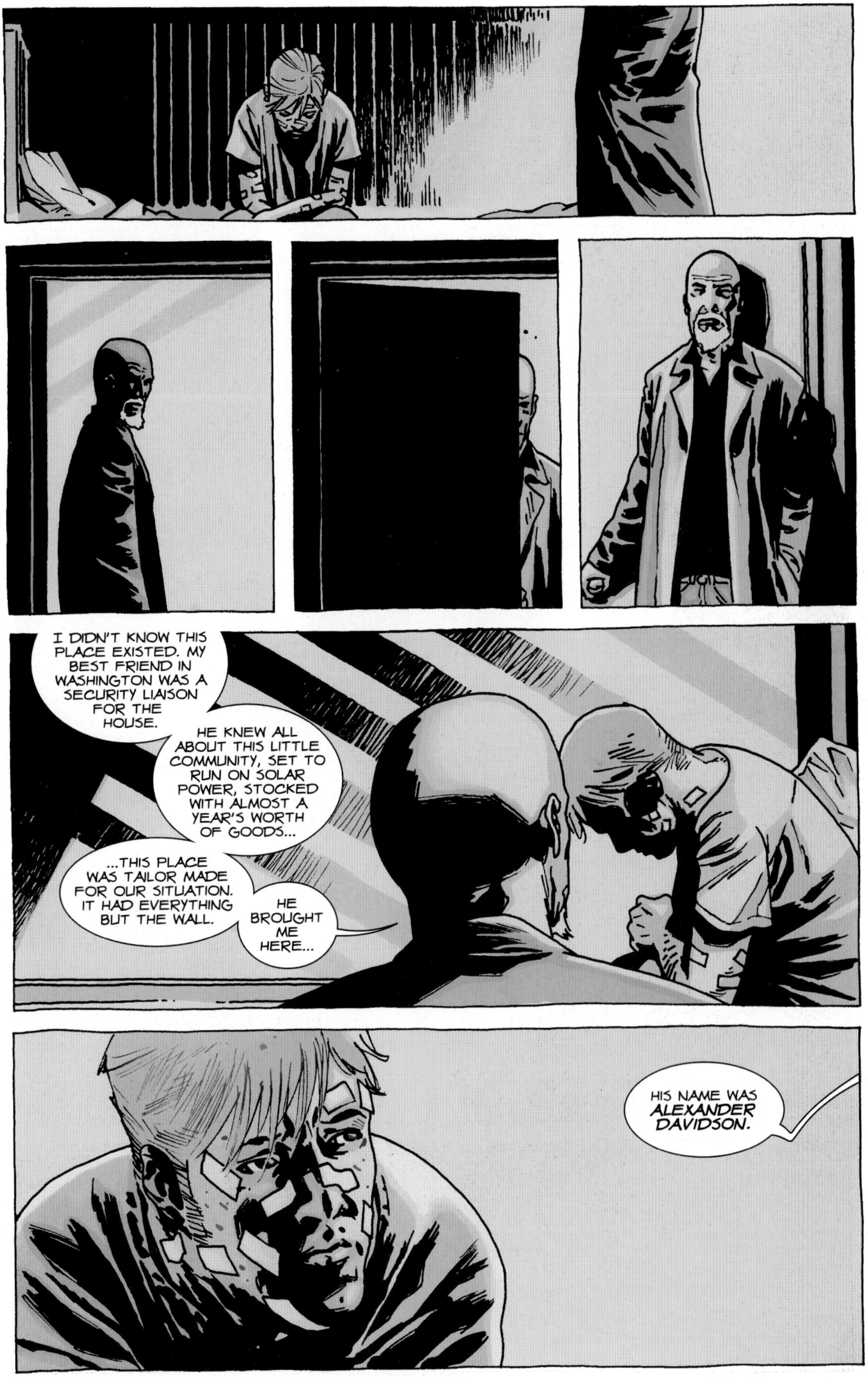

I DIDN'T KNOW THIS PLACE EXISTED. MY BEST FRIEND IN WASHINGTON WAS A SECURITY LIAISON FOR THE HOUSE.
HE KNEW ALL ABOUT THIS LITTLE COMMUNITY, SET TO RUN ON SOLAR POWER, STOCKED WITH ALMOST A YEAR'S WORTH OF GOODS...
...THIS PLACE WAS TAILOR MADE FOR OUR SITUATION. IT HAD EVERYTHING BUT THE WALL.
HE BROUGHT ME HERE...
HIS NAME WAS *ALEXANDER DAVIDSON.*

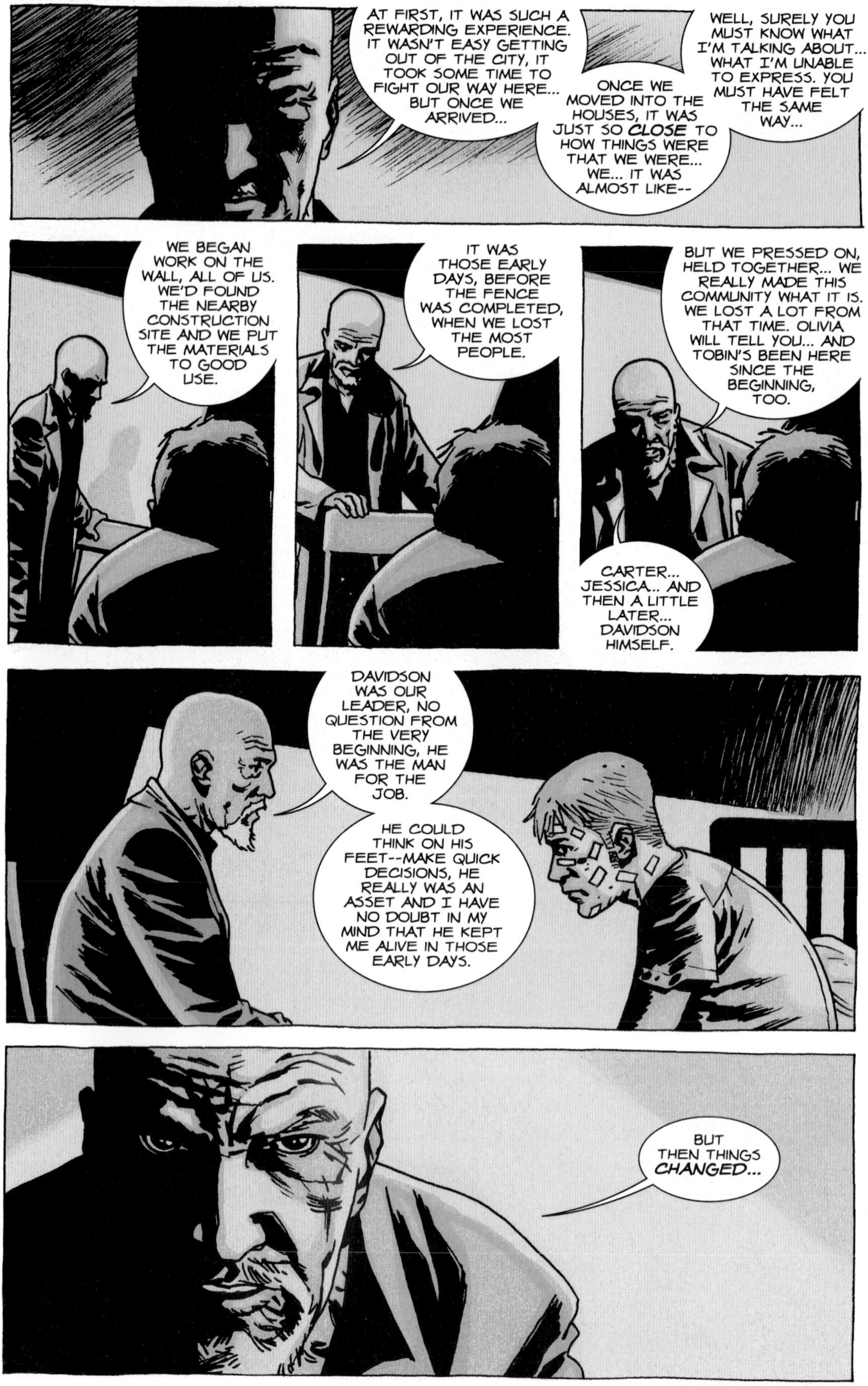
AT FIRST, IT WAS SUCH A REWARDING EXPERIENCE. IT WASN'T EASY GETTING OUT OF THE CITY, IT TOOK SOME TIME TO FIGHT OUR WAY HERE... BUT ONCE WE ARRIVED...
ONCE WE MOVED INTO THE HOUSES, IT WAS JUST SO CLOSE TO HOW THINGS WERE THAT WE WERE... WE... IT WAS ALMOST LIKE--
WELL, SURELY YOU MUST KNOW WHAT I'M TALKING ABOUT... WHAT I'M UNABLE TO EXPRESS. YOU MUST HAVE FELT THE SAME WAY...
WE BEGAN WORK ON THE WALL, ALL OF US. WE'D FOUND THE NEARBY CONSTRUCTION SITE AND WE PUT THE MATERIALS TO GOOD USE.
IT WAS THOSE EARLY DAYS, BEFORE THE FENCE WAS COMPLETED, WHEN WE LOST THE MOST PEOPLE.
BUT WE PRESSED ON, HELD TOGETHER... WE REALLY MADE THIS COMMUNITY WHAT IT IS. WE LOST A LOT FROM THAT TIME. OLIVIA WILL TELL YOU... AND TOBIN'S BEEN HERE SINCE THE BEGINNING, TOO.
CARTER... JESSICA... AND THEN A LITTLE LATER... DAVIDSON HIMSELF.
DAVIDSON WAS OUR LEADER, NO QUESTION FROM THE VERY BEGINNING, HE WAS THE MAN FOR THE JOB.
HE COULD THINK ON HIS FEET--MAKE QUICK DECISIONS, HE REALLY WAS AN ASSET AND I HAVE NO DOUBT IN MY MIND THAT HE KEPT ME ALIVE IN THOSE EARLY DAYS.
BUT THEN THINGS CHANGED...

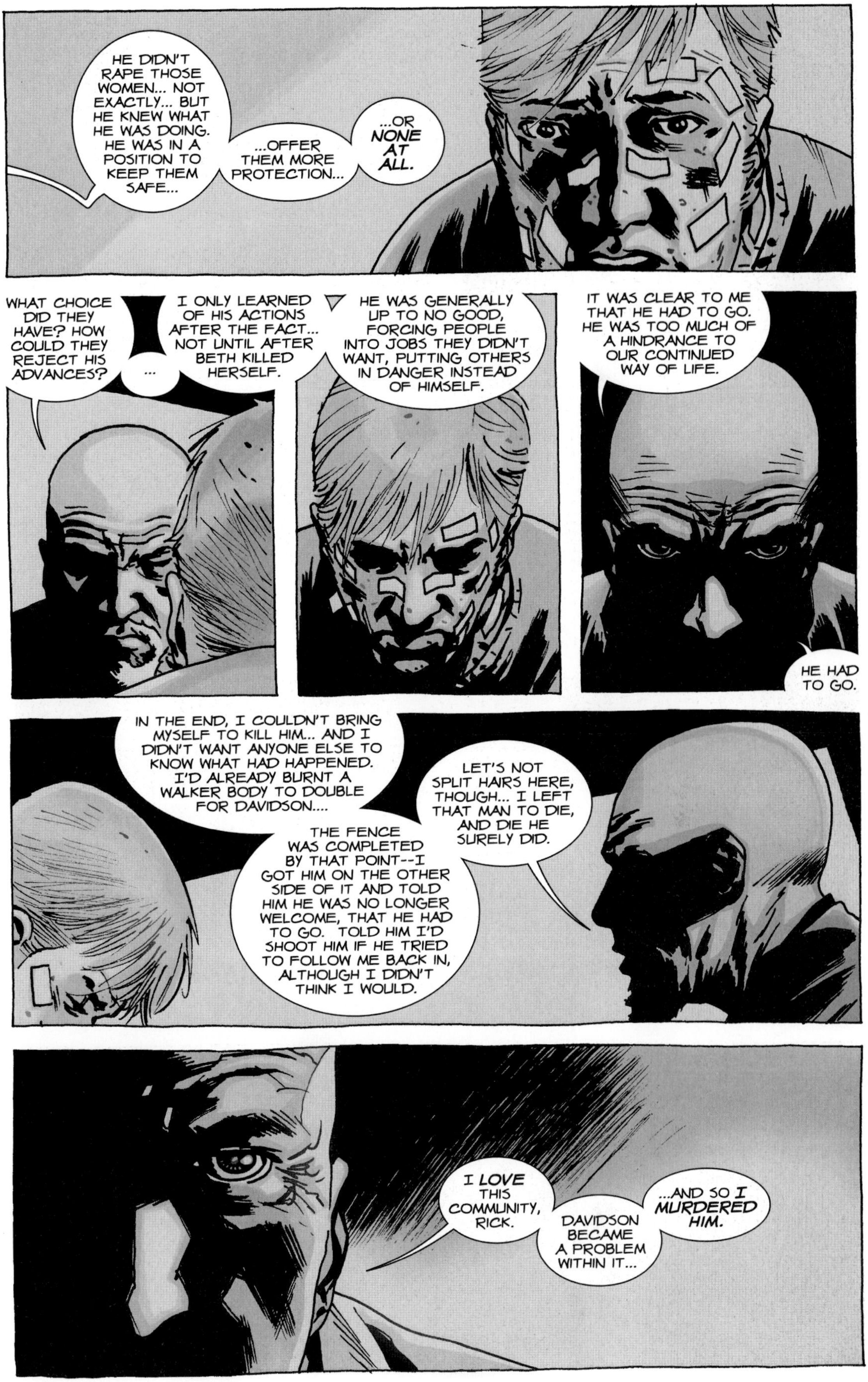

HE DIDN'T RAPE THOSE WOMEN... NOT EXACTLY... BUT HE KNEW WHAT HE WAS DOING. HE WAS IN A POSITION TO KEEP THEM SAFE...
...OFFER THEM MORE PROTECTION...
...OR NONE AT ALL.
WHAT CHOICE DID THEY HAVE? HOW COULD THEY REJECT HIS ADVANCES?
...
I ONLY LEARNED OF HIS ACTIONS AFTER THE FACT... NOT UNTIL AFTER BETH KILLED HERSELF.
HE WAS GENERALLY UP TO NO GOOD, FORCING PEOPLE INTO JOBS THEY DIDN'T WANT, PUTTING OTHERS IN DANGER INSTEAD OF HIMSELF.
IT WAS CLEAR TO ME THAT HE HAD TO GO. HE WAS TOO MUCH OF A HINDRANCE TO OUR CONTINUED WAY OF LIFE.
HE HAD TO GO.
IN THE END, I COULDN'T BRING MYSELF TO KILL HIM... AND I DIDN'T WANT ANYONE ELSE TO KNOW WHAT HAD HAPPENED. I'D ALREADY BURNT A WALKER BODY TO DOUBLE FOR DAVIDSON....
THE FENCE WAS COMPLETED BY THAT POINT--I GOT HIM ON THE OTHER SIDE OF IT AND TOLD HIM HE WAS NO LONGER WELCOME, THAT HE HAD TO GO. TOLD HIM I'D SHOOT HIM IF HE TRIED TO FOLLOW ME BACK IN, ALTHOUGH I DIDN'T THINK I WOULD.
LET'S NOT SPLIT HAIRS HERE, THOUGH... I LEFT THAT MAN TO DIE, AND DIE HE SURELY DID.
I LOVE THIS COMMUNITY, RICK.
DAVIDSON BECAME A PROBLEM WITHIN IT...
...AND SO I MURDERED HIM.

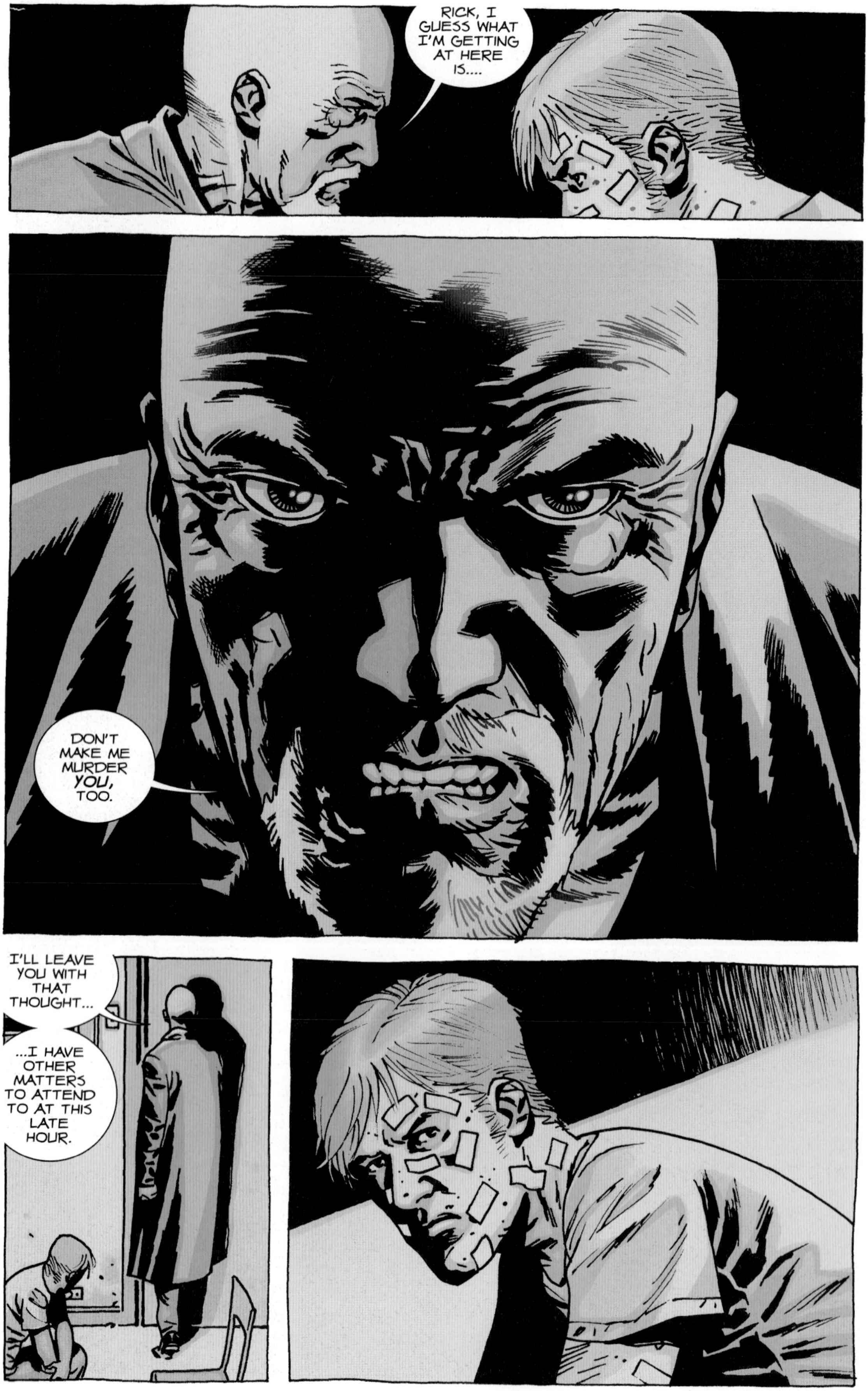

RICK, I GUESS WHAT I'M GETTING AT HERE IS....
DON'T MAKE ME MURDER *YOU,* TOO.
I'LL LEAVE YOU WITH THAT THOUGHT...
...I HAVE OTHER MATTERS TO ATTEND TO AT THIS LATE HOUR.

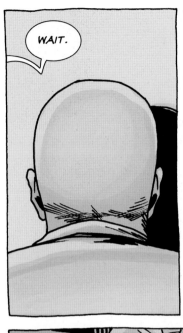

WAIT.

YES?

I NEVER WANTED TO BE A LEADER.

I DIDN'T NEED THE PRESSURE, DIDN'T *WANT* THE RESPONSIBILITY. WITH ALL THAT WAS GOING ON... I HAD OTHER THINGS ON MY MIND. MY WIFE AND SON TO PROTECT.

MY PARTNER SHANE... HE WAS THE LEADER OF OUR GROUP AT FIRST. NOT THAT WE TOOK THE TIME TO MAKE THOSE DISTINCTIONS, BUT HE WAS THE ONE EVERYONE LOOKED TO FOR ANSWERS.

IT DIDN'T REALLY MATTER TO ME UNTIL HE STARTED MAKING DECISIONS THAT WEREN'T GOOD FOR THE GROUP...

HE WANTED TO STAY ON THE OUTSKIRTS OF ATLANTA... BUT IT WAS TOO DANGEROUS. HE THOUGHT HELP WAS COMING. HE HAD HIS REASONS, BUT IT DIDN'T MAKE THINGS ANY LESS DANGEROUS.

WE BUTTED HEADS... THERE WERE A LOT OF ARGUMENTS.

THINGS EVEN GOT HEATED. HE DIDN'T LIKE THAT PEOPLE WERE STARTING TO AGREE WITH ME.

HE HELPED MY WIFE AND SON GET TO ATLANTA... I WAS IN A HOSPITAL HEALING FROM A GUNSHOT WOUND, I CAUGHT UP TO THEM LATER.

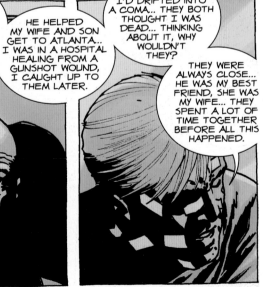

I'D DRIFTED INTO A COMA... THEY BOTH THOUGHT I WAS DEAD... THINKING ABOUT IT, WHY WOULDN'T THEY?

THEY WERE ALWAYS CLOSE... HE WAS MY BEST FRIEND, SHE WAS MY WIFE... THEY SPENT A LOT OF TIME TOGETHER BEFORE ALL THIS HAPPENED.

I KNOW SHE SLEPT WITH HIM.

NOT BEFORE... WHEN THEY WERE AT THE CAMP OUTSIDE ATLANTA, BEFORE I ARRIVED. THEY THOUGHT I WAS DEAD...

...WHO COULD BLAME THEM?

I CERTAINLY DIDN'T.

I'M ALMOST CERTAIN THAT MY DAUGHTER WAS ACTUALLY SHANE'S.

WITH ME BACK, LORI NATURALLY SHUNNED SHANE, RETURNING TO ME, PRETENDING NOTHING HAD EVER HAPPENED.

BETWEEN THAT AND SEEING THE GROUP SLOWLY TURN TO ME FOR LEADERSHIP--TAKING MY SIDE IN THE ARGUMENTS... HE STARTED TO CRACK.

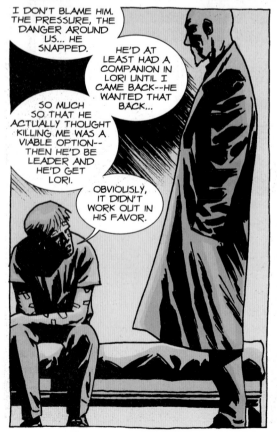

I DON'T BLAME HIM. THE PRESSURE, THE DANGER AROUND US... HE SNAPPED.

HE'D AT LEAST HAD A COMPANION IN LORI UNTIL I CAME BACK--HE WANTED THAT BACK...

SO MUCH SO THAT HE ACTUALLY THOUGHT KILLING ME WAS A VIABLE OPTION-- THEN HE'D BE LEADER AND HE'D GET LORI.

OBVIOUSLY, IT DIDN'T WORK OUT IN HIS FAVOR.

YOU KILLED YOUR BEST FRIEND, TOO?

NO.

MY SON DID IT FOR ME.

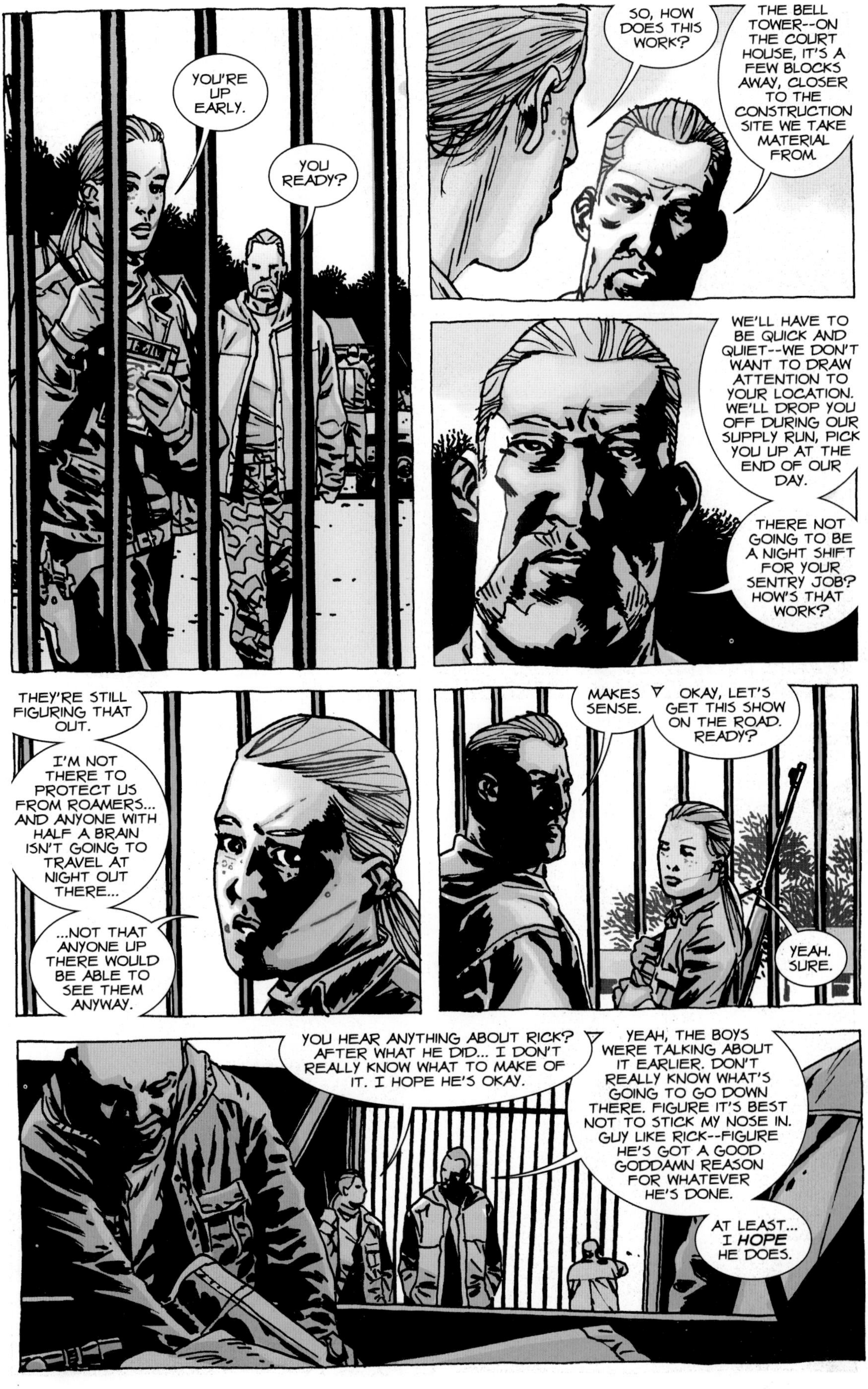
YOU'RE UP EARLY.
YOU READY?
SO, HOW DOES THIS WORK?
THE BELL TOWER--ON THE COURT HOUSE, IT'S A FEW BLOCKS AWAY, CLOSER TO THE CONSTRUCTION SITE WE TAKE MATERIAL FROM.
WE'LL HAVE TO BE QUICK AND QUIET--WE DON'T WANT TO DRAW ATTENTION TO YOUR LOCATION. WE'LL DROP YOU OFF DURING OUR SUPPLY RUN, PICK YOU UP AT THE END OF OUR DAY.
THERE NOT GOING TO BE A NIGHT SHIFT FOR YOUR SENTRY JOB? HOW'S THAT WORK?
THEY'RE STILL FIGURING THAT OUT.
I'M NOT THERE TO PROTECT US FROM ROAMERS... AND ANYONE WITH HALF A BRAIN ISN'T GOING TO TRAVEL AT NIGHT OUT THERE...
...NOT THAT ANYONE UP THERE WOULD BE ABLE TO SEE THEM ANYWAY.
MAKES SENSE.
OKAY, LET'S GET THIS SHOW ON THE ROAD. READY?
YEAH. SURE.
YOU HEAR ANYTHING ABOUT RICK? AFTER WHAT HE DID... I DON'T REALLY KNOW WHAT TO MAKE OF IT. I HOPE HE'S OKAY.
YEAH, THE BOYS WERE TALKING ABOUT IT EARLIER. DON'T REALLY KNOW WHAT'S GOING TO GO DOWN THERE. FIGURE IT'S BEST NOT TO STICK MY NOSE IN. GUY LIKE RICK--FIGURE HE'S GOT A GOOD GODDAMN REASON FOR WHATEVER HE'S DONE.
AT LEAST... I *HOPE* HE DOES.

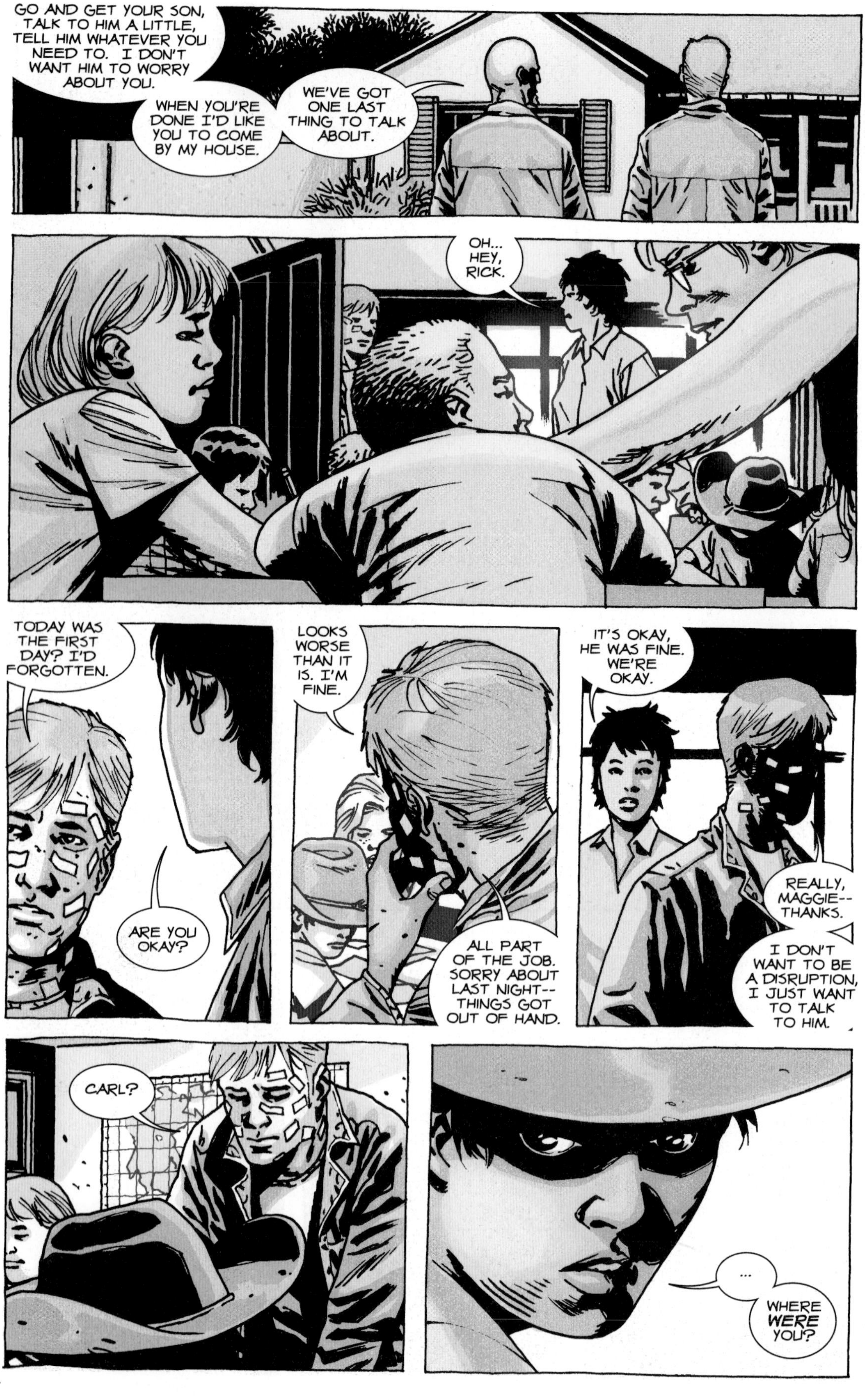
GO AND GET YOUR SON, TALK TO HIM A LITTLE, TELL HIM WHATEVER YOU NEED TO. I DON'T WANT HIM TO WORRY ABOUT YOU.
WHEN YOU'RE DONE I'D LIKE YOU TO COME BY MY HOUSE.
WE'VE GOT ONE LAST THING TO TALK ABOUT.
OH... HEY, RICK.
TODAY WAS THE FIRST DAY? I'D FORGOTTEN.
ARE YOU OKAY?
LOOKS WORSE THAN IT IS. I'M FINE.
ALL PART OF THE JOB. SORRY ABOUT LAST NIGHT-- THINGS GOT OUT OF HAND.
IT'S OKAY, HE WAS FINE. WE'RE OKAY.
REALLY, MAGGIE-- THANKS.
I DON'T WANT TO BE A DISRUPTION, I JUST WANT TO TALK TO HIM.
CARL?
...
WHERE *WERE* YOU?

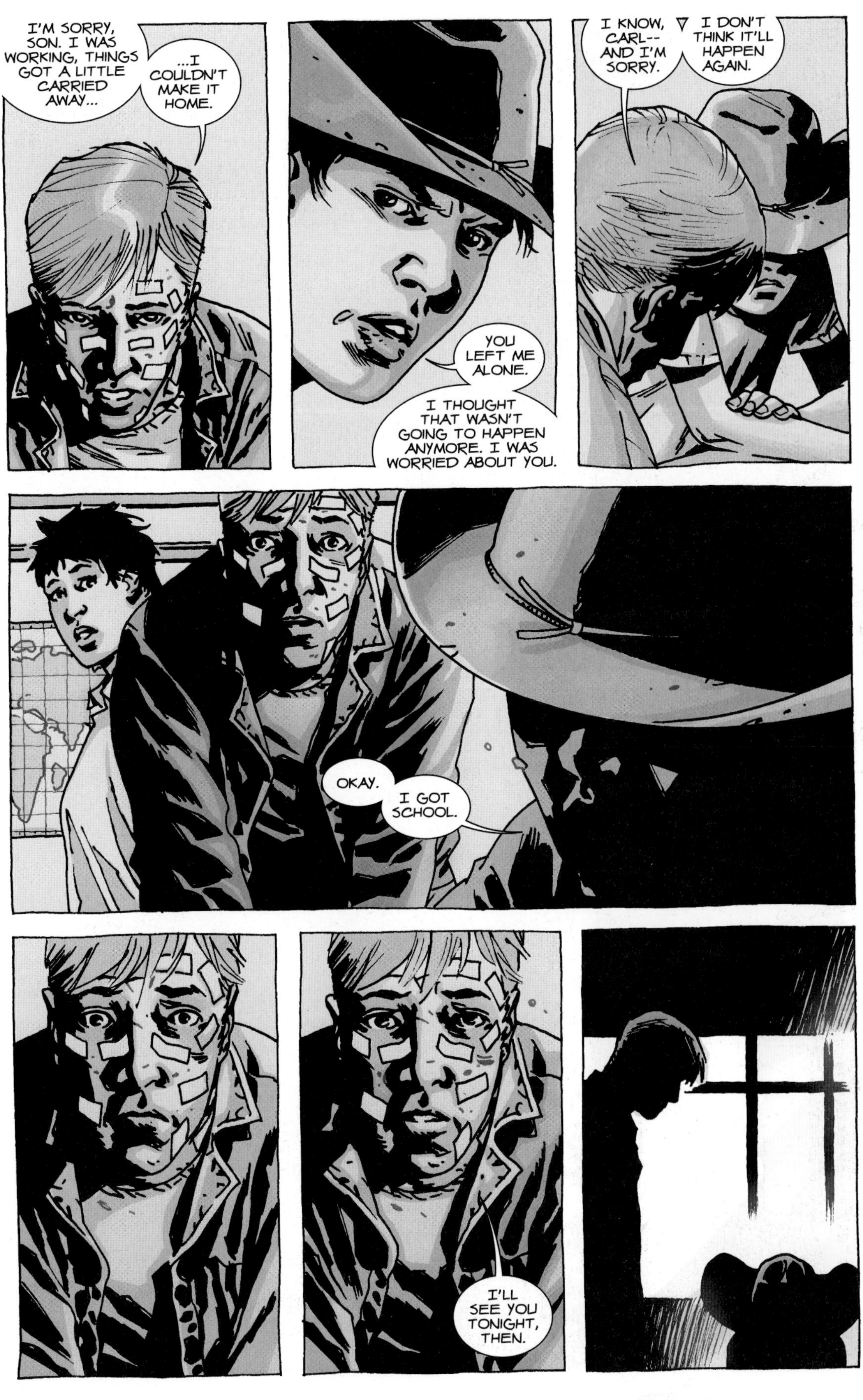
I'M SORRY, SON. I WAS WORKING, THINGS GOT A LITTLE CARRIED AWAY...
...I COULDN'T MAKE IT HOME.
YOU LEFT ME ALONE.
I THOUGHT THAT WASN'T GOING TO HAPPEN ANYMORE. I WAS WORRIED ABOUT YOU.
I KNOW, CARL-- AND I'M SORRY.
I DON'T THINK IT'LL HAPPEN AGAIN.
OKAY.
I GOT SCHOOL.
I'LL SEE YOU TONIGHT, THEN.

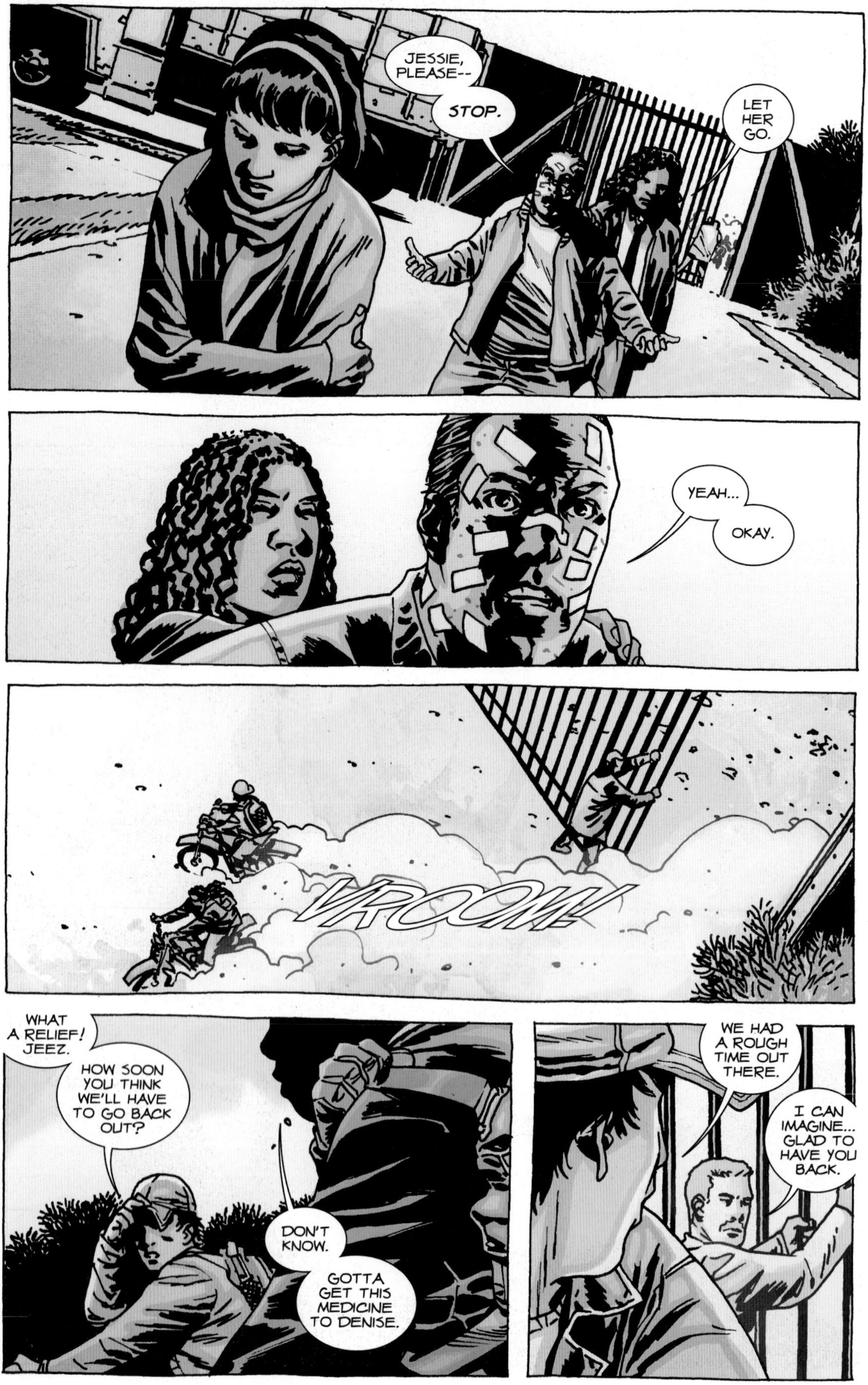
JESSIE, PLEASE--
STOP.
LET HER GO.
YEAH...
OKAY.
VROOOM!
WHAT A RELIEF! JEEZ.
HOW SOON YOU THINK WE'LL HAVE TO GO BACK OUT?
DON'T KNOW.
GOTTA GET THIS MEDICINE TO DENISE.
WE HAD A ROUGH TIME OUT THERE.
I CAN IMAGINE... GLAD TO HAVE YOU BACK.

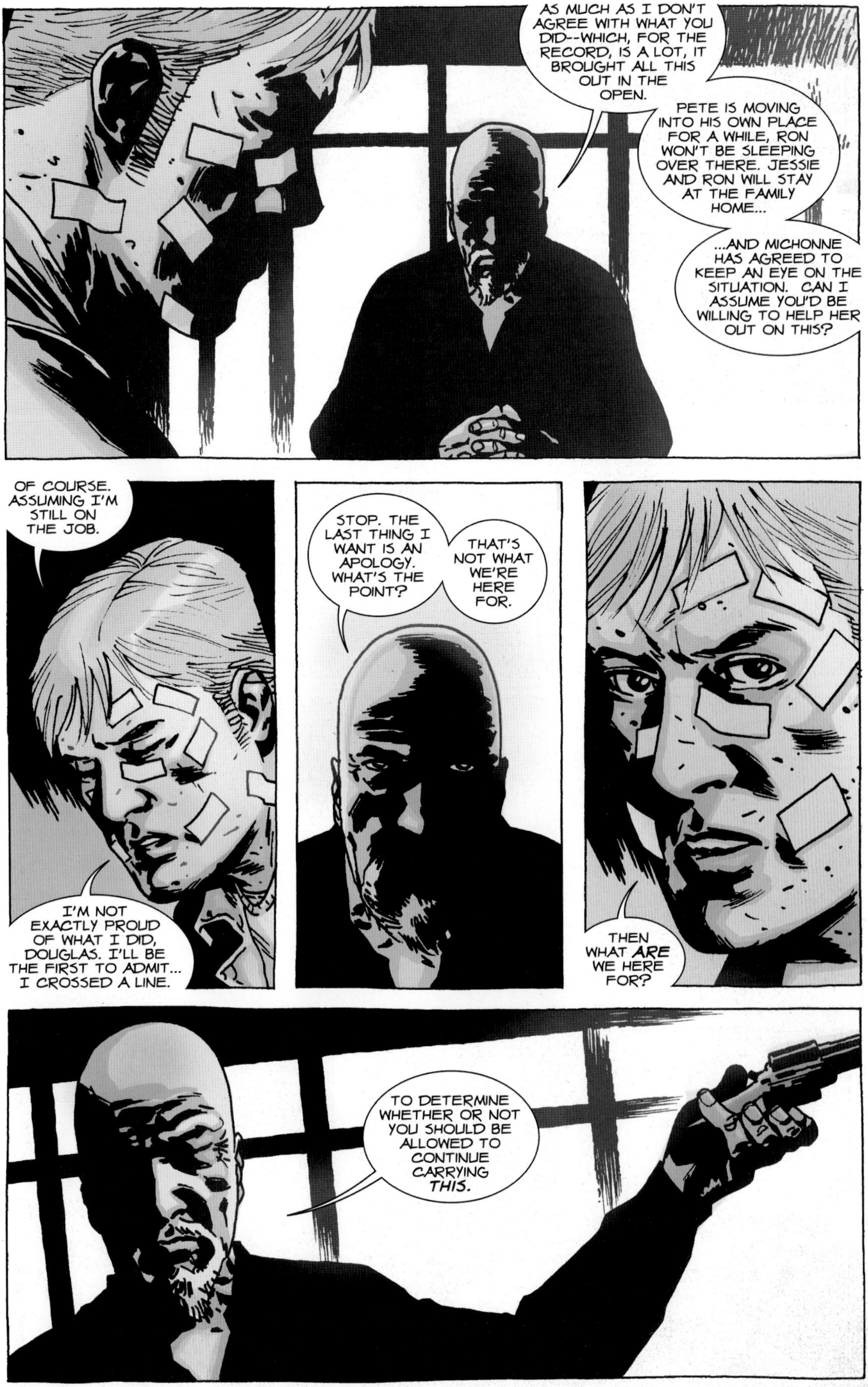
AS MUCH AS I DON'T AGREE WITH WHAT YOU DID--WHICH, FOR THE RECORD, IS A LOT, IT BROUGHT ALL THIS OUT IN THE OPEN.
PETE IS MOVING INTO HIS OWN PLACE FOR A WHILE, RON WON'T BE SLEEPING OVER THERE. JESSIE AND RON WILL STAY AT THE FAMILY HOME...
...AND MICHONNE HAS AGREED TO KEEP AN EYE ON THE SITUATION. CAN I ASSUME YOU'D BE WILLING TO HELP HER OUT ON THIS?
OF COURSE. ASSUMING I'M STILL ON THE JOB.
I'M NOT EXACTLY PROUD OF WHAT I DID, DOUGLAS. I'LL BE THE FIRST TO ADMIT... I CROSSED A LINE.
STOP. THE LAST THING I WANT IS AN APOLOGY. WHAT'S THE POINT?
THAT'S NOT WHAT WE'RE HERE FOR.
THEN WHAT *ARE* WE HERE FOR?
TO DETERMINE WHETHER OR NOT YOU SHOULD BE ALLOWED TO CONTINUE CARRYING *THIS*.

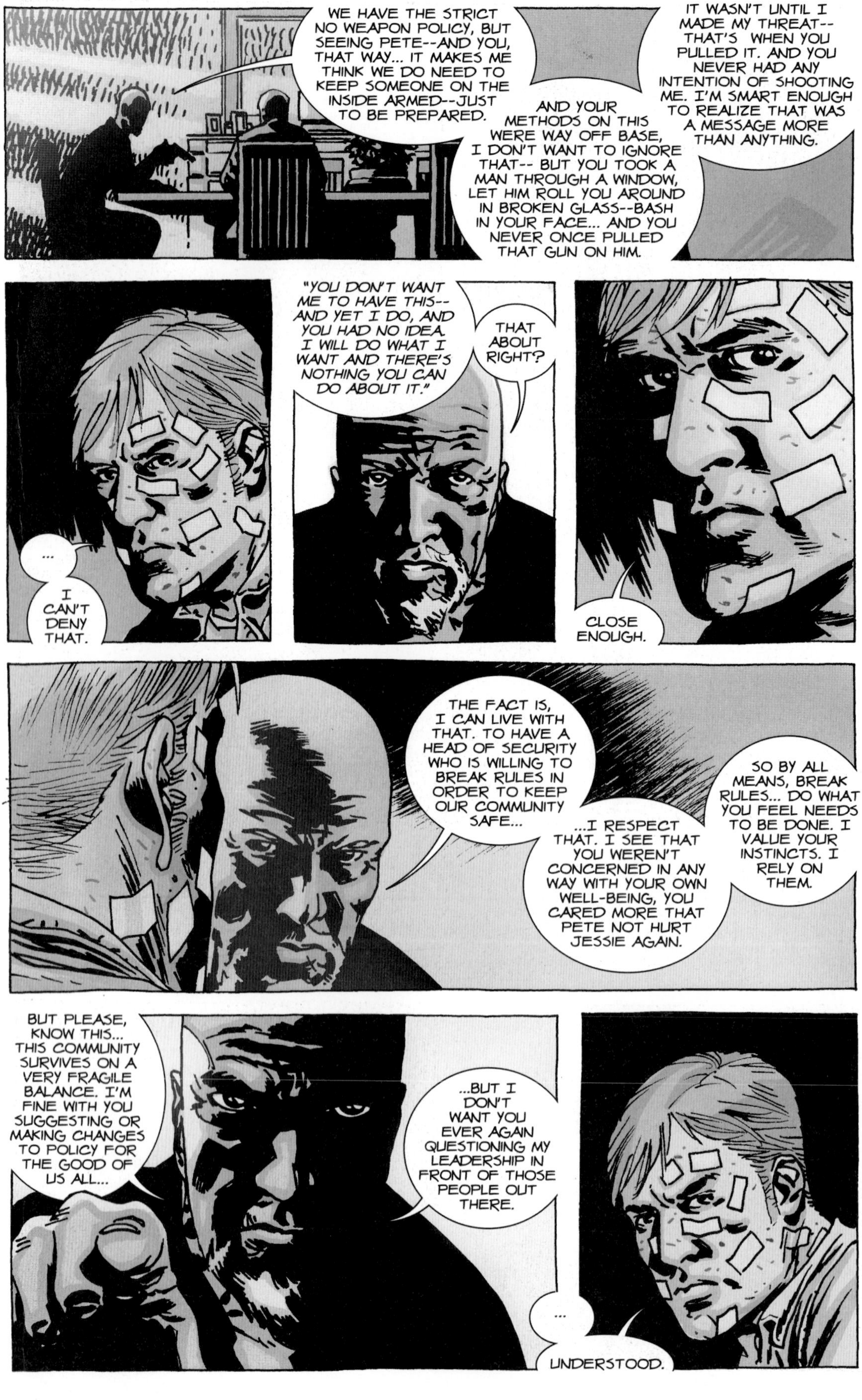

WE HAVE THE STRICT NO WEAPON POLICY, BUT SEEING PETE--AND YOU, THAT WAY... IT MAKES ME THINK WE DO NEED TO KEEP SOMEONE ON THE INSIDE ARMED--JUST TO BE PREPARED.
AND YOUR METHODS ON THIS WERE WAY OFF BASE, I DON'T WANT TO IGNORE THAT-- BUT YOU TOOK A MAN THROUGH A WINDOW, LET HIM ROLL YOU AROUND IN BROKEN GLASS--BASH IN YOUR FACE... AND YOU NEVER ONCE PULLED THAT GUN ON HIM.
IT WASN'T UNTIL I MADE MY THREAT-- THAT'S WHEN YOU PULLED IT. AND YOU NEVER HAD ANY INTENTION OF SHOOTING ME. I'M SMART ENOUGH TO REALIZE THAT WAS A MESSAGE MORE THAN ANYTHING.
...
I CAN'T DENY THAT.
"YOU DON'T WANT ME TO HAVE THIS-- AND YET I DO, AND YOU HAD NO IDEA. I WILL DO WHAT I WANT AND THERE'S NOTHING YOU CAN DO ABOUT IT."
THAT ABOUT RIGHT?
CLOSE ENOUGH.
THE FACT IS, I CAN LIVE WITH THAT. TO HAVE A HEAD OF SECURITY WHO IS WILLING TO BREAK RULES IN ORDER TO KEEP OUR COMMUNITY SAFE...
...I RESPECT THAT. I SEE THAT YOU WEREN'T CONCERNED IN ANY WAY WITH YOUR OWN WELL-BEING, YOU CARED MORE THAT PETE NOT HURT JESSIE AGAIN.
SO BY ALL MEANS, BREAK RULES... DO WHAT YOU FEEL NEEDS TO BE DONE. I VALUE YOUR INSTINCTS. I RELY ON THEM.
BUT PLEASE, KNOW THIS... THIS COMMUNITY SURVIVES ON A VERY FRAGILE BALANCE. I'M FINE WITH YOU SUGGESTING OR MAKING CHANGES TO POLICY FOR THE GOOD OF US ALL...
...BUT I DON'T WANT YOU EVER AGAIN QUESTIONING MY LEADERSHIP IN FRONT OF THOSE PEOPLE OUT THERE.
...
UNDERSTOOD.

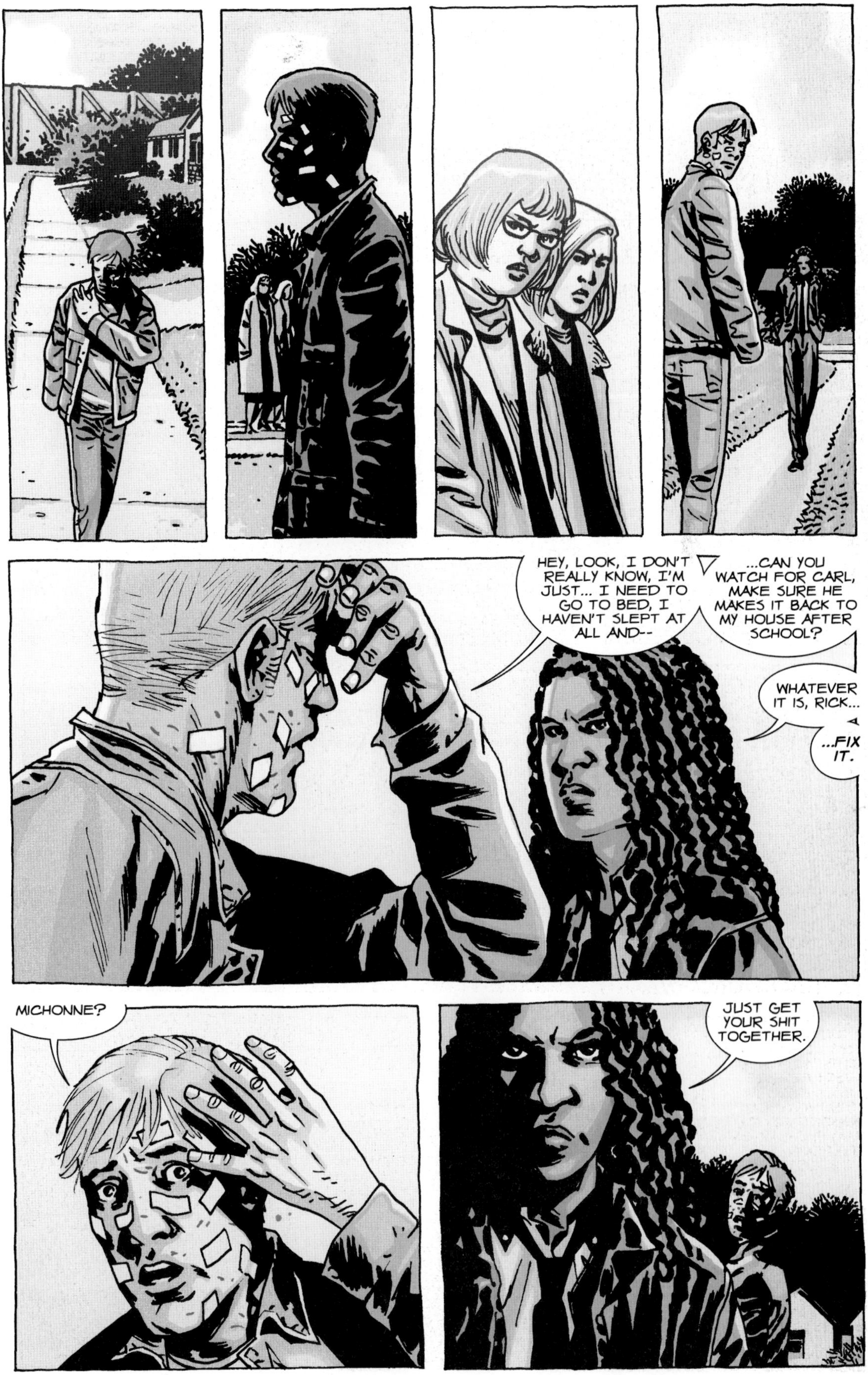
HEY, LOOK, I DON'T REALLY KNOW, I'M JUST... I NEED TO GO TO BED, I HAVEN'T SLEPT AT ALL AND--
...CAN YOU WATCH FOR CARL, MAKE SURE HE MAKES IT BACK TO MY HOUSE AFTER SCHOOL?
WHATEVER IT IS, RICK...
...FIX IT.
MICHONNE?
JUST GET YOUR SHIT TOGETHER.

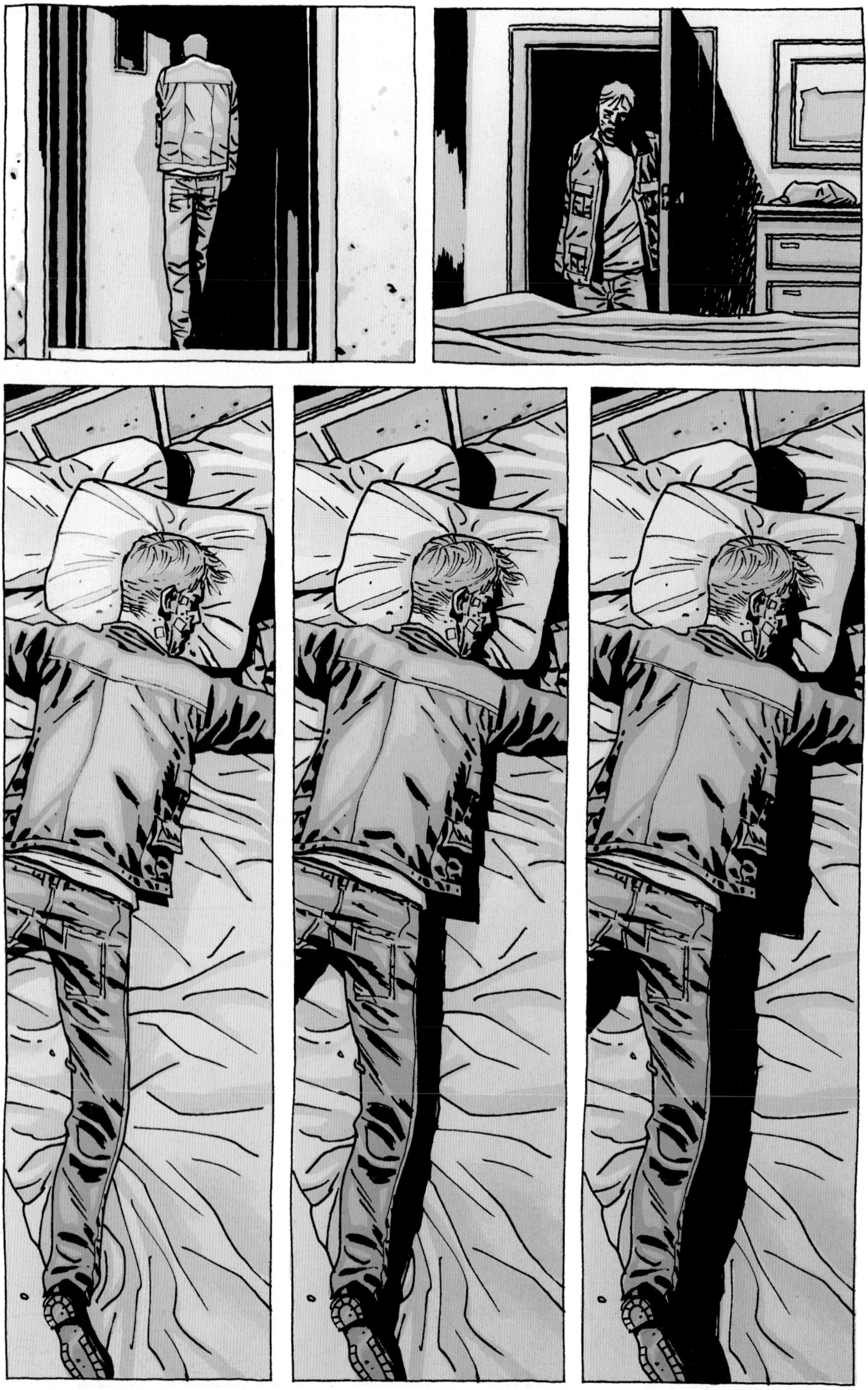

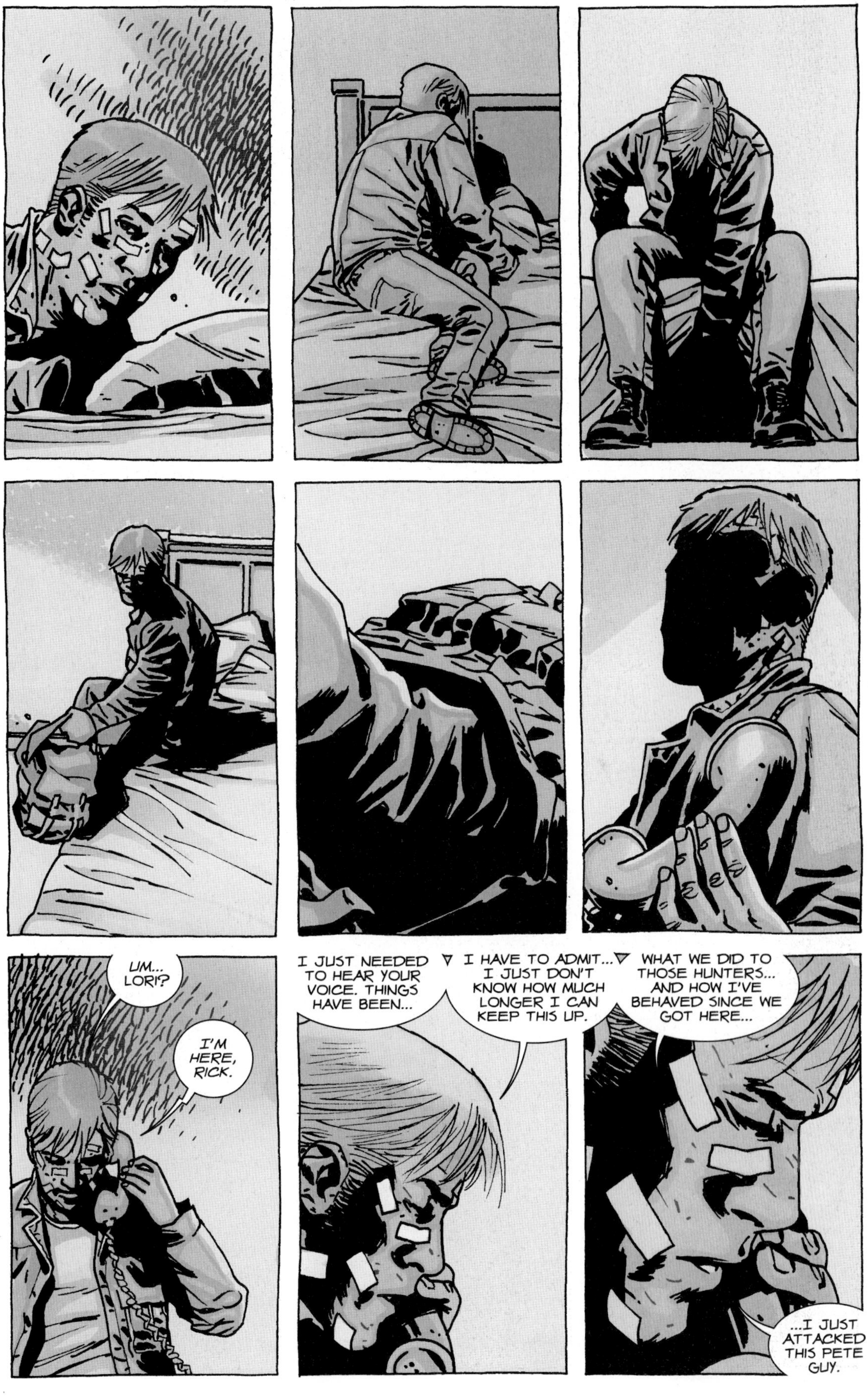

UM... LORI?
I'M HERE, RICK.
I JUST NEEDED TO HEAR YOUR VOICE. THINGS HAVE BEEN...
I HAVE TO ADMIT... I JUST DON'T KNOW HOW MUCH LONGER I CAN KEEP THIS UP.
WHAT WE DID TO THOSE HUNTERS... AND HOW I'VE BEHAVED SINCE WE GOT HERE...
...I JUST ATTACKED THIS PETE GUY.

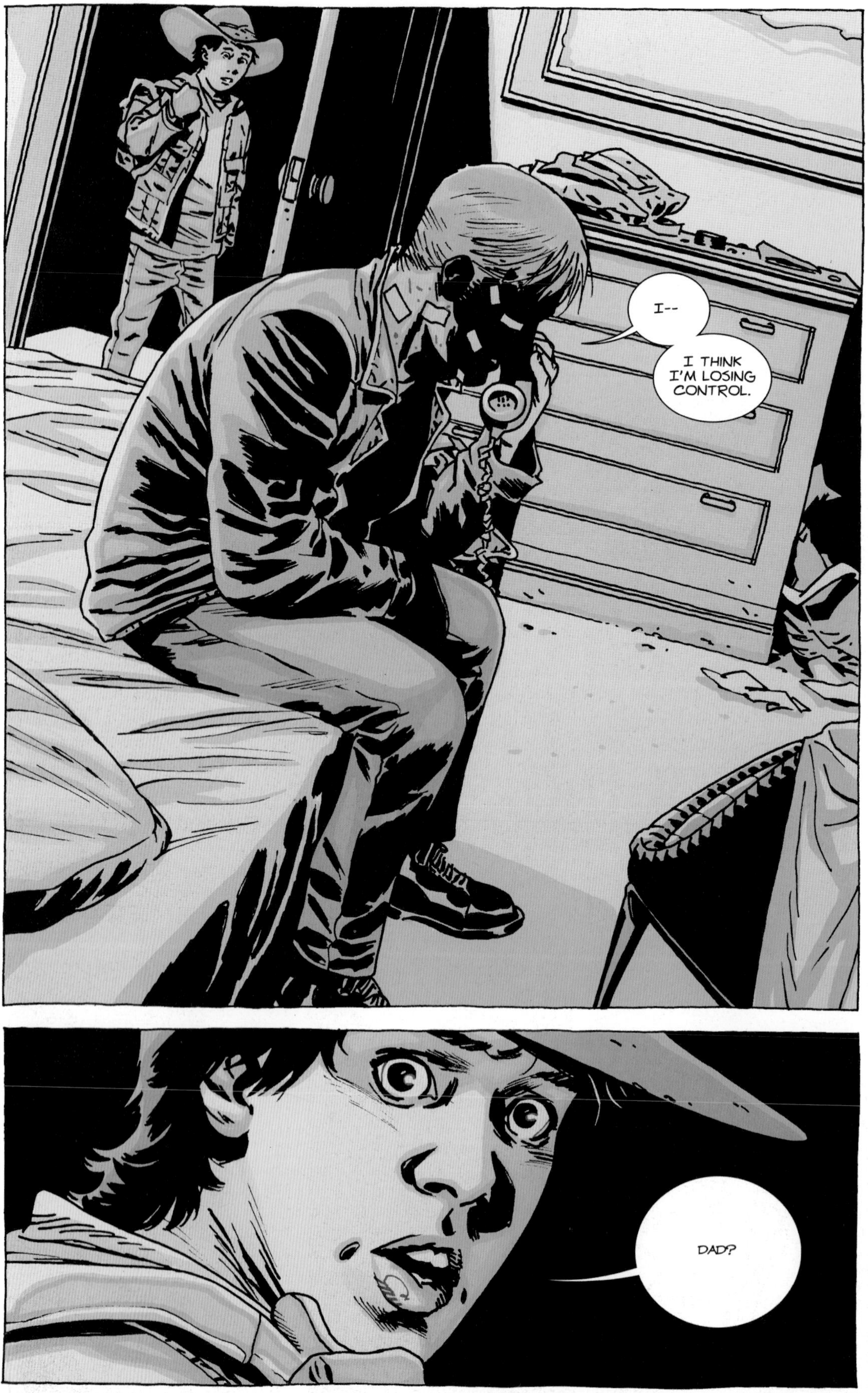
I--
I THINK I'M LOSING CONTROL.
DAD?

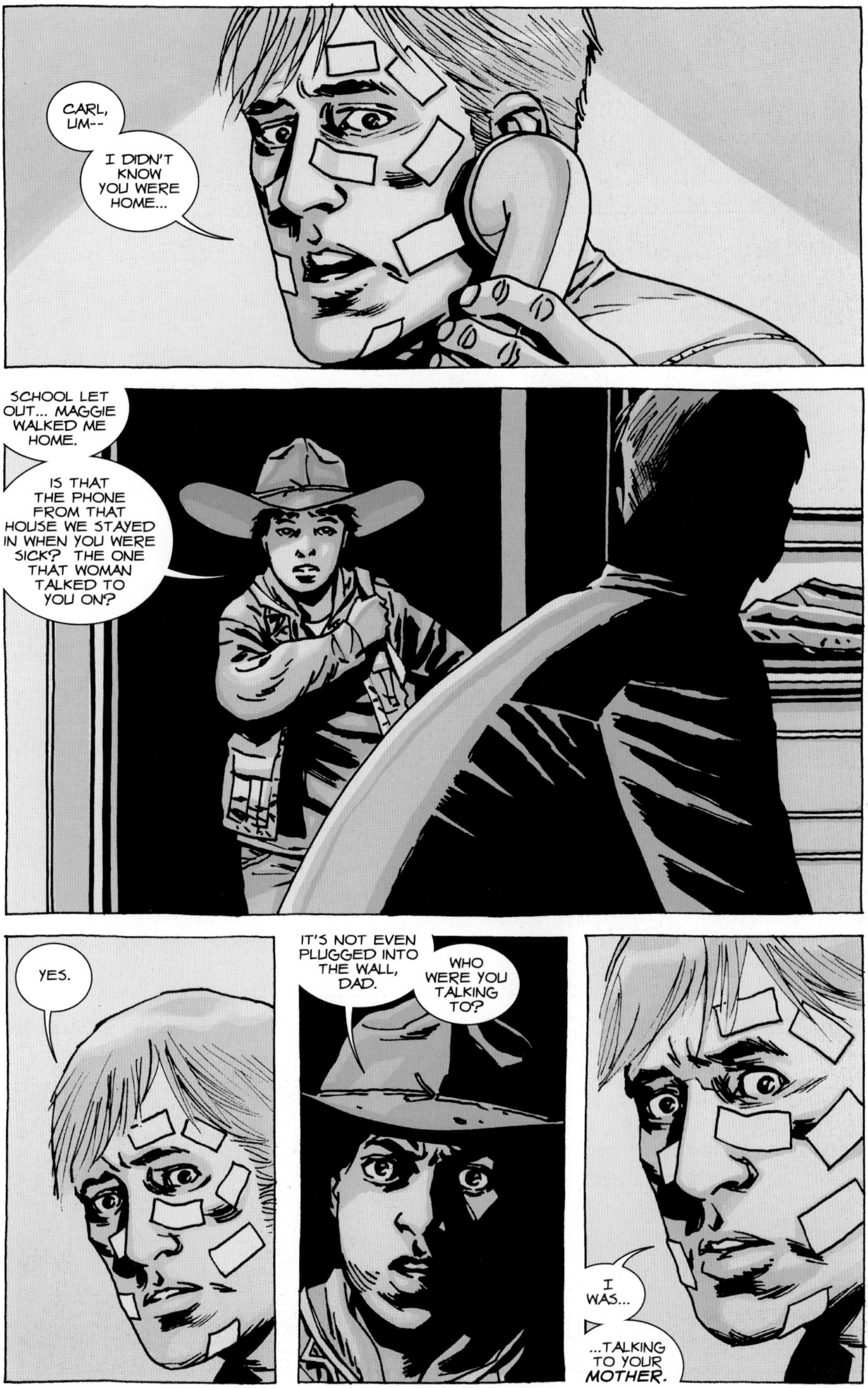
CARL, UM--
I DIDN'T KNOW YOU WERE HOME...
SCHOOL LET OUT... MAGGIE WALKED ME HOME.
IS THAT THE PHONE FROM THAT HOUSE WE STAYED IN WHEN YOU WERE SICK? THE ONE THAT WOMAN TALKED TO YOU ON?
YES.
IT'S NOT EVEN PLUGGED INTO THE WALL, DAD.
WHO WERE YOU TALKING TO?
I WAS...
...TALKING TO YOUR **MOTHER**.

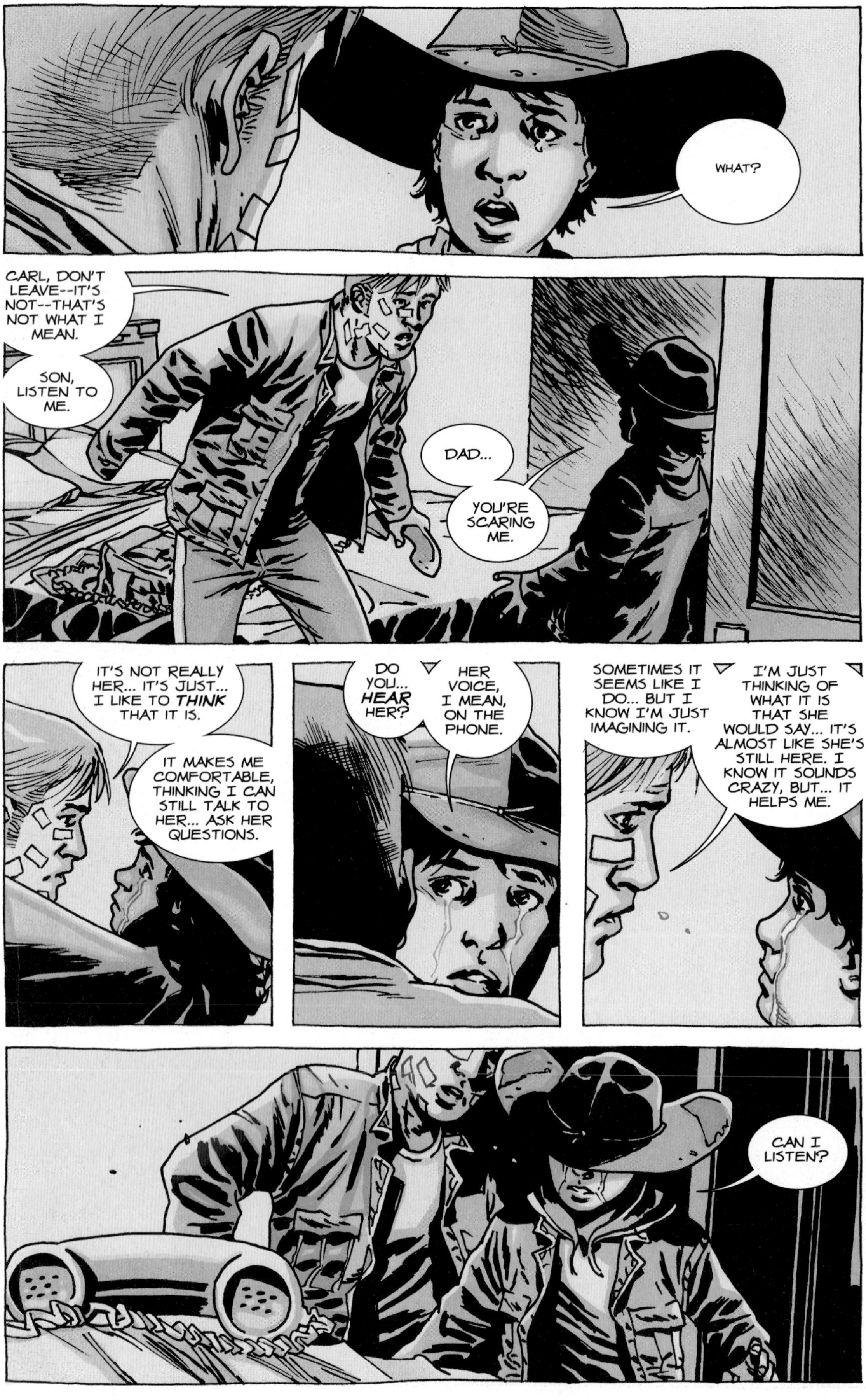
WHAT?
CARL, DON'T LEAVE--IT'S NOT--THAT'S NOT WHAT I MEAN.
SON, LISTEN TO ME.
DAD...
YOU'RE SCARING ME.
IT'S NOT REALLY HER... IT'S JUST... I LIKE TO THINK THAT IT IS.
IT MAKES ME COMFORTABLE, THINKING I CAN STILL TALK TO HER... ASK HER QUESTIONS.
DO YOU... HEAR HER?
HER VOICE, I MEAN, ON THE PHONE.
SOMETIMES IT SEEMS LIKE I DO... BUT I KNOW I'M JUST IMAGINING IT.
I'M JUST THINKING OF WHAT IT IS THAT SHE WOULD SAY... IT'S ALMOST LIKE SHE'S STILL HERE. I KNOW IT SOUNDS CRAZY, BUT... IT HELPS ME.
CAN I LISTEN?

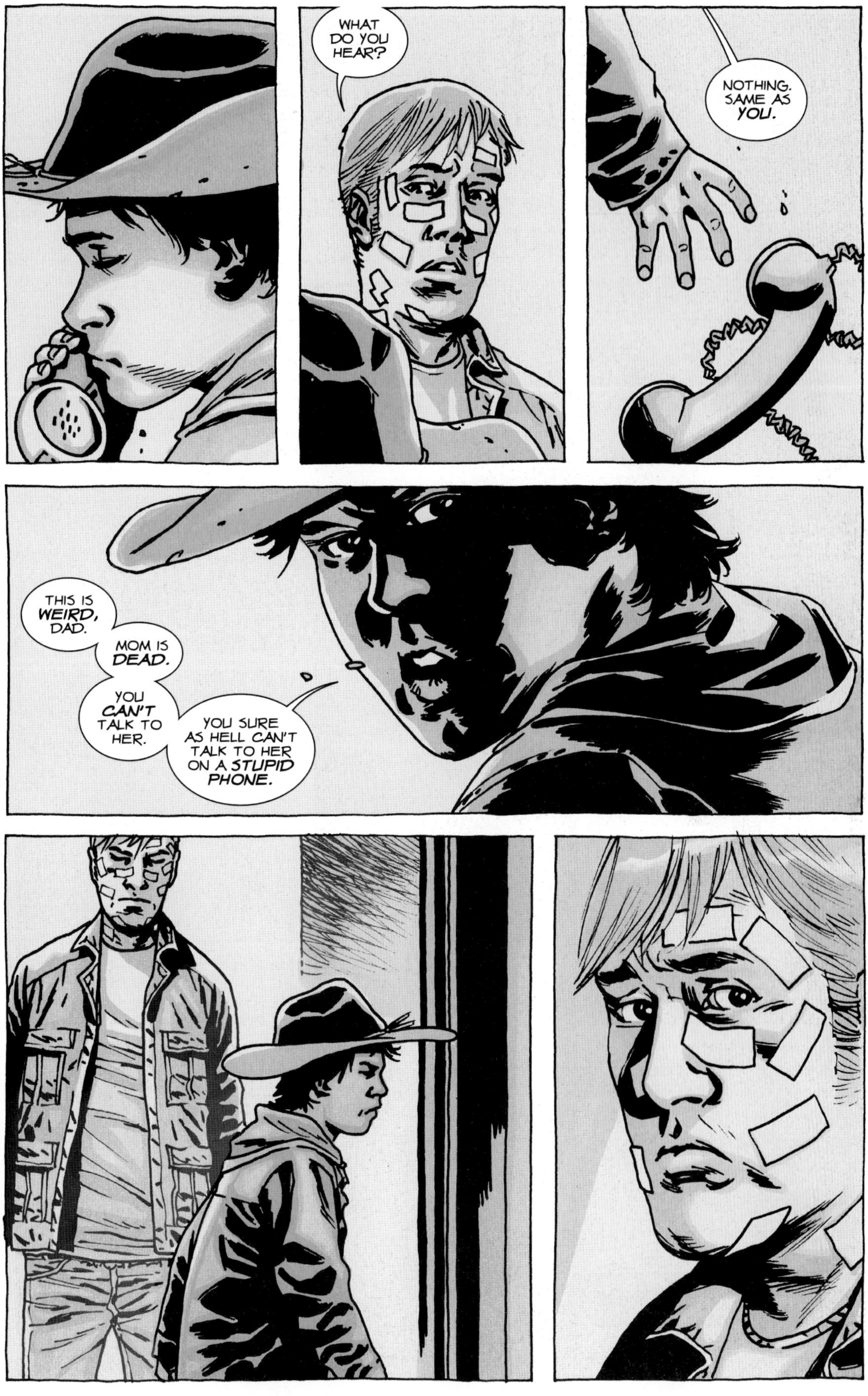
WHAT DO YOU HEAR?
NOTHING. SAME AS YOU.
THIS IS WEIRD, DAD.
MOM IS DEAD.
YOU CAN'T TALK TO HER.
YOU SURE AS HELL CAN'T TALK TO HER ON A STUPID PHONE.

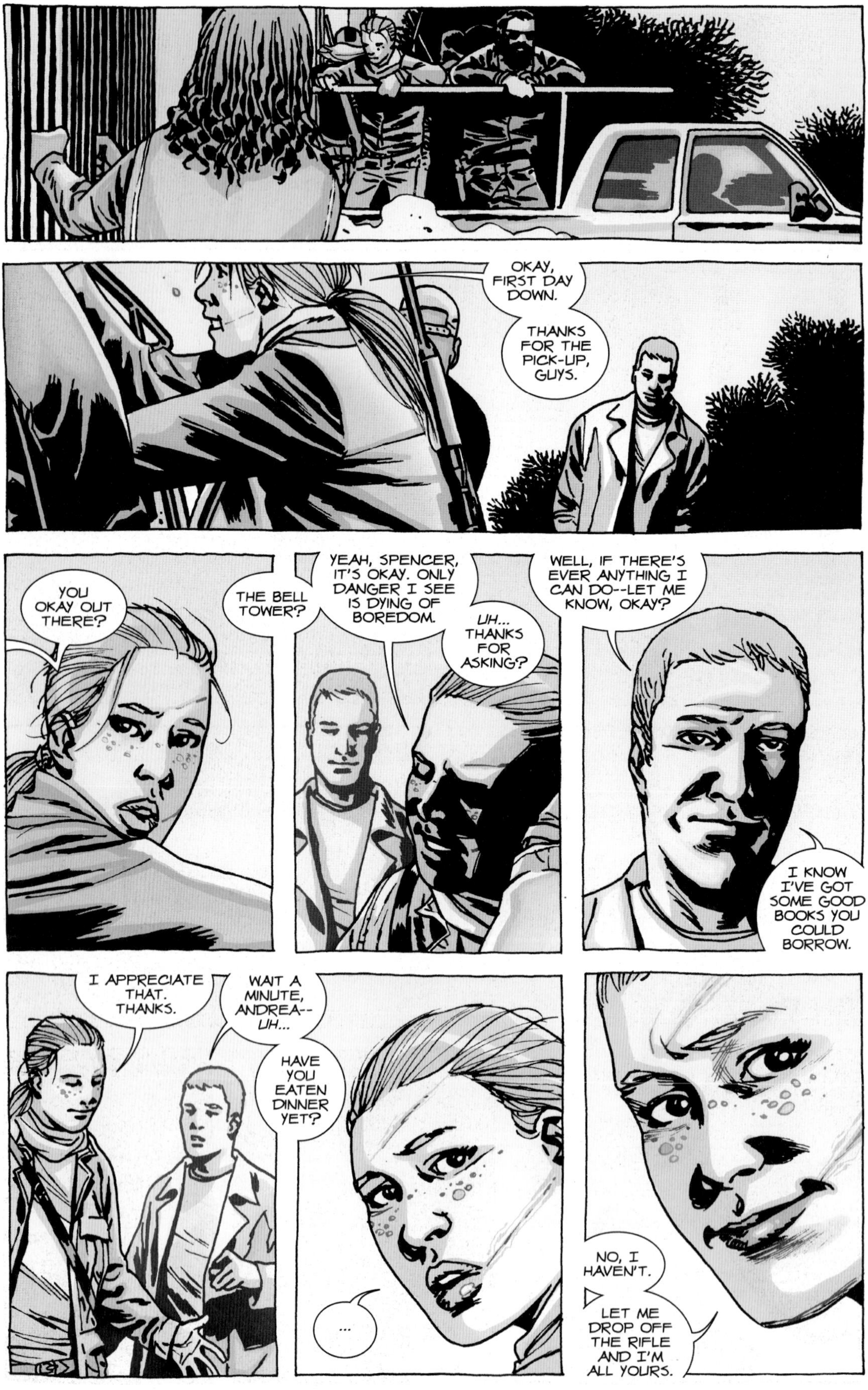
OKAY, FIRST DAY DOWN.
THANKS FOR THE PICK-UP, GUYS.
YOU OKAY OUT THERE?
THE BELL TOWER?
YEAH, SPENCER, IT'S OKAY. ONLY DANGER I SEE IS DYING OF BOREDOM.
UH... THANKS FOR ASKING?
WELL, IF THERE'S EVER ANYTHING I CAN DO--LET ME KNOW, OKAY?
I KNOW I'VE GOT SOME GOOD BOOKS YOU COULD BORROW.
I APPRECIATE THAT. THANKS.
WAIT A MINUTE, ANDREA-- UH...
HAVE YOU EATEN DINNER YET?
...
NO, I HAVEN'T.
LET ME DROP OFF THE RIFLE AND I'M ALL YOURS.

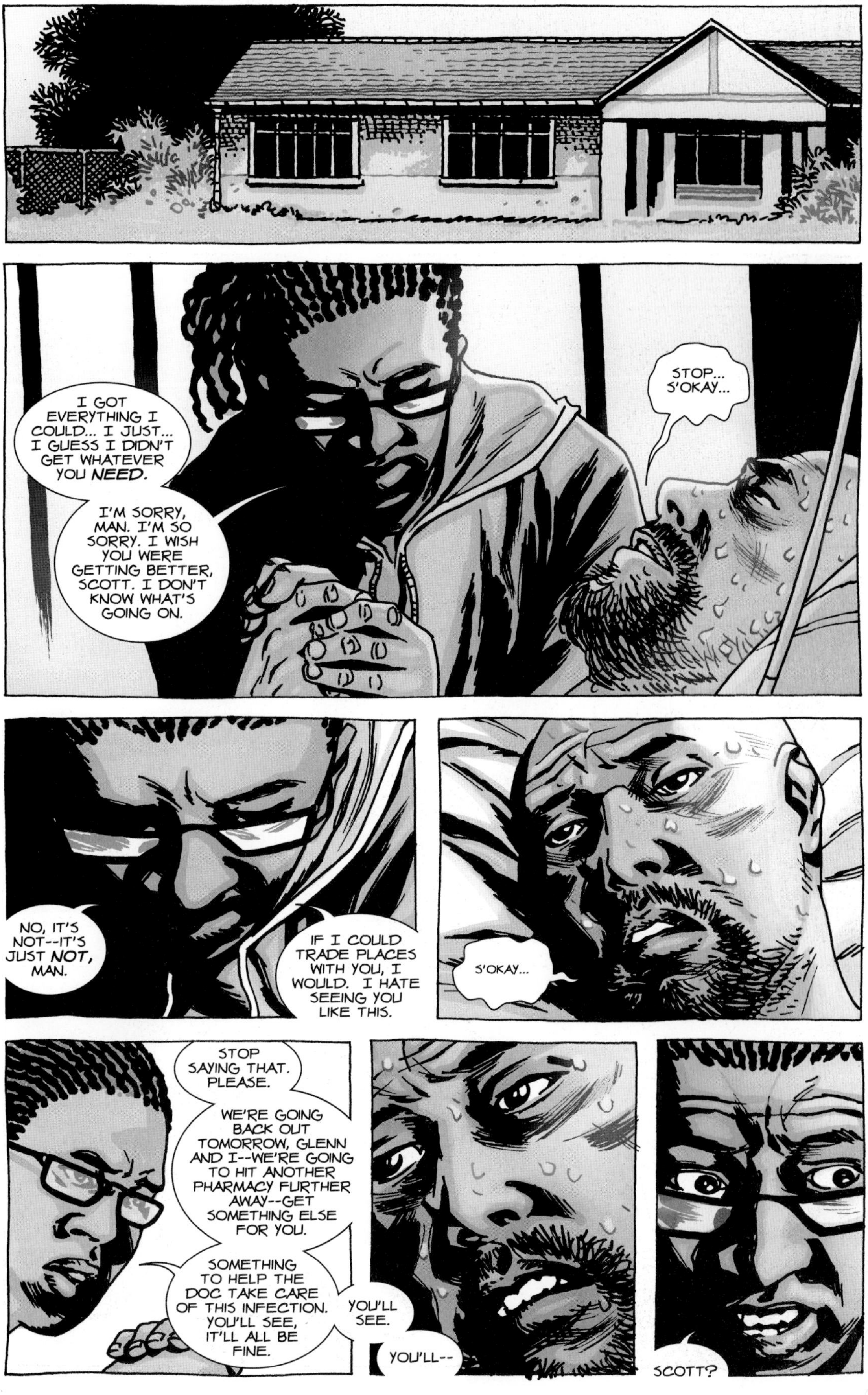
I GOT EVERYTHING I COULD... I JUST... I GUESS I DIDN'T GET WHATEVER YOU NEED.
I'M SORRY, MAN. I'M SO SORRY. I WISH YOU WERE GETTING BETTER, SCOTT. I DON'T KNOW WHAT'S GOING ON.
STOP... S'OKAY...
NO, IT'S NOT--IT'S JUST NOT, MAN.
IF I COULD TRADE PLACES WITH YOU, I WOULD. I HATE SEEING YOU LIKE THIS.
S'OKAY...
STOP SAYING THAT. PLEASE.
WE'RE GOING BACK OUT TOMORROW, GLENN AND I--WE'RE GOING TO HIT ANOTHER PHARMACY FURTHER AWAY--GET SOMETHING ELSE FOR YOU.
SOMETHING TO HELP THE DOC TAKE CARE OF THIS INFECTION. YOU'LL SEE, IT'LL ALL BE FINE.
YOU'LL SEE.
YOU'LL--
SCOTT?

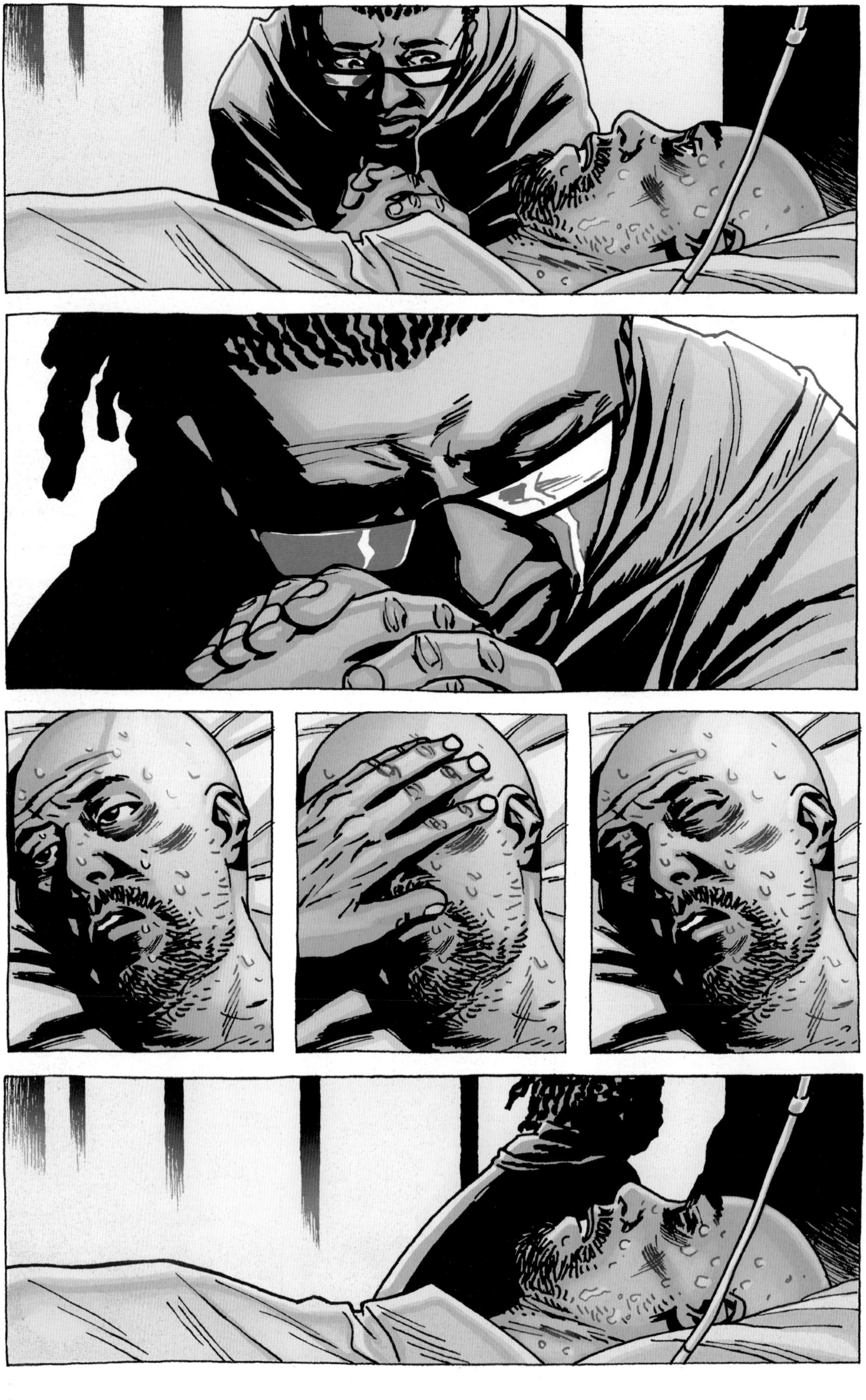

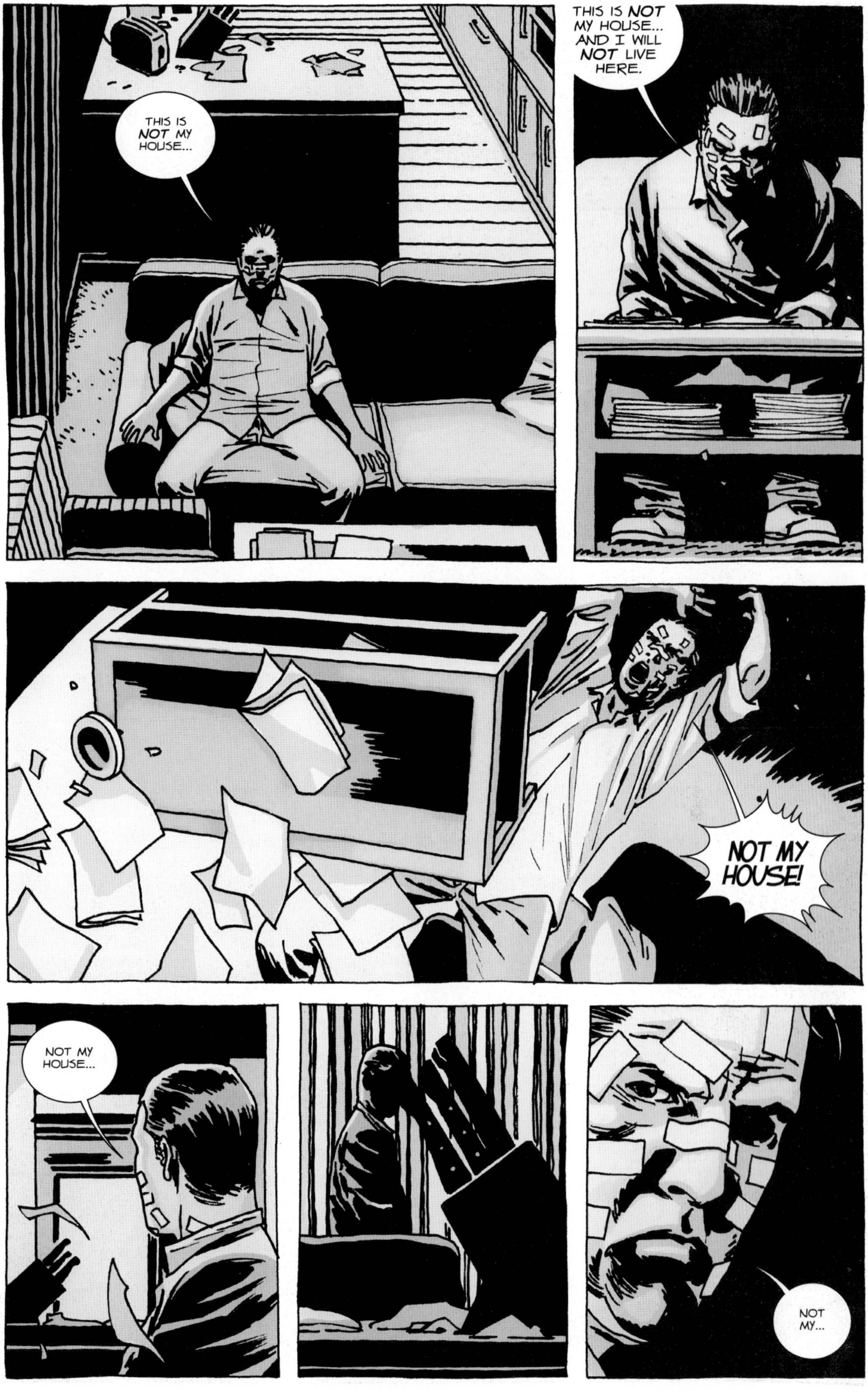
THIS IS NOT MY HOUSE...
THIS IS NOT MY HOUSE... AND I WILL NOT LIVE HERE.
NOT MY HOUSE!
NOT MY HOUSE...
NOT MY...

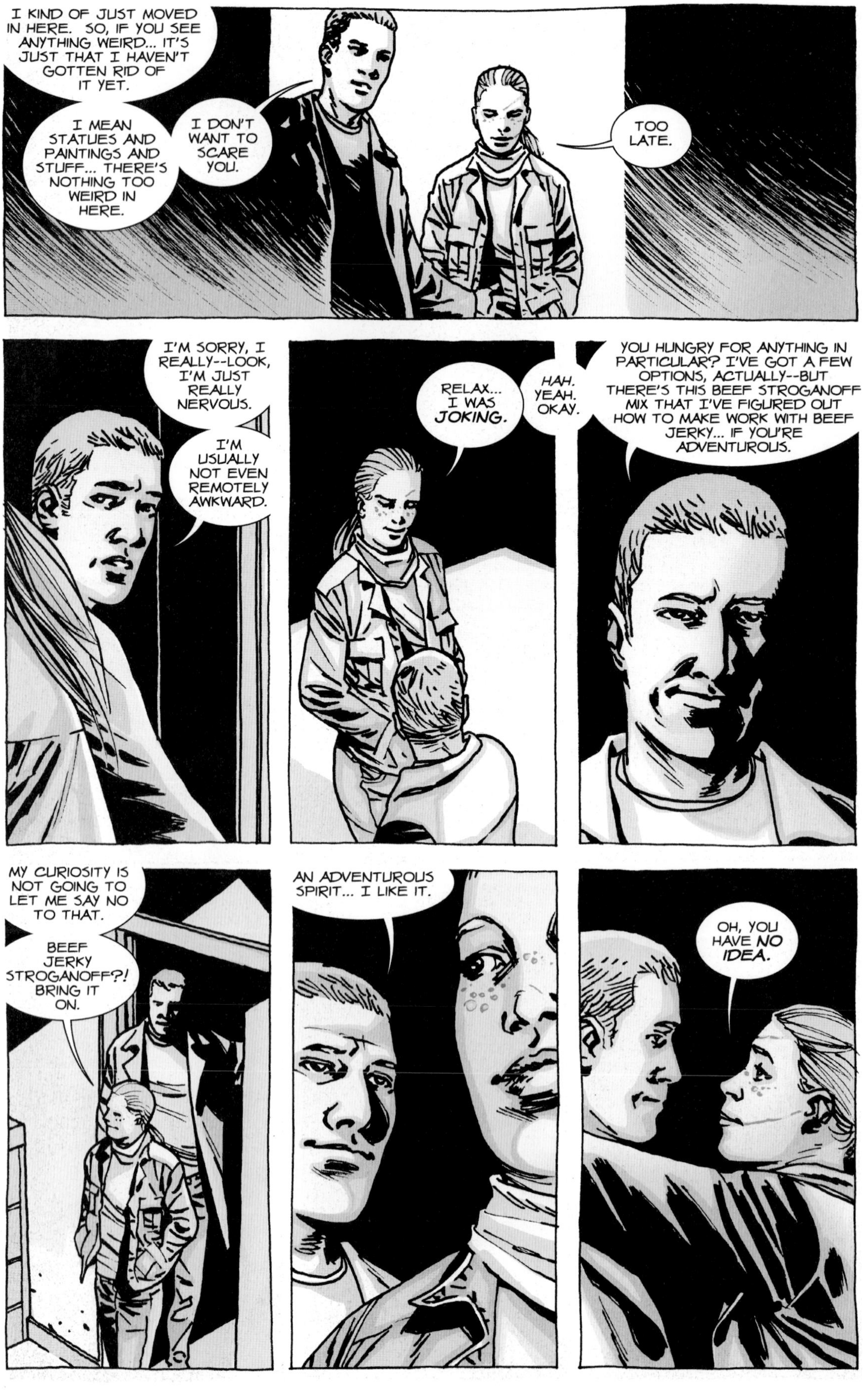
I KIND OF JUST MOVED IN HERE. SO, IF YOU SEE ANYTHING WEIRD... IT'S JUST THAT I HAVEN'T GOTTEN RID OF IT YET.
I MEAN STATUES AND PAINTINGS AND STUFF... THERE'S NOTHING TOO WEIRD IN HERE.
I DON'T WANT TO SCARE YOU.
TOO LATE.
I'M SORRY, I REALLY--LOOK, I'M JUST REALLY NERVOUS.
I'M USUALLY NOT EVEN REMOTELY AWKWARD.
RELAX... I WAS JOKING.
HAH. YEAH. OKAY.
YOU HUNGRY FOR ANYTHING IN PARTICULAR? I'VE GOT A FEW OPTIONS, ACTUALLY--BUT THERE'S THIS BEEF STROGANOFF MIX THAT I'VE FIGURED OUT HOW TO MAKE WORK WITH BEEF JERKY... IF YOU'RE ADVENTUROUS.
MY CURIOSITY IS NOT GOING TO LET ME SAY NO TO THAT.
BEEF JERKY STROGANOFF?! BRING IT ON.
AN ADVENTUROUS SPIRIT... I LIKE IT.
OH, YOU HAVE NO IDEA.

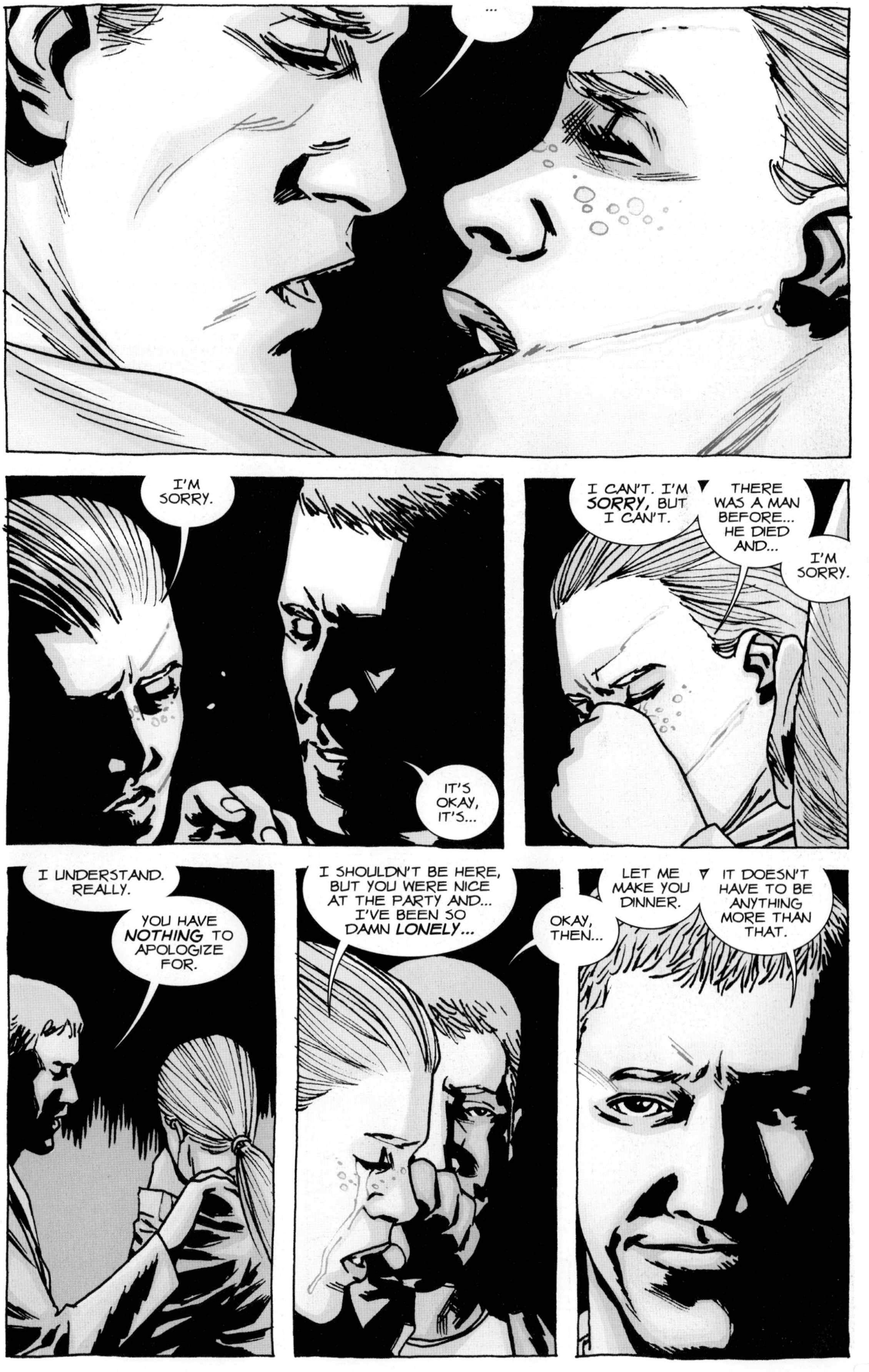
...
I'M SORRY.
IT'S OKAY, IT'S...
I CAN'T. I'M SORRY, BUT I CAN'T.
THERE WAS A MAN BEFORE... HE DIED AND...
I'M SORRY.
I UNDERSTAND. REALLY.
YOU HAVE NOTHING TO APOLOGIZE FOR.
I SHOULDN'T BE HERE, BUT YOU WERE NICE AT THE PARTY AND... I'VE BEEN SO DAMN LONELY...
OKAY, THEN...
LET ME MAKE YOU DINNER.
IT DOESN'T HAVE TO BE ANYTHING MORE THAN THAT.

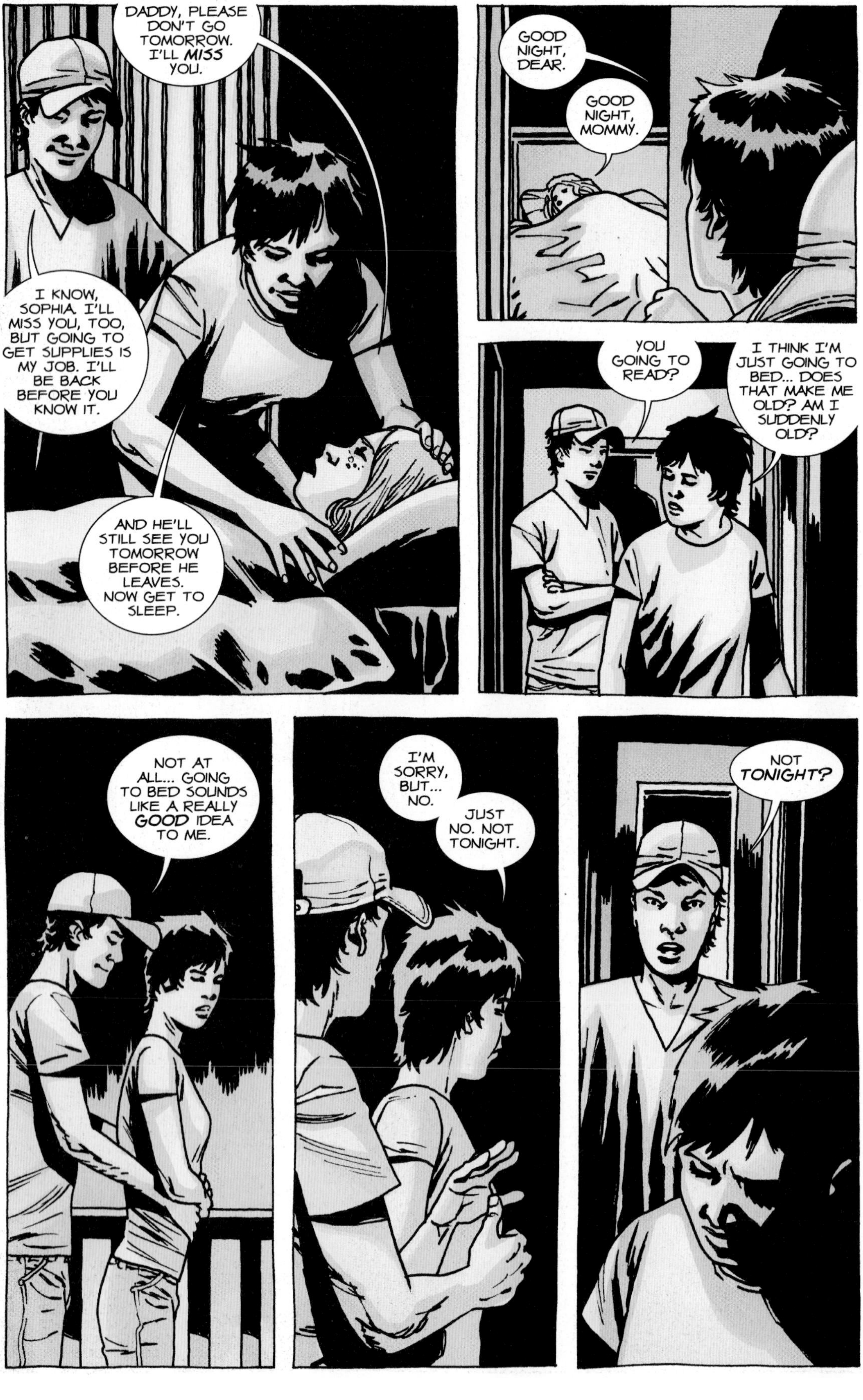
DADDY, PLEASE DON'T GO TOMORROW. I'LL *MISS* YOU.
I KNOW, SOPHIA. I'LL MISS YOU, TOO, BUT GOING TO GET SUPPLIES IS MY JOB. I'LL BE BACK BEFORE YOU KNOW IT.
AND HE'LL STILL SEE YOU TOMORROW BEFORE HE LEAVES. NOW GET TO SLEEP.
GOOD NIGHT, DEAR.
GOOD NIGHT, MOMMY.
YOU GOING TO READ?
I THINK I'M JUST GOING TO BED... DOES THAT MAKE ME OLD? AM I SUDDENLY OLD?
NOT AT ALL... GOING TO BED SOUNDS LIKE A REALLY *GOOD* IDEA TO ME.
I'M SORRY, BUT... NO.
JUST NO. NOT TONIGHT.
NOT *TONIGHT?*

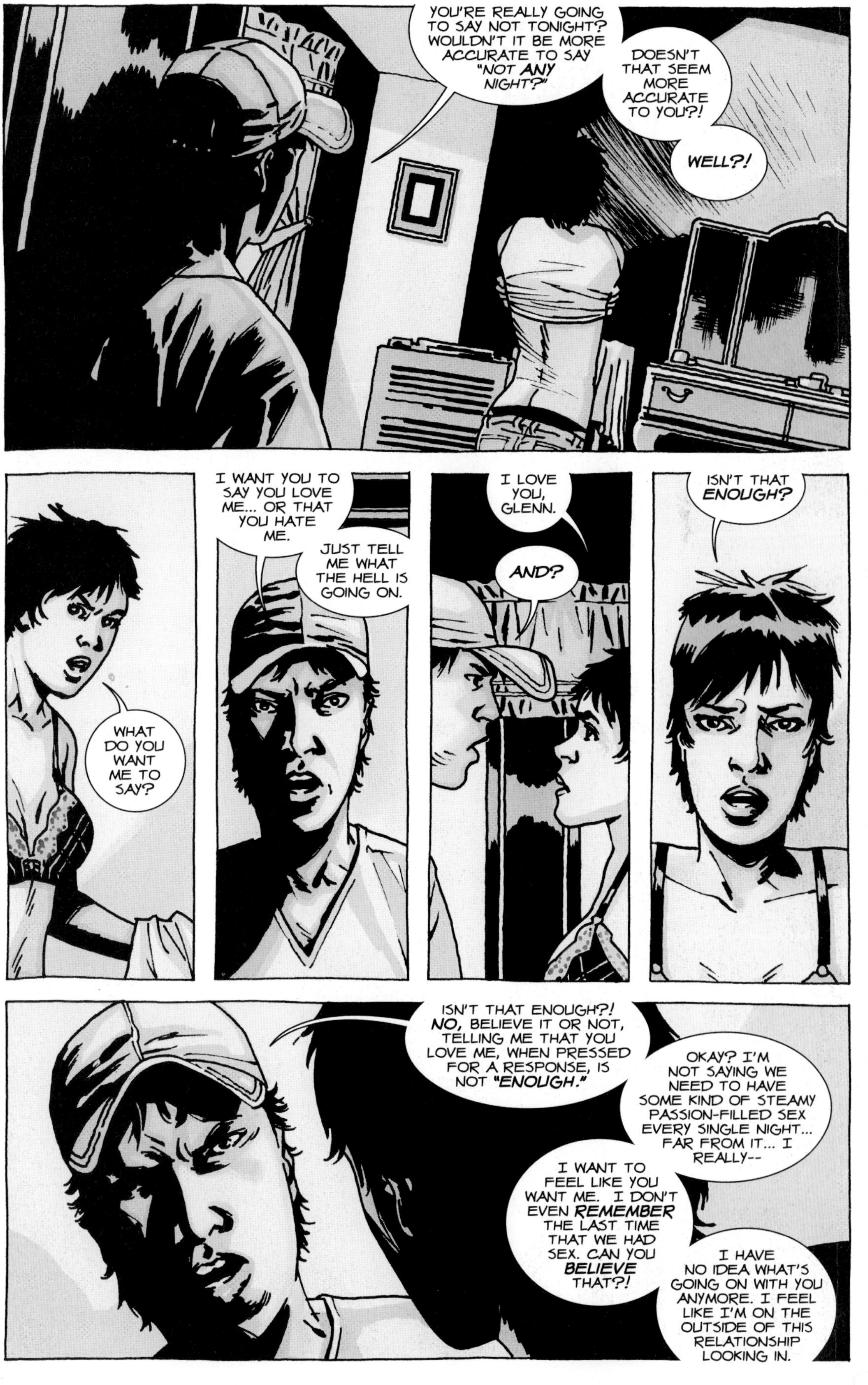
YOU'RE REALLY GOING TO SAY NOT TONIGHT? WOULDN'T IT BE MORE ACCURATE TO SAY "NOT ANY NIGHT?"
DOESN'T THAT SEEM MORE ACCURATE TO YOU?!
WELL?!
WHAT DO YOU WANT ME TO SAY?
I WANT YOU TO SAY YOU LOVE ME... OR THAT YOU HATE ME.
JUST TELL ME WHAT THE HELL IS GOING ON.
I LOVE YOU, GLENN.
AND?
ISN'T THAT ENOUGH?
ISN'T THAT ENOUGH?! NO, BELIEVE IT OR NOT, TELLING ME THAT YOU LOVE ME, WHEN PRESSED FOR A RESPONSE, IS NOT "ENOUGH."
OKAY? I'M NOT SAYING WE NEED TO HAVE SOME KIND OF STEAMY PASSION-FILLED SEX EVERY SINGLE NIGHT... FAR FROM IT... I REALLY--
I WANT TO FEEL LIKE YOU WANT ME. I DON'T EVEN REMEMBER THE LAST TIME THAT WE HAD SEX. CAN YOU BELIEVE THAT?!
I HAVE NO IDEA WHAT'S GOING ON WITH YOU ANYMORE. I FEEL LIKE I'M ON THE OUTSIDE OF THIS RELATIONSHIP LOOKING IN.

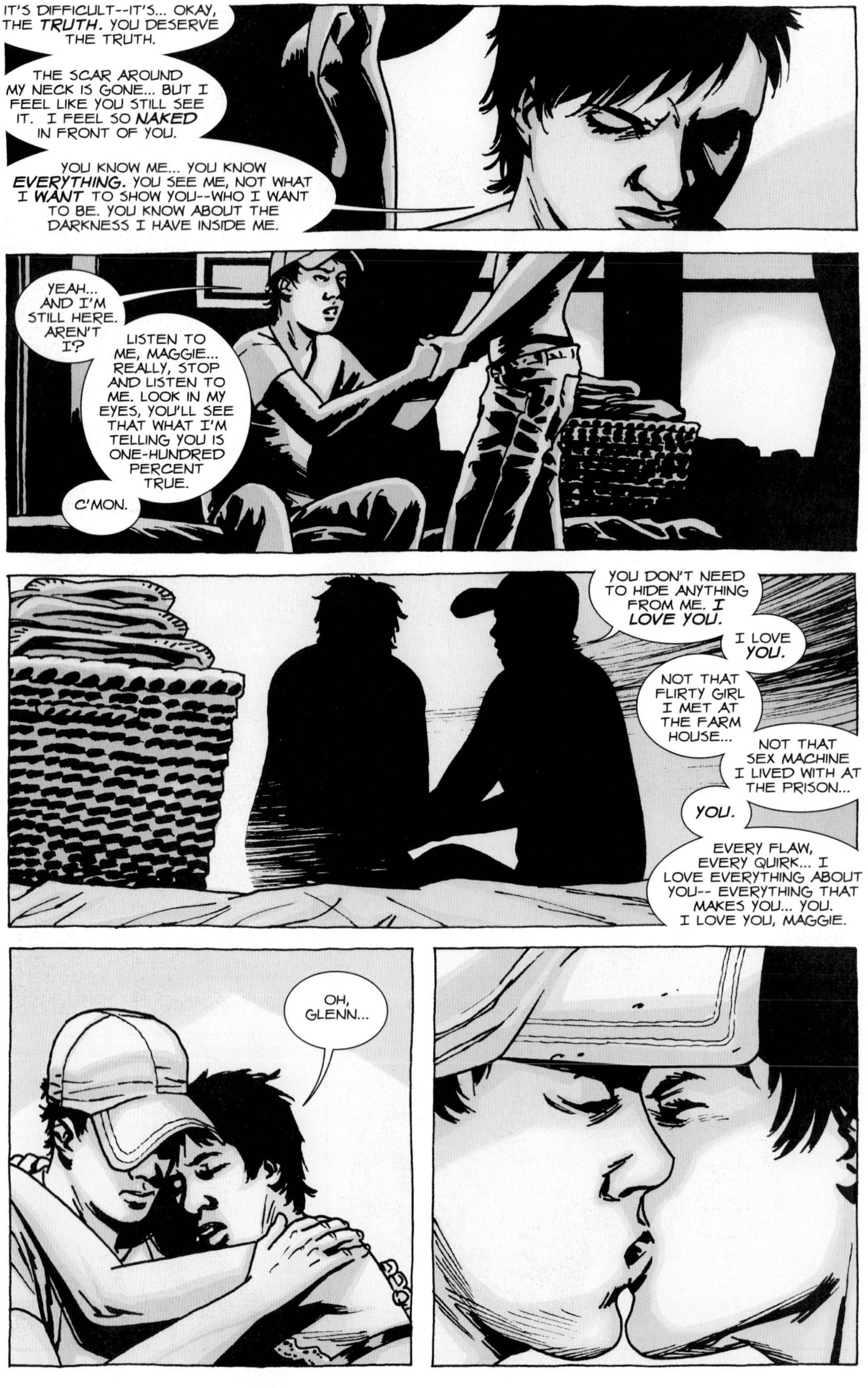
IT'S DIFFICULT--IT'S... OKAY, THE TRUTH. YOU DESERVE THE TRUTH.
THE SCAR AROUND MY NECK IS GONE... BUT I FEEL LIKE YOU STILL SEE IT. I FEEL SO NAKED IN FRONT OF YOU.
YOU KNOW ME... YOU KNOW EVERYTHING. YOU SEE ME, NOT WHAT I WANT TO SHOW YOU--WHO I WANT TO BE. YOU KNOW ABOUT THE DARKNESS I HAVE INSIDE ME.
YEAH... AND I'M STILL HERE. AREN'T I?
LISTEN TO ME, MAGGIE... REALLY, STOP AND LISTEN TO ME. LOOK IN MY EYES, YOU'LL SEE THAT WHAT I'M TELLING YOU IS ONE-HUNDRED PERCENT TRUE.
C'MON.
YOU DON'T NEED TO HIDE ANYTHING FROM ME. I LOVE YOU.
I LOVE YOU.
NOT THAT FLIRTY GIRL I MET AT THE FARM HOUSE...
NOT THAT SEX MACHINE I LIVED WITH AT THE PRISON...
YOU.
EVERY FLAW, EVERY QUIRK... I LOVE EVERYTHING ABOUT YOU-- EVERYTHING THAT MAKES YOU... YOU. I LOVE YOU, MAGGIE.
OH, GLENN...

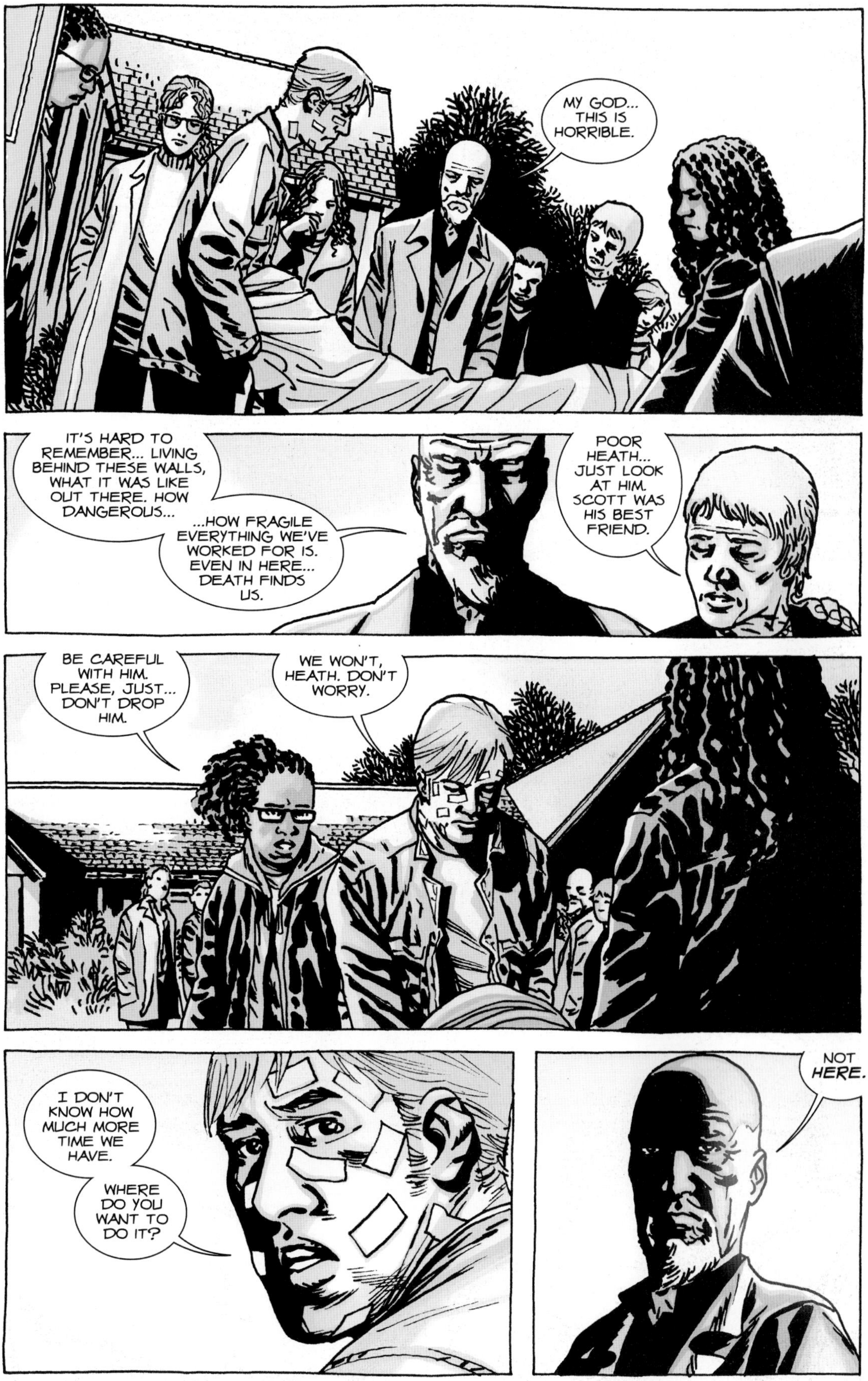
MY GOD... THIS IS HORRIBLE.
IT'S HARD TO REMEMBER... LIVING BEHIND THESE WALLS, WHAT IT WAS LIKE OUT THERE. HOW DANGEROUS...
...HOW FRAGILE EVERYTHING WE'VE WORKED FOR IS. EVEN IN HERE... DEATH FINDS US.
POOR HEATH... JUST LOOK AT HIM. SCOTT WAS HIS BEST FRIEND.
BE CAREFUL WITH HIM. PLEASE, JUST... DON'T DROP HIM.
WE WON'T, HEATH. DON'T WORRY.
I DON'T KNOW HOW MUCH MORE TIME WE HAVE.
WHERE DO YOU WANT TO DO IT?
NOT *HERE.*

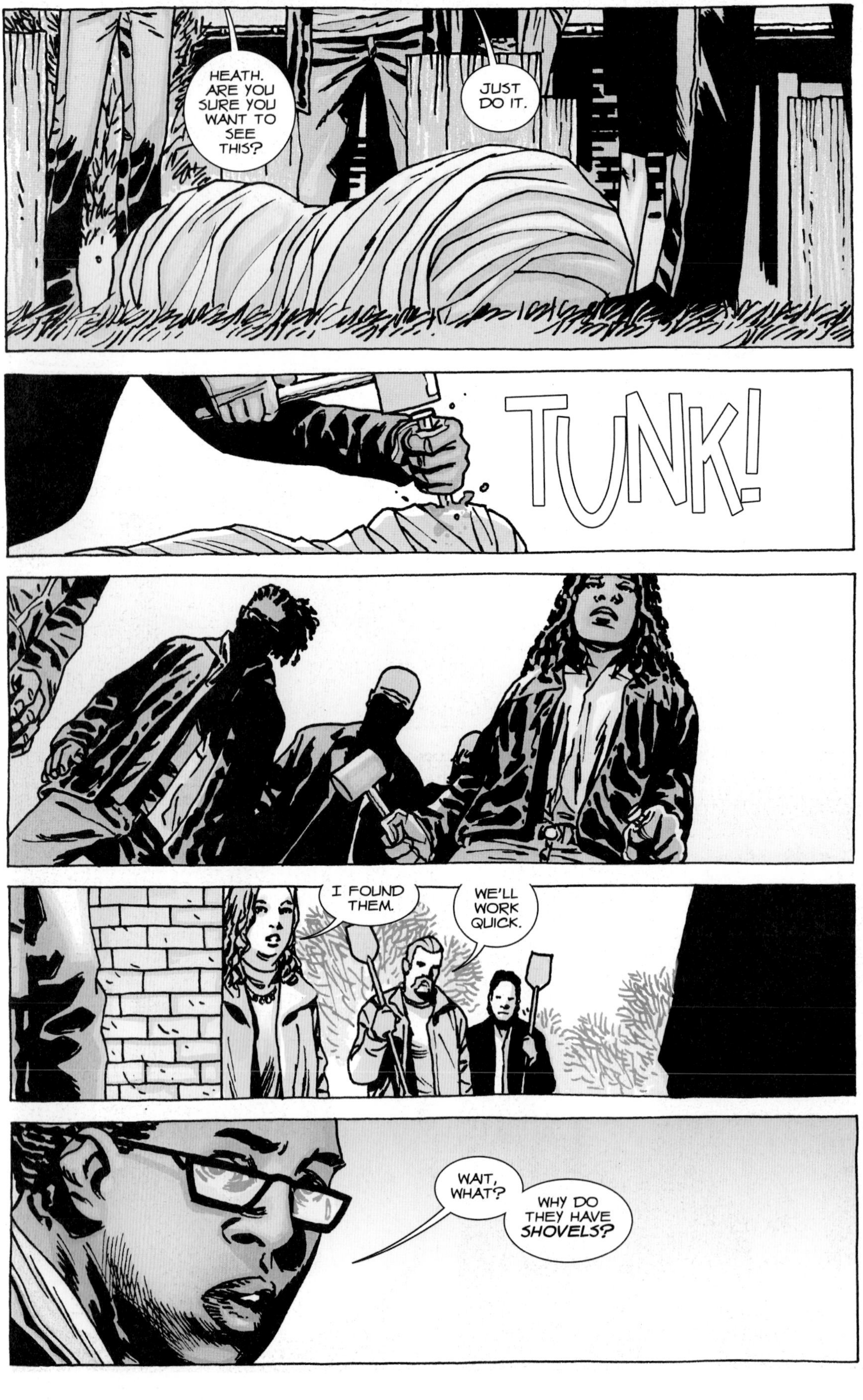
HEATH. ARE YOU SURE YOU WANT TO SEE THIS?
JUST DO IT.
TUNK!
I FOUND THEM.
WE'LL WORK QUICK.
WAIT, WHAT?
WHY DO THEY HAVE SHOVELS?

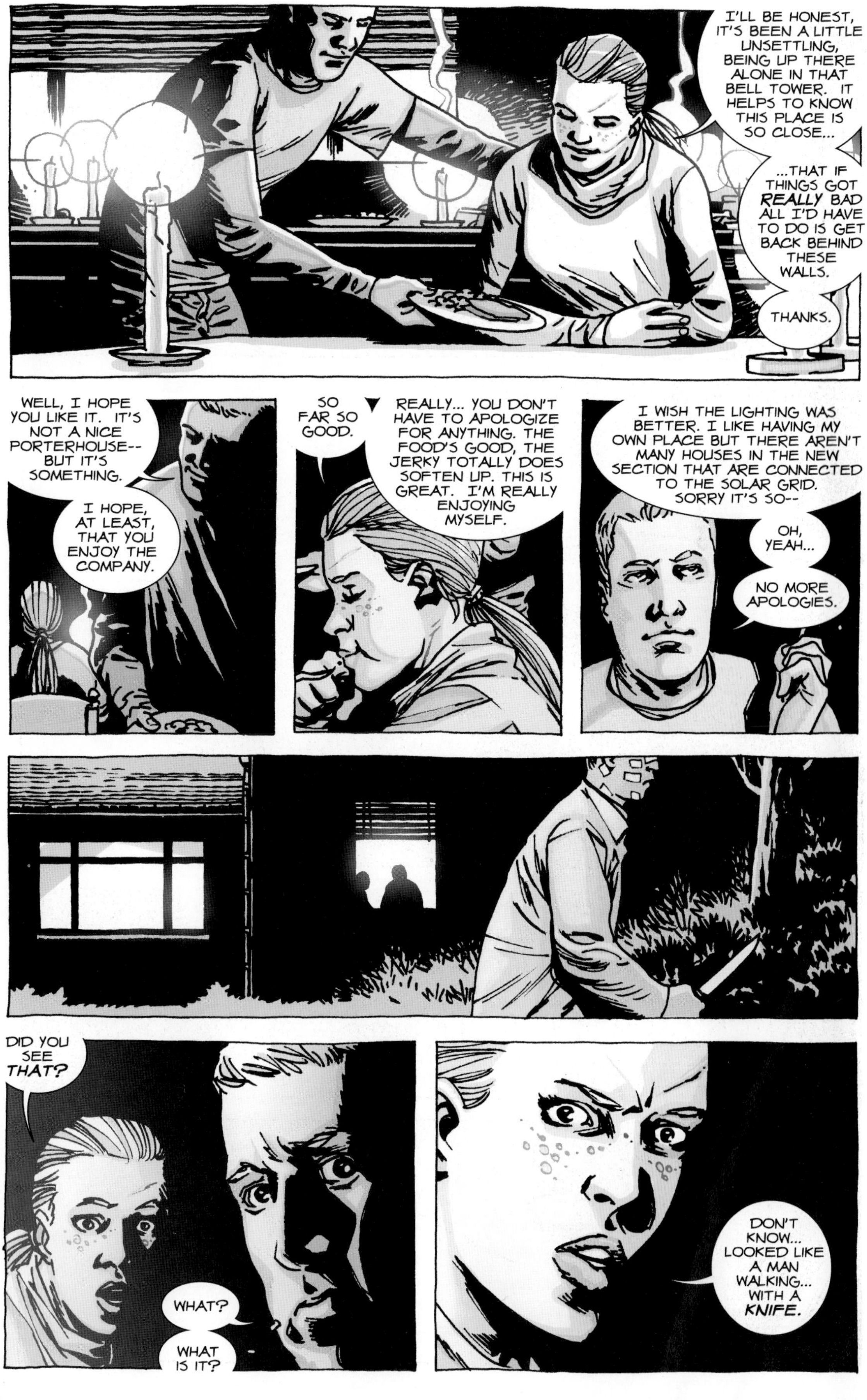

I'LL BE HONEST, IT'S BEEN A LITTLE UNSETTLING, BEING UP THERE ALONE IN THAT BELL TOWER. IT HELPS TO KNOW THIS PLACE IS SO CLOSE...
...THAT IF THINGS GOT REALLY BAD ALL I'D HAVE TO DO IS GET BACK BEHIND THESE WALLS.
THANKS.
WELL, I HOPE YOU LIKE IT. IT'S NOT A NICE PORTERHOUSE-- BUT IT'S SOMETHING.
I HOPE, AT LEAST, THAT YOU ENJOY THE COMPANY.
SO FAR SO GOOD.
REALLY... YOU DON'T HAVE TO APOLOGIZE FOR ANYTHING. THE FOOD'S GOOD, THE JERKY TOTALLY DOES SOFTEN UP. THIS IS GREAT. I'M REALLY ENJOYING MYSELF.
I WISH THE LIGHTING WAS BETTER. I LIKE HAVING MY OWN PLACE BUT THERE AREN'T MANY HOUSES IN THE NEW SECTION THAT ARE CONNECTED TO THE SOLAR GRID. SORRY IT'S SO--
OH, YEAH...
NO MORE APOLOGIES.
DID YOU SEE THAT?
WHAT?
WHAT IS IT?
DON'T KNOW... LOOKED LIKE A MAN WALKING... WITH A KNIFE.

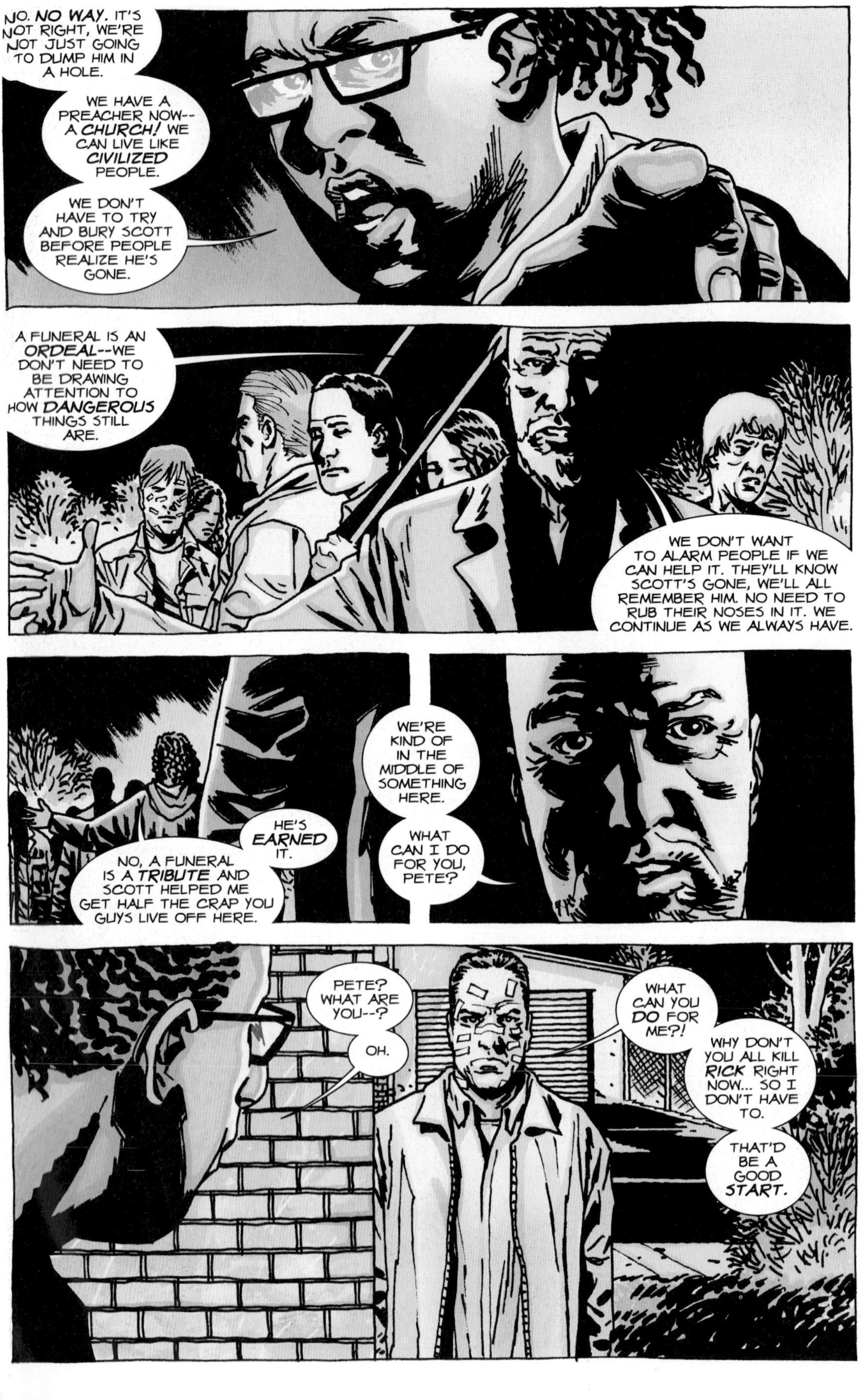
NO. NO WAY. IT'S NOT RIGHT, WE'RE NOT JUST GOING TO DUMP HIM IN A HOLE.
WE HAVE A PREACHER NOW-- A CHURCH! WE CAN LIVE LIKE CIVILIZED PEOPLE.
WE DON'T HAVE TO TRY AND BURY SCOTT BEFORE PEOPLE REALIZE HE'S GONE.
A FUNERAL IS AN ORDEAL--WE DON'T NEED TO BE DRAWING ATTENTION TO HOW DANGEROUS THINGS STILL ARE.
WE DON'T WANT TO ALARM PEOPLE IF WE CAN HELP IT. THEY'LL KNOW SCOTT'S GONE, WE'LL ALL REMEMBER HIM. NO NEED TO RUB THEIR NOSES IN IT. WE CONTINUE AS WE ALWAYS HAVE.
NO, A FUNERAL IS A TRIBUTE AND SCOTT HELPED ME GET HALF THE CRAP YOU GUYS LIVE OFF HERE.
HE'S EARNED IT.
WE'RE KIND OF IN THE MIDDLE OF SOMETHING HERE.
WHAT CAN I DO FOR YOU, PETE?
PETE? WHAT ARE YOU--?
OH.
WHAT CAN YOU DO FOR ME?!
WHY DON'T YOU ALL KILL RICK RIGHT NOW... SO I DON'T HAVE TO.
THAT'D BE A GOOD START.

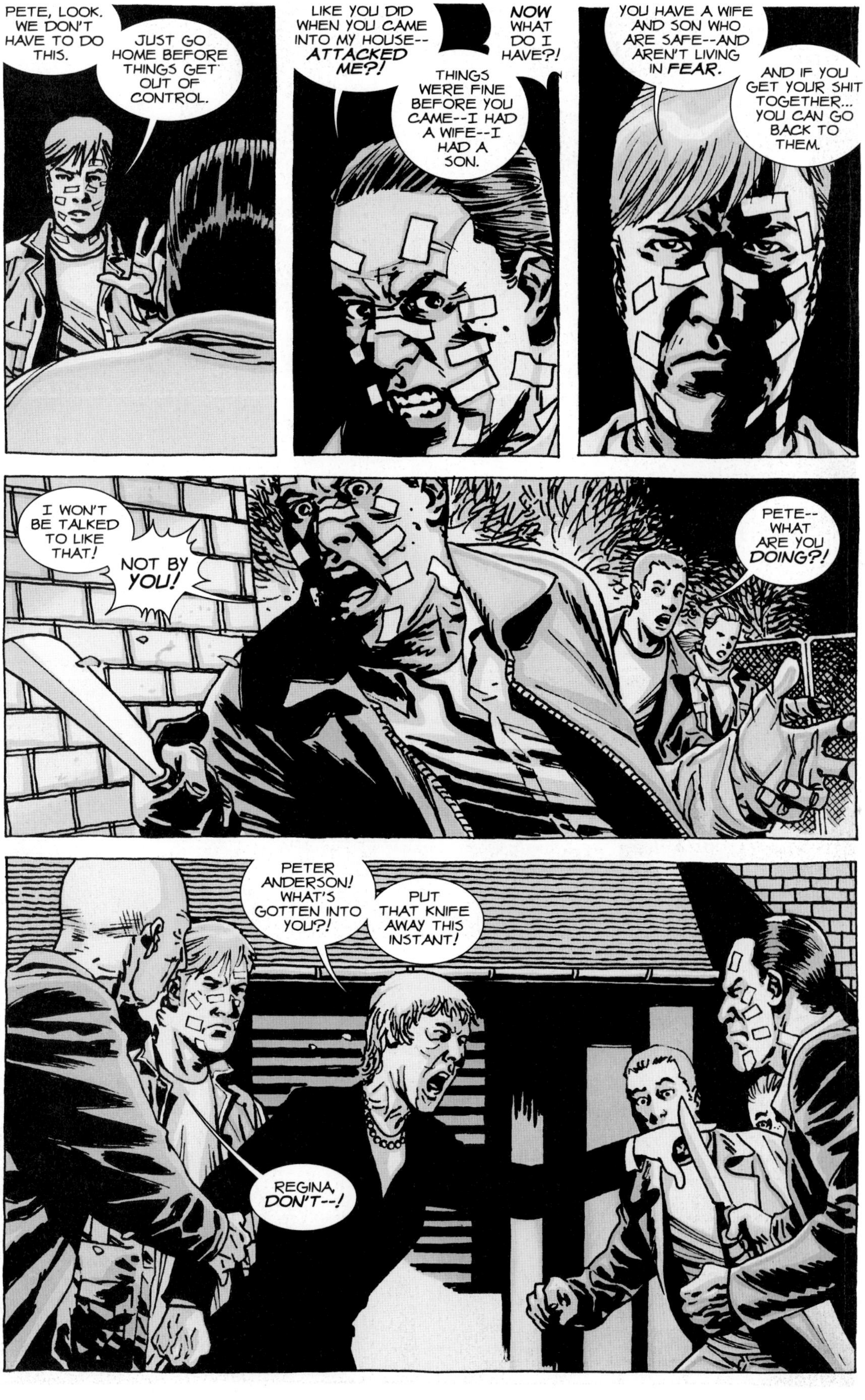
PETE, LOOK. WE DON'T HAVE TO DO THIS.
JUST GO HOME BEFORE THINGS GET OUT OF CONTROL.
LIKE YOU DID WHEN YOU CAME INTO MY HOUSE-- ATTACKED ME?!
THINGS WERE FINE BEFORE YOU CAME--I HAD A WIFE--I HAD A SON.
NOW WHAT DO I HAVE?!
YOU HAVE A WIFE AND SON WHO ARE SAFE--AND AREN'T LIVING IN FEAR.
AND IF YOU GET YOUR SHIT TOGETHER... YOU CAN GO BACK TO THEM.
I WON'T BE TALKED TO LIKE THAT!
NOT BY YOU!
PETE-- WHAT ARE YOU DOING?!
PETER ANDERSON! WHAT'S GOTTEN INTO YOU?!
PUT THAT KNIFE AWAY THIS INSTANT!
REGINA, DON'T--!

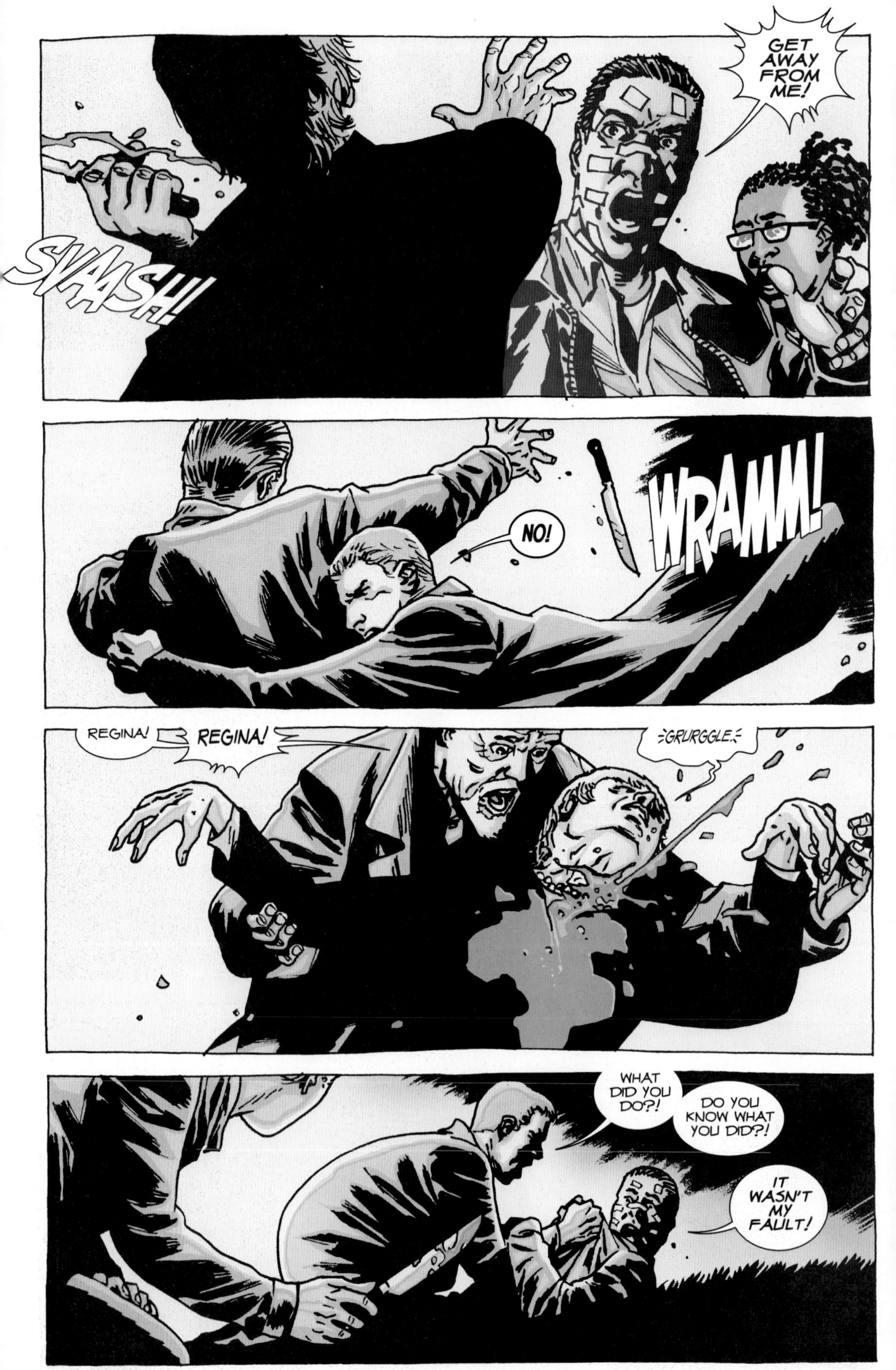
GET AWAY FROM ME!
SVAASH!
NO!
WRAMM!
REGINA!
REGINA!
GRURGGLE
WHAT DID YOU DO?!
DO YOU KNOW WHAT YOU DID?!
IT WASN'T MY FAULT!

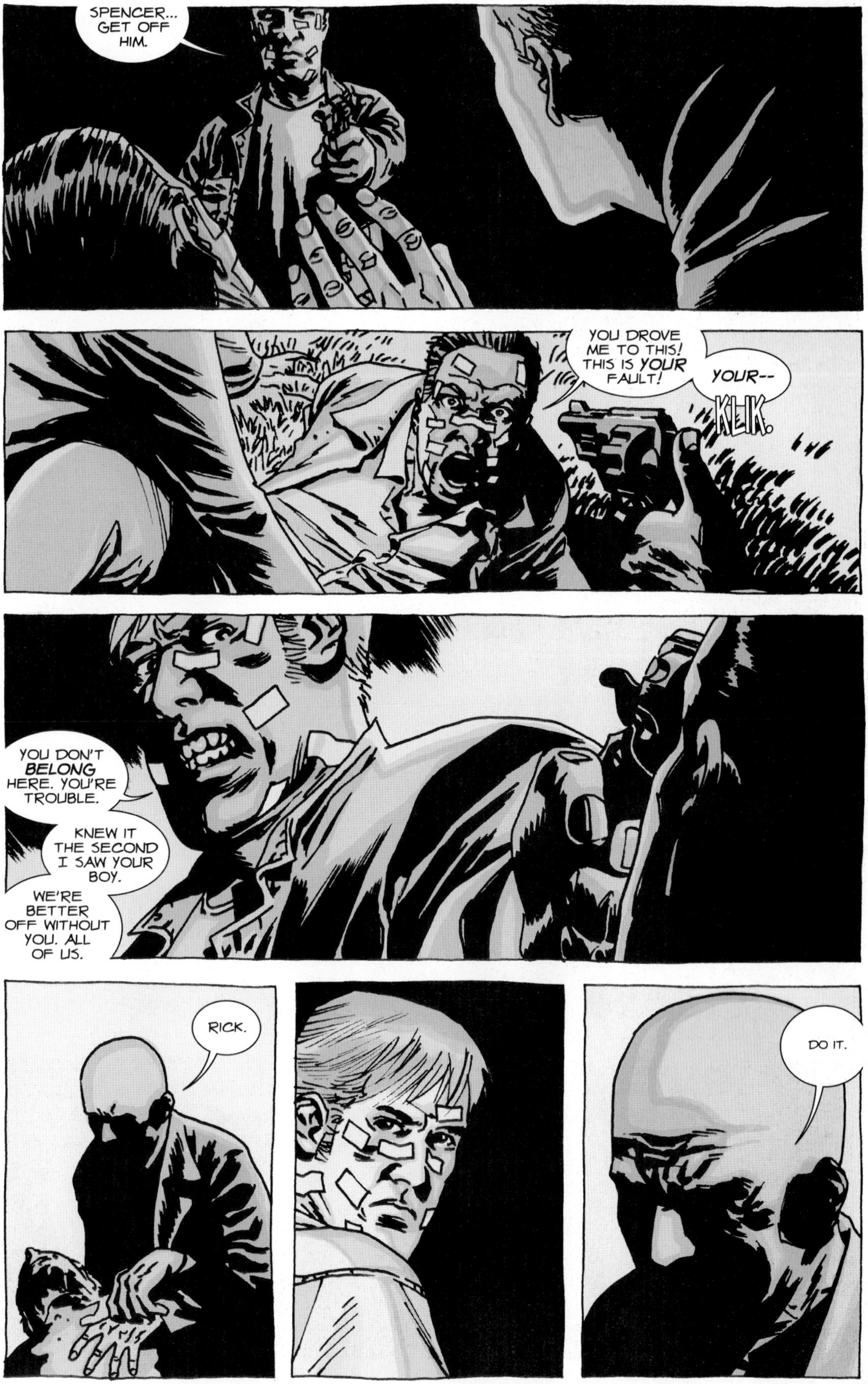
SPENCER... GET OFF HIM.
YOU DROVE ME TO THIS! THIS IS YOUR FAULT!
YOUR--
KLIK.
YOU DON'T BELONG HERE. YOU'RE TROUBLE.
KNEW IT THE SECOND I SAW YOUR BOY.
WE'RE BETTER OFF WITHOUT YOU. ALL OF US.
RICK.
DO IT.

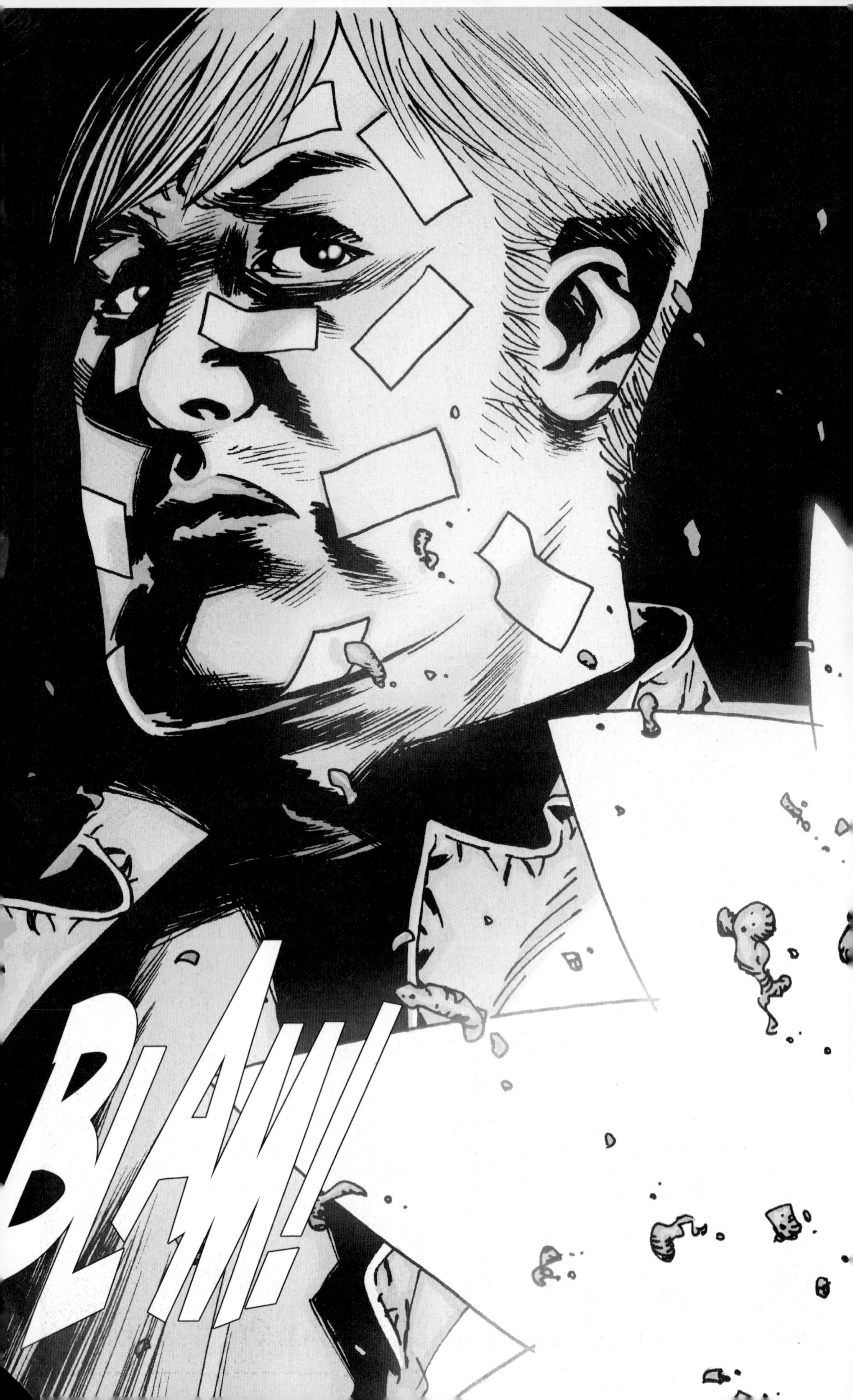
BLAM!

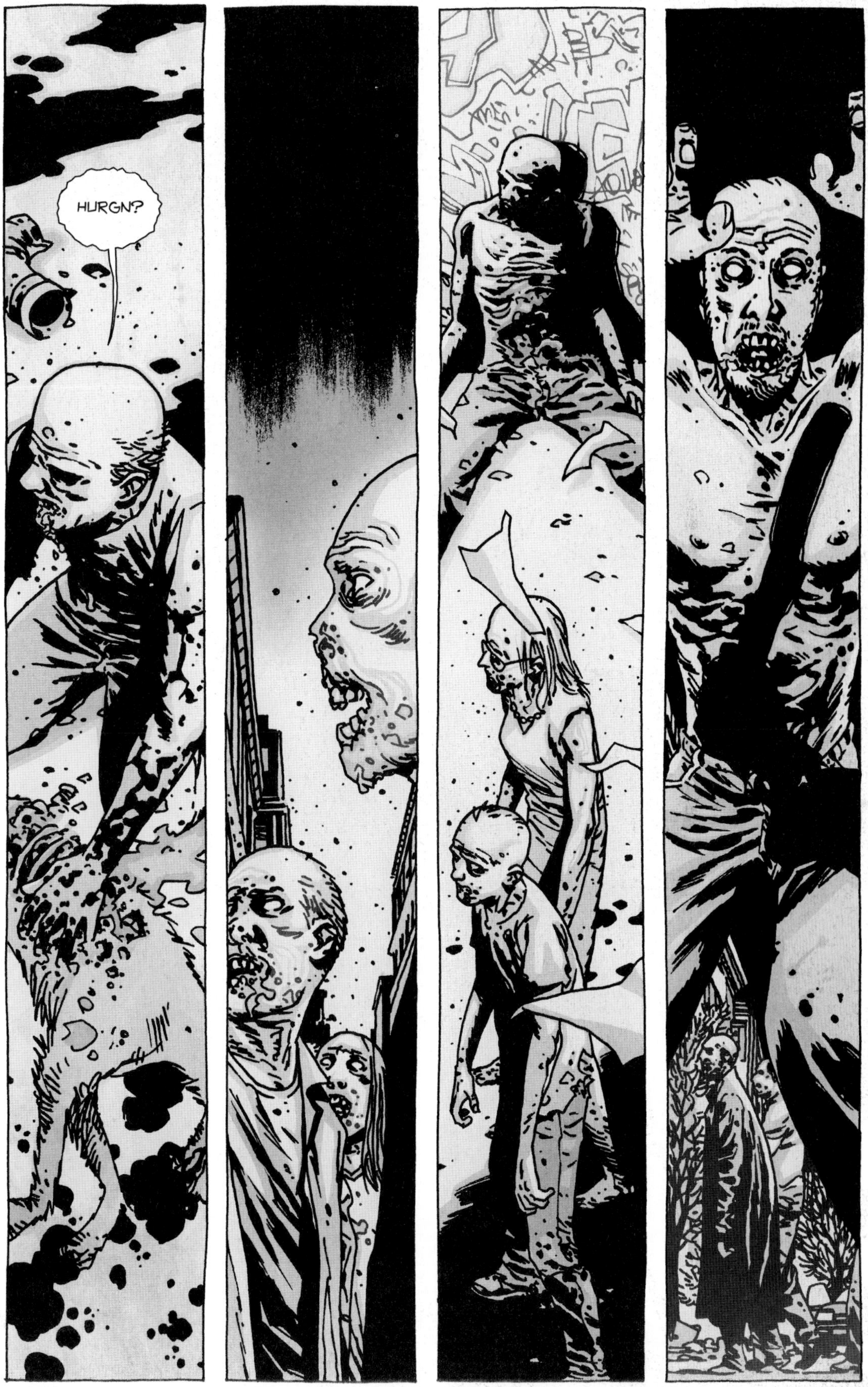
HURGN?

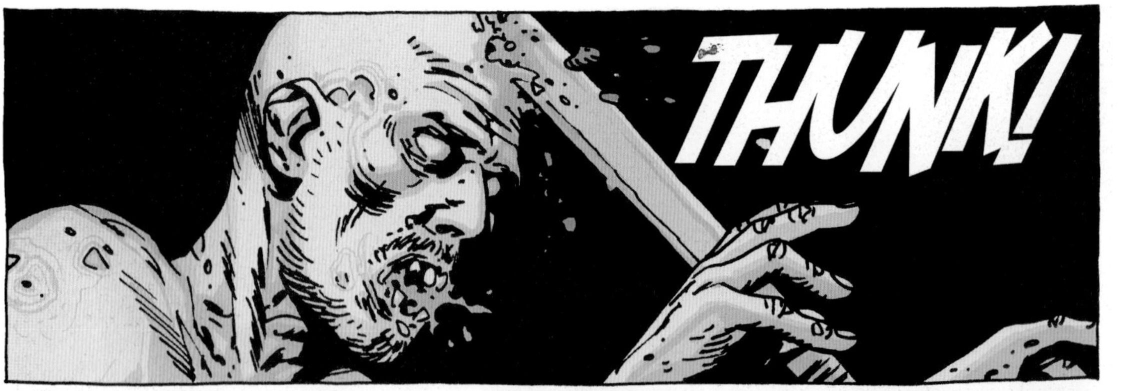
THUNK!

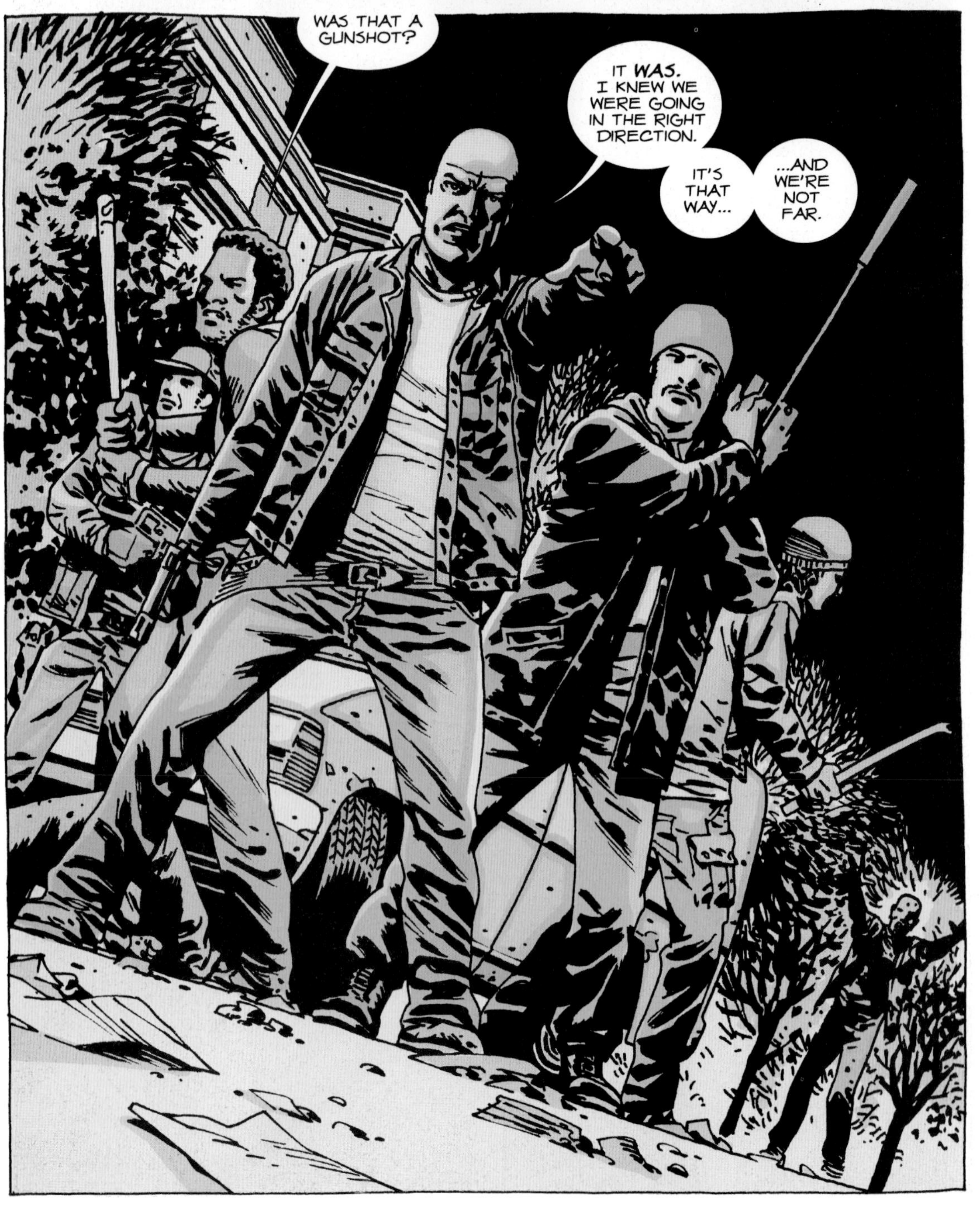
WAS THAT A GUNSHOT?
IT WAS. I KNEW WE WERE GOING IN THE RIGHT DIRECTION.
IT'S THAT WAY...
...AND WE'RE NOT FAR.

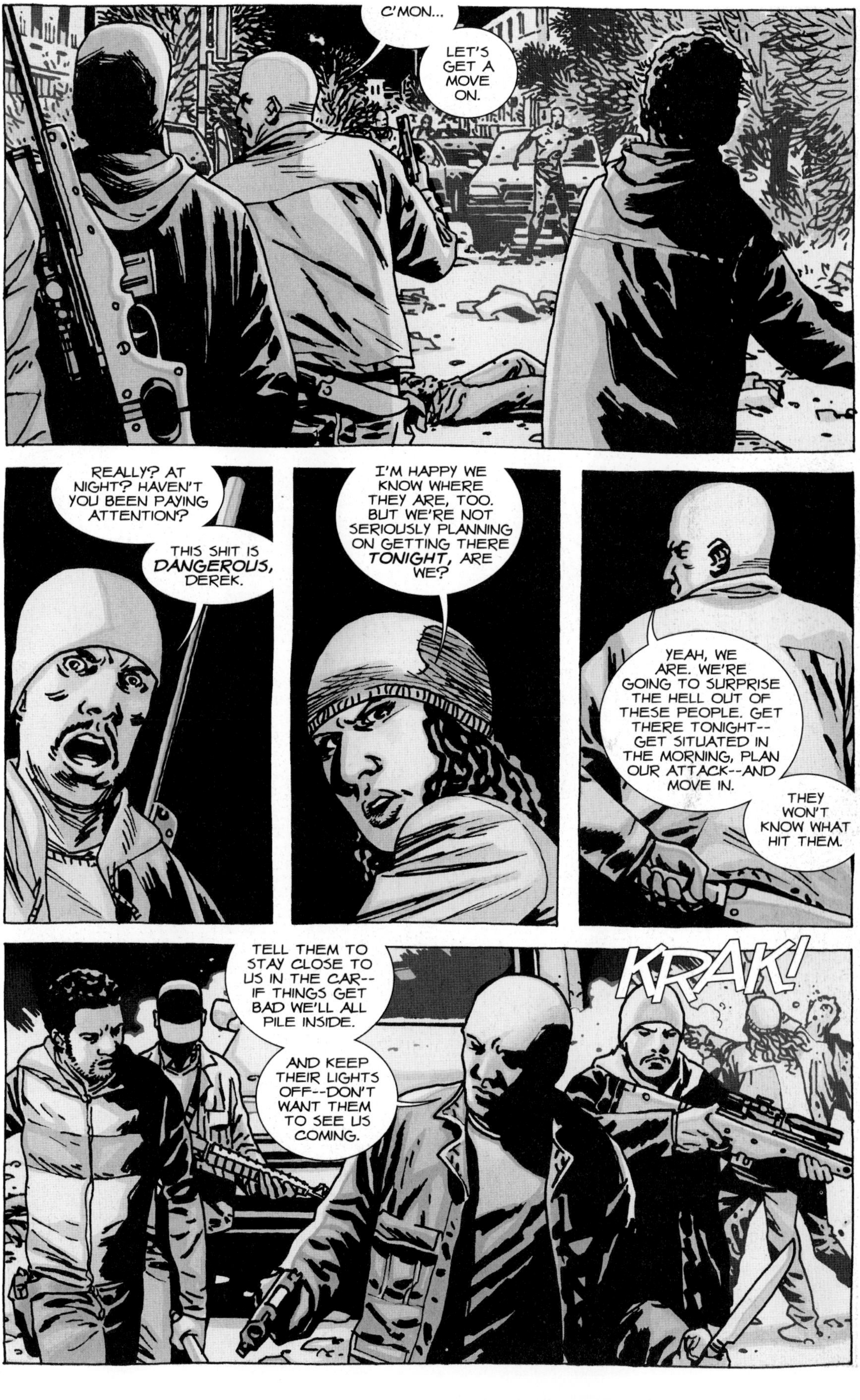
C'MON...
LET'S GET A MOVE ON.
REALLY? AT NIGHT? HAVEN'T YOU BEEN PAYING ATTENTION?
THIS SHIT IS *DANGEROUS,* DEREK.
I'M HAPPY WE KNOW WHERE THEY ARE, TOO. BUT WE'RE NOT SERIOUSLY PLANNING ON GETTING THERE *TONIGHT,* ARE WE?
YEAH, WE ARE. WE'RE GOING TO SURPRISE THE HELL OUT OF THESE PEOPLE. GET THERE TONIGHT-- GET SITUATED IN THE MORNING, PLAN OUR ATTACK--AND MOVE IN.
THEY WON'T KNOW WHAT HIT THEM.
TELL THEM TO STAY CLOSE TO US IN THE CAR-- IF THINGS GET BAD WE'LL ALL PILE INSIDE.
AND KEEP THEIR LIGHTS OFF--DON'T WANT THEM TO SEE US COMING.
KRAK!

GLENN, STOP! PLEASE!

IT'S A GUNSHOT, MAGGIE. IT COULD BE ANYTHING... THAT'S NOT SOMETHING WE HEAR A LOT.

SOMEONE COULD BE HURT. I NEED TO CHECK IT OUT.

NO, YOU *DON'T*. THIS IS A BIG PLACE--THERE ARE A LOT OF PEOPLE WHO COULD BE CHECKING THIS OUT.

STAY HERE, SOPHIA IS SCARED ENOUGH AS IT IS--WE NEED YOU *HERE*.

MAGGIE, YOU KNOW I CAN'T--

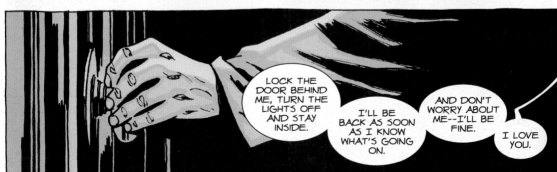

LOCK THE DOOR BEHIND ME, TURN THE LIGHTS OFF AND STAY INSIDE.

I'LL BE BACK AS SOON AS I KNOW WHAT'S GOING ON.

AND DON'T WORRY ABOUT ME--I'LL BE FINE.

I LOVE YOU.

HOLY...

WHAT HAPPENED?

NO CLUE. I THINK THAT'S WHAT EVERYONE IS TRYING TO FIGURE OUT.

I HOPE NOBODY'S HURT...

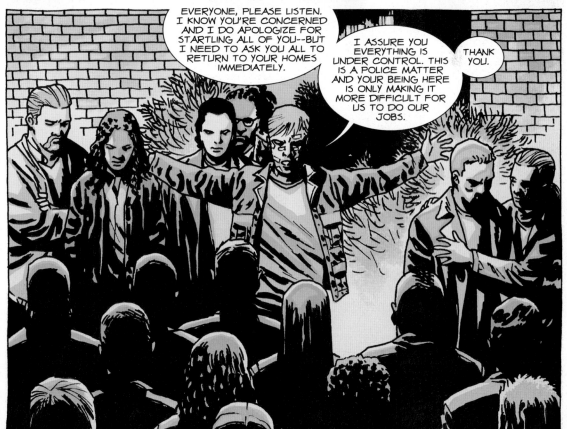

EVERYONE, PLEASE LISTEN. I KNOW YOU'RE CONCERNED AND I DO APOLOGIZE FOR STARTLING ALL OF YOU--BUT I NEED TO ASK YOU ALL TO RETURN TO YOUR HOMES IMMEDIATELY.

I ASSURE YOU EVERYTHING IS UNDER CONTROL. THIS IS A POLICE MATTER AND YOUR BEING HERE IS ONLY MAKING IT MORE DIFFICULT FOR US TO DO OUR JOBS.

THANK YOU.

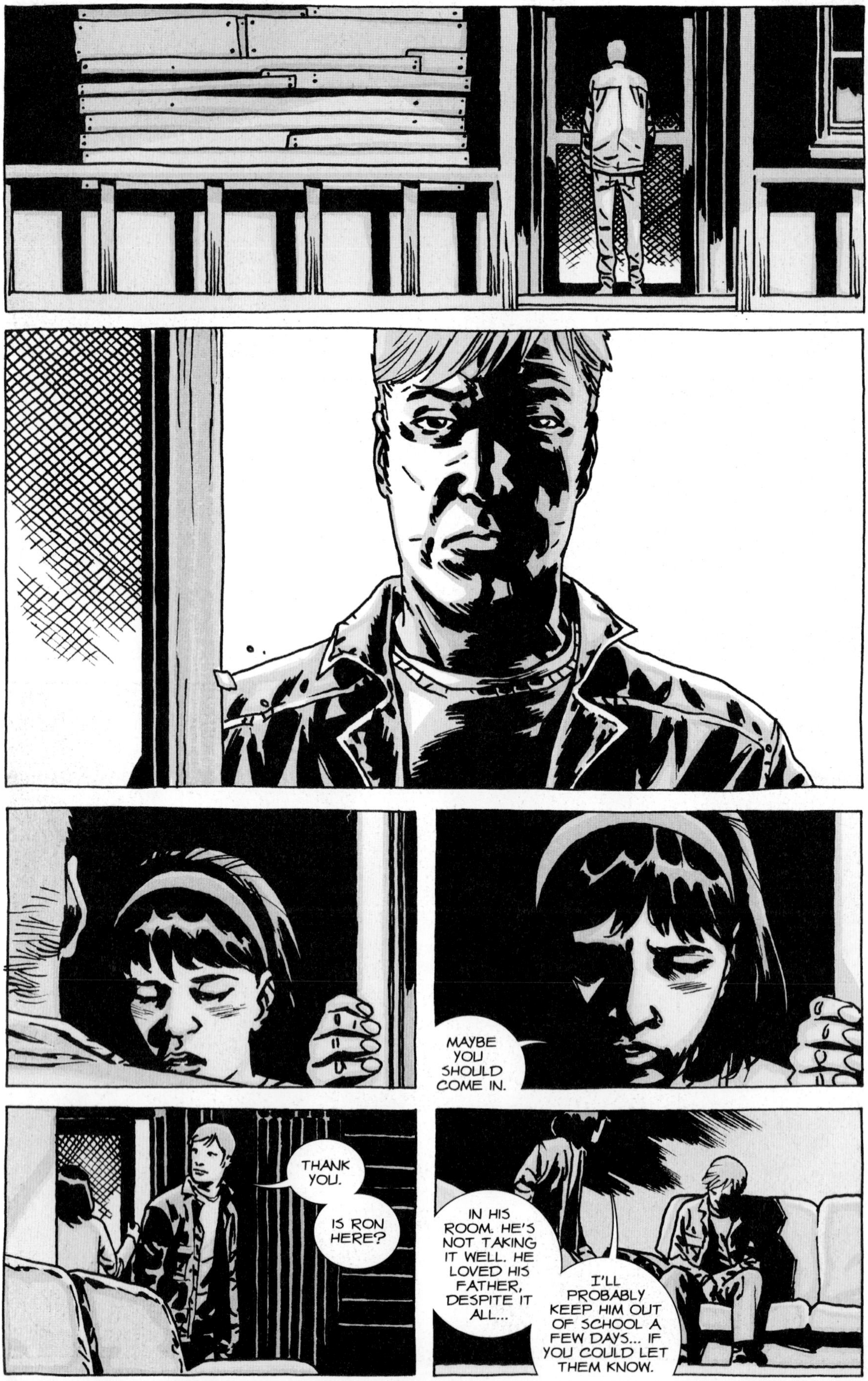

MAYBE YOU SHOULD COME IN.
THANK YOU.
IS RON HERE?
IN HIS ROOM. HE'S NOT TAKING IT WELL. HE LOVED HIS FATHER, DESPITE IT ALL...
I'LL PROBABLY KEEP HIM OUT OF SCHOOL A FEW DAYS... IF YOU COULD LET THEM KNOW.

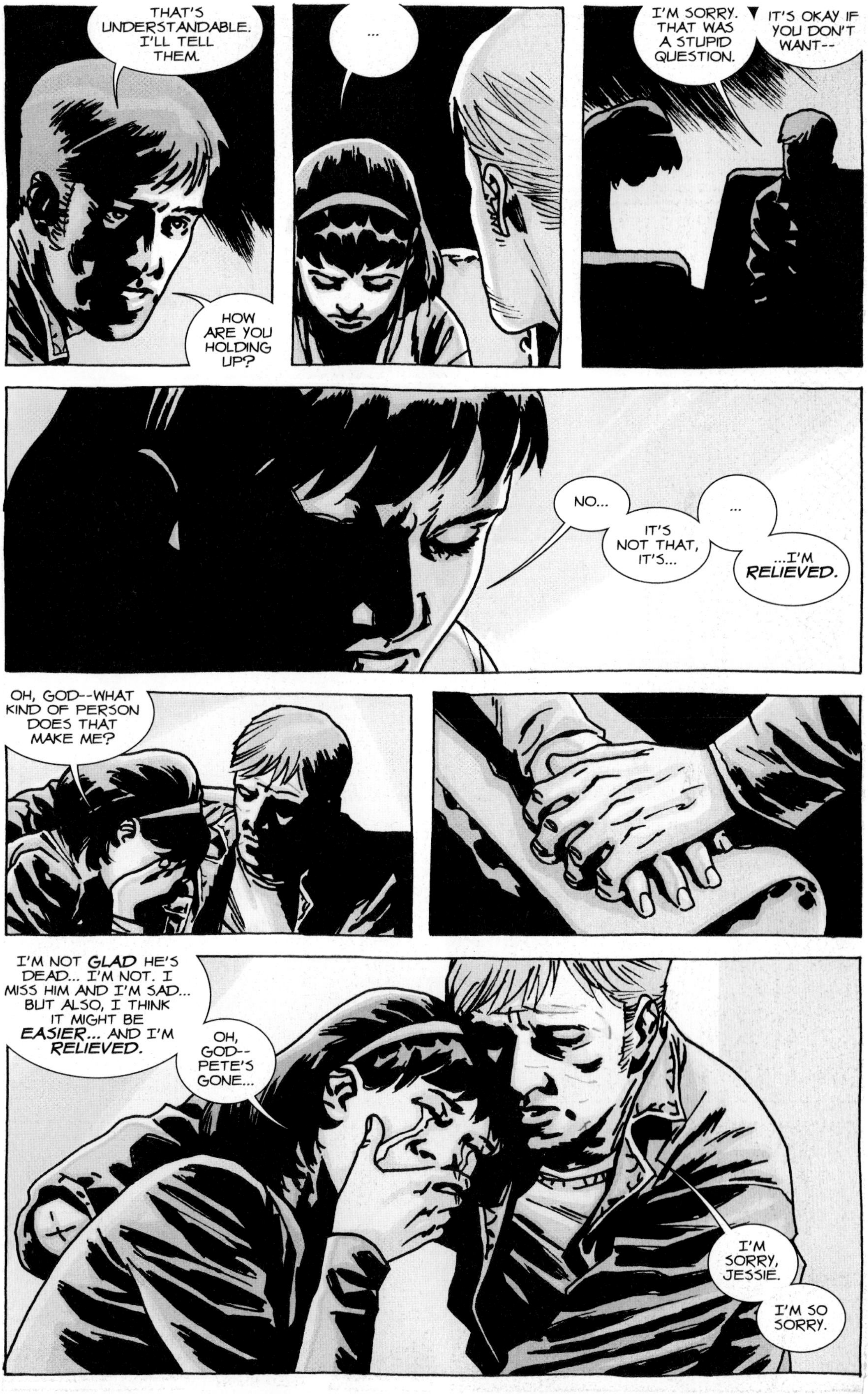
THAT'S UNDERSTANDABLE. I'LL TELL THEM.
HOW ARE YOU HOLDING UP?
...
I'M SORRY. THAT WAS A STUPID QUESTION.
IT'S OKAY IF YOU DON'T WANT--
NO...
IT'S NOT THAT, IT'S...
...
...I'M *RELIEVED.*
OH, GOD--WHAT KIND OF PERSON DOES THAT MAKE ME?
I'M NOT *GLAD* HE'S DEAD... I'M NOT. I MISS HIM AND I'M SAD... BUT ALSO, I THINK IT MIGHT BE *EASIER*... AND I'M *RELIEVED.*
OH, GOD-- PETE'S GONE...
I'M SORRY, JESSIE.
I'M SO SORRY.

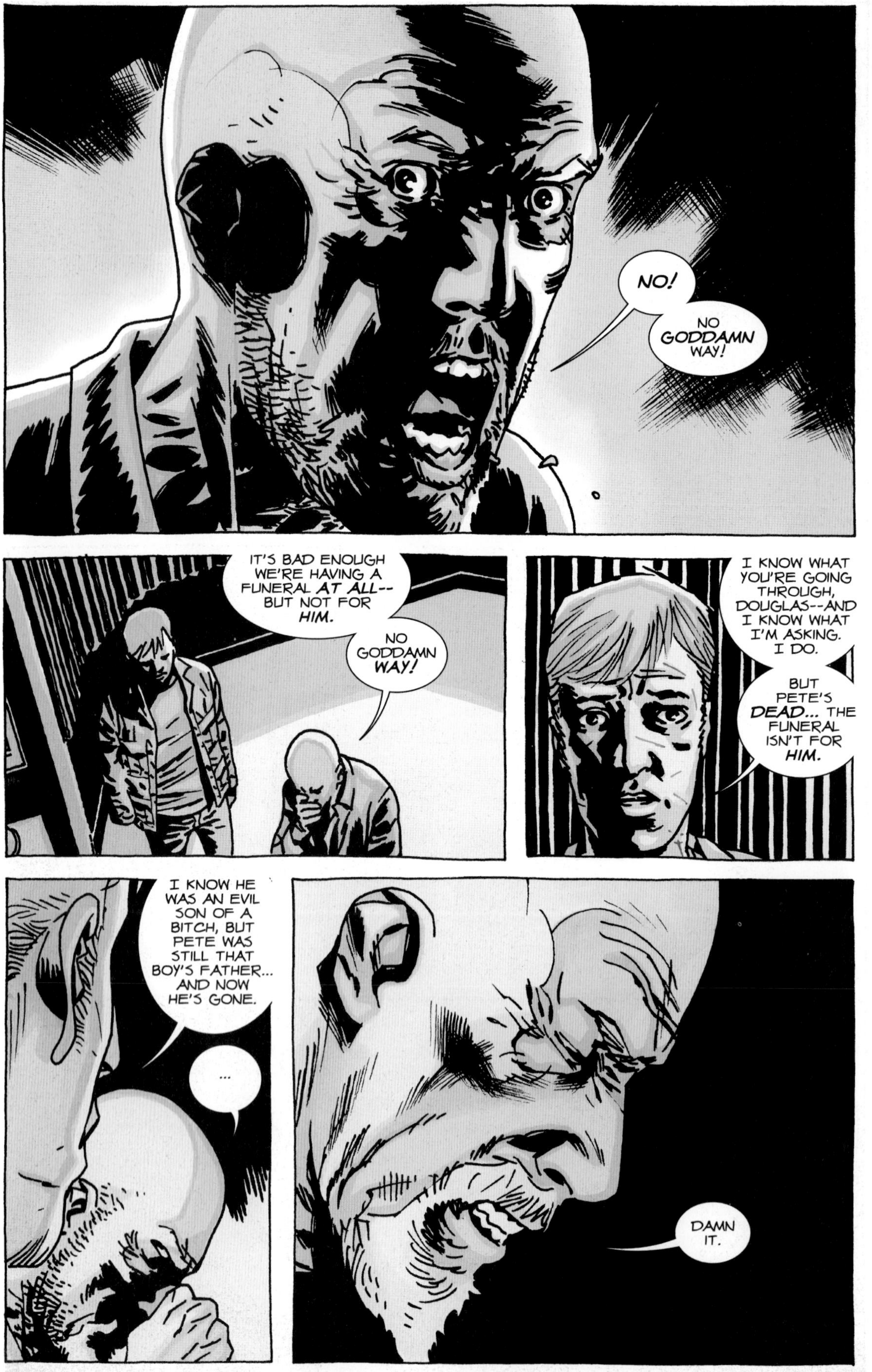
NO!
NO GODDAMN WAY!
IT'S BAD ENOUGH WE'RE HAVING A FUNERAL AT ALL-- BUT NOT FOR HIM.
NO GODDAMN WAY!
I KNOW WHAT YOU'RE GOING THROUGH, DOUGLAS--AND I KNOW WHAT I'M ASKING. I DO.
BUT PETE'S DEAD... THE FUNERAL ISN'T FOR HIM.
I KNOW HE WAS AN EVIL SON OF A BITCH, BUT PETE WAS STILL THAT BOY'S FATHER... AND NOW HE'S GONE.
...
DAMN IT.

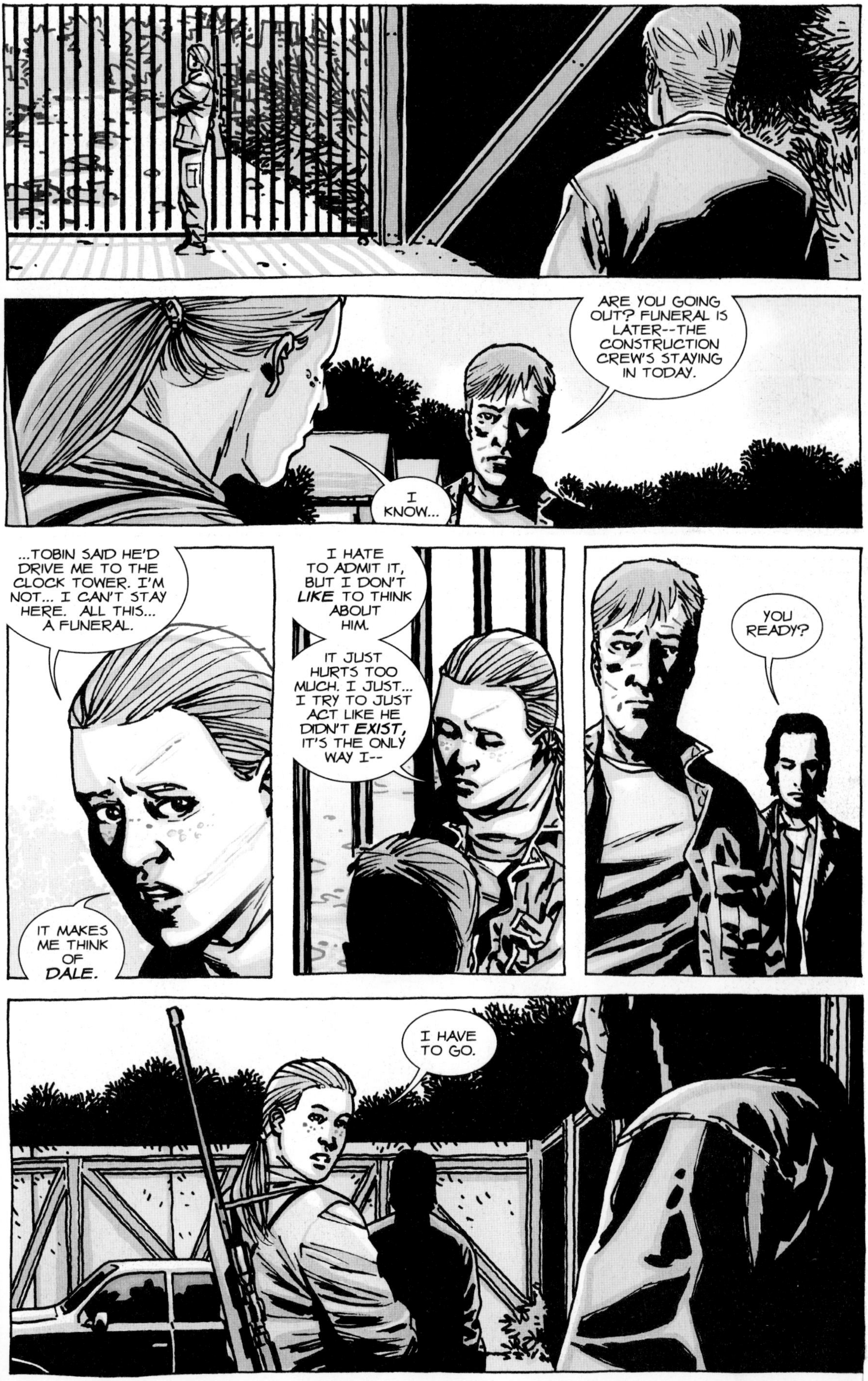
ARE YOU GOING OUT? FUNERAL IS LATER--THE CONSTRUCTION CREW'S STAYING IN TODAY.
I KNOW...
...TOBIN SAID HE'D DRIVE ME TO THE CLOCK TOWER. I'M NOT... I CAN'T STAY HERE. ALL THIS... A FUNERAL.
IT MAKES ME THINK OF DALE.
I HATE TO ADMIT IT, BUT I DON'T LIKE TO THINK ABOUT HIM.
IT JUST HURTS TOO MUCH. I JUST... I TRY TO JUST ACT LIKE HE DIDN'T EXIST, IT'S THE ONLY WAY I--
YOU READY?
I HAVE TO GO.

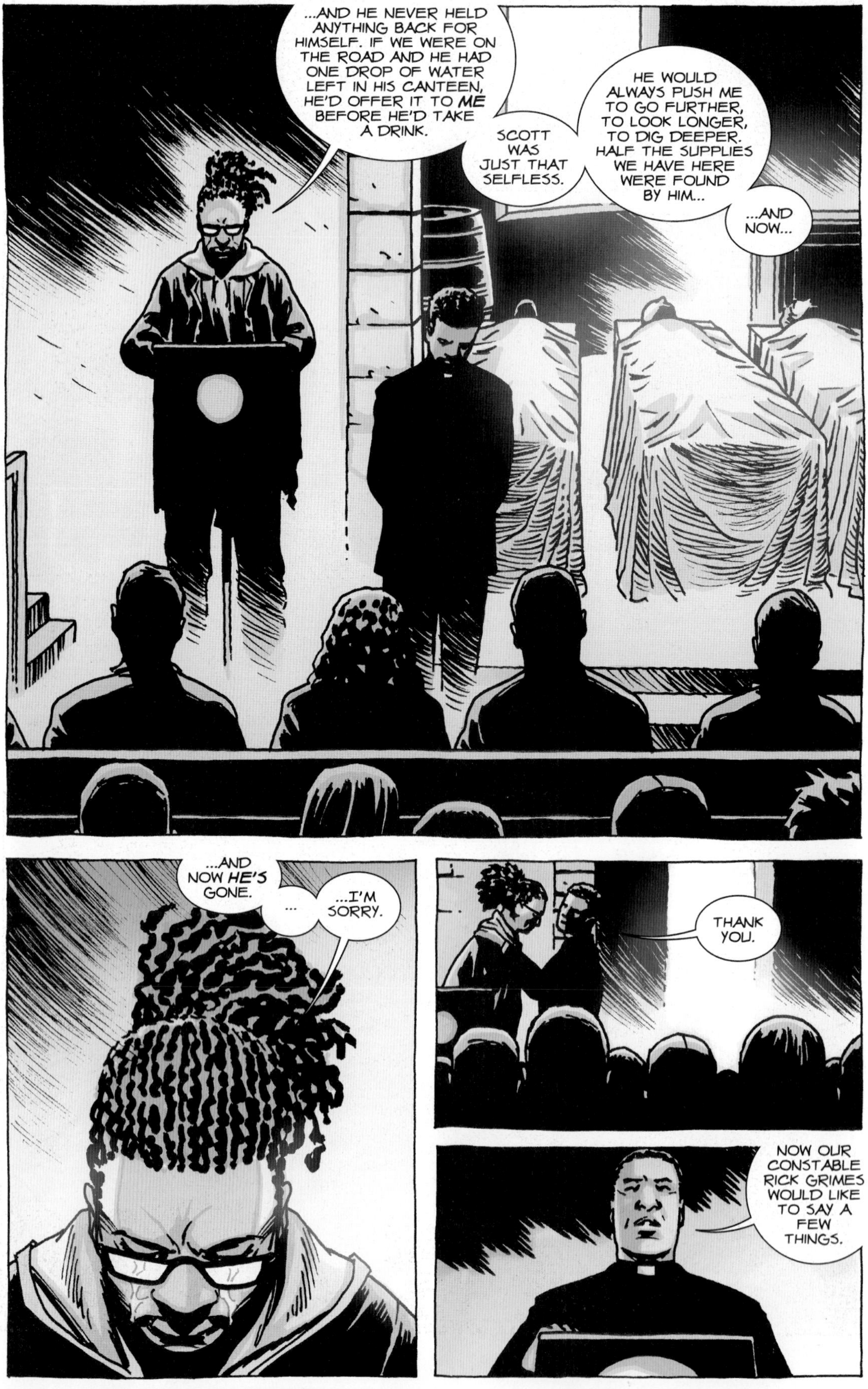

...AND HE NEVER HELD ANYTHING BACK FOR HIMSELF. IF WE WERE ON THE ROAD AND HE HAD ONE DROP OF WATER LEFT IN HIS CANTEEN, HE'D OFFER IT TO ME BEFORE HE'D TAKE A DRINK.
SCOTT WAS JUST THAT SELFLESS.
HE WOULD ALWAYS PUSH ME TO GO FURTHER, TO LOOK LONGER, TO DIG DEEPER. HALF THE SUPPLIES WE HAVE HERE WERE FOUND BY HIM...
...AND NOW...
...AND NOW HE'S GONE.
...
...I'M SORRY.
THANK YOU.
NOW OUR CONSTABLE RICK GRIMES WOULD LIKE TO SAY A FEW THINGS.

DO ANY OF US REALLY KNOW WHO WE ARE? AND EVEN IF WE DO *NOW,* DID WE KNOW BEFORE ALL THIS STARTED HAPPENING?

WITHOUT THIS ADVERSITY, THIS HARDSHIP, HOW DO WE REALLY *KNOW* WHO WE ARE, AND WHAT TRULY MATTERS TO US?

THIS IS SOMETHING I FIND MYSELF THINKING ABOUT A LOT, NOW THAT I'M LIVING HERE AND I HAVE THE LUXURY OF SPENDING TIME WITH MY THOUGHTS.

THE THINGS I'VE DONE TO SURVIVE INFORM WHO I AM AS A PERSON. I AM A MAN WHO WILL DO THINGS TO PROTECT MY FAMILY. A LOT OF THESE THINGS I'VE DONE... I'M *NOT* PROUD OF.

ARE THESE THINGS *MY FAULT?* I KNOW I WOULD NOT HAVE DONE THEM WERE THE SITUATION DIFFERENT... SO HOW AM I TO BLAME?

PETE WAS A LOVING HUSBAND AND A FATHER AND HE DID SOME BAD, UNFORGIVABLE THINGS... BUT AT THE END OF THE DAY, HOW CAN WE JUDGE HIM...

...HOW CAN I?

IS THAT WHO PETE REALLY WAS? OR IS THAT WHO HE WAS MADE INTO BY HIS SURROUNDINGS?

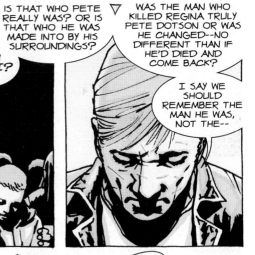

WAS THE MAN WHO KILLED REGINA TRULY PETE DOTSON OR WAS HE CHANGED--NO DIFFERENT THAN IF HE'D DIED AND COME BACK?

I SAY WE SHOULD REMEMBER THE MAN HE WAS, NOT THE--

K-POW!

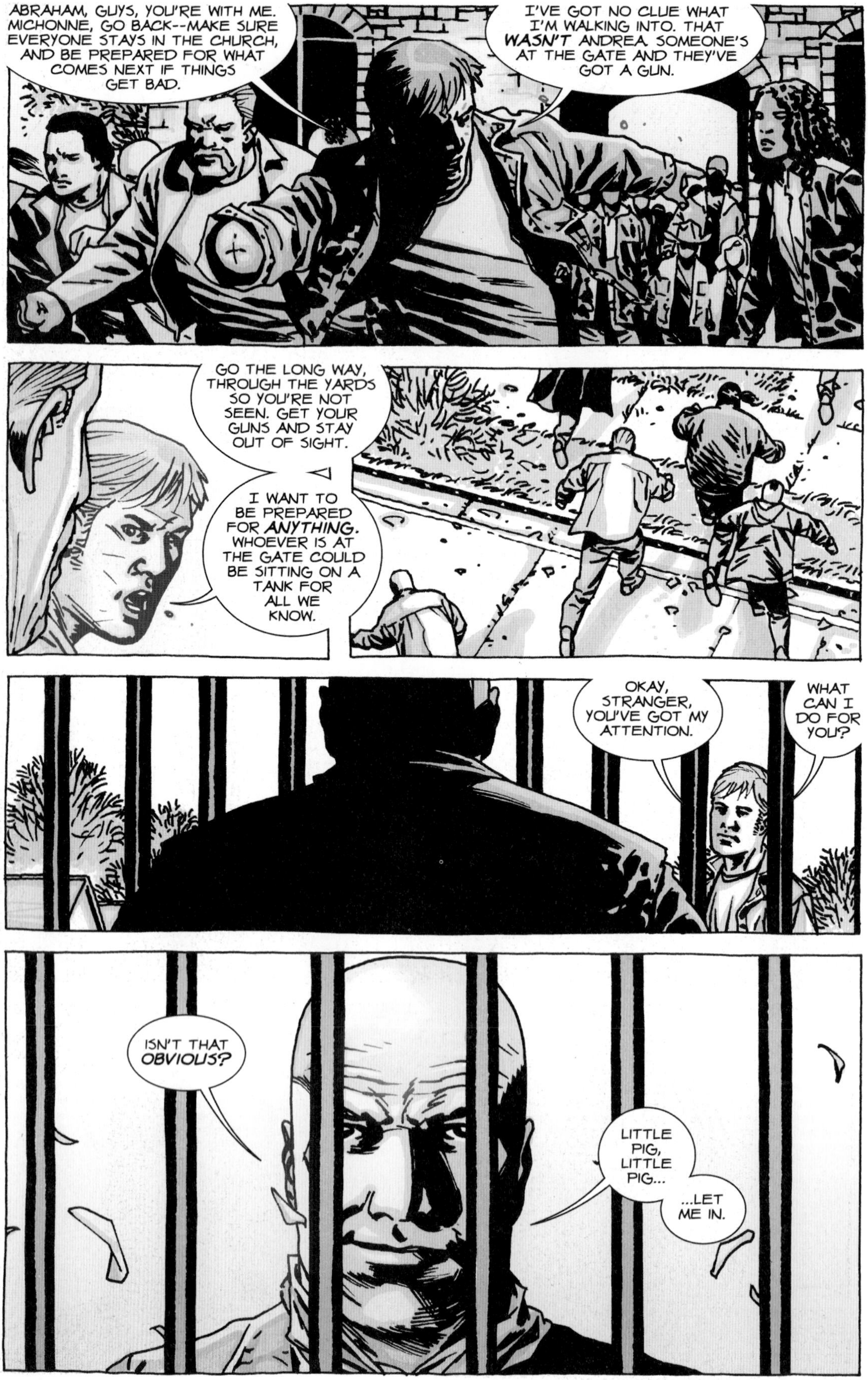
ABRAHAM, GUYS, YOU'RE WITH ME. MICHONNE, GO BACK--MAKE SURE EVERYONE STAYS IN THE CHURCH, AND BE PREPARED FOR WHAT COMES NEXT IF THINGS GET BAD.
I'VE GOT NO CLUE WHAT I'M WALKING INTO. THAT WASN'T ANDREA SOMEONE'S AT THE GATE AND THEY'VE GOT A GUN.
GO THE LONG WAY, THROUGH THE YARDS SO YOU'RE NOT SEEN. GET YOUR GUNS AND STAY OUT OF SIGHT.
I WANT TO BE PREPARED FOR ANYTHING. WHOEVER IS AT THE GATE COULD BE SITTING ON A TANK FOR ALL WE KNOW.
OKAY, STRANGER, YOU'VE GOT MY ATTENTION.
WHAT CAN I DO FOR YOU?
ISN'T THAT OBVIOUS?
LITTLE PIG, LITTLE PIG...
...LET ME IN.

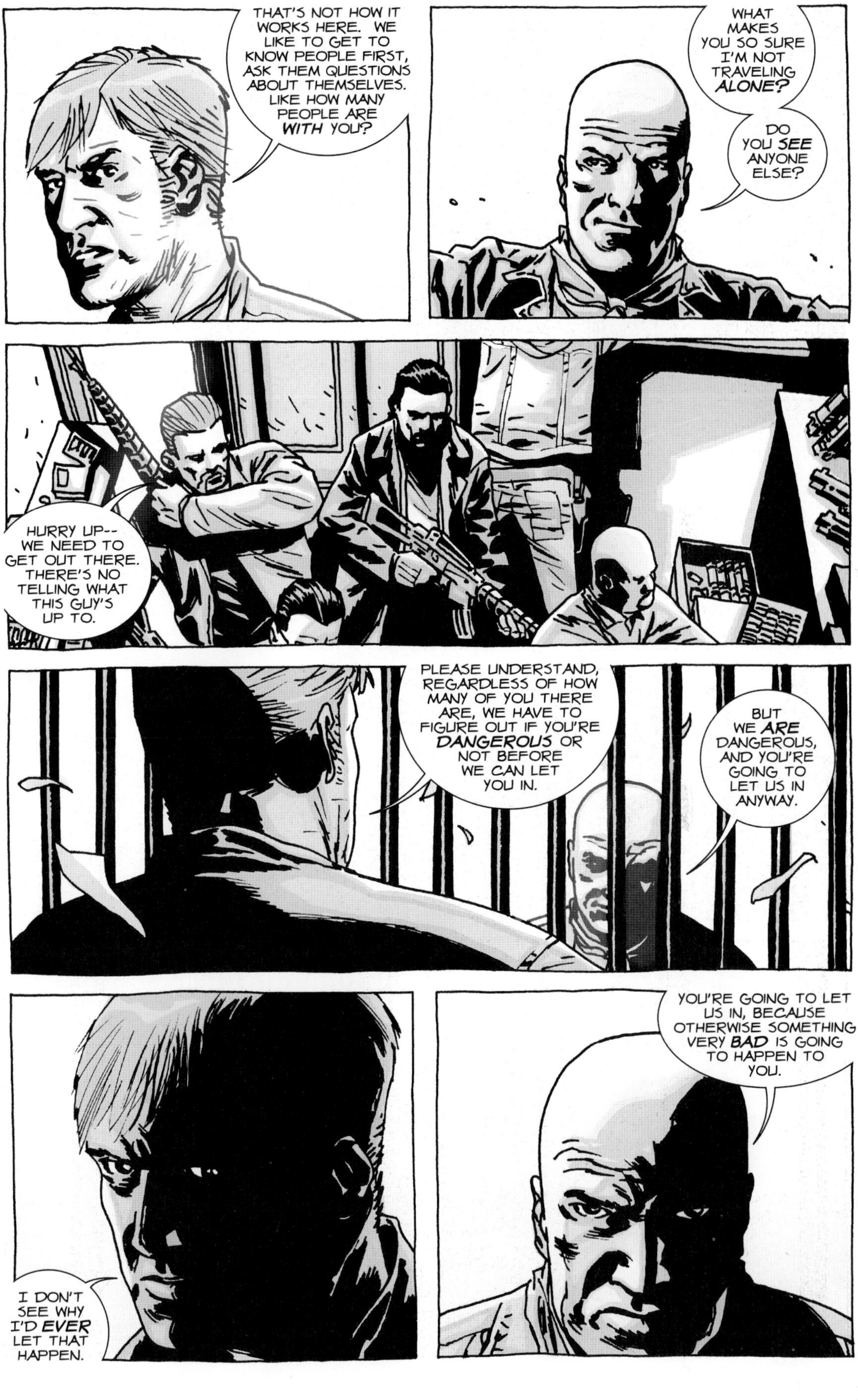
THAT'S NOT HOW IT WORKS HERE. WE LIKE TO GET TO KNOW PEOPLE FIRST, ASK THEM QUESTIONS ABOUT THEMSELVES. LIKE HOW MANY PEOPLE ARE WITH YOU?
WHAT MAKES YOU SO SURE I'M NOT TRAVELING ALONE?
DO YOU SEE ANYONE ELSE?
HURRY UP-- WE NEED TO GET OUT THERE. THERE'S NO TELLING WHAT THIS GUY'S UP TO.
PLEASE UNDERSTAND, REGARDLESS OF HOW MANY OF YOU THERE ARE, WE HAVE TO FIGURE OUT IF YOU'RE DANGEROUS OR NOT BEFORE WE CAN LET YOU IN.
BUT WE ARE DANGEROUS, AND YOU'RE GOING TO LET US IN ANYWAY.
I DON'T SEE WHY I'D EVER LET THAT HAPPEN.
YOU'RE GOING TO LET US IN, BECAUSE OTHERWISE SOMETHING VERY BAD IS GOING TO HAPPEN TO YOU.

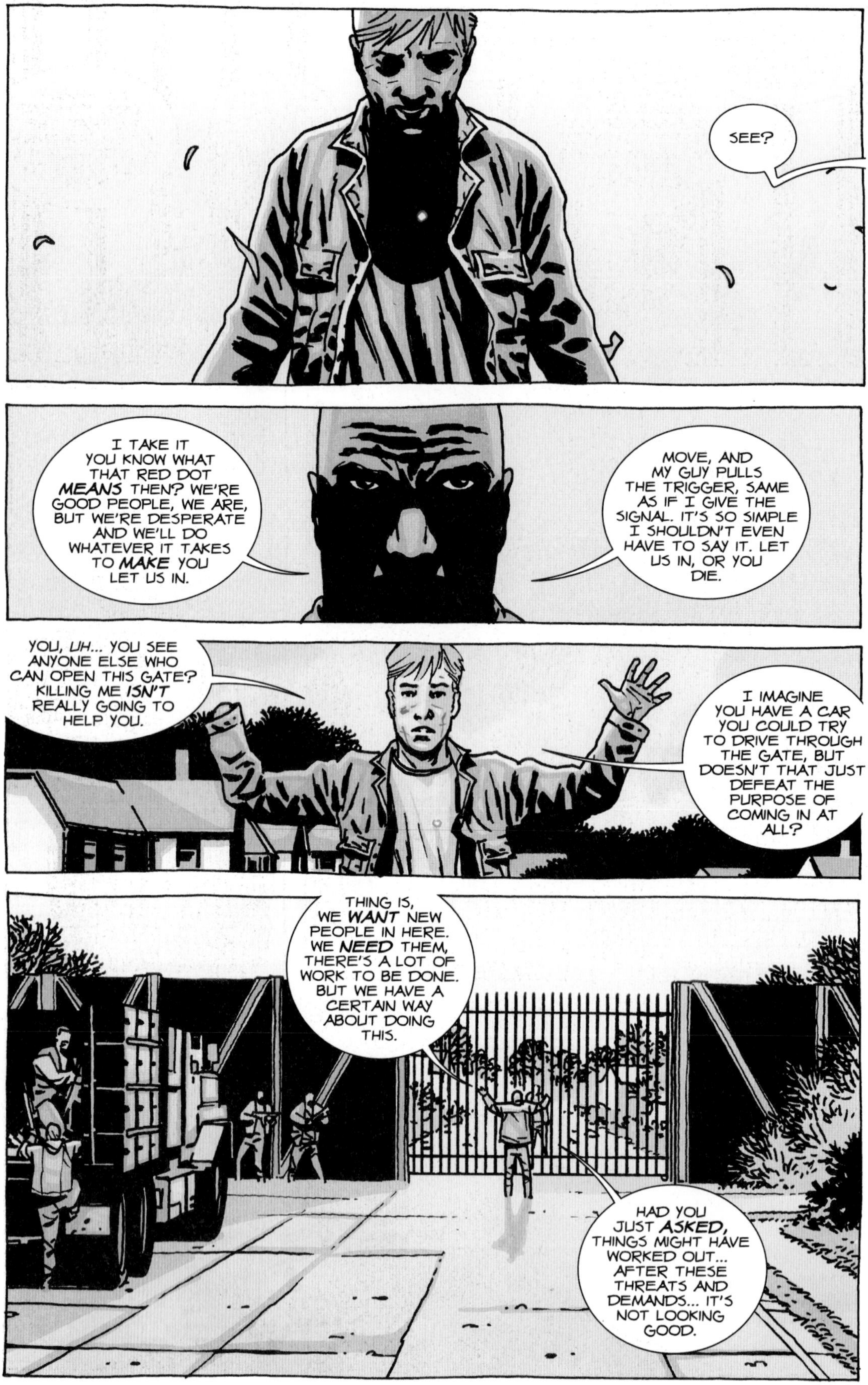

SEE?
I TAKE IT YOU KNOW WHAT THAT RED DOT MEANS THEN? WE'RE GOOD PEOPLE, WE ARE, BUT WE'RE DESPERATE AND WE'LL DO WHATEVER IT TAKES TO MAKE YOU LET US IN.
MOVE, AND MY GUY PULLS THE TRIGGER, SAME AS IF I GIVE THE SIGNAL. IT'S SO SIMPLE I SHOULDN'T EVEN HAVE TO SAY IT. LET US IN, OR YOU DIE.
YOU, UH... YOU SEE ANYONE ELSE WHO CAN OPEN THIS GATE? KILLING ME ISN'T REALLY GOING TO HELP YOU.
I IMAGINE YOU HAVE A CAR YOU COULD TRY TO DRIVE THROUGH THE GATE, BUT DOESN'T THAT JUST DEFEAT THE PURPOSE OF COMING IN AT ALL?
THING IS, WE WANT NEW PEOPLE IN HERE. WE NEED THEM, THERE'S A LOT OF WORK TO BE DONE. BUT WE HAVE A CERTAIN WAY ABOUT DOING THIS.
HAD YOU JUST ASKED, THINGS MIGHT HAVE WORKED OUT... AFTER THESE THREATS AND DEMANDS... IT'S NOT LOOKING GOOD.

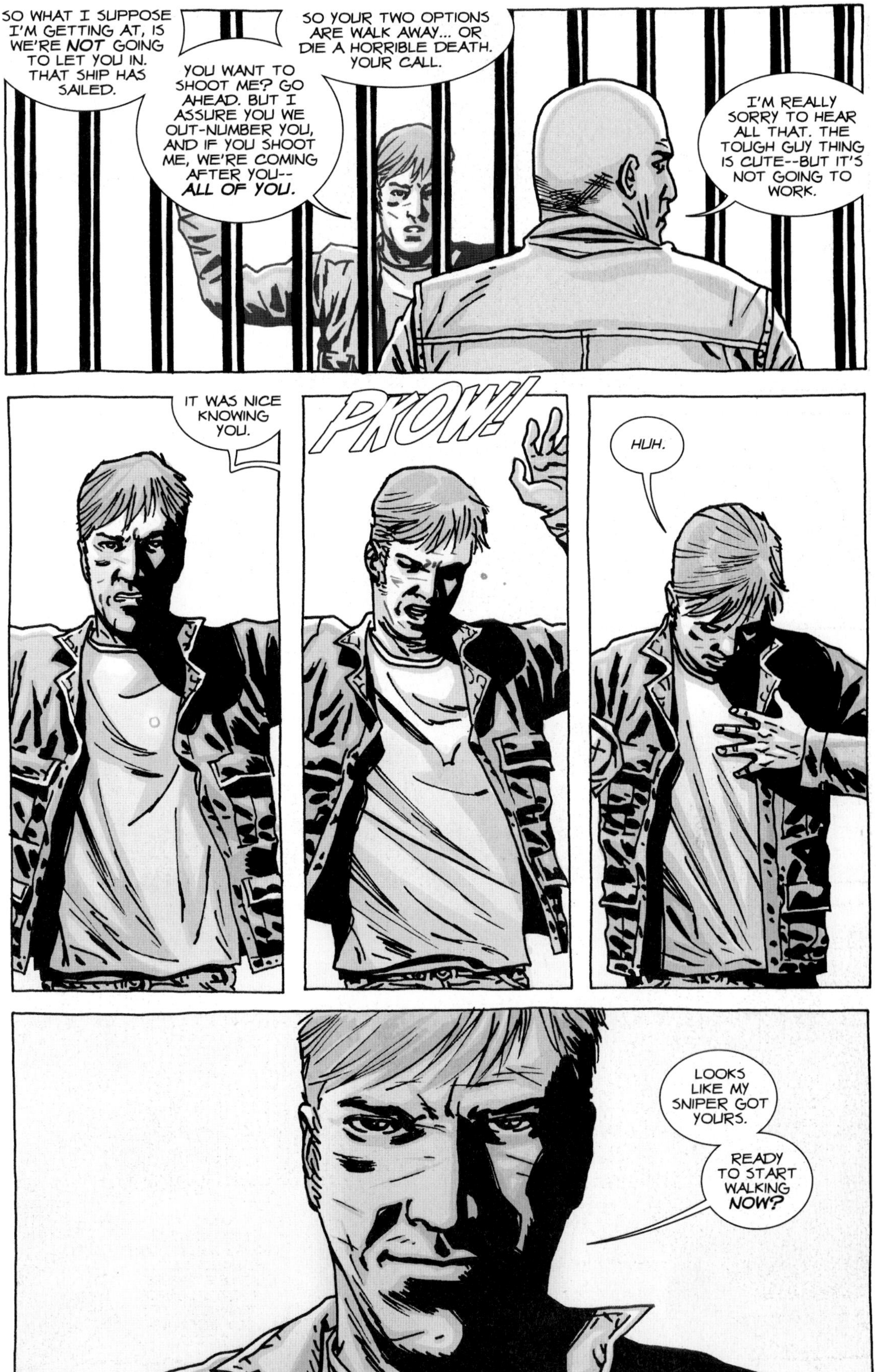

SO WHAT I SUPPOSE I'M GETTING AT, IS WE'RE NOT GOING TO LET YOU IN. THAT SHIP HAS SAILED.
SO YOUR TWO OPTIONS ARE WALK AWAY... OR DIE A HORRIBLE DEATH. YOUR CALL.
YOU WANT TO SHOOT ME? GO AHEAD. BUT I ASSURE YOU WE OUT-NUMBER YOU, AND IF YOU SHOOT ME, WE'RE COMING AFTER YOU-- ALL OF YOU.
I'M REALLY SORRY TO HEAR ALL THAT. THE TOUGH GUY THING IS CUTE--BUT IT'S NOT GOING TO WORK.
IT WAS NICE KNOWING YOU.
PKOW!
HUH.
LOOKS LIKE MY SNIPER GOT YOURS.
READY TO START WALKING NOW?

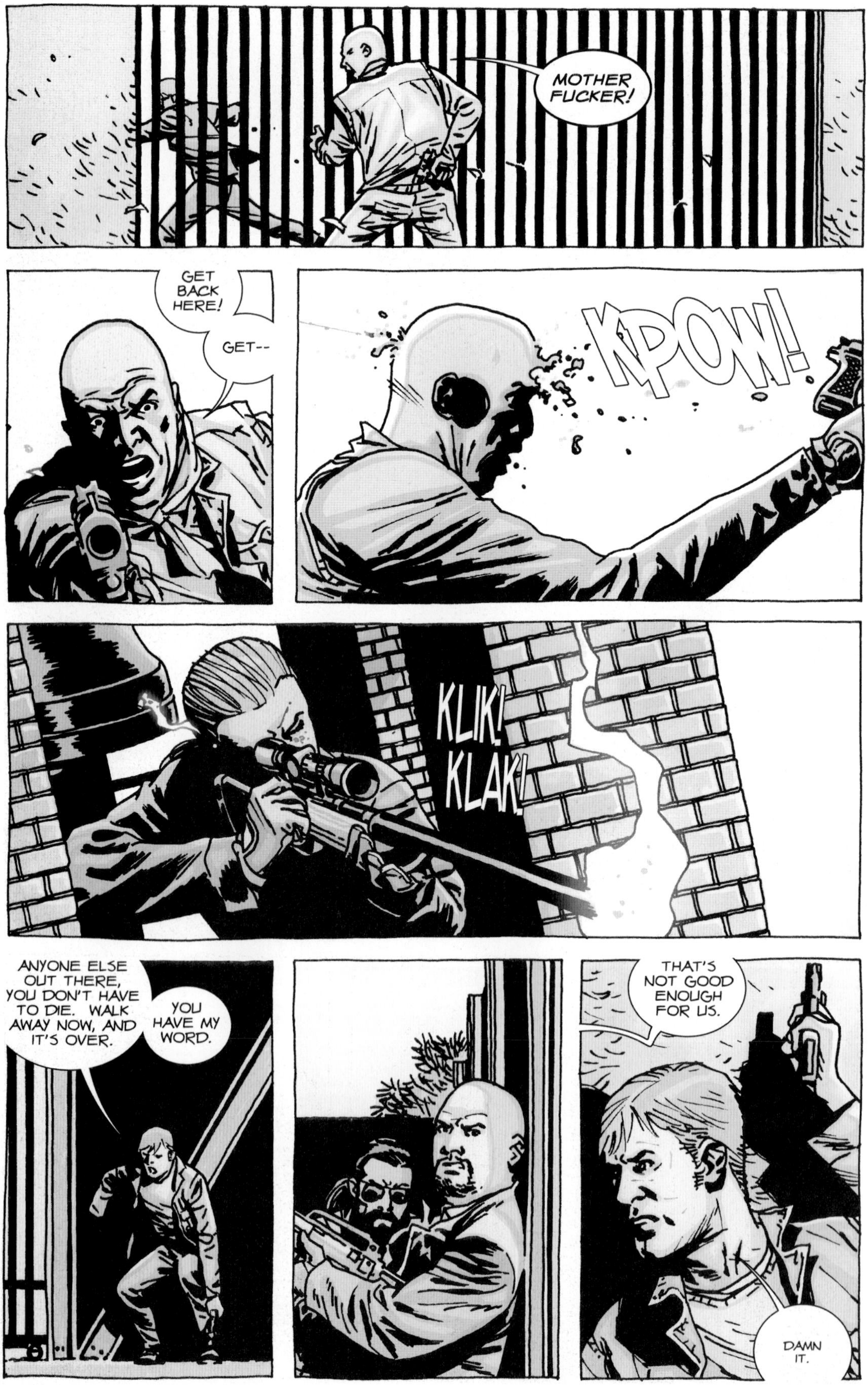
MOTHER FUCKER!
GET BACK HERE!
GET--
KPOW!
KLIK! KLAK!
ANYONE ELSE OUT THERE, YOU DON'T HAVE TO DIE. WALK AWAY NOW, AND IT'S OVER.
YOU HAVE MY WORD.
THAT'S NOT GOOD ENOUGH FOR US.
DAMN IT.

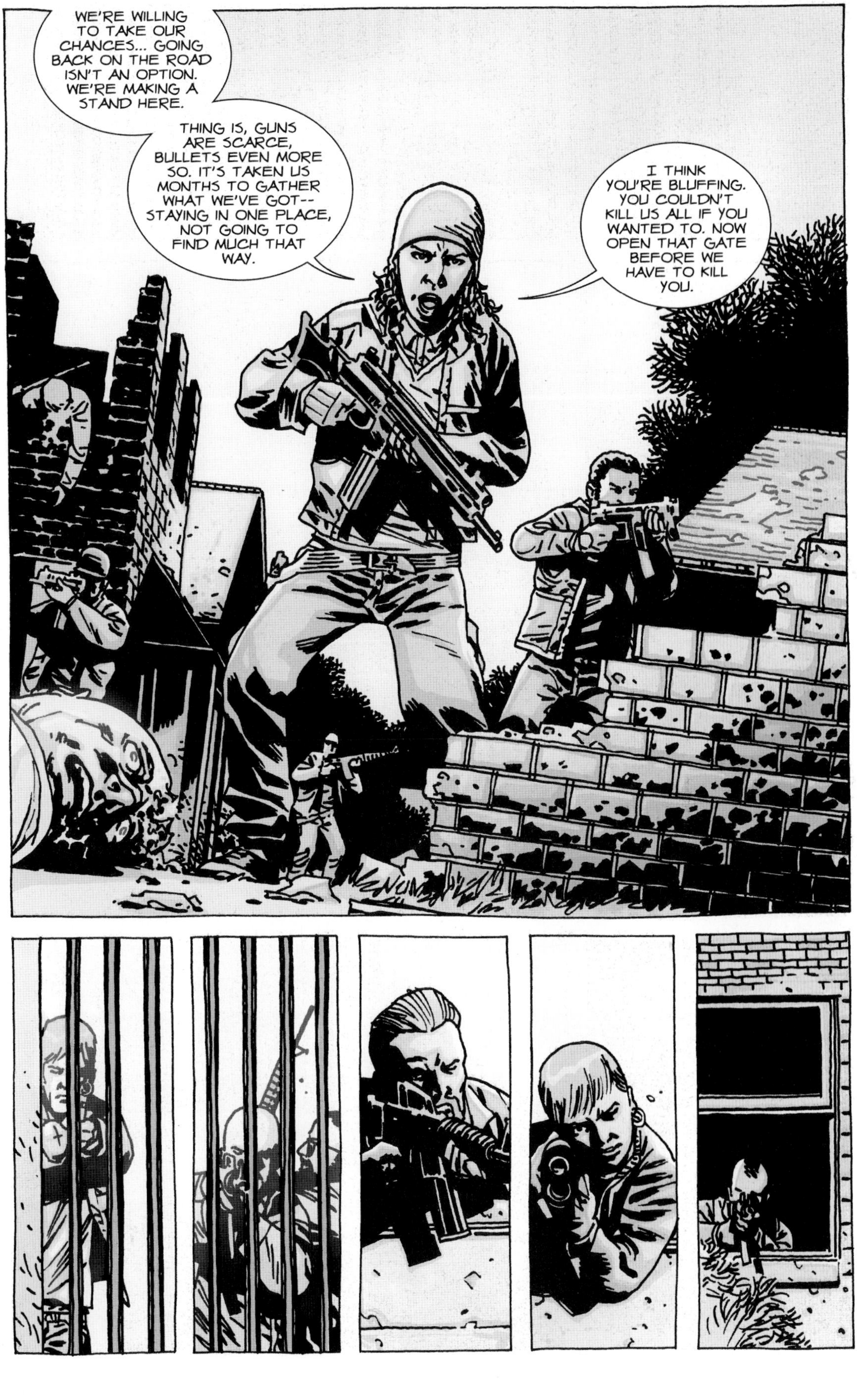
WE'RE WILLING TO TAKE OUR CHANCES... GOING BACK ON THE ROAD ISN'T AN OPTION. WE'RE MAKING A STAND HERE.
THING IS, GUNS ARE SCARCE, BULLETS EVEN MORE SO. IT'S TAKEN US MONTHS TO GATHER WHAT WE'VE GOT-- STAYING IN ONE PLACE, NOT GOING TO FIND MUCH THAT WAY.
I THINK YOU'RE BLUFFING. YOU COULDN'T KILL US ALL IF YOU WANTED TO. NOW OPEN THAT GATE BEFORE WE HAVE TO KILL YOU.

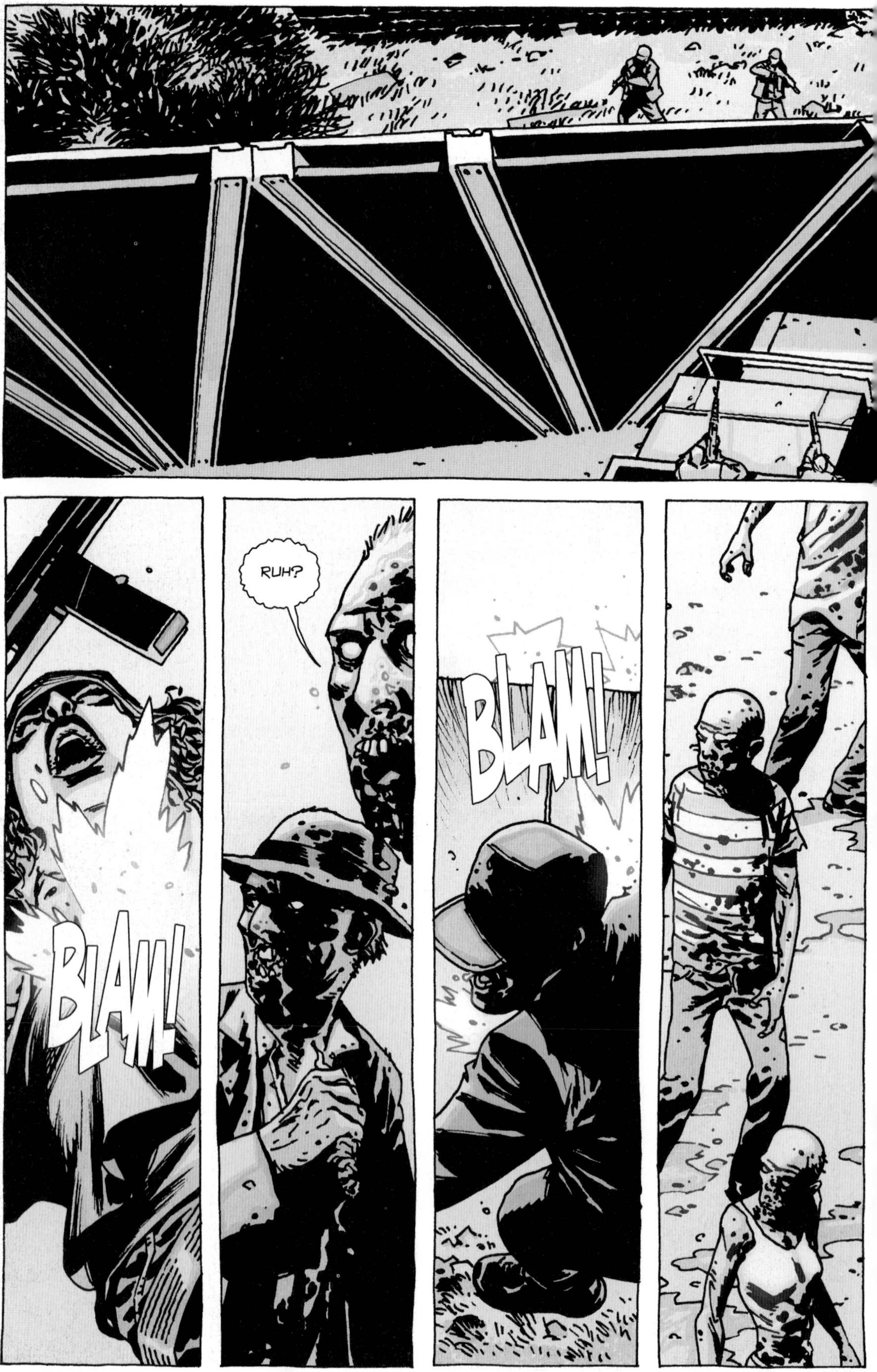
BLAM!
RUH?
BLAM!

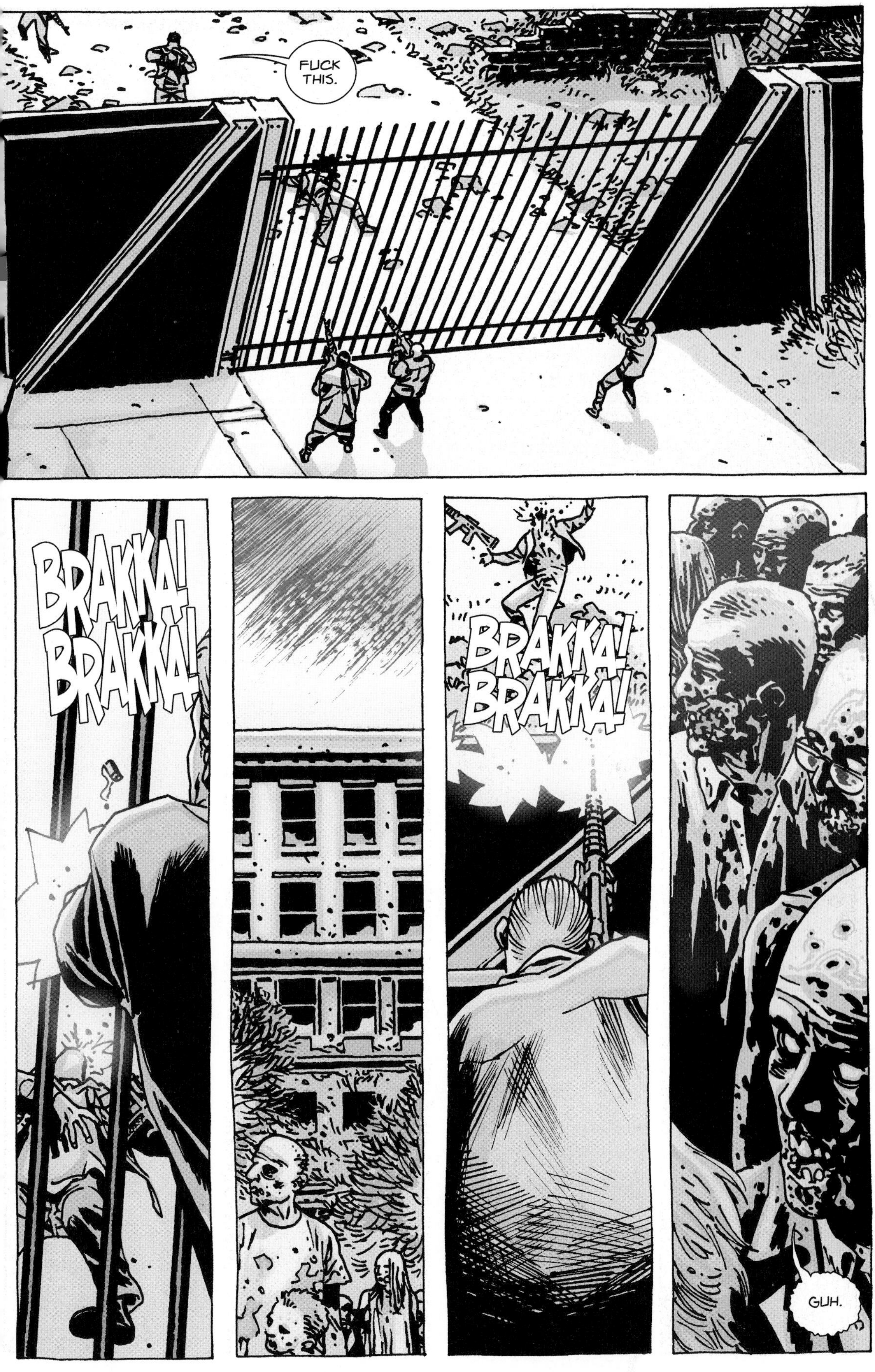
FUCK THIS.
BRAKKA! BRAKKA!
BRAKKA! BRAKKA!
GUH.

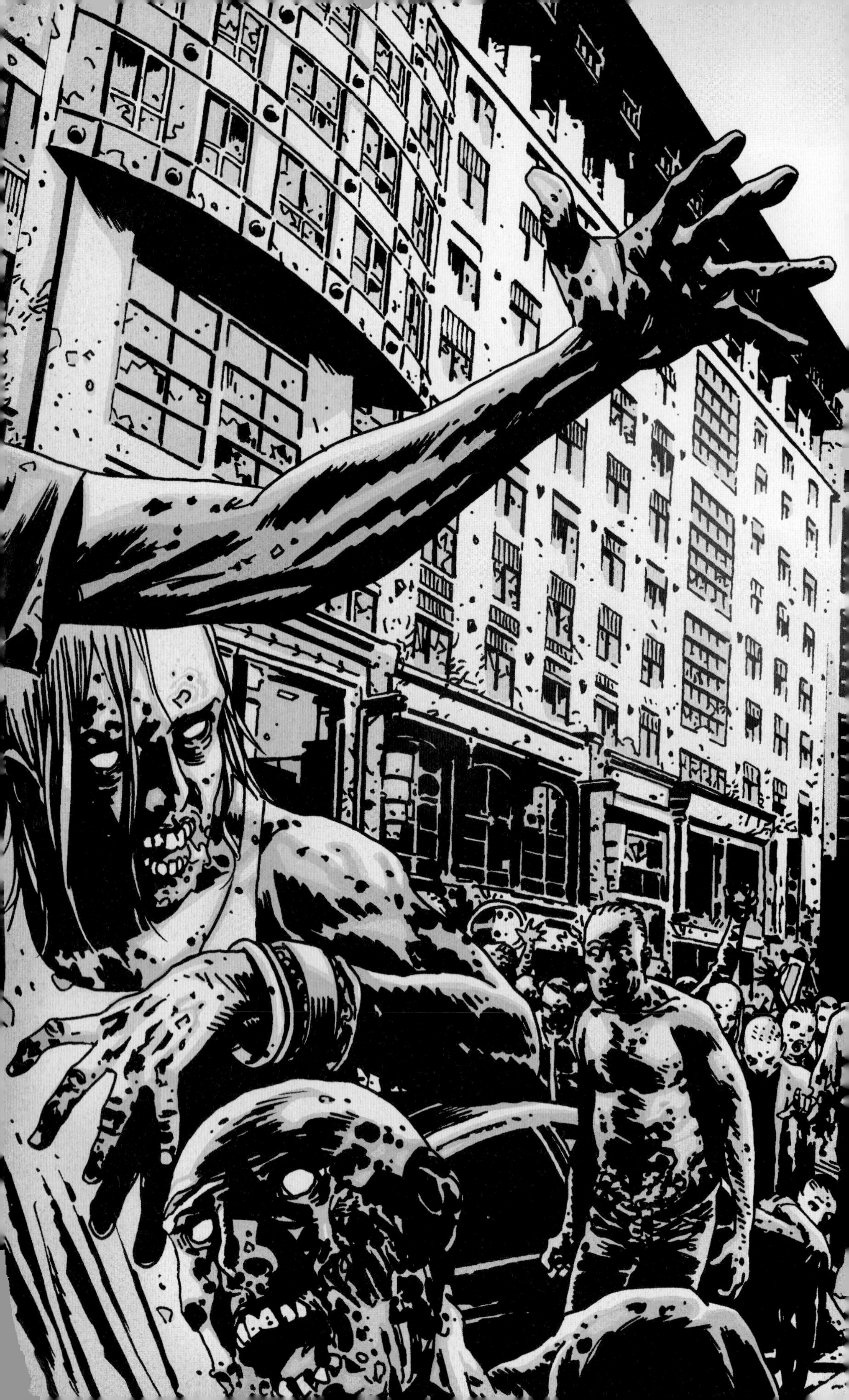

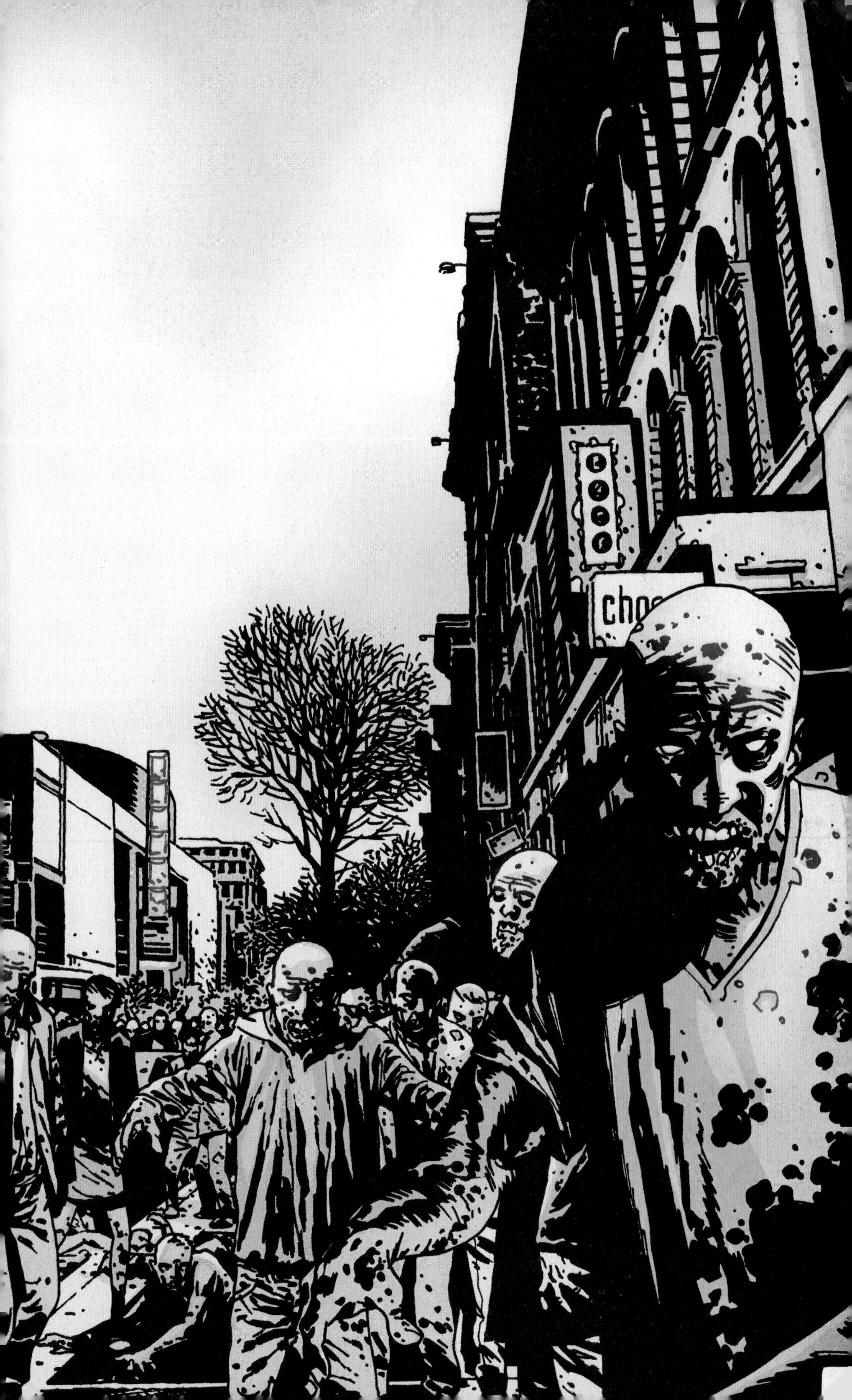

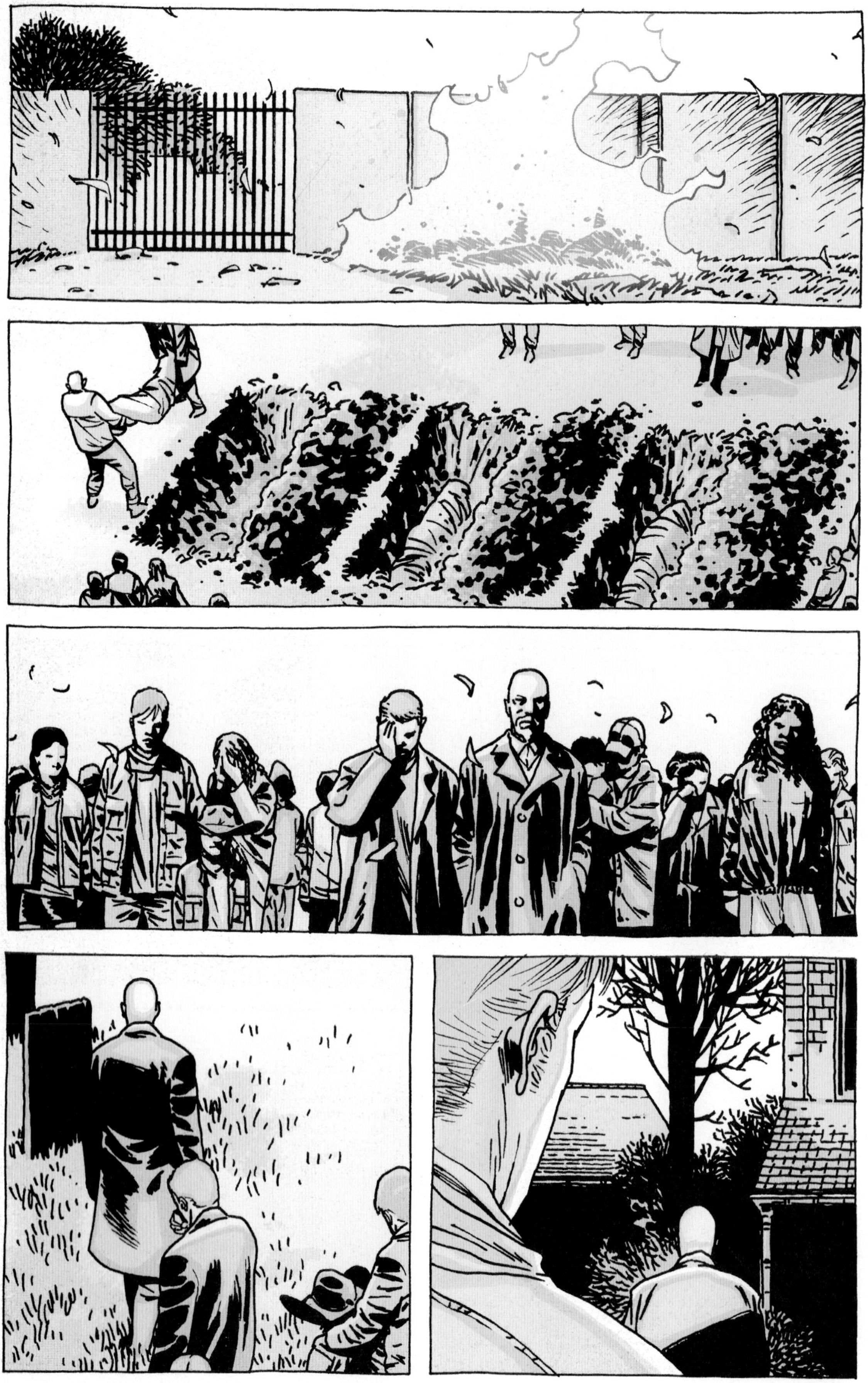

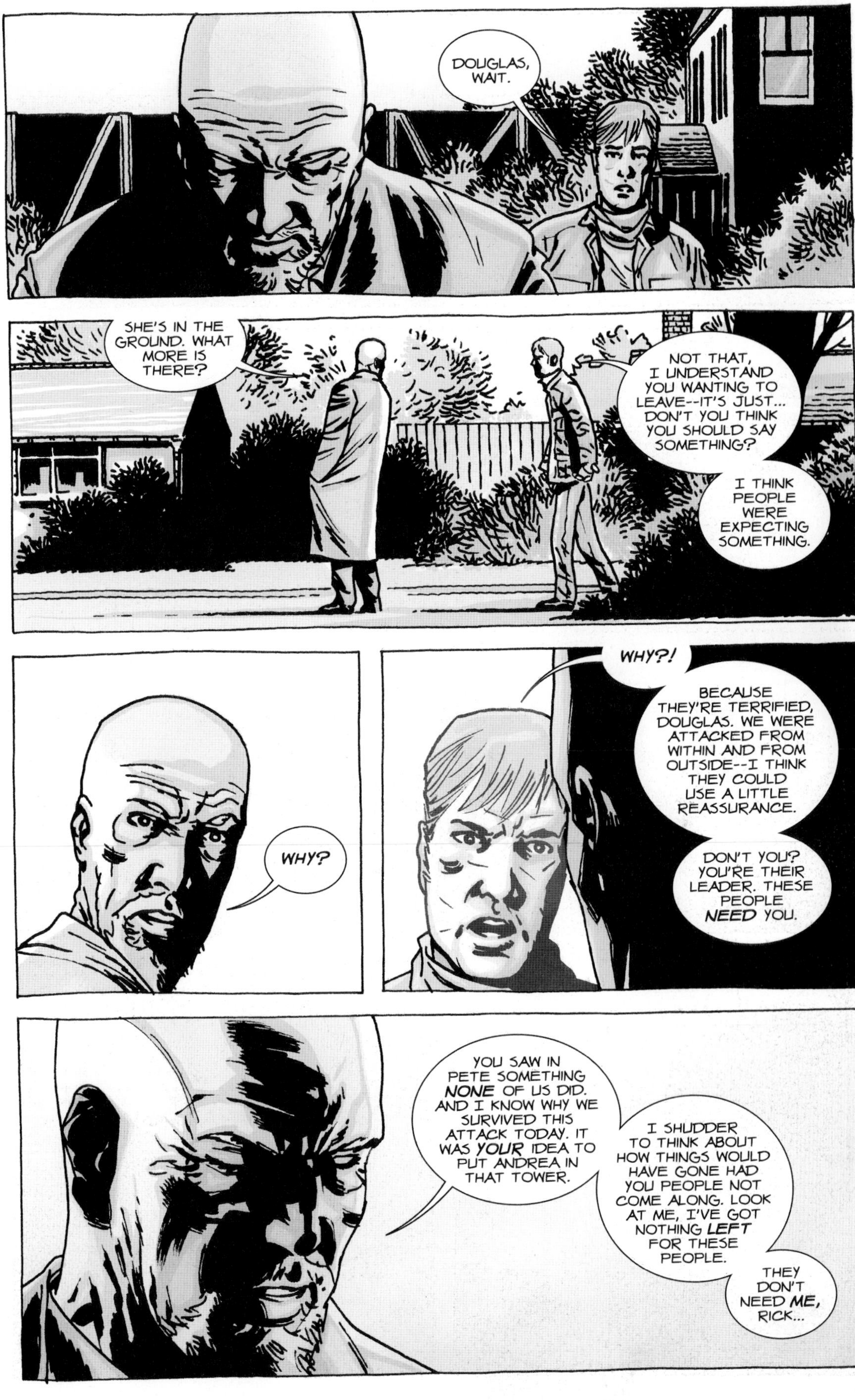
DOUGLAS, WAIT.
SHE'S IN THE GROUND. WHAT MORE IS THERE?
NOT THAT, I UNDERSTAND YOU WANTING TO LEAVE--IT'S JUST... DON'T YOU THINK YOU SHOULD SAY SOMETHING?
I THINK PEOPLE WERE EXPECTING SOMETHING.
WHY?
WHY?!
BECAUSE THEY'RE TERRIFIED, DOUGLAS. WE WERE ATTACKED FROM WITHIN AND FROM OUTSIDE--I THINK THEY COULD USE A LITTLE REASSURANCE.
DON'T YOU? YOU'RE THEIR LEADER. THESE PEOPLE **NEED** YOU.
YOU SAW IN PETE SOMETHING **NONE** OF US DID. AND I KNOW WHY WE SURVIVED THIS ATTACK TODAY. IT WAS **YOUR** IDEA TO PUT ANDREA IN THAT TOWER.
I SHUDDER TO THINK ABOUT HOW THINGS WOULD HAVE GONE HAD YOU PEOPLE NOT COME ALONG. LOOK AT ME, I'VE GOT NOTHING **LEFT** FOR THESE PEOPLE.
THEY DON'T NEED **ME,** RICK...

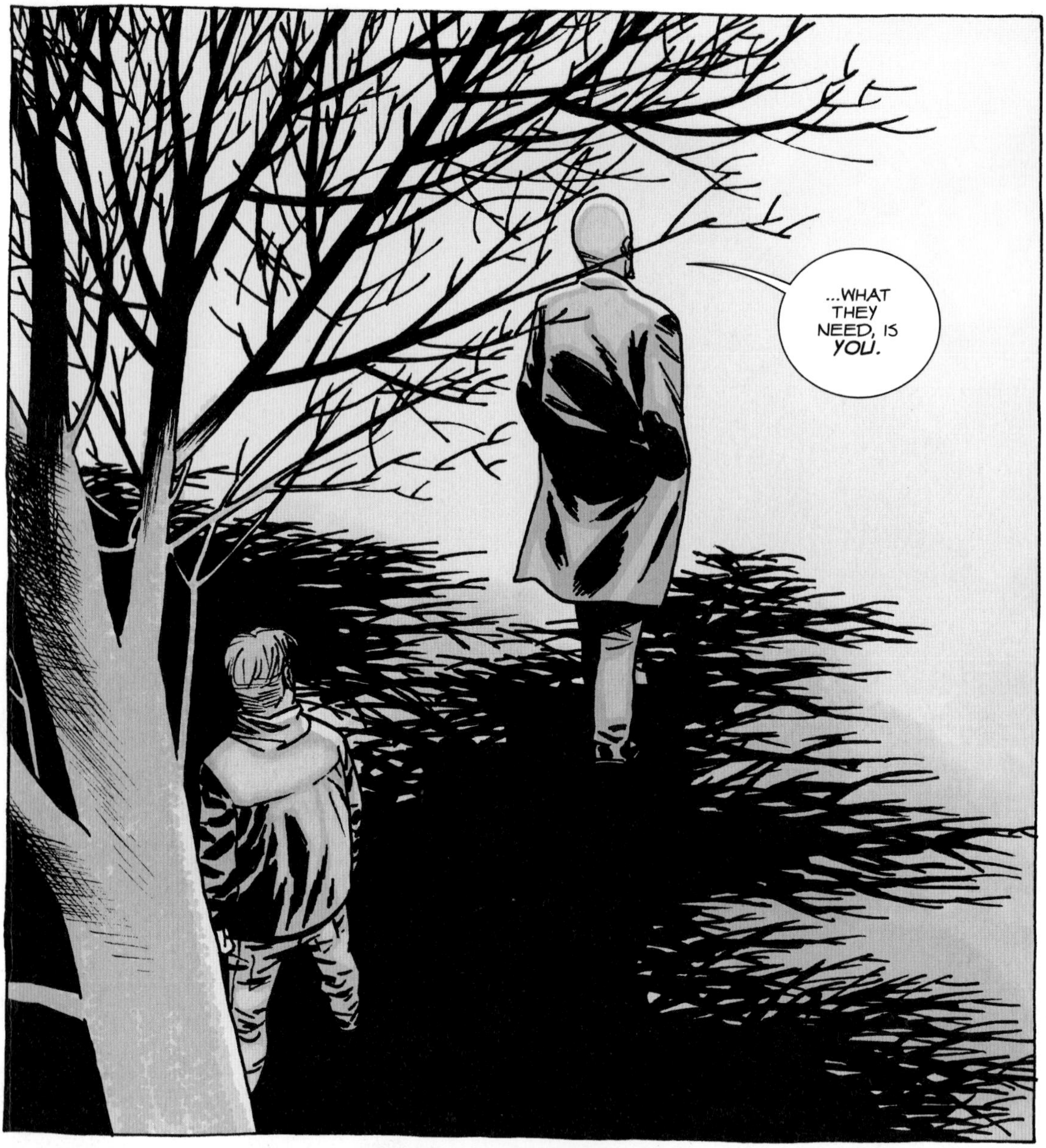
...WHAT THEY NEED, IS YOU.

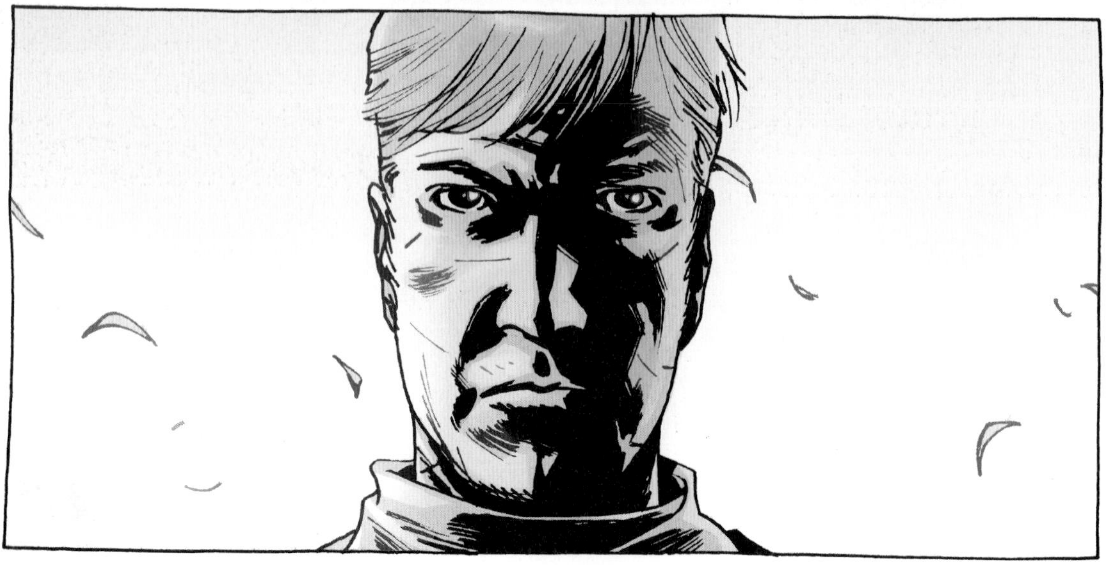

Chapter Fourteen:
No Way Out

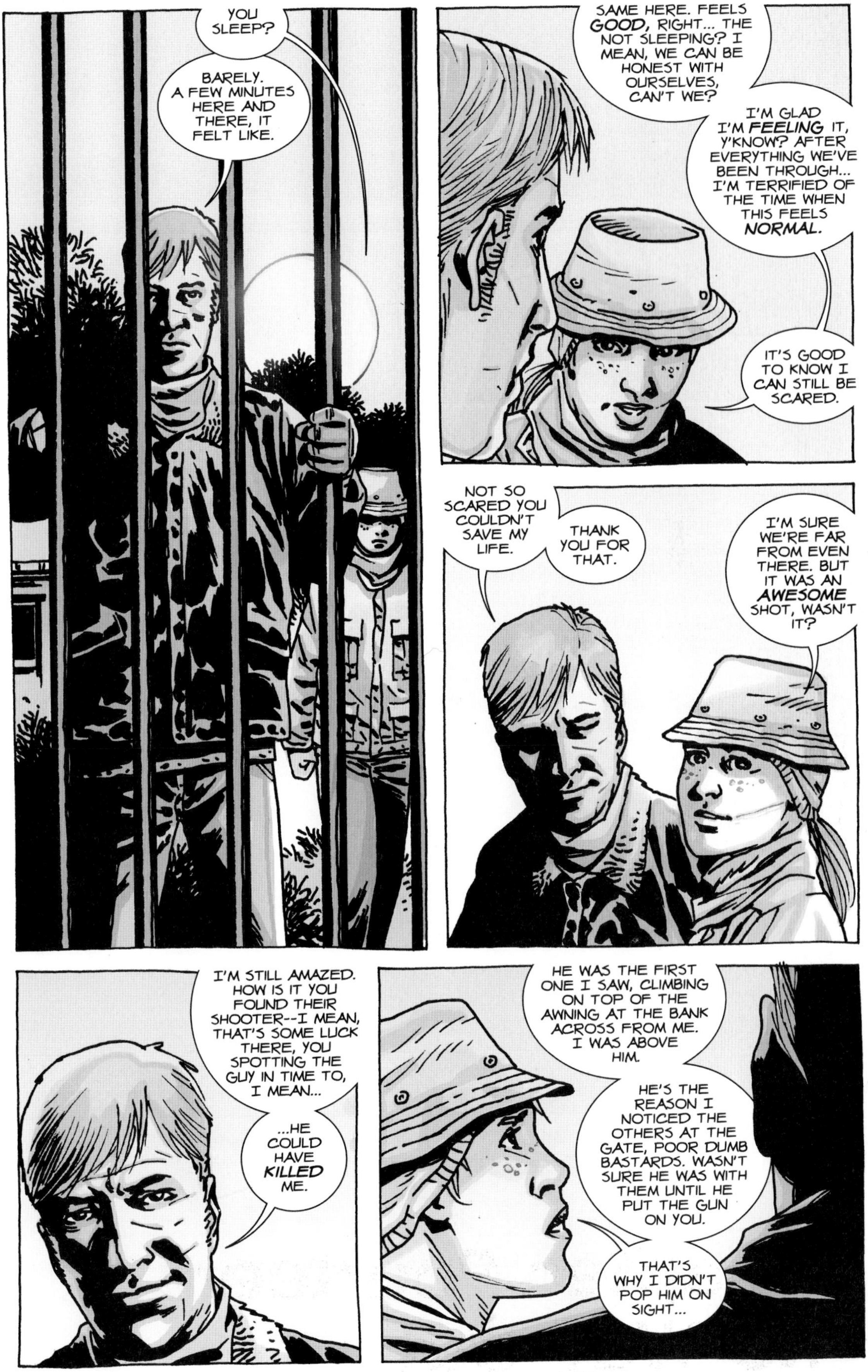
YOU SLEEP?
BARELY. A FEW MINUTES HERE AND THERE, IT FELT LIKE.
SAME HERE. FEELS GOOD, RIGHT... THE NOT SLEEPING? I MEAN, WE CAN BE HONEST WITH OURSELVES, CAN'T WE?
I'M GLAD I'M FEELING IT, Y'KNOW? AFTER EVERYTHING WE'VE BEEN THROUGH... I'M TERRIFIED OF THE TIME WHEN THIS FEELS NORMAL.
IT'S GOOD TO KNOW I CAN STILL BE SCARED.
NOT SO SCARED YOU COULDN'T SAVE MY LIFE.
THANK YOU FOR THAT.
I'M SURE WE'RE FAR FROM EVEN THERE. BUT IT WAS AN AWESOME SHOT, WASN'T IT?
I'M STILL AMAZED. HOW IS IT YOU FOUND THEIR SHOOTER--I MEAN, THAT'S SOME LUCK THERE, YOU SPOTTING THE GUY IN TIME TO, I MEAN...
...HE COULD HAVE KILLED ME.
HE WAS THE FIRST ONE I SAW, CLIMBING ON TOP OF THE AWNING AT THE BANK ACROSS FROM ME. I WAS ABOVE HIM.
HE'S THE REASON I NOTICED THE OTHERS AT THE GATE, POOR DUMB BASTARDS. WASN'T SURE HE WAS WITH THEM UNTIL HE PUT THE GUN ON YOU.
THAT'S WHY I DIDN'T POP HIM ON SIGHT...

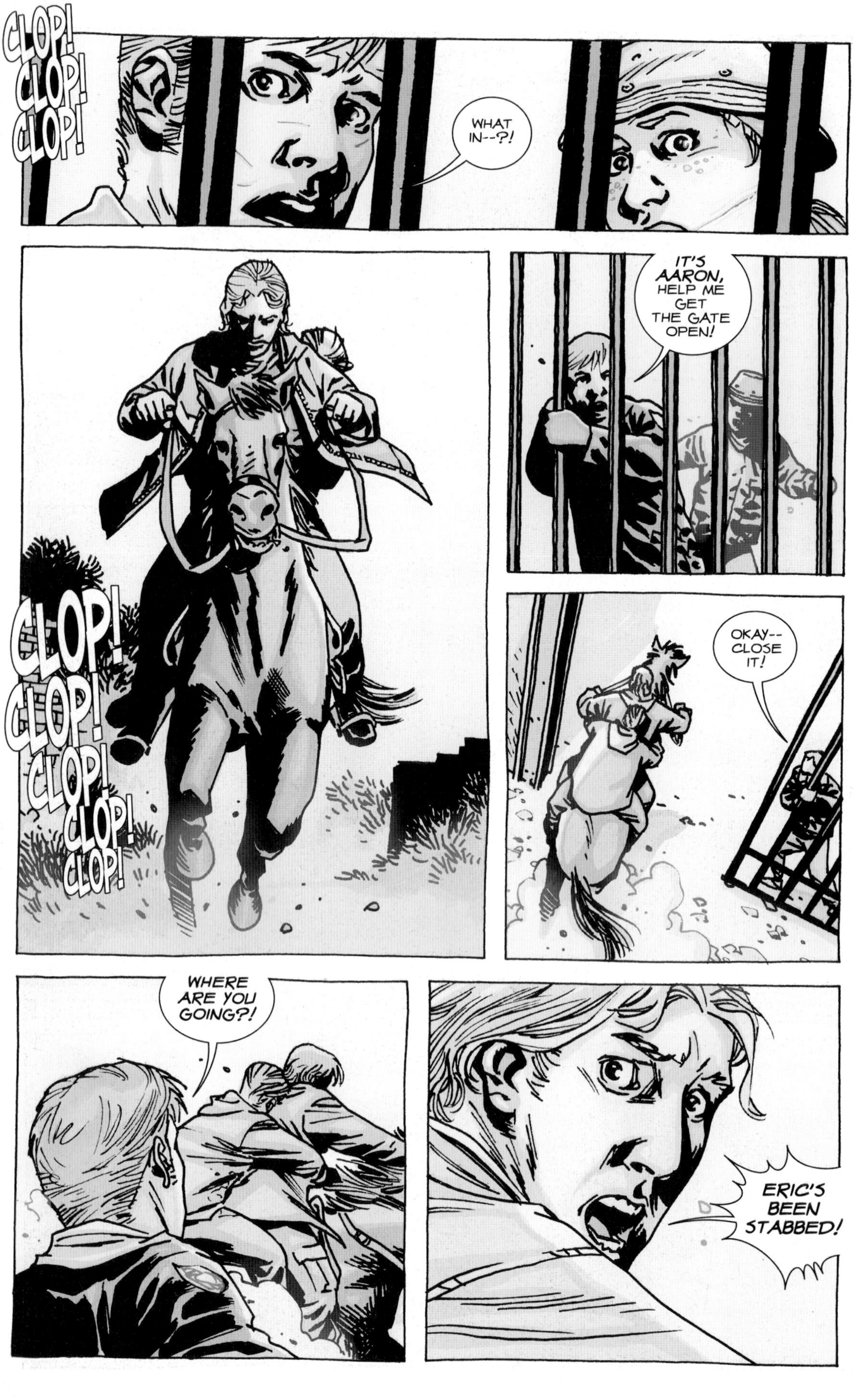

CLOP! CLOP! CLOP!
WHAT IN--?!
CLOP! CLOP! CLOP! CLOP! CLOP!
IT'S AARON, HELP ME GET THE GATE OPEN!
OKAY-- CLOSE IT!
WHERE ARE YOU GOING?!
ERIC'S BEEN STABBED!

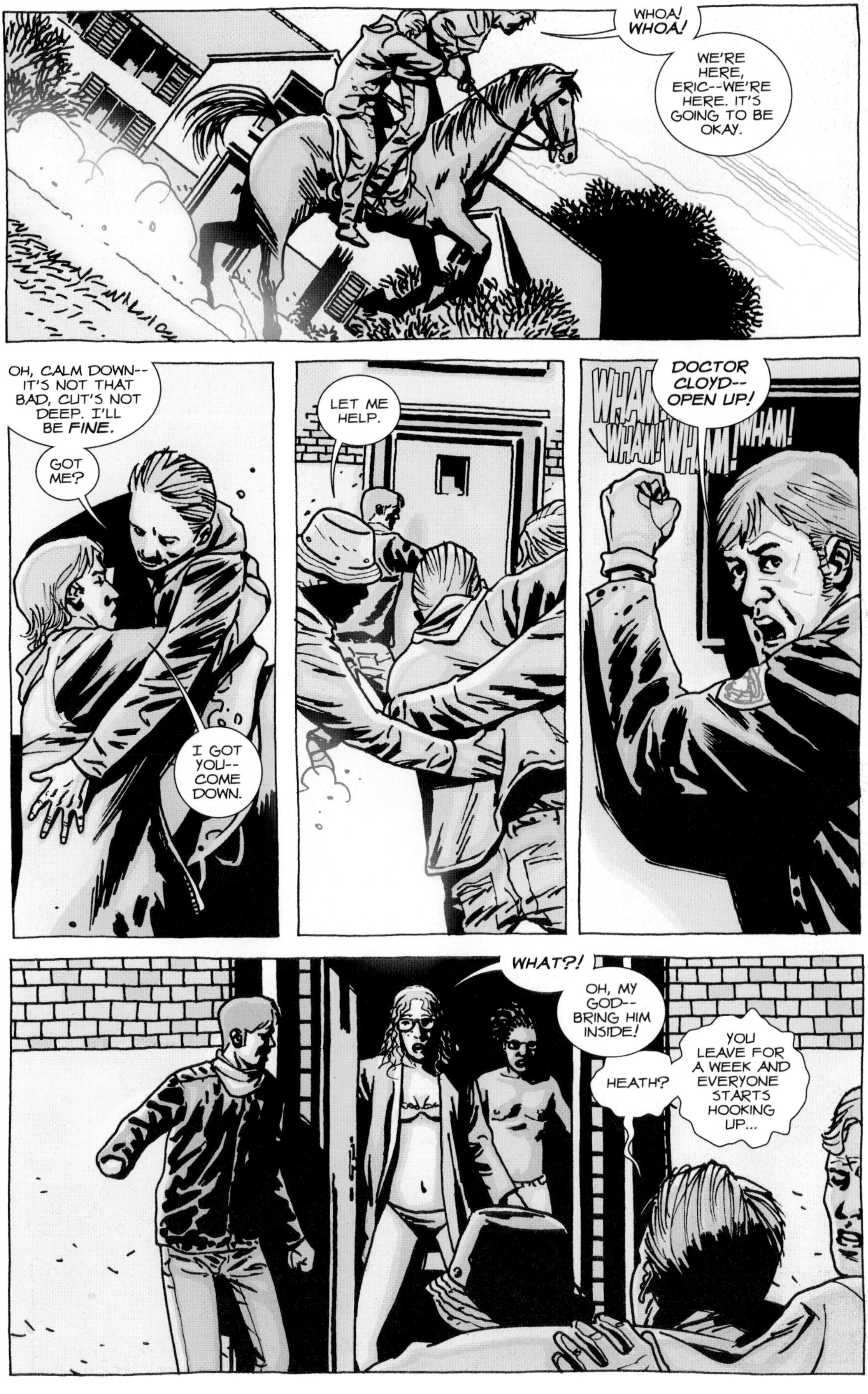

WHOA! WHOA!
WE'RE HERE, ERIC--WE'RE HERE. IT'S GOING TO BE OKAY.
OH, CALM DOWN--IT'S NOT THAT BAD, CUT'S NOT DEEP. I'LL BE FINE.
GOT ME?
I GOT YOU--COME DOWN.
LET ME HELP.
DOCTOR CLOYD--OPEN UP!
WHAM! WHAM! WHAM! WHAM!
WHAT?!
OH, MY GOD--BRING HIM INSIDE!
HEATH?
YOU LEAVE FOR A WEEK AND EVERYONE STARTS HOOKING UP...

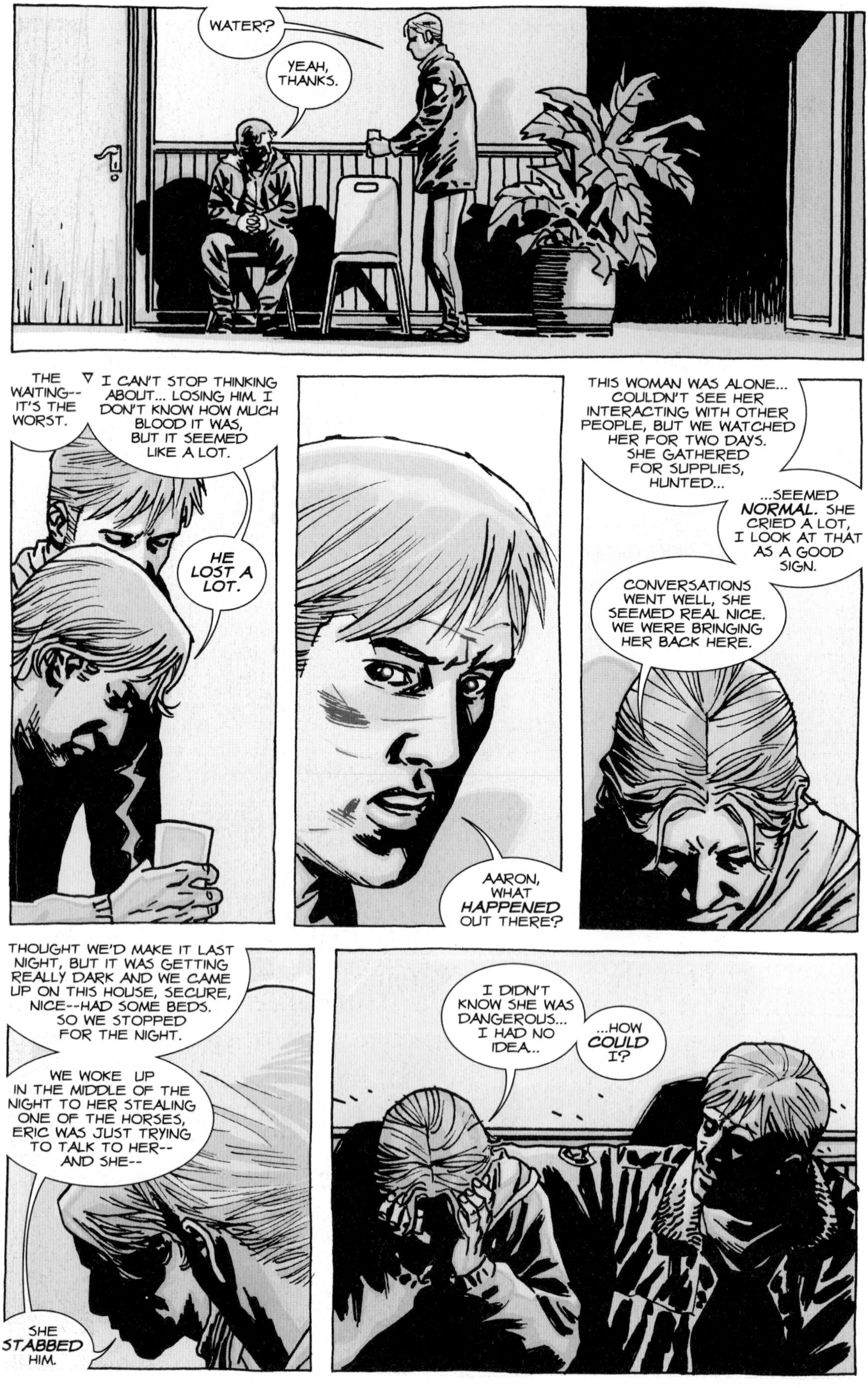
WATER?
YEAH, THANKS.
THE WAITING-- IT'S THE WORST.
I CAN'T STOP THINKING ABOUT... LOSING HIM. I DON'T KNOW HOW MUCH BLOOD IT WAS, BUT IT SEEMED LIKE A LOT.
HE LOST A LOT.
AARON, WHAT HAPPENED OUT THERE?
THIS WOMAN WAS ALONE... COULDN'T SEE HER INTERACTING WITH OTHER PEOPLE, BUT WE WATCHED HER FOR TWO DAYS. SHE GATHERED FOR SUPPLIES, HUNTED...
...SEEMED NORMAL. SHE CRIED A LOT, I LOOK AT THAT AS A GOOD SIGN.
CONVERSATIONS WENT WELL, SHE SEEMED REAL NICE. WE WERE BRINGING HER BACK HERE.
THOUGHT WE'D MAKE IT LAST NIGHT, BUT IT WAS GETTING REALLY DARK AND WE CAME UP ON THIS HOUSE, SECURE, NICE--HAD SOME BEDS. SO WE STOPPED FOR THE NIGHT.
WE WOKE UP IN THE MIDDLE OF THE NIGHT TO HER STEALING ONE OF THE HORSES, ERIC WAS JUST TRYING TO TALK TO HER-- AND SHE--
SHE STABBED HIM.
I DIDN'T KNOW SHE WAS DANGEROUS... I HAD NO IDEA...
...HOW COULD I?

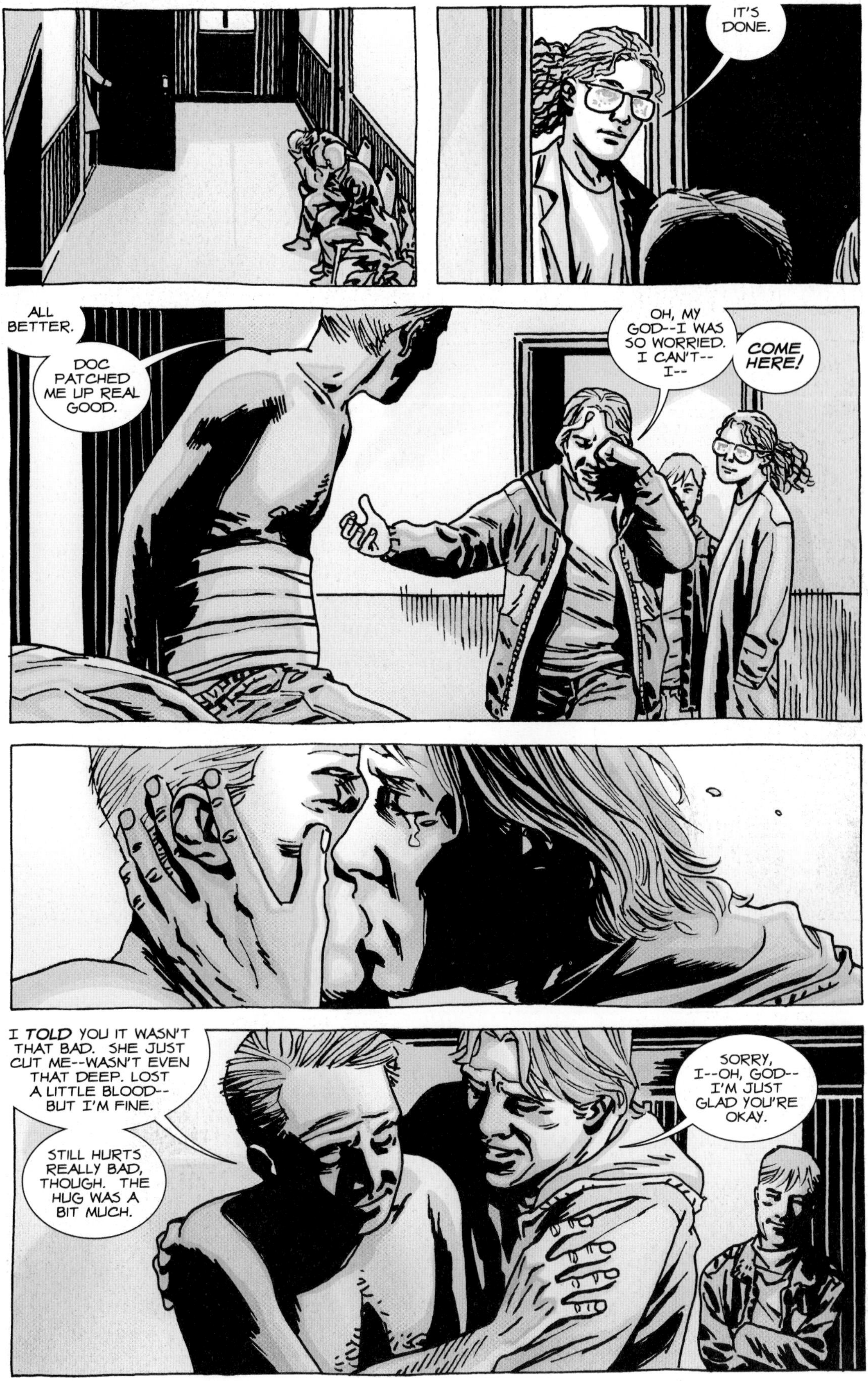
IT'S DONE.
ALL BETTER.
DOC PATCHED ME UP REAL GOOD.
OH, MY GOD--I WAS SO WORRIED. I CAN'T-- I--
COME HERE!
I TOLD YOU IT WASN'T THAT BAD. SHE JUST CUT ME--WASN'T EVEN THAT DEEP. LOST A LITTLE BLOOD--BUT I'M FINE.
STILL HURTS REALLY BAD, THOUGH. THE HUG WAS A BIT MUCH.
SORRY, I--OH, GOD-- I'M JUST GLAD YOU'RE OKAY.

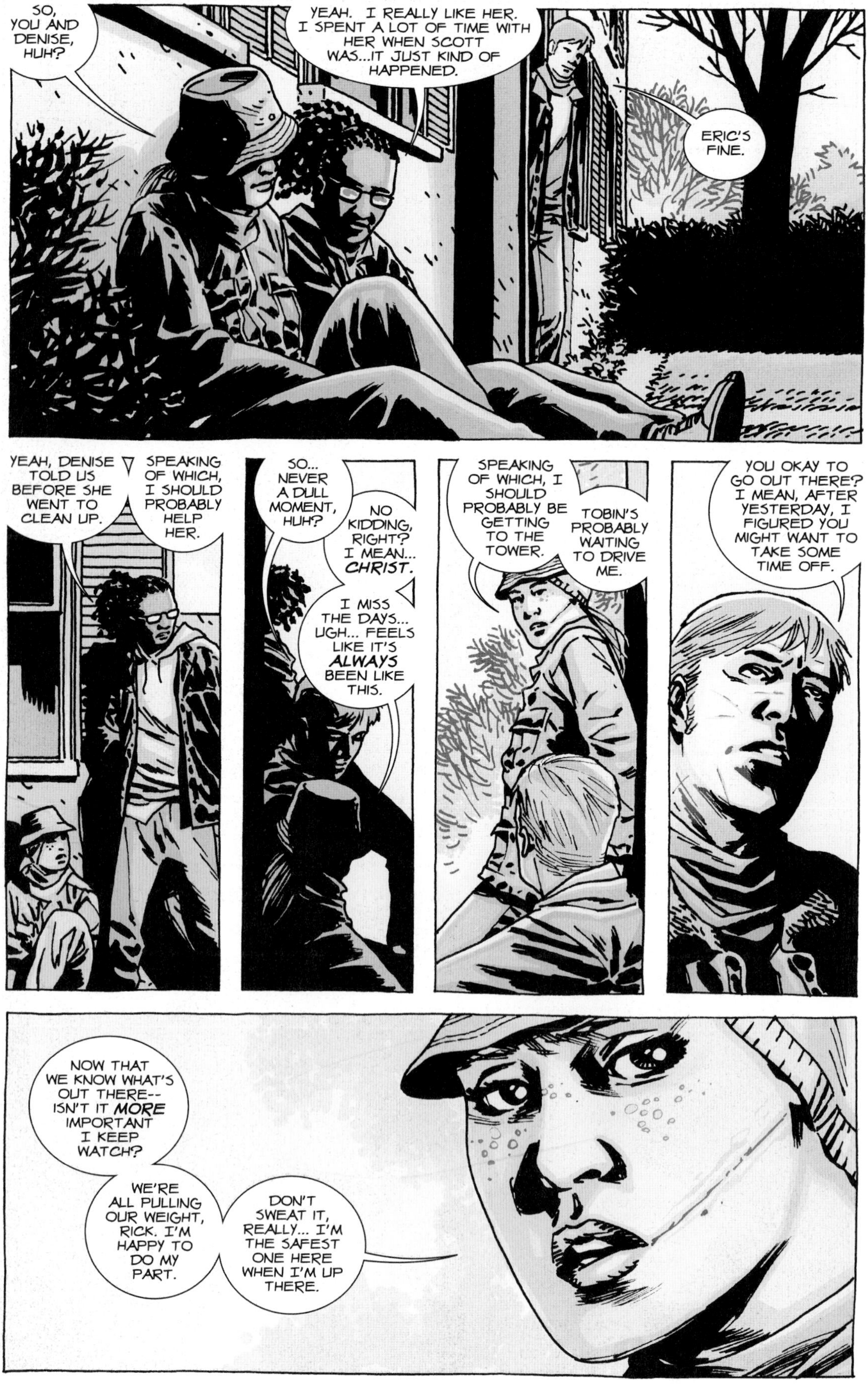
SO, YOU AND DENISE, HUH?
YEAH. I REALLY LIKE HER. I SPENT A LOT OF TIME WITH HER WHEN SCOTT WAS...IT JUST KIND OF HAPPENED.
ERIC'S FINE.
YEAH, DENISE TOLD US BEFORE SHE WENT TO CLEAN UP.
SPEAKING OF WHICH, I SHOULD PROBABLY HELP HER.
SO... NEVER A DULL MOMENT, HUH?
NO KIDDING, RIGHT? I MEAN... CHRIST.
I MISS THE DAYS... UGH... FEELS LIKE IT'S ALWAYS BEEN LIKE THIS.
SPEAKING OF WHICH, I SHOULD PROBABLY BE GETTING TO THE TOWER.
TOBIN'S PROBABLY WAITING TO DRIVE ME.
YOU OKAY TO GO OUT THERE? I MEAN, AFTER YESTERDAY, I FIGURED YOU MIGHT WANT TO TAKE SOME TIME OFF.
NOW THAT WE KNOW WHAT'S OUT THERE-- ISN'T IT MORE IMPORTANT I KEEP WATCH?
WE'RE ALL PULLING OUR WEIGHT, RICK. I'M HAPPY TO DO MY PART.
DON'T SWEAT IT, REALLY... I'M THE SAFEST ONE HERE WHEN I'M UP THERE.

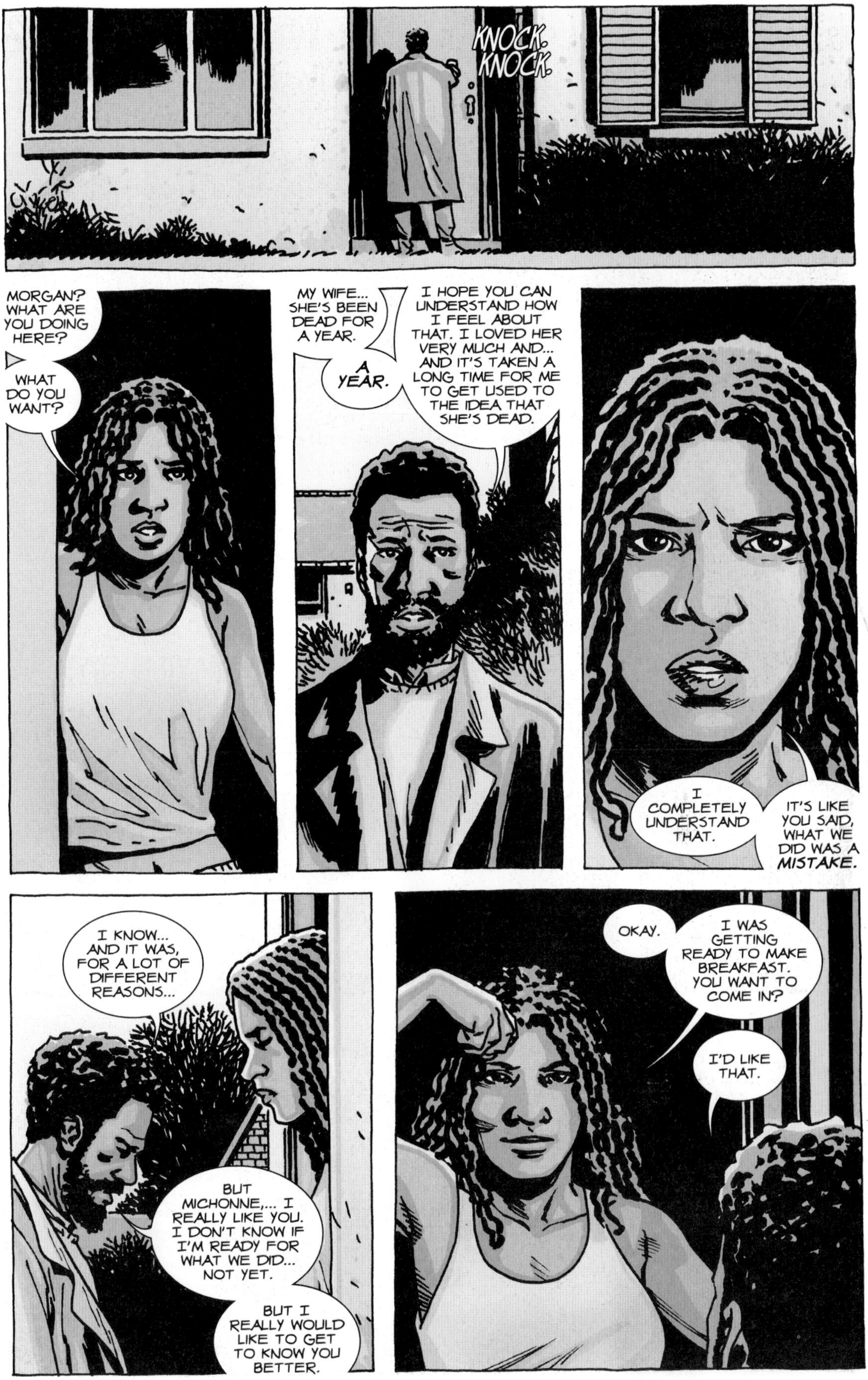
KNOCK. KNOCK.
MORGAN? WHAT ARE YOU DOING HERE?
WHAT DO YOU WANT?
MY WIFE... SHE'S BEEN DEAD FOR A YEAR.
A YEAR.
I HOPE YOU CAN UNDERSTAND HOW I FEEL ABOUT THAT. I LOVED HER VERY MUCH AND... AND IT'S TAKEN A LONG TIME FOR ME TO GET USED TO THE IDEA THAT SHE'S DEAD.
I COMPLETELY UNDERSTAND THAT.
IT'S LIKE YOU SAID, WHAT WE DID WAS A MISTAKE.
I KNOW... AND IT WAS, FOR A LOT OF DIFFERENT REASONS...
BUT MICHONNE,... I REALLY LIKE YOU. I DON'T KNOW IF I'M READY FOR WHAT WE DID... NOT YET.
BUT I REALLY WOULD LIKE TO GET TO KNOW YOU BETTER.
OKAY.
I WAS GETTING READY TO MAKE BREAKFAST. YOU WANT TO COME IN?
I'D LIKE THAT.

MORNING, SON. WHEN'D YOU GET UP?

I GOT UP WHEN YOU LEFT. I HEARD YOU CLOSING THE DOOR... WHERE'D YOU GO?

DIDN'T SLEEP WELL LAST NIGHT, WENT TO CHECK THE GATE, SEE HOW THINGS WERE ON THE OTHER SIDE OF THE FENCE.

YOU OKAY?

YEAH. WHY?

WHY? WE WERE ATTACKED YESTERDAY, I THOUGHT YOU MIGHT BE SCARED.

WELL, I'M NOT.

WHAT HAPPENED WAS A GOOD THING. NOW MAYBE EVERYONE WILL STOP PRETENDING WE'RE ALL SAFE.

CARL, I--

YEAH, DAD?

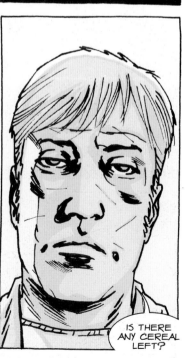

IS THERE ANY CEREAL LEFT?

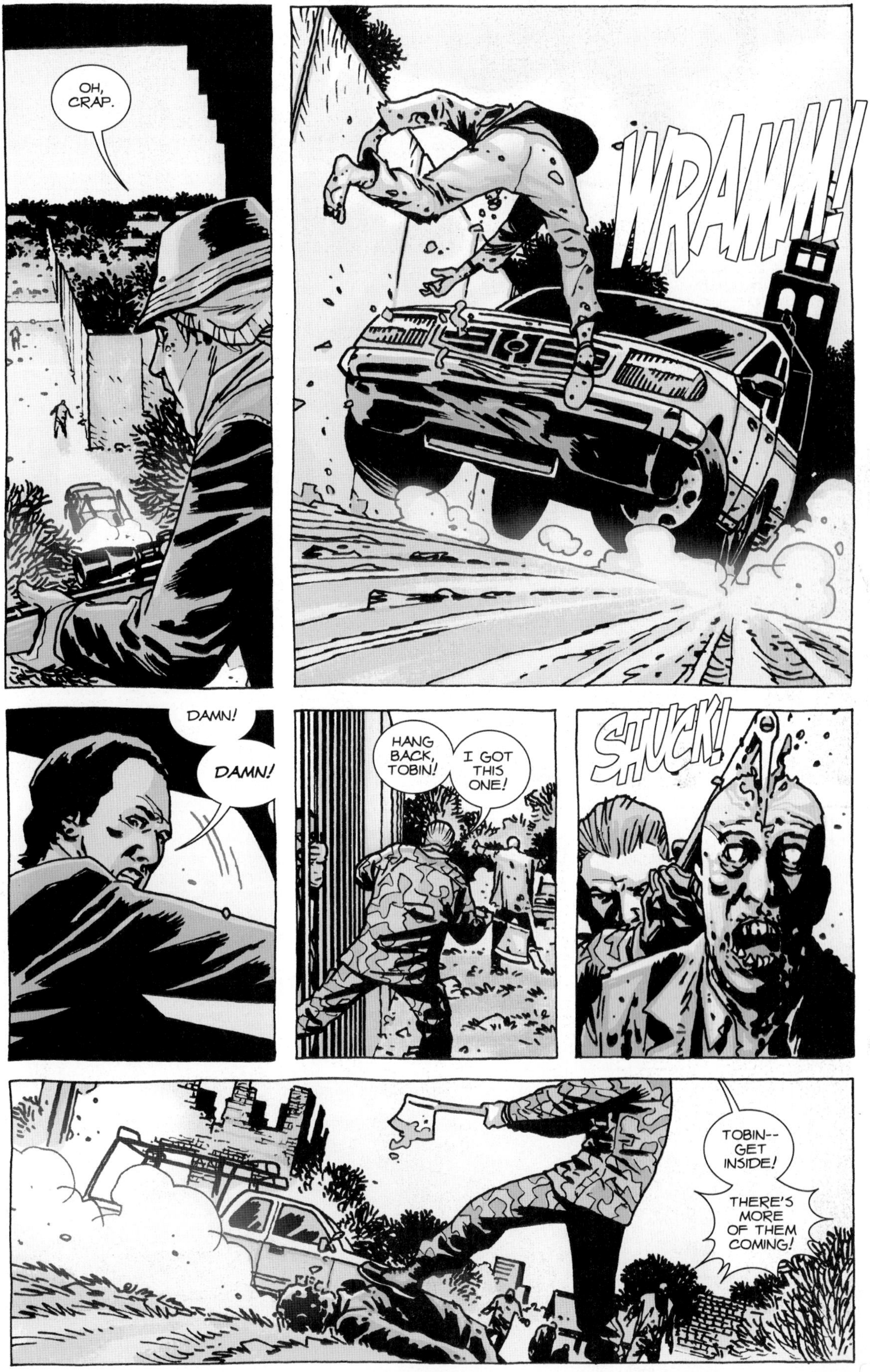
OH, CRAP.
WRAMM!
DAMN!
DAMN!
HANG BACK, TOBIN!
I GOT THIS ONE!
SHUCK!
TOBIN-- GET INSIDE!
THERE'S MORE OF THEM COMING!

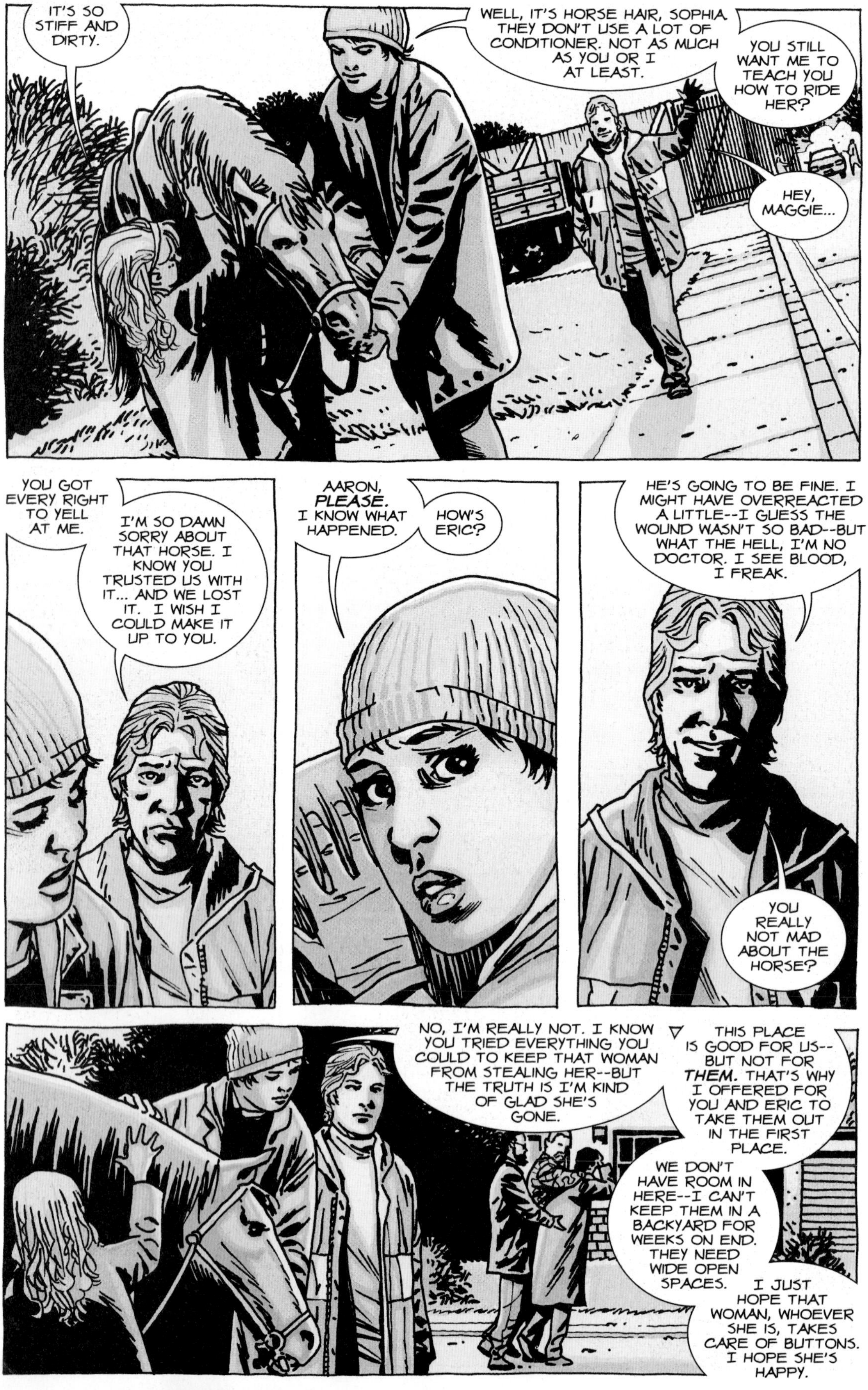
IT'S SO STIFF AND DIRTY.
WELL, IT'S HORSE HAIR, SOPHIA. THEY DON'T USE A LOT OF CONDITIONER. NOT AS MUCH AS YOU OR I AT LEAST.
YOU STILL WANT ME TO TEACH YOU HOW TO RIDE HER?
HEY, MAGGIE...
YOU GOT EVERY RIGHT TO YELL AT ME.
I'M SO DAMN SORRY ABOUT THAT HORSE. I KNOW YOU TRUSTED US WITH IT... AND WE LOST IT. I WISH I COULD MAKE IT UP TO YOU.
AARON, PLEASE. I KNOW WHAT HAPPENED.
HOW'S ERIC?
HE'S GOING TO BE FINE. I MIGHT HAVE OVERREACTED A LITTLE--I GUESS THE WOUND WASN'T SO BAD--BUT WHAT THE HELL, I'M NO DOCTOR. I SEE BLOOD, I FREAK.
YOU REALLY NOT MAD ABOUT THE HORSE?
NO, I'M REALLY NOT. I KNOW YOU TRIED EVERYTHING YOU COULD TO KEEP THAT WOMAN FROM STEALING HER--BUT THE TRUTH IS I'M KIND OF GLAD SHE'S GONE.
THIS PLACE IS GOOD FOR US--BUT NOT FOR THEM. THAT'S WHY I OFFERED FOR YOU AND ERIC TO TAKE THEM OUT IN THE FIRST PLACE.
WE DON'T HAVE ROOM IN HERE--I CAN'T KEEP THEM IN A BACKYARD FOR WEEKS ON END. THEY NEED WIDE OPEN SPACES.
I JUST HOPE THAT WOMAN, WHOEVER SHE IS, TAKES CARE OF BUTTONS. I HOPE SHE'S HAPPY.

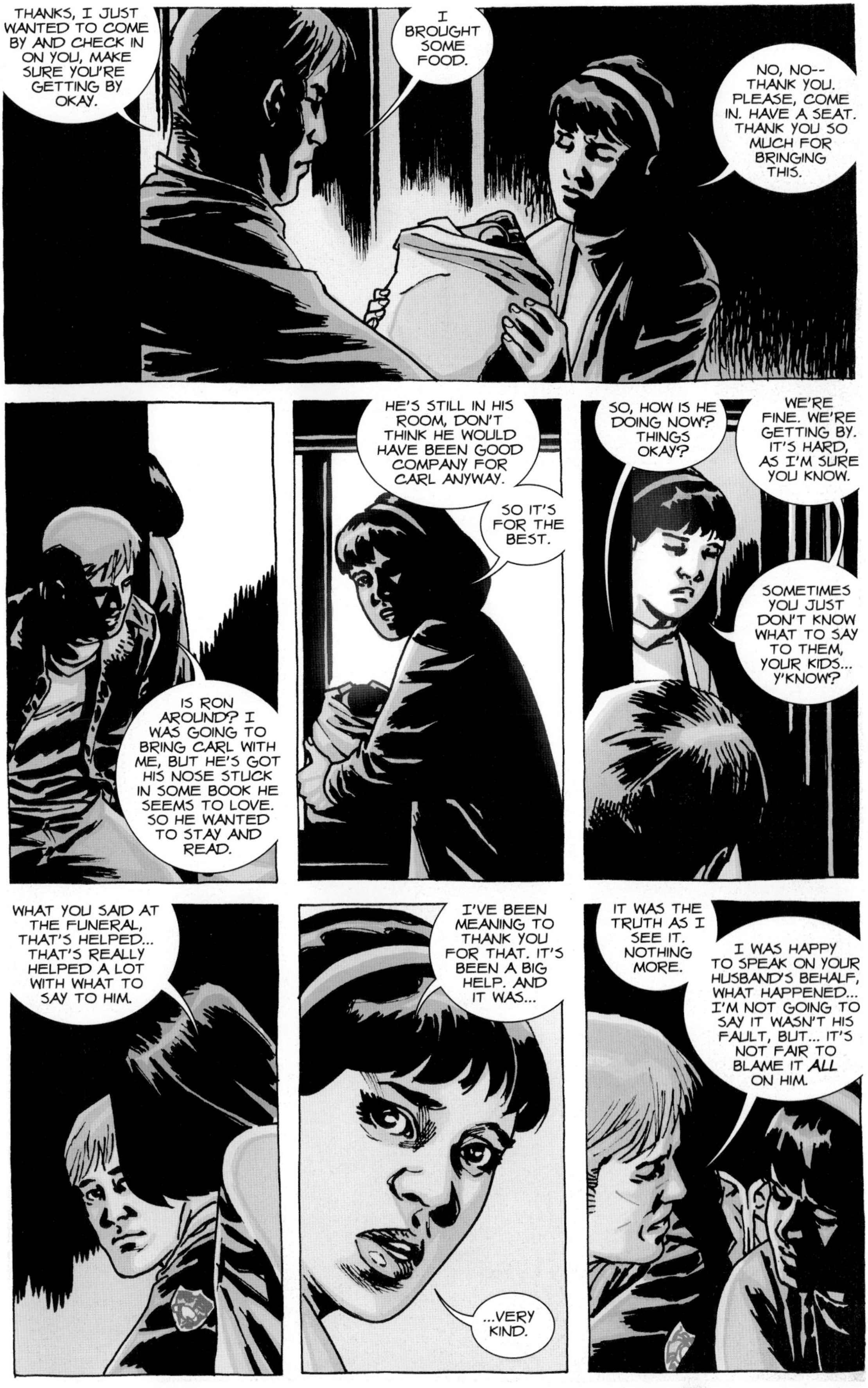
THANKS, I JUST WANTED TO COME BY AND CHECK IN ON YOU, MAKE SURE YOU'RE GETTING BY OKAY.
I BROUGHT SOME FOOD.
NO, NO-- THANK YOU. PLEASE, COME IN. HAVE A SEAT. THANK YOU SO MUCH FOR BRINGING THIS.
IS RON AROUND? I WAS GOING TO BRING CARL WITH ME, BUT HE'S GOT HIS NOSE STUCK IN SOME BOOK HE SEEMS TO LOVE. SO HE WANTED TO STAY AND READ.
HE'S STILL IN HIS ROOM, DON'T THINK HE WOULD HAVE BEEN GOOD COMPANY FOR CARL ANYWAY.
SO IT'S FOR THE BEST.
SO, HOW IS HE DOING NOW? THINGS OKAY?
WE'RE FINE. WE'RE GETTING BY. IT'S HARD, AS I'M SURE YOU KNOW.
SOMETIMES YOU JUST DON'T KNOW WHAT TO SAY TO THEM, YOUR KIDS... Y'KNOW?
WHAT YOU SAID AT THE FUNERAL, THAT'S HELPED... THAT'S REALLY HELPED A LOT WITH WHAT TO SAY TO HIM.
I'VE BEEN MEANING TO THANK YOU FOR THAT. IT'S BEEN A BIG HELP. AND IT WAS...
...VERY KIND.
IT WAS THE TRUTH AS I SEE IT. NOTHING MORE.
I WAS HAPPY TO SPEAK ON YOUR HUSBAND'S BEHALF. WHAT HAPPENED... I'M NOT GOING TO SAY IT WASN'T HIS FAULT, BUT... IT'S NOT FAIR TO BLAME IT ALL ON HIM.

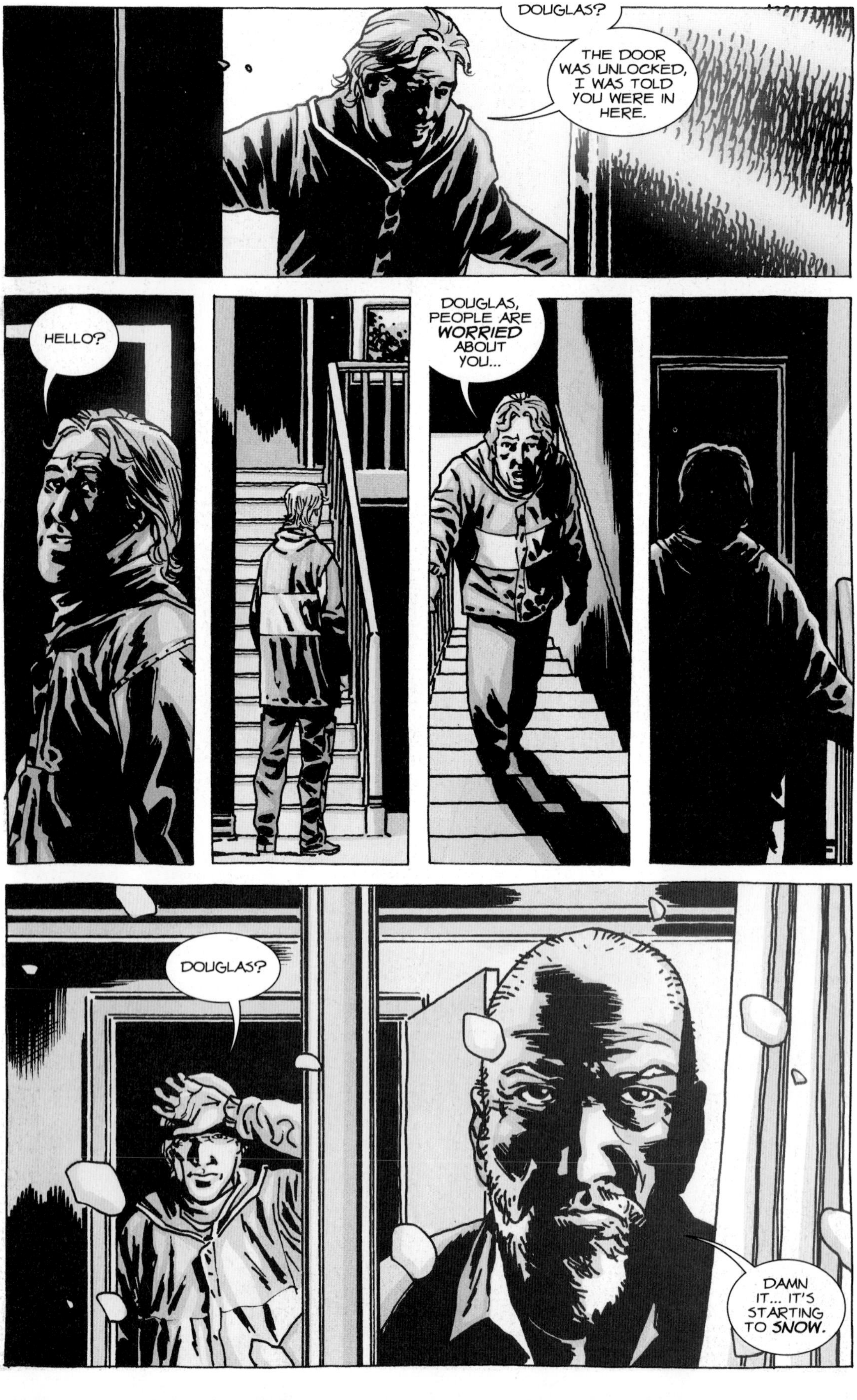

DOUGLAS?
THE DOOR WAS UNLOCKED, I WAS TOLD YOU WERE IN HERE.
HELLO?
DOUGLAS, PEOPLE ARE *WORRIED* ABOUT YOU...
DOUGLAS?
DAMN IT... IT'S STARTING TO **SNOW**.

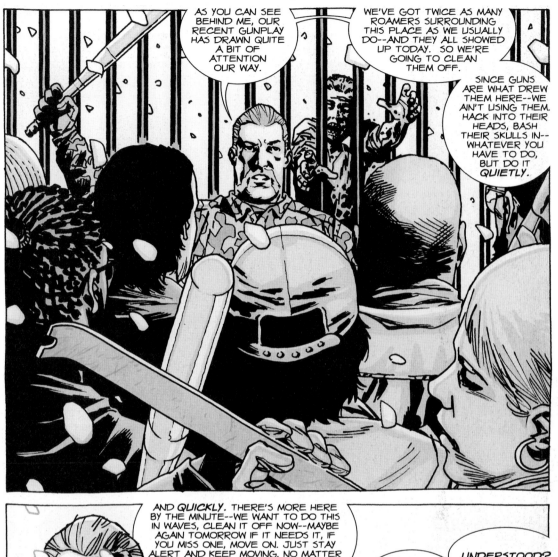

AS YOU CAN SEE BEHIND ME, OUR RECENT GUNPLAY HAS DRAWN QUITE A BIT OF ATTENTION OUR WAY.

WE'VE GOT TWICE AS MANY ROAMERS SURROUNDING THIS PLACE AS WE USUALLY DO--AND THEY ALL SHOWED UP TODAY. SO WE'RE GOING TO CLEAN THEM OFF.

SINCE GUNS ARE WHAT DREW THEM HERE--WE AIN'T USING THEM. HACK INTO THEIR HEADS, BASH THEIR SKULLS IN-- WHATEVER YOU HAVE TO DO, BUT DO IT *QUIETLY.*

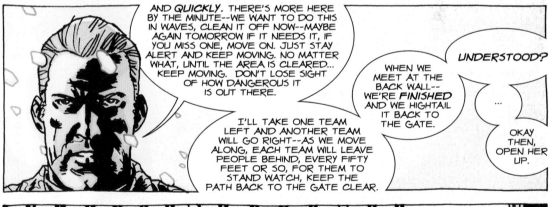

AND *QUICKLY.* THERE'S MORE HERE BY THE MINUTE--WE WANT TO DO THIS IN WAVES, CLEAN IT OFF NOW--MAYBE AGAIN TOMORROW IF IT NEEDS IT, IF YOU MISS ONE, MOVE ON. JUST STAY ALERT AND KEEP MOVING. NO MATTER WHAT, UNTIL THE AREA IS CLEARED... KEEP MOVING. DON'T LOSE SIGHT OF HOW DANGEROUS IT IS OUT THERE.

I'LL TAKE ONE TEAM LEFT AND ANOTHER TEAM WILL GO RIGHT--AS WE MOVE ALONG, EACH TEAM WILL LEAVE PEOPLE BEHIND, EVERY FIFTY FEET OR SO, FOR THEM TO STAND WATCH, KEEP THE PATH BACK TO THE GATE CLEAR.

WHEN WE MEET AT THE BACK WALL-- WE'RE *FINISHED* AND WE HIGHTAIL IT BACK TO THE GATE.

UNDERSTOOD?

...

OKAY THEN, OPEN HER UP.

HERE WE GO!

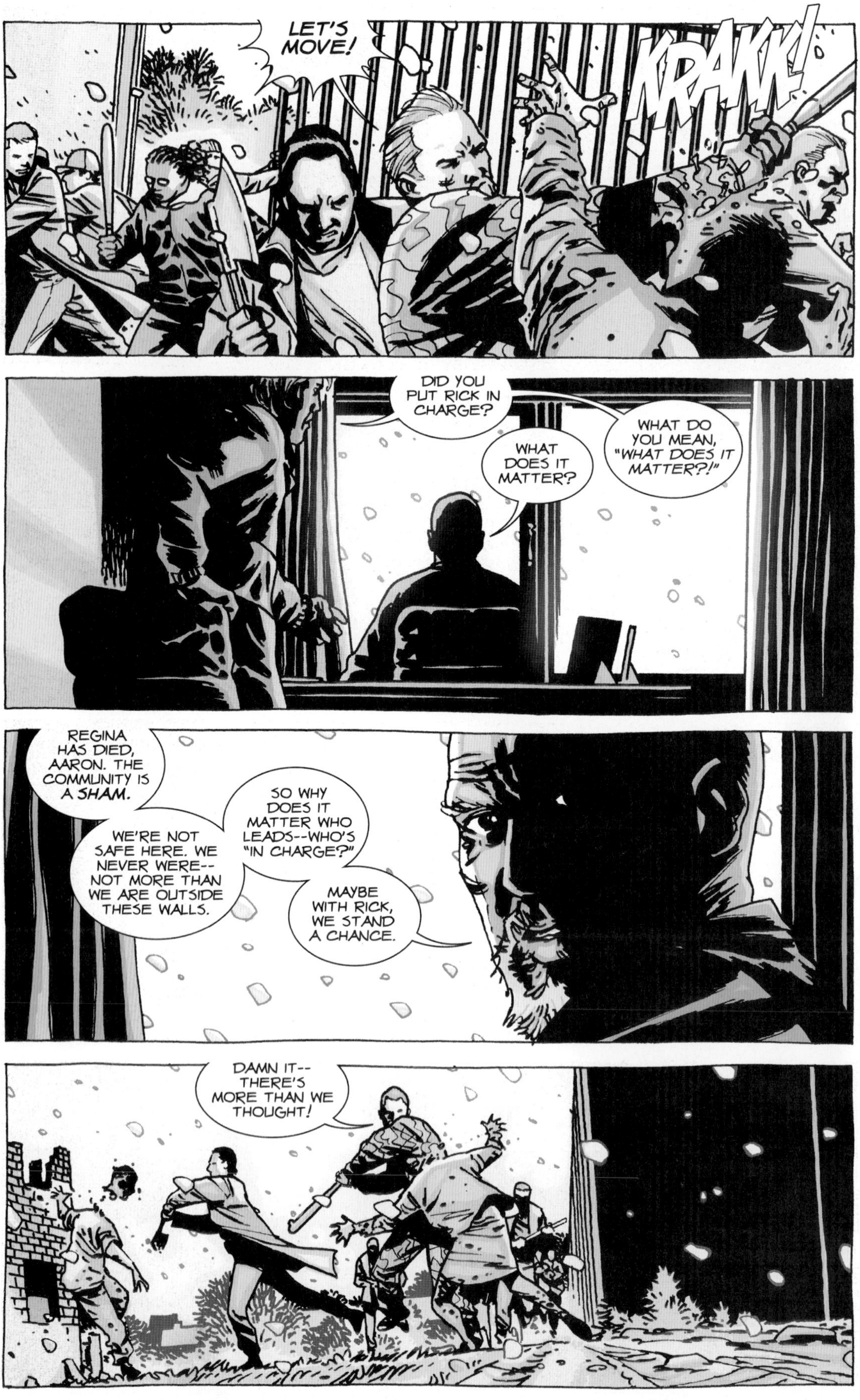

LET'S MOVE!
KRAKK!
DID YOU PUT RICK IN CHARGE?
WHAT DOES IT MATTER?
WHAT DO YOU MEAN, "WHAT DOES IT MATTER?!"
REGINA HAS DIED, AARON. THE COMMUNITY IS A SHAM.
WE'RE NOT SAFE HERE. WE NEVER WERE-- NOT MORE THAN WE ARE OUTSIDE THESE WALLS.
SO WHY DOES IT MATTER WHO LEADS--WHO'S "IN CHARGE?"
MAYBE WITH RICK, WE STAND A CHANCE.
DAMN IT-- THERE'S MORE THAN WE THOUGHT!

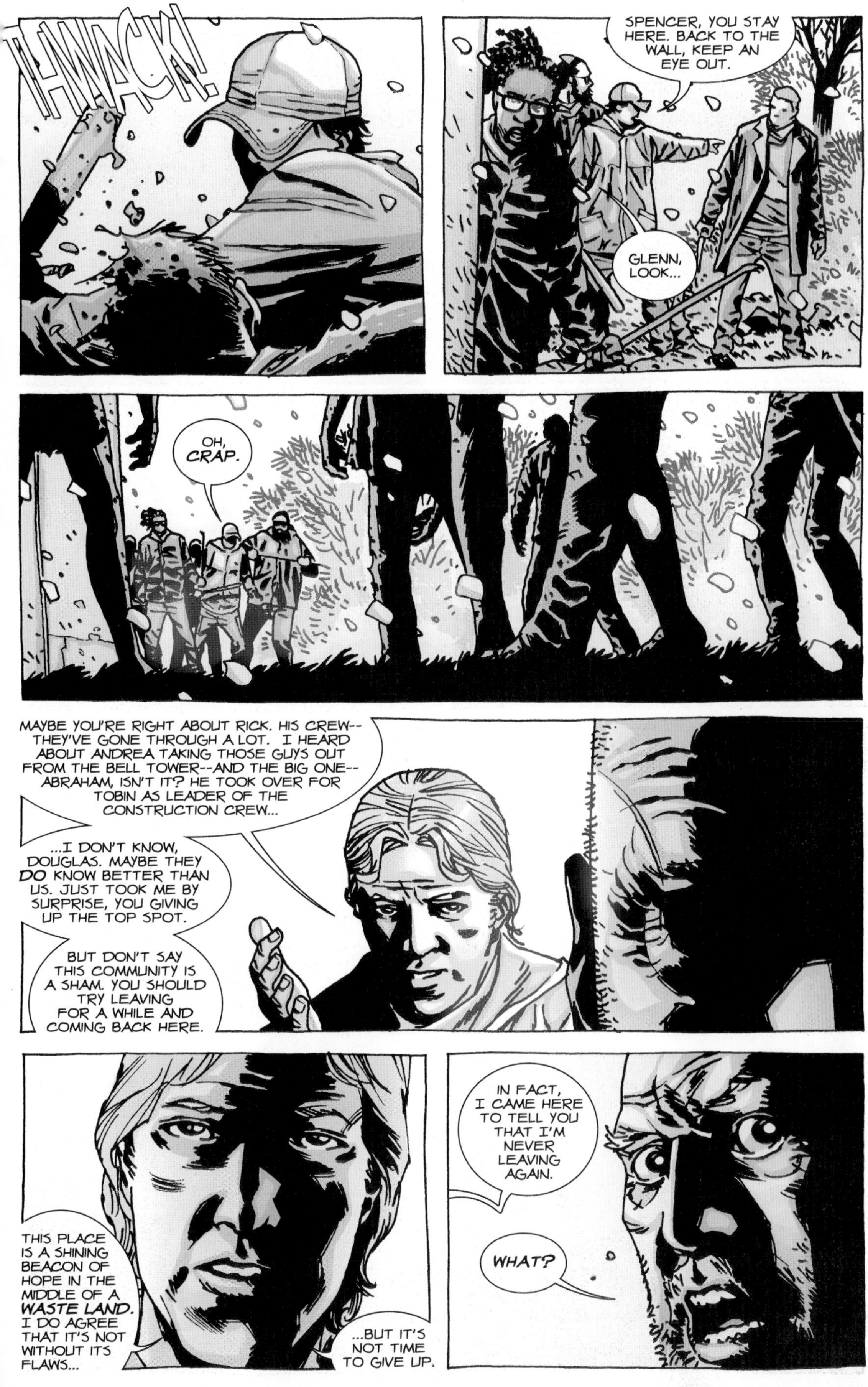
THWACK!
SPENCER, YOU STAY HERE. BACK TO THE WALL, KEEP AN EYE OUT.
GLENN, LOOK...
OH, CRAP.
MAYBE YOU'RE RIGHT ABOUT RICK. HIS CREW-- THEY'VE GONE THROUGH A LOT. I HEARD ABOUT ANDREA TAKING THOSE GUYS OUT FROM THE BELL TOWER--AND THE BIG ONE-- ABRAHAM, ISN'T IT? HE TOOK OVER FOR TOBIN AS LEADER OF THE CONSTRUCTION CREW...
...I DON'T KNOW, DOUGLAS. MAYBE THEY DO KNOW BETTER THAN US. JUST TOOK ME BY SURPRISE, YOU GIVING UP THE TOP SPOT.
BUT DON'T SAY THIS COMMUNITY IS A SHAM. YOU SHOULD TRY LEAVING FOR A WHILE AND COMING BACK HERE.
THIS PLACE IS A SHINING BEACON OF HOPE IN THE MIDDLE OF A WASTE LAND. I DO AGREE THAT IT'S NOT WITHOUT ITS FLAWS...
...BUT IT'S NOT TIME TO GIVE UP.
IN FACT, I CAME HERE TO TELL YOU THAT I'M NEVER LEAVING AGAIN.
WHAT?

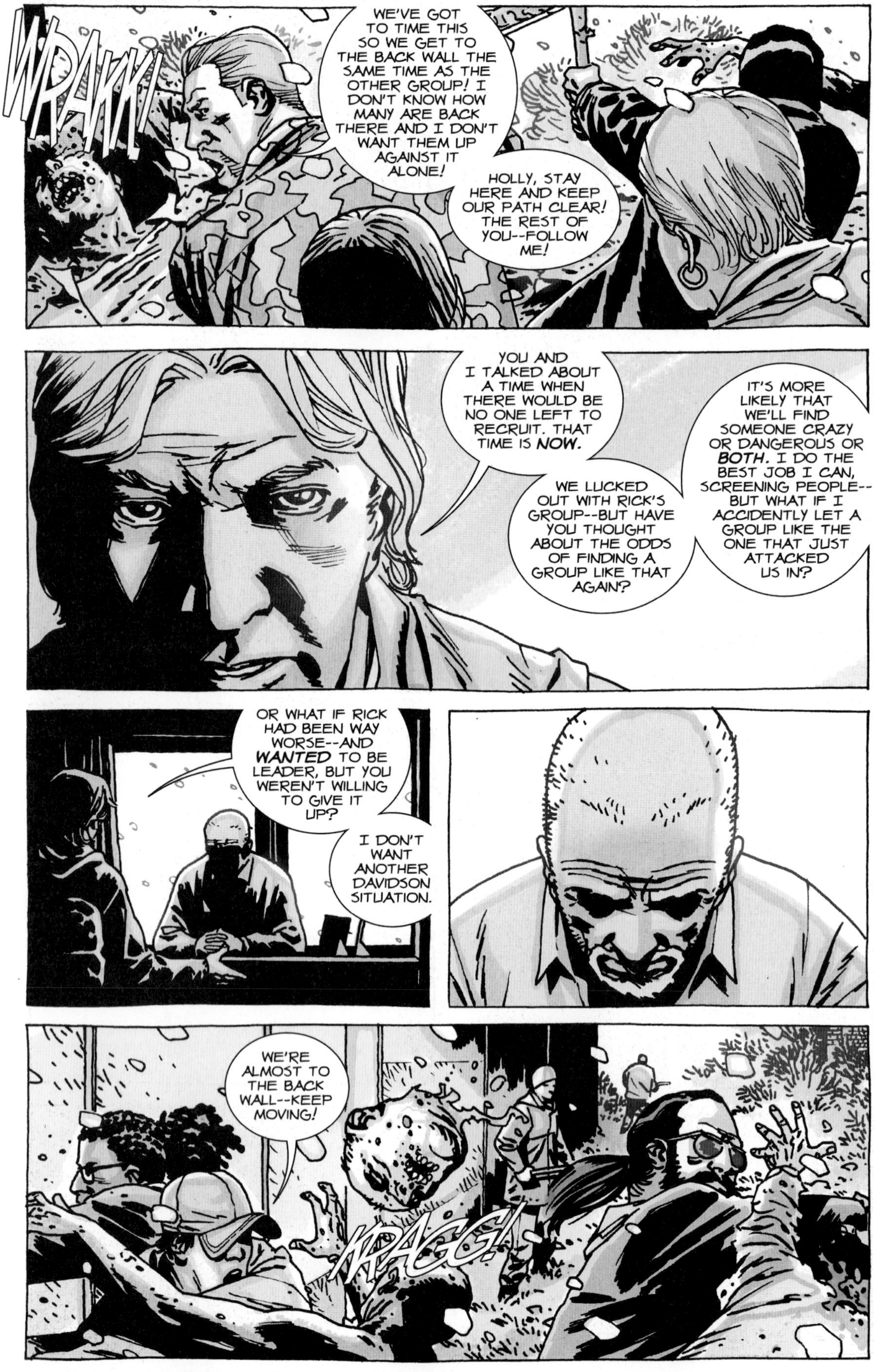

WRAKK!
WE'VE GOT TO TIME THIS SO WE GET TO THE BACK WALL THE SAME TIME AS THE OTHER GROUP! I DON'T KNOW HOW MANY ARE BACK THERE AND I DON'T WANT THEM UP AGAINST IT ALONE!
HOLLY, STAY HERE AND KEEP OUR PATH CLEAR! THE REST OF YOU--FOLLOW ME!
YOU AND I TALKED ABOUT A TIME WHEN THERE WOULD BE NO ONE LEFT TO RECRUIT. THAT TIME IS NOW.
WE LUCKED OUT WITH RICK'S GROUP--BUT HAVE YOU THOUGHT ABOUT THE ODDS OF FINDING A GROUP LIKE THAT AGAIN?
IT'S MORE LIKELY THAT WE'LL FIND SOMEONE CRAZY OR DANGEROUS OR BOTH. I DO THE BEST JOB I CAN, SCREENING PEOPLE--BUT WHAT IF I ACCIDENTLY LET A GROUP LIKE THE ONE THAT JUST ATTACKED US IN?
OR WHAT IF RICK HAD BEEN WAY WORSE--AND WANTED TO BE LEADER, BUT YOU WEREN'T WILLING TO GIVE IT UP?
I DON'T WANT ANOTHER DAVIDSON SITUATION.
WE'RE ALMOST TO THE BACK WALL--KEEP MOVING!
KRAGG!

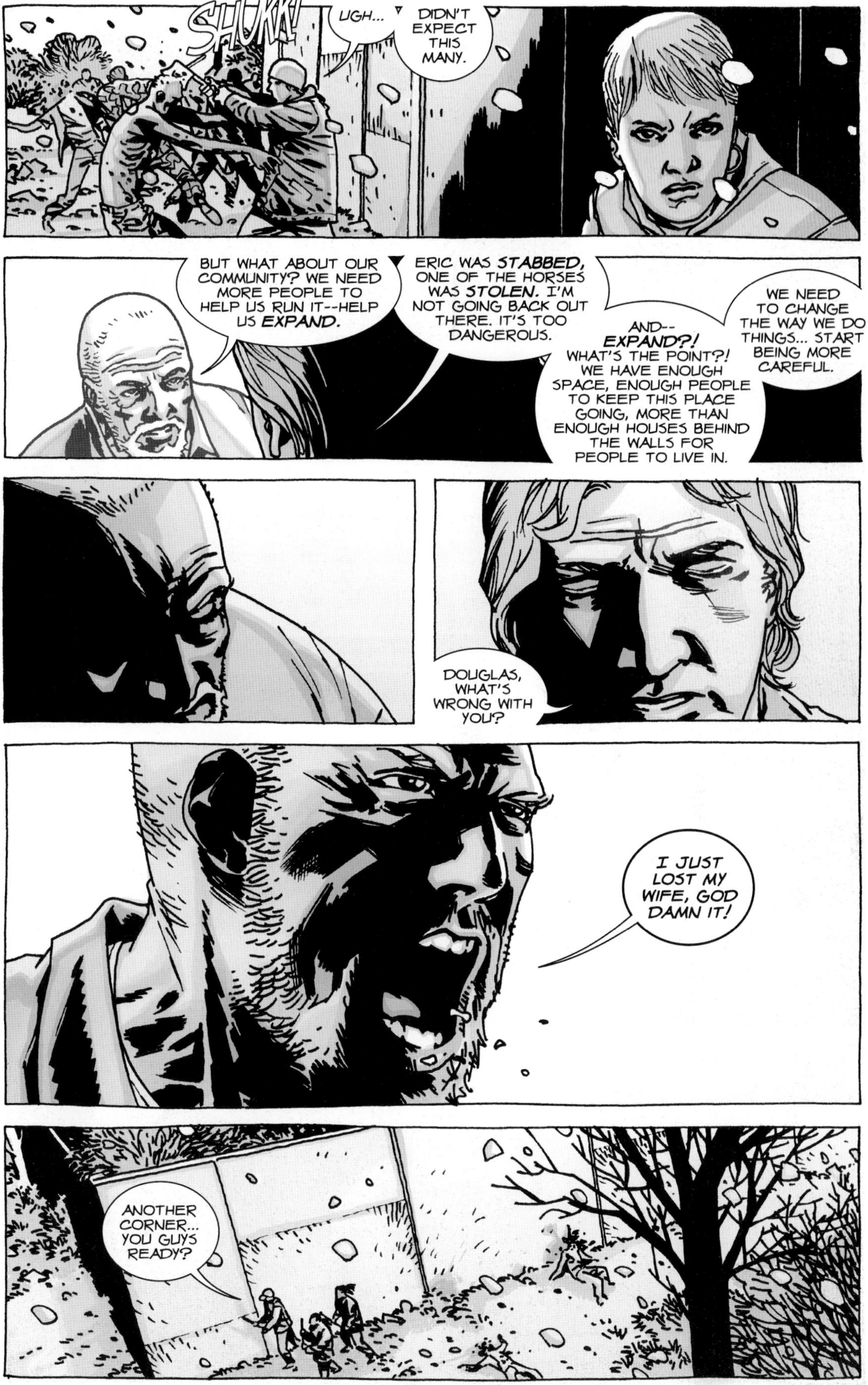
SHUKK!
UGH...
DIDN'T EXPECT THIS MANY.
BUT WHAT ABOUT OUR COMMUNITY? WE NEED MORE PEOPLE TO HELP US RUN IT--HELP US EXPAND.
ERIC WAS STABBED, ONE OF THE HORSES WAS STOLEN. I'M NOT GOING BACK OUT THERE. IT'S TOO DANGEROUS.
WE NEED TO CHANGE THE WAY WE DO THINGS... START BEING MORE CAREFUL.
AND-- EXPAND?! WHAT'S THE POINT?! WE HAVE ENOUGH SPACE, ENOUGH PEOPLE TO KEEP THIS PLACE GOING, MORE THAN ENOUGH HOUSES BEHIND THE WALLS FOR PEOPLE TO LIVE IN.
DOUGLAS, WHAT'S WRONG WITH YOU?
I JUST LOST MY WIFE, GOD DAMN IT!
ANOTHER CORNER... YOU GUYS READY?

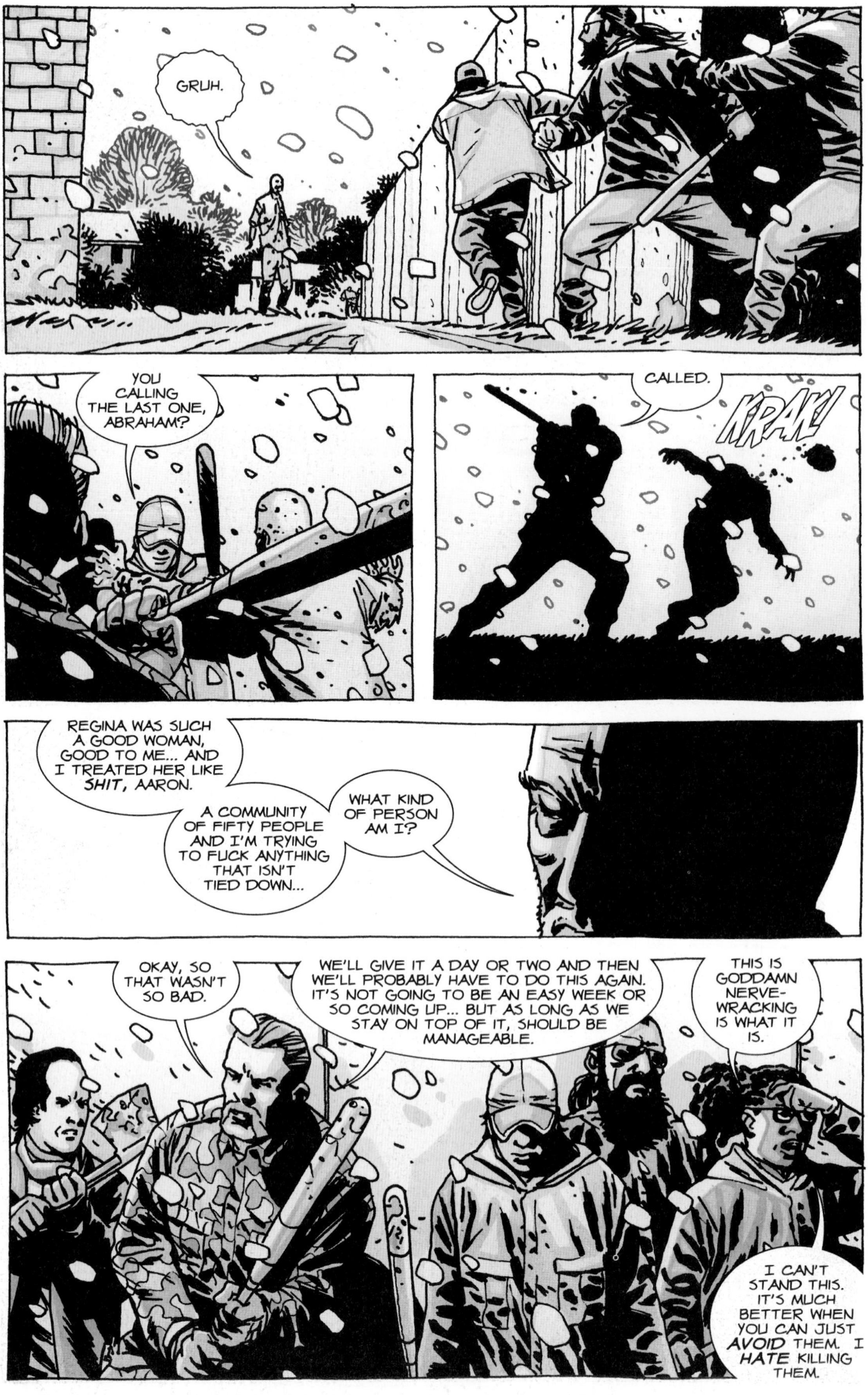
GRUH.
YOU CALLING THE LAST ONE, ABRAHAM?
CALLED.
KRAK!
REGINA WAS SUCH A GOOD WOMAN, GOOD TO ME... AND I TREATED HER LIKE SHIT, AARON.
A COMMUNITY OF FIFTY PEOPLE AND I'M TRYING TO FUCK ANYTHING THAT ISN'T TIED DOWN...
WHAT KIND OF PERSON AM I?
OKAY, SO THAT WASN'T SO BAD.
WE'LL GIVE IT A DAY OR TWO AND THEN WE'LL PROBABLY HAVE TO DO THIS AGAIN. IT'S NOT GOING TO BE AN EASY WEEK OR SO COMING UP... BUT AS LONG AS WE STAY ON TOP OF IT, SHOULD BE MANAGEABLE.
THIS IS GODDAMN NERVE-WRACKING IS WHAT IT IS.
I CAN'T STAND THIS. IT'S MUCH BETTER WHEN YOU CAN JUST AVOID THEM. I HATE KILLING THEM.

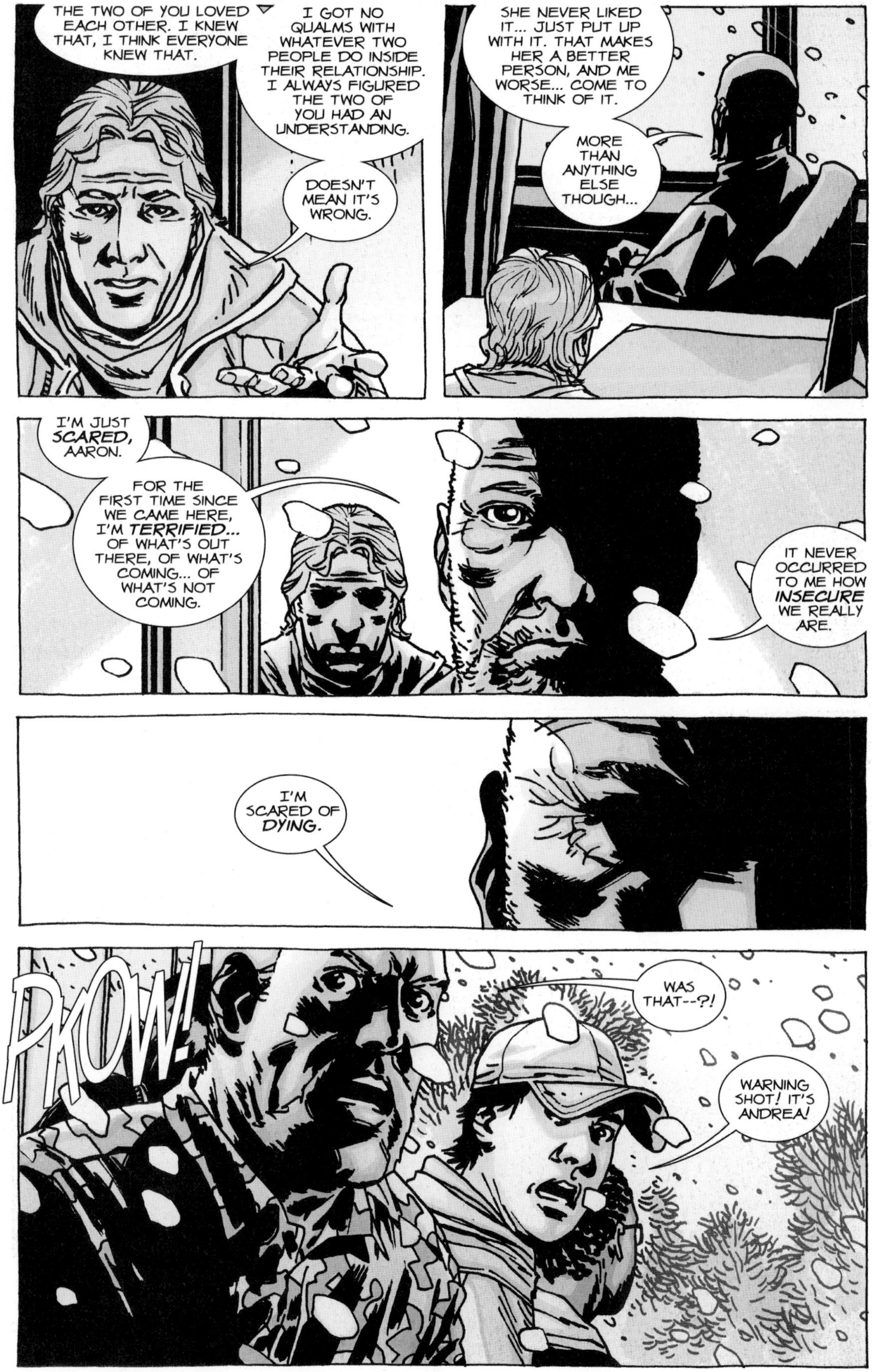
THE TWO OF YOU LOVED EACH OTHER. I KNEW THAT, I THINK EVERYONE KNEW THAT.
I GOT NO QUALMS WITH WHATEVER TWO PEOPLE DO INSIDE THEIR RELATIONSHIP. I ALWAYS FIGURED THE TWO OF YOU HAD AN UNDERSTANDING.
DOESN'T MEAN IT'S WRONG.
SHE NEVER LIKED IT... JUST PUT UP WITH IT. THAT MAKES HER A BETTER PERSON, AND ME WORSE... COME TO THINK OF IT.
MORE THAN ANYTHING ELSE THOUGH...
I'M JUST *SCARED,* AARON.
FOR THE FIRST TIME SINCE WE CAME HERE, I'M *TERRIFIED...* OF WHAT'S OUT THERE, OF WHAT'S COMING... OF WHAT'S NOT COMING.
IT NEVER OCCURRED TO ME HOW *INSECURE* WE REALLY ARE.
I'M SCARED OF *DYING.*
PKOW!
WAS THAT--?!
WARNING SHOT! IT'S ANDREA!

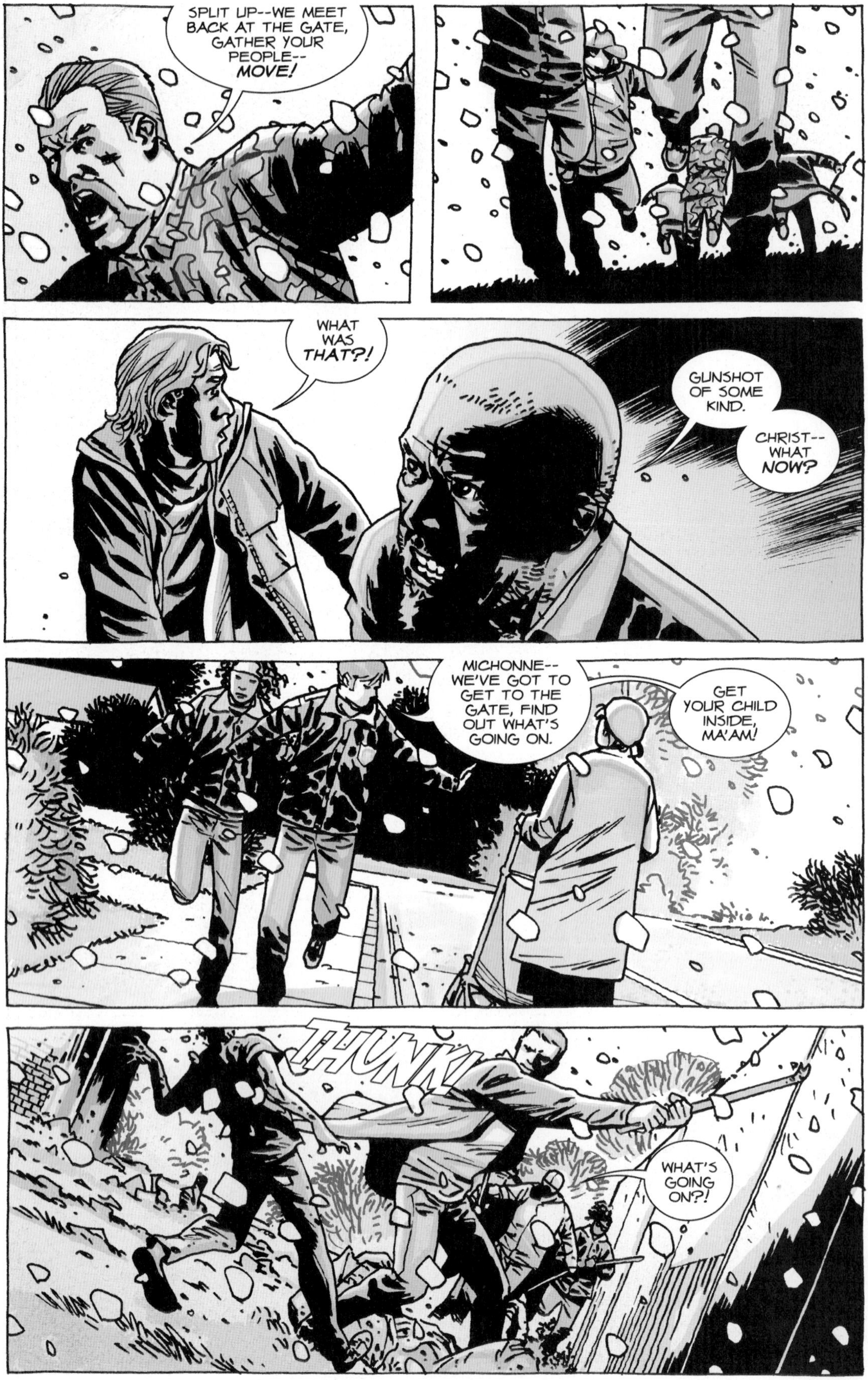

SPLIT UP--WE MEET BACK AT THE GATE, GATHER YOUR PEOPLE-- MOVE!
WHAT WAS THAT?!
GUNSHOT OF SOME KIND.
CHRIST-- WHAT NOW?
MICHONNE-- WE'VE GOT TO GET TO THE GATE, FIND OUT WHAT'S GOING ON.
GET YOUR CHILD INSIDE, MA'AM!
THUNK!
WHAT'S GOING ON?!

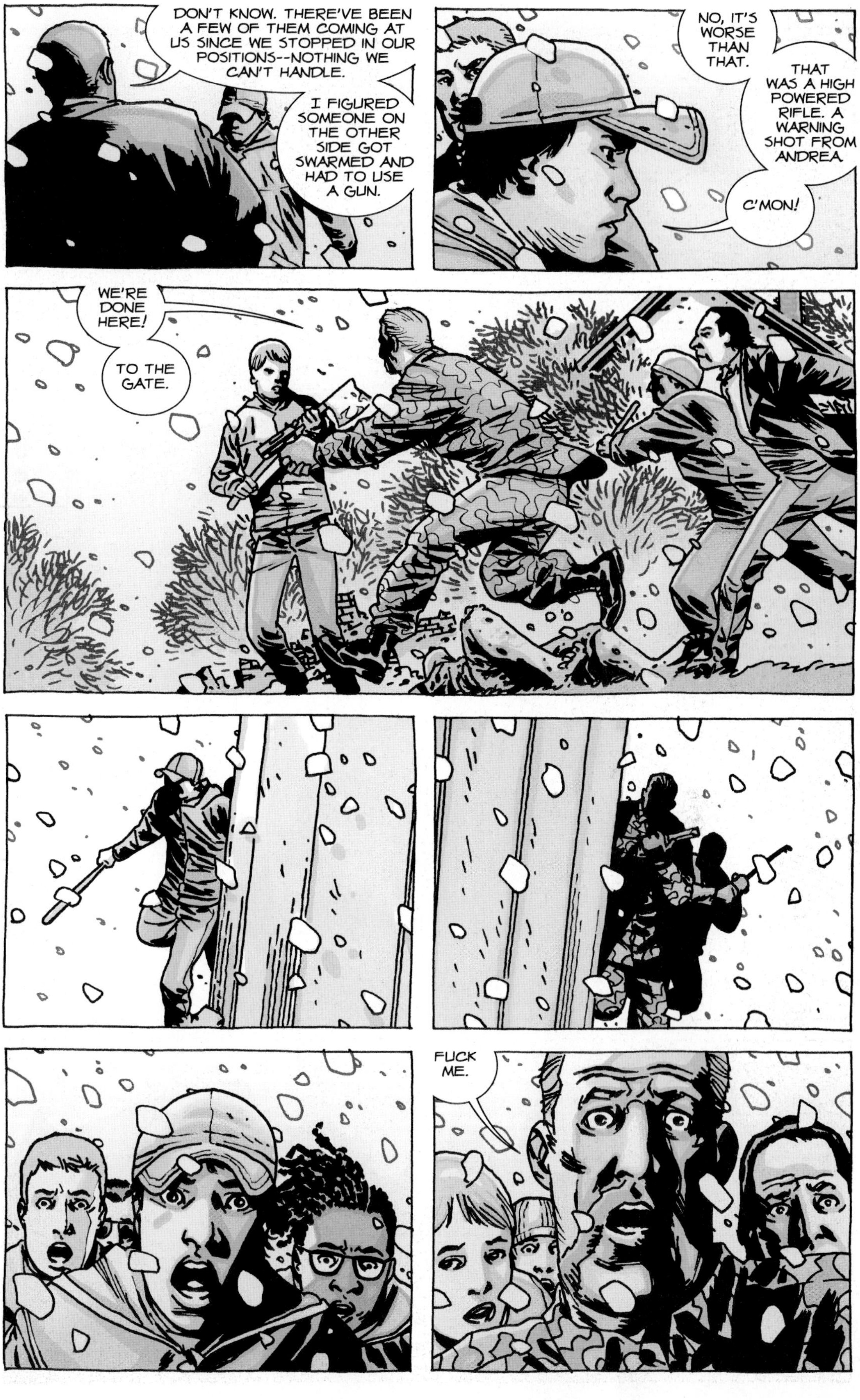
DON'T KNOW. THERE'VE BEEN A FEW OF THEM COMING AT US SINCE WE STOPPED IN OUR POSITIONS--NOTHING WE CAN'T HANDLE.
I FIGURED SOMEONE ON THE OTHER SIDE GOT SWARMED AND HAD TO USE A GUN.
NO, IT'S WORSE THAN THAT.
THAT WAS A HIGH POWERED RIFLE. A WARNING SHOT FROM ANDREA
C'MON!
WE'RE DONE HERE!
TO THE GATE.
FUCK ME.

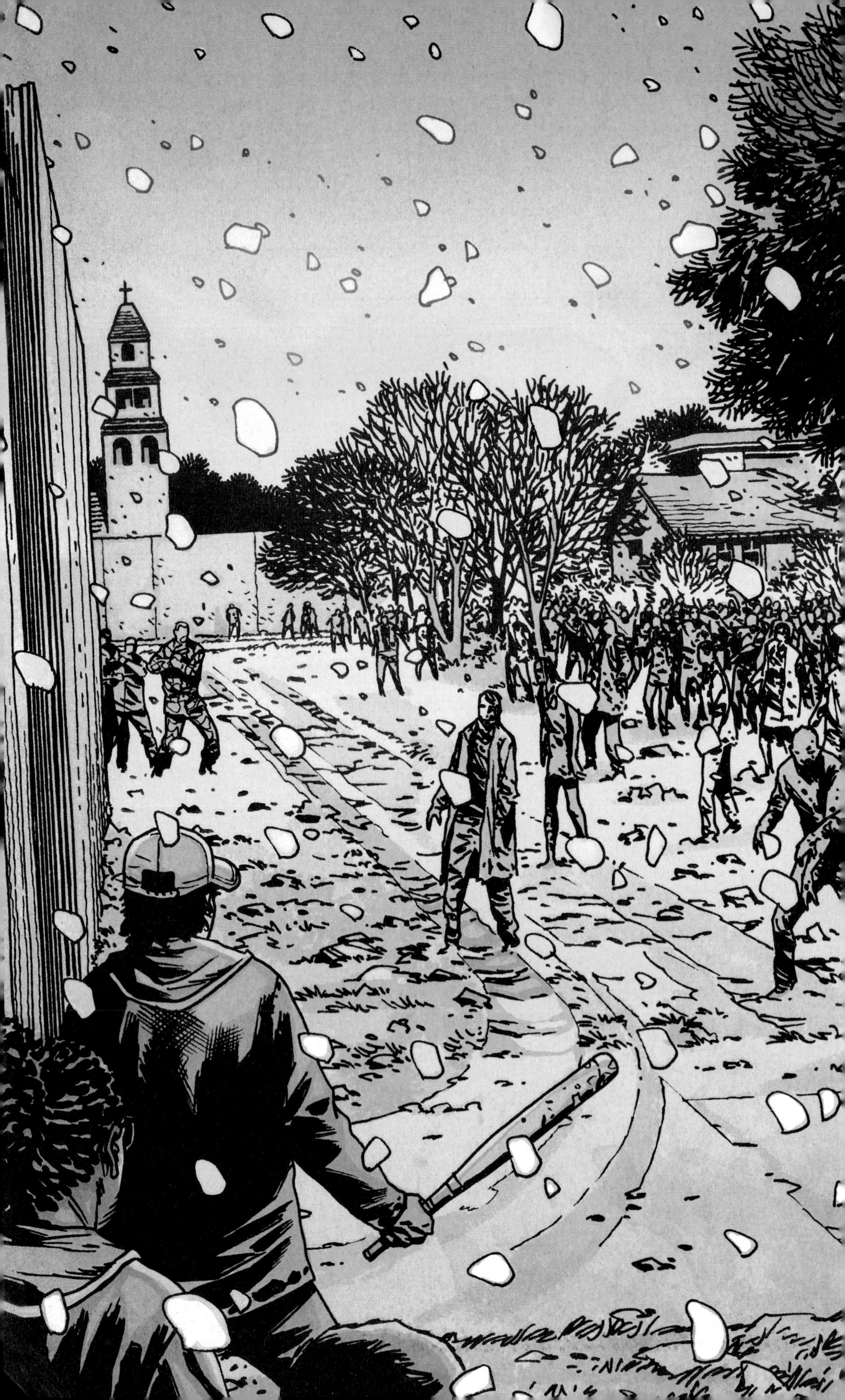

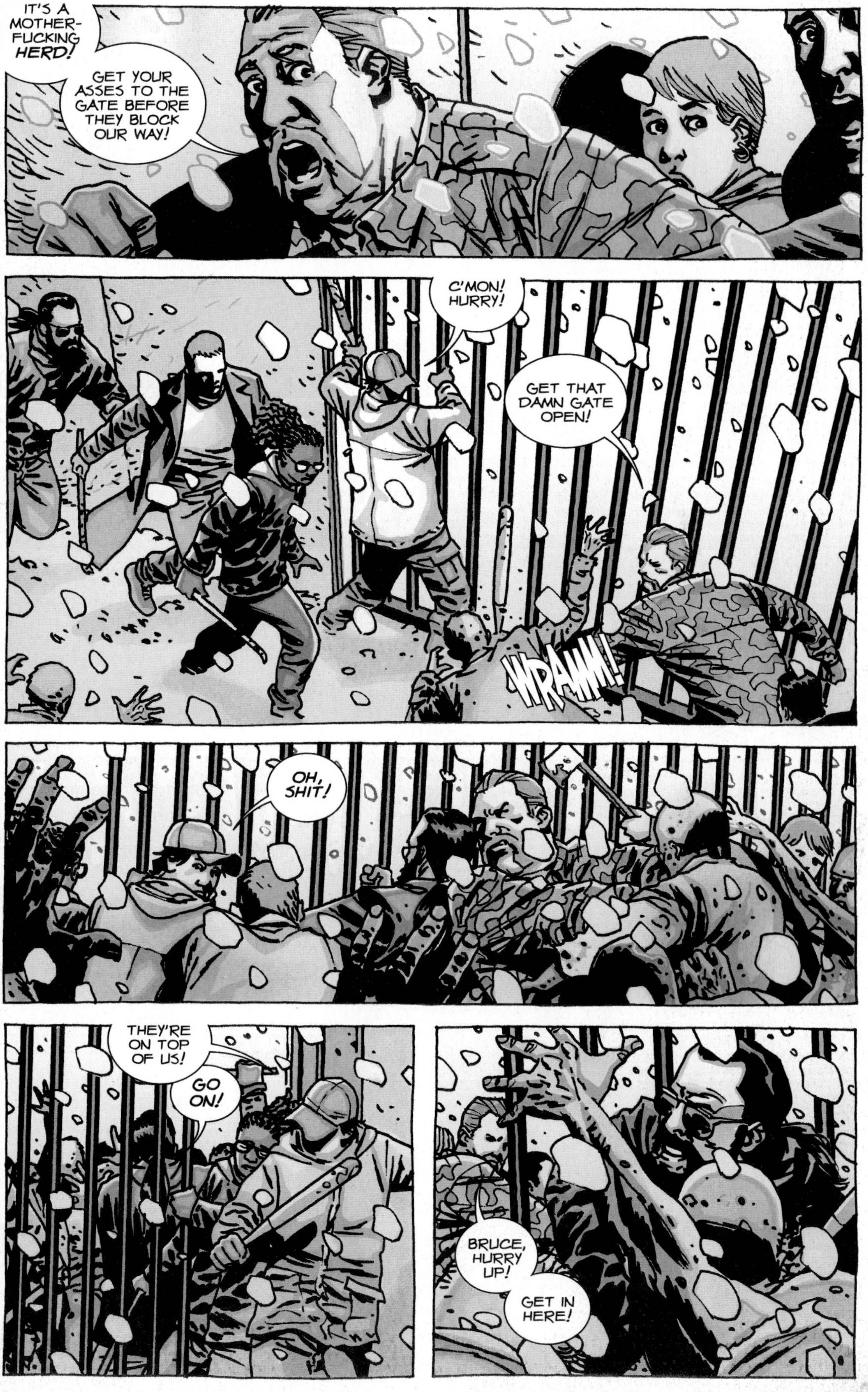
IT'S A MOTHER-FUCKING HERD!
GET YOUR ASSES TO THE GATE BEFORE THEY BLOCK OUR WAY!
C'MON! HURRY!
GET THAT DAMN GATE OPEN!
WRAMM!
OH, SHIT!
THEY'RE ON TOP OF US!
GO ON!
BRUCE, HURRY UP!
GET IN HERE!

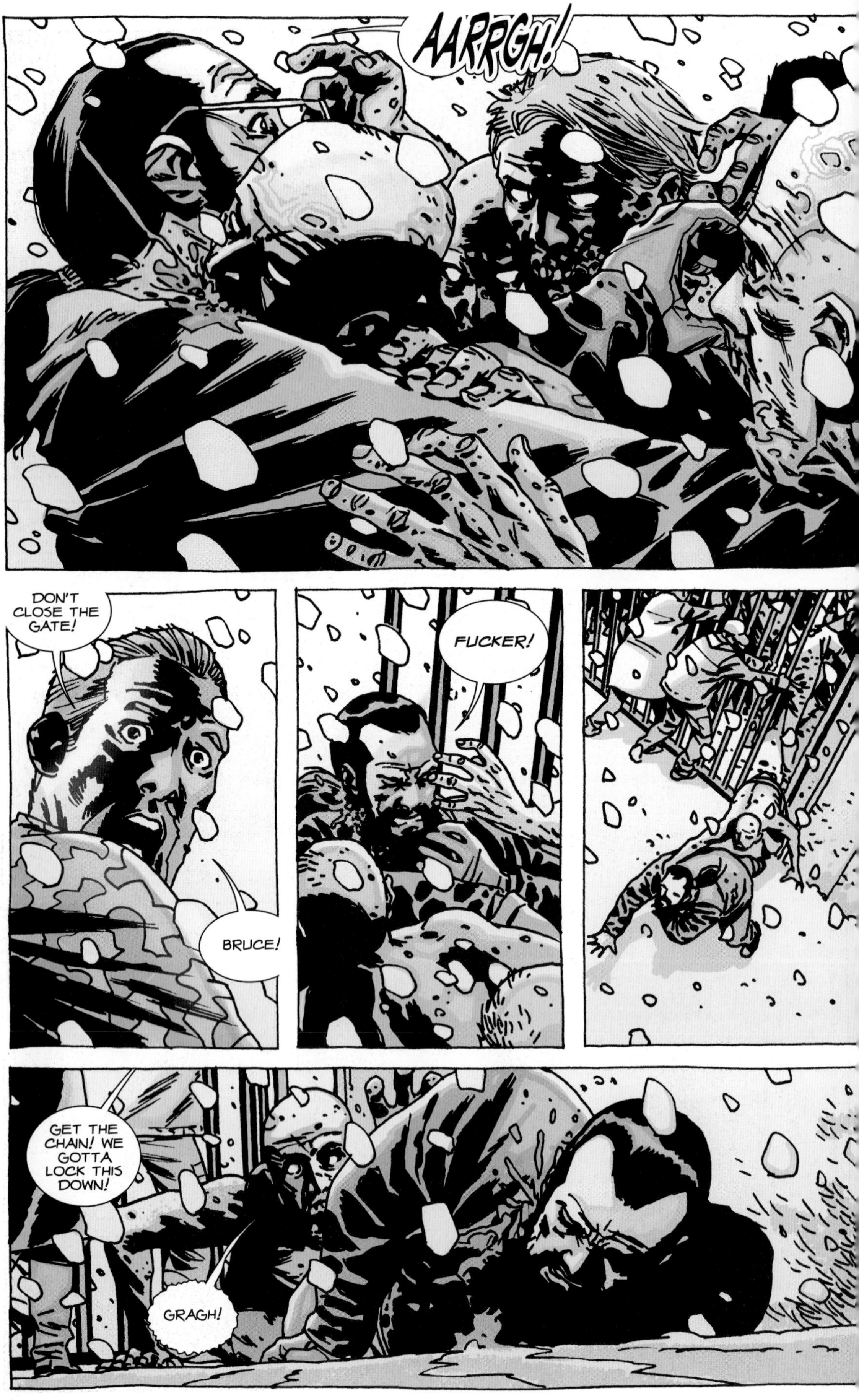
AARRGH!
DON'T CLOSE THE GATE!
BRUCE!
FUCKER!
GET THE CHAIN! WE GOTTA LOCK THIS DOWN!
GRAGH!

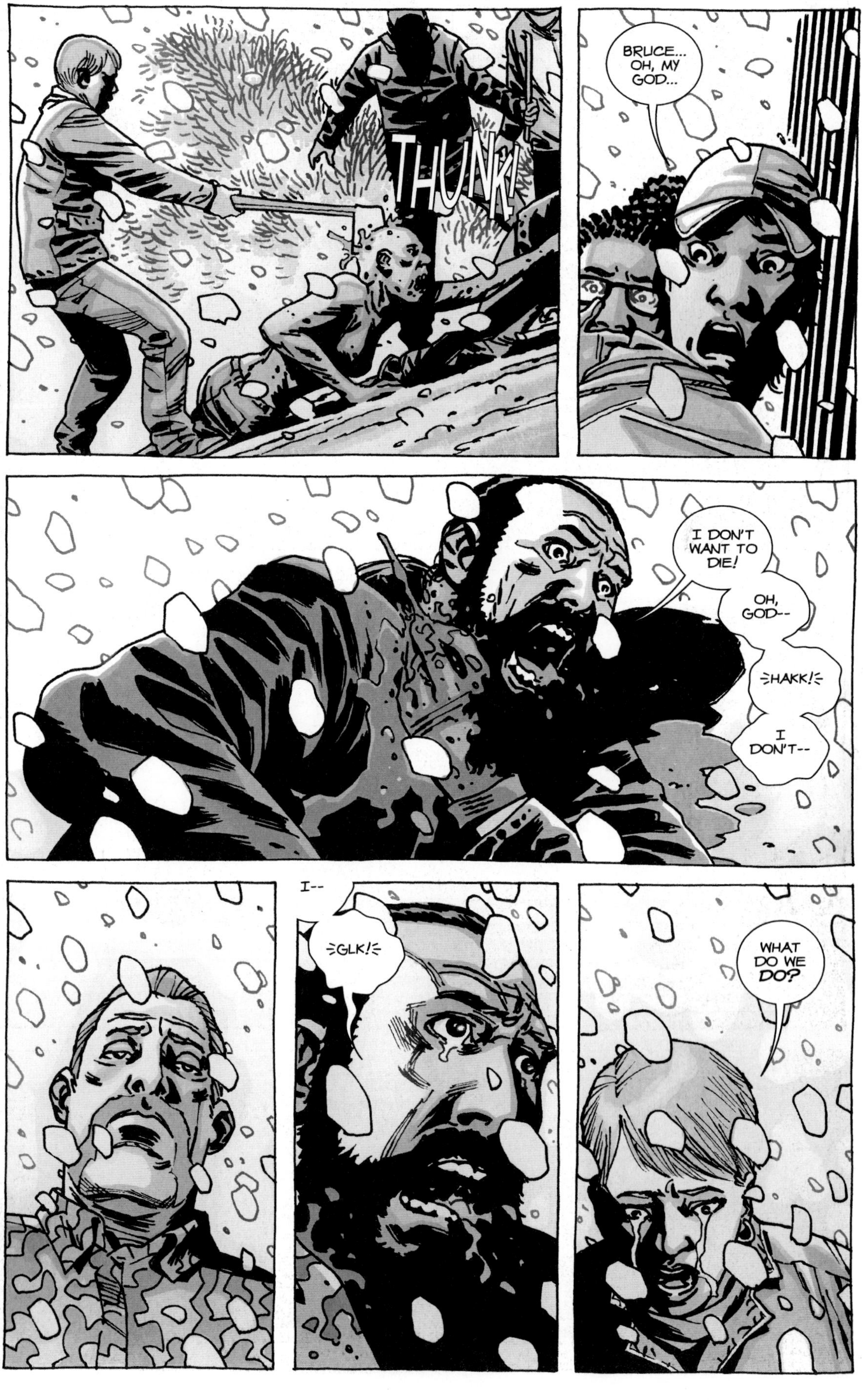
THUNK!
BRUCE... OH, MY GOD...
I DON'T WANT TO DIE!
OH, GOD--
HAKK!
I DON'T--
I--
GLK!
WHAT DO WE DO?

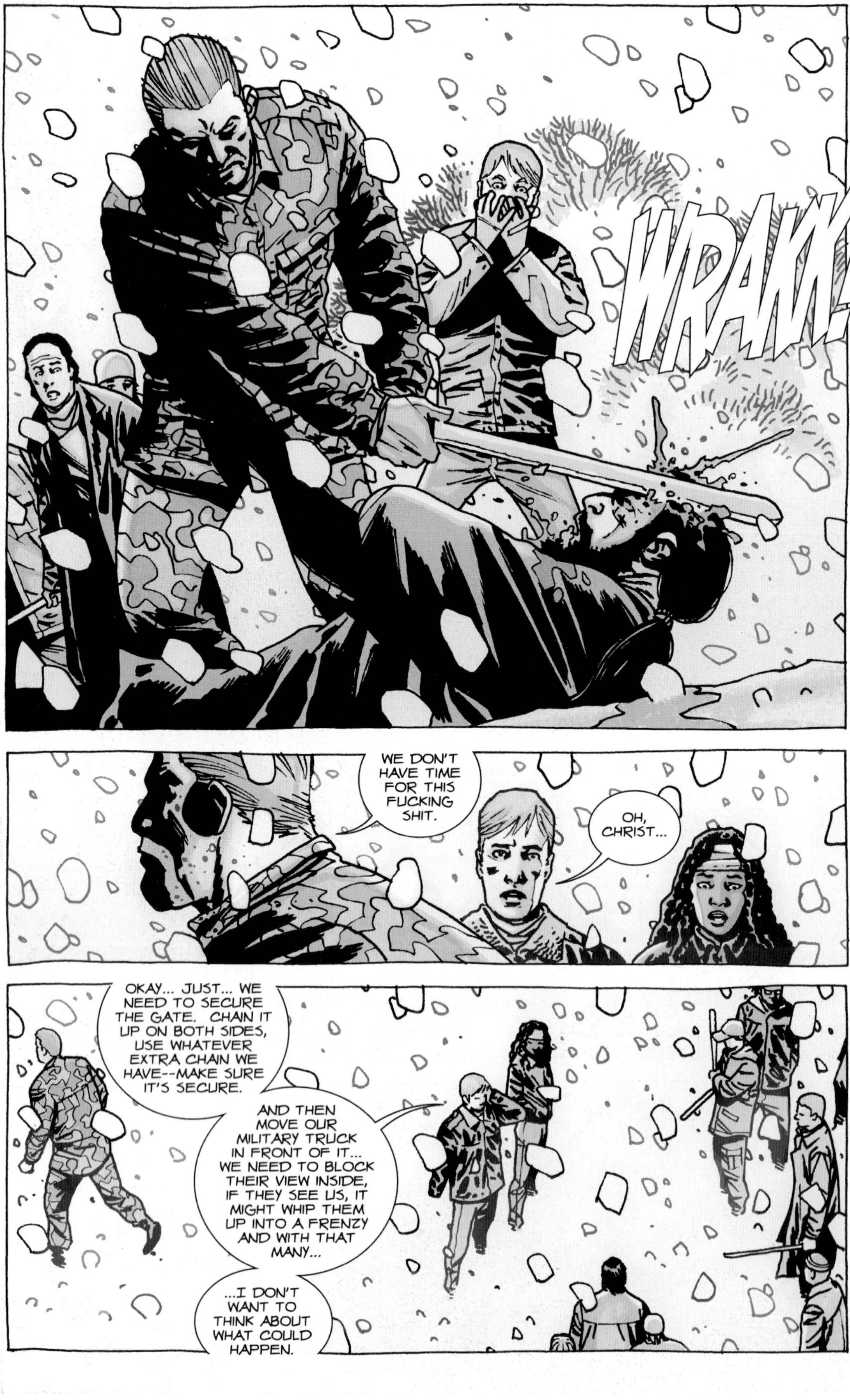
WRAKK!
WE DON'T HAVE TIME FOR THIS FUCKING SHIT.
OH, CHRIST...
OKAY... JUST... WE NEED TO SECURE THE GATE. CHAIN IT UP ON BOTH SIDES, USE WHATEVER EXTRA CHAIN WE HAVE--MAKE SURE IT'S SECURE.
AND THEN MOVE OUR MILITARY TRUCK IN FRONT OF IT... WE NEED TO BLOCK THEIR VIEW INSIDE, IF THEY SEE US, IT MIGHT WHIP THEM UP INTO A FRENZY AND WITH THAT MANY...
...I DON'T WANT TO THINK ABOUT WHAT COULD HAPPEN.

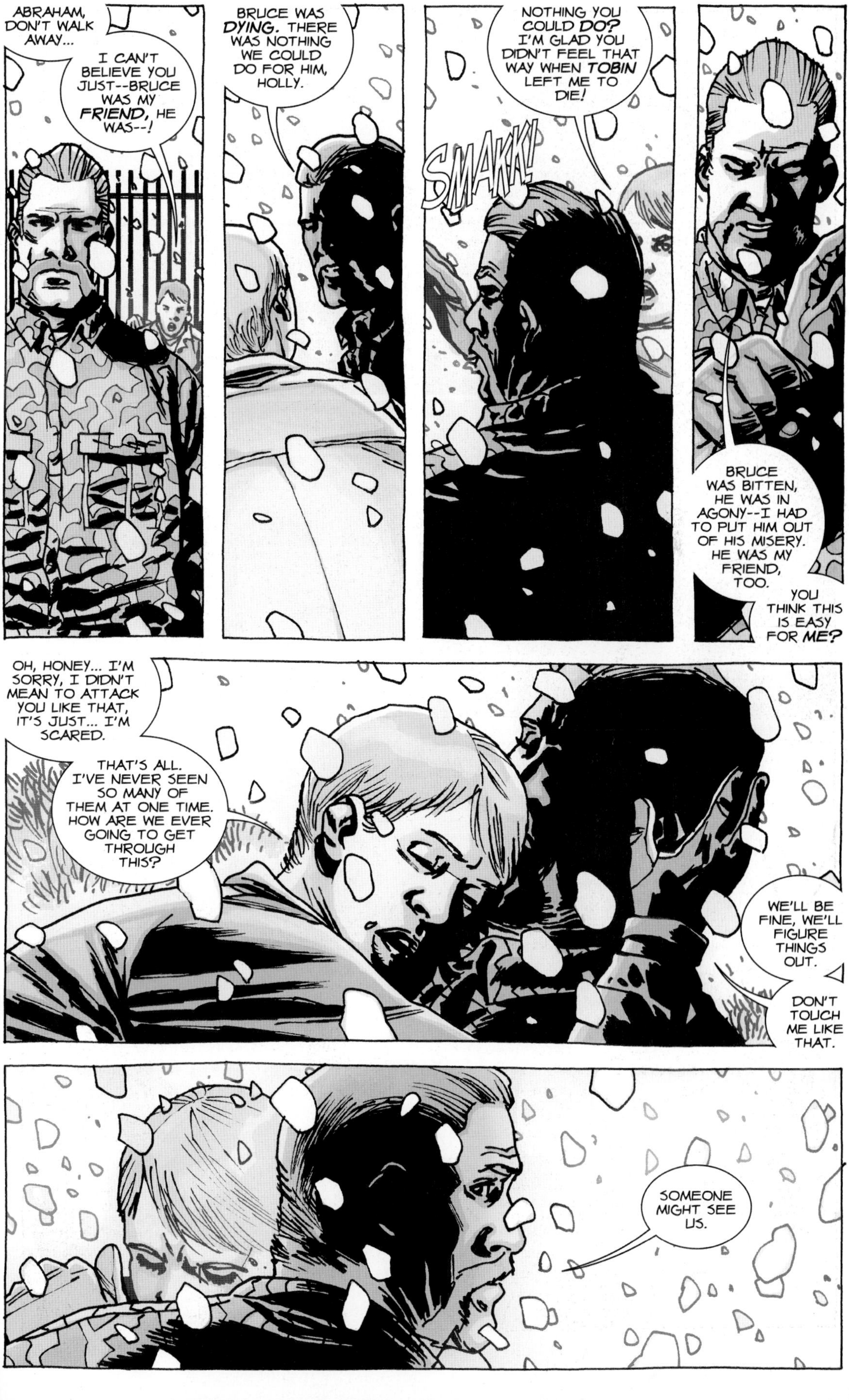
ABRAHAM, DON'T WALK AWAY...
I CAN'T BELIEVE YOU JUST--BRUCE WAS MY FRIEND, HE WAS--!
BRUCE WAS DYING. THERE WAS NOTHING WE COULD DO FOR HIM, HOLLY.
NOTHING YOU COULD DO? I'M GLAD YOU DIDN'T FEEL THAT WAY WHEN TOBIN LEFT ME TO DIE!
SMAKK!
BRUCE WAS BITTEN, HE WAS IN AGONY--I HAD TO PUT HIM OUT OF HIS MISERY. HE WAS MY FRIEND, TOO.
YOU THINK THIS IS EASY FOR ME?
OH, HONEY... I'M SORRY, I DIDN'T MEAN TO ATTACK YOU LIKE THAT, IT'S JUST... I'M SCARED.
THAT'S ALL. I'VE NEVER SEEN SO MANY OF THEM AT ONE TIME. HOW ARE WE EVER GOING TO GET THROUGH THIS?
WE'LL BE FINE, WE'LL FIGURE THINGS OUT.
DON'T TOUCH ME LIKE THAT.
SOMEONE MIGHT SEE US.

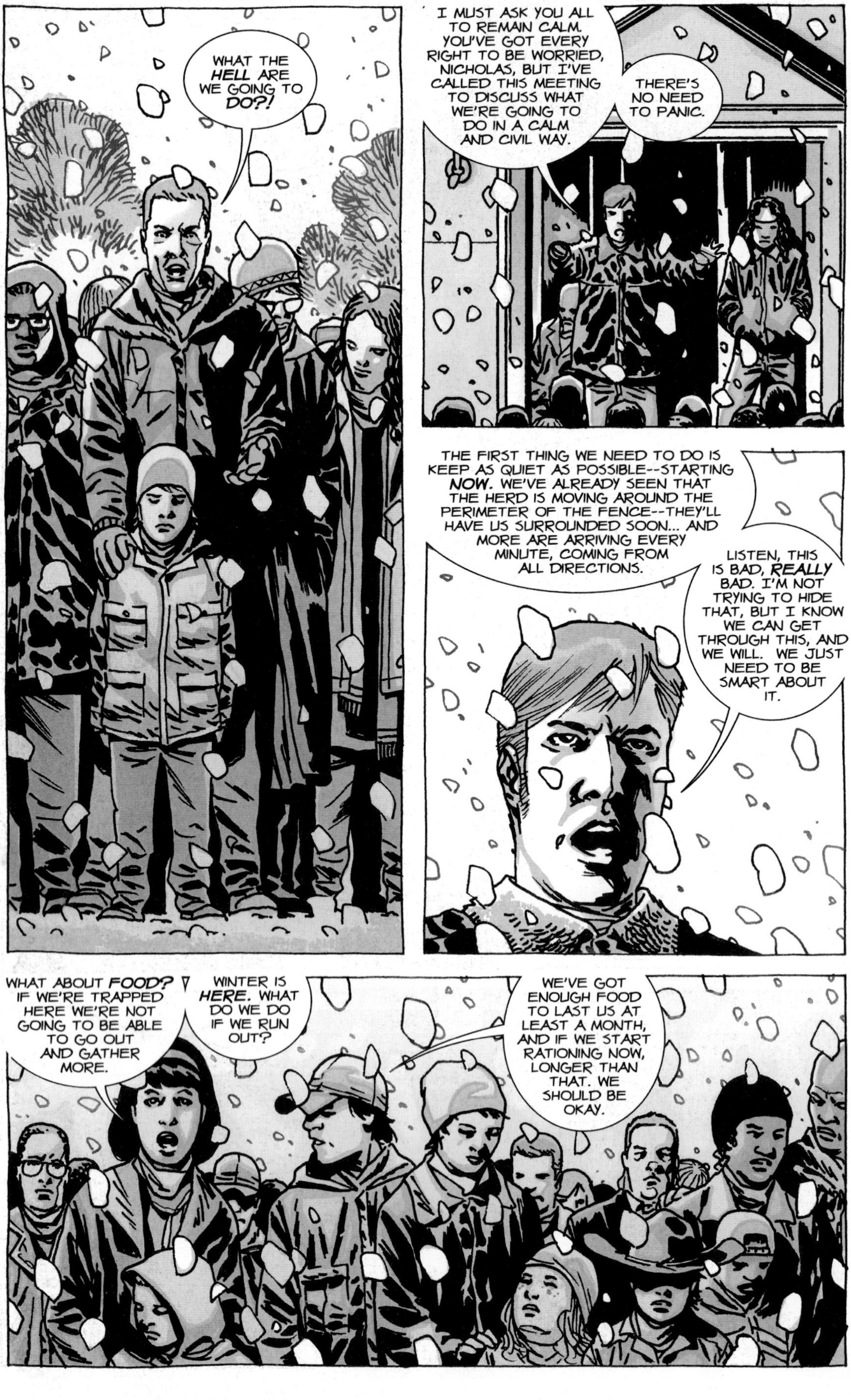
WHAT THE HELL ARE WE GOING TO DO?!
I MUST ASK YOU ALL TO REMAIN CALM. YOU'VE GOT EVERY RIGHT TO BE WORRIED, NICHOLAS, BUT I'VE CALLED THIS MEETING TO DISCUSS WHAT WE'RE GOING TO DO IN A CALM AND CIVIL WAY.
THERE'S NO NEED TO PANIC.
THE FIRST THING WE NEED TO DO IS KEEP AS QUIET AS POSSIBLE--STARTING NOW. WE'VE ALREADY SEEN THAT THE HERD IS MOVING AROUND THE PERIMETER OF THE FENCE--THEY'LL HAVE US SURROUNDED SOON... AND MORE ARE ARRIVING EVERY MINUTE, COMING FROM ALL DIRECTIONS.
LISTEN, THIS IS BAD, REALLY BAD. I'M NOT TRYING TO HIDE THAT, BUT I KNOW WE CAN GET THROUGH THIS, AND WE WILL. WE JUST NEED TO BE SMART ABOUT IT.
WHAT ABOUT FOOD? IF WE'RE TRAPPED HERE WE'RE NOT GOING TO BE ABLE TO GO OUT AND GATHER MORE.
WINTER IS HERE. WHAT DO WE DO IF WE RUN OUT?
WE'VE GOT ENOUGH FOOD TO LAST US AT LEAST A MONTH, AND IF WE START RATIONING NOW, LONGER THAN THAT. WE SHOULD BE OKAY.

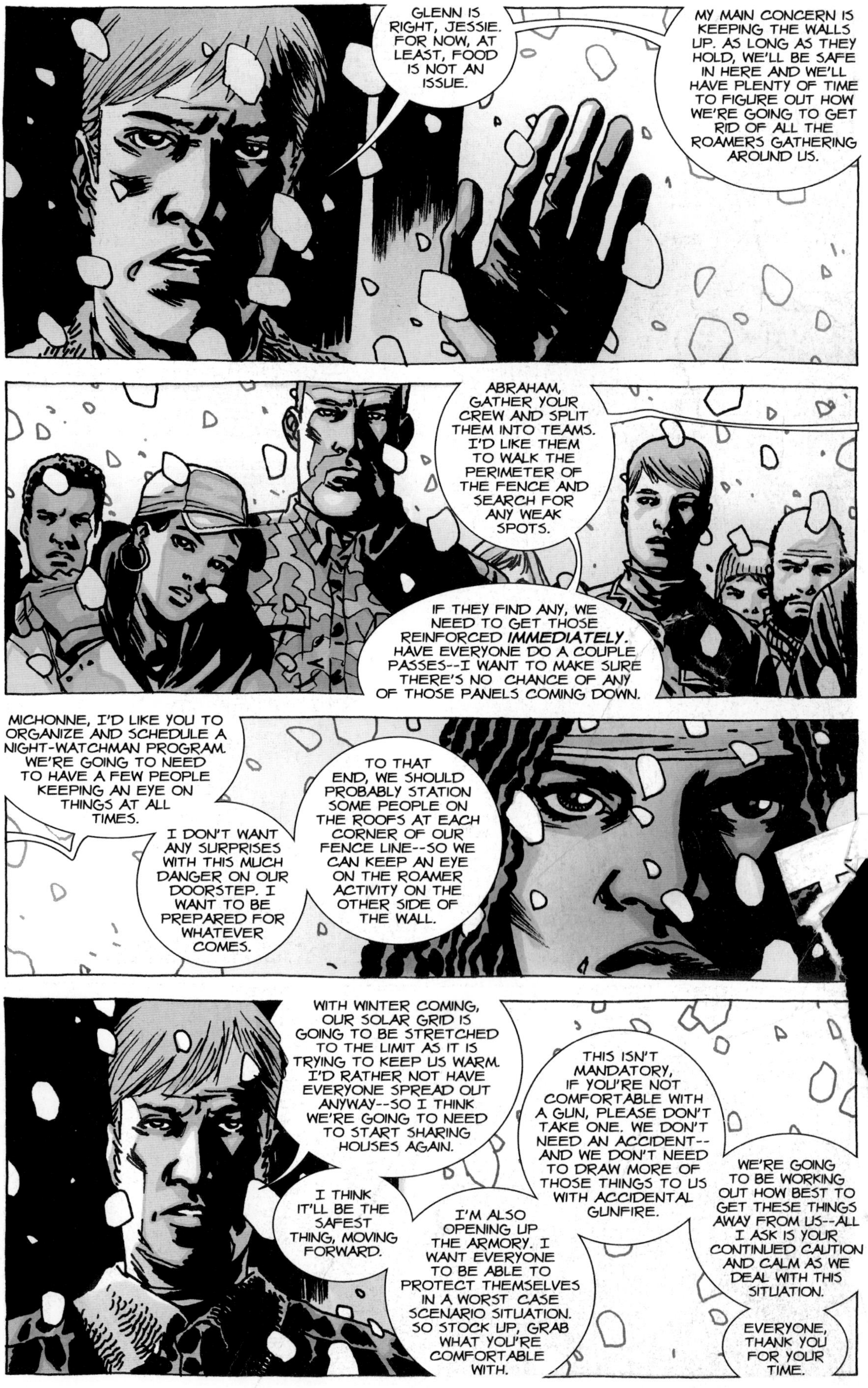
GLENN IS RIGHT, JESSIE. FOR NOW, AT LEAST, FOOD IS NOT AN ISSUE.
MY MAIN CONCERN IS KEEPING THE WALLS UP. AS LONG AS THEY HOLD, WE'LL BE SAFE IN HERE AND WE'LL HAVE PLENTY OF TIME TO FIGURE OUT HOW WE'RE GOING TO GET RID OF ALL THE ROAMERS GATHERING AROUND US.
ABRAHAM, GATHER YOUR CREW AND SPLIT THEM INTO TEAMS. I'D LIKE THEM TO WALK THE PERIMETER OF THE FENCE AND SEARCH FOR ANY WEAK SPOTS.
IF THEY FIND ANY, WE NEED TO GET THOSE REINFORCED IMMEDIATELY. HAVE EVERYONE DO A COUPLE PASSES--I WANT TO MAKE SURE THERE'S NO CHANCE OF ANY OF THOSE PANELS COMING DOWN.
MICHONNE, I'D LIKE YOU TO ORGANIZE AND SCHEDULE A NIGHT-WATCHMAN PROGRAM. WE'RE GOING TO NEED TO HAVE A FEW PEOPLE KEEPING AN EYE ON THINGS AT ALL TIMES.
I DON'T WANT ANY SURPRISES WITH THIS MUCH DANGER ON OUR DOORSTEP. I WANT TO BE PREPARED FOR WHATEVER COMES.
TO THAT END, WE SHOULD PROBABLY STATION SOME PEOPLE ON THE ROOFS AT EACH CORNER OF OUR FENCE LINE--SO WE CAN KEEP AN EYE ON THE ROAMER ACTIVITY ON THE OTHER SIDE OF THE WALL.
WITH WINTER COMING, OUR SOLAR GRID IS GOING TO BE STRETCHED TO THE LIMIT AS IT IS TRYING TO KEEP US WARM. I'D RATHER NOT HAVE EVERYONE SPREAD OUT ANYWAY--SO I THINK WE'RE GOING TO NEED TO START SHARING HOUSES AGAIN.
I THINK IT'LL BE THE SAFEST THING, MOVING FORWARD.
I'M ALSO OPENING UP THE ARMORY. I WANT EVERYONE TO BE ABLE TO PROTECT THEMSELVES IN A WORST CASE SCENARIO SITUATION. SO STOCK UP, GRAB WHAT YOU'RE COMFORTABLE WITH.
THIS ISN'T MANDATORY, IF YOU'RE NOT COMFORTABLE WITH A GUN, PLEASE DON'T TAKE ONE. WE DON'T NEED AN ACCIDENT-- AND WE DON'T NEED TO DRAW MORE OF THOSE THINGS TO US WITH ACCIDENTAL GUNFIRE.
WE'RE GOING TO BE WORKING OUT HOW BEST TO GET THESE THINGS AWAY FROM US--ALL I ASK IS YOUR CONTINUED CAUTION AND CALM AS WE DEAL WITH THIS SITUATION.
EVERYONE, THANK YOU FOR YOUR TIME.

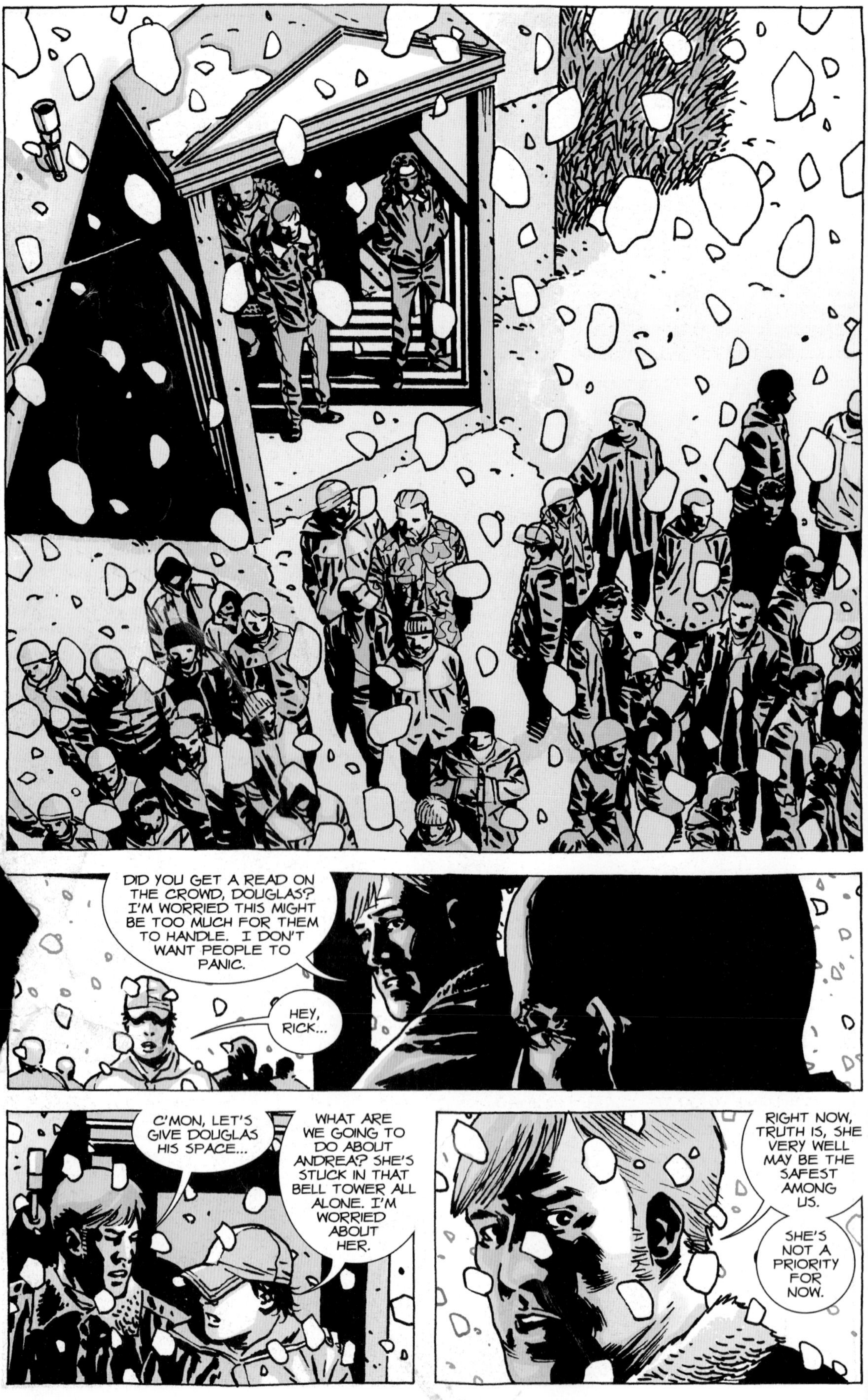
DID YOU GET A READ ON THE CROWD, DOUGLAS? I'M WORRIED THIS MIGHT BE TOO MUCH FOR THEM TO HANDLE. I DON'T WANT PEOPLE TO PANIC.
HEY, RICK...
C'MON, LET'S GIVE DOUGLAS HIS SPACE...
WHAT ARE WE GOING TO DO ABOUT ANDREA? SHE'S STUCK IN THAT BELL TOWER ALL ALONE. I'M WORRIED ABOUT HER.
RIGHT NOW, TRUTH IS, SHE VERY WELL MAY BE THE SAFEST AMONG US.
SHE'S NOT A PRIORITY FOR NOW.

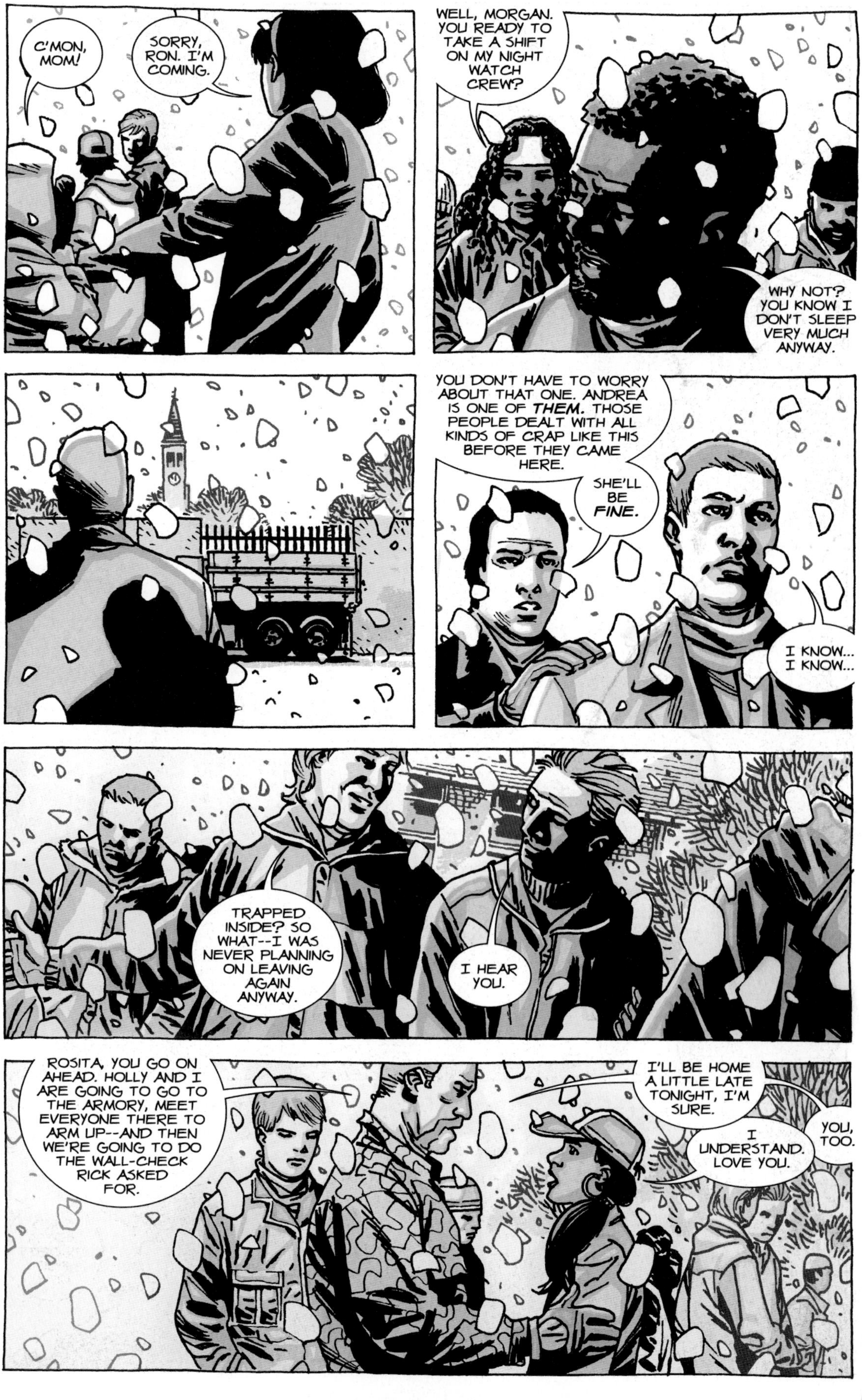
C'MON, MOM!
SORRY, RON. I'M COMING.
WELL, MORGAN. YOU READY TO TAKE A SHIFT ON MY NIGHT WATCH CREW?
WHY NOT? YOU KNOW I DON'T SLEEP VERY MUCH ANYWAY.
YOU DON'T HAVE TO WORRY ABOUT THAT ONE. ANDREA IS ONE OF THEM. THOSE PEOPLE DEALT WITH ALL KINDS OF CRAP LIKE THIS BEFORE THEY CAME HERE.
SHE'LL BE FINE.
I KNOW... I KNOW...
TRAPPED INSIDE? SO WHAT--I WAS NEVER PLANNING ON LEAVING AGAIN ANYWAY.
I HEAR YOU.
ROSITA, YOU GO ON AHEAD. HOLLY AND I ARE GOING TO GO TO THE ARMORY, MEET EVERYONE THERE TO ARM UP--AND THEN WE'RE GOING TO DO THE WALL-CHECK RICK ASKED FOR.
I'LL BE HOME A LITTLE LATE TONIGHT, I'M SURE.
I UNDERSTAND. LOVE YOU.
YOU, TOO.

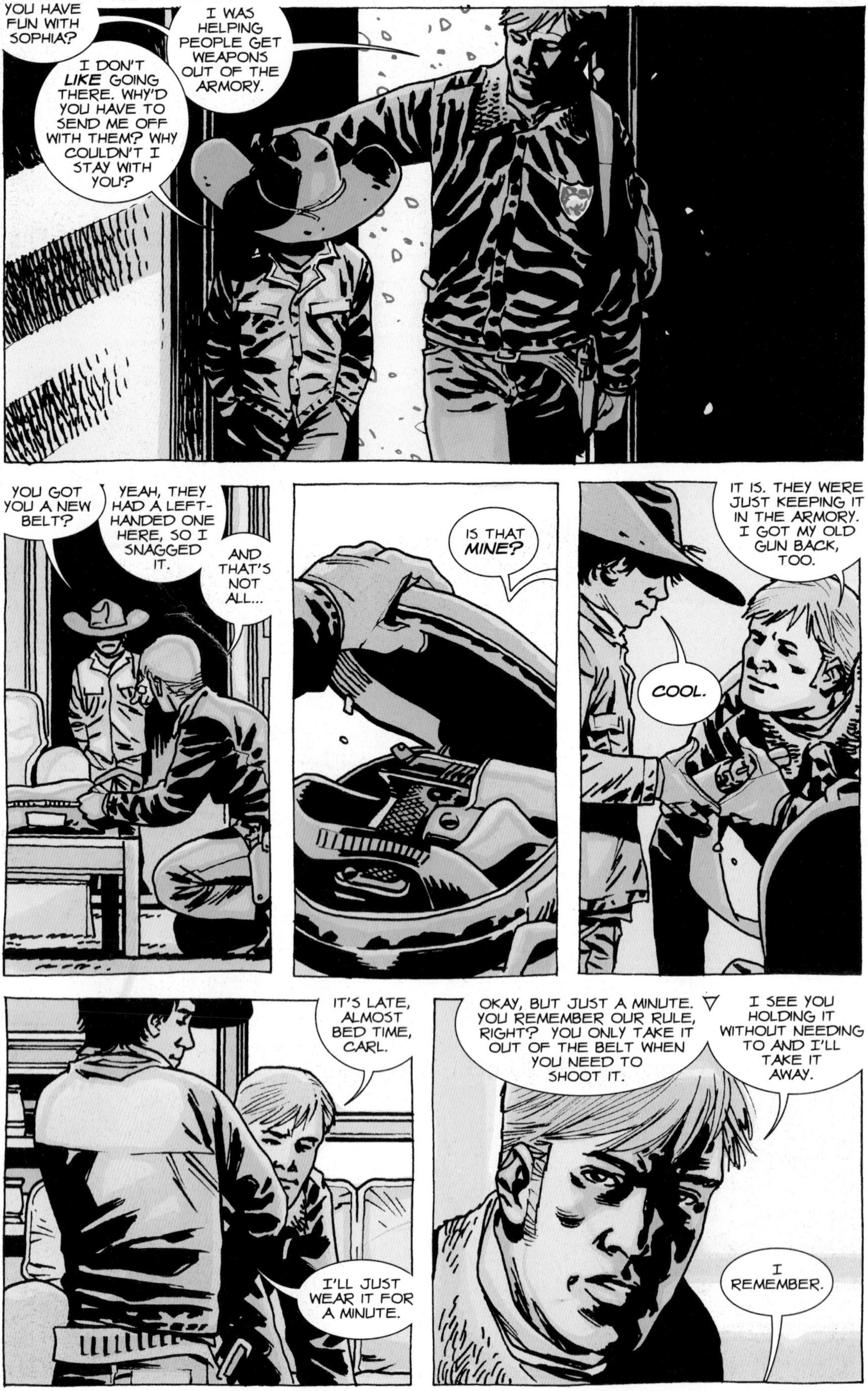
YOU HAVE FUN WITH SOPHIA?
I WAS HELPING PEOPLE GET WEAPONS OUT OF THE ARMORY.
I DON'T LIKE GOING THERE. WHY'D YOU HAVE TO SEND ME OFF WITH THEM? WHY COULDN'T I STAY WITH YOU?
YOU GOT YOU A NEW BELT?
YEAH, THEY HAD A LEFT-HANDED ONE HERE, SO I SNAGGED IT.
AND THAT'S NOT ALL...
IS THAT MINE?
IT IS. THEY WERE JUST KEEPING IT IN THE ARMORY. I GOT MY OLD GUN BACK, TOO.
COOL.
IT'S LATE, ALMOST BED TIME, CARL.
I'LL JUST WEAR IT FOR A MINUTE.
OKAY, BUT JUST A MINUTE. YOU REMEMBER OUR RULE, RIGHT? YOU ONLY TAKE IT OUT OF THE BELT WHEN YOU NEED TO SHOOT IT.
I SEE YOU HOLDING IT WITHOUT NEEDING TO AND I'LL TAKE IT AWAY.
I REMEMBER.

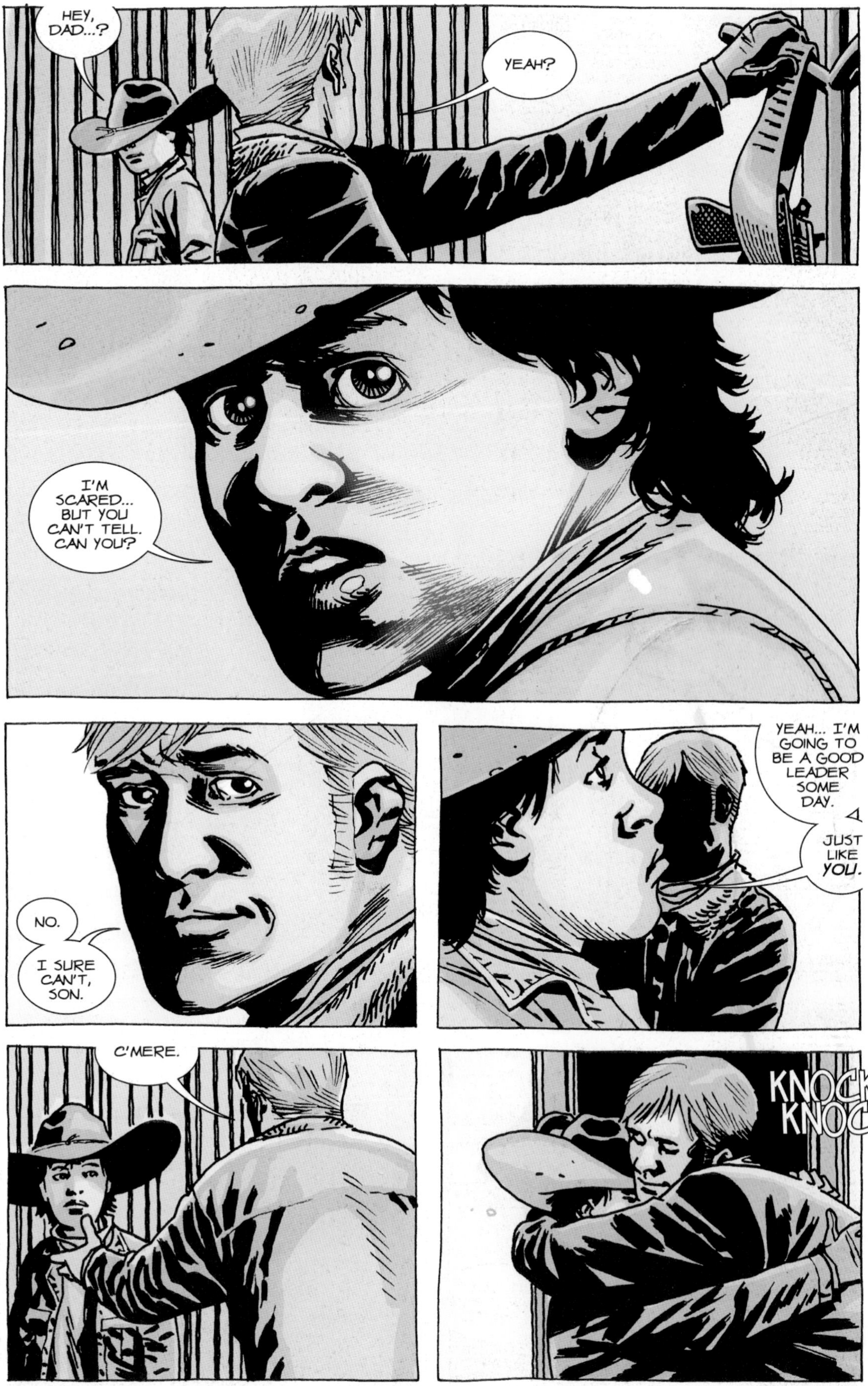

HEY, DAD...?
YEAH?
I'M SCARED... BUT YOU CAN'T TELL. CAN YOU?
NO.
I SURE CAN'T, SON.
YEAH... I'M GOING TO BE A GOOD LEADER SOME DAY.
JUST LIKE *YOU*.
C'MERE.
KNOCK. KNOCK

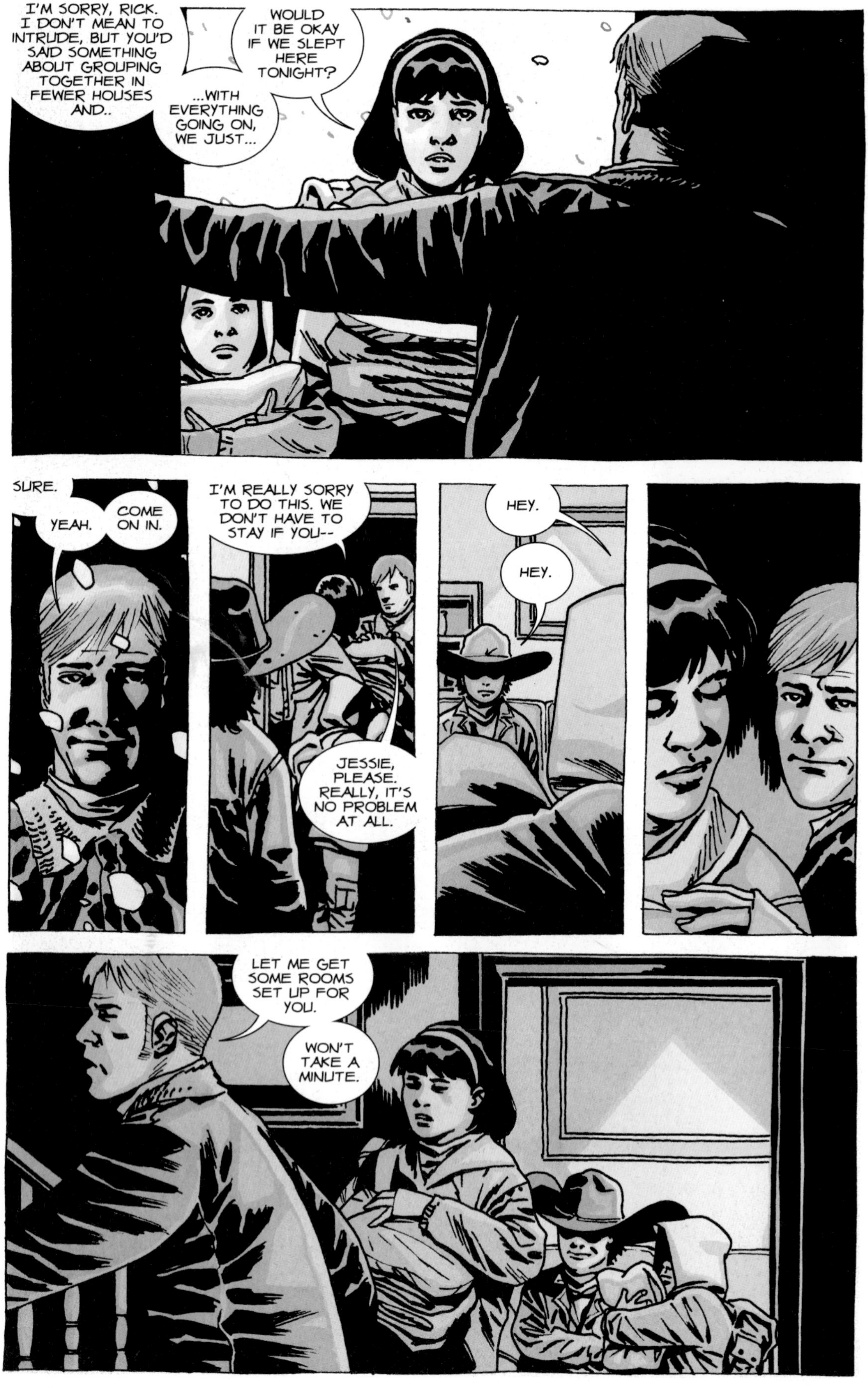
I'M SORRY, RICK. I DON'T MEAN TO INTRUDE, BUT YOU'D SAID SOMETHING ABOUT GROUPING TOGETHER IN FEWER HOUSES AND..
...WITH EVERYTHING GOING ON, WE JUST...
WOULD IT BE OKAY IF WE SLEPT HERE TONIGHT?
SURE.
YEAH.
COME ON IN.
I'M REALLY SORRY TO DO THIS. WE DON'T HAVE TO STAY IF YOU--
JESSIE, PLEASE. REALLY, IT'S NO PROBLEM AT ALL.
HEY.
HEY.
LET ME GET SOME ROOMS SET UP FOR YOU.
WON'T TAKE A MINUTE.

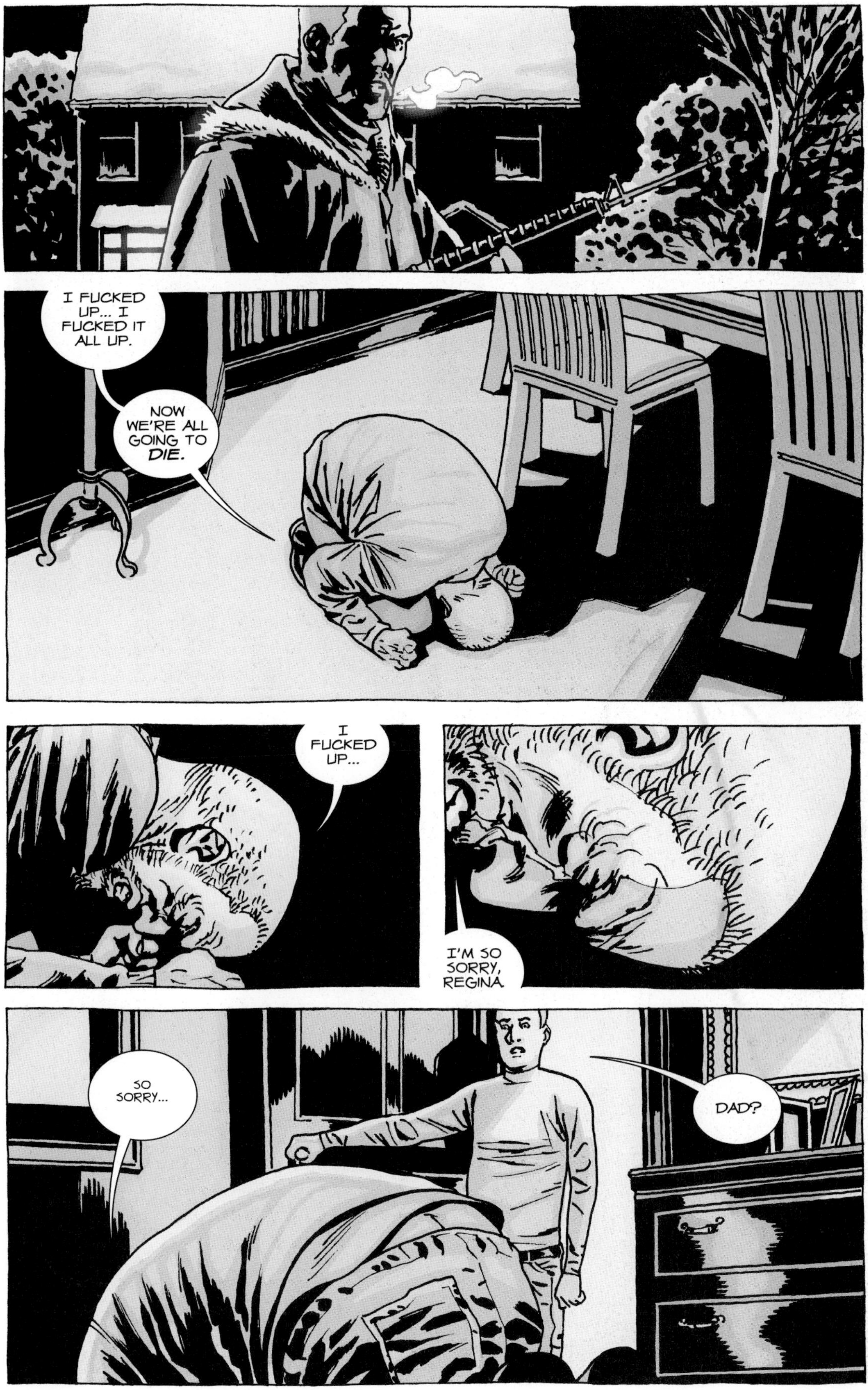
I FUCKED UP... I FUCKED IT ALL UP.
NOW WE'RE ALL GOING TO DIE.
I FUCKED UP...
I'M SO SORRY, REGINA.
SO SORRY...
DAD?

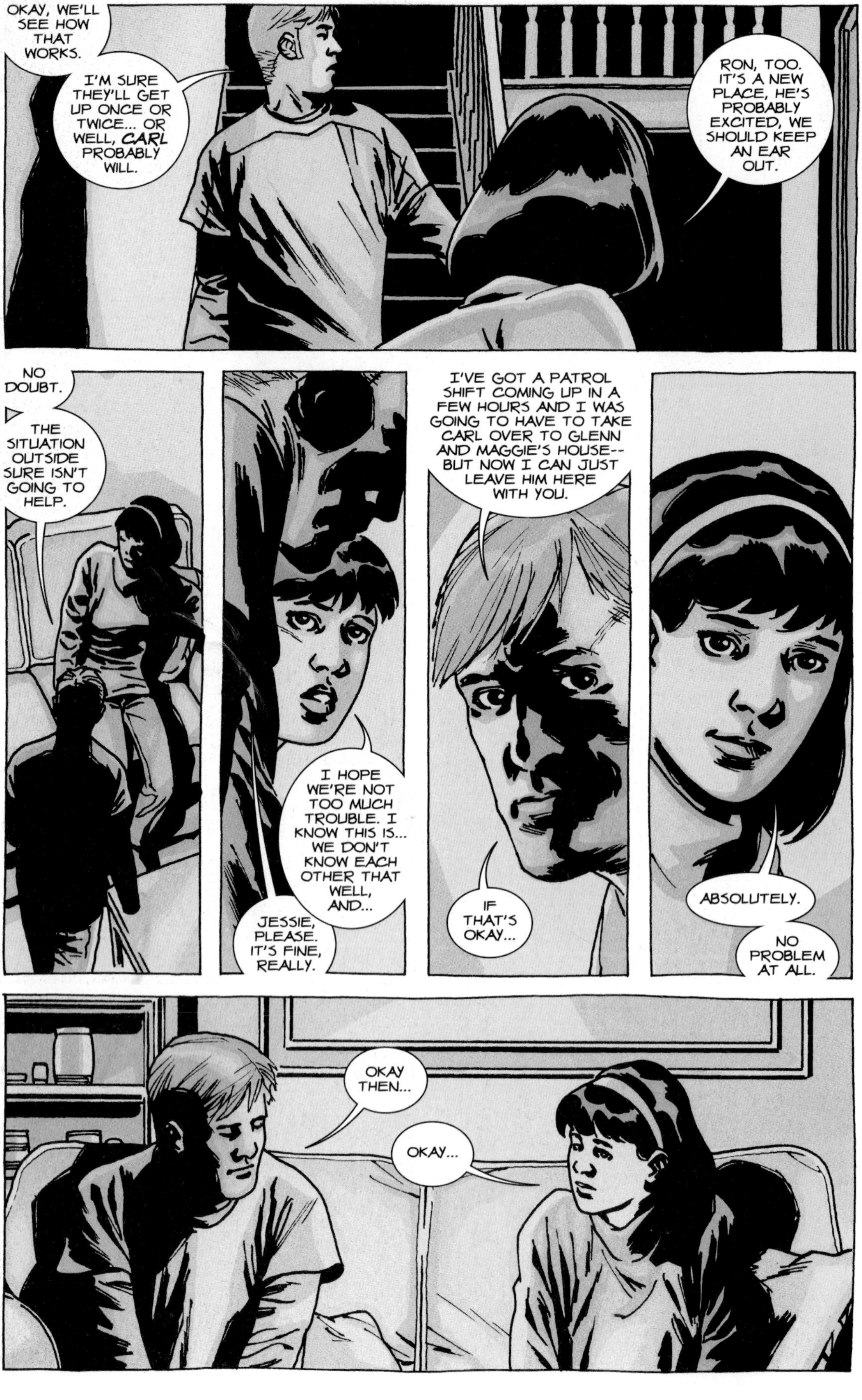

OKAY, WE'LL SEE HOW THAT WORKS.
I'M SURE THEY'LL GET UP ONCE OR TWICE... OR WELL, CARL PROBABLY WILL.
RON, TOO. IT'S A NEW PLACE, HE'S PROBABLY EXCITED, WE SHOULD KEEP AN EAR OUT.
NO DOUBT.
THE SITUATION OUTSIDE SURE ISN'T GOING TO HELP.
I HOPE WE'RE NOT TOO MUCH TROUBLE. I KNOW THIS IS... WE DON'T KNOW EACH OTHER THAT WELL, AND...
JESSIE, PLEASE. IT'S FINE, REALLY.
I'VE GOT A PATROL SHIFT COMING UP IN A FEW HOURS AND I WAS GOING TO HAVE TO TAKE CARL OVER TO GLENN AND MAGGIE'S HOUSE-- BUT NOW I CAN JUST LEAVE HIM HERE WITH YOU.
IF THAT'S OKAY...
ABSOLUTELY.
NO PROBLEM AT ALL.
OKAY THEN...
OKAY...

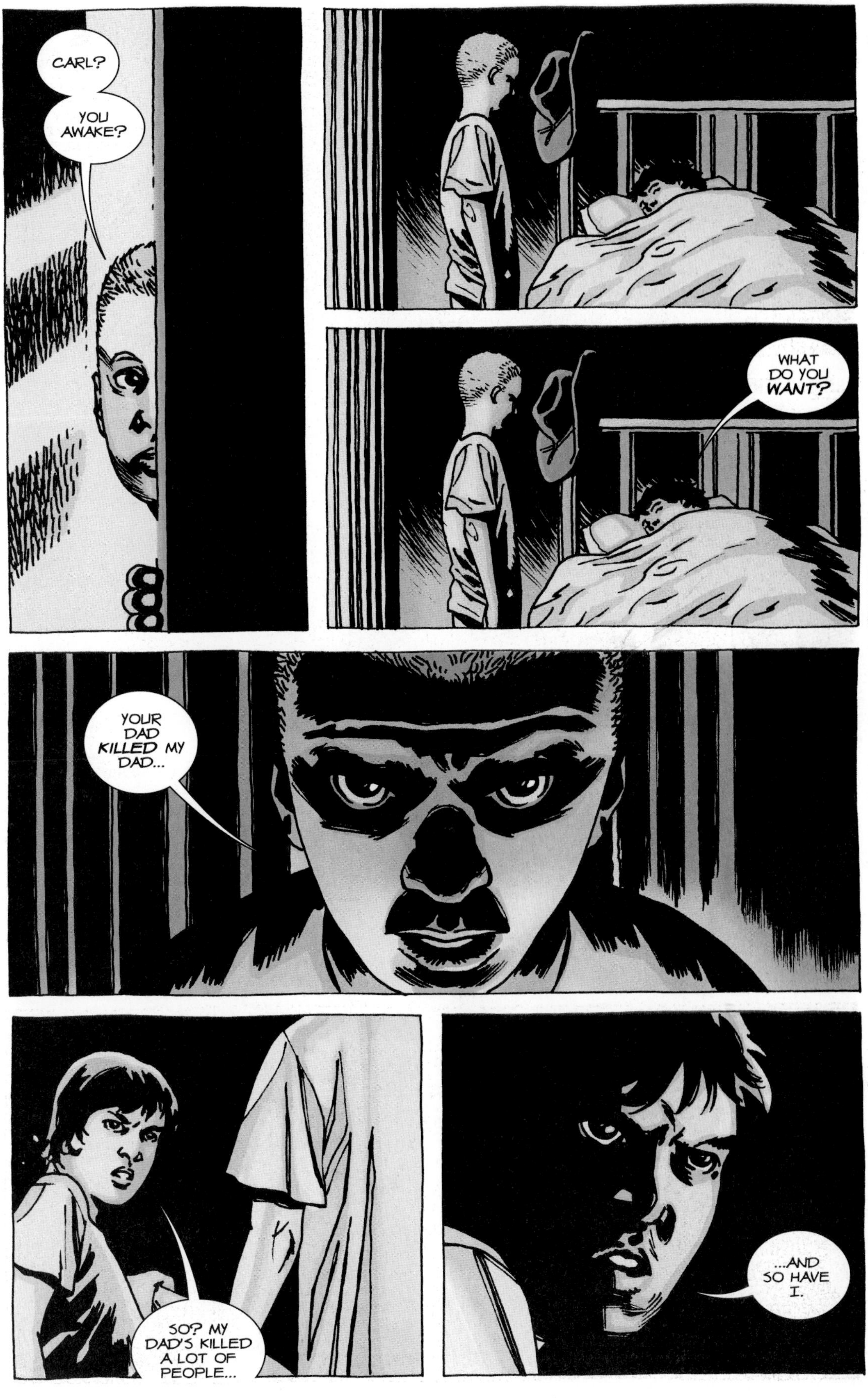
CARL?
YOU AWAKE?
WHAT DO YOU WANT?
YOUR DAD KILLED MY DAD...
SO? MY DAD'S KILLED A LOT OF PEOPLE...
...AND SO HAVE I.

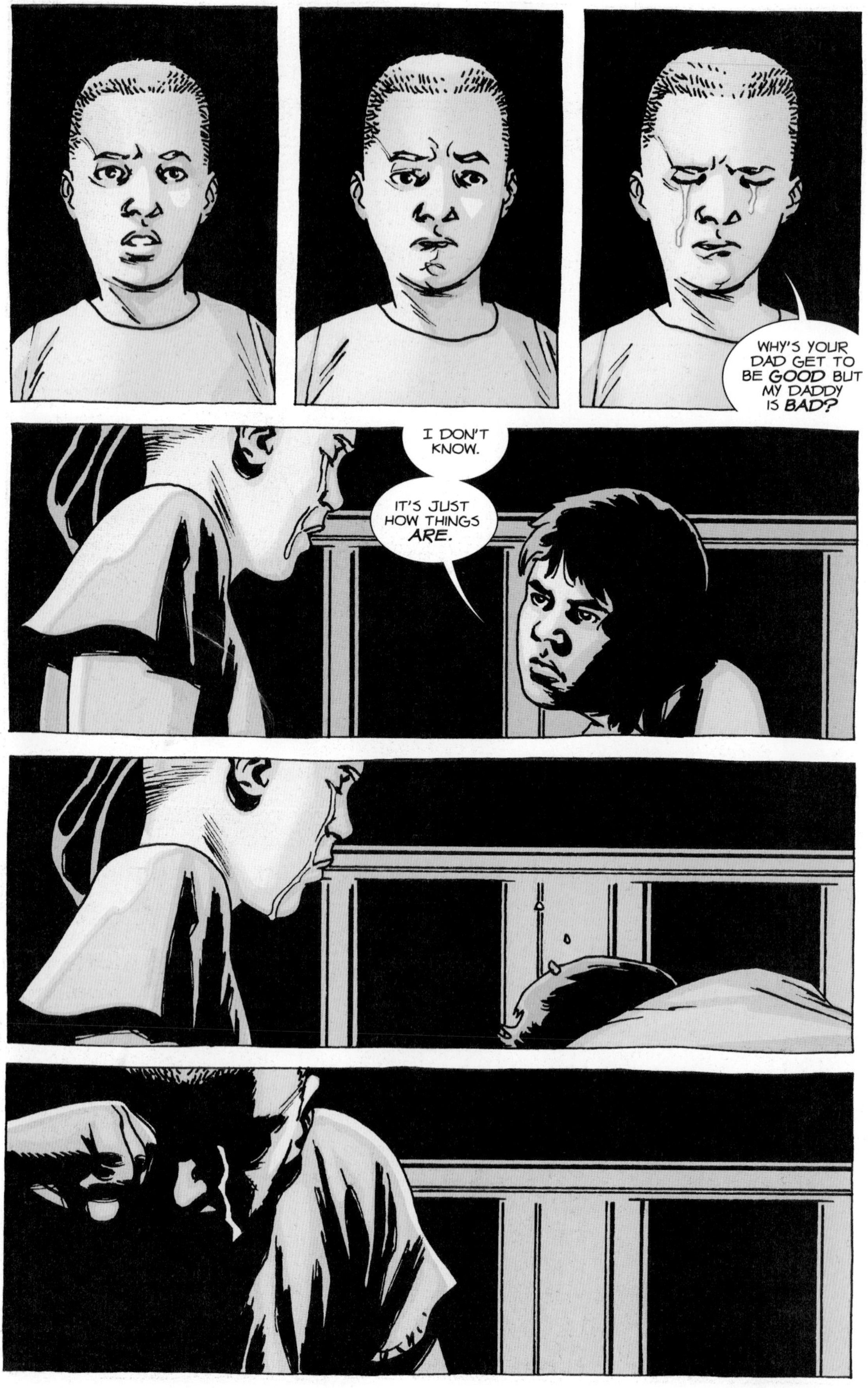
WHY'S YOUR DAD GET TO BE GOOD BUT MY DADDY IS BAD?
I DON'T KNOW.
IT'S JUST HOW THINGS ARE.

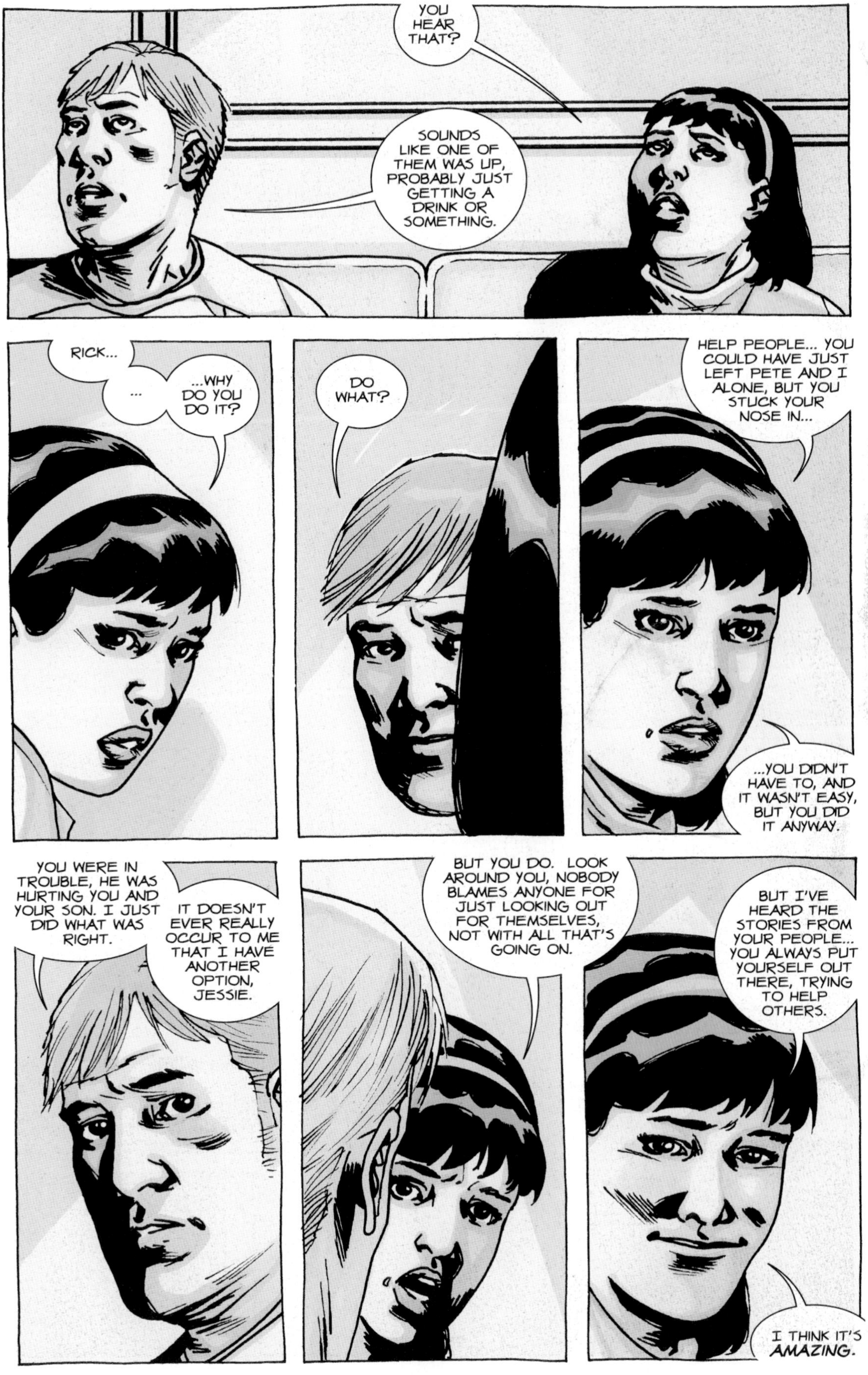
YOU HEAR THAT?
SOUNDS LIKE ONE OF THEM WAS UP, PROBABLY JUST GETTING A DRINK OR SOMETHING.
RICK...
...
...WHY DO YOU DO IT?
DO WHAT?
HELP PEOPLE... YOU COULD HAVE JUST LEFT PETE AND I ALONE, BUT YOU STUCK YOUR NOSE IN...
...YOU DIDN'T HAVE TO, AND IT WASN'T EASY, BUT YOU DID IT ANYWAY.
YOU WERE IN TROUBLE, HE WAS HURTING YOU AND YOUR SON. I JUST DID WHAT WAS RIGHT.
IT DOESN'T EVER REALLY OCCUR TO ME THAT I HAVE ANOTHER OPTION, JESSIE.
BUT YOU DO. LOOK AROUND YOU, NOBODY BLAMES ANYONE FOR JUST LOOKING OUT FOR THEMSELVES, NOT WITH ALL THAT'S GOING ON.
BUT I'VE HEARD THE STORIES FROM YOUR PEOPLE... YOU ALWAYS PUT YOURSELF OUT THERE, TRYING TO HELP OTHERS.
I THINK IT'S *AMAZING*.

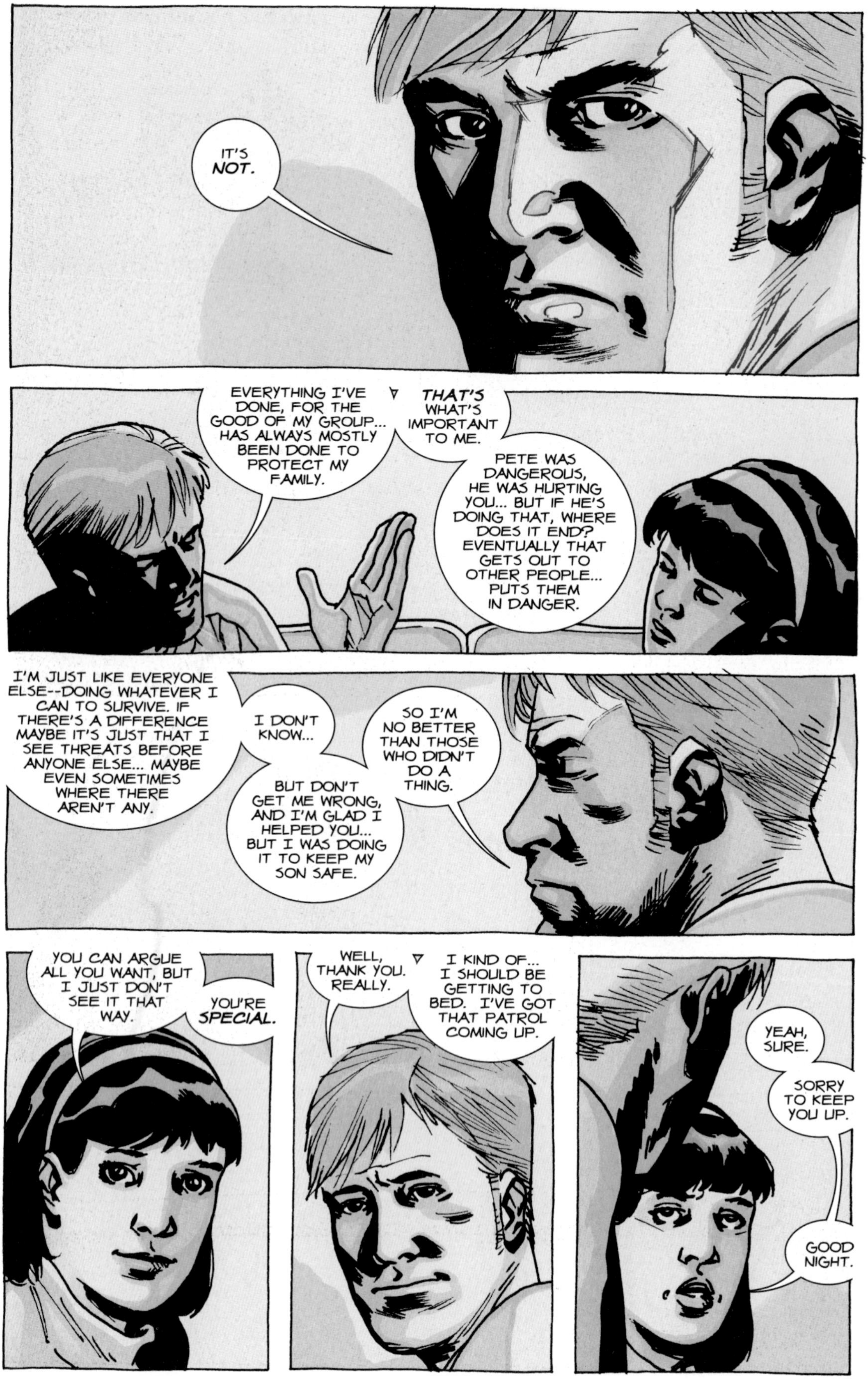
IT'S *NOT.*
EVERYTHING I'VE DONE, FOR THE GOOD OF MY GROUP... HAS ALWAYS MOSTLY BEEN DONE TO PROTECT MY FAMILY.
THAT'S WHAT'S IMPORTANT TO ME.
PETE WAS DANGEROUS, HE WAS HURTING YOU... BUT IF HE'S DOING THAT, WHERE DOES IT END? EVENTUALLY THAT GETS OUT TO OTHER PEOPLE... PUTS THEM IN DANGER.
I'M JUST LIKE EVERYONE ELSE--DOING WHATEVER I CAN TO SURVIVE. IF THERE'S A DIFFERENCE MAYBE IT'S JUST THAT I SEE THREATS BEFORE ANYONE ELSE... MAYBE EVEN SOMETIMES WHERE THERE AREN'T ANY.
I DON'T KNOW...
BUT DON'T GET ME WRONG, AND I'M GLAD I HELPED YOU... BUT I WAS DOING IT TO KEEP MY SON SAFE.
SO I'M NO BETTER THAN THOSE WHO DIDN'T DO A THING.
YOU CAN ARGUE ALL YOU WANT, BUT I JUST DON'T SEE IT THAT WAY.
YOU'RE *SPECIAL.*
WELL, THANK YOU. REALLY.
I KIND OF... I SHOULD BE GETTING TO BED. I'VE GOT THAT PATROL COMING UP.
YEAH, SURE.
SORRY TO KEEP YOU UP.
GOOD NIGHT.

I'M SORRY, DID I WAKE YOU?

MORGAN, HEY--NO, YOU DIDN'T. WHAT'S GOING ON?

I MISS MY WIFE AND I'M STILL NOT OVER HER DEATH AND I APPRECIATE YOU UNDERSTANDING ALL THAT.

BUT SOMETIMES I GET REALLY LONELY AND I JUST WANT TO BE WITH SOMEONE.

...AND THAT DOESN'T MAKE ME A BAD PERSON.

IT DOESN'T AT ALL.

COME IN. WITH ALL THAT'S GOING ON, I DON'T THINK ANYONE WANTS TO BE ALONE.

GO AHEAD, I'LL MEET YOU IN THERE.

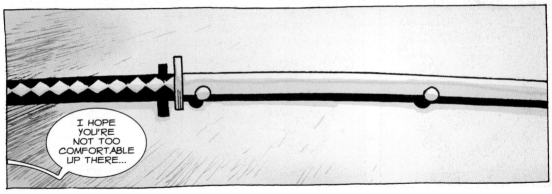

I HOPE YOU'RE NOT TOO COMFORTABLE UP THERE...

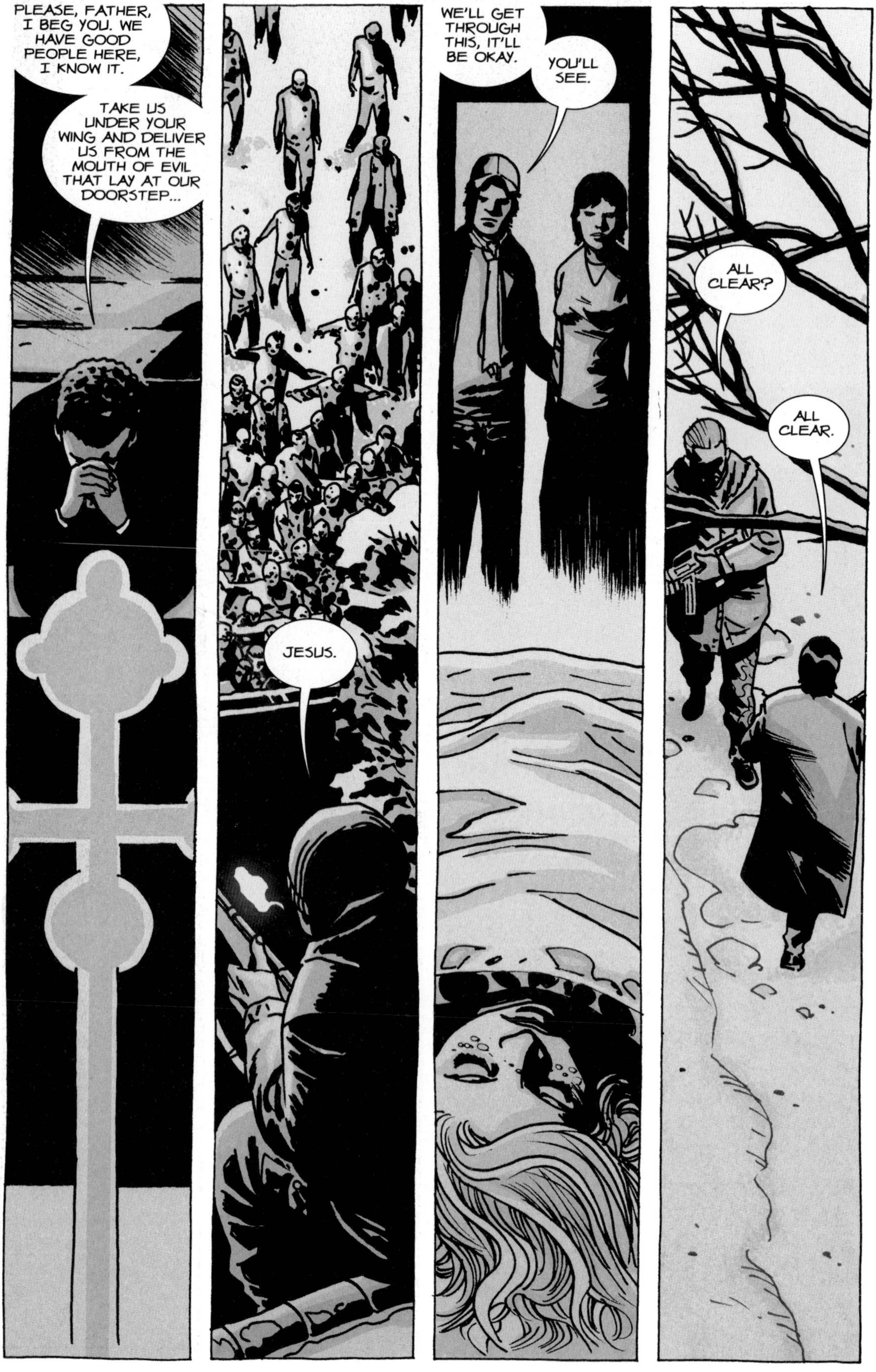
PLEASE, FATHER, I BEG YOU. WE HAVE GOOD PEOPLE HERE, I KNOW IT.
TAKE US UNDER YOUR WING AND DELIVER US FROM THE MOUTH OF EVIL THAT LAY AT OUR DOORSTEP...
JESUS.
WE'LL GET THROUGH THIS, IT'LL BE OKAY.
YOU'LL SEE.
ALL CLEAR?
ALL CLEAR.

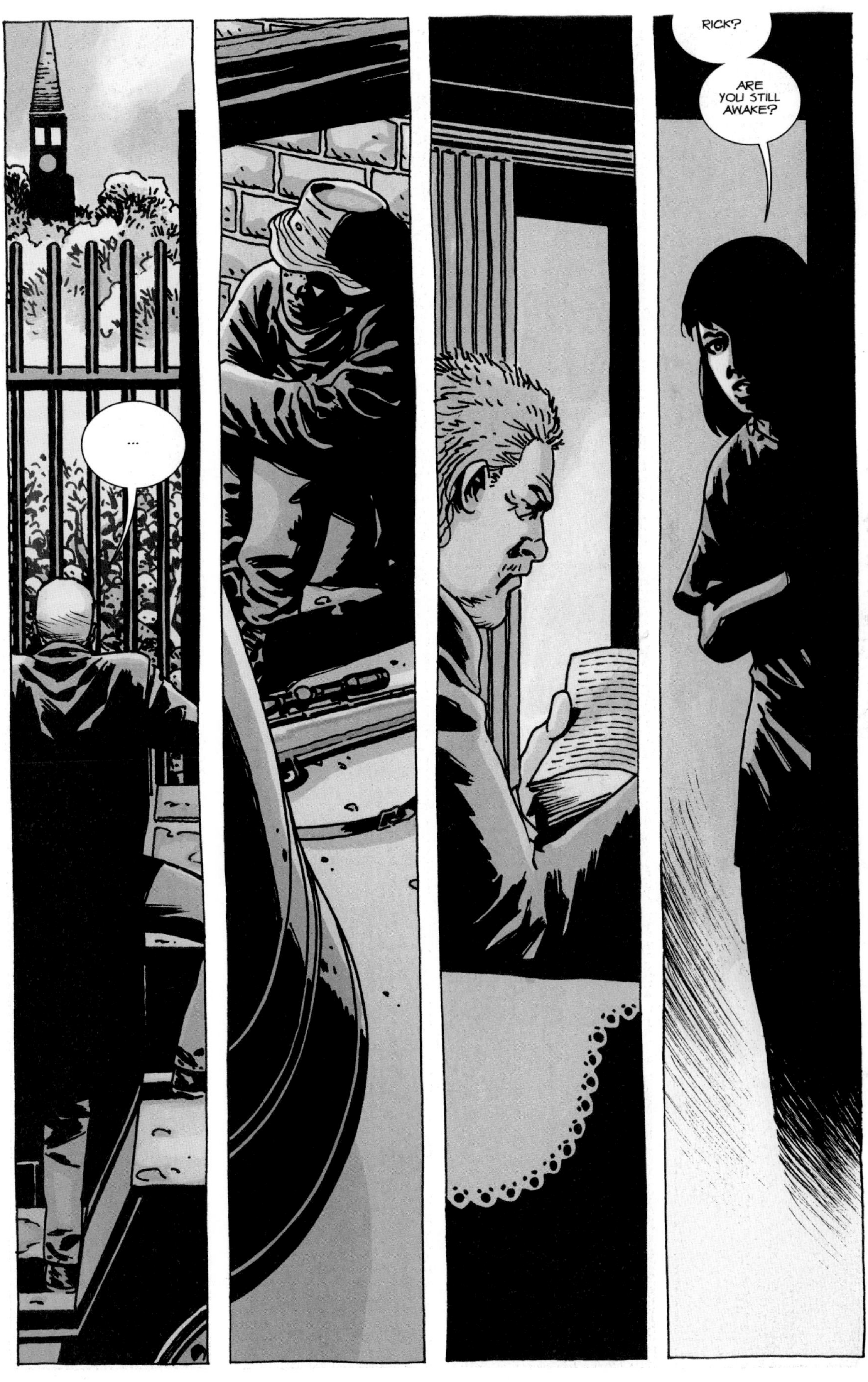
...
RICK?
ARE YOU STILL AWAKE?

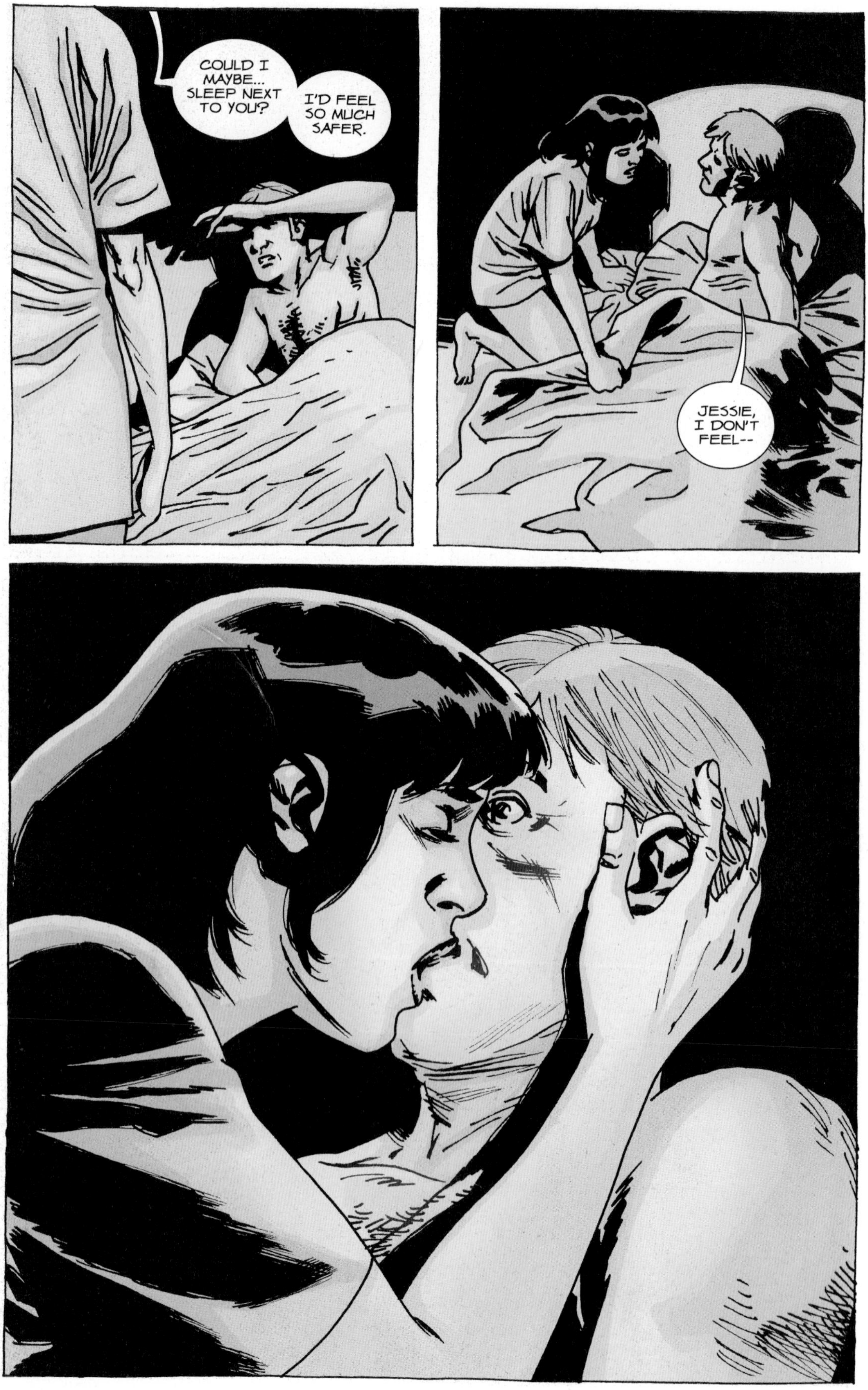
COULD I MAYBE... SLEEP NEXT TO YOU?
I'D FEEL SO MUCH SAFER.
JESSIE, I DON'T FEEL--

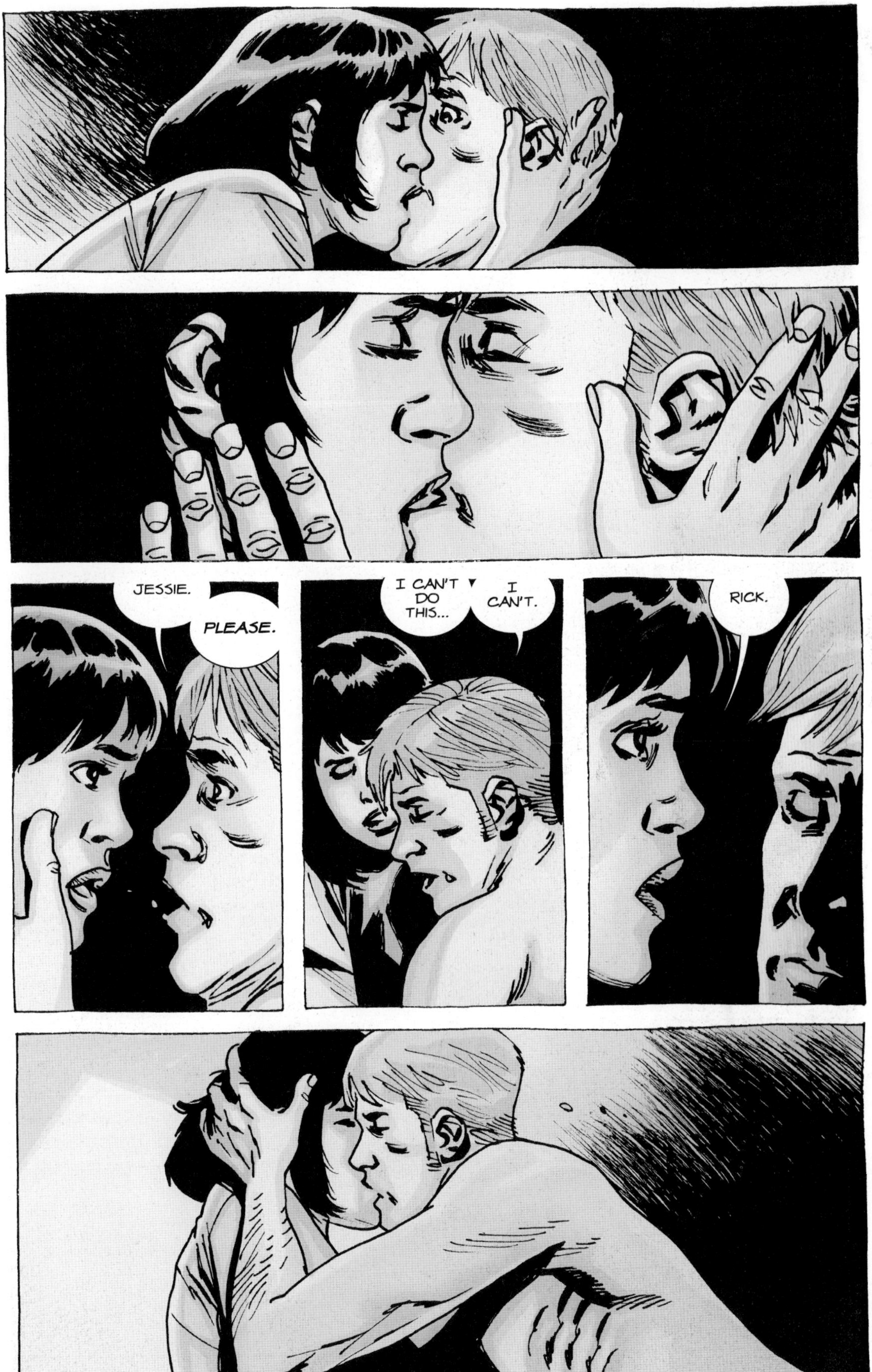
JESSIE.
PLEASE.
I CAN'T DO THIS...
I CAN'T.
RICK.

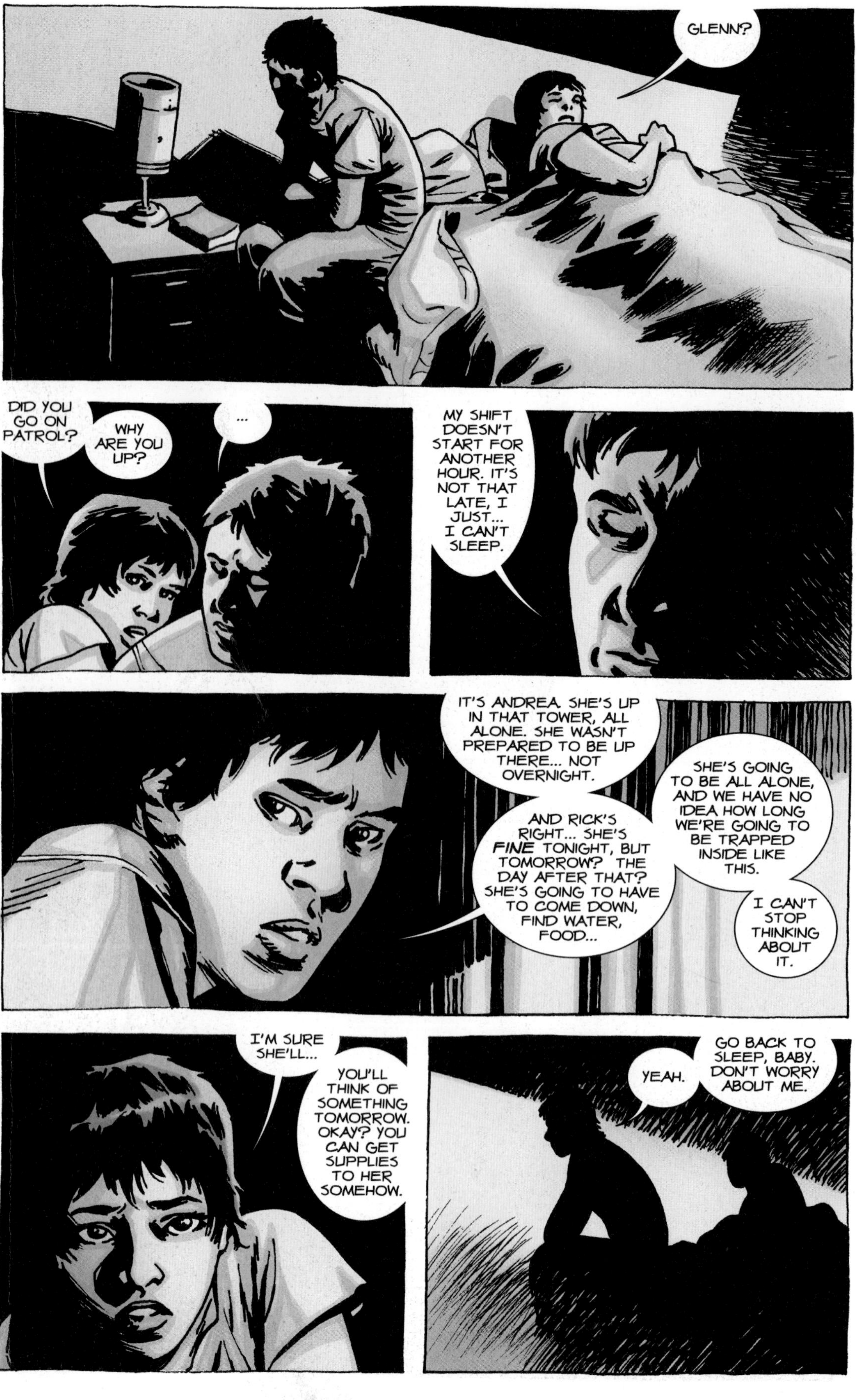
GLENN?
DID YOU GO ON PATROL?
WHY ARE YOU UP?
...
MY SHIFT DOESN'T START FOR ANOTHER HOUR. IT'S NOT THAT LATE, I JUST... I CAN'T SLEEP.
IT'S ANDREA. SHE'S UP IN THAT TOWER, ALL ALONE. SHE WASN'T PREPARED TO BE UP THERE... NOT OVERNIGHT.
AND RICK'S RIGHT... SHE'S *FINE* TONIGHT, BUT TOMORROW? THE DAY AFTER THAT? SHE'S GOING TO HAVE TO COME DOWN, FIND WATER, FOOD...
SHE'S GOING TO BE ALL ALONE, AND WE HAVE NO IDEA HOW LONG WE'RE GOING TO BE TRAPPED INSIDE LIKE THIS.
I CAN'T STOP THINKING ABOUT IT.
I'M SURE SHE'LL...
YOU'LL THINK OF SOMETHING TOMORROW. OKAY? YOU CAN GET SUPPLIES TO HER SOMEHOW.
YEAH.
GO BACK TO SLEEP, BABY. DON'T WORRY ABOUT ME.

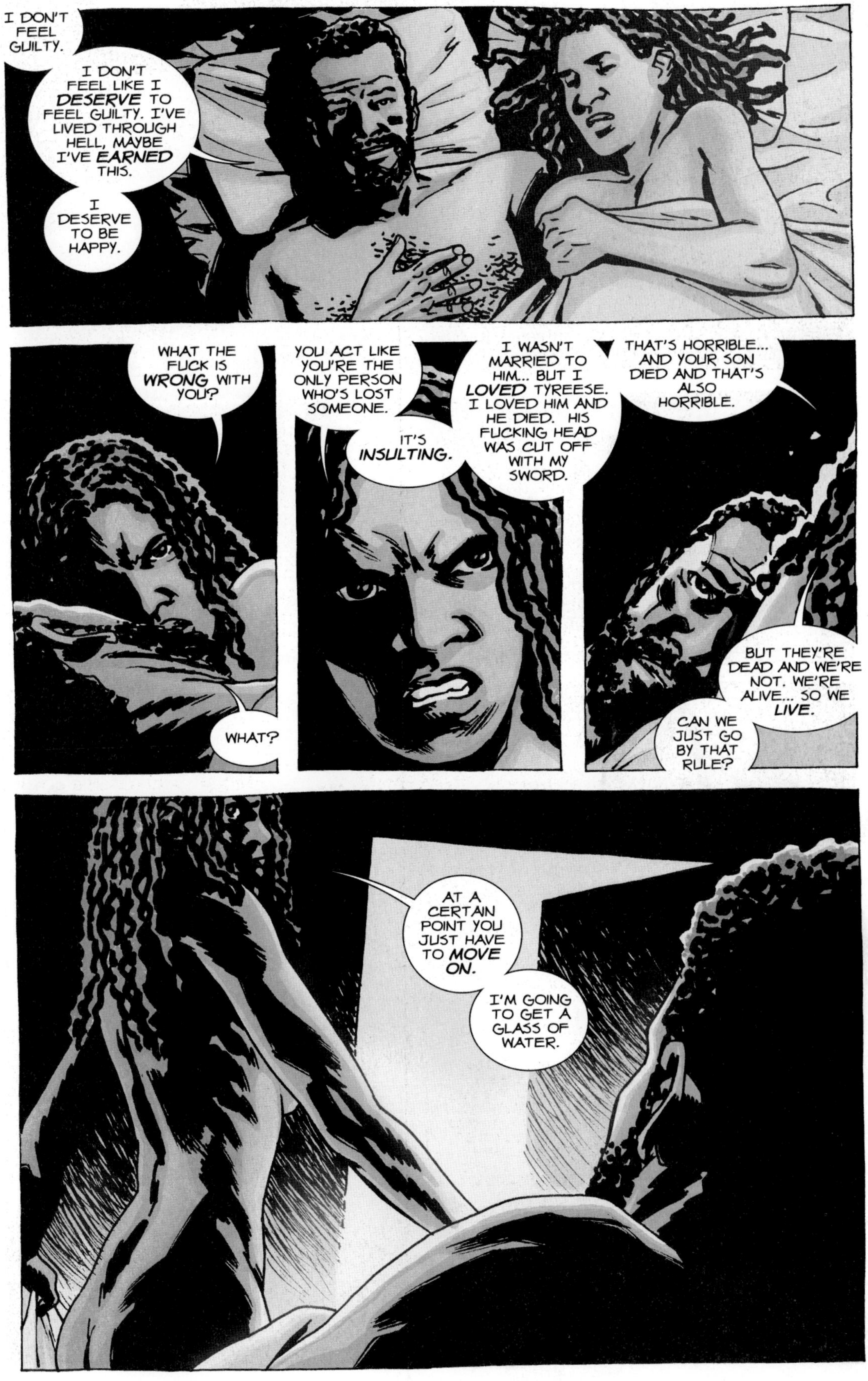
I DON'T FEEL GUILTY.
I DON'T FEEL LIKE I DESERVE TO FEEL GUILTY. I'VE LIVED THROUGH HELL, MAYBE I'VE EARNED THIS.
I DESERVE TO BE HAPPY.
WHAT THE FUCK IS WRONG WITH YOU?
WHAT?
YOU ACT LIKE YOU'RE THE ONLY PERSON WHO'S LOST SOMEONE.
IT'S INSULTING.
I WASN'T MARRIED TO HIM... BUT I LOVED TYREESE. I LOVED HIM AND HE DIED. HIS FUCKING HEAD WAS CUT OFF WITH MY SWORD.
THAT'S HORRIBLE... AND YOUR SON DIED AND THAT'S ALSO HORRIBLE.
BUT THEY'RE DEAD AND WE'RE NOT. WE'RE ALIVE... SO WE LIVE.
CAN WE JUST GO BY THAT RULE?
AT A CERTAIN POINT YOU JUST HAVE TO MOVE ON.
I'M GOING TO GET A GLASS OF WATER.

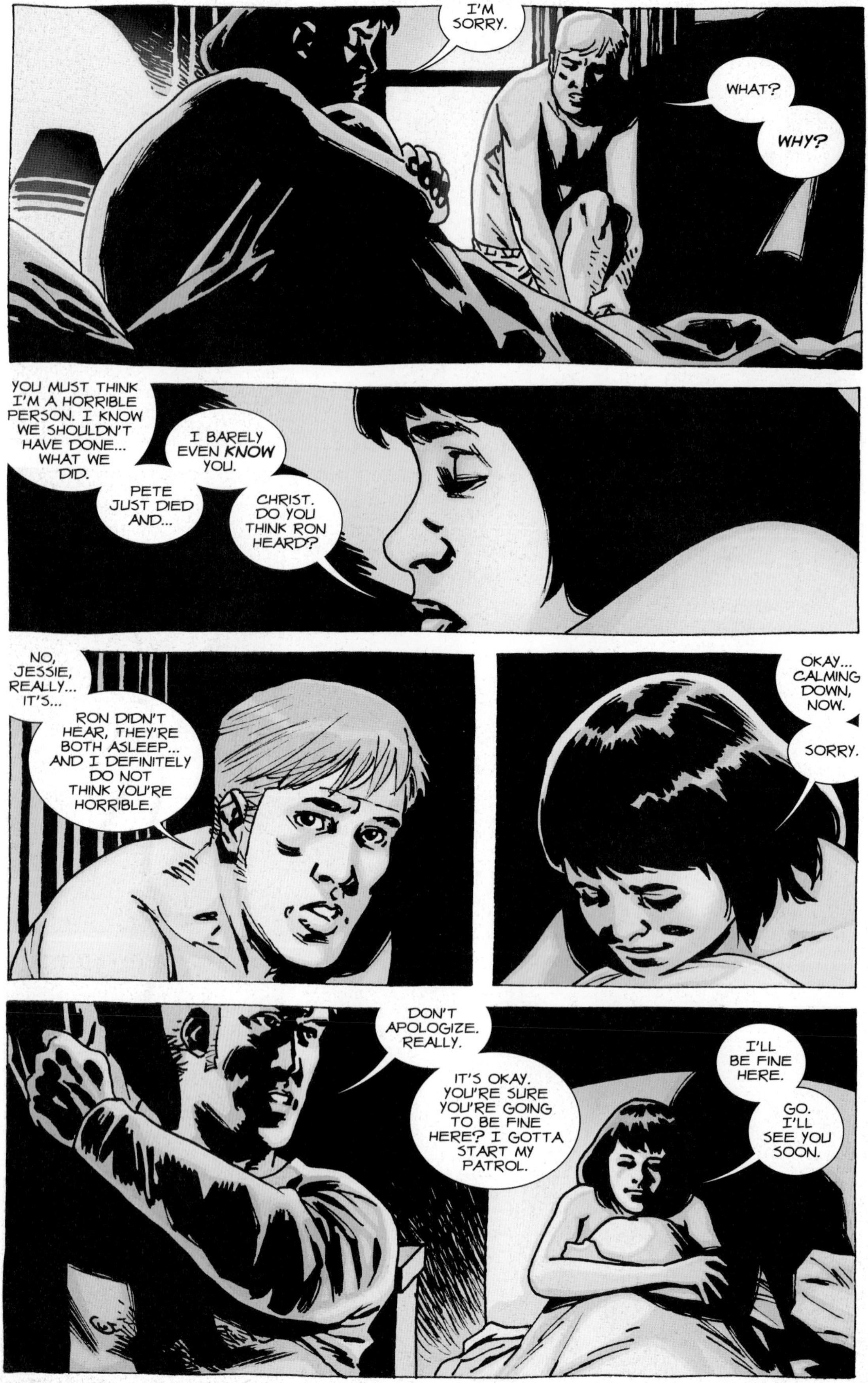
I'M SORRY.
WHAT?
WHY?
YOU MUST THINK I'M A HORRIBLE PERSON. I KNOW WE SHOULDN'T HAVE DONE... WHAT WE DID.
I BARELY EVEN KNOW YOU.
PETE JUST DIED AND...
CHRIST. DO YOU THINK RON HEARD?
NO, JESSIE, REALLY... IT'S...
RON DIDN'T HEAR, THEY'RE BOTH ASLEEP... AND I DEFINITELY DO NOT THINK YOU'RE HORRIBLE.
OKAY... CALMING DOWN, NOW.
SORRY.
DON'T APOLOGIZE. REALLY.
IT'S OKAY. YOU'RE SURE YOU'RE GOING TO BE FINE HERE? I GOTTA START MY PATROL.
I'LL BE FINE HERE.
GO. I'LL SEE YOU SOON.

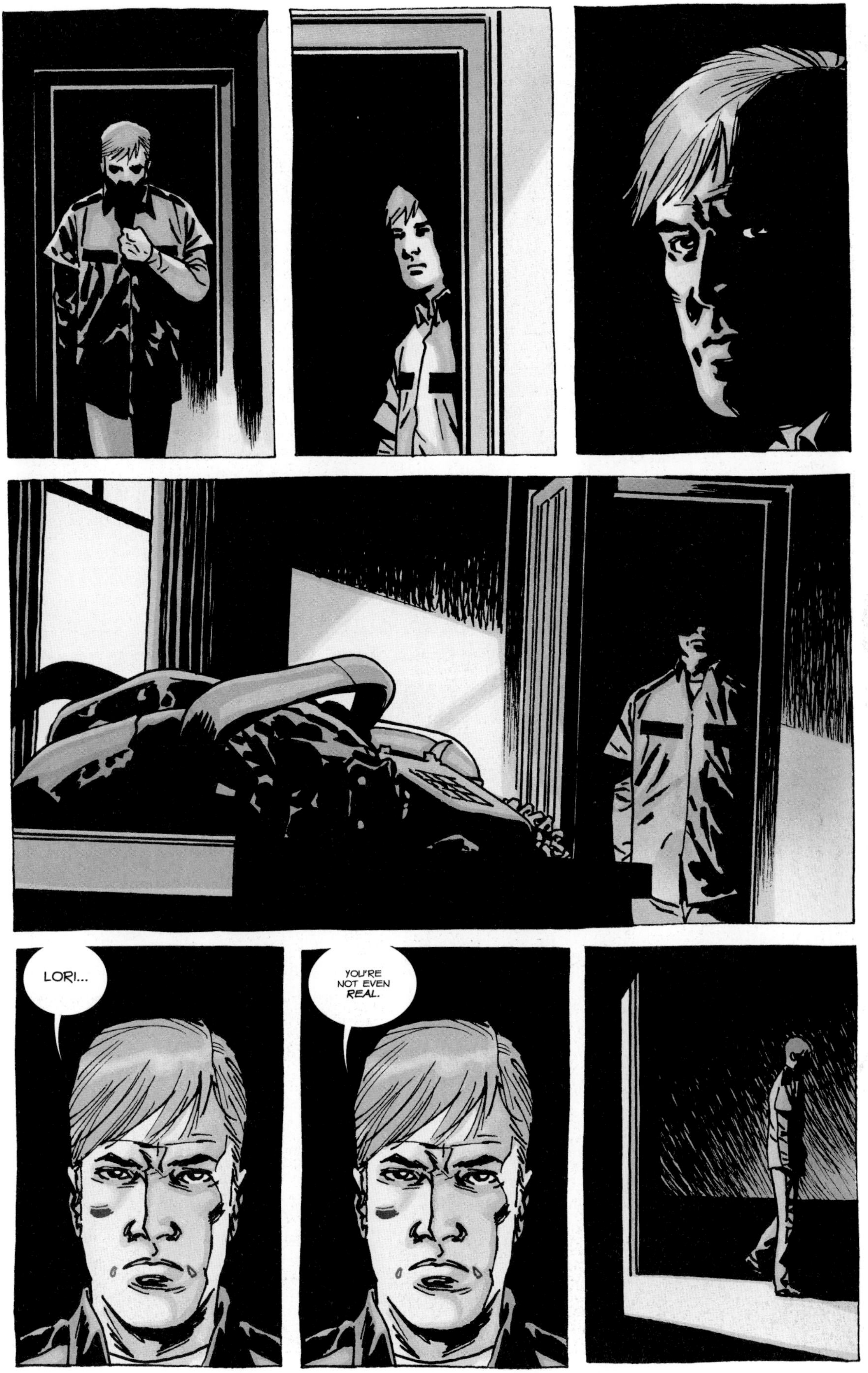
LORI...
YOU'RE NOT EVEN REAL.

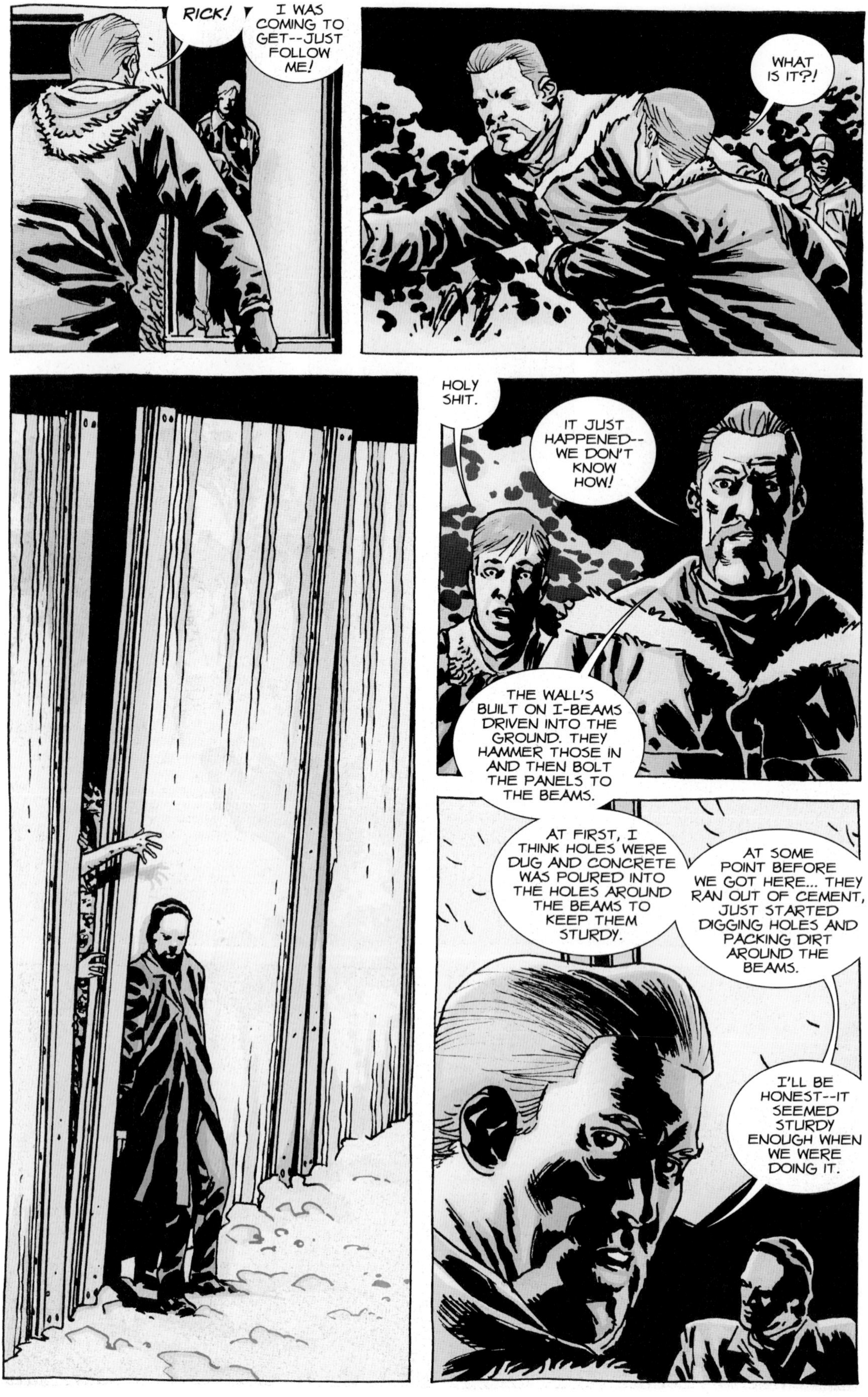
RICK!
I WAS COMING TO GET--JUST FOLLOW ME!
WHAT IS IT?!
HOLY SHIT.
IT JUST HAPPENED-- WE DON'T KNOW HOW!
THE WALL'S BUILT ON I-BEAMS DRIVEN INTO THE GROUND. THEY HAMMER THOSE IN AND THEN BOLT THE PANELS TO THE BEAMS.
AT FIRST, I THINK HOLES WERE DUG AND CONCRETE WAS POURED INTO THE HOLES AROUND THE BEAMS TO KEEP THEM STURDY.
AT SOME POINT BEFORE WE GOT HERE... THEY RAN OUT OF CEMENT, JUST STARTED DIGGING HOLES AND PACKING DIRT AROUND THE BEAMS.
I'LL BE HONEST--IT SEEMED STURDY ENOUGH WHEN WE WERE DOING IT.

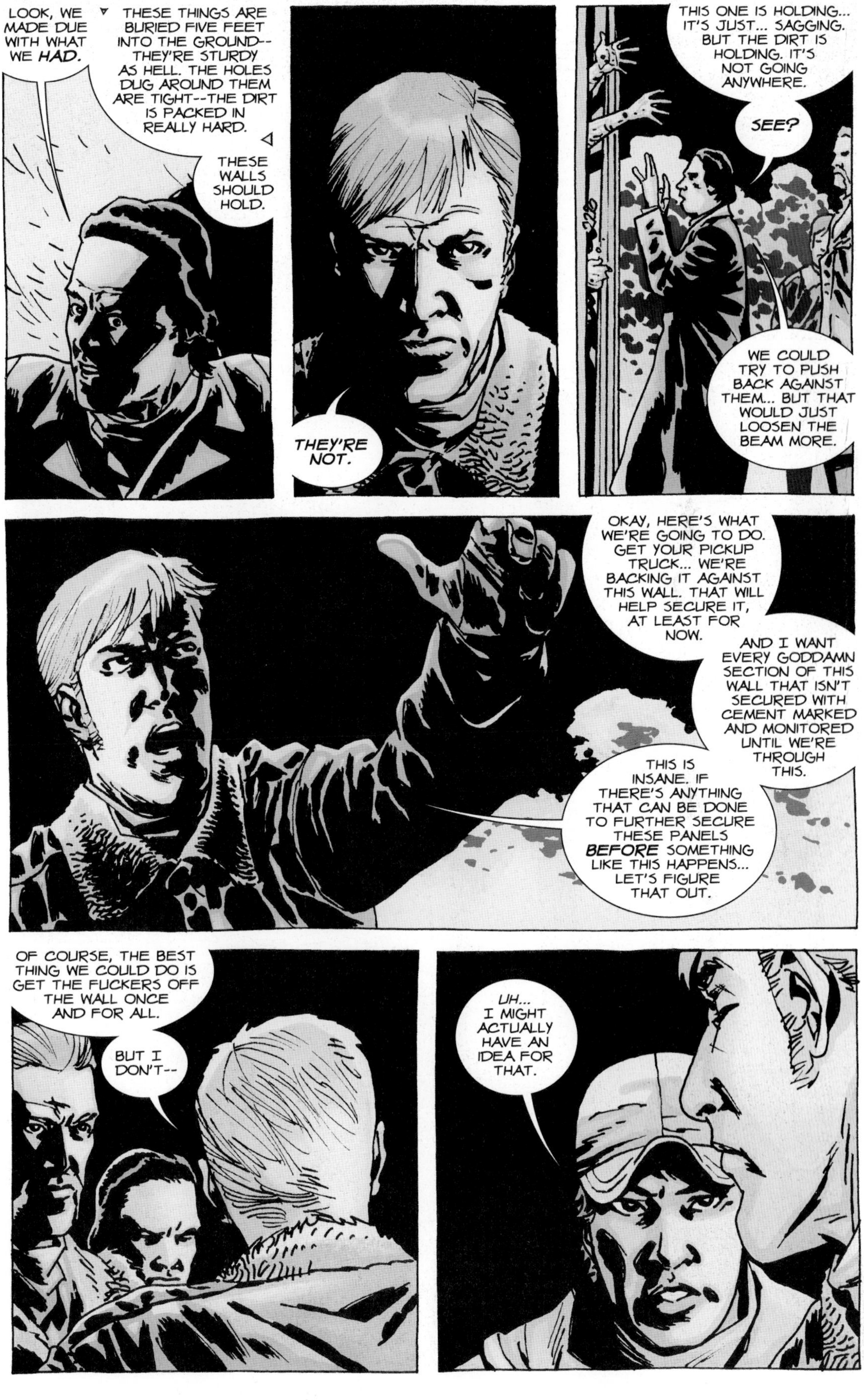
LOOK, WE MADE DUE WITH WHAT WE HAD.
THESE THINGS ARE BURIED FIVE FEET INTO THE GROUND-- THEY'RE STURDY AS HELL. THE HOLES DUG AROUND THEM ARE TIGHT--THE DIRT IS PACKED IN REALLY HARD.
THESE WALLS SHOULD HOLD.
THEY'RE NOT.
THIS ONE IS HOLDING... IT'S JUST... SAGGING. BUT THE DIRT IS HOLDING. IT'S NOT GOING ANYWHERE.
SEE?
WE COULD TRY TO PUSH BACK AGAINST THEM... BUT THAT WOULD JUST LOOSEN THE BEAM MORE.
OKAY, HERE'S WHAT WE'RE GOING TO DO. GET YOUR PICKUP TRUCK... WE'RE BACKING IT AGAINST THIS WALL. THAT WILL HELP SECURE IT, AT LEAST FOR NOW.
AND I WANT EVERY GODDAMN SECTION OF THIS WALL THAT ISN'T SECURED WITH CEMENT MARKED AND MONITORED UNTIL WE'RE THROUGH THIS.
THIS IS INSANE. IF THERE'S ANYTHING THAT CAN BE DONE TO FURTHER SECURE THESE PANELS BEFORE SOMETHING LIKE THIS HAPPENS... LET'S FIGURE THAT OUT.
OF COURSE, THE BEST THING WE COULD DO IS GET THE FUCKERS OFF THE WALL ONCE AND FOR ALL.
BUT I DON'T--
UH... I MIGHT ACTUALLY HAVE AN IDEA FOR THAT.

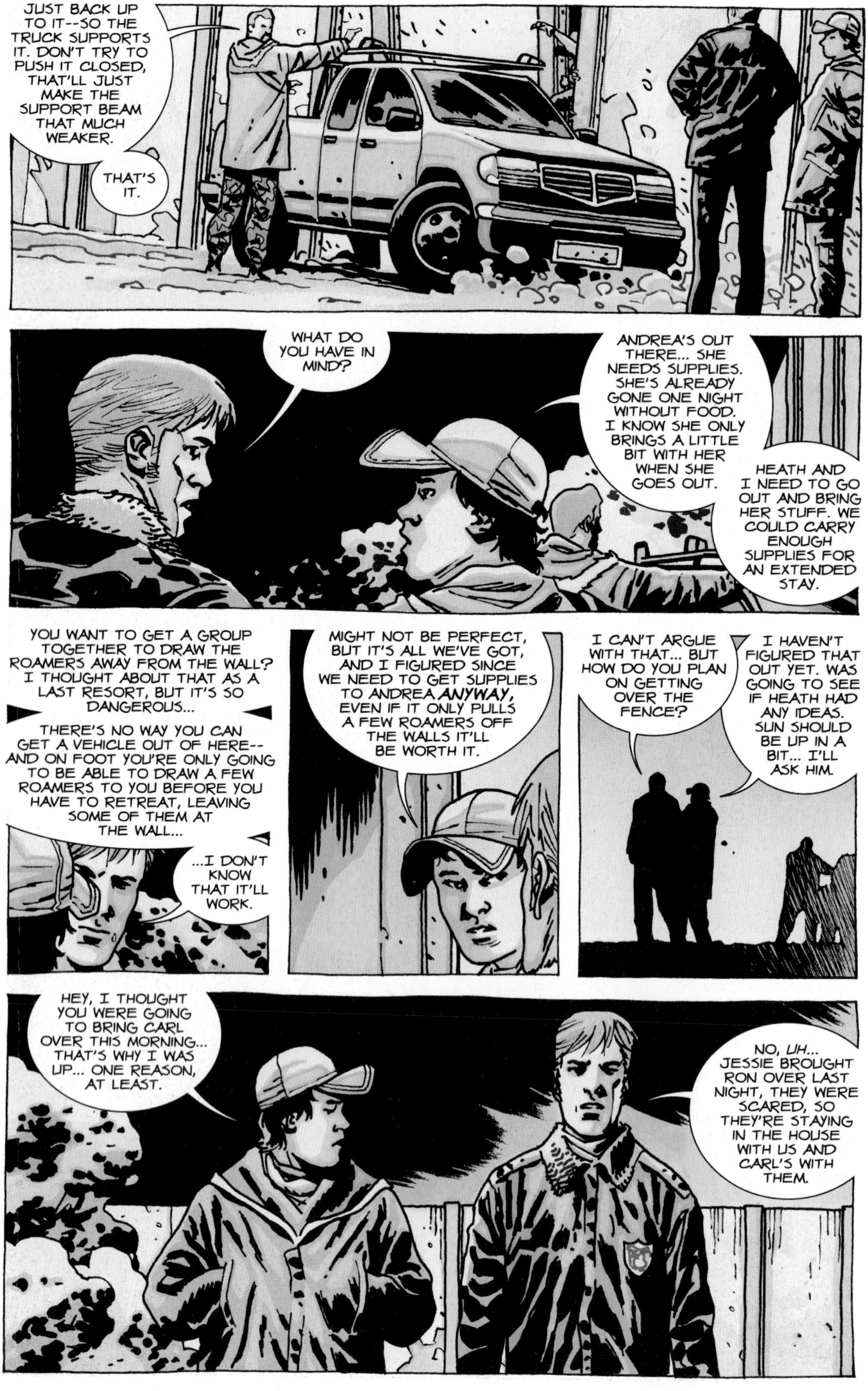
JUST BACK UP TO IT--SO THE TRUCK SUPPORTS IT. DON'T TRY TO PUSH IT CLOSED, THAT'LL JUST MAKE THE SUPPORT BEAM THAT MUCH WEAKER.
THAT'S IT.
WHAT DO YOU HAVE IN MIND?
ANDREA'S OUT THERE... SHE NEEDS SUPPLIES. SHE'S ALREADY GONE ONE NIGHT WITHOUT FOOD. I KNOW SHE ONLY BRINGS A LITTLE BIT WITH HER WHEN SHE GOES OUT.
HEATH AND I NEED TO GO OUT AND BRING HER STUFF. WE COULD CARRY ENOUGH SUPPLIES FOR AN EXTENDED STAY.
YOU WANT TO GET A GROUP TOGETHER TO DRAW THE ROAMERS AWAY FROM THE WALL? I THOUGHT ABOUT THAT AS A LAST RESORT, BUT IT'S SO DANGEROUS...
THERE'S NO WAY YOU CAN GET A VEHICLE OUT OF HERE-- AND ON FOOT YOU'RE ONLY GOING TO BE ABLE TO DRAW A FEW ROAMERS TO YOU BEFORE YOU HAVE TO RETREAT, LEAVING SOME OF THEM AT THE WALL...
...I DON'T KNOW THAT IT'LL WORK.
MIGHT NOT BE PERFECT, BUT IT'S ALL WE'VE GOT, AND I FIGURED SINCE WE NEED TO GET SUPPLIES TO ANDREA *ANYWAY,* EVEN IF IT ONLY PULLS A FEW ROAMERS OFF THE WALLS IT'LL BE WORTH IT.
I CAN'T ARGUE WITH THAT... BUT HOW DO YOU PLAN ON GETTING OVER THE FENCE?
I HAVEN'T FIGURED THAT OUT YET. WAS GOING TO SEE IF HEATH HAD ANY IDEAS. SUN SHOULD BE UP IN A BIT... I'LL ASK HIM.
HEY, I THOUGHT YOU WERE GOING TO BRING CARL OVER THIS MORNING... THAT'S WHY I WAS UP... ONE REASON, AT LEAST.
NO, *UH*... JESSIE BROUGHT RON OVER LAST NIGHT, THEY WERE SCARED, SO THEY'RE STAYING IN THE HOUSE WITH US AND CARL'S WITH THEM.

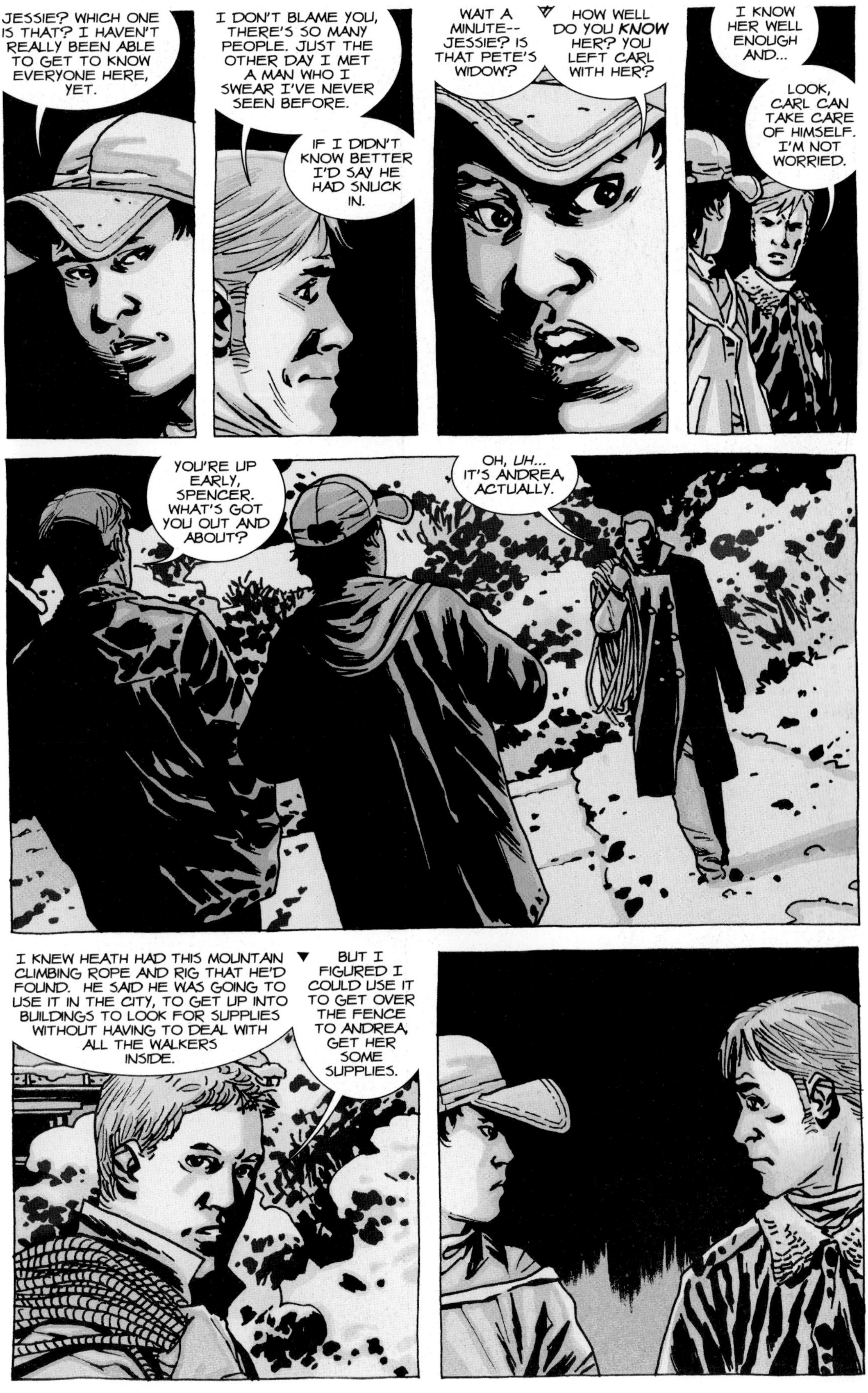

JESSIE? WHICH ONE IS THAT? I HAVEN'T REALLY BEEN ABLE TO GET TO KNOW EVERYONE HERE, YET.
I DON'T BLAME YOU, THERE'S SO MANY PEOPLE. JUST THE OTHER DAY I MET A MAN WHO I SWEAR I'VE NEVER SEEN BEFORE.
IF I DIDN'T KNOW BETTER I'D SAY HE HAD SNUCK IN.
WAIT A MINUTE-- JESSIE? IS THAT PETE'S WIDOW?
HOW WELL DO YOU *KNOW* HER? YOU LEFT CARL WITH HER?
I KNOW HER WELL ENOUGH AND...
LOOK, CARL CAN TAKE CARE OF HIMSELF. I'M NOT WORRIED.
YOU'RE UP EARLY, SPENCER. WHAT'S GOT YOU OUT AND ABOUT?
OH, *UH*... IT'S ANDREA, ACTUALLY.
I KNEW HEATH HAD THIS MOUNTAIN CLIMBING ROPE AND RIG THAT HE'D FOUND. HE SAID HE WAS GOING TO USE IT IN THE CITY, TO GET UP INTO BUILDINGS TO LOOK FOR SUPPLIES WITHOUT HAVING TO DEAL WITH ALL THE WALKERS INSIDE.
BUT I FIGURED I COULD USE IT TO GET OVER THE FENCE TO ANDREA, GET HER SOME SUPPLIES.

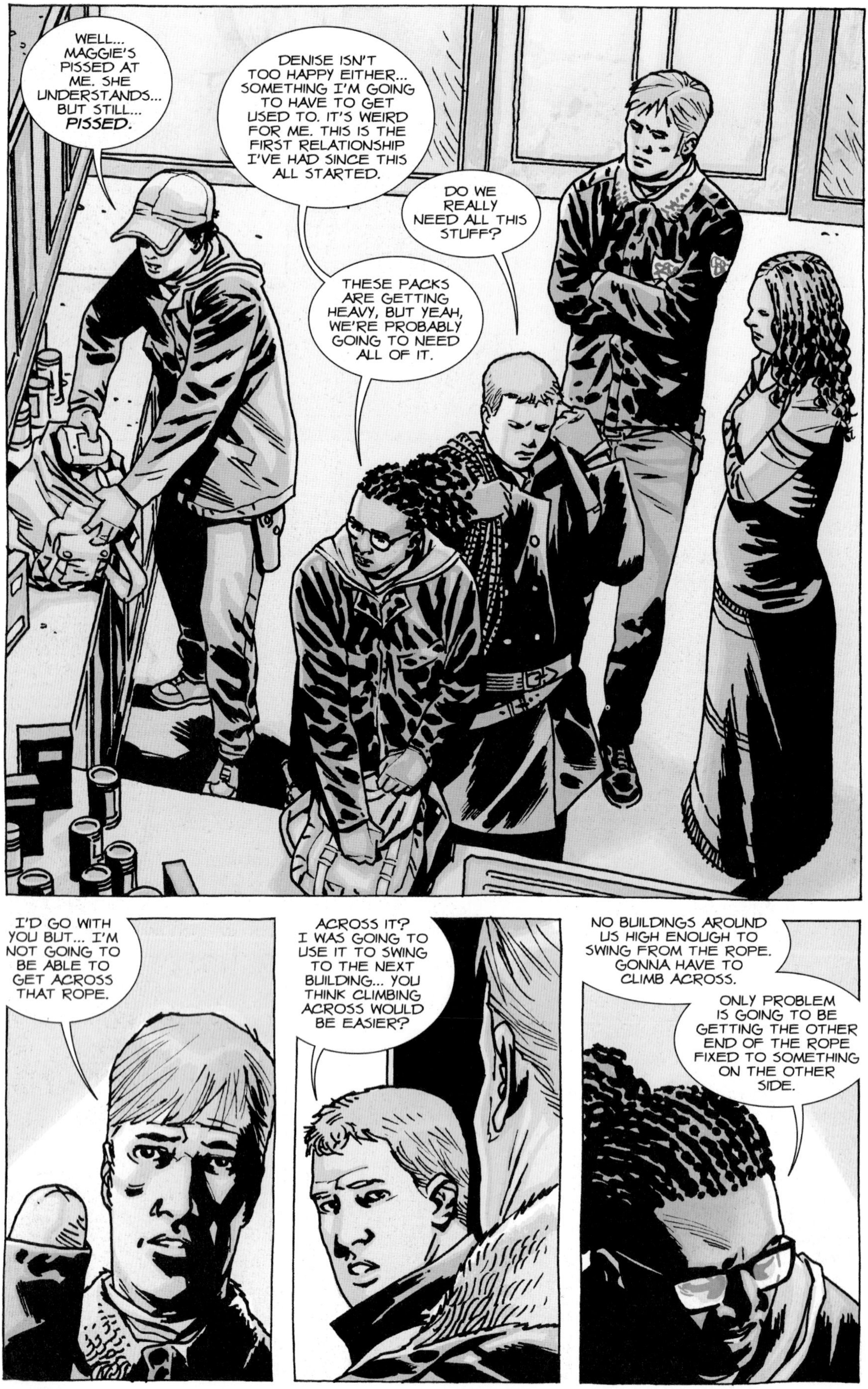
WELL... MAGGIE'S PISSED AT ME. SHE UNDERSTANDS... BUT STILL... *PISSED.*
DENISE ISN'T TOO HAPPY EITHER... SOMETHING I'M GOING TO HAVE TO GET USED TO. IT'S WEIRD FOR ME. THIS IS THE FIRST RELATIONSHIP I'VE HAD SINCE THIS ALL STARTED.
DO WE REALLY NEED ALL THIS STUFF?
THESE PACKS ARE GETTING HEAVY, BUT YEAH, WE'RE PROBABLY GOING TO NEED ALL OF IT.
I'D GO WITH YOU BUT... I'M NOT GOING TO BE ABLE TO GET ACROSS THAT ROPE.
ACROSS IT? I WAS GOING TO USE IT TO SWING TO THE NEXT BUILDING... YOU THINK CLIMBING ACROSS WOULD BE EASIER?
NO BUILDINGS AROUND US HIGH ENOUGH TO SWING FROM THE ROPE. GONNA HAVE TO CLIMB ACROSS.
ONLY PROBLEM IS GOING TO BE GETTING THE OTHER END OF THE ROPE FIXED TO SOMETHING ON THE OTHER SIDE.

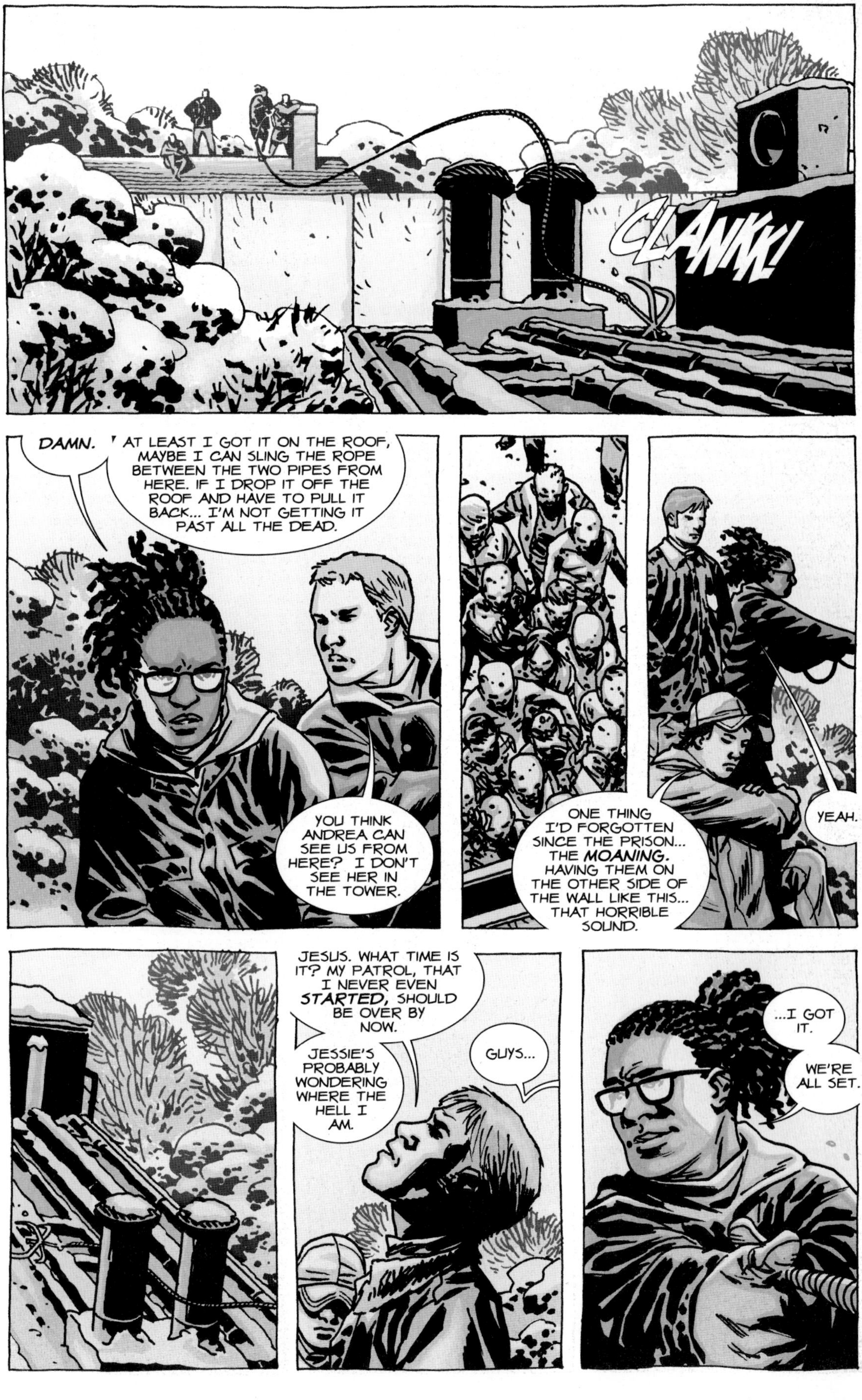

CLANKK!
DAMN.
AT LEAST I GOT IT ON THE ROOF, MAYBE I CAN SLING THE ROPE BETWEEN THE TWO PIPES FROM HERE. IF I DROP IT OFF THE ROOF AND HAVE TO PULL IT BACK... I'M NOT GETTING IT PAST ALL THE DEAD.
YOU THINK ANDREA CAN SEE US FROM HERE? I DON'T SEE HER IN THE TOWER.
ONE THING I'D FORGOTTEN SINCE THE PRISON... THE MOANING. HAVING THEM ON THE OTHER SIDE OF THE WALL LIKE THIS... THAT HORRIBLE SOUND.
YEAH.
JESUS. WHAT TIME IS IT? MY PATROL, THAT I NEVER EVEN STARTED, SHOULD BE OVER BY NOW.
JESSIE'S PROBABLY WONDERING WHERE THE HELL I AM.
GUYS...
...I GOT IT.
WE'RE ALL SET.

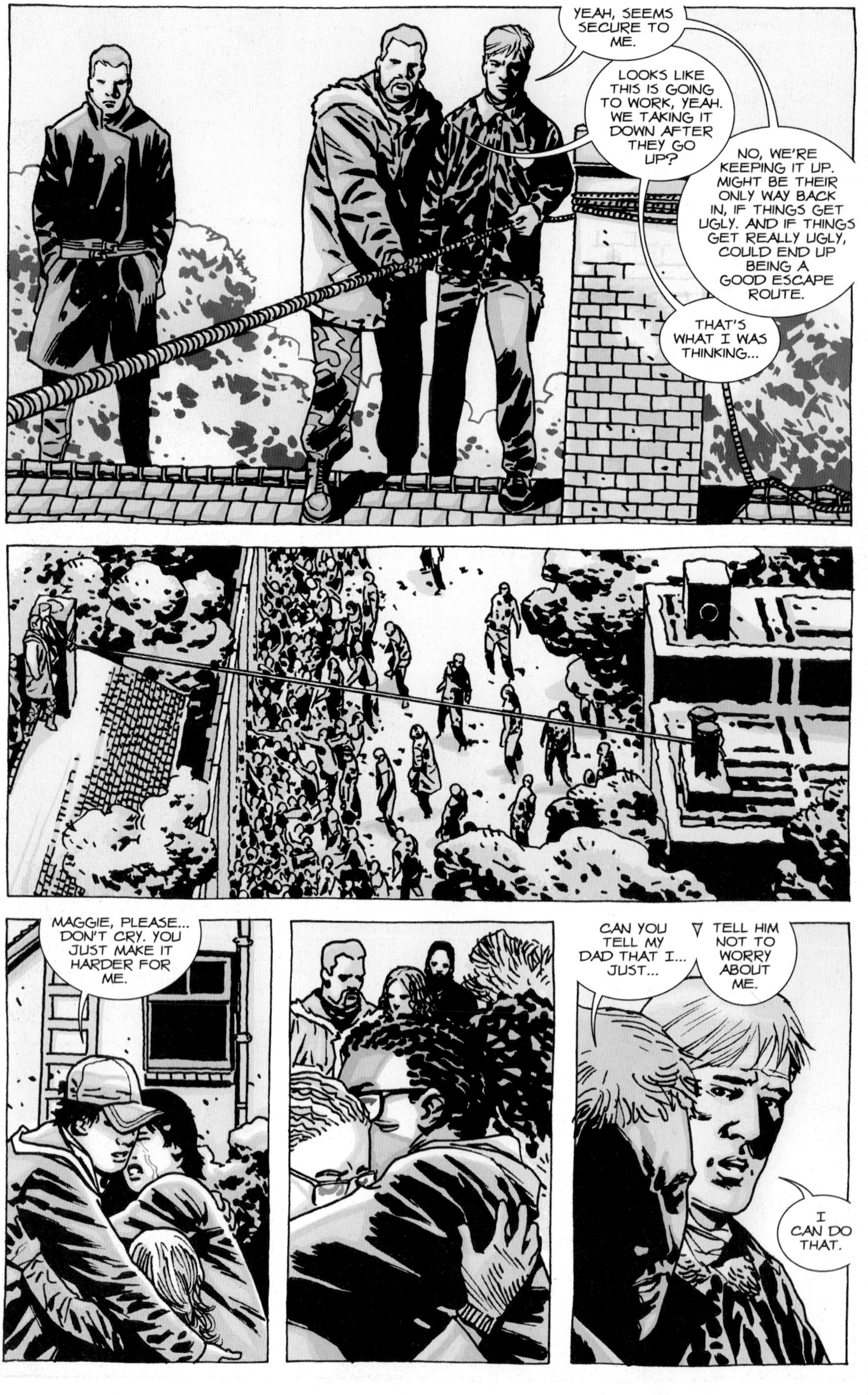
YEAH, SEEMS SECURE TO ME.
LOOKS LIKE THIS IS GOING TO WORK, YEAH. WE TAKING IT DOWN AFTER THEY GO UP?
NO, WE'RE KEEPING IT UP. MIGHT BE THEIR ONLY WAY BACK IN, IF THINGS GET UGLY. AND IF THINGS GET REALLY UGLY, COULD END UP BEING A GOOD ESCAPE ROUTE.
THAT'S WHAT I WAS THINKING...
MAGGIE, PLEASE... DON'T CRY. YOU JUST MAKE IT HARDER FOR ME.
CAN YOU TELL MY DAD THAT I... JUST...
TELL HIM NOT TO WORRY ABOUT ME.
I CAN DO THAT.

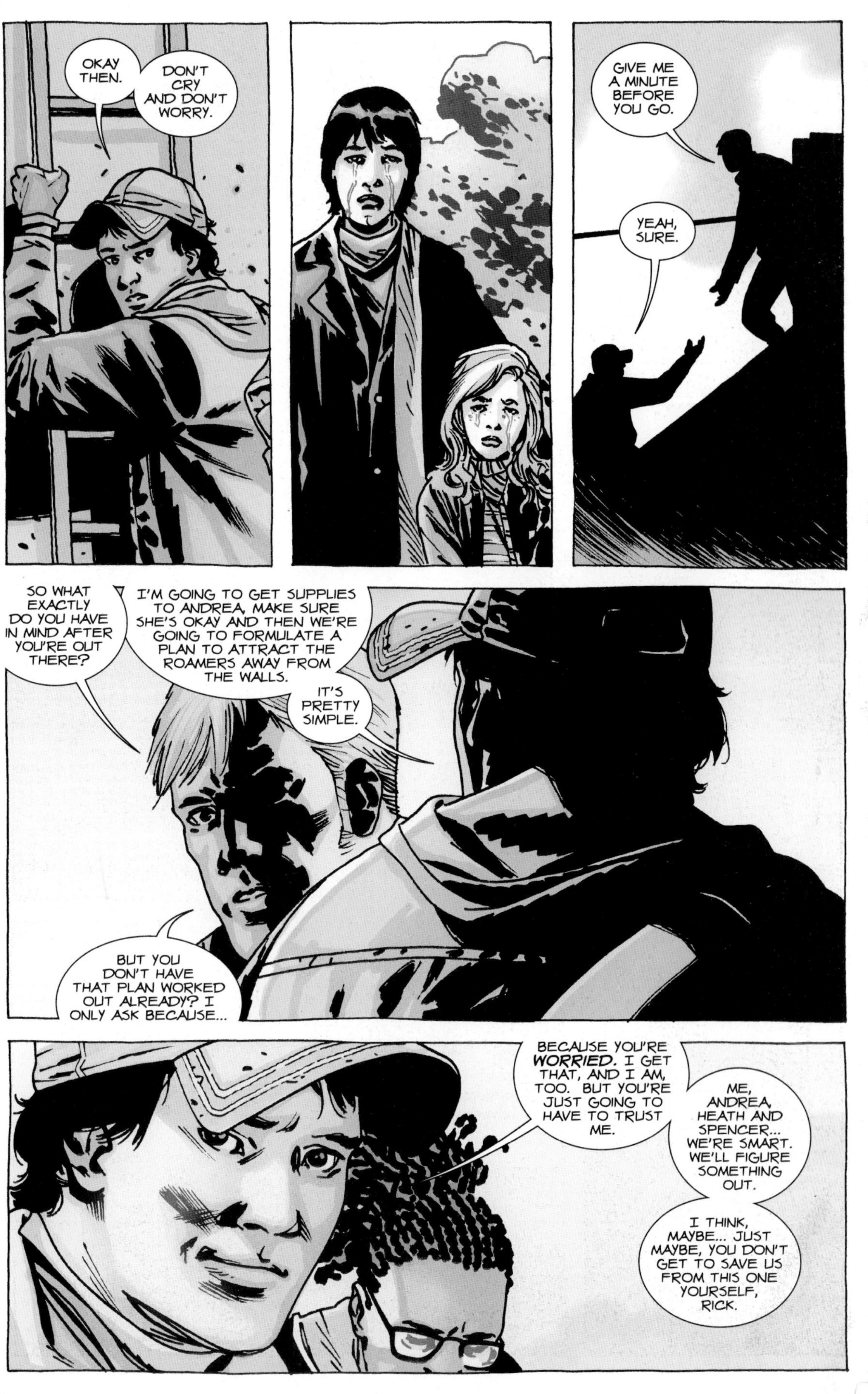
OKAY THEN.
DON'T CRY AND DON'T WORRY.
GIVE ME A MINUTE BEFORE YOU GO.
YEAH, SURE.
SO WHAT EXACTLY DO YOU HAVE IN MIND AFTER YOU'RE OUT THERE?
I'M GOING TO GET SUPPLIES TO ANDREA, MAKE SURE SHE'S OKAY AND THEN WE'RE GOING TO FORMULATE A PLAN TO ATTRACT THE ROAMERS AWAY FROM THE WALLS.
IT'S PRETTY SIMPLE.
BUT YOU DON'T HAVE THAT PLAN WORKED OUT ALREADY? I ONLY ASK BECAUSE...
BECAUSE YOU'RE WORRIED. I GET THAT, AND I AM, TOO. BUT YOU'RE JUST GOING TO HAVE TO TRUST ME.
ME, ANDREA, HEATH AND SPENCER... WE'RE SMART. WE'LL FIGURE SOMETHING OUT.
I THINK, MAYBE... JUST MAYBE, YOU DON'T GET TO SAVE US FROM THIS ONE YOURSELF, RICK.

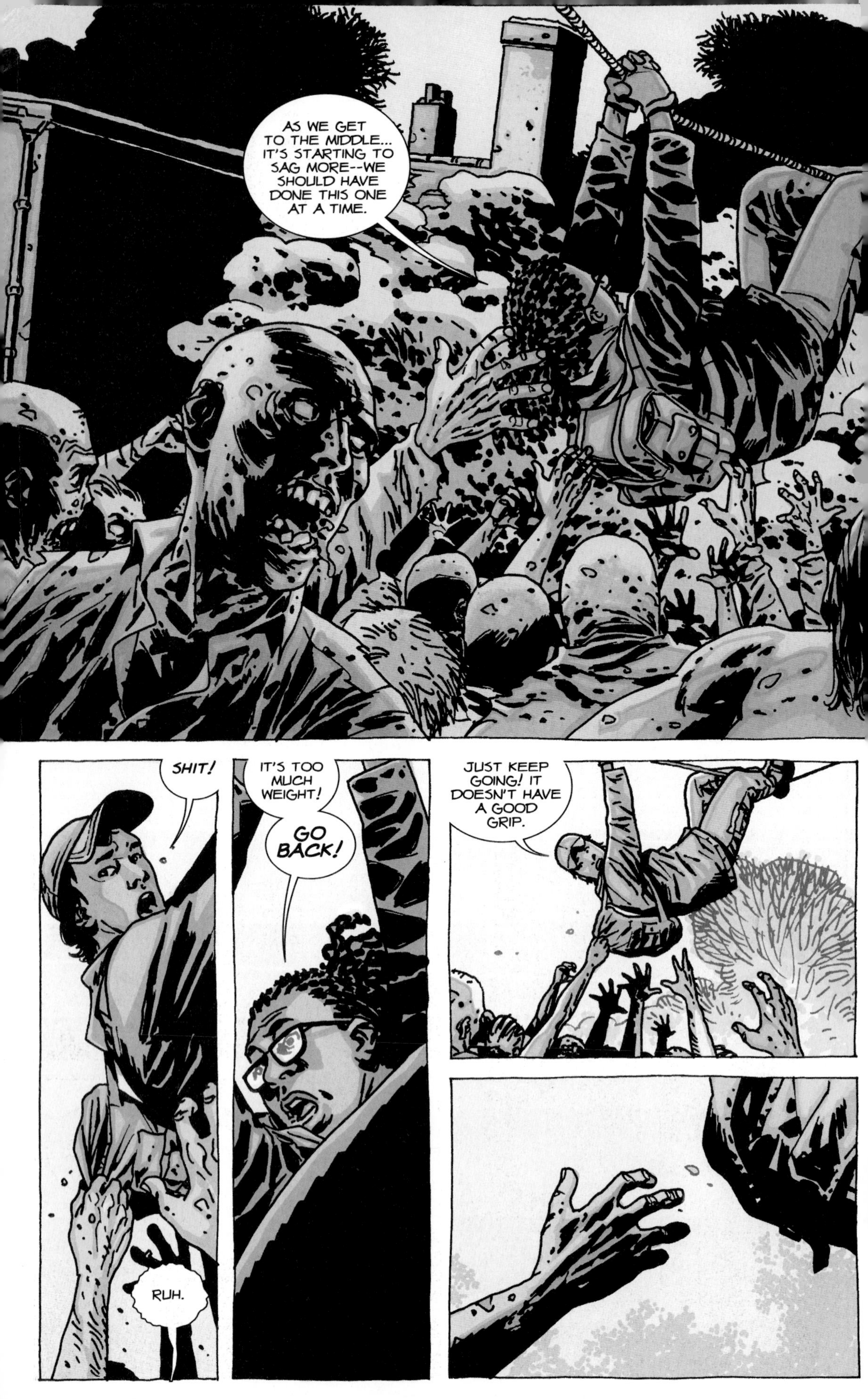
AS WE GET TO THE MIDDLE... IT'S STARTING TO SAG MORE--WE SHOULD HAVE DONE THIS ONE AT A TIME.
SHIT!
IT'S TOO MUCH WEIGHT!
GO BACK!
JUST KEEP GOING! IT DOESN'T HAVE A GOOD GRIP.
RUH.

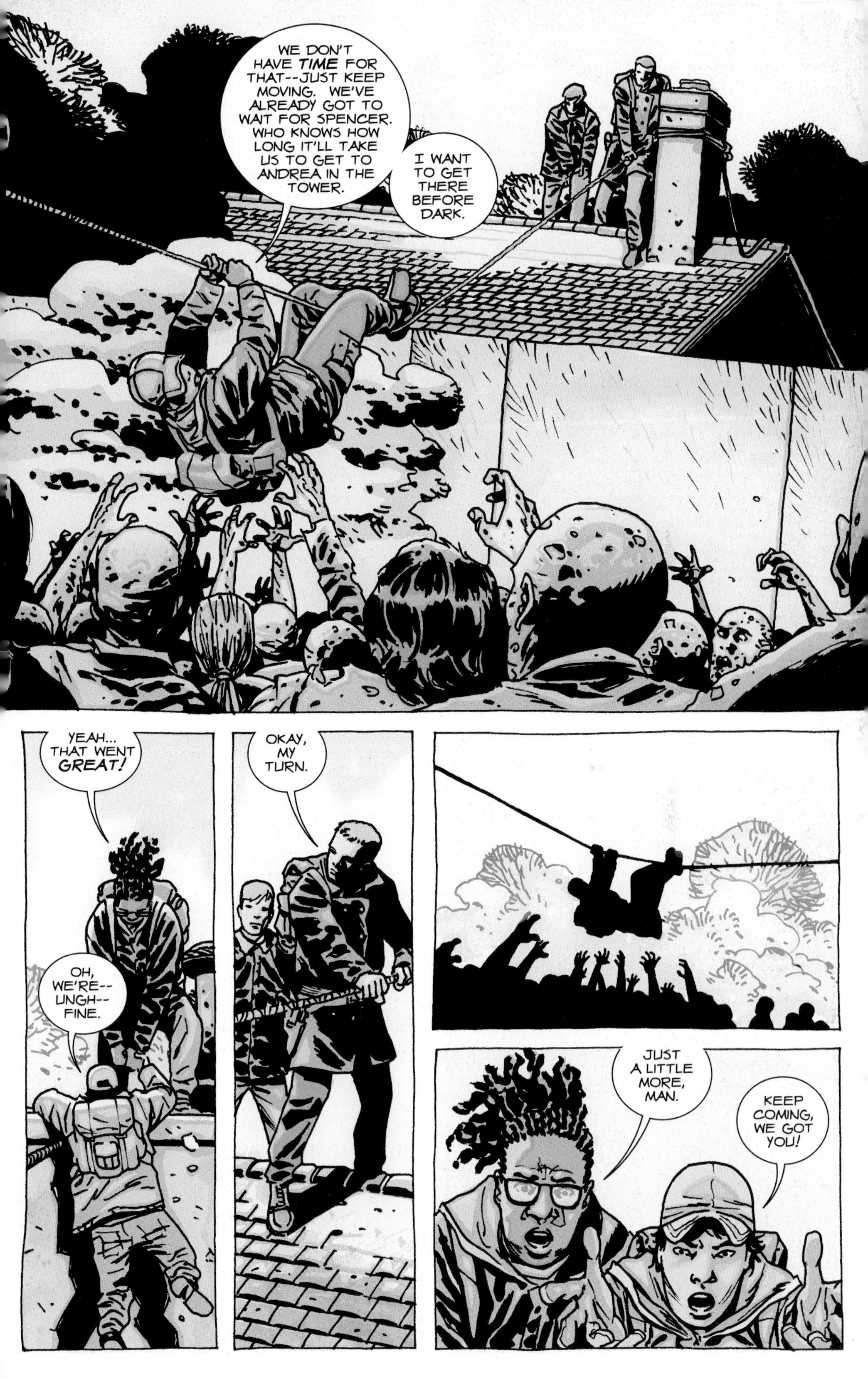
WE DON'T HAVE TIME FOR THAT--JUST KEEP MOVING. WE'VE ALREADY GOT TO WAIT FOR SPENCER. WHO KNOWS HOW LONG IT'LL TAKE US TO GET TO ANDREA IN THE TOWER.
I WANT TO GET THERE BEFORE DARK.
YEAH... THAT WENT GREAT!
OH, WE'RE-- UNGH-- FINE.
OKAY, MY TURN.
JUST A LITTLE MORE, MAN.
KEEP COMING, WE GOT YOU!

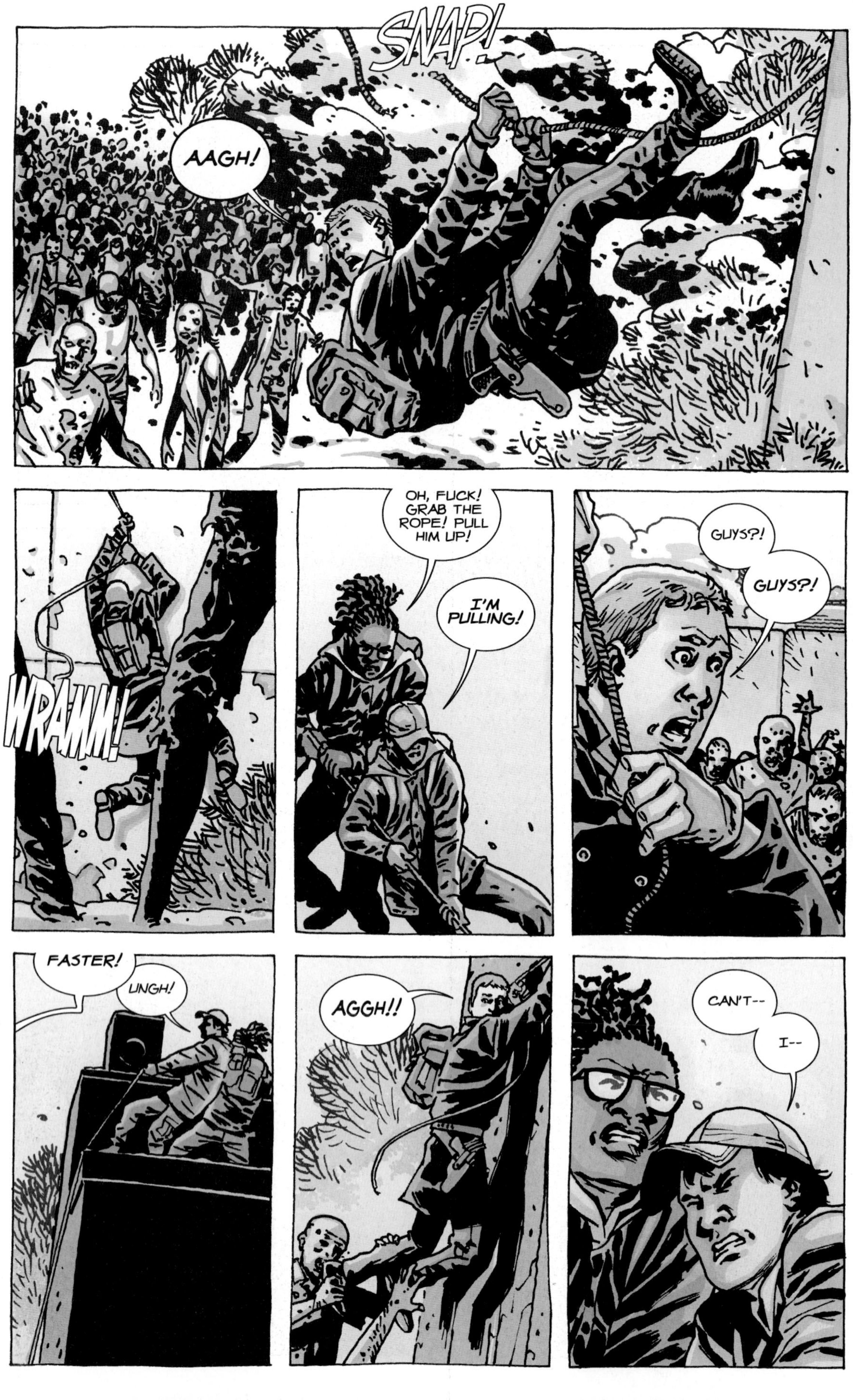
SNAP!
AAGH!
WRAMM!
OH, FUCK! GRAB THE ROPE! PULL HIM UP!
I'M PULLING!
GUYS?!
GUYS?!
FASTER!
UNGH!
AGGH!!
CAN'T--
I--

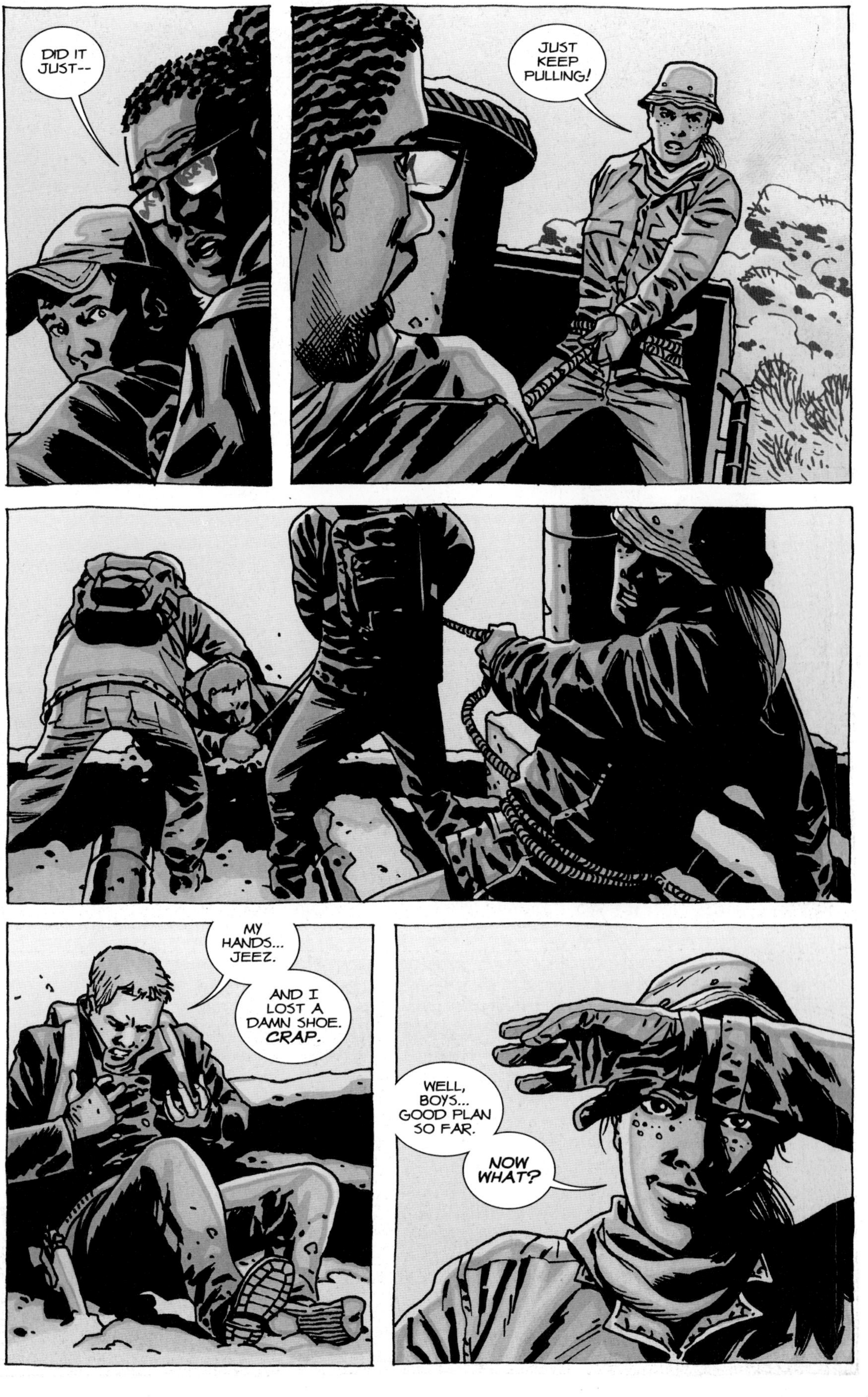
DID IT JUST--
JUST KEEP PULLING!
MY HANDS... JEEZ.
AND I LOST A DAMN SHOE. CRAP.
WELL, BOYS... GOOD PLAN SO FAR.
NOW WHAT?

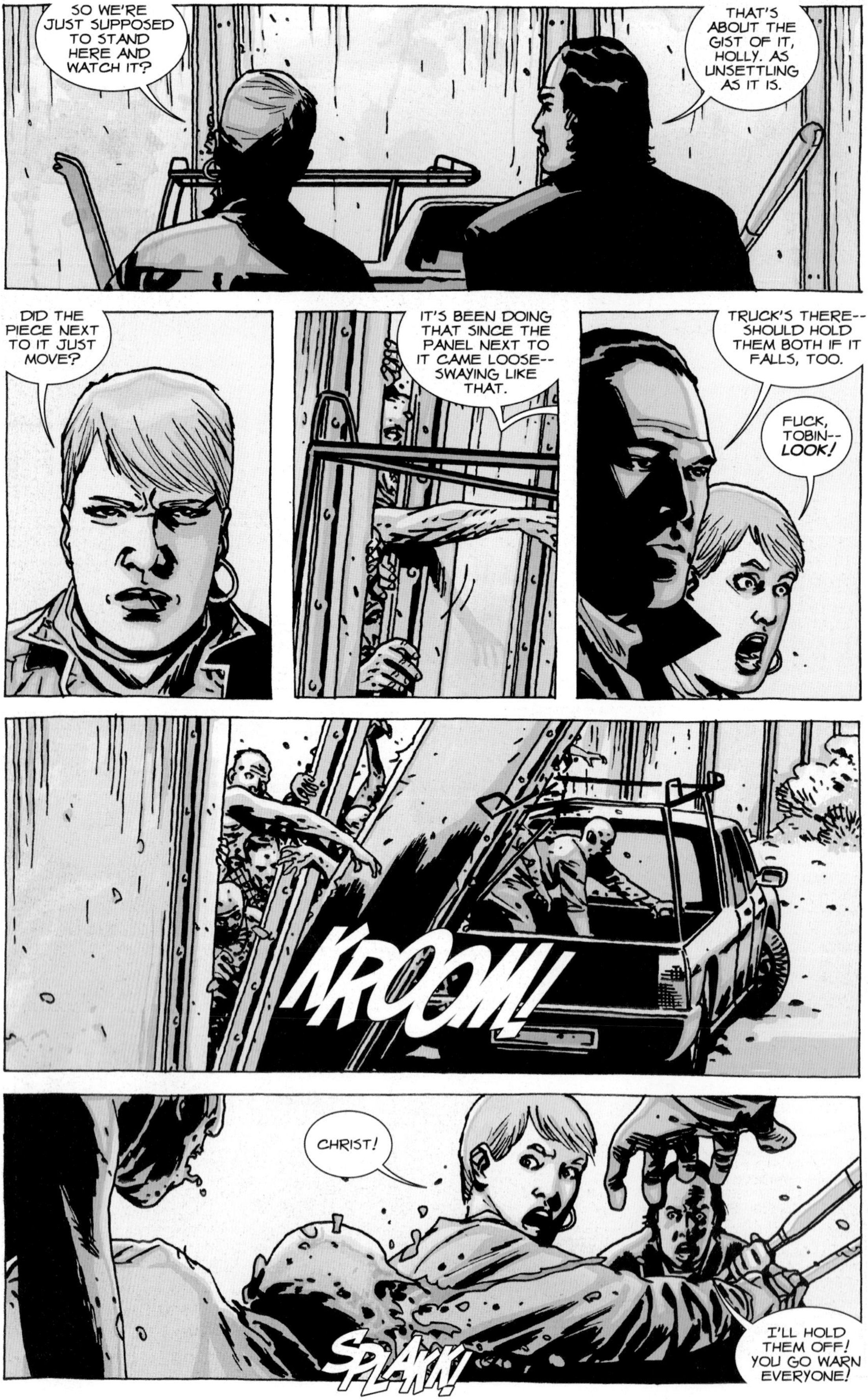
SO WE'RE JUST SUPPOSED TO STAND HERE AND WATCH IT?
THAT'S ABOUT THE GIST OF IT, HOLLY. AS UNSETTLING AS IT IS.
DID THE PIECE NEXT TO IT JUST MOVE?
IT'S BEEN DOING THAT SINCE THE PANEL NEXT TO IT CAME LOOSE-- SWAYING LIKE THAT.
TRUCK'S THERE-- SHOULD HOLD THEM BOTH IF IT FALLS, TOO.
FUCK, TOBIN-- LOOK!
KROOM!
CHRIST!
SPLAKK!
I'LL HOLD THEM OFF! YOU GO WARN EVERYONE!

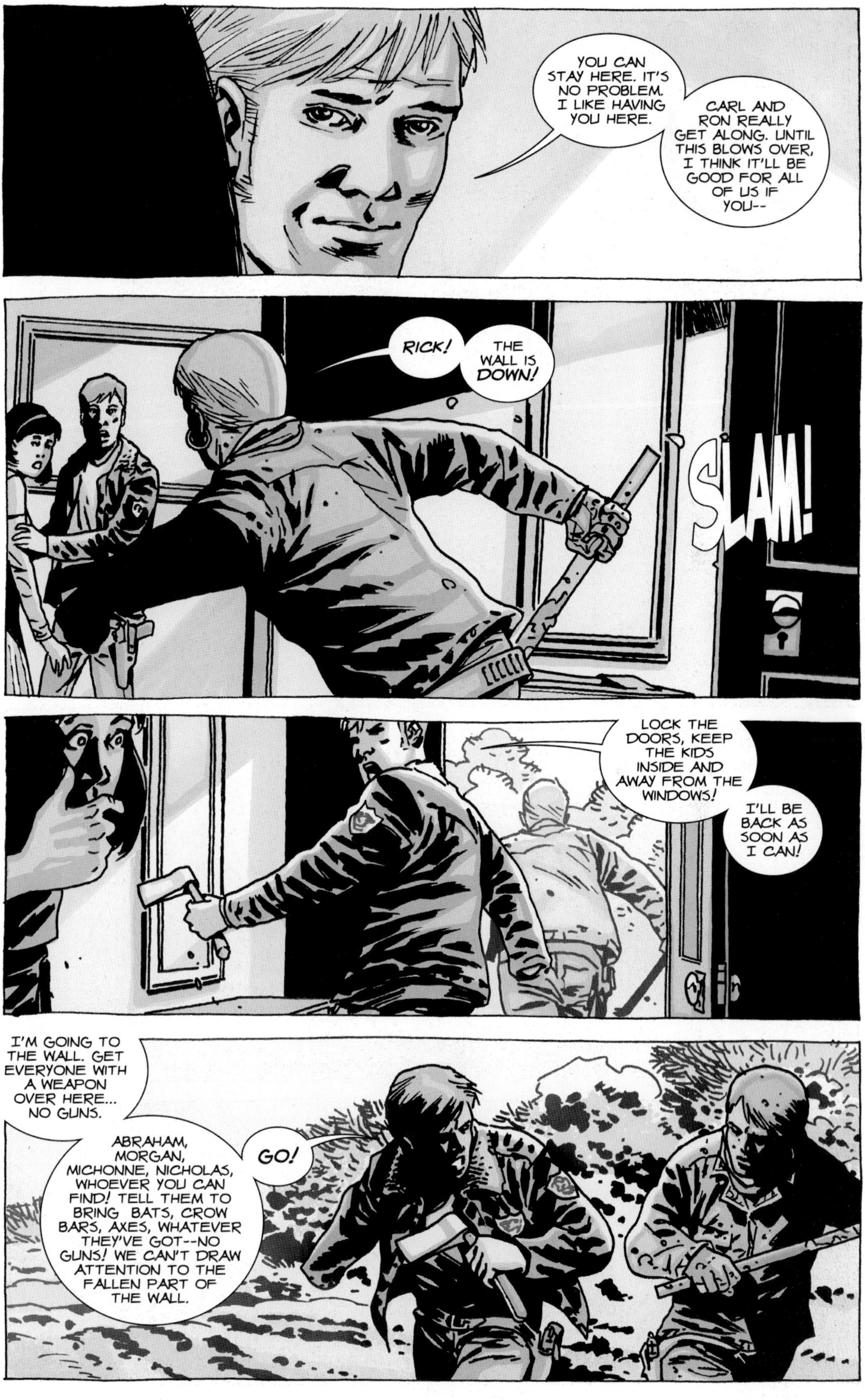
YOU CAN STAY HERE. IT'S NO PROBLEM. I LIKE HAVING YOU HERE.
CARL AND RON REALLY GET ALONG. UNTIL THIS BLOWS OVER, I THINK IT'LL BE GOOD FOR ALL OF US IF YOU--
RICK!
THE WALL IS DOWN!
SLAM!
LOCK THE DOORS, KEEP THE KIDS INSIDE AND AWAY FROM THE WINDOWS!
I'LL BE BACK AS SOON AS I CAN!
I'M GOING TO THE WALL. GET EVERYONE WITH A WEAPON OVER HERE... NO GUNS.
ABRAHAM, MORGAN, MICHONNE, NICHOLAS, WHOEVER YOU CAN FIND! TELL THEM TO BRING BATS, CROW BARS, AXES, WHATEVER THEY'VE GOT--NO GUNS! WE CAN'T DRAW ATTENTION TO THE FALLEN PART OF THE WALL.
GO!

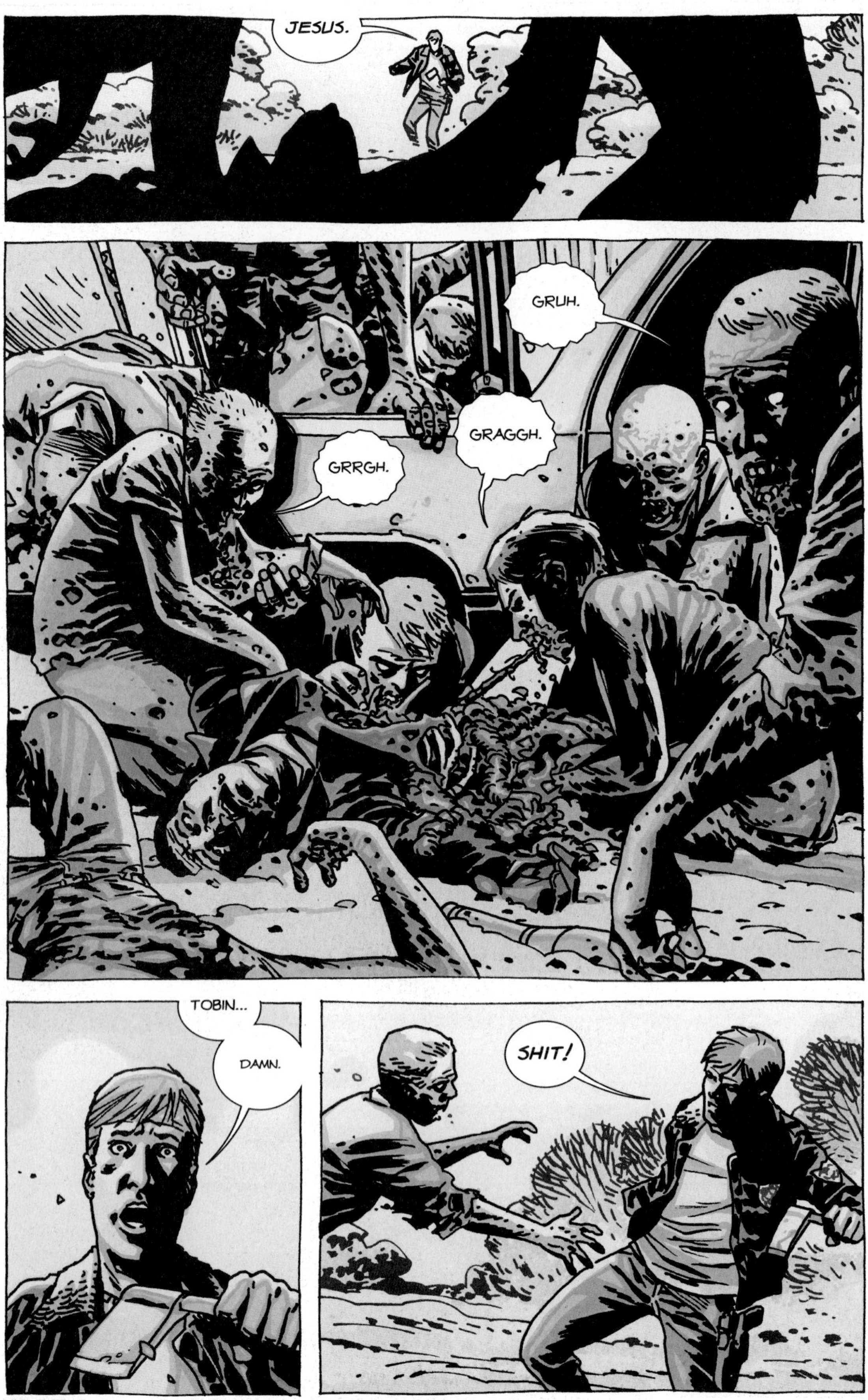
JESUS.
GRUH.
GRAGGH.
GRRGH.
TOBIN...
DAMN.
SHIT!

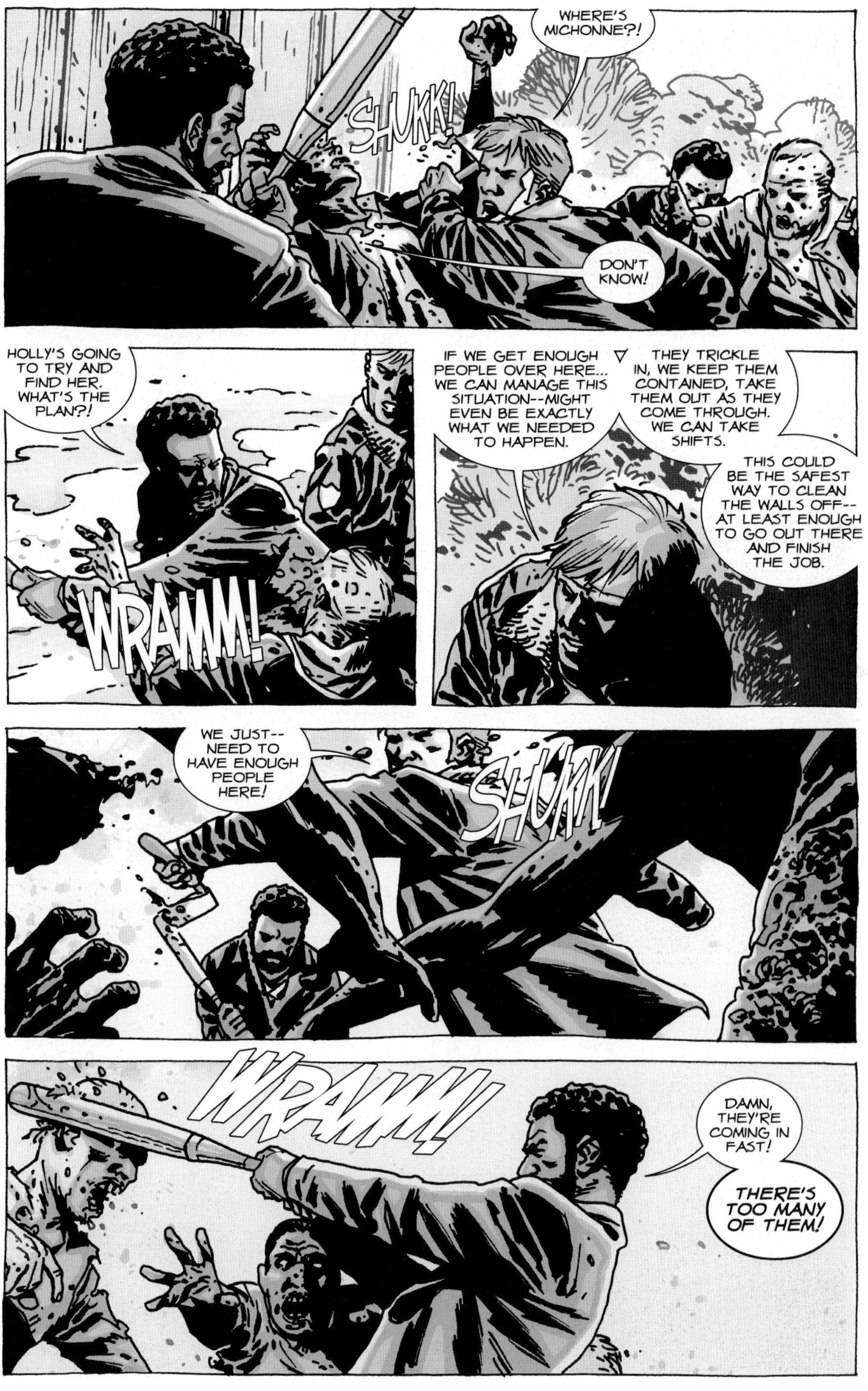
WHERE'S MICHONNE?!
SHUKK!
DON'T KNOW!
HOLLY'S GOING TO TRY AND FIND HER. WHAT'S THE PLAN?!
WRAMM!
IF WE GET ENOUGH PEOPLE OVER HERE... WE CAN MANAGE THIS SITUATION--MIGHT EVEN BE EXACTLY WHAT WE NEEDED TO HAPPEN.
THEY TRICKLE IN, WE KEEP THEM CONTAINED, TAKE THEM OUT AS THEY COME THROUGH. WE CAN TAKE SHIFTS.
THIS COULD BE THE SAFEST WAY TO CLEAN THE WALLS OFF--AT LEAST ENOUGH TO GO OUT THERE AND FINISH THE JOB.
WE JUST--NEED TO HAVE ENOUGH PEOPLE HERE!
SHUKK!
WRAMM!
DAMN, THEY'RE COMING IN FAST!
THERE'S TOO MANY OF THEM!

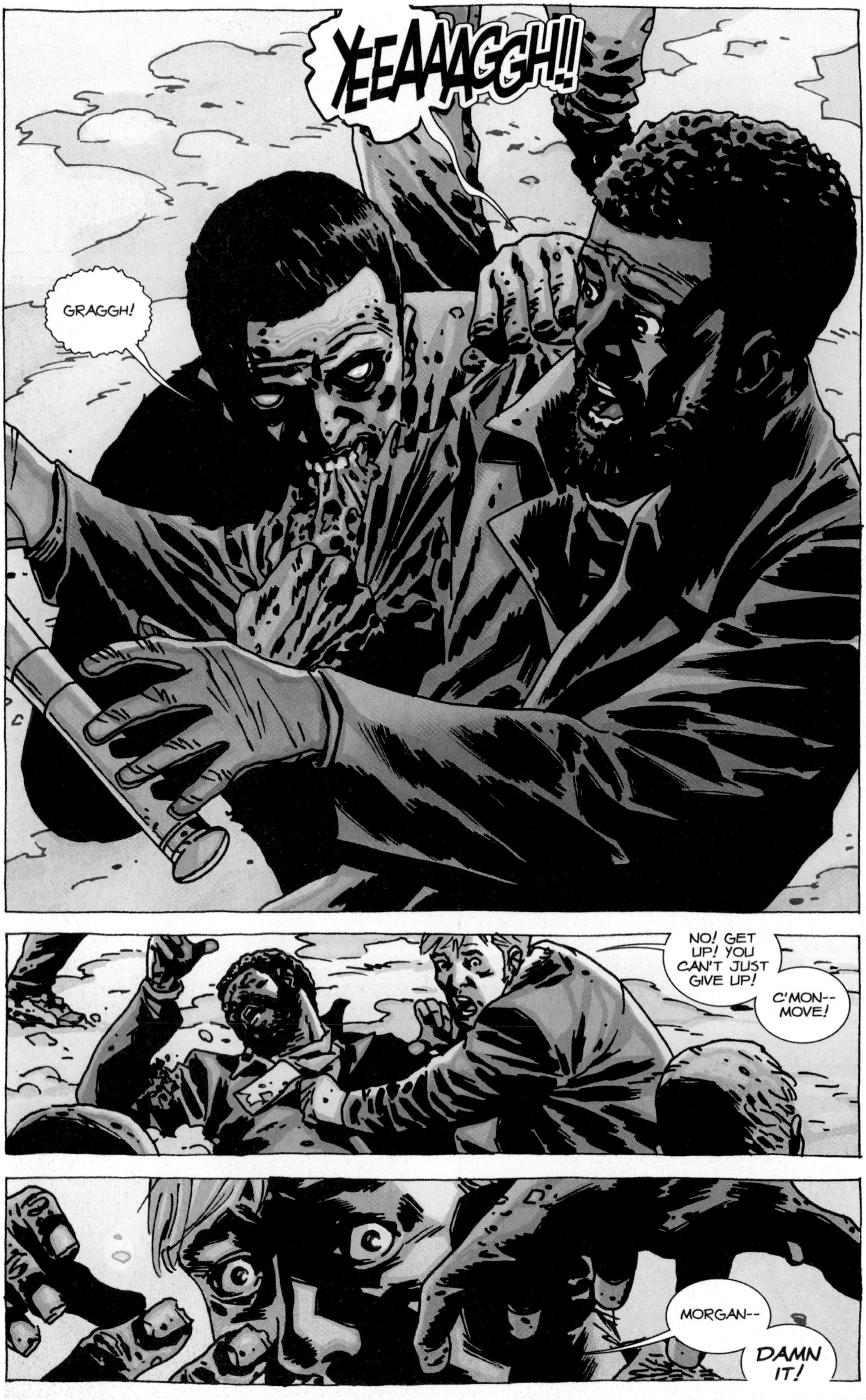
YEEAAAGGH!!
GRAGGH!
NO! GET UP! YOU CAN'T JUST GIVE UP!
C'MON-- MOVE!
MORGAN--
DAMN IT!

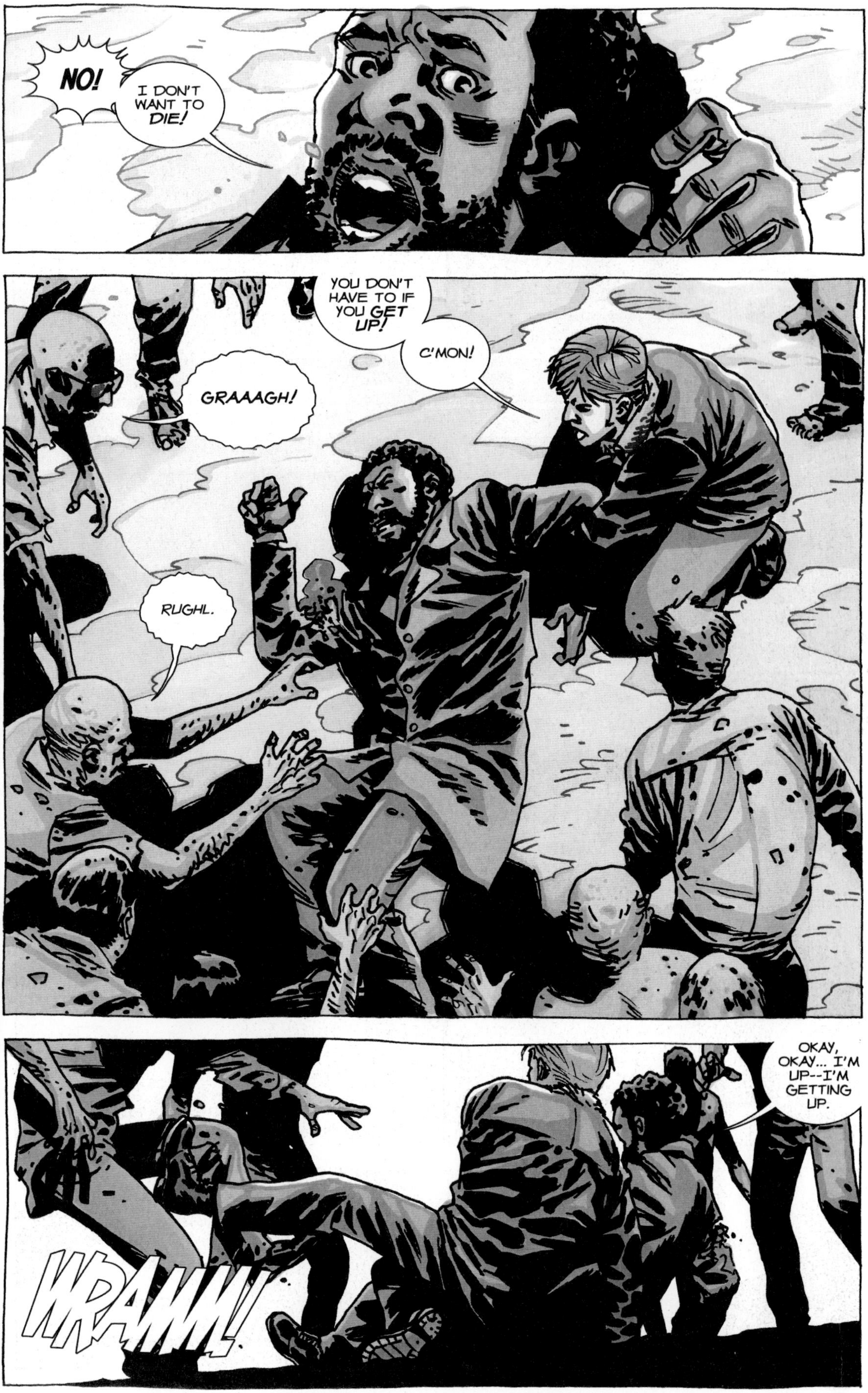
NO!
I DON'T WANT TO DIE!
YOU DON'T HAVE TO IF YOU GET UP!
C'MON!
GRAAAGH!
RUGHL.
OKAY, OKAY... I'M UP--I'M GETTING UP.
WRAMM!

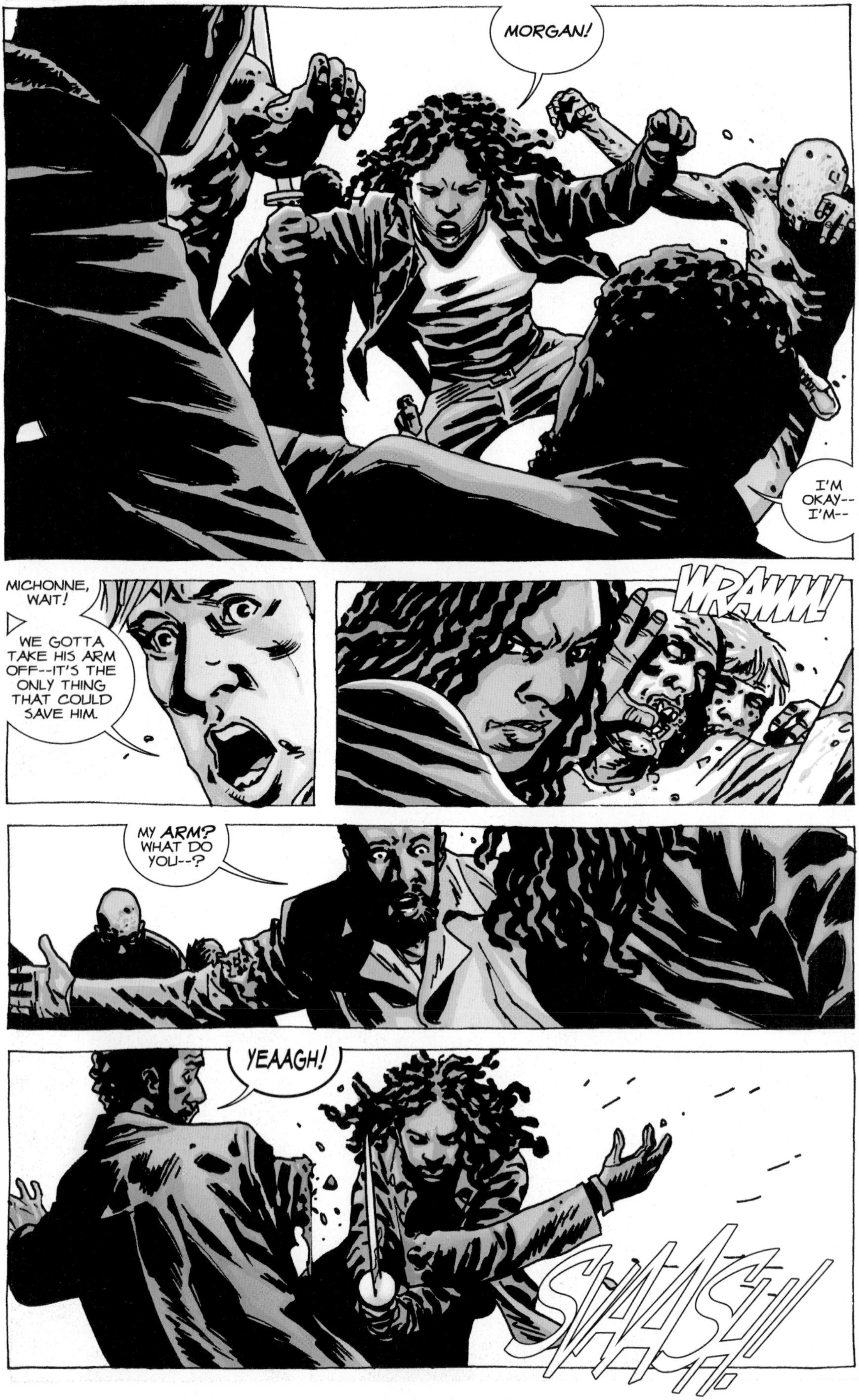
MORGAN!
I'M OKAY-- I'M--
MICHONNE, WAIT!
WE GOTTA TAKE HIS ARM OFF--IT'S THE ONLY THING THAT COULD SAVE HIM.
WRAMM!
MY ARM? WHAT DO YOU--?
YEAAGH!
SHASHH!

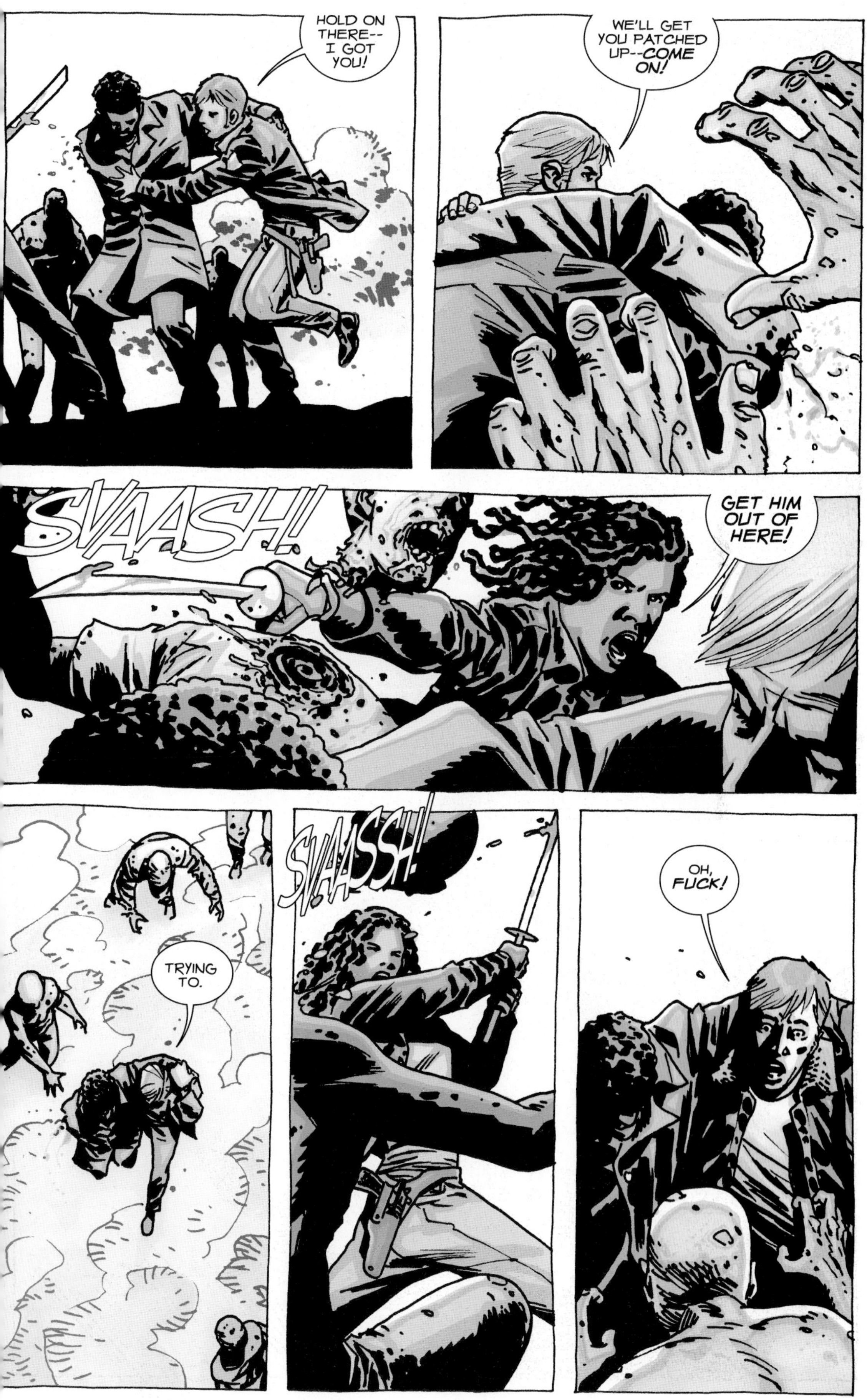
HOLD ON THERE-- I GOT YOU!
WE'LL GET YOU PATCHED UP--COME ON!
SVAASH!
GET HIM OUT OF HERE!
TRYING TO.
SVAASSH!
OH, FUCK!

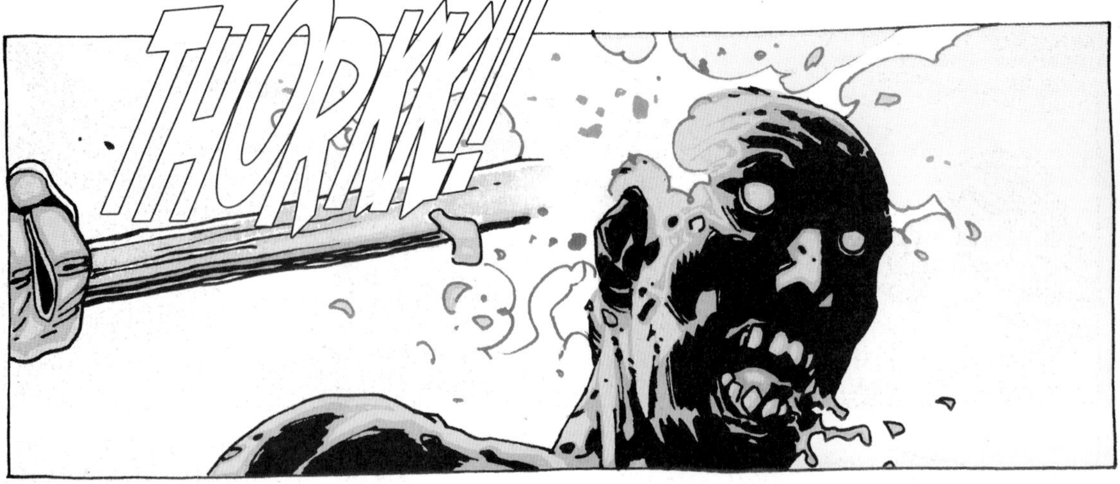
THORKK!!

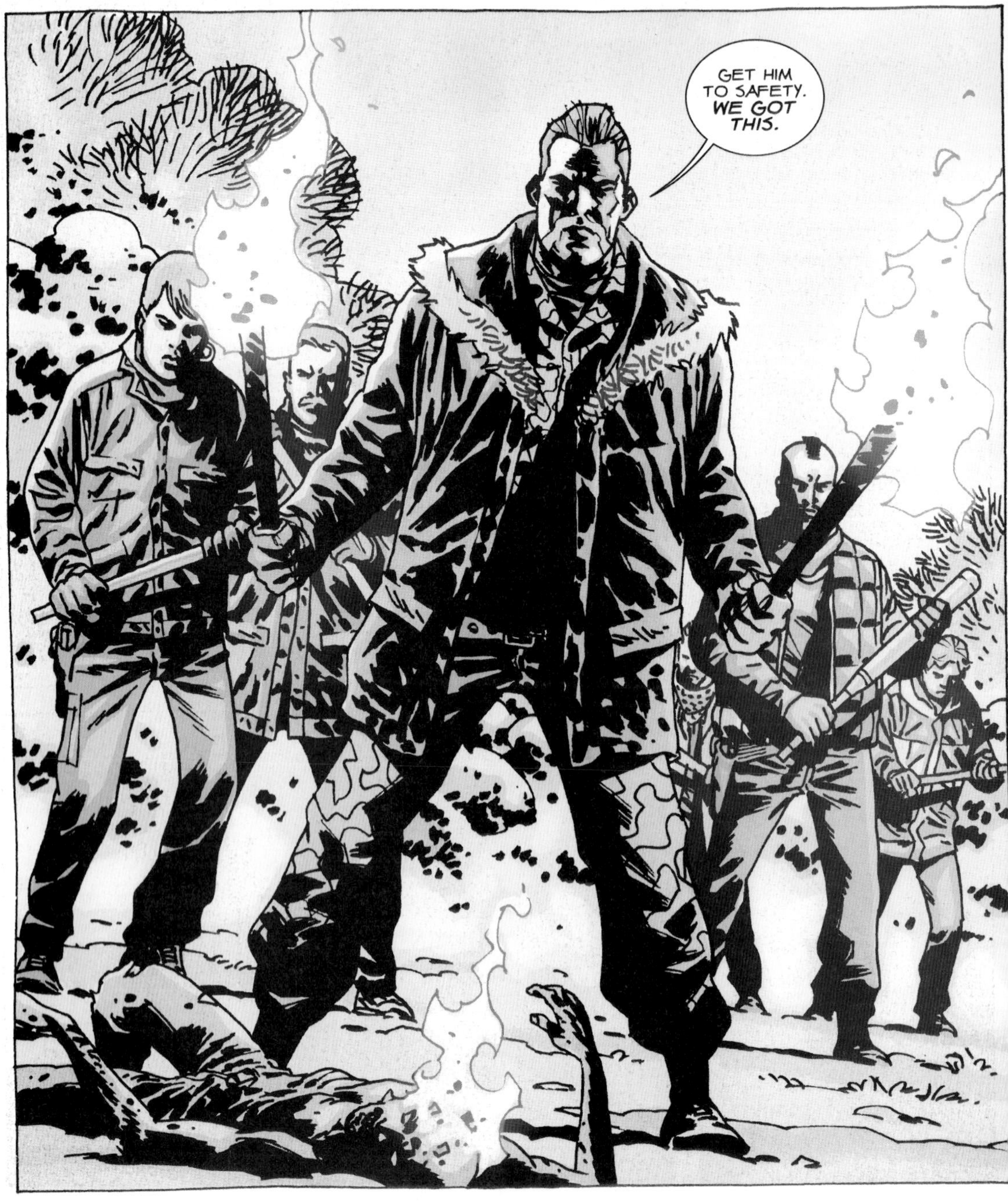
GET HIM TO SAFETY. WE GOT THIS.

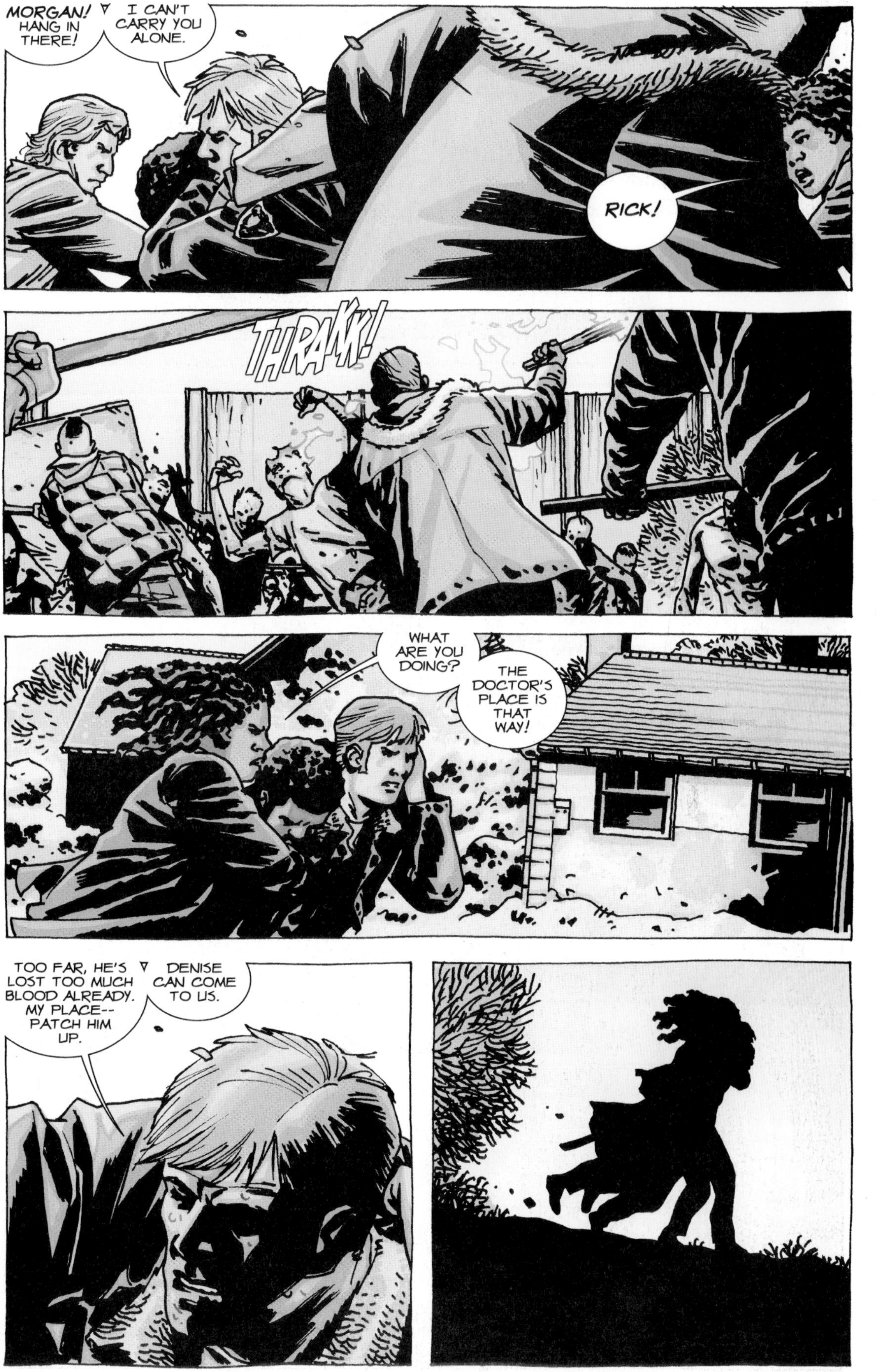

MORGAN! HANG IN THERE!
I CAN'T CARRY YOU ALONE.
RICK!
THRAKK!
WHAT ARE YOU DOING?
THE DOCTOR'S PLACE IS THAT WAY!
TOO FAR, HE'S LOST TOO MUCH BLOOD ALREADY. MY PLACE-- PATCH HIM UP.
DENISE CAN COME TO US.

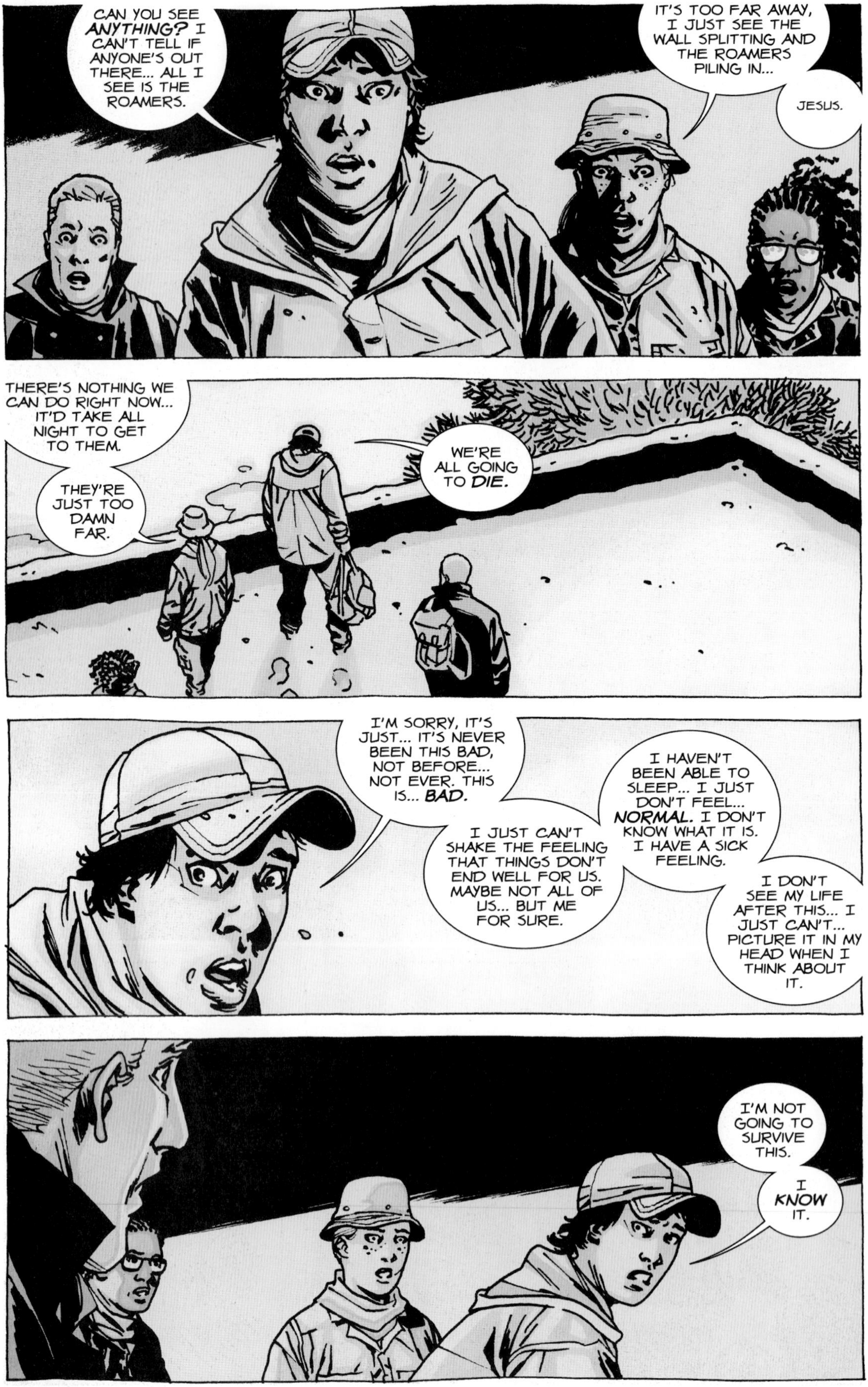
CAN YOU SEE ANYTHING? I CAN'T TELL IF ANYONE'S OUT THERE... ALL I SEE IS THE ROAMERS.
IT'S TOO FAR AWAY, I JUST SEE THE WALL SPLITTING AND THE ROAMERS PILING IN...
JESUS.
THERE'S NOTHING WE CAN DO RIGHT NOW... IT'D TAKE ALL NIGHT TO GET TO THEM.
THEY'RE JUST TOO DAMN FAR.
WE'RE ALL GOING TO DIE.
I'M SORRY, IT'S JUST... IT'S NEVER BEEN THIS BAD, NOT BEFORE... NOT EVER. THIS IS... BAD.
I JUST CAN'T SHAKE THE FEELING THAT THINGS DON'T END WELL FOR US. MAYBE NOT ALL OF US... BUT ME FOR SURE.
I HAVEN'T BEEN ABLE TO SLEEP... I JUST DON'T FEEL... NORMAL. I DON'T KNOW WHAT IT IS. I HAVE A SICK FEELING.
I DON'T SEE MY LIFE AFTER THIS... I JUST CAN'T... PICTURE IT IN MY HEAD WHEN I THINK ABOUT IT.
I'M NOT GOING TO SURVIVE THIS.
I KNOW IT.

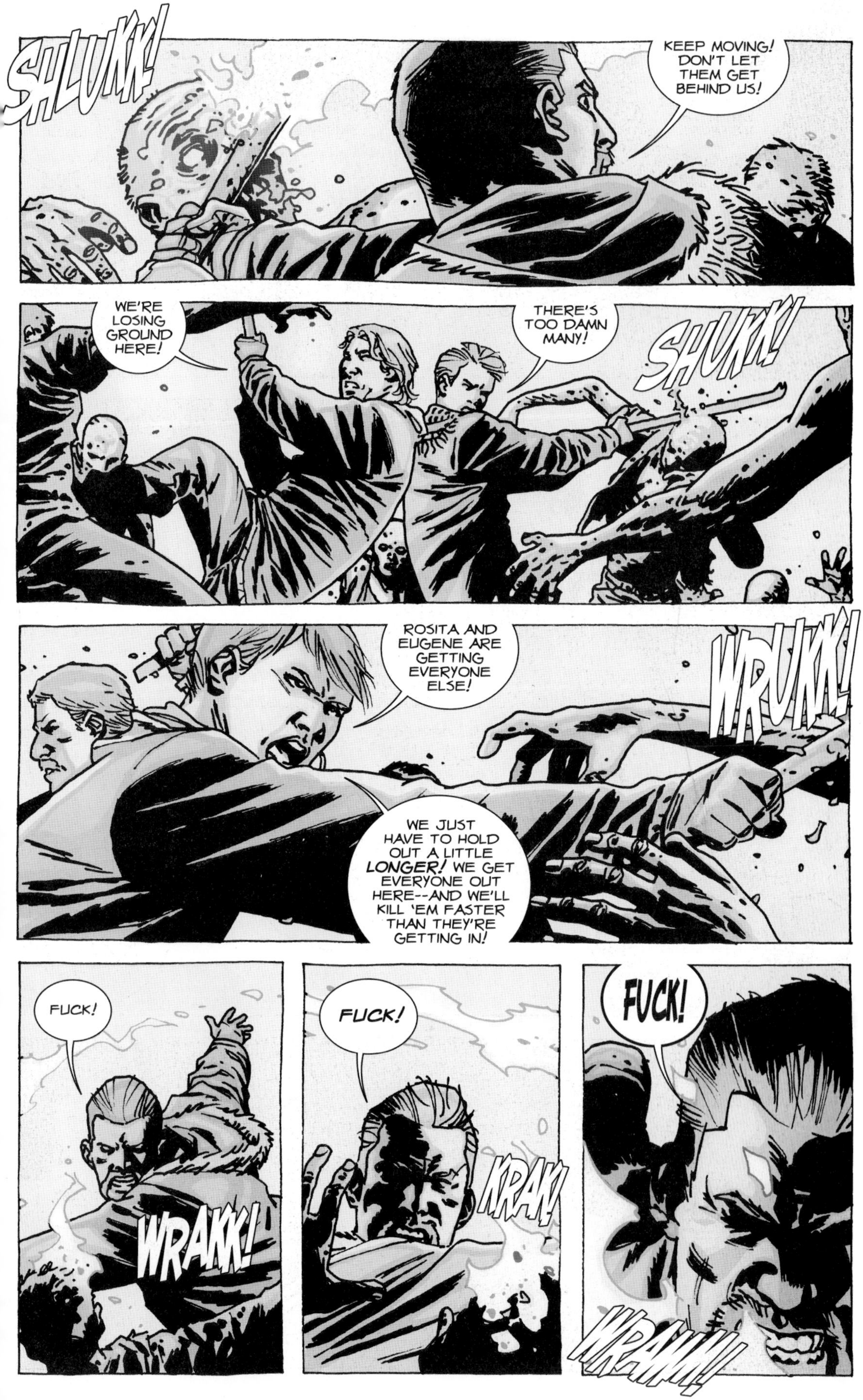
SHLUKK!
KEEP MOVING! DON'T LET THEM GET BEHIND US!
WE'RE LOSING GROUND HERE!
THERE'S TOO DAMN MANY!
SHUKK!
ROSITA AND EUGENE ARE GETTING EVERYONE ELSE!
WRUKK!
WE JUST HAVE TO HOLD OUT A LITTLE LONGER! WE GET EVERYONE OUT HERE--AND WE'LL KILL 'EM FASTER THAN THEY'RE GETTING IN!
FUCK!
WRAKK!
FUCK!
KRAK!
FUCK!
WRAMM!

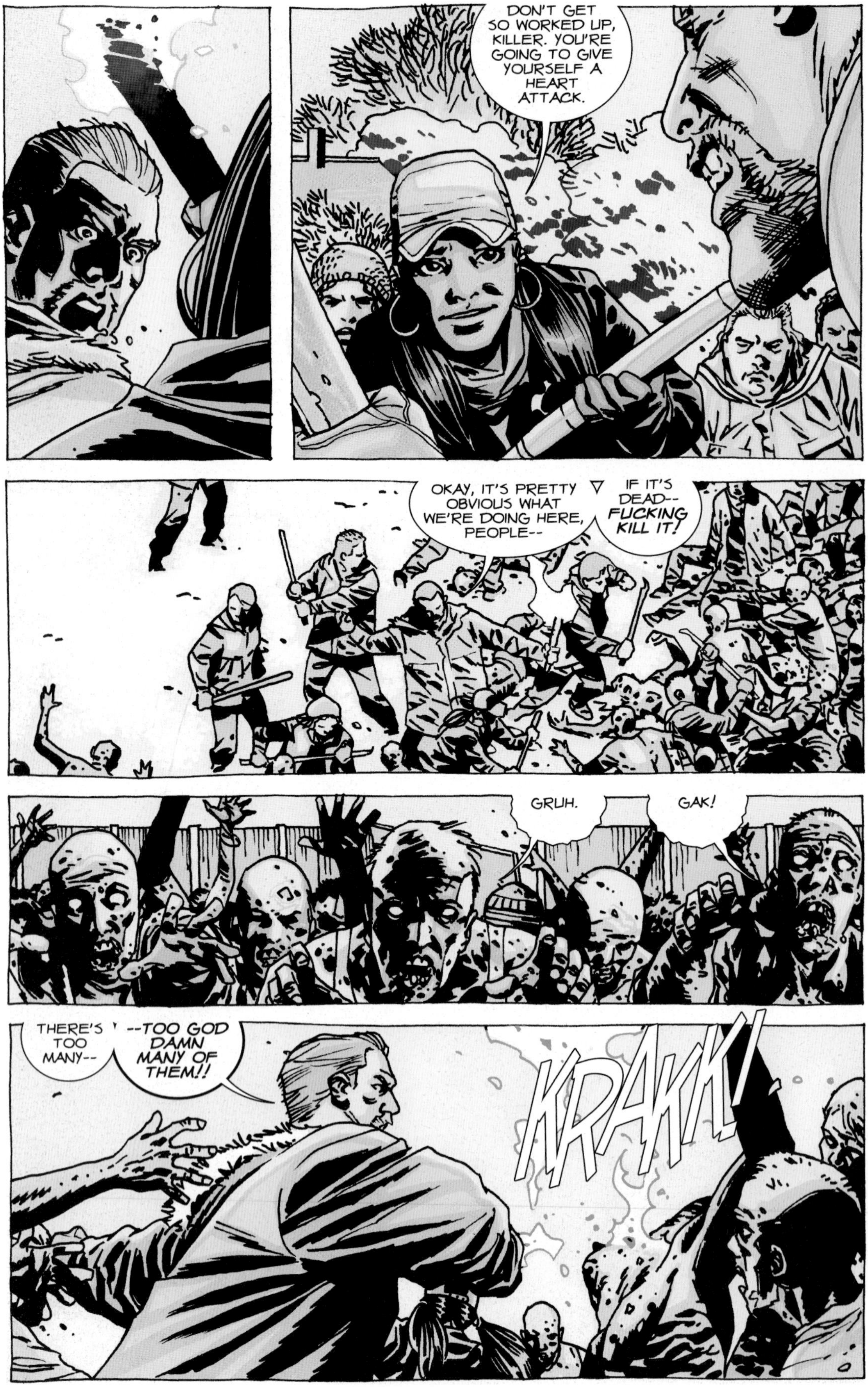
DON'T GET SO WORKED UP, KILLER. YOU'RE GOING TO GIVE YOURSELF A HEART ATTACK.
OKAY, IT'S PRETTY OBVIOUS WHAT WE'RE DOING HERE, PEOPLE--
IF IT'S DEAD-- FUCKING KILL IT!
GRUH.
GAK!
THERE'S TOO MANY--
--TOO GOD DAMN MANY OF THEM!!
KRAKK!

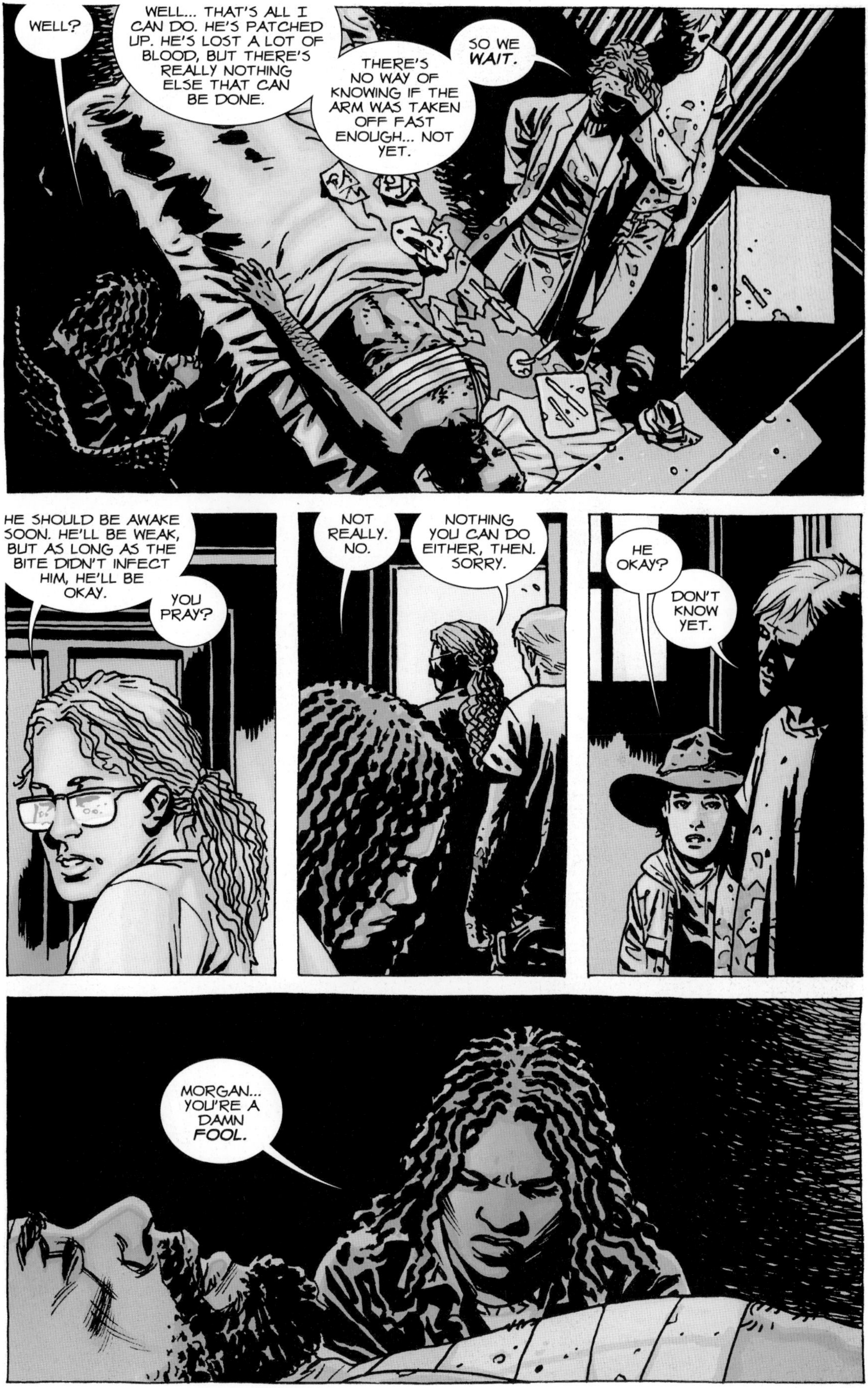
WELL?
WELL... THAT'S ALL I CAN DO. HE'S PATCHED UP. HE'S LOST A LOT OF BLOOD, BUT THERE'S REALLY NOTHING ELSE THAT CAN BE DONE.
THERE'S NO WAY OF KNOWING IF THE ARM WAS TAKEN OFF FAST ENOUGH... NOT YET.
SO WE WAIT.
HE SHOULD BE AWAKE SOON. HE'LL BE WEAK, BUT AS LONG AS THE BITE DIDN'T INFECT HIM, HE'LL BE OKAY.
YOU PRAY?
NOT REALLY. NO.
NOTHING YOU CAN DO EITHER, THEN. SORRY.
HE OKAY?
DON'T KNOW YET.
MORGAN... YOU'RE A DAMN FOOL.

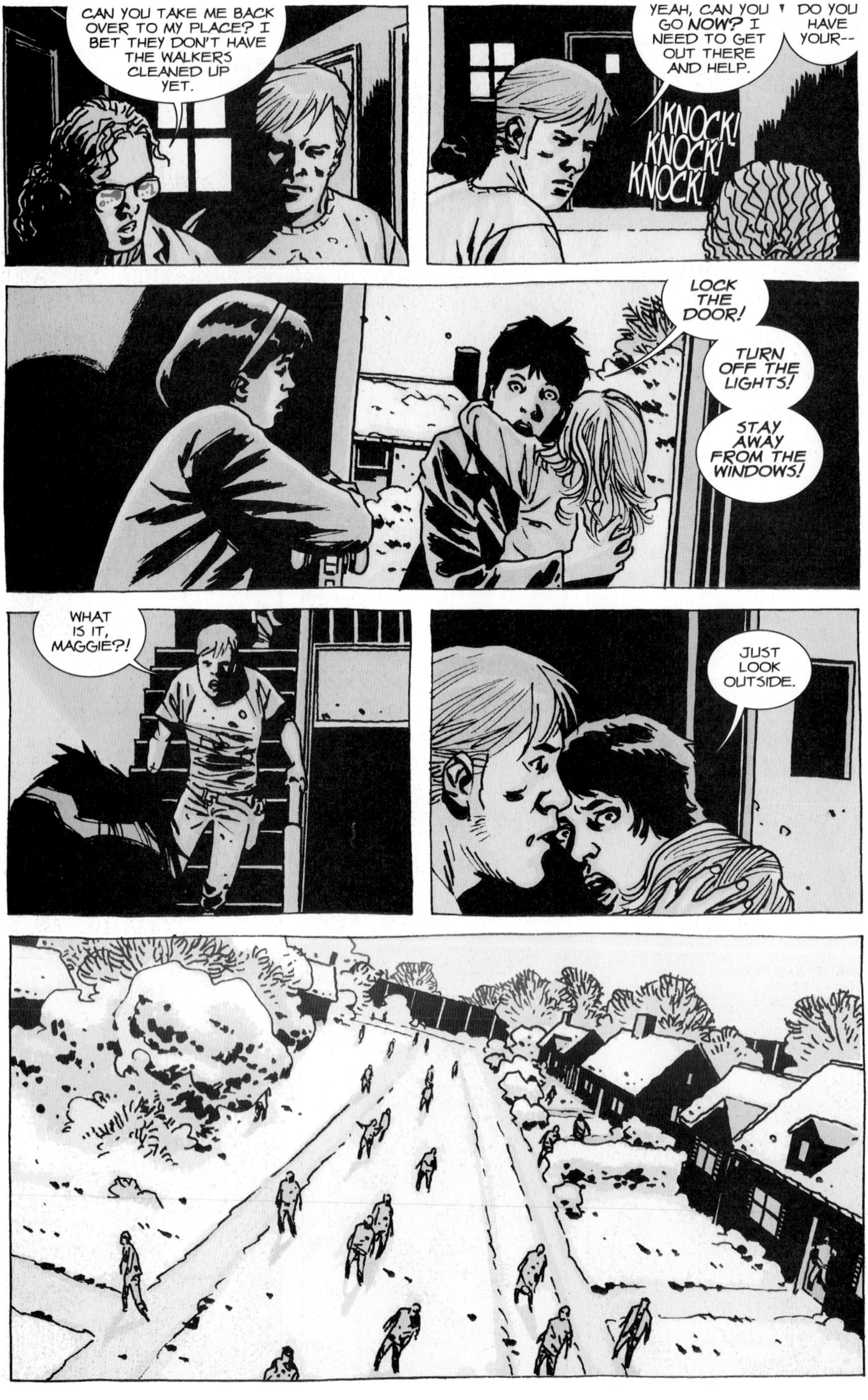

CAN YOU TAKE ME BACK OVER TO MY PLACE? I BET THEY DON'T HAVE THE WALKERS CLEANED UP YET.
YEAH, CAN YOU GO NOW? I NEED TO GET OUT THERE AND HELP.
DO YOU HAVE YOUR--
KNOCK! KNOCK! KNOCK!
LOCK THE DOOR!
TURN OFF THE LIGHTS!
STAY AWAY FROM THE WINDOWS!
WHAT IS IT, MAGGIE?!
JUST LOOK OUTSIDE.

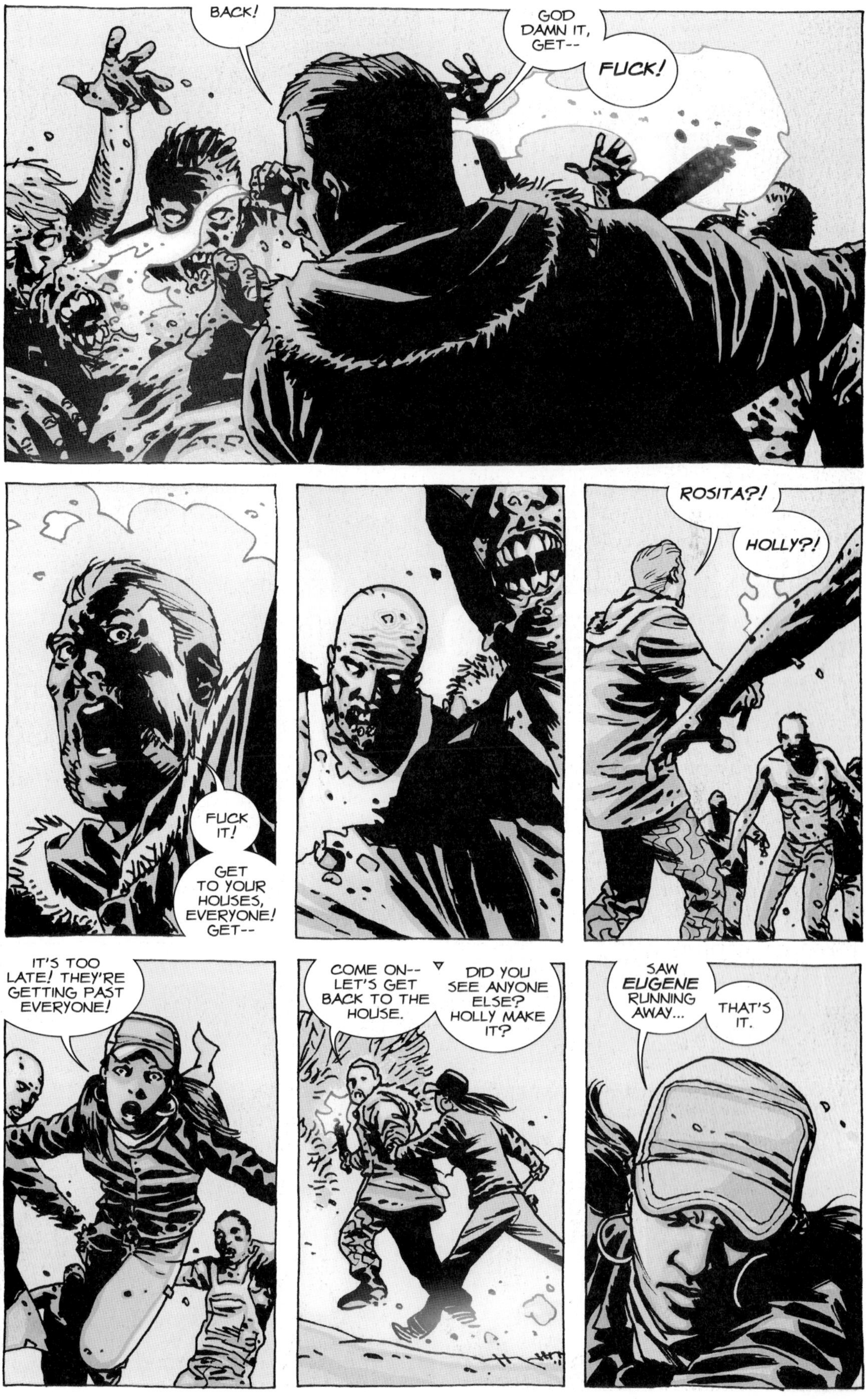
BACK!
GOD DAMN IT, GET--
FUCK!
FUCK IT!
GET TO YOUR HOUSES, EVERYONE! GET--
ROSITA?!
HOLLY?!
IT'S TOO LATE! THEY'RE GETTING PAST EVERYONE!
COME ON-- LET'S GET BACK TO THE HOUSE.
DID YOU SEE ANYONE ELSE? HOLLY MAKE IT?
SAW EUGENE RUNNING AWAY...
THAT'S IT.

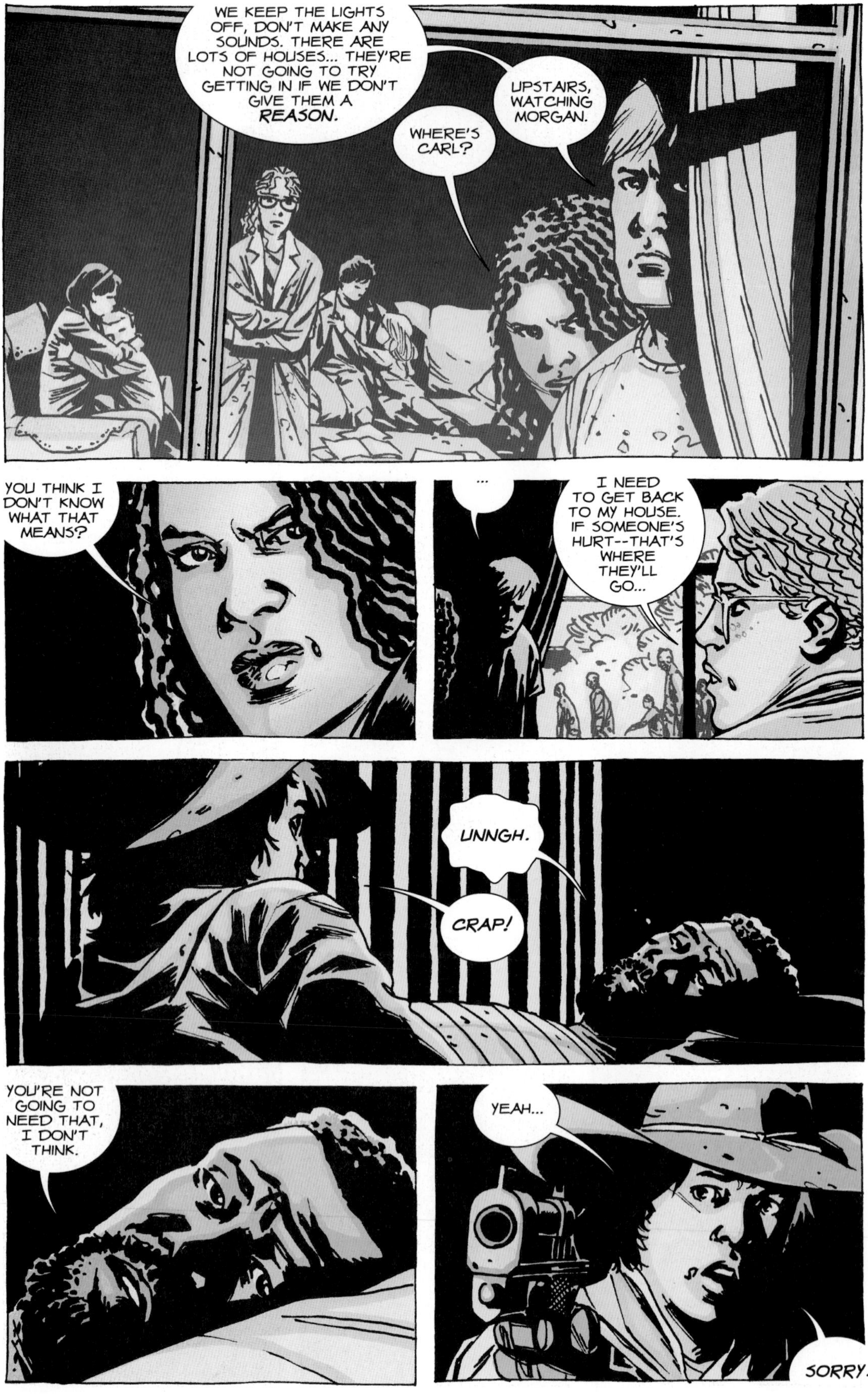
WE KEEP THE LIGHTS OFF, DON'T MAKE ANY SOUNDS. THERE ARE LOTS OF HOUSES... THEY'RE NOT GOING TO TRY GETTING IN IF WE DON'T GIVE THEM A REASON.
WHERE'S CARL?
UPSTAIRS, WATCHING MORGAN.
YOU THINK I DON'T KNOW WHAT THAT MEANS?
...
I NEED TO GET BACK TO MY HOUSE. IF SOMEONE'S HURT--THAT'S WHERE THEY'LL GO...
UNNGH.
CRAP!
YOU'RE NOT GOING TO NEED THAT, I DON'T THINK.
YEAH...
SORRY.

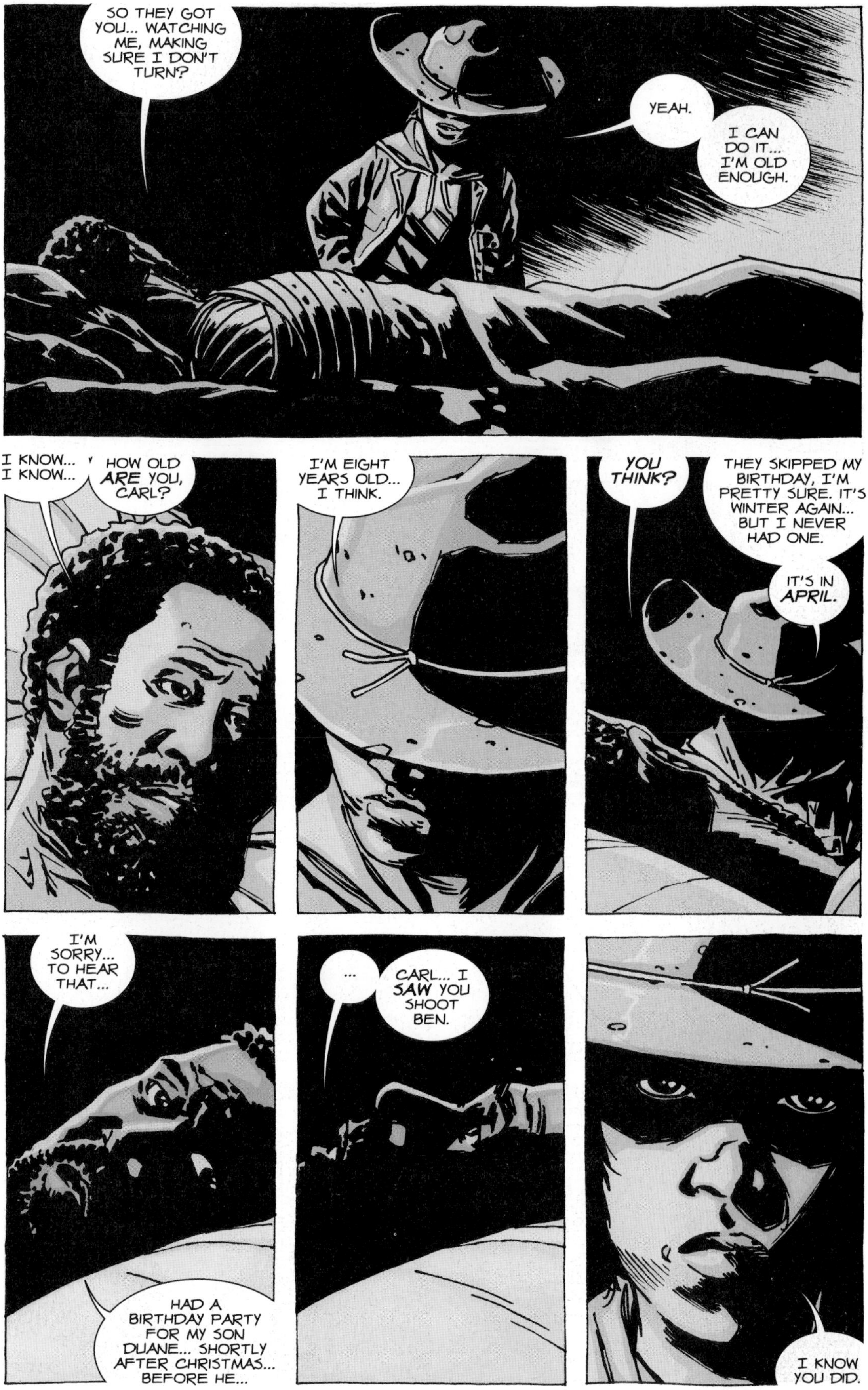
SO THEY GOT YOU... WATCHING ME, MAKING SURE I DON'T TURN?
YEAH.
I CAN DO IT... I'M OLD ENOUGH.
I KNOW... I KNOW...
HOW OLD *ARE* YOU, CARL?
I'M EIGHT YEARS OLD... I THINK.
YOU THINK?
THEY SKIPPED MY BIRTHDAY, I'M PRETTY SURE. IT'S WINTER AGAIN... BUT I NEVER HAD ONE.
IT'S IN *APRIL.*
I'M SORRY... TO HEAR THAT...
HAD A BIRTHDAY PARTY FOR MY SON DUANE... SHORTLY AFTER CHRISTMAS... BEFORE HE...
...
CARL... I *SAW* YOU SHOOT BEN.
I KNOW YOU DID.

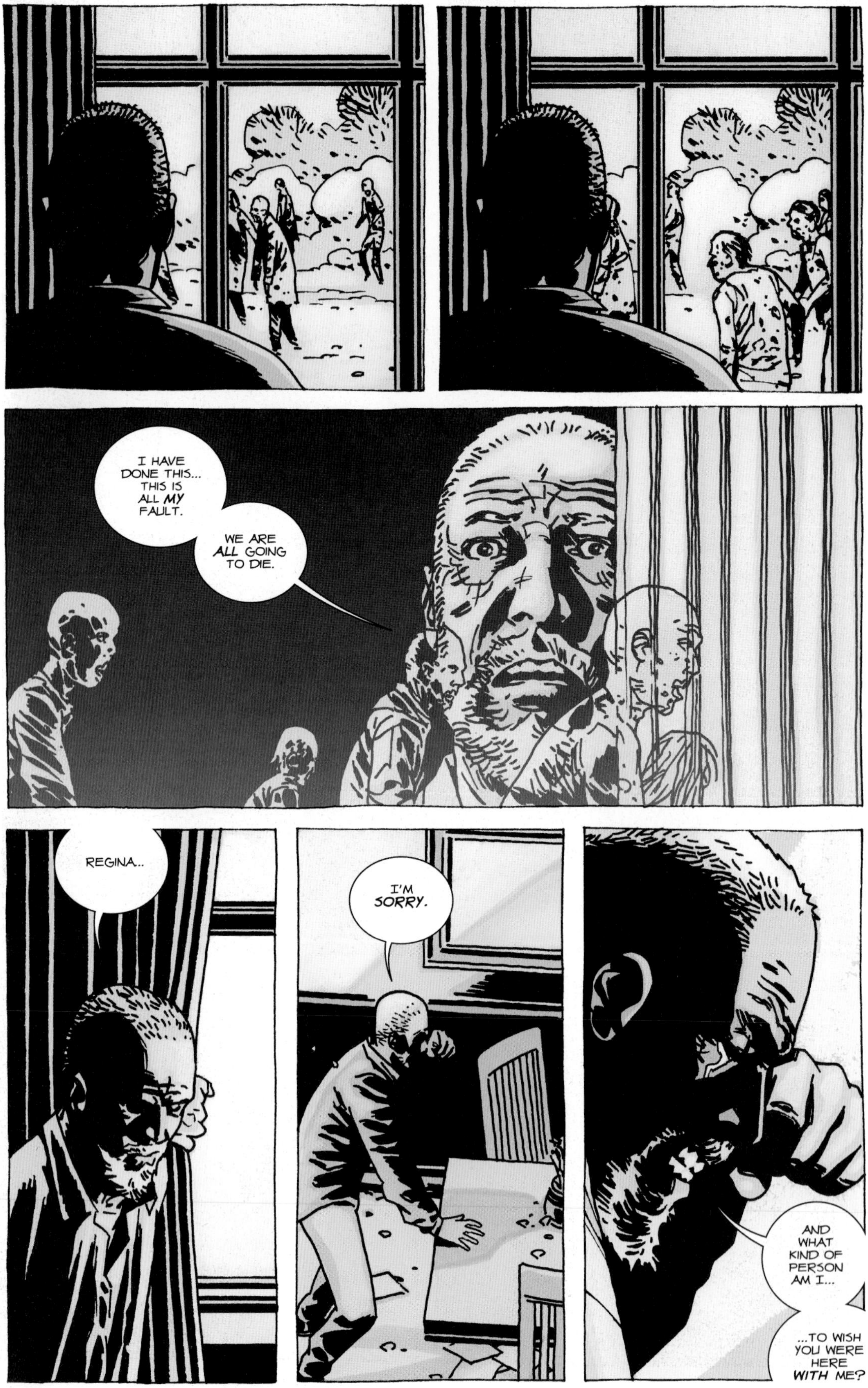
I HAVE DONE THIS... THIS IS ALL MY FAULT.
WE ARE ALL GOING TO DIE.
REGINA..
I'M SORRY.
AND WHAT KIND OF PERSON AM I...
...TO WISH YOU WERE HERE WITH ME?

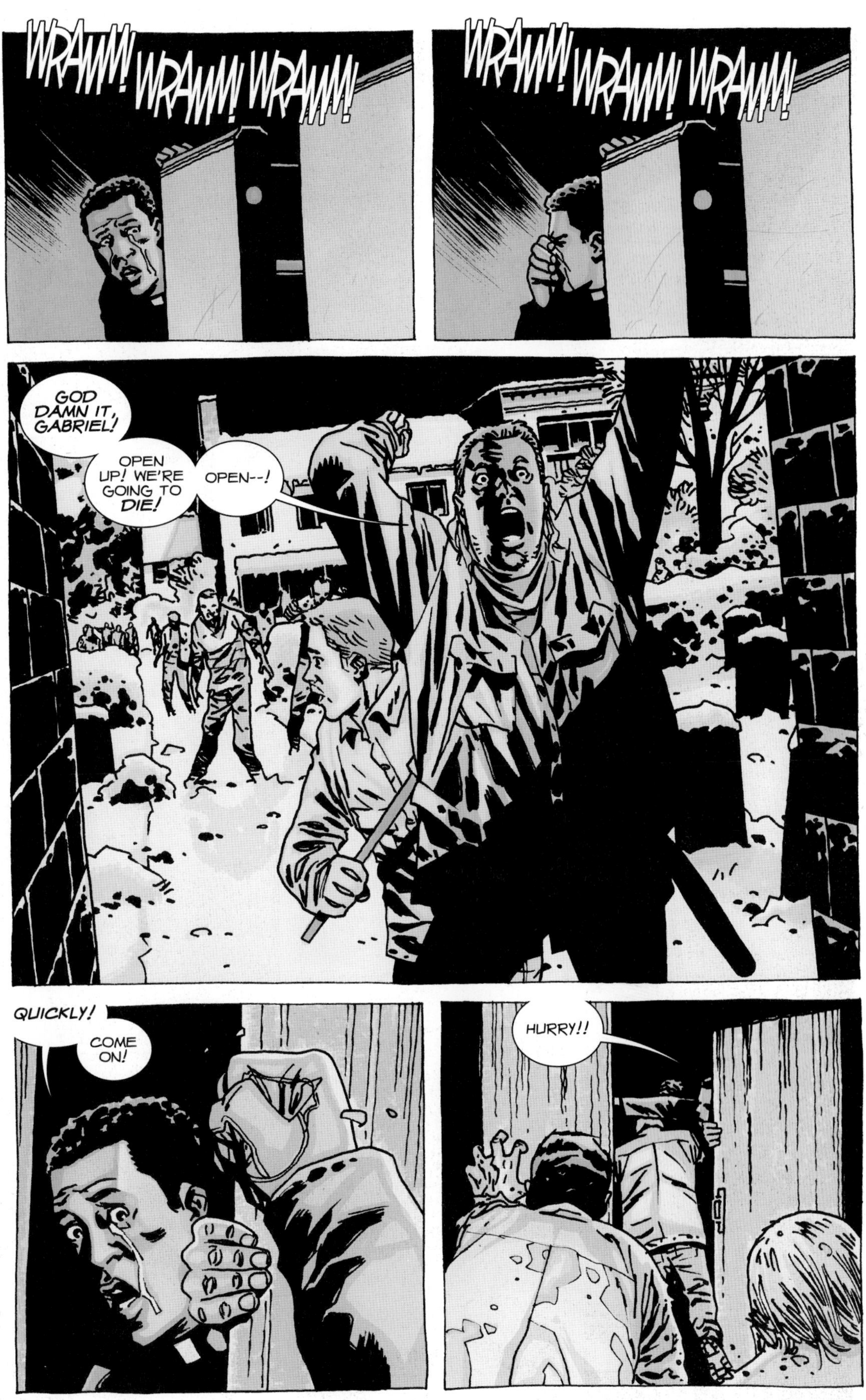
WRAMM! WRAMM! WRAMM!
WRAMM! WRAMM! WRAMM!
GOD DAMN IT, GABRIEL!
OPEN UP! WE'RE GOING TO DIE!
OPEN--!
QUICKLY!
COME ON!
HURRY!!

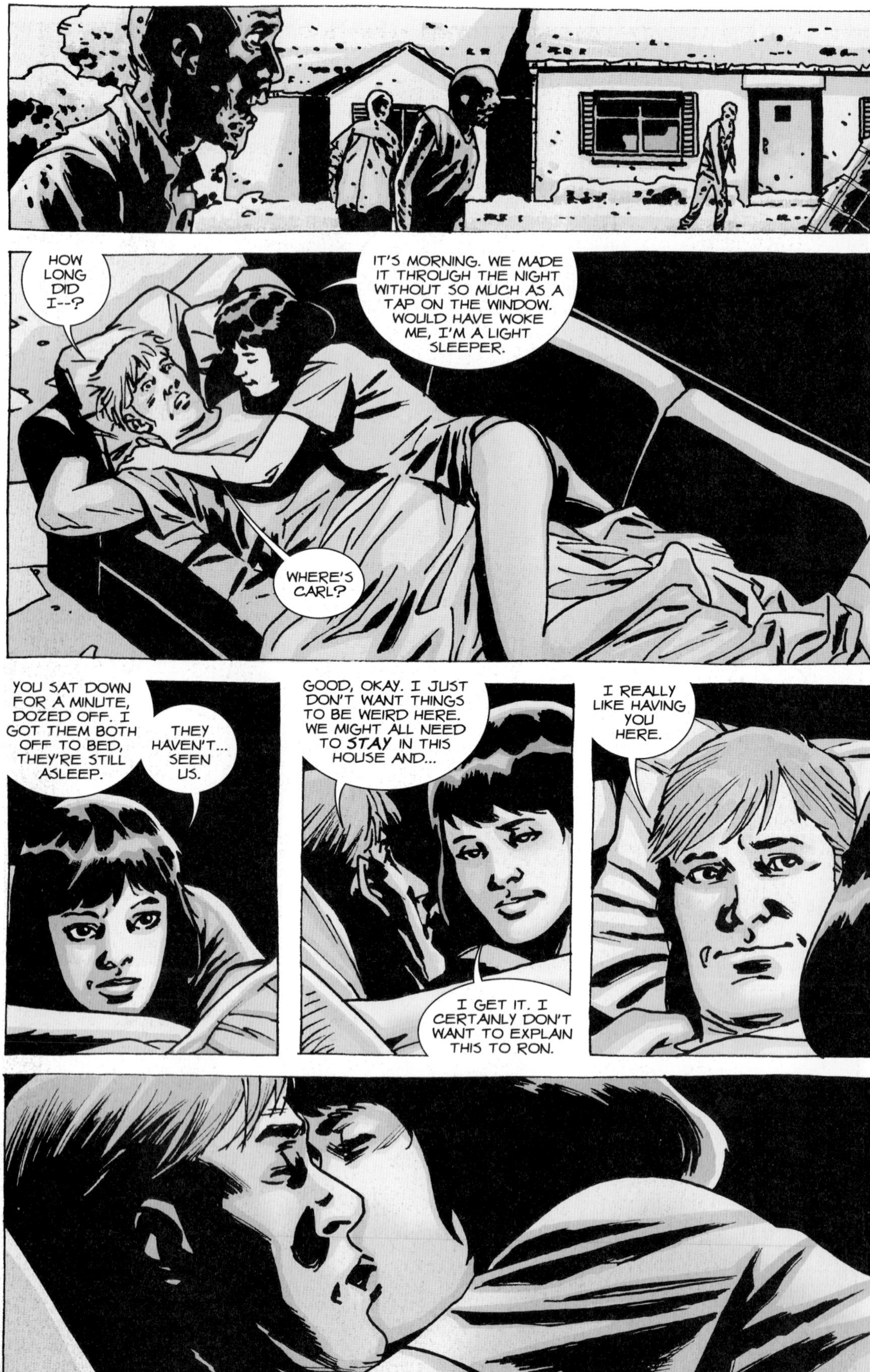
HOW LONG DID I--?
IT'S MORNING. WE MADE IT THROUGH THE NIGHT WITHOUT SO MUCH AS A TAP ON THE WINDOW. WOULD HAVE WOKE ME, I'M A LIGHT SLEEPER.
WHERE'S CARL?
YOU SAT DOWN FOR A MINUTE, DOZED OFF. I GOT THEM BOTH OFF TO BED, THEY'RE STILL ASLEEP.
THEY HAVEN'T... SEEN US.
GOOD, OKAY. I JUST DON'T WANT THINGS TO BE WEIRD HERE. WE MIGHT ALL NEED TO STAY IN THIS HOUSE AND...
I GET IT. I CERTAINLY DON'T WANT TO EXPLAIN THIS TO RON.
I REALLY LIKE HAVING YOU HERE.

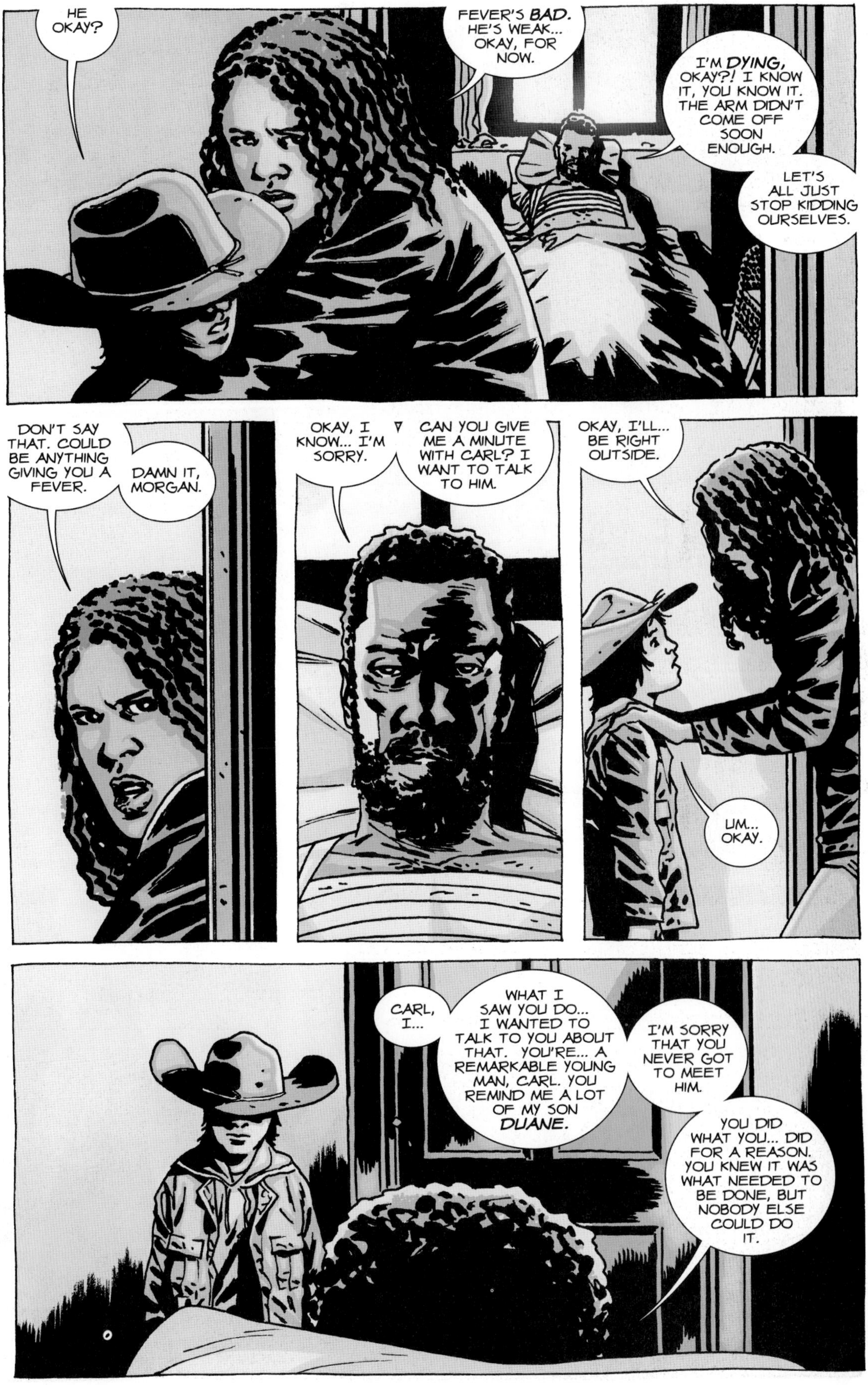
HE OKAY?
FEVER'S BAD. HE'S WEAK... OKAY, FOR NOW.
I'M DYING, OKAY?! I KNOW IT, YOU KNOW IT. THE ARM DIDN'T COME OFF SOON ENOUGH.
LET'S ALL JUST STOP KIDDING OURSELVES.
DON'T SAY THAT. COULD BE ANYTHING GIVING YOU A FEVER.
DAMN IT, MORGAN.
OKAY, I KNOW... I'M SORRY.
CAN YOU GIVE ME A MINUTE WITH CARL? I WANT TO TALK TO HIM.
OKAY, I'LL... BE RIGHT OUTSIDE.
UM... OKAY.
CARL, I...
WHAT I SAW YOU DO... I WANTED TO TALK TO YOU ABOUT THAT. YOU'RE... A REMARKABLE YOUNG MAN, CARL. YOU REMIND ME A LOT OF MY SON DUANE.
I'M SORRY THAT YOU NEVER GOT TO MEET HIM.
YOU DID WHAT YOU... DID FOR A REASON. YOU KNEW IT WAS WHAT NEEDED TO BE DONE, BUT NOBODY ELSE COULD DO IT.

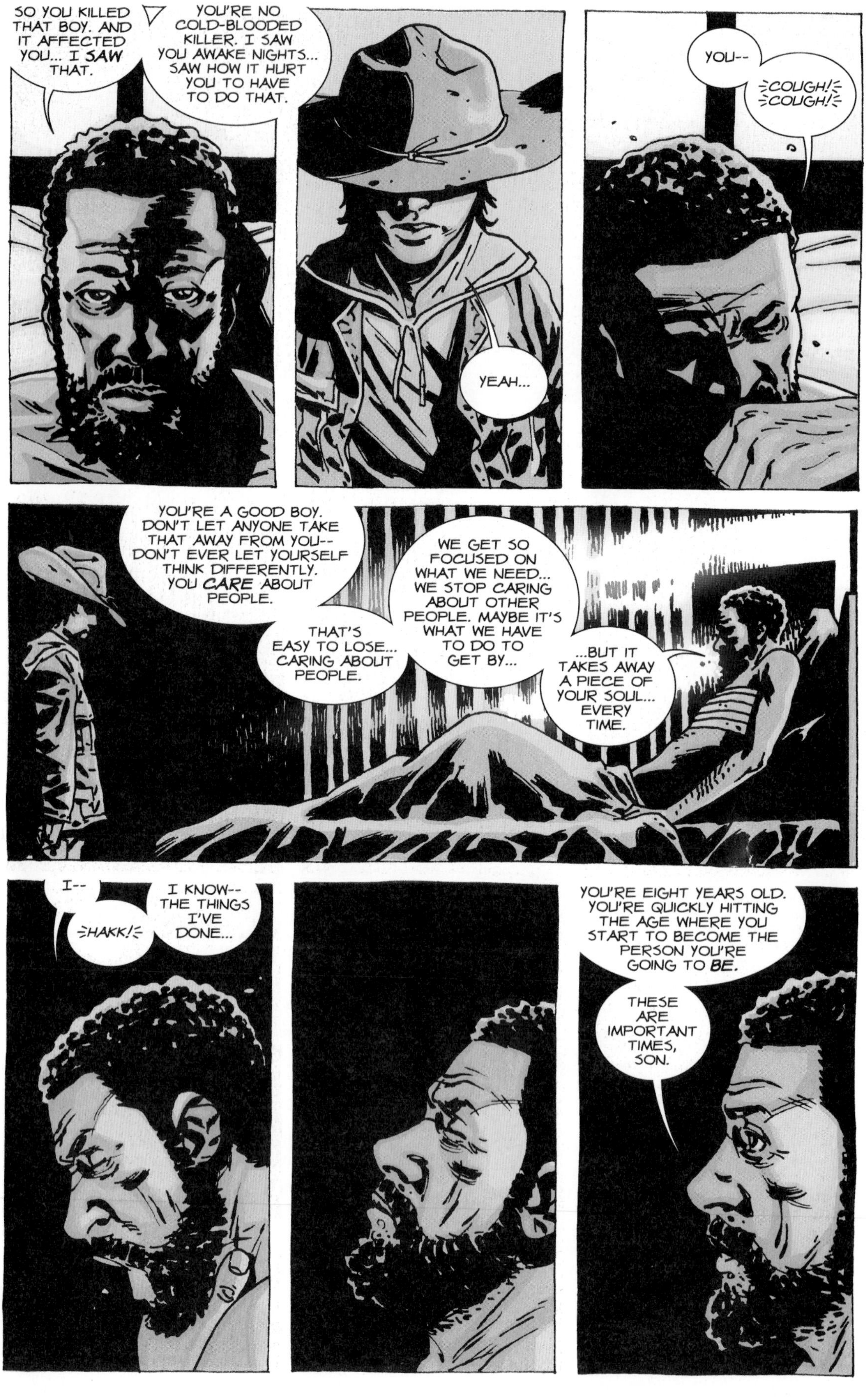
SO YOU KILLED THAT BOY. AND IT AFFECTED YOU... I SAW THAT.
YOU'RE NO COLD-BLOODED KILLER. I SAW YOU AWAKE NIGHTS... SAW HOW IT HURT YOU TO HAVE TO DO THAT.
YEAH...
YOU--
COUGH! COUGH!
YOU'RE A GOOD BOY. DON'T LET ANYONE TAKE THAT AWAY FROM YOU-- DON'T EVER LET YOURSELF THINK DIFFERENTLY. YOU CARE ABOUT PEOPLE.
THAT'S EASY TO LOSE... CARING ABOUT PEOPLE.
WE GET SO FOCUSED ON WHAT WE NEED... WE STOP CARING ABOUT OTHER PEOPLE. MAYBE IT'S WHAT WE HAVE TO DO TO GET BY...
...BUT IT TAKES AWAY A PIECE OF YOUR SOUL... EVERY TIME.
I--
HAKK!
I KNOW-- THE THINGS I'VE DONE...
YOU'RE EIGHT YEARS OLD. YOU'RE QUICKLY HITTING THE AGE WHERE YOU START TO BECOME THE PERSON YOU'RE GOING TO BE.
THESE ARE IMPORTANT TIMES, SON.

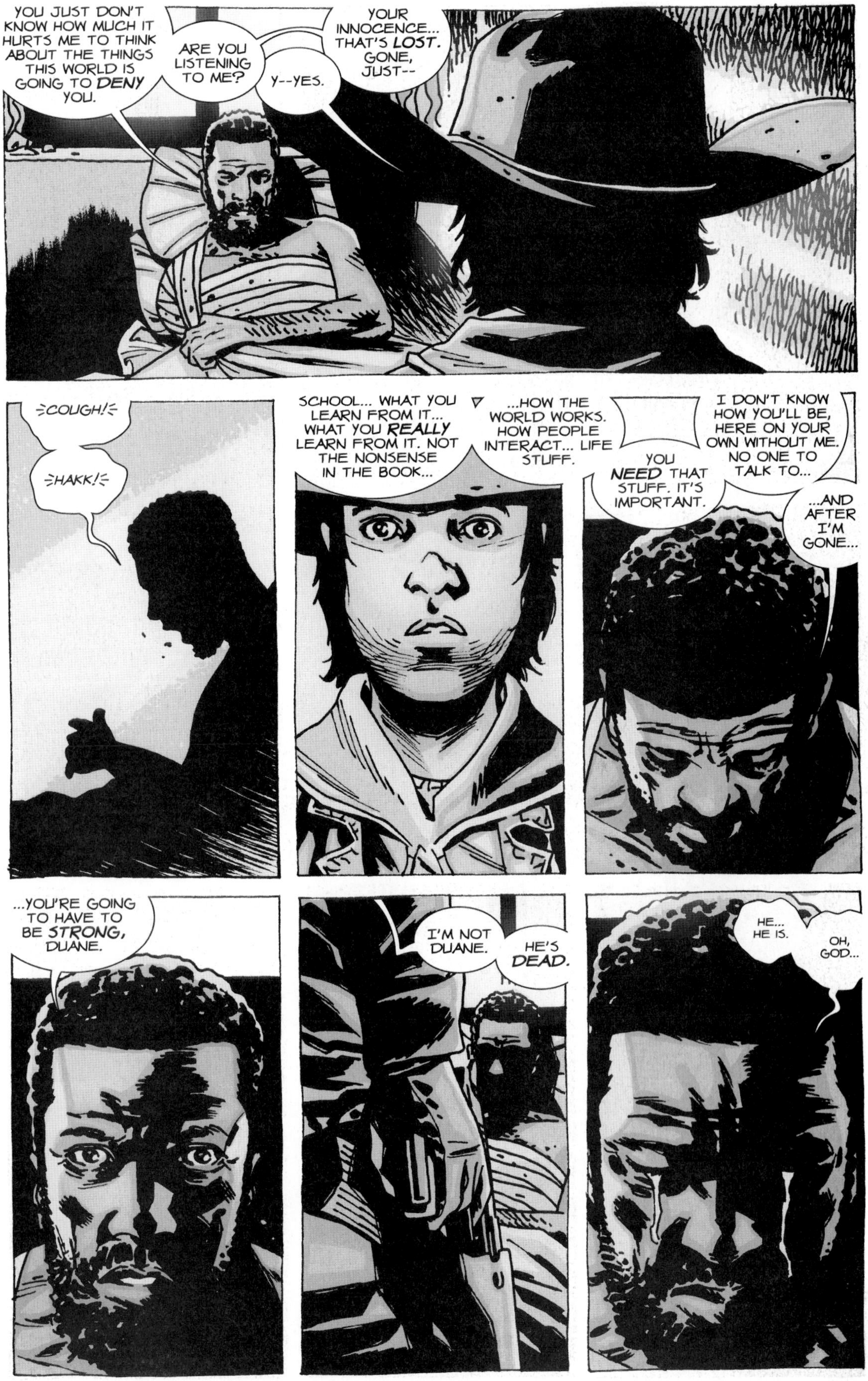

YOU JUST DON'T KNOW HOW MUCH IT HURTS ME TO THINK ABOUT THE THINGS THIS WORLD IS GOING TO DENY YOU.
ARE YOU LISTENING TO ME?
Y--YES.
YOUR INNOCENCE... THAT'S LOST. GONE, JUST--
COUGH!
HAKK!
SCHOOL... WHAT YOU LEARN FROM IT... WHAT YOU REALLY LEARN FROM IT. NOT THE NONSENSE IN THE BOOK...
...HOW THE WORLD WORKS. HOW PEOPLE INTERACT... LIFE STUFF.
YOU NEED THAT STUFF. IT'S IMPORTANT.
I DON'T KNOW HOW YOU'LL BE, HERE ON YOUR OWN WITHOUT ME. NO ONE TO TALK TO...
...AND AFTER I'M GONE...
...YOU'RE GOING TO HAVE TO BE STRONG, DUANE.
I'M NOT DUANE.
HE'S DEAD.
HE... HE IS.
OH, GOD...

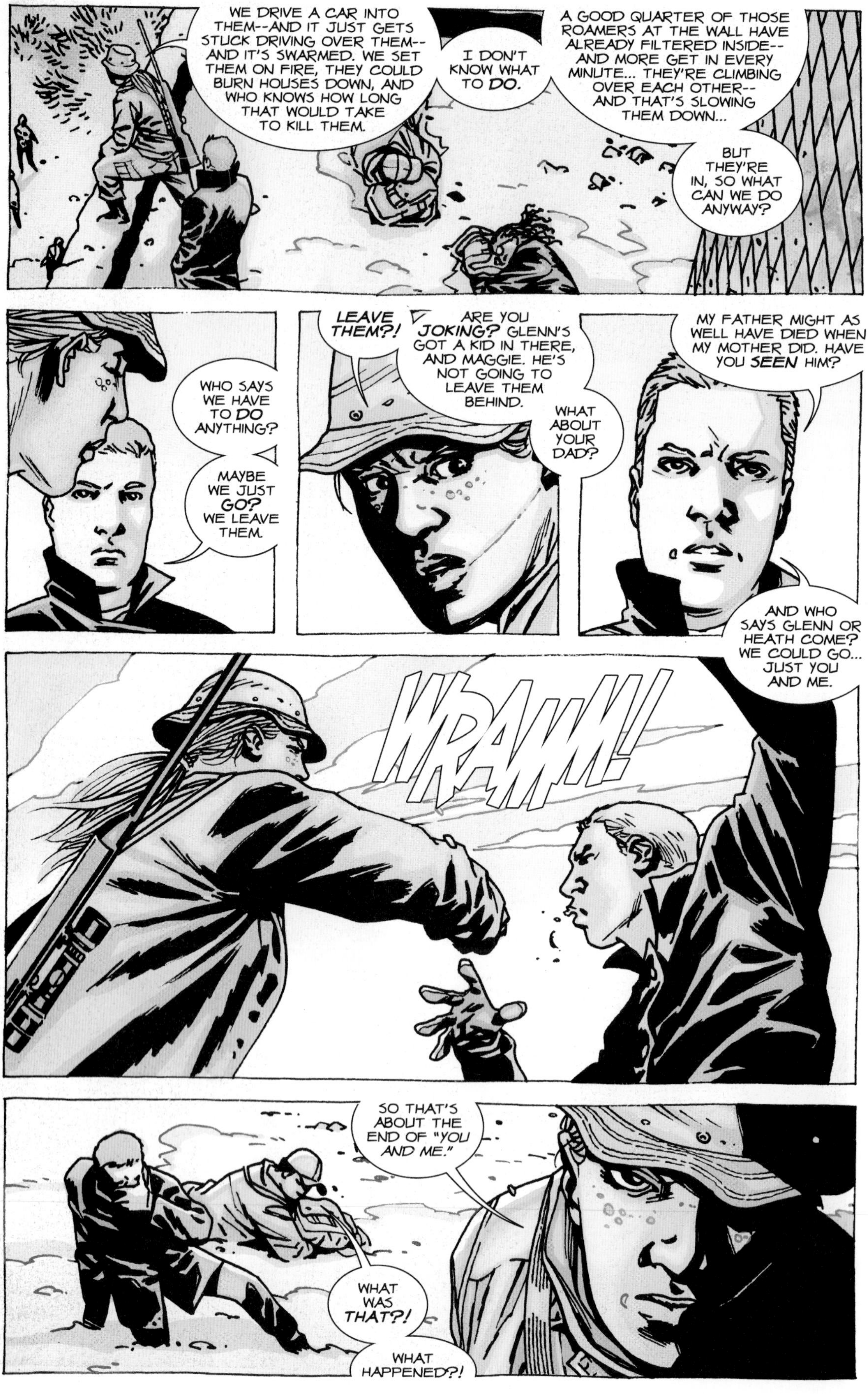
WE DRIVE A CAR INTO THEM--AND IT JUST GETS STUCK DRIVING OVER THEM--AND IT'S SWARMED. WE SET THEM ON FIRE, THEY COULD BURN HOUSES DOWN, AND WHO KNOWS HOW LONG THAT WOULD TAKE TO KILL THEM.
I DON'T KNOW WHAT TO DO.
A GOOD QUARTER OF THOSE ROAMERS AT THE WALL HAVE ALREADY FILTERED INSIDE--AND MORE GET IN EVERY MINUTE... THEY'RE CLIMBING OVER EACH OTHER--AND THAT'S SLOWING THEM DOWN...
BUT THEY'RE IN, SO WHAT CAN WE DO ANYWAY?
WHO SAYS WE HAVE TO DO ANYTHING?
MAYBE WE JUST GO? WE LEAVE THEM.
LEAVE THEM?!
ARE YOU JOKING? GLENN'S GOT A KID IN THERE, AND MAGGIE. HE'S NOT GOING TO LEAVE THEM BEHIND.
WHAT ABOUT YOUR DAD?
MY FATHER MIGHT AS WELL HAVE DIED WHEN MY MOTHER DID. HAVE YOU SEEN HIM?
AND WHO SAYS GLENN OR HEATH COME? WE COULD GO... JUST YOU AND ME.
WRAMM!
SO THAT'S ABOUT THE END OF "YOU AND ME."
WHAT WAS THAT?!
WHAT HAPPENED?!

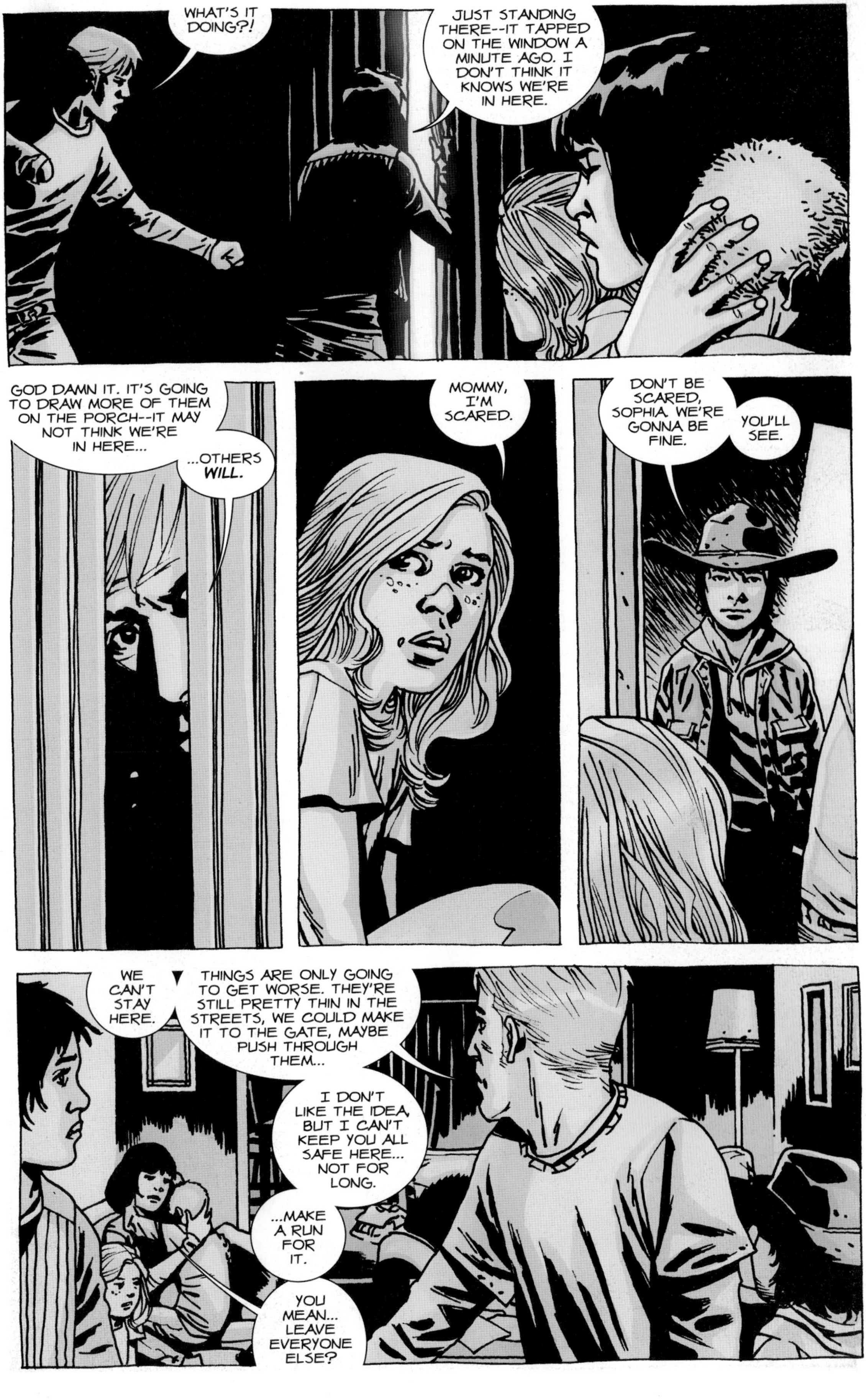
WHAT'S IT DOING?!
JUST STANDING THERE--IT TAPPED ON THE WINDOW A MINUTE AGO. I DON'T THINK IT KNOWS WE'RE IN HERE.
GOD DAMN IT. IT'S GOING TO DRAW MORE OF THEM ON THE PORCH--IT MAY NOT THINK WE'RE IN HERE...
...OTHERS WILL.
MOMMY, I'M SCARED.
DON'T BE SCARED, SOPHIA. WE'RE GONNA BE FINE.
YOU'LL SEE.
WE CAN'T STAY HERE.
THINGS ARE ONLY GOING TO GET WORSE. THEY'RE STILL PRETTY THIN IN THE STREETS, WE COULD MAKE IT TO THE GATE, MAYBE PUSH THROUGH THEM...
I DON'T LIKE THE IDEA, BUT I CAN'T KEEP YOU ALL SAFE HERE... NOT FOR LONG.
...MAKE A RUN FOR IT.
YOU MEAN... LEAVE EVERYONE ELSE?

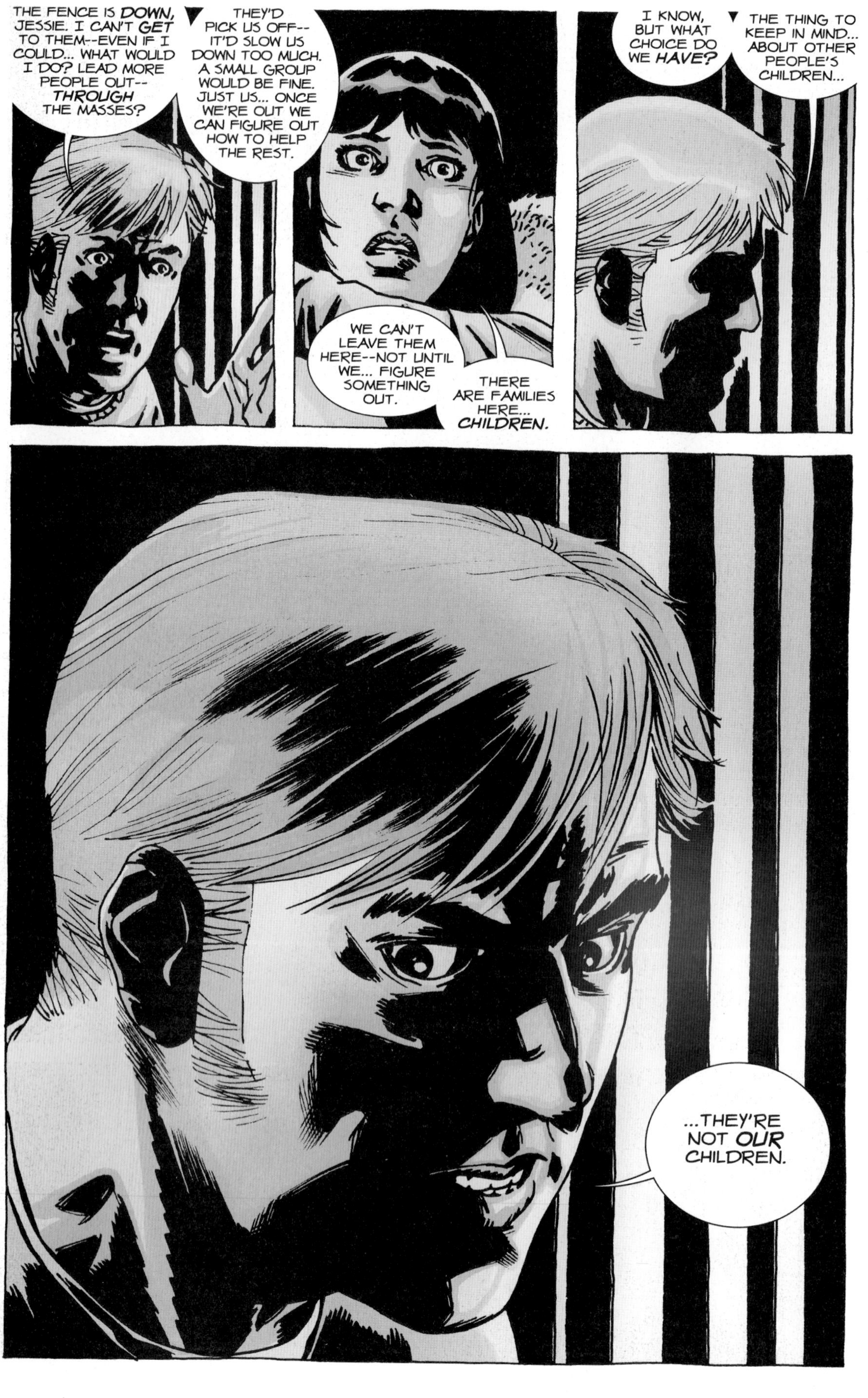
THE FENCE IS DOWN, JESSIE. I CAN'T GET TO THEM--EVEN IF I COULD... WHAT WOULD I DO? LEAD MORE PEOPLE OUT-- THROUGH THE MASSES?
THEY'D PICK US OFF-- IT'D SLOW US DOWN TOO MUCH. A SMALL GROUP WOULD BE FINE. JUST US... ONCE WE'RE OUT WE CAN FIGURE OUT HOW TO HELP THE REST.
WE CAN'T LEAVE THEM HERE--NOT UNTIL WE... FIGURE SOMETHING OUT.
THERE ARE FAMILIES HERE... CHILDREN.
I KNOW, BUT WHAT CHOICE DO WE HAVE?
THE THING TO KEEP IN MIND... ABOUT OTHER PEOPLE'S CHILDREN...
...THEY'RE NOT OUR CHILDREN.

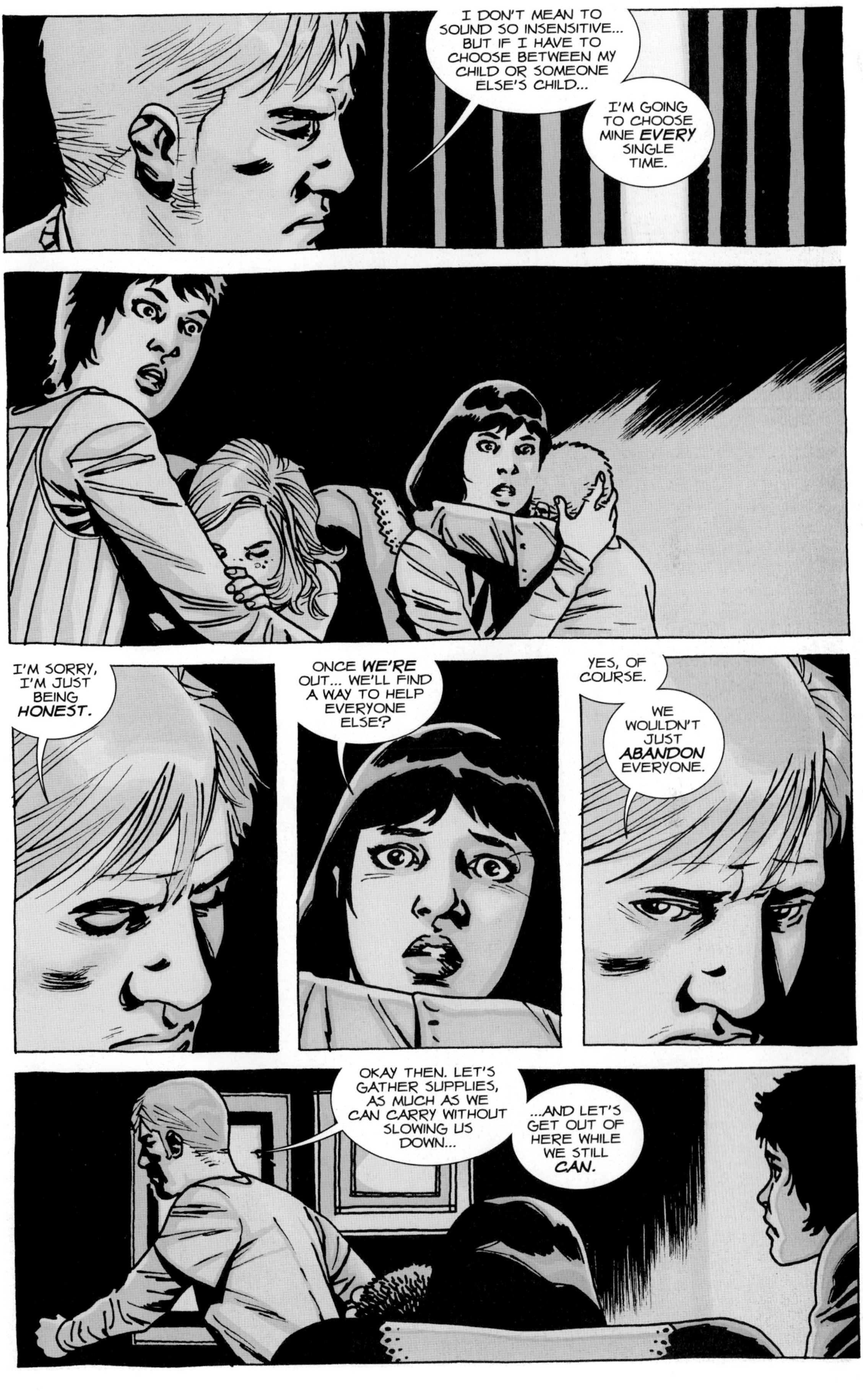
I DON'T MEAN TO SOUND SO INSENSITIVE... BUT IF I HAVE TO CHOOSE BETWEEN MY CHILD OR SOMEONE ELSE'S CHILD...
I'M GOING TO CHOOSE MINE EVERY SINGLE TIME.
I'M SORRY, I'M JUST BEING HONEST.
ONCE WE'RE OUT... WE'LL FIND A WAY TO HELP EVERYONE ELSE?
YES, OF COURSE.
WE WOULDN'T JUST ABANDON EVERYONE.
OKAY THEN. LET'S GATHER SUPPLIES, AS MUCH AS WE CAN CARRY WITHOUT SLOWING US DOWN...
...AND LET'S GET OUT OF HERE WHILE WE STILL CAN.

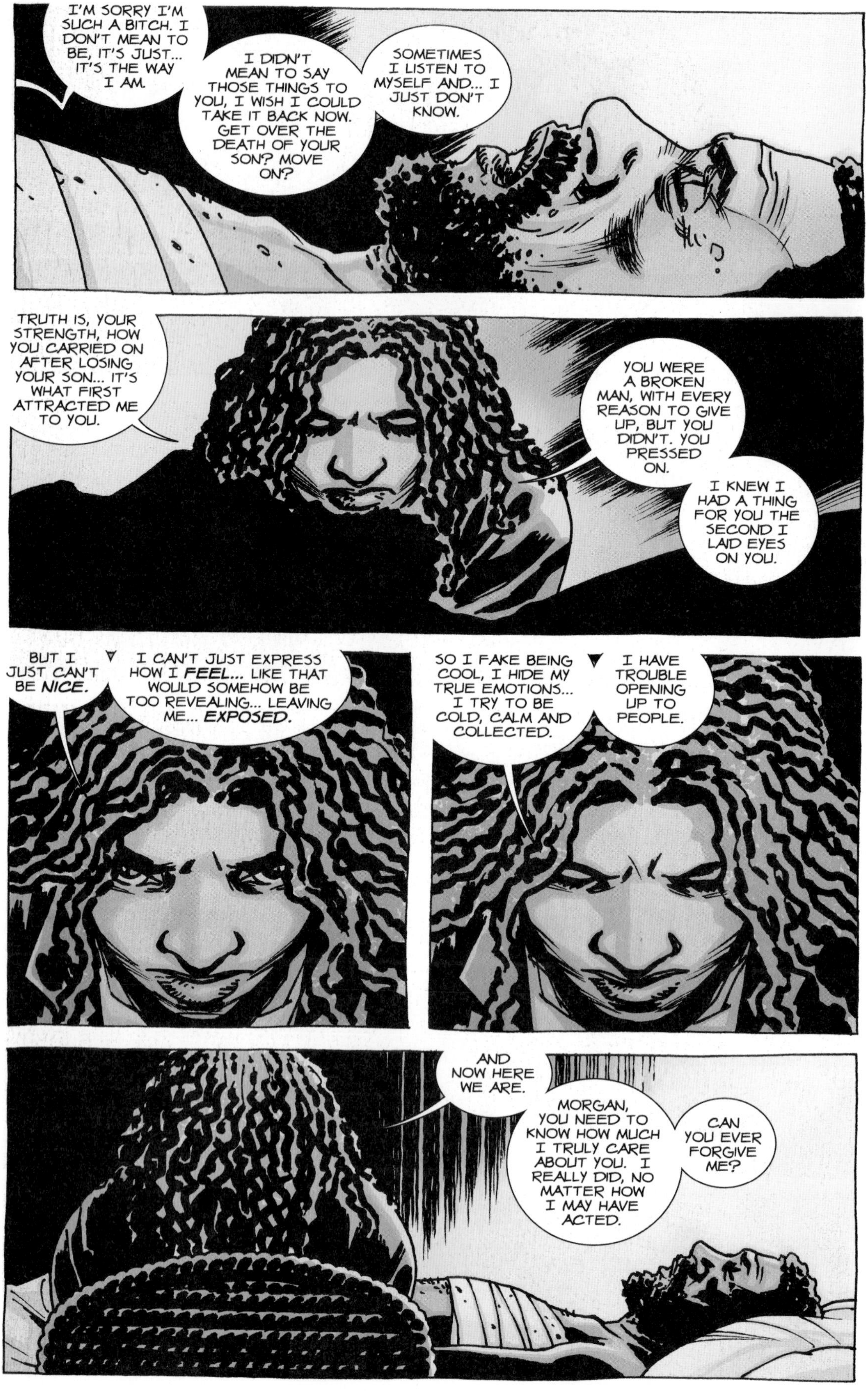
I'M SORRY I'M SUCH A BITCH. I DON'T MEAN TO BE, IT'S JUST... IT'S THE WAY I AM.
I DIDN'T MEAN TO SAY THOSE THINGS TO YOU, I WISH I COULD TAKE IT BACK NOW. GET OVER THE DEATH OF YOUR SON? MOVE ON?
SOMETIMES I LISTEN TO MYSELF AND... I JUST DON'T KNOW.
TRUTH IS, YOUR STRENGTH, HOW YOU CARRIED ON AFTER LOSING YOUR SON... IT'S WHAT FIRST ATTRACTED ME TO YOU.
YOU WERE A BROKEN MAN, WITH EVERY REASON TO GIVE UP, BUT YOU DIDN'T. YOU PRESSED ON.
I KNEW I HAD A THING FOR YOU THE SECOND I LAID EYES ON YOU.
BUT I JUST CAN'T BE NICE.
I CAN'T JUST EXPRESS HOW I FEEL... LIKE THAT WOULD SOMEHOW BE TOO REVEALING... LEAVING ME... EXPOSED.
SO I FAKE BEING COOL, I HIDE MY TRUE EMOTIONS... I TRY TO BE COLD, CALM AND COLLECTED.
I HAVE TROUBLE OPENING UP TO PEOPLE.
AND NOW HERE WE ARE.
MORGAN, YOU NEED TO KNOW HOW MUCH I TRULY CARE ABOUT YOU. I REALLY DID, NO MATTER HOW I MAY HAVE ACTED.
CAN YOU EVER FORGIVE ME?

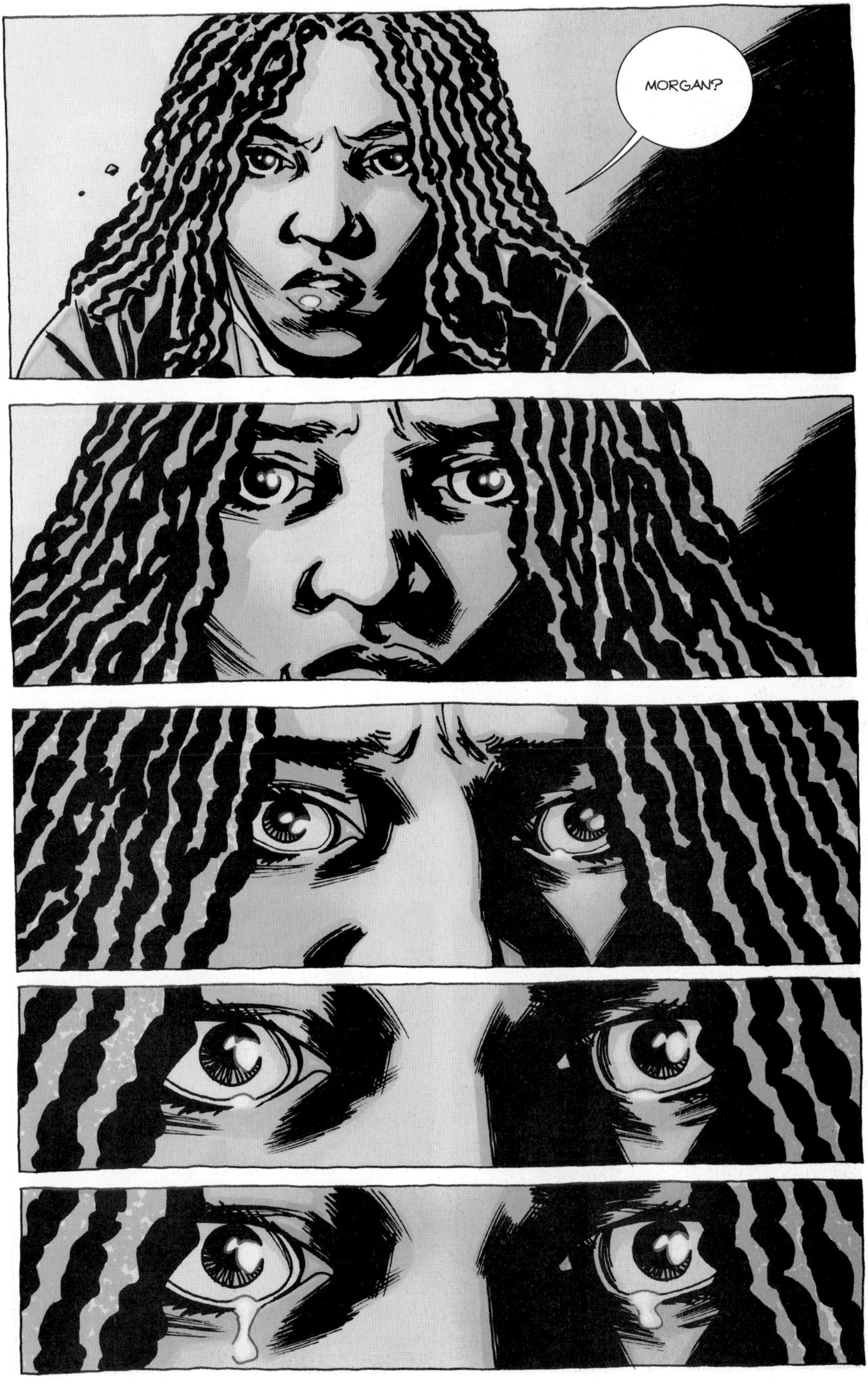
MORGAN?

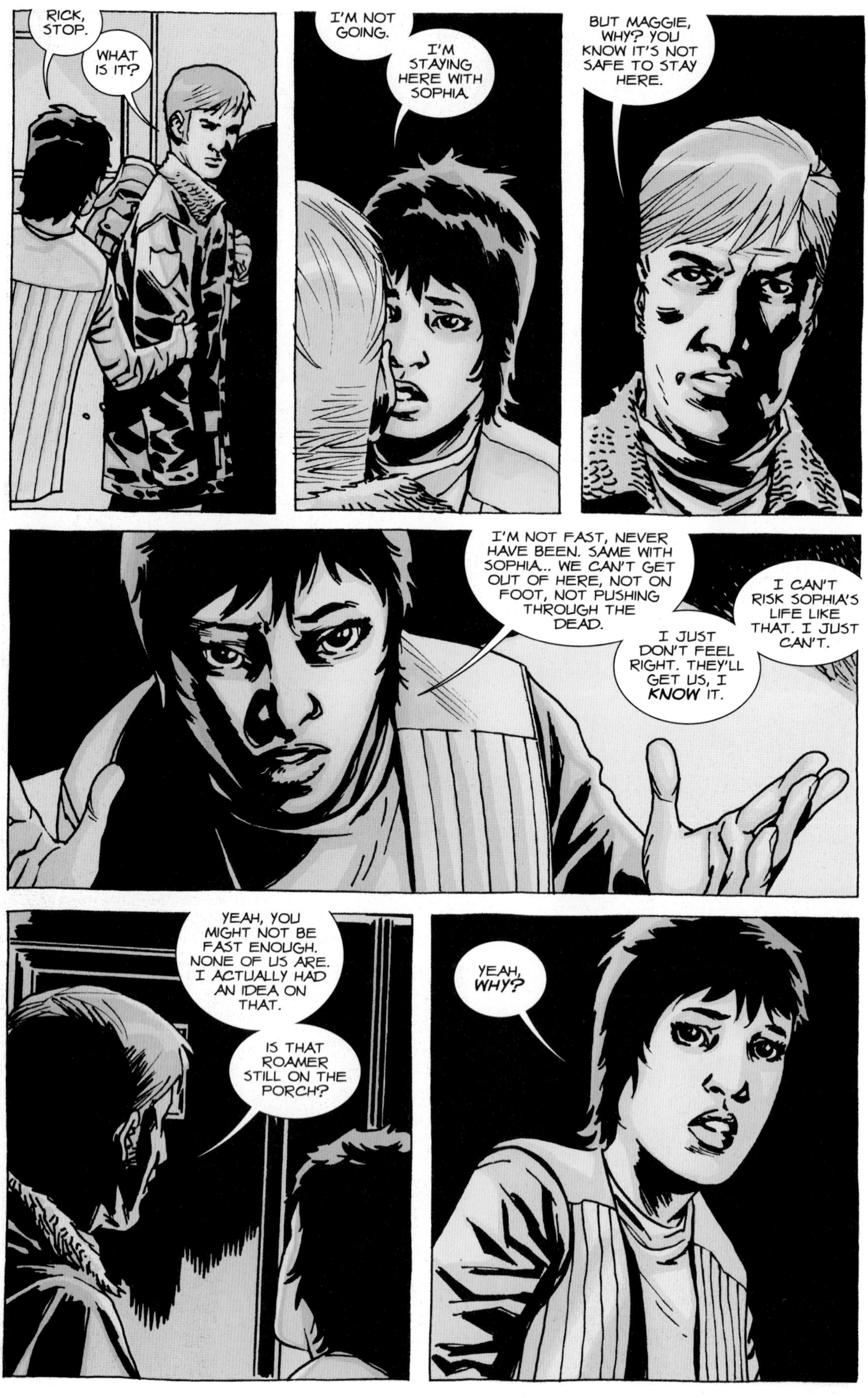
RICK, STOP.
WHAT IS IT?
I'M NOT GOING.
I'M STAYING HERE WITH SOPHIA.
BUT MAGGIE, WHY? YOU KNOW IT'S NOT SAFE TO STAY HERE.
I'M NOT FAST, NEVER HAVE BEEN. SAME WITH SOPHIA.. WE CAN'T GET OUT OF HERE, NOT ON FOOT, NOT PUSHING THROUGH THE DEAD.
I JUST DON'T FEEL RIGHT. THEY'LL GET US, I KNOW IT.
I CAN'T RISK SOPHIA'S LIFE LIKE THAT. I JUST CAN'T.
YEAH, YOU MIGHT NOT BE FAST ENOUGH. NONE OF US ARE. I ACTUALLY HAD AN IDEA ON THAT.
IS THAT ROAMER STILL ON THE PORCH?
YEAH, WHY?

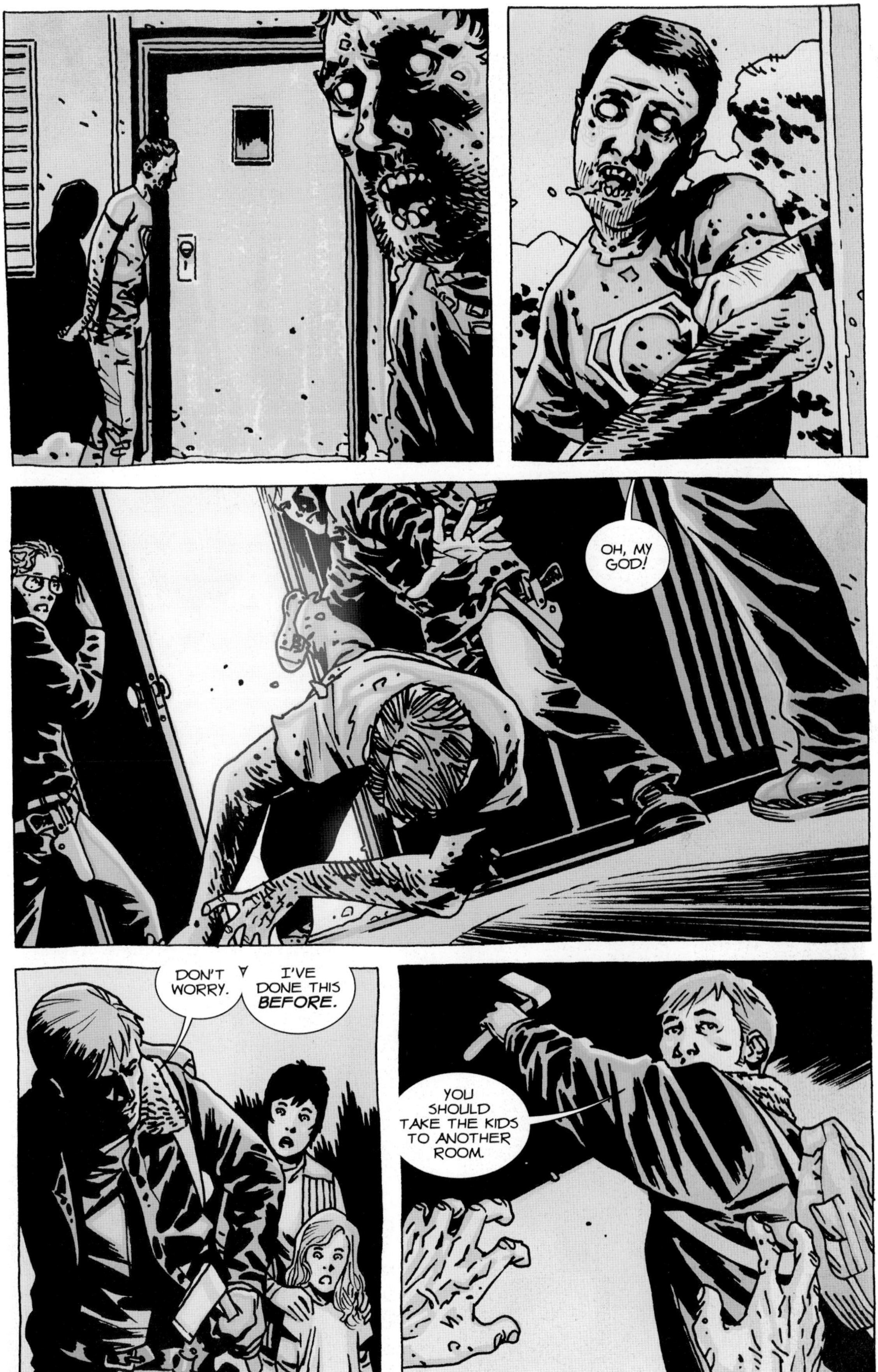
OH, MY GOD!
DON'T WORRY.
I'VE DONE THIS BEFORE.
YOU SHOULD TAKE THE KIDS TO ANOTHER ROOM.

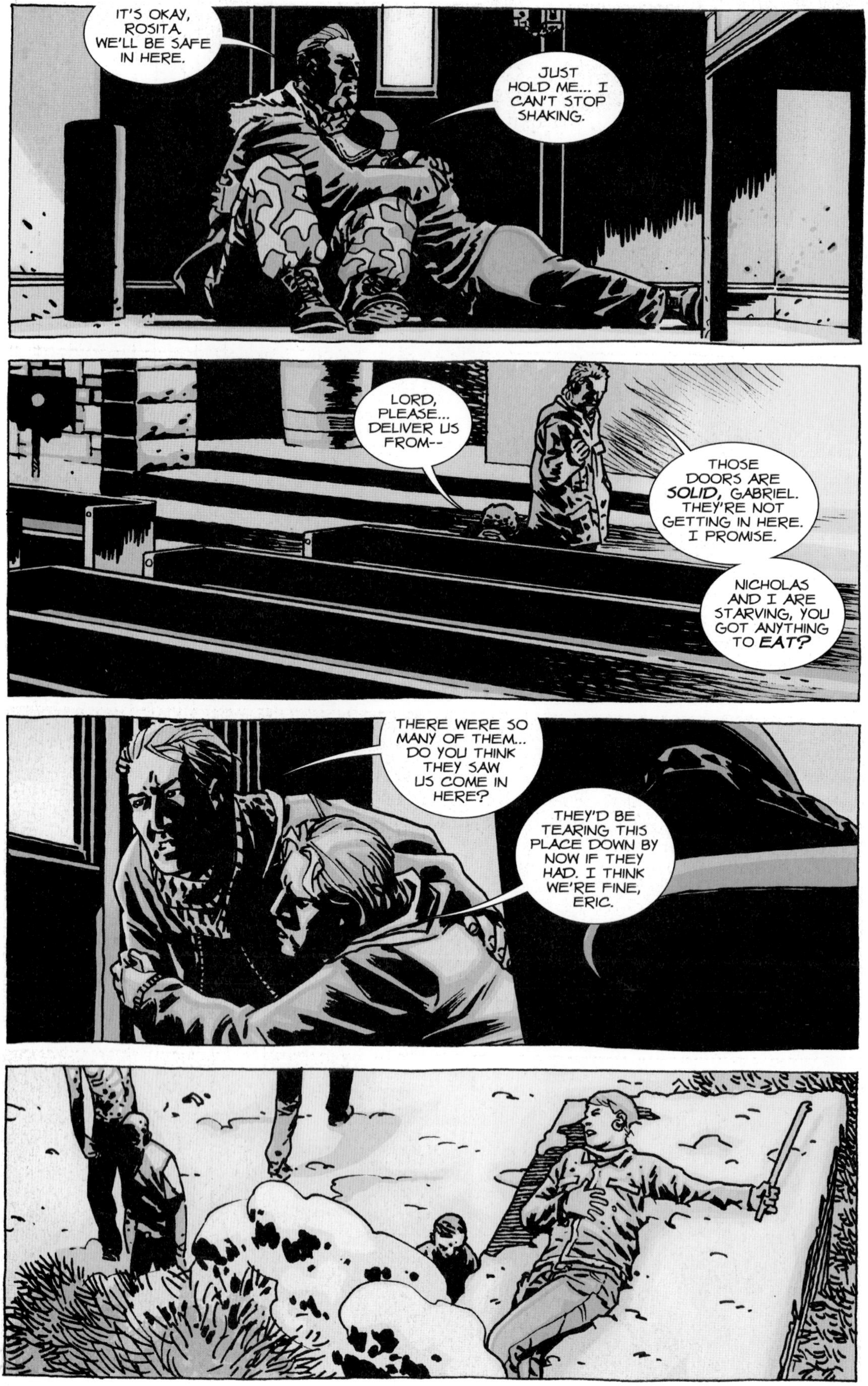
IT'S OKAY, ROSITA. WE'LL BE SAFE IN HERE.
JUST HOLD ME... I CAN'T STOP SHAKING.
LORD, PLEASE... DELIVER US FROM--
THOSE DOORS ARE SOLID, GABRIEL. THEY'RE NOT GETTING IN HERE. I PROMISE.
NICHOLAS AND I ARE STARVING, YOU GOT ANYTHING TO EAT?
THERE WERE SO MANY OF THEM... DO YOU THINK THEY SAW US COME IN HERE?
THEY'D BE TEARING THIS PLACE DOWN BY NOW IF THEY HAD. I THINK WE'RE FINE, ERIC.

C-C-C--

I CAN'T--

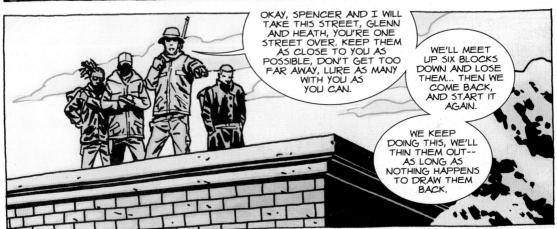

OKAY, SPENCER AND I WILL TAKE THIS STREET, GLENN AND HEATH, YOU'RE ONE STREET OVER. KEEP THEM AS CLOSE TO YOU AS POSSIBLE, DON'T GET TOO FAR AWAY, LURE AS MANY WITH YOU AS YOU CAN.

WE'LL MEET UP SIX BLOCKS DOWN AND LOSE THEM... THEN WE COME BACK, AND START IT AGAIN.

WE KEEP DOING THIS, WE'LL THIN THEM OUT-- AS LONG AS NOTHING HAPPENS TO DRAW THEM BACK.

I'M SORRY, MORGAN.

THUNK!

OH, MY GOD--WHAT ARE YOU DOING?!

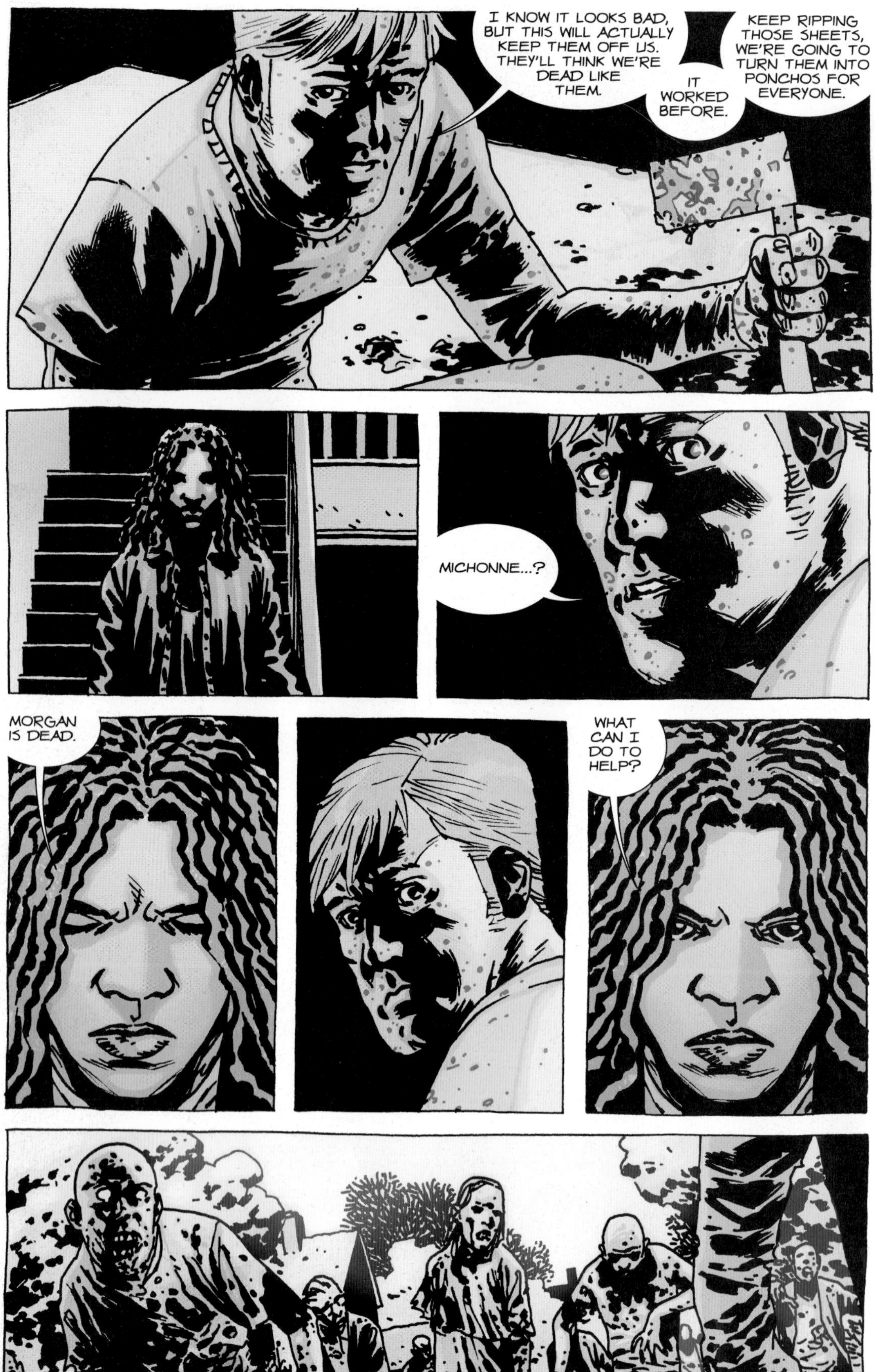

I KNOW IT LOOKS BAD, BUT THIS WILL ACTUALLY KEEP THEM OFF US. THEY'LL THINK WE'RE DEAD LIKE THEM.
IT WORKED BEFORE.
KEEP RIPPING THOSE SHEETS, WE'RE GOING TO TURN THEM INTO PONCHOS FOR EVERYONE.
MICHONNE...?
MORGAN IS DEAD.
WHAT CAN I DO TO HELP?

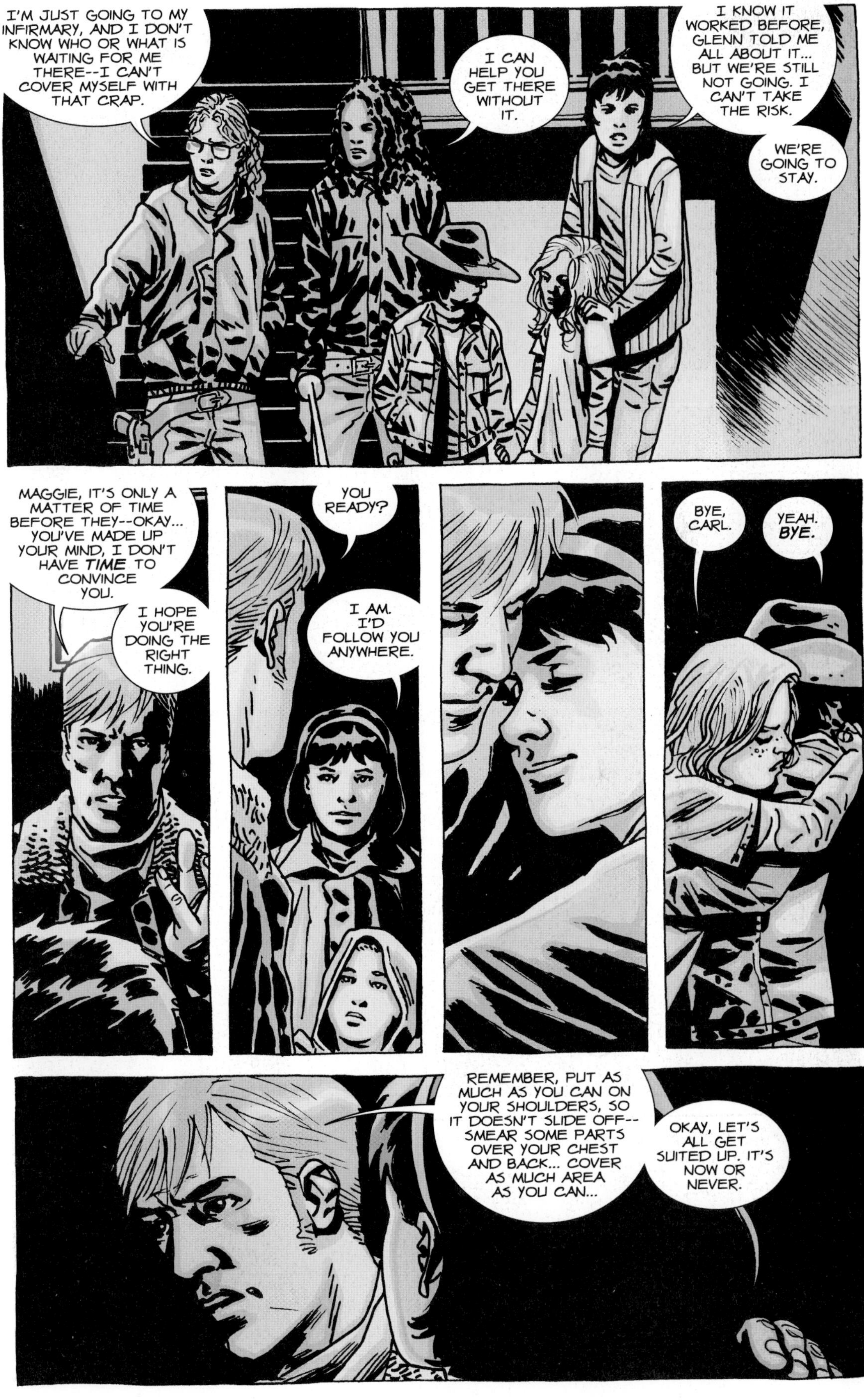

I'M JUST GOING TO MY INFIRMARY, AND I DON'T KNOW WHO OR WHAT IS WAITING FOR ME THERE--I CAN'T COVER MYSELF WITH THAT CRAP.
I CAN HELP YOU GET THERE WITHOUT IT.
I KNOW IT WORKED BEFORE, GLENN TOLD ME ALL ABOUT IT... BUT WE'RE STILL NOT GOING. I CAN'T TAKE THE RISK.
WE'RE GOING TO STAY.
MAGGIE, IT'S ONLY A MATTER OF TIME BEFORE THEY--OKAY... YOU'VE MADE UP YOUR MIND, I DON'T HAVE *TIME* TO CONVINCE YOU.
I HOPE YOU'RE DOING THE RIGHT THING.
YOU READY?
I AM. I'D FOLLOW YOU ANYWHERE.
BYE, CARL.
YEAH. ***BYE.***
REMEMBER, PUT AS MUCH AS YOU CAN ON YOUR SHOULDERS, SO IT DOESN'T SLIDE OFF-- SMEAR SOME PARTS OVER YOUR CHEST AND BACK... COVER AS MUCH AREA AS YOU CAN...
OKAY, LET'S ALL GET SUITED UP. IT'S NOW OR NEVER.

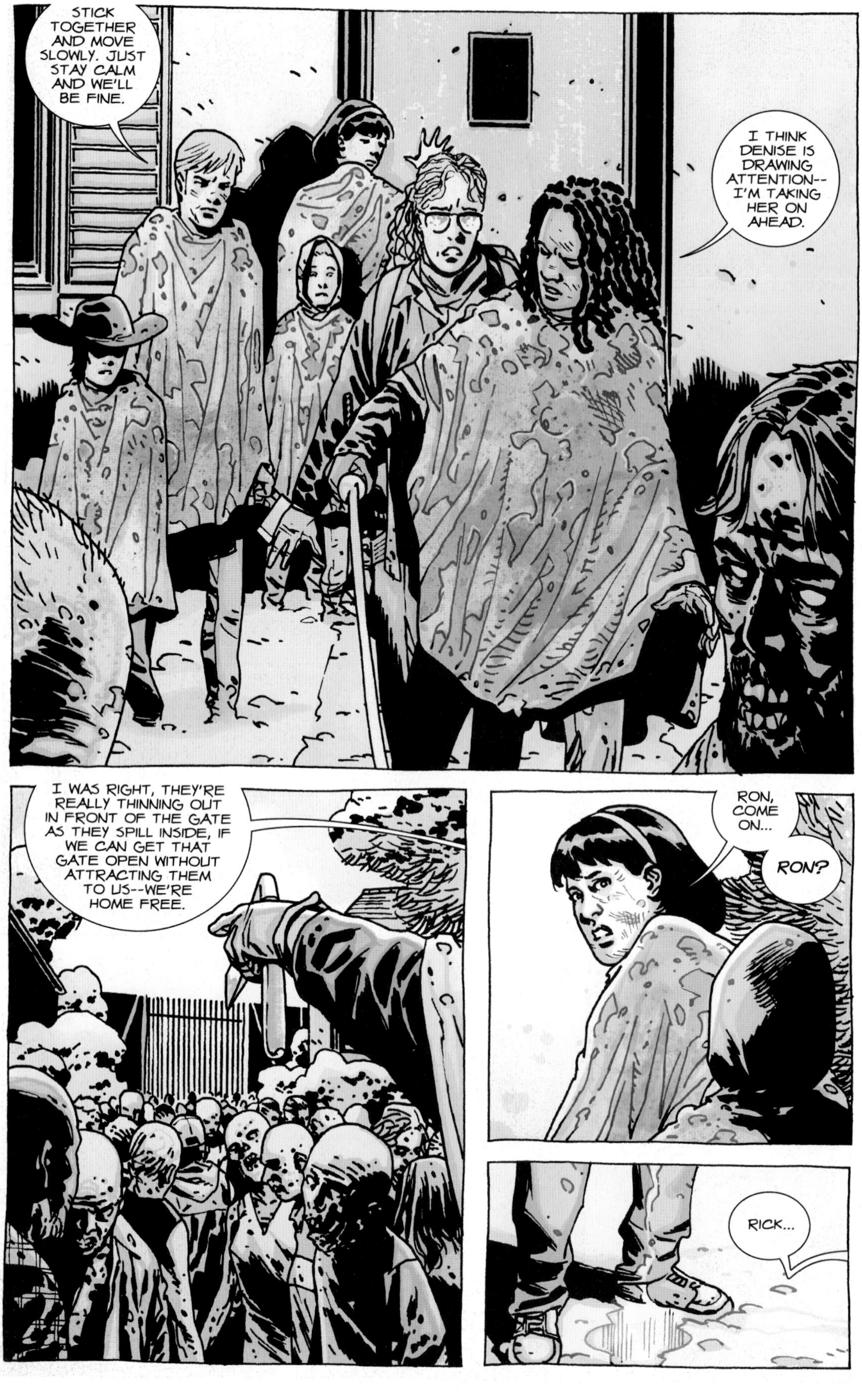
STICK TOGETHER AND MOVE SLOWLY. JUST STAY CALM AND WE'LL BE FINE.
I THINK DENISE IS DRAWING ATTENTION-- I'M TAKING HER ON AHEAD.
I WAS RIGHT, THEY'RE REALLY THINNING OUT IN FRONT OF THE GATE AS THEY SPILL INSIDE, IF WE CAN GET THAT GATE OPEN WITHOUT ATTRACTING THEM TO US--WE'RE HOME FREE.
RON, COME ON...
RON?
RICK...

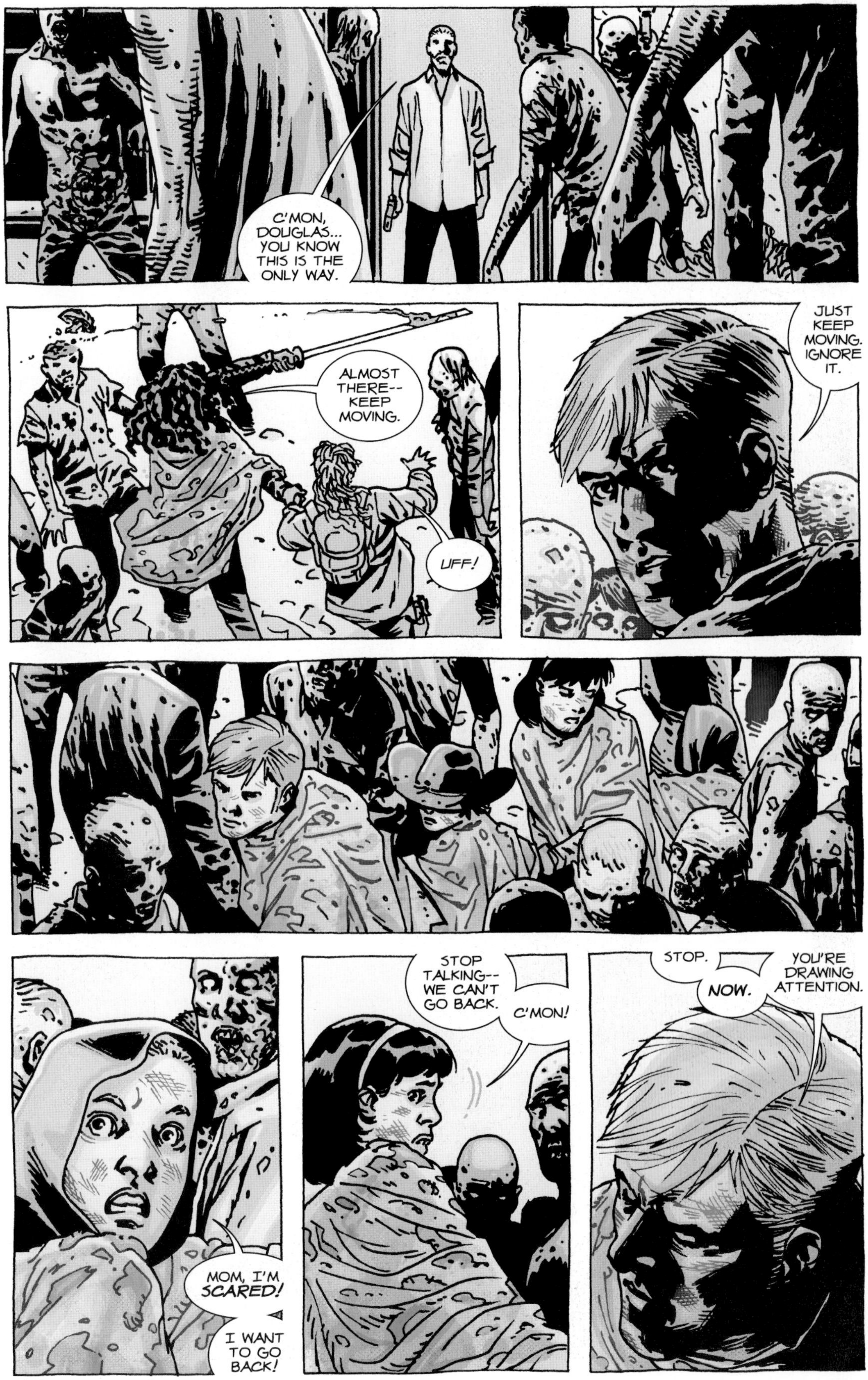
C'MON, DOUGLAS... YOU KNOW THIS IS THE ONLY WAY.
ALMOST THERE-- KEEP MOVING.
UFF!
JUST KEEP MOVING. IGNORE IT.
MOM, I'M SCARED!
I WANT TO GO BACK!
STOP TALKING-- WE CAN'T GO BACK.
C'MON!
STOP.
NOW.
YOU'RE DRAWING ATTENTION.

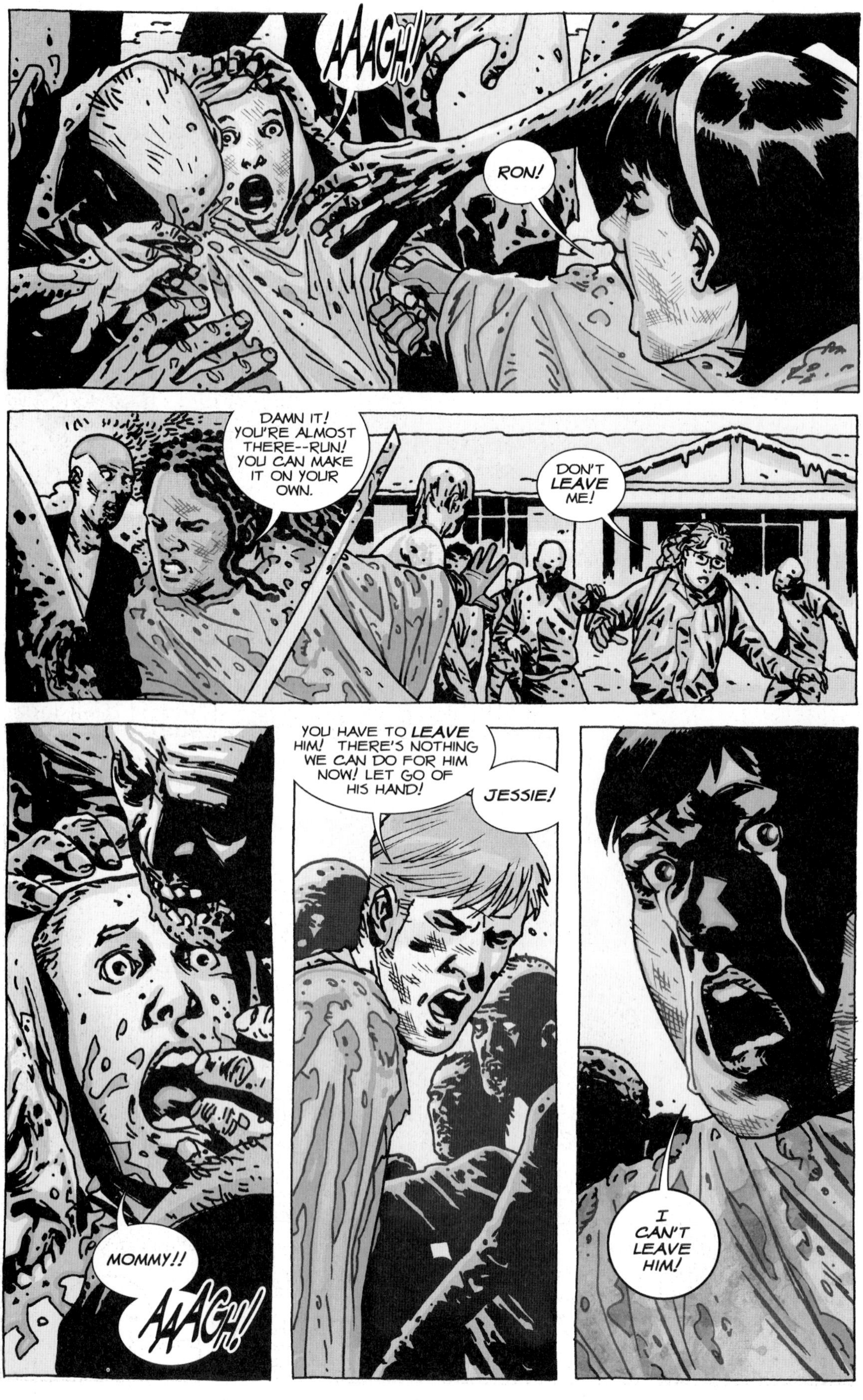
AAAGH!!
RON!
DAMN IT! YOU'RE ALMOST THERE--RUN! YOU CAN MAKE IT ON YOUR OWN.
DON'T LEAVE ME!
MOMMY!!
AAAGH!
YOU HAVE TO LEAVE HIM! THERE'S NOTHING WE CAN DO FOR HIM NOW! LET GO OF HIS HAND!
JESSIE!
I CAN'T LEAVE HIM!

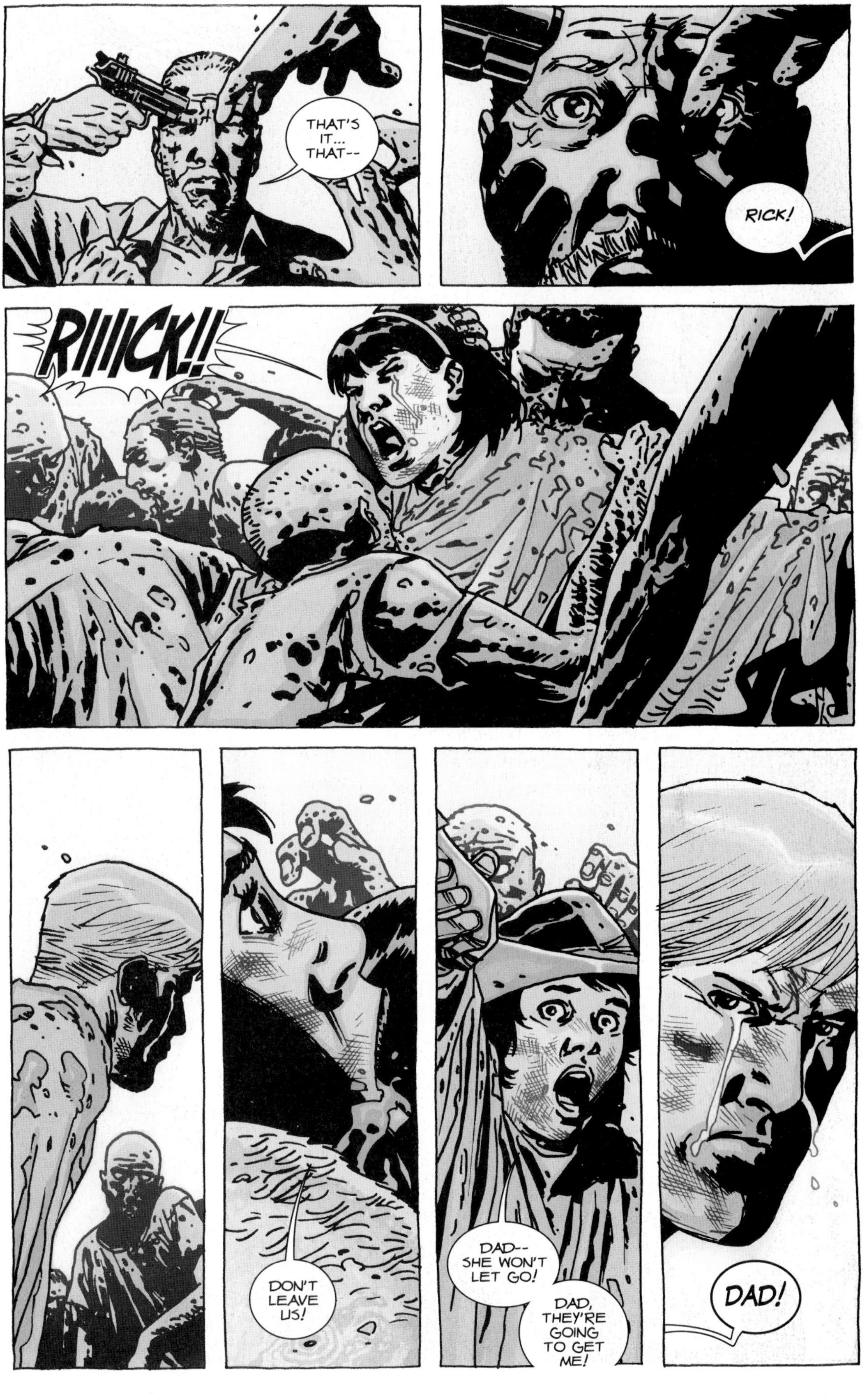

THAT'S IT... THAT--
RICK!
RIIICK!!
DON'T LEAVE US!
DAD-- SHE WON'T LET GO!
DAD, THEY'RE GOING TO GET ME!
DAD!

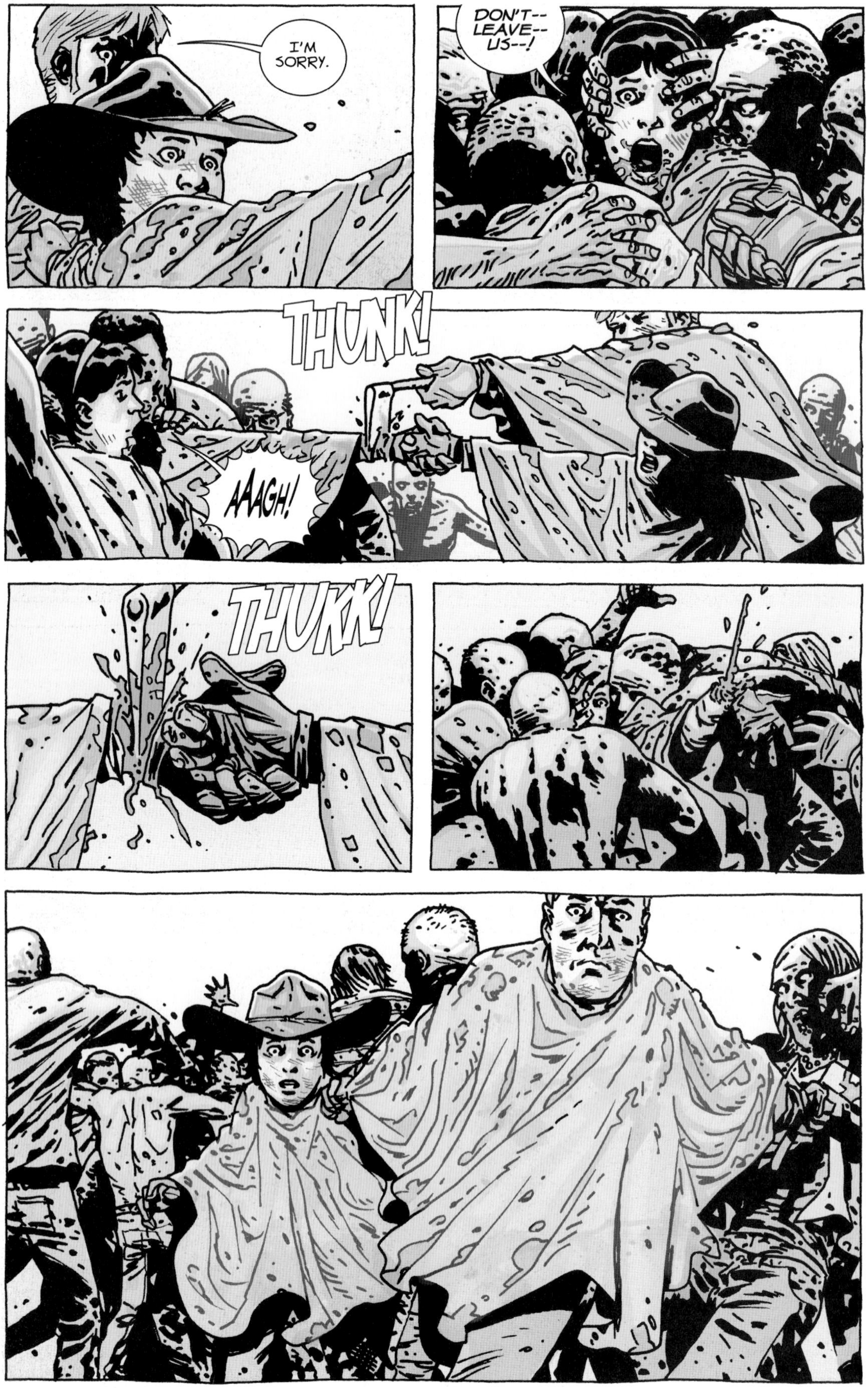
I'M SORRY.
DON'T-- LEAVE-- US--!
THUNK!
AAAGH!
THUKK!

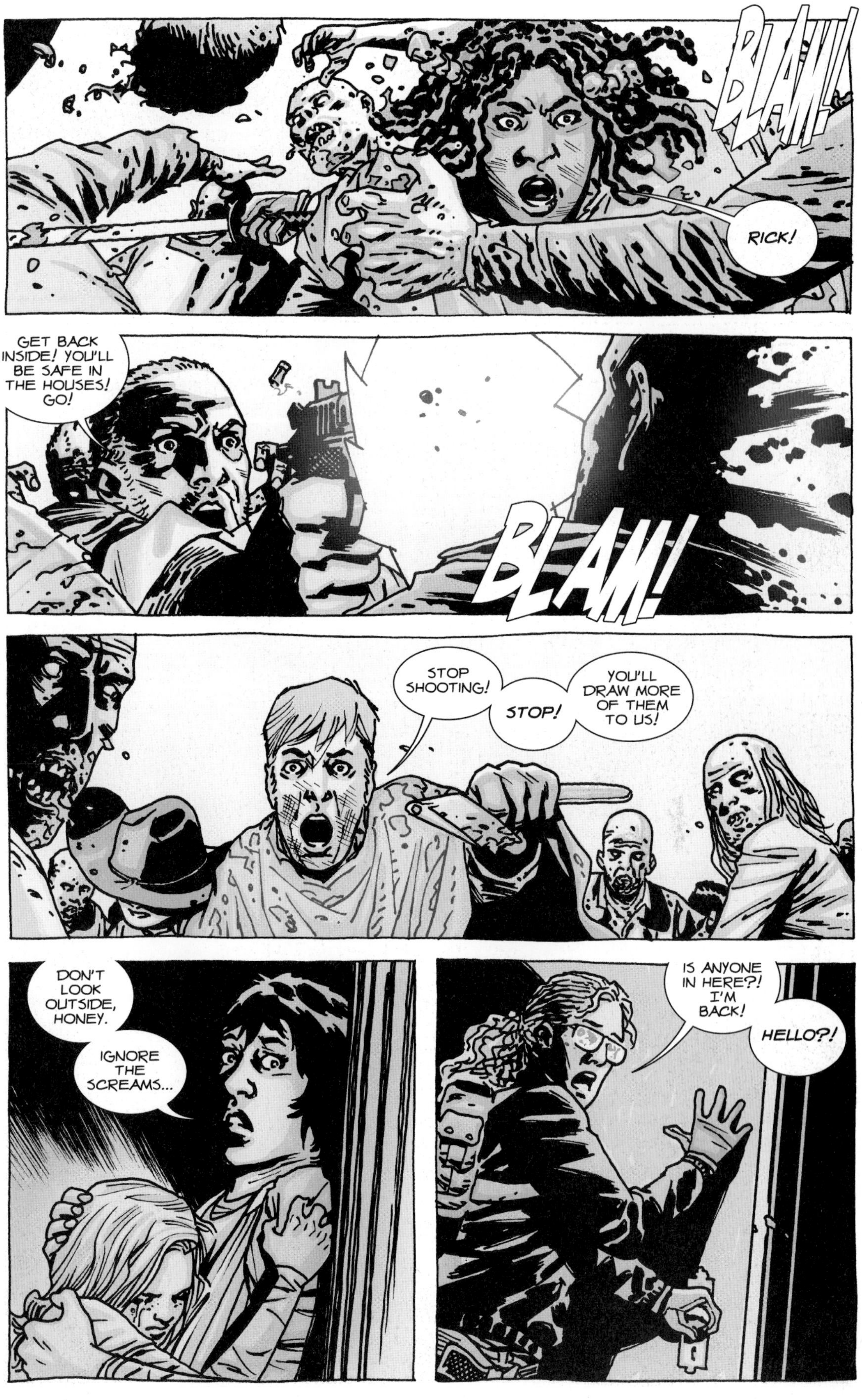
BLAM!!
RICK!
GET BACK INSIDE! YOU'LL BE SAFE IN THE HOUSES! GO!
BLAM!
STOP SHOOTING!
STOP!
YOU'LL DRAW MORE OF THEM TO US!
DON'T LOOK OUTSIDE, HONEY.
IGNORE THE SCREAMS...
IS ANYONE IN HERE?! I'M BACK!
HELLO?!

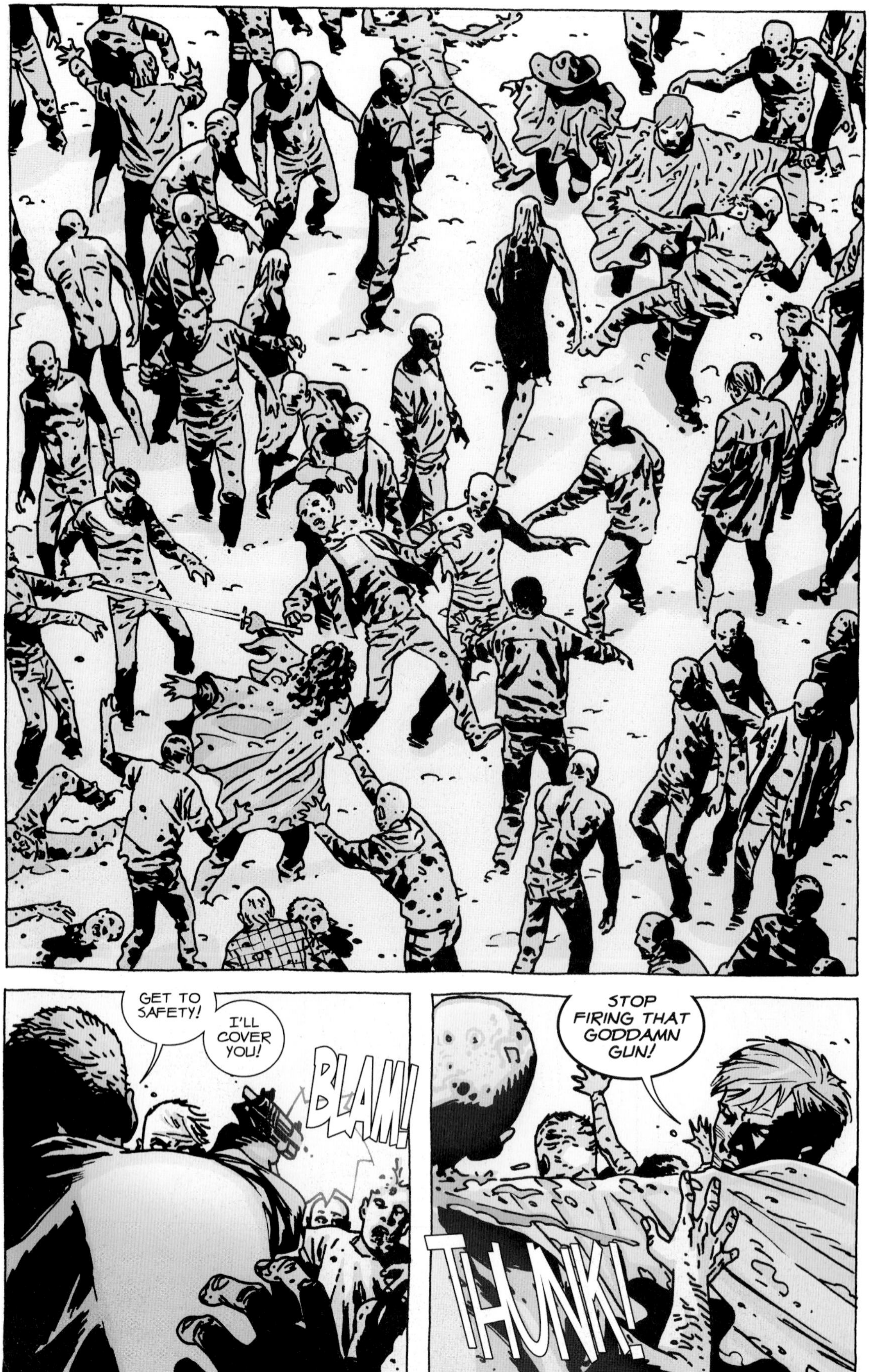
GET TO SAFETY!
I'LL COVER YOU!
BLAM!
STOP FIRING THAT GODDAMN GUN!
THUNK!

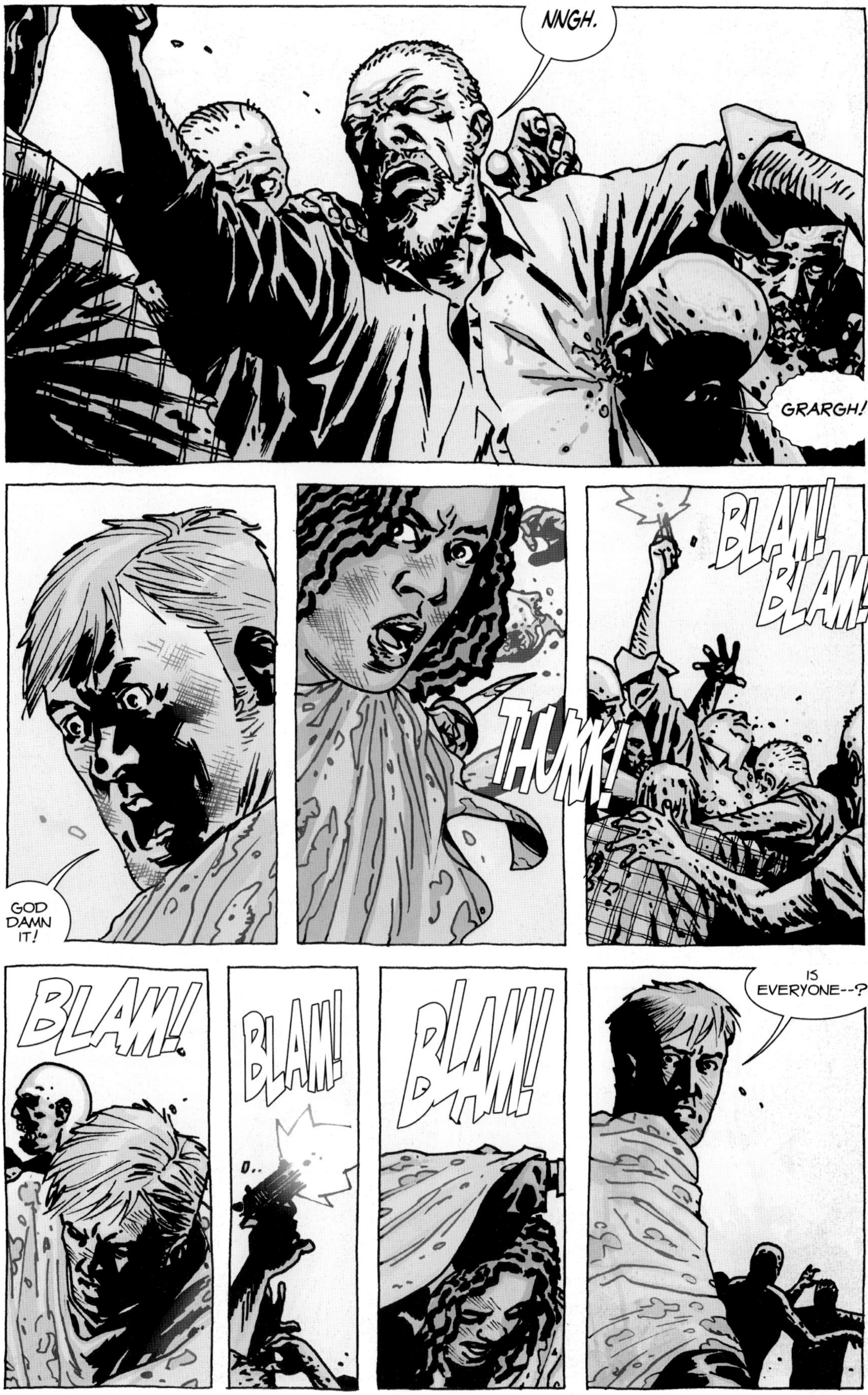
NNGH.
GRARGH!
GOD DAMN IT!
THUNK!
BLAM! BLAM!
BLAM!
BLAM!
BLAM!
IS EVERYONE--?

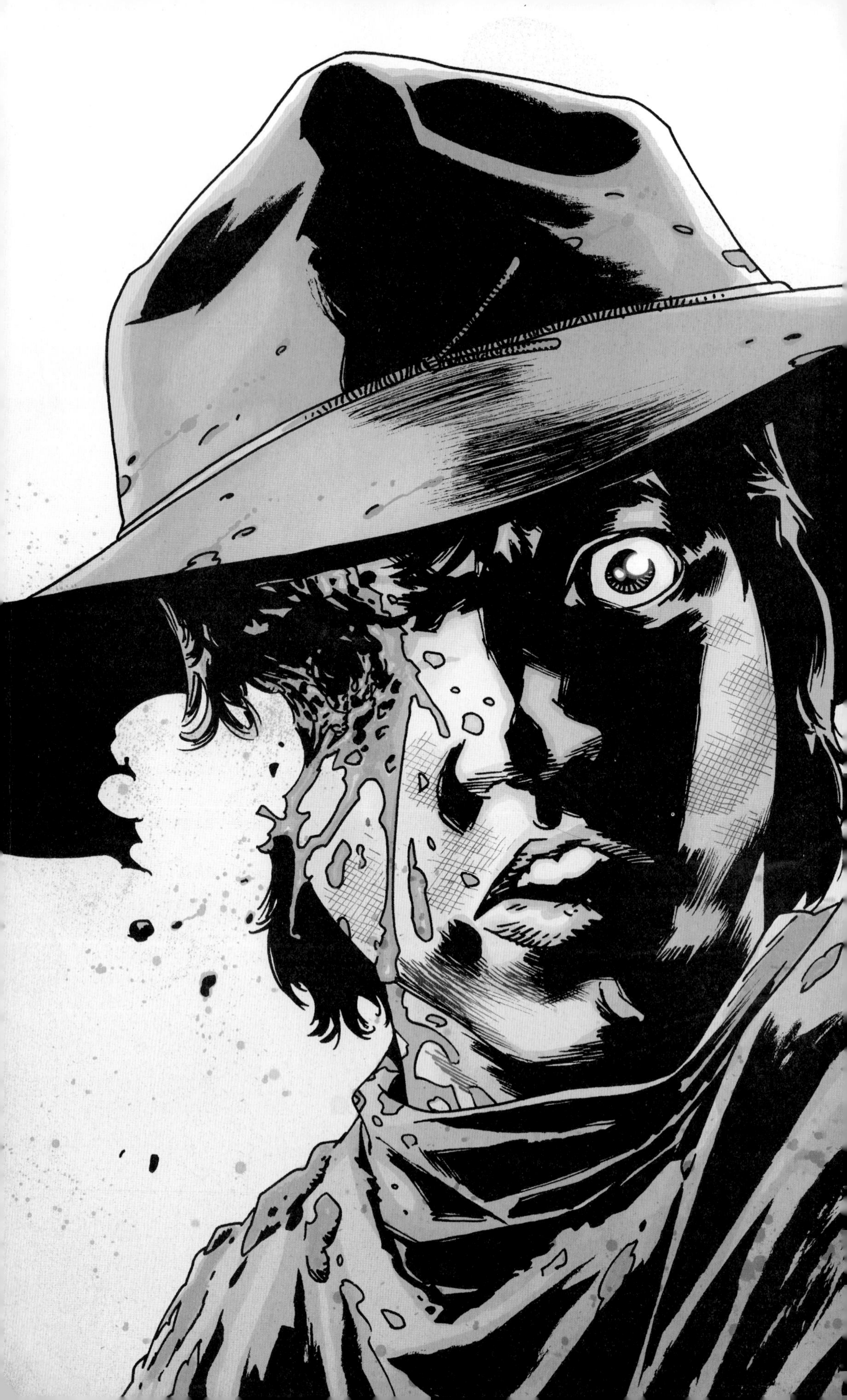

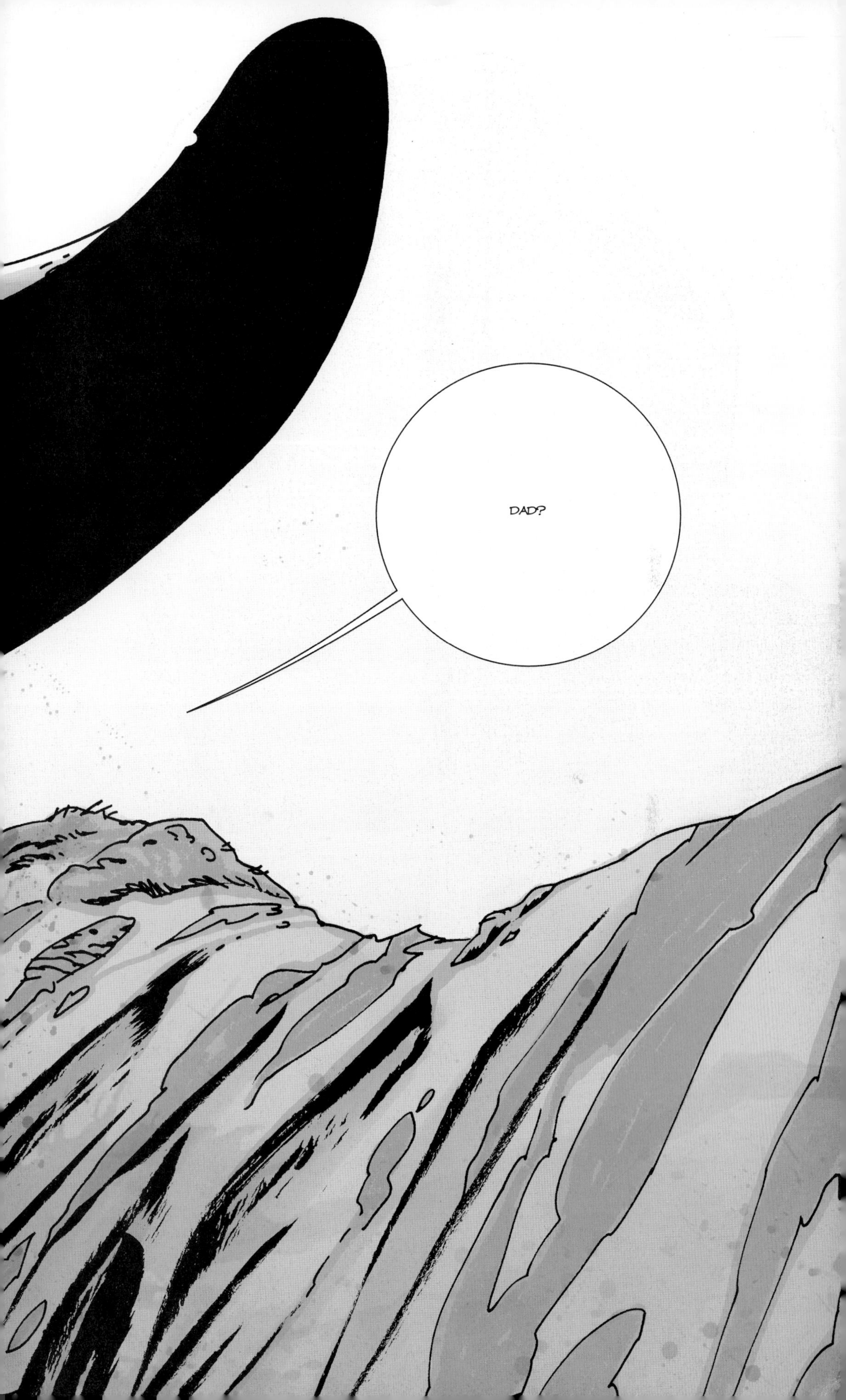
DAD?

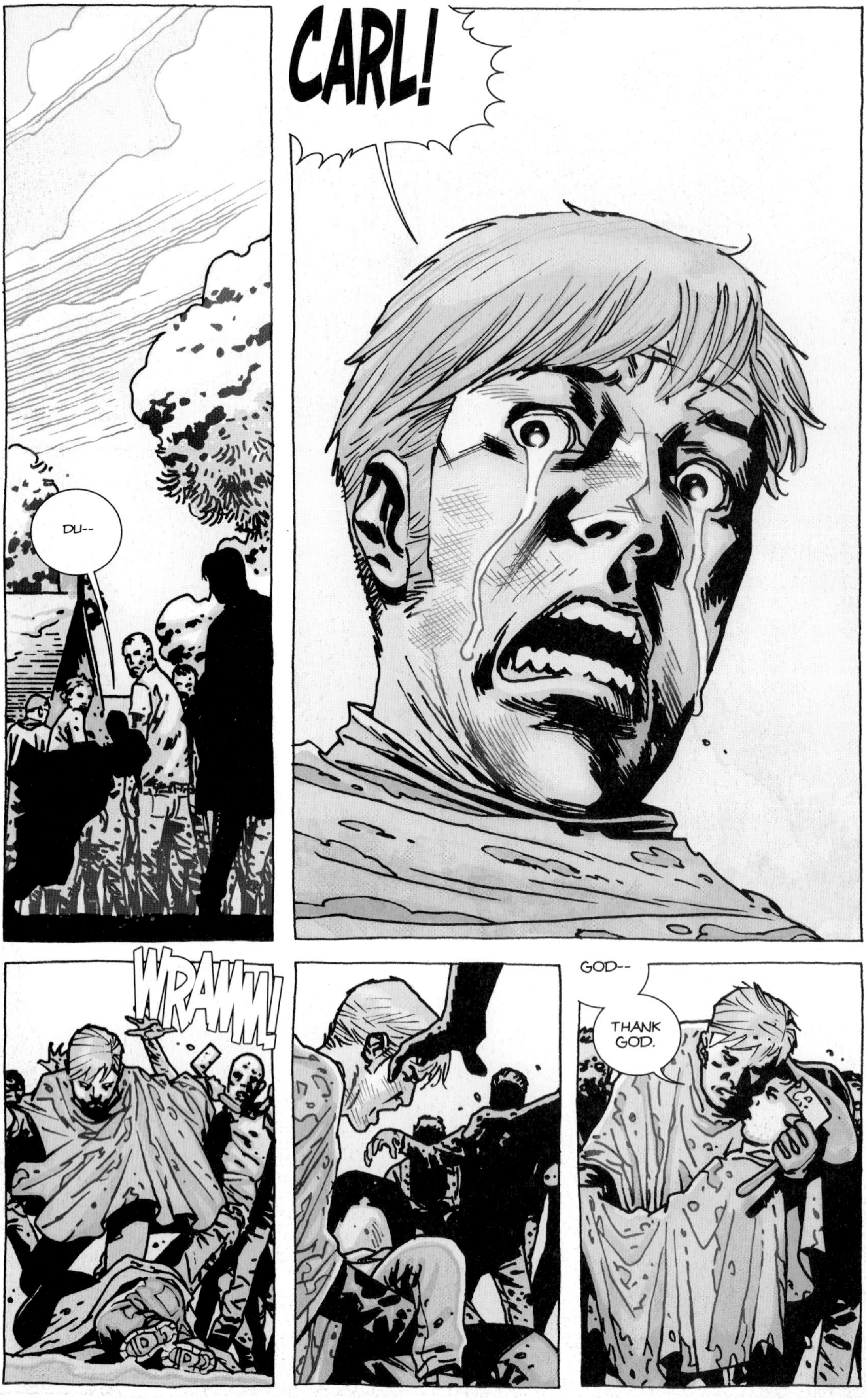
DU--
CARL!
WRAMM!
GOD--
THANK GOD.

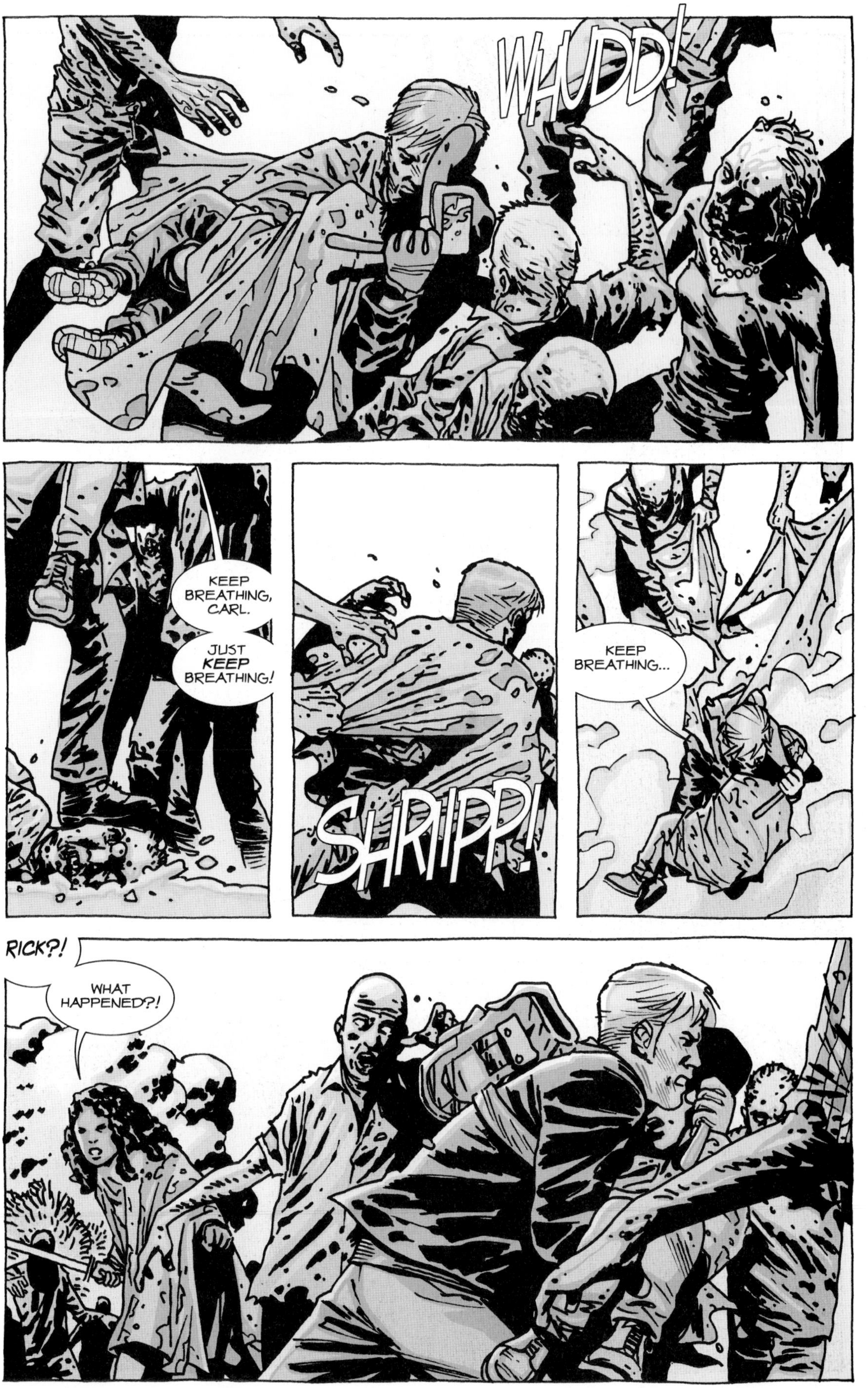

WHUDD!
KEEP BREATHING, CARL.
JUST KEEP BREATHING!
SHRIPP!
KEEP BREATHING...
RICK?!
WHAT HAPPENED?!

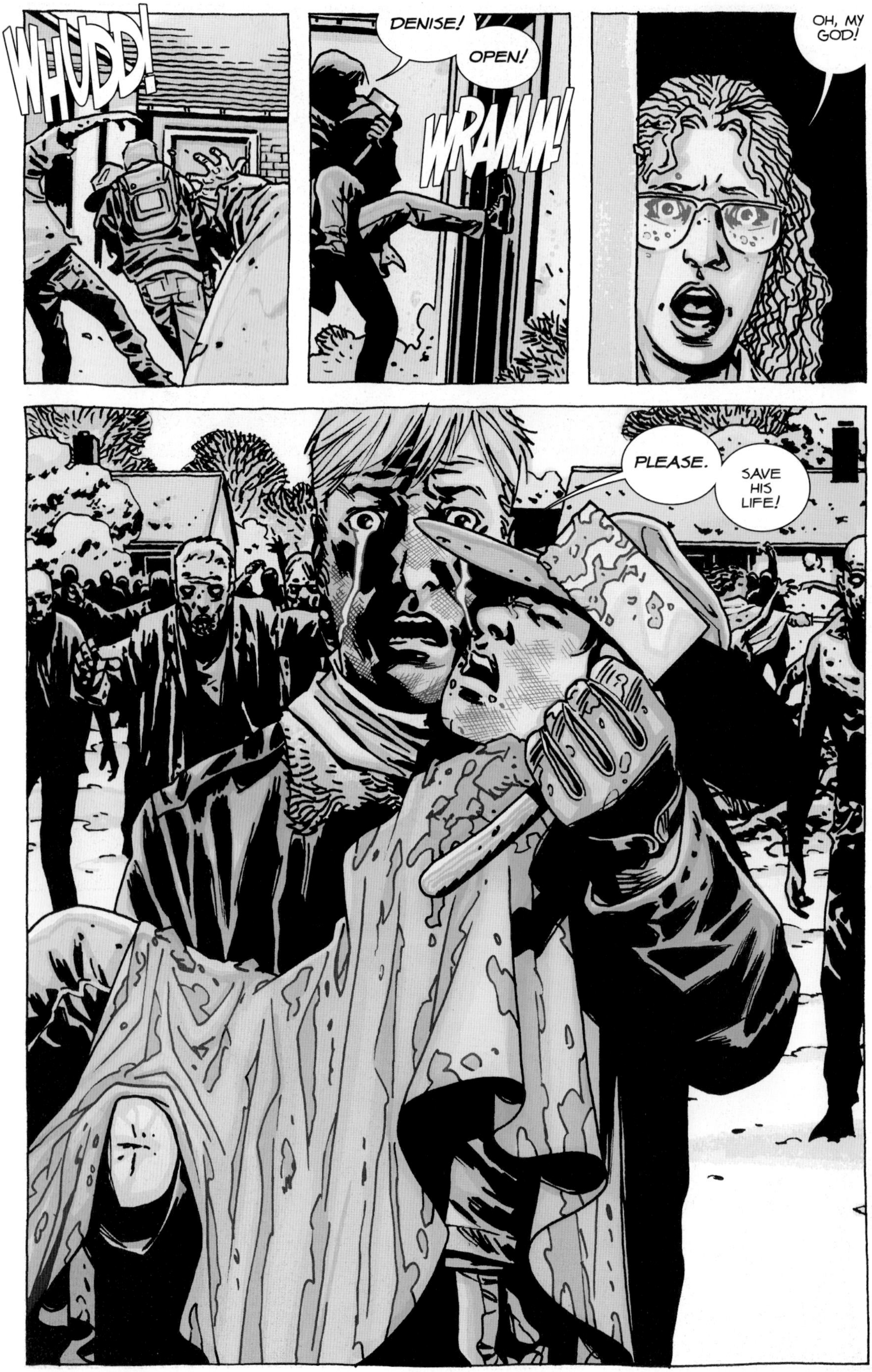
WHUDD!
DENISE!
OPEN!
WRAMM!
OH, MY GOD!
PLEASE.
SAVE HIS LIFE!

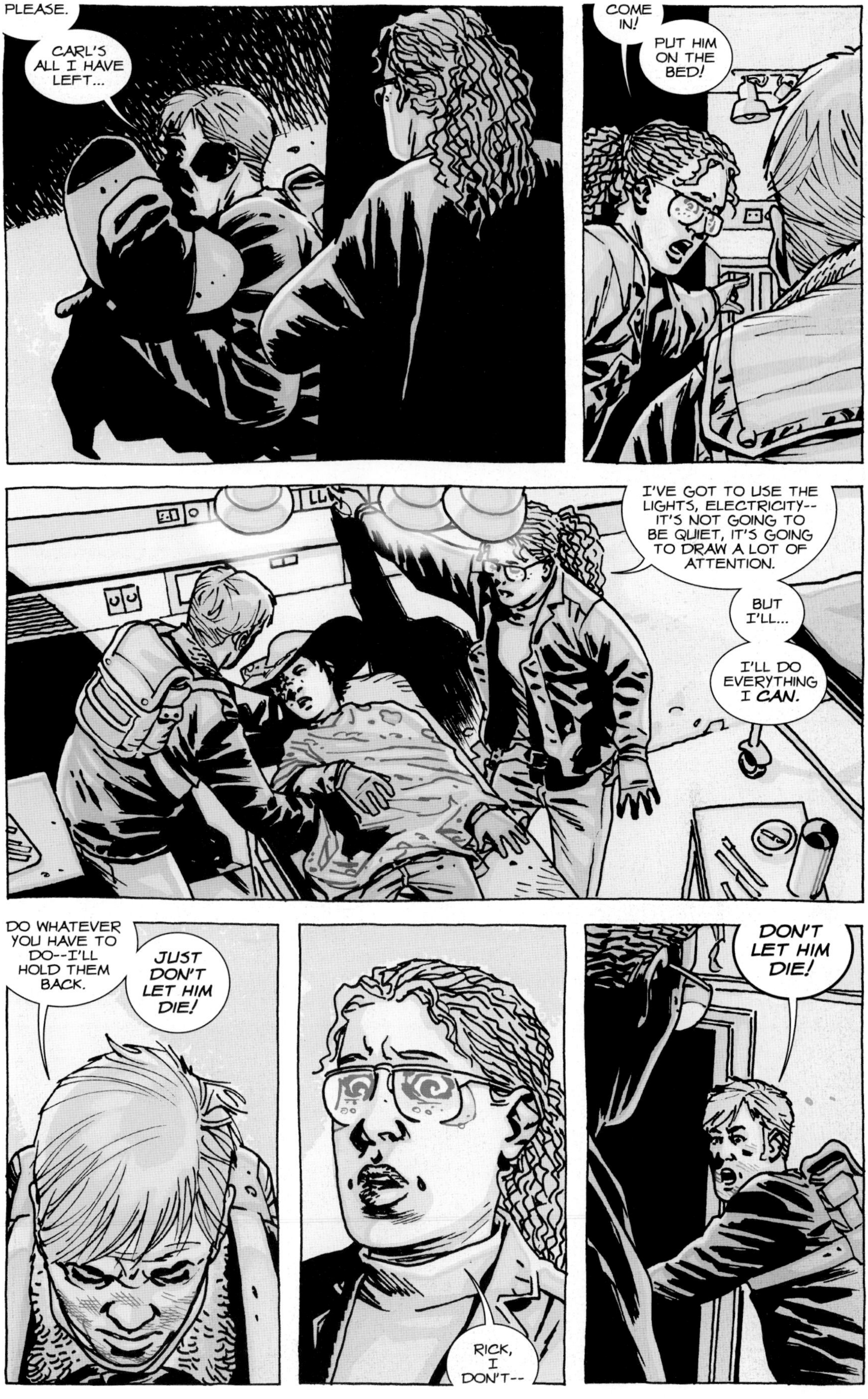
PLEASE.
CARL'S ALL I HAVE LEFT...
COME IN!
PUT HIM ON THE BED!
I'VE GOT TO USE THE LIGHTS, ELECTRICITY-- IT'S NOT GOING TO BE QUIET, IT'S GOING TO DRAW A LOT OF ATTENTION.
BUT I'LL...
I'LL DO EVERYTHING I CAN.
DO WHATEVER YOU HAVE TO DO--I'LL HOLD THEM BACK.
JUST DON'T LET HIM DIE!
RICK, I DON'T--
DON'T LET HIM DIE!

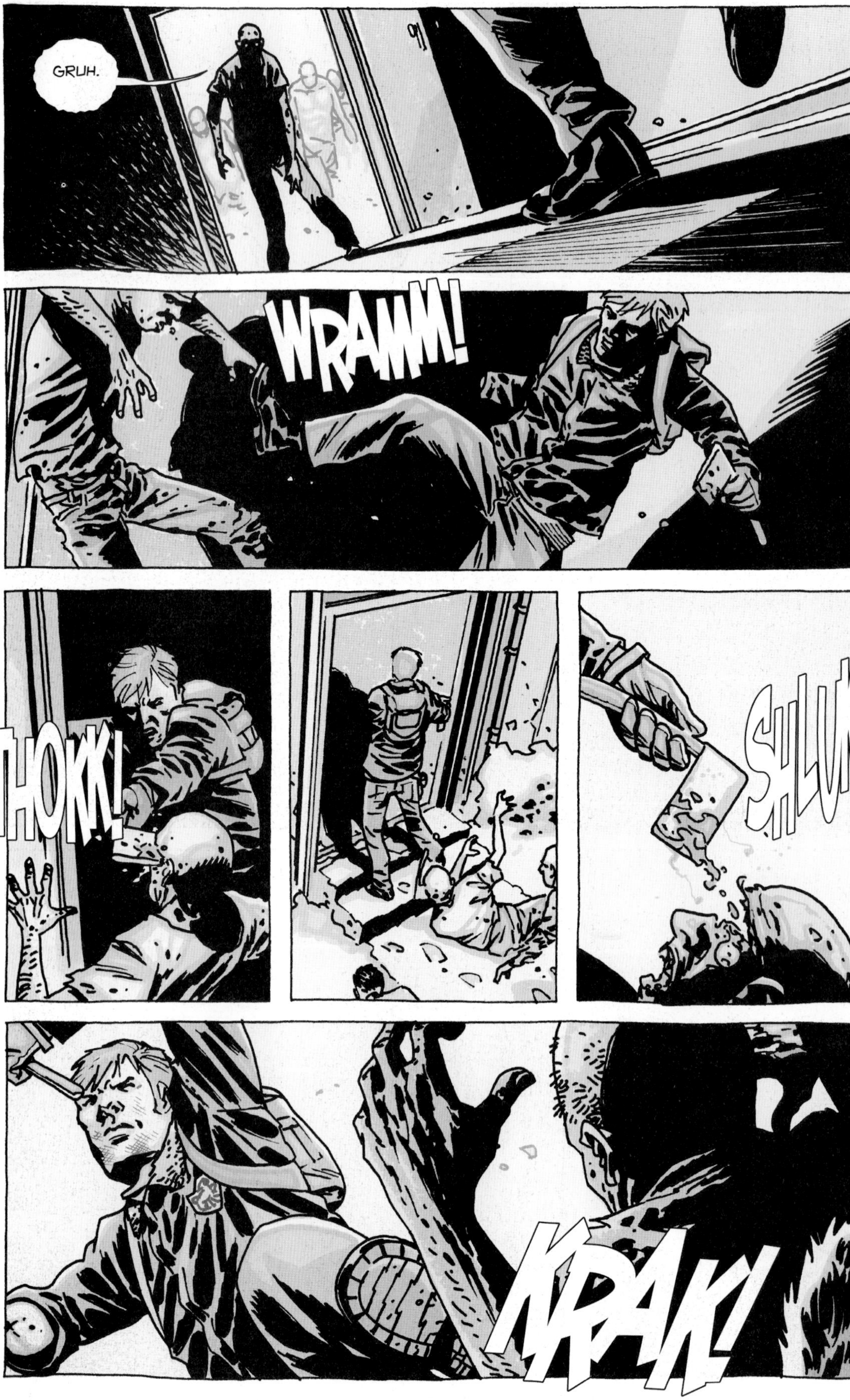
GRUH.
WRAMM!
THOKK!
SHLUK!
KRAK!

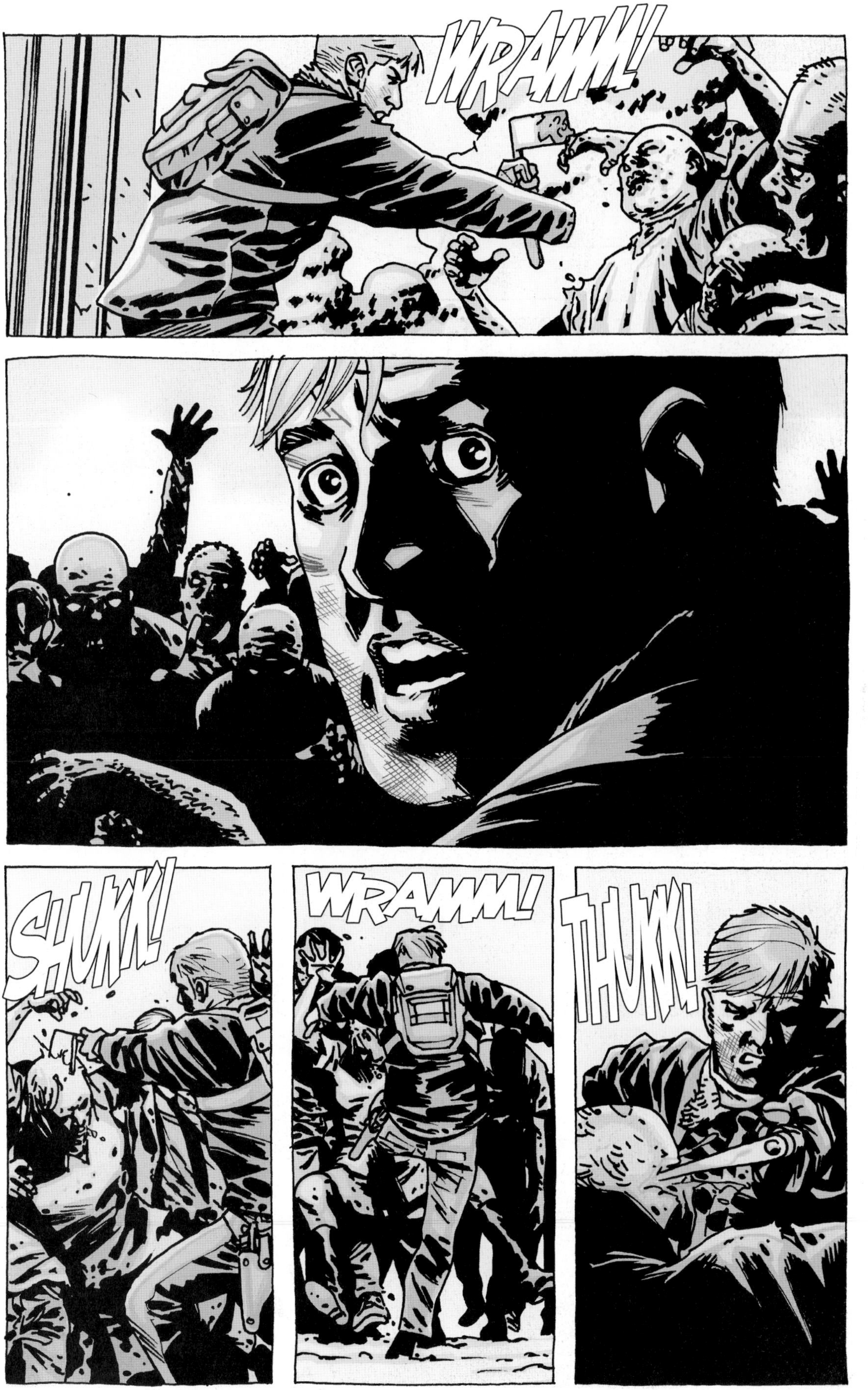
WRAMM!
SHUKK!
WRAMM!
THUNK!

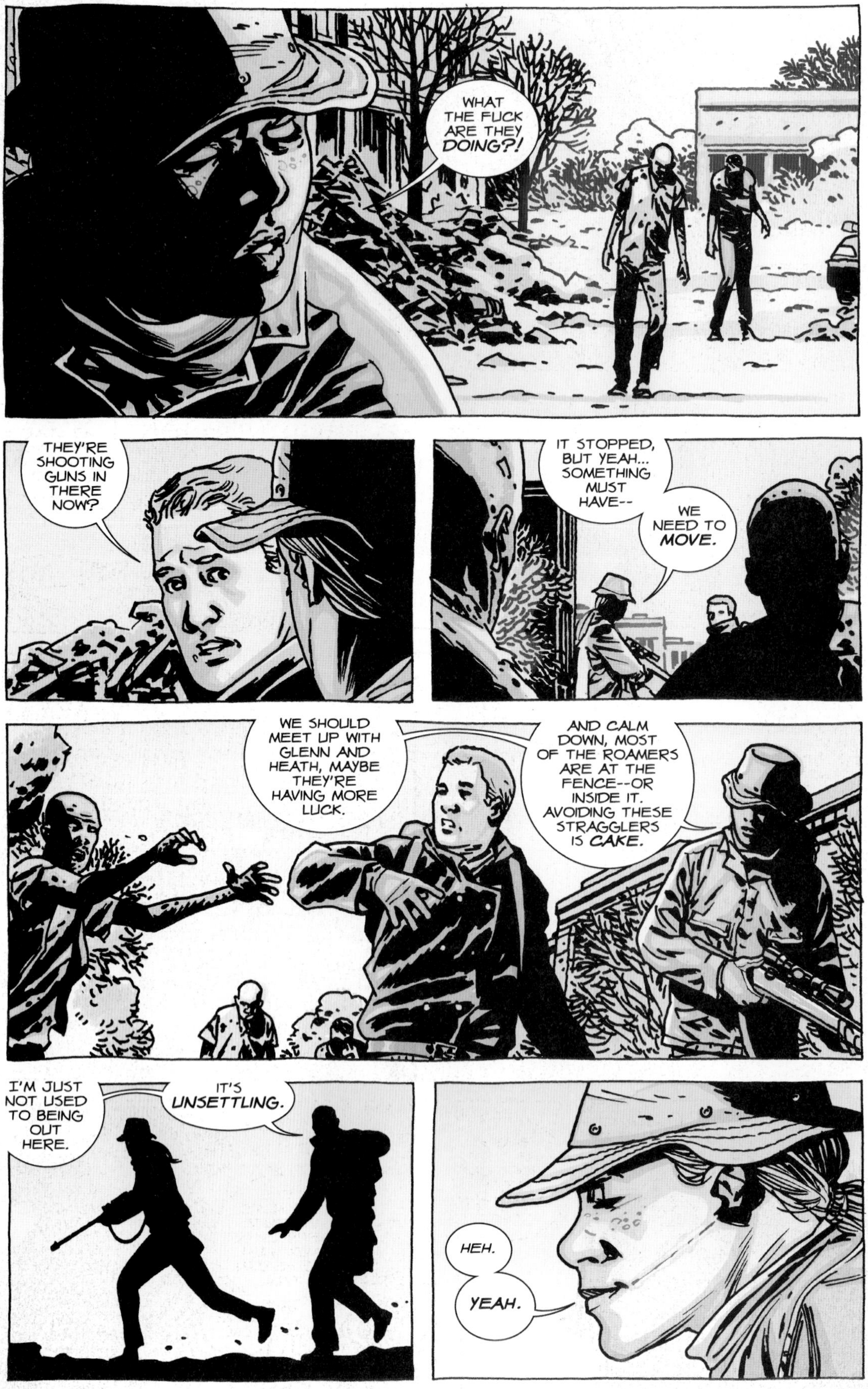
WHAT THE FUCK ARE THEY DOING?!
THEY'RE SHOOTING GUNS IN THERE NOW?
IT STOPPED, BUT YEAH... SOMETHING MUST HAVE--
WE NEED TO MOVE.
WE SHOULD MEET UP WITH GLENN AND HEATH, MAYBE THEY'RE HAVING MORE LUCK.
AND CALM DOWN, MOST OF THE ROAMERS ARE AT THE FENCE--OR INSIDE IT. AVOIDING THESE STRAGGLERS IS CAKE.
I'M JUST NOT USED TO BEING OUT HERE.
IT'S UNSETTLING.
HEH.
YEAH.

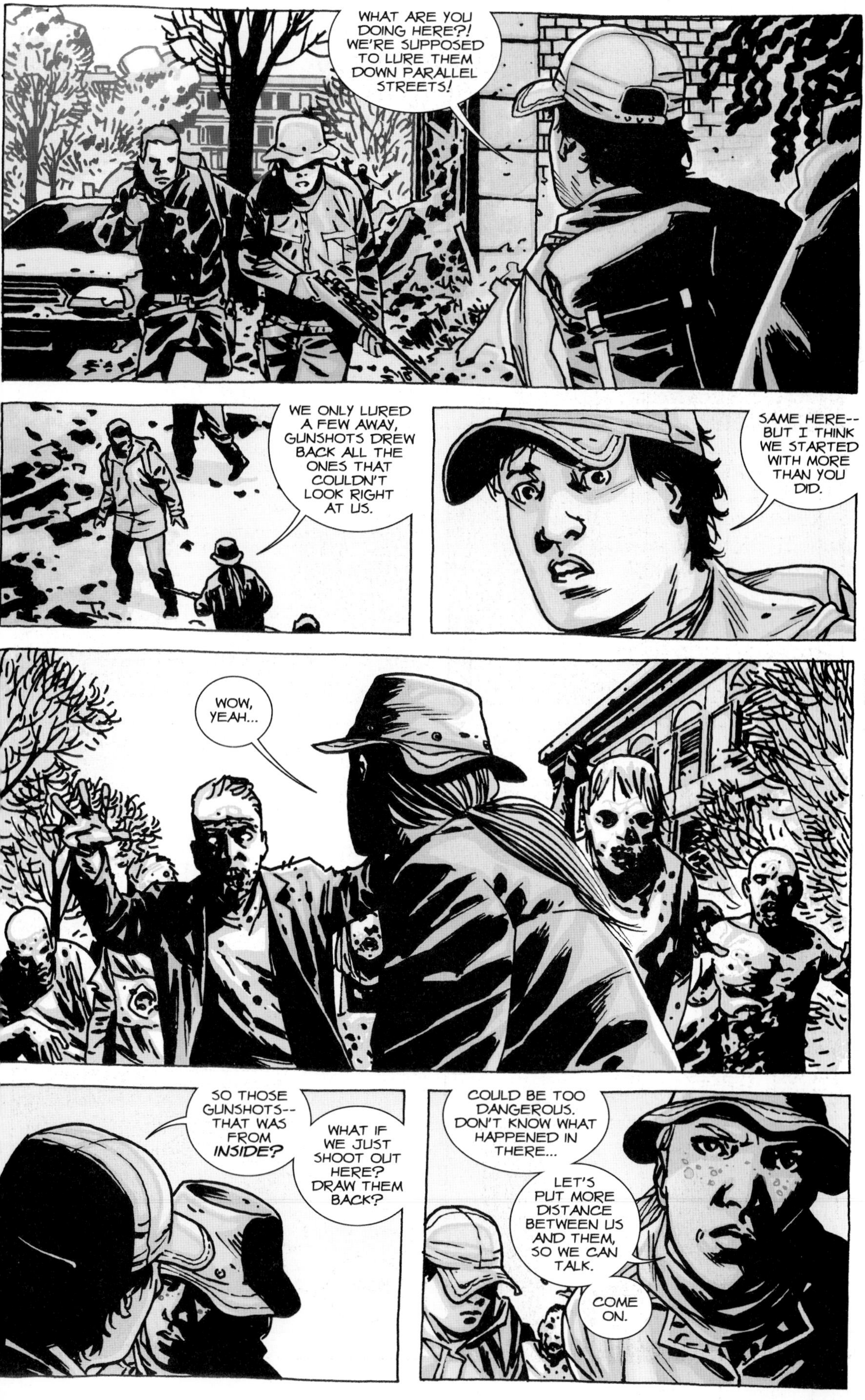
WHAT ARE YOU DOING HERE?! WE'RE SUPPOSED TO LURE THEM DOWN PARALLEL STREETS!
WE ONLY LURED A FEW AWAY, GUNSHOTS DREW BACK ALL THE ONES THAT COULDN'T LOOK RIGHT AT US.
SAME HERE-- BUT I THINK WE STARTED WITH MORE THAN YOU DID.
WOW, YEAH...
SO THOSE GUNSHOTS-- THAT WAS FROM *INSIDE?*
WHAT IF WE JUST SHOOT OUT HERE? DRAW THEM BACK?
COULD BE TOO DANGEROUS. DON'T KNOW WHAT HAPPENED IN THERE...
LET'S PUT MORE DISTANCE BETWEEN US AND THEM, SO WE CAN TALK.
COME ON.

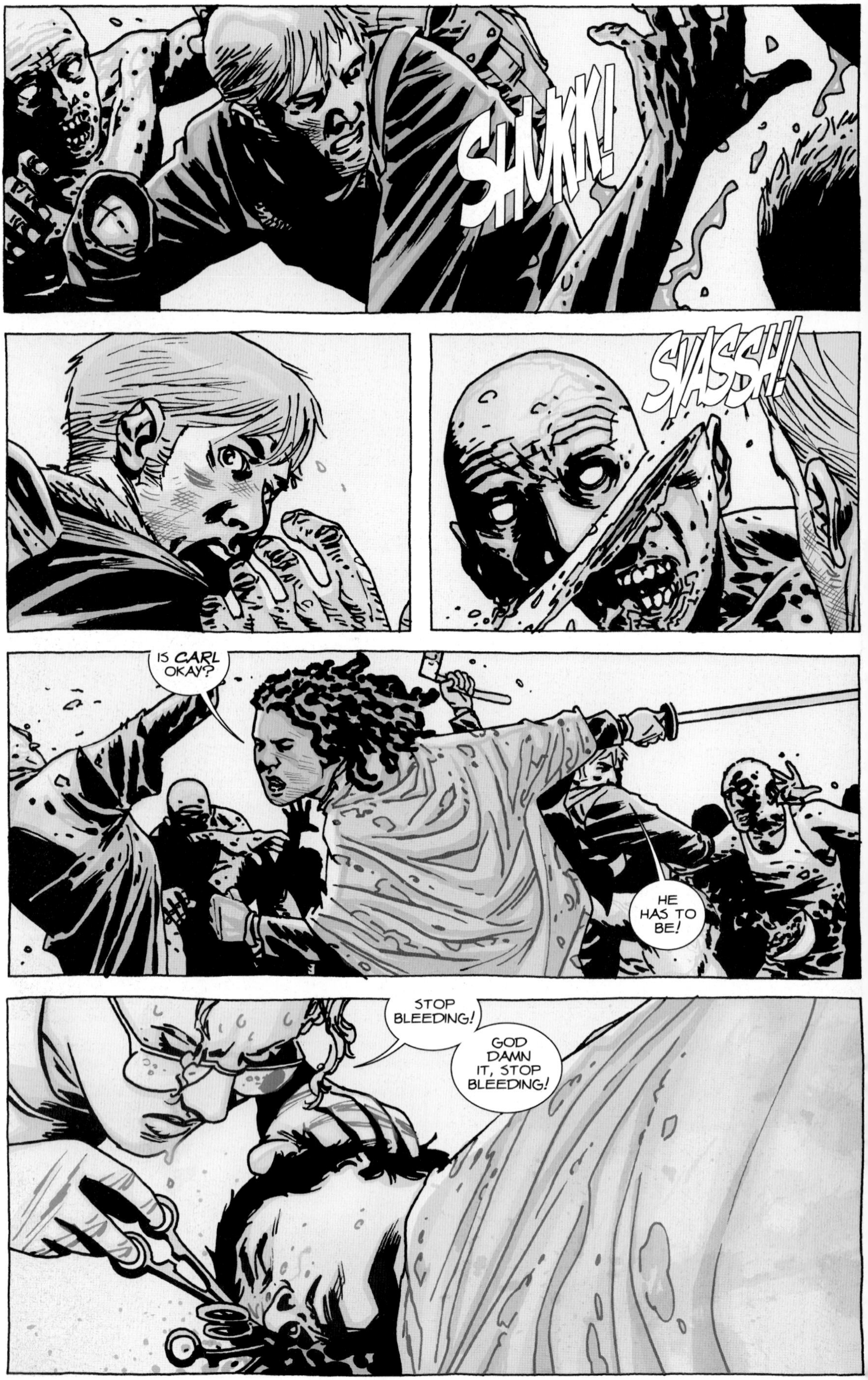
SHUKK!
SVASSH!
IS CARL OKAY?
HE HAS TO BE!
STOP BLEEDING!
GOD DAMN IT, STOP BLEEDING!

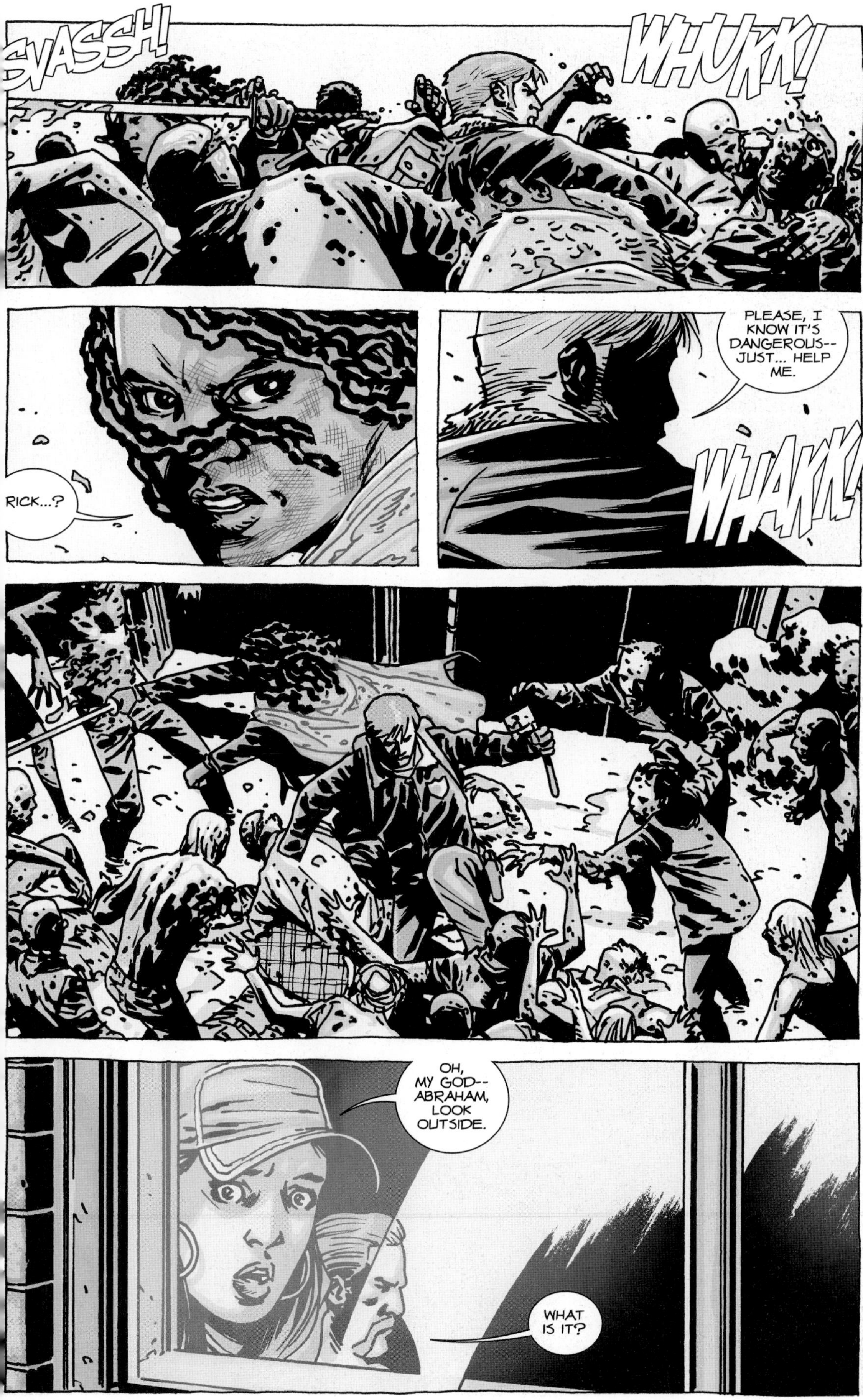
SVASSH!
WHUKK!
RICK...?
PLEASE, I KNOW IT'S DANGEROUS-- JUST... HELP ME.
WHAKK!
OH, MY GOD-- ABRAHAM, LOOK OUTSIDE.
WHAT IS IT?

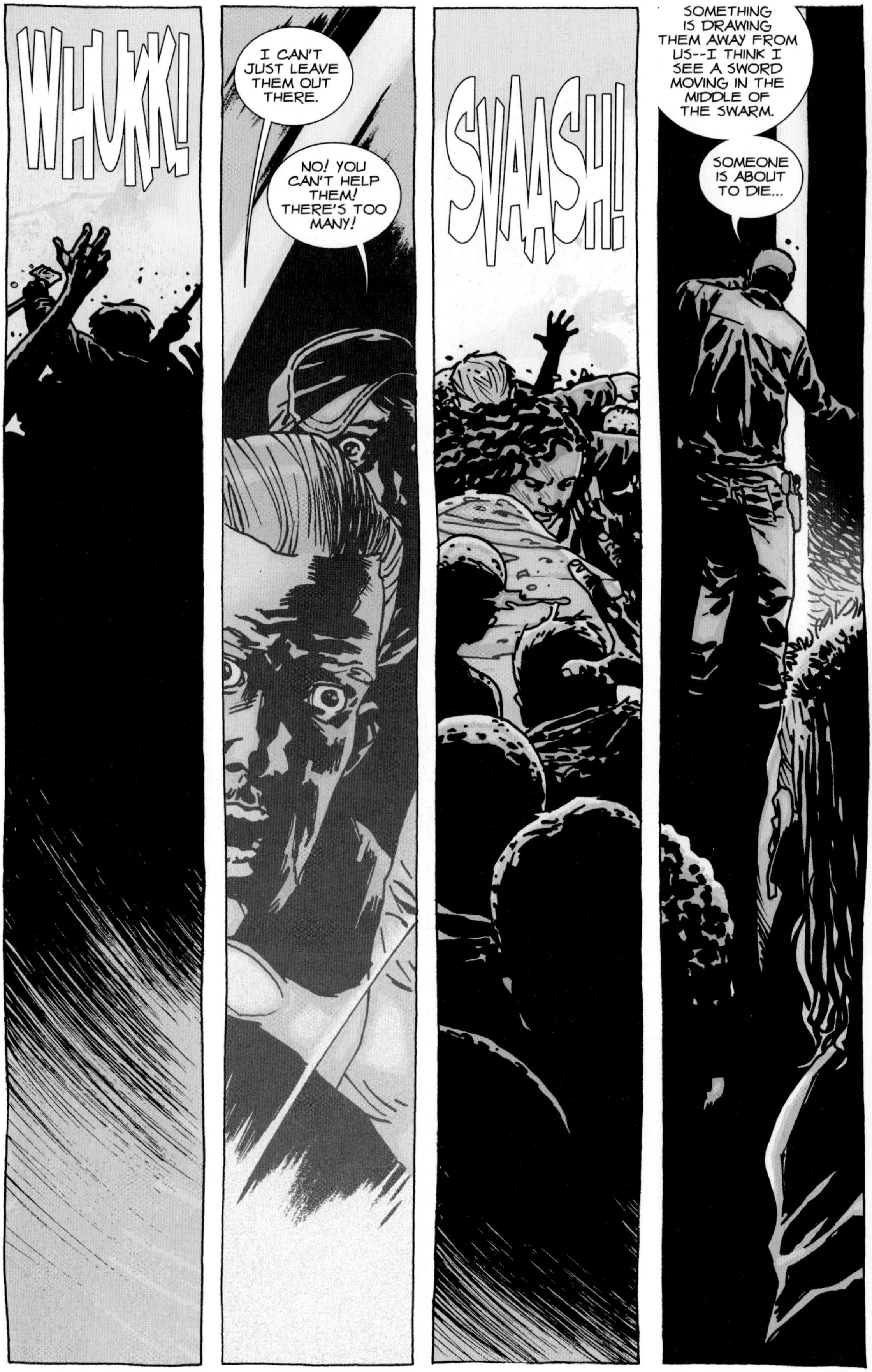
WHUKK!
I CAN'T JUST LEAVE THEM OUT THERE.
NO! YOU CAN'T HELP THEM! THERE'S TOO MANY!
SVAASH!
SOMETHING IS DRAWING THEM AWAY FROM US--I THINK I SEE A SWORD MOVING IN THE MIDDLE OF THE SWARM.
SOMEONE IS ABOUT TO DIE...

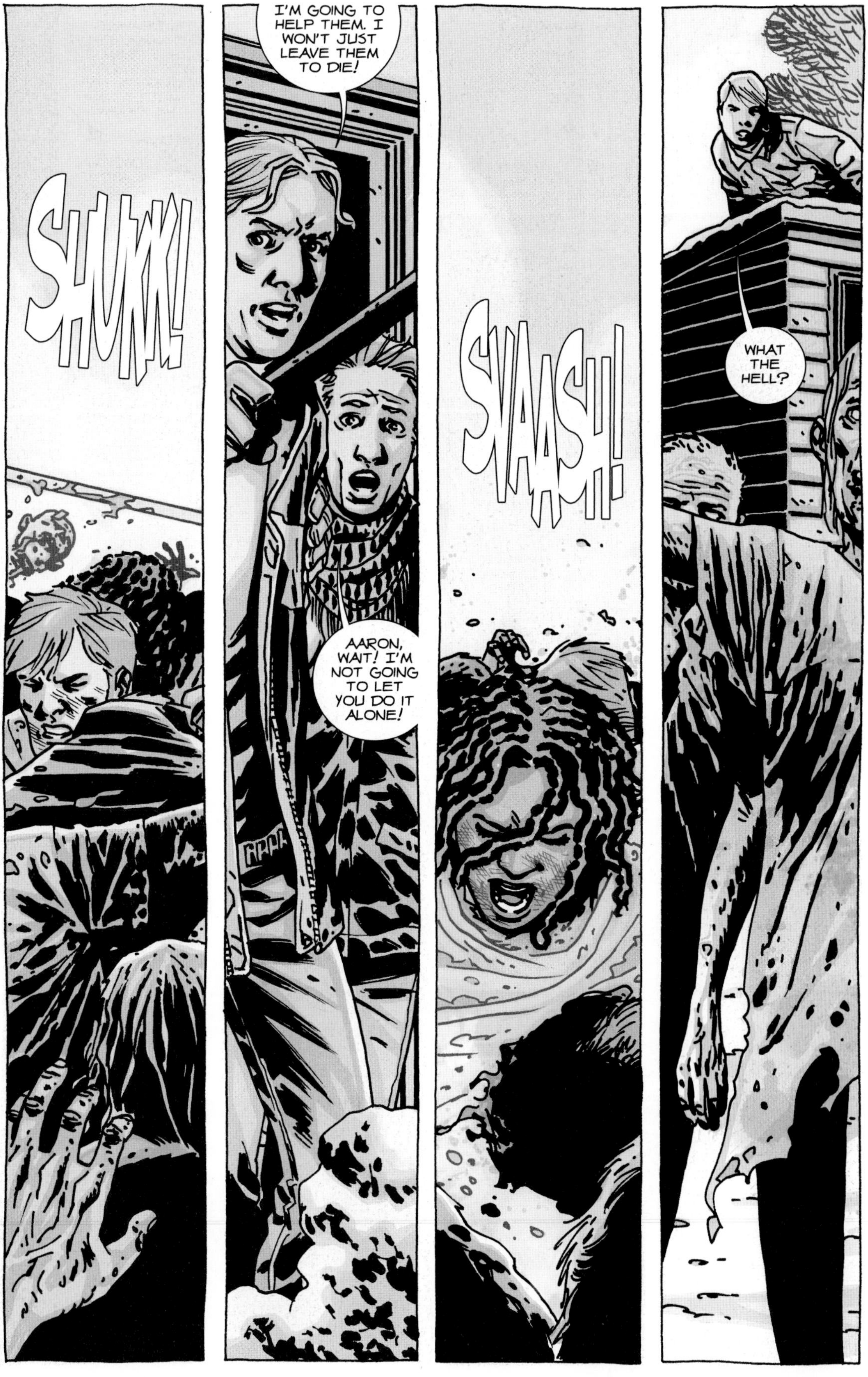
SHUNK!
I'M GOING TO HELP THEM. I WON'T JUST LEAVE THEM TO DIE!
AARON, WAIT! I'M NOT GOING TO LET YOU DO IT ALONE!
SWAASH!
WHAT THE HELL?

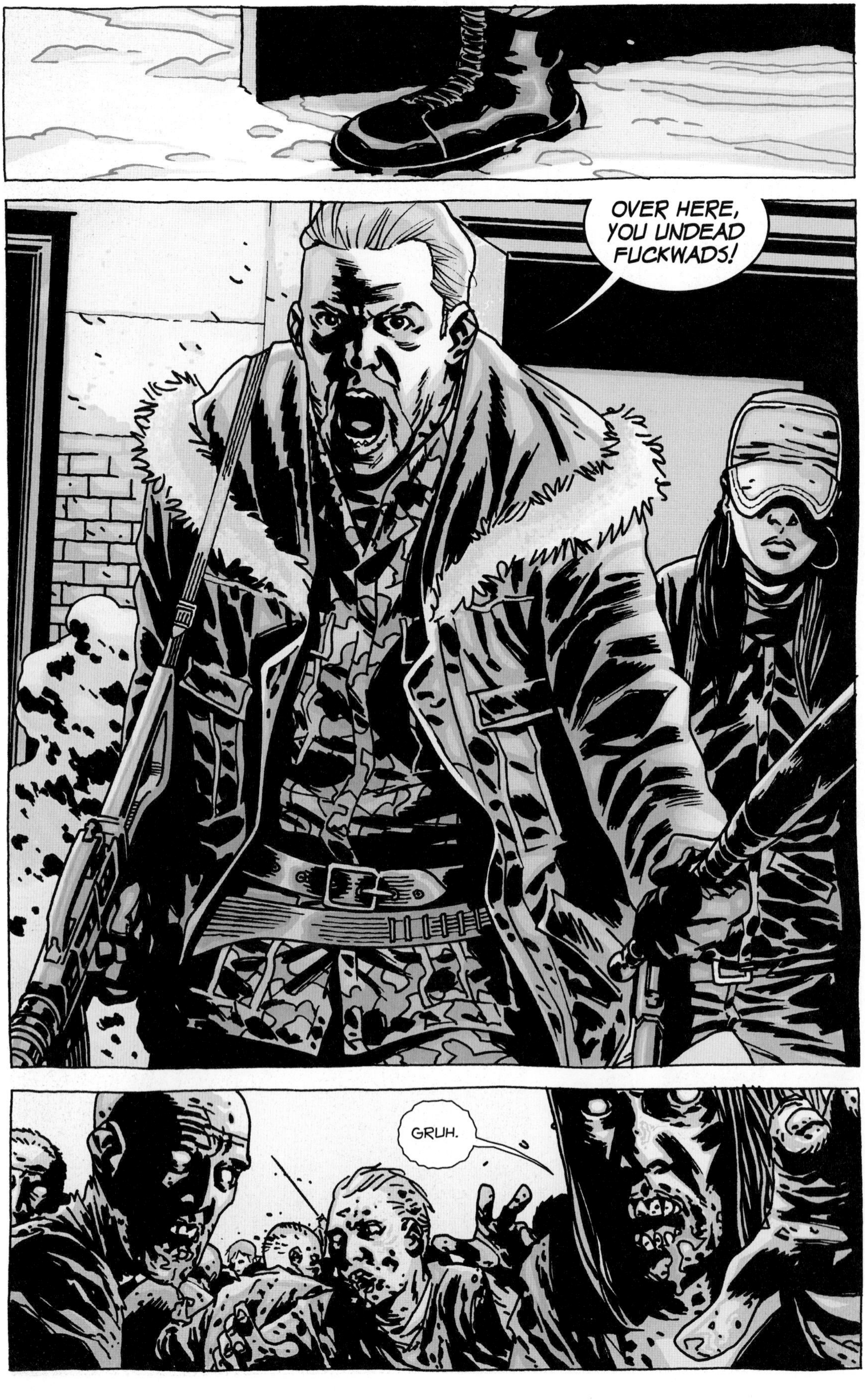
OVER HERE, YOU UNDEAD FUCKWADS!
GRUH.

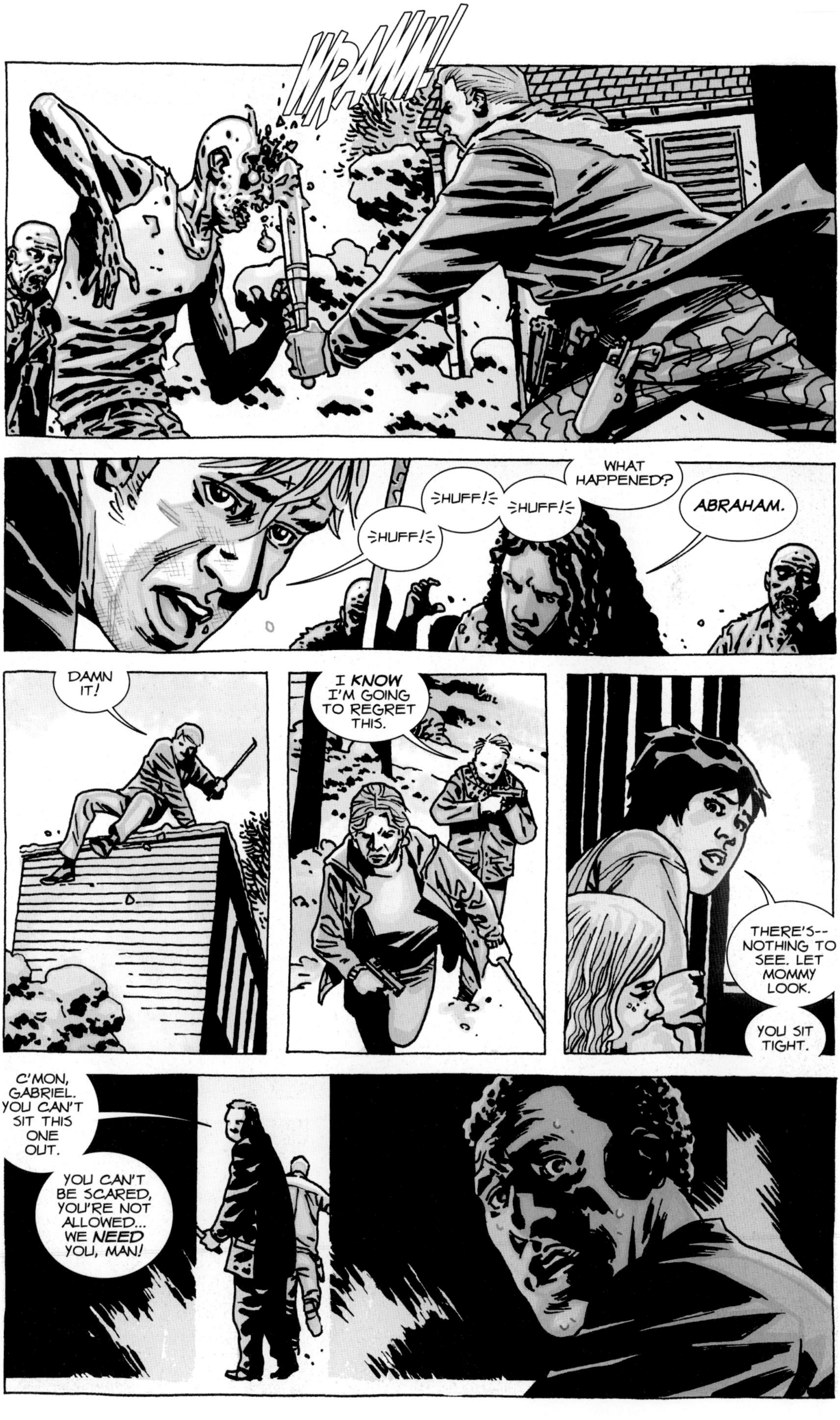

WHAMM!!
WHAT HAPPENED?
HUFF!
HUFF!
HUFF!
ABRAHAM.
DAMN IT!
I KNOW I'M GOING TO REGRET THIS.
THERE'S-- NOTHING TO SEE. LET MOMMY LOOK.
YOU SIT TIGHT.
C'MON, GABRIEL. YOU CAN'T SIT THIS ONE OUT.
YOU CAN'T BE SCARED, YOU'RE NOT ALLOWED... WE NEED YOU, MAN!

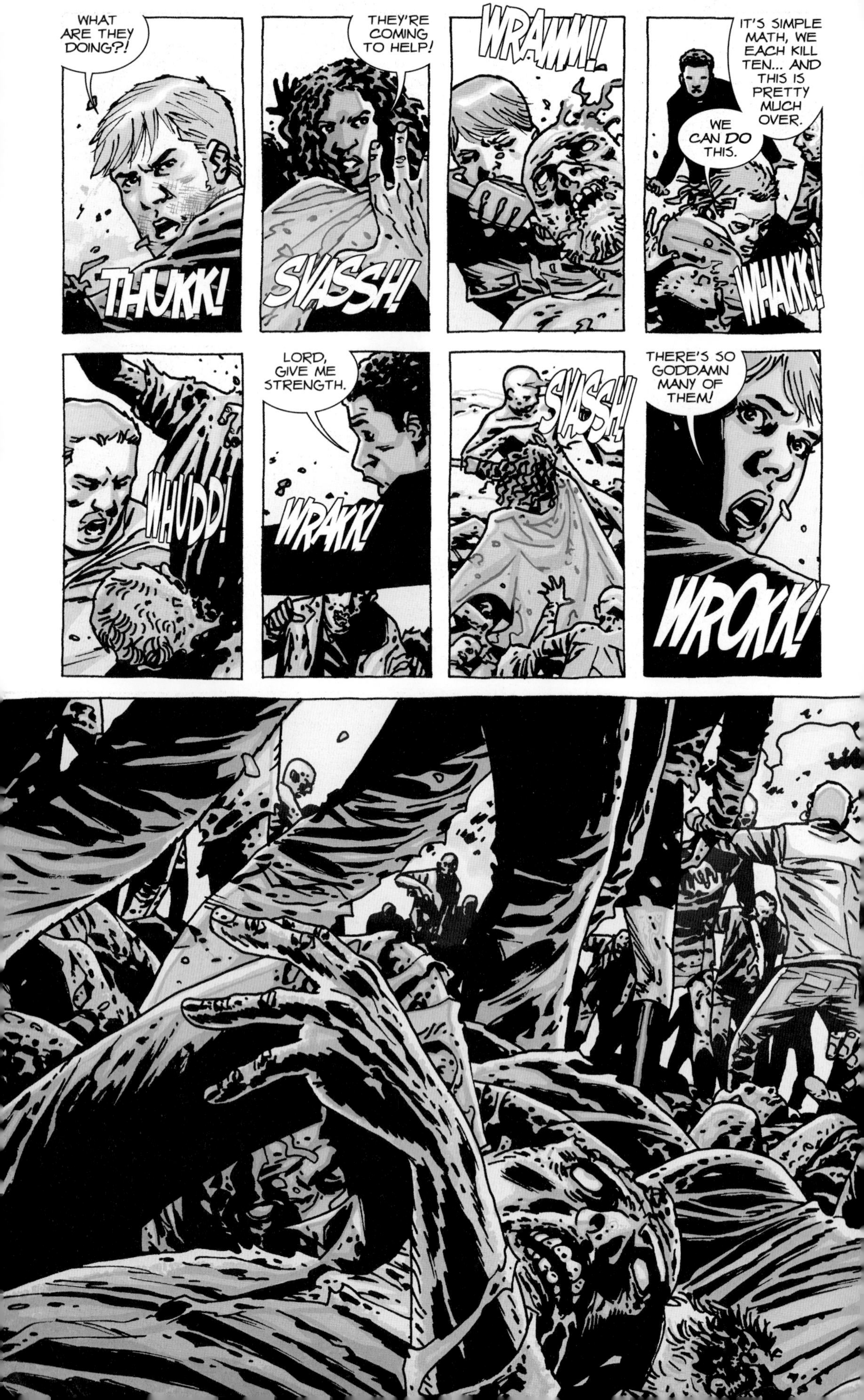

WHAT ARE THEY DOING?!
THUKK!
THEY'RE COMING TO HELP!
SVASSH!
WRAMM!!
IT'S SIMPLE MATH, WE EACH KILL TEN... AND THIS IS PRETTY MUCH OVER.
WE CAN DO THIS.
WHAKK!
WHUDD!
LORD, GIVE ME STRENGTH.
WRAKK!
SVASSH!
THERE'S SO GODDAMN MANY OF THEM!
WROKK!

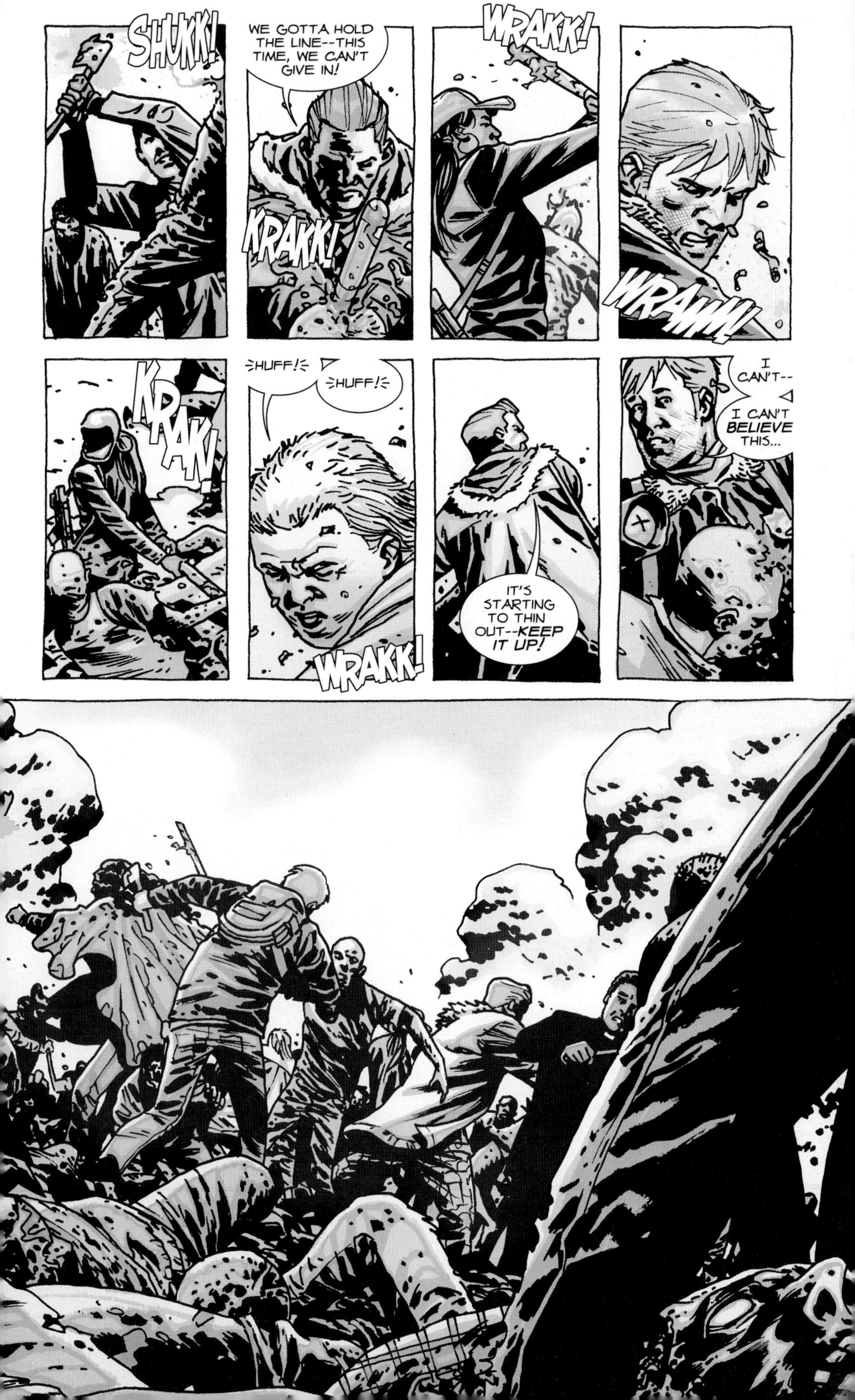

SHUKK!
WE GOTTA HOLD THE LINE--THIS TIME, WE CAN'T GIVE IN!
KRAKK!
WRAKK!
WRAMM!
KRAK!
HUFF!
HUFF!
WRAKK!
IT'S STARTING TO THIN OUT--KEEP IT UP!
I CAN'T--
I CAN'T BELIEVE THIS...

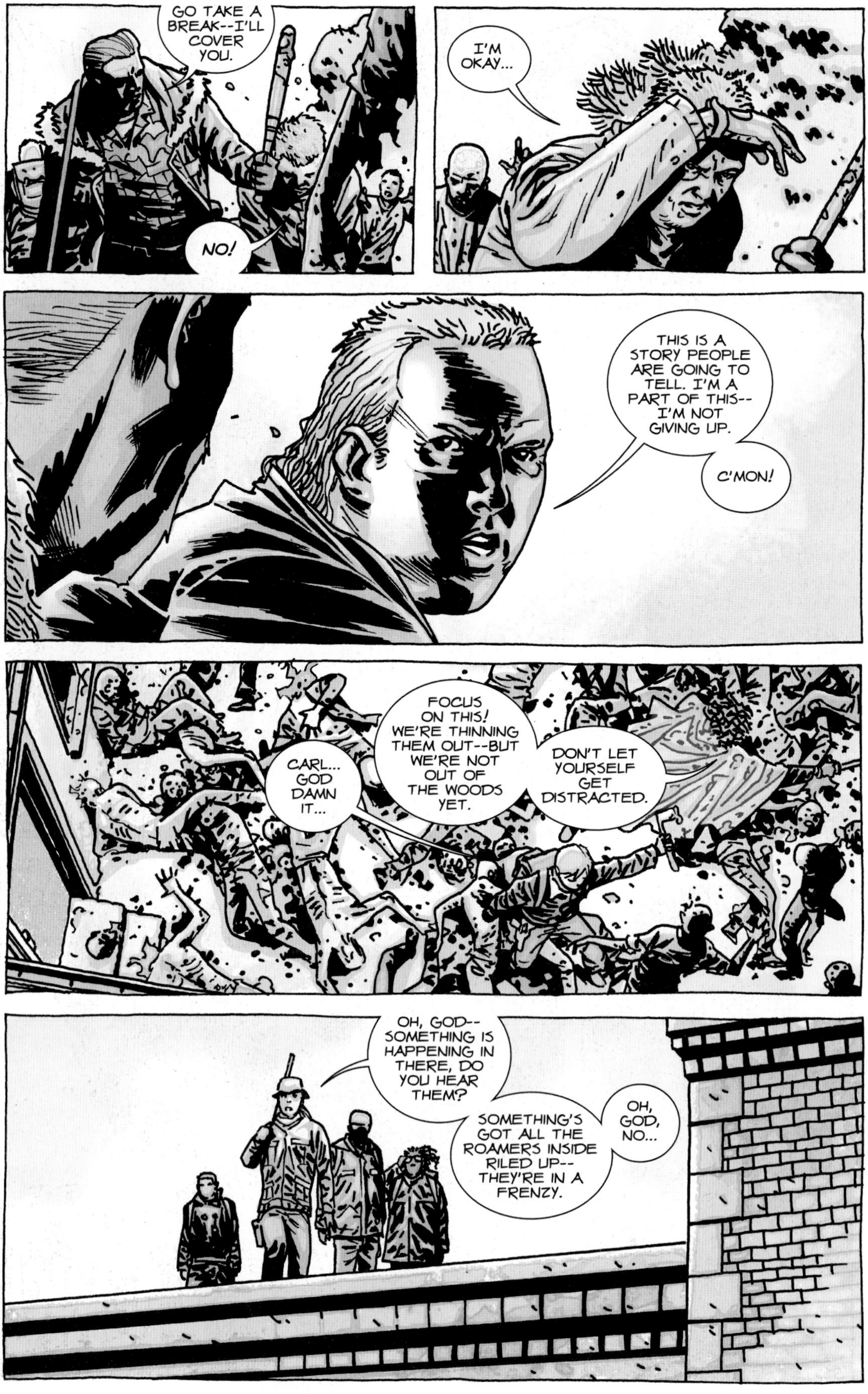
GO TAKE A BREAK--I'LL COVER YOU.
NO!
I'M OKAY...
THIS IS A STORY PEOPLE ARE GOING TO TELL. I'M A PART OF THIS--I'M NOT GIVING UP.
C'MON!
CARL... GOD DAMN IT...
FOCUS ON THIS! WE'RE THINNING THEM OUT--BUT WE'RE NOT OUT OF THE WOODS YET.
DON'T LET YOURSELF GET DISTRACTED.
OH, GOD--SOMETHING IS HAPPENING IN THERE, DO YOU HEAR THEM?
SOMETHING'S GOT ALL THE ROAMERS INSIDE RILED UP--THEY'RE IN A FRENZY.
OH, GOD, NO...

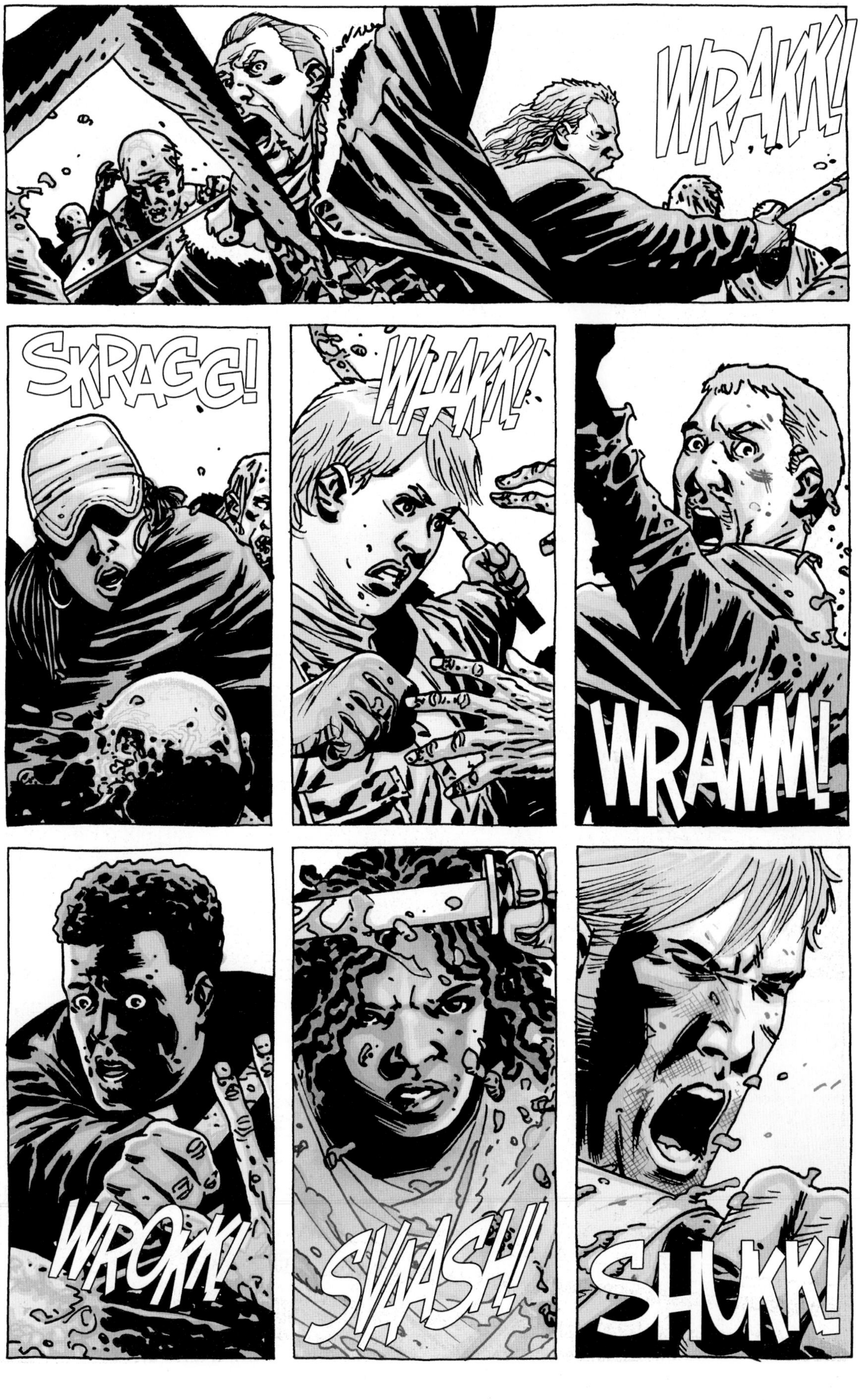
WRAKK!
SKRAGG!
WHAKK!
WRAMM!
WROKK!
SVAASH!
SHUKK!

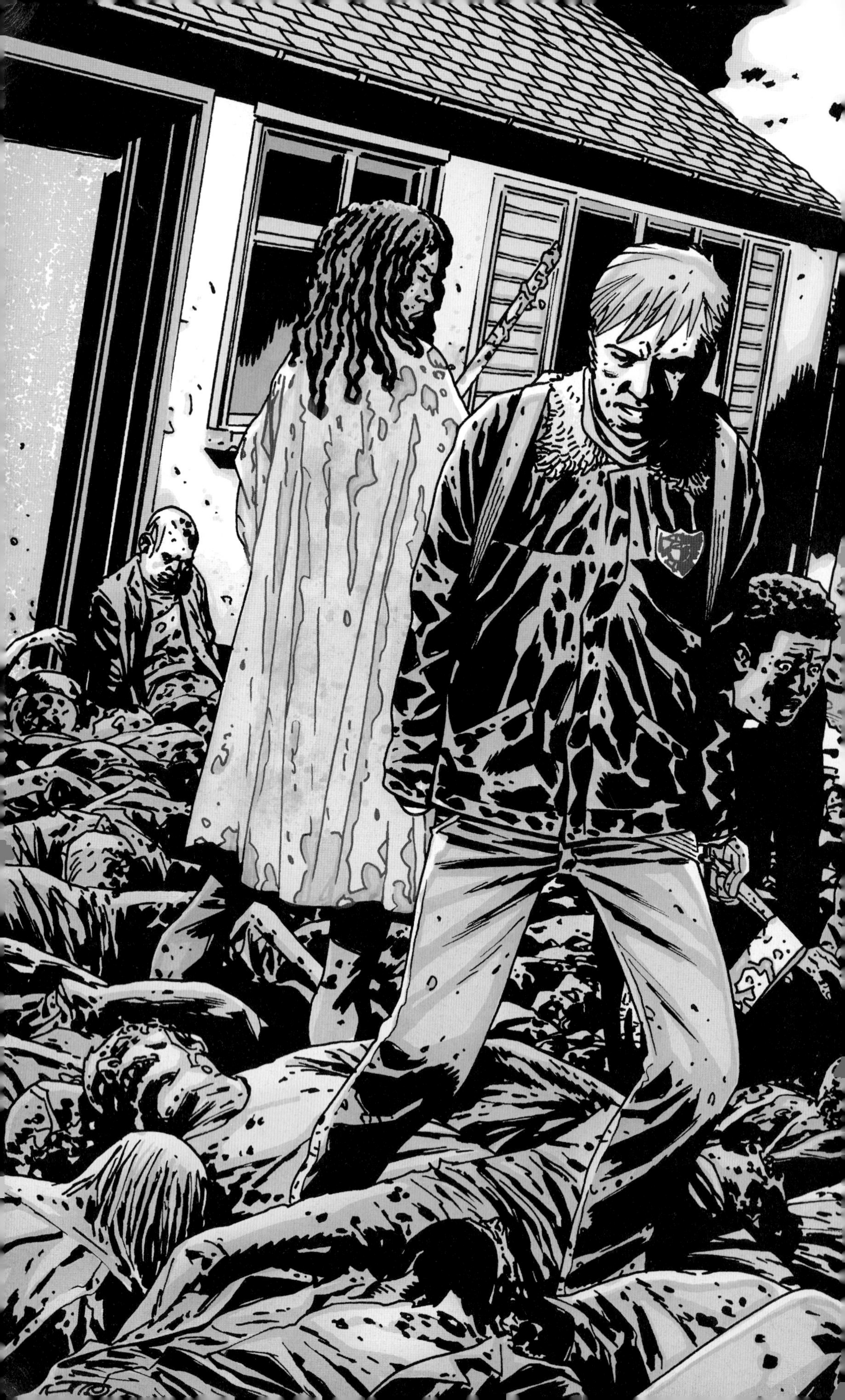

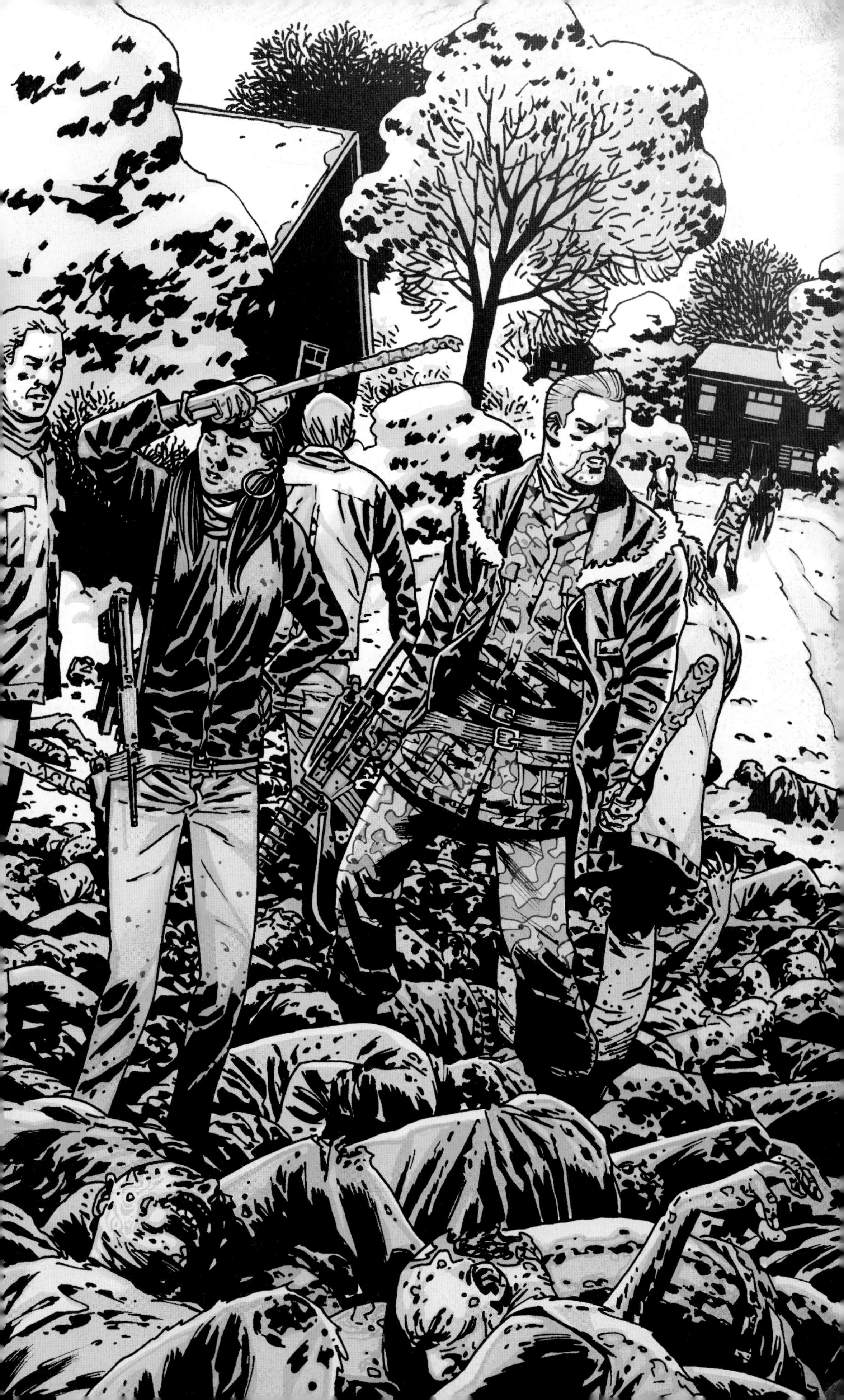

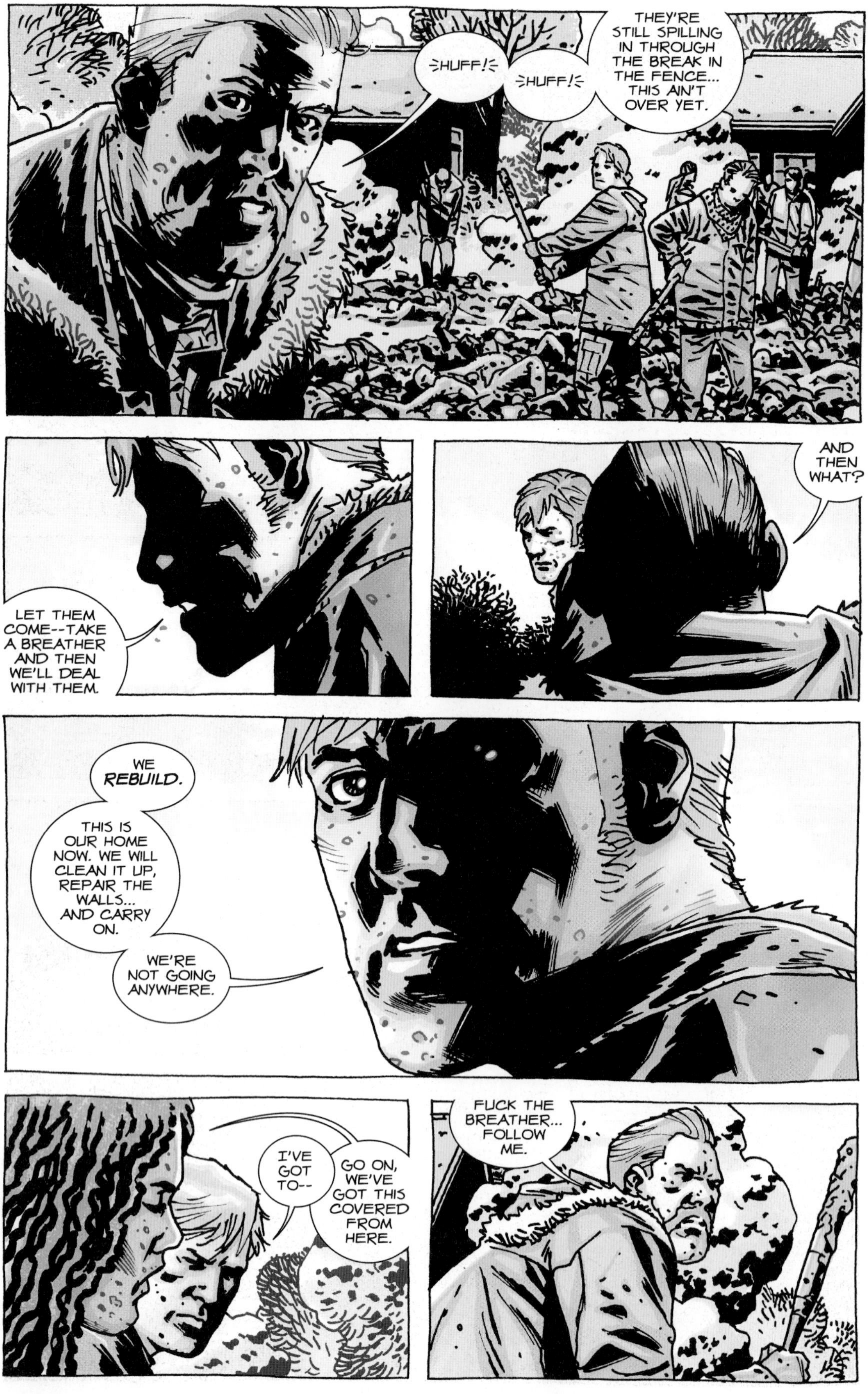

HUFF!
HUFF!
THEY'RE STILL SPILLING IN THROUGH THE BREAK IN THE FENCE... THIS AIN'T OVER YET.
LET THEM COME--TAKE A BREATHER AND THEN WE'LL DEAL WITH THEM.
AND THEN WHAT?
WE REBUILD.
THIS IS OUR HOME NOW. WE WILL CLEAN IT UP, REPAIR THE WALLS... AND CARRY ON.
WE'RE NOT GOING ANYWHERE.
I'VE GOT TO--
GO ON, WE'VE GOT THIS COVERED FROM HERE.
FUCK THE BREATHER... FOLLOW ME.

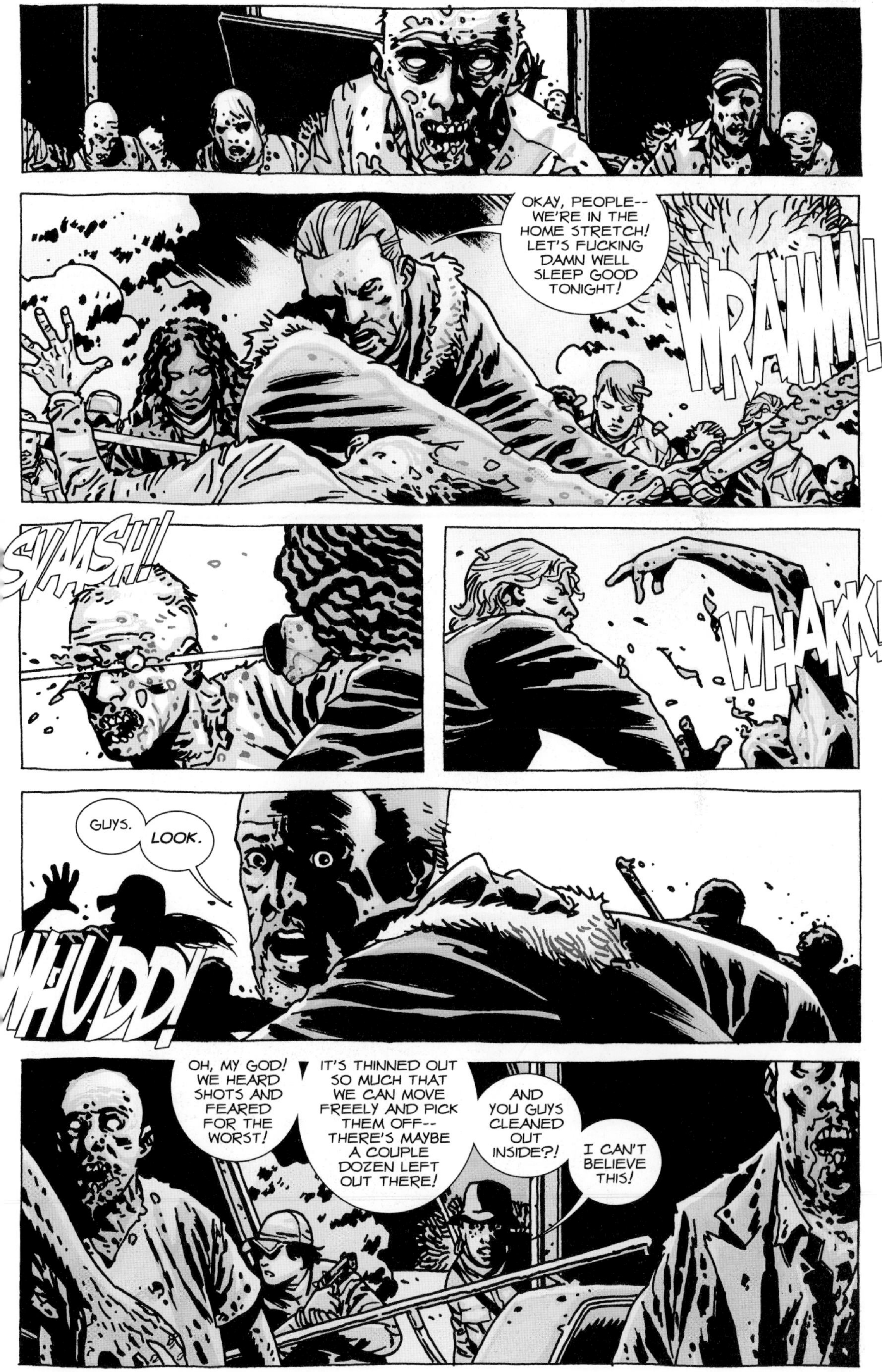

OKAY, PEOPLE-- WE'RE IN THE HOME STRETCH! LET'S FUCKING DAMN WELL SLEEP GOOD TONIGHT!
WRAMM!
SVAASH!
WHAKK!
GUYS.
LOOK.
WHUDD!
OH, MY GOD! WE HEARD SHOTS AND FEARED FOR THE WORST!
IT'S THINNED OUT SO MUCH THAT WE CAN MOVE FREELY AND PICK THEM OFF-- THERE'S MAYBE A COUPLE DOZEN LEFT OUT THERE!
AND YOU GUYS CLEANED OUT INSIDE?!
I CAN'T BELIEVE THIS!

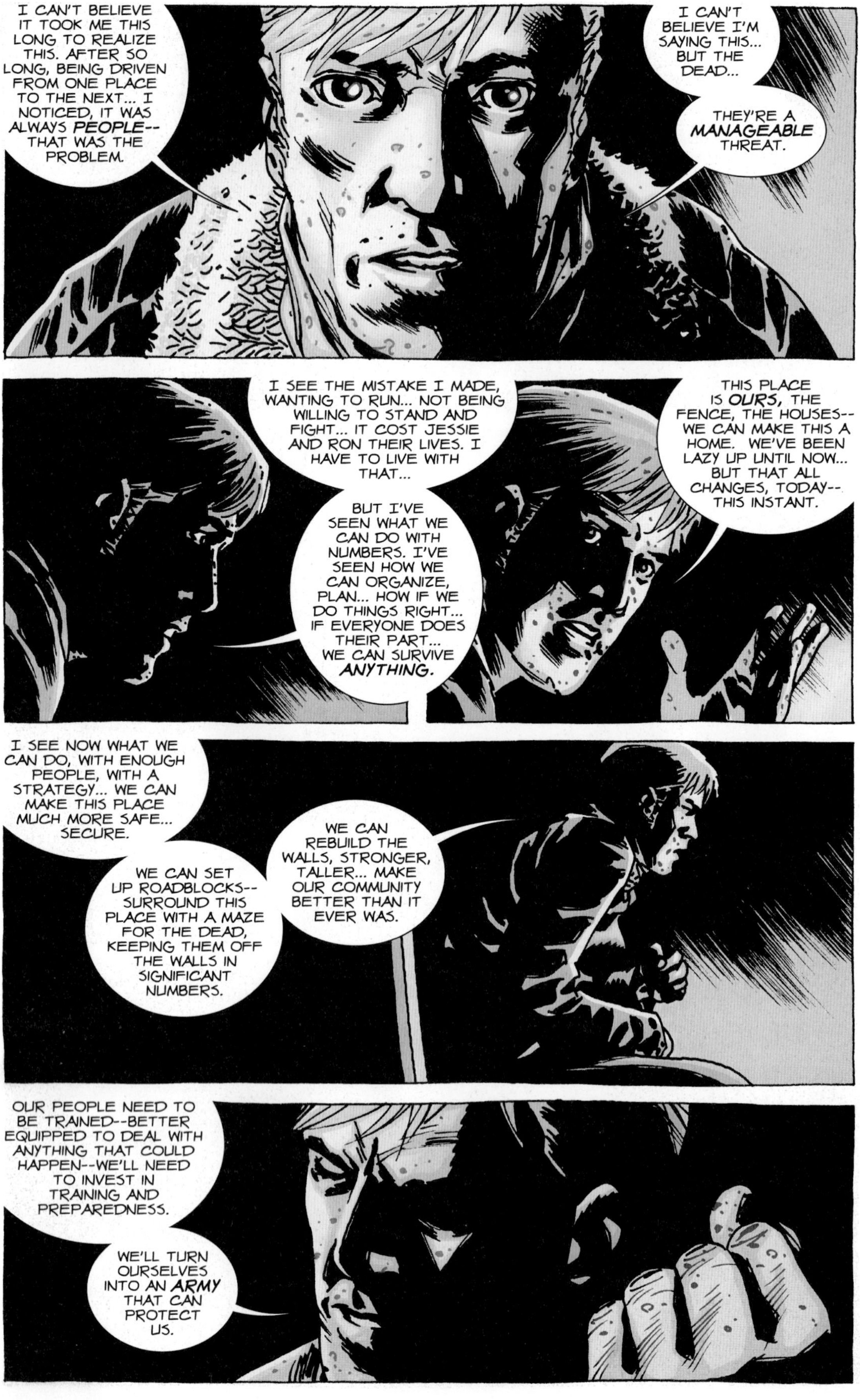
I CAN'T BELIEVE IT TOOK ME THIS LONG TO REALIZE THIS. AFTER SO LONG, BEING DRIVEN FROM ONE PLACE TO THE NEXT... I NOTICED, IT WAS ALWAYS PEOPLE-- THAT WAS THE PROBLEM.
I CAN'T BELIEVE I'M SAYING THIS... BUT THE DEAD...
THEY'RE A MANAGEABLE THREAT.
I SEE THE MISTAKE I MADE, WANTING TO RUN... NOT BEING WILLING TO STAND AND FIGHT... IT COST JESSIE AND RON THEIR LIVES. I HAVE TO LIVE WITH THAT...
BUT I'VE SEEN WHAT WE CAN DO WITH NUMBERS. I'VE SEEN HOW WE CAN ORGANIZE, PLAN... HOW IF WE DO THINGS RIGHT... IF EVERYONE DOES THEIR PART... WE CAN SURVIVE ANYTHING.
THIS PLACE IS OURS, THE FENCE, THE HOUSES-- WE CAN MAKE THIS A HOME. WE'VE BEEN LAZY UP UNTIL NOW... BUT THAT ALL CHANGES, TODAY-- THIS INSTANT.
I SEE NOW WHAT WE CAN DO, WITH ENOUGH PEOPLE, WITH A STRATEGY... WE CAN MAKE THIS PLACE MUCH MORE SAFE... SECURE.
WE CAN SET UP ROADBLOCKS-- SURROUND THIS PLACE WITH A MAZE FOR THE DEAD, KEEPING THEM OFF THE WALLS IN SIGNIFICANT NUMBERS.
WE CAN REBUILD THE WALLS, STRONGER, TALLER... MAKE OUR COMMUNITY BETTER THAN IT EVER WAS.
OUR PEOPLE NEED TO BE TRAINED--BETTER EQUIPPED TO DEAL WITH ANYTHING THAT COULD HAPPEN--WE'LL NEED TO INVEST IN TRAINING AND PREPAREDNESS.
WE'LL TURN OURSELVES INTO AN ARMY THAT CAN PROTECT US.

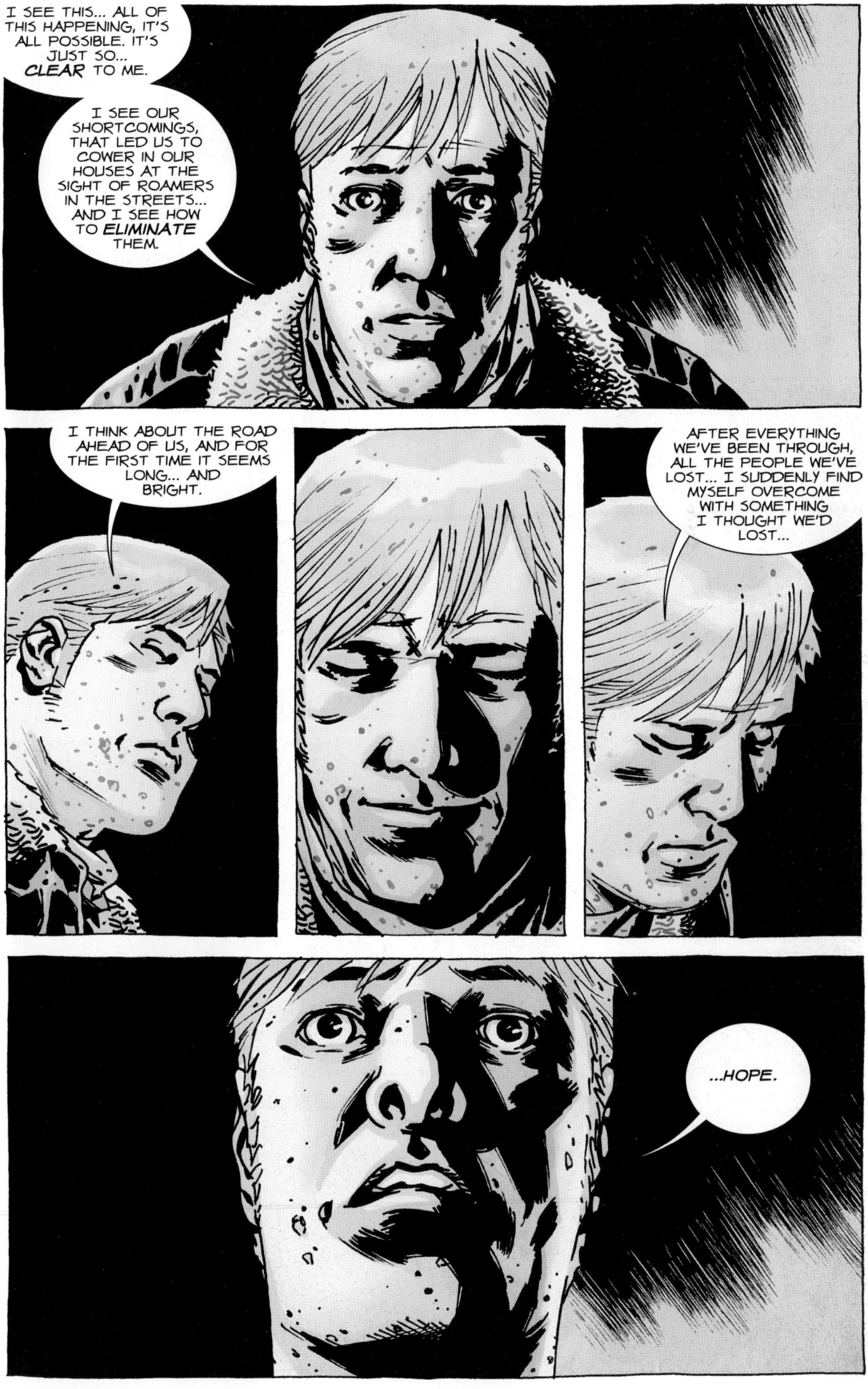
I SEE THIS... ALL OF THIS HAPPENING, IT'S ALL POSSIBLE. IT'S JUST SO... CLEAR TO ME.
I SEE OUR SHORTCOMINGS, THAT LED US TO COWER IN OUR HOUSES AT THE SIGHT OF ROAMERS IN THE STREETS... AND I SEE HOW TO ELIMINATE THEM.
I THINK ABOUT THE ROAD AHEAD OF US, AND FOR THE FIRST TIME IT SEEMS LONG... AND BRIGHT.
AFTER EVERYTHING WE'VE BEEN THROUGH, ALL THE PEOPLE WE'VE LOST... I SUDDENLY FIND MYSELF OVERCOME WITH SOMETHING I THOUGHT WE'D LOST...
...HOPE.

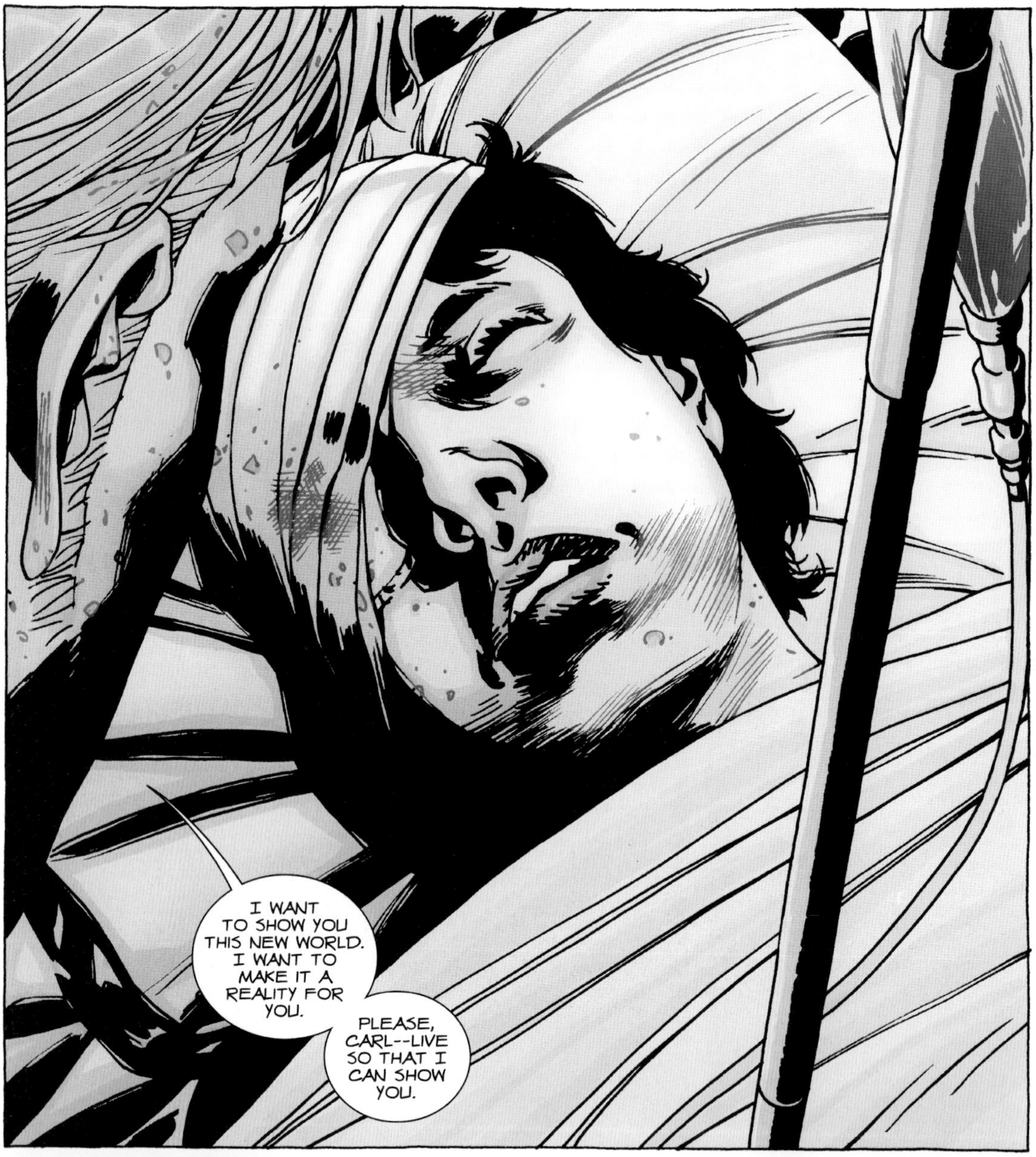
I WANT TO SHOW YOU THIS NEW WORLD. I WANT TO MAKE IT A REALITY FOR YOU.
PLEASE, CARL--LIVE SO THAT I CAN SHOW YOU.

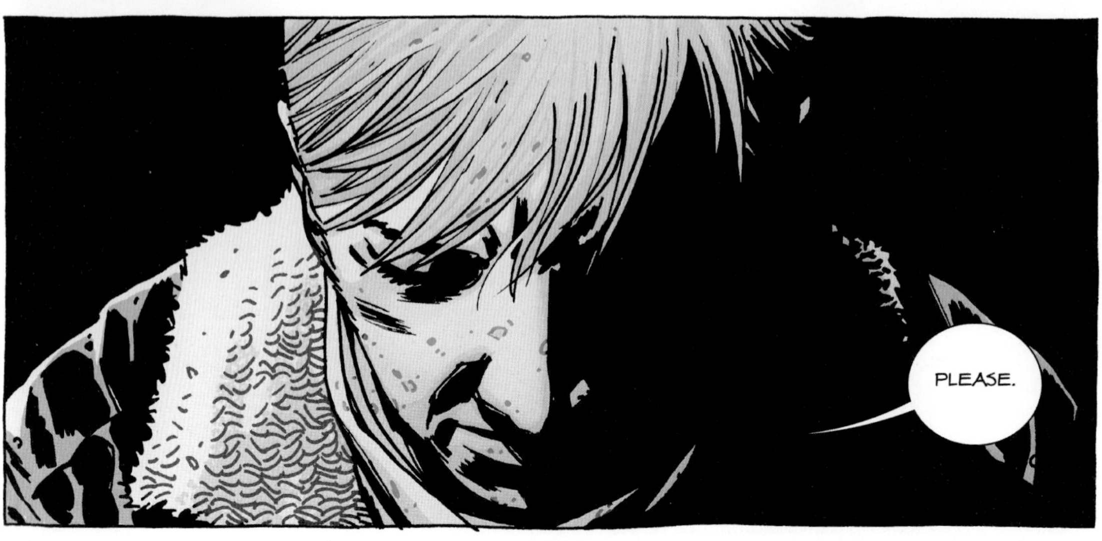
PLEASE.

Chapter Fifteen:
We Find Ourselves

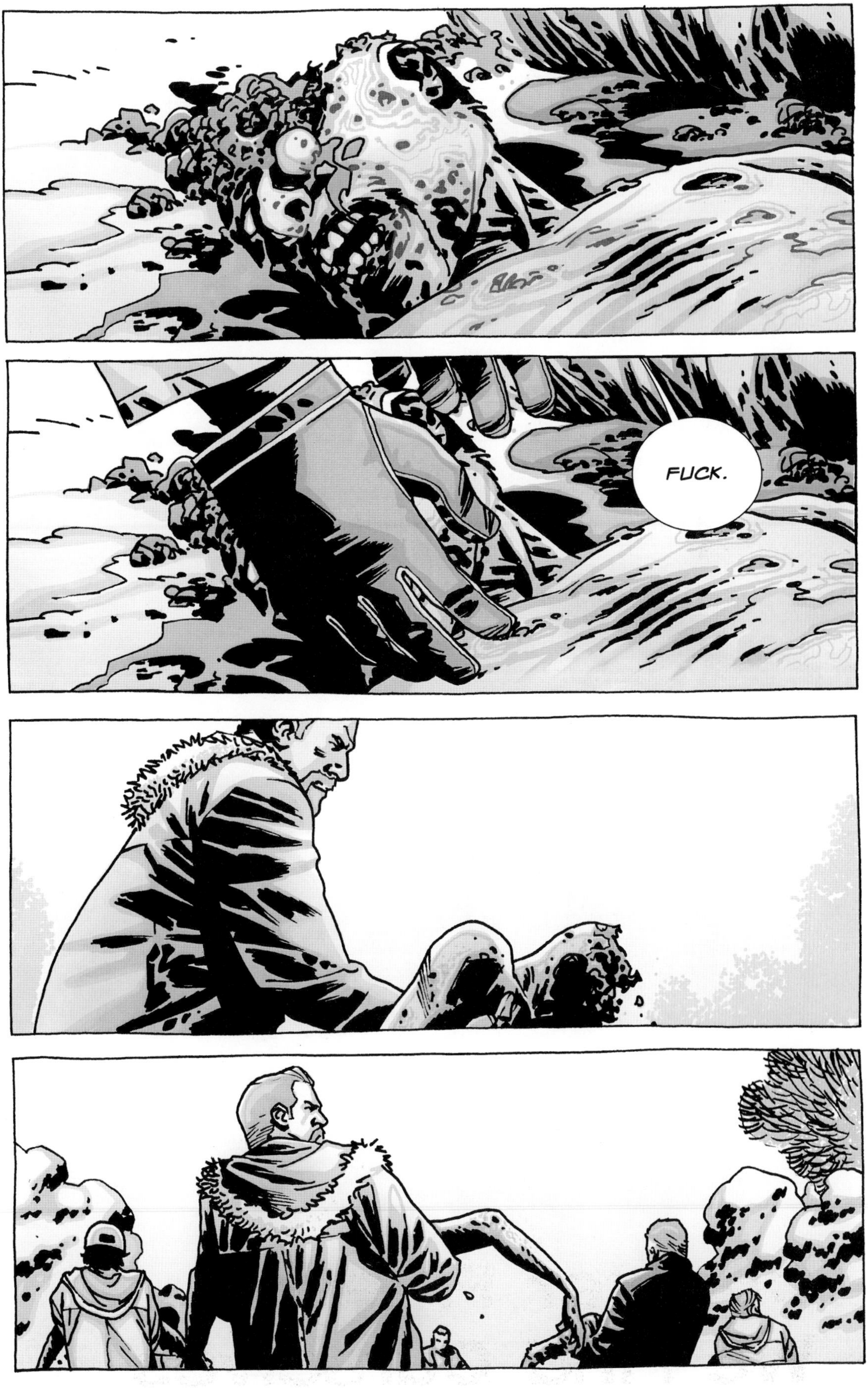
FUCK.

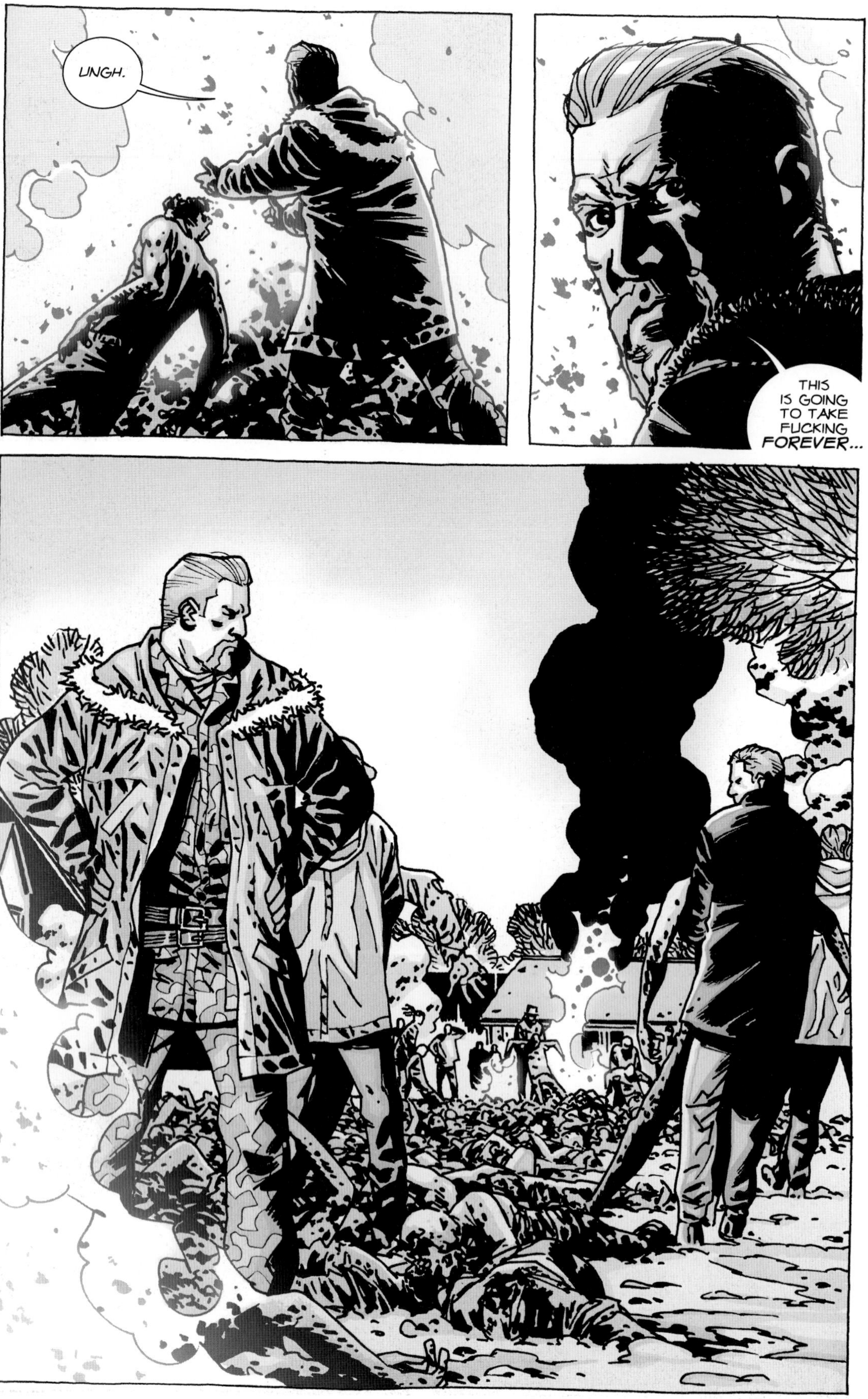
UNGH.
THIS IS GOING TO TAKE FUCKING FOREVER...

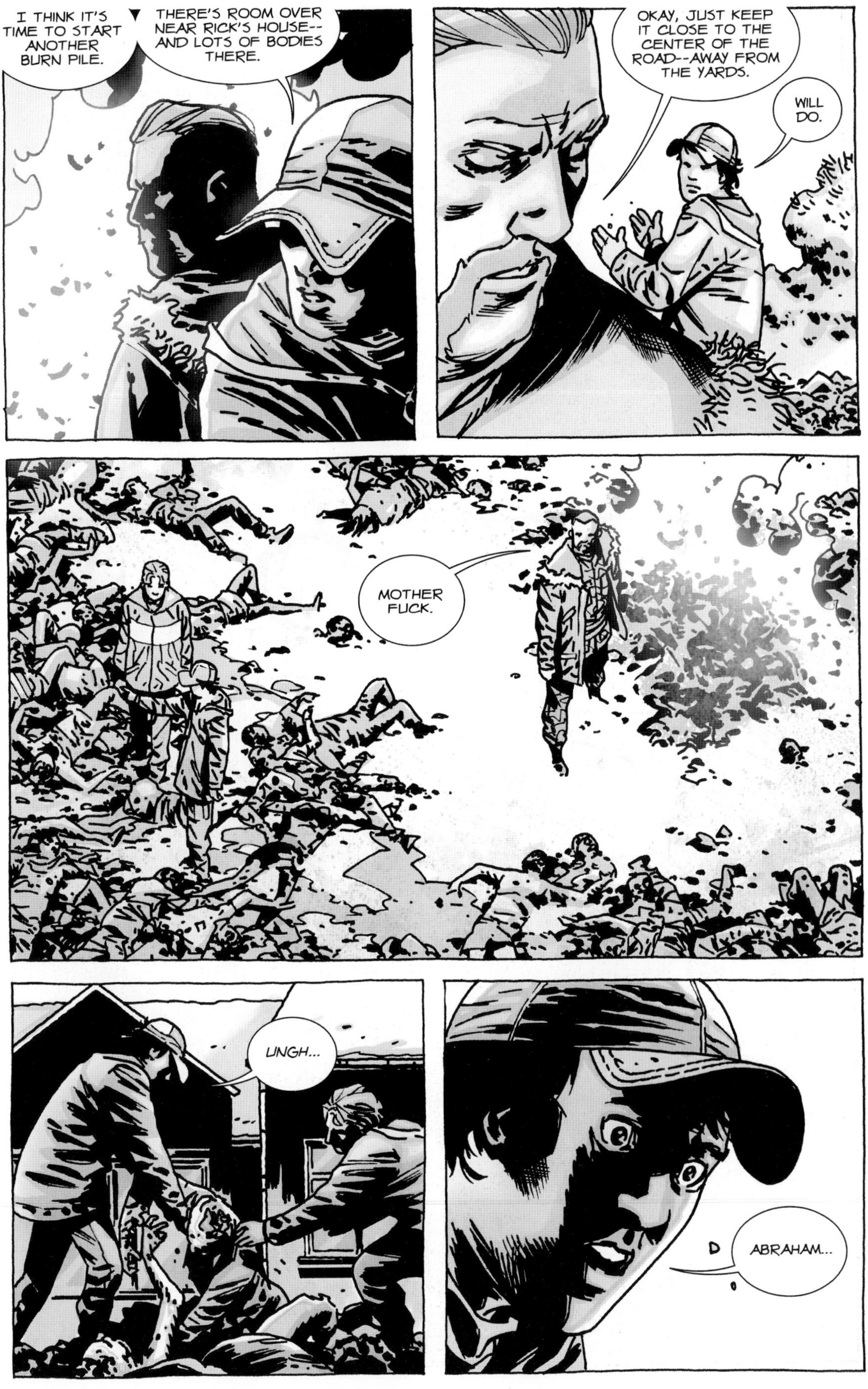
I THINK IT'S TIME TO START ANOTHER BURN PILE.
THERE'S ROOM OVER NEAR RICK'S HOUSE-- AND LOTS OF BODIES THERE.
OKAY, JUST KEEP IT CLOSE TO THE CENTER OF THE ROAD--AWAY FROM THE YARDS.
WILL DO.
MOTHER FUCK.
UNGH...
ABRAHAM...

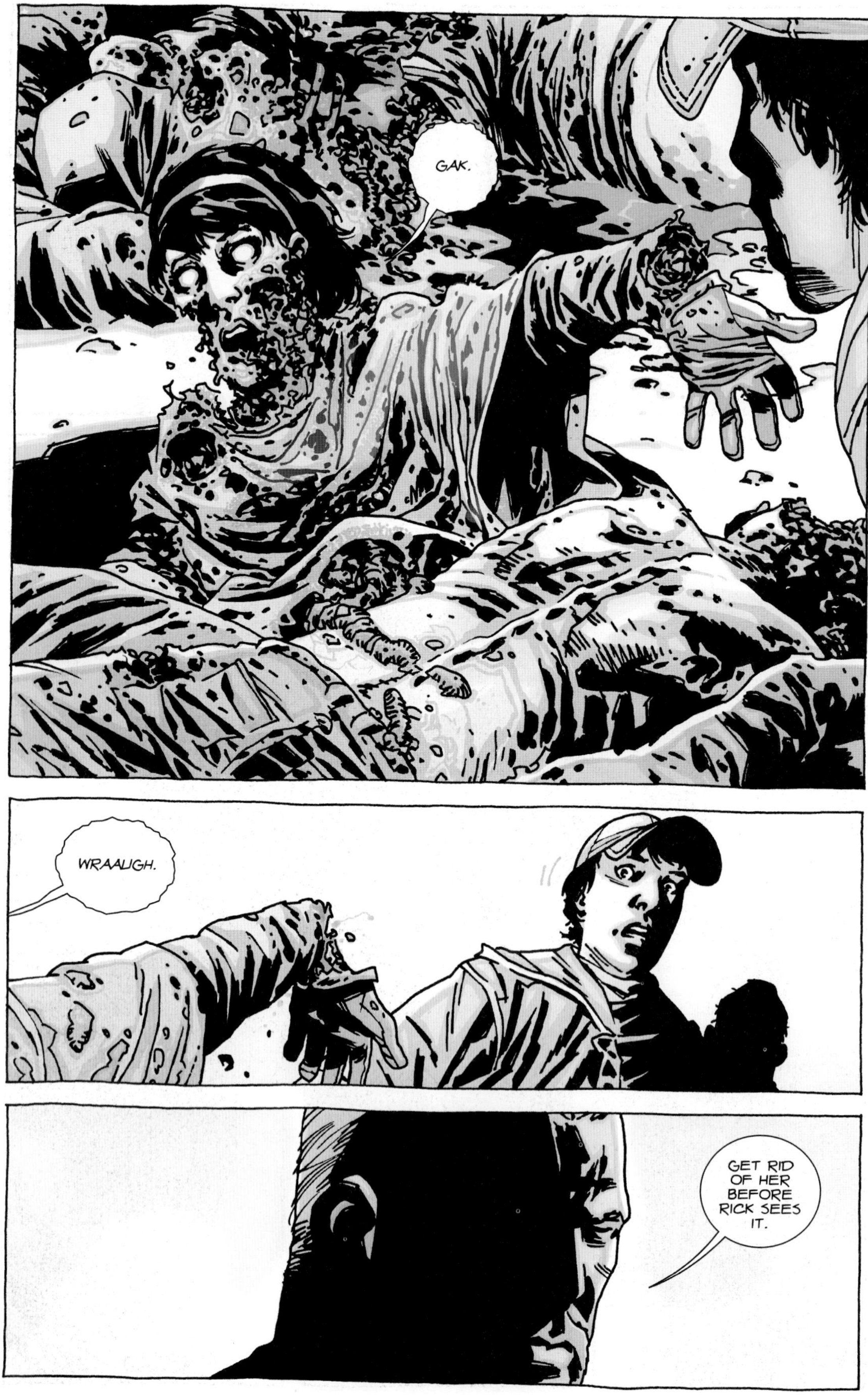
GAK.
WRAAUGH.
GET RID OF HER BEFORE RICK SEES IT.

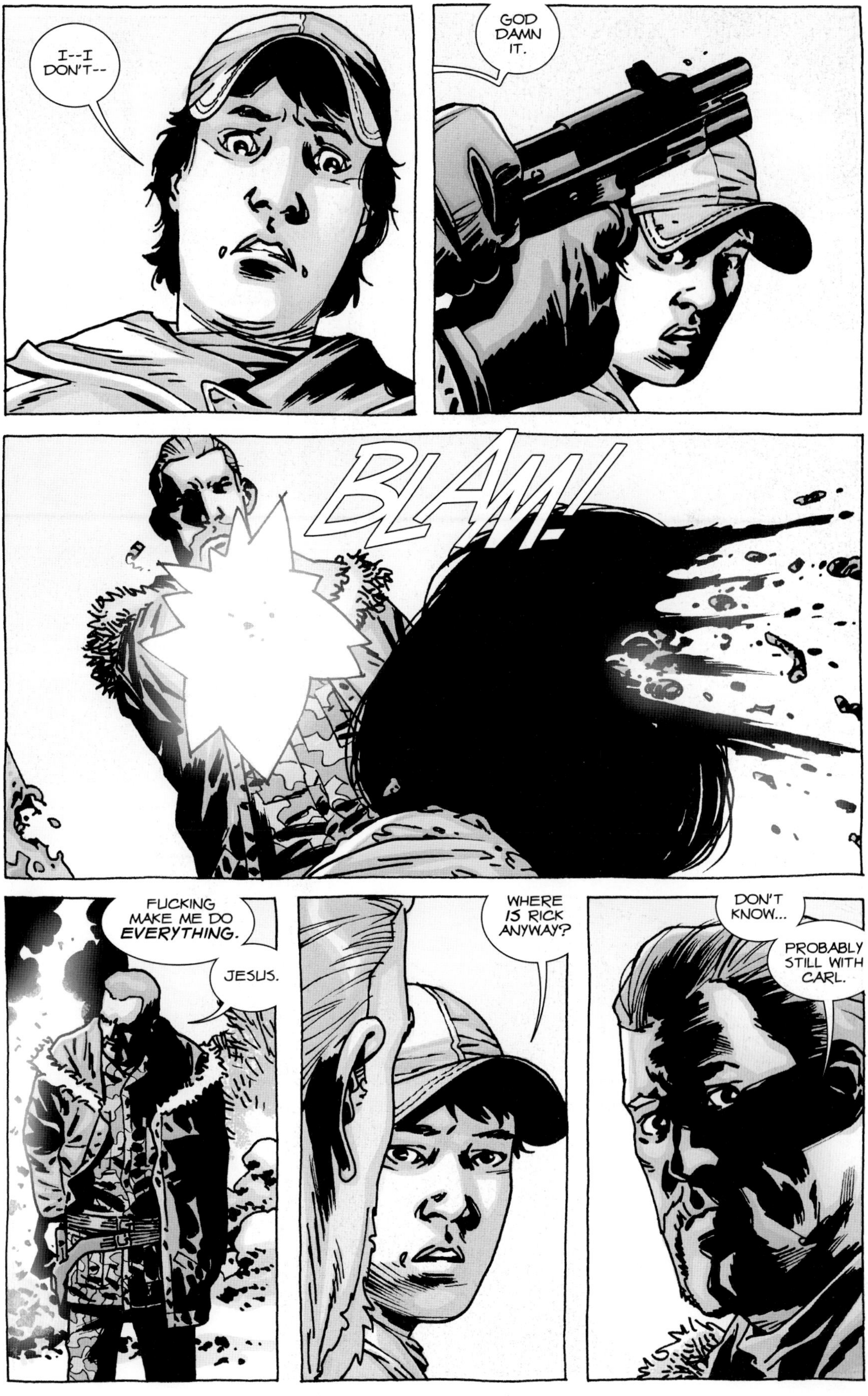
I--I DON'T--
GOD DAMN IT.
BLAM!
FUCKING MAKE ME DO *EVERYTHING*.
JESUS.
WHERE *IS* RICK ANYWAY?
DON'T KNOW...
PROBABLY STILL WITH CARL.

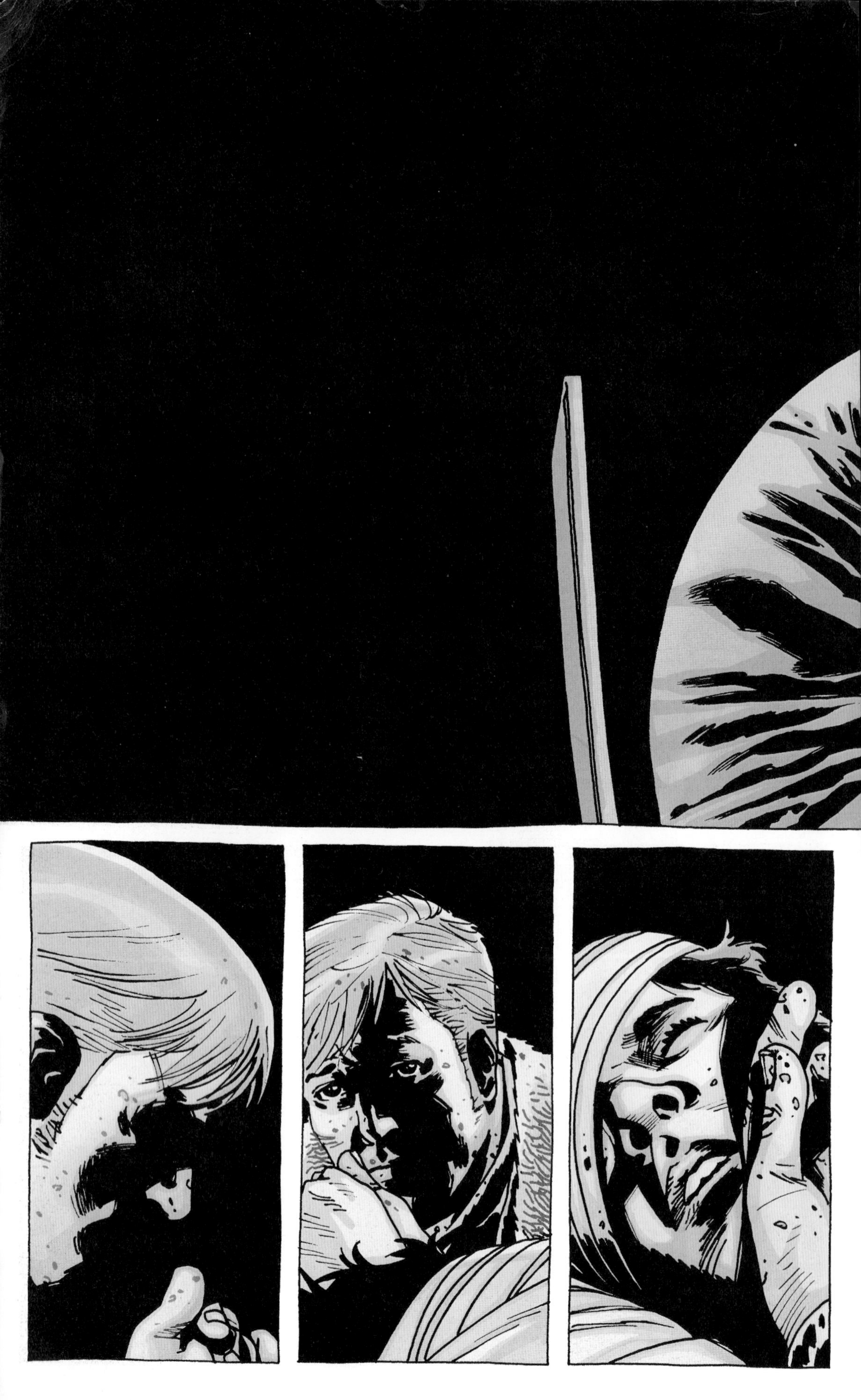

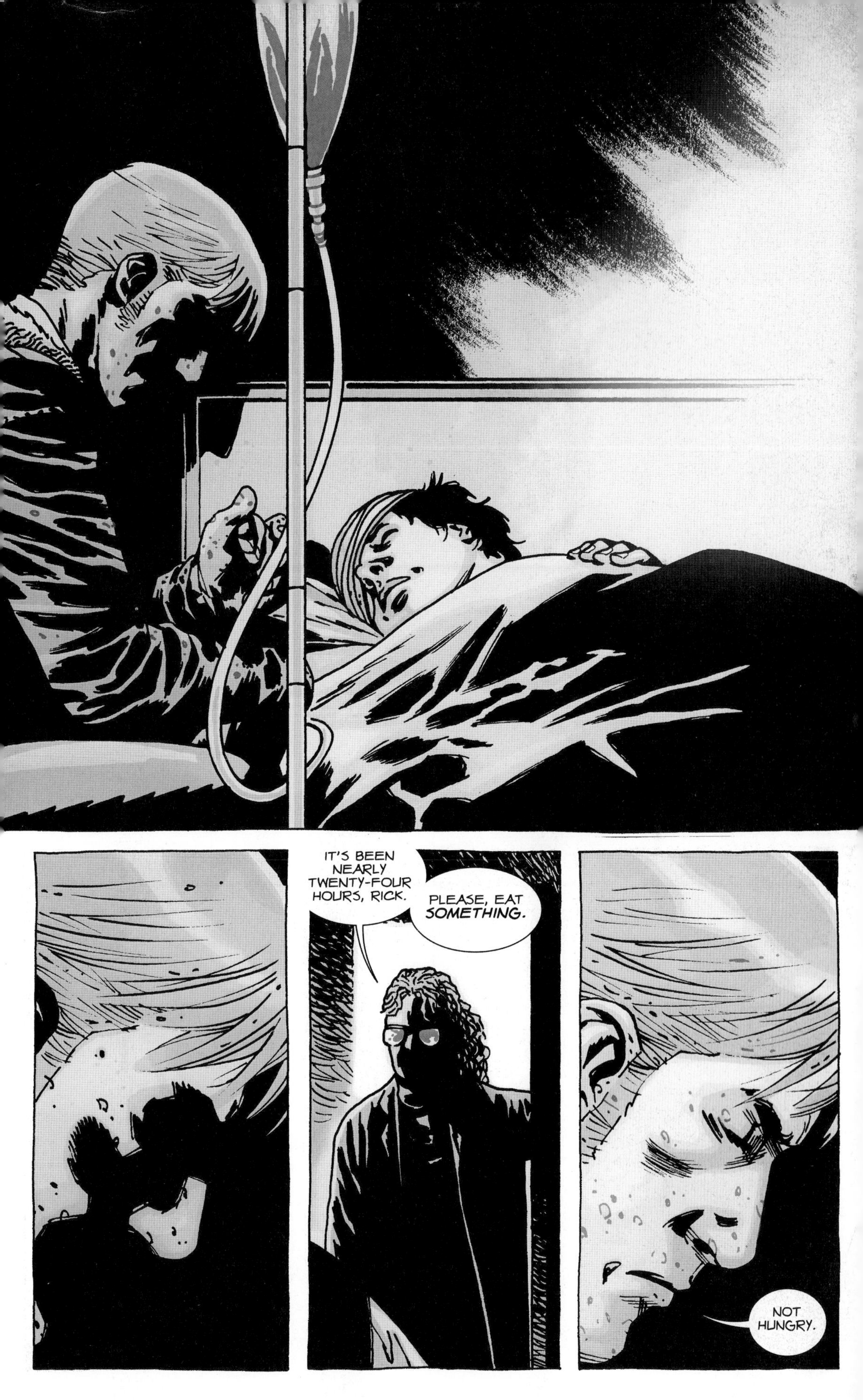
IT'S BEEN NEARLY TWENTY-FOUR HOURS, RICK.
PLEASE, EAT SOMETHING.
NOT HUNGRY.

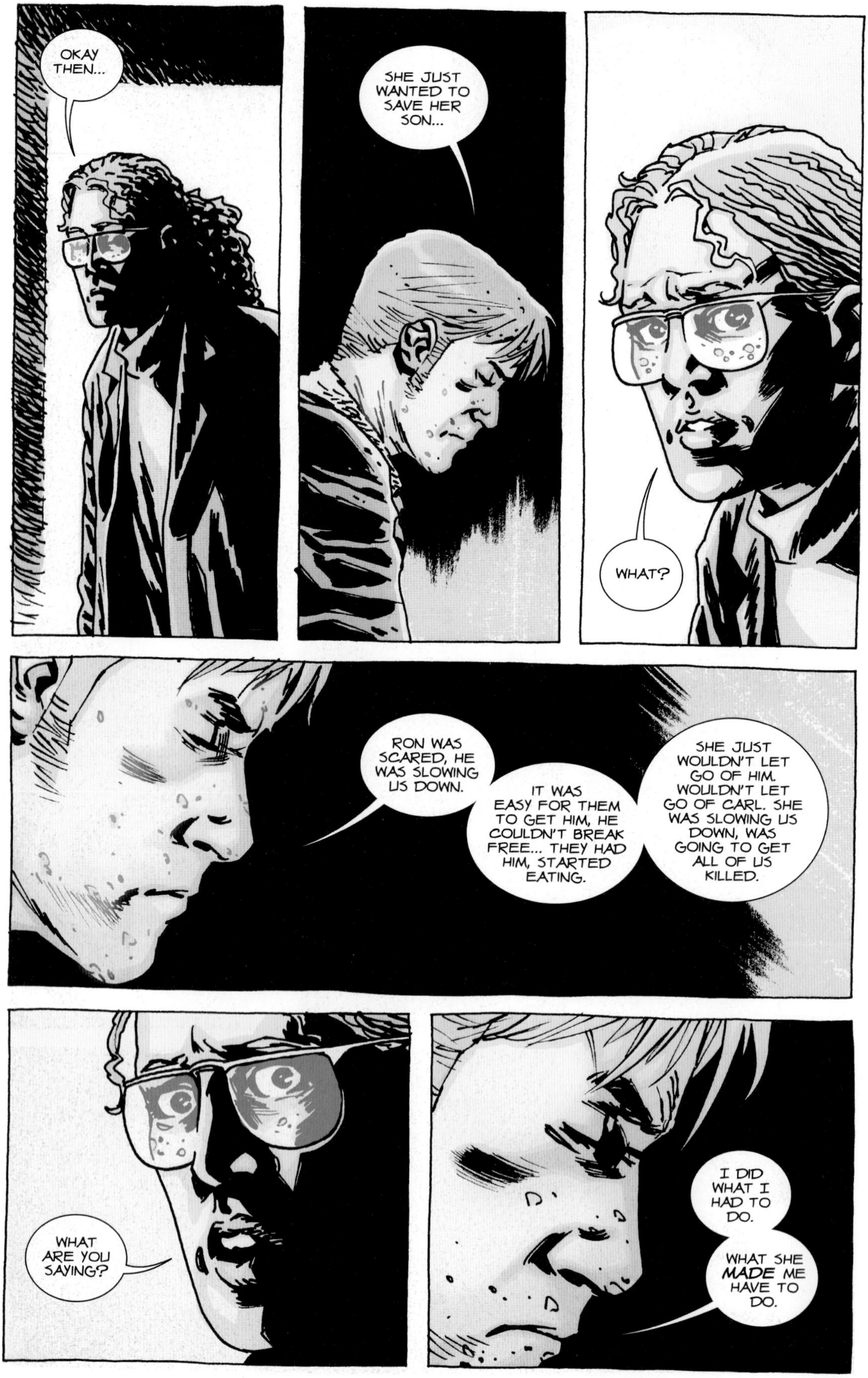

OKAY THEN...
SHE JUST WANTED TO SAVE HER SON...
WHAT?
RON WAS SCARED, HE WAS SLOWING US DOWN.
IT WAS EASY FOR THEM TO GET HIM, HE COULDN'T BREAK FREE... THEY HAD HIM, STARTED EATING.
SHE JUST WOULDN'T LET GO OF HIM. WOULDN'T LET GO OF CARL. SHE WAS SLOWING US DOWN, WAS GOING TO GET ALL OF US KILLED.
WHAT ARE YOU SAYING?
I DID WHAT I HAD TO DO.
WHAT SHE MADE ME HAVE TO DO.

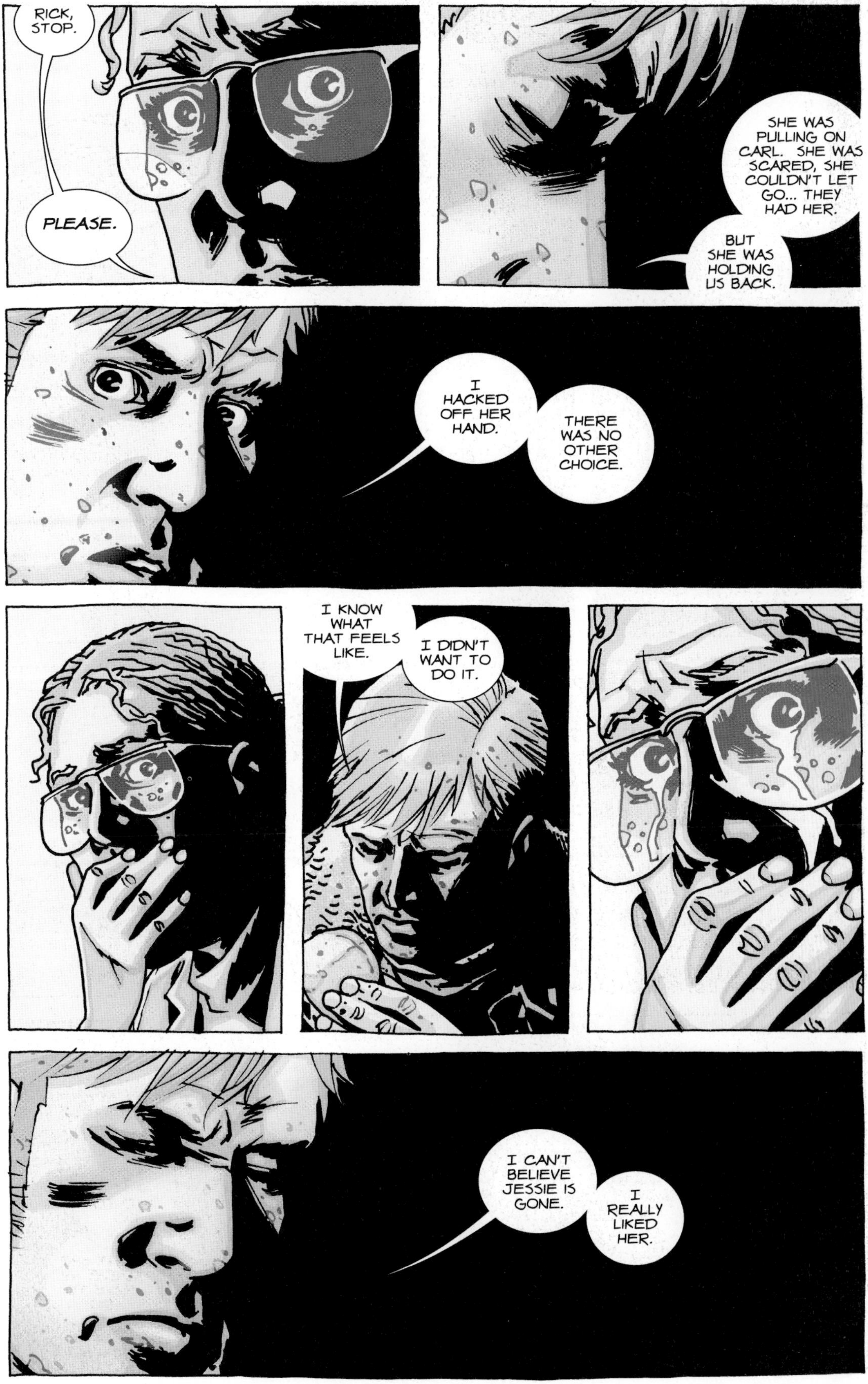
RICK, STOP.
PLEASE.
SHE WAS PULLING ON CARL. SHE WAS SCARED, SHE COULDN'T LET GO... THEY HAD HER.
BUT SHE WAS HOLDING US BACK.
I HACKED OFF HER HAND.
THERE WAS NO OTHER CHOICE.
I KNOW WHAT THAT FEELS LIKE.
I DIDN'T WANT TO DO IT.
I CAN'T BELIEVE JESSIE IS GONE.
I REALLY LIKED HER.

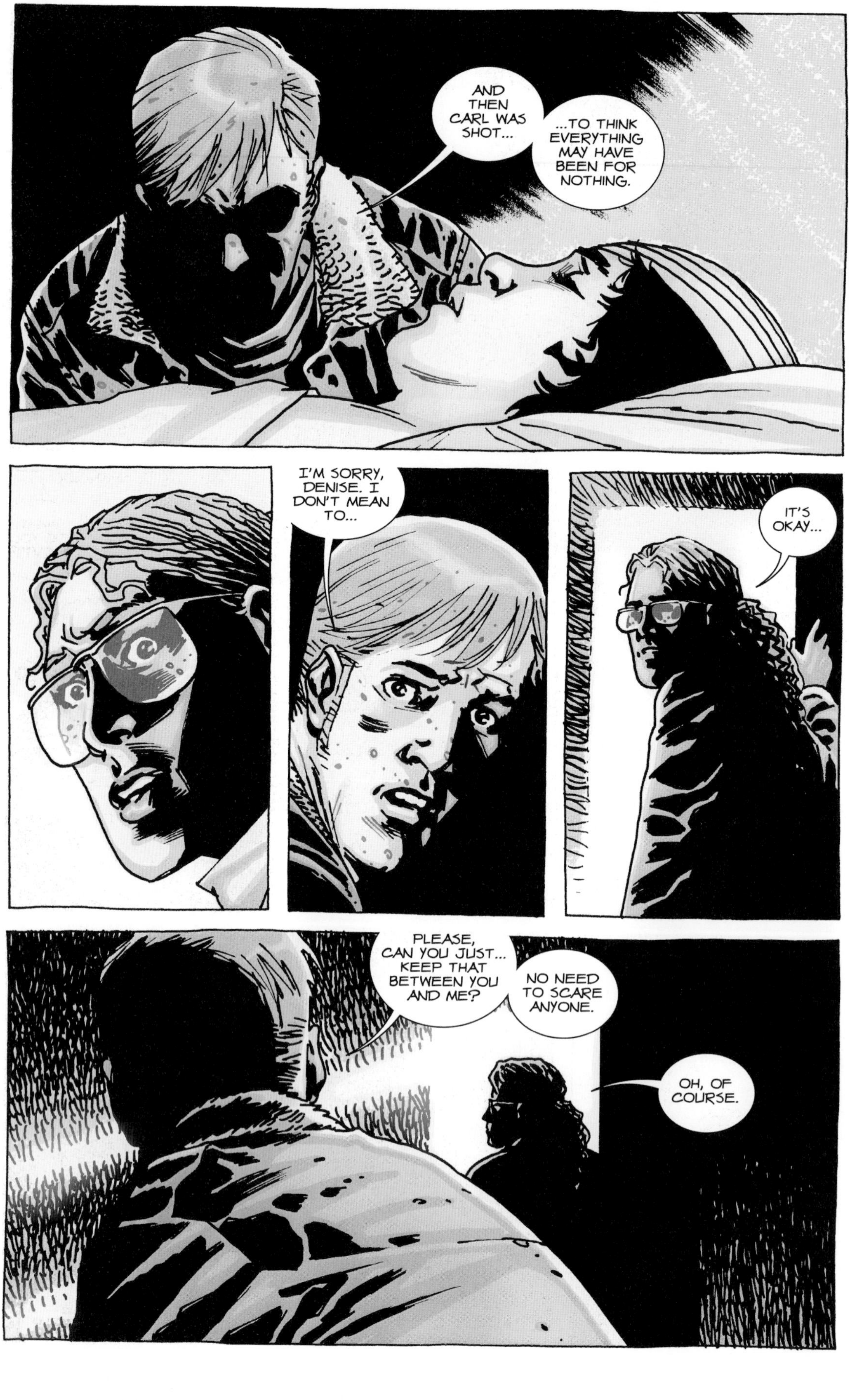
AND THEN CARL WAS SHOT...
...TO THINK EVERYTHING MAY HAVE BEEN FOR NOTHING.
I'M SORRY, DENISE. I DON'T MEAN TO...
IT'S OKAY...
PLEASE, CAN YOU JUST... KEEP THAT BETWEEN YOU AND ME?
NO NEED TO SCARE ANYONE.
OH, OF COURSE.

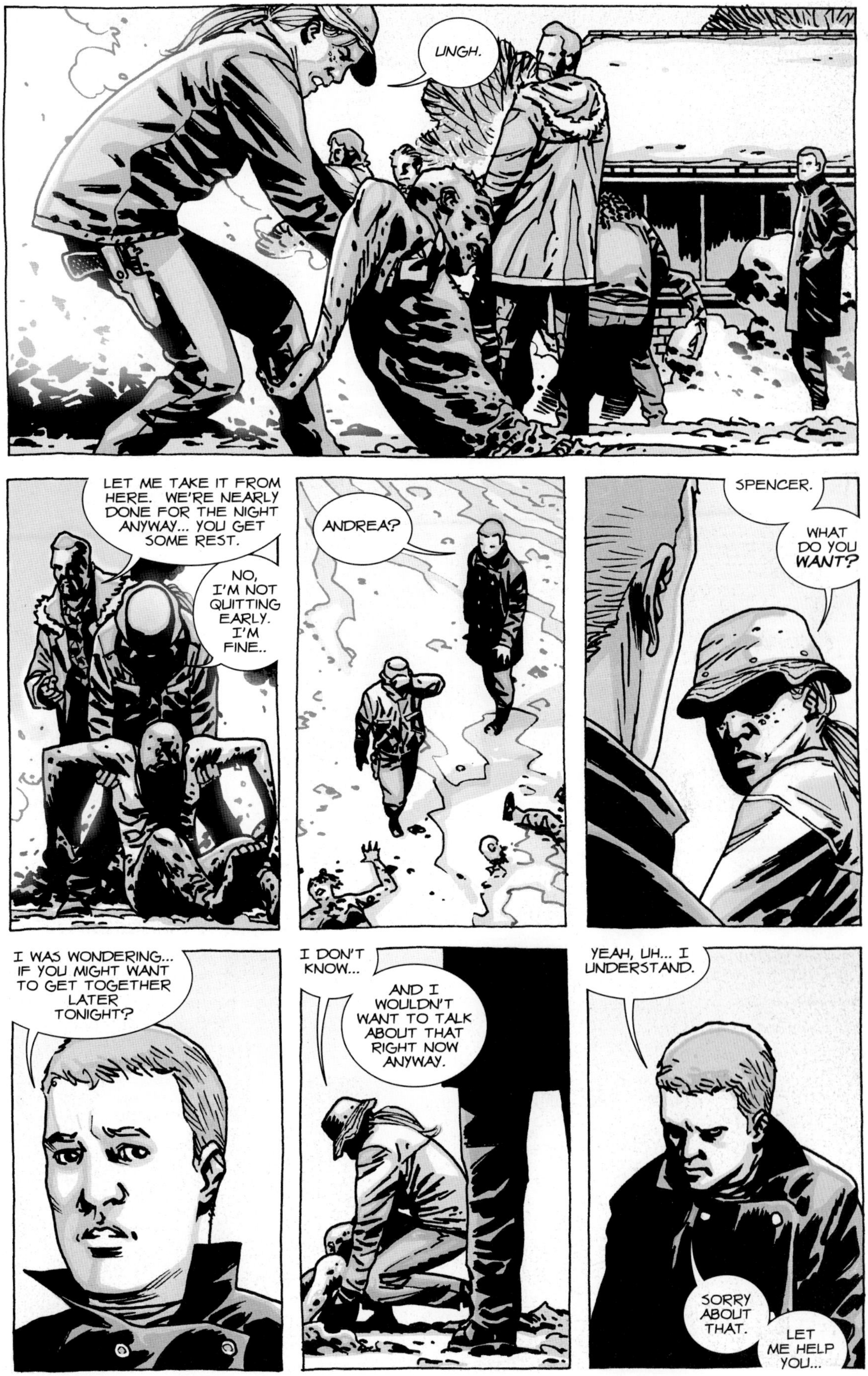
UNGH.
LET ME TAKE IT FROM HERE. WE'RE NEARLY DONE FOR THE NIGHT ANYWAY... YOU GET SOME REST.
NO, I'M NOT QUITTING EARLY. I'M FINE..
ANDREA?
SPENCER.
WHAT DO YOU WANT?
I WAS WONDERING... IF YOU MIGHT WANT TO GET TOGETHER LATER TONIGHT?
I DON'T KNOW...
AND I WOULDN'T WANT TO TALK ABOUT THAT RIGHT NOW ANYWAY.
YEAH, UH... I UNDERSTAND.
SORRY ABOUT THAT.
LET ME HELP YOU...

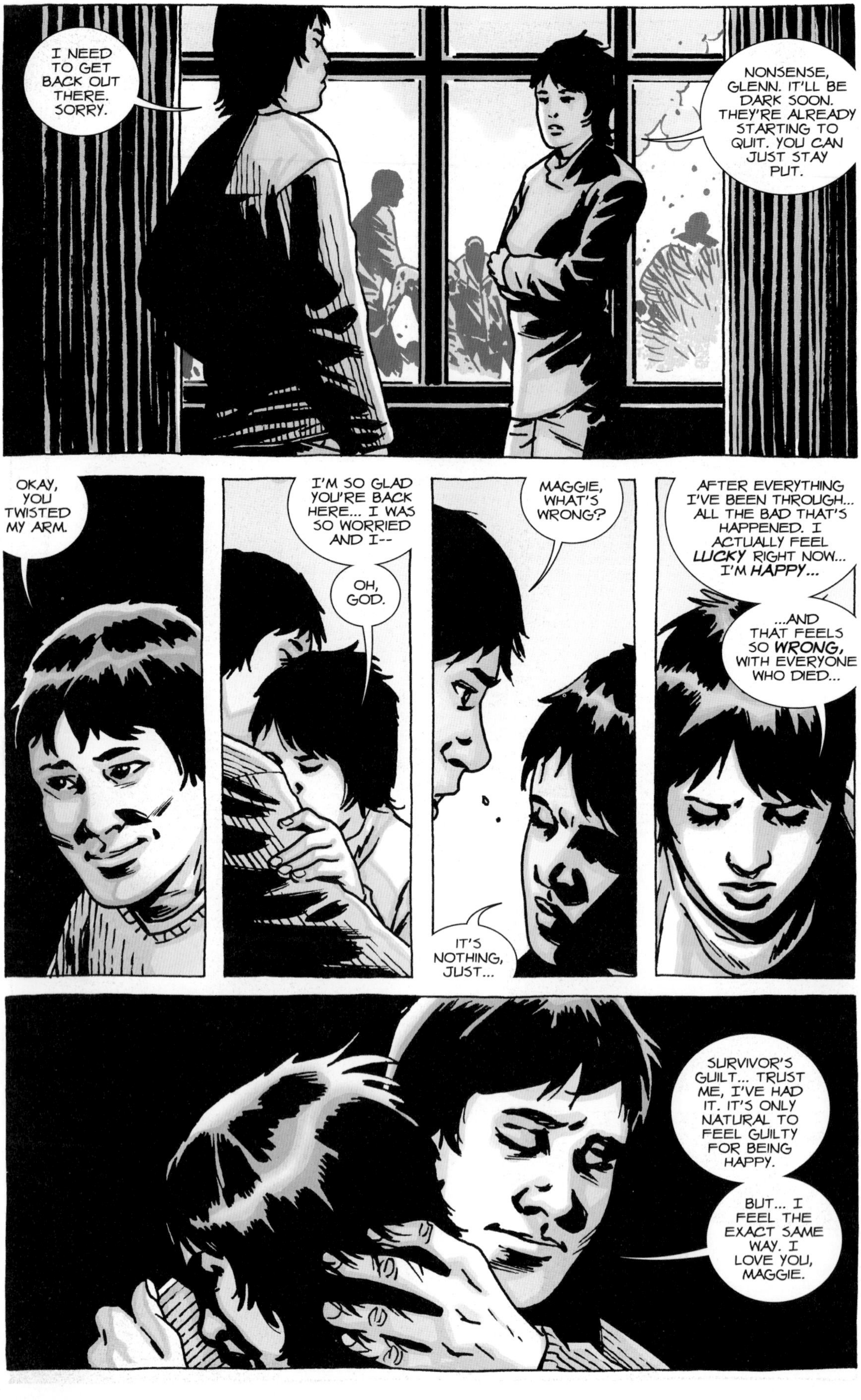
I NEED TO GET BACK OUT THERE. SORRY.
NONSENSE, GLENN. IT'LL BE DARK SOON. THEY'RE ALREADY STARTING TO QUIT. YOU CAN JUST STAY PUT.
OKAY, YOU TWISTED MY ARM.
I'M SO GLAD YOU'RE BACK HERE... I WAS SO WORRIED AND I--
OH, GOD.
MAGGIE, WHAT'S WRONG?
IT'S NOTHING, JUST...
AFTER EVERYTHING I'VE BEEN THROUGH... ALL THE BAD THAT'S HAPPENED. I ACTUALLY FEEL LUCKY RIGHT NOW... I'M HAPPY...
...AND THAT FEELS SO WRONG, WITH EVERYONE WHO DIED...
SURVIVOR'S GUILT... TRUST ME, I'VE HAD IT. IT'S ONLY NATURAL TO FEEL GUILTY FOR BEING HAPPY.
BUT... I FEEL THE EXACT SAME WAY. I LOVE YOU, MAGGIE.

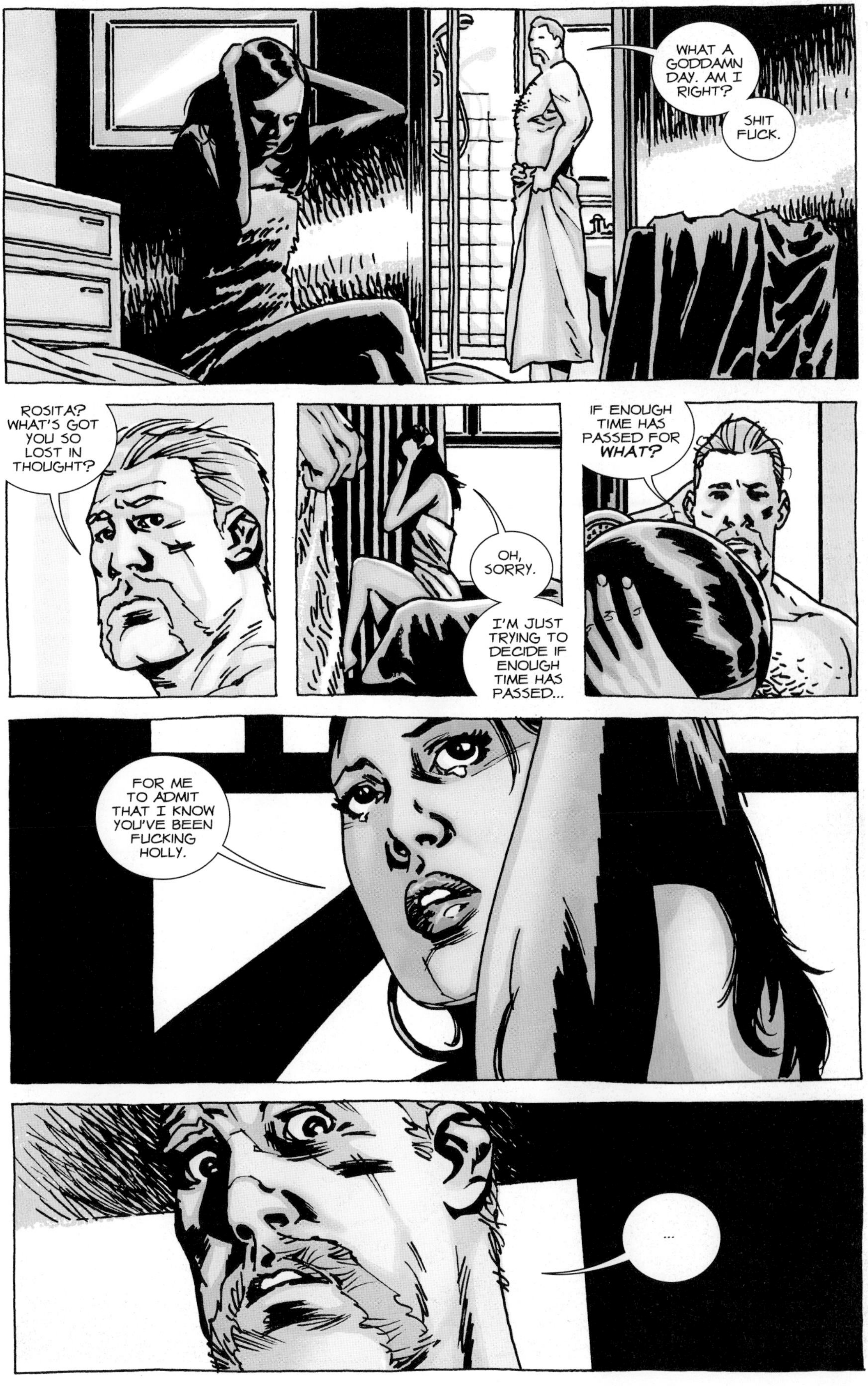
WHAT A GODDAMN DAY. AM I RIGHT?
SHIT FUCK.
ROSITA? WHAT'S GOT YOU SO LOST IN THOUGHT?
OH, SORRY.
I'M JUST TRYING TO DECIDE IF ENOUGH TIME HAS PASSED...
IF ENOUGH TIME HAS PASSED FOR WHAT?
FOR ME TO ADMIT THAT I KNOW YOU'VE BEEN FUCKING HOLLY.
...

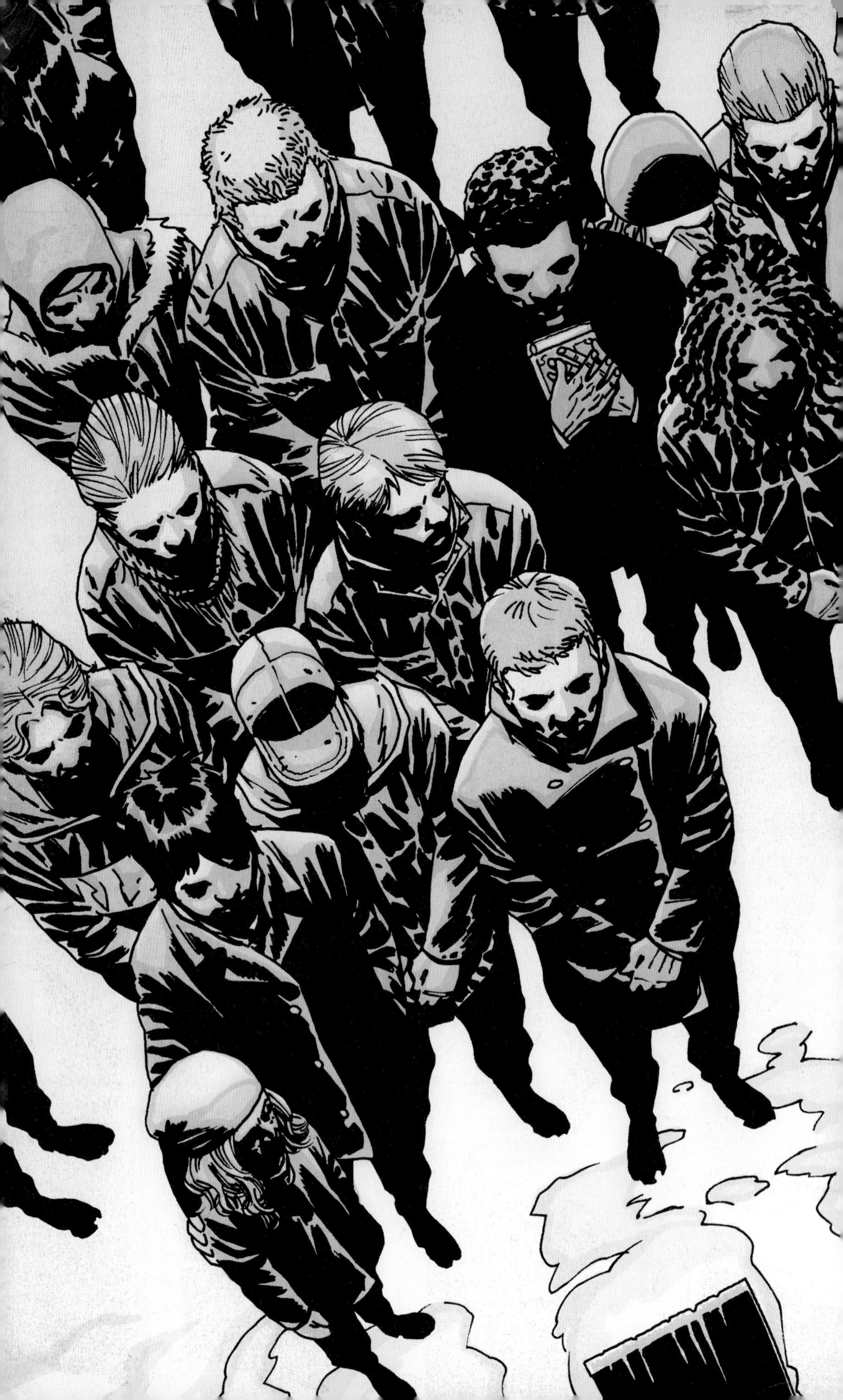

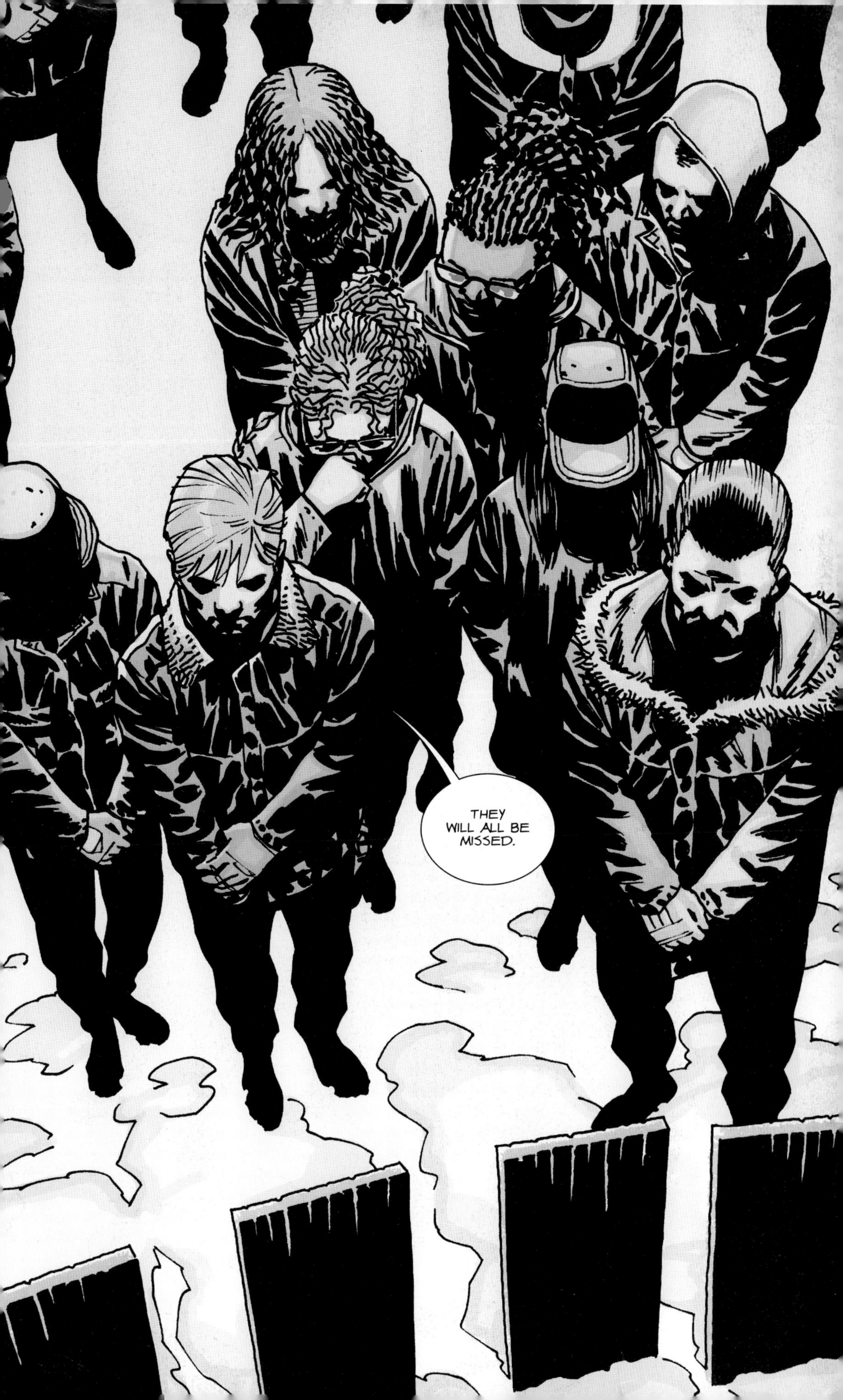
THEY WILL ALL BE MISSED.

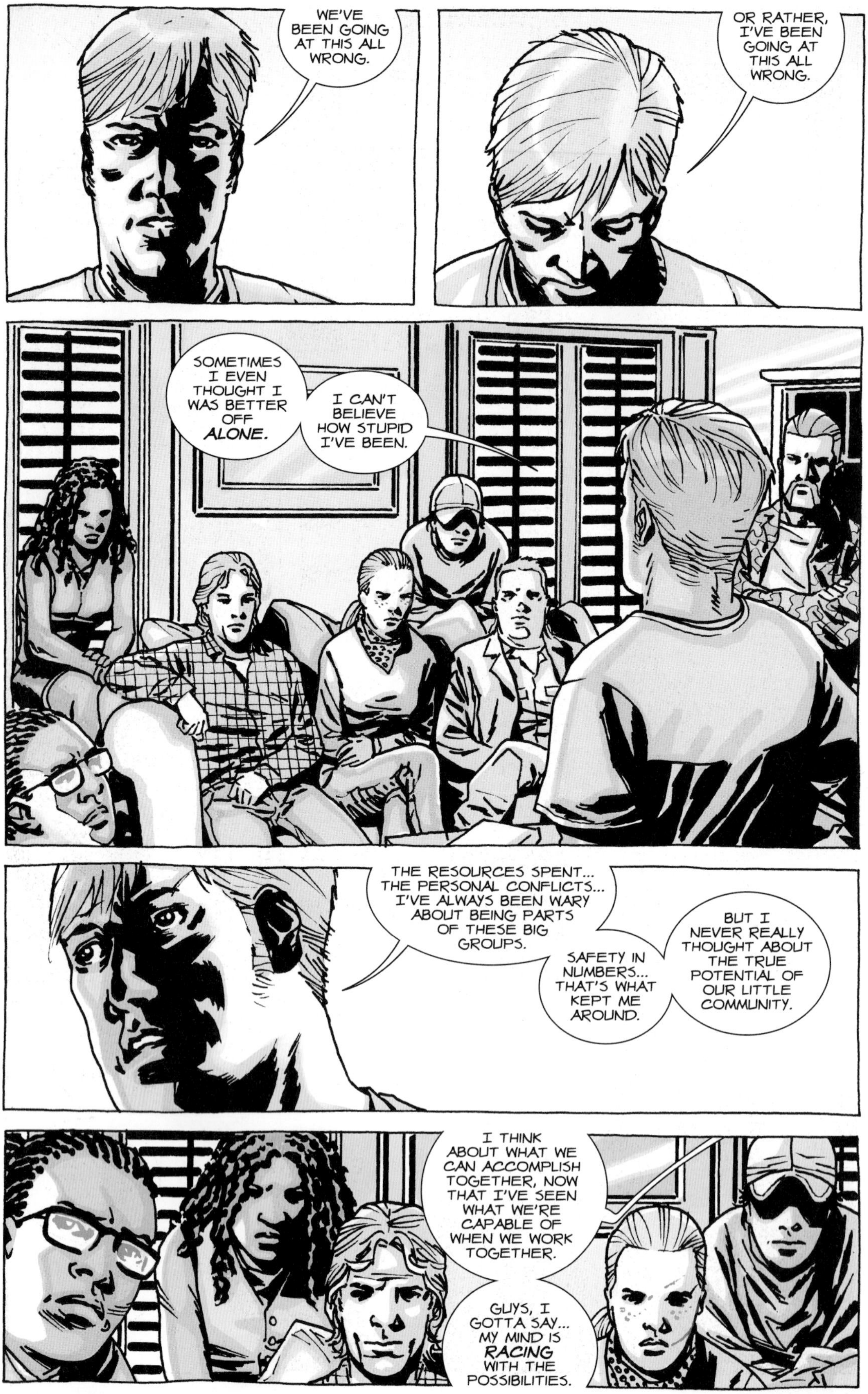

WE'VE BEEN GOING AT THIS ALL WRONG.
OR RATHER, I'VE BEEN GOING AT THIS ALL WRONG.
SOMETIMES I EVEN THOUGHT I WAS BETTER OFF *ALONE.*
I CAN'T BELIEVE HOW STUPID I'VE BEEN.
THE RESOURCES SPENT... THE PERSONAL CONFLICTS... I'VE ALWAYS BEEN WARY ABOUT BEING PARTS OF THESE BIG GROUPS.
SAFETY IN NUMBERS... THAT'S WHAT KEPT ME AROUND.
BUT I NEVER REALLY THOUGHT ABOUT THE TRUE POTENTIAL OF OUR LITTLE COMMUNITY.
I THINK ABOUT WHAT WE CAN ACCOMPLISH TOGETHER, NOW THAT I'VE SEEN WHAT WE'RE CAPABLE OF WHEN WE WORK TOGETHER.
GUYS, I GOTTA SAY... MY MIND IS *RACING* WITH THE POSSIBILITIES.

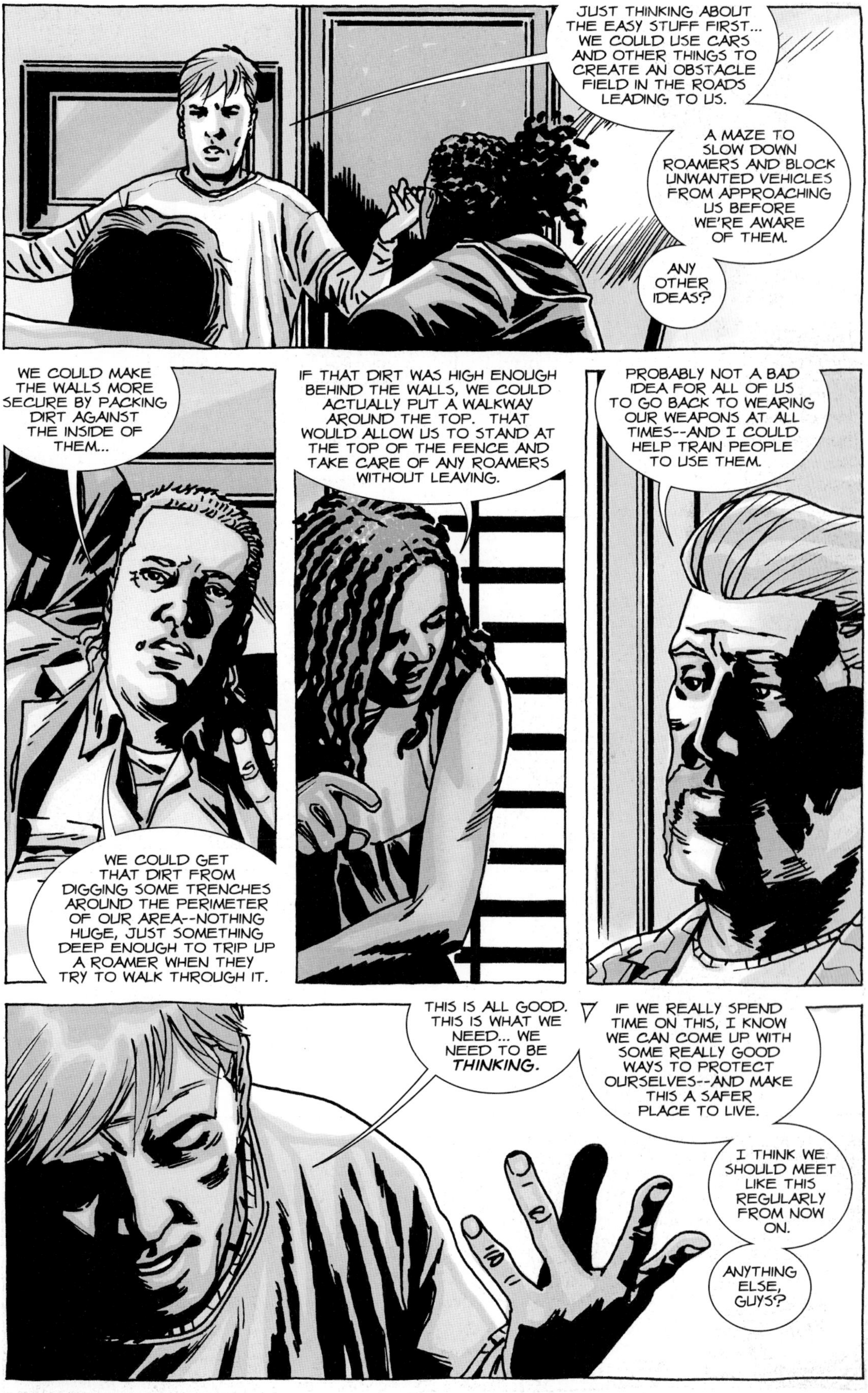
JUST THINKING ABOUT THE EASY STUFF FIRST... WE COULD USE CARS AND OTHER THINGS TO CREATE AN OBSTACLE FIELD IN THE ROADS LEADING TO US.
A MAZE TO SLOW DOWN ROAMERS AND BLOCK UNWANTED VEHICLES FROM APPROACHING US BEFORE WE'RE AWARE OF THEM.
ANY OTHER IDEAS?
WE COULD MAKE THE WALLS MORE SECURE BY PACKING DIRT AGAINST THE INSIDE OF THEM...
WE COULD GET THAT DIRT FROM DIGGING SOME TRENCHES AROUND THE PERIMETER OF OUR AREA--NOTHING HUGE, JUST SOMETHING DEEP ENOUGH TO TRIP UP A ROAMER WHEN THEY TRY TO WALK THROUGH IT.
IF THAT DIRT WAS HIGH ENOUGH BEHIND THE WALLS, WE COULD ACTUALLY PUT A WALKWAY AROUND THE TOP. THAT WOULD ALLOW US TO STAND AT THE TOP OF THE FENCE AND TAKE CARE OF ANY ROAMERS WITHOUT LEAVING.
PROBABLY NOT A BAD IDEA FOR ALL OF US TO GO BACK TO WEARING OUR WEAPONS AT ALL TIMES--AND I COULD HELP TRAIN PEOPLE TO USE THEM.
THIS IS ALL GOOD. THIS IS WHAT WE NEED... WE NEED TO BE *THINKING*.
IF WE REALLY SPEND TIME ON THIS, I KNOW WE CAN COME UP WITH SOME REALLY GOOD WAYS TO PROTECT OURSELVES--AND MAKE THIS A SAFER PLACE TO LIVE.
I THINK WE SHOULD MEET LIKE THIS REGULARLY FROM NOW ON.
ANYTHING ELSE, GUYS?

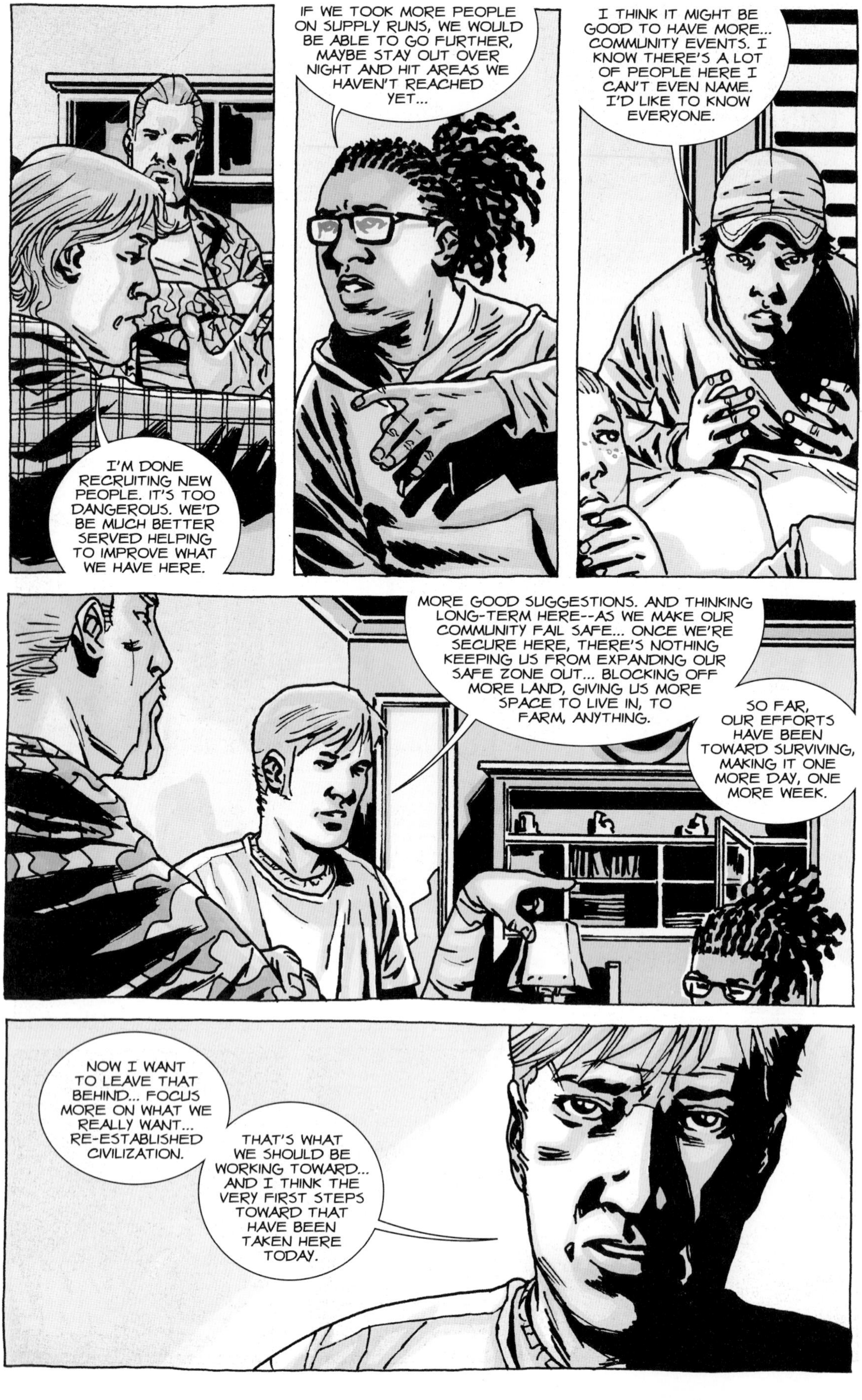
I'M DONE RECRUITING NEW PEOPLE. IT'S TOO DANGEROUS. WE'D BE MUCH BETTER SERVED HELPING TO IMPROVE WHAT WE HAVE HERE.
IF WE TOOK MORE PEOPLE ON SUPPLY RUNS, WE WOULD BE ABLE TO GO FURTHER, MAYBE STAY OUT OVER NIGHT AND HIT AREAS WE HAVEN'T REACHED YET...
I THINK IT MIGHT BE GOOD TO HAVE MORE... COMMUNITY EVENTS. I KNOW THERE'S A LOT OF PEOPLE HERE I CAN'T EVEN NAME. I'D LIKE TO KNOW EVERYONE.
MORE GOOD SUGGESTIONS. AND THINKING LONG-TERM HERE--AS WE MAKE OUR COMMUNITY FAIL SAFE... ONCE WE'RE SECURE HERE, THERE'S NOTHING KEEPING US FROM EXPANDING OUR SAFE ZONE OUT... BLOCKING OFF MORE LAND, GIVING US MORE SPACE TO LIVE IN, TO FARM, ANYTHING.
SO FAR, OUR EFFORTS HAVE BEEN TOWARD SURVIVING, MAKING IT ONE MORE DAY, ONE MORE WEEK.
NOW I WANT TO LEAVE THAT BEHIND... FOCUS MORE ON WHAT WE REALLY WANT... RE-ESTABLISHED CIVILIZATION.
THAT'S WHAT WE SHOULD BE WORKING TOWARD... AND I THINK THE VERY FIRST STEPS TOWARD THAT HAVE BEEN TAKEN HERE TODAY.

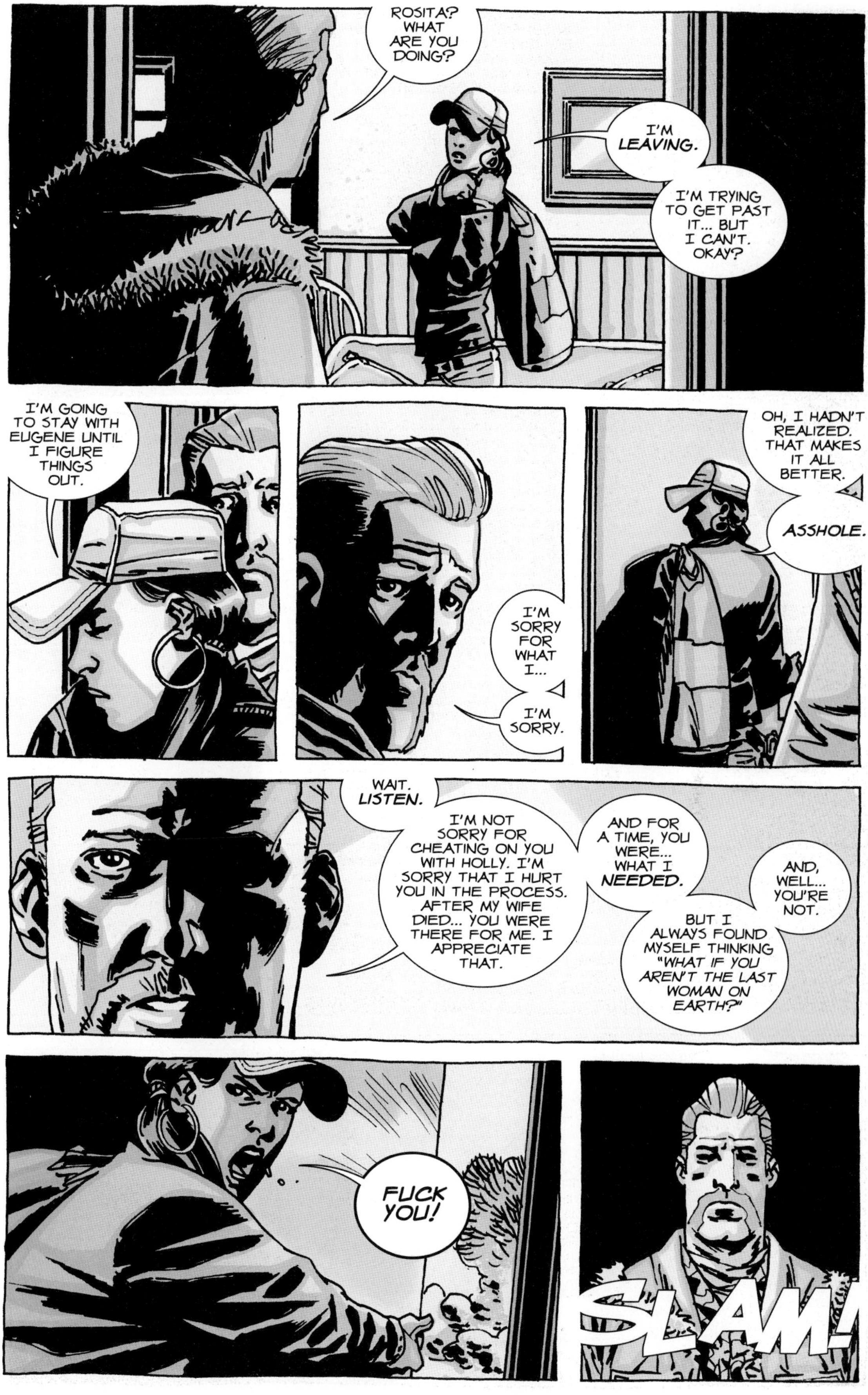

ROSITA? WHAT ARE YOU DOING?
I'M *LEAVING.*
I'M TRYING TO GET PAST IT... BUT I CAN'T. OKAY?
I'M GOING TO STAY WITH EUGENE UNTIL I FIGURE THINGS OUT.
I'M SORRY FOR WHAT I...
I'M SORRY.
OH, I HADN'T REALIZED. THAT MAKES IT ALL BETTER.
ASSHOLE.
WAIT. *LISTEN.*
I'M NOT SORRY FOR CHEATING ON YOU WITH HOLLY. I'M SORRY THAT I HURT YOU IN THE PROCESS. AFTER MY WIFE DIED... YOU WERE THERE FOR ME. I APPRECIATE THAT.
AND FOR A TIME, YOU WERE... WHAT I *NEEDED.*
BUT I ALWAYS FOUND MYSELF THINKING *"WHAT IF YOU AREN'T THE LAST WOMAN ON EARTH?"*
AND, WELL... YOU'RE NOT.
FUCK YOU!
SLAM!

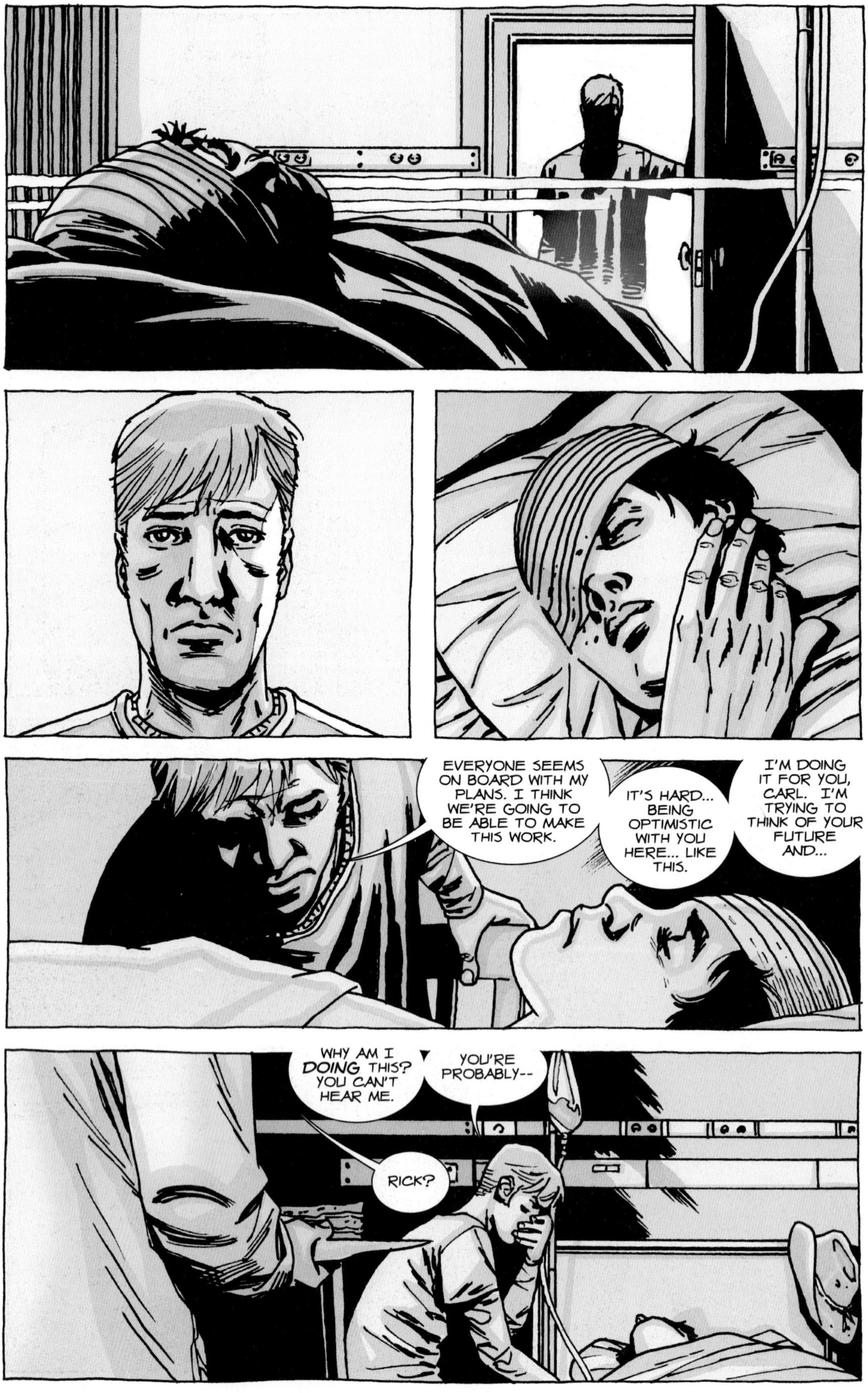
EVERYONE SEEMS ON BOARD WITH MY PLANS. I THINK WE'RE GOING TO BE ABLE TO MAKE THIS WORK.
IT'S HARD... BEING OPTIMISTIC WITH YOU HERE... LIKE THIS.
I'M DOING IT FOR YOU, CARL. I'M TRYING TO THINK OF YOUR FUTURE AND...
WHY AM I DOING THIS? YOU CAN'T HEAR ME.
YOU'RE PROBABLY--
RICK?

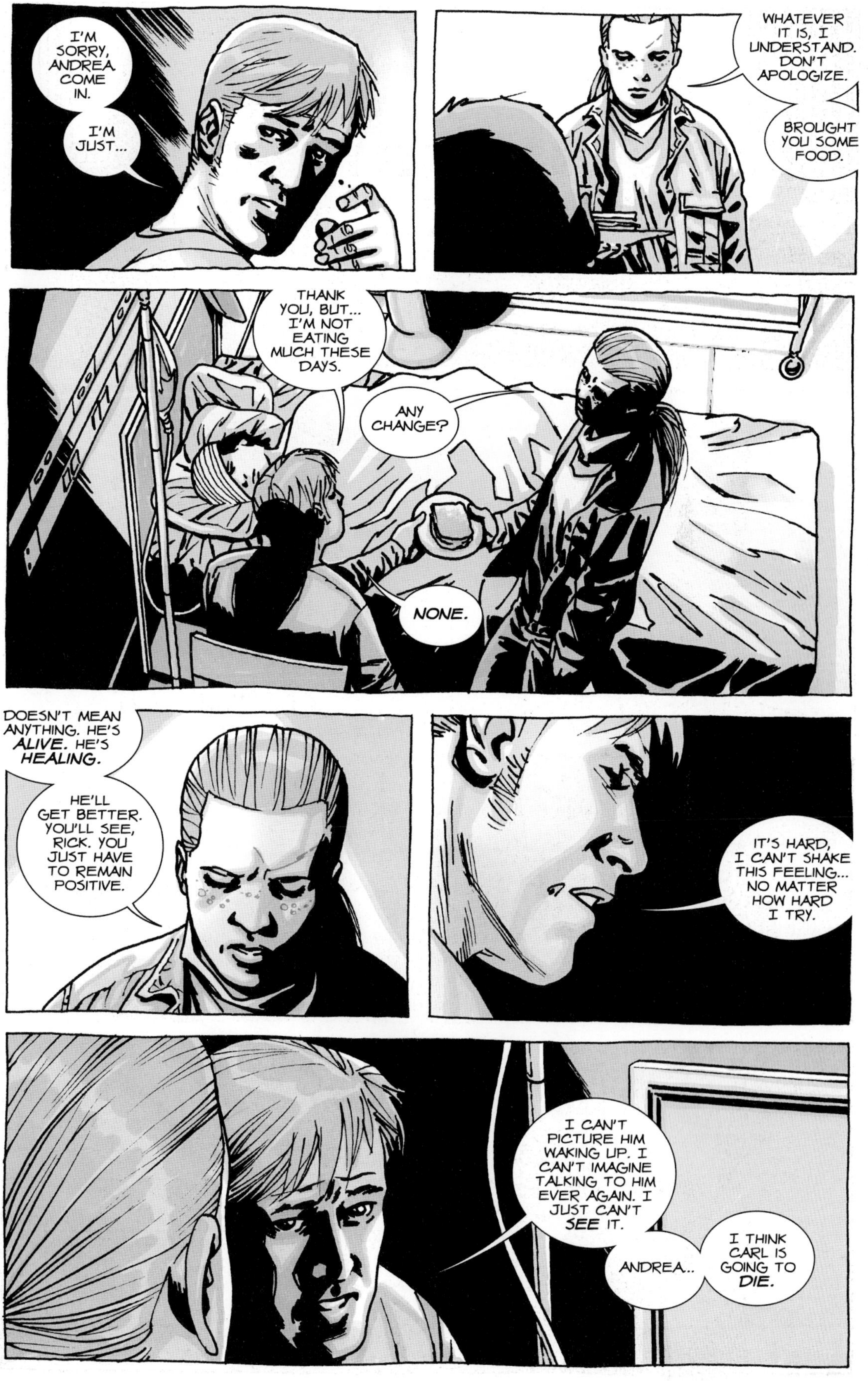
I'M SORRY, ANDREA COME IN.
I'M JUST...
WHATEVER IT IS, I UNDERSTAND. DON'T APOLOGIZE.
BROUGHT YOU SOME FOOD.
THANK YOU, BUT... I'M NOT EATING MUCH THESE DAYS.
ANY CHANGE?
NONE.
DOESN'T MEAN ANYTHING. HE'S ALIVE. HE'S HEALING.
HE'LL GET BETTER. YOU'LL SEE, RICK. YOU JUST HAVE TO REMAIN POSITIVE.
IT'S HARD, I CAN'T SHAKE THIS FEELING... NO MATTER HOW HARD I TRY.
I CAN'T PICTURE HIM WAKING UP. I CAN'T IMAGINE TALKING TO HIM EVER AGAIN. I JUST CAN'T SEE IT.
ANDREA..
I THINK CARL IS GOING TO DIE.

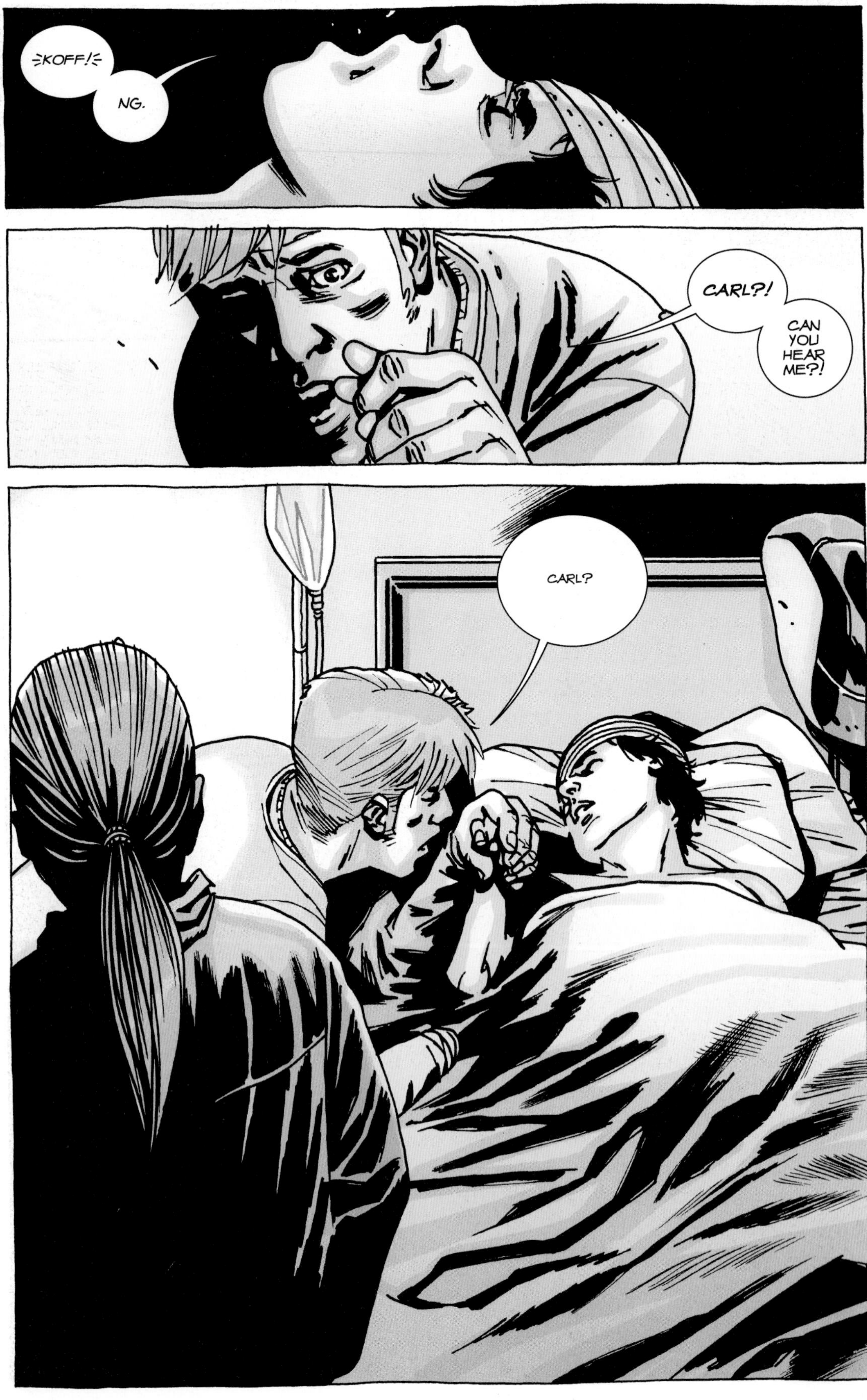

=KOFF!=
NG.
CARL?!
CAN YOU HEAR ME?!
CARL?

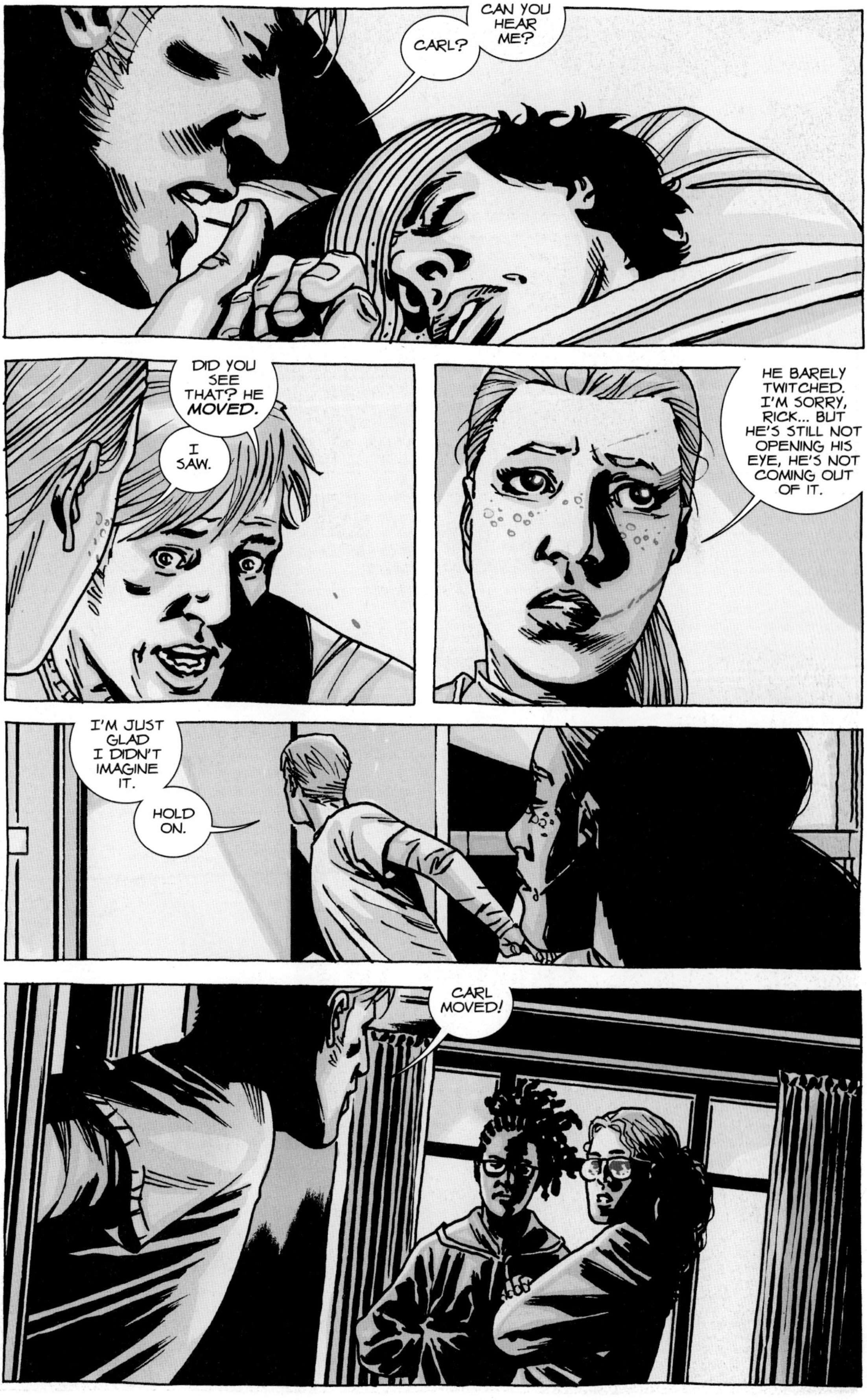

CARL?
CAN YOU HEAR ME?
DID YOU SEE THAT? HE *MOVED.*
I SAW.
HE BARELY TWITCHED. I'M SORRY, RICK... BUT HE'S STILL NOT OPENING HIS EYE, HE'S NOT COMING OUT OF IT.
I'M JUST GLAD I DIDN'T IMAGINE IT.
HOLD ON.
CARL MOVED!

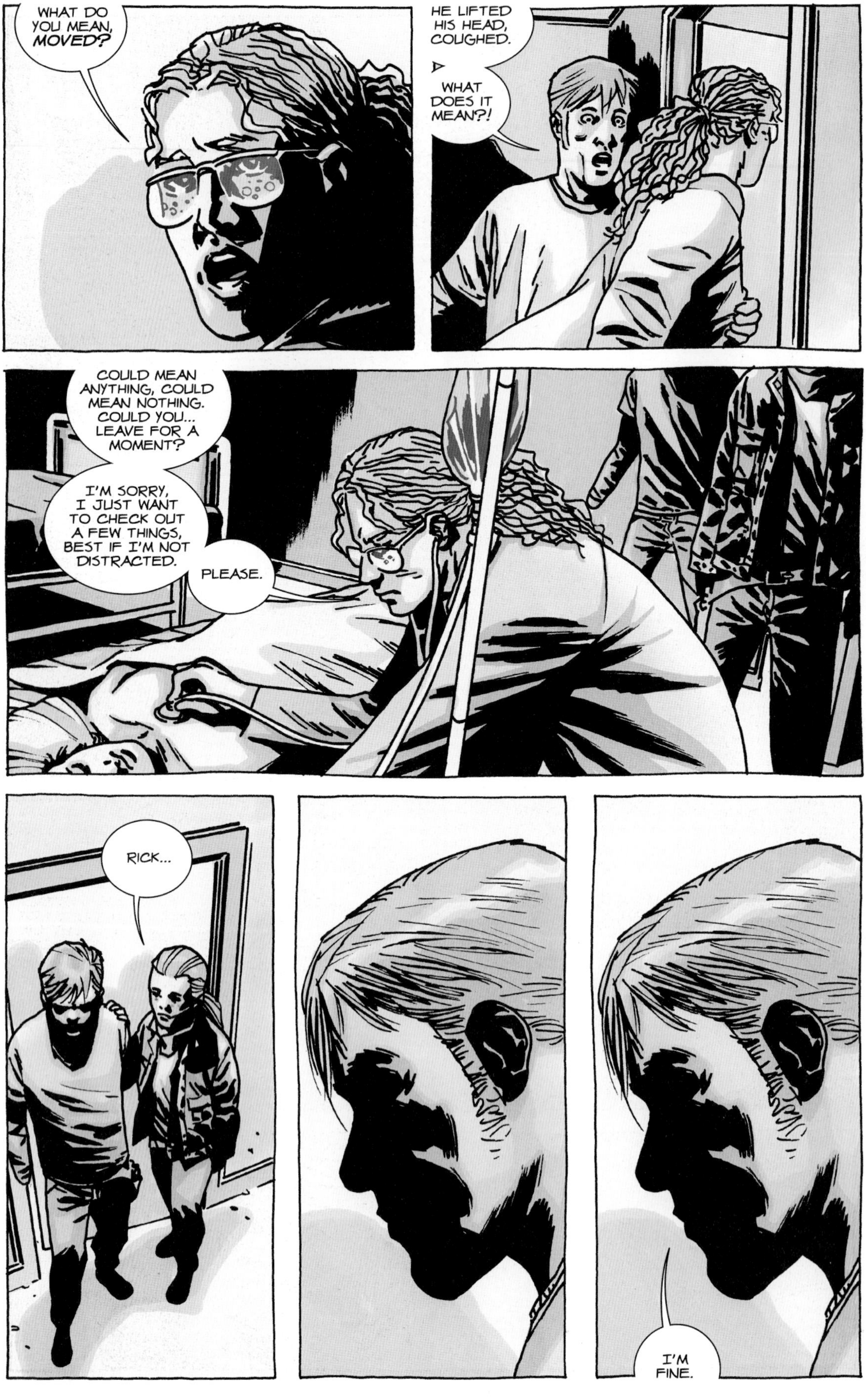

WHAT DO YOU MEAN, *MOVED?*
HE LIFTED HIS HEAD, COUGHED.
WHAT DOES IT MEAN?!
COULD MEAN ANYTHING, COULD MEAN NOTHING. COULD YOU... LEAVE FOR A MOMENT?
I'M SORRY, I JUST WANT TO CHECK OUT A FEW THINGS, BEST IF I'M NOT DISTRACTED.
PLEASE.
RICK...
I'M FINE.

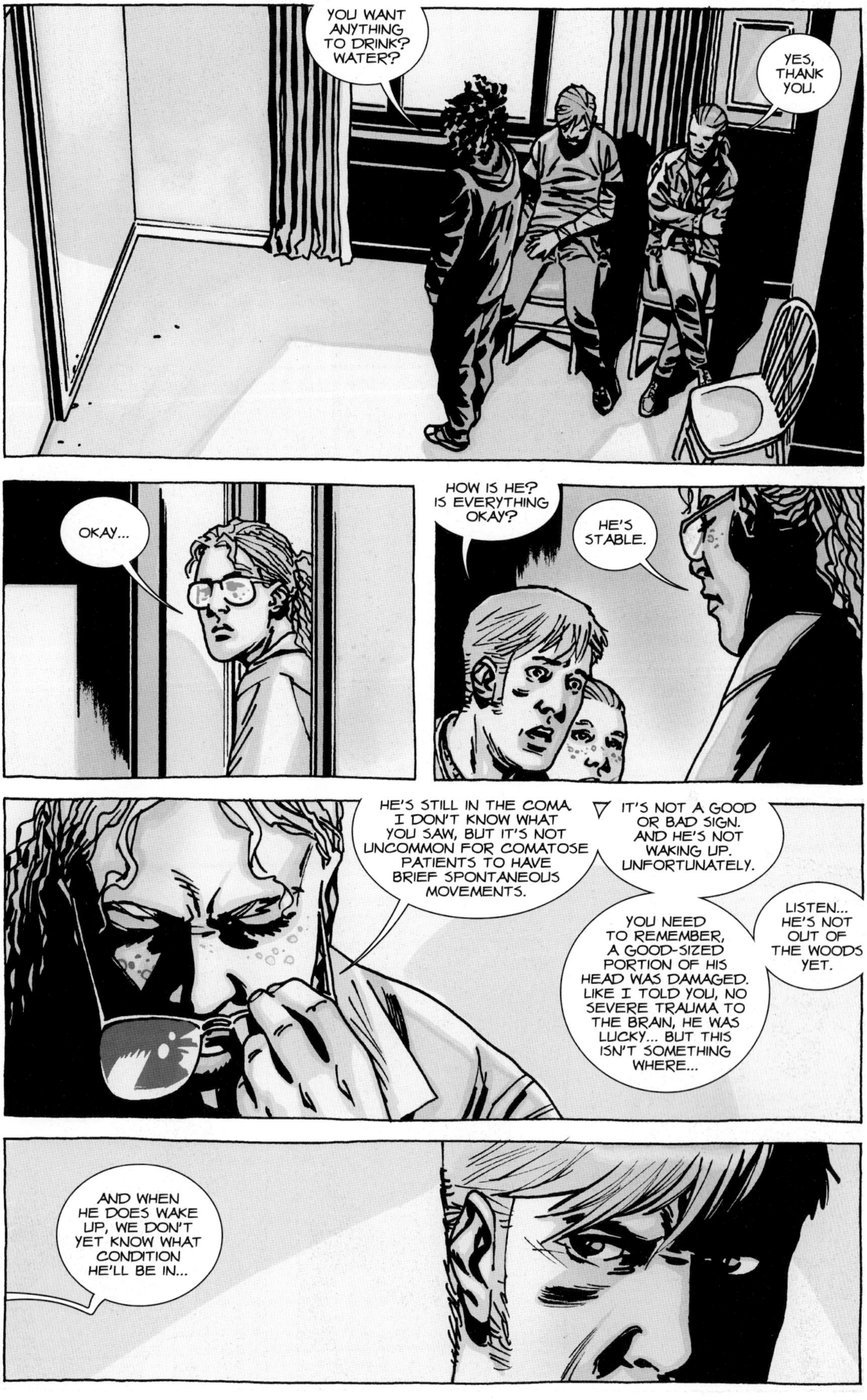
YOU WANT ANYTHING TO DRINK? WATER?
YES, THANK YOU.
OKAY...
HOW IS HE? IS EVERYTHING OKAY?
HE'S STABLE.
HE'S STILL IN THE COMA. I DON'T KNOW WHAT YOU SAW, BUT IT'S NOT UNCOMMON FOR COMATOSE PATIENTS TO HAVE BRIEF SPONTANEOUS MOVEMENTS.
IT'S NOT A GOOD OR BAD SIGN. AND HE'S NOT WAKING UP. UNFORTUNATELY.
YOU NEED TO REMEMBER, A GOOD-SIZED PORTION OF HIS HEAD WAS DAMAGED. LIKE I TOLD YOU, NO SEVERE TRAUMA TO THE BRAIN, HE WAS LUCKY... BUT THIS ISN'T SOMETHING WHERE...
LISTEN... HE'S NOT OUT OF THE WOODS YET.
AND WHEN HE DOES WAKE UP, WE DON'T YET KNOW WHAT CONDITION HE'LL BE IN...

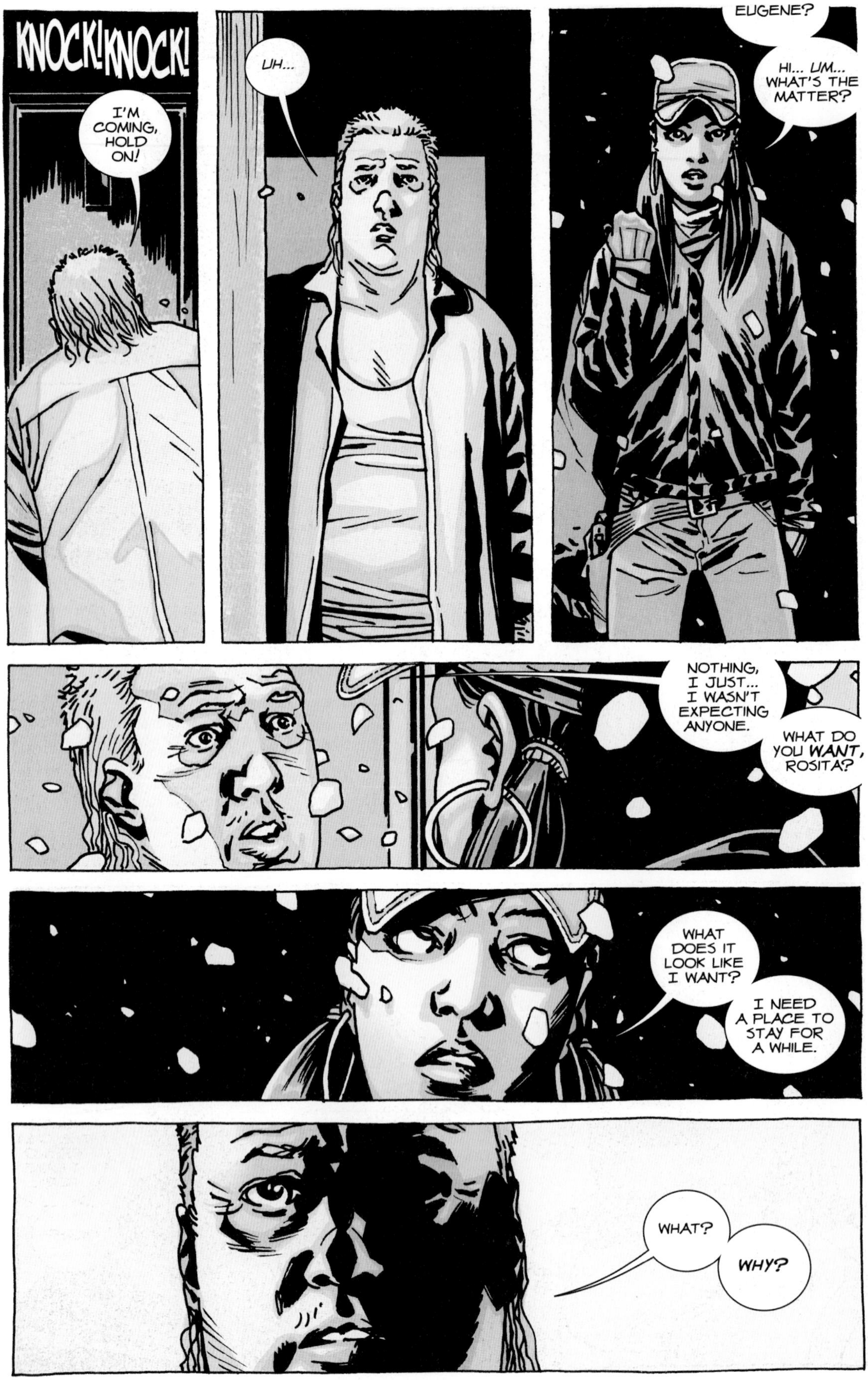
KNOCK! KNOCK!
I'M COMING, HOLD ON!
UH...
EUGENE?
HI... UM... WHAT'S THE MATTER?
NOTHING, I JUST... I WASN'T EXPECTING ANYONE.
WHAT DO YOU **WANT**, ROSITA?
WHAT DOES IT LOOK LIKE I WANT?
I NEED A PLACE TO STAY FOR A WHILE.
WHAT?
WHY?

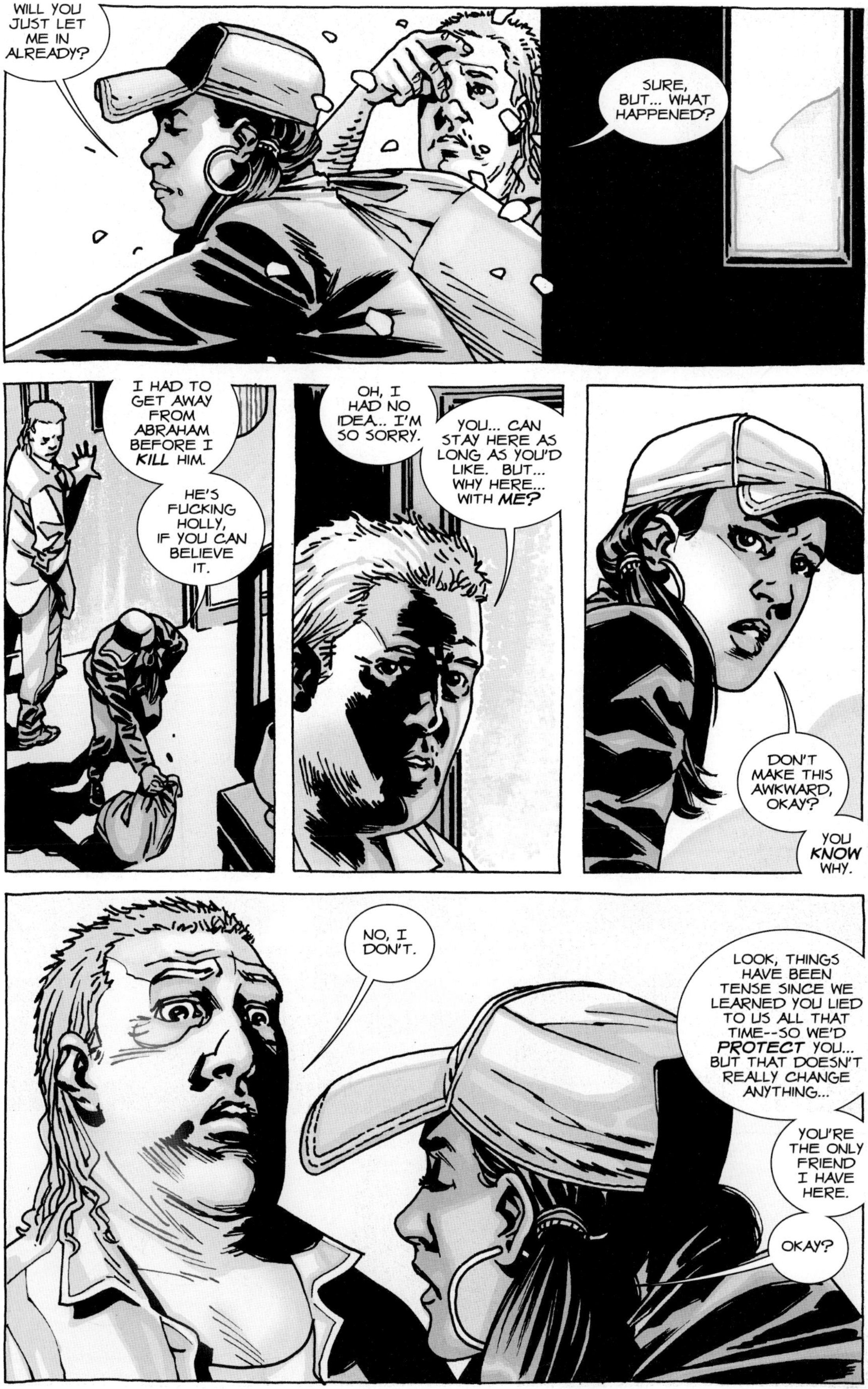
WILL YOU JUST LET ME IN ALREADY?
SURE, BUT... WHAT HAPPENED?
I HAD TO GET AWAY FROM ABRAHAM BEFORE I KILL HIM.
HE'S FUCKING HOLLY, IF YOU CAN BELIEVE IT.
OH, I HAD NO IDEA... I'M SO SORRY.
YOU... CAN STAY HERE AS LONG AS YOU'D LIKE. BUT... WHY HERE... WITH ME?
DON'T MAKE THIS AWKWARD, OKAY?
YOU KNOW WHY.
NO, I DON'T.
LOOK, THINGS HAVE BEEN TENSE SINCE WE LEARNED YOU LIED TO US ALL THAT TIME--SO WE'D PROTECT YOU... BUT THAT DOESN'T REALLY CHANGE ANYTHING...
YOU'RE THE ONLY FRIEND I HAVE HERE.
OKAY?

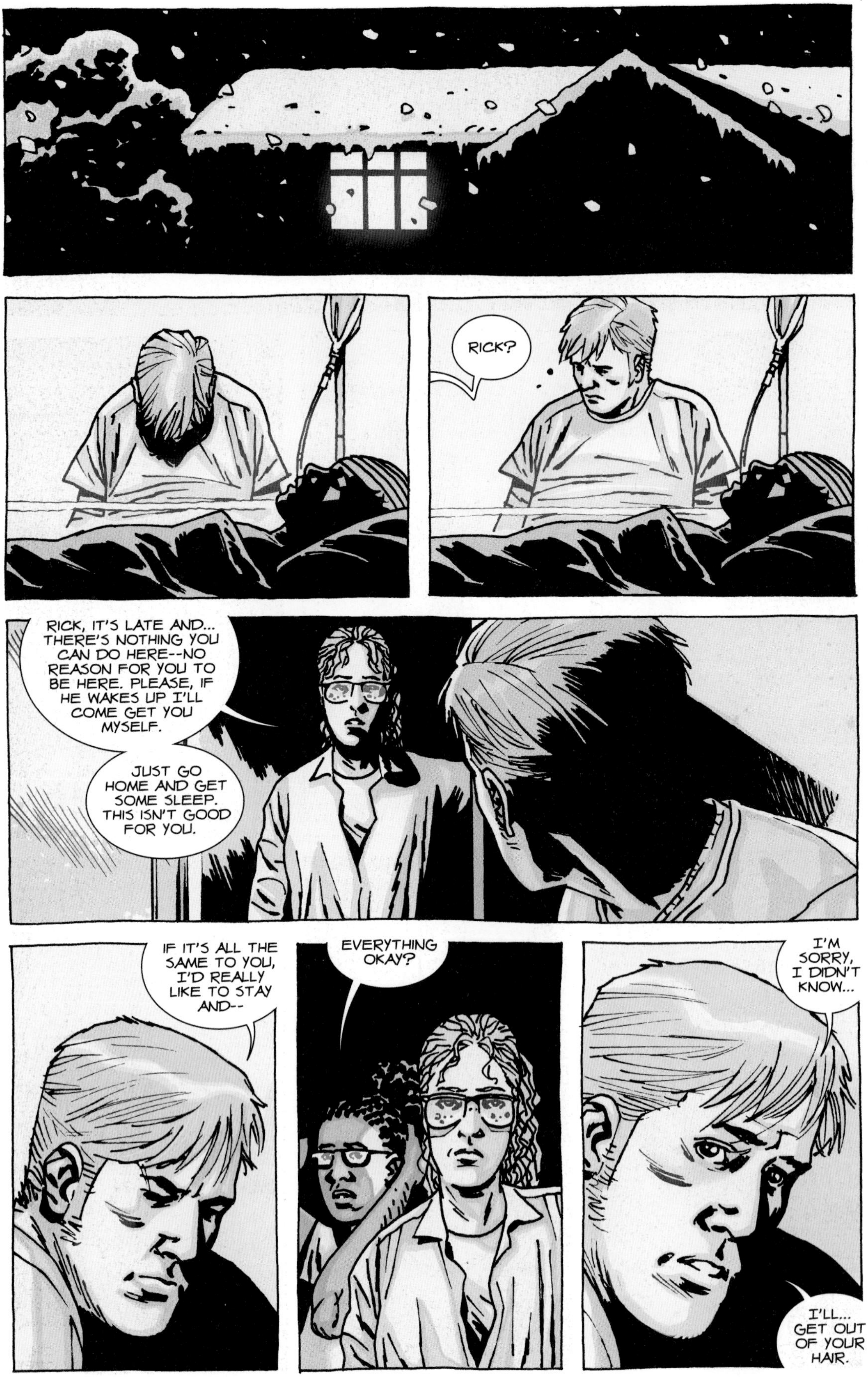
RICK?
RICK, IT'S LATE AND... THERE'S NOTHING YOU CAN DO HERE--NO REASON FOR YOU TO BE HERE. PLEASE, IF HE WAKES UP I'LL COME GET YOU MYSELF.
JUST GO HOME AND GET SOME SLEEP. THIS ISN'T GOOD FOR YOU.
IF IT'S ALL THE SAME TO YOU, I'D REALLY LIKE TO STAY AND--
EVERYTHING OKAY?
I'M SORRY, I DIDN'T KNOW...
I'LL... GET OUT OF YOUR HAIR.

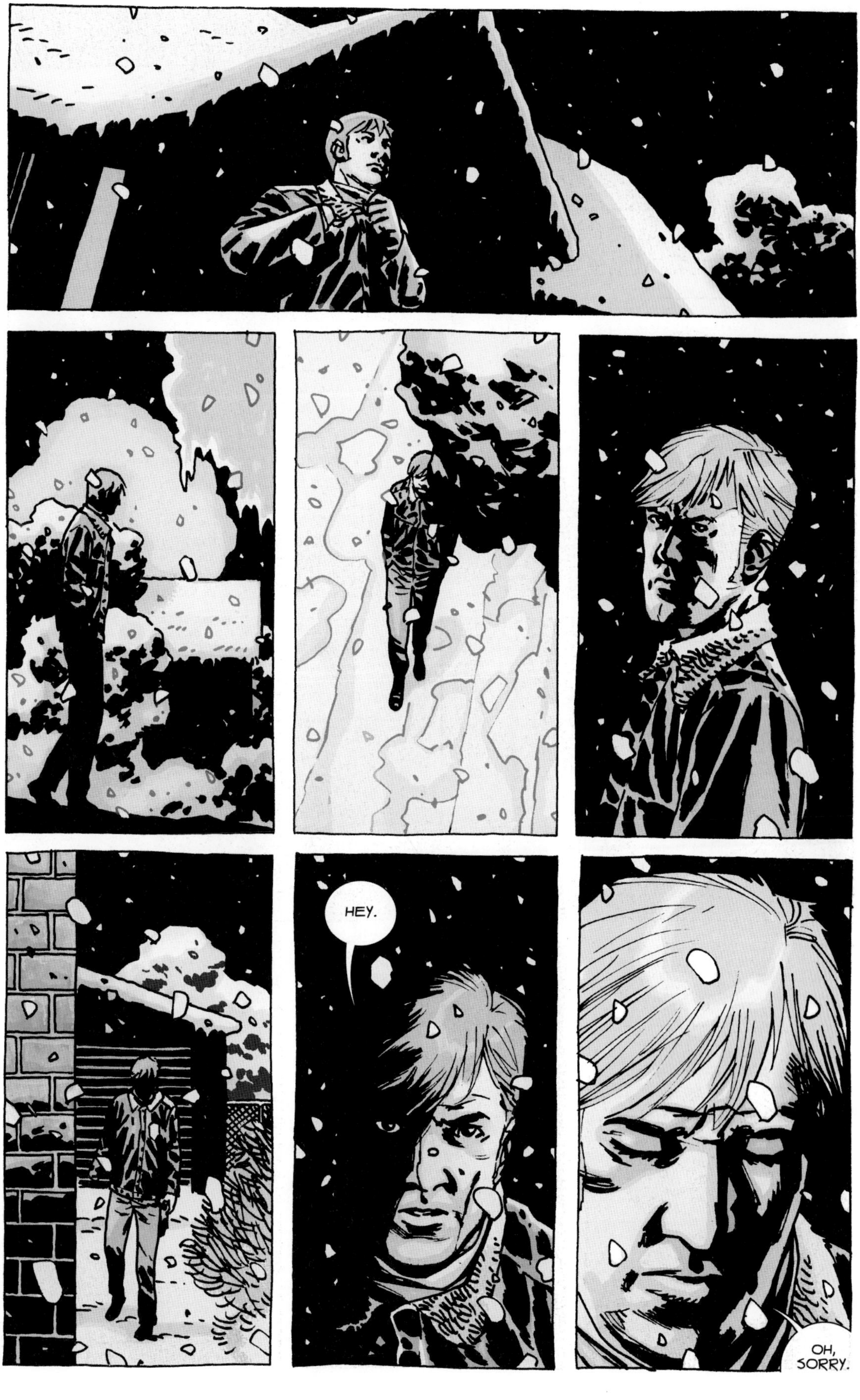
HEY.
OH, SORRY.

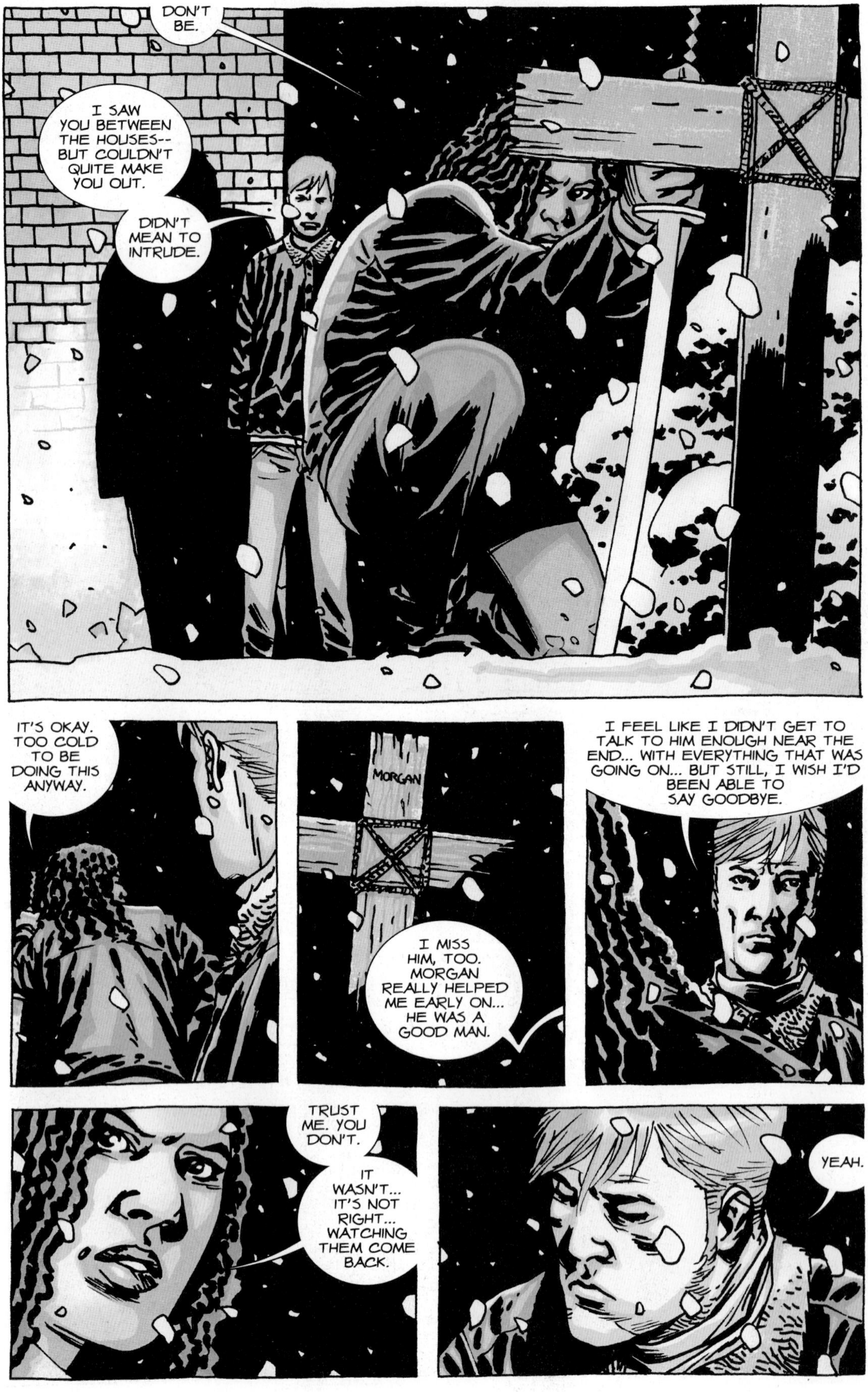
DON'T BE.
I SAW YOU BETWEEN THE HOUSES-- BUT COULDN'T QUITE MAKE YOU OUT.
DIDN'T MEAN TO INTRUDE.
IT'S OKAY. TOO COLD TO BE DOING THIS ANYWAY.
MORGAN
I MISS HIM, TOO. MORGAN REALLY HELPED ME EARLY ON... HE WAS A GOOD MAN.
I FEEL LIKE I DIDN'T GET TO TALK TO HIM ENOUGH NEAR THE END... WITH EVERYTHING THAT WAS GOING ON... BUT STILL, I WISH I'D BEEN ABLE TO SAY GOODBYE.
TRUST ME. YOU DON'T.
IT WASN'T... IT'S NOT RIGHT... WATCHING THEM COME BACK.
YEAH.

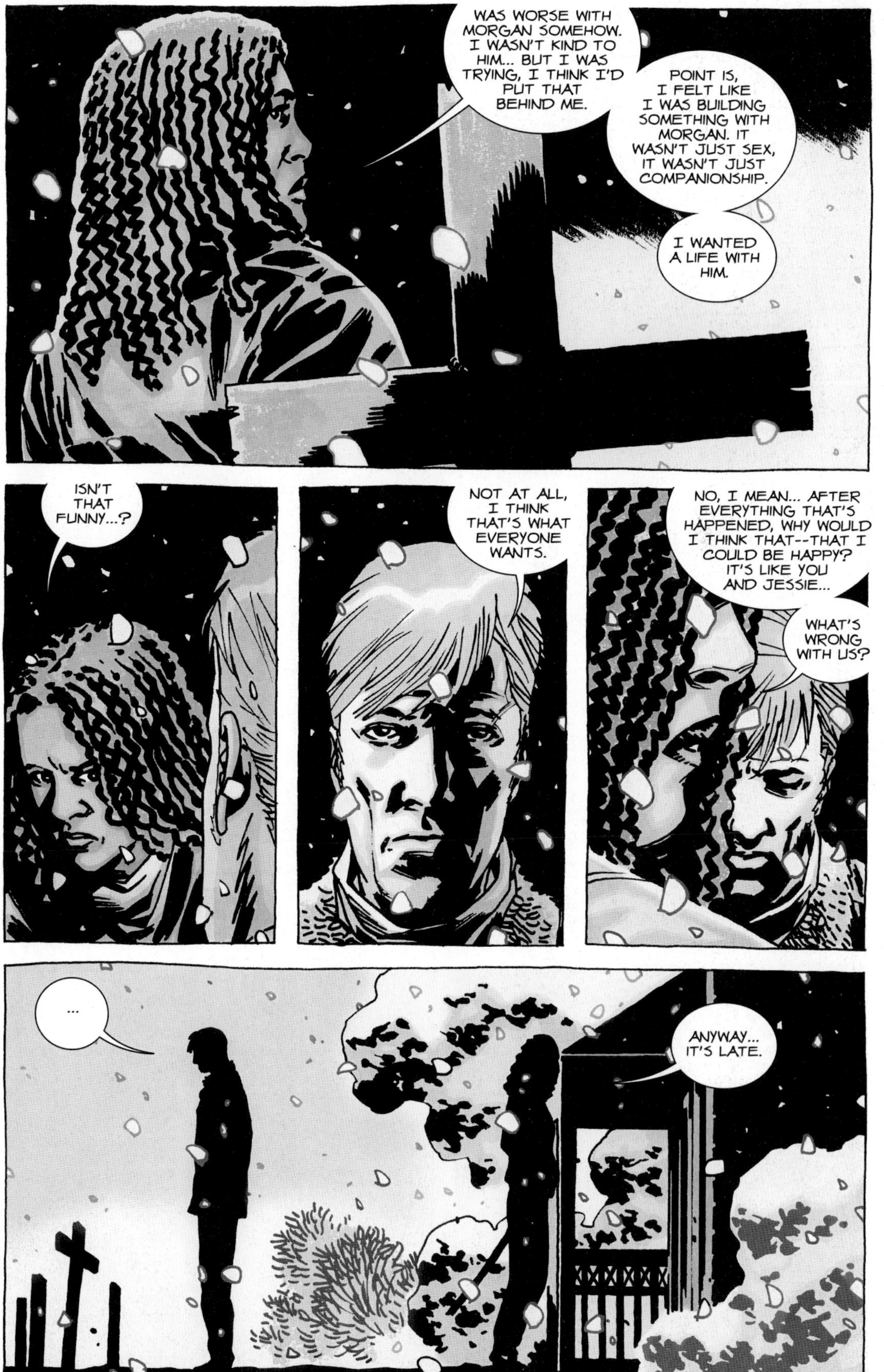
WAS WORSE WITH MORGAN SOMEHOW. I WASN'T KIND TO HIM... BUT I WAS TRYING, I THINK I'D PUT THAT BEHIND ME.
POINT IS, I FELT LIKE I WAS BUILDING SOMETHING WITH MORGAN. IT WASN'T JUST SEX, IT WASN'T JUST COMPANIONSHIP.
I WANTED A LIFE WITH HIM.
ISN'T THAT FUNNY...?
NOT AT ALL, I THINK THAT'S WHAT EVERYONE WANTS.
NO, I MEAN... AFTER EVERYTHING THAT'S HAPPENED, WHY WOULD I THINK THAT--THAT I COULD BE HAPPY? IT'S LIKE YOU AND JESSIE...
WHAT'S WRONG WITH US?
...
ANYWAY... IT'S LATE.

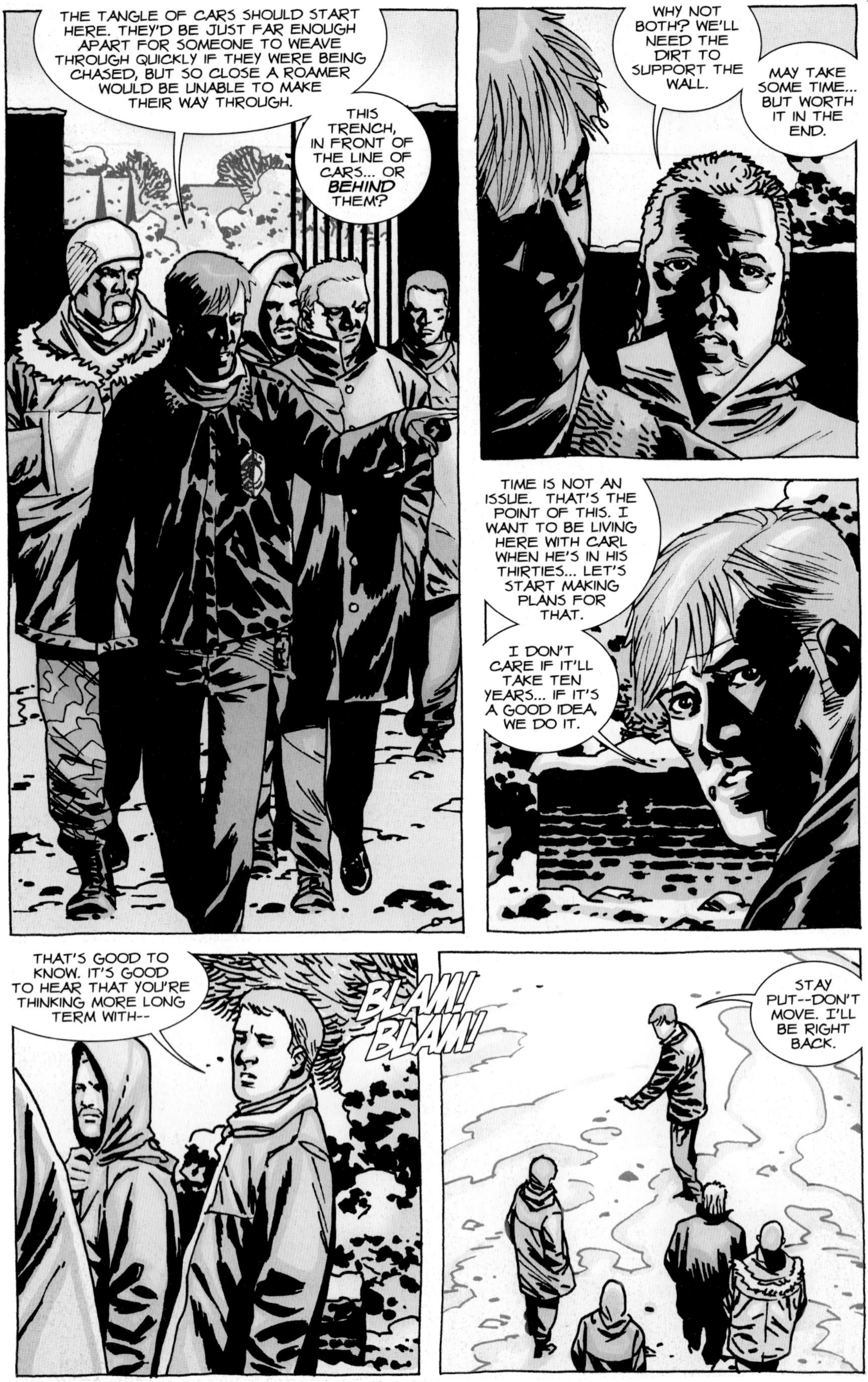
THE TANGLE OF CARS SHOULD START HERE. THEY'D BE JUST FAR ENOUGH APART FOR SOMEONE TO WEAVE THROUGH QUICKLY IF THEY WERE BEING CHASED, BUT SO CLOSE A ROAMER WOULD BE UNABLE TO MAKE THEIR WAY THROUGH.
THIS TRENCH, IN FRONT OF THE LINE OF CARS... OR *BEHIND* THEM?
WHY NOT BOTH? WE'LL NEED THE DIRT TO SUPPORT THE WALL.
MAY TAKE SOME TIME... BUT WORTH IT IN THE END.
TIME IS NOT AN ISSUE. THAT'S THE POINT OF THIS. I WANT TO BE LIVING HERE WITH CARL WHEN HE'S IN HIS THIRTIES... LET'S START MAKING PLANS FOR THAT.
I DON'T CARE IF IT'LL TAKE TEN YEARS... IF IT'S A GOOD IDEA, WE DO IT.
THAT'S GOOD TO KNOW. IT'S GOOD TO HEAR THAT YOU'RE THINKING MORE LONG TERM WITH--
BLAM! BLAM!
STAY PUT--DON'T MOVE. I'LL BE RIGHT BACK.

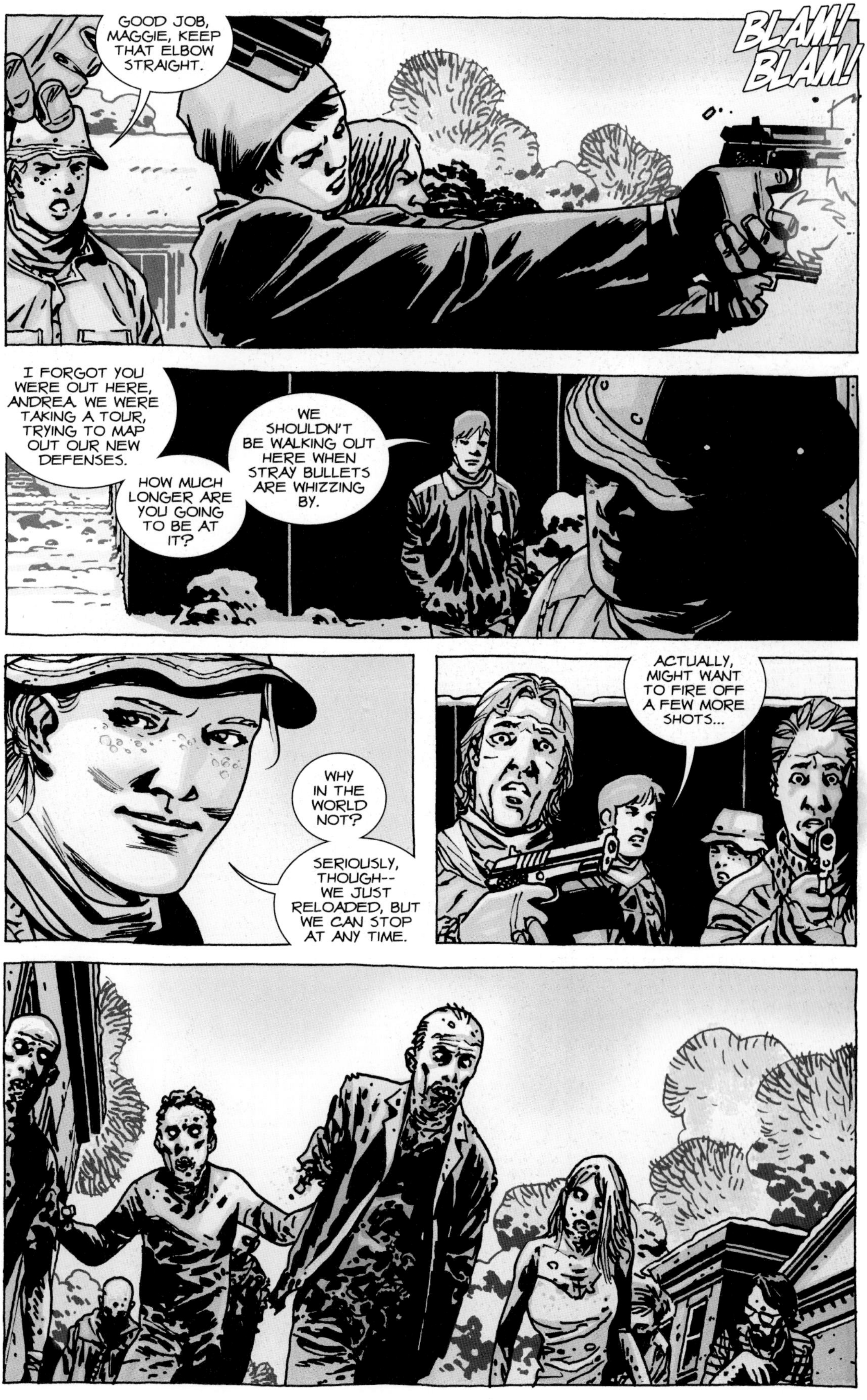
GOOD JOB, MAGGIE, KEEP THAT ELBOW STRAIGHT.
BLAM! BLAM!
I FORGOT YOU WERE OUT HERE, ANDREA. WE WERE TAKING A TOUR, TRYING TO MAP OUT OUR NEW DEFENSES.
HOW MUCH LONGER ARE YOU GOING TO BE AT IT?
WE SHOULDN'T BE WALKING OUT HERE WHEN STRAY BULLETS ARE WHIZZING BY.
WHY IN THE WORLD NOT?
SERIOUSLY, THOUGH-- WE JUST RELOADED, BUT WE CAN STOP AT ANY TIME.
ACTUALLY, MIGHT WANT TO FIRE OFF A FEW MORE SHOTS...

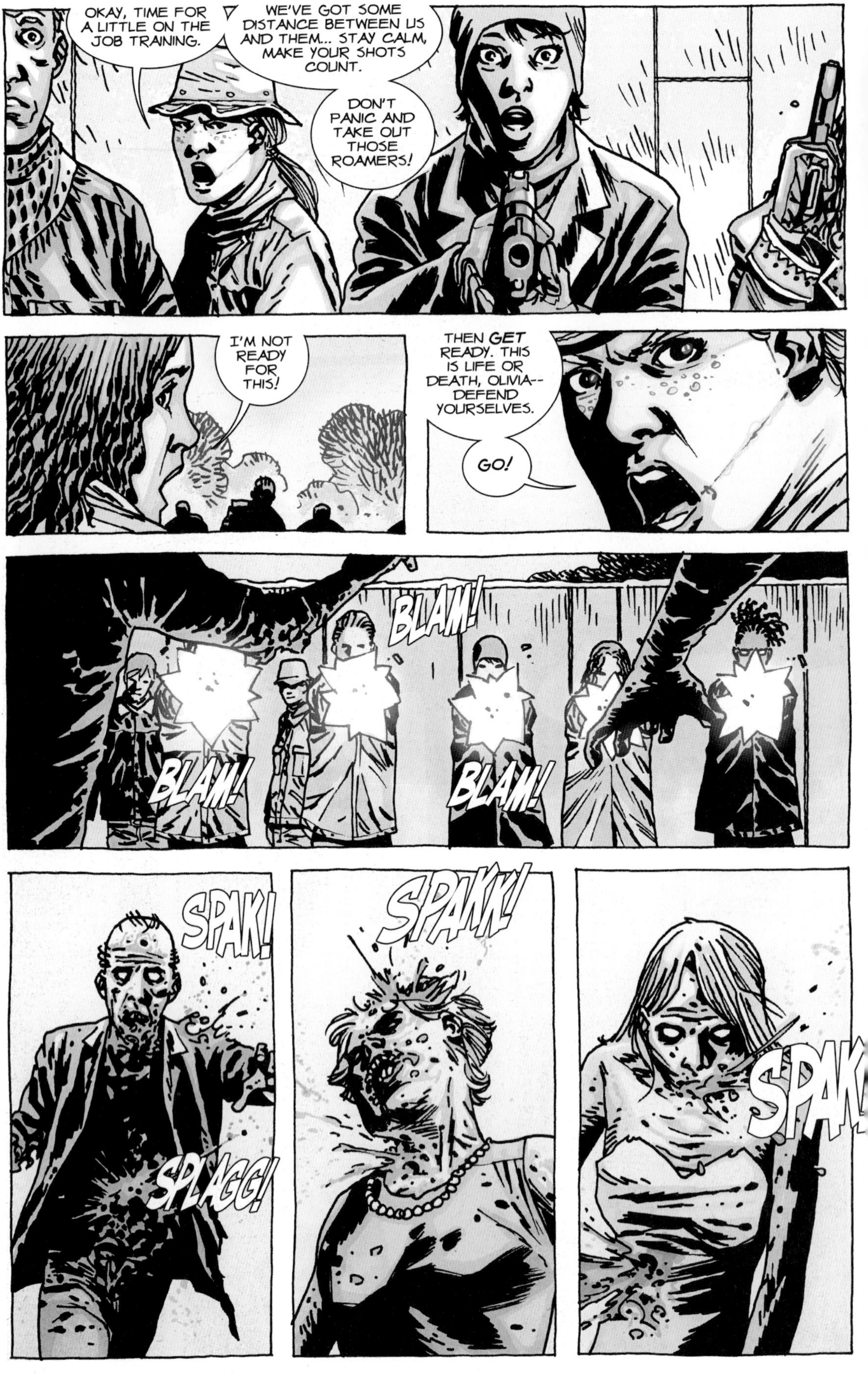
OKAY, TIME FOR A LITTLE ON THE JOB TRAINING.
WE'VE GOT SOME DISTANCE BETWEEN US AND THEM... STAY CALM, MAKE YOUR SHOTS COUNT.
DON'T PANIC AND TAKE OUT THOSE ROAMERS!
I'M NOT READY FOR THIS!
THEN GET READY. THIS IS LIFE OR DEATH, OLIVIA-- DEFEND YOURSELVES.
GO!
BLAM!
BLAM!
BLAM!
SPAK!
SPLAGG!
SPAKK!
SPAK!

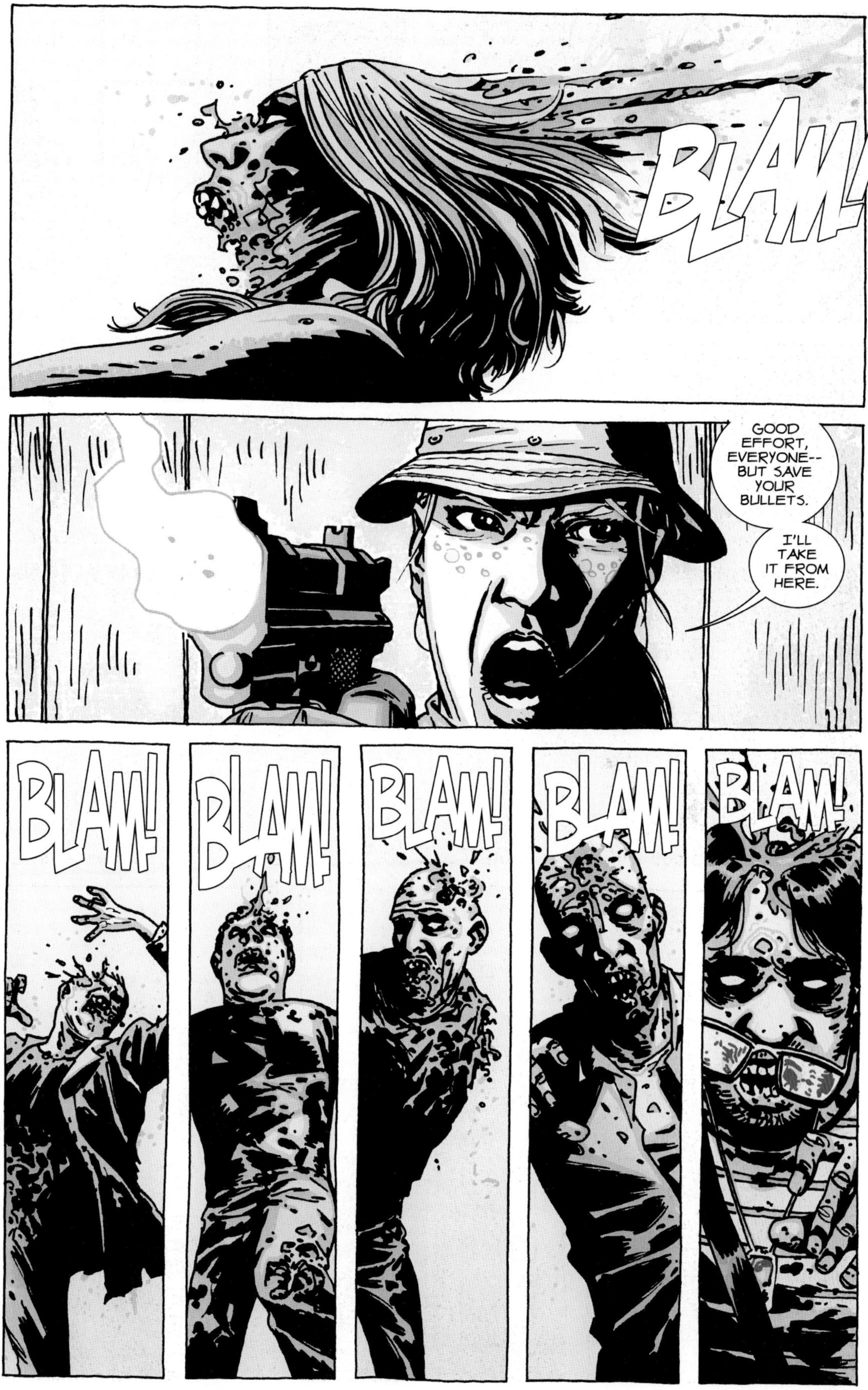

BLAM!
GOOD EFFORT, EVERYONE-- BUT SAVE YOUR BULLETS.
I'LL TAKE IT FROM HERE.
BLAM!
BLAM!
BLAM!
BLAM!
BLAM!

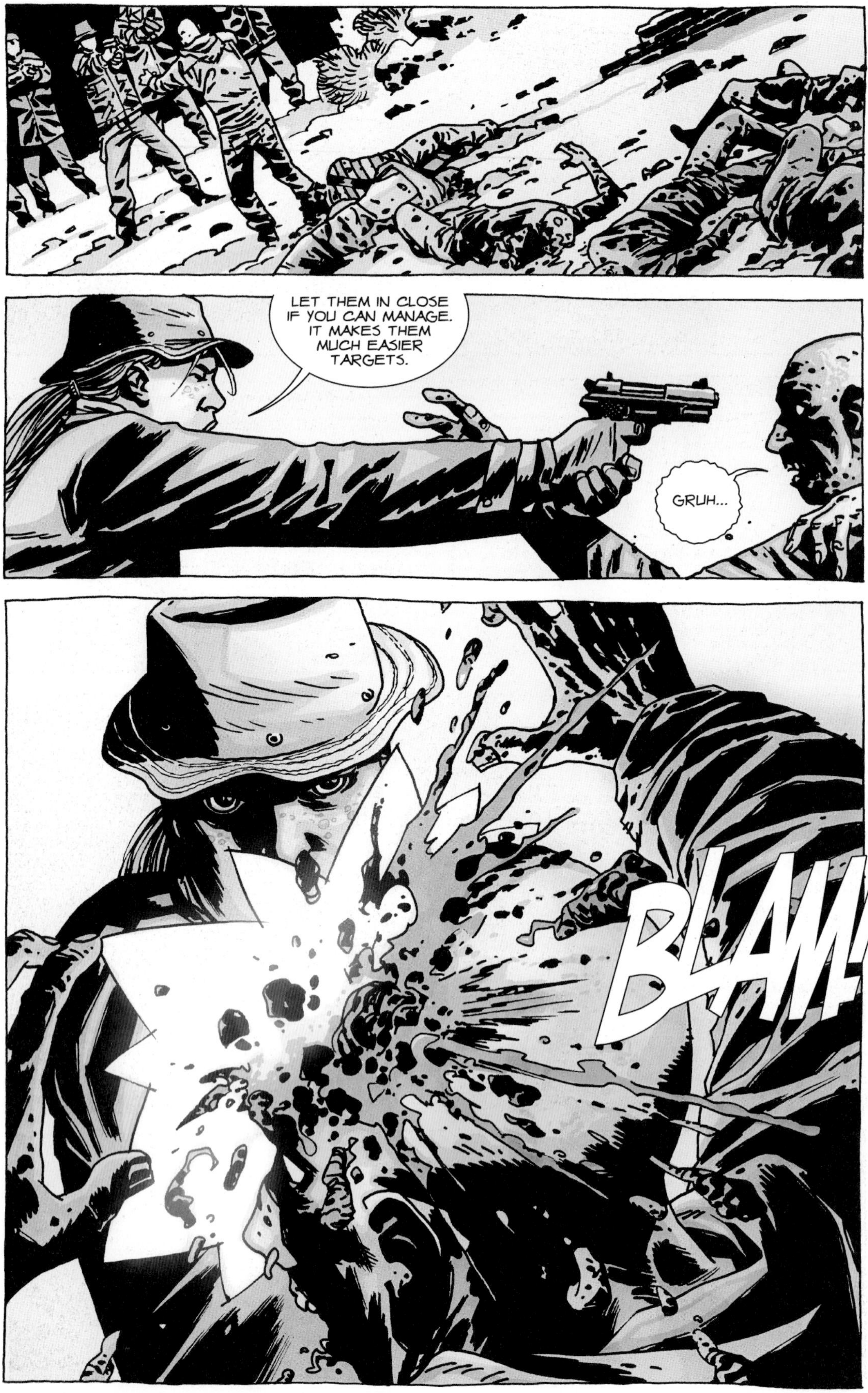
LET THEM IN CLOSE IF YOU CAN MANAGE. IT MAKES THEM MUCH EASIER TARGETS.
GRUH...
BLAM!!

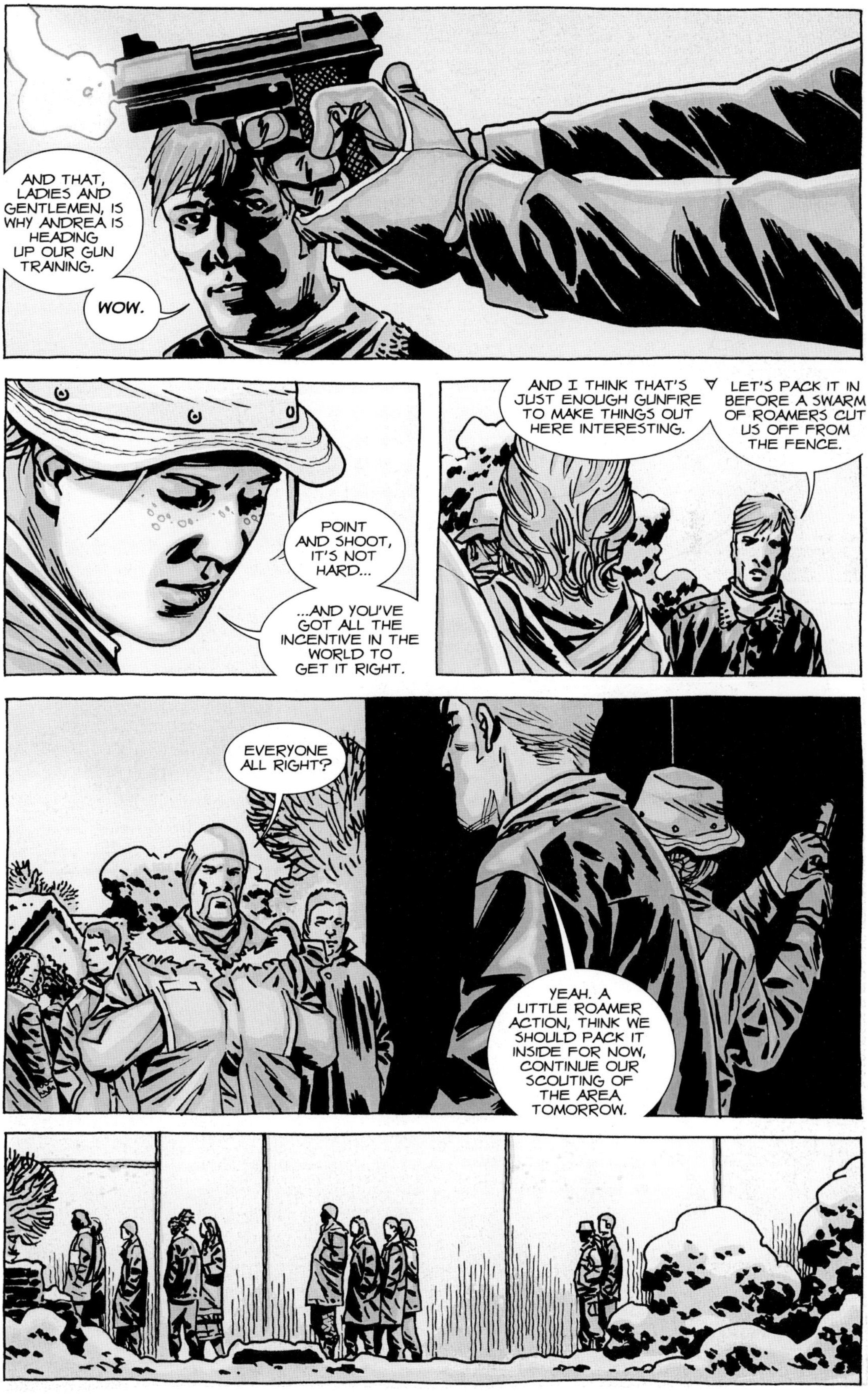
AND THAT, LADIES AND GENTLEMEN, IS WHY ANDREA IS HEADING UP OUR GUN TRAINING.
WOW.
POINT AND SHOOT, IT'S NOT HARD...
...AND YOU'VE GOT ALL THE INCENTIVE IN THE WORLD TO GET IT RIGHT.
AND I THINK THAT'S JUST ENOUGH GUNFIRE TO MAKE THINGS OUT HERE INTERESTING.
LET'S PACK IT IN BEFORE A SWARM OF ROAMERS CUT US OFF FROM THE FENCE.
EVERYONE ALL RIGHT?
YEAH. A LITTLE ROAMER ACTION, THINK WE SHOULD PACK IT INSIDE FOR NOW, CONTINUE OUR SCOUTING OF THE AREA TOMORROW.

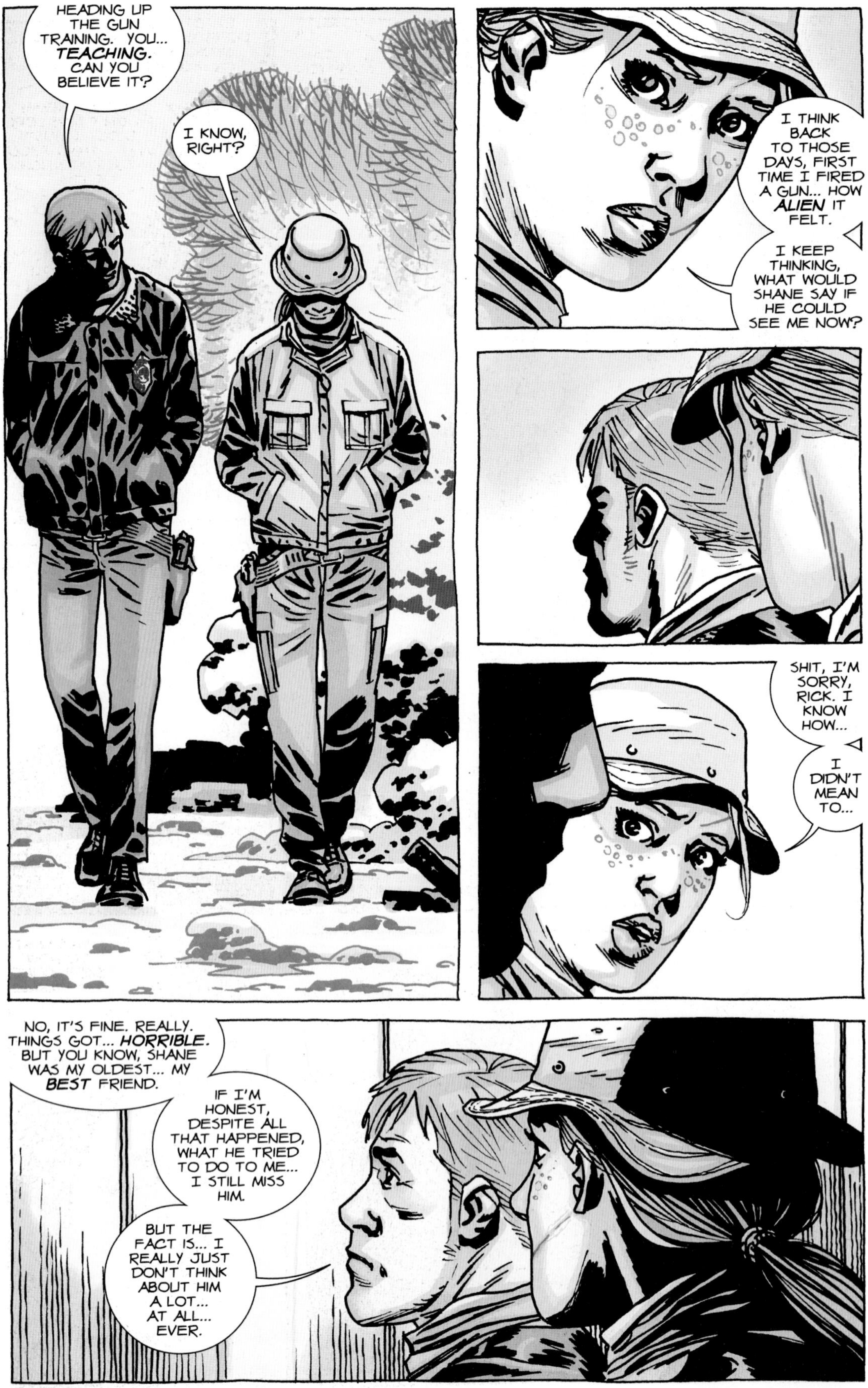
HEADING UP THE GUN TRAINING. YOU... TEACHING. CAN YOU BELIEVE IT?
I KNOW, RIGHT?
I THINK BACK TO THOSE DAYS, FIRST TIME I FIRED A GUN... HOW ALIEN IT FELT.
I KEEP THINKING, WHAT WOULD SHANE SAY IF HE COULD SEE ME NOW?
SHIT, I'M SORRY, RICK. I KNOW HOW...
I DIDN'T MEAN TO...
NO, IT'S FINE. REALLY. THINGS GOT... HORRIBLE. BUT YOU KNOW, SHANE WAS MY OLDEST... MY BEST FRIEND.
IF I'M HONEST, DESPITE ALL THAT HAPPENED, WHAT HE TRIED TO DO TO ME... I STILL MISS HIM.
BUT THE FACT IS... I REALLY JUST DON'T THINK ABOUT HIM A LOT... AT ALL... EVER.

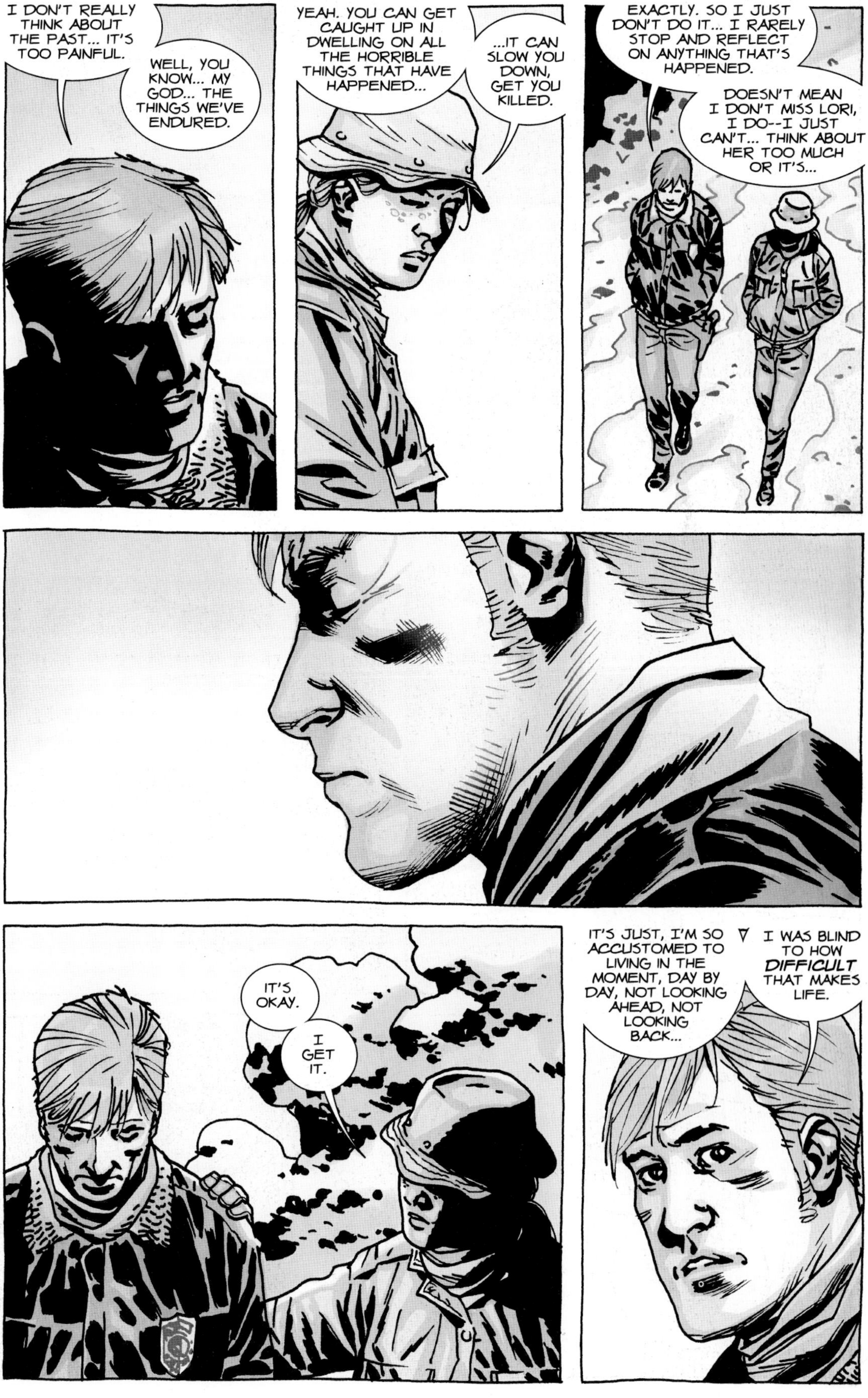
I DON'T REALLY THINK ABOUT THE PAST... IT'S TOO PAINFUL.
WELL, YOU KNOW... MY GOD... THE THINGS WE'VE ENDURED.
YEAH. YOU CAN GET CAUGHT UP IN DWELLING ON ALL THE HORRIBLE THINGS THAT HAVE HAPPENED...
...IT CAN SLOW YOU DOWN, GET YOU KILLED.
EXACTLY. SO I JUST DON'T DO IT... I RARELY STOP AND REFLECT ON ANYTHING THAT'S HAPPENED.
DOESN'T MEAN I DON'T MISS LORI, I DO--I JUST CAN'T... THINK ABOUT HER TOO MUCH OR IT'S...
IT'S OKAY.
I GET IT.
IT'S JUST, I'M SO ACCUSTOMED TO LIVING IN THE MOMENT, DAY BY DAY, NOT LOOKING AHEAD, NOT LOOKING BACK...
I WAS BLIND TO HOW DIFFICULT THAT MAKES LIFE.

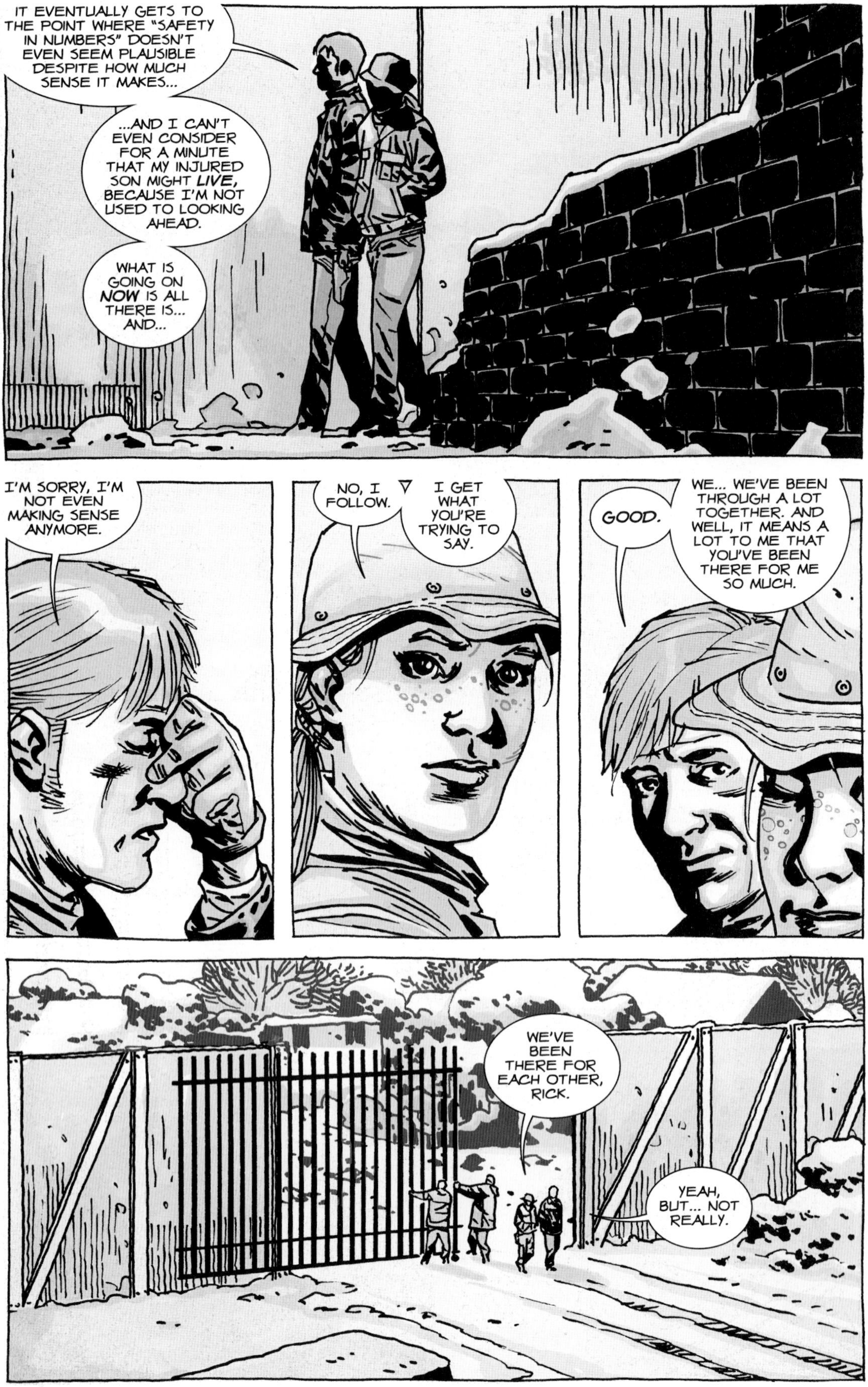
IT EVENTUALLY GETS TO THE POINT WHERE "SAFETY IN NUMBERS" DOESN'T EVEN SEEM PLAUSIBLE DESPITE HOW MUCH SENSE IT MAKES...
...AND I CAN'T EVEN CONSIDER FOR A MINUTE THAT MY INJURED SON MIGHT LIVE, BECAUSE I'M NOT USED TO LOOKING AHEAD.
WHAT IS GOING ON NOW IS ALL THERE IS... AND...
I'M SORRY, I'M NOT EVEN MAKING SENSE ANYMORE.
NO, I FOLLOW.
I GET WHAT YOU'RE TRYING TO SAY.
GOOD.
WE... WE'VE BEEN THROUGH A LOT TOGETHER. AND WELL, IT MEANS A LOT TO ME THAT YOU'VE BEEN THERE FOR ME SO MUCH.
WE'VE BEEN THERE FOR EACH OTHER, RICK.
YEAH, BUT... NOT REALLY.

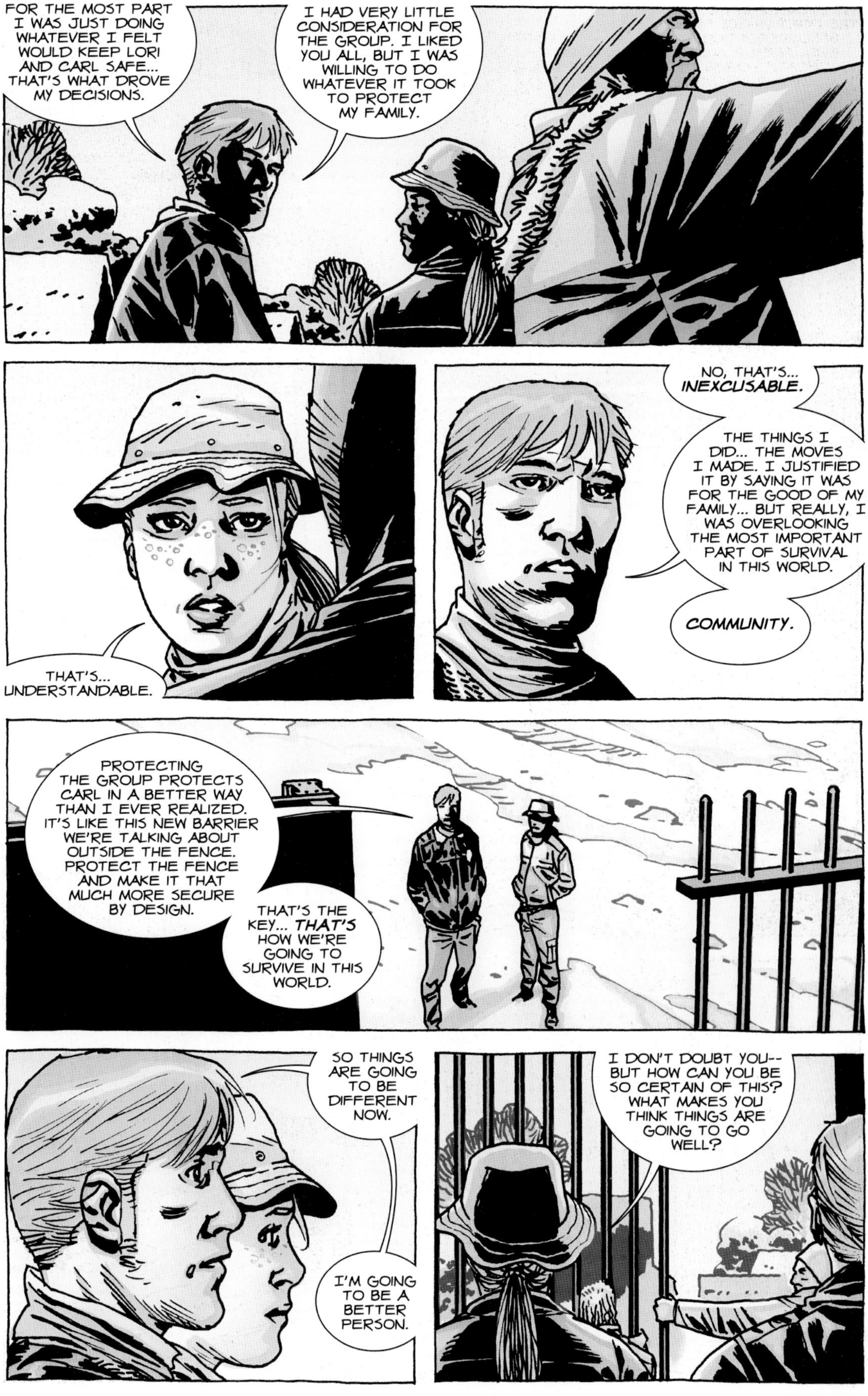
FOR THE MOST PART I WAS JUST DOING WHATEVER I FELT WOULD KEEP LORI AND CARL SAFE... THAT'S WHAT DROVE MY DECISIONS.
I HAD VERY LITTLE CONSIDERATION FOR THE GROUP. I LIKED YOU ALL, BUT I WAS WILLING TO DO WHATEVER IT TOOK TO PROTECT MY FAMILY.
THAT'S... UNDERSTANDABLE.
NO, THAT'S... *INEXCUSABLE.*
THE THINGS I DID... THE MOVES I MADE. I JUSTIFIED IT BY SAYING IT WAS FOR THE GOOD OF MY FAMILY... BUT REALLY, I WAS OVERLOOKING THE MOST IMPORTANT PART OF SURVIVAL IN THIS WORLD.
COMMUNITY.
PROTECTING THE GROUP PROTECTS CARL IN A BETTER WAY THAN I EVER REALIZED. IT'S LIKE THIS NEW BARRIER WE'RE TALKING ABOUT OUTSIDE THE FENCE. PROTECT THE FENCE AND MAKE IT THAT MUCH MORE SECURE BY DESIGN.
THAT'S THE KEY... *THAT'S* HOW WE'RE GOING TO SURVIVE IN THIS WORLD.
SO THINGS ARE GOING TO BE DIFFERENT NOW.
I'M GOING TO BE A BETTER PERSON.
I DON'T DOUBT YOU-- BUT HOW CAN YOU BE SO CERTAIN OF THIS? WHAT MAKES YOU THINK THINGS ARE GOING TO GO WELL?

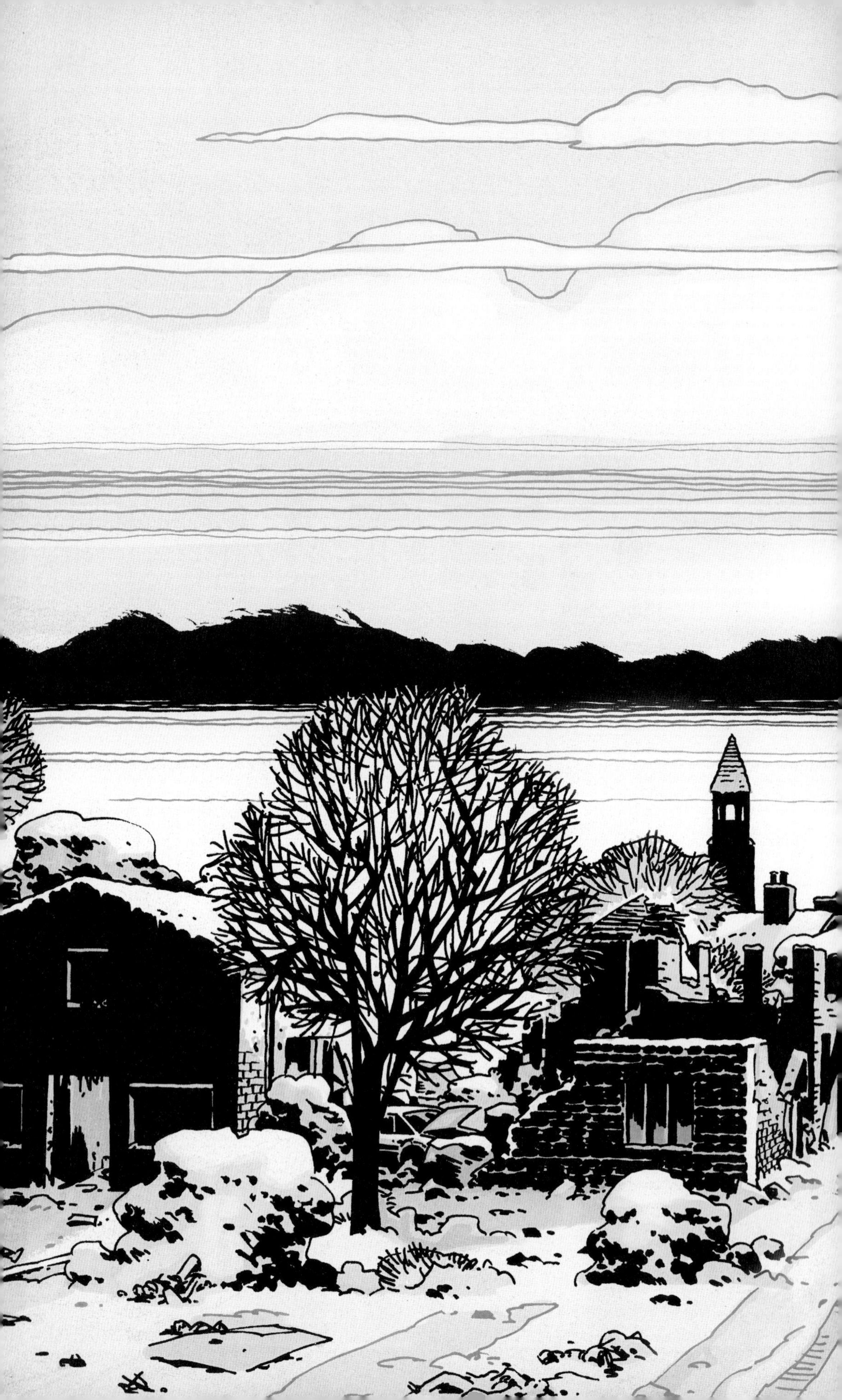

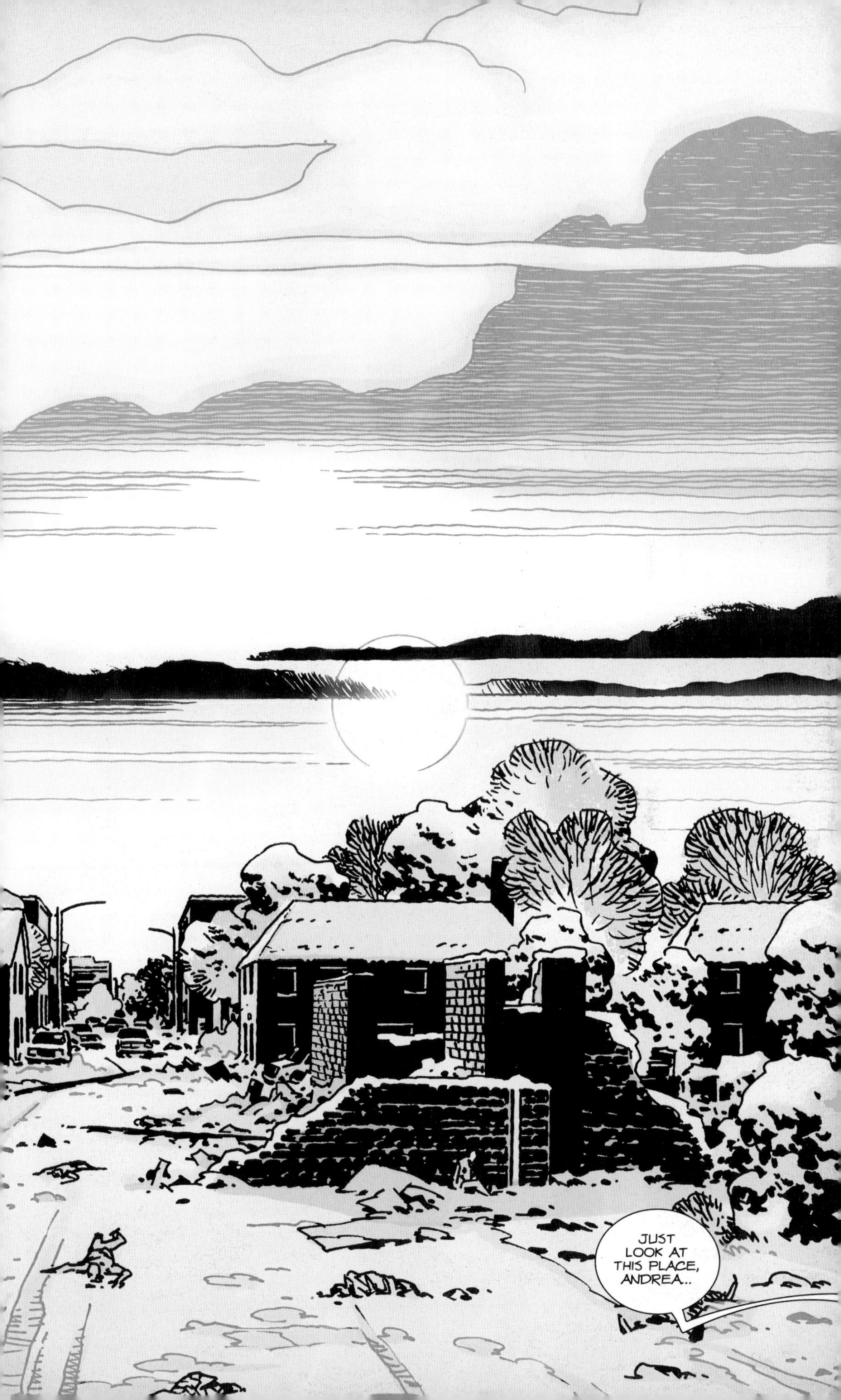
JUST LOOK AT THIS PLACE, ANDREA...

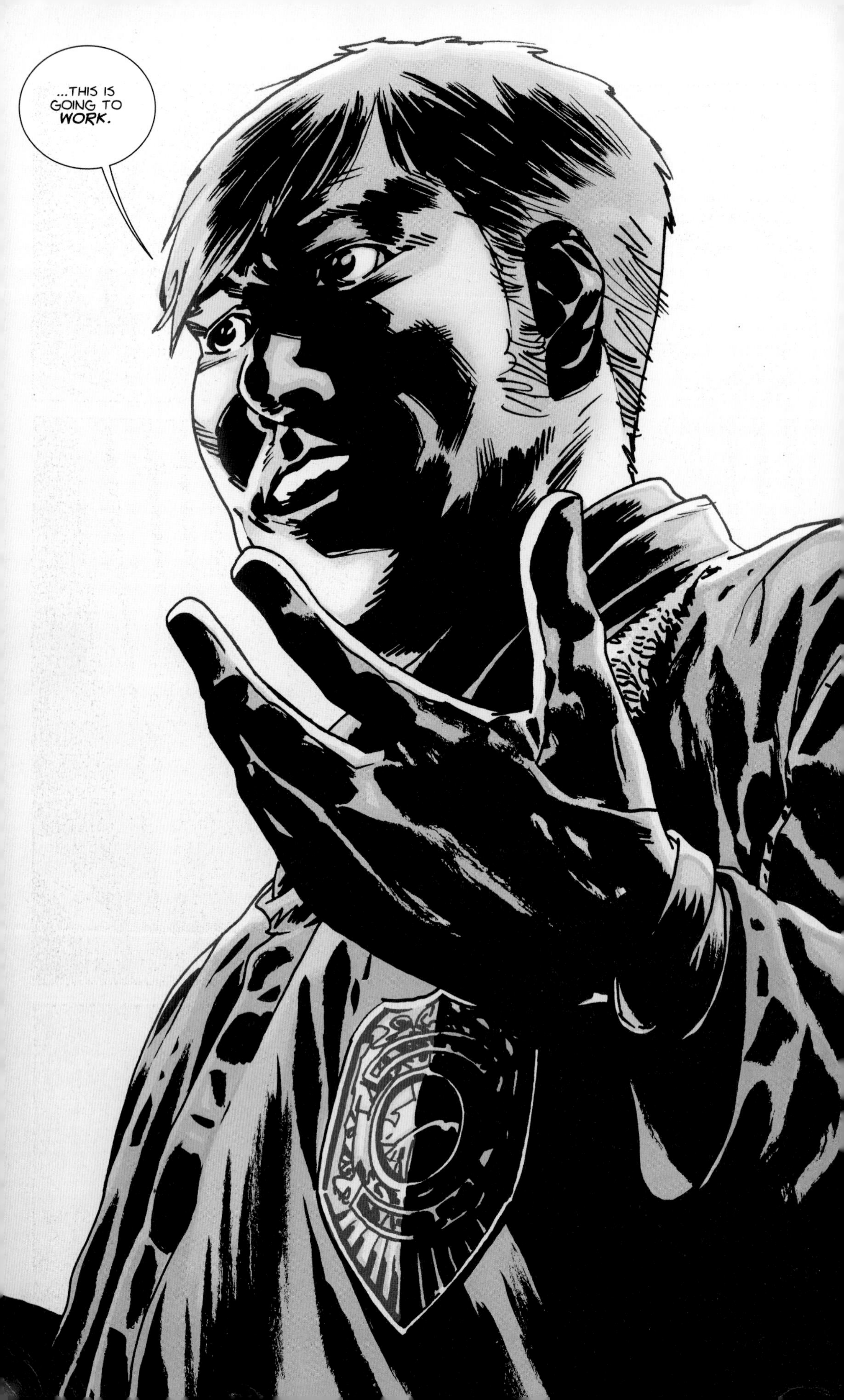
...THIS IS GOING TO WORK.

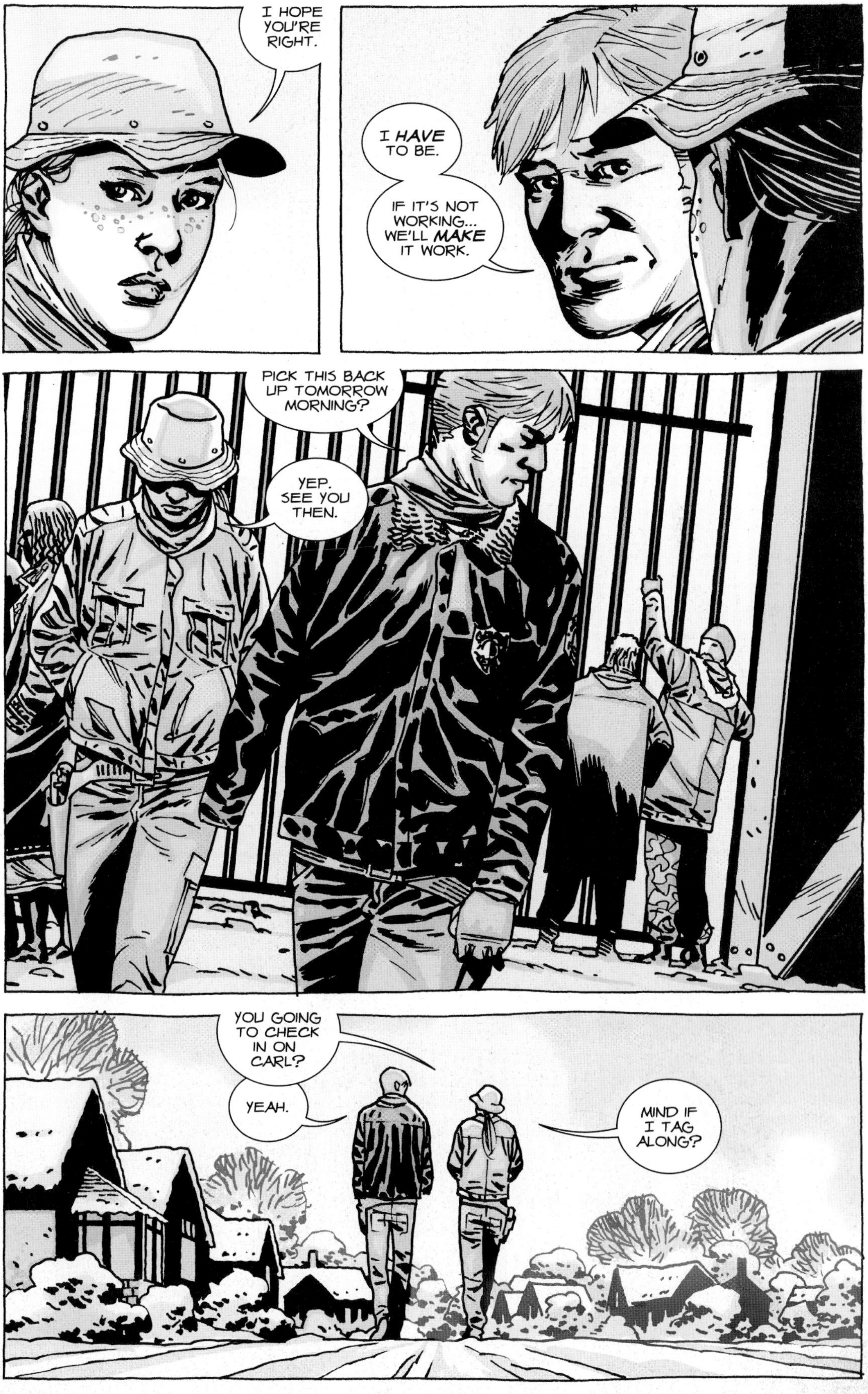
I HOPE YOU'RE RIGHT.
I *HAVE* TO BE.
IF IT'S NOT WORKING... WE'LL *MAKE* IT WORK.
PICK THIS BACK UP TOMORROW MORNING?
YEP. SEE YOU THEN.
YOU GOING TO CHECK IN ON CARL?
YEAH.
MIND IF I TAG ALONG?

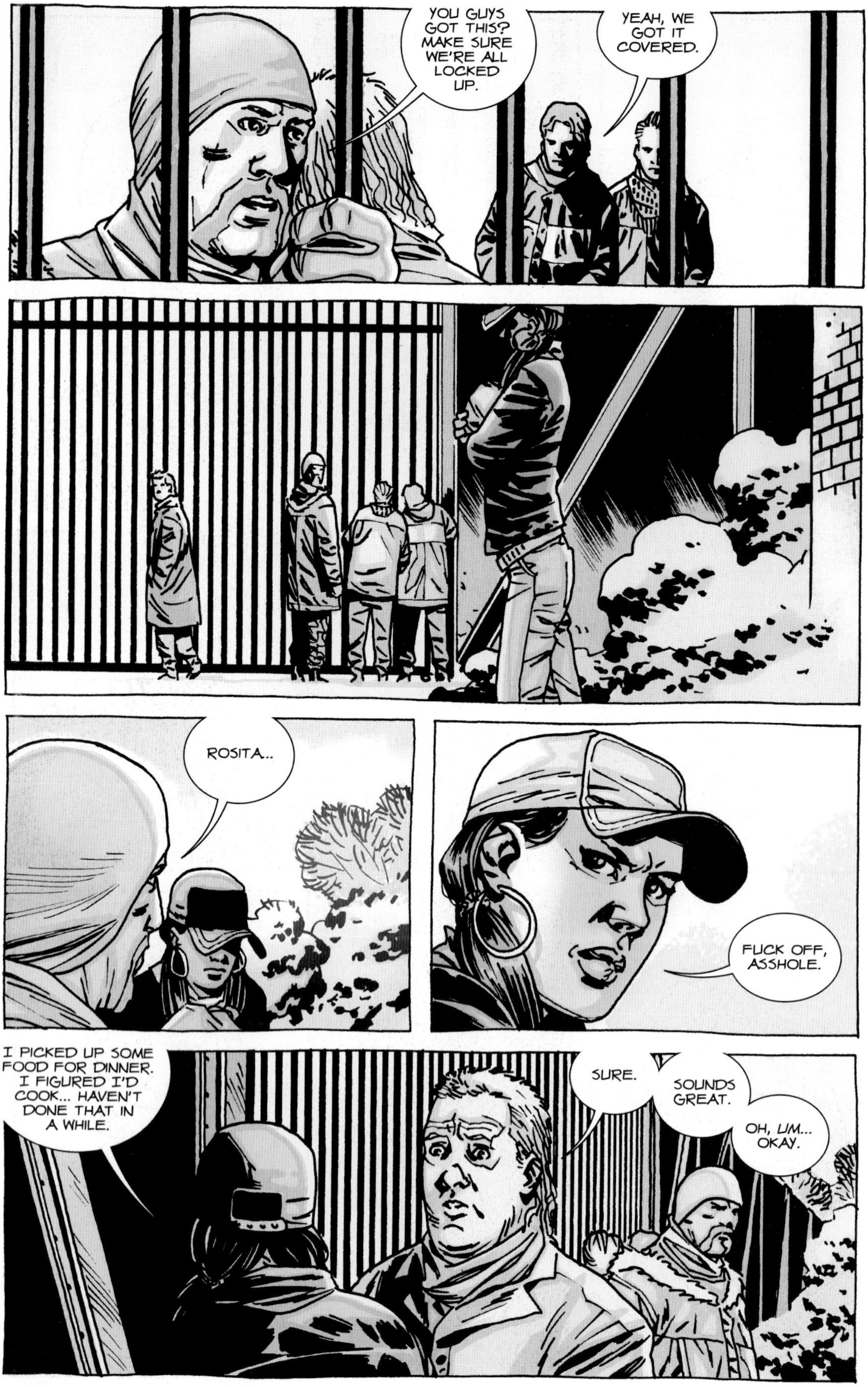
YOU GUYS GOT THIS? MAKE SURE WE'RE ALL LOCKED UP.
YEAH, WE GOT IT COVERED.
ROSITA...
FUCK OFF, ASSHOLE.
I PICKED UP SOME FOOD FOR DINNER. I FIGURED I'D COOK... HAVEN'T DONE THAT IN A WHILE.
SURE.
SOUNDS GREAT.
OH, UM... OKAY.

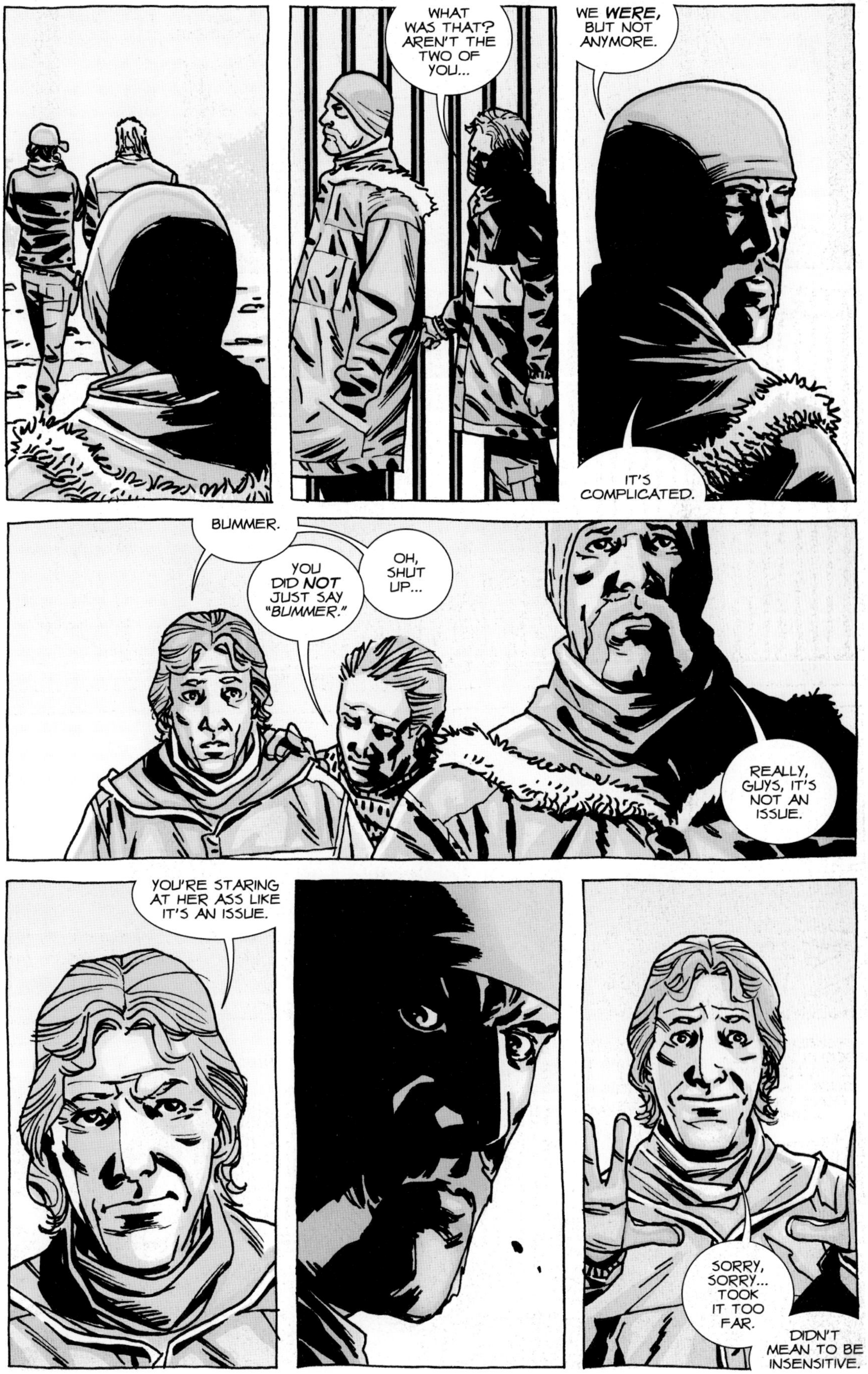
WHAT WAS THAT? AREN'T THE TWO OF YOU...
WE **WERE**, BUT NOT ANYMORE.
IT'S COMPLICATED.
BUMMER.
YOU DID **NOT** JUST SAY "*BUMMER.*"
OH, SHUT UP...
REALLY, GUYS, IT'S NOT AN ISSUE.
YOU'RE STARING AT HER ASS LIKE IT'S AN ISSUE.
SORRY, SORRY... TOOK IT TOO FAR.
DIDN'T MEAN TO BE INSENSITIVE.

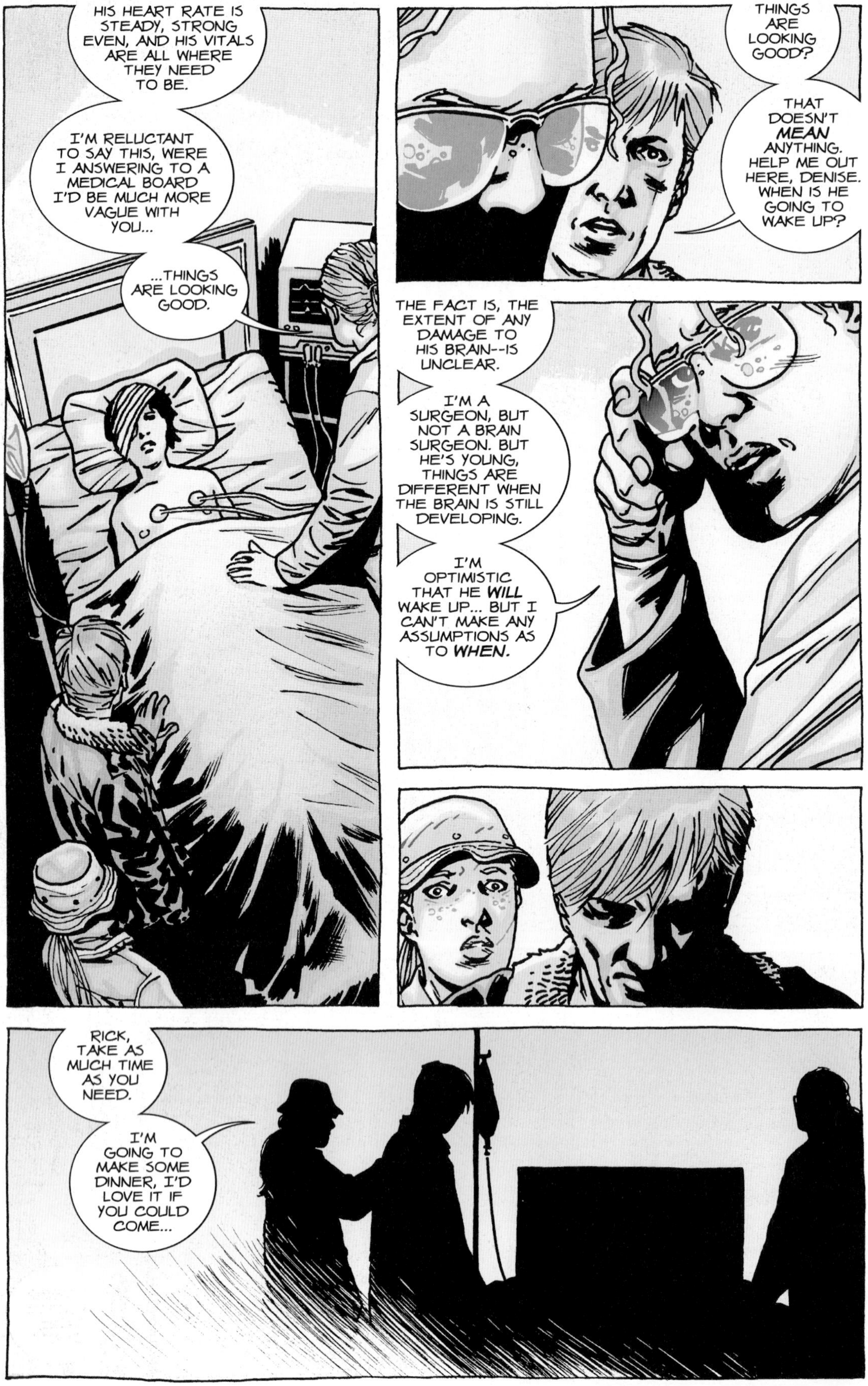
HIS HEART RATE IS STEADY, STRONG EVEN, AND HIS VITALS ARE ALL WHERE THEY NEED TO BE.
I'M RELUCTANT TO SAY THIS, WERE I ANSWERING TO A MEDICAL BOARD I'D BE MUCH MORE VAGUE WITH YOU...
...THINGS ARE LOOKING GOOD.
THINGS ARE LOOKING GOOD?
THAT DOESN'T MEAN ANYTHING. HELP ME OUT HERE, DENISE. WHEN IS HE GOING TO WAKE UP?
THE FACT IS, THE EXTENT OF ANY DAMAGE TO HIS BRAIN--IS UNCLEAR.
I'M A SURGEON, BUT NOT A BRAIN SURGEON. BUT HE'S YOUNG, THINGS ARE DIFFERENT WHEN THE BRAIN IS STILL DEVELOPING.
I'M OPTIMISTIC THAT HE WILL WAKE UP... BUT I CAN'T MAKE ANY ASSUMPTIONS AS TO WHEN.
RICK, TAKE AS MUCH TIME AS YOU NEED.
I'M GOING TO MAKE SOME DINNER, I'D LOVE IT IF YOU COULD COME...

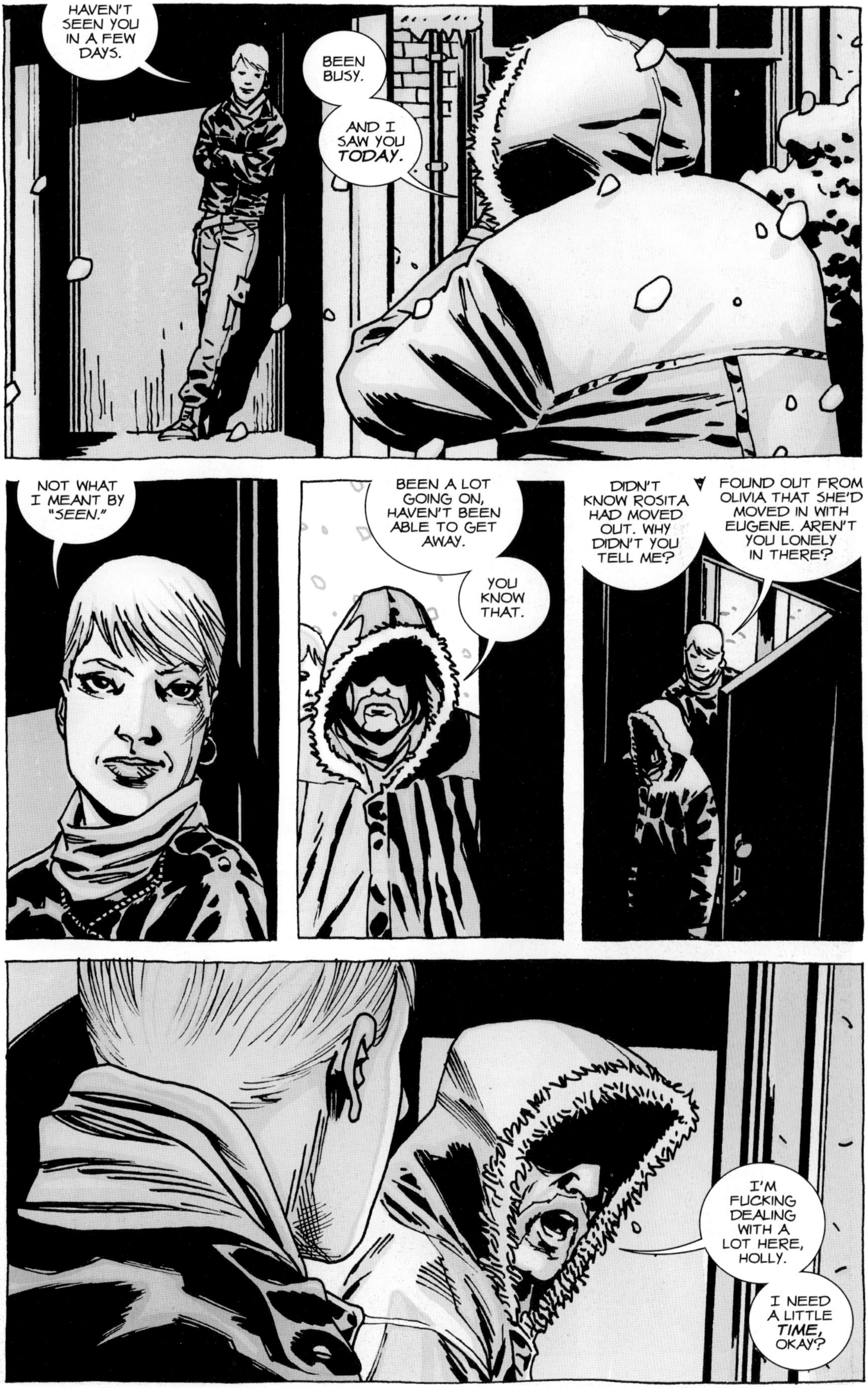
HAVEN'T SEEN YOU IN A FEW DAYS.
BEEN BUSY.
AND I SAW YOU *TODAY.*
NOT WHAT I MEANT BY "SEEN."
BEEN A LOT GOING ON, HAVEN'T BEEN ABLE TO GET AWAY.
YOU KNOW THAT.
DIDN'T KNOW ROSITA HAD MOVED OUT. WHY DIDN'T YOU TELL ME?
FOUND OUT FROM OLIVIA THAT SHE'D MOVED IN WITH EUGENE. AREN'T YOU LONELY IN THERE?
I'M FUCKING DEALING WITH A LOT HERE, HOLLY.
I NEED A LITTLE *TIME,* OKAY?

YEAH.

FINE.

TAKE ALL THE TIME YOU NEED.

HOLLY, WAIT.

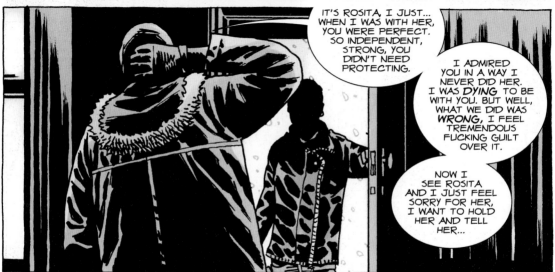

IT'S ROSITA, I JUST... WHEN I WAS WITH HER, YOU WERE PERFECT. SO INDEPENDENT, STRONG, YOU DIDN'T NEED PROTECTING.

I ADMIRED YOU IN A WAY I NEVER DID HER. I WAS *DYING* TO BE WITH YOU. BUT WELL, WHAT WE DID WAS *WRONG*, I FEEL TREMENDOUS FUCKING GUILT OVER IT.

NOW I SEE ROSITA AND I JUST FEEL SORRY FOR HER, I WANT TO HOLD HER AND TELL HER...

ARE YOU FUCKING *KIDDING* ME?!

YOU WANT HER BACK?!

NO. *FUCK.* THAT'S NOT WHAT I MEAN AT ALL.

IT'S NOT LOVE THAT I FEEL FOR HER... IT'S *PITY.* I FEEL LIKE I DID HER WRONG AND THAT MAKES ME... FEELING *GOOD* RIGHT NOW WOULDN'T BE RIGHT.

JUST...

...COME INSIDE.

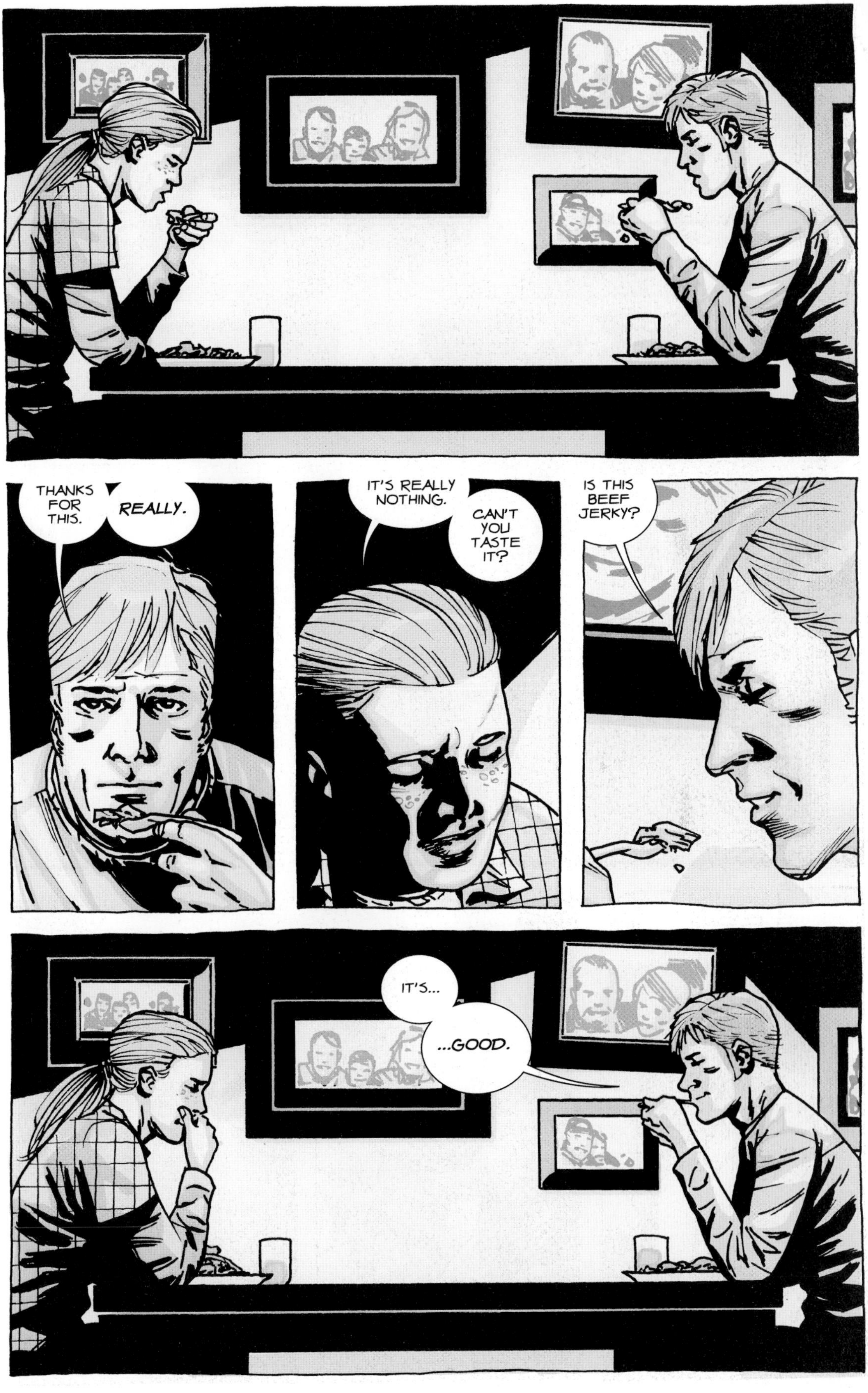
THANKS FOR THIS.
REALLY.
IT'S REALLY NOTHING.
CAN'T YOU TASTE IT?
IS THIS BEEF JERKY?
IT'S...
...GOOD.

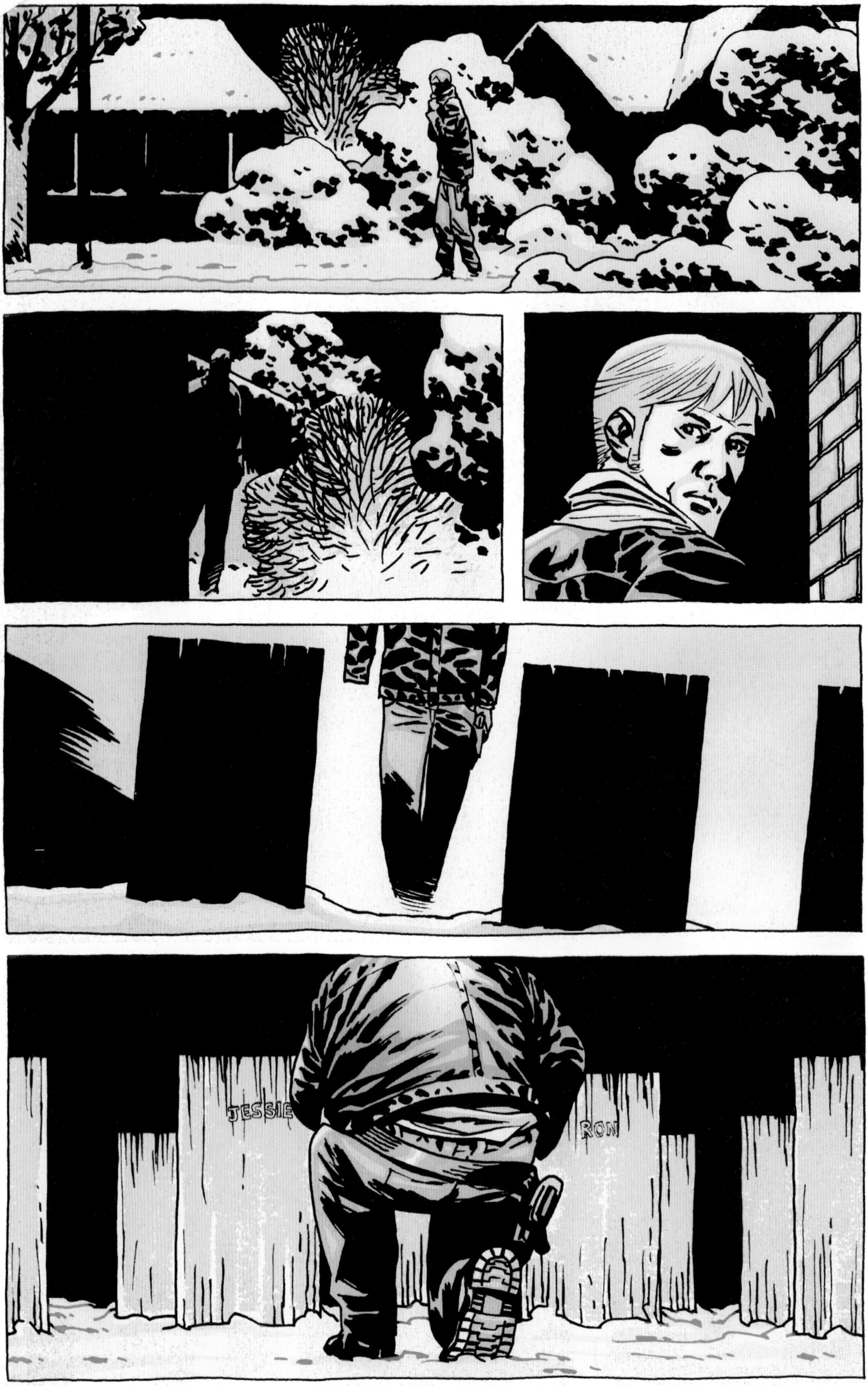
JESSIE
RON

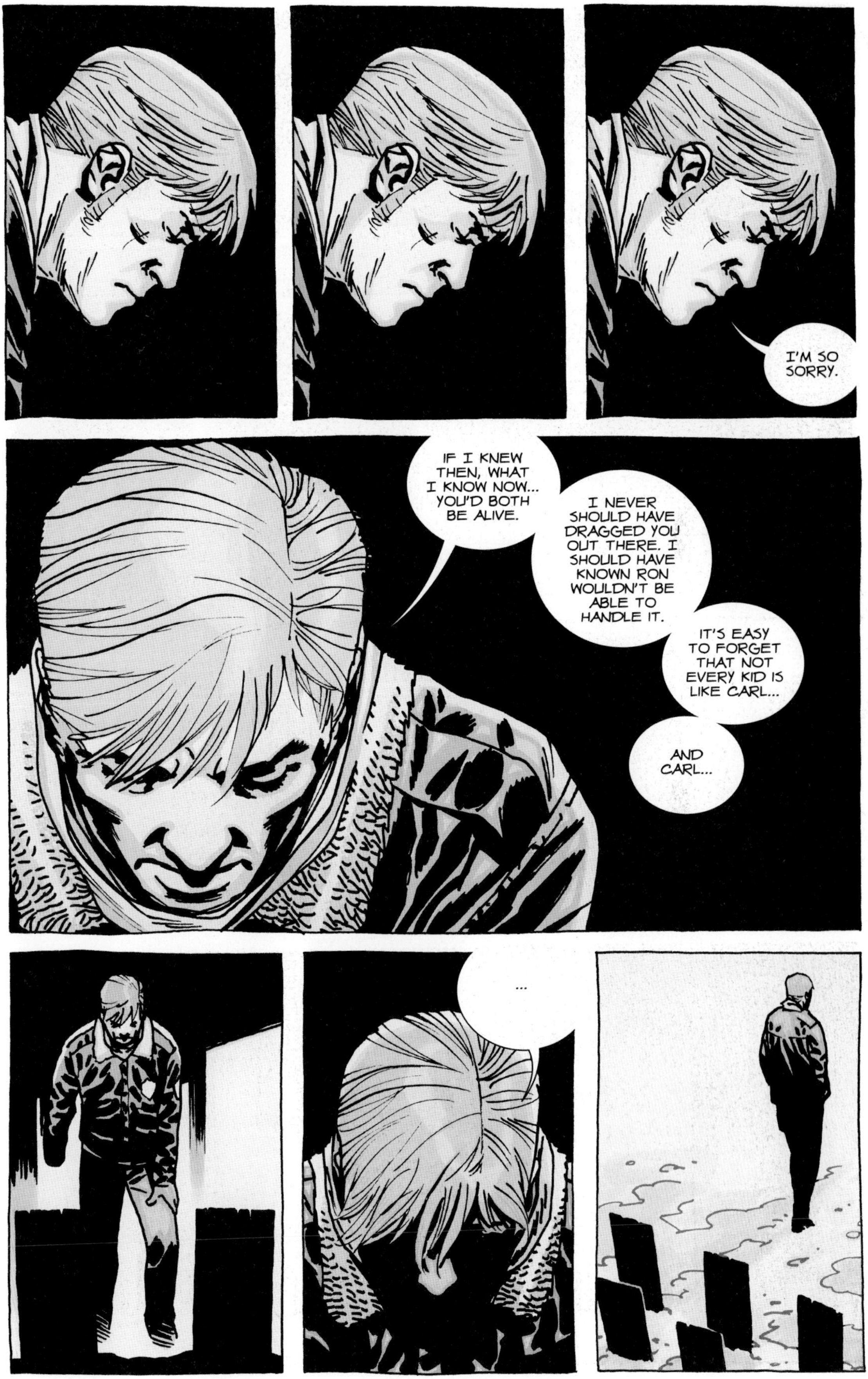

I'M SO SORRY.
IF I KNEW THEN, WHAT I KNOW NOW... YOU'D BOTH BE ALIVE.
I NEVER SHOULD HAVE DRAGGED YOU OUT THERE. I SHOULD HAVE KNOWN RON WOULDN'T BE ABLE TO HANDLE IT.
IT'S EASY TO FORGET THAT NOT EVERY KID IS LIKE CARL...
AND CARL...
...

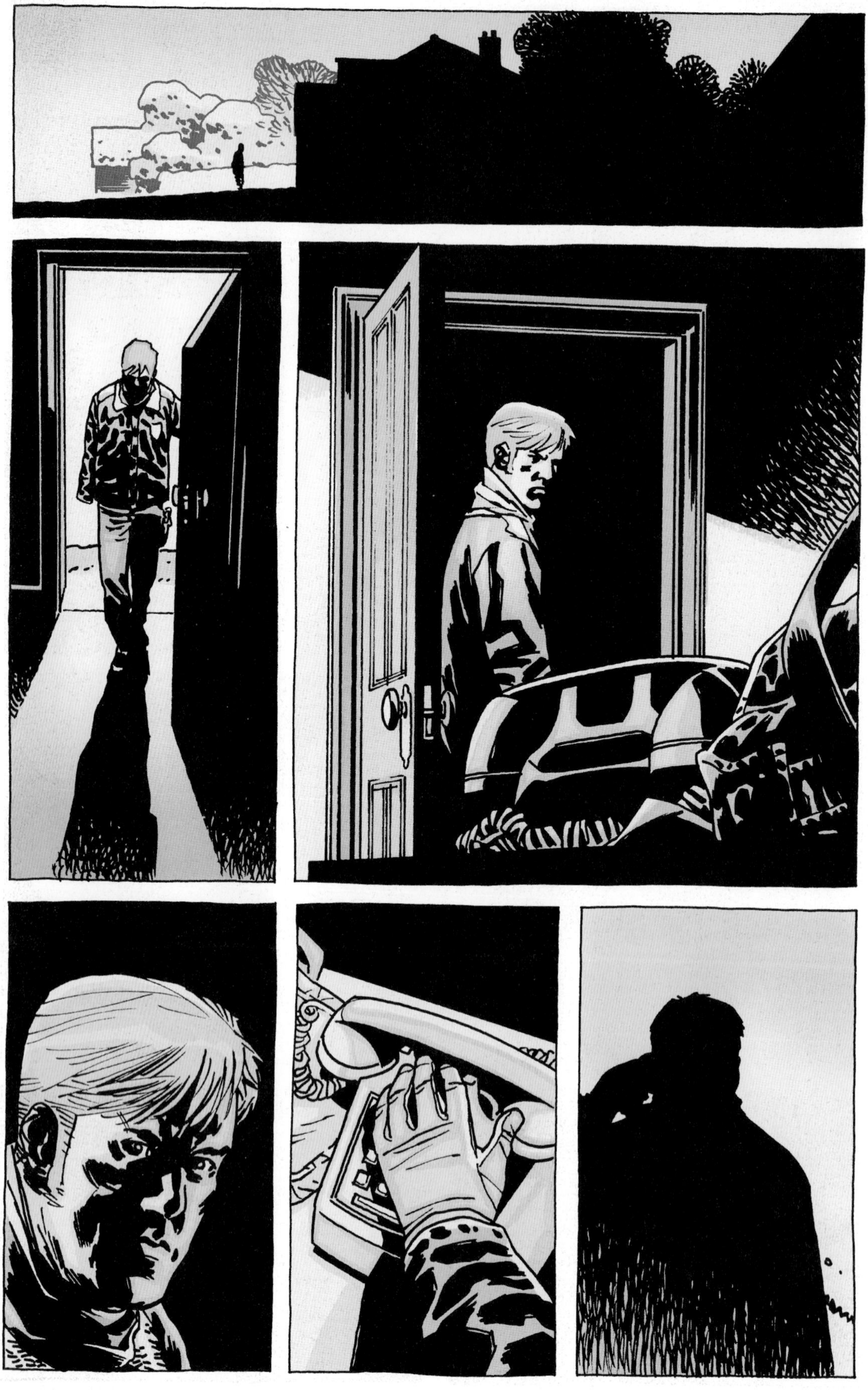

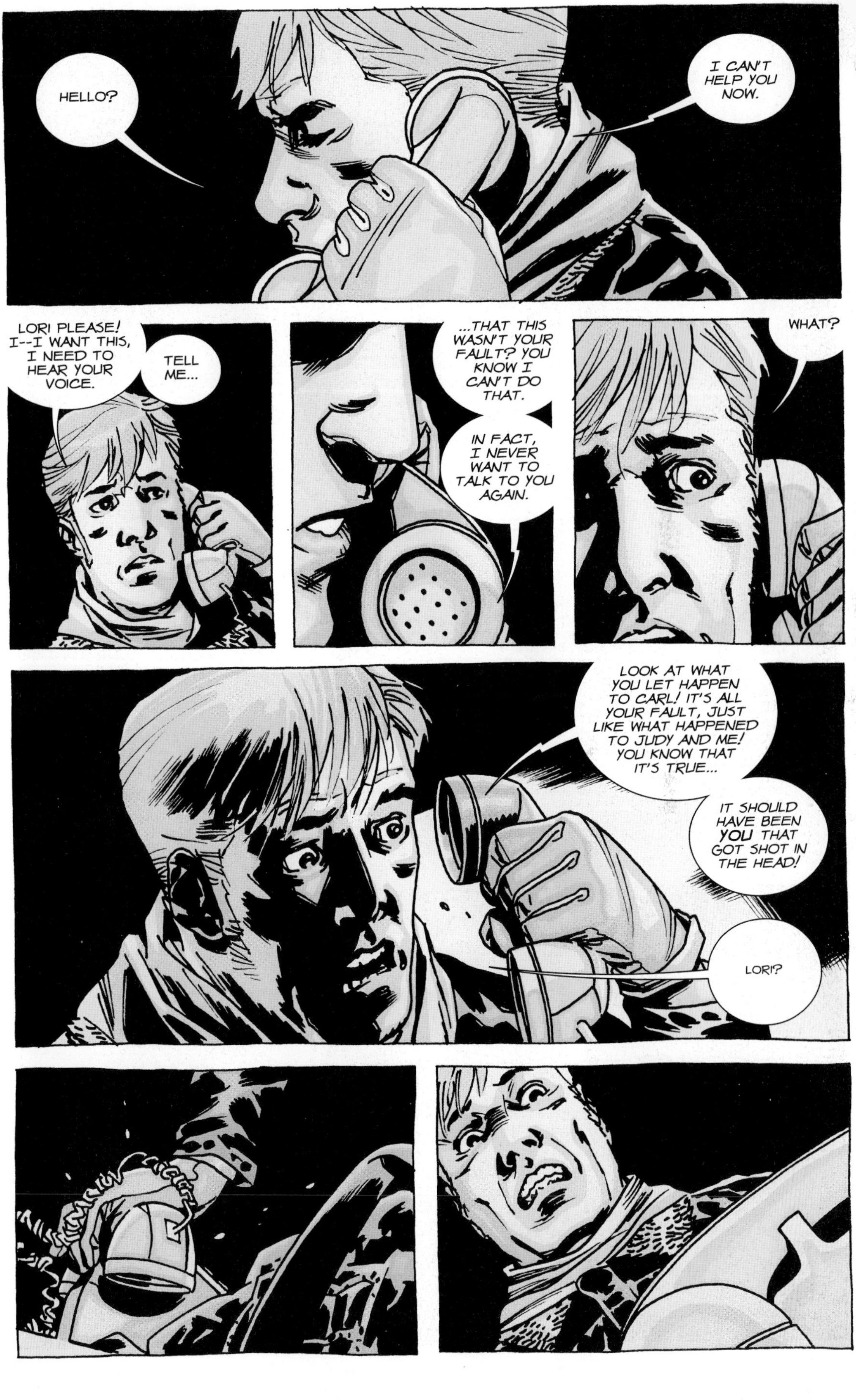
HELLO?
I CAN'T HELP YOU NOW.
LORI PLEASE! I--I WANT THIS, I NEED TO HEAR YOUR VOICE.
TELL ME...
...THAT THIS WASN'T YOUR FAULT? YOU KNOW I CAN'T DO THAT.
IN FACT, I NEVER WANT TO TALK TO YOU AGAIN.
WHAT?
LOOK AT WHAT YOU LET HAPPEN TO CARL! IT'S ALL YOUR FAULT, JUST LIKE WHAT HAPPENED TO JUDY AND ME! YOU KNOW THAT IT'S TRUE...
IT SHOULD HAVE BEEN YOU THAT GOT SHOT IN THE HEAD!
LORI!?

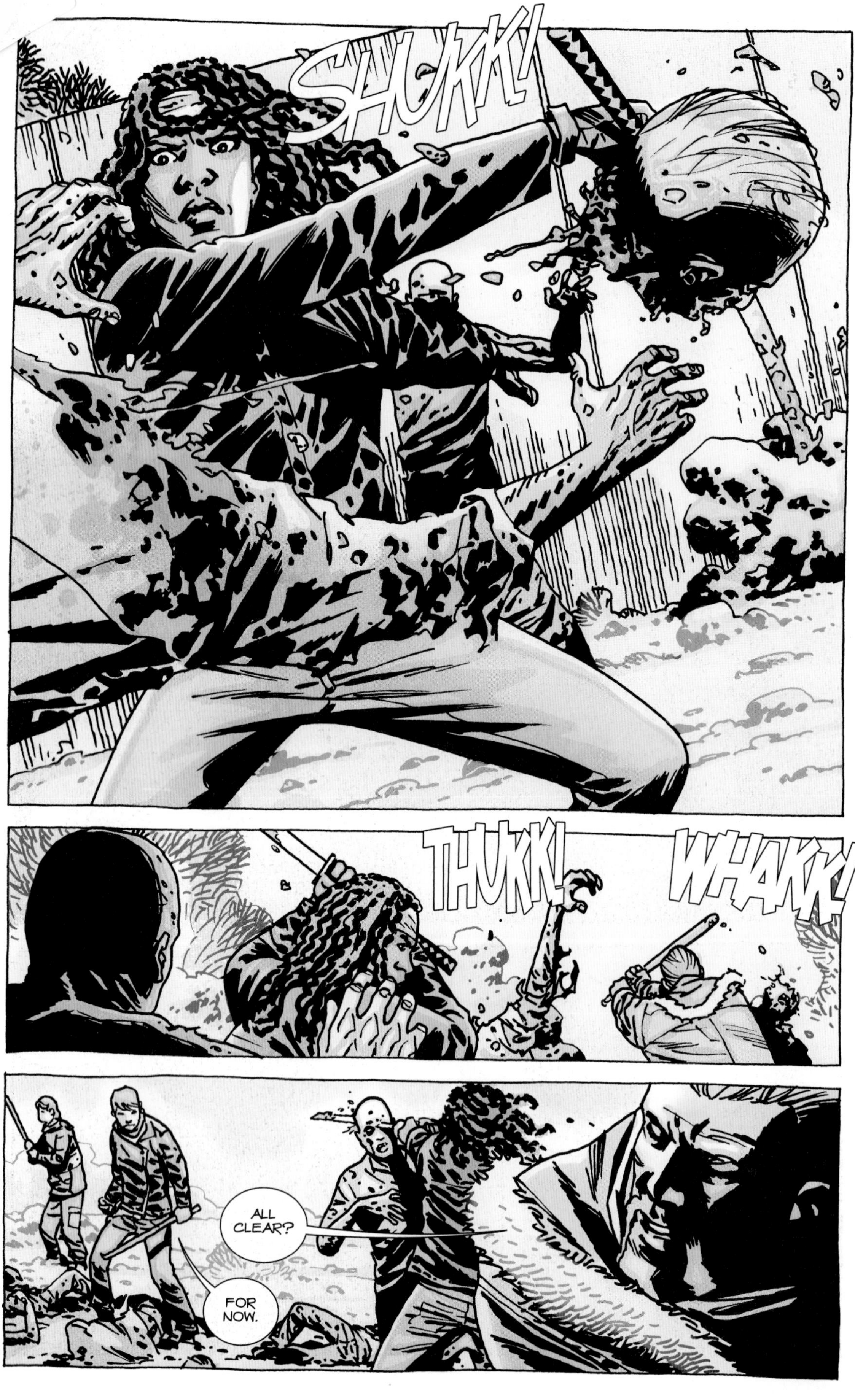
SHUKK!
THUKK!
WHAKK!
ALL CLEAR?
FOR NOW.

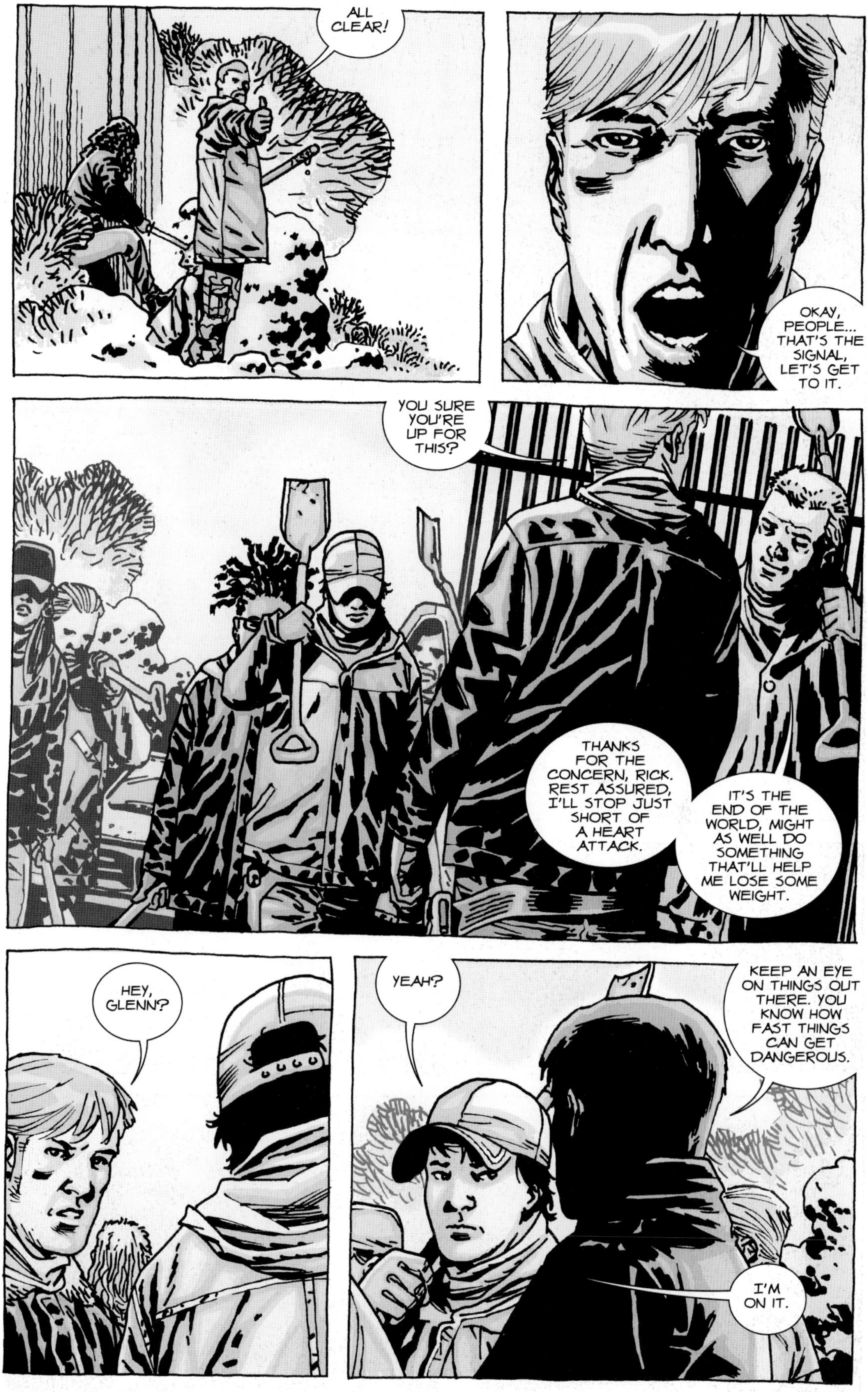
ALL CLEAR!
OKAY, PEOPLE... THAT'S THE SIGNAL, LET'S GET TO IT.
YOU SURE YOU'RE UP FOR THIS?
THANKS FOR THE CONCERN, RICK. REST ASSURED, I'LL STOP JUST SHORT OF A HEART ATTACK.
IT'S THE END OF THE WORLD, MIGHT AS WELL DO SOMETHING THAT'LL HELP ME LOSE SOME WEIGHT.
HEY, GLENN?
YEAH?
KEEP AN EYE ON THINGS OUT THERE. YOU KNOW HOW FAST THINGS CAN GET DANGEROUS.
I'M ON IT.

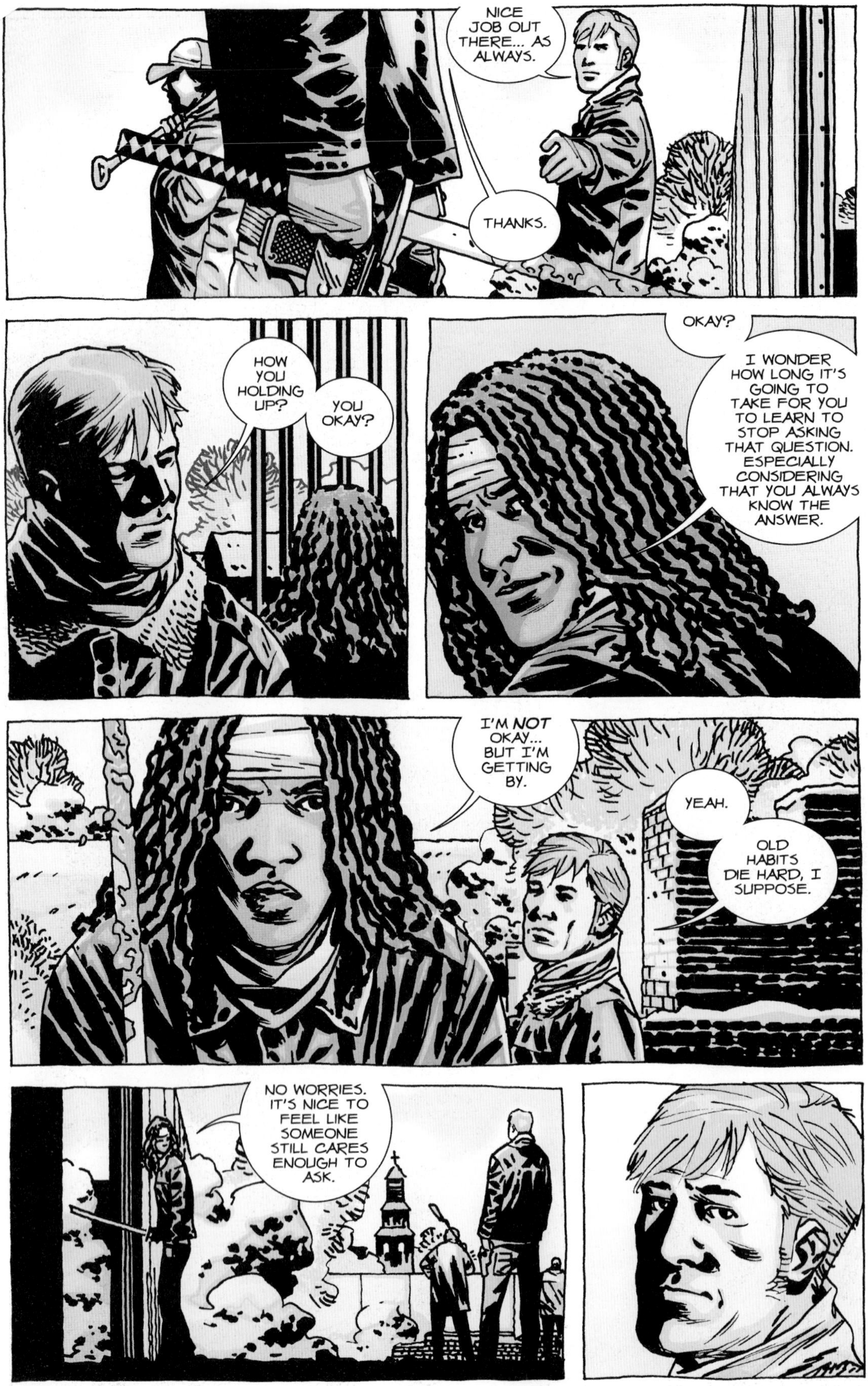
NICE JOB OUT THERE... AS ALWAYS.
THANKS.
HOW YOU HOLDING UP?
YOU OKAY?
OKAY?
I WONDER HOW LONG IT'S GOING TO TAKE FOR YOU TO LEARN TO STOP ASKING THAT QUESTION. ESPECIALLY CONSIDERING THAT YOU ALWAYS KNOW THE ANSWER.
I'M NOT OKAY... BUT I'M GETTING BY.
YEAH.
OLD HABITS DIE HARD, I SUPPOSE.
NO WORRIES. IT'S NICE TO FEEL LIKE SOMEONE STILL CARES ENOUGH TO ASK.

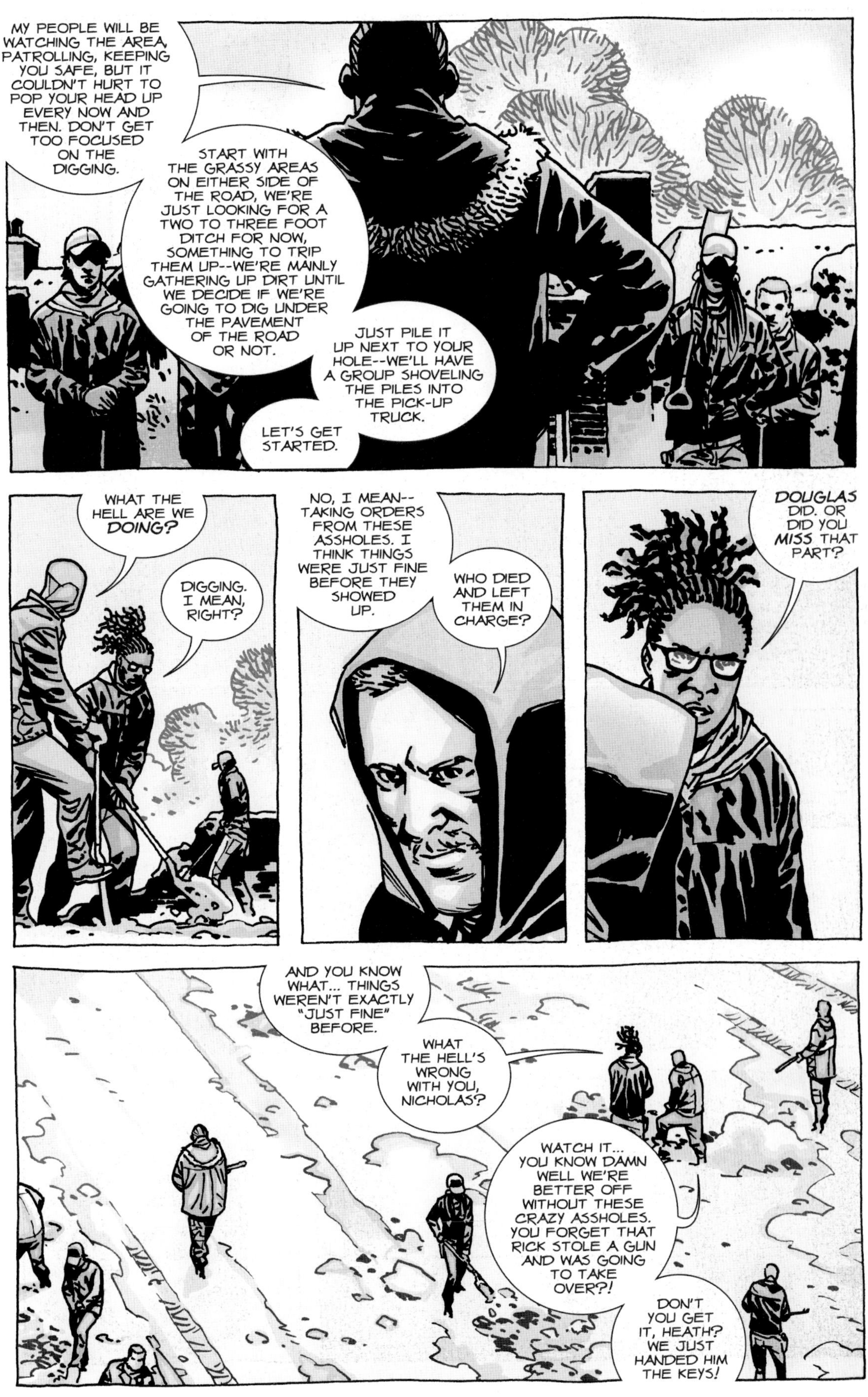
MY PEOPLE WILL BE WATCHING THE AREA, PATROLLING, KEEPING YOU SAFE, BUT IT COULDN'T HURT TO POP YOUR HEAD UP EVERY NOW AND THEN. DON'T GET TOO FOCUSED ON THE DIGGING.
START WITH THE GRASSY AREAS ON EITHER SIDE OF THE ROAD, WE'RE JUST LOOKING FOR A TWO TO THREE FOOT DITCH FOR NOW, SOMETHING TO TRIP THEM UP--WE'RE MAINLY GATHERING UP DIRT UNTIL WE DECIDE IF WE'RE GOING TO DIG UNDER THE PAVEMENT OF THE ROAD OR NOT.
JUST PILE IT UP NEXT TO YOUR HOLE--WE'LL HAVE A GROUP SHOVELING THE PILES INTO THE PICK-UP TRUCK.
LET'S GET STARTED.
WHAT THE HELL ARE WE DOING?
DIGGING. I MEAN, RIGHT?
NO, I MEAN--TAKING ORDERS FROM THESE ASSHOLES. I THINK THINGS WERE JUST FINE BEFORE THEY SHOWED UP.
WHO DIED AND LEFT THEM IN CHARGE?
DOUGLAS DID. OR DID YOU MISS THAT PART?
AND YOU KNOW WHAT... THINGS WEREN'T EXACTLY "JUST FINE" BEFORE.
WHAT THE HELL'S WRONG WITH YOU, NICHOLAS?
WATCH IT... YOU KNOW DAMN WELL WE'RE BETTER OFF WITHOUT THESE CRAZY ASSHOLES. YOU FORGET THAT RICK STOLE A GUN AND WAS GOING TO TAKE OVER?!
DON'T YOU GET IT, HEATH? WE JUST HANDED HIM THE KEYS!

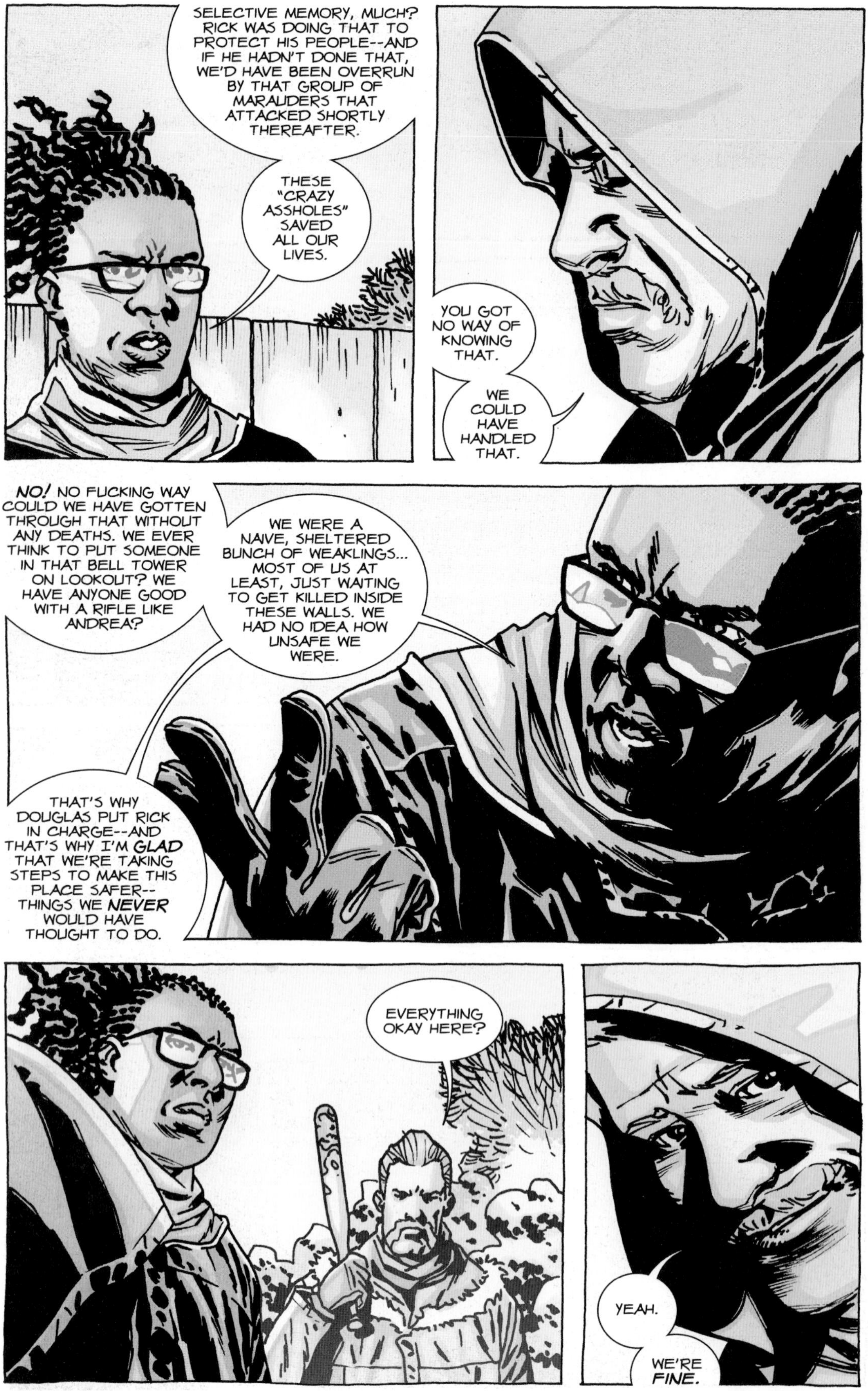
SELECTIVE MEMORY, MUCH? RICK WAS DOING THAT TO PROTECT HIS PEOPLE--AND IF HE HADN'T DONE THAT, WE'D HAVE BEEN OVERRUN BY THAT GROUP OF MARAUDERS THAT ATTACKED SHORTLY THEREAFTER.
THESE "CRAZY ASSHOLES" SAVED ALL OUR LIVES.
YOU GOT NO WAY OF KNOWING THAT.
WE COULD HAVE HANDLED THAT.
NO! NO FUCKING WAY COULD WE HAVE GOTTEN THROUGH THAT WITHOUT ANY DEATHS. WE EVER THINK TO PUT SOMEONE IN THAT BELL TOWER ON LOOKOUT? WE HAVE ANYONE GOOD WITH A RIFLE LIKE ANDREA?
WE WERE A NAIVE, SHELTERED BUNCH OF WEAKLINGS... MOST OF US AT LEAST, JUST WAITING TO GET KILLED INSIDE THESE WALLS. WE HAD NO IDEA HOW UNSAFE WE WERE.
THAT'S WHY DOUGLAS PUT RICK IN CHARGE--AND THAT'S WHY I'M GLAD THAT WE'RE TAKING STEPS TO MAKE THIS PLACE SAFER-- THINGS WE NEVER WOULD HAVE THOUGHT TO DO.
EVERYTHING OKAY HERE?
YEAH.
WE'RE FINE.

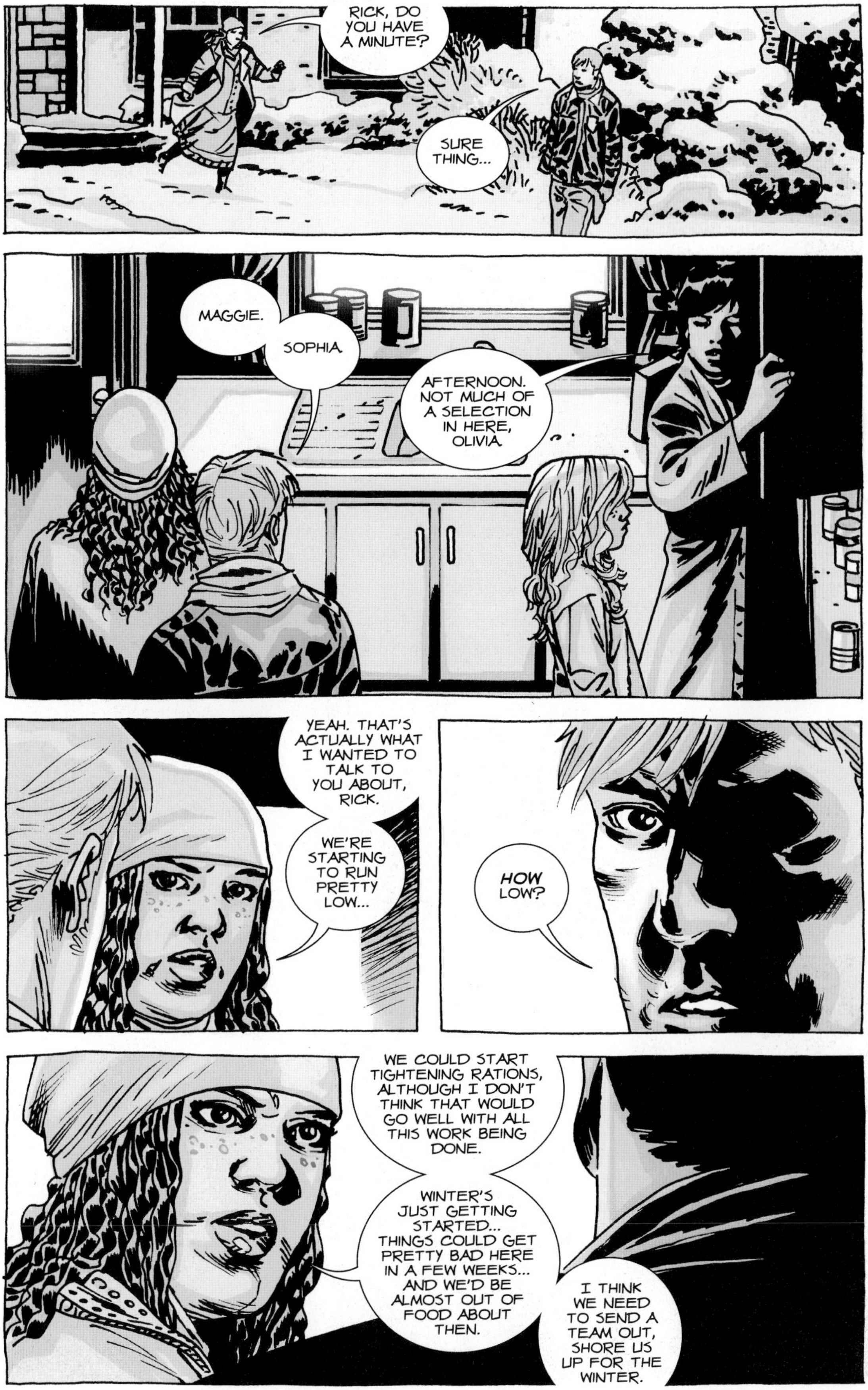
RICK, DO YOU HAVE A MINUTE?
SURE THING...
MAGGIE.
SOPHIA.
AFTERNOON. NOT MUCH OF A SELECTION IN HERE, OLIVIA.
YEAH. THAT'S ACTUALLY WHAT I WANTED TO TALK TO YOU ABOUT, RICK.
WE'RE STARTING TO RUN PRETTY LOW...
HOW LOW?
WE COULD START TIGHTENING RATIONS, ALTHOUGH I DON'T THINK THAT WOULD GO WELL WITH ALL THIS WORK BEING DONE.
WINTER'S JUST GETTING STARTED... THINGS COULD GET PRETTY BAD HERE IN A FEW WEEKS... AND WE'D BE ALMOST OUT OF FOOD ABOUT THEN.
I THINK WE NEED TO SEND A TEAM OUT, SHORE US UP FOR THE WINTER.

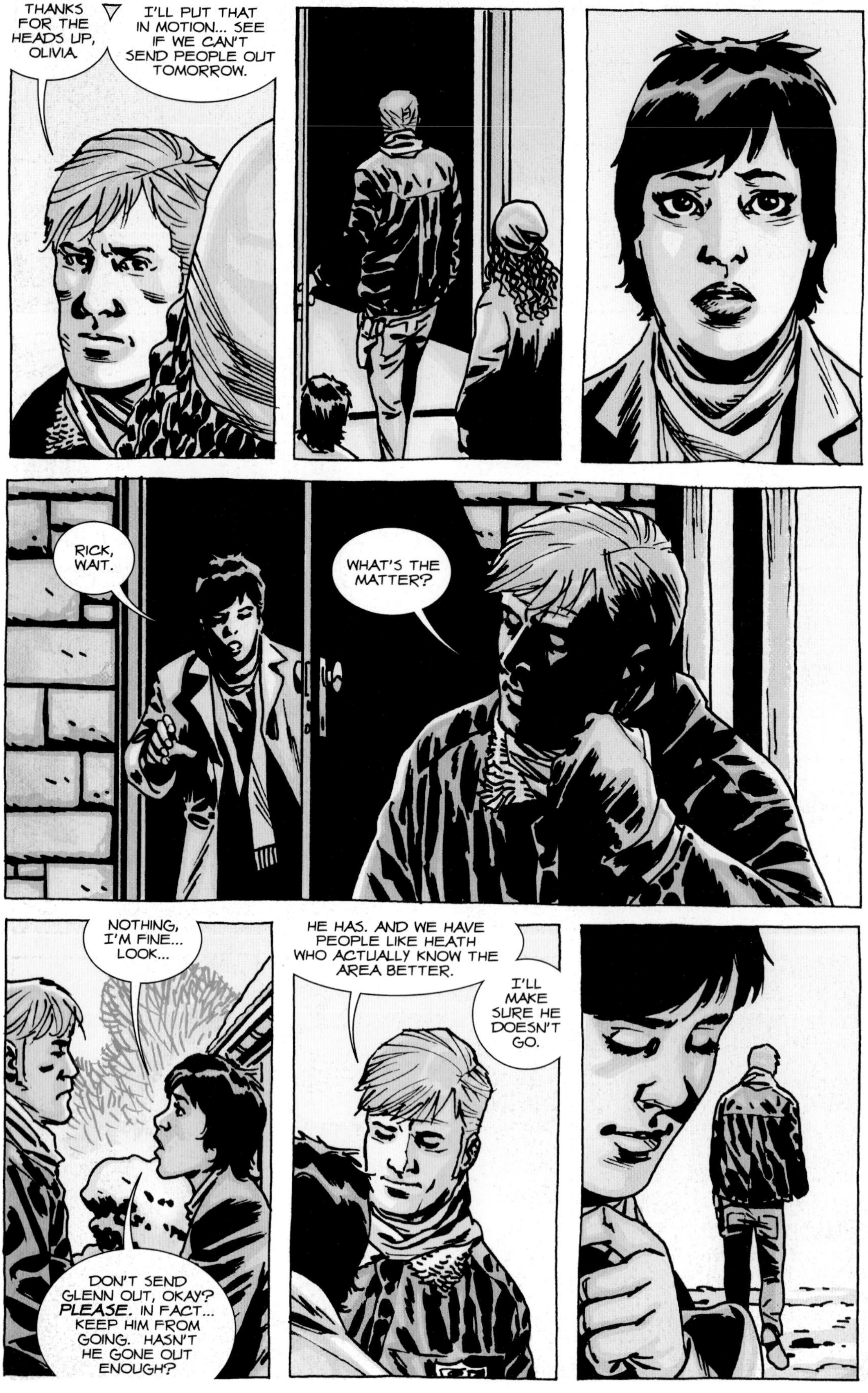
THANKS FOR THE HEADS UP, OLIVIA.
I'LL PUT THAT IN MOTION... SEE IF WE CAN'T SEND PEOPLE OUT TOMORROW.
RICK, WAIT.
WHAT'S THE MATTER?
NOTHING, I'M FINE... LOOK...
DON'T SEND GLENN OUT, OKAY? PLEASE. IN FACT... KEEP HIM FROM GOING. HASN'T HE GONE OUT ENOUGH?
HE HAS. AND WE HAVE PEOPLE LIKE HEATH WHO ACTUALLY KNOW THE AREA BETTER.
I'LL MAKE SURE HE DOESN'T GO.

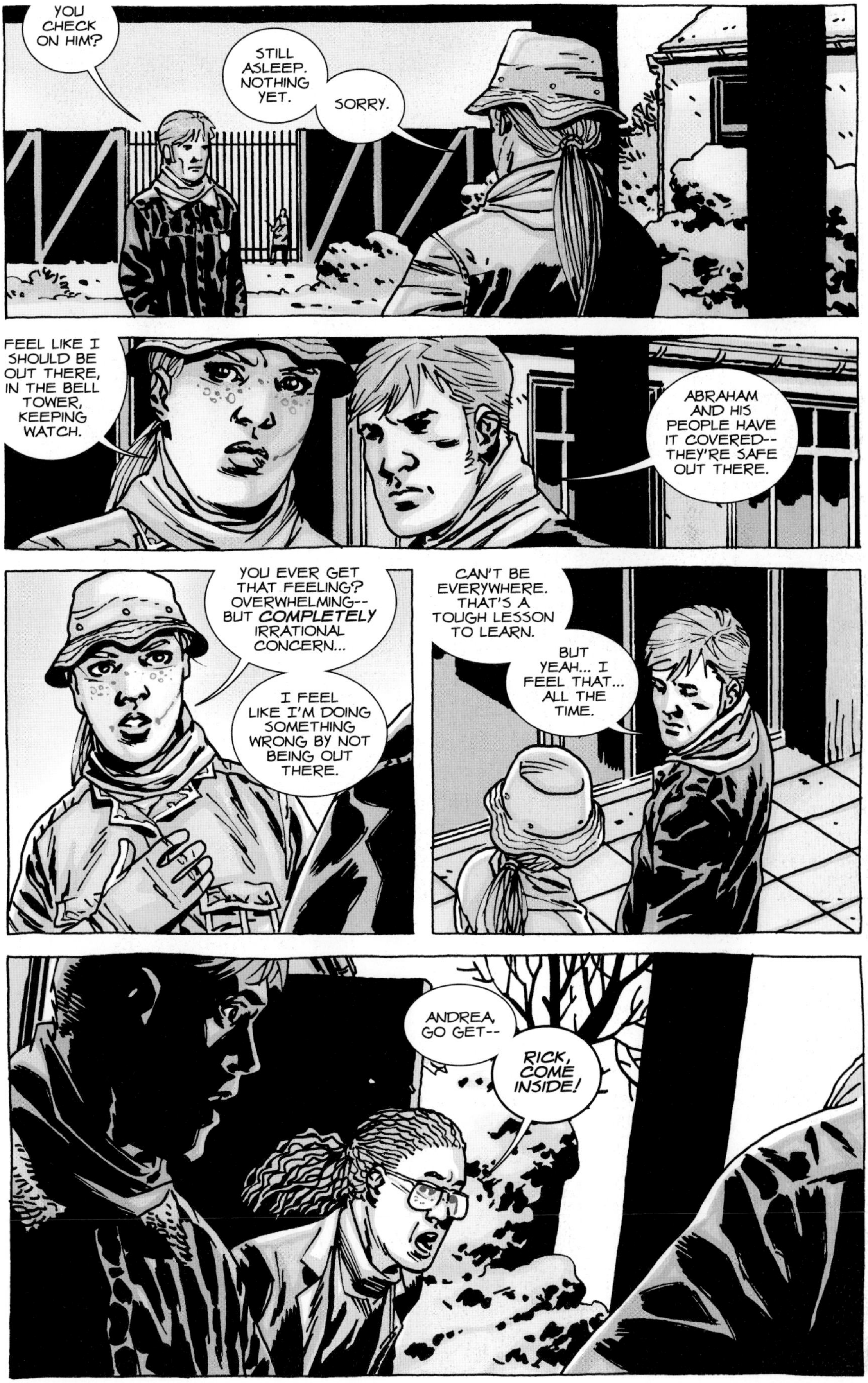

YOU CHECK ON HIM?
STILL ASLEEP. NOTHING YET.
SORRY.
FEEL LIKE I SHOULD BE OUT THERE, IN THE BELL TOWER, KEEPING WATCH.
ABRAHAM AND HIS PEOPLE HAVE IT COVERED-- THEY'RE SAFE OUT THERE.
YOU EVER GET THAT FEELING? OVERWHELMING-- BUT COMPLETELY IRRATIONAL CONCERN...
I FEEL LIKE I'M DOING SOMETHING WRONG BY NOT BEING OUT THERE.
CAN'T BE EVERYWHERE. THAT'S A TOUGH LESSON TO LEARN.
BUT YEAH... I FEEL THAT... ALL THE TIME.
ANDREA, GO GET--
RICK, COME INSIDE!

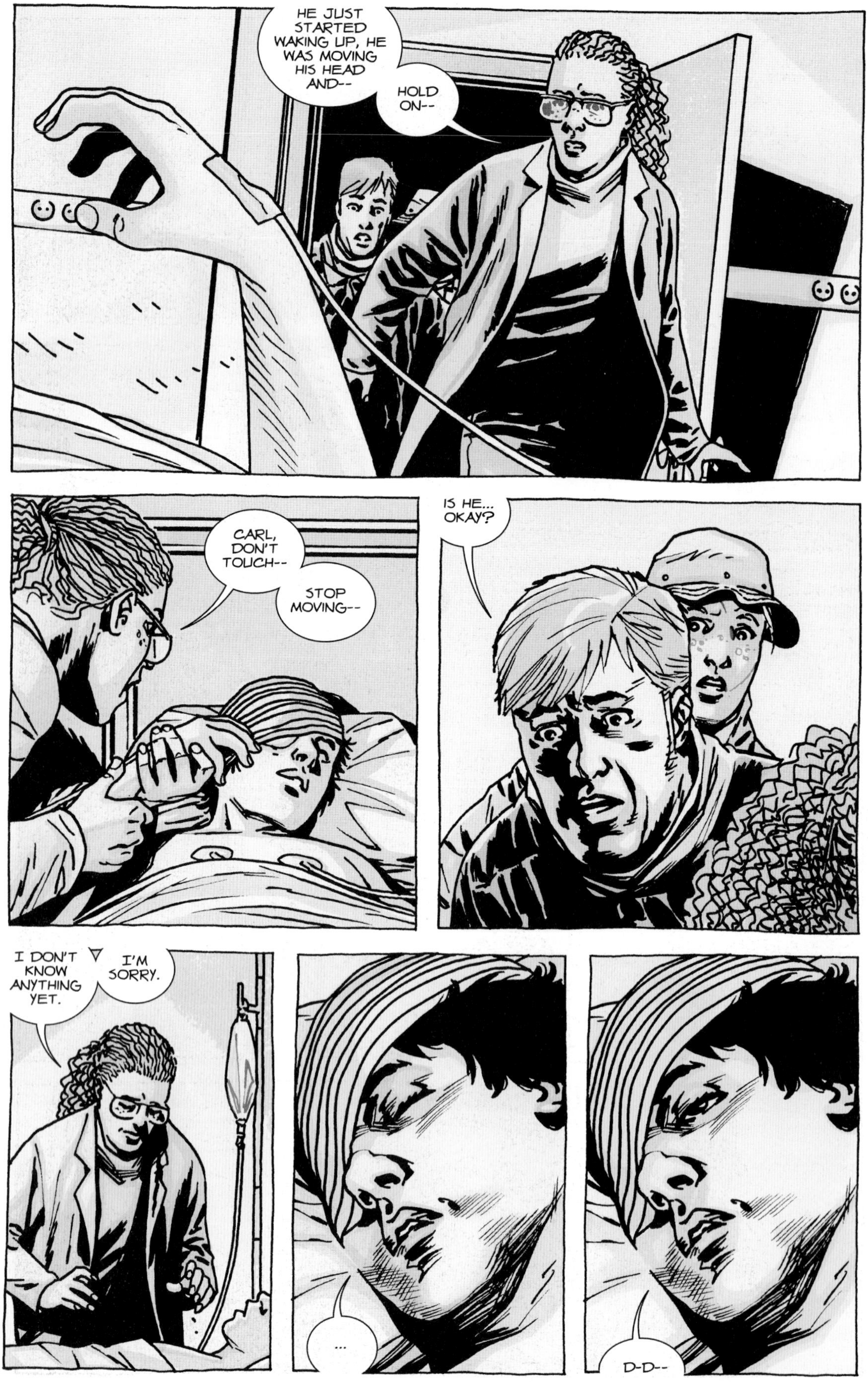
HE JUST STARTED WAKING UP, HE WAS MOVING HIS HEAD AND--
HOLD ON--
CARL, DON'T TOUCH--
STOP MOVING--
IS HE... OKAY?
I DON'T KNOW ANYTHING YET.
I'M SORRY.
...
D-D--

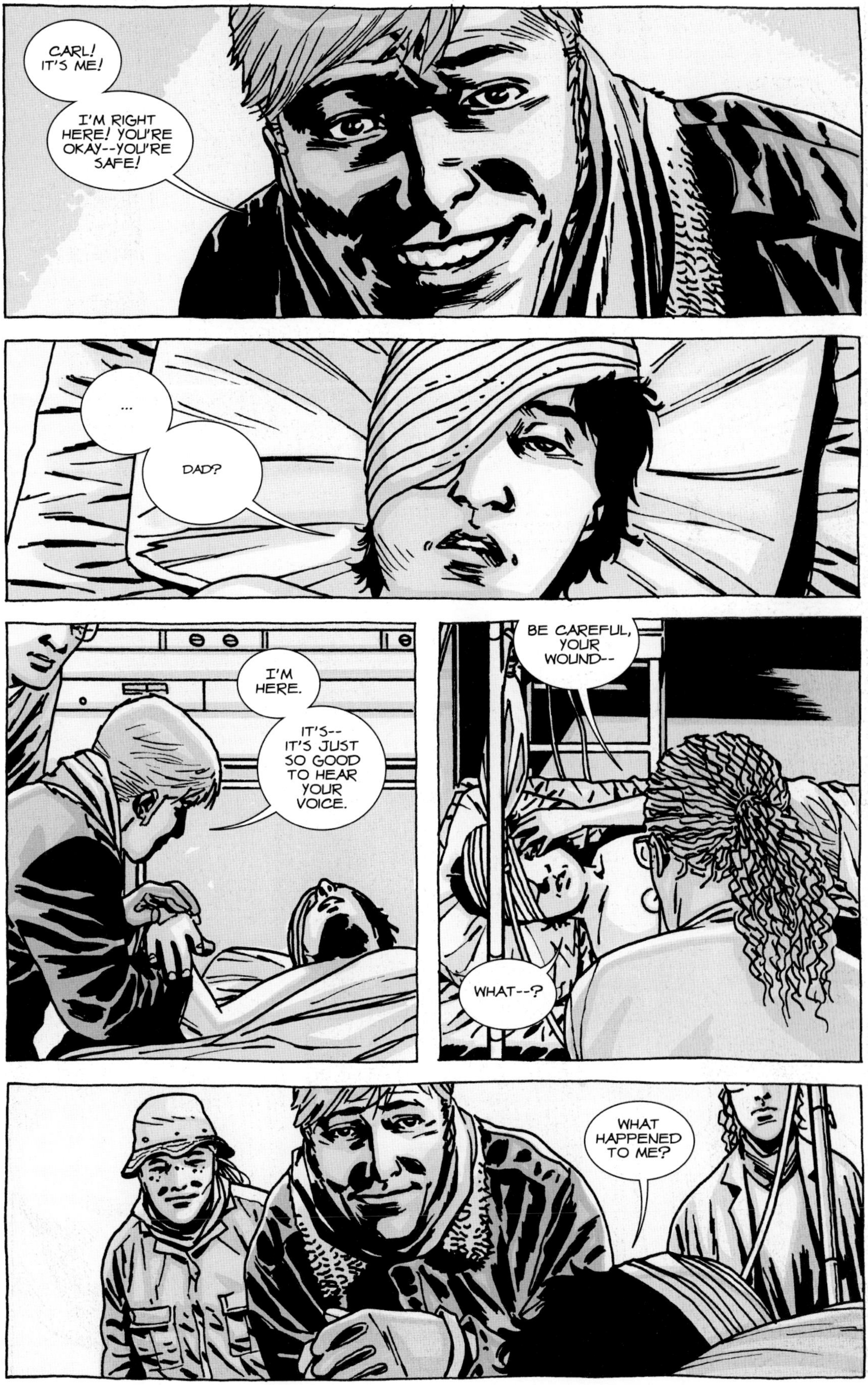
CARL! IT'S ME!
I'M RIGHT HERE! YOU'RE OKAY--YOU'RE SAFE!
...
DAD?
I'M HERE.
IT'S-- IT'S JUST SO GOOD TO HEAR YOUR VOICE.
BE CAREFUL, YOUR WOUND--
WHAT--?
WHAT HAPPENED TO ME?

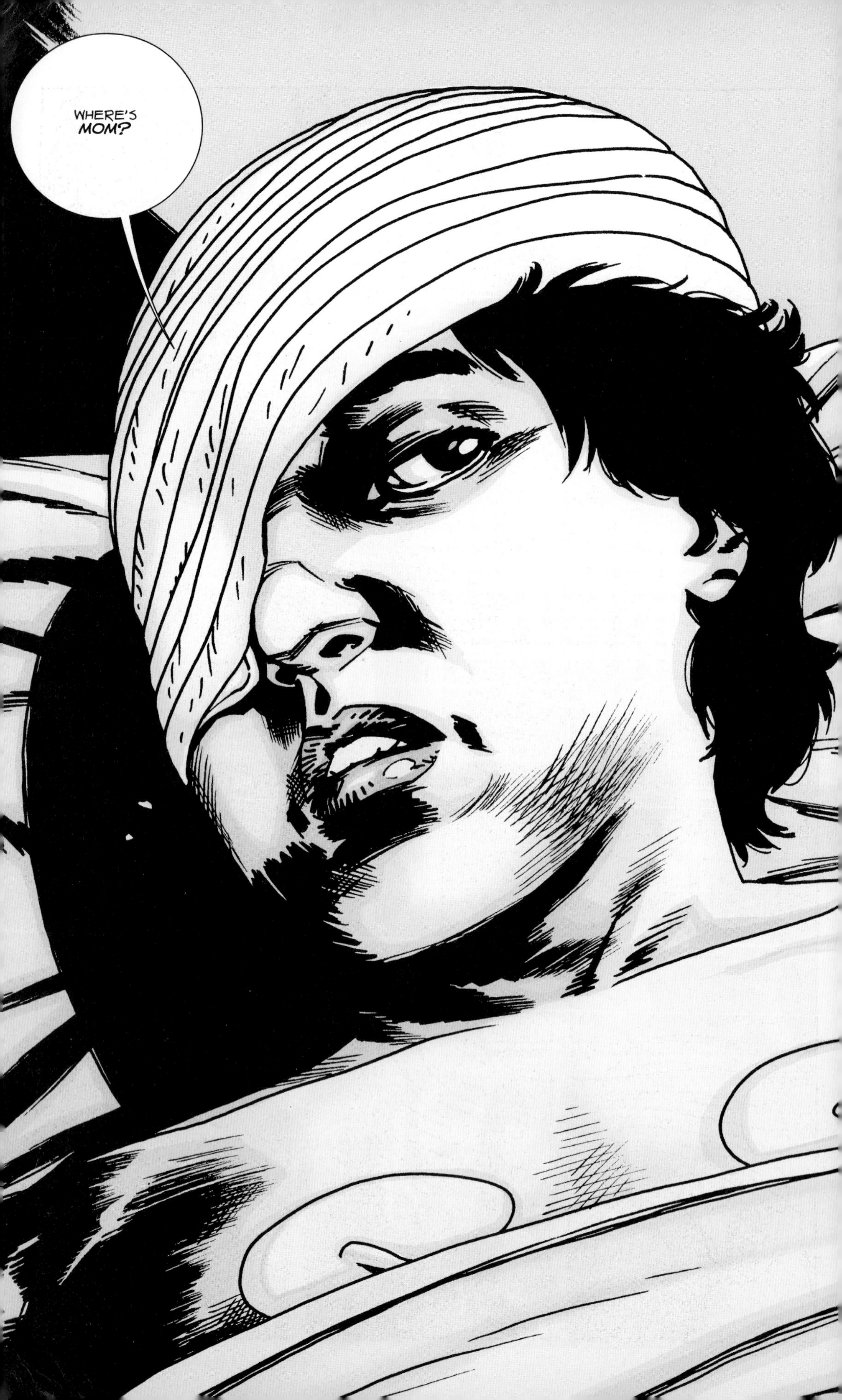
WHERE'S MOM?

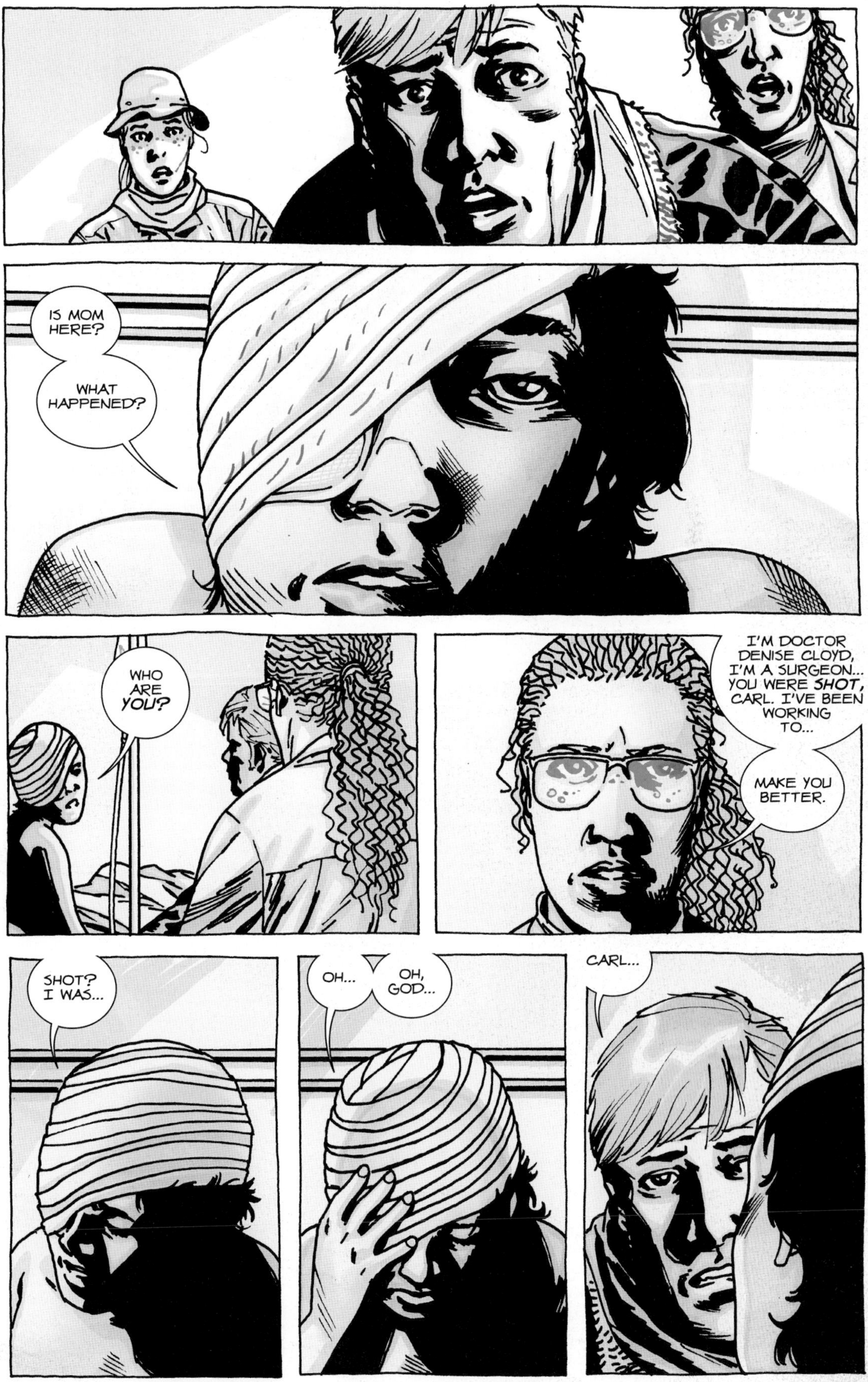
IS MOM HERE?
WHAT HAPPENED?
WHO ARE YOU?
I'M DOCTOR DENISE CLOYD, I'M A SURGEON... YOU WERE SHOT, CARL. I'VE BEEN WORKING TO...
MAKE YOU BETTER.
SHOT? I WAS...
OH...
OH, GOD...
CARL...

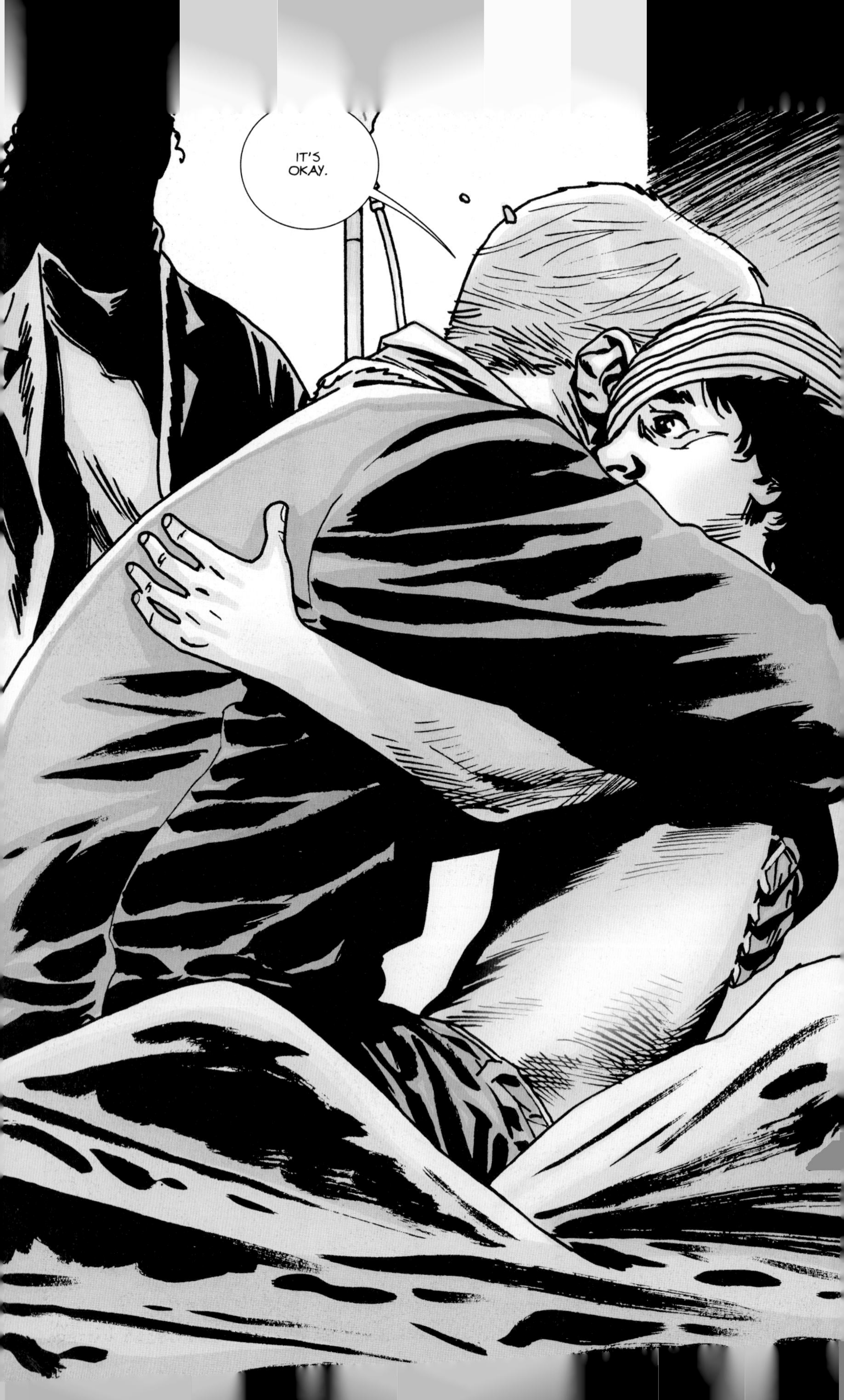
IT'S OKAY.

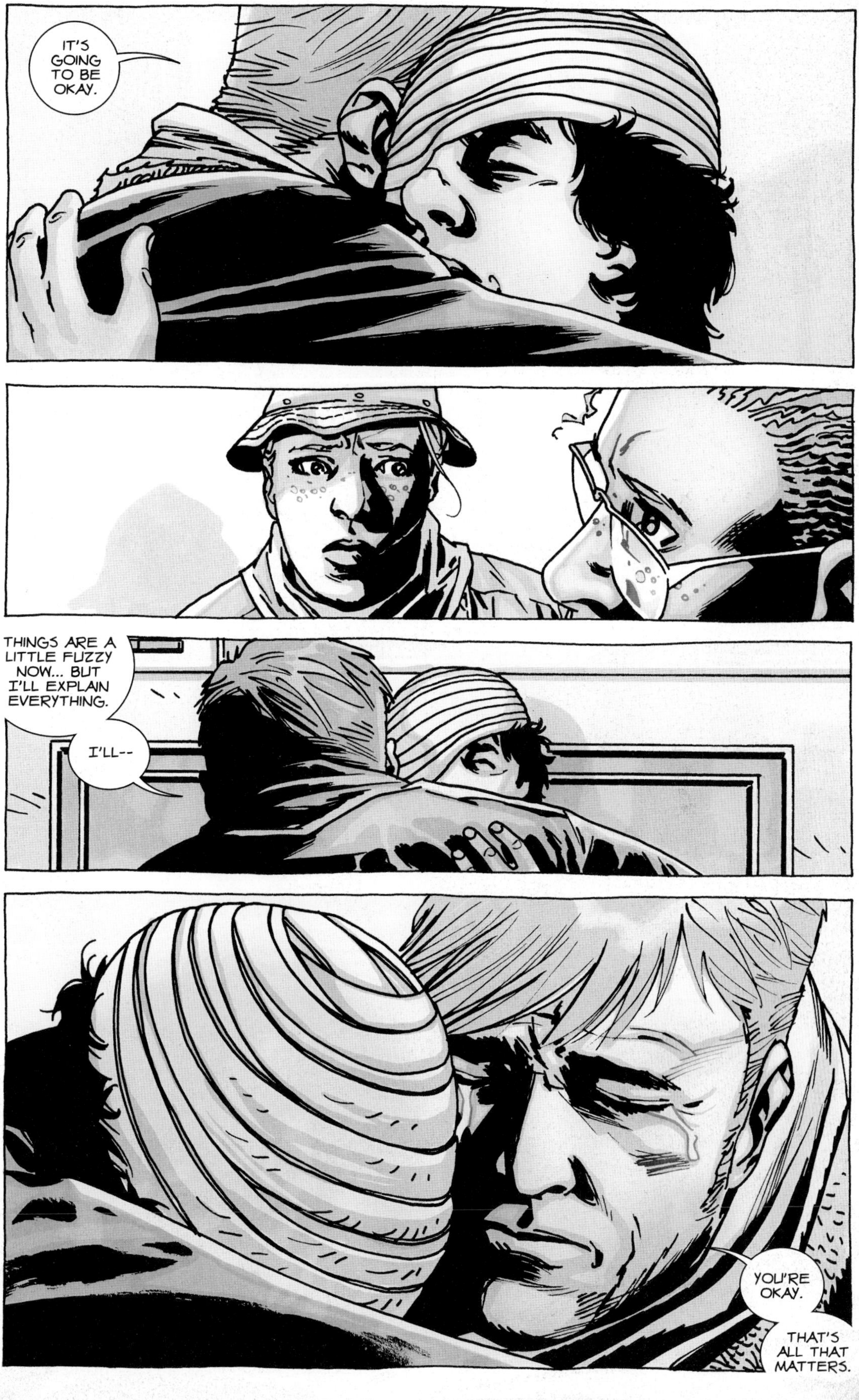
IT'S GOING TO BE OKAY.
THINGS ARE A LITTLE FUZZY NOW... BUT I'LL EXPLAIN EVERYTHING.
I'LL--
YOU'RE OKAY.
THAT'S ALL THAT MATTERS.

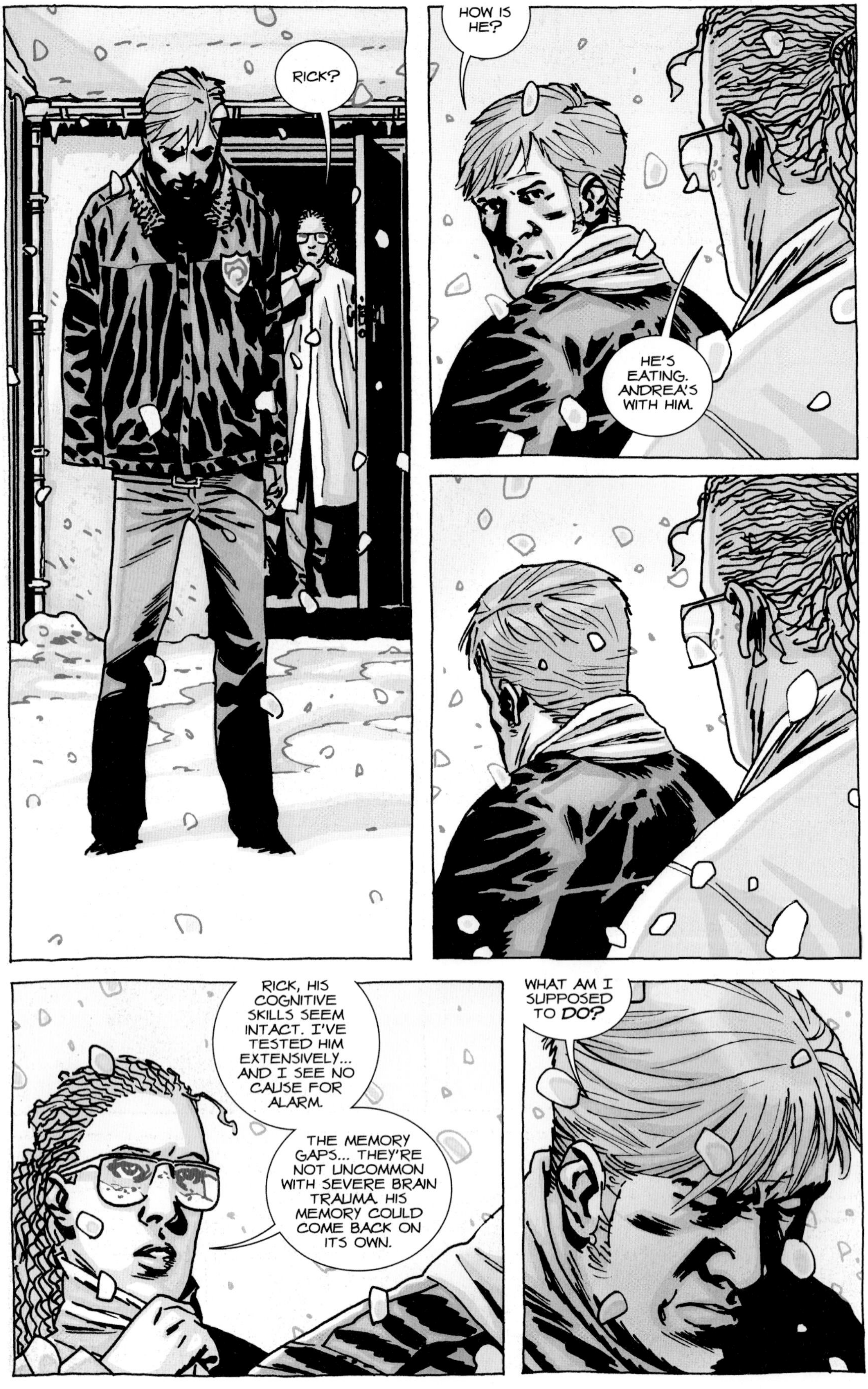
RICK?
HOW IS HE?
HE'S EATING. ANDREA'S WITH HIM.
RICK, HIS COGNITIVE SKILLS SEEM INTACT. I'VE TESTED HIM EXTENSIVELY... AND I SEE NO CAUSE FOR ALARM.
THE MEMORY GAPS... THEY'RE NOT UNCOMMON WITH SEVERE BRAIN TRAUMA. HIS MEMORY COULD COME BACK ON ITS OWN.
WHAT AM I SUPPOSED TO DO?

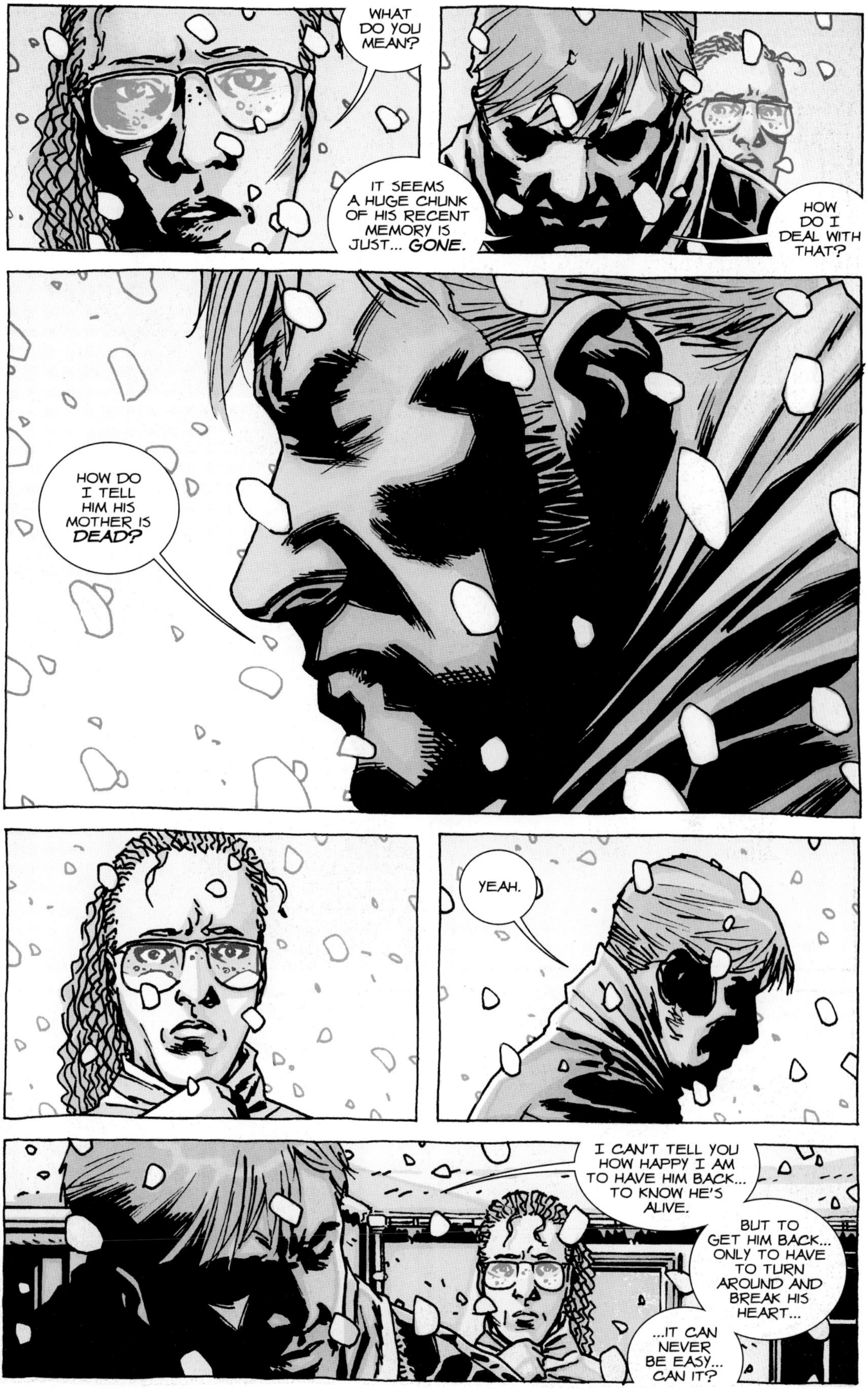
WHAT DO YOU MEAN?
IT SEEMS A HUGE CHUNK OF HIS RECENT MEMORY IS JUST... **GONE.**
HOW DO I DEAL WITH THAT?
HOW DO I TELL HIM HIS MOTHER IS ***DEAD?***
YEAH.
I CAN'T TELL YOU HOW HAPPY I AM TO HAVE HIM BACK... TO KNOW HE'S ALIVE.
BUT TO GET HIM BACK... ONLY TO HAVE TO TURN AROUND AND BREAK HIS HEART...
...IT CAN NEVER BE EASY... CAN IT?

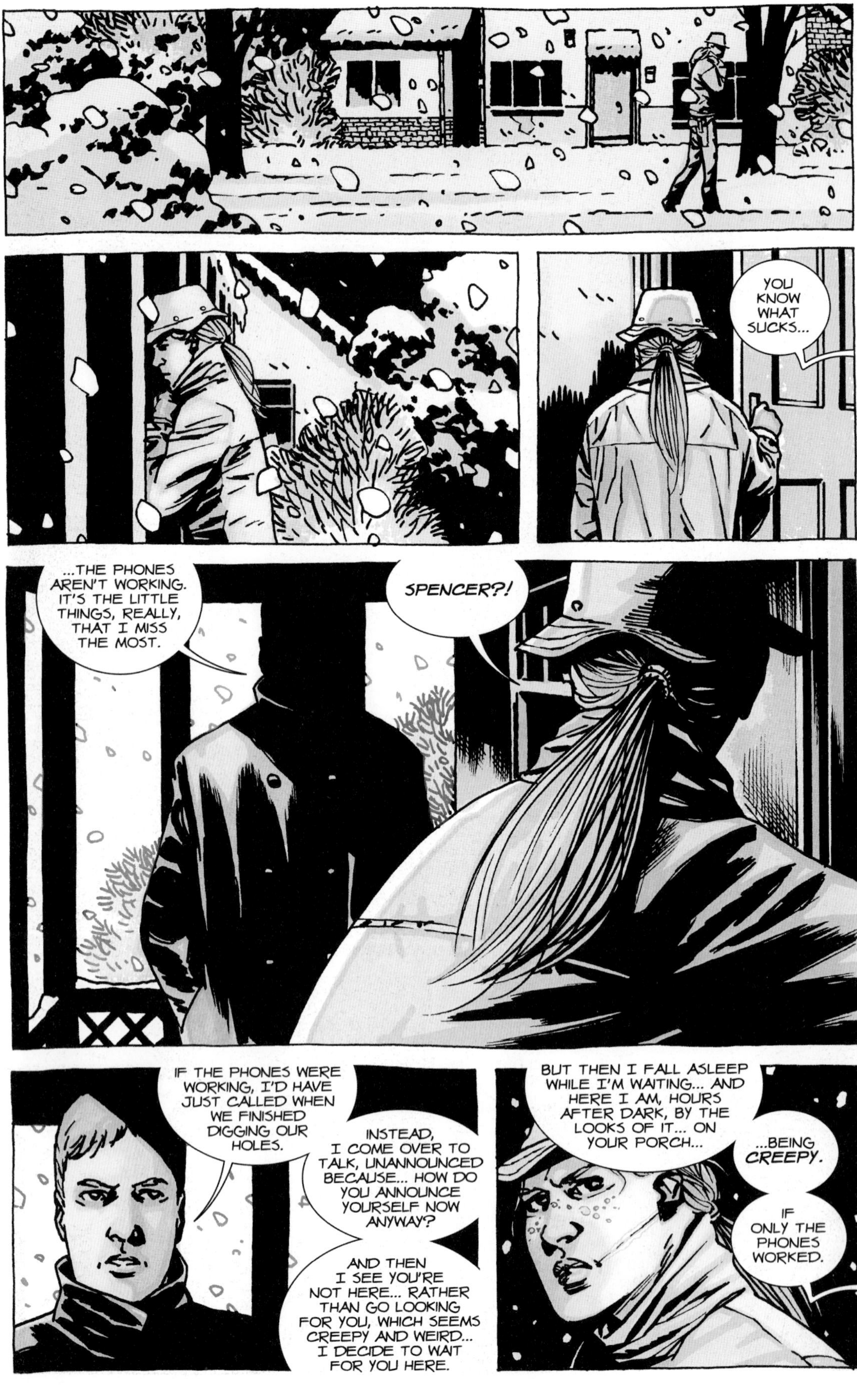
YOU KNOW WHAT SUCKS...
...THE PHONES AREN'T WORKING. IT'S THE LITTLE THINGS, REALLY, THAT I MISS THE MOST.
SPENCER?!
IF THE PHONES WERE WORKING, I'D HAVE JUST CALLED WHEN WE FINISHED DIGGING OUR HOLES.
INSTEAD, I COME OVER TO TALK, UNANNOUNCED BECAUSE... HOW DO YOU ANNOUNCE YOURSELF NOW ANYWAY?
AND THEN I SEE YOU'RE NOT HERE... RATHER THAN GO LOOKING FOR YOU, WHICH SEEMS CREEPY AND WEIRD... I DECIDE TO WAIT FOR YOU HERE.
BUT THEN I FALL ASLEEP WHILE I'M WAITING... AND HERE I AM, HOURS AFTER DARK, BY THE LOOKS OF IT... ON YOUR PORCH...
...BEING CREEPY.
IF ONLY THE PHONES WORKED.

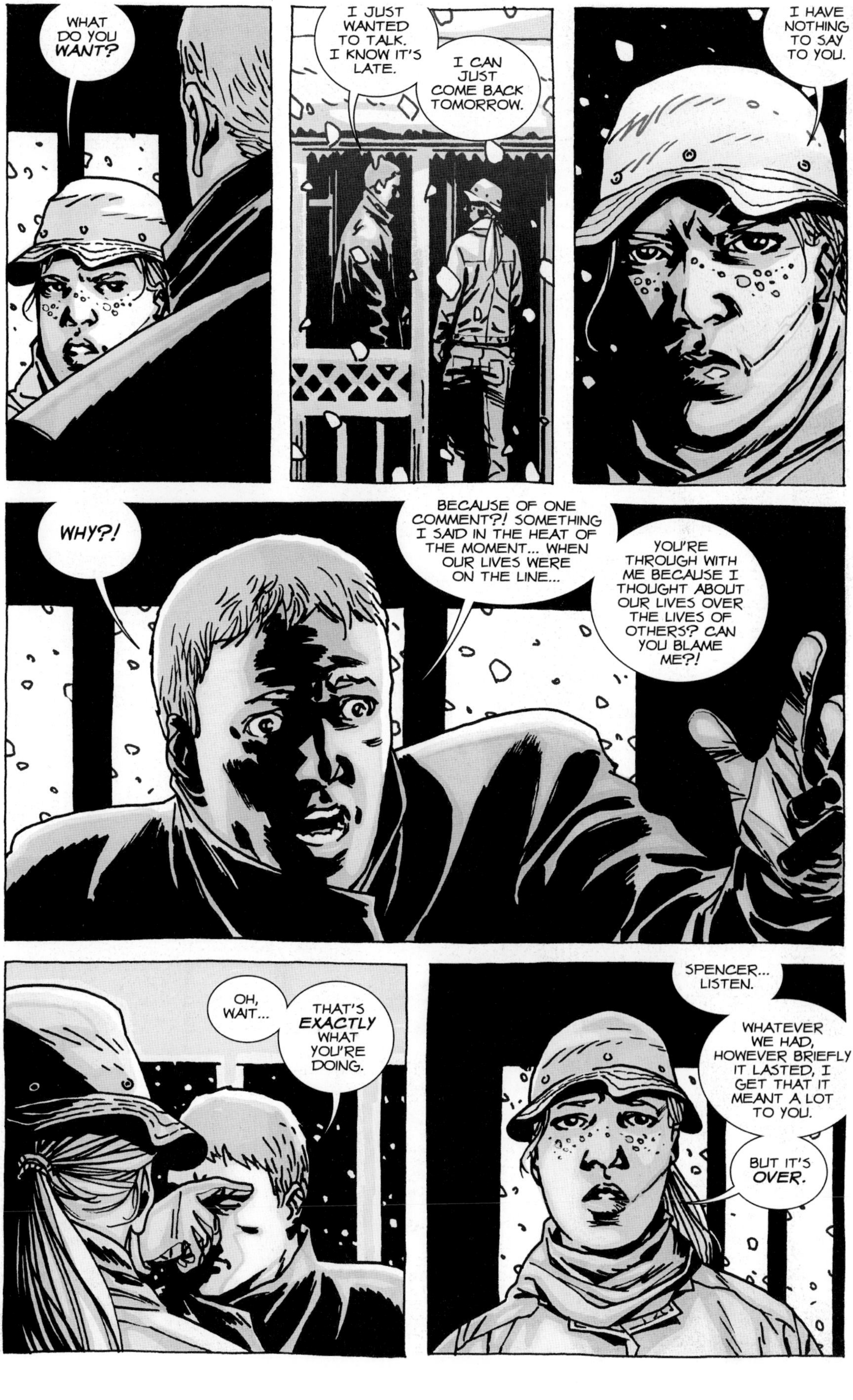
WHAT DO YOU *WANT?*
I JUST WANTED TO TALK. I KNOW IT'S LATE.
I CAN JUST COME BACK TOMORROW.
I HAVE NOTHING TO SAY TO YOU.
WHY?!
BECAUSE OF ONE COMMENT?! SOMETHING I SAID IN THE HEAT OF THE MOMENT... WHEN OUR LIVES WERE ON THE LINE...
YOU'RE THROUGH WITH ME BECAUSE I THOUGHT ABOUT OUR LIVES OVER THE LIVES OF OTHERS? CAN YOU BLAME ME?!
OH, WAIT...
THAT'S *EXACTLY* WHAT YOU'RE DOING.
SPENCER... LISTEN.
WHATEVER WE HAD, HOWEVER BRIEFLY IT LASTED, I GET THAT IT MEANT A LOT TO YOU.
BUT IT'S *OVER.*

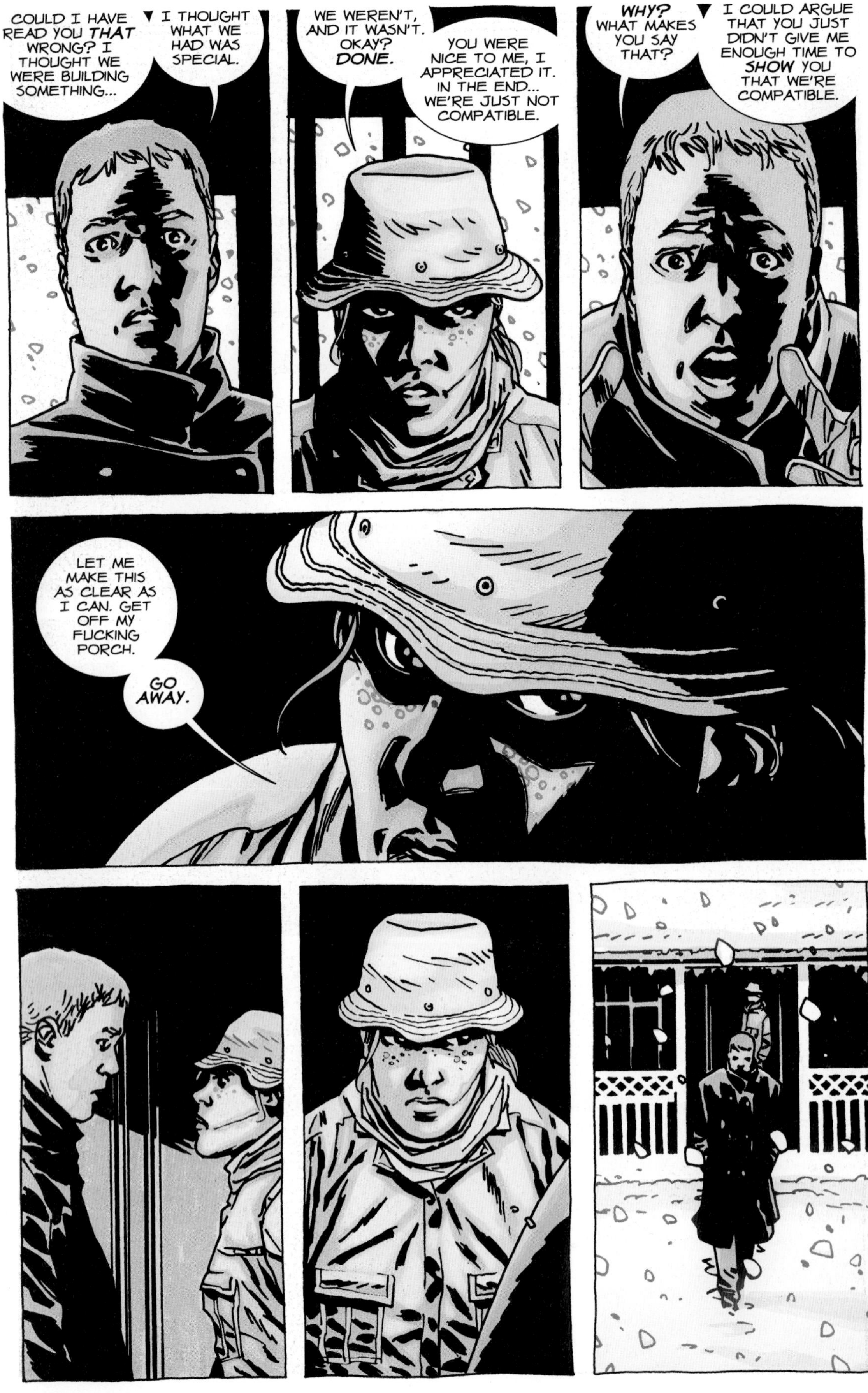

COULD I HAVE READ YOU THAT WRONG? I THOUGHT WE WERE BUILDING SOMETHING...
I THOUGHT WHAT WE HAD WAS SPECIAL.
WE WEREN'T, AND IT WASN'T. OKAY? DONE.
YOU WERE NICE TO ME, I APPRECIATED IT. IN THE END... WE'RE JUST NOT COMPATIBLE.
WHY? WHAT MAKES YOU SAY THAT?
I COULD ARGUE THAT YOU JUST DIDN'T GIVE ME ENOUGH TIME TO SHOW YOU THAT WE'RE COMPATIBLE.
LET ME MAKE THIS AS CLEAR AS I CAN. GET OFF MY FUCKING PORCH.
GO AWAY.

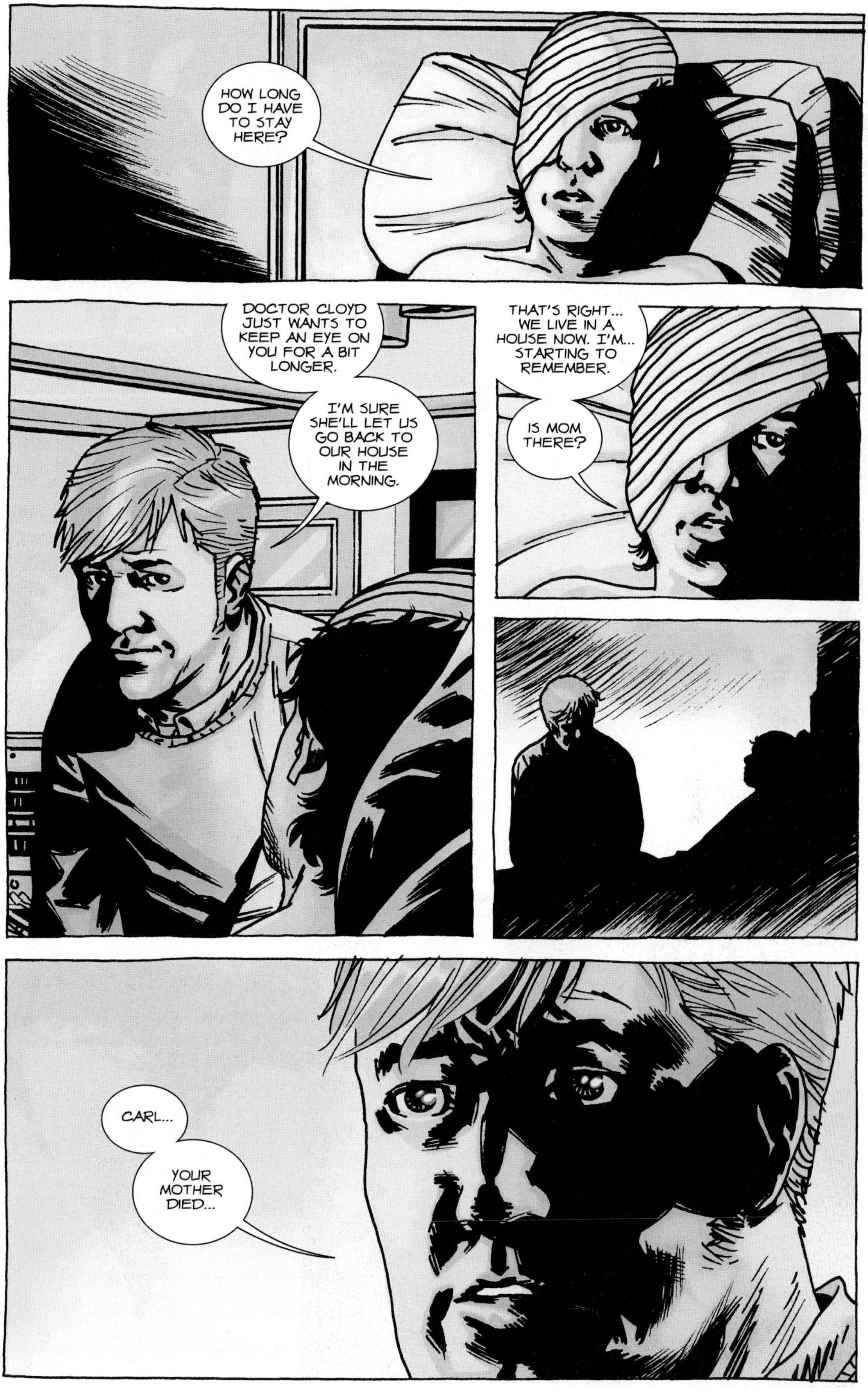
HOW LONG DO I HAVE TO STAY HERE?
DOCTOR CLOYD JUST WANTS TO KEEP AN EYE ON YOU FOR A BIT LONGER.
I'M SURE SHE'LL LET US GO BACK TO OUR HOUSE IN THE MORNING.
THAT'S RIGHT... WE LIVE IN A HOUSE NOW. I'M... STARTING TO REMEMBER.
IS MOM THERE?
CARL...
YOUR MOTHER DIED...

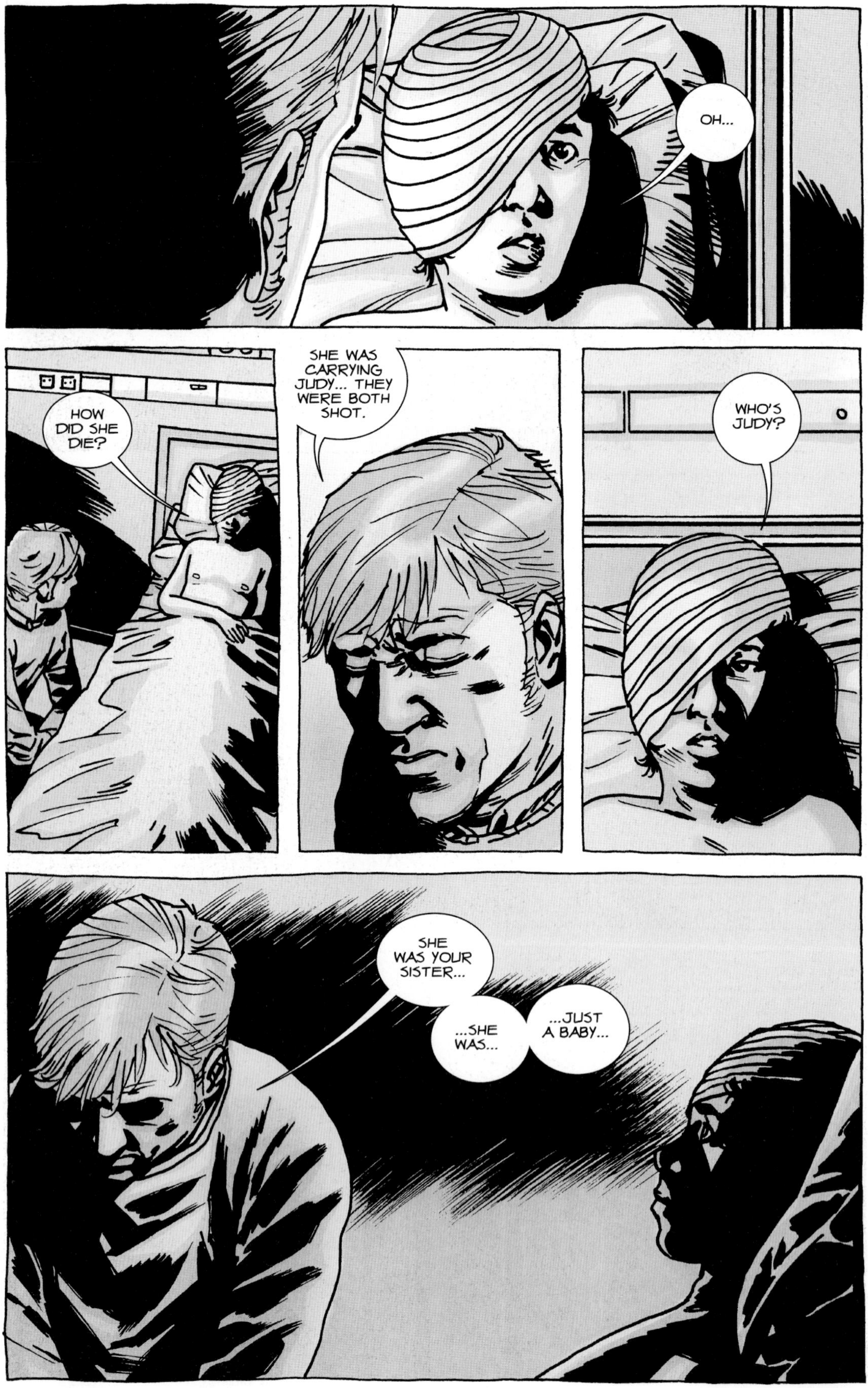
OH...
HOW DID SHE DIE?
SHE WAS CARRYING JUDY... THEY WERE BOTH SHOT.
WHO'S JUDY?
SHE WAS YOUR SISTER...
...SHE WAS...
...JUST A BABY...

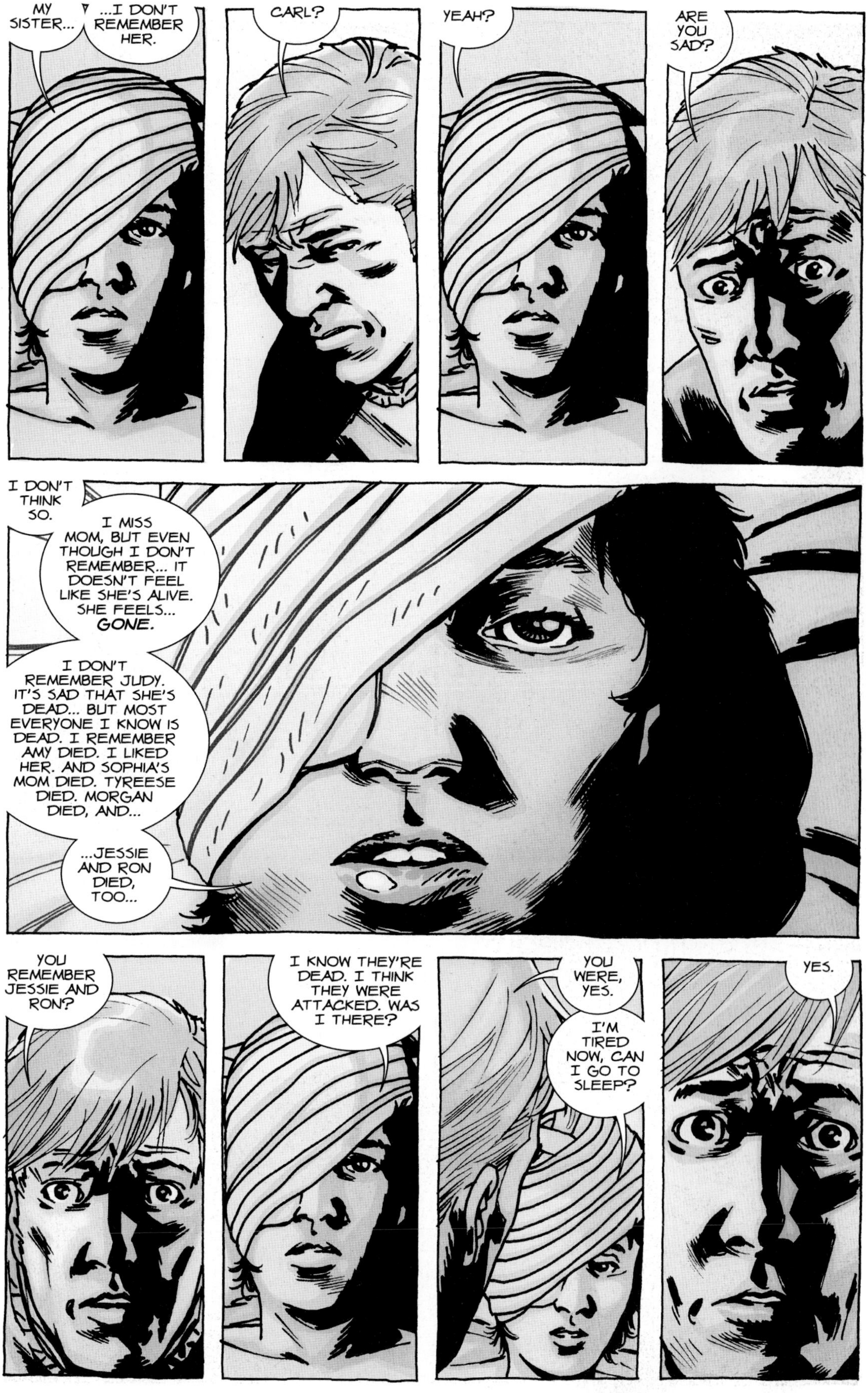
MY SISTER...
...I DON'T REMEMBER HER.
CARL?
YEAH?
ARE YOU SAD?
I DON'T THINK SO.
I MISS MOM, BUT EVEN THOUGH I DON'T REMEMBER... IT DOESN'T FEEL LIKE SHE'S ALIVE. SHE FEELS... **GONE.**
I DON'T REMEMBER JUDY. IT'S SAD THAT SHE'S DEAD... BUT MOST EVERYONE I KNOW IS DEAD. I REMEMBER AMY DIED. I LIKED HER. AND SOPHIA'S MOM DIED. TYREESE DIED. MORGAN DIED, AND...
...JESSIE AND RON DIED, TOO...
YOU REMEMBER JESSIE AND RON?
I KNOW THEY'RE DEAD. I THINK THEY WERE ATTACKED. WAS I THERE?
YOU WERE, YES.
I'M TIRED NOW, CAN I GO TO SLEEP?
YES.

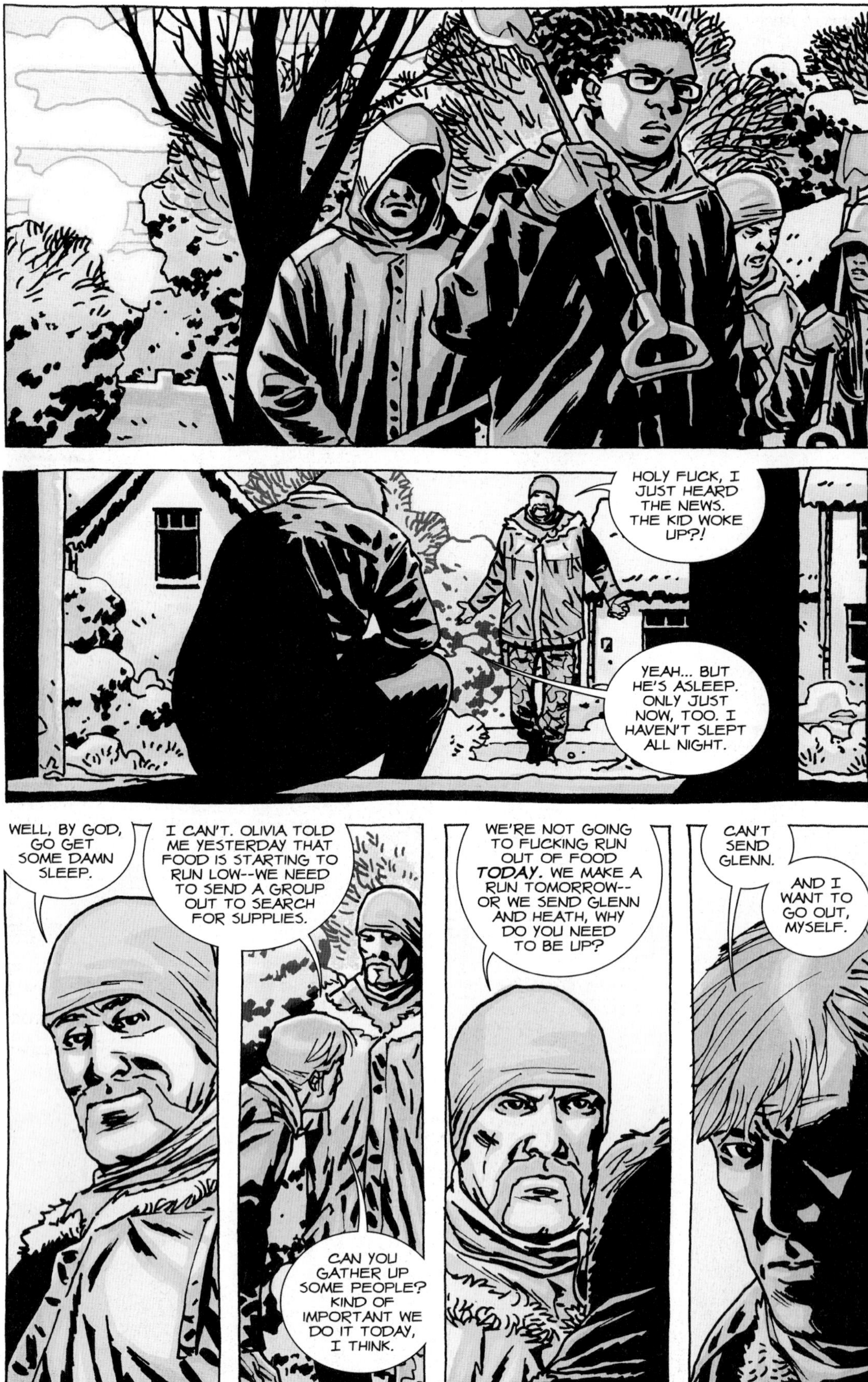
HOLY FUCK, I JUST HEARD THE NEWS. THE KID WOKE UP?!
YEAH... BUT HE'S ASLEEP. ONLY JUST NOW, TOO. I HAVEN'T SLEPT ALL NIGHT.
WELL, BY GOD, GO GET SOME DAMN SLEEP.
I CAN'T. OLIVIA TOLD ME YESTERDAY THAT FOOD IS STARTING TO RUN LOW--WE NEED TO SEND A GROUP OUT TO SEARCH FOR SUPPLIES.
CAN YOU GATHER UP SOME PEOPLE? KIND OF IMPORTANT WE DO IT TODAY, I THINK.
WE'RE NOT GOING TO FUCKING RUN OUT OF FOOD *TODAY.* WE MAKE A RUN TOMORROW--OR WE SEND GLENN AND HEATH, WHY DO YOU NEED TO BE UP?
CAN'T SEND GLENN.
AND I WANT TO GO OUT, MYSELF.

WHY NOT AND WHY THE FUCK?

BECAUSE MAGGIE ASKED ME NOT TO. GLENN ALWAYS GOES, IT'S ALWAYS KIND OF BEEN HIS THING.

SHE THINKS IT'S NOT FAIR AND SHE'S RIGHT.

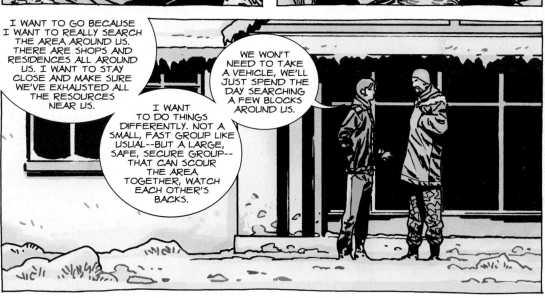

I WANT TO GO BECAUSE I WANT TO REALLY SEARCH THE AREA AROUND US. THERE ARE SHOPS AND RESIDENCES ALL AROUND US. I WANT TO STAY CLOSE AND MAKE SURE WE'VE EXHAUSTED ALL THE RESOURCES NEAR US.

I WANT TO DO THINGS DIFFERENTLY. NOT A SMALL, FAST GROUP LIKE USUAL--BUT A LARGE, SAFE, SECURE GROUP-- THAT CAN SCOUR THE AREA TOGETHER, WATCH EACH OTHER'S BACKS.

WE WON'T NEED TO TAKE A VEHICLE, WE'LL JUST SPEND THE DAY SEARCHING A FEW BLOCKS AROUND US.

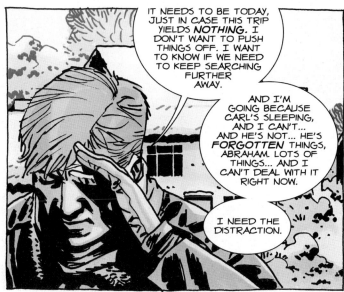

IT NEEDS TO BE TODAY, JUST IN CASE THIS TRIP YIELDS **NOTHING.** I DON'T WANT TO PUSH THINGS OFF. I WANT TO KNOW IF WE NEED TO KEEP SEARCHING FURTHER AWAY.

AND I'M GOING BECAUSE CARL'S SLEEPING, AND I CAN'T... AND HE'S NOT... HE'S *FORGOTTEN* THINGS, ABRAHAM. LOTS OF THINGS... AND I CAN'T DEAL WITH IT RIGHT NOW.

I NEED THE DISTRACTION.

OKAY.

UNDERSTOOD.

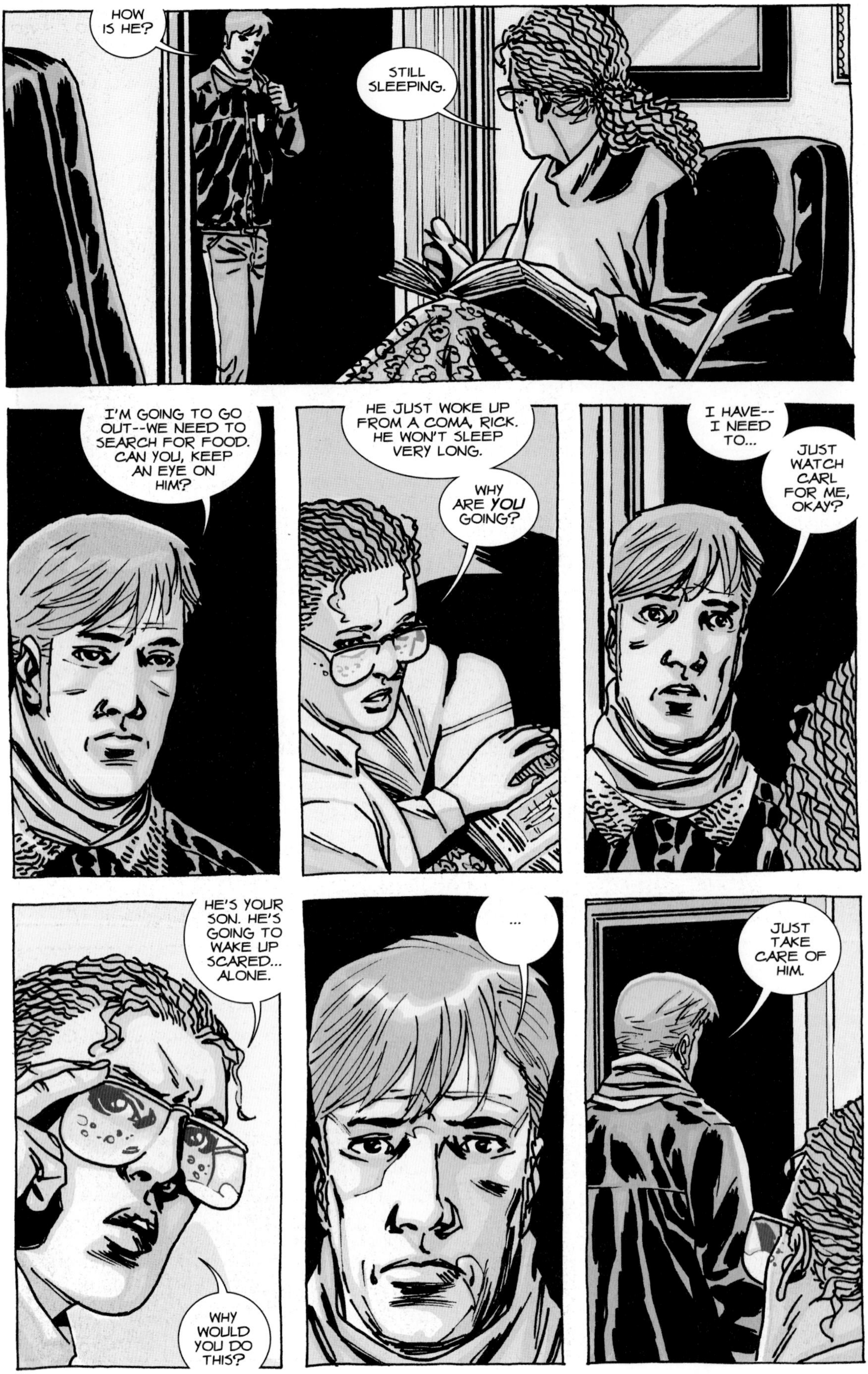
HOW IS HE?
STILL SLEEPING.
I'M GOING TO GO OUT--WE NEED TO SEARCH FOR FOOD. CAN YOU, KEEP AN EYE ON HIM?
HE JUST WOKE UP FROM A COMA, RICK. HE WON'T SLEEP VERY LONG.
WHY ARE *YOU* GOING?
I HAVE-- I NEED TO...
JUST WATCH CARL FOR ME, OKAY?
HE'S YOUR SON. HE'S GOING TO WAKE UP SCARED... ALONE.
WHY WOULD YOU DO THIS?
...
JUST TAKE CARE OF HIM.

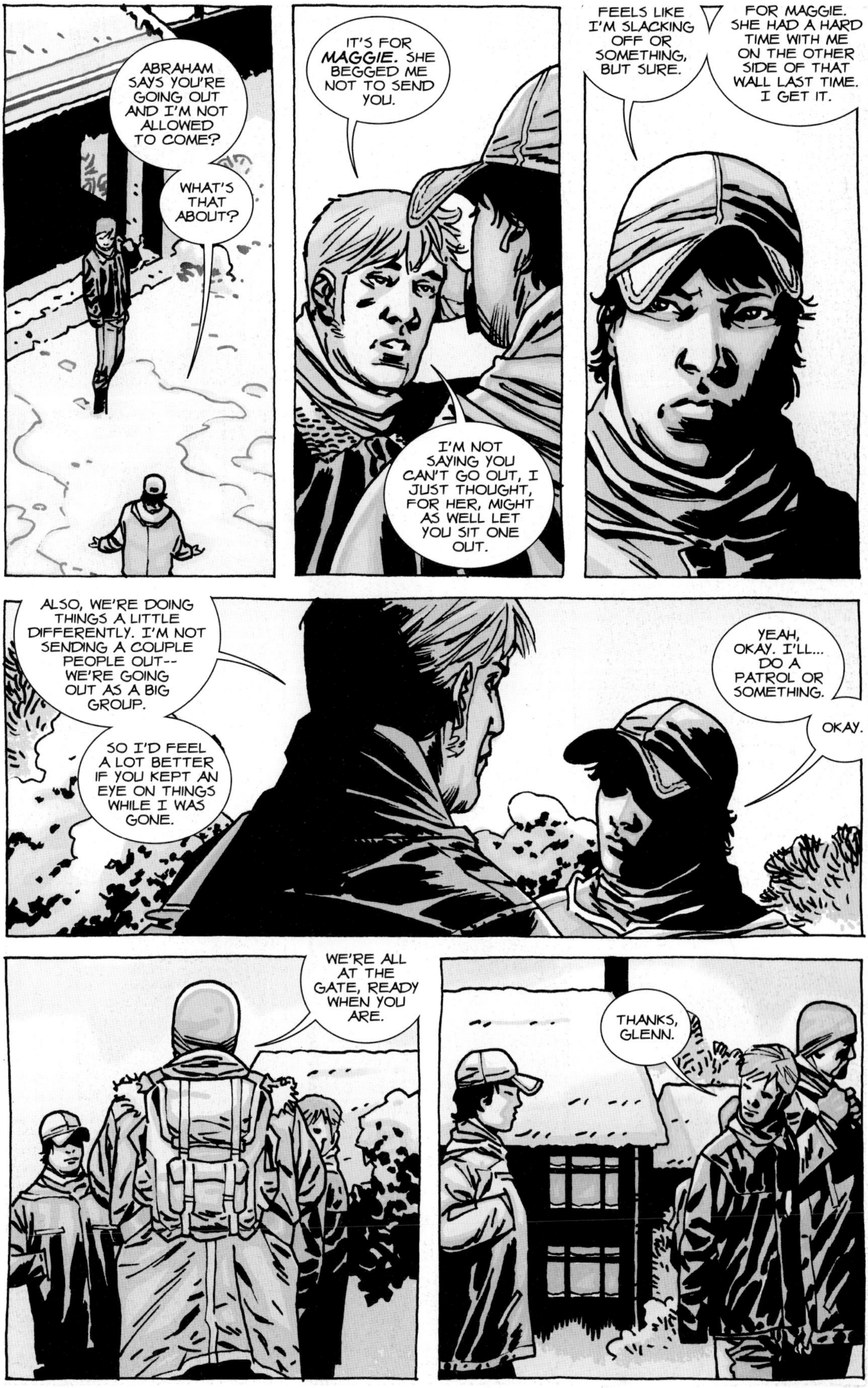

ABRAHAM SAYS YOU'RE GOING OUT AND I'M NOT ALLOWED TO COME?
WHAT'S THAT ABOUT?
IT'S FOR MAGGIE. SHE BEGGED ME NOT TO SEND YOU.
I'M NOT SAYING YOU CAN'T GO OUT, I JUST THOUGHT, FOR HER, MIGHT AS WELL LET YOU SIT ONE OUT.
FEELS LIKE I'M SLACKING OFF OR SOMETHING, BUT SURE.
FOR MAGGIE. SHE HAD A HARD TIME WITH ME ON THE OTHER SIDE OF THAT WALL LAST TIME. I GET IT.
ALSO, WE'RE DOING THINGS A LITTLE DIFFERENTLY. I'M NOT SENDING A COUPLE PEOPLE OUT-- WE'RE GOING OUT AS A BIG GROUP.
SO I'D FEEL A LOT BETTER IF YOU KEPT AN EYE ON THINGS WHILE I WAS GONE.
YEAH, OKAY. I'LL... DO A PATROL OR SOMETHING.
OKAY.
WE'RE ALL AT THE GATE, READY WHEN YOU ARE.
THANKS, GLENN.

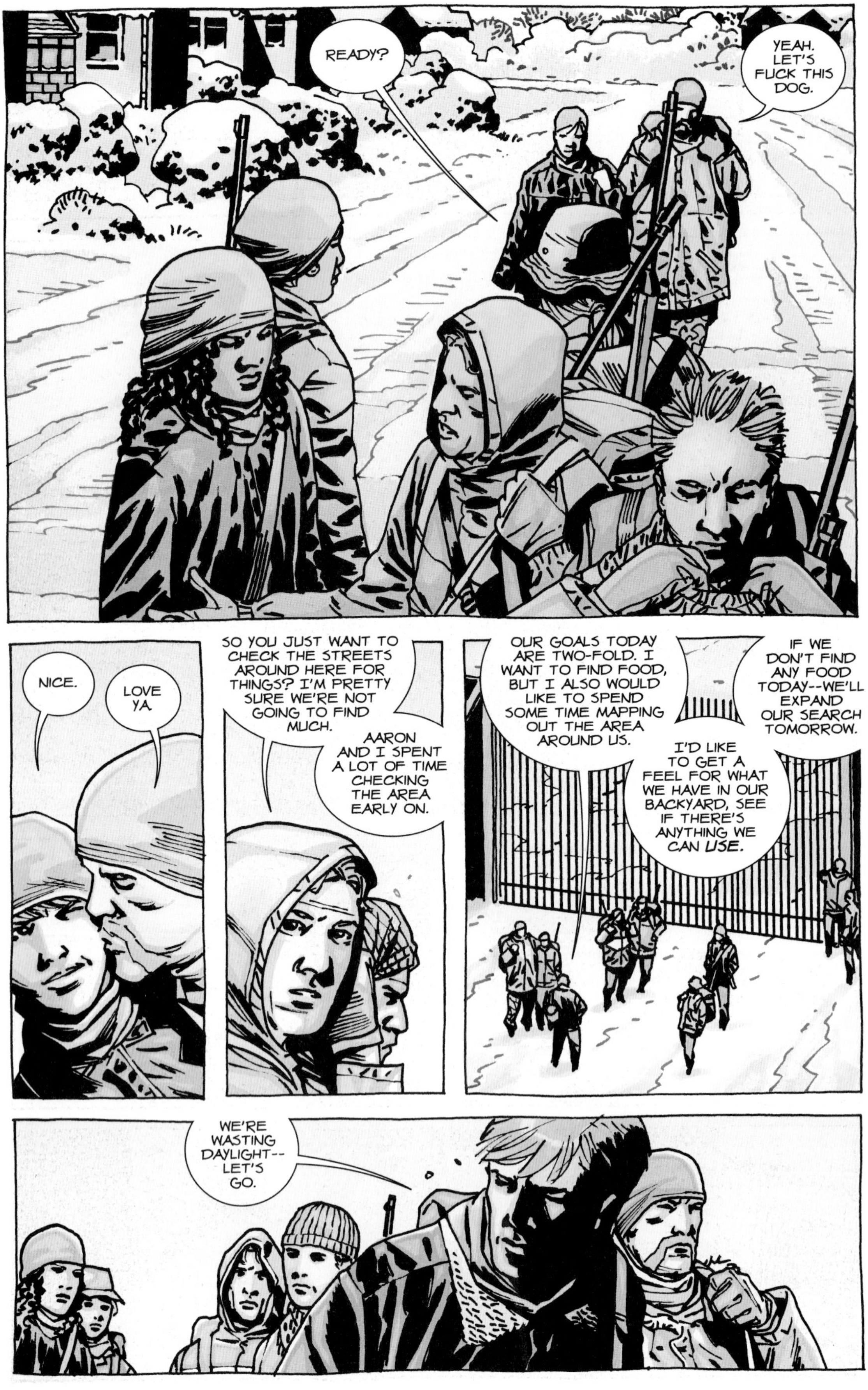
READY?
YEAH. LET'S FUCK THIS DOG.
NICE.
LOVE YA.
SO YOU JUST WANT TO CHECK THE STREETS AROUND HERE FOR THINGS? I'M PRETTY SURE WE'RE NOT GOING TO FIND MUCH.
AARON AND I SPENT A LOT OF TIME CHECKING THE AREA EARLY ON.
OUR GOALS TODAY ARE TWO-FOLD. I WANT TO FIND FOOD, BUT I ALSO WOULD LIKE TO SPEND SOME TIME MAPPING OUT THE AREA AROUND US.
I'D LIKE TO GET A FEEL FOR WHAT WE HAVE IN OUR BACKYARD, SEE IF THERE'S ANYTHING WE CAN USE.
IF WE DON'T FIND ANY FOOD TODAY--WE'LL EXPAND OUR SEARCH TOMORROW.
WE'RE WASTING DAYLIGHT-- LET'S GO.

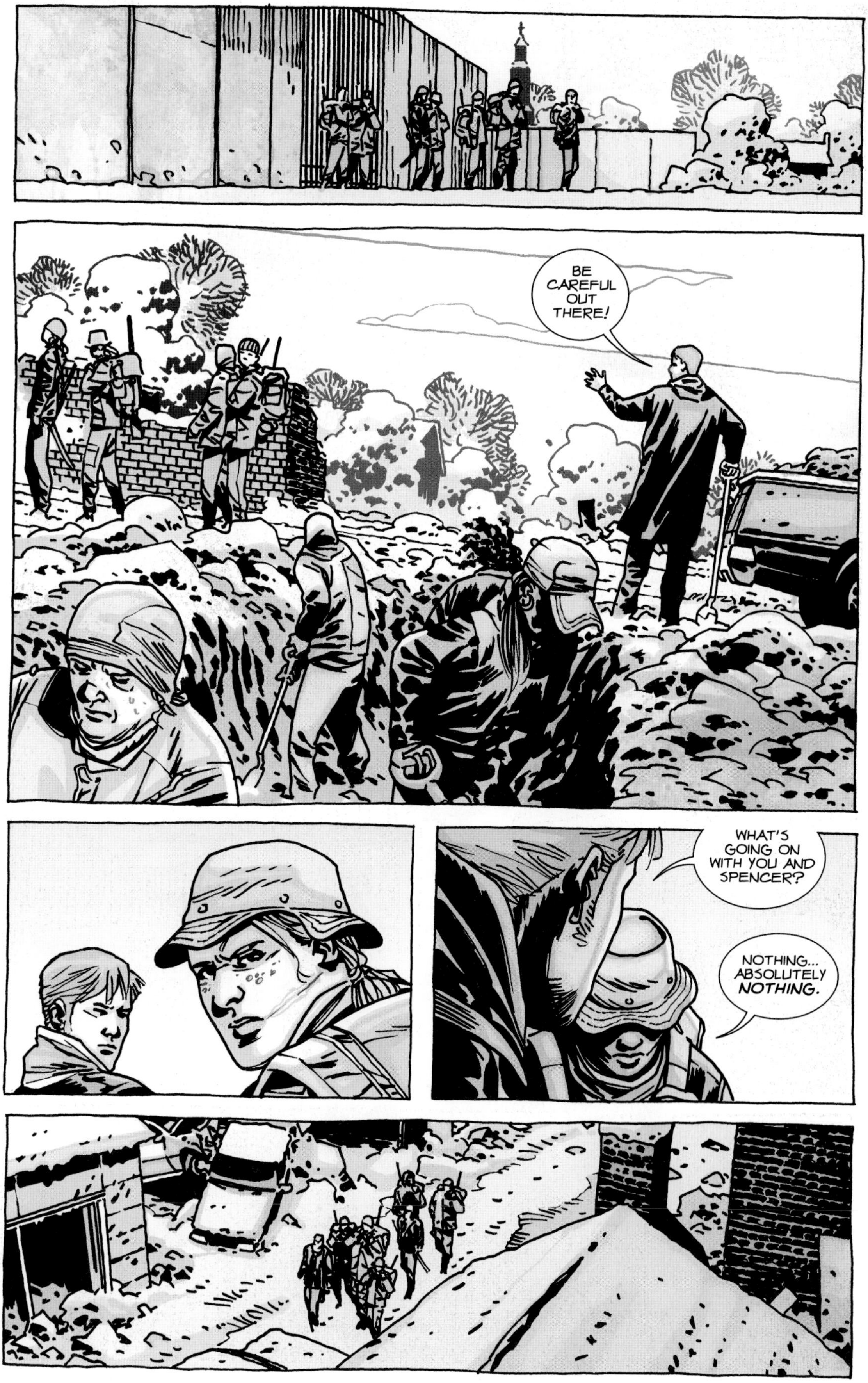
BE CAREFUL OUT THERE!
WHAT'S GOING ON WITH YOU AND SPENCER?
NOTHING... ABSOLUTELY *NOTHING.*

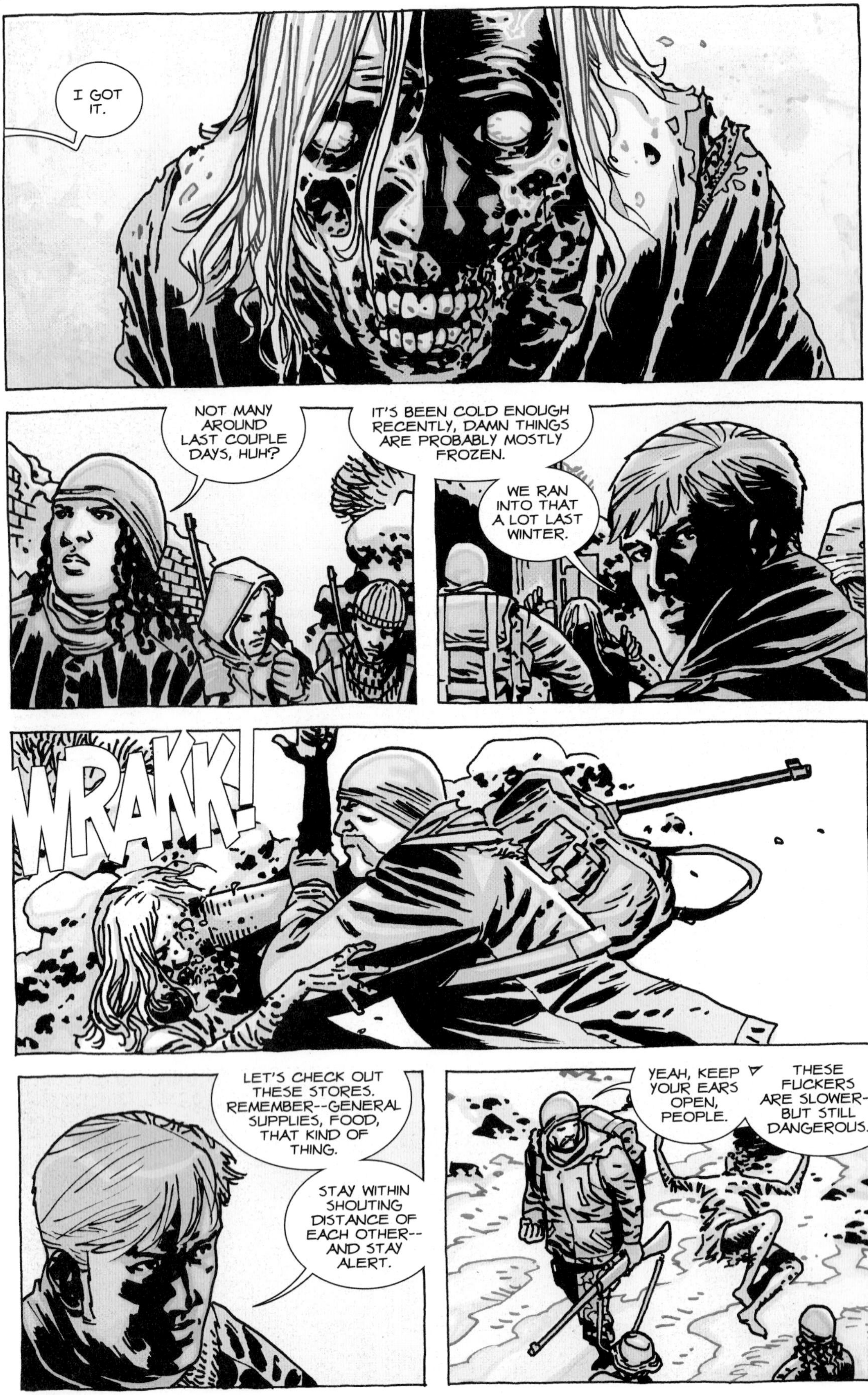
I GOT IT.
NOT MANY AROUND LAST COUPLE DAYS, HUH?
IT'S BEEN COLD ENOUGH RECENTLY, DAMN THINGS ARE PROBABLY MOSTLY FROZEN.
WE RAN INTO THAT A LOT LAST WINTER.
WRAKK!
LET'S CHECK OUT THESE STORES. REMEMBER--GENERAL SUPPLIES, FOOD, THAT KIND OF THING.
STAY WITHIN SHOUTING DISTANCE OF EACH OTHER--AND STAY ALERT.
YEAH, KEEP YOUR EARS OPEN, PEOPLE.
THESE FUCKERS ARE SLOWER--BUT STILL DANGEROUS.

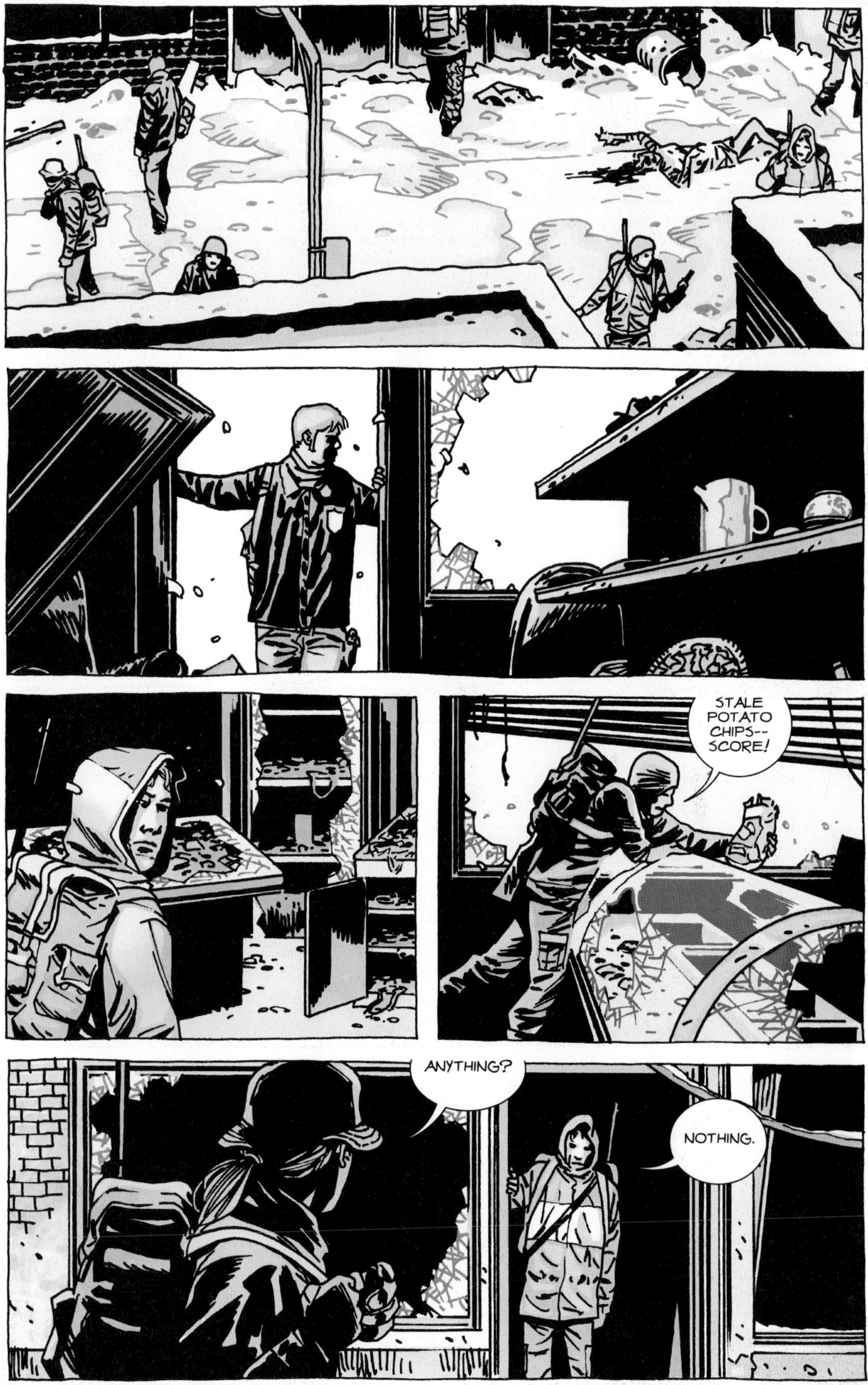
STALE POTATO CHIPS-- SCORE!
ANYTHING?
NOTHING.

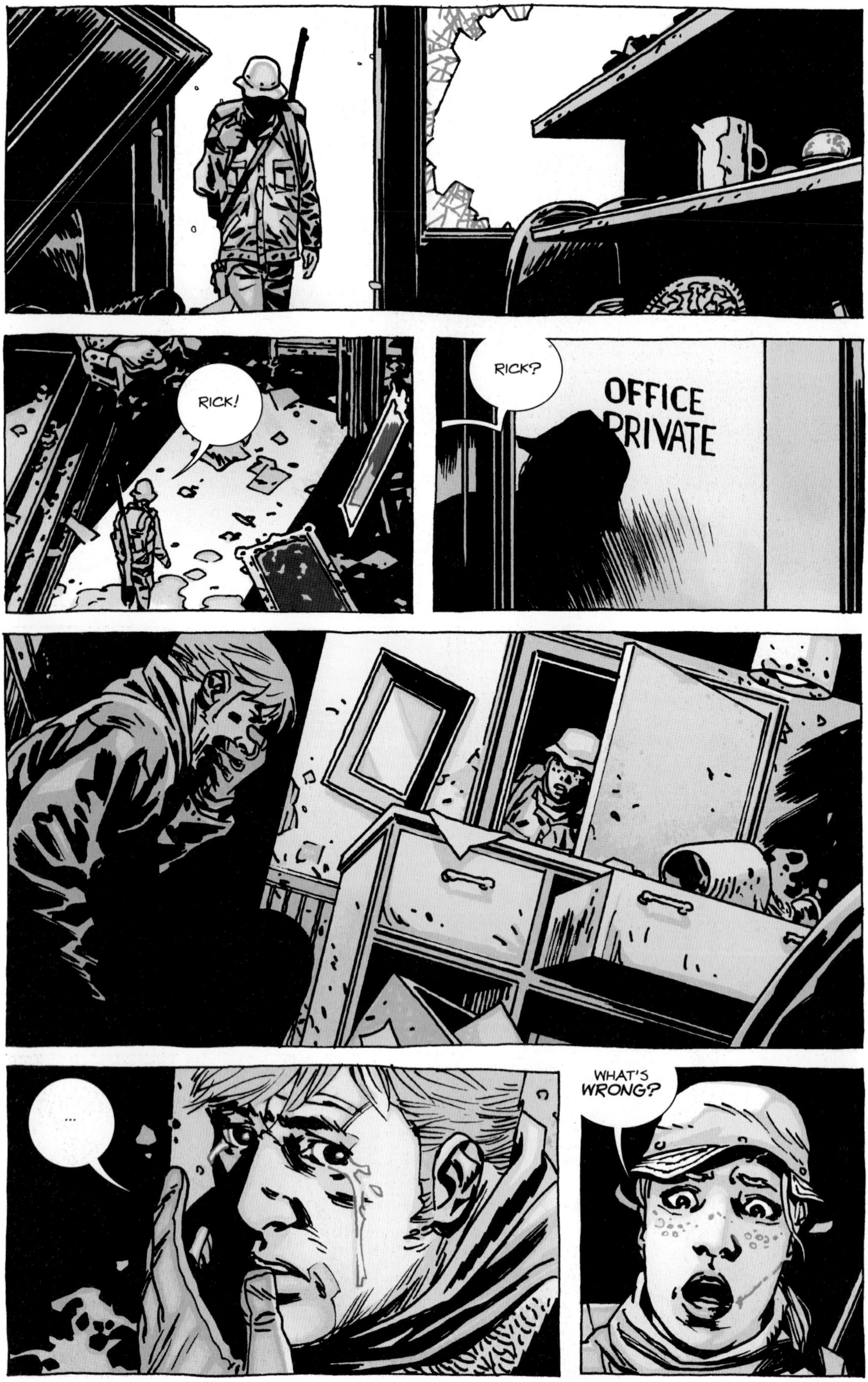

RICK!
RICK?
OFFICE
PRIVATE
...
WHAT'S WRONG?

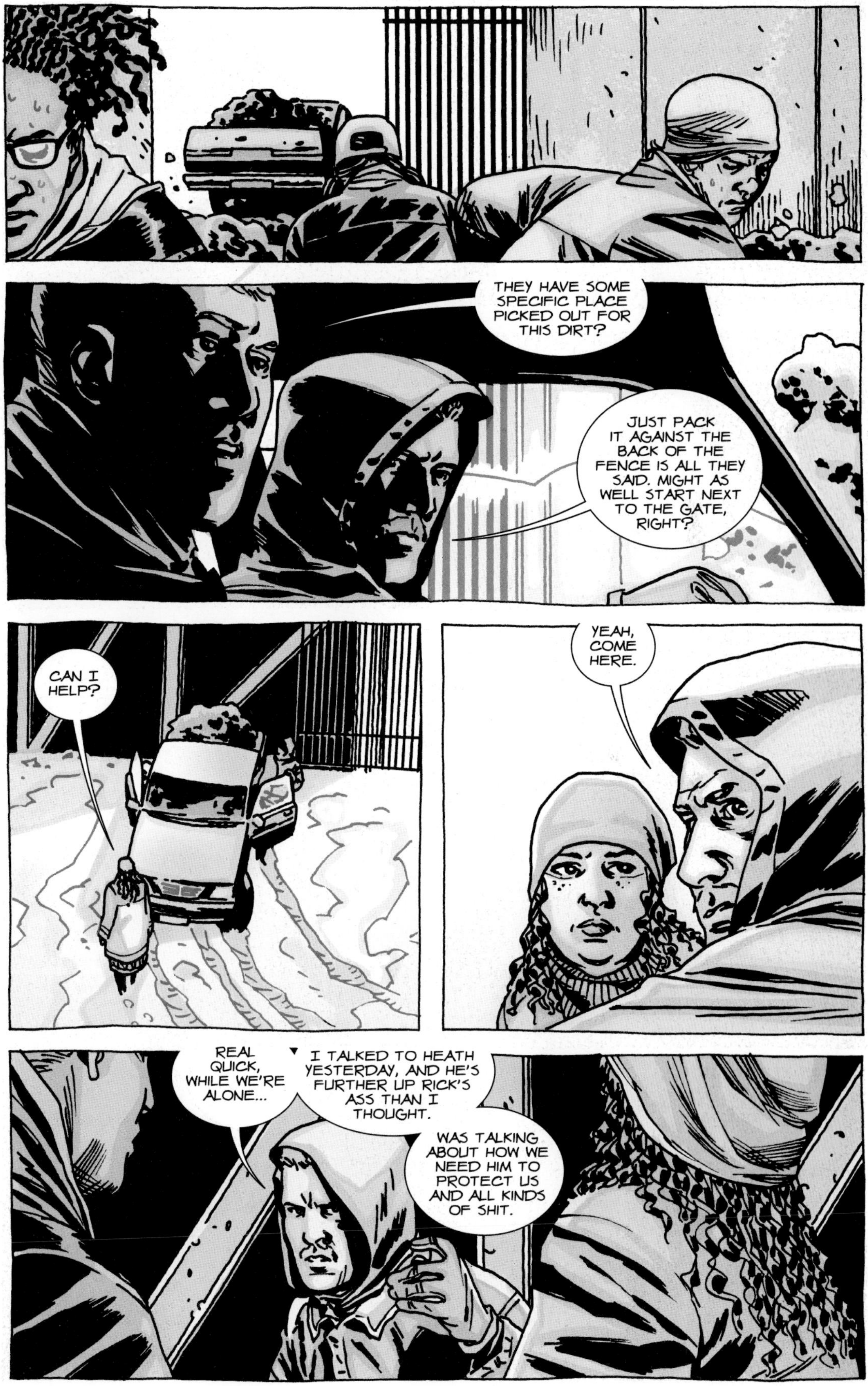
THEY HAVE SOME SPECIFIC PLACE PICKED OUT FOR THIS DIRT?
JUST PACK IT AGAINST THE BACK OF THE FENCE IS ALL THEY SAID. MIGHT AS WELL START NEXT TO THE GATE, RIGHT?
CAN I HELP?
YEAH, COME HERE.
REAL QUICK, WHILE WE'RE ALONE...
I TALKED TO HEATH YESTERDAY, AND HE'S FURTHER UP RICK'S ASS THAN I THOUGHT.
WAS TALKING ABOUT HOW WE NEED HIM TO PROTECT US AND ALL KINDS OF SHIT.

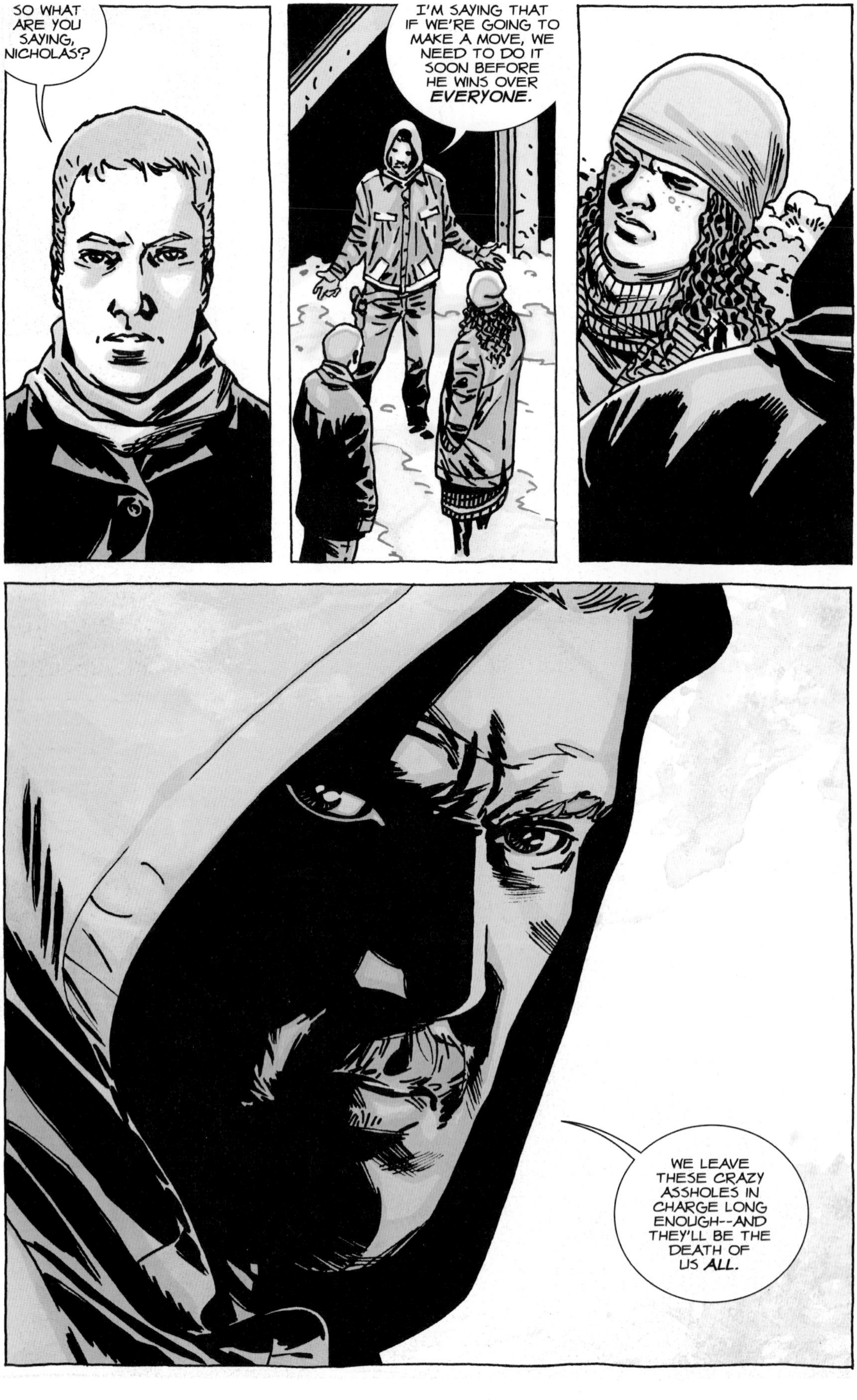
SO WHAT ARE YOU SAYING, NICHOLAS?
I'M SAYING THAT IF WE'RE GOING TO MAKE A MOVE, WE NEED TO DO IT SOON BEFORE HE WINS OVER *EVERYONE*.
WE LEAVE THESE CRAZY ASSHOLES IN CHARGE LONG ENOUGH--AND THEY'LL BE THE DEATH OF US *ALL*.

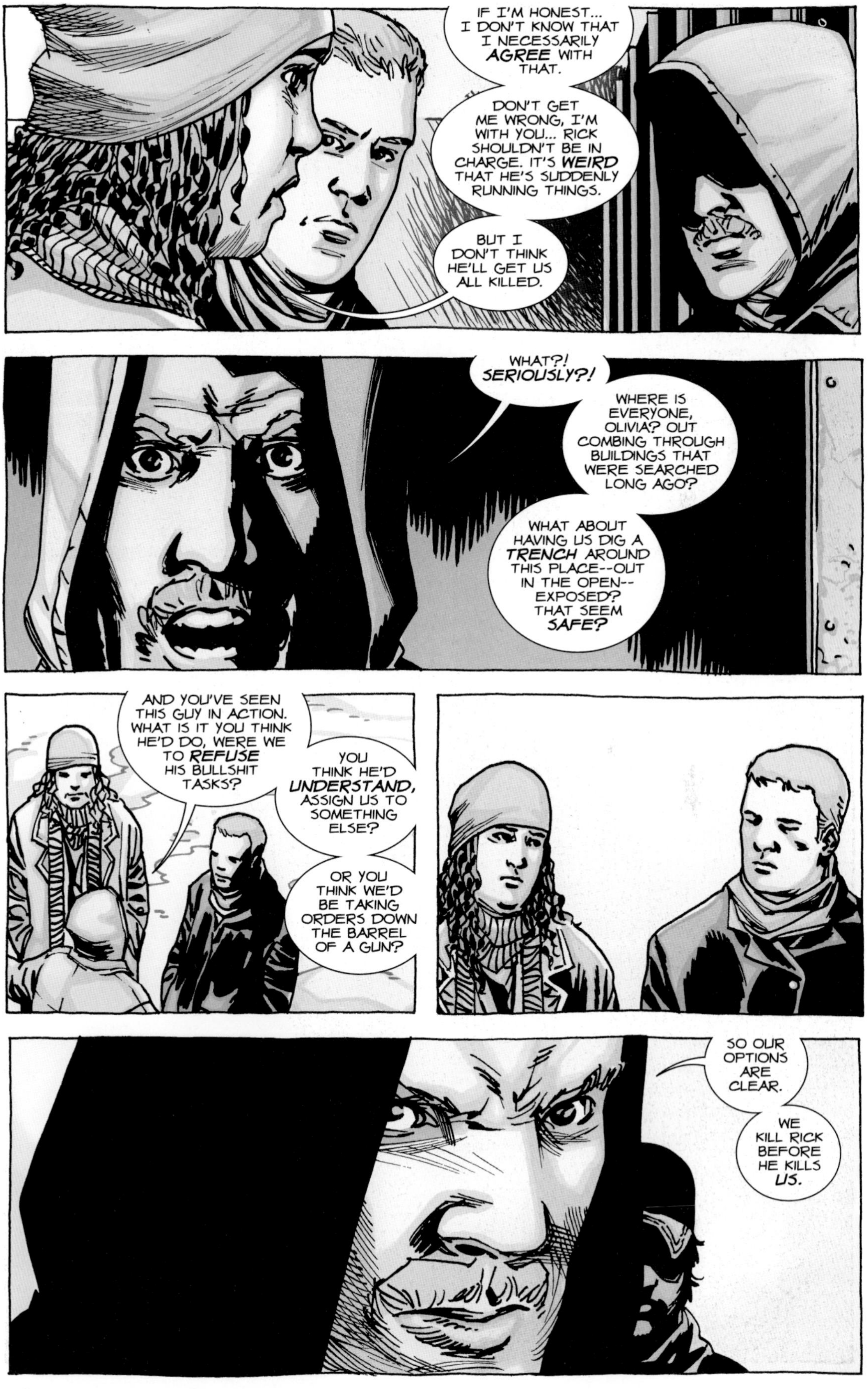
IF I'M HONEST... I DON'T KNOW THAT I NECESSARILY AGREE WITH THAT.
DON'T GET ME WRONG, I'M WITH YOU... RICK SHOULDN'T BE IN CHARGE. IT'S WEIRD THAT HE'S SUDDENLY RUNNING THINGS.
BUT I DON'T THINK HE'LL GET US ALL KILLED.
WHAT?! SERIOUSLY?!
WHERE IS EVERYONE, OLIVIA? OUT COMBING THROUGH BUILDINGS THAT WERE SEARCHED LONG AGO?
WHAT ABOUT HAVING US DIG A TRENCH AROUND THIS PLACE--OUT IN THE OPEN--EXPOSED? THAT SEEM SAFE?
AND YOU'VE SEEN THIS GUY IN ACTION. WHAT IS IT YOU THINK HE'D DO, WERE WE TO REFUSE HIS BULLSHIT TASKS?
YOU THINK HE'D UNDERSTAND, ASSIGN US TO SOMETHING ELSE?
OR YOU THINK WE'D BE TAKING ORDERS DOWN THE BARREL OF A GUN?
SO OUR OPTIONS ARE CLEAR.
WE KILL RICK BEFORE HE KILLS US.

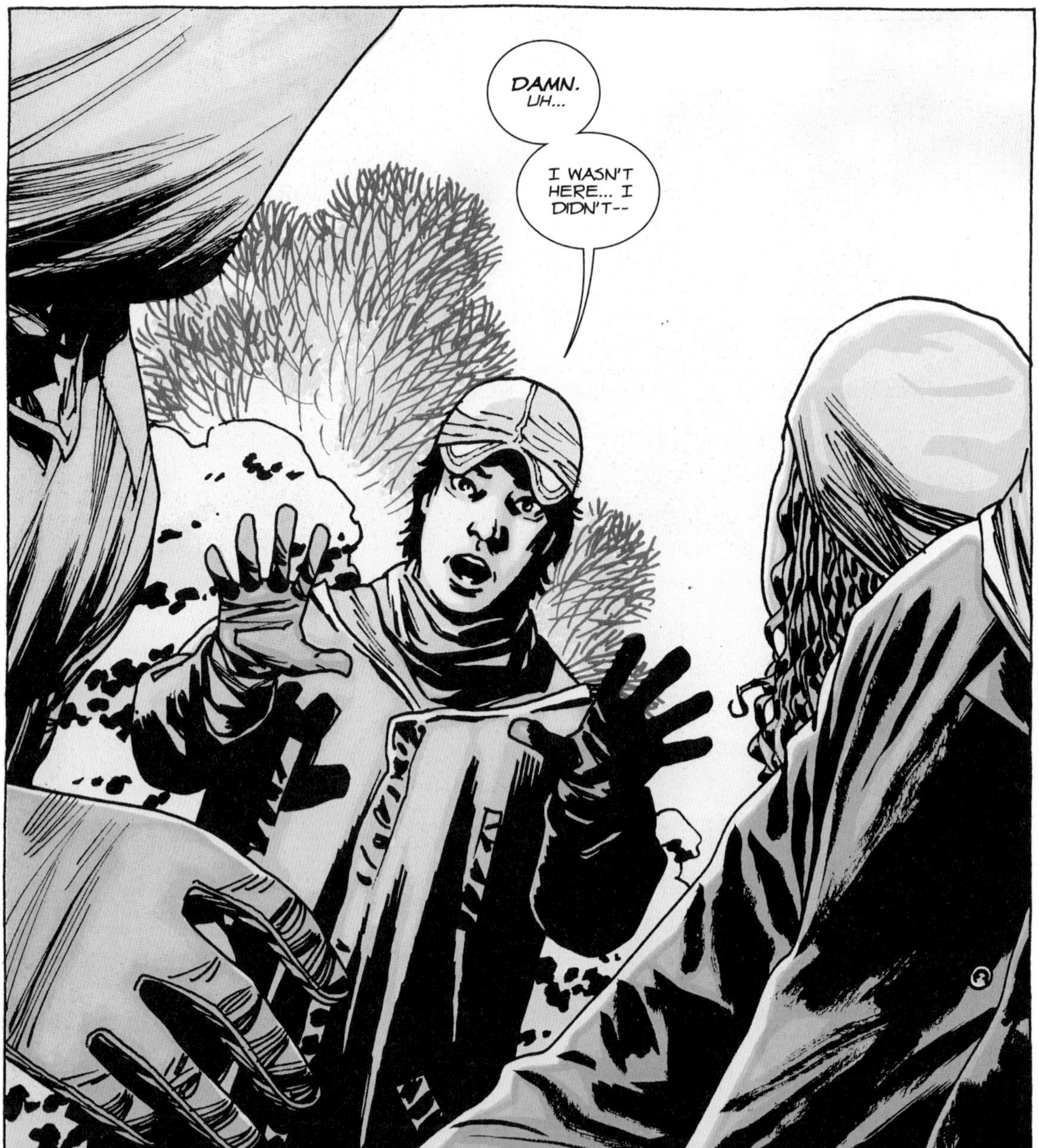
DAMN. UH...
I WASN'T HERE... I DIDN'T--

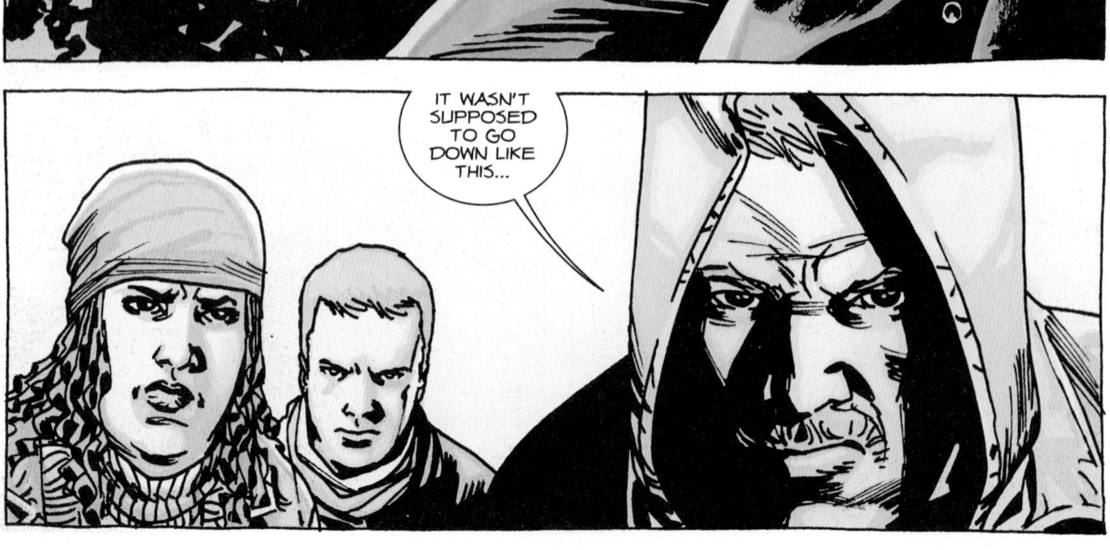
IT WASN'T SUPPOSED TO GO DOWN LIKE THIS...

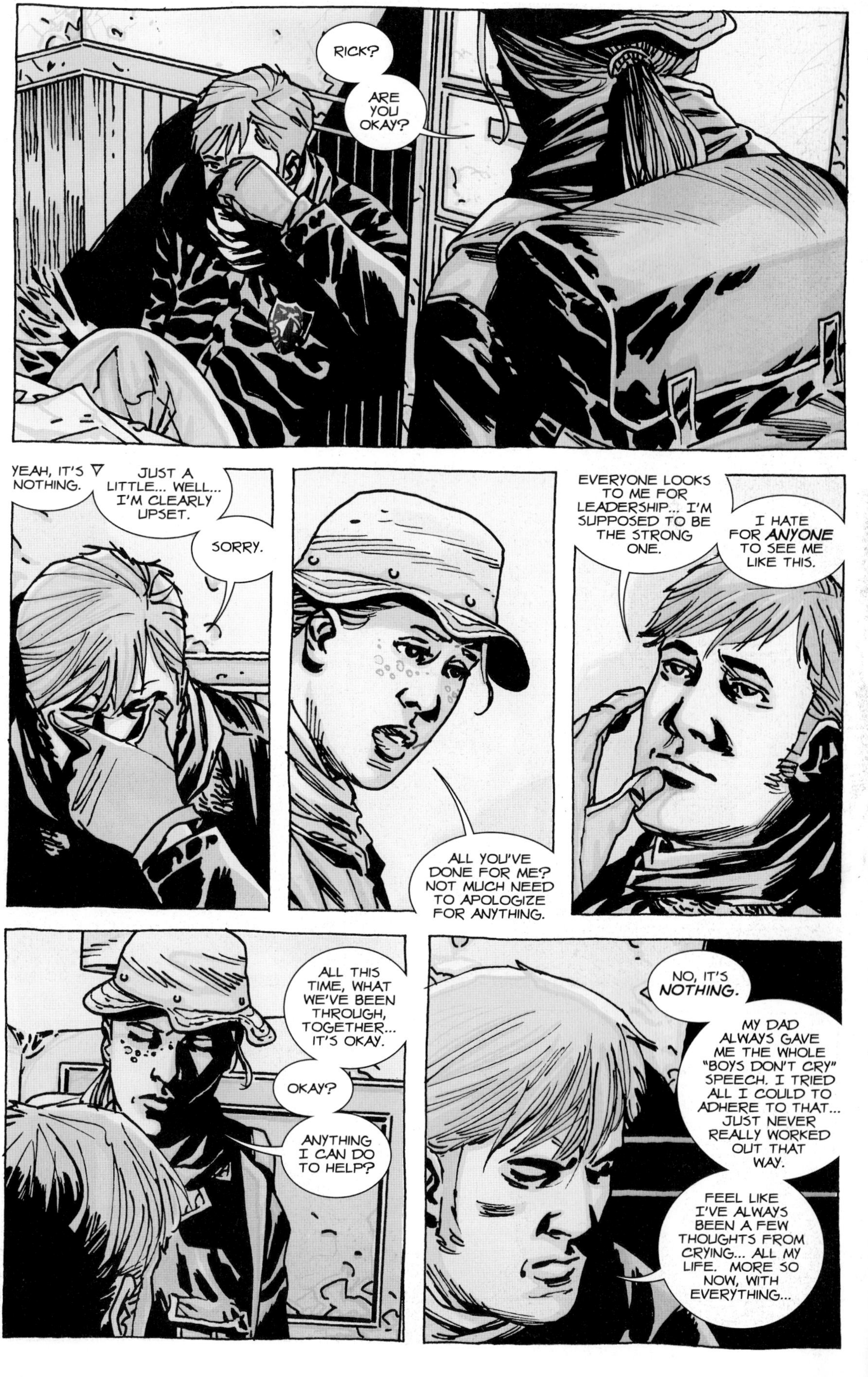
RICK?
ARE YOU OKAY?
YEAH, IT'S NOTHING.
JUST A LITTLE... WELL... I'M CLEARLY UPSET.
SORRY.
ALL YOU'VE DONE FOR ME? NOT MUCH NEED TO APOLOGIZE FOR ANYTHING.
EVERYONE LOOKS TO ME FOR LEADERSHIP... I'M SUPPOSED TO BE THE STRONG ONE.
I HATE FOR ANYONE TO SEE ME LIKE THIS.
ALL THIS TIME, WHAT WE'VE BEEN THROUGH, TOGETHER... IT'S OKAY.
OKAY?
ANYTHING I CAN DO TO HELP?
NO, IT'S NOTHING.
MY DAD ALWAYS GAVE ME THE WHOLE "BOYS DON'T CRY" SPEECH. I TRIED ALL I COULD TO ADHERE TO THAT... JUST NEVER REALLY WORKED OUT THAT WAY.
FEEL LIKE I'VE ALWAYS BEEN A FEW THOUGHTS FROM CRYING... ALL MY LIFE. MORE SO NOW, WITH EVERYTHING...

SCHOOL YARD FIGHTS NEVER WENT SO WELL FOR ME--THAT ADRENALINE RUSH ALWAYS GOT THE TEARS FLOWING... MADE IT HARD TO LOOK TOUGH.

I GOT A BETTER HANDLE ON IT WHEN I WAS OLDER... BUT NOW, IT'S JUST...

THERE'S AN AWFUL LOT WORTH CRYING ABOUT THESE DAYS.

YEAH...

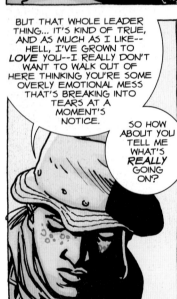

BUT THAT WHOLE LEADER THING... IT'S KIND OF TRUE, AND AS MUCH AS I LIKE-- HELL, I'VE GROWN TO *LOVE* YOU--I REALLY DON'T WANT TO WALK OUT OF HERE THINKING YOU'RE SOME OVERLY EMOTIONAL MESS THAT'S BREAKING INTO TEARS AT A MOMENT'S NOTICE.

SO HOW ABOUT YOU TELL ME WHAT'S *REALLY* GOING ON?

...

IT'S CARL...

I CAN'T IMAGINE WHAT YOU'RE GOING THROUGH RIGHT NOW... HE'S YOUR *SON*, I UNDERSTAND HOW PAINFUL THIS MUST HAVE BEEN... BUT HE'S GOING TO GET HIS MEMORY BACK.

HE'S ALIVE AND--

IT'S NOT THAT...

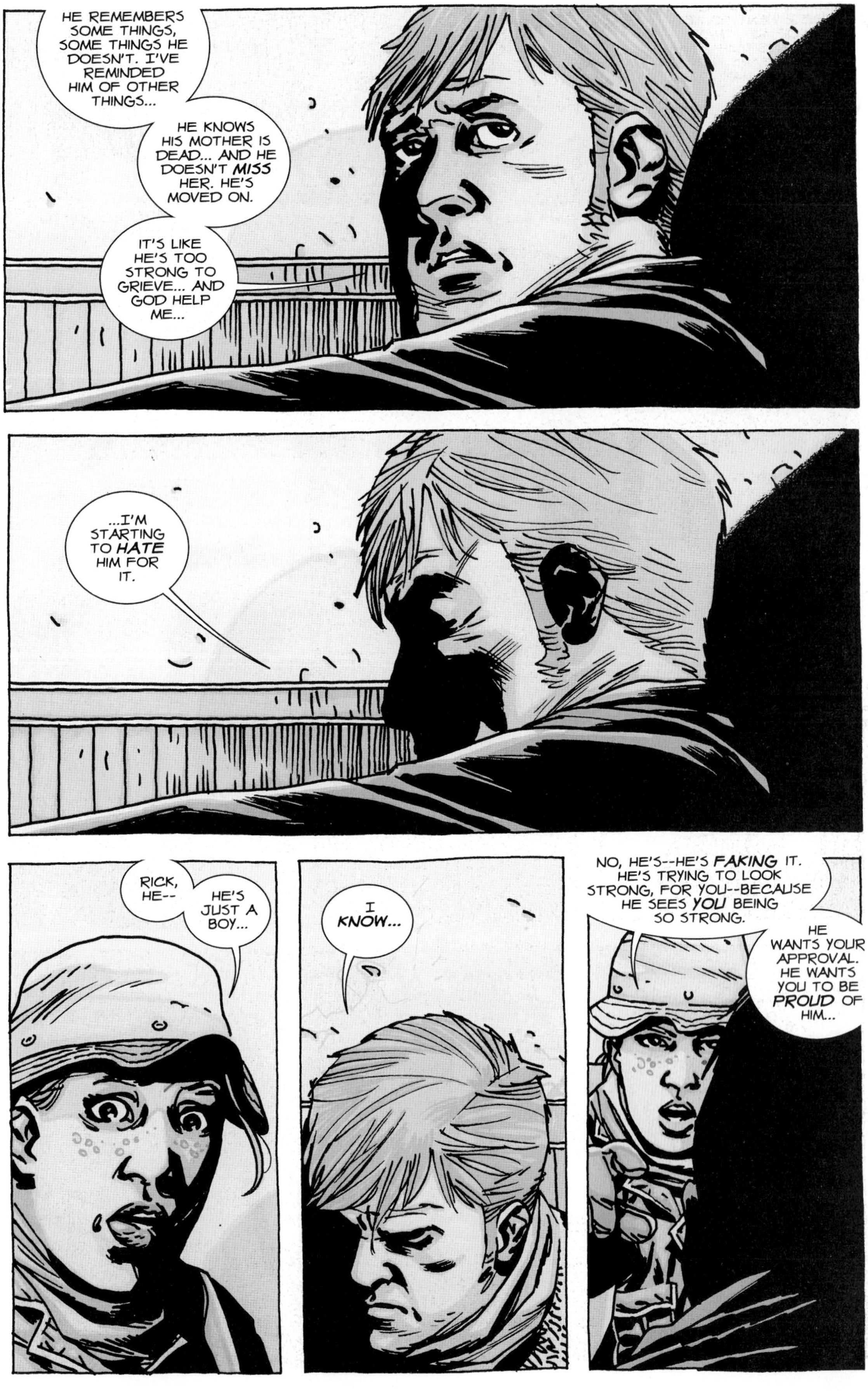

HE REMEMBERS SOME THINGS, SOME THINGS HE DOESN'T. I'VE REMINDED HIM OF OTHER THINGS...
HE KNOWS HIS MOTHER IS DEAD... AND HE DOESN'T MISS HER. HE'S MOVED ON.
IT'S LIKE HE'S TOO STRONG TO GRIEVE... AND GOD HELP ME...
...I'M STARTING TO HATE HIM FOR IT.
RICK, HE--
HE'S JUST A BOY...
I KNOW...
NO, HE'S--HE'S FAKING IT. HE'S TRYING TO LOOK STRONG, FOR YOU--BECAUSE HE SEES YOU BEING SO STRONG.
HE WANTS YOUR APPROVAL. HE WANTS YOU TO BE PROUD OF HIM...

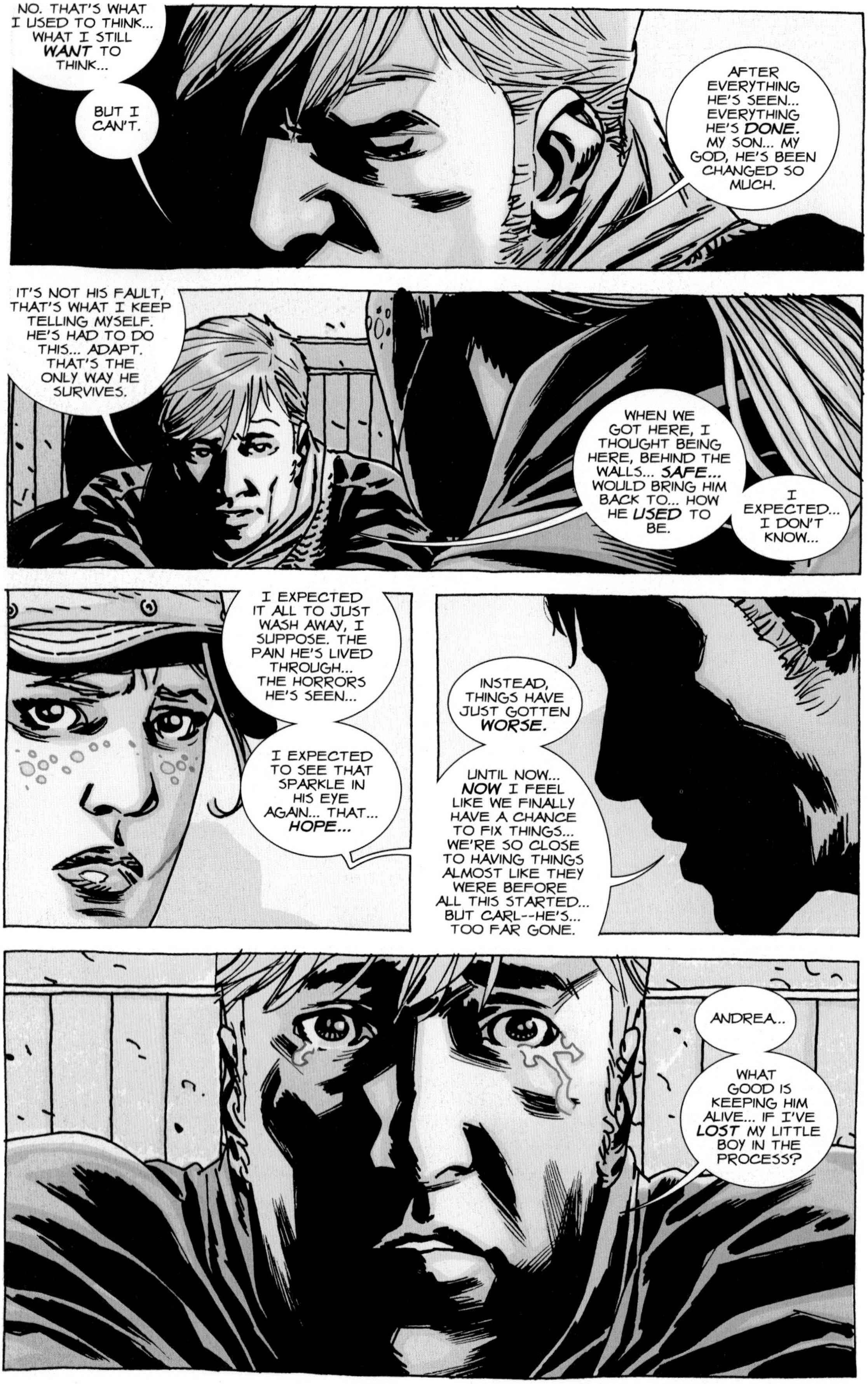

NO. THAT'S WHAT I USED TO THINK... WHAT I STILL WANT TO THINK...
BUT I CAN'T.
AFTER EVERYTHING HE'S SEEN... EVERYTHING HE'S DONE. MY SON... MY GOD, HE'S BEEN CHANGED SO MUCH.
IT'S NOT HIS FAULT, THAT'S WHAT I KEEP TELLING MYSELF. HE'S HAD TO DO THIS... ADAPT. THAT'S THE ONLY WAY HE SURVIVES.
WHEN WE GOT HERE, I THOUGHT BEING HERE, BEHIND THE WALLS... SAFE... WOULD BRING HIM BACK TO... HOW HE USED TO BE.
I EXPECTED... I DON'T KNOW...
I EXPECTED IT ALL TO JUST WASH AWAY, I SUPPOSE. THE PAIN HE'S LIVED THROUGH... THE HORRORS HE'S SEEN...
I EXPECTED TO SEE THAT SPARKLE IN HIS EYE AGAIN... THAT... HOPE...
INSTEAD, THINGS HAVE JUST GOTTEN WORSE.
UNTIL NOW... NOW I FEEL LIKE WE FINALLY HAVE A CHANCE TO FIX THINGS... WE'RE SO CLOSE TO HAVING THINGS ALMOST LIKE THEY WERE BEFORE ALL THIS STARTED... BUT CARL--HE'S... TOO FAR GONE.
ANDREA...
WHAT GOOD IS KEEPING HIM ALIVE... IF I'VE LOST MY LITTLE BOY IN THE PROCESS?

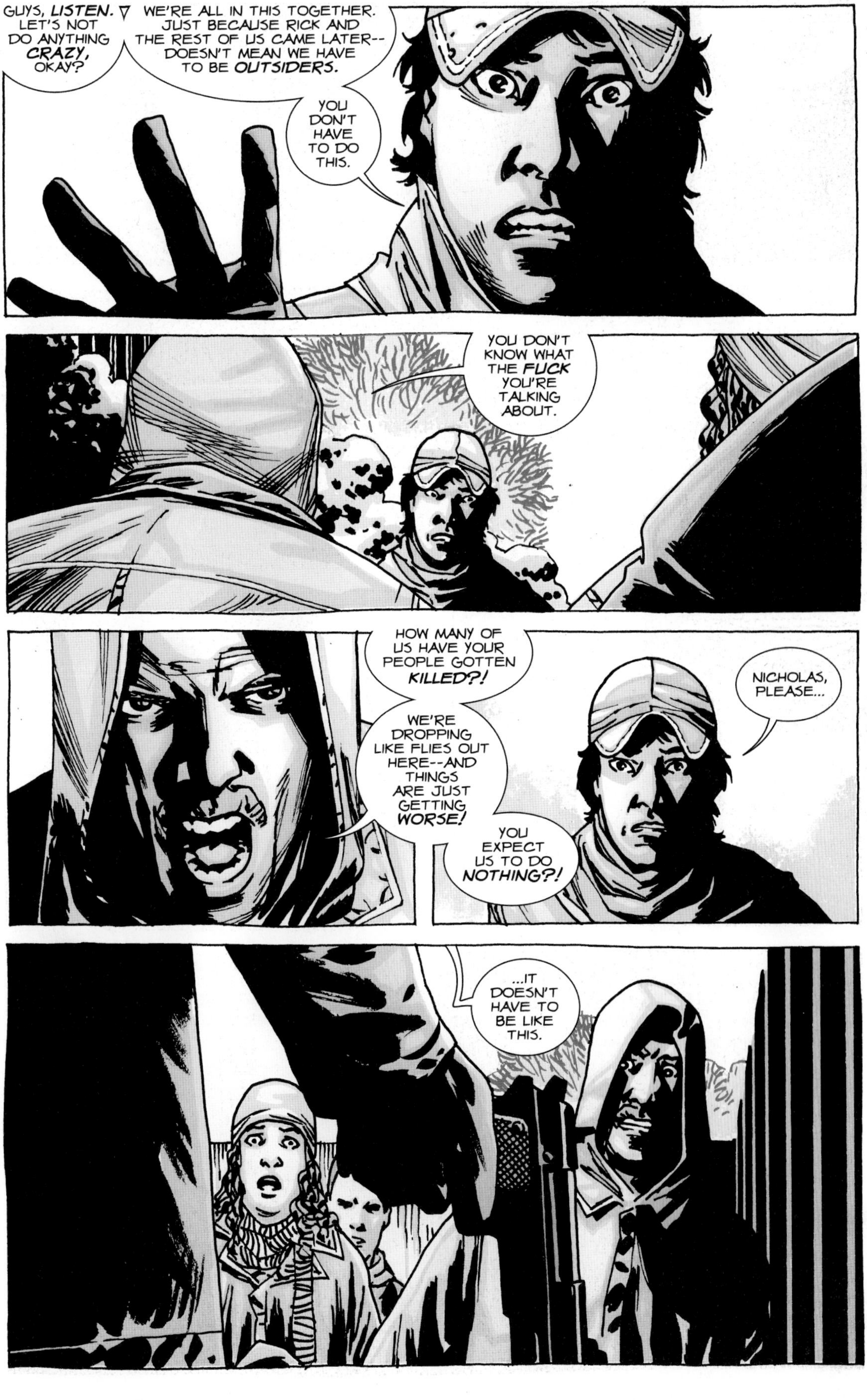
GUYS, LISTEN. LET'S NOT DO ANYTHING CRAZY, OKAY?
WE'RE ALL IN THIS TOGETHER. JUST BECAUSE RICK AND THE REST OF US CAME LATER-- DOESN'T MEAN WE HAVE TO BE OUTSIDERS.
YOU DON'T HAVE TO DO THIS.
YOU DON'T KNOW WHAT THE FUCK YOU'RE TALKING ABOUT.
HOW MANY OF US HAVE YOUR PEOPLE GOTTEN KILLED?!
WE'RE DROPPING LIKE FLIES OUT HERE--AND THINGS ARE JUST GETTING WORSE!
YOU EXPECT US TO DO NOTHING?!
NICHOLAS, PLEASE...
...IT DOESN'T HAVE TO BE LIKE THIS.

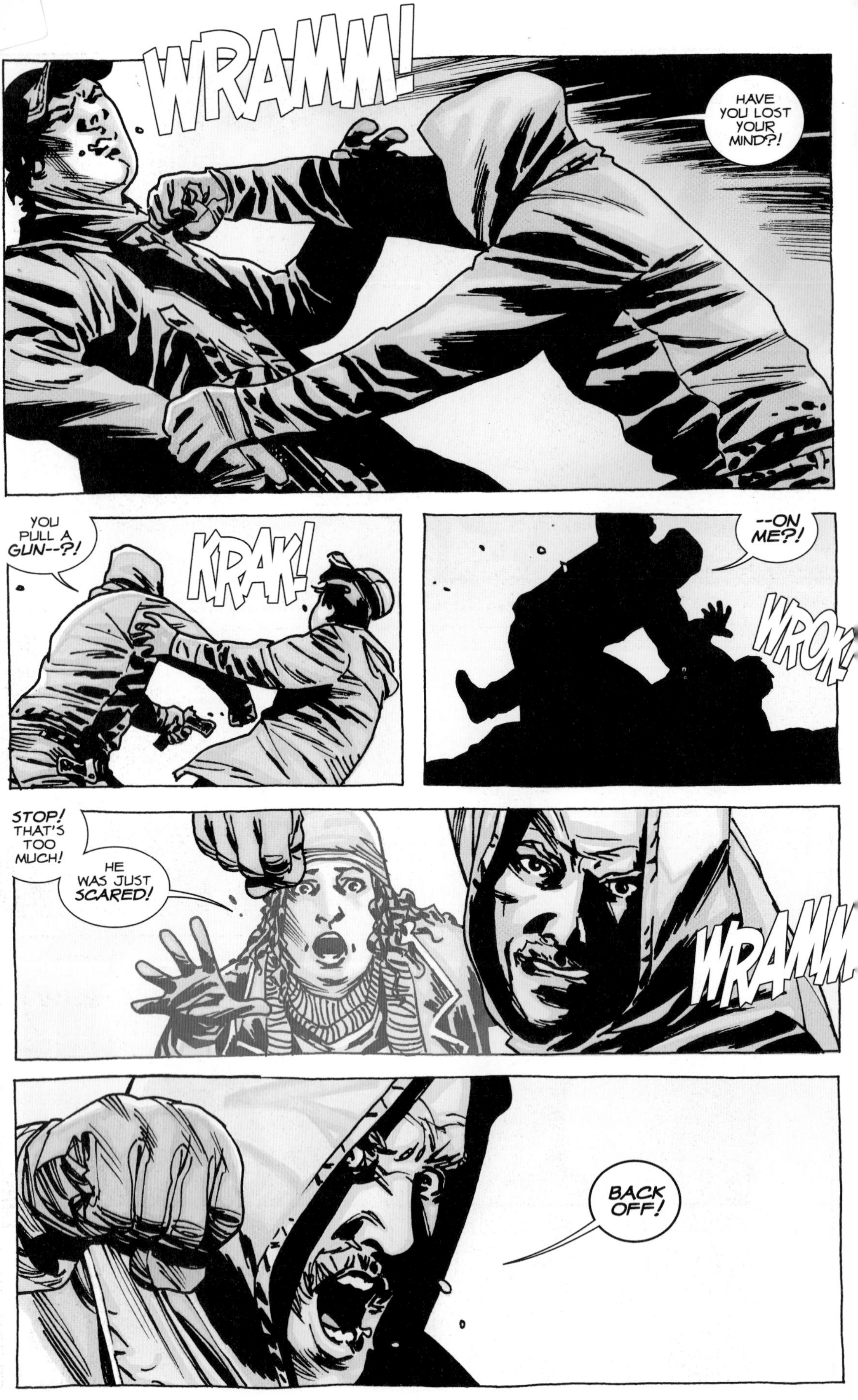

WRAMM!
HAVE YOU LOST YOUR MIND?!
YOU PULL A GUN--?!
KRAK!
--ON ME?!
WROK!
STOP! THAT'S TOO MUCH!
HE WAS JUST SCARED!
WRAMM
BACK OFF!

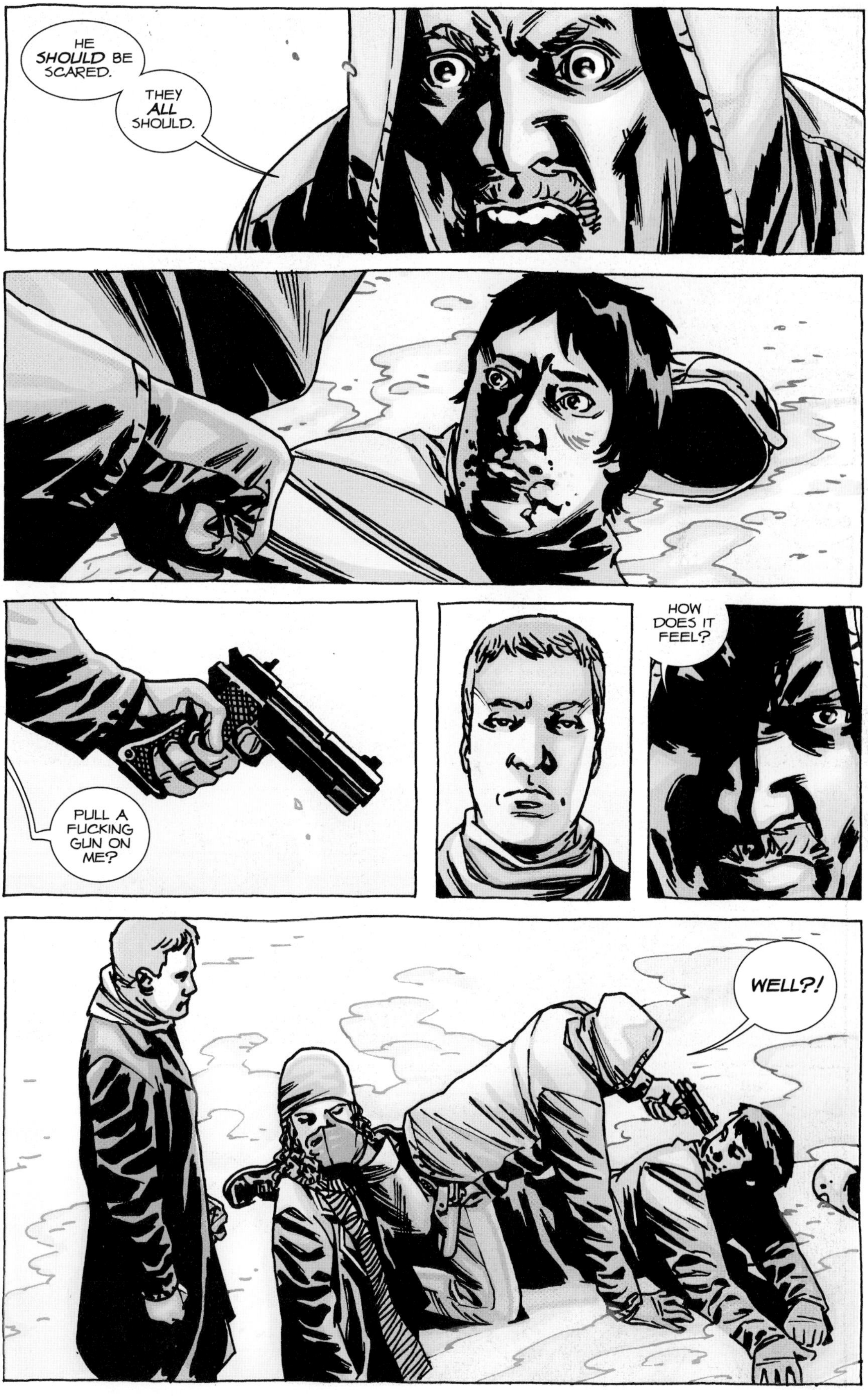
HE *SHOULD* BE SCARED.
THEY *ALL* SHOULD.
PULL A FUCKING GUN ON ME?
HOW DOES IT FEEL?
WELL?!

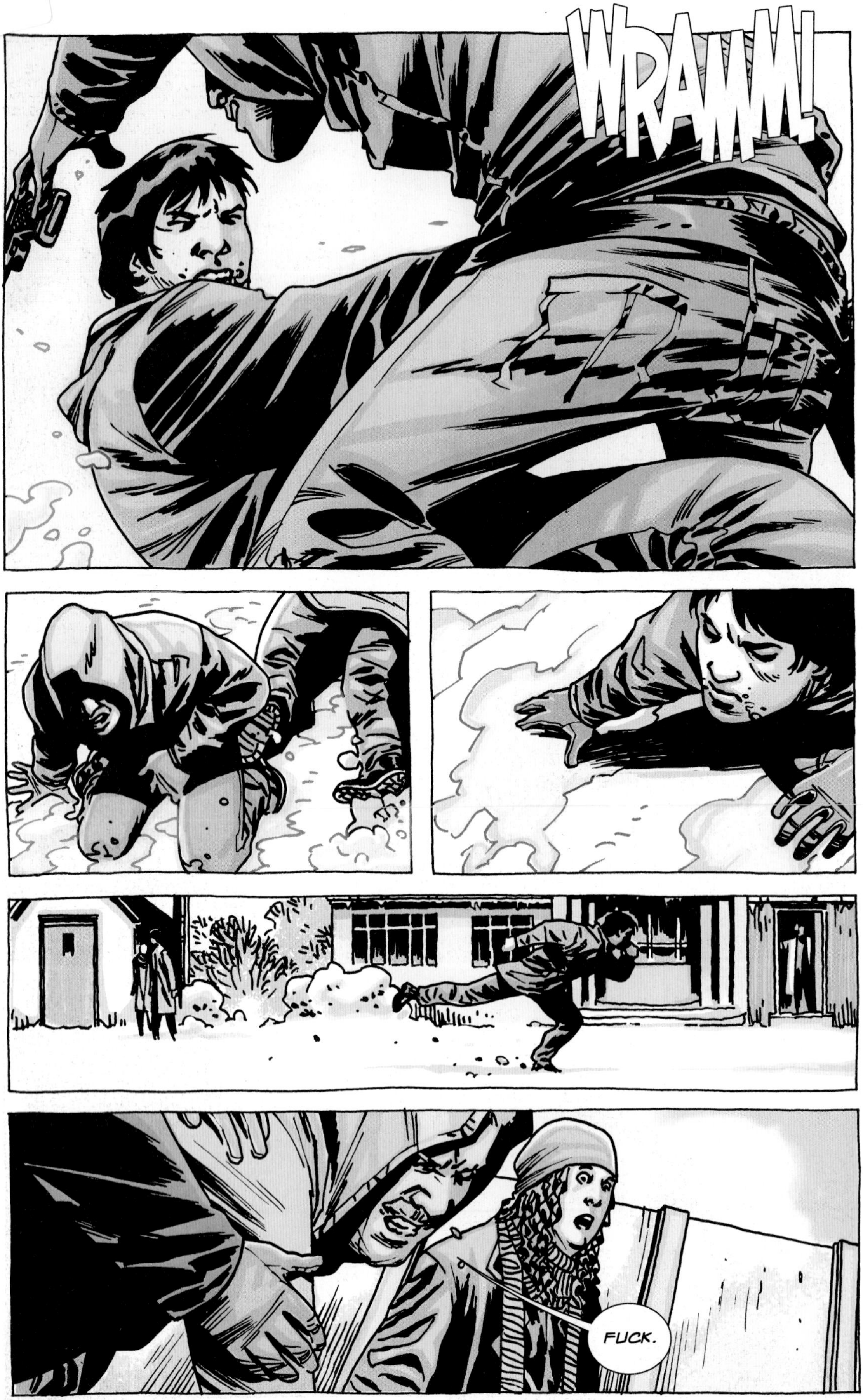
WRAMM!
FUCK.

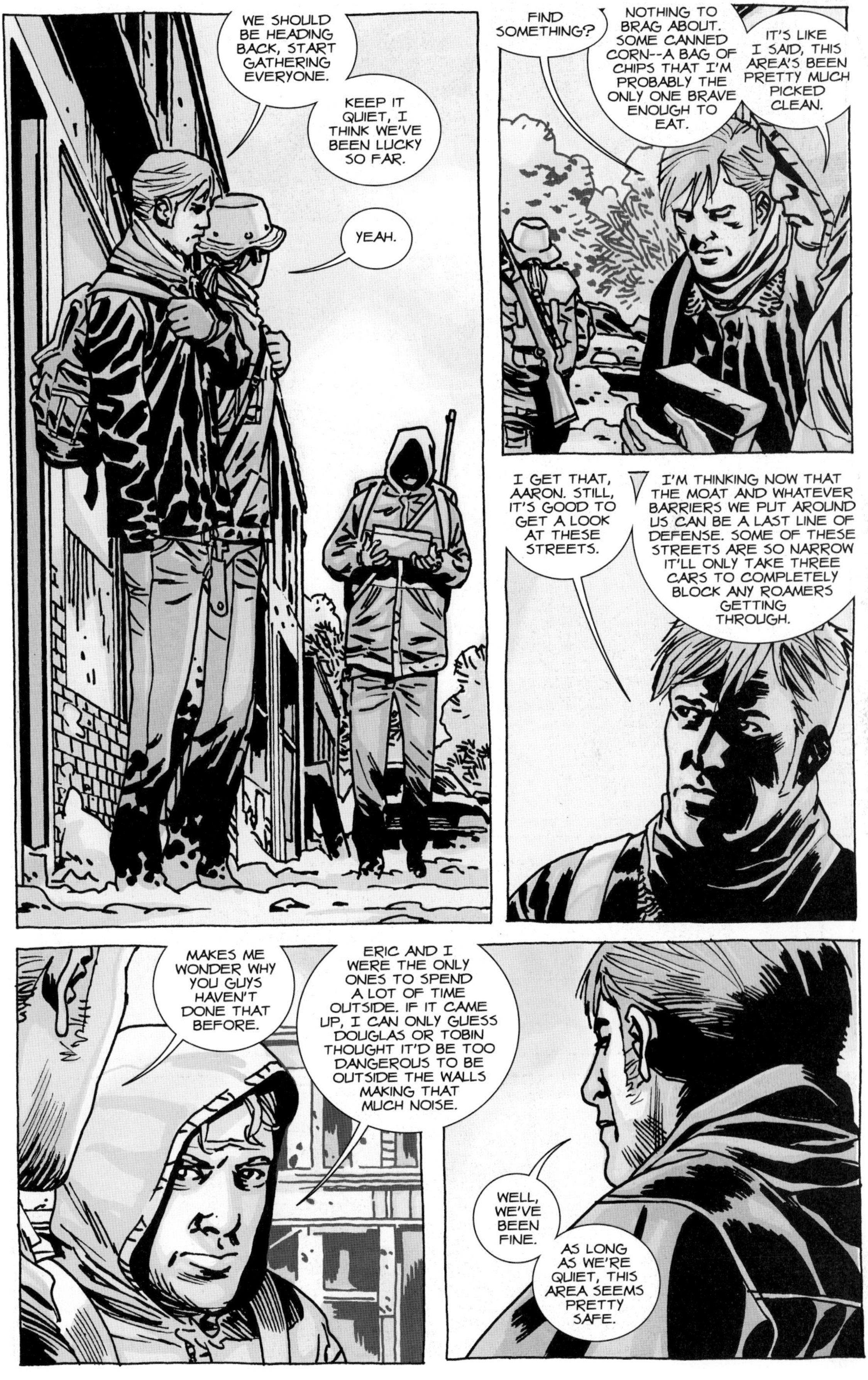
WE SHOULD BE HEADING BACK, START GATHERING EVERYONE.
KEEP IT QUIET, I THINK WE'VE BEEN LUCKY SO FAR.
YEAH.
FIND SOMETHING?
NOTHING TO BRAG ABOUT. SOME CANNED CORN--A BAG OF CHIPS THAT I'M PROBABLY THE ONLY ONE BRAVE ENOUGH TO EAT.
IT'S LIKE I SAID, THIS AREA'S BEEN PRETTY MUCH PICKED CLEAN.
I GET THAT, AARON. STILL, IT'S GOOD TO GET A LOOK AT THESE STREETS.
I'M THINKING NOW THAT THE MOAT AND WHATEVER BARRIERS WE PUT AROUND US CAN BE A LAST LINE OF DEFENSE. SOME OF THESE STREETS ARE SO NARROW IT'LL ONLY TAKE THREE CARS TO COMPLETELY BLOCK ANY ROAMERS GETTING THROUGH.
MAKES ME WONDER WHY YOU GUYS HAVEN'T DONE THAT BEFORE.
ERIC AND I WERE THE ONLY ONES TO SPEND A LOT OF TIME OUTSIDE. IF IT CAME UP, I CAN ONLY GUESS DOUGLAS OR TOBIN THOUGHT IT'D BE TOO DANGEROUS TO BE OUTSIDE THE WALLS MAKING THAT MUCH NOISE.
WELL, WE'VE BEEN FINE.
AS LONG AS WE'RE QUIET, THIS AREA SEEMS PRETTY SAFE.

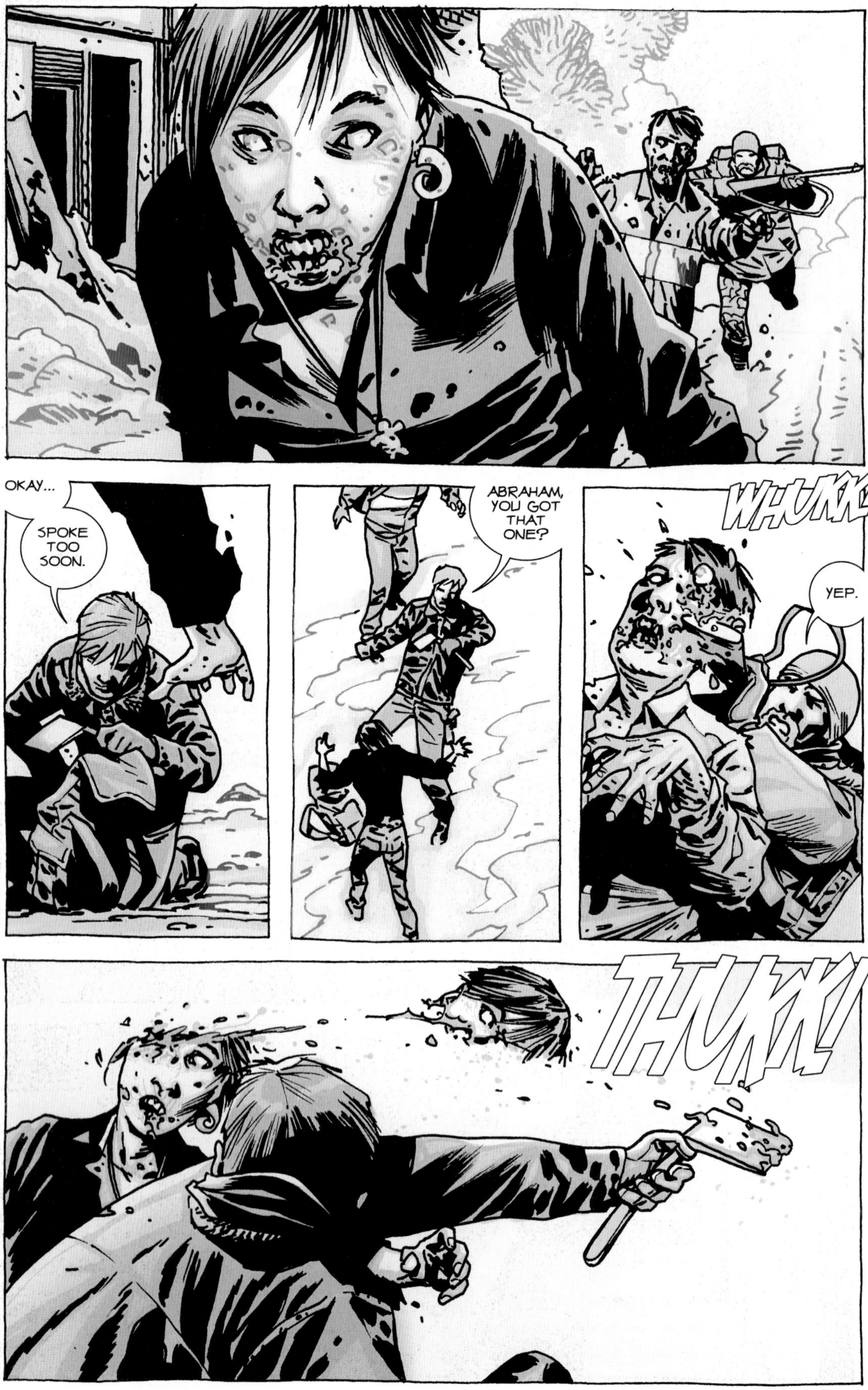
OKAY...
SPOKE TOO SOON.
ABRAHAM, YOU GOT THAT ONE?
WHUKK!
YEP.
THUKK!

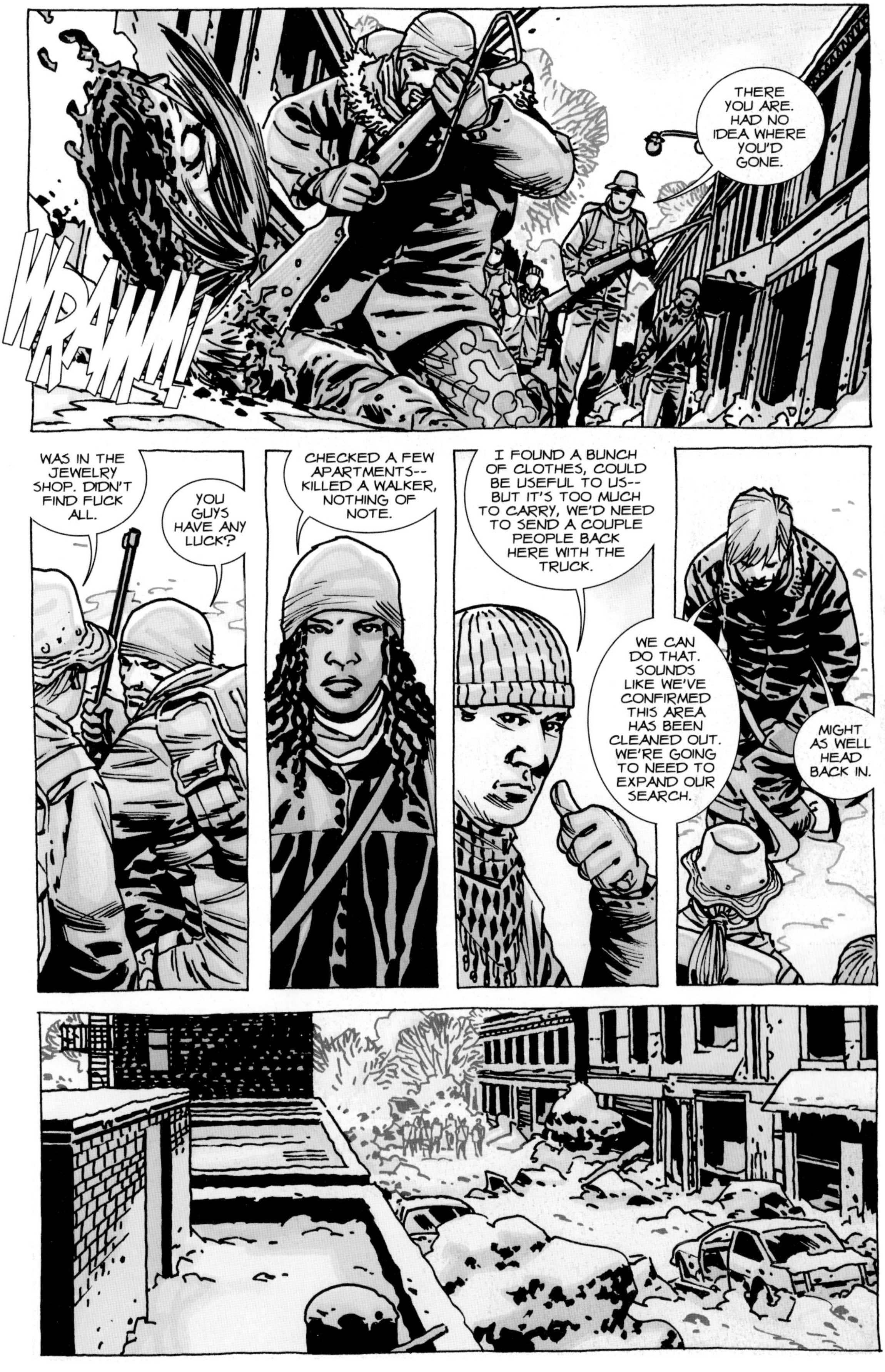
WRAMM!
THERE YOU ARE. HAD NO IDEA WHERE YOU'D GONE.
WAS IN THE JEWELRY SHOP. DIDN'T FIND FUCK ALL.
YOU GUYS HAVE ANY LUCK?
CHECKED A FEW APARTMENTS-- KILLED A WALKER, NOTHING OF NOTE.
I FOUND A BUNCH OF CLOTHES, COULD BE USEFUL TO US-- BUT IT'S TOO MUCH TO CARRY, WE'D NEED TO SEND A COUPLE PEOPLE BACK HERE WITH THE TRUCK.
WE CAN DO THAT. SOUNDS LIKE WE'VE CONFIRMED THIS AREA HAS BEEN CLEANED OUT. WE'RE GOING TO NEED TO EXPAND OUR SEARCH.
MIGHT AS WELL HEAD BACK IN.

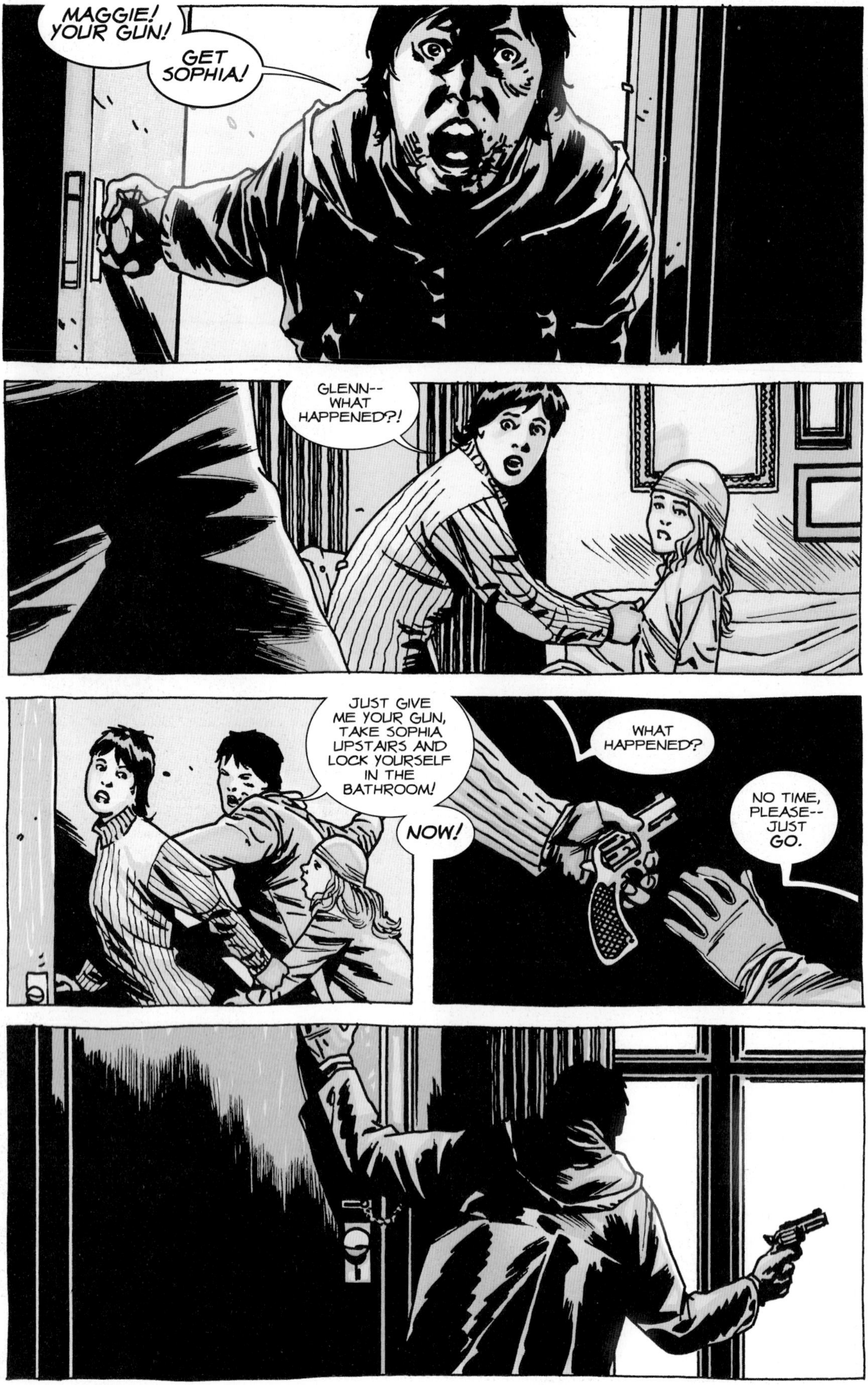
MAGGIE! YOUR GUN!
GET SOPHIA!
GLENN-- WHAT HAPPENED?!
JUST GIVE ME YOUR GUN, TAKE SOPHIA UPSTAIRS AND LOCK YOURSELF IN THE BATHROOM!
NOW!
WHAT HAPPENED?
NO TIME, PLEASE-- JUST GO.

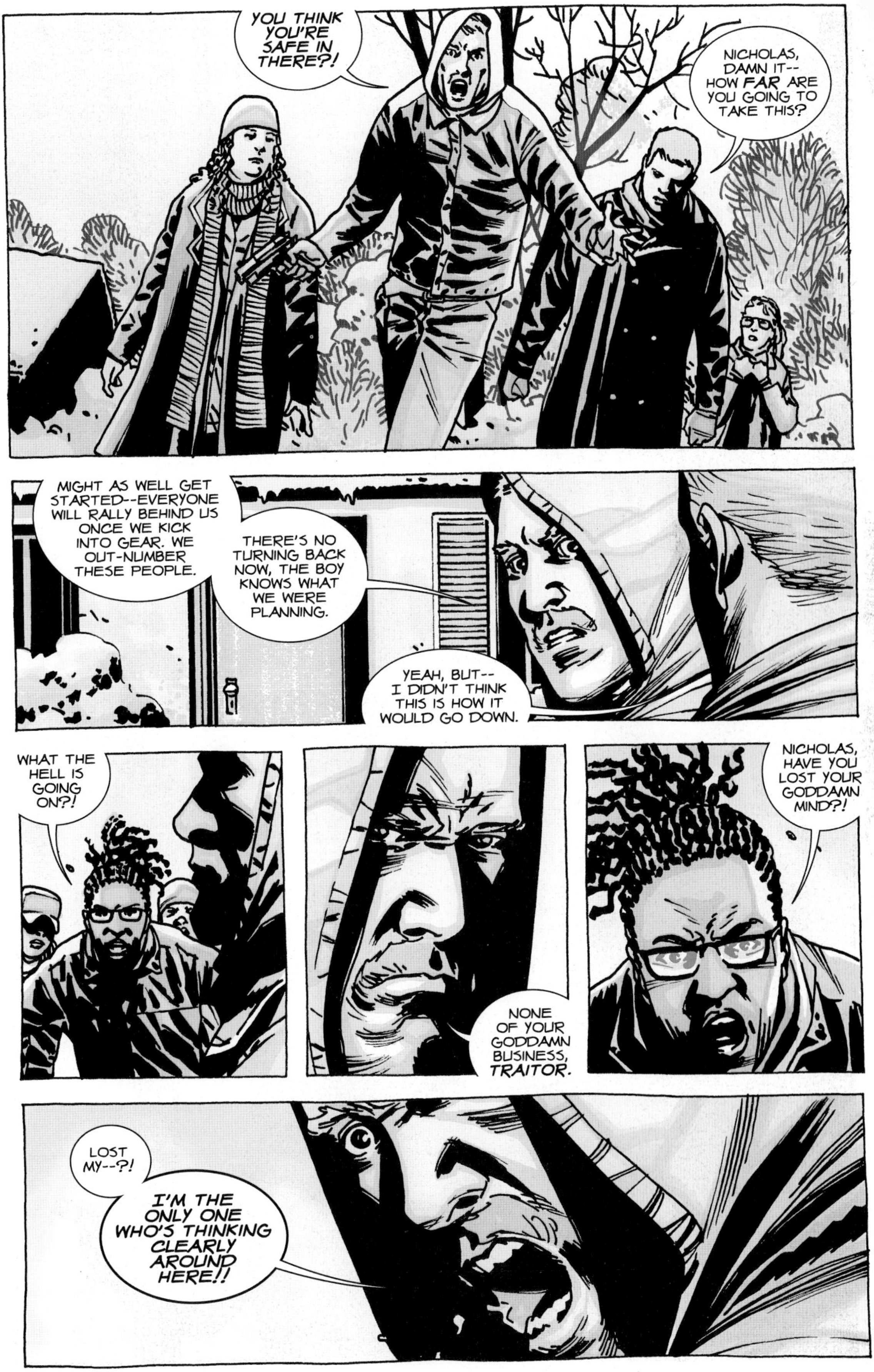
YOU THINK YOU'RE SAFE IN THERE?!
NICHOLAS, DAMN IT-- HOW FAR ARE YOU GOING TO TAKE THIS?
MIGHT AS WELL GET STARTED--EVERYONE WILL RALLY BEHIND US ONCE WE KICK INTO GEAR. WE OUT-NUMBER THESE PEOPLE.
THERE'S NO TURNING BACK NOW, THE BOY KNOWS WHAT WE WERE PLANNING.
YEAH, BUT-- I DIDN'T THINK THIS IS HOW IT WOULD GO DOWN.
WHAT THE HELL IS GOING ON?!
NONE OF YOUR GODDAMN BUSINESS, TRAITOR.
NICHOLAS, HAVE YOU LOST YOUR GODDAMN MIND?!
LOST MY--?!
I'M THE ONLY ONE WHO'S THINKING CLEARLY AROUND HERE!!

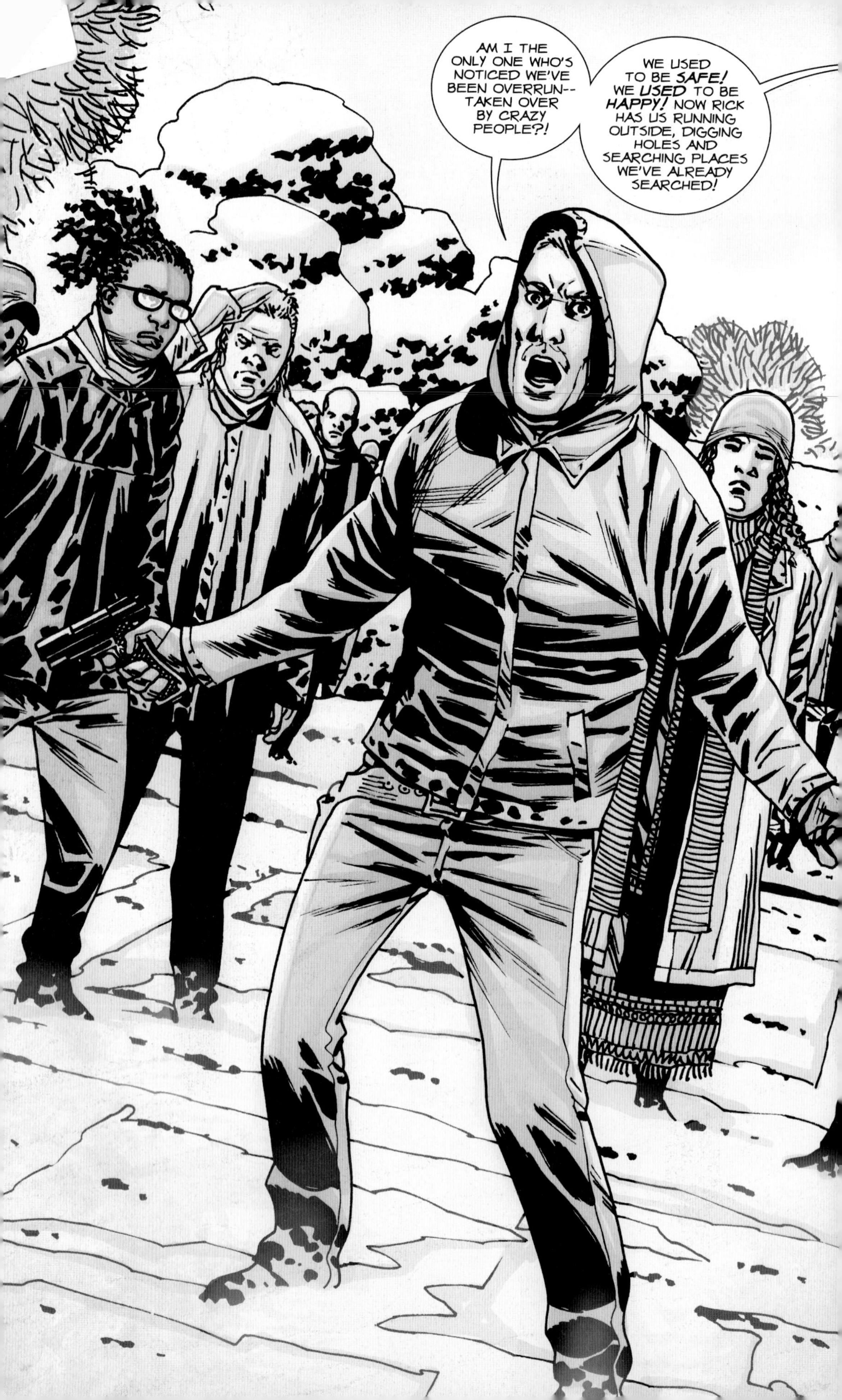
AM I THE ONLY ONE WHO'S NOTICED WE'VE BEEN OVERRUN-- TAKEN OVER BY CRAZY PEOPLE?!
WE USED TO BE SAFE! WE USED TO BE HAPPY! NOW RICK HAS US RUNNING OUTSIDE, DIGGING HOLES AND SEARCHING PLACES WE'VE ALREADY SEARCHED!

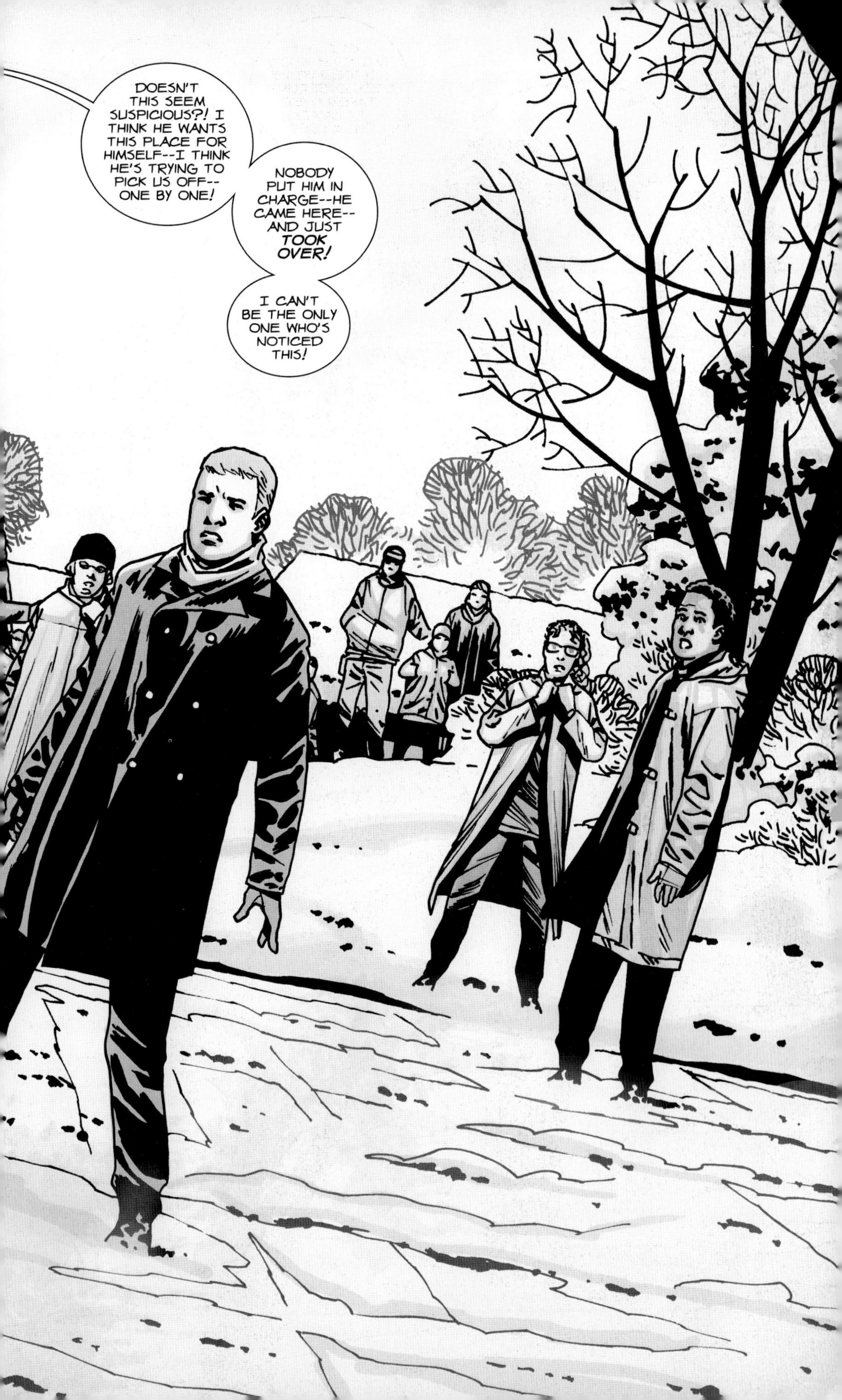
DOESN'T THIS SEEM SUSPICIOUS?! I THINK HE WANTS THIS PLACE FOR HIMSELF--I THINK HE'S TRYING TO PICK US OFF-- ONE BY ONE!
NOBODY PUT HIM IN CHARGE--HE CAME HERE-- AND JUST TOOK OVER!
I CAN'T BE THE ONLY ONE WHO'S NOTICED THIS!

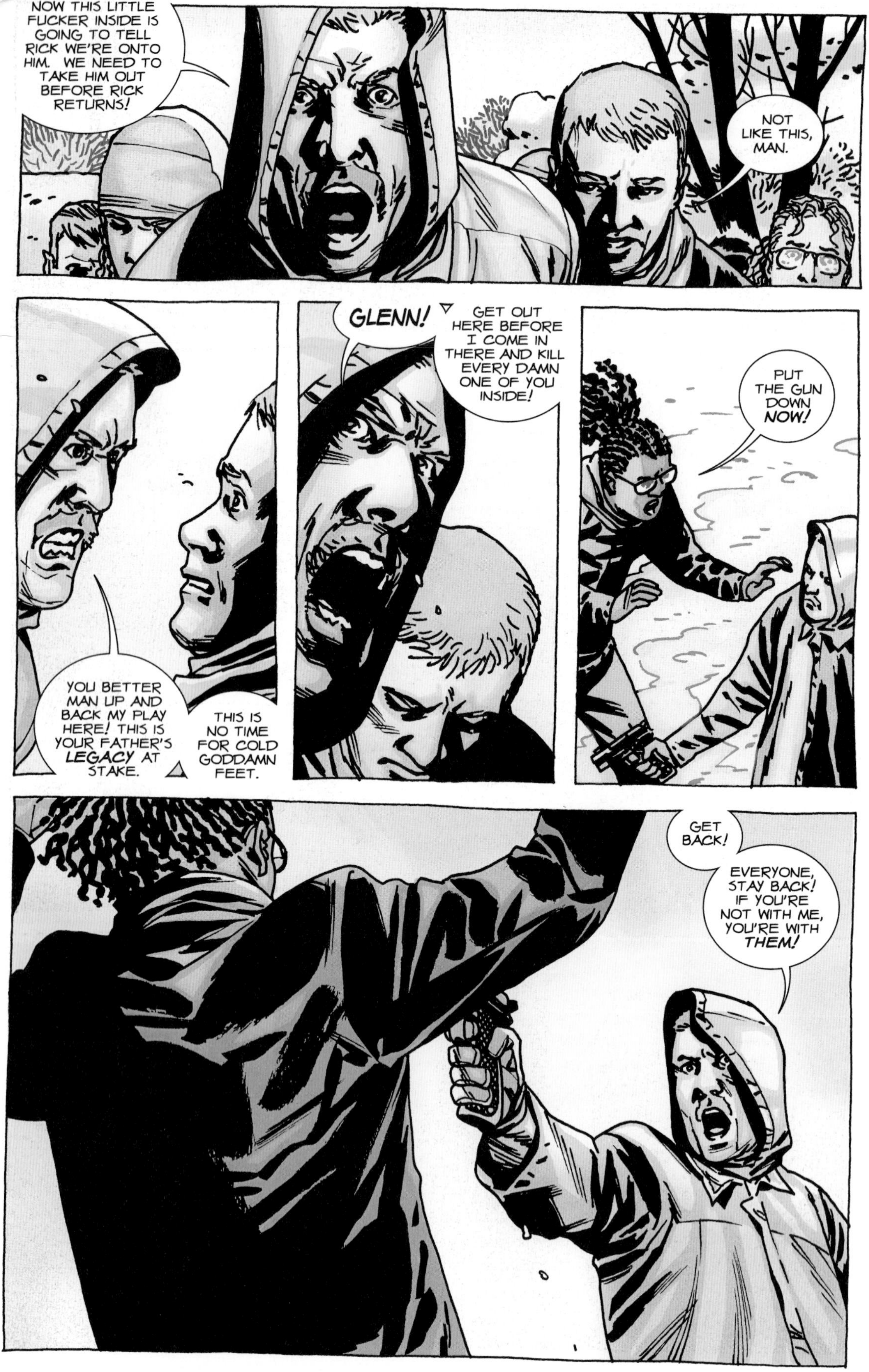

NOW THIS LITTLE FUCKER INSIDE IS GOING TO TELL RICK WE'RE ONTO HIM. WE NEED TO TAKE HIM OUT BEFORE RICK RETURNS!
NOT LIKE THIS, MAN.
YOU BETTER MAN UP AND BACK MY PLAY HERE! THIS IS YOUR FATHER'S LEGACY AT STAKE.
THIS IS NO TIME FOR COLD GODDAMN FEET.
GLENN!
GET OUT HERE BEFORE I COME IN THERE AND KILL EVERY DAMN ONE OF YOU INSIDE!
PUT THE GUN DOWN NOW!
GET BACK!
EVERYONE, STAY BACK! IF YOU'RE NOT WITH ME, YOU'RE WITH THEM!

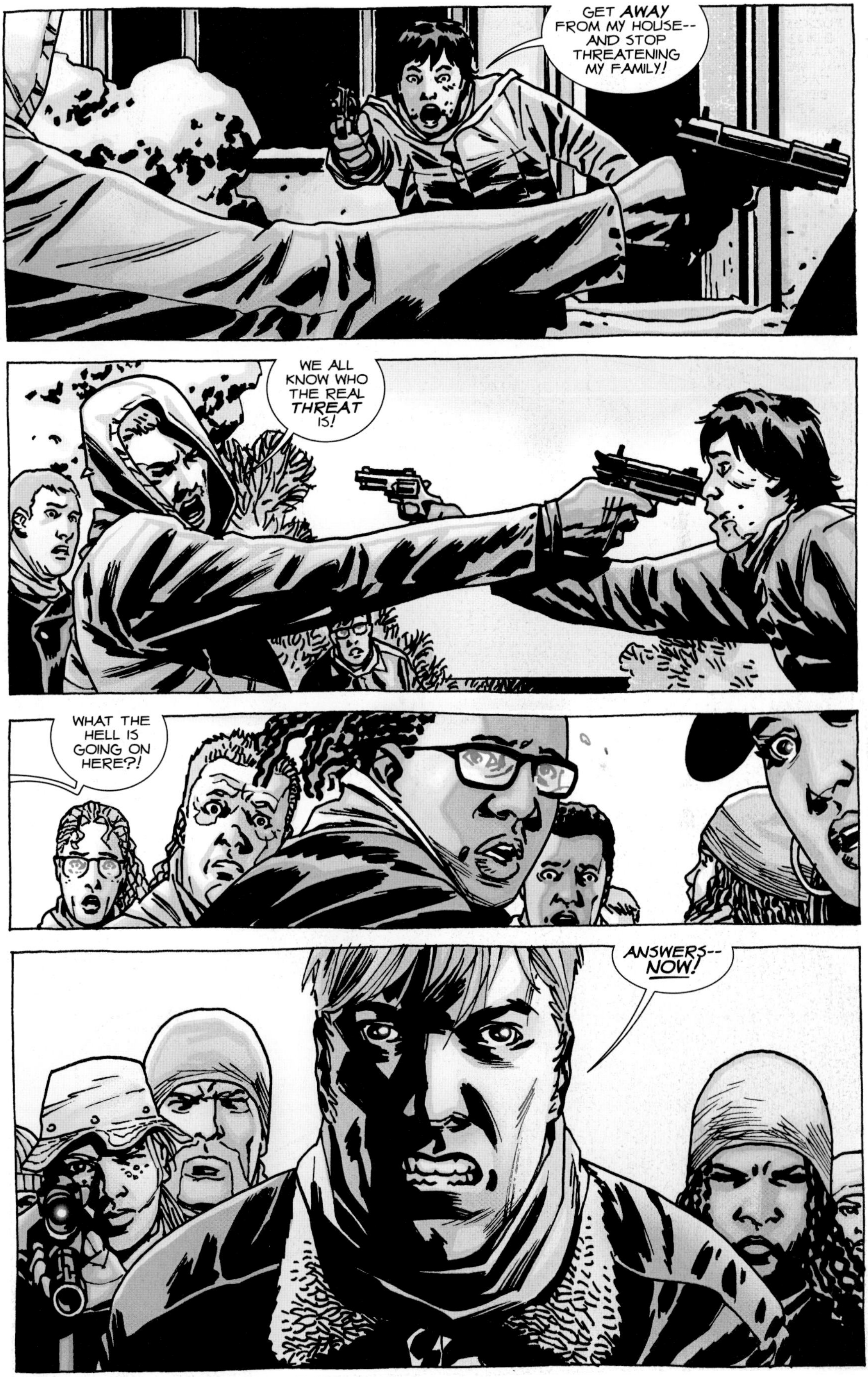
GET AWAY FROM MY HOUSE-- AND STOP THREATENING MY FAMILY!
WE ALL KNOW WHO THE REAL THREAT IS!
WHAT THE HELL IS GOING ON HERE?!
ANSWERS-- NOW!

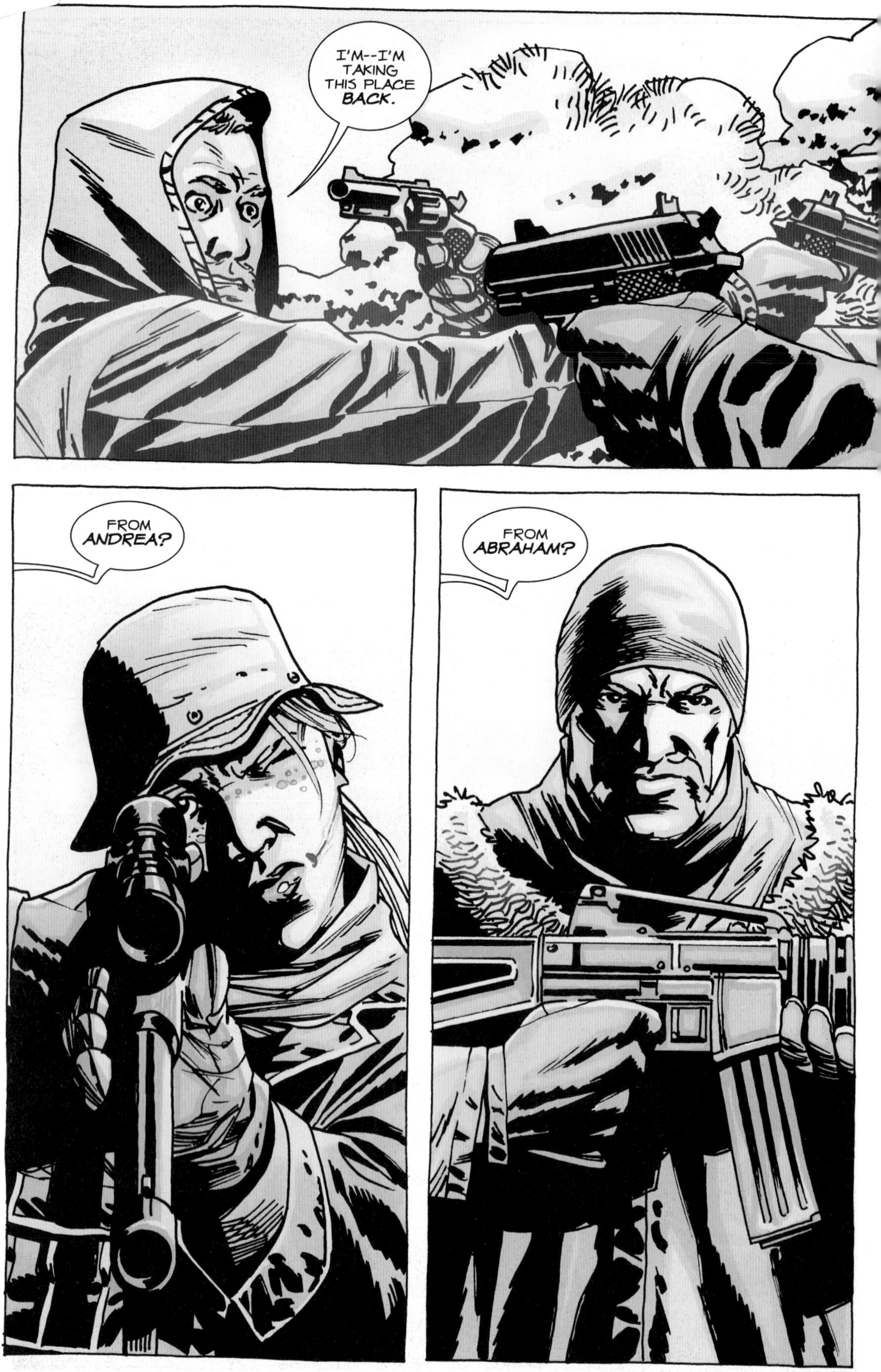
I'M--I'M TAKING THIS PLACE BACK.
FROM ANDREA?
FROM ABRAHAM?

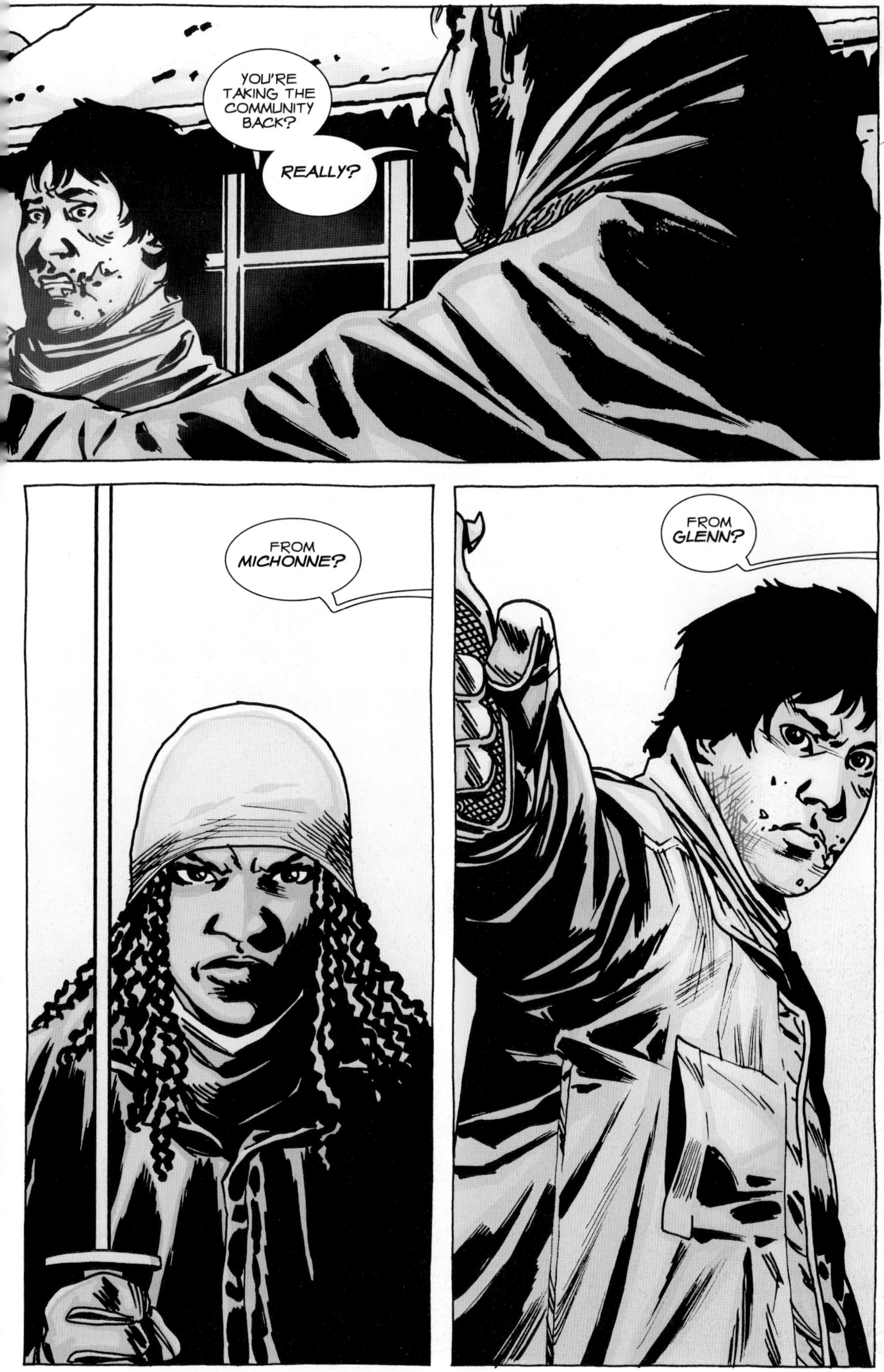
YOU'RE TAKING THE COMMUNITY BACK?
REALLY?
FROM MICHONNE?
FROM GLENN?

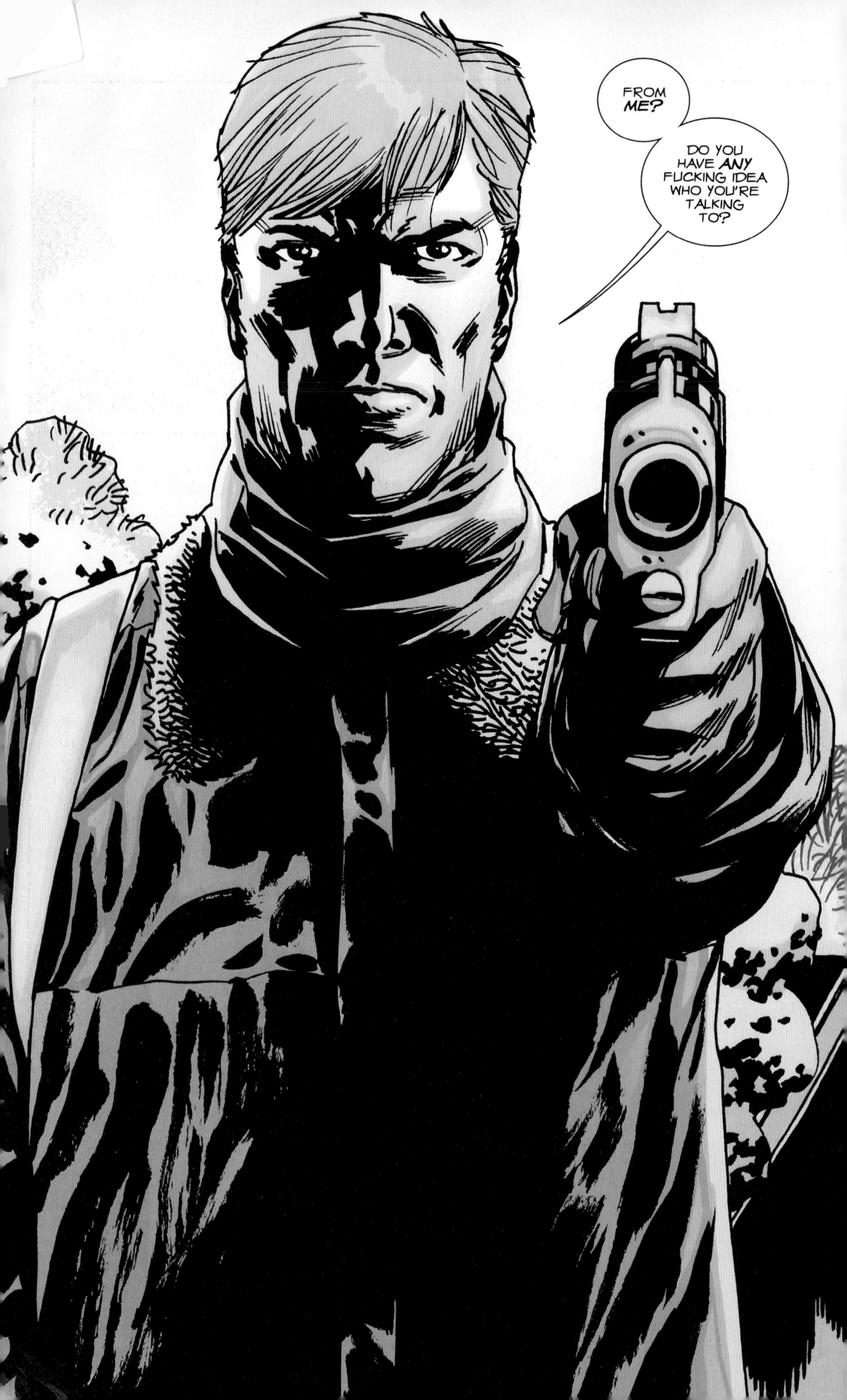
FROM ME?
DO YOU HAVE ANY FUCKING IDEA WHO YOU'RE TALKING TO?

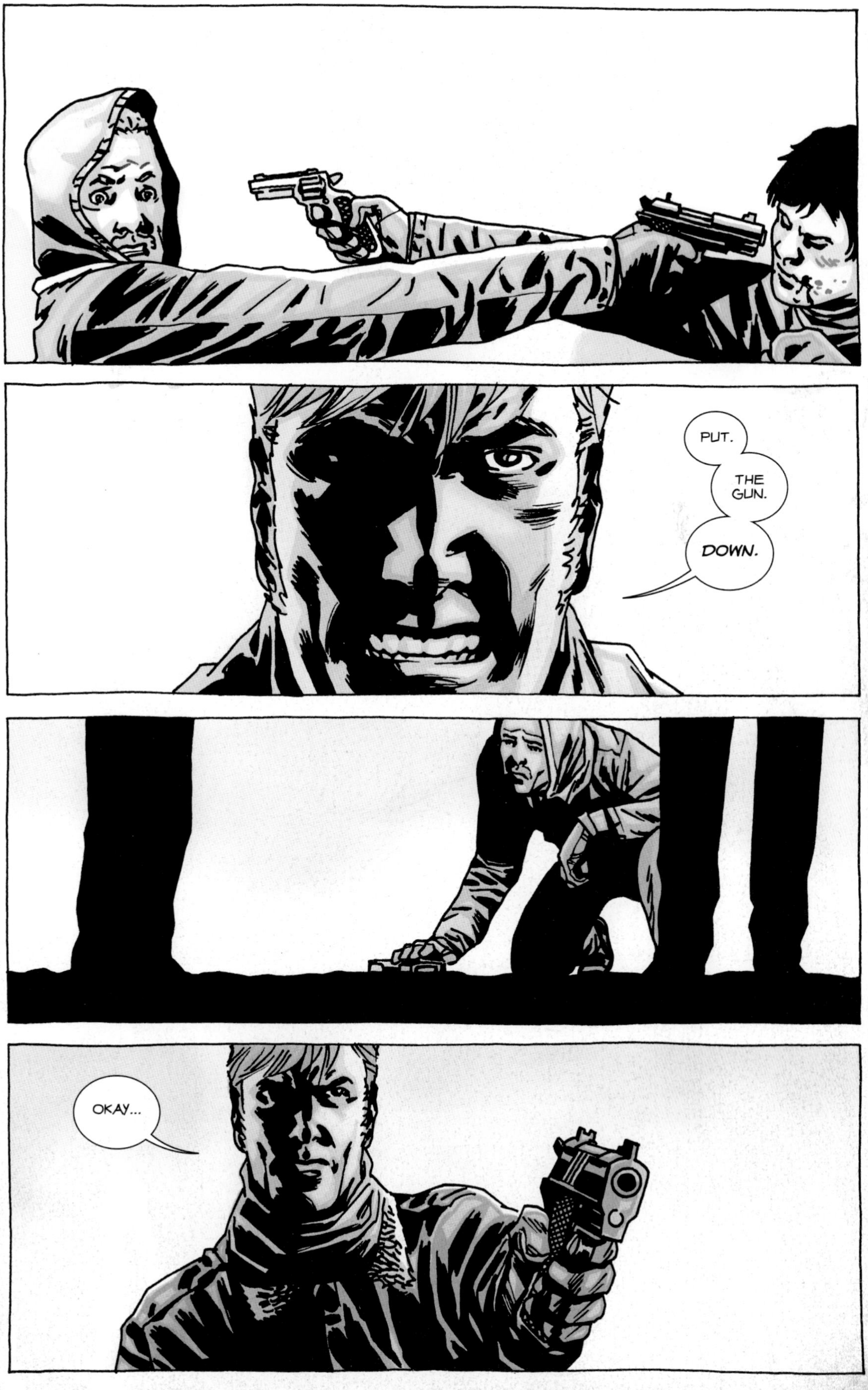
PUT.
THE GUN.
DOWN.
OKAY...

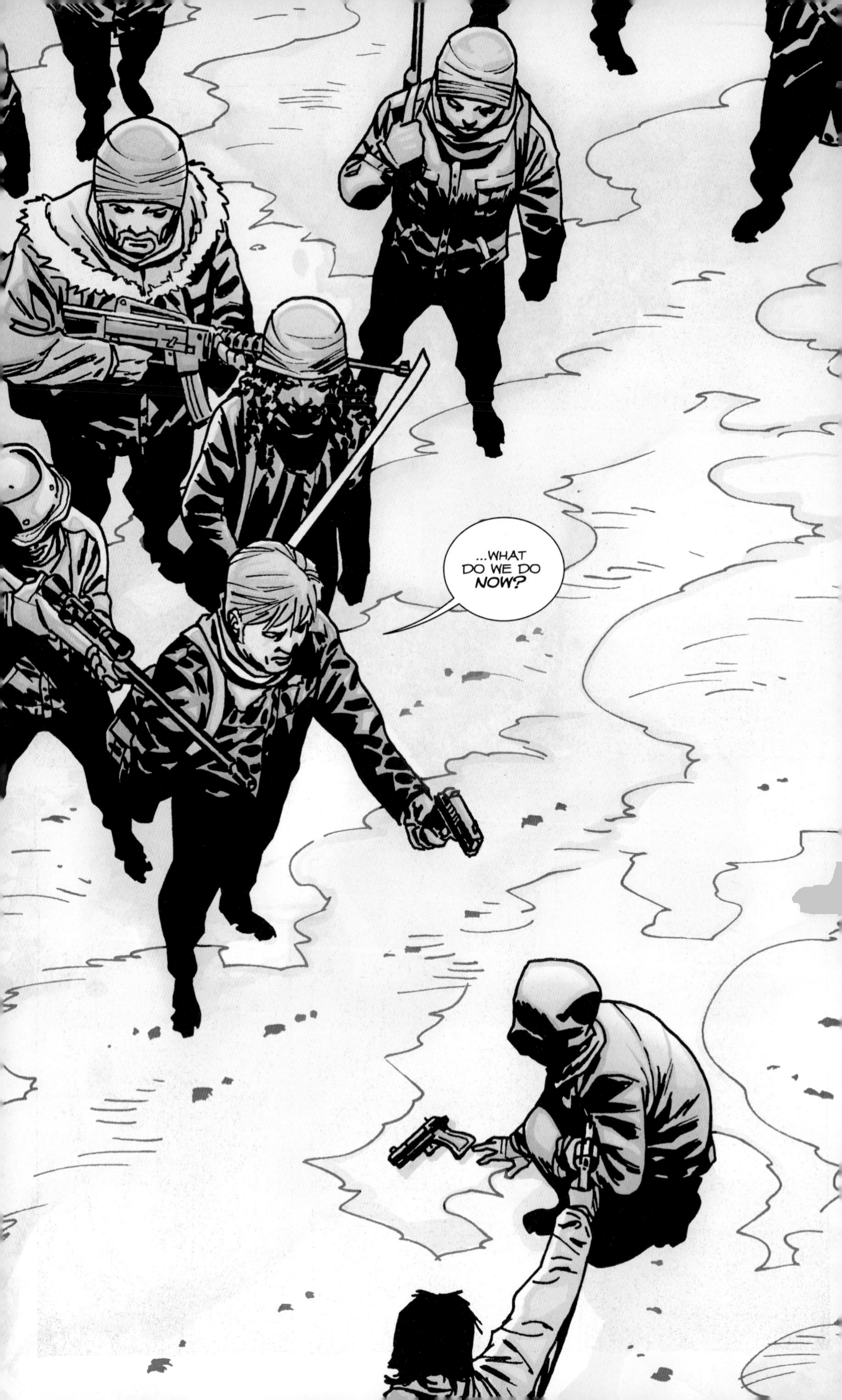
...WHAT DO WE DO NOW?

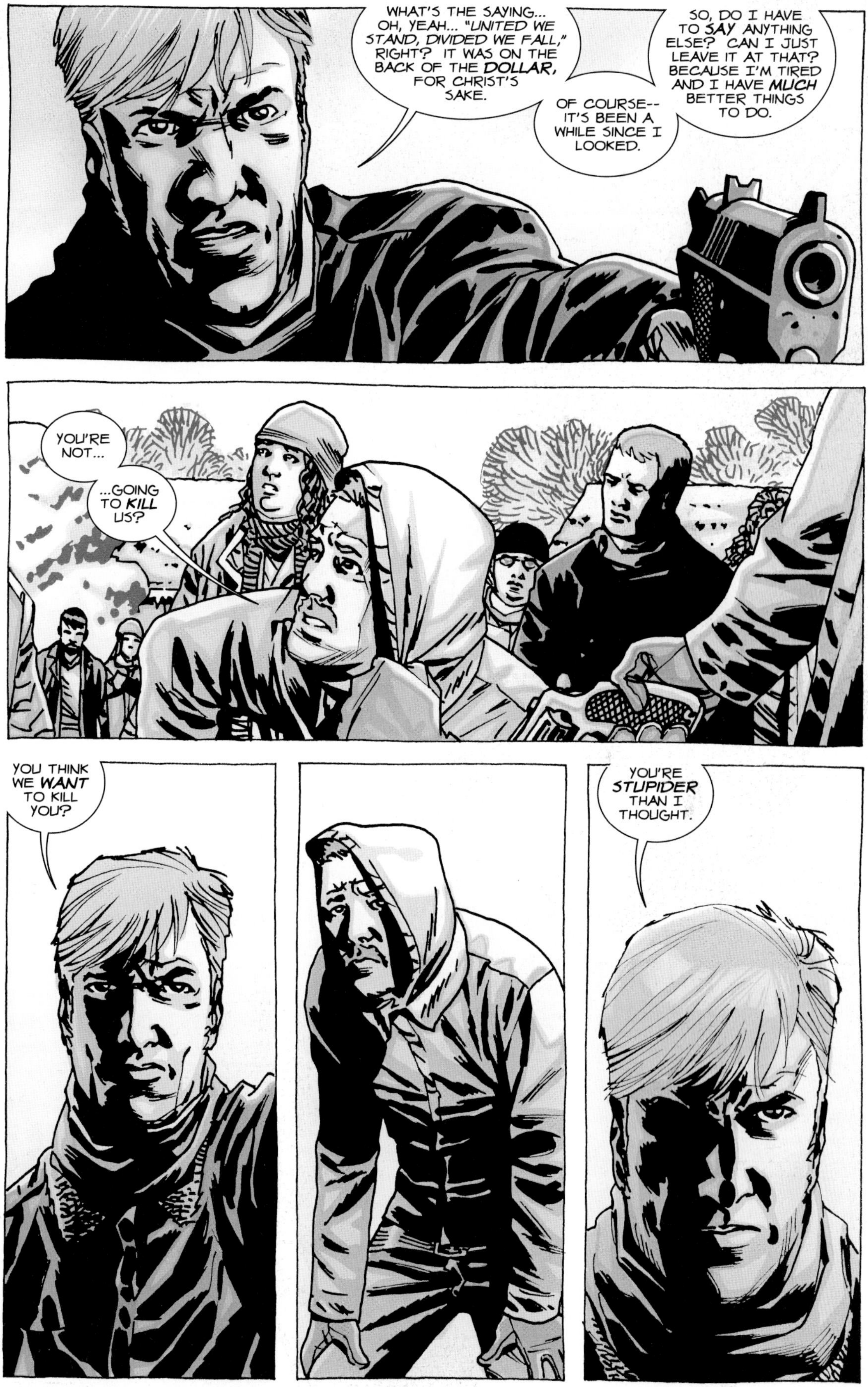
WHAT'S THE SAYING... OH, YEAH... "UNITED WE STAND, DIVIDED WE FALL," RIGHT? IT WAS ON THE BACK OF THE DOLLAR, FOR CHRIST'S SAKE.
OF COURSE-- IT'S BEEN A WHILE SINCE I LOOKED.
SO, DO I HAVE TO SAY ANYTHING ELSE? CAN I JUST LEAVE IT AT THAT? BECAUSE I'M TIRED AND I HAVE MUCH BETTER THINGS TO DO.
YOU'RE NOT...
...GOING TO KILL US?
YOU THINK WE WANT TO KILL YOU?
YOU'RE STUPIDER THAN I THOUGHT.

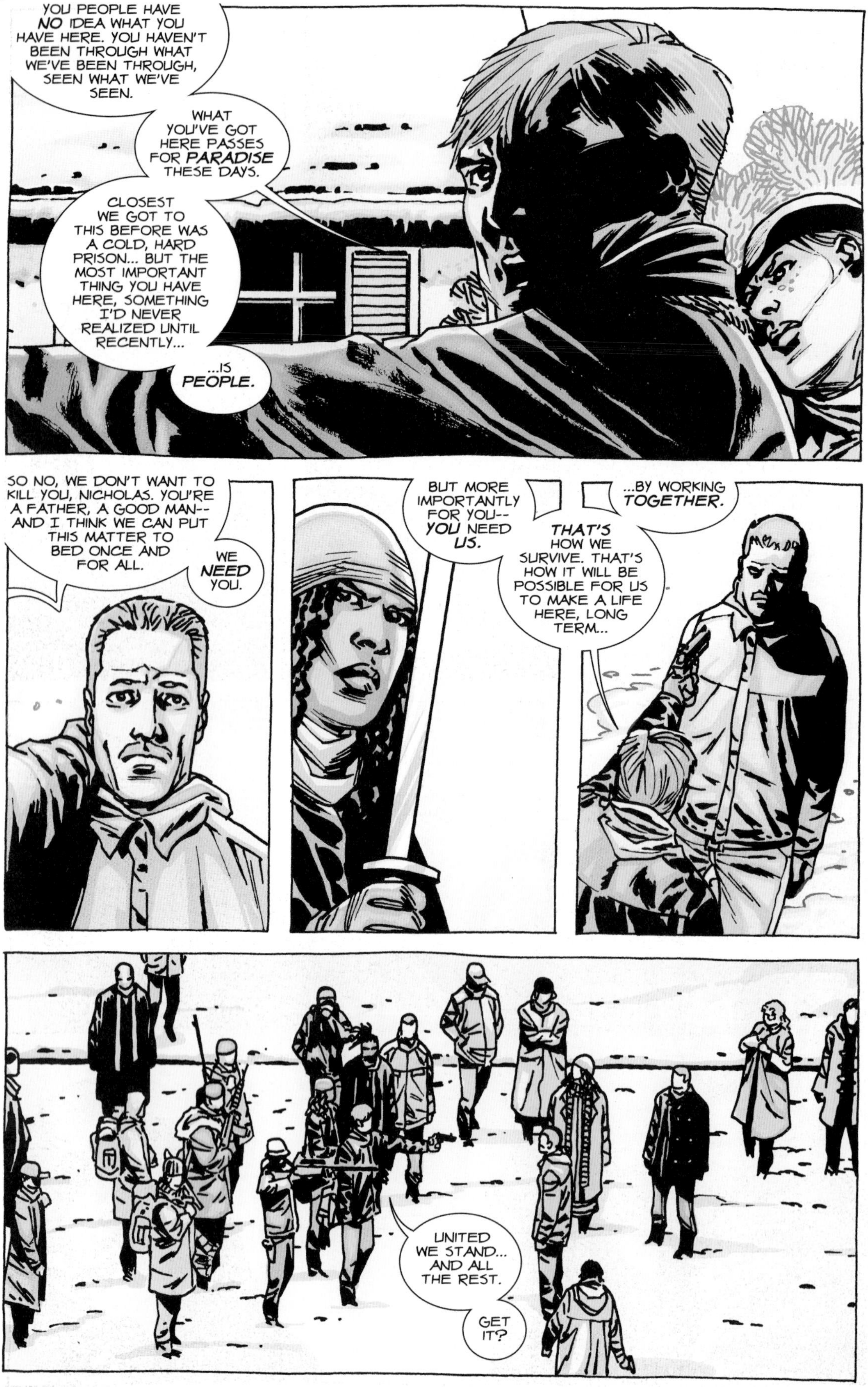
YOU PEOPLE HAVE NO IDEA WHAT YOU HAVE HERE. YOU HAVEN'T BEEN THROUGH WHAT WE'VE BEEN THROUGH, SEEN WHAT WE'VE SEEN.
WHAT YOU'VE GOT HERE PASSES FOR PARADISE THESE DAYS.
CLOSEST WE GOT TO THIS BEFORE WAS A COLD, HARD PRISON... BUT THE MOST IMPORTANT THING YOU HAVE HERE, SOMETHING I'D NEVER REALIZED UNTIL RECENTLY...
...IS PEOPLE.
SO NO, WE DON'T WANT TO KILL YOU, NICHOLAS. YOU'RE A FATHER, A GOOD MAN-- AND I THINK WE CAN PUT THIS MATTER TO BED ONCE AND FOR ALL.
WE NEED YOU.
BUT MORE IMPORTANTLY FOR YOU-- YOU NEED US.
...BY WORKING TOGETHER.
THAT'S HOW WE SURVIVE. THAT'S HOW IT WILL BE POSSIBLE FOR US TO MAKE A LIFE HERE, LONG TERM...
UNITED WE STAND... AND ALL THE REST.
GET IT?

Y--YEAH.

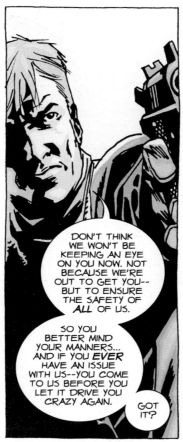

DON'T THINK WE WON'T BE KEEPING AN EYE ON YOU NOW. NOT BECAUSE WE'RE OUT TO GET YOU-- BUT TO ENSURE THE SAFETY OF *ALL* OF US.

SO YOU BETTER MIND YOUR MANNERS... AND IF YOU *EVER* HAVE AN ISSUE WITH US--YOU COME TO US BEFORE YOU LET IT DRIVE YOU CRAZY AGAIN.

GOT IT?

YES.

GOOD.

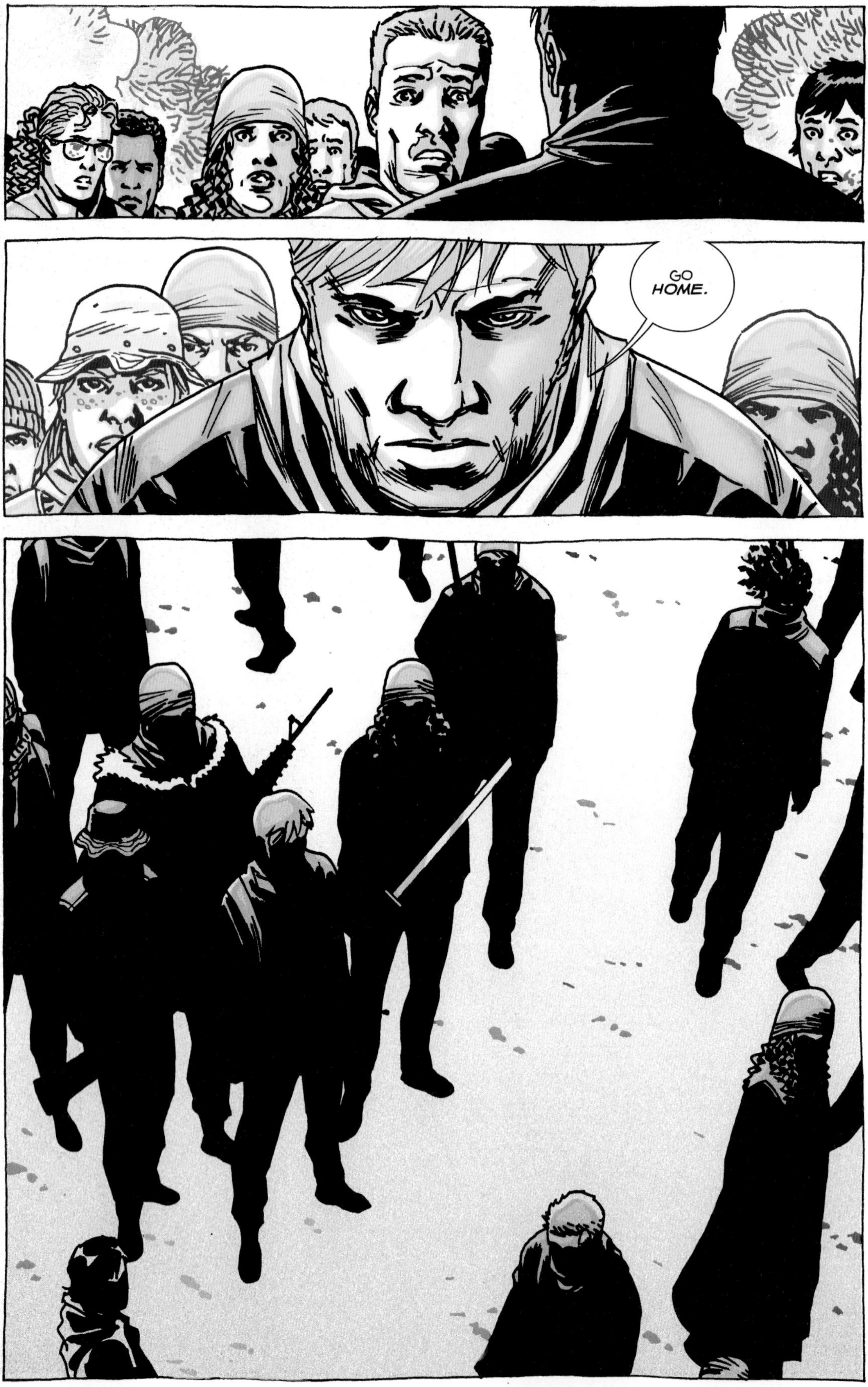
GO HOME.

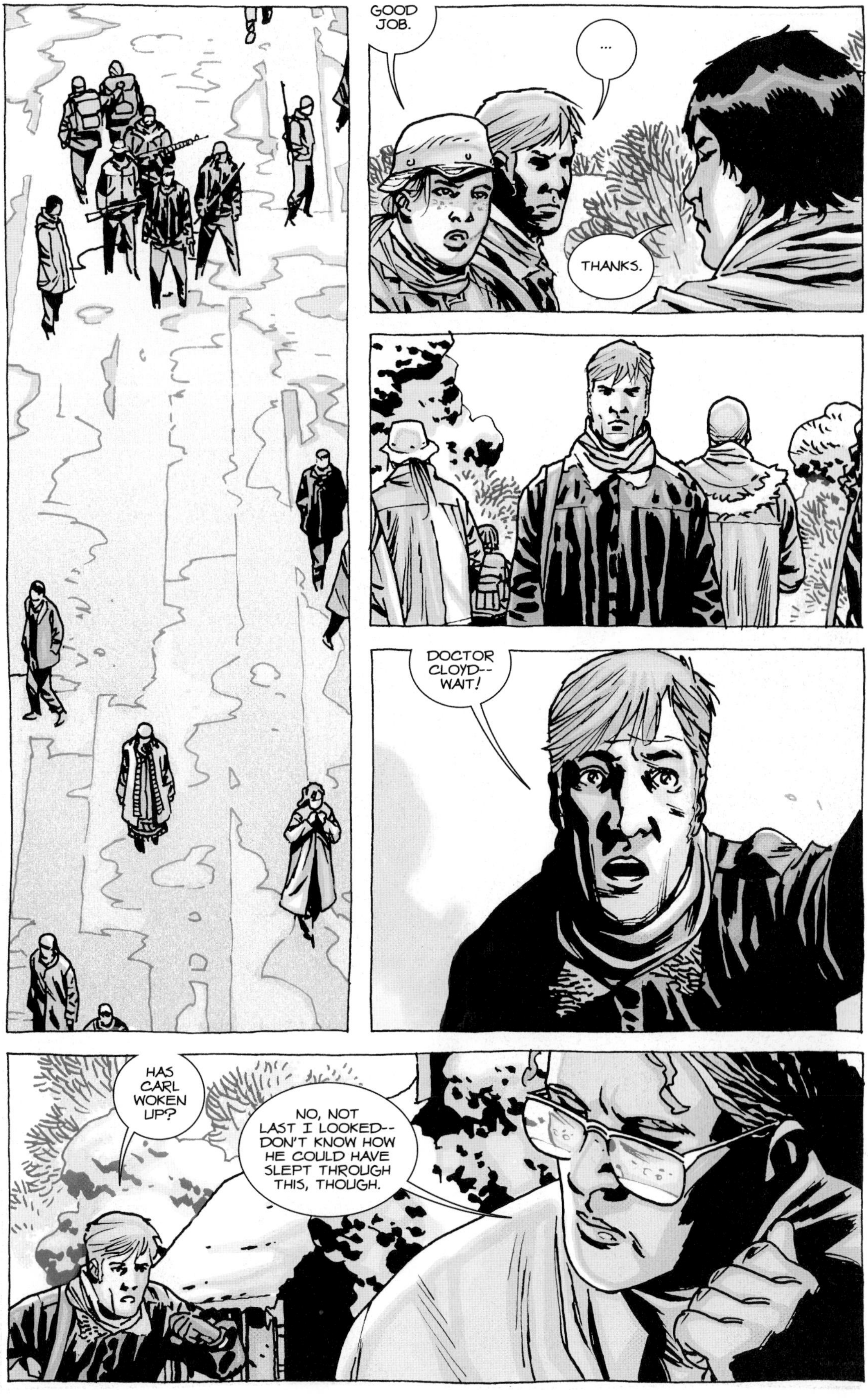
GOOD JOB.
...
THANKS.
DOCTOR CLOYD-- WAIT!
HAS CARL WOKEN UP?
NO, NOT LAST I LOOKED-- DON'T KNOW HOW HE COULD HAVE SLEPT THROUGH THIS, THOUGH.

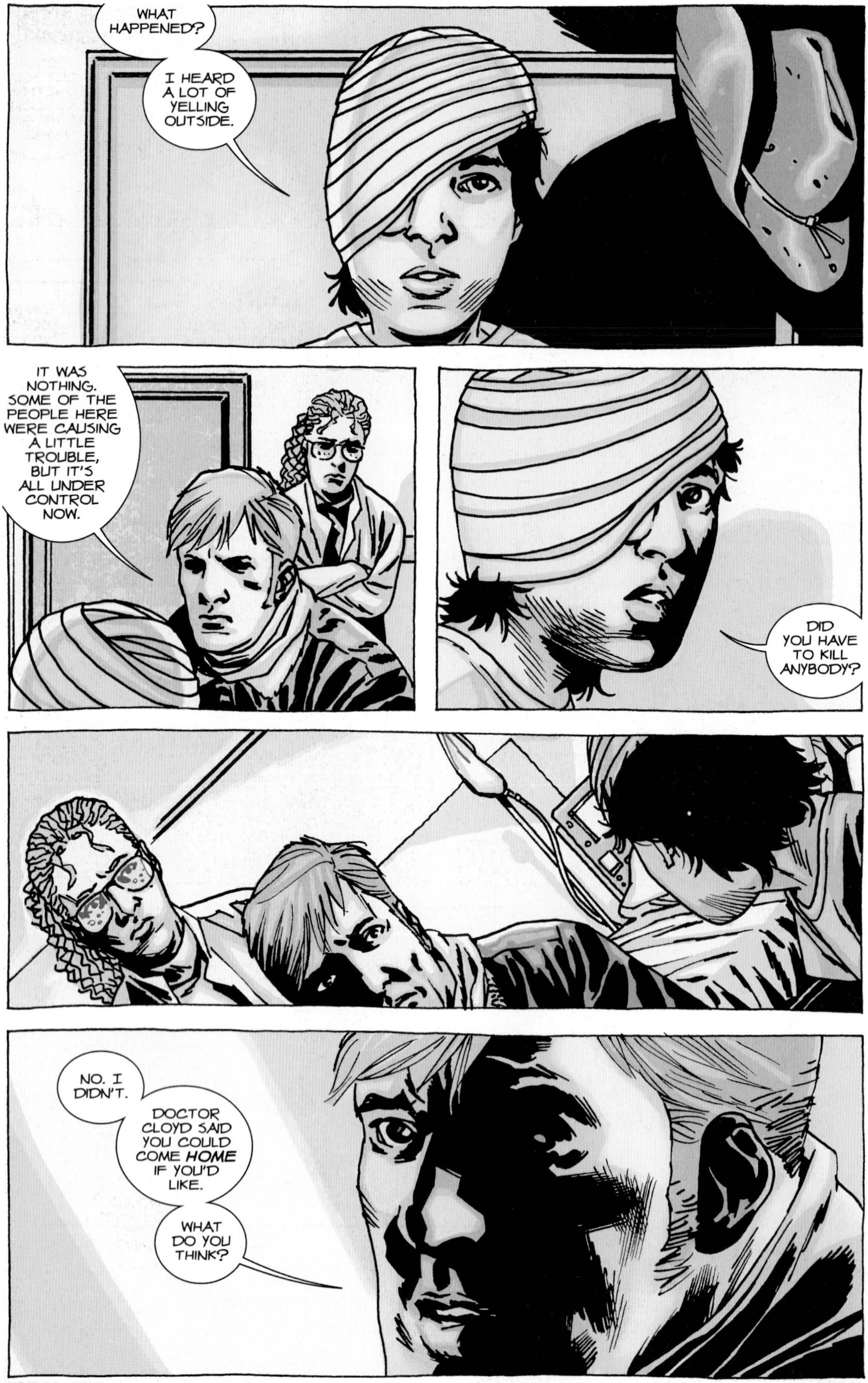
WHAT HAPPENED?
I HEARD A LOT OF YELLING OUTSIDE.
IT WAS NOTHING. SOME OF THE PEOPLE HERE WERE CAUSING A LITTLE TROUBLE, BUT IT'S ALL UNDER CONTROL NOW.
DID YOU HAVE TO KILL ANYBODY?
NO. I DIDN'T.
DOCTOR CLOYD SAID YOU COULD COME HOME IF YOU'D LIKE.
WHAT DO YOU THINK?

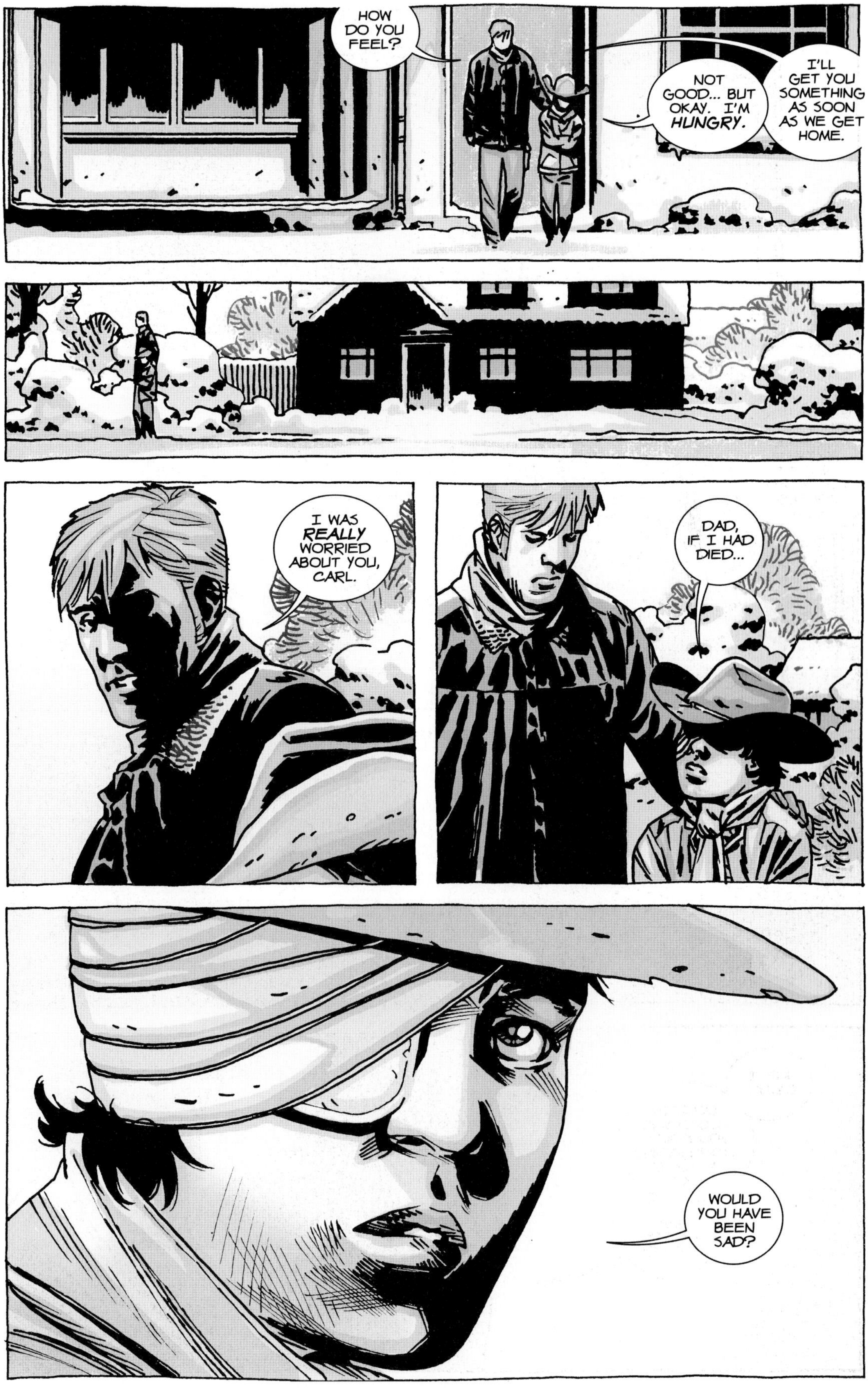
HOW DO YOU FEEL?
NOT GOOD... BUT OKAY. I'M HUNGRY.
I'LL GET YOU SOMETHING AS SOON AS WE GET HOME.
I WAS REALLY WORRIED ABOUT YOU, CARL.
DAD, IF I HAD DIED...
WOULD YOU HAVE BEEN SAD?

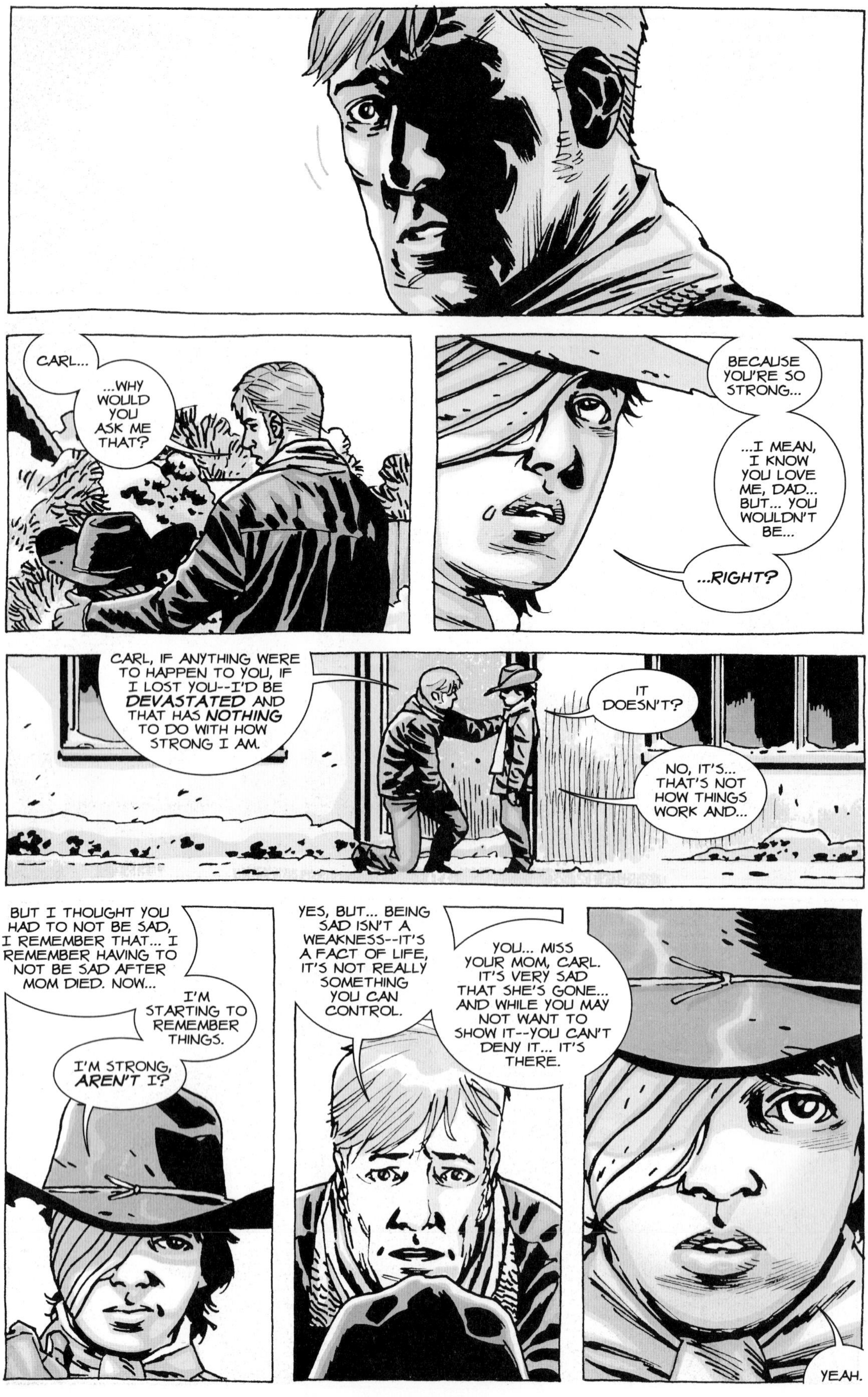

CARL...
...WHY WOULD YOU ASK ME THAT?
BECAUSE YOU'RE SO STRONG...
...I MEAN, I KNOW YOU LOVE ME, DAD... BUT... YOU WOULDN'T BE...
...RIGHT?
CARL, IF ANYTHING WERE TO HAPPEN TO YOU, IF I LOST YOU--I'D BE DEVASTATED AND THAT HAS NOTHING TO DO WITH HOW STRONG I AM.
IT DOESN'T?
NO, IT'S... THAT'S NOT HOW THINGS WORK AND...
BUT I THOUGHT YOU HAD TO NOT BE SAD, I REMEMBER THAT... I REMEMBER HAVING TO NOT BE SAD AFTER MOM DIED. NOW...
I'M STARTING TO REMEMBER THINGS.
I'M STRONG, AREN'T I?
YES, BUT... BEING SAD ISN'T A WEAKNESS--IT'S A FACT OF LIFE, IT'S NOT REALLY SOMETHING YOU CAN CONTROL.
YOU... MISS YOUR MOM, CARL. IT'S VERY SAD THAT SHE'S GONE... AND WHILE YOU MAY NOT WANT TO SHOW IT--YOU CAN'T DENY IT... IT'S THERE.
YEAH.

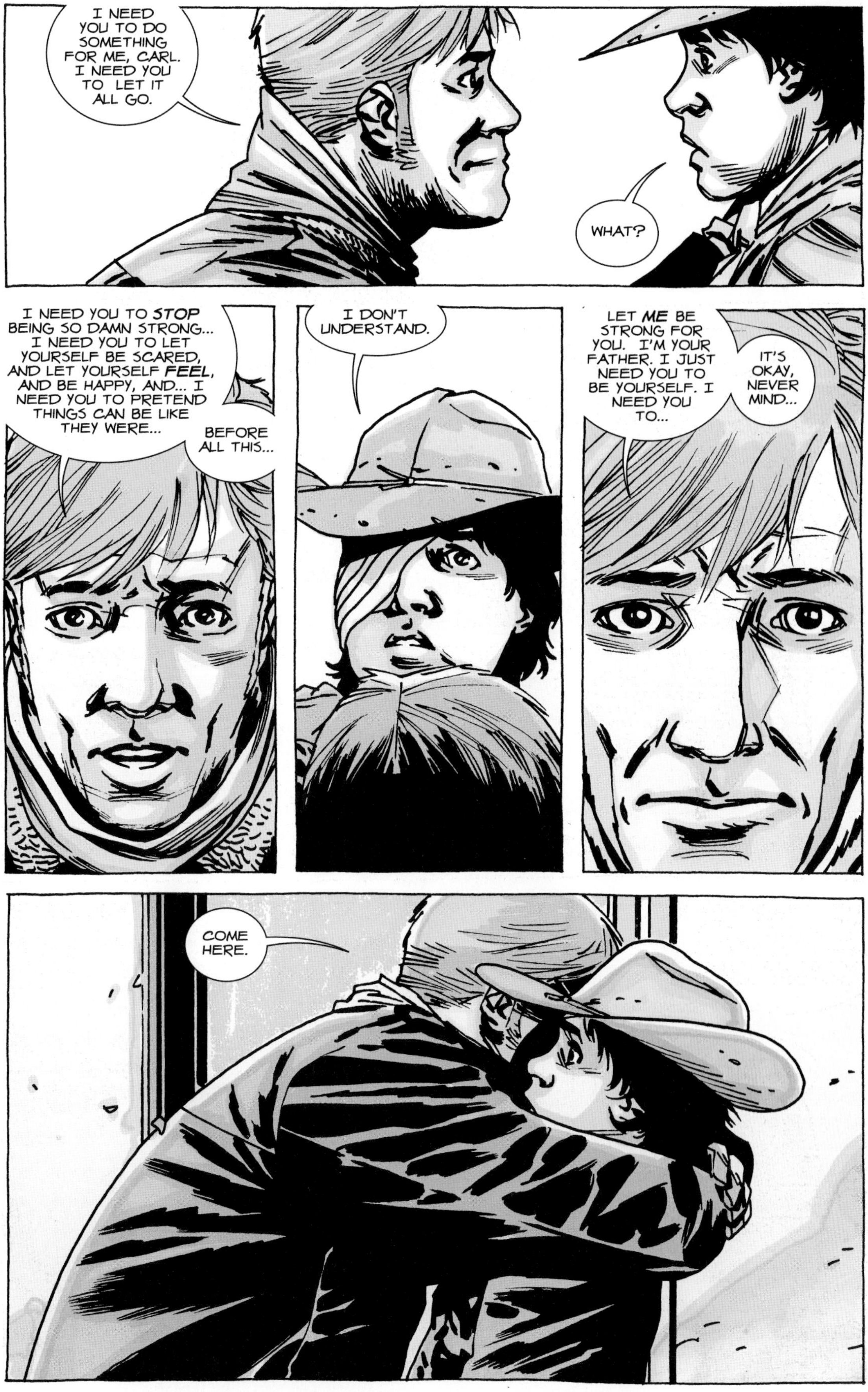
I NEED YOU TO DO SOMETHING FOR ME, CARL. I NEED YOU TO LET IT ALL GO.
WHAT?
I NEED YOU TO *STOP* BEING SO DAMN STRONG... I NEED YOU TO LET YOURSELF BE SCARED, AND LET YOURSELF *FEEL*, AND BE HAPPY, AND... I NEED YOU TO PRETEND THINGS CAN BE LIKE THEY WERE...
BEFORE ALL THIS...
I DON'T UNDERSTAND.
LET *ME* BE STRONG FOR YOU. I'M YOUR FATHER. I JUST NEED YOU TO BE YOURSELF. I NEED YOU TO...
IT'S OKAY, NEVER MIND...
COME HERE.

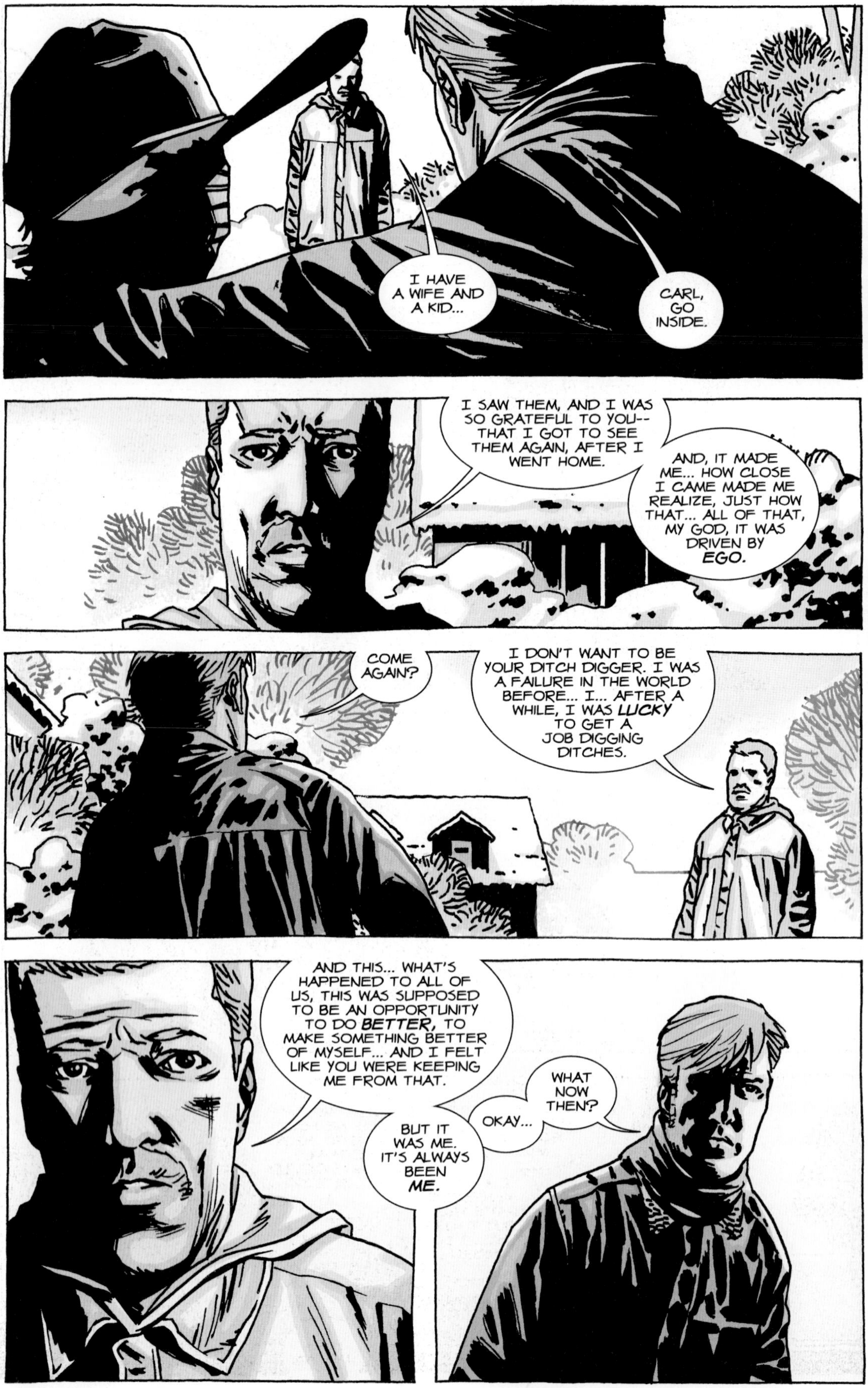
I HAVE A WIFE AND A KID...
CARL, GO INSIDE.
I SAW THEM, AND I WAS SO GRATEFUL TO YOU-- THAT I GOT TO SEE THEM AGAIN, AFTER I WENT HOME.
AND, IT MADE ME... HOW CLOSE I CAME MADE ME REALIZE, JUST HOW THAT... ALL OF THAT, MY GOD, IT WAS DRIVEN BY EGO.
COME AGAIN?
I DON'T WANT TO BE YOUR DITCH DIGGER. I WAS A FAILURE IN THE WORLD BEFORE... I... AFTER A WHILE, I WAS LUCKY TO GET A JOB DIGGING DITCHES.
AND THIS... WHAT'S HAPPENED TO ALL OF US, THIS WAS SUPPOSED TO BE AN OPPORTUNITY TO DO BETTER, TO MAKE SOMETHING BETTER OF MYSELF... AND I FELT LIKE YOU WERE KEEPING ME FROM THAT.
BUT IT WAS ME. IT'S ALWAYS BEEN ME.
OKAY...
WHAT NOW THEN?

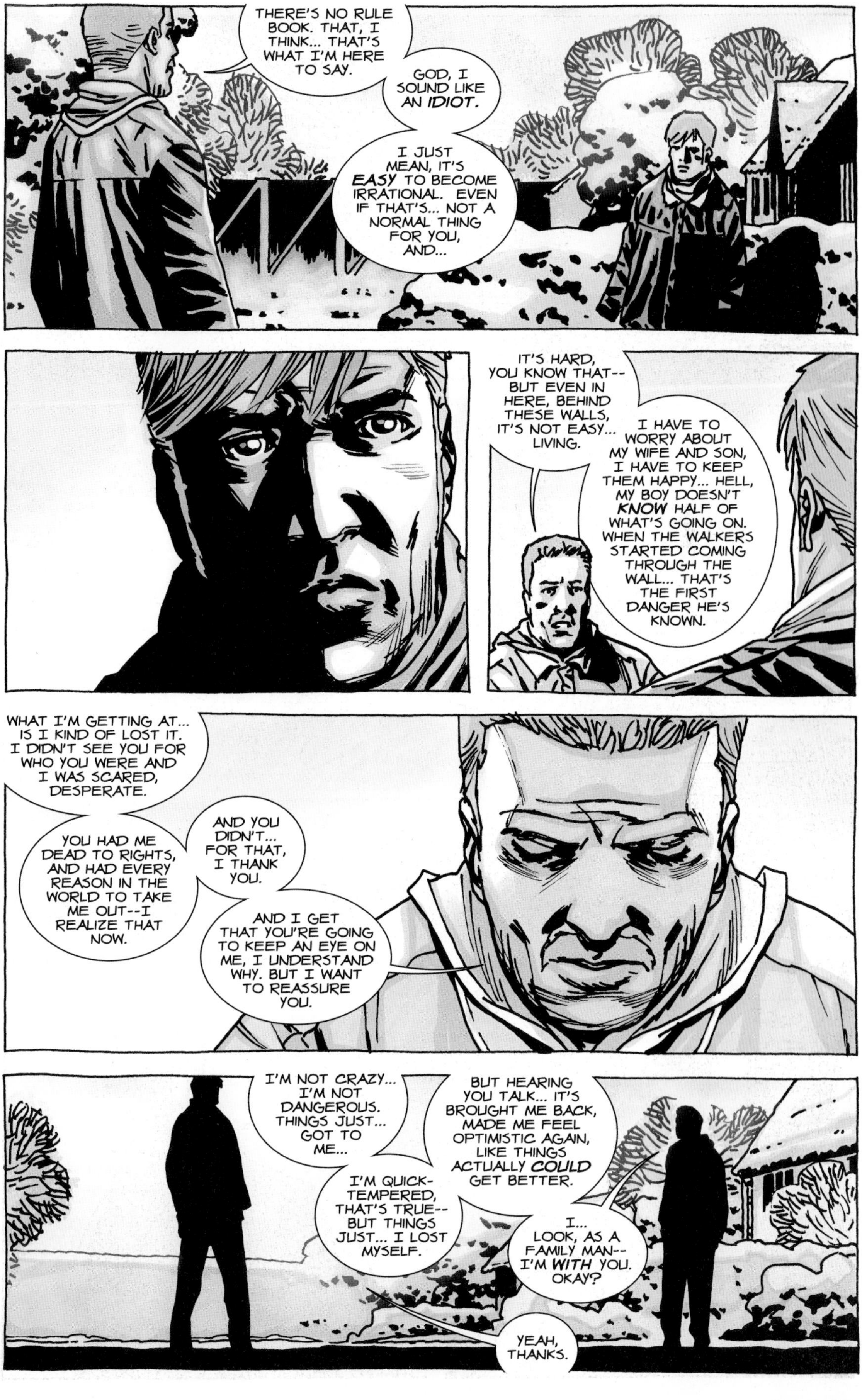
THERE'S NO RULE BOOK. THAT, I THINK... THAT'S WHAT I'M HERE TO SAY.
GOD, I SOUND LIKE AN *IDIOT.*
I JUST MEAN, IT'S *EASY* TO BECOME IRRATIONAL. EVEN IF THAT'S... NOT A NORMAL THING FOR YOU, AND...
IT'S HARD, YOU KNOW THAT-- BUT EVEN IN HERE, BEHIND THESE WALLS, IT'S NOT EASY... LIVING.
I HAVE TO WORRY ABOUT MY WIFE AND SON, I HAVE TO KEEP THEM HAPPY... HELL, MY BOY DOESN'T *KNOW* HALF OF WHAT'S GOING ON. WHEN THE WALKERS STARTED COMING THROUGH THE WALL... THAT'S THE FIRST DANGER HE'S KNOWN.
WHAT I'M GETTING AT... IS I KIND OF LOST IT. I DIDN'T SEE YOU FOR WHO YOU WERE AND I WAS SCARED, DESPERATE.
YOU HAD ME DEAD TO RIGHTS, AND HAD EVERY REASON IN THE WORLD TO TAKE ME OUT--I REALIZE THAT NOW.
AND YOU DIDN'T... FOR THAT, I THANK YOU.
AND I GET THAT YOU'RE GOING TO KEEP AN EYE ON ME, I UNDERSTAND WHY. BUT I WANT TO REASSURE YOU.
I'M NOT CRAZY... I'M NOT DANGEROUS. THINGS JUST... GOT TO ME...
I'M QUICK-TEMPERED, THAT'S TRUE-- BUT THINGS JUST... I LOST MYSELF.
BUT HEARING YOU TALK... IT'S BROUGHT ME BACK, MADE ME FEEL OPTIMISTIC AGAIN, LIKE THINGS ACTUALLY *COULD* GET BETTER.
I... LOOK, AS A FAMILY MAN-- I'M *WITH* YOU. OKAY?
YEAH, THANKS.

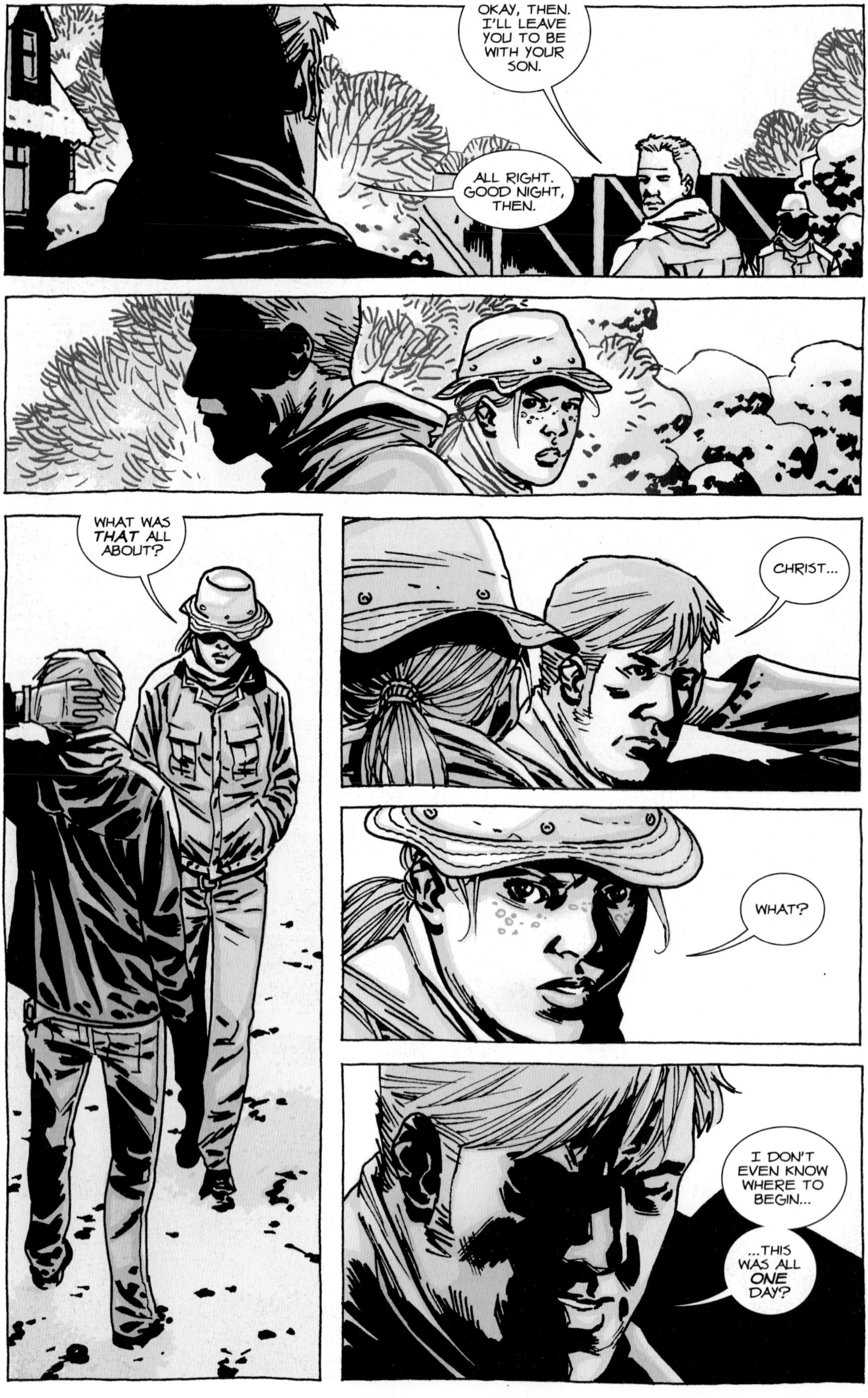
OKAY, THEN. I'LL LEAVE YOU TO BE WITH YOUR SON.
ALL RIGHT. GOOD NIGHT, THEN.
WHAT WAS THAT ALL ABOUT?
CHRIST...
WHAT?
I DON'T EVEN KNOW WHERE TO BEGIN...
...THIS WAS ALL ONE DAY?

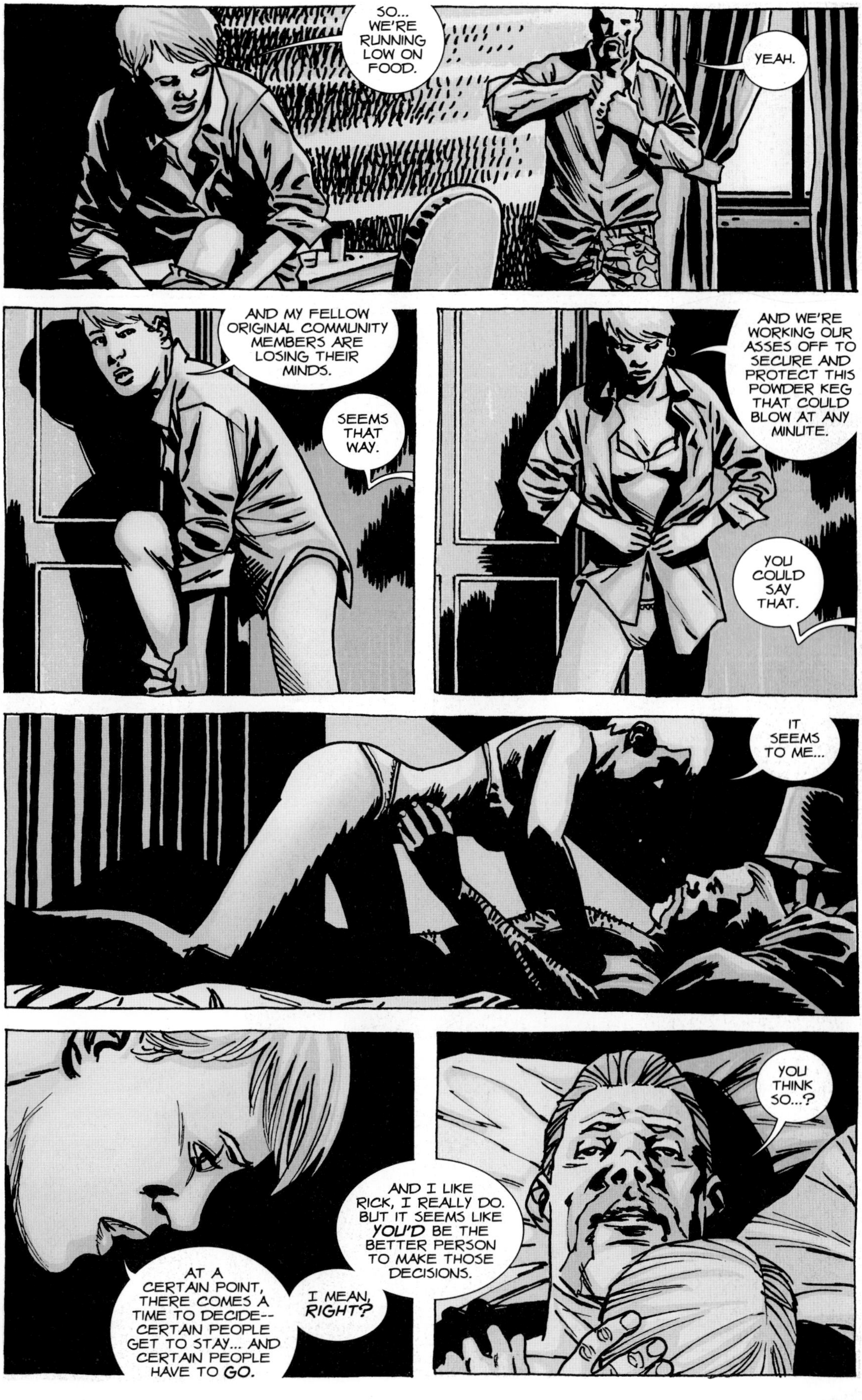
SO... WE'RE RUNNING LOW ON FOOD.
YEAH.
AND MY FELLOW ORIGINAL COMMUNITY MEMBERS ARE LOSING THEIR MINDS.
SEEMS THAT WAY.
AND WE'RE WORKING OUR ASSES OFF TO SECURE AND PROTECT THIS POWDER KEG THAT COULD BLOW AT ANY MINUTE.
YOU COULD SAY THAT.
IT SEEMS TO ME...
AT A CERTAIN POINT, THERE COMES A TIME TO DECIDE-- CERTAIN PEOPLE GET TO STAY... AND CERTAIN PEOPLE HAVE TO GO.
YOU THINK SO...?
AND I LIKE RICK, I REALLY DO. BUT IT SEEMS LIKE YOU'D BE THE BETTER PERSON TO MAKE THOSE DECISIONS.
I MEAN, RIGHT?

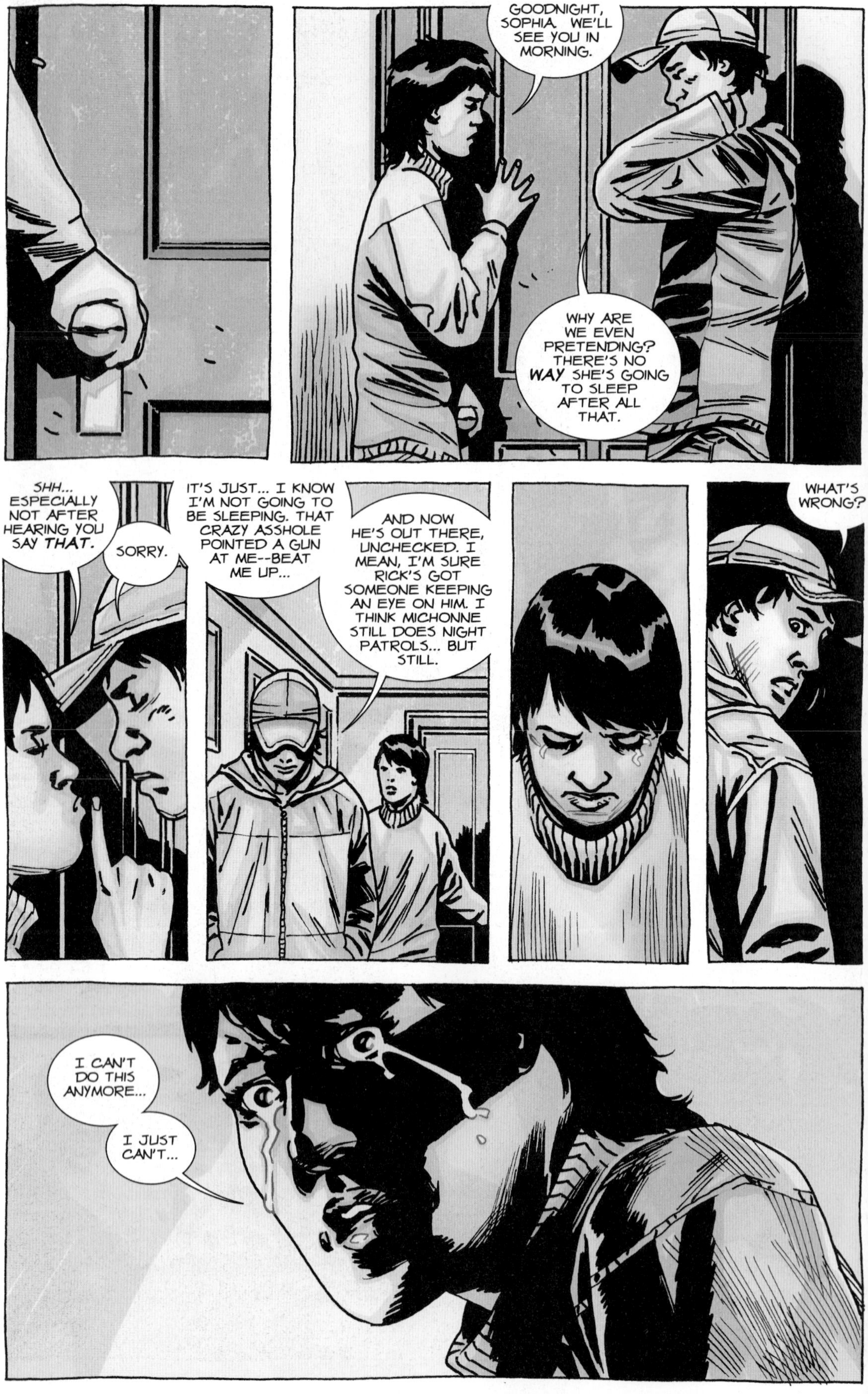
GOODNIGHT, SOPHIA. WE'LL SEE YOU IN MORNING.
WHY ARE WE EVEN PRETENDING? THERE'S NO WAY SHE'S GOING TO SLEEP AFTER ALL THAT.
SHH... ESPECIALLY NOT AFTER HEARING YOU SAY THAT.
SORRY.
IT'S JUST... I KNOW I'M NOT GOING TO BE SLEEPING. THAT CRAZY ASSHOLE POINTED A GUN AT ME--BEAT ME UP...
AND NOW HE'S OUT THERE, UNCHECKED. I MEAN, I'M SURE RICK'S GOT SOMEONE KEEPING AN EYE ON HIM. I THINK MICHONNE STILL DOES NIGHT PATROLS... BUT STILL.
WHAT'S WRONG?
I CAN'T DO THIS ANYMORE...
I JUST CAN'T...

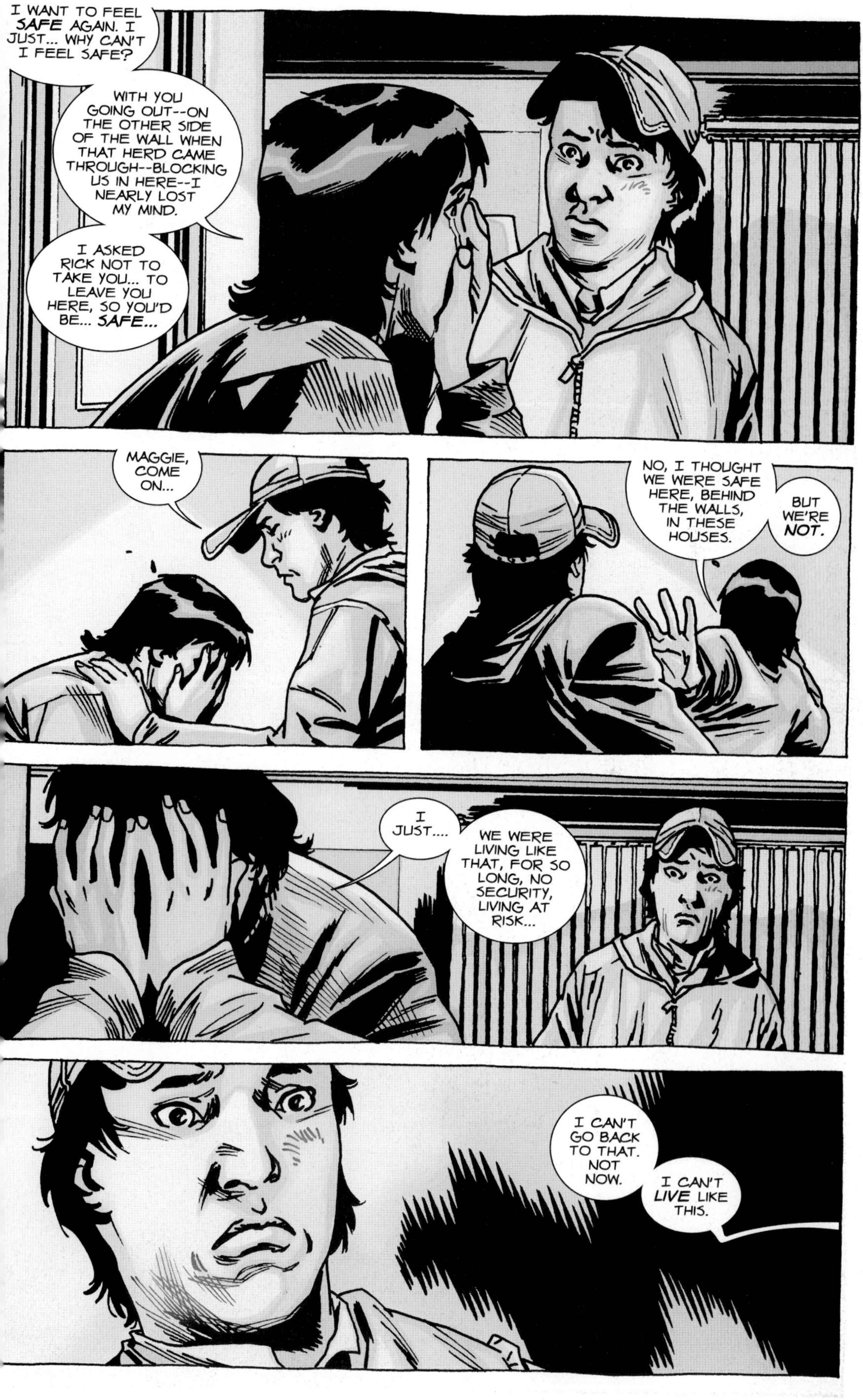
I WANT TO FEEL SAFE AGAIN. I JUST... WHY CAN'T I FEEL SAFE?
WITH YOU GOING OUT--ON THE OTHER SIDE OF THE WALL WHEN THAT HERD CAME THROUGH--BLOCKING US IN HERE--I NEARLY LOST MY MIND.
I ASKED RICK NOT TO TAKE YOU... TO LEAVE YOU HERE, SO YOU'D BE... SAFE...
MAGGIE, COME ON...
NO, I THOUGHT WE WERE SAFE HERE, BEHIND THE WALLS, IN THESE HOUSES.
BUT WE'RE NOT.
I JUST....
WE WERE LIVING LIKE THAT, FOR SO LONG, NO SECURITY, LIVING AT RISK...
I CAN'T GO BACK TO THAT. NOT NOW.
I CAN'T LIVE LIKE THIS.

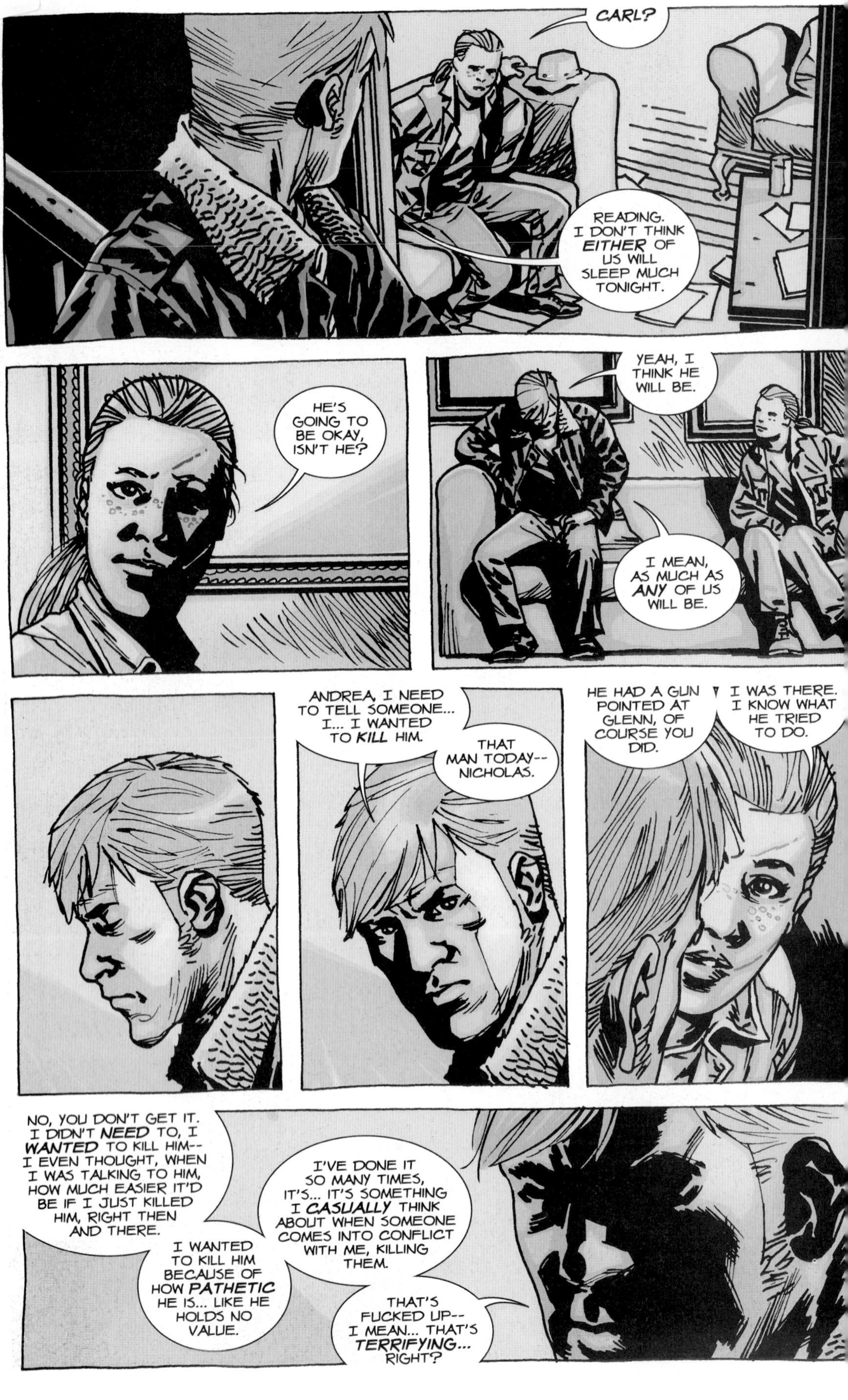
CARL?
READING. I DON'T THINK EITHER OF US WILL SLEEP MUCH TONIGHT.
HE'S GOING TO BE OKAY, ISN'T HE?
YEAH, I THINK HE WILL BE.
I MEAN, AS MUCH AS ANY OF US WILL BE.
ANDREA, I NEED TO TELL SOMEONE... I... I WANTED TO KILL HIM.
THAT MAN TODAY-- NICHOLAS.
HE HAD A GUN POINTED AT GLENN, OF COURSE YOU DID.
I WAS THERE. I KNOW WHAT HE TRIED TO DO.
NO, YOU DON'T GET IT. I DIDN'T NEED TO, I WANTED TO KILL HIM-- I EVEN THOUGHT, WHEN I WAS TALKING TO HIM, HOW MUCH EASIER IT'D BE IF I JUST KILLED HIM, RIGHT THEN AND THERE.
I WANTED TO KILL HIM BECAUSE OF HOW PATHETIC HE IS... LIKE HE HOLDS NO VALUE.
I'VE DONE IT SO MANY TIMES, IT'S... IT'S SOMETHING I CASUALLY THINK ABOUT WHEN SOMEONE COMES INTO CONFLICT WITH ME, KILLING THEM.
THAT'S FUCKED UP-- I MEAN... THAT'S TERRIFYING... RIGHT?

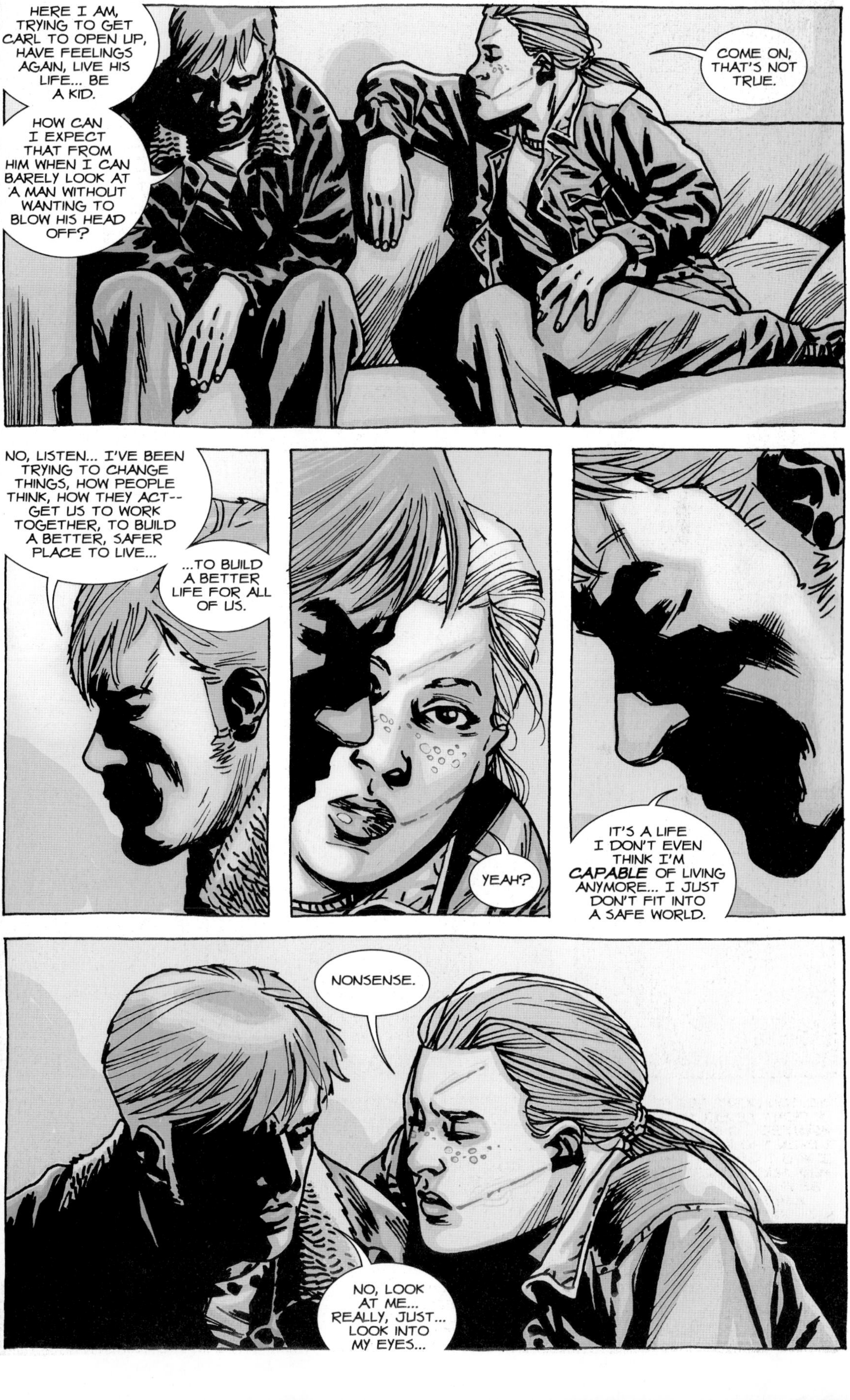
HERE I AM, TRYING TO GET CARL TO OPEN UP, HAVE FEELINGS AGAIN, LIVE HIS LIFE... BE A KID.
HOW CAN I EXPECT THAT FROM HIM WHEN I CAN BARELY LOOK AT A MAN WITHOUT WANTING TO BLOW HIS HEAD OFF?
COME ON, THAT'S NOT TRUE.
NO, LISTEN... I'VE BEEN TRYING TO CHANGE THINGS, HOW PEOPLE THINK, HOW THEY ACT-- GET US TO WORK TOGETHER, TO BUILD A BETTER, SAFER PLACE TO LIVE...
...TO BUILD A BETTER LIFE FOR ALL OF US.
YEAH?
IT'S A LIFE I DON'T EVEN THINK I'M CAPABLE OF LIVING ANYMORE... I JUST DON'T FIT INTO A SAFE WORLD.
NONSENSE.
NO, LOOK AT ME... REALLY, JUST... LOOK INTO MY EYES...

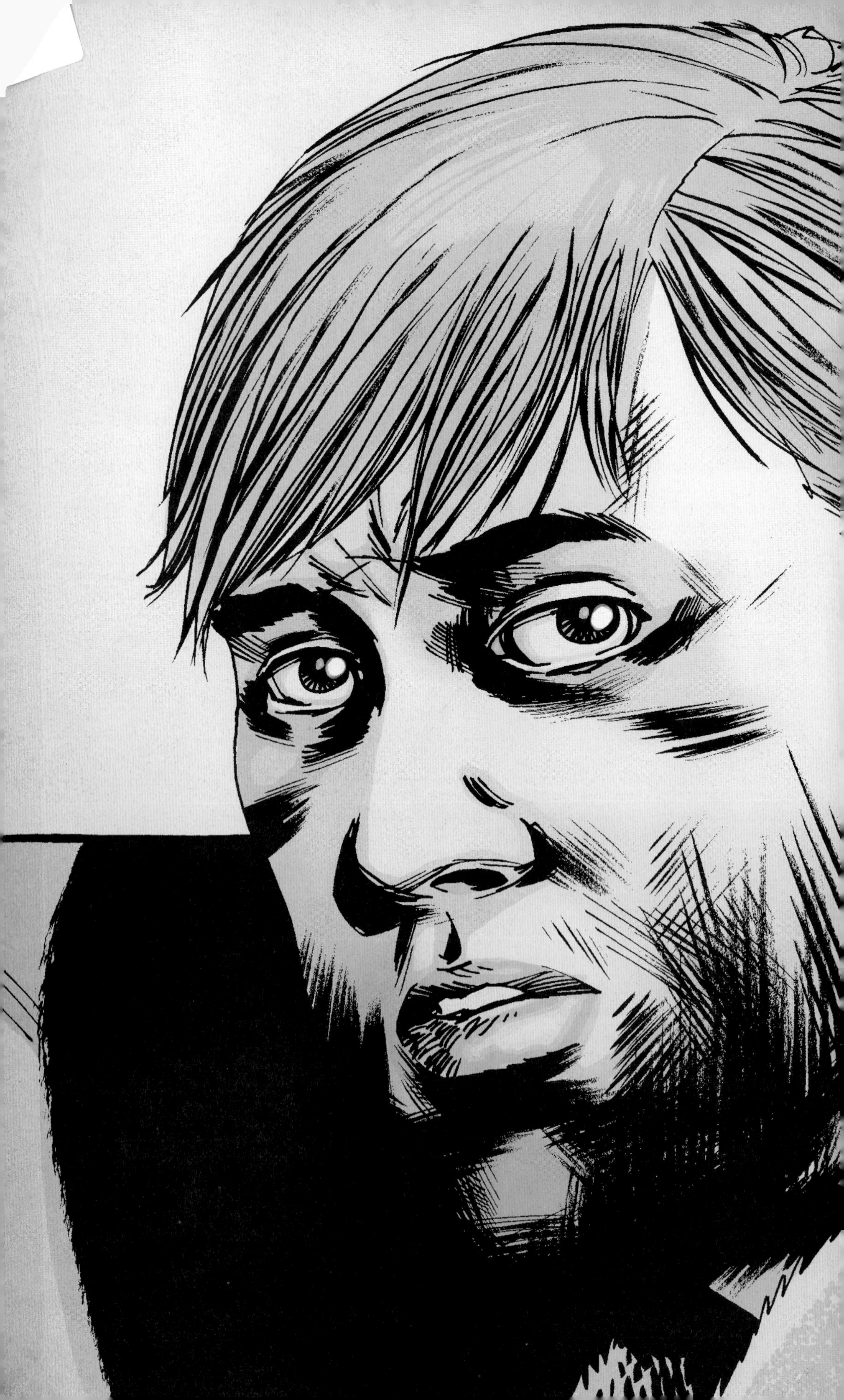

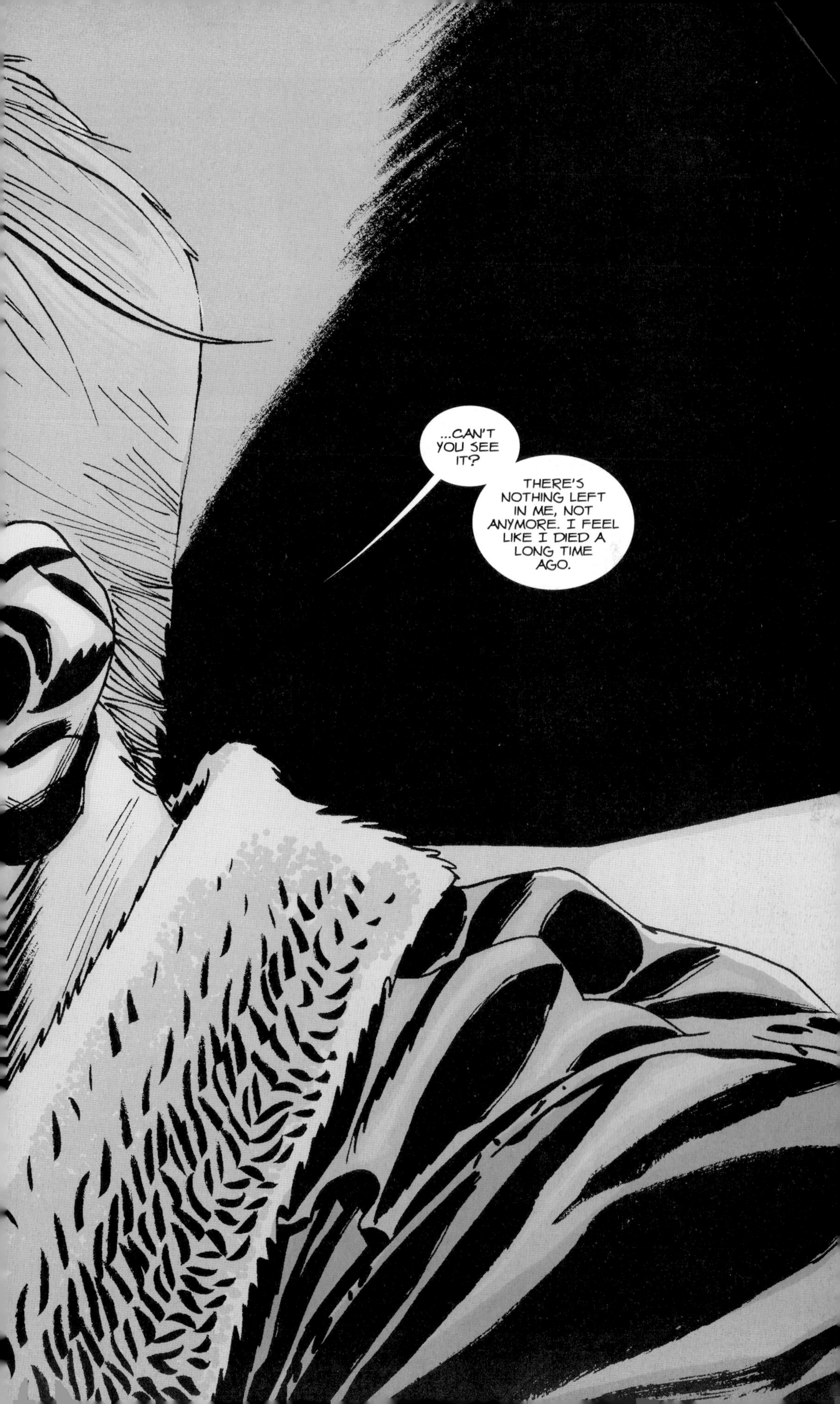
...CAN'T YOU SEE IT?
THERE'S NOTHING LEFT IN ME, NOT ANYMORE. I FEEL LIKE I DIED A LONG TIME AGO.

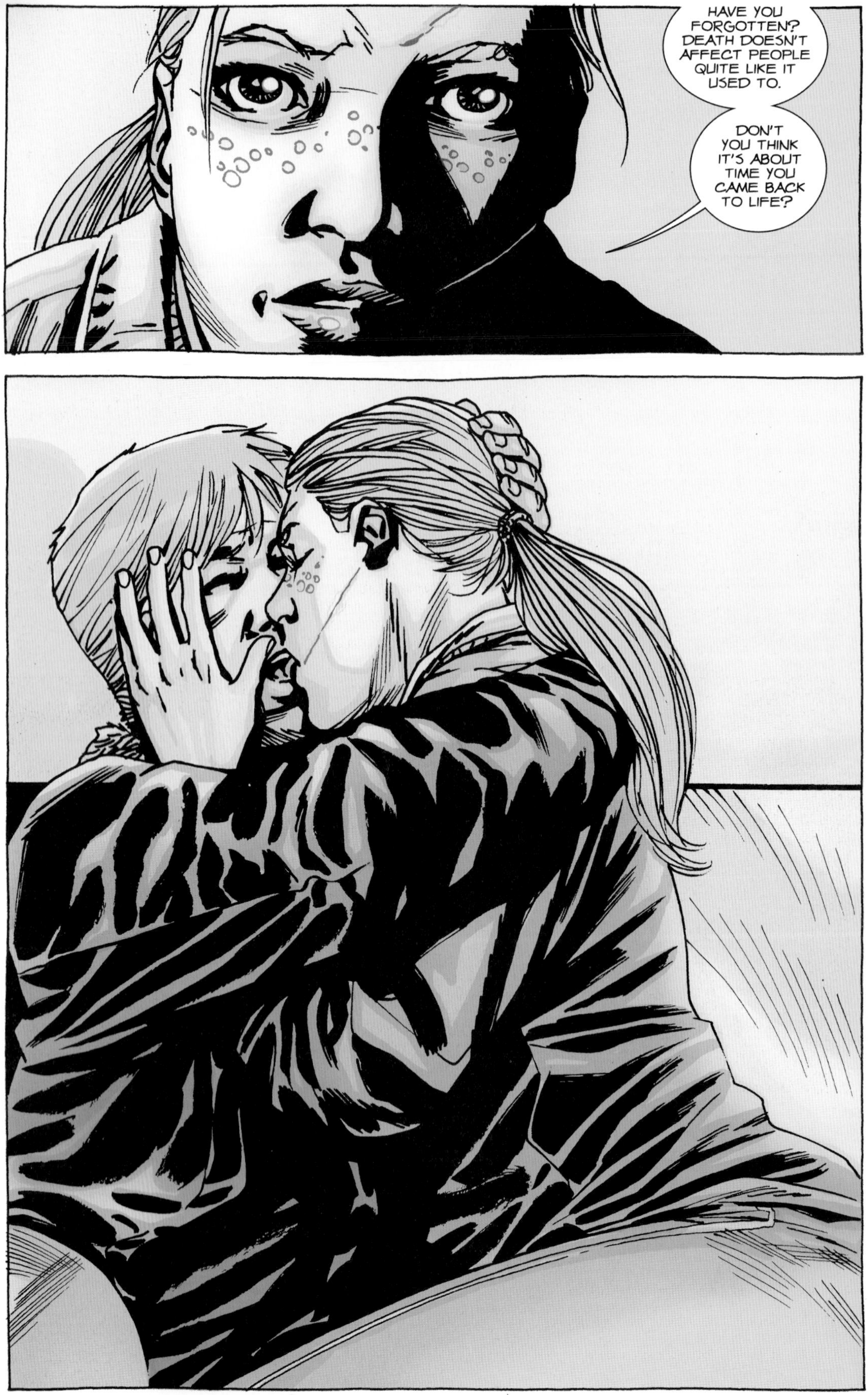
HAVE YOU FORGOTTEN? DEATH DOESN'T AFFECT PEOPLE QUITE LIKE IT USED TO.
DON'T YOU THINK IT'S ABOUT TIME YOU CAME BACK TO LIFE?

Chapter Sixteen:
A Larger World

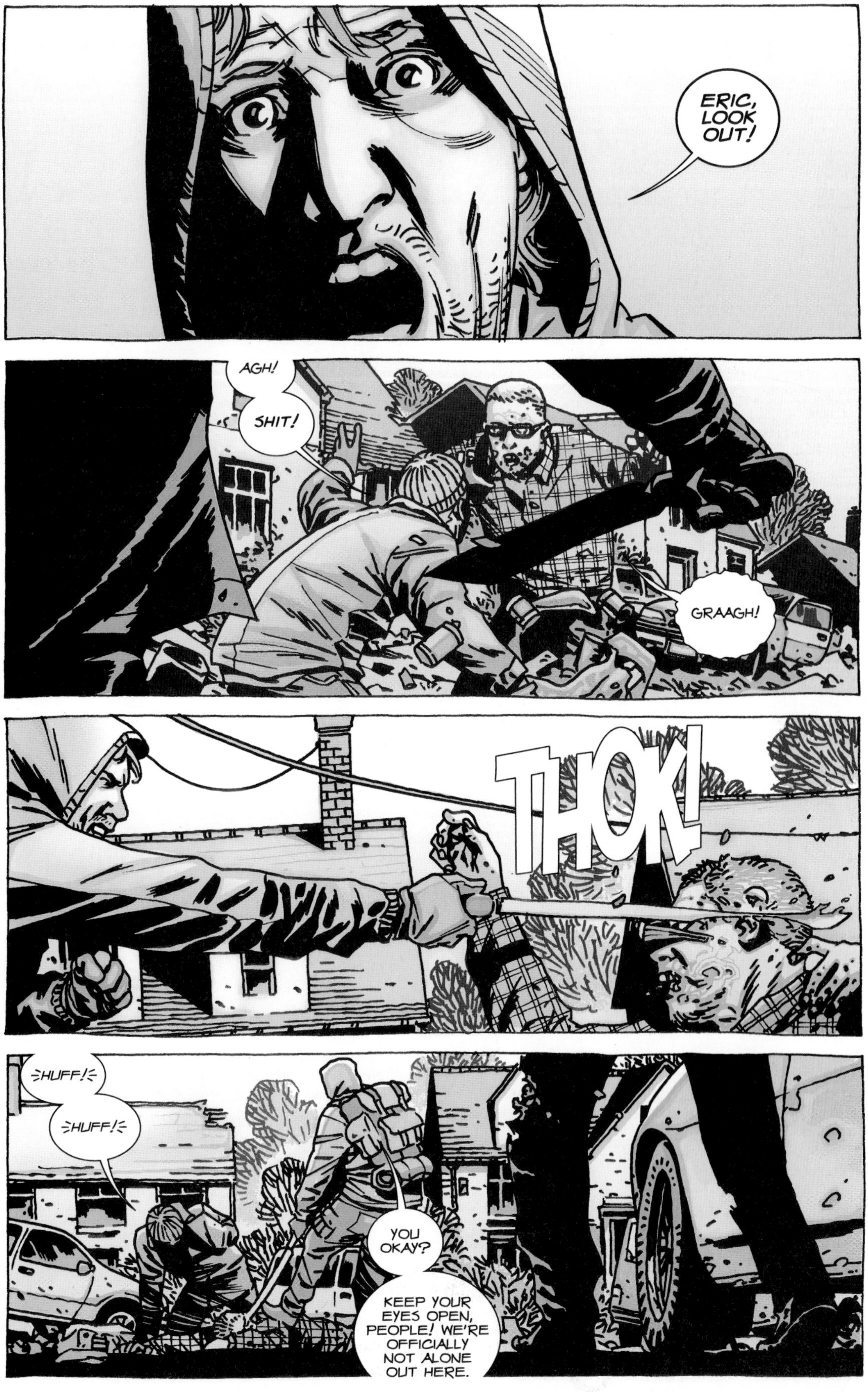

ERIC, LOOK OUT!
AGH!
SHIT!
GRAAGH!
THOK!
HUFF!
HUFF!
YOU OKAY?
KEEP YOUR EYES OPEN, PEOPLE! WE'RE OFFICIALLY NOT ALONE OUT HERE.

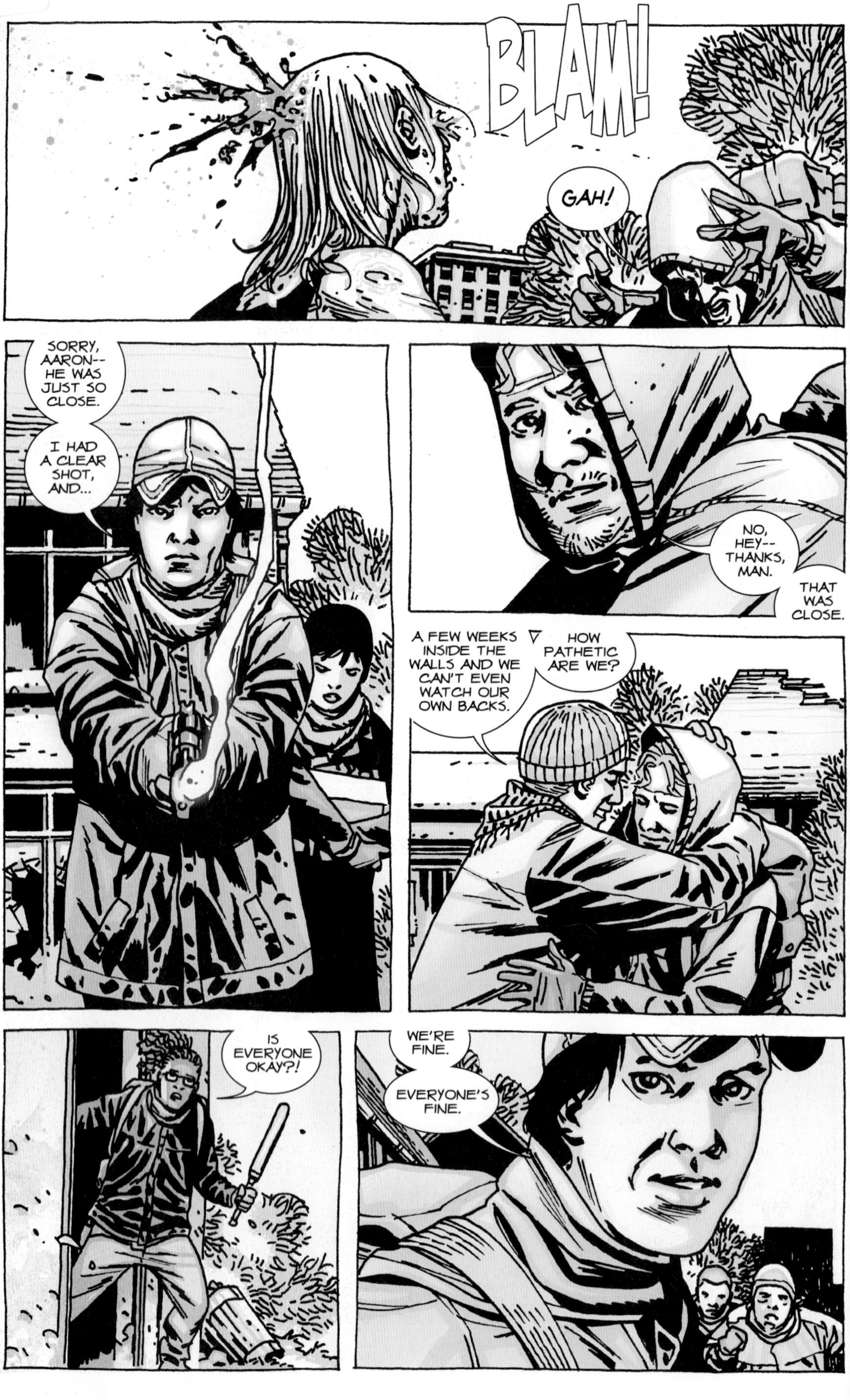
BLAM!
GAH!
SORRY, AARON-- HE WAS JUST SO CLOSE.
I HAD A CLEAR SHOT, AND...
NO, HEY-- THANKS, MAN.
THAT WAS CLOSE.
A FEW WEEKS INSIDE THE WALLS AND WE CAN'T EVEN WATCH OUR OWN BACKS.
HOW PATHETIC ARE WE?
IS EVERYONE OKAY?!
WE'RE FINE.
EVERYONE'S FINE.

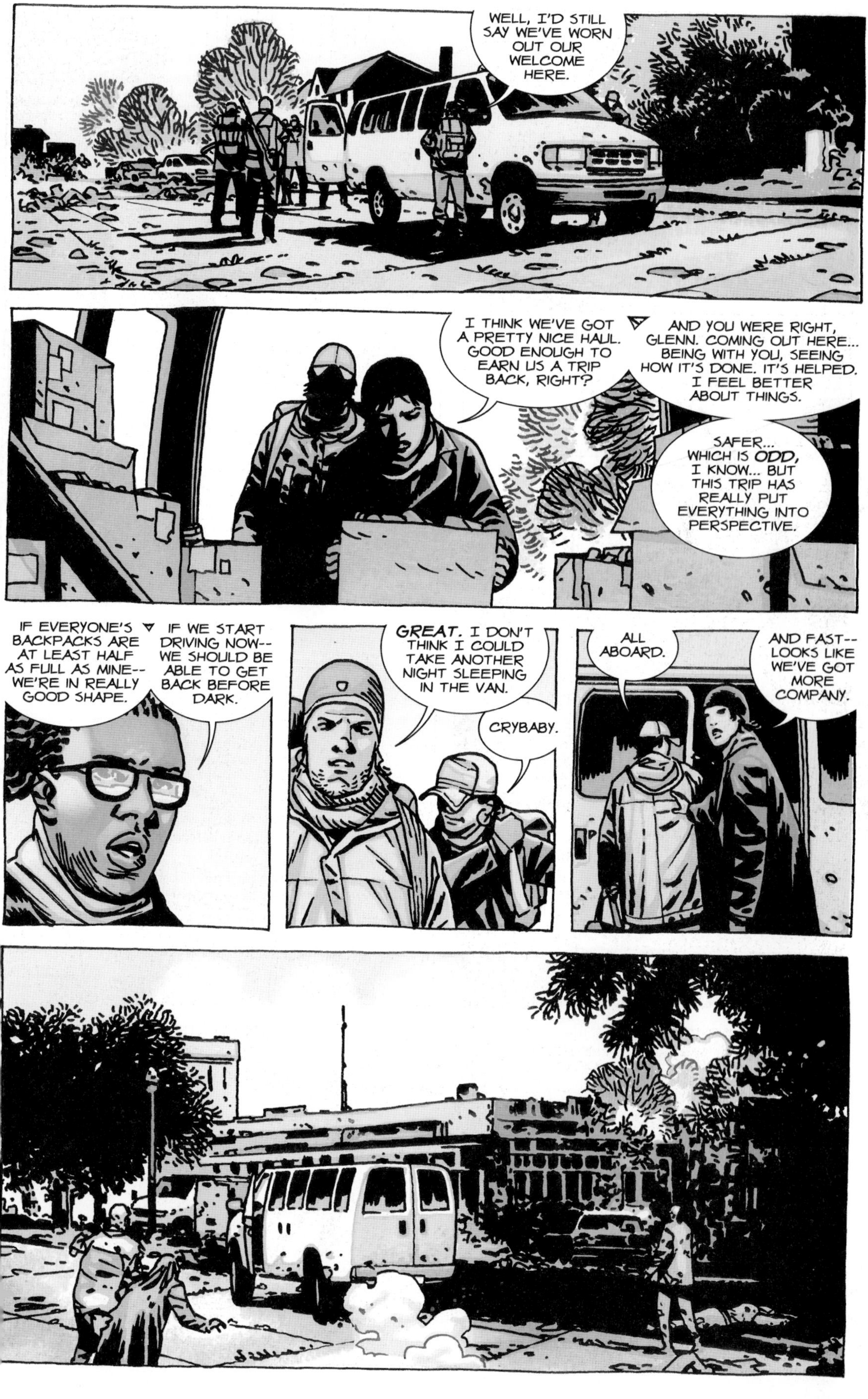
WELL, I'D STILL SAY WE'VE WORN OUT OUR WELCOME HERE.
I THINK WE'VE GOT A PRETTY NICE HAUL. GOOD ENOUGH TO EARN US A TRIP BACK, RIGHT?
AND YOU WERE RIGHT, GLENN. COMING OUT HERE... BEING WITH YOU, SEEING HOW IT'S DONE. IT'S HELPED. I FEEL BETTER ABOUT THINGS.
SAFER... WHICH IS ODD, I KNOW... BUT THIS TRIP HAS REALLY PUT EVERYTHING INTO PERSPECTIVE.
IF EVERYONE'S BACKPACKS ARE AT LEAST HALF AS FULL AS MINE-- WE'RE IN REALLY GOOD SHAPE.
IF WE START DRIVING NOW-- WE SHOULD BE ABLE TO GET BACK BEFORE DARK.
GREAT. I DON'T THINK I COULD TAKE ANOTHER NIGHT SLEEPING IN THE VAN.
CRYBABY.
ALL ABOARD.
AND FAST-- LOOKS LIKE WE'VE GOT MORE COMPANY.

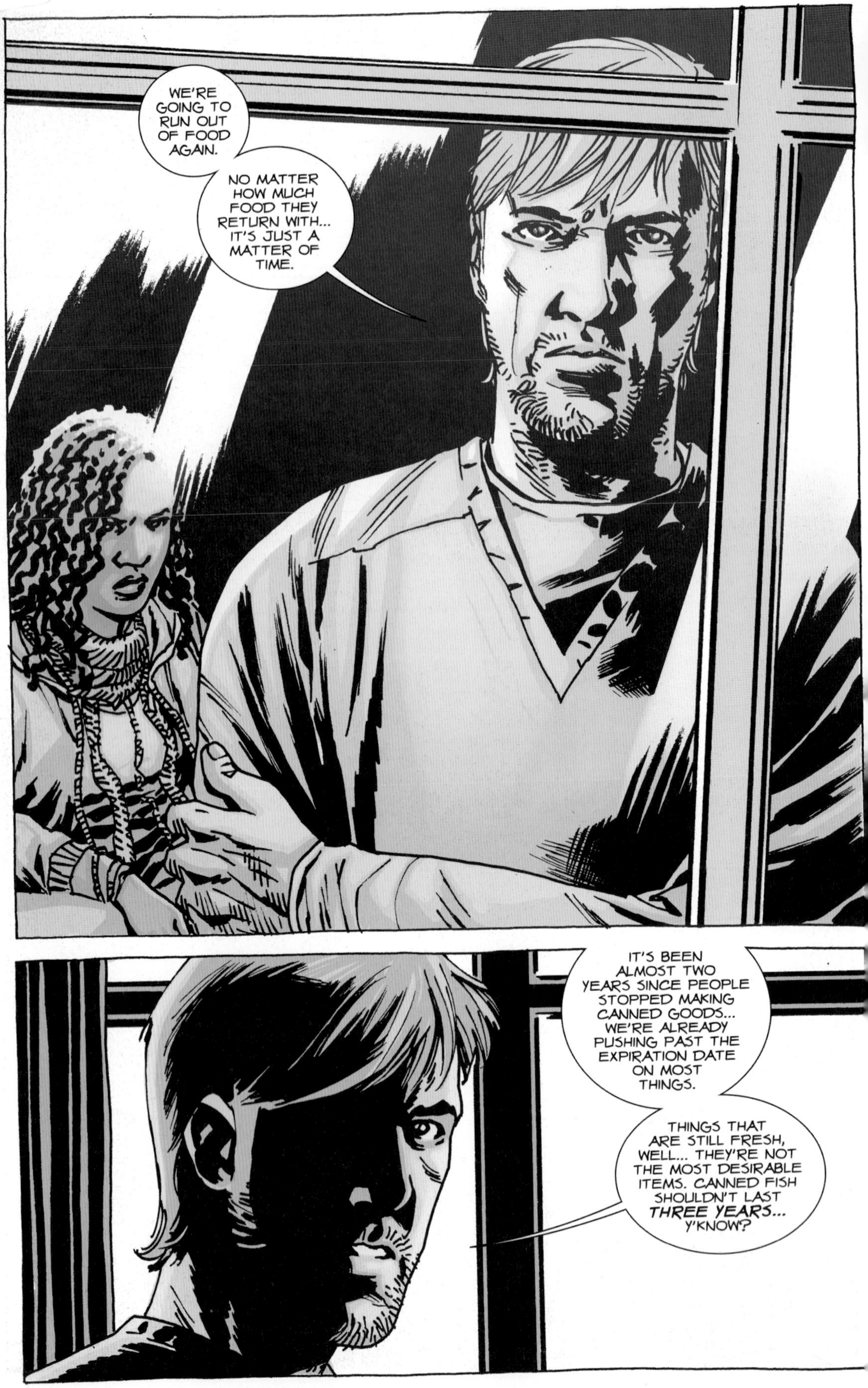
WE'RE GOING TO RUN OUT OF FOOD AGAIN.
NO MATTER HOW MUCH FOOD THEY RETURN WITH... IT'S JUST A MATTER OF TIME.
IT'S BEEN ALMOST TWO YEARS SINCE PEOPLE STOPPED MAKING CANNED GOODS... WE'RE ALREADY PUSHING PAST THE EXPIRATION DATE ON MOST THINGS.
THINGS THAT ARE STILL FRESH, WELL... THEY'RE NOT THE MOST DESIRABLE ITEMS. CANNED FISH SHOULDN'T LAST *THREE YEARS...* Y'KNOW?

I FEEL LIKE WE'LL BE HUNTING WILD DOGS BEFORE THE END OF THE WINTER. WE SIMPLY WERE NOT PREPARED.

THAT'S A MISTAKE I REFUSE TO MAKE A SECOND TIME... WE CAN'T *AFFORD* IT.

WE NEED TO GET SERIOUS ABOUT FARMING.

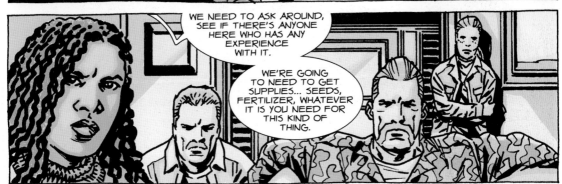

WE NEED TO ASK AROUND, SEE IF THERE'S ANYONE HERE WHO HAS ANY EXPERIENCE WITH IT.

WE'RE GOING TO NEED TO GET SUPPLIES... SEEDS, FERTILIZER, WHATEVER IT IS YOU NEED FOR THIS KIND OF THING.

AS FAR AS LAND GOES, WE COULD JUST PICK THREE OR FOUR YARDS... MORE DEPENDING ON HOW BIG AN AREA WE'D NEED.

THERE ARE STILL ENOUGH VACANT HOUSES WE WOULDN'T NEED TO TAKE OVER ANYONE'S BACKYARDS.

THAT FALLS UNDER... ZONING. SOUNDS LIKE AN ABRAHAM PROBLEM.

I CAN HANDLE THAT, EASY.

I'LL ASK AROUND, SEE IF THERE ARE ANY FARMERS IN THE MIX HERE.

GOOD, I THINK THAT'S ALL FOR TODAY. THANKS FOR COMING, EVERYONE.

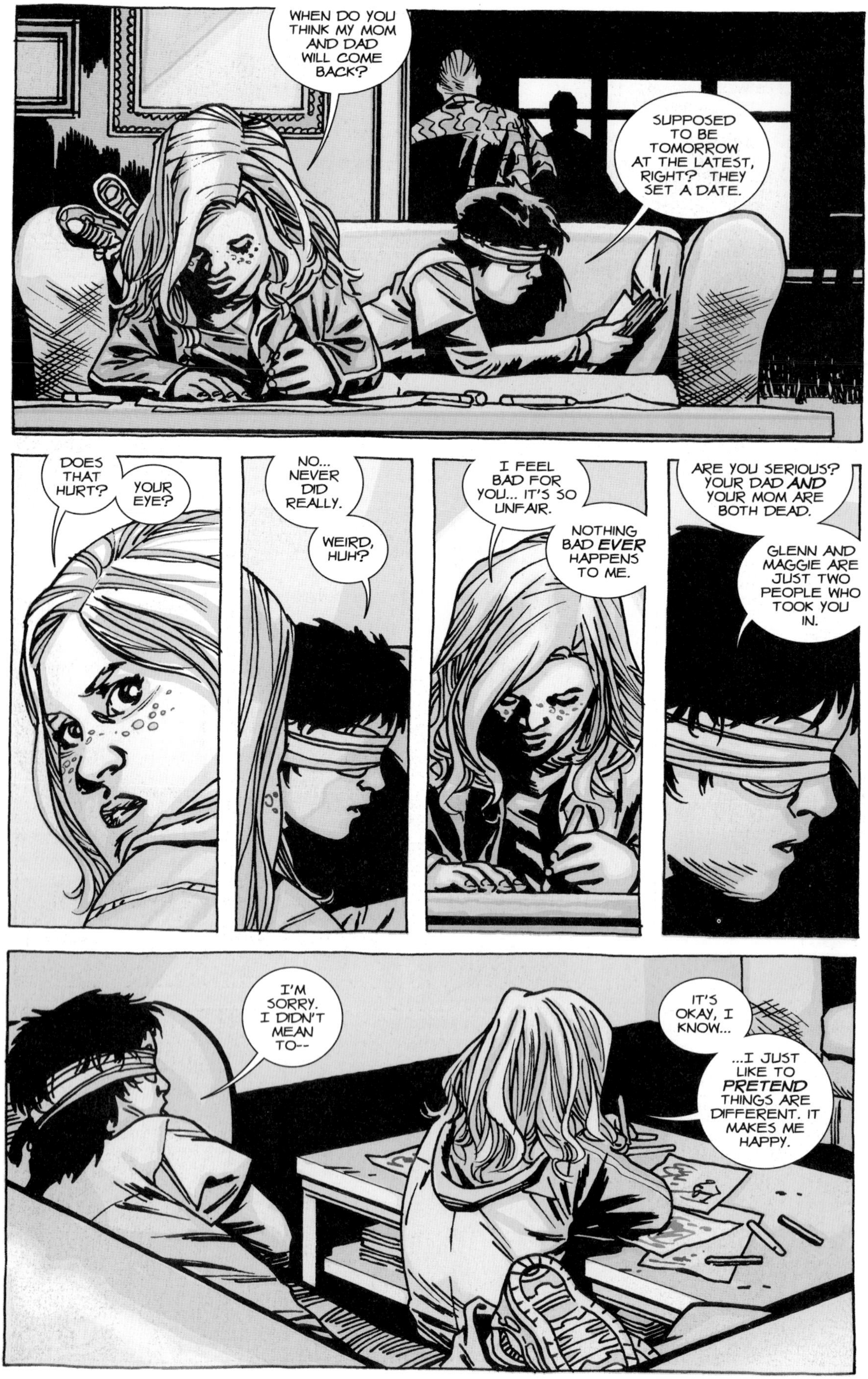
WHEN DO YOU THINK MY MOM AND DAD WILL COME BACK?
SUPPOSED TO BE TOMORROW AT THE LATEST, RIGHT? THEY SET A DATE.
DOES THAT HURT?
YOUR EYE?
NO... NEVER DID REALLY.
WEIRD, HUH?
I FEEL BAD FOR YOU... IT'S SO UNFAIR.
NOTHING BAD EVER HAPPENS TO ME.
ARE YOU SERIOUS? YOUR DAD AND YOUR MOM ARE BOTH DEAD.
GLENN AND MAGGIE ARE JUST TWO PEOPLE WHO TOOK YOU IN.
I'M SORRY. I DIDN'T MEAN TO--
IT'S OKAY, I KNOW...
...I JUST LIKE TO PRETEND THINGS ARE DIFFERENT. IT MAKES ME HAPPY.

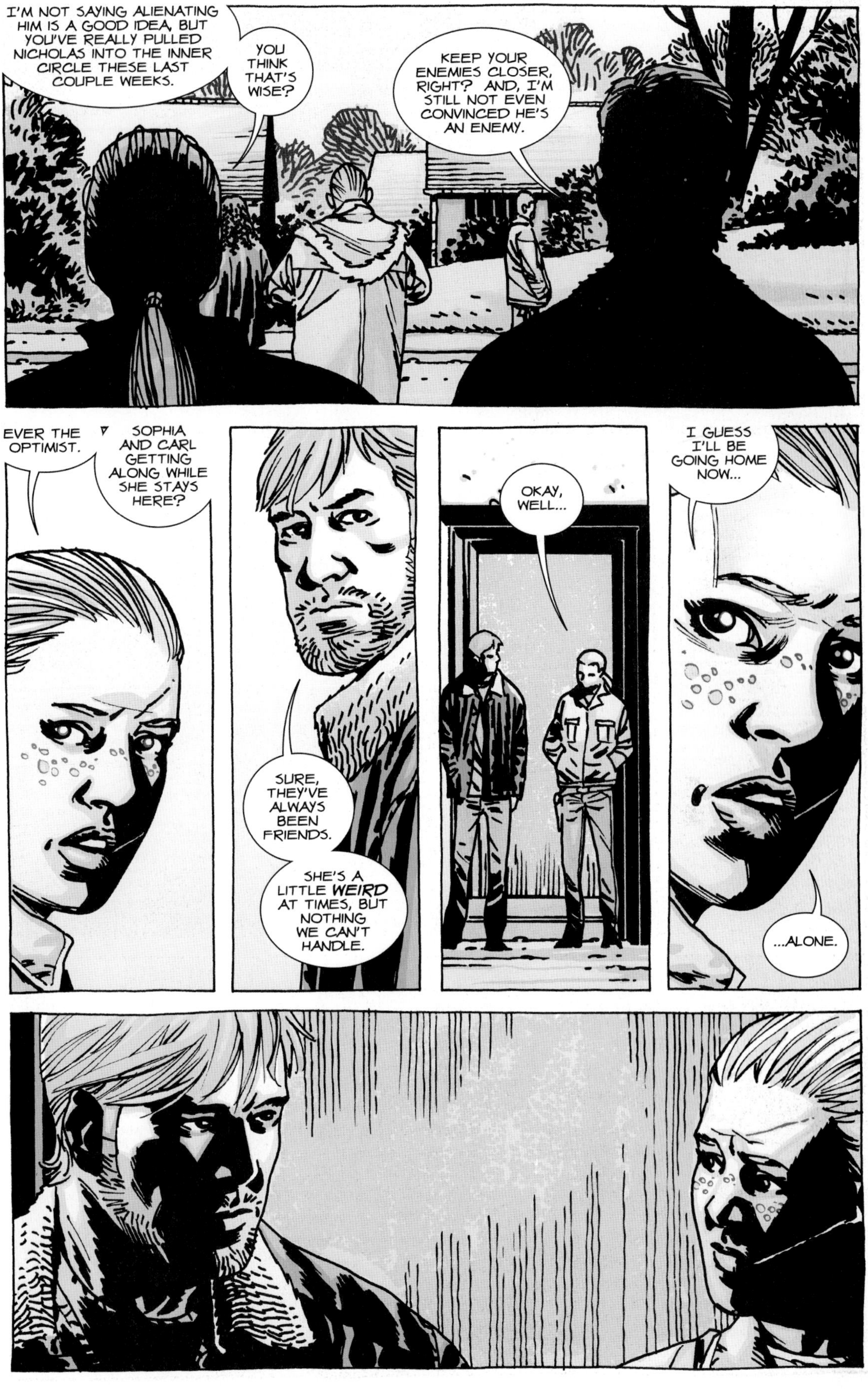

I'M NOT SAYING ALIENATING HIM IS A GOOD IDEA, BUT YOU'VE REALLY PULLED NICHOLAS INTO THE INNER CIRCLE THESE LAST COUPLE WEEKS.
YOU THINK THAT'S WISE?
KEEP YOUR ENEMIES CLOSER, RIGHT? AND, I'M STILL NOT EVEN CONVINCED HE'S AN ENEMY.
EVER THE OPTIMIST.
SOPHIA AND CARL GETTING ALONG WHILE SHE STAYS HERE?
SURE, THEY'VE ALWAYS BEEN FRIENDS.
SHE'S A LITTLE WEIRD AT TIMES, BUT NOTHING WE CAN'T HANDLE.
OKAY, WELL...
I GUESS I'LL BE GOING HOME NOW...
...ALONE.

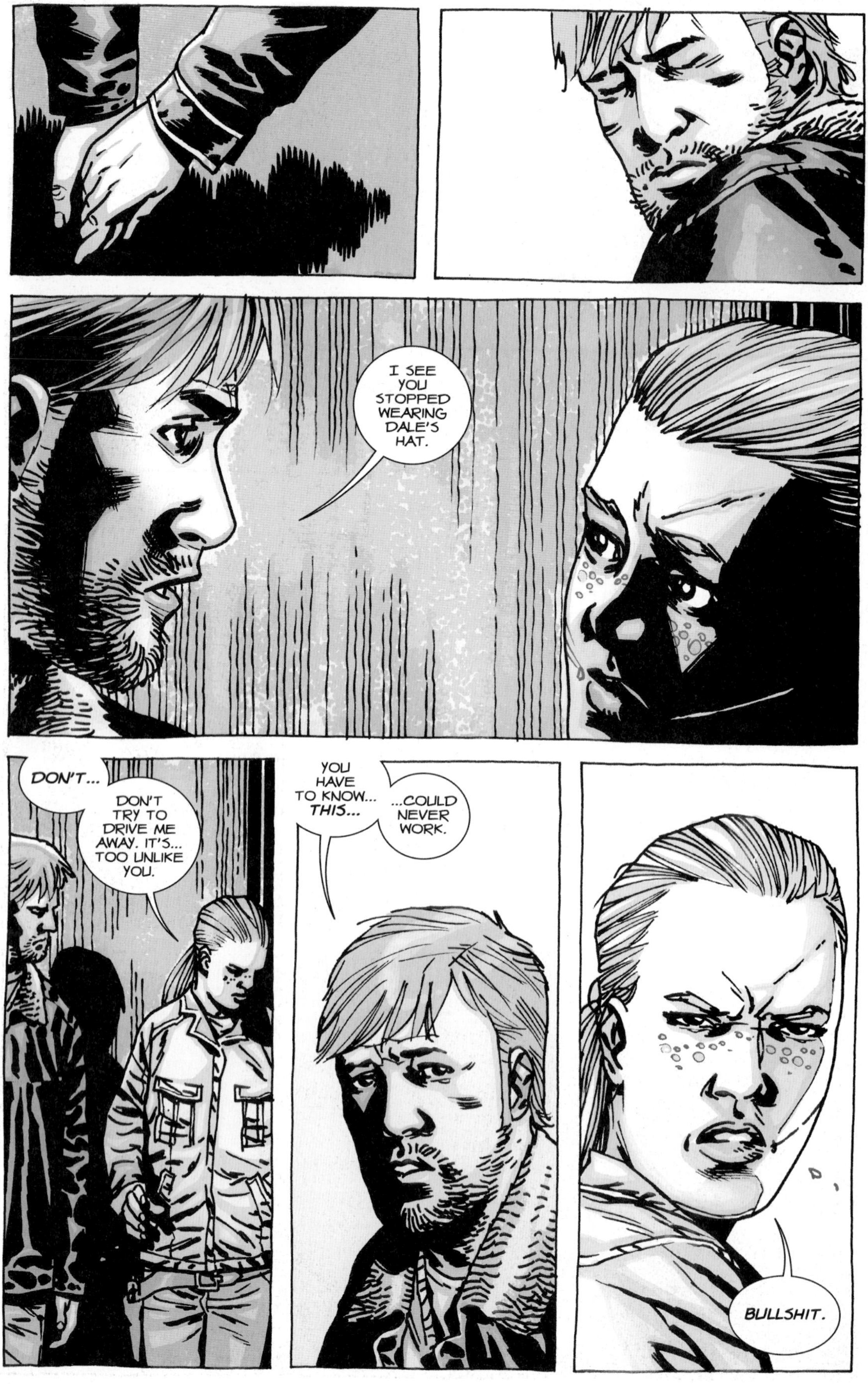
I SEE YOU STOPPED WEARING DALE'S HAT.
DON'T...
DON'T TRY TO DRIVE ME AWAY. IT'S... TOO UNLIKE YOU.
YOU HAVE TO KNOW... THIS...
...COULD NEVER WORK.
BULLSHIT.

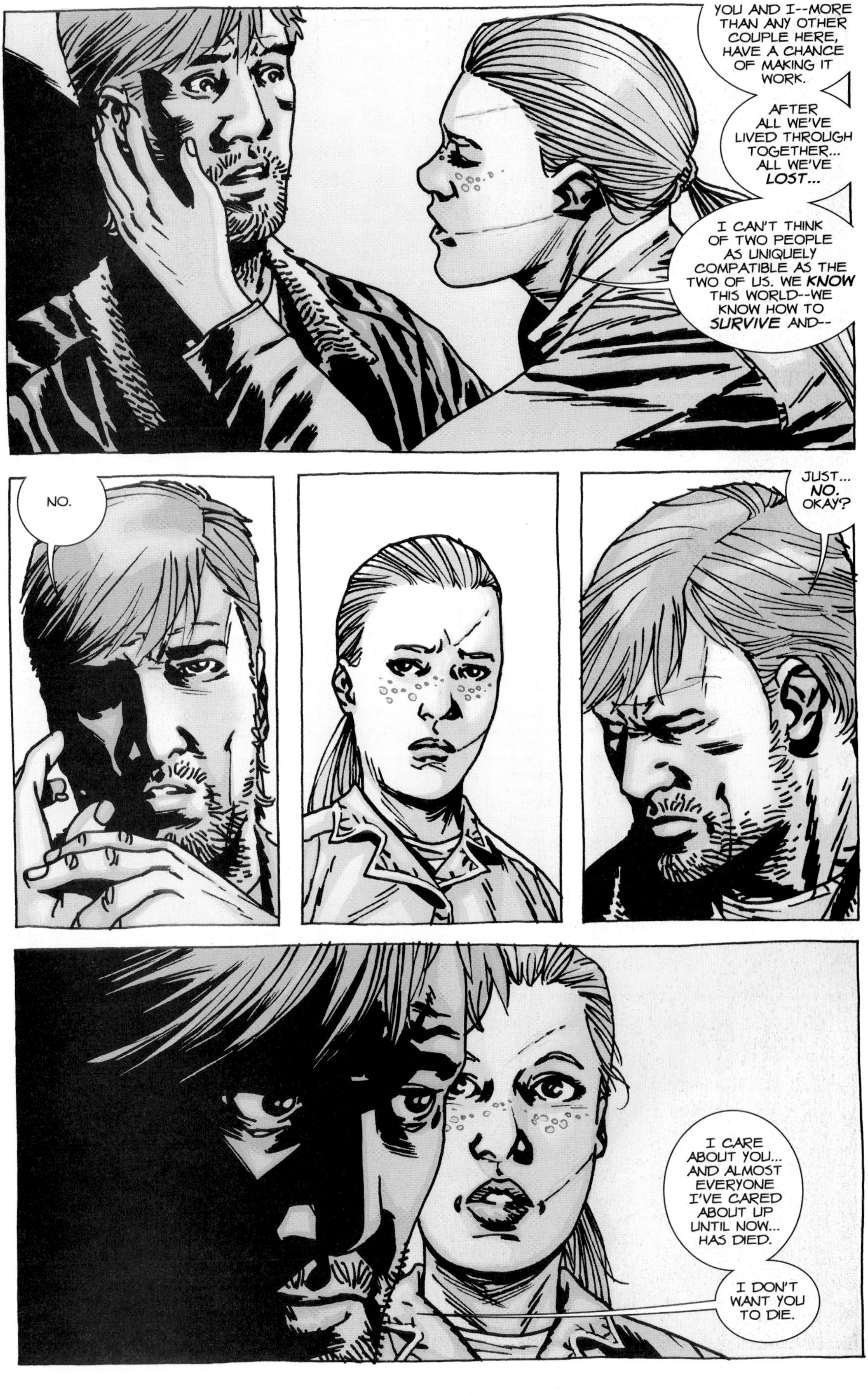
YOU AND I--MORE THAN ANY OTHER COUPLE HERE, HAVE A CHANCE OF MAKING IT WORK.
AFTER ALL WE'VE LIVED THROUGH TOGETHER... ALL WE'VE *LOST...*
I CAN'T THINK OF TWO PEOPLE AS UNIQUELY COMPATIBLE AS THE TWO OF US. WE *KNOW* THIS WORLD--WE KNOW HOW TO *SURVIVE* AND--
NO.
JUST... *NO.* OKAY?
I CARE ABOUT YOU... AND ALMOST EVERYONE I'VE CARED ABOUT UP UNTIL NOW... HAS DIED.
I DON'T WANT YOU TO DIE.

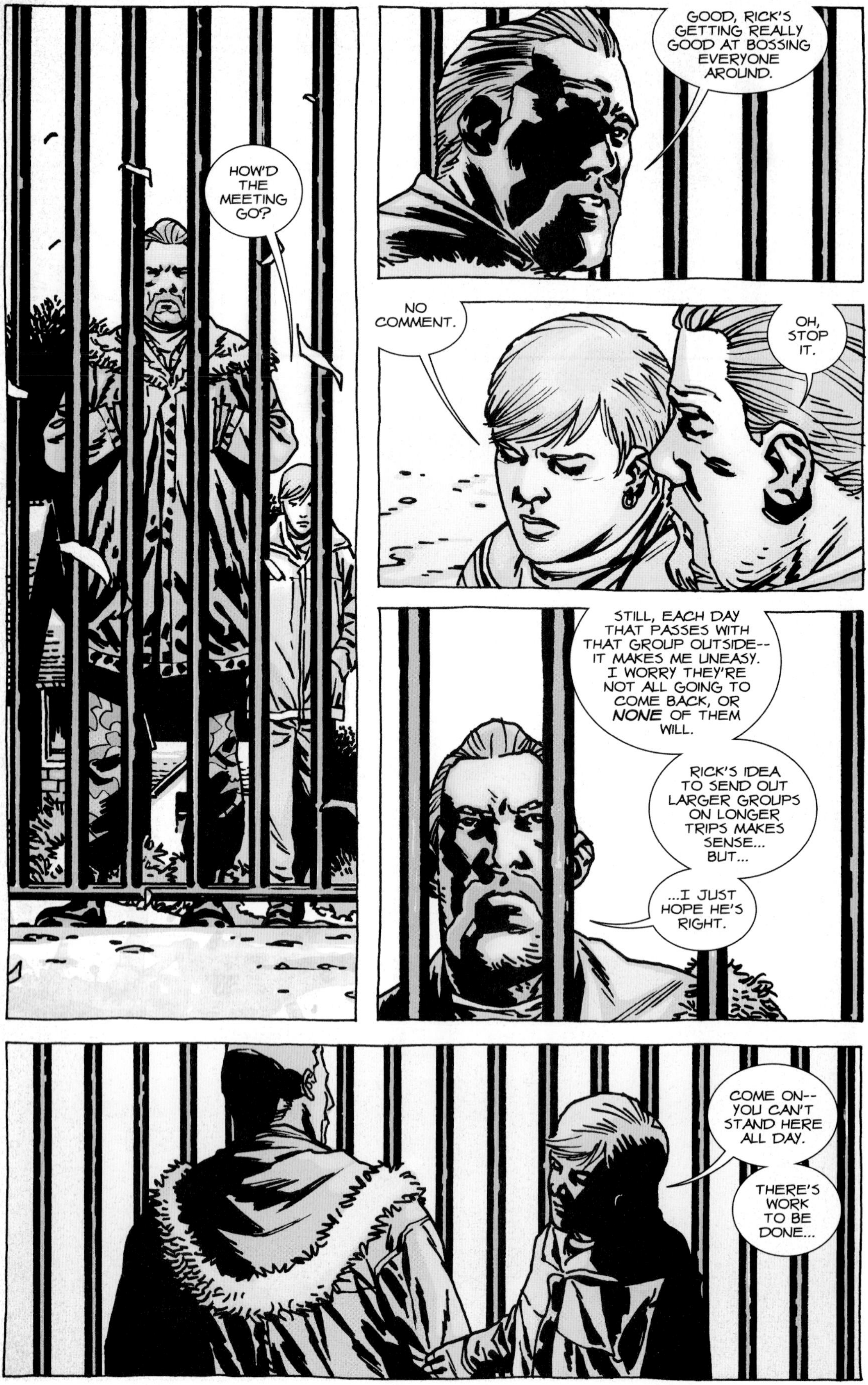
HOW'D THE MEETING GO?
GOOD, RICK'S GETTING REALLY GOOD AT BOSSING EVERYONE AROUND.
NO COMMENT.
OH, STOP IT.
STILL, EACH DAY THAT PASSES WITH THAT GROUP OUTSIDE-- IT MAKES ME UNEASY. I WORRY THEY'RE NOT ALL GOING TO COME BACK, OR NONE OF THEM WILL.
RICK'S IDEA TO SEND OUT LARGER GROUPS ON LONGER TRIPS MAKES SENSE... BUT...
...I JUST HOPE HE'S RIGHT.
COME ON-- YOU CAN'T STAND HERE ALL DAY.
THERE'S WORK TO BE DONE...

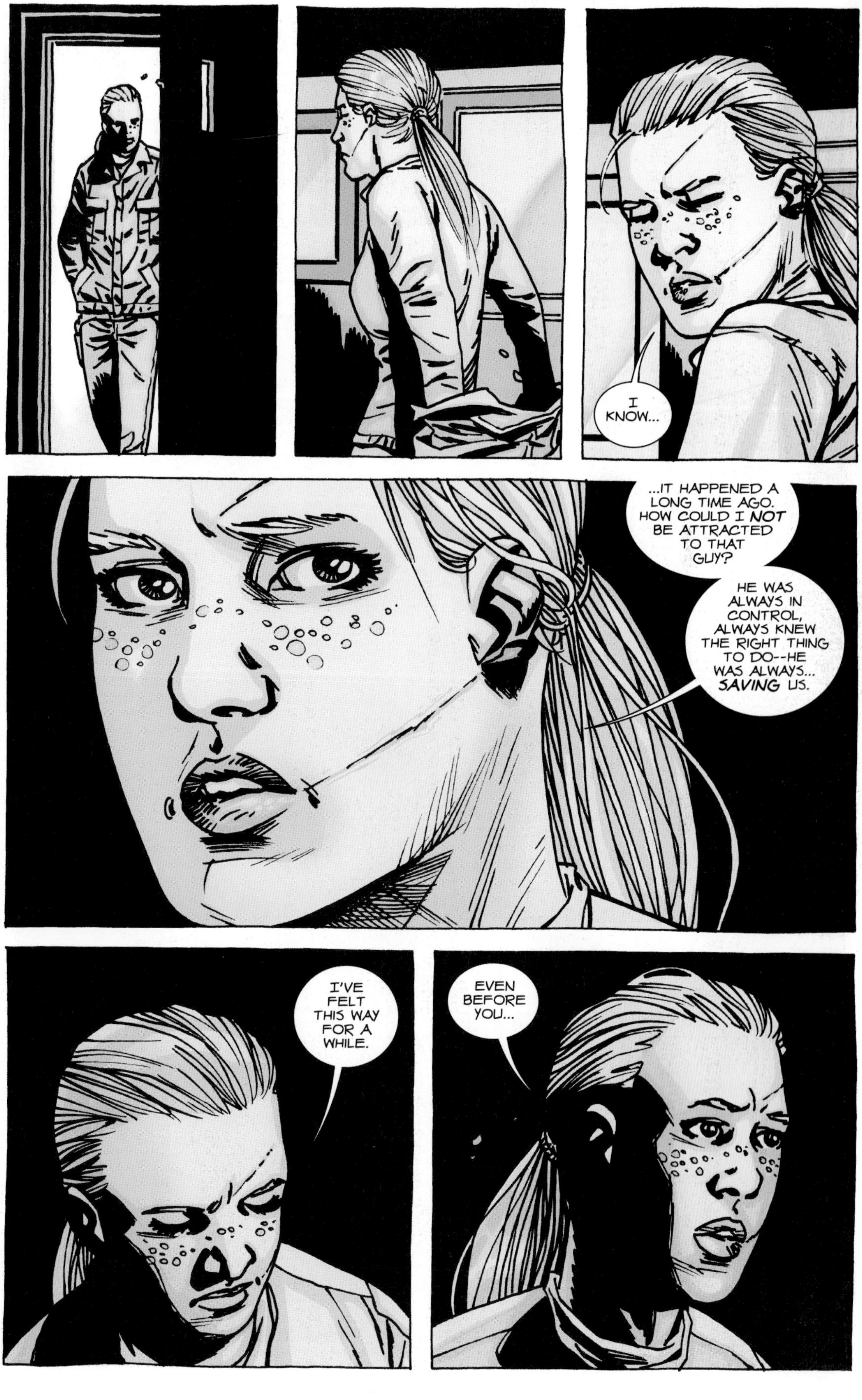
I KNOW...
...IT HAPPENED A LONG TIME AGO. HOW COULD I NOT BE ATTRACTED TO THAT GUY?
HE WAS ALWAYS IN CONTROL, ALWAYS KNEW THE RIGHT THING TO DO--HE WAS ALWAYS... SAVING US.
I'VE FELT THIS WAY FOR A WHILE.
EVEN BEFORE YOU...

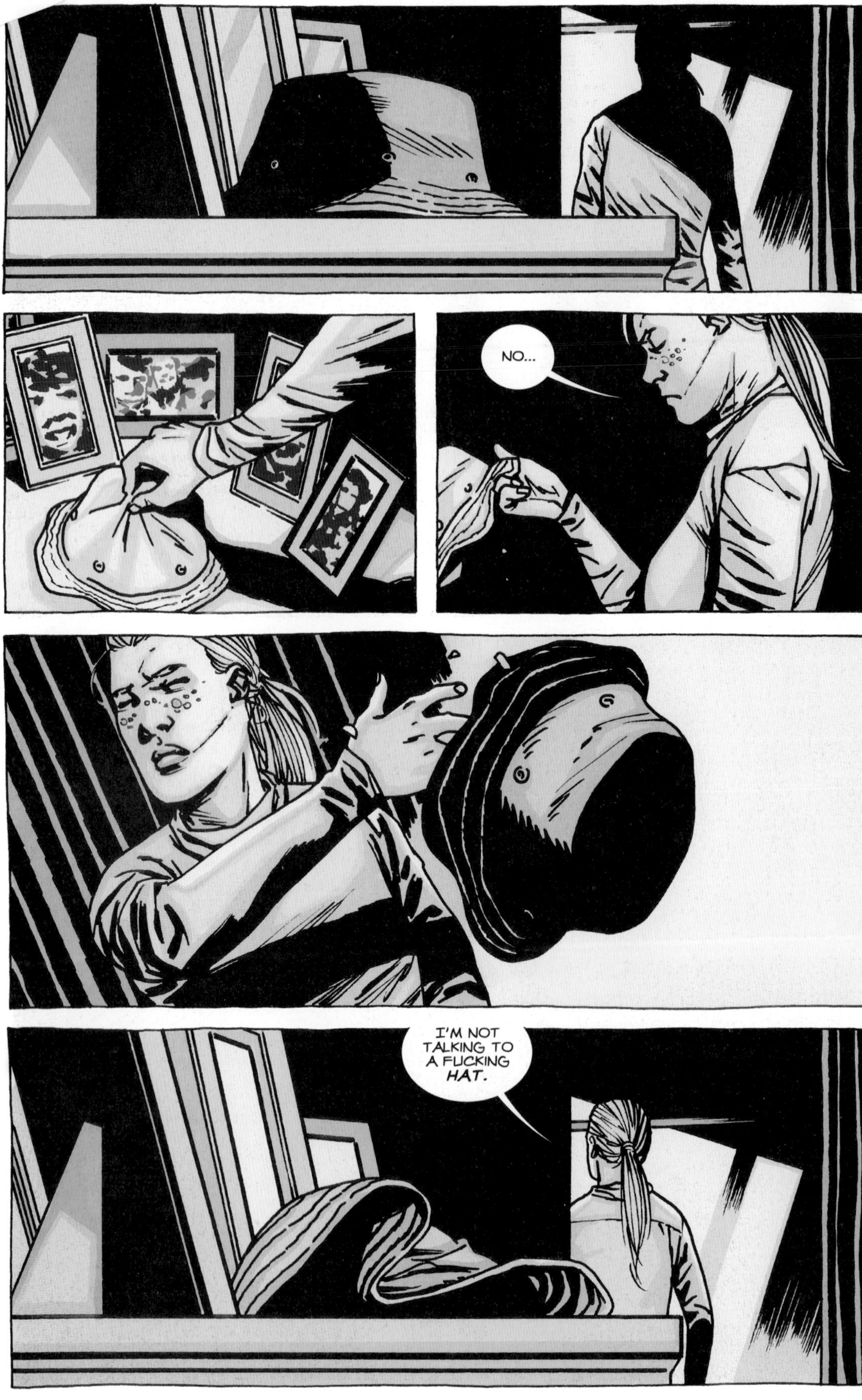
NO...
I'M NOT TALKING TO A FUCKING HAT.

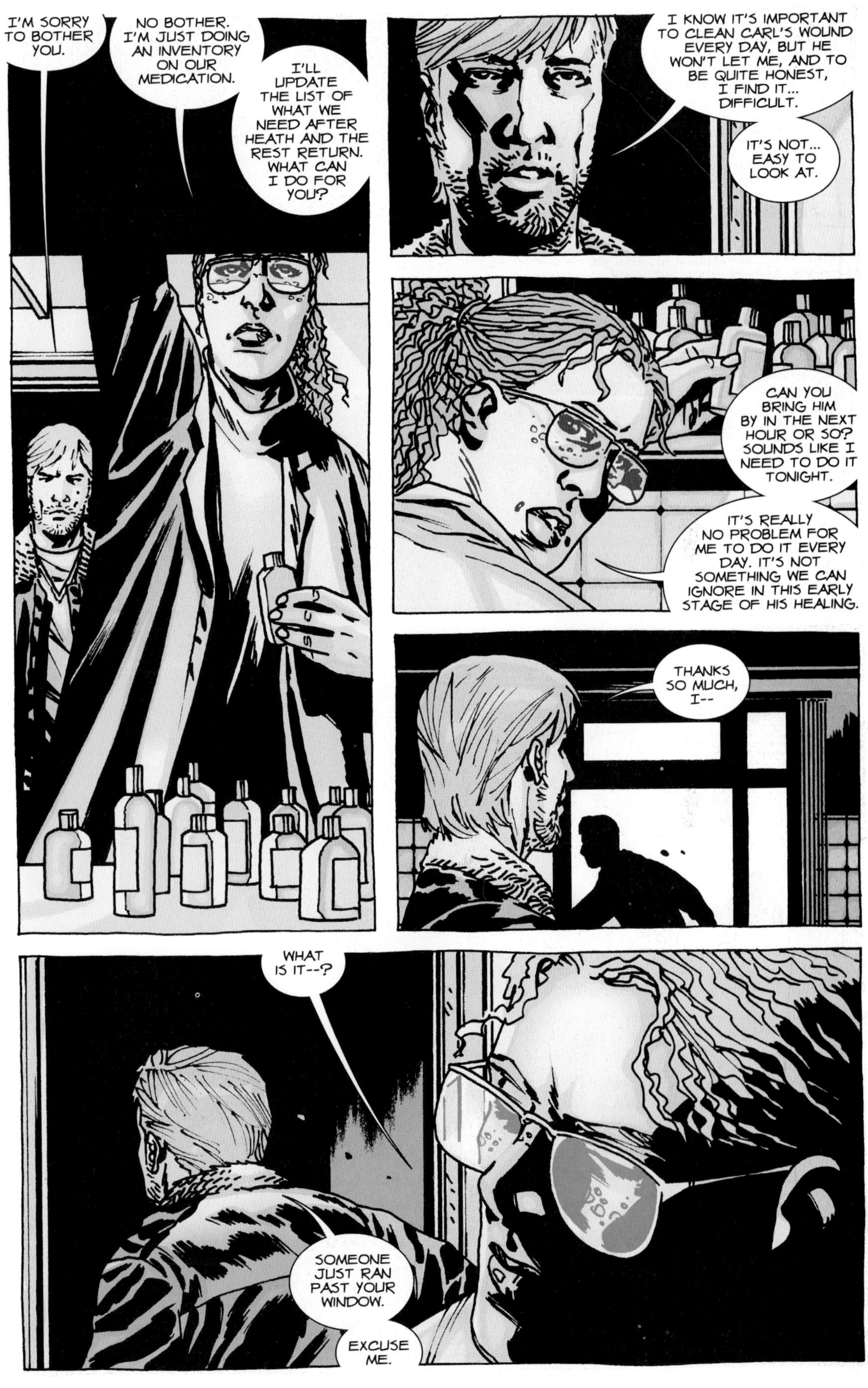
I'M SORRY TO BOTHER YOU.
NO BOTHER. I'M JUST DOING AN INVENTORY ON OUR MEDICATION.
I'LL UPDATE THE LIST OF WHAT WE NEED AFTER HEATH AND THE REST RETURN. WHAT CAN I DO FOR YOU?
I KNOW IT'S IMPORTANT TO CLEAN CARL'S WOUND EVERY DAY, BUT HE WON'T LET ME, AND TO BE QUITE HONEST, I FIND IT... DIFFICULT.
IT'S NOT... EASY TO LOOK AT.
CAN YOU BRING HIM BY IN THE NEXT HOUR OR SO? SOUNDS LIKE I NEED TO DO IT TONIGHT.
IT'S REALLY NO PROBLEM FOR ME TO DO IT EVERY DAY. IT'S NOT SOMETHING WE CAN IGNORE IN THIS EARLY STAGE OF HIS HEALING.
THANKS SO MUCH, I--
WHAT IS IT--?
SOMEONE JUST RAN PAST YOUR WINDOW.
EXCUSE ME.

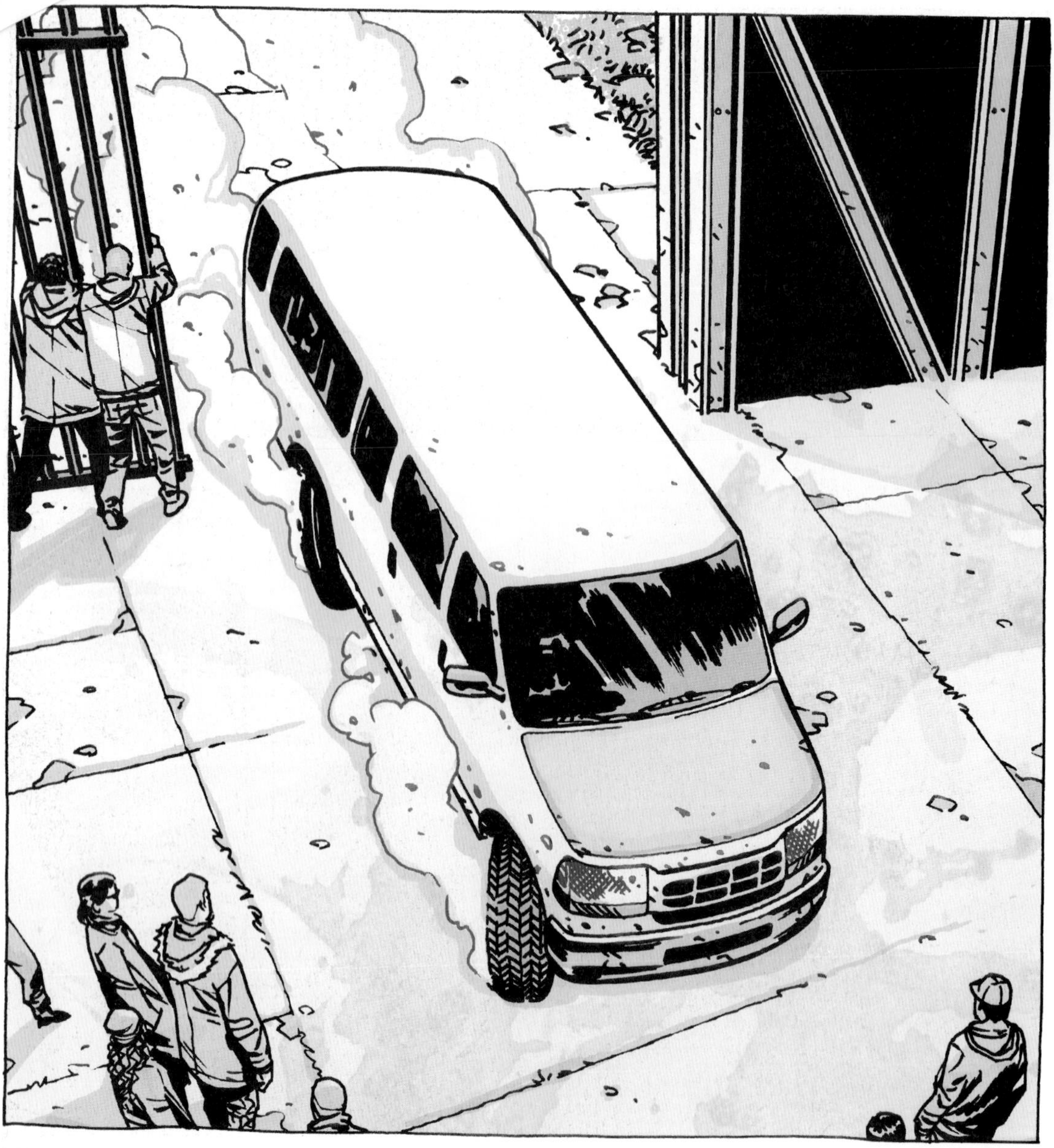

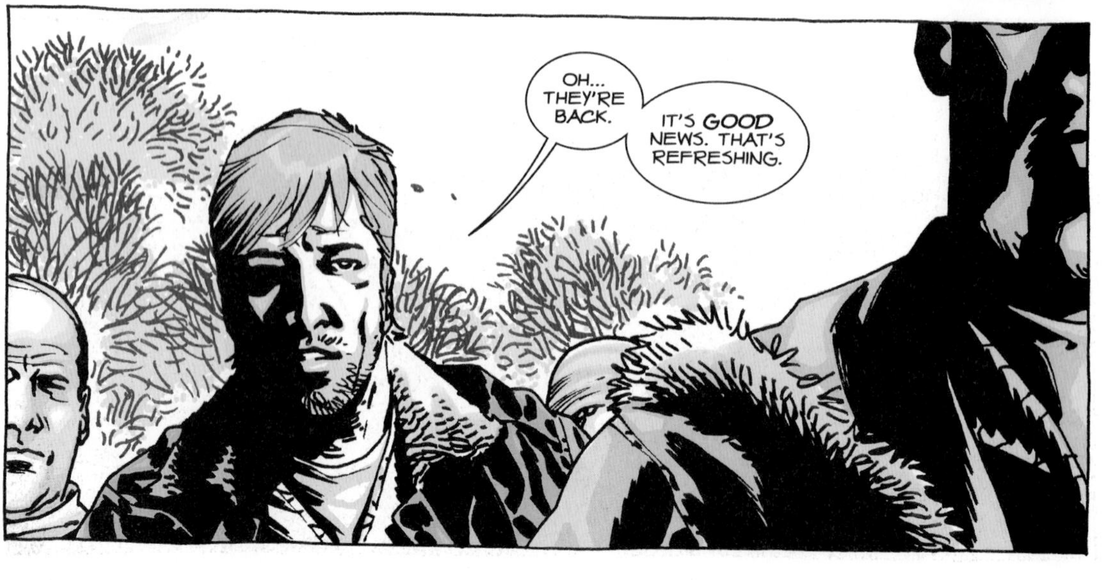

OH... THEY'RE BACK.
IT'S GOOD NEWS. THAT'S REFRESHING.

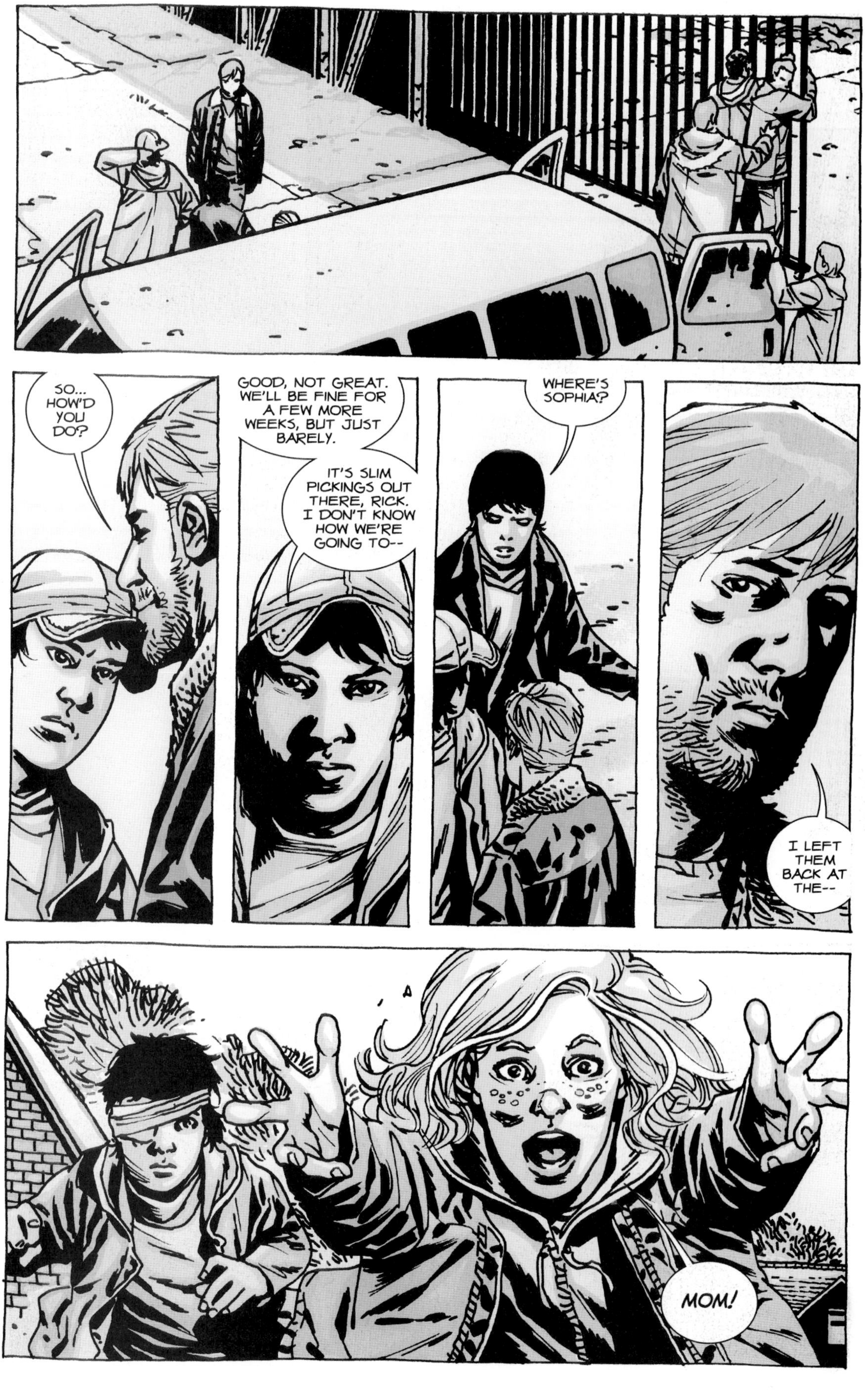
SO... HOW'D YOU DO?
GOOD, NOT GREAT. WE'LL BE FINE FOR A FEW MORE WEEKS, BUT JUST BARELY.
IT'S SLIM PICKINGS OUT THERE, RICK. I DON'T KNOW HOW WE'RE GOING TO--
WHERE'S SOPHIA?
I LEFT THEM BACK AT THE--
MOM!

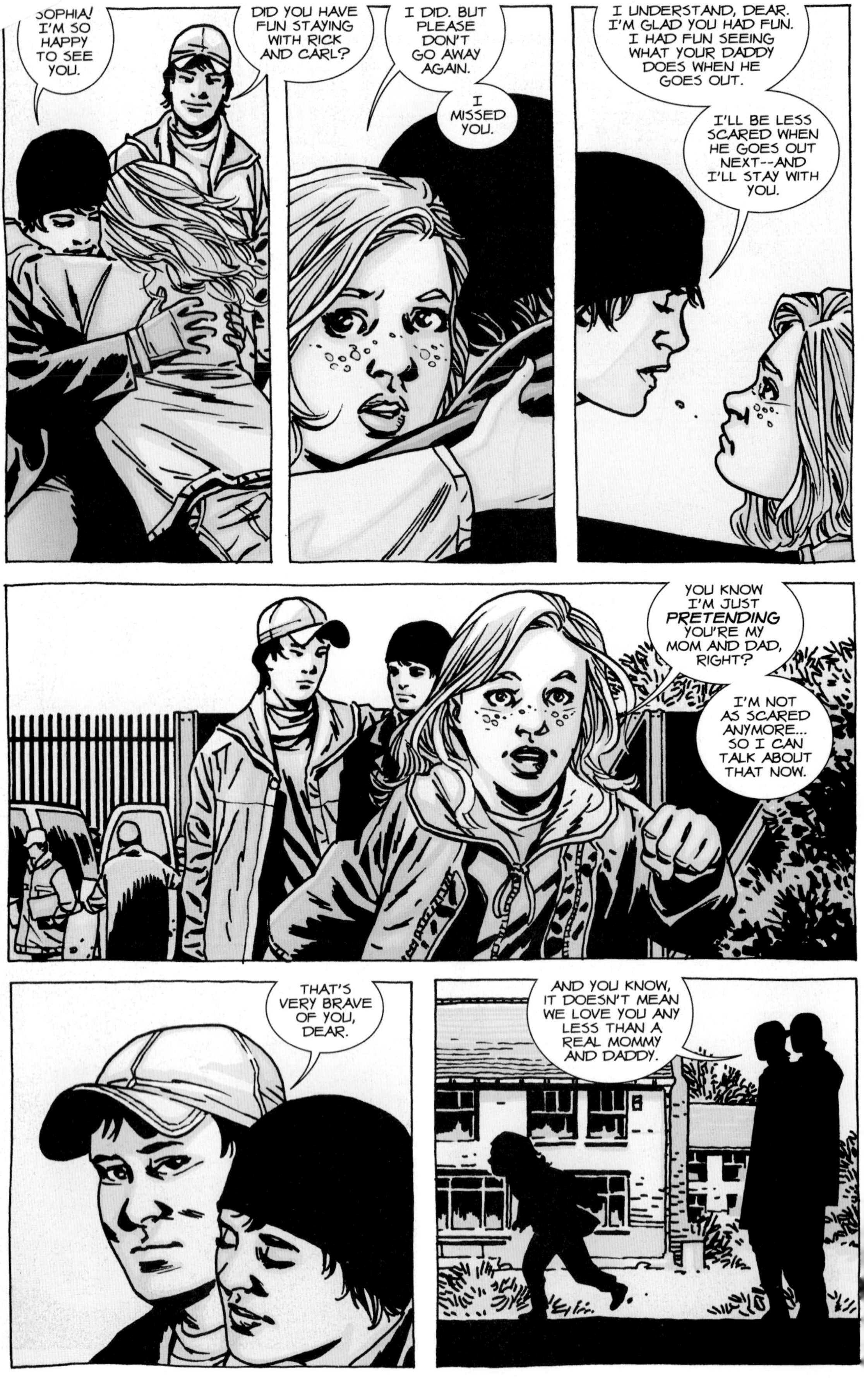
SOPHIA! I'M SO HAPPY TO SEE YOU.
DID YOU HAVE FUN STAYING WITH RICK AND CARL?
I DID. BUT PLEASE DON'T GO AWAY AGAIN.
I MISSED YOU.
I UNDERSTAND, DEAR. I'M GLAD YOU HAD FUN. I HAD FUN SEEING WHAT YOUR DADDY DOES WHEN HE GOES OUT.
I'LL BE LESS SCARED WHEN HE GOES OUT NEXT--AND I'LL STAY WITH YOU.
YOU KNOW I'M JUST PRETENDING YOU'RE MY MOM AND DAD, RIGHT?
I'M NOT AS SCARED ANYMORE... SO I CAN TALK ABOUT THAT NOW.
THAT'S VERY BRAVE OF YOU, DEAR.
AND YOU KNOW, IT DOESN'T MEAN WE LOVE YOU ANY LESS THAN A REAL MOMMY AND DADDY.

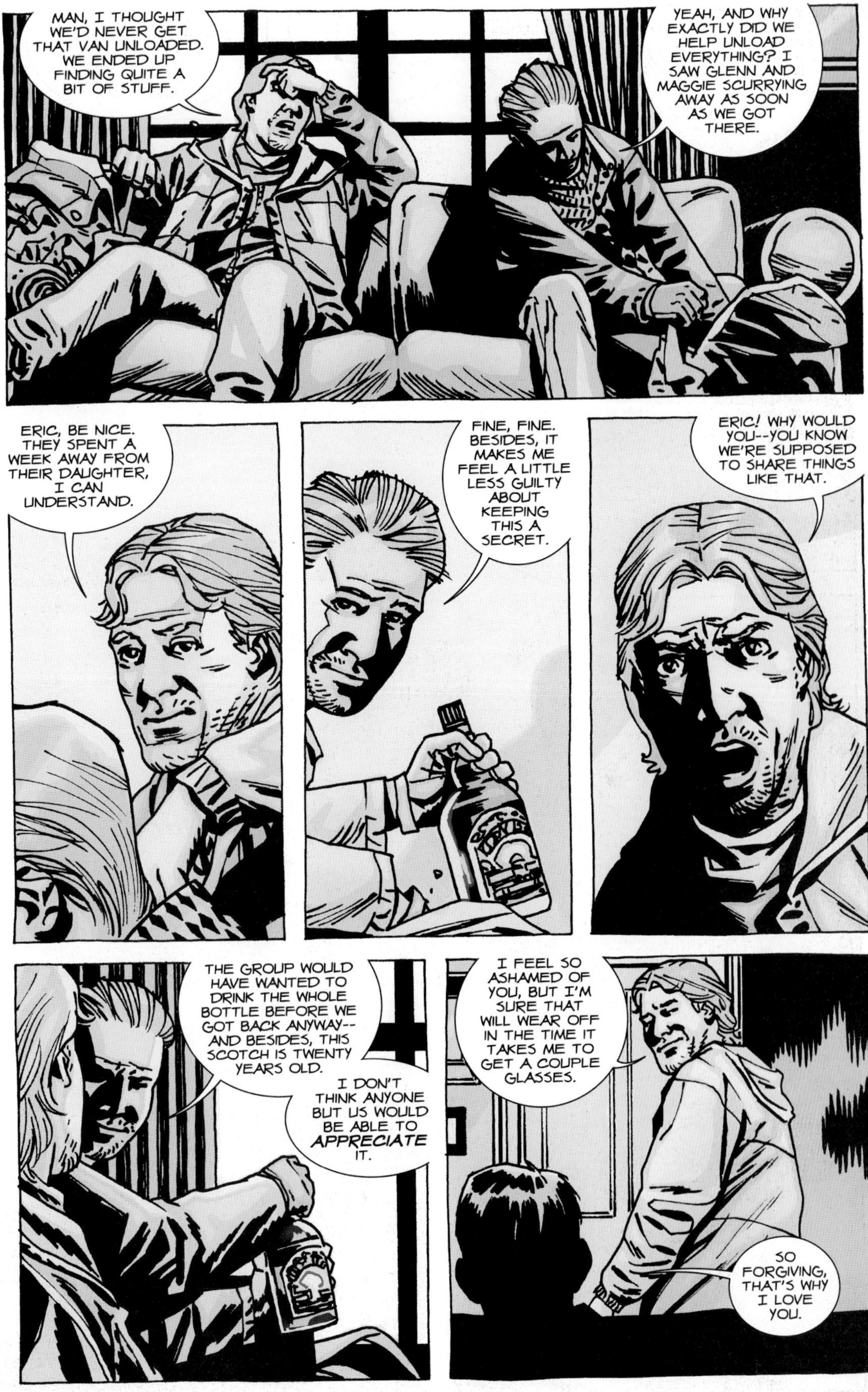
MAN, I THOUGHT WE'D NEVER GET THAT VAN UNLOADED. WE ENDED UP FINDING QUITE A BIT OF STUFF.
YEAH, AND WHY EXACTLY DID WE HELP UNLOAD EVERYTHING? I SAW GLENN AND MAGGIE SCURRYING AWAY AS SOON AS WE GOT THERE.
ERIC, BE NICE. THEY SPENT A WEEK AWAY FROM THEIR DAUGHTER, I CAN UNDERSTAND.
FINE, FINE. BESIDES, IT MAKES ME FEEL A LITTLE LESS GUILTY ABOUT KEEPING THIS A SECRET.
ERIC! WHY WOULD YOU--YOU KNOW WE'RE SUPPOSED TO SHARE THINGS LIKE THAT.
THE GROUP WOULD HAVE WANTED TO DRINK THE WHOLE BOTTLE BEFORE WE GOT BACK ANYWAY--AND BESIDES, THIS SCOTCH IS TWENTY YEARS OLD.
I DON'T THINK ANYONE BUT US WOULD BE ABLE TO *APPRECIATE* IT.
I FEEL SO ASHAMED OF YOU, BUT I'M SURE THAT WILL WEAR OFF IN THE TIME IT TAKES ME TO GET A COUPLE GLASSES.
SO FORGIVING, THAT'S WHY I LOVE YOU.

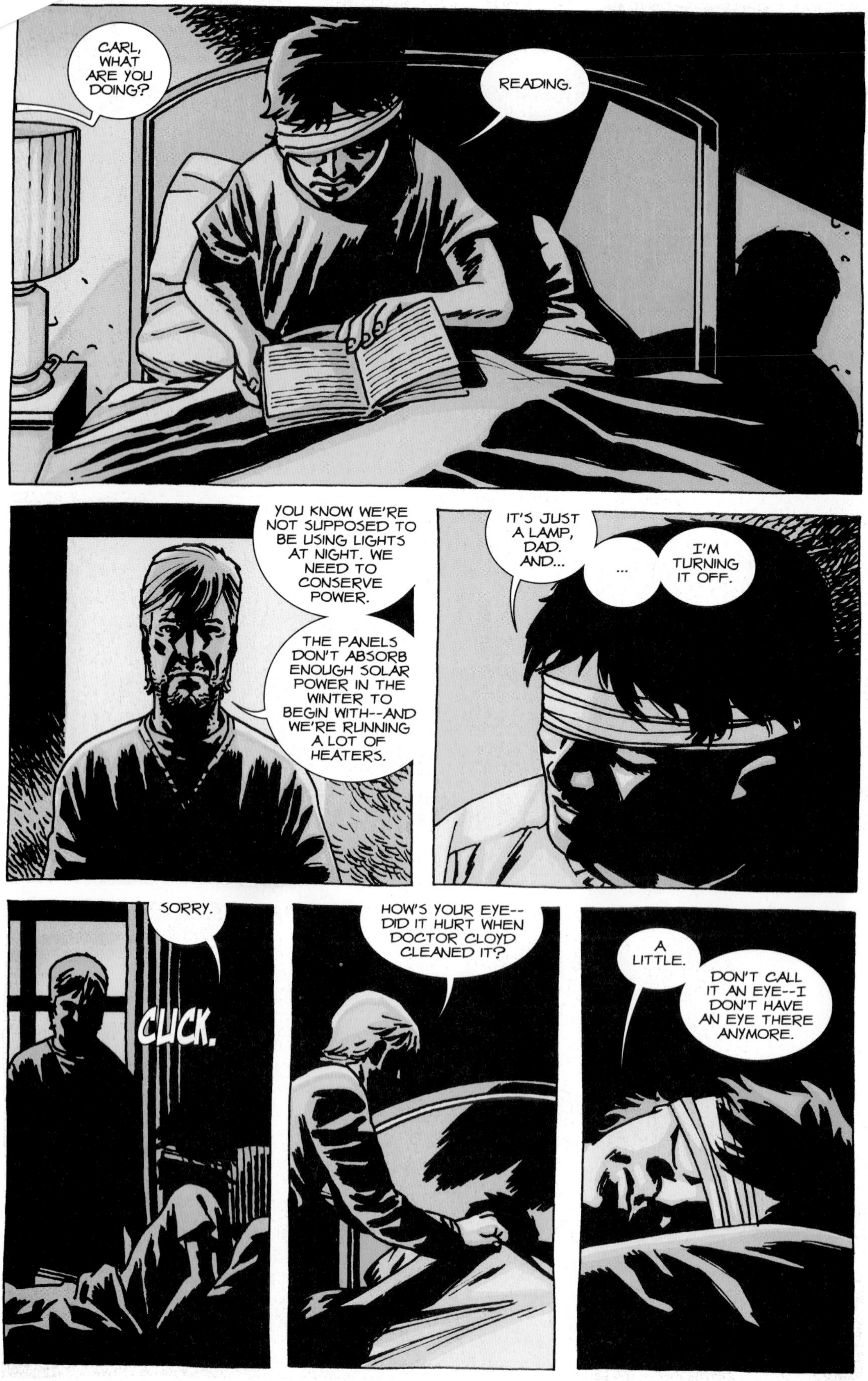
CARL, WHAT ARE YOU DOING?
READING.
YOU KNOW WE'RE NOT SUPPOSED TO BE USING LIGHTS AT NIGHT. WE NEED TO CONSERVE POWER.
THE PANELS DON'T ABSORB ENOUGH SOLAR POWER IN THE WINTER TO BEGIN WITH--AND WE'RE RUNNING A LOT OF HEATERS.
IT'S JUST A LAMP, DAD. AND...
...
I'M TURNING IT OFF.
SORRY.
CLICK.
HOW'S YOUR EYE-- DID IT HURT WHEN DOCTOR CLOYD CLEANED IT?
A LITTLE.
DON'T CALL IT AN EYE--I DON'T HAVE AN EYE THERE ANYMORE.

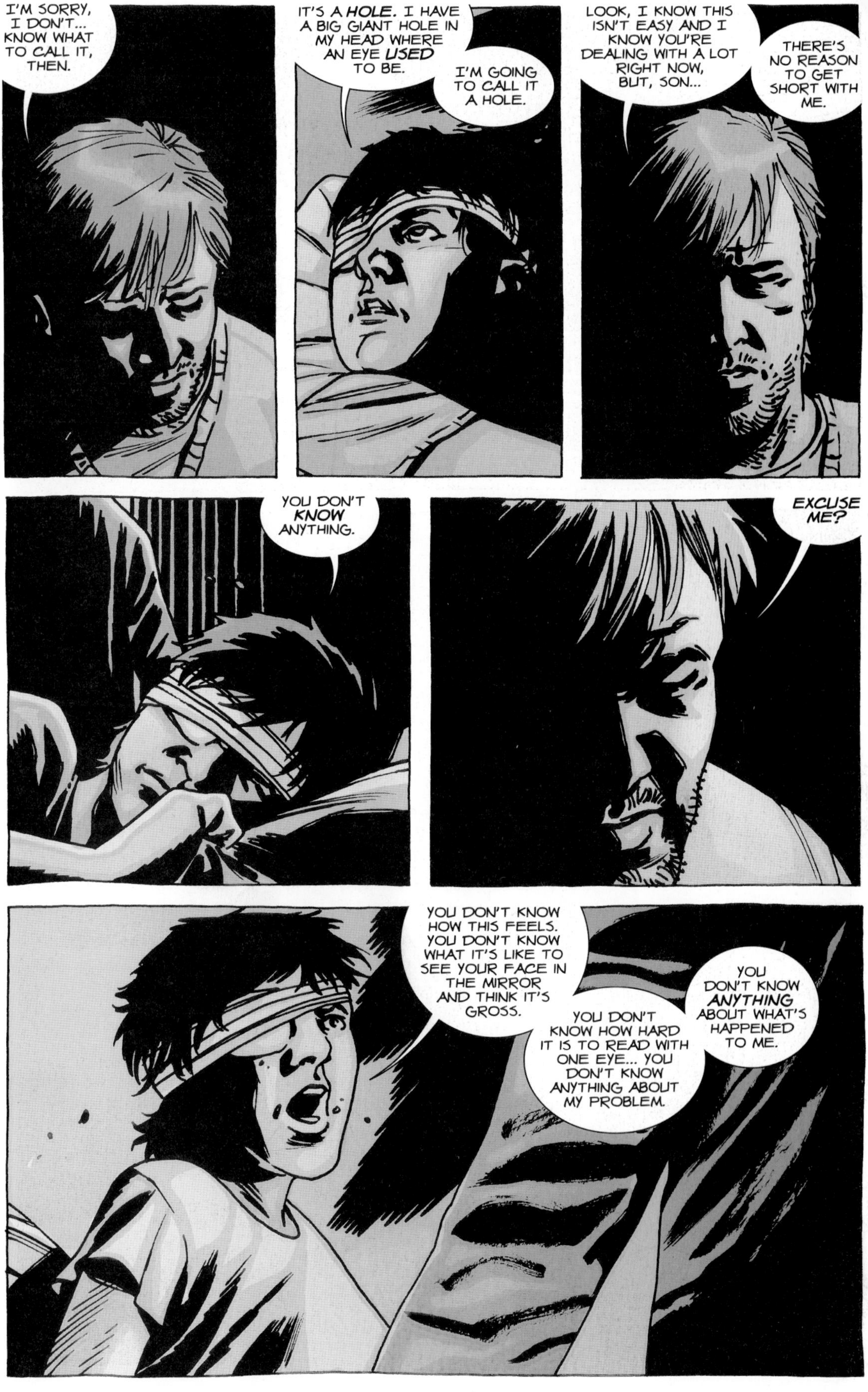
I'M SORRY, I DON'T... KNOW WHAT TO CALL IT, THEN.
IT'S A HOLE. I HAVE A BIG GIANT HOLE IN MY HEAD WHERE AN EYE USED TO BE.
I'M GOING TO CALL IT A HOLE.
LOOK, I KNOW THIS ISN'T EASY AND I KNOW YOU'RE DEALING WITH A LOT RIGHT NOW, BUT, SON...
THERE'S NO REASON TO GET SHORT WITH ME.
YOU DON'T KNOW ANYTHING.
EXCUSE ME?
YOU DON'T KNOW HOW THIS FEELS. YOU DON'T KNOW WHAT IT'S LIKE TO SEE YOUR FACE IN THE MIRROR AND THINK IT'S GROSS.
YOU DON'T KNOW HOW HARD IT IS TO READ WITH ONE EYE... YOU DON'T KNOW ANYTHING ABOUT MY PROBLEM.
YOU DON'T KNOW ANYTHING ABOUT WHAT'S HAPPENED TO ME.

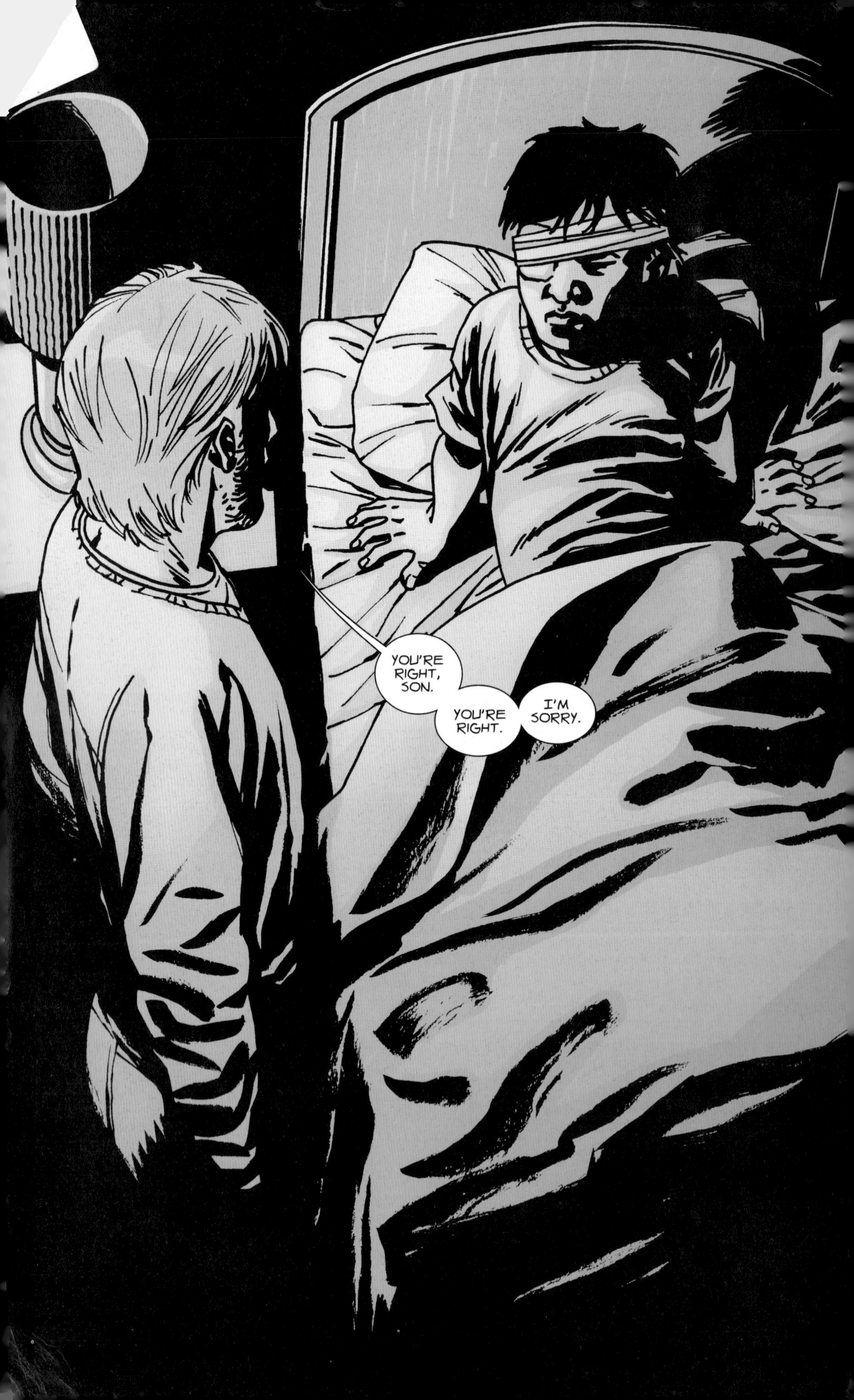

YOU'RE RIGHT, SON.
YOU'RE RIGHT.
I'M SORRY.

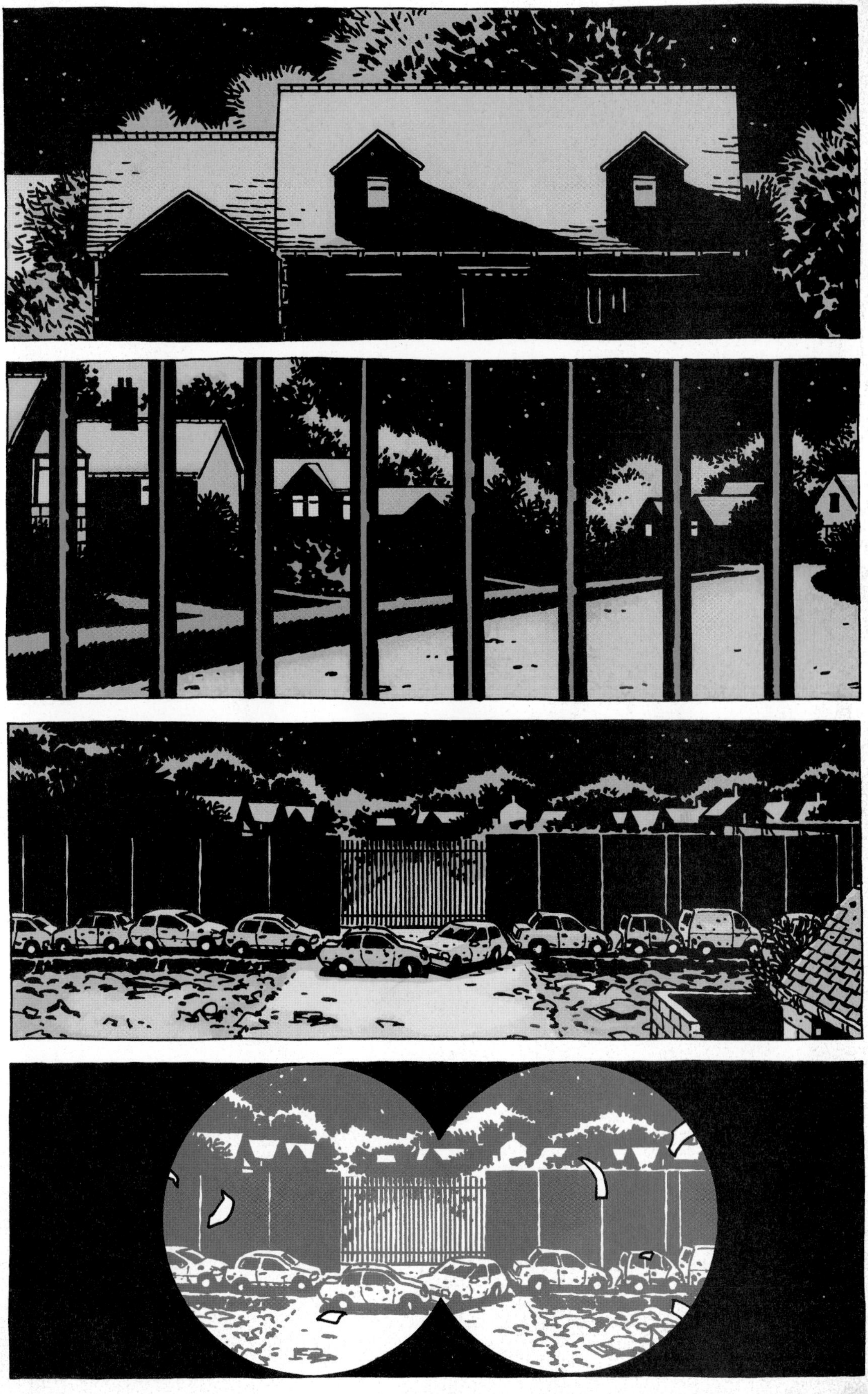

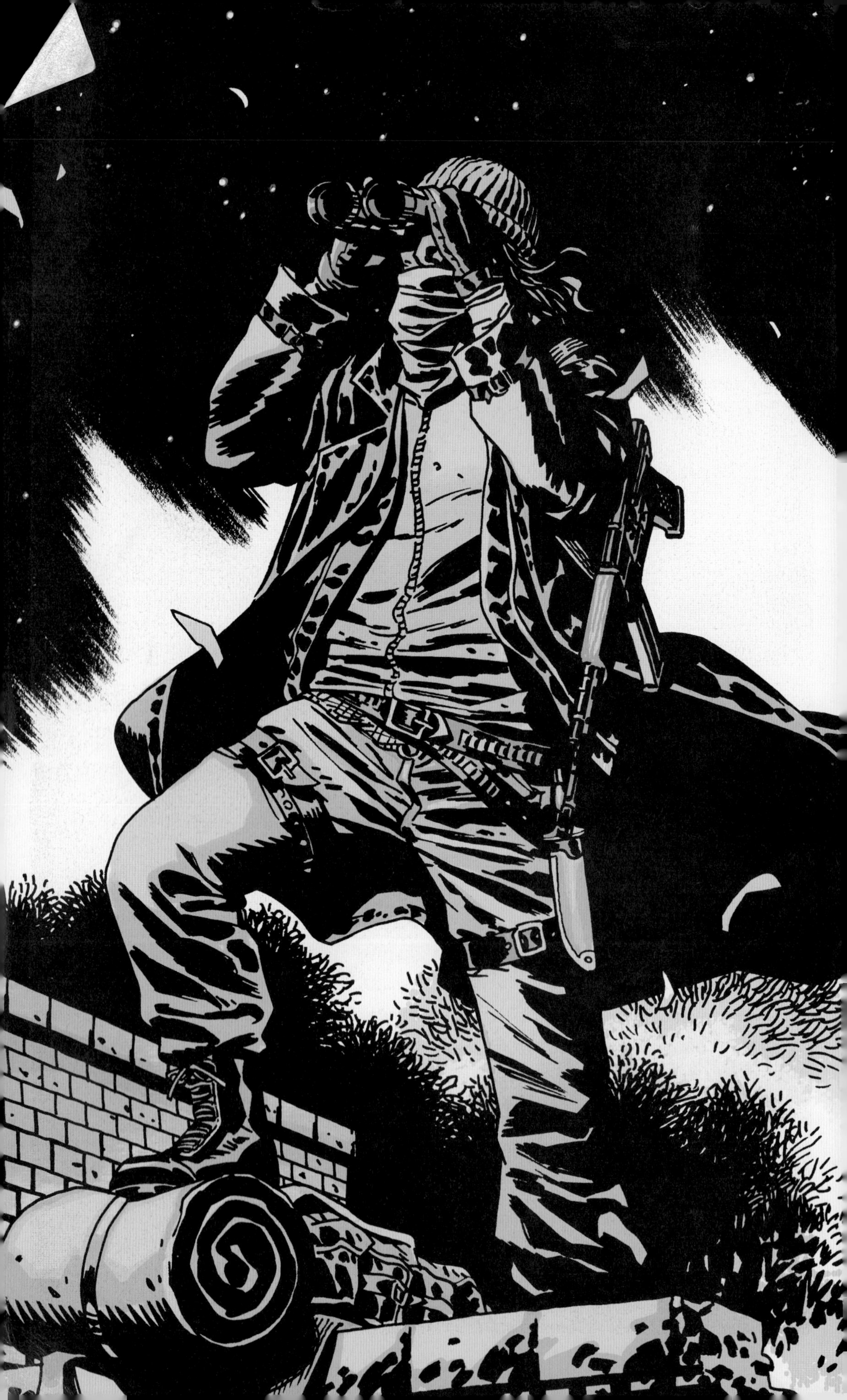

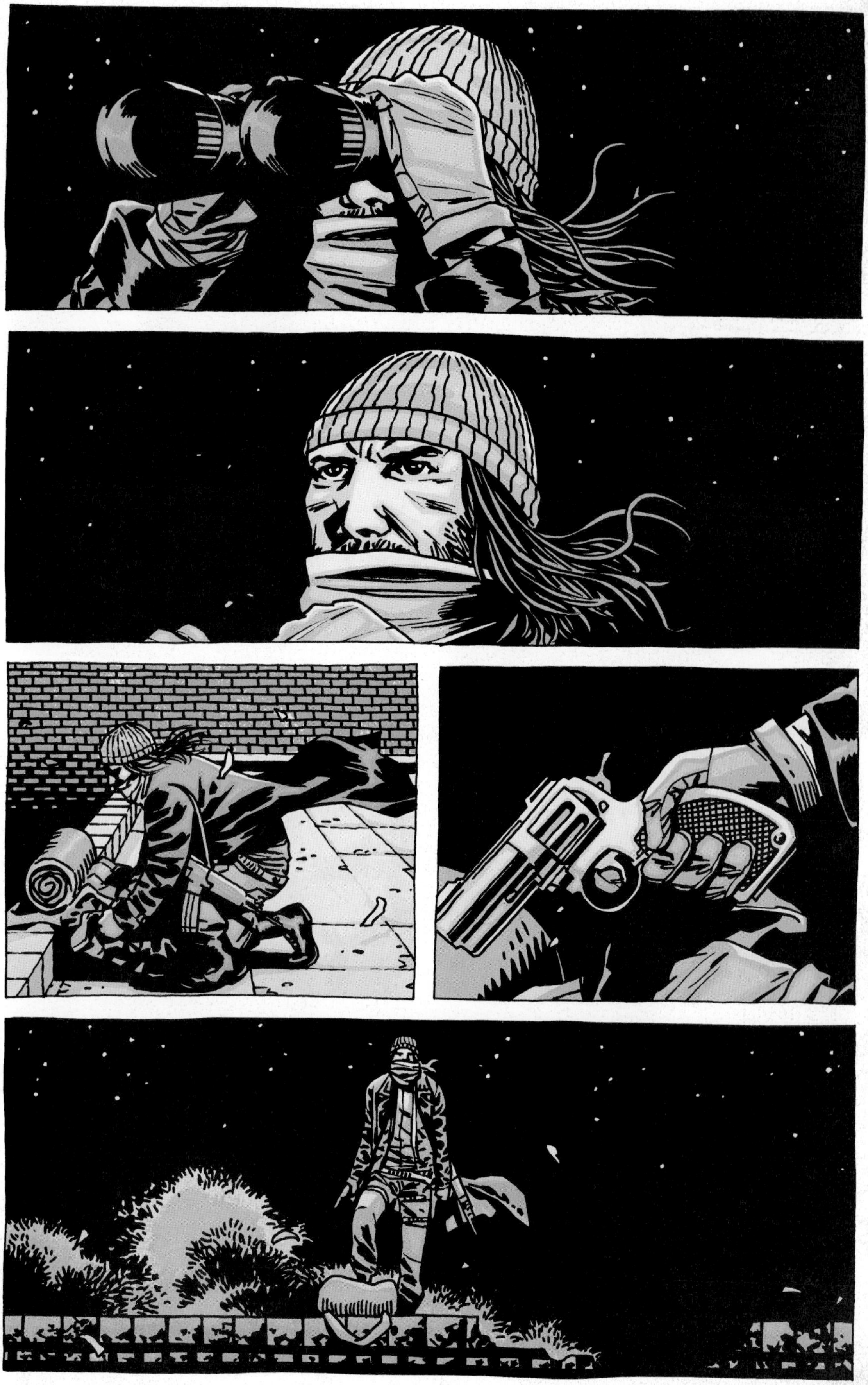

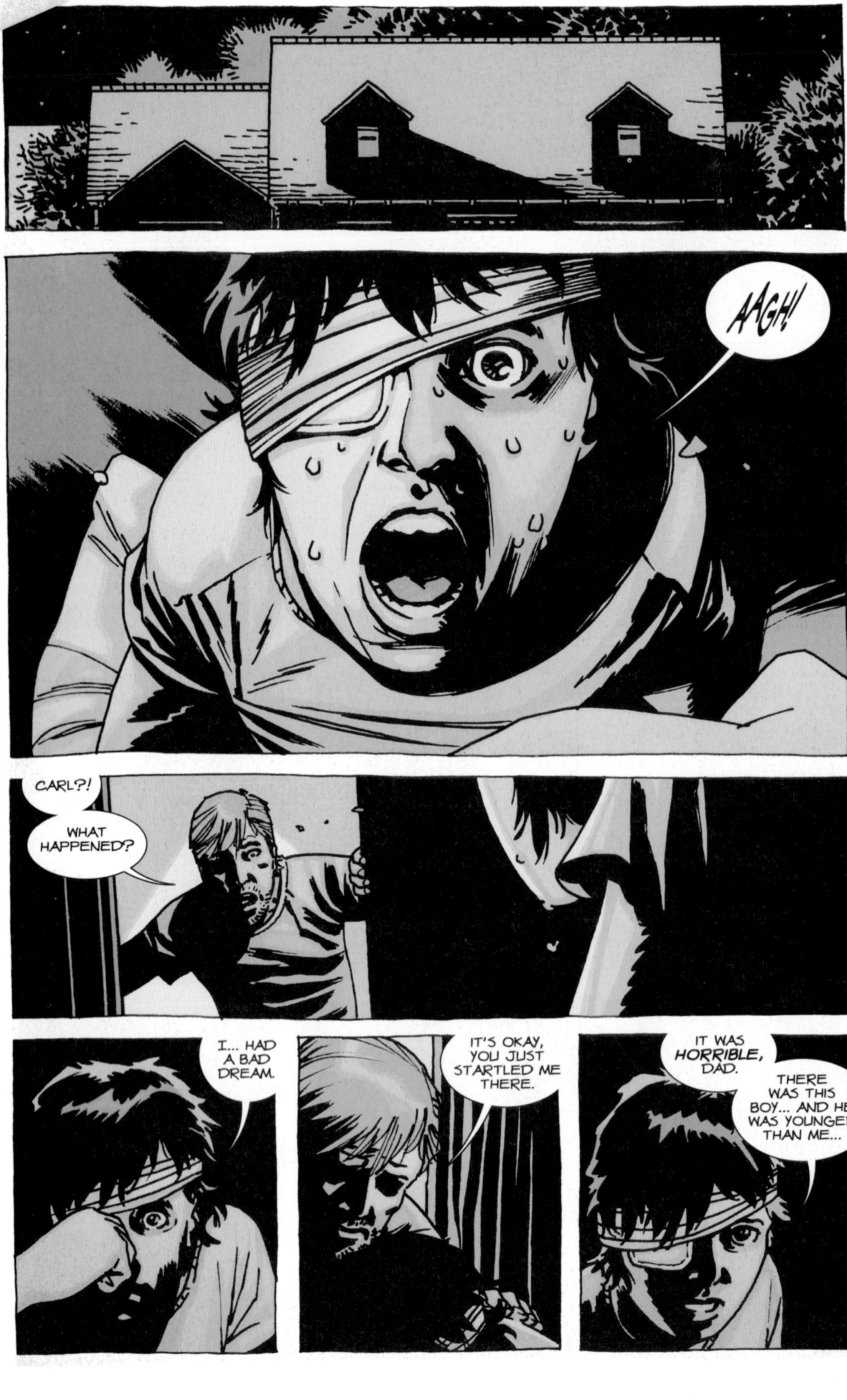
AAGH!
CARL?!
WHAT HAPPENED?
I... HAD A BAD DREAM.
IT'S OKAY, YOU JUST STARTLED ME THERE.
IT WAS *HORRIBLE*, DAD.
THERE WAS THIS BOY... AND HE WAS YOUNGER THAN ME...

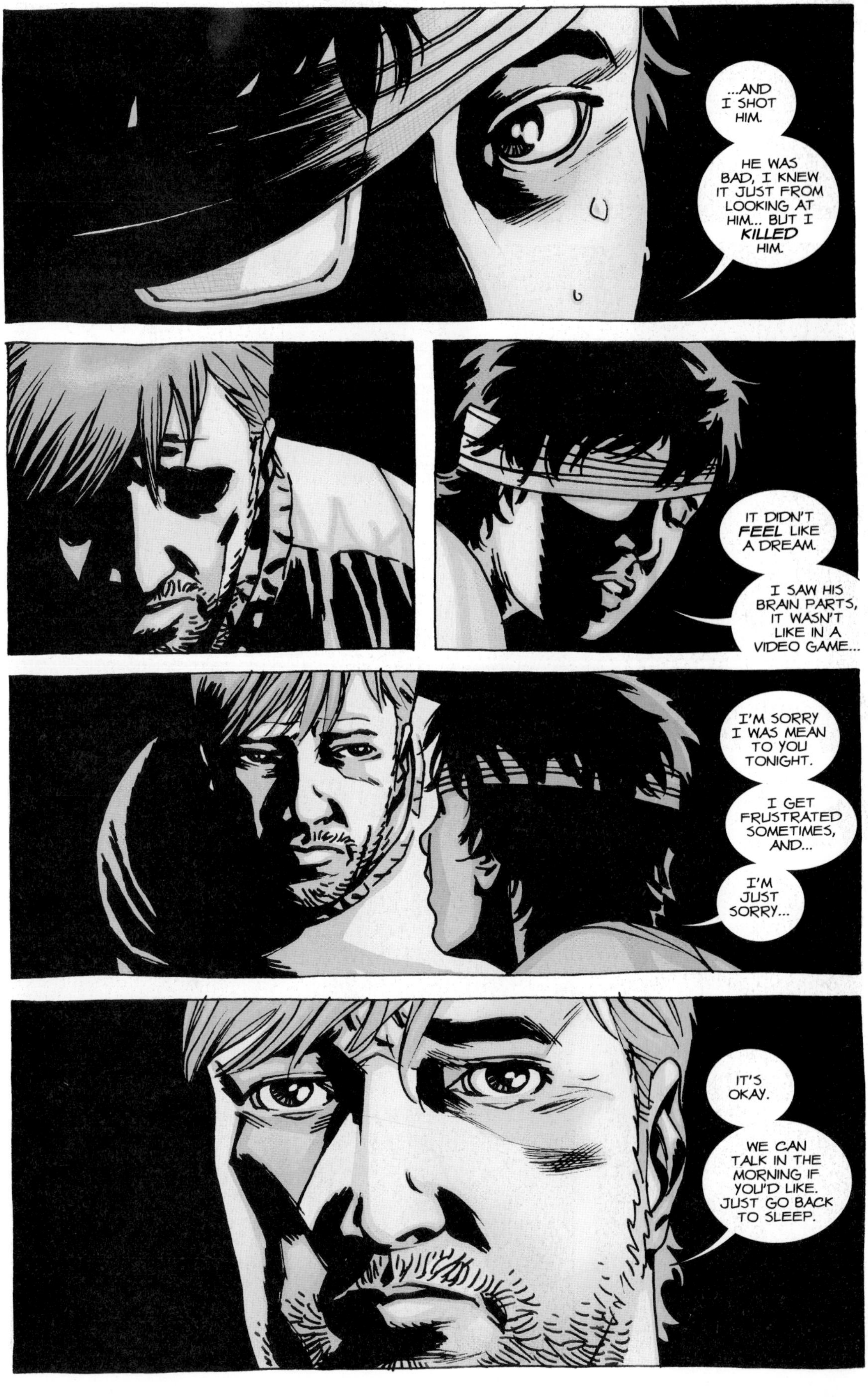
...AND I SHOT HIM.
HE WAS BAD, I KNEW IT JUST FROM LOOKING AT HIM... BUT I KILLED HIM.
IT DIDN'T FEEL LIKE A DREAM.
I SAW HIS BRAIN PARTS, IT WASN'T LIKE IN A VIDEO GAME...
I'M SORRY I WAS MEAN TO YOU TONIGHT.
I GET FRUSTRATED SOMETIMES, AND...
I'M JUST SORRY...
IT'S OKAY.
WE CAN TALK IN THE MORNING IF YOU'D LIKE. JUST GO BACK TO SLEEP.

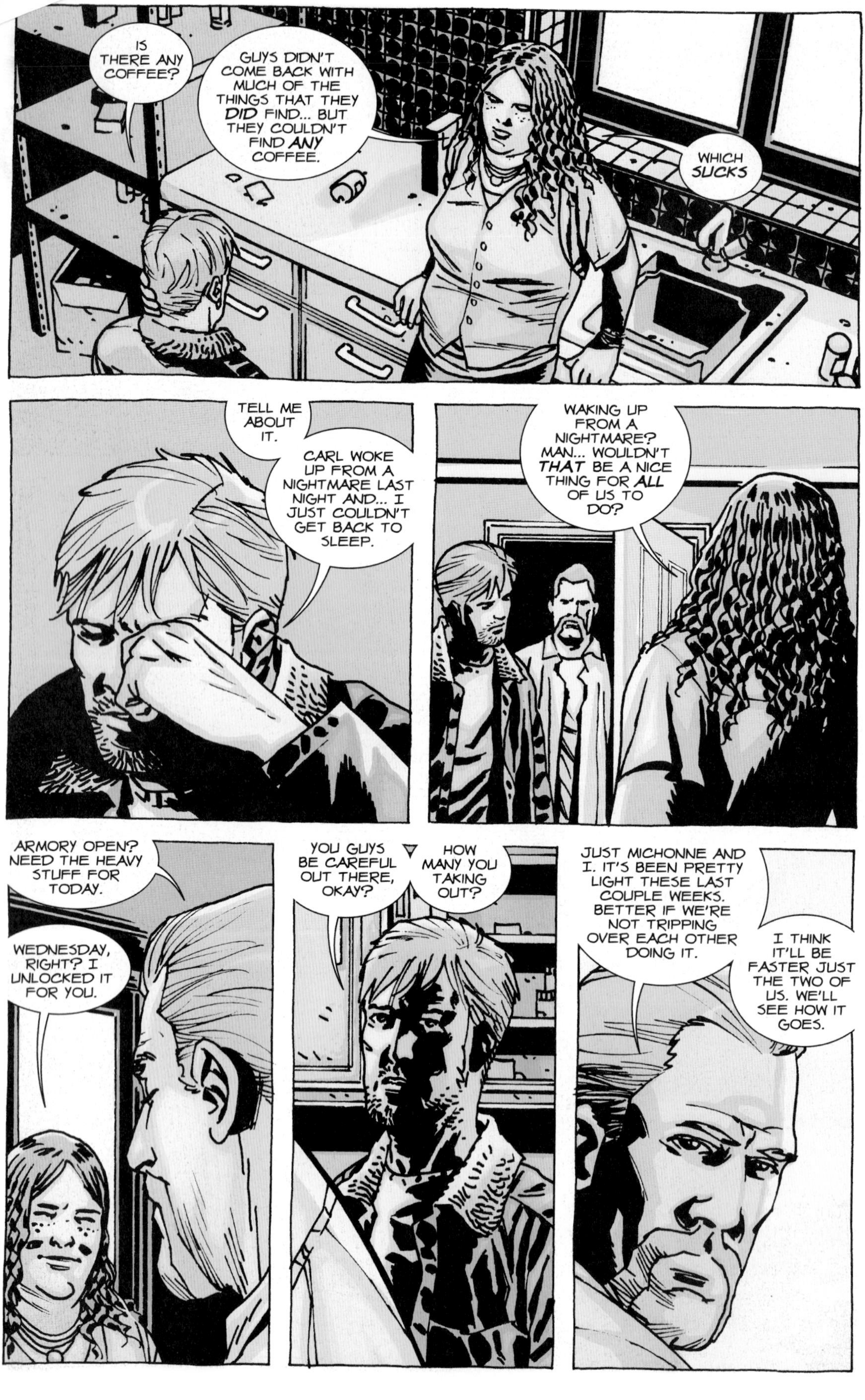
IS THERE ANY COFFEE?
GUYS DIDN'T COME BACK WITH MUCH OF THE THINGS THAT THEY DID FIND... BUT THEY COULDN'T FIND ANY COFFEE.
WHICH SUCKS
TELL ME ABOUT IT.
CARL WOKE UP FROM A NIGHTMARE LAST NIGHT AND... I JUST COULDN'T GET BACK TO SLEEP.
WAKING UP FROM A NIGHTMARE? MAN... WOULDN'T THAT BE A NICE THING FOR ALL OF US TO DO?
ARMORY OPEN? NEED THE HEAVY STUFF FOR TODAY.
WEDNESDAY, RIGHT? I UNLOCKED IT FOR YOU.
YOU GUYS BE CAREFUL OUT THERE, OKAY?
HOW MANY YOU TAKING OUT?
JUST MICHONNE AND I. IT'S BEEN PRETTY LIGHT THESE LAST COUPLE WEEKS. BETTER IF WE'RE NOT TRIPPING OVER EACH OTHER DOING IT.
I THINK IT'LL BE FASTER JUST THE TWO OF US. WE'LL SEE HOW IT GOES.

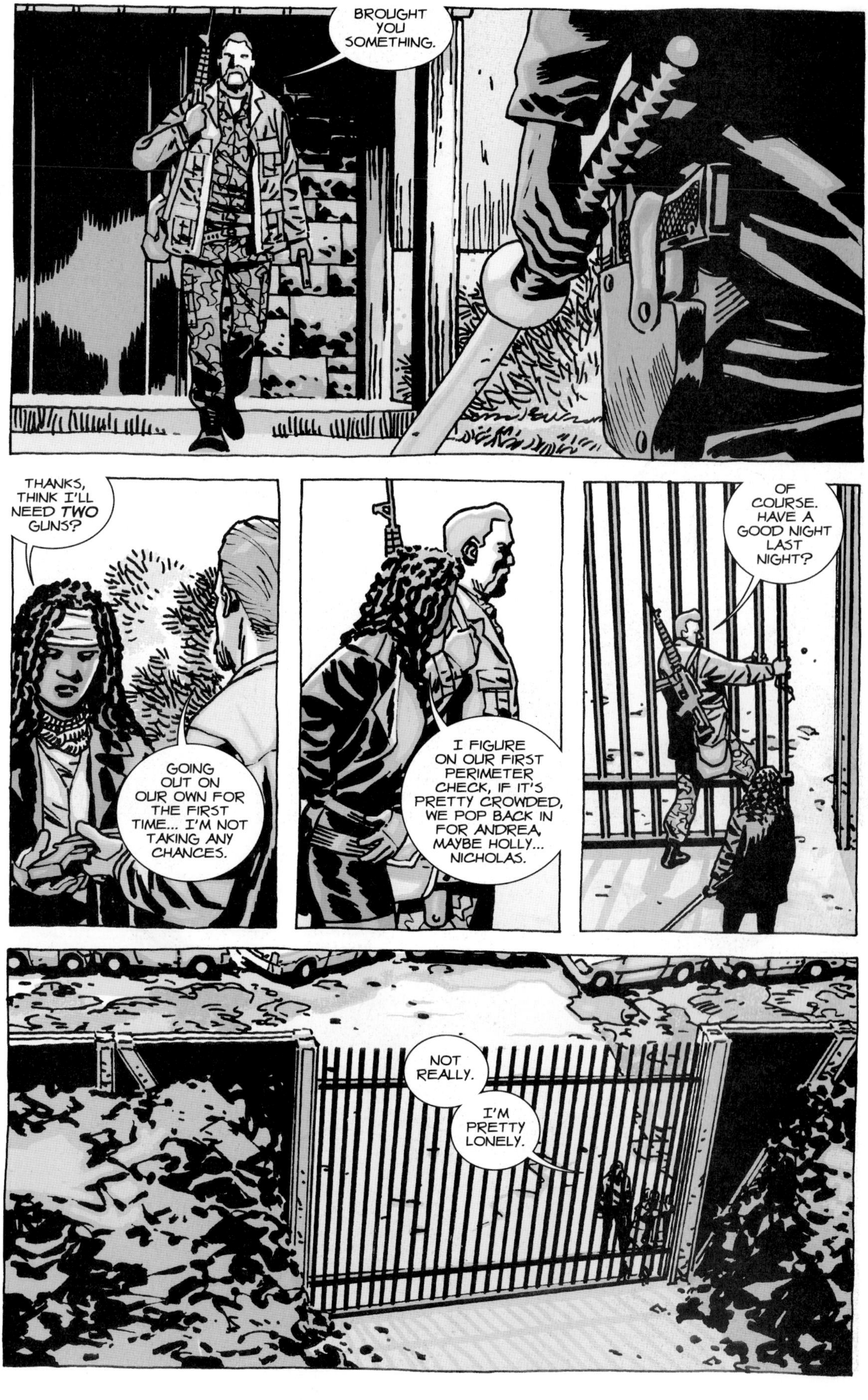
BROUGHT YOU SOMETHING.
THANKS, THINK I'LL NEED **TWO** GUNS?
GOING OUT ON OUR OWN FOR THE FIRST TIME... I'M NOT TAKING ANY CHANCES.
I FIGURE ON OUR FIRST PERIMETER CHECK, IF IT'S PRETTY CROWDED, WE POP BACK IN FOR ANDREA, MAYBE HOLLY... NICHOLAS.
OF COURSE. HAVE A GOOD NIGHT LAST NIGHT?
NOT REALLY.
I'M PRETTY LONELY.

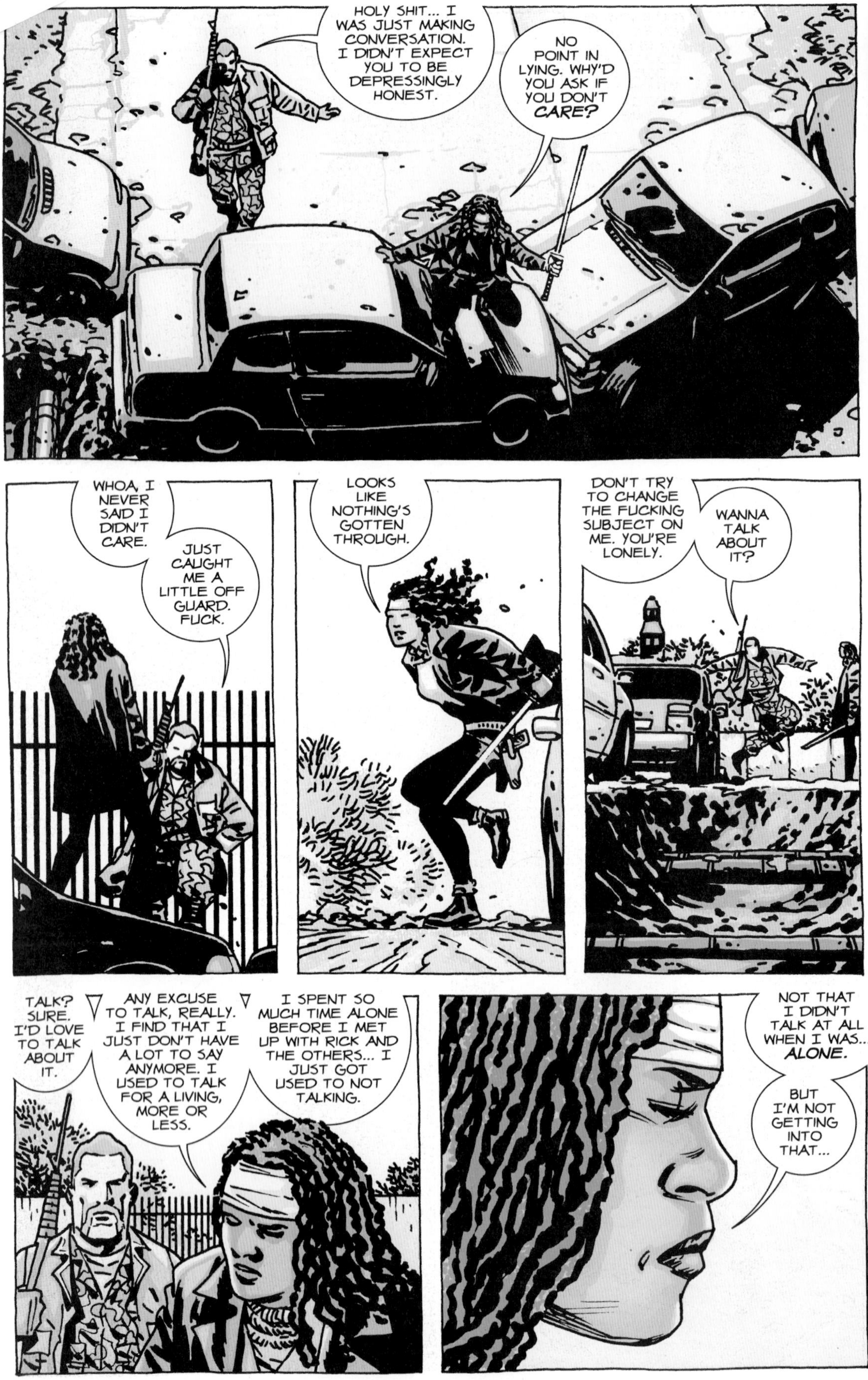
HOLY SHIT... I WAS JUST MAKING CONVERSATION. I DIDN'T EXPECT YOU TO BE DEPRESSINGLY HONEST.
NO POINT IN LYING. WHY'D YOU ASK IF YOU DON'T CARE?
WHOA, I NEVER SAID I DIDN'T CARE.
JUST CAUGHT ME A LITTLE OFF GUARD. FUCK.
LOOKS LIKE NOTHING'S GOTTEN THROUGH.
DON'T TRY TO CHANGE THE FUCKING SUBJECT ON ME. YOU'RE LONELY.
WANNA TALK ABOUT IT?
TALK? SURE. I'D LOVE TO TALK ABOUT IT.
ANY EXCUSE TO TALK, REALLY. I FIND THAT I JUST DON'T HAVE A LOT TO SAY ANYMORE. I USED TO TALK FOR A LIVING, MORE OR LESS.
I SPENT SO MUCH TIME ALONE BEFORE I MET UP WITH RICK AND THE OTHERS... I JUST GOT USED TO NOT TALKING.
NOT THAT I DIDN'T TALK AT ALL WHEN I WAS... ALONE.
BUT I'M NOT GETTING INTO THAT...

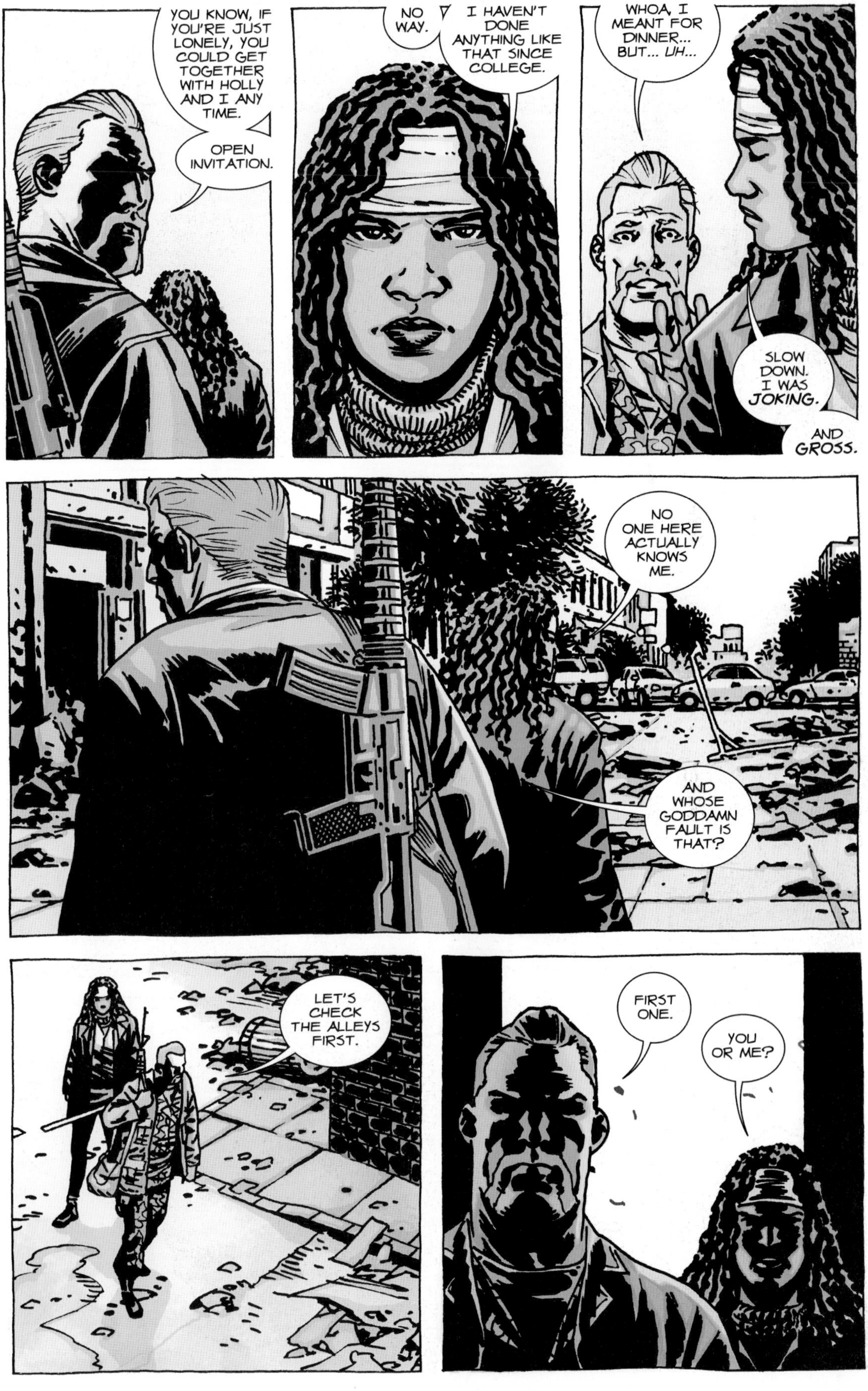
YOU KNOW, IF YOU'RE JUST LONELY, YOU COULD GET TOGETHER WITH HOLLY AND I ANY TIME.
OPEN INVITATION.
NO WAY.
I HAVEN'T DONE ANYTHING LIKE THAT SINCE COLLEGE.
WHOA, I MEANT FOR DINNER... BUT... UH...
SLOW DOWN. I WAS JOKING.
AND GROSS.
NO ONE HERE ACTUALLY KNOWS ME.
AND WHOSE GODDAMN FAULT IS THAT?
LET'S CHECK THE ALLEYS FIRST.
FIRST ONE.
YOU OR ME?

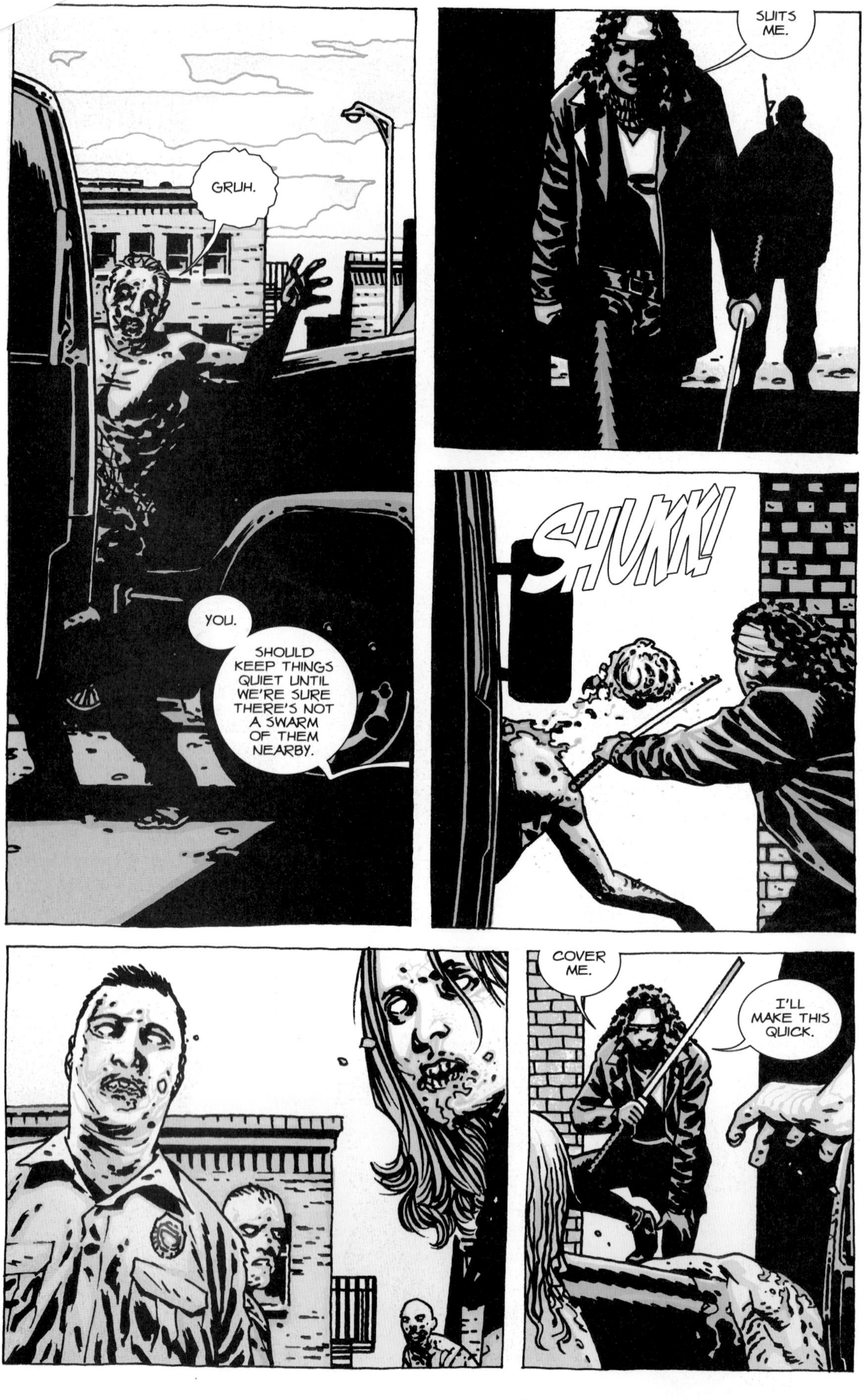
GRUH.
YOU.
SHOULD KEEP THINGS QUIET UNTIL WE'RE SURE THERE'S NOT A SWARM OF THEM NEARBY.
SUITS ME.
SHUKK!
COVER ME.
I'LL MAKE THIS QUICK.

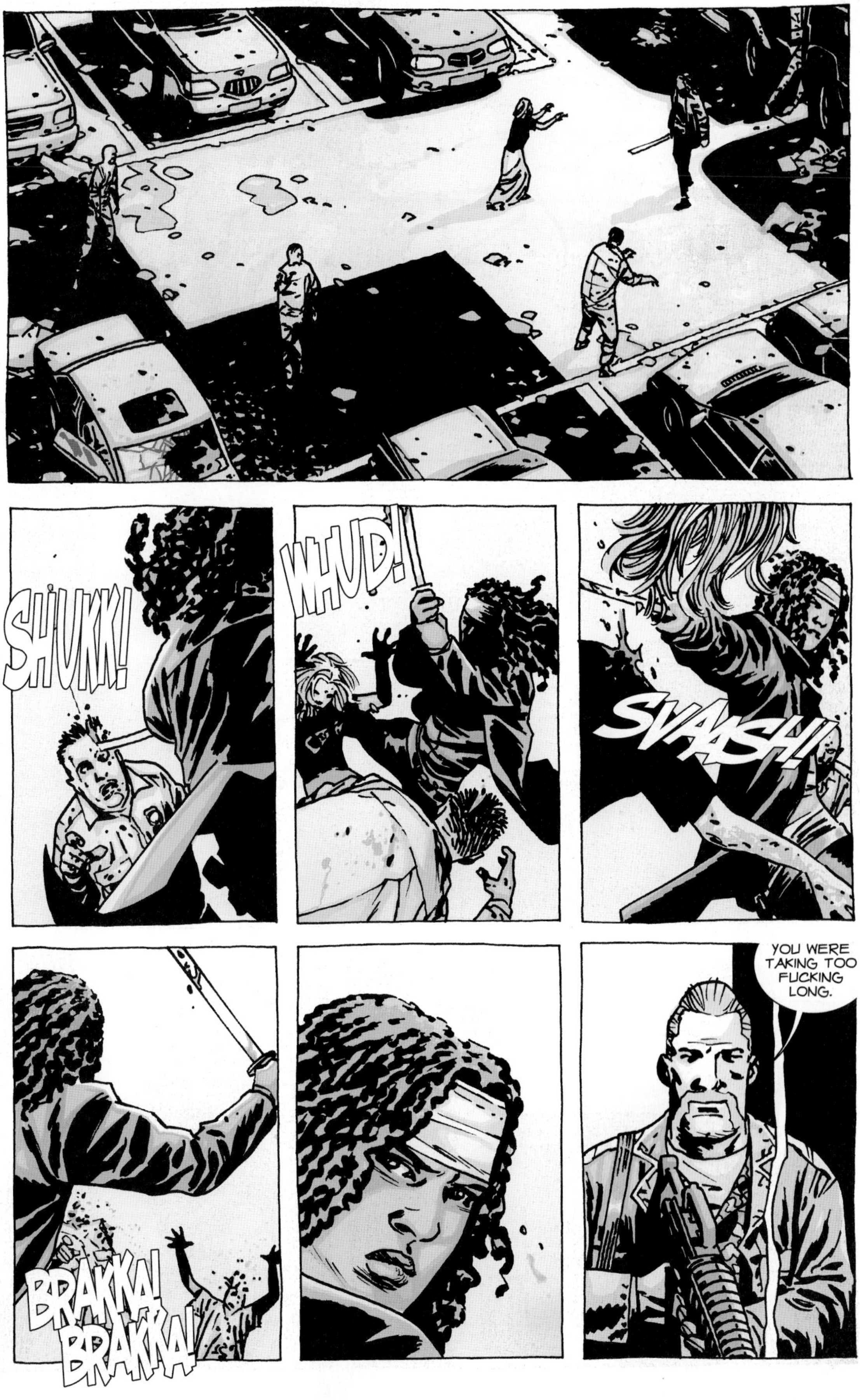
SHUKK!
WHUD!
SVAASH!
BRAKKA! BRAKKA!
YOU WERE TAKING TOO FUCKING LONG.

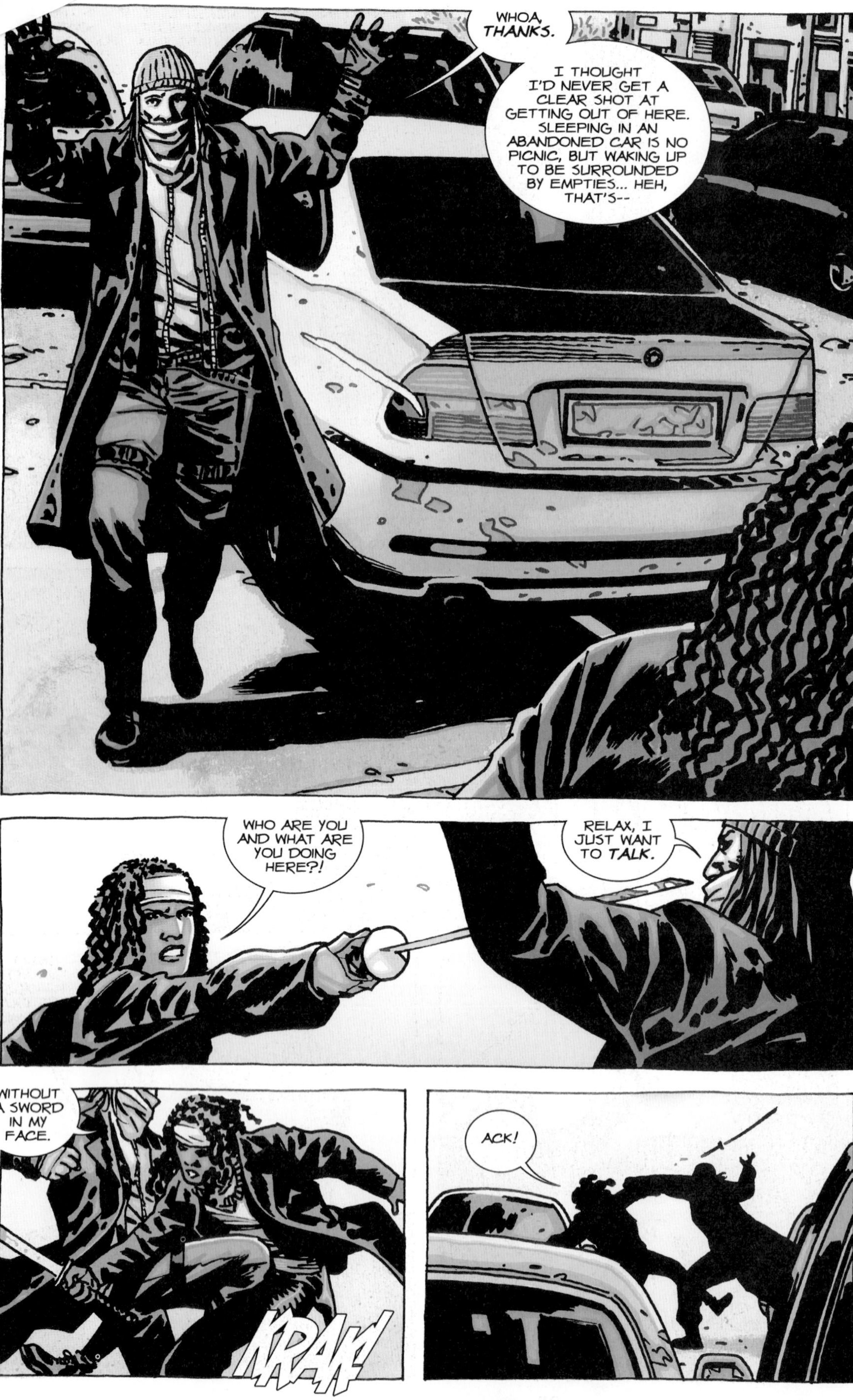
WHOA, THANKS.
I THOUGHT I'D NEVER GET A CLEAR SHOT AT GETTING OUT OF HERE. SLEEPING IN AN ABANDONED CAR IS NO PICNIC, BUT WAKING UP TO BE SURROUNDED BY EMPTIES... HEH, THAT'S--
WHO ARE YOU AND WHAT ARE YOU DOING HERE?!
RELAX, I JUST WANT TO TALK.
WITHOUT A SWORD IN MY FACE.
KRAK!
ACK!

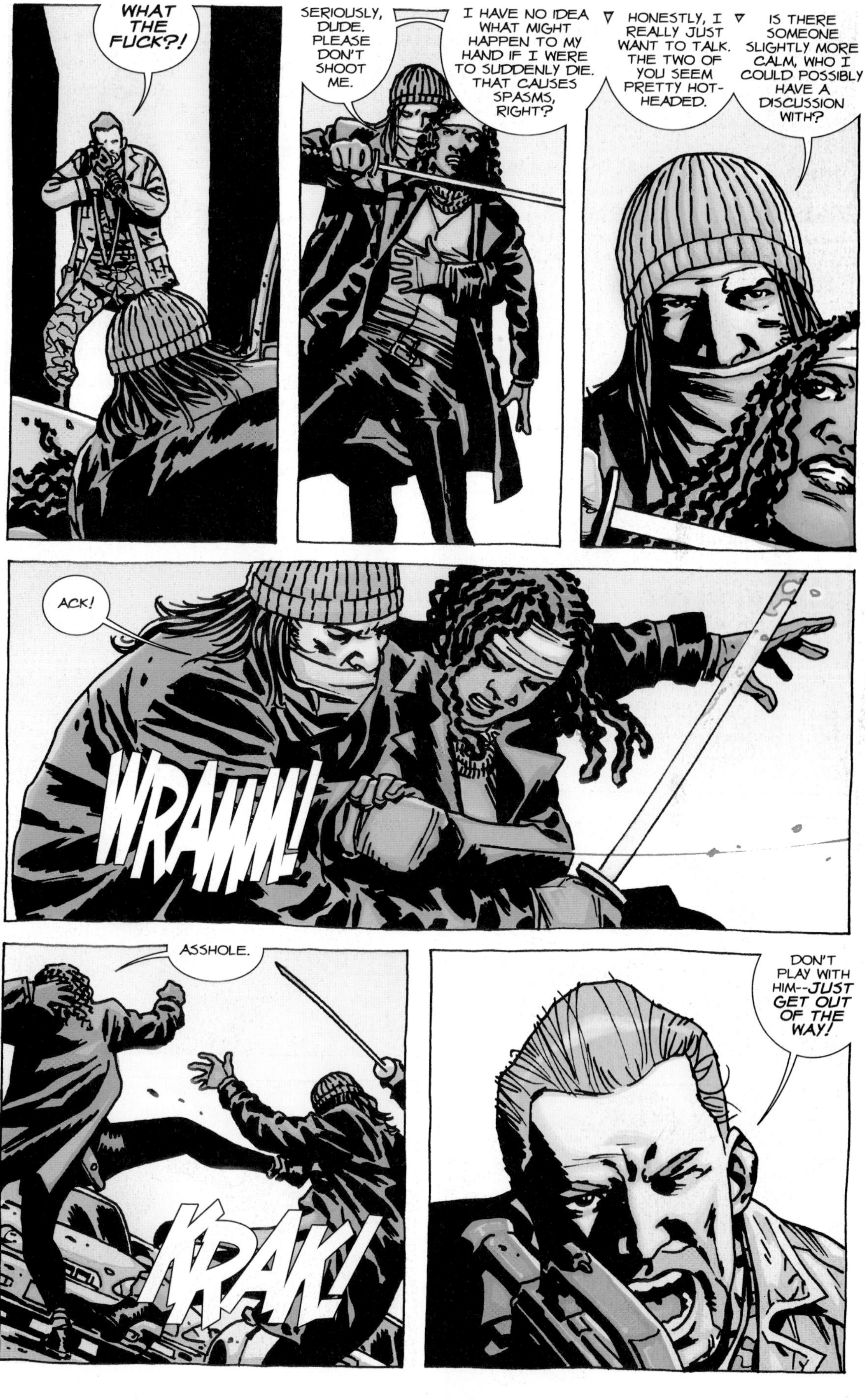
WHAT THE FUCK?!
SERIOUSLY, DUDE. PLEASE DON'T SHOOT ME.
I HAVE NO IDEA WHAT MIGHT HAPPEN TO MY HAND IF I WERE TO SUDDENLY DIE. THAT CAUSES SPASMS, RIGHT?
HONESTLY, I REALLY JUST WANT TO TALK. THE TWO OF YOU SEEM PRETTY HOT-HEADED.
IS THERE SOMEONE SLIGHTLY MORE CALM, WHO I COULD POSSIBLY HAVE A DISCUSSION WITH?
ACK!
WRAMM!
ASSHOLE.
KRAK!
DON'T PLAY WITH HIM--JUST GET OUT OF THE WAY!

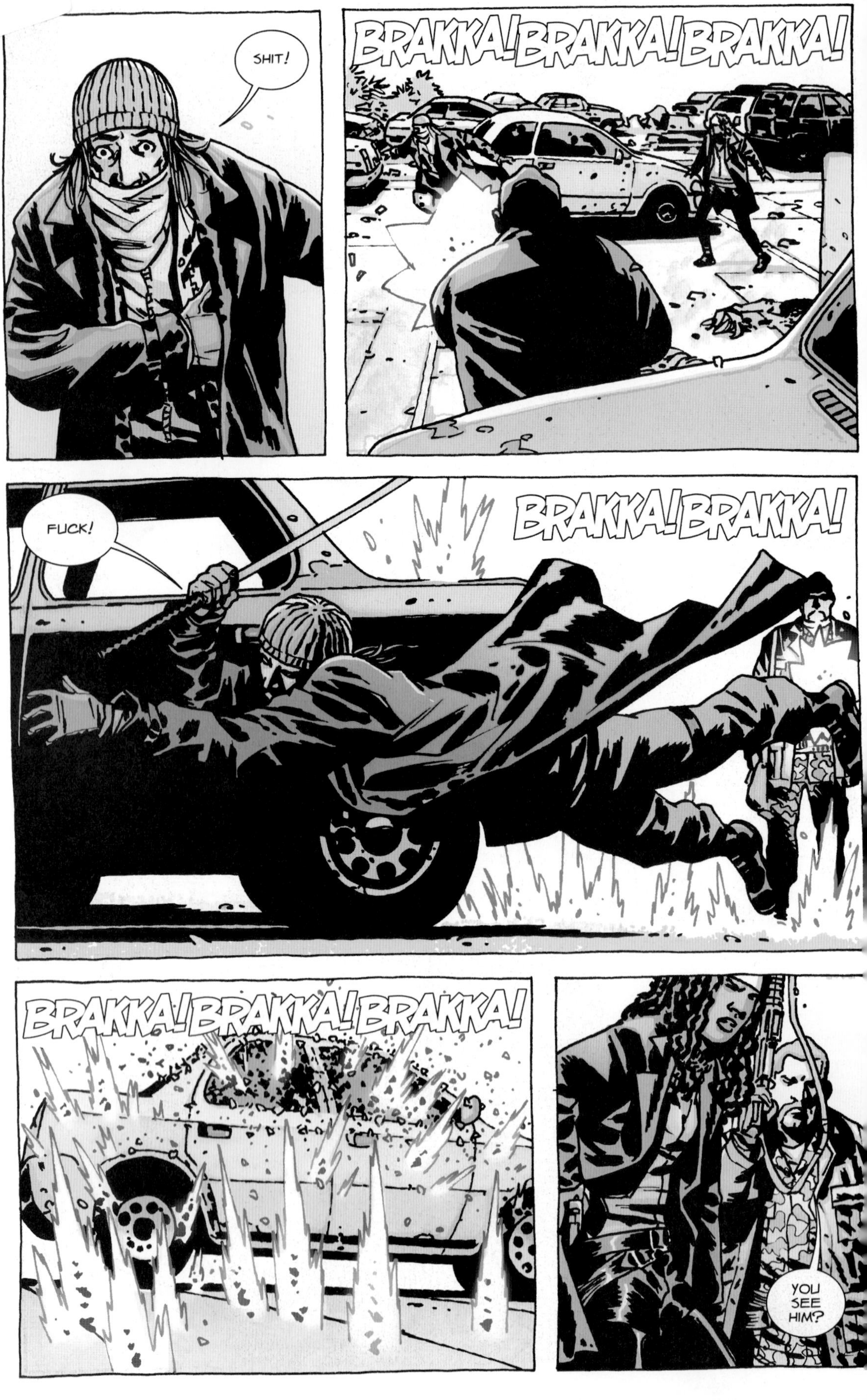
SHIT!
BRAKKA! BRAKKA! BRAKKA!
BRAKKA! BRAKKA!
FUCK!
BRAKKA! BRAKKA! BRAKKA!
YOU SEE HIM?

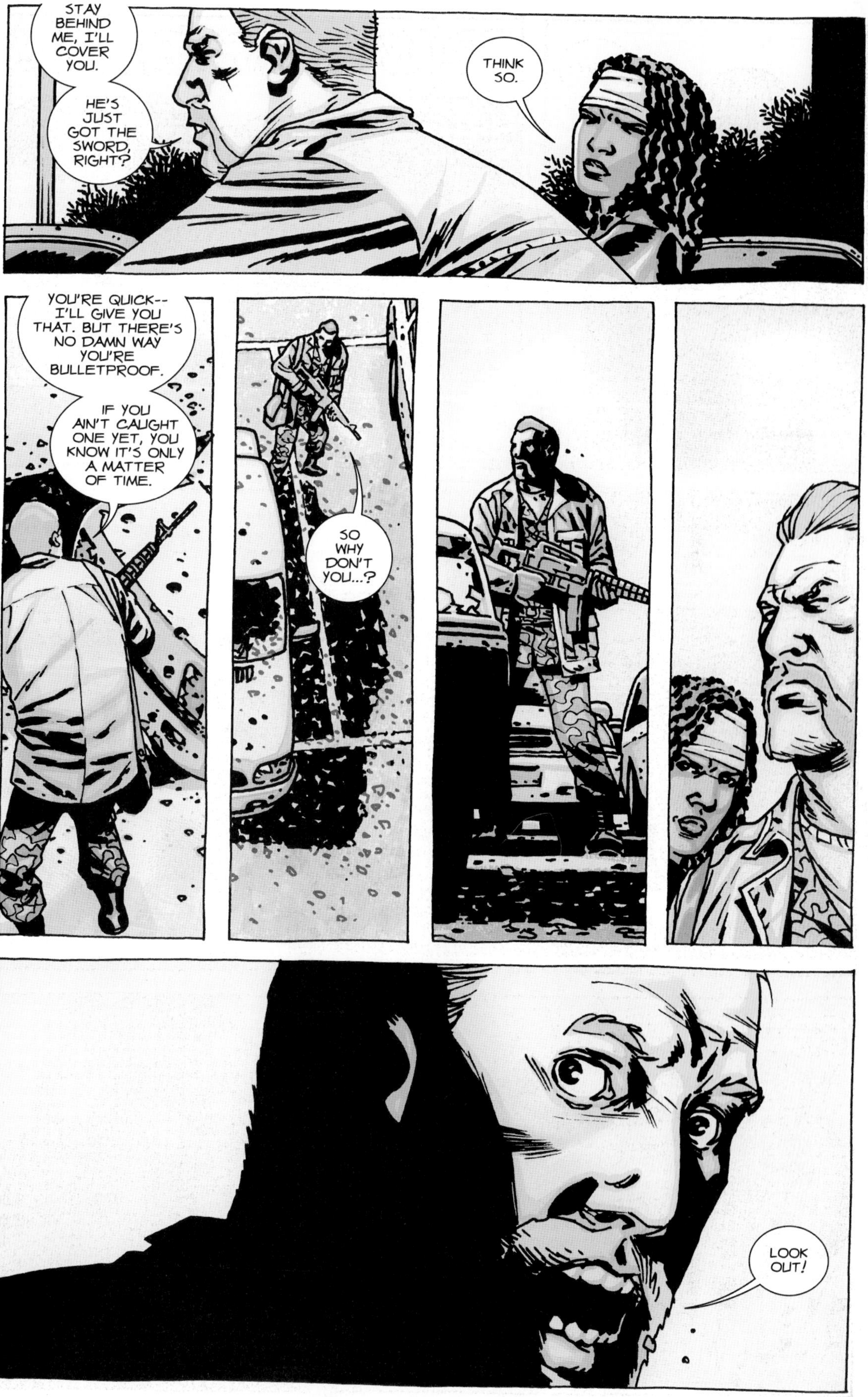
STAY BEHIND ME, I'LL COVER YOU.
HE'S JUST GOT THE SWORD, RIGHT?
THINK SO.
YOU'RE QUICK-- I'LL GIVE YOU THAT. BUT THERE'S NO DAMN WAY YOU'RE BULLETPROOF.
IF YOU AIN'T CAUGHT ONE YET, YOU KNOW IT'S ONLY A MATTER OF TIME.
SO WHY DON'T YOU...?
LOOK OUT!

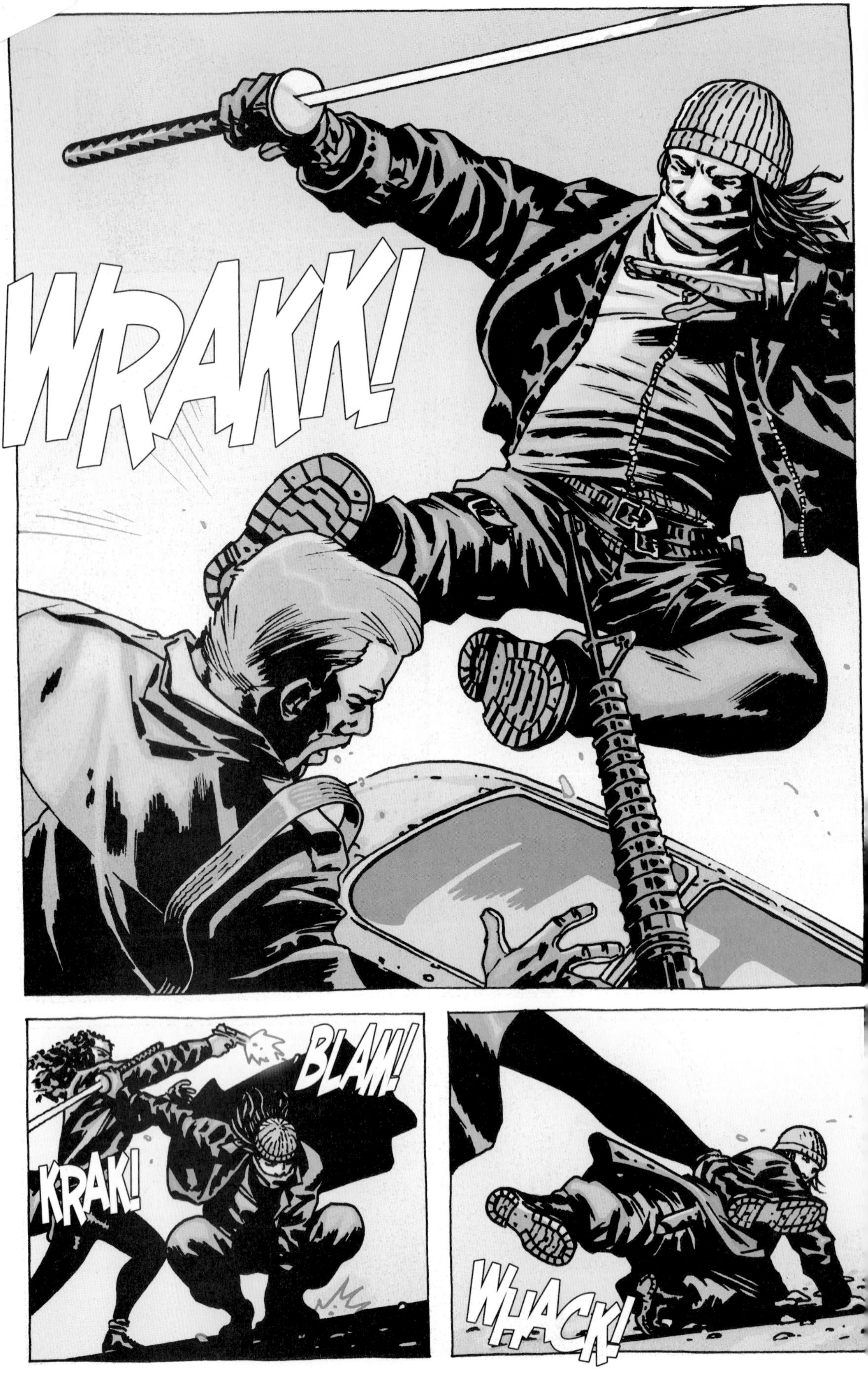
WRAKK!
BLAM!
KRAK!
WHACK!

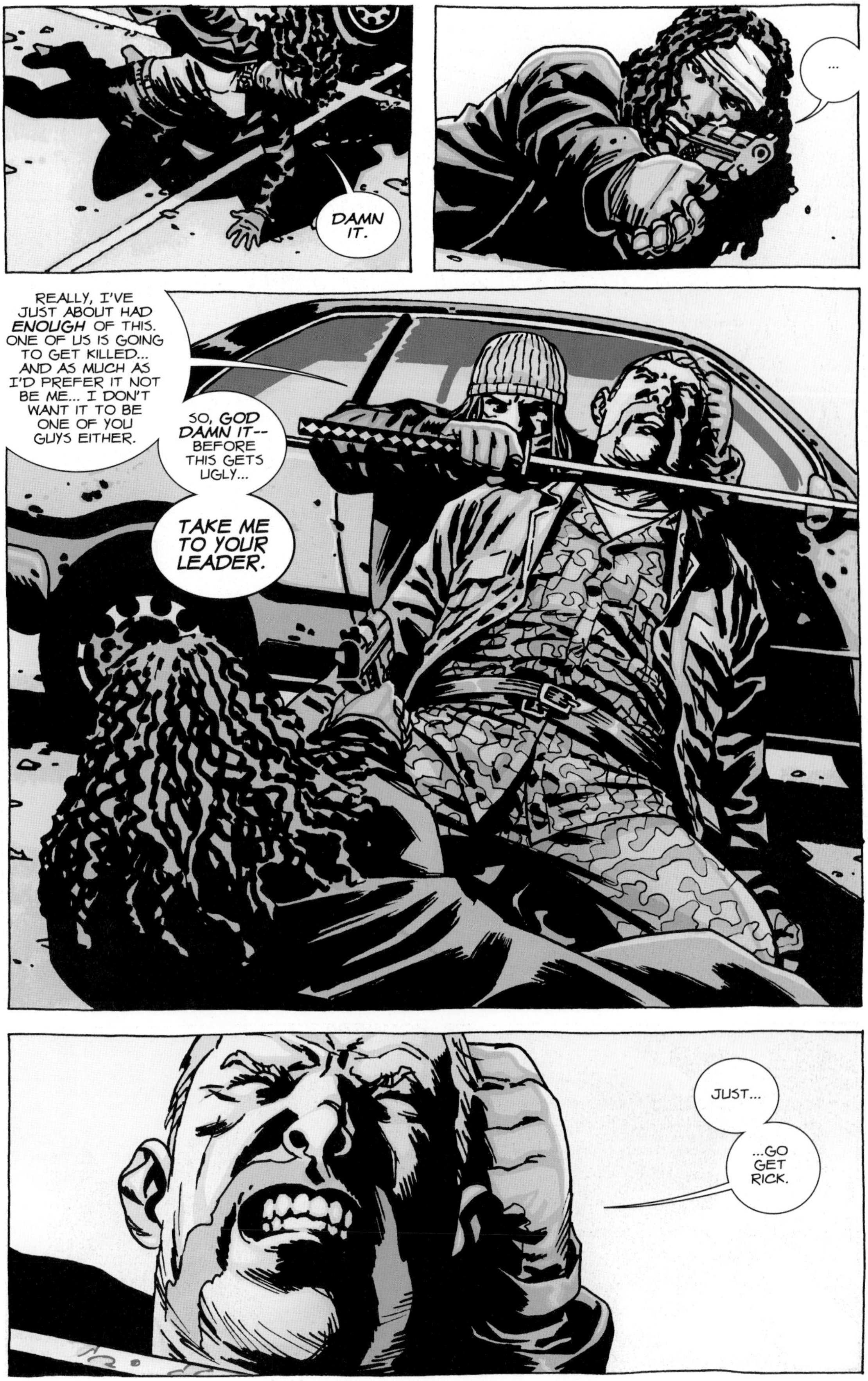
DAMN IT.
...
REALLY, I'VE JUST ABOUT HAD ENOUGH OF THIS. ONE OF US IS GOING TO GET KILLED... AND AS MUCH AS I'D PREFER IT NOT BE ME... I DON'T WANT IT TO BE ONE OF YOU GUYS EITHER.
SO, GOD DAMN IT-- BEFORE THIS GETS UGLY...
TAKE ME TO YOUR LEADER.
JUST...
...GO GET RICK.

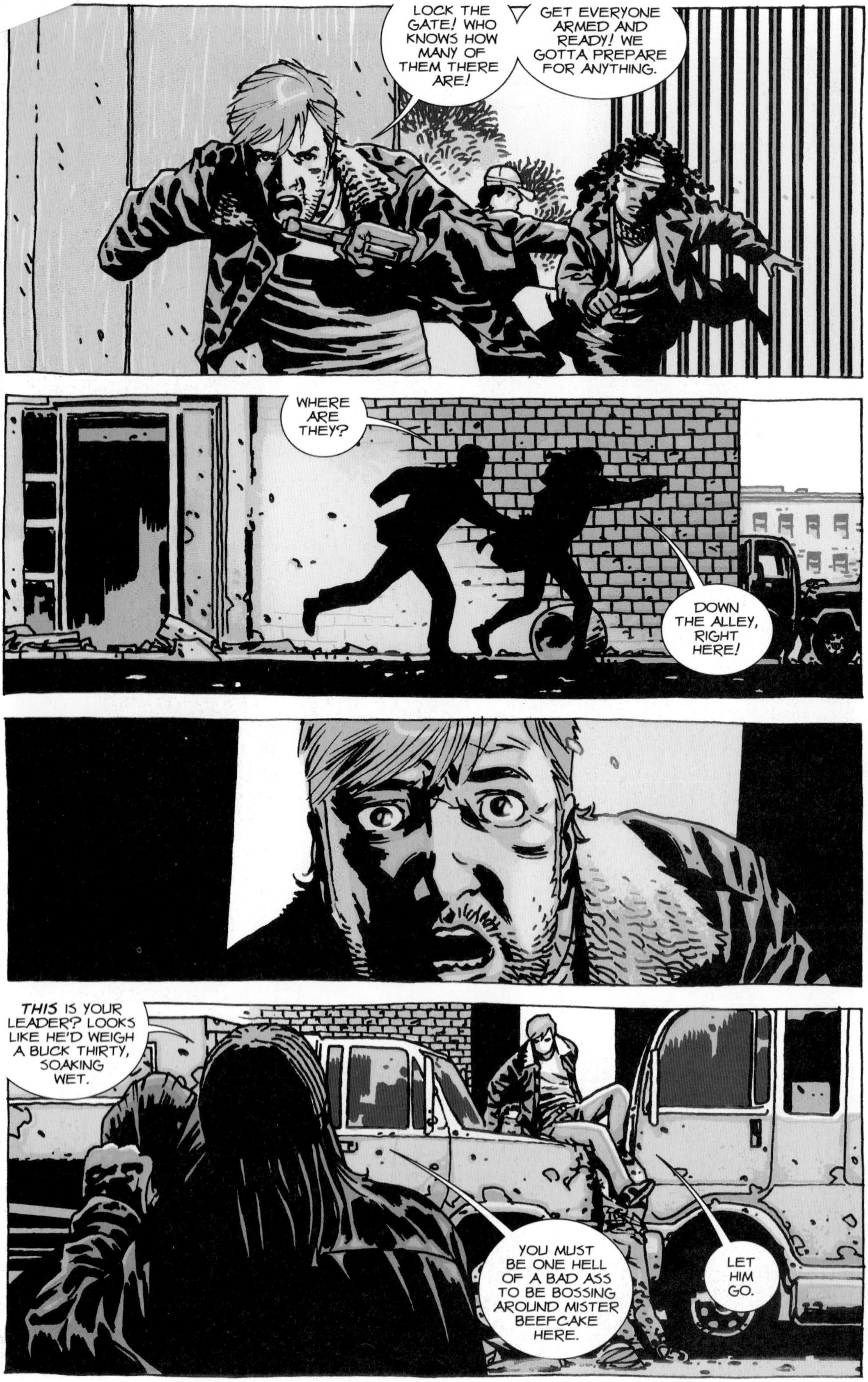
LOCK THE GATE! WHO KNOWS HOW MANY OF THEM THERE ARE!
GET EVERYONE ARMED AND READY! WE GOTTA PREPARE FOR ANYTHING.
WHERE ARE THEY?
DOWN THE ALLEY, RIGHT HERE!
THIS IS YOUR LEADER? LOOKS LIKE HE'D WEIGH A BUCK THIRTY, SOAKING WET.
YOU MUST BE ONE HELL OF A BAD ASS TO BE BOSSING AROUND MISTER BEEFCAKE HERE.
LET HIM GO.

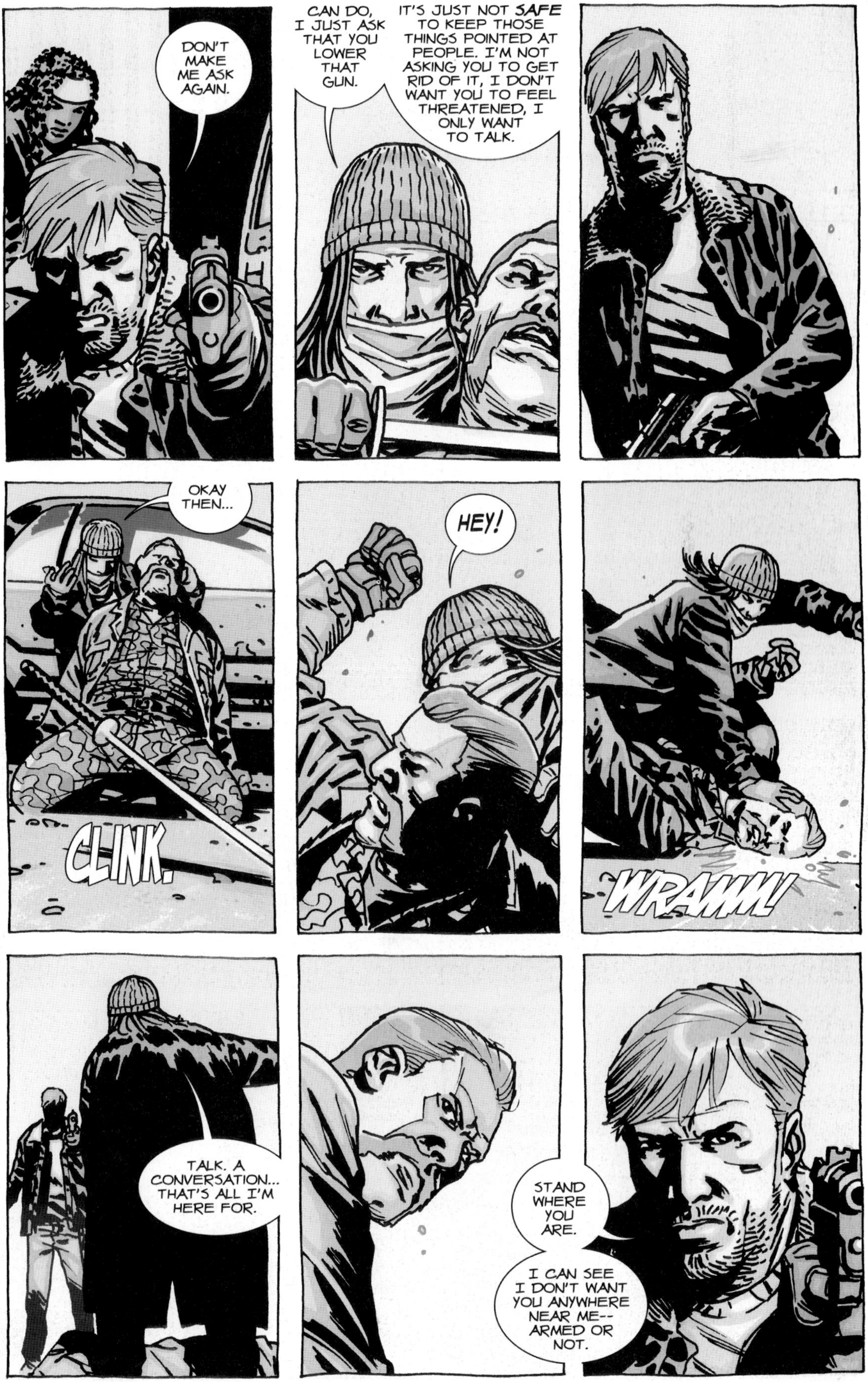

DON'T MAKE ME ASK AGAIN.
CAN DO, I JUST ASK THAT YOU LOWER THAT GUN.
IT'S JUST NOT SAFE TO KEEP THOSE THINGS POINTED AT PEOPLE. I'M NOT ASKING YOU TO GET RID OF IT, I DON'T WANT YOU TO FEEL THREATENED, I ONLY WANT TO TALK.
OKAY THEN...
CLINK.
HEY!
WRAMM!
TALK. A CONVERSATION... THAT'S ALL I'M HERE FOR.
STAND WHERE YOU ARE.
I CAN SEE I DON'T WANT YOU ANYWHERE NEAR ME-- ARMED OR NOT.

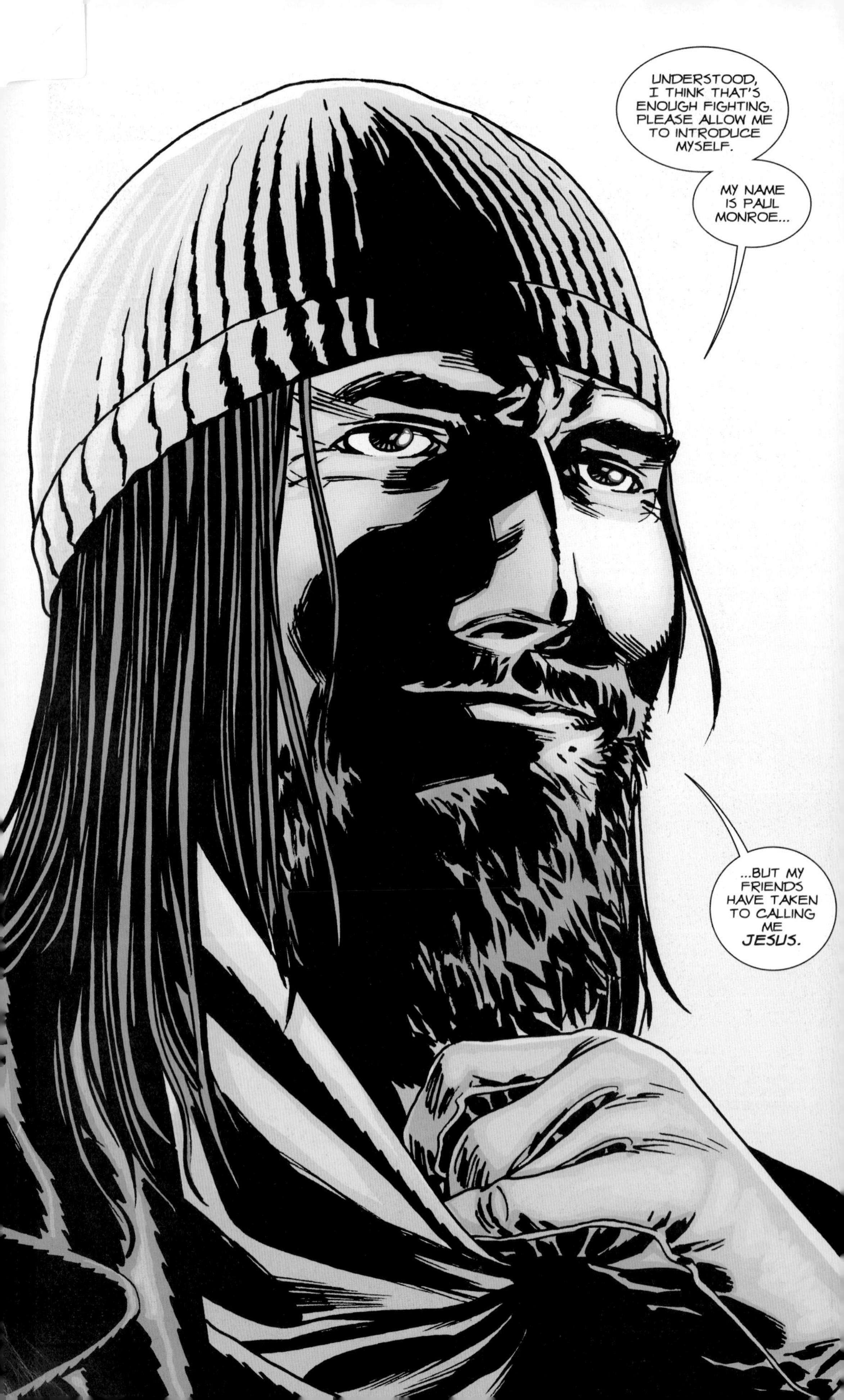
UNDERSTOOD, I THINK THAT'S ENOUGH FIGHTING. PLEASE ALLOW ME TO INTRODUCE MYSELF.
MY NAME IS PAUL MONROE...
...BUT MY FRIENDS HAVE TAKEN TO CALLING ME *JESUS*.

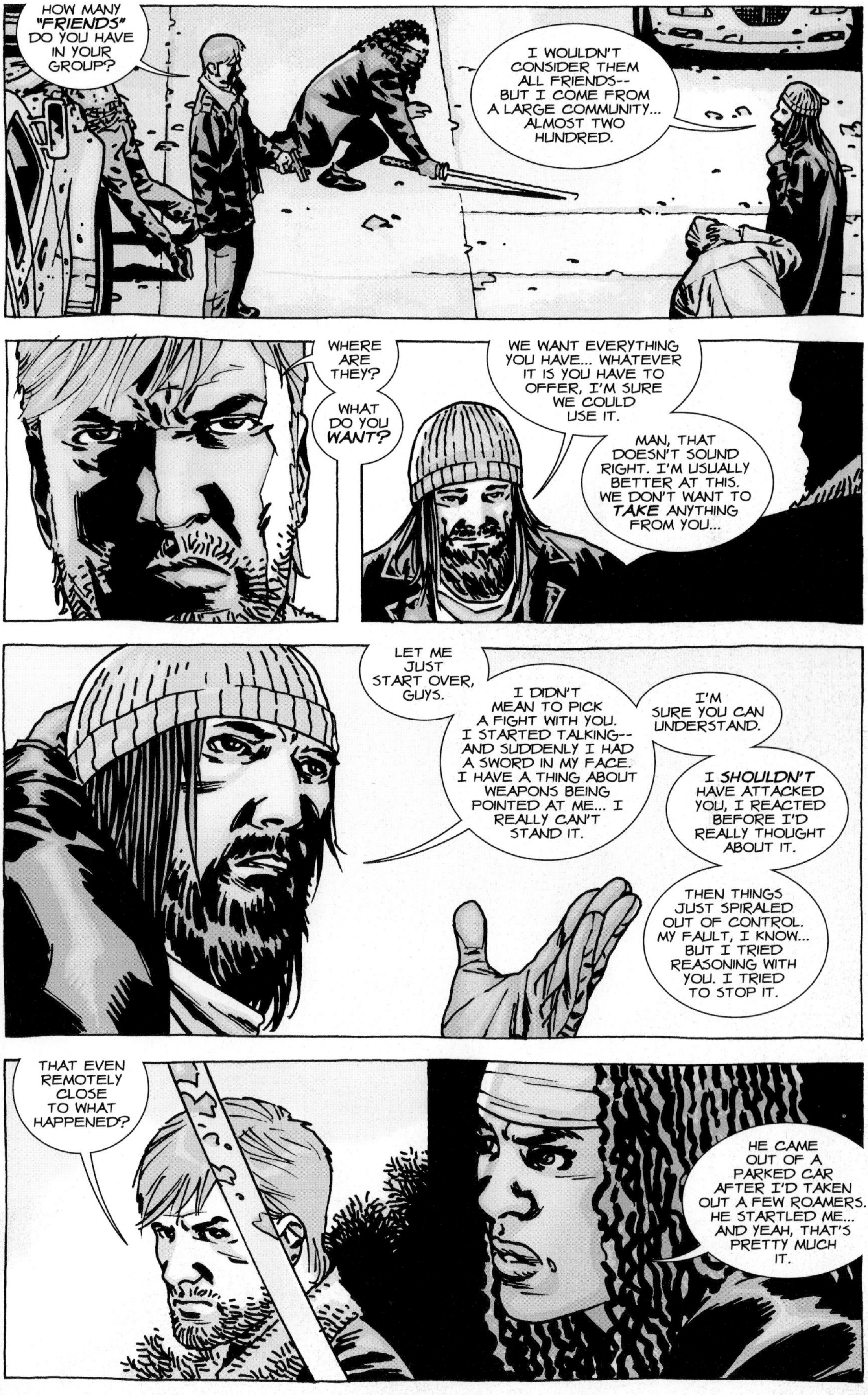
HOW MANY "FRIENDS" DO YOU HAVE IN YOUR GROUP?
I WOULDN'T CONSIDER THEM ALL FRIENDS-- BUT I COME FROM A LARGE COMMUNITY... ALMOST TWO HUNDRED.
WHERE ARE THEY?
WHAT DO YOU WANT?
WE WANT EVERYTHING YOU HAVE... WHATEVER IT IS YOU HAVE TO OFFER, I'M SURE WE COULD USE IT.
MAN, THAT DOESN'T SOUND RIGHT. I'M USUALLY BETTER AT THIS. WE DON'T WANT TO TAKE ANYTHING FROM YOU...
LET ME JUST START OVER, GUYS.
I DIDN'T MEAN TO PICK A FIGHT WITH YOU. I STARTED TALKING-- AND SUDDENLY I HAD A SWORD IN MY FACE. I HAVE A THING ABOUT WEAPONS BEING POINTED AT ME... I REALLY CAN'T STAND IT.
I'M SURE YOU CAN UNDERSTAND.
I SHOULDN'T HAVE ATTACKED YOU, I REACTED BEFORE I'D REALLY THOUGHT ABOUT IT.
THEN THINGS JUST SPIRALED OUT OF CONTROL. MY FAULT, I KNOW... BUT I TRIED REASONING WITH YOU. I TRIED TO STOP IT.
THAT EVEN REMOTELY CLOSE TO WHAT HAPPENED?
HE CAME OUT OF A PARKED CAR AFTER I'D TAKEN OUT A FEW ROAMERS. HE STARTLED ME... AND YEAH, THAT'S PRETTY MUCH IT.

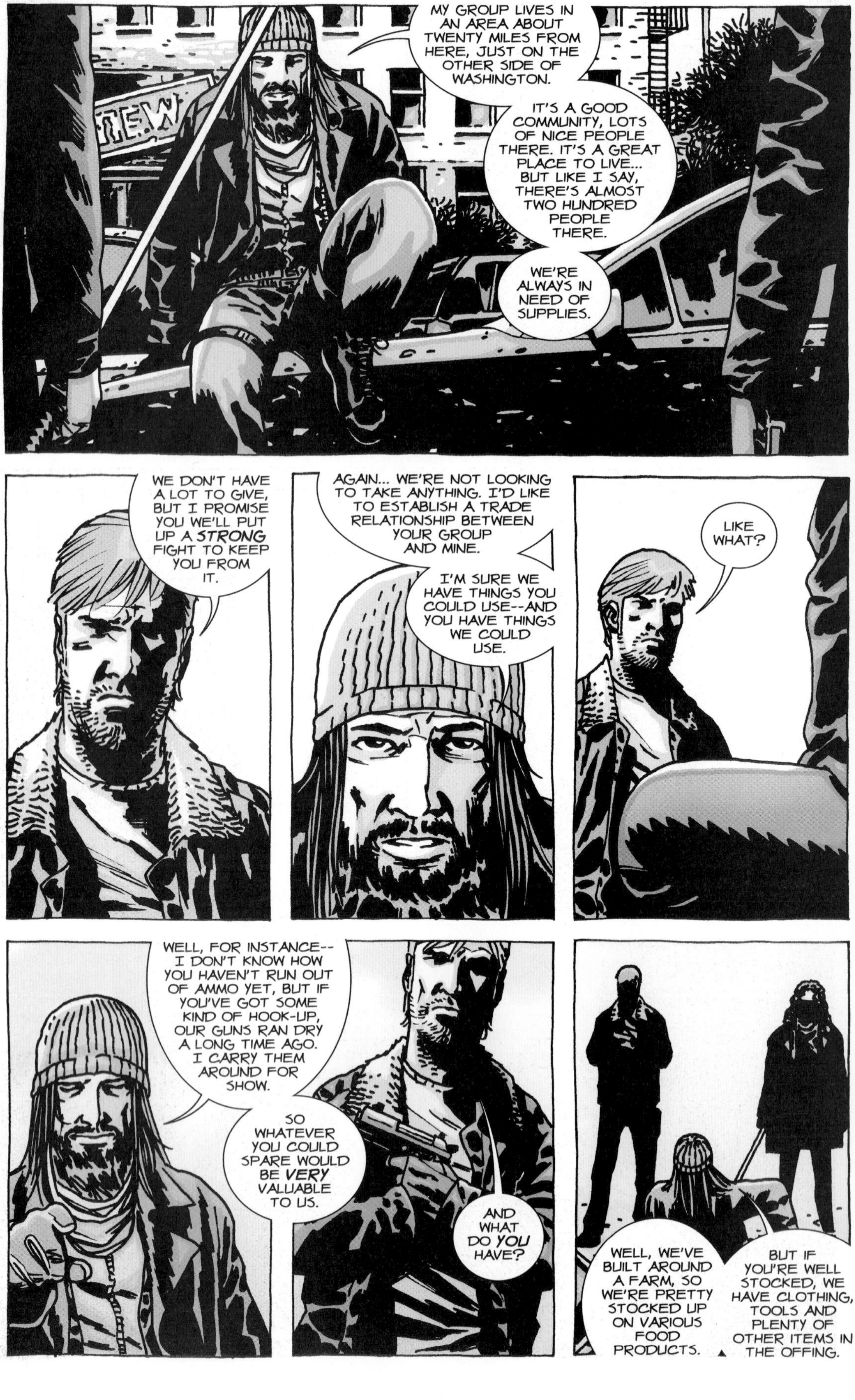
MY GROUP LIVES IN AN AREA ABOUT TWENTY MILES FROM HERE, JUST ON THE OTHER SIDE OF WASHINGTON.
IT'S A GOOD COMMUNITY, LOTS OF NICE PEOPLE THERE. IT'S A GREAT PLACE TO LIVE... BUT LIKE I SAY, THERE'S ALMOST TWO HUNDRED PEOPLE THERE.
WE'RE ALWAYS IN NEED OF SUPPLIES.
WE DON'T HAVE A LOT TO GIVE, BUT I PROMISE YOU WE'LL PUT UP A STRONG FIGHT TO KEEP YOU FROM IT.
AGAIN... WE'RE NOT LOOKING TO TAKE ANYTHING. I'D LIKE TO ESTABLISH A TRADE RELATIONSHIP BETWEEN YOUR GROUP AND MINE.
I'M SURE WE HAVE THINGS YOU COULD USE--AND YOU HAVE THINGS WE COULD USE.
LIKE WHAT?
WELL, FOR INSTANCE-- I DON'T KNOW HOW YOU HAVEN'T RUN OUT OF AMMO YET, BUT IF YOU'VE GOT SOME KIND OF HOOK-UP, OUR GUNS RAN DRY A LONG TIME AGO. I CARRY THEM AROUND FOR SHOW.
SO WHATEVER YOU COULD SPARE WOULD BE VERY VALUABLE TO US.
AND WHAT DO YOU HAVE?
WELL, WE'VE BUILT AROUND A FARM, SO WE'RE PRETTY STOCKED UP ON VARIOUS FOOD PRODUCTS.
BUT IF YOU'RE WELL STOCKED, WE HAVE CLOTHING, TOOLS AND PLENTY OF OTHER ITEMS IN THE OFFING.

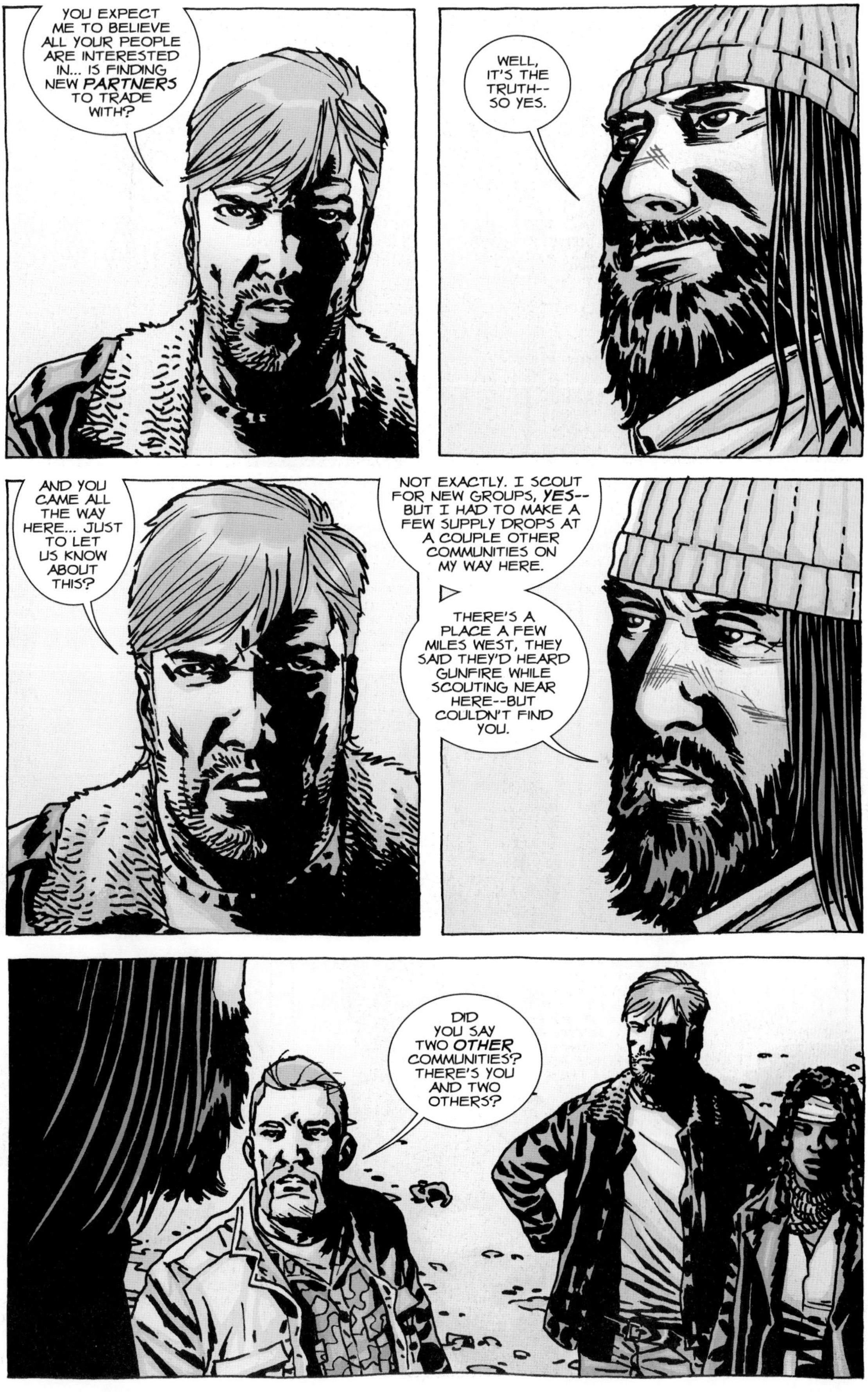
YOU EXPECT ME TO BELIEVE ALL YOUR PEOPLE ARE INTERESTED IN... IS FINDING NEW PARTNERS TO TRADE WITH?
WELL, IT'S THE TRUTH-- SO YES.
AND YOU CAME ALL THE WAY HERE... JUST TO LET US KNOW ABOUT THIS?
NOT EXACTLY. I SCOUT FOR NEW GROUPS, YES-- BUT I HAD TO MAKE A FEW SUPPLY DROPS AT A COUPLE OTHER COMMUNITIES ON MY WAY HERE.
THERE'S A PLACE A FEW MILES WEST, THEY SAID THEY'D HEARD GUNFIRE WHILE SCOUTING NEAR HERE--BUT COULDN'T FIND YOU.
DID YOU SAY TWO OTHER COMMUNITIES? THERE'S YOU AND TWO OTHERS?

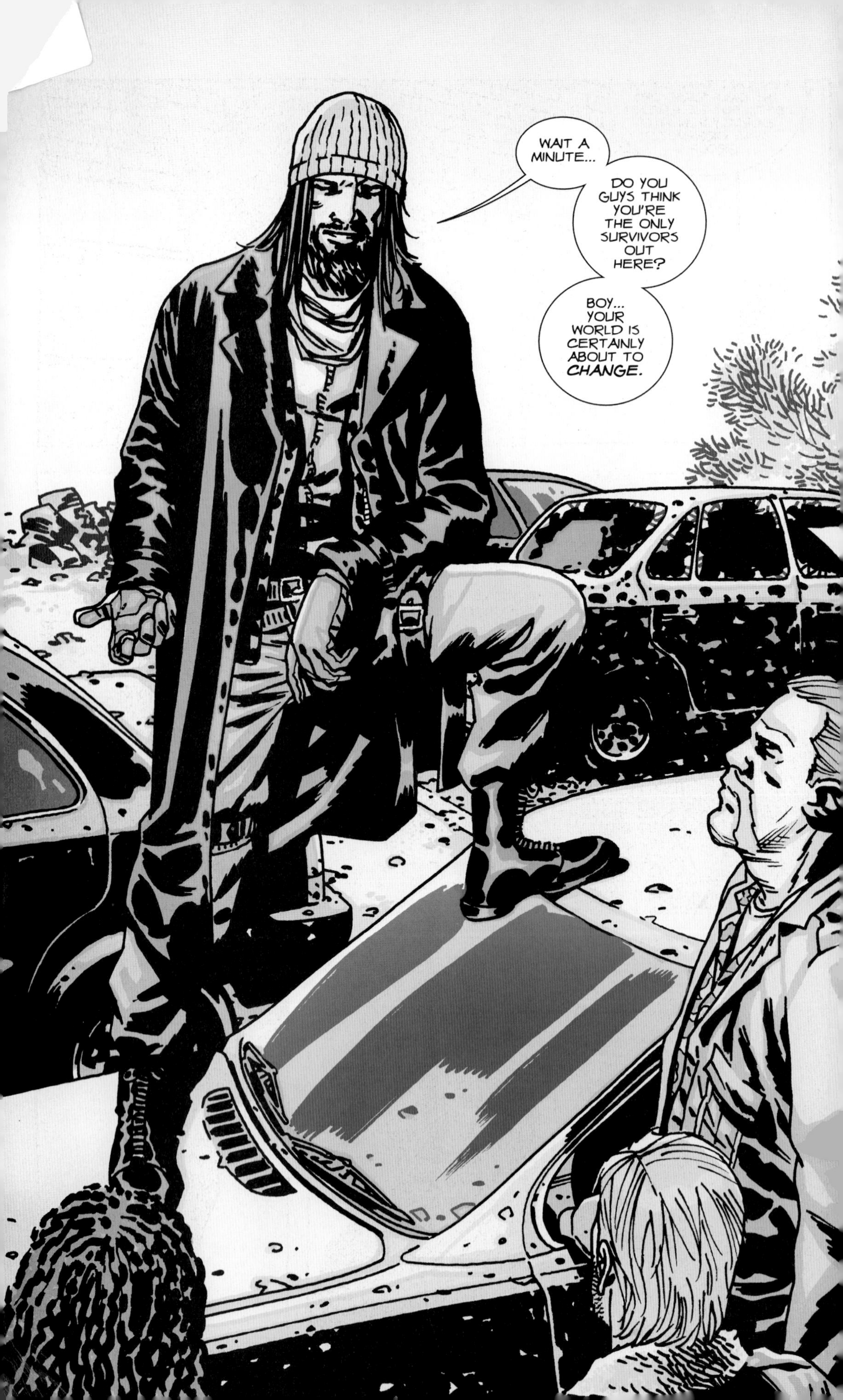
WAIT A MINUTE...
DO YOU GUYS THINK YOU'RE THE ONLY SURVIVORS OUT HERE?
BOY... YOUR WORLD IS CERTAINLY ABOUT TO *CHANGE.*

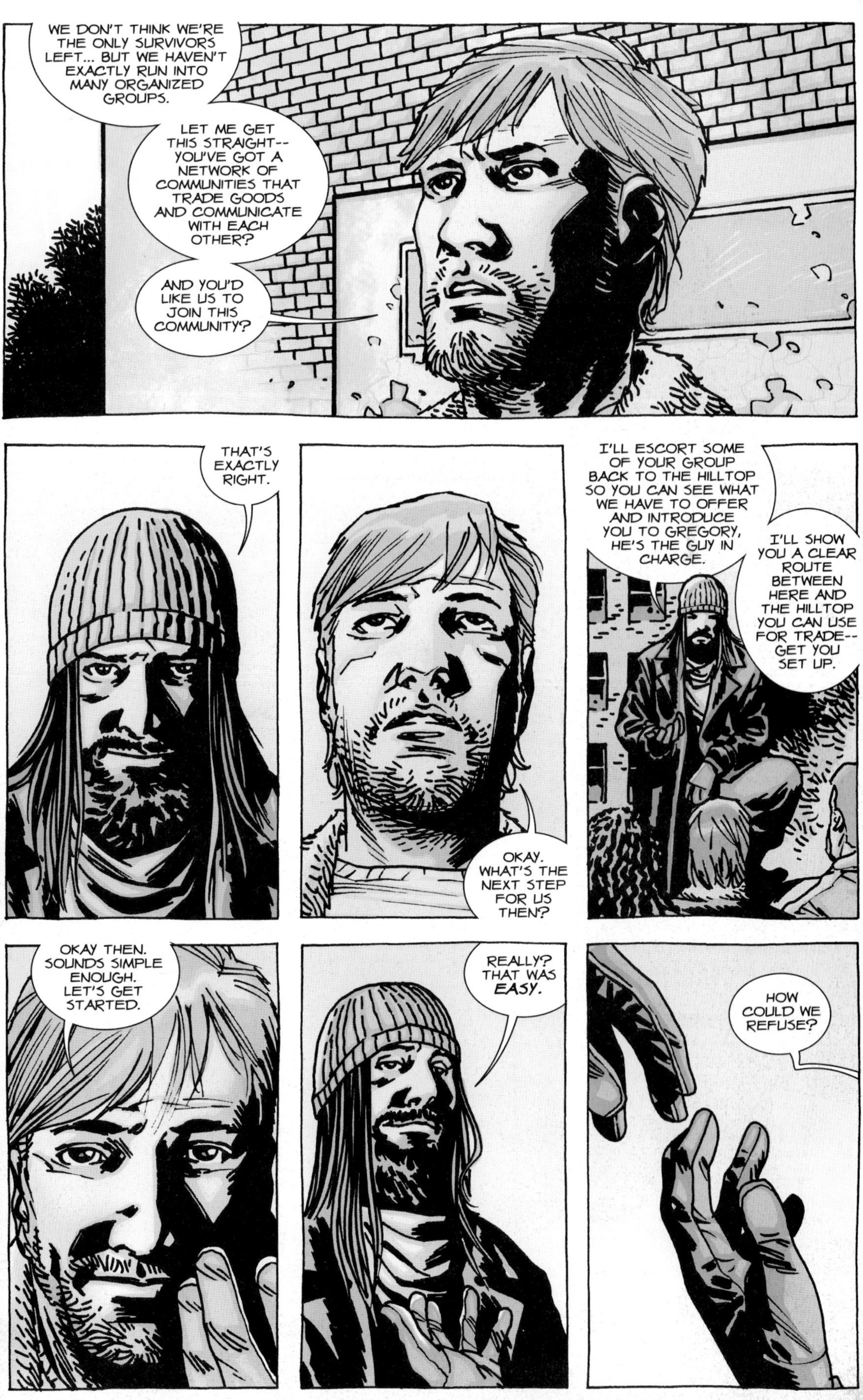
WE DON'T THINK WE'RE THE ONLY SURVIVORS LEFT... BUT WE HAVEN'T EXACTLY RUN INTO MANY ORGANIZED GROUPS.
LET ME GET THIS STRAIGHT-- YOU'VE GOT A NETWORK OF COMMUNITIES THAT TRADE GOODS AND COMMUNICATE WITH EACH OTHER?
AND YOU'D LIKE US TO JOIN THIS COMMUNITY?
THAT'S EXACTLY RIGHT.
OKAY. WHAT'S THE NEXT STEP FOR US THEN?
I'LL ESCORT SOME OF YOUR GROUP BACK TO THE HILLTOP SO YOU CAN SEE WHAT WE HAVE TO OFFER AND INTRODUCE YOU TO GREGORY, HE'S THE GUY IN CHARGE.
I'LL SHOW YOU A CLEAR ROUTE BETWEEN HERE AND THE HILLTOP YOU CAN USE FOR TRADE-- GET YOU SET UP.
OKAY THEN. SOUNDS SIMPLE ENOUGH. LET'S GET STARTED.
REALLY? THAT WAS *EASY.*
HOW COULD WE REFUSE?

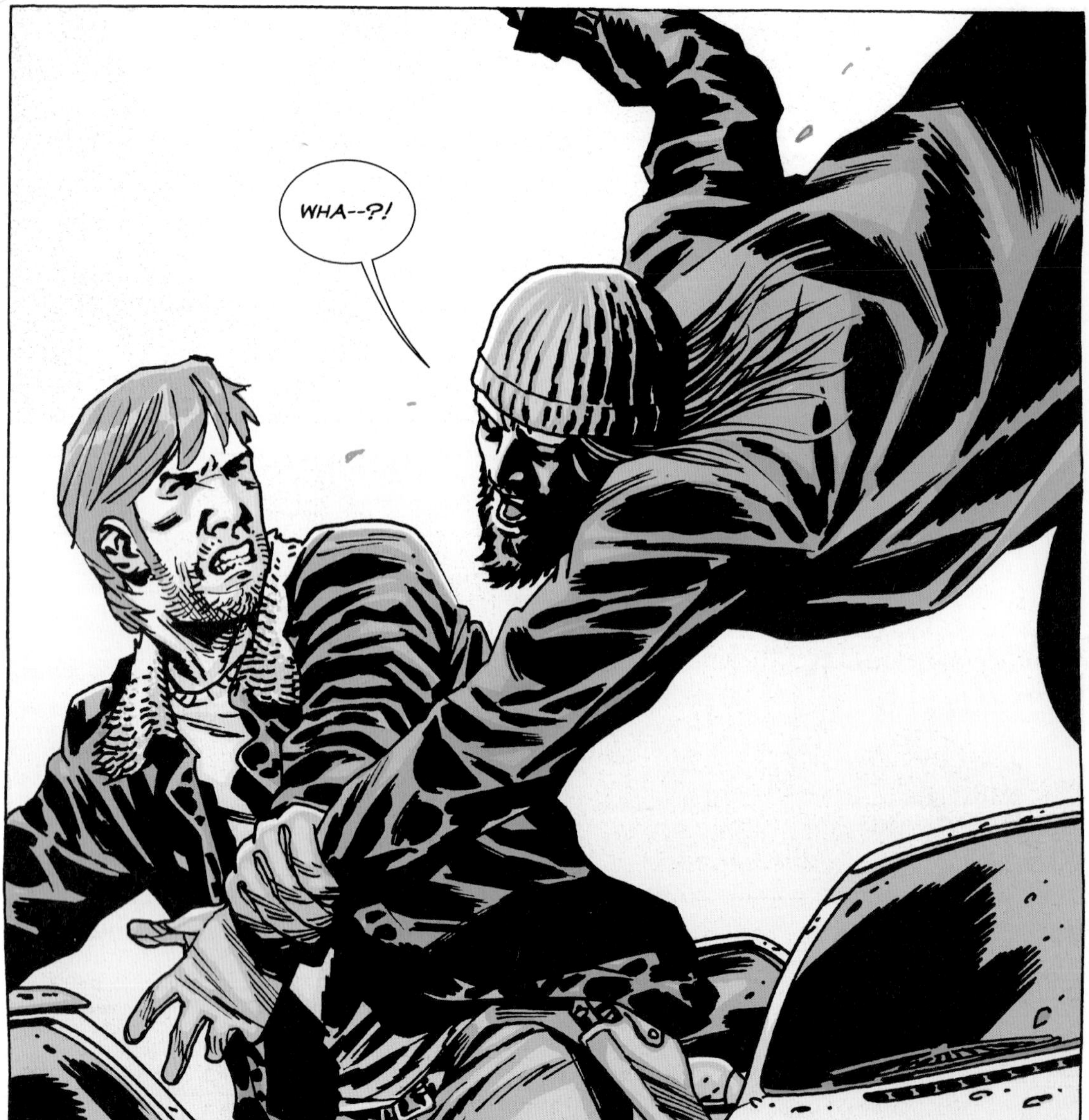
WHA--?!

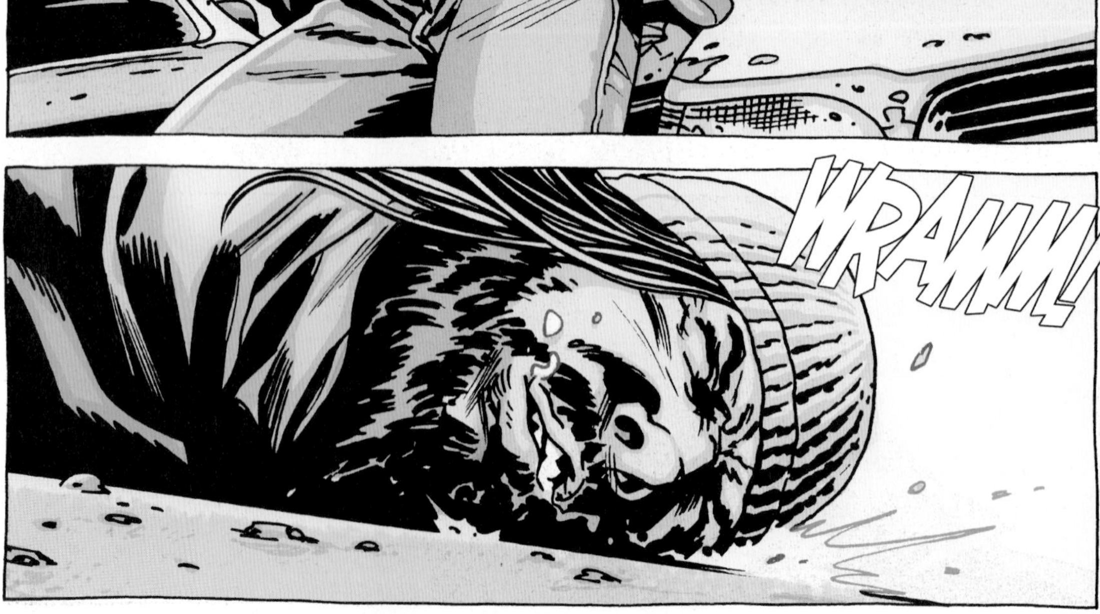
WRAMM!

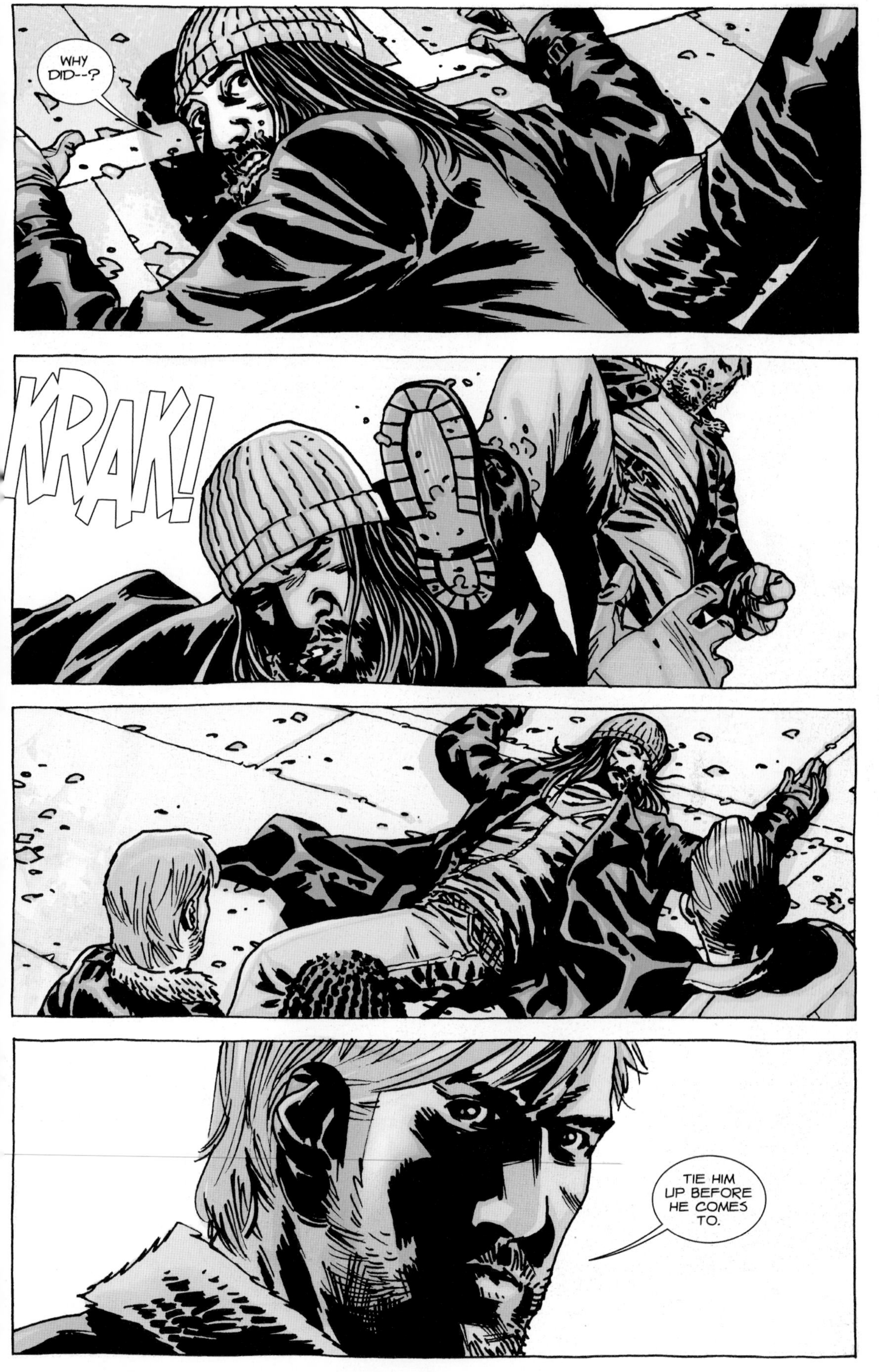
WHY DID--?
KRAK!
TIE HIM UP BEFORE HE COMES TO.

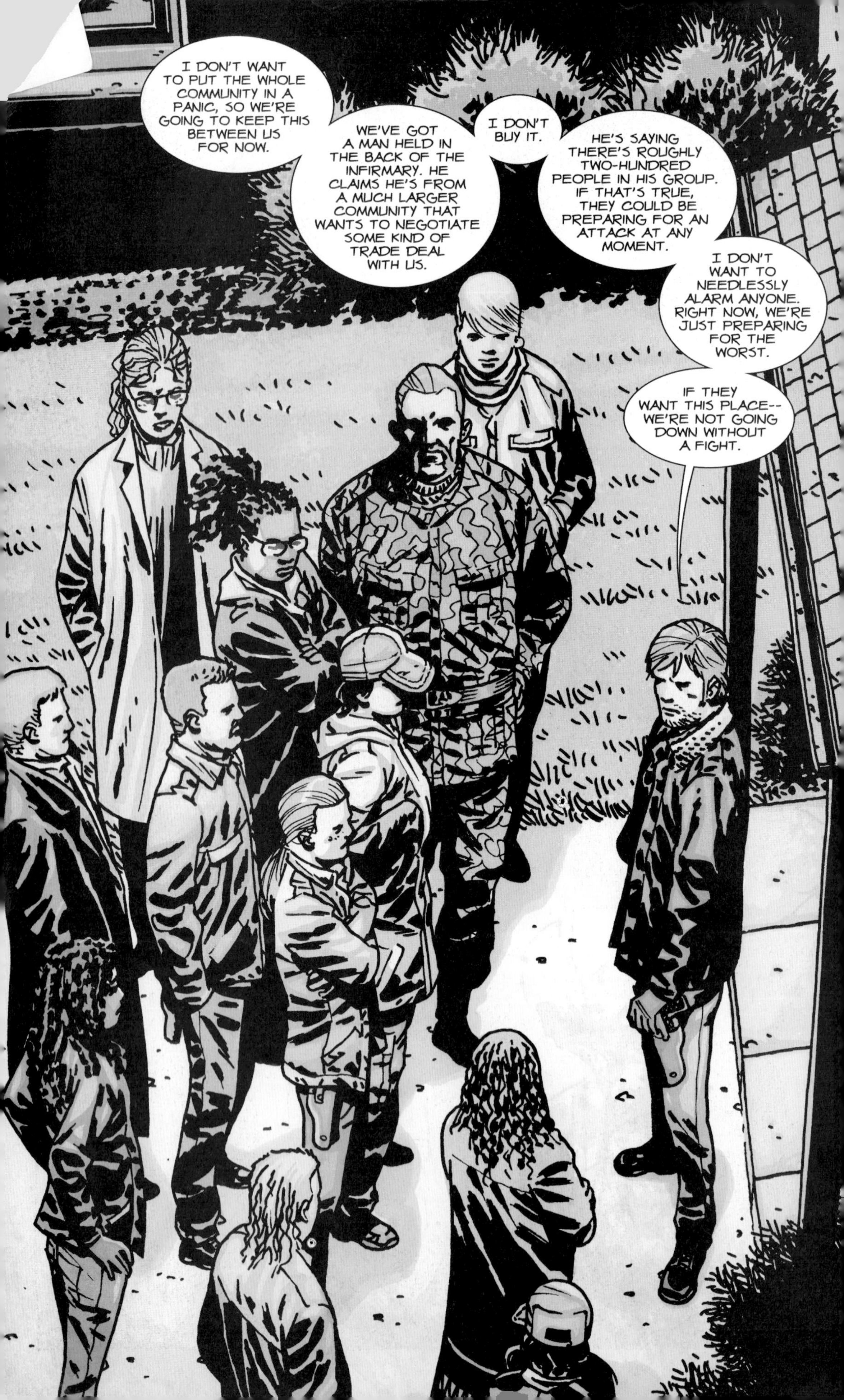
I DON'T WANT TO PUT THE WHOLE COMMUNITY IN A PANIC, SO WE'RE GOING TO KEEP THIS BETWEEN US FOR NOW.
WE'VE GOT A MAN HELD IN THE BACK OF THE INFIRMARY. HE CLAIMS HE'S FROM A MUCH LARGER COMMUNITY THAT WANTS TO NEGOTIATE SOME KIND OF TRADE DEAL WITH US.
I DON'T BUY IT.
HE'S SAYING THERE'S ROUGHLY TWO-HUNDRED PEOPLE IN HIS GROUP. IF THAT'S TRUE, THEY COULD BE PREPARING FOR AN ATTACK AT ANY MOMENT.
I DON'T WANT TO NEEDLESSLY ALARM ANYONE. RIGHT NOW, WE'RE JUST PREPARING FOR THE WORST.
IF THEY WANT THIS PLACE-- WE'RE NOT GOING DOWN WITHOUT A FIGHT.

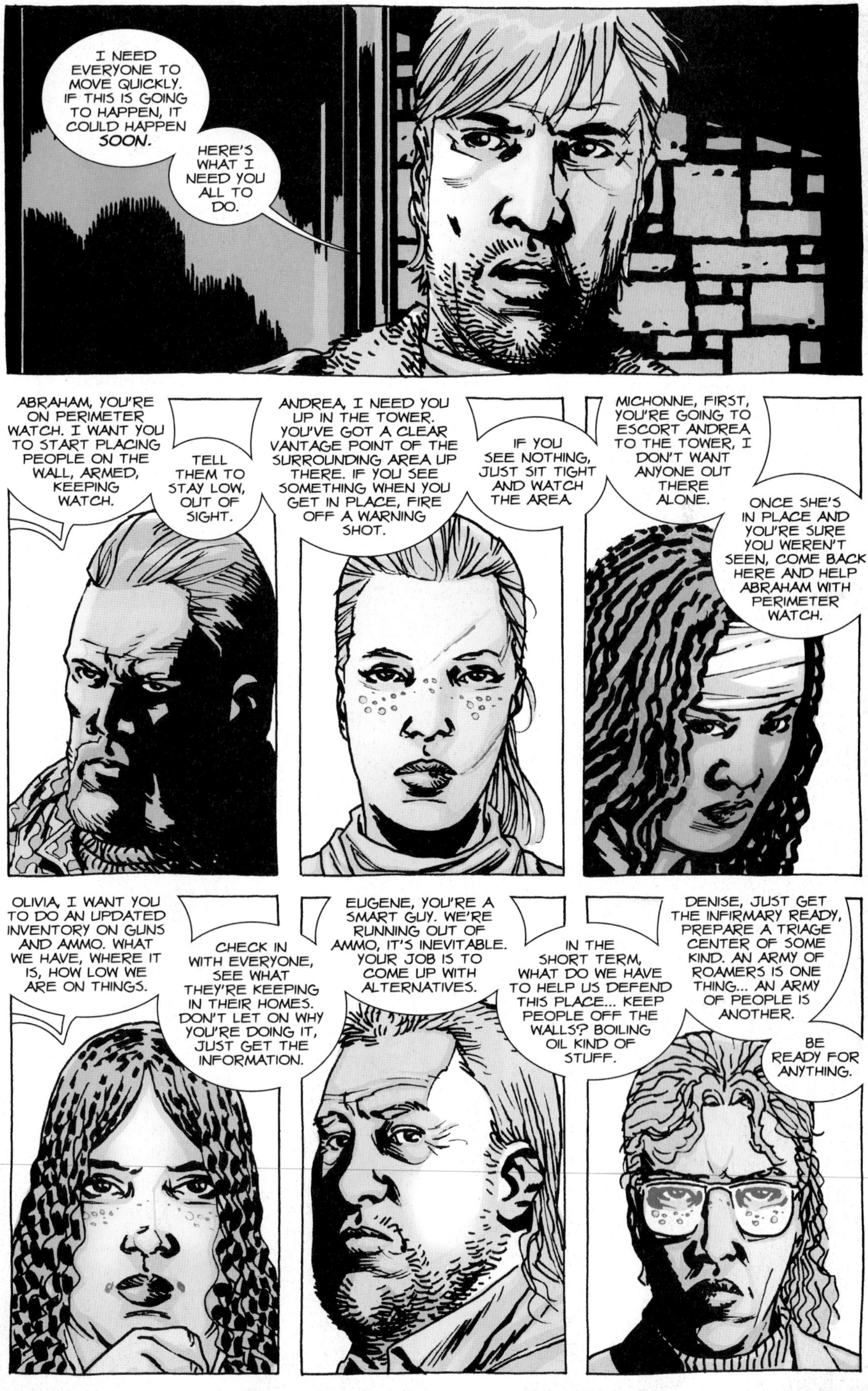

I NEED EVERYONE TO MOVE QUICKLY. IF THIS IS GOING TO HAPPEN, IT COULD HAPPEN **SOON.**
HERE'S WHAT I NEED YOU ALL TO DO.
ABRAHAM, YOU'RE ON PERIMETER WATCH. I WANT YOU TO START PLACING PEOPLE ON THE WALL, ARMED, KEEPING WATCH.
TELL THEM TO STAY LOW, OUT OF SIGHT.
ANDREA, I NEED YOU UP IN THE TOWER. YOU'VE GOT A CLEAR VANTAGE POINT OF THE SURROUNDING AREA UP THERE. IF YOU SEE SOMETHING WHEN YOU GET IN PLACE, FIRE OFF A WARNING SHOT.
IF YOU SEE NOTHING, JUST SIT TIGHT AND WATCH THE AREA.
MICHONNE, FIRST, YOU'RE GOING TO ESCORT ANDREA TO THE TOWER, I DON'T WANT ANYONE OUT THERE ALONE.
ONCE SHE'S IN PLACE AND YOU'RE SURE YOU WEREN'T SEEN, COME BACK HERE AND HELP ABRAHAM WITH PERIMETER WATCH.
OLIVIA, I WANT YOU TO DO AN UPDATED INVENTORY ON GUNS AND AMMO. WHAT WE HAVE, WHERE IT IS, HOW LOW WE ARE ON THINGS.
CHECK IN WITH EVERYONE, SEE WHAT THEY'RE KEEPING IN THEIR HOMES. DON'T LET ON WHY YOU'RE DOING IT, JUST GET THE INFORMATION.
EUGENE, YOU'RE A SMART GUY. WE'RE RUNNING OUT OF AMMO, IT'S INEVITABLE. YOUR JOB IS TO COME UP WITH ALTERNATIVES.
IN THE SHORT TERM, WHAT DO WE HAVE TO HELP US DEFEND THIS PLACE... KEEP PEOPLE OFF THE WALLS? BOILING OIL KIND OF STUFF.
DENISE, JUST GET THE INFIRMARY READY, PREPARE A TRIAGE CENTER OF SOME KIND. AN ARMY OF ROAMERS IS ONE THING... AN ARMY OF PEOPLE IS ANOTHER.
BE READY FOR ANYTHING.

I DID AN INVENTORY NOT TOO LONG AGO ON OUR AMMUNITION. WE WERE RUNNING LOW THEN. WE FOUND SOME WHEN THE GROUP WAS OUT LAST WEEK, BUT...

WE JUST DON'T HAVE ENOUGH TO HOLD OFF ANY KIND OF ASSAULT.

I KNOW.

YOU LET ME WORRY ABOUT THAT. YOU JUST FIND OUT *EXACTLY* HOW DIRE THINGS ARE.

I'M ON TOP OF IT.

RICK, JUST A MOMENT, PLEASE.

YEAH? YOU ALREADY GOT SOMETHING FOR ME?

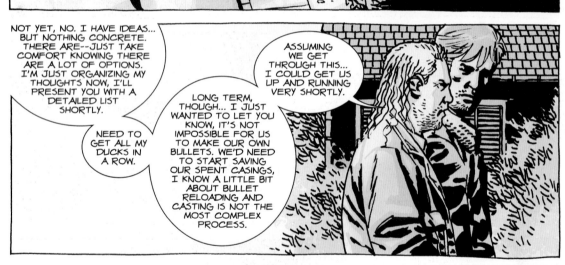

NOT YET, NO. I HAVE IDEAS... BUT NOTHING CONCRETE. THERE ARE--JUST TAKE COMFORT KNOWING THERE ARE A LOT OF OPTIONS. I'M JUST ORGANIZING MY THOUGHTS NOW, I'LL PRESENT YOU WITH A DETAILED LIST SHORTLY.

NEED TO GET ALL MY DUCKS IN A ROW.

ASSUMING WE GET THROUGH THIS... I COULD GET US UP AND RUNNING VERY SHORTLY.

LONG TERM, THOUGH... I JUST WANTED TO LET YOU KNOW, IT'S NOT IMPOSSIBLE FOR US TO MAKE OUR OWN BULLETS. WE'D NEED TO START SAVING OUR SPENT CASINGS, I KNOW A LITTLE BIT ABOUT BULLET RELOADING AND CASTING IS NOT THE MOST COMPLEX PROCESS.

BEST NEWS I'VE HEARD ALL DAY. THAT WOULD CERTAINLY FIX A FEW OF OUR PROBLEMS.

I'M LOOKING FORWARD TO HEARING MORE WHEN YOU'RE READY.

THANKS.

IT'LL FEEL GOOD... TO BE PULLING MY WEIGHT AROUND HERE.

YEAH.

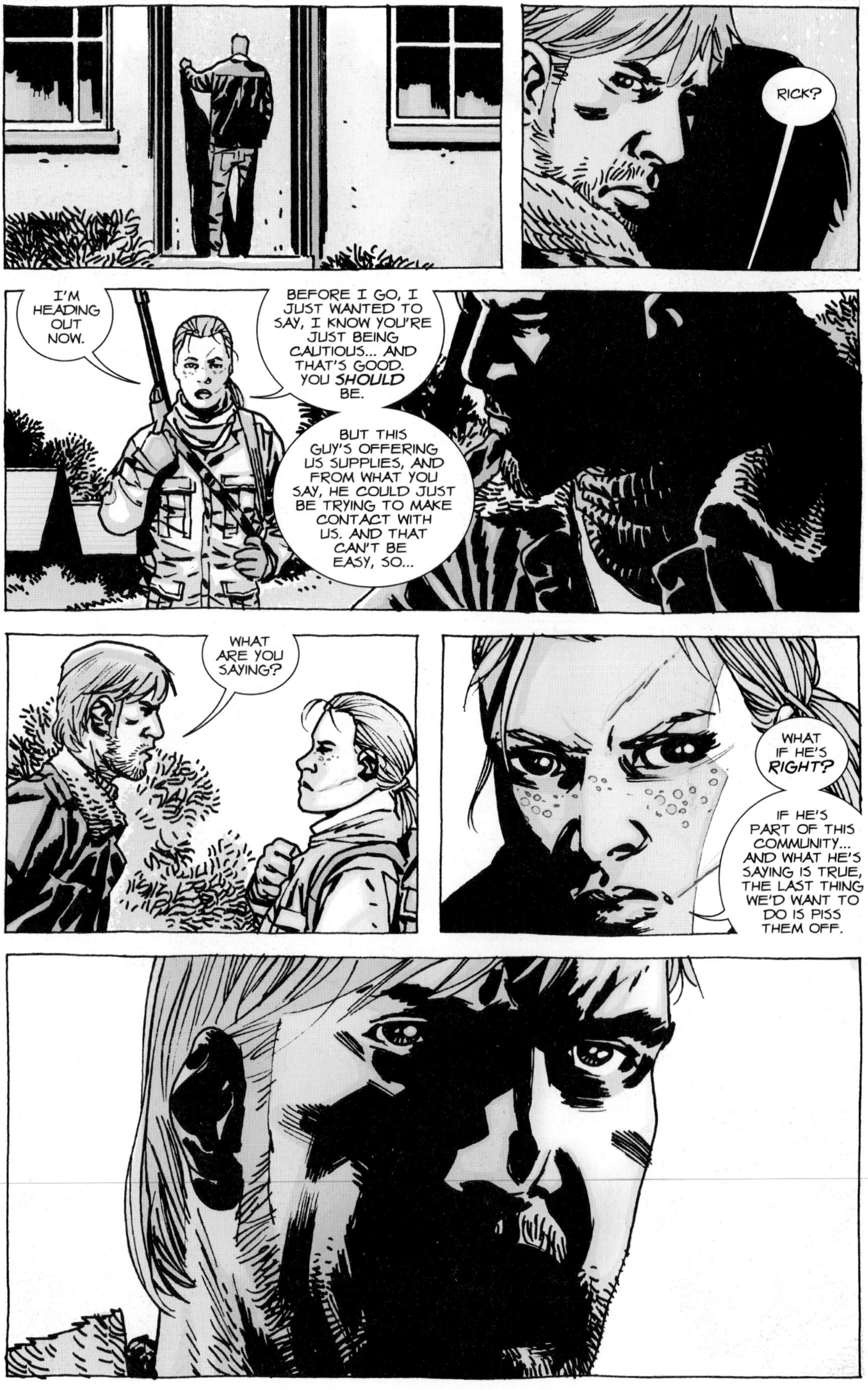
RICK?
I'M HEADING OUT NOW.
BEFORE I GO, I JUST WANTED TO SAY, I KNOW YOU'RE JUST BEING CAUTIOUS... AND THAT'S GOOD. YOU SHOULD BE.
BUT THIS GUY'S OFFERING US SUPPLIES, AND FROM WHAT YOU SAY, HE COULD JUST BE TRYING TO MAKE CONTACT WITH US. AND THAT CAN'T BE EASY, SO...
WHAT ARE YOU SAYING?
WHAT IF HE'S RIGHT?
IF HE'S PART OF THIS COMMUNITY... AND WHAT HE'S SAYING IS TRUE, THE LAST THING WE'D WANT TO DO IS PISS THEM OFF.

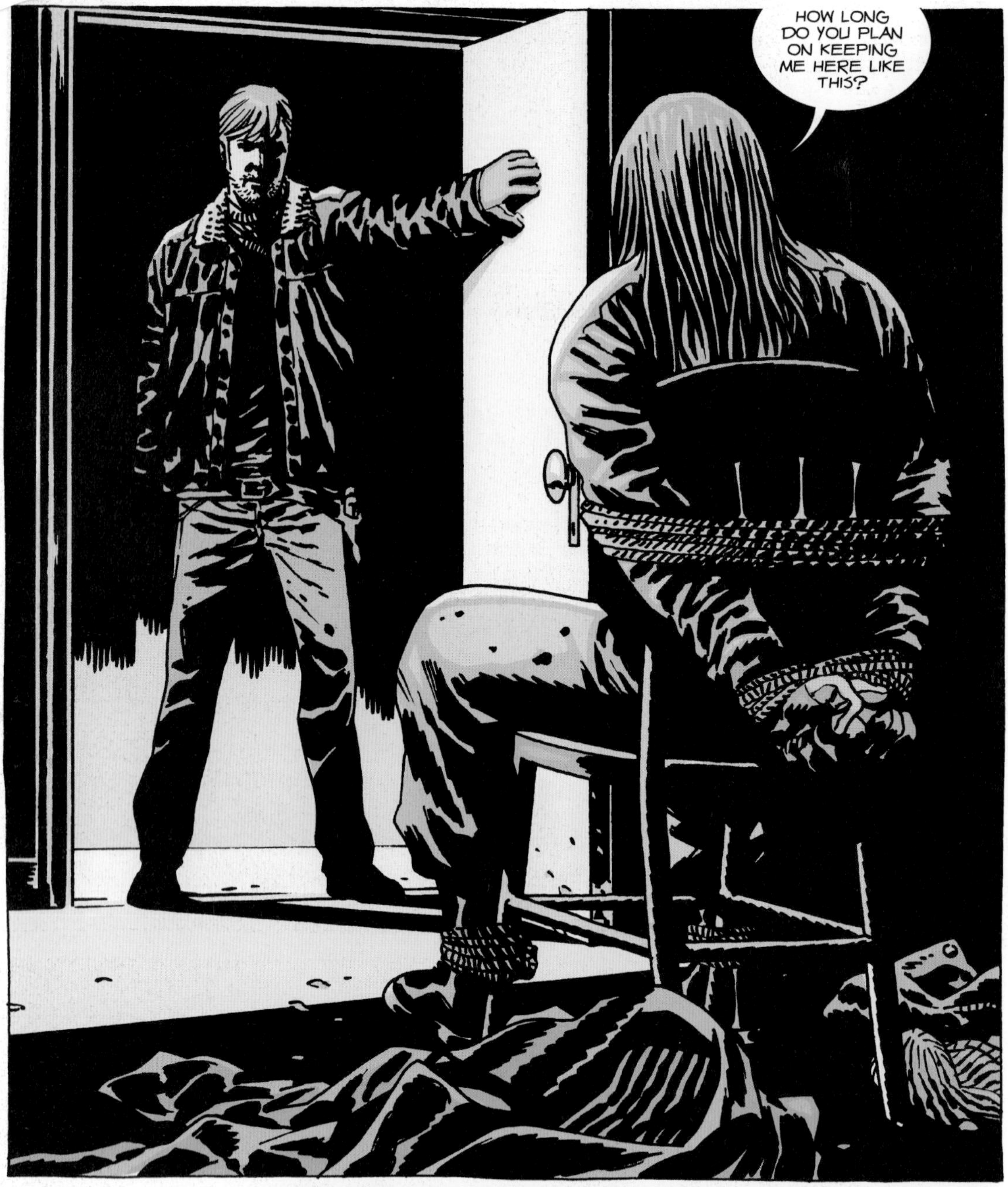
HOW LONG DO YOU PLAN ON KEEPING ME HERE LIKE THIS?
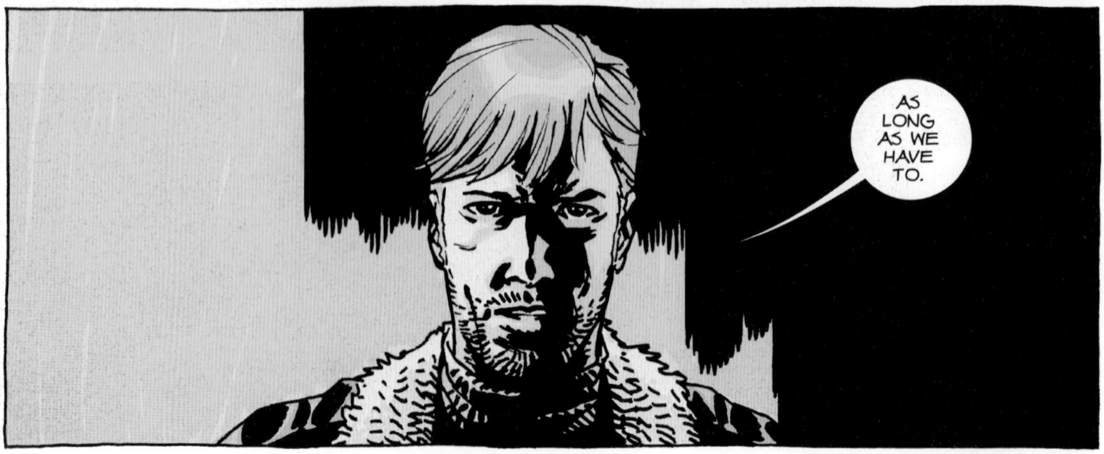
AS LONG AS WE HAVE TO.

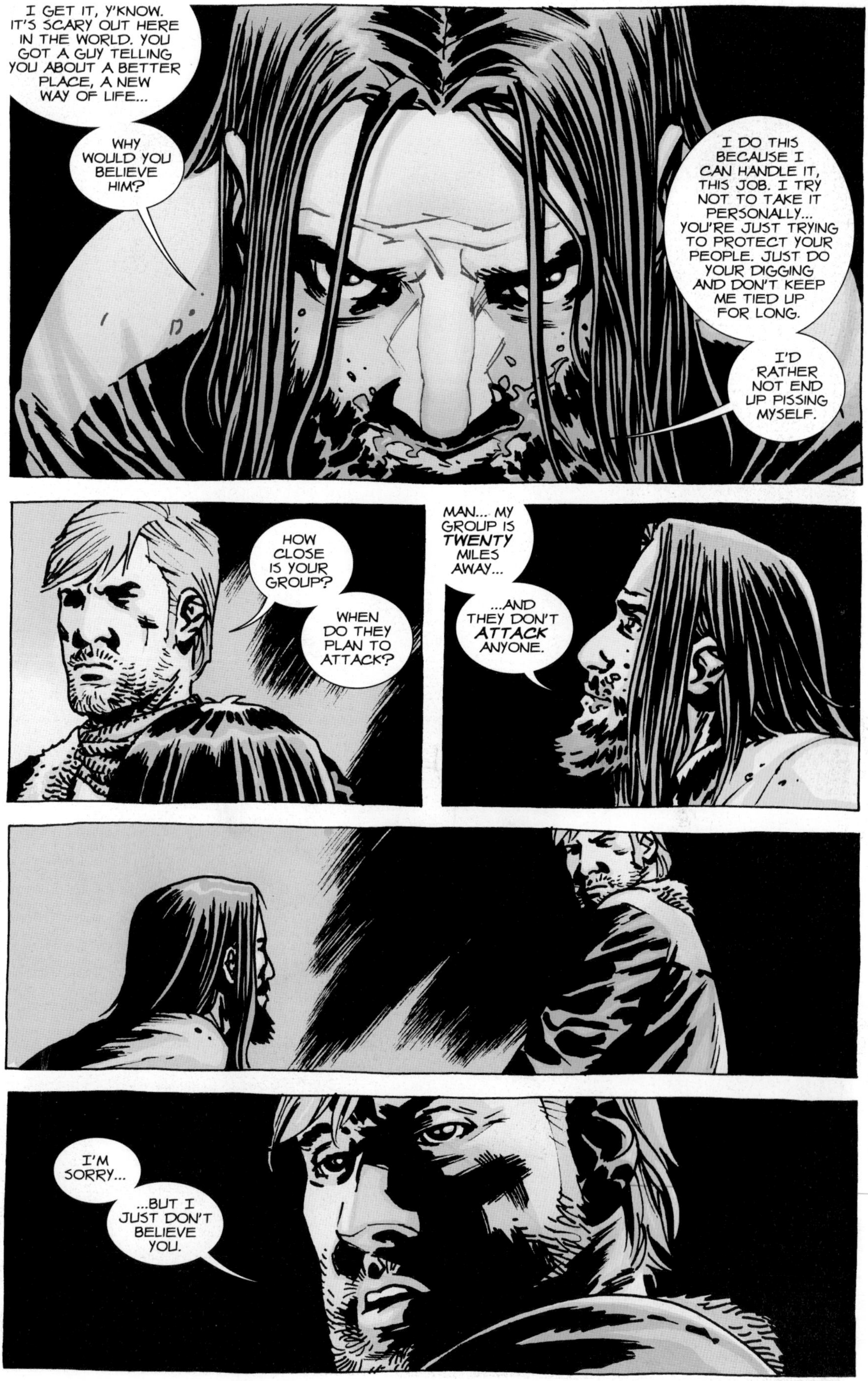
I GET IT, Y'KNOW. IT'S SCARY OUT HERE IN THE WORLD. YOU GOT A GUY TELLING YOU ABOUT A BETTER PLACE, A NEW WAY OF LIFE...
WHY WOULD YOU BELIEVE HIM?
I DO THIS BECAUSE I CAN HANDLE IT, THIS JOB. I TRY NOT TO TAKE IT PERSONALLY... YOU'RE JUST TRYING TO PROTECT YOUR PEOPLE. JUST DO YOUR DIGGING AND DON'T KEEP ME TIED UP FOR LONG.
I'D RATHER NOT END UP PISSING MYSELF.
HOW CLOSE IS YOUR GROUP?
WHEN DO THEY PLAN TO ATTACK?
MAN... MY GROUP IS *TWENTY* MILES AWAY...
...AND THEY DON'T *ATTACK* ANYONE.
I'M SORRY...
...BUT I JUST DON'T BELIEVE YOU.

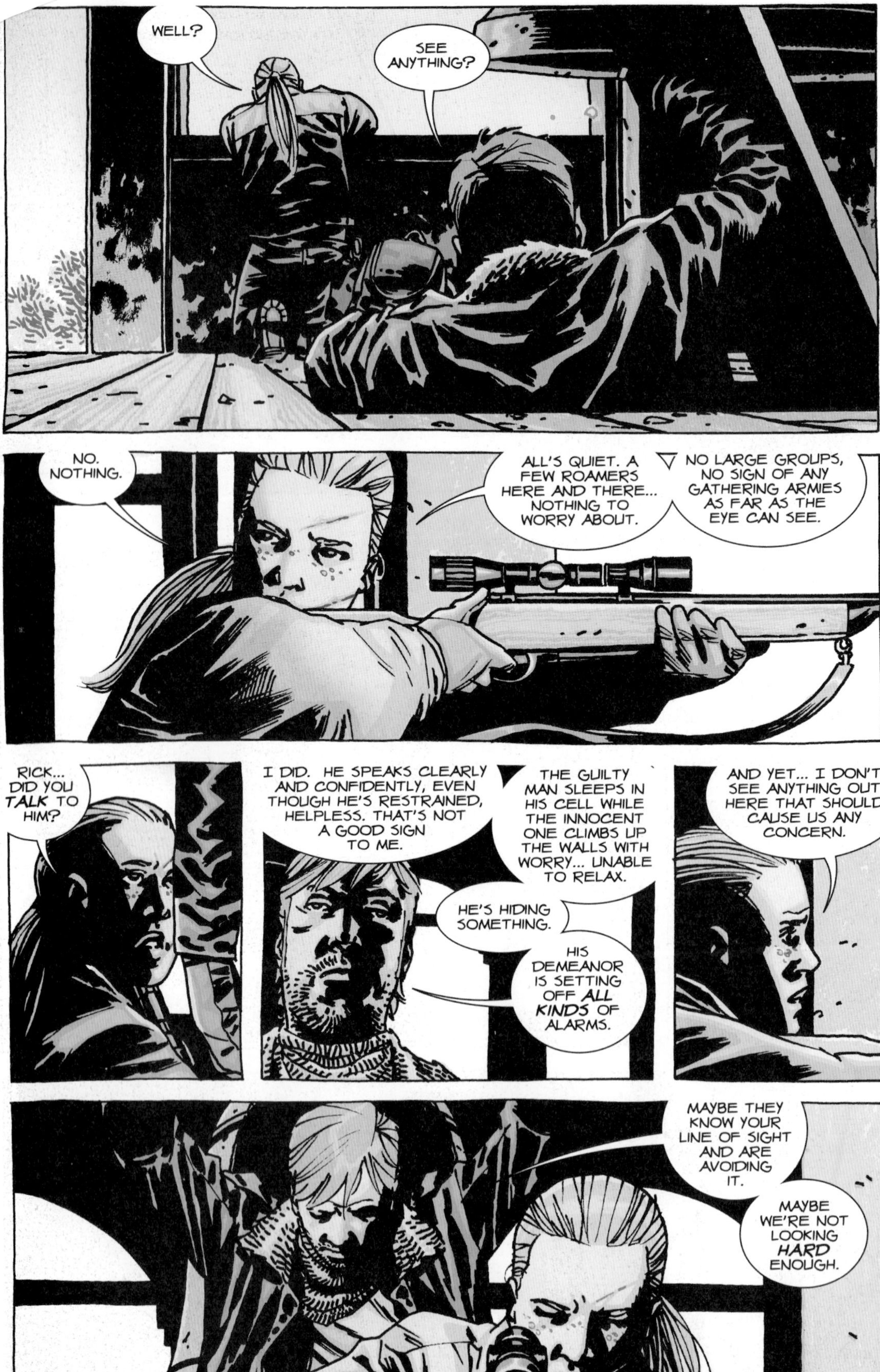
WELL?
SEE ANYTHING?
NO. NOTHING.
ALL'S QUIET. A FEW ROAMERS HERE AND THERE... NOTHING TO WORRY ABOUT.
NO LARGE GROUPS, NO SIGN OF ANY GATHERING ARMIES AS FAR AS THE EYE CAN SEE.
RICK... DID YOU *TALK* TO HIM?
I DID. HE SPEAKS CLEARLY AND CONFIDENTLY, EVEN THOUGH HE'S RESTRAINED, HELPLESS. THAT'S NOT A GOOD SIGN TO ME.
THE GUILTY MAN SLEEPS IN HIS CELL WHILE THE INNOCENT ONE CLIMBS UP THE WALLS WITH WORRY... UNABLE TO RELAX.
HE'S HIDING SOMETHING.
HIS DEMEANOR IS SETTING OFF *ALL KINDS* OF ALARMS.
AND YET... I DON'T SEE ANYTHING OUT HERE THAT SHOULD CAUSE US ANY CONCERN.
MAYBE THEY KNOW YOUR LINE OF SIGHT AND ARE AVOIDING IT.
MAYBE WE'RE NOT LOOKING *HARD* ENOUGH.

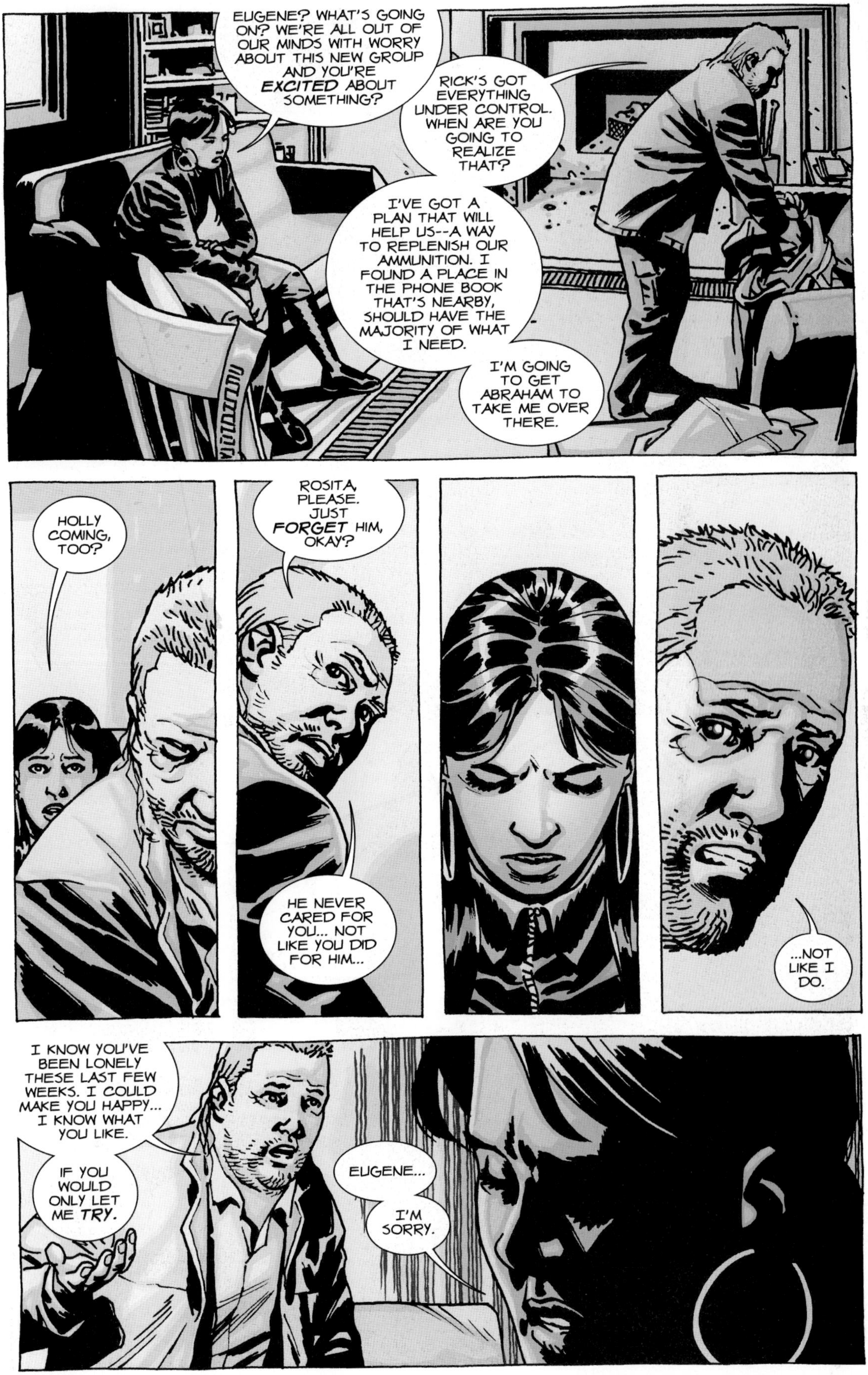
EUGENE? WHAT'S GOING ON? WE'RE ALL OUT OF OUR MINDS WITH WORRY ABOUT THIS NEW GROUP AND YOU'RE EXCITED ABOUT SOMETHING?
RICK'S GOT EVERYTHING UNDER CONTROL. WHEN ARE YOU GOING TO REALIZE THAT?
I'VE GOT A PLAN THAT WILL HELP US--A WAY TO REPLENISH OUR AMMUNITION. I FOUND A PLACE IN THE PHONE BOOK THAT'S NEARBY, SHOULD HAVE THE MAJORITY OF WHAT I NEED.
I'M GOING TO GET ABRAHAM TO TAKE ME OVER THERE.
HOLLY COMING, TOO?
ROSITA, PLEASE. JUST FORGET HIM, OKAY?
HE NEVER CARED FOR YOU... NOT LIKE YOU DID FOR HIM...
...NOT LIKE I DO.
I KNOW YOU'VE BEEN LONELY THESE LAST FEW WEEKS. I COULD MAKE YOU HAPPY... I KNOW WHAT YOU LIKE.
IF YOU WOULD ONLY LET ME TRY.
EUGENE...
I'M SORRY.

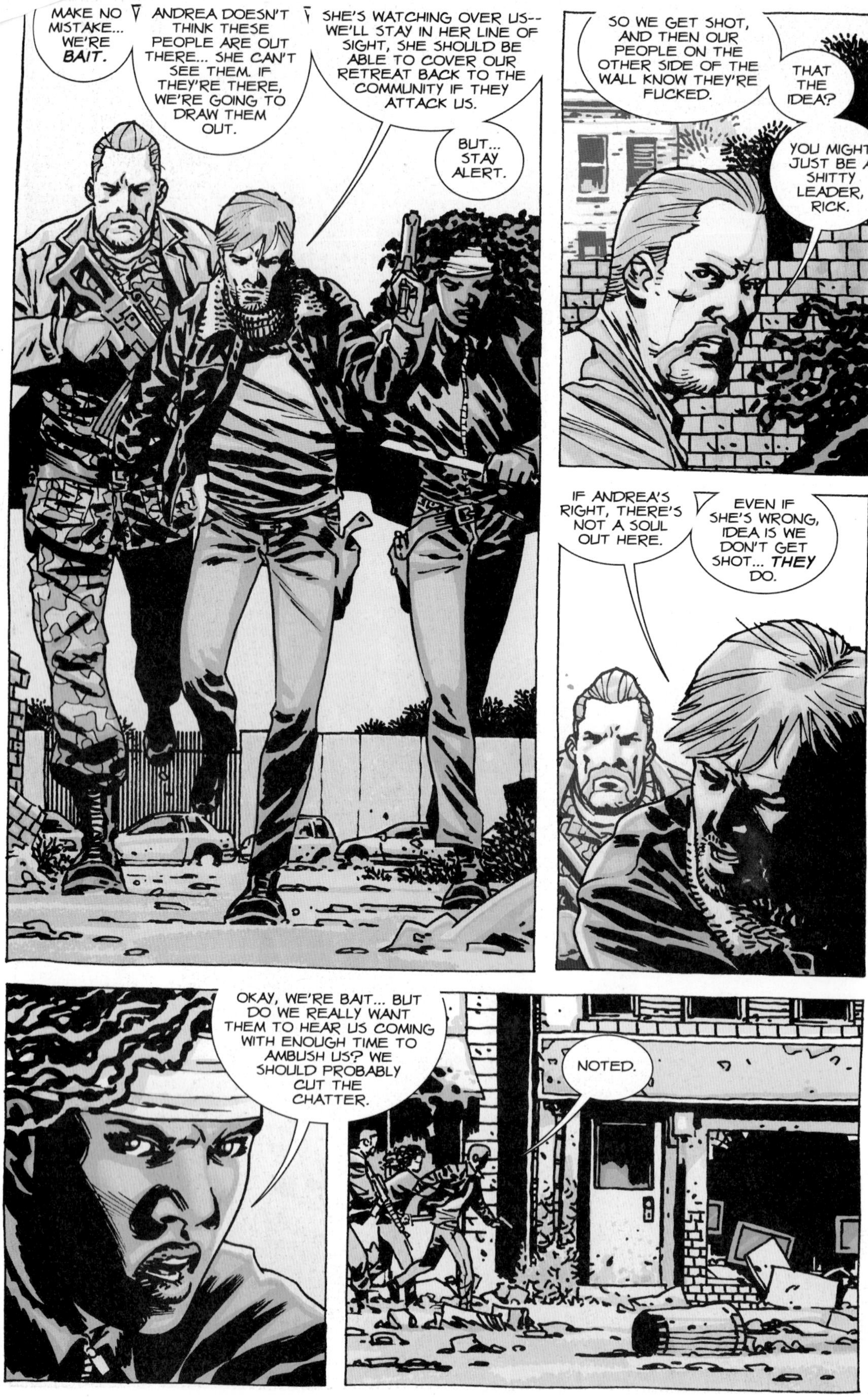
MAKE NO MISTAKE... WE'RE *BAIT.*
ANDREA DOESN'T THINK THESE PEOPLE ARE OUT THERE... SHE *CAN'T* SEE THEM. IF THEY'RE THERE, WE'RE GOING TO DRAW THEM OUT.
SHE'S WATCHING OVER US-- WE'LL STAY IN HER LINE OF SIGHT, SHE SHOULD BE ABLE TO COVER OUR RETREAT BACK TO THE COMMUNITY IF THEY ATTACK US.
BUT... STAY ALERT.
SO WE GET SHOT, AND THEN OUR PEOPLE ON THE OTHER SIDE OF THE WALL KNOW THEY'RE FUCKED.
THAT THE IDEA?
YOU MIGHT JUST BE A SHITTY LEADER, RICK.
IF ANDREA'S RIGHT, THERE'S NOT A SOUL OUT HERE.
EVEN IF SHE'S WRONG, IDEA IS WE DON'T GET SHOT... *THEY* DO.
OKAY, WE'RE BAIT... BUT DO WE REALLY WANT THEM TO HEAR US COMING WITH ENOUGH TIME TO AMBUSH US? WE SHOULD PROBABLY CUT THE CHATTER.
NOTED.

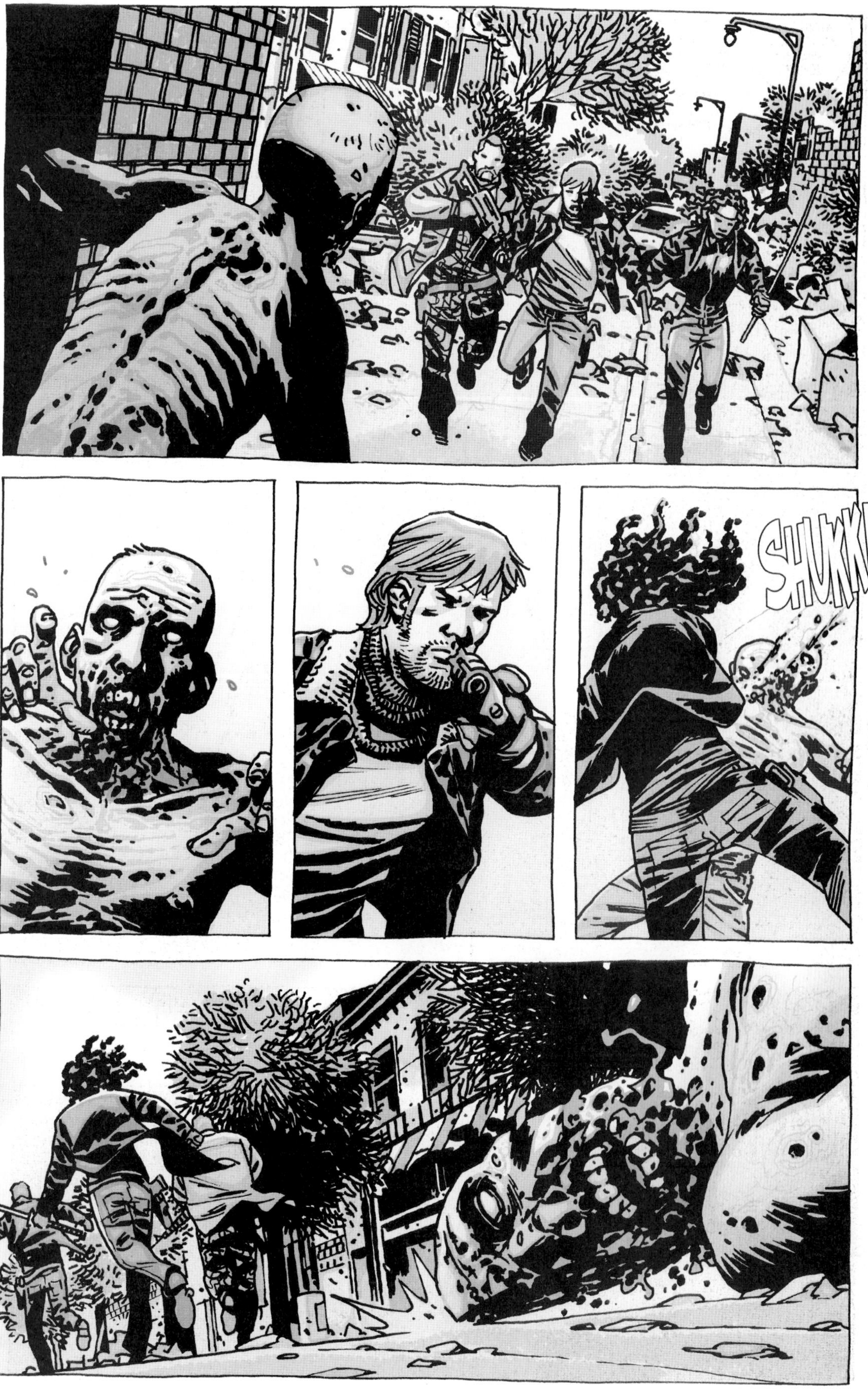
SHUKK!

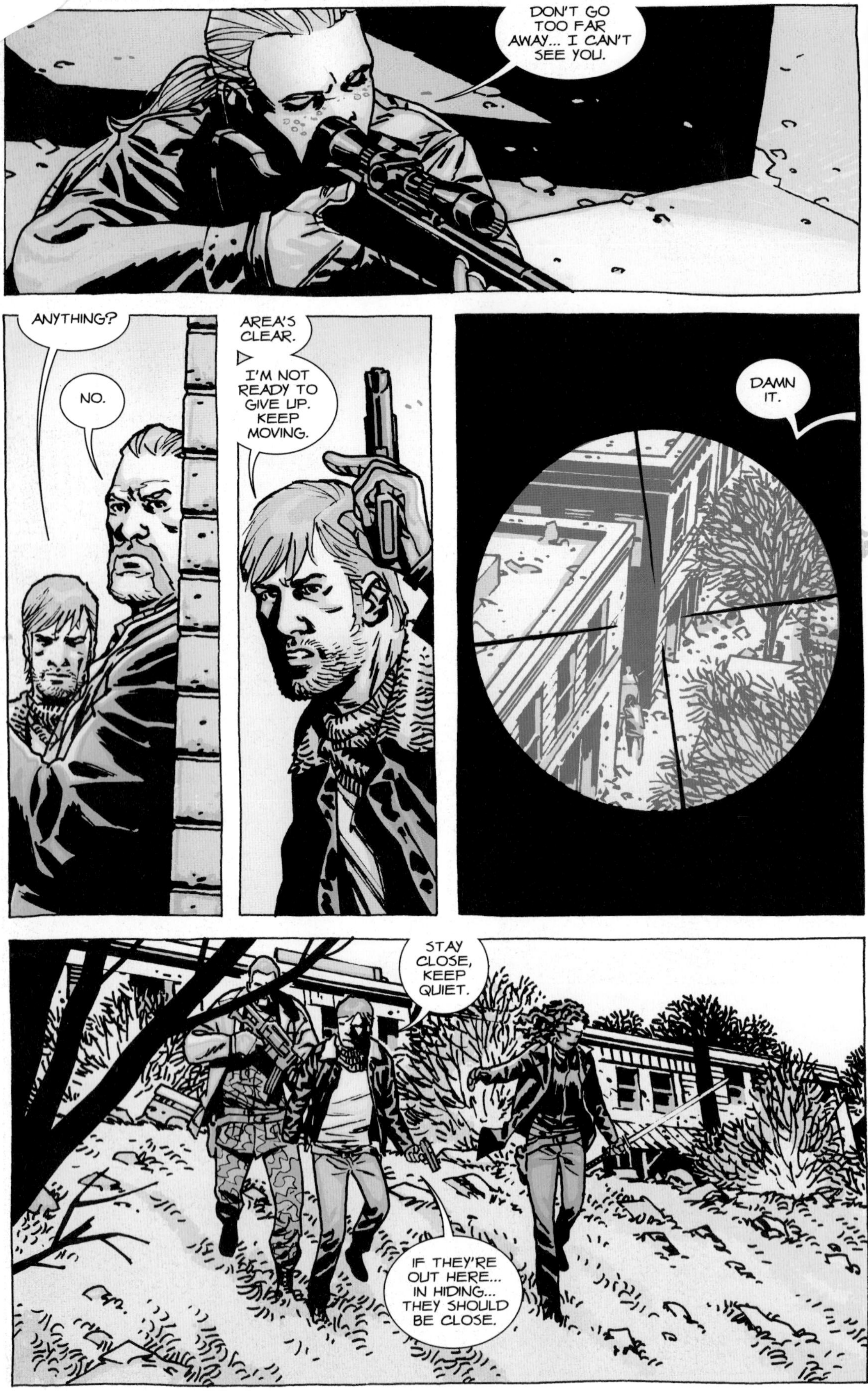
DON'T GO TOO FAR AWAY... I CAN'T SEE YOU.
ANYTHING?
NO.
AREA'S CLEAR.
I'M NOT READY TO GIVE UP. KEEP MOVING.
DAMN IT.
STAY CLOSE, KEEP QUIET.
IF THEY'RE OUT HERE... IN HIDING... THEY SHOULD BE CLOSE.

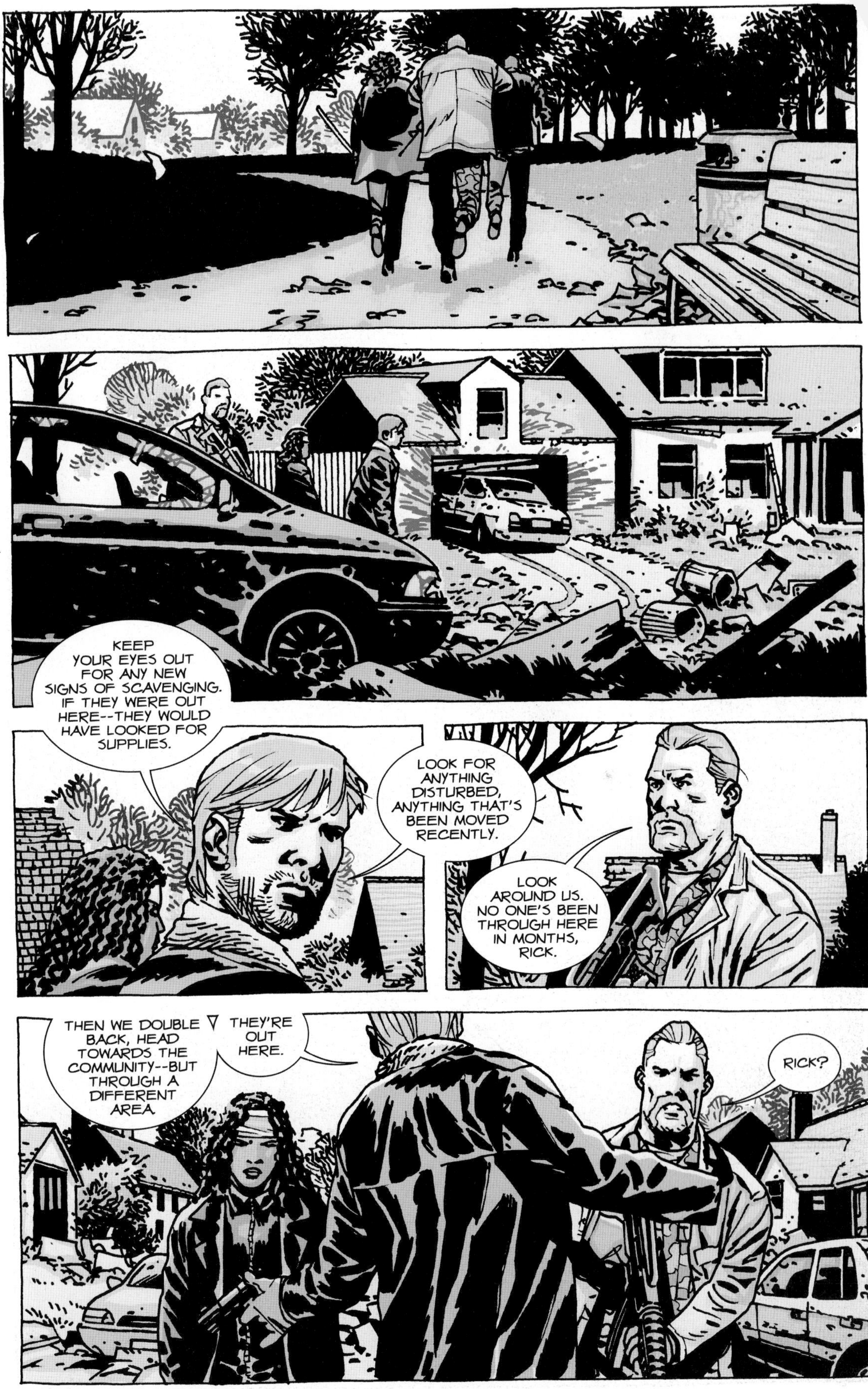
KEEP YOUR EYES OUT FOR ANY NEW SIGNS OF SCAVENGING. IF THEY WERE OUT HERE--THEY WOULD HAVE LOOKED FOR SUPPLIES.
LOOK FOR ANYTHING DISTURBED, ANYTHING THAT'S BEEN MOVED RECENTLY.
LOOK AROUND US. NO ONE'S BEEN THROUGH HERE IN MONTHS, RICK.
THEN WE DOUBLE BACK, HEAD TOWARDS THE COMMUNITY--BUT THROUGH A DIFFERENT AREA.
THEY'RE OUT HERE.
RICK?

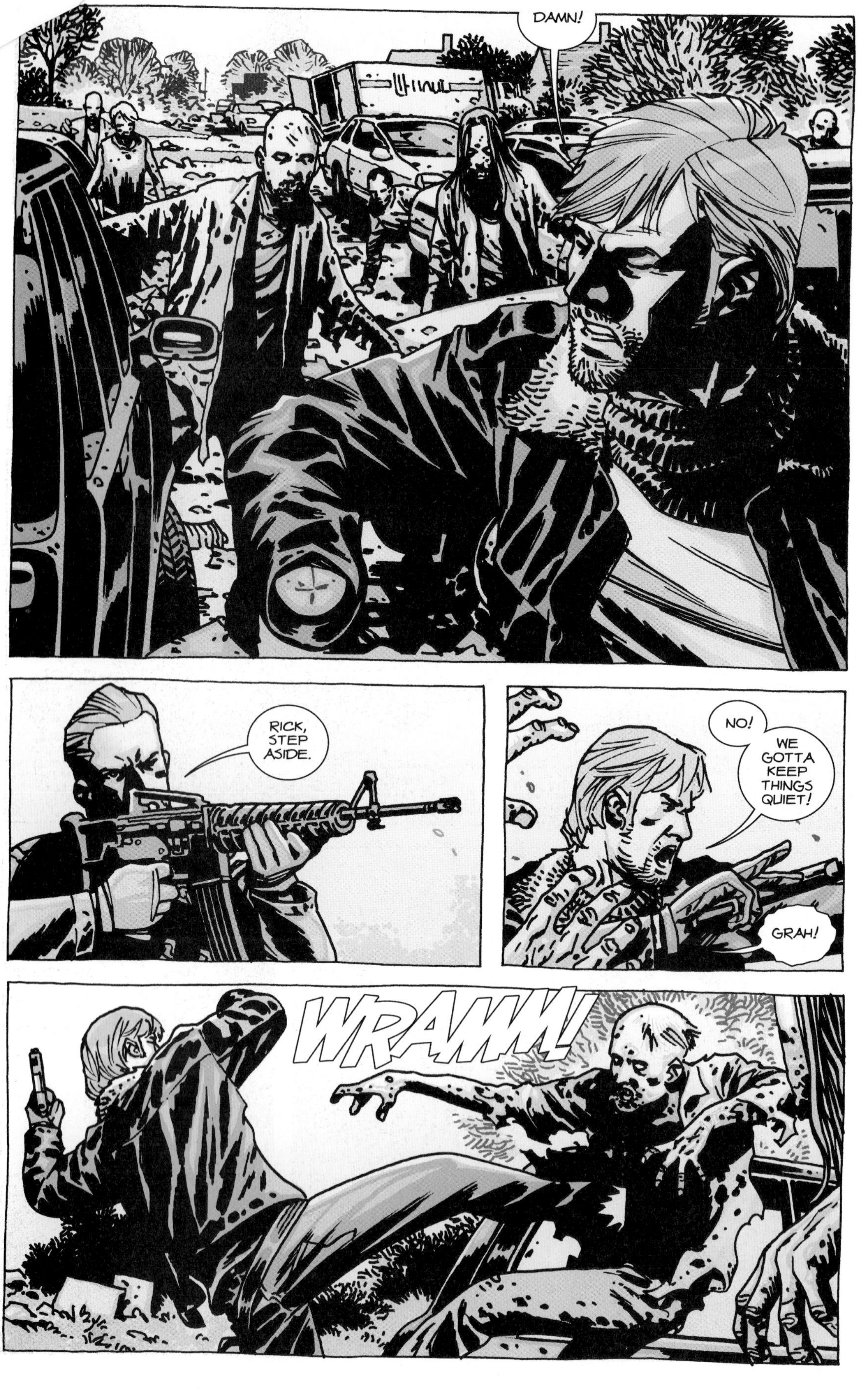
DAMN!
RICK, STEP ASIDE.
NO!
WE GOTTA KEEP THINGS QUIET!
GRAH!
WRAMM!

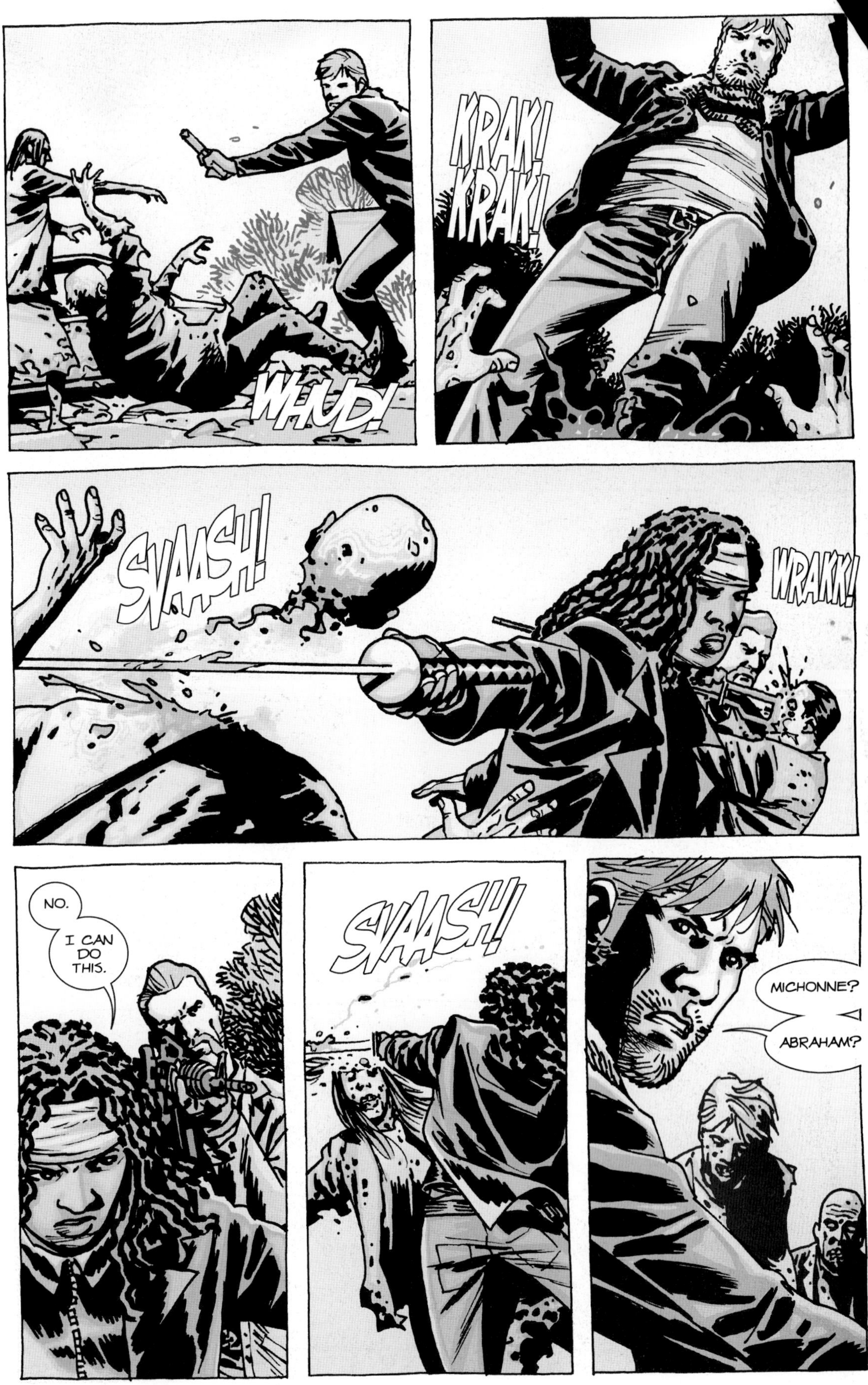
WHUD!
KRAK!
KRAK!
SVAASH!
WRAKK!
NO.
I CAN DO THIS.
SVAASH!
MICHONNE?
ABRAHAM?

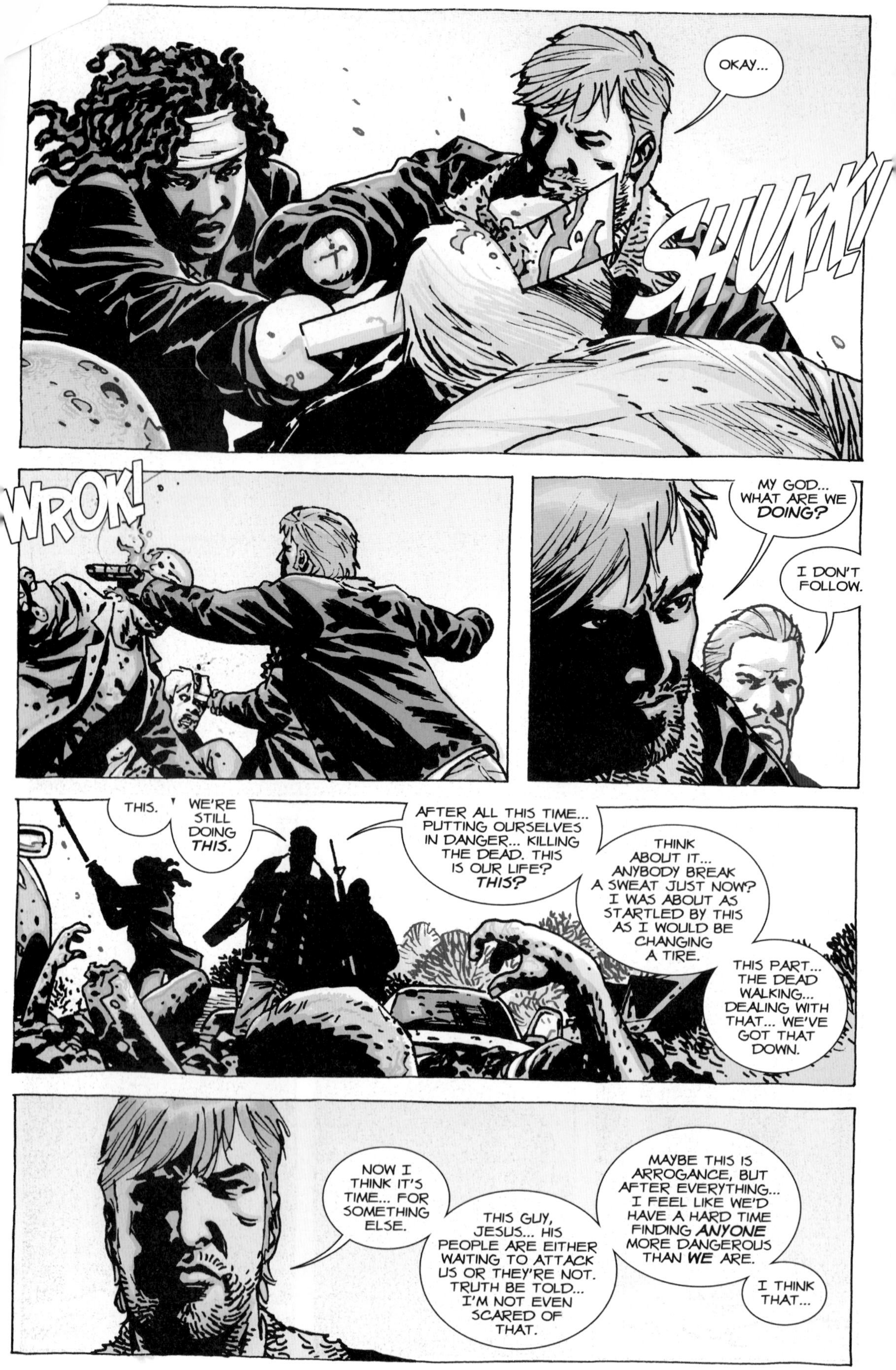
OKAY...
SHUKK!
WROK!
MY GOD... WHAT ARE WE DOING?
I DON'T FOLLOW.
THIS.
WE'RE STILL DOING THIS.
AFTER ALL THIS TIME... PUTTING OURSELVES IN DANGER... KILLING THE DEAD. THIS IS OUR LIFE? THIS?
THINK ABOUT IT... ANYBODY BREAK A SWEAT JUST NOW? I WAS ABOUT AS STARTLED BY THIS AS I WOULD BE CHANGING A TIRE.
THIS PART... THE DEAD WALKING... DEALING WITH THAT... WE'VE GOT THAT DOWN.
NOW I THINK IT'S TIME... FOR SOMETHING ELSE.
THIS GUY, JESUS... HIS PEOPLE ARE EITHER WAITING TO ATTACK US OR THEY'RE NOT. TRUTH BE TOLD... I'M NOT EVEN SCARED OF THAT.
MAYBE THIS IS ARROGANCE, BUT AFTER EVERYTHING... I FEEL LIKE WE'D HAVE A HARD TIME FINDING ANYONE MORE DANGEROUS THAN WE ARE.
I THINK THAT...

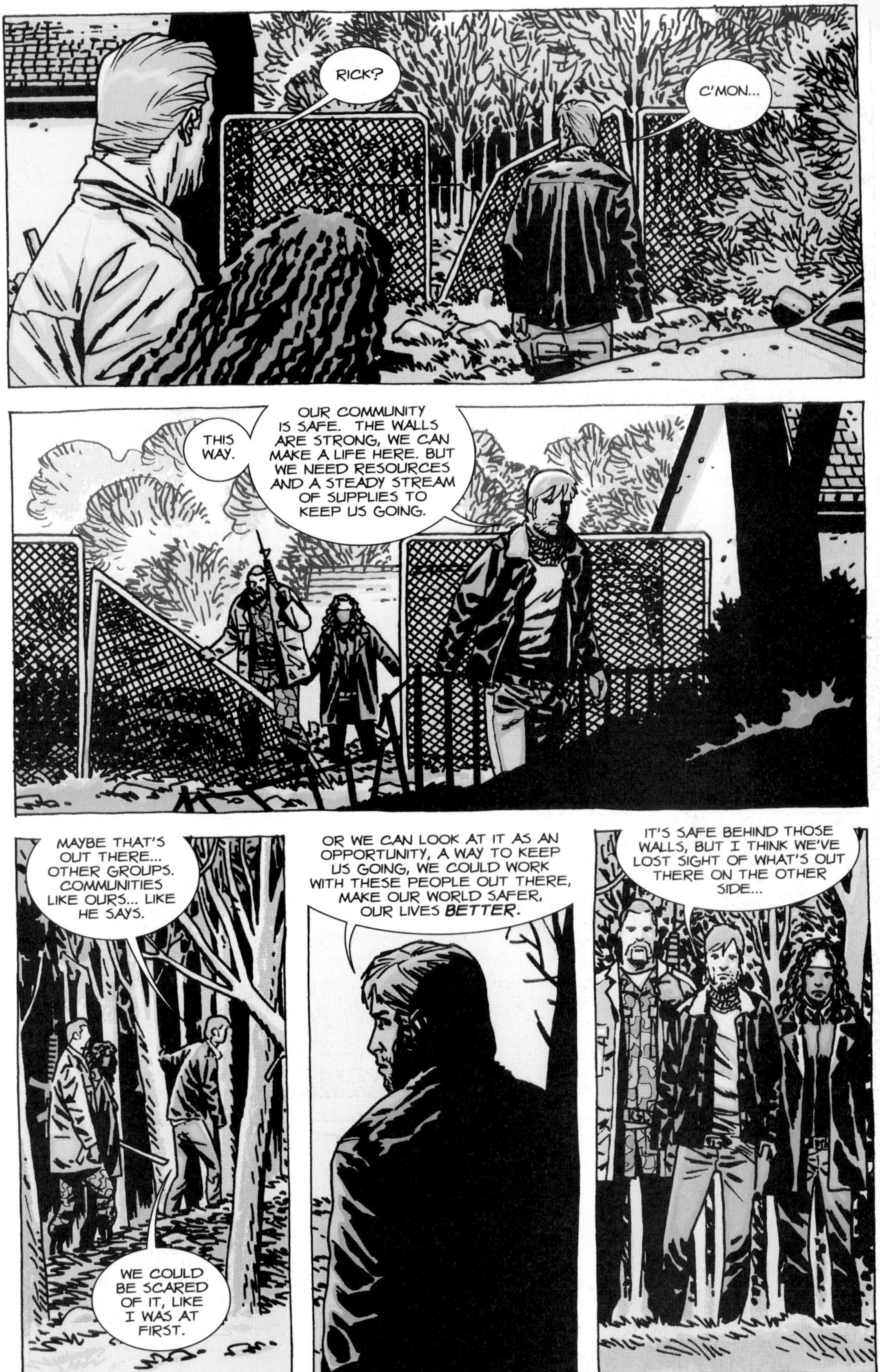
RICK?
C'MON...
THIS WAY.
OUR COMMUNITY IS SAFE. THE WALLS ARE STRONG, WE CAN MAKE A LIFE HERE. BUT WE NEED RESOURCES AND A STEADY STREAM OF SUPPLIES TO KEEP US GOING.
MAYBE THAT'S OUT THERE... OTHER GROUPS. COMMUNITIES LIKE OURS... LIKE HE SAYS.
WE COULD BE SCARED OF IT, LIKE I WAS AT FIRST.
OR WE CAN LOOK AT IT AS AN OPPORTUNITY, A WAY TO KEEP US GOING, WE COULD WORK WITH THESE PEOPLE OUT THERE, MAKE OUR WORLD SAFER, OUR LIVES BETTER.
IT'S SAFE BEHIND THOSE WALLS, BUT I THINK WE'VE LOST SIGHT OF WHAT'S OUT THERE ON THE OTHER SIDE...

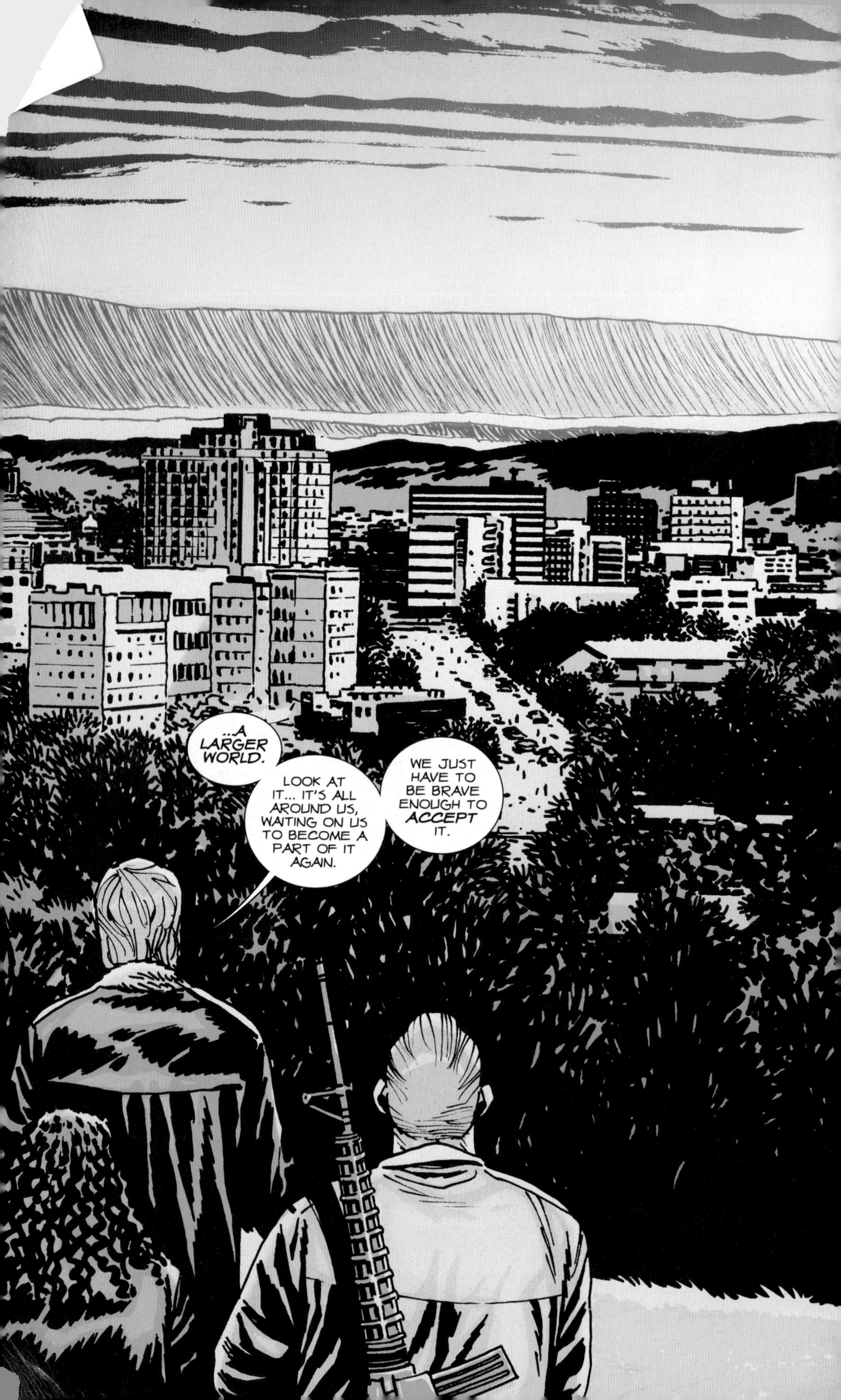
...A LARGER WORLD.
LOOK AT IT... IT'S ALL AROUND US, WAITING ON US TO BECOME A PART OF IT AGAIN.
WE JUST HAVE TO BE BRAVE ENOUGH TO ACCEPT IT.

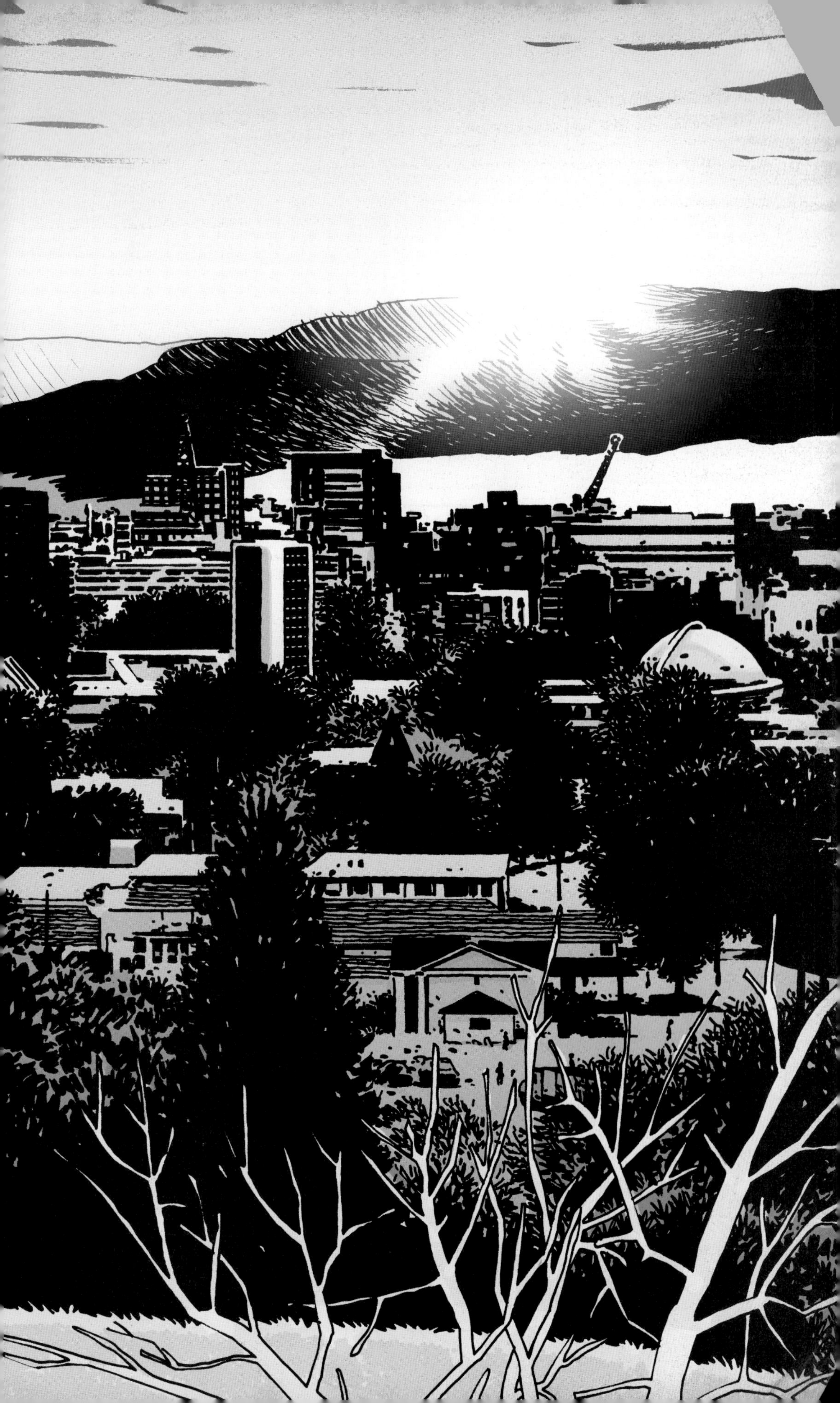

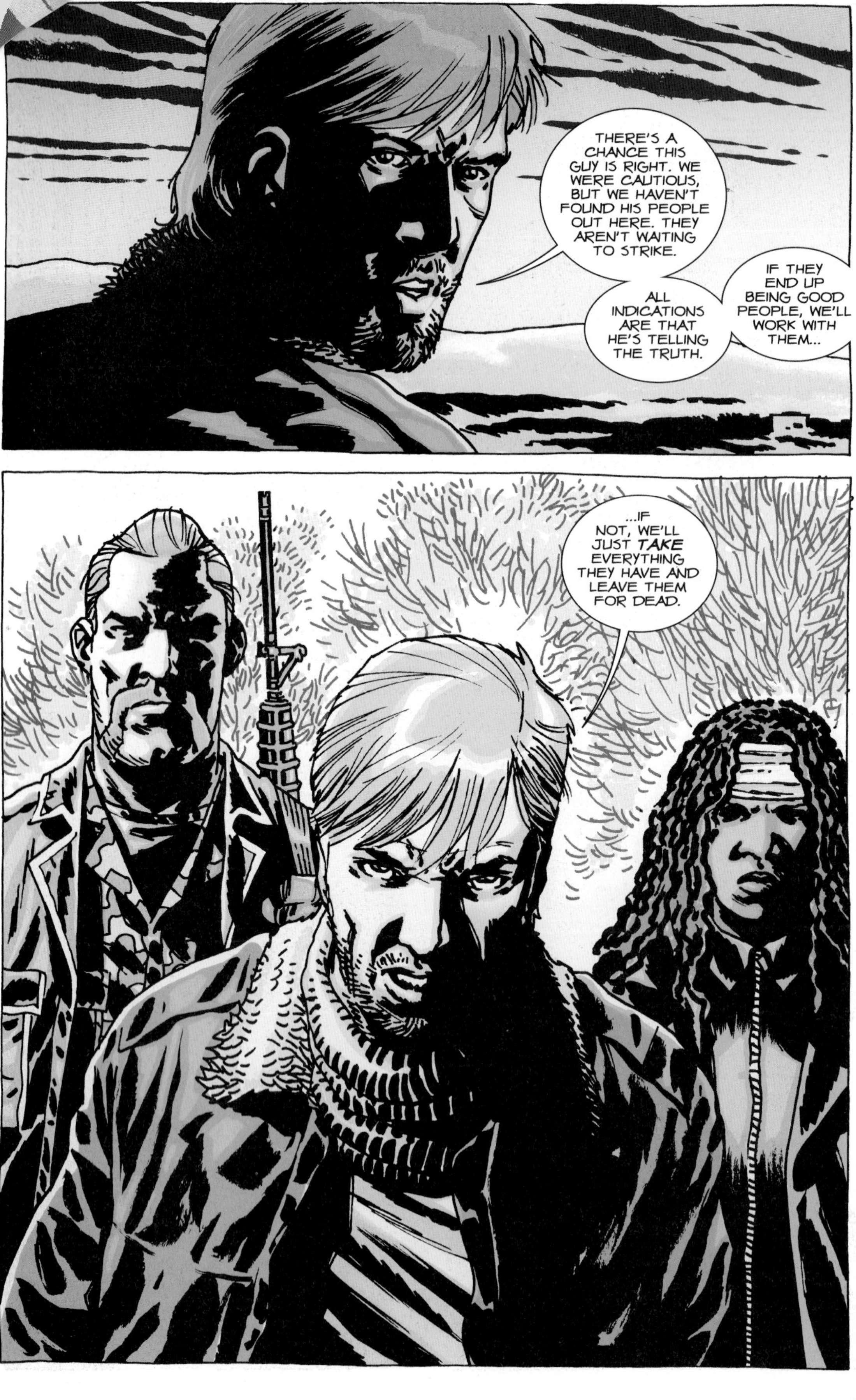
THERE'S A CHANCE THIS GUY IS RIGHT. WE WERE CAUTIOUS, BUT WE HAVEN'T FOUND HIS PEOPLE OUT HERE. THEY AREN'T WAITING TO STRIKE.
ALL INDICATIONS ARE THAT HE'S TELLING THE TRUTH.
IF THEY END UP BEING GOOD PEOPLE, WE'LL WORK WITH THEM...
...IF NOT, WE'LL JUST TAKE EVERYTHING THEY HAVE AND LEAVE THEM FOR DEAD.

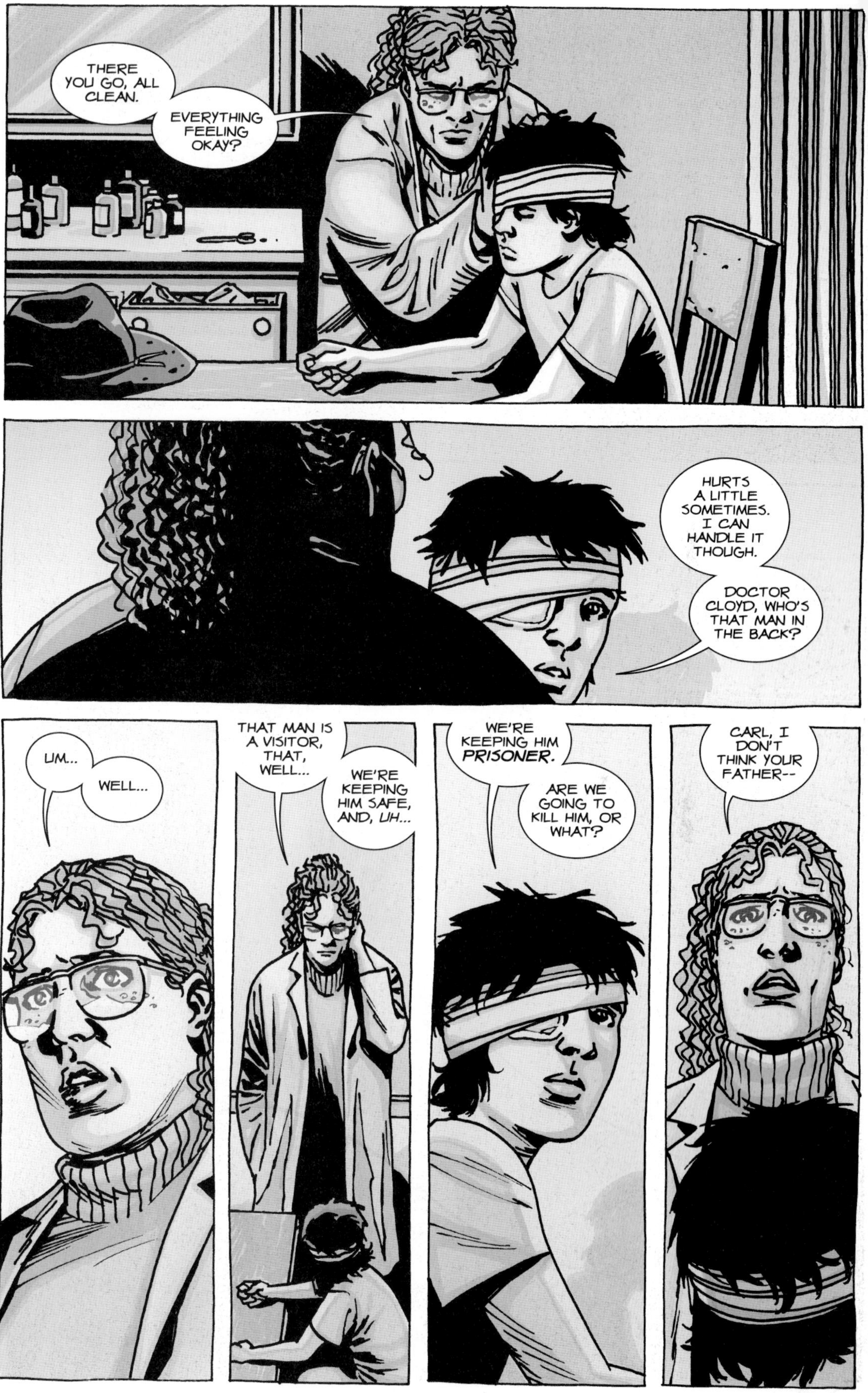
THERE YOU GO, ALL CLEAN.
EVERYTHING FEELING OKAY?
HURTS A LITTLE SOMETIMES. I CAN HANDLE IT THOUGH.
DOCTOR CLOYD, WHO'S THAT MAN IN THE BACK?
UM...
WELL...
THAT MAN IS A VISITOR, THAT, WELL...
WE'RE KEEPING HIM SAFE, AND, *UH*...
WE'RE KEEPING HIM *PRISONER*.
ARE WE GOING TO KILL HIM, OR WHAT?
CARL, I DON'T THINK YOUR FATHER--

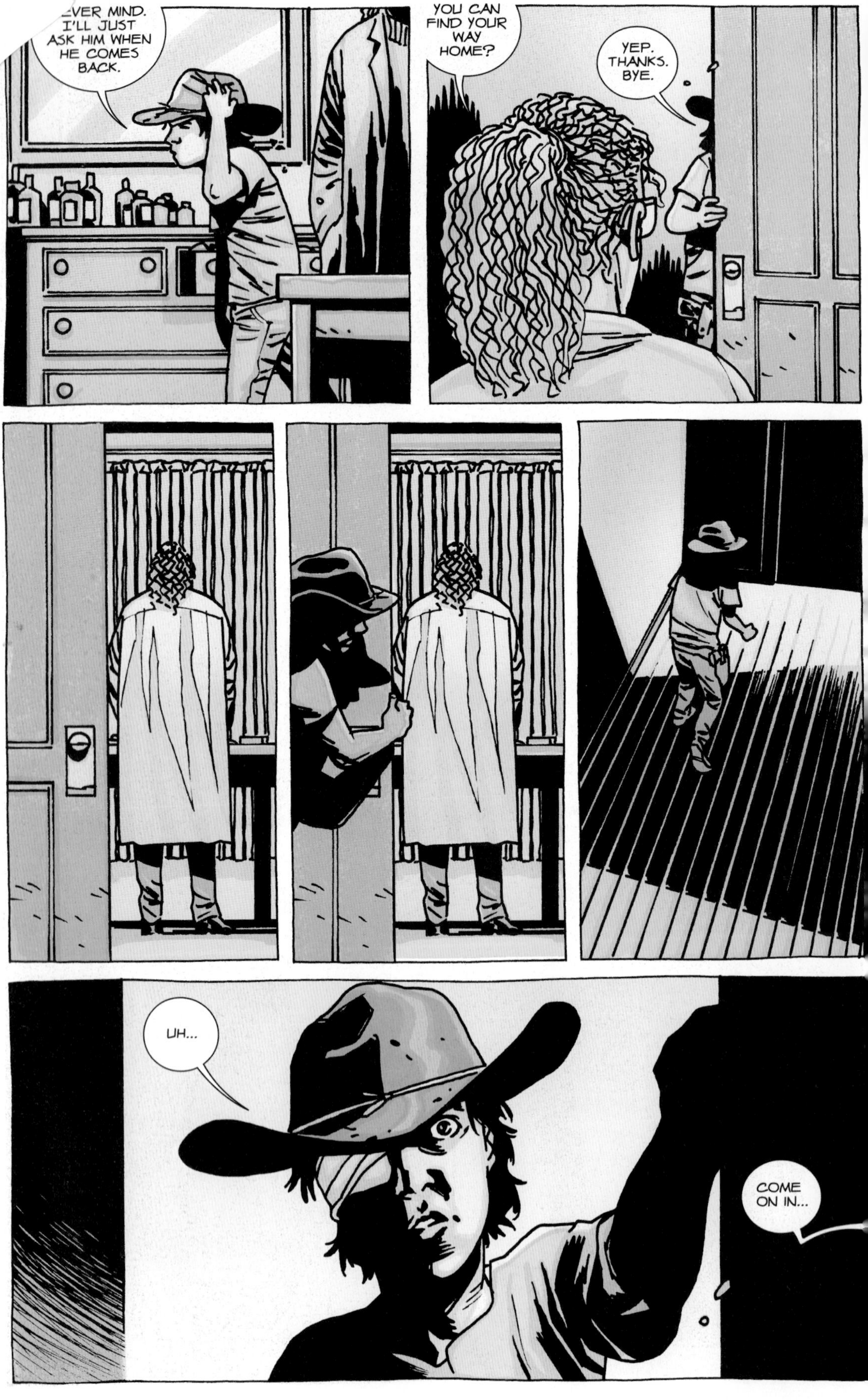

EVER MIND. I'LL JUST ASK HIM WHEN HE COMES BACK.
YOU CAN FIND YOUR WAY HOME?
YEP. THANKS. BYE.
UH...
COME ON IN...

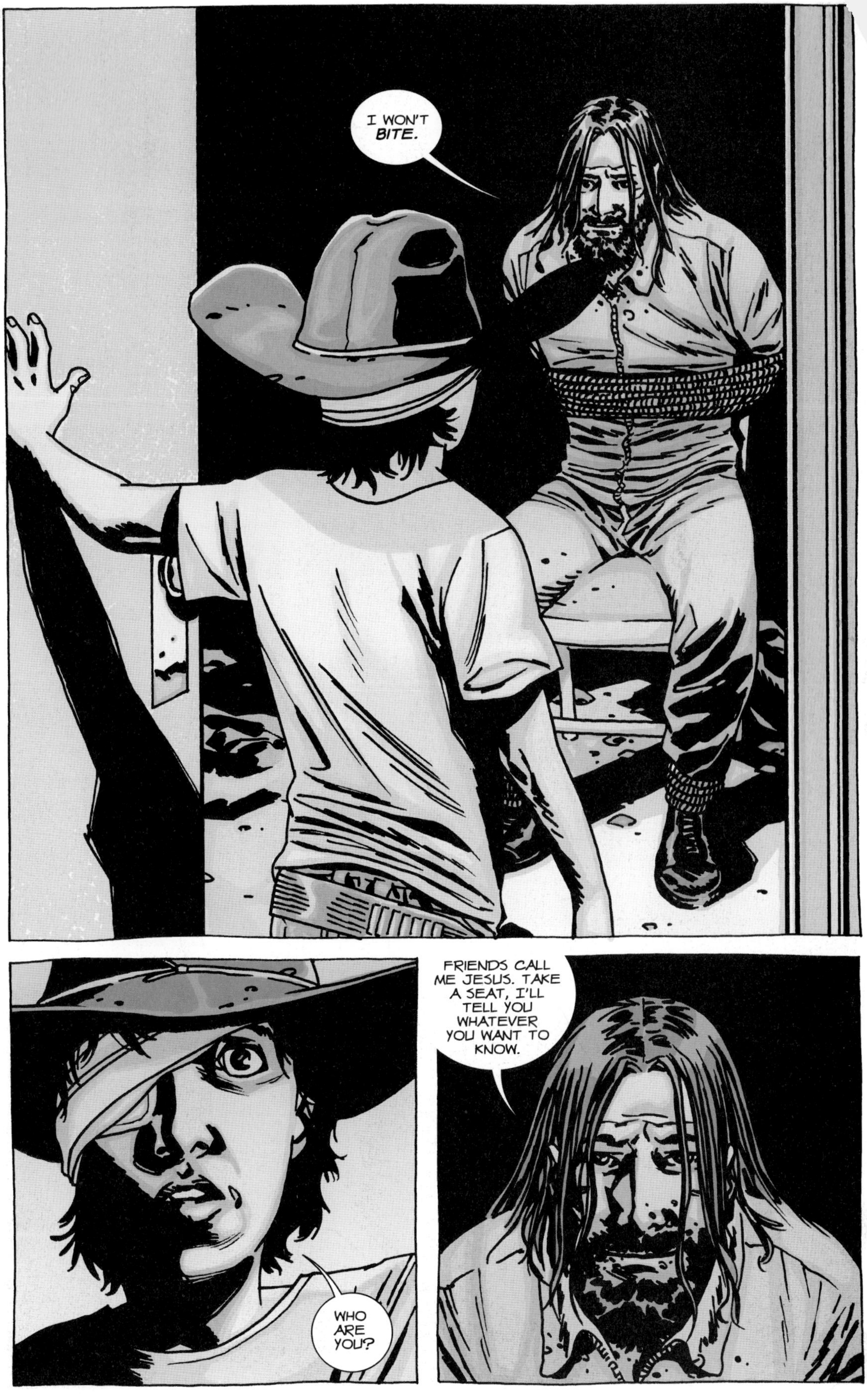
I WON'T *BITE.*
WHO ARE YOU?
FRIENDS CALL ME JESUS. TAKE A SEAT, I'LL TELL YOU WHATEVER YOU WANT TO KNOW.

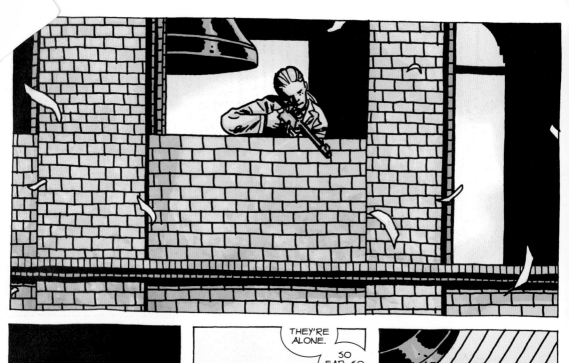

THEY'RE ALONE.

SO FAR, SO GOOD.

WHAT'S THE WORD?

WE'RE CLEAR. SEEMS LIKE THE GUY IS TELLING THE TRUTH.

RECKON WE'LL BELIEVE HIM FOR NOW. STAND DOWN, LET'S HEAD BACK.

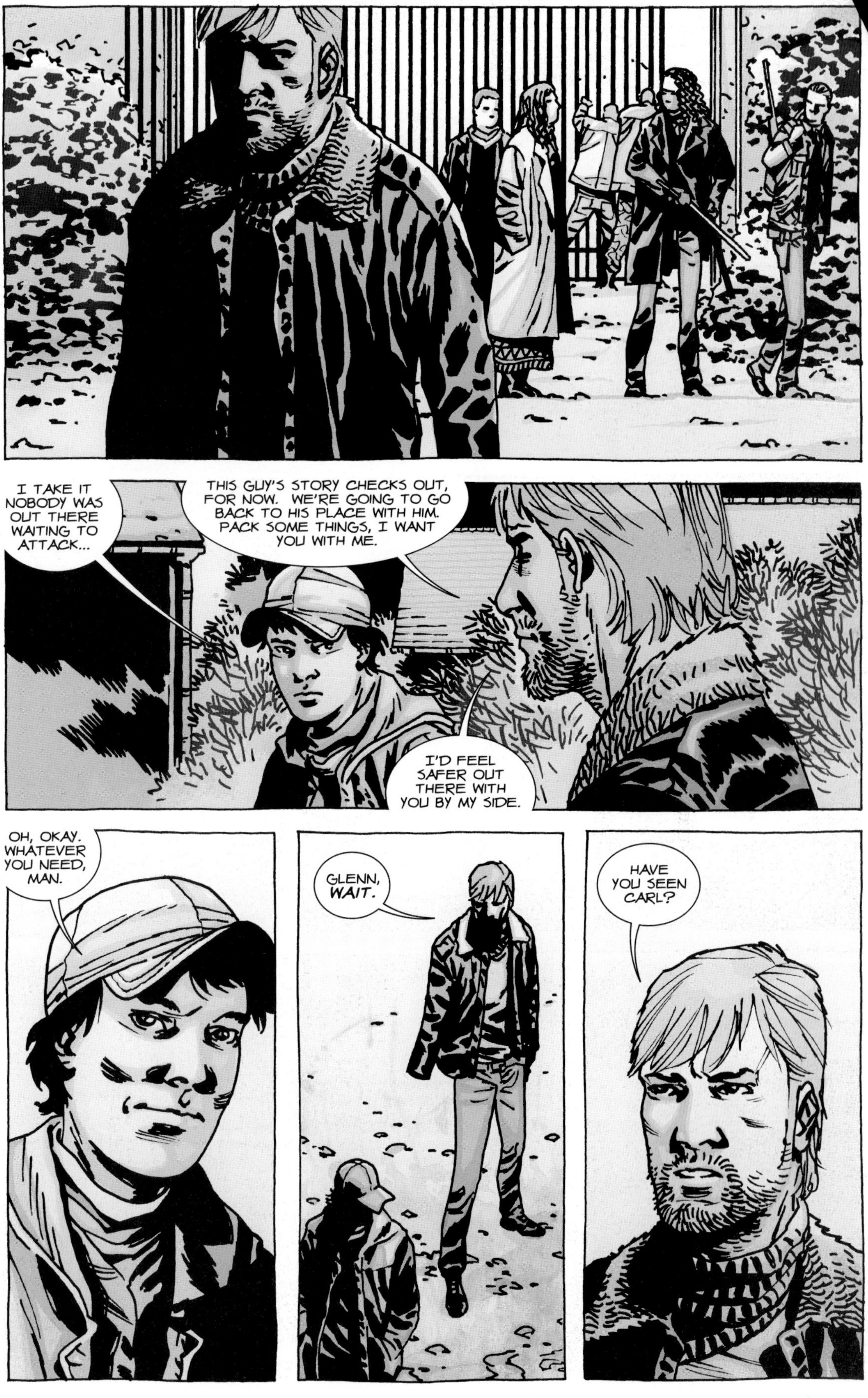
I TAKE IT NOBODY WAS OUT THERE WAITING TO ATTACK...
THIS GUY'S STORY CHECKS OUT, FOR NOW. WE'RE GOING TO GO BACK TO HIS PLACE WITH HIM. PACK SOME THINGS, I WANT YOU WITH ME.
I'D FEEL SAFER OUT THERE WITH YOU BY MY SIDE.
OH, OKAY. WHATEVER YOU NEED, MAN.
GLENN, *WAIT.*
HAVE YOU SEEN CARL?

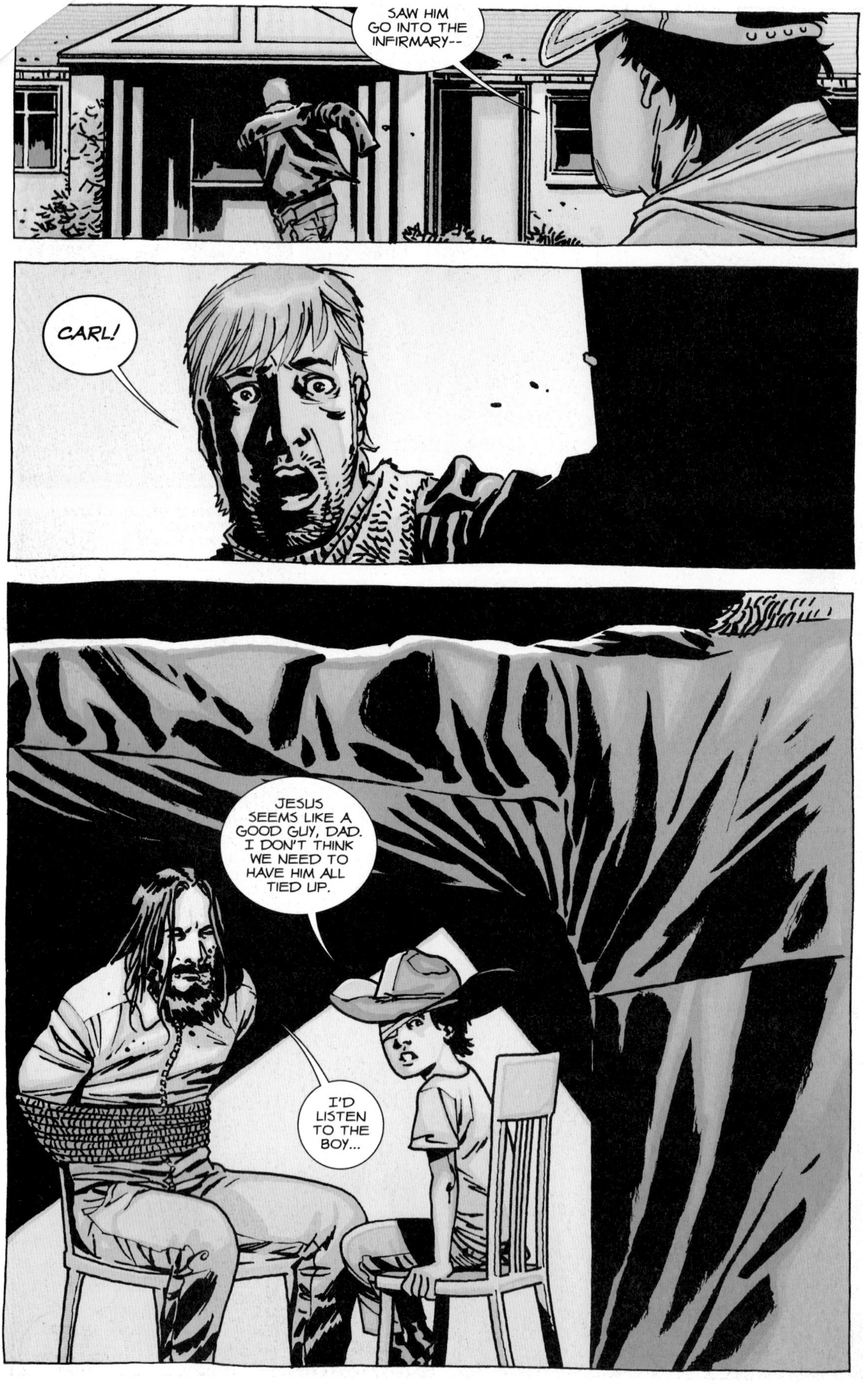
SAW HIM GO INTO THE INFIRMARY--
CARL!
JESUS SEEMS LIKE A GOOD GUY, DAD. I DON'T THINK WE NEED TO HAVE HIM ALL TIED UP.
I'D LISTEN TO THE BOY...

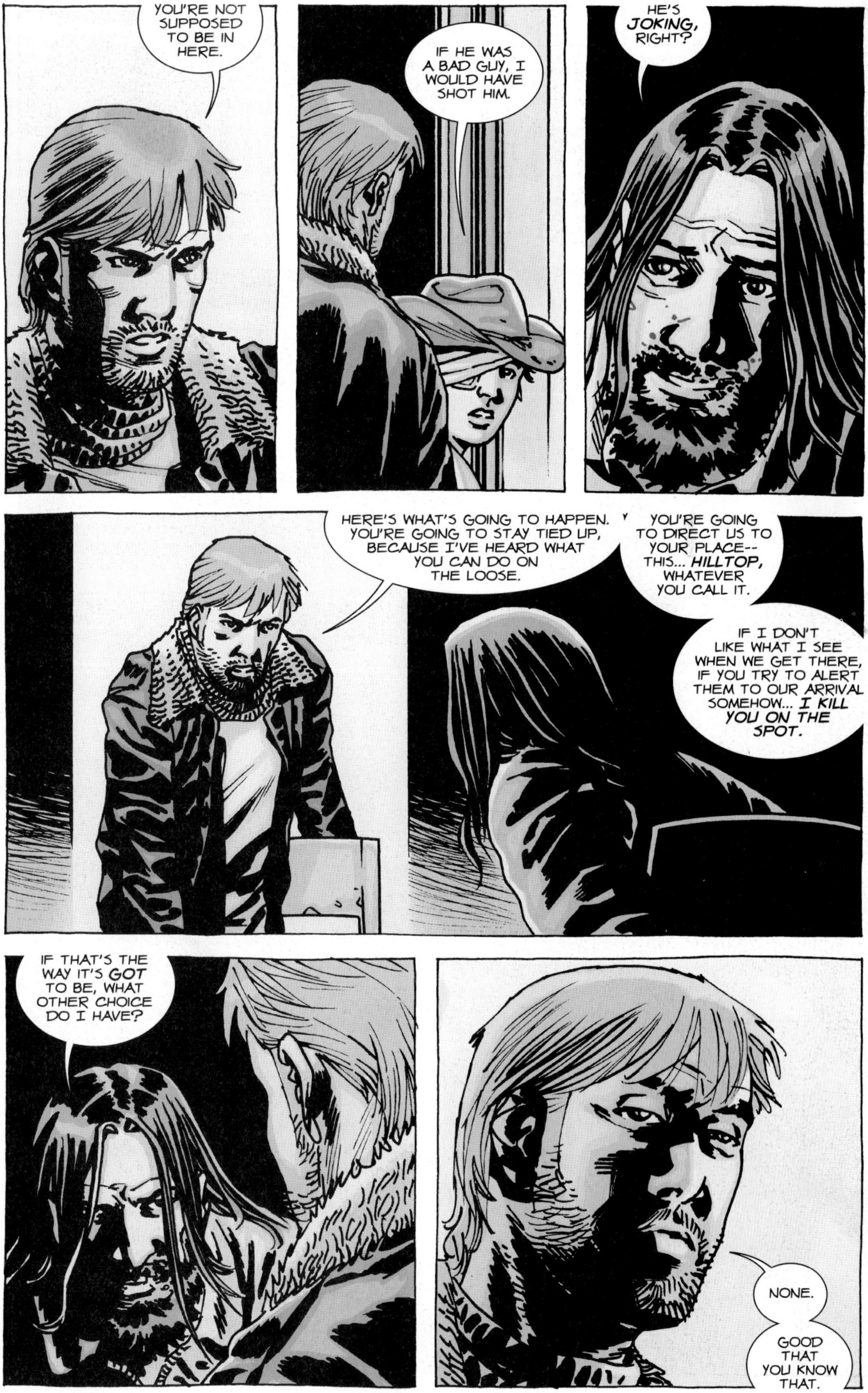
YOU'RE NOT SUPPOSED TO BE IN HERE.
IF HE WAS A BAD GUY, I WOULD HAVE SHOT HIM.
HE'S JOKING, RIGHT?
HERE'S WHAT'S GOING TO HAPPEN. YOU'RE GOING TO STAY TIED UP, BECAUSE I'VE HEARD WHAT YOU CAN DO ON THE LOOSE.
YOU'RE GOING TO DIRECT US TO YOUR PLACE-- THIS... HILLTOP, WHATEVER YOU CALL IT.
IF I DON'T LIKE WHAT I SEE WHEN WE GET THERE, IF YOU TRY TO ALERT THEM TO OUR ARRIVAL SOMEHOW... I KILL YOU ON THE SPOT.
IF THAT'S THE WAY IT'S GOT TO BE, WHAT OTHER CHOICE DO I HAVE?
NONE.
GOOD THAT YOU KNOW THAT.

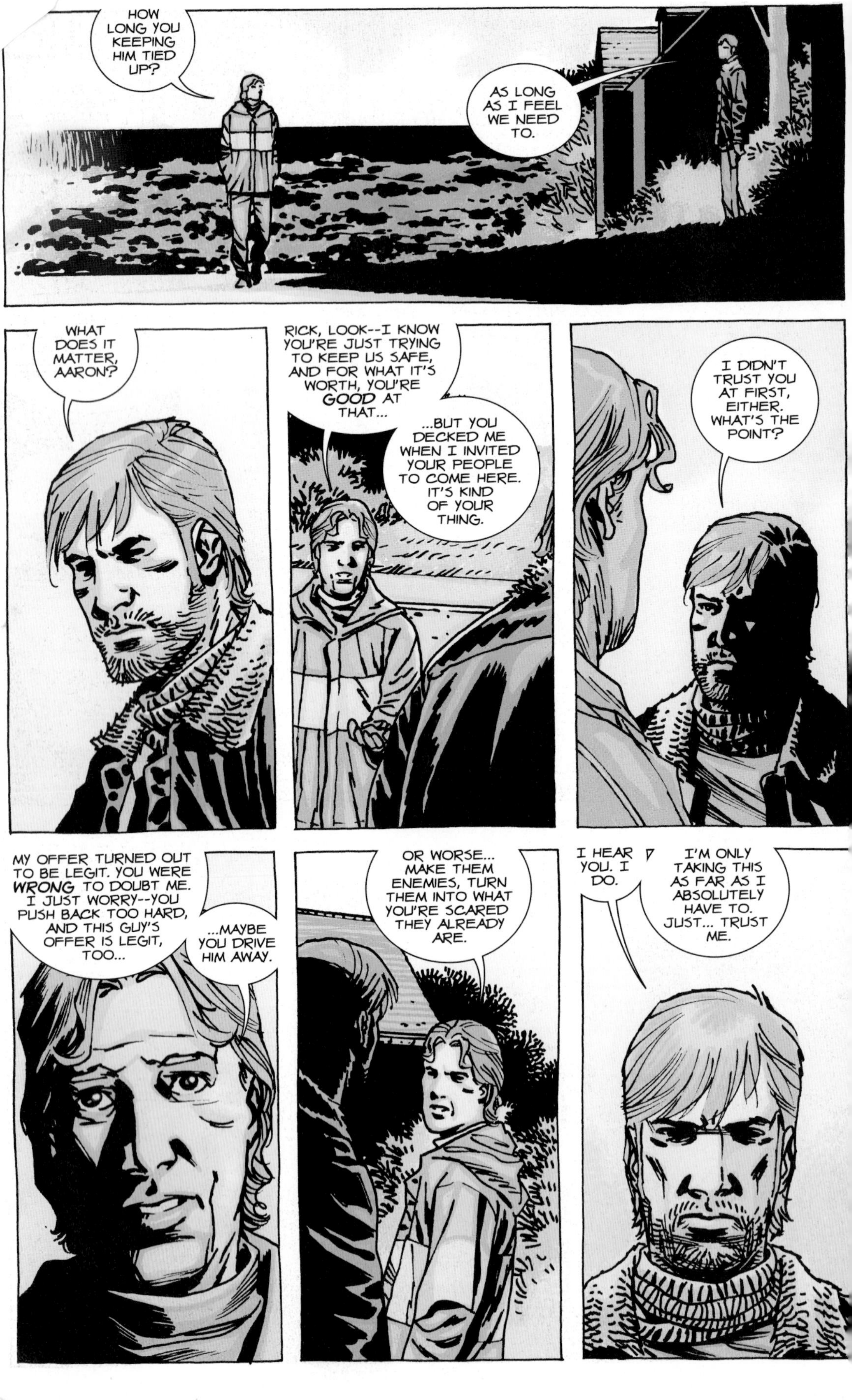
HOW LONG YOU KEEPING HIM TIED UP?
AS LONG AS I FEEL WE NEED TO.
WHAT DOES IT MATTER, AARON?
RICK, LOOK--I KNOW YOU'RE JUST TRYING TO KEEP US SAFE, AND FOR WHAT IT'S WORTH, YOU'RE GOOD AT THAT...
...BUT YOU DECKED ME WHEN I INVITED YOUR PEOPLE TO COME HERE. IT'S KIND OF YOUR THING.
I DIDN'T TRUST YOU AT FIRST, EITHER. WHAT'S THE POINT?
MY OFFER TURNED OUT TO BE LEGIT. YOU WERE WRONG TO DOUBT ME. I JUST WORRY--YOU PUSH BACK TOO HARD, AND THIS GUY'S OFFER IS LEGIT, TOO...
...MAYBE YOU DRIVE HIM AWAY.
OR WORSE... MAKE THEM ENEMIES, TURN THEM INTO WHAT YOU'RE SCARED THEY ALREADY ARE.
I HEAR YOU. I DO.
I'M ONLY TAKING THIS AS FAR AS I ABSOLUTELY HAVE TO. JUST... TRUST ME.

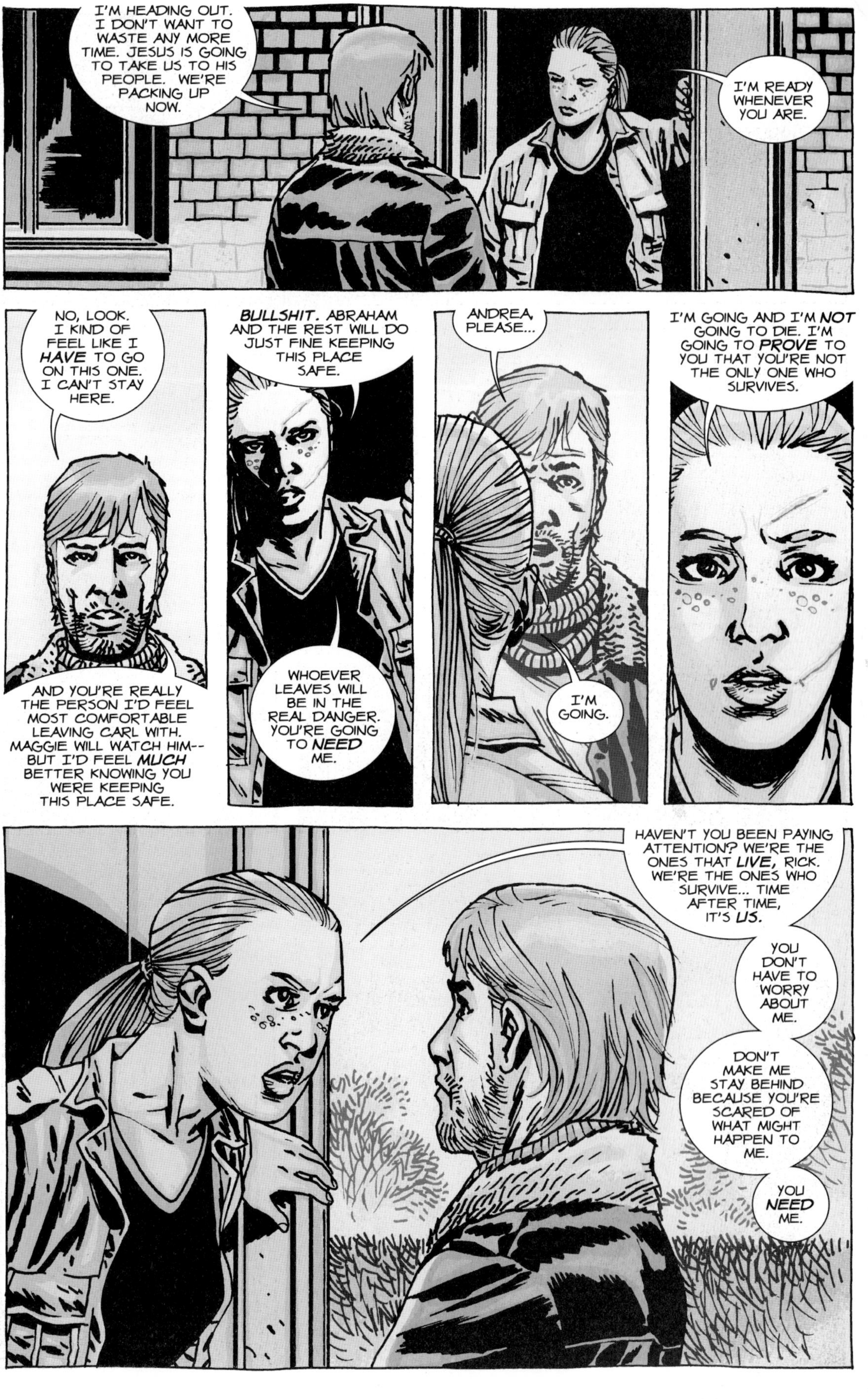
I'M HEADING OUT. I DON'T WANT TO WASTE ANY MORE TIME. JESUS IS GOING TO TAKE US TO HIS PEOPLE. WE'RE PACKING UP NOW.
I'M READY WHENEVER YOU ARE.
NO, LOOK. I KIND OF FEEL LIKE I HAVE TO GO ON THIS ONE. I CAN'T STAY HERE.
AND YOU'RE REALLY THE PERSON I'D FEEL MOST COMFORTABLE LEAVING CARL WITH. MAGGIE WILL WATCH HIM-- BUT I'D FEEL MUCH BETTER KNOWING YOU WERE KEEPING THIS PLACE SAFE.
BULLSHIT. ABRAHAM AND THE REST WILL DO JUST FINE KEEPING THIS PLACE SAFE.
WHOEVER LEAVES WILL BE IN THE REAL DANGER. YOU'RE GOING TO NEED ME.
ANDREA, PLEASE...
I'M GOING.
I'M GOING AND I'M NOT GOING TO DIE. I'M GOING TO PROVE TO YOU THAT YOU'RE NOT THE ONLY ONE WHO SURVIVES.
HAVEN'T YOU BEEN PAYING ATTENTION? WE'RE THE ONES THAT LIVE, RICK. WE'RE THE ONES WHO SURVIVE... TIME AFTER TIME, IT'S US.
YOU DON'T HAVE TO WORRY ABOUT ME.
DON'T MAKE ME STAY BEHIND BECAUSE YOU'RE SCARED OF WHAT MIGHT HAPPEN TO ME.
YOU NEED ME.

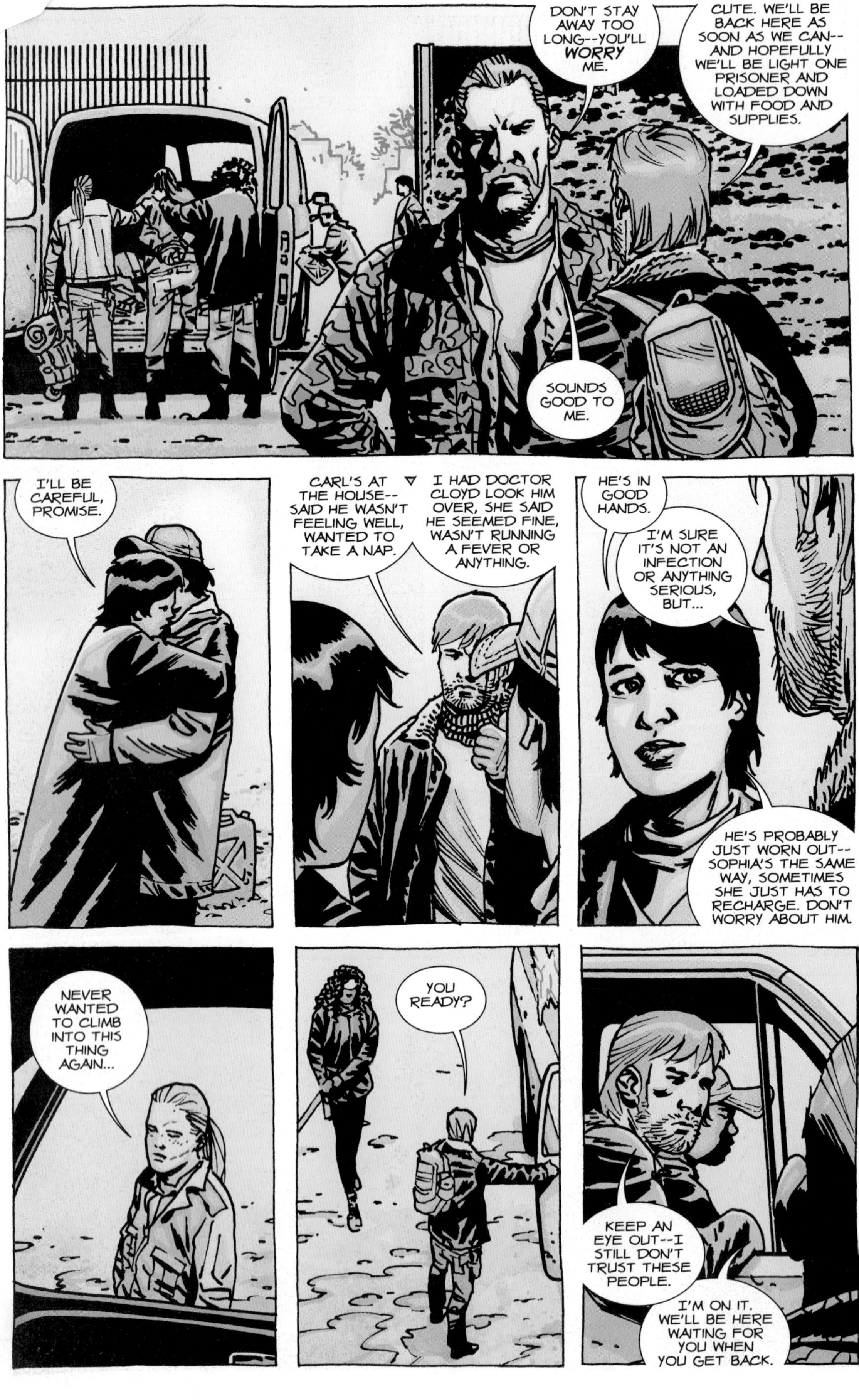
DON'T STAY AWAY TOO LONG--YOU'LL WORRY ME.
CUTE. WE'LL BE BACK HERE AS SOON AS WE CAN-- AND HOPEFULLY WE'LL BE LIGHT ONE PRISONER AND LOADED DOWN WITH FOOD AND SUPPLIES.
SOUNDS GOOD TO ME.
I'LL BE CAREFUL, PROMISE.
CARL'S AT THE HOUSE-- SAID HE WASN'T FEELING WELL, WANTED TO TAKE A NAP.
I HAD DOCTOR CLOYD LOOK HIM OVER, SHE SAID HE SEEMED FINE, WASN'T RUNNING A FEVER OR ANYTHING.
HE'S IN GOOD HANDS.
I'M SURE IT'S NOT AN INFECTION OR ANYTHING SERIOUS, BUT...
HE'S PROBABLY JUST WORN OUT-- SOPHIA'S THE SAME WAY, SOMETIMES SHE JUST HAS TO RECHARGE. DON'T WORRY ABOUT HIM.
NEVER WANTED TO CLIMB INTO THIS THING AGAIN...
YOU READY?
KEEP AN EYE OUT--I STILL DON'T TRUST THESE PEOPLE.
I'M ON IT. WE'LL BE HERE WAITING FOR YOU WHEN YOU GET BACK.

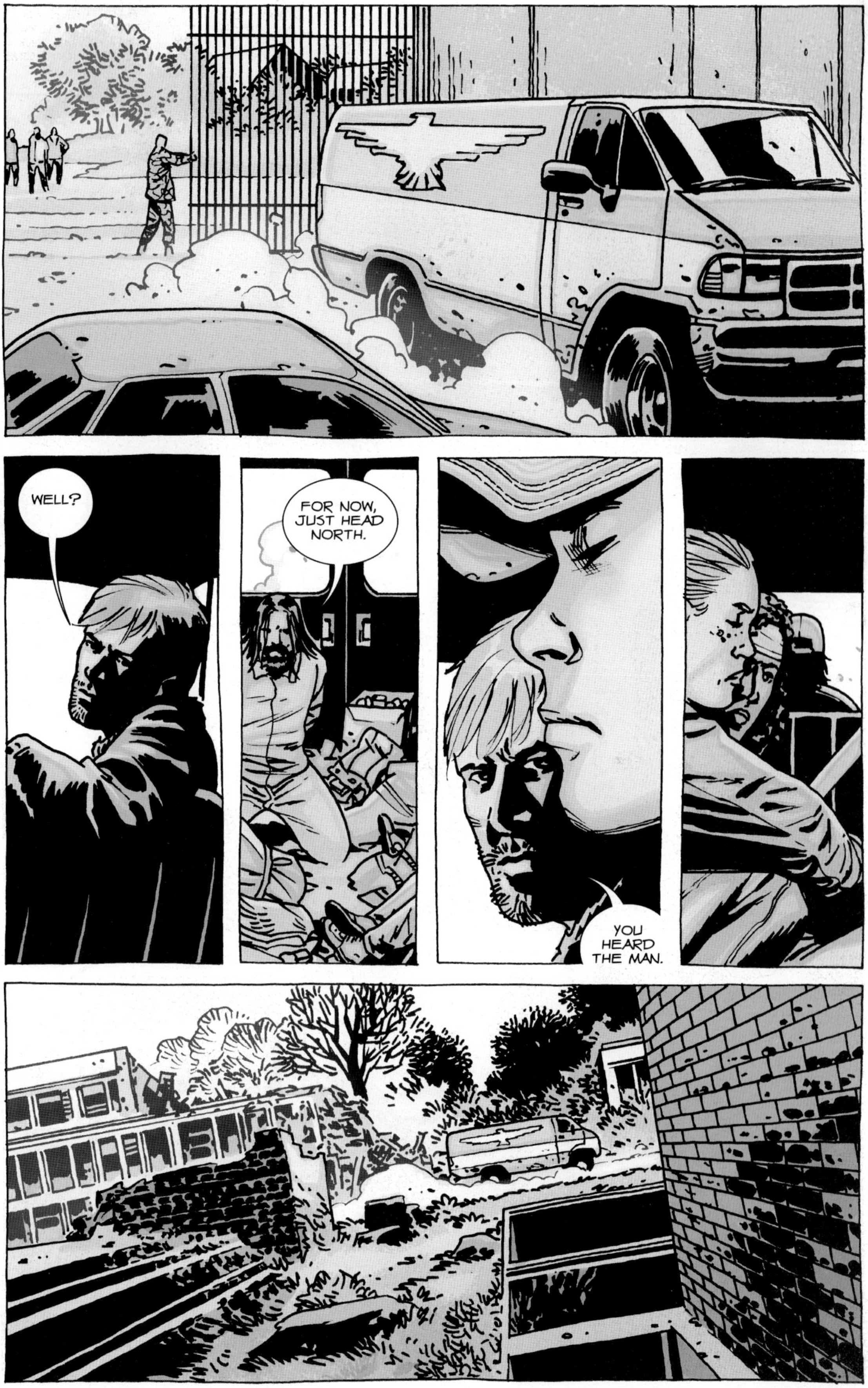
WELL?
FOR NOW, JUST HEAD NORTH.
YOU HEARD THE MAN.

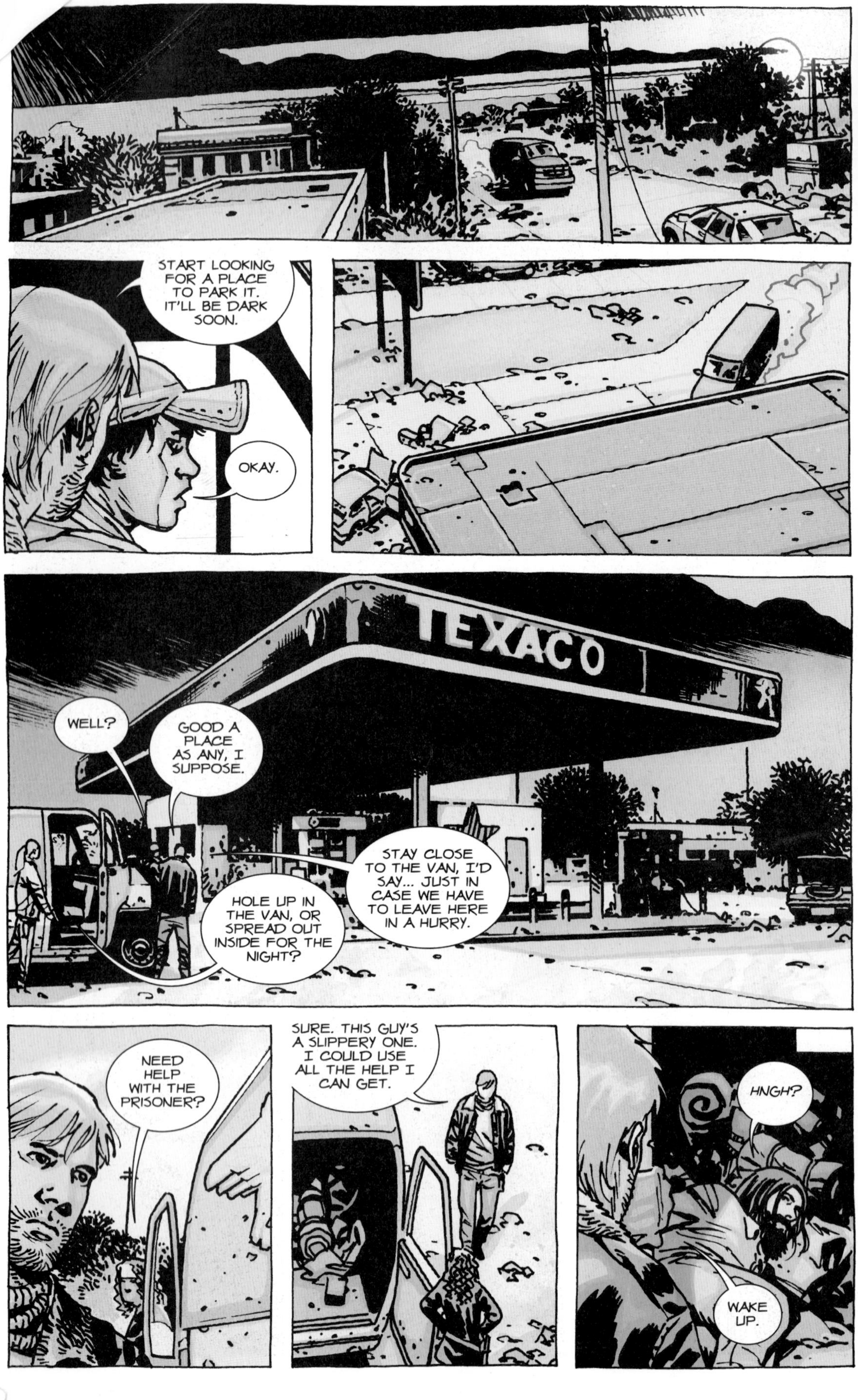

START LOOKING FOR A PLACE TO PARK IT. IT'LL BE DARK SOON.
OKAY.
TEXACO
WELL?
GOOD A PLACE AS ANY, I SUPPOSE.
HOLE UP IN THE VAN, OR SPREAD OUT INSIDE FOR THE NIGHT?
STAY CLOSE TO THE VAN, I'D SAY... JUST IN CASE WE HAVE TO LEAVE HERE IN A HURRY.
NEED HELP WITH THE PRISONER?
SURE. THIS GUY'S A SLIPPERY ONE. I COULD USE ALL THE HELP I CAN GET.
HNGH?
WAKE UP.

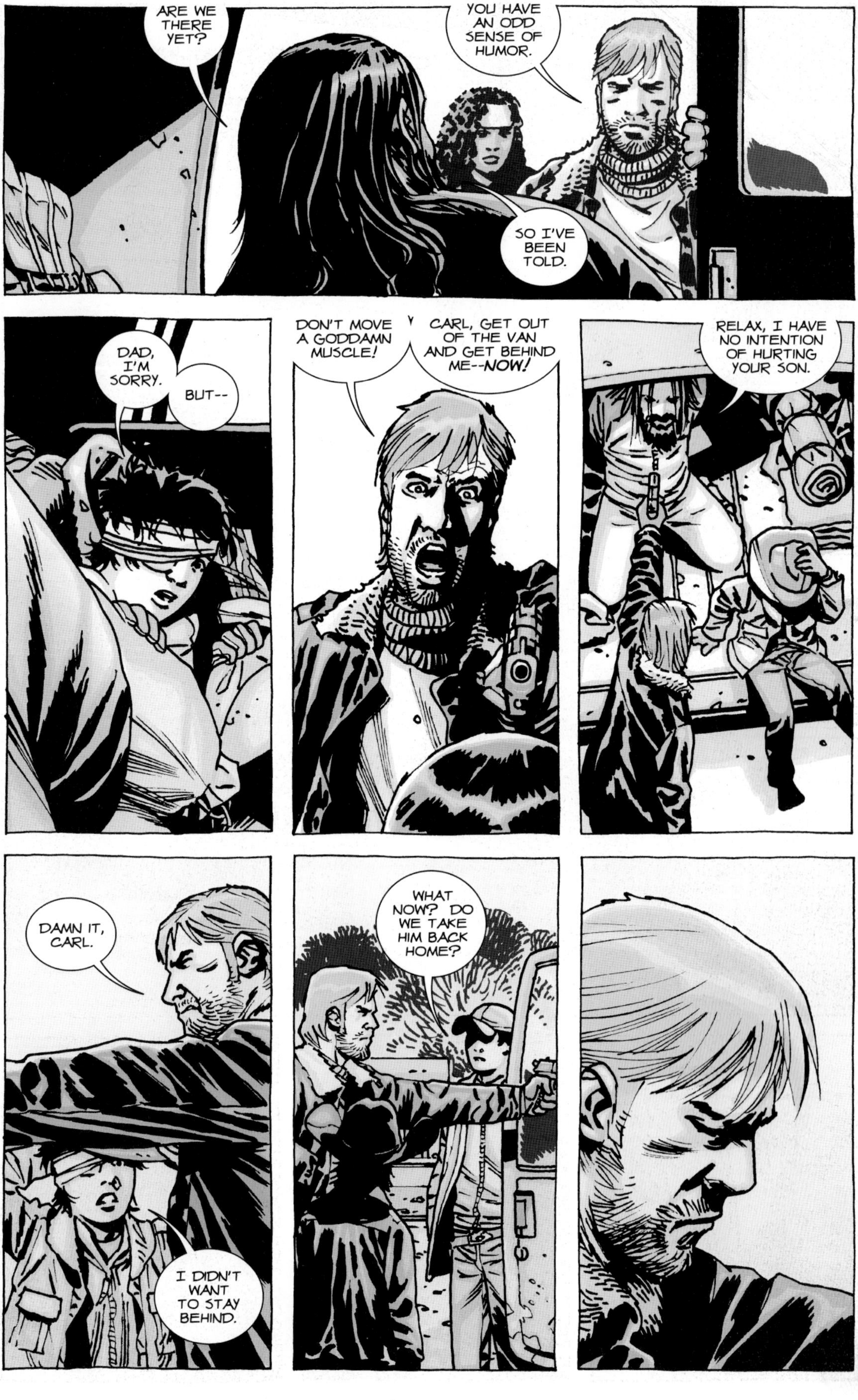
ARE WE THERE YET?
YOU HAVE AN ODD SENSE OF HUMOR.
SO I'VE BEEN TOLD.
DAD, I'M SORRY.
BUT--
DON'T MOVE A GODDAMN MUSCLE!
CARL, GET OUT OF THE VAN AND GET BEHIND ME--NOW!
RELAX, I HAVE NO INTENTION OF HURTING YOUR SON.
DAMN IT, CARL.
I DIDN'T WANT TO STAY BEHIND.
WHAT NOW? DO WE TAKE HIM BACK HOME?

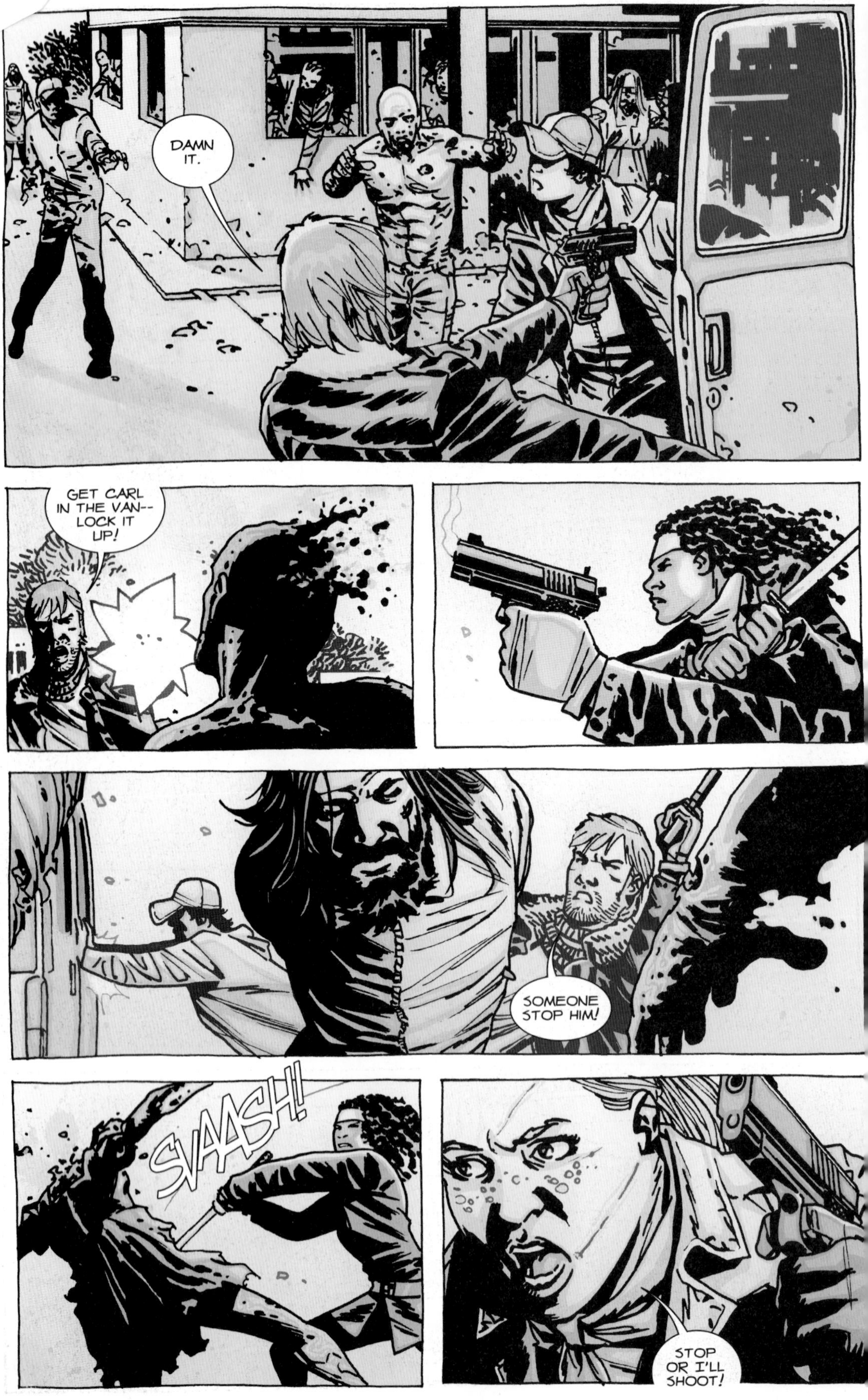
DAMN IT.
GET CARL IN THE VAN-- LOCK IT UP!
SOMEONE STOP HIM!
SVAASH!
STOP OR I'LL SHOOT!

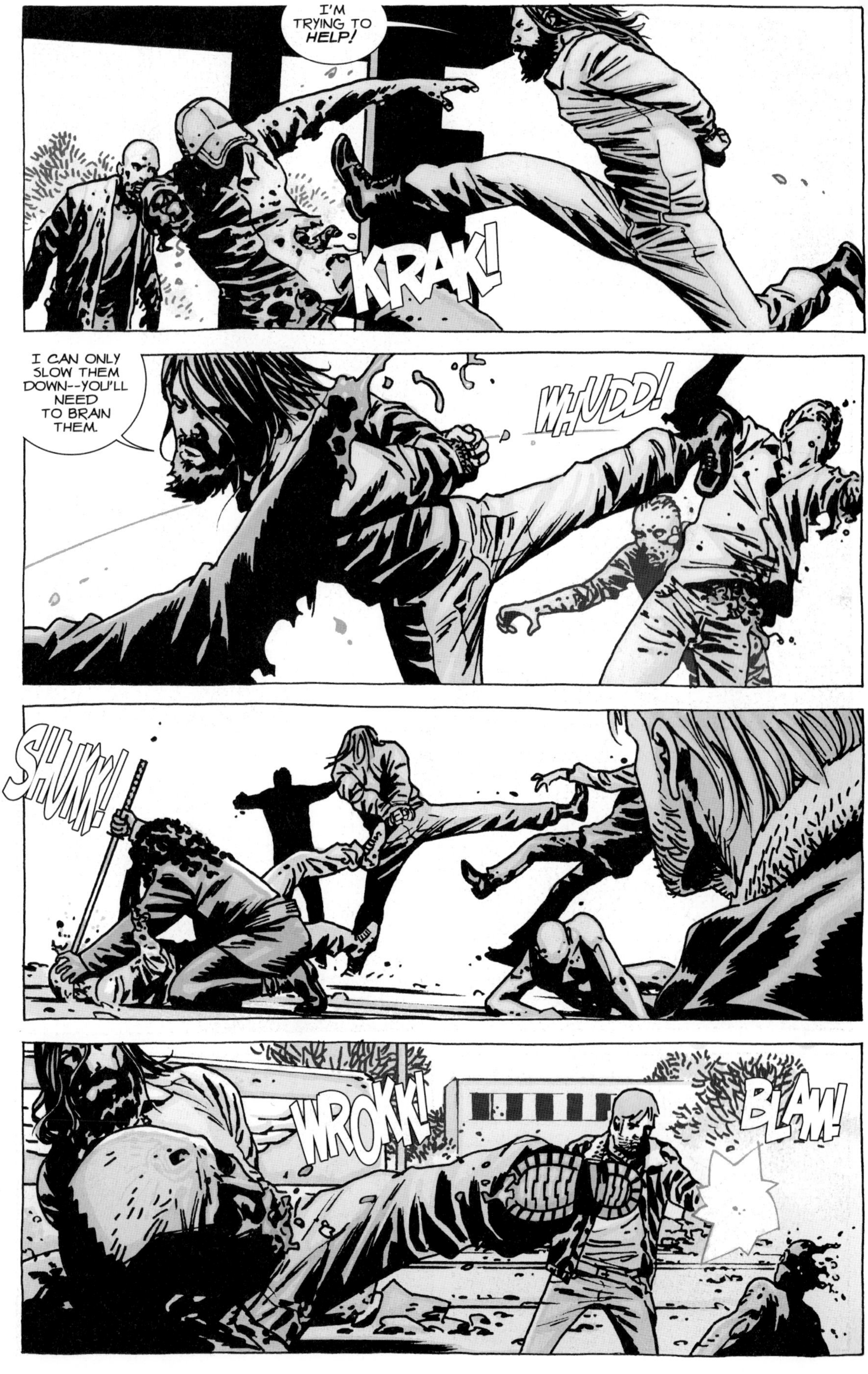

I'M TRYING TO HELP!
KRAK!
I CAN ONLY SLOW THEM DOWN--YOU'LL NEED TO BRAIN THEM.
WHUDD!
SHUKK!
WROKK!
BLAM!

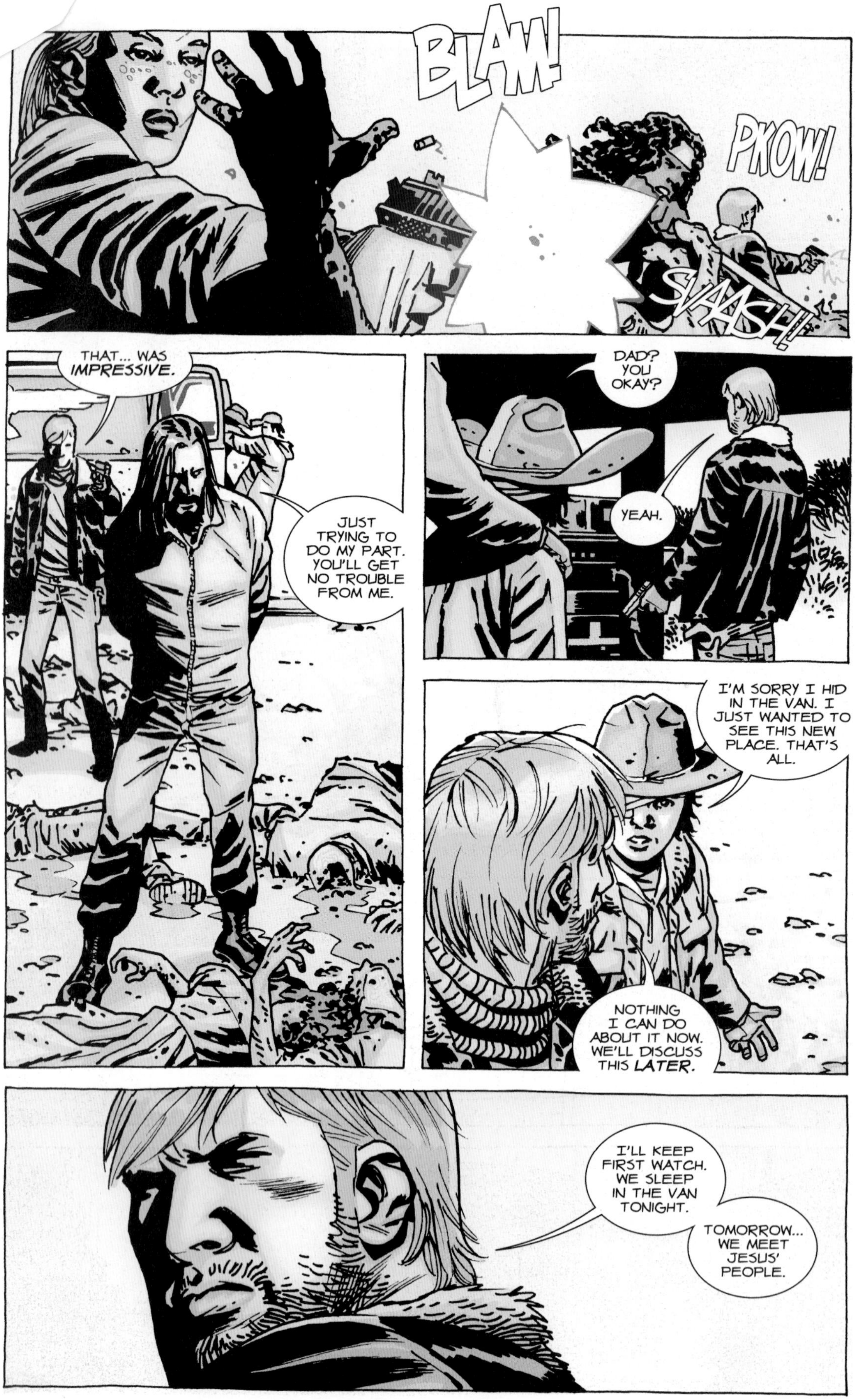
BLAM!
PKOW!
SHAASH!
THAT... WAS IMPRESSIVE.
JUST TRYING TO DO MY PART. YOU'LL GET NO TROUBLE FROM ME.
DAD? YOU OKAY?
YEAH.
I'M SORRY I HID IN THE VAN. I JUST WANTED TO SEE THIS NEW PLACE. THAT'S ALL.
NOTHING I CAN DO ABOUT IT NOW. WE'LL DISCUSS THIS LATER.
I'LL KEEP FIRST WATCH. WE SLEEP IN THE VAN TONIGHT.
TOMORROW... WE MEET JESUS' PEOPLE.

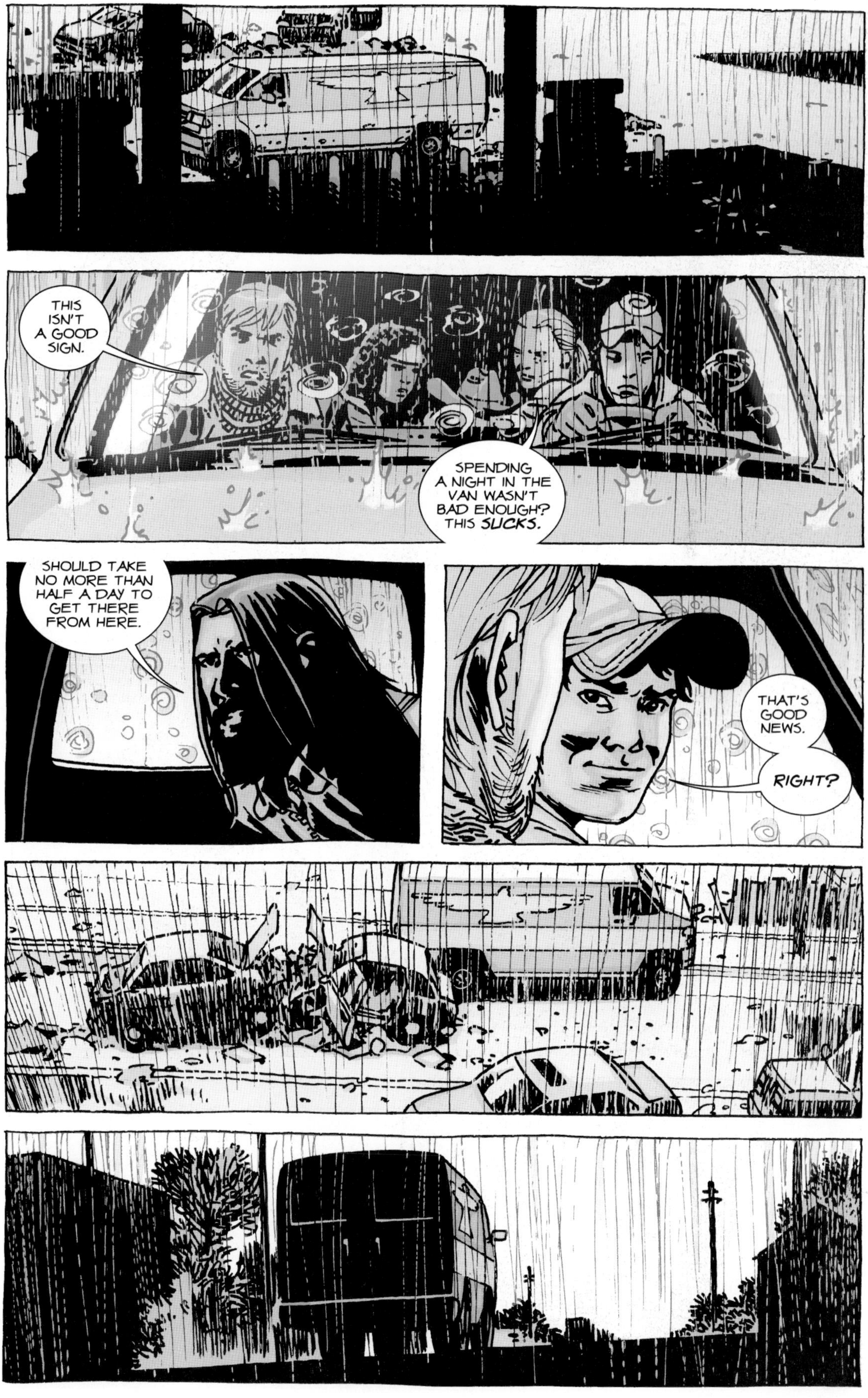
THIS ISN'T A GOOD SIGN.
SPENDING A NIGHT IN THE VAN WASN'T BAD ENOUGH? THIS SUCKS.
SHOULD TAKE NO MORE THAN HALF A DAY TO GET THERE FROM HERE.
THAT'S GOOD NEWS.
RIGHT?

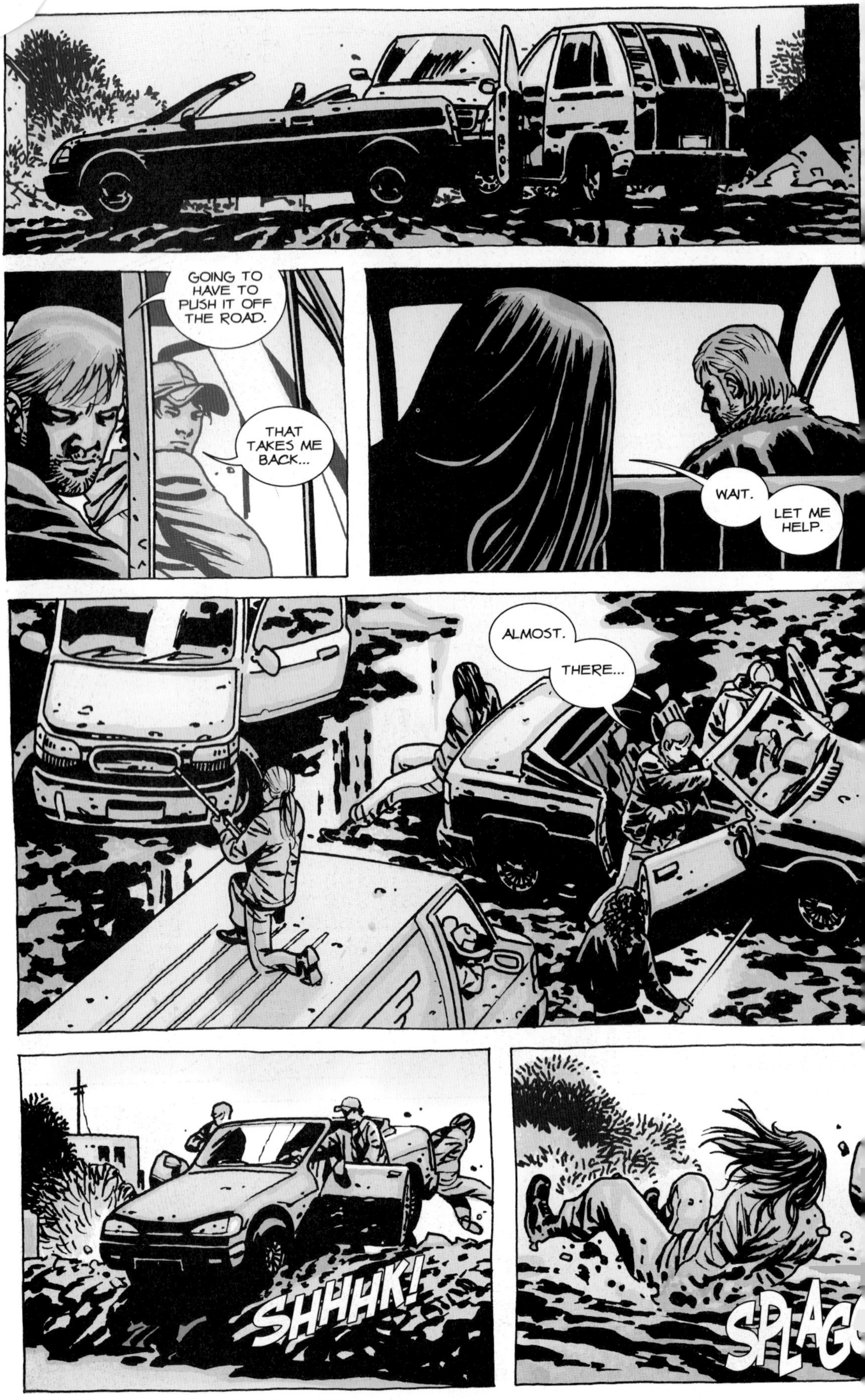
GOING TO HAVE TO PUSH IT OFF THE ROAD.
THAT TAKES ME BACK...
WAIT.
LET ME HELP.
ALMOST.
THERE...
SHHHK!
SPLAG

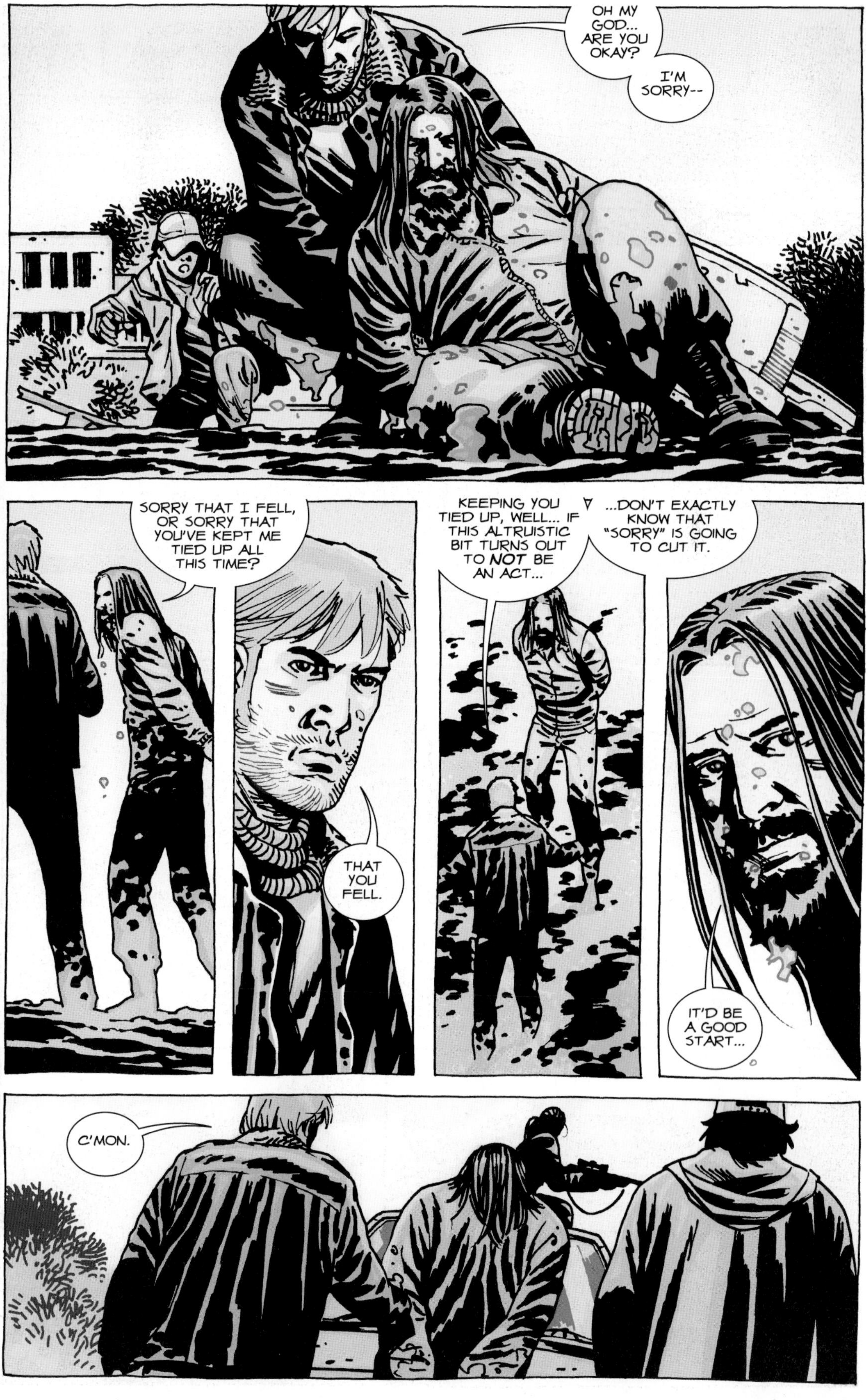

OH MY GOD... ARE YOU OKAY?
I'M SORRY--
SORRY THAT I FELL, OR SORRY THAT YOU'VE KEPT ME TIED UP ALL THIS TIME?
THAT YOU FELL.
KEEPING YOU TIED UP, WELL... IF THIS ALTRUISTIC BIT TURNS OUT TO NOT BE AN ACT...
...DON'T EXACTLY KNOW THAT "SORRY" IS GOING TO CUT IT.
IT'D BE A GOOD START...
C'MON.

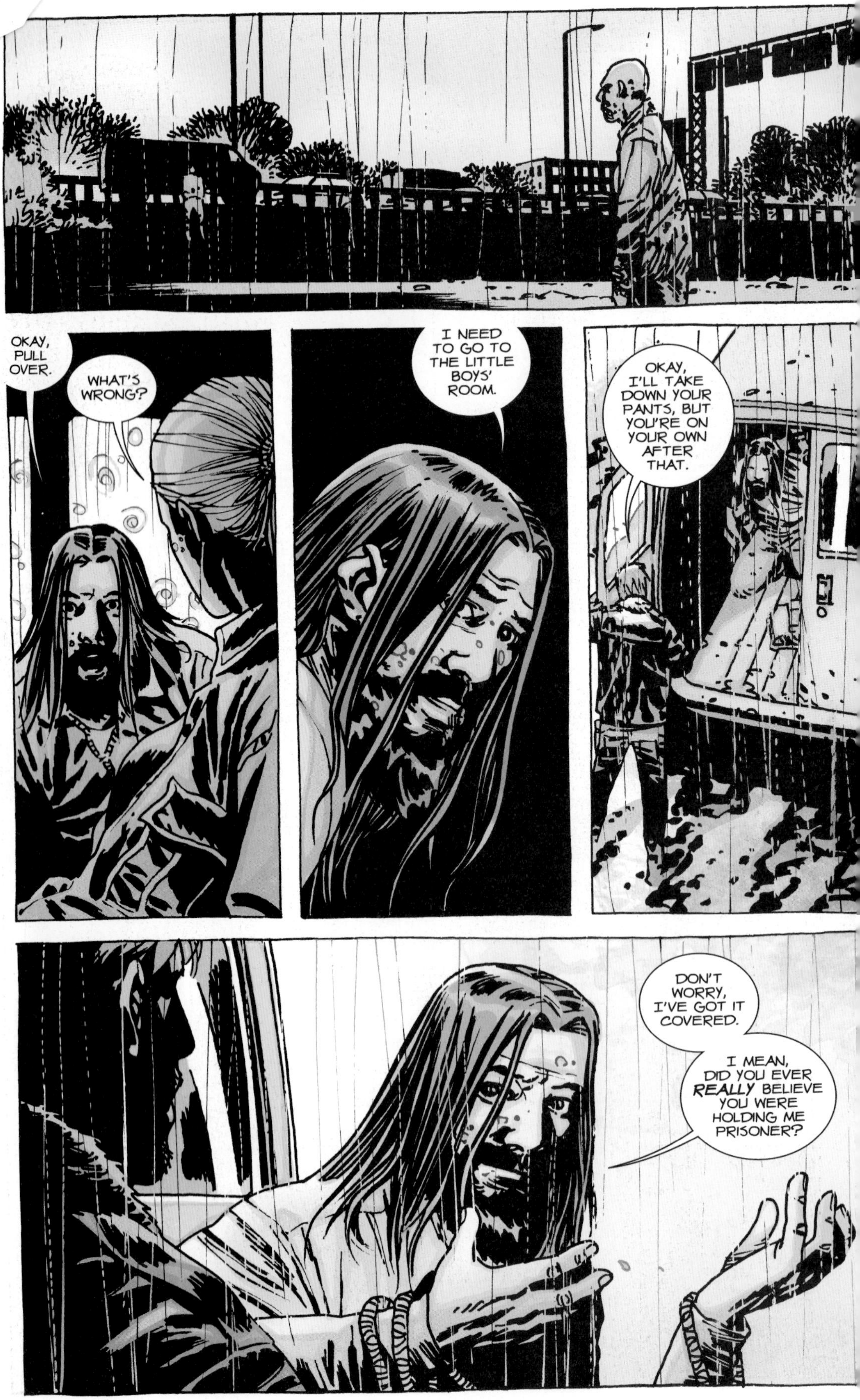
OKAY, PULL OVER.
WHAT'S WRONG?
I NEED TO GO TO THE LITTLE BOYS' ROOM.
OKAY, I'LL TAKE DOWN YOUR PANTS, BUT YOU'RE ON YOUR OWN AFTER THAT.
DON'T WORRY, I'VE GOT IT COVERED.
I MEAN, DID YOU EVER *REALLY* BELIEVE YOU WERE HOLDING ME PRISONER?

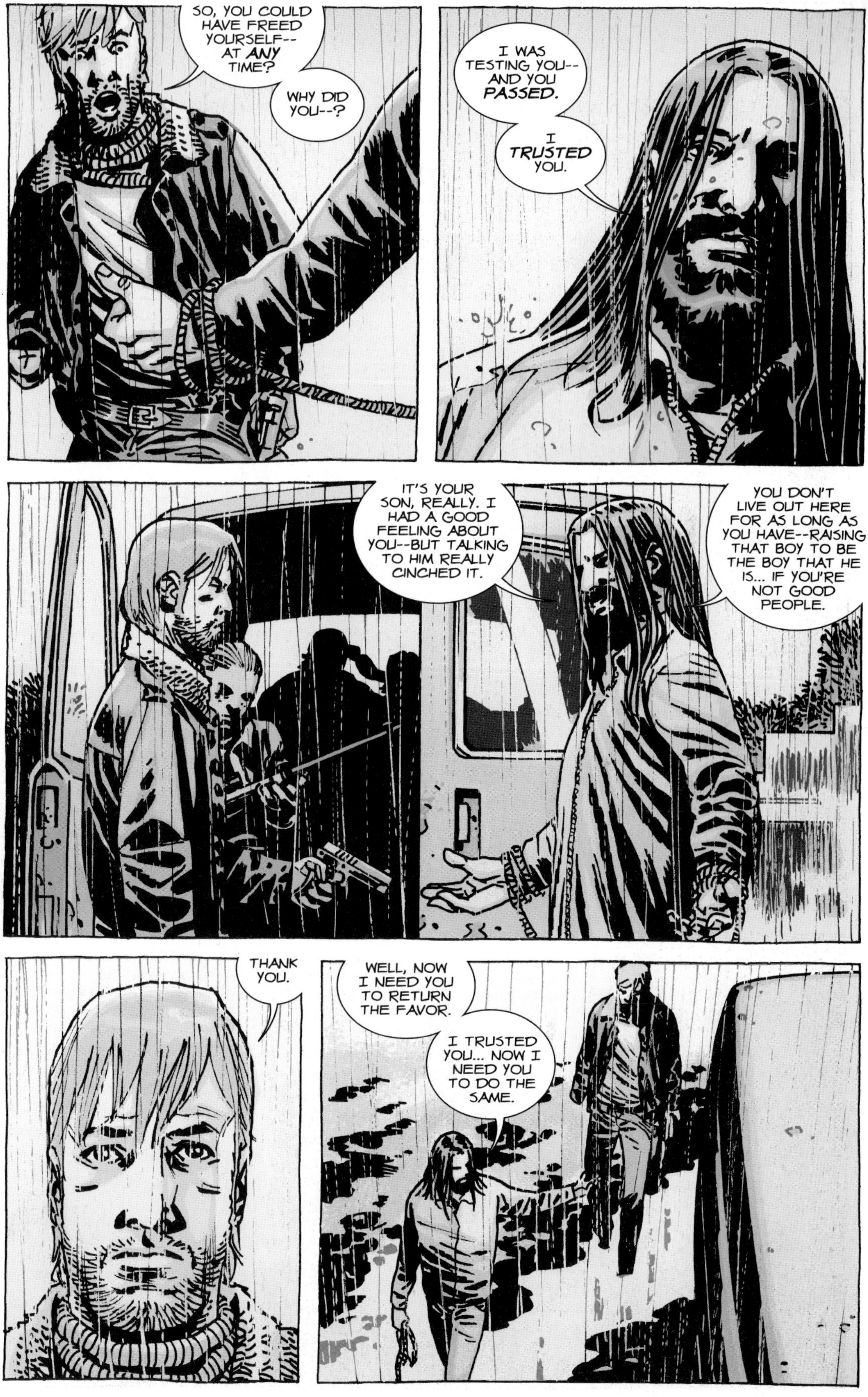
SO, YOU COULD HAVE FREED YOURSELF-- AT ANY TIME?
WHY DID YOU--?
I WAS TESTING YOU-- AND YOU PASSED.
I TRUSTED YOU.
IT'S YOUR SON, REALLY. I HAD A GOOD FEELING ABOUT YOU--BUT TALKING TO HIM REALLY CINCHED IT.
YOU DON'T LIVE OUT HERE FOR AS LONG AS YOU HAVE--RAISING THAT BOY TO BE THE BOY THAT HE IS... IF YOU'RE NOT GOOD PEOPLE.
THANK YOU.
WELL, NOW I NEED YOU TO RETURN THE FAVOR.
I TRUSTED YOU... NOW I NEED YOU TO DO THE SAME.

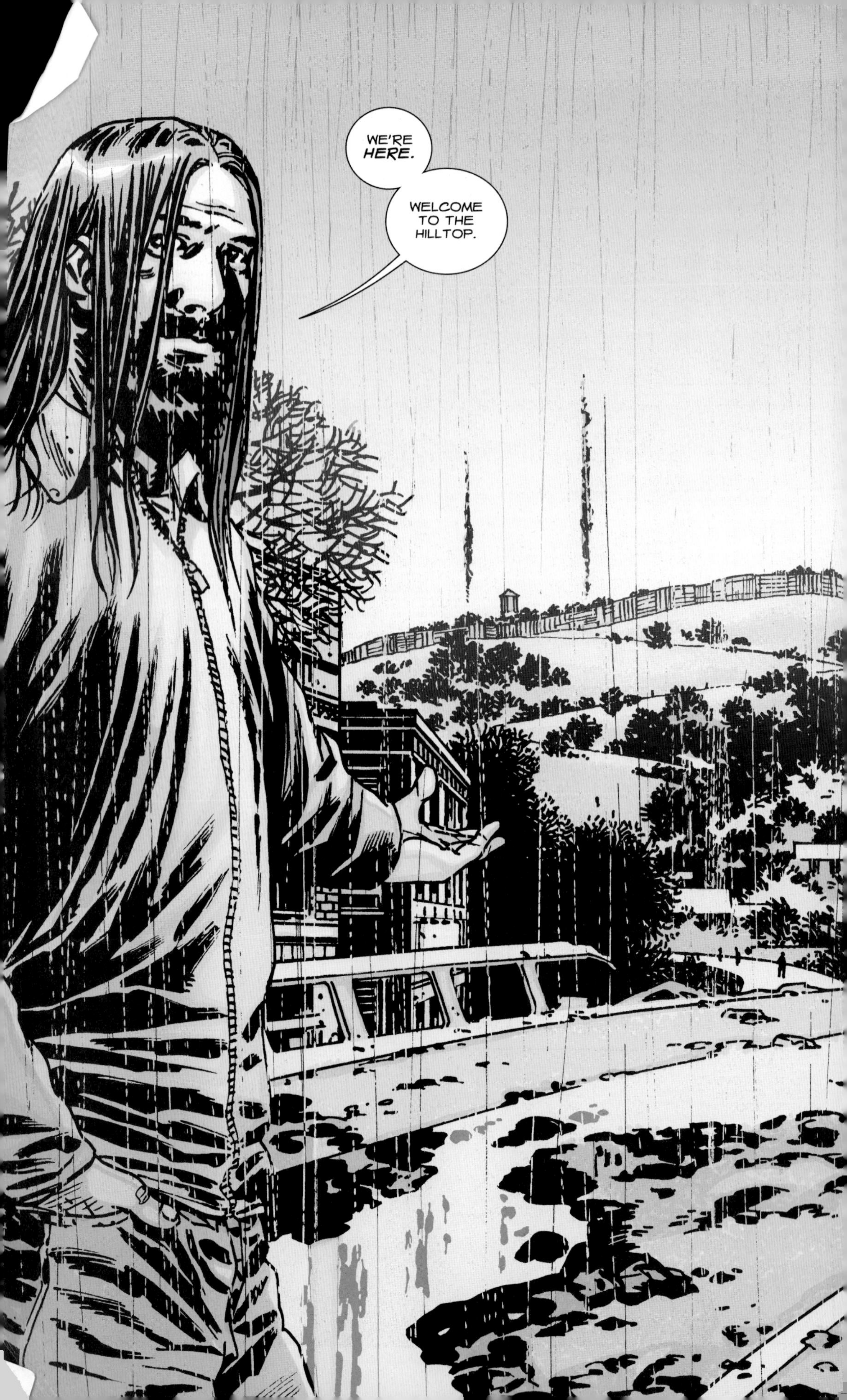
WE'RE *HERE*.
WELCOME TO THE HILLTOP.

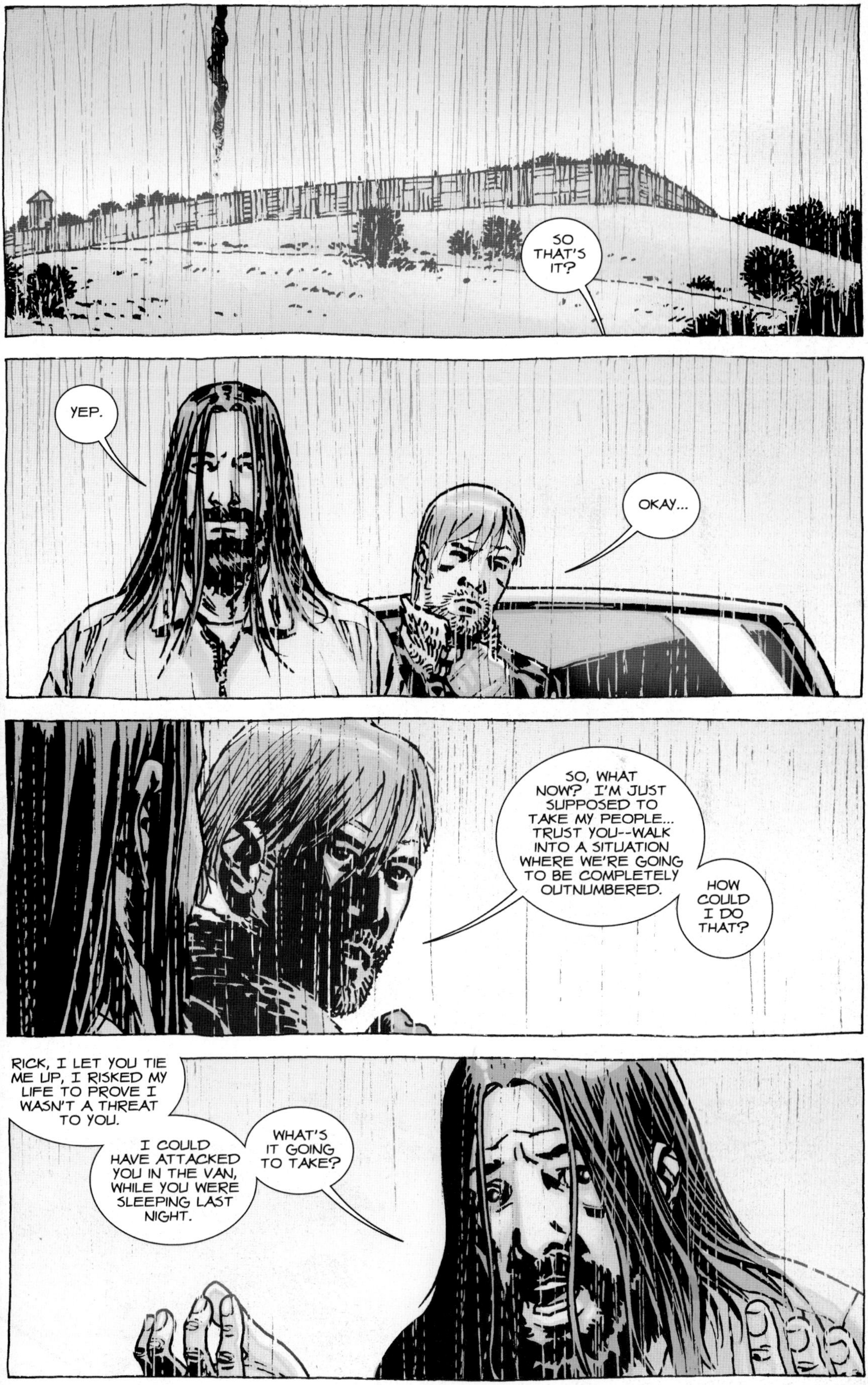
SO THAT'S IT?
YEP.
OKAY...
SO, WHAT NOW? I'M JUST SUPPOSED TO TAKE MY PEOPLE... TRUST YOU--WALK INTO A SITUATION WHERE WE'RE GOING TO BE COMPLETELY OUTNUMBERED.
HOW COULD I DO THAT?
RICK, I LET YOU TIE ME UP, I RISKED MY LIFE TO PROVE I WASN'T A THREAT TO YOU.
I COULD HAVE ATTACKED YOU IN THE VAN, WHILE YOU WERE SLEEPING LAST NIGHT.
WHAT'S IT GOING TO TAKE?

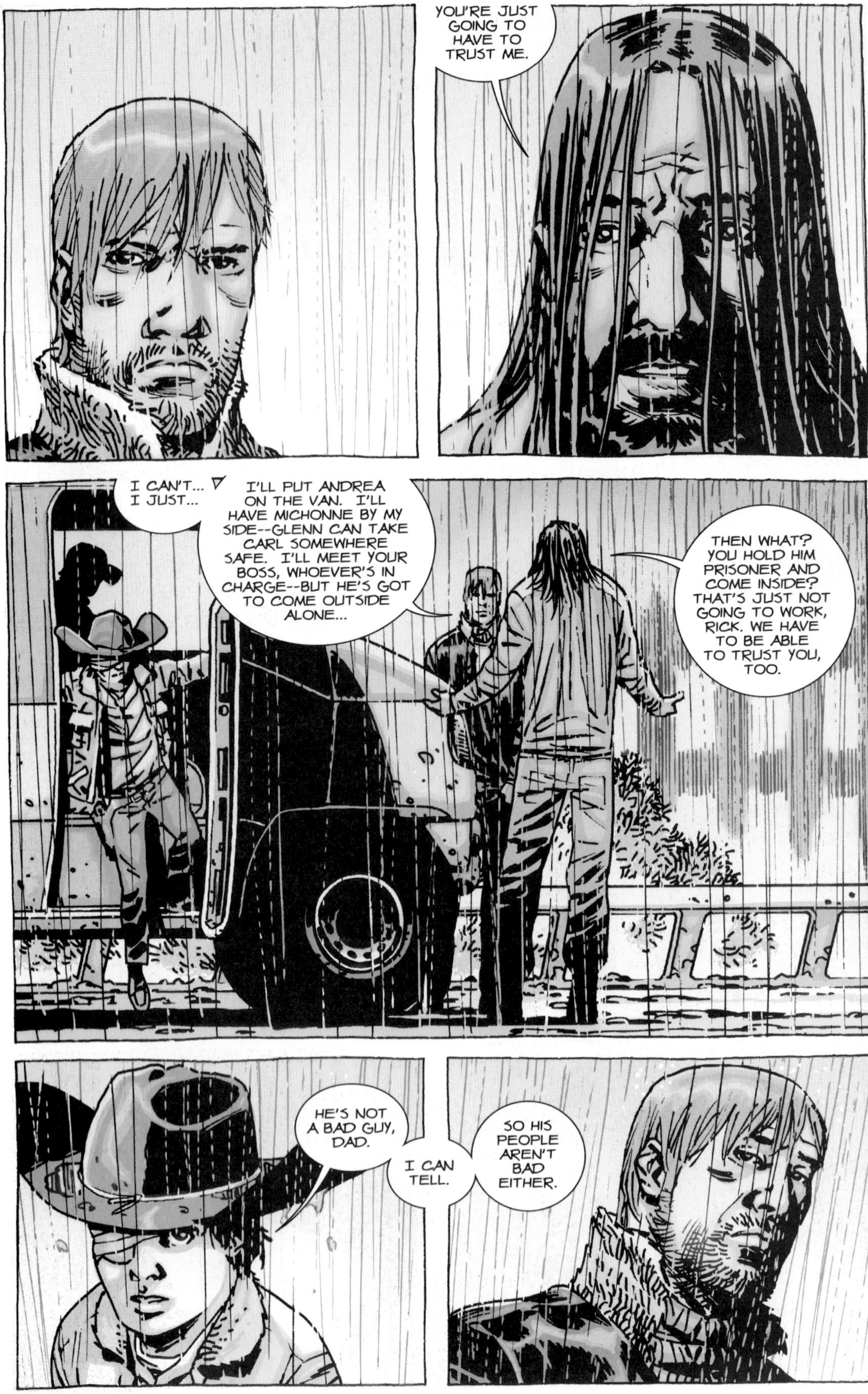
YOU'RE JUST GOING TO HAVE TO TRUST ME.
I CAN'T... I JUST...
I'LL PUT ANDREA ON THE VAN. I'LL HAVE MICHONNE BY MY SIDE--GLENN CAN TAKE CARL SOMEWHERE SAFE. I'LL MEET YOUR BOSS, WHOEVER'S IN CHARGE--BUT HE'S GOT TO COME OUTSIDE ALONE...
THEN WHAT? YOU HOLD HIM PRISONER AND COME INSIDE? THAT'S JUST NOT GOING TO WORK, RICK. WE HAVE TO BE ABLE TO TRUST YOU, TOO.
HE'S NOT A BAD GUY, DAD.
I CAN TELL.
SO HIS PEOPLE AREN'T BAD EITHER.

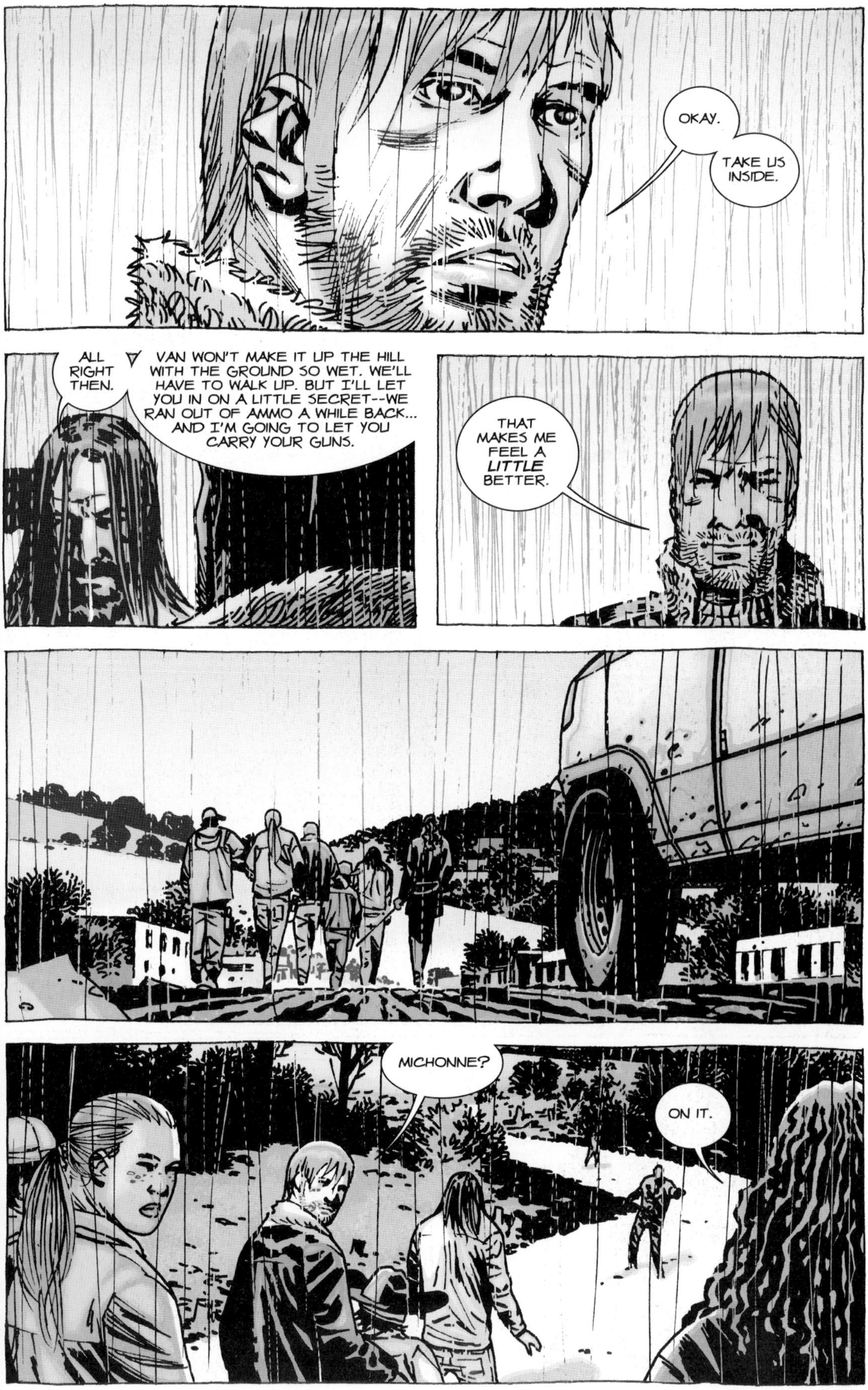
OKAY.
TAKE US INSIDE.
ALL RIGHT THEN.
VAN WON'T MAKE IT UP THE HILL WITH THE GROUND SO WET. WE'LL HAVE TO WALK UP. BUT I'LL LET YOU IN ON A LITTLE SECRET--WE RAN OUT OF AMMO A WHILE BACK... AND I'M GOING TO LET YOU CARRY YOUR GUNS.
THAT MAKES ME FEEL A *LITTLE* BETTER.
MICHONNE?
ON IT.

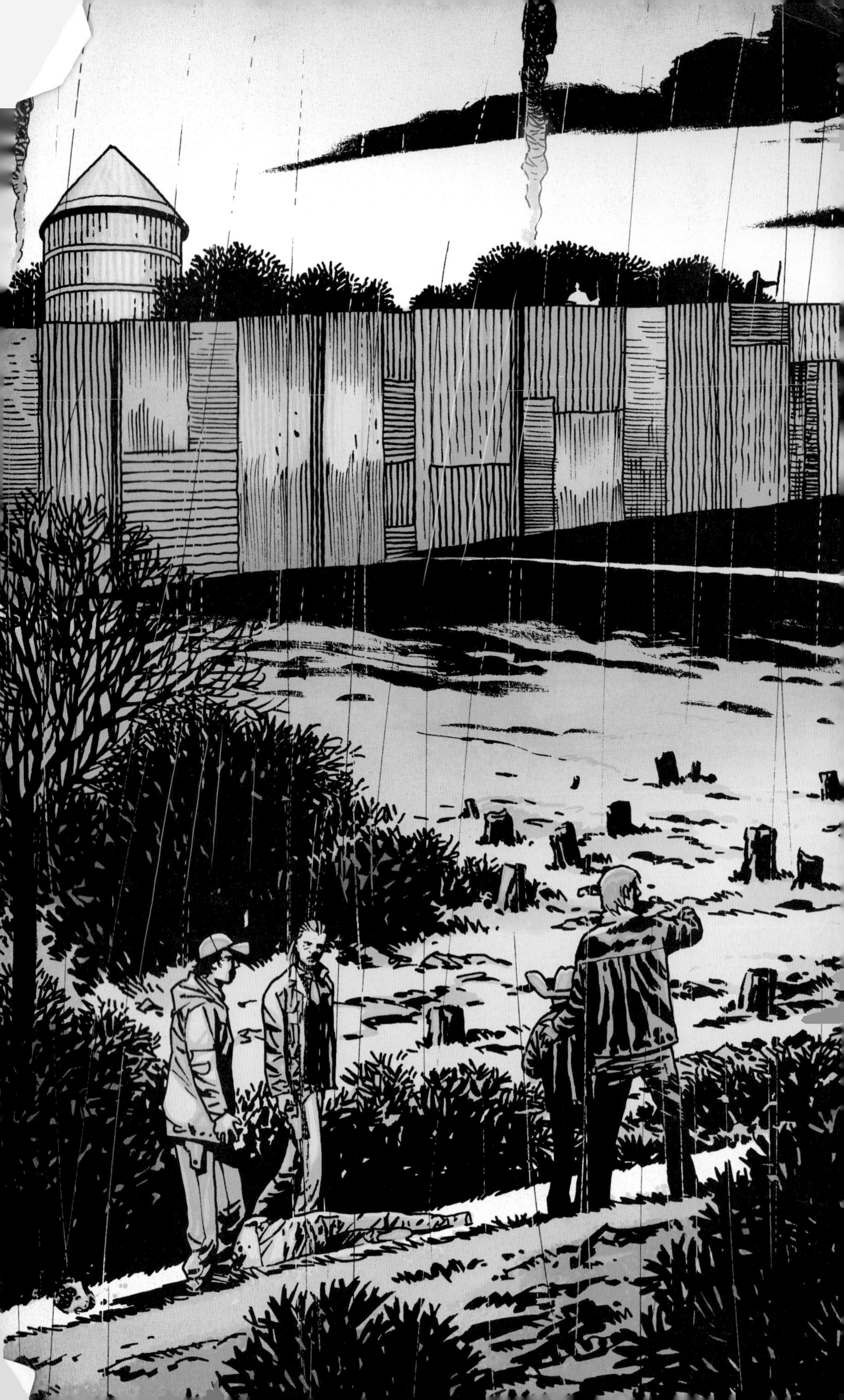

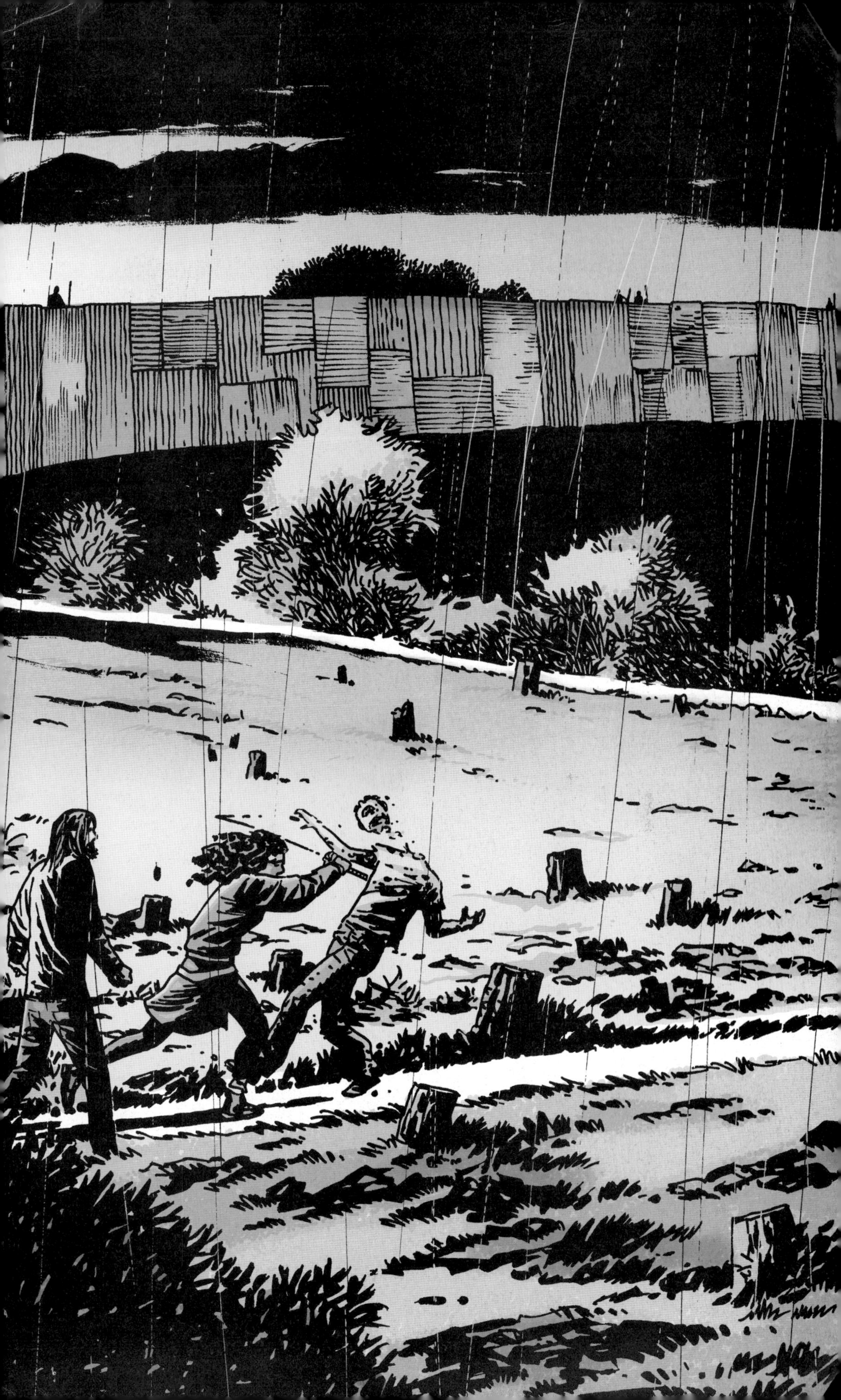

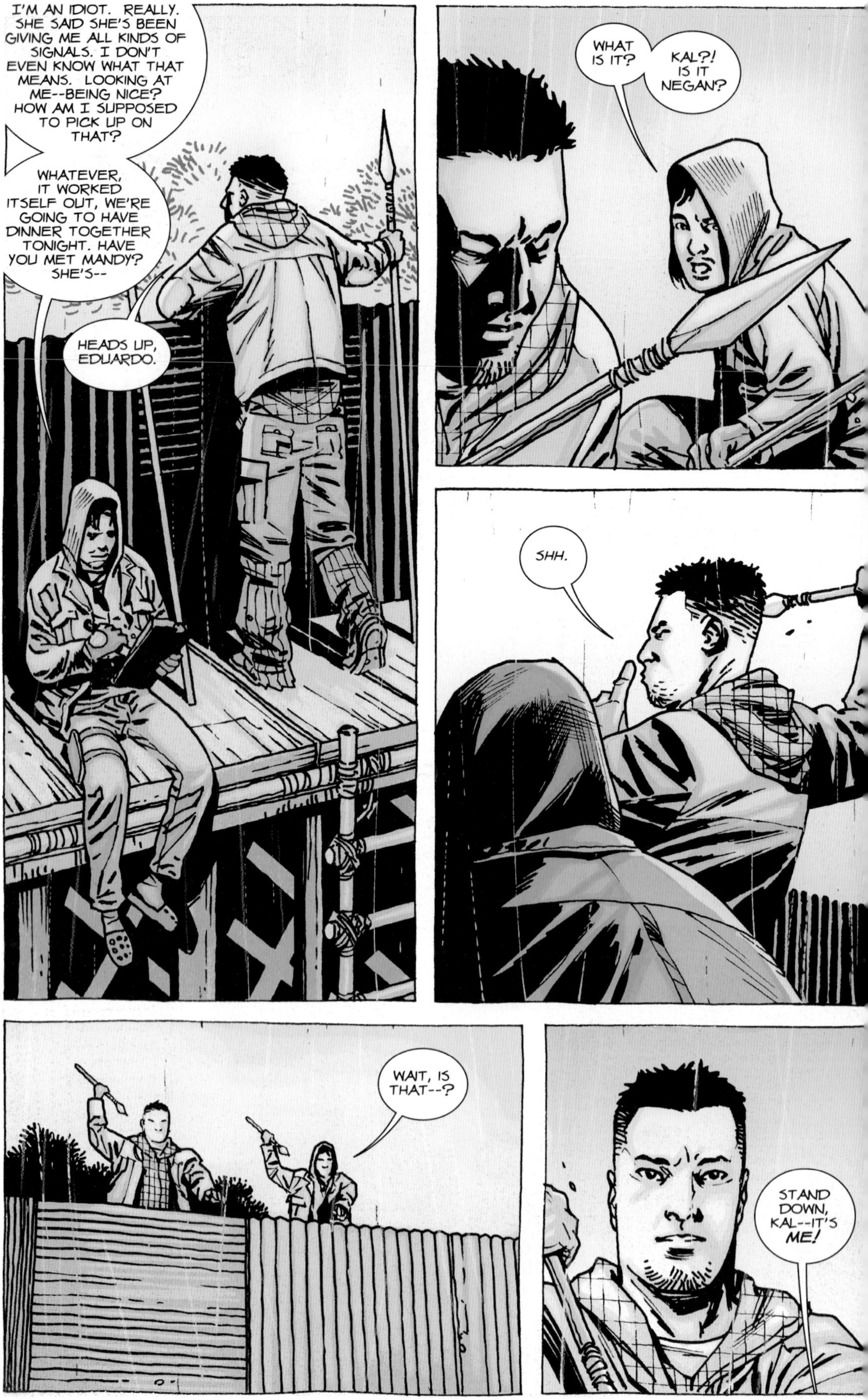
I'M AN IDIOT. REALLY. SHE SAID SHE'S BEEN GIVING ME ALL KINDS OF SIGNALS. I DON'T EVEN KNOW WHAT THAT MEANS. LOOKING AT ME--BEING NICE? HOW AM I SUPPOSED TO PICK UP ON THAT?
WHATEVER, IT WORKED ITSELF OUT, WE'RE GOING TO HAVE DINNER TOGETHER TONIGHT. HAVE YOU MET MANDY? SHE'S--
HEADS UP, EDUARDO.
WHAT IS IT?
KAL?! IS IT NEGAN?
SHH.
WAIT, IS THAT--?
STAND DOWN, KAL--IT'S *ME!*

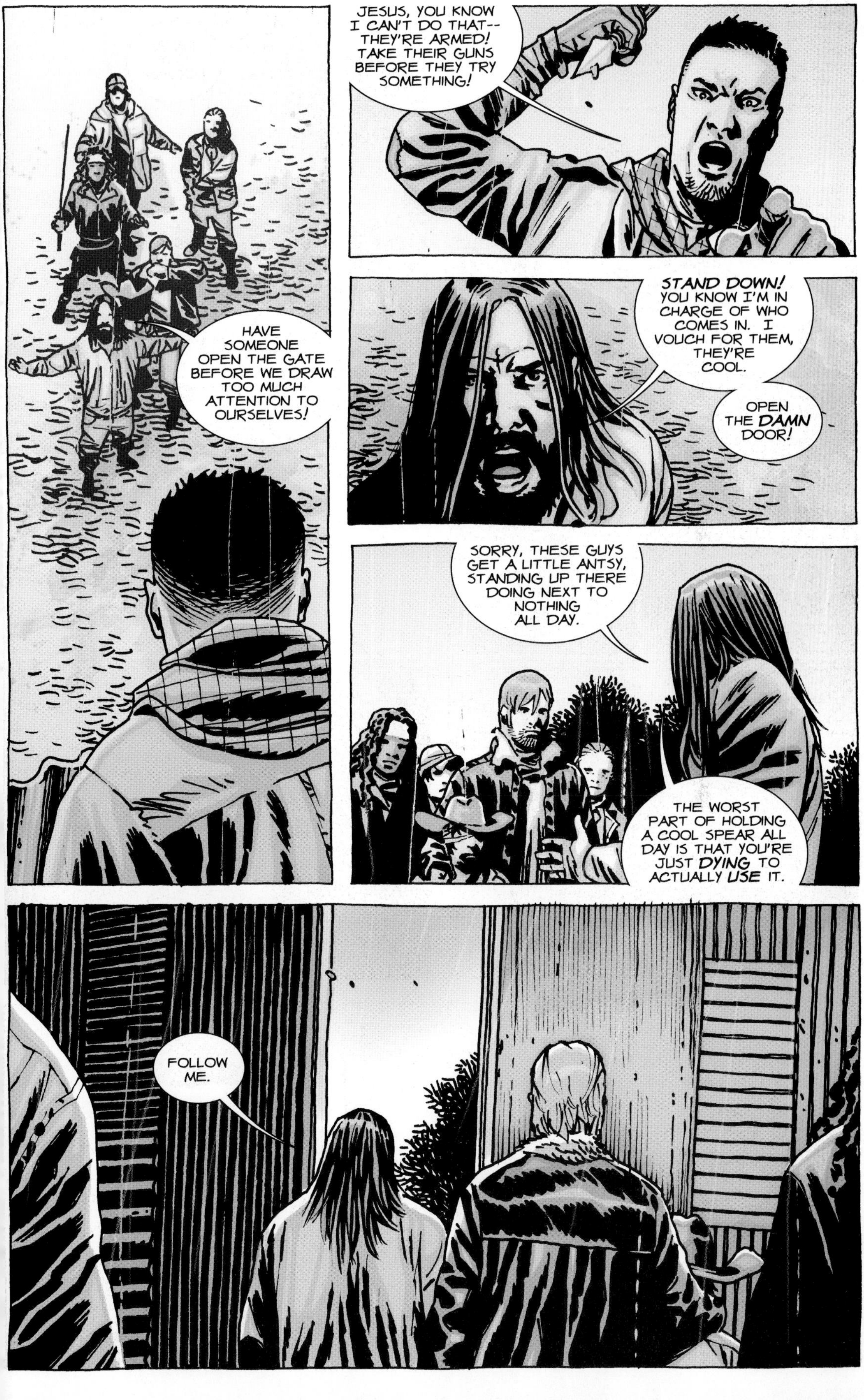
HAVE SOMEONE OPEN THE GATE BEFORE WE DRAW TOO MUCH ATTENTION TO OURSELVES!
JESUS, YOU KNOW I CAN'T DO THAT-- THEY'RE ARMED! TAKE THEIR GUNS BEFORE THEY TRY SOMETHING!
STAND DOWN! YOU KNOW I'M IN CHARGE OF WHO COMES IN. I VOUCH FOR THEM, THEY'RE COOL.
OPEN THE DAMN DOOR!
SORRY, THESE GUYS GET A LITTLE ANTSY, STANDING UP THERE DOING NEXT TO NOTHING ALL DAY.
THE WORST PART OF HOLDING A COOL SPEAR ALL DAY IS THAT YOU'RE JUST DYING TO ACTUALLY USE IT.
FOLLOW ME.

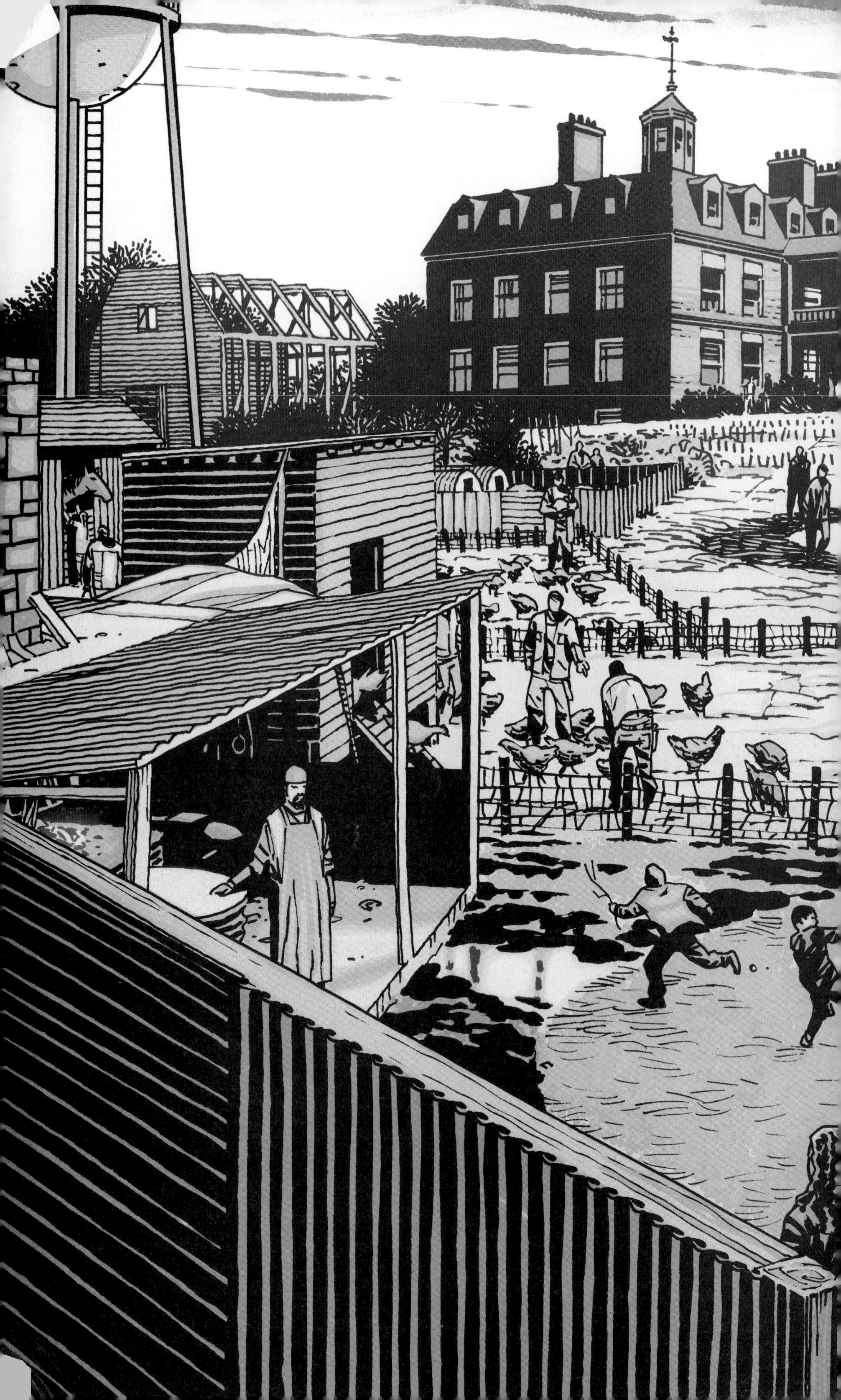

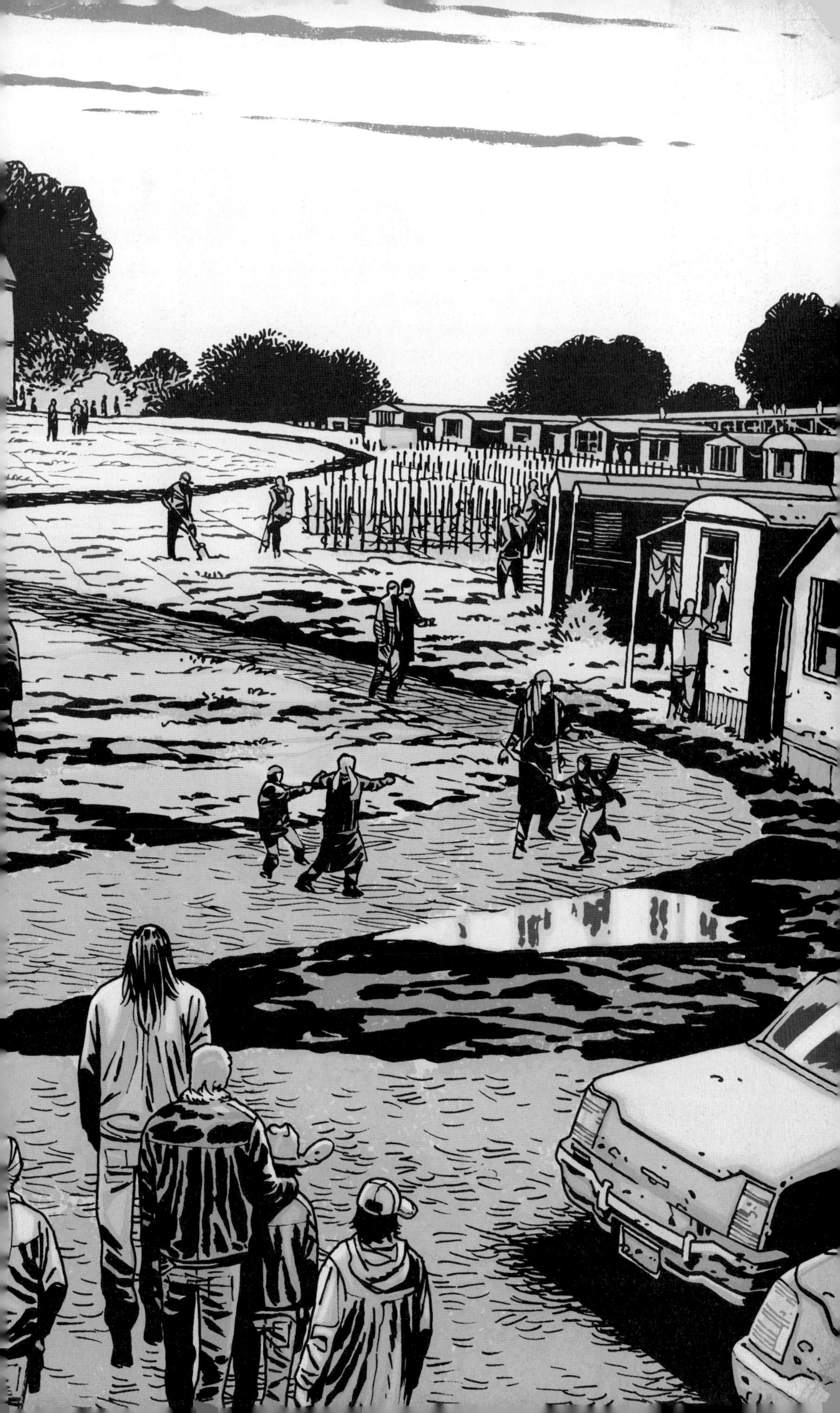

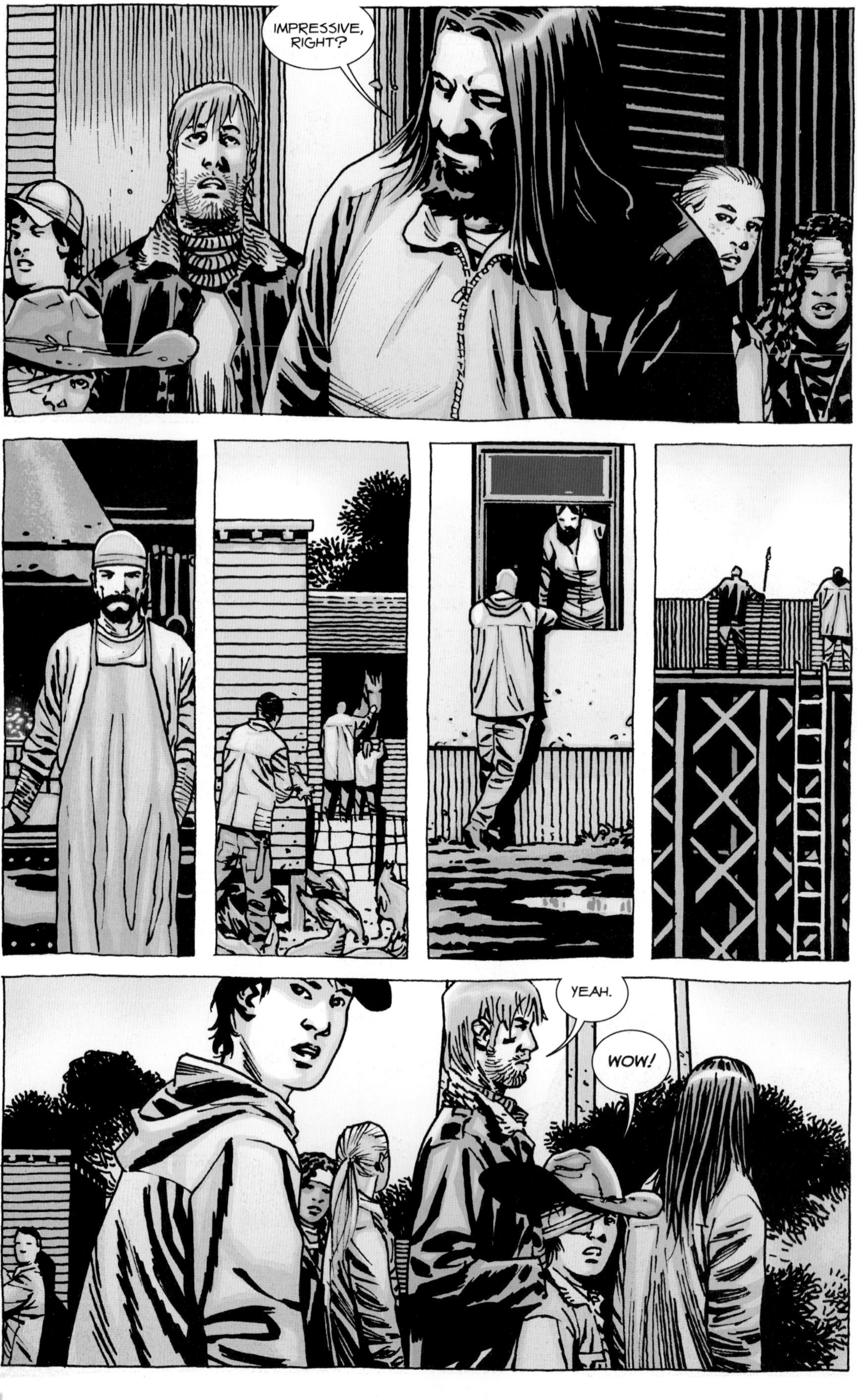
IMPRESSIVE, RIGHT?
YEAH.
WOW!

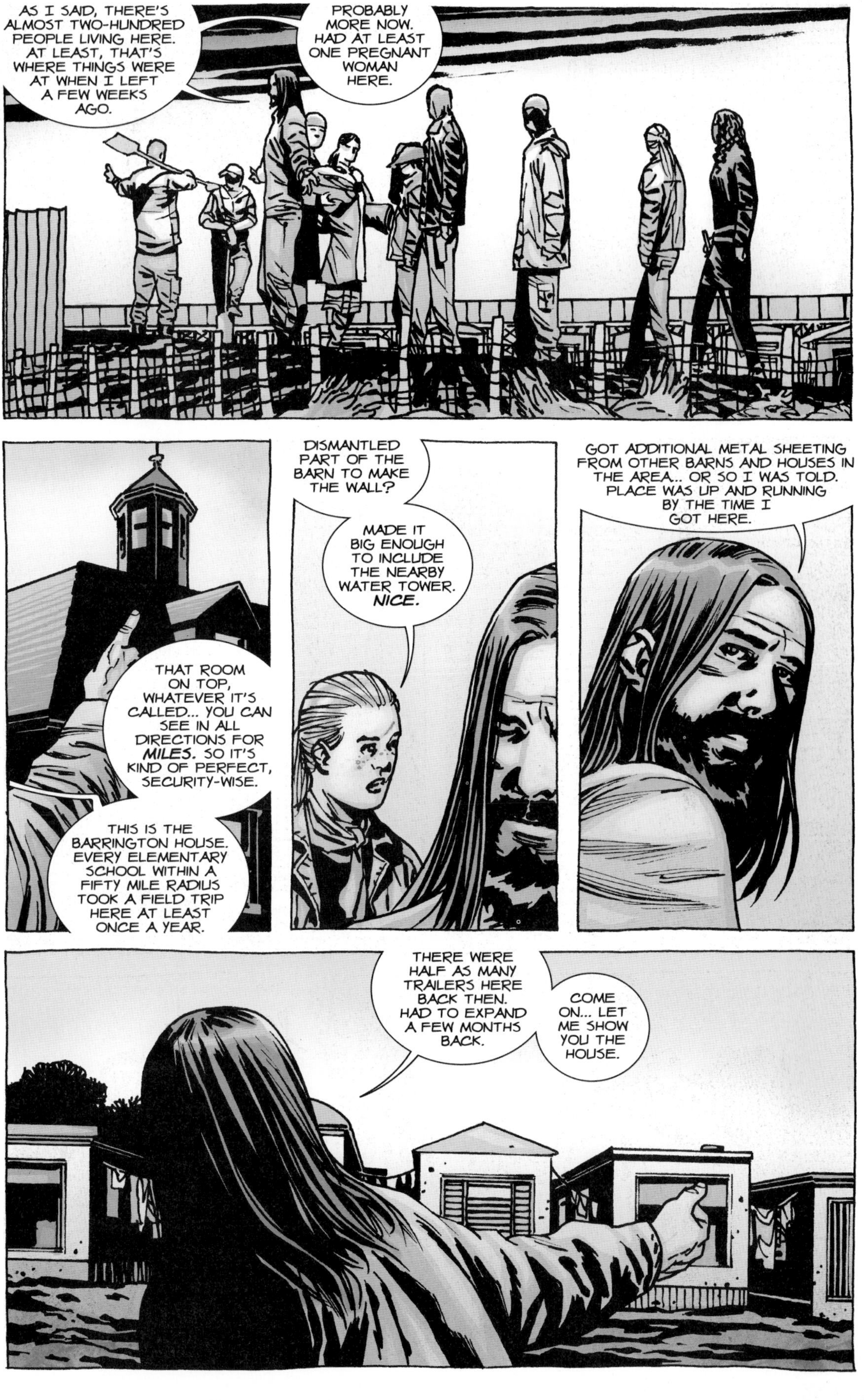
AS I SAID, THERE'S ALMOST TWO-HUNDRED PEOPLE LIVING HERE. AT LEAST, THAT'S WHERE THINGS WERE AT WHEN I LEFT A FEW WEEKS AGO.
PROBABLY MORE NOW. HAD AT LEAST ONE PREGNANT WOMAN HERE.
THAT ROOM ON TOP, WHATEVER IT'S CALLED... YOU CAN SEE IN ALL DIRECTIONS FOR MILES. SO IT'S KIND OF PERFECT, SECURITY-WISE.
THIS IS THE BARRINGTON HOUSE. EVERY ELEMENTARY SCHOOL WITHIN A FIFTY MILE RADIUS TOOK A FIELD TRIP HERE AT LEAST ONCE A YEAR.
DISMANTLED PART OF THE BARN TO MAKE THE WALL?
MADE IT BIG ENOUGH TO INCLUDE THE NEARBY WATER TOWER. NICE.
GOT ADDITIONAL METAL SHEETING FROM OTHER BARNS AND HOUSES IN THE AREA... OR SO I WAS TOLD. PLACE WAS UP AND RUNNING BY THE TIME I GOT HERE.
THERE WERE HALF AS MANY TRAILERS HERE BACK THEN. HAD TO EXPAND A FEW MONTHS BACK.
COME ON... LET ME SHOW YOU THE HOUSE.

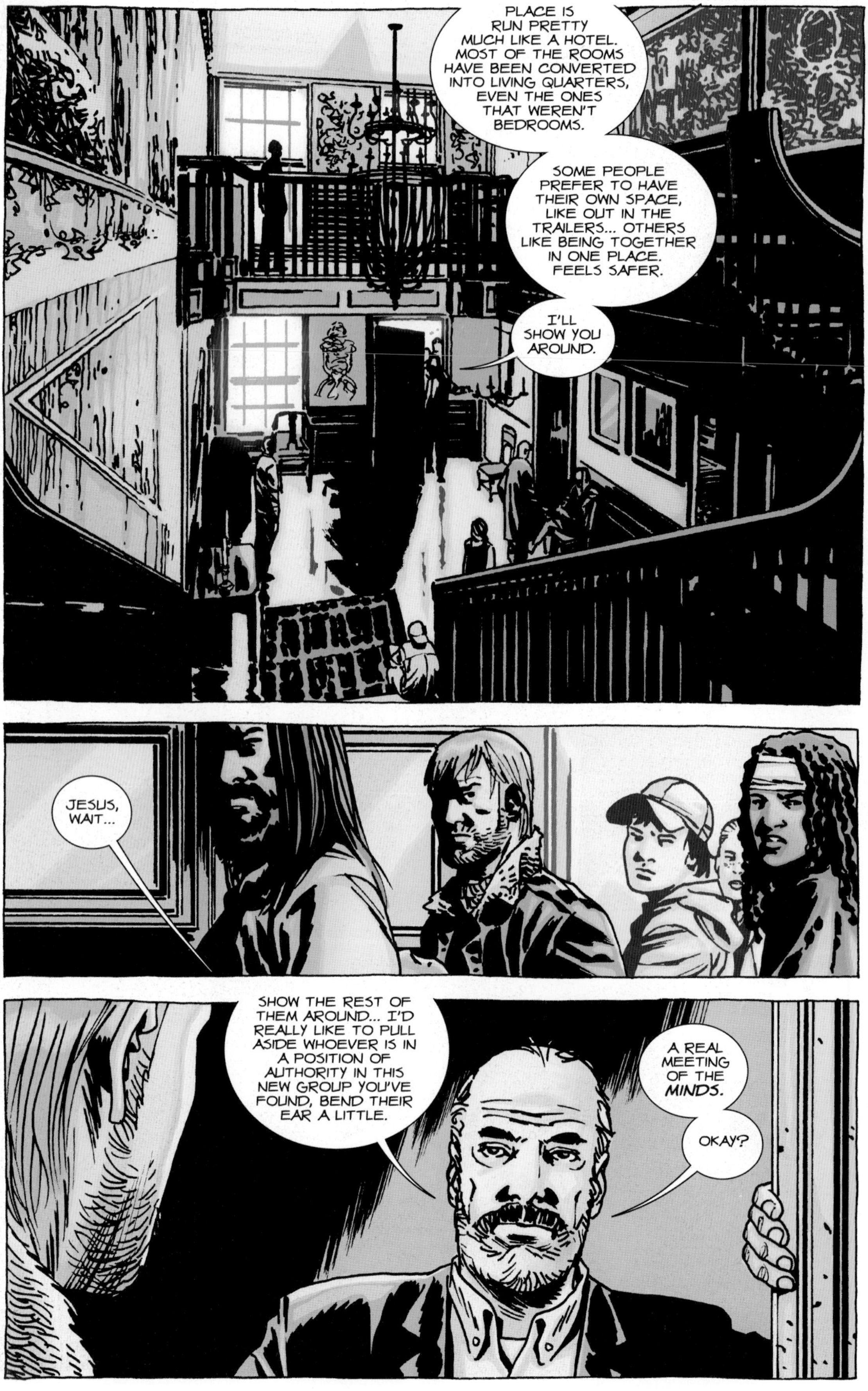
PLACE IS RUN PRETTY MUCH LIKE A HOTEL. MOST OF THE ROOMS HAVE BEEN CONVERTED INTO LIVING QUARTERS, EVEN THE ONES THAT WEREN'T BEDROOMS.
SOME PEOPLE PREFER TO HAVE THEIR OWN SPACE, LIKE OUT IN THE TRAILERS... OTHERS LIKE BEING TOGETHER IN ONE PLACE. FEELS SAFER.
I'LL SHOW YOU AROUND.
JESUS, WAIT...
SHOW THE REST OF THEM AROUND... I'D REALLY LIKE TO PULL ASIDE WHOEVER IS IN A POSITION OF AUTHORITY IN THIS NEW GROUP YOU'VE FOUND, BEND THEIR EAR A LITTLE.
A REAL MEETING OF THE *MINDS*.
OKAY?

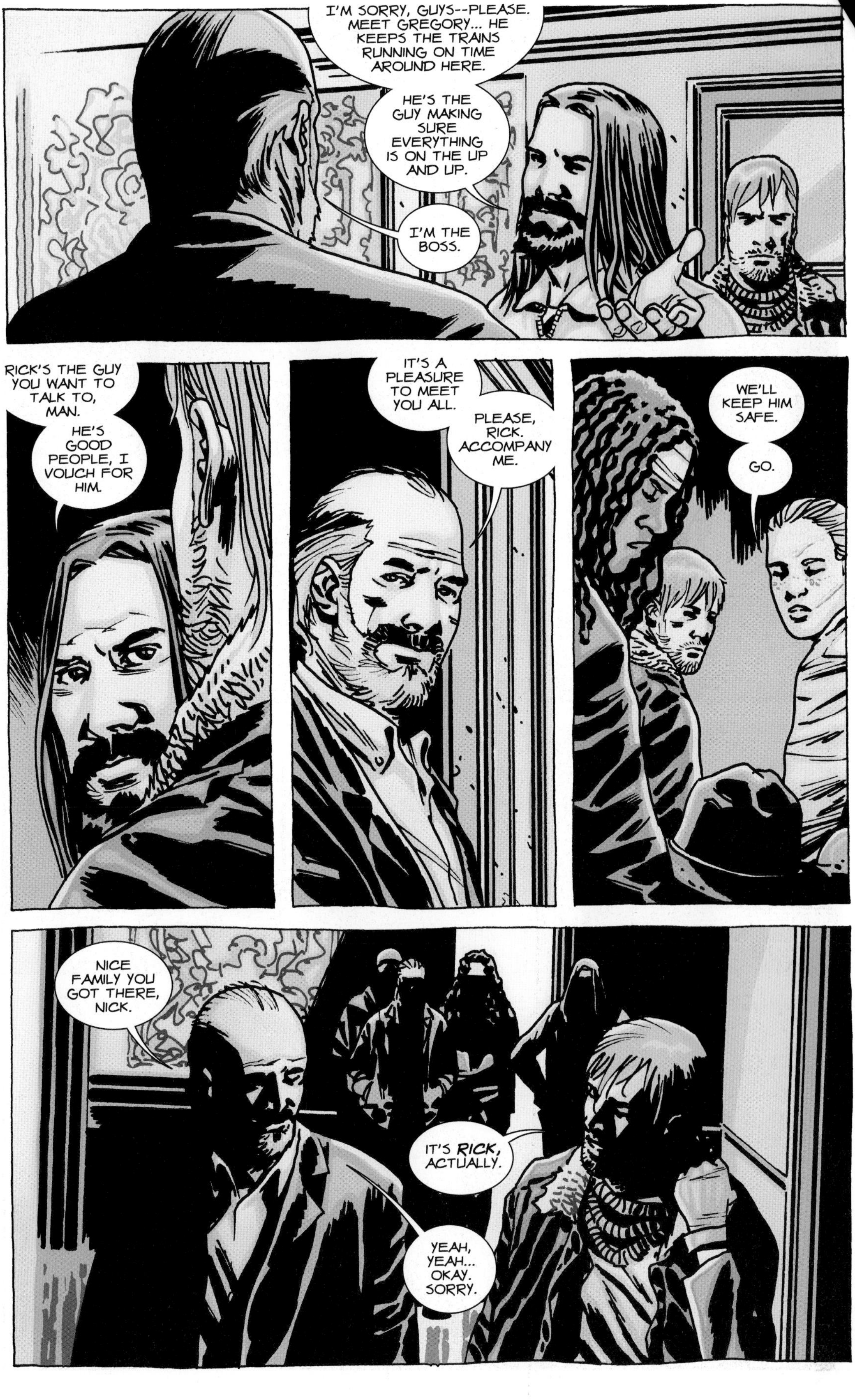
I'M SORRY, GUYS--PLEASE. MEET GREGORY... HE KEEPS THE TRAINS RUNNING ON TIME AROUND HERE.
HE'S THE GUY MAKING SURE EVERYTHING IS ON THE UP AND UP.
I'M THE BOSS.
RICK'S THE GUY YOU WANT TO TALK TO, MAN.
HE'S GOOD PEOPLE, I VOUCH FOR HIM.
IT'S A PLEASURE TO MEET YOU ALL.
PLEASE, RICK. ACCOMPANY ME.
WE'LL KEEP HIM SAFE.
GO.
NICE FAMILY YOU GOT THERE, NICK.
IT'S RICK, ACTUALLY.
YEAH, YEAH... OKAY. SORRY.

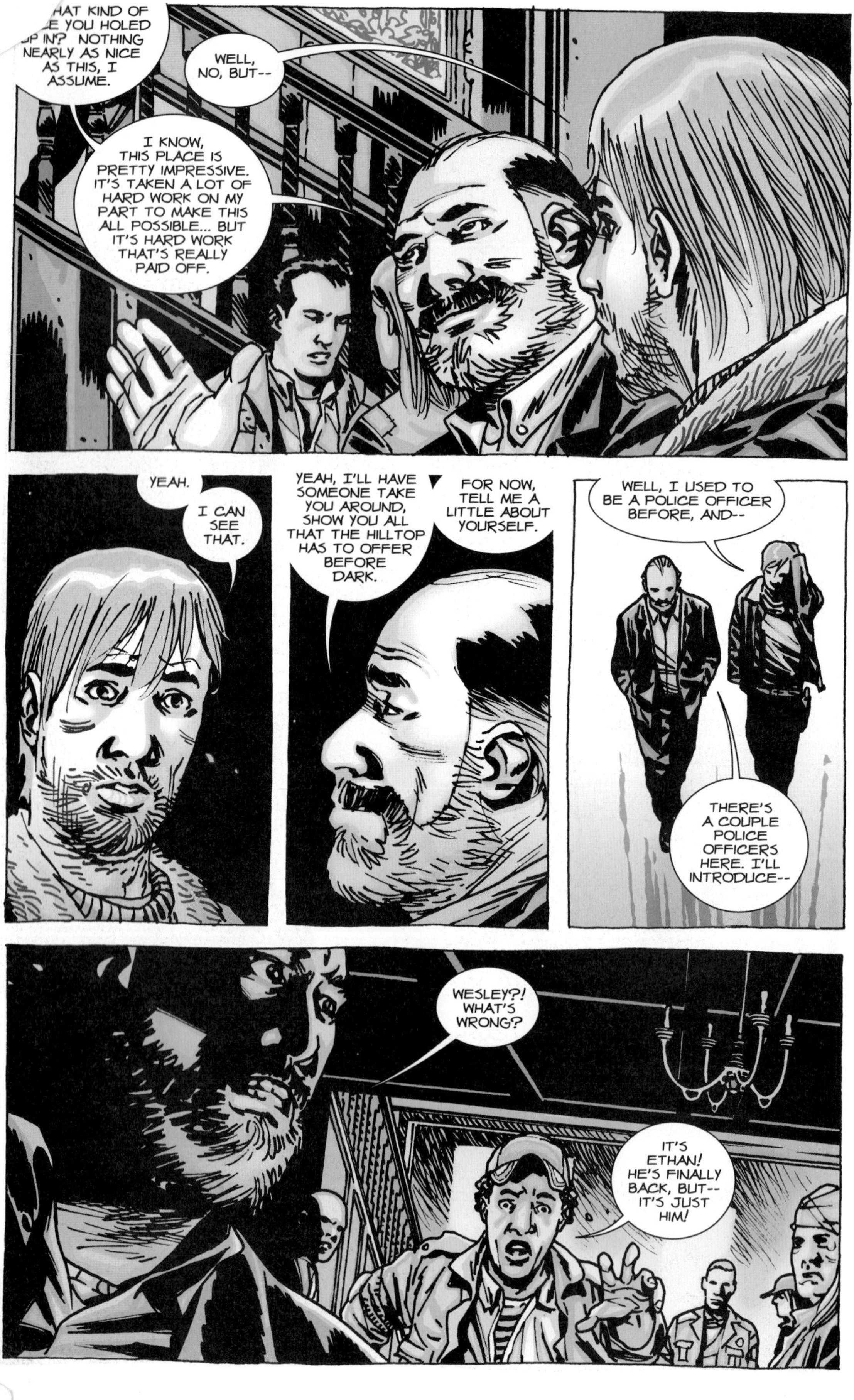
...HAT KIND OF ...CE YOU HOLED ...UP IN? NOTHING NEARLY AS NICE AS THIS, I ASSUME.
WELL, NO, BUT--
I KNOW, THIS PLACE IS PRETTY IMPRESSIVE. IT'S TAKEN A LOT OF HARD WORK ON MY PART TO MAKE THIS ALL POSSIBLE... BUT IT'S HARD WORK THAT'S REALLY PAID OFF.
YEAH.
I CAN SEE THAT.
YEAH, I'LL HAVE SOMEONE TAKE YOU AROUND, SHOW YOU ALL THAT THE HILLTOP HAS TO OFFER BEFORE DARK.
FOR NOW, TELL ME A LITTLE ABOUT YOURSELF.
WELL, I USED TO BE A POLICE OFFICER BEFORE, AND--
THERE'S A COUPLE POLICE OFFICERS HERE. I'LL INTRODUCE--
WESLEY?! WHAT'S WRONG?
IT'S ETHAN! HE'S FINALLY BACK, BUT-- IT'S JUST HIM!

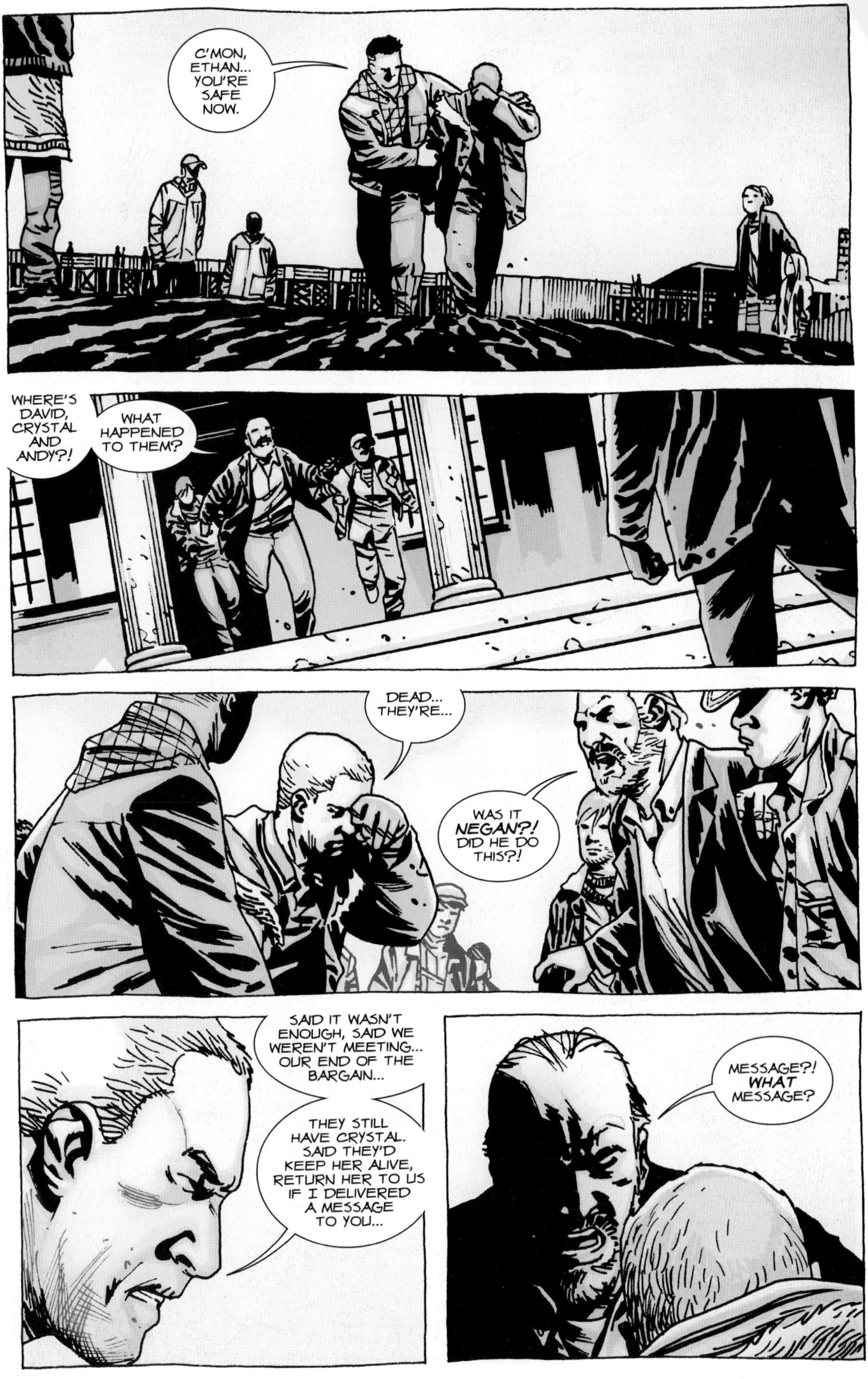
C'MON, ETHAN... YOU'RE SAFE NOW.
WHERE'S DAVID, CRYSTAL AND ANDY?!
WHAT HAPPENED TO THEM?
DEAD... THEY'RE...
WAS IT NEGAN?! DID HE DO THIS?!
SAID IT WASN'T ENOUGH, SAID WE WEREN'T MEETING... OUR END OF THE BARGAIN...
THEY STILL HAVE CRYSTAL. SAID THEY'D KEEP HER ALIVE, RETURN HER TO US IF I DELIVERED A MESSAGE TO YOU...
MESSAGE?! WHAT MESSAGE?

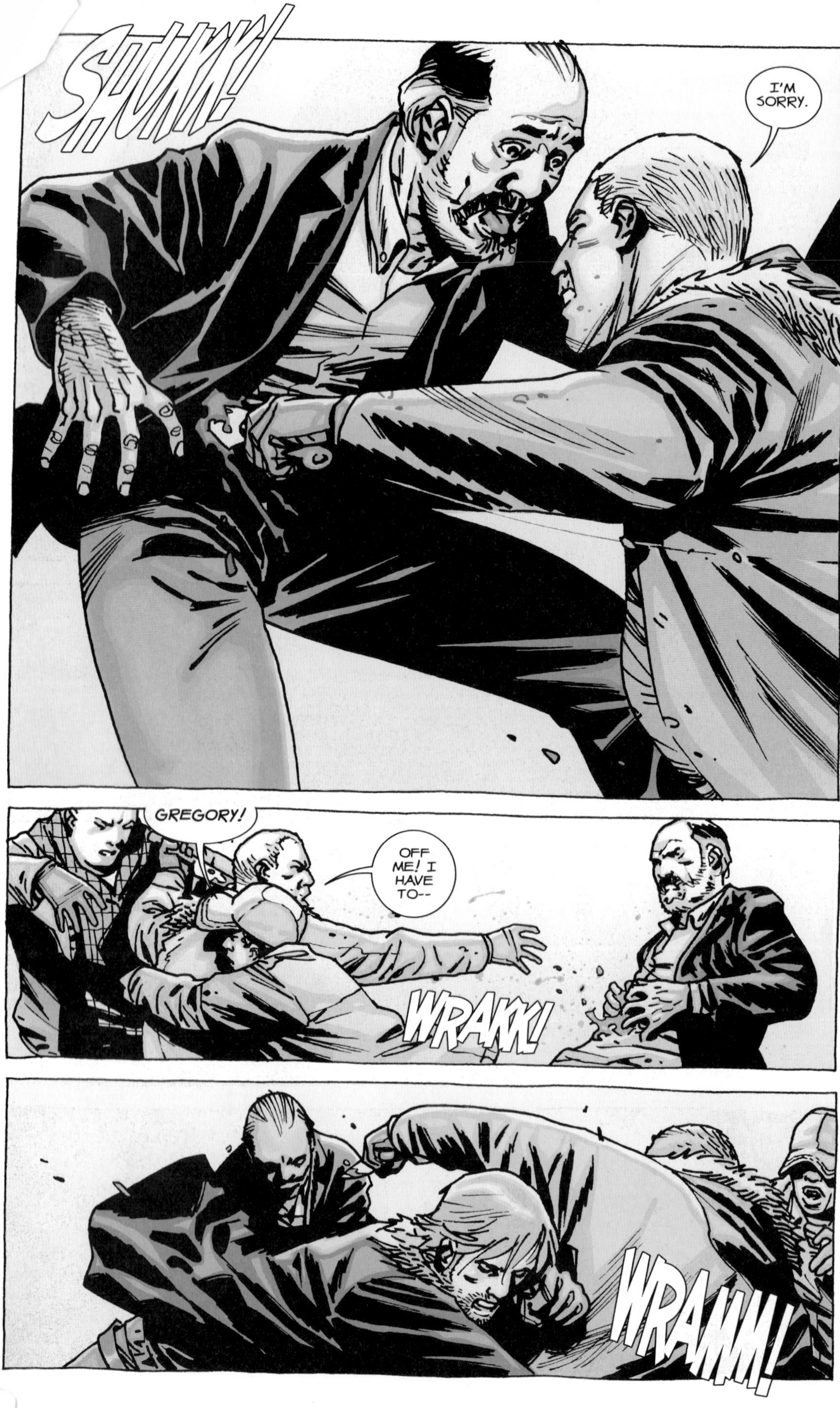
SHUNK!
I'M SORRY.
GREGORY!
OFF ME! I HAVE TO--
WRAKK!
WRAMM!

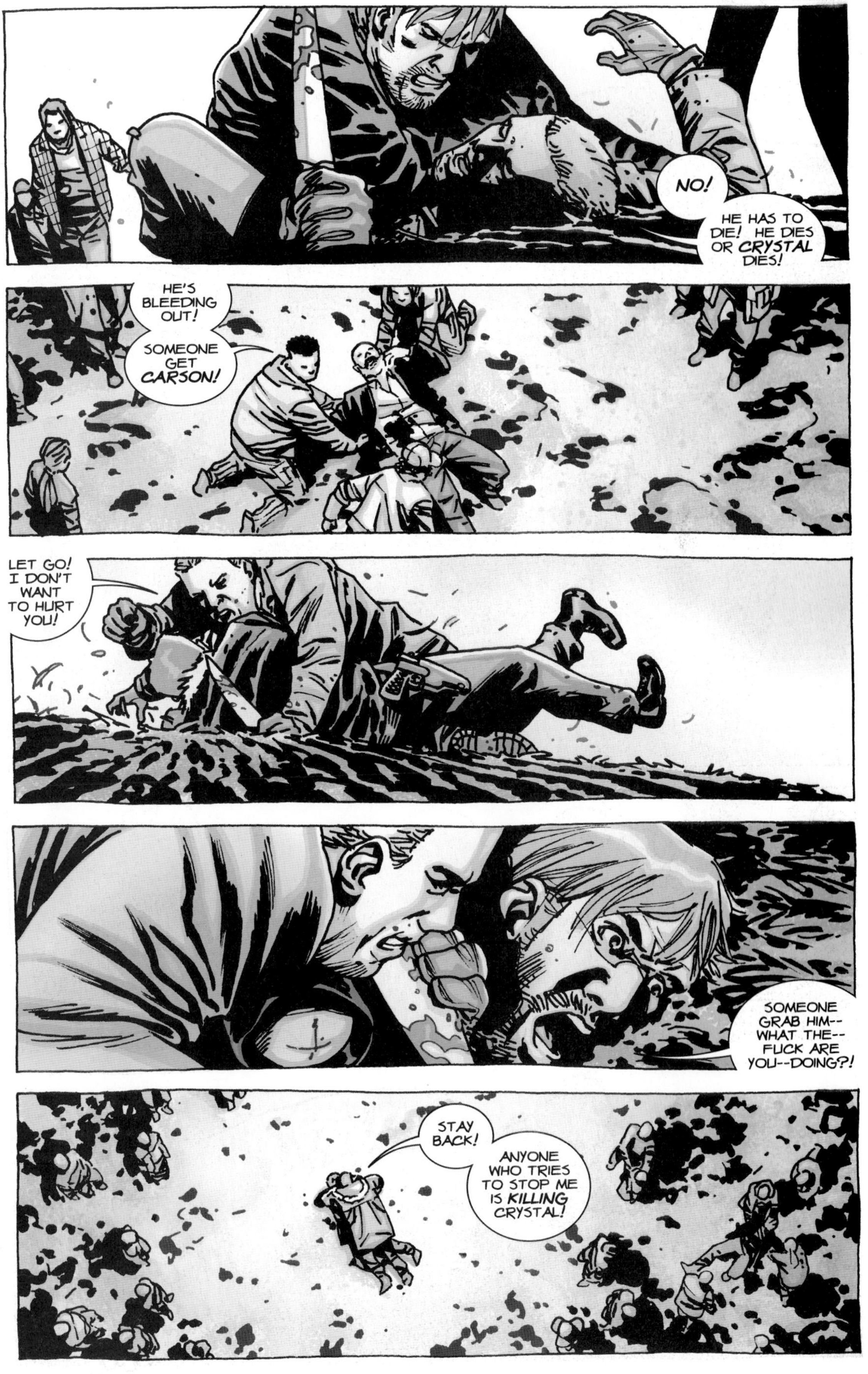
NO!
HE HAS TO DIE! HE DIES OR CRYSTAL DIES!
HE'S BLEEDING OUT!
SOMEONE GET CARSON!
LET GO! I DON'T WANT TO HURT YOU!
SOMEONE GRAB HIM-- WHAT THE-- FUCK ARE YOU--DOING?!
STAY BACK!
ANYONE WHO TRIES TO STOP ME IS KILLING CRYSTAL!

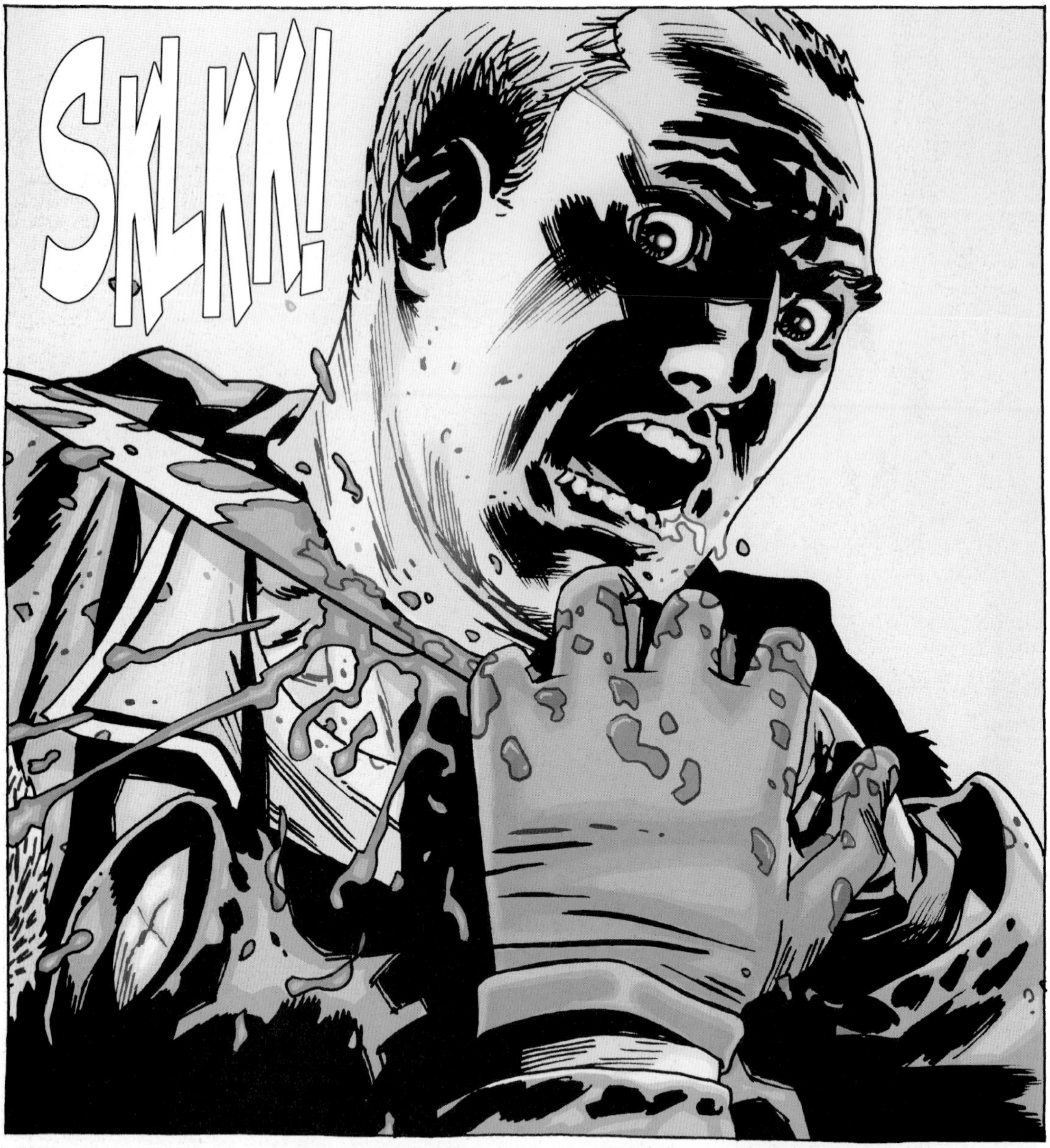
SHLKK!

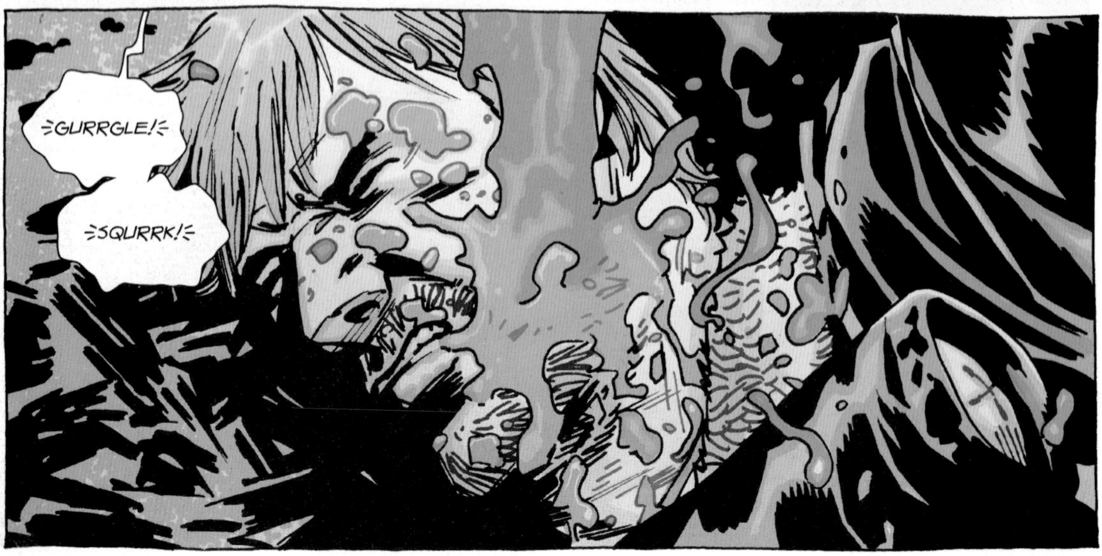
GURRGLE!
SQURRK!

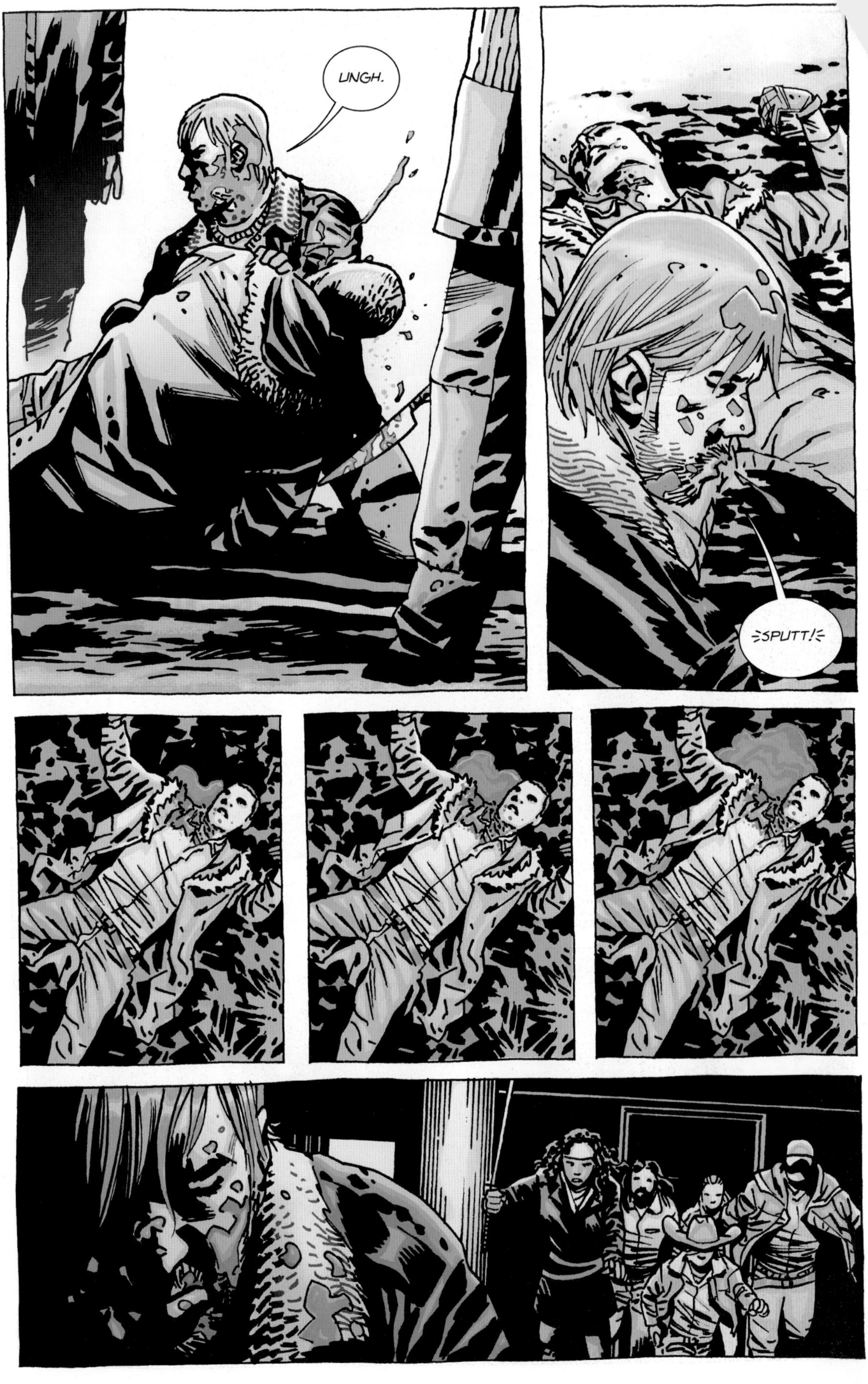
UNGH.
SPUTT!

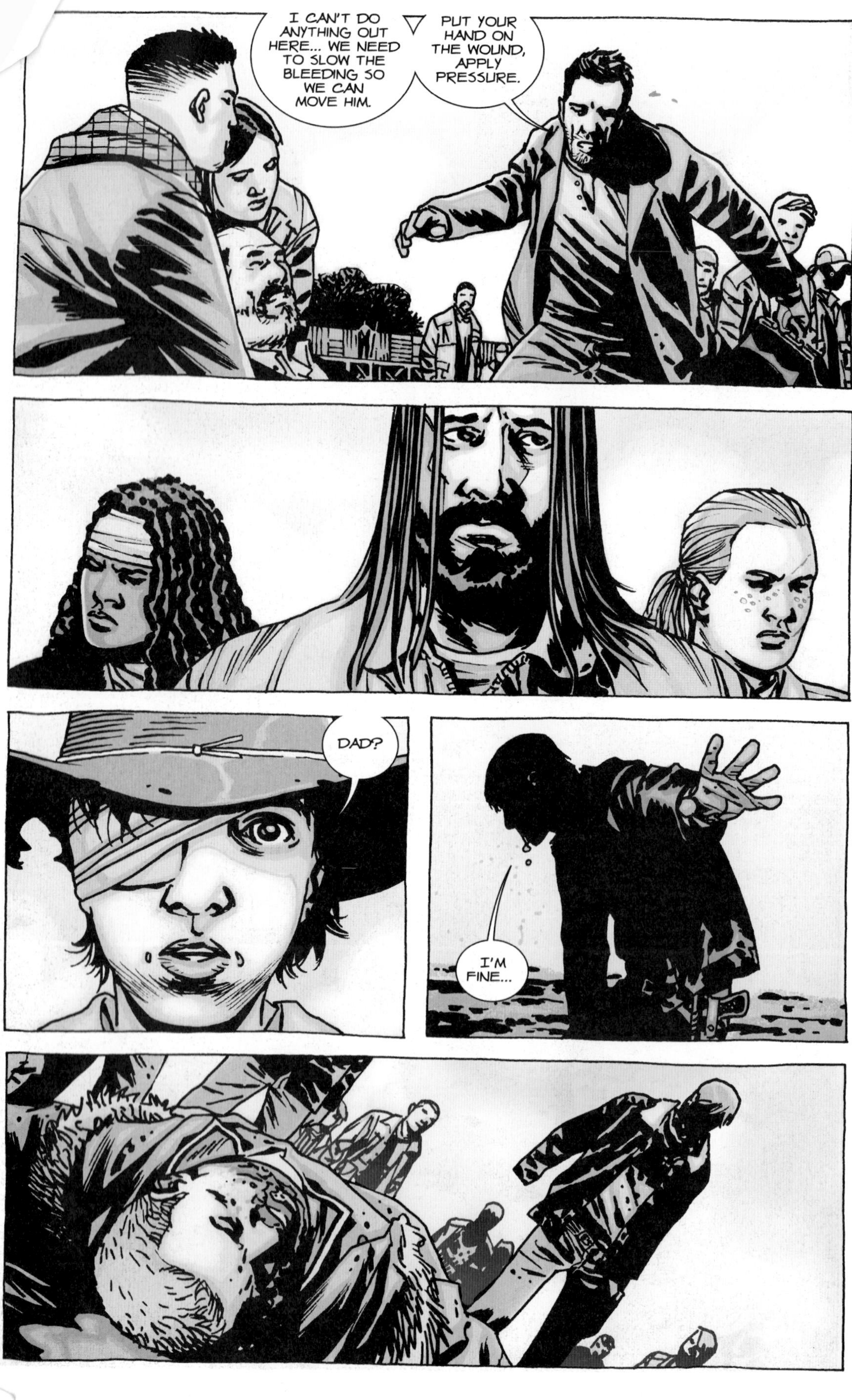
I CAN'T DO ANYTHING OUT HERE... WE NEED TO SLOW THE BLEEDING SO WE CAN MOVE HIM.
PUT YOUR HAND ON THE WOUND, APPLY PRESSURE.
DAD?
I'M FINE...

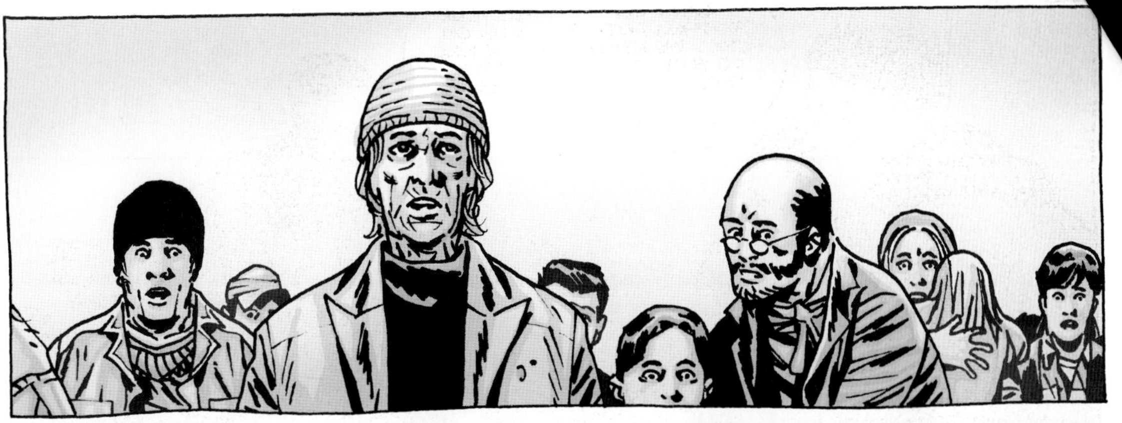

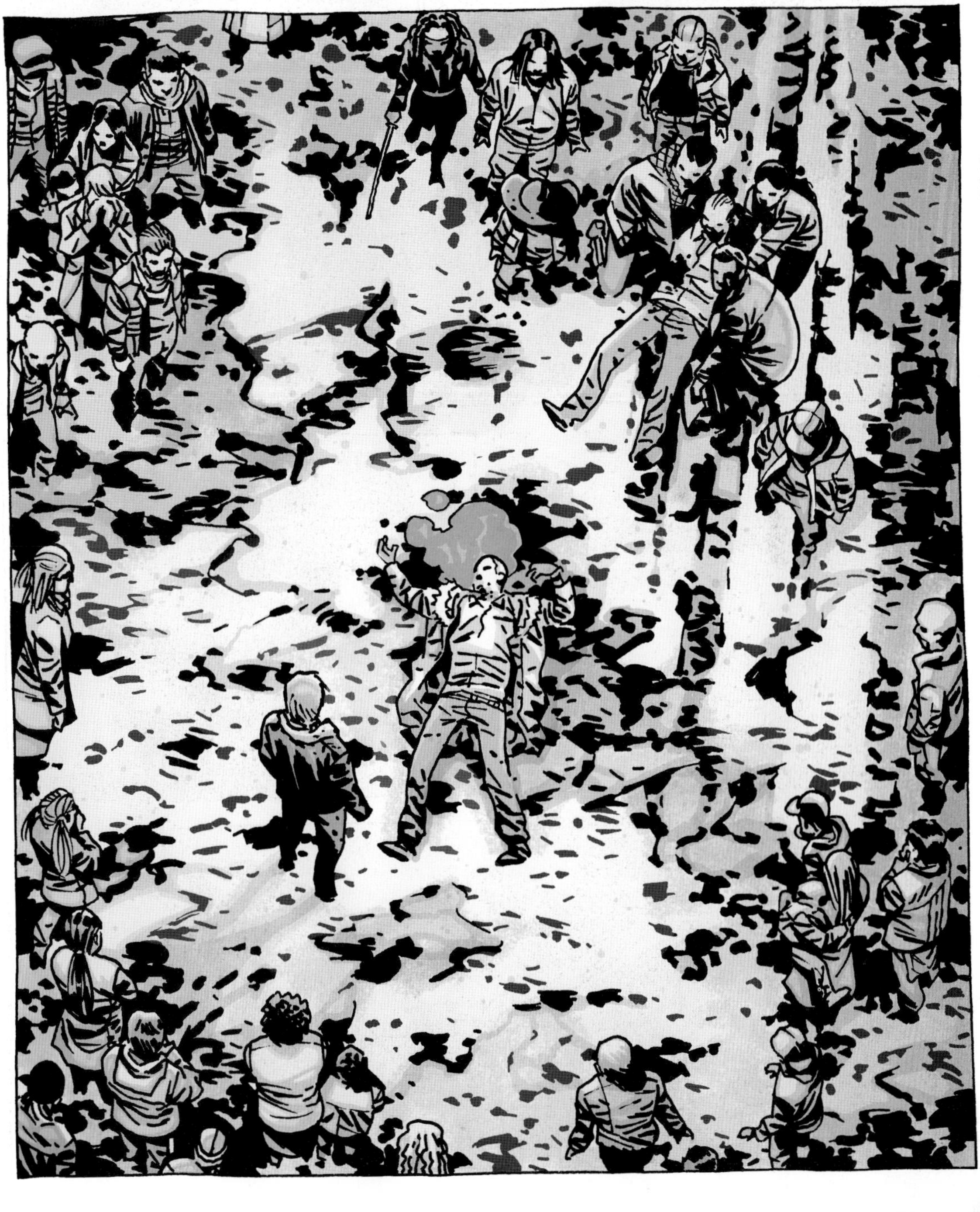

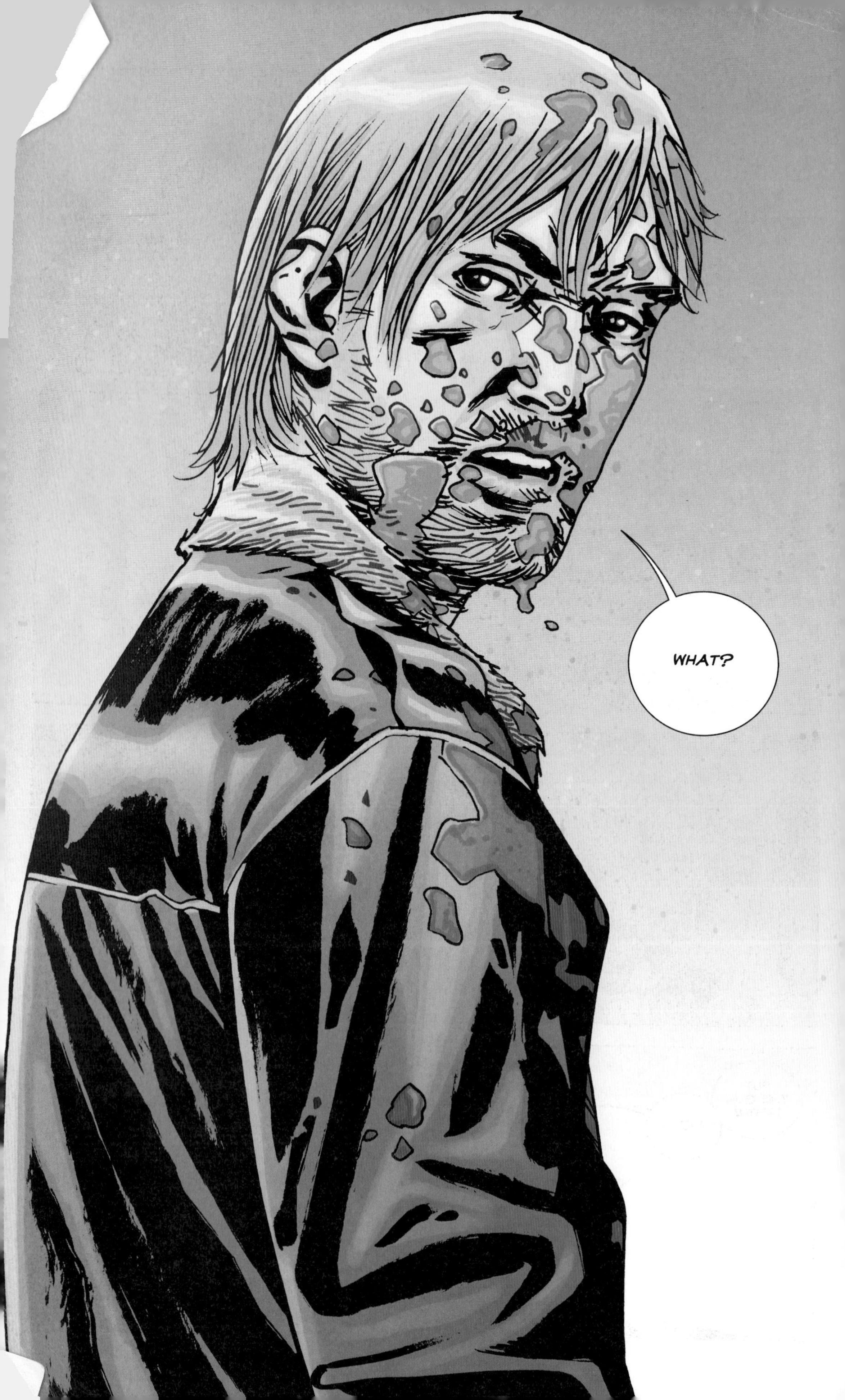
WHAT?

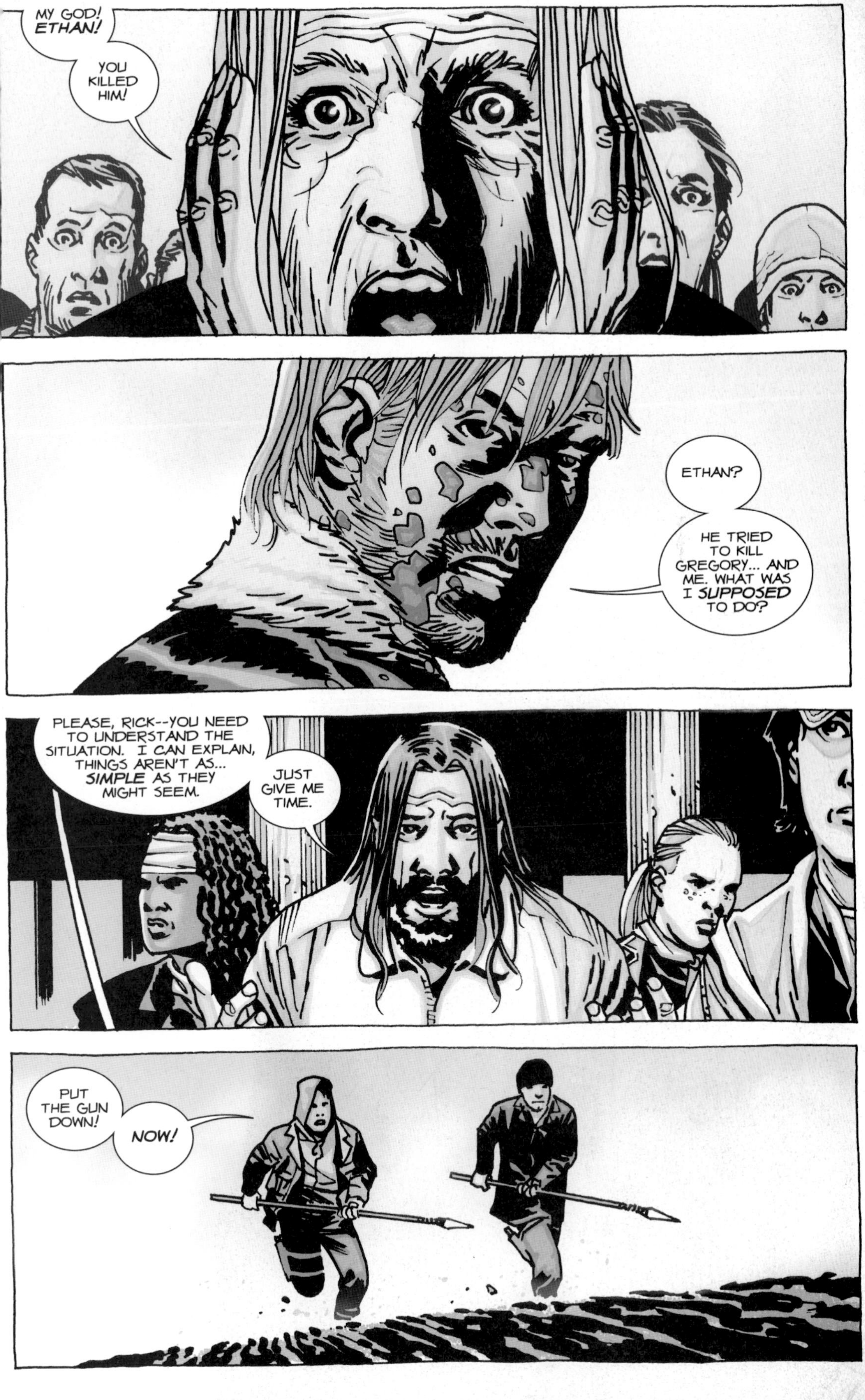
MY GOD! ETHAN!
YOU KILLED HIM!
ETHAN?
HE TRIED TO KILL GREGORY... AND ME. WHAT WAS I SUPPOSED TO DO?
PLEASE, RICK--YOU NEED TO UNDERSTAND THE SITUATION. I CAN EXPLAIN, THINGS AREN'T AS... SIMPLE AS THEY MIGHT SEEM.
JUST GIVE ME TIME.
PUT THE GUN DOWN!
NOW!

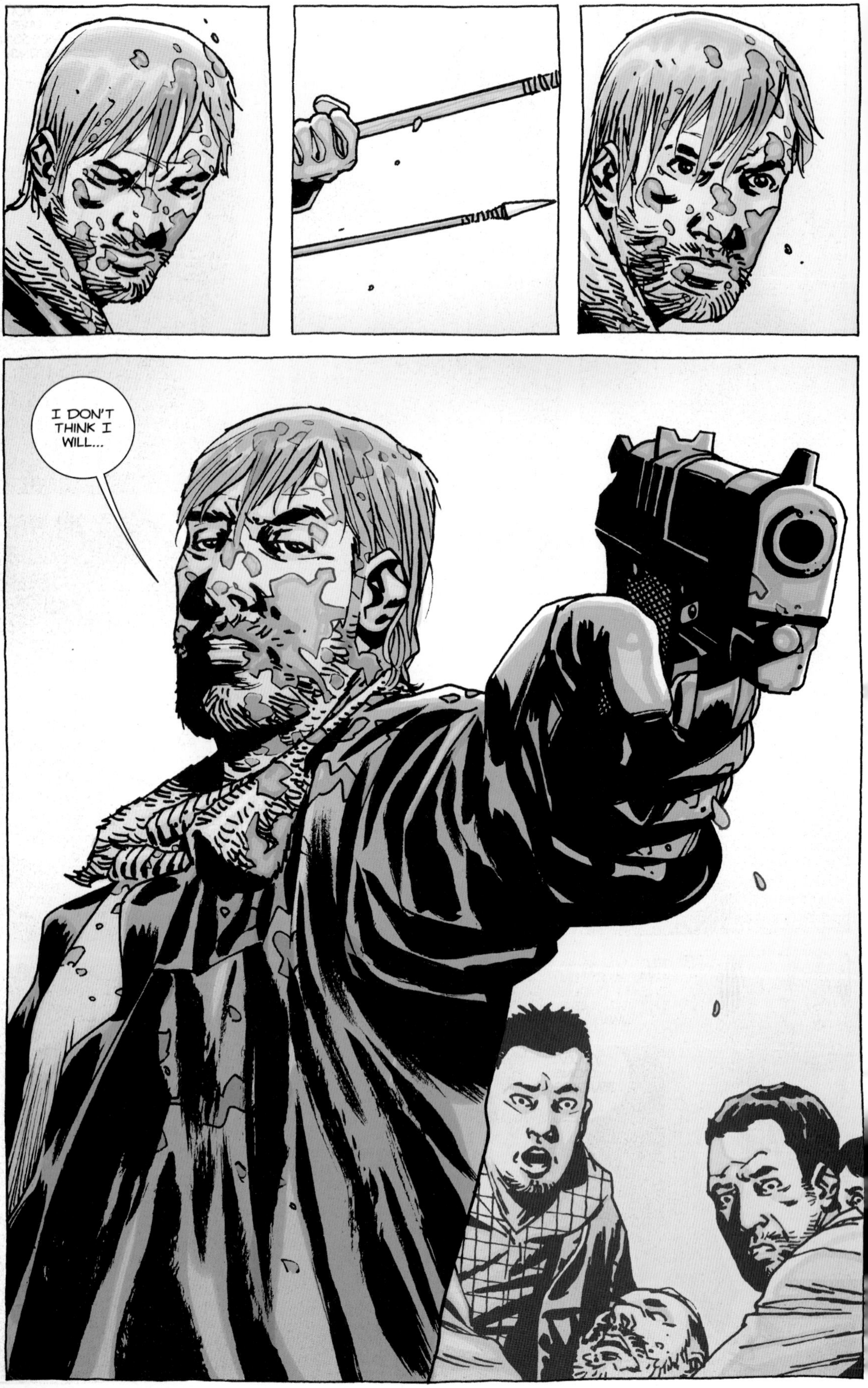
I DON'T THINK I WILL...

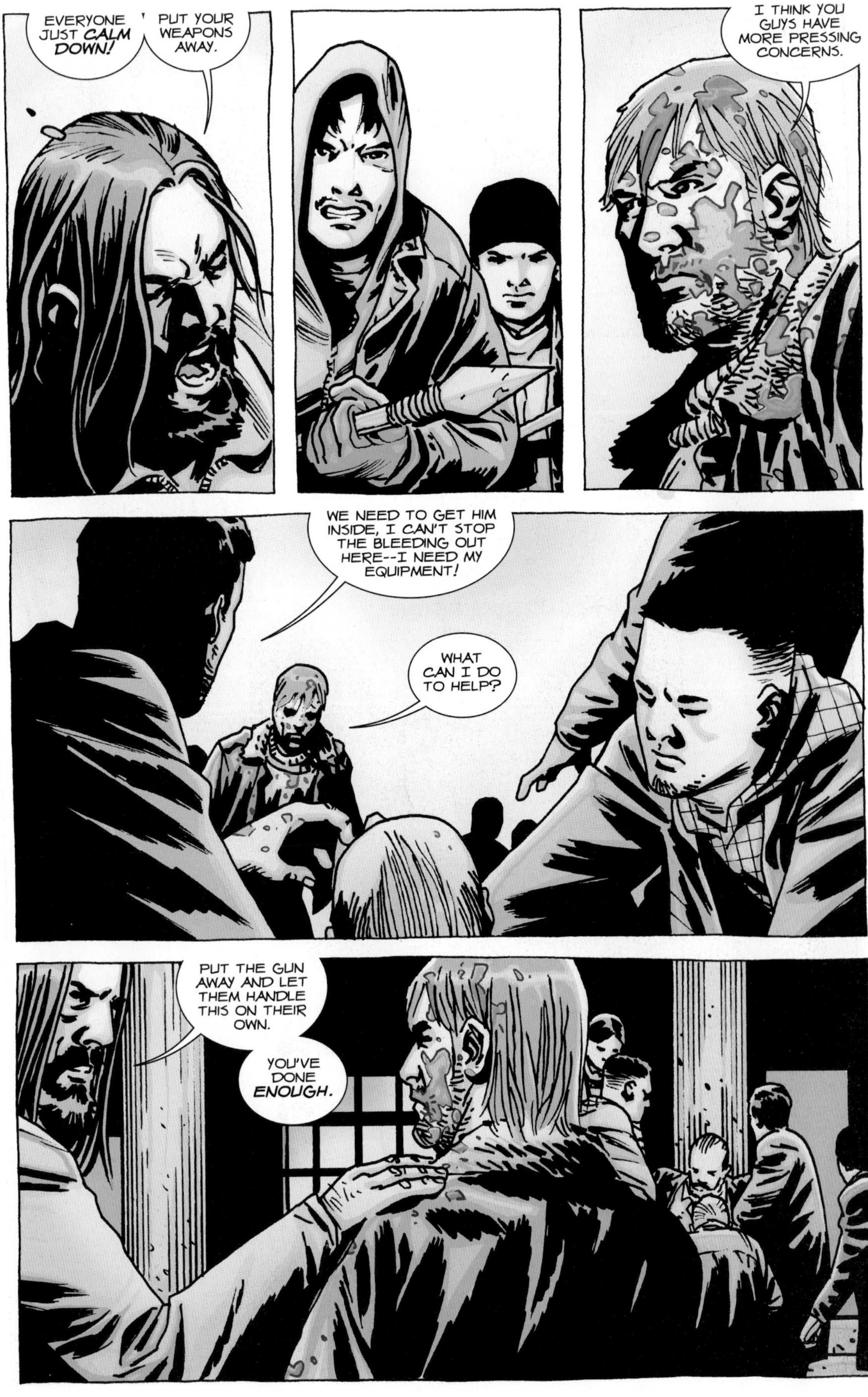
EVERYONE JUST CALM DOWN!
PUT YOUR WEAPONS AWAY.
I THINK YOU GUYS HAVE MORE PRESSING CONCERNS.
WE NEED TO GET HIM INSIDE, I CAN'T STOP THE BLEEDING OUT HERE--I NEED MY EQUIPMENT!
WHAT CAN I DO TO HELP?
PUT THE GUN AWAY AND LET THEM HANDLE THIS ON THEIR OWN.
YOU'VE DONE ENOUGH.

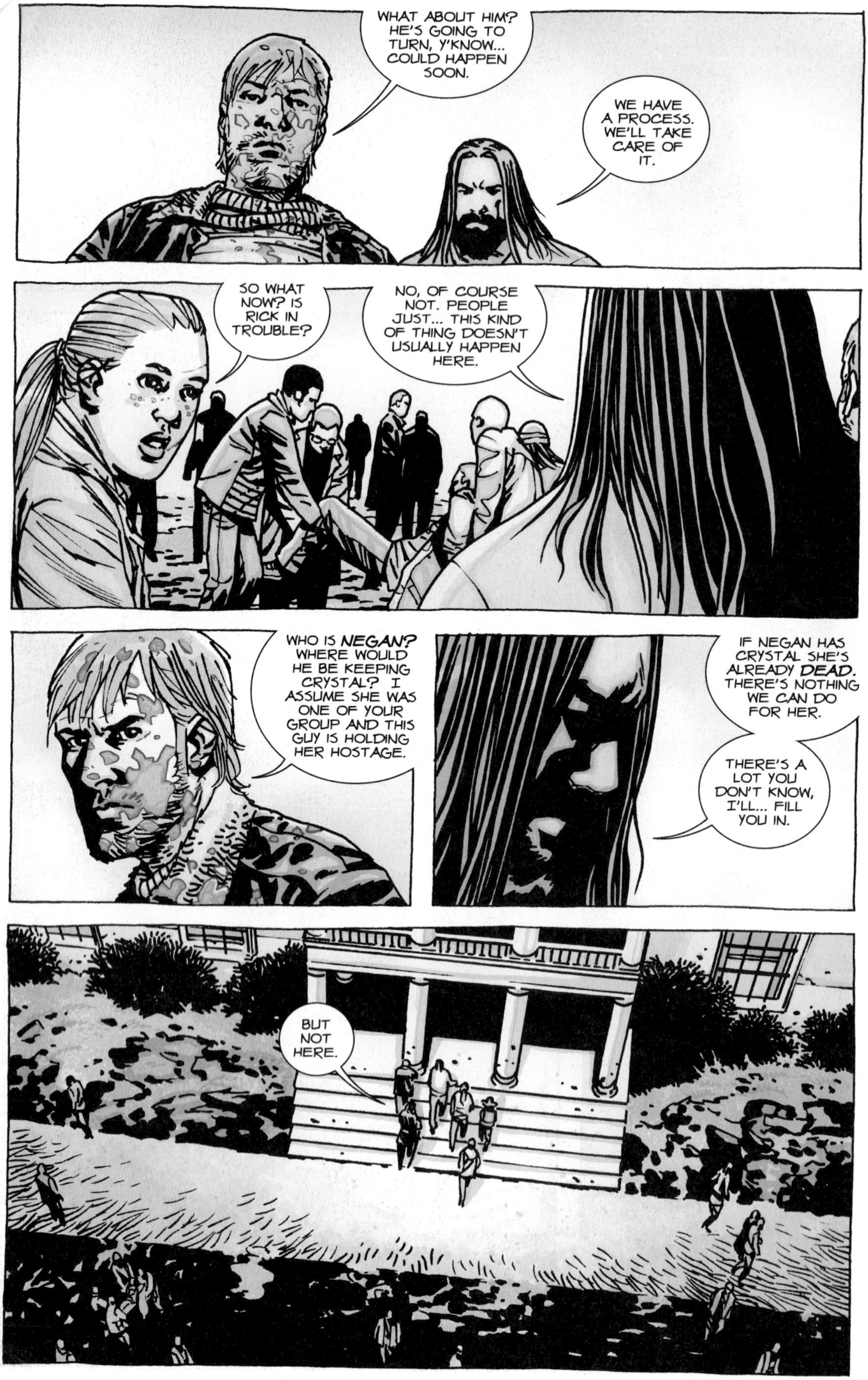
WHAT ABOUT HIM? HE'S GOING TO TURN, Y'KNOW... COULD HAPPEN SOON.
WE HAVE A PROCESS. WE'LL TAKE CARE OF IT.
SO WHAT NOW? IS RICK IN TROUBLE?
NO, OF COURSE NOT. PEOPLE JUST... THIS KIND OF THING DOESN'T USUALLY HAPPEN HERE.
WHO IS NEGAN? WHERE WOULD HE BE KEEPING CRYSTAL? I ASSUME SHE WAS ONE OF YOUR GROUP AND THIS GUY IS HOLDING HER HOSTAGE.
IF NEGAN HAS CRYSTAL SHE'S ALREADY DEAD. THERE'S NOTHING WE CAN DO FOR HER.
THERE'S A LOT YOU DON'T KNOW, I'LL... FILL YOU IN.
BUT NOT HERE.

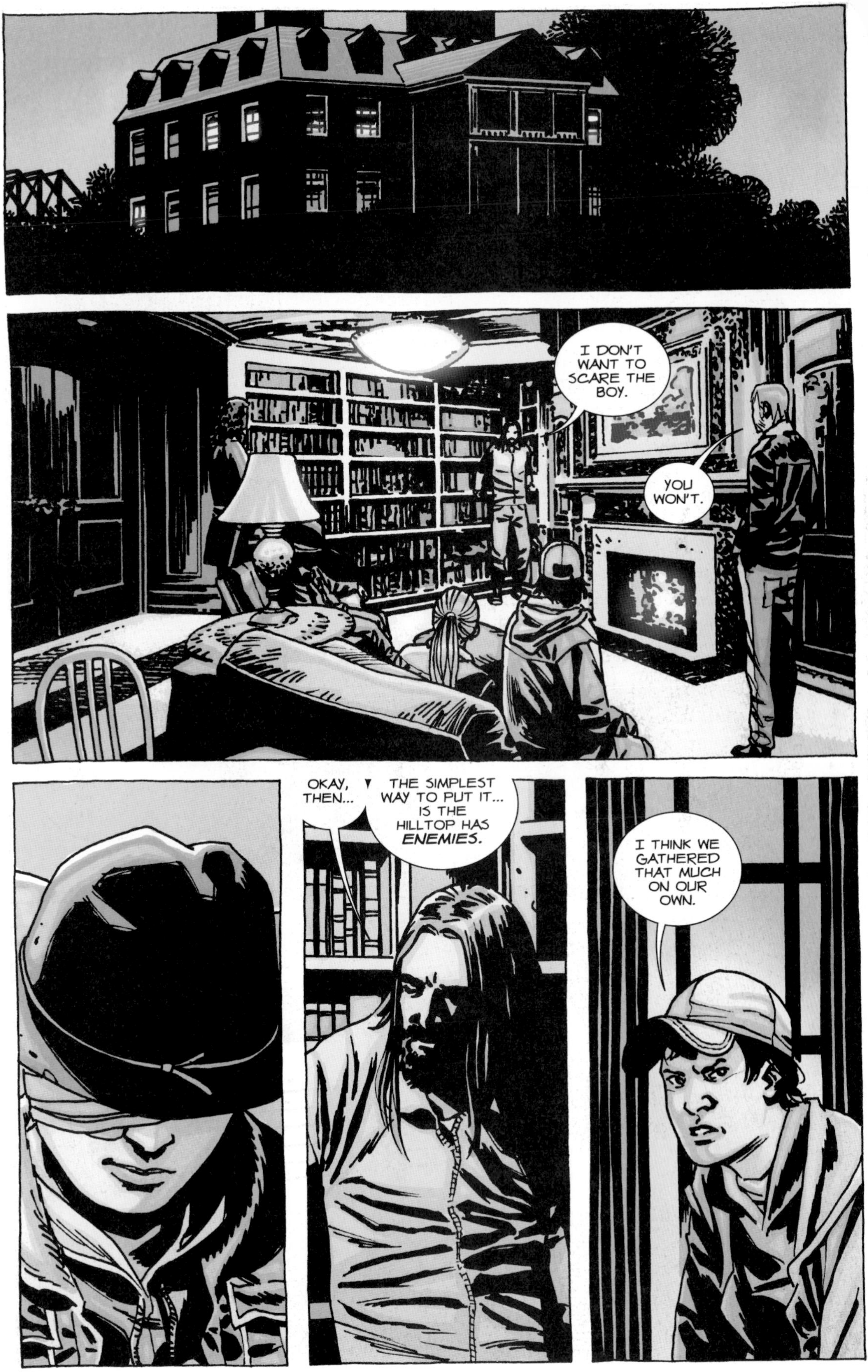
I DON'T WANT TO SCARE THE BOY.
YOU WON'T.
OKAY, THEN...
THE SIMPLEST WAY TO PUT IT... IS THE HILLTOP HAS ENEMIES.
I THINK WE GATHERED THAT MUCH ON OUR OWN.

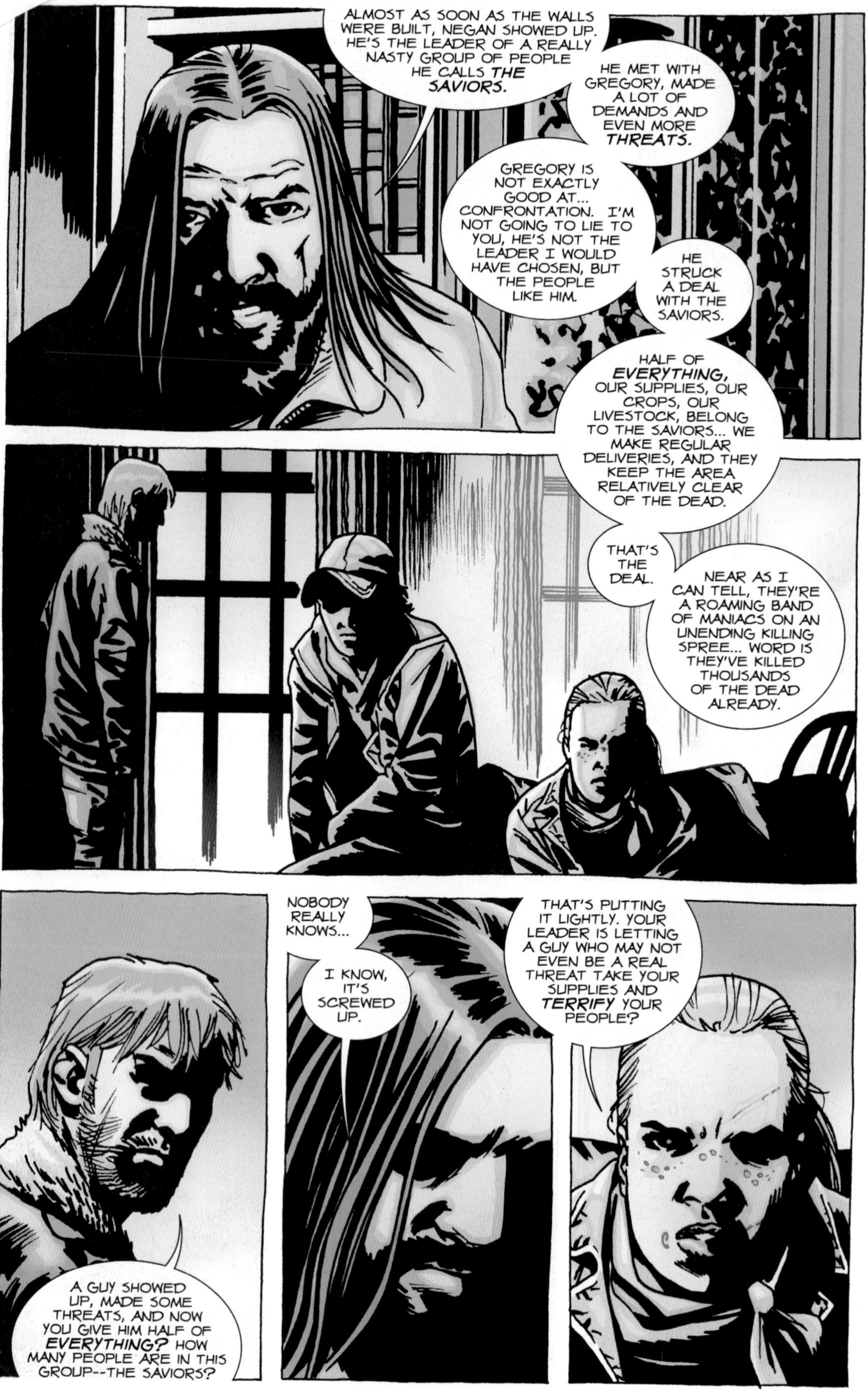

ALMOST AS SOON AS THE WALLS WERE BUILT, NEGAN SHOWED UP. HE'S THE LEADER OF A REALLY NASTY GROUP OF PEOPLE HE CALLS THE SAVIORS.
HE MET WITH GREGORY, MADE A LOT OF DEMANDS AND EVEN MORE THREATS.
GREGORY IS NOT EXACTLY GOOD AT... CONFRONTATION. I'M NOT GOING TO LIE TO YOU, HE'S NOT THE LEADER I WOULD HAVE CHOSEN, BUT THE PEOPLE LIKE HIM.
HE STRUCK A DEAL WITH THE SAVIORS.
HALF OF EVERYTHING, OUR SUPPLIES, OUR CROPS, OUR LIVESTOCK, BELONG TO THE SAVIORS... WE MAKE REGULAR DELIVERIES, AND THEY KEEP THE AREA RELATIVELY CLEAR OF THE DEAD.
THAT'S THE DEAL.
NEAR AS I CAN TELL, THEY'RE A ROAMING BAND OF MANIACS ON AN UNENDING KILLING SPREE... WORD IS THEY'VE KILLED THOUSANDS OF THE DEAD ALREADY.
A GUY SHOWED UP, MADE SOME THREATS, AND NOW YOU GIVE HIM HALF OF EVERYTHING? HOW MANY PEOPLE ARE IN THIS GROUP--THE SAVIORS?
NOBODY REALLY KNOWS...
I KNOW, IT'S SCREWED UP.
THAT'S PUTTING IT LIGHTLY. YOUR LEADER IS LETTING A GUY WHO MAY NOT EVEN BE A REAL THREAT TAKE YOUR SUPPLIES AND TERRIFY YOUR PEOPLE?

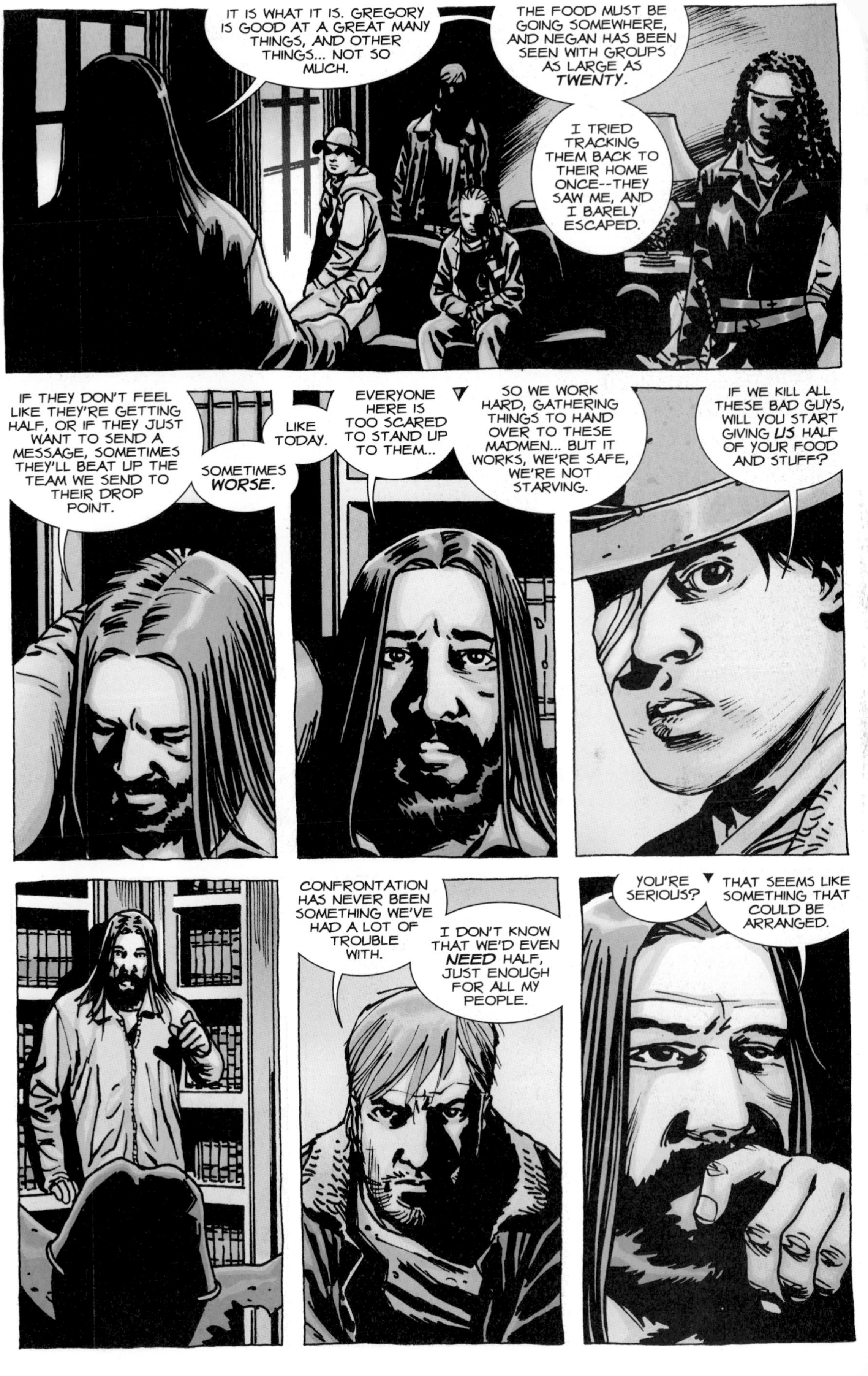
IT IS WHAT IT IS. GREGORY IS GOOD AT A GREAT MANY THINGS, AND OTHER THINGS... NOT SO MUCH.
THE FOOD MUST BE GOING SOMEWHERE, AND NEGAN HAS BEEN SEEN WITH GROUPS AS LARGE AS TWENTY.
I TRIED TRACKING THEM BACK TO THEIR HOME ONCE--THEY SAW ME, AND I BARELY ESCAPED.
IF THEY DON'T FEEL LIKE THEY'RE GETTING HALF, OR IF THEY JUST WANT TO SEND A MESSAGE, SOMETIMES THEY'LL BEAT UP THE TEAM WE SEND TO THEIR DROP POINT.
SOMETIMES WORSE.
LIKE TODAY.
EVERYONE HERE IS TOO SCARED TO STAND UP TO THEM...
SO WE WORK HARD, GATHERING THINGS TO HAND OVER TO THESE MADMEN... BUT IT WORKS, WE'RE SAFE, WE'RE NOT STARVING.
IF WE KILL ALL THESE BAD GUYS, WILL YOU START GIVING US HALF OF YOUR FOOD AND STUFF?
CONFRONTATION HAS NEVER BEEN SOMETHING WE'VE HAD A LOT OF TROUBLE WITH.
I DON'T KNOW THAT WE'D EVEN NEED HALF, JUST ENOUGH FOR ALL MY PEOPLE.
YOU'RE SERIOUS?
THAT SEEMS LIKE SOMETHING THAT COULD BE ARRANGED.

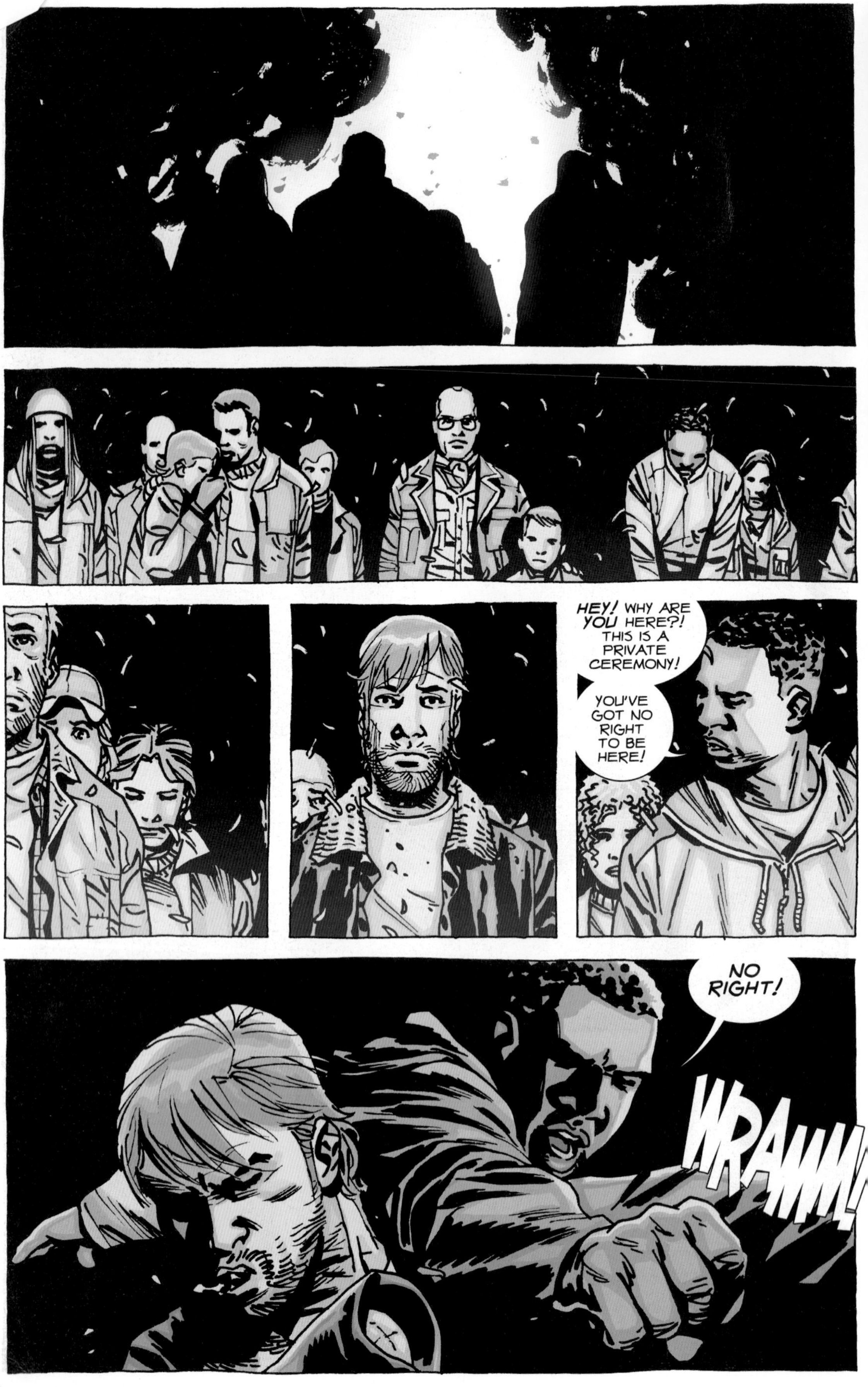
HEY! WHY ARE YOU HERE?! THIS IS A PRIVATE CEREMONY!
YOU'VE GOT NO RIGHT TO BE HERE!
NO RIGHT!
WRAMM!

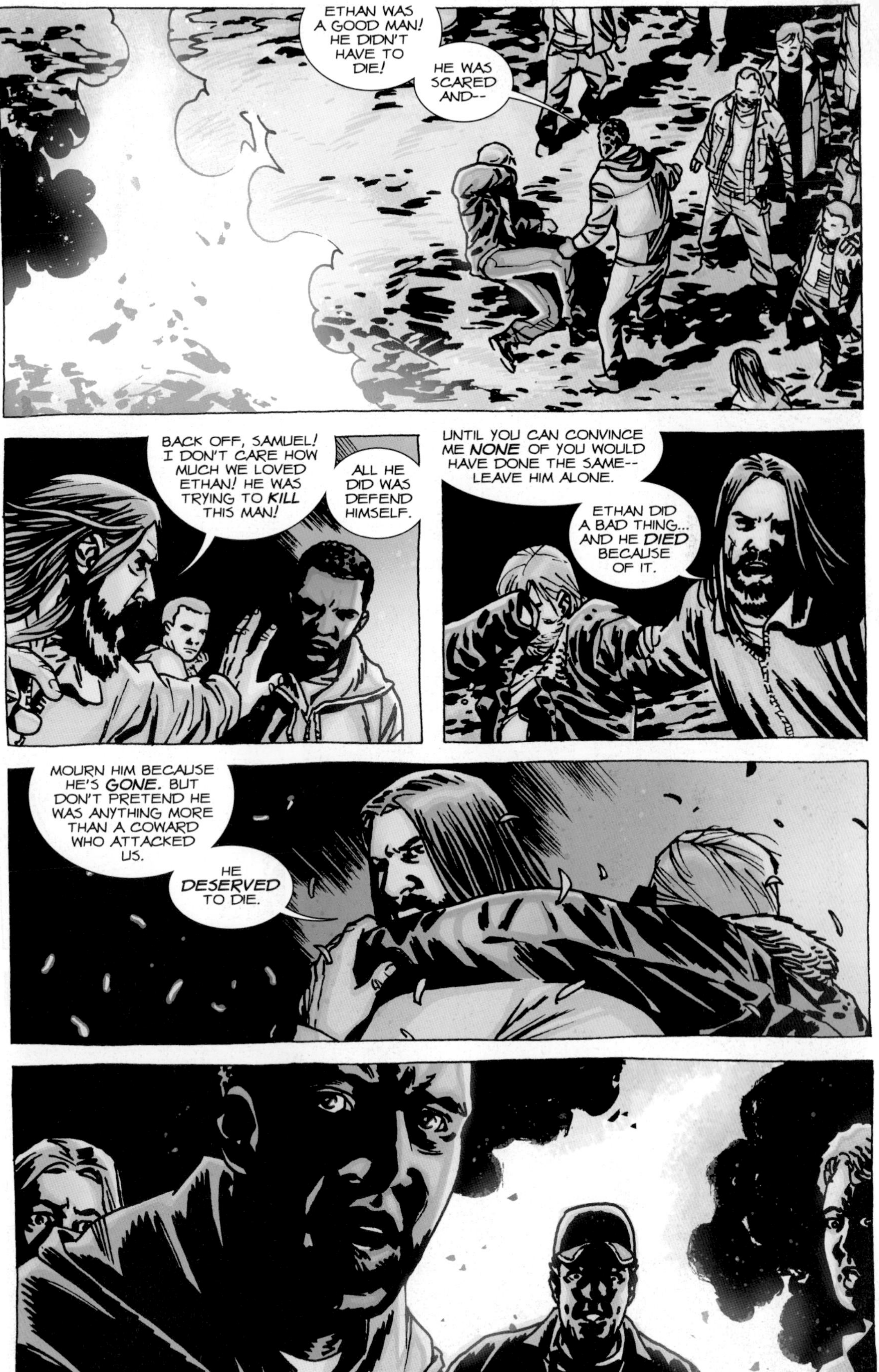
ETHAN WAS A GOOD MAN! HE DIDN'T HAVE TO DIE!
HE WAS SCARED AND--
BACK OFF, SAMUEL! I DON'T CARE HOW MUCH WE LOVED ETHAN! HE WAS TRYING TO KILL THIS MAN!
ALL HE DID WAS DEFEND HIMSELF.
UNTIL YOU CAN CONVINCE ME NONE OF YOU WOULD HAVE DONE THE SAME-- LEAVE HIM ALONE.
ETHAN DID A BAD THING... AND HE DIED BECAUSE OF IT.
MOURN HIM BECAUSE HE'S GONE. BUT DON'T PRETEND HE WAS ANYTHING MORE THAN A COWARD WHO ATTACKED US.
HE DESERVED TO DIE.

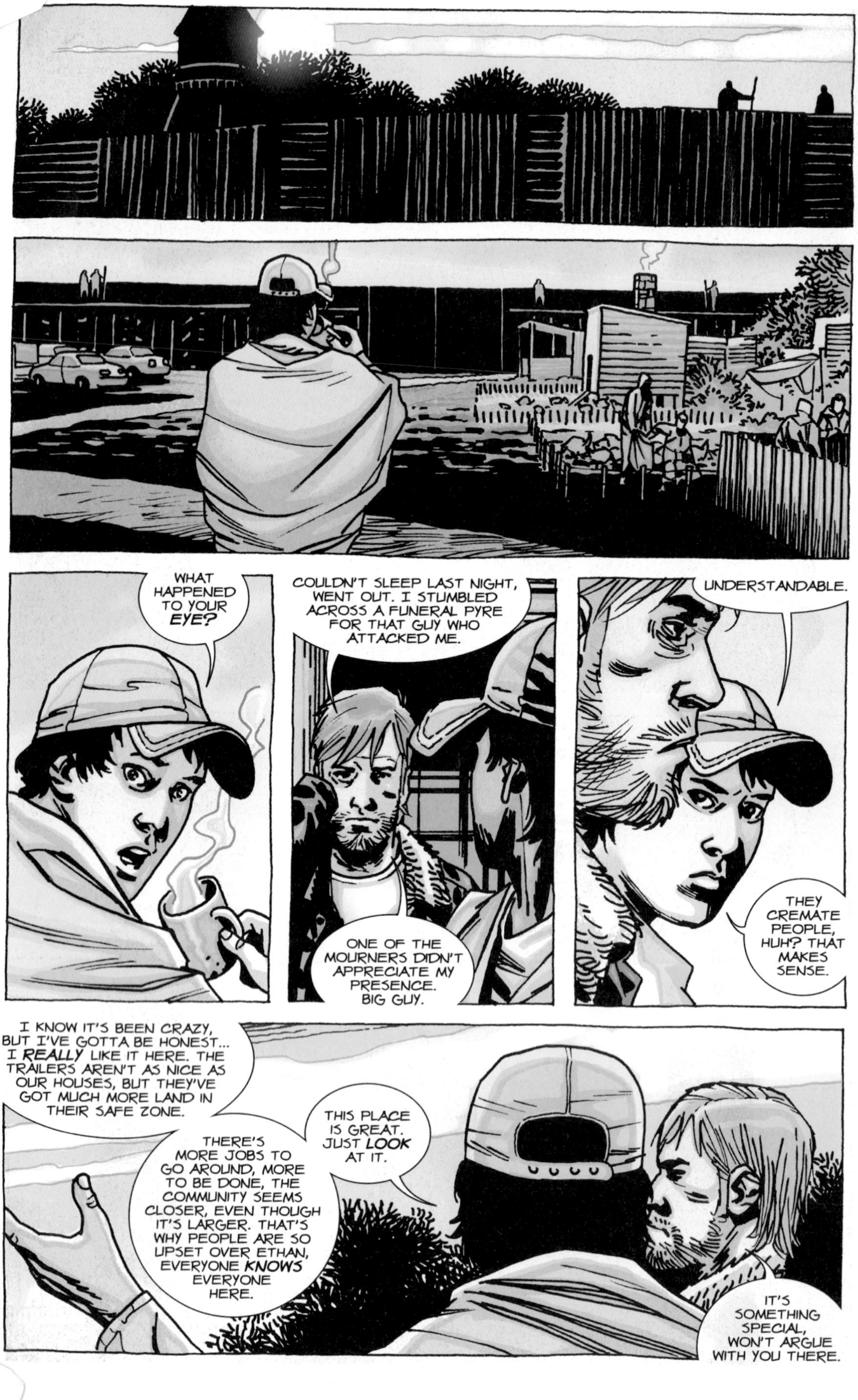
WHAT HAPPENED TO YOUR *EYE?*
COULDN'T SLEEP LAST NIGHT, WENT OUT. I STUMBLED ACROSS A FUNERAL PYRE FOR THAT GUY WHO ATTACKED ME.
ONE OF THE MOURNERS DIDN'T APPRECIATE MY PRESENCE. BIG GUY.
UNDERSTANDABLE.
THEY CREMATE PEOPLE, HUH? THAT MAKES SENSE.
I KNOW IT'S BEEN CRAZY, BUT I'VE GOTTA BE HONEST... I *REALLY* LIKE IT HERE. THE TRAILERS AREN'T AS NICE AS OUR HOUSES, BUT THEY'VE GOT MUCH MORE LAND IN THEIR SAFE ZONE.
THERE'S MORE JOBS TO GO AROUND, MORE TO BE DONE, THE COMMUNITY SEEMS CLOSER, EVEN THOUGH IT'S LARGER. THAT'S WHY PEOPLE ARE SO UPSET OVER ETHAN, EVERYONE *KNOWS* EVERYONE HERE.
THIS PLACE IS GREAT. JUST *LOOK* AT IT.
IT'S SOMETHING SPECIAL, WON'T ARGUE WITH YOU THERE.

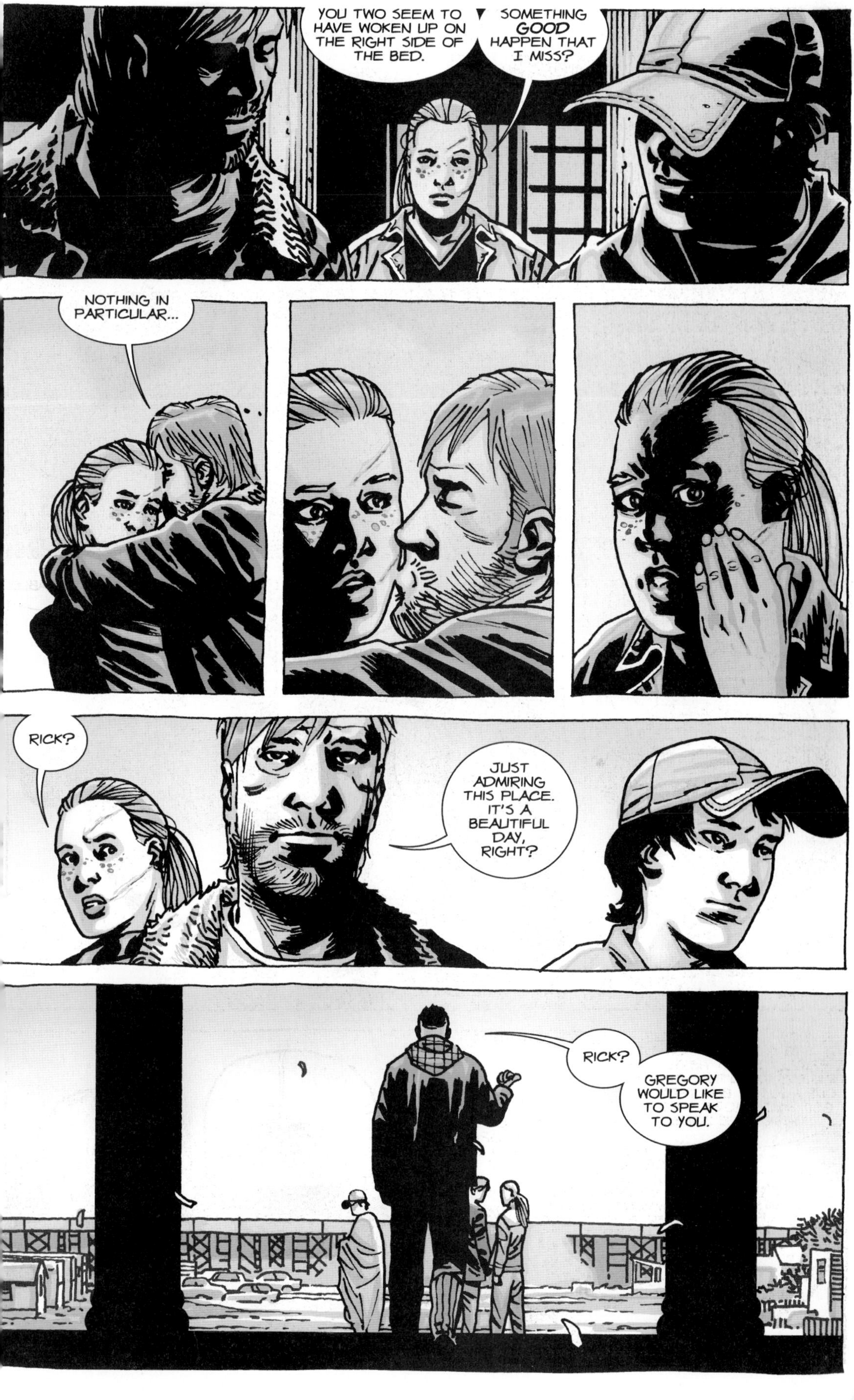
YOU TWO SEEM TO HAVE WOKEN UP ON THE RIGHT SIDE OF THE BED.
SOMETHING GOOD HAPPEN THAT I MISS?
NOTHING IN PARTICULAR...
RICK?
JUST ADMIRING THIS PLACE. IT'S A BEAUTIFUL DAY, RIGHT?
RICK?
GREGORY WOULD LIKE TO SPEAK TO YOU.

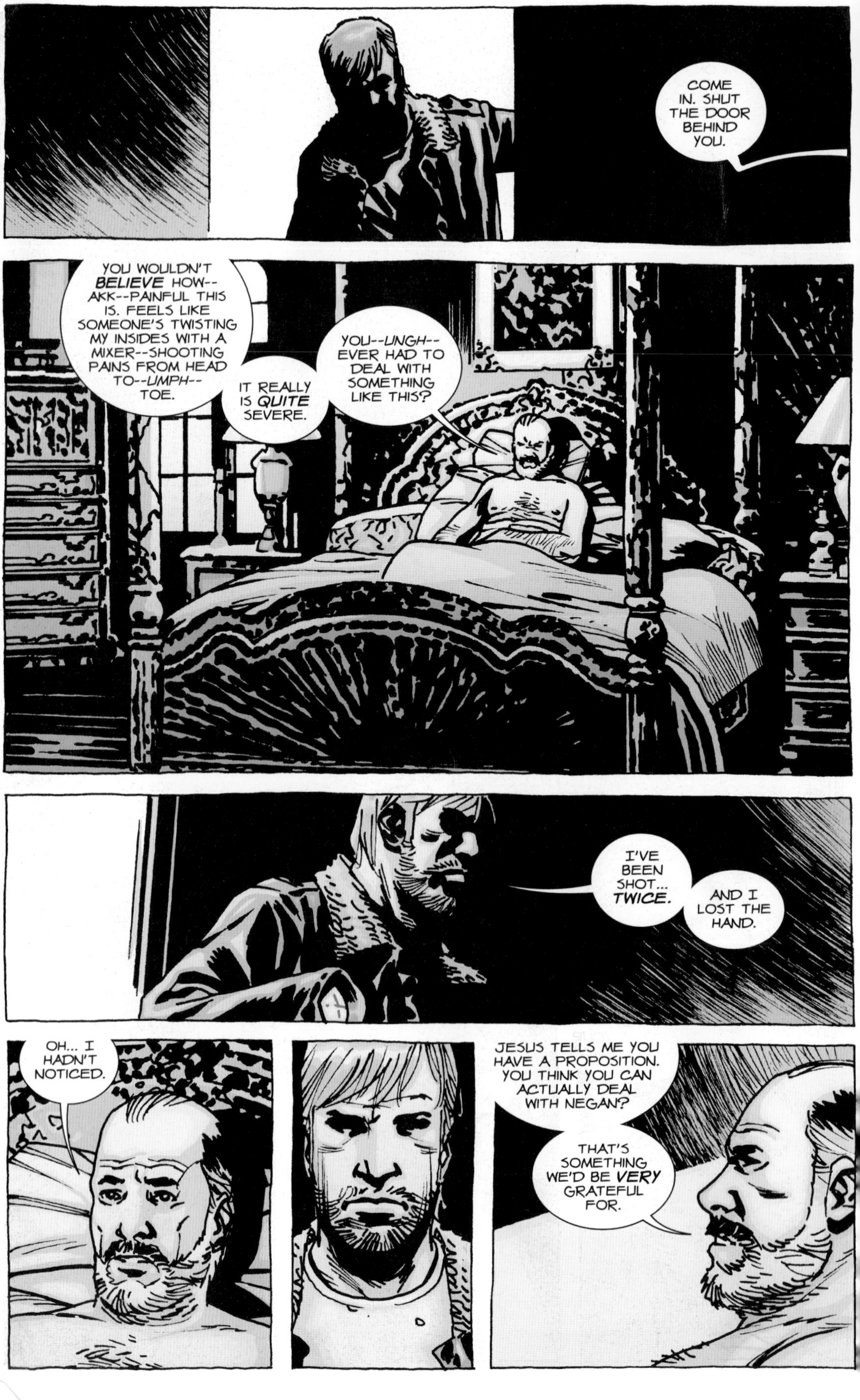
COME IN. SHUT THE DOOR BEHIND YOU.
YOU WOULDN'T *BELIEVE* HOW--AKK--PAINFUL THIS IS. FEELS LIKE SOMEONE'S TWISTING MY INSIDES WITH A MIXER--SHOOTING PAINS FROM HEAD TO--*UMPH*--TOE.
IT REALLY IS *QUITE* SEVERE.
YOU--*UNGH*--EVER HAD TO DEAL WITH SOMETHING LIKE THIS?
I'VE BEEN SHOT... *TWICE.*
AND I LOST THE HAND.
OH... I HADN'T NOTICED.
JESUS TELLS ME YOU HAVE A PROPOSITION. YOU THINK YOU CAN ACTUALLY DEAL WITH NEGAN?
THAT'S SOMETHING WE'D BE *VERY* GRATEFUL FOR.

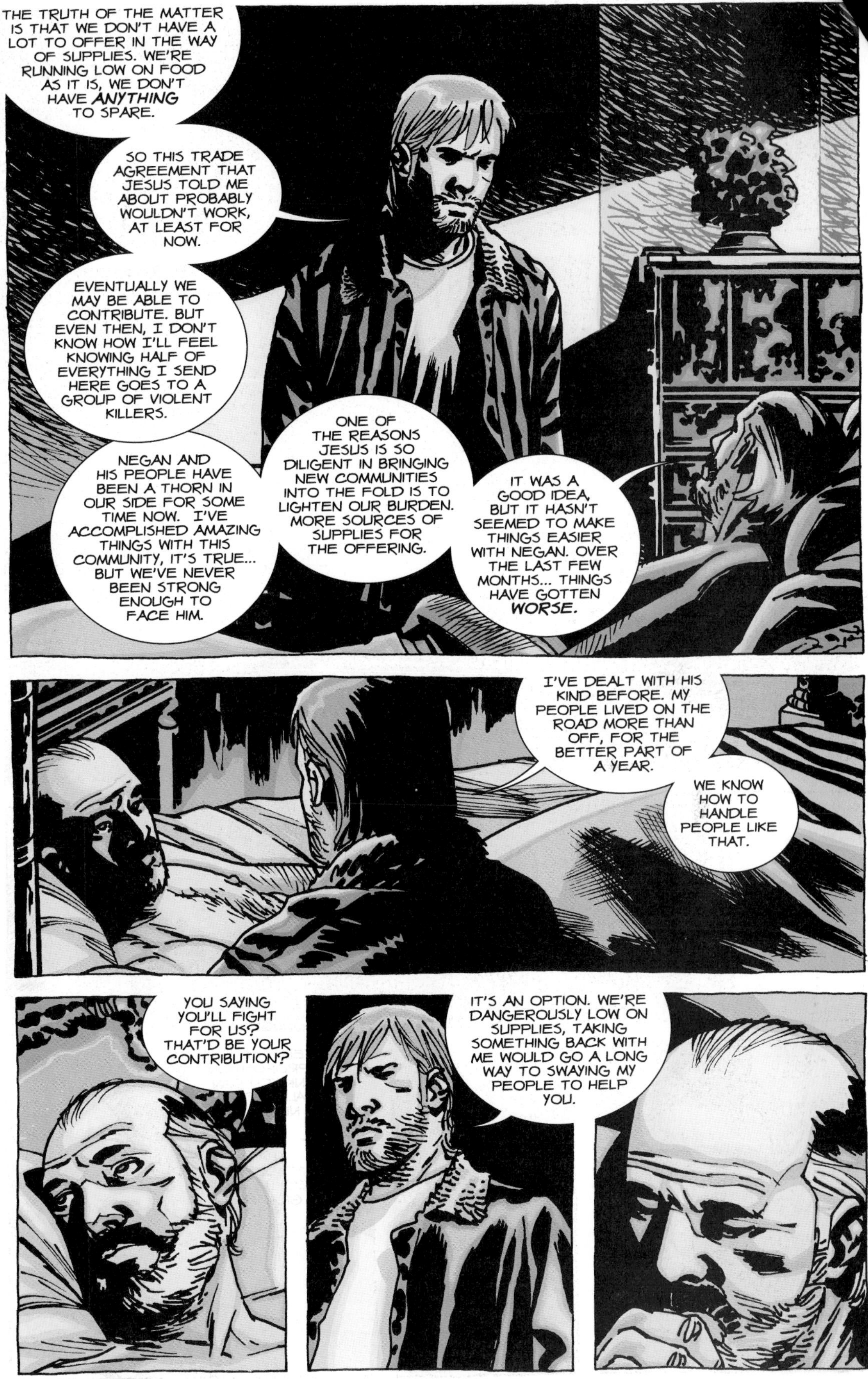
THE TRUTH OF THE MATTER IS THAT WE DON'T HAVE A LOT TO OFFER IN THE WAY OF SUPPLIES. WE'RE RUNNING LOW ON FOOD AS IT IS, WE DON'T HAVE ANYTHING TO SPARE.
SO THIS TRADE AGREEMENT THAT JESUS TOLD ME ABOUT PROBABLY WOULDN'T WORK, AT LEAST FOR NOW.
EVENTUALLY WE MAY BE ABLE TO CONTRIBUTE. BUT EVEN THEN, I DON'T KNOW HOW I'LL FEEL KNOWING HALF OF EVERYTHING I SEND HERE GOES TO A GROUP OF VIOLENT KILLERS.
NEGAN AND HIS PEOPLE HAVE BEEN A THORN IN OUR SIDE FOR SOME TIME NOW. I'VE ACCOMPLISHED AMAZING THINGS WITH THIS COMMUNITY, IT'S TRUE... BUT WE'VE NEVER BEEN STRONG ENOUGH TO FACE HIM.
ONE OF THE REASONS JESUS IS SO DILIGENT IN BRINGING NEW COMMUNITIES INTO THE FOLD IS TO LIGHTEN OUR BURDEN. MORE SOURCES OF SUPPLIES FOR THE OFFERING.
IT WAS A GOOD IDEA, BUT IT HASN'T SEEMED TO MAKE THINGS EASIER WITH NEGAN. OVER THE LAST FEW MONTHS... THINGS HAVE GOTTEN WORSE.
I'VE DEALT WITH HIS KIND BEFORE. MY PEOPLE LIVED ON THE ROAD MORE THAN OFF, FOR THE BETTER PART OF A YEAR.
WE KNOW HOW TO HANDLE PEOPLE LIKE THAT.
YOU SAYING YOU'LL FIGHT FOR US? THAT'D BE YOUR CONTRIBUTION?
IT'S AN OPTION. WE'RE DANGEROUSLY LOW ON SUPPLIES, TAKING SOMETHING BACK WITH ME WOULD GO A LONG WAY TO SWAYING MY PEOPLE TO HELP YOU.

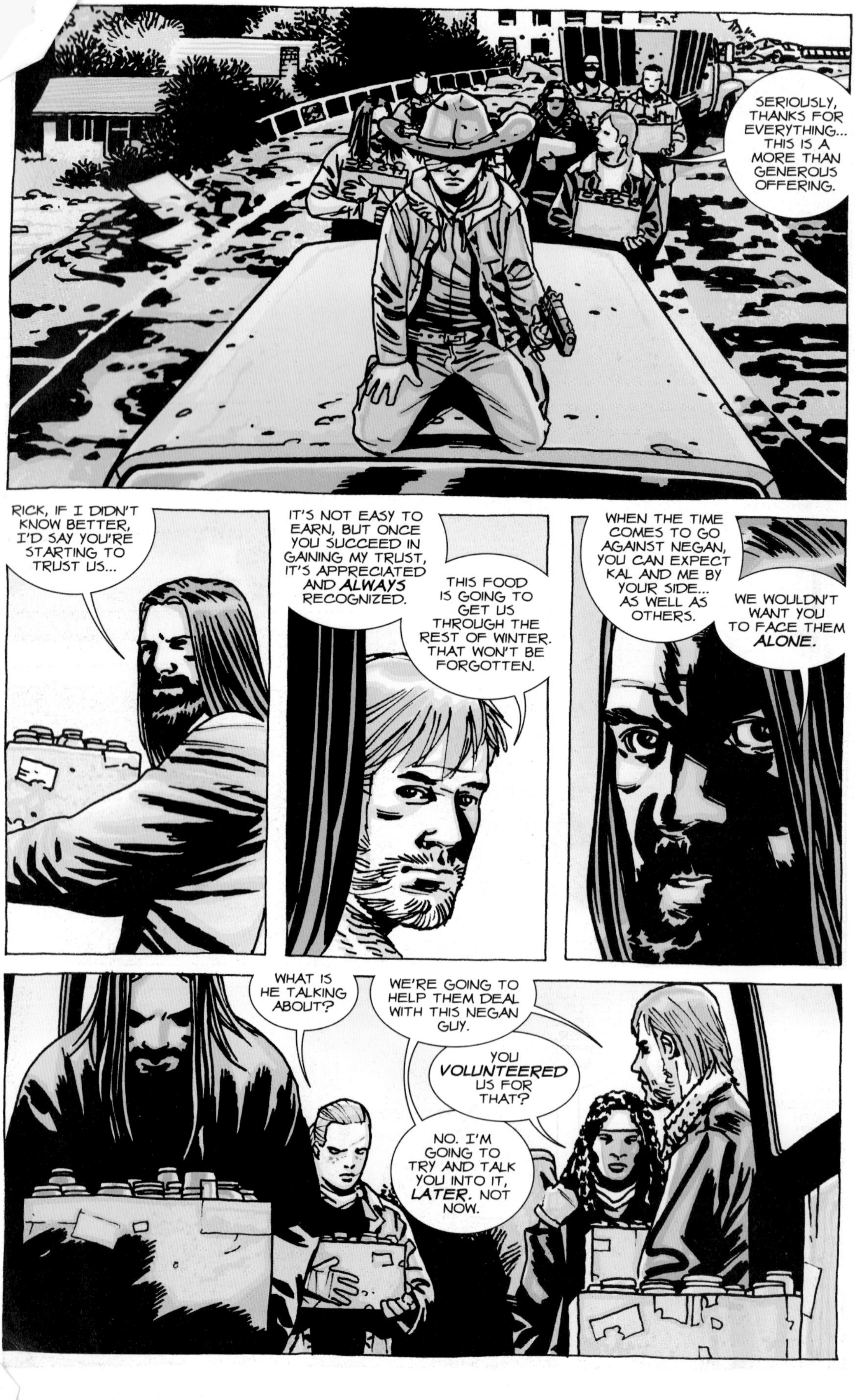
SERIOUSLY, THANKS FOR EVERYTHING... THIS IS A MORE THAN GENEROUS OFFERING.
RICK, IF I DIDN'T KNOW BETTER, I'D SAY YOU'RE STARTING TO TRUST US...
IT'S NOT EASY TO EARN, BUT ONCE YOU SUCCEED IN GAINING MY TRUST, IT'S APPRECIATED AND ALWAYS RECOGNIZED.
THIS FOOD IS GOING TO GET US THROUGH THE REST OF WINTER. THAT WON'T BE FORGOTTEN.
WHEN THE TIME COMES TO GO AGAINST NEGAN, YOU CAN EXPECT KAL AND ME BY YOUR SIDE... AS WELL AS OTHERS.
WE WOULDN'T WANT YOU TO FACE THEM ALONE.
WHAT IS HE TALKING ABOUT?
WE'RE GOING TO HELP THEM DEAL WITH THIS NEGAN GUY.
YOU VOLUNTEERED US FOR THAT?
NO. I'M GOING TO TRY AND TALK YOU INTO IT, LATER. NOT NOW.

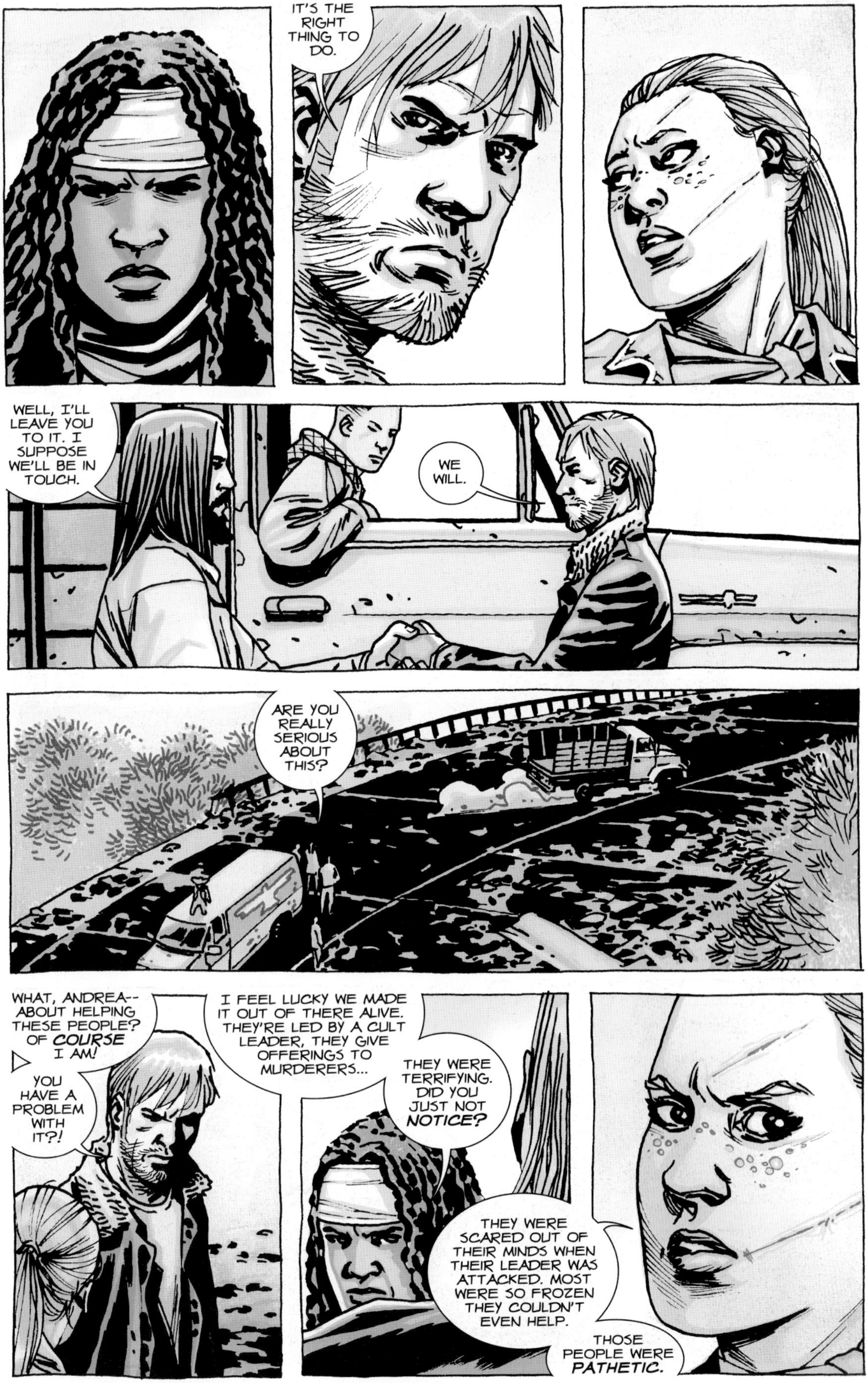
IT'S THE RIGHT THING TO DO.
WELL, I'LL LEAVE YOU TO IT. I SUPPOSE WE'LL BE IN TOUCH.
WE WILL.
ARE YOU REALLY SERIOUS ABOUT THIS?
WHAT, ANDREA-- ABOUT HELPING THESE PEOPLE? OF COURSE I AM!
YOU HAVE A PROBLEM WITH IT?!
I FEEL LUCKY WE MADE IT OUT OF THERE ALIVE. THEY'RE LED BY A CULT LEADER, THEY GIVE OFFERINGS TO MURDERERS...
THEY WERE TERRIFYING. DID YOU JUST NOT NOTICE?
THEY WERE SCARED OUT OF THEIR MINDS WHEN THEIR LEADER WAS ATTACKED. MOST WERE SO FROZEN THEY COULDN'T EVEN HELP.
THOSE PEOPLE WERE PATHETIC.

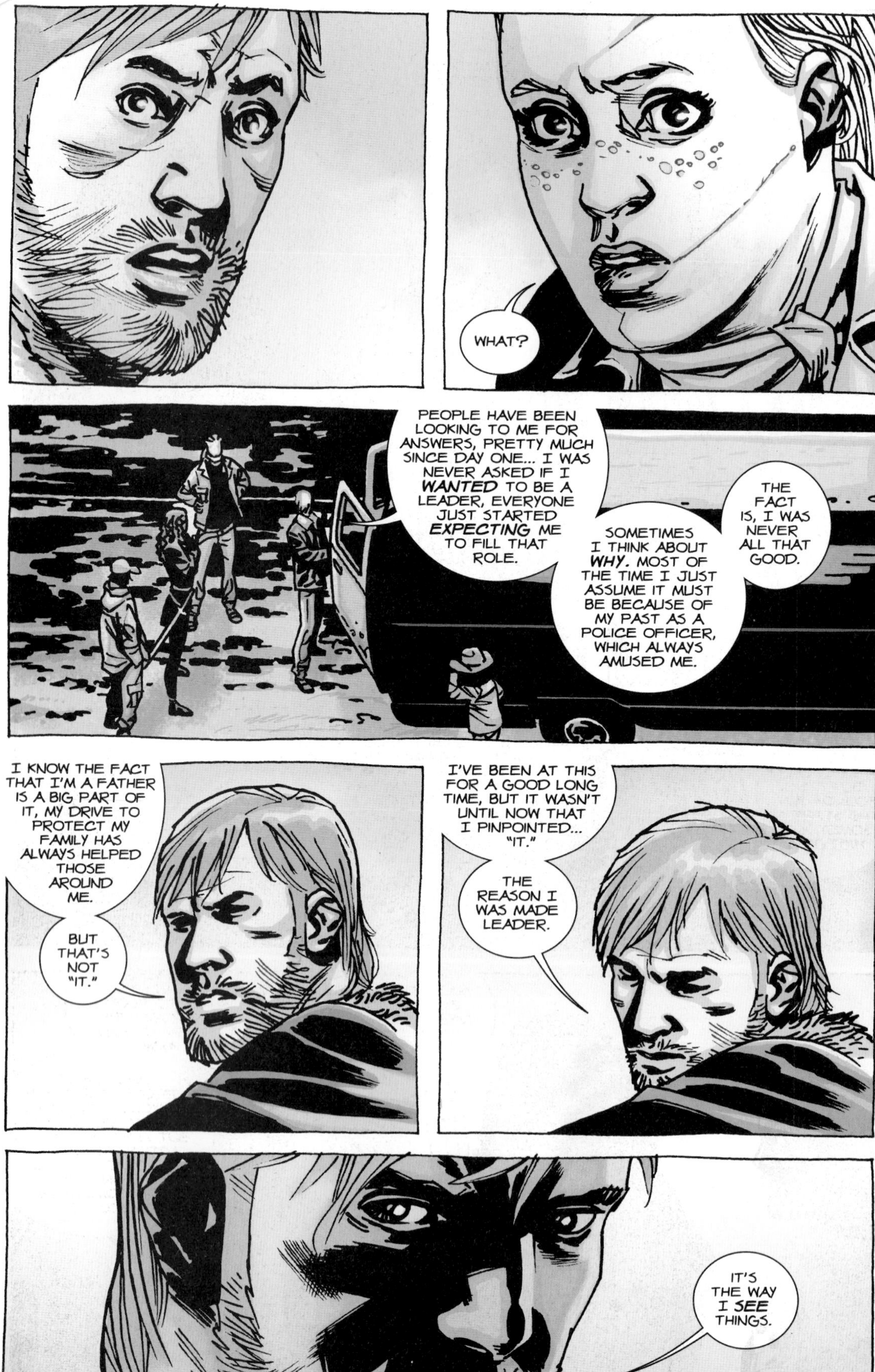
WHAT?
PEOPLE HAVE BEEN LOOKING TO ME FOR ANSWERS, PRETTY MUCH SINCE DAY ONE... I WAS NEVER ASKED IF I **WANTED** TO BE A LEADER, EVERYONE JUST STARTED ***EXPECTING*** ME TO FILL THAT ROLE.
SOMETIMES I THINK ABOUT **WHY.** MOST OF THE TIME I JUST ASSUME IT MUST BE BECAUSE OF MY PAST AS A POLICE OFFICER, WHICH ALWAYS AMUSED ME.
THE FACT IS, I WAS NEVER ALL THAT GOOD.
I KNOW THE FACT THAT I'M A FATHER IS A BIG PART OF IT, MY DRIVE TO PROTECT MY FAMILY HAS ALWAYS HELPED THOSE AROUND ME.
BUT THAT'S NOT "IT."
I'VE BEEN AT THIS FOR A GOOD LONG TIME, BUT IT WASN'T UNTIL NOW THAT I PINPOINTED... "IT."
THE REASON I WAS MADE LEADER.
IT'S THE WAY I ***SEE*** THINGS.

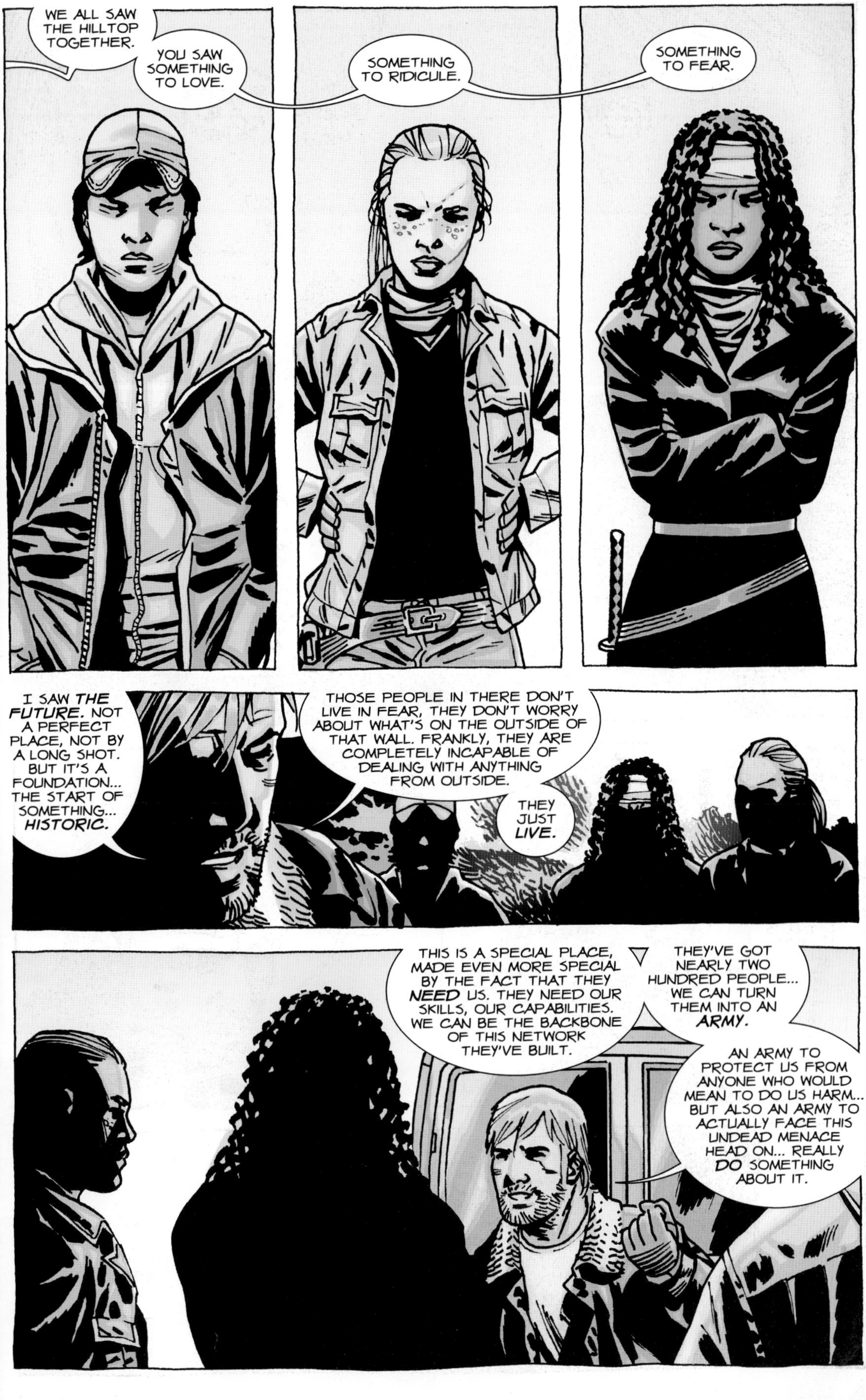

WE ALL SAW THE HILLTOP TOGETHER.
YOU SAW SOMETHING TO LOVE.
SOMETHING TO RIDICULE.
SOMETHING TO FEAR.
I SAW THE FUTURE. NOT A PERFECT PLACE, NOT BY A LONG SHOT. BUT IT'S A FOUNDATION... THE START OF SOMETHING... HISTORIC.
THOSE PEOPLE IN THERE DON'T LIVE IN FEAR, THEY DON'T WORRY ABOUT WHAT'S ON THE OUTSIDE OF THAT WALL. FRANKLY, THEY ARE COMPLETELY INCAPABLE OF DEALING WITH ANYTHING FROM OUTSIDE.
THEY JUST LIVE.
THIS IS A SPECIAL PLACE, MADE EVEN MORE SPECIAL BY THE FACT THAT THEY NEED US. THEY NEED OUR SKILLS, OUR CAPABILITIES. WE CAN BE THE BACKBONE OF THIS NETWORK THEY'VE BUILT.
THEY'VE GOT NEARLY TWO HUNDRED PEOPLE... WE CAN TURN THEM INTO AN ARMY.
AN ARMY TO PROTECT US FROM ANYONE WHO WOULD MEAN TO DO US HARM... BUT ALSO AN ARMY TO ACTUALLY FACE THIS UNDEAD MENACE HEAD ON... REALLY DO SOMETHING ABOUT IT.

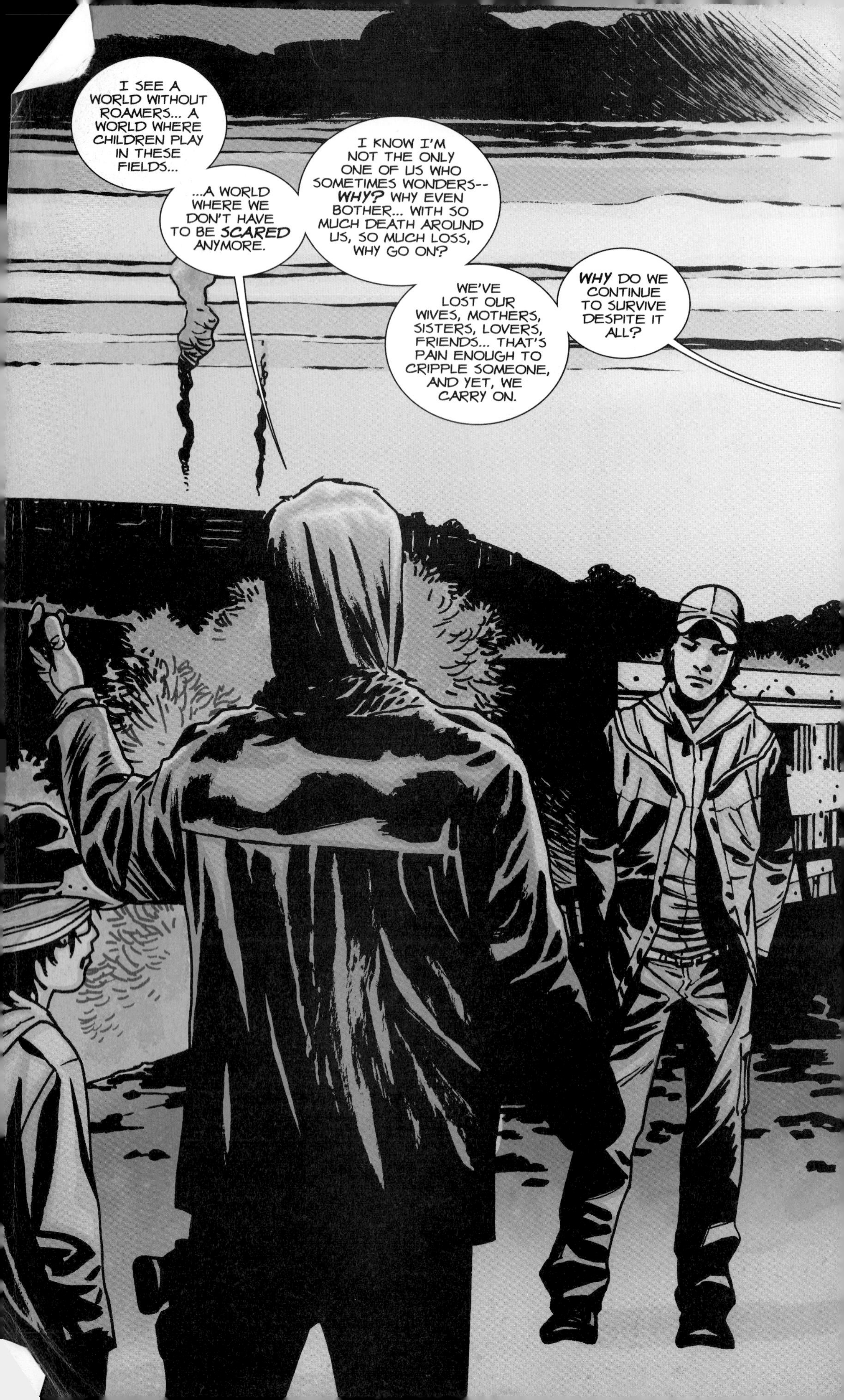
I SEE A WORLD WITHOUT ROAMERS... A WORLD WHERE CHILDREN PLAY IN THESE FIELDS...
...A WORLD WHERE WE DON'T HAVE TO BE SCARED ANYMORE.
I KNOW I'M NOT THE ONLY ONE OF US WHO SOMETIMES WONDERS-- WHY? WHY EVEN BOTHER... WITH SO MUCH DEATH AROUND US, SO MUCH LOSS, WHY GO ON?
WE'VE LOST OUR WIVES, MOTHERS, SISTERS, LOVERS, FRIENDS... THAT'S PAIN ENOUGH TO CRIPPLE SOMEONE, AND YET, WE CARRY ON.
WHY DO WE CONTINUE TO SURVIVE DESPITE IT ALL?

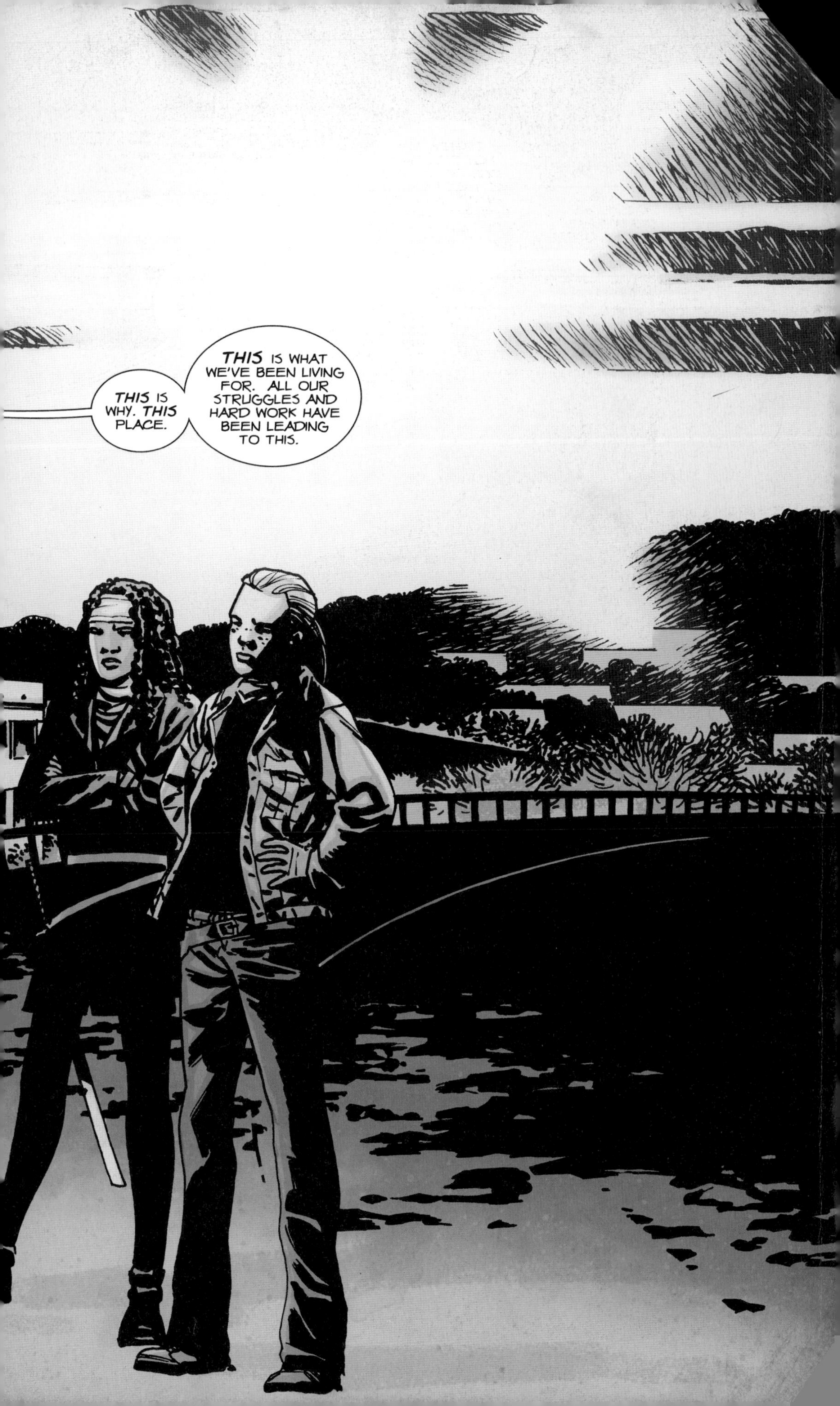
THIS IS WHY. THIS PLACE.
THIS IS WHAT WE'VE BEEN LIVING FOR. ALL OUR STRUGGLES AND HARD WORK HAVE BEEN LEADING TO THIS.

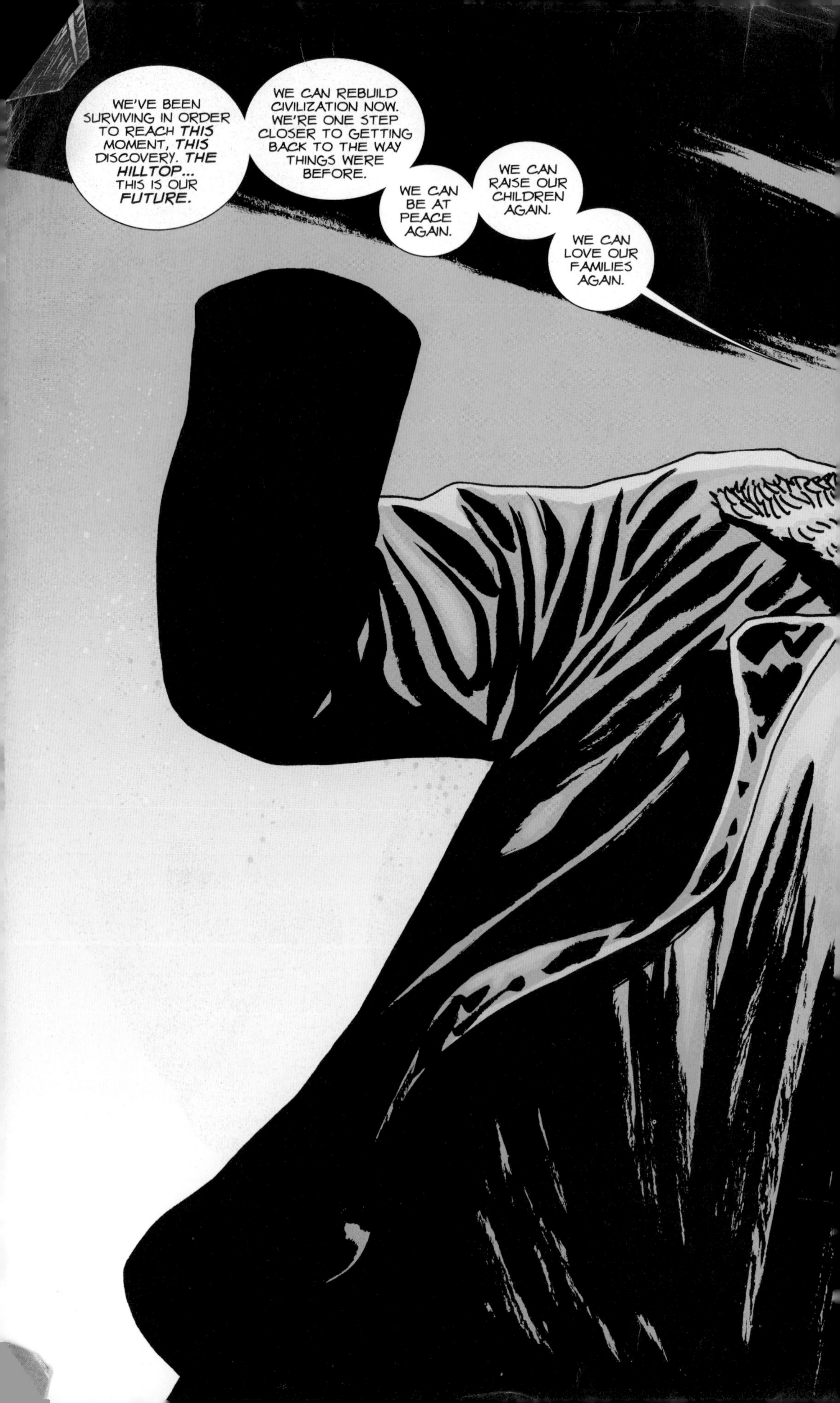
WE'VE BEEN SURVIVING IN ORDER TO REACH *THIS* MOMENT, *THIS* DISCOVERY. *THE HILLTOP...* THIS IS OUR *FUTURE.*
WE CAN REBUILD CIVILIZATION NOW. WE'RE ONE STEP CLOSER TO GETTING BACK TO THE WAY THINGS WERE BEFORE.
WE CAN BE AT PEACE AGAIN.
WE CAN RAISE OUR CHILDREN AGAIN.
WE CAN LOVE OUR FAMILIES AGAIN.

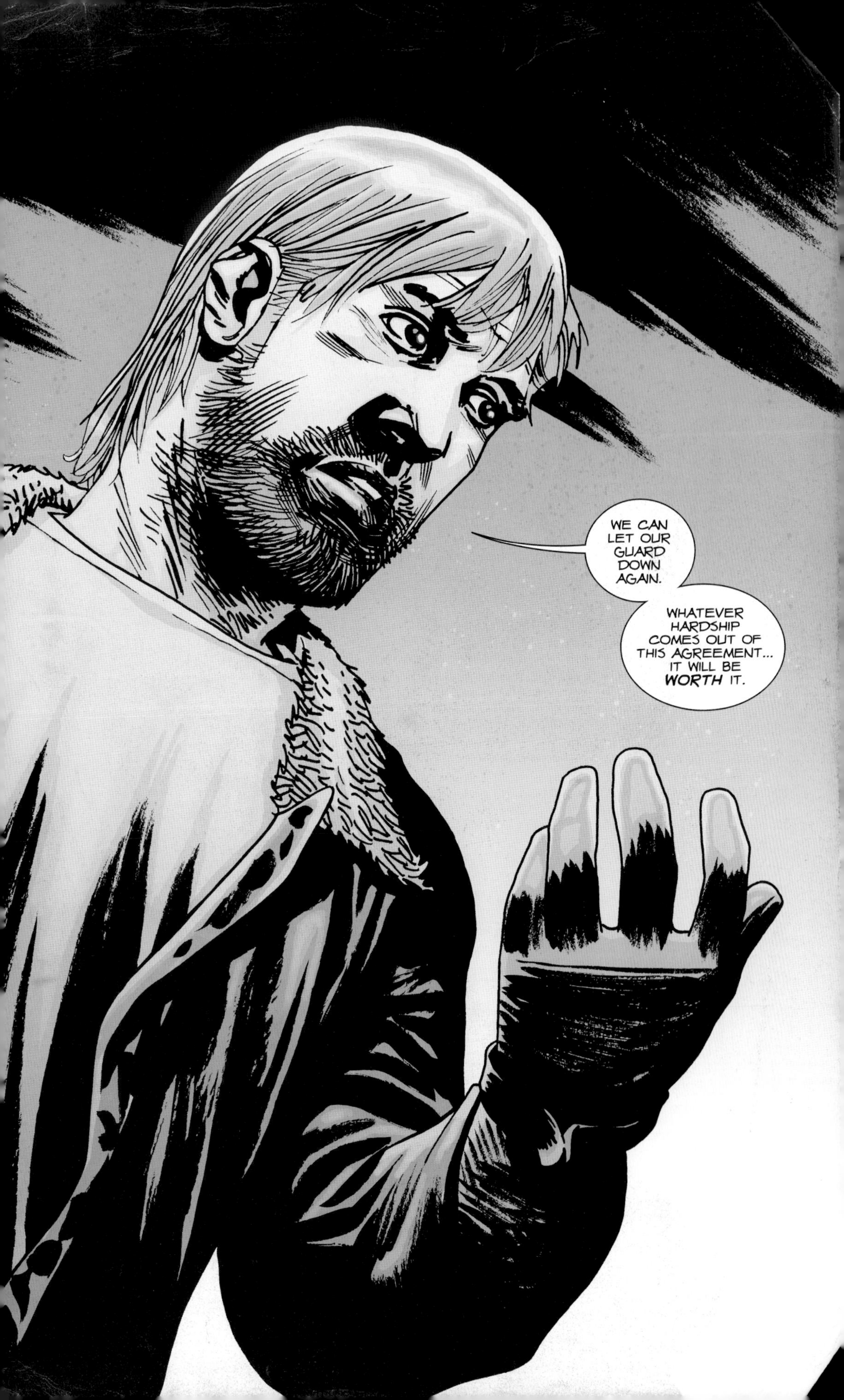
WE CAN LET OUR GUARD DOWN AGAIN.
WHATEVER HARDSHIP COMES OUT OF THIS AGREEMENT... IT WILL BE **WORTH** IT.

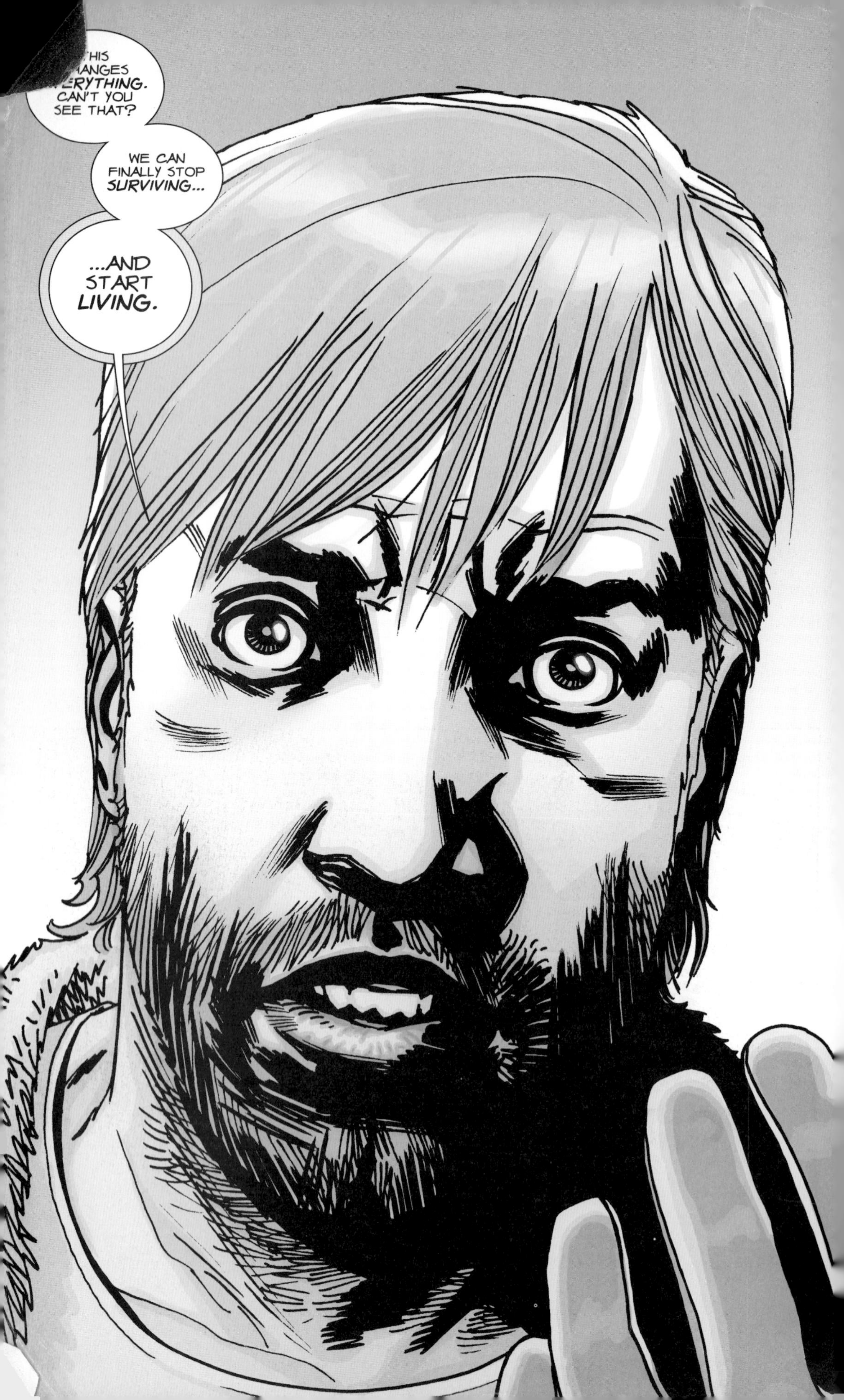
THIS HANGES ERYTHING. CAN'T YOU SEE THAT?
WE CAN FINALLY STOP SURVIVING...
...AND START LIVING.

TO BE CONTINUED...

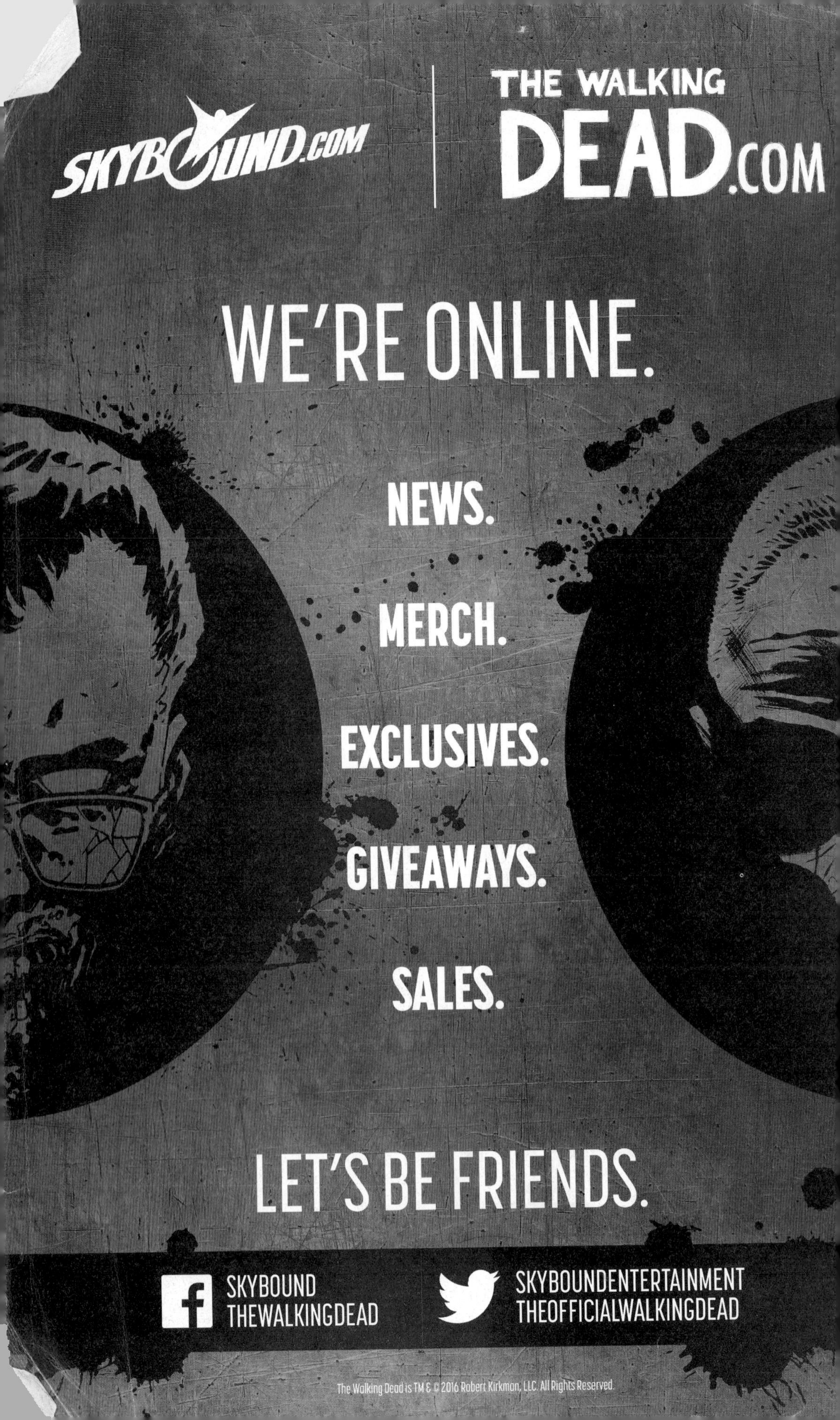
SKYBOUND.COM
THE WALKING DEAD.COM
WE'RE ONLINE.
NEWS.
MERCH.
EXCLUSIVES.
GIVEAWAYS.
SALES.
LET'S BE FRIENDS.
SKYBOUND
THEWALKINGDEAD
SKYBOUNDENTERTAINMENT
THEOFFICIALWALKINGDEAD
The Walking Dead is TM & © 2016 Robert Kirkman, LLC. All Rights Reserved.

for more tales from ROBERT KIRKMAN and SKYBOUND

VOLUME 3: THIS LITTLE LIGHT
BY KIRKMAN & AZACETA
OUTCAST

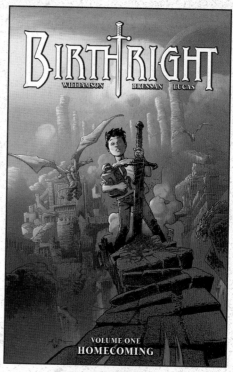

VOL. 1: A DARKNESS SURROUNDS HIM TP
ISBN: 978-1-63215-053-0
$9.99

VOL. 2: A VAST AND UNENDING RUIN TP
ISBN: 978-1-63215-448-4
$14.99

VOL. 3: THIS LITTLE LIGHT TP
ISBN: 978-1-63215-693-8
$14.99

BIRTHRIGHT
WILLIAMSON BRESSAN LUCAS
VOLUME ONE
HOMECOMING

VOL. 1: HOMECOMING TP
ISBN: 978-1-63215-231-2
$9.99

VOL. 2: CALL TO ADVENTURE TP
ISBN: 978-1-63215-446-0
$12.99

CLONE
VOLUME 4
FOURTH GENERATION

VOL. 1: FIRST GENERATION TP
ISBN: 978-1-60706-683-5
$12.99

VOL. 2: SECOND GENERATION TP
ISBN: 978-1-60706-830-3
$12.99

VOL. 3: THIRD GENERATION TP
ISBN: 978-1-60706-939-3
$12.99

VOL. 4: FOURTH GENERATION TP
ISBN: 978-1-63215-036-3
$12.99

WILLIAMSON LACI RYP MRVA
GHOSTED
VOLUME FOUR · GHOST TOWN

VOL. 1: HAUNTED HEIST TP
ISBN: 978-1-60706-836-5
$9.99

VOL. 2: BOOKS OF THE DEAD TP
ISBN: 978-1-63215-046-2
$12.99

VOL. 3: DEATH WISH TP
ISBN: 978-1-63215-051-6
$12.99

VOL. 4: GHOST TOWN TP
ISBN: 978-1-63215-317-3
$12.99

MANIFEST DESTINY

VOL. 1: FLORA & FAUNA TP
ISBN: 978-1-60706-982-9
$9.99

VOL. 2: AMPHIBIA & INSECTA TP
ISBN: 978-1-63215-052-3
$14.99

VOL. 3: CHIROPTERA & CARNIFORMAVES TP
ISBN: 978-1-63215-397-5
$14.99

THIEF OF THIEVES
VOLUME 5
"TAKE ME."

VOL. 1: "I QUIT."
ISBN: 978-1-60706-592-0
$14.99

VOL. 2: "HELP ME."
ISBN: 978-1-60706-676-7
$14.99

VOL. 3: "VENICE."
ISBN: 978-1-60706-844-0
$14.99

VOL. 4: "THE HIT LIST."
ISBN: 978-1-63215-037-0
$14.99

VOL. 5: "TAKE ME."
ISBN: 978-1-63215-401-9
$14.99

FOR MORE OF THE WALKING DEA

TRADEPAPERBACKS

ROBERT KIRKMAN TONY MOORE
THE WALKING DEAD
VOLUME 1
DAYS GONE BYE

VOL. 1: DAYS GONE BYE TP
ISBN: 978-1-58240-672-5
$14.99
VOL. 2: MILES BEHIND US TP
ISBN: 978-1-58240-775-3
$14.99
VOL. 3: SAFETY BEHIND BARS TP
ISBN: 978-1-58240-805-7
$14.99
VOL. 4: THE HEART'S DESIRE TP
ISBN: 978-1-58240-530-8
$14.99
VOL. 5: THE BEST DEFENSE TP
ISBN: 978-1-58240-612-1
$14.99
VOL. 6: THIS SORROWFUL LIFE TP
ISBN: 978-1-58240-684-8
$14.99
VOL. 7: THE CALM BEFORE TP
ISBN: 978-1-58240-828-6
$14.99
VOL. 8: MADE TO SUFFER TP
ISBN: 978-1-58240-883-5
$14.99
VOL. 9: HERE WE REMAIN TP
ISBN: 978-1-60706-022-2
$14.99
VOL. 10: WHAT WE BECOME TP
ISBN: 978-1-60706-075-8
$14.99
VOL. 11: FEAR THE HUNTERS TP
ISBN: 978-1-60706-181-6
$14.99
VOL. 12: LIFE AMONG THEM TP
ISBN: 978-1-60706-254-7
$14.99
VOL. 13: TOO FAR GONE TP
ISBN: 978-1-60706-329-2
$14.99
VOL. 14: NO WAY OUT TP
ISBN: 978-1-60706-392-6
$14.99
VOL. 15: WE FIND OURSELVES TP
ISBN: 978-1-60706-440-4
$14.99
VOL. 16: A LARGER WORLD TP
ISBN: 978-1-60706-559-3
$14.99
VOL. 17: SOMETHING TO FEAR TP
ISBN: 978-1-60706-615-6
$14.99
VOL. 18: WHAT COMES AFTER TP
ISBN: 978-1-60706-687-3
$14.99
VOL. 19: MARCH TO WAR TP
ISBN: 978-1-60706-818-1
$14.99
VOL. 20: ALL OUT WAR PART ONE TP
ISBN: 978-1-60706-882-2
$14.99
VOL. 21: ALL OUT WAR PART TWO TP
ISBN: 978-1-63215-030-1
$14.99
VOL. 22: A NEW BEGINNING TP
ISBN: 978-1-63215-041-7
$14.99
VOL. 23: WHISPERS INTO SCREAMS TP
ISBN: 978-1-63215-258-9
$14.99
VOL. 24: LIFE AND DEATH TP
ISBN: 978-1-63215-402-6
$14.99
VOL. 25: NO TURNING BACK T
ISBN: 978-1-63215-6
$14.99
VOL. 1: SPANISH EDITION
ISBN: 978-1-60706-7
$14.99
VOL. 2: SPANISH EDITION
ISBN: 978-1-60706-8
$14.99
VOL. 3: SPANISH EDITION
ISBN: 978-1-60706-8
$14.99
VOL. 4: SPANISH EDITION
ISBN: 978-1-63215-0
$14.99

HARDCOVERS

THE WALKING DEAD
BOOK ONE
a continuing story of survival horror.

BOOK ONE HC
ISBN: 978-1-58240-619-0
$34.99
BOOK TWO HC
ISBN: 978-1-58240-698-5
$34.99
BOOK THREE HC
ISBN: 978-1-58240-825-5
$34.99
BOOK FOUR HC
ISBN: 978-1-60706-000-0
$34.99
BOOK FIVE HC
ISBN: 978-1-60706-171-7
$34.99
BOOK SIX HC
ISBN: 978-1-60706-327-8
$34.99
BOOK SEVEN HC
ISBN: 978-1-60706-439-8
$34.99
BOOK EIGHT HC
ISBN: 978-1-60706-593-7
$34.99
BOOK NINE HC
ISBN: 978-1-60706-798-6
$34.99
BOOK TEN HC
ISBN: 978-1-63215-034-9
$34.99
BOOK ELEVEN HC
ISBN: 978-1-63215-271-8
$34.99
BOOK TWELVE HC
ISBN: 978-1-63215-451-4
$34.99

COMPENDIUMS

The ultimate edition of The New York Times bestseller
THE WALKING DEAD
COMPENDIUM ONE
Robert Kirkman • Charlie Adlard • Tony Moore • Cliff Rathburn

COMPENDIUM TP, VOL. 1
ISBN: 978-1-60706-076-5
$59.99
COMPENDIUM TP, VOL. 2
ISBN: 978-1-60706-596-8
$59.99
COMPENDIUM TP, VOL. 3
ISBN: 978-1-63215-456-9
$59.99

SPECIALTY BOOKS

THE WALKING DEAD
THE COVERS

THE WALKING DEAD: THE COVERS, VOL. 1 HC
ISBN: 978-1-60706-002-4
$24.99
THE WALKING DEAD SURVIVORS' GUIDE
ISBN: 978-1-60706-458-9
$12.99
THE WALKING DEAD: ALL OUT WAR HC
ISBN: 978-1-63215-038-7
$34.99

OMNIBUS

THE WALKING DEAD

OMNIBUS, VOL. 1
ISBN: 978-1-60706-503-6
$100.00
OMNIBUS, VOL. 2
ISBN: 978-1-60706-515-9
$100.00
OMNIBUS, VOL. 3
ISBN: 978-1-60706-330-8
$100.00
OMNIBUS, VOL. 4
ISBN: 978-1-60706-616-3
$100.00
OMNIBUS, VOL. 5
ISBN: 978-1-63215-042-4
$100.00
OMNIBUS, VOL. 6
ISBN: 978-1-63215-521-4
$100.00

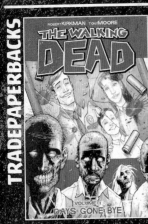

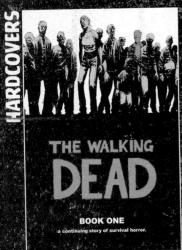

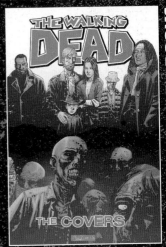

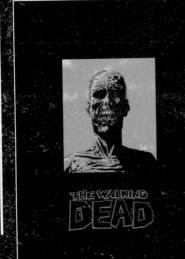